McDougal Littell

THE LANGUAGE OF
LITERATURE

ANNOTATED TEACHER'S EDITION

GRADE

8

 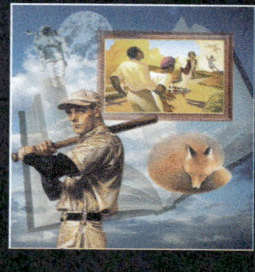    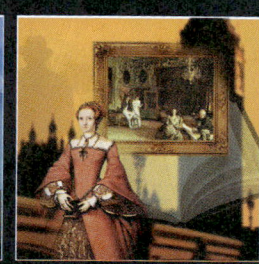

Copyright © 1997 by McDougal Littell Inc. All rights reserved.

WARNING: No part of this book may be reproduced or transmitted in any form or by any means, electronic or mechanical, including photocopying and recording, or by any information storage and retrieval system, without prior written permission of McDougal Littell Inc. unless such copying is expressly permitted by federal copyright law. Address inquiries to Manager, Rights and Permissions, McDougal Littell Inc., P.O. Box 1667, Evanston, IL 60204.

ISBN: 0-395-73710-9

Printed in the United States of America.

2 3 4 5 6 7 8 9 - DWO - 01 00 99 98 97

Table of Contents

Telling Our Story
What Is *The Language of Literature?* T4
Program Authors and Consultants T5

Overview
Core Components T6
Resource Materials/Integrated Technology T8
Assessment Package T9
Access for Students Acquiring English T9

A Closer Look

TEACHING LITERATURE
The Literature Lesson: Pupil's Edition T10
The Literature Lesson: Resource Materials T12

INTEGRATING LANGUAGE AND WRITING SKILLS
The Writing Workshops: Pupil's Edition T14
Writing and Language: Resource Materials T17
Special Features of the Pupil's Edition T18

THE TEACHER'S EDITION
Unit Support T20
Selection and Writing Workshop Support T22

ASSESSMENT
Assessment Resources T24

Advice from the Experts
Practical suggestions for planning your school year

Planning Your Year T26
Developing a Classroom Profile: Multimodal Learners T28
Developing a Classroom Profile: Students Acquiring English T29
Planning Your Instruction T30
Setting Up Your Classroom T32
New Technology and the English Classroom T34
Preparing for Assessment T36
Making Connections T39

Annotated Student Text

Additional Unit Resources
Unit 1 Resources 13a
Unit 2 Resources 147a
Unit 3 Resources 283a
Unit 4 Resources 423a
Unit 5 Resources 573a
Unit 6 Resources 695a

THE LANGUAGE OF LITERATURE
Telling Our Story

What Is *The Language of Literature*?

Is it a literature anthology? an integrated language arts series? a new approach to teaching and learning? *The Language of Literature* is all of these things—and much, much more.

CLASSIC STORIES, FRESH VOICES, AND NEW PERSPECTIVES

The powerful mix of selections in *The Language of Literature* reflects the exciting nature of our own society:

- Classic and contemporary literature
- Multicultural perspectives
- A mix of genres
- Authentic readings in a variety of media

A PROGRAM, NOT A BOOK

The Language of Literature is not simply an anthology with a collection of "extras." It is a seamlessly integrated program that links a student book to comprehensive lesson support; mini-lessons in writing, language, and communication; innovative technology; and access for students with special needs.

AN INTEGRATED APPROACH TO LANGUAGE

The selections in *The Language of Literature* become the springboard to a rich mix of language experiences:

- Writing workshops
- Grammar and vocabulary instruction
- Oral communication activities
- Critical viewing and listening
- Research skills
- Visual and media literacy

A WAY TO MAKE STUDENTS CARE

A strong student-centered approach acknowledges the differences among readers and the experiences they bring to a literary selection or writing experience. Responding options, multimodal activities, access materials for all students, and strategies for using media and technology ensure that students learn in a way that matches their individual learning styles.

A NEW WAY OF SEEING

A striking art program is only the beginning of the series's attention to visual and media literacy. Special activities and features throughout the program teach students that reading literature can be the first step toward reading the people and the world around them.

A SPRINGBOARD TO THE WORLD

Every prereading page, response section, and writing workshop provides meaningful activities and thoughtful connections that link the literature to students' own lives, to other curriculum areas, to their family and community, to other cultures, and to the situations and issues they confront every day in the "real world."

A PARTNER IN TECHNOLOGY

A rich videodisc treasury of images, audio and electronic libraries, Internet connections, and the unique Writing Coach software all support the literature and activities in this series. In addition, lessons in the pupil book model the use of technology to access information, network with others, and produce creative multimedia projects.

A WAY TO CONNECT AND REFLECT

Perhaps most importantly, *The Language of Literature* provides a way for students to connect the literature to the often confusing situations they encounter on the pathway from childhood to adulthood. The thoughtfully chosen selections, carefully crafted themes, and rich variety of learning options connect to students' lives and allow them to reflect on how universal certain experiences are.

Program Authors and Consultants

Arthur N. Applebee Professor of Education, State University of New York at Albany; Director, Center for the Learning and Teaching of Literature; Senior Fellow, Center for Writing and Literacy

Andrea B. Bermúdez Professor of Studies in Language and Culture; Director, Research Center for Language and Culture; Chair, Foundations and Professional Studies, University of Houston-Clear Lake

Sheridan Blau Senior Lecturer in English and Education and former Director of Composition, University of California at Santa Barbara; Director, South Coast Writing Project; Director, Literature Institute for Teachers; Vice President, National Council of Teachers of English

Rebekah Caplan Coordinator, English Language Arts K-12, Oakland Unified School District, Oakland, California; Teacher-Consultant, Bay Area Writing Project, University of California at Berkeley; served on the California State English Assessment Development Team for Language Arts

Franchelle S. Dorn Professor of Drama, Howard University, Washington, D.C.; Adjunct Professor, Graduate School of Opera, University of Maryland, College Park, Maryland; Co-founder of The Shakespeare Acting Conservatory, Washington, D.C.

Peter Elbow Professor of English, University of Massachusetts at Amherst; Fellow, Bard Center for Writing and Thinking

Susan Hynds Professor and Director of English Education, Syracuse University, Syracuse, New York

Judith A. Langer Professor of Education, State University of New York at Albany; Co-director, Center for the Learning and Teaching of Literature; Senior Fellow, Center for Writing and Literacy

James Marshall Professor of English and English Education, University of Iowa, Iowa City

THE LANGUAGE OF LITERATURE TEACHER'S EDITION **T5**

THE LANGUAGE OF LITERATURE
Overview

Core Components

The Language of Literature is a seamlessly integrated program that provides teachers with a common-sense system for teaching literature, language, and communication skills. The components described on these pages—the core elements of the program—provide teachers and students with all of the materials they need in a flexible, customizable format. (For more information on each element, please see pages T00 to T00.)

PUPIL EDITION
A rich mix of classic, contemporary and multicultural literature is the starting point from which your class begins its exploration of a world of ideas and experiences. Writing Workshops in each unit continue this exploration, moving students from the literature to interactions with real-world communication and technology.

ANNOTATED TEACHER'S EDITION
This comprehensive book provides all of the material you require for a successful teaching experience.

- Unit Content Overview and Planning Charts
- Student Projects
- Professional Enrichment Pages
- Family and Community Involvement
- Annotations for Literature Selections and Writing Workshops
- Bar Codes to LaserLinks
- Recommended Resources

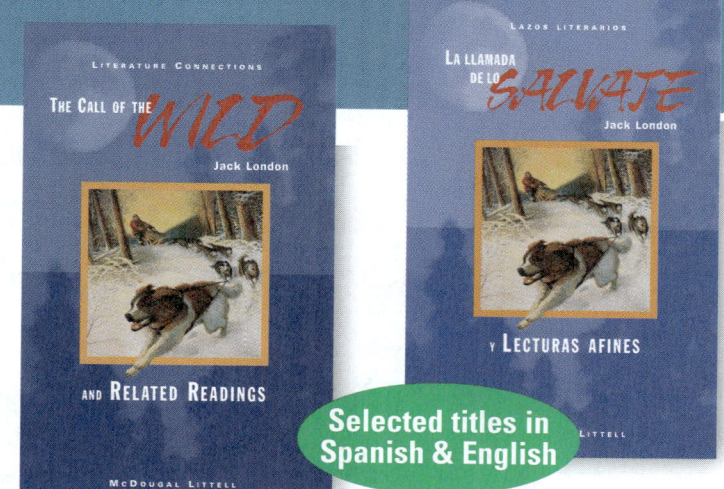

Selected titles in Spanish & English

LITERATURE CONNECTIONS

Unique to *The Language of Literature*, these stand-alone books allow you to decide which plays and novels to include in your literature class. Each longer work is accompanied by several related readings that extend the subject or theme.

SourceBook Provides you with all the information and student support materials you will need to present fresh and effective lessons.

Spanish Editions Selected titles are also available in Spanish, with corresponding Spanish SourceBook pages.

The Language of Literature Teacher's Edition **T7**

OVERVIEW (CONTINUED)

Resource Materials

UNIT RESOURCE BOOK Organized by unit and selection, these copymasters provide you with a variety of ways to build and reinforce student skills in reading comprehension, spelling, vocabulary, and writing.

GRAMMAR MINI-LESSONS WRITING MINI-LESSONS These transparency packs allow teachers to identify areas where students need help, and to teach exactly what is needed when it is needed. Corresponding grammar exercise sheets ensure that students get the practice they need on key areas of language and usage.

DAILY LANGUAGE SKILLBUILDER Through daily, literature-based exercises, this product integrates the teaching of grammar, proofreading, and punctuation skills.

Integrated Technology

 LASERLINKS
A treasury of full-motion video, photographs, and fine art, this videodisc provides the following program support:

- Selection Support: Historical and Cultural Background
- Author Interviews
- Writing Springboards
- Visual Vocabulary
- Art Galleries
- Storytelling
- Spanish Audio Track

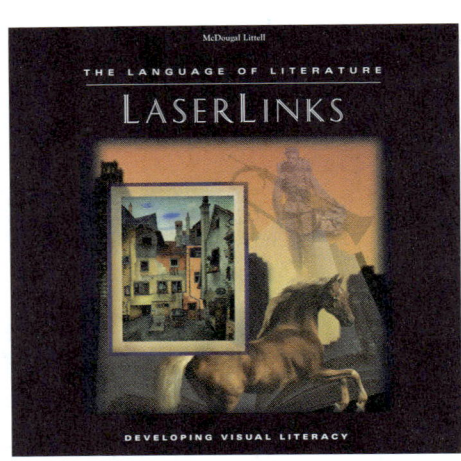

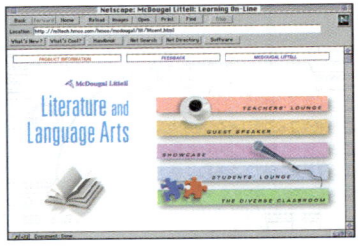

INTERNET CONNECTIONS Program-related information can be accessed through the McDougal Littell home page at http://www.hmco.com/mcdougal

AUDIO LIBRARY These tapes contain professional recordings of nearly every selection in the anthology. The performances can be used to enhance the literature or to provide support for less-proficient readers.

WRITING COACH
A comprehensive word-processing program with a unique, multi-column format and on-line writing support, the Writing Coach is a powerful tool for collaborative writing, peer response, and evaluation.

TEST GENERATOR Use this software to customize your own selection tests from hundreds of available questions.

T8 The Language of Literature Teacher's Edition

Assessment Package

TEACHER'S GUIDE TO ASSESSMENT AND PORTFOLIO USE This guide describes the types and uses of assessment and includes guidesheets, assessment forms, and checklists.

FORMAL ASSESSMENT This booklet contains selection and unit tests, writing assessment materials, and standardized test practice.

ALTERNATIVE ASSESSMENT With these materials—modeled on the authentic assessment materials used in many states and districts across the country—you can evaluate the processes students use as they read and write, as well as the products they create.

Access for Students Acquiring English

TEACHER'S SOURCEBOOK FOR LANGUAGE DEVELOPMENT A teacher handbook that includes teaching strategies and techniques.

TRANSLATIONS IN SPANISH A separate anthology that includes Spanish translations of one selection per unit.

RELATED READINGS Literature that is tied thematically to *The Language of Literature* units. Available in Spanish, Vietnamese, Cantonese, Cambodian, and Hmong.

SELECTION SUMMARIES Summaries of the literature in five languages: Spanish, Vietnamese, Cantonese, Cambodian, and Hmong.

READING AND WRITING SUPPORT Practice activities that support every literature selection and guidesheets for Writing Workshops.

FAMILY AND COMMUNITY INVOLVEMENT Available in six languages, these pages allow students to extend unit activities outside the classroom.

LITERATURE CONNECTIONS Spanish translations of selected titles for grades 6-12.

AUDIO LIBRARY These professional recordings may be used as support for Students Acquiring English.

LASERLINKS A separate Spanish audio track and Spanish captions allow students full access to the resources on these videodiscs.

A CLOSER LOOK
Teaching Literature

The Literature Lesson: Pupil's Edition

Each literature lesson is divided into three sections: Previewing, the literature selection itself, and Responding Options. This student-centered lesson offers a wide range and choice of activities.

PREVIEWING

Personal Connection Helps students explore prior experience and knowledge about topics covered in the selection.

Historical (Biographical, Cultural, Literary, Geographical, Scientific, etc.) Connection Provides important background information relevant to the selection.

Reading Connection Presents direct instruction in a reading skill designed to improve comprehension of the selection.

Writing Connection Serves as an alternative to the Reading Connection. Allows students to explore selection-related topics through writing.

Graphic Organizer Helps students explore new topics and structure their thinking.

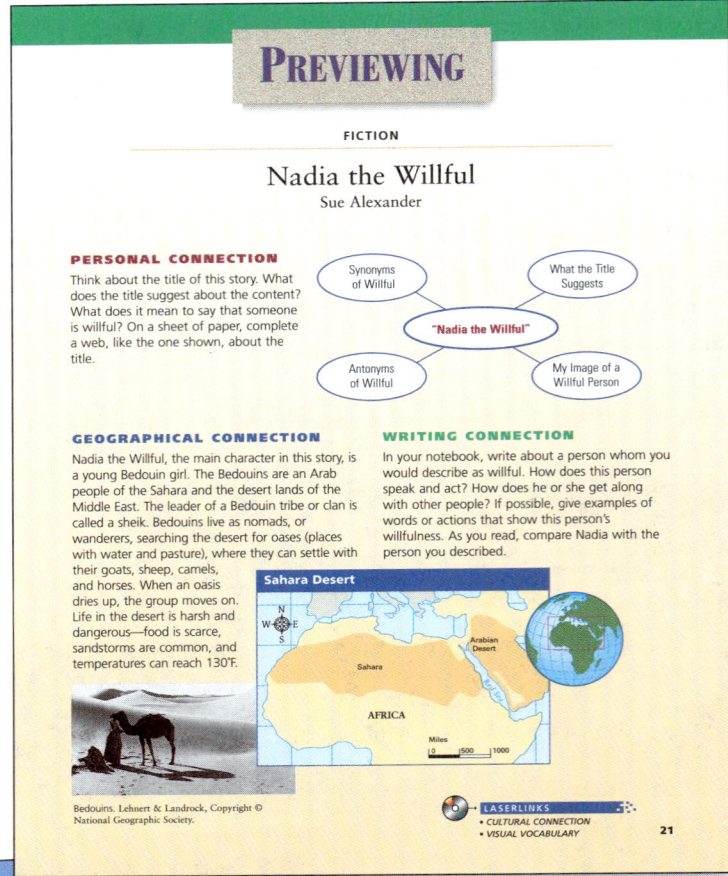

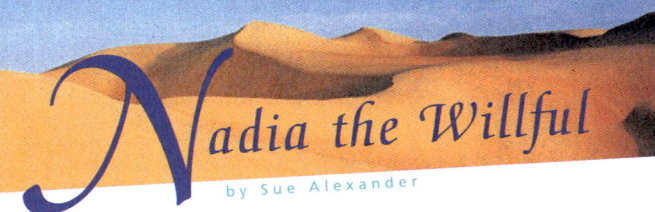

THE SELECTION

The finest literature offerings. Represented are traditional and contemporary pieces, familiar and new voices.

Natural and thematic connections. Selections are organized thematically and, where appropriate, chronologically.

Attractive, engaging design. Helps entice and motivate students.

Active reading questions. Provided as appropriate within selections to help students with comprehension of more challenging pieces.

RESPONDING OPTIONS

FROM PERSONAL RESPONSE TO CRITICAL ANALYSIS

REFLECT 1. What were your thoughts about Nadia as you finished reading? Write about her in your notebook.

RETHINK 2. Think about the word web and notebook entry about willfulness that you made for the Personal Connection on page 21. In your opinion, does Nadia deserve to be called willful? Explain.

3. How does Nadia change across time, and why?

4. Nadia's father promises to punish anyone who speaks Hamed's name. Why do you think Nadia is able to change her father's mind?
   Consider
   • Nadia's character
   • the effect of grief on her father

RELATE 5. Read "Primer Lesson" on page 27. What connections do you see between Sandburg's warning about "proud words" and Nadia the Willful?

6. Nadia and Tarik have different ways of reacting to death. Do their actions bring to mind any feelings or experiences of grief and death that you know about or have read about?

LITERARY CONCEPTS
The **setting** of a story is the time and place in which the events of the story happen. Skim the story and make a list of details about the setting. What role does the setting play in this story? How important is the setting?

Setting Details:

ANOTHER PATHWAY
Cooperative Learning
What if this story were told by Nadia or by Tarik? With a small group, choose what you consider the most important section of the story. Then rewrite that section, telling it from either Nadia's or Tarik's point of view. Share your version with the class.

QUICKWRITES
1. Compose a **narrative poem** that tells the events of this story. (For a description of narrative poetry, see page 104.)

2. Prepare a **character sketch** that would help an actor playing Tarik in a film version of "Nadia the Willful" to understand Tarik's character.

3. Imagine you are the set designer for the film version of the story. Write a **memo** to the director, describing the setting that you want to create. In your memo use details that you gathered for the Literary Concepts activity.

📁 **PORTFOLIO** Save your writing. You may want to use it later as a springboard to a piece for your portfolio.

ALTERNATIVE ACTIVITIES
Make a desert **diorama**. Cut a small square opening in one side of a shoebox. Using sand, sandpaper, paint, and other materials, create the setting of the story inside the shoebox. Then make paper figures of the characters and their animals to position within the scene. View the scene from the top or through the opening.

ACROSS THE CURRICULUM
Science Find out how deserts and oases form and change. Present your information to the class in an oral report.

WORDS TO KNOW
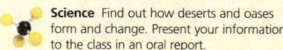
Review the Words to Know in the boxes at the bottom of the selection pages. Write the word most closely related to the idea of each sentence.

1. The sheik was angered by the theft of the horses and commanded that anyone found stealing a horse be put to death.

2. The marketplace was packed with every imaginable item—blankets, saddles, robes of woven cloth, and even wooden toys for children.

3. Looking out at the horizon, Hamed sat and thought of the extraordinary size of the hot and silent desert.

4. They camped at the oasis, all of the families of the tribe sleeping in tents and cooking food for one another over open fires.

5. There was no way he could survive in the desert alone, but he had no choice because the tribe would not let him live among them any longer.

SUE ALEXANDER

1933–

At the age of eight, Sue Alexander began writing stories for her friends. She says, "At that time I was small for my age (I still am) and very clumsy. So clumsy, in fact, that none of my classmates wanted me on their teams at recess time." One day Alexander spent recess time telling a made-up story to someone else who was not playing. Before her story was finished, all the rest of the class had come to listen. This incident sparked her love of storytelling.

Alexander says she would not trade any other profession because writing gives her a sense of fun and her need to share. Her fantasy stories all begin the same way—with how she feels about something. She writes for young people because she likes to excite their imaginations.

Alexander's short stories have been published in *My Weekly Reader* and other magazines for younger readers. The book publication of *Nadia the Willful* won many honors, including one from the American Library Association in 1983.

28 UNIT ONE PART 1: SEIZING THE MOMENT

RESPONDING OPTIONS

From Personal Response to Critical Analysis Invites student-centered discussion with the response-based approach made famous by McDougal Littell. Includes questions that help students relate the literature to their own lives.

Another Pathway Offers an alternative to typical classroom discussion. Generates full exploration of major issues in the selection.

Literary Concepts Introduces or reviews major literary terms and applies them to the selection just read.

Quickwrites Give students several innovative ways of responding to what they have read through writing.

Alternative Activities Offer opportunities to respond to their reading through multimodal activities.

Words to Know Reinforces vocabulary introduced in the selection with motivating exercises.

Author Biography Makes the authors come to life with interesting, student-friendly information. Includes listings of other works by the authors.

ADDITIONAL RESPONDING OPTIONS

Critic's Corner Gives critical commentary on an author or piece of literature and asks students to respond.

Literary Links Asks students to make connection between selection just read and another selection read at an earlier point in the book.

The Writer's Style Asks students to engage in analysis of style by focusing on stylistic traits of author being studied.

Across the Curriculum Provides cross-curricular activities that invite students to go beyond the selection to investigate new areas of study.

Art Connection Asks students to reflect on a work of fine art included in the selection.

TEACHING LITERATURE
(CONTINUED)

The Literature Lesson: Resource Materials

The literature in the Pupil's Edition is reinforced and extended by the following teaching tools for students' own use.

UNIT RESOURCE BOOK
Worksheets and tests provide support for all literature selections.

- **Strategic Reading: Literature Worksheets** reinforce reading strategies and extend the understanding of literary elements.
- **Reading SkillBuilders**
- **Vocabulary SkillBuilders**
- **Spelling SkillBuilders**
- **Selection and Unit Tests** stimulate higher order thinking skills as they assess understanding of selections, literary terms, and language skills.
- **Family and Community Involvement Worksheets** connect unit themes to students' world. A separate booklet provides these same worksheets in five languages: Spanish, Vietnamese, Cantonese, Cambodian, and Hmong.

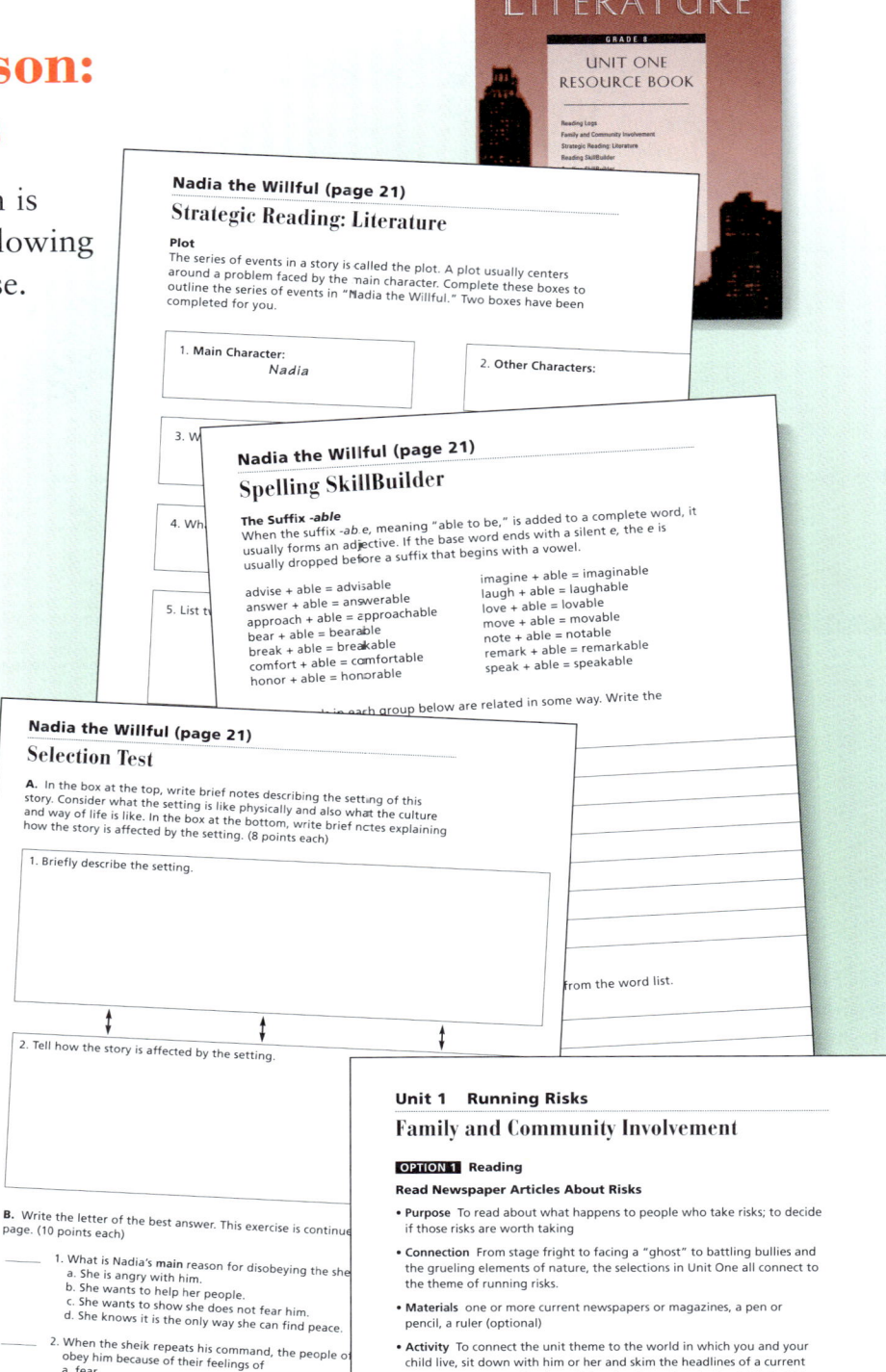

T12 The Language of Literature Teacher's Edition

LASERLINKS

A Level One videodisc program that enhances the literature curriculum, develops visual literacy, and helps students explore and interact with the literature.

- Provides historical and cultural background to strengthen interdisciplinary connections
- Helps build students' vocabulary through the Visual Vocabulary feature
- Contains author interviews
- Includes images that stimulate writing
- Presents storyteller in action

AUDIO LIBRARY

Recordings of almost all selections in each anthology. Provides easy listening, enhances and enriches students' literary experience, and helps students develop strategies for critical listening.

INTERNET CONNECTIONS

The following resources can be accessed through the McDougal Littell home page at http://www.hmco.com/mcdougal

- Literature selection support
- Links to professional materials and organizations
- Teacher discussion groups and bulletin boards

A CLOSER LOOK

Integrating Language and Writing Skills

The Writing Workshops: Pupil's Edition

Paired writing workshops in each unit offer students two distinct ways to respond to the literature and make "real world" connections.

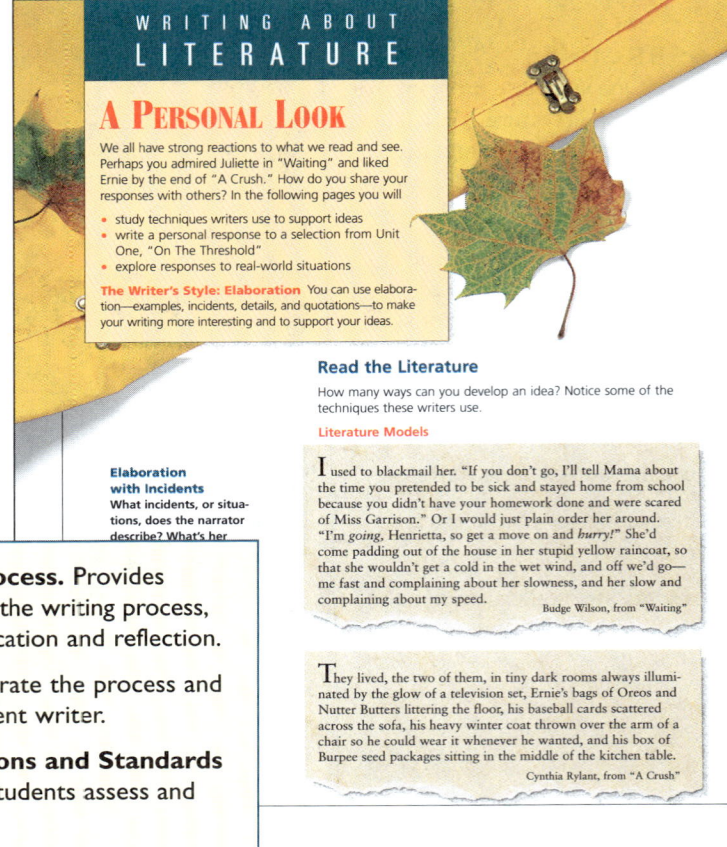

WRITING ABOUT LITERATURE
This workshop appears as a set of three related lessons.

- **The Writer's Style** lesson focuses on a writing skill such as sentence variety or elaboration. Literary excerpts and a real-world model show the technique in context.

- **The Guided Assignment** invites students to explore the literature through both creative and analytical writing.

- **Complete writing process.** Provides advice for each stage of the writing process, from prewriting to publication and reflection.

- **Student models.** Illustrate the process and choices of another student writer.

- **Peer response questions and Standards for Evaluation.** Help students assess and revise their writing.

- **Skills instruction.** Grammar in Context and Grammar SkillBuilders teach grammar concepts that relate to the writing.

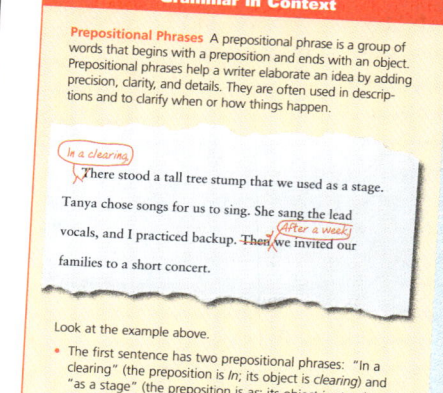

■ **Reading the World** builds visual literacy and shows students how the same skills they have just used to analyze and write about literature can also be used to observe, interpret, and understand the world around them.

WRITING FROM EXPERIENCE

The second writing workshop invites students to extend the unit theme by creating products for real purposes and real audiences in situations they encounter in the world around them.

Primary source materials. Magazine and newspaper articles, photographs, charts, and graphs provide a springboard to writing while building critical thinking and media literacy skills.

Oral communication and research skills. Used during prewriting as students gather information. Students are also encouraged to use technology—from CD-ROMs to on-line services—to access information.

Alternative forms of publishing. Visual, oral, and electronic products are suggested and modeled.

INTEGRATING LANGUAGE AND WRITING SKILLS
(CONTINUED)

SCOPE AND SEQUENCE OF WRITING INSTRUCTION

The writing workshops in *The Language of Literature* grow in sophistication as your students do, providing a rich variety of writing assignments that become more challenging in every grade. In the following chart, blue dots indicate the Writing About Literature workshops, and red dots indicate the Writing from Experience workshops. The number following each assignment represents the unit in which it appears.

Writing Strands	Grade 6	Grade 7	Grade 8
Firsthand and Expressive	• Personal Response / 1* • Anecdote / 1	• Personal Response / 1 • Firsthand Narrative / 1	• Firsthand Narrative / 1 • Personal Response / 4
Narrative and Literary	• Character Sketch / 2 • Fill in the Blanks / 4 • Writing in Kind: Poem / 5	• Short Story / 2 • Creative Response: Extending story / 4 • Writing in Kind: Fable / 6	• Creative Response: Change story element / 1 • Short Story / 2 • Creative Response: Scene from play / 6
Informative Exposition	• Interpretive: Analyze passage / 2 • Analysis: Plot devices / 3 • Problem-solution / 3 • Compare-contrast / 4 • Critical: Evaluating the message / 6	• Analysis: Imagery / 2 • Interpretive: Answering big question / 3 • Definition: Abstract idea / 3 • Critical: Review (poetry) / 5 • Compare-contrast / 6	• Interpretive: Finding the message / 2 • Critical: Evaluating ideas / 3 • Problem-solution / 3 • Eyewitness / 4 • Analysis: Poetry / 5
Persuasion	• Opinion / 5	• Opinion / 5	• Persuasive Essay / 5
Report	• I-Search / 6	• Report / 4	• Report / 6

*Denotes unit number

Writing and Language: Resource Materials

MINI-LESSONS

- The unique mini-lesson transparency packs in *The Language of Literature* allow you to decide what your students need to learn and when they need to learn it.
- Writing Mini-Lessons transparencies cover skills ranging from unity and coherence to voice and style.
- Grammar Mini-Lessons transparencies provide instruction on the most common usage problems faced by writers. Corresponding copymasters offer additional literature-based practice for students.

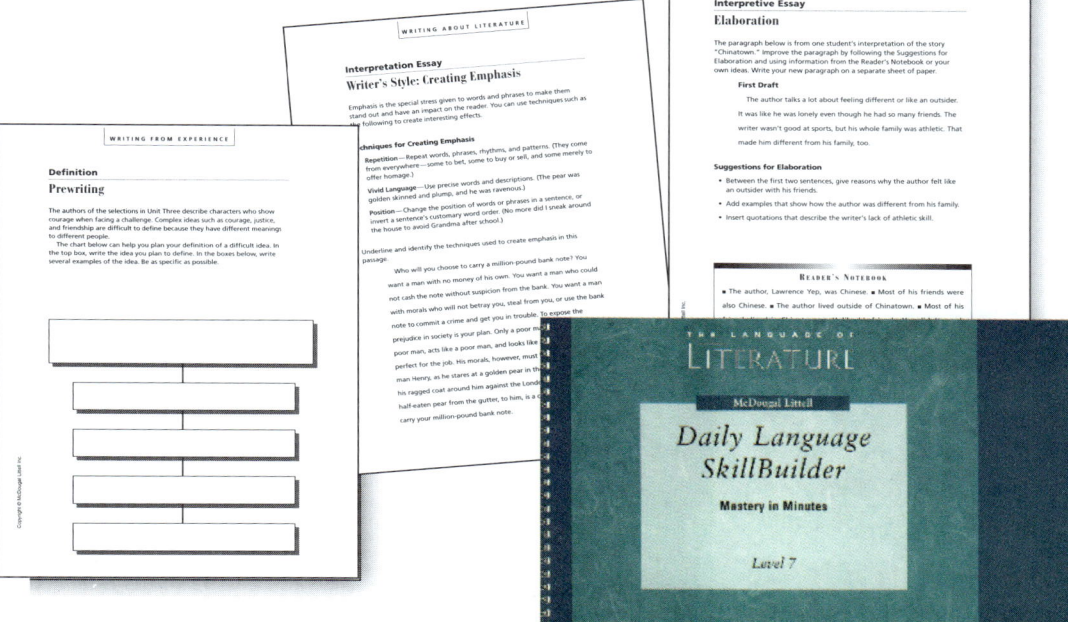

UNIT RESOURCE BOOK

In addition to support for the literature selections, the Unit Resource Book provides comprehensive practice and support for each stage of the writing process. Copymasters include the following:

Writer's Style Worksheet
Prewriting Worksheet
Elaboration Practice
Peer Response Guide
Revising and Proofreading Practice
Complete Student Model
Rubrics for Evaluation

DAILY LANGUAGE SKILLBUILDER

Through daily exercises, this product integrates grammar, proofreading, and punctuation skills with literature-based content

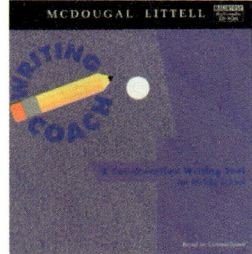

WRITING COACH
Collaborative Writing Software
This interactive, multimedia writing program on CD-ROM guides students through the writing process in a collaborative environment.

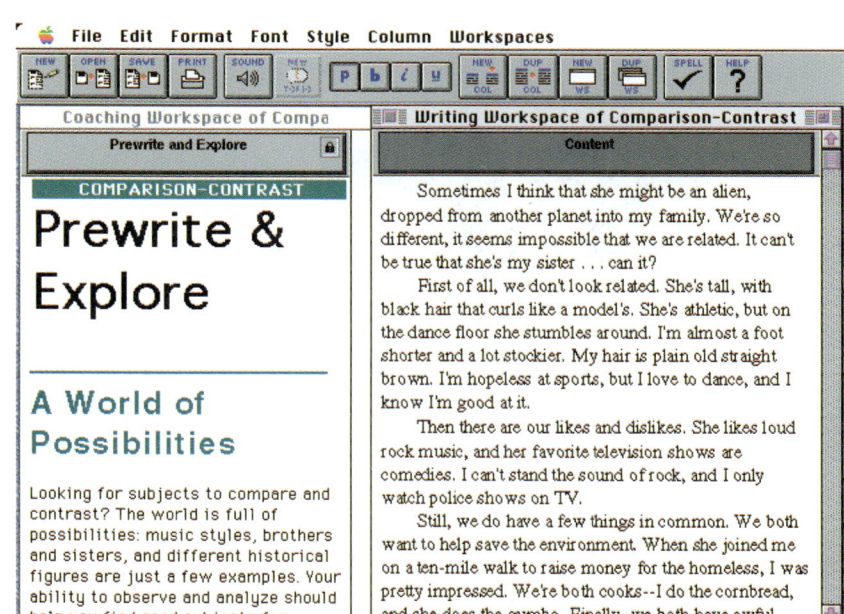

A CLOSER LOOK

Special Features of the Pupil's Edition

This book contains a wealth of special features to help enrich each student's learning experience.

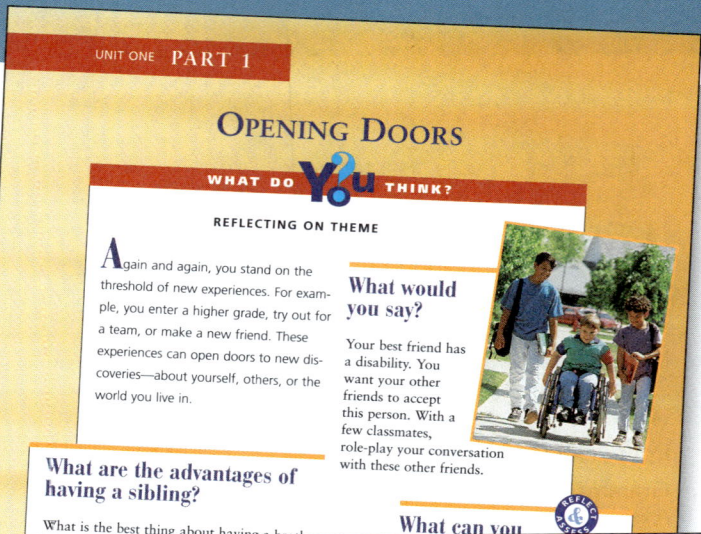

WHAT DO YOU THINK?
Motivating activities at the beginning of each unit part that help introduce students to the theme they are about to encounter in the next grouping of selections.

STRATEGIES FOR READING
Shows students how active readers read—what they think about as they read and how they make connections between the text and real-world experiences. Model provides thoughts and comments of two students engaged in the following active reading strategies:

- Question
- Connect
- Predict
- Clarify
- Evaluate

FOCUS ON FICTION/ NONFICTION/POETRY/DRAMA
Helps introduce and reinforce basic knowledge of literary elements. Also includes strategies used when reading a particular genre. Feature provides students with a strong foundation for the reading of literature.

T18

THE ORAL TRADITION
Celebrates storytelling in an entire unit devoted to folk tales from around the world. The featured storyteller also appears on LaserLinks. Activity-based response options throughout the unit tie to other curriculum areas.

REFLECT & ASSESS
Features end-of-unit activities that help students review and reflect upon what they have learned in the course of a unit. Includes options for:

- Reflecting on Theme
- Reviewing Literary Concepts
- Portfolio Building

STUDENT HANDBOOKS

- **Reading Terms and Literary Concepts**
- **Writing Handbook**
- **Multimedia Handbook**
- **Grammar Handbook**

A CLOSER LOOK

The Teacher's Edition

Unit Support

Special pages in the Teacher's Edition provide professional enrichment and help you plan your lessons, organize necessary materials, and carry out unit-related projects.

SKILLS TRACE

Allows you to see at a glance the scope and sequence of reading, writing, speaking, listening, viewing, study, research, grammar, spelling, and literary skills taught within each part of a unit. Also tracks the teaching of vocabulary words and the type and frequency of multimodal activities.

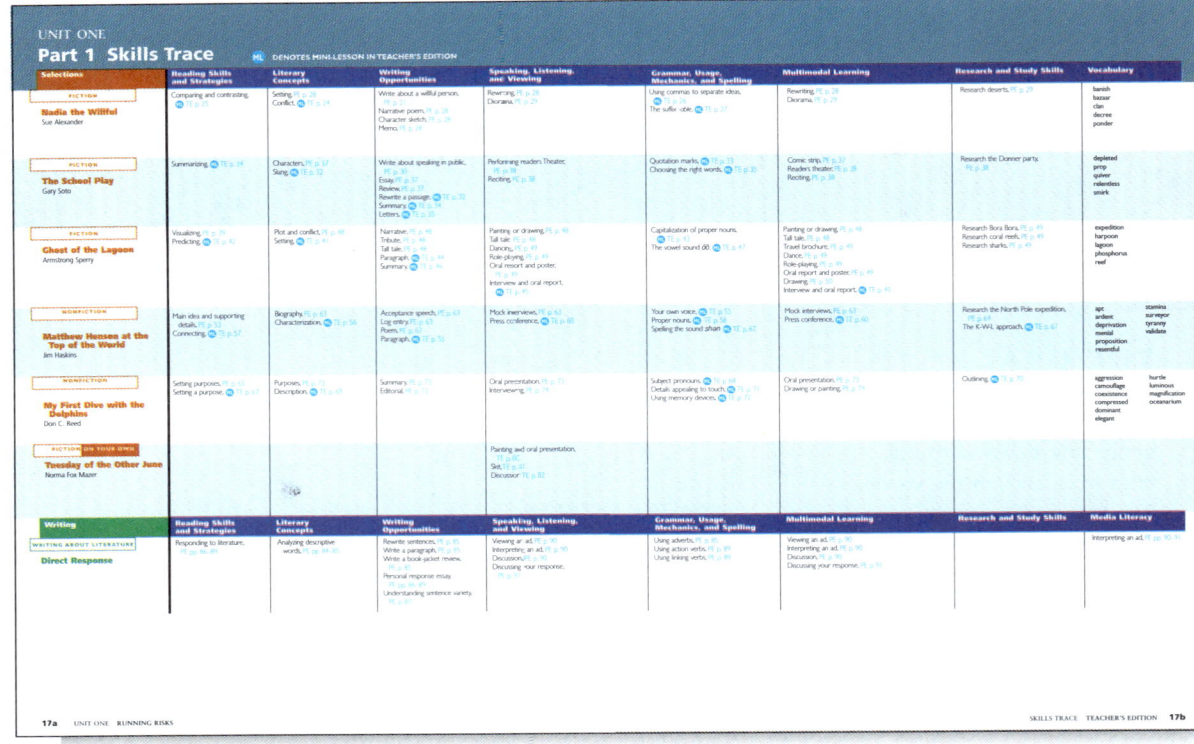

RECOMMENDED RESOURCES

Invaluable listings of unit-specific resources for both you and your students. Includes titles of novels and plays, cross-curricular readings, and media resources. Helps you extend and enrich the curriculum and enrich yourself professionally as well.

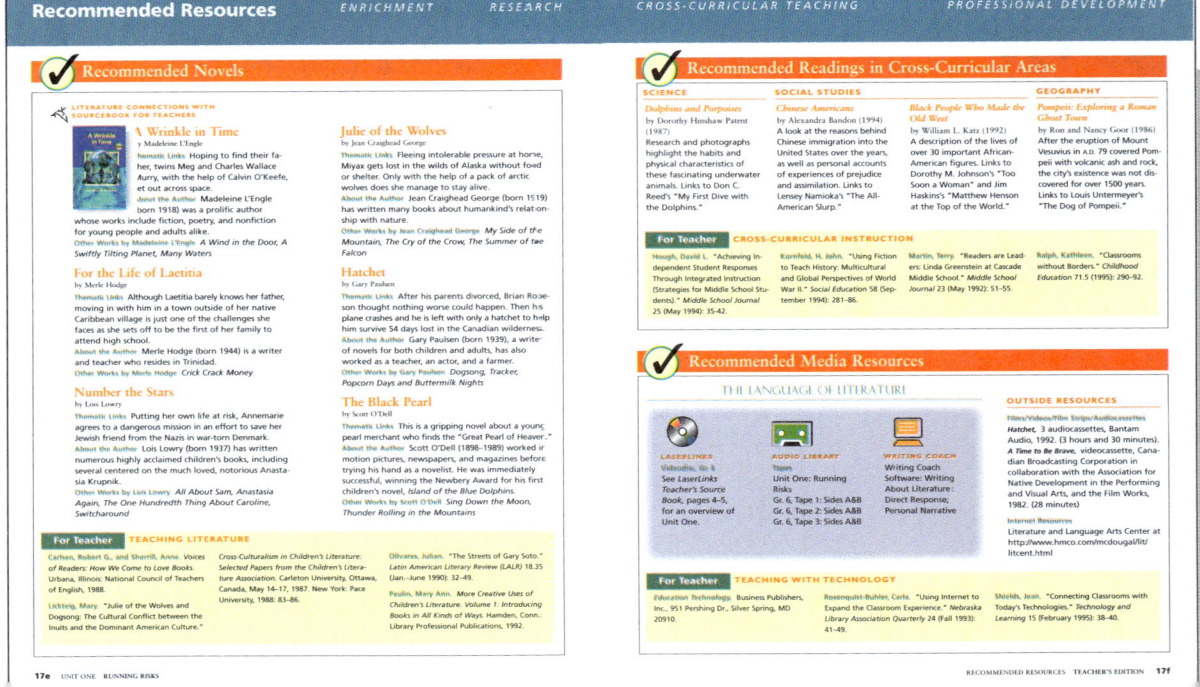

T20

UNIT ONE
Professional Enrichment

Staging a Readers Theater

"The play's the thing!" Shakespeare proclaimed in Hamlet nearly four hundred years ago.

Everyone loves a play—even the most bashful students. Creative dramatics can bring new excitement to the classroom. A readers theater is ideally suited to introduce your sixth graders to the drama of drama!

Explain to the class that a readers theater is one kind of dramatic performance. In a readers theater, actors and actresses stand on a bare stage and hold scripts. They must keep the audience's attention without props, scenery, or costumes. Readers theater is ideally suited to a classroom dramatic performance precisely because so little technical preparation is required.

Start by selecting a piece of literature—it can be a story students are already familiar with, one of the plays in this book (such as *A Shipment of Mute Fate* and *The Hobbit*), or a literary selection, easily adapted to dramatic performance, such as "The School Play." Then use the following techniques to stage a readers theater adaptation of the work.

STAGECRAFT
- Readers should step forward as they make "entrances" and step back for "exits."
- Have the main characters walk in and around the other characters.
- Use "freezes" to end scenes.
- Instruct actors to focus their delivery out toward the audience rather than toward other characters.

PREPARATION
Nothing succeeds like preparation! Explore with the class the importance of complete and thorough preparation for a successful readers theater. Try these ideas:
- Set aside time for students to read their material aloud several times before the actual performance.
- Students will rehearse with their groups as well as on their own. Encourage students to meet with their groups on their free time, perhaps before or after class.
- Make sure students know how to pronounce any difficult or foreign words.
- Be sure that students understand all the words. They cannot correctly interpret what they don't understand.
- Explain to the performers that they should pay special attention to the key points in their performance, such as excitement, tension, or flashes of humor in the script.

- Show students how to mark their scripts to cue places that require special emphasis and body language. Students can use a pencil, highlight marker, or pen to mark their cues.

PROJECTION
Help students learn to speak up. Remind them that they should not shout, but aim their voice outward, to the very back of the room. Show them how to hold their head and script up, rather than down, as they read. Good posture will improve voice projection.

VOICE CONTROL
Explain how the voice can be used as an instrument to express the nuances of the script. Model the process by reading part of the script to the class. For example, to emphasize humor, readers can increase the volume of their voice. To show tension, they can raise the volume and then lower it.

MOVEMENT
Guide students to use their whole body to express the character's personality. Their hands and face can be used to express emotion. Body language, including posture and movements, can also express emotion. Point out how posture also affects voice—both its tone and its volume.

CONCLUSION
When students are ready to stage their readers theater performance, consider inviting another class to be part of the audience. All that hard work and preparation shouldn't go unnoticed!

Related Reading
Childress, Alice. *When the Rattlesnake Sounds.* New York: Coward, 1975.

Davis, Ossie. *Escape to Freedom: A Play About Young Frederick Douglass.* New York: Viking, 1978.

Kamerman, Sylvia, ed. *Space and Science Fiction Plays for Young People.* Boston, MA: Plays, 1987.

Latrobe, Kathy Howard and Mildred Knight Laughlin. *Readers' Theatre for Young Adults: Scripts and Script Development.* Englewood, CO: Libraries Unlimited, Inc., 1989.

Family and Community Involvement

Family

From experiencing stage fright to facing a "ghost" to battling bullies and the grueling elements of nature, all of the selections in Unit One connect to the theme of taking risks.

The Copymasters listed below provide activities that students can take home and complete with a parent or other family member.

OPTION 1: READ NEWSPAPER ARTICLES
- **Connection** All of the selections in Unit One illustrate the theme of running risks.
- **Activity** Copymaster 00 Students and family members skim newspapers or magazines for articles about people who have taken risks. After they have taken turns reading the articles aloud, they decide if the risk was worth taking. A chart is provided for keeping track of the articles.

OPTION 2: WRITE AN ADVICE COLUMN
- **Connection** In both "The School Play" and "Tuesday of the Other June," the main characters must decide how to deal with bullies.
- **Activity** Copymaster 00 Students and family members write advice-column questions and answers on the topic of bullies and how to handle them.

OPTION 3: WATCH A DOCUMENTARY
- **Connection** In "My Dive With the Dolphins," the author takes a risk and finds out many things about dolphins that he never knew before.
- **Activity** Copymaster 00 Students and family members view a documentary on dolphins as a way of preparing students to read "My Dive With the Dolphins." A KWL chart is provided.

Community

OPTION 1
- **Connection** The selections in Unit One all illustrate the theme of running risks.
- **Activity** Have the class interview a psychologist to discuss personality types and why some people are more prone to take risks than other people are.

OPTION 2
- **Connection** The main character in "Nadia the Willful" is a young Bedouin girl who lives in the Middle East. She risks going against her family's beliefs as she grieves the loss of her brother.
- **Activity** Have the class interview a grief counselor to discuss the ways people deal with a death in the family.
- **Alternative Activity** Invite a former resident to discuss the Bedouin way of life in the desert lands of the Middle East.

OPTION 3
- **Connection** "The Walrus and the Carpenter," is a classic poem by Lewis Carroll; "Mean Song" and "Life Doesn't Frighten Me" are poems by two popular contemporary poets. All the poems deal with risk-taking.
- **Activity** Stage a "poetry slam." Invite a local poet to read his or her poems to the class, and then ask members of the class to share poems that they have written.

OPTION 4
- **Connection** *Woodsong* is an account of Gary Paulsen's experiences in the wildernesses of Minnesota and Alaska.
- **Activity** Have the class interview a scouting leader to discuss the risks involved in camping in the wild, as well as how to camp without leaving a trace.

PROFESSIONAL ENRICHMENT

Articles that give practical ideas for teaching literature and writing. Topics relate to unit content.

FAMILY AND COMMUNITY INVOLVEMENT

Activities designed to involve parents and other family members and to foster students' interaction with other people in their communities. Corresponding worksheets are provided.

COOPERATIVE PROJECT

Content-related projects for teachers interested in cooperative learning. Includes suggestions for how to assign and manage the projects and tells how connections might be made to other curriculum areas. Two different projects are included for each unit.

LESSON PLANNER

Helps you plan your lessons by indicating approximate length of time for each task. Allows you to accommodate a variety of classroom situations and needs.

T21

TEACHER'S EDITION
(CONTINUED)

Selection and Writing Workshop Support

The Annotated Teacher's Edition of *The Language of Literature* is a professional sourcebook designed to promote effective and efficient teaching. Each page contains features that allow you to take students into, through, and beyond the literature.

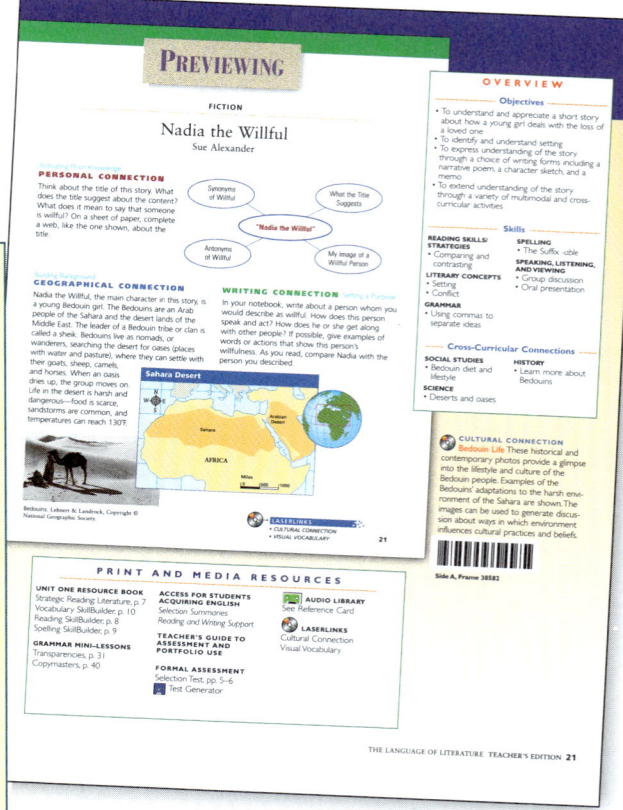

SELECTION ANNOTATIONS
Notes on literary concepts and critical thinking skills appear with each selection and its corresponding activity pages. Also included are the following features.

- **Overview** Lists objectives, key skills, and cross-curricular connections
- **Print and Media Resources**
- **Selection Summary**
- **LaserLinks bar codes**
- **Words to Know**
- **Art Notes**
- **Customizing for**
  - multiple learning styles
  - students acquiring English
  - gifted and talented students
  - less-proficient readers
- **Activities** Suggestions for whole class, small group, and individual activities
- **Mini-Lessons** Provided for grammar, spelling, reading, genre, writing, and a number of other subjects
- **Active Reading Questions**
- **Comprehension Check**
- **Assessment Options**
- **Links Across the Curriculum**
- **Links to *The Writer's Craft***
- **Activity Support and Answer Keys**

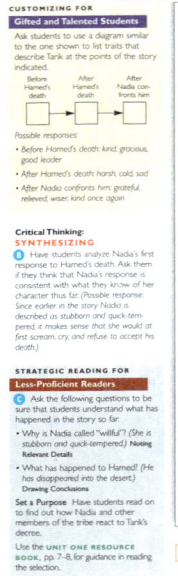

T22

WORKSHOP ANNOTATIONS

The Teacher's Edition notes for the Writing Workshops provide support similar to that provided for each literary selection. In addition, Writing Workshops contain the following:

- **Writing Springboards** Provides writing ideas from LaserLinks.
- **Modeling** Gives suggestions for using both literary models and student writing models.
- **SkillBuilder Mini-Lesson Support**
- **Visual and Media Literacy Features**
- **Research Skills**
- **Oral Communication**
- **Rubrics**
- **Standards for Evaluation**

T23

A CLOSER LOOK
Assessment

Assessment Resources

The Language of Literature provides you with material that allows you to customize assessment to best fit the activities and structure of your particular classroom. With options for formal, informal, and alternative assessment, these resources provide you with all the support you need.

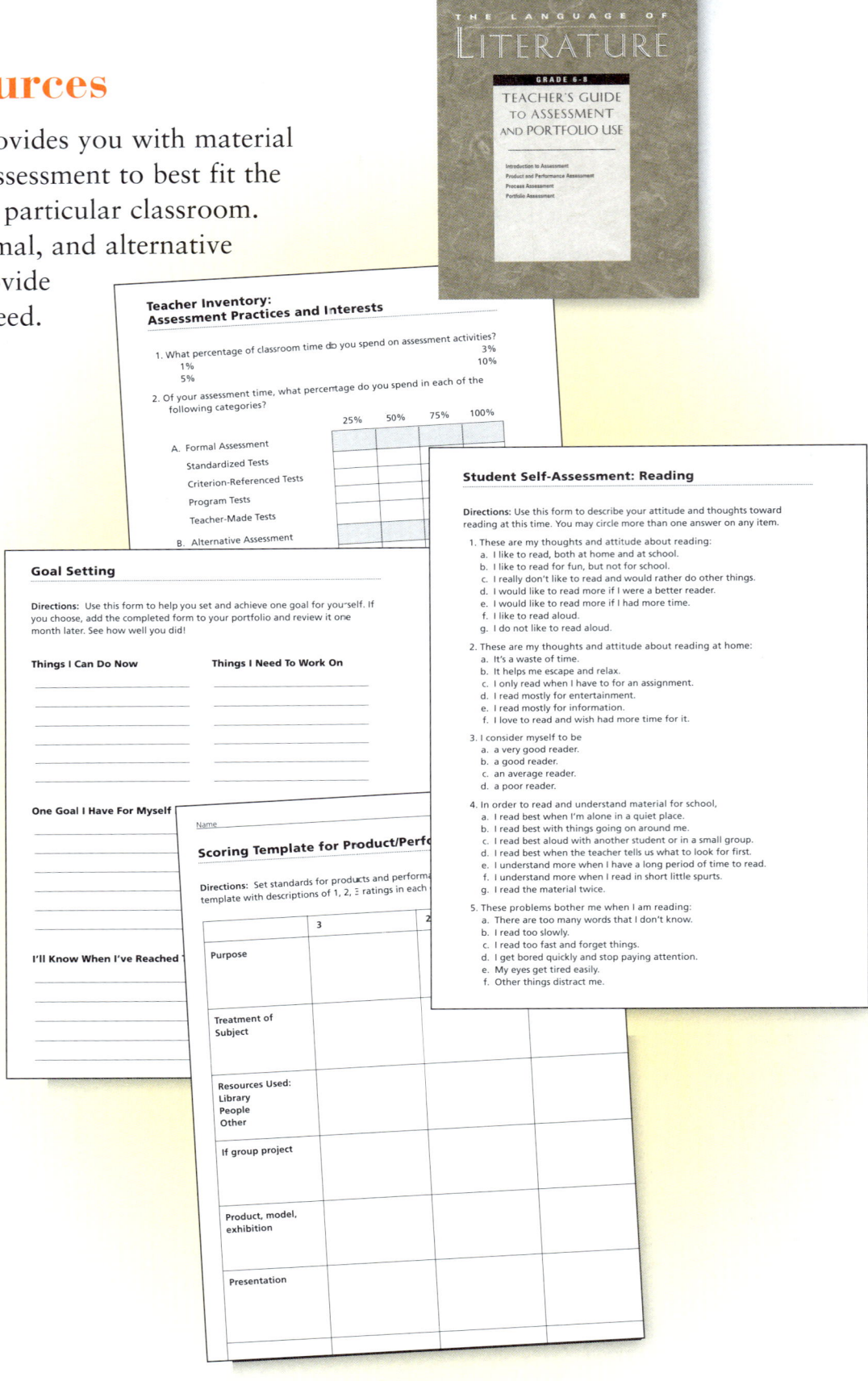

TEACHER'S GUIDE TO ASSESSMENT AND PORTFOLIO USE

This Teacher's Guide

- provides information on different types and forms of assessment: formal selection and unit tests, portfolio building, authentic assessment, reading notebooks, self-assessment, group and project assessment, and more.

- helps you decide which assessment types you wish to use and explains how to implement those approaches

- provides forms and checklists that can be used to give shape to assessment choices

T24 The Language of Literature Teacher's Edition

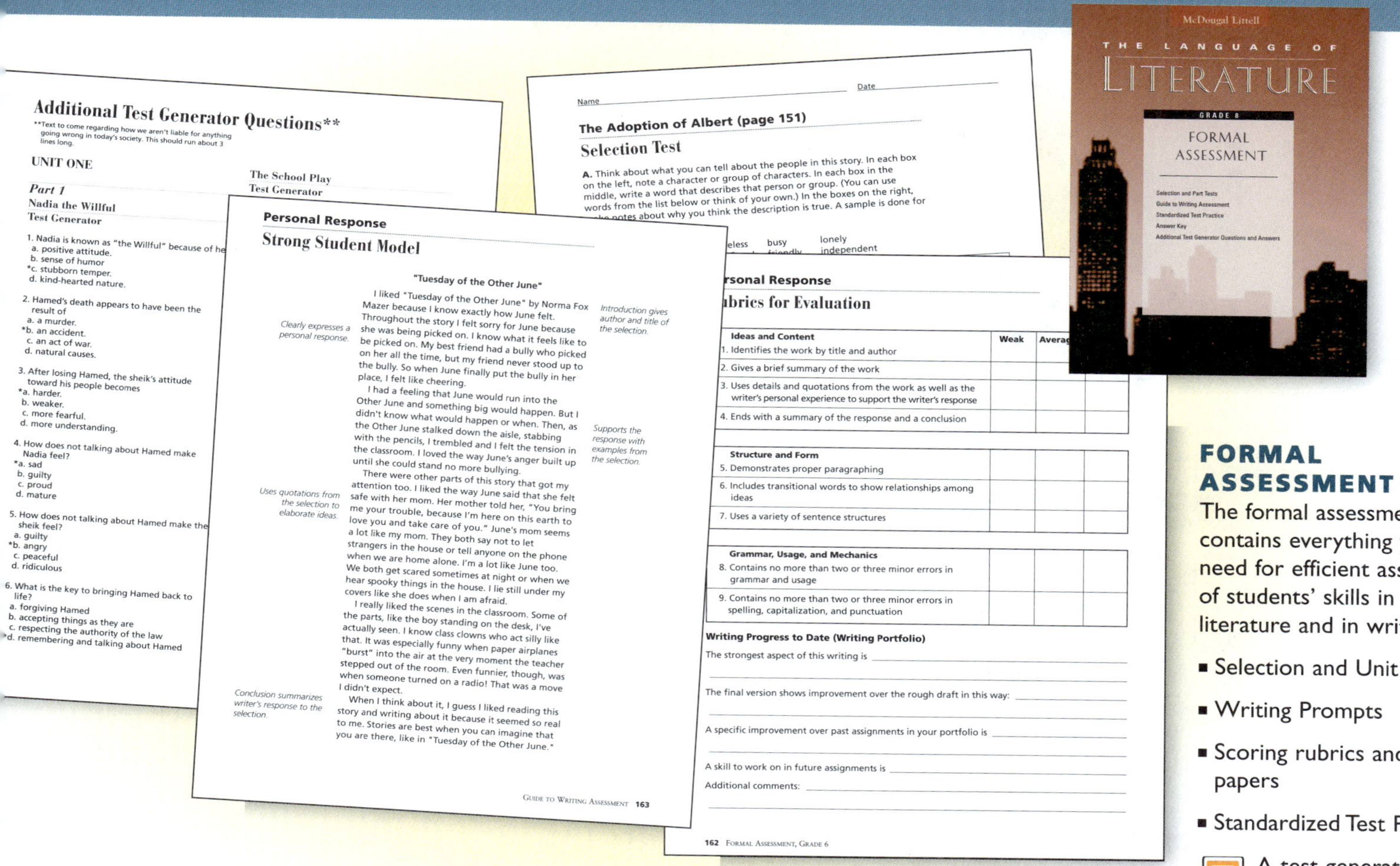

FORMAL ASSESSMENT

The formal assessment booklet contains everything you will need for efficient assessment of students' skills in reading literature and in writing.

- Selection and Unit Tests
- Writing Prompts
- Scoring rubrics and sample papers
- Standardized Test Practice

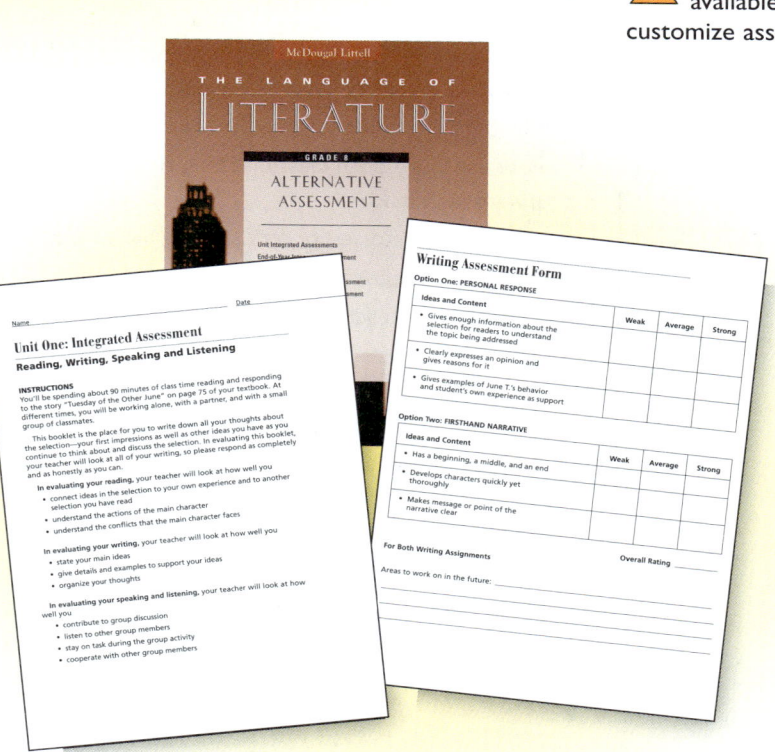 A test generator is also available to help you customize assessment.

ALTERNATIVE ASSESSMENT

These assessments integrate all of the language arts processes and are modeled on authentic assessment materials used in many states across the country.

- **Unit Integrated Assessments** are completed over two days and are based on the On Your Own selections in the student book. Prereading activities and post-reading response and discussion lead to in-depth writing options.

- The **End-of-Year Integrated Assessment** includes a reader and a Student Response Booklet. It is completed over several days and requires students to respond to three or more related selections.

The Language of Literature   Teacher's Edition   T25

GETTING STARTED...
Advice from the Experts

Planning YOUR YEAR

Every new school year requires much planning. The information and advice on these pages comes from the consultants on *The Language of Literature* and is designed to help you bring some of your plans into focus. (You may want to copy the pages and keep them in your lesson planner for easy reference.) As you begin your planning, here's a list of questions to consider. Their answers and some additional information can be found on the pages cited.

Developing a Classroom Profile   See pages T28–T29.

✔ **Who are my students?**

- ☐ What can I learn about my students from previous teachers, students, records, and portfolios— and how can I best use this information?
- ☐ What are my students' preferred learning styles, and how can I best accommodate them?
- ☐ If I have students who are not proficient in English, what will their needs be?
- ☐ Are there any other special needs represented in my class?
- ☐ What adjustments do I need to make due to tracking, mainstreaming, and other situations?

Planning My Instruction   See pages T30–T31.

✔ **What do I want to teach?**

- ☐ What are the requirements of my school, district, and state?
- ☐ What are my personal preferences?
- ☐ What are my students' preferences?
- ☐ How can I use both classic literature and young-adult literature to reflect the needs and interests of my students?
- ☐ What mix of stories, poetry, essays, and novels do I want to teach?
- ☐ How can I effectively combine writing, language, and communication skills?
- ☐ Do I want to teach a research paper and/or other longer projects?

✔ **How much collaborating do I want to do with other teachers?**

- ☐ To plan thematic units and/or projects
- ☐ To coordinate instruction

✔ **What mix of instructional styles do I want to use?**

- ☐ Lectures
- ☐ Cooperative/collaborative work
- ☐ Writing workshops/peer response groups

✔ **How will I organize the content?**

- ☐ By genre or mode
- ☐ By theme

Setting Up My Classroom
See pages T32–T33.

✔ **How will I organize my classroom?**

☐ In rows of desks
☐ With tables and chairs
☐ In paired-seating arrangements
☐ In cooperative learning groups
☐ In stations or centers

Taking Advantage of Technology
See pages T34–T35.

✔ **How large a role will technology play in my classroom?**

☐ What technological resources do I have at my disposal?
☐ For what purpose or purposes do I want to use them?
☐ How can I best set up my classroom or use a lab to take advantage of these resources?

Preparing for Assessment
See pages T36–T38.

✔ **What types of assessment do I want to use or prepare for?**

Do I want to use one or more of the following:
☐ Portfolios, journals, and/or logs
☐ Process assessment
☐ Product assessment
☐ Peer and self-assessment
☐ My own observations
☐ Tests from *The Language of Literature*
☐ District- or state-mandated tests
☐ Standardized tests

Planning Connections
See pages T39–T40.

✔ **What kinds of connections do I want to make outside the classroom?**

☐ To other curriculum areas
☐ To other classrooms or schools
☐ To my students' parents
☐ To the community
☐ To the world

DEVELOPING A Classroom PROFILE

> To avoid misunderstanding, it is critical that teachers disregard the assumption that all students have the same, or similar, frames of reference or perceptions about the world.
>
> Andrea Bermúdez
> Professor of Studies in Language and Culture, University of Houston–Clear Lake

UNDERSTANDING LEARNING STYLES

Your students are all unique. They have different sets of characteristics, abilities, and needs. It should not be surprising, therefore, to learn that they have different learning styles as well. This theory gained acceptance in the early 1980s, due in large part to the research of Harvard psychologist Howard Gardner. Gardner recognizes seven types of intelligences: linguistic, logical-mathematical, spatial, musical, bodily-kinesthetic, interpersonal, and intrapersonal. He claims that everyone has all seven of these intelligences, but in different proportions.

Understanding your students' intelligences, or learning styles, will help you teach them more effectively. How can you tell which learning style or styles your students favor? As you consider each of your students, asking yourself these questions will help.

Does the student...	Then he or she is mostly a...	So try these activities and assignments:
☐ Have good verbal skills? think in words? have highly developed auditory skills? like to read and write?	**Linguistic Learner**	Creative writing; essays; debates and speeches; oral reports; dramatic readings and performances; storytelling; joke, pun, and riddle telling
☐ Think conceptually? think and reason in a highly abstract and logical way?	**Logical-Mathematical Learner**	Graphic organizers; charts, graphs, and time lines; coded messages; prediction exercises; models; computer projects; science experiments
☐ Think in visual images and pictures? enjoy drawing, designing, building, daydreaming, inventing?	**Spatial Learner**	Drawings and paintings; comic strips; maps and flow charts; dioramas, displays, and murals; collages; drawing games; photography activities
☐ Have a sensitivity to music, nonverbal sounds, and rhythm? enjoy singing, playing, and listening to and moving to music?	**Musical Learner**	Interpretive dances; musical plays and compositions; rap songs, jingles, and melodies; rhyming games; playing a musical instrument
☐ Process knowledge through bodily sensations? have exceptional fine-motor coordination? communicate through body language?	**Bodily-Kinesthetic Learner**	Demonstration speeches; experiments; using gestures, facial expressions, and pantomime; impersonations; role-playing
☐ Understand other people? organize, communicate, and socialize well?	**Interpersonal Learner**	Discussions; cooperative and collaborative projects; peer coaching; conducting interviews; simulation activities; human graphs
☐ Prefer working alone? seem intuitive, independent, private, and self-motivated?	**Intrapersonal Learner**	Response journals, dialogue journals, learning logs; observations; photo essays; autobiographical stories; written reports

A PROFILE OF THE STUDENT ACQUIRING ENGLISH

Culturally and linguistically diverse students bring to the classroom a wealth of experiences that can enrich the learning environment of all your students. Developing multicultural sensitivity involves (a) acceptance of each student's circumstances, (b) a genuine search for information about his or her background and prior knowledge, (c) an updated bank of teaching strategies, and (d) a desire to find the best options for each student.

The Student Acquiring English

- generally focuses attention on style, not content
- is often unaware of learning strategies that could facilitate comprehension
- may become disorderly and disobedient due to an inability to relate to the learning environment
- often does not make eye contact when addressing others
- may seem to have difficulty meeting deadlines
- may not seem to understand classroom "rules"
- generally shows a different speaking and listening style
- may organize thoughts in a pattern that does not correspond to the expected linear-sequential pattern characteristic of standard English communication
- may exhibit an external locus of control, seeming overly dependent on teachers or peers for validation of responses

Common Problem Areas

The following problem areas pose special challenges to students acquiring English as they try to read and understand information.

Vocabulary Difficulty
If the student has no prior experience with the words appearing in a selection, the normal links between certain concepts and their labels will not occur. Problems often arise when a selection contains the following:
- low frequency words
- idiomatic or dialectal expressions
- jargon

Unfamiliar Content
The student may misunderstand the message in what he or she is reading if not given the proper context. This often happens as a result of the following:
- a lack of prior experience with the context
- ideas expressed in an unfamiliar or abstract way
- ideas expressed being of an unfamiliar culture

Grammatical Features of the Selection
Comprehension problems arise when the student encounters the following:
- dialectal forms
- outdated grammatical forms
- unusual word order

Effective Teaching and Learning Strategies

These instructional strategies have been shown to be successful when used with students acquiring English.

Cognitive Mapping
- Many SAE students, however, may organize and categorize information differently than English speakers would. Instruction in cognitive mapping can enable students to integrate previous experience with new knowledge.

An Integrated Approach
- The integrated approach to learning is particularly successful with students acquiring English. Students learn about reading and writing while listening, they learn about writing from reading, and they gain insights into reading from writing. Any strategy or approach based on dissecting language and mutually exclusive components jeopardizes second-language acquisition by not drawing on the prior knowledge and strengths of the learner.

Cooperative Learning
- Cooperative learning is a generic term that refers to a variety of approaches to integrating students into group activities where each participant is responsible for contributing to group outcomes and products. Cooperative learning strategies significantly improve students' achievement and productivity for a wide range of subjects and grade levels. This approach also improves self-esteem and respect for others. For more detailed information, see the *Teacher's SourceBook for Language Development*.

Planning YOUR INSTRUCTION

Just as your students all have their own preferred learning styles, you have your own preferred teaching styles. Understanding when and where your most comfortable style really works—and when another method would reach your goals and the goals of your students more effectively—will help you plan just the right type of instruction for every situation.

Here are some questions to ask yourself as you make decisions about your instruction:

- ☐ What is my objective for the lesson . . . today, this week, this month, this term?
- ☐ What is my time frame . . . 45 minutes, 90 minutes, three class periods, longer?
- ☐ Who are my students (refer to your classroom profiles, pages T28 and T29)?
- ☐ What teaching styles am I most comfortable with?
- ☐ What additional teaching techniques would be effective with these students and this material?

Consider these options . . .

WHOLE-CLASS INSTRUCTION

Lecture

EXAMPLES:
- ☐ Introducing a new unit of study
- ☐ Providing instruction for a project
- ☐ Introducing grammatical principles or definitions of literary elements

Teacher-led Discussion

EXAMPLES:
- ☐ Exploring students' ideas about and responses to literature selections and themes
- ☐ Examining complex issues and problems

Viewing

EXAMPLES:
- ☐ Viewing a filmstrip or a videotape
- ☐ Watching demonstrations, performances, and project presentations

COLLABORATIVE LEARNING

Pairs or Partners

EXAMPLES:
- ☐ Sharing responses to literature
- ☐ Interviewing and reciprocal questioning
- ☐ Brainstorming for project or writing ideas
- ☐ Peer tutoring
- ☐ Writing workshops

Small Groups (3-8 students)

EXAMPLES:
- ☐ Discussing literature or other topics
- ☐ Planning and problem-solving activities
- ☐ Writing workshops
- ☐ Cooperative work on reports, projects, and presentations
- ☐ Cooperative planning and producing of larger projects such as plays, panel discussions or debates, and videotapes

INDEPENDENT LEARNING

Students Working Individually

EXAMPLES:
- ☐ Independent reading and writing
- ☐ Drawing, painting, and collages
- ☐ Listening to audiotapes

... for meeting these instructional goals ...	... with these guidelines and cautions:
☐ Developing critical listening and note-taking skills ☐ Providing unknown historical or cultural background ☐ Introducing new concepts or skills	☐ Lectures appeal to linguistic learners with highly developed auditory skills. Other students may tune you out because this style lacks interactivity. ☐ Lectures are most effective if no longer than 20 minutes. Research shows that immediately after a 10-minute presentation, average adult listeners retain less than 50% of what they hear—and 48 hours later, they only recall 25%.
☐ Developing critical listening, responding, and conversational skills ☐ Introducing or reviewing skills	☐ Not all students are comfortable speaking in front of their peers. Highly verbal students can drown out students who favor other learning styles. ☐ When you lead the discussion, students may tend to direct their comments to you rather than to other students. Encourage students to speak directly to one another as well as to you.
☐ Supporting and improving visual literacy ☐ Developing evaluative skills ☐ Encouraging appreciation for music, art, and various kinds of performances	☐ Although viewing is a comfortable activity for most students, it's essentially passive. You'll want to choose occasions carefully. ☐ To help students remain focused, agree on goals ahead of time and provide standards and forms for evaluating what students are watching.
☐ Reinforcing cooperative learning skills ☐ Providing support for students acquiring English ☐ Encouraging peer feedback for writing	☐ It's important to cultivate a classroom atmosphere of support and trust so that pair interactions are effective and productive. ☐ You may want to pair students differently for different purposes. Strong students may be paired with weaker students, native English speakers with students acquiring English, talkative students with more reserved students, and so on.
☐ Developing problem solving skills ☐ Encouraging peer feedback for writing ☐ Reinforcing cooperative learning skills ☐ Providing opportunities for students to explore various points of view ☐ Improving social skills and promoting self-esteem in students of all abilities	☐ Some students will lean too hard on other members of the group. Both groups and individual students need to be accountable. ☐ Some students can get lost in the shuffle of a larger group. Individual students should have specific responsibilities. ☐ Group size can be determined by the task. Small groups are appropriate for sharing personal writing and receiving individual attention; larger groups are effective when the task is large or complex. ☐ The "jigsaw" method may be useful for groups working on complex tasks. The group divides the assignment into pieces and assigns each student a piece. Then students work together to meld the pieces into a coherent whole.
☐ Providing opportunities for reflection and self-assessment ☐ Providing support for students acquiring English	☐ Individual learning tasks require a quiet classroom atmosphere. Highly developed interpersonal learners may distract other students. ☐ Using independent learning too frequently can hinder students' development of collaborative and cooperative skills.

Setting Up YOUR CLASSROOM

Are you planning to try some new instructional approaches this year? If so, you also may want to consider some new classroom setups. Moving away from the traditional arrangement of desks in rows will provide you and your students a welcome change—and will be more conducive to different teaching and learning situations. Here are a few pointers:

If you teach in the same room all day, the ideas on these pages will provide ways to set up your room for a variety of purposes.

If you switch rooms, team teach, or share your room, you can find an arrangement that best meets everyone's needs. Some options:

☐ One arrangement that works for everyone

☐ Different classrooms for different purposes

☐ A resource room or common area that could be used for specific types of activities

Before you arrange your classroom, draw a scale floor plan of it. Then add furniture and design a setting that will best accommodate your instructional plans.

When you have your floor plan firmed up, post lists of procedures in the different areas of your classroom. Encourage students to add new procedures as needs arise in the future.

Don't be afraid to experiment with different arrangements throughout the year. You may find that some arrangements work better than others for specific projects or assignments.

> The ideal literature classroom is a literary community where students... have room to respond, interpret, think critically, and contrast their ideas with those of other readers.
>
> Judith Langer and Arthur Applebee
> Professors of Education, State University of New York at Albany

A LOOK AT THREE CLASSROOM SETUPS
Lectures and Demonstrations

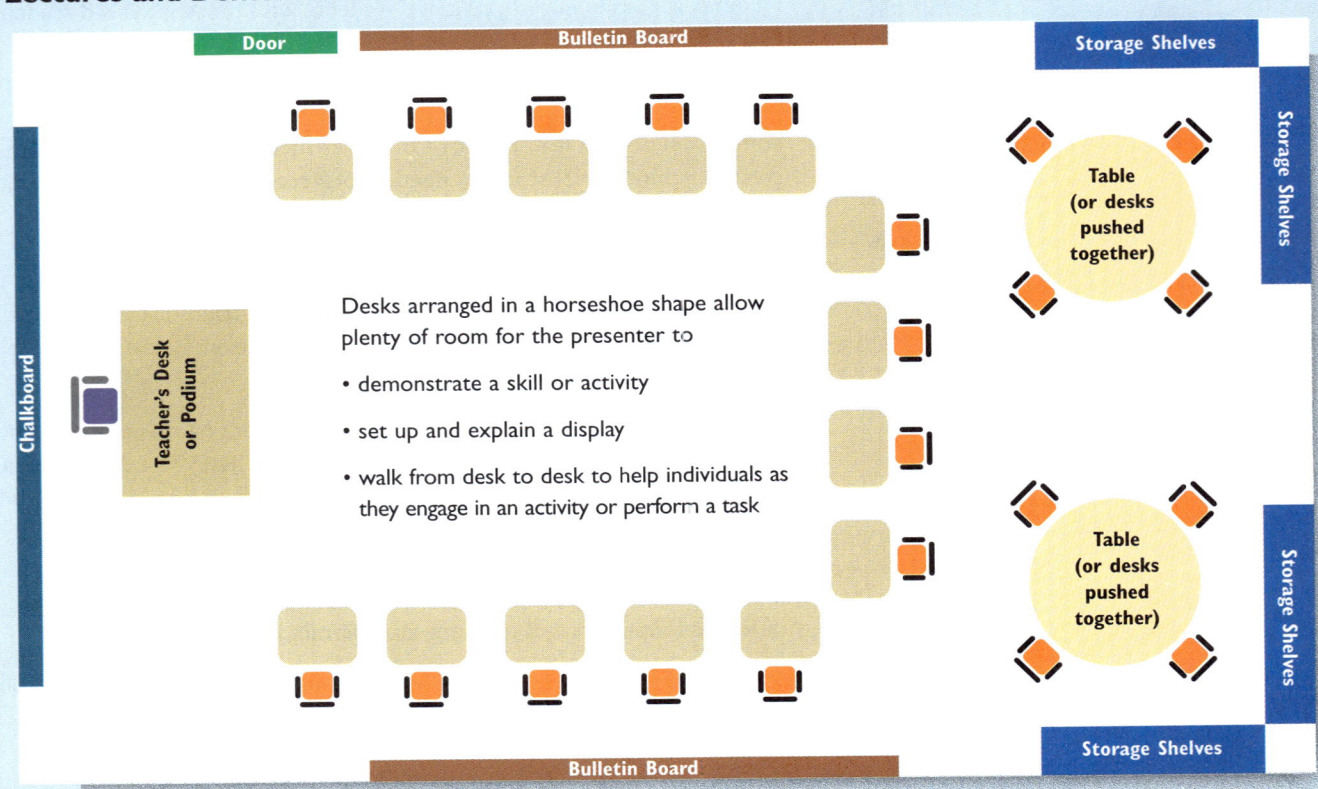

Desks arranged in a horseshoe shape allow plenty of room for the presenter to

- demonstrate a skill or activity
- set up and explain a display
- walk from desk to desk to help individuals as they engage in an activity or perform a task

Peer Tutoring & Cooperative Learning

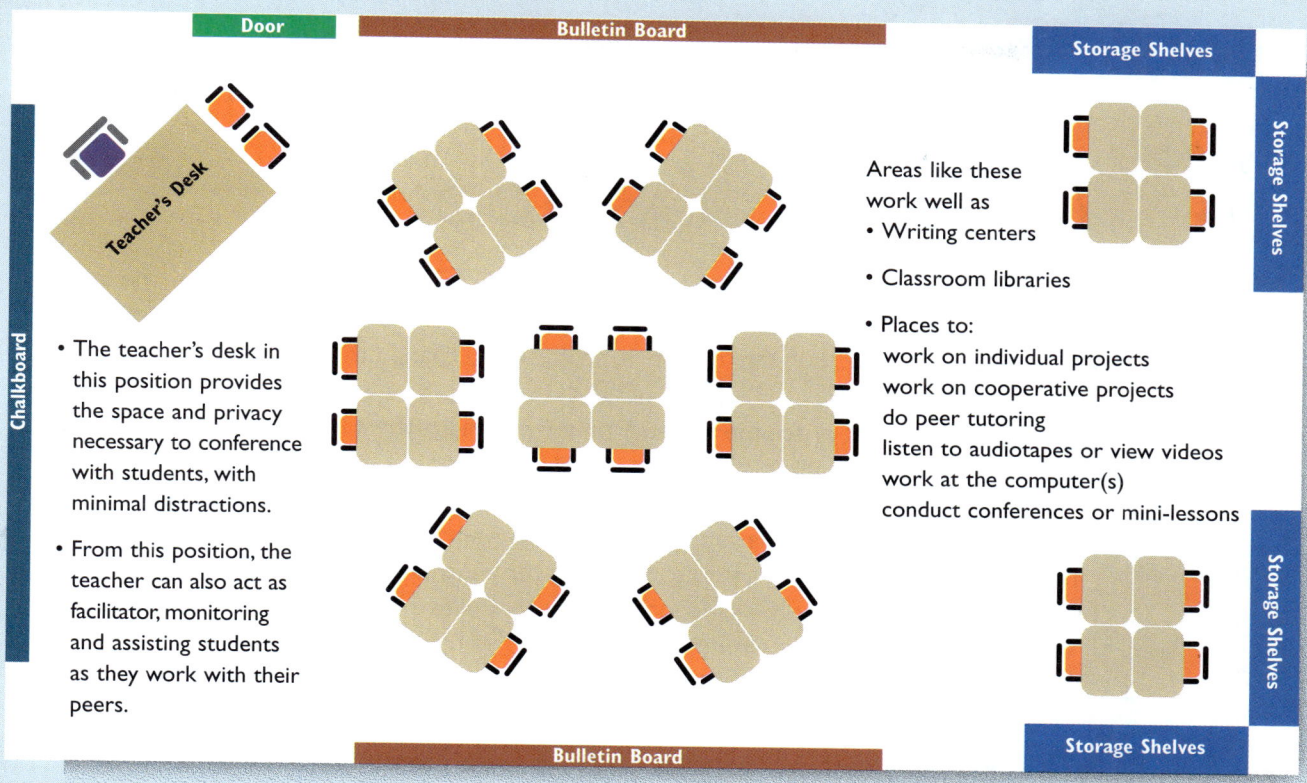

- The teacher's desk in this position provides the space and privacy necessary to conference with students, with minimal distractions.
- From this position, the teacher can also act as facilitator, monitoring and assisting students as they work with their peers.

Areas like these work well as
- Writing centers
- Classroom libraries
- Places to:
  work on individual projects
  work on cooperative projects
  do peer tutoring
  listen to audiotapes or view videos
  work at the computer(s)
  conduct conferences or mini-lessons

Work Stations

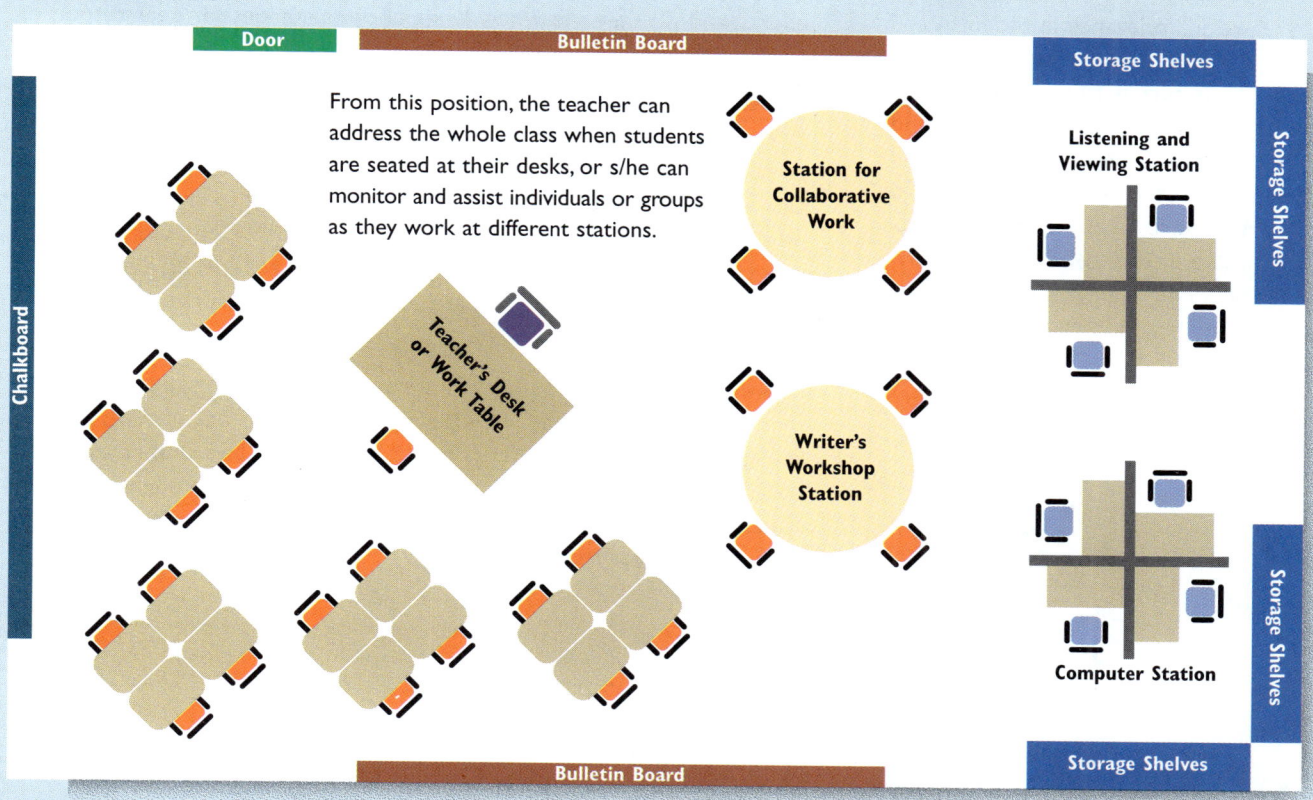

From this position, the teacher can address the whole class when students are seated at their desks, or s/he can monitor and assist individuals or groups as they work at different stations.

THE LANGUAGE OF LITERATURE TEACHER'S EDITION T33

NEW Technology AND THE ENGLISH CLASSROOM

> Technology enables students to become active participants in their own learning.
> Jeffrey N. Golub
> Assistant Professor of English Education, University of South Florida, Tampa

The idea of using technology as part of your instructional plan is not simply the latest passing fad. Instead, it reflects continuing revelations about what is worth knowing and how students learn. For this reason, it promises to change the nature of classroom instruction.

Why is technology so important? Primarily because the use of computers is not a "spectator sport." Rather, computers require users to do the work themselves instead of passively sitting back and watching or listening to someone else—typically a teacher—dispense information. Thus, using technology enables students to become active participants in their own learning. Similarly, the teacher's role changes to that of a "designer" and "director"—one who *designs* innovative and worthwhile instructional activities and then *directs* students as they work through these activities.

Let's look for a moment at how technology is being used in English classrooms across the country.

Bringing Literature to Life

Teachers are always striving to make connections between literature and students' lives by providing "real-world" relevance in the form of historical and biographical information, cross-curricular ties, and connections to current issues. Recordings and films have always been the primary resources used to achieve this goal, but more recent technology—such as video discs and CD-ROM's—is providing teachers with new worlds of information to draw from.

Taking the Fear Out of Writing

In probably their most familiar function, computers offer terrific opportunities for writing because (1) they provide students with more efficient and effective means of drafting, revising, editing, and publishing their writing efforts, and (2) they allow new kinds of opportunities for peer response, collaboration, and sharing.

More Enthusiastic Writers   Research has shown repeatedly that students tend to be more fluent and less inhibited when they work at computers: the many editing features and on-line resources make revision easy. In addition, publishing programs allow students to create products far more exciting than words on paper have ever been. Computers can also make portfolio building simpler and cleaner: journal entries, drafts and revisions, and finished products are easy to store, categorize, and retrieve on computers or disks.

Easier Collaboration   If you have access to a writing lab, you will find that, with readily available software programs and by networking, or linking, the computers, students can be more easily encouraged to collaborate on their planning and writing efforts. When students can compose and comment on-screen, they often become much more articulate and less reserved.

Making Connections

One of the most commonly heard complaints among teachers is that they seldom have a chance to network with each other and share ideas. Through the wonders of the Internet, this problem has all but disappeared. Education sites exist where teachers can find information ranging from developments in state assessments to projects that have worked well in other classrooms. Through the Internet, teachers can also set up classroom exchanges with other schools across the country, allow their students to go on electronic field trips, and plan interactions between the class and famous authors, scientists, and other professionals.

Developing Information Literacy

The use of technology in the English classroom enables teachers to help their students develop what will become one of the most basic skills needed for the 21st century—media and information literacy. Students need to learn how to access information from a wide variety of both print and electronic sources; how to select appropriate information from the vast array of available resources; how to analyze and evaluate information that they read, see, and hear daily; and how to communicate their conclusions and insights clearly, completely, ethically, and persuasively. In particular, the growth of telecommunications opportunities in the form of information webs presents students with the opportunity to actively seek pertinent information and to engage in the processes of selection, analysis, and evaluation.

Conclusion These are just some of the ways in which technology can make learning happen for your students. But they help demonstrate that, if used creatively, technology can bring new excitement and levels of success to any English classroom—even while helping us achieve the same goals we have always had: to make our students solid readers, thinkers, and communicators.

Technology	Uses in the English Classroom	The Language of Literature
Videodisc A 12-inch disc, used with a videodisc player, that can store thousands of still images as well as full-motion video. Images can be accessed immediately through the use of bar codes.	• To provide background information and cross-curricular connections for selection enrichment • For presenting real-world situations and images that can be used as writing springboards • To bring movies, archival material, and recordings of live performances into the classroom • To teach visual literacy	**LASERLINKS** Support for lessons in the student book, including • Author and Selection Background • Visual Vocabulary • Professional Storyteller • Writing Springboards
Floppy Disks and CD-ROM's Both are information storage devices that can hold text, still images, and full-motion video. Compact discs, however, are able to store encyclopedic amounts of information.	• As sources of additional or enhanced selections • As a reference tool: encyclopedias, atlases, and almanacs are all available in CD-ROM form • For writing: publishing software, image banks, and word processing programs all enhance student writing	**THE ELECTRONIC LIBRARY** Additional classic selections to expand program options **WRITING COACH** Special word-processing program with on-line writing tips and handbooks, multiple text columns for revision and peer response, and a multimedia Idea Generator
Internet/World Wide Web/ On-line Services A connected system of on-line computer networks through which mail and data can be transferred.	• To obtain additional information on a selection, author, or topic • To teach information-access skills • To gather professional materials, project ideas, research articles • To network with other teachers and set up classroom exchanges • To interact with authors, public figures, scientists, and other professionals	**THE MCDOUGAL LITTELL HOME PAGE** Can be accessed on the World Wide Web at http://www.hmco.com/mcdougal and contains the following resources: • Internet links for specific selections in *The Language of Literature* • Teacher discussion groups/ bulletin boards • Links to professional organizations • Guest speakers

PREPARING FOR Assessment

The word *assessment* conjures up many different images and raises just as many questions in teachers' minds. Although assessment options are often categorized as either formal or alternative, assessment activities usually embrace qualities of both kinds. Most teachers use a combination of many types of assessment in determining what a student knows or is able to do. The overview on these three pages will introduce you to the types of assessment used in *The Language of Literature* and will help you decide which ones you might want to try with your students this year. (For teacher resources and information on implementing these types of assessment, see the following three booklets: *Teacher's Guide to Assessment and Portfolio Use*, *Formal Assessment*, and *Alternative Assessment*.)

WHAT TYPES OF ASSESSMENT ARE THERE?

TYPES OF ASSESSMENT

FORMAL
Asks "What do you know?"

PURPOSES
Usually paper-and-pencil tests; helps teachers
- measure students' achievement against students in their own class, district, state, or country
- report students' achievement to parents and administrators
- make appropriate instructional and grouping decisions

FORMATS
Test formats are commonly
- true-false
- multiple choice
- matching
- essay
- standardized
- norm-referenced
- criterion-referenced
- objective

ALTERNATIVE
Asks "What can you do?"

PURPOSES
Usually tasks that emulate real-life situations; helps teachers
- get a broad picture of each student as a problem solver, critical thinker, and acquirer of knowledge
- measure student growth over time

TASKS
Tasks are commonly
- authentic
- products or performances
- processes

WHAT FORMS CAN ALTERNATIVE ASSESSMENT TAKE?

For more information on implementing these types of assessment, see the *Teacher's Guide to Assessment and Portfolio Use*.

> Portfolios offer one of the best vehicles for classroom-based assessment because they typically contain a variety of student work and they make it easy to separate evaluation from the process of instruction.
>
> Judith Langer and Arthur Applebee
> Professors of Education, State University of New York at Albany

✓ Product and Performance Assessment

- Requires students to produce tangible products or create performances that demonstrate their understanding of skills and concepts
- Focuses teacher's attention on the end product rather than on the processes, behaviors, or strategies students used to create it
- Is based on judgment and observation guided by criteria

TYPES OF EVALUATION CRITERIA USED
Can include rubrics, formal scales and checklists, and peer and self-evaluations

POSSIBLE PRODUCTS
- scripts, dialogues
- audiotapes, videotapes
- charts, maps, graphs
- games, puzzles
- puppet shows
- plays, skits, talent shows
- interviews, debates
- role-playing
- dances
- mock trials
- cooking or sports demonstrations
- recipes, menus
- children's books
- museum exhibits
- research papers
- inventions
- book or movie reviews
- questionnaires, surveys
- print or TV ads
- poems, riddles, jokes
- time capsules
- awards
- oral histories
- murals, collages
- computer programs
- scale models, dioramas
- essays, editorials
- family trees

✓ Portfolio Assessment

- Is a purposeful collection of student work that exhibits overall efforts, progress, and achievement over time in one or more areas of the curriculum
- Is a combination of process and product assessment, with a strong measure of self-evaluation and self-reflection

TYPES OF EVALUATION CRITERIA USED
Can include inventories, conference notes, rubrics, formal scales and checklists, anecdotal records, observations, and peer evaluations

POSSIBLE PRODUCTS TO INCLUDE IN THE PORTFOLIO
- interest inventories
- outlines
- written assignments
- videotapes
- reading records
- audiotapes
- performance plans
- photographs
- logs
- sketches or drawings
- journal entries
- works in progress
- textbook tasks
- research findings
- reports
- book reports or reviews
- project evaluations
- standardized tests

✓ Process Assessment

- Requires students to demonstrate or share their processes, behaviors, strategies, and critical thinking abilities as they work to understand skills and concepts
- Focuses teacher's attention on student processes, behaviors, and strategies rather than on the final results
- Is based on judgment and observation guided by criteria

TYPES OF EVALUATION CRITERIA USED
Can include rubrics, formal scales and checklists, anecdotal records, observations, and self- and peer evaluations

POSSIBLE PROCESSES
While the evaluator observes students' abilities to apply higher-order thinking skills during certain processes, he or she focuses on the following:

- the use of reading strategies to develop interpretations of a text
- behavior during peer review
- evidence of investment in a task
- the ability to work in a collaborative group
- drafts created while writing an essay
- the ability to participate in class discussions
- the use of conferences to refine work
- evolving personal criteria and standards

> If criteria for evaluation are consistent with those stressed during instruction, and if response is shared between student and teacher, assessment can become an effective complement to any learning situation.
>
> Judith Langer and Arthur Applebee
> Professors of Education, State University of New York at Albany

HOW CAN I PREPARE MY STUDENTS FOR THESE TYPES OF ASSESSMENT?

A major difference between formal assessment and alternative assessment is what you choose to assess and how you choose to assess it. Alternative assessment is a natural outgrowth and extension of classroom practices. Therefore, it is important to establish an effective learning—and testing—environment right away. Following are a few pointers to help you get started.

✓ Establish an environment based on trust.

Because alternative assessment makes students much more in charge of their own learning, and much more responsible for demonstrating their learning in a variety of ways, it is important to establish a classroom environment that is based on trust. Many of the activities students will be engaging in will be unfamiliar to them—and to you. Let them see that you are right in there with them, taking risks and trying new experiences. Help them understand that it's all right to try and fail—even seemingly unsuccessful experiences bring about growth and learning.

✓ Establish a tone of reflection and self-evaluation.

At the beginning of the year, ask your students to write letters describing themselves as readers, writers, and classroom participants. Also have them describe what they hope to accomplish during the coming year. Have them keep their letters in their notebooks, journals, or portfolios; encourage them to reread the letters regularly. Reflecting on their performance will help them acknowledge and evaluate their growth over the year. It will also help them see that learning and evaluating are ongoing and ever-changing processes.

✓ Help your students set goals and make commitments.

In order to grow as learners, your students must become actively involved in setting goals and making commitments. Their goals can be for a day, a week, a project, or the year; but whatever their duration, encourage students to consider their strengths and limitations so that the goals they set will be realistic.

✓ Help students view assessment in a new light.

One of the best things you can do for your students is help them break away from the notion that a "test" is something to study for the night before and then to forget. Help them see that alternative assessment involves a demonstration of what they know at a particular moment, but that what they know is bound to keep changing as new knowledge builds on old.

✓ Help your students discover their individual learning styles and preferences.

Chances are, most of your students are not fully aware of their own learning styles and preferences. Why not help them recognize which tasks and situations suit them best and help them learn more effectively? (See page T28.) After all, the better your students understand themselves, the better you'll understand how to teach and assess them.

✓ Encourage peer review as a regular part of the assessment process.

Sometimes it's easier for students to "get inside the minds" of their peers. And sometimes it's easier for them to take instruction or criticism from their peers. This is an excellent strategy, as long as growth and learning are taking place.

✓ Help your students learn to operate independently of you.

As students get comfortable with their learning environment, they'll probably want to do more and more without your help. Try to provide as many opportunities as possible for them to develop into independent learners—you'll be doing one of the best things you can do to prepare them for life in the real world!

✓ Improve and increase your own assessment tools.

As an evaluator, your goal should be to get as broad a view as possible of each of your students. Increasing your ability to provide situations in which you can observe your students will help you get more complete pictures of them. It will also help you learn more about yourself!

MAKING Connections

The Language of Literature bases all of its instruction on a "connected" approach to learning. On every page—from the Previewing pages to the Writing Workshops and Reading the World feature—students are encouraged to find the links between the literature, other subject areas, their own lives, and the world around them.

Of course, there are always more connections to be made, and certain themes and selections are particularly rich with possibilities. When you identify a selection or idea that you feel might have particular interest for your students, you may want to involve the class, as well as other teachers, in expanding the lesson into a more customized exploration. The following chart describes one way to accomplish this.

STEP 1 What Will We Explore?

As a class, or in small groups, have students ask questions such as the following:
- What really excited me or fascinated me about this selection?
- What questions did I have as I read this?
- What didn't I understand?
- What would I like to find out more about?
- What people, experiences, issues, or situations did this remind me of that might be interesting to explore?

TIP: Clustering, discussion, brainstorming, freewriting, and notebooks and logs are among the methods that can be used to generate ideas.

STEP 2 What Skills or Information Will We Need?

Once the questions are in place, have students identify the skills needed to find the answers. For example, the story "The Circuit" might prompt questions about the life of the migrant worker. Will students need certain map-reading or geographical skills to learn the answers? Would information about farming or economics be important?

STEP 3 What Resources Will We Use?

At this point, students can be encouraged to plan the kinds of resources they might use to continue their exploration. Remind them of the following possibilities:
- print resources
- interviews
- surveys and questionnaires
- CD-ROM
- the Internet and other on-line resources

TIP: This is also the point at which you might collaborate with other teachers to take advantage of team teaching and block scheduling to coordinate overlapping topics. Classroom exchanges within or between schools may also be useful to arrange at this point. Technology can provide exciting options for networking as well.

STEP 4 How Will the Results Be Shared?

The methods for sharing information will be as varied as the projects themselves. Following are just a few of the possibilities students might consider:

- essays
- photo journals
- dramas
- videos
- speeches
- oral histories
- paintings
- music
- multimedia
- panel
- fairs
- community program

See page T40 for an example of the explorations generated from the selection "The Moustache."

> Teachers need to help their students feel integral and involved in their community and the larger world.
>
> Susan Hynds
> Professor of English Education,
> Syracuse University, Syracuse, New York

A SAMPLE PLANNING MAP

Below is an example of the different explorations that were generated from one story by a teacher following the approach outlined on page T39.

SELECTION: "THE MOUSTACHE"

SUMMARY: a boy gains a new understanding of his grandmother when he visits her in a nursing home.

COMMUNITY
- Visit a nursing home/hospital
- Write a letter to the American Association of Retired Persons (AARP)
- Plan community involvement doing volunteer work with the elderly, in nursing homes or hospitals

FIRSTHAND EXPERIENCE
- Interview an elderly member of your own family
- Create a family history

WORLD
- Study the representation of the elderly in our media
- Observe and discuss social attitudes toward elderly
- Carry out survey on attitudes to elderly (Internet, print)
- Interview care worker
- Research legislation regarding the elderly

CROSS-CURRICULAR LINKS
- Math: Plot the changes in life expectancy over the past century
- Social studies: Discuss the effect of the Great Depression on society
- Art: Consider the portrayal of the elderly in fine art

T40 THE LANGUAGE OF LITERATURE TEACHER'S EDITION

McDougal Littell

THE LANGUAGE OF
LITERATURE

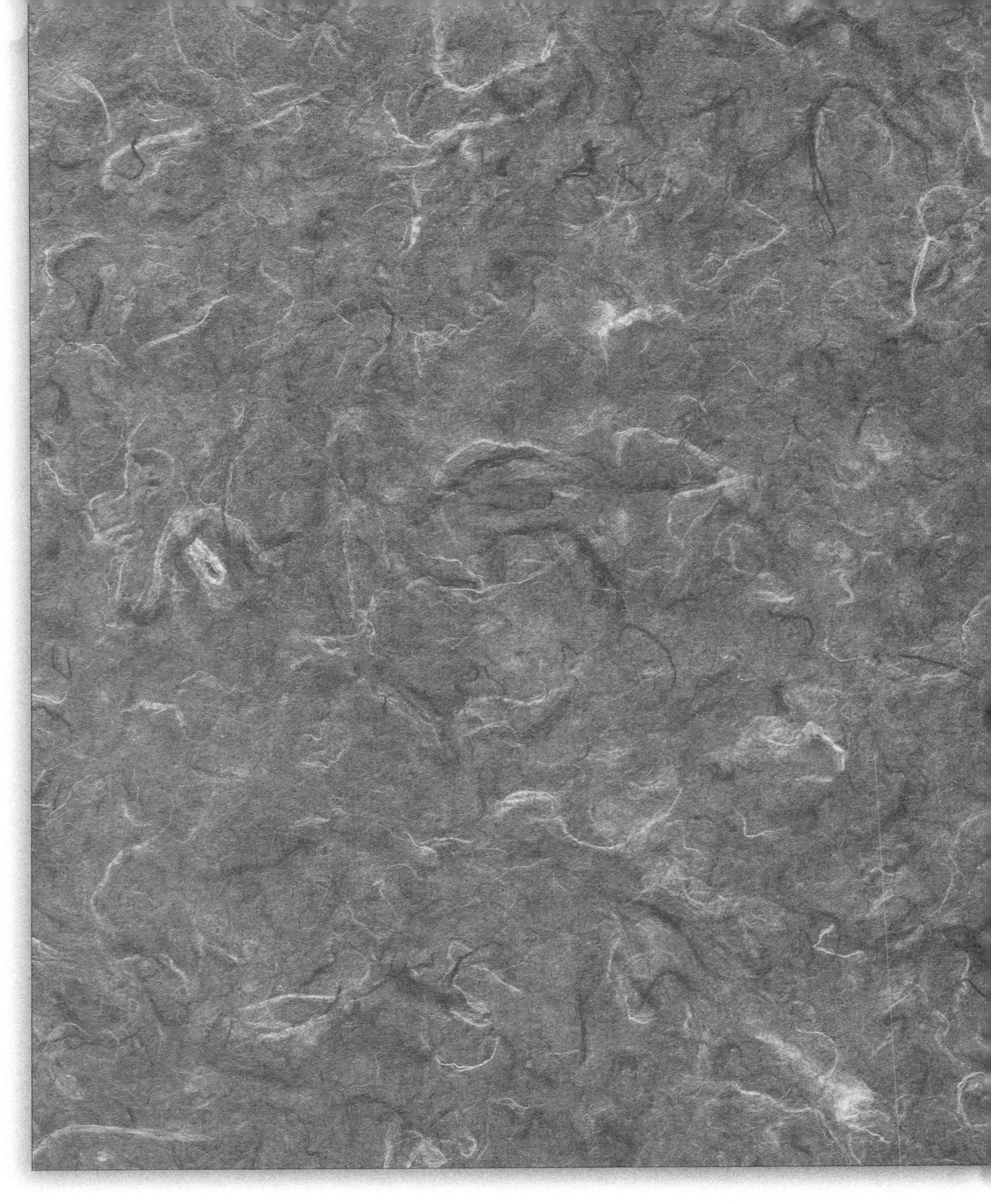

McDougal Littell

THE LANGUAGE OF
LITERATURE

Arthur N. Applebee
Andrea B. Bermúdez
Sheridan Blau
Rebekah Caplan
Franchelle Dorn
Peter Elbow
Susan Hynds
Judith A. Langer
James Marshall

McDougal Littell
A HOUGHTON MIFFLIN COMPANY

Evanston, Illinois ▪ Boston ▪ Dallas

Acknowledgments

Unit One

Susan Bergholz Literary Services: "Three Wise Guys" by Sandra Cisneros; Copyright © 1990 by Sandra Cisneros. First published by *Vista Magazine*, December 23, 1990. By permission of Susan Bergholz Literary Services, New York.

Miriam Altshuler: "The Treasure of Lemon Brown" by Walter Dean Myers, from *Boys' Life Magazine*, March 1983; Copyright © 1983 by Walter Dean Myers. By permission of Miriam Altshuler Literary Agency on behalf of Walter Dean Myers.

Delacorte Press/Seymour Lawrence: "The Lie," from *Welcome to the Monkey House* by Kurt Vonnegut, Jr.; Copyright © 1962 by Kurt Vonnegut, Jr. By permission of Delacorte Press/Seymour Lawrence, a division of Bantam Doubleday Dell Publishing Group, Inc.

Doubleday Books: "Country Boys," from *Reflections on the Civil War* by Bruce Catton; Copyright © 1981 by Gerald Dickler as the executor of the estate of Bruce Catton and John Leckley. By permission of Doubleday Books, a division of Bantam Doubleday Dell Publishing Group, Inc.

Elizabeth Barnett, literary executor: "Dirge Without Music" from *Collected Poems*, by Edna St. Vincent Millay, published by HarperCollins. Copyright 1928, 1955 by Edna St. Vincent Millay and Norma Millay Ellis. By permission of Elizabeth Barnett, literary executor.

Continued on page 918

Cover Art

Background photo: Atlanta skyline, Copyright © Phyllis Picadi / Uniphoto Stock Agency. **Village scene:** *Old Houses in Lindau* (1928), Rudolf Wacker. Statliche Kunstsammulunger, Dresden, Germany, Photo © Erick Lessing / Art Resource, New York. **Soldier:** Reproduced from the Collections of the Library of Congress. **Bugle:** Courtesy Steve and Patricia Mullinaz Collection; Photo by J. Stoll. **Horse:** *Whistlejacket* (1762), George Stubbs. Kenwood House, Hampstead, London / Bridgeman Art Library, London / Superstock. **Book:** Photo by Alan Shortall. **Frame:** Photo by Sharon Hoogstraten.

Warning: No part of this work may be reproduced or transmitted in any form or by any means, electronic or mechanical, including photocopying and recording, or by any information storage or retrieval system without prior written permission of McDougal Littell Inc. unless such copying is expressly permitted by federal copyright law. Address inquiries to Manager, Rights and Permissions, McDougal Littell Inc., P.O. Box 1667, Evanston, IL 60204

ISBN 0-395-73703-6

Copyright © 1997 by McDougal Littell Inc. All rights reserved. Printed in the United States of America.

3 4 5 6 7 8 9 – RRD – 01 00 99 98 97

Senior Consultants

The senior consultants guided the conceptual development for *The Language of Literature* series. They participated actively in shaping prototype materials for major components, and they reviewed completed prototypes and/or completed units to ensure consistency with current research and the philosophy of the series.

Arthur N. Applebee Professor of Education, State University of New York at Albany; Director, Center for the Learning and Teaching of Literature; Senior Fellow, Center for Writing and Literacy

Andrea B. Bermúdez Professor of Studies in Language and Culture; Director, Research Center for Language and Culture; Chair, Foundations and Professional Studies, University of Houston-Clear Lake

Sheridan Blau Senior Lecturer in English and Education and former Director of Composition, University of California at Santa Barbara; Director, South Coast Writing Project; Director, Literature Institute for Teachers; Vice President, National Council of Teachers of English

Rebekah Caplan Coordinator, English Language Arts K-12, Oakland Unified School District, Oakland, California; Teacher-Consultant, Bay Area Writing Project, University of California at Berkeley; served on the California State English Assessment Development Team for Language Arts

Franchelle Dorn Professor of Drama, Howard University, Washington, D.C.; Adjunct Professor, Graduate School of Opera, University of Maryland, College Park, Maryland; Co-founder of The Shakespeare Acting Conservatory, Washington, D.C.

Peter Elbow Professor of English, University of Massachusetts at Amherst; Fellow, Bard Center for Writing and Thinking

Susan Hynds Professor and Director of English Education, Syracuse University, Syracuse, New York

Judith A. Langer Professor of Education, State University of New York at Albany; Co-director, Center for the Learning and Teaching of Literature; Senior Fellow, Center for Writing and Literacy

James Marshall Professor of English and English Education, University of Iowa, Iowa City

Contributing Consultants

Tommy Boley Associate Professor of English, University of Texas at El Paso

Jeffrey N. Golub Assistant Professor of English Education, University of South Florida, Tampa

William L. McBride Reading and Curriculum Specialist; former middle and high school English instructor

Multicultural Advisory Board

The multicultural advisors reviewed literature selections for appropriate content and made suggestions for teaching lessons in a multicultural classroom.

Dr. Joyce M. Bell, Chairperson, English Department, Townview Magnet Center, Dallas, Texas

Dr. Eugenia W. Collier, author; lecturer; Chairperson, Department of English and Language Arts; teacher of Creative Writing and American Literature, Morgan State University, Maryland

Kathleen S. Fowler, President, Palm Beach County Council of Teachers of English, Boca Raton Middle School, Boca Raton, Florida

Noreen M. Rodriguez, Trainer for Hillsborough County School District's Staff Development Division, independent consultant, Gaither High School, Tampa, Florida

Michelle Dixon Thompson, Seabreeze High School, Daytona Beach, Florida

Teacher Review Panels

The following educators provided ongoing review during the development of the tables of contents, lesson design, and key components of the program.

CALIFORNIA

Steve Bass, 8th Grade Team Leader, Meadowbrook Middle School, Ponway Unified School District

Cynthia Brickey, 8th Grade Academic Block Teacher, Kastner Intermediate School, Clovis Unified School District

Karen Buxton, English Department Chairperson, Winston Churchill Middle School, San Juan School District

continued on page 928

Manuscript Reviewers

The following educators reviewed prototype lessons and tables of contents during the development of *The Language of Literature* program.

William A. Battaglia, Herman Intermediate School, San Jose, California

Hugh Delle Broadway, McCullough High School, The Woodlands, Texas

Robert M. Bucan, National Mine Middle School, Ishpeming, Michigan

Ann E. Clayton, Department Chair for Language Arts, Rockway Middle School, Miami, Florida

Linda C. Dahl, National Mine Middle School, Ishpeming, Michigan

Shirley Herzog, Reading Department Coordinator, Fairfield Middle School, Fairfield, Ohio

continued on page 929

Student Board

The student board members read and evaluated selections to assess their appeal for eighth-grade students.

Iruma Bello, Henry H. Filer Middle School, Hialeah, Florida

Leslie M. Blaha, Walnut Springs Middle School, Westerville, Ohio

Osvelia Cantoran, Chester W. Nimitz Middle School, Huntington Park, California

Elizabeth Donaldson, Bettendorf Middle School, Bettendorf, Iowa

Patricia Ernst, East Aurora Middle School, East Aurora, New York

Theresa Ernst, East Aurora Middle School, East Aurora, New York

Aaron Fitzstephens, Fairfield Middle School, Fairfield, Ohio

Stephen Tremayne Johnson, Lincoln College Prep School, Kansas City, Missouri

John Paul Marshall, RAA Middle School, Tallahassee, Florida

Meghan McGuire, St. John of the Cross School, Western Springs, Illinois

Jaret Heath Radford, Fondren Middle School, Houston, Texas

Erick Strauss, Cobb Middle School, Tallahassee, Florida

Christine Warner, Keith Valley Middle School, Horsham, Pennsylvania

The Language of Literature

CORE COMPONENTS

Student Anthology
A rich mix of classic and contemporary literature

& Literature Connections
Longer works with related readings

FREE!
Choose from a variety of *Literature Connections* titles when you adopt *The Language of Literature* from McDougal Littell
Call 800-323-5435 for details

viii THE LANGUAGE OF LITERATURE TEACHER'S EDITION

Literature Connections

Each hardback volume contains

- Novel or Play
- Related Readings—poems, stories, plays, and articles that provide new perspectives on the longer works
- Teacher's SourceBook filled with background information and activities

Additional Literature Connections such as:

Across Five Aprils
Irene Hunt

The Call of the Wild*
Jack London

The Clay Marble
Minfong Ho

The Contender
Robert Lipsyte

The Diary of Anne Frank
Frances Goodrich and Albert Hackett

Dogsong
Gary Paulsen

Dragonwings
Laurence Yep

The Giver
Lois Lowry

The Glory Field
Walter Dean Myers

The House of Dies Drear
Virginia Hamilton

I, Juan de Pareja*
Elizabeth Borton de Treviño

Johnny Tremain
Esther Forbes

Maniac Magee
Jerry Spinelli

Nothing but the Truth
Avi

Roll of Thunder, Hear My Cry*
Mildred D. Taylor

So Far from the Bamboo Grove
Yoko Kawashima Watkins

Tuck Everlasting*
Natalie Babbitt

Where the Red Fern Grows
Wilson Rawls

The Witch of Blackbird Pond
Elizabeth George Speare

A Wrinkle in Time
Madeleine L'Engle

*A Spanish version is also available.

The Diary of Anne Frank
by Frances Goodrich and Albert Hackett
and Related Readings

from **Anne Frank: The Diary of a Young Girl** / DIARY
Anne Frank

from **Anne Frank Remembered** / MEMOIR
Miep Gies with Alison Leslie Gold

Elegy for Anne Frank / POEM
Jessica Smith

Bubili: A Young Gypsy's Fight for Survival / ORAL HISTORY
Ina R. Friedman

The Bracelet / PERSONAL NARRATIVE
Yoshiko Uchida

from **Rescue: the Story of How Gentiles Saved Jews in the Holocaust** / NONFICTION
Milton Meltzer

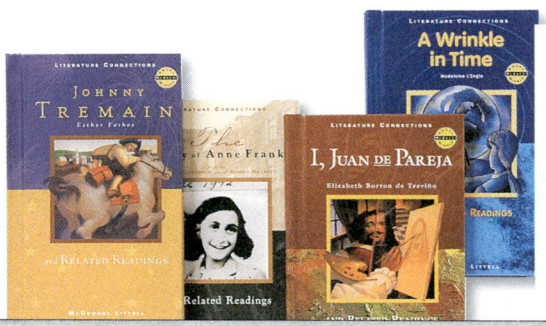
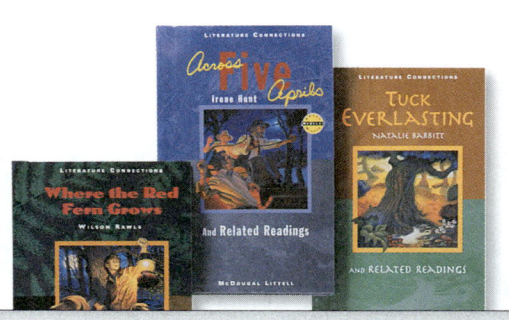

UNIT ONE *Changing Perceptions* 12

Part 1 Taught by Experience

WHAT DO YOU THINK? Reflecting on Theme 14

▶ FOCUS ON FICTION 15

Walter Dean Myers — **The Treasure of Lemon Brown** .... FICTION 17
HISTORICAL INSIGHT / Blues Music

Kurt Vonnegut, Jr. — **The Lie** .... FICTION 29

▶ FOCUS ON NONFICTION 43

Bruce Catton — from **Reflections on the Civil War** .... NONFICTION 45

Edna St. Vincent Millay — **Dirge Without Music** / LITERARY INSIGHT .... POETRY 53

Patrick F. McManus — **The Clown** .... NONFICTION 57

Dorothy Canfield Fisher — **The Apprentice**
ON YOUR OWN / ASSESSMENT OPTION .... FICTION 64

✏️ WRITING ABOUT LITERATURE **Creative Response**

Writer's Style: Point of View 74
Guided Assignment: Changing a Story Element 76
Grammar in Context: Sentence Fragments and Run-on Sentences 79
  SKILLBUILDERS: Using Pronouns, Writing Introductions,
                Avoiding Fragments

READING THE WORLD: VISUAL LITERACY 80
Close-Up on Perspective
SKILLBUILDER: Analyzing Perspective

Part 2 Fooled by Appearances

WHAT DO YOU THINK? Reflecting on Theme 82

James Herriot	*from* **All Things Bright and Beautiful**	NONFICTION	83
Lensey Namioka	**The Inn of Lost Time**	FICTION	90
Robert Silverberg	**Collecting Team**	FICTION	107
	HISTORICAL INSIGHT / Space Exploration		

▶ **FOCUS ON POETRY** 123

David Nava Monreal	**Moco Limping**	POETRY	125
Arnold Adoff	**Mixed Singles**	POETRY	125
Eve Merriam	**Simile: Willow and Ginkgo**	POETRY	131
Elinor Wylie	**Sea Lullaby**	POETRY	131

✏️ **WRITING FROM EXPERIENCE** Firsthand and Expressive Writing

Guided Assignment: Write Your Family History 136
Prewriting: Exploring the Past
Drafting: Shaping Your History
Revising and Publishing: Finishing Your Narrative
  SKILLBUILDERS: Asking Questions, Using Descriptive Language,
    Punctuating Introductory Phrases

UNIT REVIEW: Reflect & Assess 144

THE LANGUAGE OF LITERATURE TEACHER'S EDITION xi

UNIT TWO *Critical Adjustments* 146

Part 1 Twinges of Conscience

WHAT DO YOU THINK? Reflecting on Theme 148

Gerald Haslam	**The Horned Toad**	FICTION	149
Francisco X. Alarcón	**In a Neighborhood in Los Angeles** / LITERARY INSIGHT	POETRY	158
Beryl Markham	**The Splendid Outcast**	FICTION	161
Alice Walker	**We Alone**	POETRY	175
Margaret Tsuda	**Hard Questions**	POETRY	175
Naoshi Koriyama	**oil crisis**	POETRY	175

HISTORICAL INSIGHT / The Oil Crisis of the 1970s

▸FOCUS ON DRAMA: Reading Strategies 181

Mark Twain, dramatized by Walter Hackett	**The Million-Pound Bank Note**	DRAMA	183
Gary Soto	**Mother and Daughter** ON YOUR OWN / ASSESSMENT OPTION	FICTION	203

WRITING ABOUT LITERATURE Interpretation

Writer's Style: Creating Emphasis 210
Guided Assignment: Interpret a Selection's Meaning 212
Grammar in Context: Subject-Verb Agreement 215
 SKILLBUILDERS: Using Interjections, Organizing Your Interpretive Essay, Using Inverted Sentences

READING THE WORLD: VISUAL LITERACY 216
What's the Message?
SKILLBUILDER: Analyzing for Meaning

Part 2 Unexpected Developments

WHAT DO YOU THINK? Reflecting on Theme 218

Marjorie Kinnan Rawlings	**A Mother in Mannville** .... FICTION 219		
Nikki Giovanni	**The World Is Not a Pleasant Place to Be** / LITERARY INSIGHT .... POETRY 225		
Rubén Sálaz-Márquez	**White Mice** .... FICTION 228		
Anton Chekhov	**The Bet** .... FICTION 240
	▸ Reading Strategies: Cause and Effect
Clifton L. Taulbert	from **Once Upon a Time When We Were Colored** ..... NONFICTION 252
Hazel Shelton Abernethy	**The Home Front: 1941–1945** .... NONFICTION 259
	HISTORICAL INSIGHT / The Military Draft
Norman Russell	**my enemy was dreaming** .... POETRY 267
Bruce Ignacio	**Lost** .... POETRY 267

WRITING FROM EXPERIENCE Narrative and Literary Writing

Guided Assignment: Write a Short Story 272
Prewriting: Working Out Your Ideas
Drafting: Telling the Story
Revising and Publishing: Polishing Your Story
   SKILLBUILDERS: Ordering Events, Planning the Climax, Using Precise Verbs

UNIT REVIEW: REFLECT & ASSESS 280

ACROSS TIME AND PLACE: The Oral Tradition

For more stories related to the unit theme, see page 716.

UNIT THREE *Battle for Control* 282

Part 1 Struggling for Survival

	WHAT DO YOU THINK? Reflecting on Theme		284
Paulette Childress White	**Getting the Facts of Life**	FICTION	285
Robert H. Abel	**Appetizer**	FICTION	298
	▶ Reading Strategies: Evaluating		
Langston Hughes	**Mother to Son**	POETRY	313
Don Marquis	**the lesson of the moth**	POETRY	313
"Von," a Vietnamese youth interviewed by Janet Bode	**Von**	NONFICTION	319
Barbara B. Robinson	**Foreign Student** / LITERARY INSIGHT	POETRY	329
Lucille Fletcher	**The Hitchhiker**	DRAMA	332
	HISTORICAL INSIGHT / Route 66		
Ralph Helfer (REFLECT & ASSESS)	**The Flood** ON YOUR OWN / ASSESSMENT OPTION	NONFICTION	347

WRITING ABOUT LITERATURE Criticism

Writer's Style: Elaboration 360
Guided Assignment: Write a Critical Essay 362
Grammar in Context: Complex Sentences 365
   SKILLBUILDERS: Using Appositives, Creating Effective Paragraphs, Using Commas with Subordinate Clauses

READING THE WORLD: VISUAL LITERACY 366
   Elaborate Details
   SKILLBUILDER: Establishing Criteria for Evaluation

Part 2 Going to Extremes

	WHAT DO YOU THINK? Reflecting on Theme		368
James Berry	**The Banana Tree**	FICTION	369
Luis Palés Matos	**The Hurricane** / LITERARY INSIGHT	POETRY	377
Edgar Allan Poe	**The Tell-Tale Heart**	FICTION	380
Norah Roper, as told to Alice Marriott	**Tsali of the Cherokees** HISTORICAL INSIGHT / The Trail of Tears	NONFICTION	390
Dave Barry	**Painful Memories of Dating**	NONFICTION	400
Robert Frost	**The Runaway**	POETRY	406
T. S. Eliot	**Macavity: The Mystery Cat**	POETRY	406

✏️ **WRITING FROM EXPERIENCE**   Informative Exposition

  Guided Assignment: Write a Problem-Solution Essay 412
  Prewriting: Exploring Solutions
  Drafting: Writing Your Ideas
  Revising and Publishing: Finishing Your Essay
    SKILLBUILDERS: Conducting Group Discussions,
        Elaborating on Ideas, Using Direct Objects

UNIT REVIEW: REFLECT & ASSESS 420

ACROSS TIME AND PLACE: The Oral Tradition

For more stories related to the unit theme, see page 732.

THE LANGUAGE OF LITERATURE TEACHER'S EDITION **XV**

UNIT FOUR *Facing the Enemy* 422

Part 1 So Much at Stake

WHAT DO YOU THINK? Reflecting on Theme 424

O. Henry	**The Gift of the Magi**	FICTION	425
Gwendolyn Brooks	**Speech to the Young / Speech to the Progress-Toward**	POETRY	434
Nina Cassian	**A Man**	POETRY	434
Russell Freedman	from **Lincoln: A Photobiography**	NONFICTION	439
Walt Whitman	**O Captain! My Captain!**	POETRY	439

HISTORICAL INSIGHT / Presidential Assassinations

Ben Carson, M.D., with Cecil Murphey	from **Gifted Hands**	NONFICTION	450
Alfred Brenner	**Survival**	DRAMA	459
Theodore J. Waldeck	**Battle by the Breadfruit Tree** ON YOUR OWN / ASSESSMENT OPTION	NONFICTION	483

WRITING ABOUT LITERATURE   Direct Response

Writer's Style: Show, Don't Tell 490
Guided Assignment: Write a Personal Response 492
Grammar in Context: Pronoun and Antecedent Agreement 495
   SKILLBUILDERS: Using Descriptive Language, Achieving Sentence Variety, Using Indefinite Pronouns

READING THE WORLD: VISUAL LITERACY 496
   Speaking Without Words
   SKILLBUILDER: Interpreting Nonverbal Cues

Part 2 Unlikely Heroes

WHAT DO YOU THINK? Reflecting on Theme ... 498

Jack C. Haldeman II	**Playing for Keeps**	FICTION	499
Mona Gardner	**The Dinner Party**	FICTION	507
Daniel Keyes	**Flowers for Algernon**	FICTION	512
	▸ Reading Strategies: Making Inferences		
Henry Wadsworth Longfellow	**Paul Revere's Ride**	POETRY	542
	HISTORICAL INSIGHT / Paul Revere: The Man		
Ann Petry	from **Harriet Tubman: Conductor on the Underground Railroad**	NONFICTION	550
Frederick Douglass	**Letter to Harriet Tubman** / LITERARY INSIGHT	NONFICTION	559

> **WRITING FROM EXPERIENCE**   Informative Exposition
> **Guided Assignment:** Write an Eyewitness Report ... 562
> **Prewriting:** Uncovering the Story
> **Drafting:** Sharing Your Experience
> **Revising and Publishing:** Finishing Your Report
> SKILLBUILDERS: Selecting Relevant Information, Relating Incidents, Sentence Combining

UNIT REVIEW: REFLECT & ASSESS ... 570

ACROSS TIME AND PLACE: The Oral Tradition
For more stories related to the unit theme, see page 760.

xvii

UNIT FIVE *Personal Discoveries* — 572

Part 1 Finding Your Place

WHAT DO YOU THINK? Reflecting on Theme 574

Vickie Sears	**Dancer**	FICTION	575
Alonzo Lopez	**Celebration** / LITERARY INSIGHT	POETRY	580
Robert Cormier	**The Moustache**	FICTION	583
Roberto Félix Salazar	**The Other Pioneers**	POETRY	594
Diana Chang	**Saying Yes**	POETRY	594
Edward Everett Hale, dramatized by Walter Hackett	**The Man Without a Country**	DRAMA	600

▶ Reading Strategies: Sequencing

HISTORICAL INSIGHT / Aaron Burr: Portrait of a Sly Man

REFLECT & ASSESS

Stephen Crane	**Think As I Think**	POETRY	620
Dorothy Parker	**The Choice**	POETRY	621
A. Whiterock	**I Belong**	POETRY	622
John Kieran	**There's This That I Like About Hockey, My Lad**	POETRY	624
Diane Mei Lin Mark	**Rice and Rose Bowl Blues**	POETRY	626

ON YOUR OWN / ASSESSMENT OPTION

✏ WRITING ABOUT LITERATURE | Analysis

Writer's Style: Sentence Variety 628
Guided Assignment: Analyze a Poem 630
Grammar in Context: Verb Tense 633
  SKILLBUILDERS: Using Adverb and Adjective Phrases, Punctuating Poetry, Using Verb Tense with Quotations

READING THE WORLD: VISUAL LITERACY 634
  Breaking It Down
  SKILLBUILDER: Analyzing Parts of a Whole

Part 2 Vital Connections

WHAT DO YOU THINK? Reflecting on Theme 636

Gary Paulsen	**Stop the Sun**	FICTION	637
	HISTORICAL INSIGHT / The Vietnam War		
Toni Cade Bambara	**Raymond's Run**	FICTION	648
Bill Meissner	**Keeping Time**	FICTION	659
Christopher de Vinck	**Power of the Powerless: A Brother's Lesson**	NONFICTION	668
Leroy V. Quintana	**A Fairy Tale**	POETRY	674
Wing Tek Lum	**My Mother Really Knew**	POETRY	674
John Masefield	**Sea-Fever**	POETRY	679
Pat Mora	**Mi Madre**	POETRY	679

WRITING FROM EXPERIENCE Persuasion

Guided Assignment: Write a Persuasive Essay 684
Prewriting: Building Your Case
Drafting: Making Your Point
Revising and Publishing: Finishing Your Essay
SKILLBUILDERS: Evaluating Sources, Avoiding Loaded Language, Avoiding Double Negatives

UNIT REVIEW: REFLECT & ASSESS 692

ACROSS TIME AND PLACE: The Oral Tradition

For more stories related to the unit theme, see page 784.

UNIT SIX
Across Time and Place: The Oral Tradition 694

STORYTELLERS PAST AND PRESENT 696
KEEPING THE PAST ALIVE 698

Links to Unit One
retold by Paul Robert Walker

retold by Guadalupe Baca-Vaughn

retold by Maureen Scott

Changing Perceptions 700
Paul Bunyan and the Winter of the Blue Snow .... NORTH AMERICAN TALL TALE 702
The Souls in Purgatory .... MEXICAN FOLK TALE 706

The Girl in the Lavender Dress ... URBAN LEGEND 710
CROSS-CURRICULAR PROJECTS 714

Links to Unit Two
traditional

retold by Jackie Torrence

retold by Judith Ortiz Cofer

retold by J.J. Reneaux

Critical Adjustments 716
John Henry .... NORTH AMERICAN FOLK BALLAD 718
Brer Possum's Dilemma .... AFRICAN-AMERICAN FABLE 721
Aunty Misery .... PUERTO RICAN FOLK TALE 724
M'su Carencro and Mangeur de Poulet .... CAJUN FOLK TALE 727
CROSS-CURRICULAR PROJECTS 730

Links to Unit Three
retold by Mary Pope Osborne

retold by Frank Henius

retold by Gail Robinson and Douglas Hill

retold by Jenny Leading Cloud

Battle for Control 732
Pecos Bill .... SOUTHWESTERN TALL TALE 734
The Five Eggs .... ECUADORIAN FOLK TALE 740
Raven and the Coming of Daylight .... HAIDA MYTH 742

Spotted Eagle and Black Crow ... OGLALA LEGEND 745
CROSS-CURRICULAR PROJECTS 750

WRITING ABOUT LITERATURE Creative Response

Writer's Style: Using Dialogue 752
Guided Assignment: Write a Play 754
Grammar in Context: Formatting a Script 757
SKILLBUILDERS: Using Commas in Quotations, Giving a Performance, Showing Direct Address

READING THE WORLD: VISUAL LITERACY 758
Real or Ideal?
SKILLBUILDER: Separating Fiction from Reality

Links to Unit Four	**Facing the Enemy**		760
retold by Joseph Bruchac	**Racing the Great Bear**	IROQUOIS LEGEND	762
retold by Robert D. San Souci	**Otoonah**	ESKIMO LEGEND	769
retold by Patricia C. McKissack	**The Woman in the Snow**	AFRICAN-AMERICAN LEGEND	775
	CROSS-CURRICULAR PROJECTS		782
Links to Unit Five	**Personal Discoveries**		784
retold by Gayle Ross	**Strawberries**	CHEROKEE MYTH	786
retold by Connie Regan-Blake and Barbara Freeman	**No News**	NORTH AMERICAN FOLK TALE	789
retold by Dorothy Sharp Carter	**The First Flute**	GUATEMALAN MYTH	791
	CROSS-CURRICULAR PROJECTS		796

WRITING FROM EXPERIENCE Report

Guided Assignment: Write a Research Report 798
Prewriting: Researching Folklore
Drafting: Reporting the Facts
Revising and Publishing: Finishing Your Report
  SKILLBUILDERS: Taking Notes, Crediting Sources, Capitalizing Titles of Created Works

UNIT REVIEW: REFLECT AND ASSESS 806

xxi

THE LANGUAGE OF LITERATURE TEACHER'S EDITION xxi

Selections by Genre, Writing Workshops

Fiction

Three Wise Guys: *Un Cuento de Navidad* / A Christmas Tale	.6
The Treasure of Lemon Brown	.17
The Lie	.29
The Apprentice	.64
The Inn of Lost Time	.90
Collecting Team	.107
The Horned Toad	.149
The Splendid Outcast	.161
Mother and Daughter	.203
A Mother in Mannville	.219
White Mice	.228
The Bet	.240
Getting the Facts of Life	.285
Appetizer	.298
The Banana Tree	.369
The Tell-Tale Heart	.380
The Gift of the Magi	.425
Playing for Keeps	.499
The Dinner Party	.507
Flowers for Algernon	.512
Dancer	.575
The Moustache	.583
Stop the Sun	.637
Raymond's Run	.648
Keeping Time	.659

Nonfiction

from Reflections on the Civil War	.45
The Clown	.57
from All Things Bright and Beautiful	.83
from Once Upon a Time When We Were Colored	.252
The Home Front: 1941–1945	.259
Von	.319
The Flood	.347
Tsali of the Cherokees	.390
Painful Memories of Dating	.400
from Lincoln: A Photobiography	.439
from Gifted Hands	.450
Battle by the Breadfruit Tree	.483
from Harriet Tubman: Conductor on the Underground Railroad	.550
Letter to Harriet Tubman	.559
Power of the Powerless: A Brother's Lesson	.668

Drama

The Million-Pound Bank Note	.183
The Hitchhiker	.332
Survival	.459
The Man Without a Country	.600

Poetry

Dirge Without Music	.53
Moco Limping	.125
Mixed Singles	.125
Simile: Willow and Ginkgo	.131
Sea Lullaby	.131
In a Neighborhood in Los Angeles	.158
We Alone	.175
Hard Questions	.175
oil crisis	.175
The World Is Not a Pleasant Place to Be	.225
my enemy was dreaming	.267
Lost	.267
Mother to Son	.313
the lesson of the moth	.313

Foreign Student	329
The Hurricane	377
The Runaway	406
Macavity: The Mystery Cat	406
Speech to the Young / Speech to the Progress-Toward	434
A Man	434
O Captain! My Captain!	439
Paul Revere's Ride	542
Celebration	580
The Other Pioneers	594
Saying Yes	594
Think As I Think	620
The Choice	621
I Belong	622
There's This That I Like About Hockey, My Lad	624
Rice and Rose Bowl Blues	626
A Fairy Tale	674
My Mother Really Knew	674
Sea-Fever	679
Mi Madre	679

The Oral Tradition
Myths, Legends, Folk Tales, and Fables

Paul Bunyan and the Winter of the Blue Snow	702
The Souls in Purgatory	706
The Girl in the Lavender Dress	710
John Henry	718
Brer Possum's Dilemma	721
Aunty Misery	724
M'su Carencro and Mangeur de Poulet	727
Pecos Bill	734
The Five Eggs	740
Raven and the Coming of Daylight	742
Spotted Eagle and Black Crow	745
Racing the Great Bear	762
Otoonah	769
The Woman in the Snow	775
Strawberries	786
No News	789
The First Flute	791

Writing About Literature

Creative Response	74
Interpretation	210
Criticism	360
Direct Response	490
Analysis	628
Creative Response	752

Writing From Experience

Firsthand and Expressive Writing	136
Narrative and Literary Writing	272
Informative Exposition	412
Informative Exposition	562
Persuasion	684
Report	798

Reading the World: Visual Literacy

Close-Up on Perspective	80
What's the Message?	216
Elaborate Details	366
Speaking Without Words	496
Breaking It Down	634
Real or Ideal?	758

LEARNING THE LANGUAGE OF LITERATURE

Objectives

Designed to help students realize that their encounters with the literature in this book will challenge them to discover new ways of reading, learning and understanding, this section has the following purposes:

- To involve students in an activity that will help them perceive the study of literature in a new way
- To help students discover how literature connects to their own lives and the world around them
- To introduce students to the parts of the book
- To familiarize students with the tools necessary for learning, such as a reading log, a notebook, and strategies for reading
- To provide a model of real students using reading strategies to become involved with literature

LEARNING THE LANGUAGE OF LITERATURE

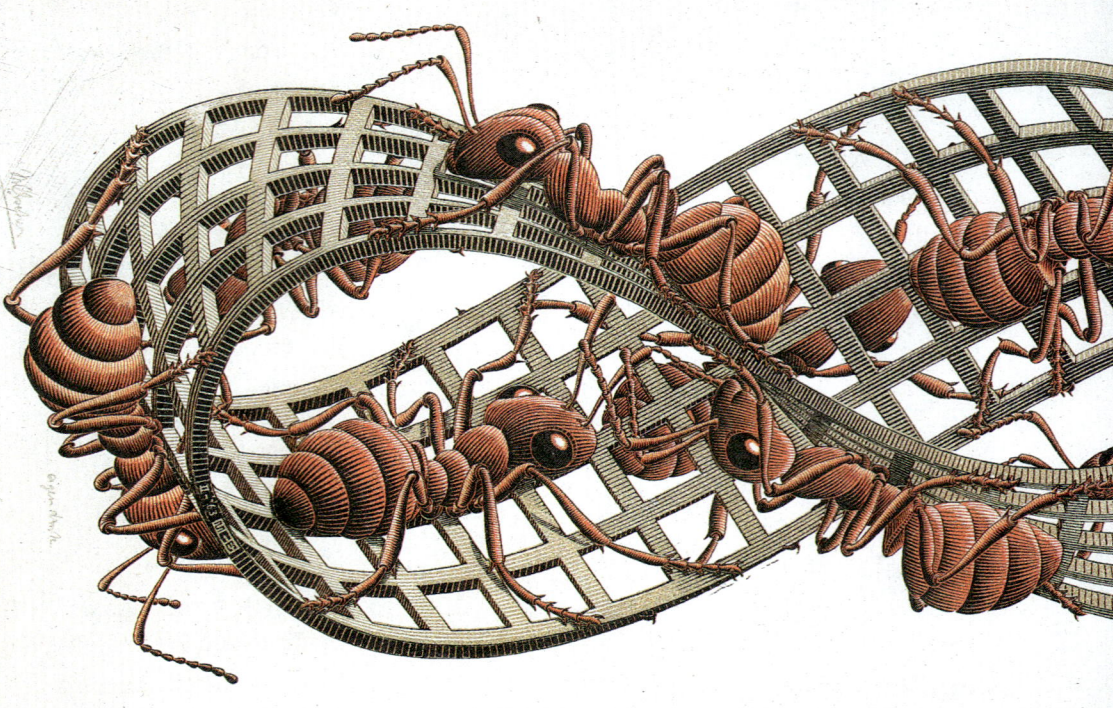

Möbius II, M. C. Escher. Copyright © M. C. Escher/Cordon Art, Baarn, Holland, all rights reserved.

Where Are They Going?

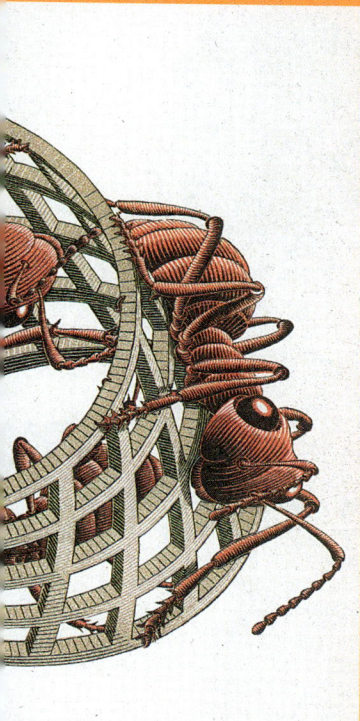

Nine ants are busily walking along this oddly shaped figure. How many ants are on each side? Before you try to answer that question, look at the activity below.

LOOK AGAIN

A German mathematician discovered the figure at the left during the 1800s. The Möbius strip can turn your thoughts inside out.

1. Make your own Möbius strip. Cut out a rectangular strip of paper about 17 inches long and 1 inch wide. How many sides does the strip of paper have?

2. Turn over one end of the strip, twisting it 180 degrees, and join the ends with a staple or tape.

3. Examine your strip. Now how many sides do you think it has?

4. Draw a line down the middle of the strip. Stop when you've made a continuous line running all the way around your Möbius strip. What have you learned?

5. What happens when you cut the Möbius strip in two along the line that you have drawn? What do these exercises tell you about the Möbius strip? Do you know anything you didn't know before?

6. Tell your friends how many sides the Möbius strip has and explain why you think this is the right number.

CONNECT TO LITERATURE

Did your examination of the Möbius strip confirm your expectation, or did you discover something new? Like a Möbius strip, literature can have many twists and turns that surprise and challenge you. The next pages will show you how to follow literature's lead to eye-opening destinations.

Look Again
Students should say that the strip of paper has two sides before they create the Möbius strip. Most students will say that the Möbius strip also has two sides. After drawing the line around the strip, students will say that the strip appears to have only one side. When students cut the strip along the line, they should end up with one longer strip.

Connect to Literature
Encourage students to understand the reason for this activity by stressing the idea that studying literature often involves unexpected challenges and discoveries, just as they experienced with their Möbius strips.

Where Can Literature Take You?

These two pages are designed both to extend the explanation of literature that was introduced in the opening activity, and to provide an overview of the pupil book for students.

You can help students work through this page by first generating a class discussion. Ask students to describe how literature currently affects their lives:

- What does the word "literature" mean to you?
- What kinds of literature do you like to read? Why?
- Do you think studying literature is important? Why or why not?
- Do you think literature, or the study of literature, can affect people's lives? How?
- Do you think literature can broaden your horizons by taking you on journeys both far away and into yourself? If so, are these journeys fun to take?

Where Can Literature Take You?

Everyday life can sometimes be routine. When you enter the world of literature, put your expectations aside. Literature can turn you inside out, flip you upside down, and zip you around the world. Are you ready to go?

ON A FAR JOURNEY

Reading is like entering a kind of cosmic internet—you can move backward and forward in time and worlds away in space. With a little help from your imagination, you can experience almost anything. The **literature selections** in this book will take you to a planet in the future, to the United States during World War II, and to the English countryside with a veterinarian. So get ready! The journey is about to begin.

INTO YOURSELF

Thinking about what you read casts a spotlight on your own personality. Most selections in this book begin with a **Previewing** page. This page taps into what you already know about a subject and gives you background information. For example, on page 149 you'll explore the subject of extended families before reading "The Horned Toad," a story about a boy learning how to understand his family. The **Responding** pages help you develop your ideas after you've read a selection. For a look at some responding activities, see page 159.

THROUGH OTHER DOORS

Literature opens many doorways, introducing you to new people and other ways of life. The **Writing About Literature** workshops help you share your discoveries. For example, in the workshop on page 490 you'll explore the special message one story brings to you. The **Writing from Experience** workshops help you connect unit themes to your life. In Unit Three for example, you will see how some people triumph over their problems. In the workshop on page 412, you will write an essay tackling a problem important to you.

TOWARD A NEW OUTLOOK

As you read literature, you may find yourself questioning things you have never questioned before, which can lead you to see the world and yourself in a new way. As you will see in the **Reading the World** features, the knowledge you gain while studying literature can help you develop a better understanding of the world you live in. For example, the lesson on page 80 helps you see why an event, idea, or object can be interpreted in many different ways.

LEARNING THE LANGUAGE OF LITERATURE **3**

You may wish to have students read these two pages on their own, with a partner, or as a class. Encourage students to turn to the specific pages and examples suggested. Also suggest that they write down any comments or questions they think of while reading. Once students have read the two pages, discuss the questions they have recorded and ask them if their expectations about the book or the study of literature have changed. (For further information about each of the book sections that are mentioned, please turn to pages T10, T11, T14 and T15 at the front of this Teacher's Edition.)

MULTIPLE PATHWAYS

Help students to understand the concept of multiple pathways by explaining to them that there is more than one correct way to learn. Tell them that learning can take different forms and can involve different approaches which tap into a variety of their skills, abilities, and talents.

PORTFOLIO

Students will use their portfolios to file the work they will carry out in the projects and activities throughout the book. You can determine the way in which students use their portfolios. For instance, you may wish to have students include not only their completed work, but also outlines, drafts, and revisions. These portfolios can also be used to help students reflect on and assess what they learned from these projects.

NOTEBOOK

Students will use their notebooks to record their responses to and notes for some items on the Previewing and Responding pages. At various times, you may wish to have students use their notes to help them participate in paired or group discussions. You also may wish to return to these previewing notes after students have finished reading a selection to allow them to reflect and assess whether any of their thoughts have changed.

READING LOG

Students will use their reading logs to record their thoughts and responses while reading. At times, students will be responding to questions incorporated in the selections, but they should also be encouraged to record their ideas and questions whenever they read independently.

You can use these three tools in any number of ways that best suit the needs of your class. Refer to the *Teacher's Guide to Assessment and Portfolio Use* for more information on using these tools, and to the *Unit Resource Book* for copymasters of different examples of reading logs.

How Do You Get There from Here?

Your pencils are sharp and so is your mind. You are almost ready to enter the world of literature. In this world your unique personality can help you find rewards that are all your own.

MULTIPLE PATHWAYS

Do you learn better when working alone or with a friend? Do your strengths lie in writing, speaking, acting, or art? This book contains a wide variety of learning options. You can choose the activities that suit you best. In addition, you will be given opportunities to collaborate with classmates to share ideas, improve your writing, and make connections to other subject areas. Perhaps you will use technological tools such as the LaserLinks and the Writing Coach software program to further customize your learning.

Notebook

Portfolio

PORTFOLIO

Artists, photographers, designers, and writers often keep samples of their work in a portfolio that they show to others. This year you also will be collecting samples of your work in a portfolio—writing samples, records of activities, artwork. You probably won't put all your work in your portfolio, just carefully chosen pieces. Discuss with your teacher portfolio options for this year. Suggestions for using your portfolio occur throughout this book.

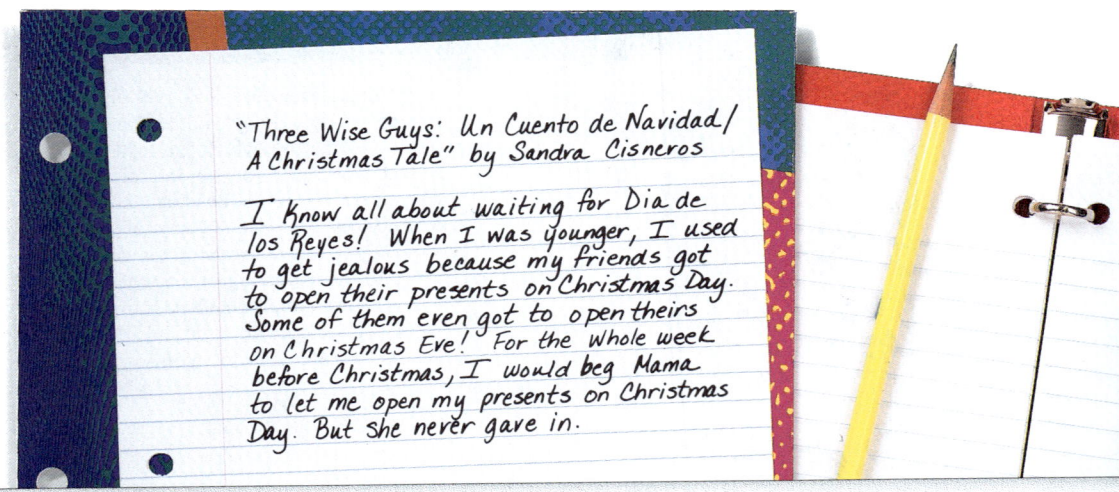

board. ...understood, I saw something... was Clifford Slick again with pencils stuck in... ink dribbling from his mouth. He wasn't imitating me this time. He was putting on another of his stupid comic routines, disturbing students who were trying to work. I rushed back to Clifford to get him out of my classroom before he completely ruined the lesson. However, when I grabbed his hair to propel him down to the office, my fingers slid through the greasiest slime.

Teachers always send bad students to the office. It's just the normal thing to do. When you think about it, though, you have to ask yourself what happens to a kid in the office. Sure, they probably get yelled at or made to stay...

NOTEBOOK

Choose any type of notebook and dedicate it to your study of literature. Divide the notebook into three sections. Use the first section to jot down ideas, describe personal experiences, take notes, and express your thoughts before, while, and after you read a selection. Also include any charts, diagrams, and drawings that help you connect your reading to your life. The second section is for your reading log, which is described below. Use the third section as a writer's notebook to record ideas and inspirations that you might use later in your writing.

READING LOG

In your reading log you will record a special kind of response to literature—your direct comments as you read a selection. The reading strategies detailed at the right will help you think about what you read. Experiment with recording your own comments in your reading log as you read. Specific opportunities to use your reading log appear throughout this book.

Reading Log

> "Three Wise Guys: Un Cuento de Navidad / A Christmas Tale" by Sandra Cisneros
>
> The mother introduced in the first paragraph reminds me of my mother. I wonder if I'll be able to relate to the rest of the story so well.

Strategies for Reading

When you get involved in reading, literature will take you far. How can you get involved? Simply get into the habit of thinking about what you read. The strategies below describe some of the ways that active readers think as they read.

QUESTION

Question what's happening while you read. Searching for reasons behind events and characters' feelings can help you feel more involved in what you're reading. Make notes about confusing words or statements, but don't worry if you don't understand everything. As you read further, you will probably begin to see things more clearly.

CONNECT

Connect personally with what you're reading. Think of similarities between the descriptions in the selection and what you have personally experienced, heard about, or read about.

PREDICT

Try to figure out what will happen next and how the selection might end. Then read on to see if you made good guesses.

CLARIFY

Stop occasionally to review what you understand so far, and expect to have your understanding change and develop as you read on. Also, watch for answers to questions you had earlier.

EVALUATE

Form opinions about what you read, both while you're reading and after you've finished. Try to visualize characters and develop your ideas about events.

Now turn the page to see how two student readers put these strategies to work.

LEARNING THE LANGUAGE OF LITERATURE 5

Reading Strategies

Ask volunteers to talk about a time they read a very exciting story. Ask students to describe their reading experiences of being actively involved in a story. Tell students that when they are involved in reading they are probably using some of the strategies described on this page. Explain that these strategies are ways that active readers get more pleasure and understanding from what they read and that using these strategies can make reading easier and more enjoyable.

Invite students to read aloud and discuss the descriptions of the strategies for reading on this page. Ask students to share occasions when they have used these strategies. Explain that the model they are about to read shows what some readers thought as they were reading the story. Suggest that they cover the remarks in the margin while they read each page; then they can go back and compare their thoughts with the printed ones. Stress that these readers' thoughts are not "right" answers but rather a set of possible active responses.

READING MODEL
Objectives

This model can be used in several ways.

- You may wish to have students cover the sidebar notes and read "Three Wise Guys" as they practice recording their thoughts in a reading log. Afterwards, students can compare their responses to those of other classmates and to the student readers to illustrate how different readers respond to the same selection.

- You might read the selection aloud, pausing to have students record their ideas and reactions. You may wish to pause and have students discuss Philip and Lindsay's comments.

READING MODEL

Alongside "Three Wise Guys: *Un Cuento de Navidad*/A Christmas Story" are comments made by Philip Colas and Lindsay Iversen, two eighth-grade students, as they read the story for the first time. Their comments show how different readers made use of active reading strategies while reading this story. (A label after each comment identifies the strategy the comment reflects.) To benefit most from the students' comments, read the story first, using the strategies of active reading yourself. Then review Philip's and Lindsay's comments, comparing their responses with your own.

three wise guys
UN CUENTO DE NAVIDAD 🌿 A CHRISTMAS TALE
BY SANDRA CISNEROS

Three Kings (about 1950), unknown Puerto Rican artist. Museum of New Mexico Collections, Museum of International Folk Art, Santa Fe. Photo by Blair Clark.

The big box came marked DO NOT OPEN TILL XMAS, but the mama said not until the Day of the Three Kings. Not until *Día de los Reyes*, the 6th of January, do you hear. That is what the mama said exactly, only she said it all in Spanish. Because in Mexico where she was raised it is the custom for boys and girls to receive their presents on January 6th, and not Christmas, even though they were living on the Texas side of the river now. Not until the 6th of January.

Yesterday the mama had risen in the dark same as always to reheat the coffee in a tin saucepan and warm the breakfast tortillas. The papa had gotten up coughing and spitting up the night, complaining how the evening before the buzzing of the *chicharras* had kept him from sleeping. By the time the mama had the house smelling of oatmeal and cinnamon the papa would be gone to the fields, the sun already tangled in the trees and the urracas screeching their rubber-screech cry. The boy Rubén and the girl Rosalinda would have to be shaken awake for school. The mama would give the baby Gilberto his bottle, and then she would go back to sleep before getting up again to the chores that were always waiting. That is how the world had been.

But today the big box had arrived. When the boy Rubén and the girl Rosalinda came home from school, it was already sitting in the living room in front of the television set that no longer worked. Who had put it there? Where had it come from? A box covered with red paper with green Christmas trees and a card on top that said: Merry Christmas to the González Family. Frank, Earl, and Dwight Travis. P.S. DO NOT OPEN TILL XMAS. That's all.

Two times the mama was made to come into the living room, first to explain to the children and later to their father how the brothers Travis had arrived in the blue pickup, and how it had taken all three of those big men to lift the box off the back of the truck and bring it inside, and how she had had to nod and say thank-you thank-you thank-you over and over because those were the only words she knew in English. Then the brothers Travis had nodded as well the way they always did when they came and brought the boxes of clothes, or the turkey each November, or the canned ham on Easter ever since the children had begun to earn high grades at the school where Dwight Travis was the principal.

But this year the Christmas box was bigger than usual. What could be in a box so big? The boy Rubén and the girl Rosalinda begged all afternoon to be allowed to open it, and that is when the

Philip: This story reminds me of a story I heard in storytelling club.
CONNECTING

Lindsay: The mama seems like a 1950s housewife.
EVALUATING

Lindsay: Why did they keep a TV set that didn't work?
QUESTIONING

Philip: The suspense is building: "Don't open till Christmas." I wonder what's going to be in the box.
QUESTIONING, PREDICTING

Lindsay: Maybe it's a box full of food.
PREDICTING

 Readers sometimes recognize situations in stories that remind them of personal experiences. Such prior knowledge can add depth and richness to a reader's understanding of a selection. Here Philip connects the selection to his own experience by noting his familiarity with this type of story.

 The opinions that readers often form when evaluating a story are based on personal judgments. Lindsay makes a judgment about the mother's character and behavior by comparing her to a 1950s housewife. In this selection, the details and descriptions through which the writer characterizes the mother can lead to an interesting class discussion.

 Lindsay questions a moment in the story. However, she notes her question and continues reading. Students should be encouraged to learn when to stop and reread for important information and when to read ahead for information that answers their questions.

 Philip's comment about the suspense in the story indicates his growing interest in the selection. He questions a moment in the passage, but continues reading. Students should be encouraged to keep track of their questions and to return to those left unanswered at the end of the selection. Usually these unanswered questions can be used to generate class discussions.

 Readers often make predictions as they read about what will happen next in a selection. Based on information she has just read, Lindsay makes a prediction about what is in the box. She will then continue reading to see if her prediction is correct.

F At this point in the selection, Lindsay evaluates the actions of the children and forms an opinion of their behavior. Readers often use their judgments about characters in a selection to enrich their understanding and appreciation of a story.

G Philip's comment indicates his growing interest in the story. Here he evaluates the way in which the writer communicates story information to the reader. Students should be encouraged to form opinions, not only about characters and events in the story, but also about a writer's particular style.

H Lindsay contemplates information not stated directly in the passage. While certain information may not be crucial to a reader's understanding of the story, students should be encouraged to ask questions in order to sustain interest in what they read.

I Philip once again notes his growing interest in finding out what is hidden in the box. Students should be encouraged to use questions of this nature to make predictions about characters and events in a story. However, students will find that they often have to revise their predictions as they read.

F *Lindsay:* The kids poured iced tea into the TV! What a dumb thing to do!
EVALUATING

G *Philip:* Telling what different people think might be in the box keeps the story interesting.
EVALUATING

H *Lindsay:* Why does the father spread newspapers on the cot?
QUESTIONING

I *Philip:* I'm even more curious about what's in the box. Everybody's guessing but the baby. I'm just wondering what's in the box.
QUESTIONING, PREDICTING

8   READING MODEL

---

mama had said the 6th of January, the Day of the Three Kings. Not a day sooner.

It seemed the weeks stretched themselves wider and wider since the arrival of the big box. The mama got used to sweeping around it because it was too heavy for her to push into a corner, but since the television no longer worked ever since the afternoon the children had poured iced tea through the little grates in the back, it really didn't matter if it obstructed the view. Visitors who came inside the house were told and told again the story of how the box had arrived, and then each was made to guess what was inside.

It was the *comadre* Elodia who suggested over coffee one afternoon that the big box held a portable washing machine that could be rolled away when not in use, the kind she had seen in her Sears Roebuck catalogue. The mama said she hoped so because the wringer washer she had used for the last ten years had finally gotten tired and quit. These past few weeks she had had to boil all the clothes in the big pot she used for cooking the Christmas tamales. Yes. She hoped the big box was a portable washing machine. A washing machine, even a portable one, would be good.

But the neighbor man Cayetano said, What foolishness, *comadre*. Can't you see the box is too small to hold a washing machine, even a portable one? Most likely God has heard your prayers and sent a new color TV. With a good antenna you could catch all the Mexican soap operas, the neighbor man said. You could distract yourself with the complicated troubles of the rich and then give thanks to God for the blessed simplicity of your poverty. A new TV would surely be the end to all your miseries.

Each night when the papa came home from the fields he would spread newspapers on the cot in the living room where the boy Rubén and the girl Rosalinda slept, and sit facing the big box in the center of the room. Each night he imagined the box held something different. The day before yesterday he guessed a new record player. Yesterday an ice chest filled with beer. Today the papa sat with his bottle of beer, fanning himself with a magazine, and said in a voice as much a plea as a prophecy: air conditioner.

But the boy Rubén and the girl Rosalinda were sure the big box was filled with toys. They had even punctured a hole in one corner with a pencil when their mother was busy cooking, although they could see nothing inside but blackness.

Only the baby Gilberto remained uninterested in the contents of the big box and seemed each day more fascinated with the exterior of the box rather than the interior. One afternoon he tore off a fistful of paper which he was chewing when his mother swooped him up with one arm, rushed him to the kitchen sink, and forced him to swallow handfuls of lukewarm water in case the red dye of the wrapping paper might be poisonous.

When Christmas Eve finally came, the family González put on their good clothes and went to midnight mass. They came home to a house that smelled of tamales and atole, and everyone was allowed to open one present before going to sleep, but the big box was to remain untouched until the 6th of January.

On New Year's Eve the little house was filled with people, some related, some not, coming in and out. The friends of the papa came with bottles, and the mama set out a bowl of grapes to count off the New Year. That night the children did not sleep on the living room cot as they usually did because the living room was crowded with big-fannied ladies and fat-stomached men sashaying to the accordion music of the midget twins from McAllen. Instead, the children fell asleep on a lump of handbags and crumpled suit jackets on top of the mama and the papa's bed, dreaming of the contents of the big box.

Finally the 5th of January. And the boy Rubén and the girl Rosalinda could hardly sleep. All night they whispered last-minute wishes. The boy thought perhaps if the big box held a bicycle, he would be the first to ride it since he was the oldest. This made his sister cry until the mama had to yell from her bedroom on the other side of the plastic curtains, Be quiet or I'm going to give you each the stick, which sounds worse in Spanish than it does in English. Then no one said anything. After a very long time, long after they heard the mama's wheezed breathing and the papa's piped snoring, the children closed their eyes and remembered nothing.

The papa was already in the bathroom coughing up the night before from his throat when the *urracas* began their clownish chirping. The boy Rubén awoke and shook his sister. The mama frying the potatoes and beans for breakfast nodded permission for the box to be opened.

With a kitchen knife the boy Rubén cut a careful edge along the top. The girl Rosalinda tore the Christmas wrapping with her fingernails. The papa and the mama lifted the cardboard flaps, and everyone peered inside to see what it was the brothers Travis had brought them on the Day of the Three Kings.

There were layers of balled newspaper packed on top. When these had been cleared away, the boy Rubén looked inside. The

---

Lindsay: What do grapes have to do with the new year?
QUESTIONING

Philip: That's like my family. If your little sister wants something and starts crying, your parents get mad—I know how the boy is feeling.
CONNECTING

Lindsay: The father is coughing again. Is he sick?
QUESTIONING

THREE WISE GUYS **9**

J Lindsay questions information stated directly in the passage. She makes note of her question and continues reading. Again, while certain information may not be crucial to a reader's understanding, students should be encouraged to sustain their interest in a story by forming questions.

K Here Philip relates an event in the passage to his own experience to enrich his understanding of characters in the story.

L Lindsay uses details from the passage to formulate a question about the father's health. However, she notes her question and continues reading.

M Philip uses details from the passage to form an opinion about the characters' reactions to the contents of the box and to clarify what has just occurred in the story. Readers must often make inferences in order to clarify their understanding of events in a story as well as to make judgments about these events. Students should also be aware that readers often use more than one strategy to enrich their understanding of characters and events in a story.

N At this point in the story, Lindsay evaluates the gift based on what she has learned from the selection and forms her own opinion about its appropriateness for a Spanish-speaking family.

O Lindsay clarifies this event in the story by using details from the passage to make inferences about what is going on. She then forms an opinion of the family's actions based on this inference.

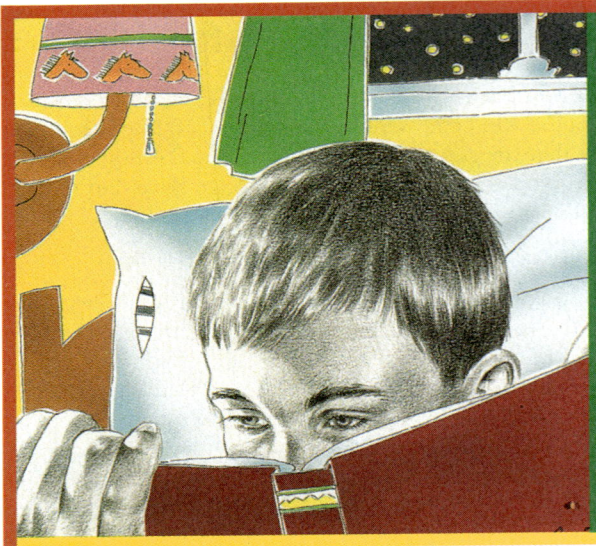

Copyright © Lisa Adams / SIS

M *Philip:* Strange that it's Encyclopaedia Britannica. *I thought it would be something they wanted. Now everyone's disappointed.*
EVALUATING, CLARIFYING

N *Lindsay:* A set of encyclopedias isn't a good gift for a family who can't speak English.
EVALUATING

O *Lindsay:* They're not going to read the encyclopedias. They're going to sit on them!
CLARIFYING, EVALUATING

girl Rosalinda looked inside. The papa and the mama looked.

This is what they saw: the complete Encyclopaedia Britannica Junior, 24 volumes in red imitation leather with gold-embossed letters beginning with Volume I, Aar-Bel, and ending with Volume XXIV, Yel-Zyn. The girl Rosalinda let out a sad cry as if her hair was going to be cut again. The boy Rubén pulled out Volume IV, Ded-Fem. There were many pictures and many words, but there were more words than pictures. The papa flipped through Volume XXII, but because he could not read English words, simply put the book back and grunted, What can we do with this? No one said anything, and shortly after, the screen door slammed.

Only the mama knew what to do with the contents of the big box. She withdrew Volumes VI, VII, and VIII, marched off to the dinette set in the kitchen, placed two on Rosalinda's chair so she could better reach the table and put one underneath the plant stand that danced.

When the boy and the girl returned from school that day, they found the books stacked into squat pillars against one living room wall and a board placed on top. On this were arranged several plastic doilies and framed family photographs. The rest of the volumes the baby Gilberto was playing with, and he was already rubbing his sore gums along the corners of Volume XIV.

10 READING MODEL

The girl Rosalinda also grew interested in the books. She took out her colored pencils and painted blue on the eyelids of all the illustrations of women, and with a red pencil dipped in spit she painted their lips and fingernails red-red. After a couple of days when all the pictures of women had been colored in this manner, she began to cut out some of the prettier pictures and paste them on loose-leaf paper.

One volume suffered from being exposed to the rain when the papa improvised a hat during a sudden shower. He forgot it on the hood of the car when he drove off. When the children came home from school, they set it on the porch to dry. But the pages puffed up and became so fat, the book was impossible to close.

Only the boy Rubén refused to touch the books. For several days he avoided the principal because he didn't know what to say in case Mr. Travis were to ask how they were enjoying the Christmas present.

On the Saturday after New Year's the mama and the papa went into town for groceries and left the boy in charge of watching his sister and baby brother. The girl Rosalinda was stacking books into spiral staircases and making her paper dolls descend them in a fancy manner.

Perhaps the boy Rubén would not have bothered to open the volume left on the kitchen table if he had not seen his mother wedge her name-day corsage in its pages. On the page where the mama's carnation lay pressed between two pieces of Kleenex was a picture of a dog in a spaceship. FIRST DOG IN SPACE the caption said. The boy turned to another page and read where cashews came from. And then about the man who invented the guillotine. And then about Bengal tigers. And about clouds. All afternoon the boy read, even after the mama and the papa came home. Even after the sun set, until the mama said time to sleep, and put the light out.

In their bed on the other side of the plastic curtain the mama and the papa slept. Across from them in the crib slept the baby Gilberto. The girl Rosalinda slept on her end of the cot. But the boy Rubén watched the night sky turn from violet. To blue. To grey. And then from grey. To blue. To violet once again. ❖

Philip: They think they have no use for the books. Mother is using them like a household utensil. They really don't know what to do with them and really don't care for them.
CLARIFYING

Philip: They cared for books so little that they left one on top of the car when it was raining, and now it's so wet they can't even close it.
CLARIFYING, EVALUATING

Philip: The boy is starting to show interest in reading the book, and he's learning things too.
CLARIFYING

Lindsay: I guess at least the boy will use the encyclopedias.
EVALUATING, PREDICTING

P Philip takes careful note of the mother's actions at this point in the story and clarifies what has just occurred.

Q Again, Philip clarifies information in the story and develops his own ideas about the characters based on their actions.

R As an active reader, Philip continues to reflect on what he has just read by clarifying the boy's actions in the story.

S Lindsay has finished reading the selection and forms an opinion of the boy's behavior. Her evaluation also involves a prediction of what the boy will do with the encyclopedias.

BIOGRAPHY

SANDRA CISNEROS

Sandra Cisneros (1954–) grew up with six brothers in a Mexican-American family in Chicago. As a shy child, she escaped into her reading. One biographer learned that the young Cisneros "viewed her life as a story in which she was the main character manipulated by a romantic narrator."

Cisneros wrote secretly at home, openly expressing her creativity only in high school. She later graduated from college, and in the late 1970s enrolled in the Iowa Writers' Workshop, where she found herself an outsider. "My classmates . . . had been bred as fine hothouse flowers," she has said. "I was a yellow weed among the city's cracks." This realization about being different from others in her writing classes helped define her own literary voice: "I knew I was a Mexican woman . . . . My race, my gender, my class! That's when I decided I would write about something my classmates couldn't write about."

What she wrote first was *The House on Mango Street,* a series of 44 related stories told by Esperanza Cordero, a young girl growing up in a Latino neighborhood of Chicago. The book, considered by some a novel and by others a collection of prose poems, has been read by students in classes ranging from Chicago studies to psychology. Since then, Cisneros has worked as a teacher and a poet-in-residence at schools. She remains "nobody's mother and nobody's wife."

UNIT ONE

UNIT THEMES

Unit One

Changing Perceptions In this unit, students will read selections that explore how and why people's viewpoints undergo transformation. The unit contains two parts: Part 1, "Taught by Experience," and Part 2, "Fooled by Appearances." Selections in both parts contribute to the unit theme by detailing how the experiences of a variety of characters affect their perceptions of the world around them.

Part 1

Taught by Experience Selections in Part 1 emphasize characters' changing points of view based on the experiences they have, such as the experience of the boy who comes to understand his father better in "The Treasure of Lemon Brown."

Part 2

Fooled by Appearances Selections in Part 2 emphasize how characters' perceptions of people and events around them are influenced by initial appearances. In "The Collecting Team," for example, the members of a space exploration team sent to collect alien life forms learn an ironic lesson about deceptive appearances.

Links to Unit Six

The Oral Tradition Unit Six contains literature from the oral tradition—specifically, folklore from the Americas—that connects with the themes in Unit One. You may wish to begin or end Unit One by using the following selections from Unit Six that relate to the theme "Changing Perceptions":
- "Paul Bunyan and the Winter of the Blue Snow," p. 702
- "The Souls in Purgatory," p. 706
- "The Girl in the Lavender Dress," p. 710

UNIT ONE

Copyright © John Martin.

Changing Perceptions

Things don't pass for what they are, but for what they seem. Most things are judged by their jackets.

Baltasar Gracián
17th-century Spanish writer

Exploring Theme

To help students explore the connections between the art, the quotation, and the unit theme, have them consider the following questions:

1. Do you think the theme "Changing Perceptions" is an important one to explore? Why or why not? *(Possible response: yes, because we constantly undergo changes in our opinions and perceptions of the people, places, and events around us)*

2. Restate Baltasar Gracián's remark in your own words. *(Possible responses: People usually judge things on the basis of appearance. There is an important difference between how something appears on the outside and what is contained on the inside, and most people wrongly judge others on the basis of initial and sometimes superficial appearances.)*

3. How well does the painting capture the idea of changing perceptions? *(Possible responses: The painting is a good example of the idea of changing perceptions because it's a kind of visual trick that shows how looks can be deceiving and how we often have to change our initial perceptions of things. The chameleon is a good subject because its coloring can change.)*

4. What kinds of stories do you expect to read in this unit? *(Possible response: stories about people who have had to alter the way they perceive the world around them)*

5. Discuss a personal experience in which your perception of another person or an event changed. What changed your perception? What did you learn from the experience? *(Responses will vary.)*

Art Note

Illustration by John Martin Andrew Marvell wrote in his poem "The Garden" of "a green thought in a green shade." In this illustration, the artist John Martin shows a green creature in a green shade—a chameleon that has the same coloring as its surroundings. As we look at the picture, our perceptions of it change.
Reading the Art *What are some of the ways in which the artist blurs the distinction between the chameleon in the foreground and the forest in the background?*

UNIT ONE
Part 1 Skills Trace

 DENOTES MINI-LESSON IN TEACHER'S EDITION

Selections	Reading Skills and Strategies	Literary Concepts	Writing Opportunities	Speaking, Listening, and Viewing
FICTION **The Treasure of Lemon Brown** Walter Dean Myers	Appreciating dialogue, PE p. 17 Making inferences, ML p. 21	Characterization, PE p. 27 Conflict, ML TE p. 20	Dialogue, PE p. 27 Character sketch, PE p. 27 Compose a letter, ML TE p. 24	Song lyrics, PE p. 27 Radio play, PE p. 28 Map reading, PE p. 28 Listening to the blues, ML TE p. 23
FICTION **The Lie** Kurt Vonnegut, Jr.	Questioning, ML TE p. 36	Third-person point of view, PE p. 41 Irony, PE p. 41 Short story, ML TE p. 31 Characterization, ML TE p. 32	Writer's notebook, PE p. 29 Personal narrative, PE p. 41 Quatrain, PE p. 41 Letter of advice, PE p. 41 Rewrite short story from alternative point of view, ML TE p. 39	Classroom discussion, PE p. 29 Panel discussion, PE p. 41 Dramatization, PE p. 42 Dramatic reading, ML TE p. 33
NONFICTION *from* **Reflections on the Civil War** Bruce Catton	Finding the main idea, PE p. 45 Finding the main idea, ML TE p. 48	Anecdote, PE p. 54 Description, ML TE p. 47	Letter, PE p. 54 Anecdote, PE p. 54 Newspaper article, PE p. 54 Complete chart from Personal Connection, PE p. 54 Report, PE p. 55	Classroom discussion, PE p. 54 Research and organize a concert, PE p. 55 Create a poster, PE p. 55 Oral report, PE p. 55 Listening to music from the Civil War, ML TE p. 52
NONFICTION **The Clown** Patrick F. McManus	Exaggeration, PE p. 57 Making judgments and appreciating exaggeration, ML TE p. 59	Humor, PE p. 62 Irony, PE p. 62 Autobiography, ML TE p. 60	Poem, PE p. 62 Brief narrative, PE p. 62 Rewrite section with alternative point of view, PE p. 62	Oral storytelling, PE p. 62 Caricature, PE p. 63 Comparison of different forms of humor, PE p. 63
FICTION ON YOUR OWN **The Apprentice** Dorothy Canfield Fisher			Dialogue journals, TE p. 64 Writing a poem, TE p. 68	Individual and group reading, TE p. 64 Readers theater presentation, TE p. 71

Writing	Reading Skills and Strategies	Literary Concepts	Writing Opportunities	Speaking, Listening, and Viewing
WRITING ABOUT LITERATURE **Creative Response**	Analyzing point of view, PE pp. 74–75 Responding to literature, PE pp. 76–79	Analyzing point of view, PE pp. 74–75 Story elements, PE pp. 76–77	Write a paragraph, PE p. 75 Revise a QuickWrite, PE p. 75 Rewrite a scene, PE p. 75 Personal response essay, PE pp. 76–79 Writing introductions, PE p. 77	Viewing a scene, PE p. 80 Interpreting a scene, PE p. 80 Discussion, PE p. 80 Discussing perspectives, PE p. 81

Grammar, Usage, Mechanics, and Spelling	Multimodal Learning	Research and Study Skills	Vocabulary	
Action and linking verbs, ML TE p. 22 Writing dialogue, ML TE p. 25 Spelling the schwa, ML TE p. 26	Song lyrics, PE p. 27 Radio play, PE p. 27 Map reading, PE p. 28	Research the distance between New York City and East St. Louis, PE p. 28 Note-taking, ML TE p. 19	ajar commence gnarled impromptu ominous tentatively vault	
Punctuating dialogue, ML TE p. 34 Denotation and connotation, ML TE p. 37 Using suffixes, ML TE p. 40	Classroom discussion, PE p. 29 Panel discussion, PE p. 41 Dictionary study, PE p. 42 Dramatization, PE p. 42	Research the meaning and usage of a word, PE p. 42 Taking essay tests: Planning your answers, ML TE p. 38	bureaucrat deter excess inconceivable incredulity	reserve resignation subdued tuition unrepentant
Complex sentences, ML TE p. 49 Stating ideas clearly, ML TE p. 50 Adverbs that end in -ly, ML TE p. 53	Classroom discussion, PE p. 54 Research and organize a concert, PE p. 55 Create a poster, PE p. 55 Design a comparison chart, PE p. 55 Circle graph, PE p. 55 Oral report, PE p. 55	Research Civil War songs, PE p. 55 Research Civil War uniforms, PE p. 55 Research nutritional values, PE p. 55 Research women soldiers during the Civil War, PE p. 55 Research Civil War battles, PE p. 55 Skimming, ML TE p. 51	abominably adulterate appalling apt ardent	devastating infested laudable repertoire soberly
Endmarks, ML TE p. 61	Oral storytelling, PE p. 62 Caricature, PE p. 63 Comparison of different forms of humor, PE p. 63 Individual and group reading, TE p. 64 Readers theater presentation TE p. 71	Research a situation comedy, PE p. 63	copious inducing malevolent mirth motivation	nuance ricochet sarcasm writhe

Grammar, Usage, Mechanics, and Spelling	Multimodal Learning	Research and Study Skills	Media Literacy
Using pronouns, PE p. 75 Avoiding clause fragments, PE p. 79 Run-on sentences, PE p. 79	Viewing a scene, PE p. 80 Interpreting a scene, PE p. 80 Discussion, PE p. 80 Discussing perspectives, PE p. 81	Analyzing literature, PE pp. 76–79 Analyzing perspectives, PE p. 81	Interpreting a scene, PE pp. 80–81

SKILLS TRACE TEACHER'S EDITION **13b**

UNIT ONE
Part 2 Skills Trace

 DENOTES MINI-LESSON IN TEACHER'S EDITION

Selections	Reading Skills and Strategies	Literary Concepts	Writing Opportunities	Speaking, Listening, and Viewing
NONFICTION from **All Things Bright and Beautiful** James Herriot	Context clues, PE p. 83 Using context clues, ML TE p. 85	Style, PE p. 88 Description, ML TE p. 86	Rewrite an ending, PE p.88 Personal essay, PE p. 88 Evaluation of a character, PE p. 88	Discussion with a partner, PE p. 88 Draw a picture, PE p. 89 Oral report, PE p. 89
FICTION **The Inn of Lost Time** Lensey Namioka	Frame story, PE p. 90 Evaluating, ML TE p. 95	Setting, PE p. 104 Plot, ML TE p. 92	Contemporary version of a folktale, PE p. 104 Rewrite story ending, PE p. 104 Interior monologue, PE p. 104 Summary statement of theme, PE p. 104 Rewrite short story from alternative point of view, TE p. 100	Group discussion, PE p. 104 Screen painting, PE p. 105 Video viewing, PE p. 105 Storytelling, ML TE p. 102
FICTION **Collecting Team** Robert Silverberg	Visualizing, ML TE p. 112	Climax, PE p. 121 Science fiction, ML TE p. 109 Irony, ML TE p. 111	Description, PE p. 107 Additional episode, PE p. 120 Log entries, PE p. 120 Science journal entry, PE p. 120	Compile a list of clues, PE p. 120 Make an audiotape, PE p. 121 Oral reading, PE p. 121 Scientific observation, ML TE p. 115
POETRY **Moco Limping** David Nava Monreal **Mixed Singles** Arnold Adoff	Speaker, PE p. 125	Form, PE p. 129 Free verse, ML TE p. 126 Metaphor, ML TE p. 127	Poem, PE p. 129 Newspaper article, PE p. 129	Poetry reading, PE p. 129 Create illustrations, PE p. 130 Presenting a poem, ML TE p. 128
POETRY **Simile: Willow and Ginkgo** Eve Merriam **Sea Lullaby** Elinor Wylie	Comparisons in poetry: similes and personification, PE p. 131	Rhyme and rhythm, PE p. 134 Personification, ML TE p. 133 Figurative language, TE p. 132	Explanatory paragraph, PE p. 134 List of similes, PE p. 134 Poem, PE p. 134	Read aloud with music, PE p. 135 Draw human versions of willow and ginkgo trees, PE p. 135
Writing	**Reading Skills and Strategies**	**Literary Concepts**	**Writing Opportunities**	**Speaking, Listening, and Viewing**
WRITING FROM EXPERIENCE **Firsthand and Expressive Writing**			Writing a family history, PE pp. 136–43 Drafting, PE pp. 140–41 Using descriptive language, PE p. 141 Revising and publishing, PE pp. 142–43	Oral histories, PE p. 138 Asking questions, PE p. 139 Family video, PE p. 143 Interviewing, ML TE p. 138

Grammar, Usage, Mechanics, and Spelling	Multimodal Learning	Research and Study Skills	Vocabulary
Verb phrases, ML TE p. 87	Draw a picture, PE p. 89 Oral report, PE p. 89	Research veterinary programs, PE p. 89	catastrophic docile malice placid vain
Avoiding clichés, ML TE p. 94 Direct and indirect questioning, ML TE p. 97 The letters *qu*, ML TE p. 103	Design a classified ad, PE p. 105 Screen painting, PE p. 105 Video viewing, PE p. 105 Create a time line, PE p. 105	Research 16th-century Japan, PE p. 105 Research Japanese screen painting, PE p. 105 Outlining, ML TE p. 96	compensate qualm decrepit rapt delusion reluctant desolate remit gilded tantalizing implication traumatic inconsistency unwary poignant
Idioms, PE p. 121 Adjectives, ML TE p. 110 Stating ideas clearly, ML TE p. 114 Words ending in *-al* and *-ly*, ML TE p. 118	Diorama, PE p. 121 Make an audiotape, PE p. 121 Oral reading, PE p. 121 Write an equation, PE p. 121 Research ecosystems, PE p. 121	Research ecosystems, PE p. 121 Using the library, ML TE p. 113	blithe preliminaries bonanza preposterous ecologically repress futile sabotaged hodgepodge nebulous
	Poetry reading, PE p. 129 Create illustrations, PE p. 130 Compile a poetry anthology, PE p. 130	Research unusual poems, PE p. 130	
	Read aloud with music, PE p. 135 Draw human versions of willow and ginkgo trees, PE p. 135		

Grammar, Usage, Mechanics, and Spelling	Multimodal Learning	Research and Study Skills	Media Literacy
Using descriptive language, PE p. 141 Punctuating introductory phrases, PE p. 143	Analyzing letters, PE p. 136 Interpreting memorabilia, PE pp. 136–37	On-line sources, PE p. 138	Analyzing letters, PE p. 136 Interpreting memorabilia, PE pp. 136–37 Using on-line sources, PE p. 138

UNIT ONE
Recommended Resources

ENRICHMENT *RESEARCH*

✓ Recommended Novels, Nonfiction, and Collections

 LITERATURE CONNECTIONS WITH SOURCEBOOK FOR TEACHERS

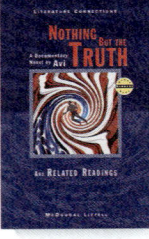

Nothing But the Truth
by Avi

Thematic Links In this "documentary" novel, a teenage boy learns some important lessons after he finds himself in the center of an ever-growing storm of media attention due to incorrect perceptions.
About the Author Avi (born 1937) writes about young people both in history and in the contemporary world. He is highly acclaimed and has won several awards for his young-adult writing.
Other Works by Avi *The Man Who Was Poe, The True Confessions of Charlotte Doyle, S.O.R. Losers, Romeo and Juliet—Together (and Alive!) At Last*

American Dragons, Twenty-five Asian American Voices
edited by Laurence Yep

Thematic Links Teens will identify with the book's theme of a homeward search and how this search can change one's perceptions.
About the Author Yep (born 1948) published his first short story when he was a college freshman. Many of his stories feature Chinese-American children learning to identify with their Chinese heritage.
Other Works by Laurence Yep *Dragonwings, Sweetwater, Child of the Owl*

Where I Want to Be
by Cara DeVito

Thematic Links A 14-year-old relates the adventures with her older brother before her mother returns to claim her.
About the Author DeVito (born 1956) is a lawyer who thought of a story one day and decided to write a book. She continues to practice law and write novels for young adults.
Other Works by Cara DeVito *Our Last Best Chance, Fifty*

Hannah In Between
by Colby Rodowsky

Thematic Links Hannah is experiencing a desperate struggle between childhood and adulthood as she tries to hide her mother's alcoholism.
About the Author Rodowsky (born 1932) didn't begin her writing career until she was about forty and raising her six children. Many of her stories are about family relationships and communication within families.
Other Works by Colby Rodowsky *H, My Name Is Henley; The Gathering Room; What About Me?*

Kids at Work: Lewis Hine and the Crusade Against Child Labor
by Russell Freedman

Thematic Links A school teacher's photographs sparked a crusade against the dangerous and cruel child labor practices of the early 20th century.
About the Author Freedman (born 1929) has written over three dozen nonfiction books for children and young adults. In addition to writing history books, Freedman writes about animal behavior.
Other Works by Russell Freedman *Immigrant Kids, Franklin Delano Roosevelt, Eleanor Roosevelt*

With Every Drop of Blood: A Novel of the Civil War
by James L. Collier and Christopher Collier

Thematic Links A black Union soldier captures a 14-year-old white rebel soldier in this novel with a "my enemy, my friend" theme.
About the Authors James Collier (born 1928) and Christopher Collier (born 1930) have written separately, as well as together. James had been writing professionally for about 15 years before teaming up with his brother to write historical novels.
Other Works by James L. Collier and Christopher Collier *The Winter Hero, War Comes to Willy Freeman, Who is Carrie?, Jump Ship to Freedom*

For Teacher — TEACHING LITERATURE

Bodart-Talbot, Joni. *Booktalk! Three.* New York: H. W. Wilson, 1988.

Ellenwood, Stephen. "Literature-based Character Education." *Middle School Journal* 26.2 (November 1994).

Scott, J. "Literature Circles in the Middle School Classroom: Developing Reading, Responding, and Responsibility." *Middle School Journal* 26.2 (November 1994): 37–41.

Wood, K. D., Lapp, D., & Flood, J. *Guiding Readers Through Text: A Review of Study Guides.* Newark, DE: International Reading Association, 1992.

13e UNIT ONE CHANGING PERCEPTIONS

CROSS-CURRICULAR TEACHING   PROFESSIONAL DEVELOPMENT

Recommended Readings in Cross-Curricular Areas

MUSIC

Black Music in America: A History Through Its People by James Haskins (1987) Provides a historical overview of African-American music from its beginnings up to Michael Jackson. Links to Walter Dean Meyers's "The Treasure of Lemon Brown."

HISTORY

A Nation Torn: The Story of How the Civil War Began by Delia Ray (1990) Relates the history of the Civil War, focusing on the years 1860 and 1861. Includes newspaper articles, speeches, photographs, diaries, and letters. Links to Bruce Catton's *Reflections on the Civil War.*

SCIENCE

They Work with Wildlife: Jobs for People Who Want to Work with Animals by Edward R. Ricciuti (1983) Discusses a variety of jobs that enable people to work with all kinds of animals. Links to James Herriot's *All Things Bright and Beautiful.*

SOCIAL STUDIES

Japan: From Shogun to Sony 1543–1984 by John R. Roberson (1985) Gives comprehensive coverage on the history and development of Japan. Links to Lensey Namioka's "The Inn of Lost Time."

For Teacher — CROSS-CURRICULAR INSTRUCTION

Beane, James A., ed. *Toward a Coherent Curriculum.* Alexandria, VA: Association for Supervision and Curriculum Development, 1995.

Vars, G. *Interdisciplinary Teaching in the Middle Grades.* Columbus, OH: National Middle School Association, 1993.

Lounsbury, Jon H., ed. *Connecting the Curriculum Through Interdisciplinary Instruction.* Columbus, OH: National Middle School Association, 1992.

Meinbach, Anita Meyer, et al. *The Complete Guide to Thematic Units: Creating the Integrated Curriculum.* Norwood, MA: Christopher-Gordon 1995.

Recommended Media Resources

THE LANGUAGE OF LITERATURE

LASERLINKS
Videodisc, Gr. 8
See *LaserLinks Teacher's Source Book,* pages 4–5, for an overview of Unit One.

AUDIO LIBRARY
Tapes
Unit One: Changing Perceptions
Gr. 8, Tape 1: Sides A & B
Gr. 8, Tape 2: Sides A & B
Gr. 8, Tape 3: Sides A & B

WRITING COACH
Writing Coach Software: Writing About Literature: Interpretive Response; Personal Narrative

OUTSIDE RESOURCES

Films/Videos/Film Strips/Audiocassettes
Kurt Vonnegut, Jr. Audiocassette. American Audio Prose Library. (56 min.)
The Civil War. 9 videocassettes. Florentine Films in association with WETA TV; produced by Ken and Ric Burns, 1989. (70 min. each)
Big City Blues. 1 videocassette. Rhapsody Film; produced by St. Claire Bourne, 1986. (28 min.)

Internet Resources
Worldwide Web at
http://www.hmco.com/mcdougal

For Teacher — TEACHING WITH TECHNOLOGY

Olson, Renee. "The Way Things Ought to Work: David Macaulay Talks About the Problems and the Promise of CD-ROM." *School Library Journal* (May 1995).

McAlister, Brian K. "Accessing Resources Over the Internet." *The Technology Teacher* 54 (November 1994): 12–14.

Peterson, Norman K., and Orde, Barbara J. "Implementing Multimedia in the Middle School Curriculum: Pros, Cons, and Lessons Learned." *T.H.E. Journal* 22 (February 1995).

RECOMMENDED RESOURCES   TEACHER'S EDITION   **13f**

UNIT ONE
Professional Enrichment

Make a Little Classroom Magic

Presto change-o . . . a short story becomes a radio play!

Few activities are as challenging and fun as recasting one genre into another. This activity is also a great way to teach students the conventions of dialogue, plot, and pacing. Try a little magic in your classroom by having students transform the short story "The Treasure of Lemon Brown" into a radio play. All you need are a few tricks up your sleeve to help students pull this rabbit out of a hat!

Be sure students understand that a radio play is an oral interpretation of a story, poem, or play. The performers use voice, music, and sound effects to tell the story and convey the mood. Because of the nature of the medium, the story is told largely through dialogue.

Explain that in a short story such as "The Treasure of Lemon Brown," dialogue helps launch and propel the plot, define the characters, and make the story more interesting. In a radio play, however, dialogue most often tells the entire story. As a result, your students will first have to recast the plot of "The Treasure of Lemon Brown" into dialogue. Provide them with the following guidelines.

MECHANICS OF DIALOGUE
- Tell students to capitalize the first word of a quotation. Also remind them to capitalize the first word of a new sentence within a quotation.
- Have students use "speaker's tags," short explanations such as *she yelled* and *I whispered,* to identify the speaker and tell how things are said. This is especially important in a radio play, where the speaker's tags can function as stage directions.
- Remind students to put quotation marks around a speaker's exact words.
- Be sure students use a comma to set off quoted words from the speaker's tags. Remind students that this rule holds whether the explanatory words come before, between, or after the quoted words.
- Explain that commas and periods go *inside* quotation marks. Question marks and exclamation points go *inside* quotation marks if they belong to the quotation itself. They go *outside* the quotation marks if they do not belong to the quotation.
- Remind students to begin a new paragraph each time the speaker changes.

RECASTING "LEMON BROWN" INTO A RADIO PLAY
- Tell students that dialogue is the exact words that a character says. Explore with the class how effective dialogue sounds realistic. Point out that, like real conversation, dialogue often contains slang, informal language, and sentence fragments.
- As students write their radio scripts, encourage them to read their dialogue aloud to check whether the characters' conversation sounds realistic.
- While they draft, students should also talk about different ways the characters could deliver their lines. Explore how these different deliveries might change listeners' attitudes toward the characters. Encourage students to incorporate their discussion into their stage directions.

STAGING THE RADIO PLAY
The importance of voice and sound effects in a radio play cannot be overestimated. Remind students that the listeners of a radio play can't see the actors. As a result, radio performers must rely on other techniques to spark their listeners' imaginations. Here are some tried-and-true methods that are well suited for eighth graders:
- Instruct students to vary their rate of speaking. Reading lines quickly, for instance, can show that a character is in a hurry or excited. Conversely, using a less hurried rate can indicate sadness or thoughtfulness.
- Model for the class how pausing can help create suspense or show surprise.
- Teach students how to vary the pitch of their voices to reveal more about their characters. For example, a medium pitch is well-suited for the narrator.

SOUND EFFECTS
- Explain how a radio play also relies heavily on the skillful use of sound effects. Have students brainstorm how they might create the sound effects they need. Remind them that realistic sound effects can be created from simple objects. For instance, crumbling plastic wrap can sound like a crackling fire and a finger popping from a mouth full of air can sound like water dripping.

Related Reading

 Conford, Ellen. *If This is Love, I'll Take Spaghetti.* New York: Macmillan, 1983.

 Rockwell, Thomas. *How to Eat Fried Worms and Other Plays.* New York: Delacorte, 1980.

 Serling, Rod. *The Monsters are Due on Maple Street.* The Rod Serling Trust, 1960.

 Wicks, Keith. *Sound and Recordings.* New York: Watts, 1982.

Family and Community Involvement

 Family

The selections in Unit One connect to the theme of proving oneself. By completing some of the following activities, your students and their families can make important connections outside the classroom as they explore real-life examples of people who prove themselves.

OPTION 1: READ AN EDITORIAL
- **Connection** All of the selections in Unit One connect to the theme of changing perceptions.
- **Activity** *Copymaster, p. 4* Students and family members discuss their thoughts about particular issues both before and after reading editorials to see if their perceptions of these issues have changed. A chart is provided for students and family members to keep track of their thoughts.

OPTION 2: WHAT DO YOU SEE?
- **Connection** In all of the selections in Unit One, characters' perceptions change because of their experiences.
- **Activity** *Copymaster, p. 5* Students work with family members to create random drawings and to find out what different people see in the drawings. A chart is provided to keep track of people's responses.

OPTION 3: WRITE A LETTER TO A STRANGER
- **Connection** Some of the selections in Unit One, such as "The Treasure of Lemon Brown," deal with characters who discover that looks can be deceiving.
- **Activity** *Copymaster, p. 6* Students imagine that family members are mysterious, reclusive strangers and write letters about their first impressions. Then, in another letter, family members write their replies in which they address their children's mistaken first impressions.

 Community

OPTION 1
- **Connection** The selection "The Inn of Lost Time" is set in the samurai period of Japan's history.
- **Activity** Invite students to visit their local library to find books about the samurai period in Japan's history.

OPTION 2
- **Connection** A number of the selections in Unit One, such "Moco Limping" and "Mixed Singles," are poems dealing with mistaken first impressions.
- **Activity** Invite a poet to read his or her work to the class and discuss with students the importance of writing and appreciating poetry.

OPTION 3
- **Connection** The selection excerpted from *All Things Bright and Beautiful* describes the experiences of a town veterinarian.
- **Activity** Invite a veterinarian to the class to speak with students about animal medicine.

OPTION 4
- **Connection** The selection "The Collecting Team" is a science fiction tale of space exploration and alien life forms.
- **Activity** Invite an expert on space exploration to discuss with students the history and importance of space exploration. Encourage students to prepare questions before the speaker visits the class.

UNIT ONE
Part 1 Cooperative Project

A Mentor Program

Overview

Students will create and implement a mentor program aimed at offering advice and guidance for younger children in their school or community.

PROJECT AT A GLANCE
The selections in Unit One, Part 1 are about people who have set examples for others, as well as those who have learned from such examples. For this project, students will discover how they can be examples for younger children, learning the responsibilities that come with being a mentor. Students will work in small groups to outline a program that allows them to spend time with a selected group of children, acting as big brothers and sisters. The program will be put into effect and the results analyzed and discussed. The project might culminate in a picnic or party for the class and their new friends, if time and the school administration allow.

OBJECTIVES
- To learn how people set examples for others and what is considered a "good" example
- To plan and put into effect a mentor program for younger children
- To discover the responsibilities inherent in such a program

SUGGESTED GROUP SIZE
3–4 students

MATERIALS
- Paper and writing utensils

 **Getting Started**

Arranging the Project
Find a group of children whose families and teachers are willing to cooperate with the formation of a mentor program. Review the makeup of your own class before deciding on an appropriate age level of children. Students who show marked maturity may be able to handle older children or very young children, while others will do best with children three to four years younger than themselves. Contact the school administration and be sure they have contacted families for their permission before proceeding.

If your school does not include children of the appropriate age(s), look around in the community. Other schools, day-care centers, church groups, and community organizations (such as Scouts or the YMCA) might be willing to let you "borrow" their children. Again, be sure both administration and families are aware of the project and have given their permission. You also will have to coordinate times when visits may be arranged, paying attention to students' extracurricular activities, travel distances to and from the facility, and the level of supervision necessary during these times. It might be possible to arrange whole-class field trips for this purpose.

Arranging for Visiting
Students will need a good deal of one-on-one visiting with the children, without interference from adults. At the same time, supervision is a must. How remote that supervision can be is a decision you will need to make.

 Creating the Program

Introducing the Project
Explain that students will be working in small groups to plan a mentor program that can be put into effect in their school or community. They will have a chance to put it to the test as they make friends with a child and try to follow the guidelines they have set forth. You may be able to get informational brochures from the Big Brothers and Big Sisters organizations to help students get an understanding of the goals of the project.

Initiate a class discussion about people students look up to. Point out that you are referring to personal ethics and behavior, and not Hollywood stardom or athletic ability. Some students may have difficulty making this distinction. Ask them to name someone they know personally, such as a relative or neighbor. Discuss how these people have set examples for others.

Students who have younger siblings might discuss how they have tried to set good examples for their siblings.

Group Investigations
Divide the students into groups of three or four. Ask members to brainstorm how they plan to reach younger children, and to come up with a list of important ideas they think these children should be taught. Explain that students will be able to try out their plans and ideas on a one-to-one basis and will then meet again to analyze and discuss the results.

Creating a Project Description
After students have brainstormed, they should write a brief report of their plans and goals. Meet individually with each group to discuss the reports and to offer suggestions. This will give you an opportunity to help the groups keep the projects within the confines of the guidelines.

OPTION 1: INTERVIEWING A MENTOR
Students can interview the person they most admire in the neighborhood or community. They might learn what difficult decisions that person has made, how he or she made them, and the results. Reports should also explain why the student looks up to that person.

OPTION 2: FINDING A MENTOR Groups can interview three or four senior citizens about their lives and any difficult decisions they have made. Each student should then write a brief description of which person they would chose for a mentor and why. Eldercare facilities and senior citizen centers would likely welcome the diversion of the interviews, provided you have made necessary arrangements in advance.

OPTION 3: MENTORS BY MAIL Make arrangements with another school. Groups can set down guidelines and then maintain individual correspondences with children at the other school. Groups should meet frequently to discuss how the correspondence is going, and to help one another with any problems that arise. Letters may be collected and sent through school channels or through a computer networking system.

3 Sharing the Results

The project could culminate in a class picnic or party for the children. Ask students to note how the established relationships function in a social setting. Groups should offer a final analysis of the project, including its successes and failures.

Assessing the Project

The following rubric can be used for group or individual assessment.

3 Full Accomplishment Students followed directions and produced a plan for a mentor program that was successfully put into action.

2 Substantial Accomplishment Students formulated a plan that was not viable or formulated a plan but failed to follow up on establishing mentor relationships.

1 Little or Partial Accomplishment Students' plan was incomplete or did not fulfill the requirements of the project.

For the Portfolio
Master copies of the groups' plans can be photocopied for inclusion in each member's personal portfolio. Include your observation notes of each relationship's progress, as well.

Note: For other assessment options, see the *Teacher's Guide to Assessment and Portfolio Use.*

Cross-Curricular Options

PHYSICAL EDUCATION
Have students focus on teaching a sport they like to a younger child. Nonathletic students might concentrate on teaching the rules of a sport and encouraging the child to play. Special emphasis should be placed on good sportsmanship, both in teaching and by example.

SOCIAL STUDIES

Ask students to select a child from another race, religion, or place of origin. Mentors should concentrate on learning about the child's race, religion, or culture while they teach the child about their own.

FOREIGN LANGUAGE
Students can offer their services as foreign-language tutors to younger children needing assistance in almost any school subject. Monitor the needs of the children to match them with the academic and language abilities of the tutors. Encourage the tutors to pass on good study habits as well as knowledge of the chosen subject.

Resources

Contact local chapters of:
Boy Scouts of America
Girls Scouts of the United States of America
Big Brothers/Big Sisters
Department for the Aging's Foster Grandparent Program

UNIT ONE
Part 1 Lesson Planner

TIME ALLOTMENTS SHOWN ARE APPROXIMATE. DEPENDING ON YOUR GOALS AND THE NEEDS OF YOUR STUDENTS, YOU MAY WISH TO ALLOW MORE OR LESS TIME FOR CERTAIN PORTIONS OF THE LESSON.

Table of Contents	Discussion	Previewing the Selection	Reading the Selection
PART OPENER **TAUGHT BY EXPERIENCE** **What Do You Think?** page 14	**20 MINUTES** • Reflect on the part theme		
GENRE LESSON **Focus on Fiction** page 15	**20 MINUTES** • Discuss characteristics of fiction • Discuss strategies for reading fiction		
SELECTION **The Treasure of Lemon Brown** page 18 AVERAGE		**20 MINUTES** • PERSONAL CONNECTION • SOCIAL STUDIES CONNECTION • READING CONNECTION: Appreciating dialogue	**30 MINUTES** • INTRODUCE VOCABULARY • Read pp. 18–26 (9 pp.)
SELECTION **The Lie** page 30 AVERAGE		**20 MINUTES** • PERSONAL CONNECTION • SOCIAL STUDIES CONNECTION • WRITING CONNECTION	**40 MINUTES** • INTRODUCE VOCABULARY • Read pp. 30–40 (11 pp.)
GENRE LESSON **Focus on Nonfiction** page 43	**20 MINUTES** • Discuss characteristics of nonfiction • Discuss strategies for reading nonfiction		
SELECTION *from* **Reflections on the Civil War** page 46 AVERAGE		**20 MINUTES** • PERSONAL CONNECTION • HISTORICAL CONNECTION • READING CONNECTION: Finding the main idea/Topic sentence	**30 MINUTES** • INTRODUCE VOCABULARY • Read pp. 46–53 (8 pp.)
SELECTION **The Clown** page 58 EASY		**20 MINUTES** • PERSONAL CONNECTION • BIOGRAPHICAL CONNECTION • READING CONNECTION: Exaggeration	**20 MINUTES** • INTRODUCE VOCABULARY • Read pp. 58–61 (4 pp.)
FICTION ON YOUR OWN **The Apprentice** page 64 CHALLENGING			**30 MINUTES** • Read pp. 64–73 (10 pp.)

Writing	Writer's Style	Prewriting	Drafting and Revising
WRITING ABOUT LITERATURE **Creative Response*** * Time estimates assume in-class work. You may wish to assign some of these stages as homework.	**20 MINUTES**	**25 MINUTES**	**80-MINUTES**

Responding to the Selection

FROM PERSONAL RESPONSE TO CRITICAL ANALYSIS	OR	ANOTHER PATHWAY	LITERARY CONCEPTS	QUICKWRITES
35 MINUTES				
• Discussion questions	OR	• Blues lyrics	• Characterization	• Dialogue • Character sketch
50 MINUTES				
• Discussion questions	OR	• Panel discussion	• Third-person point of view • Irony	• Personal narrative • Quatrain • Letter of advice
45 MINUTES				
• Discussion questions	OR	• Complete chart	• Anecdote	• Letter • Anecdote • Article
30 MINUTES				
• Discussion questions	OR	• Rewriting	• Humor • Irony	• Poem • Narrative

Extension Activities

Columns: • ALTERNATIVE ACTIVITIES • LITERARY LINKS • CRITIC'S CORNER • THE WRITER'S STYLE • ACROSS THE CURRICULUM • ART CONNECTION • WORDS TO KNOW • BIOGRAPHY

Alternative Activities	Literary Links	Critic's Corner	The Writer's Style	Across the Curriculum	Art Connection	Words to Know	Biography
40 MINUTES							
✓				GEOGRAPHY		✓	✓
40 MINUTES							
✓						✓	✓
50 MINUTES							
✓		✓		SOCIAL STUDIES / MATH		✓	✓
20 MINUTES							
✓				MEDIA		✓	✓
							✓

Publishing and Reflecting
30 MINUTES

Grammar in Context
10 MINUTES

Reading the World
30 MINUTES

LESSON PLANNER TEACHER'S EDITION 13I

PART 1

WHAT DO YOU THINK?
Objectives

The activities on this page can be used to
- introduce the Part 1 theme, "Taught by Experience," since each activity is connected to one or more of the selections in Part 1
- create materials for students' personal portfolios that they can later reconsider or revise
- build an understanding of theme that can be reviewed and revised as students progress through the unit

Whom would you picture?
Be sure that students select photos or draw illustrations that capture the reasons why these people are important to them. When students have completed the activity, you might have them speak before the class about why the people in their collages are important to them and how these people helped changed their perceptions of the world. (See "The Treasure of Lemon Brown," p. 17.)

Were you surprised?
Tell students that their letters can be addressed to someone they know or someone they have read about or seen in the media. Encourage students to read their letters aloud to the class when they have completed the activity. (See "The Clown," p. 57.)

Who knows you?
After the class has completed the activity, you may wish to discuss why people often worry about others' perceptions of them. For example, students might think about why a person might choose to reveal certain skills, talents, or interests but keep others a secret. (See "The Lie," p. 29.)

How would you handle this?
Encourage students to jot down some ideas for dialogue before they begin to role-play. They can refer to their notes during the role play, if necessary. In addition, you may wish to have students role-play other situations in which children and parents disagree. (See "The Treasure of Lemon Brown," p. 17, and "The Apprentice," p. 64.)

UNIT ONE **PART 1**

TAUGHT BY EXPERIENCE

WHAT DO YU THINK?

REFLECTING ON THEME

Has someone or something ever caused you to change completely the way you view things? Use the activities on this page to begin exploring ways in which experience can be one of the greatest teachers. Keep a record of your impressions, ideas, or results. Later you can compare them with the lessons the characters in this unit learn.

Were you surprised?

Have you ever learned something about a person that surprised you and caused you to revise completely your opinion of that individual? Write a letter addressed to that person, telling her or him what surprised you.

Who knows you?

Do people really know what you're about? As a class, play hangman or a game of charades in which you reveal a skill or an interest people may not know you have.

Whom would you picture?

Think of people who have caused you to change your attitudes and your perception of the world. They could be people you know or people whom you admire, such as writers or world leaders. Create a collage of photos or drawings featuring these people. Be sure to identify the people in the collage.

How would you handle this?

Imagine you really want to spend the night at a friend's house. The friend's parents are away, and so your parents say no. What would you say? Role-play the situation with a partner. After a few minutes, switch roles and continue the role play. Discuss whether the role play gave you a better understanding of the other side of the argument.

Cross-Curricular Connections

Social Studies Have students carry out research projects in which they explore the work of individuals who have had a major impact on the way people think about the world. Students can research civil rights leaders, Nobel Prize winners, human rights activists, or environmental activists. When they have completed the activity, students can share their reports with classmates.

COMMUNITY OUTREACH

To help students explore the benefits of changing people's perceptions of the world and the difficulties involved in doing so, invite members from a variety of community-based organizations to speak to the class. For example, you may wish to have political lobbyists, activists from health care organizations, or local journalists speak about their experiences in attempting to change your community's perceptions of important issues.

Focus on Fiction

A story is a work of fiction. **Fiction** is writing that comes from an author's imagination—whether the author made the whole idea up or based it on real events.

Depending on its length, a work of fiction may be classified as a short story or as a novel. A **short story** usually revolves around a single idea and is short enough to be read at one sitting. The fiction selections that you will read in this book are short stories. A **novel** is much longer and more complex.

Fiction writing contains four main elements: **character, setting, plot,** and **theme.**

CHARACTER Characters are the people, animals, or imaginary creatures that take part in the action of a story. Usually, a short story centers on events in the life of one person, animal, or creature. This is the story's **main character.**

Generally, there are also one or more **minor characters** in the story. Minor characters interact with the main character and with one another, sometimes providing part of the background for the story. Their words and actions help to move the plot along.

SETTING A story's setting is the time and place in which the action of the story happens. The time may be in the past, the present, or the future; in daytime or in the night; at any season. The story may be set in a small town or a large city, in outer space, in a desert, or in an empty room.

PLOT The sequence of events in a story is called the story's plot. The plot is the writer's plan for what happens, when it happens, and to whom it happens. One event causes another, which causes another, and so on until the end of the story.

Generally, a plot is built around a **conflict**—a problem or struggle involving two or more opposing forces. A conflict can be as serious as a boy's attempt to cope with a lie he told or as frivolous as a boy's game of marbles with aliens.

Although the development of each plot is different, traditional works of fiction generally follow a pattern that includes the following stages:

Exposition Exposition sets the stage for a story. Characters are introduced, the setting is described, and the conflict begins to unfold.

FOCUS ON FICTION **15**

FOCUS ON FICTION

This feature defines *fiction* and provides an explanation of the terms used to discuss it. It also introduces students to the conventions of the genre and suggests strategies for reading fiction. The terms introduced here are covered in depth in the fiction selections that follow.

Objectives

- To understand and appreciate fiction
- To understand the elements of fiction: character, setting, plot, and theme
- To learn effective strategies for reading fiction

Teaching Strategies:
ELEMENTS OF FICTION

Character Read the description of characters to the class. Then create a chart with two headings: *main characters* and *minor characters*. Invite students to name characters from books, movies, and television that fit these categories. As a class, complete the chart.

Setting Have students list real and imaginary places they would like to visit. Challenge them to explain the easiest way to visit all of these places—through reading. Have students list memorable settings they have visited through fiction.

Plot Draw on the chalkboard the plot diagram shown and use it to explain standard plot development.

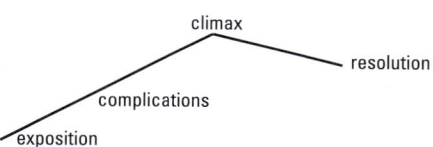

Then invite students to complete the chart by explaining the plot of a familiar story such as "The Boy Who Cried Wolf" or a short story the entire class has read.

Theme Have a volunteer read the description of theme aloud. Then explore with the class why it is important to discover a story's theme. *(To understand and appreciate the story; to learn more about ourselves and others)*

Reading Strategies: MODELING
Invite volunteers to read aloud the Strategies for Reading Fiction. Tell students they will be using these strategies as they read "The Treasure of Lemon Brown" on page 17 and other fiction selections throughout the book. Then model the strategies as students read "The Treasure of Lemon Brown." You may wish to use the models provided or create your own.

- **Preview** *"From the title and pictures, I think the story is about an elderly man with some sort of treasure."*
- **Visualize the setting and the characters** *"I imagine Lemon Brown to be an old, wrinkled man with a sad face who lives in a dark, wet, abandoned building that is filled with garbage."*
- **Make connections** *"I've had a similar experience to Greg's. I remember that my parents used to urge me to spend more time studying."*
- **Question as you read** *"I wonder why Greg stays to talk to Lemon Brown? Doesn't he know it's dangerous to be in that abandoned building?"*
- **Make predictions** *"I think Greg is going to learn something from Lemon Brown that will help him deal with his father."*
- **Clarify** *"I realized while reading that Lemon Brown is not just some crazy homeless man. He's had a very difficult life and has lost the only people he loved."*
- **Evaluate** *"This story is written very vividly in a way that kept my attention. Lemon Brown is an interesting character who taught me that you can't simply judge a person by his or her appearance."*
- **Discuss** Have students discuss the story in pairs. You may wish to have them first prepare a few questions or opinions about the story, such as assessing whether they agree with Lemon Brown's idea of what makes something a treasure.

16 THE LANGUAGE OF LITERATURE TEACHER'S EDITION

Complications As the story continues, the plot becomes more complex. While the characters struggle to find solutions to the conflict, suspense and a feeling of excitement and energy build.

Climax The climax is the point of greatest interest or suspense in the story. It is the turning point, when the action reaches a peak and the outcome of the conflict is decided. The climax may occur because of a decision the characters reach or because of a discovery or an event that changes the situation. The climax usually results in a change in the characters or a solution to the conflict.

Resolution The resolution occurs at the conclusion of the story. Loose ends are tied up, and the story comes to a close.

THEME The theme of a story is the main message the writer conveys to the reader. This message might be a lesson about life or a belief about people and their actions. In most cases, the theme is not stated directly; it is like a hidden message that the reader must decode. As you discuss literature, however, you will find that different readers can discover different themes in the same story. The following suggestions will help you unlock a theme:

- Review what happened to the main character. Did he or she change during the story? What did he or she learn about life?
- Skim the story for key phrases and sentences—statements that go beyond the action of the story to say something important about life or people.
- Think about the story's title. Does it have a special meaning that could lead you to the main idea of the work?

STRATEGIES FOR READING FICTION

To really "get inside" a story, try the following strategies:

- **Preview the story.** Before you read, look at the title and the pictures. Perhaps even skim through the pages and read some words here and there.
- **Visualize the setting and the characters.** Can you picture a similar place in your mind? Can you "see" the action and the characters?
- **Make connections.** Do any of the characters have thoughts or experiences that you have had? Does any character remind you of someone you know? Does the story remind you of an event you've heard of or read about?
- **Question as you read.** Ask questions about the events, characters, and ideas in the story. "Why isn't she able to tell the truth?" "Why is he so angry?" Asking good questions is at the heart of good reading.
- **Make predictions.** During your reading, stop occasionally to predict what might happen next and how the story will end.
- **Clarify your understanding.** As you read, build on what you learn about the characters and events in the story, and let your thoughts change and grow as you learn more.
- **Evaluate the story.** Think about your feelings about the characters and their actions. Also consider how well the author is telling his or her story.
- **Discuss the story.** When you have finished reading, talk about the story with someone else.

Remember, a story never tells you everything; it leaves room for your own ideas. After you read a story, you are left with first impressions, but you need to be able to elaborate and explain them on the basis of the story itself, your own experiences, and other stories you have read.

16 UNIT ONE PART 1: TAUGHT BY EXPERIENCE

PREVIEWING

FICTION

The Treasure of Lemon Brown
Walter Dean Myers

PERSONAL CONNECTION Activating Prior Knowledge

"Every man got a treasure," claims Lemon Brown in the story you are about to read. With your classmates, discuss what kinds of things people treasure. Then, in a chart like the one shown, list five of your treasures and have a parent or another adult list five of his or hers. In the third column, write ways in which your treasures and the other person's are similar or different.

My Treasures	Other Person's Treasures	Ways They Are Similar or Different

Building Background
SOCIAL STUDIES CONNECTION

This story deals with the treasure of a character named Lemon Brown—a homeless person living in an abandoned, decaying tenement in New York City. Tenements are buildings designed to house low-income families in small, usually poorly maintained apartments.

Today, many homeless people like Lemon Brown live in abandoned tenements. Others live on the streets or in emergency shelters. Estimates of the number of homeless people in the United States range from 250,000 to 3,000,000. With few possessions to their name, what do you suppose homeless people might keep and treasure?

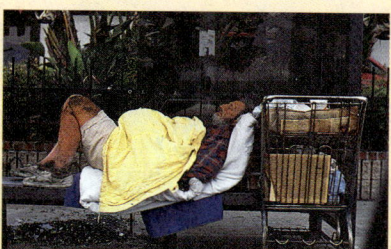

Active Reading/Setting a Purpose
READING CONNECTION

Appreciating Dialogue One way writers help readers get to know characters is through dialogue, or conversation between two or more characters. When Lemon Brown says, "You ain't one of them bad boys looking for my treasure, is you?" (page 21), we learn that he is suspicious and not highly educated. As you read, notice what other things Lemon Brown's words reveal about his personality and about what he treasures.

 LASERLINKS
- SOCIAL STUDIES CONNECTION
- VISUAL VOCABULARY

17

OVERVIEW

Objectives
- To understand and appreciate a short story about a man and what he values
- To understand and appreciate the use of dialogue
- To identify and understand characterization
- To express understanding of the story through a choice of writing forms, including a dialogue and a character sketch
- To extend understanding of the story through a variety of multimodal and cross-curricular activities

Skills

READING SKILLS/ STRATEGIES
- Appreciating dialogue
- Making inferences

THE WRITER'S STYLE
- Writing dialogue

GRAMMAR
- Action and linking verbs

LITERARY CONCEPTS
- Characterization
- Conflict

GENRE STUDY
- Fiction: short story

SPELLING
- Spelling the schwa

SPEAKING, LISTENING, AND VIEWING
- Music
- Group discussion
- Oral presentation

Cross-Curricular Connections

SOCIAL STUDIES
- The Salvation Army

HISTORY
- Blues music

GEOGRAPHY
- Calculating distance on a map

MATHEMATICS
- Calculating alternate routes

 **SOCIAL STUDIES CONNECTION**
Homeless in the United States
Life without a home becomes a reality for thousands of Americans each year. These images show the human face of homelessness in the United States.

Side A, Frame 52548

PRINT AND MEDIA RESOURCES

UNIT ONE RESOURCE BOOK
Strategic Reading: Literature, p. 7
Vocabulary SkillBuilder, p. 10
Reading SkillBuilder, p. 8
Spelling SkillBuilder, p. 9

GRAMMAR MINI-LESSONS
Transparencies, p. 17

WRITING MINI-LESSONS
Transparencies, p. 48

ACCESS FOR STUDENTS ACQUIRING ENGLISH
Selection Summaries
Reading and Writing Support

TEACHER'S GUIDE TO ASSESSMENT AND PORTFOLIO USE

FORMAL ASSESSMENT
Selection Test, pp. 5–6
 Test Generator

 **AUDIO LIBRARY**
See Reference Card

 **LASERLINKS**
Social Studies Connection
Visual Vocabulary
Music Connection

THE LANGUAGE OF LITERATURE **TEACHER'S EDITION** **17**

The Treasure of Lemon Brown
by Walter Dean Myers

Study of Williams (1976), Hubert Shuptrine. Copyright © 1976 Hubert Shuptrine. All rights reserved, used with permission of the S. Hill Corporation.

18 UNIT ONE PART 1: TAUGHT BY EXPERIENCE

SUMMARY

The father of fourteen-year-old Greg Ridley won't let him play basketball because his schoolwork is poor. One night Greg escapes to an abandoned building rather than hear another lecture at home. There Greg meets Lemon Brown, a homeless man who was once a noted blues musician. After a scuffle with some local thugs, Brown shows Greg an old harmonica and newspaper reviews of his past performances. Brown's son was carrying this "treasure" when he died in the war. Brown is comforted to know that his son had valued his heritage. As Greg goes home, he awaits his father's lecture with new understanding.

Thematic Link: *Taught by Experience*
A boy learns about the valuable connections between parents and children from an old musician who lost his son in the war.

STRATEGIC READING FOR
Less-Proficient Readers

Set a Purpose Encourage students to become involved in the story by having them role-play one of the opening scenes. Then ask students to read to find out what Greg does during the evening instead of studying math.

Use **UNIT ONE RESOURCE BOOK**, p. 7, for guidance in reading the selection.

Art Note

Study of Williams by Hubert Shuptrine
Hubert Shuptrine's affectionate portrait conveys the personality of his subject in gentle watercolors. By painting Williams up close, Shuptrine encourages the viewer to notice physical details that show something of his age and personality.

Reading the Art *What other details suggest what Williams's life and personality are like?*

WORDS TO KNOW

ajar (ə-jär′) *adj.* partially open (p. 19)
commence (kə-měns′) *v.* to begin; start (p. 21)
gnarled (närld) *adj.* rugged and roughened, as from old age or work (p. 22)
impromptu (ĭm-prŏmp′tōō) *adj.* done on the spur of the moment; unplanned (p. 19)
ominous (ŏm′ə-nəs) *adj.* menacing; threatening (p. 23)
tentatively (těn′tə-tĭv-lē) *adv.* with uncertainty or hesitation (p. 19)
vault (vôlt) *v.* to jump or leap (p. 19)

 VISUAL VOCABULARY
- **bodega** (bō-dā′gə)
- **stoop** (stōōp)
- **tenement** (těn′ə-mənt)

Side A, Frame 52555

18 THE LANGUAGE OF LITERATURE TEACHER'S EDITION

The dark sky, filled with angry, swirling clouds, reflected Greg Ridley's mood as he sat on the stoop[1] of his building. His father's voice came to him again, first reading the letter the principal had sent to the house, then lecturing endlessly about his poor efforts in math.

"I had to leave school when I was thirteen," his father had said. "That's a year younger than you are now. If I'd had half the chances that you have, I'd . . ."

Greg had sat in the small, pale green kitchen listening, knowing the lecture would end with his father saying he couldn't play ball with the Scorpions. He had asked his father the week before, and his father had said it depended on his next report card. It wasn't often the Scorpions took on new players, especially 14-year-olds, and this was a chance of a lifetime for Greg. He hadn't been allowed to play high school ball, which he had really wanted to do, but playing for the community center team was the next best thing. Report cards were due in a week, and Greg had been hoping for the best. But the principal had ended the suspense early when she sent that letter saying Greg would probably fail math if he didn't spend more time studying.

"And you want to play *basketball*?" His father's brows knitted over deep brown eyes. "That must be some kind of a joke. Now you just get into your room and hit those books."

That had been two nights before. His father's words, like the distant thunder that now echoed through the streets of Harlem,[2] still rumbled softly in his ears.

It was beginning to cool. Gusts of wind made bits of paper dance between the parked cars. There was a flash of nearby lightning, and soon large drops of rain splashed onto his jeans. He stood to go upstairs, thought of the lecture that probably awaited him if he did anything except shut himself in his room with his math book, and started walking down the street instead. Down the block there was an old tenement that had been abandoned for some months. Some of the guys had held an impromptu checker tournament there the week before, and Greg had noticed that the door, once boarded over, had been slightly ajar.

Pulling his collar up as high as he could, he checked for traffic and made a dash across the street. He reached the house just as another flash of lightning changed the night to day for an instant, then returned the graffiti-scarred building to the grim shadows. He vaulted over the outer stairs and pushed tentatively on the door. It was open, and he let himself in.

The inside of the building was dark except for the dim light that filtered through the dirty windows from the street lamps. There was a room a few feet from the door, and from where he stood at the entrance, Greg could see a squarish patch of light on the floor. He entered the room, frowning at the musty smell. It was a large room that might have been someone's parlor at one time. Squinting, Greg could see an old table on its side against one wall, what looked like a pile of rags or a torn mattress in the corner, and a couch, with one side broken, in front of the window.

---

1. **stoop:** a small porch or staircase at the entrance of a building.
2. **Harlem:** a section of New York City; since about 1910, it has been one of the largest African-American communities in the United States.

WORDS TO KNOW
impromptu (ĭm-prŏmp'tōō) *adj.* done on the spur of the moment; unplanned
ajar (ə-jär') *adj.* partially open
vault (vôlt) *v.* to jump or leap
tentatively (tĕn'tə-tĭv-lē) *adv.* with uncertainty or hesitation

---

CUSTOMIZING FOR Students Acquiring English

- Use **ACCESS FOR STUDENTS ACQUIRING ENGLISH,** *Reading and Writing Support.*
- Students may have trouble picturing the setting of this story. Make them aware of descriptive passages and check for comprehension as they read.

CUSTOMIZING FOR Gifted and Talented Students

As students read, have them note the author's use of setting. Ask them to explain how Myers presents details of setting (including the weather) as a reflection or echo of some events and conflicts in the story.

Possible responses:

- Page 19—"The dark sky . . . building"/ Greg feels angry and turbulent about his father's rules.
- Pages 19–23—many references to darkness and inability to see. Greg does not truly understand why his father has told him he can't play basketball.
- Page 26—"The night had warmed, and the rain had stopped"/Greg has made a discovery that allows him to smile, not scowl, as he nears his home.

Literary Concept: CONFLICT

A Ask students to explain which two forces had come into conflict before the story begins. *(Possible responses: Greg and his father; Greg and his principal.)*

STRATEGIC READING FOR Less-Proficient Readers

B Check to see that students are clear about the setting and the order of events.

- What events occurred before the story begins? *(Greg wanted to play basketball, but the principal had written a letter saying Greg was failing math. His father said he must study instead.)*
Summarizing

Set a Purpose Have students read to learn what happens to Greg in the large room.

Mini-Lesson — Study Skills

NOTE TAKING Remind students that taking good notes takes both time and practice. Point out that good note taking can provide a record of important information in writing. Taking notes allows a person to organize ideas, discover aspects of a subject he or she doesn't understand, and see how the different parts of a subject relate to one another. The following are some note-taking strategies:

- Keep your notes in one place in a notebook.
- Write key facts and ideas, rather than details.
- Take notes as if you were making an outline.
- Review your notes regularly to keep the ideas fresh in your mind.

Application Read part of the selection aloud to the class or have students read to themselves. Have students take notes about the selection. Take breaks while reading to make sure students are organizing their notes in a clear and logical manner. When you have finished reading, encourage students to discuss the decisions they made while taking notes; for instance, how did they choose what to leave out, and how did they decide to organize their notes?

Active Reading: PREDICT

C Ask students to predict what they think is causing the noises Greg hears.

CUSTOMIZING FOR
Students Acquiring English

1 Students should be made aware that Lemon uses a nonstandard dialect of English and many colorful expressions. More-fluent students could help others to paraphrase the unusual expressions.

2 Students can read aloud the dialogues between Lemon and Greg to help them see and understand the personalities of the characters more clearly.

STRATEGIC READING FOR
Less-Proficient Readers

D Ask students the following questions to make sure they are following the story:

- What objects does Greg see inside the room? *(He sees an old table, a pile of rags or torn mattress, a couch, and an old newspaper on the floor.)* Noting Relevant Details

- What does Greg hear as he stands near the window? *(He hears a voice say, "Don't try nothin' 'cause I got a razor here sharp enough to cut a week into nine days!")* Noting Relevant Details

Set a Purpose Have students read to find out what Greg learns about Lemon Brown and why Lemon Brown and Greg go up the dark stairs of the tenement.

Literary Concept:
CHARACTERIZATION

E Ask students what they learn about Lemon Brown from the author's physical description of him. *(Possible response: Brown is an old, poor African-American man who wears dirty clothes and rags.)*

He went to the couch. The side that wasn't broken was comfortable enough, though a little creaky. From this spot he could see the blinking neon sign over the bodega³ on the corner. He sat awhile, watching the sign blink first green, then red, allowing his mind to drift to the Scorpions, then to his father. His father had been a postal worker for all Greg's life and was proud of it, often telling Greg how hard he had worked to pass the test. Greg had heard the story too many times to be interested now.

For a moment Greg thought he heard something that sounded like a scraping against the wall. He listened carefully, but it was gone.

Outside, the wind had picked up, sending the rain against the window with a force that shook the glass in its frame. A car passed, its tires hissing over the wet street and its red taillights glowing in the darkness.

Greg thought he heard the noise again. His stomach tightened as he held himself still and listened intently. There weren't any more scraping noises, but he was sure he had heard something in the darkness—something breathing!

He tried to figure out just where the breathing was coming from; he knew it was in the room with him. Slowly he stood, tensing. As he turned, a flash of lightning lit up the room, frightening him with its sudden brilliance. He saw nothing, just the overturned table, the pile of rags, and an old newspaper on the floor. Could he have been imagining the sounds? He continued listening but heard nothing and thought that it might have just been rats. Still, he thought, as soon as the rain let up he would leave. He went to the window and was about to look out when he heard a voice behind him.

"Don't try nothin' 'cause I got a razor here sharp enough to cut a week into nine days!"

Greg, except for an involuntary tremor in his knees, stood stock-still. The voice was high and brittle, like dry twigs being broken, surely not one he had ever heard before. There was a shuffling sound as the person who had been speaking moved a step closer. Greg turned, holding his breath, his eyes straining to see in the dark room.

The upper part of the figure before him was still in darkness. The lower half was in the dim rectangle of light that fell unevenly from the window. There were two feet, in cracked, dirty shoes from which rose legs that were wrapped in rags.

> *"Don't try nothin' 'cause I got a razor here sharp enough to cut a week into nine days!"*

"Who are you?" Greg hardly recognized his own voice.

"I'm Lemon Brown," came the answer. "Who're you?"

"Greg Ridley."

"What you doing here?" The figure shuffled forward again, and Greg took a small step backward.

"It's raining," Greg said.

"I can see that," the figure said.

The person who called himself Lemon Brown peered forward, and Greg could see him clearly. He was an old man. His black, heavily wrinkled face was surrounded by a halo of crinkly white hair and whiskers that seemed to separate his head from the layers of dirty coats piled on his smallish frame. His pants were bagged to the knee, where they were met with rags that went down to the old shoes. The rags were held on with strings, and

---

3. **bodega** (bō-dā′gə): a small grocery store.

20 UNIT ONE PART 1: TAUGHT BY EXPERIENCE

Mini-Lesson Literary Concept

REVIEWING CONFLICT Remind students that conflict is a struggle between two opposing forces. In an external conflict, a character struggles against some outside person or force. Internal conflict occurs when the struggle is within a character.

Application Ask students to think about the conflicts that Greg Ridley faces. Have them reread page 19 to see evidence of his external conflict with his father over whether he will be allowed to play basketball. Also have them reread pages 20 and 21 to see how Greg is thrust into conflict with Lemon Brown.

there was a rope around his middle. Greg relaxed. He had seen the man before, picking through the trash on the corner and pulling clothes out of a Salvation Army box. There was no sign of the razor that could "cut a week into nine days."

"What are you doing here?" Greg asked.

"This is where I'm staying," Lemon Brown said. "What you here for?"

"Told you it was raining out," Greg said, leaning against the back of the couch until he felt it give slightly.

"Ain't you got no home?"

"I got a home," Greg answered.

"You ain't one of them bad boys looking for my treasure, is you?" Lemon Brown cocked his head to one side and squinted one eye. "Because I told you I got me a razor."

"I'm not looking for your treasure," Greg answered, smiling. "*If* you have one."

"What you mean, *if* I have one," Lemon Brown said. "Every man got a treasure. You don't know that, you must be a fool!"

"Sure," Greg said as he sat on the sofa and put one leg over the back. "What do you have, gold coins?"

"Don't worry none about what I got," Lemon Brown said. "You know who I am?"

"You told me your name was orange or lemon or something like that."

"Lemon Brown," the old man said, pulling back his shoulders as he did so. "They used to call me Sweet Lemon Brown."

"Sweet Lemon?" Greg asked.

"Yessir. Sweet Lemon Brown. They used to say I sung the blues so sweet that if I sang at a funeral, the dead would <u>commence</u> to rocking with the beat. Used to travel all over Mississippi and as far as Monroe, Louisiana, and east on over to Macon, Georgia. You mean you ain't never heard of Sweet Lemon Brown?"

"Afraid not," Greg said. "What . . . what happened to you?"

"Hard times, boy. Hard times always after a poor man. One day I got tired, sat down to rest a spell, and felt a tap on my shoulder. Hard times caught up with me."

"Sorry about that."

"What you doing here? How come you didn't go on home when the rain come? Rain don't bother you young folks none."

"Just didn't." Greg looked away.

"I used to have a knotty-headed boy just like you." Lemon Brown had half walked, half shuffled back to the corner and sat down against the wall. "Had them big eyes like you got. I used to call them moon eyes. Look into them moon eyes and see anything you want."

"How come you gave up singing the blues?" Greg asked.

"Didn't give it up," Lemon Brown said. "You don't give up the blues; they give you up. After a while you do good for yourself, and it ain't nothing but foolishness singing about how hard you got it. Ain't that right?"

"I guess so."

"What's that noise?" Lemon Brown asked, suddenly sitting upright.

Greg listened, and he heard a noise outside. He looked at Lemon Brown and saw the old man was pointing toward the window.

Greg went to the window and saw three men, neighborhood thugs, on the stoop. One was carrying a length of pipe. Greg looked back toward Lemon Brown, who moved quietly across the room to the window. The old man looked out, then beckoned frantically for Greg to follow him. For a moment Greg couldn't move. Then he found himself following Lemon Brown into the hallway and up dark-

WORDS TO KNOW

commence (kə-mĕns′) *v.* to begin; start

STRATEGIC READING FOR
Less-Proficient Readers

I Have students summarize what Greg has learned.

- What has Greg found out about the man who confronts him in the abandoned building? *(Greg has learned that the man is Lemon Brown, an old man dressed in rags and dirty clothes who was once a successful blues singer. Lemon may have a razor; he has a son and "a treasure.")* **Summarizing**

- What causes Greg and Lemon Brown to flee up the dark stairs? *(They see three thugs through the window, one armed with a length of pipe.)* **Relating Cause and Effect**

Set a Purpose Have students continue reading to find out what Lemon Brown keeps tied beneath the rags on his right leg.

Literary Concept: SUSPENSE

J Writers create suspense, the growing tension and excitement felt by a reader, by raising questions in the reader's mind about what might happen in the plot. Have students notice the way Myers uses dialogue, vivid descriptive words, and short sentences to create suspense in this passage. Ask them what effect the author achieves by focusing on the movements of the neighborhood thugs and by rarely mentioning Greg and Lemon Brown's location. *(Possible response: This creates anxiety and suspense because the reader senses the thugs getting closer but doesn't know exactly how close they are.)*

Critical Thinking: HYPOTHESIZING

K Ask students why Lemon Brown has decided to stand at the top of the stairs with his hands over his head. *(Possible response: He is going to attempt to frighten or attack the thugs.)*

---

ened stairs. Greg followed as closely as he could. They reached the top of the stairs, and Greg felt Lemon Brown's hand, first lying on his shoulder, then probing down his arm until he finally took Greg's hand into his own as they crouched in the darkness.

> "One day I got tired, sat down to rest a spell. . . . Hard times caught up with me."

"They's bad men," Lemon Brown whispered. His breath was warm against Greg's skin.

"Hey! Rag man!" a voice called. "We know you in here. What you got up under them rags? You got any money?"

Silence.

"We don't want to have to come in and hurt you, old man, but we don't mind if we have to."

Lemon Brown squeezed Greg's hand in his own hard, <u>gnarled</u> fist.

There was a banging downstairs and a light as the men entered. They banged around noisily, calling for the rag man.

"We heard you talking about your treasure." The voice was slurred. "We just want to see it, that's all."

"You sure he's here?" One voice seemed to come from the room with the sofa.

"Yeah, he stays here every night."

"There's another room over there; I'm going to take a look. You got that flashlight?"

"Yeah, here, take the pipe too."

Greg opened his mouth to quiet the sound of his breath as he sucked it in uneasily. A beam of light hit the wall a few feet opposite him, then went out.

"Ain't nobody in that room," a voice said. "You think he gone or something?"

"I don't know," came the answer. "All I know is that I heard him talking about some kind of treasure. You know they found that shopping-bag lady with that money in her bags."

"Yeah. You think he's upstairs?"

"HEY, OLD MAN, ARE YOU UP THERE?"

Silence.

"Watch my back. I'm going up."

There was a footstep on the stairs, and the beam from the flashlight danced crazily along the peeling wallpaper. Greg held his breath. There was another step and a loud crashing noise as the man banged the pipe against the wooden banister. Greg could feel his temples throb as the man slowly neared them. Greg thought about the pipe, wondering what he would do when the man reached them—what he *could* do.

Then Lemon Brown released his hand and moved toward the top of the stairs. Greg looked around and saw stairs going up to the next floor. He tried waving to Lemon Brown, hoping the old man would see him in the dim light and follow him to the next floor. Maybe, Greg thought, the man wouldn't follow them up there. Suddenly, though, Lemon Brown stood at the top of the stairs, both arms raised high above his head.

"There he is!" a voice cried from below.

"Throw down your money, old man, so I won't have to bash your head in!"

Lemon Brown didn't move. Greg felt himself near panic. The steps came closer, and still Lemon Brown didn't move. He was an eerie sight, a bundle of rags standing at the top of the stairs, his shadow on the wall looming over him. Maybe, the thought came to Greg, the scene could be even eerier.

WORDS TO KNOW
gnarled (närld) *adj.* rugged and roughened, as from old age or work

22

Mini-Lesson Grammar

ACTION AND LINKING VERBS Action verbs express actions. Linking verbs express a state of being or link the verb with one or more words describing the subject.

Linking Verbs
Greg felt scared.

The wallpaper looked old.

Action Verbs
Greg felt his temples throb.

Greg looked at the wallpaper.

Application Invite students to find two linking verbs and six action verbs in the  highlighted passage on page 22. *(was, was; danced, held, banged, feel, throb, neared)*

Have students write a description of Lemon Brown and his treasure, using linking verbs.

Reteaching/Reinforcement
- *Grammar Handbook*, anthology p. 903
- *Grammar Mini-Lessons* transparencies, p. 17

The Writer's Craft

Action and Linking Verbs, pp. 474, 516

Greg wet his lips, put his hands to his mouth, and tried to make a sound. Nothing came out. He swallowed hard, wet his lips once more, and howled as evenly as he could.

"What's that?"

As Greg howled, the light moved away from Lemon Brown, but not before Greg saw him hurl his body down the stairs at the men who had come to take his treasure. There was a crashing noise and then footsteps. A rush of warm air came in as the downstairs door opened, then there was only an ominous silence.

Greg stood on the landing. He listened, and after a while there was another sound on the staircase.

"Mr. Brown?" he called.

"Yeah, it's me," came the answer. "I got their flashlight."

Greg exhaled in relief as Lemon Brown made his way slowly back up the stairs.

"You O.K.?"

"Few bumps and bruises," Lemon Brown said.

"I think I'd better be going," Greg said, his breath returning to normal. "You'd better leave, too, before they come back."

"They may hang around outside for a while," Lemon Brown said, "but they ain't getting their nerve up to come in here again. Not with crazy old rag men and howling spooks. Best you stay awhile till the coast is clear. I'm heading out west tomorrow, out to East St. Louis."[4]

"They were talking about treasures," Greg said. "You *really* have a treasure?"

"What I tell you? Didn't I tell you every

Sitting In at Baron's (1980), Romare Bearden. Courtesy of the Estate of Romare Bearden.

man got a treasure?" Lemon Brown said. "You want to see mine?"

"If you want to show it to me," Greg shrugged.

"Let's look out the window first, see what them scoundrels be doing," Lemon Brown said.

They followed the oval beam of the flashlight into one of the rooms and looked out the window. They saw the men who had tried to take the treasure sitting on the curb near the

---

4. **East St. Louis:** a city in southwestern Illinois, across the Mississippi River from St. Louis, Missouri.

WORDS TO KNOW

ominous (ŏm′ə-nəs) *adj.* menacing; threatening

23

Literary Concept:
CHARACTERIZATION

N What does this speech by Lemon Brown tell you about his character? *(Possible response: Lemon Brown has had much experience with pain, and he has learned to acknowledge and then ignore it. He has a sense of humor about life and its burdens.)*

STRATEGIC READING FOR
Less-Proficient Readers

O Have students describe what Lemon Brown keeps concealed beneath the rags on his right leg. *(Lemon Brown keeps his "treasure" stored there—a harmonica and some old newspaper reviews of his music performances.)* **Clarifying**

Set a Purpose Have students read to find out how what happens to Greg and Lemon Brown at the end of the story.

Critical Thinking: ANALYZING

P Ask students what they thought Lemon Brown's treasure was. Then ask them how their guess compares with the truth.

CUSTOMIZING FOR
Students Acquiring English

4 Many different experiences will come to students' minds when they read that Jesse went off to fight in a war. Explain that Americans in this century have fought wars only in other places, not in the United States, so Jesse fought in another country. Explain that the phrase "saw fit to go off and fight" means Jesse volunteered to fight.

CUSTOMIZING FOR
Multiple Learning Styles

Q **Spatial or Graphic Learners** Have students explain how the Romare Bearden collage *Midtown Sunset* relates to the selection. Encourage students to discuss the kind of place Bearden's city is.

---

corner. One of them had his pants leg up, looking at his knee.

"You sure you're not hurt?" Greg asked Lemon Brown.

"Nothing that ain't been hurt before," Lemon Brown said. "When you get as old as me, all you say when something hurts is 'Howdy, Mr. Pain, sees you back again.' Then when Mr. Pain see he can't worry you none, he go on mess with somebody else."

Greg smiled.

"Here, you hold this." Lemon Brown gave Greg the flashlight.

He sat on the floor near Greg and carefully untied the strings that held the rags on his right leg. When he took the rags away, Greg saw a piece of plastic. The old man carefully took off the plastic and unfolded it. He revealed some yellowed newspaper clippings and a battered harmonica.

"There it be," he said, nodding his head. "There it be."

Greg looked at the old man, saw the distant look in his eye, then turned to the clippings. They told of Sweet Lemon Brown, a blues singer and harmonica player who was appearing at different theaters in the South. One of the clippings said he had been the hit of the show, although not the headliner. All of the clippings were reviews of shows Lemon Brown had been in more than 50 years ago. Greg looked at the harmonica. It was dented badly on one side, with the reed holes on one end nearly closed.

"I used to travel around and make money for to feed my wife and Jesse—that's my boy's name. Used to feed them good, too. Then his mama died, and he stayed with his mama's sister. He growed up to be a man, and when the war come, he saw fit to go off and fight in it. I didn't have nothing to give him except these things that told him who I was and what he come from. If you know your pappy did something, you know you can do something too.

"Anyway, he went off to war, and I went off still playing and singing. 'Course by then I wasn't as much as I used to be, not without

Midtown Sunset (1981), Romare Bearden. Courtesy of the Estate of Romare Bearden.

24 UNIT ONE PART 1: TAUGHT BY EXPERIENCE

Assessment ✓ Option

INFORMAL ASSESSMENT
Describing To assess students' understanding of the story and their ability to describe, have them compose a letter that Lemon Brown might have sent to Greg (or vice versa) after some time had passed. Tell students that in the letter they should at some point describe or otherwise refer to the events that occurred in the abandoned tenement.

Rubric
3 Full Accomplishment Students write a vivid letter in the style of a character and review or discuss events from the story.
2 Substantial Accomplishment Students write a letter in the style of a character and review or discuss some events from the story.
1 Little or Partial Accomplishment Students have difficulty writing a letter in the style of a character and discuss few events from the story.

somebody to make it worth the while. You know what I mean?"

"Yeah," Greg nodded, not quite really knowing.

"I traveled around, and one time I come home, and there was this letter saying Jesse got killed in the war. Broke my heart, it truly did.

"They sent back what he had with him over there, and what it was is this old mouth fiddle and these clippings. Him carrying it around with him like that told me it meant something to him. That was my treasure, and when I give it to him, he treated it just like that, a treasure. Ain't that something?"

"Yeah, I guess so," Greg said.

"You *guess* so?" Lemon Brown's voice rose an octave as he started to put his treasure back into the plastic. "Well, you got to guess 'cause you sure don't know nothing. Don't know enough to get home when it's raining."

"I guess . . . I mean, you're right."

"You O.K. for a youngster," the old man said as he tied the strings around his leg, "better than those scalawags what come here looking for my treasure. That's for sure."

"You really think that treasure of yours was worth fighting for?" Greg asked. "Against a pipe?"

"What else a man got 'cepting what he can pass on to his son, or his daughter if she be his oldest?" Lemon Brown said. "For a big-headed boy you sure do ask the foolishest questions."

Lemon Brown got up after patting his rags in place and looked out the window again.

"Looks like they're gone. You get on out of here and get yourself home. I'll be watching from the window so you'll be all right."

Lemon Brown went down the stairs behind Greg. When they reached the front door, the old man looked out first, saw the street was clear, and told Greg to scoot on home.

"You sure you'll be O.K.?" Greg asked.

"Now didn't I tell you I was going to East St. Louis in the morning?" Lemon Brown asked. "Don't that sound O.K. to you?"

THE TREASURE OF LEMON BROWN **25**

Mini-Lesson The Writer's Style

WRITING DIALOGUE Help students understand that throughout this story Walter Dean Myers lets characters speak for themselves in dialogue. Dialogue provides important information about characters—they reveal who they are by what they say and how they say it. For example, in the passage highlighted on page 25, the dialogue shows young Greg Ridley's uncertainty and inexperience as well as Lemon Brown's wisdom and personal bravado.

Application Have students write a short dialogue between two people. Encourage them to let the two characters reveal their personalities through the things they say and how they say them. You might recommend that they focus the dialogue on some disagreement or conflict.

Reteaching/Reinforcement
- Writing Handbook, anthology pp. 836–837
- *Writing Mini-Lessons* transparencies, p. 48

The Writer's Craft
Guidelines for Writing Dialogue, p. 327

Art Note

Midtown Sunset **by Romare Bearden**
In this collage, Romare Bearden shows the way a modern city can play on a person's eyes and emotions. By placing shapes representing various buildings in a jumbled arrangement, the artist creates the sense of excitement, possibility, and anxiety that many people feel in cities.

Reading the Art Would the effect of this collage be different if it showed the city on a rainy day? If so, how?

Active Reading: CLARIFY

Ask students what Lemon Brown means by the statement "I wasn't as much as I used to be, not without somebody to make it worth the while." *(Possible response: Lemon means that his playing and singing were not as good as they used to be because he did not have anyone important in his life to share it with, such as his son or wife.)*

Critical Thinking: ANALYZING

Ask students to explain why Greg first says, "Yeah, I guess so," and then says, "I guess . . . I mean, you're right." *(Possible response: Greg may express doubt because he is uncomfortable with Brown's emotional story. After Lemon scolds him, Greg responds more directly to the truth of what the old man has said.)*

CUSTOMIZING FOR
Students Acquiring English

Explain to students that a scalawag is a dishonest or bad person.

Literary Concept: CONFLICT

Ask students what evidence there is of conflict in this paragraph. *(Greg's question elicits a somewhat irritated question in response from Lemon Brown, who then tells Greg he asks foolish questions. They seem to disagree about what is worth fighting for.)*

STRATEGIC READING FOR
Less-Proficient Readers

Have students explain what Lemon Brown and Greg are doing at the end of the story. *(Brown is staying in the tenement until he leaves for East St. Louis the next morning. Greg returns home with a new insight on fathers, and he readies himself for a lecture from his own father.)* Summarizing/Evaluating

CUSTOMIZING FOR
Gifted and Talented Students

When Greg asks Lemon if his treasure was worth fighting for, he replies, "What else a man got 'cepting what he can pass on to his son, or his daughter if she be his oldest?" Have students discuss Brown's reasoning, given that his son is dead. Does his statement make sense in light of this fact? Why or why not? *(Possible response: It does still make sense. The objects provide Lemon with a concrete link to his son.)*

COMPREHENSION CHECK
1. What is the condition of the building Greg enters? *(It is an abandoned tenement littered with trash and old furniture.)*
2. Why did Lemon travel so much as a young man? *(He was a musician.)*
3. Why do the thugs try to attack him? *(They have heard of his treasure.)*
4. What did Lemon's son carry with him in the war? *(He had Lemon's harmonica and reviews of his shows.)*

INSIGHT
1. Why do you think blues music has been so popular and influential? *(Possible response: The blues deal with experiences of suffering and hard luck that most people understand.)*
2. What are the historical reasons for the development of the blues? *(Possible responses: The former slaves had no political or economic resources; those were "hard times"; it was a way to express their difficult situation.)*

"Sure it does," Greg said. "Sure it does. And you take care of that treasure of yours."

"That I'll do," Lemon said, the wrinkles about his eyes suggesting a smile. "That I'll do."

The night had warmed, and the rain had stopped, leaving puddles at the curbs. Greg didn't even want to think how late it was. He thought ahead of what his father would say and wondered if he should tell him about Lemon Brown. He thought about it until he reached his stoop, and decided against it. Lemon Brown would be O.K., Greg thought, with his memories and his treasure.

Greg pushed the button over the bell marked Ridley, thought of the lecture he knew his father would give him, and smiled. ❖

HISTORICAL INSIGHT
BLUES MUSIC

In "The Treasure of Lemon Brown," Lemon Brown tells Greg, "I sung the blues so sweet that if I sang at a funeral, the dead would commence to rocking with the beat." Blues music had its origins in West African musical traditions brought to the United States by slaves. Blues songs were first sung in the late 1800s by African Americans living in the Mississippi Delta. These recently freed slaves, many of whom worked on cotton plantations, had no economic or political power. The misery of their daily lives was reflected in the lyrics of their songs. Their distinctive music featured "blue," or flattened, notes and a beat that seemed to conflict with the melody. In time, instrumental accompaniment—at first a banjo and later a guitar—was added to the songs.

In the early 1900s, as African Americans migrated from the country to the cities, the blues became more widely known. By the 1920s, blues music had become a craze, and orchestras were playing versions of it in many popular nightclubs. In later years, blues influenced the development of jazz, rock, and country music.

In the 1920s, one famous blues singer, Blind Lemon Jefferson, became widely known throughout the South. He recorded 81 songs but spent nearly all of his earnings and died poor at the age of 32. The last stanza of one of his songs, "Tin Cup Blues," illustrates the sad and tragic tone of the blues:

> Now gather 'round me people and let me tell you a true fact
> Now gather 'round me people and let me tell you a true fact
> That tough luck has sunk me and the rats is getting in my hat.

26 UNIT ONE PART 1: TAUGHT BY EXPERIENCE

Mini-Lesson Spelling

SPELLING THE SCHWA Tell students that the schwa (ə) is a common vowel sound in unstressed syllables but that it can represent several different vowels or vowel combinations.

ajar (ə-jär′)
tentatively (těn′tə-tǐv-lē)
commence (kə-měns′)
ominous (ŏm′ə-nəs)
treasure (trězh′ər)
lemon (lěm′ən)
harmonica (här-mŏn′ĭ-kə)
Harlem (här′ləm)

Application Have students examine the highlighted sentences above, find examples of the schwa sound, and identify the letters responsible for the sound.

Ask students to look for more words with the schwa sound and record them in their personal word lists.

Reteaching/Reinforcement
• *Unit One Resource Book*, p. 9

26 THE LANGUAGE OF LITERATURE TEACHER'S EDITION

RESPONDING OPTIONS

FROM PERSONAL RESPONSE TO CRITICAL ANALYSIS

REFLECT 1. What are your impressions of Lemon Brown? Jot down your thoughts in your notebook.

RETHINK 2. Why does Greg smile at the end of the story?

Thematic Link **Consider**
- what he has learned from Lemon Brown
- how his perception of his father may have changed

3. Why do you think Lemon Brown decides to show his treasure to Greg?

RELATE 4. In your opinion, does society have a responsibility to protect homeless people? If so, what should be done?

Multimodal Learning
ANOTHER PATHWAY
Cooperative Learning

Most blues songs have slow, emphatic rhythms and express sad thoughts. In small groups, try creating the lyrics of a blues song about Lemon Brown's life and his treasure. You might include his encounter with Greg. Share your group's lyrics with other groups.

LITERARY CONCEPTS

The techniques that writers use to bring characters to life are known as **characterization.** The basic methods of characterization are physical description of a character; the character's speech, thoughts, or actions; the dialogue, thoughts, or actions of other characters; and the writer's direct comments about the character's personality. Make a chart like the one below, adding at least one more example of each of the three methods used to make Lemon Brown seem real.

QUICKWRITES

1. Write a **dialogue** that might take place between Greg and his father during their next encounter. Remember what concerns Greg's father has about him and how Greg's perceptions may have changed.

2. Look at the chart you made for the Literary Concepts activity. Use your entries in the chart to help you write a **character sketch** of Lemon Brown.

📁 **PORTFOLIO** Save your writing. You may want to use it later as a springboard to a piece for your portfolio.

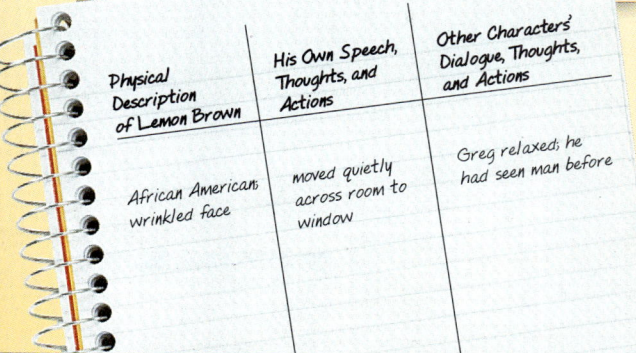

THE TREASURE OF LEMON BROWN 27

From Personal Response to Critical Analysis

1. Responses will vary. Encourage students to be specific about aspects of Brown's behavior and personality.
2. Possible responses: Some students may say that Greg smiles because he understands that his father's lectures come out of love. Others may say that it is because he has learned about the importance of family and pride in who you are and where you come from.
3. Possible responses: Some students may say that Brown shows his treasure because he senses that Greg is unhappy with his life. Others may say that the fact that they helped each other through a dangerous situation helped him begin to trust the boy.
4. Possible responses: Students may mention that we must provide basic human needs—food, shelter, medical care. Students may note that homeless people need help to function in society again.

Another Pathway

Cooperative Learning In small groups, one student can read aloud the blues lyrics from the Historical Insight (page 26). One or two others can identify passages in the story where Lemon Brown refers to things that might sadden him. Another student can examine Brown's words and behavior with Greg for possible use in the lyrics. All group members can help draft the actual lyrics.

Rubric
3 Full Accomplishment Students' lyrics vividly express Brown's painful experiences.
2 Substantial Accomplishment Students' lyrics express some facet of Brown's life.
1 Little or Partial Accomplishment Students have difficulty composing lyrics in the blues form and focusing on the sadder aspects of Brown's life.

Literary Concepts

Point out that the author rarely makes direct comments about the characters' personalities. Have students form small groups to come up with examples of the methods of characterization used. Other physical descriptions include "There were two feet, in cracked, dirty shoes from which rose legs that were wrapped in rags." Possible additions to the second column include: "'...if I sang at a funeral, the dead would commence to rocking with the beat.'" Possible additions to the third column include "Lemon Brown would be O.K., Greg thought, with his memories and treasure."

QuickWrites

1. Students can refer to the story to help them match the way each character speaks. They might say each line of dialogue out loud as they write it, to test that it sounds like real speech.
2. Have students begin with a clear statement that characterizes Brown. Then they can use vivid details from each column in the Literary Concepts activity to flesh out their sketches.

The Writer's Craft
Guidelines for Writing Dialogue, p. 327

Across the Curriculum

Geography Have students work in groups of three. Two group members can locate each city, and a third member can find the map's distance scales. All members can help calculate the distance between East St. Louis and New York City. *(about 975 miles)*

ADDITIONAL SUGGESTION

 **Math** *Travel Plans* Lemon Brown says that his next destination is East St. Louis. Imagine that a friend convinces him to come to Memphis first. Ask students to determine the difference in mileage between New York and these two cities. *(Memphis is 1,100 miles from New York—125 miles farther than East St. Louis.)*

Words to Know

1. vault	6. gnarled
2. ajar	7. tentatively
3. tentatively	8. commence
4. impromptu	9. gnarled
5. ominous	10. ominous

Reteaching/Reinforcement
• *Unit One Resource Book*, p. 10

WALTER DEAN MYERS

Walter Dean Myers writes not only from a need to discover himself but also from what he sees as his obligation to fellow African Americans. He believes that children and adults "must have role models with which they can identify," so he tries to "deliver images upon which [they] could build and expand their own worlds." He says, "I want to talk about my people. . . . There is always one more story to tell, one more person whose life needs to be held up to the sun."

MUSIC CONNECTION

The Blues The American music form called the blues has a long history. Students can listen and watch as the blues unfold in images and music.

Side A, Frame 904

Multimodal Learning
ALTERNATIVE ACTIVITIES

Cooperative Learning With a group of classmates, create a **radio play** version of this story. Keep in mind that a radio play relies on dialogue more than narration. Perform the play for your class.

Multimodal Learning
ACROSS THE CURRICULUM

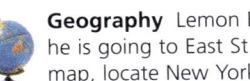 **Geography** Lemon Brown says that he is going to East St. Louis. On a map, locate New York City, where the story takes place, and East St. Louis. Then use the map's distance scale to calculate how far Lemon will travel.

WORDS TO KNOW

Review the Words to Know at the bottom of the selection pages. On your paper, write the word that is most clearly related to each description below. Some words will be used twice.

1. mountain goats leaping from rock to rock
2. an open refrigerator
3. how to enter a tiger's den
4. an unrehearsed show
5. an oncoming storm with heavy clouds and high winds
6. the arthritic hands of an old person
7. a nervous amateur singing a solo
8. the only way to get going
9. the bark of an old, twisted tree
10. a stranger approaching in a dark alley

WALTER DEAN MYERS

Walter Dean Myers was born into a large, poor family in Martinsburg, West Virginia. After the death of his mother, he was raised by the Deans, friends of his family, with whom he moved to Harlem, where most of his stories take place. "Compared to Martinsburg," he says, "I found Harlem a marvel, an exotic land with an inexhaustible supply of delights and surprises."

Myers began to write fiction on a regular basis when he was only 10 or 11, but he did not imagine that writing might become his career. "I was from a family of laborers . . . Writing had no practical value for a Black child."

1937–

Nevertheless, Myers wrote stories throughout his high school years, during his three years in the army, and after his discharge. Finally, several of his stories were published, and in the late 1960s he won a contest with his text for a children's picture book. Since 1975, Myers has written more than 20 novels and many short stories, most of them for young adults. He has won two Newbery Awards and four Coretta Scott King Awards.

OTHER WORKS *Malcolm X: By Any Means Necessary, The Glory Field, Brown Angels*

Extended Reading

28 UNIT ONE PART 1: TAUGHT BY EXPERIENCE

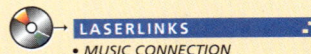
• MUSIC CONNECTION

Alternative Activities

Remind students that they will need to gather sections of dialogue for the following characters: Mr. Ridley, Greg Ridley, Lemon Brown, and at least two of the three neighborhood thugs. Students can establish both the setting and the background of the story's conflict in a short section of narration at the start of the radio play.

Have students consider how each character's voice can be performed to express that character's personality. Despite the lack of female characters in Myers's story, encourage female students to perform in the play.

28 THE LANGUAGE OF LITERATURE **TEACHER'S EDITION**

PREVIEWING

FICTION

The Lie
Kurt Vonnegut, Jr.

Activating Prior Knowledge/Setting a Purpose
PERSONAL CONNECTION

Teenagers often feel pressure to meet their parents' expectations. The pressure is usually created by the parents' desire to see their children succeed, whether in simply cleaning their rooms or in earning college scholarships.

With your classmates, discuss the most common expectations parents have. Of these expectations, which do you think result in the most pressure on teenagers? On the chalkboard, rank the expectations on a diagram like the one shown.

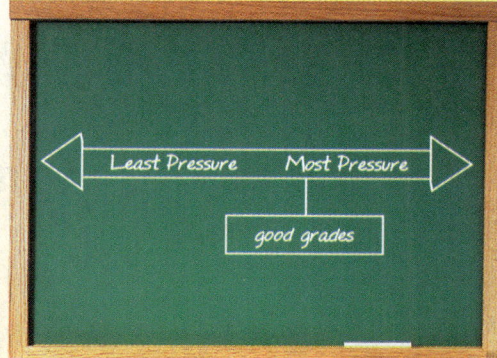

Building Background
SOCIAL STUDIES CONNECTION

In this story, Eli Remenzel is faced with the expectations of his parents. They pressure him to attend the preparatory school that many generations of Remenzels have attended.

Prep schools are expensive private high schools that prepare students for college. Many provide a high-quality education with a great deal of individual attention. Because of the high cost of a prep school education, and because admission to these schools usually involves passing difficult entrance examinations, most of their students are bright children from wealthy families. Families develop strong loyalties to prep schools, sometimes donating large sums of money to the schools.

Setting a Purpose
WRITING CONNECTION

Think about the discussion you had about parental expectations and pressure. In your notebook, jot down your ideas about how teenagers react to those pressures. Then, as you read, evaluate Eli's way of reacting to the pressure he faces.

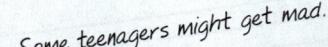

• EDUCATIONAL CONNECTION

OVERVIEW
Objectives

- To understand and appreciate a short story about a boy who hides the truth due to parental pressure
- To enrich reading by using active-reading strategies
- To identify and understand the third-person point of view and the use of irony
- To express understanding of the story through a choice of writing forms, including a personal narrative, a quatrain, and a letter of advice
- To extend understanding of the story through a variety of multimodal and cross-curricular activities

Skills

READING SKILLS/STRATEGIES
• Questioning

THE WRITER'S STYLE
• Denotation and connotation

GRAMMAR
• Punctuating dialogue

LITERARY CONCEPTS
• Third-person point of view

• Irony
• Characterization

GENRE STUDY
• Fiction: short story

SPELLING
• Using suffixes

SPEAKING, LISTENING, AND VIEWING
• Dramatic reading
• Group discussion
• Oral presentation

Cross-Curricular Connections

SOCIAL STUDIES
• College preparatory schools

SCIENCE
• Signs of spring

MATHEMATICS
• Calculating percentage of college applicants

 **EDUCATIONAL CONNECTION**
Prep School Life Some parents choose to send their children to preparatory schools to prepare them for college. These images offer a glimpse into prep school life.

Side A, Frame 52559

PRINT AND MEDIA RESOURCES

UNIT ONE RESOURCE BOOK
Strategic Reading: Literature, p. 13
Vocabulary SkillBuilder, p. 16
Reading SkillBuilder, p. 14
Spelling SkillBuilder, p. 15

GRAMMAR MINI-LESSONS
Transparencies, p. 33
Copymasters, p. 42

WRITING MINI-LESSONS
Transparencies, p. 37

ACCESS FOR STUDENTS ACQUIRING ENGLISH
Selection Summaries
Reading and Writing Support

FORMAL ASSESSMENT
Selection Test, pp. 7–8
 Test Generator

 AUDIO LIBRARY
See Reference Card

LASERLINKS
Educational Connection
Author Background

THE LANGUAGE OF LITERATURE TEACHER'S EDITION **29**

The LIE

SUMMARY

The Remenzels take their son, Eli, to enroll at the Whitehill School, which has been attended by generations of Remenzels. Only Eli knows that Whitehill has refused him admission because of low test scores. Doctor Remenzel warns his family not to ask for any special treatment at Whitehill. When Eli's lie is revealed, his mother sympathizes with him; the doctor pressures members of the Whitehill board to admit the boy, but they refuse. Eli scolds his father for tarnishing the family's honor by asking for special treatment, and Doctor Remenzel apologizes to Eli.

Thematic Link: *Taught by Experience*
In the face of failure, a schoolboy learns a valuable lesson about truth and teaches his father the importance of honor.

CUSTOMIZING FOR
Students Acquiring English

- Use **ACCESS FOR STUDENTS ACQUIRING ENGLISH**, *Reading and Writing Support.*
- Guide students to an understanding of the personalities of the characters through their actions and language. Be sure that they see the importance of what is said and what is implied throughout the story.
- ① Some students from warmer climates may not know what the change of seasons is like in New England. If appropriate, have students imagine a long, cold, snowy winter, and then how they would feel as spring begins.

STRATEGIC READING FOR
Less-Proficient Readers

Set a Purpose To help students get into the selection, have them draw the scene described on the first two pages. Then ask them to notice what each of the three main characters is engaged in on the drive to Whitehill.

Use **UNIT ONE RESOURCE BOOK**, p. 13, for guidance in reading the selection.

Copyright © Fred Lynch.

30 UNIT ONE PART 1: TAUGHT BY EXPERIENCE

It was early springtime. Weak sunshine lay cold on old gray frost. Willow twigs against the sky showed the golden haze of fat catkins about to bloom. A black Rolls-Royce streaked up the Connecticut Turnpike from New York City. At the wheel was Ben Barkley, a colored chauffeur.

"Keep it under the speed limit, Ben," said Doctor Remenzel. "I don't care how ridiculous any speed limit seems; stay under it. No reason to rush—we have plenty of time."

Ben eased off on the throttle. "Seems like in the springtime she wants to get up and go," he said.

"Do what you can to keep her down—O.K.?" said the doctor.

"Yes, sir!" said Ben. He spoke in a lower voice to the thirteen-year-old boy who was riding beside him, to Eli Remenzel, the doctor's son. "Ain't just people and animals feel good in the springtime," he said to Eli. "Motors feel good too."

"Um," said Eli.

"Everything feels good," said Ben. "Don't you feel good?"

"Sure, sure I feel good," said Eli emptily.

"Should feel good—going to that wonderful school," said Ben.

The wonderful school was the

WORDS TO KNOW

bureaucrat (byŏŏr′ə-krăt′) *n.* an official who deals with details of administrative procedure (p. 35)
deter (dĭ-tûr′) *v.* to discourage; prevent from acting (p. 34)
excess (ĭk-sĕs′) *n.* an amount greater than necessary; surplus (p. 32)
inconceivable (ĭn′kən-sē′və-bəl) *adj.* impossible to understand; unbelievable (p. 34)
incredulity (ĭn′krĭ-dōō′lĭ-tē) *n.* an unwillingness to accept what is offered as true; disbelief (p. 38)

reserve (rĭ-zûrv′) *n.* a keeping of one's feelings and thoughts to oneself (p. 32)
resignation (rĕz′ĭg-nā′shən) *n.* an unresisting acceptance of what seems unavoidable (p. 38)
subdued (səb-dōōd′) *adj.* toned down; diminished in intensity (p. 40)
tuition (tōō-ĭsh′ən) *n.* the fee charged for instruction at a college or private school (p. 34)
unrepentant (ŭn′rĭ-pĕn′tənt) *adj.* feeling or showing no regret (p. 33)

30 THE LANGUAGE OF LITERATURE TEACHER'S EDITION

by Kurt Vonnegut, Jr.

Whitehill School for Boys, a private preparatory school in North Marston, Massachusetts. That was where the Rolls-Royce was bound. The plan was that Eli would enroll for the fall semester while his father, a member of the class of 1939, attended a meeting of the board of overseers of the school.

"Don't believe this boy's feeling so good, doctor," said Ben. He wasn't particularly serious about it. It was more genial springtime blather.

"What's the matter, Eli?" said the doctor absently. He was studying blueprints, plans for a thirty-room addition to the Eli Remenzel Memorial Dormitory—a building named in honor of his great-great-grandfather. Doctor Remenzel had the plans draped over a walnut table that folded out of the back of the front seat. He was a massive, dignified man, a physician, a healer for healing's sake, since he had been born as rich as the Shah of Iran.[1]

"Worried about something?" he asked Eli without looking up from the plans.

"Nope," said Eli.

Eli's lovely mother, Sylvia, sat next to the doctor, reading the catalogue of the Whitehill School.

"If I were you," she said to Eli, "I'd be so excited I could hardly stand it. The best four years of your whole life are just about to begin."

"Sure," said Eli. He didn't show her his face. He gave her only the back of his head, a pinwheel of coarse brown hair above a stiff white collar, to talk to.

"I wonder how many Remenzels have gone to Whitehill," said Sylvia.

"That's like asking how many people are dead in a cemetery," said the doctor. He gave the answer to the old joke, and to Sylvia's question too. "All of 'em."

"If all the Remenzels who went to Whitehill were numbered, what number would Eli be?" said Sylvia. "That's what I'm getting at."

The question annoyed Doctor Remenzel a little. It didn't seem in very good taste. "It isn't the sort of thing you keep score on," he said.

"Guess," said his wife.

"Oh," he said, "you'd have to go back through all the records, all the way back to the end of the eighteenth century, even, to make any kind of a guess. And you'd have to decide whether to count the Schofields and

---

1. **Shah of Iran:** one of the wealthy former monarchs of Iran.

THE LIE 31

STRATEGIC READING FOR
Less-Proficient Readers

C Check to see that students clearly understand who the characters are, how they are related, and what is happening on the drive to Whitehill School.

- What is Doctor Remenzel doing as he rides in the car to Massachusetts? *(He is studying plans for an addition to a Whitehill School building.)* **Noting Relevant Details**

- How does Eli behave in the car? *(He is quiet and seems out of sorts.)* **Making Generalizations**

- Why does Eli's mother say he is number thirty-one? *(Eli may be the thirty-first Remenzel to attend Whitehill.)* **Restating**

Set a Purpose Have students read to find out if Eli passed his entrance exams and if his parents know the results of the exams.

Active Reading: QUESTION

D Have students discuss Mrs. Remenzel's excitement about the prospect of Eli's enrollment. Encourage them to note her interest in carving out an identity for Eli as the thirty-first Remenzel attending Whitehill.

CUSTOMIZING FOR
Students Acquiring English

2 The phrase *a simple-minded country girl at heart* implies information about Mrs. Remenzel's background. Ask students to guess what her childhood was like and how it was different from the doctor's. Explain that she probably did not grow up with the wealth that her husband did. Doctor Remenzel probably received superior schooling and was exposed to more of the world than his wife was.

Active Reading: EVALUATE

E Invite students to share their early impressions and opinions of Eli's mother. Urge them to point to particular passages in the text to support their statements.

---

the Haleys and the MacLellans as Remenzels."

"Please make a guess—" said Sylvia, "just people whose last names were Remenzel."

"Oh—" The doctor shrugged, rattled the plans. "Thirty maybe."

"So Eli is number thirty-one!" said Sylvia, delighted with the number. "You're number thirty-one, dear," she said to the back of Eli's head.

Doctor Remenzel rattled the plans again. "I don't want him going around saying something asinine, like he's number thirty-one," he said.

"Eli knows better than that," said Sylvia. She was a game, ambitious woman, with no money of her own at all. She had been married for sixteen years but was still openly curious and enthusiastic about the ways of families that had been rich for many generations.

"Just for my own curiosity—not so Eli can go around saying what number he is," said Sylvia, "I'm going to go wherever they keep the records and find out what number he is. That's what I'll do while you're at the meeting and Eli's doing whatever he has to do at the admissions office."

"All right," said Doctor Remenzel, "you go ahead and *do* that."

QUESTION
Why does Sylvia care what number Eli is?

"I will," said Sylvia. "I think things like that are interesting, even if you don't." She waited for a rise[2] on that but didn't get one. Sylvia enjoyed arguing with her husband about her lack of <u>reserve</u> and his <u>excess</u> of it, enjoyed saying, toward the end of arguments like that, "Well, I guess I'm just a simple-minded country girl at heart, and that's all I'll ever be, and I'm afraid you're going to have to get used to it."

But Doctor Remenzel didn't want to play that game. He found the dormitory plans more interesting.

"Will the new rooms have fireplaces?" said Sylvia. In the oldest part of the dormitory, several of the rooms had handsome fireplaces.

"That would practically double the cost of construction," said the doctor.

"I want Eli to have a room with a fireplace, if that's possible," said Sylvia.

"Those rooms are for seniors."

"I thought maybe through some fluke—"[3] said Sylvia.

"What kind of fluke do you have in mind?" said the doctor. "You mean I should demand that Eli be given a room with a fireplace?"

"Not *demand*—" said Sylvia.

"Request firmly?" said the doctor.

"Maybe I'm just a simple-minded country girl at heart," said Sylvia, "but I look through this catalogue, and I see all the buildings named after Remenzels, look through the back and see all the hundreds of thousands of dollars given by Remenzels for scholarships, and I just can't help thinking people named Remenzel are entitled to ask for a little something extra."

EVALUATE
What is your impression of Sylvia?

"Let me tell you in no uncertain terms," said Doctor Remenzel, "that you are not to ask for anything special for Eli—not anything."

"Of course I won't," said Sylvia. "Why do you always think I'm going to embarrass you?"

"I don't," he said.

"But I can still think what I think, can't I?" she said.

---

2. **rise:** an angry reaction to teasing or provoking.
3. **fluke:** a stroke of luck.

WORDS TO KNOW
reserve (rĭ-zûrv′) *n.* a keeping of one's feelings and thoughts to oneself
excess (ĭk-sĕs′) *n.* an amount greater than necessary; surplus

32

Mini-Lesson  Literary Concepts

REVIEWING CHARACTERIZATION
Remind students that characterization is the technique a writer uses to create and develop a character. There are four basic means of developing a character: (1) a physical description of the character; (2) the character's thoughts, speech, and actions; (3) the thoughts, speech, and actions of other characters; and (4) direct comments on a character's nature.

Application Have students think about the different means that Kurt Vonnegut uses to reveal the character of Eli's father in "The Lie." For example, have them find the physical descriptions and direct comments about the personality of Doctor Remenzel on page 31. Then have them note on pages 30–32 his actions and words to the other three people in the car. Students can also see on page 32 a comment of Mrs. Remenzel's that says something about her husband's character.

"If you have to," he said.

"I have to," she said cheerfully, utterly unrepentant. She leaned over the plans. "You think those people will like those rooms?"

"What people?" he said.

"The Africans," she said. She was talking about thirty Africans who, at the request of the State Department, were being admitted to Whitehill in the coming semester. It was because of them that the dormitory was being expanded.

"The rooms aren't for them," he said. "They aren't going to be segregated."

"Oh," said Sylvia. She thought about this awhile, and then she said, "Is there a chance Eli will have one of them for a roommate?"

"Freshmen draw lots[4] for roommates," said the doctor. "That piece of information's in the catalogue too."

"Eli?" said Sylvia.

"H'm?" said Eli.

"How would you feel about it if you had to room with one of those Africans?"

Eli shrugged listlessly.

"That's all right?" said Sylvia.

Eli shrugged again.

"I guess it's all right," said Sylvia.

"It had better be," said the doctor.

The Rolls-Royce pulled abreast of an old Chevrolet, a car in such bad repair that its back door was lashed shut with clothesline. Doctor Remenzel glanced casually at the driver, and then, with sudden excitement and pleasure, he told Ben Barkley to stay abreast of the car.

The doctor leaned across Sylvia, rolled down his window, yelled to the driver of the old Chevrolet, "Tom! Tom!"

The man was a Whitehill classmate of the doctor. He wore a Whitehill necktie, which he waved at Doctor Remenzel in gay recognition. And then he pointed to the fine young son who

Jerry (1955, repainted 1975), Fairfield Porter. Private collection.

sat beside him, conveyed with proud smiles and nods that the boy was bound for Whitehill.

Doctor Remenzel pointed to the chaos of

---

4. **draw lots:** pick numbers or names from a container to assure a random outcome.

WORDS TO KNOW

unrepentant (ŭn'rĭ-pĕn'tənt) *adj.* feeling or showing no regret

STRATEGIC READING FOR
Less-Proficient Readers

H Make sure that students are following the story by asking the following questions.

- Why can't Eli attend the Whitehill School for Boys? *(He failed the entrance examinations.)* **Noting Relevant Details**

- Why are his parents taking him to Whitehill? *(They don't know that he failed the exams, because Eli tore up the rejection letter from the school.)* **Restating**

- Now that you know the facts about Eli's exams, how would you explain his behavior in the car? *(He is very uncomfortable, because he has deceived his parents. He is anticipating his lie being found out.)* **Relating Cause and Effect**

Set a Purpose Have students read to find out about Whitehill School, its students, and Doctor Remenzel's feelings about privilege.

Literary Concept: IRONY

I Have students read the paragraph and explain why it is ironic. *(Possible response: It is ironic because Eli's parents are confident about Eli's acceptance, when in fact he has already failed the entrance exam.)*

Active Reading: PREDICT

J Invite students to predict the effects of Eli's deception on his parents. If students need help, you might wish to share the following thought processes with them:

Think-Aloud Model *I think that Eli's father will have a really bad reaction. He seems uptight and cranky, and I'm afraid he might lose his temper and get very angry with Eli. I think Eli's mother's reaction could be even worse. She seems excitable and much more impressed with the idea of Eli's actually being at the school, so her disappointment might be even greater.*

---

the back of Eli's head, beamed that his news was the same. In the wind blustering between the two cars they made a lunch date at the Holly House in North Marston, at the inn whose principal business was serving visitors to Whitehill.

"All right," said Doctor Remenzel to Ben Barkley, "drive on."

"You know," said Sylvia, "somebody really ought to write an article—" And she turned to look through the back window at the old car now shuddering far behind. "Somebody really ought to."

"What about?" said the doctor. He noticed that Eli had slumped way down in the front seat. "Eli!" he said sharply. "Sit up straight!" He returned his attention to Sylvia.

"Most people think prep schools are such snobbish things, just for people with money," said Sylvia, "but that isn't true." She leafed through the catalogue and found the quotation she was after.

"*The Whitehill School operates on the assumption,*" she read, "*that no boy should be deterred from applying for admission because his family is unable to pay the full cost of a Whitehill education. With this in mind, the Admissions Committee selects each year from approximately 3,000 candidates the 150 most promising and deserving boys, regardless of their parents' ability to pay the full $2,200 tuition. And those in need of financial aid are given it to the full extent of their need. In certain instances, the school will even pay for the clothing and transportation of a boy.*"

Sylvia shook her head. "I think that's perfectly amazing. It's something most people don't realize at all. A truck driver's son can come to Whitehill."

"If he's smart enough," he said.

"Thanks to the Remenzels," said Sylvia with pride.

"And a lot of other people too," said the doctor.

Sylvia read out loud again: "*In 1799, Eli Remenzel laid the foundation for the present Scholarship Fund by donating to the school forty acres in Boston. The school still owns twelve of those acres, their current evaluation being $3,000,000.*"

"Eli!" said the doctor. "Sit up! What's the matter with you?"

Eli sat up again but began to slump almost immediately, like a snowman in hell. Eli had good reason for slumping, for actually hoping to die or disappear. He could not bring himself to say what the reason was. He slumped because he knew he had been denied admission to Whitehill. He had failed the entrance examinations. Eli's parents did not know this, because Eli had found the awful notice in the mail and had torn it up.

Doctor Remenzel and his wife had no doubts whatsoever about their son's getting into Whitehill. It was inconceivable to them that Eli could not go there, so they had no curiosity as to how Eli had done on the examinations, were not puzzled when no report ever came.

"What all will Eli have to do to enroll?" said Sylvia as the black Rolls-Royce crossed the Rhode Island border.

"I don't know," said the doctor. "I suppose they've got it all complicated now with forms to be filled out in quadruplicate and punch-

> **PREDICT**
> What is going to happen when Eli's parents find out the truth?

WORDS TO KNOW
deter (dĭ-tûr') *v.* to discourage; prevent from acting
tuition (to͞o-ĭsh'ən) *n.* the fee charged for instruction at a college or private school
inconceivable (ĭn'kən-sē'və-bəl) *adj.* impossible to understand; unbelievable

34

Mini-Lesson Grammar

PUNCTUATING DIALOGUE Remind students that quotation marks are used at the beginning and end of direct quotations. Direct quotations always begin with a capital letter. Commas and periods are placed inside the quotation marks, and exclamation points and question marks are placed outside the quotation marks unless they belong to the quotation. Invite students to find examples of each of the above rules in the dialogue on page 34.

Application Have students correctly punctuate the following sentences.

1. When was the letter mailed asked Sylvia. *("When was the letter mailed?" asked Sylvia.)*
2. Did you hear me say how awful *(Did you hear me say "How awful"?)*

Reteaching/Reinforcement
- *Grammar Handbook,* anthology pp. 898–899
- *Grammar Mini-Lessons* copymasters p. 42, transparencies p. 33

Punctuating Dialogue, pp. 38, 666

34 THE LANGUAGE OF LITERATURE **Teacher's Edition**

card machines and bureaucrats. This business of entrance examinations is all new too. In my day a boy simply had an interview with the headmaster. The headmaster would look him over, ask him a few questions, and then say, 'There's a Whitehill boy.'"

"Did he ever say, 'There isn't a Whitehill boy'?" said Sylvia.

"Oh, sure," said Doctor Remenzel, "if a boy was impossibly stupid or something. There have to be standards. There have always been standards. The African boys have to meet the standards, just like anybody else. They aren't getting in just because the State Department wants to make friends. We made that clear. Those boys had to meet the standards."

"And they did?" said Sylvia.

"I suppose," said Doctor Remenzel. "I heard they're all in, and they all took the same examination Eli did."

"Was it a hard examination, dear?" Sylvia asked Eli. It was the first time she'd thought to ask.

"H'm," said Eli.

"What?" she said.

"Yes," said Eli.

"I'm glad they've got high standards," she said, and then she realized that this was a fairly silly statement. "Of course they've got high standards," she said. "That's why it's such a famous school. That's why people who go there do so well in later life."

Sylvia resumed her reading of the catalogue again, opened out a folding map of the Sward, as the campus of Whitehill was traditionally called. She read off the names of features that memorialized Remenzels—the Sanford Remenzel Bird Sanctuary, the George MacLellan Remenzel Skating Rink, the Eli Remenzel Memorial Dormitory—and then she read out loud a quatrain⁵ printed on one corner of the map:

> *When night falleth gently*
> *Upon the green Sward,*
> *It's Whitehill, dear Whitehill,*
> *Our thoughts all turn toward.*

"You know," said Sylvia, "school songs are so corny when you just read them. But when I hear the Glee Club sing those words, they sound like the most beautiful words ever written, and I want to cry."

"Um," said Doctor Remenzel.

"Did a Remenzel write them?"

"I don't think so," said Doctor Remenzel. And then he said, "No—wait. That's the *new* song. A Remenzel didn't write it. Tom Hilyer wrote it."

"The man in that old car we passed?"

"Sure," said Doctor Remenzel. "Tom wrote it. I remember when he wrote it."

"A scholarship boy wrote it?" said Sylvia. "I think that's awfully nice. He *was* a scholarship boy, wasn't he?"

"His father was an ordinary automobile mechanic in North Marston."

"You hear what a democratic school you're going to, Eli?" said Sylvia.

Half an hour later Ben Barkley brought the limousine to a stop before the Holly House, a rambling country inn twenty years older than the Republic. The inn was on the edge of the Whitehill Sward, glimpsing the school's rooftops and spires over the innocent wilderness of the Sanford Remenzel Bird Sanctuary.

Ben Barkley was sent away with the car for an hour and a half. Doctor Remenzel shepherded

---

5. **quatrain** (kwŏt′rān′): a four-line poem or stanza.

WORDS TO KNOW

bureaucrat (byŏŏr′ə-krăt′) *n.* an official who deals with details of administrative procedure

Art Note

Amherst Campus No. 1 by Fairfield Porter This work emphasizes the way in which human beings and nature coexist in the academic setting of Amherst College in Amherst, Massachusetts. The beauty and grandeur of the forested mountains sweep across the background of the painting. Yet Porter places in the foreground the corners and partial faces of buildings, three richly colored automobiles, and a lone human figure. The painting's composition stresses not the disjuncture but rather the harmony of the human and natural worlds.

Reading the Art Why do you think Porter chose to place a single human being in this painting? Why might he have decided against painting more than one person? Would the effect of this painting be any different if the automobiles and parking lot had been left out? Why or why not?

Amherst Campus No. 1 (1969), Fairfield Porter. Oil on canvas, 62″ × 46″, The Parrish Art Museum, Southampton, New York, gift of the Estate of Fairfield Porter. Photo by Jim Strong.

36 UNIT ONE PART 1: TAUGHT BY EXPERIENCE

Mini-Lesson  Reading Skills/Strategies

ACTIVE READING: QUESTIONING
Remind students that active readers use strategies as they read. Asking questions about what is happening when you read is one useful strategy. Exploring possible reasons for what is going on in the story and how characters feel can help you better understand the selection.

Application Ask students to reread the selection, keeping a list of questions about the main characters as they read. When students have finished reading, invite several volunteers to adopt the identities of the main characters. Then encourage the class to ask the characters questions from their lists. Have the students who are pretending to be the characters attempt to answer these questions based on information in the story. Encourage these students to try to speak and behave as they imagine the characters might.

Reteaching/Reinforcement
• *Unit One Resource Book*, p. 14

Sylvia and Eli into a familiar, low-ceilinged world of pewter,[6] clocks, lovely old woods, agreeable servants, elegant food and drink.

Eli, clumsy with horror of what was surely to come, banged a grandmother clock with his elbow as he passed, made the clock cry.

Sylvia excused herself. Doctor Remenzel and Eli went to the threshold of the dining room, where a hostess welcomed them both by name. They were given a table beneath an oil portrait of one of the three Whitehill boys who had gone on to become president of the United States.

The dining room was filling quickly with families. What every family had was at least one boy about Eli's age. Most of the boys wore Whitehill blazers[7]—black, with pale blue piping, with Whitehill seals on their breast pockets. A few, like Eli, were not yet entitled to wear blazers, were simply hoping to get in.

The doctor ordered a martini, then turned to his son and said, "Your mother has the idea that you're entitled to special privileges around here. I hope you don't have that idea too."

"No, sir," said Eli.

"It would be a source of the greatest embarrassment to me," said Doctor Remenzel with considerable grandeur, "if I were ever to hear that you had used the name Remenzel as though you thought Remenzels were something special."

"I know," said Eli wretchedly.

"That settles it," said the doctor. He had nothing more to say about it. He gave abbreviated salutes to several people he knew in the room, speculated as to what sort of party had reserved a long banquet table that was set up along one wall. He decided that it was for a visiting athletic team. Sylvia arrived, and Eli had to be told in a sharp whisper to stand when a woman came to a table.

Sylvia was full of news. The long table, she related, was for the thirty boys from Africa. "I'll bet that's more colored people than have eaten here since this place was founded," she said softly. "How fast things change these days!"

"You're right about how fast things change," said Doctor Kemenzel. "You're wrong about the colored people who've eaten here. This used to be a busy part of the Underground Railroad."[8]

"Really?" said Sylvia. "How exciting." She looked all about herself in a birdlike way. "I think everything's exciting here. I only wish Eli had a blazer on."

Doctor Remenzel reddened. "He isn't entitled to one," he said.

"I know that," said Sylvia.

"I thought you were going to ask somebody for permission to put a blazer on Eli right away," said the doctor.

"I wouldn't do that," said Sylvia, a little offended now. "Why are you always afraid I'll embarrass you?"

"Never mind. Excuse me. Forget it," said Doctor Remenzel.

Sylvia brightened again, put her hand on Eli's arm, and looked radiantly at a man in the dining-room doorway. "There's my favorite person in all the world, next to my son and husband," she said. She meant Dr. Donald Warren, headmaster of the Whitehill School. A thin gentleman in his early sixties, Doctor Warren was in the doorway with the manager of the inn, looking over the arrangements for the Africans.

It was then that Eli got up abruptly, fled the dining room, fled as much of the nightmare as

---

6. **pewter** (pyo͞o′tər): a metal—consisting mainly of tin—formerly used for the making of fine kitchen utensils and tableware.
7. **blazers:** lightweight single-breasted jackets, often used as part of school uniforms.
8. **Underground Railroad:** a secret system, created by antislavery forces before the Civil War, to help slaves escape to free states or Canada.

THE LIE **37**

Mini-Lesson The Writer's Style

DENOTATION AND CONNOTATION Help students understand that words have two types of meanings. A denotation is the way a word is defined in the dictionary. A connotation is a feeling or thought that a word suggests. Two words may have similar denotations but very different connotations. For instance, the words *confident* and *cocky* have similar denotations. However, *confident* has a positive connotation, whereas *cocky* has a negative connotation.

Application Have students write a short description of Eli, first using words with positive connotations. Then have students rewrite the description, this time using words with negative connotations.

Reteaching/Reinforcement
- *Writing Handbook*, anthology pp. 832–833
- *Writing Mini-Lessons* transparencies, p. 37

Denotation and Connotation, pp. 314, 696

Literary Concept:
THIRD-PERSON POINT OF VIEW

P Help students understand that Kurt Vonnegut's use of the third-person point of view in "The Lie" allows his narrator to give a bird's-eye view of the activities of several characters at once. Ask students how this part of the story would be different if the story had been told from Doctor Remenzel's point of view only. *(The reader probably would not know about the failed exam at this point and therefore would not understand Eli's behavior.)*

Literary Concept:
CHARACTERIZATION

Q Ask students to explain what this speech by Doctor Warren tells them about his character. *(Possible response: His words seem sincere, and they show him to be a straightforward, frank man with a strong sense of loyalty and integrity.)*

Active Reading: CLARIFY

R Discuss the questions and comments students have at this point in the selection. Have them consider what Eli, having fled the scene, might be feeling as his parents talk to Doctor Warren. *(Doctor Warren and Eli know that Eli has not been invited to enroll at the Whitehill School for Boys, because he failed the exam.)*

---

he could possibly leave behind. He brushed past Doctor Warren rudely, though he knew him well, though Doctor Warren spoke his name. Doctor Warren looked after him sadly.

"I'll be damned," said Doctor Remenzel. "What brought that on?"

"Maybe he really *is* sick," said Sylvia.

The Remenzels had no time to react more elaborately, because Doctor Warren spotted them and crossed quickly to their table. He greeted them, some of his perplexity about Eli showing in his greeting. He asked if he might sit down.

"Certainly, of course," said Doctor Remenzel expansively. "We'd be honored if you did. Heavens."

"Not to eat," said Doctor Warren. "I'll be eating at the long table with the new boys. I would like to talk, though." He saw that there were five places set at the table. "You're expecting someone?"

"We passed Tom Hilyer and his boy on the way," said Doctor Remenzel. "They'll be along in a minute."

"Good, good," said Doctor Warren absently. He fidgeted, looked again in the direction in which Eli had disappeared.

"Tom's boy will be going to Whitehill in the fall?" said Doctor Remenzel.

"H'm?" said Doctor Warren. "Oh—yes, yes. Yes, he will."

"Is he a scholarship boy, like his father?" said Sylvia.

"That's not a polite question," said Doctor Remenzel severely.

"I beg your pardon," said Sylvia.

"No, no—that's a perfectly proper question these days," said Doctor Warren. "We don't keep that sort of information very secret any more. We're proud of our scholarship boys, and they have every reason to be proud of themselves. Tom's boy got the highest score anyone's ever got on the entrance examinations. We feel privileged to have him."

"We never *did* find out Eli's score," said Doctor Remenzel. He said it with good-humored <u>resignation</u>, without expectation that Eli had done especially well.

"A good strong medium, I imagine," said Sylvia. She said this on the basis of Eli's grades in primary school, which had ranged from medium to terrible.

The headmaster looked surprised. "I didn't tell you his scores?" he said.

"We haven't seen you since he took the examinations," said Doctor Remenzel.

CLARIFY
What do Eli and Dr. Warren know that Dr. and Mrs. Remenzel don't know?

"The letter I wrote you—" said Doctor Warren.

"What letter?" said Doctor Remenzel. "Did we get a letter?"

"A letter from me," said Doctor Warren, with growing <u>incredulity</u>. "The hardest letter I ever had to write."

Sylvia shook her head. "We never got any letter from you."

Doctor Warren sat back, looking very ill. "I mailed it myself," he said. "It was definitely mailed—two weeks ago."

Doctor Remenzel shrugged. "The U.S. mails don't lose much," he said, "but I guess that now and then something gets misplaced."

Doctor Warren cradled his head in his hands. "Oh, dear—oh, my, oh, Lord," he said. "I was surprised to see Eli here. I wondered that he would want to come along with you."

"He didn't come along just to see the scenery,"

WORDS TO KNOW
resignation (rĕz′ĭg-nā′shən) *n.* an unresisting acceptance of what seems unavoidable
incredulity (ĭn′krĭ-doo′lĭ-tē) *n.* an unwillingness to accept what is offered as true; disbelief

38

Mini-Lesson — Study Skills

TAKING ESSAY TESTS: PLANNING YOUR ANSWERS Remind students that essay questions contain writing prompts, which ask students to write a short composition. A writing prompt gives information on the form an essay should take or the audience one should write for. Planning an essay involves carefully studying the writing prompt to know exactly what the topic of the essay should be. Tell students to look for key words in the prompt that tell them what to do, such as *identify, describe, explain,* or *compare and contrast*. They should organize their ideas on scrap paper before beginning to write their essay.

Application Encourage students to plan an essay in response to the following writing prompt:

Write a brief essay about whether or not you think "The Lie" would make a good movie. In your essay, use specific details from the story to explain your opinion.

said Doctor Remenzel. "He came to enroll."

"I want to know what was in the letter," said Sylvia.

Doctor Warren raised his head, folded his hands. "What the letter said was this, and no other words could be more difficult for me to say: 'On the basis of his work in primary school and his scores on the entrance examinations, I must tell you that your son and my good friend Eli cannot possibly do the work required of boys at Whitehill.'" Doctor Warren's voice steadied, and so did his gaze. "To admit Eli to Whitehill, to expect him to do Whitehill work," he said, "would be both unrealistic and cruel."

The chaos that followed this statement was not only emotional. It was real as well. Thirty African boys, escorted by several faculty members, State Department men, and diplomats from their own countries, filed into the dining room.

And Tom Hilyer and his boy, having no idea that something had just gone awfully wrong for the Remenzels, came in, too, and said hello to the Remenzels and Doctor Warren gaily, as though life couldn't possibly be better.

"I'll talk to you more about this later, if you like," Doctor Warren said to the Remenzels, rising. "I have to go now, but later on—" He left quickly.

"My mind's a blank," said Sylvia. "My mind's a perfect blank."

Tom Hilyer and his boy sat down. Hilyer looked at the menu before him, clapped his hands, and said, "What's good? I'm hungry." And then he said, "Say—where's your boy?"

"He stepped out for a moment," said Doctor Remenzel evenly.

"We've got to find him," said Sylvia to her husband.

"In time, in due time," said Doctor Remenzel.

"That letter," said Sylvia; "Eli knew about it. He found it and tore it up. Of course he did!"

She started to cry, thinking of the hideous trap Eli had caught himself in.

"I'm not interested right now in what Eli's done," said Doctor Remenzel. "Right now I'm a lot more interested in what some other people are going to do."

"What do you mean?" said Sylvia.

Doctor Remenzel stood impressively, angry and determined. "I mean," he said, "I'm going to see how quickly people can change their minds around here."

"Please," said Sylvia, trying to hold him, trying to calm him, "we've got to find Eli. That's the first thing."

"The first thing," said Doctor Remenzel quite loudly, "is to get Eli admitted to Whitehill. After that we'll find him, and we'll bring him back."

"But darling—" said Sylvia.

"No 'but' about it," said Doctor Remenzel. "There's a majority of the board of overseers in this room at this very moment. Every one of them is a close friend of mine, or a close friend of my father. If they tell Doctor Warren Eli's in, that's it—Eli's in. If there's room for all these other people," he said, "there's damn well room for Eli too."

e strode quickly to a table nearby, sat down heavily, and began to talk to a fierce-looking and splendid old gentleman who was eating there. The old gentleman was chairman of the board.

Sylvia apologized to the baffled Hilyers and then went in search of Eli.

Asking this person and that person, Sylvia found him. He was outside—all alone on a bench in a bower of lilacs that had just begun to bud.

Eli heard his mother's coming on the gravel path, stayed where he was, resigned. "Did you find out," he said, "or do I still have to tell you?"

THE LIE **39**

STRATEGIC READING FOR
Less-Proficient Readers

- Make sure that students are clear about the events that follow the revelation of Eli's secret.

- How do the Remenzels find out about Eli's lie? *(Dr. Warren informs them that Eli did not pass his entrance examinations.)* **Reviewing**

- What does Doctor Remenzel attempt to do? *(He tries to persuade the board of overseers to admit Eli anyway.)* **Summarizing**

- Why does Eli feel ashamed and his father feel obliged to apologize? *(His father has asked for special treatment, just as he had instructed Eli never to do.)* **Drawing Conclusions and Making Inferences**

CUSTOMIZING FOR
Gifted and Talented Students

Have students discuss the idea of preferential treatment. Was Eli right to feel ashamed of his father's actions? Is it unfair to think that an institution might reward a family's generous donation? Challenge students to debate this example of privilege.

COMPREHENSION CHECK

1. Where are the Remenzels taking their son? *(the Whitehill School for Boys, a private preparatory school in Massachusetts)*

2. Why didn't Eli tell his parents that he failed the entrance exams? *(He knew his parents had always expected him to go to Whitehill, and he couldn't bear the thought of telling them that he would not be attending the school.)*

3. What difficult news does Doctor Warren deliver to Doctor and Mrs. Remenzel? *(He tells them that Eli was not accepted at Whitehill.)*

4. Why is Eli ashamed at the end of the story? *(Because his father has asked the school board to make an exception and let Eli in despite his poor grades and test scores.)*

"About you?" she said gently. "About not getting in? Doctor Warren told us."

"I tore his letter up," said Eli.

"I can understand that," she said. "Your father and I have always made you feel that you had to go to Whitehill, that nothing else would do."

"I feel better," said Eli. He tried to smile, found he could do it easily. "I feel so much better now that it's over. I tried to tell you a couple of times—but I just couldn't. I didn't know how."

"That's my fault, not yours," she said.

"What's Father doing?" said Eli.

Sylvia was so intent on comforting Eli that she'd put out of her mind what her husband was up to. Now she realized that Doctor Remenzel was making a ghastly mistake. She didn't want Eli admitted to Whitehill, could see what a cruel thing that would be.

She couldn't bring herself to tell the boy what his father was doing, so she said, "He'll be along in a minute, dear. He understands." And then she said, "You wait here, and I'll go get him and come right back."

But she didn't have to go to Doctor Remenzel. At that moment the big man came out of the inn and caught sight of his wife and son. He came to her and to Eli. He looked dazed.

"Well?" she said.

"They—they all said no," said Doctor Remenzel, very <u>subdued</u>.

"That's for the best," said Sylvia. "I'm relieved. I really am."

"Who said no?" said Eli. "Who said no to what?"

"The members of the board," said Doctor Remenzel, not looking anyone in the eye. "I asked them to make an exception in your case—to reverse their decision and let you in."

Eli stood, his face filled with incredulity and shame that were instant. "You what?" he said, and there was no childishness in the way he said it. Next came anger. "You shouldn't have done that!" he said to his father.

Doctor Remenzel nodded. "So I've already been told."

"That isn't done!" said Eli. "How awful! You shouldn't have."

"You're right," said Doctor Remenzel, accepting the scolding lamely.

"Now I *am* ashamed," said Eli, and he showed that he was.

Doctor Remenzel, in his wretchedness, could find no strong words to say. "I apologize to you both," he said at last. "It was a very bad thing to try."

"Now a Remenzel *has* asked for something," said Eli.

"I don't suppose Ben's back yet with the car?" said Doctor Remenzel. It was obvious that Ben wasn't. "We'll wait out here for him," he said. "I don't want to go back in there now."

"A Remenzel asked for something—as though a Remenzel were something special," said Eli.

"I don't suppose—" said Doctor Remenzel, and he left the sentence unfinished, dangling in the air.

"You don't suppose what?" said his wife, her face puzzled.

"I don't suppose," said Doctor Remenzel, "that we'll ever be coming here anymore." ❖

WORDS TO KNOW

subdued (səb-dōōd′) *adj.* toned down; diminished in intensity **subdue** *v.*

Mini-Lesson Spelling

USING SUFFIXES Tell students one important rule for adding suffixes: When adding a suffix beginning with a vowel to a word ending in silent e, drop the e.

inconceive	+ able	= inconceivable
ridicule	+ ous	= ridiculous
ride	+ ing	= riding
subdue	+ ed	= subdued
ramble	+ ing	= rambling

Application Have students write each word using the suffix shown.

1. lose + ing
2. frustrate + ion
3. execute + ive
4. serve + ant
5. move + able
6. write + ing
7. arrive + al
8. accuse + ation
9. loose + er
10. sincere + ity

Ask students to look for more words in the selection that fit this pattern and to write them in their personal word lists.

Reteaching/Reinforcement
- *Unit One Resource Book*, p. 15

RESPONDING OPTIONS

FROM PERSONAL RESPONSE TO CRITICAL ANALYSIS

REFLECT
1. What were your reactions to Eli? Record your thoughts in your notebook. Share your reactions with a partner.

RETHINK
2. Who do you think deserves blame for the lie? Explain your answer.
3. Which characters feel pressure in this story? What kinds of pressure do they feel? Give reasons to support your answer.
4. What do you think of Dr. and Mrs. Remenzel?

Close Textual Reading

Consider
- their expectations of Eli
- their remarks about the African students
- how they respond when they discover the lie
- their reactions at the end of the story

5. Do you sympathize with any of the characters in the story? Why or why not?

RELATE
6. Compare and contrast the way teenagers facing today's pressures react to them with the way Eli reacts. Do you consider his reaction normal? Explain your opinion.

LITERARY CONCEPTS

An author must decide from whose perspective a story will be told. A story told from the **third-person point of view** is narrated by a person outside the story, who uses pronouns such as *he, she,* and *it*. Why do you think Kurt Vonnegut chose to tell "The Lie" from the third-person point of view? How would the story be different if Eli narrated it?

A contrast between what is expected and what actually happens in a story is called **irony**. For example, the Remenzels' snobbish attitude about the school's high standards makes it ironic that their own son can't meet them. What do you think is ironic about Dr. Remenzel's actions at the end of the story?

Multimodal Learning

ANOTHER PATHWAY
Cooperative Learning
The members of the Remenzel family have trouble communicating with one another. Plan and conduct a panel discussion in which you and other students analyze the Remenzels' problems and offer suggestions to help them.

QUICKWRITES

1. Write a **personal narrative** about a time when you disappointed someone else or when you were disappointed by someone. Try to judge whether anyone's expectations were too high.
2. Compose a **quatrain** that could be the start of a song about your school, or add four lines to the one about Whitehill on page 35.
3. What different way of handling his situation might you suggest to Eli? Write a **letter of advice** to him.

 **PORTFOLIO** *Save your writing. You may want to use it later as a springboard to a piece for your portfolio.*

THE LIE 41

From Personal Response to Critical Analysis

1. Remind students to be specific about aspects of Eli's character and behavior.
2. Possible responses: Eli deserves the blame, because he was the one who was dishonest; Eli's parents deserve the blame, because they have placed unfair pressure on Eli.
3. Possible responses: Eli feels pressure to be an academic success. Mrs. Remenzel feels constant pressure from her husband to be different from the way she is. Doctor Remenzel feels the pressure to carry on family tradition.
4. Possible response: Eli's parents are both out of touch with Eli. However, they are quite different from each other: his father is proper and restrained, whereas his mother is more frank but unpredictable.
5. Be sure students explain their responses.
6. Answers will vary.

Another Pathway
Cooperative Learning Several students might pinpoint specific problem areas in the Remenzels' relationships as another student records what is presented. Another student could lead a discussion in which a list of suggestions for solving the problems is made. Throughout the activity, all group members should participate in a freeform exchange of ideas.

Rubric
3 Full Accomplishment Students identify the Remenzels' key problems and offer reasonable suggestions in an organized panel discussion.
2 Substantial Accomplishment Students identify some problems and offer some suggestions in a fairly organized panel discussion.
1 Little or Partial Accomplishment Students have difficulty identifying problems and offering suggestions.

Literary Concepts

Third-Person Point of View Vonnegut may have chosen the third-person point of view so he would have an objective narrator. In this way the narrator has no obvious bias that affects the reader's judgment. If Eli narrated, there would be little or no suspense about the nature of the lie and Eli's feelings.

Irony His actions are ironic because he made such a big deal out of lecturing Eli on not asking for special treatment.

QuickWrites

1. Encourage students to make notes about the experience before they write. Have them consider what information they need to give the reader.
2. Before students write, have them jot down what it is they wish to say. It may help them to say their lines aloud.
3. Have students think about adopting a diplomatic attitude before they begin. Remind them to outline two or three points they wish to make before they start.

The Writer's Craft
Autobiographical Incident, pp. 27–39
Writing a Poem, pp. 72–83

THE LANGUAGE OF LITERATURE TEACHER'S EDITION 41

Words to Know

Exercise A
1. office; deals with administrative matters
2. no; fighting and being resigned, or accepting, are opposites
3. schools
4. probably not, because the sharing of thoughts and ideas are fundamental to teaching and learning
5. anxious to explain myself

Exercise B
1. synonym, antonym
2. synonym, antonym
3. antonym, antonym
4. antonym, antonym
5. synonym, antonym

Reteaching/Reinforcement
- *Unit One Resource Book*, p. 16

KURT VONNEGUT, JR.

For many years Kurt Vonnegut, Jr., was saddled with the reputation of being a writer only of science fiction. This caused his first several novels to go unreviewed and unappreciated by the literary community. In the 1970s, he became a cult favorite among high school and college students.

Across the Curriculum

Math *Getting a Whitehill Education* Have students study the first italicized passage on page 34 and calculate the percentage of applicants to Whitehill who gain admission each year *(150 out of 3,000 is 5 percent)*. Then have them determine the amount of money Whitehill would receive if an entire year's students paid the full tuition *($330,000)*.

Science *Signs of Spring* Vonnegut includes references to willows and lilacs about to bloom in the early spring. Have students research the life cycles and varieties of either of these two forms of plant life. You may wish to have students work in groups of three or four to complete the activity cooperatively.

AUTHOR BACKGROUND
Kurt Vonnegut, Jr. In this film, the author tells a writers' workshop about the changes technology has caused in the arts. He also discusses the social issues dealt with in his work.

Side A, Frame 4276

Multimodal Learning

ALTERNATIVE ACTIVITIES

1. **Cooperative Learning** With a small group of classmates, look up and discuss the definition of the term *stereotype*. Then **list** stereotypes of rich people that you've heard. Finally, look through the story to locate behaviors that seem stereotypical of the rich.

2. With other students, **dramatize** the conversation that might take place between the Remenzels and Ben Barkley, the chauffeur, when the family returns to the car.

WORDS TO KNOW

EXERCISE A Answer the questions on your paper.

1. Would you be more likely to find a **bureaucrat** in an office or on a playground? Why?
2. If you fight a school policy, are you acting with **resignation**? Why or why not?
3. Who or what receives **tuition**?
4. Do principals want their teachers to act with **reserve**? Why or why not?
5. If a teacher looked at you with **incredulity**, how would you feel? Explain.

EXERCISE B Copy the following items on your paper. Label each word that follows a boldfaced word as a synonym or antonym of the boldfaced word, as in the example.

Example: **large** big *synonym* small *antonym*

1. **excess**	surplus	shortage
2. **inconceivable**	unimaginable	understandable
3. **subdued**	intense	excited
4. **unrepentant**	sorry	remorseful
5. **deter**	prevent	encourage

KURT VONNEGUT, JR.

The Great Depression of the 1930s made a lasting impression on Kurt Vonnegut and strongly influenced his writing. During that period, his architect father faced ten years of unemployment, while his mother unsuccessfully tried writing fiction. Although Vonnegut's parents had attended private schools, they could not afford to send their son to a private school.

After college, Vonnegut served in the U.S. infantry during World War II and was awarded a Purple Heart. Captured by the Germans, he was sheltered in an underground meat locker in Dresden during the Allied firebombing of that city, in which 135,000 people died. Afterward, he was set to work digging corpses from the ruins. Twenty-three years passed before he could write about what he had seen.

1922–

Vonnegut's books, with their strongly antiwar, antitechnology, and antiscience themes, have sold in the millions. There are no heroes and villains in his stories, but he says, "I have always rigged my stories as to include myself."

OTHER WORKS "The Kid Nobody Could Handle," "Long Walk to Forever," "Harrison Bergeron"

Extended Reading

- AUTHOR BACKGROUND

42 UNIT ONE PART 1: TAUGHT BY EXPERIENCE

Alternative Activities

1. Remind students to consider both positive and negative characteristics as they think about stereotypes of wealthy people. Students may find it helpful to make separate columns for these two general categories. As students examine the story for examples of stereotypical behavior, it will be instructive for them to note also any examples of the Remenzels' behavior that go against the stereotype.

2. Encourage students to reread the first few pages of the story to familiarize themselves with the way Ben Barkley and the Remenzels interact. It might help students to improvise the scene and have this dialogue jotted down. This improvised script could serve as a first draft or as a springboard for the final dramatization.

Focus on Nonfiction

What many readers enjoy reading most is **nonfiction**—writing about real people, places, and events. Nonfiction falls into two broad categories. One category, called **informative nonfiction,** is mainly written to provide factual information. Nonfiction of this type includes history and science books, encyclopedias, pamphlets, and most of the articles in magazines and newspapers. An example of informative nonfiction that you will read in this book is the Historical Insight on page 119, which gives information about developments in space exploration.

The other category of nonfiction is called **literary nonfiction** because it is written to be read and experienced in much the same way as fiction. However, literary nonfiction differs from fiction in that it deals with real people rather than fictional characters and with settings and plots that are not imagined but are actual places and true events.

The selections of literary nonfiction you will read in this book include **autobiographies, biographies,** and **essays.**

AUTOBIOGRAPHY An autobiography is the true story of a person's life, told by that person. It is almost always written from the first-person point of view. In this book, you will read an excerpt from an autobiography by Clifton L. Taulbert, in which Taulbert describes an influential person in his life.

An autobiography is usually book length because it covers a long period of the writer's life. However, there are shorter types of autobiographical writing, such as **journals, diaries,** and **memoirs.**

BIOGRAPHY A biography is the true story of a person's life, told by someone else. The writer, or **biographer,** interviews the subject if possible and also researches the subject's life by reading letters, books, diaries, and any other information he or she can find. In this book, you will read an excerpt from a biography of Harriet Tubman, a famous runaway slave who helped other slaves escape from the United States to Canada.

As you will see, biographies and autobiographies often contain many elements that fiction contains, such as character, setting, and plot.

FOCUS ON NONFICTION

This feature defines *nonfiction* and provides an explanation of the terms used to discuss it. It also introduces students to the conventions of the genre and suggests strategies for reading nonfiction. The terms introduced here are covered in depth in the nonfiction selections that follow.

Objectives

- To understand and appreciate nonfiction
- To understand the categories of nonfiction: informative nonfiction and literary nonfiction (including autobiographies, biographies, and essays)
- To learn effective strategies for reading nonfiction

Teaching Strategies:
CATEGORIES OF NONFICTION
Autobiography Have a volunteer read the description of autobiography aloud. Then draw on the chalkboard the web shown and use it to show the characteristics of an autobiography.

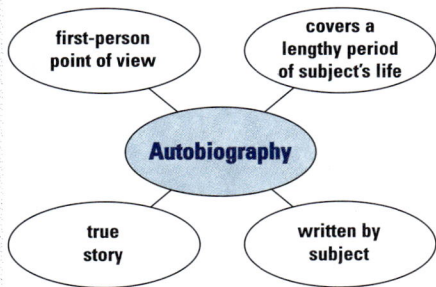

Biography After students read the passage, invite them to list people who would be good subjects for a biography. Spark discussion with these names: Dr. Martin Luther King, Jr., Hillary Rodham Clinton, Mohandes Gandhi, Pocahontas.

Essay Read some essays from newspapers and magazines. Have students explain why each selection is classified as an essay.

Reading Strategies: MODELING
Invite volunteers to read aloud the Strategies for Reading Nonfiction. Tell students they will be using these strategies as they read an excerpt from *Reflections on the Civil War* on page 45 and other nonfiction selections throughout the book. Then model the strategies as students read the excerpt. You may wish to use the models provided or create your own.

- **Preview** *"This selection appears to be about the soldiers from both the North and South who fought in the Civil War."*

- **Figure out the organization** *"This is a historical selection that is not really organized chronologically. The author organizes it around certain topics and stories that he shares with the reader."*

- **Separate facts and opinions** *"The author presents many facts about the Civil War such as statistics about Northern and Southern soldiers. Sometimes the author forms opinions about these facts as when he says that the boys from the country made better fighters because they were more self-reliant."*

- **Question as you read** *"I wonder where the author found some of this information and stories about the Civil War?"*

- **Make predictions** *"I think the writer will end the selection with another story that shows how both Northern and Southern soldiers were very similar."*

- **Clarify your understanding** *"It seems that the Civil War did not involve as clear a split between North and South as I thought."*

- **Continually evaluate what you read** *"This piece was very interesting. I liked the way the author used so many anecdotes about the soldiers to make some of his points."*

ESSAY An essay is a short piece of nonfiction that deals with one subject. Essays are often found in newspapers and magazines. The writer might share an opinion, try to entertain or persuade the reader, or simply describe an incident that has special significance. Essays that explain how the author feels about a subject are called **informal essays** or **personal essays.** In this book, the selection "The Power of the Powerless" is an example of an informal essay. **Formal essays** are scholarly and serious and are rarely found in literature textbooks.

STRATEGIES FOR READING NONFICTION

Nonfiction can be read as literature or as a source of information. The nonfiction selections in this book will provide you with opportunities both to learn new information and to enjoy the true stories and opinions the authors have to share.

Use the following strategies when you read nonfiction:

- **Preview the selection.** Before you read a selection, look at the title, the pictures or diagrams, and any subtitles or terms in boldface or italic type. All of these will give you an idea of what the selection is about.

- **Figure out the organization.** If the work is a biography, an autobiography, or a historical selection, the organization is probably chronological—that is, events are told in the order they happened. Other selections may be organized around ideas the author wants to discuss.

- **Separate facts and opinions.** Facts are statements that can be proved, such as "The letter written by Frederick Douglass is the shortest nonfiction selection in this book." Opinions are statements that cannot be proved. They simply express a person's beliefs, such as "'The Clown' is the funniest nonfiction selection in this book." Writers sometimes present opinions as if they were facts. Be sure you can recognize the difference.

- **Question as you read.** "Why did things happen the way they did?" "Who or what caused this event?" "How did people feel?" "What is the writer's opinion?" Try to decide whether you share the writer's opinion or have different ideas on the subject.

- **Make predictions.** During your reading, stop now and then and try to predict what will come next. Sometimes you will be surprised by what happens or by what an author has to say about an issue.

- **Clarify your understanding.** As you read, add new information to what you have already learned, and see if your ideas and opinions change.

- **Continually evaluate what you read.** Form opinions about the people, events, and ideas that are presented. Decide whether you like the way the piece was written.

Finally, it is important to recognize that your understanding of a selection does not end when you stop reading. As you think more about what you have read and discuss it with others, you will find that your understanding continues to grow.

PREVIEWING

NONFICTION

from Reflections on the Civil War
Bruce Catton

PERSONAL CONNECTION Activating Prior Knowledge
This selection tells about young soldiers during the Civil War. What do you already know about Civil War soldiers? What do you want to know? With your classmates, make a chart like the one shown here and fill in the first two columns. You will complete the third column after you read the selection.

What We Know About Civil War Soldiers	What We Want to Know About Them	What We Learned About Them

Building Background

HISTORICAL CONNECTION

Confederate cap worn during the Battle of Gettysburg.

During the American Civil War (1861–1865), the Northern states, called the Union, and the Southern states, called the Confederacy, fought each other in the bloodiest war in U.S. history. More than 600,000 American soldiers died, nearly as many as have been killed in all our nation's other wars combined.

A young man who joined the army during the Civil War had a hard life. He was issued a poorly made uniform, ill-fitting shoes, and unappetizing food rations. His only weapon was a musket, a gun that required reloading after each shot. As part of a regiment—a large unit of soldiers—he experienced a daily life quite different from anything he may have known or imagined before.

READING CONNECTION Active Reading/Setting a Purpose

Finding the Main Idea Authors of nonfiction often organize each paragraph around a main idea. The main idea is often stated in a **topic sentence** at the beginning of the paragraph, although it may be stated anywhere in the paragraph. Other sentences in the paragraph give details about the main idea. Look for topic sentences as you read this selection to help you understand the organization of Catton's thoughts about young soldiers and the lives they led during the Civil War.

LASERLINKS
- HISTORICAL CONNECTION
- VISUAL VOCABULARY

45

OVERVIEW

Objectives
- To understand and appreciate a historical essay about Civil War soldiers
- To understand how to find the main idea
- To identify and understand the use of anecdotes
- To appreciate the use of colloquial expressions in creating an informal style
- To express understanding of the selection through a choice of writing forms, including a letter, an anecdote, and an article
- To extend understanding of the selection through a variety of multimodal and cross-curricular activities

Skills

READING SKILLS/STRATEGIES
- Finding the main idea

THE WRITER'S STYLE
- Stating ideas clearly
- Colloquial expressions

GRAMMAR
- Complex sentences

LITERARY CONCEPTS
- Anecdote
- Description

SPELLING
- Adverbs that end in -ly

SPEAKING, LISTENING, AND VIEWING
- Music
- Group discussion
- Oral presentation

Cross-Curricular Connections

SOCIAL STUDIES
- Women in the Civil War
- Civil War battles

MATHEMATICS
- Circle graphs

SCIENCE
- Malaria

HISTORY
- The Underground Railroad

GEOGRAPHY
- Location of cities

HISTORICAL CONNECTION
Civil War Soldiers The Civil War was the bloodiest war in U.S. history. Here students will see Mathew Brady's photographs of the young men who endured unbearable conditions during the four-year conflict.

Side A, Frame 52563

PRINT AND MEDIA RESOURCES

UNIT ONE RESOURCE BOOK
Strategic Reading: Literature, p. 19
Vocabulary SkillBuilder, p. 22
Reading SkillBuilder, p. 20
Spelling SkillBuilder, p. 21

GRAMMAR MINI–LESSONS
Transparencies, p. 47

WRITING MINI–LESSONS
Transparencies, p. 45

ACCESS FOR STUDENTS ACQUIRING ENGLISH
Selection Summaries
Reading and Writing Support

FORMAL ASSESSMENT
Selection Test, pp. 9–10
 Test Generator

 **AUDIO LIBRARY**
See Reference Card

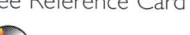 **LASERLINKS**
Historical Connection
Visual Vocabulary

INTERNET RESOURCES
McDougal Littell Literature Center at http://www.hmco.com/mcdougal/lit

---

THE LANGUAGE OF LITERATURE TEACHER'S EDITION **45**

SUMMARY

Most Civil War soldiers were rural teenagers. They lived on hardtack, salt pork, and coffee, tolerated inadequate provisions, and battled disease in their crowded camps. Often young soldiers held informal truces. Opposing troops traded coffee or stopped fighting so that brothers could confer across enemy lines. After one battle, a Union band played requests from Confederate troops, and homesick soldiers in both armies sang along.

Thematic Link: *Taught by Experience*
Union and Confederate soldiers learned that their enemies were a lot like themselves.

CUSTOMIZING FOR
Students Acquiring English

- Use **ACCESS FOR STUDENTS ACQUIRING ENGLISH,** *Reading and Writing Support.*

- This selection does not explain why the American Civil War was fought. Be sure that the causes of the war (slavery; threat of secession by the Southern states) are explained to students before the selection is read.

- Using a map, ask students to indicate the Northern and Southern states. Ask near-fluent and fluent students to guess at the border states. Have a volunteer check an encyclopedia to verify the map and to find the western border between the states and the territories at the start of the Civil War.

- As you guide students through the selection, you may want to use the suggestions in these boxes as well as the suggestions under Strategic Reading for Less-Proficient Readers.

46 UNIT ONE PART 1: TAUGHT BY EXPERIENCE

WORDS TO KNOW

abominably (ə-bŏm'ə-nə-blē) *adv.* in a thoroughly disagreeable way (p. 49)

adulterate (ə-dŭl'tə-rāt') *v.* to make impure by adding inferior ingredients (p. 49)

appalling (ə-pô'lĭng) *adj.* causing horror or dismay; frightful (p. 50)

apt (ăpt) *adj.* likely; inclined (p. 51)

ardent (är'dnt) *adj.* enthusiastic; devoted (p. 48)

devastating (dĕv'ə-stā'tĭng) *adj.* causing great destruction (p. 50)

infested (ĭn-fĕs'tĭd) *adj.* overrun or swarming, as with insects (p. 49)

laudable (lô'də-bəl) *adj.* deserving approval; praiseworthy (p. 50)

repertoire (rĕp'ər-twär') *n.* the stock of songs, plays, or other pieces that a person or group is prepared to perform (p. 53)

soberly (sō'bər-lē) *adv.* in a serious or solemn way (p. 50)

 **VISUAL VOCABULARY**

- **haversack** (hăv'ər-săk')
- **outpost** (out'pōst')
- **picket lines** (pĭk'ĭt līnz')
- **skirmish lines** (skûr'mĭsh līnz')

Side A, Frame 52571

46 THE LANGUAGE OF LITERATURE **TEACHER'S EDITION**

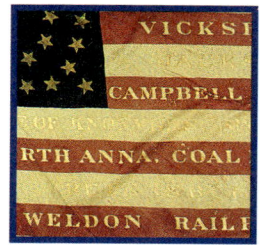

In the Civil War, the common soldiers of both sides were the same sort of people: untrained and untaught young men, mostly from the country. There weren't many cities then, and they weren't very large, so the average soldier generally came either from a farm or from some very small town or rural area. He had never been anywhere; he was completely unsophisticated. He joined up because he wanted to, because his patriotism had been aroused. The bands were playing, the recruiting officers were making speeches, so he got stirred up and enlisted. Sometimes, he was not altogether dry behind the ears.

Mini-Lesson — Literary Concepts

REVIEWING DESCRIPTION Remind students that description is a picture in words of a scene, a character, or an object. A description might appeal to the reader's senses or provide detailed information about characters or events.

Application Have students work in small groups to identify places in the text where Catton uses descriptions that appeal to the senses. Three or four people might each be responsible for finding examples for one or two of the senses. Another person might record the findings of the others. Groups might present their findings in a chart that illustrates how each of the five senses is addressed by specific text.

Linking to Geography

A Refer to a map. Help students to find the Middle West (or Northwest, as it was called during the Civil War). Where were the big cities in the United States at that time? *(Northeast)* Why were there cities in the Northeast and rural areas to the west? *(westward expansion in progress)*

Literary Concept: ANECDOTE

B Ask students what point Catton is making by telling the anecdote about the teenagers' methods of getting enlisted into the army. *(Possible response: The anecdote illustrates the teenagers' eagerness to enlist and their code of ethics.)*

STRATEGIC READING FOR
Less-Proficient Readers

C Check to see that students are clear about the rural and youthful background of most Confederate and Union soldiers.

- Where did most soldiers come from—the city or the country? *(the country)* **Making Generalizations**
- Which soldiers does the author say were more likely to have used weapons before enlisting in the army? *(the soldiers from rural areas)* **Noting Relevant Details**
- What did the piece of paper with the figure 18 in a teenager's shoe allow him to do? *(It allowed him to say honestly that he was "over eighteen.")* **Restating**

Set a Purpose Have students read to find out more about the soldiers' daily lives and what cause other than battles resulted in so many deaths.

When the boy joined the army, he would, of course, be issued clothing. He would get his uniform—pants, coat, shoes, and underwear. In the frontier regions, the quartermasters discovered that quite a lot of these young men picked up the underwear and looked at it and said, "What is this?" They had never seen any before. They hadn't worn it back home. Well, they caught on. They were fresh out of the backwoods, most of them.

A The boys from the country and the very small towns seemed to have made better soldiers than the boys from the cities. In the North, for instance, the boys from the rural areas, and especially from the Middle West, which they then called the Northwest, were a little tougher than the boys from the big cities. They could stand more; they were more self-reliant; perhaps they were more used to handling weapons. In any case, they made very good soldiers. On the Southern side, the same was true—even more so. A larger percentage of the men came from rural areas because there were fewer cities in the South. A number of them didn't even bother with shoes, but they were very, very bad boys to get into a fight with.

The war was greeted in its first few weeks almost as a festival. Everybody seemed relieved. People went out and celebrated, both in the North and in the South. There were parades, bands playing, flags flying; people seemed almost happy. Large numbers of troops were enlisted; as a matter of fact, again in both the North and the South, more men offered themselves than could be handled. Neither the Union nor the Confederate government had the weapons, uniforms, or anything else to equip all of the men who tried to enlist.

Both armies contained a number of very ardent teenagers who had lied about their age in order to get into the army in the first place. Legal age, of course, was eighteen. It turned out that, in the North at least, a very common little gag had been developed. A boy who was under eighteen and wanted to enlist would take a piece of paper and scribble the figure eighteen on it. Then he would take off his shoe, placing the piece of paper into the sole of his shoe, put it back on and tie it up. He would go to the recruiting station, and since he would obviously be looking rather young, sooner or later the recruiting officer would look at him and say, "How old are you, son?" Then the boy, in perfect honesty, could say, "I am over eighteen." **B**

The point about that is not so much that young men were lying about their age in order to get into the army but that they would go to the trouble of working out a gag like that. A man simply wouldn't dream of taking an oath that he was eighteen when he wasn't. Lying to the government was a little beyond him, but he would work out a thing like this and could say honestly, "I'm over eighteen," and that made it quite all right. **C**

A set of statistics were compiled about the average Northern soldier that are rather interesting. They apply pretty much to the South as well. An average soldier was 5 feet 8¼ inches tall; he weighed just over 143 pounds. Forty-eight percent were farmers, 24 percent were mechanics, 15 percent were laborers, 5 percent were businessmen, and 3 percent were professional men. That was really a kind of cross-section of the population of the United States at that time: about one-half farmers, about 40 percent working men, and 10 percent businessmen or professionals.

When a man joined the Union army, he was given shoes that must have been a little bit of a trial to wear. In a great many cases, army

WORDS TO KNOW **ardent** (är′dnt) *adj.* enthusiastic; devoted

---

Mini-Lesson Reading Skills/Strategies

ACTIVE READING: FINDING THE MAIN IDEA Remind students that the main idea is the central idea that a writer expresses in his or her work. Also remind them that, in most cases, each paragraph has its own main idea.

Application Encourage students to choose one paragraph per page, review it, and write the author's main idea in a single sentence, as shown in the chart. The chart shows the main idea of the highlighted paragraph.

Reteaching/Reinforcement
- *Unit One Resource Book*, p. 20

Paragraph Location	Main Idea
p. 48, paragraph 2	Rural boys were better soldiers than city boys.

48 THE LANGUAGE OF LITERATURE TEACHER'S EDITION

contractors simply made the right and left shoes identical. They were squared off at the toe, and it didn't matter which one you put on which foot; they were supposed to work either way. They must have been very uncomfortable, and I imagine they account for a great many of the cases of footsore soldiers who fell out on the march and stumbled into camp long after everybody else had gone to bed.

The Civil War soldier, on the Northern side at least, got a great deal to eat; the trouble was that most of it was not very good. The Union army enlisted no cooks or bakers during the entire war. Originally, each man was supposed to cook for himself. It happened, of course, practically immediately that company kitchens were established. Men were detailed from the ranks to act as cooks; some of them cooked fairly well, and some of them, of course, cooked abominably. But whatever they cooked, the boys ate.

The basic ration for the Civil War soldier, particularly on the march, where it was not possible to carry along vegetables, was salt pork or bacon and hardtack. The hardtack was a big soda cracker, quite thick and, as the name implies, very tough—made tough so that it wouldn't fall into pieces while it was joggling about in a man's haversack.[1] When the hardtack was fresh, it was apparently quite good to eat. The trouble is that it was very rarely fresh. Boxes of hardtack would sit on railroad platforms or sidetracked in front of warehouses for weeks and months at a time, and by the time the soldier got them, they were often infested and not very good.

Every soldier carried some sort of a tin can in which he could boil coffee. Coffee was issued in the whole bean, for when the government issued ground coffee, they could never quite trust the contractors not to adulterate it. When the soldier made coffee, he would put a handful of beans in a bucket and grind them with the butt of his musket. In the morning, in camp, you could tell when the boys were getting up by the rhythmic clinking, grinding noise that came up from in front of every tent.

The soldier also had sugar to go with his coffee, and he would boil his coffee in his little tin can and then dump in some sugar. He would usually have a skillet in which to fry his bacon. Sometimes he would crumble up hardtack and drop the crumbs in the sizzling bacon fat and make a rather indescribable mess—I guess a healthy young man who got a good deal of exercise could digest it without too much difficulty.

In the Civil War, which lasted four years, about 600,000 young Americans, North and

---

1. **haversack:** a bag carried over one shoulder and used to carry supplies or personal belongings.

WORDS TO KNOW

abominably (ə-bŏm′ə-nə-blē) *adv.* in a thoroughly disagreeable way
infested (ĭn-fĕs′tĭd) *adj.* overrun or swarming, as with insects **infest** *v.*
adulterate (ə-dŭl′tə-rāt′) *v.* to make impure by adding inferior ingredients

49

CUSTOMIZING FOR
Multiple Learning Styles

G **Bodily-Kinesthetic Learners** Have students study the illustrations that depict various young soldiers. Then have students demonstrate how these soldiers might have carried themselves—their posture and gestures—during the course of a routine day in the early 1860s.

STRATEGIC READING FOR
Less-Proficient Readers

H Check to see that students are clear about some aspects of Civil War soldiers' daily lives.

- Who cooked for the soldiers? *(They cooked for themselves; sometimes certain soldiers were designated to be cooks.)* **Noting Relevant Details**
- What caused more than one-half of the deaths in the war? *(diseases)* **Relating Cause and Effect**

Set a Purpose Have students read to find out the ways in which soldiers from the North and the South behaved with each other.

Linking to Science

 **I** The great Greek physician Hippocrates discussed malaria and other types of fever as early as the fifth century B.C. Yet it was not until 1898 that four Italian scientists proved that malaria was transmitted only by infected mosquitoes.

Critical Thinking:
SPECULATING

J Ask students if they think that young Northerners and Southerners would have been so eager to enlist if they had realized what their chances for survival were. *(Possible responses: Most young soldiers would still have been willing to enlist because they were willing to risk their lives for their beliefs. If they had known about the risks of disease and death, most soldiers would not have enlisted.)*

South together, lost their lives. That is not the total casualty list; it is the number that actually went under the sod.[2] The wounded, the missing, the prisoners, were in another list. Six hundred thousand is the number of lives that were actually lost.

If you want to understand what a terrible drain that was on the country, reflect that the total population in the United States in the 1860s was about an eighth or a ninth of what it is today. The number of men killed in that war, if you interpret it in today's terms, would come to something between four and four and one-half million. In other words, a perfectly frightful toll of American lives was taken.

There are a good many reasons why the toll was so high. More than *one-half* of the men who died were not killed in action; they simply died of camp diseases: typhoid fever, pneumonia, dysentery, and childhood diseases like measles and chicken pox.

To begin with, medical science then was woefully inadequate. Doctors simply did not know what caused such devastating camp diseases as typhoid fever, which accounted for about one-fourth of all deaths in army hospitals. Malaria, a plague of the Virginia swamp country, was attributed to "miasmic vapors" arising from stagnant waters and not to the pestiferous mosquitoes bred therein. (The vapors were also largely blamed for typhoid and dysentery.) Nothing was known about how and why wounds became infected, and so nothing much was done to prevent infection; surgeons talked soberly about "laudable pus" which was expected to appear a few days after an operation or a gunshot wound, its laudable character arising because it showed that the body was discharging poisons.

The number of men who simply got sick and died, or who got a minor scratch or cut and then could do nothing to check the infection, was appalling. Just to be in the army in the 1860s was much more dangerous than anything we know about today, even though many a man in the army never got into action. It was a very common thing—in fact, almost the rule—for a Civil War regiment on either side to lose about half of its strength in men who either became sick and died or became so ill they had to get medical discharges before the regiment ever saw action. Whereas a Civil War regiment, on paper, contained about one thousand men, in actual fact, a regiment that went into battle with as many as five hundred men was quite fortunate.

---

2. **went under the sod:** died and were buried—literally, "went beneath the grass."

WORDS TO KNOW	**devastating** (dĕv′ə-stā′tĭng) *adj.* causing great destruction **devastate** *v.*
	soberly (sō′bər-lē) *adv.* in a serious or solemn way
	laudable (lô′də-bəl) *adj.* deserving approval; praiseworthy
	appalling (ə-pô′lĭng) *adj.* causing horror or dismay; frightful

---

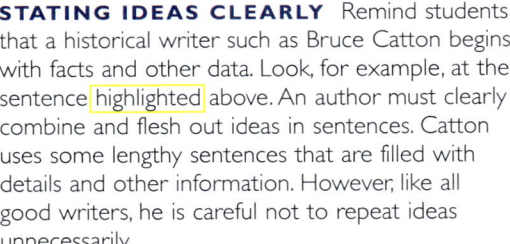

Mini-Lesson • The Writer's Style

STATING IDEAS CLEARLY Remind students that a historical writer such as Bruce Catton begins with facts and other data. Look, for example, at the sentence highlighted above. An author must clearly combine and flesh out ideas in sentences. Catton uses some lengthy sentences that are filled with details and other information. However, like all good writers, he is careful not to repeat ideas unnecessarily.

Application Have students rewrite the following sentences by eliminating repetition and adding interesting details.

1. Some diseases killed many soldiers, and a shocking number of them died.
2. Some teenagers lied to get into the army, and they deceived the enlistment officers.

Reteaching/Reinforcement
- *Writing Handbook*, anthology, p. 828
- *Writing Mini-Lessons* transparencies, p. 45

Revising Empty Sentences, p. 299

Not long after the war began, whenever a Northern army and a Southern army were camped fairly close to each other, the men on the picket lines³ would get acquainted with one another and would call little informal truces.⁴ The Northern soldiers would bring in coffee to trade. Along the Rappahannock River, they made quite a thing of constructing little toy boats out of planks. A boat would be maybe two feet long, with a mast and a sail. Loaded with coffee, it would be sent out into the stream, pointed south, and when it would get across the river, the Confederate soldiers would unload the coffee, stock it with tobacco, and send it back.

This led to some rather odd happenings, since men who are stopping to trade with each other are apt to get a little friendly along the way. There was one rather famous occasion, again along the Rappahannock River, when in a building not far behind the Confederate lines back of the outposts,⁵ there was going to be a dance one evening, and the Confederate pickets invited their Yankee friends to come over and go to the dance.

Half a dozen Yankee soldiers, leaving their guns behind them, crossed the river in the darkness, went to the dance, and had a very good time—until a Confederate officer appeared just when festivities were at their height. He was, of course, horrified and ordered the Yankee soldiers arrested and thrown into prison, at which point the Confederates begged him not to do this. They said they had given the Yankees their word that everything would be all right if they came to the dance, and asked that the officer let them go.

Well, the officer saw some point to that appeal. He couldn't violate or cause his men to violate their honor, so after giving all hands a don't-let-it-happen-again lecture, he released the Yankee prisoners, and they went home, with a good dance under their belts.

Along the Rapidan River during the winter of 1863 and 1864, the armies for a number of miles had outposts that were drawn up very close to each other. In fact, in one or two places, they actually overlapped. The Yankees had a way of advancing their picket lines in the night and pulling them back in the daytime. The Confederates did it just the other way around; their picket lines were a little farther forward by day than by night. Pretty soon it turned out that there was a picket post, with a log cabin and a fireplace, that was used at night by the Yankees and in the daytime by the Confederates. The boys worked out a deal: each party would leave a stack of firewood on hand and be sure to get out before the other one got there. They kept on that way quite pleasantly for some months.

At the great Battle of Fredericksburg, down at the far end of the line where the fighting was not very heavy, there was a woodland stretch held by the Confederates on one side and the Yankees on the other. The pickets, again, were quite close together, and the skirmish lines⁶ not much farther apart. The men got to catcalling and jeering at each other and making insulting remarks. This went on for quite a while in much the same way that a couple of high school football cheering

---

3. **picket lines:** lines of soldiers posted around encampments to guard against surprise attack.
4. **truces:** agreements to temporarily stop fighting.
5. **outposts:** places where troops are stationed away from a main force.
6. **skirmish lines:** lines of opposing troops attacking each other.

WORDS TO KNOW
apt (ăpt) *adj.* likely; inclined

51

Literary Concept:
DESCRIPTION

N Have students imagine that they have been asked to draw an illustration to accompany the writer's description of this scene. Ask them what details from the description they would use in their illustrations. *(Possible responses: "all along the line . . . of the woodland; the riled-up Yankee and Southerner . . . had a very fine, soul-satisfying fistfight; the men went to a nearby stream and washed the blood off their faces and shook hands.")*

Critical Thinking: ANALYZE

O What message does this anecdote convey about the complications and passions that existed during the Civil War? *(Possible response: Individuals on both sides of the conflict passionately believed in what they were fighting for. Sometimes even family ties were not enough to prevent fighting.)*

STRATEGIC READING FOR
Less-Proficient Readers

P Check that students are clear about the unusual ways Northern and Southern soldiers behaved with each other.

- What message does the anecdote about the Confederate dance illustrate? *(The Northern and Southern soldiers often had friendly or at least "normal" contact with each other.)* **Drawing Conclusions**

- What surprising thing does the Union band do for the Confederate soldiers across the Rappahannock River? *(They play several Southern tunes at the request of the Confederate soldiers.)* **Summarizing**

---

sections might yell back and forth at each other. Finally, a couple of soldiers, a Confederate and a Yankee, got really angry. They got so angry that they had to have a fight. So all along the line in this particular section of the woodland, the soldiers called an informal truce, and the riled-up Yankee and Southerner got out and had a very fine, soul-satisfying fistfight. I don't know who came out on top, but at last the fight ended, as all such fights do, and the men went to a nearby stream and washed the blood off their faces and shook hands. Then both sides went back, picked up their weapons, and started shooting at each other again.

It was that kind of war—rather informal, and fought between men who, when left alone, got along together beautifully. You've often heard it spoken of as the War Between Brothers. Actually, it really was that.

The siege⁷ of Vicksburg was another case where the picket lines were so close together that on one occasion the Southerners and the Northerners had a little meeting and came to an agreement as to just where the picket lines ought to go, so they wouldn't trespass on each other's territory.

During this siege, one of the Confederates out on the picket line asked if there were any Missouri regiments in the army immediately opposing his section. He was a Missourian himself and was looking for his brother. The Yankees made inquiry, and pretty soon they came forward with the Confederate soldier's brother—both boys from Missouri, one of them in Confederate gray and the other in Federal blue. The Confederate had a roll of bills in his hand and gave them to his brother to send to their mother, who was peaceably at home in Missouri. He couldn't get things out from Vicksburg through the Union lines, Vicksburg being completely surrounded, so he asked his brother to send them to her, and the brother did. There was no shooting while these arrangements were made, then the brothers shook hands and retired to their individual lines, and the shooting started up again.

During the fighting at Crampton's Gap in Maryland in the fall of 1862, the Confederates were slowly withdrawing. They were fighting a rear-guard action rather than a regular battle. One Yankee soldier got a little too far forward, slipped, and accidentally slid down the side of the steep hill on which he had been posted, winding up at the bottom of the hill in a thicket. There he confronted a Confederate soldier who wasn't ready to retreat yet. The two men grabbed their guns. But eventually they figured there was no point in shooting each other here, off in a quiet corner where there wasn't much going on, so they laid down their weapons and made an agreement. They would stay where they were with no shooting. At the end of the day if the Confederates had advanced, the Yankee would be the Confederate soldier's prisoner. If the Yankees had advanced, then the Confederate would be the Yankee's prisoner. Meanwhile, there wasn't any sense in getting shot. The Confederates eventually withdrew, and the Yankee soldier found he had taken a prisoner.

One of the most touching stories I know involving this acquaintanceship—friendship, really—between the rival soldiers took place at Fredericksburg, Virginia, along the Rappahannock, a couple of months after the big battle there. The Rappahannock River is not very wide, and the men on the northern bank could easily talk with the men on the southern bank if they raised their voices a little. One winter afternoon when nothing much was going on, a

---

7. **siege** (sēj): the blockading of a city or fort by a hostile surrounding army.

52 UNIT ONE PART 1: TAUGHT BY EXPERIENCE

Mini-Lesson: Speaking, Listening, and Viewing

MUSIC Explain to students that listening to popular music from the American Civil War can help us appreciate the war firsthand. Remind students that some songs were written to inspire patriotic zeal in listeners, whereas other songs were written to commemorate the sober and melancholy side of war.

Application Have students listen to any available recordings of songs that were written or popularized during the Civil War, such as "Dixie," "The Battle Hymn of the Republic," "The Bonnie Blue Flag," "Tramp, Tramp, Tramp, the Boys Are Marching," "Just Before the Battle, Mother," "Marching Through Georgia," and "The Battle Cry of Freedom." Invite them to analyze and respond to the music in as much detail as possible.

number of the Federal army bands were massed on the hillside overlooking the river valley to give a little informal concert. They played all of the Northern patriotic songs, and the Northern soldiers crowded around to listen. On the opposite shore, the Confederate soldiers gathered to enjoy the concert.

After a while, the band had pretty well run through its repertoire, and there was a pause, whereupon some of the Confederates shouted, "Now play some of ours." So the band began to play Southern tunes. They played "Dixie" and "Bonnie Blue Flag" and "Yellow Rose of Texas" and I don't know what all. They played Southern tunes while the Southern and Northern armies sat in the quiet and listened.

It was getting on toward dusk by this time, so the band, to signal the end of the concert, went into "Home, Sweet Home." Both armies together tried to sing it, and it was rather a sentimental occasion. After all, these boys were a long way from home. They knew perfectly well that a great many of them were never going to see home again; as soon as the warm weather came, they would be fighting each other. The song got to be a little too much for them, and pretty soon they choked up and couldn't sing, and the band finished the music all by itself.

A couple of months later, the troops faced each other in the terrible Battle of Chancellorsville. ❖

LITERARY INSIGHT

Dirge Without Music
BY EDNA ST. VINCENT MILLAY

I am not resigned to the shutting away of
  loving hearts in the hard ground.
So it is, and so it will be, for so it has been,
  time out of mind:
Into the darkness they go, the wise and the
  lovely. Crowned
With lilies and with laurel they go; but I am
  not resigned.

Lovers and thinkers, into the earth with
  you.
Be one with the dull, the indiscriminate
  dust.
A fragment of what you felt, of what you
  knew,
A formula, a phrase remains,—but the best
  is lost.

The answers quick and keen, the honest
  look, the laughter, the love,—
They are gone. They are gone to feed the
  roses. Elegant and curled
Is the blossom. Fragrant is the blossom. I
  know. But I do not approve.
More precious was the light in your eyes
  than all the roses of the world.

Down, down, down into the darkness of
  the grave
Gently they go, the beautiful, the tender, the
  kind;
Quietly they go, the intelligent, the witty,
  the brave.
I know. But I do not approve. And I am not
  resigned.

WORDS TO KNOW
repertoire (rĕp′ər-twär′) *n.* the stock of songs, plays, or other pieces that a person or group is prepared to perform

---

Mini-Lesson Spelling

ADVERBS THAT END IN -LY Remind students that they can easily turn many adjectives into adverbs by adding the suffix *-ly*. When this suffix is added, the spelling of the adjective usually does not change. (Remind students that a final silent *e* is sometimes dropped before the *ly* is added, as in *abominably*.)

abominably	(abominabl[e] + ly)
soberly	(sober + ly)
practically	(practical + ly)
pleasantly	(pleasant + ly)
perfectly	(perfect + ly)
woefully	(woeful + ly)

Application Have students turn the following adjectives, taken from Catton's essay, into correctly spelled adverbs.
1. regular *(regularly)*
2. fortunate *(fortunately)*
3. informal *(informally)*
4. simple *(simply)*

Reteaching/Reinforcement
• *Unit One Resource Book,* p. 21

CUSTOMIZING FOR
Gifted and Talented Students

Have students create detailed maps that illustrate key facts and details from the selection. For instance, their maps might indicate not only the identity of Union and Confederate states but also the precise locations of battle sites, rivers, and the capitals of the Union (Washington, D.C.) and the Confederacy (Richmond, Virginia).

COMPREHENSION CHECK
1. How did some underage boys enlist in the army? *(They put a piece of paper bearing the number 18 in their shoes so they could say they were "over eighteen.")*
2. What were the main causes of death among soldiers during the Civil War? *(diseases and battlefield injuries)*
3. What other name for the Civil War does Catton cite. *(the War Between Brothers)*
4. What surprising thing did the Union army band do at Fredericksburg? *(They played Southern songs for Confederate soldiers.)*

INSIGHT
1. What seem to be some of the most treasured aspects of human life to the speaker? *(Possible responses: intelligence, wit, bravery, beauty, kindness, tenderness)*
2. Why might the poet use present, future, and past tenses in the third line of the poem? *(Possible responses: She is suggesting that death is universal; she is suggesting that wars have been fought in the past, were being fought at the time this poem was written, and will be fought in the future.)*
3. How might the speaker's lack of resignation show itself in the way she lives her life? *(Responses will vary.)*

EDNA ST. VINCENT MILLAY

Edna St. Vincent Millay was born in Rockland, Maine, in 1892. She began to write poetry at an early age and went on to write more than 20 volumes of poetry, plays, an opera, and essays. In 1923 she won a Pulitzer Prize for her poem "The Ballad of the Harp-Weaver." Millay, who died in 1950, was not afraid to cause controversy or to take strong political stands.

From Personal Response to Critical Analysis

1. Answers will vary. Accept all reasonable responses.
2. Possible response: An eager youth might have been unprepared for uncomfortable shoes, bad food, disease, exhaustion, and homesickness.
3. Encourage students to make specific comparisons and contrasts to the soldiers in Catton's text.
4. Answers will vary. Examples include "Hard Young Lives" and "Sick and Tired of War."
5. Possible response: Catton would probably agree with Millay's sentiments. Although his tone is lighter and less gloomy, throughout his work he indicates that war and death are hardly worth glorifying.
6. Possible response: Certain things would be similar—the strain on a soldier's body and mind, the homesickness, the horror. The biggest difference would be in the weapons: technology has changed hand-to-hand combat and has introduced bombs that are more powerful.

Another Pathway

Cooperative Learning One or more students could serve as moderator of a class discussion, choosing a handful of students to review the kinds of entries they made in their charts' first two columns. As a group, all students can then consider what entries to make in the third column.

Rubric

3 Full Accomplishment Students actively review their charts and accurately report what they learned.

2 Substantial Accomplishment Students review their charts and report a few things that they learned.

1 Little or Partial Accomplishment Students have difficulty identifying or expressing what they learned.

RESPONDING OPTIONS

FROM PERSONAL RESPONSE TO CRITICAL ANALYSIS

REFLECT 1. What surprised you about Civil War soldiers? Jot down the most surprising facts in your notebook.

RETHINK
Thematic Link 2. How might the perceptions of a soldier who was eager to enlist have changed once he was in the army?

3. Do you think you would be as eager to enlist in a war as the young men Catton describes? Give reasons for your answer.

4. What title would you give this selection to indicate the kinds of facts it contains?

Literary Link 5. Do you think Catton would agree with the sentiments expressed in Edna St. Vincent Millay's "Dirge Without Music" (page 53)? Why or why not?

Consider
Close Textual Reading
- the feelings about war that "Dirge Without Music" conveys
- how you think Catton feels about war

RELATE 6. Compare and contrast what you have learned about the life of Civil War soldiers with what you envision as the life of a soldier today. Share your thoughts with your class.

LITERARY CONCEPTS

An **anecdote** is a brief story told to entertain or to make a point. What point do you think Catton makes by means of the anecdotes he tells about encounters between Union and Confederate soldiers? What else do the anecdotes add to the presentation of factual information?

Multimodal Learning

ANOTHER PATHWAY

Cooperative Learning

Look at the chart you created for the Personal Connection on page 45. With your classmates, discuss what you learned about Civil War soldiers from this selection. Write those facts in the third column of your chart.

QUICKWRITES

1. Imagine that you are a common soldier in the Civil War, and write a **letter** about your experiences to your family or girlfriend back home.

2. Rewrite an **anecdote** in this selection from the point of view of a soldier involved in the incident.

3. Imagine that you are a newspaper reporter given the assignment of observing firsthand a day in the life of a Confederate or Union soldier. Write an **article** that presents the events of the day.

📁 **PORTFOLIO** Save your writing. You may want to use it later as a springboard to a piece for your portfolio.

54 UNIT ONE PART 1: TAUGHT BY EXPERIENCE

Literary Concepts

Students should first review the selection and compile a list of Catton's anecdotes. His anecdotes illustrate the fact that underneath the animosity stirred up by the Civil War, soldiers from both the North and the South (often friends and family fighting on opposing sides) were able to reach out across their differences and to realize they were the same. Besides presenting factual information, the anecdotes entertain and give the reader a glimpse into the personalities of Civil War soldiers.

QuickWrites

1. Encourage students to imagine a day in the life of a soldier before they write. Then have them think about how they would express themselves to the individual to whom they are writing.
2. Ask students to think about details that Catton did not include in his anecdote.
3. Ask students if a journalist's feelings should be included in his or her article.

 **The Writer's Craft**

Letter Form, p. 684
Point of View, pp. 322–323

Multimodal Learning

ALTERNATIVE ACTIVITIES

1. **Cooperative Learning** Research the tunes and lyrics of some Confederate and Union songs and of "Home, Sweet Home." With a small group of classmates, organize a **concert** in which half the class sings Confederate songs, half sings Union songs, and all sing "Home, Sweet Home."
2. Create a Confederate or Union army **recruitment poster** that includes a full-length portrait of a soldier in uniform with a haversack and a musket. Research the details of his outfit.
3. Find out what food today's soldiers carry. List some of the foods and their nutritional value. Design and fill in a **comparison chart** that shows the nutritional value of these foods alongside the nutritional value of soda crackers and bacon, the foods mentioned in the selection.

ACROSS THE CURRICULUM

Mathematics Make a **circle graph** that shows, in percentages, the kinds of jobs the soldiers held before they enlisted. Keep in mind that the percentages given in the selection add up to 95, rather than 100. Once you have completed your circle graph, design another type of graph to display the same data.

Social Studies Some women disguised themselves as men in order to fight in the Civil War. Find out about some of these women and share what you learn with the class in an **oral report**.

Cooperative Learning Catton mentions the battles of Fredericksburg, Vicksburg, and Chancellorsville. With a small group of classmates, research one of these battles, then write a short **report** about it. Include pictures or illustrations if possible.

THE WRITER'S STYLE

By his use of colloquial expressions—like "not altogether dry behind the ears," meaning "young and inexperienced," in the first paragraph of the selection—Catton creates an informal style. Find another such expression that Catton uses, and explain its relationship to the soldiers' experiences.

The Battle of Fredericksburg. The Bettmann Archive.

Across the Curriculum

Mathematics Have students begin by reviewing the text and making notes on the statistics. Then they can make their circle graph. Encourage them to think carefully about which other kind of graph would be especially effective for this data. Then they can create that type of graph. (bar graph)

Social Studies You may want to direct students' attention both to books about the Civil War and to books and articles about women in history. Encourage students to find out as much as possible about the background of these women, whether they were more likely to enlist for the Confederacy or for the Union, and whether their trick was apt to be discovered by their fellow soldiers.

Social Studies *Cooperative Learning* Have students work in groups of three or four. Groups might focus their research on casualties, the geography of the battle, the military leaders involved, and the specific reasons for and results of the battle. One student should act as facilitator to organize the group's research, and a second student can act as recorder of the group's information. The remaining students can either clarify and paraphrase the research to create a report or present the group's findings to the class.

ADDITIONAL SUGGESTION
History *The Underground Railroad* The Underground Railroad was organized by sympathetic Northerners and Southerners to help escaped slaves travel from the slave states to the free states of the North and sometimes to other countries. Have students research the routes of the railroad and prepare maps detailing the locations of stops.

The Writer's Style

Encourage students to identify such phrases as "fresh out of the backwoods" (page 48), "a good dance under their belts" (page 51), and "I don't know what all" (page 53). In each case, the language reflects the informality of rural American speech.

Informal English, p. 315

Alternative Activities

1. Encourage students to use both books and recordings to research the music of the Civil War period. Have them be alert for specific characteristics (such as the song's lyrics or history) that identify it geographically.
2. Have students look for models of recruitment posters, or illustrations of particular items a soldier might wear or carry.
3. Students might need to use periodicals and newspapers to research the diet of contemporary soldiers. Encourage them to consult diet and nutrition books about these foods' nutritional values.

Words to Know

1. b   6. a
2. c   7. a
3. a   8. c
4. b   9. b
5. a   10. b

Reteaching/Reinforcement
• *Unit Resource One Book*, p. 22

BRUCE CATTON

Bruce Catton was a journalist in Cleveland, Boston, and Washington, D.C., early in his career. The combination of his journalist's discipline and his innate ability to tell an engaging story produced a host of books that vividly chronicled the Civil War.

Catton believed that "history ought to be a good yarn," but he was also aware of its grandeur. He wrote that history "extends far back into the past, and it will go on . . . far into the future. Our American heritage is greater than any of us. It can express itself in very homely truths; in the end, it can lift up our eyes beyond the glow in the sun-set skies."

WORDS TO KNOW

On your paper, write the letter of the best answer.

1. Which person would be *least* likely to speak **soberly**?
   a. a victorious general   b. an injured soldier   c. a surgeon
2. An officer whose soldiers behaved **abominably** would feel
   a. relieved.   b. proud.   c. angry.
3. At which of these places would you most likely hear a **repertoire**?
   a. a concert hall   b. an army hospital   c. a battlefield
4. Which one of these behaviors is most **appalling**?
   a. tripping on steps   b. abandoning a baby   c. singing
5. Food that has been **infested** may be
   a. full of bugs.   b. undercooked.   c. cooked to perfection.
6. Which one of these people could *not* be described as **ardent**?
   a. a bored student   b. a heroic soldier   c. an avid sports fan
7. A person who is **apt** to enlist in the army is
   a. likely to enlist.   b. not likely to enlist.   c. refusing to enlist.
8. A soldier who performed a **laudable** act would most likely be
   a. ridiculed.   b. arrested.   c. praised.
9. If someone made a **devastating** remark to you, you would probably feel
   a. elated.   b. upset.   c. confident.
10. Something that is **adulterated** is
    a. purified.   b. contaminated.   c. used only by adults.

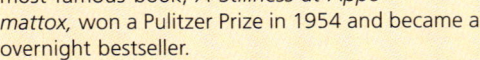

BRUCE CATTON

1899–1978

With the publication of 13 books in the last third of his life, Bruce Catton became the Civil War's most famous chronicler. His historical narratives, highly respected for their accuracy, have been credited with starting a renewed interest in the Civil War in the 1950s. Written from the enlisted man's point of view, they are dramatic, personal, and realistic. His most famous book, *A Stillness at Appomattox*, won a Pulitzer Prize in 1954 and became an overnight bestseller.

Catton's interest in the Civil War began in the small northern Michigan town of Benzonia, where he was raised. "All the old men," he explained, "were Civil War veterans. We boys used to sit around and listen to their yarns." As a result of that experience, Catton became a master of storytelling.

The Civil War was Catton's lifelong interest, but it wasn't until the age of 50 that he began writing about the war. When he was not writing, Catton enjoyed studying Central American archaeology, whittling wooden soldiers, fishing, and walking in the northern Michigan woods.

OTHER WORKS *This Hallowed Ground* (young readers' edition), *Glory Road*   Extended Reading

56   UNIT ONE   PART 1: TAUGHT BY EXPERIENCE

WHAT DO YOU THINK?
Reflecting on Theme

Have students think back to the photo collage they did on p. 14 before they began reading the selections in Part One. Ask students what they learned by creating a collage of people who caused them to change their attitudes. Have students imagine they must choose one of the pictures of a Civil War soldier from this selection to add to their collage. Which one would it be, and why?

PREVIEWING

NONFICTION

The Clown
Patrick F. McManus

Activating Prior Knowledge/Setting a Purpose
PERSONAL CONNECTION

Have you ever turned blue in the face or almost passed out trying to keep from laughing in class? Think back to the crazy moments you have had in the classroom during your school career. Share any comical stories that come to mind. If you remember a class clown, tell how your teacher and your classmates reacted to this student. Did he or she cause you to burst out laughing or simply to roll your eyes? Use your notebook to jot down what you recall.

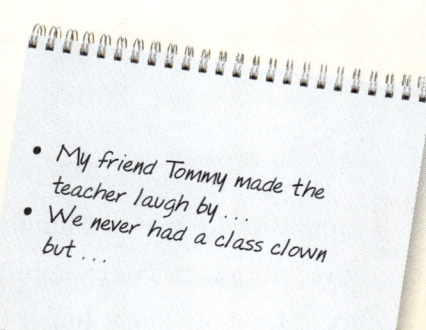

- My friend Tommy made the teacher laugh by . . .
- We never had a class clown but . . .

Building Background
BIOGRAPHICAL CONNECTION

Like many of us, the humorist Patrick McManus enjoys reminiscing about his life experiences. Most of his stories are based on actual incidents, with exaggeration added for humorous effect. McManus explains, "If I stick to the unembellished truth for too long at a stretch, I tend to tense up, get a headache."

This kind of humorous writing is usually categorized as nonfiction, which, as you recall, tells about real people, places, and events. In this account, McManus starts with a true incident in his own classroom experience and then magnifies it somewhat. He confides, "Although I may base a story on an actual experience I've had, I usually will use characters who will produce the best comic effect."

Active Reading/Setting a Purpose
READING CONNECTION

Exaggeration As you have learned, humorists use exaggeration to make readers laugh. An exaggeration is a statement that something is much more than it actually is. For example, in "The Clown," the narrator claims Miss Bindle, his teacher, has "an eighty-year-old face and twenty-year old red hair." If you saw her, it is doubtful that you would find this to be true. As you read McManus's account, look for and enjoy his exaggeration of the truth.

THE CLOWN **57**

OVERVIEW

Objectives

- To understand and appreciate an autobiographical essay about the author, his class-clown friend, and their no-nonsense teacher
- To appreciate the use of exaggeration
- To identify and understand humor and review the concept of irony
- To express understanding of the autobiographical essay story through a choice of writing forms, including a poem and a narrative
- To extend understanding of the selection through a variety of cross-curricular and multimodal activities

Skills

READING SKILLS/ STRATEGIES
- Making judgments and appreciating exaggeration

GRAMMAR
- End marks

LITERARY CONCEPTS
- Humor
- Irony
- Autobiography

SPEAKING, LISTENING, AND VIEWING
- Group discussion
- Oral presentation

Cross-Curricular Connections

HISTORY
- Writing inks

SOCIAL STUDIES
- Comparing today's classroom with the 1940s classroom

MEDIA
- Humor and television

ALTERNATIVE
Previewing

Instead of writing about a comical situation in the classroom, students can choose partners and discuss the topic.

Personal Connection

Discussion Prompts *With your partner, discuss a humorous experience you had in a classroom setting. The following questions might help you get started:*

- What was humorous about the situation?
- If the situation involved a class clown, how did the student behave?
- How did the class react to the situation?
- Why do you think it's so easy to make people laugh in class?

As you read "The Clown," pay attention to the class clown's effect on the classroom.

PRINT AND MEDIA RESOURCES

UNIT ONE RESOURCE BOOK
Strategic Reading: Literature, p. 25
Vocabulary SkillBuilder, p. 27
Reading SkillBuilder, p. 26

ACCESS FOR STUDENTS ACQUIRING ENGLISH
Selection Summaries
Reading and Writing Support

FORMAL ASSESSMENT
Selection Test, pp. 11–12
Test Generator

 **AUDIO LIBRARY**
See Reference Card

THE LANGUAGE OF LITERATURE TEACHER'S EDITION **57**

The Clown

by Patrick F. McManus

I admit it: my sense of humor is a bit weird. It's caused me some trouble over the years. For example, the only time I ever got sent to the principal's office at Delmore Blight Junior High was because I laughed in the wrong place at the wrong time—Miss Bindle's math class.

They don't make teachers like Miss Bindle anymore. At least, I hope they don't. She was tiny, scrawny, and fierce, with an eighty-year-old face and twenty-year-old red hair. Her wrinkles were permanently fused into a frown beneath the glowing halo of frizzy hair. Miss Bindle was the Jesse James of <u>sarcasm</u>: she could quick-draw a sarcastic remark and drill you between the eyes with it at thirty paces. She once hit Mort Simmons with a slug of sarcasm that spun him around half out of his desk. Then she walked over and coolly finished him off with two shots to the head. Mort recovered, but he was never the same afterward. His was a sad case.

Mort had always been dumb. The reason Miss Bindle drilled him was that he had been sneaking a look at one of my answers during a test; that's how dumb he was, or so Miss Bindle remarked, catching me with a <u>ricochet</u> from her shot at Mort. She never coddled us dumb kids, as did some of the kinder, more merciful teachers. She made us learn the same stuff as the smart kids. A few teachers took pity on us and let us relax in the cozy vacuum of our dumbness, but Miss Bindle forced us to learn everything the smart kids did, even though it took us three times as long. Everybody hated her for it, even the smart kids, who were cheated out of the satisfaction of knowing more than the dumb ones. Anybody could see that wasn't fair.

But I started to tell about Mort. He couldn't do arithmetic without counting on his fingers.

WORDS TO KNOW
sarcasm (sär′kăz′əm) *n.* humor intended to hurt, criticize, or ridicule a person
ricochet (rĭk′ə-shā′) *n.* a rebound, as from a surface

WORDS TO KNOW

copious (kō′pē-əs) *adj.* in great quantity; abundant (p. 60)
inducing (ĭn-dōō′sĭng) *n.* bringing about the occurrence of (p. 59)
malevolent (mə-lĕv′ə-lənt) *adj.* showing ill will; evil (p. 60)
mirth (mûrth) *n.* merriment shown in the form of laughter (p. 61)
motivator (mō′tə-vā′tər) *n.* a spur to action (p. 59)

nuance (nōō′äns′) *n.* a slight shade of difference (p. 60)
psyche (sī′kē) *n.* a mind or soul (p. 59)
ricochet (rĭk′ə-shā′) *n.* a rebound, as from a surface (p. 58)
sarcasm (sär′kăz′əm) *n.* humor intended to hurt, criticize, or ridicule a person (p. 58)
writhe (rīth) *v.* to twist or squirm (p. 61)

Miss Bindle said she didn't care what parts of his anatomy he had to count on, he was going to learn just as much math as anybody else. Mort did, too, but it was a terrible strain on him, dumb as he was. When we got to multiplying and dividing fractions, his fingers moved so fast he had to keep a glass of ice water on his desk to cool them off. It was a good thing we didn't do algebra in seventh grade, because somebody would have had to stand next to Mort with a fire extinguisher.

It is my understanding that modern educational theory dismisses the use of fear as a means of inducing learning in adolescents. Educators now take a more civilized approach and try to make learning an enjoyable experience. I agree with that. I know that all my children enjoyed school much more than I did. On the other hand, none of them knows how to multiply and divide fractions. I suppose that's part of the trade-off.

Fear was Miss Bindle's one and only motivator. It was as though she had done her teacher training at Marine boot camp. She would stick her face an inch from yours and, snarling and snapping, rearrange the molecules of your brain to suit her fancy. It was clearly evident to the person whose brain molecules were being rearranged that breath mints either hadn't been invented or hadn't come in a flavor pleasing to Miss Bindle. The oral hygiene of an executioner, however, is scarcely a matter of great concern to the potential victim.

Miss Bindle preferred psychological violence—whipping your psyche into a pink froth—to physical violence. Physical violence was direct and straightforward, something all of us youngsters thoroughly understood. There was no mystery to it. Given a choice, we would have taken the teacher's physical violence, which consisted of snatching the culprit by the hair and dragging him off to the principal's office. As I say, Miss Bindle was extremely short, only about half the size of some of the larger boys. When Miss Bindle grabbed them by the hair and took off for the office, they had to trail along behind her in a bent-over posture, which didn't do a lot for the macho image of some of the guys, particularly if they were saying, "Ow ow ow," as they went out the door. On the other hand, if they had stood erect, in order to depart from the room in a dignified fashion, Miss Bindle would have dangled from their hair, her feet swinging a good six inches off the floor. It was a no-win situation, and wisdom dictated the less painful of the two modes of being escorted to the office. In contrast to Miss Bindle, other teachers merely pointed toward the door and ordered, "Go to the office!" This method allowed the typical louts, some of whom were near voting age, to leave the room swaggering and sneering. No lout ever left Miss Bindle's room swaggering and sneering.

I was a fairly timid fellow and took great care never to attract the wrath of Miss Bindle. I studied ways to make myself invisible in her class, with such success that a couple of times she marked me absent when I was there. Pitiful victims were snatched from their desks on all sides of me, but month after month I escaped unsnatched, making myself increasingly invisible, until finally there were only a few weeks left of my seventh-grade sentence. I thought I was going to make it safely through to the end of the school year, but I hadn't taken into

WORDS TO KNOW
inducing (ĭn-dōō'sĭng) n. bringing about the occurrence of **induce** v.
motivator (mō'tə-vā'tər) n. a spur to action
psyche (sī'kē) n. a mind or soul

59

CUSTOMIZING FOR
Gifted and Talented Students

As students read, have them evaluate how Miss Bindle disciplines her class. Ask students if they think her methods for disciplining are successful, and have them suggest other ways Miss Bindle might handle the situations described.

Literary Concept:
AUTOBIOGRAPHY

A Have students use the text to explain how they know that "The Clown" is an example of autobiography. (*Possible response: The story is based on facts that happened in the life of the author, who uses pronouns such as* my, I, *and* we.)

CUSTOMIZING FOR
Students Acquiring English

I Explain that boot camp is where new soldiers are instructed and trained. Ask students what sort of training they think people receive at boot camp. Then have them explain how Miss Bindle behaves like a soldier.

Active Reading: QUESTION

B Ask students what is meant by "psychological violence." You may wish to use the following model to give them ideas of what they might be thinking about.

Think-Aloud Model *Instead of actually spanking or striking students, Miss Bindle does things that frustrate, annoy, and humiliate them. For example, she ridicules the students with sarcasm, she gets right in their face and yells, and she grabs troublemakers by the hair, dragging them—stripped of their dignity—to the principal's office.*

Mini-Lesson — Reading Skills/Strategies

MAKING JUDGMENTS AND APPRECIATING EXAGGERATION Remind students that making a judgment involves understanding the quality or value of something. It is important that a judgment be backed up by concrete facts. In literature, for example, judgments must be supported by evidence in the text. In this mini-lesson, students can make judgments about the use of exaggeration in "The Clown."

Remind students that writers (and other storytellers) use exaggeration to create humor. A writer can exaggerate certain details (some aspect of a person's personality, for example) to make readers laugh. Two examples of exaggeration are highlighted on this page.

Application As students read this autobiographical essay, encourage them to make judgments as to when they think McManus is exaggerating and have them give evidence by listing these exaggerations in their notebooks.

Reteaching/Reinforcement
- *Unit One Resource Book,* p. 26

Critical Thinking: SPECULATING

C Ask students to speculate on why the narrator says bragging to Slick was a mistake. *(Possible response: Slick should take it as a dare to put the narrator at risk for being "snatched.")*

CUSTOMIZING FOR
Students Acquiring English

2 Students may know the words *come into* as meaning "enter" and may be confused by this usage. Point out that in this case, *come into* means "receive."

Literary Concept: HUMOR

D Have students comment on McManus's techniques for creating humor in this paragraph. *(Possible response: He exaggerates Miss Bindle's age and the history of her classroom. The author's perception of himself as "a profoundly fearful and insecure person" is also humorous in the context of this narrative.)*

Linking to History

E Writing inks were first used in ancient Egypt and China beginning in about 2500 B.C. Unlike today's synthetic inks, the ancient writing inks were made from natural materials, such as linseed oil, berries, bark, and soot. Even galls (abnormal growths) on oak trees were used to make an early form of ink. Over many hundreds of years, thousands of different formulas have been created for inks.

Literary Concept: AUTOBIOGRAPHY

F Ask students to find the real-life detail in these sentences that Pat McManus probably exaggerated somewhat. *(Possible response: It's doubtful that his classmate's name was Olga Bonemarrow.)*

---

account my weird sense of humor—or my friend Slick.

Clifford Slick was the class clown. Ol' Slick felt his purpose in life was to make people laugh, and he was pretty good at it. Everybody liked Slick. We would gather around him during lunch hour to watch his routines and laugh ourselves sick. He did a wonderful impression of Miss Bindle snatching a kid by the hair and dragging him off. He did both parts alternately, the kid and Miss Bindle, and it was hilarious. One of the reasons Slick got the routine down so well was that he got snatched about once a week. It was as though he had researched the act. He knew every little nuance of a snatching, and how to exaggerate it just enough to turn the horror into humor. It was a gift.

C One day before school, I made the mistake of bragging to Slick that I was going to make it all the way through the year without getting snatched by Miss Bindle. Slick was concentrating on combing his hair into a weird shape. **2** His father had shot a bear, and Slick had come into a quantity of bear grease. He slathered a copious amount of bear grease on his hair and was delighted to see that he could now comb it into any shape he wanted. He combed it flat down against his skull, so that it looked as though he were wearing a shiny, tight leather helmet.

"How's that look?" he asked me. "Funny?"

I grinned. "Yeah, pretty funny, Cliff. I like the one best, though, where you comb it straight out from your forehead. It looks like a duck bill. Ha!"

"Okay, good," he said. "I'll go with that. Should get some laughs. Now what was that you were saying?"

"I said I've never been snatched by Miss Bindle. I'm going to make it all the way through the year without getting snatched."

Slick turned a <u>malevolent</u> smile on me. "No you ain't. Today you're going to bust out laughing right in old Bindle's class!"

"Not a chance!" The mere thought of bursting out laughing in Miss Bindle's class would totally paralyze my entire laughing apparatus. It was like having a fail-safe mechanism.

"You'll laugh," Slick said. "I'll make you laugh."

I shook my head. "No way."

In the whole hundred or so years that Miss Bindle had taught, I was reasonably sure that not so much as a snicker had ever been heard in her class, let alone a laugh. It was absolutely insane for Slick to think that I, a profoundly fearful and insecure person, would achieve fame as the one kid ever to burst out laughing within snatching range of Miss Bindle.

s soon as Miss Bindle's back was turned to scratch some fractions on the blackboard, Slick went into his routine. He took a dainty sip from his ink bottle and then made a terrible face. His greasy duck-bill hair contributed considerably to the comedy. I felt a laugh coming on but easily strangled it. Slick looked disappointed. Then he stuck two yellow pencils up his nose, his impression of a walrus. I felt a major laugh inflating inside me. Slick next imitated a walrus taking a dainty sip of tea. That almost got me, but the laugh exploded deep in my interior with a muffled *whump!* Suspicious, Olga Bonemarrow, in the next row, glared at me. Feeling as though I had suffered major internal injuries, I wiped some

> **WORDS TO KNOW**
> **nuance** (nōō'äns') *n.* a slight shade of difference
> **copious** (kō'pē-əs) *adj.* in great quantity; abundant
> **malevolent** (mə-lĕv'ə-lənt) *adj.* showing ill will; evil

60

Mini-Lesson • Literary Concepts

REVIEWING AUTOBIOGRAPHY Remind students that an autobiography is a form of nonfiction in which one person tells the story of his or her life. Some autobiographies are serious, whereas others are designed to be humorous.

Application In small groups, have students discuss their ideas about what makes a good autobiography. What kinds of material are readers interested in? Is an incident like the one in "The Clown" good material for an autobiography?

tears from my eyes. Slick took this as an encouraging sign and pulled out all the stops. He was doing his duck-bill walrus daintily sipping tea while wiggling its ears when Miss Bindle turned to face the class.

He was doing his duck-bill walrus daintily sipping tea while wiggling its ears.

"Clifford!" she roared, hurtling down the aisle like a tiny, ancient, redheaded dreadnought.[1] Slick's ears ceased to wiggle; the pencils in his nose quivered; a bit of inky drool dribbled from his gaping mouth. He clenched his eyes in preparation for a major-league snatching. Miss Bindle grabbed at his hair and headed off down the aisle, obviously expecting Slick to be firmly in tow. But Slick was still seated at his desk, eyes clenched, pencils up nose. Miss Bindle rushed back and made another pass at his hair, but again her hand slipped off. She snatched again and again, with even less effect. Apparently, it was the first time she had ever encountered bear-greased hair on one of her snatchees.

All the while, Slick sat there numbly, the yellow pencils poking out of his nose and a terrible expression on his face. Maybe it was Slick's expression that got to me, or maybe it was the way the teacher stared down at her greasy palms, her eyes full of rage and disgust and incomprehension. Whatever the trigger, it bypassed the fail-safe mechanism. My wild, booming laugh detonated like a bomb in the frozen silence of the room. I could scarcely believe it was my own laugh. I hoped it might be Mort's: only he might possibly be stupid enough to laugh in Miss Bindle's math class. But no, the laugh, now diminishing from a roar into a sort of breathless squealing, was none other than my own. I had been betrayed by my weird sense of humor! By Clifford Slick and his bear grease! And yes, even by Miss Bindle! As I writhed in an agony of mirth, half hilarity and half terror, I could feel Miss Bindle's stiletto[2] eyes piercing my living—for the moment—flesh. My stunned classmates failed to find my laughter infectious. He who laughed in Miss Bindle's class laughed alone.

And then it happened. "Clifford! Pat!" snarled Miss Bindle. "Go to the office!" She pointed the way with a finger shiny with bear grease.

I left the classroom erect and dignified. Cliff went out the door sideways, doing his comical little vaudeville[3] dance. It didn't get a laugh.

After the principal, Mr. Wiggens, gave us his bored lecture on the importance of discipline in a learning environment, he ordered us back to class. As I was passing the entrance of the cloakroom, I heard strange sounds emanating from the far end. A quick glance revealed that it was Miss Bindle. At first I thought she was crying, possibly over the disappointment of failing to snatch Cliff's and my hair. But no! She was laughing! Cackling, actually, quietly and to herself. It struck me that Miss Bindle had a weird sense of humor, too. ❖

---

1. **dreadnought** (drĕd′nôt′): a heavily armed battleship.
2. **stiletto**: a small dagger with a slender blade.
3. **vaudeville** (vôd′vĭl′): a stage performance made up of song-and-dance numbers and slapstick comedy.

WORDS TO KNOW
writhe (rīth) *v.* to twist or squirm
mirth (mûrth) *n.* merriment shown in the form of laughter

Mini-Lesson Grammar

END MARKS Review with students the three ways to punctuate the end of a sentence: with a period, a question mark, or an exclamation point. A period is used at the end of a sentence that makes a statement or a command. A question mark is used at the end of a question. An exclamation point is used after a statement or phrase that expresses strong feeling.

Application Invite students to find examples of each of the three end marks in "The Clown." Then have them correctly punctuate the ends of the following sentences.

1. Will you come to my party (?)
2. Oh, my goodness (!)
3. Write your name on the paper (.)

Reteaching/Reinforcement
• Grammar Handbook, anthology p. 903

End Marks, pp. 638–639

From Personal Response to Critical Analysis

1. Responses will vary. Encourage students to explain what they define as humorous.
2. Possible response: The narrator considers Miss Bindle a challenging, a difficult, and, finally, a surprising person. His description of her at the beginning of the story says a lot about how he feels about her. Certainly he feels afraid of her personality and her punishments, and he is not very comfortable in her classroom. At the end of the story, he sees a more human side of Miss Bindle.
3. Possible response: Miss Bindle is a good teacher in the sense that students respect her and listen to her. But Miss Bindle's teaching methods are not very positive, and she relies too much on creating fear in her students. The author says at one point, "Fear was Miss Bindle's one and only motivator."
4. Encourage students to give honest appraisals and expressive demonstrations of Slick's behavior.
5. Encourage students to have fun with the question rather than deliver the "right" answer.
6. Answers will vary.

Another Pathway

One student can read aloud the section from McManus's essay as the other jots down details that Miss Bindle would see differently. Then both students can help draft the actual sentences from Miss Bindle's point of view.

Rubric

3 Full Accomplishment Students accurately and entertainingly capture Miss Bindle's voice and point of view.

2 Substantial Accomplishment Students rewrite part of the essay from Miss Bindle's point of view but include few details that make her outlook lively and interesting.

1 Little or Partial Accomplishment Students have difficulty expressing Miss Bindle's voice and recasting the section from her point of view.

RESPONDING OPTIONS

FROM PERSONAL RESPONSE TO CRITICAL ANALYSIS

REFLECT 1. Did you find this selection funny? Why or why not?

RETHINK 2. What is the narrator's opinion of Miss Bindle? Give evidence to support your answer.

Consider
Close Textual Reading
- the two teaching methods he mentions
- his own behavior

Thematic Link
- whether his perceptions of Miss Bindle have changed by the end of the selection

3. Use details from the selection to evaluate Miss Bindle as a teacher.
4. What do you think of Slick's behavior? Use pantomime to show what you think his behavior is like.
5. Could the events described in this selection occur in your classroom? Why or why not?

RELATE 6. The narrator seems to believe that modern teaching methods are more enjoyable but result in inferior learning. Do you agree with him? Do you feel that harsher discipline would improve students' performance? Explain your opinion.

Multimodal Learning
ANOTHER PATHWAY

With another student, choose a section of "The Clown" that you would enjoy telling from Miss Bindle's point of view. Then rewrite that section in Miss Bindle's words. Don't forget about her "weird sense of humor," and feel free to exaggerate as McManus did. Tell your story to the class.

LITERARY CONCEPTS

McManus uses several methods to create **humor,** or make his writing funny. How does he use repetition in the third paragraph? What comical actions does he describe? What names of people and places add humor? What examples of exaggeration did you notice as you read?

CONCEPT REVIEW: Irony As you know, irony is a contrast between what is expected and what actually happens. Explain how the end of this selection is ironic and why the irony is amusing.

QUICKWRITES

1. Pretend that you are Miss Bindle and create an amusing rhyming **poem** about Clifford Slick.
2. Imagine other antics that Clifford Slick might perform in class. Write a brief **narrative** of new trouble he gets into. You may wish to include other characters, like Olga Bonemarrow.

📁 **PORTFOLIO** Save your writing. You may want to use it later as a springboard to a piece for your portfolio.

62 UNIT ONE PART 1: TAUGHT BY EXPERIENCE

Literary Concepts

McManus repeatedly stresses the idea of "dumb" students to make the passage humorous. He also describes actions in a comical way, such as Miss Bindle's grabbing students by the hair. Descriptions are exaggerated for humorous effect, such as the description of Mort's needing a glass of water to cool his fingers and of Pat's laugh, which detonates like a bomb.

Concept Review The ending is both humorous and ironic because the truly unexpected happens: Miss Bindle laughs and reveals herself to have a "weird" sense of humor.

QuickWrites

1. Ask students to focus on McManus's descriptions of Slick's actions, which Miss Bindle has seen many times. Remind them to imagine her manner of speaking as they write.
2. Encourage students to reread the descriptions of Cliff's behavior to help them come up with other ideas. What other physical things might he do without making noise in a classroom? What "other side" of Olga might students be able to reveal?

The Writer's Craft

Writing a Poem, pp. 71–83

Multimodal Learning

ALTERNATIVE ACTIVITIES

A caricature is a drawing of a person in which certain physical characteristics and mannerisms are exaggerated for the sake of humor. Using the descriptions in the selection, draw a **caricature** of Miss Bindle or Clifford Slick. If you have an art program on your computer, here is a chance to use it.

ACROSS THE CURRICULUM

Media Watch a situation comedy or a standup comedian on television. Compare the ways in which humor is created on the television show with the techniques that McManus uses in "The Clown." Which methods work more easily in visual media, and which seem more appropriate for speaking or writing? Discuss your findings with the class.

WORDS TO KNOW

Review the Words to Know at the bottom of the selection pages. Decide which word is described in each riddle below, and write the answer on your paper.

1. Bullets, balls, and smart remarks can do this and come back at you!
2. I am a lot—maybe more than you need, like a great deal of homework.
3. Sticks and stones can break your bones, but I can hurt your feelings.
4. I can be money, praise, or a spanking; I'll make you do what I want!
5. Just a shade of me can make all the difference!
6. I'm more than naughty; I'm evil, and I wish you harm!
7. I'm what you might do if you laugh really hard or feel terrible pain.
8. Belly laughs, chuckles, howls, guffaws—these are all signs of me.
9. A girl in mythology is named for me; she really knew her own mind!
10. I'm making things happen.

PATRICK F. MCMANUS

The humor and practical jokes that sustained the young Patrick McManus and his family through tragedy and hardship resurface in his humorous stories. McManus's father and stepfather died when he was young, and his family lost their first home to fire.

He claims that his entire family had a weird sense of humor. For example, his mother told him that after his birth in Sandpoint, Idaho, she paid the attending doctor in homemade preserves and canned vegetables.

When McManus was in the first grade, his mother taught in a rundown, one-room schoolhouse, and the family slept on beds in the back of

1933–

the classroom. McManus attended the school where his mother taught until the eighth grade. He says that she flunked him in second grade. If it had not been for his love of reading about such heroes as Huck Finn and Tom Sawyer, the author claims, "I might have run totally wild."

McManus began his writing career while attending college. He published his first book of humorous stories in 1978 and later was an editor for *Field and Stream* and *Outdoor Life* magazines.

OTHER WORKS *Real Ponies Don't Go Oink!; Kid Camping from Aaaaiii! to Zip*

Extended Reading

THE CLOWN **63**

Words to Know

1. ricochet
2. copious
3. sarcasm
4. motivator
5. nuance
6. malevolent
7. writhe
8. mirth
9. psyche
10. inducing

Reteaching/Reinforcement
- *Unit One Resource Book*, p. 27

Across the Curriculum

Media Have students work in pairs. Both students should watch the television show and jot down observations about how humor is used. Ask them to compare notes and then to contrast their findings with the exaggerated verbal humor of McManus's essay.

ADDITIONAL SUGGESTION

 **Social Studies** *The Changing Classroom* The selection makes reference to things not found in modern classrooms, such as ink bottles. Students can interview an older relative or friend to find out other ways in which today's classroom differs from that of the 1940s. What new equipment can be found in the modern classroom? Are class sizes similar? How do content and length of lessons compare? What about other classroom conditions?

PATRICK MCMANUS

Patrick McManus has some strong opinions about writing humor. He believes that humor writers should not take themselves too seriously. He writes that "as soon as the humor writer starts thinking of himself as a person of letters, as soon as he perceives his purpose as something other than seeking the ultimate, base, vulgar, gut-busting, psyche-wrenching laugh, he is done for."

Alternative Activities

As students begin their caricatures, encourage them to focus on one or two of the subject's physical (or behavioral) characteristics. Some students might choose to concentrate on Slick's greased hair or perhaps his wiggling ears. Others might choose to focus on Miss Bindle's small size, her wrinkles or frown, or her hands as she is about to "snatch" a student by the hair.

OBJECTIVES

- To promote independent active reading
- To practice and apply skills learned in previous selections
- To provide an opportunity to assess students' performance through an alternative assessment instrument

Reading Pathways

- Have students read independently and write in dialogue journals.
- Encourage groups of students to do a choral reading, choosing parts for each individual to read.
- Invite students to choose passages to read aloud.
- Evaluate how well students can read, interpret, discuss, and write about the selection on their own by using the Integrated Assessment for Unit One, located in the Alternative Assessment booklet. Administer the assessment at the end of the unit after students have read all the selections and completed all the writing that was assigned. Set aside two class periods, or about two hours, for the assessment.

Art Note

The Garden Road by Fairfield Porter
As an American figurative painter, Porter (1907–1975) was known for his landscapes, seascapes, and portraits. A friend of Willem de Kooning, Porter blends elements of abstract painting into his figurative works. The dense shapes and textures of the trees overhead (as well as the shade they cast) underscore the division between the house and the girl's location. The composition suggests she has left the house and is in the process of entering and exploring another landscape on her own.

Reading the Art What does the girl's expression convey? Do you imagine that she has a particular destination in mind? As you read, think about whether this painting is an apt illustration for "The Apprentice."

The Garden Road (1962), Fairfield Porter. Oil on canvas, 62" × 48", collection of the Whitney Museum of American Art, New York, gift of the Greylock Foundation (62.55). Copyright © 1995 Whitney Museum of American Art. Photo by Geoffrey Clements, New York.

64 UNIT ONE PART 1: TAUGHT BY EXPERIENCE

PRINT AND MEDIA RESOURCES

UNIT ONE RESOURCE BOOK
Strategic Reading: Literature, p. 31

FORMAL ASSESSMENT
Selection Test, pp. 13–14
Part Test, pp. 15–16
Test Generator

ALTERNATIVE ASSESSMENT
Unit One Integrated Assessment, pp. 1–6

ACCESS FOR STUDENTS ACQUIRING ENGLISH
Selection Summaries

AUDIO LIBRARY
See Reference Card

ON YOUR OWN

The Apprentice

BY DOROTHY CANFIELD FISHER

> **SUMMARY**
>
> As 13-year-old Peg reflects on her conflicts with her strict parents, she realizes that Rollie, her collie puppy, is missing. She worries that he is chasing sheep, because a neighbor once shot a collie caught killing sheep. Peg panics and runs wildly through the dusk, calling for Rollie and sobbing. She finds him in the woods, lectures him sternly, and finally comforts him. As the pair heads home together, Peg feels the burden of adult responsibility. At home, she is filled with love for her mother and with contentment at being her own age.
>
> **Thematic Link: *Taught by Experience***
> The search for an exuberant puppy helps a teenage girl learn a lesson about the reasons behind her parents' stern rules.

The day had been one of the unbearable ones, when every sound had set her teeth on edge like chalk creaking on a blackboard, when every word her father or mother said to her or did not say to her seemed an intentional injustice. And of course it would happen, as the fitting end to such a day, that just as the sun went down back of the mountain and the long twilight began, she noticed that Rollie was not around.

Tense with exasperation[1] at what her mother would say, she began to call him in a carefully casual tone—she would simply explode if mother got going: "Here Rollie! He-ere boy! Want to go for a walk, Rollie?" Whistling to him cheerfully, her heart full of wrath at the way the world treated her, she made the rounds of his haunts: the corner of the woodshed, where he liked to curl up on the wool of father's discarded old sweater; the hay barn, the cow barn, the sunny spot on the side porch. No Rollie.

Perhaps he had sneaked upstairs to lie on her bed, where he was not supposed to go—not that *she* would have minded! That rule was part of mother's fussiness, part, too, of mother's bossiness. It was *her* bed, wasn't it? But was she allowed the say-so about it? Not on your life. They *said* she could have things the way she wanted in her own room, now she was in her teens, but—her heart burned at unfairness as she took the stairs stormily, two steps at a time, her pigtails flopping up and down on her back. If Rollie was there, she was just going to let him stay there, and mother could say what she wanted to.

But he was not there. The bedspread and pillow were crumpled, but that was where she

---

1. **exasperation** (ĭg-zăs′pə-rā′shən): frustrated annoyance.

THE APPRENTICE **65**

Science

Collies are intelligent, obedient dogs that are famous for being gentle with children. The breed originated hundreds of years ago in Scotland, where they tended sheep in the mountains. Distinctive qualities of the collie include a thin, almost wedge-shaped head and a thick coat of hair.

---

had flung herself down to cry that afternoon. Every nerve in her had been twanging discordantly, but she couldn't cry. She could only lie there, her hands doubled up hard, furious that she had nothing to cry about. Not really. She was too big to cry just over father's having said to her, severely, "I told you if I let you take the chess set, you were to put it away when you got through with it. One of the pawns was on the floor of our bedroom this morning. I stepped on it. If I'd had my shoes on I'd have broken it."

Well, he *had* told her that. And he hadn't said she mustn't ever take the set again. No, the instant she thought about that, she knew she couldn't cry about it. She could be, and was, in a rage about the way father kept on talking, long after she'd got his point: "It's not that I care so much about the chess set. It's because if you don't learn how to take care of things, you yourself will suffer for it. You'll forget or neglect something that will be really important, for *you*. We *have* to try to teach you to be responsible for what you've said you'll take care of. If we—" on and on.

She stood there, dry eyed, by the bed that Rollie had not crumpled and thought, *I hope mother sees the spread and says something about Rollie—I just hope she does.*

She heard her mother coming down the hall, and hastily shut her door. She had a right to shut the door to her own room, hadn't she? She had *some* rights, she supposed, even if she was only thirteen and the youngest child. If her mother opened it to say, "What are you doing in here that you don't want me to see?" she'd say—she'd just say—

But her mother did not open the door. Her feet went steadily on along the hall, and then, carefully, slowly, down the stairs. She probably had an armful of winter things she was bringing down from the attic. She was probably thinking that a tall, thirteen-year-old daughter was big enough to help with a chore like that. But she wouldn't *say* anything. She would just get out that insulting look of a grownup silently putting up with a crazy unreasonable kid. She had worn that expression all day; it was too much to be endured.

Up in her bedroom behind her closed door the thirteen-year-old stamped her foot in a gust of uncontrollable rage, nonetheless savage and heart-shaking because it was mysterious to her.

But she had not located Rollie. She would be cut into little pieces before she would let her father and mother know she had lost sight of him, forgotten about him. They would not scold her, she knew. They would do worse; they would look at her. And in their silence she would hear, droning on reproachfully, what they had said when she had been begging to keep for her own the sweet, woolly collie puppy in her arms.

How warm he had felt! Astonishing how warm and alive a puppy was compared with a doll! She had never liked her dolls much after she had held Rollie, feeling him warm against her breast, warm and wriggling, bursting with life, reaching up to lick her face. He had loved her from that first instant. As he felt her arms around him his liquid, beautiful eyes had melted in trusting sweetness. And they did now, whenever he looked at her. Her dog was the only creature in the world who *really* loved her, she thought passionately.

And back then, at the very minute when, as a darling baby dog, he was beginning to love her, her father and mother were saying, so cold, so reasonable—gosh, how she *hated* reasonableness!— "Now, Peg, remember that, living where we do, with sheep on the farms around us, it is a serious responsibility to have a collie dog. If you keep him, you've got to be the one to take care of him. You'll have to be the one to train him to stay at home. We're too busy with you children to start bringing up a puppy too."

Rollie, nestling in her arms, let one hind leg drop awkwardly. It must be uncomfortable. She looked down at him tenderly, tucked his leg up under him and gave him a hug. He laughed up in her face—he really did laugh, his mouth stretched wide in a cheerful grin. Now he was snug in a warm little ball.

Her parents were saying, "If you want him, you can have him. But you must be responsible for him. If he gets to running sheep, he'll just have to be shot, you know that."

They had not said, aloud, "Like the Wilsons' collie." They never mentioned that awfulness—her racing unsuspectingly down across the fields just at the horrible moment when Mr. Wilson shot their collie, caught in the very act of killing sheep. They probably thought that if they never spoke about it, she would forget it—*forget* the crack of that rifle, and the collapse of the great beautiful dog! Forget the red red blood spurting from the hole in his head. She hadn't forgotten. She never would. She knew as well as they did how important it was to train a collie puppy about sheep. They didn't have to rub it in like that. They always rubbed everything in. She had told them, fervently, indignantly, that of *course* she would take care of him, be responsible for him, teach him to stay at home. Of course. Of course. *She* understood!

> "If he gets to running sheep, he'll just have to be shot, you know that."

And now, when he was six months old, tall, rangy,[2] powerful, standing up far above her knee, nearly to her waist, she didn't know where he was. But of course he must be somewhere around. He always was. She composed her face to look natural and went downstairs to search the house. He was probably asleep somewhere. She looked every room over carefully. Her mother was nowhere visible. It was safe to call him again, to give the special piercing whistle which always brought him racing to her, the white-feathered plume of his tail waving in elation that she wanted him.

But he did not answer. She stood still on the front porch to think.

Could he have gone up to their special place in the edge of the field where the three young pines, their branches growing close to the ground, made a triangular, walled-in space, completely hidden from the world? Sometimes he went up there with her, and when she lay down on the dried grass to dream he, too, lay down quietly, his head on his paws, his beautiful eyes fixed adoringly on her. He entered into her every mood. If she wanted to be quiet, all right, he did too. It didn't seem as though he would have gone alone there. Still—she loped up the steep slope of the field rather fast, beginning to be anxious.

No, he was not there. She stood irresolutely[3] in the roofless, green-walled triangular hide-out, wondering what to do next.

Then, before she knew what thought had come into her mind, its emotional impact knocked her down. At least her knees

---

2. **rangy** (rān'jē): slender and long-limbed.
3. **irresolutely** (ĭ-rĕz'ə-lo͞ot'lē): in an undecided way.

THE APPRENTICE **67**

OPTION 1

Individual Activity
WRITING A POEM

Have students think about notable experiences they have had with animals. It might be a relationship they had with a pet or even an event that occurred with some wild animal. Invite students to brainstorm a list of words and phrases that in some way describe or evoke that experience or animal. Then have them turn their impressions into a poem.

Teacher's Role Remind students that their poems might relate a story, evoke a mood or a personality, or celebrate a certain animal or trait. Encourage students to experiment, either with free verse or through a more structured arrangement of the poem's lines or stanzas.

Rubric

3 Full Accomplishment Student composes a stylistically interesting poem that clearly evokes an experience with an animal.

2 Substantial Accomplishment Student composes a poem that evokes an experience with an animal in some way.

1 Little or Partial Accomplishment Student has difficulty composing a poem that relates or evokes any experience he or she has had with an animal.

---

crumpled under her. The Wilsons had, last Wednesday, brought their sheep down from the far upper pasture, to the home farm. They were—she herself had seen them on her way to school, and like an idiot had not thought of Rollie—on the river meadow.

She was off like a racer at the crack of the starting pistol, her long, strong legs stretched in great leaps, her pigtails flying. She took the short cut, regardless of the brambles. Their thorn-spiked, wiry stems tore at her flesh, but she did not care. She welcomed the pain. It was something she was doing for Rollie, for her Rollie.

She was in the pine woods now, rushing, down the steep, stony path, tripping over roots, half falling, catching herself just in time, not slackening her speed. She burst out on the open knoll above the river meadow, calling wildly, "Rollie, here Rollie, here, boy! Here! Here!" She tried to whistle, but she was crying too hard to pucker her lips.

There was nobody to see or hear her. Twilight was falling over the bare, grassy knoll. The sunless evening wind slid down the mountain like an invisible river, engulfing her in cold. Her teeth began to chatter. "Here, Rollie, here, boy, here!" She strained her eyes to look down into the meadow to see if the sheep were there. She could not be sure. She stopped calling him as she would a dog, and called out his name despairingly, as if he were her child, "Rollie! Oh, *Rollie,* where are you?"

The tears ran down her cheeks in streams. She sobbed loudly, terribly; she did not try to control herself, since there was no one to hear. "Hou! Hou! Hou!" she sobbed, her face contorted grotesquely. "Oh, Rollie! Rollie! Rollie!" She had wanted something to cry about. Oh, how terribly now she had something to cry about.

She saw him as clearly as if he were there beside her, his muzzle and gaping mouth all smeared with the betraying blood (like the Wilsons' collie). "But he didn't *know* it was wrong!" she screamed like a wild creature. "Nobody *told* him it was wrong. It was my fault. I should have taken better care of him. I will now. I will!"

But no matter how she screamed, she could not make herself heard. In the cold gathering darkness, she saw him stand, poor, guiltless victim of his ignorance, who should have been protected from his own nature, his beautiful soft eyes looking at her with love, his splendid plumed tail waving gently. "It was my fault. I promised I would bring him up. I should have *made* him stay at home. I was responsible for him. It was my fault."

But she could not make his executioners hear her. The shot rang out, Rollie sank down, his beautiful liquid eyes glazed, the blood spurting from the hole in his head—like the Wilsons' collie. She gave a wild shriek, long, soul-satisfying, frantic. It was the scream at sudden, unendurable tragedy of a mature, full-blooded woman. It drained dry the girl of thirteen. She came to herself. She was standing on the knoll, trembling and quaking with cold, the darkness closing in on her.

Her breath had given out. For once in her life she had wept all the tears there were in her body. Her hands were so stiff with cold she could scarcely close them. How her nose was running, simply streaming down her upper lip! And she had no handkerchief. She lifted her skirt, fumbled for her slip, stooped, blew her nose on it, wiped her eyes, drew a long quavering breath—and heard something! Far off in the distance, a faint sound, like a dog's muffled bark.

She whirled on her heels and bent her head to

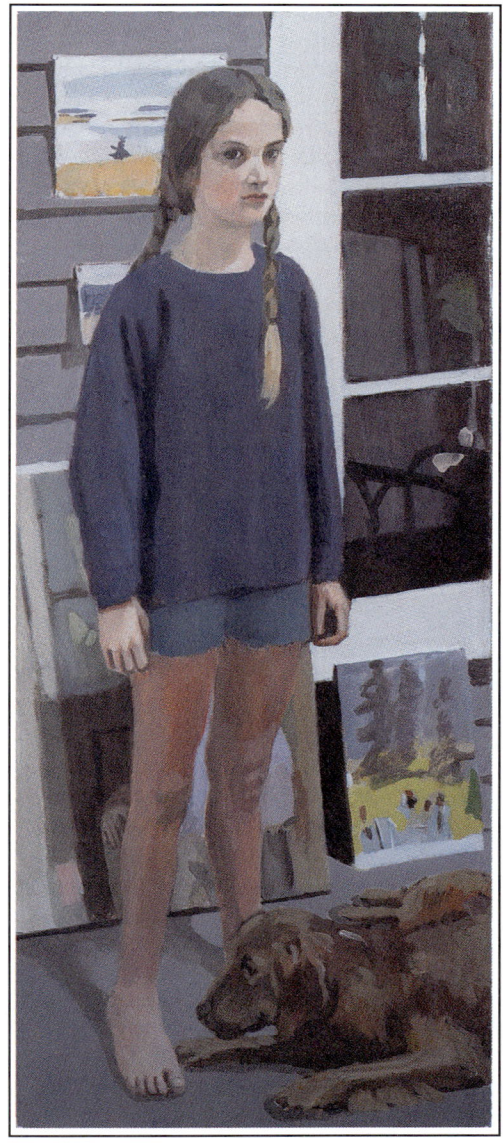

Lizzie and Bruno (1970), Fairfield Porter. Collection of Dr. and Mrs. Joseph Del Gaudio. Photo by Affiliated Photographic Services, Inc.

listen. The sound did not come from the meadow below the knoll. It came from back of her, from the Wilsons' maple grove higher up. She held her breath. Yes, it came from there. She began to run again, but now she was not sobbing. She was silent, absorbed in her effort to cover ground. If she could only live to get there, to see if it really were Rollie. She ran steadily till she came to the fence, and went over this in a great plunge. Her skirt caught on a nail. She impatiently pulled at it, not hearing or not heeding the long sibilant tear as it came loose. She was in the dusky maple woods, stumbling over the rocks as she ran. As she tore on up the slope she knew it was Rollie's bark.

She stopped short and leaned weakly against a tree, sick with the breathlessness of her straining lungs, sick in the reaction of relief, sick with anger at Rollie, who had been here having a wonderful time while she had been dying, just dying in terror about him.

For she could now not only hear that it was Rollie's bark; she could hear, in the dog language she knew as well as he, what he was saying in those excited yips: that he had run a woodchuck into a hole in the tumbled stone wall, that he almost had him, that the intoxicating wild animal smell was as close to him—almost—as if he had his jaws on his quarry. Yip! Woof! Yip! Yip!

The wild, joyful quality of the dog talk enraged the girl. She was trembling in exhaustion, in indignation. So that was where he had been, when she was killing herself trying to take care of him. Plenty near enough to hear her calling and whistling to him, if he had paid attention. Just so set on having his foolish good time, he never thought to listen for her call.

She stooped to pick up a stout stick. She would teach him! It was time he had something to make him remember to listen. She started forward.

Art Note

Lizzie and Bruno by Fairfield Porter In this painting, as in Porter's *The Garden Road*, the central figure is a teenage girl who is looking directly at the viewer. Her facial expression is ambiguous—perhaps anxious, worried, angry, or gloomy. Note Porter's inclusion of unframed art against the wall behind the girl.

Reading the Art *In your opinion, what kind of a person might Lizzie be? Does her appearance suggest what she might be thinking or feeling? What details from the painting help show this?*

But she stopped, stood thinking. One of the things to remember about collies—everybody knew that—was their sensitiveness. A collie who had been beaten was never "right" again. His spirit was broken. "Anything but a broken-spirited collie," the farmers often said. They were no good after that.

She threw down her stick. Anyhow, she thought, he was too young to know, really, that he had done wrong. He was still only a puppy. Like all puppies, he got perfectly crazy over wild-animal smells. Probably he really and truly hadn't heard her calling and whistling.

All the same, all the same— she stared intently into the twilight—he couldn't be let to grow up just as he wanted to. She would have to make him understand that he mustn't go off this way by himself. He must be trained to know how to do what a good dog does— not because *she* wanted him to, but for his own sake.

She walked on now, steady, purposeful, gathering her inner strength together, Olympian⁴ in her understanding of the full meaning of the event.

When he heard his own special young god approaching, he turned delightedly and ran to meet her, panting, his tongue hanging out. His eyes shone. He jumped up on her in an ecstasy of welcome and licked her face.

But she pushed him away. Her face and voice were grave. "No, Rollie, *no!*" she said severely. "You're *bad.* You know you're not to go off in the woods without me! You are—a— bad—dog."

He was horrified, stricken into misery. He stood facing her, frozen, the gladness going out of his eyes, the erect waving plume of his tail slowly lowered to slinking, guilty dejection.

"I know you were all wrapped up in that woodchuck. But that's no excuse. You *could* have heard me, calling you, whistling for you, if you'd paid attention," she went on. "You've got to learn, and I've got to teach you."

With a shudder of misery he lay down, his tail stretched out limp on the ground, his head flat on his paws, his ears drooping—ears ringing with the doomsday awfulness of the voice he so loved and revered.⁵ He must have been utterly wicked. He trembled, and turned his head away from her august look of blame, groveling in remorse⁶ for whatever mysterious sin he had committed.

She sat down by him, as miserable as he. "I don't *want* to scold you. But I have to! I have to bring you up right, or you'll get shot, Rollie. You *mustn't* go away from the house without me, do you hear, *never!*"

Catching, with his sharp ears yearning for her approval, a faint overtone of relenting affection in her voice, he lifted his eyes to her, humbly, soft in imploring⁷ fondness.

"Oh, Rollie!" she said, stooping low over him. "I *do* love you. I do. But I *have* to bring you up. I'm responsible for you, don't you see?"

He did not see. Hearing sternness, or

---

4. **Olympian:** godlike; from the name of Mount Olympus, the dwelling place of the gods in Greek mythology.
5. **revered** (rĭ-vîrd′): regarded with awe and devotion.
6. **groveling in remorse:** lying submissively as a sign of guilt or regret.
7. **imploring:** begging; appealing.

something else he did not recognize, in the beloved voice, he shut his eyes tight in sorrow, and made a little whimpering lament in his throat.

She had never heard him cry before. It was too much. She sat down by him and drew his head to her, rocking him in her arms, soothing him with inarticulate small murmurs.

He leaped in her arms and wriggled happily as he had when he was a baby; he reached up to lick her face as he had then. But he was no baby now. He was half as big as she, a great, warm, pulsing, living armful of love. She clasped him closely. Her heart was brimming full, but calmed, quiet. The blood flowed in equable gentleness all over her body. She was deliciously warm. Her nose was still running a little. She sniffed and wiped it on her sleeve.

It was almost dark now. "We'll be late to supper, Rollie," she said responsibly. Pushing him gently off, she stood up. "Home, Rollie, home!"

Here was a command he could understand. At once he trotted along the path toward home. His plumed tail, held high, waved cheerfully. His short dog memory had dropped into oblivion the suffering just back of him.

Her human memory was longer. His prancing gait was as carefree as a young child's. Plodding heavily like a serious adult, she trod behind him. Her very shoulders seemed bowed by what she had lived through. She felt, she thought, like an old, old woman of thirty. But it was all right now. She knew she had made an impression on him.

When they came out into the open pasture, Rollie ran back to get her to play with him. He leaped around her in circles, barking in cheerful yawps, jumping up on her, inviting her to run a race with him, to throw him a stick, to come alive.

His high spirits were ridiculous but infectious. She gave one little leap to match his. Rollie pretended that this was a threat to him, planted his forepaws low and barked loudly at her, laughing between yips. He was so funny, she thought, when he grinned that way. She laughed back, and gave another mock-threatening leap at him. Radiant that his sky was once more clear, he sprang high on his steel-spring muscles in an explosion of happiness, and bounded in circles around her.

Following him, not noting in the dusk where she was going, she felt the grassy slope drop steeply. Oh, yes, she knew where she was. They had come to the rolling-down hill just back of the house. All the kids rolled down there, even the little ones, because it was soft grass without a stone. She had rolled down that slope a million times—years and years ago, when she was a kid herself. It was fun. She remembered well the whirling dizziness of the descent, all the world turning over and over crazily. And the delicious giddy staggering when you first stood up, the earth still spinning under your feet.

"All right, Rollie, let's go," she cried, and flung herself down in the rolling position, her arms straight up over her head.

Rollie had never seen this skylarking before. It threw him into almost hysterical amusement. He capered around the rapidly rolling figure, half scared, mystified, enchanted.

His wild frolicsome barking might have come from her own throat, so accurately did it sound the way she felt—crazy, foolish, like a little kid, no more than five years old, the age she had been when she had last rolled down that hill.

At the bottom she sprang up, on muscles as steel-strong as Rollie's. She staggered a little, and laughed aloud.

The living room windows were just before

THE APPRENTICE 71

Art Note

***Hilltop—Farmhouse* by Marie Atkinson Hull** This study of a verdant rural landscape conveys a sense of space, of freedom, and of a rich natural world. Hull's strong brushstrokes, bold use of color, and soft, sensuous lines draw the viewer's attention to both the human habitations and the fertile land around them.

Reading the Art *How would you describe the subject of this painting? Do you think the painter lived mainly in the city or the country? What makes you say so?*

Hilltop—Farmhouse (1929), Marie Atkinson Hull. Oil on canvas board, 24″ × 20″, Lauren Rogers Museum of Art, Laurel, Mississippi, Lauren Rogers Museum Purchase, 1984 (84.3).

them. How yellow lighted windows looked when you were in the darkness going home. How nice and yellow. Maybe mother had waffles for supper. She was a swell cook, mother was, and she certainly gave her family all the breaks, when it came to meals.

"Home, Rollie, home!" She burst open the door to the living room. "Hi, mom, what you got for supper?"

From the kitchen her mother announced coolly, "I hate to break the news to you, but its waffles."

"Oh, *mom!*" she shouted in ecstasy.

Her mother could not see her. She did not need to. "For goodness' sakes, go and wash," she called.

In the long mirror across the room she saw herself, her hair hanging wild, her long bare legs scratched, her broadly smiling face dirt-streaked, her torn skirt dangling, her dog laughing up at her. Gosh, was it a relief to feel your own age, just exactly thirteen years old! ❖

DOROTHY CANFIELD FISHER

1879–1958

Dorothy Canfield Fisher's novels and short stories, both those for children and those for adults, were inspired by the ordinary events and human problems she saw around her. Major elements of "The Apprentice" were part of her life: her collie, her daughter Sally, and her country home.

Fisher was born in Lawrence, Kansas. Her father taught at a college, and her mother was an artist. She attended Ohio State University, planning to be a violinist or a language teacher. Soon after receiving her doctorate from Columbia University, with her stories selling, she decided on a writing career.

During World War I, Fisher took her children to France while her husband served with an ambulance unit there. She wrote stories that were translated into Braille for blinded soldiers and started a fund to aid French children affected by the war. Later, in 1940, she started the Children's Crusade for Children, in which American children donated pennies to help refugee children.

A member of the first Book-of-the-Month Club selection panel, and the only woman on the panel, Fisher read and critiqued more than 4,000 books for 25 years before failing eyesight forced her to resign.

So popular were Fisher's compassionate stories and her nonfiction about children, parenting, and education, that she received many awards and honorary degrees. The Dorothy Canfield Fisher Children's Book Award was established in her honor, and a group of Indiana women named their literary club after her. Eleanor Roosevelt placed Fisher among the ten American women who had had the most influence on women's lives.

THE APPRENTICE 73

OVERVIEW

In the Guided Assignment for this section, students will rewrite a scene from a selection. By changing one of the story's elements in their rewritten version, students will better understand how elements—such as point of view, setting, character, or plot—function in a literary work. As preparation for this assignment, The Writer's Style will help students understand how different points of view can change the effect of a story. In Reading the World, students will explore the ways we encounter different points of view in the world around us every day.

Objectives

- To recognize how authors use different points of view effectively
- To write introductions
- To use pronouns appropriate to the point of view
- To rewrite a story by changing one of its elements
- To analyze an event seen from several points of view

Skills

LITERATURE
- Identifying point of view

GRAMMAR AND USAGE
- Using pronouns
- Avoiding clause fragments

MEDIA LITERACY
- Analyzing perspectives

ORAL COMMUNICATION
- Giving peer feedback
- Group conferencing

CRITICAL THINKING
- Analyzing perspective
- Classifying
- Speculating

Teaching Strategy: MODELING

In the following models, the author's point of view affects how the reader understands characters and events.

A McManus Possible responses: The narrator seems shy, anxious, careful, and a bit sly; the first-person point of view encourages the reader to see Miss Bindle as the narrator does—someone to be feared.

B Myers Possible responses: The narrator is not part of the story. In this passage, the reader does not get any direct, personal sense of what the characters are thinking or feeling.

WRITING ABOUT LITERATURE

Exploring Perspectives

In literature, as in life, looking at an event from another point of view can change your understanding. For example, if Miss Bindle narrated "The Clown" or if Greg narrated "The Treasure of Lemon Brown," imagine how the stories would change! In the following pages you will

- look at how authors use point of view in stories
- explore how changing a story element affects a story
- notice how people react differently to an experience

The Writer's Style: Point of View In literature, point of view refers to the perspective from which the story is told. Two common types of point of view are first person and third person. In first-person point of view, the narrator is a character in the story. In third-person, the narrator describes the action but doesn't take part in it.

Read the Literature

Notice the point of view in each of the following excerpts.

Literature Models

A First-Person Point of View
What does the point of view allow you to learn about the narrator? How does it affect your view of Miss Bindle?

> I was a fairly timid fellow and took great care never to attract the wrath of Miss Bindle. I studied ways to make myself invisible in her class, with such success that a couple of times she marked me absent when I was there. Pitiful victims were snatched from their desks on all sides of me, but month after month I escaped unsnatched, making myself increasingly invisible . . .
>
> Patrick F. McManus, from "The Clown"

B Third-Person Point of View
Is the narrator part of this story? What kind of information did you get in the first model that you do not get here?

> Greg went to the window and saw three men, neighborhood thugs, on the stoop. One was carrying a length of pipe. Greg looked back toward Lemon Brown, who moved quietly across the room to the window. The old man looked out, then beckoned frantically for Greg to follow him. For a moment Greg couldn't move.
>
> Walter Dean Myers, from "The Treasure of Lemon Brown"

74 UNIT ONE: CHANGING PERCEPTIONS

PRINT AND MEDIA RESOURCES

UNIT ONE RESOURCE BOOK
The Writer's Style, p. 35
Prewriting, p. 36
Elaboration, p. 37
Peer Response Guide, pp. 38–39
Revising and Proofreading, p. 40
Rubric, p. 42

GRAMMAR MINI-LESSONS
Transparencies, pp. 10–11
Copymasters, pp. 12–14

ACCESS FOR STUDENTS ACQUIRING ENGLISH
Reading and Writing Support

FORMAL ASSESSMENT
Guidelines for Writing Assessment

Connect to Life
Newspaper, magazine, television, and radio writers and reporters use both first-person and third-person point of view. When might a reporter want to write in the first person? When might third person be better?

Magazine Article

I'm a mediator, and I carry what I learn into the street. One time, there was something going on, and I told the guys, "Look, you're not talking, you're arguing. You're not listening, all you're doing is yelling. You don't get along. Just forget about it. You go your way, you go yours. Because, whatcha gonna do? You're gonna fight. *Boom!* . . . and it never ends. Just let it be."

Janet Gonzales, 19, New York City
from "Fresh Voices"
Parade, January 8, 1995

First-Person Point of View
Would this paragraph be more or less interesting written in the third person? Why do you think so?

Try Your Hand: Understanding Point of View

1. **Use Point of View** Use first-person or third-person point of view to develop one of these ideas into a paragraph.
   - A teenager attends a concert.
   - A child finds a stray pet.

2. **Revise a QuickWrite** Look through your QuickWrites to find a story idea that you can develop by using the point of view of one of the characters. Visualize one event as this person would experience it. Think about how this character would feel and how he or she would express these feelings. Then write a scene based on your idea.

3. **Rewrite a Scene** Choose a paragraph from one of the selections you have read so far in this unit and rewrite it, changing its point of view. Consider what information you will need to add or leave out depending on the point of view you are using.

SkillBuilder

 GRAMMAR FROM WRITING

Using Pronouns

The pronouns you use in a story will depend on the point of view you're telling the story from. Notice how authors Patrick F. McManus and Walter Dean Myers use pronouns to show the story's point of view.

I thought I was going to make it safely through to the end of the school year. (first-person point of view: I)

He hadn't been allowed to play high school ball, which he had really wanted to do. (third-person point of view: he)

APPLYING WHAT YOU'VE LEARNED
Rewrite the following sentences so that the speaker's point of view changes.

1. Greg knew he would fail math if he didn't study.
2. When I saw Miss Bindle laughing, I realized that she had a sense of humor, too.
3. Lemon Brown untied the strings around his leg and revealed his treasure.

 GRAMMAR HANDBOOK

For more information on pronouns, see page 870 in the Grammar Handbook.

WRITING ABOUT LITERATURE 75

SkillBuilder  GRAMMAR FROM WRITING

USING PRONOUNS Use the chart shown to remind students that the first-person point of view uses first-person pronouns and the third-person point of view uses third-person pronouns.

First Person	Third Person
I, me	he, him, his
my, mine	she, her, hers
us, we, ours	them, theirs

Applying What You've Learned Possible responses:

1. *I* knew *I* would fail math if *I* didn't study.
2. When *she* saw Miss Bindle laughing, *she* realized that the teacher had a sense of humor, too.
3. *I* untied the strings around *my* leg and revealed *my* treasure.

Reteaching/Reinforcement
Grammar Mini-Lessons copymasters, pp. 12–14, transparencies, pp. 10–11

The Writer's Craft
Pronouns, pp. 435–69

Teaching Strategy: MODELING
C Gonzales Possible responses: It would probably be less interesting because the narrator's vivid personality wouldn't be conveyed as clearly.

Teaching Strategy: USING THE SKILLBUILDER
D You can help students understand point of view by teaching the SkillBuilder on Using Pronouns at this time. Students will see how consistent use of pronouns helps them stay focused on the point of view they have chosen.

Try Your Hand

1. Responses will vary. Students' paragraphs should adhere to the first- or third-person point of view by using the correct perspective.
   Note the following examples:
   - I couldn't believe that I was finally going to see my favorite band perform!
   - The small boy pushed aside the boxes and discovered the source of the strange noise—a kitten!
2. Students' first-person scenes should employ pronouns such as *I*, *me*, and *my* and should convey the thoughts, feelings, and personality of the first-person narrator. If students are having trouble visualizing the character's point of view, they can review the selection.
3. Suggest that students first think about what a given character could know and not know about other characters and events.

Teaching Strategy:
STUMBLING BLOCK

E Students might benefit from help in choosing which scene to rewrite and which element to change. Remind students that the process of changing a story element will put them in the position of the original story writer. It will require that they ask the questions that led to the story being one way instead of another.

You might wish to have students choose a favorite scene. If some students seem reluctant to change any element in a "perfect" scene, you could ask them to choose a scene that they would like to see changed in some way. Remind them that they can think of the change as improving the story or as taking it in some new direction.

Critical Thinking: CLASSIFYING

F Be sure students understand that classifying requires placing specific story elements into categories. Point out that when they list the differences between Pat's and Miss Bindle's point of view, they are classifying.

WRITING ABOUT LITERATURE

Creative Response

One way to explore how the elements of a story work together is to change one element, such as the point of view. Then watch what happens to the story.

GUIDED ASSIGNMENT
Changing a Story Element In this assignment you will rewrite a scene from a story by changing the point of view or by changing another story element, such as the story's setting, characters, or plot.

1 Prewrite and Explore

Reexamine the stories you have read in Unit One. Examine the role of the elements in each one. Which story might be the most interesting to experiment with?

CHOOSING A SCENE AND A NEW STORY ELEMENT

Choose a story that you think would be fun to rework. Consider these questions:

- What scene in the story would be interesting to change?
- If you changed the story's setting (either the time period or the place), how would that affect the characters and what they do?
- If a key event didn't happen, how would that affect the plot?
- How would the scene change with a new narrator or different point of view?

Decision Point Now that you have thought about it, which scene would you like to retell? Which story element change would have the most impact?

Student's Prewriting Chart

"The Clown"	Event: Pat Laughs in Class	
Point of View	First Person Pat	First Person Miss Bindle
Feelings	Mirth, Terror	Frustration
Thoughts	I can't believe I'm laughing	I'll never get through this lesson
Observations	Miss Bindle's stiletto eyes glaring	Pat's flushed face

GATHERING INFORMATION

Think about how changing one story element would affect the scene you've selected. For example, suppose you had Miss Bindle narrate "The Clown." How would her view of characters and events differ from Pat's? What new information would Miss Bindle give the reader? What details would her point of view *not* include? Jot down your ideas.

Assessment ✓ Option

SELF-ASSESSMENT After students have completed the Gathering Information activity, they can assess their understanding of how changing a story element can change a story. Students should consider the following questions:

- *Does changing a story element affect how I will retell that story?*
- *Does changing point of view affect how the story will be told? What information is included?*
- *Do I have enough information to begin to write, or should I review the scene for more ideas?*

② Try a Draft

Before you write, visualize the scene. Then begin drafting new descriptions, dialogue, and events. If you're rewriting the story's opening, the SkillBuilder on writing introductions may help you. When you've finished, ask yourself a few questions:

- Does this scene reveal a change in a story element?
- Have I stuck with this new element throughout?
- What dialogue and descriptions can I add?

Student's Draft

Once I caught Mort looking at Pat's paper. I thought Pat, at least, knew better. I guess I lost my temper, and I said something sarcastic about Pat being a poor source for answers. Maybe I also wanted to get some response from Pat. He'd improved in spelling and arithmetic, but he was so quiet that I worried about him.

Introduction: Tell what Miss B. thinks of Pat. Make it sound like a teacher talking.

Describe what Clifford was doing and how he looked. Add more details about the scene.

I was used to Clifford's antics, but the bear grease was a surprise. At first I was furious. But when Pat started laughing, I saw how funny it was. And Pat was finally acting like a normal boy. I controlled myself until the boys left. Then I went into the cloakroom and laughed.

③ Share Your Work

After you have completed your draft, use these questions to help a classmate give you feedback.

PEER RESPONSE

- What story element have I changed? How could you tell?
- What are some ideas I might include?
- How can I make my introduction better?

SkillBuilder

WRITER'S CRAFT

Writing Introductions

As you draft, keep in mind that your introduction should capture your audience's attention and should present the change in a story element.

- You might begin with a vivid description of the setting, the characters, or the events of your scene.
- You could start with a question to get your readers thinking about the change in the story element.
- You might begin with an interesting or humorous incident to draw your readers into your scene.
- You could begin with dialogue between characters in your scene.

APPLYING WHAT YOU'VE LEARNED

Look at the introduction to the scene you're retelling and answer these questions:

- How does the introduction engage the attention of my readers?
- What information about the change of setting, point of view, characters, or events is provided?
- What effect will the introduction have on readers?

WRITING HANDBOOK

For more information on introductions, see pages 826 in the Writing Handbook.

WRITING ABOUT LITERATURE **77**

Writing Skill: REWRITING

The draft gives students an opportunity to familiarize themselves with ideas and to sort through the information they've gathered. Suggest that students think in terms of making adjustments to the existing text, as well as adding new material. Help them see that changing a story's point of view will require them to change some pronouns. In addition, as they reimagine the story through the eyes of the new narrator, they may need to take out or add certain images, phrases, descriptions, or events.

Teaching Strategy: USING THE SKILLBUILDER

You can help students rewrite a story's opening by teaching the SkillBuilder on Writing Introductions at this time. This SkillBuilder helps students understand the techniques they can use to write an effective and attention-grabbing introduction.

SkillBuilder WRITER'S CRAFT

WRITING INTRODUCTIONS Explain that a writer chooses the best way to begin a story based on what the story is about and how he or she wants to tell the story. Have students analyze the beginning of their stories as they are written and consider why the writer began exactly that way. Then have them consider how their change of one story element might affect the story's beginning. Remind them that the effect on the introduction might be dramatic or subtle.

Applying What You've Learned Students should explain what information they have decided to change and then identify whether this information is conveyed through dialogue, description, a question, an unusual or humorous fact, or an incident.

Additional Suggestions If students need more practice writing introductions, they can rewrite the introduction to another selection from Unit 1.

Reteaching/Reinforcement

The Writer's Craft
Introductions, pp. 278–80

Teaching Strategy:
USING THE SKILLBUILDER

I By teaching the SkillBuilder on Avoiding Clause Fragments, you can help students to understand how to avoid or to correct sentence fragments and run-on sentences.

Critical Thinking: ANALYZING

J To evaluate their work, students should make sure that the scene reflects the change of one story element, the element is consistently developed, and the descriptions fit with the new element.

Teaching Tip: MODELING

K Invite students to discuss how the two samples on this page meet the Standards for Evaluation. In the first paragraph the writer establishes Miss Bindle as the first-person narrator in the first sentence. In the second paragraph the writer adds details about the lesson ("turned around to make sure the students understood") and the pupils ("He wasn't imitating me this time") that could come only from Miss Bindle's point of view.

Standards for Evaluation

Ideas and Content
- Retells a scene from a story by changing a story element: point of view, plot, setting, or character
- Keeps new element the same throughout scene
- Changes other story elements and adds or removes information to make sense with new element
- Begins with an introduction that catches the reader's attention and makes clear what element has changed

Structure and Form
- Displays a clear order of events
- Demonstrates proper and effective paragraphing
- Includes sentences with a variety of structures

Grammar, Usage, and Mechanics
- Contains no more than two or three minor errors in grammar and usage
- Contains no more than two or three minor errors in spelling, capitalization, and punctuation

---

WRITING ABOUT LITERATURE

4 Revise and Edit

I Use the information from Grammar in Context on the opposite page along with your peer comments as you revise and edit your draft. Reflect on how your change of a story element affects the scene you chose. Think about how you might share your final draft with the class.

The Quiet One

Pat sat in the back of my seventh grade classroom. He was a nice-looking boy, but he never said anything. No matter what subject the class was working on, he never volunteered to answer a question. He did his homework and never made any trouble. If I called on him, he usually had the right answer, so I knew he wasn't stupid.

How does this paragraph introduce the change of a story element (in this case, Miss Bindle as the narrator)?

What information does the writer add here that could only come through the point of view of the teacher?

I was explaining a problem and writing on the chalkboard. When I turned around to make sure the students understood, I saw something that made my blood boil. It was Clifford Slick again with pencils stuck in his nose and ink dribbling from his mouth. He wasn't imitating me this time. He was putting on another of his stupid comic routines, disturbing students who were trying to work. I rushed back to Clifford to get him out of my classroom before he completely ruined the lesson.

Standards for Evaluation

A creative response
- retells one scene from a story by changing a story element: point of view, setting, character, or plot
- keeps the new element the same throughout the scene
- changes other story elements and adds or removes information to make sense with the new element
- begins with an introduction that catches readers' attention and makes clear what element has changed

78 UNIT ONE: CHANGING PERCEPTIONS

Assessment Option

SELF-ASSESSMENT To help students assess their own writing, they should ask themselves the following questions:
- *What scene have I rewritten? What story element have I changed?*
- *Have I kept the new element the same throughout the scene?*
- *Have I made adjustments in other story elements to make sense with the new element?*
- *Have I begun my rewrite with an introduction that grabs the reader's attention and makes clear which element I've changed?*
- *Have I incorporated comments from my classmates?*

Grammar in Context

 Sentence Fragments and Run-on Sentences As you turn your rough notes into a story, pay particular attention to correcting sentence fragments or run-ons.

A **sentence fragment** is a group of words that does not express a complete thought. A sentence fragment can be corrected by adding the missing subject or predicate or by combining the incomplete thought with another sentence.

A **run-on sentence** is two or more sentences incorrectly written as one. Sometimes a run-on sentence can be corrected by separating the two complete thoughts with an end mark or with a conjunction and a comma.

> Clifford was my problem student, ~~B~~ecause his only interest was in making others laugh. Clifford would do anything to disrupt my class, ^he never was concerned about hurting my feelings or making me angry. ^He d~~D~~elighted in making me look like an ogre. ~~W~~when I would have to take him to the principal's office.

In the example above, the sentence fragments and run-on sentence are corrected.

Try Your Hand: Writing Correct Sentences

Revise the following paragraph by correcting any sentence fragments or run-on sentences.

> The year was almost over. When I learned that Pat actually had a sense of humor. I was anxious to cover the last chapter of the arithmetic text that morning. (Every student had learned to multiply and divide fractions some of them still needed to work on word problems.) I wasn't thinking. When I turned my back on Clifford.

SkillBuilder

 GRAMMAR FROM WRITING

Avoiding Fragments

Sentence fragments can often be eliminated in your writing by combining them with another sentence.

If I called on him, he usually had the right answer.

Be careful, however, that you are not putting two simple sentences together with a comma and creating a run-on sentence. Two simple sentences can correctly be combined with a comma and conjunction such as *and*, *but*, or *or*.

I was used to Clifford's antics, but the bear grease was a surprise.

Sometimes two simple sentences can be joined with a semicolon if they are very closely related.

He wasn't imitating me this time; he was putting on a comic routine.

APPLYING WHAT YOU'VE LEARNED

Combine the fragments below into complete sentences.

When Pat started laughing. I saw how funny it was. And how Pat was finally acting like a normal boy. I controlled myself. Until the boys left.

 **GRAMMAR HANDBOOK**

For more information about writing complete sentences, see page 860 of the Grammar Handbook.

WRITING ABOUT LITERATURE **79**

CUSTOMIZING FOR
Students Acquiring English

L Before you introduce this page, make sure that students understand the requirements of a complete sentence: It must contain a subject and a verb and express a complete thought. Help students understand that sentence fragments and run-on sentences are two of the most common errors in writing sentences.

Critical Thinking: ANALYZING

M Challenge students to explain the rationale for each of the corrections in the sample. (Possible responses: first change—the second sentence did not express a complete thought; second change—two sentences were incorrectly written as one; third change—sentence contained no subject; fourth change—final sentence did not express a complete thought)

Try Your Hand

Below is one possible revision of the paragraph:

The year was almost over when I learned that Pat actually had a sense of humor. I was anxious to cover the last chapter of the arithmetic text that morning. (Every student had learned to multiply and divide fractions, but some of them still needed to work on word problems.) I wasn't thinking when I turned my back on Clifford.

SkillBuilder GRAMMAR FROM WRITING

AVOIDING CLAUSE FRAGMENTS Remind students that writers often use fragments in informal, spoken language. However, it is important to identify and correct fragments in our writing. Point out to students that saying a thought aloud sometimes can help them decide if it is a complete sentence or a fragment.

Applying What You've Learned Possible response: When Pat started laughing, I saw how funny it was and how Pat was finally acting like a normal boy. I controlled myself until the boys left.

Additional Suggestions Have students separate the following compound sentences into two complete sentences.
1. Clifford always laughed in class, but Pat never did.
2. It was nice to see Pat laugh, and I was relieved to see that he could enjoy himself.

Reteaching/Reinforcement
Grammar Mini-Lessons copymasters, p. 1, transparencies, p. 1

The Writer's Craft
Fragments, pp. 296, 382, 386, 561

THE LANGUAGE OF LITERATURE TEACHER'S EDITION **79**

READING THE WORLD

On pages 74–79 students explored how changing one story element—such as point of view—would affect the story as a whole. In this lesson, students will consider how they can use their awareness of different points of view in their dealings with friends, family, and others.

Critical Thinking: SPECULATING

N Students may say that the scene is portraying a group of people riding in a roller coaster. They may have a number of different descriptions for the people represented. For instance, students may describe some of the facial expressions as fearful, surprised, or terrified. However, other passengers look like they are having fun.

Media Literacy: INTERPRETING SITUATIONS

O Students might mention age, personality, and experience as reasons for the riders' different reactions. A person who had never ridden on a roller coaster before might be more surprised or frightened than a person who had ridden many times. Students might interpret the riders' facial expressions as showing joy, excitement, pleasure, fear, apprehension, or wonder.

Speaking and Listening: GROUP DISCUSSION

P Have students work in small groups to discuss the riders' different perspectives on their experience. As these people retell the event later, they might focus on the aspects of the ride that made the deepest impression on them. Of course, each person's experience of the ride would be unique. Thus one person might focus on details about how the sounds of the roller coaster frightened him or her, whereas another person's retelling might stress the exhilarating speed of the roller coaster's descent.

READING THE WORLD

CLOSE-UP ON PERSPECTIVE

Like characters you read about in literature, people that you see every day have different ways of looking at the same experience. Look at the faces of the people in this situation and think about each person's response.

N **View** In your journal, describe what you think is happening here and how people are reacting.

O **Interpret** Using the observations in your journal, continue writing about the scene. Why do you think the riders' reactions are different? How would you interpret what they are feeling, based on their expressions?

P **Discuss** Discuss this situation in a small group. Say why you think the riders' reactions are different. Imagine each of these people retelling the event later. How might their versions differ? Now use the SkillBuilder on the opposite page for help in evaluating perspectives.

SkillBuilder

 CRITICAL THINKING

Analyzing Perspective

Perspective refers to the way we look at events and people around us. Because we have different likes and dislikes and because we come from different backgrounds, our perspectives are often different. Conflicts can occur when we don't take the time to think about what the other person sees. For example, you may think the new student is stuck-up. If you look at the situation through her eyes, however, you may see that she is shy and unsure of herself.

Point of view also affects the information you receive from others. What does this tell you about how you might judge news stories, political speeches, and other kinds of information you receive? Be sure you consider any event, idea, or person from different perspectives.

APPLYING WHAT YOU'VE LEARNED

In a small group, discuss one or more of the following.

- List situations in which seeing someone else's perspective would be important.
- What problems can occur when someone insists that his or her perspective is more important than someone else's?
- Can you think of a time when considering someone else's point of view helped you solve a problem?

READING THE WORLD **81**

SkillBuilder CRITICAL THINKING

ANALYZING PERSPECTIVE Point out to students that just as they and their classmates have different perspectives on some issues, so do adults. You might wish to discuss with students the mistake of assuming that things in the newspaper, on television, or on radio are factual. Remind them that the newspaper reporter and the radio commentator have their own perspectives. It will serve students well to develop the habit of reflecting on the particular perspective from which various public figures speak.

Applying What You've Learned

- Students might mention situations such as mediating an argument between two other people, getting advice before making an important decision, or accepting a newcomer into a neighborhood or a class.
- Students might note that this situation can cause the other person to feel resentment, anger, or hopelessness because it does not allow for any compromise.
- Responses will vary. Encourage students to explain carefully the cause-and-effect relationship between listening to the other person and solving the problem.

UNIT ONE
Part 2 Lesson Planner

TIME ALLOTMENTS SHOWN ARE APPROXIMATE. DEPENDING ON YOUR GOALS AND THE NEEDS OF YOUR STUDENTS, YOU MAY WISH TO ALLOW MORE OR LESS TIME FOR CERTAIN PORTIONS OF THE LESSON.

Table of Contents	Discussion	Previewing the Selection	Reading the Selection
PART OPENER **FOOLED BY APPEARANCES** What Do You Think? page 82	**20 MINUTES** • Reflect on the part theme		
SELECTION *from* **All Things Bright and Beautiful** page 84 AVERAGE		**20 MINUTES** • PERSONAL CONNECTION • SCIENCE CONNECTION • READING CONNECTION: Context clues	**25 MINUTES** • Introduce vocabulary • Read pp. 84–87 (4 pp.)
SELECTION **The Inn of Lost Time** page 91 CHALLENGING		**20 MINUTES** • PERSONAL CONNECTION • HISTORICAL CONNECTION • READING CONNECTION: Frame story	**50 MINUTES** • Introduce vocabulary • Read pp. 91–103 (13 pp.)
SELECTION **Collecting Team** page 108 AVERAGE		**20 MINUTES** • PERSONAL CONNECTION • LITERARY CONNECTION • WRITING CONNECTION	**40 MINUTES** • Introduce vocabulary • Read pp. 108–119 (12 pp.)
GENRE LESSON **Focus on Poetry** page 123	**20 MINUTES** • Discuss characteristics of poetry • Discuss strategies for reading poetry		
SELECTIONS **Moco Limping** **Mixed Singles** page 126 CHALLENGING		**20 MINUTES** • PERSONAL CONNECTION • LITERARY CONNECTION • READING CONNECTION: Speaker	**15 MINUTES** • Read pp. 126–128 (3 pp.)
SELECTIONS **Simile: Willow and Ginkgo** **Sea Lullaby** page 132 CHALLENGING		**20 MINUTES** • PERSONAL CONNECTION • SCIENCE CONNECTION • READING CONNECTION: Comparisons in poetry	**10 MINUTES** • Read pp. 132–133 (2 pp.)

Writing	Exploring Topics	Prewriting	Drafting and Revising
WRITING ABOUT EXPERIENCE **Firsthand and Expressive Writing*** * Time estimates assume in-class work. You may wish to assign some of these stages as homework.	**20 MINUTES**	**25 MINUTES**	**80 MINUTES**

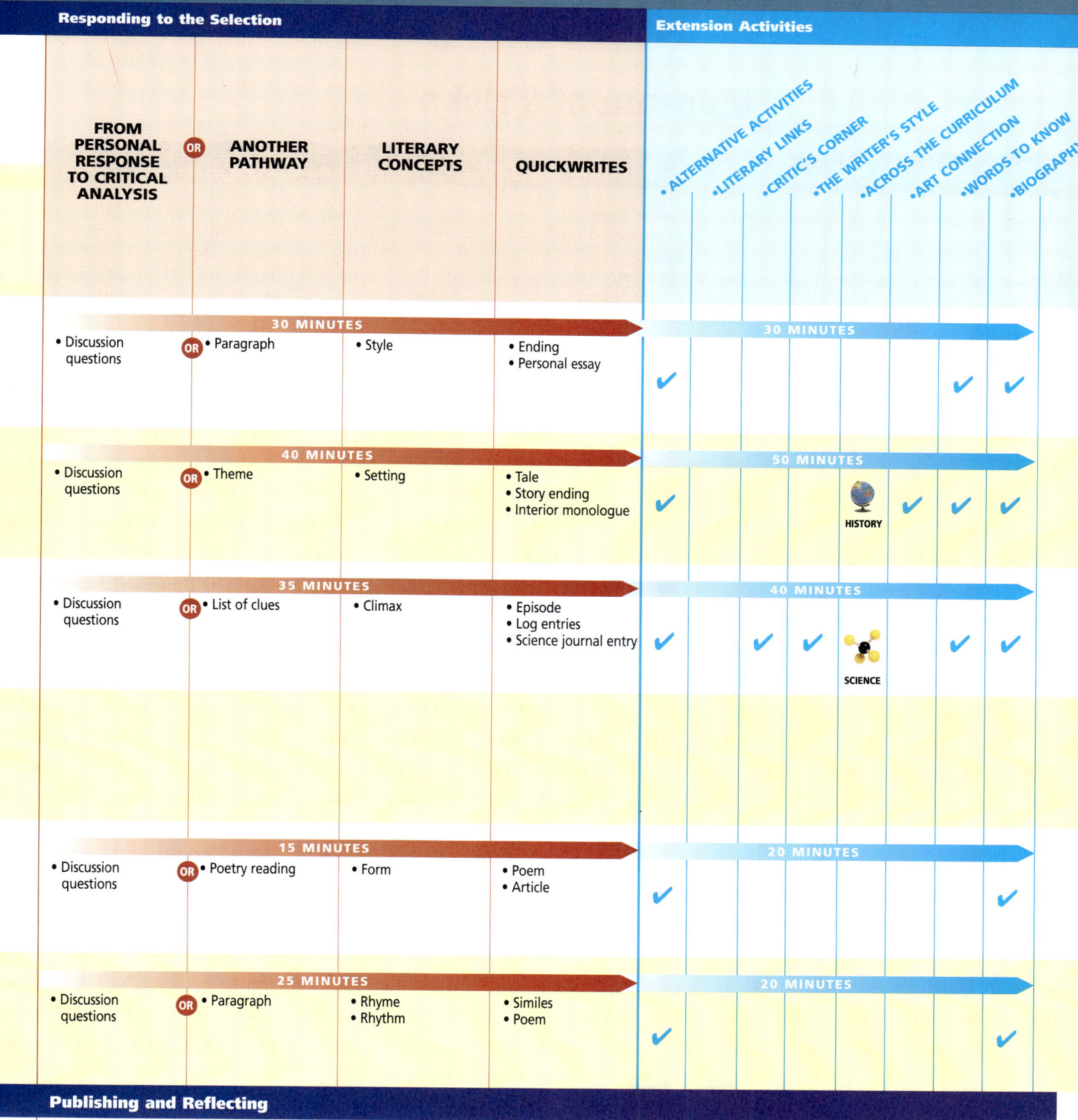

UNIT ONE
Part 2 Cooperative Project

Museum of Tricks

Overview

Students will create a "museum" of optical illusions, magic tricks, and famous hoaxes and frauds, each designed to show how people can be fooled by appearances.

PROJECT AT A GLANCE
The selections in Unit One, Part 2 are about how people have been fooled, some by judging the outside appearance of a person and some by blatant trickery. For this project, students will investigate how often and in how many different ways people can be duped into believing that something is what it is not. Students will work in pairs to research a deception by optical illusion, magic, hoax, or fraud. They will then re-create the act or produce a display reporting on the act for a Museum of Tricks. Other students or classes can be invited to walk through the museum.

OBJECTIVES
- To learn that appearances can be deceiving and that you must always look beneath the surface before judging
- To research, plan, and demonstrate or report on a form of deception for a Museum of Tricks
- To relate deception by appearance to how it can affect human relations

SUGGESTED GROUP SIZE
2–3 students

MATERIALS
- General art supplies (paper, glue, markers, and so on)
- Other props as needed

 **Getting Started**

Arranging the Project
Make arrangements for the final Museum of Tricks by arranging for the use of an empty classroom or someplace where the museum can be set up for an extended period of time. Some groups will need to spend a fair amount of time putting together their demonstration, so allow for advance time in the room, as well. Construction should be away from the prying eyes of other students so that tricks will not be revealed. If other teachers are assigning the same project, you might consult from time to time to ensure that deceptions are not being duplicated and to coordinate for the final museum display.

Arranging for Demonstrations and Displays
Students who plan magic tricks may need some props. It is up to you to limit such demonstrations to the practical. For instance, students who plan to make the Empire State Building disappear should be discouraged. Students who want to do card tricks may need help finding a suitable deck of cards.

Students who plan displays may need poster board and other art supplies. Encourage them to bring unusual items from home, or suggest where these items can be found in the community.

 **Creating the Demonstrations and Displays**

Introducing the Project
Tell students they will be working in pairs or small groups to develop a trick or illusion, and explain that their tricks and illusions will be combined into a Museum of Tricks.

To spark interest, ask students if they have ever seen optical illusions or distorted images. Students may have seen their reflections in fun-house mirrors or in the curved security mirrors used in stores.

Group Investigations
Divide students into pairs or small groups. Have them work together to research some magic tricks, optical illusions, or famous historical hoaxes or frauds. Their research should include a study of how the ruses were uncovered, as well as an explanation of the fate of the perpetrators. Encourage students to interview professional magicians (who may be listed in the Yellow Pages) or to interview art experts and scientists about optical illusions. They should discover the general theories behind these "tricks" to gain an understanding of how people can be deceived.

Creating a Project Description
Pairs or groups should write a brief description of their selected trick and how they plan to exhibit it at the Museum of Tricks. This will give you a chance to monitor the ideas and check on students' progress while helping them solidify their ideas. You may wish to confer privately with each pair or group, rather than reveal any secrets in a general class discussion of specific tricks.

OPTION 1: LEARNING FROM AN EXPERT
Invite a member of the police fraud division to speak to the class. Students should research the fraud division as well as some famous crimes of deception and should prepare questions for the visitor. They can submit a written report after the visit, offering suggestions about some ways to prevent fraud.

OPTION 2: SECRETS OF MAGIC TRICKS
Groups can contact the International Society of American Magicians (P.O. Box 368, Mango, FL 34262-0368) for more information about magic tricks.

The society promotes magicianship as an art and is interested in its instruction, performance, and advancement. They offer a free publication, answer inquiries, and may be able to refer you to one or more magicians in your area. Encourage students to maintain a correspondence with the society or an individual magician.

3 Sharing the Tricks

This project can be finalized in several ways, ranging from group demonstrations and reports to the class to a major Museum of Tricks, open to the entire school. If you want to establish a museum, you might invite a professional magician or a school administrator to judge students' work along the lines of a science fair. In this event, categorize the tricks and award prizes in each category. The museum should remain in place for several days so that families and students can all have a chance to see it.

Assessing the Project

The following rubric can be used for group or individual assessment.

3 Full Accomplishment Students follow directions and produce a demonstration or report that accurately illustrates or describes trickery or deception.

2 Substantial Accomplishment Students produce a demonstration or report, but it is not an accurate illustration or description of deception.

1 Little or Partial Accomplishment Students' work is incomplete or does not fulfill the requirements of the assignment.

For the Portfolio

If possible, take a photograph of the demonstration or report for each student's portfolio. Include a copy of your written assessment. You might want to make a master list of the demonstrations and reports for reference in future years.

Note: For other assessment options, see the *Teacher's Guide to Assessment and Portfolio Use.*

Cross-Curricular Options

SCIENCE

You might invite a high school physics teacher to demonstrate some "magic" with light or sound. Students can then research similar "tricks" and be prepared to demonstrate them for the class.

SOCIAL STUDIES

Students can research some famous frauds or hoaxes and investigate the aftermath of the events. They should look to see if laws were changed or societal behavior was modified after people were made aware of such deceptions.

PHYSICAL EDUCATION

Athletically inclined students might investigate how deception is used legally in various sports. For instance, football includes plays known as "fakes" and the "quarterback sneak." Basketball players use "feints" as players try to score. Students should find as many references to deception as possible.

ART

Students may enjoy researching the life and illusions of the artist M.C. Escher. Some students may be inspired to make an original sketch imitating his style.

Resources

Illusions Illustrated: A Professional Magic Show for Young Performers by James W. Baker reveals and explains ten baffling magic tricks.

Magic . . . Naturally! Science Entertainments and Amusements by Vicki Cobb describes 30 magic tricks based on principles of science.

Magic Tricks, Science Facts by Bob Friedhoffer demonstrates mathematical and scientific principles through magic.

PART 2

WHAT DO YOU THINK?
Objectives

The activities on this page can be used to
- introduce the Part 2 theme, "Fooled by Appearances," since each activity is connected to one or more of the selections in Part 2
- create materials for students' personal portfolios that they can later reconsider or revise
- build an understanding of theme that can be reviewed and revised as students progress through the unit

What would you do?
Encourage students to discuss why people might avoid telling the truth in these situations. Make sure students are able to support their opinions. Then ask them whether they agree or disagree with the common saying "Honesty is the best policy." (See "All Things Bright and Beautiful," p. 83.)

How would you handle this?
Encourage students to sketch or outline the dialogue for the skit. When all pairs have had a chance to perform their skits, you may wish to have the class discuss why common misperceptions like this one arise. (See "The Inn of Lost Time," p. 90, and "The Collecting Team," p. 107.)

What do you see in nature?
Encourage students to be as creative as possible in making their works of art. They can use a variety of media, including found objects—for example, cotton balls to represent a cloudy sky. When students have completed the activity, you may wish to have them present their works of art to the class. (See "Simile: Willow and Ginkgo" and "Sea Lullaby," p. 131.)

UNIT ONE PART 2

FOOLED BY APPEARANCES

WHAT DO YOU THINK?

REFLECTING ON THEME

Looks can be deceiving. Have you ever read a terrific book that had a dull and uninteresting cover? The activities on this page will help you to begin investigating how things may not always be as they first appear. Keep a record of your impressions, ideas, and results.

How would you handle this?
Things aren't always what they seem. You start talking to someone you think is a new kid in your school. In fact, he or she is a student teacher, who looks much younger than he or she really is. With a partner, develop a skit about the confusions that might arise.

What would you do?
Is a white lie, or deception, ever justified? Would you tell the truth in these situations?
A Your boyfriend or girlfriend has a new hairstyle, which you think is awful.
B A friend has written a song, which you absolutely hate! Working in groups, think of three other situations in which some people might avoid telling the truth. Survey your classmates to see how they would react in each situation.

Situation A
definitely
probably
possibly
definitely not

What do you see in nature?
We can be fooled by changing appearances in nature. Sometimes the sky is calm and clear, at other times gloomy and threatening. Brainstorm elements of nature that can have more than one aspect or face. Then choose one element and create a work of art that shows several of its faces.

Looking back
At the beginning of this unit, you thought about ways in which people or events have caused you to change your perceptions. Did your ideas change as you read the selections in Part 1? Test this by choosing one of the selections and considering the ways in which it connects to events and people in your life. In what ways is it different from your life? Convey your thoughts in a diagram or picture.

82

Looking Back
Before students create their diagram or picture, have them make a chart of the ways in which the selection they chose connects with and departs from their own experiences. Students can then use details from their chart to depict their thoughts in their diagram or picture. Suggest a Venn diagram as one graphic organizer to help them see the connections between the selection and their own life.

Cross-Curricular Connections

 Science Invite students to research types of animals that rely on deceptive appearances to protect themselves from predators. Students can research animals such as chameleons, whose bodies change color to blend with their environment, or stick insects, whose bodies resemble small twigs and thus enable them to hide from their enemies. Encourage students to bring in photos or illustrations and to present their findings to the class.

82 THE LANGUAGE OF LITERATURE TEACHER'S EDITION

PREVIEWING

NONFICTION

from All Things Bright and Beautiful
James Herriot

Activating Prior Knowledge/Setting a Purpose
PERSONAL CONNECTION
This selection was written by British country veterinarian and author James Herriot, known for his accounts of his funny and often unusual dealings with a wide variety of animals and their owners. Have you ever had a comical, unusual, or even dangerous experience with an animal? Share with the class any interesting encounters you can remember.

Building Background
SCIENCE CONNECTION
As a veterinarian, Herriot treated all kinds of animals with much less knowledge and technology than is available today. Today's veterinarians use new drugs and new technologies and techniques that are nearly as advanced as those used in medicine for humans. These days, veterinarians are more specialized: country vets chiefly treat farm animals, while city vets care mainly for pets. Some vets treat zoo animals, and others conduct research on diseases and new drugs.

Active Reading/Setting a Purpose
READING CONNECTION

Word	Clues	Probable Meaning
pelt		
flank		

Context Clues As Herriot discusses the animals he treats and their human owners, he may use terms unfamiliar to you. You can infer the general meaning of a word by using context clues, which are hints in the words or sentences around the word. For example, on page 84, you can infer the meaning of the word *calipers* from the way they are used on the animal, the number that Herriot calls out, and the statement about the animal's size. Calipers must be an instrument used to measure thickness.

As you read, keep track of unfamiliar words on a chart like the one shown.

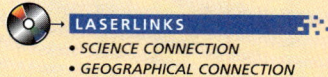
- SCIENCE CONNECTION
- GEOGRAPHICAL CONNECTION

OVERVIEW

Objectives
- To understand and appreciate an autobiographical essay about a country veterinarian
- To understand context clues
- To identify and understand the elements of a writer's style
- To express understanding of the selection through a choice of writing forms, including fiction writing and a personal essay
- To extend understanding of the selection through a variety of multimodal and cross-curricular activities

Skills

READING SKILLS/STRATEGIES
- Using context clues

GRAMMAR
- Verb phrases

LITERARY CONCEPTS
- Style
- Description

SPEAKING, LISTENING, AND VIEWING
- Group discussion
- Oral presentation

Cross-Curricular Connections

SOCIAL STUDIES
- Sacred animals

GEOGRAPHY
- Yorkshire, England

SCIENCE
- Veterinary science
- Education of veterinarians

SCIENCE CONNECTION
Veterinary Work The profession of veterinary medicine involves the care of a wide variety of animals, as students will see in these images of veterinarians at work.

Side A, Frame 52576

GEOGRAPHICAL CONNECTION
James Herriot's World These images of rural Yorkshire, England, offer students a visual context for Herriot's account of his veterinary work.

Side A, Frame 52583

PRINT AND MEDIA RESOURCES

UNIT ONE RESOURCE BOOK
Strategic Reading: Literature, p. 45
Vocabulary SkillBuilder, p. 47
Reading SkillBuilder, p. 46

GRAMMAR MINI-LESSONS
Transparencies, p. 38

ACCESS FOR STUDENTS ACQUIRING ENGLISH
Selection Summaries
Reading and Writing Support

FORMAL ASSESSMENT
Selection Test, pp. 17–18
 Test Generator

 **AUDIO LIBRARY**
See Reference Card

 **LASERLINKS**
Science Connection
Geographical Connection

INTERNET RESOURCES
McDougal Littell Literature Center at http://www.hmco.com/mcdougal/lit

SUMMARY

Herriot offers a personal account of his experiences as a veterinarian in rural Yorkshire, England. First, Herriot's life was threatened when an enormous but docile bull innocently pinned him against a wall. Although he was not seriously hurt, Herriot appeared foolish in front of the farmer and the farmer's young daughter. Herriot also reminisces about his attempt to trim the beak of an elderly woman's budgie, a kind of parakeet. The bird died of fright when Herriot took it from the cage, and he quickly purchased a younger bird to take its place. The woman, both nearsighted and deaf, never noticed the switch. She was delighted by the bird's new, sprightly personality.

Thematic Link: *Fooled by Appearances*
James Herriot's reminiscences about a bull and a budgie illustrate how appearances can be deceptive.

CUSTOMIZING FOR
Students Acquiring English

- Use **ACCESS FOR STUDENTS ACQUIRING ENGLISH**, *Reading and Writing Support.*
- Ask students to think about their native countries and to list which of the country's animals are often kept as pets, which animals are kept as livestock or farm animals, and which are wild. Invite students to discuss whether people have different feelings toward pets than toward farm animals or wild animals.

STRATEGIC READING FOR
Less-Proficient Readers

Set a Purpose To help students become involved in the action of the story, encourage them to sketch their favorite barnyard animals. Then ask them to read to find out what happens between Herriot and the bull.

Use **UNIT ONE RESOURCE BOOK**, p. 45, for guidance in reading the selection.

from All Things Bright & Beautiful
by James Herriot

"Move over, Bill!" Mr. Dacre cried some time later as he tweaked the big bull's tail.

Nearly every farmer kept a bull in those days and they were all called Billy or Bill. I suppose it was because this was a very mature animal that he received the adult version. Being a <u>docile</u> beast he responded to the touch on his tail by shuffling his great bulk to one side, leaving me enough space to push in between him and the wooden partition against which he was tied by a chain.

I was reading a tuberculin test and all I wanted to do was to measure the intradermal[1] reaction. I had to open my calipers very wide to take in the thickness of the skin on the enormous neck.

"Thirty," I called out to the farmer.

He wrote the figure down on the testing book and laughed.

"By heck, he's got some pelt on 'im."

"Yes," I said, beginning to squeeze my way out. "But he's a big fellow, isn't he?"

Just how big he was was brought home to me immediately because the bull suddenly swung round, pinning me against the partition. Cows did this regularly and I moved them by bracing my back against whatever was behind me and pushing them away. But it was different with Bill.

Gasping, I pushed with all my strength against the rolls of fat which covered the vast roan-colored flank, but I might as well have tried to shift a house.

The farmer dropped his book and seized the tail again but this time the bull showed no response. There was no <u>malice</u> in his behavior—he was simply having a comfortable lean

---
1. **intradermal** (ĭn′trə-dûr′məl): inside the layers of skin.

> **WORDS TO KNOW**
> **docile** (dŏs′əl) *adj.* easy to handle or train; tame
> **malice** (măl′ĭs) *n.* a feeling of wanting to hurt others or see them suffer

WORDS TO KNOW

catastrophic (kăt′ə-strŏf′ĭk) *adj.* disastrous (p. 85)
docile (dŏs′əl) *adj.* easy to handle or train; tame (p. 84)
malice (măl′ĭs) *n.* a feeling of wanting to hurt others or see them suffer (p. 84)

placid (plăs′ĭd) *adj.* calm and quiet; peaceful (p. 86)
vain (vān) *adj.* having too high an opinion of oneself (p. 86)

against the boards and I don't suppose he even noticed the morsel of puny humanity wriggling frantically against his rib cage.

Still, whether he meant it or not, the end result was the same; I was having the life crushed out of me. Popeyed, groaning, scarcely able to breathe, I struggled with everything I had, but I couldn't move an inch. And just when I thought things couldn't get any worse, Bill started to rub himself up and down against the partition. So that was what he had come round for; he had an itch and he just wanted to scratch it.

The effect on me was catastrophic. I was certain my internal organs were being steadily ground to pulp and as I thrashed about in complete panic the huge animal leaned even more heavily.

I don't like to think what would have happened if the wood behind me had not been old and rotten, but just as I felt my senses leaving me there was a cracking and splintering and I fell through into the next stall. Lying there like a stranded fish on a bed of shattered timbers I looked up at Mr. Dacre, waiting till my lungs started to work again.

The farmer, having gotten over his first alarm, was rubbing his upper lip vigorously in a polite attempt to stop himself laughing. His little girl who had watched the whole thing from her vantage point in one of the hayracks had no such inhibitions. Screaming with delight, she pointed at me.

"Ooo, Dad, Dad, look at that man! Did you see him, Dad, did you see him? Ooo what a funny man!" She went into helpless convulsions.[2] She was only about five but I had a feeling she would remember my performance all her life.

At length I picked myself up and managed to brush the matter off lightly, but after I had driven a mile or so from the farm I stopped the car and looked myself over. My ribs ached pretty uniformly as though a light road roller had passed over them and there was a tender area on my left buttock where I had landed on my calipers but otherwise I seemed to have escaped damage. I removed a few spicules of wood from my trousers, got back into the car and consulted my list of visits.

And when I read my next call a gentle smile of relief spread over my face. "Mrs. Tompkin, 14, Jasmine Terrace. Clip budgie's[3] beak."

Thank heaven for the infinite variety of veterinary practice. After that bull I needed something small and weak and harmless and really you can't ask for much better in that line than a budgie.

Number 14 was one of a row of small mean houses built of the cheap bricks so beloved of the jerrybuilders[4] after the first world war. I armed myself with a pair of clippers and stepped on to the narrow strip of pavement which separated the door from the road. A pleasant looking red-haired woman answered my knock.

"I'm Mrs. Dodds from next door," she said. "I keep an eye on t'old lady. She's over eighty and lives alone. I've just been out gettin' her pension[5] for her."

She led me into the cramped little room. "Here y'are, love," she said to the old woman who sat in a corner. She put the pension book and money on the mantelpiece. "And here's Mr. Herriot come to see Peter for you."

Mrs. Tompkin nodded and smiled. "Oh that's good. Poor little feller can't hardly eat with 'is long beak and I'm worried about him. He's me

---

2. **convulsions:** violent fits of laughter.
3. **budgie:** shortened form of *budgerigar*, an Australian parakeet.
4. **jerrybuilders:** builders who make poorly constructed, cheap houses.
5. **pension:** money paid regularly by a company or government to a retired person.

WORDS TO KNOW
catastrophic (kăt′ə-strŏf′ĭk) *adj.* disastrous

85

Mini-Lesson   Reading Skills/Strategies

USING CONTEXT CLUES Remind students that they can infer the meaning of unfamiliar words by looking for context clues. The words or phrases that surround an unfamiliar word often provide hints or clues to its probable meaning. In this situation, try substituting the unfamiliar word with a different word thought to have a similar meaning. If the substituted word makes sense within the context, then the inference is probably correct.

Application Have students return to the charts they made for the Reading Connection on page 83. Encourage volunteers to share a few of the unfamiliar words and their contexts from their charts. Write these words on the chalkboard and read aloud the surrounding text. Have the class discuss probable meanings for the words. If there is disagreement, make sure each student gives an explanation for the meaning he or she is suggesting.

Reteaching/Reinforcement
• *Unit One Resource Book*, p. 46

CUSTOMIZING FOR
Gifted and Talented Students

In Herriot's writing, he shows great affection for the individual quirks of the people whose animals he treats. Encourage students, as they read, to take note of how Herriot describes his characters' appearances and behavior. Then examine how Herriot's feelings and actions are influenced by the personalities of the characters he encounters.

Possible responses:

• Page 85—"The farmer . . . was rubbing his upper lip vigorously in a polite attempt to stop himself from laughing."/After noticing the farmer's merriment over his situation, Herriot, although quite shaken, "managed to brush the matter off lightly."

• Page 86—"Mrs. Dodds and I looked at each other in horror . . . she was still nodding and smiling."/Because Mrs. Tompkin appears not to have noticed the bird's death, Herriot decides to replace the budgie rather than upset the woman.

STRATEGIC READING FOR
Less-Proficient Readers

A Ask students what the bull did that put Herriot in danger. Also ask why Herriot wasn't hurt. *(It leaned on him, but then the wall broke, and he fell away from the bull.)* **Noting Relevant Details/Relating Cause and Effect**

Set a Purpose Have students think about what could happen as Herriot attempts to clip a small bird's beak, and then read to see what actually occurs.

CUSTOMIZING FOR
Students Acquiring English

I Have students paraphrase the expression "to brush the matter off lightly." *(to let it go; not to make a fuss over it)*

THE LANGUAGE OF LITERATURE TEACHER'S EDITION **85**

Linking to Social Studies

 B In many societies, certain domesticated animals were and are considered sacred. In ancient Egypt, for example, cats were not only a favored pet but a sacred animal. A number of cultures today believe that cats bring good fortune. Cows are considered sacred by India's millions of Hindus.

Critical Thinking:
MAKING JUDGMENTS

C Have students review Herriot's handling of the bird to decide whether the bird's death could have been avoided. *(Possible responses: Knowing the bird was old, Herriot could have had its owner lift him out of the cage. It is likely that the bird would have died anyway when Herriot tried to cut its beak.)*

STRATEGIC READING FOR
Less-Proficient Readers

D Ask students to explain what happens to the budgie. *(It dies of fright while Herriot is holding it.)* **Summarizing**

- Why does Herriot go to buy a new bird, and what happens when he gets there? *(He goes to find a green bird that looks like the bird that died. Jack Almond does not like Herriot's rush to find a matching bird, but he sells Herriot one anyway.)* **Summarizing**

Set a Purpose As students read, have them watch for how Mrs. Tompkin feels about her bird when Herriot visits her months later. *(She thinks old Peter, which of course is actually a replacement bird, is wonderfully chatty and lively ever since Herriot cut his beak.)*

---

only companion, you know."

"Yes, I understand, Mrs. Tompkin." I looked at the cage by the window with the green budgie perched inside. "These little birds can be wonderful company when they start chattering."

She laughed. "Aye, but it's a funny thing. Peter never has said owt much. I think he's lazy! But I just like havin' him with me."

"Of course you do," I said. "But he certainly needs attention now."

The beak was greatly overgrown, curving away down till it touched the feathers of the breast. I would be able to revolutionize his life with one quick snip from my clippers. The way I was feeling this job was right up my street.

I opened the cage door and slowly inserted my hand.

"Come on, Peter," I wheedled as the bird fluttered away from me. And I soon cornered him and enclosed him gently in my fingers. As I lifted him out I felt in my pocket with the other hand for the clippers, but as I poised them I stopped.

The tiny head was no longer poking cheekily[6] from my fingers but had fallen loosely to one side. The eyes were closed. I stared at the bird uncomprehendingly for a moment then opened my hand. He lay quite motionless on my palm. He was dead.

Dry mouthed, I continued to stare; at the beautiful iridescence[7] of the plumage,[8] the long beak which I didn't have to cut now, but mostly at the head dropping down over my forefinger. I hadn't squeezed him or been rough with him in any way, but he was dead. It must have been sheer fright.

Mrs. Dodds and I looked at each other in horror and I hardly dared turn my head toward Mrs. Tompkin. When I did, I was surprised to see that she was still nodding and smiling.

I drew her neighbor to one side. "Mrs. Dodds, how much does she see?"

"Oh she's very shortsighted but she's right <u>vain</u> despite her age. Never would wear glasses. She's hard of hearin', too."

"Well look," I said. My heart was still pounding. "I just don't know what to do. If I tell her about this the shock will be terrible. Anything could happen."

Mrs. Dodds nodded, stricken faced. "Aye, you're right. She's that attached to the little thing."

"I can only think of one alternative," I whispered. "Do you know where I can get another budgie?"

Mrs. Dodds thought for a moment. "You could try Jack Almond at t'town end. I think he keeps birds."

I cleared my throat but even then my voice came out in a dry croak. "Mrs. Tompkin, I'm just going to take Peter along to the surgery to do this job. I won't be long."

I left her still nodding and smiling and, cage in hand, fled into the street. I was at the town end and knocking at Jack Almond's door within three minutes.

"Mr. Almond?" I asked of the stout, shirt-sleeved man who answered.

"That's right, young man." He gave me a slow, <u>placid</u> smile.

"Do you keep birds?"

He drew himself up with dignity. "I do, and I'm t'president of the Darrowby and Houlton Cage Bird Society."

"Fine," I said breathlessly. "Have you got a green budgie?"

"Ah've got canaries, budgies, parrots, parakeets. Cockatoos . . ."

---

6. **cheekily:** without respect.
7. **iridescence** (ĭr′ĭ-dĕs′əns): shifting, rainbowlike colors.
8. **plumage** (plōō′mĭj): feathers.

| WORDS TO KNOW | **vain** (vān) *adj.* having too high an opinion of oneself |
| | **placid** (plăs′ĭd) *adj.* calm and quiet; peaceful |

86

Mini-Lesson Literary Concepts

REVIEWING DESCRIPTION Remind students that description is a picture in words of a scene, a character, or an object. A description may appeal to the reader's senses or may provide additional information about a character or event.

Application Have students form groups of four or five and develop lists of the descriptions Herriot provides of the people and events of his daily practice. For example, have them read page 86 and make a list of the words and details Herriot uses in his description of Peter, Mrs. Tompkin's bird, as well as of Mrs. Dodds's and his own responses to the bird's death. Then have students make a similar list of the words and details in Herriot's description of the replacement budgie or of Herriot's interaction with Jack Almond.

86 THE LANGUAGE OF LITERATURE TEACHER'S EDITION

"I just want a budgie."

"Well ah've got albinos, blue-greens, barreds, Lutinos . . ."

"I just want a green one."

A slightly pained expression flitted across the man's face as though he found my attitude of haste somewhat unseemly.

"Aye . . . well, we'll go and have a look," he said.

I followed him as he paced unhurriedly through the house into the back yard which was largely given over to a long shed containing a bewildering variety of birds.

Mr. Almond gazed at them with gentle pride and his mouth opened as though he was about to launch into a dissertation[9] then he seemed to remember that he had an impatient chap to deal with and dragged himself back to the job in hand.

"There's a nice little green 'un here. But he's a bit older than t'others. Matter of fact I've got 'im talkin'."

"All the better, just the thing. How much do you want for him?"

"But . . . there's some nice 'uns along here. Just let me show you . . ."

I put a hand on his arm. "I want that one. How much?"

He pursed his lips in frustration then shrugged his shoulders.

"Ten bob."[10]

"Right. Bung[11] him in this cage."

As I sped back up the road I looked in the driving mirror and could see the poor man regarding me sadly from his doorway.

Mrs. Dodds was waiting for me back at Jasmine Terrace.

"Do you think I'm doing the right thing?" I asked her in a whisper.

"I'm sure you are," she replied. "Poor awd[12] thing, she hasn't much to think about and I'm sure she'd fret over Peter."

"That's what I thought." I made my way into the living room.

Mrs. Tompkin smiled at me as I went in. "That wasn't a long job, Mr. Herriot."

"No," I said, hanging the cage with the new bird up in its place by the window. "I think you'll find all is well now."

It was months before I had the courage to put my hand into a budgie's cage again. In fact to this day I prefer it if the owners will lift the birds out for me. People look at me strangely when I ask them to do this; I believe they think I am scared the little things might bite me.

It was a long time, too, before I dared go back to Mrs. Tompkin's but I was driving down Jasmine Terrace one day and on an impulse I stopped outside Number 14.

The old lady herself came to the door.

"How . . . ," I said, "How is . . . er . . . ?"

She peered at me closely for a moment then laughed. "Oh I see who it is now. You mean Peter, don't you, Mr. Herriot. Oh 'e's just grand. Come in and see 'im."

In the little room the cage still hung by the window and Peter the Second took a quick look at me then put on a little act for my benefit; he hopped around the bars of the cage, ran up and down his ladder and rang his little bell a couple of times before returning to his perch.

His mistress reached up, tapped the metal and looked lovingly at him.

"You know, you wouldn't believe it," she said. "He's like a different bird."

I swallowed. "Is that so? In what way?"

"Well he's so active now. Lively as can be. You know 'e chatters to me all day long. It's wonderful what cuttin' a beak can do." ❖

---

9. **dissertation** (dĭs'ər-tā'shən): a long speech.
10. **bob:** slang for *shilling*, a silver British coin no longer minted.
11. **bung:** to toss.
12. **awd:** *dialect*, old.

ALL THINGS BRIGHT AND BEAUTIFUL **87**

From Personal Response to Critical Analysis

1. Students can review details that describe Herriot.
2. Some students may say that deceiving the elderly Mrs. Tompkin caused her no harm and spared her grief. Others may say that Herriot should have been honest with Mrs. Tompkin.
3. Some students will note that Herriot does not take himself too seriously and is respectful of other people's feelings. Others may point out that Herriot avoids conflict, to the point of dishonesty.
4. Some students may want Herriot as their veterinarian because he appears to be very caring about the animals he treats. Others may not want a vet who accidentally kills pets.
5. Possible responses: Herriot's characters are very lifelike. He has a good sense of humor—a quality that everybody can relate to.

Literary Links

Compare how Herriot is fooled by appearances with the way Greg is fooled in "The Treasure of Lemon Brown." (*Herriot is fooled by the budgie, who looks far from death by all appearances. Greg is fooled by Lemon Brown's appearance into thinking that he doesn't have any history, background, or even "treasure."*)

Another Pathway

Have students work in pairs. Before they begin writing, encourage partners to discuss their opinions of Herriot's bedside manner. Have one student make a list of what they agree on. The other student can make a list of their disagreements. They should incorporate both lists as they write.

Rubric
3 Full Accomplishment Students write a well-balanced paragraph that details their agreements and explains why they disagree.
2 Substantial Accomplishment Students describe their agreements, but there is little or no discussion of the reasons why they disagree.
1 Little or Partial Accomplishment Students have difficulty expressing their opinions or fail to provide any reasons to support them.

RESPONDING OPTIONS

FROM PERSONAL RESPONSE TO CRITICAL ANALYSIS

REFLECT 1. What is your impression of James Herriot? Jot down any phrases that come to mind.

RETHINK
Thematic Link 2. When Mrs. Tompkin's budgie dies, Herriot fools her by buying one similar in appearance. Do you agree or disagree with his action? Explain.

3. Judging from the incidents he reports and the way he relates them, how would you describe Herriot's attitude toward himself and others?

Close Textual Reading **Consider**
- his response in the bull's stall
- his reaction to the incident at Mrs. Tompkin's
- his feelings toward the animals he cares for

RELATE 4. Would you want Herriot to be your animal's veterinarian? Why or why not?

5. Based on your reading of this selection, why do you think Herriot's books are so popular?

> **Multimodal Learning**
> **ANOTHER PATHWAY**
> How important do you think Herriot's "bedside manner" toward the animals' owners is? Write a paragraph in which you evaluate his behavior toward the humans in this selection. Then discuss your evaluation with a partner.

LITERARY CONCEPTS

The particular way in which an author uses words and sentences is known as **style**. Style refers to *how* something is said, rather than *what* is said. Herriot's style is lighthearted, down-to-earth, and engaging. Find examples of humor, descriptive detail, dialect, and choice of words that illustrate his style.

QUICKWRITES

1. Reread the passage in which the budgie dies in Herriot's hand. How might the outcome have been different if Herriot had admitted what happened? Rewrite the **ending** from this point on.

2. Based on this selection and your experiences with animals, would you want to be a veterinarian? Write a **personal essay** explaining why or why not.

📁 **PORTFOLIO** Save your writing. You may want to use it later as a springboard to a piece for your portfolio.

88 UNIT ONE PART 2: FOOLED BY APPEARANCES

Literary Concepts

Make sure students focus on *how* Herriot describes events in the story rather than *what* he is describing. Students should pay attention to Herriot's choice of words, details, and tone in discussing his style. For instance, when writing about his near-death experience with the bull, Herriot describes himself as "a morsel of puny humanity" rather than simply saying "he didn't notice me." Also, Herriot's use of dialect doesn't just tell the reader what people are saying, but helps to describe *how* these people sound when they speak.

QuickWrites

1. Remind students of Mrs. Tompkin's advanced age and that this is the first time she has met Herriot. The characters' unfamiliarity will affect how students choose to rewrite the story.
2. Have students draw upon their own experiences with animals as well as upon relevant details from Herriot's life to support their choice of becoming or not becoming a veterinarian.

Autobiographical Incident, pp. 27–39

Multimodal Learning

ALTERNATIVE ACTIVITIES

1. The scene in which the bull pins Herriot against the wall is vivid with description. Use this detail to draw a **picture** of the scene.
2. Research the four-year program a student must complete to become a veterinarian, and the two-year program required for veterinary technology. What schools offer each kind of training? What courses does one take? If you have access to an encyclopedia program or an on-line service, use your computer to start your research. Share your information in an **oral report** to the class.

WORDS TO KNOW

Create a word map for each of the five Words to Know and three of the unfamiliar words that you identified in the Reading Connection on page 83. Include a synonym, an antonym, and an example of the word. A sample map, using the word *aggressive*, is provided.

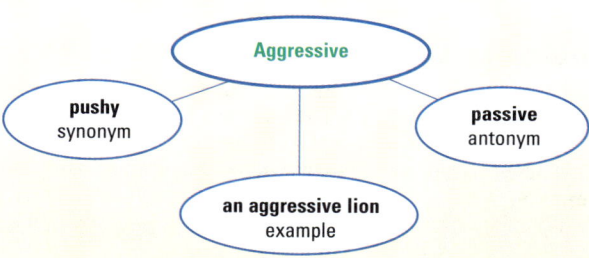

JAMES HERRIOT

1916–1995

For most of his career, James Herriot had talked to his wife about writing a book concerning his veterinary experiences in Yorkshire, England. Herriot explained, "One day, when I was fifty, she said: 'Who are you kidding? Vets of fifty don't write first books.' Well, that did it. I stormed out and bought some paper and taught myself to type."

Because of the British veterinary system's ban on advertising, Herriot changed the names of people and communities in his books and wrote under a pseudonym, or pen name. James Alfred Wight was the author's real name.

Herriot wrote more than a dozen books, including his bestsellers—*All Creatures Great and Small, All Things Bright and Beautiful, All Things Wise and Wonderful,* and *The Lord God Made Them All.*

Several of his works were adapted for film and television. The author received many awards and honors, including the James Herriot Award established by the Humane Society of America.

Said Herriot, "The life of a country vet was dirty, uncomfortable, sometimes dangerous. It was terribly hard work and I loved it." He continued to see patients, but his veterinarian son eventually took over his practice. He convinced his daughter, Rosemary, who he said was "mad keen to be a country vet," to be a doctor of humans, "which," he added, "is the next best thing."

OTHER WORKS *James Herriot's Cat Stories, It Shouldn't Happen to a Vet, James Herriot's Yorkshire, Every Living Thing* Extended Reading

ALL THINGS BRIGHT AND BEAUTIFUL **89**

Words to Know

Word maps will vary. Be sure each map includes a synonym, an antonym, and an appropriate example of how the word can be used correctly.

Reteaching/Reinforcement
• *Unit One Resource Book*, p. 47

Across the Curriculum

Science Have students research the history of veterinary science. Encourage them to pay particular attention to the technical advances being made in the field and whether this has resulted in veterinarians' performing new and different work.

Geography *Cooperative Learning* Divide students into groups of four or five. Have students research Yorkshire, England, where Herriot lived and worked. Different groups can each research one particular aspect, such as location, population, wildlife, economy, or exported products. Encourage each group to use maps or charts to support its topic. Groups can present their research to the class.

JAMES HERRIOT

As a second career, writing was very difficult for James Herriot at first. It took him more than four years to write and publish his first book, *If Only They Could Talk*, which sold only 1,200 copies. It was later incorporated into Herriot's hugely successful third book, *All Creatures Great and Small*. Of his experience at learning the craft of writing, Herriot said, "I started to put it all down and the story didn't work. All I managed to pick out on the machine was a very amateur school essay. So I spent a year or two learning my craft, as real writers say."

Alternative Activities

1. Have students review pages 84 and 85, noting Herriot's use of details to describe his experience. Encourage them to utilize these details when drawing their versions of the scene.
2. Have students work in groups of four. Each student can research a different area of veterinary training and work. Have one student serve as facilitator, overseeing the group's research. Another student can record assignments and findings. One student should summarize results, and another student should present these findings to the class.

OVERVIEW

Objectives

- To understand and appreciate a short story about a samurai
- To enrich reading by using active reading strategies
- To identify and understand the use of a frame story
- To identify and understand the influence of a story's setting
- To express understanding of the story through a choice of writing forms including a tale, alternative story endings, and an interior monologue
- To extend understanding of the story through a variety of multimodal and cross-curricular activities

Skills

READING SKILLS/STRATEGIES
- Evaluating
- Frame story

THE WRITER'S STYLE
- Avoiding clichés

SPEAKING, LISTENING, AND VIEWING
- Group discussion
- Oral report

GRAMMAR
- Direct and indirect questioning

LITERARY CONCEPTS
- Plot
- Setting

SPELLING
- The letters *qu*

Cross-Curricular Connections

HISTORY
- Samurai codes of honor
- 16th-century Japan

MATH
- Writing a fraction

SOCIAL STUDIES
- Feudal warriors

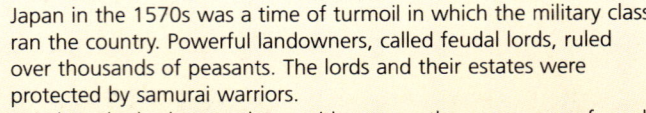

FICTION

The Inn of Lost Time
Lensey Namioka (nä′mē-ō′kə)

Activating Prior Knowledge
PERSONAL CONNECTION

What does the saying "Things aren't always what they appear to be" mean to you? For example, have you ever formed an impression of someone, only to change it after you got to know the person better? Perhaps you attended an event that turned out to be different than you expected. With your classmates, discuss situations you have experienced in which things or people did not turn out to be what you expected.

Building Background
HISTORICAL CONNECTION

Japan in the 1570s was a time of turmoil in which the military class ran the country. Powerful landowners, called feudal lords, ruled over thousands of peasants. The lords and their estates were protected by samurai warriors.

When the lords waged war with one another, some were forced to dismiss both workers and warriors. The unemployed samurai, or *ronin*, roamed the countryside looking for adventure and work. Contrary to the code of honor of the samurai, some ronin preyed upon defenseless farmers.

Active Reading / Setting a Purpose
READING CONNECTION

Frame Story A frame story is a story that contains one or more other stories. In the selection two stories are told within the structure of the frame story. The first is the tale of Urashima Taro. The second is the tale of Zenta and Tokubei. To keep the stories straight, ask questions as you read: Who tells each story? Why is it told? What does the story reveal? Jot down your answers in a chart like the one shown.

	Frame Story	Tale of Urashima Taro	Tale of Zenta and Tokubei
Who tells it?			
Why is it told?			
What does it reveal?			

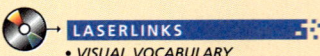
- VISUAL VOCABULARY

PRINT AND MEDIA RESOURCES

UNIT ONE RESOURCE BOOK
Strategic Reading: Literature, p. 51
Vocabulary SkillBuilder, p. 54
Reading SkillBuilder, p. 52
Spelling SkillBuilder, p. 53

GRAMMAR MINI-LESSONS
Transparencies, p. 33
Copymasters, p. 43

ACCESS FOR STUDENTS ACQUIRING ENGLISH
Selection Summaries
Reading and Writing Support

FORMAL ASSESSMENT
Selection Test, pp. 19–20
 Test Generator

 LASERLINKS
Visual Vocabulary
Art Gallery

INTERNET RESOURCES
McDougal Littell Literature Center at http://www.hmco.com/mcdougal/lit

The Inn of Lost Time

BY LENSEY NAMIOKA

Detail of *Portrait of Sato Issai* (1824), Watanabe Kazan. Ink and color on silk, Japan, Edo Period, Nanga School, 113.0 cm × 51.5 cm, courtesy of the Freer Gallery of Art, Smithsonian Institution, Washington, D.C. (68.66).

SUMMARY

A farmer tells his young boys and two visiting samurai, Zenta and Matsuzo, the story of a man who lost 72 years of his life under the sea. Afterward, Zenta tells a story from his own youth. While he was employed as a bodyguard for a wealthy merchant, he and his employer stayed the night at a remote inn. The innkeeper and his helper, a young six-fingered woman, drugged their two guests and then fooled them into believing that 50 years had passed overnight. The swindlers claimed that a local priestess could restore the lost years at the cost of one gold piece per year. Zenta saw through the hoax before the merchant paid. It is revealed that the farmer's wife was the innkeeper's six-fingered helper who is now living an honest life.

Thematic Link: *Fooled by Appearances*
When a young woman tries to make Zenta believe she has aged overnight, he sees through her hoax by noticing details that contradict her claims.

Art Note

Portrait of Satō Issai by **Watanabe Kazan** Watanabe Kazan was a famous artist and patriot of 19th-century Japan. This portrait of Kazan's teacher presents the Confucian scholar as an austere man, clothed in a vest and a colorful robe.

Reading the Art What does this painting tell you about Satō Issai? What details, such as the clothes he is wearing and the scar on the side of his neck, influence your opinion?

WORDS TO KNOW

compensate (kŏm′pən-sāt) *v.* to make up for (p. 95)
decrepit (dĭ-krĕp′ĭt) *adj.* weakened by old age (p. 92)
delusion (dĭ-lōō′zhən) *n.* a false belief or opinion (p. 98)
desolate (dĕs′ə-lĭt) *adj.* miserable; very unhappy (p. 92)
gilded (gĭl′dĭd) *adj.* as if covered with a thin layer of gold (p. 95)
implication (ĭm′plĭ-kā′shən) *n.* a possible meaning or significance (p. 100)

inconsistency (ĭn′kən-sĭs′tən-sē) *n.* something that is not in agreement or harmony (p. 102)
poignant (poin′yənt) *adj.* very touching or moving; painful (p. 92)
qualm (kwäm) *n.* a sudden disturbing feeling (p. 103)
rapt (răpt) *adj.* deeply interested (p. 92)
reluctant (rĭ-lŭk′tənt) *adj.* unwilling (p. 100)
remit (rĭ-mĭt′) *v.* to send in payment (p. 101)
tantalizing (tăn′tə-lī′zĭng) *adj.* desirable but out of reach **tantalize** *v.* (p. 94)

traumatic (trou-măt′ĭk) *adj.* emotionally shocking (p. 100)
unwary (ŭn-wâr′ē) *adj.* not alert or cautious (p. 100)

 VISUAL VOCABULARY

• **samurai** (săm′ə-rī′)   • **scabbard** (skăb′ərd)

Side A, Frame 52588

CUSTOMIZING FOR
Students Acquiring English

- Use **ACCESS FOR STUDENTS ACQUIRING ENGLISH**, Reading and Writing Support.
- The Tale of Urashima Taro is a folk tale—a simple story that has been handed down by word of mouth from one generation to another. The characters in folk tales may be animals, humans, or superhumans. Ask students to share folk tales from their native cultures with the class.

STRATEGIC READING FOR
Less-Proficient Readers

Set a Purpose To help students understand the importance of folk tales in the story, have them think of other folk and fairy tales they already know. Then have them compare their tales to the farmer's tale of Urashima Taro.

Use **UNIT ONE RESOURCE BOOK**, p. 51, for guidance in reading the selection.

CUSTOMIZING FOR
Gifted and Talented Students

As students read the selection, ask them to draw comparisons between the story of Urashima Taro and Zenta's account of his experiences. Have students explain the ways Zenta's story is more than a simple retelling of the folk tale.

Possible responses:

- Page 95 —"Youth and inexperience should not have prevented me from wondering why an inn should be found hidden away from the highway"/Just as the turtle's taking Urashima to the bottom of the ocean only appears to be a reward, the finding of an inn in a remote place, while appearing to be a blessing, should have caused Zenta and the merchant to pause and examine the situation.

- Page 96 —"On the ground? . . . My last memory was of staying at an inn with a merchant called Tokubei"/ Whereas Urashima's underwater experiences are fantasy, the experiences of Zenta, although containing fantastic elements, remain in the real world.

"Will you promise to sleep if I tell you a story?" said the father. He pretended to put on a stern expression.

"Yes! Yes!" the three little boys chanted in unison. It sounded like a nightly routine.

The two guests smiled as they listened to the exchange. They were wandering ronin, or unemployed samurai, and they enjoyed watching this cozy family scene.

The father gave the guests a helpless look. "What can I do? I have to tell them a story, or these little rascals will give us no peace." Clearing his throat, he turned to the boys. "All right. The story tonight is about Urashima Taro."

Instantly the three boys became still. Sitting with their legs tucked under them, the three little boys, aged five, four, and three, looked like a descending row of stone statuettes. Matsuzo, the younger of the two ronin, was reminded of the wayside half-body statues of Jizo, the god of travelers and protector of children.

Behind the boys the farmer's wife took up a pair of iron chopsticks and stirred the ashes of the fire in the charcoal brazier.[1] A momentary glow brightened the room. The lean faces of the two ronin, lit by the fire, suddenly looked fierce and hungry.

The farmer knew that the two ronin were supposed to use their arms in defense of the weak. But in these troubled times, with the country torn apart by civil wars, the samurai didn't always live up to their honorable code.

Then the fire died down again, and the subdued red light softened the features of the two ronin. The farmer relaxed and began his story.

The tale of Urashima Taro is familiar to every Japanese. No doubt the three little boys had heard their father tell it before—and more than once. But they listened with <u>rapt</u> attention.

Urashima Taro, a fisherman, rescued a turtle from some boys who were battering it with stones. The grateful turtle rewarded Taro by carrying him on his back to the bottom of the sea, where he lived happily with the princess of the undersea. But Taro soon became home-sick for his native village and asked to go back on land. The princess gave him a box to take with him but warned him not to peek inside.

When Taro went back to his village, he found the place quite changed. In his home he found his parents gone, and living there was another old couple. He was stunned to learn that the aged husband was his own son, whom he had last seen as a baby! Taro thought he had spent only a pleasant week or two under-sea with the princess. On land, seventy-two years had passed! His parents and most of his old friends had long since died.

<u>Desolate</u>, Taro decided to open the box given him by the princess. As soon as he looked inside, he changed in an instant from a young man to a <u>decrepit</u> old man of more than ninety.

At the end of the story the boys were close to tears. Even Matsuzo found himself deeply touched. He wondered why the farmer had told his sons such a <u>poignant</u> bedtime story. Wouldn't they worry all evening instead of going to sleep?

But the boys recovered quickly. They were soon laughing and jostling each other, and they made no objections when their mother shooed them toward bed. Standing in order of age,

---
1. **brazier** (brā′zhər): a metal pan holding burning charcoal or coals for cooking.

WORDS TO KNOW	**rapt** (răpt) *adj.* deeply interested **desolate** (dĕs′ə-lĭt) *adj.* miserable; very unhappy **decrepit** (dĭ-krĕp′ĭt) *adj.* weakened by old age **poignant** (poin′yənt) *adj.* very touching or moving; painful

92

Mini-Lesson  Literary Concepts

REVIEWING PLOT Remind students that plot is the sequence of related events that make up the story; it is the action, or what happens in the story. Most plots follow a regular progression, as shown by the flow chart at the right.

Application Draw the flow chart on the chalkboard and use it to explain the elements of plot progression. Encourage students to copy it into their notebooks. Invite them to apply the chart to both of the stories in order to map the development of the plot in each one.

EXPOSITION: Characters are introduced. They face a conflict. As they try to resolve conflict, complications arise.

↓

CLIMAX: The highest point of interest with the most suspense. Will characters solve their problem?

↓

RESOLUTION: Loose ends are tied up, and the story is brought to a close.

they bowed politely to the guests and then lay down on the mattresses spread out for them on the floor. Within minutes the sound of their regular breathing told the guests that they were asleep.

Zenta, the older of the two ronin, sighed as he glanced at the peaceful young faces. "I wish I could fall asleep so quickly. The story of Urashima Taro is one of the saddest that I know among our folk tales."

The farmer looked proudly at his sleeping sons. "They're stout lads. Nothing bothers them much."

The farmer's wife poured tea for the guests and apologized. "I'm sorry this is only poor tea made from coarse leaves."

Zenta hastened to reassure her. "It's warm and heartening on a chilly autumn evening."

"You know what I think is the saddest part of the Urashima Taro story?" said Matsuzo, picking up his cup and sipping the tea. "It's that Taro lost not only his family and friends but a big piece of his life as well. He had lost the most precious thing of all: time."

The farmer nodded agreement. "I wouldn't sell even one year of my life for money. As for losing seventy-two years, no amount of gold will make up for that!"

CLARIFY
A How do Matsuzo and the farmer feel about the loss of time?
Using a Reading Log

Zenta put his cup down on the floor and looked curiously at the farmer. "It's interesting that you should say that. I had an opportunity once to observe exactly how much gold a person was willing to pay for some lost years of his life." He smiled grimly. "In this case the man went as far as one gold piece for each year he lost."

"That's bizarre!" said Matsuzo. "You never told me about it."

"It happened long before I met you," said Zenta. He drank some tea and smiled ruefully. "Besides, I'm not particularly proud of the part I played in that strange affair."

"Let's hear the story!" urged Matsuzo. "You've made us all curious."

The farmer waited expectantly. His wife sat down quietly behind her husband and folded her hands. Her eyes looked intently at Zenta.

"Very well, then," said Zenta. "Actually, my story bears some resemblance to that of Urashima Taro. . . ."

It happened about seven years ago, when I was a green, inexperienced youngster not quite eighteen years old. But I had had a good training in arms, and I was able to get a job as a bodyguard for a wealthy merchant from Sakai.

As you know, wealthy merchants are relatively new in our country. Traditionally the rich have been noblemen, landowners, and warlords with thousands of followers. Merchants, considered as parasites in our society, are a despised class. But our civil wars have made people unusually mobile and stimulated trade between various parts of the country. The merchants have taken advantage of this to conduct businesses on a scale our fathers could not imagine. Some of them have become more wealthy than a warlord with thousands of samurai under his command.

The man I was escorting, Tokubei, was one of this new breed of wealthy merchants. He was trading not only with outlying provinces but even with the Portuguese[2] from across the sea. On this particular journey he was not carrying much gold with him. If he had, I'm sure he would have hired an older and more experienced bodyguard. But if the need should arise, he could always write a message to his clerks at home and have money forwarded to him. It's important to remember this.

---

2. **Portuguese:** here, merchants from Portugal; the first Europeans to reach Japan.

THE INN OF LOST TIME 93

Art Note

The actor Onoe Baiko VII as Mokuzume* in Tamamo no Mae Kumoi no Hareginu *by Tsuruya Kokei The colorful woodblock prints of contemporary artist Tsuruya Kokei mark a revival of portraits of Kabuki theater actors. In this portrait, Kokei depicts a Kabuki actor playing a traditional onnagata (female impersonator) role.

Reading the Art What details in the print suggest that the actor's appearance may be deceiving?

Literary Concept: PLOT

E Have students discuss the exposition of the plot at this point in Zenta's story. How far has the plot progressed? *(Possible response: The young Zenta and the merchant Tokubei have been introduced. A conflict arises when both characters are tired and hungry, but the merchant refuses to pay for expensive accommodations.)*

CUSTOMIZING FOR
Students Acquiring English

2 Ask students to paraphrase the expression, "We followed our noses." *(We smelled something good and used our sense of smell to find it.)* What did they smell? *(freshly cooked rice)*

The actor Onoe Baikō VII as Mokuzume in Tamamo no Mae Kumoi no Hareginu *(1984), Tsuruya Kokei. Color woodblock print, 39.8 cm × 27.5 cm. Copyright © British Museum.*

The second day of our journey was a particularly grueling one, with several steep hills to climb. As the day was drawing to its close, we began to consider where we should spend the night. I knew that within an hour's walking was a hot-spring resort known to have several attractive inns.

But Tokubei, my employer, said he was already very tired and wanted to stop. He had heard of the resort and knew the inns there were expensive. Wealthy as he was, he did not want to spend more money than he had to.

While we stood talking, a smell reached our noses, a wonderful smell of freshly cooked rice. Suddenly I felt ravenous. From the way Tokubei swallowed, I knew he was feeling just as hungry.

We looked around eagerly, but the area was forested, and we could not see very far in any direction. The tantalizing smell seemed to grow, and I could feel the saliva filling my mouth.

"There's an inn around here, somewhere," muttered Tokubei. "I'm sure of it."

We followed our noses.

WORDS TO KNOW — **tantalizing** (tăn′tə-lī′zĭng) *adj.* desirable but out of reach **tantalize** *v.*

94

Mini-Lesson The Writer's Style

AVOIDING CLICHÉS Characters and settings can be so overused that they become clichéd. In this selection, Namioka uses familiar characters, a common setting (a family and guests gathered near a fire), and a familiar situation (a host and visitors exchanging their stories). However, the characters' stories and their relationship to one another allow Namioka to use established conventions in unique and interesting ways.

Application Have students work in small groups to make a list of the common characters (farmer, wife, merchant, bodyguard) and the setting of the story (farmhouse, hearth, inn, nightfall). After making their list, have students brainstorm possible ways these same characters or setting might be used in a fresh or innovative manner.

Reteaching/Reinforcement

Avoiding Clichés, p. 320

We had to leave the well-traveled highway and take a narrow, winding footpath. But the mouth-watering smell of the rice and the vision of fluffy, freshly aired cotton quilts drew us on.

The sun was just beginning to set. We passed a bamboo grove,³ and in the low evening light the thin leaves turned into little golden knives. I saw a gilded clump of bamboo shoots. The sight made me think of the delicious dish they would make when boiled in soy sauce.

We hurried forward. To our delight we soon came to a clearing with a thatched house standing in the middle. The fragrant smell of rice was now so strong that we were certain a meal was being prepared inside.

Standing in front of the house was a pretty girl beaming at us with a welcoming smile. "Please honor us with your presence," she said, beckoning.

There was something a little unusual about one of her hands, but being hungry and eager to enter the house, I did not stop to observe closely.

You will say, of course, that it was my duty as a bodyguard to be suspicious and to look out for danger. Youth and inexperience should not have prevented me from wondering why an inn should be found hidden away from the highway. As it was, my stomach growled, and I didn't even hesitate but followed Tokubei to the house.

Before stepping up to enter, we were given basins of water to wash our feet. As the girl handed us towels for drying, I saw what was unusual about her left hand: she had six fingers.

Tokubei had noticed it as well. When the girl turned away to empty the basins, he nudged me. "Did you see her left hand? She had—" He broke off in confusion as the girl turned around, but she didn't seem to have heard.

The inn was peaceful and quiet, and we soon discovered the reason why. We were the only guests. Again, I should have been suspicious. I told you that I'm not proud of the part I played.

Tokubei turned to me and grinned. "It seems that there are no other guests. We should be able to get extra service for the same amount of money."

The girl led us to a spacious room which was like the principal chamber of a private residence. Cushions were set out for us on the floor, and we began to shed our traveling gear to make ourselves comfortable.

The door opened, and a grizzled-haired man entered. Despite his vigorous-looking face his back was a little bent, and I guessed his age to be about fifty. After bowing and greeting us he apologized in advance for the service. "We have not always been innkeepers here," he said, "and you may find the accommodations lacking. Our good intentions must make up for our inexperience. However, to compensate for our inadequacies, we will charge a lower fee than that of an inn with an established reputation."

Tokubei nodded graciously, highly pleased by the words of our host, and the evening began well. It continued well when the girl came back with some flasks of wine, cups, and dishes of salty snacks.

---

3. **bamboo grove:** a group of tall, tropical grasses with woody stems.

PREDICT
What do you think might happen at the inn?
Using a Reading Log

WORDS TO KNOW
gilded (gĭl′dĭd) *adj.* as if covered with a thin layer of gold **gild** *v.*
compensate (kŏm′pən-sāt) *v.* to make up for

95

CUSTOMIZING FOR
Multiple Learning Styles

F **Linguistic Learners** Read this section of Zenta's story aloud. Invite students to write the images and details they feel are the most important. Then have students write an explanation of why they selected particular images and details.

Active Reading: PREDICT

G Invite students to tell what they think will happen next in the story. If they need help, you may want to share the following model with them.

Think-Aloud Model *I'm not really sure what is going to happen next, but if I were Zenta and Tokubei, I would be suspicious. It seems strange that this inn is so far away from everything. It's also strange that they are the only guests—how can the inn stay in business?*

STRATEGIC READING FOR
Less-Proficient Readers

H Have students discuss the details about the setting of the inn and also details about the owners that strike Zenta as odd or peculiar. (*The inn is off the beaten track; the girl who greets them has six fingers; there are no other guests at the inn.*) **Noting Relevant Details**

Set a Purpose Have students continue reading to find out more about the stay of Zenta and Tokubei at the inn.

Mini-Lesson   Reading Skills/Strategies

ACTIVE READING: EVALUATING Remind students that active readers use strategies as they read. Evaluating means to form opinions about what we read, both during and after reading. It means to develop our own images of and ideas about characters and events.

Application Ask students what they think of Zenta as a storyteller. Encourage students to record their responses in a chart like the one shown.

Reteaching/Reinforcement
• *Unit One Resource Book,* p. 52

Why Zenta Is a Good Storyteller		
Literary Technique	Example from Story	Reason It Is Interesting
Setting	"To our delight we soon came to a clearing with a thatched house . . . we were certain a meal was being prepared inside."	The appearance of the inn and the intoxicating smell of the food anticipate an upcoming meal.
Description	"The door opened, and a grizzled-haired man entered . . . I guessed his age to be about fifty."	Zenta gives a clear picture of the man's arrival. Readers can easily visualize the innkeeper's appearance.

Linking to History

 Explain to students that there was a strict social hierarchy during the feudal period in Japan. Both former samurai (the innkeeper and Zenta) were not working as traditional samurai and so were of a lower social status than true samurai. Merchants were traditionally at the bottom of the social ladder, lower even than farmers, although many merchants were wealthy, as was Tokubei in this story.

Literary Concept: SETTING

J Have students notice the details of setting (such as the vase and the sliding doors) provided in these three paragraphs. They will become important later in the story.

Critical Thinking: HYPOTHESIZING

K Before students read further, ask them to hypothesize about how much time has actually passed. Have years passed, or only one night? *(Possible responses: Because of the farmer's telling of Urashima's story, it is likely that many years have passed. Or, it is unlikely that many years have passed because the story Zenta is telling happened only seven years earlier.)*

Active Reading: QUESTION

L Have students discuss their ideas of what has happened to Zenta and Tokubei. Remind students of the reason why Zenta is telling the story.

CUSTOMIZING FOR
Students Acquiring English

3 Act out the expression "my head was swimming" as if it had a literal meaning. Have students guess the expression's figurative meaning. *(I felt dizzy and confused.)*

While the girl served the wine, the host looked with interest at my swords. From the few remarks he made, I gathered that he was a former samurai, forced by circumstances to turn his house into an inn.

I Having become a bodyguard to a tight-fisted merchant, I was in no position to feel superior to a ronin turned innkeeper. Socially, therefore, we were more or less equal.

We exchanged polite remarks with our host while we drank and tasted the salty snacks. I looked around at the pleasant room. It showed excellent taste, and I especially admired a vase standing in the alcove.

 My host caught my eyes on it. "We still have a few good things that we didn't have to sell," he said. His voice held a trace of bitterness. "Please look at the panels of these doors. They were painted by a fine artist."

Tokubei and I looked at the pair of sliding doors. Each panel contained a landscape painting, the right panel depicting a winter scene and the left one the same scene in late summer. Our host's words were no idle boast. The pictures were indeed beautiful.

Tokubei rose and approached the screens for a closer look. When he sat down again, his eyes were calculating. No doubt he was trying to estimate what price the paintings would fetch.

After my third drink I began to feel very tired. Perhaps it was the result of drinking on an empty stomach. I was glad when the girl brought in two dinner trays and a lacquered container of rice. Uncovering the rice container, she began filling our bowls.

Again I noticed her strange left hand with its six fingers. Any other girl would have tried to keep that hand hidden, but this girl made no effort to do so. If anything, she seemed to use that hand more than her other one when she served us. The extra little finger always

96 UNIT ONE PART 2: FOOLED BY APPEARANCES

stuck out from the hand, as if inviting comment.

The hand fascinated me so much that I kept my eyes on it and soon forgot to eat. After a while the hand looked blurry. And then everything else began to look blurry. The last thing I remembered was the sight of Tokubei shaking his head, as if trying to clear it.

When I opened my eyes again, I knew that time had passed, but not how much time. My next thought was that it was cold. It was not only extremely cold but damp.

I rolled over and sat up. I reached immediately for my swords and found them safe on the ground beside me. *On the ground? What was I doing on the ground?* My last memory was of staying at an inn with a merchant called Tokubei.

The thought of Tokubei put me into a panic. I was his bodyguard, and instead of watching over him, I had fallen asleep and had awakened in a strange place.

I looked around frantically and saw that he was lying on the ground not far from where I was. Had he been killed?

I got up shakily, and when I stood up, my head was swimming. But my sense of urgency gave some strength to my legs. I stumbled over to my employer and to my great relief found him breathing—breathing heavily, in fact.

When I shook his shoulder, he grunted and finally opened his eyes. "Where am I?" he asked thickly.

It was a reasonable question. I looked around and saw that we had been lying in a bamboo grove. By the light I guessed that it was early morning, and the reason I felt cold and damp was because my clothes were wet with dew.

"It's cold!" said Tokubei, shivering and

> **QUESTION**
> What do you think has happened to them?
> *Using a Reading Log*

Mini-Lesson Study Skills

OUTLINING Outlines help organize information. In creating outlines, use key ideas or events as headings. The details that support the main ideas or events are the subpoints. Students may also want to use a modified outline form when taking notes.

Application In order to sort out the complex plots of the two stories, have students make an outline of the major events of each.

OUTLINE EXAMPLE—Second Story

I. Zenta and Tokubei initially enjoy dinner (key idea)
  A. They talk to their host (subpoint for I)
  B. They eat and drink
  C. They enjoy the pleasant things in the room
    1. the vase (detail for C)
    2. the winter/summer landscape paintings
II. The meal changes
  A. Zenta becomes very tired (subpoint for II)
  B. Zenta notices the six-fingered girl
    1. She doesn't hide her hand (detail for B)
    2. Zenta can't stop looking at it
  C. The two men feel strange
    1. Zenta's vision becomes blurred
    2. Tokubei tries to clear his head

96 THE LANGUAGE OF LITERATURE TEACHER'S EDITION

climbing unsteadily to his feet. He looked around slowly, and his eyes became wide with disbelief. "What happened? I thought we were staying at an inn!"

His words came as a relief. One of the possibilities I had considered was that I had gone mad and that the whole episode with the inn was something I had imagined. Now I knew that Tokubei had the same memory of the inn. I had not imagined it.

But why were we out here on the cold ground, instead of on comfortable mattresses in the inn?

"They must have drugged us and robbed us," said Tokubei. He turned and looked at me furiously. "A fine bodyguard you are!"

There was nothing I could say to that. But at least we were both alive and unharmed. "Did they take all your money?" I asked.

Tokubei had already taken his wallet out of his sash and was peering inside. "That's funny! My money is still here!"

This was certainly unexpected. What did the innkeeper and his strange daughter intend to do by drugging us and moving us outside?

At least things were not as bad as we had feared. We had not lost anything except a comfortable night's sleep, although from the heaviness in my head I had certainly slept deeply enough—and long enough too. Exactly how much time had elapsed since we drank wine with our host?

All we had to do now was find the highway again and continue our journey. Tokubei suddenly chuckled. "I didn't even have to pay for our night's lodging!"

As we walked from the bamboo grove, I saw the familiar clump of bamboo shoots, and we found ourselves standing in the same clearing again. Before our eyes was the thatched house. Only it was somehow different. Perhaps things looked different in the daylight than at dusk.

But the difference was more than a change of light. As we approached the house slowly, like sleepwalkers, we saw that the thatching was much darker. On the previous evening the thatching had looked fresh and new. Now it was dark with age. Daylight should make things appear brighter, not darker. The plastering of the walls also looked more dingy.

Tokubei and I stopped to look at each other before we went closer. He was pale, and I knew that I looked no less frightened. Something was terribly wrong. I loosened my sword in its scabbard.[4]

e finally gathered the courage to go up to the house. Since Tokubei seemed unable to find his voice, I spoke out. "Is anyone there?"

After a moment we heard shuffling footsteps, and the front door slid open. The face of an old woman appeared. "Yes?" she inquired. Her voice was creaky with age.

What set my heart pounding with panic, however, was not her voice. It was the sight of her left hand holding on to the frame of the door. The hand was wrinkled and crooked with the arthritis[5] of old age—and it had six fingers.

I heard a gasp beside me and knew that Tokubei had noticed the hand as well.

The door opened wider, and a man appeared beside the old woman. At first I thought it was our host of the previous night. But this man was much younger, although the resemblance was strong. He carried himself straighter, and his hair was black, while the innkeeper had been grizzled and slightly bent with age.

---

4. **scabbard** (skăb′ərd): a sheath or case for a sword.
5. **arthritis:** an inflammation of joints resulting in pain and swelling.

THE INN OF LOST TIME 97

Linking To History

Samurai practiced a code of fierce loyalty and obedience to their warlords. They valued honor above all other things, including money and even life itself. When a samurai dishonored himself, he committed suicide, or hara-kiri. The practice of samurai officially ended in 1871 when feudalism was abolished in Japan, but the cultural influence of the samurai continues.

STRATEGIC READING FOR
Less-Proficient Readers

Ask students why Tokubei, as a wealthy merchant, is so happy that he did not have to pay for his night's lodging. *(Possible responses: He has been characterized as stingy. He thought he had been robbed and now considers himself lucky not to have paid for the inn at all.)* **Making Inferences**

Set a Purpose As students continue to read, have them pay attention to how Tokubei's attitude toward money influences how he acts.

Literary Concept: PLOT

Ask students how the characters' awareness of the passage of time relates to the climax—or turning point—of the story. *(Possible response: The plot has moved closer to its climax because the characters' growing awareness of the passage of time makes them increasingly suspicious and increases the suspense for the reader.)*

Mini-Lesson  Grammar

DIRECT AND INDIRECT QUESTIONING
Point out to students that questions can be either direct or indirect. An indirect question is a statement that tells what someone asked without using the person's direct words and ends with a period. A direct question uses the exact words of a person's question, and it ends with a question mark inside the quotation marks, as in the highlighted examples.

Application Read the following sentences aloud. Have students copy and punctuate the sentences properly. Then have students identify the sentences that ask direct and indirect questions.

1. Zenta questioned whether one night or many years had passed. *(indirect)*
2. "Did they take all your money?" Zenta asked. *(direct)*

Reteaching/Reinforcement
- *Grammar Handbook*, anthology p. 898
- *Grammar Mini-Lessons* copymasters p. 43, transparencies p. 33

The Writer's Craft
End Marks, pp. 638–639

THE LANGUAGE OF LITERATURE TEACHER'S EDITION 97

Art Note

***Mountain Landscape* by Sesshū Tōyō**
Sesshū Tōyō was a Japanese artist who lived from 1420 to 1506. This landscape was created using ink and color on a folded five-panel screen. Japanese art has a strong tradition of using landscapes, often on room screens, sliding panels, and hanging scrolls.

Reading the Art *Compare this landscape with the description of the sliding doors on page 96. What do the two have in common? What are their differences?*

Literary Concept: CONFLICT

P Explain to students that it is common for conflict between characters to increase as the plot moves closer to a climax. The clash between Tokubei and the innkeeper is an example of external conflict, which involves one character's struggle with another person. Ask students how it is possible to tell that the conflict between characters is increasing. *(Possible responses: The merchant and the innkeeper are so mad they are almost shouting at each other; the exclamation marks indicate the rising emotion of the characters.)*

Detail of mountain landscape (15th–16th century), Sesshū Tōyō. Six-fold screen, ink and color on paper, Japan, Muromachi Period, 161.0 cm × 351.2 cm, courtesy of the Freer Gallery of Art, Smithsonian Institution, Washington, D.C. (58.5).

"Please excuse my mother," said the man. "Her hearing is not good. Can we help you in some way?"

Tokubei finally found his voice. "Isn't this the inn where we stayed last night?"

The man stared. "Inn? We are not innkeepers here!"

"Yes, you are!" insisted Tokubei. "Your daughter invited us in and served us with wine. You must have put something in the wine!"

The man frowned. "You are serious? Are you sure you didn't drink too much at your inn and wander off?"

"No, I didn't drink too much!" said Tokubei, almost shouting. "I hardly drank at all! Your daughter, the one with six fingers in her hand, started to pour me a second cup of wine . . ." His voice trailed off, and he stared again at the left hand of the old woman.

"I don't have a daughter," said the man slowly. "My mother here is the one who has six fingers in her left hand, although I hardly think it polite of you to mention it."

"I'm getting dizzy," muttered Tokubei and began to totter.

"I think you'd better come in and rest a bit," the man said to him gruffly. He glanced at me. "Perhaps you wish to join your friend. You don't share his delusion about the inn, I hope?"

WORDS TO KNOW — **delusion** (dĭ-lōō′zhən) *n.* a false belief or opinion

Multicultural Perspectives

JAPANESE LITERATURE Lensey Namioka was born in China and came to the United States as a teenager. However, many of her stories are set in 16th-century Japan—her husband's country of origin—and they often reflect themes common in Japanese literature.

The Japanese produced their first written literature during the A.D. 500s. However, the tradition remained unknown outside Japan until the 1900s, most likely as a result of Japan's relative isolation and the difficulty of mastering the Japanese language.

During the early 11th century, Murasaki Shikibu, a lady-in-waiting to a famous empress, wrote *The Tale of Genji*. This is considered to be one of the greatest works in the literary tradition of Japan, as well as one of the world's first novels.

"I wouldn't presume to contradict my elders," I said carefully. Since both Tokubei and the owner of the house were my elders, I wasn't committing myself. In truth I didn't know what to believe, but I did want a look at the inside of the house.

The inside was almost the same as it was before, but the differences were there when I looked closely. We entered the same room with the alcove and the pair of painted doors. The vase I had admired was no longer there, but the doors showed the same landscapes painted by a master. I peered closely at the pictures and saw that the colors looked faded. What was more, the left panel, the one depicting a winter scene, had a long tear in one corner. It had been painstakingly mended, but the damage was impossible to hide completely.

Tokubei saw what I was staring at, and he became even paler. At this stage we had both considered the possibility that a hoax of some sort had been played on us. The torn screen convinced Tokubei that our host had not played a joke: the owner of a valuable painting would never vandalize it for a trivial reason.

As for me, I was far more disturbed by the sight of the sixth finger on the old woman's hand. Could the young girl have disguised herself as an old crone?[6] She could put rice powder in her hair to whiten it, but she could not transform her pretty straight fingers into old fingers twisted with arthritis. The woman here with us now was genuinely old, at least fifty years older than the girl.

It was this same old woman who finally gave us our greatest shock. "It's interesting that you should mention an inn, gentlemen," she croaked. "My father used to operate an inn. After he died, my husband and I turned this back into a private residence. We didn't need the income, you see."

"Your . . . your . . . f-father?" stammered Tokubei.

"Yes," replied the old woman. "He was a ronin, forced to go into innkeeping when he lost his position. But he never liked the work. Besides, our inn had begun to acquire an unfortunate reputation. Some of our guests disappeared, you see."

Even before she finished speaking, a horrible suspicion had begun to dawn on me. Her *father* had been an innkeeper, she said, her father who used to be a ronin. The man who

---

6. **crone:** an ugly, withered old woman.

Active Reading: QUESTION

S Ask students to question how Zenta and Tokubei could have slept 50 years. *(Possible responses: They could not have slept 50 years and so they must have been deceived. Or they might have been the victims of a magic spell.)*

Active Reading: EVALUATE

T Have students compare the different responses of Tokubei and Zenta to the loss of time. How does Tokubei's response alter Zenta's feelings toward Tokubei? *(Possible response: Zenta does not have a wife or business to lose, so he is not as upset as Tokubei by the passage of years. Although Zenta never respected Tokubei, he now feels sorry for him.)*

---

had been our host was a ronin turned innkeeper. Could this mean that this old woman was actually the same person as the young girl we had seen?

I sat stunned while I tried to absorb the <u>implications</u>. What had happened to us? Was it possible that Tokubei and I had slept while this young girl grew into a mature woman, got married, and bore a son, a son who was now an adult? If that was the case, then we had slept for fifty years!

> **QUESTION**
> How could they have slept for 50 years?
> *Using a Reading Log*

The old woman's next words confirmed my fears. "I recognize you now! You are two of the lost guests from our inn! The other lost ones I don't remember so well, but I remember *you* because your disappearance made me so sad. Such a handsome youth, I thought, what a pity that he should have gone the way of the others!"

A high wail came from Tokubei, who began to keen[7] and rock himself back and forth. "I've lost fifty years! Fifty years of my life went by while I slept at this accursed inn!"

The inn was indeed accursed. Was the fate of the other guests similar to ours? "Did anyone else return as we did, fifty years later?" I asked.

The old woman looked uncertain and turned to her son. He frowned thoughtfully. "From time to time wild-looking people have come to us with stories similar to yours. Some of them went mad with the shock."

Tokubei wailed again. "I've lost my business! I've lost my wife, my young and beautiful wife! We had been married only a couple of months!"

A gruesome chuckle came from the old woman. "You may not have lost your wife. It's just that she's become an old hag like me!"

That did not console Tokubei, whose keening became louder. Although my relationship with my employer had not been characterized by much respect on either side, I did begin to feel very sorry for him. He was right: he had lost his world.

s for me, the loss was less <u>traumatic</u>. I had left home under extremely painful circumstances and had spent the next three years wandering. I had no friends and no one I could call a relation. The only thing I had was my duty to my employer. Somehow, some way, I had to help him.

"Did no one find an explanation for these disappearances?" I asked. "Perhaps if we knew the reason why, we might find some way to reverse the process."

The old woman began to nod eagerly. "The priestess! Tell them about the shrine priestess!"

"Well," said the man, "I'm not sure if it would work in your case. . . ."

"What? What would work?" demanded Tokubei. His eyes were feverish.

"There was a case of one returning guest who consulted the priestess at our local shrine," said the man. "She went into a trance and revealed that there was an evil spirit dwelling in the bamboo grove here. This spirit would put <u>unwary</u> travelers into a long, unnatural sleep. They would wake up twenty, thirty, or even fifty years later."

"Yes, but you said something worked in his case," said Tokubei.

The man seemed <u>reluctant</u> to go on. "I don't like to see you cheated, so I'm not sure I should be telling you this."

---

7. **keen:** to wail or cry out loudly.

WORDS TO KNOW
implication (ĭm′plĭ-kā′shən) *n.* a possible meaning or significance
traumatic (trou-măt′ĭk) *adj.* emotionally shocking
unwary (ŭn-wâr′ē) *adj.* not alert or cautious
reluctant (rĭ-lŭk′tənt) *adj.* unwilling

100

Assessment ✓ Option

INFORMAL ASSESSMENT

Comparing and Contrasting Have students rewrite Zenta's story from a different point of view. Invite them to choose from one of the following options or come up with their own alternative:

1. Rewrite the story from the point of view of the six-fingered woman. Compare and contrast how her perspective differs from that of Zenta.
2. Imagine that Matsuzo is retelling the tale to a friend several years later. What elements of Zenta's story might he emphasize or downplay? Compare and contrast the two versions.

Rubric

3 Full Accomplishment Students incorporate all the major components of the plot and retell the story from another character's point of view in a consistent, insightful way.

2 Substantial Accomplishment Students cover the basic events of the plot but do not have enough mastery to move from Zenta's perspective to another point of view.

1 Little or Partial Accomplishment Students cover some elements of the plot but have little understanding of the characters or issues involved.

"Tell me! Tell me!" demanded Tokubei. The host's reluctance only made him more impatient.

"The priestess promised to make a spell that would undo the work of the evil spirit," said the man. "But she demanded a large sum of money, for she said that she had to burn some very rare and costly incense before she could begin the spell."

At the mention of money Tokubei sat back. The hectic flush died down on his face, and his eyes narrowed. "How much money?" he asked.

The host shook his head. "In my opinion the priestess is a fraud and makes outrageous claims about her powers. We try to have as little to do with her as possible."

"Yes, but did her spell work?" asked Tokubei. "If it worked, she's no fraud!"

"At least the stranger disappeared again," cackled the old woman. "Maybe he went back to his own time. Maybe he walked into a river."

Tokubei's eyes narrowed further. "How much money did the priestess demand?" he asked again.

"I think it was one gold piece for every year lost," said the host. He hurriedly added, "Mind you, I still wouldn't trust the priestess."

"Then it would cost me fifty gold pieces to get back to my own time," muttered Tokubei. He looked up. "I don't carry that much money with me."

"No, you don't," agreed the host.

Something alerted me about the way he said that. It was as if the host knew already that Tokubei did not carry much money on him.

Meanwhile Tokubei sighed. He had come to a decision. "I do have the means to obtain more money, however. I can send a message to my chief clerk, and he will <u>remit</u> the money when he sees my seal."

"Your chief clerk may be dead by now," I reminded him.

"You're right!" moaned Tokubei. "My business will be under a new management, and nobody will even remember my name!"

"And your wife will have remarried," said the old woman, with one of her chuckles. I found it hard to believe that the gentle young girl who had served us wine could turn into this dreadful harridan.[8]

"Sending the message may be a waste of time," agreed the host.

"What waste of time!" cried Tokubei. "Why shouldn't I waste time? I've wasted fifty years already! Anyway, I've made up my mind. I'm sending that message."

"I still think you shouldn't trust the priestess," said the host.

That only made Tokubei all the more determined to send for the money. However, he was not quite resigned to the amount. "Fifty gold pieces is a large sum. Surely the priestess can buy incense for less than that amount?"

"Why don't you try giving her thirty gold pieces?" cackled the old woman. "Then the priestess will send you back thirty years, and your wife will only be middle-aged."

While Tokubei was still arguing with himself about the exact sum to send for, I decided to have a look at the bamboo grove. "I'm going for a walk," I announced, rising and picking up my sword from the floor beside me.

The host turned sharply to look at me. For an instant a faint, rueful smile appeared on his lips. Then he looked away.

---

8. **harridan** (hăr′ĭ-dn): a scolding, vicious woman.

WORDS TO KNOW
remit (rĭ-mĭt′) *v.* to send in payment

STRATEGIC READING FOR
Less-Proficient Readers

W What has Zenta learned, beginning with his investigation of the bamboo grove? *(Possible responses: He and Tokubei had slept overnight, not 50 years. This enables him to figure out the hoax.)*
Summarizing

Set a Purpose Have students read on to find out what happens to the innkeeper and his daughter.

Critical Thinking: ANALYZING

X Have students analyze why Tokubei agrees so quickly with Zenta that he has been the victim of a hoax. *(Possible responses: Tokubei does not want to accept that he actually has lost 50 years; Tokubei believes Zenta because he seems so confident that the innkeeper has played a hoax.)*

Outside, I went straight to the clump of shoots in the bamboo grove. On the previous night—or what I perceived as the previous night—I had noticed that clump of bamboo shoots particularly, because I had been so hungry that I pictured them being cut up and boiled.

The clump of bamboo shoots was still in the same place. That in itself proved nothing, since bamboo could spring up anywhere, including the place where a clump had existed fifty years earlier. But what settled the matter in my mind was that the clump looked almost exactly the way it did when I had seen it before, except that every shoot was about an inch taller. That was a reasonable amount for bamboo shoots to grow overnight.

vernight. Tokubei and I had slept on the ground here overnight. We had not slept here for a period of fifty years.

Once I knew that, I was able to see another inconsistency: the door panels with the painted landscapes. The painting with the winter scene had been on the *right* last night, and it was on the *left* this morning. It wasn't simply a case of the panels changing places, because the depressions in the panel for the handholds had been reversed. In other words, what I saw just now was not a pair of paintings faded and torn by age. They were an entirely different pair of paintings.

But how did the pretty young girl change into an old woman? The answer was that if the screens could be different ones, so could the women. I had seen one woman, a young girl, last night. This morning I saw a different woman, an old hag.

The darkening of the thatched roof? Simply blow ashes over the roof. The grizzled-haired host of last night could be the same man who claimed to be his grandson today. It would be a simple matter for a young man to put gray in his hair and assume a stoop.

And the purpose of the hoax? To make Tokubei send for fifty pieces of gold, of course. It was clever of the man to accuse the shrine priestess of fraud and pretend reluctance to let Tokubei send his message.

I couldn't even feel angry toward the man and his daughter—or mother, sister, wife, whatever. He could have killed me and taken my swords, which he clearly admired. Perhaps he was really a ronin and felt sympathetic toward another one. **W**

When I returned to the house, Tokubei was looking resigned. "I've decided to send for the whole fifty gold pieces." He sighed.

"Don't bother," I said. "In fact we should be leaving as soon as possible. We shouldn't even stop here for a drink, especially not of wine."

Tokubei stared. "What do you mean? If I go back home, I'll find everything changed!"

"Nothing will be changed," I told him. "Your wife will be as young and beautiful as ever."

"I don't understand," he said. "Fifty years . . ."

"It's a joke," I said. "The people here have a peculiar sense of humor, and they've played a joke on us."

Tokubei's mouth hung open. Finally he closed it with a snap. He stared at the host, and his face became first red and then purple. "You—you were trying to swindle me!" He turned furiously to me. "And you let them do this!" **X**

"I'm not letting them," I pointed out. "That's why we're leaving right now."

"Are you going to let them get away with this?" demanded Tokubei. "They might try to swindle someone else!"

"They only went to this much trouble when they heard of the arrival of a fine fat fish like you," I said. I looked deliberately at the host.

WORDS TO KNOW	**inconsistency** (ĭn′kən-sĭs′tən-sē) *n.* something that is not in agreement or harmony

---

Mini-Lesson: Speaking, Listening, and Viewing

STORYTELLING Explain to students that storytelling is a way to entertain listeners with unique interpretations of a story.

In preparation for their storytelling, tell students that an effective storyteller
- presents a meaningful and interesting story
- includes necessary introductory information so listeners can follow the story
- performs the story using appropriate voices and gestures

Application "The Inn of Lost Time" provides an opportunity for students to tell their own stories. Students may want to create their own version of Zenta's story, find another folk tale, or write an original story.

Have students work in small groups, with each student reviewing his or her ideas for the story with the group. Encourage each group to develop different voices or gestures that would bring each member's story to life. Finally, the groups should take turns presenting their story to the class.

"I'm sure they won't be tempted to try the same trick again."

nd that's the end of your story?" asked Matsuzo. "You and Tokubei just went away? How did you know the so-called innkeeper wouldn't try the trick on some other luckless traveler?"

Zenta shook his head. "I didn't know. I merely guessed that once the trick was exposed, they wouldn't take the chance of trying it again. Of course I thought about revisiting the place to check if the people there were leading an honest life."

"Why didn't you?" asked Matsuzo. "Maybe we could go together. You've made me curious about that family now."

"Then you can satisfy your curiosity," said Zenta, smiling. He held his cup out for more tea, and the farmer's wife came forward to pour.

Only now she used both hands to hold the pot, and for the first time Matsuzo saw her left hand. He gasped. The hand had six fingers.

"Who was the old woman?" Zenta asked the farmer's wife.

"She was my grandmother," she replied. "Having six fingers is something that runs in my family."

At last Matsuzo found his voice. "You mean this is the very house you visited? This is the inn where time was lost?"

"Where we *thought* we lost fifty years," said Zenta. "Perhaps I should have warned you first. But I was almost certain that we'd be safe this time. And I see that I was right."

He turned to the woman again. "You and your husband are farmers now, aren't you? What happened to the man who was the host?"

"He's dead," she said quietly. "He was my brother, and he was telling you the truth when he said that he was a ronin. Two years ago he found work with another warlord, but he was killed in battle only a month later."

Matsuzo was peering at the pair of sliding doors, which he hadn't noticed before. "I see that you've put up the faded set of paintings. The winter scene is on the left side."

The woman nodded. "We sold the newer pair of doors. My husband said that we're farmers now and that people in our position don't need valuable paintings. We used the money to buy some new farm implements."

She took up the teapot again. "Would you like another cup of tea?" she asked Matsuzo.

Staring at her left hand, Matsuzo had a sudden qualm. "I—I don't think I want any more."

Everybody laughed. ❖

WORDS TO KNOW
qualm (kwäm) *n.* a sudden disturbing feeling

103

STRATEGIC READING FOR
Less-Proficient Readers

Y Ask students if there is any relation between the daughter of the innkeeper in Zenta's story and the farmer's wife. *(They are the same person.)* Drawing Conclusions

Literary Concept: PLOT

Z Have students discuss the resolution of the story. How does the six-fingered woman bring Zenta's story and the frame story together? *(Possible response: The six-fingered woman is present in both Zenta's story and the frame story: She explains who the innkeeper and old woman were, as well as why she has six fingers.)*

CUSTOMIZING FOR
Gifted and Talented Students

Have students discuss the role of the six-fingered woman in the story. Challenge students to debate whether the story would have been more effective if she had played a larger role from the beginning.

COMPREHENSION CHECK

1. Who is visiting the farmer and his family at the opening of the story? *(Zenta and Matsuzo, two unemployed samurai)*
2. How is Zenta's story similar to the farmer's tale of Urashima Taro? *(Both stories are about the loss of many years of someone's life.)*
3. Why does Tokubei not pay to have 50 years of his life restored to him? *(Zenta realizes the innkeeper is trying to swindle him.)*
4. Why is it so important that Matsuzo notices that the farmer's wife has six fingers? *(We learn what happened to the people that ran the inn.)*

Mini-Lesson Spelling

THE LETTERS qu Explain to students that the letter *q* is almost always followed by the vowel *u*. In most words, *qu* is pronounced /kw/. When *qu* is pronounced /kw/, it can appear at the beginning or in the middle of a word:

qualm = kwäm   *equation* = ē-kwā′ zhən

In some words, *qu* is pronounced /k/. Then it may appear in the middle or at the end of a word.

conquer = kän′kər   *plaque* = plăk

Application Write the following words on the board. Have students identify the words in which *qu* has the sound of *k* and words in which it has the sound of *kw*.

1. quaint *(kw)*
2. equinox *(kw)*
3. masquerade *(k)*
4. clique *(k)*
5. banquet *(kw)*
6. quizzical *(kw)*
7. quench *(kw)*
8. sequel *(kw)*
9. conquest *(kw)*
10. lacquer *(k)*

Ask students to look for more words that fit this pattern and to add these words to their personal word lists.

Reteaching/Reinforcement
- *Unit One Resource Book*, p. 53

Personal Response to Critical Analysis

1. Students' responses will vary. Accept all reasonable responses.
2. Possible responses: Some students may say that Zenta follows a strict code of honor, which demands that he serve his employer to the best of his ability. Others might point out that he is paid to protect and defend Tokubei and so is skeptical and cautious.
3. Possible responses: Some students may think that the innkeepers' offenses are minor and not deserving of punishment. Others may think that some sort of punishment is in order.
4. Possible response: Some students might suggest that Zenta knew that this was the same house that he had come to years before, so he wanted everyone who lived in the house to know why he had returned.
5. Possible responses: Some students may argue that Tokubei did not act rationally by planning to send for money. Others might suggest that considering the shock of his losing 50 years, Tokubei's desperation is understandable.
6. Students' responses will vary. Accept all reasonable responses.

Another Pathway

Cooperative Learning Groups should exchange and compare their charts. One student should record how the charts are similar, while another student develops a theme statement from the similarities in the charts. A third student should report the group's findings to the class. After listening to the theme statements of each group, have students revise or rework their group's statements, taking into account what other groups have said.

Rubric

3 Full Accomplishment Students indicate complete understanding of story elements.

2 Substantial Accomplishment Students show only partial understanding of the story.

1 Little or Partial Accomplishment Students show little or no understanding of story.

RESPONDING OPTIONS

FROM PERSONAL RESPONSE TO CRITICAL ANALYSIS

REFLECT 1. What are your thoughts about Zenta's story of the hoax? Write your reactions in your notebook. Share your thoughts with a partner.

RETHINK 2. Why do you think the hoax worked on other people, but not on Zenta?
Consider
- the nature of Zenta's profession
- his relationship with Tokubei
- why Zenta questioned appearances

3. If you had been Zenta or Tokubei, would you have punished the innkeepers? Why or why not?

4. Why do you think Zenta told the story to the farmer's family?

5. Tokubei thought that he had lost several years of his life. How realistic was his reaction to this loss? Explain your opinion.

RELATE 6. Suppose both Tokubei and Zenta lived in our country today. What professions would each have? How might the problems they had in the story be similar to or different from what they would encounter today?

LITERARY CONCEPTS

Setting is the time and place of the action of a story. A setting may be real or imaginary. In some stories, such as "Collecting Team" on page 107, the setting has a major influence on the story. Is the setting of "The Inn of Lost Time" real or imaginary? In what ways is the setting important to the story?

Multimodal Learning
ANOTHER PATHWAY
Cooperative Learning
In small groups, using the chart you made on page 90, try to figure out the **theme** of this story—or the author's message about life. Summarize your group's finding in a statement. Then compare and discuss the theme statements that each group decided on.

QUICKWRITES

1. The Urashima Taro folktale could be adapted to any setting. Write a contemporary or futuristic version of this **tale,** placing it in the setting of your choice.

2. Imagine that Zenta and Tokubei really did age 50 years. How might their story be different? Rewrite the **story ending** as if the men actually had grown older.

3. The farmer's wife appeared calm as she sat listening to Zenta. Do you think she was really calm, or was her appearance deceiving? With another student, write an **interior monologue** that shows what she might have been thinking and feeling.

📁 **PORTFOLIO** Save your writing. You may want to use it later as a springboard to a piece for your portfolio.

104 UNIT ONE PART 2: FOOLED BY APPEARANCES

Literary Concepts

Students may be confused by the selection's use of multiple settings: the farmhouse where the selection begins, the undersea world of Urashima Taro, and the inn. Have students describe each of the three settings to determine which one is real *(farmhouse)*, which one is fantastical *(undersea world)*, and which combines both *(the inn—real setting but fantastical experience)*. The multiple settings are important to the structure of the story because the frame story contains two other stories and each of the three has its own setting.

QuickWrites

1. Encourage students to use their imagination when creating a new setting for the folk tale.
2. Point out to students that if Zenta and Tokubei are actually 50 years older, the plot of both Zenta's story and the frame story will change.
3. Explain to students than an interior monologue takes place solely in the mind of a character.

The Writer's Craft
Guidelines for Writing Dialogue, p. 327

Multimodal Learning

ALTERNATIVE ACTIVITIES

1. Imagine that you are Zenta and that you are looking for a new job. Design a **classified ad** in which you describe the job you want and your qualifications for it. Consider your training and experience. Also think about including various graphic elements for grabbing the reader.
2. During the time of this story, Japanese screen painting was popular. Artists used bold colors, gold leaf, and details to depict scenes such as samurai at war. Find examples of 16th-century Japanese **screen painting** and share them with the class.
3. Rent and watch the **videos** of the Japanese classic *Seven Samurai* and the American classic *The Magnificent Seven*. What differences and what similarities between the two cultures do you notice? How are the movies' heroes alike, and how are they different? With other viewers, compare and contrast the two movies.

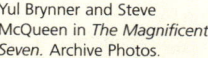

Yul Brynner and Steve McQueen in *The Magnificent Seven*. Archive Photos.

ART CONNECTION

Look again at the painting on page 94. Does the painting match the image you had of the female character in the story? What details add or detract from your own mental picture of the character?

Detail of *The actor Onoe Baikō VII as Mokuzume* in Tamamo no Mae Kumoi no Hareginu (1984), Tsuruya Kokei. Color woodblock print, 39.8 cm × 27.5 cm. Copyright © British Museum.

ACROSS THE CURRICULUM

History Investigate Japan's history during the late 1500s, including the role of the samurai during this period. Create a time line that highlights major events. Use pictures or your own drawings to illustrate the key dates on your time line.

THE INN OF LOST TIME **105**

Across the Curriculum

History Have students work in small groups. Ask them to plan cooperatively the tasks necessary to complete the project. One student should be responsible for researching Japan's history. Another student should organize the information into a time line. A third student should be responsible for finding or drawing pictures to illustrate the time line.

ADDITIONAL SUGGESTION

Social Studies *Warriors* Have students research how a warrior class developed in different feudal societies. For example, students could compare the 16th-century Japanese samurai to their knightly counterparts in 13th- and 14th-century England and France. Students should note the similarities and differences between how knights and samurai related among themselves, as well as their respective styles of armor and complex codes of honor.

Art Connection

Some students will say that the painting shares similarities with their mental image of the woman. Other students will say that the abstract qualities of the painting detract from their more realistic mental images of the woman.

ART GALLERY

Japanese Art These images of Japanese screen paintings reveal some of the perceptions and themes that Japanese painters have sought to express in their work.

Side A, Frame 52591

Alternative Activities

1. Refer students to the classified ads in the newspaper to find models for the kind of ads they will be writing. Urge them to link Zenta's training as a warrior to the new job for which they are applying.
2. Before beginning this activity, refer students to the reproduction of a screen painting shown on pages 98–99. Have students use their school or local library to find additional sourcebooks for Japanese art.
3. Arrange for a collective screening of the films. Both films should be readily available from most libraries and video stores. Invite students to take notes while watching. You may wish to preselect clips for students to watch and compare. Then divide the class into small groups to share their notes and thoughts.

Words to Know

Exercise A
1. rapt
2. poignant
3. decrepit
4. reluctant
5. unwary
6. compensate
7. traumatic
8. remit
9. gilded
10. tantalizing
11. qualm
12. inconsistency
13. delusion
14. implication
15. desolate

Exercise B
Students' drawings will vary. If partners have difficulty guessing the correct word, allow students to revise their drawings.

Reteaching/Reinforcement
• *Unit One Resource Book*, p. 54

LENSEY NAMIOKA

Lensey Namioka spent many years as a mathematician. However, she feels she has managed to keep her writing career quite separate. As she has said, "My long years of training in mathematics have little influence on my writing," though she does credit her training with helping her write more concisely and economically.

WORDS TO KNOW

EXERCISE A Review the Words to Know at the bottom of the selection pages. Then, on your paper, write the word that fills each blank below. Use each word once.

The children listened with __1__ attention as the samurai began the moving, __2__ story of the crippled, __3__ old feudal lord.

"The fearful old man, living in poverty, was __4__ to leave his home because he knew that poor and hungry ronin would set upon any __5__ travelers and take their belongings. To __6__ for his fear and to avoid any __7__ or upsetting experiences with robbers, the man wanted to hire me as a bodyguard. He offered to __8__ payment in the form of a special kimono covered with shimmering gold threads, his only valuable possession.

"Even though the __9__ kimono was __10__ to me, I suddenly felt an unusual __11__ about this assignment. I sensed an unexplained __12__ in such a poor man's owning such a splendid garment. I started to wonder if I was suffering from some sort of __13__.

However, the __14__ of this situation soon became clear to me. The old man looked so __15__ that I knew there was more to this than met the eye. The lord then revealed that he was a shogun who was disguised to protect himself from ruthless ronin. The lord's desperation made me want to help him, so I became the best dressed bodyguard in all of Japan in my splendid new kimono!"

EXERCISE B Select six of the Words to Know in this selection. Draw pictures to illustrate or represent each one. Have a partner guess the words.

LENSEY NAMIOKA

1929–

Lensey Namioka was born in Beijing, China, and spent most of her childhood there. It wasn't until she was a teenager that she and her parents came to the United States.

Namioka began writing professionally during the 1960s. At that time, China was beginning its Cultural Revolution, and the Communist government attempted to eliminate counterrevolutionaries. Because of this situation, Namioka was afraid to write about China. "I had relatives who could have been harmed," she says. Therefore, she chose her husband's country, Japan, as the setting of her stories—specifically, late 16th-century Japan because it was "rich ground for conflict."

After the Cultural Revolution, when Namioka felt "safe," she wrote about the Chinese-American immigrant experience in *Yang the Youngest and His Terrible Ear*, which is based on her own childhood experience. Namioka's latest book, set in Japan, is her seventh book about the two samurai Zenta and Matsuzo. She has received awards for several of these books.

OTHER WORKS *White Serpent Castle, Valley of the Broken Cherry Trees, Phantom of Tiger Mountain, Who's Hu?* Extended Reading

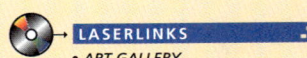
• ART GALLERY

106 UNIT ONE PART 2: FOOLED BY APPEARANCES

WHAT DO YOU THINK?
Reflecting on Theme

Ask students to look back at the skits they developed before they began reading the selections in Part 2. The point of the skits was to show that people and things aren't always what they seem. Ask students to compare their thoughts then to their thoughts now about how appearances can be deceiving. Have them write a brief paragraph explaining how their thoughts about this topic have changed.

PREVIEWING

FICTION

Collecting Team
Robert Silverberg

PERSONAL CONNECTION Activating Prior Knowledge/Setting a Purpose

The story you are about to read involves travel to distant planets and suggests the idea of life beyond our solar system. Some people believe there is life elsewhere in the universe. What do you think? Discuss your thoughts with the class.

Building Background
LITERARY CONNECTION

On Halloween Eve in 1938, thousands of people panicked when a radio broadcast announced a Martian invasion of New Jersey. One woman nearly committed suicide when she learned of the alien attack. Rather than a news report, however, listeners had actually heard a science fiction radio play produced by Orson Welles and based on H.G. Wells's novel *The War of the Worlds*.

Modern **science fiction**—stories about real or imagined scientific developments—emerged during the late 1800s with the works of H. G. Wells and Jules Verne. At this time, advancements in science and technology were occurring rapidly and having a significant effect on the development of science fiction. Verne's novel *From the Earth to the Moon,* written in 1863, describes a moon launch with surprising scientific accuracy. He was one of the first writers to draw attention to science fiction as a distinct branch of literature.

Setting a Purpose
WRITING CONNECTION

Suppose that there were living creatures on other planets. How frightening would they be? Use your imagination to write a brief description of such a creature in your notebook. Add a sketch of the creature and share it with classmates if you wish. Then read to see how Silverberg's tale of alien life compares to your mental image.

Orson Welles performs in one of his radio productions during the 1930s. Archive Photos.

LASERLINKS
• LITERARY CONNECTION

OVERVIEW

Objectives

- To understand and appreciate a short story in the science fiction genre about humans collecting alien zoo specimens
- To identify the climax of a story
- To appreciate the writer's use of idiom
- To express understanding of the story through a choice of writing forms including an episode, log entries, and a science journal entry
- To extend understanding of the story through a variety of multimodal and cross-curricular activities

Skills

READING SKILLS/STRATEGIES
- Visualizing

THE WRITER'S STYLE
- Stating ideas clearly

GRAMMAR
- Adjectives

SPEAKING, LISTENING, AND VIEWING
- Scientific observation
- Group discussion
- Oral presentation

LITERARY CONCEPTS
- Irony
- Allusion
- Climax

GENRE STUDY
- Science fiction

SPELLING
- Words ending in *al* + *ly*

Cross-Curricular Connections

SCIENCE
- The branches of zoology
- Ecological systems
- Animal classification

 **LITERARY CONNECTION**
The History of Science Fiction
These images will acquaint students with the extensive history of science fiction in books and movies.

Side A, Frame 8764

PRINT AND MEDIA RESOURCES

UNIT ONE RESOURCE BOOK
Strategic Reading: Literature, p. 57
Vocabulary SkillBuilder, p. 60
Reading SkillBuilder, p. 58
Spelling SkillBuilder, p. 59

GRAMMAR MINI-LESSONS
Transparencies, pp. 12, 13, 14, 39
Copymasters, pp. 19, 20, 22

WRITING MINI-LESSONS
Transparencies, p. 45

ACCESS FOR STUDENTS ACQUIRING ENGLISH
Selection Summaries
Reading and Writing Support

FORMAL ASSESSMENT
Selection Test, pp. 21–22
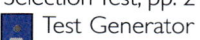 Test Generator

AUDIO LIBRARY
See Reference Card

LASERLINKS
Literary Connection

INTERNET RESOURCES
McDougal Littell Literature Center at http://www.hmco.com/mcdougal/lit

SUMMARY

Three men—the pilot and narrator, Gus, and the zoologists Lee Davison and Clyde Holdreth—are on a space mission to collect alien animal specimens for a research bureau on Earth. They land on an uncharted planet teeming with a variety of animal life. After capturing a few specimens, the men are unable to leave because the ship is repeatedly and mysteriously sabotaged. They discover that they have landed on a planet that is an interstellar zoo. They have been added to the collection of the zoo's alien owners.

Thematic Link: *Fooled by Appearances*
Although the pilot and the zoologists believe they are successfully collecting alien life forms, in reality the men themselves have been captured as specimens for an alien zoo, along with the animal life they think they've been collecting.

CUSTOMIZING FOR
Students Acquiring English

- Use **ACCESS FOR STUDENTS ACQUIRING ENGLISH**, Reading and Writing Support.
- This selection may prove difficult because of the use of scientific or fantasy-based language, such as "acceleration cradles." Reassure students that science fiction often uses made-up words.
- In addition to these boxes, you may want to use the suggestions under Strategic Reading for Less-Proficient Readers.

STRATEGIC READING FOR
Less-Proficient Readers

Set a Purpose To help students become immersed in the story, have them discuss missions in space and the various reasons people might explore the universe, such as investigating other planets to colonize or searching for new life forms. Then invite them to read to find out the crew's mission.

Use **UNIT ONE RESOURCE BOOK**, p. 57, for guidance in reading the selection.

COLLECTING TEAM
by Robert Silverberg

Return from the Stars, Gregory Manchess. Copyright © Gregory Manchess.

108 UNIT ONE PART 2: FOOLED BY APPEARANCES

WORDS TO KNOW

blithe (blĭth) *adj.* showing a lack of concern; casual (p. 111)
bonanza (bə-năn′zə) *n.* source of great wealth (p. 110)
ecologically (ĕk′ə-lŏj′ĭ-klē) *adv.* having to do with the biological relationships between organisms and their environment (p. 111)
futile (fyo͞ot′l) *adj.* having no useful result; useless (p. 109)
hodgepodge (hŏj′pŏj) *n.* a mixture of unlike ingredients; a jumble (p. 113)

nebulous (nĕb′yə-ləs) *adj.* not clear or definite; vague (p. 113)
preliminaries (prĭ-lĭm′ə-nĕr′ēz) *n.* preparations for the main matter, action, or business (p. 114)
preposterous (prĭ-pŏs′tər-əs) *adj.* contrary to nature; absurd (p. 110)
repress (rĭ-prĕs′) *v.* to keep down or hold back (p. 109)
sabotaged (săb′ə-täzhd′) *adj.* harmed with the purpose of producing failure or damage **sabotage** *v.* (p. 113)

108 THE LANGUAGE OF LITERATURE TEACHER'S EDITION

From fifty thousand miles up, the situation looked promising. It was a middle-sized, brown-and-green, inviting-looking planet, with no sign of cities or any other such complications. Just a pleasant sort of place, the very sort we were looking for to redeem what had been a pretty <u>futile</u> expedition.

I turned to Clyde Holdreth, who was staring reflectively at the thermocouple.

"Well? What do you think?"

"Looks fine to me. Temperature's about seventy down there—nice and warm, and plenty of air. I think it's worth a try."

Lee Davison came strolling out from the storage hold, smelling of animals, as usual. He was holding one of the blue monkeys we picked up on Alpheraz, and the little beast was crawling up his arm. "Have we found something, gentlemen?"

"We've found a planet," I said. "How's the storage space in the hold?"

"Don't worry about that. We've got room for a whole zooful more before we get filled up. It hasn't been a very fruitful trip."

"No," I agreed. "It hasn't. Well? Shall we go down and see what's to be seen?"

"Might as well," Holdreth said. "We can't go back to Earth with just a couple of blue monkeys and some anteaters, you know."

"I'm in favor of a landing too," said Davison. "You?"

I nodded. "I'll set up the charts, and you get your animals comfortable for deceleration."

Davison disappeared back into the storage hold, while Holdreth scribbled furiously in the logbook, writing down the coordinates of the planet below, its general description, and so forth. Aside from being a collecting team for the zoological department of the Bureau of Interstellar Affairs, we also double as a survey ship, and the planet down below was listed as *unexplored* on our charts.

I glanced out at the mottled brown-and-green ball spinning slowly in the view port and felt the warning twinge of gloom that came to me every time we made a landing on a new and strange world. <u>Repressing</u> it, I started to figure out a landing orbit. From behind me came the furious chatter of the blue monkeys as Davison strapped them into their acceleration cradles, and under that the deep, unmusical honking of the Rigelian anteaters, noisily bleating their displeasure.

The planet was inhabited, all right. We hadn't had the ship on the ground more than a minute before the local fauna[1] began to congregate. We stood at the view port and looked out in wonder.

"This is one of those things you dream about," Davison said, stroking his little beard nervously. "Look at them! There must be a thousand different species out there."

"I've never seen anything like it," said Holdreth.

I computed how much storage space we had left and how many of the thronging creatures outside we would be able to bring back with us. "How are we going to decide what to take and what to leave behind?"

"Does it matter?" Holdreth said gaily. "This is what you call an embarrassment of riches, I guess. We just grab the dozen most bizarre creatures and blast off—and save the rest for another trip. It's too bad we wasted all that time wandering around near Rigel."

"We *did* get the anteaters," Davison pointed

---

1. **fauna** (fô′nə): animals of a particular region.

| WORDS TO KNOW | **futile** (fyōōt′l) *adj.* having no useful result; useless
repress (rĭ-prĕs′) *v.* to keep down or hold back |

109

STRATEGIC READING FOR
Less-Proficient Readers

B Have students identify the purpose of the spacecraft's mission. *(To find and collect new animals from space and survey unknown planets)* Summarizing

- How does the mission of the spacecraft explain why the characters are so excited? *(The number and uniqueness of the animals on this planet mean their mission to collect new animals will be a success.)* Drawing Conclusions

Set a Purpose Have students read to see what it is about the planet's habitats that Gus seems to find noteworthy.

CUSTOMIZING FOR
Students Acquiring English

2 If students are unfamiliar with the phrase *whole kit and caboodle*, help them use context clues to find the meaning. *(Davison wants to take everything back to Earth.)*

3 Encourage a volunteer to define *on the level*. *(without deception; honest)* Invite several students to use the phrase in a sentence. *(For example: Rashad is on the level about his travels to Siberia.)* Have students discuss whether they think that things are on the level at this point in the story.

Active Reading: PREDICT

C Point out to students that Gus is uneasy about the planet, given its unusual variety of wildlife. Ask students to predict what might happen, keeping Gus's suspicions in mind. *(Possible responses: The animals seem cooperative now, but they might end up turning on the crew; some other species the crew has yet to encounter will attack and harm the crew.)*

---

out. They were his find, and he was proud of them.

I smiled sourly. "Yeah. We got the anteaters there." The anteaters honked at that moment, loud and clear. "You know, that's one set of beasts I think I could do without."

"Bad attitude," Holdreth said. "Unprofessional."

"Whoever said I was a zoologist, anyway? I'm just a spaceship pilot, remember. And if I don't like the way those anteaters talk—and smell—I see no reason why I—"

"Say, look at that one," Davison said suddenly.

I glanced out the view port and saw a new beast emerging from the thick-packed vegetation in the background. I've seen some fairly strange creatures since I was assigned to the zoological department, but this one took the grand prize.

It was about the size of a giraffe, moving on long, wobbly legs and with a tiny head up at the end of a <u>preposterous</u> neck. Only it had six legs and a bunch of writhing snakelike tentacles as well, and its eyes, great violet globes, stood out nakedly on the ends of two thick stalks. It must have been twenty feet high. It moved with exaggerated grace through the swarm of beasts surrounding our ship, pushed its way smoothly toward the vessel, and peered gravely in at the view port. One purple eye stared directly at me, the other at Davison. Oddly, it seemed to me as if it were trying to tell us something.

"Big one, isn't it?" Davison said finally. "I'll bet you'd like to bring one back, too."

"Maybe we can fit a young one aboard," Davison said. "If we can find a young one." He turned to Holdreth. "How's that air analysis coming? I'd like to get out there and start collecting. God, that's a crazy-looking beast!"

The animal outside had apparently finished its inspection of us, for it pulled its head away and, gathering its legs under itself, squatted near the ship. A small doglike creature with stiff spines running along its back began to bark at the big creature, which took no notice. The other animals, which came in all shapes and sizes, continued to mill around the ship, evidently very curious about the newcomer to their world. I could see Davison's eyes thirsty with the desire to take the whole kit and caboodle back to Earth with him. I knew what was running through his mind. He was dreaming of the umpteen thousand species of extraterrestrial wildlife roaming around out there, and to each one he was attaching a neat little tag: *Something-or-other davisoni.*

"The air's fine," Holdreth announced abruptly, looking up from his test tubes. "Get your butterfly nets, and let's see what we can catch."

There was something I didn't like about the place. It was just too good to be true, and I learned long ago that nothing ever is. There's always a catch someplace.

Only this seemed to be on the level. The planet was a <u>bonanza</u> for zoologists, and Davison and Holdreth were having the time

WORDS TO KNOW	**preposterous** (prĭ-pŏs′tər-əs) *adj.* contrary to nature; absurd **bonanza** (bə-năn′zə) *n.* source of great wealth

110

Mini-Lesson — Grammar

EXAMPLE Types of Adjectives		
What Kind	**How Many**	**Which One(s)**
long, tiny	six, two	its, our

ADJECTIVES Remind students that adjectives modify nouns or pronouns. Adjectives are used to tell
- what kind (*beautiful* colors)
- how many (*many* animals)
- which one (*my* computer)
- which ones (*those* giraffes)

Explain to students that *my* (a possessive pronoun) and *those* (a demonstrative pronoun) function as adjectives here.

Application Have students make a list of the adjectives in the  highlighted paragraph on page 110. Then have them organize their lists under the appropriate headings of "what kind," "how many," or "which one(s)" as shown in the example.

Reteaching/Reinforcement
- *Grammar Handbook,* anthology p. 878
- *Grammar Mini-Lessons* copymasters pp. 19, 20, 22, transparencies pp. 12, 13, 14, 39

The Writer's Craft
Adjectives, pp. 507–10, 696

of their lives, hip deep in obliging specimens.

"I've never seen anything like it," Davison said for at least the fiftieth time as he scooped up a small purplish squirrel-like creature and examined it curiously. The squirrel stared back, examining Davison just as curiously.

"Let's take some of these," Davison said. "I like them."

"Carry 'em on in, then," I said, shrugging. I didn't care which specimens they chose, so long as they filled up the storage hold quickly and let me blast off on schedule. I watched as Davison grabbed a pair of the squirrels and brought them into the ship.

Holdreth came over to me. He was carrying a sort of dog with insect-faceted[2] eyes and gleaming furless skin. "How's this one, Gus?"

THE PLANET WAS TOO FLATLY INCREDIBLE FOR ME TO ACCEPT AT FACE VALUE.

"Fine," I said bleakly. "Wonderful."

He put the animal down—it didn't scamper away, just sat there smiling at us—and looked at me. He ran a hand through his fast-vanishing hair. "Listen, Gus, you've been gloomy all day. What's eating you?"

"I don't like this place," I said.

"Why? Just on general principles?"

"It's too *easy*, Clyde. Much too easy. These animals just flock around here waiting to be picked up."

Holdreth chuckled. "And you're used to a struggle, aren't you? You're just angry at us because we have it so simple here!"

"When I think of the trouble we went through just to get a pair of miserable vile-smelling anteaters, and—"

"Come off it, Gus. We'll load up in a hurry if you like. But this place is a zoological gold mine!"

I shook my head. "I don't like it, Clyde. Not at all."

Holdreth laughed again and picked up his faceted-eyed dog. "Say, know where I can find another of these, Gus?"

"Right over there," I said, pointing. "By that tree. With its tongue hanging out. It's just waiting to be carried away."

Holdreth looked and smiled. "What do you know about that!" He snared his specimen and carried both of them inside.

I walked away to survey the grounds. The planet was too flatly incredible for me to accept at face value, without at least a look-see, despite the blithe way my two companions were snapping up specimens.

For one thing, animals just don't exist this way—in big miscellaneous quantities, living all together happily. I hadn't noticed more than a few of each kind, and there must have been five hundred different species, each one stranger looking than the next. Nature doesn't work that way.

For another, they all seemed to be on friendly terms with one another, though they acknowledged the unofficial leadership of the giraffelike creature. Nature doesn't work *that* way, either. I hadn't seen one quarrel between the animals yet. That argued that they were all herbivores,[3] which didn't make sense ecologically.

I shrugged my shoulders and walked on.

---

2. **insect-faceted:** having eyes like insects, with many simple eyes functioning together.
3. **herbivores** (hûr′bə-vôrz): grass-eating and plant-eating animals.

| WORDS TO KNOW | **blithe** (blīth) *adj.* showing a lack of concern; casual
ecologically (ĕk′ə-lŏj′ĭ-kə-lē) *adv.* having to do with the biological relationships between organisms and their environment |

111

STRATEGIC READING FOR
Less-Proficient Readers

F Point out to students that Gus notices nearly every imaginable habitat as existing on the planet. Ask them what is noteworthy about this fact. *(Possible response: The great variety of habitats exist in a very small area. Students might say that only a very large land mass would have many habitats, which backs up Gus's uneasiness about the planet.)* **Drawing Conclusions**

Set a Purpose Have students continue reading to find out what happens to the crew's spacecraft.

Critical Thinking:
SPECULATING

G This is the second time that Gus believes the giraffe is trying to communicate with him. Have students speculate on what the giraffe is trying to tell him. *(Possible responses: The giraffe is warning him about an impending danger. As the leader of the animals, the giraffe is asking the pilot not to capture additional animals.)*

Half an hour later, I knew a little more about the geography of our bonanza. We were on either an immense island or a peninsula of some sort, because I could see a huge body of water bordering the land some ten miles off. Our vicinity was fairly flat, except for a good-sized hill from which I could see the terrain.

There was a thick, heavily wooded jungle not too far from the ship. The forest spread out all the way toward the water in one direction but ended abruptly in the other. We had brought the ship down right at the edge of the clearing. Apparently most of the animals we saw lived in the jungle.

On the other side of our clearing was a low, broad plain that seemed to trail away into a desert in the distance; I could see an uninviting stretch of barren sand that contrasted strangely with the fertile jungle to my left. There was a small lake to the side. It was, I saw, the sort of country likely to attract a varied fauna, since there seemed to be every sort of habitat within a small area.

And the fauna! Although I'm a zoologist only by osmosis,[4] picking up both my interest and my knowledge secondhand from Holdreth and Davison, I couldn't help but be astonished by the wealth of strange animals. They came in all different shapes and sizes, colors and odors, and the only thing they all had in common was their friendliness. During the course of my afternoon's wanderings a hundred animals must have come marching boldly right up to me, given me the once-over, and walked away. This included half a dozen kinds that I hadn't seen before, plus one of the eye-stalked, intelligent-looking giraffes and a furless dog. Again, I had the feeling that the giraffe seemed to be trying to communicate.

I didn't like it. I didn't like it at all.

I returned to our clearing and saw Holdreth and Davison still buzzing madly around, trying to cram as many animals as they could into our hold.

"How's it going?" I asked.

"Hold's all full," Davison said. "We're busy making our alternate selections now." I saw him carrying out Holdreth's two furless dogs and picking up instead a pair of eight-legged penguinish things that uncomplainingly allowed themselves to be carried in. Holdreth was frowning unhappily.

"What do you want *those* for, Lee? Those doglike ones seem much more interesting, don't you think?"

"No," Davison said, "I'd rather bring along these two. They're curious beasts, aren't they? Look at the muscular network that connects the—"

"Hold it, fellows," I said. I peered at the animal in Davison's hands and glanced up. "This *is* a curious beast," I said. "It's got eight legs."

"You becoming a zoologist?" Holdreth asked, amused.

---

4. **osmosis** (ŏz-mō′ sĭs): a gradual process of absorption.

Mini-Lesson — **Reading Skills/Strategies**

VISUALIZING Explain that visualizing is the process of forming a mental picture from a written description. Good readers use details supplied by the writer to picture in their minds characters, settings, and events. These "mental pictures" allow readers to understand and experience the action of the story.

Application Have students make a mental picture of two of the following:
- the pilot
- a crew member
- an animal in the ship's hold
- an animal on the planet
- a habitat found on the planet

After creating their mental pictures, encourage students to share their images with a classmate, either by writing a descriptive paragraph or by making a sketch of their composite image.

Reteaching/Reinforcement
- *Unit One Resource Book,* p. 58

---

112 THE LANGUAGE OF LITERATURE TEACHER'S EDITION

"No—but I am getting puzzled. Why should this one have eight legs, some of the others here six, and some of the others only four?"

They looked at me blankly, with the scorn of professionals.

"I mean, there ought to be some sort of logic to evolution here, shouldn't there? On Earth we've developed a four-legged pattern of animal life; on Venus, they usually run to six legs. But have you ever seen an evolutionary hodgepodge like this place before?"

"There are stranger setups," Holdreth said. "The symbiotes[5] on Sirius Three, the burrowers of Mizar—but you're right, Gus. This *is* a peculiar evolutionary dispersal.[6] I think we ought to stay and investigate it fully."

Instantly I knew from the bright expression on Davison's face that I had blundered, had made things worse than ever. I decided to take a new tack.

"I don't agree," I said. "I think we ought to leave with what we've got and come back with a larger expedition later."

Davison chuckled. "Come on, Gus, don't be silly! This is a chance of a lifetime for us—why should we call in the whole zoological department on it?"

I didn't want to tell them I was afraid of staying longer. I crossed my arms. "Lee, I'm the pilot of this ship, and you'll have to listen to me. The schedule calls for a brief stopover here, and we have to leave. Don't tell me I'm being silly."

"But you are, man! You're standing blindly in the path of scientific investigation, of—"

"Listen to me, Lee. Our food is calculated on a pretty narrow margin, to allow you fellows more room for storage. And this is strictly a collecting team. There's no provision for extended stays on any one planet. Unless you want to wind up eating your own specimens, I suggest you allow us to get out of here."

They were silent for a moment. Then Holdreth said, "I guess we can't argue with that, Lee. Let's listen to Gus and go back now. There's plenty of time to investigate this place later, when we can take longer."

"But—oh, all right," Davison said reluctantly. He picked up the eight-legged penguins. "Let me stash these things in the hold, and we can leave." He looked strangely at me, as if I had done something criminal.

As he started into the ship, I called to him. "What is it, Gus?"

"Look here, Lee. I don't *want* to pull you away from here. It's simply a matter of food," I lied, masking my nebulous suspicions.

"I know how it is, Gus." He turned and entered the ship.

I stood there thinking about nothing at all for a moment, then went inside myself to begin setting up the blastoff orbit.

I got as far as calculating the fuel expenditure when I noticed something. Feed wires were dangling crazily down from the control cabinet. Somebody had wrecked our drive mechanism, but thoroughly.

For a long moment, I stared stiffly at the sabotaged drive. Then I turned and headed into the storage hold.

"Davison?"

"What is it, Gus?"

"Come out here a second, will you?"

---

5. **symbiotes** (sĭm′bē-ōts): organisms that live very close together and depend on one another for survival.
6. **evolutionary dispersal:** distribution or pattern according to the laws of evolution.

WORDS TO KNOW	**hodgepodge** (hŏj′pŏj) *n.* a mixture of unlike ingredients; a jumble
	nebulous (nĕb′yə-ləs) *adj.* not clear or definite; vague
	sabotaged (săb′ə-täzhd) *adj.* harmed with the purpose of producing failure or damage **sabotage** *v.*

113

Active Reading: CLARIFY

H Ask students what makes the evolutionary pattern of animals on this planet unique. You may wish to use the following model to give them ideas of what they might be thinking about.

Think-Aloud Model *I think that what makes these animals unique is that the number of legs they have varies widely. This goes against patterns of evolution on Earth.*

Literary Concept: CONFLICT

I Ask students to identify the source of conflict between the pilot and his crew. *(Possible response: The pilot thinks that the docility of the animals is too good to be true, so he wants to leave as soon as possible before anything bad happens. The crew thinks the pilot is being too cautious and is preventing them from successfully completing their mission.)* How is this conflict temporarily resolved? *(When the pilot manages to fool the crew into believing they do not have enough food to continue on the planet, the crew reluctantly agree to put their personal safety before science.)*

Mini-Lesson Study Skills

USING THE LIBRARY Encourage students to investigate the resources in their school and local libraries. Point out that many libraries now offer videotapes, artwork, compact discs, photographs, laser discs, and computers. To help make the library more accessible, have students locate the sections of the library listed in the checklist shown.

Application After students have completed their checklists, have them select one of the sections listed to use as a resource to complete any of the research activities suggested on page 121.

CHECKLIST

___ **The Stacks** are where nonfiction and fiction books are shelved.

___ **Catalogs and Indexes** may be found on file cards or computers; they tell where to find a book or magazine.

___ **Reference** materials include encyclopedias, atlases, and other resources.

___ **Periodicals** are the library's magazines, journals and newspapers.

___ **Audio-visual** resources may include audiotapes, records, videotapes, films, CD's, and videodiscs.

___ The **Children/Young Adult** area is a special section for materials specifically for children and teenagers.

THE LANGUAGE OF LITERATURE TEACHER'S EDITION 113

Literary Concept: SUSPENSE

J Remind students that suspense is the growing tension or excitement felt by a reader. Writers create suspense by raising questions in the reader's mind about what might happen in the plot. Ask students how Silverberg creates added suspense in this part of the story. (Possible response: After the pilot and crew argue about whether to stay or leave the planet, the drive mechanism of the spacecraft is found to be sabotaged. None of the crew members admits to having done the damage, which adds suspense to the story.)

Critical Thinking: MAKING JUDGMENTS

K Have students discuss whether the pilot takes adequate precautions to protect himself and the crew after the sabotage. (Possible responses: The pilot is doing all he can to get the ship repaired without alarming the other crew members more than he needs to; the pilot is not taking the fact of the damaged drive mechanism seriously enough.)

CUSTOMIZING FOR
Students Acquiring English

4 The use of scientific jargon can make science fiction difficult. In this case, *lead, input, transistor,* and *potentiometer* are all components in an electrical circuit. Reassure students that knowing exactly what these are is not necessary to understanding the story.

I waited, and a few minutes later he appeared, frowning impatiently. "What do you want, Gus? I'm busy and I—" His mouth dropped open. *"Look at the drive!"*

"You look at it," I snapped. "I'm sick. Go get Holdreth, on the double."

While he was gone, I tinkered with the shattered mechanism. Once I had the cabinet panel off and could see the inside, I felt a little better; the drive wasn't damaged beyond repair, though it had been pretty well scrambled. Three or four days of hard work with a screwdriver and solder beam[7] might get the ship back into functioning order.

But that didn't make me any less angry. I heard Holdreth and Davison entering behind me, and I whirled to face them.

"All right, you idiots. Which one of you did this?"

They opened their mouths in protesting squawks at the same instant. I listened to them for a while, then said, "One at a time!"

"If you're implying that one of us deliberately sabotaged the ship," Holdreth said, "I want you to know—"

"I'm not implying anything. But the way it looks to me, you two decided you'd like to stay here a while longer to continue your investigations and figured the easiest way of getting me to agree was to wreck the drive." I glared hotly at them. "Well, I've got news for you. I can fix this, and I can fix it in a couple of days. So go on—get about your business! Get all the zoologizing you can in, while you still have time. I—"

Davison laid a hand gently on my arm. "Gus," he said quietly, *"we didn't do it.* Neither of us."

Suddenly all the anger drained out of me and was replaced by raw fear. I could see that Davison meant it.

"If you didn't do it, and Holdreth didn't do it, and *I* didn't do it—then who did?"

Davison shrugged.

"Maybe it's one of us who doesn't know he's doing it," I suggested. "Maybe—" I stopped. "Oh, that's nonsense. Hand me that tool kit, will you, Lee?"

They left to tend to the animals, and I set to work on the repair job, dismissing all further speculations and suspicions from my mind, concentrating solely on joining Lead A to Input A and Transistor F to Potentiometer K, as indicated. It was slow, nerve-harrowing work, and by mealtime I had accomplished only the barest preliminaries. My fingers were starting to quiver from the strain of small-scale work, and I decided to give up the job for the day and get back to it tomorrow.

I slept uneasily, my nightmares punctuated by the moaning of the accursed anteaters and the occasional squeals, chuckles, bleats, and hisses of the various other creatures in the hold. It must have been four in the morning before I dropped off into a really sound sleep, and what was left of the night passed swiftly. The next thing I knew, hands were shaking me, and I was looking up into the pale, tense faces of Holdreth and Davison.

I pushed my sleep-stuck eyes open and blinked. "Huh? What's going on?"

Holdreth leaned down and shook me savagely. "Get up, Gus!"

I struggled to my feet slowly. "Hell of a thing to do, wake a fellow up in the middle of the—"

I found myself being propelled from my cabin and led down the corridor to the control room. Blearily, I followed where Holdreth pointed, and then I woke up in a hurry.

---

7. **solder** (sŏd′ər) **beam**: an imaginary device used to repair wiring.

WORDS TO KNOW
preliminaries (prĭ-lĭm′ə-nĕr′ēz) *n.* preparations for the main matter, action, or business

114

 Mini-Lesson The Writer's Style

STATING IDEAS CLEARLY Explain to students that in order to state their ideas clearly, writers should avoid padding sentences with unnecessary words that may confuse or mislead the reader.

Application Point out to students that the author of "Collecting Team," while often using long and complex sentences, does not pad his writing with extraneous or irrelevant information. Have the students revise the following padded sentence by crossing out excess details, words, and phrases.

1. It would seem that the other animals were tranquil, placid, and more or less peaceful when the pilot and the crew all tried to capture them near where their spaceship was. (~~It would seem that~~ The other animals were ~~tranquil, placid, and more or less~~ peaceful when the pilot and the crew ~~all~~ tried to capture them near ~~where~~ their spaceship ~~was~~.)

Reteaching/Reinforcement
• *Writing Mini-Lessons* transparencies, p. 45

 The Writer's Craft

Padded Sentences, pp. 300–301

---

114 THE LANGUAGE OF LITERATURE **Teacher's Edition**

The drive was battered again. Someone—or *something*—had completely undone my repair job of the night before.

If there had been bickering among us, it stopped. This was past the category of a joke now; it couldn't be laughed off, and we found ourselves working together as a tight unit again, trying desperately to solve the puzzle before it was too late.

"Let's review the situation," Holdreth said, pacing nervously up and down the control cabin. "The drive has been sabotaged twice. None of us knows who did it, and on a conscious level each of us is convinced *he* didn't do it."

He paused. "That leaves us with two possibilities. Either, as Gus suggested, one of us is doing it unaware of it even himself, or someone else is doing it while we're not looking. Neither possibility is a very cheerful one."

"We can stay on guard, though," I said. "Here's what I propose: first, have one of us awake at all times—sleep in shifts, that is, with somebody guarding the drive until I get it fixed. Two—jettison[8] all the animals aboard ship."

"What?"

"He's right," Davison said. "We don't know what we may have brought aboard. They don't seem to be intelligent, but we can't be sure. That purple-eyed baby giraffe, for instance—suppose he's been hypnotizing us into damaging the drive ourselves. How can we tell?"

"Oh, but—" Holdreth started to protest, then stopped and frowned soberly. "I suppose we'll have to admit the possibility," he said, obviously unhappy about the prospect of freeing our captives. "We'll empty out the hold, and you see if you can get the drive fixed. Maybe later we'll recapture them all if nothing further develops."

We agreed to that, and Holdreth and Davison cleared the ship of its animal cargo while I set to work determinedly at the drive mechanism. By nightfall, I had managed to accomplish as much as I had the day before.

THE EXPEDITION HAD TURNED INTO A NIGHTMARE.

I sat up as watch the first shift, aboard the strangely quiet ship. I paced around the drive cabin, fighting the great temptation to doze off, and managed to last through until the time Holdreth arrived to relieve me.

Only—when he showed up, he gasped and pointed at the drive. It had been ripped apart a third time.

Now we had no excuse, no explanation. The expedition had turned into a nightmare.

I could only protest that I had remained awake my entire spell on duty and that I had seen no one and no thing approach the drive panel. But that was hardly a satisfactory explanation, since it either cast guilt on me as the saboteur or implied that some unseen external power was repeatedly wrecking the drive. Neither hypothesis made sense, at least to me.

By now we had spent four days on the planet, and food was getting to be a major problem. My carefully budgeted flight schedule called for us to be two days out on our return journey to Earth by now. But we still were no closer to departure than we had been four days ago.

The animals continued to wander around outside, nosing up against the ship, examining it, almost fondling it, with those damned pseudo-giraffes[9] staring soulfully at us always. The beasts were as friendly as ever, little

---

8. **jettison:** to cast overboard or off.
9. **pseudo-giraffes** (sōō′dō): false giraffes in the sense that they look something like, but are not, the giraffes found on Earth.

COLLECTING TEAM **115**

Mini-Lesson: Speaking, Listening, and Viewing

SCIENTIFIC OBSERVATION Explain to students that making detailed observations and accurately reporting what they observe is an important skill in many professions, particularly science. Point out that noting an observation is only the first step. In order to be effective, students must also analyze and interpret their information to decide which details are relevant and which can be discarded.

Application At the opening of the story, we are told that "Holdreth scribbled furiously in the logbook, writing down the coordinates of the planet below, its general description, and so forth." The scientists also probably keep records of the mission. Have students work in groups of five or six. Using details from the story, have each member make a list of what he or she feels are the relevant details about the animals on the planet. Each group should review and compare student lists to compile a log of scientific data, which can be written by the group's recorder. Then have groups compare their logs. What details did every group decide were important? Were there any details the group left out or could have eliminated?

CUSTOMIZING FOR
Students Acquiring English

6 Explain that *knock off* is an expression meaning "to stop doing something." Ask students if the narrator slept on this night. *(no)* Why or why not? *(He was keeping watch to be sure the drive wasn't destroyed again.)*

Active Reading: CONNECT

N Ask students if they have ever been in a situation that they felt they could not change. Did they give up and accept the situation as Gus did, or did they try to discover alternatives as Holdreth did?

Literary Concept: ALLUSION

O Remind students that an allusion is a reference to a famous person, place, event, or other work of literature. Have students explain how the allusion to manna relates to the action of the story. *(Possible response: The reference to manna is an allusion to a biblical story where manna fell from the sky to feed the starving Israelites. It seems appropriate that the team should find manna at the same time that they are desperate for food.)*

Critical Thinking: MAKING JUDGMENTS

P The pilot and crew have been on the planet for eight days and are already very thin and hungry. Have students decide how desperate the crew's situation is. *(Possible responses: Their situation is very desperate because one cannot go much longer than eight days without food before getting seriously ill; their situation is not that desperate because the space agency they work for will probably send a rescue party, or they will start to eat some of the animals on the planet.)*

---

knowing how the tension was growing within the hull. The three of us walked around like zombies, eyes bright and lips clamped. We were scared—all of us.

Something was keeping us from fixing the drive.

Something didn't want us to leave this planet.

I looked at the bland face of the purple-eyed giraffe staring through the view port, and it stared mildly back at me. Around it was grouped the rest of the local fauna, the same incredible hodgepodge of improbable genera[10] and species.

That night, the three of us stood guard in the control room together. The drive was smashed anyway. The wires were soldered in so many places by now that the control panel was a mass of shining alloy, and I knew that a few more such sabotagings and it would be impossible to patch it together anymore—if it wasn't so already.

The next night, I just didn't knock off. I continued soldering right on after dinner (and a pretty skimpy dinner it was, now that we were on close rations) and far on into the night.

By morning, it was as if I hadn't done a thing.

"I give up," I announced, surveying the damage. "I don't see any sense in ruining my nerves trying to fix a thing that won't stay fixed."

Holdreth nodded. He looked terribly pale. "We'll have to find some new approach."

"Yeah. Some new approach."

I yanked open the food closet and examined our stock. Even figuring in the synthetics[11] we would have fed to the animals if we hadn't released them, we were low on food. We had overstayed even the safety margin. It would be a hungry trip back—if we ever did get back.

I clambered through the hatch and sprawled down on a big rock near the ship. One of the furless dogs came over and nuzzled in my shirt. Davison stepped to the hatch and called down to me.

"What are you doing out there, Gus?"

"Just getting a little fresh air. I'm sick of living aboard that ship." I scratched the dog behind his pointed ears and looked around.

The animals had lost most of their curiosity about us and didn't congregate the way they used to. They were meandering all over the plain, nibbling at little deposits of a white doughy substance. It precipitated every night. Manna,[12] we called it. All the animals seemed to live on it.

I folded my arms and leaned back.

We were getting to look awfully lean by the eighth day. I wasn't even trying to fix the ship anymore; the hunger was starting to get me. But I saw Davison puttering around with my solder beam.

"What are you doing?"

"I'm going to repair the drive," he said. "You don't want to, but we can't just sit around, you know." His nose was deep in my repair guide, and he was fumbling with the release on the solder beam.

I shrugged. "Go ahead if you want to." I didn't care what he did. All I cared about was the gaping emptiness in my stomach, and about the dimly grasped fact that somehow we were stuck here for good.

"Gus?"

"Yeah?"

"I think it's time I told you something. I've

---

10. **genera:** plural of *genus*; categories of living organisms that are made up of groups of species with similar traits.
11. **synthetics:** artificial food produced by chemical means.
12. **manna:** in the Bible, the food miraculously provided for the Israelites in the wilderness during their flight from Egypt.

116   UNIT ONE   PART 2: FOOLED BY APPEARANCES

been eating the manna for four days. It's good. It's nourishing stuff."

"You've been eating—the manna? Something that grows on an alien world? You crazy?"

"What else can we do? Starve?"

I smiled feebly, admitting that he was right. From somewhere in the back of the ship came the sounds of Holdreth moving around. Holdreth had taken this thing worse than any of us. He had a family back on Earth, and he was beginning to realize that he wasn't ever going to see them again.

"Why don't you get Holdreth?" Davison suggested. "Go out there and stuff yourselves with the manna. You've got to eat something."

"Yeah. What can I lose?" Moving like a mechanical man, I headed toward Holdreth's cabin. We would go out and eat the manna and cease being hungry, one way or another.

"Clyde?" I called. "Clyde?"

I entered his cabin. He was sitting at his desk, shaking convulsively, staring at the two streams of blood that trickled in red spurts from his slashed wrists.

"Clyde!"

He made no protest as I dragged him toward the infirmary cabin and got tourniquets around his arms, cutting off the bleeding. He just stared dully ahead, sobbing.

I slapped him, and he came around. He shook his head dizzily, as if he didn't know where he was.

"I—I—"

"Easy, Clyde. Everything's all right."

"It's *not* all right," he said hollowly. "I'm still alive. Why didn't you let me die? Why didn't you—"

Davison entered the cabin. "What's been happening, Gus?"

"It's Clyde. The pressure's getting him. He tried to kill himself, but I think he's all right now. Get him something to eat, will you?"

We had Holdreth straightened around by evening. Davison gathered as much of the manna as he could find, and we held a feast.

"I wish we had nerve enough to kill some of the local fauna," Davison said. "Then we'd have a feast—steaks and everything!"

"The bacteria," Holdreth pointed out quietly. "We don't dare."

"I know. But it's a thought."

"No more thoughts," I said sharply. "Tomorrow morning we start work on the drive panel again. Maybe with some food in our bellies we'll be able to keep awake and see what's happening here."

Holdreth smiled. "Good. I can't wait to get out of this ship and back to a normal existence. God, I just can't wait!"

"Let's get some sleep," I said. "Tomorrow we'll give it another try. We'll get back," I said with a confidence I didn't feel.

The following morning I rose early and got my tool kit. My head was clear, and I was trying to put the pieces together without much luck. I started toward the control cabin.

And stopped.

And looked out the view port.

I went back and awoke Holdreth and Davison. "Take a look out the port," I said hoarsely.

They looked. They gaped.

STRATEGIC READING FOR
Less-Proficient Readers

S Have students explain where the house comes from at the end of the story. *(Possible responses: The house came from the mind of Holdreth, who was thinking of his house on Earth; the house came from the aliens so that the captured crew could live in their "natural" environment as specimens in the zoo.)*

Literary Concept: IRONY

T Ask students to discuss the end of the story. How is the crew's imprisonment ironic? *(The ending of the story is ironic because the purpose of the mission was to gather animal specimens to bring back to Earth. The tables were turned, and the pilot and crew became specimens in an alien zoo.)*

CUSTOMIZING FOR
Gifted and Talented Students

Have students debate the purpose of the space mission. Do the pilot and crew get what they deserve, or should readers sympathize with their situation? Challenge students to apply this debate to our current practices of keeping animals in zoos and using animals for research.

COMPREHENSION CHECK

1. What is the crew excited about when it first lands on the planet? *(the great variety of animal life and the ease with which the crew seems to be able to collect whichever animal specimens they want)*
2. Why do the pilot and crew fight about remaining on the planet? *(The crew wants to stay because of the unique animal specimens; the pilot wants to leave because he doesn't trust the animals' docility and the strange evolutionary patterns.)*
3. Why can't the team leave the planet? *(The drive mechanism of their ship is destroyed.)*
4. What happens to the team at the end of the story? *(They become a permanent exhibit in the alien zoo.)*

"It looks just like my house," Holdreth said. "My house on Earth."

"With all the comforts of home inside, I'll bet." I walked forward uneasily and lowered myself through the hatch. "Let's go look at it."

We approached it, while the animals frolicked around us. The big giraffe came near and shook its head gravely. The house stood in the middle of the clearing, small and neat and freshly painted.

I saw it now. During the night, invisible hands had put it there. Had assembled and built a cozy little Earth-type house and dropped it next to our ship for us to live in.

"Just like my house," Holdreth repeated in wonderment.

"It should be," I said. "They grabbed the model from your mind, as soon as they found out we couldn't live on the ship indefinitely."

Holdreth and Davison asked as one, "What do you mean?"

"You mean you haven't figured this place out yet?" I licked my lips, getting myself used to the fact that I was going to spend the rest of my life here. "You mean you don't realize what this house is intended to be?"

They shook their heads, baffled. I glanced around, from the house to the useless ship to the jungle to the plain to the little pond. It all made sense now.

"They want to keep us happy," I said. "They knew we weren't thriving aboard the ship, so they—they built us something a little more like home."

"*They?* The giraffes?"

"Forget the giraffes. They tried to warn us, but it's too late. They're intelligent beings, but they're prisoners just like us. I'm talking about the ones who run this place. The super-aliens who make us sabotage our own ship and not even know we're doing it, who stand someplace up there and gape at us. The ones who dredged together this motley assortment of beasts from all over the galaxy. Now we've been collected too. This whole damned place is just a zoo—a zoo for aliens so far ahead of us we don't dare dream what they're like."

I looked up at the shimmering blue-green sky, where invisible bars seemed to restrain us, and sank down dismally on the porch of our new home. I was resigned. There wasn't any sense in struggling against *them*.

I could see the neat little placard now:

EARTHMEN. Native Habitat, Sol III. ❖

Mini-Lesson — Spelling

SPELLING WORDS ENDING IN -AL AND -LY Remind students that when adding -ly to a word that ends in al, the word is spelled keeping both l's.

ecological + ly = ecologically
final + ly = finally
geographical + ly = geographically
hypothetical + ly = hypothetically
historical + ly = historically

Application Read the following words aloud. Have students spell the words, adding -ly.

1. physical
2. psychological
3. additional
4. logical
5. theatrical
6. exceptional
7. temporal
8. spatial
9. social
10. numerical

Ask students to look for more words that fit this pattern, in their own writing and in things that they read, and to add these words to their personal word lists.

Reteaching/Reinforcement
• *Unit One Resource Book*, p. 59

HISTORICAL INSIGHT

SPACE EXPLORATION

"Collecting Team" was published just one year before the space age began. It was on October 4, 1957, that space exploration took off, and the line between science fiction and science fact started to blur. The former Soviet Union launched *Sputnik*, the first artificial satellite to orbit the earth, forever changing the relationship between human beings and outer space. This impressive show of scientific might spurred the United States on to launch its first two satellites, *Explorer 1* and *Vanguard 1*, in 1958.

These necessary first steps in the quest for space would eventually lead to the launching of human beings into orbit. Yuri A. Gagarin, a Soviet cosmonaut, was the first human being in space. Gagarin orbited the earth on April 12, 1961. Following him, in 1962, John H. Glenn, Jr., was hailed as the first American to orbit the earth. Then, beginning with Neil A. Armstrong's historic first "small step," U.S. Apollo astronauts explored the surface of the moon six times between 1969 and 1972.

During the 1970s, astronauts and cosmonauts developed technology for living in space aboard the Skylab and Salyut space stations. Between 1983 and 1992, the National Aeronautics and Space Administration (NASA) achieved a number of firsts in the sending of astronauts into space: Sally K. Ride became the first U.S. woman in space; Guion S. Bluford, Jr., the first African American; Marc Garneau, the first Canadian; and Mae C. Jemison, the first African-American woman in space.

The crew of the space shuttle Endeavor on an 8-day mission in 1992. Mae Jemison is on the right.

Researchers are now investigating ways to manufacture products in space, studying the possibility of identifying other intelligent life in the universe, and planning bases to be set up on the moon and Mars. Some scientists are even looking to a time when people might be born, live, and die on space colonies.

HISTORICAL INSIGHT

1. "Collecting Team" was written before humans actually traveled in space. How does Silverberg's vision of space exploration in 1957 compare with yours today? *(Student responses will vary.)*

2. In light of what you know about space exploration, what aspects of "Collecting Team" would you consider to be science fiction, rather than fact? *(Possible responses: The writer's description of alien life forms is still science fiction, because I do not believe that these kinds of aliens and animals exist. In addition, I would consider the super-aliens' powers to be science fiction, because I do not believe that the ability to control someone's mind or to make objects materialize out of thin air are really possible.)*

3. Why do you think space exploration is important? Explain your answer. *(Possible response: Space exploration is important because it is a significant way for us to know more about the universe in which we live. Scientists can learn a great deal more about the earth by studying other planets, stars, and galaxies.)*

4. Do you think space exploration should be a priority in terms of government spending, or should the money that goes to space exploration be budgeted in other ways? Explain your answer. *(Possible responses: Yes, money should continue to be spent on space exploration because our future may very well depend on it. There may come a time when humans will need to colonize other planets, and space exploration will help in making sure this is possible in the future. No, it is more important to spend money to improve the conditions of life here on Earth. We should not be concerned with outer space until we take care of our own problems on Earth.)*

From Personal Response to Critical Analysis

1. Students' responses will vary.
2. Possible responses: Students who agree may say Gus's explanation, that advanced alien beings have taken the crew as specimens for an alien zoo, is entirely reasonable, especially considering the aliens' reading of Holdreth's mind to duplicate his house. Those who disagree might argue that Gus is so tired and hungry that he is blowing all out of proportion the predicament they are in. It could very well be that help will arrive soon.
3. Possible response: Gus has been nervous about the planet all along, so he is the first to notice that he has been fooled. Holdreth and Davison are too excited by everything on the planet to be critical observers.
4. Encourage students to use specific details from the story in developing their pictures.
5. Possible responses: It is unlikely that there is alien life on other planets, so the story is not scary to me at all; I can imagine there being more intelligent life in the universe that would want to capture humans for specimens, so the story really scares me.
6. Possible response: The title is ironic because the men who are sent to collect animals end up being collected themselves.
7. Accept all reasonable responses.

Another Pathway

Have students list their clues in a chart with one column showing the clue and the other column explaining how it links to the story's climax. These lists will make the compiling of a class list easier.

Rubric

3 Full Accomplishment Student's list illustrates understanding of clues and story ending.
2 Substantial Accomplishment Student's list is missing some clues or misreads relationship to ending.
1 Little or Partial Accomplishment Student's list is missing important story clues and misinterprets ending.

RESPONDING OPTIONS

FROM PERSONAL RESPONSE TO CRITICAL ANALYSIS

REFLECT 1. What is your reaction to the ending of the story?

RETHINK 2. How does the narrator, Gus, explain what has happened? Do you agree with him? Why or why not?

Thematic Link 3. Why do you think Gus, rather than Davison or Holdreth, realizes that they have been fooled by appearances?
Consider
Close Textual Reading
- his role in the expedition
- how Gus feels as they land on a new planet
- what he observes while the others collect specimens

4. If you were with the men, what would you do next? Draw a picture that shows what you would do.

5. In your opinion, how frightening is this tale?
Consider
- what events and details are believable
- how your concept of life on other planets compares with that shown in the story

6. What is ironic about the title of the story?

RELATE 7. Just as the team does in this story, people on earth remove animals from their natural habitats for scientific study and for placement in zoos. Do you think both reasons justify the removal of animals? Explain your answer.

ANOTHER PATHWAY

Carefully reread "Collecting Team" and gather clues that hint at how the story ends. Combine your listed clues with those of your classmates to compile a complete list.

QUICKWRITES

1. Gus seems resigned to living in his new home. How do you think Holdreth and Davison feel? What might they do? Write the next **episode** of the story.

2. As the spaceship approaches the planet, Holdreth scribbles what he sees in the ship's logbook, the daily record of data and events. Write a series of **log entries** that reflect highlights of the story.

3. Imagine that you are one of the "super-aliens" who collect the space travelers. Write observations of your specimens in the form of a **science journal entry**.

 PORTFOLIO Save your writing. You may want to use it later as a springboard to a piece for your portfolio.

120 UNIT ONE PART 2: FOOLED BY APPEARANCES

QuickWrites

1. Encourage students to imagine what it would be like to lose all contact with their family and friends forever. Have them identify the role family plays in the different responses of Holdreth and the rest of the men.
2. Explain to students that log entries are relatively short and include only the most important facts. Encourage students to isolate the most important events of the story before writing.
3. Ask students to write detailed observations of the space travelers both before and after they realize they are captured. Remind students that these notes should include observations of physical characteristics and behavioral traits.

The Writer's Craft

Eyewitness Report, pp. 49–61
Chronological Order, pp. 240–41

LITERARY CONCEPTS

The **climax** of a story is the moment at which the action is at a peak, the readers are most interested, and the conflict is resolved. The climax may involve a change, a decision, or a new understanding. At what point do you think the climax of "Collecting Team" occurs? Explain your answer.

Multimodal Learning

ALTERNATIVE ACTIVITIES

1. Make a **diorama** of the planet in the story. Use Gus's descriptions of the geography and animals to create the three-dimensional scene.
2. If this story were made into a movie, what music would you choose as background for the drama? Make an **audiotape** to accompany an oral reading of the story by taping a combination of sound bites from music you select. Have someone read parts of the story aloud as you share your music with the class.
3. The narrator guesses that there are 500 species on the planet. Skim the selection and count how many are referred to. Count the species, not the number of individual animals, and be careful not to include the animals already on the ship. What percentage of the narrator's estimate is this sample? Write an **equation** to show how you arrived at the results.

WRITER'S STYLE

On page 110, Silverberg uses an idiom in the expression "whole kit and caboodle," which means *the entire collection*. An idiom is a phrase or an expression that has a meaning different from what the words usually suggest. Use of such idioms enables Silverberg to create an informal style. Find a couple of other examples of idioms in the story. Then, for these idiomatic phrases, think of other idioms with roughly the same meaning, or invent your own. For example, "the whole shootin' match" has a meaning similar to "whole kit and caboodle."

CRITIC'S CORNER

One student board reviewer, Iruma Bello, said this about the ending of this story: "It would have been better if they could have returned to their home on Earth and gone back with their families." Do you agree with this statement? Give reasons for your opinion.

ACROSS THE CURRICULUM

Science The story tells us that many different animal species would never live together in a real ecosystem. Research ecosystems on the earth to find out exactly what they are and how they function. Then look more closely at the ecological facts in "Collecting Team," and explain what does and does not make sense, considering how ecosystems actually work.

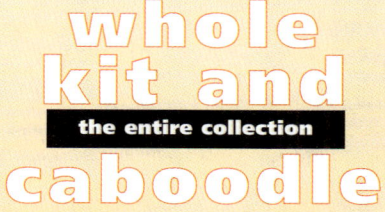

whole kit and caboodle — the entire collection

COLLECTING TEAM 121

Literary Concepts

In order to help students identify the climax of the story, encourage them to think about the dramatic event that affected them the most. Explain to students that there is not necessarily one correct answer here. For this reason encourage them to explain their answers. (*Possible responses: Holdreth's attempted suicide; Gus's realization that they have been collected themselves.*)

Across the Curriculum

Science *Cooperative Learning* Have students work in groups of six. Have one half of the group research ecosystems and their function. The other half can be responsible for examining the ecological facts in the story. Then, as a whole group, they should compare the story to their research in order to assess what elements do or do not make sense. Students may also want to prepare visual aids as part of their research.

ADDITIONAL SUGGESTION
Science *Name Game* Point students to Gus's joke on page 110 about Davison naming each animal species "*Something-or-other davisoni.*" This is a reference to the standard use of two Latin words to classify organisms. The first word is the genus, the second is the species name. For example, the domestic cat is *Felis catus*. Ask students to find the genus names for monkey, anteater, giraffe, dog, and squirrel. Then have them invent the species label that might go with the genus name for each animal in the story, given how it is described in the story. *Giraffa preposteralis* is an example of a name students might invent.

Alternative Activities

1. Explain to students that a diorama is a three-dimensional scene that pictures figures in a natural setting. In creating their diorama, students might create one habitat that the pilot sees, and then put imaginary animals in the diorama to fit the habitat.
2. Invite students to visit their library and check out science fiction soundtracks as sources for their audiotape. Encourage students to make their own music if they cannot find taped music that they like.
3. The species collected on the planet by the team are the squirrel-like creature, the furless dog, and the eight-legged penguin. Students should work out that 3 species out of a total of 500 species is 0.6 percent. ($3/500 \times 100 = 0.6$ percent)

The Writer's Style

Have students record their thoughts in a chart like the one shown. The first column should contain idioms from the story, the second column should contain paraphrases, and the third column should contain an idiom with a similar meaning.

the whole kit and caboodle	everything	the whole shootin' match

Words to Know

1. futile
2. preposterous
3. repress
4. blithe
5. preliminaries
6. sabotaged
7. nebulous
8. hodgepodge
9. bonanza
10. ecologically

The boxed letters spell *furless dog*.

Reteaching/Reinforcement
- *Unit One Resource Book*, p. 60

ROBERT SILVERBERG

Robert Silverberg is a prolific author: at one time he published an average of at least 12 books each year—more than 2 million words. His many nonfiction works deal with such diverse subjects as conservation, history, natural science, and archaeology, including his 1968 classic *Mound Builders of Ancient America: The Archeology of Myth*.

WORDS TO KNOW

Review the Words to Know at the bottom of the selection pages. Identify the word that is most closely related to the situation described in each sentence below. The boxed letters will spell the name of one of the animals in the story.

1. Gus tried again and again to repair the spaceship before giving up. ☐ _ _ _ _ _
2. The space travelers must have looked as silly to the super-aliens as the animals looked to the men. _ _ _ _ _ _ _ _ _ _ ☐ _
3. With food low and the spaceship damaged, Gus could no longer ignore his anxiety. ☐ _ _ _ _ _ _
4. Davison and Holdreth seemed unconcerned about their safety. _ ☐ _ _ _ _
5. The many preparations needed to repair the spaceship took a long time. _ _ ☐ _ _ _ _ _ _ _ _ _
6. Gus suspected that the damage was not accidental but was done on purpose. ☐ _ _ _ _ _ _ _ _
7. Gus did not fully understand his uneasy feelings about the planet. _ _ _ _ _ _ _ ☐
8. The odd mixture of animals was unnatural. _ _ ☐ _ _ _ _ _ _ _
9. The zoologists never expected to find this rich source of animals all in one place. _ ☐ _ _ _ _ _
10. The animal life did not fit Gus's knowledge of how animals live in their environment. _ _ _ _ _ ☐ _ _ _ _ _

ROBERT SILVERBERG

1935–

For over 40 years, Robert Silverberg has produced a great body of varied work, ranging from science fiction to diverse nonfiction topics. Silverberg started preparing for this impressive career at age 6, when he began writing stories in addition to editing his school newspaper. He loved science fiction and wrote his first science fiction tale when he was 12 years old. Silverberg explains, "We worked on it in class, I recall, whispering details of the plot to each other despite our teacher's scowls."

Silverberg has won science fiction's Nebula and Hugo awards and has received more award nominations for his work than any other writer in the field. Silverberg says he writes science fiction stories because "I couldn't not write them. There are plenty of other things I'd rather be doing—tidying up the garden, taking a trip, or just sitting in the sunshine and giggling quietly to myself. But story first, sunshine afterward. I won't allow it to be any other way. I can't."

OTHER WORKS *Nightwings, Lost Race of Mars, Lord Valentine's Castle* Extended Reading

FOCUS ON POETRY

Almost everyone, young or old, knows at least one poem. Poetry is the most compact form of literature, and often the most memorable. A poem packs all kinds of ideas, feelings, and sounds into a few carefully chosen words. The words, the sounds—even the form of a poem—all work together to create a total effect.

FORM The way a poem looks—or its arrangement on the page—is its form. Poetry is written in lines, which may or may not be sentences. Sometimes the lines are combined into groups called **stanzas**. Poets deliberately choose the arrangements of words and lines. Some poets even plan the spaces between words and letters to create the form, as in "Mixed Singles" on page 125.

SOUND Poems are meant to be read aloud. Therefore, poets choose and arrange words to create the sounds they want the listener to hear. There are many techniques poets can use to achieve different sounds. Three of these techniques are described below.

Rhyme Words that end with the same sound rhyme. In Western cultures, traditional poems, such as "Sea Lullaby" on page 131, often contain rhyming words at the ends of the lines.

> The old moon is tarnished
> With smoke of the flood,
> The dead leaves are varnished
> With color like blood,

Rhythm A poem's rhythm is sometimes called its beat. The rhythm is the pattern of stressed and unstressed syllables in a line of poetry. Stressed syllables are those word parts that are read with more emphasis; they can be indicated with a ´ mark. Unstressed syllables are those word parts that are read with less emphasis; they can be indicated with a ˇ mark. In these lines from "Paul Revere's Ride," listen for the beat that makes the lines sound like the pounding of horses' hooves.

> In the hour of darkness and peril and need,
> The people will waken and listen to hear
> The hurrying hoof-beats of that steed,
> And the midnight message of Paul Revere.

Poems that do not have a regular rhythm and that sound more like conversation are called **free verse**. The poem "Lost" on page 267 is written in free verse.

Repetition Poets often choose to repeat sounds, words, phrases, or whole lines in a poem.

FOCUS ON POETRY **123**

Imagery Have students create their own images of nature based on the model in "Simile: Willow and Ginkgo" shown here. Guide students to craft images that appeal to all five senses.

Figurative Language Ask students to create similes, metaphors, and personification to describe the weather. Provide them with some examples to spark ideas:

- **Simile** The rain crashed down on the village like a tidal wave.
- **Metaphor** The snow was a thick blanket over the fields.
- **Personification** The wind growled in the trees.

Theme Have students work in small groups to brainstorm a list of themes or messages about life that a poet might choose to write about. Invite volunteers to list these themes on the chalkboard. Then ask students if they know any poems or song lyrics that express one of these themes.

Reading Strategies: MODELING
Invite volunteers to read aloud the Strategies for Reading Poetry. Tell students they will be using these strategies as they read "Moco Limping" and "Mixed Singles" on page 125 and other poems throughout the book. Then model the strategies as students read "Moco Limping" and "Mixed Singles." You may wish to use the following models or create your own.

- **Preview the poem** "The poem 'Mixed Singles' has an interesting and irregular form. It's short and is divided unevenly into three stanzas."
- **Read the poem aloud** "In 'Moco Limping' I knew to pause at commas, such as after 'beautiful' in line 8, and to come to a full stop at the period after 'pet' in line 9."
- **Visualize the images** "In 'Moco Limping' I picture in my mind a frail, old dog with a bad leg but one that is warm and friendly."
- **Think about the words and phrases** "The author uses very vivid details to make the poem interesting, such as 'savage grace of his gait' in lines 14–15."
- **Try to figure out the theme** "Both poems are about people being fooled by appearances. In the first poem, the speaker is unhappy about the way in which his dog looks, but he loves him anyway. In the second poem, the speaker is surprised by his opponent's tennis ability and seems to fall in love with her."
- **Let your understanding grow** "After reading 'Mixed Singles' again, I realized that the last line has a double meaning. 'Love' can mean both an emotion and a score in tennis."
- **Allow yourself to enjoy poetry** "I enjoyed 'Moco Limping' because, like the speaker in 'Moco', I had an old pet that sometimes embarrassed me, but I loved it dearly."

Repetition helps the poet emphasize an idea or convey a certain feeling.

IMAGERY Imagery refers to words and phrases that appeal to the five senses. Poets use imagery to create a picture in the reader's mind or to remind the reader of a familiar sensation. Notice how these lines from "Simile: Willow and Ginkgo" on page 131 give you a visual picture as well as appealing to your sense of touch:

> The willow is sleek as a velvet-nosed calf;
> The ginkgo is leathery as an old bull,

FIGURATIVE LANGUAGE Poets use figurative language when they choose words and phrases that help the reader to picture ordinary things in new ways. The following are three kinds of these special descriptions, called **figures of speech.**

Simile A comparison that uses the word *like* or *as* is called a simile. This simile from "Simile: Willow and Ginkgo" compares the willow tree to a nymph:

> The willow is like a nymph with streaming hair;

Metaphor A comparison that does not use the word *like* or *as* is called a metaphor. To what does the speaker compare herself in these lines from "I Belong" on page 622?

> I am the mountain, to stand
>   with pride, strength, and faith.

Personification When a poet describes an animal or an object as if it were human or had human qualities, he or she is using personification. In these lines from "Sea Lullaby," the poet gives human characteristics to the sea:

> Her bright locks were tangled,
> She shouted for joy,
> With one hand she strangled
> A strong little boy.

THEME All the poetic elements you have read about help the poet establish the theme. Just as in fiction, the message about life that the poem conveys is its theme.

STRATEGIES FOR READING POETRY

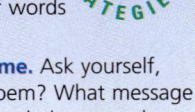

- **Preview the poem.** Notice the poem's form: its shape, its length, the length of the lines, and whether or not it has stanzas.
- **Read the poem aloud.** Pause at the ends of complete thoughts, not necessarily at the ends of lines. Look for end punctuation to help you find the end of a complete thought. As you read, listen for rhyme and listen for rhythm as well as the overall sound of the words in the poem.
- **Visualize the images.** In your mind's eye, picture the images and comparisons in the poem. Do the images remind you of feelings or experiences you have had?
- **Think about the words and phrases.** Allow yourself to wonder about any words or phrases that seem to stand out. Think about what that choice of words adds to the poem.
- **Try to figure out the theme.** Ask yourself, What's the point of the poem? What message is the poet trying to send or help me understand?
- **Let your understanding grow.** When you finish reading, you are left with first impressions of the poem. Reread the poem; each time you read it, you will find new meanings that add to your understanding and appreciation of the poem.
- **Allow yourself to enjoy poetry.** Remember that poetry is about feelings. You may connect with a particular poem because it expresses feelings that you have felt.

PREVIEWING

POETRY

Moco Limping
David Nava Monreal

Mixed Singles
Arnold Adoff

PERSONAL CONNECTION
Activating Prior Knowledge

Have you ever made a surprising discovery about someone familiar to you? For example, you might suddenly realize that your brother has an annoying habit you overlooked before or that your friend has a talent you never noticed. In your notebook, jot down something you have learned recently about someone whom you've known a long time.

- I just recently noticed that my sister Kathleen cracks her knuckles—she's driving me crazy!
- I didn't know my friend Ricardo could play the cello. He even performs on stage.

Building Background
LITERARY CONNECTION

Poems often enable readers to picture familiar things in new ways. Sometimes poets even use the spacing of words and lines to help the reader visualize the idea. In the two poems you are about to read, the spacing of words and lines reflects the subject matter of the poem. Before you read each poem, look at its shape on the page. As you read "Moco Limping," think about why the lines are short and irregular. As you read "Mixed Singles," think about how the lines reflect what is happening in the poem.

READING CONNECTION
Active Reading/Setting a Purpose

Speaker In poetry, the voice that "talks" to the reader is called the speaker. The speaker is like a narrator in a work of fiction. In some poems, the speaker expresses the feelings of the poet. In other poems, the speaker and the poet are not the same.

In "Moco Limping" and "Mixed Singles," look for clues to the personality of the speaker, the qualities the speaker notices in his subject, and the speaker's reactions to the subject. Record your findings in a chart like the one below.

Poem	Speaker's Personality	Subject's Qualities	Speaker's Reactions
"Moco Limping"			
"Mixed Singles"			

MOCO LIMPING/MIXED SINGLES **125**

OVERVIEW

Objectives
- To analyze and appreciate two poems that reflect the subjective nature of the perception of outward appearances
- To examine form in poetry
- To express understanding of the poems through a choice of writing forms, including a poem and an article
- To extend understanding of the poems through a variety of multimodal and cross-curricular activities

Skills

LITERARY CONCEPTS
- Form
- Metaphor

GENRE STUDY
- Poetry: free verse

SPEAKING, LISTENING, AND VIEWING
- Presenting a poem
- Group discussion

Cross-Curricular Connections

SCIENCE
- Dogs

ALTERNATIVE

Previewing

Students can choose partners and use the following prompts to discuss a surprising discovery.

Personal Connection

Discussion Prompts *Think about the last time you were surprised by someone you've known a long time. In as much detail as possible, describe this event to your partner. Then listen as your partner describes a similar situation. Ask each other these questions:*

- What surprised you about the person?
- Was there something the person said or did that you didn't expect?
- Did the surprise teach you something new about this person? What?

PRINT AND MEDIA RESOURCES

UNIT ONE RESOURCE BOOK
Strategic Reading: Literature, p. 63

ACCESS FOR STUDENTS ACQUIRING ENGLISH
Reading and Writing Support

FORMAL ASSESSMENT
Selection Test, pp. 23–24
 Test Generator

AUDIO LIBRARY
See Reference Card

THE LANGUAGE OF LITERATURE TEACHER'S EDITION **125**

Thematic Link: *Fooled by Appearances*
Although the speaker of the first poem seems to criticize everything about his dog, particularly his appearance, he actually loves him. The speaker in the second poem is impressed by his female tennis opponent's skill and finds a game of tennis is more than it seems.

CUSTOMIZING FOR
Students Acquiring English
- Use **ACCESS FOR STUDENTS ACQUIRING ENGLISH,** Reading and Writing Support.
- This selection may prove difficult because of the format of the poems and the use of figurative language.

STRATEGIC READING FOR
Less-Proficient Readers
Set a Purpose To engage students in the poems, have them predict what they think they are about, based on the poems' titles. Then have them read the poems to see if their predictions are correct.
Use **UNIT ONE RESOURCE BOOK,** p. 63, for guidance in reading the selection.

Literary Concept: METAPHOR

A Have students discuss what the metaphor "a stick of a leg" suggests is wrong with the dog. *(Possible response: His leg is as stiff as a stick, so he drags it.)*

Critical Thinking: SPECULATING

B Ask students why they think the speaker of the poem would like his dog to be strong and capture attention when he walks. *(Possible response: His friends have strong, graceful dogs, and he wants his dog to measure up to theirs; his idea of a "noble" pet is a pet with strength and grace.)*

Moco Limping

UNIT ONE PART 2: FOOLED BY APPEARANCES

Mini-Lesson Genre Study

POETRY Tell students that **free verse** is a type of poetry with the following characteristics:
- It has no regular patterns of rhyme, rhythm, or line length.
- It often is used to capture the sounds and rhythms of ordinary language.
- It often experiments with form, the way a poem looks on the page.

Application Have students copy the web into their notebooks. Ask them to refer to it as they continue to read additional poetry selections to decide which poems are free verse. Invite students to name which characteristics of free verse "Moco Limping" and "Mixed Singles" contain.

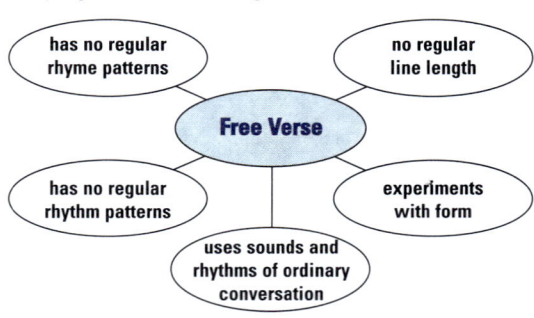

by david nava monreal

A My dog hobbles
with a stick
of a leg that
he drags behind
5   him as he moves.
And I was a man
that wanted a
beautiful, noble
animal as a pet.
10 I wanted him
to be strong and
capture all the
B attention by
the savage grace
15 of his gait.
I wanted him to
be the first
dog howling in
the pack.

20 The leader,
C the brutal hunter
that broke through
the woods with
thunder.
25 But, instead he's
this rickety
little canine
that leaves trails
in the dirt
30 with his club foot.
He's the stumbler
that trips while
chasing lethargic
bees and butterflies.
35 It hurts me to
see him so
D abnormal,
so clumsy and
stupid.

40 My vain heart weeps
knowing he
is mine.
But then he turns
my way and
45 looks at me with
eyes that cry out
with life.
He jumps at me with
E his feeble paws,
50 I feel his warm fur
and his imperfection is
forgotten.

FROM PERSONAL RESPONSE TO CRITICAL ANALYSIS

REFLECT 1. In this poem, did you react more strongly to the speaker or to the dog? Why? Jot down your thoughts in your notebook.

RETHINK 2. Could you identify with the speaker's thoughts and feelings in this poem? Explain your answer.
   Consider
   • how Moco's appearance contrasted with the speaker's expectations
   • the speaker's opinion of himself
   • how you would feel if Moco were your dog

3. Did your ideas about the speaker change as you read the poem? Give reasons for your answer.

MOCO LIMPING **127**

CUSTOMIZING FOR
Gifted and Talented Students

C Have students keep note of the contrast between the poet's ideal dog and the reality of Moco. For example, these lines suggest the speaker wanted him to be an aggressive hunting dog that is a leader.

Active Reading: EVALUATE

D Have students discuss their responses to the speaker's characterization of Moco. If they need help, share the following thought process with them:

Think-Aloud Model *Just because Moco does not meet his owner's expectations doesn't mean that the dog cannot be a good pet in other ways. I think the speaker is too rough on Moco. However, he also seems to have a soft spot for the dog.*

Critical Thinking:
SYNTHESIZING

E Ask students what changes at the end of the poem. *(how the speaker feels about the dog)* Have students discuss reasons for the change. *(Possible response: The dog jumps up to greet the speaker, causing him to change his mind when he sees how full of life the dog is.)*

From Personal Response to Critical Analysis

1. Responses will vary.
2. Possible responses: I could not identify with the speaker because I don't like aggressive or strong dogs; I could identify because I want a big dog.
3. Possible response: My ideas changed because I did not like how poorly he spoke about his dog, but by the end the speaker showed he had a heart and really cared about Moco.

Mini-Lesson Literary Concepts

REVIEWING METAPHOR Remind students that a metaphor is a comparison of two unlike things that have something in common. A metaphor, unlike a simile, does not use direct words of comparison such as *like*, *as*, or *resembles*. In "Moco Limping," the speaker's description of the pack leader's gait *(broke through the woods with thunder)* is an example of a metaphor.

Application Have students think of other animals and/or pets they have had or known. Ask them to list details describing the animal. Then have students develop metaphors to describe the distinct qualities of the animal. Students may find it helpful to make a chart like the one shown.

Animal/Pet	Qualities	Descriptive Metaphor

THE LANGUAGE OF LITERATURE **TEACHER'S EDITION** **127**

Literary Concept: FORM

F Ask students to discuss why the author arranged the lines this way. *(Possible response: in order to illustrate the movements of the woman and ball)*

Active Reading: CONNECT

G Ask students if they have ever been caught off guard by how skilled another person was at an activity. Ask how they responded to the other person's talent.

CUSTOMIZING FOR
Students Acquiring English

1. Explain to students that chalk is sometimes used to mark the boundaries on a tennis court.
2. Point out to students unfamiliar with the game that in tennis, *love* means "the score of zero."

STRATEGIC READING FOR
Less-Proficient Readers

Have students explain the relationship of the speaker to his tennis partner. *(He is surprised that she can hit the ball so hard; he is impressed by her abilities; he is attracted to her.)* **Clarifying**

CUSTOMIZING FOR
Gifted and Talented

Be sure students understand the double meaning of *love* that the poem uses. It may also mean the start of a romantic relationship.

Literary Concept: METAPHOR

Have students consider what is being compared in the poem. *(Possible response: a game of tennis and falling in love)* How does the speaker relate the two? *(Possible response: through the title of the poem and the term* love, *which can refer both to emotions and to a tennis score)*

Mixed Singles.

BY ARNOLD ADOFF

F She tosses the tennis ball   high
                               into   the   air.
Her
racket comes down harder   than I e v e r
G   k n e w
a
racket could hit.

It
is a serve into the inside corner,
that I barely see: kicking   chalk
1 as
it flies away, untouched   by   me.

2 I know this will be love.

Mini-Lesson: Speaking,  Listening, and Viewing

PRESENTING A POEM Explain to students that most poems are meant to be read aloud. However, because students are often unfamiliar with poetic conventions, reading poetry is often intimidating. Tell students that presenting a poem is different from giving an oral report or reading aloud from a prose work. Many students do not realize that when reading poetry, regardless of how the words are positioned on the page, you usually pause at a punctuation mark, not at the end of a line. Advise students that they may want to use self-stick notes to mark places where to pause or to mark the parts of the poem they think should be given particular emphasis. Students should also note the rhythm of the poem when reading.

Application Encourage students to read either "Moco Limping" or "Mixed Singles" aloud to the class. Have them prepare the poems by noting appropriate places to pause and the parts that deserve special emphasis.

RESPONDING OPTIONS

FROM PERSONAL RESPONSE TO CRITICAL ANALYSIS

REFLECT 1. What was your first thought when you finished reading "Mixed Singles"?

RETHINK 2. What is the speaker's opinion of his opponent? Give reasons to support your answer.

Consider

Close Textual Reading
- the speaker's description of her tennis playing
- the meaning of the title and of the last line of the poem

3. What outcome(s) does the speaker expect from the tennis match?

Thematic Link 4. What do the speakers in the two poems have in common?

RELATE 5. Look back at the chart you made for the Reading Connection on page 125. Compare and contrast how the speakers reacted to the subjects in the poems. Did their perceptions of the subjects change? Explain your answer.

Multimodal Learning
ANOTHER PATHWAY
Cooperative Learning
Practice reading one of the two poems aloud. Then make an audiotape of your reading. The class can critique the presentations of each poem, noticing the varied interpretations that different readers give the same poem.

LITERARY CONCEPTS

The **form** of a poem is the way it looks, or its arrangement on the page. A poet chooses this arrangement deliberately. How do you think the forms the poets chose for "Moco Limping" and "Mixed Singles" reflect the subject matter and what is happening in those poems? Use a chart like the one shown to organize your thoughts.

Form	
"Moco Limping"	"Mixed Singles"

QUICKWRITES

1. Try your hand at writing a **poem** about someone or something very familiar to you, such as your best friend, your favorite sport, or a pet. Create a form for your poem that reflects its meaning.

2. Imagine that you are a sportswriter who attended the tennis match described in "Mixed Singles." Write an **article** for your newspaper in which you tell how the rest of the match was played.

📁 **PORTFOLIO** Save your writing. You may want to use it later as a springboard to a piece for your portfolio.

MOCO LIMPING/MIXED SINGLES **129**

From Personal Response to Critical Analysis
1. Responses will vary.
2. Possible responses: He is impressed by her strength and skill; he is attracted to her.
3. Possible response: Based on the speaker's surprise at his opponent's skill, he expected an easy victory.
4. Possible response: The speakers of both poems are fooled by the appearance of the poems' subjects. In the first poem, the speaker disliked Moco's appearance but loved him anyway. The speaker of the second poem is impressed by his opponent's skill at tennis and is attracted to her.
5. Responses will vary.

Another Pathway
Cooperative Learning Ask students to form small groups of five or six and to take turns reading the poem. Direct students to the mini-lesson on presenting a poem for techniques they can use in their reading. Have students make notes of which readings were most effective and why. Then encourage them to compare notes before making a recording of the poem. Remind students critiquing the readings that there is no right or wrong way to read a poem.

Rubric
3 Full Accomplishment Students read the poem with careful attention to the rhythm and interpret the lines creatively.
2 Substantial Accomplishment Students read the poem with emotion and enthusiasm but may miss the rhythm.
1 Little or Partial Accomplishment Students have difficulty reading the poem or have no sense of its rhythm.

Literary Concepts
If students have difficulty discussing the relationship between form and subject, have them first list a few short ideas about what each poem is trying to convey. Then have them describe the form each poem uses. Comparing these two lists should help students see the relationship. (Possible responses: "Moco Limping" is written in short lines with a varying number of syllables in each line; this imitates Moco's uneven walk. "Mixed Singles" breaks its lines of poetry with words shifting up and down. This is like the quick movement of the tennis ball.)

QuickWrites
1. Encourage students to write their poem in a form that reflects their overall impressions or feelings on their subjects.
2. Invite students who are less familiar with tennis to go to the library and research tennis in newspaper and magazines articles, or on videotape, before writing their articles.

 **The Writer's Craft**

Writing a Poem, pp. 71–83
Informative Writing: Explaining How, pp. 93–109

THE LANGUAGE OF LITERATURE TEACHER'S EDITION **129**

Literary Links

Ask students to compare the way the speaker appears to treat his dog in "Moco Limping" with the way Mrs. Tompkin treats her pet in "All Things Bright and Beautiful" (p. 84). *(Possible response: The speaker in "Moco Limping" loves his dog but he is disappointed by Moco's appearance and ill health. Mrs. Tompkin loves and coddles her pet parakeet. She is not disappointed by him even when he gets old and sick.)*

Across the Curriculum

Science *Cooperative Learning* Have students work in groups of four or five to research a particular breed of dog. Groups should write brief reports on their chosen breed. One student should act as facilitator to organize the group's research. Another student should act as recorder of facts. Of the remaining students, one should summarize the group's findings and the others should present the information to the class.

DAVID NAVA MONREAL

The poetry of David Nava Monreal reflects the range of experiences and hardships faced by Mexican Americans, especially the poor. He is well known for the colorful and diverse characters that appear in his poems, from broken-down prizefighters, to teenage weight lifters, to struggling college students.

ARNOLD ADOFF

Arnold Adoff is, by his own admission, a very particular and demanding editor. Says Adoff of his anthologies of African-American literature, "The material selected must be the finest in literary terms as well as in content/message/racial vision."

Multimodal Learning

ALTERNATIVE ACTIVITIES

1. Create a pair of **illustrations** of Moco, first showing the dog the speaker wanted and then showing Moco as he is.
2. Look for other poems whose unusual shape or form reflects their meaning. Copy the poems and compile a **booklet** of them to share in class.

DAVID NAVA MONREAL

David Nava Monreal (1935–) wrote about his own dog in "Moco Limping," a poem that was part of his 55-piece poetry collection appearing in *Sighs and Songs of Aztlan,* a collection of Chicano literature published in 1975. That same year, he won a nationwide contest sponsored by the Chicano Cultural Center of Bakersfield College for his works.

Monreal's poetry is personal, expressing his deep feelings about nature, peasants, love, jealousy, and poverty. Without bitterness, he writes poems of protest against injustice. Monreal's idea of peace is rolling fields under a warm sun, an April shower, or a duck floating like a leaf.

A California native, Monreal has worked on the staff of a public library and as a group supervisor in a county probation department. Extended Reading

ARNOLD ADOFF

Arnold Adoff was born in New York City, in the East Bronx. As a youngster, he enjoyed exploring both his neighborhood and the rest of the city. After attending City College and Columbia University, he taught in Harlem for 12 years. While teaching his African-American students, Adoff, a poet himself, realized how hard it was to find books of African-American poetry to share with them. He decided to do something about it. Adoff gathered African-American poetry into an anthology and published it under the title *I Am the Darker Brother.* The book won an American Library Association Notable Book Award in 1968.

1935–

Besides compiling several more anthologies of African-American poetry, Adoff has continued to write his own poetry. He married the writer Virginia Hamilton in 1960, and they later had two children. Many of his poems for young people celebrate the joys of loving families like his own. Adoff has long championed the need for relevant and exciting poetry for children. Besides writing and teaching, he lectures and is part of a multicultural center that promotes the writing of poetry by young people.

OTHER WORKS *Slow Dance Heartbreak Blues, All the Colors of the Race, Sports Pages, Chocolate Dreams*

130 UNIT ONE PART 2: FOOLED BY APPEARANCES

Alternative Activities

1. Before students begin to draw, have them make a two-column chart that lists the speaker's ideal dog and Moco as he is. Encourage them to include as many specific details as possible to use later in their illustrations.
2. Encourage students to consult a librarian or an on-line computer service before looking for poems for their booklets. You might wish to have students look for examples of concrete poems, poems that use very obvious shapes that directly relate to the subject. For example, Lewis Carroll writes a poem about a mouse that looks like a mouse's tail in *Alice's Adventures in Wonderland.*

PREVIEWING

POETRY

Simile: Willow and Ginkgo
Eve Merriam

Sea Lullaby
Elinor Wylie

PERSONAL CONNECTION Activating Prior Knowledge
You are probably aware that the weather has an effect on your mood, but have you ever noticed how objects in nature influence you? For example, how do you feel when you look at a lake or the ocean? How do you feel when you see a desolate landscape, a huge tree, a tiny flower, or a rocky cliff? Sketch or describe one or two scenes or objects from nature that have affected you the most.

SCIENCE CONNECTION Building Background
The poems you are about to read describe objects in nature—two kinds of trees and the sea. The willow is a graceful tree with slender, drooping branches and narrow, pointed leaves. Willow trees generally grow near water, and their network of roots prevents soil erosion. Many of the 300 species of willow are planted for their beauty.

The ginkgo tree, on the other hand, is a relic from the past—the only survivor of a species of prehistoric plants. Its squat shape and fan-shaped leaves make it look quite different from the willow. The female tree yields a nasty-smelling nut that fouls the air around it.

READING CONNECTION Active Reading/Setting a Purpose
Comparisons in Poetry In these poems, the poets make comparisons to help you picture objects or scenes from nature using two literary devices: **simile** and **personification**. A simile is a comparison that usually uses the word *like* or *as*. "The willow is *like* an etching" is a simile from "Simile: Willow and Ginkgo." Using personification, a poet gives human qualities to an object, animal, or idea. In "Sea Lullaby," the words *smiler* and *teeth* make the sea seem human.

As you read the poems, record other comparisons, using a web like the one shown. Label each comparison with a tree or a wave to show which poem it came from.

SIMILE: WILLOW AND GINKGO/SEA LULLABY **131**

OVERVIEW

Objectives
- To understand and appreciate two poems about objects in nature
- To identify and understand simile and personification
- To examine the use of rhyme and rhythm in a poem
- To express understanding of the poems through a choice of writing forms, including similes and a poem
- To extend understanding of the poems through a variety of multimodal and cross-curricular activities

Skills

LITERARY CONCEPTS
- Figurative language
- Rhyme and rhythm

THE WRITER'S STYLE
- Personification

SPEAKING, LISTENING, AND VIEWING
- Group discussion
- Oral presentation

Cross-Curricular Connections
SCIENCE
- Seas and oceans

ALTERNATIVE Previewing
Students can choose partners and use the following prompts to preview these poems orally.

Personal Connection
Discussion Prompts: *Think about a time you were in natural surroundings, such as a beach, a forest, or a desert. Describe the place to your partner, and tell how the place made you feel. The following questions might help you get started:*

- *What is the one thing you remember most vividly?*
- *Was it day or night?*
- *What smells can you remember?*
- *What sounds can you remember?*

As you read these poems, notice the details the poets use to describe nature.

PRINT AND MEDIA RESOURCES

UNIT ONE RESOURCE BOOK
Strategic Reading: Literature, p. 67

WRITING MINI–LESSONS
Transparencies, p. 39

ACCESS FOR STUDENTS ACQUIRING ENGLISH
Reading and Writing Support

FORMAL ASSESSMENT
Selection Test, pp. 25–26
Part Test, pp. 27–28
 Test Generator

 **AUDIO LIBRARY**
See Reference Card

 **LASERLINKS**
Author Background

THE LANGUAGE OF LITERATURE **Teacher's Edition** **131**

Simile: Willow and Ginkgo
by Eve Merriam

The willow is like an etching,
Fine-lined against the sky.
The ginkgo is like a crude sketch,
Hardly worthy to be signed.

5   The willow's music is like a soprano
Delicate and thin.
The ginkgo's tune is like a chorus
With everyone joining in.

The willow is sleek as a velvet-nosed calf;
10 The ginkgo is leathery as an old bull.
The willow's branches are like silken thread;
The ginkgo's like stubby rough wool.

The willow is like a nymph with streaming hair;
Wherever it grows, there is green and gold and fair.
15 The willow dips to the water,
Protected and precious, like the king's favorite daughter.

The ginkgo forces its way through gray concrete:
Like a city child, it grows up in the street.
Thrust against the metal sky,
20 Somehow it survives and even thrives.

Ⓐ My eyes feast upon the willow,
But my heart goes to the ginkgo.

FROM PERSONAL RESPONSE TO CRITICAL ANALYSIS

REFLECT   1. What images came to mind as you read this poem?
RETHINK   2. Why does the speaker's heart go to the ginkgo? Would yours? Explain.
             3. How does the poet appeal to the reader's senses? Give examples.

132   UNIT ONE PART 2: FOOLED BY APPEARANCES

Mini-Lesson Literary Concepts

REVIEWING FIGURATIVE LANGUAGE
Remind students that figurative language goes beyond the dictionary meaning of words to create fresh and original descriptions. The three most common forms of figurative language are simile, metaphor, and personification.

Application Have students review the two poems and make a list of the poets' use of similes, metaphors, and personification. Then have students write additional comparisons using new similes, metaphors, or personification. For example:
- The sea was like a wise, caring woman who cradled children in her arms.
- Ginkgo, the crusty old man, shuffled from side to side as he grumpily made his way down the street.

After students have completed the task, encourage them to share their comparisons.

Thematic Link: *Fooled by Appearances*
These two poems illustrate how we can be fooled by nature's appearance. First, the willow may appear more beautiful than the ginkgo, but the latter has its own kind of appeal. Second, the sea often appears beautiful, but it can be very dangerous.

CUSTOMIZING FOR
Students Acquiring English
- Use **ACCESS FOR STUDENTS ACQUIRING ENGLISH,** *Reading and Writing Support.*
- Students may know fables and stories that use personification from their first countries. Ask them to share with the class examples of how this literary device is used.

STRATEGIC READING FOR
Less-Proficient Readers
Set a Purpose To immerse students in the selection, have them draw or sketch a willow and a ginkgo tree. Then as they read the selection, have them keep track of the similes Merriam uses to compare the willow and the ginkgo.

Use **UNIT ONE RESOURCE BOOK,** p. 67, for guidance in reading the poem.

Critical Thinking:
SYNTHESIZING
Ⓐ Ask students to think about the speaker's conclusion that her "heart goes to the ginkgo." Have them discuss the qualities or attributes the speaker values most. *(Possible response: The speaker values the ginkgo's ruggedness and its survival skills.)*

From Personal Response to Critical Analysis
1. Accept all reasonable responses. Encourage students to use sensory details in their answers.
2. Possible response: She admires the ability of the ginkgo to survive—even though it isn't pretty, it is tough.
3. Possible response: The poet appeals to the reader's senses through the use of imagery, sensory detail, and figurative language, as in the third stanza.

Sea Lullaby

by Elinor Wylie

The old moon is tarnished
With smoke of the flood,
The dead leaves are varnished
With color like blood,

5 A treacherous smiler
With teeth white as milk,
A savage beguiler
In sheathings of silk,

The sea creeps to pillage,
10 She leaps on her prey;
A child of the village
Was murdered today.

She came up to meet him
In a smooth golden cloak,
15 She choked him and beat him
To death, for a joke.

Her bright locks were tangled,
She shouted for joy,
With one hand she strangled
20 A strong little boy.

Now in silence she lingers
Beside him all night
To wash her long fingers
In silvery light

Literary Concept: RHYME

B Ask students to locate the end rhymes in this stanza. *(tarnished/varnished, flood/blood)* Ask them how the rhyming pattern for this poem differs from "Willow and Ginkgo" *(the rhyme varies from stanza to stanza in "Willow and Ginkgo," whereas in "Sea Lullaby" the first and third and second and fourth lines rhyme in each stanza).*

Literary Concept: FIGURATIVE LANGUAGE

C Have students discuss the way the sea is personified. *(Possible response: The sea is a woman who stalks her prey and delights in death.)*

CUSTOMIZING FOR
Gifted and Talented Students

D Have students think about why this poem is shocking. What is the sea's attitude toward the crime she commits? *(Possible response: The poem is shocking not so much because of the little boy's death as because of the delight the sea takes in murdering him. The poet's frankness in describing the murderer's delight is what really shocks the reader.)*

Mini-Lesson The Writer's Style

PERSONIFICATION The giving of human qualities to an animal, object, or idea is called personification. Help students understand that in both these poems, the poets use personification as the basis for many of the similes.

Application Have students write a list of animals or inanimate objects. Next to each item, have students identify which human quality they would attribute to it. Then have them write a personification around that human quality, as in the chart shown.

Reteaching/Reinforcement
• *Writing Mini-Lessons* transparencies, p. 39

Personification, pp. 319–320

Animal/Object	Human Quality	Personification
spring	youthful	Crying with screams of delight, spring was born on a cold winter's morning.

From Personal Response to Critical Analysis

1. Responses will vary.
2. Possible response: Because the title included the word *lullaby*, I expected the poem to be about the sea's calming effect.
3. Possible responses: I would describe her as cruel and heartless. I would describe her as beautiful but deadly.
4. Possible responses: The poet chose the title because the boy's death is similar to his being put to sleep; and to create a strong contrast between title and poem to reveal another aspect of the sea.
5. Possible response: The personification of the sea who "choked him and beat him/To death, for a joke" makes me angry and sad. In contrast, the "protected and precious" willow is beautiful and tranquil.
6. Accept all reasonable responses.

Another Pathway

Cooperative Learning Have groups make a list of the similes, metaphors, and personification each poet uses. Ask the group to review the student lists to identify the items that deal with appearance. One student should record those that fit the theme "Fooled by Appearances." After the members of each group are done, have them compare their findings with those of at least one other group.

Rubric

3 Full Accomplishment Students find all uses of figurative language and correctly identify those that fit the theme.

2 Substantial Accomplishment Students can identify similes, metaphors, and personification but have trouble relating them to the theme.

1 Little or Partial Accomplishment Students have difficulty finding the poets' use of figurative language.

RESPONDING OPTIONS

FROM PERSONAL RESPONSE TO CRITICAL ANALYSIS

REFLECT
1. How did this poem affect you? Jot down your reactions in your notebook. Share your thoughts with a partner.

RETHINK
2. How is the portrayal of the sea different from what you expected? Explain your answer. *Thematic Link*

3. As you have learned, the sea is personified in this poem. If the sea in the poem were actually a woman, how would you describe her personality? To support your answer, include relevant phrases from the web you made for the Reading Connection on page 131.

4. Why do you think the poet chose the title she did?

RELATE
5. Compare and contrast how the two poems make you feel. Use words and phrases from each in your comparison.

6. Which poem do you like better? Why?

ANOTHER PATHWAY

Cooperative Learning
In a paragraph, explain how "Simile: Willow and Ginkgo" and "Sea Lullaby" fit the theme, "Fooled by Appearances." Look for examples of figurative language in each poem that fit the theme.

LITERARY CONCEPTS

In contrast to "Moco Limping" and "Mixed Singles," Merriam's and Wylie's poems use rhyme and rhythm. **Rhyme** involves the repetition of the same or similar sounds, with matching sounds often falling at the ends of lines.

Rhythm, sometimes called the "beat" of the poem, is the pattern of stressed and unstressed syllables. Stressed syllables are read with more emphasis, unstressed syllables with less emphasis.

Read both poems aloud. Which poem has a more consistent end-rhyme pattern? Which one has a stronger, more even rhythm? How does that regularity reflect the subject of the poem?

QUICKWRITES

1. In the Personal Connection on page 131, you described or sketched a scene or an object from nature. Now write a list of **similes** that compare that scene or object to other things familiar to readers.

2. "Sea Lullaby" reminds us that nature can seem cruel. Choose another natural killer, such as a hurricane, and write a **poem** about it. Include comparisons in your poem.

📁 **PORTFOLIO** Save your writing. You may want to use it later as a springboard to a piece for your portfolio.

134 UNIT ONE PART 2: FOOLED BY APPEARANCES

Literary Concepts

Have student volunteers read each poem aloud. If necessary, remind students about using the poem's punctuation marks to know whether or not to pause at the end of a line. Use the oral reading to show students that "Sea Lullaby" has a more consistent end-rhyme pattern and a more even rhythm. Ask them why an even rhythm would be important to a poem about the sea. *(It gives the reader a sense of waves crashing.)*

QuickWrites

1. Remind students that similes are direct comparisons using *like* or *as*. Before students write their nature similes, have them list the particular qualities or attributes they wish to relate about the scene or object.

2. Invite students to use a regular rhythm or end-rhyme pattern in writing their poems. Encourage students to create a rhythm pattern that evokes nature's movement.

Using Poetic Devices, pp 318–319

Multimodal Learning

ALTERNATIVE ACTIVITIES

1. Arrange a **read-aloud** of "Sea Lullaby" that includes appropriate musical accompaniment.
2. Find the personification in "Simile: Willow and Ginkgo." Then draw or paint a **picture** of the willow and the ginkgo trees as if they were human.

Eve Merriam

1916–1992

The daughter of Russian immigrants, Eve Merriam grew up in small Pennsylvania towns. As a child, she enjoyed reading poetry, and she began writing her own poems when she was seven or eight. She went on to become one of the most respected poets in the United States, publishing more than 25 volumes of adult's and children's poetry.

Merriam won the Yale Younger Poets Prize in 1946, and the National Council of Teachers of English honored her poetry for children in 1981. One of her volumes of poetry, *The Inner City Mother Goose*, published in 1969, became controversial when law enforcement officials claimed it glamorized crime. It was later adapted into an award-winning play.

About her craft, Merriam said, "There is a special magic about rhyme, the chime that rings in time. It's like the little bell at the end of the typewriter line." It was not unusual for her to have "spent weeks looking for precisely the right word. It's like having a tiny marble in your pocket; you can just feel it."

OTHER WORKS *It Doesn't Always Have to Rhyme, Out Loud, Fresh Paint: New Poems*   Extended Reading

Elinor Wylie

1885–1928

Free-spirited Elinor Wylie chose to ignore the social conventions of her day. As a teenager, she was an outstanding student, but chose to enjoy the social life of Washington, D.C., rather than attend college. In 1905, she married Philip Hichborn. However, the marriage soon fell apart over Hichborn's violent fits of jealousy. They had one child together before Elinor left him and began a romantic relationship with Horace Wylie.

The scandal surrounding Elinor and Horace's behavior forced them to move to England, where Elinor published her first collection of poems. In response to the loss of her second baby, Elinor went blind for a number of weeks. Meanwhile, back in the United States, Hichborn committed suicide, and Horace Wylie's wife agreed to a divorce. Elinor and Horace returned to the United States in 1916 and were finally married in 1917. Soon after, Elinor joined a New York literary group that included William Rose Benét and Sinclair Lewis. Nine years after publication of her first book, she published her second collection of poems, *Nets to Catch the Wind*, which she considered her first significant work.

In 1923, William Rose Benét became her third husband. During the next five years, until her death, Wylie published four novels, three volumes of poetry, and short stories.

OTHER WORKS *Incidental Numbers, Black Armour*

Extended Reading

SIMILE: WILLOW AND GINKGO/SEA LULLABY   **135**

Across the Curriculum

Science *Cooperative Learning* Divide students into groups of three or four. Have groups research the seas and oceans of the world. Each group can choose a particular sea or ocean to research. Besides an atlas or map, students may be able to find documentary videos or CD-ROMs that provide visually stimulating resources. One student may be the facilitator to ensure all students are participating and to organize the group's research. Another student should record the group's findings, and the remaining students may present the group's findings to the class.

Eve Merriam

Eve Merriam found that listening to or reading poetry was a very physical experience. She said, "I find it difficult to sit still when I hear poetry or read it out loud. I feel a tingling feeling all over, particularly in the tips of my fingers and in my toes, and it just seems to go right from my mouth all the way through my body."

Elinor Wylie

Although Elinor Wylie's writing sometimes received mixed reviews, one critic was so enthusiastic about her first novel that he led a torchlight parade through New York City in Wylie's honor. Many critics have appreciated Wylie's work for its beauty, vivid imagery, and understanding of life.

AUTHOR BACKGROUND
Eve Merriam In this film, Eve Merriam offers her ideas about the goals of poets and the purposes of poetry.

Side A, Frame 12644

Alternative Activities

1. Students may want to use some of the following materials in their accompaniment: seashells, sand, water, whistle/horn, bird sounds, wind chimes.
2. Have students find specific examples of personification before they begin. Invite students to present multiple versions of the personified image.

OVERVIEW

To gain a deeper appreciation of the selections they have read in this unit, students will explore the characteristics of a narrative and then create their own well-developed example in this lesson.

Objectives

- To plan a firsthand narrative by considering elements such as resources, research, and sequence of events
- To draft a firsthand narrative and solicit a response
- To revise, edit, and publish a firsthand narrative
- To reflect on the process of writing a firsthand narrative

Skills

LITERATURE
- Identifying the focus

WRITING AND LANGUAGE
- Gathering details
- Organizing research
- Creating vivid images
- Using descriptive language

GRAMMAR AND USAGE
- Punctuating introductory phrases

MEDIA LITERACY
- Analyzing letters
- Interpreting memorabilia

- Reading family trees
- Using on-line sources
- Using a time line

SPEAKING, LISTENING, AND VIEWING
- Gathering oral histories
- Interviewing
- Asking questions
- Giving dramatic readings
- Reading aloud

Teaching Strategy: STUMBLING BLOCK

A Be sure that students understand that a firsthand narrative is a true story told from the first-person point of view. Stress that this is factual writing, not fiction.

Teaching Strategy: MODELING

B Show students how to use authentic sources such as souvenirs, letters, family trees, and other memorabilia as springboards for writing ideas by directing them to study the examples on these two pages. Then ask students how they might use this material to spark their own writing ideas, such as asking family members more about these items and constructing stories from their memories.

WRITING FROM EXPERIENCE

A — Writing a Firsthand Narrative

How do you view your parents or guardians and other relatives? What do you know about them? What were they like when they were your age? We may think we know everything about the people in our families. Often our perceptions change as we learn more about one another, as you discovered in Unit One, "Changing Perceptions."

GUIDED ASSIGNMENT

Write Your Family History Exploring family history can help you understand your background and maybe where some of your beliefs and attitudes come from. It might also change your perceptions about yourself and the people you live with. The next few pages will help you find ways to write about your family history.

1 Find the Clues

To learn about what sorts of materials can be clues to your family history, take a look at the letter and the other family items on these pages.

B — **Examine the Items** What story do they tell? Suppose these items were in your family. What clues do you see that could help you make connections from one item to another? Write your ideas.

Souvenir

To Davis Best Wishes Jackie Robinson

Letter

December 5, 1975
177-20 105th Street
Jamaica, NY 11433

Preston Washington
651 Riverside Drive
Pontiac, Michigan 48058

Dear Preston,

Mama is thrilled that we're getting married. (You were always her favorite.) Daddy didn't say anything about our wedding, the last time I saw him. Now that he and Mama are divorced, I hardly ever see him. When we have children, I'd hate for them not to know their grandfather.

I miss you. I'm glad we'll be getting married soon, now that your tour of duty is over.

Love always,
Susie

I wonder how Preston and Susie met.

136   UNIT ONE: CHANGING PERCEPTIONS

PRINT AND MEDIA RESOURCES

UNIT ONE RESOURCE BOOK
Prewriting Activity, p. 71
Elaboration, p. 72
Peer Response Guide, pp. 73–74
Revising and Proofreading, p. 75
Student Model, p. 76
Rubric p. 77

GRAMMAR MINI-LESSONS
Transparencies, p. 29
Copymasters, p. 39

WRITING MINI-LESSONS
Transparencies, pp. 38, 46

ACCESS FOR STUDENTS ACQUIRING ENGLISH
Reading and Writing Support

FORMAL ASSESSMENT
Guidelines for Writing Assessment

LASERLINKS
Writing Springboard

 WRITING COACH

Family Tree

Washington/Edwards Family Tree

Is there a connection between the family tree and the other items?

- Emilene Thigpen
- Tobias Williams
- Hattie James
- Davis Williams
- Willie Edwards
- Marie Williams
- Daisy Williams
- Preston Washington
- Susie Edwards
- Ozell Edwards
- Margaret Johnson
- Linda Washington
- Stan Washington
- Tecela Edwards

Military Decoration (Purple Heart)

② Collect Family Keepsakes

Keepsakes are things that serve as reminders about a place, an event, a person, and so on. Ask to see family keepsakes, such as journals, diaries, old letters, newspaper clippings, military and cemetery records, and photo albums. In your journal or notebook, sketch out a rough chart that combines this information with what you already know about your family. Make connections between the items.

- LASERLINKS
  - WRITING SPRINGBOARD
- WRITING COACH

WRITING FROM EXPERIENCE 137

Teaching Strategy: MODELING

C Have a volunteer answer the question in the margin by explaining how an analysis of the family tree and surrounding items might help someone understand who got the baseball and who earned the Purple Heart. For instance, the inscription on the baseball indicates it belonged to Davis Williams. In the letter, Susie's reference to Preston's tour of duty suggests that the military decorations may have been awarded to Preston Washington.

Then model for students how to use the samples on this page as springboards for firsthand narratives by brainstorming story ideas from the family tree. Possibilities include the following:
- I wonder what Willie Edwards' life was like.
- Who could give me firsthand information?

Teaching Strategy: STUMBLING BLOCK

D Approach the collection of family keepsakes with sensitivity. Foster children, adopted children, and students living in nontraditional families may have a difficult time gathering such artifacts. Further, the people who can explain the artifacts' meaning may not be available for assistance or willing to cooperate. As an alternative, students can select a contemporary or historical figure they admire, such as Eleanor Roosevelt or Martin Luther King, Jr., and research information about this person's life. This can be the basis for a narrative.

WRITING SPRINGBOARD
An Oral History ... on Video Two students—one from Cambodia and one from Ukraine—tell of the experiences and emotions they had when they came to the United States.

Side B, Frame 606

Writing Prompt Think of an interesting family incident you have been involved in or can learn about. Interview a family member about the event. Then write down the story so that it can be preserved among your family's records

THE LANGUAGE OF LITERATURE TEACHER'S EDITION 137

CUSTOMIZING FOR

Students Acquiring English

E Tell students that when the subject of an interview speaks a language other than English, writers sometimes quote a few important phrases in the subject's own language. This helps the reader hear the subject's real voice. Remind students that such quotations should be brief and clear. Guide students to set the quotations in context or provide translations so English-speaking audiences can understand them.

Speaking and Listening:
COLLABORATIVE OPPORTUNITY

F Suggest that students practice their interviews to polish their techniques. Have students work in pairs to write and edit their questions and then interview each other. This also allows students to practice operating a tape recorder and taking useful notes.

Research Skills:
USING THE COMPUTER

G To avoid expensive telephone bills or delays as material travels though the mail, suggest that students telephone long-distance sources to obtain their E-mail addresses. Then have students download any information they need from the E-mail into their word-processing programs.

PREWRITING

Exploring the Past

Researching Your Family When it comes to researching the history of a family, there are a lot of people and events to consider. You'll need to go to many different sources for the information you need. As you begin to discover more about your family, you may be surprised by what you learn.

Linda and Stan at Ozell's wedding

Grandma Edwards

❶ Gather Oral Histories

The best way to start gathering information is to talk to your family. Here are some possible resources for gathering oral histories— the stories that have been handed down by word of mouth from generation to generation.

Talk to Older Relatives Older relatives can be a rich source of information on family history. Take time to talk to your parents or guardians, grandparents, aunts, uncles, and other family members about their lives. Use the phone to talk to relatives who live far away. **E**

Record What Relatives Say The SkillBuilder on the following page can help you develop good questions. Taking notes on your conversations will help you remember key events and the people involved in them. You might want to tape-record your interviews so that later you can check your memory or clarify a point. If you can, make a duplicate copy to share with other members of your family. **F**

❷ Use a Variety of Resources

There are many ways to go about finding information to use in your family history. **G**

Community Resources Your local library has books and pamphlets that can help you trace your family history. Other sources include courthouse records, military records, adoption records, and state records of births, marriages, and land titles.

On-line Services The Census Bureau has genealogy services records on Internet. Other on-line services are as follows:

- The International Genealogical Index of the Latter Day Saints Family History Library at Salt Lake City, Utah
- The National Archives in Washington, D.C., which has Ante-Bellum Plantation Records and the Freedmen's Bureau records

Use the Multimedia Handbook for tips on conducting computerized searches.

138

Mini-Lesson: Speaking, Listening, and Viewing

INTERVIEWING Provide students with the following guidelines for planning and conducting an interview:

Planning an Interview
1. Contact the person to be interviewed. Arrange a time and place to meet at the subject's convenience.
2. Beforehand, find out something about the subject.
3. Plan effective questions. See the SkillBuilder on page 139 for more details.
4. Gather paper, pencils, and a tape recorder.

Conducting an Interview
1. Listen carefully and take accurate notes.
2. Ask permission to tape-record the interview. Never tape-record an interview without getting the subject's approval.
3. Ask questions to clarify anything you don't understand.
4. Go over your notes immediately after the interview.
5. Send a thank-you note to the subject.

Application Have students follow these guidelines as they conduct interviews to gather oral histories.

138 THE LANGUAGE OF LITERATURE TEACHER'S EDITION

3. Organize Your Research

Keep Track of Your Facts Consider using one of these organizing methods to help you keep track of the information you collect through research.

- Record your information on numbered note cards.
- Store family keepsakes in labeled boxes.
- List dates and other important information about a person or event. Make a time line of events, showing the order in which they occurred.

Decision Point What will you focus on? What details do you want to stress? Will you write about one person, time period, or event? You might consider focusing on an event or a person about which you have a strong feeling.

Family Time Line

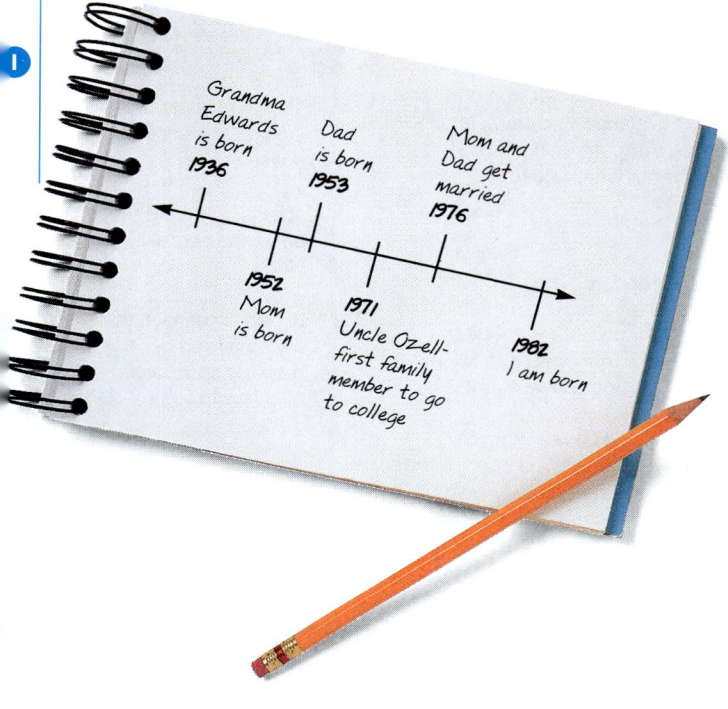

SkillBuilder

SPEAKING & LISTENING

Asking Questions
The tips below will help you develop effective questions to use as you collect oral histories.

- Avoid questions that can be answered yes or no. Try to ask more open-ended questions—for example: "What did you think about Dad when the two of you first met?"
- Ask questions that can be answered with details that appeal to the senses—for example: "What did you see when you stepped out your front door?"
- Ask follow-up questions to aid your understanding of a point. ("And then what happened?")

APPLYING WHAT YOU'VE LEARNED
With a partner, brainstorm a list of questions to ask relatives. Share your questions with another set of partners. Which of their questions might you use in your interviews?

THINK & PLAN

Reflecting on Your Ideas

1. What other information do you need? Where might you look for what you need?
2. Has something you learned changed the way you look at family members? How will you describe your discoveries in your report?

WRITING FROM EXPERIENCE **139**

Research Skill: DOCUMENTING SOURCES

Explain to students that it is important that they keep track of the resources they used. Doing so enables them to document facts, check information, and extend their work. Use these guidelines to show students how to keep bibliographic information on index cards, one source per card.

Books: Include the call number, author, title, place of publication, publisher, and date.

Periodicals: Include the author, article title, periodical name, volume, date, and page numbers.

Interviews: Include the subject's name and identification and the interview date and place.

Remind students that if they use a computer information service to locate sources, they should credit the book or magazine where the information was published originally, not the name of the information service.

Media Literacy: USING A TIME LINE

Explain to students that a time line is a graphic organizer that presents events in chronological order (the order in which events happened). Explore with students how time lines enable writers to organize events and see how the narrative will unfold. Have students work in pairs to arrange their details in chronological order to decide what to include and what to delete.

Mini-Lesson: Speaking, Listening, and Viewing

ASKING QUESTIONS To help students learn how to write effective questions, have them identify the problems with each of the following questions and then rewrite the questions to make them more effective.

1. Do you like your work? *(yes/no question)*
2. What was your favorite food as a child? *(does not require sensory details)*
3. Did you retire at age 65? *(yes/no question)*
4. Do you remember when Grandma was the grand prize winner on the quiz show? *(yes/no question)*

Applying What You've Learned Have partners make sure that the questions are open-ended and can be answered with sensory details.

Additional Suggestions Students may wish to submit their questions to the interview subject ahead of time. This will give the subject time to review the questions and jot down written responses, if he or she wishes.

THE LANGUAGE OF LITERATURE TEACHER'S EDITION **139**

Writing Skill:
USING THE COMPUTER

J Point out that the model draft was written on a computer. Explore with students how computer drafting can make composing easier. Then describe to the class how the writer of the student draft used the detailed, specific guidelines for drafting provided by The Writing Coach. Discuss each of the comments on the right-hand side of the screen. Invite students to generate additional comments that could help the student writer.

Writing Skill:
USING THE COMPUTER

K To help students concentrate on their thoughts and feelings, they can write on a computer with the monitor screen turned off. Then have students turn the screen on to see what they have written, adding and deleting material as desired.

CUSTOMIZING FOR
Less-Proficient Writers

L Students who are having difficulty getting started might write about the most important part of the narrative first. Then guide students to imagine what details their readers need to know in order to understand how the situation began and ended.

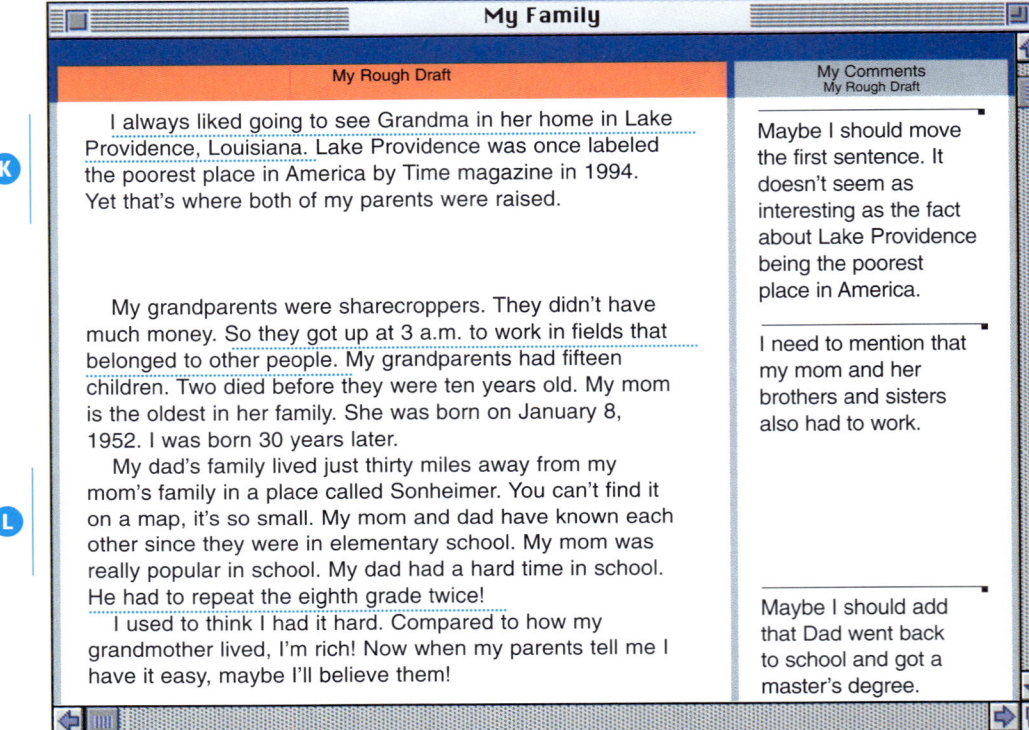

DRAFTING

Shaping Your History

Getting It All Down Once you have organized your notes and decided on a focus, begin getting your ideas on paper. The steps on these two pages will help you develop a draft of your family history.

❶ Write a Rough Draft

Try not to edit yourself while you write. Just concentrate on getting the facts down in a way that makes sense. The Writing Coach can give you drafting ideas. Afterward, read your draft out loud. What do you like about what you've written? What do you need to change?

Student's Rough Draft

My Family

My Rough Draft	My Comments My Rough Draft
I always liked going to see Grandma in her home in Lake Providence, Louisiana. Lake Providence was once labeled the poorest place in America by Time magazine in 1994. Yet that's where both of my parents were raised.	Maybe I should move the first sentence. It doesn't seem as interesting as the fact about Lake Providence being the poorest place in America.
My grandparents were sharecroppers. They didn't have much money. So they got up at 3 a.m. to work in fields that belonged to other people. My grandparents had fifteen children. Two died before they were ten years old. My mom is the oldest in her family. She was born on January 8, 1952. I was born 30 years later. My dad's family lived just thirty miles away from my mom's family in a place called Sonheimer. You can't find it on a map, it's so small. My mom and dad have known each other since they were in elementary school. My mom was really popular in school. My dad had a hard time in school. He had to repeat the eighth grade twice! I used to think I had it hard. Compared to how my grandmother lived, I'm rich! Now when my parents tell me I have it easy, maybe I'll believe them!	I need to mention that my mom and her brothers and sisters also had to work. Maybe I should add that Dad went back to school and got a master's degree.

140   UNIT ONE: CHANGING PERCEPTIONS

Nouns: words that name people, places, things, and ideas

Verbs: words that state an action or link the subject with a word that describes it

Adjectives: words that modify or describe nouns and pronouns

Adverbs: words that modify or describe a verb, an adjective, or another adverb

140   THE LANGUAGE OF LITERATURE   TEACHER'S EDITION

❷ Rework Your Draft

The following guidelines can help you develop a more formal draft.

Strengthen the Shape of Your Story These points can help you develop a smooth flow of ideas:

- As you write your draft, you might need to refer to your time line to check the order of events. One way you can order events is through the use of words that show the passing of time. Some transitional words that show time order are *later, meanwhile, first, then, soon,* and *immediately*—for example: "My mom is the oldest in her family. She was born on January 8, 1952. I was born 30 years *later.*"
- Most effective narratives have an attention-grabbing beginning. If you don't grab your readers at the beginning, they may not stick around for the end. The middle of the narrative should develop the thought you expressed at the beginning and lead to a conclusion or concluding thought.

Create Vivid Images The SkillBuilder at the right and the techniques below can help you create vivid images for your readers.

- Use descriptions to enliven dry facts. What did the person you are writing about see, hear, taste, smell, or feel?
- Dialogue can help readers understand the excitement and significance of an event. Include remembered conversations whenever possible.

 **PEER RESPONSE**

When you are ready to share what you have written with others, ask a peer reviewer for feedback. You can ask questions such as the following to get the kind of feedback you need to revise your draft.

- What was the most memorable point for you?
- Were you able to understand the sequence of events? If not, where did you become confused?

SkillBuilder

 WRITER'S CRAFT

Using Descriptive Language

Read the following two sentences. Which sentence gives you a clearer picture of the action?

We went to Lake Providence.

One cold winter evening, Mom and I boarded a plane traveling to Lake Providence.

The first sentence is vague, while the second sentence includes more precise details to help readers picture the scene. Using more descriptive nouns, verbs, adjectives, and adverbs can make your writing clearer to your readers.

APPLYING WHAT YOU'VE LEARNED
You can use descriptive nouns, verbs, adjectives, or adverbs to make your writing more precise. What do you need to add to your draft?

 WRITING HANDBOOK

For more information on descriptive language, see page 832 of the Writing Handbook.

RETHINK & EVALUATE

Preparing to Revise

1. What details do you need to add to strengthen the organization of your family history?
2. What changes do you want to make to your draft as a result of peer response?

CUSTOMIZING FOR Less-Proficient Writers

M If students have trouble writing conclusions, they can think about the endings to popular television shows. Discuss with students how episodes of their favorite shows are resolved. Point out that there is usually a final scene in which the characters reflect on what has happened. Invite students to think about some concluding scenes they have watched and analyze how they might use the same techniques in their narrative.

Teaching Strategy: MODELING

N Consider drafting your own family history. Ask a group of students to read it and make suggestions for revision. Read the suggestions to the entire class and model the thinking process used in evaluating the readers' comments. Explain why you accepted some and not others.

SkillBuilder WRITER'S CRAFT

USING DESCRIPTIVE LANGUAGE
Students may have difficulty distinguishing among nouns, verbs, adjectives, and adverbs. Provide students with the definitions on the chart on p. 140.

Applying What You've Learned Arrange students in pairs. Have partners read each other's narratives and underline all the descriptive nouns, verbs, adjectives, and adverbs.

Additional Suggestions Suggest that students draw sketches to accompany their draft. These sketches can help students see where more detail is needed and how to add it.

Reteaching/Reinforcement
Writing Mini-Lesson transparencies, pp. 38, 46

Sensory Details, p. 256

Writing Skill: REVISING

O Tell students that when they come back to their writing after a break, they should begin by reading aloud what they have written to help them focus again on their work. At the same time, they now may notice things they want to change.

Teaching Strategy: MODELING

P Use the student's final draft to walk students through the revision process. Invite a volunteer to read the essay aloud while students follow along silently. Then work as a class to isolate the words and phrases that show time order. Possibilities include *3 A.M., before, since, later,* and *now.*

Help students analyze what the writer reveals in the last paragraph about what she learned from her family. Guide students to see that she learned she has a relatively easy, affluent life. Be sure that students understand that she learned this lesson by comparing her life to her parents' childhood and adolescence.

REVISING AND PUBLISHING

Finishing Your Narrative

Making It Final Make any changes you think are necessary based on your readers' responses. Pay special attention to any suggestions made by family members who are mentioned in your narrative. Make sure you've presented them fairly and accurately. As you revise, though, don't lose sight of the focus of your family history.

❶ Revise and Edit Your Draft

Use the following guidelines as you revise your draft:

- Refer to the comments made by your peer reviewers.
- Use the Standards for Evaluation and the Editing Checklist on page 143 to be sure that you've presented events of your family history in the correct order.
- This model will help you see how one student revised her draft. How did she make use of the notes she wrote to herself during the drafting stage?

Which words or phrases indicate a sense of time order?

What does the last paragraph tell you about what the student learned from her family?

Student's Final Draft

My Family

According to an August 1994 issue of *Time* magazine, Lake Providence, Louisiana, is one of the poorest places in America. Yet this is where both of my parents grew up.

My mother's parents were sharecroppers. They didn't have much money. They had to get up at 3 A.M. to go to work in fields they didn't own.

Fifteen children were born into my mom's family. My mom is the oldest. Two of her siblings died before they reached the age of ten. The kids who survived also had to work in the fields to get the crops ready for harvest.

My parents have known each other since they were in elementary school. My mom was popular in school and did well. Dad had a harder time in school. He had to repeat the eighth grade twice! Later he went to college and received a master's degree.

I used to think I had it hard. Compared to how my parents lived, I'm rich! Now when my parents tell me I have it easy, maybe I'll believe them.

142 UNIT ONE: CHANGING PERCEPTIONS

WRITING SPRINGBOARD
Family Memories Every family's history contains memorable milestones. These video clips of events like a child's learning to ride a bicycle and people's celebrating a grandparent's birthday will spark students' memories of family experiences.

Writing Prompt Choose a large or small event in your family's history. Write an account of the event, explaining why you think it is important.

Side B, Frame 3518

Making a video is one way to share your family history with others.

❷ Share Your Work

The format your writing takes may be determined by your reason for writing your family history. Below are some possible formats you can use for your family history. What do you like best about each format?

PUBLISHING IDEAS

- Make a family video, with narration. A storyboard like the one above can help you plan each scene.
- Use family photos in a photo essay with captions.
- Collect family recipes passed down from generation to generation, and include them with your history.

Standards for Evaluation

The firsthand narrative
- shows the writer's strong personal interest in the topic
- presents events in a clear order
- includes vivid imagery to give the reader a clear impression of the events
- concludes with the writer's personal reactions and observations

---

SkillBuilder

 GRAMMAR FROM WRITING

Punctuating Introductory Phrases
Use a comma after a participial phrase at the beginning of a sentence.

According to an August 1994 issue of Time *magazine, Lake Providence, Louisiana, is one of the poorest places in America.*

Editing Checklist Check the following as you revise your draft:
- Did you use transitional words to show the order of events?
- Did you use vivid images to create a clear picture of your family?

 GRAMMAR HANDBOOK

For more information on punctuating introductory phrases, see page 892 of the Grammar Handbook.

REFLECT & ASSESS

Evaluating the Experience

1. How did peer comments help you improve your narrative?
2. Share with the class something important you learned about yourself while writing your family history.

📁 **PORTFOLIO** Consider including photos or drawings you made to accompany your family history.

WRITING FROM EXPERIENCE 143

Writing Skill: PUBLISHING

Q Share these other possibilities for publication with students.
- Publish an oral history magazine. Students can work in small groups to link several histories together based on a common theme. Students can publish their magazines on paper or on-line.
- Donate copies of the oral histories to the community's public library, historical society, or town hall. This method is best suited for narratives that provide information about the community and its members.
- Give dramatic readings of their oral histories. Students may wish to read their oral histories in a small group, in front of the class, or at a historical society meeting.

Portfolio

Invite students to select the writing pieces they wish to include in their portfolio. If students select the narrative, they should also include all their research and a copy of any tape recordings they made.

Standards for Evaluation

Have students review their firsthand narratives for the following:

Ideas and Content
- Recounts a personal experience vividly
- Uses an interesting introduction
- Gives a sense of time, place, and characters
- Shows why the event is important

Structure and Form
- Displays a clear order of events
- Presents a single focus in each paragraph
- Uses a variety of sentence structures

Grammar, Usage, and Mechanics
- Contains only a few minor errors in grammar and usage
- Contains only a few minor errors in spelling, capitalization, and punctuation

---

SkillBuilder GRAMMAR FROM WRITING

PUNCTUATING INTRODUCTORY PHRASES First, be sure that students understand that a participle is a form of a verb that acts as an adjective. Present these examples:

A *buzzing* sound came from the toaster.

Smiling, the man shook my hand.

Then explain that a participial phrase is a present or past participle that is modified by an adverb or has a complement. The entire phrase acts as an adjective in the sentence. Share these examples:

Walking slowly, we did not notice the neighbor waving at us.

Using the loudspeaker, the principal announced a fire drill.

Applying What You've Learned Guide students to use the Editing Checklist as they revise their work. Remind students to pay special attention to using commas after introductory phrases.

Reteaching/Reinforcement
Grammar Mini-Lessons copymasters p. 39, transparencies, p. 29

THE LANGUAGE OF LITERATURE TEACHER'S EDITION 143

UNIT REVIEW

This feature allows students to reflect on what they have learned in Unit One and to assess how well they understand what they have learned. This feature provides students with multiple opportunities for self-assessment, although you may wish to use some of the activities to informally assess specific skills such as speaking and listening or cooperative work.

Objectives

- To allow students to reflect on and assess their understanding of theme
- To allow students to reflect on and assess their understanding of literary concepts such as characterization and climax
- To provide students with the opportunity to assess and build their portfolios

Reflecting on Theme

OPTION 1

Have students first review the selections by recording in their notebooks their impressions of each character and the lessons they learned. Make sure students write their letters in a manner consistent with their chosen characters.

OPTION 2

Encourage students to review the selections by writing a brief summary for each one. Students can use this information to decide which story connects the most to their own lives. Students should outline first their paragraphs and then jot down their impressions and organize their thoughts before they begin writing.

OPTION 3

Suggest to students that they first jot down in their notebooks some ideas that they can refer to in their discussions. You may wish to assign the role of monitor to one student in each group to insure that all students get a chance to share their ideas.

 Self-Assessment
Encourage students to review their reading logs to help them reflect on what they learned while reading the selections. Suggest that their assessments include their responses to any of the activities on this page that they completed.

REFLECT & ASSESS

UNIT ONE: CHANGING PERCEPTIONS

In this unit, many of the characters experience situations and encounters that change the way they view things. As you read the selections, did your own perceptions change in any way? Did any of the selections lead you to think that things may not be as you once believed? Explore these questions by completing one or more of the options in each of the following sections.

REFLECTING ON THEME

OPTION 1 Reading from Within The characters in Unit One, "Changing Perceptions," learn important lessons as a result of their experiences. Which character do you think learns the most valuable lesson? Whose life will change the most as a result of what he or she has learned? Pretend that you are that character and write a letter to a friend, explaining how your perceptions have changed and what you plan to do from now on.

OPTION 2 Connecting to Experience Which situation or encounter in this unit's selections reminds you the most of an event in your own life? Write a few paragraphs, stating the similarities and telling whether your views changed as a result of your experience.

OPTION 3 Discussion With a small group of classmates, discuss the different ways in which people learn that things are not as they once believed. Use examples from your own experiences and from the selections. You might consider the following factors:

- friends
- society
- family
- parents
- human nature
- the natural world

Self Assessment: What new ways of looking at things have you developed as a result of reading the selections in Unit One? Jot down your thoughts in a chart like the one shown, naming the selection that influenced your thinking.

What I Thought	What I Think Now
My parents were too strict about homework.	They have my best interests at heart. ("The Treasure of Lemon Brown")

REVIEWING LITERARY CONCEPTS

OPTION 1 Looking at Characterization Which characters in Unit One do you think you came to know best? What methods of characterization did the writers use to make those characters so memorable? Create a chart like the one shown. For each character you chose, fill in details from the story that show how the writer developed the character.

Character	Physical Description	Own Speech, Thoughts, and Actions	Others' Speech, Thoughts, and Actions	Direct Comments About Character
Dr. Remenzel ("The Lie")	a large man	". . . you are not to ask for anything special for Eli—not anything."	Mrs. Remenzel: "Why do you always think I'm going to embarrass you?"	dignified, wealthy

144 UNIT ONE: CHANGING PERCEPTIONS

OPTION 2 **Thinking About Climax** As you know, the climax of a plot is the moment when the reader's interest is at its highest point. Look back over the short stories you have read, and summarize the climax of each in a single sentence. Discuss your summaries with a classmate. See if you agree on exactly where each climax occurs. If you don't, try to persuade your partner to adopt your views.

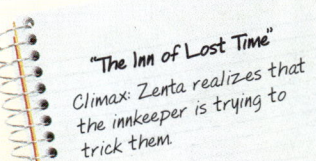

"The Inn of Lost Time"
Climax: Zenta realizes that the innkeeper is trying to trick them.

 Self-Assessment: On a sheet of paper, copy this list of other literary terms that were introduced in this unit. Next to each term, indicate whether you feel you understand it well, somewhat, or not at all. Review the terms you are not sure about by looking them up in The Handbook of Reading Terms and Literary Concepts (page 812).

irony	frame story	form
anecdote	setting	simile
humor	third-person	personification
style	point of view	rhyme
	speaker	rhythm

PORTFOLIO BUILDING

- **QuickWrites** Several of the QuickWrites in this unit asked you to write continuations of stories, new endings for stories, and narratives involving characters from stories. Choose the piece of writing in which you think you most successfully portrayed characters, wrote in an appropriate style, and reflected the theme of the unit. In a cover note, explain why you think you were successful. Add the piece and the cover note to your portfolio.

- **Writing About Literature** In this unit, you responded to a story by changing one of its elements. Look back at the scene you rewrote. Think about your changes and the way they affected the story. Before you add the scene to your portfolio, write a letter to the story's author, briefly describing what changes you made and why you made them. Tell whether you think you were successful, giving reasons for your opinion. Ask the author to read and respond to your scene.

- **Writing from Experience** Reread the family history that you prepared, and begin to list some of its highlights on a sheet of paper. Who was the most interesting person you wrote about? What do you think was the most interesting period in your family's history? What was the most interesting thing that you discovered about your family?

Add any other highlights that you wish to include, then attach your list to your family history.

- **Personal Choice** Look back through your records and evaluations of the activities you completed in this unit. Also look at any activities and writing you have done on your own. Are there any activities you would do differently in the light of what you have learned since doing them? Write a brief paragraph outlining the changes you would make, attach it to the evaluation or writing, and add both to your portfolio.

 Self-Assessment: At this point, you are just beginning your portfolio. Do you think the pieces of writing that you have included are the ones you'll keep, or do you think you will be replacing them as the year goes on?

SETTING GOALS

As you completed the reading and writing activities in this section, you probably identified certain skills on which you need work. Look back through your writing folder, worksheets, and notebook. Create a list of skills or concepts you'd like to work on in the next unit.

REFLECT & ASSESS **145**

Reviewing Literary Concepts

OPTION 1

Students also can use the information in their charts to write a brief description that communicates their impressions of each character. In addition, you may wish to have students compare and discuss their charts with a partner.

OPTION 2

Be sure that students can support their choices with details from the selections if they are trying to persuade their partners.

Self-Assessment For terms that students need to understand better, have them write, in their own words, a definition for each term after checking in the Handbook. Then have students apply each term to a selection they have read. For instance, a student can identify a use of irony or an example of personification in one of the selections.

Portfolio Building

You may wish to help students choose options or modify options for them that best suit the needs you have established for the class. Encourage students to incorporate in their portfolios drafts in addition to final products so that they can reflect on and assess their development and progress.

Self-Assessment Students should consider with which pieces in their portfolios they feel most comfortable and with which kinds of pieces they would like to have more practice. Students can create charts that list each piece in their portfolios and rate their success for each.

Setting Goals

In order to help students answer these questions and set future goals, suggest that students review their work and look at the areas which involved the most revision. Ask students to identify any patterns in their revising that might reveal problems or areas in which they need more work. Students should use this information to construct their lists of skills and concepts they feel need more work in the future.

UNIT TWO

UNIT THEMES

Unit Two

Critical Adjustments In this unit, students will read selections that explore the necessary changes people make in order to adapt to various situations in their lives. The unit contains two parts: Part 1, "Twinges of Conscience," and Part 2, "Unexpected Developments." Selections in both parts contribute to the unit theme by detailing the kinds of changes various characters make in their lives—sometimes as a result of determining what is right and wrong, and sometimes as a result of unforeseen circumstances.

Part 1

Twinges of Conscience Selections in Part 1 focus on experiences that impel characters to change from within and adjust their attitudes and actions. For example, the death of a feisty grandmother in "The Horned Toad" leads her young grandson to finally understand the importance of home.

Part 2

Unexpected Developments Selections in Part 2 emphasize how a variety of characters adjust to the unpredictability of their lives, such as the Americans in "The Home Front: 1941–1945," who must adjust to the unforeseen events of war.

Links to Unit Six

The Oral Tradition Unit Six contains literature from the oral tradition—specifically, folklore from the Americas—that connects with the themes in Unit Two. You may wish to begin or end Unit Two by using the following selections from Unit Six that relate to the theme of "Critical Adjustments":
- "John Henry," p. 718
- "Brer Possum's Dilemma," p. 721
- "Aunty Misery," p. 724
- "M'su Carencro and Mangeur de Poulet," p. 727

UNIT TWO

Critical Adjustments

There are two ways

of meeting difficulties.

You alter the difficulties

or you alter yourself to

meet them.

Phyllis Bottome
British novelist and short story writer

Zwei Köpfe [Two heads] (1932), Paul Klee. Encaustic on canvas, 31 ⅞" × 33 ½", Norton Simon Museum, Pasadena, California, The Blue Four Galka Scheyer Collection, 1953.

Exploring Theme

To help students explore the connections between the art, the quotation, and the unit theme, have them consider the following questions:

1. What does the phrase "critical adjustments" mean to you? *(Possible response: An adjustment is a change or an adaptation that a person makes in response to a situation in his or her life. A critical adjustment would be a change or an adaptation that involves a great deal of thought—a change that is very important.)*

2. Clarify Phyllis Bottome's statement by explicating the two ways of dealing with a difficulty. *(Possible response: A person can deal with a difficult situation in life in one of two ways: by attempting to change the situation itself so that it is no longer difficult or by changing oneself in a way that prepares one to overcome the difficult situation.)*

3. In your opinion, how does Klee's painting connect to the unit theme of critical adjustments? *(Possible response: The two faces represent the need to change or alter oneself to meet difficulties.)*

4. What kinds of stories do you expect to read in this unit? *(Possible response: stories about people who have had to change their attitudes in response to an experience or a situation)*

5. Discuss a personal experience that led you to adjust your attitude toward another person. Why did you have to change your attitude? How did you go about changing your attitude? *(Responses will vary.)*

Art Note

Zwei Köpfe [Two Heads] by Paul Klee
Paul Klee (1879–1940) was one of the most original painters of modern art. Many of Klee's thousands of paintings, drawings, and prints are considered to be witty and imaginative works of consummate skill. His sensitive use of line and color contributes to the fantastic and humorous quality of many of his works.

Reading the Art *How does Klee's use of line and color help create a sense of depth in this painting?*

UNIT TWO
Part 1 Skills Trace

ML DENOTES MINI-LESSON IN TEACHER'S EDITION

Selections	Reading Skills and Strategies	Literary Concepts	Writing Opportunities	Speaking, Listening, and Viewing
FICTION **The Horned Toad** Gerald Haslam	Connecting, PE p. 149 Connecting, ML TE p. 153	First-person point of view, PE p. 159 Setting, ML TE p. 151	List of personality traits, PE p. 159 Epitaph, PE p. 159 Letter, PE p. 159	Create a game, PE p. 160 Eulogy, ML TE p. 156
FICTION **The Splendid Outcast** Beryl Markham	Challenging vocabulary, PE p. 161 Clarifying, ML TE p. 166	Allusions, PE p. 173 Setting, PE p. 173 Similes, ML TE p. 164 Short story, ML TE p. 165	Newspaper headlines, PE p. 173 Poem, PE p. 173 Short paragraph with allusions, PE p. 173 Rewrite a scene, TE p. 169	Group discussion, PE p. 173 Dramatic reading, PE p. 174 Dramatic reading, ML TE p. 171
POETRY **We Alone** Alice Walker **Hard Questions** Margaret Tsuda **oil crisis** Naoshi Koriyama		Theme, PE p. 179 Imagery, ML TE p. 177	Brief explanation of environmental issues, PE p. 175 Poem, PE p. 179 Description, PE p. 179 Paraphrase a poem, TE p. 178	Brainstorming session, PE p. 179 Oral interpretation, ML TE p. 176
DRAMA **The Million-Pound Bank Note** Mark Twain, dramatized by Walter Hackett	Setting changes, PE p. 183 Noting relevant details, ML TE p. 186	Resolution, PE p. 200 Dramatization of a story, ML TE p. 189 Characterization, ML TE p. 190	Script, PE p. 200 Society-page report, PE p. 200 Character sketch, PE p. 200 Letter asking for charity, PE p. 201 Venn diagram, PE p. 202 Letter from one character to another, TE p. 197	Stage production, PE p. 200 Oral report, PE p. 201 Survey of class, PE p. 201 Evaluate art work, PE p. 201 Dramatic reading, ML TE p. 188 Evaluating art, ML TE p. 192
FICTION ON YOUR OWN **Mother & Daughter** Gary Soto			Dialogue journals, TE p. 203 Writing a personal narrative, TE p. 208	Paired reading, TE p. 203 Role-playing a scene, TE p. 207

Writing	Reading Skills and Strategies	Literary Concepts	Writing Opportunities	Speaking, Listening, and Viewing
WRITING ABOUT LITERATURE **Interpretation**	Analyzing emphasis, PE pp. 210–11 Interpreting literature, PE pp. 212–15	Analyzing emphasis, PE pp. 210–11 Finding the meaning, PE pp. 212–13	Describe a scene, PE p. 211 Write lyrics, PE p. 211 Revise a QuickWrite, PE p. 211 Interpretive essay, PE pp. 212–15 Rewriting a paragraph, PE p. 215	Viewing a photograph, PE p. 216 Interpreting a photograph, PE p. 216 Discussion, p. 216 Discussing meaning, PE p. 217

147a UNIT TWO CRITICAL ADJUSTMENTS

Grammar, Usage, Mechanics, and Spelling	Multimodal Learning	Research and Study Skills	Vocabulary
Commas after introductory elements, ML TE p. 152 The letter combination *ph*, ML TE p. 157	Choose a picture that captures personality traits, PE p. 159 Create a game, PE p. 160 Display information on horned toads, PE p. 160	Research horned toads, PE p. 160 Summarizing, ML TE p. 155	incongruously inter millennium periphery verdancy
Adverbs, ML TE p. 168 Connecting ideas, ML TE p. 170 Words ending in *-ant/-ance* and *-ent/-ence*, ML TE p. 172	Group discussion, PE p. 173 Graph events leading to climax, PE p. 173 Dramatic reading, PE p. 174 Create a drawing, painting, or sculpture, PE p. 174	Using general reference books, ML TE p. 163	adversary imposing cow insolence disdainfully novice homage retribution impeccable zealot
	Brainstorming session, PE p. 179 Illustrate a poem with drawings or pictures, PE p. 179		
Dialogue in plays, ML TE p. 185 Sentence fragments, ML TE p. 187 Spelling with suffixes, ML TE p. 199	Stage production, PE p. 200 Oral report, PE p. 201 Survey of class, PE p. 201 Evaluate art work, PE p. 201 Calculate exchange rates, PE p. 201	Taking objective tests: Short-answer questions, ML TE p. 198	accommodation diversion ad-libbing eccentric competent judicious consequence precarious discreet rebuke

Grammar, Usage, Mechanics, and Spelling	Multimodal Learning	Research and Study Skills	Media Literacy
Using interjections, PE p. 211 Using inverted sentences, PE p. 215 Subject-verb agreement, PE p. 215	Viewing a photograph, PE p. 216 Interpreting a photograph, PE p. 216 Discussion, p. 216 Discussing meaning, PE p. 217	Organizing notes, PE p. 212	Interpreting a photograph, PE p. 216

UNIT TWO
Part 2 Skills Trace

(ML) DENOTES MINI-LESSON IN TEACHER'S EDITION

Selections	Reading Skills and Strategies	Literary Concepts	Writing Opportunities	Speaking, Listening, and Viewing
FICTION **A Mother in Mannville** Marjorie Kinnan Rawlings	Visualizing, PE p. 219 Visualizing, (ML) TE p. 221	Conflict, PE p. 226 Setting, PE p. 226 Tone, (ML) TE p. 224 Motivation, (ML) TE p. 222	Personal ad, PE p. 226 Epilogue, PE p. 226 Poem, PE p. 226	Group discussion, PE p. 226 Videotaped role-playing, PE p. 227
FICTION **White Mice** Rubén Sálaz-Márquez	Predicting, PE p. 228 Predicting, (ML) TE p. 231	Surprise ending, PE p. 238 Theme, PE p. 238 Show, don't tell, (ML) TE p. 232 Humor, (ML) TE p. 230	Rewrite incident, PE p. 238 Narrative, PE p. 238 Description of event from alternative point of view, TE p. 234	Dramatization, PE p. 238 Spanish-language music, (ML) TE p. 236
FICTION **The Bet** Anton Chekhov	Cause and effect, PE p. 241 Clarifying, (ML) TE p. 243	Flashback, PE p. 249 Climax, PE p. 249 Theme, (ML) TE p. 242	Complete chart, PE p. 249 Diary entries, PE p. 249 Graffiti, PE p. 249 Compile list of books, PE p. 250	Group discussion, PE p. 249 Sketch or paint pictures, PE p. 250 Dramatic performance, PE p. 250 Role-playing, TE p. 245
NONFICTION **from Once Upon a Time When We Were Colored** Clifton L. Taulbert	Setting a purpose, (ML) TE p. 254	Autobiography, PE p. 257 Description, (ML) TE p. 255	Diagram, PE p. 252 Emotions graph, PE p. 257 Dialogue, PE p. 257 Paragraphs, PE p. 257	Presentation, PE p. 258
NONFICTION **The Home Front: 1941–1945** Hazel Shelton Abernethy	Questioning, PE p. 259 Questioning, (ML) TE p. 261	Memoir, PE p. 265 Point of view, (ML) TE p. 260 Memoir, TE p. 262	Paragraph, PE p. 265 Encyclopedia entry, PE p. 265 Public service announcement, PE p. 265	Poster, PE p. 265 Interview, PE p. 266
POETRY **my enemy was dreaming** Norman Russell **Lost** Bruce Ignacio	Free verse, PE p. 267	Mood, PE p. 270 Alliteration, (ML) TE p. 269 Repetition, (ML) TE p. 268	Stanza, PE p. 270 Character analysis, PE p. 270	Roleplay, PE p. 270 Group reading, PE p. 271
Writing	Reading Skills and Strategies	Literary Concepts	Writing Opportunities	Speaking, Listening, and Viewing
WRITING FROM EXPERIENCE **Narrative and Literary Writing**		Story elements, PE pp. 272–79	Writing a short story, PE pp. 276-79 Drafting, PE pp. 276–77 Revising and publishing, PE pp. 278–79	Storytelling, (ML) TE p. 274

Grammar, Usage, Mechanics, and Spelling	Multimodal Learning	Research and Study Skills	Vocabulary	
Compound sentences, ML TE p. 223 Spelling hard and soft *c*, ML TE p. 225	Group discussion, PE p. 226 Montage, PE p. 227 Videotaped role-playing, PE p. 227		blunt clarity communion ecstasy	impel inadequate instinctive kindling
Commas that separate ideas, ML TE p. 233 Indistinct vowels, ML TE p. 237	Dramatization, PE p. 238 Prepare an ethnic food, PE p. 239		ardor component gusto intimidate palate	persevering prone scrutinize transitional vigilant
Chronological order, ML TE p. 246 Subject-verb agreement, ML TE p. 247 Prefixes *in-/im-*, ML TE p. 248	Group discussion, PE p. 249 Sketch or paint pictures, PE p. 250 Dramatic performance, PE p. 250 Compile a list of books, PE p. 250 Determine hourly wage, PE p. 250 Role-playing, ML TE p. 245	Research capital punishment, PE p. 250	capricious haphazardly humane immoral incessantly	obsolete posterity rapture renunciation stipulated
Nonstandard English, PE p. 258 Prefixes and roots, ML TE p. 256	Draw a map, PE p. 258 Presentation, PE p. 258	Research Mississippi, PE p. 258 Research child labor laws, PE p. 258	conservative impact meticulously responsive vogue	
	Poster, PE p. 265 Shared research, PE p. 266 Interview, PE p. 266	Research unanswered questions, PE p. 266 Research internment camps, PE p. 266 Research World War II, PE p. 266 Research ratio, PE p. 266 SQ3R, ML TE p. 264		
	Role-play, PE p. 270 Group reading, PE p. 271 Illustrations, PE p. 271	Research a Native American group, PE p. 271		

Grammar, Usage, Mechanics, and Spelling	Multimodal Learning	Research and Study Skills	Media Literacy
Ordering events, PE p. 275 Planning the climax, PE p. 277 Using precise verbs, PE p. 279	Diagram story action, PE p. 277	Making a time line, PE p. 275	

UNIT TWO
Recommended Resources

ENRICHMENT   RESEARCH

Recommended Novels

LITERATURE CONNECTIONS WITH SOURCEBOOK FOR TEACHERS

The Giver
by Lois Lowry

Thematic Links As Jonas trains for his new role as The Giver, his perceptions of himself and his seemingly perfect community change, and he must decide how to meet the challenges brought about by his new knowledge.

About the Author Newbery Award-winning author Lois Lowry (born 1937), whose memories were the inspiration for *The Giver*, uses her writing to share with others her beliefs about the importance of communication and interdependence between people.

Other Works by Lois Lowry *A Summer to Die; Number the Stars; Find a Stranger, Say Goodbye; Anastasia Krupnik; The One Hundredth Thing About Caroline; Taking Care of Terrific*

Dealing with Dragons
by Patricia Wrede

Thematic Links Bored with her life as a princess, Cimorene makes some serious adjustments in her life when she joins the powerful dragon Kazul in a battle against wicked wizards.

About the Author Patricia Wrede (born 1953), the eldest of five children, often told stories to her younger siblings. She published her first book in 1980 and continues her storytelling with her nieces as the audience.

Other Works by Patricia Wrede *Searching for Dragons, Mairelon the Magician, Caught in Crystal*

The Alien Game
by Catherine Dexter

Thematic Links A game of tag unexpectedly develops a sinister effect in this science fiction thriller.

About the Author Catherine Dexter's stories for young adults have been recognized and honored by the Junior Literary Guild and the Child Study Association Book Committee.

Other Works by Catherine Dexter *The Oracle Doll, The Guilded Cat, Mazemaker*

The Prince and the Pauper
by Mark Twain

Thematic Links When a royal member and a poor boy trade places, both must learn to make critical adjustments.

About the Author Mark Twain (1835–1910) often places his characters in unfamiliar settings, where the rich and the poor, the free and the enslaved, the royal and the common learn how the other lives.

Other Works by Mark Twain *The Adventures of Tom Sawyer, The Adventures of Huckleberry Finn, Life on the Mississippi, A Connecticut Yankee in King Arthur's Court*

The Barn
by Avi

Thematic Links Ben is forced to make a critical life adjustment when he is called home from school to take care of his severely disabled father.

About the Author Avi (born 1937) writes about young people both historically and in the contemporary world. Tales of mystery, hauntings, adventures, sorrow, and fun are all trademarks of this popular author.

Other Works by Avi *The Man Who Was Poe, The True Confessions of Charlotte Doyle, S.O.R. Losers, Romeo and Juliet—Together (and Alive!) At Last*

Taking Sides
by Gary Soto

Thematic Links Lincoln Mendoza's world changes when he has to move from San Francisco to the suburbs.

About the Author Gary Soto (born 1952) often writes about the experiences of Mexican Americans, especially the difficult decisions young people face.

Other Works by Gary Soto *The Skirt, Local News, Baseball in April and Other Stories, Black Hair*

For Teacher   TEACHING LITERATURE

Barber, Ray. "Books in the Middle: Outstanding Books of 1994." *VOYA* (June 1995).

Diegmueller, Karen. "California Plotting: New Tack on Language Arts." *Network News and Views* (August 1995).

Freedman, Morris. "Making the Classics Available to Students." *Education Week* (September 27, 1995).

Twain, Mark. "How to Tell a Story," *Selected Shorter Writings of Mark Twain.* Boston: MA: Houghton Mifflin, 1962.

147e   UNIT TWO   CRITICAL ADJUSTMENTS

CROSS-CURRICULAR TEACHING   PROFESSIONAL DEVELOPMENT

Recommended Readings in Cross-Curricular Areas

MUSIC
A Day at the Races
by Harold Roth (1983)
Provides a behind-the-scenes look at horse racing. Links to Beryl Markham's "The Splendid Outcast."

HISTORY
Energy
by Robin McKie (1989)
Introduces and illustrates various power resources. Links to Naoshi Koriyama's "oil crisis."

SCIENCE
V Is for Victory: America Remembers World War II
by Kathleen Krull (1995)
Book is both informative and visually interesting. Links to Hazel Shelton Abernethy's "The Home Front: 1941–1945."

SOCIAL STUDIES
The Hidden Children
by Howard Greenfield (1993)
Contains stories of children who saved themselves during World War II. Links to Hazel Shelton Abernethy's "The Home Front: 1941–1945."

For Teacher — CROSS-CURRICULAR INSTRUCTION

Davis, Vivian I. "Working Toward Language-Centered Writing and Literature Courses." *English Journal* 84:1 (January 1995) 35.

Rebore, Nancy. "Board Games as Research Projects." *The Book Report* (November/December 1993).

Reinhartz, Dennis, and Judy Reinhartz. *Geography Across the Curriculum.* Washington, D.C.: National Education Association, 1990.

Recommended Media Resources

THE LANGUAGE OF LITERATURE

LASERLINKS
Videodisc, Gr. 8
See *LaserLinks Teacher's Source Book*, pages 14–15, for an overview of Unit Two.

AUDIO LIBRARY
Tapes
Unit Two: Critical Adjustments
Gr. 8, Tape 4: Sides A & B
Gr. 8, Tape 5: Sides A & B
Gr. 8, Tape 6: Sides A & B

WRITING COACH
Writing Coach Software: Writing About Literature: Interpretive Response; Short Story

OUTSIDE RESOURCES

Films/Videos/Film Strips/Audiocassettes
America Goes to War: The Home Front—WWII. 5 videocassettes. PBS Video.
Mark Twain—A Musical Biography. videocassette. WMHT/Monterey Home Video, 1992. (87 min.)
Visions of the Spirit: a Portrait of Alice Walker. videocassette. New York, 1989. (58 min.)

Internet Resources
WorldWide Web at
http://www.hmco.com/mcdougal

For Teacher — TEACHING WITH TECHNOLOGY

Computing Teacher. International Society for Technology in Education (ISTE), 1787 Agate St. Eugene, OR 97403–1923.

Hahn, Harley. *The Internet Yellow Pages.* Third Ed. Berkeley, CA: Osborne McGraw-Hill, 1996.

Sheingold, K., and Hadley, M. *Accomplished Teachers: Integrating Computers into Classroom Practice.* New York: Center for Technology in Education, Bank Street College of Education, 1990.

UNIT TWO
Professional Enrichment

Showing, Not Telling

by Rebekah Caplan, Coordinator, English Language Arts K–12, Oakland Unified School District, Oakland, California

Many of the selections in this unit contain very descriptive writing—writing that "shows, not tells" what is happening. "Showing, not telling" is beneficial in that it works to move students away from generalized and clichéd thinking to an appreciation of the richness and complexity of language.

The notion of "showing" an idea—revealing thinking through examples and specifics—carries infinite possibilities. Some think of "showing" as purely descriptive writing, but description is only one prospect a writer might consider as he or she strives for specificity. Depending on the purpose, a writer might also explain through analogy, defend through metaphor, characterize through dialogue, or appeal through anecdote.

Sensitizing students to the possibilities takes more, however, than simply passing out a list. Imagine your classroom as a studio, similar to the teaching atmosphere of a music, drama, art, or dance class. There are periods of improvising and creating, of learning and applying technique, of examining one another's work, and of preparing for major performances. Built into instruction is also an expectation of regular and disciplined practice. Teachers can train students to become effective readers, writers, and thinkers who practice and appreciate the art of "showing" by structuring language arts classrooms similarly.

IMPROVISING AND CREATING
Showing, not telling, as disciplined practice for writing As a homework assignment several times a week, assign a "telling" sentence for expansion into a "showing" paragraph. Vary the kinds of sentences you assign to include narrative, informative, and persuasive writing modes so that students practice being specific in a range of fictional and nonfictional forms. Challenge students not to use the assigned sentence in the body of the paragraph but to reveal the idea through specifics alone. Later, you can challenge students to reduce ideas to single sentences that "show" instead of "tell."

Showing, not telling, as disciplined practice for reading As a follow-up, have students exchange papers with partners. Partners should read each other's version, looking for especially interesting or successful "showing" techniques. Partners should then select an appealing area and write an evaluative response, "showing" why the particular section made an impact. As students choose and respond to effective lines or techniques, they act as critical readers and, in effect, practice the kind of interpretive thinking they will use to analyze literature.

LEARNING FROM ONE ANOTHER'S WORK
To pull the lessons together, invite volunteer partners to take the "author's chair" and "reader's chair" in front of the room. Ask the writer to read his or her paragraph and the partner to share his or her written response. Conclude by offering additional feedback of your own.

LEARNING AND APPLYING TECHNIQUE
Showing, not telling, as directed instruction: Studying the techniques of masters A third feature of the training is the use of professional models taken from selections students are studying. Selections in this unit such as "The Splendid Outcast," "Mother and Daughter," "White Mice," "Once Upon a Time When We Were Colored," and "Home Front" might work especially well. After students have experimented with their own development of a "telling" sentence, they can examine how a published author deals with a similar idea. Additionally, students can compose commentaries to the author, selecting impressive areas for critical response. As a reverse exercise, students can read a professional model and invent a "telling" sentence that captures the main idea that the author is "showing."

PREPARING FOR "PERFORMANCE," OR PUBLICATION
Showing, not telling, in the revision process As students prepare major essays and compositions for publication, have them scrutinize their own and each other's papers for generalities or clichés that need development. Have them extract their own "telling" sentences from first-draft writing and "show" them for homework. Expanded sentences and paragraphs can be inserted into original drafts to enrich the writing. Peer readers can serve as critics, offering insight into the effectiveness of individual revisions.

Related Reading

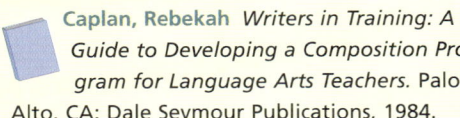
Caplan, Rebekah *Writers in Training: A Guide to Developing a Composition Program for Language Arts Teachers.* Palo Alto, CA: Dale Seymour Publications, 1984.

The Writer's Craft. Evanston, IL: McDougal Littell, 1995.

Family and Community Involvement

 Family

All of the selections in Unit Two connect to the theme of proving oneself. By completing some of the following Copymasters, your students, their families, and other community members can explore real-life examples of people who prove themselves.

OPTION 1: LEARNING YOUR WAY THROUGH A MAZE
- **Connection** All of the selections in Unit Two connect to the theme of critical adjustments.
- **Activity** *Copymaster, p. 1* Family members design a maze and students attempt to successfully complete it. Students and family members can then discuss their experience with the maze in terms of making critical adjustments in the course of one's life.

OPTION 2: WHAT WOULD YOU GIVE UP FOR A MILLION DOLLARS?
- **Connection** The main character in *The Million Pound Bank Note* withstands a test of morals after receiving a large sum of money.
- **Activity** *Copymaster, p. 2* Students and family members imagine that they have just received a million dollars on the condition that they give up something very important to them. They then complete a chart to list those things they would not give up and those things that they would consider giving up for the money.

OPTION 3: WRITE A SONG ABOUT LIFE'S UNPREDICTABILITY
- **Connection** Many of the selections in Unit Two explore characters' experiences with and reactions to unpredictable events in their lives.
- **Activity** *Copymaster, p. 3* Students and family members collaborate to write a song exploring their feelings about the unpredictability of life. A word web is provided to help organize thoughts and ideas.

 Community

OPTION 1
- **Connection** In "White Mice," the children in Mrs. Teubbes's class bring in various ethnic foods for a "cultural day" celebration.
- **Activity** Invite other classes in your school to a multicultural potluck festival. You might also invite students' parents to share stories about their cultures.

OPTION 2
- **Connection** One of the selections in Unit Two, "The Home Front: 1941–1945," discusses the adjustments Americans made in their daily lives during wartime.
- **Activity** Invite grandparents of students to speak to the class about their experiences of living through World War II.

OPTION 3
- **Connection** *The Million Pound Bank Note* is a drama selection in Unit Two that deals with the world of banking and finance.
- **Activity** Invite a bank manager or professional investor to speak to the class about the role of banking and finance in American society.

UNIT TWO
Part 1 Cooperative Project

A Radio Play of Changes

Overview

Students will create a radio play of dramatic monologues where the characters explain how their consciences led them to change in some way.

PROJECT AT A GLANCE
The selections in Unit Two, Part 1 are about people who have been led to change their attitudes, beliefs, or lives in some way. For this project, students will create a radio play in which the main characters in the selections explain how their consciences led them to make a change. Students will work cooperatively to decide what event, realization, or knowledge caused the change in the characters' behavior and script a dramatic speech around that reason. Monologues should be written in the same style as the original selection, with the narrator remaining "in character" throughout. The monologues may be read by students in the classroom or taped and played during a class session.

OBJECTIVES
- To discover the reason behind a character's change of heart
- To script and read a dramatic monologue that tells the change and the reason or reasons for it
- To write a script following the author's style in the original selection

SUGGESTED GROUP SIZE
2–4 students

MATERIALS
- Audiotape player and tapes (if available)

1 Getting Started

Arranging the Project
Before the project begins, there is very little you need to do. If you want to audiotape the monologues, look into getting a tape player and some tapes. You might use one tape for each group or a single tape for the entire class, in which case you will have to remember to include vocal introductions to identify each group.

Decide how the performances will be presented. Will students read their monologues in front of the class? Will they memorize the monologues? For a real "radio" effect, you can also ask students to perform from behind a screen or a sheet hung in a corner of the room. Make decisions like these now, so you can inform students exactly what is expected of them. If you choose to have groups tape their monologues outside of class for a later presentation, you will have to find a place and a time for this to be done. Stress good diction to students, and encourage them to speak into the microphone clearly and with a reasonable volume.

Arranging the Performances
Having made all the important decisions in advance, you can sit back and enjoy the performances.

2 Creating the Monologues

Introducing the Project
Explain that students will be working in small groups to write and read monologues based on the characters in the selections they have been reading. They should brainstorm to decide how and why each character changed by the end of the selection. Each group should select as many characters as they have members and should collaborate to write a monologue for each character that will be read by a member of the group. The monologues should explain, in the character's own words, the change and the reason for it. Students might also be inspired by listening to a few old radio plays, such as Orson Welles's *War of the Worlds*, or an old episode of *The Green Hornet* (such tapes are often available at your local library). Many students today have never had any experience with radio plays and may pick up some interesting ideas from listening to the masters of the genre.

Students should also investigate the difference between a monologue and a soliloquy. Some might immediately think of Hamlet's "To be or not to be . . ." soliloquy (in which he wrestles with his conscience, basically talking to himself) and confuse it with a dramatic monologue (in which a character explains something to someone else). Be sure all students understand the assignment and what is expected of them.

Group Investigations
Divide students into groups of two to four. Groups should meet to discuss the selections and determine which ones interest them most. They should agree on how the character in the chosen selection changes and the motive behind the change. Each member should select a specific character and write a monologue for him or her. Groups can meet later to review the monologues, make changes, offer suggestions, and rehearse for the final performances. Class meetings can help you monitor progress as students work toward the big day.

Creating a Project Description
After groups have selected specific characters and before they start writing the monologues, each group should submit a brief description of the characters selected, the determined reasons for change, and who will be giving the final monologue for each character. In this way you can steer groups away from too much duplication and offer other helpful suggestions to keep them on the right track. Drop in on rehearsals from time to time to monitor progress.

147i UNIT TWO CRITICAL ADJUSTMENTS

OPTION 1: PANEL INTERVIEW Students can arrange to interview a character in the manner of a *Meet the Press* interview. Group members can take turns being interviewed and asking questions. Questions should be well thought out and prepared ahead of time. Characters' answers can be written ahead of time or given extemporaneously, according to your directions.

OPTION 2: ORIGINAL SCENARIO Groups can create an original scenario during which a character shows change. Scenarios should be briefly explained in writing, and the monologues should evolve from those scenarios.

OPTION 3: THE OLD FRIEND Groups can write a dialogue between a character who has changed and an old friend he or she has not seen in a while. The two characters can discuss what has happened in their lives, including the main character's explanation of the changes in his or her life.

OPTION 4: A TOTAL PRODUCTION If you are taping the performances, you can ask groups to add sound effects and background or dramatic music to the production. Again, refer groups to old radio shows for ideas. As always, a good, well-mannered audience is a must for any production. You may encourage other students to take notes for future discussions, but caution them to listen respectfully. Comments can be shared after the performances.

3 Sharing the Productions

If you think the monologues created can stand by themselves (that is, if there is no need to be familiar with the selections the monologues are based on), you may arrange for the tapes to be broadcast over the school public address system. This can be done during morning announcements or at special times arranged by you and school officials. If the monologues do require a certain amount of background information and knowledge, you can offer to share them with other teachers using the same program. Tapes also can be played for other sections of your class.

Assessing the Project

The following rubric can be used for group or individual assessment.

3 Full Accomplishment Students follow directions and produce a monologue using the author's style of writing that describes how and why the character changed.

2 Substantial Accomplishment Students produce a monologue, but it does not fully describe the change or the reason, or it is not in the author's style of writing.

3 Little or Partial Accomplishment Students' monologue is incomplete or does not fulfill the requirements of the assignment.

For the Portfolio
Students can submit written copies of the monologues to include in their portfolios along with a copy of the project description. Include a copy of your written assessment, too. Tapes may be returned to students or kept in the classroom or library for future reference.

Note: For other assessment options, see the *Teacher's Guide to Assessment and Portfolio Use*.

Cross-Curricular Options

SOCIAL STUDIES

Students can interview adults in the neighborhood to find out if they ever went through a change like one of those experienced by the characters in the selections. Changes described can be summarized and compared within the class.

ART
Ask students to design a promotional poster for a selection that is to be made into a movie. They may even enjoy "casting" famous actors and actresses in the leading roles.

LANGUAGE ARTS
Students can write a new ending to one of the selections they have been reading that shows what might have happened if the character did not undergo a change. Be sure writers retain the original style of the author.

Resources

Speak Up! A Guide to Public Speaking by Patricia Sternberg provides tips, from preparing a speech to overcoming stage fright.

On the Air: Radio Broadcasting by Robert Hawkins gives a brief historical overview of broadcasting and discusses available broadcasting careers.

UNIT TWO
Part 1 Lesson Planner

TIME ALLOTMENTS SHOWN ARE APPROXIMATE. DEPENDING ON YOUR GOALS AND THE NEEDS OF YOUR STUDENTS, YOU MAY WISH TO ALLOW MORE OR LESS TIME FOR CERTAIN PORTIONS OF THE LESSON.

Table of Contents	Discussion	Previewing the Selection	Reading the Selection
PART OPENER **TWINGES OF CONSCIENCE** **What Do You Think?** page 148	**20 MINUTES** • Reflect on the part theme		
SELECTION **The Horned Toad** page 150 CHALLENGING		**20 MINUTES** • PERSONAL CONNECTION • CULTURAL CONNECTION • READING CONNECTION: Connecting	**40 MINUTES** • Introduce vocabulary • Read pp. 150–158 (9 pp.)
SELECTION **The Splendid Outcast** page 162 AVERAGE		**20 MINUTES** • PERSONAL CONNECTION • CULTURAL CONNECTION • READING CONNECTION: Challenging vocabulary	**40 MINUTES** • Introduce vocabulary • Read pp. 162–172 (11 pp.)
SELECTIONS **We Alone** **Hard Questions** **oil crisis** page 176 AVERAGE		**20 MINUTES** • PERSONAL CONNECTION • SCIENCE CONNECTION • WRITING CONNECTION	**15 MINUTES** • Read pp. 176–178 (3 pp.)
GENRE LESSON **Focus on Drama** page 181	**20 MINUTES** • Discuss characteristics of drama • Discuss strategies for reading drama		
SELECTION **The Million-Pound Bank Note** page 184 AVERAGE		**20 MINUTES** • PERSONAL CONNECTION • CULTURAL CONNECTION • READING CONNECTION: Setting changes	**45 MINUTES** • Introduce vocabulary • Read pp. 184–199 (16 pp.)
FICTION ON YOUR OWN **Mother and Daughter** page 203 EASY			**20 MINUTES** • Read pp. 203–209 (7 pp.)
Writing **WRITING ABOUT LITERATURE** **Interpretation**	**Writer's Style** **20 MINUTES**	**Prewriting** **25 MINUTES**	**Drafting and Revising** **80 MINUTES**

Time estimates assume in-class work. You may wish to assign some of these stages as homework.

147k   UNIT TWO   CRITICAL ADJUSTMENTS

Responding to the Selection

FROM PERSONAL RESPONSE TO CRITICAL ANALYSIS	OR	ANOTHER PATHWAY	LITERARY CONCEPTS	QUICKWRITES
35 MINUTES				
• Discussion questions	OR	• List of personality traits	• First-person point of view	• Epitaph • Letter
45 MINUTES				
• Discussion questions	OR	• Graph	• Allusions • Setting	• Newspaper headlines • Poem • Paragraph
30 MINUTES				
• Discussion questions	OR	• Illustration	• Theme	• Poem • Description
60 MINUTES				
• Discussion questions	OR	• Stage production	• Resolution	• Script • Society-page report • Character sketch

Extension Activities

• ALTERNATIVE ACTIVITIES • LITERARY LINKS • CRITIC'S CORNER • THE WRITER'S STYLE • ACROSS THE CURRICULUM • ART CONNECTION • WORDS TO KNOW • BIOGRAPHY

ALTERNATIVE ACTIVITIES	LITERARY LINKS	CRITIC'S CORNER	THE WRITER'S STYLE	ACROSS THE CURRICULUM	ART CONNECTION	WORDS TO KNOW	BIOGRAPHY
40 MINUTES							
✓			✓	SCIENCE		✓	✓
35 MINUTES							
✓						✓	✓
15 MINUTES							✓
60 MINUTES							
✓	✓			MATH	✓	✓	✓
							✓

Publishing and Reflecting	Grammar in Context	Reading the World
30 MINUTES	10 MINUTES	30 MINUTES

PART 1

WHAT DO YOU THINK?
Objectives

The activities on this page can be used to
- introduce the Part 1 theme, "Twinges of Conscience," since each activity is connected to one or more of the selections in Part 1
- create materials for students' personal portfolios that they can later reconsider or revise
- build an understanding of theme that can be reviewed and revised as students progress through the unit

What can you do?
Have students choose three things that they are not doing now to help the environment. Encourage them to discuss the impact that doing these things might have on their daily lives. (See "We Alone," "Hard Questions," and "oil crisis," p. 175.)

How do you view your changing relationships?
Suggest that students write brief descriptions of the critical changes they have experienced in the past as well as the changes they expect to experience over the next ten years. Students can use these descriptions as a basis for their drawings. (See "The Horned Toad," p. 149.)

What would you say now?
Encourage students to draft a short outline of their letter first. Ask them to think about the reasons for their change of heart and to incorporate these thoughts in their letter. (All selections are connected to this activity.)

How would you react?
Have students complete this activity in small groups. One student can play the host, and the others can be the millionaires. Before students stage the talk show, encourage students to brainstorm a list of some of the negative aspects of being a millionaire. (See "The Million-Pound Bank Note," p. 183.)

UNIT TWO **PART 1**

TWINGES OF CONSCIENCE

WHAT DO You THINK?

REFLECTING ON THEME

What causes people to change their behavior? The following activities will help you to think about the critical adjustments that people make in their lives. Keep a record of your impressions and ideas. As you read this part of Unit Two, you can compare them with the characters' shifts in behavior.

What can you do?
Mother Earth's health weighs on many consciences. Name three things you could do to help save the environment. Then gather into a booklet all of the class's ideas. Create illustrations and a cover design for your notebook.

How do you view your changing relationships?
Think about your relationships with your parents or grandparents. How have these relationships changed since you were younger? Pinpoint two or three critical changes you can identify. For example, perhaps you've only recently begun to enjoy thoughtful conversations with your grandfather. Make a series of drawings to convey the changes. In other drawings, predict what the relationships might be like ten years from now.

How would you react?
Sudden wealth requires a number of adjustments—and not all of them are happy ones. Imagine you've just won a million dollars! Your new-found wealth is, however, making you miserable. Stage a mock talk show in which the host interviews you about the negative side of becoming a millionaire.

What would you say now?
Have you ever felt guilty about something you did or said to someone, wishing you could make up for it? Think of a particularly memorable example. Then write the letter of apology that you never sent but wish you had.

148

Cross-Curricular Connections

Science Have students work in small groups to do some research on the environment. They might focus their research on some aspect of the oil industry. For example, they might investigate the steps oil companies have taken to avoid oil spills and the strategies they have devised to deal with spills should they occur. When groups have completed their research, encourage them to present their findings to the class.

PARENTAL INVOLVEMENT
Have students work with their families to write a brief dialogue in which a child asks his or her parents for advice about making a critical decision or a change in behavior. Tell students that before they write the dialogue, they should choose a topic, such as how to deal with a friend who has treated them badly or done something they think is wrong. Each student can perform his or her dialogue with a classmate.

148 THE LANGUAGE OF LITERATURE **TEACHER'S EDITION**

PREVIEWING

FICTION

The Horned Toad
Gerald Haslam

Activating Prior Knowledge
PERSONAL CONNECTION

This story is about an extended family—a boy, his parents, and relatives from several generations. Talk about some of the people in your extended family. What are their ethnic backgrounds? Are any of them recent immigrants? In a word map like the one shown here, jot down what you know about these relatives.

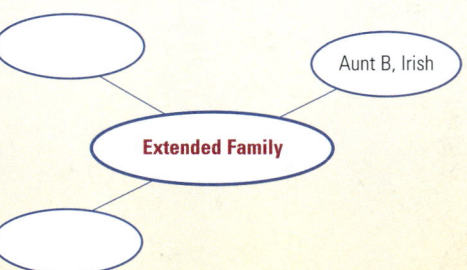

Building Background
CULTURAL CONNECTION

Gerald Haslam's great-great-grandparents immigrated to California from Mexico in the 1850s, just after California became the 31st state of the United States. A great many Hispanics immigrated to the United States at that time. They brought with them a heritage that emphasizes the importance of the extended family and the community in daily life.

Despite the changes that modern living and marriage to members of other ethnic groups have brought, many Hispanic families still manage to maintain intense feelings of loyalty and cooperation among their members.

Mexican family crossing the international bridge at the border between Brownsville, Texas, and Mexico. UPI/Bettmann.

Active Reading / Setting a Purpose
READING CONNECTION

Connecting One way to become a better reader is by consciously connecting your personal experiences with what you read. Reading is much more enjoyable when you make associations between what you are reading and what you already know.

Try connecting to a key aspect of "The Horned Toad" by considering how your life might change if an older relative came to stay with you. What would be good and bad about such a situation? Share your thoughts with the class. Then, as you read this story, look for other connections you have with the characters. You might jot them down in your notebook.

- GEOGRAPHICAL CONNECTION

OVERVIEW

Objectives
- To understand and appreciate a short story about the meaning of home
- To enrich reading by using connecting strategies
- To identify and understand the use of first-person point of view
- To appreciate and understand the use of Spanish words and phrases in the story
- To express understanding of the story through a choice of writing forms, including an epitaph and a letter
- To extend understanding of the story through a variety of multimodal and cross-curricular activities

Skills

READING SKILLS/STRATEGIES
- Connecting

GRAMMAR
- Commas after introductory elements

LITERARY CONCEPTS
- First-person point of view
- Setting

SPELLING
- The letter combination *ph*

SPEAKING, LISTENING, AND VIEWING
- Speeches
- Group discussion
- Oral presentation

Cross-Curricular Connections

GEOGRAPHY
- *Las Ciudades*

SCIENCE
- The truth about horned toads

GEOGRAPHICAL CONNECTION
The California Desert These photographs of desert plants and animals will help students envision the desert environment Haslam describes.

Side A, Frame 52602

PRINT AND MEDIA RESOURCES

UNIT TWO RESOURCE BOOK
Strategic Reading: Literature, p. 4
Vocabulary SkillBuilder, p. 7
Reading SkillBuilder, p. 5
Spelling SkillBuilder, p. 6

GRAMMAR MINI-LESSONS
Transparencies, p. 29
Copymasters, p. 38

ACCESS FOR STUDENTS ACQUIRING ENGLISH
Selection Summaries
Reading and Writing Support

FORMAL ASSESSMENT
Selection Test, pp. 29–30
 Test Generator

 **AUDIO LIBRARY**
See Reference Card

LASERLINKS
Geographical Connection
Author Background

THE LANGUAGE OF LITERATURE **TEACHER'S EDITION** 149

SUMMARY

When his great-grandmother comes to stay, the narrator—a boy of Anglo and Hispanic heritage—stays clear of her. She hates city life and yearns for the ranch where she once lived with her late husband. Although at first Grandma spurns the boy and his Anglo father, the three eventually grow close. The boy tries to keep a horned toad as a pet and feels guilty when it is killed returning to its true home. When Grandma dies, the boy and his father insist that she be buried not in the city but at the ranch she loved.

Thematic Link: *Twinges of Conscience*
A boy's guilt after the death of a toad helps him learn a valuable lesson about the importance of family and home.

STRATEGIC READING FOR
Less-Proficient Readers

Set a Purpose Encourage students to become involved in the story by sketching part of the landscape described on page 151. Then ask them to read to find out about the story's setting and the narrator's relatives.

Use **UNIT TWO RESOURCE BOOK**, pp. 4–5, for guidance in reading the selection.

CUSTOMIZING FOR
Students Acquiring English

- Use **ACCESS FOR STUDENTS ACQUIRING ENGLISH**, *Reading and Writing Support*.

- Encourage students from different backgrounds to discuss the importance of extended families, especially elderly relatives, in their native countries. You may also wish to have them explain how their families express affection. Ask students to note how the family of the narrator's mother shows affection as compared to his father.

WORDS TO KNOW

incongruously (ĭn-kŏng′grōō-əs-lē) *adv.* in a way that is not appropriate or fitting (p. 151)
inter (ĭn-tûr′) *v.* to place in a grave; bury (p. 157)
millennium (mə-lĕn′ē-əm) *n.* a period of 1000 years; *plural*—**millennia** (mə-lĕn′ē-ə) (p. 151)
periphery (pə-rĭf′ə-rē) *n.* a region on an outer boundary; outskirts (p. 151)
verdancy (vûr′dn-sē) *n.* the greenness of vegetation (p. 151)

150 THE LANGUAGE OF LITERATURE **TEACHER'S EDITION**

"*Expectoran su sangre!*"¹ exclaimed Great-grandma when I showed her the small horned toad I had removed from my breast pocket. I turned toward my mother, who translated: "They spit blood."

"*De los ojos,*"² Grandma added. "From their eyes," mother explained, herself uncomfortable in the presence of the small beast.

I grinned, "Awwwwww."

But my great-grandmother did not smile. "*Son muy toxicos,*"³ she nodded with finality. Mother moved back an involuntary step, her hands suddenly busy at her breast. "Put that thing down," she ordered.

"His name's John," I said.

"Put John down and not in your pocket, either," my mother nearly shouted. "Those things are very poisonous. Didn't you understand what Grandma said?"

I shook my head.

"Well . . ." mother looked from one of us to the other—spanning four generations of California, standing three feet apart—and said, "of course you didn't. Please take him back where you got him, and be careful. We'll all feel better when you do." The tone of her voice told me that the discussion had ended, so I released the little reptile where I'd captured him.

During those years in Oildale, the mid-1940s, I needed only to walk across the street to find a patch of virgin desert. Neighborhood kids called it simply "the vacant lot," less than an acre without houses or sidewalks. Not that we were desperate for desert then, since we could walk into its scorched skin a mere half-mile west, north, and east. To the south, incongruously, flowed the icy Kern River, fresh from the Sierras and surrounded by riparian forest.⁴

Ours was rich soil formed by that same Kern River as it ground Sierra granite and turned it into coarse sand, then carried it down into the valley and deposited it over millennia along its many changes of channels. The ants that built miniature volcanoes on the vacant lot left piles of tiny stones with telltale markings of black on white. Deeper than ants could dig were pools of petroleum that led to many fortunes and lured men like my father from Texas. The dry hills to the east and north sprouted forests of wooden derricks.

Despite the abundance of open land, plus the constant lure of the river where desolation and verdancy met, most kids relied on the vacant lot as their primary playground. Even with its bullheads and stinging insects, we played everything from football to kick-the-can on it. The lot actually resembled my father's head, bare in the middle but full of growth around the edges: weeds, stickers, cactuses, and a few bushes. We played our games on its sandy center, and conducted such sports as ant fights and lizard hunts on its brushy periphery.

That spring, when I discovered the lone horned toad near the back of the lot, had been rough on my family. Earlier, there had been quiet, unpleasant tension between Mom and Daddy. He was a silent man, little given to emotional displays. It was difficult for him to

---

1. *Expectoran su sangre* (ĕs-pĕk-tô′rän sōō säng′grĕ) *Spanish*.
2. *de los ojos* (dĕ lôs ô′hôs) *Spanish*.
3. *Son muy toxicos* (sôn mwē tôk′sē-kôs) *Spanish*: They are very poisonous.
4. *riparian* (rĭ-pâr′ē-ən) **forest**: a forest along the banks of a river.

WORDS TO KNOW
incongruously (ĭn-kŏng′grōō-əs-lē) *adv.* in a way that is not appropriate or fitting
millennium (mə-lĕn′ē-əm) *n.* a period of 1000 years; *plural—* **millennia** (mə-lĕn′ē-ə)
verdancy (vûr′dn-sē) *n.* the greenness of vegetation
periphery (pə-rĭf′ə-rē) *n.* a region on an outer boundary; outskirts

151

CUSTOMIZING FOR
Gifted and Talented Students

As students read, have them discuss the ways in which they think the horned toad's situation compares to the grandmother's situation. *(Possible responses: The horned toad's situation parallels the grandmother's situation. The narrator is told that the toad is poisonous and dangerous, and the grandmother is presented at first as scary and frightening to the narrator. Both perceptions are found to be untrue. From his experiences with his grandmother and the toad, the narrator learns the meaning of family and home.)*

Literary Concept: SETTING

A Have students note the many details of setting the author includes at the beginning of the story. Then ask them to consider whether the contrast between some details (for instance, "rich soil" and the "scorched skin" of the desert) surprises them.

CUSTOMIZING FOR
Students Acquiring English

I Find out how many students know the rules to kick-the-can. Ask those who don't know to think about the game's name and to say how they think it is played. If possible, have a volunteer clarify the rules for the class.

Literary Concept: FIGURATIVE LANGUAGE

B Ask students what elements are being compared in the figure of speech in this sentence. *(The vacant lot is compared to a head that is bald on top but has a growth of hair around the sides.)*

Mini-Lesson Literary Concepts

REVIEWING SETTING Remind students that the setting is the time and place of the action of a story, poem, or play. Setting may include geographic location, the historical period (past, present, or future), season, and time of day.

Application Draw on the chalkboard the web shown on the right, and encourage students to use it to scan this page to identify specifics of the story's setting. *(California, Oildale, the mid-1940s, the icy Kern River, the dry hills to the east and north, wooden derricks, spring, and descriptions of the vacant lot)*

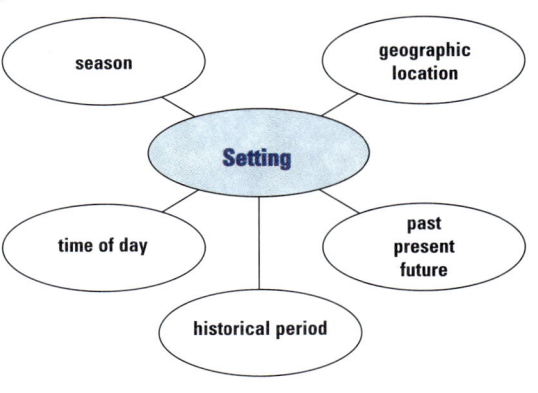

THE LANGUAGE OF LITERATURE TEACHER'S EDITION **151**

CUSTOMIZING FOR
Multiple Learning Styles

C **Intrapersonal Learners** Ask individual students to locate Oildale (on the outskirts of Bakersfield) and Los Angeles on a map of southern California. Also have them note the Kern River, the Sierra Nevadas to the north and east of Oildale, and the barren tracts of land surrounding it in Kern County.

CUSTOMIZING FOR
Students Acquiring English

2 Encourage Spanish-speaking students to discuss when a nickname like *ese gringo* would be used. Ask them if it is possible that such a nickname could be used either positively or affectionately.

STRATEGIC READING FOR
Less-Proficient Readers

D Check to see that students are clear about the setting and the narrator's family.

- Where and when does the story take place? *(Oildale, California, in the mid-1940s)* Noting Relevant Details
- Where do many of the narrator's relatives live? *(Los Angeles)* Summarizing
- Why does the narrator's great-grandmother want to live in Oildale? *(It is near the open country, where she grew up, and she wants to be near the narrator's mother, whom she raised.)* Restating

Set a Purpose Have students read to find out about Grandma's background and her behavior with other characters in the story.

Active Reading: CLARIFY

E What do Uncle Manuel and Aunt Toni deliver? *(the narrator's great-grandmother)*

---

show affection and I guess the openness of Mom's family made him uneasy. Daddy had no kin[5] in California and rarely mentioned any in Texas. He couldn't understand my mother's large, intimate family, their constant noisy concern for one another, and I think he was a little jealous of the time she gave everyone, maybe even me.

I heard her talking on the phone to my various aunts and uncles, usually in Spanish. Even though I couldn't understand—Daddy had warned her not to teach me that foreign tongue because it would hurt me in school—I could sense the stress. I had been afraid they were going to divorce, since she only used Spanish to hide things from me. I'd confronted her with my suspicion, but she comforted me, saying, no, that was not the problem. They were merely deciding when it would be our turn to care for Grandma. I didn't really understand, although I was relieved.

I later learned that my great-grandmother—whom we simply called "Grandma"—had been moving from house to house within the family, trying to find a place she'd accept. She hated the city, and most of my aunts and uncles lived in Los Angeles. Our house in Oildale was much closer to the open country where she'd dwelled all her life. She had wanted to come to our place right away because she had raised my mother from a baby when my own grandmother died. But the old lady seemed unimpressed with Daddy, whom she called "*ese gringo*."[6]

In truth, we had more room, and my dad made good money in the oil patch. Since my mother was the closest to Grandma, our place was the logical one for her, but Ese Gringo didn't see it that way, I guess, at least not at first. Finally, after much debate, he relented.

In any case, one windy afternoon, my Uncle Manuel and Aunt Toni drove up and deposited four-and-a-half feet of bewigged, bejeweled Spanish spitfire: a square, pale face topped by a tightly curled black wig that hid a bald head—her hair having been lost to typhoid[7] nearly sixty years before—her small white hands veined with rivers of blue. She walked with a prancing bounce that made her appear half her age, and she barked orders in Spanish from the moment she emerged from Manuel and Toni's car. Later, just before they left, I heard Uncle Manuel tell my father, "Good luck, Charlie. That old lady's dynamite."

Daddy only grunted.

She had been with us only two days when I tried to impress her with my horned toad. In fact, nothing I did seemed to impress her, and she referred to me as *el malcriado*,[8] causing my mother to shake her head. Mom explained to me that Grandma was just old and lonely for Grandpa and uncomfortable in town. Mom told me that Grandma had lived over half a century in the country, away from the noise, away from clutter, away from people. She would not accompany my mother on shopping trips, or anywhere else. She even refused to climb into a

> *four-and-a-half feet of bewigged, bejeweled Spanish spitfire*

---

5. **kin:** relatives; family.
6. ***ese gringo*** (ĕ´sĕ grēng´gô) *Spanish:* that Yankee; that American.
7. **typhoid:** typhoid fever—a very serious disease that is transmitted by contaminated food or water.
8. ***el malcriado*** (ĕl mäl-kryä´dô) *Spanish:* the rude fellow.

152 UNIT TWO PART 1: TWINGES OF CONSCIENCE

Mini-Lesson Grammar

COMMAS AFTER INTRODUCTORY ELEMENTS Point out to students that commas are used to separate an introductory word, phrase, or clause from the rest of a sentence. If the pause after a very short introductory element is brief, it is possible to omit the comma.

Application Have students look at page 152 and identify at least three examples of a comma separating an introductory element from the rest of the sentence. *(In truth, . . . ; Finally, after much debate, . . . ; In any case, . . . ; Later, just before they left, . . . ; In fact, . . .)* Then have them add commas to the following sentences.

1. Because she had lived most of her life in the country Grandma did not like city living.
2. When Grandma arrived it seemed as if Mom and Dad grew closer.

Reteaching/Reinforcement
- *Grammar Handbook*, anthology pp. 892
- *Grammar Mini-Lessons* copymasters p. 38, transparencies p. 29

Commas After Introductory Elements, p. 646

---

152 THE LANGUAGE OF LITERATURE TEACHER'S EDITION

Nito Herrera in Springtime (1960), Peter Hurd. Denver Art Museum (1961.24).

car, and I wondered how Uncle Manuel had managed to load her up in order to bring her to us.

She disliked sidewalks and roads, dancing across them when she had to, then appearing to wipe her feet on earth or grass. Things too civilized simply did not please her. A brother of hers had been killed in the great San Francisco earthquake and that had been the end of her tolerance of cities. Until my great-grandfather died, they lived on a small rancho near Arroyo Cantua, north of Coalinga. Grandpa, who had come north from Sonora as a youth to work as a *vaquero*,[9] had bred horses and cattle, and cowboyed for other ranchers, scraping together enough of a living to raise eleven children.

He had been, until the time of his death, a dark-skinned man with wide shoulders, a large nose, and a sweeping handlebar mustache that was white when I knew him. His Indian blood darkened all his progeny[10] so that not even I was as fair-skinned as my great-grandmother, Ese Gringo for a father or not.

As it turned out, I didn't really understand very much about Grandma at all. She was old, of course, yet in many ways my parents treated

---

9. **vaquero** (vä-kĕ′rô) *Spanish:* cowboy.
10. **progeny:** children and other descendants.

THE HORNED TOAD 153

her as though she were younger than me, walking her to the bathroom at night and bringing her presents from the store. In other ways—drinking wine at dinner, for example—she was granted adult privileges. Even Daddy didn't drink wine except on special occasions. After Grandma moved in, though, he began to occasionally join her for a glass, sometimes even sitting with her on the porch for a premeal sip.

She held court[11] on our front porch, often gazing toward the desert hills east of us or across the street at kids playing on the lot. Occasionally, she would rise, cross the yard and sidewalk and street, skip over them, sometimes stumbling on the curb, and wipe her feet on the lot's sandy soil, then she would slowly circle the boundary between the open middle and the brushy sides, searching for something, it appeared. I never figured out what.

One afternoon I returned from school and saw Grandma perched on the porch as usual, so I started to walk around the house to avoid her sharp, mostly incomprehensible tongue. She had already spotted me. "*Venga aquí!*"[12] she ordered, and I understood.

I approached the porch and noticed that Grandma was vigorously chewing something. She held a small paper bag in one hand. Saying "*Qué deseas tomar?*"[13] she withdrew a large orange gumdrop from the bag and began slowly chewing it in her toothless mouth, smacking loudly as she did so. I stood below her for a moment trying to remember the word for candy. Then it came to me: "*Dulce*," I said.

Still chewing, Grandma replied, "*Mande?*"[14]

Knowing she wanted a complete sentence, I again struggled, then came up with "*Deseo dulce.*"[15]

She measured me for a moment, before answering in nearly perfect English, "Oh, so you wan' some candy. Go to the store an' buy some."

I don't know if it was the shock of hearing her speak English for the first time, or the way she had denied me a piece of candy, but I suddenly felt tears warm my cheeks and I sprinted into the house and found Mom, who stood at the kitchen sink. "Grandma just talked English," I burst between light sobs.

"What's wrong?" she asked as she reached out to stroke my head.

"Grandma can talk English," I repeated.

"Of course she can," Mom answered. "What's wrong?"

I wasn't sure what was wrong, but after considering, I told Mom that Grandma had teased me. No sooner had I said that than the old woman appeared at the door and hiked her skirt. Attached to one of her petticoats by safety pins were several small tobacco sacks, the white cloth kind that closed with yellow drawstrings. She carefully unhooked one and opened it, withdrawing a dollar, then handed the money to me. "*Para su dulce,*"[16] she said. Then, to my mother, she asked, "Why does he bawl like a motherless calf?"

"It's nothing," Mother replied.

"Do not weep, little one," the old lady comforted me, "Jesus and the Virgin love you." She smiled and patted my head. To my mother she said as though just realizing it, "Your baby?"

Somehow that day changed everything. I wasn't afraid of my great-grandmother any longer and, once I began spending time with

---

11. **held court:** sat as the center of attention, like a ruler on a throne.
12. ***Venga aquí!*** (věng'gä ä-kē') *Spanish:* Come here!
13. ***Qué deseas tomar?*** (kě dě-sě'äs tô-mär') *Spanish:* What would you like to have?
14. ***Mande?*** (män'dě) *Spanish:* What did you say?
15. ***Deseo dulce*** (dě-sě'ô dōōl'sě) *Spanish:* I want candy.
16. ***para su dulce*** (pä'rä sōō dōōl'sě) *Spanish:* for your candy.

154 UNIT TWO PART 1: TWINGES OF CONSCIENCE

her on the porch, I realized that my father had also begun directing increased attention to the old woman. Almost every evening Ese Gringo was sharing wine with Grandma. They talked out there, but I never did hear a real two-way conversation between them. Usually Grandma rattled on and Daddy nodded. She'd chuckle and pat his hand and he might grin, even grunt a word or two, before she'd begin talking again. Once I saw my mother standing by the front window watching them together, a smile playing across her face.

No more did I sneak around the house to avoid Grandma after school. Instead, she waited for me and discussed my efforts in class gravely, telling mother that I was *"muy inteligente,"*[17] and that I should be sent to the nuns who would train me. I would make a fine priest. When Ese Gringo heard that, he smiled and said, "He'd make a fair-to-middlin' Holy Roller preacher,[18] too." Even Mom had to chuckle, and my great-grandmother shook her finger at Ese Gringo. "Oh you debil, Sharlie!" she cackled.

Frequently, I would accompany Grandma to the lot where she would explain that no fodder[19] could grow there. Poor pasture or not, the lot was at least unpaved, and Grandma greeted even the tiniest new cactus or flowering weed with joy. "Look how beautiful," she would croon. "In all this ugliness, it lives." Oildale was my home and it didn't look especially ugly to me, so I could only grin and wonder.

Because she liked the lot and things that grew there, I showed her the horned toad when I captured it a second time. I was determined to keep it, although I did not discuss my plans with anyone. I also wanted to hear more about the bloody eyes, so I thrust the small animal nearly into her face one afternoon. She did not flinch. *"Ola señor sangre de ojos,"*[20] she said with a mischievous grin. *"Qué tal?"*[21] It took me a moment to catch on.

"You were kidding before," I accused.

"Of course," she acknowledged, still grinning.

"But why?"

"Because the little beast belongs with his own kind in his own place, not in your pocket. Give him his freedom, my son."

"Give him his freedom, my son."

I had other plans for the horned toad, but I was clever enough not to cross Grandma. "Yes, Ma'am," I replied. That night I placed the reptile in a flower bed cornered by a brick wall Ese Gringo had built the previous summer. It was a spot rich with insects for the toad to eat, and the little wall, only a foot high, must have seemed massive to so squat an animal.

Nonetheless, the next morning when I searched for the horned toad it was gone. I had no time to explore the yard for it, so I trudged off to school, my belly troubled. How could it have escaped? Classes meant little to me that day. I thought only of my lost pet—I had changed his name to Juan, the same as my great-grandfather—and where I might find him.

I shortened my conversation with Grandma

---

17. *muy inteligente* (mwē ēn-tĕ-lē-hĕn′tĕ) *Spanish:* very intelligent.
18. **Holy Roller preacher:** a preacher who leads services that include shouting, singing, and movement.
19. **fodder:** plants grown as food for livestock.
20. *Ola señor sangre de ojos* (ô′lä sĕ-nyôr′ säng′grĕ dĕ ô′hôs) *Spanish:* Hi, Mr. Bloody Eyes.
21. *Qué tal?* (kĕ täl) *Spanish:* How are you?

THE HORNED TOAD 155

Art Note

A medio día (At High Noon) by Carmen Lomas Garza This image is part of the series *Pedacito de mi corazón (A Little Piece of My Heart)* in which Garza (1948–) expresses her memories of growing up in Chicano culture. Garza often organizes paintings around some visual repetition. For instance, in *A medio día* she juxtaposes one repetition (soft, round plant shapes) with a second one (sharp prickles) to mimic the twin realities of the desert landscape.

Reading the Art What effect do you think the artist wishes to achieve with her juxtaposition of the desert lizards with the cacti? What emotions does this landscape stir in you?

Literary Concept: SETTING

N Draw students' attention to these sharply contrasting aspects of the story's setting: the road and the vacant lot at its edge. Have students contrast these two adjacent landscapes, one of which is fatal to the toad. *(Possible responses: The vacant lot is filled with life—bushes, cacti, weeds, toads, insects—whereas the road is used by motorized vehicles. The road is a very dangerous setting for living things, especially those as small as a toad. Although there may be predators of the toad in the "miniature desert" of the vacant lot, none is as dangerous as an automobile.)*

CUSTOMIZING FOR
Multiple Learning Styles

O **Spatial or Graphic Learners** Have students draw, paint, or construct a model of the area surrounding the narrator's home in Oildale. Have them review the narrator's descriptions of the area. Invite them to pay special attention to the vacant lot, the garden by the narrator's house, and the road separating the two places.

---

that afternoon so I could search for Juan. "What do you seek?" the old woman asked me as I poked through flower beds beneath the porch. "Praying mantises,"[22] I improvised, and she merely nodded, surveying me. But I had eyes only for my lost pet, and I continued pushing through branches and brushing aside leaves. No luck.

N Finally, I gave in and turned toward the lot. I found my horned toad nearly across the street, crushed. It had been heading for the miniature desert and had almost made it when an automobile's tire had run over it. One notion immediately swept me: If I had left it on its lot, it would still be alive. I stood rooted there in the street, tears slicking my cheeks, and a car honked its horn as it passed, the driver shouting at me.

O Grandma joined me, and stroked my back. "The poor little beast," was all she said, then she bent slowly and scooped up what remained of the horned toad and led me out of the street. "We must return him to his own place," she explained, and we trooped, my eyes still clouded, toward the back of the vacant lot. Carefully, I dug a hole with a piece of wood. Grandma placed Juan in it and covered him. We said an Our Father and a Hail Mary,[23] then Grandma walked me back to the house. "Your little Juan is safe with God, my son," she comforted. We kept the horned toad's death a secret, and we visited his small grave frequently.

Grandma fell just before school ended and summer vacation began. As was her habit, she had walked alone to the vacant lot but this time, on her way back, she tripped over the curb and broke her hip. That following week, when Daddy brought her home from the hospital, she seemed to have shrunken. She sat hunched in a wheelchair on the porch, gazing with faded eyes toward the hills or at the lot, speaking rarely. She still sipped wine every evening with Daddy and even I could tell how concerned he was about her. It got to where he'd look in on her before leaving for work every morning and again at night before turning in. And if Daddy was home, Grandma always wanted him to push her chair when she needed moving, calling, "Sharlie!" until he arrived.

A Medio Día/Pedacito de mi Corazón [At high noon/A little piece of my heart] (1986), Carmen Lomas Garza. Gouache on cotton rag paper, 28" × 20". Copyright © 1986 Carmen Lomas Garza. Photo by Wolfgang Dietze.

---

22. **praying mantises:** long, slender insects that feed on other insects and, when at rest, hold their front legs as if praying.
23. **an Our Father and a Hail Mary:** the Lord's Prayer and a prayer to the Virgin Mary.

156 UNIT TWO PART 1: TWINGES OF CONSCIENCE

Mini-Lesson: Speaking, Listening, and Viewing

SPEECHES Explain to students that a eulogy is a formal speech praising a person who has recently died. In a eulogy, the speaker describes the individual's special qualities and tells about the person's life and his or her effect on others.

Application Have students imagine that they are the narrator of "The Horned Toad" (or his mother or father). Invite them to write a eulogy for Grandma and deliver it to the class as if they were at her funeral.

I was tugged from sleep on the night she died by voices drumming through the walls into darkness. I couldn't understand them but was immediately frightened by the uncommon sounds of words in the night. I struggled from bed and walked into the living room just as Daddy closed the front door and a car pulled away.

Mom was sobbing softly on the couch and Daddy walked to her, stroked her head, then noticed me. "Come here, son," he gently ordered.

I walked to him and, uncharacteristically, he put an arm around me.

"What's wrong?" I asked, near tears myself. Mom looked up, but before she could speak, Daddy said, "Grandma died." Then he sighed heavily and stood there with his arms around his weeping wife and son.

The next day my Uncle Manuel and Uncle Arnulfo, plus Aunt Chinta, arrived and over food they discussed with my mother where Grandma should be <u>interred</u>. They argued that it would be too expensive to transport her body home and, besides, they could more easily visit her grave if she was buried in Bakersfield. "They have such a nice, manicured grounds at Greenlawn," Aunt Chinta pointed out. Just when it seemed they had agreed, I could remain silent no longer: "But Grandma has to go home," I burst. "She has to! It's the only thing she really wanted. We can't leave her in the city."

Uncle Arnulfo, who was on the edge, snapped to Mother that I belonged with the other children, not interrupting adult conversation. Mom quietly agreed, but I refused. My father walked into the room then. "What's wrong?" he asked.

"They're going to bury Grandma in Bakersfield, Daddy. Don't let 'em, please."

"Well, son . . ."

"When my horny toad got killed and she helped me to bury it, she said we had to return him to his place."

"Your horny toad?" Mother asked.

"He got squished and me and Grandma buried him in the lot. She said we had to take him back to his place. Honest she did."

No one spoke for a moment, then my father, Ese Gringo, who stood against the sink, responded: "That's right . . ." he paused, then added, "We'll bury her." I saw a weary smile cross my mother's face. "If she wanted to go back to the ranch then that's where we have to take her," Daddy said.

I hugged him and he, right in front of everyone, hugged back.

No one argued. It seemed, suddenly, as though they had all wanted to do exactly what I had begged for. Grownups baffled me. Late that week the entire family, hundreds it seemed, gathered at the little Catholic church in Coalinga for Mass, then drove out to Arroyo Cantua and buried Grandma next to Grandpa. She rests there today.

My mother, father, and I drove back to Oildale that afternoon across the scorching westside desert, through sand and tumbleweeds and heat shivers. Quiet and sad, we knew we had done our best. Mom, who usually sat next to the door in the front seat, snuggled close to Daddy, and I heard her whisper to him, "Thank you, Charlie," as she kissed his cheek.

Daddy squeezed her, hesitated as if to clear his throat, then answered, "When you're family, you take care of your own." ❖

> **WORDS TO KNOW**
> **inter** (ĭn-tûr′) *v.* to place in a grave; bury

Mini-Lesson Spelling

THE LETTER COMBINATION *ph* Explain to students that one sound may be spelled different ways. Tell students that the letter combination *ph* is pronounced like *f*. An example from the selection is *periphery*.

Application Have students identify the word that contains the letter combination *ph* in each sentence and then write the word:
1. Grandma had typhoid fever 60 years ago.
2. She never talks to her friends on the phone.
3. A horned toad is an amphibian.
4. I looked at old photographs of Oildale.
5. I want to make a graph that shows the toad's growth.
6. Do you think the toad will get enough physical exercise?

Have students find more words that fit this pattern, in their own writing and in things they read, and to add these words to their personal word lists.

Reteaching/Reinforcement
- *Unit Two Resource Book*, p. 6

Active Reading: EVALUATE

P Ask students what is significant about the ranch. (*The ranch was where Grandma and her husband lived for more than 50 years.*)

STRATEGIC READING FOR
Less-Proficient Readers

Q Check that students understand the narrator's feeling of responsibility for the toad's death and how it affects his response to Grandma's death.

- What does Grandma tell the narrator to do with the toad? (*set it free*) **Restating**
- Why does the narrator put the toad in the flower bed? (*so that he can find it the next morning*) **Making Inferences**
- Where and in what condition does he find the toad? (*He finds it dead in the road.*) **Summarizing**
- Why does the narrator insist that Grandma be buried at her home? (*He believes that she would have wanted to go back to the ranch where she had spent her life.*) **Drawing Conclusions**

CUSTOMIZING FOR
Gifted and Talented Students

Ask students to discuss the value of learning about their cultures. How can a sense of an ethnic culture add to their identities as individuals? How does the entire community benefit from a mixture of cultures? Invite students to share their personal experiences with the class.

COMPREHENSION CHECK
1. Who comes to live at the narrator's house? (*his great-grandmother*)
2. Whom does Grandma call "ese gringo"? (*the narrator's father*)
3. Where does the horned toad live? (*in the vacant lot*)
4. What does the narrator learn from Grandma's help in his burial of the toad? (*She wants to be returned to where she came from when her own time comes.*)

INSIGHT

1. Do you think the speaker's grandmother is imaginative? Why or why not? *(Possible response: She shows that she is imaginative by the way she brings chairs to life and creates lively, interesting situations to entertain the speaker as a baby.)*
2. Explain how the speaker might have seen the mountains or deserts of Mexico in his grandmother's eyes or heard them in her voice. *(Possible responses: The speaker does not mean this literally, but since his grandmother is thoroughly Mexican, her heritage is visible in the color and texture of her hair, as well as in her accent and language.)*

FRANCISCO X. ALARCÓN

Born in 1954, Francisco X. Alarcón moved back and forth between California and Mexico during his youth. In this way he received a bilingual and bicultural education. Alarcón has written fiction as well as essays and poetry, and he is a noted showman at his own poetry readings. His volume *Quake Poems* considers the lives and actions of the thousands of people affected by the 1989 earthquakes in California.

LITERARY INSIGHT

IN A NEIGHBORHOOD IN LOS ANGELES

BY FRANCISCO X. ALARCÓN

I learned
Spanish
from my grandma

mijito[1]
don't cry
she'd tell me

on the mornings
my parents
would leave

to work
at the fish
canneries

my grandma
would chat
with chairs

sing them
old
songs

dance
waltzes with them
in the kitchen

when she'd say
niño barrigón[2]
she'd laugh

with my grandma
I learned
to count clouds

to point out
in flowerpots
mint leaves

my grandma
wore moons
on her dress

Mexico's mountains
deserts
ocean

in her eyes
I'd see them
in her braids

I'd touch them
in her voice
smell them

one day
I was told:
she went far away

but still
I feel her
with me

whispering
in my ear
mijito

---

1. *mijito:* (mē-hē′tô): a contraction of Spanish *mi hijito,* "my little child."
2. *niño barrigón* (nē′nyô bä-rē-gôn′) *Spanish:* big-bellied baby.

158 UNIT TWO PART 1: TWINGES OF CONSCIENCE

Multicultural Perspectives

SPANISH IN THE UNITED STATES

Students may not be aware that Spanish has been spoken longer than English in what is now called the United States. The language was first brought to these shores by the Spanish settlers of San Agustín (now called St. Augustine) in what is now Florida. San Agustín, established in 1565, is the oldest permanent city in the United States. Due to emigration from various parts of Latin America, Spanish is the second most widely spoken language in the nation today. The areas of the country with the most Spanish speakers are Texas, California, New Mexico, Florida, and metropolitan areas such as Chicago and New York City.

RESPONDING OPTIONS

FROM PERSONAL RESPONSE TO CRITICAL ANALYSIS

REFLECT 1. What is your impression of the grandmother in this story? Write your reactions in your notebook.

RETHINK 2. Why is the horned toad important?
Consider
- the boy's treatment of the animal, and its escape
- the grandmother's feelings about her new home, and the circumstances surrounding her death
- the significance of the vacant lot to the boy, the grandmother, and the horned toad

3. How does the boy's relationship with his grandmother change?

4. How do the father and the grandmother adjust to each other?

RELATE 5. Consider the Insight poem on page 158 and "The Horned Toad" together. What do you think older relatives bring to a family? Share your ideas with the class.
Literary Link

Multimodal Learning
ANOTHER PATHWAY
Cooperative Learning

Grandma's personality has many facets. In small groups, find and list her personality traits, supported with examples from the story. Then find a picture that captures her personality.

QUICKWRITES

1. An epitaph is a brief statement inscribed on a tombstone to honor the memory of the person buried there. Write an **epitaph** for the grandmother in this story. Before writing, think about what was important to her in life.

2. Suppose the grandmother were describing her family to a friend. Write a **letter** that describes her impression of "Ese Gringo" and her grandson after she has lived with them awhile.

📁 **PORTFOLIO** Save your writing. You may want to use it later as a springboard to a piece for your portfolio.

LITERARY CONCEPTS

A story told from the **first-person point of view** is told by a narrator who is one of the characters. In "The Horned Toad," the first-person narrator is the boy. He tells everything that happens in his own words, using such pronouns as *I* and *we*. How might his mother's account of what happens differ from his own account?

THE HORNED TOAD   159

From Personal Response to Critical Analysis

1. Responses will vary.
2. Possible response: The toad's situation and experiences provide an echo of Grandma's. Both are out of place around the narrator's home, and both die and are given final rest in their real homes.
3. Possible response: The relationship changes from being distant to intimate. At first they treat each other warily, but then the narrator stops being afraid of Grandma.
4. Possible response: The father and grandmother adjust to each other slowly. They begin to know and trust each other and to enjoy each other's company.
5. Possible response: Older relatives can give a family wisdom gained from time and experience.

Another Pathway

Cooperative Learning Divide the class into groups of four. One student might list the personality traits that are brainstormed by the group. Two students might be responsible for finding examples of these traits in the selection, while another student researches pictures that capture her personality.

Rubric
3 Full Accomplishment Students list a full range of traits, each supported by examples, and identify a picture that accurately captures Grandma's personality.
2 Substantial Accomplishment Students list several traits, most supported by examples, and identify a picture that captures some part of Grandma's personality.
1 Little or Partial Accomplishment Students have difficulty identifying traits and examples, and are unable to find a picture that captures Grandma's personality.

Literary Concepts

Make sure students understand that first-person narration affects the information communicated to the reader in a story. Students should understand that if the mother narrated the story, a great deal of the information provided by the boy might be left out. For example, the boy's thoughts and feelings about the toad and his grandmother probably would not be known to his mother.

QuickWrites

1. Ask students what they consider to be Grandma's best character trait and have them use this in their epitaphs. How might the boy's mother, his father, and his late great-grandfather describe her?
2. Encourage students to review the scenes in which Grandma interacts with the boy or his father and to consider how these relationships changed over time.

The Writer's Craft
Analyzing a Story, pp. 163–169
Letter, p. 684

THE LANGUAGE OF LITERATURE TEACHER'S EDITION **159**

Words to Know

1. inter
2. incongruously
3. periphery
4. verdancy
5. millennium

Reteaching/Reinforcement
• *Unit Two Resource Book*, p. 7

Across the Curriculum

Science Have students display or otherwise report information about these lizards, which live in desert or semidesert sandy country in the western sections of North America. Students may be surprised to discover that horned toads can, although rarely, spurt blood from their eyes in order to protect themselves.

ADDITIONAL SUGGESTION

Geography *Las Ciudades* Have students study a map of southern California in order to make a list of towns and cities with Spanish names. Encourage Spanish-speaking students (or have students use a Spanish-English dictionary) to translate as many of these names as possible.

GERALD HASLAM

Gerald Haslam admits that he "can't wait to face the typewriter each morning. I'm always amazed at what's in there." He tries to find the particular details and textures of life in the American West that will give his work universal appeal. He attributes his success at storytelling partly to the fact that he has always been a good listener.

AUTHOR BACKGROUND

Gerald Haslam The author discusses the rich cultural history of the San Joaquin Valley, the setting of "The Horned Toad," in this informative video clip.

Side A, Frame 14565

Multimodal Learning

ALTERNATIVE ACTIVITIES

Cooperative Learning As you have learned, the Spanish word for a cowboy is *vaquero*. Use an English-Spanish dictionary to find the Spanish equivalents of some of the key English nouns in this story. Then create a **Spanish match game**. On a sheet of poster board, display a list of the Spanish words, along with magazine pictures of the things they name. Have classmates try to match each word with the appropriate picture.

ACROSS THE CURRICULUM

Science Using the library or a computer data base, find out what you can about horned toads. Present your findings in the form of a poster display or in any other inventive form that comes to mind.

GERALD HASLAM

Gerald Haslam (1937–) was born and raised in California's San Joaquin Valley. He describes it as a richly varied environment, where "oral tale-telling was a fine art." About his mixed Anglo-Hispanic heritage, Haslam has written, "I am more openly and proudly Hispanic than my pale skin and fair hair might suggest (I am three-quarters Anglo and equally pleased with that). At home, however, Spanish was our secret language, Catholicism our church, *la familia* our real religion. I tell my children (who add Cree, French, Polish, and German to the mix) that we are what America is becoming."

Before beginning his writing and teaching career, Haslam was a jack-of-all-trades. He worked as a roustabout (a person who performs odd jobs in oil fields); he picked, plowed, irrigated, and packed crops in the San Joaquin Valley; he worked in banks and stores. Haslam graduated from San Francisco State College in 1963.

Haslam has published six collections of stories, including his most recent, the award-winning *That Constant Coyote*. He has also written essays, other nonfiction, and a novel and has compiled anthologies. He has said, "It is a continuing source of both wonder and satisfaction to me that I have evolved into a storyteller."

OTHER WORKS *Okies: Selected Stories*, *The Man Who Cultivated Fire*, *Voices of a Place*   Extended Reading

160   UNIT TWO   PART 1: TWINGES OF CONSCIENCE

• AUTHOR BACKGROUND

THE WRITER'S STYLE

Haslam sprinkles this story with Spanish words and phrases. Why do you think he uses Spanish in an English-language story? What does his use of Spanish add to the story?

WORDS TO KNOW

Review the Words to Know at the bottom of the selection pages. Then, on your paper, write the vocabulary word that is related to each rhyming phrase below.

1. put to rest in her best
2. a lizard caught in a blizzard
3. all around the lot's vacant ground
4. a scene lush and green
5. hundreds of years make the climb with this measure of time

---

The Writer's Style

Encourage students to understand that Spanish words (such as *ese gringo*, *vaquero*, and *venga aquí*) give immediacy and texture to the portrayal of the characters' Spanish heritage. In this case, the use of Spanish words allows many readers to connect with the monolingual narrator.

Personal Voice, pp. 316–317
Word Choice, pp. 314–315

Alternative Activities

You might have groups of students look for key English nouns in the story. Then have the groups compare lists of the words they find. Have the class choose which words to find in the dictionary and display on the poster.

PREVIEWING

FICTION

The Splendid Outcast
Beryl Markham

Activating Prior Knowledge
PERSONAL CONNECTION

The narrator of this story travels from Africa to England to purchase a special racehorse for breeding purposes. Have you ever wanted something so much that you went to extraordinary lengths to get it? What did you do to get what you wanted? Did you succeed? Write about the experience in your notebook.

Building Background
CULTURAL CONNECTION

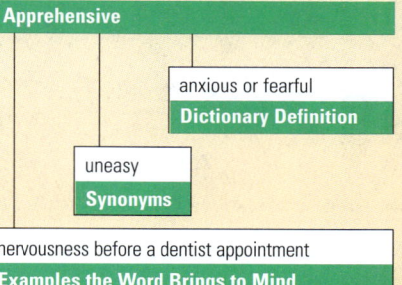

Raising racehorses is big business in many countries. Stallions (male horses) and mares (female horses) are carefully selected for mating in the hope of producing champion racers. Breeders take into account the horses' racing records, ancestry, and physical traits. A champion racing stallion can earn millions of dollars in stud fees—money paid to the stallion's owner when it sires foals.

In England, the setting of this story, records of horses' ancestry have been kept since the early 17th century. Rigel, the Thoroughbred stallion that the narrator is so keen to purchase, is a known winner with an outstanding ancestry. His sire (father) was unbeaten, and his dam (mother) was a superior steeplechaser, or runner of obstacle races.

Active Reading/Setting A Purpose
READING CONNECTION

Challenging Vocabulary Remember that you do not need to understand every word to enjoy the story. The footnotes and the definitions of the Words to Know will help you with the meanings of the difficult words and phrases that are most important for your understanding.

To help you keep track of the plot, questions have been inserted at various points in the story for you to answer in your reading log. After you finish the story, you can go back and enrich your vocabulary by using organizers like the one shown here to analyze unfamiliar words.

Apprehensive
anxious or fearful — **Dictionary Definition**
uneasy — **Synonyms**
nervousness before a dentist appointment — **Examples the Word Brings to Mind**

• CULTURAL CONNECTION

THE SPLENDID OUTCAST   **161**

OVERVIEW

Objectives

- To understand and appreciate a short story about a woman's attempt to purchase an outcast stallion
- To enrich reading by using active reading strategies
- To identify and understand the use of allusions
- To express understanding of the story through a choice of writing forms, including newspaper headlines, a poem, and a paragraph
- To extend understanding of the story through a variety of multimodal and cross-curricular activities

Skills

READING SKILLS/STRATEGIES
- Clarifying
- Challenging vocabulary

THE WRITER'S STYLE
- Connecting ideas

GRAMMAR
- Adverbs

LITERARY CONCEPTS
- Allusions
- Similes

GENRE STUDY
- Fiction: short story

SPELLING
- Words ending in *ant/ance* and *ent/ence*

SPEAKING, LISTENING, AND VIEWING
- Dramatic Reading
- Group discussion
- Oral presentation

Cross-Curricular Connections

SOCIAL STUDIES
- Auctions

HISTORY
- The Republic of Kenya

MATHEMATICS
- Converting currency

 **CULTURAL CONNECTION**
Raising Racehorses These colorful photographs will introduce students to the high-stakes world of breeding and racing horses.

Side A, Frame 52610

PRINT AND MEDIA RESOURCES

UNIT TWO RESOURCE BOOK
Strategic Reading: Literature, p. 11
Vocabulary SkillBuilder, p. 14
Reading SkillBuilder, p. 12
Spelling SkillBuilder, p. 13

GRAMMAR MINI–LESSONS
Transparencies, p. 12, p. 40
Copymasters, p. 19

WRITING MINI–LESSONS
Transparencies, p. 33

ACCESS FOR STUDENTS ACQUIRING ENGLISH
Selection Summaries
Reading and Writing Support

FORMAL ASSESSMENT
Selection Test, pp. 31–32
 Test Generator

 **AUDIO LIBRARY**
See Reference Card

 **LASERLINKS**
Cultural Connection
Art Gallery

THE LANGUAGE OF LITERATURE TEACHER'S EDITION   **161**

SUMMARY

The narrator travels from Kenya to England to attend a horse auction in the hopes of buying a champion racehorse named Rigel. Rigel has been banned from racing for attacking several people and killing a man, but the narrator plans to use the horse for breeding. The other bidder for Rigel is a mild-mannered (and not wealthy) jockey. As the narrator is poised to outbid the jockey, Rigel breaks loose. The jockey skillfully quiets the stallion. After witnessing these events, the narrator decides not to outbid the jockey.

Thematic Link: *Twinges of Conscience*
A gentle man's mastery of a dangerous stallion leads the narrator to reconsider her intention to outbid him for the horse.

Art Note

Whistlejacket by George Stubbs This British painter (1724–1806), a master of anatomical drawing, was uninterested in popular Romantic ideas about making imaginative and emotionally expressive paintings. Instead, his belief in the power and importance of observation led Stubbs to paint what he had learned from dissecting horses. In *Whistlejacket* Stubbs captures the lean, muscular grace of a racehorse in great detail. The absence of any background forces the viewer to see the subject clinically and without distraction.

Reading the Art *What words would you use to describe the feeling or mood the horse exudes? Which details of the animal's body and position convey this feeling or mood to the viewer?*

Whistlejacket (1762), George Stubbs. Kenwood House, Hampstead, London/Bridgeman Art Library, London/Superstock.

162 UNIT TWO PART 1: TWINGES OF CONSCIENCE

WORDS TO KNOW

adversary (ăd′vər-sĕr′ē) *n.* an opponent (p. 168)
cow (kou) *v.* to frighten by a show of force (p. 168)
disdainfully (dĭs-dān′fə-lē) *adv.* in a manner showing contempt or aloofness; scornfully (p. 165)
homage (hŏm′ĭj) *n.* an expression of honor or respect (p. 163)
impeccable (ĭm-pĕk′ə-bəl) *adj.* without flaws; perfect (p. 164)

imposing (ĭm-pō′zĭng) *adj.* impressive in size or strength (p. 166)
insolence (ĭn′sə-ləns) *n.* arrogance; disrespect (p. 170)
novice (nŏv′ĭs) *n.* a person new to an activity; beginner (p. 168)
retribution (rĕt′rə-byōō′shən) *n.* punishment for wrongdoing (p. 169)
zealot (zĕl′ət) *n.* a person who shows intense devotion to a cause; a fanatic (p. 164)

THE SPLENDID OUTCAST

by
· BERYL MARKHAM ·

The stallion was named after a star, and when he fell from his particular heaven, it was easy enough for people to say that he had been named too well. People like to see stars fall, but in the case of Rigel, it was of greater importance to me. To me and to one other—to a little man with shabby cuffs and a wilted cap that rested over eyes made mild by something other than time.

It was at Newmarket, in England, where, since Charles I instituted the first cup race, a kind of court has been held for the royalty of the turf.[1] Men of all classes come to Newmarket for the races and for the December sales.[2] They come from everywhere—some to bet, some to buy or sell, and some merely to offer homage to the resplendent peers of the Stud Book,[3] for the sport of kings[4] may, after all, be the pleasure of every man.

December can be bitterly cold in England, and this December was. There was frozen sleet on buildings and on trees, and I remember that the huge Newmarket track lay on the downs below the village like a noose of diamonds on a tarnished mat. There was a festive spirit everywhere, but it was somehow lost on me. I had come to buy new blood for my stable in Kenya, and since my stable was my living, I came as serious buyers do, with figures in my mind and caution in my heart. Horses are hard to judge at best, and the thought of putting your hoarded pounds[5] behind that judgment makes it harder still.

I sat close on the edge of the auction ring and held my breath from time to time as the bidding soared. I held it because the casual mention of ten thousand guineas in payment for a horse or for anything else seemed to me

---

1. **turf:** the grass track on which horses race.
2. **December sales:** end-of-year auctions of horses.
3. **resplendent peers of the Stud Book:** outstanding racehorses whose family trees are carefully preserved like those of the nobility.
4. **sport of kings:** horseracing, so called because many British monarchs and noblemen have owned racehorses.
5. **pounds:** British units of money. At the time of this story, one pound (£1) was equivalent to $5.00 in U.S. currency; today a pound is worth considerably less than this.

WORDS TO KNOW
homage (hŏm′ĭj) *n.* an expression of honor or respect

163

Mini-Lesson — Study Skills

USING GENERAL REFERENCE BOOKS
Remind students that an atlas is a valuable reference book. If possible, show them the different sections of a good atlas: world maps, as well as maps of continents, countries, and sections of countries; charts, tables, and maps giving information on topics such as climate, natural resources, population, languages, and religions.

Application Have students use the index of an atlas to locate the African country of Kenya and the town of Newmarket in England (just outside Cambridge). Encourage students to use all sections of the atlas to learn any other details about these two areas of the world, for instance, population, climate, and economy.

CUSTOMIZING FOR
Gifted and Talented Students

As students read the selection, have them think about the desirability of owning a horse, or any animal, that behaves as Rigel does. Ask them to discuss the responses of different characters in the selection and whether they agree or disagree with these characters. *(Responses will vary but should include an assessment of the behavior of the narrator, the old jockey, the auctioneer, and other participants at the auction.)*

Active Reading: CLARIFY

A Help students focus on Rigel's violent history. The horse has not only hurt people but has even killed a man. *(The narrator believes Rigel can be bought cheaply because no one wants to buy a violent horse.)*

Literary Concept: SIMILE

B Encourage students to note this simile. In what way is the jockey like a "stone of granite"? What or whom does "the glitter" refer to? *(Possible response: Using the word* like, *Markham compares the little man's drab appearance to "a stone of granite." This comparison is followed by an implied comparison of the monied people with "the glitter" [i.e., precious stones] in the jeweler's window.)*

STRATEGIC READING FOR
Less-Proficient Readers

C Check that students are aware of who Rigel is and why he is considered an outcast.

- Who is Rigel? *(a stallion named after a star)* **Restating**
- Why does the narrator want to buy Rigel? *(She wishes to breed the horse at her stable in Kenya.)* **Restating**
- What sets Rigel apart from most horses? *(He has an impressive pedigree, yet he has killed a man and wounded other men.)* **Comparing and Contrasting**

Set a Purpose Have students read to find out what happens at the auction.

---

wildly beyond the realm of probable things. For myself, I had five hundred pounds to spend and, as I waited for Rigel to be shown, I remember that I felt uncommonly maternal about each pound. I waited for Rigel because I had come six thousand miles to buy him, nor was I apprehensive lest anyone should take him from me; he was an outcast.

Rigel had a pedigree that looked backward and beyond the pedigrees of many Englishmen— and Rigel had a brilliant record. By all odds, he should have brought ten thousand guineas[6] at the sale, but I knew he wouldn't, for he had killed a man.

He had killed a man—not fallen upon him, nor thrown him in a playful moment from the saddle, but killed him dead with his hooves and with his teeth in a stable. And that was not all, though it was the greatest thing. Rigel had crippled other men and, so the story went, would cripple or kill still more, so long as he lived. He was savage, people said, and while he could not be hanged for his crimes, like a man, he could be shunned as criminals are. He could be offered for sale. And yet, under the implacable rules of racing, he had been warned off the turf for life—so who would buy?

Well, I for one—and I had supposed there would not be two. I would buy if the price were low enough, because I had youth then, and a corresponding contempt for failure. It seemed probable that in time and with luck and with skill, the stallion might be made manageable again, if only for breeding—especially for breeding. He could be gentled, I thought. But I found it hard to believe what I saw that day. I had not known that the mere touch of a hand could, in an instant, extinguish the long-burning anger of an angry heart.

I first noticed the little man when the sale was already well on its way, and he caught my attention at once, because he was incongruous there. He sat a few benches from me and held his lean, interwoven fingers upon his knees. He started down upon the arena as each horse was led into it, and he listened to the dignified encomiums[7] of the auctioneer with the humble attention of a parishioner at mass. He never moved. He was surrounded by men and women, who, by their impeccable clothes and by their somewhat bored familiarity with pounds and guineas, made him conspicuous. He was like a stone of granite in a jeweler's window, motionless and grey against the glitter.

You could see in his face that he loved horses—just as you could see, in some of the faces of those around him, that they loved the idea of horses. They were the cultists, he the votary,[8] and there were, in fact, about his grey eyes and his slender lips, the deep, tense lines so often etched in the faces of zealots and of lonely men. It was the cast of his shoulders, I think, the devotion of his manner that told me he had once been a jockey.

A yearling came into the ring and was bought, and then another, while the pages of catalogues were quietly turned. The auctioneer's voice, clear but scarcely lifted, intoned the virtues of his magnificent merchandise as other voices, responding to this magic, spoke

CLARIFY
A Why does the narrator think she can buy Rigel cheaply?
Using a Reading Log

---

6. **ten thousand guineas** (gĭn'ēz): a sum of money equivalent to $52,500 at the time the story was written. A guinea, a British monetary unit no longer in use, was equal to £1.05.
7. **encomiums** (ĕn-kō'mē-əmz): expressions of enthusiastic praise.
8. **cultists . . . votary:** Here, *cultists* refers to people attracted to something because it is fashionable, in contrast to the *votary*, who is intensely devoted to something for its own sake.

WORDS TO KNOW
impeccable (ĭm-pĕk'ə-bəl) *adj.* without flaws; perfect
zealot (zĕl'ət) *n.* a person who shows intense devotion to a cause; a fanatic

164

Mini-Lesson Literary Concepts

REVIEWING SIMILES Remind students that figurative language goes beyond dictionary meanings of words to create fresh and original descriptions. The three most common forms of figurative language are simile, metaphor, and personification.

A simile is a comparison of two unlike things that have some quality in common. Similes make a direct comparison, using words such as *like, as,* or *resembles.*

Application Have students try to find the similes in the selection. ("Newmarket lay . . . like a noose of diamonds"—p. 163; "He was like a stone of granite"—p. 164; "looks . . . as a captured king may look"—p. 165; "golden mane lifted like a flag"—p. 166; "spirit flares like fire"—p. 168; "shrill as the cry of winter"—p. 169; "Rigel's neck is . . . straight as a saber"—p. 169) Then have them devise three similes of their own that describe something or someone from the selection in an interesting way by comparing it to some unlike thing.

reservedly of figures: "A thousand guineas . . . two thousand . . . three . . . four! . . ."

The scene at the auction comes to me clearly now, as if once again it were happening before my eyes.

"Five, perhaps?" The auctioneer scans the audience expectantly as a groom[9] parades a dancing colt around the arena. There is a moment of near silence, a burly voice calls, "Five!" and the colt is sold while a murmur of polite approval swells and dies.

And so they go, one after another, until the list is small; the audience thins, and my finger traces the name, Rigel, on the last page of the catalogue. I straighten on my bench and hold my breath a little, forgetting the crowd, the little man, and a part of myself. I know this horse. I know he is by Hurry On out of Bounty[10]—the sire unbeaten, the dam a great steeplechaser—and there is no better blood than that. Killer or not, Rigel has won races and won them clean. If God and Barclays Bank stay with me, he will return to Africa when I do.

And there, at last, he stands. In the broad entrance to the ring, two powerful men appear with the stallion between them. The men are not grooms of ordinary size; they have been picked for strength, and in the clenched fist of each is the end of a chain. Between the chain and the bit there is on the near side a short rod of steel, close to the stallion's mouth—a rod of steel, easy to grasp, easy to use. Clenched around the great girth of the horse, and fitted with metal rings, there is a strap of thick leather that brings to mind the restraining harness of a madman.

Together, the two men edge the stallion forward. Tall as they are, they move like midgets beside his massive shoulders. He is the biggest thoroughbred I have ever seen. He is the most beautiful. His coat is chestnut, flecked with white, and his mane and tail are close to gold. There is a blaze on his face—wide and straight and forthright, as if by this marking he proclaims that he is none other than Rigel, for all his sins, for all the hush that falls over the crowd.

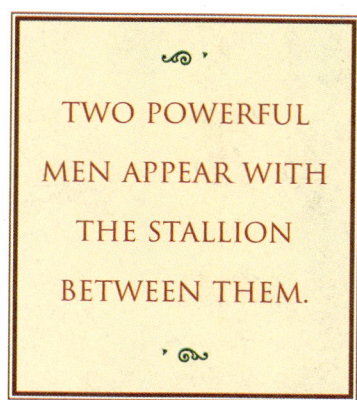

> TWO POWERFUL MEN APPEAR WITH THE STALLION BETWEEN THEM.

He is Rigel, and he looks upon the men who hold his chains as a captured king may look upon his captors. He is not tamed. Nothing about him promises that he will be tamed. Stiffly, on reluctant hooves, he enters the ring and flares his crimson nostrils at the crowd, and the crowd is still. The crowd whose pleasure is the docile beast of pretty paddocks,[11] the gainly horse of cherished prints that hang upon the finest walls, the willing winner of the race—upon the rebel this crowd stares, and the rebel stares back.

His eyes are lit with anger or with hate. His head is held <u>disdainfully</u> and high, his neck an

---

9. **groom:** a man or boy whose job it is to care for horses.
10. **he is by Hurry On out of Bounty:** Hurry On was his father, and Bounty was his mother.
11. **paddocks:** fenced-in areas where horses are saddled before they race.

WORDS TO KNOW

disdainfully (dĭs-dān′fə-lē) *adv.* in a manner showing contempt or aloofness; scornfully

165

Mini-Lesson Genre Study

FICTION Explain to students that a short story is a kind of fiction with many of the same characteristics of longer fictional works. Both contain characters, plots, settings, and themes. However, short stories usually revolve around a single idea and can be read in one sitting.

Application Have students create a chart like the one shown. Have them fill in the chart with details summarizing the selection. You may wish to have students reread the selection, filling in the chart as they reread.

Characters	Plot	Setting	Theme

Art Note

Portrait of Mrs. Whelan by Harold Gilman The work of Harold Gilman (1876–1919) and of several other English painters in the early years of this century hovers between abstraction and clear representation. For instance, *Portrait of Mrs. Whelan* is not painted with the clarity of detail that would allow the viewer to see (and make judgments about) minute aspects of her physical appearance. Rather, the image suggests the subject's intelligence and hints at a strain of pensiveness or anxiety in her.

Reading the Art *Do you think this portrait is an apt illustration for "The Splendid Outcast"? Why or why not? Does the painting contain any information that hints at the subject's social position?*

Active Reading: CLARIFY

G Help students focus on the fact that Rigel is rearing back on his hind legs and beating the air with his front hooves. The narrator suggests that the animal does this because it has just realized what is happening.

Literary Concept: ALLUSION

H Beryl Markham uses an allusion in naming the racehorse Rigel. Tell students that one of the brightest stars in the sky also goes by this name. Thought to be about 20,000 times brighter than our sun, Rigel (also called Beta Orionis) appears in the constellation Orion (the giant hunter). Have students discuss why the author might have given this name to the horse. *(Possible response: Before Rigel's character changed, he was one of the brightest stars of racing.)* Then ask students why Markham's allusion to *Gulliver's Travels* is especially appropriate. *(Rigel is huge, and Gulliver was a giant compared to the tiny Lilliputians.)*

Detail of *Portrait of Mrs. Whelan* (about 1911), Harold Gilman. Courtesy of the Fine Art Society, London.

arc of arrogance. He prances now—impatience in the thudding of his hooves upon the tanbark, defiance in his manner—and the chains jerk tight. The long stallion reins are tightly held—apprehensively held—and the men who hold them glance at the auctioneer, an urgent question in their eyes.

The auctioneer raises his arm for silence, but there is silence. No one speaks. The story of Rigel is known—his breeding, his brilliant victories, and finally his insurgence and his crimes. Who will buy the outcast? The auctioneer shakes his head as if to say that this is a trick beyond his magic. But he will try. He is an <u>imposing</u> man, an experienced man, and now he clears his throat and confronts the crowd, a kind of pleading in his face.

"This splendid animal—" he begins—and does not finish. He cannot finish.

Rigel has scanned the silent audience and smelled the unmoving air, and he—a creature of the wind—knows the indignity of this skyless temple. He seems aware at last of the chains that hold him, of the men who cling forlornly to the heavy reins. He rears from the tanbark, higher and higher still, until his golden mane is lifted like a flag unfurled and defiant. He beats the air. He trembles in his rising anger, and the crowd leans forward.

CLARIFY
What is Rigel doing?
Using a Reading Log

A groom clings like a monkey to the tightened chain. He is swept from his feet while his partner, a less tenacious man, sprawls ignobly below, and men—a dozen men—rush to the ring, some shouting, some waving their arms. They run and swear in lowered voices; they grasp reins, chains, rings, and swarm upon their towering Gulliver.[12] And he subsides.

With something like contempt for this hysteria, Rigel touches his forehooves to the tanbark once more. He has killed no one, but they are jabbing at his mouth now, they are surrounding him, adding fuel to his fiery reputation, and the auctioneer is a wilted man.

He sighs, and you can almost hear it. He raises both arms and foregoes his speech.

---

[12] **Gulliver:** the first-person narrator of Jonathan Swift's satire *Gulliver's Travels*. One of the places Gulliver visits is the island of Lilliput, where he is a giant among the six-inch-tall Lilliputians.

WORDS TO KNOW
imposing (ĭm-pō′zĭng) *adj.* impressive in size or strength

Mini-Lesson Reading Skills/Strategies

ACTIVE READING: CLARIFY Remind students that, in order to understand a story fully, it can be useful to stop occasionally to review what is going on. This strategy may by particularly useful in texts that contain challenging vocabulary. For instance, students can analyze an unfamiliar vocabulary word and clarify its meaning by looking at its context, learning its dictionary definition, identifying its synonyms, and considering what examples from their own experience they can apply to the word.

Application If students have not noted unfamiliar vocabulary as they read, have them skim the selection and jot down any words that confused them when they read it the first time. Then have them apply the steps explained above to each of the words. Refer students to the organizer on page 161 to use for this activity.

Reteaching/Reinforcement
• *Unit Two Resource Book*, p. 12

"What," he asks with weariness, "am I offered?" And there is a ripple of laughter from the crowd. Smug in its wisdom, it offers nothing.

But I do, and my voice is like an echo in a cave. Still there is triumph in it. I will have what I have come so far to get—I will have Rigel.

> SUDDENLY I AM AWARE THAT I HAVE A COMPETITOR, AND I AM CAUTIOUS.

"A hundred guineas!" I stand as I call my price, and the auctioneer is plainly shocked—not by the meagerness of the offer, but by the offer itself. He stares upward from the ring, incredulity in his eyes.

He lifts a hand and slowly repeats the price. "I am offered," he says, "one hundred guineas."

There is a hush, and I feel the eyes of the crowd and watch the hand of the auctioneer. When it goes down, the stallion will be mine.

But it does not go down. It is still poised in midair, white, expectant, compelling, when the soft voice, the gently challenging voice is lifted. "Two hundred!" the voice says, and I do not have to turn to know that the little jockey has bid against me. But I do turn.

He has not risen from the bench, and he does not look at me. In his hand he holds a sheaf of bank notes. I can tell by their color that they are of small denomination, by their rumpled condition that they have been hoarded long. People near him are staring—horrified, I think—at the vulgar spectacle of cash at a Newmarket auction.

I am not horrified, nor sympathetic. Suddenly I am aware that I have a competitor, and I am cautious. I am here for a purpose that has little to do with sentiment, and I will not be beaten. I think of my stable in Kenya, of the feed bills to come, of the syces[13] to be paid, of the races that are yet to be won if I am to survive in this unpredictable business. No, I cannot now yield an inch. I have little money, but so has he. No more, I think, but perhaps as much.

I hesitate a moment and glance at the little man, and he returns my glance. We are like two gamblers bidding against the other's unseen cards. Our eyes meet for a sharp instant—a cold instant.

I straighten, and my catalogue is crumpled in my hand. I moisten my lips and call, "Three hundred!" I call it firmly, steadily, hoping to undo my opponent at a stroke. It is a wishful thought.

He looks directly at me now but does not smile. He looks at me as a man might look at one who bears false witness against him, then soundlessly he counts his money and bids again, "Three fifty!"

The interest of the crowd is suddenly aroused. All these people are at once conscious of being witnesses, not only before an auction, but before a contest, a rivalry of wills. They shift in their seats and stare as they might stare at a pair of duelists, rapiers in hand.[14]

---

13. **syces** (sī′səz): stablemen or grooms.
14. **duelists, rapiers** (rā′pē-ərz) **in hand:** two people fighting with swords.

THE SPLENDID OUTCAST 167

Active Reading: EVALUATE

L Ask students for their opinions of the narrator's behavior here. How do they feel about her smothering her natural sympathy for the underdog in this bidding contest? You may wish to use the following model to give them ideas of what they might be thinking about.

Think-Aloud Model *I definitely can see why the narrator feels sympathetic toward the little jockey. On the other hand, it really is necessary for her to smother her feelings if she wants to purchase Rigel for her business. I'm glad I don't have to make the decision.*

Active Reading: CLARIFY

M Help students recognize that the narrator concentrates on presenting a cool, confident manner as she bids on the horse. She forces herself to remain clinical and mimics the behavior of the monied men and women around her.

CUSTOMIZING FOR
Students Acquiring English

I Pronounce *entrance* (ĕn-trăns′) and elicit its meaning from a near-fluent student. *(to delight; to fill with wonder; to put in a trance)* Be sure students can distinguish the pronunciation of this verb from the pronunciation of the noun *entrance*.

But money is the weapon, Rigel the prize. And prize enough, I think, as does my adversary.

I ponder and think hard, then decide to bid a hundred more. Not twenty, not fifty, but a hundred. Perhaps by that I can take him in my stride. He need not know there is little more to follow. He may assume that I am one of the casual ones, impatient of small figures. He may hesitate, he may withdraw. He may be cowed.

Still standing, I utter, as indifferently as I can, the words, "Four fifty!" and the auctioneer, at ease in his element of contention, brightens visibly.

I am aware that the gathered people are now fascinated by this battle of pounds and shillings over a stallion that not one of them would care to own. I only hope that in the heat of it some third person does not begin to bid. But I need not worry; Rigel takes care of that.

The little jockey has listened to my last offer, and I can see that he is already beaten—or almost, at least. He has counted his money a dozen times, but now he counts it again, swiftly, with agile fingers, as if hoping his previous counts had been wrong.

L I feel a momentary surge of sympathy, then smother it. Horse training is not my hobby. It is my living. I wait for what I am sure will be his last bid, and it comes. For the first time, he rises from his bench. He is small and alone in spirit, for the glances of the well-dressed people about him lend him nothing. He does not care. His eyes are on the stallion, and I can see that there is a kind of passion in them. I have seen that expression before—in the eyes of sailors appraising a comely ship, in the eyes of pilots sweeping the clean, sweet contours of a plane. There is reverence in it, desire—and even hope.

The little man turns slightly to face the expectant auctioneer, then clears his throat and makes his bid. "Four eighty!" he calls, and the slight note of desperation in his voice is unmistakable, but I force myself to ignore it.

CLARIFY
How does the narrator get the upper hand in the bidding process?
Using a Reading Log

Now, at last, I tell myself, the prize is mine.

The auctioneer receives the bid and looks at me, as do a hundred people. Some of them, no doubt, think I am quite mad or wholly inexperienced, but they watch while the words "Five hundred" form upon my lips. They are never uttered.

Throughout the bidding for Rigel, Rigel has been ignored. He has stood quietly enough after his first brief effort at freedom; he has scarcely moved. But now, at the climax of the sale, his impatience overflows, his spirit flares like fire, his anger bursts through the circle of men who guard him. Suddenly, there are cries, shouts of warning, the ringing of chains and the cracking of leather, and the crowd leaps to its feet. Rigel is loose. Rigel has hurled his captors from him, and he stands alone.

It is a beautiful thing to see, but there is terror in it. A thoroughbred stallion with anger in his eyes is not a sight to entrance anyone but a novice. If you are aware of the power and the speed and the intelligence in that towering symmetrical body, you will hold your breath as you watch it. You will know that the teeth of a horse can crush a bone, that hooves can crush a man. And Rigel's hooves have crushed a man.

He stands alone, his neck curved, his golden tail a battle plume, and he turns, slowly, deliberately, and faces the men he has flung away. They are not without courage, but they

M

I

WORDS TO KNOW	**adversary** (ăd′vər-sĕr′ē) *n.* an opponent
	cow (kou) *v.* to frighten by a show of force
	novice (nŏv′ĭs) *n.* a person new to an activity; beginner

168

Mini-Lesson  Grammar

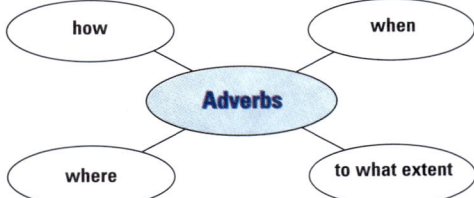

ADVERBS Point out to students that an adverb modifies a verb, an adjective, or another adverb. Adverbs help make meaning clear by telling how, when, where, or to what extent something is true.

Application Invite students to copy the web shown into their notebooks and use it to find the adverbs in the highlighted passage on page 168. *(still, indifferently, visibly, now, only)* Then have them identify the adverbs in the following sentences:

1. I felt *somewhat* sad when I outbid the little jockey.
2. She *finally* arrived at the horse auction.

Reteaching/Reinforcement
- *Grammar Handbook*, anthology p. 878
- *Grammar Mini-Lessons* copymasters p. 19, transparencies p. 12, p. 40

Adverbs, pp. 511–512

168 THE LANGUAGE OF LITERATURE **TEACHER'S EDITION**

are without resource. Horses are not tamed by whips or by blows. The strength of ten men is not so strong as a single stroke of a hoof; the experience of ten men is not enough, for this is the unexpected, the unpredictable. No one is prepared. No one is ready.

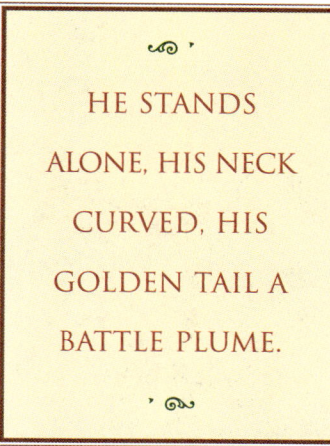

HE STANDS ALONE, HIS NECK CURVED, HIS GOLDEN TAIL A BATTLE PLUME.

The words "Five hundred" die upon my lips as I watch, as I listen. For the stallion is not voiceless now. His challenging scream is shrill as the cry of winter wind. It is bleak and heartless. His forehooves stir the tanbark. The auction is forgotten.

A man stands before him—a man braver than most. He holds nothing in his hands save an exercise bat; it looks a feeble thing, and is. It is a thin stick bound with leather—enough only to enrage Rigel, for he has seen such things in men's hands before. He knows their meaning. Such a thing as this bat, slight as it is, enrages him because it is a symbol that stands for other things. It stands, perhaps, for the confining walls of a darkened stable, for the bit of steel, foreign, but almost everpresent in his mouth, for the tightened girth, the command to gallop, to walk, to stop, to parade before the swelling crowds of gathered people, to accept the measured food gleaned from forbidden fields. It stands for life no closer to the earth than the sterile smell of satin on a jockey's back or the dead wreath hung upon a winner. It stands for servitude. And Rigel has broken with his overlords.

He lunges quickly, and the man with a bat is not so quick. He lifts the pathetic stick and waves it in desperation. He cries out, and the voice of the crowd drowns his cry. Rigel's neck is outstretched and straight as a saber.[15] There is dust and the shouting of men and the screaming of women, for the stallion's teeth have closed on the shoulder of his forlorn enemy.

The man struggles and drops his bat, and his eyes are sharp with terror, perhaps with pain. Blood leaves the flesh of his face, and it is a face grey and pleading, as must be the faces of those to whom <u>retribution</u> is unexpected and swift. He beats against the golden head while the excitement of the crowd mounts against the fury of Rigel. Then reason vanishes. Clubs, whips, and chains appear like magic in the ring, and a regiment of men advance upon the stallion. They are angry men, brave in their anger, righteous and justified in it. They advance, and the stallion drops the man he has attacked, and the man runs for cover, clutching his shoulder.

I am standing, as is everyone. It is a strange and unreal thing to see this trapped and frustrated creature, magnificent and alone, away from his kind, remote from the things he understands, face the punishment of his minuscule masters. He is, of course, terrified, and the terror is a mounting madness. If he could run, he would leave this place, abandoning his fear and his hatred to do it. But he cannot run. The

---

15. **saber** (sā′bər): a dueling or fencing sword.

WORDS TO KNOW
retribution (rĕt′rə-byōō′shən) *n.* punishment for wrongdoing

Active Reading: CLARIFY

Q Encourage students to describe the reasons for Rigel's actions. If they need help, you can share the following thought process with them.

Think-Aloud Model *At first I wondered whether Rigel fights back simply because he's mean. After all, he has a history of hurting people. But now I'm not so sure. The author goes into great detail about the big men, the chains, the rods, and the leather strap used to keep Rigel under control. I'm sure all of these restraints scare him. I think that Rigel fights back because he's afraid.*

STRATEGIC READING FOR Less-Proficient Readers

R Check to see that students clearly understand what happens as the auction continues.

- What strategy does the narrator use to outbid the jockey? *(She bids in 100-guinea increments and tries to convey a casual, powerful attitude.)* **Noting Relevant Details**

- What does Rigel do as the narrator is about to bid 500 guineas? *(He breaks loose and stands alone.)* **Noting Sequence of Events**

- After men approach Rigel with chains and whips, who approaches Rigel "like a ghost"? *(the jockey)* **Clarifying**

Set a Purpose Have students read to find out what happens to the horse, the jockey, and the narrator.

Literary Concept: ALLUSION

S Ask students to identify the author's use of allusion in this passage. *(The story of David and Goliath; the small jockey approaching Rigel is like David going against Goliath.)*

---

walls of the arena are high. The doors are shut, and the trap makes him blind with anger. He will fight, and the blows will fall with heaviness upon his spirit, for his body is a rock before these petty weapons.

The men edge closer, ropes and chains and whips in determined hands. The whips are lifted, the chains are ready; the battle line is formed, and Rigel does not retreat. He comes forward, the whites of his eyes exposed and rimmed with carnelian fire, his nostrils crimson.

CLARIFY
Q Why does Rigel fight back?
Using a Reading Log

There is a breathless silence, and the little jockey slips like a ghost into the ring. His eyes are fixed on the embattled stallion. He begins to run across the tanbark and breaks through the circle of advancing men and does not stop. Someone clutches at his coat, but he breaks loose without turning, then slows to an almost casual walk and approaches Rigel alone. The men do not follow him. He waves them back. He goes forward, steadily, easily and happily, without caution, without fear, and Rigel whirls angrily to face him.

Rigel stands close to the wall of the arena. He cannot retreat. He does not propose to. Now he can focus his fury on this insignificant David[16] who has come to meet him, and he does. He lunges at once as only a stallion can—swiftly, invincibly, as if escape and freedom can be found only in the destruction of all that is human, all that smells human, and all that humans have made.

He lunges and the jockey stops. He does not turn or lift a hand or otherwise move. He stops, he stands, and there is silence everywhere. No one speaks; no one seems to breathe. Only Rigel is motion. No special

hypnotic power emanates from the jockey's eyes; he has no magic. The stallion's teeth are bared and close, his hooves are a swelling sound when the jockey turns. Like a matador of nerveless skill and studied <u>insolence</u>, the

---
16. **David:** the shepherd boy who, according to the Bible, killed the giant warrior Goliath with only a slingshot.

WORDS TO KNOW
insolence (ĭn′sə-ləns) *n.* arrogance; disrespect

170

Mini-Lesson The Writer's Style

CONNECTING IDEAS Explain to students that if a sentence expresses more than one idea, a good writer connects them with a word that shows the relationship between the ideas. For example:

Someone clutches at his coat, <u>but</u> he breaks loose without turning, <u>then</u> slows to an almost casual walk <u>and</u> approaches Rigel alone.

On the other hand, a sentence that loosely connects two or more ideas with the word *and* is called a stringy sentence.

Example I went to the race, and it started to rain, and the race went on, and I got soaked.

Application Have students revise the following stringy sentence:

1. The crowd started yelling, and the horse had reared up, and the jockey moved toward the horse, and finally the horse became still.

Reteaching/Reinforcement
- *Writing Handbook,* anthology pp. 829–830
- *Writing Mini-Lessons* transparencies, p. 33

 The Writer's Craft

Stringy Sentences, pp. 298–299

Showing at Tattersall's, Robert Bevan. Copyright © Ashmolean Museum, Oxford, United Kingdom, all rights reserved.

jockey turns his back on Rigel and does not walk away, and the stallion pauses.

Rigel rears high at the back of the little man, screaming his defiant scream, but he does not strike. His hooves are close to the jockey's head but do not touch him. His teeth are sheathed. He hesitates, trembles, roars wind from his massive lungs. He shakes his head, his golden mane, and beats the ground. It is frustration—but of a new kind. It is a thing he does not know—a man who neither cringes in fear nor threatens with whips or chains. It is a thing beyond his memory perhaps—as far beyond it as the understanding of the mare that bore him.

Rigel is suddenly motionless, rigid, suspicious. He waits, and the grey-eyed jockey turns to face him. The little man is calm and smiling. We hear him speak, but cannot understand his words. They are low and they are lost to us—an incantation. But the stallion seems to understand at least the spirit if not the sense of them. He snorts but does not move. And now the jockey's hand goes forward to the golden mane—neither hurriedly nor with hesitance, but unconcernedly, as if it had rested there a thousand times. And there it stays.

There is a murmur from the crowd, then silence. People look at one another and stir in their seats—a strange self-consciousness in their stirring, for people are uneasy before the proved worth of their inferiors, unbelieving of the virtue of simplicity. They watch with open mouths as the giant Rigel, the killer Rigel, with no harness save a head collar, follows his Lilliputian master, his new friend, across the ring.

All has happened in so little time—in moments. The audience begins to stand, to

CLARIFY

How does the jockey gain control of Rigel?

Using a Reading Log

THE SPLENDID OUTCAST **171**

Art Note

Showing at Tattersall's by Robert Bevan This image by Robert Bevan (1865–1925) is especially interesting when contrasted with *Whistlejacket*. Whereas Stubbs painted a portrait of a majestic animal, Bevan's subject is the business of showing and purchasing horses. Thus Bevan's work features two fine animals (one positioned in the center of the canvas), but the viewer cannot see them clearly. In fact, every person and animal in the painting is partially obstructed from the viewer. Instead, it is the *process* of looking, buying, and selling that is the focus of Bevan's painting.

Reading the Art *What other details in the painting suggest that these horses are part of a highly controlled environment? In your opinion, does the artist convey a point of view about the activity in the painting?*

CUSTOMIZING FOR
Multiple Learning Styles

T **Bodily-Kinetic Learners** Have volunteers mime the movements of the jockey and Rigel, beginning with the horse's lunge and ending with the jockey's touching Rigel's mane.

Active Reading: **CLARIFY**

U Help students understand that the jockey's fearlessness and lack of aggression seem to surprise the horse. Ultimately, the jockey's calm presence, words, and touch instill a sense of trust in the animal.

Mini-Lesson: Speaking, Listening, and Viewing

DRAMATIC READING Explain to students that good writers convey the excitement of action by choosing certain words (sometimes for their sound) and by adjusting the length of their sentences. Sometimes a writer juxtaposes one or more short sentences with a longer one to heighten the scene's tension or suspense. This variety contributes to the dramatic quality of a selection, which can be especially apparent if the selection, or parts of it, is read aloud.

For example, on page 170, Markham uses the following combination of sentences to describe Rigel readying himself to meet the little jockey: *Rigel stands close to the wall of the arena. He cannot retreat. He does not propose to.*

Application Encourage students to appreciate Markham's masterful descriptions of the motions of Rigel and the jockey as you or a volunteer read aloud the two paragraphs at the bottom of pages 170–171.

THE LANGUAGE OF LITERATURE TEACHER'S EDITION **171**

STRATEGIC READING FOR
Less-Proficient Readers

▼ Check that students clearly understand the resolution of the story.

- What happens to Rigel? *(The jockey, not the narrator, purchases Rigel.)* Summarizing
- Why doesn't the narrator continue bidding? *(The narrator feels the jockey and Rigel belong together.)* Drawing Conclusions

CUSTOMIZING FOR
Gifted and Talented Students

Have students discuss the narrator's thoughts, feelings, and behavior during the auction. What is their opinion of the narrator's suppression of sympathy for the jockey? How do they view the narrator's decision to allow the jockey to purchase Rigel? Have students discuss similar situations where they wanted to have something that someone else also wanted.

COMPREHENSION CHECK

1. Where is the setting of the story? *(a horse auction in Newmarket, England)*
2. Which two people bid on Rigel? *(the narrator and a jockey)*
3. Why is Rigel being sold? *(The horse has a history of violent behavior.)*
4. Who buys the horse for 480 guineas? *(the jockey)*
5. Who is considered an outcast? *(Rigel for his violent behavior; also the jockey, who has been barred from racing)*

---

leave. But they pause at the lift of the auctioneer's hand. He waves it and they pause. It is all very well, his gestures say, but business is, after all, business, and Rigel has not been sold. He looks up at me, knowing that I have a bid to make—the last bid. And I look down into the ring at the stallion I have come so far to buy. His head is low and close to the shoulder of the man who would take him from me. He is not prancing now, not moving. For this hour, at least, he is changed.

I straighten and then shake my head. I need only say "Five hundred," but the words won't come. I can't get them out. I am angry with myself—a sentimental fool—and I am disappointed. But I cannot bid. It is too easy—twenty pounds too little, and yet too great an advantage.

No. I shake my head again, the auctioneer shrugs and turns to seal his bargain with the jockey.

On the way out, an old friend jostles me. "You didn't really want him then," he says.

"Want him? No. No, I didn't really want him."

"It was wise," he says. "What good is a horse that's warned off every course in the Empire? You wouldn't want a horse like that."

"That's right, I wouldn't want a horse like that."

We move to the exit, and when we are out in the bright cold air of Newmarket, I turn to my friend and mention the little jockey. "But he wanted Rigel," I say.

And my old friend laughs. "He would," he says. "That man has himself been barred from racing for fifteen years. Why, I can't remember. But it's two of a kind, you see—Rigel and Sparrow. Outlaws, both. He loves and knows horses as no man does, but that's what we call him around the tracks—the Fallen Sparrow."

172 UNIT TWO PART 1: TWINGES OF CONSCIENCE

Mini-Lesson Spelling

WORDS ENDING IN *ANT/ANCE* AND *ENT/ENCE* Tell students that adjectives ending in *ant* or *ent* are related to nouns ending in *ance* or *ence*.

insolent *adj.*   insolence *n.*
important *adj.*   importance *n.*

If students know how to spell one form, they should be able to correctly spell the other, because *ant* and *ance* always go together, as do *ent* and *ence*.

Application Ask students to look at the following words and give the related noun or adjective:

expectant   indifference
reluctance   reverent
arrogant   impatience
intelligent   silent
insignificance   brilliance
insolent   insurgent

Ask students to look for more words that fit this pattern in their own reading and writing and add these words to their personal word lists.

Reteaching/Reinforcement
• *Unit Two Resource Book,* p. 13

RESPONDING OPTIONS

FROM PERSONAL RESPONSE TO CRITICAL ANALYSIS

REFLECT 1. What is your reaction to the narrator's decision at the end? Share your thoughts with a partner.

RETHINK 2. After being so intent on purchasing Rigel, why does the narrator give up her chance?

3. Do you think the narrator makes the right decision? Why or why not?
   Consider
   - Rigel's reputation and his behavior at the auction
   - Rigel's reaction to the jockey
   - the narrator's financial situation

4. Compare Rigel, the jockey, and the narrator. What characteristics do they share?

Thematic Link 5. How does this story relate to the Unit Two theme, "Critical Adjustments," and the theme of this part of the unit, "Twinges of Conscience"?

RELATE 6. Even though Rigel's actions have made him an outcast, the narrator considers him valuable. What kinds of actions make a human being an outcast? What human outcasts do you consider valuable? Explain your answers.

LITERARY CONCEPTS

Markham includes **allusions,** or references to famous people, places, and works of literature. Understanding the allusions can help a reader better appreciate the story. For example, when the narrator calls the jockey Lilliputian, she is alluding to a nation of tiny people in the book *Gulliver's Travels*. Find two other allusions to fictional or historical people in the story. What idea does each allusion add?

CONCEPT REVIEW: Setting The setting of a story involves not only the time and place of the action but also the customs, manners, and attitudes of that time and place. In this story, what attitudes and manners are characteristic of the majority of people who come to Newmarket to buy horses?

Multimodal Learning
ANOTHER PATHWAY
Cooperative Learning
A dramatic series of events leads up to the climax of this story. With a group of classmates, decide at what point the climax of the story occurs. Then work with the group to create a graph that shows the main events leading up to the climax.

QUICKWRITES

1. Compose a series of **newspaper headlines** that relate events in the lives of Rigel and the jockey before the story begins.

2. Write a **poem** about Rigel. Take into account the subject matter and mood of the story as you decide whether to use rhyme and a regular rhythm.

3. Write a short **paragraph,** including at least two allusions, about a time when you felt like an outcast. You may wish to review the Literary Concepts for this selection before you start.

📁 **PORTFOLIO** *Save your writing. You may want to use it later as a springboard to a piece for your portfolio.*

From Personal Response to Critical Analysis

1. Responses will vary.
2. Possible response: After watching the jockey's behavior and the horse's extraordinary response, she realizes that the jockey needs and deserves Rigel more than she does.
3. Possible responses: I think that the narrator makes the right decision; the narrator acts from the heart, and in certain situations this is the best thing to do. I think the narrator makes the wrong decision: the narrator feels sympathy for the jockey, but it is the narrator's business to breed good horses.
4. Possible response: The behavior of all three shows their independence and their sensitivity to the world around them.
5. Possible response: The narrator repeatedly feels "twinges of conscience"—that is, sympathy for the jockey. The narrator initially suppresses these feelings, but after making a "critical adjustment," the narrator stops bidding.
6. Students might mention actions ranging from crimes to extreme social or political views. Encourage them to be specific about the reasons they consider certain outcasts valuable, such as people who follow their beliefs even if it makes them unpopular.

Another Pathway

Cooperative Learning Each group member might begin by instinctively describing what moment in the story holds the greatest drama and tension. Then students can make a more disciplined analysis by charting the plot's causes and effects, conflicts, and resolution.

Rubric
3 Full Accomplishment Students accurately identify and clearly illustrate the main events and climax of the plot.
2 Substantial Accomplishment Students identify and illustrate most of the events and the climax of the plot.
1 Little or Partial Accomplishment Students have difficulty identifying and charting the plot's main events and climax.

Literary Concepts

Help students appreciate allusions to the biblical story of David and Goliath (which emphasizes the discrepancy in size between the jockey and the horse and suggests the ultimate outcome) and to the star Rigel (which gives the horse an aura of excellence).

Concept Review Help students see the festive spirit of the people attending the auction, most of whom are well-off, well-dressed, and perhaps somewhat arrogant in their sense of privilege.

QuickWrites

1. Have students review the text for information about Rigel's history. Then have them transform these events into short, interesting headlines.
2. You might suggest that students make some notes of their impressions before beginning their poems.
3. Have students choose the event or experience they will use in their paragraph. Then have them think of two well-known allusions that would help their readers appreciate the experience.

The Writer's Craft

Paragraphs, pp. 244–254
Poetry, pp. 71–83

Words to Know

Accept all answers that in some way make a figurative comparison with the boldfaced word.

Literary Links

Ask students to compare how certain experiences have changed the characters' point of view in "The Treasure of Lemon Brown" and "The Splendid Outcast." *(Possible response: In "Lemon Brown," Greg learns to appreciate his father after speaking to Lemon Brown. In "The Splendid Outcast," the narrator learns about the bond between animals and humans once she has watched the jockey and Rigel.)*

Across the Curriculum

Social Studies *Going Once, Twice—Sold!* Have students find out about the history and traditions of auctions in America. Encourage them to investigate how auctions are conducted, as well as who attends them. Also, suggest to students that they check classified newspaper advertisements for current auctions in the area.

History *The Republic of Kenya* Have students research and report on highlights of the history of Kenya, the home of the narrator and the place where Markham raced her stallion. Students might wish to focus their report on the period since 1895 (when the British took control of the country), including information about Kenyan independence in 1963. See also the Study Skills application on atlases on page 163.

BERYL MARKHAM

After being out of print for many years, *West with the Night*—Beryl Markham's book about her famous 1936 solo flight across the Atlantic—was reissued in 1983 to huge critical and popular acclaim.

ART GALLERY

Horses in Art Students will better appreciate the excitement of horseracing and show jumping after seeing these paintings by Edgar Degas and Lance Richbourg.

Side A, Frame 52618

Multimodal Learning

ALTERNATIVE ACTIVITIES

1. Select a passage from this story and give a **dramatic reading** of it for the class. You may wish to include a brief introduction and conclusion to clarify the context of your passage in the story.
2. Create a **drawing, painting,** or **sculpture** of Rigel in his most defiant moment. Refer to the narrator's vivid descriptions of Rigel's size, appearance, and behavior before you begin.

WORDS TO KNOW

On your paper, complete each simile below. Use a word or phrase that helps illustrate the meaning of the word in bold. Be creative!

1. The **novice** breeder was as inexperienced as …
2. The frightened yearling acted as **cowed** as …
3. The official offered **homage** to the first cup winner like …
4. The jockey's **insolence** was as bold as …
5. The great white stallion's appearance was as **imposing** as …
6. The face of the **zealot** was as wild as …
7. The bidder approached his **adversary** like …
8. Once the mare was groomed, she looked as **impeccable** as …
9. When the horse thief was caught, the owner's **retribution** was as severe as …
10. The horse acted as **disdainfully** as …

BERYL MARKHAM

Markham's fictitious Rigel is similar to a real horse she owned and tamed. Messenger Boy, a stallion with an excellent pedigree, had killed a groom and attacked another man before Markham bought the horse and trained him to become one of the best racers in Kenya.

Born in England, Beryl Markham moved to East Africa with her father when she was three years old. There she learned African languages and customs as she watched her father turn wilderness into a working farm. As a girl, she suffered a leg injury from a lion attack, remembering "an immense roar that encompassed the world and dissolved me in it."

Before turning to the training and breeding of horses, which she learned from her father, Markham became the first woman to obtain a commercial pilot's license in East Africa. Flying a flimsy, fabric-covered plane with no radio, she spotted game for safari parties and carried passengers, mail, and supplies to remote areas. She spent most of her later life training racehorses. Eight of her horses were winners of the prestigious Kenya Derby.

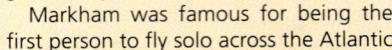

1902–1986

Markham was famous for being the first person to fly solo across the Atlantic Ocean from east to west. Her 1936 flight, which took 21 hours 25 minutes, ended in Canada, where she ran out of fuel and crash-landed. Although her plane was severely damaged, she walked away with only minor injuries.

OTHER WORKS *West with the Night,* "Something I Remember"

Extended Reading

174 UNIT TWO PART 1: TWINGES OF CONSCIENCE

• ART GALLERY

Alternative Activities

1. Encourage students to review the entire story before they choose particular scenes that appeal to them. After they decide on a passage, have them consider its qualities. Ask the students if it contains dialogue. If so, they might wish to change their voice slightly for these lines. Are there one or more specific moments that need to be stressed for special effect? Are there any vocabulary words whose meaning or pronunciation is not clear? After students have rehearsed, have them present their readings to the class.
2. Encourage students to focus on a single moment in the story that they believe reflects Rigel at his most defiant. As students think about ways of communicating the horse's defiance, you might remind them that they are not limited to a realistic portrayal of Rigel. Encourage students to use a variety of media: pencil, crayon, paint, marker, magazine cutouts, and so forth.

PREVIEWING

POETRY

We Alone
Alice Walker

Hard Questions
Margaret Tsuda

oil crisis
Naoshi Koriyama

Activating Prior Knowledge/Setting a Purpose
PERSONAL CONNECTION

Imagine that you and your family are moving to a remote cabin to live close to nature. You cannot take much with you, and you will not be able to use anything that runs on electricity. What do you think will be the advantages and the disadvantages of your new life? Jot down your ideas in a web like the one shown.

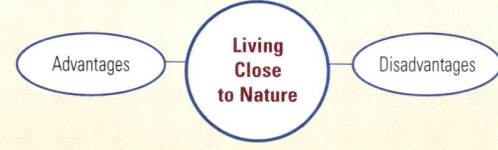

SCIENCE CONNECTION Building Background

You may find it difficult to imagine life without things like televisions, VCRs, and cars. However, there is a high price to pay for such luxuries. Increased industrialization is eliminating more and more of our natural environment, draining the earth's supply of mineral resources, and polluting our air and water.

The debate rages between those who want to use the earth's resources to provide jobs, thus improving or maintaining people's standard of living, and those who say we have to cut back our use of natural resources no matter what the effect on our lifestyles.

Settlers clearing rainforest in northern Guatemala. Copyright © David Hiser / Tony Stone Images.

Setting a Purpose
WRITING CONNECTION

The writers of the three poems you are about to read feel that we should value and take care of our natural environment. What do you think is the greatest environmental problem facing our world today? Write your thoughts in a few sentences. Then read to discover the environmental problems the poets point out.

LASERLINKS
• SCIENCE CONNECTION

OVERVIEW

Objectives
- To understand and appreciate three poems about humanity's relationship with the environment
- To identify and understand the concept of theme
- To express understanding of the poems through a choice of writing forms, including a poem and a description
- To extend understanding of the poems through a variety of multimodal and cross-disciplinary activities

Skills

LITERARY CONCEPTS
- Theme
- Imagery

SPEAKING, LISTENING, AND VIEWING
- Oral tradition
- Group discussion
- Oral presentation

Cross-Curricular Connections

SCIENCE
- Researching environments

HISTORY
- OPEC

ALTERNATIVE

Previewing
Instead of writing their opinions about the greatest environmental problem facing the world today, partners can discuss their opinions.

Writing Connection
Discussion Prompts What do you think is the greatest environmental problem facing our world today? State your opinion, in detail, to your partner. Then listen as your partner states his or her opinion. The following questions might help you get started:
- What are the environmental problems or controversies in your town or county?
- What are your views on issues such as the destruction of the ozone layer, air pollution, or acid rain? As you read "We Alone," "Hard Questions," and "oil crisis," notice the environmental problems the three poets point out.

SCIENCE CONNECTION
Nature and Technology The three poems in this lesson raise the question, Which is more important—conservation of nature or technological progress? These images of polluted and unpolluted environments can spark a discussion about conservation versus progress.

Side A, Frame 52625

PRINT AND MEDIA RESOURCES

UNIT TWO RESOURCE BOOK
Strategic Reading: Literature, p. 17

ACCESS FOR STUDENTS ACQUIRING ENGLISH
Reading and Writing Support

FORMAL ASSESSMENT
Selection Test, pp. 33–34
Test Generator

LASERLINKS
Science Connection

INTERNET RESOURCES
McDougal Littell Literature Center at http://www.hmco.com/mcdougal/lit

THE LANGUAGE OF LITERATURE TEACHER'S EDITION **175**

Thematic Link: *Twinges of Conscience*
All three poets feel a pang of conscience at the thought of humanity's treatment of our natural resources.

CUSTOMIZING FOR
Students Acquiring English

- Use **ACCESS FOR STUDENTS ACQUIRING ENGLISH**, Reading and Writing Support.
- The qualities of poetry vary from language to language. Traditional poetry in English depends on rhythm and rhyme, but this is not necessarily true of poetry in other languages. Help students appreciate the poems by listening as you read them aloud.

STRATEGIC READING FOR
Less-Proficient Readers

Set a Purpose Have students make a list of environmental issues that people are concerned about. Then have them read to find out what issues these three poems focus on.

Use **UNIT TWO RESOURCE BOOK**, p. 17, for guidance in reading the selections.

Critical Thinking: ANALYZING

 Invite students to share what they know about gold and the economy. Then ask them their interpretations of the poem's first four lines. *(When the price of gold goes up, it becomes more valuable to people. But the only reason gold has any value at all is that people want it. By ignoring its value and standing in the marketplace—and not buying it—people could conceivably turn gold into a valueless metal.)*

From Personal Response to Critical Analysis

1. Responses will vary.
2. Possible response: The speaker feels that gold imprisons people; also, the value of the substance is dictated by the very people whom it imprisons.
3. Possible response: convincing people to love plentiful natural resources as much as rare ones
4. Encourage students to supply detailed explanations.

We Alone

by Alice Walker

Copyright © Roxana Villa/SIS.

 We alone can devalue gold
by not caring
if it falls or rises
in the marketplace.
5 Wherever there is gold
there is a chain, you know,
and if your chain
is gold
so much the worse
10 for you.

Feathers, shells
and sea-shaped stones
are all as rare.

This could be our revolution:
15 To love what is plentiful
as much as
what is scarce.

FROM **PERSONAL RESPONSE** *TO* **CRITICAL ANALYSIS**

REFLECT 1. What were your thoughts as you read this poem? Record them in your notebook.

RETHINK 2. What problems does the speaker associate with gold?

Close Textual Reading

Consider
- how the price of gold is influenced by buyers and sellers
- the double meaning of *chain* in the poem
- why a gold chain might be a problem

3. What is the speaker's solution to the problems associated with the value of gold?
4. What is your opinion of the speaker's solution? Explain your answer.

176   UNIT TWO   PART 1: TWINGES OF CONSCIENCE

Mini-Lesson: Speaking, **Listening, and Viewing**

ORAL INTERPRETATION Explain to students that poets pay special attention to various sound devices because they intend poems to be spoken as well as read silently. Many poems convey an overall mood or attitude. In an oral interpretation, the reader can convey the mood that the poem creates.

Application Encourage students to analyze the sound devices of one poem: rhyme, notable rhythms, repetition, or particular consonant or vowel sounds. Have students practice conveying any of these devices with their voices. Then have them decide what mood the poem instills in them and deliver the poem accordingly.

Hard Questions
by Margaret Tsuda

Why not mark out the land
into neat rectangles
squares and clover leafs?

Put on them cubes of
5   varying sizes
according to use—
dwellings
      singles/multiples
complexes
10   commercial/industrial.

Bale them together with
bands of roads.

What if a child shall cry
"I have never known spring!
15 I have never seen autumn!"

What if a man shall say
"I have never heard
silence fraught with living as
in swamp or forest!"
20 What if the eye shall never see
marsh birds and muskrats?

Does not the heart need
wildness?
Does not the thought need
25 something
to rest upon
not self-made by man,
a bosom
not his own?

FROM PERSONAL RESPONSE TO CRITICAL ANALYSIS

REFLECT 1. What does this poem mean to you? Write your thoughts in your notebook.

RETHINK 2. Summarize the hard questions asked by the speaker in lines 13–21. Why does the speaker ask these questions?

3. How do the questions in lines 22–29 serve as the speaker's answer to the hard questions?

4. Do you agree or disagree with the speaker's answer? Why?

WE ALONE\HARD QUESTIONS   **177**

Mini-Lesson — Literary Concepts

REVIEWING IMAGERY Remind students that imagery refers to words and phrases that appeal to the reader's five senses. Writers use details to help the reader imagine how things look, feel, smell, sound, and taste.

Application Have students think about the images that these three poets use to convey positive images of the natural world. Then invite them to consider the negative side of nature. Encourage them to work in small groups to generate lists of images that convey the more destructive, violent side of nature and record them in a chart like the one shown. Have students include the sense or senses each image appeals to.

Force from Nature	Imagery
hurricane	howling winds (sound, touch)
	driving rains (sight, touch)
winter	freezing temperatures (touch)
	blinding blizzards (sight, sound, touch)

CUSTOMIZING FOR
Students Acquiring English

I Describe to students what a clover leaf looks like. You might also wish to point out, given the ecological focus of this poem, that "cloverleaf" is the term used for the curving ramps in the shape of a four-leaf clover at the crossing of two highways.

CUSTOMIZING FOR
Gifted and Talented Students

B Ask students to contrast the images in lines 1–10 with those in lines 14–21. (*Possible response: Images such as "rectangles," "squares," "cubes," "dwellings," "complexes," and even—in this context—"clover leafs" are cold and abstract; they suggest a spare world possibly without nature. In contrast, images such as "spring," "swamp," "forest," and "marsh birds and muskrats" are rich images of the natural world.*)

Literary Concept: THEME

Ask students to identify the theme of this poem, and then to explain how the theme is conveyed. (*Possible responses: by focusing on the importance of nature to humanity; contrasting soulless images of human society with vivid images of nature; by asking direct questions*)

From Personal Response to Critical Analysis

1. Responses will vary.
2. Possible response: The speaker asks what would happen if a child could not see changing seasons, if a man could not hear the "silence" in a natural environment, and if the human eye could not see wild animals. The questions stress the emptiness of a world without these sensations and experiences.
3. Possible response: The speaker's final questions are rhetorical and suggest that "wildness" and natural landscapes are essential for human existence.
4. Responses will vary.

oil crisis

by Naoshi Koriyama

when our last drop
of oil
has been used up
and all our cars
5   come to a stop
and all our planes
begin to rust
on the runway
in the rain
10 and the lights
go out

from the soaring sky-
    scrapers
we will walk
to the hill
15 to pick
raspberries wild
and steal
dappled eggs
from quails' nests
20 and then
we will walk

down to a stream
and catch eels
and by night
25 we will sit
by the river's bank
looking up
into the clear silent sky
reading poetry
30 in the stars

HISTORICAL INSIGHT

The Oil Crisis of the 1970s

The oil crisis Koriyama writes about struck the world in 1973. Arab countries of the Middle East, in protest against certain countries' support for Israel, reduced or stopped oil exports to Japan and some Western countries, including the United States. Heightening the crisis, the main association of oil-producing countries began to raise oil prices, which increased from less than $3 a barrel in 1973 to $30 a barrel in 1980. These events caused serious problems for the United States. Even though the United States was a major oil producer, in the early 1970s the cost of producing oil was greater than the cost of importing it. The United States was importing nearly half of the oil it needed and was therefore dependent on Middle Eastern oil.

The oil crisis led to fuel shortages and increases in fuel prices, which in turn caused some U.S. businesses and schools to close or lay off workers, to lower thermostats, and to dim lights. Drivers formed long lines to buy expensive gasoline, gas stations were closed on Sundays, and speed limits were lowered. Industrial production decreased, and the stock market fell.

In response to the crisis, Congress worked to boost domestic oil production, reduce the demand for imported oil, and control domestic oil prices, while oil companies searched for new sources of oil and cheaper and better ways to recover and refine it.

Today, because of the depletion of the earth's supply of fossil fuels and the air and water pollution caused by the production, transfer, and use of these fuels, many people have come to advocate the use of alternative sources of energy, such as synthetic fuels, solar energy, and nuclear power.

178   UNIT TWO   PART 1: TWINGES OF CONSCIENCE

RESPONDING OPTIONS

FROM PERSONAL RESPONSE TO CRITICAL ANALYSIS

REFLECT
1. What feeling were you left with at the end of "oil crisis"? What caused you to have that feeling? Jot down your thoughts in your notebook.

RETHINK
2. The speaker assumes that the world's oil will eventually be used up. Does the speaker see this outcome as a crisis? Use evidence from the poem to support your answer.
3. Do the activities the speaker describes in lines 13–30 appeal to you? Why or why not?
4. Do you think that most people would react to an oil crisis as the speaker does? Explain.

RELATE
5. Compare and contrast the speakers' attitudes toward our natural resources in the poems.
6. Which of the three poems do you think gives the strongest advice about humanity's relationship with the earth? Present your choice to a partner in the form of pantomime.

Multimodal Learning
ANOTHER PATHWAY

Note the contrast in each poem between human-made objects and natural objects or scenes. Choose one of the poems and illustrate the contrast by drawing or using magazine pictures.

QUICKWRITES

1. These poets have strong feelings about nature. Write a **poem** in which you give advice on the subject of using natural resources.
2. Imagine that there is a severe oil crisis. Write a **description** of a day in your life without oil or oil products. Before writing, brainstorm with a classmate or a parent to think of some of the many ways in which oil affects your daily life.

📁 **PORTFOLIO** Save your writing. You may want to use it later as a springboard to a piece for your portfolio.

LITERARY CONCEPTS

A poem's **theme** is a message about life that the poem conveys to a reader. For example, "Moco Limping" (page 125) might be said to have the theme "It's what's inside that counts." Since themes are not directly stated and must be inferred by readers, different readers may discover different themes in a poem. What do you think is the theme of each of these three poems? How does each theme relate to the unit theme, "Critical Adjustments"?

WE ALONE / HARD QUESTIONS / OIL CRISIS **179**

From Personal Response to Critical Analysis

1. Encourage students to use sensory details in their answers.
2. Possible response: The speaker does not see it as a crisis because one outcome envisioned by the speaker is a return to the pleasures of nature.
3. Responses will vary.
4. Possible responses: No, they would not, because most people don't see the positive aspects of a world without technology; yes, it is possible that the lack of oil would force people to appreciate the natural world more, as people did before the invention of automobiles and planes.
5. Possible response: In "We Alone," the speaker conveys that we should learn to value a wider range of our natural resources. The speakers of the other two poems are more direct in saying that natural resources deepen and enrich our lives.
6. Encourage students to look for specific descriptive details that would give definition to their performances.

Another Pathway

Cooperative Learning Have students work in groups of three. Each group can make a two-column list of the artificial and natural objects for each of the three poems. Then each student should choose one list and create an illustration of the contrasting imagery, like a rusty airplane contrasted with a quail's egg.

Rubric
3 Full Accomplishment Students accurately identify and effectively illustrate contrasting imagery.
2 Substantial Accomplishment Students identify and illustrate most images in the poems.
1 Little or Partial Accomplishment Students identify and illustrate only a few images from the poems.

Literary Concepts

Draw students' attention to the title in "We Alone" as well as the final four lines, so that they recognize the adjustment humanity must make to appreciate how precious earth's natural resources really are. Help them see that, in "Hard Questions," the last two rhetorical questions express the theme that human beings need nature in order to thrive. Urge students to find the theme of "oil crisis" in the juxtaposition of artificial and natural images. The critical adjustment needed in both "Hard Questions" and "oil crisis" serves to bring human beings into contact with nature again.

QuickWrites

1. Have students begin by brainstorming and jotting down thoughts and feelings about the earth's resources. After students have generated ideas, have them consider how to express them poetically with rhythm and/or rhyme.
2. Encourage students to use chronological order for their descriptions. Remind them that they do not have to account for every minute in the day.

The Writer's Craft
Field Notes, pp. 64–65
Poetry, pp. 76–80

Across the Curriculum

Science *Researching Environments* Have students research either of the two environments in "Hard Questions" mentioned in the lines "silence fraught with living as in swamp or forest!" Ask students what kinds of sounds a listener would be likely to hear in this environment. Invite them to present their research to the class in the form of an oral report.

History *OPEC* Have students research and report on the Organization of Petroleum Exporting Countries (OPEC), the group formed in 1960 to protect and further the interests of oil-producing nations. Have students focus special attention on events during the 1970s (when OPEC dramatically raised the price of oil) and the early 1980s (when an oversupply of oil caused a large drop in the price).

ALICE WALKER

In thinking about how the experience of writing poems has changed since her teenage years, Walker says, "My poems today are more about the world outside myself. It is more definitely a poetry of reclaiming ancient, global connections that I wasn't aware of when I was younger. I love writing beautifully—it must be the next best thing to singing beautifully." Walker's poem "We Alone" was inspired by her experiences witnessing the effects on blacks of gold mining in South Africa.

NAOSHI KORIYAMA

Koriyama was born in Kikai Island, Kagoshima Prefecture, in the southern part of Japan. Years ago he set for himself the professional challenge of writing poetry not in his native language, but in English. His *Selected Poems 1945–1985* was recently published.

SCIENCE CONNECTION
New Energy Sources A variety of alternative sources of energy are available today. These images show innovations like a solar powered car and windmills that can generate power from a breeze.

Side A, Frame 52632

ALICE WALKER

1944–

"To me, writing really is magic, and I want people to feel rather than just know," says Alice Walker—a novelist, short story writer, poet, and essayist. Her writings about family relationships, poverty, women's issues, and civil rights have touched the hearts and minds of her readers.

Walker was born in Eatonton, Georgia, to share-cropper parents who did not go to school beyond fifth grade. She has said, "Sometimes I thought I'd gotten into the family by mistake. I always seemed to need more peace and quiet than anybody else."

At the age of eight, Walker was blinded in her right eye after being shot accidentally with a BB gun. She began to express her thoughts and feelings in poetry that she recorded in a personal notebook. However, she says, "I think the poetry that I actually *call* poetry didn't start coming until I was a teenager."

One of Walker's best-known novels is *The Color Purple,* a story about growing up in the South. It won a Pulitzer Prize and an American Book Award and was made into a movie.

OTHER WORKS *Horses Make a Landscape Look More Beautiful; Langston Hughes, American Poet; Once: Poems; Five Poems; Revolutionary Petunias and Other Poems; Goodnight, Willie Lee, I'll See You in the Morning*

Extended Reading

MARGARET TSUDA

Margaret Tsuda (1921–) is a poet and artist whose poems have been translated into eight languages, including Hindi. She drew the illustrations for her books *Cry Love Aloud* and *Urban River,* using a bamboo pen. Her poems have been published in many anthologies and in the *Christian Science Monitor,* the *Sentinel,* and the magazines *Living Wilderness* and *Bodhi.* Tsuda graduated from Hunter College in New York City and lives in Newark, New Jersey.

NAOSHI KORIYAMA

1926–

Naoshi Koriyama studied English in Japan before coming to the United States to complete his college education. Since 1967 he has been a professor of English, teaching American poetry, at Toyo University in Tokyo.

Koriyama says that he writes about "any subject that may happen to interest me in the course of my daily life." He has published eight volumes of poetry in English, including his latest collection, *Eternal Grandeur and Other Poems.* His poems have appeared in high school textbooks in the United States, Canada, and Australia.

Koriyama also made translations into English of Japanese poetry and of folk songs from the Amami Islands in southern Japan, where he was born and raised.

OTHER WORKS *We Wrote These Poems* (trans.), *Coral Reefs, Songs from Sagamihara, Plum Tree in Japan and Other Poems, By the Lakeshore and Other Poems*

Extended Reading

• SCIENCE CONNECTION

WHAT DO YOU THINK?
Reflecting on Theme

Invite students to reconsider the save-the-environment booklet they made before reading the selections in Part 1. Ask them if they would make additions or changes to the booklet after reading these poems. If so, encourage them to make revisions.

FOCUS ON DRAMA

Have you watched any good movies lately? If you have, you are already familiar with drama. A **drama,** or **play,** is a work of literature that is performed for an audience, either on stage or before a camera. People see dramas on television, in movies, and on stage. Occasionally people listen to dramas in the form of radio plays, which were a very popular form of entertainment before the coming of television.

The elements of drama are similar to the elements of fiction. Like a work of fiction, a drama usually tells a story with characters, a plot, and a setting. Unlike fiction, drama is written to be performed for an audience. For this reason, drama is written in a special form called a **script,** in which lines are written out for the characters to speak. The various parts of a script are described below.

CAST OF CHARACTERS A script usually begins with a list of the characters in the play, presented in the order of their appearance. Often a short description appears next to each character's name.

DIALOGUE Most plays consist almost entirely of dialogue—conversation between the characters. Both the plot of the play and the characters' personalities are revealed through the dialogue. The words spoken by each character are preceded by the character's name, as in this example from *The Million-Pound Bank Note* (page 185):

Henry. I'd like to discuss the matter.

Gordon. There is nothing to discuss at the moment.

Henry. Is this a joke?

Abel. Not at all. And now good day.

Gordon. And good luck.

STAGE DIRECTIONS In addition to dialogue, a play almost always includes instructions for the director, the performers, and the stage crew. These are called stage directions and are printed in italics in this book; often they are also enclosed in parentheses. Many stage directions tell actors how to speak or move. Others describe **sound effects,** which are especially important in radio plays, since the success of such plays depends entirely on dialogue and sound. Notice how the stage directions in this excerpt from *The Hitchhiker* (page 337) describe sound effects and tell how the actors should speak:

FOCUS ON DRAMA **181**

Acts and Scenes Describe to the class how dramas are divided into scenes and acts just as novels often are divided into chapters. Then invite volunteers to explain how the end of an act is shown on the stage. *(The curtains are closed; the lights are dimmed; the setting or scenery changes.)*

Reading Strategies: MODELING
Invite volunteers to read aloud the Strategies for Reading Drama. Tell students they will be using these strategies as they read *The Million-Pound Bank Note* and other dramas throughout the book. Then model the strategies as students read *The Million-Pound Bank Note*. You may wish to use the models provided or create your own.

- **Read the play silently** Before they begin the play, students can set a purpose for reading, such as finding out the importance of the million-pound note.

- **Figure out what is happening** *"After reading the first few pages I realize that this drama is about an American who is given a million-pound note by two elderly brothers. He isn't yet sure why they have given it to him, but he knows it has something to do with a bet."*

- **Read the stage directions carefully** *"The stage directions indicate how characters should deliver their lines, how they should behave, and the sound effects the audience should hear."*

- **Get to know the characters** *"From his dialogue and behavior, Henry seems to be a well-mannered, confident young man. Although he seems to be taking advantage of some people who think he's a millionaire, I don't think he's a bad person."*

- **Keep track of the plot** *"Henry has received a million-pound note as a bet from two old men. If he returns all the money in 30 days, they will give him a job. Henry gets preferential treatment from people who think he's a millionaire, he helps his former employer, and falls in love."*

- **Read the play aloud with others** Arrange students in small groups to read portions of the play aloud to the class. Be sure everyone who wishes gets a chance to read.

Voice (*closer*). Going to California?
(*Sound: starter starting … gears jamming*)
Adams (*as though sweating blood*). No. Not today. The other way. Going to New York. Sorry … sorry …
(*Sound: Car starts with squeal of wheels on dirt … into auto hum.*)

Stage directions are also used to describe the **scenery**—stage decorations that represent the setting. Some stage directions describe **props**—the objects used by the actors.

ACTS AND SCENES The action of a play is sometimes divided into scenes. A new scene begins whenever the setting—time, place, or both time and place—changes. Sometimes scenes are grouped into acts, especially in long plays. *Survival*, on pages 459–479, is an example of a three-act play.

STRATEGIES FOR READING DRAMA

- **Read the play silently.** Before you try to read a play aloud, read it to yourself. You need to know the entire plot and understand the characters before you can perform a part in the play.

- **Figure out what is happening.** When you watch a movie, it usually takes you a while to understand exactly what the movie is about. The same is true when you read a play. Since the plot and the characters are revealed through dialogue, you will need to read several pages to understand what is happening.

- **Read the stage directions carefully.** If you were watching a drama on stage or on television, you would see the action and the scenery. When you read a drama, you have to imagine both. The stage directions tell where and when each scene is happening and help you visualize the action. If you skip the stage directions, you will miss important information.

- **Get to know the characters.** Drama does not usually contain descriptions of characters' personalities. You get to know the characters through their actions and through the dialogue—both what the characters say themselves and what others say to and about them. Analyze each character's words carefully and try to discover the feelings behind them, just as if you were reading fiction.

- **Keep track of the plot.** As in fiction, the plot of a drama usually centers on a main conflict. Look for the conflict and let yourself become involved in the story. Watch for the action to build to a climax, and evaluate the way in which the conflict is resolved.

- **Read the play aloud with others.** When drama is performed, it takes on a whole new aspect; it becomes almost like real life. When you read the part of a character, you become an actor. Your reading of the part will be different from anyone else's because you will bring your own interpretation to the role. Let yourself "get into" the part and become that character for a while. React to what other characters say and do. Be ready with your character's lines, and read only the words your character says; do not read the stage directions aloud. You may find that you really enjoy playing the part of someone different from yourself.

PREVIEWING

DRAMA

The Million-Pound Bank Note
Mark Twain
Dramatized by Walter Hackett

Activating Prior Knowledge
PERSONAL CONNECTION

Imagine a man dressed in a designer suit and driving a $50,000 sports car. Then picture a bag lady getting on a city bus. What different assumptions would you make about these people? In other words, how much does the appearance of wealth affect your judgment of people? Discuss your thoughts with your classmates.

Building Background
CULTURAL CONNECTION

Most of this play is set in England in the late 1800s. Then as now, the pound was the main British monetary unit, similar to our dollar. In 1893, when Mark Twain published the story on which this play is based, the million-pound bank note was worth 5 million U.S. dollars. Today, however, the British pound is worth less than two dollars in U.S. currency.

Respectability guided the lives of the British upper and middle classes; the keeping up of appearances was extremely important. Fine clothes, polished manners, an attractive home, financial success, and influential friends were common goals.

Active Reading/Setting a Purpose
READING CONNECTION

Setting Changes This selection is a rewriting of Mark Twain's original story as a radio play. The setting changes are described in very little detail, making them somewhat difficult to spot. The play opens in a restaurant in San Francisco and then moves to a London street. While you read about the changing fortunes of the American in London, note the changes of setting on a setting tracker like the one started here.

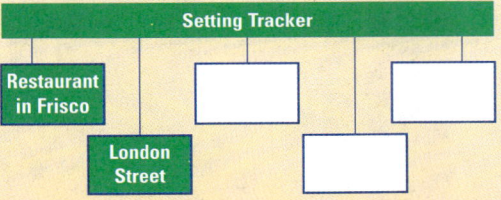

• CULTURAL CONNECTION   183

OVERVIEW
Objectives

- To understand and appreciate a drama about a man who must use his wits to keep up his end of a mysterious bargain
- To recognize and understand setting changes
- To identify and understand the use of a plot resolution
- To express understanding of the drama through a choice of writing forms, including a script, a society-page report, and a character sketch
- To extend understanding of the story through a variety of multimodal and cross-disciplinary activities

Skills

READING SKILLS/STRATEGIES
- Setting changes
- Noting relevant details

THE WRITER'S STYLE
- Dialogue in plays

GRAMMAR
- Sentence fragments

LITERARY CONCEPTS
- Resolution
- Characterization

GENRE STUDY
- Dramatization of a story

SPELLING
- Spelling with suffixes

SPEAKING, LISTENING, AND VIEWING
- Drama
- Art
- Group discussion
- Oral presentation

Cross-Curricular Connections

SOCIAL STUDIES
- "Taking an Option"
- *The Arabian Nights*

HISTORY
- Prospecting for gold

GEOGRAPHY
- Mapping the gold rush

MATHEMATICS
- Exchange rates

CULTURAL CONNECTION
London, Late 1800s These photographs will help students understand the tremendous differences between upper-class and working class life in the London of the late 1800s.

Side A, Frame 52637

PRINT AND MEDIA RESOURCES

UNIT RESOURCE BOOK
Strategic Reading: Literature, p. 21
Vocabulary SkillBuilder, p. 24
Reading SkillBuilder, p. 22
Spelling SkillBuilder, p. 23

GRAMMAR MINI–LESSONS
Transparencies, p. 1
Copymasters, p. 1

WRITING MINI–LESSONS
Transparencies, p. 48

ACCESS FOR STUDENTS ACQUIRING ENGLISH
Selection Summaries
Reading and Writing Support

FORMAL ASSESSMENT
Selection Test, pp. 35–36
 Test Generator

 AUDIO LIBRARY
See Reference Card

LASERLINKS
Cultural Background
Author Background

 INTERNET RESOURCES
McDougal Littell Literature Center at http://www.hmco.com/mcdougal/lit

SUMMARY

Henry Adams, a young clerk working for a San Francisco mine broker, is stranded penniless in London. On a bet, two wealthy brothers give him a bank note worth 1 million pounds; if he returns all the money in 30 days, the pair will give him any job he likes. Thenceforth, Henry is treated preferentially. He fulfills the terms of the bet, helps his American employer out of a financial crisis, earns £200,000 of his own, and wins the hand of a woman with whom he has fallen in love.

Thematic Link: *Twinges of Conscience*
Thrust unexpectedly into the role of a millionaire, a man battles to maintain his sense of truth and identity as people lavish him with special treatment.

Art Note

Going to the City, Hansom Cab by James J. Tissot   The painting by Tissot (1836–1902) is oddly shaped (17 inches tall by 10 inches wide), and this shape is echoed by the image's dominant vertical lines, which draw the viewer's eye to the cab driver, the cathedral, and the sky.

Reading the Art   *What do the details in the picture tell you about the person being transported "to business"?*

CUSTOMIZING FOR
Students Acquiring English

- Use **ACCESS FOR STUDENTS ACQUIRING ENGLISH**, *Reading and Writing Support*.
- Point out that sometimes Henry Adams is in conversation with people, while at other times he is simply acting as the narrator.

STRATEGIC READING FOR
Less-Proficient Readers

Set a Purpose   Have students read to find out why the narrator finds himself in London.

Use **UNIT TWO RESOURCE BOOK**, pp. 21–22, for guidance in reading the selection.

The Million-Pound Bank Note

by Mark Twain

Dramatized by Walter Hackett

Going to the City, Hansom Cab (1879), James J. Tissot. Private collection, Bridgeman Art Library, London/Superstock.

184   UNIT TWO   PART 1: TWINGES OF CONSCIENCE

WORDS TO KNOW

accommodation (ə-kŏm′ə-dā′shən) *n.* a favor or convenience (p. 189)

ad-libbing (ăd-lĭb′ĭng) *v.* speaking spontaneously, without preparation (p. 191)

competent (kŏm′pĭ-tənt) *adj.* qualified; capable (p. 188)

consequence (kŏn′sĭ-kwĕns′) *n.* importance (p. 187)

discreet (dĭ-skrēt′) *adj.* showing caution in speech and behavior (p. 196)

diversion (dĭ-vûr′zhən) *n.* a distraction, entertainment, or relaxation (p. 186)

eccentric (ĭk-sĕn′trĭk) *adj.* very unusual in behavior; odd (p. 190)

judicious (jōō-dĭsh′əs) *adj.* careful; showing sound judgment (p. 198)

precarious (prĭ-kâr′ē-əs) *adj.* not secure; risky (p. 194)

rebuke (rĭ-byōōk′) *n.* a sharp scolding or criticism (p. 190)

CAST OF CHARACTERS

Henry Adams	Servant	Second Man
Lloyd Hastings	Tod	Woman
First Cockney	Mr. Smedley	Third Man
Gordon Featherstone	Hotel Manager	Butler
Abel Featherstone	Second Cockney	Portia Langham
Albert Hawkins	First Man	Sir Alfred

Henry. When I was twenty-seven years old, I was a mining broker's[1] clerk in San Francisco. I was alone in the world and had nothing to depend upon but my wits and a clean reputation. These were setting my feet in the road to eventual fortune, and I was content with the prospect. During my spare time, I did outside work. One of my part-time employers was Lloyd Hastings, a mining broker. During this period I was helping Hastings to verify the Gould and Curry Extension papers, covering what seemed to be a highly valuable gold mine. One morning at two, after six hard hours of work on these papers, Lloyd Hastings and I went to the What Cheer restaurant in Frisco.[2] As we lingered over our coffee, he offered me a proposition.

Hastings. Henry, how would you like to go to London?

Henry. Thank you, no.

Hastings. Listen to me. I'm thinking of taking a month's option on the Gould and Curry Extension for the locators.

Henry. And—?

Hastings. They want one million dollars for it.

Henry. Not too much—if the claim works out the way it appears it may.

Hastings. I'm going to try to sell it to London interests, which means a trip there, and I want you to go with me, because you know more about these papers than I.

Henry. No, thanks.

Hastings. I'll make it well worth your while. I'll

---

1. **mining broker's:** relating to a person who acts as an agent in the buying or selling of mineral rights.
2. **Frisco:** short for "San Francisco."

THE MILLION-POUND BANK NOTE 185

Linking To Social Studies

C When Hastings says he is willing to gamble, he implies that he is thinking of "taking an option." An option gives its owner the right to buy a property or stock at a certain price on a certain date. If that price is less than what the property or stock is worth at the later date, the owner of the option makes a profit. Hastings's option would entitle him to buy the Gould and Curry claim for $1 million within one month. If he could presell the mine for more than that sum, the difference would be his profit.

STRATEGIC READING FOR
Less-Proficient Readers

D Check that students understand the series of events that lead Henry to London.

- Why does Henry refuse Hastings's offer to go to London? *(Henry doesn't want to disrupt his present job. Also, he doubts that Hastings will be able to sell the claim.)* **Noting Relevant Details**
- What happens when Henry is carried out to sea? *(He is picked up by a London-bound freighter and arrives in London penniless.)* **Noting Sequence of Events**

Set a Purpose Have students read to find out who Gordon and Abel are and what they give Henry.

Literary Concept: DRAMA

E Remind students that this dramatization was created for radio. Encourage them to think about what the particular benefits and limitations of radio might be. Also have them discuss what the stage directions *fading* and *away* might mean. ("Fading" indicates that the actor's voice should grow softer until it is no longer heard. "Away" indicates that the actor's voice is faint, as if it is coming from a distance.)

Critical Thinking: SPECULATING

F Invite students to speculate on why Gordon and Abel are behaving in this peculiar way.

---

pay all your expenses and give you something over if I make the sale.

Henry. I have a job.

Hastings. I'll arrange for you to get a leave of absence. What do you say?

Henry. No.

Hastings. Why?

Henry. If I go to London, I'll get out of touch with my work and with mining conditions here, and that means months getting the hang of things again.

Hastings. That's a pretty slim excuse, Henry.

Henry. More important, perhaps, I think you're doomed to failure.

Hastings. But you just said the claim is valuable.

Henry. It may well turn out that way, but right now its real value can't be proved. And even so, a month's option may leave you too little time to sell it; unless you sell it within the option time, you'll go stone broke.

C **Hastings.** I'm willing to gamble.

Henry. Well, I'm not.

Hastings. Think—a free trip to London.

Henry. I've no desire to go to London. I'll remain right here in Frisco.

Hastings (*fading*). Very well, but I know you're making a mistake, Henry.

Henry. One of my few <u>diversions</u> was sailing in the bay. One day I ventured too far and was carried out to sea. Late that night, I was picked up by a freighter which was bound for London. It was a long voyage, and the captain made me work my passage without pay, as a common sailor. When I stepped ashore at London, my clothes were ragged and shabby, and I had only a dollar in my pocket. This money fed and sheltered me for twenty-four hours. During the next twenty-four I went without food and shelter. I tried to get a job, doing manual labor. But the reply was always the same.

First Cockney. I'm not sure you'd do. You ain't the sort. (*suspiciously*) Look, 'ere, you're a Yank, ain't you?

Henry. The next morning, seedy and hungry, I was dragging myself along Portland Place when my desiring eye fell on a tempting treasure lying in the gutter. It was a luscious big pear—minus one bite. My mouth watered for it. But every time I made a move to get it, some passing eye detected my purpose. I was just getting desperate enough to brave all the shame when a window behind me was raised.

Gordon (*away*). I say, you there, will you step in here, please?

Henry. It was a very sumptuous house and an equally sumptuous room into which I was ushered by a servant. A couple of elderly gentlemen were sitting by the window. At that moment if I had known what they had in mind, undoubtedly I would have bolted for the door. They looked me over very thoroughly.

Gordon. He looks poor enough, don't you think, Brother?

Abel. Very. Er, young man, you are poor?

Henry. Extremely!

Abel. Good! And honest, too?

Henry. Honesty is about all I have left; that and character.

WORDS TO KNOW
diversion (dĭ-vûr′zhən) *n.* a distraction, entertainment, or relaxation

---

Mini-Lesson — Reading Skills/Strategies

NOTING RELEVANT DETAILS Remind students that good readers notice details that provide important information about a story when they read. By noting these details, readers can learn more information about a story's plot, its setting, and the characters.

Application Have students refer to the setting trackers they made while reading the story (see page 183). Ask them to identify the relevant details they used to locate the various changes in setting. You may wish to have the class discuss the changes in settings, how easy or difficult it was to locate these changes, and what they used to detect them.

Reteaching/Reinforcement
- *Unit Two Resource Book*, p. 22

---

186 THE LANGUAGE OF LITERATURE TEACHER'S EDITION

Abel. Splendid!

Gordon. If my brother and I are judges of people, we'd say you are just the man for whom we have been searching. By the way, you are also intelligent, I would say.

Henry. Yes, sir, I am. But what do you mean by saying that I appear to be just the man for whom you have been searching?

Gordon. And we don't know you. You're a perfect stranger. And better still, an American.

Henry. It's very kind of you gentlemen to call me into your home, but I'm a bit puzzled. Could you tell me what you have in mind?

Abel. Might we inquire into your background?

Henry. Pretty soon they had my full story. Their questions were complete and searching, and I gave them straightforward answers. Finally one said:

Gordon. Oh, yes, we're certain you will do, eh, Brother?

Abel. Definitely! He is elected.

Henry. To what am I elected, please?

Gordon. This envelope will explain everything. Here, take it. (*hastily*) No, don't open it now. Take it to your lodgings and look it over carefully.

Abel. Being sure not to be rash or hasty.

Henry. I'd like to discuss the matter.

Gordon. There is nothing to discuss at the moment.

Henry. Is this a joke?

Abel. Not at all. And now good day.

Gordon. And good luck.

Abel. Cheerio!

Henry. As soon as I was out of sight of the house, I opened my envelope and saw it contained money. I lost not a moment but shoved note and money into my pocket and broke for the nearest cheap eating house. How I did eat! Finished, I took out my money and unfolded it. I took one glimpse and nearly fainted. It was a single million-pound bank note. Five millions of dollars! It made my head swim. The next thing I noticed was the owner of the eating house. His eyes were on the note, and he was petrified. He couldn't stir hand or foot. I tossed the note toward him in careless fashion.

Hawkins. I-is it real, sir? A million-pound note?

Henry (*casually*). Certainly. Let me have my change, please.

Hawkins. Oh, I'm very sorry, sir, but I can't break the bill.

Henry. Look here—

Hawkins. Hawkins is the name, Albert Hawkins, proprietor. It's only a matter of two shillings[3] you owe, a trifling sum. Please owe it to me.

Henry. I may not be in this neighborhood again for a good time.

Hawkins. It's of no consequence, sir. And you can have anything you want, any time you choose, and let the account run as long as you please. I'm not afraid to trust as rich a gentleman as you just because you choose to play larks[4] by dressing as a tramp.

---

3. **shillings:** former British coins; a shilling was equal to a twentieth of a pound.
4. **play larks:** joke around; engage in harmless pranks.

WORDS TO KNOW
consequence (kŏn'sĭ-kwĕns') *n.* importance

187

Literary Concept: PLOT

Ask students what Henry's conflict is. (*He is penniless and away from home.*) Then have them comment on whether Gordon and Abel offer a solution to Henry's conflict or whether they complicate it. (*Possible response: Inviting Henry in and giving him the envelope indicates that they may somehow help him. But their refusal to answer his questions causes him anxiety and suggests there may be complication ahead.*)

Active Reading: PREDICT

Ask students to make predictions about what problems Henry might encounter in the near future. You may wish to use the following model to give them ideas.

Think-Aloud Model *I really don't think that Henry should be waving the note around the way he does. Advertising the fact that he has so much money can only cause him to come to a bad end.*

Active Reading: CONNECT

Ask students to comment on the restaurant owner's reaction to the bank note. If they were presented with a million-dollar bank note, how would they respond? (*Possible responses: I think his response is natural, because it's an enormous sum of money, and it seems safe to assume that a wealthy person will be able to pay his bill. I think his response is embarrassing and phony, because it is so obvious that he is trying to win favor with a rich person.*)

Mini-Lesson Grammar

SENTENCE FRAGMENTS Point out to students that a sentence fragment does not express a complete thought. The subject or the verb—or sometimes both—are missing.

Help students appreciate that playwrights (and other writers of dialogue) are keenly interested in capturing the way people really speak. Thus plays are often filled with grammatical fragments. For instance, the highlighted passage above contains a fragment, "And better still, an American." There is no subject or verb in this sentence fragment.

Application Have students identify other examples of sentence fragments in the dialogue between Henry, Abel, and Gordon and rewrite one or two of them as complete sentences.

Reteaching/Reinforcement
- *Grammar Handbook*, anthology p. 860
- *Grammar Mini-Lessons* copymasters p. 1, transparencies p. 1

The Writer's Craft
Sentence Fragments, p. 382

Active Reading: EVALUATE

J Ask students to explain their opinions about Gordon and Abel's absence. Should Henry worry? *(Possible response: The fact that they seem to have left intentionally—since they anticipated that Henry would come to the house—is in keeping with their earlier playful and mysterious behavior. Their departure seems designed to make Henry uncomfortable and uncertain, so it might be natural for him to worry.)*

STRATEGIC READING FOR
Less-Proficient Readers

K Check that students understand what leads Henry to return to the old men's house and what he learns there.

- Who are Gordon and Abel? *(They are elderly gentlemen who invite Henry into their home and involve him in a bet.)* **Noting Relevant Details**
- What is inside the envelope they give Henry? *(a million-pound note and a letter)* **Noting Relevant Details**

Set a Purpose Have students read to find out what happens to Henry after he receives the million-pound note.

Active Reading: CONNECT

L Ask students to consider how they would feel if they were in Henry's position at this point. Would they feel excited, nervous, or trapped?

Henry. Well, thank you. I shall take advantage of your kindness.

Hawkins. Not at all, sir, *(fading)* and please, sir, enter my humble restaurant place any time you wish. I shall be honored to receive you.

Henry. I was frightened, afraid that the police might pick me up. I was afraid of the two brothers' reaction when they discovered they had given me a million-pound note instead of what they must have intended giving—a one-pound note. I hurried to their house and rang the bell. The same servant appeared. I asked for the brothers.

Servant. They are gone.

Henry. Gone! Where?

Servant. On a journey.

Henry. But whereabouts?

Servant. To the Continent,⁵ I think.

Henry. The Continent?

Servant. Yes, sir.

Henry. Which way—by what route?

Servant. I can't say, sir.

Henry. When will they be back?

Servant. In a month, they said.

Henry. A month! This is awful! Tell me how to get word to them. It's of great importance.

Servant. I can't, indeed. I've no idea where they've gone, sir.

Henry. Then I must see some member of the family.

Servant. Family's been away too; been abroad months—in Egypt and India, I think.

Henry. There's been an immense mistake made. They'll be back before night. Tell them I've been here, and that I'll keep coming till it's all made right, and they needn't worry.

Servant. I'll tell them, if they come back, but I'm not expecting them. They said you'd be here in an hour to make inquiries, but I must tell you it's all right, they'll be here on time to meet you. *(fading)* And that's all they said.

Henry *(slowly).* I had to give it up and go away. What a riddle it all was! They would be here "on time." What could that mean? Then I thought of the letter. I got it out and read it. It said: "You are an intelligent and honest man, as one can see by your face. We conceive you to be poor and a stranger. Enclosed you will find a sum of money. It is lent to you for thirty days, without interest. Report to this house at the end of that time. I have a bet on you. If I win it, you shall have any situation that is in my gift, any, that is, that you shall be able to prove yourself familiar with and <u>competent</u> to fill." That was all. No signature, no address, no date. I hadn't the least idea what the game was, nor whether harm was meant me or kindness. The letter said there was a bet on me. What kind of a bet? Was the bet that I would abscond with the million-pound bank note? Which brother was betting on my honesty? I reasoned this way: if I ask the Bank of England to deposit it to the credit of the man it belongs to, they'll ask me how I came by it, and if I tell the truth, they'll put me in the asylum; on the other hand, if I lie, they'll put me in jail. The same result would follow if I try to bank it anywhere or borrow money on it. Therefore, I have to carry this burden around until those

---

5. **the Continent:** mainland Europe.

WORDS TO KNOW
competent (kŏm′pĭ-tənt) *adj.* qualified; capable

Mini-Lesson: Speaking, Listening, and Viewing

DRAMA Have you ever been listening to the radio when suddenly there was an unnatural silence? Radio broadcasters dread this phenomenon, which they call "dead air." During these unintentional moments of silence, listeners realize that the pause is a mistake. However, radio dramas such as "The Million-Pound Bank Note" contain intentional short pauses that serve a purpose—for example, conveying a character's thoughtfulness or a mood of suspense.

Application Challenge pairs or small groups of students to perform a passage of dialogue, including significant pauses, from this radio play. (The conversation between Henry and the servant on this page is a good example.) Begin by discussing the importance of really listening and responding to one another. Students must come in right on cue but without cutting one another off. Invite students to present their passages to the class.

Liverpool Quay by Moonlight (1887), John Atkinson Grimshaw. Tate Gallery, London/Art Resource, New York.

men come back. A month's suffering without wages or profit—unless I help win that bet, whatever it may be. If I do, I will get the situation I am promised. My hopes began to rise high. Then I looked at my rags. Could I afford a new suit? No, for I had nothing in the world but a million pounds. Finally I gave in and entered a fashionable tailor shop. The clerk looked at me very arrogantly.

Tod (*icily*). No chores to be done here. Get out!

Henry. Perhaps you have a misfit suit.

Tod. We don't give away suits, even misfits.

Henry. I can pay for it.

Tod. Follow me.

Henry. He took me into a back room and overhauled a pile of rejected suits. He tossed the rattiest-looking one at me. I put it on. It didn't fit. It wasn't in any way attractive.

Tod. You may have that for four pounds, cash.

Henry. It would be an <u>accommodation</u> to me if you could wait some days for the money. I haven't any small change about me.

Tod (*sarcastically*). Oh, you haven't? Well, of course, I didn't expect it. I'd only expect gentlemen like you to carry large change.

Henry (*nettled*[6]). My friend, you shouldn't judge

---

6. **nettled:** irritated; annoyed.

WORDS TO KNOW
accommodation (ə-kŏm′ə-dā′shən) *n.* a favor or convenience

189

Literary Concept:
CHARACTERIZATION

O What does Henry's behavior with Tod and with Smedley tell you about his character? *(Possible response: Henry is not only smart but also sly; he has a good poker face and a good sense of humor. By remaining calm, proper, and understated as Tod insults him, Henry shows a sporting side to his nature.)*

Literary Concept:
EXAGGERATION

P Ask students to comment on how Twain uses exaggeration for comedic effect in the scene with Smedley, Tod, and Henry. *(Possible response: In his efforts to impress Henry and apologize for Tod by putting him in his place, Smedley implies that millionaires often shop at his store and instructs Tod to burn an inelegant suit.)*

Critical Thinking:
MAKING JUDGMENTS

Q Ask students for their opinions of Henry's behavior as people spin out of control around him. Is he taking advantage of the innocence of these people? *(Possible responses: Henry's behavior is perfectly acceptable, because it is the people around him who are acting stupidly and falsely. Henry should explain the situation to these people rather than take advantage of them.)*

---

a stranger always by the clothes he wears. I am quite able to pay for this suit.

Tod. Hah!

Henry. I simply don't wish to put you to the trouble of changing a large note.

Tod. As long as <u>rebukes</u> are going around, I might say that it wasn't quite your affair to infer that we couldn't change any note that you might happen to be carrying around. On the contrary, we can.

Henry. Oh, very well. I apologize. Here you are.

Tod. Thank you. (*A complete change. He stutters and fumbles.*) Ah—it's—ah—that is—we—ah—you see— It's— (*quickly*) Take it back, please. (*raising voice*) Mr. Smedley! Mr. Smedley! Help! Oh, Mr. Smedley.

Smedley (*coming in; a fussy man*). What is it, Tod, what is it? Stop shouting!

Tod. Oh, but Mr. Smedley, I can't control myself.

Smedley. What's up? What's the trouble? What's wanting? Who's this?

Henry. I am a customer, and I am waiting for my change.

Smedley. Change, change! Tod, give him his change. Get it for him.

Tod. Get him his change! It's easy for you to say that, Mr. Smedley, but look at the bill yourself.

Smedley. Bill, bill! Let me see it! (*pause*) Tod, you ass, selling an <u>eccentric</u> millionaire such an unspeakable suit as that. Tod, you're a fool—a born fool! Drives every millionaire away from this place, because he can't tell a millionaire from a tramp. Here, sir, are some suits more in keeping with your position.

Henry. Thank you, but this one will do.

Smedley. Of course it won't do! I shall burn it. Tod, burn this suit at once.

Tod. Yes, Mr. Smedley.

Smedley. We shall be honored to outfit you completely, sir . . . morning clothes, evening dress, sack suits, tweeds, shetlands[7]—everything you need. Come, Tod, book and pen. Now—length of leg, 32 inches; sleeve—

Henry. But look here. I can't give you an order for suits unless you can wait indefinitely or change this bill.

Smedley. Indefinitely, sir. It's a weak word, a weak word. *Eternally, that's* the word, sir. Tod, rush these things through. Let the minor customers wait. Set down the gentleman's address and—

Henry. I'm changing my quarters. I'll drop in and leave the new address.

Smedley. Quite right, sir, quite right. One moment—allow me to show you out, sir. And don't worry about paying us. (*fading*) Your credit is the highest. Good day, sir, good day. You honor us greatly, sir.

Henry (*as though sighing*). Well, don't you see what was bound to happen? I drifted naturally into whatever I wanted. Take my hotel, for example. I merely showed the resident manager my million-pound note, and he said:

Manager. We are honored to have you as a guest, sir. Now, I have just the suite for you. It con-

---

7. **morning clothes … sack suits … shetlands:** men's garments—formal daytime dress, business suits with loose-fitting jackets, and suits made of wool from the Shetland Islands.

WORDS TO KNOW
rebuke (rĭ-byōōk′) *n.* a sharp scolding or criticism
eccentric (ĭk-sĕn′trĭk) *adj.* very unusual in behavior; odd

190

 Mini-Lesson Literary Concepts

REVIEWING CHARACTERIZATION
Remind students that the techniques a writer uses to create and develop a character are called characterization. Point out that a playwright is usually restricted to three methods of developing a character. A playwright can develop a character through:
• the character's speech, thoughts, or actions
• the speech and actions of other characters
• a physical description in the stage directions

Application Have students copy the web shown and use it to think about the ways Walter Hackett develops Mark Twain's characters. For example, discuss with them how Tod's character is developed in his dialogue and actions (fumbling and stuttering) on page 190.

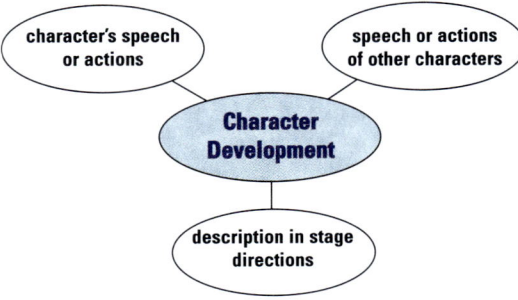

sists of a bedroom, a sitting room, a dressing room, a dining room, two baths, and—

Henry. I'll pay you a month in advance with this.

Manager (*laughing*). You honor our simple hotel, sir. Pray, don't worry about the bill.

Henry. But it may be several months before I can pay you.

Manager. We're not worried, Mr.—er—

Henry. Henry Adams.

Manager. Mr. Adams, you are a most distinguished guest. (*fading*) Anything you desire, please name it, and we shall procure it for you immediately. Thank you, sir.

Henry. And there I was, sumptuously housed in an expensive hotel in Hanover Square. I took my dinners there, but for breakfast I stuck by Hawkins's humble feeding-house, where I had got my first meal on my million-pound bank note. I was the making of Hawkins.

(*Rattle of dishes and silver. Customers' voices ad-libbing in background.*)

Hawkins. Business is brisk, sir, very brisk, indeed, and has been ever since you and your million-pound bank note became patrons of my humble establishment. I've had to hire extra help, put in additional tables. Look for yourself, sir. There's a long queue[8] waiting to get in. Why, I'm famous and fair on my way to becoming wealthy.

Second Cockney. Pardon me, Guv'ner, but aren't you the gentleman what owns the million-pound bank note?

Hawkins. Look here, you, go away and stop bothering Mr.—Mr.—

Henry. Adams.

Hawkins. Mr. Adams.

Second Cockney. I was just anxious to get a look at him.

Hawkins. Who? Mr. Adams?

Second Cockney. No. The bank note.

Henry. Glad to oblige. There you are.

Second Cockney. By george, it *is* real. (*fading*) Now I can go home and tell me old lady I've seen it with me own eyes. I hopes she believes me, but she won't.

Hawkins. Mr. Adams, I wonder if I couldn't force upon you a small loan—even a large one.

Henry. Oh, no.

Hawkins. Please allow me, sir.

Henry (*relenting*). Well, as a matter of fact, I haven't gotten around to changing this note.

Hawkins. Fifty pounds might help tide you over. You know, a little spending money?

Henry. It would help, a bit.

Hawkins. I consider it a great honor. (*fading*) Indeed, a very great honor. Here you are, Mr. Adams, fifty pounds it is. (*fading*) And don't worry about repaying me.

Henry. I was in, now, and must sink or swim. I walked on air. And it was natural, for I had become one of the notorieties[9] of London. It turned my head, not just a little, but a great deal. The newspapers referred to me as the Vest-Pocket Millionaire. Then came the climaxing stroke: *Punch*[10] caricatured me!

---

8. **queue** (kyōō): a line of people.
9. **notorieties** (nō′tə-rī′ĭ-tēz): famous people; celebrities.
10. ***Punch***: An English humor magazine, known for its cartoons poking fun at famous people.

WORDS TO KNOW
ad-libbing (ăd-lĭb′ĭng) *adj.* speaking spontaneously, without preparation **ad-lib** *v.*

Art Note

Lord Ribblesdale by John Singer Sargent
John Singer Sargent (1856–1925) is best known for his elegant portraits of internationally prominent and wealthy people. This portrait shows a well-to-do gentleman whose stern gaze and self-assured posture give him an imposing presence.

Reading the Art *Which character in the play might this painting represent? How would you use words or phrases to describe this man's appearance or attitude?*

Critical Thinking: MAKING JUDGMENTS

V Ask students to comment on Henry's assertion that he fell in love with Portia "in two minutes, and she with me." Do you believe him? Why or why not? *(Possible responses: I think Henry can be trusted here, because it can be really obvious when people fall in love with each other. In my opinion, this seems hasty of Henry, especially his presuming that Portia immediately loves him.)*

Active Reading: CLARIFY

W Ask students to clarify the details of Hastings and Henry's relationship. *(Possible response: Hastings is a mining broker who was one of Henry's part-time employers. He offered to take Henry to London on business, but Henry refused.)*

Lord Ribblesdale (1902), John Singer Sargent. Tate Gallery, London/A.K.G., Berlin/Superstock.

Wherever I went, people cried:

First Man. There he goes!

Second Man. That's him!

Woman. Morning, Guv'ner.

Third Man. He's a bit of all right, he is.

Henry. Why, I just swam in glory all day long. About the tenth day of my fame I fulfilled my duty to my country by calling upon the American ambassador. He received me with enthusiasm and insisted that I attend a dinner party he was giving the following night. Two important things happened at that dinner. I met two people who were to play important roles in the little drama I was living. Among the guests was a lovely English girl, named Portia Langham, whom I fell in love with in two minutes, and she with me; I could see it without glasses. And just before dinner, the butler announced:

(*Guests ad-libbing in background, very politely.*)

Butler (*calling out*). Mr. Lloyd Hastings.

Henry. I stared at Hastings, and he at me, his mouth open in surprise.

Hastings. I, er—pardon me, but are you?—no, of course you can't be.

Henry (*chuckling*). But I am, Lloyd.

Hastings. Henry, I'm speechless. (*suddenly*) Don't tell me that you're also the Vest-Pocket Millionaire?

Henry. Correct!

Hastings. I've seen your own name coupled with the nickname, but it never occurred to me you were *the* Henry Adams. Why, it isn't six months since you were clerking in Frisco and sitting up nights helping me verify the Gould and Curry Extension papers. The

192 UNIT TWO PART 1: TWINGES OF CONSCIENCE

Mini-Lesson: Speaking, Listening, and Viewing

ART Explain to students that asking certain questions about technical details in a painting can offer clues to understanding and appreciating those works. Two questions are: "Where is the highest concentration of light in the image?" and "What are the dominant lines in the image?" Using light and line, painters draw the viewer's eye to certain (often surprising) areas of the canvas. For instance, in *Lord Ribblesdale,* John Singer Sargent uses light to guide the viewer to the subject's face and to the area of his trousers just above the knee, where he holds a riding whip. With one exception, the dominant lines in the painting are vertical and accentuate the subject's literal height and figurative stature. There is one strong diagonal line, which draws attention once again to the riding whip, a class symbol that does much to characterize Ribblesdale.

Application Invite students to choose another painting from this selection and apply these two questions to those images.

idea of your being in London, and a vast millionaire, and a colossal celebrity! It's out of the *Arabian Nights!*

Henry. I can't realize it myself.

Hastings. It was just three months ago that we were eating together and I tried to persuade you to come to London with me. You turned me down, and now here you are. How did you happen to come, and what gave you this incredible start?

Henry. I'll tell you all about it, but not now.

Hastings. When?

Henry. The end of this month.

Hastings. Make it a week.

Henry. I can't. How's your business venture coming along?

Hastings (*sighing*). You were a true prophet, Henry. I wish I hadn't come.

Henry. Stop with me, when we leave here, and tell me all about it. I want to hear the whole story.

Hastings. You'll hear it, every last dismal word. (*fading a bit*) I'm so grateful to find a willing and sympathetic ear.

(*Background ad-libbing out. A pause, then piano playing semiclassical tune in background.*)

Henry. After dinner there was coffee and an informal piano recital and dear Miss Langham—lovely Portia Langham, the English girl. I eased her away from the music and the guests to the library, where we talked.

(*Piano out.*)

Portia. I'm really quite excited, Mr. Adams, meeting you like this. A millionaire!

Henry. But I'm not one.

Portia. B-but of course you are.

Henry. You're wrong.

Portia. I don't understand.

Henry. You will! You will, that is, if you allow me to see you tomorrow.

Portia (*as though smiling*). Well, Mr. Adams—

Henry. Henry.

Portia. Henry, then. I will give the invitation serious thought.

Henry. Tomorrow is going to be a sunny day, just right for a picnic in the country. Yes?

Portia. Yes.

Henry. I'll tell you the whole story then.

Portia. Do you think you should?

Henry. Certainly! After all, we're going to be married.

Portia (*amazed*). We—we're—going to—marry!

Henry. Absolutely! I'll call for you at noon. Where?

Portia. Meet me here.

Henry. You're a guest here?

Portia. N—no, but it will be more convenient.

Henry. Do you like me?

Portia. Yes, Henry. (*fading*) You're a very unusual young man, even if you are a millionaire, and even if you claim you aren't.

Henry. All the way home I was in the clouds, Hastings talking and I not hearing a word. When we reached my suite, he said to me:

Hastings. This luxury makes me realize how poor, how defeated I am. Even the drippings of your daily income would seem like a tremendous fortune to me.

Henry. Unreel your story, Lloyd.

Critical Thinking: ANALYZING

BB Why, do you think, does Hackett include this short scene between Henry and Hastings? *(Possible response: It demonstrates that Henry was being honest with Portia about his feelings for her. He seems really to be in love.)*

Active Reading: CONNECT

CC Invite volunteers to describe what their thoughts and feelings would be if they were in Hastings's place in this scene. How would their feelings be different if they were in Henry's position? Which position would they prefer?

STRATEGIC READING FOR
Less-Proficient Readers

DD Check that students understand Henry's responses to Portia Langham and Lloyd Hastings.

- What two people does Henry meet at the home of the American ambassador? *(an Englishwoman named Portia Langham, and Lloyd Hastings, Henry's former part-time employer)* **Summarizing**

- What plans does Henry have for Portia and himself? *(He has planned a picnic and a marriage.)* **Summarizing**

- How does Henry let down Hastings? *(Henry feels that he cannot erase Hastings's debts by buying his option for a million dollars and assuring his friend's passage home.)* **Clarifying**

Set a Purpose Have students read to find out how Henry helps Hastings and what happens at the Featherstones' home.

Hastings. I told you the whole story on the way over here.

Henry. You did?

Hastings. Yes.

Henry. I'll be hanged if I heard a word of it.

Hastings. Are you well?

Henry. Yes. I'm in love.

Hastings. That English girl you were speaking to?

Henry. Yes. I'm going to marry her.

Hastings. Small wonder you didn't hear a word I said.

Henry. Now I'm all attention.

Hastings. I came here with what I thought was a grand opportunity. I have an option to sell the Gould and Curry Mine and keep all I can get over a million dollars.

Henry. Sounds like a good proposition.

Hastings. Yes, it's a fine claim.

Henry. Well?

Hastings. The parties here whom I tried to interest have backed down. And so here I am, trying to peddle a gold mine but with nary a[11] buyer in sight. In addition, I am almost penniless.

Henry. Surely you'll find a buyer.

Hastings. My option on the mine expires in a matter of days—in fact, at the end of this month.

Henry. You *are* in a fix.

Hastings. Henry, you can save me. Will you do it?

Henry. I? How?

Hastings. Give me a million dollars and my passage home for my option.

Henry. I can't.

Hastings. But you're wealthy.

Henry. I—I—not really.

Hastings. You have a million pounds—five millions of dollars. Buy the mine and you'll double, maybe triple, your investment.

Henry. I'd like to help, but I can't.

Hastings. You know the value of this mine as well as I do.

Henry (*tired*). Oh, Lloyd, I wish I could explain, but I can't. What you ask is impossible.

Hastings. That's quite all right. I'm sorry to have bothered you, Henry. (*fading*) You must have a good reason in turning me down, I'm sure.

Henry. It hurt me to have to refuse Lloyd, but it made me comprehend my delicate and <u>precarious</u> position. Here I was, deep in debt, not a cent in the world, in love with a lovely girl, and nothing in front of me but a promise of a position if, *if,* I won the bet for the nameless brother. Nothing could save me. The next day, Portia and I went on our picnic in the country. I told her the whole story, down to the last detail. Her reaction wasn't exactly what I thought it would be.

(*Sound of bird singing in background, weaving in and out of this scene.*)

Portia (*laughs*). Oh, Henry, that's priceless.

Henry (*a bit stiffly*). I fail to see the humor.

Portia. But I do, more than you can imagine.

---

11. **nary a:** not one.

WORDS TO KNOW
precarious (prĭ-kâr′ē-əs) *adj.* not secure; risky

Henry. Here I am, mixed up in a bet between two eccentric old men, and for all they care I might well be in jail.

Portia (*still laughing*). Wonderful, the funniest thing I've ever heard.

Henry. Pardon me if I don't laugh.

Portia (*stops laughing*). Sorry, but it is both funny and pathetic. But you say that one of the men is going to offer you a position?

Henry. If I win the bet.

Portia. Which one is he?

Henry. I don't know. But I have one solution. If I win, I get the position. Now, I've kept very careful track of every cent I either owe or have borrowed, and I'm going to pay it back from my salary. If the position pays me six hundred pounds a year, I'll—I'll—

Portia. You'll what?

Henry. I'll— (*He whistles.*) To date I owe exactly six hundred pounds, my whole year's salary.

Portia. And the month isn't ended.

Henry. If I'm careful, my second year's salary may carry me through. Oh, dear, that is going to make it difficult for us to get married immediately, isn't it?

Portia (*dreamily*). Yes, it is. (*suddenly*) Henry, what are you talking about? Marriage! You don't know me.

Henry. I know your name, your nationality, your age, and most important, I know that I love you. I also know that you love me.

Portia. Please be sensible.

Henry. I can't. I'm in love.

Portia. All this sounds like a play.

Henry. It is—a wonderful one. I'll admit my owing my first two years' pay is going to pose a problem insofar as our getting married is concerned. (*suddenly*) I have it! The day I confront those two old gentlemen, I'll take you with me.

Portia. Oh, no. It wouldn't be proper.

Henry. But so much depends upon that meeting. With you there, I can get the old boys to raise my salary—say, to a thousand pounds a year. Perhaps fifteen hundred. Say you'll go with me.

Portia. I'll go.

Henry. In that case, I'll demand two thousand a year, so we can get married immediately.

Portia. Henry.

Henry. Yes?

Portia. Keep your expenses down for the balance of the month. Don't dip into your third year's salary.

Henry. And that is how matters stood at that point. Thoughts raced through my mind. What if I lost the bet for my nameless benefactor?[12] What if he failed to give me a position? Then the answer came to me like a flash of lightning. I roused Lloyd Hastings from bed. He was a bit bewildered.

Hastings. I don't understand you. What are you getting at?

Henry. Lloyd, I'm going to save you. Save you—understand?

Hastings. No.

Henry. I'll save you, but not in the way you ask, for that wouldn't be fair after your hard work and the risks you've run. Now, I don't need to buy a mine. I can keep my capital

---

12. **benefactor:** a person who provides money or help.

THE MILLION-POUND BANK NOTE **195**

moving without that; it's what I'm doing all the time. I know all about your mine; I know its immense value and can swear to it if anybody wishes it. You shall sell it inside of the fortnight[13] for three million cash.

Hastings. Three million!

Henry. Right!

Hastings. But how?

Henry. By using my name freely—and right now my name is on the tip of everybody's tongue. We'll divide the profits, share and share alike.

Hastings (*overjoyed*). I may use your name! Your name—think of it! Man, they'll flock in droves,[14] these rich English. They'll fight for that stock. I'm a made man, a made man forever. (*fading*) I'll never forget you as long as I live . . . never, never . . .

Henry. In less than twenty-four hours, London was abuzz! I hadn't anything to do, day after day, but sit home and wait for calls.

Sir Alfred. Then I may assume, Mr. Adams, that you consider this mining property a sound investment?

Henry. A very sound investment, Sir Alfred.

Sir Alfred. And what of this American chap, Hastings?

Henry. I know him very well, and he is as sound as the mine.

Sir Alfred. Then I think I shall invest in this property. Your recommendation does it.

(*Sound of telephone bell.*)

Henry. Excuse me, Sir Alfred.

(*Sound of receiver lifted from hook.*)

Henry (*into phone*). Yes, this is Henry Adams. Who? Sir John Hardcastle. Yes, Sir John. The Gould and Curry Extension? Yes, I know a great deal about it. I certainly would recommend it as a shrewd investment. The mine is worth far more than the asking price. Yes, Mr. Hastings is very well known in the States. Honest as the day is long, as they say. Yes, I suggest you contact Mr. Hastings. Thank you. Not at all. Good day, Sir John.

(*Sound of receiver replaced onto hook.*)

Sir Alfred. That clinches it. If Sir John is in, so am I. Do you suppose that your Mr. Hastings would mind if I brought in a few discreet friends on this venture?

Henry. Er, no, in fact I'm sure he wouldn't. Mr. Hastings is a very democratic chap.

Sir Alfred. Directly I shall go and call upon Mr. Hastings. By the way, exactly where is this mine?

Henry. California.

Sir Alfred. Is that near Washington, D.C.?

Henry. Not exactly.

Sir Alfred. A pity, for I had thought of asking the British ambassador to look at it. (*fading*) Well, I'm off. Thank you for your advice. Good day, Mr. Adams.

Henry. And that's the way it went—a steady stream of wealthy Londoners asking my advice, which, of course, I gave freely. Meanwhile I said not a word to Portia about the possible sale of the mine. I wanted to save it as a surprise; and then there always was the

---

13. **fortnight:** two weeks.
14. **droves:** mobs; crowds.

WORDS TO KNOW

discreet (dĭ-skrēt′) *adj.* showing caution in speech and behavior possibility the sale might fall through. The day the month was up, she and I, dressed in our best, went to the house on Portland Place. As we waited for the two old gentlemen to enter, we talked excitedly.

Portia. You're certain you have the bank note with you?

Henry. Right here. Portia, dearest, the way you look it's a crime to ask for a salary a single penny under three thousand a year.

Portia. You'll ruin us.

Henry. Just trust in me. It'll come out all right.

Portia (*worried*). Please remember, if we ask for too much, we may get no salary at all; and then what will become of us, with no way in the world to earn our living? (*fading*) Please handle this delicately, Henry.

Henry. When the two old gentlemen entered, of course they were surprised to see Portia with me. I asked them to introduce themselves, which they did.

Gordon. I am Gordon Featherstone.

Abel. And I am Abel Featherstone.

Henry. Gentlemen, I am ready to report, but first may I ask which of you bet on me?

Gordon. It was I. Have you the million-pound note?

Henry. Here it is, sir.

Gordon. Ah! I've won. *Now* what do you say, Abel?

Abel. I say he did survive, and I've lost twenty thousand pounds. I never would have believed it.

Henry. Perhaps you might enlighten me as to the terms of the bet.

Les adieux [The good-bye] (1871), James J. Tissot. City of Bristol Museum and Art Gallery, England/Bridgeman Art Library, London/Superstock.

THE MILLION-POUND BANK NOTE **197**

Art Note

Les Adieux (The Good-bye) by James J. Tissot In this painting, completed in 1871, two lovers in formal dress hold hands on either side of a wrought-iron fence. Their hands are clasped, and their faces exude the powerful emotion of their parting. The painting is full of a sense of struggle and restraint.

Reading the Art What purpose do the iron bars serve in the painting? What details in the painting add to the sense of a lack of freedom or space?

STRATEGIC READING FOR
Less-Proficient Readers

Check that students are following the story by asking these questions:

- How does Henry help Hastings? (*He convinces wealthy London businessmen to buy Hastings's mine.*) **Relating Cause and Effect**

- Why does Portia join Henry at the Featherstones' home? (*Henry plans to ask for a larger salary so that he can support his future wife, and he thinks her presence will help his cause.*) **Drawing Conclusions**

- Who bet on Henry? (*Gordon Featherstone*)

Set a Purpose Have students read to find out how the plot is resolved.

Assessment  Option

INFORMAL ASSESSMENT You can informally assess students' understanding of "The Million-Pound Bank Note" and of the literary concept characterization by having students compose a letter from one character to another. Although major characters such as Henry, Portia, Hastings, or Gordon or Abel might be the best choices, students could also choose a vividly drawn minor character such as Smedley. Urge students to make word choices that are appropriate to their chosen character. Suggest that in their letter students report and explain the details of some scene from the play.

Rubric

3 Full Accomplishment Student's letter accurately explains events in a vivid style appropriate to the chosen character.

2 Substantial Accomplishment Student's letter explains events in a style approximating that of the chosen character.

1 Little or Partial Accomplishment Student has difficulty writing a letter that explains events from the play and that features the style of a character from the play.

THE LANGUAGE OF LITERATURE TEACHER'S EDITION **197**

Active Reading: CLARIFY

LL Encourage students to discuss the circumstances surrounding "that pear incident." What did Henry do at the time? *(Possible response: Recently arrived in England—and penniless and starving—Henry was tempted by a partially eaten and discarded pear in the gutter. However, he was too embarrassed to pick it up while others watched him.)*

Critical Thinking: MAKING JUDGMENTS

MM Ask students whether they agree with the Featherstones' belief that if a person had boldly picked up the pear, it would be proof that that person was "nothing but a tramp." *(Possible responses: I agree because the only person who would boldly pick up food on the street would be a person who has lost all self-respect. I disagree because these rich Englishmen don't understand that a hungry person living on the streets would have to pick up the fruit before someone else beat him or her to it.)*

Active Reading: EVALUATE

NN Remind students that Henry turned an uncomfortable situation to his advantage. A series of events occurred between his offering the bill for trifles and his earning £200,000. Ask students to reconstruct this cause-and-effect chain. You may wish to use the following model to give them ideas of what they might be thinking about.

Think-Aloud Model *I think that his offering the bill caused people to believe he was a wealthy man; their opinions gave Henry a reputation for being a "Vest-Pocket Millionaire," and this reputation caused people to trust his advice. His advice led wealthy Londoners to invest in the mine, which caused Henry to earn £200,000.*

Gordon. Gladly! The Bank of England once issued two notes of a million pounds each. Only one of these had been used and canceled; the other lay in the vaults. Well, Abel and I got to wondering what would happen to a perfectly honest and intelligent stranger turned adrift in London without a friend and with no money in the world but the million-pound bank note. Abel said he would starve to death, and I claimed he wouldn't. My brother said he would be arrested if he offered the note at a bank. Well, we went on arguing until I bet him twenty thousand pounds that the man would live thirty days, *anyway,* on that million, and keep out of jail, too.

Abel. And I took him up.

Henry. How did you know I was the right choice?

Abel. After talking with you, we decided you had all the qualifications.

Gordon. And that pear incident—if you had picked it up very boldly, it would have proved to us you were nothing but a tramp.

Henry. You don't know how tempted I was to do just that.

Gordon. And so you shall receive your reward—a choice of any position you can fill.

Henry. First I ask that you look at this scrap of paper, all of you. You, too, Portia.

Gordon. A certificate of deposit in the London and County Bank—

Abel. In the sum of—

Gordon. Two hundred thousand pounds.

Portia. Henry, is it yours?

Henry. It is. It represents my share of the sale of a mining property in California, sold by my friend Lloyd Hastings—a sort of commission, as it were. It all came about by thirty days' judicious use of that little loan you gentlemen let me have. And the only use I made of it was to buy trifles and offer the bill in change.

Abel. Come, this is astonishing.

Gordon. It's incredible.

Henry (*laughing*). I can prove it.

Portia. Henry, is that really your money? Have you been fibbing to me?

Henry. I have, indeed. But you'll forgive me, I know.

Portia (*half smiling*). Don't you be so sure.

Henry. Oh, you'll get over it. Come, let's be going.

Gordon. Wait! I promised to give you a situation, you know.

Henry. Thank you, but I really don't want one.

Portia. Henry, I'm ashamed of you. You don't even thank the good gentleman. May I do it for you?

Henry. If you can improve upon it.

Portia. I shall. Uncle Abel, first, thank you for making this possible. And, dear Father—

Henry. Hold on. You're her uncle?

Abel. I am.

Henry. And you—

Gordon. Yes, I'm her stepfather.

Portia. And the dearest one that ever was. You understand now, don't you, Henry, why I was able to laugh when you told me the story of the bet with the two nameless gentlemen. Of course I couldn't miss knowing that it was

---

WORDS TO KNOW
judicious (jōō-dĭsh′əs) *adj.* careful; showing sound judgment

198

Mini-Lesson Study Skills

TAKING OBJECTIVE TESTS: SHORT-ANSWER QUESTIONS Explain to students that classroom tests on literature such as "The Million-Pound Bank Note" often contain short-answer questions. These questions are used to test specific knowledge and general comprehension of the story. A short-answer question asks students to provide information in a brief written answer. Some strategies for writing accurate, concise answers include:

- read the directions completely;
- answer in carefully phrased complete sentences;
- make sure that your grammar, spelling, punctuation, and capitalization are correct.

Application Have students practice their skills by answering a short-answer question such as, "Why is it ironic that Henry is introduced to Hastings in London?" *(It is ironic because Hastings asked Henry in San Francisco to accompany him to London and Henry turned him down.)*

this house and that the two men were Father and Uncle Abel.

Henry. Sir, you *have* got a situation open that I want.

Gordon. Name it.

Henry. Son-in-law.

Gordon. Well, well, well! But if you haven't ever served in that capacity, you of course can't furnish satisfactory recommendations to satisfy the conditions of the contract.

Henry. Only just try me for thirty or forty years.

Gordon. What do you think, Abel?

Abel. Well, he does look to be a satisfactory sort.

Gordon. And you, Portia?

Portia. I agree—heartily.

Gordon. Very well. Take her along. If you hurry, you can reach the license bureau before it closes. (*fading*) Hop to it now.

Henry. Happy, we two? Indeed, yes! And when London got the whole history of my adventure for a month, how it did talk. My Portia's father took the million-pound bank note to the Bank of England, cashed it, had it canceled; and he gave it to us at our wedding. Framed, it now hangs in our home. It gave me my Portia; but for it I could not have remained in London, would not have appeared at the American ambassador's, never should have met her. And so I always say: Yes, it's a million-pounder, but it made but one purchase in its life and then got the article for only about a tenth part of its value. ❖

STRATEGIC READING FOR
Less-Proficient Readers

OO Ask students to explain how the plot is resolved. (*Henry discovers that the two gentlemen are Portia's stepfather and uncle. The two men are so impressed with Henry that they agree to his desire to marry Portia.*) Summarizing/Drawing Conclusions

Active Reading: QUESTION

PP Ask students if any unanswered questions remain in their own minds, despite the fact that the plot is completely resolved.

CUSTOMIZING FOR
Gifted and Talented Students

The British are famous for their ability to make subtle class distinctions on the basis of someone's accent. Ask students to consider the issue of socioeconomic class in American society. Are there classes in the United States? If so, what defines and separates them? How are the poor viewed and treated in this country? How are the wealthy viewed and treated? Who are the people between these two groups? Challenge students to discuss and debate the thorny issue of class in America.

COMPREHENSION CHECK
1. Where does the story begin? (*San Francisco*)
2. What is Henry's condition when he gets to London? (*He is hungry and tired and has only one dollar.*)
3. What do two Englishmen give Henry? (*a million-pound bank note*)
4. With whom does Henry fall in love? (*Portia Langham*)
5. How does Henry end up helping Lloyd Hastings? (*Henry convinces rich Englishmen to buy Hastings's mine.*)
6. What does Henry learn about the identity of Abel and Gordon? (*They are Portia's uncle and stepfather.*)

Mini-Lesson Spelling

SPELLING WITH SUFFIXES Tell students that suffixes such as *-ion* and *-ous* can be added to base words. Adding *-ion* to a verb forms a noun. Adding *-ous* to a noun forms an adjective. If the base word ends in a consonant, simply add the suffix. If the base word ends in silent e, usually drop the e before adding the suffix.

accommodat[e] + ion = **accommodation**

Application Have students add suffixes to the following base words:
1. fame + ous
2. desire + ous
3. frustrate + ion
4. riot + ous
5. accelerate + ion
6. situate + ion

Ask students to look for more words that fit this pattern in their own writing and in things they read, and add these words to their personal word lists.

Reteaching/Reinforcement
- *Unit Two Resource Book,* p. 23

From Personal Response to Critical Analysis

1. Ask students to be specific about aspects of Henry Adams's character and behavior.
2. Possible response: At first, he panics, but gradually he adjusts and learns to use his wits and take advantage of people's assumption that he is rich.
3. Possible responses: They want some of his money; they associate wealth with excellence or prestige.
4. Possible response: Henry is an admirable person. He knows himself and what he wants (whether it is staying in California or marrying Portia). His intelligent response to the bet shows that he can rise above adversity without hurting anybody.
5. Possible response: The scheme made for an interesting tale, because it put Henry in a comical bind. But also, the scheme was essentially hateful and manipulative because it was carried out on a real person.
6. Possible response: Sudden wealth can put a lot of stress on people, as well as offer opportunities. Money could help people pay off debts or help family members who were struggling. On the other hand, a lottery winner would probably get a lot of new "friends" looking for a handout.

Another Pathway

Cooperative Learning Small groups of students might be in charge of researching costumes, the play's setting, and British accents, while others list and gather necessary props or arrange for videotaping. After the play is cast, students should learn their lines, rehearse their scenes, and prepare for a performance in front of their peers.

Rubric
- **3 Full Accomplishment** Students do ample research and enthusiastically participate in the production of the play.
- **2 Substantial Accomplishment** Students do research and participate in the production of the play.
- **1 Little or Partial Accomplishment** Students have difficulty doing research and participating in the production of the play.

RESPONDING OPTIONS

FROM PERSONAL RESPONSE TO CRITICAL ANALYSIS

REFLECT
1. What are your impressions of Henry? Jot down your thoughts in your notebook. Draw a series of sketches showing how Henry makes use of the bank note.

RETHINK
Thematic Link

2. How does having the million-pound note affect Henry? What adjustments does he make?
3. Why do you think people's attitudes toward Henry change when he appears rich?
4. How would you evaluate Henry as a person?
   Consider
   - why he declines to go to London with Hastings
   - how he responds initially to receiving the bank note, and how he uses it
   - his response to Portia
5. What is your opinion of the scheme devised by the two brothers? Explain your answer.

RELATE
Thematic Link

6. Like Henry, people who win big lottery jackpots suddenly become fabulously wealthy, forcing them to make critical adjustments in their lives. How do you imagine winning a lottery might affect a person's life? What might be the good and the bad effects of instant wealth?

Multimodal Learning
ANOTHER PATHWAY

Cooperative Learning
With your classmates, present a full-scale stage production of this play. To make your production authentic, research the setting and the costumes of late 19th-century England. Divide tasks among the members of the class, assigning one to videotape the production.

QUICKWRITES

1. The Vest-Pocket Millionaire is big news in London. Write a **script** for a TV-news-show feature about this lucky young man's experiences.
2. The biggest social event in London is the wedding of the Vest-Pocket Millionaire to his English bride. Write a **society-page report** of the event for a San Francisco newspaper.
3. Put yourself in the shoes of one of the characters who encounters the Vest-Pocket Millionaire in the play. Write a **character sketch** of Henry from that character's point of view.

📁 **PORTFOLIO** *Save your writing. You may want to use it later as a springboard to a piece for your portfolio.*

LITERARY CONCEPTS

As in fiction, the climax or turning point of a drama is usually followed by a **resolution** that shows how the conflict or conflicts are resolved and how the story ends. This is the time when loose ends are tied up and the story comes to a close. Summarize what happens in the resolution of this play.

200 UNIT TWO PART 1: TWINGES OF CONSCIENCE

Literary Concepts

Help students focus on the loose ends that are tied up after Henry and the Featherstones clear up their business. Students should understand that in the resolution Henry reveals his new income, Portia reveals her identity, Henry turns down the Featherstones' job offer, and he secures Portia's hand in marriage.

Multimodal Learning

ALTERNATIVE ACTIVITIES

1. **Cooperative Learning** With other students, research the political leaders and the royalty of Great Britain in the 1890s using the library or an on-line service. Find out how British society was changing during this time and what caused the changes. Present your findings in an **oral report.**

2. Suppose Henry regularly donates a portion of his earnings to special causes or to individuals in need. Write a letter to Henry, telling him why your cause or need deserves his help. The class can read its letters aloud and vote to select the three **special causes** or needs to which Henry should donate money.

3. Take a **survey** or **poll** to find out what each of your classmates would do with a million dollars. Plot the responses on a chart or graph.

ACROSS THE CURRICULUM

Mathematics Exchange rates are ratios used to compare the values of different currencies. These rates change daily. Find out how exchange rates are determined and what a U.S. dollar is worth in the currencies listed below. What is the current dollar equivalent of 1 million British pounds?

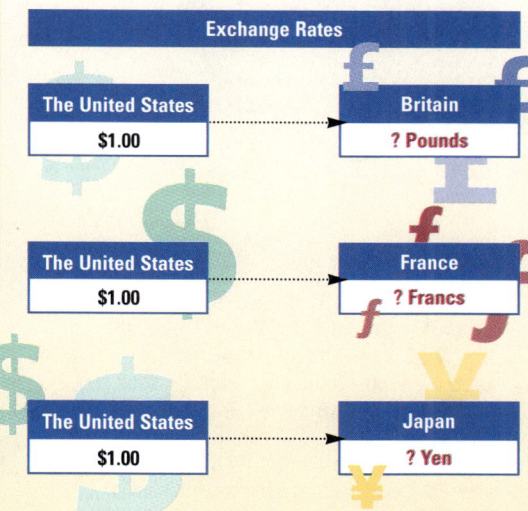

Exchange Rates

The United States $1.00	→	Britain ? Pounds
The United States $1.00	→	France ? Francs
The United States $1.00	→	Japan ? Yen

ART CONNECTION

Examine all of the artwork in the selection. What can you say about the use of color and the style of painting across these four works? Evaluate their effectiveness in grabbing the reader's attention and conveying time and place.

Across the Curriculum

Mathematics Have students consult library reference books to learn about exchange rates. Also encourage them to check the financial pages of a newspaper to see current rates.

ADDITIONAL SUGGESTIONS

Geography *Gold Fever* Have students research and create a map that shows where prospectors mined for gold during the California gold rush. Encourage them to illustrate and label the map with information showing where prospectors traveled from to find their fortune.

Art Connection

Answers will vary, but should include specific references to the four paintings. Students might note Tissot's use of the bright colors of the female's skirt and the male's arm sleeve in *Les Adieux*, which draws the viewer's eye to the farewell hand clasp.

QuickWrites

1. Have students think about feature stories they have seen on TV news shows. Suggest that students outline the feature before scripting it.
2. Have students study the society pages of a local newspaper to find out which details are typically included in announcements.
3. Before students begin to make notes for their sketch, urge them to focus on the parts of Henry's personality that were evident during the time spent with their chosen character.

The Writer's Craft
Details, pp. 249–250
Script Writing, pp. 86–88

Alternative Activities

1. Students could use a time line as part of their presentation. To put this information in context, the time line could show events in the United States as well as in Great Britain.
2. Remind students to present their particular charity in the best light possible, in order to convince Mr. Adams that it is worth his attention. You might wish to review with students the form of a business letter.
3. Urge students to prepare questions that have multiple-choice or yes or no answers. This will make the responses easier to chart.

Words to Know

1. A	6. S
2. A	7. S
3. A	8. S
4. S	9. S
5. A	10. A

Reteaching/Reinforcement
• *Unit Two Resource Book*, p. 24

Literary Link

Possible responses:

"The Lie": Vonnegut portrays the wealthy as sometimes generous and fair-minded but at other times frivolous, insensitive, and apt to use their wealth to gain special treatment.

"The Million-Pound Bank Note": Twain portrays the wealthy largely as foolish, bored, and shallow, although the Featherstones are also ultimately generous.

SAMUEL CLEMENS

Samuel Clemens went to Nevada and California and prospected for gold during the years 1862–1865. In 1864 he moved to San Francisco, hoping to sell some silver mining stock he had acquired. The mines failed, and Clemens went broke. He supported himself during these years with occasional work as a newspaper reporter. In 1865 he published "The Celebrated Jumping Frog of Calaveras County" and began a remarkable writing career.

 **AUTHOR BACKGROUND**
The celebrated and illustrious life of Samuel Langhorne Clemens, better known as Mark Twain, is the subject of these photographs and illustrations.

Side A, Frame 52644

LITERARY LINKS

Using a Venn diagram like the one below, compare and contrast Kurt Vonnegut's attitude toward the wealthy in "The Lie" with the attitude shown in this play.

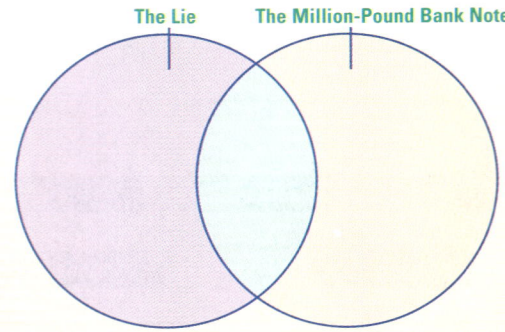

WORDS TO KNOW

Review the Words to Know at the bottom of the selection pages. Then decide whether the words in each pair below are synonyms or antonyms. On your paper, write *S* for *Synonyms* or *A* for *Antonyms*.

1. judicious—foolish
2. rebuke—compliment
3. competent—unfit
4. accommodation—favor
5. precarious—secure
6. consequence—importance
7. diversion—amusement
8. discreet—guarded
9. eccentric—strange
10. ad-lib—recite

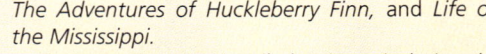

SAMUEL CLEMENS (MARK TWAIN)

Samuel Clemens took his pen name, Mark Twain, from a cry used by boatmen on the Mississippi River. They would call out "Mark twain!" when they had measured the water to be two fathoms deep —deep enough for travel. Traveling the Mississippi River in makeshift rafts as a child and piloting riverboats as an adult inspired Twain to write his most famous books, *The Adventures of Tom Sawyer*, *The Adventures of Huckleberry Finn*, and *Life on the Mississippi*.

1835–1910

Twain grew up in Hannibal, Missouri, during the mid-1800s. As an adult, he headed west, mining for gold and silver and eventually working for newspapers in San Francisco. Like the character Hastings in this play, he also invested in mines, but these ventures failed.

Twain's courtship was perhaps even more romantic than Henry and Portia's. In 1867, he fell in love with a picture of Olivia Langdon. When he finally met "Livy," he was determined to marry her, but his busy lecture schedule kept them apart. In one year, Twain wrote her well over 100 love letters. They were finally married in 1870.

In the 1890s, Twain and his family were plagued with tragedy. One daughter died after contracting meningitis, a disease of the brain and spine. Her daughter's death resulted in emotional and physical problems for Livy, who died soon afterward. Four years later, another daughter drowned in the bath during an epileptic seizure. A third daughter suffered a nervous collapse.

Although Twain grew increasingly bitter and mean-spirited during the final decade of his life, he is remembered for his love of fun, his frontier spirit, and his commitment to democracy.

OTHER WORKS *The Prince and the Pauper*, "The Celebrated Jumping Frog of Calaveras County," "The $30,000 Bequest," *A Connecticut Yankee in King Arthur's Court*

202 UNIT TWO PART 1: TWINGES OF CONSCIENCE

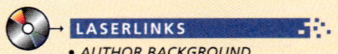
• AUTHOR BACKGROUND

WHAT DO YOU THINK?
Reflecting on Theme

Ask students to think back to the mock talk show they staged before reading the selections in Part One. Having read about Henry's experience with the million-pound note, ask students to discuss whether their impressions of newfound wealth have changed. Encourage students to re-stage their mock talk shows to take into consideration any new thoughts on the subject.

ON YOUR OWN

Mother & Daughter

by GARY SOTO

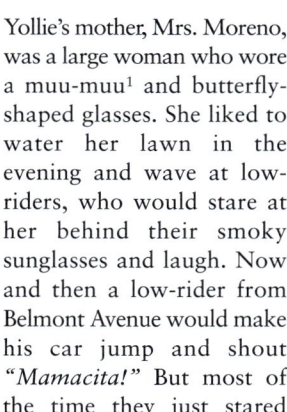

Yollie's mother, Mrs. Moreno, was a large woman who wore a muu-muu[1] and butterfly-shaped glasses. She liked to water her lawn in the evening and wave at low-riders, who would stare at her behind their smoky sunglasses and laugh. Now and then a low-rider from Belmont Avenue would make his car jump and shout *"Mamacita!"* But most of the time they just stared and wondered how she got so large.

Mrs. Moreno had a strange sense of humor. Once, Yollie and her mother were watching a late-night movie called *They Came to Look*. It was about creatures from the underworld who had climbed through molten lava to walk the earth. But Yollie, who had played soccer all day with the kids next door, was too tired to be scared. Her eyes closed but sprang open when her mother screamed, "Look, Yollie! Oh, you missed a scary part. The guy's face was all ugly!"

But Yollie couldn't keep her eyes open. They fell shut again and stayed shut, even when her mother screamed and slammed a heavy palm on the arm of her chair.

"Mom, wake me up when the movie's over so I can go to bed," mumbled Yollie.

"OK, Yollie, I wake you," said her mother through a mouthful of popcorn.

But after the movie ended, instead of waking her daughter, Mrs. Moreno laughed under her breath, turned the TV and lights off, and tiptoed to bed. Yollie woke up in the middle of the night and didn't know where she was. For a moment she thought she was dead. Maybe something from the underworld had lifted her from her house and carried

---

1. **muu muu** (mōō′mōō′): a long, loose dress, often brightly colored.

MOTHER AND DAUGHTER **203**

OBJECTIVES

- To promote independent active reading
- To practice and apply skills learned in previous selections
- To provide an opportunity to assess students' performance through an alternative assessment instrument

Reading Pathways

- Have students read independently and write in dialogue journals.
- Encourage students to read silently for enjoyment.
- Invite students to choose passages to read aloud to a partner.
- Evaluate how well students can read, interpret, discuss, and write about the selection on their own by using the Integrated Assessment for Unit Two, located in the Alternative Assessment booklet. Administer the assessment at the end of the unit after students have read all the selections and completed all the writing that was assigned.

PRINT AND MEDIA RESOURCES

UNIT TWO RESOURCE BOOK
Strategic Reading: Literature, p. 27

FORMAL ASSESSMENT
Selection Test, p. 37
Part Test, pp. 39–40
Test Generator

ALTERNATIVE ASSESSMENT
- *Unit Two Integrated Assessment*, pp. 7–12

ACCESS FOR STUDENTS ACQUIRING ENGLISH
Selection Summaries

AUDIO LIBRARY
See Reference Card

THE LANGUAGE OF LITERATURE TEACHER'S EDITION **203**

SUMMARY

Mrs. Moreno, the struggling daughter of migrant farm workers, wants her bright daughter, Yollie, to value education. She uses hard-earned money to buy Yollie a desk, lamp, and typewriter but does not have the money to spend on new clothes for her. Yollie attends a special dance wearing an old dress her mother spruced up with black dye. However, the pigment runs during a rainstorm, and Yollie feels humiliated. The next day, Mrs. Moreno gets money from a secret college fund and takes Yollie shopping for new clothes.

Thematic Link: *Twinges of Conscience*
A mother dips into the money she has saved for her daughter's college education in order to buy her some new clothes after the girl is humiliated by the old clothing she has had to wear.

---

her into the earth's belly. She blinked her sleepy eyes, looked around at the darkness, and called, "Mom? Mom, where are you?" But there was no answer, just the throbbing hum of the refrigerator.

Finally, Yollie's grogginess cleared, and she realized her mother had gone to bed, leaving her on the couch. Another of her little jokes.

But Yollie wasn't laughing. She tiptoed into her mother's bedroom with a glass of water and set it on the night stand next to the alarm clock. The next morning, Yollie woke to screams. When her mother reached to turn off the alarm, she had overturned the glass of water.

Yollie burned her mother's morning toast and gloated. "Ha! Ha! I got you back. Why did you leave me on the couch when I told you to wake me up?"

Despite their jokes, mother and daughter usually got along. They watched bargain matinees together and played croquet[2] in the summer and checkers in the winter. Mrs. Moreno encouraged Yollie to study hard because she wanted her daughter to be a doctor. She bought Yollie a desk, a typewriter, and a lamp that cut glare so her eyes would not grow tired from hours of studying.

Yollie was slender as a tulip, pretty, and one of the smartest kids at Saint Theresa's. She was captain of crossing guards, an altar girl, and a whiz in the school's monthly spelling bees.

"*Tienes que estudiar mucho,*"[3] Mrs. Moreno said every time she propped her work-weary feet on the hassock. "You have to study a lot, then you can get a good job and take care of me."

"Yes, Mama," Yollie would respond, her face buried in a book. If she gave her mother any sympathy, she would begin her stories about how she had come with her family from Mexico with nothing on her back but a sack with three skirts, all of which were too large by the time she crossed the border because she had lost weight from not having enough to eat.

Everyone thought Yollie's mother was a riot. Even the nuns laughed at her antics. Her brother Raul, a nightclub owner, thought she was funny enough to go into show business.

But there was nothing funny about Yollie needing a new outfit for the eighth-grade fall dance. They couldn't afford one. It was late October, with Christmas around the corner, and their dented Chevy Nova had gobbled up almost one hundred dollars in repairs.

> Everyone thought Yollie's mother was a riot.

"We don't have the money," said her mother, genuinely sad because they couldn't buy the outfit, even though there was a little money stashed away for college. Mrs. Moreno remembered her teenage years and her hard-working parents, who picked grapes and oranges and chopped beets and cotton for meager pay around Kerman. Those were the days when "new clothes" meant limp and out-of-style dresses from Saint Vincent de Paul.[4]

The best Mrs. Moreno could do was buy Yollie a pair of black shoes with velvet bows and fabric dye to color her white summer dress black.

---

2. **croquet** (krō-kā′): an outdoor game in which players use mallets to hit wooden balls through a series of wire arches.
3. ***Tienes que estudiar mucho*** (tyĕ′nĕs kĕ ĕs-tōō-dyär′ mōō′chô) *Spanish.*
4. **Saint Vincent de Paul:** a reference to the Society of Saint Vincent de Paul, a Roman Catholic organization that operates stores where donated goods are sold cheaply.

Colombiane (1978), Fernando Botero. Copyright ©1995 Fernando Botero/Licensed by VAGA, New York.

Art Note

Colombiane by Fernando Botero The image that Colombian artist Fernando Botero (1932–) chose to paint challenges viewers' perceptions of attractiveness and obesity. It shows a large woman whose size is underscored by her sleeveless dress. Although Botero uses humor and exaggeration, the viewer is left with the feeling that the artist is neither ridiculing nor pitying the woman. Rather he is straightforwardly presenting the way she looks.

Reading the Art *How does the subject's facial expression affect your experience of the painting? What do her fingers (and her body language generally) tell you about her sense of herself emotionally and physically? How would you describe the tone of this painting?*

Art Note

Yucateca Sentada (Seated Yucatan Woman) by Alfredo Zalce Mexican artist Alfredo Zalce (1908–) presents his subject with a provocative simplicity and forthrightness. In the strong lines, vivid textures, and clear contrasts of the image, the artist seems to see the world as a place where basic elements—human beings, dirt, fabric, walls, air, and light—exist together in a kind of unity.

Reading the Art In your opinion, what (if anything) is the woman doing? Why, do you think, did the artist paint her in this physical position? Do you think this painting is suited to the selection? Why or why not?

"We can color your dress so it will look brand-new," her mother said brightly, shaking the bottle of dye as she ran hot water into a plastic dish tub. She poured the black liquid into the tub and stirred it with a pencil. Then, slowly and carefully, she lowered the dress into the tub.

Yollie couldn't stand to watch. She *knew* it wouldn't work. It would be like the time her mother stirred up a batch of molasses for candy apples on Yollie's birthday. She'd dipped the apples into the goo and swirled them and seemed to taunt Yollie by singing "*Las Mañanitas*" to her. When she was through, she set the apples on wax paper. They were hard as rocks and hurt the kids' teeth. Finally they had a contest to see who could break the apples open by throwing them against the side of the house. The apples shattered like grenades, sending the kids scurrying for cover, and in an odd way the birthday party turned out to be a success. At least everyone went home happy.

To Yollie's surprise, the dress came out shiny black. It looked brand-new and sophisticated, like what people in New York wear. She beamed at her mother, who hugged Yollie and said, "See, what did I tell you?"

Yucateca Sentada (1979), Alfredo Zalce. Acrylic on wood, 60 cm × 80 cm, courtesy of the Mexico Fine Arts Center Museum, Chicago.

206 UNIT TWO PART 1: TWINGES OF CONSCIENCE

Multicultural Perspectives

BORDER CROSSINGS In "Mother & Daughter" Yollie's mother repeatedly tells the story of how she and her family traveled across the border to the United States. Explain to students that until the mid-1800s much of the southwestern United States, from California to Texas, was actually part of Mexico. In 1836 Mexico lost the land that is now Texas and, after defeat by the United States in the Mexican War (1846–1848), lost what is now California, Nevada, and Utah, and parts of Arizona, Colorado, New Mexico, and Wyoming.

The dance was important to Yollie because she was in love with Ernie Castillo, the third-best speller in the class. She bathed, dressed, did her hair and nails, and primped until her mother yelled, "All right already." Yollie sprayed her neck and wrists with Mrs. Moreno's Avon perfume and bounced into the car.

Mrs. Moreno let Yollie out in front of the school. She waved and told her to have a good time but behave herself, then roared off, blue smoke trailing from the tail pipe of the old Nova.

Yollie ran into her best friend, Janice. They didn't say it, but each thought the other was the most beautiful girl at the dance; the boys would fall over themselves asking them to dance.

The evening was warm but thick with clouds. Gusts of wind picked up the paper lanterns hanging in the trees and swung them, blurring the night with reds and yellows. The lanterns made the evening seem romantic, like a scene from a movie. Everyone danced, sipped punch, and stood in knots of threes and fours, talking. Sister Kelly got up and jitterbugged[5] with some kid's father. When the record ended, students broke into applause.

Janice had her eye on Frankie Ledesma, and Yollie, who kept smoothing her dress down when the wind picked up, had her eye on Ernie. It turned out that Ernie had his mind on Yollie, too. He ate a handful of cookies nervously, then asked her for a dance.

"Sure," she said, nearly throwing herself into his arms.

They danced two fast ones before they got a slow one. As they circled under the lanterns, rain began falling, lightly at first. Yollie loved the sound of the raindrops ticking against the leaves. She leaned her head on Ernie's shoulder, though his sweater was scratchy. He felt warm and tender. Yollie could tell that he was in love, and with her, of course. The dance continued successfully, romantically, until it began to pour.

"Everyone, let's go inside—and, boys, carry in the table and the record player," Sister Kelly commanded.

The girls and boys raced into the cafeteria. Inside, the girls, drenched to the bone, hurried to the restrooms to brush their hair and dry themselves. One girl cried because her velvet dress was ruined. Yollie felt sorry for her and helped her dry the dress off with paper towels, but it was no use. The dress was ruined.

Yollie went to a mirror. She looked a little gray now that her mother's makeup had washed away but not as bad as some of the other girls. She combed her damp hair, careful not to pull too hard. She couldn't wait to get back to Ernie.

> Drip, black drip. Drip, black drip. The dye was falling from her dress like black tears.

Yollie bent over to pick up a bobby pin, and shame spread across her face. A black puddle was forming at her feet. Drip, black drip. Drip, black drip. The dye was falling from her dress like black tears. Yollie stood up. Her dress was now the color of ash. She looked around the room. The other girls, unaware of Yollie's problem, were busy grooming themselves. What could she do? Everyone would laugh. They would know she dyed an old dress because she couldn't afford a new one. She hurried from the restroom with her head down, across the

---
5. **jitterbugged:** danced in a lively, acrobatic style popular in the early 1940s.

OPTION 2

Individual Activity

WRITING A PERSONAL NARRATIVE

Have students brainstorm about their own embarrassing experiences. What are some of the most embarrassing things that have happened to them? Invite students to consider exactly why these experiences embarrassed them. Then have them focus on one experience and relate it in a personal narrative. Remind students to include details that help the reader understand the scene and the progression of their thoughts and feelings.

Teacher's Role Some students may be reluctant to write about embarrassing moments. Encourage them to see that embarrassing moments are universal, often filled with humor (if seen from a different point of view or after some time has passed), and usually don't cause any serious or lasting damage.

Rubric

3 Full Accomplishment Student writes a vivid, cohesive personal narrative that describes an embarrassing experience.

2 Substantial Accomplishment Student writes a somewhat detailed personal narrative that describes an embarrassing experience.

1 Little or Partial Accomplishment Student has difficulty focusing on a personal narrative that describes an embarrassing experience.

---

cafeteria floor and out the door. She raced through the storm, crying as the rain mixed with her tears and ran into twig-choked gutters.

When she arrived home, her mother was on the couch eating cookies and watching TV.

"How was the dance, *m'ija*?[6] Come watch the show with me. It's really good."

Yollie stomped, head down, to her bedroom. She undressed and threw the dress on the floor.

Her mother came into the room. "What's going on? What's all this racket, baby?"

"The dress. It's cheap! It's no good!" Yollie kicked the dress at her mother and watched it land in her hands. Mrs. Moreno studied it closely but couldn't see what was wrong. "What's the matter? It's just little bit wet."

"The dye came out, that's what."

Mrs. Moreno looked at her hands and saw the grayish dye puddling in the shallow lines of her palms. Poor baby, she thought, her brow darkening as she made a sad face. She wanted to tell her daughter how sorry she was, but she knew it wouldn't help. She walked back to the living room and cried.

The next morning, mother and daughter stayed away from each other. Yollie sat in her room turning the pages of an old *Seventeen,* while her mother watered her plants with a Pepsi bottle.

"Drink, my children," she said loud enough for Yollie to hear. She let the water slurp into pots of coleus and cacti. "Water is all you need. My daughter needs clothes, but I don't have no money."

Yollie tossed her *Seventeen* on her bed. She was embarrassed at last night's tirade. It wasn't her mother's fault that they were poor.

When they sat down together for lunch, they felt awkward about the night before. But Mrs. Moreno had made a fresh stack of tortillas and cooked up a pan of *chile verde,* and that broke the ice. She licked her thumb and smacked her lips.

"You know, honey, we gotta figure a way to make money," Yollie's mother said. "You and me. We don't have to be poor. Remember the Garcias. They made this stupid little tool that fixes cars. They moved away because they're rich. That's why we don't see them no more."

> *"Water is all you need. My daughter needs clothes, but I don't have no money."*

"What can we make?" asked Yollie. She took another tortilla and tore it in half.

"Maybe a screwdriver that works on both ends? Something like that." The mother looked around the room for ideas but then shrugged. "Let's forget it. It's better to get an education. If you get a good job and have spare time, then maybe you can invent something." She rolled her tongue over her lips and cleared her throat. "The county fair hires people. We can get a job there. It will be here next week."

Yollie hated the idea. What would Ernie say if he saw her pitching hay at the cows? How could she go to school smelling like an armful of chickens? "No, they wouldn't hire us," she said.

The phone rang. Yollie lurched from her chair to answer it, thinking it would be Janice wanting to know why she had left. But it was Ernie wondering the same thing. When he

---

6. **m'ija** (mē′ hä) *Spanish*: a shortened version of *mi hija,* meaning "my daughter."

208 UNIT TWO PART 1: TWINGES OF CONSCIENCE

found out she wasn't mad at him, he asked if she would like to go to a movie.

"I'll ask," Yollie said, smiling. She covered the phone with her hand and counted to ten. She uncovered the receiver and said, "My mom says it's OK. What are we going to see?"

After Yollie hung up, her mother climbed, grunting, onto a chair to reach the top shelf in the hall closet. She wondered why she hadn't done it earlier. She reached behind a stack of towels and pushed her chubby hand into the cigar box where she kept her secret stash of money.

"I've been saving a little every month," said Mrs. Moreno. "For you, *m'ija.*" Her mother held up five twenties, a blossom of green that smelled sweeter than flowers on that Saturday. They drove to Macy's and bought a blouse, shoes, and a skirt that would not bleed in rain or any other kind of weather. ❖

GARY SOTO

1952–

A native of Fresno, California, Gary Soto writes about the experiences of Mexican Americans. As a child, Soto worked as a field laborer, but he dreamed of becoming a priest, a hobo, and a paleontologist. Once in college, he planned to study geography until he discovered poetry. "I don't think I had any literary aspirations when I was a kid," says Soto. "In fact, we were pretty much an illiterate family. We didn't have books, and no one encouraged us to read. So my wanting to write poetry was a sort of fluke." He graduated with high honors from California State University, Fresno.

Since college, Soto has been writing novels, short stories, and essays in addition to poetry. His first book of poems, *The Elements of San Joaquin*, won the United States Award of the International Poetry Forum. In 1985, his collection of autobiographical pieces *Living up the Street* won the American Book Award of the Before Columbus Foundation.

Among young readers, Soto is best known for his short story collections. However, he has also written a one-act play, *Novio Boy*, that is frequently staged in high schools and has produced three films for Spanish-speaking children. Soto currently teaches English and Chicano studies at the University of California, Berkeley.

OTHER WORKS *The Skirt, Local News, The Pool Party, Crazy Weekend, Neighborhood Odes, Baseball in April and Other Stories, A Summer Life, The Tale of Sunlight, Where Sparrows Work Hard, Black Hair*

GARY SOTO

In explaining the vitality of his work, Gary Soto speaks of his sense of play. "I think I'm very childlike, and I often write youthful poems," he says. "It's sort of a silly act, writing itself. I don't know why anyone would pay attention to these half-schooled, half-literate poets. But when I write I like the youth in my poetry, sort of a craziness. For me that's really important. I don't want to take a dreary look at the world and then start writing. I left that somewhere along the line."

OVERVIEW

In the Guided Assignment for this section, students will write an essay interpreting the message of a selection. By interpreting the meaning or message, students will become more familiar with the ways writers express their ideas in literary works. As preparation for this assignment, The Writer's Style will help students understand the three primary ways that writers emphasize their ideas. In Reading the World, students will interpret the messages conveyed in real-world images.

Objectives

- To recognize how authors emphasize their ideas
- To organize an interpretive essay
- To use interjections to add emphasis to ideas or emotions
- To interpret the message or meaning of a selection
- To interpret the messages in real-world images

Skills

LITERATURE
- Recognizing and analyzing writers' techniques for creating emphasis

GRAMMAR AND USAGE
- Using interjections
- Using inverted sentences

MEDIA LITERACY
- Interpreting media images

ORAL COMMUNICATION
- Giving peer feedback
- Group conferencing

CRITICAL THINKING
- Analyzing elements
- Synthesizing
- Analyzing
- Classifying

Teaching Strategy: MODELING

In the following models, the authors emphasize the message and meaning of their stories in different ways.

A Twain Encourage students to note that Twain emphasizes his message—love is worth more than money—by placing it at the end of this paragraph.

B Markham Possible responses: *overflows; spirit flares like fire; anger bursts; cries; shouts of warning, the ringing of chains and the cracking of leather; crowd leaps*. The language conveys the scene's violence, surprise, and excitement.

WRITING ABOUT LITERATURE

FINDING THE MESSAGE

What was *The Million-Pound Bank Note* really about? What made "The Splendid Outcast" splendid? Stories have messages, and uncovering them can help you understand and appreciate the stories. To find a story's message, notice the ways the writer emphasizes, or draws attention to, his or her ideas. On the next few pages, you will

- discover how writers emphasize a message
- write an interpretive essay on a story's message
- take a closer look at the messages around you

The Writer's Style: Creating Emphasis Writers emphasize their ideas in several ways—by using placement, vivid language, and repetition.

Read the Literature

Notice how these authors create emphasis.

Literature Models

A **Emphasis Through Placement**
An important message may appear at the beginning of a work or at the end, as it does in this example.

> Henry. Happy, we two? Indeed yes! And when London got the whole history of my adventure for a month, how it did talk. My Portia's father took the million-pound bank note to the Bank of England, cashed it, had it cancelled; and he gave it to us at our wedding. Framed, it now hangs in our home. It gave me my Portia; but for it I could not have remained in London, would not have appeared at the American ambassador's, never should have met her. And so I always say: Yes, it's a million-pounder, but it made but one purchase in its life and then got the article for only about a tenth part of its value.
>
> Mark Twain, from *The Million-Pound Bank Note*

B **Emphasis Through Vivid Language**
What examples of word choice make this scene vivid? What effect does the language have?

> But now, at the climax of the sale, his impatience overflows, his spirit flares like fire, his anger bursts through the circle of men who guard him. Suddenly, there are cries, shouts of warning, the ringing of chains and the cracking of leather, and the crowd leaps to its feet.
>
> Beryl Markham, from "The Splendid Outcast"

210   UNIT TWO: CRITICAL ADJUSTMENTS

PRINT AND MEDIA RESOURCES

UNIT TWO RESOURCE BOOK
The Writer's Style, p. 31
Prewriting Guide, p. 32
Elaboration, p. 33
Peer Response Guide, p. 34–35
Revising and Editing, p. 36
Student Model, p. 37
Rubric, p. 38

FORMAL ASSESSMENT
Guidelines for Writing Assessment

GRAMMAR MINI-LESSONS
Transparencies, pp. 7, 43
Copymasters, p. 7

WRITING MINI-LESSONS
Transparencies, p. 59

ACCESS FOR STUDENTS ACQUIRING ENGLISH
Reading and Writing Support

Connect to Music

Do you have favorite song lyrics that you know by heart? What is it about them that draws you to them? In the lyrics to a popular song below, the writers use repetition to get across a key idea.

Song Lyrics

> I see trees of green, red roses too,
> I see them bloom for me and you,
> and I think to myself
> What a wonderful world.
>
> I see skies of blue and clouds of white,
> the bright blessed day, the dark sacred night,
> and I think to myself
> What a wonderful world.
>
> — recorded by Louis Armstrong from "What a Wonderful World" written by George David Weiss and Bob Thiele

Emphasis Through Repetition
What words are repeated in this passage? What main idea does the repetition emphasize?

Try Your Hand: Creating Emphasis

1. **Describe a Scene** Write a paragraph describing a scene based on one of these situations: a race, a surprise party, a friend moving away. Emphasize the mood with vivid language.

2. **Write New Lyrics** Use the lyrics for "What a Wonderful World" above as a model. Think of a simple, short message you could repeat as a refrain. Then write song lyrics that emphasize your song's message.

3. **Revise a QuickWrite** Choose one of your QuickWrites or another piece of writing in which you tried to make a point or get across an important idea. Revise the piece, using placement, vivid language, or repetition for emphasis.

SkillBuilder

 GRAMMAR FROM WRITING

Using Interjections

An **interjection** is a word or group of words that can add emphasis to a sentence by expressing a feeling or emotion. An interjection that expresses strong emotion is followed by an exclamation point. One that expresses mild emotion is usually followed by a comma. Notice how this sentence changes when interjections are added.

I'm going to change my vote.

Wow! No way! Well, I'm going to change my vote.

Find the interjections in these lines from *The Million-Pound Bank Note* by Mark Twain. What emotional changes in the character are expressed by the interjections?

Tod. Thank you. (*A complete change. He stutters and fumbles.*) Ah—it's—ah—that is—we—ah—you see—It's— (*quickly*) Take it back, please. (*raising voice*) Mr. Smedley! Mr. Smedley! Help! Oh, Mr. Smedley.

APPLYING WHAT YOU'VE LEARNED
Rewrite these sentences. Use interjections to add emphasis.

1. I'm drowning.
2. I won't help you.
3. Where are you going?
4. I was only joking.

WRITING ABOUT LITERATURE **211**

Teaching Strategy: MODELING

C **Weiss and Thiele** Possible responses: *I see; of [color]; and I think to myself; what a wonderful world.* The repetition emphasizes the idea that the world is filled with colorful and marvelous things.

Try Your Hand

1. Responses will vary. Students' paragraphs should use vivid language—especially nouns, verbs, and precise adjectives and adverbs—to describe the mood.
2. Students' song lyrics should express a simple, straightforward idea. They should include at least one example of repetition but should not rely entirely on that repeated phrase to convey their message.
3. Encourage students to analyze their existing draft before they begin to revise. Ask them to identify the main idea of the writing and to decide which of the three techniques for emphasizing ideas would work best in this piece of writing.

SkillBuilder  GRAMMAR FROM WRITING

USING INTERJECTIONS Help students understand that overuse of interjections can reduce their effectiveness. Interjections are appropriate in a special circumstance—when a speaker is expressing an unusual amount of emotion or feeling. The interjections in the Twain excerpt are *"Ah," "Mr. Smedley!," "Help!,"* and *Oh,"*.

Applying What You've Learned Possible responses:
1. Help! I'm drowning!
2. No way, I won't help you. No! I won't help you.
3. Say, where are you going?
4. Aw, I was only joking.

Additional Suggestions You may wish to add these sentences to the exercise:
1. I won't stand for it.
2. Are you kidding me?

Reteaching/Reinforcement
Grammar Mini-Lessons transparencies, p. 43

 The Writer's Craft

Interjections, pp. 543–544

THE LANGUAGE OF LITERATURE TEACHER'S EDITION **211**

CUSTOMIZING FOR
Less-Proficient Writers

D Some students may be intimidated by the task of interpreting the meaning of a selection. Invite them to think in terms of their own responses to the literature rather than attempting to formulate a right answer. You might suggest that they think about how they would describe the selection to a friend. If the person asked them, "What is the story about?" how would they answer?

Critical Thinking:
SYNTHESIZING

E Remind students that some questions require them to think about two or more parts of a literary work. When readers do this, they are synthesizing information. Explain that interpreting the meaning of a selection requires synthesis because students must look at many different parts of the selection in order to infer and restate the writer's message.

WRITING ABOUT LITERATURE

Interpretation

You've studied some of the techniques writers use to create emphasis. Now you can use your knowledge of those techniques to uncover key ideas and meanings in literature.

GUIDED ASSIGNMENT

Interpret a Selection's Meaning For this assignment, you'll choose one selection and look for its message or meaning. You'll write your interpretation of the message and support it with details and examples from the selection.

❶ Prewrite and Explore

Which selection in this unit did you think about long after you finished reading it? Which led to the most interesting discussions with your friends or classmates? These may be clues as to which story carried the most powerful message for you. Choose a selection you would like to explore more deeply.

D

EXPLORING THE SELECTION

Reread the selection carefully, taking notes about your questions, your thoughts, and your interpretation of what is happening. You might use a chart like the one here to keep track of your thinking. Consider the following questions as you reread:

E

- What makes this selection intriguing?
- What parts of the selection are puzzling or unclear?
- What does the author seem to be emphasizing through placement, vivid language, or repetition?

Discuss your impressions and findings with others who chose the same selection. Keep in mind that your interpretation may differ from someone else's. You may need to reread all or parts of the selection to answer questions or to understand someone else's impressions.

Student's Prewriting Chart

Scenes from the Selection	My Interpretation or Thoughts
Two men give Henry a million-pound note.	The two men are betting on how people will react to the note.
Restaurant, clothing store, and hotel all give Henry credit.	Henry gets treated better just because he appears rich.
Henry helps Hastings sell his mine.	People trust Henry because he's rich and famous. Is this a fair judgment?
Gordon says if Henry had picked up the pear, they wouldn't have trusted him.	

Assessment ✓ Option

SELF-ASSESSMENT After students have completed the Exploring the Selection discussion, they should assess their understanding of the selection's message. Students might consider the following questions:

- Have I identified the important events of the selection? Does the author convey any important idea in the description of these events?

- Have I clarified any confusing passages and answered any outstanding questions that I had?
- Have I noted the way the author uses vivid language, repetition, or placement to emphasize a particular idea?

---

212 THE LANGUAGE OF LITERATURE TEACHER'S EDITION

2 Write and Analyze a Discovery Draft

Once you have reread and discussed the selection, write a discovery draft to help sort through your ideas. Explore these questions as you write.

- Which parts of the selection seem to tell me something?
- Which details or events still puzzle me? How important are these puzzling parts?

Student's Discovery Draft

I wonder if the gentlemen judged Henry fairly when they chose him.

The gentlemen say they picked Henry because he seemed intelligent and honest. Why did they think so? One of the men says it's because he didn't pick the pear up boldly. But Henry was just about to do that.

One thing that keeps happening is that Henry gets stuff free when he waves that bank note around. The clothing store salesman is rude to him until he sees the note. Then the store gives him a whole wardrobe for free. Also, the hotel gives him a luxury room, and the restaurant feeds him. Everyone says he shouldn't worry about paying them back.

Maybe the story's message is something about the way people treat the rich and the poor.

3 Draft and Share

Remember that the message you discovered may not be the same as someone else's. Look back through your notes for supporting details to use as you write your draft. See the SkillBuilder at the right for help in organizing your essay. Then use these questions to get feedback from other students.

PEER RESPONSE

- Restate what you think my interpretation is.
- What other details would support my ideas?

SkillBuilder

WRITER'S CRAFT

Organizing Your Interpretive Essay

A well-organized interpretive essay will make it easy for readers to understand your thinking. Your interpretive essay should include the following sections:

- An introduction that gives the author and title and familiarizes your reader with the selection. You don't need to tell the whole story. Just give a brief summary of the work.
- A body that states your interpretation of the message supported with details from the selection.
- A conclusion that summarizes your interpretation and the reasons for it.

APPLYING WHAT YOU'VE LEARNED

Evaluate your draft against the guidelines above. Make sure you have an introduction, a body, and a conclusion and that your writing is clear and easy to follow.

WRITING HANDBOOK

For help in writing introductions and conclusions, see pages 826; 834–835 of the Writing Handbook.

Writing Skill: ELABORATION

 The Discovery Draft gives students a chance to explore their own ideas and to sort through the information they gathered. Encourage them to identify any scenes or passages that seem to contain a "message." Remind them to put in their own words what they think the message is. Students should elaborate their points by using any of the scene's details that support their interpretation.

Invite students to pursue any details that they don't understand as they write. Thinking about these details may help them discover a variation on the writer's message or a new way of looking at their own interpretation.

Teaching Strategy:
USING THE SKILLBUILDER

 You can help students write their interpretation of a selection's message by teaching the SkillBuilder on Organizing Your Interpretive Essay at this time. This SkillBuilder helps students understand how to shape their essay into an introduction, a body, and a conclusion.

Teaching Strategy:
STUMBLING BLOCK

Students often have trouble getting started writing. If the idea of writing an introduction is intimidating, they might want to write the body of the essay first and then go back and write the introduction.

SkillBuilder — WRITER'S CRAFT

ORGANIZING YOUR INTERPRETIVE ESSAY Remind students that organization is as important in an interpretive essay as it is in an expository essay.

Explain that the introduction gives the reader a sense of what he or she will be reading about. The essay's body contains the writer's ideas about the selection. The conclusion briefly reviews the ideas in the essay.

Applying What You've Learned Encourage students to check that they express a clear interpretation of the selection in this section. Remind them also to look for supporting details and examples in the body of the essay. Then they can check their introductory and concluding paragraphs.

Additional Suggestions Have students draft outlines that indicate the elements included in the introduction, body, and conclusion of their essays.

Reteaching/Reinforcement
Writing Mini-Lessons transparencies, p. 59

Outlining, pp. 200, 683

Critical Thinking: ANALYZING

I To evaluate and revise their essays, students should check that their introduction is clear, the examples support the main idea, and that the word placement and sentence structure are varied.

Teaching Strategy: MODELING

J Discuss with students how this sample meets the Standards for Evaluation on this page. The first sentence of the first paragraph gives the author and title, and the following four sentences provide a brief summary of the play. In the final sentence of the first paragraph, the writer states the main point that the essay will explore. The second paragraph offers two or three sentences of support for the main idea. The final sentence summarizes it for the reader.

Standards for Evaluation

Ideas and Content
- Gives the author, title, and brief summary of the literature
- Explains what the writer thinks a passage means
- Is supported with quotes, reasons, and other evidence
- Shows why the writer thinks the passage is important

Structure and Form
- Uses well-organized paragraphs and a clear organization.
- Includes transitional words and phrases to show relationships among ideas
- Uses a variety of sentence structures

Grammar, Usage, and Mechanics
- Contains no more than two or three minor errors in grammar and usage
- Contains no more than two or three minor errors in spelling, capitalization, and punctuation

---

WRITING ABOUT LITERATURE

4 Revise and Edit

I Before revising, reflect on your draft. Have you explained the selection's meaning clearly? Have you supported your ideas with enough details and examples? Use your peer comments and the Standards for Evaluation below as you finalize your draft.

Student's Final Draft

The Million-Pound Bank Note by Mark Twain tells the story of a young broker's clerk named Henry. Henry finds himself in London without money or friends. Two elderly gentlemen bet on whether he can survive a month with nothing but a million-pound bank note. Henry finds out that trying to cash the note would land him in prison. Instead, he uses the note just to make people think he is rich. In this story, Twain shows how the way people treat someone depends on whether the person appears to be rich or poor.

What information makes the essay topic clear? What main point will the essay make?

What evidence supports the statement made in the first sentence of this paragraph?

Henry is treated much differently as a poor man than he is as a rich one. When he enters a clothing store in rags, the clerk speaks to him rudely. "We don't give away suits, even misfits," says the clerk. When Henry displays the million-pound note, the salesmen suddenly fall all over themselves trying to please him. While they wouldn't give away a useless suit to a ragged man, they offer a millionaire a complete wardrobe for nothing.

Standards for Evaluation

An interpretive essay
- has an introduction that gives the author, title, and a brief summary of the selection
- has a logical organization and a clear focus
- summarizes the interpretation in its conclusion
- supports its interpretation with reasons, examples, quotations, or other evidence

---

Assessment Option

SELF-ASSESSMENT Students can assess their own writing by asking themselves the following questions:
- *What selection am I discussing?*
- *Have I clearly explained my interpretation of the story's message?*
- *Have I discussed how the writer has emphasized the selection's message, and have I elaborated on these points?*
- *Have I clearly summarized my points in my conclusion?*

Grammar in Context

Subject-Verb Agreement Whenever you interpret literature, you are likely to be discussing several characters and events. As you write, keep in mind the rules of subject-verb agreement. The subject and the verb in a sentence must agree in number. If the subject is singular, the verb should be singular. If the subject is plural, the verb should be plural as well.

> Sir Alfred, as well as many other wealthy men, trust [trusts] Henry's opinion of the mine because he thinks he is rich. One of the men invite [invites] his friends to invest. Henry and Hastings becomes [become] rich.

As in the example above, be careful that the verb agrees with its subject, not with the nearest noun. The verb and its subject may be separated by other words or phrases.

Try Your Hand: Subject-Verb Agreement

Imagine that the following article appeared in the local newspaper. Read the article, and then use a separate sheet of paper to correct any subject-verb agreement problems.

Vest-Pocket Millionaire Takes London by Storm

London's Miss Portia Langham and Henry Adams, better known as the Vest-Pocket Millionaire, is happily married. They met after Miss Langham's stepfather, Gordon Featherstone, and his younger brother, Abel, chose Adams for a now-famous experiment. The elder of the brothers are quick to praise Adams's cleverness. He says that both he and his brother is impressed by the 200,000 pounds Adams raised without ever cashing the million-pound bank note.

Miss Portia Langham, granddaughter of the Cambridge Langhams, agree with her stepfather, Gordon. "My family and I am so proud of Henry," she says.

SkillBuilder

GRAMMAR FROM WRITING

Using Inverted Sentences
In most sentences, the subject comes before the verb. In sentences with inverted order, the verb comes before the subject. The rules of subject-verb agreement still apply, however. For example:

In the park were two trees.

First, look for the verb. (*were*) Ask yourself who or what goes with the verb. What was in the park? (*two trees*) Then put the sentence in its natural order to check the subject-verb agreement. (*Two trees were in the park.*)

APPLYING WHAT YOU'VE LEARNED

Copy the sentences below in your journal or on a sheet of paper. Be sure the subject and verb in each sentence agree. Then check the subject-verb agreement in your draft.

1. Abel said, "There is several honest men in London."
2. Through Henry's recommendation comes investors for the gold mine.
3. In Portia's lovely hands rest Henry's future.

GRAMMAR HANDBOOK

For more information on inverted sentences and subject-verb agreement, see pages 863, 866–869 of the Grammar Handbook.

WRITING ABOUT LITERATURE 215

CUSTOMIZING FOR
Students Acquiring English

Before you introduce this page, make sure that students understand that subjects, and verbs must agree in number. Point out that verbs in the present tense have endings that show whether they are singular or plural.

Teaching Strategy: USING THE SKILLBUILDER

You can help students familiarize themselves with sentence constructions that often pose problems involving subject-verb agreement by teaching the SkillBuilder on Using Inverted Sentences.

Critical Thinking: ANALYZING

Have students explain the rationale for each of the corrections in the sample. (*Possible responses: first change—the subject, "Sir Alfred," is singular, so the singular verb "trusts" is correct; second change—the subject, "one," is singular, so the singular verb "invites" is correct; third change—the subject, "Henry and Hastings," is plural, so the plural verb "become" is correct.*)

Try Your Hand

Corrections: *Millionaire,* <u>are</u> *happily married*

elder of the brothers <u>is</u> *quick to praise*

he and his brother <u>are</u> *impressed*

Cambridge Langhams, <u>agrees</u> *with her stepfather*

My family and I <u>are</u> *so proud*

SkillBuilder — GRAMMAR FROM WRITING

USING INVERTED SENTENCES Point out to students that inverting the order of the subject and verb is fairly unusual in declarative sentences. However, it is extremely common in questions. In fact, most questions are phrased with the verb preceding the subject.

Applying What You've Learned

1. Abel said, "There <u>are</u> several honest men in London."
2. Through Henry's recommendation <u>come</u> investors for the gold mine.
3. In Portia's lovely hands <u>rests</u> Henry's future.

Additional Suggestions Have students correct the subject-verb agreement in these sentences.
1. *Lying in the gutter were a pear.* (<u>was</u>)
2. *Comfortable is the lives of Gordon and Abel Featherstone.* (<u>are</u>)
3. *To the bank race Henry.* (<u>races</u>)

Reteaching/Reinforcement

Grammar Mini-Lessons copymasters p. 7, transparencies, p.7

The Writer's Craft

Inverted Sentences, p 584

READING THE WORLD

On pages 210–215 students explored how to identify and interpret the message in a literary work. They should also be aware that they are surrounded by messages everywhere they look and that interpreting these messages is very similar to interpreting literature. In this lesson, students will interpret messages that appear in the media and other aspects of the real world.

Critical Thinking: CLASSIFYING

N Students might note how the differences between elements in the photograph are conveyed in its composition. For instance, the soldiers, with their uniforms and guns, are on the left and top of the photo. The young people, wearing casual clothes and bearing flowers, are in the lower right-hand portion of the photo. In this composition, the soldiers are given more space in the photo. Some students also may note how prominently the guns figure in the photo.

Media Literacy: INTERPRETING A PHOTOGRAPH

O Possible responses: There is a stand-off between a group of soldiers and a group of young people. The soldiers are sending the message that they are armed and powerful. The space they take up in the photo suggests an overwhelming force faced by the young people. By placing flowers in the policemen's gun barrels, the young person in the sweater seems to be sending a message of nonviolence.

Speaking and Listening: GROUP DISCUSSION

P Have students work in groups to discuss their interpretations. Remind students to elaborate on their points by referring to specific details from the photograph.

READING THE WORLD

WHAT'S THE MESSAGE?

Messages are sent to us every day—on television, in magazines, in school. These messages may be words, images, even actions. Some are direct, some subtle. It's important to be aware of these possibilities so you don't miss anything.

N **View** Take notes on the details you see in this photograph. What kinds of contrasts can you find here?

O **Interpret** What's going on? What are the messages and meanings? Who is sending a message? If there is more than one message, do the messages agree?

P **Discuss** Share your ideas about the messages with your group. Discuss how different messages are possible here. Then look at the SkillBuilder at the right for more help in finding the messages in the real world.

SkillBuilder

 CRITICAL THINKING

Analyzing for Meaning
When you analyze something, you can begin by identifying separate elements. In this picture, the separate elements include the military police, their guns, the young man in the sweater, the people with him, the flowers, and his gesture of placing a flower in a gun.

Once you've identified what you feel are the most important elements, you can begin to analyze each element for meaning. Start listing words and phrases you associate with each element. For the military police, you might list *combat, uniform, defend,* and so on. When you have a similar list for each element, review each list for meanings and messages. As you look over all your lists, look for an overall meaning or message. You may find that your analysis has led you to new insights.

APPLYING WHAT YOU'VE LEARNED
With a small group, discuss one of the following items.

- Find and discuss an ad that sends both visual and verbal messages. Explain how the messages are alike or different from each other.
- Where else can you use what you've learned here about interpreting messages?

READING THE WORLD 217

SkillBuilder CRITICAL THINKING

ANALYZING ELEMENTS Encourage students to brainstorm associations with each of the elements in the photograph. You might wish to have them brainstorm as a class, in small groups, or in pairs. Invite them to put into words the meaning of the action of the person placing the flowers in the gun barrel. Ask them for their opinions about the perspective of the photographer. Ask if they think the photographer supports the young man or the police. Encourage them to explain their answers.

Applying What You've Learned
- Encourage students to analyze the elements of the image and express its meaning in a single sentence. Then have them put the meaning of the text into their own words. Invite them to compare and contrast the messages.
- Students might mention such everyday activities as reading or watching advertisements, watching the news, watching music videos, or spending time on the Internet.

UNIT TWO
Part 2 Lesson Planner

TIME ALLOTMENTS SHOWN ARE APPROXIMATE. DEPENDING ON YOUR GOALS AND THE NEEDS OF YOUR STUDENTS, YOU MAY WISH TO ALLOW MORE OR LESS TIME FOR CERTAIN PORTIONS OF THE LESSON.

Table of Contents	Discussion	Previewing the Selection	Reading the Selection
PART OPENER **UNEXPECTED DEVELOPMENTS** What Do You Think? page 218	**20 MINUTES** • Reflect on the part theme		
SELECTION A Mother in Mannville page 220 AVERAGE		**20 MINUTES** • PERSONAL CONNECTION • HISTORICAL CONNECTION • READING CONNECTION: Visualizing	**20 MINUTES** • Introduce vocabulary • Read pp. 220–224 (5 pp.)
SELECTION White Mice page 229 CHALLENGING		**20 MINUTES** • PERSONAL CONNECTION • LANGUAGE ARTS CONNECTION • READING CONNECTION: Predicting	**40 MINUTES** • Introduce vocabulary • Read pp. 229–237 (9 pp.)
SELECTION The Bet page 242 AVERAGE		**20 MINUTES** • PERSONAL CONNECTION • HISTORICAL CONNECTION • READING CONNECTION: Cause and effect	**30 MINUTES** • Introduce vocabulary • Read pp. 242–248 (7 pp.)
SELECTION from Once Upon a Time When We Were Colored page 253 AVERAGE		**20 MINUTES** • PERSONAL CONNECTION • HISTORICAL CONNECTION • WRITING CONNECTION	**20 MINUTES** • Introduce vocabulary • Read pp. 253–256 (4 pp.)
SELECTION The Home Front: 1941–1945 page 260 AVERAGE		**20 MINUTES** • PERSONAL CONNECTION • HISTORICAL CONNECTION • READING CONNECTION: Questioning	**25 MINUTES** • Introduce vocabulary • Read pp. 260–264 (5 pp.)
SELECTIONS my enemy was dreaming Lost page 268 CHALLENGING		**20 MINUTES** • PERSONAL CONNECTION • HISTORICAL CONNECTION • READING CONNECTION: Free verse	**15 MINUTES** • Read pp. 268–269 (2 pp.)
Writing	Exploring Topics	Prewriting	Drafting and Revising
WRITING FROM EXPERIENCE Narrative and Literary Writing	**20 MINUTES**	**25 MINUTES**	**80 MINUTES**

Time estimates assume in-class work. You may wish to assign some of these stages as homework.

Responding to the Selection

FROM PERSONAL RESPONSE TO CRITICAL ANALYSIS	OR	ANOTHER PATHWAY	LITERARY CONCEPTS	QUICKWRITES
		40 MINUTES		
• Discussion questions	OR	• Group discussion	• Conflict • Setting	• Personal ad • Epilogue • Poem
		45 MINUTES		
• Discussion questions	OR	• Dramatization	• Surprise ending • Theme	• Rewrite • Narrative
		40 MINUTES		
• Discussion questions	OR	• Character chart	• Flashback • Climax	• Diary entries • Graffiti
		35 MINUTES		
• Discussion questions	OR	• Emotions graph	• Autobiography	• Dialogue • Paragraphs
		40 MINUTES		
• Discussion questions	OR	• Poster	• Memoir	• Paragraph • Encyclopedia entry • Radio/TV Public Service Announcement
		30 MINUTES		
• Discussion questions	OR	• Role-play	• Mood	• Stanza • Character analysis

Extension Activities

ALTERNATIVE ACTIVITIES	LITERARY LINKS	CRITIC'S CORNER	THE WRITER'S STYLE	ACROSS THE CURRICULUM	ART CONNECTION	WORDS TO KNOW	BIOGRAPHY
40 MINUTES							
	✓				✓	✓	
35 MINUTES							✓
✓	✓				✓		
50 MINUTES							
✓	✓			SOCIAL STUDIES / MATH	✓	✓	✓
60 MINUTES							
✓			✓	SOCIAL STUDIES		✓	✓
40 MINUTES							
✓				SOCIAL STUDIES		✓	✓
20 MINUTES							
✓				SOCIAL STUDIES			✓

Publishing and Reflecting

30 MINUTES

UNIT TWO
Part 2 Cooperative Project

Life's Little Surprises

Overview

Students will design a board game that assigns good and bad conditions randomly as participants play the game.

PROJECT AT A GLANCE

The selections in Unit Two, Part 2 show the unpredictability of life and how people can be forced to change even their best-laid plans. For this project, students will create, design, produce, and play a board game that reflects this unpredictability. Students will work in small groups to find a setting for the game, choose a goal, and create a pathway to the goal. They will then add stumbling blocks and helpful events that might change the players' courses through the game. Final versions of the games can be played by classmates or other students in the school.

OBJECTIVES
- To recognize that unexpected developments can create the need for change
- To design and create a board game that mimics the unpredictability of life
- To exchange and play the games produced by other groups

SUGGESTED GROUP SIZE
4–6 students

MATERIALS
- 1 large sheet of poster board per group
- Index cards (about 20 per group)
- Small objects for use as markers (buttons, stones, and so on)
- Art supplies (rulers, pencils, paints, markers)
- Spinners or number cubes (1 spinner or 2 number cubes per group)
- Commercial board games (optional)

1 Getting Started

Arranging the Project
Assemble all the supplies students will need to use during the project. You will need to find a place for groups to work on the artistic portion of the project. If students have art supplies at home, you might allow them to take the project home, providing all group members can still participate. If all work must be done in school, schedule time for students to work in an appropriate room, or limit materials to those that can be easily cleaned up and stored.

You will also need to schedule a place where students can play the completed games. Card tables would be ideal, but desks pushed together or larger tables can also be used. If possible, arrange a separate table for each game.

Arranging for Playing the Games
Decide how you would like the groups to share their games. If they will try out the games in the classroom, you will have little to do except rearrange a bit of furniture. If they will share the games with other students, or if there will be a full-fledged round-robin game period, you will want to arrange for the class (or classes) to meet in a larger room with appropriate playing surfaces. Tournament or elimination play might be interesting with some of the games, in which case you should make a wall chart to keep track of winners.

2 Creating the Games

Introducing the Project
Explain that students will be working in small groups to create, design, produce, and play a board game that reflects the unpredictability of life. They will decide on a general life goal and will create a path toward that goal. An integral part of play is the element of chance, which may result in good things happening to the participant or may result in serious setbacks. The game should be thoughtfully laid out on a sheet of poster board and artistically decorated. A full set of rules covering all possible situations should be written in language that all participants can understand.

If you have brought in commercial board games to show as examples, allow students time to examine them. Invite students to point out how each makes use of unpredictable events to keep the game interesting. Students who have played these games can share recollections of games that included surprises for them or for an opponent.

Discuss with students the various elements of the games that are controlled by the player and those that are not. Note that the uncontrolled events in the game contain both good and bad elements.

Group Investigations
Divide students into groups of four or five (four is better for most board games). Groups will work together to set a game goal and to make suggestions about the kinds of events that might help or a hinder attaining that goal. Stress that games' goals and events should be fairly realistic. For example, more than one "You have won the Lottery" card is probably unrealistic.

Encourage groups to decorate the game boards and to be inventive about markers and surprise cards or spaces. Remind them that people play games for fun.

Creating a Project Description
After each group has set the game goal and decided on a path and a set of "surprises," they should write a brief summary describing the game and how it is played. You can use these summaries to scan for obvious flaws in the planning or to make suggestions that would help the game move faster or be more fun to play. Meet with each group after reading their summary and discuss how they plan to create the actual game board.

OPTION 1: WILL YOU GET OUT OF SCHOOL? Students can create a game set in high school that has graduation as its goal. Surprises can range from a "You've got a pop quiz in science class!" to "You've just made the varsity team!" All elements should have a basis in school life. Groups can personalize the game further by mentioning teachers, principals, and actual school events.

OPTION 2: AN ADVENTURE GAME Students might enjoy creating an adventure game that is still set in reality. While the goal might be something along the line of "climbing the Matterhorn," surprises should be events ranging from "Oops! Your piton came loose!" to "Congratulations! You have found shelter for the night in a cave." Bigfoot should not be in the picture.

OPTION 3: YOUNGSTERS OR OLDSTERS Groups can design games for young children or senior citizens. Encourage them to arrange to play their game at the children's ward of a local hospital or at a senior citizens' center. They may want to donate their game to the institution.

3 Sharing the Games

Although this project can culminate in game play within your class, it would be nice to share the games with others. Your class could challenge another class or just invite them to visit for a bit of game playing. At least allow groups to examine and try out each others' games. Discuss the games as a class, having students point out some of the surprise events in each and how they might affect play. Game boards can be displayed for the entire school to view.

Assessing the Project

The following rubric can be used for group or individual assessment.

3 Full Accomplishment Students follow directions and design, create, and make a board game that reflects some of life's unexpected developments.

2 Substantial Accomplishment Students produce a board game, but the game does not reflect the uncertainties in life, or the rules of play are indefinite.

1 Little or Partial Accomplishment Students' game is incomplete or does not fulfill the requirements of the assignment.

For the Portfolio
Your written assessment of the project should be copied and placed in each student's portfolio. You might also insert a copy of the project description or the written rules of the game. The games themselves can be placed in individual boxes and kept in the classroom for further play. At the end of the year, they may be returned to students or placed in the library.

Note: For other assessment options, see the *Teacher's Guide to Assessment and Portfolio Use*.

Cross-Curricular Options

SOCIAL STUDIES
Students interested in history can create a game set in another time period. Ask them to research what life was like in the selected era and to establish goals and events that are true to the times.

LANGUAGE ARTS
Have students write a description of a trip through the game board from the marker's point of view.

HEALTH AND SAFETY
Ask students to center the game on finding and maintaining good health. Events such as "Great news! You have lost 5 pounds!" and "Too bad! You're sitting next to a smoker at lunch!" might be included as surprises.

MEDIA
Challenge students to design a video game. They can outline how the game works, write its rules, and create their own playing strategies.

Resources

Ultimate Unauthorized Nintendo Game Strategies by Corey Sanderland and Tom Badgett gives tips to over 100 games.

PART 2

WHAT DO YOU THINK?

Objectives

The activities on this page can be used to
- introduce the Part 2 theme, "Unexpected Developments," since each activity is connected to one or more of the selections in Part 2
- create materials for students' personal portfolios that they can later reconsider or revise
- build an understanding of theme that can be reviewed and revised as students progress through the unit

What would you do?
Have students generate a list of events they might experience in a war, as well as possible ways of dealing with these events. Students can use this list to help them develop their diary entries. You may wish to have students read firsthand accounts of life during wartime, such as *The Diary of Anne Frank* or *Zlata's Diary*. (See "The Home Front: 1941–1945," p. 259.)

What would you argue?
Encourage students to write a brief outline of the arguments they will use in their editorial. Suggest that they read some newspaper editorials to get a sense of the style and tone used in an editorial. (See "White Mice," p. 228, and "The Bet," p. 240.)

What if . . .
Have students list important events or turning points to use in their flow charts. Encourage students to spend time imagining how their lives would have turned out if each turning point or event had not occurred. To extend this activity, you may wish to have students write brief "alternative" autobiographies in which they talk about "what might have been." (See "A Mother in Mannville," p. 219, and the excerpt from *Once Upon a Time When We Were Colored*, p. 252. All selections in Part 2 can be connected to this activity.)

UNIT TWO **PART 2**

UNEXPECTED DEVELOPMENTS

WHAT DO You THINK?

REFLECTING ON THEME

Life is unpredictable—people are often faced with unexpected developments. Use the activities on this page to help you examine how unexpected developments push human beings to make critical changes in their lives. Keep a record of your impressions, ideas, and results in your notebook.

What would you argue?
Strong feelings about a cause can inspire people to make critical changes in their lives. Is there any cause you feel especially enthusiastic about, like saving endangered species or improving the quality of television? Write a newspaper editorial that argues the important points of your case.

What would you do?
War demands that people make swift adjustments in their lives. If war broke out, how would you feel? Try to imagine what might go on around you in a war. Present your response in a series of diary entries.

What if . . .
Life is full of twists and turns. Think back to an important turning point in your life. Imagine how things might have been different if that event had not happened. Design a flow chart like the one at left, showing what really occurred and what might have been.

Looking Back
At the beginning of this unit, you thought about ways in which people make critical adjustments in their lives. After reading the selections in Part 1, do you have a better sense of the kinds of choices people make when their circumstances change? Recall the characters' twinges of conscience. For each major character in Part 1, think of one word that best describes what troubles his or her conscience.

Looking Back
Suggest that students create a chart in which they list each major character in the Part 1 selections and describe what troubles the conscience of that character. You may wish to have students write a short summary of each selection to help them organize their thoughts about each character.

COMMUNITY OUTREACH
Invite physical therapists from your local hospital to speak to students about the critical changes people must make in their lives after unexpected accidents or illnesses. These guest speakers can help students think about the challenges that seriously injured people must face.

PREVIEWING

FICTION

A Mother in Mannville
Marjorie Kinnan Rawlings

Activating Prior Knowledge
PERSONAL CONNECTION

The main characters in this story are a lonely orphan boy and a writer who seeks time alone. What do you think is the difference between being lonely and being alone? Using examples from your own life and the lives of people you know, discuss the differences in meaning with your classmates. Use a chart like the one shown to help you organize your thoughts.

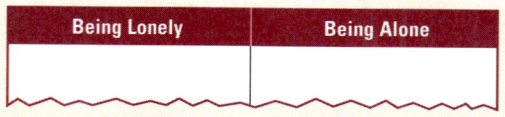

Being Lonely	Being Alone

HISTORICAL CONNECTION
Building Background

This story takes place in the North Carolina mountains, near an orphanage. An orphanage is an institution for the care of children who are alone because their parents have died, have abandoned them, or can no longer care for them. Orphanages for large groups of children were more prevalent in the past than they are today. Nowadays, orphaned children are often cared for by foster families until permanent adoptive families are found. When neither foster nor adoptive parents are available, children are placed in group homes, where small numbers of children are cared for by professionals.

An orphan boy at a New York mission repairs toys for the young, December, 1948. UPI/Bettmann.

Active Reading/Setting A Purpose
READING CONNECTION

Visualizing You can enjoy a story more when you picture its characters, setting, and events. When you use descriptive details to form a picture in your mind as you read, you are visualizing. "A Mother in Mannville" contains vivid description of the isolated setting. As you read, visualize the details of the surroundings. Think about why the narrator, a writer, might have chosen such a setting in which to work. You might sketch a few of your mental pictures in your notebook.

 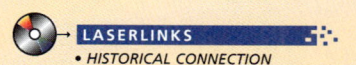
LASERLINKS
• HISTORICAL CONNECTION

OVERVIEW
Objectives

- To understand and appreciate a short story about the relationship between a woman and an orphan boy she employs
- To understand visualizing strategies
- To identify and understand conflict
- To express understanding of the short story through a choice of writing forms, including a personal ad, an epilogue, and a poem
- To extend understanding of the story through a variety of multimodal and cross-curricular activities

Skills

READING SKILLS/STRATEGIES	GRAMMAR
• Visualizing	• Compound sentences
LITERARY CONCEPTS	**SPELLING**
• Conflict	• Spelling hard and soft c
• Motivation	
THE WRITER'S STYLE	**SPEAKING, LISTENING, AND VIEWING**
• Tone	• Group discussion
	• Oral presentation

Cross-Curricular Connections

SCIENCE	MEDIA
• The flora of Carolina	• *Cross Creek*

HISTORICAL CONNECTION
Orphanages These photographs of orphans engaging in daily activities and going on special outings will help students comprehend what life in an orphanage was like at the beginning of the 20th century.

Side A, Frame 52651

ALTERNATIVE
Previewing

Instead of writing their impressions of the differences between being lonely and being alone, students can choose partners and discuss their opinions.

Personal Connection

Discussion Prompts Think of times when you have either felt lonely or wanted to be alone. Using as much detail as possible, describe your feelings to your partner and then listen as your partner describes his or her experiences. The following questions might help you get started:

- Where were you when you felt lonely?
- Were you with other people or alone?
- How did being lonely make you feel?

PRINT AND MEDIA RESOURCES

UNIT TWO RESOURCE BOOK
Strategic Reading: Literature, p. 41
Vocabulary SkillBuilder, p. 44
Reading SkillBuilder, p. 42
Spelling SkillBuilder, p. 43

GRAMMAR MINI-LESSONS
Transparencies, p. 46
Copymasters, p. 37

WRITING MINI-LESSONS
Transparencies, p. 26

ACCESS FOR STUDENTS ACQUIRING ENGLISH
Selection Summaries
Reading and Writing Support

FORMAL ASSESSMENT
Selection Test, pp. 41–42
 Test Generator

AUDIO LIBRARY
See Reference Card

 LASERLINKS
Historical Connection

A Mother in Mannville

by Marjorie Kinnan Rawlings

The orphanage is high in the Carolina mountains. Sometimes in winter the snowdrifts are so deep that the institution is cut off from the village below, from all the world. Fog hides the mountain peaks, the snow swirls down the valleys, and a wind blows so bitterly that the orphanage boys who take the milk twice daily to the baby cottage reach the door with fingers stiff in an agony of numbness.

"Or when we carry trays from the cook house for the ones that are sick," Jerry said, "we get our faces frostbit, because we can't put our hands over them. I have gloves," he added. "Some of the boys don't have any."

He liked the late spring, he said. The rhododendron was in bloom, a carpet of color, across the mountainsides, soft as the May winds that stirred the hemlocks. He called it laurel.

"It's pretty when the laurel blooms," he said. "Some of it's pink and some of it's white."

I was there in the autumn. I wanted quiet, isolation, to do some troublesome writing. I wanted mountain air to blow out the malaria from too long a time in the subtropics. I was homesick, too, for the flaming of maples in October, and for corn shocks and pumpkins and black-walnut trees and the lift of hills. I found them all, living in a cabin that belonged to the orphanage, half a mile beyond the orphanage farm. When I took the cabin, I asked for a boy or man to come and chop wood for the fireplace. The first few days were warm, I found what wood I needed about the cabin, no one came, and I forgot the order.

I looked up from my typewriter one late afternoon, a little startled. A boy stood at the door, and my pointer dog, my companion, was at his side and had not barked to warn me. The boy was probably twelve years old, but undersized. He wore overalls and a torn shirt, and was barefooted.

He said, "I can chop some wood today."

I said, "But I have a boy coming from the orphanage."

"I'm the boy."

"You? But you're small."

"Size don't matter, chopping wood," he said. "Some of the big boys don't chop good. I've been chopping wood at the orphanage a long time."

220 UNIT TWO PART 2: UNEXPECTED DEVELOPMENTS

WORDS TO KNOW

blunt (blŭnt) *adj.* abrupt; rudely straightforward or honest (p. 221)

clarity (klăr´ĭ-tē) *n.* the quality of being easily seen; clearness (p. 221)

communion (kə-myōōn´yən) *n.* close relationship in which deep feelings are shared; intimacy (p. 222)

ecstasy (ĕk´stə-sē) *n.* intense joy or delight; bliss (p. 225)

impel (ĭm-pĕl´) *v.* to drive, force, or urge to action (p. 223)

inadequate (ĭn-ăd´ĭ-kwĭt) *adj.* not good enough for what is needed (p. 221)

instinctive (ĭn-stĭngk´tĭv) *adj.* having a natural tendency; spontaneous (p. 222)

kindling (kĭnd´lĭng) *n.* pieces of dry wood or other material that can be easily lighted to start a fire; tinder (p. 221)

I visualized mangled and <u>inadequate</u> branches for my fires. I was well into my work and not inclined to conversation. I was a little <u>blunt</u>.

"Very well. There's the ax. Go ahead and see what you can do."

I went back to work, closing the door. At first, the sound of the boy dragging brush annoyed me. Then he began to chop. The blows were rhythmic and steady, and shortly I had forgotten him, the sound no more of an interruption than a consistent rain. I suppose an hour and a half passed, for when I stopped and stretched, and heard the boy's steps on the cabin stoop, the sun was dropping behind the farthest mountain, and the valleys were purple with something deeper than the asters.

The boy said, "I have to go to supper now. I can come again tomorrow evening."

I said, "I'll pay you now for what you've done," thinking I should probably have to insist on an older boy. "Ten cents an hour?"

"Anything is all right."

We went together back of the cabin. An astonishing amount of solid wood had been cut. There were cherry logs and heavy roots of rhododendron, and blocks from the waste pine and oak left from the building of the cabin.

"But you've done as much as a man," I said. "This is a splendid pile."

B I looked at him, actually, for the first time. His hair was the color of the corn shocks, and his eyes, very direct, were like the mountain sky when rain is pending—gray, with a shadowing of that miraculous blue. As I spoke, a light came over him, as though the setting sun had touched him with the same suffused glory with which it touched the mountains. I gave him a quarter.

"You may come tomorrow," I said, "and thank you very much."

He looked at me, and at the coin, and seemed to want to speak, but could not, and turned away.

"I'll split <u>kindling</u> tomorrow," he said over his thin ragged shoulder. "You'll need kindling and medium wood and logs and backlogs."

At daylight I was half wakened by the sound of chopping. Again it was so even in texture that I went back to sleep. When I left my bed in the cool morning, the boy had come and gone, and a stack of kindling was neat against the cabin wall. He came again after school in the afternoon and worked until time to return to the orphanage. His name was Jerry; he was twelve years old, and he had been at the orphanage since he was four. I could picture him at four, with the same grave gray-blue eyes and the same—independence? No, the word that comes to me is "integrity."

C The word means something very special to me, and the quality for which I use it is a rare one. My father had it—there is another of whom I am almost sure—but almost no man of my acquaintance possesses it with the <u>clarity</u>, the purity, the simplicity of a mountain stream. But the boy Jerry had it. It is bedded on courage, but it is more than brave. It is honest, but it is more than honesty. The ax handle broke one day. Jerry said the wood shop at the orphanage would repair it. I brought money to pay for the job, and he refused it.

"I'll pay for it," he said. "I broke it. I brought the ax down careless."

D "But no one hits accurately every time," I told him. "The fault was in the wood of the handle. I'll see the man from whom I bought it."

It was only then that he would take the money. He was standing back of his own carelessness. He was a free-will agent, and he

WORDS TO KNOW	**inadequate** (ĭn-ăd′ĭ-kwĭt) *adj.* not good enough for what is needed **blunt** (blŭnt) *adj.* abrupt; rudely straightforward or honest **kindling** (kĭnd′lĭng) *n.* pieces of dry wood or other material that can be easily lighted to start a fire; tinder **clarity** (klăr′ĭ-tē) *n.* the quality of being easily seen; clearness

Art Note

Gathering Autumn Leaves by Winslow Homer Homer (1836–1910) was a U.S. painter and pictorial journalist who covered the Civil War for *Harper's Weekly*. In this painting, much of the work's drama is conveyed by the natural scene in the background. Homer contrasts this thick, heavy imagery with the boy's slight figure and the single maple branch he holds.

Reading the Art *In your opinion, what kind of person is the boy in this painting? Why do you feel this way?*

Active Reading: CLARIFY

E Ask students what the narrator says is done "only by the great of heart"? *("the unnecessary thing, the gracious thing")* Have students give examples of how Jerry demonstrates these acts. *(he puts dry wood in a cubbyhole; he steadies a loose stone)*

CUSTOMIZING FOR
Students Acquiring English

1 Ask students why "medium" is in quotation marks in this sentence. *(Possible response: It is Jerry's own term for a certain-size log.)* Ask them to think of another way quotation marks are used. *(in dialogue)*

2 Ask a more fluent student to paraphrase the difficult sentence that begins, "I could no more have turned him away." *(Possible response: I could not tell him to leave now, just as I could not tell him to leave if he needed food.)*

Literary Concept: CONFLICT

F Have students identify the external conflict faced by the narrator in this paragraph. *(The fog represents an outside force.)* Ask what internal conflict might be brought on by the external conflict. *(Possible response: indecision about whether to travel)*

Autumn Leaves (1873), Winslow Homer. Cooper-Hewitt, National Design Museum, Smithsonian Institution/Art Resource, New York.

---

chose to do careful work, and if he failed, he took the responsibility without subterfuge.¹

And he did for me the unnecessary thing, the gracious thing, that we find done only by the great of heart. Things no training can teach, for they are done on the instant, with no predicated experience. He found a cubbyhole beside the fireplace that I had not noticed. There, of his own accord, he put kindling and "medium" wood, so that I might always have dry fire material ready in case of sudden wet weather. A stone was loose in the rough walk to the cabin. He dug a deeper hole and steadied it, although he came, himself, by a shortcut over the bank. I found that when I tried to return his thoughtfulness with such things as candy and apples, he was wordless. "Thank you" was, perhaps, an expression for which he had had no use, for his courtesy was <u>instinctive</u>. He only looked at the gift and at me, and a curtain lifted, so that I saw deep into the clear well of his eyes, and gratitude was there, and affection, soft over the firm granite of his character.

He made simple excuses to come and sit with me. I could no more have turned him away than if he had been physically hungry. I suggested once that the best time for us to visit was just before supper, when I left off my writing. After that, he waited always until my typewriter had been some time quiet. One day I worked until nearly dark. I went outside the cabin, having forgotten him. I saw him going up over the hill in the twilight toward the orphanage. When I sat down on my stoop, a place was warm from his body where he had been sitting.

He became intimate, of course, with my pointer, Pat. There is a strange <u>communion</u> between a boy and a dog. Perhaps they possess the same singleness of spirit, the same kind of wisdom. It is difficult to explain, but it exists. When I went across the state for a weekend, I left the dog in Jerry's charge. I gave him the dog whistle and the key to the cabin and left sufficient food. He was to come two or three times a day and let out the dog and feed and exercise him. I should return Sunday night, and Jerry would take out the dog for the last time Sunday afternoon and then leave the key under an agreed hiding place.

My return was belated, and fog filled the mountain passes so treacherously that I dared

---

1. **subterfuge** (sŭb′tər-fyōōj′): anything used to hide one's true purpose or avoid a difficult situation.

WORDS TO KNOW
instinctive (ĭn-stĭngk′tĭv) *adj.* having a natural tendency; spontaneous
communion (kə-myōōn′yən) *n.* close relationship in which deep feelings are shared; intimacy

222

Mini-Lesson  Literary Concepts

REVIEWING MOTIVATION Remind students that motivation is the reason a character acts, feels, or thinks a certain way. The narrator's motivation for coming to the North Carolina mountains is to find quiet to write and to "blow out the malaria from too long a time in the subtropics."

Application Have students think about Jerry's motivation for filling the cubbyhole with wood, then have them write his motivation in a single sentence. Ask students to explain Jerry's motivations for telling the tale about his mother in Mannville and for disappearing when he learns of the narrator's imminent departure. Encourage them to record their thoughts in a chart like the one shown.

Character	Event	Motivation
Narrator	comes to cabin	to find quiet to write and to leave behind the atmosphere of the tropics
Jerry	fills cubbyhole with wood	desire to please and be accepted by the narrator

222 THE LANGUAGE OF LITERATURE TEACHER'S EDITION

not drive at night. The fog held the next morning, and it was Monday noon before I reached the cabin. The dog had been fed and cared for that morning. Jerry came early in the afternoon, anxious.

"The superintendent said nobody would drive in the fog," he said. "I came just before bedtime last night and you hadn't come. So I brought Pat some of my breakfast this morning. I wouldn't have let anything happen to him."

"I was sure of that. I didn't worry."

"When I heard about the fog, I thought you'd know."

He was needed for work at the orphanage, and he had to return at once. I gave him a dollar in payment, and he looked at it and went away. But that night he came in the darkness and knocked at the door.

"Come in, Jerry," I said, "if you're allowed to be away this late."

"I told maybe a story," he said. "I told them I thought you would want to see me."

"That's true," I assured him, and I saw his relief. "I want to hear about how you managed with the dog."

He sat by the fire with me, with no other light, and told me of their two days together. The dog lay close to him and found a comfort there that I did not have for him. And it seemed to me that being with my dog, and caring for him, had brought the boy and me, too, together, so that he felt that he belonged to me as well as to the animal.

"He stayed right with me," he told me, "except when he ran in the laurel. He likes the laurel. I took him up over the hill and we both ran fast. There was a place where the grass was high, and I lay down in it and hid. I could hear Pat hunting for me. He found my trail and he barked. When he found me, he acted crazy, and he ran around and around me, in circles."

We watched the flames.

"That's an apple log," he said. "It burns the prettiest of any wood."

We were very close.

He was suddenly impelled to speak of things he had not spoken of before, nor had I cared to ask him.

"You look a little bit like my mother," he said. "Especially in the dark, by the fire."

"But you were only four, Jerry, when you came here. You have remembered how she looked, all these years?"

"My mother lives in Mannville," he said.

For a moment, finding that he had a mother shocked me as greatly as anything in my life has ever done, and I did not know why it disturbed me. Then I understood my distress. I was filled with a passionate resentment that any woman should go away and leave her son. A fresh anger added itself. A son like this one— The orphanage was a wholesome place, the executives were kind, good people, the food was more than adequate, the boys were healthy, a ragged shirt was no hardship, nor the doing of clean labor. Granted, perhaps, that the boy felt no lack, what blood fed the bowels of a woman who did not yearn over this child's lean body that had come in parturition out of her own? At four he would have looked the same as now. Nothing, I thought, nothing in life could change those eyes. His quality must be apparent to an idiot, a fool. I burned with questions I could not ask. In any, I was afraid, there would be pain.

"Have you seen her, Jerry—lately?"

"I see her every summer. She sends for me."

I wanted to cry out, "Why are you not with her? How can she let you go away again?"

He said, "She comes up here from Mannville whenever she can. She doesn't have a job now."

His face shone in the firelight.

WORDS TO KNOW
impel (ĭm-pĕl′) *v.* to drive, force, or urge to action

223

Art Note

After the Chase by Andrew Wyeth
Andrew Wyeth (1917–) is known for his precise, realistic appraisals of human involvement with the natural world. In this painting he tucks into a wooded setting the partial images of a sporting dog and a barn. Wyeth's attention to detail gives the image an almost photographic authenticity.

Reading the Art How would your opinion of the painting change if you didn't know its title?

CUSTOMIZING FOR
Students Acquiring English

5 Be sure that students understand the analogy between physical nourishment and emotional nourishment.

Critical Thinking:
MAKING JUDGMENTS

J Have students comment on the narrator's strong reaction to Jerry's comments about his mother. Ask if they think her feelings are fair. *(Possible response: While the narrator hates to think of Jerry being in pain, her feelings are not necessarily fair because she doesn't know the mother's circumstances or motives.)*

STRATEGIC READING FOR
Less-Proficient Readers

K Have students explain what the narrator plans to do before leaving. *(The narrator plans on seeing Jerry's mother and learning why she did not keep him with her.)* **Summarizing**

- Ask students if the narrator follows through on these plans. *(No, the narrator's work and travel plans distract her, and she never meets Jerry's mother.)* **Making Generalizations**

Set a Purpose *Have students read on to find out what the narrator learns about Jerry's mother.*

"She wanted to give me a puppy, but they can't let any one boy keep a puppy. You remember the suit I had on last Sunday?" He was plainly proud. "She sent me that for Christmas. The Christmas before that"—he drew a long breath, savoring the memory—"she sent me a pair of skates."

"Roller skates?"

My mind was busy, making pictures of her, trying to understand her. She had not, then, entirely deserted or forgotten him. But why, then— I thought, "I must not condemn her without knowing."

"Roller skates. I let the other boys use them. They're always borrowing them. But they're careful of them."

What circumstance other than poverty—

"I'm going to take the dollar you gave me for taking care of Pat," he said, "and buy her a pair of gloves."

I could only say, "That will be nice. Do you know her size?"

"I think it's 8½," he said. He looked at my hands.

"Do you wear 8½?" he asked.

"No. I wear a smaller size, a 6."

"Oh! Then I guess her hands are bigger than yours."

I hated her. Poverty or no, there was other food than bread, and the soul could starve as quickly as the body. He was taking his dollar to buy gloves for her big stupid hands, and she lived away from him, in Mannville, and contented herself with sending him skates.

"She likes white gloves," he said. "Do you think I can get them for a dollar?"

"I think so," I said.

After the Chase (1965), Andrew Wyeth. Wichita (Kansas) Art Museum.

I decided that I should not leave the mountains without seeing her and knowing for myself why she had done this thing.

The human mind scatters its interests as though made of thistledown, and every wind stirs and moves it. I finished my work. It did not please me, and I gave my thoughts to another field. I should need some Mexican material.

I made arrangements to close my Florida place. Mexico immediately, and doing the writing there, if conditions were favorable. Then, Alaska with my brother. After that, heaven knew what or where.

I did not take time to go to Mannville to see Jerry's mother, nor even to talk with the orphanage officials about her. I was a trifle abstracted about the boy, because of my work and plans. And after my first fury at her— we did not speak of her again—his having a mother, any sort at all, not far away, in Mannville, relieved me of the ache I had had about him. He did not question the anomalous[2] relation. He was not lonely. It was none of my concern.

He came every day and cut my wood and did small helpful favors and stayed to talk. The days had become cold, and often I let him come inside the cabin. He would lie on the floor in front of the fire, with one arm across

---

2. **anomalous** (ə-nŏm′ə-ləs): differing from the general rule; abnormal.

224 UNIT TWO PART 2: UNEXPECTED DEVELOPMENTS

Mini-Lesson The Writer's Style

TONE Remind students that tone shows a writer's attitude toward his or her subject. A writer's tone may convey many different attitudes. Caution students that while the writer's tone is reflected in the words and actions of characters (including the narrator), the writer doesn't necessarily share the attitude of the characters.

Application Have students read several short passages of narration on page 224 and describe the tone in a word or phrase. *(Possible responses:*

intelligent, generous, caring, serious, unsentimental) Then ask students to rewrite one passage to convey a completely different tone.

Reteaching/Reinforcement
- *Writing Handbook*, anthology p. 821
- *Writing Mini-Lessons* transparencies, p. 26

 **The Writer's Craft**

Audience, pp. 234–235
Meaning and Word Choice, pp. 314–315

224 THE LANGUAGE OF LITERATURE **TEACHER'S EDITION**

the pointer, and they would both doze and wait quietly for me. Other days they ran with a common ecstasy through the laurel, and since the asters were now gone, he brought me back vermilion maple leaves, and chestnut boughs dripping with imperial yellow. I was ready to go.

I said to him, "You have been my good friend, Jerry. I shall often think of you and miss you. Pat will miss you too. I am leaving tomorrow."

He did not answer. When he went away, I remember that a new moon hung over the mountains, and I watched him go in silence up the hill. I expected him the next day, but he did not come. The details of packing my personal belongings, loading my car, arranging the bed over the seat, where the dog would ride, occupied me until late in the day. I closed the cabin and started the car, noticing that the sun was in the west and I should do well to be out of the mountains by nightfall. I stopped by the orphanage and left the cabin key and money for my light bill with Miss Clark.

"And will you call Jerry for me to say goodbye to him?"

"I don't know where he is," she said. "I'm afraid he's not well. He didn't eat his dinner this noon. One of the other boys saw him going over the hill into the laurel. He was supposed to fire the boiler this afternoon. It's not like him; he's unusually reliable."

I was almost relieved, for I knew I should never see him again, and it would be easier not to say goodbye to him.

I said, "I wanted to talk with you about his mother—why he's here—but I'm in more of a hurry than I expected to be. It's out of the question for me to see her now too. But here's some money I'd like to leave with you to buy things for him at Christmas and on his birthday. It will be better than for me to try to send him things. I could so easily duplicate— skates, for instance."

She blinked her honest spinster's eyes.

"There's not much use for skates here," she said.

Her stupidity annoyed me.

"What I mean," I said, "is that I don't want to duplicate things his mother sends him. I might have chosen skates if I didn't know she had already given them to him."

She stared at me.

"I don't understand," she said. "He has no mother. He has no skates." ❖

LITERARY INSIGHT

The World Is Not a Pleasant Place to Be

by Nikki Giovanni

the world is not a pleasant place
to be without
someone to hold and be held by

a river would stop
its flow if only
a stream were there
to receive it

an ocean would never laugh
if clouds weren't there
to kiss her tears

the world is not
a pleasant place to be without
someone

WORDS TO KNOW
ecstasy (ĕk'stə-sē) *n.* intense joy or delight; bliss

225

Mini-Lesson Spelling

SPELLING HARD AND SOFT c Review with students the basic rules that govern spelling of words containing the soft and hard c sounds.
- When the letter c has a soft sound, it is usually followed by *e, i,* or *y*.
- When the letter c has a hard sound, it is usually followed by the vowels *a, o,* or *u,* or by any consonant except *y*.

clarity (klăr'ĭ-tē)
instinctive (ĭn-stĭngk'tĭv)
communion (kə-myōōn'yən)
ecstasy (ĕk'stə-sē)

Application Have students spell the following words as you recite them.
1. Carolina
2. circles
3. companion
4. cents
5. courtesy

Ask students to look for more words with hard and soft c sounds, in their own reading and writing. Have them add these words to their personal word lists.

Reteaching/Reinforcement
- *Unit Two Resource Book,* p. 43

STRATEGIC READING FOR Less-Proficient Readers

L Ask students what the narrator learns about Jerry and his mother just before leaving. *(He has no mother.)*
Noting Relevant Details

Literary Concept: MOTIVATION

M Ask students to comment on Jerry's motivation for misleading the narrator about his mother. *(Possible responses: He may have felt desperate to appear "normal" and loved; the fondness he felt for the narrator might have led him to try to hide his feelings of loneliness about being an orphan.)*

COMPREHENSION CHECK
1. What two friendships does Jerry develop at the cabin? *(He becomes friends with the narrator and her dog, Pat.)*
2. What unexpected discovery does the narrator make about Jerry? *(He has lied about his relationship with his mother.)*

INSIGHT
1. According to the poem, in what way is a flowing river like a lonely person? *(Possible response: Both are in search of something to make them complete.)*
2. What natural elements are personified in this poem? *(Possible responses: a river and a stream; the ocean and clouds)*
3. What does this poem tell you about Jerry's world? *(Possible response: It is not a pleasant place for him without family.)*

NIKKI GIOVANNI

Born in 1943 in Knoxville, Tennessee, and raised in Cincinnati, Ohio, Nikki Giovanni emerged in the 1970s as a leading American poet. Her books of poetry include *Black Feeling, Black Talk,* and *Cotton Candy on a Rainy Day.*

From Personal Response to Critical Analysis

1. Responses will vary.
2. Possible response: I believe that Jerry spends a lot of time fantasizing about having a mother. He probably wishes he had a mother, or is embarrassed that he doesn't have one.
3. Possible response: The narrator believes Jerry's story because of her strong sense of his integrity. She feels that he is so honest in his daily life that he must be telling the truth about his mother.
4. Possible response: Jerry needs someone to call his own—a parent, foster parent, or guardian. In contrast, the narrator seems to have a deep need for independence, solitude, and professional accomplishment.
5. Possible response: I think that Jerry would agree with the poem more than the narrator would. In my opinion, the poem is about being lonely, and Jerry seems more lonely than the narrator.

Another Pathway

Cooperative Learning In order to fuel the discussion, one student might write each phrase or sentence that the narrator uses to define the term. One or two other students might be responsible for paraphrasing the narrator's words. Another student might write dictionary definitions of the words *integrity*, *honesty*, and *courage*.

Rubric

3 Full Accomplishment Students coherently discuss the narrator's ideas and come to a conclusion about whether either character behaves with "integrity."

2 Substantial Accomplishment Students discuss some of the narrator's ideas and come to a conclusion about whether either character behaves with "integrity."

1 Little or Partial Accomplishment Students have difficulty grasping the narrator's ideas and coming to a conclusion.

RESPONDING OPTIONS

FROM PERSONAL RESPONSE TO CRITICAL ANALYSIS

REFLECT
Thematic Link

1. What was your reaction to learning the truth behind Jerry's story?

RETHINK

2. In your opinion, why does Jerry make up the story about his mother?

3. Why do you think the narrator believes Jerry?

4. The narrator and Jerry seem to have very different needs. How do their needs differ? Explain.

   Consider
   - Jerry's life in an orphanage
   - Jerry's response to the narrator and her dog
   - why the narrator comes to the cabin and then leaves
   - what the narrator says about Jerry

RELATE
Literary Link

5. Which character, the narrator or Jerry, might agree more with the view expressed in the poem "The World Is Not a Pleasant Place to Be"? Does the poem relate more to being lonely or to being alone?

Multimodal Learning
ANOTHER PATHWAY
Cooperative Learning

In a small group, discuss what the narrator means by *integrity* as she defines it on page 221. Then decide if either Jerry or the narrator behaves with integrity.

QUICKWRITES

1. Use clues in the story to compose a **personal ad** Jerry might write to find a new mother.
2. Write an **epilogue**, or closing section, for the story that tells what the narrator says and does after she learns that Jerry has no mother.
3. Write a **poem** Jerry might send to the narrator as a memento of their friendship.

📁 **PORTFOLIO** Save your writing. You may want to use it later as a springboard to a piece for your portfolio.

LITERARY CONCEPTS

The plot of a story almost always revolves around a **conflict** between opposing forces. An **external conflict** involves a character's struggle against an outside person or force. An **internal conflict** occurs when a struggle is within a character. In the story, Jerry struggles internally with the loneliness he feels. What is the narrator's internal conflict? Are these conflicts ever resolved?

CONCEPT REVIEW: Setting In Rawlings's story, what role does the setting play in bringing the narrator to the cabin? How does the setting affect the narrator's general view of Jerry?

226 UNIT TWO PART 2: UNEXPECTED DEVELOPMENTS

Literary Concepts

Help students infer from the narrator's changing emotions toward Jerry that she is experiencing an internal conflict between her stated desire to be alone and her fondness for the boy.

CONCEPT REVIEW Ask students to look for any comparisons the narrator makes between Jerry and the setting provided by the surrounding environment. *(Page 221—hair color of corn shocks, eyes like a mountain sky)* Students should conclude that the narrator's positive view of the nature around her extends to Jerry as well.

QuickWrites

1. Urge students to identify passages in which Jerry describes the qualities he values in a parent.
2. Encourage students to ponder the question of the narrator's reaction to the news about Jerry's mother and her own professional commitments.
3. Have students think about whether they would like to write a poem that refers to specific events or that describes Jerry's thoughts and feelings.

 **The Writer's Craft**

Analyzing a Story, pp. 163–177
Poetry, pp. 71–83

Multimodal Learning

ALTERNATIVE ACTIVITIES

1. A montage is an image created from a series of overlapping pictures. Use pictures and drawings to create a **montage** that suggests the mood of the story's setting.
2. With a partner, practice playing the role of Jerry and then record each other for a **videotape** that an adoption agency might show to adoptive parents.

WORDS TO KNOW

EXERCISE A On your paper, write the letter of the word that is closest in meaning to the boldfaced Word to Know.

1. It appears that the attention the narrator paid Jerry was **inadequate**.
   a. insufficient   b. unhappy   c. effective
   d. forceful
2. The narrator was **impelled** to seek isolation.
   a. moved   b. uninspired   c. driven
   d. expected
3. Jerry did not notice the **blunt** way she spoke.
   a. delicate   b. short   c. curious   d. abrupt
4. The dog's bonding was **instinctive**.
   a. intentional   b. abnormal   c. natural
   d. healthy
5. The narrator saw the scenery with more **clarity** than she saw Jerry.
   a. intelligence   b. integrity   c. clearness
   d. understanding

EXERCISE B Draw a picture to portray the meaning of each Word to Know listed below.

kindling   clarity   communion   ecstasy   impel

CRITIC'S CORNER

Christine Warner, an eighth-grade student, said of this story: "The story is sad. A boy, not unlike the other orphans, deprived of love and affection, invents things he wants in his mind, for all his friends are temporary." Do you agree with her analysis? Do you think that Jerry is very different from children who live with their parents? Explain.

MARJORIE KINNAN RAWLINGS

1896–1953

A boy whom Marjorie Kinnan Rawlings met in North Carolina was the model for Jerry in "A Mother in Mannville." This story and others she wrote about farmers, trappers, and fishermen were collected in a book titled *When the Whippoorwill—*.

As a child growing up in Washington, D.C., Rawlings entertained neighborhood children with stories, and at age 11 she won her first award for writing. After graduating from the University of Wisconsin, Rawlings worked as a newspaper reporter in Kentucky and New York while writing stories at night.

Like the narrator in "A Mother in Mannville," Rawlings eventually felt the need for a quiet place in which to write.

Rawlings is considered one of America's outstanding regional writers, one who carefully portrays nature, dialect, and local culture. Her most famous novel, *The Yearling*, won a Pulitzer Prize in 1939.
OTHER WORKS *Mountain Prelude, Cross Creek*

Extended Reading

A MOTHER IN MANNVILLE 227

Words to Know

Exercise A
1. a   4. c
2. c   5. c
3. d

Exercise B
Pictures will vary. Remind students that their drawings, particularly these depicting emotions, need not be realistic.

Reteaching/Reinforcement
- *Unit Two Resource Book*, p. 44

MARJORIE KINNAN RAWLINGS

Rawlings believed that human happiness was directly connected to place. She felt that in order for a person to be content, he or she needs to find a place to which he or she feels a natural connection. For Rawlings that place was the tiny village of Cross Creek, Florida. At age 32, she bought and settled on a farm there. She later titled one of her most famous books after the village.

Across the Curriculum

Science Cooperative Learning *The Flora of Carolina* Ask students to form groups of four and to find out more information about the climate and flora of the story's setting. Have them investigate what trees and plants (besides hemlocks, black walnuts, corn, pumpkins, and rhododendrons) are indigenous to the area. Individual groups might choose to focus on one type of flora. In each group, two students can research the scientific information while the others look for visual representations or, if possible, actual samples of flora. Have groups share their information with the class.

Media *Cross Creek* Have students watch a video of *Cross Creek*, the 1983 film of one of Rawlings's most famous works. Encourage students to take special note of the film's attention to the rural setting.

Alternative Activities

1. Remind students to consider both the general aspects of setting as described by the narrator—"high in the Carolina mountains," "autumn," and so forth—and the specific descriptions surrounding the story's actions and events. Encourage students to review the entire story to collect words and phrases to be illustrated before they begin to research and assemble their montage. Then have them decide on a word or phrase that describes the story's overall mood.
2. Help students decide what to put on tape by having them refer to the story to look at Jerry's words. They might consider adapting Jerry's description of his weekend with Pat, for instance. Alternatively, they might simply reacquaint themselves with Jerry's thought and speech patterns in order to write (or improvise) a new scene.

OVERVIEW

Objectives

- To understand and appreciate a short story about a teacher's experiences with her bilingual students
- To understand predicting
- To identify and analyze a surprise ending
- To express understanding of the story through a choice of writing forms, including rewriting and narratives
- To extend understanding of the story through a variety of multimodal and cross-curricular activities

Skills

READING SKILLS/STRATEGIES
- Predict

THE WRITER'S STYLE
- Show, don't tell

GRAMMAR
- Commas that separate ideas

LITERARY CONCEPTS
- Surprise ending
- Humor

SPEAKING, LISTENING, AND VIEWING
- Spanish Music
- Group discussion
- Oral presentation

Cross-Curricular Connections

SOCIAL STUDIES
- Researching unfamiliar cultures

HISTORY
- Bilingual education

PREVIEWING

FICTION

White Mice
Rubén Sálaz-Márquez

PERSONAL CONNECTION
Activating Prior Knowledge

Most of us have ancestors who were born in another country. From them, we have inherited customs, recipes, and treasured possessions that reflect our cultural heritage. Choose something that your family inherited from your ancestors and describe it in your notebook. Explain what that item or custom represents in your ethnic background.

Building Background
LANGUAGE ARTS CONNECTION

The Hispanic children in this story are part of a bilingual education program in a U.S. school. They learn their school subjects partly in English and partly in Spanish, their native language.

Learning a second language is not easy. A common mistake that bilingual students tend to make is code switching—that is, combining their native language with English within a single phrase or sentence. For example, a Hispanic child might say *red corazón* instead of *corazón de roja* for "red heart."

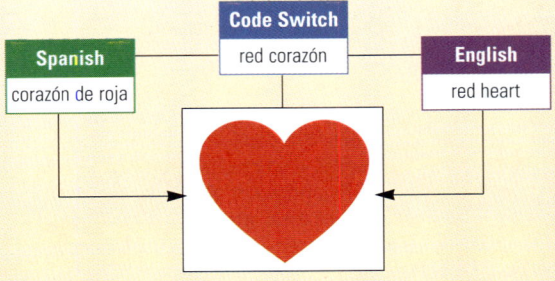

Active Reading/Setting a Purpose
READING CONNECTION

Predicting Using what you already know from a story to guess what will happen later is called predicting. Sometimes your prediction will be correct; sometimes what happens will be unexpected. Regardless of the actual outcome, predicting keeps you involved in the story.

You already know that cultural heritage plays a role in this story. As you read, look for clues that help you predict what may happen as the story progresses. As you make a prediction, jot it down in your notebook. Then read on to see what actually happens.

228 UNIT TWO PART 2: UNEXPECTED DEVELOPMENTS

PRINT AND MEDIA RESOURCES

UNIT TWO RESOURCE BOOK
Strategic Reading: Literature, p. 47
Vocabulary SkillBuilder, p. 50
Reading SkillBuilder, p. 48
Spelling SkillBuilder, p. 49

GRAMMAR MINI-LESSONS
Transparencies, pp. 28–31
Copymasters, pp. 37–40

WRITING MINI-LESSONS
Transparencies, p. 46

ACCESS FOR STUDENTS ACQUIRING ENGLISH
Selection Summaries
Reading and Writing Support

FORMAL ASSESSMENT
Selection Test, pp. 43–44
 Test Generator

AUDIO LIBRARY
See Reference Card

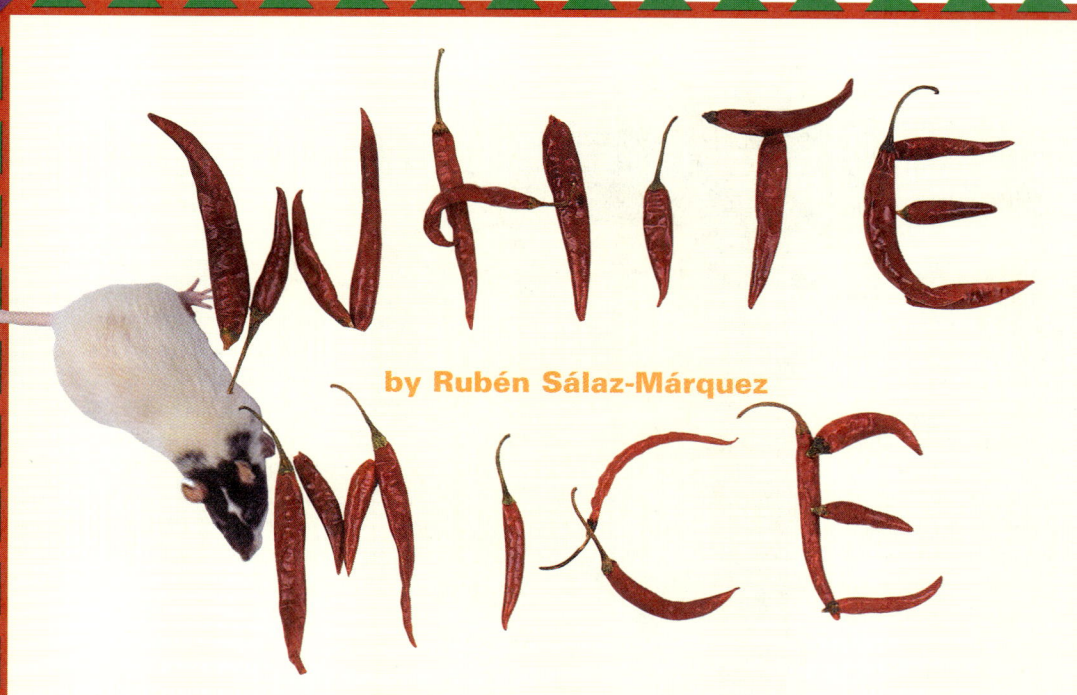

WHITE MICE

by Rubén Sálaz-Márquez

Mrs. Teubbes thrust her key into the knob, unlocked the door and swung it open. Her great bulk reacted against bending over to engage the stopper, but the motion was completed without undue strain for a woman her size. The classroom was pleasantly quiet as she walked to her desk and set down the papers she had graded last night. She pulled out another key, the smaller one for her desk drawer, unlocked it and deposited her purse within, shoved it shut and locked it once more. She glanced at the clock. Kids would start coming in after a spell. She sat at her desk and relaxed, as everything was ready for the coming day. *Two more days before Christmas vacation*, she thought. She would weather the storm of student anticipation. She was confident, and all she needed now was the students. Tomorrow she would meet some of the parents for the cultural day her aide, Mrs. Archunde, had set up. Now there was a gem. If Archunde had a college education, she would be a top teacher . . . *too*, she added quietly in her mind. These Hispanics, or Latins or Chicanos or whatever they were going by these days, had as much talent as anybody; they just didn't, well, apply themselves at the proper time or in gainful ways. There were exceptions, of course, nothing being one hundred percent, but Mrs. Archunde could be excellently qualified with a degree. Teubbes wondered why she didn't go to college now, for it was never too late. It wasn't that she couldn't speak English. She knew both languages and used them well. At least Teubbes thought

WORDS TO KNOW

ardor (är′dər) *n.* strong enthusiasm (p. 230)
component (kəm-pō′nənt) *n.* one part of a whole unit or system (p. 230)
gusto (gŭs′tō) *n.* vigorous enjoyment; zest (p. 233)
intimidate (ĭn-tĭm′ĭ-dāt) *v.* to fill with fear (p. 231)
palate (păl′ĭt) *n.* sense of taste (p. 236)
persevering (pûr′sə-vîr′ĭng) *adj.* determined to continue (p. 234)
prone (prōn) *adj.* having a strong tendency toward; inclined (p. 230)
scrutinize (skrōōt′n-īz′) *v.* to observe carefully (p. 231)
transitional (trăn-zĭsh′ə-nəl) *adj.* passing from one state or stage to another (p. 230)
vigilant (vĭj′ə-lənt) *adj.* on the alert; watchful (p. 232)

STRATEGIC READING FOR
Less-Proficient Readers

A Have students explain how Mrs. Teubbes and her assistant, Mrs. Archunde, teach their fourth-grade class. *(Mrs. Teubbes teaches in English and Mrs. Archunde teaches the Spanish component.)* **Restating**

Set a Purpose Ask students to note, as they continue to read, how Mrs. Teubbes feels about her Hispanic students.

CUSTOMIZING FOR
Gifted and Talented Students

Ask students to discuss which is more important: preserving one's cultural and linguistic heritage or assimilating into a new culture. Invite them to weigh both sides of the issue.

Art Note

***Pleased With Herself* by Marjorie McDonald** McDonald (1898–) did not begin painting until she was in her seventies. She was 91 years old when she created this collage made of dyed rice paper. The childlike innocence and humor of the collage suggest a youthful love of life.

Reading the Art *What impression do you get from the colors and the figure's expression?*

CUSTOMIZING FOR
Students Acquiring English

2 Explain that a bilingual conference is a meeting at which many teachers involved in bilingual education talk about their classroom experiences and learn more about bilingual education.

3 Ask more fluent students to try to infer the meaning of *lark* from the context clues. Point out that the people to whom the conference was a lark had not gone to any presentations—they were goofing off. Students should then be able to infer that a *lark* is a fun time, something not taken seriously.

A Archunde used Spanish well because she taught the Spanish **component** for all fourth graders in the school.

Thus far Mrs. Teubbes was enjoying the bilingual component, something new for her classroom, and she was picking up the language right along with the kids. Of course, the students already had a background in it, but the teachers could learn too. If the component would help the kids learn English better, then Teubbes was in favor of it. She had even attended the entire bilingual conference last month in an effort to learn firsthand how to combat code switching and maybe even cultural switching,[1] both of which her students were **prone** to. Her **ardor** cooled somewhat when she saw the conference was just a lark for a number of the participants. Some of them must have spent all their time at the lounge, for they weren't seen at any of the presentations. And she had seen some of them getting rather chummy. Well, no matter. You get out what you put in. But the real tragedy was that the *bilingual* conference had been conducted totally in English. Yes, after a few *Buenos días's* and such, not a word was spoken in Spanish. Kathy Teubbes had gone prepared to make a herculean[2] effort to catch what would be said, but precious little turned up in Spanish. She still hadn't decided if she was relieved or disappointed, for it was her nature to take up new challenges, whether she conquered all of them or not. *After all, nobody's perfect.* But now she was quite certain the bilingual program was soft government money[3] being put to use until it ran out. If the language wasn't going to be used all through life, including bilingual conferences, it was just as well to teach the children English and forget about Spanish in school except as a **transitional** tool. If these were the facts of life, and the English bilingual conference proved they were, she didn't feel bad that she had never picked up much Spanish over the years. If Hispanic adults and intellectual leaders didn't use the language in conferences

Pleased with Herself (1989), Marjorie McDonald. Stevenson's Gallery, Corvallis, Oregon.

---

1. **cultural switching:** changing back and forth between two sets of cultural beliefs as one thinks and acts.
2. **herculean** (hûr′kyə-lē′ən): of exceptional strength.
3. **soft government money:** government funds that are not budgeted for a specific purpose.

WORDS TO KNOW
component (kəm-pō′nənt) *n.* one part of a whole unit or system
prone (prōn) *adj.* having a tendency toward; inclined
ardor (är′dər) *n.* strong enthusiasm
transitional (trăn-zĭsh′ə-nəl) *adj.* passing from one state or stage to another

230

Mini-Lesson  Literary Concepts

REVIEWING HUMOR Remind students that humor is the quality that makes writing funny or amusing. Some techniques writers use to create humor are shown in the web.

Application Have students copy the word web into their notebooks, leaving space under each technique. Ask students to review the story to find examples of Sálaz-Márquez's use of humor, and have them record the examples under the appropriate headings.

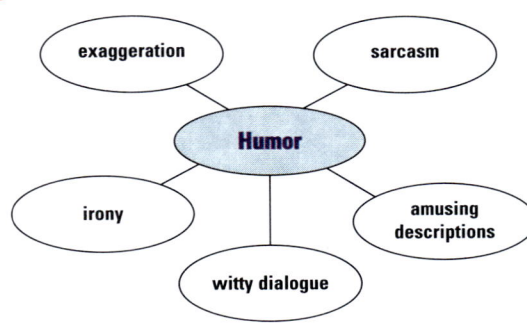

and whatever, they themselves were admitting Spanish isn't necessary in the good old U.S.A. *Why waste taxpayers' money?* Besides, mixing the two languages often trapped students in hilariously embarrassing code and cultural switching.

"Good morning, Mrs. Teubbes," said Ricardo as he bounced into the room.

"Good morning, Richard," replied the teacher as she came out of her reverie. Oh, that little imp had more energy than anyone, but the only thing he could do right was say good morning when he charged in ahead of everyone else. "Are you ready for another day of learning?"

Ricardo didn't answer. Instead he sat at his desk and looked intently at his teacher.

"Well?" she said.

"Two more days of school," he said, "and tomorrow is our cultural day, huh?"

"Yes, and I'm looking forward to it. We've never done that in this room."

"You like to eat, huh?" observed Ricardo as other students began to fill the room. That impish look was in his eyes, as usual. "I'll bring something good!"

"You like Mexican food?" asked Becky.

"Of course," said Mrs. Teubbes. "Now why don't you review your vocabulary words?" What children! Ah well, at least Richard wasn't vicious. *Of course, none of the children are,* she thought as they trooped into the room. She felt most of them had very good manners, actually, and were quite nice. They were followers more than leaders, but then followers were important too. She wished very sincerely these students were more interested in schoolwork, for the sake of their future.

"Good morning Mrs. Teubbes!" rang out a happy, feminine voice.

"Well, good morning, America!" returned the teacher. Now there was a jewel if there ever was one. That Martinez girl was in a class by herself as far as Kathy Teubbes was concerned. Indeed, it could almost be said the teacher was in awe of America Martinez. She <u>scrutinized</u> the girl as she went over to the cages of gerbils and white mice even before putting down her books. How she loved those little animals! And when there were some to give away, America was sure to take them. The teacher often wondered what she did with them. They couldn't be made into hamburger. Teubbes had worked with such critters for several years, but down deep she had a revulsion for rodents as a species, and even the thought of "hamburger mice" almost turned her stomach. She wondered how the Martinez family could put up with them at home.

"Everybody made it through the night," said America as she went to her desk.

Mrs. Teubbes smiled at the girl. If the teacher were ever to adopt one of her students, it would be America Martinez. Not that she was underprivileged or anything like that, of course. She was always clean, well dressed, polite. Her skin was a bit on the olive side, but her jet black hair and pearly teeth went well with her complexion. But what impressed Teubbes the most was America's determined spirit. When she didn't understand something, she'd march right up to the teacher's desk and get help. And if she didn't get it right the next time, she'd come right back with another thoughtful question. She was good at language and had to work harder on her math, but she was usually equal to the task. Teubbes remembered once when she had been outside on recess duty, a couple of little nasties thought they were going to <u>intimidate</u> America. The two had each grabbed an arm,

WORDS TO KNOW
scrutinize (skrōōt'n-īz') *v.* to observe carefully
intimidate (ĭn-tĭm'ĭ-dāt') *v.* to fill with fear

231

Active Reading: EVALUATE

B Ask students to discuss how Mrs. Teubbes feels about the Spanish and English language. Does she consider one superior to the other? *(She does make the effort to attend the bilingual conference, but Mrs. Teubbes really is concerned only with how to help students learn English; she believes that teaching in a foreign language is just a waste of taxpayers' money.)*

Critical Thinking: ANALYZING

C Have students explain why the boy's name is given as Ricardo, yet Mrs. Teubbes refers to him as Richard. *(Possible response: Mrs. Teubbes's preference for the English language is so strong that she changes students' Hispanic names to their English equivalents.)*

STRATEGIC READING FOR
Less-Proficient Readers

D Have students describe what Mrs. Teubbes thinks of her students. *(Possible responses: She sees them as generally well mannered and friendly but as followers rather than leaders. She does not think they are interested enough in schoolwork.)* **Drawing Conclusions**

Set a Purpose Have students read on to find out how a person's unfamiliarity with another language can lead to misunderstandings.

Mini-Lesson — Reading Skills/Strategies

ACTIVE READING: PREDICT Remind students that good readers use certain strategies as they read. Predicting strategies are used to try to figure out what will happen next and how the story might turn out. It does not matter if the prediction turns out to be accurate; predicting is a way to remain interested in the story. If predictions are wrong, it only adds to the surprise at the ending.

Application Have students work in groups to compare the reading logs they started at the beginning of the story. Have members of each group answer the following questions:

- What clues did students record in their reading logs?
- Did students make the same predictions?
- If predictions were different, which one does the group think is most likely to be true?
- Which predictions actually came true in the story?

After groups compare their logs, have each group select a reporter to share the group's findings with the class.

Reteaching/Reinforcement
• *Unit Two Resource Book,* p. 48

THE LANGUAGE OF LITERATURE TEACHER'S EDITION **231**

Critical Thinking: ANALYZING

E Ask students what Mrs. Teubbes thinks of America's name. *(She feels it is disrespectful.)* Ask why Mrs. Teubbes is disturbed by America's confidence. *(Possible responses: She expects children to be more dependent and less ready to defend themselves; Mrs. Teubbes does not think it fair that a young minority student should have the confidence she herself lacks.)*

CUSTOMIZING FOR
Students Acquiring English

4 Ask students why Mrs. Teubbes refers to her student America as a "minority." *(The student is Hispanic.)* Then have them describe what groups are considered to be "minorities" in the United States. *(Possible response: some ethnic and racial groups that are under-represented in politics and business, such as African Americans, Hispanics, Asians, and Native Americans)*

Literary Concept: HUMOR

F Have students decide whether America's father misunderstood the type of "borrowing" she was studying in class or if he was making a joke. *(Possible responses: America's father was joking because he knew he was helping her with her math homework. America's father misunderstood the type of borrowing involved, otherwise he would not have bothered to explain the process of cosigning for a loan.)*

---

but America broke loose, made a fist and whacked each one on the nose, causing them to bleed profusely. Later in the principal's office America was a picture of confidence and contentment. Lord! Most fourth graders would have been quaking in their little shoes.

"What would you do in my place?" the principal had asked.

"I'd send you back to class," America had replied matter-of-factly.

"What if those girls jump you again?"

"I'll bloody their noses again."

Heavens! Mrs. Teubbes now began to consider something she had been unable to define before. Something, perhaps bordering on the ineffable, *bothered* her about America. Was it the child's name? How could any parents name their daughter *America*? That was rather sacrilegious, wasn't it? She had heard children teasing "Miss America!" and "God Bless America!" on the playground. It never seemed to bother the little girl. Or maybe that's what disturbed Mrs. Teubbes: *nothing* seemed to bother America, such was her confidence and aplomb. Why, she could put many an eighteen-year-old to the blush. Somehow it just wasn't fair that a mere child, of a minority at that—

"*Buenos días, Señora Teubbes,*" repeated Mrs. Archunde.

"Oh, yes, *buenos días,* Magdalena. How are you today?"

"Fine, thank you. You seem to have been lost in thought."

"Not lost, just thinking. I'm looking forward to the cultural day tomorrow." Teubbes looked up at the wall clock just as the bell rang for classes to begin.

"You'll enjoy it," assured Archunde, "and unless I miss my guess, a number of parents will be here."

"Will America's be here, do you know?"

"We can ask her."

"Yes, of course," said Teubbes. "All right children, let's take out your mathematics workbooks." There was an audible groan from the class. "Come on, borrowing is not hard, and you have to learn it. How many of you worked on it at home and had your parents help you?" A couple of hands went up, including America's. "And what did your parents have to say about borrowing, America?"

"My Dad said it was what you did after you found a cosigner,"[4] replied the girl. Mrs. Archunde chuckled.

"Oh, I see," continued Mrs. Teubbes, "but that's not the kind of borrowing we mean, of course. Well, let's get busy. Richard, stay in your seat. Mrs. Archunde and I will walk around, then you come to the desk when you need help."

The students fell to working quickly, for Mrs. Teubbes believed in discipline and no one was allowed to clown it up. After a vigilant walk around the room, the teacher and her aide sat at their respective desks and tutored one-on-one. Mrs. Teubbes saw America look up with confusion wrinkled into her pretty face. "Come on up if you need help." The girl did. "Yes, dear?"

"Mrs. Teubbes, can you borrow from the dollar sign?"

Now it was the teacher who broke out

---

4. **cosigner:** a person who signs a loan along with another person, thus becoming responsible for the debt if the first signer fails to pay back the money.

WORDS TO KNOW
vigilant (vĭj′ə-lənt) *adj.* on the alert; watchful

232

Mini-Lesson The Writer's Style

SHOW, DON'T TELL Help students understand that throughout this selection, Sálaz-Márquez uses specific verbs, nouns, adverbs, and adjectives to give his readers the clearest possible picture of Mrs. Teubbes and her fourth-grade class. Point out, as an example, the sentence highlighted above, and explain that rather than merely telling readers, "America was confused," the author shows how the confusion was "wrinkled" into her face.

Application After the math lesson is over, the students have a bilingual lesson on English and Spanish vocabulary. Have students describe the bilingual lesson, the teacher and aide, and the students, by using words that show rather than tell how the bilingual lesson is conducted.

Reteaching/Reinforcement
- *Writing Handbook,* anthology p. 833
- *Writing Mini-Lessons* transparencies, p. 46

Show, Don't Tell, pp. 262–266

laughing, everyone stopping what he or she had been doing and staring. "No, dear," said a chuckling Mrs. Teubbes. "The dollar sign just informs us we are dealing with dollars and cents. You can't borrow from it. Now let's take a look at your paper . . ." The problem was discovered and explained away.

After mathematics Mrs. Archunde drilled the class on vocabulary in both English and Spanish. She reviewed the old words and carefully introduced the new. ". . . and what do you buy when you go to the movies?"

"POPCORN!"

"Isn't it beautiful, children, to be able to use two languages?"

"And how do you say that in Spanish?"

"*Maíz*,"⁵ said Caroline.

"Yes," encouraged Archunde, "that's part of it. Anybody know the rest?" No one did, so she told them: "*Palomitas de maíz.*"⁶

"Pigeon corn?" asked Martin.

"Yes," encouraged Archunde further, "and can anybody tell me why they call it that in Mexico?" She could tell the kids were trying hard to figure out the riddle, but no hands were up. "Now let's imagine as we think . . . the corn pops up and flies into the air, almost like little . . . white . . . pigeons."

"Ooooh!" chorused the class, impressed with the imagery.

"Yes, now let's review our vegetables quickly," said Archunde as she pointed to a chart on the wall. "Besides *maíz*, what do we have?"

"Cowcumbers!" said Martin.

Mrs. Teubbes almost interrupted to correct the code switching mistake which so many students were prone to make.

"Cucumbers," said Mrs. Archunde.

"My grandfather's are big!" explained Martin. Then to Mrs. Teubbes: "Remember those he sent you?"

"Yes, Martin." His grandfather, Mr. De La O, had sent her some very large cucumbers in September.

"He's coming tomorrow."

"Fine," said Archunde, "now let's get back to work." When all the vegetables were mentioned in English, they were reviewed in Spanish with equal *gusto*. "Isn't it beautiful, children, to be able to use two languages? Each one of you is worth two people if you learn both languages. Your lives will be that much richer. Now I want to teach you three new words. Maybe some of you know them; we'll see. What do you call a person who knows three languages?"

The children concentrated but couldn't come up with an answer.

"Trilingual," said Archunde, then she had everyone repeat it several times. She wrote it on the board and underlined the prefix. "Remember, *tri*- means 'three,' 'three.'" Most of the students wrote it down.

"Now who can tell me the word for a person who speaks *two* languages? You should know that one, children." But no one came up with it. "Bilingual!" said Archunde, then she repeated the procedure as before. "And don't forget: *bi*- means 'two.' Yes, I don't have to tell you to put it in your notebooks. Don't forget it over the Christmas vacation." Mrs. Teubbes walked up and down the rows verifying the notebook work.

---

5. *maíz* (mä-ēs′) *Spanish.*
6. *palomitas de maíz* (päl-ô-mē′täs dĕ mä-ēs′) *Spanish.*

WORDS TO KNOW

gusto (gŭs′tō) *n.* vigorous enjoyment; zest

233

Mini-Lesson — Grammar

COMMAS THAT SEPARATE IDEAS Explain to students that commas are usually used to separate ideas in two ways:
- before the conjunction in a compound sentence
- to separate items in a series

Application Have students find at least two sentences in the selection in which commas are used either before a conjunction or after items in a series. Then write the following sentences on the board, omitting the commas. Have students copy the sentences in their notebooks with commas in the correct places.

1. America, Martin, and Ricardo were eager to learn, and they tried hard to excel in class.
2. Mrs. Teubbes did her best, but her lack of Spanish, her unspoken biases, and her stereotyping were major problems.

Reteaching/Reinforcement
- *Grammar Handbook,* anthology pp. 891–896
- *Grammar Mini-Lessons* copymasters pp. 37–40, transparencies, pp. 28–31

The Writer's Craft

Compound Sentences, pp. 556–557
Series of Sentence Parts, pp. 112–113

STRATEGIC READING FOR
Less-Proficient Students

J Have students explain how America's answer shows that she does not understand Mrs. Archunde's question. *(Possible responses: America says the answer is "gringo," a derogatory reference to Anglo Americans; Mrs. Archunde is looking for the word monolingual to describe a person who speaks only one language.)* **Making Generalizations**

Set a Purpose Have students look, as they continue to read, for how Mrs. Teubbes's lack of knowledge of Spanish leads her to misunderstand America.

Critical Thinking: ANALYZING

K Ask students to explain what Ricardo's questioning of the word "gringo" reveals about the students' awareness of acquiring a new language. *(Possible response: Ricardo's "mischievous" question shows he is aware that many Anglo Americans are not bilingual and do not encourage the learning of secondary languages; as America first volunteered the answer, her response suggests that many other students are aware of the political aspects of learning new languages.)*

Active Reading: CLARIFY

L Ask: What does the students' ability to move between Spanish and English suggest about their mastery of each of language? *(Possible response: Moving between languages suggests that although the students sometimes confuse particular words or codes, they can typically switch back and forth with ease. Thus, they demonstrate a good working knowledge of both languages.)*

"Now," said Archunde, "what is the word for a person who speaks just one language?" One hand instantly went up in the air. "America?"

"Gringo!" said the girl.

Archunde burst out laughing, but she controlled it quickly. "No, not quite," said the aide, who trembled mirthfully as she used to do as a young girl when she got the giggles in church. "The word I was looking for is *monolingual. Mono-* means 'one,' 'one,'" she said as she wrote it on the board.

Ricardo's hand went up. "Mrs. Archunde, what's gringo?" he asked mischievously.

Archunde felt like hitting him with a "cowcumber." She was momentarily at a loss for words.

"*Gringo,*" said Mrs. Teubbes, "is a word used to describe someone who is of American-English descent. It is not the nicest word to use."

"My grandmother uses it all the time and she's nice," said Ricardo.

"It depends on how you use it, how you say it," volunteered Archunde. "Technically it comes from the Spanish word *griego*,[7] which means 'Greek.' *Gringo* just means 'foreigner.' Now let's get back to our lesson so we can finish the details for the cultural day."

Other vocabulary words were introduced, written down, and drilled. When that was done, the aide reinforced the cultural unit from three days before. "All right, now let's see who can lead the class in a little Christmas carol. Who wants to do it?"

"In English or Spanish?" asked a student.

"Well, let me see, how should I do it?"

"I know," said Martin, "eenie, meenie, minie, moe."

"I like the way you taught it to us in Spanish," said America.

"All right, go ahead," encouraged the aide.

America got up from her desk and turned to face the class. She pointed to a different student with each syllable she uttered: "*Tela mela, teplatí, como sal que es para ti!*[8] Becky is it!" She sat down again.

Becky put on a persevering face, shrugged her shoulders a bit, and went up in front of the class. "But which one shall we sing?" she asked in mild protestation. Other students called out a number of carols.

"You pick it, dear," said Mrs. Archunde.

"Well, let's do 'Alarrú,' but you all have to sing!"

The class was enthusiastic as Archunde picked up her guitar and everyone joined voices with the Christmas lullaby:

No temas a Herodes
Que nada te ha de hacer;
Duérmete, Niño lindo,
No tienes que temer.

Alarrú, alamé,
Alarrú, alamé, mi Señor.[9]

The class finished the carol; contentment was expressed on the children's faces. They felt good about themselves, a sentiment the two professionals had labored strenuously to achieve.

"That was beautiful, children!" said Mrs. Teubbes. "I could listen to you all day. But let's take some time to review who is going to bring

---

7. *griego* (grē-ĕ′gô) *Spanish.*
8. *Tela mela, teplatí, como sal que es para ti!* (tĕ′lä mĕ′lä tĕ-plä-tē′ kô′mô säl kĕ ĕs pä′rä tē): a Spanish counting-out rhyme, similar to "One potato, two potato . . . ."
9. *No temas . . . mi Señor Spanish:* Have no fear of Herod/Who has nothing to do with you;/Fall asleep, beautiful boy,/You have nothing to fear./Lullaby, lullay,/Lullaby, lullay, my Lord.

WORDS TO KNOW **persevering** (pûr′sə-vîr′ĭng) *adj.* determined to continue **persevere** *v.*

234

Assessment Option

SELF-ASSESSMENT Have each student choose one of the following characters: Mrs. Archunde, Mrs. Teubbes, or Ricardo. Ask students to describe to a friend, in writing, the episode involving the word *gringo*, from the point of view of the character he or she chose. Students should write the story in the ways that the character would say it. Encourage students to think about the personality of the chosen character and his or her position in the classroom. To help students assess their own work, you may wish to have them ask themselves the following questions:

- Why did I choose the character I did?
- What information in the story helped me decide how my character would describe the incident?
- Which part of this assignment was the most difficult? Why?
- Which part of this assignment was the most enjoyable? Why?

234 THE LANGUAGE OF LITERATURE TEACHER'S EDITION

Empanadas [Turnovers] (1991), Carmen Lomas Garza. Gouache painting, 20" × 28". Collection of Romeo Montalvo, Brownsville, Texas. Copyright © 1991 Carmen Lomas Garza. Photo by Judy Reed.

what for tomorrow. I am so excited about our cultural day!" Quickly she wrote the students' names on the board, then gave the chalk to Mrs. Archunde to jot down the names of the foods, since she was more familiar with the spelling. When the task was completed, Mrs. Teubbes said, "Children, I'm looking forward to seeing your parents tomorrow, those who can come, and everything sounds so good I'm not even going to eat breakfast at home."

"That's okay; I'll bring you some *atole*,"[10] said Ricardo.

"Wonderful, Richard," Mrs. Teubbes sighed. One never knew what that boy was going to say.

"I'm a wonderful boy," admitted Ricardo as the bell sounded for recess. "I can hardly wait for tomorrow!"

---

10. **atole** (ä-tô′lĕ) *Spanish:* a Mexican drink made of cornmeal.

WHITE MICE **235**

Multicultural Perspectives

TURNOVERS, THE WORLD OVER The pastries depicted in the art shown are called empanadas. A person preparing these Mexican turnovers will roll out pastry dough and cut it into circles. The circles are filled with meat or cheese for main course empanadas or with fruit and nuts for dessert empanadas. Then the dough is folded in half and sealed. Empanadas are usually fried, but they also can be baked. Many other cultures make similar turnovers—*ravioli* (Italy), *pierogi* (Poland), *gyoza* (Japan), *pot stickers* (China), *burek* (Turkey), *samosas* (India), and *pasties* (England).

Active Reading: PREDICT

O The author hints that something memorable is about to happen. Ask students to predict what may happen next in the story. If necessary, help students by reading the following model.

Think-Aloud Model *I'm not sure what will make the cultural day memorable, but the title refers to white mice, and, so far, mice have not played an important part in the story. I think that white mice will be a big part of the cultural day, perhaps getting out of their cage and ruining the students' food.*

Active Reading: CONNECT

P Have students make a top-ten list of foods they most enjoy. Then have them identify the culture in which each food originated. Ask them to find out which foods come from their own cultural background and which are borrowed from another culture.

Literary Concept: HUMOR

Q Point out that Mrs. Teubbes has mispronounced a Spanish name as "De La Zero" rather than "De La Oh." Have students discuss what this humorous mistake reveals about Mrs. Teubbes. *(Possible responses: She has again inadvertently shown her lack of understanding of the Spanish language—this time turning a real person into a zero. She is trying to do her best, but she reveals her hidden biases.)*

O The following day no one realized how memorable the cultural day would be as the students got to class earlier than usual because of the food they brought. By the time the final bell rang to start the day, the food table was covered with all sorts of aromatic steaming crockpots, ovenware, and gaily painted dishes, which lent even more personality to the foods **P** with which Mrs. Teubbes was becoming acquainted. Indeed, this experience would do a tremendous job of broadening her cultural perspectives, as well as her <u>palate</u>.

"Oh-oh, if it's no good, they'll throw us out for sure."

The children were remarkably well-behaved, especially with so much temptation at hand. Archunde put on a tape of Spanish-language Christmas carols to start the festivities. A choir of angels couldn't sound more heavenly, thought Mrs. Teubbes. She was glad she was able to make a contribution, for she had taken the time to go out and purchase the tape by José Feliciano, and afterward she would play it for everyone and maybe even lead them in his *"Feliz Navidad!"*[11]

Mrs. Teubbes saw Martin's grandfather, Mr. De La O, entering the room. Immediately she went to thank him for his gift from back in September. "I'm so glad you could come, Mr. **Q** De La Zero," she blurted as she shook the man's hand. "I wanted to express in person how much my family and I appreciated your thoughtfulness."

"Thank you, *señora*," said the old gentleman, warmly receptive to the woman's intent. "I'm glad you enjoyed our little gift."

"We have a chair for you right over here," she said as she led him across the room.

Mrs. Archunde was mixing with everyone, but she went to America and her father when they walked into the room.

"I hope you won't throw us out for being fashionably late," said the man to Mrs. Archunde.

"Of course not," she replied.

"I brought the *pozole*,"[12] chirped America. "We even grew the corn that's in it."

"Oh-oh, if it's no good, they'll throw us out for sure," said the father, making Archunde smile. Little wonder America had such a sense of humor. "I'll put it right over here," he said as he placed the large pot on the last remaining space on the table.

"We were saving it for you," said Archunde.

"I guess we're ready to start," said Mrs. Teubbes. "Children, you all make a line on that side of the table, with your parents, and Mrs. Archunde and I will serve from this side if you need help." A second invitation was unnecessary, but everyone cooperated in an orderly fashion.

Mrs. Teubbes had not eaten breakfast, usually a very large meal for her, so she was quite hungry to begin with; and as she helped serve the different dishes, her mouth literally watered in expectation. She controlled herself by making pleasant comments on how good everything looked, but she could hardly wait to begin her own meal.

"Is this porridge or cement?" asked Denise as she looked at a white crockpot full of light blue *atole*.

---

11. *"Feliz Navidad!"* (fĕ-lēs′ nä-vē-däd′): the title of a popular song, from the Spanish for "Merry Christmas."
12. *pozole* (pô-sô′lĕ) *Spanish:* a Mexican stew.

WORDS TO KNOW
palate (păl′ĭt) *n.* sense of taste

236

Mini-Lesson · Listening

SPANISH MUSIC Remind students that the theme of "White Mice" centers around issues of cross-cultural communication. Explain that different cultures develop their own traditions and styles of music, yet audiences from all over the world can share in the appreciation and enjoyment of different musical styles. Even if listeners don't understand the meanings of lyrics, they can relate to the expressive ways the music is played and the lyrics are sung.

Application Play for students a recording of popular music sung in Spanish. Ask students to write, as they listen, their impressions of the music and what mood the song evokes. When the song is over, have students share their impressions. Then, if possible, have a Spanish-speaking volunteer translate the lyrics. Ask students if their understanding of the music changed after learning the translation. Spanish-speaking students may also include comparisons to other Spanish songs performed in a similar style or on a similar topic.

The people talked, music played, and when everyone had been through the line once, the two teachers finally served themselves. Mrs. Teubbes was not shy about sampling a little of everything, starting with the items familiar to her, devouring them in as dainty a fashion as possible. Then she began with the unfamiliar dishes, and this is where she got herself into a bit of difficulty. A *relleno*[13] had some hot chili in it, and the unsuspecting woman had to make a quick exit to the drinking fountain for some cold water. Undaunted, she returned to the food table and continued her adventures amid the happiness and jovial spirit which everyone shared. The good food, beautiful music, and happy people enriched the holiday season as nothing else could.

"Mrs. Teubbes, have you tasted my *pozole* yet?" asked America of her teacher.

"Your what?"

"This dish over here," said the girl, "the *pozole*."

"No, dear," admitted Mrs. Teubbes, "but hand me a bowl and it will be next. I've never had such delicious food in my life!"

"Really?" said the smiling girl.

"Can you imagine that?" continued Mrs. Teubbes. "Of course, I grew up in a different part of the country. But they couldn't drag me away now." She took the bowl America handed to her and filled it generously. "Hmm, smells delicious." She was ever so slightly wary because of the chili relleno, but the woman was unable to discover anything potentially deleterious to her palate as she tasted a little. "Hmm, it's good." She looked at America, put a hand on her shoulder momentarily, and said, "You know, my dear, I've been wondering something for a long time . . . I mean, I have a question for you." She continued to eat the tasty *pozole*.

"I have always wondered, what do you do with all those little rodents you take home?"

"We put them to good use; we don't waste anything," replied America as she smiled.

"Heavens, this has such flavor!" said Mrs. Teubbes as she ate the *pozole*. "Quite unlike anything I've ever eaten. What do you call it again?"

After America told her, Mrs. Teubbes waxed rather poetic and said happily, "One thing is certain: this taste is not a waste! What is this that gives it such flavor?"

America couldn't see the bits of white pork meat the teacher was moving about with her spoon, so she assumed Mrs. Teubbes was referring to the white corn, for to her that was the best part of the *pozole*.

"Oh, *that's* the white *maíz!*" replied America.

Mrs. Teubbes's eyes opened wide as saucers, and an expression of terror swept into her face as she blurted: "WHITE MICE?!" She dropped the leprous bowl of *pozole*, clamped a hand over her mouth, and raced out of the room. ❖

---

13. **relleno** (rĕ-yĕ′nô) *Spanish:* stuffing; commonly refers to a chile relleno, or stuffed pepper.

WHITE MICE **237**

Literary Concept:
SURPRISE ENDING

R Have students explain what makes the ending of the story a surprise. (*Possible responses: Even though Mrs. Teubbes doesn't understand many Hispanic customs, it is surprising that she would think the stew is made from mice.*)

STRATEGIC READING FOR
Less-Proficient Students

S Ask students why Mrs. Teubbes runs from the classroom after eating America's *pozole*. (*She misunderstands what America has said; she thinks the pozole is flavored with white mice rather than white maíz.*) **Drawing Conclusions/Summarizing**

CUSTOMIZING FOR
Gifted and Talented Students

Have students explain how the title of the story is symbolic. Ask them to identify the larger meaning of the title beyond its foreshadowing of the surprise ending. (*Possible response: White mice are often used in laboratory experiments, where their behavior in a controlled setting is observed and analyzed. Mrs. Teubbes's students are like "white mice" who are subject to her experimenting with bilingual education.*)

COMPREHENSION CHECK

1. What special day is the class planning? (*a cultural day*)
2. What is Mrs. Archunde's responsibility in the classroom? (*She teaches the Spanish component.*)
3. What animals in Mrs. Teubbes's classroom is America particularly interested in? (*the mice and gerbils*)
4. How does Mrs. Archunde feel about children learning two languages? (*She thinks it is beneficial.*)
5. What does Mrs. Teubbes think is the main ingredient in America's *pozole*? (*white mice*)

Mini-Lesson Spelling

INDISTINCT VOWELS Explain to students that unstressed vowels preceding the letter *r* are often difficult to identify.

ard<u>o</u>r

Application Read each word aloud. Have students write each word with the correct vowel.

1. temporary
2. victory
3. similar
4. memorandum
5. cultural
6. editor
7. necessary
8. history
9. popular
10. familiar
11. ordinary
12. conqueror

Ask students to look for more words that fit this pattern, in their own writing and in things that they read, and to add these words to their personal word lists.

Reteaching/Reinforcement
- *Unit Two Resource Book*, p. 49

THE LANGUAGE OF LITERATURE TEACHER'S EDITION **237**

RESPONDING OPTIONS

FROM PERSONAL RESPONSE TO CRITICAL ANALYSIS

REFLECT
1. What was your reaction to the unexpected development on the cultural day? Did you predict what happened? Jot down your answer in your notebook and share it with a partner.

RETHINK
2. What are the causes of the incident at the end of the story?
   Consider
   - Mrs. Teubbes's knowledge of Spanish
   - America's knowledge of English
   - Mrs. Teubbes's attitude toward Hispanics
3. A **stereotype** is an oversimplified mental picture of a person, a group, or an institution. How does Mrs. Teubbes stereotype Hispanics?
4. How do you think Mrs. Archunde and the students feel about Mrs. Teubbes as a teacher? Would you like Mrs. Teubbes for a teacher? Why or why not?

RELATE
5. People have different opinions about the value of bilingual education. What do you think are the benefits and the drawbacks of this approach?

LITERARY CONCEPTS

An unexpected twist in the plot at the end of a story can provide a **surprise ending.** For a surprise ending to be effective, it must be based on facts and clues provided earlier in the story. Find at least two facts or clues that lead up to the surprise ending in this story.

CONCEPT REVIEW: Theme The theme of a story is the message about life that the writer wants to share with the reader. What do you think is the theme of "White Mice"?

238 UNIT TWO PART 2: UNEXPECTED DEVELOPMENTS

Multimodal Learning
ANOTHER PATHWAY
Cooperative Learning
What do you think will happen when Mrs. Teubbes returns to the classroom? What might she say and do? What might the others say and do? With a group of classmates, dramatize the scene that might take place.

QUICKWRITES

1. How do you think America would have described her encounter with Mrs. Teubbes at the cultural day celebration? Rewrite this **incident** from America's point of view.
2. Imagine that you are a visitor to a foreign country. You have been handed a bowl of steaming hot food that, to you, is rather strange looking. Write a **narrative** that tells what you do next.

📁 **PORTFOLIO** Save your writing. You may want to use it later as a springboard to a piece for your portfolio.

From Personal Response to Critical Analysis

1. Responses will vary.
2. Possible responses: Mrs. Teubbes has not made an attempt to learn even basic Spanish, which leads to her confusion; she is so focused on her own culture that she thinks it conceivable that America would use white mice for her *pozole.*
3. Possible responses: Mrs. Teubbes stereotypes Hispanic students as less capable than other students; she stereotypes Mrs. Archunde as not applying herself.
4. Responses will vary.
5. Possible responses: Bilingual education allows students to learn more about their own heritage as well as American culture. It may take bilingual students longer to learn English.

Another Pathway

Cooperative Learning Have students form large groups of at least seven to play the roles of Mrs. Teubbes, Mrs. Archunde, America, America's father, Mr. De La O, Ricardo, and Martin. Additional students may wish to play other students or parents. Have the group discuss what the response of each character might be to Mrs. Teubbes's return. After one student records the group's ideas, the group should cooperatively plan who will write the script of the scene. Encourage students to practice the scene before performing in front of the class.

Rubric

3 Full Accomplishment Students create a scene that accurately details the characters and follows the events in the story.

2 Substantial Accomplishment Students develop roles to fit the events of the story, but responses do not correspond to the characters presented by Sálaz-Márquez.

1 Little or Partial Accomplishment Students have difficulty relating the return of Mrs. Teubbes to the events of the story.

Literary Concepts

Remind students that the title is the first clue to the surprise ending. In addition, the coding error involving "pigeon corn," the translation of the Spanish words for *popcorn,* anticipates the mix-up that occurs at the end of the story.

CONCEPT REVIEW To help students focus on the theme of cross-cultural exchange and hidden biases, ask them how the story might have been different if Mrs. Teubbes had had a better understanding of Hispanic culture.

QuickWrites

1. Before students begin to write, remind them to keep in mind America's sincerity as well as her awareness of Mrs. Teubbes's biases.
2. Point out to students that as visitors to a foreign country, their response to the different food must also be respectful of the host—what appears strange may in fact be a special dish reserved for only the most important guests.

 **The Writer's Craft**
Analyzing a Story, pp. 163–177

238 THE LANGUAGE OF LITERATURE TEACHER'S EDITION

LITERARY LINKS

Compare and contrast Mrs. Teubbes in "White Mice" with Miss Bindle in "The Clown." Who do you think is the better teacher? Explain.

ALTERNATIVE ACTIVITIES

Prepare a homemade food that represents your ethnic background, and bring it to class for your classmates to sample. Tell them the name of the food, its ingredients, and the country it comes from.

Thai Chicken with Cellophane Noodles

- 6 ounces Thai noodles
- 1 pound chicken
- 2 tbsp. vegetable oil
- 1 cup sliced carrots
- 4 serrano chilis
- 2 cups chopped cabbage
- 1 cup sliced celery
- 3 green onions
- 1/3 cup soy sauce
- 2 tsp. grated lime peel

WORDS TO KNOW

Review the Words to Know at the bottom of the selection pages. Then, on your paper, revise each sentence by substituting a Word to Know for each boldfaced word or phrase.

1. Mrs. Teubbes showed a **great enthusiasm** for pleasing her **taste buds.**
2. Mrs. Teubbes was **inclined** to show **great enjoyment** when eating.
3. She was **watchful** toward the children and **carefully studied** their every move.
4. Mrs. Teubbes's **determined** attitude could **frighten** the more timid students.
5. Mrs. Archunde had no doubts about the **part** of the curriculum that was meant to be an **intermediate** step from Spanish-speaking to English-speaking.

RUBÉN SÁLAZ-MÁRQUEZ

Rubén Sálaz-Márquez says that his inspiration for "White Mice" came from an anecdote he once heard: "A woman told me that her daughter had been asked to name her favorite food and the little girl answered, 'At my house, we like white maiz best of all.' The surprised questioner wanted to know how they cooked the mice—and whether they ate gray mice too!"

In addition to teaching for more than 20 years, Sálaz-Márquez has written several books, including *Cosmic: The La Raza Sketchbook* and *Heartland: Stories of the Southwest.*

A lifelong native of New Mexico, Sálaz-Márquez enjoys his home state's unique blend of Native American, Hispanic, and European-American cultures. "Living in New Mexico is a tremendous experience," he says, "because we have a long history of getting along without racial hatred."

1935–

WHITE MICE 239

Alternative Activities

The dishes that students bring to class do not have to be elaborate or expensive to prepare. Be aware that some students might identify themselves as "American" and bring typically American food, such as peanut butter and jelly, hot dogs, and apple pie. Ask these students to explain why the food they selected is representative of "America." You may wish to point out that even these foods often have origins in other cultures. For instance, hot dogs are an adaptation of German *wursts* (sausages).

Words to Know

1. ardor, palate
2. prone, gusto
3. vigilant, scrutinized
4. persevering, intimidate
5. component, transitional

Reteaching/Reinforcement
- *Unit Two Resource Book,* p. 50

Literary Links

Possible responses: Miss Bindle is the better teacher because she seems more at ease with her students and can even laugh privately at their antics. Mrs. Teubbes, despite her biases, is the better teacher because she teaches through interaction, not intimidation.

RUBÉN SÁLAZ-MÁRQUEZ

Sálaz-Márquez's work belongs to a tradition of New Mexican literature that laments the passing of time-honored ways of living, whether Native American or Hispanic. In particular, his diverse historical and fictional writings focus on the difficulty of maintaining one's cultural and individual identity in the face of rapid change and the pressure to assimilate into the larger culture.

Across the Curriculum

Social Studies *Cooperative Learning* Have students work in groups of four or five. Have each group choose one culture about which they know little, but would like to know more. Students should begin to research their topic, each member focusing on a specific aspect of the culture such as language, music, arts, food, geography, or religious beliefs. Have groups present their findings to the class. If possible, students may also wish to invite someone from that cultural background to speak to the class.

History *Tu y yo (You and I)* Bilingual education in public schools is largely the result of the civil rights movement of the 1960s. Have students research the development of bilingual education in the United States and the continuing debates over its effectiveness.

OVERVIEW

Objectives

- To understand and appreciate a short story about the nature of long-term imprisonment
- To enrich reading by using active reading strategies
- To understand cause and effect
- To identify and analyze the use of flashbacks
- To express understanding of the story through a choice of writing forms, including diary entries and graffiti
- To extend understanding of the story through a variety of multimodal and cross-curricular activities

Skills

READING SKILLS/STRATEGIES
- Cause and effect
- Clarify

THE WRITER'S STYLE
- Chronological order

SPEAKING, LISTENING, AND VIEWING
- Group discussion
- Oral presentation

GRAMMAR
- Subject-verb agreement

LITERARY CONCEPTS
- Flashbacks
- Theme

SPELLING
- Prefixes in-/im-

Cross-Curricular Connections

SOCIAL STUDIES
- Capital punishment

HISTORY
- Russian Revolution

MATHEMATICS
- Hourly rates

GEOGRAPHY
- Mountain ranges

HISTORICAL CONNECTION
Russia in the 1800s These photographs and illustrations capture the turmoil over land reform and tax reform in late-19th-century Russia. Also included are photographs of the famous writers who supported expanded rights for peasants.

Side A, Frame 52657

PREVIEWING

FICTION

The Bet
Anton Chekhov

Activating Prior Knowledge
PERSONAL CONNECTION
Whether to condemn a murderer to death or to life in prison is a question that has plagued societies for a long time. With your classmates, discuss arguments you have heard for and against capital punishment, or the death penalty. Use a chart like the one shown to organize your thoughts.

Capital Punishment	
Arguments For	Arguments Against

Building Background/Setting a Purpose
HISTORICAL CONNECTION
This story is about a bet made on the issue of capital punishment. Just as this issue is hotly debated in our country today, so was it a controversial issue in Russia in the late 1800s. At that time, Russia was going through a period of tremendous change. Peasants, artists, writers, and others were pressuring the czar, Nicholas II, to free the peasants from forced labor and military service, unfair taxes, and unjust treatment in courts. Among the leaders of this reform movement were the popular writers Leo Tolstoy, Maxim Gorky, and Anton Chekhov. As you read Chekhov's story, see if you can figure out where he stands on the issue of capital punishment.

Czar Nicholas II. UPI/Bettmann.

240   UNIT TWO   PART 2: UNEXPECTED DEVELOPMENTS

- HISTORICAL CONNECTION

PRINT AND MEDIA RESOURCES

UNIT TWO RESOURCE BOOK
Strategic Reading: Literature, p. 53
Vocabulary SkillBuilder, p. 56
Reading SkillBuilder, p. 54
Spelling SkillBuilder, p. 55

GRAMMAR MINI-LESSONS
Transparencies, p. 3
Copymasters, p. 3

WRITING MINI-LESSONS
Transparencies, p. 33

ACCESS FOR STUDENTS ACQUIRING ENGLISH
Selection Summaries
Reading and Writing Support

FORMAL ASSESSMENT
Selection Test, pp. 45–46
Test Generator

 **AUDIO LIBRARY**
See Reference Card

 **LASERLINKS**
Historical Connection

240   THE LANGUAGE OF LITERATURE   TEACHER'S EDITION

Active Reading

READING CONNECTION

Cause and Effect

Imagine that you are at a football game. Your team is only one yard away from the winning touchdown. The teams line up for the final play, and your fullback dives through the line and scores. Overjoyed fans run onto the field, cheering wildly.

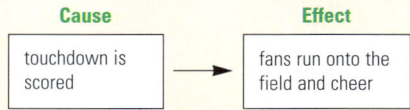

In this situation, the touchdown is the reason why the fans run onto the field. In other words, the touchdown is the cause. The fans' running onto the field is the effect. A cause happens first in time; what follows is the effect.

Events in stories have a similar cause-and-effect relationship. However, in a story, an effect is not always described after its cause. The effect might be presented first, and you read on to discover the cause. Furthermore, an event might have multiple causes or multiple effects. Notice the several causes and one effect in the passage shown on the right:

To recognize causes and effects in all your reading, look for ways that events are connected. Mentally keep track of the order of events. The cause must precede the effect, even if you learn about them in a different order. Be aware, too, that an effect can become the cause of another effect. In addition, look for key words, such as *because*, *since*, and *therefore*, that point out cause-and-effect relationships.

As you read "The Bet," jot down causes and effects in a chart like the one below. For example, the bet is an effect; what is its cause?

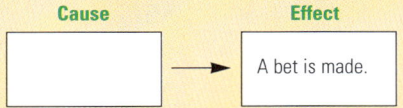

You learn the **effect** first.

An unspeakable dread filled the heart of the murderer. His weapon had been badly damaged, and he had lost all contact with his accomplices. He felt cut off and isolated.

As you continue to read, several **causes** become apparent.

THE BET 241

SUMMARY

A wealthy banker bets a poor young lawyer that if the lawyer can endure living in solitary confinement for 15 years, he'll make him a millionaire. The lawyer spends the time reading and thinking while confined to a room in the banker's house. Just before the lawyer is to be released, the banker, who has fallen on hard times, decides to kill the lawyer to avoid financial ruin. He finds the lawyer asleep and a note that expresses the lawyer's contempt for society. The lawyer plans to leave five minutes before the bet is up. The banker is filled with self-loathing, but he allows the lawyer to leave. The banker keeps the lawyer's note and his money.

Thematic Link: *Unexpected Developments* The banker's plan to kill a man rather than make good on a bet becomes unnecessary when the man unexpectedly runs away and forfeits his winnings.

STRATEGIC READING FOR
Less-Proficient Readers

Set a Purpose Before students begin reading, have them list what they would be willing to do to win two million dollars. Have them compare their lists with other students' lists. Then ask them to read to identify the exact terms of the bet.

Use **UNIT TWO RESOURCE BOOK**, p.53, for guidance in reading the selection.

CUSTOMIZING FOR
Students Acquiring English

- Use **ACCESS FOR STUDENTS ACQUIRING ENGLISH**, Reading and Writing Support.
- Students may have trouble with Chekhov's use of complex sentences and difficult writing style, but they should be able to follow the general story line. To check understanding, frequently ask students to paraphrase what they have read.

WORDS TO KNOW

capricious (kə-prĭsh′əs) *adj.* unpredictable (p. 243)

haphazardly (hăp-hăz′ərd-lē) *adv.* in a random manner (p. 245)

humane (hyōō-mān′) *adj.* merciful; showing the best qualities of humans (p. 243)

immoral (ĭ-môr′əl) *adj.* contrary to what is considered to be correct behavior (p. 243)

incessantly (ĭn-sĕs′ənt-lē) *adv.* continually, without interruption (p. 243)

obsolete (ŏb′sə-lēt′) *adj.* out-of-date (p. 243)

posterity (pŏ-stĕr′ĭ-tē) *n.* future generations (p. 247)

rapture (răp′chər) *n.* a feeling of ecstasy; great joy (p. 243)

renunciation (rĭ-nŭn′sē-ā′shən) *n.* a declaration in which something is given up (p. 248)

stipulated (stĭp′yə-lā′tĭd) *adj.* arranged in an agreement **stipulate** *v.* (p. 248)

Art Note

Portrait de Matisse by André Derain
This work by French painter Derain (1880–1954) dates to a famous art show in the autumn of 1905 that announced the arrival of fauvism. Led by Matisse and Derain, painters in this style used bold tints of primary colors in order to give full expression to their vision.

Reading the Art How do the thick brush strokes and heavy color combine to give a sense of Matisse's character? What aspects of his personality come through in the painting?

CUSTOMIZING FOR
Gifted and Talented Students

Have students note, as they read the selection, how Chekhov shows the influence of money on people's actions.

Possible responses:

- Page 243—"'You stake . . . my freedom,' said the lawyer." The lawyer is willing to give up the most productive years of his career in order to win the two million.
- Page 246—"'If I have the courage . . . first of all.'" Not only is the banker willing to commit murder to keep his money, he is willing to let an innocent person take the blame.

Literary Concept: FLASHBACK

A Ask students how they know that the story will describe events that occurred earlier. *(Possible response: The description of the party occurs in the memory of the old banker.)*

CUSTOMIZING FOR
Students Acquiring English

I Be sure that less fluent students understand the phrases *not a few* (many) and *for the most part* (mostly).

THE BET

by Anton Chekhov

It was a dark autumn night. The old banker was pacing from corner to corner of his study, recalling to his mind the party he gave in the autumn fifteen years ago. There were many clever people at the party and much interesting conversation. They talked among other things of capital punishment. The guests, among them not a few scholars and journalists, for the most part disapproved of capital punishment.

242

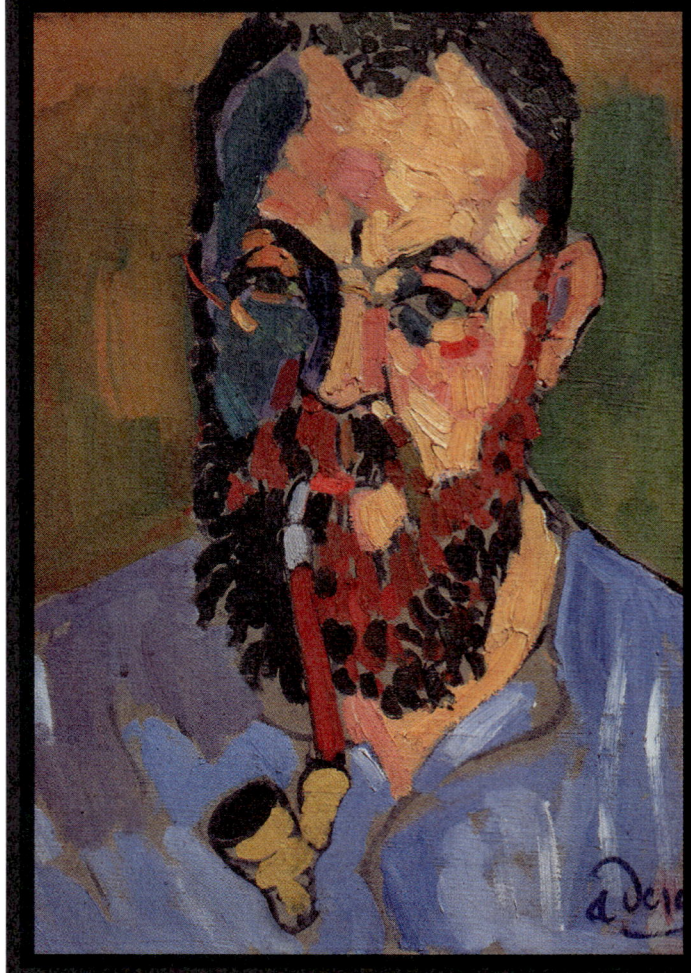

Portrait of Henri Matisse (1905), André Derain. Tate Gallery, London/Art Resource, New York. Copyright © 1996 Artists Rights Society (ARS), New York/ADAGP, Paris.

Mini-Lesson — Literary Concepts

REVIEWING THEME Remind students that theme refers to the message about life or human nature communicated by a work of literature. In most cases, the reader must infer the theme. One way to figure out a theme is to apply to all people the lessons learned by the main characters.

Application Have students work in small groups to discuss the theme of "The Bet." In developing their answers, each group should answer the following questions:

- What are the banker and the lawyer most concerned about at the opening of the story?
- How do the concerns of the banker and the lawyer change?
- What concern remains constant for both characters?

When students have finished responding to these questions, have each group identify the theme of the story (*the value of human freedom; greed*) and what Chekhov is saying about human nature (*humans cannot be solitary creatures; people's greed outweighs their morals; those quick to condemn others should look inward*). Invite groups to share their conclusions with the rest of the class.

242 THE LANGUAGE OF LITERATURE TEACHER'S EDITION

They found it obsolete as a means of punishment, unfitted to a Christian state and immoral. Some of them thought that capital punishment should be replaced universally by life imprisonment.

"I don't agree with you," said the host. "I myself have experienced neither capital punishment nor life imprisonment, but if one may judge a priori,[1] then in my opinion capital punishment is more moral and more humane than imprisonment. Execution kills instantly; life imprisonment kills by degrees. Who is the more humane executioner, one who kills you in a few seconds or one who draws the life out of you incessantly, for years?"

"They're both equally immoral," remarked one of the guests, "because their purpose is the same, to take away life. The state is not God. It has no right to take away that which it cannot give back, if it should so desire."

Among the company was a lawyer, a young man of about twenty-five. On being asked his opinion, he said:

"Capital punishment and life imprisonment are equally immoral; but if I were offered the choice between them, I would certainly choose the second. It's better to live somehow than not to live at all."

There ensued a lively discussion. The banker, who was then younger and more nervous, suddenly lost his temper, banged his fist on the table, and turning to the young lawyer, cried out:

"It's a lie. I bet you two millions you wouldn't stick in a cell even for five years."

"If you're serious," replied the lawyer, "then I bet I'll stay not five but fifteen."

"Fifteen! Done!" cried the banker. "Gentlemen, I stake two millions."

"Agreed. You stake two millions, I my freedom," said the lawyer.

So this wild, ridiculous bet came to pass. The banker, who at that time had too many millions to count, spoiled and capricious, was beside himself with rapture. During supper he said to the lawyer jokingly:

"Come to your senses, young man, before it's too late. Two millions are nothing to me, but you stand to lose three or four of the best years of your life. I say three or four, because you'll never stick it out any longer. Don't forget either, you unhappy man, that voluntary is much heavier than enforced imprisonment. The idea that you have the right to free yourself at any moment will poison the whole of your life in the cell. I pity you."

And now the banker, pacing from corner to corner, recalled all this and asked himself:

CLARIFY
Why do the banker and the lawyer make the bet?
Using a Reading Log

"Why did I make this bet? What's the good? The lawyer loses fifteen years of his life and I throw away two millions. Will it convince people that capital punishment is worse or better than imprisonment for life? No, no! all stuff and rubbish. On my part, it was the caprice of a well-fed man; on the lawyer's, pure greed of gold."

He recollected further what happened after the evening party. It was decided that the lawyer must undergo his imprisonment under

---
1. **a priori** (ä′prē-ôr′ē): based on a theory rather than on experience.

WORDS TO KNOW
obsolete (ŏb′sə-lēt′) *adj.* out-of-date
immoral (ĭ-môr′əl) *adj.* contrary to what is considered to be correct behavior
humane (hyōō-mān′) *adj.* merciful; showing the best qualities of humans
incessantly (ĭn-sĕs′ənt-lē) *adv.* continually, without interruption
capricious (kə-prĭsh′əs) *adj.* unpredictable
rapture (răp′chər) *n.* a feeling of ecstasy; great joy

243

Mini-Lesson  Reading Skills/Strategies

ACTIVE READING: CLARIFY Remind students that active readers often pause in their reading to clarify any confusing plot points. Encourage students to clarify which elements of the plot cause other events to happen, and which actions are the effects of other occurrences. Explain that one of the best ways to organize this information is to develop a cause-and-effect chart. Refer students to the cause-and-effect charts on page 241.

Application Draw a cause-and-effect chart like the one shown. Point out that some causes may have multiple effects and some effects are the result of multiple causes. Encourage students to create their own charts to track the causes and effects of other major events such as:
- the banker's impending financial ruin
- the decision to murder the lawyer

After students complete their charts, have them compare their charts with other students.

Cause	Effect
Bet is made.	Lawyer is imprisoned.

Critical Thinking: MAKING JUDGMENTS
B Have students consider whether money is ever sufficient payment for the loss of years of a life, and if so, what price they would place on one year of their own lives. Ask them to focus on contemporary issues such as malpractice or accidental injury.

CUSTOMIZING FOR
Students Acquiring English
2 Ask a more fluent student to paraphrase *stick in a cell.* (*stay or remain in a cell*) Then have students find the expression used later on this page, *you'll never stick it out,* and ask them to explain what it means. (*You'll never stay or remain.*)

STRATEGIC READING FOR
Less-Proficient Readers
C Have students explain the terms of the bet. (*The banker will pay the lawyer two million if the lawyer can voluntarily stay confined for 15 years. The banker will lose a lot of money, while the lawyer will lose his freedom.*) Restating

Set a Purpose Have students follow the progression of the bet. Ask them to pay particular attention to what will happen to the banker if the lawyer wins the bet.

Active Reading: CLARIFY
D Ask students to refer back to the discussion of capital punishment versus life imprisonment and to discuss how the different financial situations of the lawyer and banker affect the terms of the bet. (*Possible responses: The lawyer and the banker are young and hotheaded and make the bet without thinking it through. The banker has so much money that two million doesn't matter to him, but the lawyer will give up years of his life to get it.*)

Active Reading: CONNECT

E Ask students to decide whether they think they could survive 15 years of solitary confinement if they were provided with the same items as the banker supplies for the lawyer.

Literary Concept: THEME

F Have students discuss how the terms of the bet relate to the overall theme of the story. *(Possible responses: The story is concerned with how the desire for money can imprison people, and the behavior of the lawyer and the banker shows the lengths to which people will go for money. The story is concerned with the value of human freedom, and the terms of the bet reveal unexpected information about each of the main characters.)*

CUSTOMIZING FOR
Students Acquiring English

3 Explain that classics are literary works that have been considered important for many centuries (especially works from ancient Greece and Rome). Also, some students may not be familiar with the New Testament, which is mentioned later on this page.

Active Reading: PREDICT

G Have students discuss whether it is likely that the lawyer will keep his side of the bet. You may use the following model to help students make predictions.

Think-Aloud Model *At first, it seemed unlikely that the lawyer could stay locked up for 15 years, but he seems very serious about winning the bet. Also, because the story opens with a flashback to 15 years earlier, it is clear that the lawyer has either won the bet or is about to.)*

---

the strictest observation, in a garden wing of the banker's house. It was agreed that during the period he would be deprived of the right to cross the threshold, to see living people, to hear human voices, and to receive letters and newspapers. He was permitted to have a musical instrument, to read books, to write letters, to drink wine and smoke tobacco. By the agreement he could communicate, but only in silence, with the outside world through a little window specially constructed for this purpose. Everything necessary, books, music, wine, he could receive in any quantity by sending a note through the window. The agreement provided for all the minutest details, which made the confinement strictly solitary, and it obliged the lawyer to remain exactly fifteen years from twelve o'clock of November 14th, 1870, to twelve o'clock of November 14th, 1885. The least attempt on his part to violate the conditions, to escape if only for two minutes before the time, freed the banker from the obligation to pay him the two millions.

During the first year of imprisonment, the lawyer, as far as it was possible to judge from his short notes, suffered terribly from loneliness and boredom. From his wing day and night came the sound of the piano. He rejected wine and tobacco. "Wine," he wrote, "excites desires, and desires are the chief foes of a prisoner; besides, nothing is more boring than to drink good wine alone," and tobacco spoiled the air in his room. During the first year, the lawyer was sent books of a light character; novels with a complicated love interest, stories of crime and fantasy, comedies, and so on.

In the second year, the piano was heard no longer and the lawyer asked only for classics. In the fifth year, music was heard again, and the prisoner asked for wine. Those who watched him said that during the whole of that year he was only eating, drinking, and lying on his bed. He yawned often and talked angrily to himself. Books he did not read. Sometimes at nights he would sit down to write. He would write for a long time and tear it all up in the morning. More than once he was heard to weep.

In the second half of the sixth year, the prisoner began zealously to study languages, philosophy, and history. He fell on these subjects so hungrily that the banker hardly had time to get books enough for him. In the space of four years about six hundred volumes were bought at his request. It was while that passion lasted that the banker received the following letter from the prisoner: "My dear jailer, I am writing these lines in six languages. Show them to experts. Let them read them. If they do not find one single mistake, I beg you to give orders to have a gun fired off in the garden. By the noise I shall know that my efforts have not been in vain. The geniuses of all ages and countries speak in different languages; but in them all burns the same flame. Oh, if you knew my heavenly happiness now that I can understand them!" The prisoner's desire was fulfilled. Two shots were fired in the garden by the banker's order.

Later on, after the tenth year, the lawyer sat immovable before his table and read only the New Testament. The banker found it strange that a man who in four years had mastered six hundred erudite² volumes, should have spent nearly a year in reading one book, easy to understand and by no means thick. The New Testament was then replaced by the history of religions and theology.

During the last two years of his confinement the prisoner read an extraordinary amount,

PREDICT
Will the lawyer stay for 15 years?
Using a Reading Log

---

2. **erudite** (ĕr′yə-dīt′): scholarly.

244 UNIT TWO PART 2: UNEXPECTED DEVELOPMENTS

Multicultural  Perspectives

LAND AND MONEY In Chekhov's time, one-third of the Russian population was made up of free serfs or peasants who were forced to work the land of wealthy people. Chekhov's plays and writings were financially successful, but he never forgot that he was the grandson of a serf and the son of a grocer. Throughout his life he ran a free clinic for peasants (he was also a physician) and supported relief organizations concerned with famines and epidemics.

Taking into account these cultural circumstances, one can see that "The Bet" addresses issues larger than the pride of two men. It questions the role of money in society. Whether the banker or the lawyer wins the bet, the outcome is the same: greed is a prison.

244 THE LANGUAGE OF LITERATURE TEACHER'S EDITION

quite haphazardly. Now he would apply himself to the natural sciences, then would read Byron³ or Shakespeare. Notes used to come from him in which he asked to be sent at the same time a book on chemistry, a textbook of medicine, a novel, and some treatise on philosophy or theology. He read as though he were swimming in the sea among broken pieces of wreckage, and in his desire to save his life was eagerly grasping one piece after another.

The banker recalled all this, and thought:

"Tomorrow at twelve o'clock he receives his freedom. Under the agreement, I shall have to pay him two millions. If I pay, it's all over with me. I am ruined forever. . . ."

Fifteen years before he had too many millions to count, but now he was afraid to ask himself which he had more of, money or debts. Gambling on the stock exchange, risky speculation, and the recklessness of which he could not rid himself even in old age, had gradually brought his business to decay; and the fearless, self-confident, proud man of business had become an ordinary banker, trembling at every rise and fall in the market.

"That cursed bet," murmured the old man clutching his head in despair. . . . "Why didn't the man die? He's only forty years old. He will take away my

CLARIFY
Why might the banker be ruined?
Using a Reading Log

He yawned often and talked angrily to himself. . . . More than once he was heard to weep.

3. **Byron:** George Gordon Byron (1788–1824), a leading English poet of the Romantic movement.

WORDS TO KNOW
haphazardly (hăp-hăz´ərd-lē) *adv.* in a random manner

Critical Thinking: ANALYZING
H Have students explain why the banker recalls the details of the lawyer's education. *(Possible responses: The banker's thoughts reveal how the lawyer was able to survive 15 years cut off from people; through the banker the reader learns how the lawyer's mind was shaped.)*

STRATEGIC READING FOR
Less-Proficient Readers
I Have students describe what might happen if the banker loses the bet. *(Possible response: The banker faces financial disaster if he has to pay two million to the lawyer.)* **Noting Relevant Details**

Set a Purpose Ask students to continue reading to find out how the banker attempts to avoid financial ruin.

Active Reading: CLARIFY
J Ask students to think about the passage of time in the story. Have them compare the banker's financial situation when he made the bet with his situation 15 years later. *(Possible responses: Over 15 years, the banker made bad business decisions and gambled. As a result, his fortune decreased dramatically.)*

Assessment Option

INFORMAL ASSESSMENT You can informally assess students' understanding of the selection by having them role-play a U.S. TV news correspondent. Read the following scenario to the class:

You are assigned to cover the mysterious outcome of a 15-year bet in Russia for the viewers of your news program. Be sure your viewers understand the terms of the bet, how it originated, what the banker and lawyer did for 15 years, and the outcome of the bet..

Invite students to read their written broadcasts to the class in the manner of reporters.

Rubric
3 Full Accomplishment Students carefully recount the events of the story and make clear the causes and effects.
2 Substantial Accomplishment Students cover most of the main points of the plot but do not clearly show cause-and-effect relationships.
1 Little or Partial Accomplishment Students have difficulty covering the basic components of the plot.

STRATEGIC READING FOR
Less-Proficient Readers

K Have students discuss how they feel about the banker's decision to kill the lawyer in order to keep from paying the bet. *(Possible responses: The banker thinks he is saving himself from disgrace, but he must resort to murder to keep the lawyer from winning. Although the bet was about life imprisonment and capital punishment, the banker's decision to kill the lawyer shows he is not really concerned with the issues involved.)*

Making Judgments

Set a Purpose Have students read on to find out the banker's response to winning the bet.

Critical Thinking:
SPECULATING

L Have students speculate about what the lawyer will look like after 15 years alone. *(Possible responses: Because he can eat and drink as much as he wishes he will be overweight and out of shape. He may be healthy because there was nothing to distract him from staying in shape.)*

Literary Concept:
METAPHOR

M Have students discuss how the comparison of the lawyer to a skeleton with women's hair shows what has happened to him. *(Possible responses: Like a skeleton, the lawyer is "dead" to this world. He has grown thin and has long hair.)*

---

last penny, marry, enjoy life, gamble on the exchange, and I will look on like an envious beggar and hear the same words from him every day: 'I'm obliged to you for the happiness of my life. Let me help you.' No, it's too much! The only escape from bankruptcy and disgrace—is that the man should die."

The clock had just struck three. The banker was listening. In the house everyone was asleep, and one could hear only the frozen trees whining outside the windows. Trying to make no sound, he took out of his safe the key of the door which had not been opened for fifteen years, put on his overcoat, and went out of the house. The garden was dark and cold. It was raining. A keen damp wind hovered howling over all the garden and gave the trees no rest. Though he strained his eyes, the banker could see neither the ground, nor the white statues, nor the garden wing, nor the trees. Approaching the place where the garden wing stood, he called the watchman twice. There was no answer. Evidently the watchman had taken shelter from the bad weather and was now asleep somewhere in the kitchen or the greenhouse.

"If I have the courage to fulfil my intention," thought the old man, "the suspicion will fall on the watchman first of all."

In the darkness he groped for the stairs and the door and entered the hall of the garden wing, then poked his way into a narrow passage and struck a match. Not a soul was there. Someone's bed, with no bedclothes on it, stood there, and an iron stove was dark in the corner. The seals on the door that led into the prisoner's room were unbroken.

When the match went out, the old man, trembling from agitation, peeped into the little window.

In the prisoner's room a candle was burning dim. The prisoner himself sat by the table. Only his back, the hair on his head, and his hands were visible. On the table, the two chairs, and on the carpet by the table, open books were strewn.

Five minutes passed and the prisoner never once stirred. Fifteen years' confinement had taught him to sit motionless. The banker tapped on the window with his finger, but the prisoner gave no movement in reply. Then the banker cautiously tore the seals from the door and put the key into the lock. The rusty lock gave a hoarse groan and the door creaked. The banker expected instantly to hear a cry of surprise and the sound of steps. Three minutes passed and it was as quiet behind the door as it had been before. He made up his mind to enter.

Before the table sat a man, unlike an ordinary human being. It was a skeleton, with tight-drawn skin, with a woman's long curly hair, and a shaggy beard. The color of his face was yellow, of an earthy shade; the cheeks were sunken, the back long and narrow, and the hand upon which he leaned his hairy head was so lean and skinny that it was painful to look upon. His hair was already silvering with grey, and no one who glanced at the senile

246 UNIT TWO PART 2: UNEXPECTED DEVELOPMENTS

Mini-Lesson The Writer's Style

LIST OF EVENTS
5 the lawyer gives up the money
1 a party was held
4 the banker decides to kill the lawyer
3 the banker loses most of his money
2 the lawyer and the banker made a bet

CHRONOLOGICAL ORDER Although much of the action of the story is told through flashbacks, Chekhov keeps the events in chronological order by using transitional words, dates, and time references.

Application Write on the board the list of events from the chart shown. Have students copy the list into their notebooks and number the items in the correct chronological order. Then ask students to combine their list with the following transition words and phrases in a paragraph that outlines the major story events:

- later that evening (2)
- then (4)
- 15 years ago (1)
- finally (5)
- over time (3)

Reteaching/Reinforcement
- *Writing Handbook*, anthology p. 829
- *Writing Mini-Lessons* transparencies, p. 33

 **The Writer's Craft**

Chronological Order, pp. 240–241

emaciation[4] of the face would have believed that he was only forty years old. On the table, before his bent head, lay a sheet of paper on which something was written in a tiny hand.

"Poor devil," thought the banker, "he's asleep and probably seeing millions in his dreams. I have only to take and throw this half-dead thing on the bed, smother him a moment with the pillow, and the most careful examination will find no trace of unnatural death. But, first, let us read what he has written here."

The banker took the sheet from the table and read:

"Tomorrow at twelve o'clock midnight, I shall obtain my freedom and the right to mix with people. But before I leave this room and see the sun I think it necessary to say a few words to you. On my own clear conscience and before God who sees me, I declare to you that I despise freedom, life, health, and all that your books call the blessings of the world.

"For fifteen years I have diligently studied earthly life. True, I saw neither the earth nor the people, but in your books I drank fragrant wine, sang songs, hunted deer and wild boar in the forests, loved women . . . And beautiful women, like clouds ethereal,[5] created by the magic of your poets' genius, visited me by night and whispered to me wonderful tales, which made my head drunken. In your books I climbed the summits of Elbruz and Mont Blanc and saw from there how the sun rose in the morning, and in the evening overflowed the sky, the ocean and the mountain ridges with a purple gold. From there I saw how above me lightnings glimmered, cleaving the clouds; I saw green forests, fields, rivers, lakes, cities; I heard sirens[6] singing, and the playing of the pipes of Pan;[7] I touched the wings of beautiful devils who came flying to me to speak of God . . . In your books I cast myself into bottomless abysses,[8] worked miracles, burned cities to the ground, preached new religions, conquered whole countries . . .

"Your books gave me wisdom. All that unwearying human thought created in the centuries is compressed to a little lump in my skull. I know that I am more clever than you all.

"And I despise your books, despise all worldly blessings and wisdom. Everything is void, frail, visionary and delusive as a mirage. Though you be proud and wise and beautiful, yet will death wipe you from the face of the earth like the mice underground; and your <u>posterity</u>, your history, and the immortality of your men of genius will be as frozen slag, burnt down together with the terrestrial globe.

"You are mad, and gone the wrong way. You take lie for truth and ugliness for beauty. You would marvel if by certain conditions frogs and lizards should suddenly grow on apple and orange trees, instead of fruit, and if roses should begin to breathe the odor of a sweating horse. So do I marvel at you, who have bartered heaven for earth. I do not want to understand you.

"That I may show you in deed my contempt for that by which you live, I waive the two millions of which I once dreamed of as paradise, and which I now despise. That I may deprive myself of my right to them, I shall

---

4. **emaciation** (ĭ-mā′shē-ā′shən): abnormal thinness, usually caused by starvation.
5. **ethereal** (ĭ-thîr′ē-əl): delicate; heavenly.
6. **sirens**: from Greek mythology, sea goddesses whose sweet singing lured sailors to their deaths on rocky coasts.
7. **pipes of Pan**: Pan, the Greek god of woods, fields, and flocks, played a flutelike pipe instrument.
8. **abysses** (ə-bĭs′ĭz): deep gulfs, gorges, or chasms in the earth.

WORDS TO KNOW
posterity (pŏ-stĕr′ĭ-tē) *n.* future generations

247

Literary Concept: THEME

N Have students discuss how dreaming of millions and planning to murder the lawyer relate to the theme. *(Possible response: The linking of money and murder shows how people can be so concerned with money that they disregard human life.)*

Critical Thinking: MAKING JUDGMENTS

O Ask students to decide how comprehensive the lawyer's study of "earthly life" is. *(Possible responses: After 15 years of reading, the lawyer is thoroughly educated in the ways of the world. Even though he has read a lot, this does not mean that the lawyer really understands people.)*

Linking to Geography

P Elbruz is a mountain range in northern Iran that reaches to a height of 18,603 feet. Mont Blanc, a mountain in the Alps on the French-Italian border, reaches 15,781 feet, Europe's highest point.

Literary Concept: IRONY

Q Have students explain the irony of the prisoner's claims that the banker and the world he represents are mad. *(Possible response: The lawyer himself has gone mad after being cut off from human contact for so many years.)*

Mini-Lesson Grammar

SUBJECT-VERB AGREEMENT Remind students that the subject and the verb in a sentence must agree in number. Tell students to be careful of words and phrases that come between the subject and the verb. Point out that the subject of a sentence is never found in a prepositional phrase or an appositive.

Application Read the following sentences aloud and have students write the correct form of the verb in each.
1. The lawyer, one of the guests, (disagree, <u>disagrees</u>) with the host.
2. The banker, still in the prime of life, (<u>fears</u>, fear) financial ruin.
3. The seals on the door (has, <u>have</u>) not been opened in 15 years.

Reteaching/Reinforcement
- *Grammar Handbook*, anthology p. 863
- *Grammar Mini-Lessons* copymasters p. 3, transparencies p. 3

The Writer's Craft
Subject-Verb Agreement, pp. 577–592

THE LANGUAGE OF LITERATURE TEACHER'S EDITION **247**

Active Reading: EVALUATE

R Have students refer to the lawyer's letter for reasons that might explain his feelings and actions. *(Possible response: The lawyer believes he has acquired wisdom during his years in prison that has enabled him to see through the world's illusions to what is really important in life.)*

STRATEGIC READING FOR
Less-Proficient Readers

S Have students describe the banker's feelings after winning the bet. *(Possible response: The banker is shamed by the realization that he was so concerned with money that he was willing to kill another man for it.)* Drawing Conclusions

CUSTOMIZING FOR
Gifted and Talented Students

Have students discuss the importance and preconditions of freedom. Ask them if freedom is something given to the individual, or if it is something each person must strive to achieve. Encourage students to use examples from the story in their responses.

Art Note

Gauguin's Armchair by Vincent van Gogh Although van Gogh's art is respected throughout the world, during his lifetime he sold only one painting and received no critical recognition.

Reading the Art *What details create a sense of introspection and isolation in the painting?*

COMPREHENSION CHECK
1. How much time has elapsed since the lawyer and banker made the bet? *(almost 15 years)*
2. What will happen to the banker if the lawyer wins? *(He will be destroyed financially.)*
3. What does the banker decide to do to stop the lawyer from winning? *(murder him)*
4. Why does the banker win the bet? *(The lawyer runs away minutes before the 15 years are up.)*

---

come out from here five minutes before the <u>stipulated</u> term, and thus shall violate the agreement."

When he had read, the banker put the sheet on the table, kissed the head of the strange man, and began to weep. He went out of the wing. Never at any other time, not even after his terrible losses on the Exchange, had he felt such contempt for himself as now. Coming home, he lay down on his bed, but agitation and tears kept him long from sleep. . . .

It EVALUATE
What causes the lawyer's bitterness?

The next morning the poor watchman came running to him and told him that they had seen the man who lived in the wing climbing through the window into the garden. He had gone to the gate and disappeared. With his servants the banker went instantly to the wing and established the escape of his prisoner. To avoid unnecessary rumors he took the paper with the <u>renunciation</u> from the table and, on his return, locked it in his safe. ❖

Gauguin's Armchair (1888), Vincent van Gogh. Van Gogh Museum, Amsterdam, the Netherlands. Art Resource/New York.

WORDS TO KNOW
stipulated (stĭp′yə-lā′tĭd) *adj.* arranged in an agreement **stipulate** *v.*
renunciation (rĭ-nŭn′sē-ā′shən) *n.* a declaration in which something is given up

---

Mini-Lesson TM Spelling

PREFIXES *in-/im-* Explain to students that the prefix *in-* means "not" or "in." Tell them that *in-* becomes *im-* before roots or words beginning with *b, m,* and *p.*

in- + cessantly

im- + moral

Application Have students add the prefix *in-* or *im-* to the following roots or base words.

1. tuition
2. sulation
3. mediate
4. mortality
5. practical
6. fection
7. patient
8. digestion
9. migration
10. competent
11. nate
12. ject
13. position
14. vasion
15. balance
16. perfect

Ask students to look for more words that fit this pattern, in their own writing and in things that they read, and to add these words to their personal word lists.

Reteaching/Reinforcement
• *Unit Two Resource Book,* p. 55

RESPONDING OPTIONS

FROM PERSONAL RESPONSE TO CRITICAL ANALYSIS

REFLECT 1. Did you have stronger feelings about the banker or the lawyer? Jot down your thoughts in your notebook and share them with the class.

RETHINK 2. What do you think of the lawyer for walking away from the money?
Consider
- what he could have gained by not leaving early
- the effects of long-term isolation on him

3. If the banker and the lawyer had foreseen the effects of this bet, do you think they would have agreed to it? Why or why not?

4. What do you think the bet proved? Explain your answer.

5. What does this story show about Chekhov's viewpoint on life imprisonment?

RELATE 6. After reading this story and considering your discussion with classmates for the Personal Connection on page 240, how do you think a murderer should be punished? Explain.

Thematic Link

Multimodal Learning
ANOTHER PATHWAY
Cooperative Learning
In a small group, discuss what the lawyer and the banker were like at the time the bet was made and after the 15 years had passed. Record the changes in these characters in a chart like the one below.

How the Characters Change		
	Lawyer	Banker
Before		
After		

QUICKWRITES

1. Write three **diary entries** the lawyer might have written—one during his first year of imprisonment, one during the middle years, and one near the end. Make sure your entries show changes in his personality and thinking.

2. Write at least three pieces of **graffiti** that the lawyer might have written on the walls of his room.

📁 **PORTFOLIO** Save your writing. You may want to use it later as a springboard to a piece for your portfolio.

LITERARY CONCEPTS

A scene from an earlier time that interrupts the ongoing action in a story is called a **flashback.** Flashbacks provide information that helps readers understand a character's present situation. In "The Bet," the banker's recollection of a party he gave 15 years earlier is a flashback. Look for a second flashback the banker experiences. What does he recall in that flashback?

CONCEPT REVIEW: Climax You know that the climax is the most dramatic moment in a story, the point at which an important event, decision, or discovery takes place. What do you think is the climax of "The Bet"?

THE BET **249**

From Personal Response to Critical Analysis

1. Responses will vary.
2. Possible responses: He was foolish to walk away from so much money, even if he thought he was making a statement. He was wise to walk away because he realized that money and greed corrupt people.
3. Possible responses: The lawyer would not have made the bet because it cost him his sanity. The banker would not have made the bet because he lost his self-respect.
4. Possible response: The bet proved that long-term imprisonment, even under the best conditions, destroys human beings.
5. Possible response: Chekhov is opposed to life imprisonment, as it can drive people insane.
6. Responses will vary.

Another Pathway
Cooperative Learning Groups should cooperatively plan which members will be responsible for each section of the chart. One student may record the group's general impressions, while other members fill in specific information. After each group completes its chart, have members share their charts with the class.

Rubric
3 Full Accomplishment The group identifies the changes in the characters from the beginning to the end of the short story.
2 Substantial Accomplishment The group partially completes the chart but cannot describe either what the characters were like at first or how they evolved.
1 Little or Partial Accomplishment The group fails to identify how the lawyer and banker changed.

Literary Concepts

The second flashback refers to the events that took place while the lawyer was in prison (p. 245). Have students brainstorm a list of signal words that help them recognize a flashback. *(Possible responses: recalled, recounted, recollected, remembered)*

CONCEPT REVIEW Have students work in small groups to list the major events of the story and to decide which is the climax. Remind students that the climax occurs before the resolution, so the watchman's discovery of the lawyer's escape cannot be the climax. The banker's discovery of the lawyer's note is the climax.

QuickWrites

1. Have students review, before they write their diary entries, the account of the lawyer's 15 years of imprisonment. Students may wish to make a list of the different items the lawyer asked for to include in their diary.

2. Point out that graffiti often consists of elaborate designs that illustrate words and sentiments. Graffiti can be a form of social commentary and criticism without being vulgar or explicit.

Autobiographical Incident, pp. 27–39
Journal Writing, pp. 222–223

Literary Links

Possible response: The lawyer in "The Bet" must have felt comfortable being alone, or else he would not have agreed to solitary confinement for such a long period of time. On the other hand, Jerry in "A Mother in Mannville" was really never willingly alone, since he lived in an orphanage with many other children. Still, being surrounded by other people did not stop him from yearning for close human contact, the kind of companionship he felt when he was with the narrator of the story.

Across the Curriculum

Social Studies *Cooperative Learning* Have students work in small groups. You may want to assign each group a region of the country to research, such as the Southwest or the Northeast. Be sure students have a map of the United States or a listing of the states to help them divide the task among members of the group. When groups have completed their research, you may want the class to compile a color-coded map that shows the states that allow or prohibit capital punishment.

Mathematics You may wish to simplify this exercise by having students use 365 days for each year and ignore leap years. *(24 hours a day ¥ 365 days = 8,760 hours a year; 8,760 ¥ 15 years = 131,400 total hours. $2,000,000 ÷ 131,400 = $15.22 per hour.)*

ADDITIONAL SUGGESTION

History *From Reform to Revolution* Have students research how the reform movements of the late nineteenth century eventually led to the Russian Revolution at the beginning of the twentieth century. Have them prepare a time line charting important developments and display the chart in the classroom.

Art Connection

The portrait of Matisse shows a young, vigorous man. At the end of the lawyer's imprisonment, the lawyer's appearance would be older, paler, and weaker than that of Matisse.

Multimodal Learning

ALTERNATIVE ACTIVITIES

1. Sketch or paint a series of three **pictures** that the lawyer might have created at the beginning, the middle, and the end of his imprisonment. In planning your pictures, consider the lawyer's activities, thoughts, and feelings at those times.
2. With a small group of classmates, plan a **performance** of the scene in which the bet is made. You might want to expand the discussion about the death penalty with additional arguments for and against it. Act out the scene for your class.
3. Suppose that like the lawyer, you have agreed to imprisonment. What books would you most want to have with you—romance novels, mysteries, textbooks, poetry, science fiction? Make a **list** of titles and explain your choices.

LITERARY LINKS

When you read "A Mother in Manville," you were asked to think about the difference between "alone" and "lonely." Compare and contrast Jerry's experience with the lawyer's experience in "The Bet." Were these two characters alone, lonely, or both? Explain your answer.

ACROSS THE CURRICULUM

 Social Studies Find out which states in the United States have a law that permits the use of capital punishment. If possible, use an encyclopedia program or an on-line computer service to start your research. Share your findings with your class.

 Mathematics If the lawyer had received two million dollars for his fifteen years, how much would he have earned per hour?

ART CONNECTION

Look at the portrait on page 242. What do you notice about the artist's style? If this artist painted a portrait of the lawyer at the end of the lawyer's 15 years of imprisonment, how might that portrait look different from this one?

Detail of *Portrait of Henri Matisse* (1905), André Derain. Tate Gallery, London/Art Resource, New York. Copyright © 1996 Artists Rights Society (ARS), New York/ADAGP, Paris.

250 UNIT TWO PART 2: UNEXPECTED DEVELOPMENTS

Alternative Activities

1. Remind students as they begin their paintings that the lawyer had no contact with other human beings for 15 years, a fact that would have a profound effect on the subject matter the lawyer might have painted over the course of his imprisonment.
2. Have students review the opening passages of the story before they begin to plan their performance. Ask them to note the type of people who attended the party when they designate the roles to be played. Additionally, students should keep in mind when they stage their performance the tempers, age, and spontaneity of the characters and events involved.
3. Point out that the lawyer has access to any book he chooses, so students should not feel limited in their choices.

WORDS TO KNOW

EXERCISE A Review the Words to Know at the bottom of the selection pages. On your paper, write the word that is most closely related to each situation described below.

1. In some states, capital punishment is no longer used.
2. That judge is unpredictable in sentencing criminals.
3. The defendant felt thrilled when he was acquitted.
4. The corrupt politician stole government funds.
5. The judge laid down specific rules for the convict's parole.
6. A merciful judge treated the boy kindly.
7. The debaters argue on endlessly.
8. Both sides worry about future generations.
9. Is legalizing the death penalty a giving up of morality?
10. Could the death penalty be administered at random?

EXERCISE B Working in small groups, retell the plot of a popular movie using as many of the Words to Know as possible. Each student should provide a few sentences and try to use at least one of the words in each.

Words to Know

Exercise A
1. obsolete
2. capricious
3. rapture
4. immoral
5. stipulated
6. humane
7. incessantly
8. posterity
9. renunciation
10. haphazardly

Exercise B
All retellings that use words taken from Words to Know are acceptable.

Reteaching/Reinforcement
• *Unit Two Resource Book,* p. 56

ANTON CHEKHOV

1860–1904

Anton Chekhov was the third of six children born to a peasant family in Taganrog, Russia, near the Black Sea. "Childhood was sheer suffering," he once said. "My father began my education, or, to put it more simply, began to beat me, before I reached the age of five."

When Chekhov was 15, his father's business failed, and Chekhov began to help support his family. He sold household goods and tutored younger students in Taganrog. In 1879 he entered medical school in Moscow. He later abandoned medicine for a career in writing.

Chekhov wrote for comic magazines before turning to longer and more serious stories and plays. His style of writing focuses on a character's mood rather than on action; Chekhov believed that writers should portray life as it really is and should raise questions about it. As a result of his masterful stories and plays, he became known as the father of the modern short story and of the modern play. Several decades after his death from tuberculosis, Chekhov's stories and plays were translated, and they continue to be popular throughout the world today.

OTHER WORKS *A Marriage Proposal,* "The Confession," "A Slander"

Extended Reading

ANTON CHEKHOV

In addition to his short stories, Chekhov is most famous for his plays *The Seagull* (1895), *Uncle Vanya* (1899), *The Three Sisters* (1901), and *The Cherry Orchard* (1904). The unique combination of comedy and pathos in these plays revolutionized modern dramatic writing.

WHAT DO YOU THINK?
Reflecting on Theme

Refer students to the newspaper editorials and letters of response they wrote before reading the selections in Part Two. Ask students if, after reading about the bet between the lawyer and the banker, they would change how they argued their case. If so, invite students to revise their editorials or letters of response. If this selection prompts students to debate the issues of capital punishment, life imprisonment, or greed, invite them to draft additional editorials and/or letters of response explaining their opinions.

OVERVIEW

Objectives

- To understand and appreciate an autobiographical account of life in segregated Mississippi
- To identify and understand the concept of autobiography
- To understand the use of nonstandard English
- To express understanding of the autobiographical essay through a choice of writing forms, including a dialogue and paragraph writing
- To extend understanding of the autobiographical essay through a variety of multimodal and cross-curricular activities

Skills

READING SKILLS/STRATEGIES
- Setting a purpose

SPEAKING, LISTENING, AND VIEWING
- Group discussion
- Oral presentation

LITERARY CONCEPTS
- Autobiography
- Description

SPELLING
- Prefixes and roots

Cross-Curricular Connections

SOCIAL STUDIES
- Child labor laws

SCIENCE
- Iceboxes

HISTORICAL CONNECTION
Segregation These thought-provoking images show how segregation separated the residents of many areas in the 1950s and early 1960s.

Side A, Frame 52666

PREVIEWING

NONFICTION

from Once Upon a Time When We Were Colored
Clifton L. Taulbert

Activating Prior Knowledge
PERSONAL CONNECTION

Clifton L. Taulbert writes about an uncle he greatly admired in this autobiographical account of his childhood, which involves an unexpected encounter with racial discrimination. Share with the class any unexpected obstacles that you remember encountering in your life. These obstacles might be anything from discrimination to family crises, physical problems, or surprising disappointments.

Building Background
HISTORICAL CONNECTION

The term *colored* in the title of this selection bluntly points to an earlier era in the United States when different standards and ideals governed people's lives. For example, segregation—the forced separation of races—was legal in the Mississippi of Taulbert's childhood, during the 1950s. However, laws passed by Congress in 1965 ended legal segregation.

The selection also reveals other aspects of this era that no longer exist. For example, the minstrel show described in this account is rarely, if ever, performed today. It was a traveling comic variety show featuring white performers who blackened their faces in order to appear African American.

Segregated drinking fountain in use in the American South. The Bettmann Archive.

Setting a Purpose
WRITING CONNECTION

In this selection, Taulbert tells how he had been waiting to grow up enough to work with his uncle. Think about some things you have been waiting to be old enough or big enough to do. What obstacles are preventing you from doing them? Use a diagram, like the one below, to organize your thoughts.

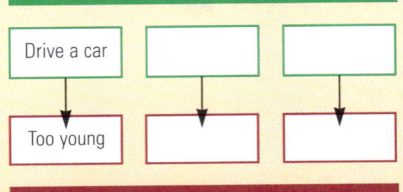

252 UNIT TWO PART 2: UNEXPECTED DEVELOPMENTS

- HISTORICAL CONNECTION

PRINT AND MEDIA RESOURCES

UNIT TWO RESOURCE BOOK
Strategic Reading: Literature, p. 59
Vocabulary SkillBuilder, p. 62
Reading SkillBuilder, p. 60
Spelling SkillBuilder, p. 61

ACCESS FOR STUDENTS ACQUIRING ENGLISH
Selection Summaries
Reading and Writing Support

FORMAL ASSESSMENT
Selection Test, pp. 47–48
Test Generator

 **AUDIO LIBRARY**
See Reference Card

 **LASERLINKS**
Historical Connection

 **INTERNET RESOURCES**
McDougal Littell Literature Center at http://www.hmco.com/mcdougal/lit

252 THE LANGUAGE OF LITERATURE TEACHER'S EDITION

FROM

ONCE UPON A TIME WHEN WE WERE COLORED

Courtesy, Council Oak Books.

by CLIFTON L. TAULBERT

WORDS TO KNOW

conservative (kən-sûr′və-tĭv) *adj.* traditional in style and manner (p. 254)
impact (ĭm′păkt′) *n.* a strong effect (p. 254)
meticulously (mĭ-tĭk′yə-ləs-lē) *adv.* very carefully (p. 256)
responsive (rĭ-spŏn′sĭv) *adj.* quick to react or reply to another (p. 254)
vogue (vōg) *n.* style; fashion (p. 254)

SUMMARY

Cliff recalls the summer when (at age 12) he helped his Uncle Cleve, the respected owner of an icehouse in Glen Allan, Mississippi. Cliff, proud to be handling 300-pound ice blocks with his uncle, is rewarded at the end of the summer with a 150-mile trip to Jackson to see a traveling tent show with Cleve. Twenty minutes into the show, an usher directs a racial slur at them and the two drive home in silence.

Thematic Link: *Unexpected Developments* A boy's reward for a summer's work is ruined by an act of racism.

STRATEGIC READING FOR Less-Proficient Readers

Set a Purpose Encourage students to become involved in the story by asking them how they usually spend their summers. Then invite students to read to find out what Cliff must do to prove that he is big enough to work at Uncle Cleve's icehouse.

Use **UNIT TWO RESOURCE BOOK,** p. 59, for guidance in reading the selection.

CUSTOMIZING FOR Students Acquiring English

- Use **ACCESS FOR STUDENTS ACQUIRING ENGLISH,** Reading and Writing Support.

- Using the Historical Connection as a springboard, ask students to share what they know about segregation in the Southern United States in the mid-20th century. Explain to students, before they begin reading, that most African Americans and whites lived in separate neighborhoods or towns. Tell them that Cliff, the child in the story, notices the race of the people he meets because, regrettably, at that time and place, race played a role in determining a person's social standing.

Surely if my Uncle Cleve were alive today, he'd find a reason to be a black Republican. He was short, neatly dressed, and conservative. Uncle Cleve came from Coldwater, Mississippi. I know very little about his early life with my great-aunt Willie, but I do recall his strong personality and the impact he had on my life growing up in Glen Allan.

I never heard him raise his voice. When he talked, he always talked politics and demonstrated a real business sense. Independence and nonconversance[1] were his most notable characteristics. I called him Uncle Cleve, Ma Ponk called him Bro. Cleve and every other colored person called him Mr. Cleve. The white community with which he had contact called him Mormon, his last name, their badge of respect.

Uncle Cleve, Mr. Cleve, Bro. Cleve, or Mormon—he was my first employer. From him, I learned a sense of responsibility that undergirds my approach today. He ran the only icehouse in town. Refrigerators were a rarity in the colored community and among the poor whites, and nearly all the small businesses used ice to keep their goods from spoiling. Only Mr. Cleve provided the ice needed in Glen Allan. Twice daily, we'd see him driving the red flatbed truck up and down the streets, announcing "The iceman is here." For years, I would run alongside the truck as Uncle Cleve stopped at each house and chipped his sales of fifteen or thirty pounds of ice. Occasionally someone would buy fifty pounds, but that was rare. He was always quick, responsive, and very polite—not given to extra conversation when waiting on his customer. His business made our lives better, and he was always received as a welcome sight.

Being an assistant to Mr. Cleve was viewed as a good job, and I couldn't wait until I was old enough to work with my cousin Joe, Uncle Cleve's son. Uncle Cleve had been training me by taking me with him to Hollandale, Mississippi, to buy ice from the ice factory. We would ride to Hollandale together, just the two of us. I recall the trip taking hours, but really it was very short. We'd drive down the road eating salami and crackers, and every once in a while he would talk to me about life.

"Yes, git you a good pattern and follow it. Always be early for work, and save fifty cents out of every dollar you make."

I didn't try to answer. I just sat in the cab of the truck and listened as he continued talking. All I wanted was the chance to show him that I could handle the big three-hundred-pound blocks of ice. If I could prove my ability to handle the big blocks, he would let me work at his icehouse.

Finally one Saturday, he gave me the chance. I must have been about twelve years old. Child-labor laws weren't in vogue in Glen Allan, and when you were strong enough to handle the job, nobody worried about how old you were. I could hardly sleep the Friday night before, although Ma Ponk had no problem getting me into bed on my little cot by the front windows.

"Boy, git to bed early, 'cause Bro. Cleve will leave you if you ain't ready to go when he comes by," Ma Ponk told me as she securely tucked me in bed.

Saturday morning didn't come soon enough. I found myself waking up nearly every hour, straining my eyes to see the hands on the clock. Finally I heard Ma Ponk's voice through the quilts. "Cliff, git up and git some food in you, 'cause you know Bro. Cleve ain't gonna stop."

---

1. **nonconversance** (nŏn′kən-vûr′səns): a term used here to describe Uncle Cleve's habit of saying very little.

| WORDS TO KNOW | **conservative** (kən-sûr′və-tĭv) *adj.* traditional in style and manner
impact (ĭm′păkt′) *n.* a strong effect
responsive (rĭ-spŏn′sĭv) *adj.* quick to react or reply to another
vogue (vōg) *n.* style; fashion |

254

Mini-Lesson — Reading Skills/Strategies

SETTING A PURPOSE Remind students that just as there are many different types of things to read, there are also many different reasons for reading. Explain to students that sometimes people read in order to learn how to do something or to obtain information, and other times people read to be entertained. Point out to students that people usually read biographies and autobiographies to learn about another person's life and times.

Application Have students imagine that they want a friend or family member to read this selection. Ask students to think about what they want the other person to learn from the story. Have students quickly review the selection by scanning its title, the photograph, and boxed callout. Then have them set a purpose for their intended reader by writing a single sentence. You may wish to have students repeat this activity by setting a purpose for their next reading. Have them quickly preview the selection, as they reviewed this one, and write their purpose in their reading logs.

Reteaching/Reinforcement
• *Unit Two Resource Book*, p. 60

No sooner had she spoken than I jumped from bed and ran to get the wash pan so I could wash up before eating my breakfast. The smell of hot oil sausages and grits[2] floated through the house, and I could hardly wait. How lucky could I be—a trip to Hollandale with Uncle Cleve, *and* my favorite breakfast. The food went fast, and I found myself ready and waiting when Uncle Cleve came by. True to form, he was a little early.

"Bye, Ma Ponk!" I yelled as I jumped from the porch to the ground.

Our trip was not unusual, but this time I would have the chance to show my uncle that I was big enough to help him with the business.

"Cleve, pull your truck in next," a colored man yelled as we pulled up to the Hollandale Icehouse.

Uncle Cleve let me out of the cab and told me to take the steps to the dock; he'd meet me there. He never made suggestions. You simply did what he told you, and quickly. After parking the truck so the bed would be against the dock, Uncle Cleve came around to the side where I was standing.

"OK, Cliff, we'll see if you can handle the big one."

As we walked into the icehouse, all I could see was a cold vapor rising from hundreds of blocks of ice. Each block weighed three hundred pounds. Standing inside the door, I felt the chill as Uncle Cleve took the giant ice hook off the wall.

"Cliff, pay attention." Uncle Cleve proceeded to show me how to put the ice hook securely into the block while using my knee as an anchor.

I watched and I watched and I watched. Finally, it was my turn. I walked over to a huge block of ice and carefully repeated what I had been shown many times. I securely hooked my ice, carefully placed my knee, and began to gently pull the block to the floor. Before I could get fearful, I had finished. The three-hundred-pound block of ice was on the floor, and I was pulling it out to the trucks.

"New helper you got, Mormon?" one of the white men asked.

"Yes, sir," Uncle Cleve nodded as he watched me load the truck for the very first time.

My ride home could not have been sweeter. Uncle Cleve stopped by a local store and bought me a large grape soda and a moon pie[3]—my reward. We didn't say much on the way back, but we both knew it had been a good day.

Many months later, nearing the end of the summer, Uncle Cleve promised to take me with him to Jackson as a gift for having done a good job for him. The day of our trip finally arrived. It started out as one of the happiest days of my life. My uncle was taking me to Jackson to the biggest tent show that had ever come our way. Ma Ponk got me all dressed up in my Sunday church clothes, combed my hair until my scalp was sore, and had me ready at least two hours early. Uncle Cleve was a slow driver, so we were going to leave in plenty of time to get to the seven o'clock grand opening.

I was ready at three o'clock and sitting out on the front steps waiting for the familiar sound of Uncle's 1947 green International truck that purred like a kitten. Ma Ponk and I were waiting, and there was absolutely no way

---

2. **grits**: short for *hominy grits*, a popular Southern breakfast dish made of coarsely ground dry corn.
3. **moon pie**: a chocolate-covered cookie that has a marshmallow filling sandwiched between two round graham crackers.

Literary Concept:
DESCRIPTION

G Ask students to explain what this description conveys about Uncle Cleve's character. *(Possible response: Cleve is a steady, sober, self-disciplined man who believes in thoroughness and doing things right.)*

STRATEGIC READING FOR
Less-Proficient Readers

H Ask the following questions to be sure that students understand the reason for—and the climax of—the trip to Jackson.

- Why do Cliff and Uncle Cleve set out for Jackson? *(Going to see a show there is Cliff's reward for doing a good job at the icehouse over the summer.)*
  Summarizing

- What happens to the two of them during the show? *(They are asked to leave because of their skin color.)*
  Noting Relevant Details

CUSTOMIZING FOR
Gifted and Talented Students

Encourage students to discuss the use of racial epithets. Ask them why some people refuse to stop using these words. Have students debate the truthfulness of the saying "Sticks and stones may break my bones, but names will never hurt me."

COMPREHENSION CHECK

1. What is Cleve's business? *(He owns an icehouse and delivers ice to area residents.)*
2. How does Cliff prove himself to his uncle? *(He moves a 300-pound block of ice.)*
3. What is Cliff's reward for working the whole summer? *(His uncle takes him to a show in Jackson.)*
4. Why is their trip cut short? *(They are told to leave the tent show because of their skin color.)*

---

of missing Uncle Cleve. When the truck pulled up, I almost jumped out of my pants, but Uncle Cleve only smiled slightly as I ran around to the passenger's side and tucked myself firmly in, secure with the knowledge that tonight was going to be a really big night for me. Uncle Cleve was very confident, only telling me that he never messed with the small-town minstrel shows that came to Glen Allan to rob you blind. If he was going to waste his time and spend his money, it would be at something like the big show that we were going to in Jackson.

G I know I counted every tree and rock between Glen Allan and Jackson, because Uncle drove so slowly. He never hurried about anything. Moving <u>meticulously</u>, like a well-greased snail, he'd get the work of two men done in half the time. His driving was the same, perfect execution of the rules, never speeding, just fast enough to beat running.

It was almost 150 miles to Jackson. Ma Ponk didn't even pack me a lunch, because Uncle Cleve had promised to buy my lunch. Packed lunches in greasy brown paper bags were for old church ladies, not the two of us.

Finally we reached Jackson. There were more bright lights than I had ever seen. This was a large city, not like Glen Allan. Uncle Cleve took the city in stride. After all, he had been to Memphis, and Jackson was just another city to him. To me, however, Jackson was the biggest and the brightest. It even had uniformed policemen directing the traffic, and I saw my first traffic jam.

I was so excited about being in a city I didn't realize we had gotten near the show grounds. There seemed to be hundreds of cars and people. But my uncle knew where we were going. He parked the truck and held my hand tightly as we followed the crowd. Finally we got to the main gate, where a big curly-headed white man reached down and took our tickets. We were ushered in with the crowds of other people to a tent that seemed big enough to cover the whole world.

White people were everywhere, laughing and talking and eating popcorn and pulling their children behind them, as we all headed toward the big tent.

It was so crowded in the tent and we were so far back that I could hardly see, but I remember when those gigantic curtains opened and I saw all those beautiful ladies in sequined stockings.[4] I could hardly sit still. I know I was too small to fully appreciate that beauty, but the glitter I understood. The music was loud all around us, and sweaty men were yelling and whistling; but my uncle just smiled slightly, ate one piece of popcorn at a time, and watched.

We couldn't have been there any more than twenty minutes when the usher came over to us and said, "I am sorry, but this ain't the night for niggers."[5]

My uncle's smile dropped from his face, and his warm eyes became cold as steel as he jerked me up and we walked out. We hadn't even seen half the show. **H**

The long trip back was completely silent. I sat in the car, miserable, trying not to cry. I was too young to understand why this had happened to us, and my uncle would not explain. ❖

---

4. **sequined** (sē′kwĭnd) **stockings:** stockings decorated with small shiny disks.
5. **niggers:** derogatory slang term for African Americans. The word is considered to be extremely offensive.

WORDS TO KNOW
meticulously (mĭ-tĭk′yə-ləs-lē) *adv.* very carefully

256

Mini-Lesson Spelling

PREFIXES AND ROOTS Point out to students that a root is a word part that cannot stand alone. It must be joined to other parts—such as a prefix, a suffix, or both—to form a complete word. You might wish to review with students the following prefixes and their meanings:

con- = with, together	pro- = forward, forth
re- = again, back	dis- = lack of
im-/in- = in, into, not	sub- = below, lower
ex- = from, out	pre- = before
de- = down, away	per- = through by

Application Have students spell words using combinations of the roots shown below and the list of prefixes shown above.

1. sponsible *(responsible)*
2. tinue *(continue)*
3. tinguish *(distinguish, extinguish)*
4. sist *(consist, desist, resist, subsist, persist)*

Ask students to look for more words that fit this pattern, and to add these words to their personal word lists.

Reteaching/Reinforcement
- *Unit Two Resource Book*, p. 61

256 THE LANGUAGE OF LITERATURE TEACHER'S EDITION

RESPONDING OPTIONS

FROM PERSONAL RESPONSE TO CRITICAL ANALYSIS

REFLECT
1. What questions does the selection raise in your mind? Jot them down in your notebook.

RETHINK

Thematic Link

2. Why do you think Uncle Cleve chooses not to explain the discrimination he and Cliff encounter in Jackson?
3. Uncle Cleve seems able to handle certain obstacles in his life. How well does he handle the obstacle of racial discrimination at the tent show? Explain your answer.
4. How would you describe Uncle Cleve's personality?
5. Cliff is about 12 years old at the time of the incident, and yet he seems to have had little experience with racial prejudice. Do you think that is possible? Use as evidence examples from the account and from your own experience.

RELATE
6. The type of discrimination that Cliff and his uncle encounter is illegal today. However, discrimination still exists in a number of forms. Describe the kinds of discrimination you are aware of.

Multimodal Learning
ANOTHER PATHWAY

Cliff shows many emotions, ranging from extreme happiness to misery. Make an "emotions graph." Plot at least three events on the horizontal line, and Cliff's emotions, from low to high, on the vertical line.

[Graph: Emotions (vertical) vs. Events (horizontal)]

QUICKWRITES

1. If Uncle Cleve had talked to Cliff about the incident in Jackson, what might he have said? How might Cliff have responded? Write the **dialogue** that you imagine might have occurred.
2. Uncle Cleve advises Cliff to get in the habit of being early for work and saving money. Write two **paragraphs** explaining the best and worst advice you have received.

 **PORTFOLIO** Save your writing. You may want to use it later as a springboard to a piece for your portfolio.

LITERARY CONCEPTS

This account is part of Taulbert's **autobiography**, or the true story of his life. Written from the first-person point of view, an autobiography provides insight into the writer's personality and development. Taulbert prefers to call his books "cultural biographies" because they reflect what it was like growing up African American before the civil rights movement. In this selection, how do Cliff's and his uncle's reactions reflect attitudes of the times? How might they react to the incident at the tent show if it happened today?

ONCE UPON A TIME WHEN WE WERE COLORED **257**

From Personal Response to Critical Analysis

1. Responses will vary.
2. Possible responses: He is too angry and/or too humiliated to discuss the experience; he may think that Cliff is not old enough for a thorough discussion of racism and discrimination.
3. Possible responses: Considering the society in which he is living, he handles it pretty well—there's nothing he can do to change the situation. Perhaps talking about the experience with Cliff would have been a better way for Cleve to handle the situation.
4. Possible response: He is a serious, fair, thoughtful, independent man who believes in hard work, dependability, and politeness.
5. Responses will vary. Some students might note that the separation of races meant that Cliff's limited contact with whites might have left him unprepared for racial prejudice.
6. Responses will vary. Students may be more aware of recent discrimination cases based on gender, sexual orientation, or disabilities. Some may say that while segregation is illegal, some people still have racial prejudices.

Another Pathway

Consider having students work on this activity in pairs. One student might be responsible for identifying two events in the text, while the partner might find one event and create the actual chart. The students could decide together how to plot the events on the graph.

Rubric

3 Full Accomplishment Students accurately identify passages that show Cliff's emotional journey and chart them clearly.

2 Substantial Accomplishment Students identify passages, some of which show Cliff's emotional journey, and chart them clearly.

1 Little or Partial Accomplishment Students have difficulty identifying and charting passages that show Cliff's emotional journey.

Literary Concepts

Discuss with students some of the changes brought about by the civil rights movement, such as the Civil Rights Act of 1964, a law banning discrimination based on a person's color, race, national origin, religion, or sex. Students may respond that while Cliff and his uncle felt compelled to leave the tent show, people nowadays have legal rights and could fight back. Some students may claim that the situation has not changed greatly and that people might react the same way because they fear violent consequences.

QuickWrites

1. Have students begin by imagining themselves in Cleve's shoes. Ask them to jot down words and phrases that express their emotional reactions to the situation. You might wish to remind them about Uncle Cleve's basic "nonconversance."
2. Encourage students to explore memories of not only adults' advice but also peers' advice. Then have them focus on a piece of advice and explain why it turned out to be helpful.

The Writer's Craft

Dialogue, pp. 324–327
Elaboration, pp. 255–261

Words to Know

Possible responses: **conservative**—conventional, cautious, traditional, moderate, tame, restrained; **impact**—force, reaction, effect, blow, collision, crash; **responsive**—sensitive, sympathetic, reactive, attentive, understanding, alert; **vogue**—style, fashion, popularity, taste, in favor, up-to-date; **meticulously**—carefully, particularly, painstakingly, thoroughly, exactly, precisely

Reteaching/Reinforcement
- *Unit Two Resource Book*, p. 62

Across the Curriculum

Social Studies *Cooperative Learning*
Divide students into groups of four or five. Individual groups may elect to focus on child labor laws of a specific era or region. Have students use a general encyclopedia or reference books of American social history. You might suggest that students display some of their findings in a time line or other chart. One student in each group can act as a note taker, another as a facilitator, a third as a presenter, and the remaining members as designers of visuals.

ADDITIONAL SUGGESTION
Science *Iceboxes* Invite students to research and explain how iceboxes worked. Students might also explain heat transfer—the process by which ice reduces the temperature of a substance below its own melting point.

CLIFTON TAULBERT

At age 17, Clifton Taulbert left family and friends behind to make his mark in the world. Today he is a leading businessman in Tulsa, Oklahoma, where he heads the Freemount Corporation, a marketing and consulting firm. He makes frequent visits to his hometown to visit friends and relatives.

Multimodal Learning

ALTERNATIVE ACTIVITIES

Draw a **map** of Mississippi that highlights the towns and cities mentioned in the selection: Coldwater, Glen Allan, Hollandale, and Jackson.

ACROSS THE CURRICULUM

Social Studies Taulbert suggests that no one in Glen Allan paid attention to child labor laws. Research the history of child labor laws in the United States. Share your findings.

THE WRITER'S STYLE

Taulbert writes dialogue using nonstandard English. **Nonstandard English** is a form of language that does not follow some of the standard rules of grammar. It shows how some people naturally talk and can lend an earthy, conversational style to writing. For example, Uncle Cleve says to Cliff, "Yes, git you a good pattern and follow it." He means, "Get yourself a good pattern and follow it." Go to page 254, and rewrite Ma Ponk's dialogue in standard English. What is the effect of your rewrite?

CLIFTON L. TAULBERT

Clifton L. Taulbert was raised in small-town Mississippi, where he graduated first in his high school class. He served in the U.S. Air Force and graduated from Oral Roberts University with a degree in sociology and history.

Of his childhood in segregated Mississippi he writes: "I would never want to return to forced segregation, but I also have a deeply felt sense that important values were conveyed to me in my colored childhood, values we're in danger of losing in our integrated world." The author expresses concern that his own children not lose these values: "Today

1945–

my children are growing up in a world where 'color' is something that comes in a box of crayons.... I want my children to know of the life-style that gave them their father and their mother."

In 1993, for the second of his three autobiographical works, *The Last Train North*, Taulbert was nominated for a Pulitzer Prize and received a Mississippi Institute of Arts and Letters Award for Nonfiction. He shared the Mississippi honor with another writer and was the first African American to win the award.

OTHER WORKS *The Season Our Crops Came In*

Extended Reading

258 UNIT TWO PART 2: UNEXPECTED DEVELOPMENTS

WORDS TO KNOW

Review the Words to Know at the bottom of the selection pages. Using the sample as a guide, create a word map containing at least six other related words for each of the five Words to Know.

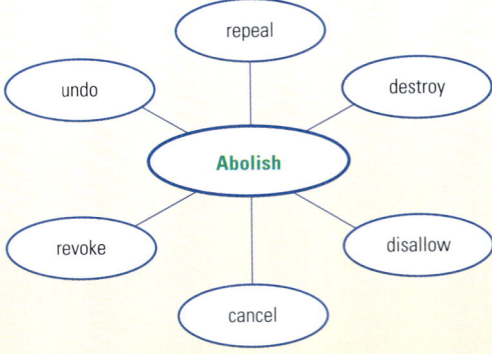

Alternative Activities

Point out to students that Glen Allan is in west central Mississippi, just a few miles from the Arkansas and the Louisiana borders. Coldwater is about 140 miles northeast of Glen Allan; Hollandale is about 15 miles northeast of Glen Allan; and Jackson, the state capital, is about 100 miles (150 by road) southeast of Glen Allan.

The Writer's Style

Possible responses: "Boy, go to bed early, because Uncle Cleve will leave you if are not ready to go when he comes by"; "Cliff, get up and get some food in you, because you know Uncle Cleve is not going to wait for you." Help students to see that the rewrite weakens Ma Ponk's language and personality. It sounds less conversational, and no longer reflects her regional dialect.

 The Writer's Craft
Formal and Informal English, p. 315

258 THE LANGUAGE OF LITERATURE TEACHER'S EDITION

PREVIEWING

NONFICTION

The Home Front: 1941–1945
Hazel Shelton Abernethy

Activating Prior Knowledge
PERSONAL CONNECTION

"I'll never forget what I was doing when . . ." Do these words remind you of a major event in your personal life or one that you heard about on the news? Can you picture the event? How did it affect you? Write down what you remember, using a chart or a creative organizer like the one shown here.

Building Background
HISTORICAL CONNECTION

Like many others of her generation, Hazel Shelton Abernethy vividly remembers where she was and what she was doing on December 7, 1941. That was the day the Japanese bombed the U.S. naval base at Pearl Harbor, in Oahu, Hawaii. This attack caused the United States to enter World War II.

The impact of the war was keenly felt by the whole country. Almost immediately, men went overseas to fight, and many women took factory jobs helping to produce enormous numbers of ships, airplanes, tanks, and weapons. Products needed by the military were rationed, including metal, gasoline, and nylon. Read this account to find out other ways the war affected the lives of citizens at home.

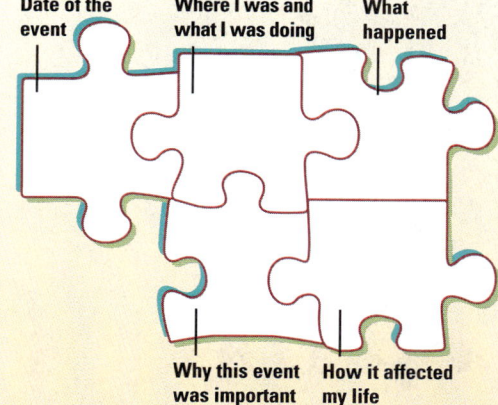

READING CONNECTION
Active Reading/Setting a Purpose

Questioning The process of raising questions while reading is called questioning. Good readers ask themselves questions in an effort to understand and think about what they're reading. Sometimes, but not always, their questions are answered later in the selection. As you read "Home Front," ask yourself questions and look for answers. For example, you might wonder why clothing was never rationed.

- HISTORICAL CONNECTION

259

OVERVIEW

Objectives

- To understand and appreciate a work of nonfiction about the effects of World War II on a town in Texas
- To understand the process of questioning
- To identify the characteristics of a memoir
- To express understanding of the story through a choice of writing forms, including paragraph writing, encyclopedia entries, and public service announcements
- To extend understanding of the story through a variety of multimodal and cross-curricular activities

Skills

READING SKILLS/STRATEGIES
- Questioning

LITERARY CONCEPTS
- Point of view
- Memoir

SPEAKING, LISTENING, AND VIEWING
- Group discussion
- Oral presentation

GENRE STUDY
- Nonfiction: memoir

Cross-Curricular Connections

GEOGRAPHY
- Identifying the battle sites of World War II and locating the countries involved

SOCIAL STUDIES
- Important places and events of World War II

HISTORICAL CONNECTION
Life During Wartime Some students may never have considered what wartime is like for people *not* on the battlefield. This informative video montage will familiarize them with the efforts American civilians made to help soldiers during World War II.

Side A, Frames 17822

PRINT AND MEDIA RESOURCES

UNIT RESOURCE BOOK
Strategic Reading: Literature, p. 65
Reading SkillBuilder, p. 66

ACCESS FOR STUDENTS ACQUIRING ENGLISH
Selection Summaries
Reading and Writing Support

FORMAL ASSESSMENT
Selection Test, pp. 49–50
 Test Generator

 AUDIO LIBRARY
See Reference Card

LASERLINKS
Historical Connection

INTERNET RESOURCES
McDougal Littell Literature Center at http://www.hmco.com/mcdougal/lit

SUMMARY

When the United States entered World War II, Hazel Abernethy was 14 and attending high school in Nacogdoches, Texas. She writes of the changes that took place at home during the war years, from war-bond and scrap-metal drives, to an ethic of "make it do, wear it out, and do without." She also recalls rationing, victory gardens, and the departure of young men, many of whom never returned. Abernethy concludes her recollection describing the jubilation the country felt as the soldiers returned from war.

Thematic Link: *Unexpected Developments* Abernethy's memoir of life during World War II provides a first-person account of the developments following the unexpected attack on Pearl Harbor.

CUSTOMIZING FOR
Students Acquiring English

- Use **ACCESS FOR STUDENTS ACQUIRING ENGLISH**, Reading and Writing Support.
- This story describes how World War II affected people in a small Texas town. Be sure that all students realize that World War II was fought overseas, and that the bombing of Pearl Harbor in the territory of Hawaii was a rare attack on U.S. land. Some students may know about the war from the perspective of their native countries or from relatives, and they should be encouraged to describe how the war affected people in other countries.

STRATEGIC READING FOR
Less-Proficient Readers

Set a Purpose To immerse students in the selection, have them imagine how their lives would change if the United States were now involved in a major war. Then have them look through the selection for ways the high-school students raised money for the war.

Use **UNIT TWO RESOURCE BOOK**, p. 65, for guidance in reading the selection.

The Home Front
1941–1945
BY HAZEL SHELTON ABERNETHY

I was fourteen years old and a sophomore at Nacogdoches High School on Sunday, December 7, 1941. Like all people old enough to have any memory of that day, I can tell you exactly where I was and what I was doing when I heard the news about Pearl Harbor. A group of friends and I had gone to the double-feature movie at the Stone Fort Theatre on the west side of the square. The movies were *Till We Meet Again* with George Brent and Merle Oberon and one of the "Maisie" movies with Ann Southern and Robert Sterling. When we came out of the theater, about 4:30, they were selling "extra" editions of the *Sentinel* that announced the Japanese attack. Most people were not completely sure at that time just where Pearl Harbor was, but our geographical knowledge widened significantly over the next few months.

On Monday, December 8, we gathered in the high school auditorium, the present-day middle school, and heard President Roosevelt ask for a declaration of war against Japan. When "The Star-Spangled Banner" was played, there were few dry eyes.

Almost immediately our lives began to change in response to the national war effort.

At school we had war-bond drives and scrap drives.[1] Tuesday was Stamp Day, and students

---
1. **war-bond drives and scrap drives:** nationwide campaigns to encourage U.S. citizens to buy government bonds and save recyclable materials to aid the war effort.

Mini-Lesson  Literary Concepts

REVIEWING POINT OF VIEW Remind students that a selection is usually told from one of three perspectives:
- **First person** The narrator is part of the action of the selection and uses the pronouns *I, me,* or *we*.
- **Third-person omniscient** The narrator is not involved in the action but can reveal the thoughts of other people in the selection; the pronouns *he, she,* and *it* are used.
- **Third-person limited** Uses the same pronouns as third-person omniscient, but the narrator brings the reader into the mind of only one person.

Application Have students work in groups of three or four. Ask half the class to rewrite a section of "The Home Front" from the third-person-omniscient point of view, taking into account the thoughts of other people in the memoir. The other half of the class should rewrite the same section of the selection from a third-person-limited point of view, providing only Abernethy's thoughts. Invite students to share their rewrites and to compare the third-person-limited and third-person-omniscient points of view, as well as the first-person point of view.

saved their pennies to buy savings stamps. The stamp books came in denominations of ten and twenty-five cents. When a student had bought $18.75 worth of stamps, he or she could purchase a savings bond that would mature in ten years at $25.00. There was competition between home rooms, and the room that sold the most stamps each week would receive some special recognition.

We had a scrap-metal drive that could have competed with any school in the country. The entire Mound Street campus was covered with metal scrap. High school students responded enthusiastically with discarded pots and pans, junked jalopies, an entire old bus "carcass," and parts of a locomotive. The drive lasted for six weeks and dominated our activities. This, too, was conducted as a home-room competition. We were in Miss Dora Grant's home room, and we won the prize—an entire page in the school annual.

At the government's request we began to save everything. Paper, tin cans, and bacon grease headed the list of vital "recyclables." We also learned to "make it do, wear it out, and do without." When clothing wore out completely, we saved everything salvageable. Buttons, snaps, and hooks and eyes were hoarded away. Silk stockings were a thing of the past, and nylons were a treasure rarely to be found, so we painted our legs with pancake makeup and drew a seam up the back with eyebrow pencil and prayed we wouldn't get caught out in the rain.

With the exception of shoes, clothing was never rationed, but there were shortages, especially of quality clothes. As wartime weddings increased, mothers of brides searched frantically for white satin or tulle.[2] My mother bought three pre-war evening dresses at the Episcopal Church rummage sale and constructed two semi-new formals for my freshman year in college. Shoe rationing allowed each person one pair of shoes for each season. This was particularly hard on families with young children whose growth was not seasonal, so there was pooling of shoe stamps among people according to need. Many a grandparent contributed his shoe stamp to a grandchild.

We worked for the Red Cross and rolled bandages and knitted socks and mufflers, and even Nacogdoches, with a population under 10,000, had a USO.[3] The high school and college girls acted as hostesses and gave dances there. It alternated as a youth center. The social clubs at the college went to Harmon Military Hospital in Longview and gave programs to entertain the recovering wounded. If they survived that entertainment, they were considered fit for active duty. We wrote letters, baked cookies to send to the boys in service, took strangers in uniform home for dinner, and never passed up a serviceman thumbing a ride on the highway. We followed the war news in the newspapers, radio, and newsreels with anxious hearts.

Do with less— so they'll have enough!

RATIONING GIVES YOU YOUR FAIR SHARE

Courtesy of the War Memorial Museum of Virginia.

---

2. **tulle** (tōōl): a fine, stiff netting used for veils and gowns.
3. **USO**: United Service Organizations, volunteer-staffed groups offering recreational and other services to U.S. military personnel and their families.

Literary Concept:
POINT OF VIEW

C Refer students to this passage and ask them which point of view is used. Ask them how they can tell. (*It is the first-person point of view, because the pronouns* my *and* we *are used.*)

Critical Thinking: MAKING JUDGMENTS

D Have students evaluate the effect of placing blue and gold star banners in the windows of schools, homes, and businesses. (*Possible response: The effect would have been tremendous, since visual reminders of the war and its casualties would have been everywhere.*)

CUSTOMIZING FOR
Students Acquiring English

4 Be sure that students understand that *red tape* refers to government rules and regulations.

Active Reading: CLARIFY

E Have students describe how driving was restricted during the war years. (*Gasoline was rationed; the speed limit was lowered to 35 miles per hour; driving was limited to a maximum of 60 miles a week; and all pleasure driving was prohibited.*)

C Sometimes we would catch a glimpse of a loved one in a newsreel. Once we saw my cousin's face on the screen, and we came to the theater everytime the newsreel appeared. Who knew when or if we would see him again?

D The real cost of the war was being brought sharply home by blue star banners, which were hung in the windows of businesses, schools, and homes. Each of these stars represented a hometown boy who was serving in the military. More and more gold stars began to appear on these banners. Gold stars represented the boys who would not come home again.

Our lives revolved around the comings and goings of our friends in the service. As my own group of friends began to leave in 1944, we developed almost a ritual of their leaving. We would give an all-day picnic for them at Fern Lake, and the night before they left we would have a family party for them. Our parents, brothers and sisters, and friends would all go with them to the station to see them off. The train to Houston left at two o'clock in the morning, and there were some emotional send-offs down at that old depot. We were lucky; all of those boys did come home.

The restrictions on transportation probably had the most immediate effect on the conduct of our daily lives. On January 1, 1942, an order was issued banning the production of civilian cars. The last civilian car rolled off the assembly line on February 10, 1942. A limit of five tires for each automobile was strictly enforced; garages and basements were checked for hoarding. Only retread tires could be purchased, and dire need had to be proved through many miles of red tape.

Gasoline rationing began on December 1, 1942, and the national speed limit was set at 35 miles an hour to conserve fuel. Stickers were placed on cars to show how much gas we were allowed to buy, and we were issued books of ration stamps to obtain our quota. Everyone with a car qualified for an A sticker, which allowed us to buy four gallons of gas a week, which was enough to drive about sixty miles a week. B and C stamps allowed more gas for salesmen, delivery men, essential war workers, and for carpools. About one-half the drivers in the country qualified for these stamps. E stamps were for doctors, emergency vehicles, ambulances, and Home Guard vehicles, and a T sticker for trucks approved unlimited gasoline mileage.

In 1943 all pleasure driving was banned—"Is this trip really necessary?"—and the use of public transportation greatly increased. A bus or train trip was never certain. Trains, especially, frequently were sidetracked for more essential uses. All public transportation was cramped and crowded.

In 1943, with SFA's[4] enrollment dipping dangerously low, the Board of Regents obtained a contract to establish the first WAAC school in the nation on our local campus. The Women's Army Auxiliary Corps

Collection of the National Archives.

---
4. **SFA**: Stephen F. Austin State University in Nacogdoches, Texas.

262   UNIT TWO   PART 2: UNEXPECTED DEVELOPMENTS

Mini-Lesson Genre Study

NONFICTION Explain to students that a **memoir**, a type of nonfiction writing, is a first-person recollection of an experience. Usually a memoir details an event that the writer participated in or witnessed. Memoirs often span an identifiable period of time and tend toward anecdotal incidents.

Application Explain to students that Abernethy's recollections involve both historical events and personal experiences during World War II. Ask students to construct a time line that details the historical events mentioned in Abernethy's memoir. Then have students go back and add to the time lines the personal events from Abernethy's life. Encourage students to discuss the relationship between the historical and personal events on their time lines.

was on the SFA campus for about twelve months, and two thousand WACs were graduated there. My father, who was the basketball coach at SFA, was not happy. He said we were the only school in the Lone Star Conference who did not get some sort of military unit with men who could play basketball. The high school girls and college girls were not very happy either.

The last thing this community needed was more females injected into the population. When the high school class of 1944 entered SFA in the fall, there were about 25 or 30 men on campus out of a school population of around 300-350. It was bleak.

Food rationing came in gradually. There were periodical sugar and coffee shortages, and sugar was rationed in April of 1942. Food ration books were issued in May of 1942, one to each family member. Prices were frozen on sixty percent of all food items that same spring. As time went on, almost every item that we ate, wore, used, or lived in was subject to rationing or price controls.

Victory gardens[5] grew on almost every vacant lot. One of the best ones was on the corner of King and Raguet where the Raguet Apartments are now. Every family in the neighborhood took its turn tending to this garden. The Demonstration School children dug up the backyard of SFA President Dr. Birdwell's on the SFA Campus and had a flourishing garden. One summer a group of ladies in Central Heights canned vegetables for a nickel a can and no ration stamps if the customer furnished the vegetables. My mother and I used precious gasoline scouring the county for vegetables. They made a delicious soup mix at those kitchens, and my father said we still had some of those canned vegetables in our attic in the late 1950's.

There were several prisoner-of-war camps in the area. Prisoners worked primarily in the forest areas harvesting wood for the lumber companies. There were always rumors of escaped POW's at large but most of these internees did not want to escape. At the camp in Chireno one evening, two prisoners were missing, but when the truck went back to the work area, there they were.

They had been left behind, and they were waiting for the truck to return and take them to supper. Several years after the war some of these men returned to visit; they had very warm memories of their treatment here.

For three-and-a-half years our lives revolved around the comings and goings of our servicemen. After D-Day[6] and the rapid advance of the Allies toward Germany, we were sure the boys would be home to stay, maybe even by Christmas, but the German breakthrough that developed into the Battle of the Bulge[7] ended that hope. The American forces suffered 77,000 casualties, and that was the grimmest Christmas of the war. As the spring of 1945 arrived, our hopes for victory increased, and even the blow of President Roosevelt's death could not completely dim our optimism. When VE Day[8] came we rejoiced, but the total victory was a few months away.

In the early morning of August 14, 1945, we heard the civil defense siren sound, along with the fire trucks and all five of the mill whistles going full blast. People dressed and went down to the Square and just hugged each other. Just as on the day that began the war, there were

---

5. **victory gardens:** vegetable gardens cultivated during World War II to help relieve food shortages.
6. **D-Day:** June 6, 1944, the day Allied forces landed in western France.
7. **Battle of the Bulge:** a World War II battle that began in December 1944, when the German army advanced into Belgium, temporarily causing a bulge in the line of the Allied military forces.
8. **VE Day:** short for Victory in Europe Day, May 8, 1945, when Germany officially surrendered and the European phase of World War II ended.

THE HOME FRONT: 1941–1945 **263**

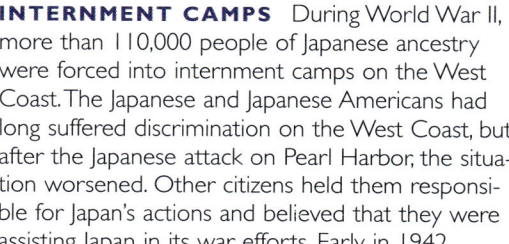

Multicultural Perspectives

INTERNMENT CAMPS During World War II, more than 110,000 people of Japanese ancestry were forced into internment camps on the West Coast. The Japanese and Japanese Americans had long suffered discrimination on the West Coast, but after the Japanese attack on Pearl Harbor, the situation worsened. Other citizens held them responsible for Japan's actions and believed that they were assisting Japan in its war efforts. Early in 1942, President Roosevelt gave in to growing pressure and, under the guise of national security, Japanese Americans were rounded up and relocated to camps on the West Coast. They lost their homes, jobs, and businesses, and were confined in camps under the watchful eyes of armed guards. It was not until after the presidential elections of 1944 that the U.S. government changed its policy and released these people.

CUSTOMIZING FOR
Gifted and Talented Students

J Tell students that to bring about a quick end to the war, U.S. leaders decided to drop the first atomic bombs on August 6, and August 9, 1945, on the Japanese cities of Hiroshima and Nagasaki. Have students research the debate over the dropping of the atomic bombs and their aftermath to decide whether they think these bombs were needed to end the war.

COMPREHENSION CHECK

1. What unexpected event begins this memoir? *(the bombing of Pearl Harbor)*
2. How did the schools help raise money for the war effort? *(by holding competitions for the most war bonds and scrap metal)*
3. What items were rationed during World War II? *(gasoline, food, shoes, tires)*
4. Why did people celebrate on August 14, 1945? *(The war was finally over.)*

INSIGHT

1. What were some of the pros and cons of the draft? *(Possible responses: All men registered had an equal chance of being sent to fight. Men should not have been forced to fight if they didn't wish to.)*
2. Should the draft be continued when the country is not at war? *(Possible responses: No, a volunteer army is sufficient. Yes, everyone should have an equal responsibility for defending the country.)*

J extra editions of the *Sentinel* being distributed that said the war was over.

Since the military point system provided for a gradual demobilization,[9] the real impact of the returning veterans was not felt until 1946. On the campus of SFA, the change was dramatic. The enrollment jumped to one thousand that fall, and the ratio of men to women was over three to one. For those girls who had attended school while it was almost an all-girl campus, this was nothing short of miraculous. College life was what it was meant to be. Dances—with MEN, and stag lines, football games and MEN, normal college life and MEN. Life was wonderful! ❖

---

9. **point system . . . demobilization:** a system used to release U.S. military personnel from active duty after World War II, based on an accumulation of points awarded for time overseas, especially time in combat.

HISTORICAL INSIGHT

THE MILITARY DRAFT

In 1940, for the first time in U.S. history and just one year before the United States entered World War II, men were drafted for required military service in peacetime. As a result, the beginnings of a fighting force were in place when the Japanese attacked Pearl Harbor.

Passions ran high during the congressional debate over the peacetime draft. Six women dressed in widows' clothes kept a silent vigil at the Capitol. Two congressmen got into a fistfight over the issue. Despite the controversy, Congress finally passed the Selective Training and Service Act. The law required men between the ages of 21 and 35 to sign up for one year of service overseas.

The 16.5 million men who registered for the draft were given numbers between 1 and 9,000. Each of these numbers was placed in a capsule, which was put in a ten-gallon fishbowl. Blindfolded, Secretary of War Henry Stimson drew a capsule and handed it to President Franklin D. Roosevelt, who opened it and read "158." The lottery continued in this way until all of the numbers were drawn, establishing a selection order. All registered men holding the number 158 were the first to report.

American men have been drafted during wartime since the Revolutionary War. Today, the United States uses volunteer military forces; however, since 1980, all men have been required to register for the draft when they reach 18. In the event of an emergency, they may be required to serve in the armed forces.

Secretary of War Henry Stimson draws the first capsule in the draft lottery in October 1940.

---

264 UNIT TWO PART 2: UNEXPECTED DEVELOPMENTS

Mini-Lesson Study Skills

SQ3R Point out to students that acquiring and using basic study skills—such as SQ3R (Survey, Question, Read, Recite, Review)—will help make their studying easier and possibly cut down on their study time. SQ3R is especially helpful when reading nonfiction because this type of literature often involves a great deal of detailed information and facts. SQ3R allows readers not only to understand the material but also to remember it.

Survey the selection quickly, noting the general ideas.

Question what you would like to find out when you read the passage.

Read the selection carefully, keeping in mind the questions you raised.

Recite the main points of what you have just read by putting the information in your own words.

Review the entire selection. What questions have been left unanswered?

Application Have students apply the SQ3R approach to their research for the Across the Curriculum activity on page 266. You might also have them compare their questions and answers with those of other students in the class.

RESPONDING OPTIONS

FROM PERSONAL RESPONSE TO CRITICAL ANALYSIS

REFLECT
1. What effect of World War II on the home front surprises you most? Why?

RETHINK
2. If you had been living during World War II, what part of rationing would have been the most difficult adjustment for you? Explain your answer.

3. What effects do you think rationing had on civilians at home, other than forcing people to make do with less?

RELATE
4. "Make it do, wear it out, and do without." How would environmentalists today view this World War II slogan? What parallels do you see between what the U.S. government urged citizens to do during World War II and what modern environmentalists urge today's citizens to do? Present your response in the form of a print ad campaign for both the past and present.

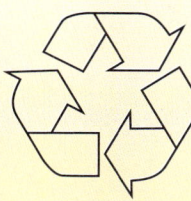

Multimodal Learning
ANOTHER PATHWAY
Cooperative Learning
Using the information in the selection, work in small groups to create a "How to Adjust" poster for citizens living in the United States during World War II. Visually portray what citizens could do to cope with shortages.

QUICKWRITES

1. Write a **paragraph** contrasting life in the United States during World War II with life as it is now.

2. Write a concise **encyclopedia entry** about rationing during World War II, using the information in the selection. Before beginning, refer to an encyclopedia to get a sense of style.

3. Create a **radio or television public service announcement** urging people to buy war bonds or save scrap metal. Explain the purpose of buying bonds or saving metal and tell how to do one or the other. Be sure to grab your listeners' attention.

📁 **PORTFOLIO** *Save your writing. You may want to use it later as a springboard to a piece for your portfolio.*

LITERARY CONCEPTS

A **memoir** is a first-person recollection of an experience. It relates the details of an event that the writer participated in or witnessed. Often, the writer describes the impact of the event on his or her personal life. How successfully do you think Abernethy conveys the impact of World War II on civilian life and on her personal life? Give evidence from the story to support your answer.

From Personal Response to Critical Analysis

1. Responses will vary.
2. Possible response: Food rationing would have been the most difficult adjustment because, being used to abundant food supplies, it would be hard to change eating habits.
3. Possible responses: It forces people to work together toward a common goal; it makes people try to get along under difficult conditions.
4. Print ads will vary. Students may make the following points in their responses: Environmentalists encourage recycling and saving energy just as the government did during the war, so they would like the slogan. However, environmentalists do not have the same popular or government support as the war effort did.

Another Pathway
Cooperative Learning Have groups of three to four students cooperatively plan the tasks necessary to complete the poster. Ask each group to review the selection, before beginning the poster, to find out the particular shortages experienced. One student should act as a recorder and note these details. Have spatial learners create the illustrations for the poster, while linguistic learners come up with captions.

Rubric
3 Full Accomplishment Students create a well-designed poster that fully represents details from Abernethy's account.
2 Substantial Accomplishment Details from the story are carefully selected, but the representation of these details is poorly executed in the poster.
1 Little or Partial Accomplishment Students fail to select shortages that correspond to the selection.

Literary Concepts
Ask students to make a chart with the headings "Civilian Life" and "Personal Life." Have them fill in details that correspond to each heading after they review Abernethy's memoir. After the charts are complete, have students exchange their charts with partners and compare the details in each chart. Invite pairs to decide where Abernethy could have added more information and where she provided a complete account of life during World War II.

QuickWrites
1. Encourage students to make a "Then/Now" chart before they begin writing.
2. Point out to students that an encyclopedia entry is objective and contains only facts.
3. If students are not familiar with public service announcements, discuss with them commercials about topics such as wearing seat belts, preventing forest fires, or saying no to drugs.

The Writer's Craft

Comparison and Contrast, pp. 115–127
Main Idea and Supporting Details, pp. 249–250
Persuasion, pp. 137–158

Words to Know

Responses will vary. *Ratio* means the relation in degree or number between two similar things. It comes from a Latin word that means "to reckon or consider." Other words with the same root are *ratiocinate, rational,* and *rationale.*

Across the Curriculum

Social Studies Encourage students to look, as they gather their research, at the many documentaries, photographic essays, and films that deal with the major events of World War II. Suggest that they ask their librarian for any alternative resources they may want to examine before beginning to do research.

ADDITIONAL SUGGESTION

Geography *Battlegrounds* Some students may not be familiar with the location of many of the major countries and battle sites of World War II. Students should use an atlas or map to locate the following:

The Allied Powers—France, Great Britain, the former Soviet Union, the United States

The Axis Powers—Germany, Japan, and Italy

Major Battles—Pearl Harbor: Oahu Island, Hawaii; Iwo Jima: volcanic island, western Pacific; D-Day: Normandy, southern France

---

ALTERNATIVE ACTIVITIES

1. **Cooperative Learning** Assemble the unanswered questions that individuals in your group had when reading this selection. Divide up the task of doing **research** to answer those questions. Share both questions and answers with the rest of the class.

2. Interview a grandparent or another older person who lived during World War II, asking about his or her memories of the war overseas and of the home front. You might want to videotape or audiotape the **interview** or orally report what you learned to the class.

ACROSS THE CURRICULUM

 Social Studies Abernethy mentions prisoner-of-war camps in the United States as well as three major military events of World War II—the Japanese attack on Pearl Harbor, D-Day, and the Battle of the Bulge. Research the details of one of these places or events. Share your research with the class.

D-Day assault by Americans on the northern coast of France.

WORDS TO KNOW

The root word of *rationing* is the Latin word *ratio.* Use a dictionary to find the meaning of *ratio;* then list as many other words as you can that have the same root. Show how those words reflect the meaning of *ratio.*

HAZEL SHELTON ABERNETHY

Hazel Shelton Abernethy is pleased to have received national recognition with the publication of "The Home Front: 1941–1945," as well as recognition from her family: "I have six wonderful grandchildren and being published increases my credibility and stature with them and the rest of the family!"

Abernethy sees herself not as a writer, but as a wife, mother, grandmother, college teacher, public speaker, actress, and—believe it or not—stagehand. She has spent her life in Nacogdoches, where she graduated from Stephen F. Austin University in 1948. That same year she married her high school sweetheart, a Navy man. "Twenty years and five children later," Abernethy went back to SFA, where she received her master's degree in history and taught until 1992.

Abernethy is head of production for Nacogdoches Lamplite Community Theater. She also speaks on local history for the East Texas Historical Association and other groups.

For Abernethy, the greatest impact of World War II was hearing the news and then seeing her friends leave. This "crystallized for me what the world was about," she recalls. "As teenagers we were certainly influenced by the drama and romance and excitement of wartime. For most of us the war was the defining period of our lives. 'Before the war' and 'after the war' are standard introductions of our remembering."

1927–

266 UNIT TWO PART 2: UNEXPECTED DEVELOPMENTS

Alternative Activities

1. Have students compare the lists of questions they created on page 261. Ask one student to act as a recorder and assemble a master list of questions. Then encourage students to review this list to select the questions they will research. After each group has completed its research, have the members of the groups review the answers before sharing them with the rest of the class.

2. Encourage students to contact a local Veteran's Association or community organization to find people who lived during World War II. Also suggest that family members may have pictures or diaries from this time that they would be willing to share. Be sure students tell their informants the nature and the purpose of the assignment before they begin their interview.

PREVIEWING

POETRY

my enemy was dreaming
Norman Russell

Lost
Bruce Ignacio

Activating Prior Knowledge
PERSONAL CONNECTION

Have you ever thought that it would be more fun to live as your ancestors did? Would life be more exciting? Were the "good old days" really better?

Imagine yourself in the place of one of your ancestors. When and where would you be living? What problems would you face? What would be the pluses and minuses of your life? List them on a chart like the one shown here.

Time:_____	Place:_____
+ Pluses of that life	− Minuses of that life

Building Background
HISTORICAL CONNECTION

The two poems you are about to read describe the thoughts and feelings of two Native Americans, one a warrior from the past, and the other a modern-day descendant. Early Native Americans faced situations and had to make decisions that affected not only their survival but also their status within their tribes.

Modern Native Americans have lifestyles that are very different from those of their ancestors. Yet they, like most other people, sometimes think that their ancestors' lives were better than theirs are. In "Lost," the speaker looks at the pluses and minuses of his life as opposed to his ancestors' lives.

Active Reading/Setting a Purpose
READING CONNECTION

Free Verse These two poems are written in free verse, which is poetry that has no regular pattern of rhythm, rhyme, or line length. Such poetry is written in a conversational style. Therefore, read each poem the way you think the speaker would express his thoughts in a conversation.

Native Americans dance during a celebration at the Blackfeet Indian Reservation in Montana. Copyright © Pat and Tom Leeson/Photo Researchers.

MY ENEMY WAS DREAMING / LOST **267**

OVERVIEW

Objectives
- To understand and appreciate two free-verse poems about Native American experiences
- To understand and appreciate the use of mood
- To express understanding of the poems through a choice of writing forms, including rewriting stanzas and character analysis
- To extend understanding of the poems through a variety of multimodal and cross-curricular activities

Skills

LITERARY CONCEPTS
- Repetition
- Mood

THE WRITER'S STYLE
- Alliteration

SPEAKING, LISTENING, AND VIEWING
- Group discussion
- Oral presentation

Cross-Curricular Connections

HISTORY
- Expansion of U.S. cities

SOCIAL STUDIES
- Modern-day Native Americans

Thematic Link: *Unexpected Developments* In these two poems, the speakers confront developments in their lives that are related to their Native American identities.

CUSTOMIZING FOR
Students Acquiring English

- Use **ACCESS FOR STUDENTS ACQUIRING ENGLISH,** Reading and Writing Support.
- Find out what students already know about Native American history and culture from movies, books, or personal experience. Point out that Native Americans experienced an abrupt change in only a few generations from a typically nomadic, subsistent tribal existence to living in an urban, industrialized society that was no longer their own.

PRINT AND MEDIA RESOURCES

UNIT TWO RESOURCE BOOK
Strategic Reading: Literature, p. 69

ACCESS FOR STUDENTS ACQUIRING ENGLISH
Reading and Writing Support

FORMAL ASSESSMENT
Selection Test, p. 51
Part Test, pp. 53-54
 Test Generator

AUDIO LIBRARY
See Reference Card

THE LANGUAGE OF LITERATURE TEACHER'S EDITION **267**

CUSTOMIZING FOR
Gifted and Talented Students

After students have read both poems, discuss the cultural values that the poems communicate. For instance, ask students whether the speaker's Native American identity in "my enemy was dreaming" might have shaped his decision to spare the life of his sleeping enemy.

Literary Concept: REPETITION

A Have students discuss the effect of the repetition of the word *i* throughout the poem. *(Possible response: It connects the actions of the speaker throughout the poem; it produces a rhythmic effect .)*

Art Note

The Branch by Lee Teter This depiction of an Iroquois warrior suggests a close relationship between the warrior and the natural world.

Reading the Art *What impression does the look on the warrior's face and his position on the branch create?*

From Personal Response to Critical Analysis

1. Responses will vary.
2. Possible response: The speaker does not kill his enemy because he is moved by the peaceful expression on the sleeping enemy's face.
3. Possible response: He does not tell his companions of his decision not to kill the enemy.
4. Possible responses: There are more pluses because the speaker chose not to dishonor himself by killing a sleeping man. There are more minuses because the enemy will awaken and may later harm the speaker or his people.

MY ENEMY WAS DREAMING
by Norman Russell

The Branch (1993), Lee Teter. Copyright © 1993 Somerset House Publishing.

when i found my enemy sleeping
i stood over him and as still
as the owl at night
as the heron waiting fish
5   i raised my knife to kill him

then i saw my enemy was dreaming
his mouth made a little smile
his legs trembled

he made small sleep sounds
10 a happy dream was in his mind

only i will have this memory
i will show the others
only the horse of my enemy
i will not tell the others
15 i left my enemy dreaming his dream.

FROM PERSONAL RESPONSE TO CRITICAL ANALYSIS

REFLECT 1. Were you surprised by the speaker's actions in "my enemy was dreaming"? Why or why not?

RETHINK 2. Why does the speaker choose not to kill his enemy?

3. What evidence in the poem suggests that the speaker has done something different from what is expected of him?

4. Do you think the pluses of his decision outweigh its minuses? Explain your answer.

268   UNIT TWO   PART 2: UNEXPECTED DEVELOPMENTS

Mini-Lesson  Literary Concepts

REVIEWING REPETITION Remind students that repetition is the repeated use of any element of language. A sound, a word, a phrase, a grammatical structure, or an entire line can be repeated in a poem to stress important ideas or to create sound effects. Explain to students that because free verse lacks regular rhythm, rhyme, and form, repetition is often crucial to the coherence of the poem.

Application Have students copy the web and use it to identify examples of the poet's use of repetition in the poem. (For example, sounds—long *i* in *i, night, knife;* words—*i*; phrases—*i will*) Invite them to discuss how the repetition of particular elements works to convey the overall mood of the poem.

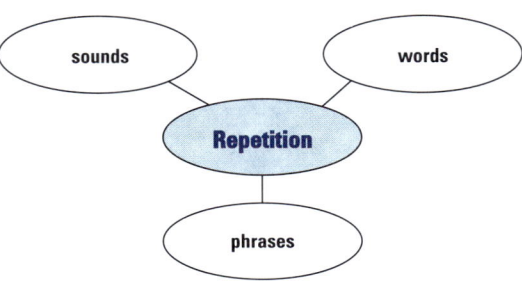

LOST

by Bruce Ignacio

Cheyenne in New Mexico (1993), Malcolm Furlow. Courtesy of the artist.

I know not of my forefathers
nor of their beliefs
For I was brought up in the city.
Our home seemed smothered and surrounded
as were other homes on city sites.
When the rain came
I would slush my way to school
as though the street were a wading pool.
Those streets were always crowded.
I brushed by people with every step,
Covered my nose once in awhile,
Gasping against the smell of perspiration on humid days.
Lights flashed everywhere
until my head became a signal, flashing on and off.
Noise so unbearable
I wished the whole place would come to a standstill,
leaving only peace and quiet

And still, would I like this kind of life? . . .
The life of my forefathers
who wandered, not knowing where they were going,
but just moving, further and further
from where they had been,
To be in quiet,
to kind of be lost in their dreams and wishing,
as I have been to this day,
I awake.

Mini-Lesson — The Writer's Style

ALLITERATION Tell students that the repetition of consonant sounds at the beginnings of words is known as alliteration. Alliteration is used to emphasize certain words and to create a musical quality in a poem or prose piece. Students are probably most familiar with examples of alliteration used in tongue-twisters, such as "Peter Piper picked a peck of pickled peppers."

Application Have students find examples of alliteration in "my enemy was dreaming." Ask them to discuss how alliteration relates to the overall mood of the poem. (Possible response: The repetition of s sounds throughout the poem helps to create a sense of silence.)

Reteaching/Reinforcement

The Writer's Craft
Alliteration, p. 321

From Personal Response to Critical Analysis

1. Responses will vary.
2. Possible responses: The city is overcrowded and smells foul; it is much too busy and lacks peace and quiet.
3. Possible responses: He is critical of his forefathers' constant movement; he thinks that his forefathers were just as dissatisfied with where they were living as he now is.
4. Possible responses: With his present awareness that peace and quiet are not to be found, he would remain in the city; for all of its negatives, the city offers a permanent home, which is preferable to a life of constant wandering.
5. Responses will vary.

Another Pathway

Before pairs begin their conversation, have them decide which speaker they will represent. Then have each student jot down a few opinions his or her speaker would probably have about dreaming and about the other speaker's lifestyle. Challenge students to include both positive and negative comments in their conversations.

Rubric

3 Full Accomplishment Student comments indicate a precise understanding of the speaker's views and lifestyle.

2 Substantial Accomplishment Student comments indicate a partial understanding of the speaker's views and lifestyle.

1 Little or Partial Accomplishment Students do not comprehend the views and/or lifestyle of the chosen speaker.

RESPONDING OPTIONS

FROM PERSONAL RESPONSE TO CRITICAL ANALYSIS

REFLECT
1. What might you say to the speaker in "Lost" if you met him? Share your ideas with a partner.

RETHINK
2. What "minuses" does the speaker find in modern life in the city?
3. What does he think are the "minuses" of the lives of his ancestors?
4. If the speaker were able to choose between the two lifestyles, which do you think he would pick?

RELATE
5. Whose life would you rather live, that of the first speaker or the second? Explain your choice.

Multimodal Learning
ANOTHER PATHWAY

With a partner, act out a conversation the speakers of the two poems might have if they met. Include the subject of dreaming, and allow both speakers to comment on each other's lifestyle.

LITERARY CONCEPTS

The **mood** of a poem or story is the emotional effect it has on its reader. The sound and rhythm of the language, descriptive words, and figurative language all contribute to the mood in these two poems. Describe the mood of each poem. What details help to create that mood?

QUICKWRITES

1. Compose several different versions of the first **stanza** of "my enemy was dreaming." Use the poet's first line and replace the similes and lines 2 and 5. Keep the meaning of the stanza in your versions.

2. Choose the speaker in either poem and write a **character analysis** of him. Infer what you can about his personality through his words and actions.

📁 **PORTFOLIO** Save your writing. You may want to use it later as a springboard to a piece for your portfolio.

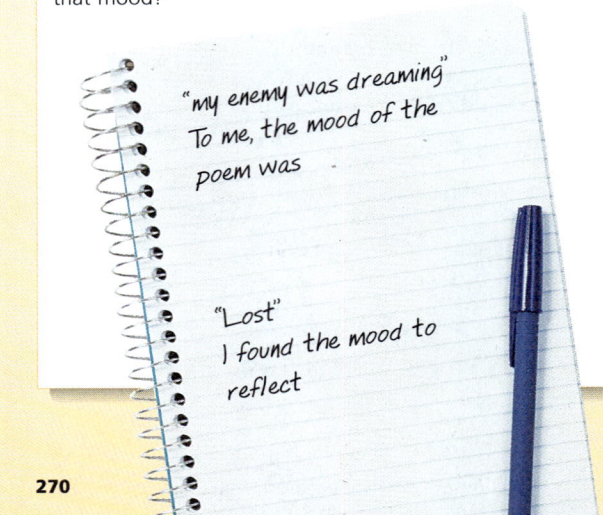

"my enemy was dreaming"
To me, the mood of the poem was

"Lost"
I found the mood to reflect

270

Literary Concepts

Students' descriptions will vary. Possible responses: "My enemy was dreaming" created a sense of quiet and suspense. The poet's use of the lowercase *i* seemed to indicate that the speaker was making himself as small as possible to go undetected. "Lost" uses descriptive language to express the sound, the smells, and the feel of the noisy, dirty, and overcrowded city. This contrasts greatly with the quieter, open spaces experienced by his forefathers.

QuickWrites

1. Suggest that students use similes from their own experiences to replace those of the speaker. For example, "I stood over him as still / as an unplugged telephone / as an empty parking lot at night."
2. Be sure students take into account the very different social and historical circumstances of the two speakers. Point out to students that their character analysis should include both positive and negative qualities.

Using Poetic Devices, pp. 318–321

ALTERNATIVE ACTIVITIES

1. **Cooperative Learning** With a small group of classmates, do a **group reading** of either of the two poems. Work on the appropriate tone of voice for each part of the poem in order to reflect its mood. Perform the reading for your class.
2. Design your own **illustrations** for each of the poems. Focus on the poems' titles for your inspiration.

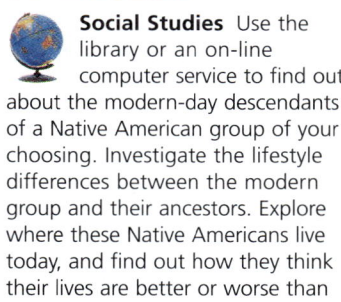

ACROSS THE CURRICULUM

Social Studies Use the library or an on-line computer service to find out about the modern-day descendants of a Native American group of your choosing. Investigate the lifestyle differences between the modern group and their ancestors. Explore where these Native Americans live today, and find out how they think their lives are better or worse than their ancestors.

NORMAN RUSSELL

Norman Russell (1921–) says he does not write his Native American poems because he is part Cherokee, but because he feels "there is much we might learn today from a re-examination of the Indian's respect for his environment." Russell is a part-time poet—his training and career are in teaching and biology. He has done research, written textbooks, and taught biology at several colleges and universities.

Russell has had six volumes of poetry published, and his poems have appeared in numerous magazines and anthologies.

OTHER WORKS *At the Zoo, Indian Thoughts: The Small Songs of God, Open the Flower*
Extended Reading

BRUCE IGNACIO

A Native American of northern Ute ancestry, Bruce Ignacio was born in Fort Duchesne, Utah. From 1967 through 1970, he attended the Institute of American Indian Arts in Santa Fe, New Mexico, where he studied creative writing and jewelry making. He made jewelry for a living until 1985, when he became a carpenter. Ignacio now lives with his wife and three daughters on the Wampanoag Indian Reservation, Martha's Vineyard, Massachusetts. There, he makes jewelry and small carvings known as fetishes.

MY ENEMY WAS DREAMING / LOST **271**

Literary Links

Compare the speaker's views of human-made objects in "Lost" with the speaker's views in "Hard Questions." *(Possible response: Both speakers have a similar disdain for human-made objects: the noise, smell, and business of the city in "Lost" and the absence of nature in "Hard Questions." However, the speaker in "Lost" seems to be more accepting of the inevitability of the encroachment of technology.)*

NORMAN RUSSELL

Born in Big Stone Gap, Virginia, Russell graduated from Slippery Rock State Teachers College, now part of Pennsylvania State University. After serving in India with the United States Army during World War II, he did graduate work at the Universities of Tennessee and Minnesota. About his writing, Russell says, "I write separately in science and in poetry, and sometimes combine them. But my science is not poetry, and my poetry is not science."

Across the Curriculum

Social Studies Students may also wish to consider using community resources such as local Native American organizations or cultural events. If possible, invite a Native American speaker to discuss with the class how contemporary Native Americans incorporate traditional ways into their present lifestyles.

ADDITIONAL SUGGESTIONS

History *Cooperative Learning* Have students research the expansion of U.S. cities following World War II. Divide students into groups of four or five and have each group examine one the following topics: migration to urban areas; the development of suburbs; the changing ethnic composition of the city; the quality of life for new immigrants. Students' research should focus on the multiple ways the city has changed and developed over time. Encourage students to include charts, maps, and other visuals in their research.

Alternative Activities

1. Have each group reread the poem together to get a feel for the flow of the language and to identify any difficult words or rhythmic patterns. Then have each student pick one stanza or section of the poem they will be responsible for interpreting. Be sure to have the groups practice their readings as a whole before performing for the class.
2. Many illustrations are possible. Students should be able to identify aspects of each poem that inspired them. Encourage students to use a variety of media—paint, marker, pencil, chalk—to create their illustrations. Students may wish to research common Native American iconography before planning their designs.

THE LANGUAGE OF LITERATURE TEACHER'S EDITION **271**

OVERVIEW

To gain a deeper appreciation of the short stories they have read in this unit, students will explore the characteristics of a short story and then create their own well-developed story in this lesson.

Objectives

- To plan a short story by considering elements such as plot, character, conflict, and setting
- To draft a short story and solicit a response
- To revise, edit, and publish a short story
- To reflect on the process of writing a short story

Skills

LITERATURE
- Identifying plot
- Creating characters
- Analyzing conflict
- Establishing setting

WRITING AND LANGUAGE
- Ordering events
- Planning the climax
- Using precise verbs

MEDIA LITERACY
- Interpreting magazine articles
- Studying advice columns
- Inferring from photographs

SPEAKING, LISTENING, AND VIEWING
- Conferencing
- Storytelling
- Reading aloud
- Performing dialogue

Teaching Strategy: STUMBLING BLOCK

A Students may not fully understand the term fiction. Explain that fiction is writing that tells about made-up events and characters. Fiction that contains imaginary situations and characters that are very similar to real life is called realistic fiction.

Teaching Strategy: MODELING

B To show students how to generate story ideas from real-life prompts such as photographs, articles, and letters, direct them to study the samples on pages 272 and 273. Next, have students write freely for one minute, using any of the prompts as a springboard. Explain to the class that there is no one right response and that their freewriting will not be graded. Then invite students to share their ideas and explain how they used the visuals as a springboard for writing ideas.

WRITING FROM EXPERIENCE

WRITING A FICTIONAL NARRATIVE

Have you ever finished reading a story or watching a movie and said to yourself, "That seemed so real!"? Some of the best fiction stories are based on struggles that real people experience. The stories in Unit Two, "Critical Adjustments," deal with such real-life issues.

GUIDED ASSIGNMENT
Write a Short Story The events of your life can inspire you to write your own short stories. You'll explore how to write a short fictional story in the next few pages.

1 Look for Inspiration

In a short story, writers explore an idea, event, or feeling that's important to them. Have you ever wondered how they get these ideas?

Getting Ideas from Experience Sometimes writers find inspiration in their own experiences. What are some of the most interesting situations you've faced in your life? Start a list of story ideas.

Getting Ideas from Reading Reading fiction, poetry, news articles, advertising, or even graffiti can give writers ideas for stories of their own. Reread a favorite story or poem and add story ideas to your list.

Finding the Story Good writers are observant and interested in the things they read and see. What story ideas do you see in these excerpts and pictures?

Maybe I can write a story about the photo and this article about twins.

Magazine Photo

These guys look like they're from outer space! A story about aliens would be fun.

Magazine Article

Why Do You Act That Way?

Barbara Parker was 36 when she met her genetic double. Returning home from the chiropractor one afternoon, she found a neighbor at her door. "Remember you told me you were adopted and an only child?" the neighbor asked. "Well, your identical twin is in my living room."

There she was—Parker's unknown, unimagined twin. Separated from her at birth, Parker had never dreamed the woman existed. But there, unmistakably, were Parker's cheekbones, smile, curly brown hair—even, the neighbor gasped, Parker's gestures and her laugh.

"The instant I saw her, I believed yes, she was my twin," said Parker, a 45-year-old landscape designer and mother of two living in Canyon Country. "But shock became disbelief. I began grilling her: Who was our mother? When is our birthday?"

Janny Scott
from *Los Angeles Times*, April 18, 1992

272 UNIT TWO: CRITICAL ADJUSTMENTS

PRINT AND MEDIA RESOURCES

UNIT TWO RESOURCE BOOK
Prewriting Activity, p. 73
Elaboration, p. 74
Peer Response Guide, pp. 75–76
Revising and Proofreading, p. 77
Student Model, pp. 78–79
Rubric, p. 80

GRAMMAR MINI-LESSONS
Transparencies, p. 38

WRITING MINI-LESSONS
Transparencies, pp. 6–7, 38, 46

ACCESS FOR STUDENTS ACQUIRING ENGLISH
Reading and Writing Support

FORMAL ASSESSMENT
Guidelines for Writing Assessment

 **WRITING COACH**

 **LASERLINKS**
Writing Springboard

Volcanologists studying lava in Ethiopia.

Advice Column Letters

Dear Aggie:
A friend of mine in my history class has cut class a couple of times and blows off some of the assignments. Now a big essay test is coming up and she wants to copy my notes. This is the third time she's done this. What should I do?
—Trying to Decide

Dear Aggie:
My older sister threw a party at our house while our parents were away. During the party, a valuable vase got broken. My sister told my parents that the dog broke it, but I know one of her friends broke it. They believe her. Should I tell them the truth?
—Wondering

② Explore Your Ideas

Once you have a few good ideas, explore them for a while before you decide which one to write about.

What If? Choose two of the story ideas you've listed. Ask yourself "what if" questions to find possible story beginnings. For example, one student read the twins article, looked at the photo, and asked, "What if one twin was from outer space?"

> LASERLINKS
> • WRITING SPRINGBOARD
>
> WRITING COACH

WRITING FROM EXPERIENCE **273**

CUSTOMIZING FOR
Less-Proficient Writers

C Many students find it difficult to generate story ideas, especially from visual prompts. Suggest that they instead write a scratch outline of a familiar story, substitute different characters, and change the plot a little bit. Then guide students to use this outline to spark further story ideas.

Writing Skill:
FINDING WRITING IDEAS

D Explain to students that story ideas can also spring from any element in a narrative, such as setting, character, or conflict. Encourage students to consider all elements of fiction as they brainstorm ideas.

Teaching Strategy:
STUMBLING BLOCK

E Students often feel that a story idea is not valid if they do not have the entire plot worked out at this early stage of the writing process. Reassure students that there is no need to know how a story will end at this point. Suggest that they develop the story as they go.

WRITING SPRINGBOARD
Moving On Members of a family literally pick up the pieces after a devastating tornado and talk about seeking a new place to live.

Side B, Frame 5470

Writing Prompt Think about how unexpected developments can cause changes in families. Write a short story about the adjustments that a family makes when faced with such a situation. If you like, you may base your story on an experience your family has had.

CUSTOMIZING FOR
Less-Proficient Writers

F For students who are unable to develop plot, character, conflict, and setting show them this method of developing a plot outline:
- Take a character.
- Get the character in trouble.
- Make the problem worse.
- Solve the problem.

Writing Skill:
USING THE COMPUTER

G Encourage students to do their prewriting on a computer. Tell students that many writers brainstorm ideas about different story elements at the same time, and the computer makes recording such ideas particularly easy. Explain that if they think of an idea for another part of their story while prewriting on a computer, they can write it in capital letters, boldface, or italics to set it off. When they go back over their prewriting, they can decide what to do with the idea. If they decide to use it, they can easily remove the special printing and place the idea where it belongs. Otherwise, they can delete the idea.

Writing Skill:
DEVELOPING CONFLICT

H Explain to students that conflicts can be internal or external. Internal conflicts occur when the character struggles with a problem such as fear, jealously, or anger. External conflicts occur when the character struggles with an outside force, such as nature or another character. Encourage students to consider both internal and external conflicts as they plot their stories.

PREWRITING

Working Out Your Ideas

Using Your Imagination Most of the work of writing occurs before you even set pen to paper. The more time you spend developing your ideas and mining your imagination, the more you'll have to work with when you begin to write.

❶ Choose a Topic
Look at the list of topic ideas you wrote earlier. Which one will you choose to write about? Write a brief explanation telling why you think this will make the best story.

❷ Think About Story Elements
A good story has a balance of several elements that can bring a conflict to life on the page. These are plot, setting, character, and conflict.

Plot A story's plot is the sequence of events that occur. Plot is the "what happens" of your story. The SkillBuilder at the right explains the different ways to order the events in your story.

Student's Planning Chart

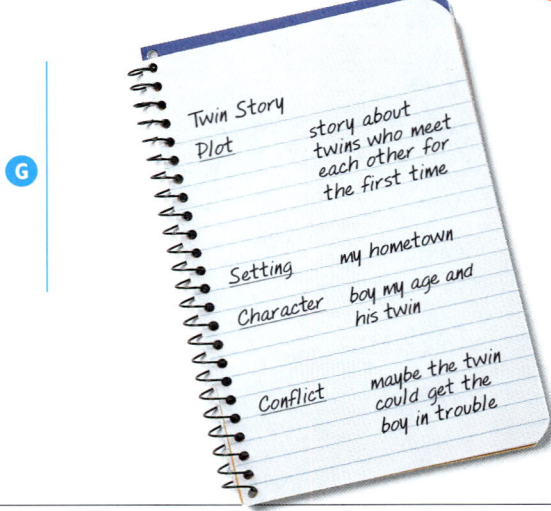

Character Characters are the people in your story. Who will be the main characters in your story? What qualities will each character have?

Conflict Conflict is the central problem your characters face. What problems will your main character have to deal with?

Setting Setting is the "where" and "when" of your story. Will your story take place in the city? in the country? on another planet? Will your story take place in the 1800s? today? in the future?

❸ Plan Your Story
Here are some suggestions to help you plan your story.

Sketch It Out Stories usually have a beginning, a middle, and an end. Making sketches of your ideas can help you to plan your setting and to order the details of your plot. Look at the drawings on the next page to see how one student planned his story.

Write Character Sketches Write brief descriptions, giving details about characters in your story. It might even help to draw sketches of each character.

274 UNIT TWO: CRITICAL ADJUSTMENTS

Mini-Lesson: Speaking, Listening, and Viewing

STORYTELLING Explain to students that professional writers often use models to spark ideas. Elicit from students that reading fiction such as short stories can help them learn how to structure plot, character, setting, and conflict. As a class, brainstorm a list of short story writers whose work might prompt ideas and structure. Possibilities include the stories of Anton Chekhov, Sandra Cisneros, O. Henry, and Toni Cade Bambara.

Application Invite students to select a short story they believe would be a good writing model for this assignment. Have students work in pairs to share the stories, each partner reading his or her story to the other. Then have partners discuss the story elements and how the model can be used as a guideline for their own story's content and structure.

4 Let the Story Unfold

These strategies may help you plan ways you can get your plot moving from the beginning to the end.

Take Time to Discover You won't know everything when you first start writing. Give yourself time to work through your ideas.

Plan the Conflict How will the main character try to resolve his or her problem?

Use Dialogue You can use dialogue to help move your plot along. For example: "Why did you break Steve's bike last week, Zolar?" Jakim asked. "Because I wanted you to get blamed for it," Zolar replied.

Show, Don't Tell Readers like to see things for themselves. Instead of telling them that a character is angry, why not let his actions show his anger?

Sketch a Story

SkillBuilder

 WRITER'S CRAFT

Ordering Events

As you think about the plot of your story, consider the order of events. If you choose to tell them in chronological order, you'll need to use time adverbs to cue your reader. For example:

On Tuesday evening, Jakim's life seemed normal. But two days later, his life totally changed.

You might also use flashback to tell your story. In a flashback, the reader is taken back in time, then back to the present. For example, you could interrupt your story to have your character reflect on a past event and then you could return to your present narration.

APPLYING WHAT YOU'VE LEARNED
Try making a time line of the events in your story to check the order of events.

 WRITING HANDBOOK

For more information on ordering events, see page 829 of the Writing Handbook.

THINK & PLAN

Reflecting on Your Ideas

1. What strategies might you use to keep your plot moving?
2. How will you use dialogue to create realistic characters?
3. How will you order the events in your story?

WRITING FROM EXPERIENCE **275**

Writing Skill:
USING DIALOGUE

Give students these guidelines to make it easier for them to use dialogue in their short stories:

- Use a speaker's tag—such as "I yelled" or "he whispered"—to identify the speaker and make the dialogue more descriptive and precise.
- Put quotation marks around the speaker's exact words.
- Capitalize the first word of a quotation and the first word of a new sentence within a quotation.
- Place commas and periods inside quotation marks.
- Begin a new paragraph each time the speaker changes.

Writing Skill:
USING GRAPHIC DEVICES

In addition to sketching a story, students can use plot diagrams, story charts, and other graphic devices to organize the plot and conflict. Encourage all students to use some type of graphic device to make sure their plot is logical and well-developed.

 **SkillBuilder** **WRITER'S CRAFT**

ORDERING EVENTS Explain to students that stories are more exciting and fun to read if the events are suspenseful. Be sure students understand that, to make their stories suspenseful, they should not reveal the ending too early. At the same time, they must present hints that suggest what the outcome might be in order to make sure the climax and ending seem logical. Have students select one or two stories in this unit that they feel are most suspenseful. As a class, analyze how the writers create suspense through the order of events.

Applying What You've Learned Encourage students to include time adverbs on their time line to show when events occurred.

Additional Suggestions Have students share their order of events with partners. Advise partners to determine whether any events are in the wrong order or would be more effective if rearranged.

Reteaching/Reinforcement
Writing Mini-Lessons transparencies, pp. 6–7

 The Writer's Craft
Chronological Order, pp. 240–241

THE LANGUAGE OF LITERATURE TEACHER'S EDITION **275**

Writing Skill:
USING THE COMPUTER

K Encourage students to draft on a computer. Have students use the Writing Coach, which provides specific guidelines for the drafting stage.

Speaking, Listening, and Viewing:
PERFORMING DIALOGUE

L Creating realistic-sounding dialogue is difficult. Suggest that students first read their dialogue aloud to themselves to see if it reflects the character portrayed. Then have students work in pairs or small groups to perform the dialogue as a skit. Guide the author and readers to evaluate the dialogue using questions such as the following:
- Can I identify each speaker? Should I add speakers' tags?
- Does the dialogue sound like real speech?
- Does it reflect the character's personality?
- Is the dialogue correctly punctuated?

Critical Thinking: ANALYZING

M Have students make up an individual checklist to evaluate their drafts, incorporating the story elements discussed previously. Possible checklist items include:
- Are my characters realistic?
- Have I included enough sensory details to establish the time and place?
- Are all the events arranged in a logical order?
- Is the conflict realistic?

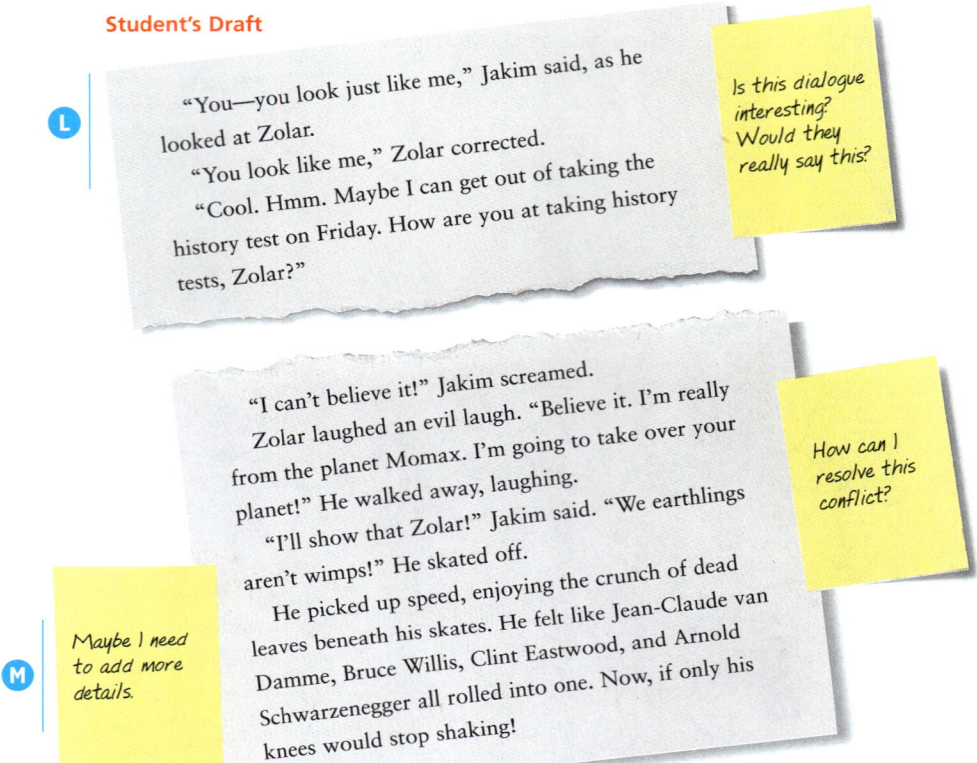

WRITING SPRINGBOARD
Gary Paulsen The noted author Gary Paulsen tells about a librarian who made a tremendous difference in his life.

Side B, Frame 7613

Writing Prompt This video shows the impact a person can have on another person's life. Imagine a situation in which a person turns another person's life around. Then write a story about those people and what happens between them.

276 THE LANGUAGE OF LITERATURE TEACHER'S EDITION

2 Analyze Your Draft

Step back from the story. Asking yourself questions like these can help you evaluate your story ideas.

- Who will my readers be?
- How can I make the story flow more smoothly?
- Where are the characters and events leading me?
- What can I do to make my characters seem more real?
- What details can I add to help show the scene?
- Is it better to tell the story from the first-person point of view, with the narrator using the words *I, my,* and *me* to refer to himself or herself? Or should I use the third-person point of view, with the narrator using *he, she,* and *they* to describe what happens to all the characters?
- Should I present my story as a play? a comic strip? a story in a class booklet?

3 Rework and Share

The following tips can help you rework your draft.

Descriptions You could describe a scene in several ways. Maybe you could start with sounds, then add smells and sights. It might be better to describe what's most important first, or to describe something in the order a movie camera might record it as the camera moves from one end to the other.

Sensory Details It's a good idea to involve your readers' eyes, ears, and nose by including sensory details. Look at the model on the previous page. The sentence "He picked up speed, enjoying the crunch of dead leaves beneath his skates" uses details of sight and sound to create a strong impression.

Dialogue Dialogue can be used to give information about the characters, show their personalities, and provide excitement and suspense in a scene. Try to make every line of dialogue add something to the story.

PEER RESPONSE

Getting feedback from your peers will help you evaluate your story. Ask questions like the following:

- How did my story make you feel?
- What made you care about the characters?
- What was the most interesting part? the most boring part?

SkillBuilder

 WRITER'S CRAFT

Planning the Climax

The climax, or turning point, of a story occurs at the point of most tension. The climax leads to the conclusion of a story. At the beginning of a story, the problem is presented. Toward the middle, the action begins to build until a climax is reached. The action slows down and then evens out at the end. Think of the rising and falling action as being like a roller coaster.

APPLYING WHAT YOU'VE LEARNED
Use a diagram like the one above to chart the events of one of the selections in Unit Two. What events lead to the climax?

RETHINK & EVALUATE

Preparing to Revise

1. Make a list of what you need to do to improve your story.
2. Read your story again, this time aloud. What parts do you need to rethink? What parts do you like the best?

WRITING FROM EXPERIENCE **277**

Writing Skill: POINT OF VIEW

N Explain to students that in addition to deciding between the first-person and third-person point of view, they can make choices about the narrator. For example, the narrator can be a person, an animal, or even an inanimate object. Invite students to try different narrators to see which one helps them create the most interesting story.

Teaching Strategy: STUMBLING BLOCK

O Students sometimes have difficulty distinguishing between reworking a draft and merely recopying the same draft over to make it look neater. In addition, novice writers are often unsure if suggested changes are really appropriate. To alleviate these problems, check students' work during this stage in the writing process. Circulate around the room to see whether students are indeed making the required changes. If they are off track, pair less- and more-proficient writers to encourage each other's efforts.

Speaking, Listening, and Viewing: STORYTELLING

P Suggest storytelling to students who are unable to completely revise their papers. Have students set aside their drafts and tell a partner their story's plot in their own words. As students retell their stories, partners can prompt revisions with questions about character, plot, and conflict. Then have partners switch roles.

SkillBuilder WRITER'S CRAFT

PLANNING THE CLIMAX Be sure that students understand that generally all the story events logically build to the climax. Explain that stories that climax illogically, such as "I woke up and it was all a dream!" often leave the reader feeling cheated and unhappy. Encourage students to talk with a partner to make sure that their story's turning point is logical and interesting.

Applying What You've Learned Invite volunteers to share their diagrams and conclusions with the class. Have students explain how they determined the story's climax.

Additional Suggestions Suggest that students also describe the turning points in favorite novels, movies, and episodes of television shows.

Reteaching/Reinforcement
Writing Mini-Lessons transparencies, p. 6–7

THE LANGUAGE OF LITERATURE TEACHER'S EDITION **277**

Writing Skill:
CHOOSING A TITLE

Q Tell students that the title of a short story should make the audience want to read on. Point out the clever pun in the student model on this page. Discuss with students how this title successfully attracts the reader's attention.

Teaching Strategy: MODELING

R Use the student model to help students understand the importance of thorough editing and revising. Start by inviting a volunteer to read the short story aloud while students follow along silently. Then work as a class to isolate vivid words and images. Possibilities include the feeling of swimming in and out, the taste of maple syrup, the feeling of gliding along on in-line skates, the smell of burning leaves, and hearing the crunch of dead leaves.

Ask volunteers to point out how the writer's choice of details helps support the plot. Possible responses include listing famous actors to suggest to the reader who Jakim felt like and using sensory details like burning leaves to help the reader become part of the action.

Have students suggest a climax, falling action, and resolution based on the rising action of the student's model. Have students share their hypotheses about "Double Trouble," and then have the class vote to decide which ones are the most logical and interesting.

REVISING AND PUBLISHING

Polishing Your Story

Coming to the End It's time to take a look at your story with a fresh eye. Review your readers' responses and your own notes for your story. Use the feedback you received to make your story work.

Student's Final Draft

Double Trouble

"Why did I ever go on that stupid hike in the first place?" Jakim complained to his two goldfish. Blue and Sea swam in and out of their castle, not bothering to answer. "I wish I had never seen that Zolar!"

To think that he had once thought having a twin would be cool! But he had never dreamed that his twin would turn out to be a trouble-making alien from the planet Momax!

Jakim slipped two bottles of maple syrup into his jacket pocket. He was glad he had discovered that Zolar was allergic to maple syrup. He quickly put on his in-line skates and set off for Pointers Hill.

A slight breeze smelling of burning leaves carried him along. He felt like Jean-Claude van Damme, Bruce Willis, Clint Eastwood, and Arnold Schwarzenegger all rolled into one.

"I just wish my knees would stop shaking!" he thought.

He picked up speed, enjoying the crunch of dead leaves beneath his skates.

---

❶ Revise and Edit

What do you like about your story? What needs to change?

- Consider comments made by your peers concerning the effect your story had on them. If there are comments you don't understand, ask reviewers to explain what they mean.
- **Q** Pretend you're the reader. Does the beginning of your story grab your attention? If not, go back and rethink it.
- Use the Standards for Evaluation and the Editing Checklist to be sure that the point of view in your story is consistently first person or third person.
- Read the excerpt of one student's draft to see how he used sensory details to make his descriptions vivid.

What do you feel, hear, taste, or smell through the character's senses?

R

How do the details support the plot?

---

278 THE LANGUAGE OF LITERATURE TEACHER'S EDITION

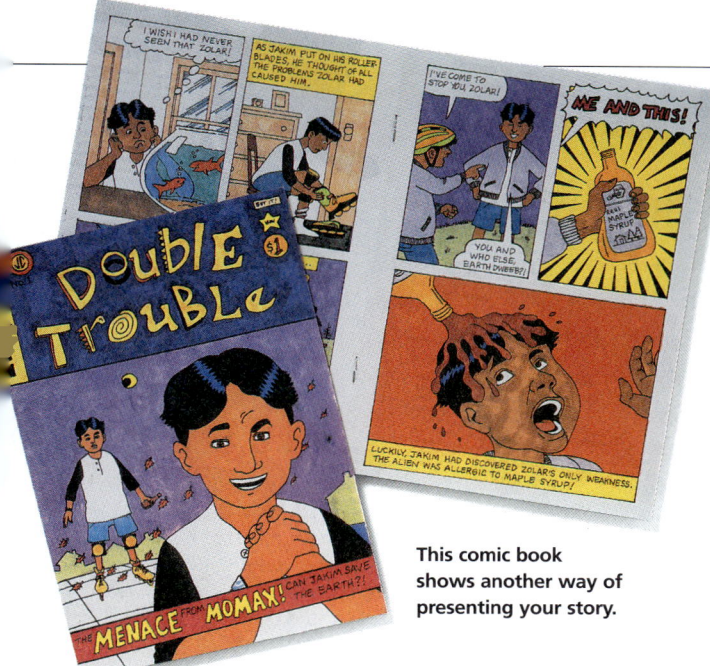

This comic book shows another way of presenting your story.

SkillBuilder

WRITER'S CRAFT

Using Precise Verbs
Action verbs express action. Good writers use a variety of descriptive verbs *(stroll, amble)* rather than using the same verb over and over *(walk)*. They also avoid using weak verbs with adverbs *(said slowly)*. Verbs that show specific action *(stumbled)* create a strong impression.

GRAMMAR HANDBOOK

For more information on using action verbs, see page 883 of the Grammar Handbook.

Editing Checklist Review the following list as you revise your draft.

- Did you check for spelling and punctuation errors?
- Did you use transition words to show time order?
- Did you use action verbs?

2 Share Your Work

The format you use for your writing may depend on your audience and purpose for writing. You may decide on a more imaginative way to present your story. Below are some possibilities. What do you like best about each one?

PUBLISHING IDEAS

- You might turn your story into a play script. Include sound effects.
- A poem or ballad might also fit the mood of your story.
- You might choose to make a comic strip or comic book.
- You could use the story events to make a gameboard.

Standards for Evaluation

A short story
- has fully developed plot, character, and setting
- uses sensory details
- presents events in a clear order
- maintains a consistent point of view
- uses realistic dialogue

REFLECT & ASSESS

Evaluating the Experience

1. How was writing a fiction story similar to or different from writing your family history?
2. How did your prewriting notes help you develop your story?

 PORTFOLIO Draw some illustrations for your story and add them to your portfolio.

WRITING FROM EXPERIENCE **279**

Critical Thinking: ANALYZING
 Invite students to explain what purposes publishing their short stories serves. Guide students to suggest that publishing stories entertains readers and gives writers a sense of accomplishment and completion. Point out that publishing also provides additional feedback students can use the next time they write.

Writing Skill: USING THE COMPUTER
 Invite students to consider publishing their short stories on an on-line bulletin board. Suggest that students solicit feedback through e-mail or set up an on-line conversation in a "chat room" about the story. Then suggest students download comments about their stories and publish these comments as critical reviews with the manuscript.

Portfolio
Invite students to select the writing pieces they wish to include in their portfolio. Suggest that students include any artwork that goes with their story.

Standards for Evaluation

Have students review their short stories for the following:

Ideas and Content
- creates believable characters who use natural-sounding dialogue
- introduces, develops, and resolves conflict through a realistic plot
- uses sensory details and description to create a setting readers can picture in their minds
- maintains a consistent point of view: first or third person

Structure and Form
- demonstrates proper and effective paragraphing
- includes transitional words and phrases to show relationships among ideas
- uses variety of sentence structures

Grammar, Usage, and Mechanics
- contains no more than two or three minor errors in grammar and usage
- contains no more than two or three minor errors in spelling, capitalization, and punctuation

SkillBuilder WRITER'S CRAFT

USING PRECISE VERBS When encouraged to include specific action verbs in their writing, some students may take the advice too literally. They comb the pages of a thesaurus seeking the most precise verbs English offers. Unfortunately, they often end up with a long string of unsuitable and awkward words. To avoid this, encourage students to act out their actions and then find the verb that gives the most precise meaning. Be sure students understand that the most precise verb is rarely the longest, most obscure one. Rather, it is the one that conveys the most vivid sensory image.

Applying What You've Learned Guide students to use the Editing Checklist as they revise their work. Have students focus on replacing trite or inappropriate verbs with precise, descriptive ones.

Reteaching/Reinforcement
Grammar Mini-Lessons transparencies, p. 38
Writing Mini-Lessons transparencies, pp. 38, 46

Action Verbs, pp. 60, 474, 516

THE LANGUAGE OF LITERATURE TEACHER'S EDITION **279**

UNIT REVIEW

This feature allows students to reflect on what they have learned in Unit Two and to assess how well they understand what they have learned. This feature provides students with multiple opportunities for self-assessment, although you may wish to use some of the activities to informally assess specific skills such as speaking and listening or cooperative work.

Objectives

- To allow students to reflect on and assess their understanding of theme
- To allow students to reflect on and assess their understanding of literary concepts such as point of view and theme
- To provide students with the opportunity to assess and build their portfolios

Reflecting on Theme

OPTION 1

Students should review each selection, paying attention to the ways in which each character faces his or her challenges. Make sure that students support their choices with details from the selections. You may also wish to encourage students to jot down notes about their chosen characters that they can refer to when role-playing.

OPTION 2

Encourage students to think about their own experiences and the extent to which the selections in Unit Two connect to these experiences. Students may wish to write brief outlines in which they provide support for their decisions which they can refer to when discussing their choices with partners.

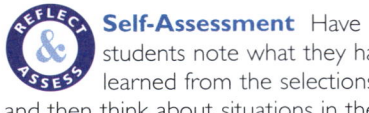 **Self-Assessment** Have students note what they have learned from the selections and then think about situations in the past that they would handle differently now on the basis of what they have learned. Students should refer to this information when outlining their plans for future adjustments.

REFLECT & ASSESS

UNIT TWO: CRITICAL ADJUSTMENTS

As you read the selections in this unit, what did you discover about the adjustments that people make in their lives? What new insights did you gain into the causes and results of such changes? Use one or more of the options in each of the following sections to help you reflect on what you have learned.

REFLECTING ON THEME

OPTION 1 Looking at Character Think about the quotation that begins this unit: "There are two ways of meeting difficulties. You alter the difficulties or you alter yourself to meet them." Create a chart showing which of the two ways each major character in this unit chooses. Working with a partner, select one character from each column of your chart, and imagine a situation in which those two characters meet. Role-play a dialogue in which the characters discuss the quotation.

Alter the Difficulties	Alter Yourself

OPTION 2 Learning a Lesson Which selections in Unit Two do you think will cause you to alter your own actions or attitudes in the future? Which have had little effect on you? Rank the selections in order of the impact they have had on you. Put the selection that has influenced you the most at the top; the selection that has influenced you the least should come last. Explain to a classmate the reasons for your rankings.

Self-Assessment: Now that you have seen several characters adjust to new circumstances, write a few short paragraphs in which you describe what you have learned about dealing with change. Outline any adjustments that you plan to make as a result of what you have learned, noting the titles of the selections that have influenced your decisions.

REVIEWING LITERARY CONCEPTS

OPTION 1 Thinking About Point of View Work with a partner, one of you listing the stories in this unit that are told from the first-person point of view and the other listing the stories that are told from the third-person point of view. Compare your lists, then discuss the following questions:
- Why do you think the author of each story chose the point of view that he or she used?
- How would each story be different if it were told from a different point of view?

OPTION 2 Exploring Theme As you know, a work's theme is a message about life that the work conveys to the reader. Summarize in a phrase or two the theme of each selection you have read in this unit. Then look for ways of grouping the selections according to their themes—you might put selections together because they convey similar messages or because they convey opposite messages. In each case, say what the link is.

280   UNIT TWO: CRITICAL ADJUSTMENTS

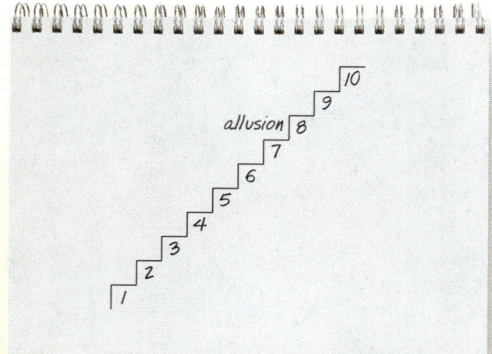

Self-Assessment: *In your notebook, draw a step diagram like the one shown. After looking at the list of literary terms introduced in this unit, write each term in an appropriate place on the diagram. If you think you have a good knowledge of the term, write it on the top step. If you have little or no understanding of the term, write it on the bottom step. Then work with a small group of classmates to clarify the meanings of the terms you are least sure about.*

allusion	surprise ending	memoir
setting	flashback	free verse
resolution	climax	mood
conflict	autobiography	

PORTFOLIO BUILDING

- **QuickWrites** Look back at your work for the QuickWrites that asked you to write as a character from a selection. Choose the piece that you think best captures a character's personality and feelings about the changes in his or her life. Then write a note explaining why you think you were able to impersonate that character well. Add the piece and the note to your portfolio.

- **Writing About Literature** Earlier in this unit, you wrote an interpretive essay about one of the selections. Write a brief note about your essay. Do you feel now that your essay offers a reasonable interpretation? Why or why not? Did you find the assignment difficult? Why or why not? What would you do differently if you could do the assignment over? Decide whether to include your note in your portfolio.

- **Writing from Experience** Reread the fictional narrative you wrote earlier in this unit. Imagine that a student arts magazine wants to publish your story in the next issue. The editor wishes to include some background information about your story and your writing process. In a brief note, tell how you came to write the story, what steps you took to get it down on paper, and how successful you think it is.

- **Personal Choice** Look back through your records and evaluations of the activities you completed in this unit. Also look at the activities and writing you did on your own. Which of these pieces do you think best reflected the theme of this unit, "Critical Adjustments"? Write a note that explains the reasons for your choice, attach it to the piece, and add both to your portfolio.

 Self-Assessment: Review the work you have added to your portfolio as you completed the first two units. Which pieces might you want to rework so that you can share them with a larger audience?

SETTING GOALS

As you completed the reading and writing activities in this section, you probably identified certain stories that you particularly liked. What kinds of stories would you like to read more of? What kinds of writing would you like to become more skillful at?

REFLECT & ASSESS **281**

Reviewing Literary Concepts

OPTION 1
Remind students to look for clues in each selection that reveal which point of view is being used. Suggest to students that they think about how the point of view used in each selection affects both the way in which story information is communicated to the reader and the amount of story information communicated.

OPTION 2
Remind students that a selection's theme can often be determined from the lesson learned by a character in the story. Encourage students to think of other ways to link the selections according to their themes in addition to their either being similar or different.

 **Self-Assessment** For terms that students put near the bottom of their step diagrams, have them write, in their own words, a definition for each term after checking in the Handbook. Then have students apply each term to a selection they have read. For instance, a student can identify a use of flashback or describe the mood in a particular selection.

Portfolio Building
You may wish to help students choose options or modify options for them that best suit the needs you have established for the class. Encourage students to incorporate in their portfolios drafts, in addition to final products, so that they can reflect on and assess their development and progress.

 **Self-Assessment** Students should consider with which pieces in their portfolios they feel most comfortable and with which kinds of pieces they would like to have more practice. Suggest that students also review their portfolio work and look at the areas which involved the most revision. Ask students to identify any patterns to their revising processes that might reveal problems or areas in which they need more work.

Setting Goals
In order to help students answer these questions and set future goals, have students consider which selections had the greatest impact on them and why they were affected by them. In addition, have students review their written work to determine the areas in which they had the most difficulty.

UNIT THREE

UNIT THREE

UNIT THEMES

Unit Three

Battle for Control In this unit, students will read selections that detail the various kinds of battles in which people engage—battles against each other, against nature, against society, or even against themselves. This unit contains two parts: Part 1, "Struggling for Survival," and Part 2, "Going to Extremes." Selections in both parts contribute to the unit theme by exploring the different forms that the struggle for survival can take and by revealing what happens when people go to extremes to control their lives.

Part 1

Struggling for Survival Selections in Part 1 emphasize the conflicts faced by characters trying to survive a typical day and by characters whose very lives are in danger, such as the young boy who undertakes a dangerous flight from war-torn Saigon to the United States in "Von."

Part 2

Going to Extremes Selections in Part 2 explore the extremes to which people can sometimes go in a battle for control, such as in the struggle on the part of a Jamaican boy to save a tree from a deadly hurricane in "The Banana Tree."

Links to Unit Six

The Oral Tradition Unit Six contains literature from the oral tradition that connects with the themes in Unit Three. You may wish to begin or end Unit Three by using the following selections from Unit Six that relate to the theme "Battle for Control":
- "Pecos Bill," p. 734
- "The Five Eggs," p. 740
- "Raven and the Coming of Daylight," p. 742
- "Spotted Eagle and Black Crow," p. 745

Prairie Fire (about 1953), Blackbear Bosin (Kiowa-Comanche people). The Philbrook Museum of Art, Tulsa, Oklahoma.

Battle for CONTROL

When you get to the end of your rope, tie a knot and hang on.

Franklin Delano Roosevelt
President of the United States
1933–1945

Art Note

Prairie Fire by Blackbear Bosin This painting by Blackbear Bosin (1921–1980) is one of the best-known watercolors by a Native American artist. The painting suggests the continuation of the natural world in the face of impending destruction.
Reading the Art How would you describe the effects of the painter's use of color? How does the painter suggest a sense of dynamic movement?

Exploring Theme

To help students explore the connections between the art, the quotation, and the unit theme, have them consider the following questions:

1. In what ways do you think people must battle for control in their lives? *(Possible response: Some people must fight battles to earn money, so that they can provide for their families; some have to fight against natural disasters, such as tornadoes or earthquakes, that threaten their homes or their lives; some people fight political battles in order to have more control over public policy that affects their lives.)*

2. Explain what you think Franklin Delano Roosevelt's statement means in terms of battling for control. *(Possible response: When people say that they are "at the end of their rope," they mean that they are close to giving up. The quotation urges people not to give up but to hang on and keep struggling.)*

3. In what ways do you think the painting represents a battle or struggle for control? *(Possible response: The painting shows humans and animals confronting a fire, which seems to be out of control and threatening their lives. Rather than fighting the fire, the humans and animals attempt to save themselves by escaping.)*

4. What kinds of stories do you think you will read in this unit? *(Possible response: The stories will be about the different kinds of battles people have to face. Some of the stories will be about battles that are won, and some will be about those that are lost.)*

5. Discuss a personal experience in which you had to struggle for control. What did this struggle involve? What was the outcome? What did you learn from the experience? *(Responses will vary.)*

UNIT THREE
Part 1 Skills Trace

 DENOTES MINI-LESSON IN TEACHER'S EDITION

Selections	Reading Skills and Strategies	Literary Concepts	Writing Opportunities	Speaking, Listening, and Viewing
FICTION **Getting the Facts of Life** Paulette Childress White	Character changes, PE p. 285 Clarifying, ML TE p. 287	Realistic fiction, PE p. 296 First-person point of view, PE p. 296 Conflict, ML TE p. 290	Poem, PE p. 295 Character sketch, PE p. 295 Dialogue, PE p. 295 Rewrite, ML TE p. 293	Readers theater, PE p. 295 Telephone conversation, PE p. 296 Debate, PE p. 296 Film music, ML TE p. 291 Pantomime, ML TE p. 292
FICTION **Appetizer** Robert H. Abel	Evaluating, PE p. 299 Evaluating, ML TE p. 300	Tone, PE p. 311 Humor, ML TE p. 301	News article, PE p. 311 Dialogue, PE p. 311 Self-assessment questions, ML TE p. 307	Interviews, ML TE p. 308
POETRY **Mother to Son** Langston Hughes **the lesson of the moth** Don Marquis		Extended metaphor, PE p. 317 Form, ML TE p. 316	Aphorism, PE p. 313 Poem, PE p. 317 Monologue, PE p. 317	Group discussion, PE p. 317 Rap song, PE p. 318
NONFICTION **Von** Von, as told to Janet Bode	Predicting, PE p. 319 Predicting, ML TE p. 321	Oral history, PE p. 330 Motivation, ML TE p. 322	Journal entry, PE p. 330 Letter, PE p. 330	Oral summary, PE p. 330 Critical viewing, ML TE p. 325
DRAMA **The Hitchhiker** Lucille Fletcher	Making inferences, ML TE p. 334	Foreshadowing, PE p. 345 Suspense, ML TE p. 335 Radio drama, ML TE p. 336	Prediction, PE p. 332 Additional scene, PE p. 345 Introduction, PE p. 345	Radio play, PE p. 346 Drama performance, ML TE p. 340 Oral reading, ML TE p. 341
NONFICTION ON YOUR OWN **The Flood** Ralph Helfer			Note-taking, TE p. 347 Listing, TE p. 358	Reading aloud, TE p. 347 Class discussion, TE p. 359

Writing	Reading Skills and Strategies	Literary Concepts	Writing Opportunities	Speaking, Listening, and Viewing
WRITING ABOUT LITERATURE **Criticism**	Evaluating literature, PE pp. 362–65	Elaboration, PE pp. 360–61 Story elements, PE pp. 362–63	Writing a paragraph, PE p. 361 Revising a sentence, PE p. 361 Evaluating literature, PE pp. 362–65 Creating effective paragraphs, PE p. 363	Viewing setting, PE p. 367 Interpreting setting, PE p. 367 Discussion, PE p. 367 Discussing criteria for evaluation, PE p. 367

Grammar, Usage, Mechanics, and Spelling	Multimodal Learning	Research and Study Skills	Vocabulary
Stating ideas clearly, ML TE p. 288 Sensory details, ML TE p. 289 Prefixes *com-*, *col-*, and *con-*, ML TE p. 294	Readers theater, PE p. 295 Picture or song, PE p. 296 Telephone conversation, PE p. 296 Debate, PE p. 296 Film music, ML TE p. 291 Pantomime, ML TE p. 292	Research the AFDC, PE p. 296	comply median partitioned reside verify
Adverb clauses, ML TE p. 302 Show, don't tell, ML TE p. 306 Words ending in *-ate* and *-ion*, ML TE p. 310	Comic strip, PE p. 311 Interviews, ML TE p. 308	Research the Alaskan brown bear, PE p. 312 Card catalogs, ML TE p. 304	assess profound burly resort dubious smug furtively speculation nostalgia superfluous
	Group discussion, PE p. 317 Rap song, PE p. 318	Research moths, PE p. 318	
Using quotation marks, ML TE p. 323 Point of view, ML TE p. 324 Y words with suffixes, ML TE p. 329	Oral summary, PE p. 330 Storyboard, PE p. 331 Collage, PE p. 331 Critical viewing, ML TE p. 325	Reference books, ML TE p. 328	ambassador visa
Sensory details, ML TE p. 337 Interjections, ML TE p. 339 Final silent e with suffixes, ML TE p. 343	Map of route traveled, PE p. 345 Radio play, PE p. 346 Drama performance, ML TE p. 340 Oral reading, ML TE p. 341	Calculate the number of miles traveled, PE p. 346 Graphic organizers, ML TE p. 338	assurance lark menacing nondescript sinister
	Creating a narrative mural, TE p. 357		

Grammar, Usage, Mechanics, and Spelling	Multimodal Learning	Research and Study Skills	Media Literacy
Using appositives, PE p. 361 Complex sentences, PE p. 365 Using commas with subordinate clauses, PE p. 365	Organizational chart, PE p. 362 Viewing setting, PE p. 367 Interpreting setting, PE p. 367 Discussion, PE p. 367 Discussing criteria for evaluation, PE p. 367	Analyzing for elaboration, PE p. 361 Establishing criteria for evaluation, PE p. 367	Analyzing details in settings, PE pp. 366–67

UNIT THREE
Part 2 Skills Trace

ML DENOTES MINI-LESSON IN TEACHER'S EDITION

Selections	Reading Skills and Strategies	Literary Concepts	Writing Opportunities	Speaking, Listening, and Viewing
FICTION **The Banana Tree** James Berry	Understanding dialect, PE p. 369 Using context clues, ML TE p. 371	Protagonist/antagonist, PE p. 378 Allusion, ML TE p. 372	Dialogue, PE p. 378 Personal narrative, PE p. 378	News interview, PE p. 378 Directing a videotape, ML p. 376
FICTION **The Tell-Tale Heart** Edgar Allan Poe	Evaluating, PE p. 380 Evaluating, ML TE p. 382	Denotation & connotation, ML TE p. 385 Mood, PE p. 387 Tone, ML TE p. 383 Horror fiction, ML TE p. 384	Alternative ending, PE p. 387 Lead paragraph, PE p. 387	Mock trial, PE p. 387 Audiotape, PE p. 388 Painting or drawing, PE p. 388
NONFICTION **Tsali of the Cherokees** Norah Roper, as told to Alice Marriott	Contrasting, PE p. 390 Comparing & contrasting, ML TE p. 392	Author's purpose, PE p. 398 Oral history, PE p. 398 Conflict, ML TE p. 393	Paragraph, PE p. 398 Epitaph, PE p. 398	Role-playing, PE p. 399 Oral storytelling, PE p. 399
NONFICTION **Painful Memories of Dating** Dave Barry	Hyperbole, PE p. 400	Humor, ML TE p. 403	Diary entry, PE p. 404 Advice column, PE p. 404	Situation-comedy episode, PE p. 404 How-to video, PE p. 405 Group discussion, TE p. 402
POETRY **The Runaway** Robert Frost **Macavity: the Mystery Cat** T.S. Eliot		Personification, ML TE p. 407 Rhyme scheme, PE p. 410 Rhythm, ML TE p. 408	Short narrative, PE p. 406 Poem, PE p. 410 Prose or poem, PE p. 410	Read-aloud, PE p. 410 Poetry reading, ML TE p. 409
Writing	**Reading Skills and Strategies**	**Literary Concepts**	**Writing Opportunities**	**Speaking, Listening, and Viewing**
WRITING FROM EXPERIENCE **Informative Exposition**			Writing a problem-solution essay, PE pp. 412–19 Journal entry, PE p. 413 Drafting, PE pp. 416–17 Elaborating on ideas, PE p. 417 Revising and publishing, PE pp. 418–19 Article or letter, PE p. 419	Brainstorm, PE p. 414 Conducting group discussions, PE p. 415 Speech, PE p. 419

Grammar, Usage, Mechanics, and Spelling	Multimodal Learning	Research and Study Skills	Vocabulary
Sentence variety, ML TE p. 374 Verb tenses, ML TE p. 375 Words from the French language, ML TE p. 377	News interview, PE p. 378 Drawing or painting, PE p. 379 Directing a videotape, ML TE p. 376	Research banana-producing countries, PE p. 379	debris grimace refuse torso turbulent
Adverbs, ML TE p. 386	Mock trial, PE p. 387 House of horrors plans, PE p. 388 Audiotape, PE p. 388 Painting or drawing, PE p. 388	Research the effects of sudden fright, PE p. 388	acute hypocritical audacity stealthily conceived stifled crevice vehemently derision vex
Possessive and plural nouns, ML TE p. 396	Illustrations, PE p. 398 Role-play, PE p. 399 Oral storytelling, PE p. 399	Research the Cherokee of the Great Smoky Mountains, PE p. 399 Taking essay tests, ML TE p. 394	askew encroaching plunder smolder sulkily
	Situation-comedy episode, PE p. 404 How-to video, PE p. 405 Group discussion, ML TE p. 402		spontaneity
	Read-aloud, PE p. 410 Portrait, PE p. 411 Poetry reading, ML TE p. 409		

Grammar, Usage, Mechanics, and Spelling	Multimodal Learning	Research and Study Skills	Media Literacy
Using direct objects, PE p. 419	Taking a poll, PE p. 412 Brainstorm, PE p. 414 Conducting group discussions, PE p. 415 Speech, PE p. 419	Research solutions, PE p. 414	Analyzing the news, PE p. 412 Ad campaign, PE p. 419

UNIT THREE
Recommended Resources

ENRICHMENT　　　RESEARCH

✓ Recommended Novels

LITERATURE CONNECTIONS WITH SOURCEBOOK FOR TEACHERS

The Diary of Anne Frank
by Frances Goodrich and Albert Hackett

Thematic Links In this dramatic adaptation of Anne Frank's diary, eight people battle for control of their safety and sanity as they hide in a secret annex in Amsterdam. Their challenge is to survive the Nazi extermination of Jews.

About the Author Frances Goodrich (1891–1984) and Albert Hackett (1900–1995) were a highly successful husband-and-wife writing team who wrote screenplays, many of which were made into popular Hollywood movies, and stage plays.

Other Works by Frances Goodrich and Albert Hackett *Up Pops the Devil, Bridal Wise, The Great Big Doorstep*

The Electric Kid
by Garry Kilworth

Thematic Links Blindboy and Hotwire are city orphans who survive in the year 2061 by robbing and stealing.

About the Author Garry Kilworth (born 1941) was born in England. He writes science fiction novels and short stories for adults as well as young readers.

Other Works by Garry Kilworth *The Rain Ghost*

Zlata's Diary: A Child's Life in Sarajevo
by Zlata Filipovic

Thematic Links A young girl keeps a diary documenting her struggle to survive in war-torn Bosnia-Hercegovina from 1991 to 1993.

About the Author Zlata Filipovic (born 1980) put a moving human face on the daily life of a teenager living under the constant dangers of war. When her diary entries, which are often compared to Anne Frank's, were published, Filipovic found herself unexpectedly at the center of international media attention.

Shadow of the Dragon
by Sherry Garland

Thematic Links This is a coming-of-age story set in the two conflicting worlds of America and Vietnam.

About the Author Sherry Garland (born 1948) has helped families from Vietnam adjust to living in the United States. She has written both fiction and nonfiction works about Vietnam.

Other Works by Sherry Garland *Song of the Buffalo Boy*

LITERATURE CONNECTIONS WITH SOURCEBOOK FOR TEACHERS

The Witch of Blackbird Pond
by Elizabeth George Speare

Thematic Links Kit Tyler's life is not as she imagined it would be when she left Barbados. Her attitude keeps her at odds with the people she meets, except for Hannah, the so-called "Witch of Blackbird Pond." After Kit, too, is tried for witchcraft, she is forced to face up to the realities of her life.

About the Author Elizabeth George Speare (born 1908) is best known for her award-winning historical fiction. Although she begins by researching the history of a place or incident, her ideas for stories come from the characters themselves.

Other Works by Elizabeth George Speare *The Sign of the Beaver; The Bronze Bow; Calico Captive; Child Life in New England, 1790–840; Life in Colonial America*

So Far from the Bamboo Grove
by Yoko Kawashima Watkins

Thematic Links A Japanese family must flee Korea following World War II. They face the enemy daily as they try to return to Japan and regain control of their lives.

About the Author The books of Yoko Kawashima Watkins (born 1934) are largely based on her experiences as a young girl in northern Korea.

Other Works by Yoko Kawashima Watkins *My Brother, My Sister and I, Tales from the Bamboo Grove*

For Teacher — TEACHING LITERATURE

Farivar, S. H. *Intergroup Relations in Cooperative Learning Groups.* Washington, D.C.: American Educational Research Association, 1991.

O'Connor, John S. "Seeking Truth in Fiction: Teaching Unreliable Narrators." *English Journal* 83:2 (February 1994) 48–50.

Wood, K. D. *Bringing Learning to Life: Cross-Curricular Integration Through the Communication Processes.* New York: Macmillan, 1993.

CROSS-CURRICULAR TEACHING   PROFESSIONAL DEVELOPMENT

Recommended Readings in Cross-Curricular Areas

SCIENCE

Can Bears Predict Earthquakes? Unsolved Mysteries of Animal Behavior
by Russell Freedman (1982)
How smart are dolphins? Are there really elephant burial grounds? These questions about animal behavior and more are answered. Links to Robert Abel's "Appetizer" and Ralph Helfer's "The Flood."

SOCIAL STUDIES

The Cherokee
by Theda Perdue (1988)
Gives an overview of the tribe's history, including contemporary federal regulations. Links to Norah Roper's telling of "Tsali of the Cherokees."

HISTORY

Native American Testimony
edited by Peter Nabokov (1987)
This anthology contains original source materials covering more than 400 years of Native American history. Links to Norah Roper's telling of "Tsali of the Cherokees."

For Teacher CROSS-CURRICULAR INSTRUCTION

Dilg, Mary A. "The Opening of the American Mind: Challenges in the Cross-Cultural Teaching of Literature." *English Journal* 84 (March 1995) 18–26.

Fagan, Edward R. "Interdisciplinary English: Science, Technology, and Society." *English Journal* 76 (September 1987) 81–83.

James, Michael, and James Zarillo. "Teaching History with Children's Literature: A Concept-based Interdisciplinary Approach." *Social Studies* 80:4 (July 1989) 153–58.

Wood, Karen D. "Linking the Disciplines through Literature." *Middle School Journal* (May 1995).

Recommended Media Resources

THE LANGUAGE OF LITERATURE

LASERLINKS
Videodisc, Gr.8
See *LaserLinks Teacher's Source Book*, pages 26–27, for an overview of Unit Three.

AUDIO LIBRARY
Tapes
Unit Three: Battle for Control
Gr. 8, Tape 7: Sides A & B
Gr. 8, Tape 8: Sides A & B
Gr. 8, Tape 9: Sides A & B
Gr. 8, Tape 10: Sides A & B

WRITING COACH
Writing Coach Software: Writing About Literature: Interpretive Response; Problem-and-Solution Essay

OUTSIDE RESOURCES

Films/Videos/Film Strips/Audiocassettes
Edgar Allan Poe: Architect of Dreams. videocassette. Direct Cinema, 1992.
Langston Hughes. filmstrip. Eye Gale Media, 1989. (15 min.)
The Land I Lost. Huynh Quang Nhuong. audiocassette. American Prose Library, 1986.
The Tell-Tale Heart and Other Terrifying Tales. audiocassette. Syd Lieberman Production, 1991. (52 min.)

Internet Resources
WorldWide Web at http://www.hmco.com/mcdougal

For Teacher TEACHING WITH TECHNOLOGY

"Whenever You Call: How to Provide Teachers with Training and Support When and Where They Need It." *Electronic Learning* (November/December 1995).

Courtney, Tim, et al. "The Impact of Computer Technology on the Teaching of English (The Round Table)." *English Journal* 82:8 (December 1993) 68–70.

Fulton, Kathleen. "Teaching Matters: The Role of Technology in Education." *Ed Tech Review* (Fall-Winter 1993) 510.

UNIT THREE
Professional Enrichment

Teaching Sensitive Issues

It's Friday afternoon and your students are dreaming of the weekend. If truth be told, so are you.

The lesson is going well; the short story is interesting. Suddenly, a student says, "The handicapped kid in this story is such a spaz. Why are cripples so stupid?" Everyone in the classroom freezes, staring at the one child in a wheelchair. What do you do?

Sensitive issues in literature take many forms. Here are some of the most common, which you already may have encountered:
- personal questions
- cultural issues
- moral issues
- questions of race, gender, class
- differences in size and appearance
- issues dealing with differently-abled individuals

Exploring the needs and characteristics of eighth-grade students makes it clear why sensitive issues are bound to arise in an eighth-grade language arts classroom, no matter how carefully literature is selected.

Emotionally, eighth graders are
- anxious about whether they are "normal"
- easily angered and often slow to calm down
- sometimes erratic
- learning to identify and relate to the behaviors linked to their sex roles.

Socially, eighth-graders are
- concerned with presenting a positive image to their peer group
- anxious to conform in order to be accepted by their friends
- beginning to explore different aspects of their sexuality.

Physically, eighth-graders are
- growing at different rates from their friends, which may be cause for great anxiety
- often very upset if they do not conform to standards of beauty in their peer group
- easily tired but rarely admit it
- restless and need to release energy.

Intellectually, eighth-graders are
- easily discouraged if they do not meet their own or their peers' standards for achievement
- varied in their levels of interests and abilities
- capable of critical thinking.

CLASSROOM OPTIONS

It's apparent from this profile that sensitive issues and eighth graders go hand-in-hand! As your students begin to look more seriously at themselves and their lives, they will inevitably turn the conversation to the issues at the center of their concerns. Try the following methods of dealing with sensitive issues when you read selections in this unit such as "Getting the Facts of Life," "Von," or "Painful Memories of Dating."

- **Role-playing** Invite volunteers to role-play or pantomime the sensitive issues raised in the literature. Role-playing the issues provides what 20th century poet Ezra Pound called a "personae," or mask, that allows students the distance they need to grapple with the issues in a less passionate way.
- **Recasting the Selection** Suggest that students rewrite a portion of the selection from a different point of view, such as shifting from the third-person to the first-person. Seeing different sides of an issue can often diffuse a tense situation while teaching adolescents the value of considering other vantage points.
- **Debate** Divide the class in half to debate sensitive issues. Remind students to attack the issues, never individuals. You may wish to have each team select a Criticizer of Ideas to intellectually challenge teammates by criticizing their ideas while communicating respect for them as individuals.
- **Journals** Some students need time and privacy to explore their feelings about touchy subjects. Suggest that these learners voice their reactions in a private journal. Offer students the option of sharing their journals with you.
- **Art** Suggest that some students explore their feelings about sensitive issues in other modes, such as drawing, painting, sculpture, or music.

Related Reading

 Bode, Janet. *New Kids on the Block: Oral Histories of Immigrant Teens.* Franklin Watts, 1989.

 Delisle, James R., and Galbraith, Judy. *The Gifted Kids Survival Guide II: A Sequel to the Original Gifted Kids Survival Guide.* Minneapolis: Free Spirit, 1987.

 Dunning, Stephen, et. al., eds. *Reflections on a Gift of Watermelon Pickle and Other Modern Verse.* Lothrop, 1966.

 Rinzler, Jane. *Teens Speak Out.* New York: Donald I. Fine, 1986.

Family and Community Involvement

Family

The following Copymasters provide activities that students can take home and complete with a parent or other family member.

OPTION 1: DESIGN A COLLAGE
- **Connection** All of the selections in Unit Three connect to the theme of battling for control.
- **Activity** *Copymaster, p. 1* Students work with family members to plan and design a collage that represents someone who has battled for control of his or her life. A word web is provided to organize their thoughts and ideas.

OPTION 2: TO WHAT EXTREMES WOULD YOU GO?
- **Connection** In many of the selections in Unit Three, characters go to extremes in their battles for control of their lives.
- **Activity** *Copymaster, p. 2* Students work with family members to make a list of several situations which involve a battle for control of one's life. For each situation, students and family members discuss the extremes to which they would go to win the battle. A chart is provided to record their thoughts and responses.

OPTION 3: READ ABOUT THE VIETNAM WAR
- **Connection** One of the selections in Unit Three, "Von," deals with a young Vietnamese boy's flight to freedom from his war-torn country.
- **Activity** *Copymaster, p. 3* Students and family members work together to read about Vietnam and the Vietnam War as a way of preparing students to read "Von." A K-W-L chart is provided.

Community

OPTION 1
- **Connection** In some of the selections in this unit, such as "Getting the Facts of Life," characters living in poverty must struggle with bureaucratic red tape in order to survive.
- **Activity** Invite a politician from your local government to discuss ways in which your local government helps people in need of assistance.

OPTION 2
- **Connection** The selection "Von" details the experiences of a young boy as he escapes to freedom from war-torn Vietnam.
- **Activity** Invite a recent immigrant to the United States to share his or her experiences with the class.

OPTION 3
- **Connection** In the selection "The Banana Tree," a young Jamaican boy battles a hurricane to save his beloved tree.
- **Activity** Invite a meteorologist to discuss hurricanes with the class. If possible, have students visit a weather museum.
- **Alternative Activity** Invite an immigrant from Jamaica, possibly a student's parent, to speak to the class about Jamaican culture.

OPTION 4
- **Connection** In "Appetizer" a man is threatened by a hungry bear.
- **Activity** Encourage students to visit a zoo to learn more about bears. You may also wish to have a zoo employee speak to the class about bear behavior in the wild and the risk of bear attacks on humans.

UNIT THREE
Part 1 Cooperative Project

A Guidebook for Survival

Overview

Students write and produce a booklet for other students describing ways to survive difficult situations.

PROJECT AT A GLANCE
The selections in Unit Three, Part 1 concern people struggling for survival in some form. For this project, students will work in cooperative groups to produce the chapters of a class booklet on survival. They will select a common situation at school, will interview those who have gone through the situation, and will develop sound advice on coping with the inherent problems, or "surviving." The chapters will be bound into a single volume and will be placed in the school library as inspiration for other students.

OBJECTIVES
- To identify difficulties or obstacles that commonly arise at school
- To interview students who have survived these or similar situations
- To gather information about ways to avoid or surmount these difficulties or obstacles
- To write a chapter condensing the advice into a coherent plan
- To bind the chapters together into a class book

SUGGESTED GROUP SIZE
4–6 students

MATERIALS
- Paper and writing utensils
- Binders or colored paper to make covers
- A variety of how-to books

1 Getting Started

Arranging the Project
Before students begin, alert the guidance counselor and other school officials that they may be getting requests for interviews from students in your class. Explain the project to them in detail and enlist their cooperation.

Gather a selection of how-to books for students to use for reference. Be sure to select a variety of topics.

Generally speaking, this project is student-driven and you need only fill a supervisory position.

Arranging for the Guidebook
If your school has computers that groups can use to create their chapters, you may want to schedule computer time well in advance.

If computers are unavailable, request that all groups write their final chapters neatly on regulation-size paper so they can be bound together.

2 Creating the Guidebook

Introducing the Project
Explain that students will be working in small groups to produce the chapters for a book on survival. The theme of the book is surviving difficult situations or overcoming obstacles, and the target audience is their fellow students. Situations and obstacles discussed should be common to the school environment or the surrounding area—ones apt to be experienced by several rather than just a few students.

Open a discussion with the class about some of the difficulties they have experienced in school. Examples might range from serious racial bigotry to finding one's way around the school building; from avoiding drug peddlers on the way home to losing a math paper; from having no handicapped-accessible restroom facilities to not liking the food in the cafeteria. In each case, discuss how the obstacle might be overcome and whether or not this is a viable solution for everyone. Stress that this must be a guidebook for as many students as possible. Students cannot assume that every person is in a position to beat up a bully—or that this is even a "good" solution. Help them recognize that a more universal solution might be to report the bully to the principal and ask for assistance from other teachers and staff.

Allow students some time to examine the selection of how-to books. Help them note that the books are organized in a step-by-step manner rather than in a haphazard one. This is an important part of any guidebook.

Group Investigations
Divide students into groups of four to six. Each group will select a particular obstacle or situation to write about. Group members will conduct individual investigations, research, and interviews among the school population. Then they'll meet to discuss and develop a plan of action for surviving the situation. Stress that the solutions must be violence-free and within school regulations. Devote a few minutes of class time each day, if possible, to a discussion of the groups' progress as they move toward writing their chapter.

Creating a Project Description
After the preliminary meeting, ask each group to write a brief description of the obstacle or situation they have selected to investigate. Talk with each group about what they plan to do. If you find too much duplication of efforts, suggest some other topics that might be pursued.

OPTION 1: SURVIVING EIGHTH GRADE
Students can base all the survival strategies on obstacles and situations common to eighth graders. They will probably want to interview some high school students for their memories of eighth grade, as well as current eighth graders.

OPTION 2: DIFFERENT ABILITIES Guidebooks can be devoted to obstacles for students who are physically challenged. Students will need to interview other students who use wheelchairs, crutches, and the like. Some of the interviewees might be willing to speak to the class.

OPTION 3: SURVIVAL WITH A SENSE OF HUMOR Students may enjoy writing a survival guide to the trivial, inane situations they encounter in everyday life. Subjects covered might be those such as "How to Survive Lunch with Aunt Matilda" or "How to Survive When the TV Set is Broken."

OPTION 4: HOW OTHERS SURVIVED Students can interview respected individuals in the community and ask them what obstacles they met in their lives and how they overcame those obstacles.

Because survival is a broad concept, don't be surprised if some of the subject matter seems trivial to you. Try to remember when a pimple was a major trauma. Many students will sympathize with and be eager to know how to survive this horrible situation. On the other hand, some students may want to tackle something like racial bias or inequality. Be sure to gauge the chapters on their content and merit, not only on their subject matter.

3 Sharing the Guidebook

If possible, make several copies of the guidebook and share them with other classes. Otherwise, you might arrange the pages of each chapter on sheets of posterboard and display them in the school corridors or donate the master guidebook to the school library for students' use.

Assessing the Project

The following rubric can be used for group or individual assessment.

3 Full Accomplishment Students produce a chapter of the guidebook that identifies a real problem and gives a viable plan for overcoming that problem.

2 Substantial Accomplishment Students produce a chapter of the guidebook, but the problem is not as perceived or the given solution is not well thought out.

1 Little or Partial Accomplishment Students' chapter is incomplete or does not fulfill the requirements of the assignment.

For the Portfolio
You may want to include a copy of the group project description in each member's portfolio, along with a written copy of your final project assessment.

Note: For other assessment options, see the *Teacher's Guide to Assessment and Portfolio Use.*

Cross-Curricular Options

SCIENCE

Students can research what human beings really do need to survive, such as food, water, air, shelter, and so on. Each item should also mention the specific quantity or range of quantities needed.

PHYSICAL EDUCATION
Interested students can research the philosophy of several martial arts. Some of these were developed as a means of defense rather than offense, which is continued in today's form of the discipline and in what is expected of the practitioners.

FOREIGN LANGUAGE
Students studying or familiar with a foreign language can write a chapter specifically for non-English speaking students. This may require enlisting the assistance of the language teacher, or can be used as a cooperative project.

Resources

The Martial Arts by Susan Ribner and Richard Chin provides an introduction to the history and philosophy behind the martial arts.

UNIT THREE
Part 1 Lesson Planner

TIME ALLOTMENTS SHOWN ARE APPROXIMATE. DEPENDING ON YOUR GOALS AND THE NEEDS OF YOUR STUDENTS, YOU MAY WISH TO ALLOW MORE OR LESS TIME FOR CERTAIN PORTIONS OF THE LESSON.

Table of Contents	Discussion	Previewing the Selection	Reading the Selection
PART OPENER **STRUGGLING FOR SURVIVAL** What Do You Think? page 284	**20 MINUTES** • Reflect on the part theme		
SELECTION Getting the Facts of Life page 286 AVERAGE		**20 MINUTES** • PERSONAL CONNECTION • SOCIAL STUDIES CONNECTION • READING CONNECTION: Character changes	**35 MINUTES** • Introduce vocabulary • Read pp. 286–94 (9 pp.)
SELECTION Appetizer page 300 CHALLENGING		**25 MINUTES** • PERSONAL CONNECTION • SCIENCE CONNECTION • READING CONNECTION: Evaluating	**50 MINUTES** • Introduce vocabulary • Read pp. 300–10 (11 pp.)
SELECTIONS Mother to Son page 314 AVERAGE the lesson of the moth page 315 AVERAGE		**20 MINUTES** • PERSONAL CONNECTION • LITERARY CONNECTION • WRITING CONNECTION	**15 MINUTES** • Read pp. 314–16 (3 pp.)
SELECTION Von page 320 AVERAGE		**20 MINUTES** • PERSONAL CONNECTION • HISTORICAL CONNECTION • READING CONNECTION: Predicting	**40 MINUTES** • Introduce vocabulary • Read pp. 320–29 (10 pp.)
SELECTION The Hitchhiker page 333 AVERAGE		**20 MINUTES** • PERSONAL CONNECTION • HISTORICAL CONNECTION • WRITING CONNECTION	**45 MINUTES** • Introduce vocabulary • Read pp. 333–44 (12 pp.)
NONFICTION ON YOUR OWN The Flood page 347 AVERAGE			**45 MINUTES** • Read pp. 347–59 (13 pp.)
Writing WRITING ABOUT LITERATURE Criticism	**Writer's Style** **25 MINUTES**	**Prewriting** **20 MINUTES**	**Drafting and Revising** **70 MINUTES**

Time estimates assume in-class work. You may wish to assign some of these stages as homework.

Responding to the Selection

FROM PERSONAL RESPONSE TO CRITICAL ANALYSIS	OR	ANOTHER PATHWAY	LITERARY CONCEPTS	QUICKWRITES
		55 MINUTES		
• Discussion questions	OR	• Readers theater presentation	• Realistic fiction • First-person point of view	• Poem • Character sketch • Dialogue
		40 MINUTES		
• Discussion questions	OR	• Comic strip	• Tone	• News article • Dialogue
		35 MINUTES		
• Discussion questions	OR	• Group discussion	• Extended metaphor	• Poem • Monologue
		40 MINUTES		
• Discussion questions	OR	• Oral Summary	• Oral history	• Journal entry • Letter
		40 MINUTES		
• Discussion questions	OR	• Map	• Foreshadowing	• Additional scene • Introduction

Extension Activities

• ALTERNATIVE ACTIVITIES • LITERARY LINKS • CRITIC'S CORNER • THE WRITER'S STYLE • ACROSS THE CURRICULUM • ART CONNECTION • WORDS TO KNOW • BIOGRAPHY

ALT	LIT	CRIT	WRIT	ACROSS	ART	WORDS	BIO
45 MINUTES							
✓	✓			✓ (SOCIAL STUDIES)	✓	✓	✓
40 MINUTES							
✓	✓			✓ (SCIENCE)		✓	✓
30 MINUTES							
✓				✓ (SCIENCE)			✓
30 MINUTES							
✓	✓					✓	✓
45 MINUTES							
✓				✓ (MATH)		✓	✓

Publishing and Reflecting	Grammar in Context	Reading the World
30 MINUTES	**10 MINUTES**	**30 MINUTES**

PART 1

WHAT DO YOU THINK?
Objectives

The activities on this page can be used to
- introduce the Part 1 theme, "Struggling for Survival," since each activity is connected to one or more of the selections in Part 1
- create materials for students' personal portfolios that they can later reconsider or revise
- build an understanding of theme that can be reviewed and revised as students progress through the unit

What went wrong?
Encourage students to begin by brainstorming a list of possible things that could go wrong on a camping trip. Then have students spend time thinking of ways to describe these things humorously. (See "Appetizer," p. 298.)

Can you remember?
Suggest that students create a chart that details their views and feelings before, during, and after the experience. (See "Getting the Facts of Life," p. 285.)

What would you include?
Make sure students pay attention to the way in which they organize the information in their outline. Tell them to list supporting details under each main topic. (All selections are connected to this activity.)

How could you help?
Have students generate a list of problems new immigrants might face. Encourage native-born students to think about the things they usually take for granted, such as speaking the language. Encourage foreign-born students to share some of their own experiences, which they might like to include in the guidebook. Have all students think about ways in which to organize all of this information in a guidebook. (See "Von," p. 319.)

UNIT THREE **PART 1**

STRUGGLING FOR SURVIVAL

WHAT DO Y?u THINK?

REFLECTING ON THEME

In order to get control of our lives, we sometimes have to "battle" other people, forces of nature, pressures of society, and even ourselves. Sometimes we have to struggle for our very lives. Use the activities on this page to explore the forms the struggle for survival can take.

Can you remember?
Difficult experiences often help people to mature. Think about an experience of yours that caused you to gain insight into yourself and the adult world. Design a chart that shows how your views or feelings changed as a result of the experience.

What went wrong?
Sometimes you can look back and laugh at events that were unpleasant, or even dangerous, at the time. Imagine that you are involved in a camping trip on which everything has gone haywire. Write a postcard, describing the trip.

How could you help?
Sometimes survival is a matter of adjusting to a new culture. If someone your age were immigrating to the United States from a country such as Vietnam or China, what problems might he or she face? Write a short guidebook designed to help immigrants adjust to life in the United States.

What would you include?
Work with a small group to prepare an outline for a television documentary entitled "Teenage Survival Skills." Include advice on how teenagers can cope with the various demands placed upon them today.

284

Cross-Curricular Connections

History Have students work in small groups to research a particular natural disaster in history and its effects. Groups should include a description of the disaster and focus on how the community it affected dealt with the damage and loss that resulted.

COMMUNITY OUTREACH

Invite an official from your local government's welfare service or a member of a local welfare organization to speak to the class about some of the difficulties faced by people living in poverty. After the speaker's visit, you may wish to discuss with students the ways in which people must struggle daily to support their families and survive in today's society.

PREVIEWING

FICTION

Getting the Facts of Life
Paulette Childress White

Activating Prior Knowledge
PERSONAL CONNECTION

You probably know something about the welfare system, either from media reports or from personal experience. Welfare is government aid that provides needy people with regular financial help, and the future of the welfare system is a hotly debated issue. What attitudes does society have about the welfare system and people who receive welfare payments? Discuss what you know with your classmates.

Building Background
SOCIAL STUDIES CONNECTION

In this story, 12-year-old Minerva learns about welfare at first hand. Welfare is not just a single U.S. government program but a group of programs funded by federal, state, and local governments. Assistance is based on need. Most cash payments come from a program called Aid to Families with Dependent Children (AFDC), which provides financial aid primarily to children and to their parents or the other adults who care for them. In 1994, AFDC distributed $22.5 billion to 14 million people, compared with $4 billion in 1974 and $8 billion in 1984.

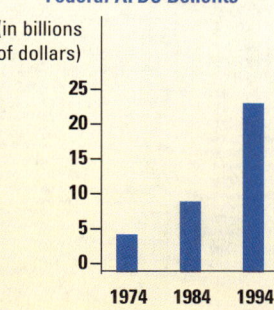

Federal AFDC Benefits (in billions of dollars)

Active Reading/Setting a Purpose
READING CONNECTION

Character Changes Minerva changes as she gains insight into herself and the adult world by visiting a welfare office with her mother. As you read this story, look for signs of change in Minerva's attitude. When you finish reading, record the changes in a chart like the one shown here.

Minerva's Feelings	At the Beginning	At the End
About welfare		
About her mother		
About herself		

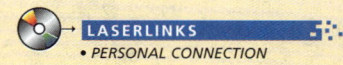
• PERSONAL CONNECTION   285

OVERVIEW

Objectives
- To understand and appreciate a short story about a girl's coming of age
- To enrich reading by using active reading strategies
- To enrich reading by understanding character changes
- To identify and understand realistic fiction and to review first-person point of view
- To express understanding of the story through a choice of writing forms, including a poem, a character sketch, and a dialogue
- To extend understanding of the story through a variety of multimodal and cross-curricular activities

Skills

READING SKILLS/STRATEGIES
- Clarify
- Character changes

LITERARY CONCEPTS
- Realistic fiction
- First-person point of view
- Conflict

THE WRITER'S STYLE
- Sensory details

GRAMMAR
- Stating ideas clearly

SPELLING
- The prefixes com-, col-, and con-

SPEAKING, LISTENING, AND VIEWING
- Film Music
- Pantomime
- Group discussion
- Oral presentation

Cross-Curricular Connections

SOCIAL STUDIES
- Aid to Families with Dependent Children
- The Motown sound

MATHEMATICS
- American basics

PERSONAL CONNECTION
The Welfare Debate In this video clip, Delaware governor Pierre "Pete" du Pont, a Republican, and Arizona governor Bruce Babbitt, a Democrat, debate the issue of welfare reform. Their clashing opinions may spark a debate in your classroom.

Side A, Frame 21415

PRINT AND MEDIA RESOURCES

UNIT THREE RESOURCE BOOK
Strategic Reading: Literature, p. 4
Vocabulary SkillBuilder, p. 7
Reading SkillBuilder, p. 5
Spelling SkillBuilder, p. 6

GRAMMAR MINI-LESSONS
Transparencies, p. 1
Copymasters, p. 1

WRITING MINI-LESSONS
Transparencies, p. 38

ACCESS FOR STUDENTS ACQUIRING ENGLISH
Selection Summaries
Reading and Writing Support

TEACHER'S GUIDE TO ASSESSMENT AND PORTFOLIO USE

FORMAL ASSESSMENT
Selection Test, pp. 55–56
 Test Generator

AUDIO LIBRARY
See Reference Card

LASERLINKS
Personal Connection

THE LANGUAGE OF LITERATURE TEACHER'S EDITION **285**

SUMMARY

Twelve-year-old Minerva Blue and her mother walk through dangerous neighborhood streets to the welfare office. After waiting for three hours, Mrs. Blue is condescendingly interviewed by a welfare officer as Minerva looks on. Trying to provide for eight children and a jobless husband, Mrs. Blue endures bad treatment to get food and clothing for her family. Walking home, Minerva is further shaken when her mother tells her "the facts of life"; however, her mother's courage and her own strong spirit steady Minerva. They enjoy sodas and plan how to get through the next week.

Thematic Link: *Struggling for Survival* A preadolescent girl sees firsthand how her mother must struggle to keep her poverty-stricken family intact.

STRATEGIC READING FOR
Less-Proficient Readers

Set a Purpose Encourage students to become involved in the story by having them describe experiences that made them feel grown-up. Then have them read to find out where Minerva and her mother are going and what thought upsets Minerva when she sees the welfare building.

Use **UNIT THREE RESOURCE BOOK**, p. 4, for guidance in reading the selection.

CUSTOMIZING FOR
Students Acquiring English

- Use **ACCESS FOR STUDENTS ACQUIRING ENGLISH**, *Reading and Writing Support*.
- Explain to students that the parents in this story are unemployed, and the family is on welfare. Ask them to describe what happens to a family in this situation in an American city. Then encourage them to discuss what would happen to this family in their native countries.

Getting the Facts of Life

The August morning was ripening into a day that promised to be a burner. By the time we'd walked three blocks, dark patches were showing beneath Momma's arms, and inside tennis shoes thick with white polish, my feet were wet against the cushions. I was beginning to regret how quickly I'd volunteered to go.

by Paulette Childress White

Main Street (1968), Billy Morrow Jackson. Photo courtesy of the artist.

WORDS TO KNOW

comply (kəm-plī′) *v.* to obey a rule or command (p. 290)

median (mē′dē-ən) *adj.* relating to the middle value in a series (p. 292)

partitioned (pär-tĭsh′ənd) *adj.* divided by interior walls **partition** *v.* (p. 289)

reside (rĭ-zīd′) *v.* to occupy a home (p. 290)

verify (vĕr′ə-fī′) *v.* to prove to be true by providing evidence (p. 291)

"Dog. My feet are getting mushy," I complained.

"You should've wore socks," Momma said, without looking my way or slowing down.

I frowned. In 1961, nobody wore socks with tennis shoes. It was bare legs, Bermuda shorts[1] and a sleeveless blouse. Period.

Momma was chubby but she could really walk. She walked the same way she washed clothes—up-and-down, up-and-down until she was done. She didn't believe in taking breaks.

This was my first time going to the welfare office with Momma. After breakfast, before we'd had time to scatter, she corralled everyone old enough to consider and announced in her serious-business voice that someone was going to the welfare office with her this morning. Cries went up.

Junior had his papers to do. Stella was going swimming at the high school. Dennis was already pulling the *Free Press*[2] wagon across town every first Wednesday to get the surplus food—like that.

"You want clothes for school, don't you?" That landed. School opened in two weeks.

"I'll go," I said.

"Who's going to baby-sit if Minerva goes?" Momma asked.

Stella smiled and lifted her small golden nose. "I will," she said. "I'd rather baby-sit than do *that*."

That should have warned me. Anything that would make Stella offer to baby-sit had to be bad.

---

1. **Bermuda shorts:** short pants that end just above the knee.
2. ***Free Press:*** a daily newspaper published in Detroit, Michigan.

Art Note

Main Street by Billy Morrow Jackson
This image is one of the most notable street scenes Jackson (1926–) has painted since the 1960s. It is dominated by a late-Victorian building that stretches horizontally across the canvas. Four figures combine with the empty spaces around the building, possibly to suggest that the people (and the neighborhood) are waiting for some kind of change in their lives.

Reading the Art *What details in the painting suggest that this area of the city is not thriving? What effect or mood is created by the figure barely visible in the distance through the corner windows?*

CUSTOMIZING FOR
Gifted and Talented Students

As students read the selection, invite them to discuss whether the Blues are treated in a certain manner because of their race or because of their poverty. You might draw students' attention to the passage in which Minerva expresses her surprise at seeing white faces among the welfare recipients.

CUSTOMIZING FOR
Students Acquiring English

① Point out to students that Momma's using a washboard, rather than a washing machine, to clean clothes indicates that the story takes place some time in the past.

② Ask students to explain what it means to say that Momma's comment "landed." *(Her comment was heard and understood by the children.)*

Mini-Lesson — Reading Skills/Strategies

ACTIVE READING: CLARIFY Remind students that clarifying is the process of making clear important information about characters and events in a story. When readers clarify, they stop and quickly review what has happened so far.

Application Ask students to clarify the relationship between Minerva and her mother as well as that between her mother and the social services officer. You may wish to have students complete a chart like the one shown. If students are having difficulty, you may want to ask the following questions:
- How would you describe the relationship between the two characters?
- How do the two characters feel about each other?
- How does the relationship change over the course of the story?

Reteaching/Reinforcement
- *Unit Three Resource Book,* p. 5

Relationship	
Minerva and mother	Mother and social services officer

Literary Concept:
POINT OF VIEW

A Ask students what point of view is being used. How can they tell? *(Possible response: The first-person point of view is being used. The narrator is a character in the story, a 12-year-old girl.)*

Cultural Note
B In the 1960s and 1970s, Stevie Wonder became an internationally famous musician and songwriter. His first records were released in 1961 under the name "Little Stevie Wonder." He had been signed to Motown Records after a member of the Miracles singing group heard him play harmonica at age 10. Detroit's Motown Records was owned and managed by African Americans, and it released much of the soul, rhythm-and-blues, and popular music that helped define the American music scene of the 1960s and early 1970s. Music from this time period still influences popular music today.

CUSTOMIZING FOR
Students Acquiring English

3 Students may be confused by this description of Ecorse. The comparison to a closet indicates that Ecorse is on the edge of Detroit, much as a closet is on the edge of a room.

Literary Concept:
REALISTIC FICTION

C Ask students to identify realistic details the narrator mentions about Salliotte Street. *(Possible responses: a white side and a black side separated by train tracks, closed offices, empty fields, the hotel block with its "bad boys and drunks," a field of weeds)*

A small cheer probably went up among my younger brothers in the back rooms, where I was not too secretly known as "The Witch" because of the criminal licks I'd learned to give on my rise to power. I was twelve, third oldest under Junior and Stella, but I had long established myself as first in command among the kids. I was chief baby sitter, biscuit maker and broom wielder. Unlike Stella, who'd begun her development at ten, I still had my girl's body and wasn't anxious to have that changed. What would it mean but a loss of power? I liked things just the way they were. My interest in bras was even less than my interest in boys, and that was limited to keeping my brothers—who seemed destined for wildness—from taking over completely.

Even before we left, Stella had Little Stevie Wonder turned up on the radio in the living room, and suspicious jumping-bumping sounds were beginning in the back. They'll tear the house down, I thought, following Momma out the door.

We turned at Salliotte, the street that would take us straight up to Jefferson Avenue where the welfare office was. Momma's face was pinking in the heat, and I was huffing to keep up. From here, it was seven more blocks on the colored side, the railroad tracks, five blocks on the white side and there you were. We'd be cooked.

"Is the welfare office near the Harbor Show?" I asked. I knew the answer; I just wanted some talk.

"Across the street."

"Umm. Glad it's not way down Jefferson somewhere."

"Nothing." Momma didn't talk much when she was outside. I knew that the reason she wanted one of us along when she had far to go was not for company but so she wouldn't have to walk by herself. I could understand that. To me, walking alone was like being naked or deformed—everyone seemed to look at you harder and longer. With Momma, the feeling was probably worse because you knew people were wondering if she were white, Indian maybe or really colored. Having one of us along, brown and clearly hers, probably helped define that. Still, it was like being a little parade, with Momma's pale skin and straight brown hair turning heads like the clang of cymbals. Especially on the colored side.

"Well," I said, "here we come to the bad part."

Momma gave a tiny laugh.

Most of Salliotte was a business street, with Old West-looking storefronts and some office places that never seemed to open. Ecorse, hinged onto southwest Detroit like a clothes closet, didn't seem to take itself seriously. There were lots of empty fields, some of which folks down the residential streets turned into vegetable gardens every summer. And there was this block where the Moonflower Hotel raised itself to three stories over the poolroom and Beaman's drugstore. Here, bad boys and drunks made their noise and did an occasional stabbing. Except for the cars that lined both sides of the block, only one side was busy—the other bordered a field of weeds. We walked on the safe side.

If you were a woman or a girl over twelve, walking this block—even on the safe side—could be painful. They usually hollered at you, and never mind what they said. Today, because it was hot and early, we made it by with only one weak *Hey baby* from a drunk sitting in the poolroom door.

"Hey baby yourself," I said, but not too loudly, pushing my flat chest out and stabbing my eyes in his direction.

"Minerva girl, you better watch your mouth with grown men like that," Momma said, her eyes catching me up in real warning, though I could see that she was holding down a smile.

288 UNIT THREE PART 1: STRUGGLING FOR SURVIVAL

Mini-Lesson Grammar

STATING IDEAS CLEARLY Point out to students that the meaning of a sentence fragment is unclear because a fragment does not express a complete thought. The subject, the verb, or sometimes both are missing. Fragments are easily corrected by adding the missing element. Here is a sentence fragment the author uses in the dialogue between Minerva and her mother:

Fragment Across the street. (*What* is across the street?)

Sentence The welfare office is across the street.

Application Have students find other sentence fragments on this page. (Several are highlighted above.) Encourage them to identify the missing elements and to rewrite the fragments as complete sentences.

Reteaching/Reinforcement
- *Grammar Handbook*, pp. 860–861
- *Grammar Mini-Lessons* copymasters, p. 1, transparencies, p. 1

 **The Writer's Craft**

Sentence Fragments, pp. 382, 386

"Well, he can't do nothing to me when I'm with you, can he?" I asked, striving to match the rise and fall of her black pumps.

> We had been on welfare for almost a year. I didn't have any strong feelings about it—my life went on pretty much the same.

She said nothing. She just walked on, churning away under a sun that clearly meant to melt us. From here to the tracks it was mostly gardens. It felt like the Dixie Peach I'd used to help water-wave my hair was sliding down with the sweat on my face, and my throat was tight with thirst. Boy, did I want a pop. I looked at the last little store before we crossed the tracks without bothering to ask.

Across the tracks, there were no stores and no gardens. It was shady, and the grass was June green. Perfect-looking houses sat in unfenced spaces far back from the street. We walked these five blocks without a word. We just looked and hurried to get through it. I was beginning to worry about the welfare office in earnest. A fool could see that in this part of Ecorse, things got serious.

We had been on welfare for almost a year. I didn't have any strong feelings about it—my life went on pretty much the same. It just meant watching the mail for a check instead of Daddy getting paid, and occasional visits from a social worker that I'd always managed to miss. For Momma and whoever went with her, it meant this walk to the office and whatever went on there that made everyone hate to go.

For Daddy, it seemed to bring the most change. For him, it meant staying away from home more than when he was working and a reason not to answer the phone.

At Jefferson, we turned left and there it was, halfway down the block. The Department of Social Services. I discovered some strong feelings. That fine name meant nothing. This was the welfare. The place for poor people. People who couldn't or wouldn't take care of themselves. Now I was going to face it, and suddenly I thought what I knew the others had thought, *What if I see someone I know?* I wanted to run back all those blocks to home.

I looked at Momma for comfort, but her face was closed and her mouth looked locked.

Inside, the place was gray. There were rows of long benches like church pews facing each other across a middle aisle that led to a central desk. Beyond the benches and the desk, four hallways led off to a maze of partitioned offices. In opposite corners, huge fans hung from the ceiling, humming from side to side, blowing the heavy air for a breeze.

Momma walked to the desk, answered some questions, was given a number and told to take a seat. I followed her through, trying not to see the waiting people—as though that would keep them from seeing me.

CONNECT
How would you feel if you were Minerva?
Using a Reading Log

Gradually, as we waited, I took them all in. There was no one there that I knew, but somehow they all looked familiar. Or maybe I only thought they did, because when your eyes connected with someone's, they didn't quickly look away and they usually smiled. They were mostly women and children, and a few low-looking men. Some of them were white, which surprised me. I hadn't expected to see them in there.

Directly in front of the bench where we sat,

WORDS TO KNOW
partitioned (pär-tĭsh'ənd) *adj.* divided by interior walls **partition** *v.*

289

Mini-Lesson — The Writer's Style

SENSORY DETAILS Bring to students' attention the fact that Paulette Childress White helps her readers experience what she is writing about by showing how things look, sound, smell, taste, or feel. These sensory details bring White's descriptions and narrative to life. For example, in the highlighted passage on page 289, White uses specific verbs and nouns (*churning, melt, sliding, gardens, sweat, throat*) and adjectives (*tight, little*) to convey sensory details to the reader.

Application Have students write a paragraph about an unpleasant trip they've taken. Remind them to refer to the chart shown and include sensory details in their descriptions.

Reteaching/Reinforcement
- *Writing Handbook,* anthology, p. 831
- *Writing Mini-Lessons* transparencies, p. 38

Sensory Details, pp. 256, 698

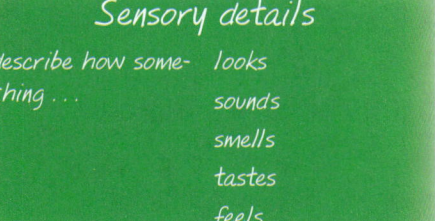

Critical Thinking: SPECULATING

G Ask students to speculate about what Minerva means when she says "...if I could make myself rise and walk to [the water fountain]." Why might she need to force herself to do this? *(Possible responses: She is embarrassed and doesn't want to be seen. She is tired and cranky because of the office's atmosphere.)*

CUSTOMIZING FOR
Students Acquiring English

5 Ask students what "never cracked a smile" means. *(She never smiled.)* Point out that the expression is more colorful than simply stating that the woman never smiled.

Critical Thinking: HYPOTHESIZING

H Ask students why Mrs. Blue might want Minerva to stay in her seat and why the social services employee might encourage her to come inside. *(Possible response: Mrs. Blue has been through the interviews before and she may not want Minerva to have to see the way poor people are treated. The welfare lady may want her to come inside to pressure Mrs. Blue to be direct and honest.)*

Literary Concept: CONFLICT

I Have students identify what forces are in conflict in this scene. Would students describe the conflicts as internal or external? *(Possible responses: Mrs. Blue is in conflict with the social services employee; the Blue family is in conflict with the Department of Social Services; Mrs. Blue feels in conflict with her husband; Minerva and Mrs. Blue feel in conflict with their guilt about Mr. Blue's lack of responsibility. All except the last are external conflicts.)*

---

a little girl with blond curls was trying to handle a bottle of Coke. Now and then, she'd manage to turn herself and the bottle around and watch me with big gray eyes that seemed to know quite well how badly I wanted a pop. I thought of asking Momma for fifteen cents so I could get one from the machine in the back, but I was afraid she'd still say no, so I just kept planning more and more convincing ways to ask. Besides, there was a water fountain near the door if I could make myself rise and walk to it.

We waited three hours. White ladies dressed like secretaries kept coming out to call numbers, and people on the benches would get up and follow down a hall. Then more people came in to replace them. I drank water from the fountain three times and was ready to put my feet up on the bench before us—the little girl with the Coke and her momma got called—by the time we heard Momma's number.

"You wait here," Momma said as I rose with her.

I sat down with a plop.

The lady with the number looked at me. Her face reminded me of the librarian's at Bunch school. Looked like she never cracked a smile. "Let her come," she said.

"She can wait here," Momma repeated, weakly.

"It's OK. She can come in. Come on," the lady insisted at me.

I hesitated, knowing that Momma's face was telling me to sit.

"Come on," the woman said.

Momma said nothing.

I got up and followed them into the maze. We came to a small room where there was a desk and three chairs. The woman sat behind the desk and we before it.

For a while, no one spoke. The woman studied a folder open before her, brows drawn together. On the wall behind her there was a calendar with one heavy black line drawn slantwise through each day of August, up to the twenty-first. That was today.

"Mrs. Blue, I have a notation here that Mr. Blue has not reported to the department on his efforts to obtain employment since the sixteenth of June. Before that, it was the tenth of April. You understand that department regulations require that he report monthly to this office, do you not?" Eyes brown as a wren's belly came up at Momma.

"Yes," Momma answered, sounding as small as I felt.

"Can you explain his failure to do so?"

Pause. "He's been looking. He says he's been looking."

"That may be. However, his failure to report those efforts here is my only concern."

Silence.

"We cannot continue with your case as it now stands if Mr. Blue refuses to comply with departmental regulations. He is still residing with the family, is he not?"

"Yes, he is. I've been reminding him to come in . . . he said he would."

"Well, he hasn't. Regulations are that any able-bodied man, head-of-household and receiving assistance, who neglects to report to this office any effort to obtain work for a period of sixty days or more is to be cut off for a minimum of three months, at which time he may reapply. As of this date, Mr. Blue is over sixty days delinquent, and officially, I am obliged to close the case and direct you to other sources of aid."

WORDS TO KNOW	
comply (kəm-plī′) *v.* to obey a rule or command	
reside (rĭ-zīd′) *v.* to occupy a home	

290

Mini-Lesson • Literary Concepts

REVIEWING CONFLICT Remind students that conflict is a struggle between two opposing forces. In an external conflict, a character struggles against some outside person or force. Internal conflict occurs when the struggle is within a character.

Application Have students think about the conflicts faced by Minerva and Mrs. Blue. Invite them to look through the story to identify both external conflicts and internal conflicts, and encourage them to place their findings in a chart like the one shown. Remind students to label whether the conflict is faced by Minerva, Mrs. Blue, or both characters.

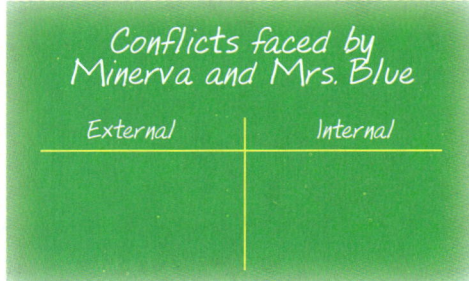

Conflicts faced by Minerva and Mrs. Blue

External	Internal

Art Note

Pink Lace by Stephen Scott Young
In this arresting watercolor image by Young (1957–), the uncompromising gaze of an African-American girl confronts the viewer. The stark contrast between her dress and the painting's dark background serves to frame the frankness of her eyes and her tightly closed mouth.

Reading the Art *What do you think the girl is thinking or feeling? Which details make you think this? Why do you think the artist chose this title for the painting? What other titles do you think would be appropriate?*

Active Reading: CONNECT

J Encourage students to imagine what they would be thinking and feeling if they were in Minerva's position at this point in the story.

CUSTOMIZING FOR
Multiple Learning Styles

K **Linguistic Learners** Have students study this and other speeches by the unnamed welfare-agency employee. Ask students to read the speech or speeches out loud, using a vocal style they think the character might use.

Pink Lace (1993), Stephen Scott Young. Photo courtesy of The John H. Surovek Gallery, Palm Beach, Florida. Copyright © Stephen Scott Young.

"What is that?"

"Aid to Dependent Children would be the only source available to you. Then, of course, you would not be eligible unless it was <u>verified</u> that Mr. Blue was no longer residing with the family."

J Another silence. I stared into the gray steel front of the desk, everything stopped but my heart.

"Well, can you keep the case open until Monday? If he comes in by Monday?"

"According to my records, Mr. Blue failed to come in May, and such an agreement was made then. In all, we allowed him a period of seventy days. You must understand that what happens in such cases as this is not wholly my decision." She sighed and watched Momma with hopeless eyes, tapping the soft end of her **K**

| WORDS TO KNOW | **verify** (vĕr′ə-fī′) *v.* to prove to be true by providing evidence |

291

Mini-Lesson: Speaking,  Listening, and Viewing

FILM MUSIC Invite students to consider the importance of music in films and television dramas. If this story were filmed or staged, the impact of certain scenes could be underscored by the use of music. If possible, you might wish to show scenes from one or two films in which the soundtrack helps establish a mood or period. Possibilities include *To Sir With Love* (1967) or *A Raisin in the Sun* (1961). You might play a scene once without sound and once with sound to have students appreciate the effect of the musical soundtrack on an audience.

Application Have students choose one scene from the short story and investigate what music would be best suited to it. Encourage them to research music from the time period in which the selection is set, paying special attention to songs released by Little Stevie Wonder and other Motown recording artists from the time. Have students play the music as the scene is read aloud for the class.

THE LANGUAGE OF LITERATURE TEACHER'S EDITION **291**

STRATEGIC READING FOR
Less-Proficient Readers

L Ask students to describe what the welfare official reads off "like items in a grocery list." *(the names of the eight Blue children)* **Noting Relevant Details**

Set a Purpose Have students read to find out how the Blues' case is left at the end of the interview and what Minerva and her mother discuss on their way home.

Literary Concept: CONFLICT

M Draw students' attention to the conflict between Mrs. Blue and the welfare employee. What makes this moment distinctive? What effect does Mrs. Blue's answer have on her opponent? *(Possible response: This is the first time that Mrs. Blue has not replied with resignation—she creates friction with an answer that implies the question was stupid. The welfare employee responds by growing even chillier than she was before.)*

Active Reading: EVALUATE

N Have students explain their opinions of the way the social services employee is treating Mrs. Blue. *(Possible responses: She is pushy and obnoxious. The welfare employee is just doing her job—she doesn't make the rules, but she is the one who has to enforce them.)*

---

pencil on the papers before her. "Mrs. Blue, I will speak to my superiors on your behalf. I can allow you until Monday next . . . that's the"—she swung around to the calendar—"twenty-sixth of August, to get him in here."

"Thank you. He'll be in," Momma breathed. "Will I be able to get the clothing order today?"

> Then I heard our names and ages—all eight of them—being called off like items in a grocery list.

Hands and eyes searched in the folder for an answer before she cleared her throat and tilted her face at Momma. "We'll see what we can do," she said, finally.

My back touched the chair. Without turning my head, I moved my eyes down to Momma's dusty feet and wondered if she could still feel them; my own were numb. I felt bodyless—there was only my face, which wouldn't disappear, and behind it, one word pinging against another in a buzz that made no sense. At home, we'd have the house cleaned by now, and I'd be waiting for the daily appearance of my best friend, Bernadine, so we could comb each other's hair or talk about stuck-up Evelyn and Brenda. Maybe Bernadine was already there, and Stella was teaching her to dance the bop.

Then I heard our names and ages—all eight of them—being called off like items in a grocery list.

"Clifford, Junior, age fourteen." She waited.

"Yes."

"Born? Give me the month and year."

"October 1946," Momma answered, and I could hear in her voice that she'd been through these questions before.

"Stella, age thirteen."

"Yes."

"Born?"

"November 1947."

"Minerva, age twelve." She looked at me. "This is Minerva?"

"Yes."

No. I thought, no, this is not Minerva. You can write it down if you want to, but Minerva is not here.

"Born?"

"December 1948."

The woman went on down the list, sounding more and more like Momma should be sorry or ashamed, and Momma's answers grew fainter and fainter. So this was welfare. I wondered how many times Momma had had to do this. Once before? Three times? Every time?

More questions. How many in school? Six. Who needs shoes? Everybody.

"Everybody needs shoes? The youngest two?"

"Well, they don't go to school . . . but they walk."

My head came up to look at Momma and the woman. The woman's mouth was left open. Momma didn't blink.

The brown eyes went down. "Our allowances are based on the <u>median</u> costs for moderately priced clothing at Sears, Roebuck." She figured on paper as she spoke. "That will mean thirty-four dollars for children over ten . . . thirty dollars for children under ten. It comes to one hundred ninety-eight dollars. I can allow eight dollars for two additional pairs of shoes."

"Thank you."

WORDS TO KNOW
median (mē′dē-ən) *adj.* relating to the middle value in a series

292

Mini-Lesson: Speaking, Listening, and Viewing

PANTOMIME Explain to students that pantomime is a type of dramatic performance that uses no speech or sound. Performers express themselves with body language, facial expressions, and gestures. Remind them that viewing a pantomime allows them to see the emotional essence of some character, action, or scene.

Application Have four students (three performers and a director) plan, develop, rehearse, and perform a pantomime of the scene in the welfare office. Encourage students to begin by analyzing the text to discover the overall shape of the scene. Then have them identify details needed to convey the scene's meaning. Help students understand that choosing a few physical characteristics of a person, such as posture or style of walking, can be enough to bring a character to life without speech.

292 THE LANGUAGE OF LITERATURE **Teacher's Edition**

"You will present your clothing order to a salesperson at the store, who will be happy to assist you in your selections. Please be practical, as further clothing requests will not be considered for a period of six months. In cases of necessity, however, requests for winter outerwear will be considered beginning November first."

Momma said nothing.

The woman rose and left the room.

For the first time, I shifted in the chair. Momma was looking into the calendar as though she could see through the pages to November first. Everybody needed a coat.

I'm never coming here again, I thought. If I do, I'll stay out front. Not coming back in here. Ever again.

CLARIFY
Why does Minerva have such strong feelings about the welfare office?
Using a Reading Log

She came back and sat behind her desk. "Mrs. Blue, I must make it clear that, regardless of my feelings, I will be forced to close your case if your husband does not report to this office by Monday, the twenty-sixth. Do you understand?"

"Yes. Thank you. He'll come. I'll see to it."

"Very well." She held a paper out to Momma.

We stood. Momma reached over and took the slip of paper. I moved toward the door.

"Excuse me, Mrs. Blue, but are you pregnant?"

"What?"

"I asked if you were expecting another child."

"Oh. No, I'm not," Momma answered, biting down on her lips.

"Well, I'm sure you'll want to be careful about a thing like that in your present situation."

"Yes."

I looked quickly to Momma's loose white blouse. We'd never known when another baby was coming until it was almost there.

"I suppose that eight children are enough for anyone," the woman said, and for the first time her face broke into a smile.

Momma didn't answer that. Somehow, we left the room and found our way out onto the street. We stood for a moment as though lost. My eyes followed Momma's up to where the sun was burning high. It was still there, blazing white against a cloudless blue. Slowly, Momma put the clothing order into her purse and snapped it shut. She looked around as if uncertain which way to go. I led the way to the corner. We turned. We walked the first five blocks.

I was thinking about how stupid I'd been a year ago, when Daddy lost his job. I'd been happy.

"You-all better be thinking about moving to Indianapolis," he announced one day after work, looking like he didn't think much of it himself. He was a welder with the railroad company. He'd worked there for eleven years. But now, "Company's moving to Indianapolis," he said. "Gonna be gone by November. If I want to keep my job, we've got to move with it."

We didn't. Nobody wanted to move to Indianapolis—not even Daddy. Here, we had uncles, aunts and cousins on both sides. Friends. Everybody and everything we knew. Daddy could get another job. First came unemployment compensation.³ Then came welfare. Thank goodness for welfare, we said, while we waited and waited for the job that hadn't yet come.

The problem was that Daddy couldn't take it. If something got repossessed⁴ or somebody took sick or something was broken or another kid was coming, he'd carry on terribly until things got better—by which time things were always worse. He'd always been that way. So when the railroad left, he began to do everything wrong. Stayed out all hours. Drank and drank

---

3. **unemployment compensation:** a regular payment of money to an unemployed worker for a limited time.
4. **repossessed:** taken back by a seller because of the buyer's failure to make payment.

Active Reading: CLARIFY

R Ask students why Minerva and her mother are enjoying a happy conversation. If students need help, you might wish to share the following thought process with them.

Think-Aloud Model *Just moments ago Minerva and her mother were anxious and upset, but now they're cheerful. They were both humiliated at the welfare office, but Minerva brings up a topic that they've enjoyed speaking about before. She probably knows it'll reassure them both.*

STRATEGIC READING FOR
Less-Proficient Readers

S Have students explain how the Blues' case is left at the end of the interview at the welfare office. *(Their case will be closed if Mr. Blue does not report on Monday.)* Relating Cause and Effect

- Then ask them to describe what Minerva and her mother discuss on the way home. *(Mrs. Blue's girlhood in Alabama and the facts of life)* Summarizing

CUSTOMIZING FOR
Gifted and Talented Students

Have students look through the story for examples of dialect. After they have developed a list of examples, have them consider why the author chose to use a regional dialect. Have them discuss whether the dialect is effective or makes meaning harder to understand.

COMPREHENSION CHECK
1. What two parts of Ecorse do Minerva and her mother walk through? *(the white section and the "colored" section)*
2. Why does the welfare official threaten to close the Blues' case? *(Mr. Blue has failed to report to the office.)*
3. What is Mr. Blue's employment situation? *(Mr. Blue is unemployed; he had been a welder for the railroad company.)*
4. What important information does Mrs. Blue tell her daughter on the way home? *("the facts of life")*

---

some more. When he was home, he was so grouchy we were afraid to squeak. Now when we saw him coming, we got lost. Even our friends ran for cover.

At the railroad tracks, we sped up. The tracks were as far across as a block was long. Silently, I counted the rails by the heat of the steel bars through my thin soles. On the other side, I felt something heavy rise up in my chest, and I knew that I wanted to cry. I wanted to cry or run or kiss the dusty ground. The little houses with their sun-scorched lawns and backyard gardens were mansions in my eyes. "Ohh, Ma . . . look at those collards!"

"Umm-humm," she agreed, and I knew that she saw it too.

"Wonder how they grew so big?"

"Cow dung, probably. Big Poppa used to put cow dung out to fertilize the vegetable plots, and everything just grew like crazy. We used to get tomatoes this big"—she circled with her hands—"and don't talk about squash or melons."

"I bet y'all ate like rich people. Bet y'all had everything you could want."

"We sure did," she said. "We never wanted for anything when it came to food. And when the cash crops were sold, we could get whatever else that was needed. We never wanted for a thing."

"What about the time you and cousin Emma threw out the supper peas?"

"Oh! Did I tell you about that?" she asked. Then she told it all over again. I didn't listen. I watched her face and guarded her smile with a smile of my own.

R We walked together, step for step. The sun was still burning, but we forgot to mind it. We talked about an Alabama girlhood in a time and place I'd never know. We talked about the wringer washer⁵ and how it could be fixed, because washing every day on a scrub board was something Alabama could keep. We talked about how to get Daddy to the Department of Social Services.

Then we talked about having babies. She began to tell me things I'd never known, and the idea of womanhood blossomed in my mind like some kind of suffocating rose.

"Momma," I said, "I don't think I can be a woman."

> She began to tell me things I'd never known, and the idea of womanhood blossomed in my mind like some kind of suffocating rose.

"You can," she laughed, "and if you live, you will be. You gotta be some kind of woman."

"But it's hard," I said, "sometimes it must be hard."

S

"Umm-humm," she said, "sometimes it is hard."

When we got to the bad block, we crossed to Beaman's drugstore for two orange crushes. Then we walked right through the groups of men standing in the shadows of the poolroom and the Moonflower Hotel. Not one of them said a word to us. I supposed they could see in the way we walked that we weren't afraid. We'd been to the welfare office and back again. And the facts of life, fixed in our minds like the sun in the sky, were no burning mysteries. ❖

---

5. **wringer washer:** an old-fashioned washing machine in which laundry is pressed between rollers to remove water.

294   UNIT THREE PART 1: STRUGGLING FOR SURVIVAL

Mini-Lesson Spelling

THE PREFIXES COM-, COL-, AND CON-
Explain to students that the prefixes *com-*, *col-*, and *con-* all mean "together" or "with." Most often, you use *com-* with words beginning with *b, p,* or *m; col-* with words beginning with *l;* and *con-* with words beginning with all other letters.

com- + ply = **comply**

col- + lapse = **collapse**

con- + clave = **conclave**

Application Have students complete the following words using one of the prefixes *com-, col-,* or *con-*.

1. -cave
2. -bine
3. -lateral
4. -mingle
5. -figure
6. -lide
7. -pound
8. -join
9. -lect
10. -clusion

Ask students to look for more words that fit this pattern, in their own writing and in things they read, and to add these words to their personal word lists.

Reteaching/Reinforcement
- *Unit Three Resource Book,* p. 6

RESPONDING OPTIONS

FROM PERSONAL RESPONSE TO CRITICAL ANALYSIS

REFLECT
1. What are your reactions to Minerva's experiences? Share your thoughts with the class.

RETHINK
Close Textual Reading

2. Which change in Minerva do you think is the most important? Support your opinion with evidence from the story.

3. Evaluate the welfare worker's attitude toward Mrs. Blue. Do you think her attitude is justified? Why or why not?

4. Do you think that Minerva's father will report to the welfare office on the appointed day? Give reasons for your prediction.

5. In your opinion, is a trip to the welfare office, like that in the story, an appropriate or useful experience for a child? Why or why not?
   Consider
   - the conversation between Mrs. Blue and the welfare worker
   - Minerva's feelings about becoming an adult and her mother's response
   - what Minerva and her mother share on the walk home

Thematic Link
6. How does the Blue family's experience relate to the unit theme, "Battle for Control"?

RELATE
7. Supporters of the welfare system say that financial assistance is a necessary "safety net" for families who are struggling to survive. Critics of the system claim that welfare discourages recipients from seeking employment. Consider your class's prereading discussion about society's attitudes toward welfare. What do you think about the welfare system now?

Multimodal Learning
ANOTHER PATHWAY
Cooperative Learning
The action of this story can be divided into three or four scenes. With a group of classmates, stage a Readers Theater presentation of one of these scenes for the rest of the class.

QUICKWRITES

1. Compose a **poem** in which Minerva is the speaker. Write either about her reactions to the visit to the welfare office or about her thoughts on approaching adulthood.

2. Write a **character sketch** of one person in the story. Describe three of the character's prominent traits and explain how each is shown.

3. Near the end of the story, Minerva says that she and her mother "talked about how to get Daddy to the Department of Social Services." Write the **dialogue** that they might have had.

📁 **PORTFOLIO** Save your writing. You may want to use it later as a springboard to a piece for your portfolio.

GETTING THE FACTS OF LIFE **295**

From Personal Response to Critical Analysis

1. Responses will vary.
2. Possible responses: The most important change in Minerva is from her seeing herself as a child to her seeing herself with adult responsibilities. Minerva's realization of what her mother goes through is the biggest change.
3. Possible responses: The way she looks down on Mrs. Blue is not justified, because she has no idea of the Blues' lives beyond the facts and figures printed on the welfare forms. The worker's opinion about Mrs. Blue not having any more babies is completely justified, because it's not fair to the Blue children (or other children) to bring them into poverty.
4. Possible response: He probably will not report, because he has proven with his actions that he can't stand the humiliation. He will show up, because he is committed to his family.
5. Possible response: It is a very valuable experience because it takes away romantic ideas about what it means to be an adult. It's not appropriate because Minerva sees her mother humiliated.
6. Possible response: The family battles against poverty every day, and it also battles against the loss of self-respect.
7. Responses will vary.

Another Pathway
Cooperative Learning While two or more students read narration or dialogue, another student might ask in-depth questions of the readers to elicit deeper understanding of the scene and of the characters' points of view.

Rubric
3 Full Accomplishment Students plan and perform a presentation that accurately and dramatically conveys the scene's characters, events, and themes.
2 Substantial Accomplishment Students plan and perform a presentation that accurately and dramatically conveys some of the scene's characters, events, and themes.
1 Little or Partial Accomplishment Students have trouble planning and performing a presentation that conveys the scene's characters, events, and themes.

QuickWrites
1. Encourage students to brainstorm words and phrases in response to either of the topics before they begin.
2. Remind students that they can find character traits in the character's words, in another character's words, or in descriptions of the character's thoughts, appearance, and actions.
3. You might suggest that students read possible lines of dialogue aloud as they write them. Often it is best to compose dialogue "in the air" and then write it down.

The Writer's Craft
Poetry, pp. 76–80
Analyzing a Story, pp. 170–174
Dialogue, pp. 324–327

Across the Curriculum

Social Studies *Aid to Families with Dependent Children* After students learn the amount of money a family like the Blues would receive, you might encourage them to find out how much money such a family would have to spend on rent, food, and basic services and to present these findings to the class. Students might do their research on prices by reading ads in the local newspapers.

ADDITIONAL SUGGESTION

Math *American Basics* Have students research how much the average American family spends annually on basics such as food, clothing, and shelter. Have them present their findings in a pie chart or graph. Much data about costs of commodities can be found in *Statistical Abstracts of the United States*.

Art Connection

The setting seems somewhat lonely and gloomy, and this is in part because of the isolation of the four figures in the scene, the dilapidated buildings, and the glistening surface of the street, still wet from a recent rain.

Literary Links

Possible responses:

Minerva and her mother
- family strongly affected by poverty
- Minerva one of many siblings; father not around very much
- close relationship with mother

Yollie and her mother
- family strongly affected by poverty
- Yollie an only child; father elsewhere
- often battling, but close relationship with mother

LITERARY CONCEPTS

Realistic fiction is imaginative writing set in the real, modern world. In such fiction, the characters act like real people, using ordinary human abilities to cope with problems and conflicts typical of modern life. In what ways is "Getting the Facts of Life" realistic? What conflicts do the characters face?

CONCEPT REVIEW: First-Person Point of View The author uses a first-person point of view in this story. Why do you think she chose Minerva rather than her mother to tell the story?

ART CONNECTION

Look at the painting on page 286–287. What mood does the painting evoke? How does the painter achieve that mood? Does the mood match that of the story? Explain your opinions.

296 UNIT THREE PART 1: STRUGGLING FOR SURVIVAL

Literary Concepts

Students should understand that the story is realistic in its details of life in city neighborhoods. The characters face conflicts stemming from poverty—external ones such as the need for food, clothing, and shelter, as well as abuse or condescension from other people; and internal conflicts such as nagging self-doubt and hopelessness.

Concept Review Having Minerva tell the story gives the reader an opportunity to experience things for the first time, just as Minerva does. This increases the story's dramatic effect.

Multimodal Learning

ALTERNATIVE ACTIVITIES

1. Think about the way this story made you feel. Then draw a **picture** or compose a **song** that reflects your feelings.
2. How might Minerva's mother have viewed the events of this story? With a classmate, act out a **telephone conversation** in which she discusses her trip with a friend.
3. Choose a classmate who disagrees with you on a topic related to the welfare system. Research the topic on your own. Then **debate** the topic with your classmate in front of your class.

ACROSS THE CURRICULUM

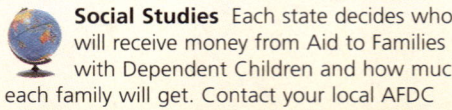

Social Studies Each state decides who will receive money from Aid to Families with Dependent Children and how much each family will get. Contact your local AFDC office to learn how much a family of two unemployed adults and eight children, like the Blue family, would receive.

LITERARY LINKS

Compare and contrast the relationship between Minerva and her mother with that of Yollie and her mother in "Mother and Daughter" (page 203). How do circumstances affect each relationship?

Alternative Activities

1. Students may wish to browse through art books as inspiration for their drawings. They might consider working in small groups to write a song in the Motown style.
2. You might urge students to perform the telephone conversation as an improvisation. Other students might prefer to script a conversation, which could then be read or performed from memory.
3. Encourage students to use books and current periodicals to get facts and figures about welfare.

296 THE LANGUAGE OF LITERATURE TEACHER'S EDITION

WORDS TO KNOW

EXERCISE A Review the Words to Know at the bottom of the selection pages, and list them on your paper. Write the Word to Know that best completes the sentence.

1. In 1993, the average monthly AFDC payment to families ranged from $120 a month to $762. Eleven states gave benefits above the _____, or midpoint, of these two figures.
2. A government welfare office may be a large room with many _____ offices.
3. A welfare worker must ask questions in order to _____ that the recipient is still unemployed and qualifies for aid.
4. If a welfare recipient cannot _____ with the department's rules, the recipient may lose his or her benefits.
5. Public-housing programs allow needy families to _____ in low-cost rental apartments.

EXERCISE B For each of the five Words to Know, make a word map like the example shown.

Word Map	Context Sentence I never divulge a secret that a friend has entrusted to me.
Word divulge	Association or Symbol
Best Guess speak out	
	One Good Sentence She will soon divulge the location of the treasure.
	Verified Definition to reveal; make public

Words to Know

Exercise A
1. median
2. partitioned
3. verify
4. comply
5. reside

Exercise B
Ensure that word maps contain the word, a context sentence, a graphic association or symbol, a "best guess," one "good sentence," and a verified definition.

Reteaching/Reinforcement
• *Unit Three Resource Book*, p. 7

PAULETTE CHILDRESS WHITE

In addition to her literary work, Paulette Childress White has spent time pursuing the visual arts. She remarks, "I am also a painter. I write and paint because I have a need to give substance to my ideas, feelings, and experiences, and because I believe it is good and important work." White has also written *Love Poem to a Black Junkie* and *The Blue Woman*.

PAULETTE CHILDRESS WHITE

1948–

Like Minerva Blue, the 12-year-old narrator of "Getting the Facts of Life," Paulette Childress White grew up in Ecorse, Michigan, a town that was racially divided by railroad tracks. Now the mother of five grown children, White lives in Detroit with her husband. She is working on a doctorate in literature while teaching at Henry Ford Community College and Wayne State University.

White often writes about contemporary African-American women in an urban environment. She has written a collection of poetry entitled *The Watermelon Dress* and has contributed to such magazines as *Essence*, *Redbook*, and *Callaloo*. Short stories by her have appeared in the anthologies *Midnight Birds* and *Memory of Kin: Stories About Family by Black Writers*, from which "Getting the Facts of Life" was taken.

About her writing the author says, "I write from a sense of irony, because I want to make sense of my experience of life."

WHAT DO YOU THINK?
Reflecting on Theme

Have students think about the chart they designed before they began reading the selections in Part One. The charts showed how their feelings changed as a result of a difficult experience. Ask them to compare their thoughts then with their thoughts now about how difficult experiences help people to mature. If their thoughts are different, invite them to design a new chart.

OVERVIEW

Objectives

- To understand and appreciate a short story about a fisherman's memorable encounter with a pair of bears
- To enrich reading by evaluating
- To identify and understand the tone of a work of literature
- To express understanding of the story through a choice of writing forms, including a news article and a dialogue
- To extend understanding of the story through a variety of multimodal and cross-curricular activities

Skills

READING SKILLS/STRATEGIES
- Evaluate

LITERARY CONCEPTS
- Tone
- Humor

SPEAKING, LISTENING, AND VIEWING
- Interview
- Group discussion
- Oral presentation

THE WRITER'S STYLE
- Show, don't tell

GRAMMAR
- Adverb clauses

SPELLING
- Words ending in *-ate* and *-ion*

STUDY SKILLS
- Card catalogs

Cross-Curricular Connections

SCIENCE
- The Alaskan brown bear

GEOGRAPHY
- The 49th state

MATHEMATICS
- Calculating pounds of fish

SCIENCE CONNECTION
Bears in the Wild These photographs of adult bears and cubs in their natural habitat will help students visualize the bears in the story.

Side A, Frame 52675

VISUAL VOCABULARY
- cast
- Chinook (shĭ-nŏŏk′)
- fly
- waders (wā′dərz)

Side A, Frame 52681

PREVIEWING

FICTION

Appetizer
Robert H. Abel

Activating Prior Knowledge
PERSONAL CONNECTION

Imagine that you are hiking in a beautiful, peaceful wilderness. Suddenly, you hear the heavy breathing of a wild animal that is creeping up behind you. Slowly you turn. The animal you see is the one you fear most. What animal is it? What will you do to survive? Jot down the ending of this story in your notebook. Then share it with your classmates.

Building Background
SCIENCE CONNECTION

Perhaps the wild animal you fear most is a bear. If so, you have good reason. The size, strength, fierceness, and unpredictability of a bear make it a serious threat to the survival of anyone it encounters in the wild. The bear in this story, an Alaskan brown bear, is certainly no exception. The Alaskan brown bear is the largest carnivore, or meat eater, that lives on land. It can grow up to nine feet long, can weigh 1,800 pounds, and, when standing, can reach the rim of a basketball hoop. Found chiefly on the mainland of Alaska and on nearby islands, Alaskan brown bears dine on, among other things, the salmon in Alaska's rivers and coastal waters.

Like other species of bears, brown bears are usually peaceful animals, but if their safety, their cubs, or their homes are threatened, they will attack. Their powerful front paws and long, thick claws are dangerous weapons. As you read this story, see what happens when a fisherman encounters "Ms. Bear."

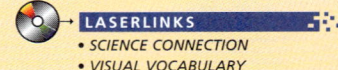
- SCIENCE CONNECTION
- VISUAL VOCABULARY

298 UNIT THREE PART 1: STRUGGLING FOR SURVIVAL

PRINT AND MEDIA RESOURCES

UNIT THREE RESOURCE BOOK
Strategic Reading: Literature, p. 11
Vocabulary SkillBuilder, p. 14
Reading SkillBuilder, p. 12
Spelling SkillBuilder, p. 13

GRAMMAR MINI–LESSONS
Transparencies, p. 44

WRITING MINI–LESSONS
Transparencies, p. 46

ACCESS FOR STUDENTS ACQUIRING ENGLISH
Selection Summaries
Reading and Writing Support

FORMAL ASSESSMENT
Selection Test, pp. 57–58
Test Generator

 **AUDIO LIBRARY**
See Reference Card

 **LASERLINKS**
Science Connection
Visual Vocabulary

---

298 THE LANGUAGE OF LITERATURE TEACHER'S EDITION

Activating Reading/Setting a Purpose
READING CONNECTION

Evaluating

The skill of making judgments about people, things, and situations is the skill of evaluating. For instance, as you watch a movie, you automatically evaluate the actors, the filming, and the action. You might decide that you like or dislike certain characters. You might think that the story line is believable or that it is absolutely absurd. As the movie progresses and more information is presented to you, you probably make additional evaluations or change evaluations you made earlier. Later, when someone asks you whether you liked the movie, you base your overall evaluation on the criteria that are most important to you.

Fiction Evaluating a story is similar to evaluating a movie. As you read, you make judgments about the story's elements—its characters, setting, and plot. You might decide, for example, that one character is really smart and another is stupid or selfish. You might judge the setting to be confusing or clear, or the plot to be exciting or dull. You might consider the ending of the story touching or disappointing. All these individual judgments combine to form your evaluation of the story as a whole.

Poetry and Nonfiction You can evaluate the elements of poetry and nonfiction as well. When reading a poem, ask yourself such questions as, Can I picture the images? Does the sound of the poem appeal to me? Does the poem say anything important to me? For nonfiction, evaluate the work's organization. Decide how much of the work is opinion and how much is fact, and whether you agree with the writer's conclusions.

Author's Purpose Another aspect of a work to evaluate is how well the author has achieved his or her purpose. Keep in mind that authors write for four main reasons: to entertain, to inform, to express opinions, and to persuade. After you determine an author's main purpose in a work, evaluate how well he or she has achieved that purpose.

As you read "Appetizer," jot down your evaluations in your notebook as you find yourself making them. When you finish the story, determine what you think Robert H. Abel's main purpose for writing it was and how well he has achieved that purpose. Finally, evaluate the story as a whole on the basis of your evaluations of its individual elements. Give it a rating of one to five stars, with five stars being the best.

APPETIZER 299

SUMMARY

Fishing in Alaska, the narrator is joined by a huge female brown bear. He distracts the bear by catching and feeding her salmon as he edges closer to the trail that leads back to his camper. When a male bear appears, the narrator desperately removes his waders, holds them in front of him like two extra legs, and tramps along the trail singing "Jingle Bells." The female bear follows him to his camper, climbs on the hood, and falls asleep. Unable to dislodge her, the narrator drives to a nearby fish cannery, where the bear rushes toward the smell of fish. After leaving the scene, the narrator takes a shower and a nap in a local hotel.

Thematic Link: *Struggling for Survival* A person needs physical endurance and mental ingenuity to survive an encounter with hungry bears.

CUSTOMIZING FOR
Students Acquiring English

- Use **ACCESS FOR STUDENTS ACQUIRING ENGLISH**, *Reading and Writing Support.*
- Point out Alaska on a map. Ask students to describe what they think Alaska is like. Some may know about the state from television or books. Be sure students understand that much of Alaska is wild and uninhabited by humans.
- In addition to these boxes, you may want to use the suggestions under Strategic Reading for Less-Proficient Readers.

WORDS TO KNOW

assess (ə-sĕs′) *v.* to determine or judge (p. 300)
burly (bûr′lē) *adj.* big and muscular (p. 305)
dubious (dōō′bē-əs) *adj.* of questionable value or quality (p. 309)
furtively (fûr′tĭv-lē) *adv.* in a sneaky way (p. 302)
nostalgia (nŏ-stăl′jə) *n.* homesickness; a longing for something distant in space or time (p. 302)
profound (prə-found′) *adj.* deep (p. 306)

resort (rĭ-zôrt′) *v.* (followed by *to*) to turn to (p. 308)
smug (smŭg) *adj.* self-satisfied (p. 305)
speculation (spĕk′yə-lā′shən) *n.* a thought or idea (p. 306)
superfluous (sōō-pûr′flōō-əs) *adj.* unnecessary; extra (p. 308)

Appetizer

by Robert H. Abel

I'm fishing this beautiful stream in Alaska, catching salmon, char and steelhead, when this bear lumbers out of the woods and down to the stream bank. He fixes me with this half-amused, half-curious look which says: You are meat.

The bear's eyes are brown, and his shiny golden fur is standing up in spikes, which shows me he has been fishing, too, perhaps where the stream curves behind the peninsula of woods he has just trudged through. He's not making any sound I can hear over the rumble of the water in the softball-sized rocks, but his presence is very loud.

I say "his" presence because temporarily I am not interested in or able to assess the creature's sex. I am looking at a head that is bigger around than my steering wheel, a pair of paws, awash in river bubbles, that could cover half my windshield. I am glad that I am wearing polarized fishing glasses so the bear cannot see the little teardrops of fear that have crept into the corner of my eyes. To assure him/her I am not the least bit intimidated, I make another cast.

Immediately I tie into a fat Chinook.[1] The

---

1. **Chinook** (shǐ-nŏŏk′): Chinook salmon, a large fish of northern Pacific waters.

WORDS TO KNOW

assess (ə-sĕs′) *v.* to determine or judge

300

Copyright © Halstead Hannah.

splashing of the fish in the stream engages the bear's attention, but he/she registers this for the moment only by shifting his/her glance. I play the fish[2] smartly, and when it comes gliding in, tired, pink-sided, glittering and astonished, I pluck it out of the water by inserting a finger in its gill—something I normally wouldn't do in order not to injure the fish before I set it free, and I do exactly what you would do in the same situation— throw it to the bear.

The bear's eyes widen, and she—for I can see now, past her huge shoulder and powerful haunches, that she is a she—turns and pounces on the fish with such speed and nimbleness that I am numbed. There is no chance that I, in my insulated waders,[3] am going to outrun her, dodge her blows, escape her jaws. While she is occupied devouring the fish—I can hear

---

2. **play the fish:** keep the hooked fish on the line until it tires.
3. **waders:** a waterproof combination of trousers and boots, used for walking in water.

APPETIZER **301**

CUSTOMIZING FOR
Gifted and Talented Students

Invite students to make a detailed chart that shows the plot development of "Appetizer." As they read, students can identify the story's exposition, conflict, complications, rising action, climax, and resolution by citing specific sentences or paragraphs from the text. You might encourage students to illustrate their charts with drawings or photographs that capture various aspects of the story.

CUSTOMIZING FOR
Students Acquiring English

② Tell students that the narrator is sport fishing: he catches fish for the challenge and then releases them, rather than killing and eating them. He carefully unhooks the fish and throws them back in the stream.

Literary Concept: HUMOR

Ⓑ Point out to students that the story's humor would not be possible if the reader did not understand that the narrator survived to tell the tale of his dangerous encounter. Ask students how they can be sure the fisherman was not killed by the bear. *(The fact that the story is told in the first-person point of view proves that the narrator survived this experience.)*

Mini-Lesson   Literary Concepts

REVIEWING HUMOR Remind students that humor is the quality that makes a story funny or amusing. Writers create humor through a number of methods, including exaggeration, sarcasm, amusing descriptions, irony, and witty and insightful dialogue.

Application Have students look at the first few pages of "Appetizer" and list examples of humor in the narrative. After they have identified several examples, have them identify the method—exaggeration, irony, and so on—the author uses to create the comic effect. You may wish to have students share their findings with the class.

THE LANGUAGE OF LITERATURE TEACHER'S EDITION **301**

Literary Concept: REPETITION

C Explain that authors often use repetition of a word, a phrase, or an idea to create humor. Ask students what Abel repeats at the end of this paragraph for humorous effect. *(Possible response: The author repeats from the end of the preceding paragraph the idea that he reacted to the bear exactly the same way that the reader or anyone else would have.)*

CUSTOMIZING FOR
Students Acquiring English

3 Spanish-speaking students in particular may not hear a difference between the pronunciation of *Miss* and *Ms.* and may think that *Ms.* is the abbreviation for *Miss*. Explain the differences among *Ms.*, *Miss*, and *Mrs.*

4 Ask a more fluent student to use context clues to explain what *bereft of* means. *(without)*

Literary Concept: HUMOR

D Invite students to explain the humor of this passage. Ask them why the image of an Alaskan brown bear leaning against a fisherman is funny. *(Possible response: The image of an enormous bear leaning casually against the man and watching him fish is funny because it is not what you would expect from a wild animal.)*

Critical Thinking: ANALYZING

E Ask students why the narrator might describe his nostalgia as "terrible." *(Possible response: He wants desperately to be safe at home rather than fishing next to a dangerous animal.)*

---

her teeth clacking together—I do what you or anyone else would do and cast again.

God answers my muttered prayer, and I am blessed with the strike of another fat salmon, like the others, on its way to spawning grounds upstream. I would like this fish to survive and release its eggs or sperm to perpetuate the salmon kingdom, but Ms. Bear has just licked her whiskers clean and has now moved knee-deep into the water and, to my consternation,[4] leans against me rather like a large and friendly dog, although her ears are at the level of my shoulder and her back is broader than that of any horse I have ever seen. Ms. Bear is intensely interested in the progress of the salmon toward us, and her head twists and twitches as the fish circles, darts, takes line away, shakes head, rolls over, leaps.

With a bear at your side, it is not the simplest thing to play a fish properly, but the presence of this huge animal, and especially her long snout, thick as my thigh, wonderfully concentrates the mind. She smells like the forest floor, like crushed moss and damp leaves, and she is as warm as a radiator back in my Massachusetts home, the thought of which floods me with a terrible nostalgia. Now I debate whether I should just drift the salmon in under the bear's nose and let her take it that way, but I'm afraid she will break off my fly and leader,[5] and right now that fly—a Doctor Wilson number eight—is saving my life. So, with much anxiety, I pretend to take charge and bring the fish in on the side away from the bear, gill and quickly unhook it, turn away from the bear and toss the fish behind me to the bank.

The bear wheels and clambers upon it at once, leaving a vortex of water pouring into the vacuum of the space she has left, which almost topples me. As her teeth snack away, I quickly and furtively regard my poor Doctor Wilson, which is fish-mauled now, bedraggled, almost unrecognizable. But the present emergency compels me to zing it out once again. I walk a few paces downstream, hoping the bear will remember an appointment or become distracted and I can sneak away.

But a few seconds later she is leaning against me again, raptly watching the stream for any sign of a salmon splash. My luck holds; another fish smacks the withered Wilson, flings sunlight and water in silver jets as it dances its last dance. I implore the salmon's forgiveness: something I had once read revealed that this is the way of all primitive hunters, to take the life reluctantly and to pray for the victim's return. I think my prayer is as urgent as that of any Mashpee or Yoruban, or Tlingit or early Celt,[6] for not only do I want the salmon to thrive forever, I want a superabundance of them now, right now, to save my neck. I have an idea this hungry bear, bereft of fish, would waste little time in conducting any prayer ceremonies before she turned me into the main course my salmon were just the appetizer for. When I take up this fish, the bear practically rips it from my hand and the sight of those teeth so close and the truly persuasive power of those muscled, pink-rimmed jaws cause a wave of fear in me so great that I nearly faint.

---

4. **consternation:** confusion; dismay.
5. **fly and leader:** a fishing lure made to look like an insect, and the part of the line to which it is attached.
6. **Mashpee or Yoruban** (yôr′ə-bən), **or Tlingit** (tlĭng′gĭt) **or early Celt:** member of an early people of North America, Africa, or Europe.

| WORDS TO KNOW | **nostalgia** (nŏ-stăl′jə) *n.* homesickness; a longing for something distant in space or time |
| | **furtively** (fûr′tĭv-lē) *adv.* in a sneaky way |

302

Mini-Lesson Grammar

ADVERB CLAUSES Remind students that adverbs are words that modify verbs, adjectives, or other adverbs. An adverb clause is a subordinate clause used as an adverb. Like adverbs, adverb clauses modify words by telling *where*, *when*, *how*, or *to what extent*. Sometimes an adverb tells *why*. Like any other clause, an adverb clause contains a subject and a verb and is always introduced by a subordinating conjunction. In "Appetizer," Abel uses adverb clauses (for example, *"As her teeth snack away, I quickly and furtively regard my poor Doctor Wilson . . ."*) to create vivid pictures.

Application Have students identify the adverb in the highlighted passage on page 302. Also ask students what word the clause modifies. *("... as the fish circles, darts, takes line away, shakes head, rolls over, leaps" modifies the verbs twists and twitches)*

Reteaching/Reinforcement
• *Grammar Mini-Lessons* transparencies, p. 44

Adverb Clauses, p. 567

302 THE LANGUAGE OF LITERATURE TEACHER'S EDITION

My vertigo[7] subsides as Ms. Bear munches and destroys the salmon with hearty shakes of her head, and I sneak a few more paces downstream, rapidly also with trembling fingers tie on a new Doctor Wilson, observing the utmost care (as you would, too) in making my knots. I cast and stride downstream, wishing I could just plunge into the crystalline water and bowl away like a log. My hope and plan is to wade my way back to the narrow trail a few hundred yards ahead and, when Ms. Bear loses interest or is somehow distracted, make a heroic dash for my camper. I think of the thermos of hot coffee on the front seat, the six-pack of beer in the cooler, the thin rubber mattress with the blue sleeping bag adorning it, warm wool socks in a bag hanging from a window crank, and almost burst into tears; these simple things, given the presence of Ms. Hungry Bear, seem so miraculous, so emblematic of the life I love to live. I promise the gods—American, Indian, African, Oriental—that if I survive, I will never complain again, not even if my teenage children leave the caps off the toothpaste tubes or their bicycles in the driveway at home.

"Oh, home," I think, and cast again.

Ms. Bear rejoins me. You may or may not believe me, and perhaps after all it was only my imagination worked up by terror, but two things happened which gave me a particle of hope. The first was that Ms. Bear actually belched—quite noisily and unapologetically, too, like a rude uncle at a Christmas dinner. She showed no signs of having committed any impropriety,[8] and yet it was clear to me that a belching bear is probably also a bear with a pretty-full belly. A few more salmon and perhaps Ms. Bear would wander off in search of a berry dessert.

Now the second thing she did, or that I imagined she did, was to begin—well, not *speaking* to me exactly, but *communicating* somehow. I know it sounds foolish, but if you were in my shoes—my waders, to be more precise—you might have learned bear talk pretty quickly, too. It's not as if the bear were speaking to me in complete sentences and English words such as "Get me another fish, pal, or you're on the menu," but in a much more indirect and subtle way, almost in the way a stream talks through its bubbling and burbling and rattling of rocks and gurgling along.

Believe me, I listened intently, more with my mind than with my ears, as if the bear were telepathizing[9] and—I know you're not going to believe this, but it's true, I am normally not what you would call an egomaniac with an inflated self-esteem such that I imagine that every bear which walks out of the woods falls in love with me—but I really did truly believe now that this Ms. Bear was expressing feelings of, well, *affection*. Really, I think she kinda liked me. True or not, the feeling made me less afraid. In fact, and I don't mean this in any erotic or perverse kind of way, but I had to admit, once my fear had passed, my feelings were kinda mutual. Like you might feel for an old pal of a dog. Or a favorite horse. I only wish she weren't such a big eater. I only wish she were not a carnivore, and I, carne.

---

7. **vertigo:** dizziness.
8. **impropriety** (ĭm′prə-prī′ĭ-tē): improper behavior.
9. **telepathizing:** communicating mentally, without speaking or gesturing.

APPETIZER 303

CUSTOMIZING FOR
Multiple Learning Styles

Musical Learners Have students think about how a movie version of "Appetizer" might look and sound. Encourage them to proceed on the assumption that a director of the film would wish to retain the humorous tone of Robert Abel's prose. Invite students to design a soundtrack for this film. Urge them to begin by analyzing the story's plot structure and identifying the causes and effects of events. This will help them break down the narrative into distinct scenes, which may have unique sound requirements. Remind students that they will be responsible not only for incidental "mood" music but also for sound effects. Students can plan the soundtrack by listing each scene and then suggesting the type of music and sound effects they think the scene requires.

Copyright © Bob Crofut.

304 UNIT THREE PART 1: STRUGGLING FOR SURVIVAL

Mini-Lesson Study Skills

CARD CATALOGS Remind students that a card catalog is a file of cards for all the materials in a library. These cards can be found (filed alphabetically) in drawers in the library. Each book in the library's collection is represented by three separate cards that are filed under the book's author, its title, and its subject. Each of these "entry cards" contains basic information including the book's title, author, call number, publisher, copyright date, and length—as well as a brief summary or description. Sometimes you will also find a cross-reference card that recommends related books or information; these cards usually invite you to "see" or "see also" another title or subject. In many libraries, card catalogs have been computerized, and people search through a series of computer menus. Although the method of search is different, the computerized catalog contains the same information as the older file-drawer format.

Application Have students use a library card catalog to research Alaska or one of the various animals mentioned in "Appetizer."

Now she nudges me with her nose.

"All right, all right," I say. "I'm doing the best I can."

Cast in the glide behind that big boulder, the bear telepathizes me. *There's a couple of whoppers in there.*

I do as I'm told and wham! The bear is right! Instantly I'm tied into a granddaddy Chinook, a really burly fellow who has no intention of lying down on anybody's platter beneath a blanket of lemon slices and scallion shoots, let alone make his last wiggle down a bear's gullet. Even the bear is excited and begins shifting weight from paw to paw, a little motion for her that nevertheless has big consequences for me as her body slams against my hip, then slams again.

Partly because I don't want to lose the fish, but partly also because I want to use the fish as an excuse to move closer to my getaway trail, I stumble downstream. This fish has my rod bent into an upside-down *U,* and I'm hoping my quick-tied knots are also strong enough to take this salmon's lurching and his intelligent, broadside swinging into the river current—a very smart fish! Ordinarily I might take a long time with a fish like this, baby it in, but now I'm putting on as much pressure as I dare. When the salmon flips into a little side pool, the bear takes matters into her own hands, clambers over the rocks, pounces, nabs the salmon smartly behind the head and lumbers immediately to the bank. My leader snaps at once, and while Ms. Bear attends to the destruction of the fish, I tie on another fly and make some shambling headway downstream.

Yes, I worry about the hook still in the fish, but only because I do not want this bear to be irritated by anything. I want her to be replete[10] and smug and doze off in the sun. I try to telepathize as much. Please, Bear, sleep.

Inevitably, the fishing slows down, but Ms. Bear does not seem to mind. Again she belches. Myself, I am getting quite a headache and know that I am fighting exhaustion. On a normal morning of humping along in waders over these slippery, softball-sized rocks, I would be tired in any case. The added emergency is foreclosing on my energy reserves. I even find myself getting a little angry, frustrated at least, and I marvel at the bear's persistence, her inexhaustible doggedness. And appetite. I catch fish; I toss them to her. At supermarket prices, I calculate she has eaten about six hundred dollars' worth of fish. The calculating gives me something to think about besides my fear.

At last I am immediately across from the opening to the trail which twines back through the woods to where my camper rests in the dapple shade of mighty pines. Still, five hundred yards separate me from this imagined haven. I entertain the notion perhaps someone else will come along and frighten the bear away, maybe someone with a dog or a gun, but I have already spent many days here without seeing another soul, and in fact have chosen to return here for that very reason. I have told myself for many years that I really do love nature, love being among the animals, am restored by wilderness adventure. Considering that right now I would like nothing better than to be nestled beside my wife in front of a blazing fire, this seems to be a sentiment in need of some revision.

---
10. **replete:** well-filled.

WORDS TO KNOW
burly (bûr′lē) *adj.* big and muscular
smug (smŭg) *adj.* self-satisfied

305

Critical Thinking: ANALYZING

K Students might be unclear about the reference to "bear-poaching Indians." If so, help them understand that poaching is trapping or killing wild animals illegally. Given the Alaskan setting, it is possible that there could be Native Americans in the vicinity of the river. However, the phrase seems to owe as much to stereotypical notions of Indians as it does to realism.

Active Reading: PREDICT

L Ask students to make predictions about how the story will unfold. If they need help, share the following thought processes with them:

Think-Aloud Model *I'm really not sure what will happen next. The narrator was lucky to distract one bear with fish, but two might prove too much. And he's already said how tired he's getting. Maybe this will push him to make some sort of getaway.*

CUSTOMIZING FOR
Students Acquiring English

7 The narrator makes a pun with the word *bear*. A pun is the humorous use of a word that suggests two meanings. *Bearing* refers to the way someone stands and presents himself or herself. When the narrator says "pardon the expression," he points out the pun.

Copyright © Charles Reid.

Now, as if in answer to my speculations, the bear turns beside me, her rump pushing me into water deeper than I want to be in, where my footing is shaky, and she stares into the woods, ears forward. She has heard something I cannot hear, or smelled something I cannot smell, and while I labor back to shallower water and surer footing, I hope some backpackers or some bear-poaching Indians are about to appear and send Ms. Bear a-galloping away. Automatically, I continue casting, but I also cannot help glancing over my shoulder in hopes of seeing what Ms. Bear sees. And in a moment I do.

It is another bear.

Unconsciously, I release a low moan, but my voice is lost in the guttural warning of Ms. Bear to the trespasser. The new arrival answers with a defiant cough. He—I believe it is a he—can afford to be defiant because he is half again as large as my companion. His fur seems longer and coarser, and though its substance is as golden as that of the bear beside me, the tips are black, and this dark surface ripples and undulates over his massive frame. His nostrils are flared, and he is staring with profound concentration at me.

Now I am truly confused and afraid. Would it be better to catch another salmon or not? I surely cannot provide for two of these beasts and in any case Mister Bear does not seem the type to be distracted by or made friendly by any measly salmon tribute. His whole bearing—pardon the expression—tells me my intrusion into this bear world is a personal affront[11] to his bear honor. Only Ms. Bear stands between us and, after all, whose side is she really on? By bear standards, I am sure a rather regal and handsome fellow has made his appearance. Why should the fur-covered heart of furry Ms. Bear go out to me? How much love can a few hundred dollars' worth of salmon buy? Most likely, this couple even have a history, know and have known each other from other seasons, even though for the

---

11. **affront:** insult.

WORDS TO KNOW	
speculation (spĕk′yə-lā′shən) *n.* a thought or idea
profound (prə-found′) *adj.* deep

306

Mini-Lesson The Writer's Style

SHOW, DON'T TELL Explain that good writers know that it is not enough to tell a reader that an event occurred or that an emotion was felt. Rather, a writer must *show* the reader the feeling or event (or the opinion, idea, comparison and contrast, or cause and effect) in action. For example, Abel does not merely tell the reader that the fisherman is frightened when the second bear appears. Instead he uses sensory details that show the reader his fear: "Unconsciously, I release a low moan, but my voice is lost in the guttural warning of Ms. Bear to the trespasser."

Application Have students identify other examples of the author's use of sensory details to show the reader a feeling, event, or idea. Then have them write a few paragraphs describing a humorous event they experienced. Before students begin writing, they can brainstorm a list of sensory details and vivid adjectives and adverbs.

Reteaching/Reinforcement
- Writing Handbook, anthology, p. 833
- *Writing Mini-Lesson* transparencies, p. 46

Show, Don't Tell, pp. 262–266

moment they prefer to pretend to regard each other as total strangers.

How disturbed I am is well illustrated by my next course of action. It is completely irrational, and I cannot account for it, or why it saved me—if indeed it did. I cranked in my line and laid my rod across some rocks, then began the arduous process of pulling myself out of my waders while trying to balance myself on those awkward rocks in that fast water. I tipped and swayed as I tugged at my boots, pushed my waders down, my arms in the foaming, frigid water, then the waders also filling, making it even more difficult to pull my feet free.

I emerged like a nymph from a cocoon, wet and trembling. The bears regarded me with clear stupefaction, as if one of them had casually stepped out of his or her fur. I drained what water I could from the waders, then dropped my fly rod into them and held them before me. The rocks were brutal on my feet, but I marched toward the trail opening, lifting and dropping first one, then the other leg of my waders as if I were operating a giant puppet. The water still in the waders gave each footfall an impressive authority, and I was half thinking that, well, if the big one attacks, maybe he'll be fooled into chomping the waders first and I'll at least now be able to run. I did not relish the idea of pounding down the trail in my nearly bare feet, but it was a better way to argue with the bear than being sucked from my waders like a snail from its shell. Would you have done differently?

Who knows what the bears thought, but I tried to make myself look as much as possible like a camel or some other extreme and inedible form of four-footedness as I plodded along the trail. The bears looked at each other, then at me as I clomped by, the water in the waders making an odd gurgling sound, and me making an odd sound, too, on remembering just then how the Indians would, staring death in the eye, sing their death song. Having no such melody prepared, and never having been anything but a bathtub singer, I chanted forth the only song I ever committed to memory: "Jingle Bells."

Yes, "Jingle Bells," I sang, "jingle all the way," and I lifted first one, then the other wader leg and dropped it stomping down. "Oh what fun it is to ride in a one-horse open sleigh-ay!"

APPETIZER **307**

Literary Concept: PLOT

P Urge students to note that the narrative's action is rising to its climax. Invite students to comment on what they are most interested in finding out at this point. *(Possible responses: Does the narrator get away safely? If so, how does he do it? What happens to the bears?)*

Critical Thinking: ANALYZING

Q Ask students to share their ideas about why Robert Abel chose to make this question a separate paragraph. *(Possible responses: The sentence on its own really stands out, so the reader is especially curious about what the author saw. The question works like a pause—the reader can sit with the narrator in the camper for a moment and stare at the bear fur covering the windshield.)*

The exercise was to prove to me just how complicated and various is the nature of the bear. The male reared up, blotting out the sun, bellowed, then twisted on his haunches and crashed off into the woods. The female, head cocked in curiosity, followed at a slight distance, within what still might be called striking distance whether I was out of my waders or not. Truly, I did not appreciate her persistence. Hauling the waders half full of water before me was trying work, and the superfluous thought struck me: suppose someone sees me now, plumping along like this, singing "Jingle Bells," a bear in attendance? Vanity, obviously, never sleeps. But as long as the bear kept her distance, I saw no reason to change my modus operandi.[12]

When I came within about one hundred feet of my camper, its white cap gleaming like a remnant of spring snow and beckoning me, I risked everything, dropped the waders and sped for the cab. The bear broke into a trot, too, I was sure, because although I couldn't see her, had my sights locked on the gleaming handle to the pickup door, I sure enough could hear those big feet slapping the ground behind me in a heavy rhythm, a terrible and elemental beat that sang to me of my own frailty, fragile bones and tender flesh. I plunged on like a madman, grabbed the camper door and hurled myself in.

I lay on the seat panting, curled like a child, shuddered when the bear slammed against the pickup's side. The bear pressed her nose to the window, then, curiously, unceremoniously licked the glass with her tongue. I know (and you know) she could have shattered the glass with a single blow, and I tried to imagine what I should do if indeed she resorted to this simple expedient. Fisherman that I am, I had nothing in the cab of the truck to defend myself with except a tire iron, and that not readily accessible behind the seat I was cowering on. My best defense, obviously, was to start the pickup and drive away.

Just as I sat up to the steering wheel and inserted the key, however, Ms. Bear slammed her big paws onto the hood and hoisted herself aboard. The pickup shuddered with the weight of her, and suddenly the windshield was full of her golden fur. I beeped the horn loud and long numerous times, but this had about the same effect as my singing, only caused her to shake her huge head, which vibrated the truck terribly. She stomped around on the hood and then lay down, back against the windshield, which now appeared to have been covered by a huge shag rug.

Could I believe my eyes?

No, I could not believe my eyes. My truck was being smothered in bear. In a moment I also could not believe my ears—Ms. Bear had decided the camper hood was the perfect place for a nap, and she was snoring, snoring profoundly, her body twitching like a cat's. Finally, she had responded to my advice and desires, but at the most inappropriate time. I was trapped. Blinded by bear body!

12. **modus operandi** (mōʹdəs ŏpʹə-rănʹdē): a way of doing something.

WORDS TO KNOW
superfluous (so͞o-pûrʹflo͞o-əs) *adj.* unnecessary; extra
resort (rĭ-zôrtʹ) *v.* (followed by *to*) to turn to

308

Mini-Lesson: Speaking, Listening, and Viewing

INTERVIEWS Point out to students that by interviewing people, they can learn a great deal about other people's frightening experiences with animals. Remind students how important good listening is to the interview process. Really listening to the speaker allows an interviewer to ask questions that occur to him or her on the spot. However, remind students that it is always useful to prepare a few questions before the interview. By doing this, an interviewer will never be without questions to ask.

Application Have students interview their peers and others to collect several narratives about frightening or unusual encounters with animals. Students can transcribe parts of the completed interviews or play the recording of the interview for classmates.

My exhaustion had been doubled by my sprint for the camper, and now that I was not in such a desperate panic, I felt the cold of the water that had soaked my clothes, and I began to tremble. It also crossed my mind that perhaps Mister Bear was still in the vicinity, and if Ms. Bear was not smart enough, or cruel enough, to smash my window to get at me, he just might be.

Therefore, I started the engine—which disturbed Ms. Bear not a whit—and rolled down the window enough to stick my head out and see down the rocky, limb-strewn trail. I figured a few jolts in those ruts and Ms. Bear would be off like a shot.

This proved a smug assumption. Ms. Bear did indeed awaken and bestir herself to a sitting position, a bit like an overgrown hood ornament, but quickly grew quite adept at balancing herself against the lurching and jolting of my truck, which, in fact, she seemed to enjoy. Just my luck, I growled, to find the first bear in Alaska who wanted a ride into town. I tried some quick braking and sharp-turn maneuvers I thought might send her tumbling off, but her bulk was so massive, her paws so artfully spread, that she was just too stable an entity. She wanted a ride, and there was nothing I could do about it.

When I came out of the woods to the gravel road known locally as the Dawson Artery, I had an inspiration. I didn't drive so fast that if Ms. Bear decided to clamber down, she would be hurt, but I did head for the main road which led to Buckville and the Buckville Cannery. Ms. Bear swayed happily along the whole ten miles to that intersection and seemed not to bat an eye when first one big logging truck, then another, plummeted by. I pulled out onto the highway, and for the safety of both of us—those logging trucks have dubious brakes, and their drivers get paid by the trip—I had to accelerate considerably.

I couldn't see much of Ms. Bear except her back and rump, as I had to concentrate on the road, some of which is pretty curvy in that coastal area, shadowed also by the giant pines. But from the attitude expressed by her posture, I'd say she was having a whale, or should I say a salmon, of a time. I saw a few cars and pickups veering out of the oncoming lane onto the shoulder as we swept by, but I didn't have time, really, to appreciate the astonishment of their drivers. In this way, my head out the window, Ms. Bear perched on the hood, I drove to the Buckville Cannery and turned into the long driveway.

Ms. Bear knew right away something good was ahead, for she rose on all fours now and stuck her nose straight out like a bird dog on a pheasant. Her legs quivered with nervous anticipation as we approached, and as soon as I came out of the trees into the parking area, she went over the front of the camper like someone plunging into a pool.

Don't tell me you would have done any differently. I stopped right there and watched Ms. Bear march down between the rows of cars and right up the truck ramp into the cannery itself. She was not the least bit intimidated by all the noise of the machines and the grinders and stampers in there, or the shouting of the workers.

Now the Buckville Cannery isn't that big—I imagine about two dozen people work there on any given day—and, since it is so remote, has no hurricane fence around it and no security guard. After all, what's anybody going to steal out of there besides a few cases of canned salmon or some bags of frozen fish parts that will soon become some company's cat food? The main

WORDS TO KNOW
dubious (dōō′bē-əs) *adj.* of questionable value or quality

309

Critical Thinking: ANALYZING

U Ask students to explain why this action of the bear's is ironic. *(Possible response: It is ironic because the bear is driven away by the lunch whistle after two solid hours of eating fish.)*

STRATEGIC READING FOR
Less-Proficient Readers

V Have students explain what happened at the cannery. *(The bear ate fish for two hours before being driven away by the lunch whistle. The narrator slipped away to a hotel in all the confusion and chose not to tell anyone what happened.)* Summarizing/Drawing Conclusions

CUSTOMIZING FOR
Gifted and Talented Students

Invite students to rewrite an event from Robert Abel's story with a different tone. Have them consider how the effect of the story would be different if they adopted a sad, serious, or angry tone.

COMPREHENSION CHECK
1. What does the narrator throw to the bear in hopes that it won't attack him? *(fish)*
2. Why does the narrator compare the bear to "a rude uncle at a Christmas dinner"? *(The bear belches after consuming a large quantity of food.)*
3. What new arrival makes the narrator change his strategy? *(a second, larger bear)*
4. How does the narrator get rid of the bear? *(He drives it to a cannery where the bear leaves him in search of more fish.)*

---

building is up on a little hill, and conveyors run down from there to the docks where the salmon boats pull in—the sea is another half mile away—and unload their catch.

I would say that in about three minutes after Ms. Bear walked into the cannery, twenty of the twenty-four workers were climbing out down the conveyors, dropping from open windows, or charging out the doors. The other four just hadn't got wind of the event yet, but in a little while they came bounding out, too, one fellow pulling up his trousers as he ran. They all assembled on the semicircular drive before the main office and had a union meeting of some vigor.

Myself, I was too tired to participate, and in any case did not want to be held liable for the disturbance at the Buckville Cannery, and so I made a U-turn and drove on into Buckville itself, where I took a room above the Buckville Tavern and had a hot shower and a really nice nap. That night in the Tap and Lounge I got to hear many an excited story about the she-bear who freeloaded at the cannery for a couple of hours before she was driven off by blowing, ironically enough, the lunch whistle loud and long. I didn't think it was the right time or place to testify to my part in that historical event, and for once kept my mouth shut. You don't like trouble any more than I do, and I'm sure you would have done about the same. ❖

310 UNIT THREE PART 1: STRUGGLING FOR SURVIVAL

Mini-Lesson Spelling

WORDS ENDING IN -ate AND -ion Explain to students that -ate is a verb ending, whereas -ion is a noun ending. Often the noun endings can be added to the verb form (dropping the silent e) to create the noun form. For instance, the ending -ion can be added to the verb *irritate* to create the noun *irritation*. When this suffix is added, the hard t sound softens so that the suffix is pronounced *shun*.

Application Have students change verbs into nouns or nouns into verbs as needed to complete this chart.

Verb	Noun
concentrate	
	speculation
	situation
perpetuate	
frustrate	
	communication
accelerate	

Reteaching/Reinforcement
• *Unit Three Resource Book*, p. 13

RESPONDING OPTIONS

FROM PERSONAL RESPONSE TO CRITICAL ANALYSIS

REFLECT
1. How many stars did you give this story? Compare your evaluation with those of your classmates.

RETHINK
Thematic Link

2. What do you think was the author's main purpose for writing this story? How well has he achieved that purpose?

3. What is your evaluation of the narrator as he struggles to survive?
   Consider
   - his response to the presence of "Ms. Bear"
   - his decision to leave "Ms. Bear" at the cannery
   - his decision to keep quiet about his adventure

4. The narrator repeatedly suggests that he is doing what you would do if you were in his situation. Do you agree with him? Why or why not?

5. In your opinion, is this story believable? Why or why not?

RELATE
6. What kinds of problems arise when wild animals venture into areas inhabited mostly by people or when people venture into areas inhabited mostly by wild animals? Discuss examples you've heard or read about.

Multimodal Learning
ANOTHER PATHWAY

Create a comic strip that shows the events of this story. Before drawing, skim the story to plan how many frames you will need and what image each frame will show.

LITERARY CONCEPTS

The **tone** of a work of literature is an expression of the writer's attitude toward his or her subject. The tone might be admiring, joyful, humorous, sad, or angry. The tone of "Appetizer" is humorous—almost tongue-in-cheek. How does Abel achieve this tone?

LITERARY LINKS

Compare the narrator's situation in this story with that of the narrator in "Collecting Team" or the narrator in "The Inn of Lost Time." Evaluate which situation is the most threatening. Do the narrators have control over the outcome?

QUICKWRITES

1. Write a **news article** for a local paper about the bear's sudden appearance at the cannery. Answer the questions *who, what, when, where, why,* and *how* in your article.

2. When the narrator returns home, his wife will undoubtedly ask him about the damage to the truck. Write a **dialogue** that might take place between the narrator and his wife.

📁 **PORTFOLIO** Save your writing. You may want to use it later as a springboard to a piece for your portfolio.

APPETIZER **311**

Eyewitness Report, pp. 54–59
Dialogue, pp. 324–327

From Personal Response to Critical Analysis

1. Answers should range from one to five stars.
2. Possible response: I think that the author wanted to entertain his readers. He succeeded because the story's mixture of humor and suspense makes it enjoyable to read.
3. Possible responses: The narrator shows courage, discipline, and self-control as he calmly continues fishing and feeding the bear. Also, his escape and his dropping the bear off at the cannery show ingenuity and boldness.
4. Responses will vary.
5. Encourage students to cite specific passages from the text.
6. Possible response: Problems arise when animals wander into inhabited areas because they are disoriented and scared. People often use poor judgment about wild animals and get too close to them and try to feed them or befriend them.

Another Pathway

Before they begin, remind students that they should identify the story's most important scenes, images, and events and make a plan that outlines them. Then they can begin to draw the comic strip.

Rubric

3 Full Accomplishment Student creates a comic strip that conveys the major events of the narrative.

2 Substantial Accomplishment Student creates a comic strip that conveys most major events.

1 Little or Partial Accomplishment Student has difficulty identifying the story's major events.

Literary Links

The fisherman knows his adversary, whereas Gus and his peers in "Collecting Team" do not know theirs until it is too late. The narrator in "The Inn of Lost Time" is also unsure of his adversary. None of the narrators has control over his situation, but the space travelers' situation is possibly the most threatening because they are in conflict with beings that are vastly more powerful.

Literary Concepts

Suggest that students look through the selection to find examples of Abel's use of exaggerations and wisecracks, similes and other descriptive details, and names such as "Ms. Bear." Ask students to explain how these techniques help to achieve a humorous tone.

QuickWrites

1. Students can role-play the reporter and various cannery employees to help them imagine details of the encounter with the bear.
2. Encourage students to improvise the dialogue out loud and jot down any ideas that seem especially promising. Point out that the narrator may not want to come clean with the story at the start of the conversation.

THE LANGUAGE OF LITERATURE TEACHER'S EDITION **311**

Words to Know

1. c   6. b
2. d   7. c
3. a   8. a
4. a   9. d
5. c   10. b

Reteaching/Reinforcement
• *Unit Three Resource Book*, p. 14

Across the Curriculum

Science Cooperative Learning
Groups may choose to divide research efforts by subject (hibernation, food) or by source (books, magazines, CD-ROM). As they create the pamphlet, individual group members should take the roles of writer, illustrator, mapmaker, layout designer, and project coordinator.

ADDITIONAL SUGGESTION

Geography *The 49th State* Have students research and report on the climatic, geographical, and geological aspects of Alaska. Students might include information on glaciers, various lakes and mountains, wildlife, and permafrost.

ROBERT H. ABEL

One of Robert H. Abel's missions in life was "to teach my children to be good and kind people." Abel once quipped that "writing is painfully hard work—instant backaches, sudden needs for a cup of tea . . . but there are lovely moments when the moon is right or something, and it all comes out right."

Multimodal Learning

ACROSS THE CURRICULUM

Science *Cooperative Learning* With a small group of classmates, gather additional information about the Alaskan brown bear—including its period of hibernation, its food, its behavior, and its relationship with humans. Using a desktop computer program if possible, create a pamphlet about the brown bear. Include drawings, maps, and copies of photographs.

WORDS TO KNOW

On a separate sheet of paper, write the letter of the word or phrase that is most closely associated with each word or phrase in dark print.

1. **burly:** (a) skinny, (b) curly, (c) strong, (d) handsome
2. **nostalgia:** (a) forgetfulness, (b) goals, (c) cleverness, (d) memories
3. **assess:** (a) judge, (b) panic, (c) regret, (d) hesitate
4. **furtively:** (a) secretively, (b) properly, (c) uncontrollably, (d) proudly
5. **smug:** (a) polluted, (b) photographed, (c) proud, (d) insecure
6. **speculation:** (a) escape, (b) idea, (c) statement, (d) condition
7. **profound:** (a) discovered, (b) favorable, (c) intense, (d) skilled
8. **superfluous:** (a) extra, (b) persistent, (c) scientific, (d) required
9. **resort to:** (a) commune with, (b) talk to, (c) attach to, (d) turn to
10. **dubious:** (a) unintelligent, (b) unreliable, (c) inactive, (d) threatening

ROBERT H. ABEL

Like the narrator of "Appetizer," Robert H. Abel is an avid fisherman, although he has competed for stream space with a bear only in his fiction. Abel recalls a happy small-town childhood in Ohio, where he was surrounded by relatives, including an uncle who taught him to fish. In elementary school he rewrote fairy tales "so the ending would turn out to my liking."

"I had my eyes on becoming a writer by the time I went to college," Abel says. After college, his work as a journalist and a college English teacher left him little time to write. Now, however,

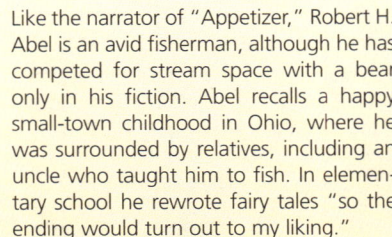

1941–

having settled in North Hadley, Massachusetts, he writes most of the time and teaches only occasionally.

Abel has published two volumes of short stories, one of which won the 1989 Flannery O'Connor Award for Short Fiction. He has also written a radio play, two novels, and many articles. Abel's work has appeared in several anthologies and literary magazines.

OTHER WORKS *Full-Tilt Boogie and Other Stories, Freedom Dues; or, A Gentleman's Progress in the New World* *Extended Reading*

Alternative Activities

Invite students to research salmon fishing as both a commercial industry and as a private sport. Encourage students to consider the various debates surrounding fishing. For instance, animal rights groups view sport fishing as cruel. At the same time, environmentalists are concerned that commercial fishing depletes the supply of fish too quickly. Industrialists and private fishermen are in conflict over the use of waterways. Students may choose to present their research in the form of an oral presentation, how-to guidebook, or annotated fishing supply catalog.

PREVIEWING

POETRY

Mother to Son
Langston Hughes

the lesson of the moth
Don Marquis

Activating Prior Knowledge
PERSONAL CONNECTION

How do you approach life? Use the scales shown here to illustrate your basic attitudes. On a sheet of paper, copy the words expressing opposing attitudes and the lines that connect them. Then place an X on each line to show where your attitude lies. For example, are you usually optimistic, expecting the best to happen, or pessimistic, bracing for the worst? Compare your attitude scales with those of a few classmates.

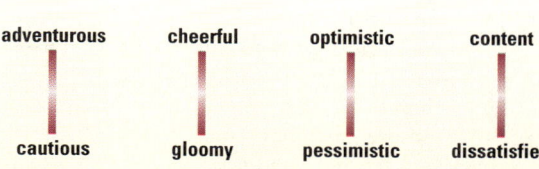

Building Background
LITERARY CONNECTION

In the poems you are about to read, Langston Hughes and Don Marquis make effective use of two very different speakers to express attitudes toward life. The speaker of Hughes's "Mother to Son" is a woman who has had a hard life. The poet presents her speech in her own dialect—a form of presentation he employed from the start of his career.

An insect is the speaker of much of Marquis's verse, including "the lesson of the moth." Marquis humorously insisted that his poems were written by a cockroach named archy. Unable to use the shift key, archy could type no capital letters, quotation marks, or question marks. Without these, and without other punctuation, the poem engagingly presents two contrasting philosophies of life.

Setting a Purpose
WRITING CONNECTION

An **aphorism** is a short sentence that expresses a truth or a clever observation. Marquis uses an aphorism in his poem to present one attitude toward life—"come easy go easy." Write an aphorism that expresses one of your basic attitudes.

MOTHER TO SON / THE LESSON OF THE MOTH **313**

OVERVIEW

Objectives
- To understand and appreciate two poems about two very different ways to live
- To identify and understand extended metaphor
- To express understanding of the poems through a choice of writing forms, including a poem and a monologue
- To extend understanding of the poems through a variety of multimodal and cross-curricular activities

Skills

LITERARY CONCEPTS
- Extended metaphor
- Form

SPEAKING, LISTENING, AND VIEWING
- Group discussion
- Oral presentation

Cross-Curricular Connections

SCIENCE
- Moths

GEOGRAPHY
- Harlem

PRINT AND MEDIA RESOURCES

UNIT THREE RESOURCE BOOK
Strategic Reading: Literature, p. 17

ACCESS FOR STUDENTS ACQUIRING ENGLISH
Reading and Writing Support

FORMAL ASSESSMENT
Selection Test, pp. 59–60
 Test Generator

 AUDIO LIBRARY
See Reference Card

 INTERNET RESOURCES
McDougal Littell Literature Center at http://www.hmco.com/mcdougal/lit

Mother to Son

by Langston Hughes

Stairs, Provincetown (1920), Charles Demuth. Gouache and pencil on cardboard, 23½ × 19½ (59.7 × 49.5 cm). The Museum of Modern Art, New York. Gift of Abby Aldrich Rockefeller. Photograph Copyright © 1995 The Museum of Modern Art, New York.

Well, son, I'll tell you:
Life for me ain't been no crystal stair.
It's had tacks in it,
And splinters,
And boards torn up,   5
And places with no carpet on the floor—
Bare.
But all the time
I'se been a-climbin' on,
And reachin' landin's,   10
And turnin' corners,
And sometimes goin' in the dark
Where there ain't been no light.
So boy, don't you turn back.
Don't you set down on the steps   15
'Cause you finds it's kinder hard.
Don't you fall now—
For I'se still goin', honey,
I'se still climbin',
And life for me ain't been no crystal stair.   20

FROM PERSONAL RESPONSE TO CRITICAL ANALYSIS

REFLECT   1. What is your first reaction to the mother in this poem? Write your thoughts in your notebook.

RETHINK   2. Do you agree with the advice the mother gives her son? Why or why not?

3. What does the mother suggest by the image of a "crystal staircase"? By contrast, what kind of staircase has her life been?
   Consider
   - what crystal (very clear, brilliant glass) brings to mind
   - the kind of life the mother has lived
   - how she has handled the obstacles in her life

the lesson of the moth

by Don Marquis

i was talking to a moth
the other evening
he was trying to break into
an electric light bulb
5 and fry himself on the wires

why do you fellows
pull this stunt i asked him
because it is the conventional
thing for moths or why
10 if that had been an uncovered
candle instead of an electric
light bulb you would
now be a small unsightly cinder
have you no sense

15 plenty of it he answered
but at times we get tired
of using it
we get bored with the routine
and crave beauty
20 and excitement
fire is beautiful
and we know that if we get
too close it will kill us
but what does that matter
25 it is better to be happy

Multicultural Perspectives

HUGHES AND THE HARLEM RENAISSANCE There was an extraordinary flowering of culture and art by African Americans in the 1920s. Langston Hughes was perhaps the leading literary figure in this movement, which was centered in New York City's Harlem and came to be known as the Harlem Renaissance.

Other important figures were the poets Jean Toomer, Claude McKay, and Countee Cullen; visual artists James Van Der Zee, Aaron Douglas, and Jacob Lawrence; novelists Zora Neale Hurston and Wallace Thurman; musicians Paul Robeson and Marian Anderson; and the scholar Alain Locke.

The Harlem Renaissance gave African-American artists a valuable sense of community. They found an environment that supported and strengthened them personally and professionally. This sense of solidarity was something African-American artists had rarely felt before in America.

Art Note

Candle, Eigg by Winifred Nicholson
This vibrant, abstract image by British artist Winifred Nicholson (1893–1981) suggests the heat, light, and vitality of a flame. The painting's candle—which burns yellow and orange—is positioned in the canvas's center and is framed by lines that could represent a window. The blue and violet hues of the foreground contrast with the remaining two-thirds of the canvas and suggest night and the absence of light and heat. The title refers to the Isle of Eigg, where the artist had a house.

Reading the Art *How would you describe this painting to someone who had never seen it? In your opinion, what is it "about"? How does the candle in Nicholson's painting resemble the flame in Marquis's poem?*

CUSTOMIZING FOR
Students Acquiring English

2 Ask a student to paraphrase "you would now be a small unsightly cinder." *(Possible response: The moth would have burned itself in the flame.)*

Literary Concept: FORM

B The form of this poem—the arrangement of the words and lines on the page—is somewhat unusual. Ask students to describe the effect of Marquis's technique of continuing a single thought over several short lines without punctuation. *(Possible response: This technique keeps the reader alert and interested, for the poem "moves" very fast—it skitters around like a moth. The technique also tends to make the language sound like real speech.)* Ask students how the form of "the lesson of the moth" compares with the form of "Mother to Son." *(Possible response: In both poems the unique voice of the speaker is important, and short lines and irregular stanzas give both poems an easy, natural sound and appearance.)*

THE LANGUAGE OF LITERATURE TEACHER'S EDITION **315**

CUSTOMIZING FOR
Gifted and Talented Students

Ask students to think about how the effect of the poems would be different if they were more formal—if, for instance, they were written as sonnets.

CUSTOMIZING FOR
Multiple Learning Styles

C **Interpersonal Learners** Have pairs of students discuss their reactions to archy's and the moth's approaches to life. Have them address the question of whether they believe it is better to "be burned up with beauty/than to live a long time/and be bored all the while."

CUSTOMIZING FOR
Students Acquiring English

3 Explain that *shoot the roll* means "to try for it all."

4 Mention the expression "easy come, easy go." Show students how the poet varies the expression here.

Critical Thinking:
MAKING JUDGMENTS

D Ask students whether they agree that human beings are "too civilized to enjoy themselves." *(Possible responses: Human beings have lost touch with their instincts, and they are too worried about being polite and "acceptable." The moth is wrong, because I know human beings who have exactly his philosophy of life—they're not too civilized to enjoy themselves.)*

COMPREHENSION CHECK
1. What has the speaker of "Mother to Son" done even when "there ain't been no light"? (climbed the "staircase")
2. What happens to the moth? (It dies in the flame of a lighter.)

Candle, Eigg (1980), Winifred Nicholson. 58 × 43 cm, private collection. Photo by John Webb. Copyright © The artist's family.

for a moment
and be burned up with beauty
than to live a long time
and be bored all the while
30 so we wad all our life up
into one little roll
and then we shoot the roll
that is what life is for
it is better to be a part of beauty
35 for one instant and then cease to
exist than to exist forever
and never be a part of beauty
our attitude toward life
is come easy go easy
40 we are like human beings
used to be before they became
too civilized to enjoy themselves

and before i could argue him
out of his philosophy
45 he went and immolated[1] himself
on a patent cigar lighter
i do not agree with him
myself i would rather have
half the happiness and twice
50 the longevity[2]

but at the same time i wish
there was something i wanted
as badly as he wanted to fry himself
archy

---
1. **immolated** (ĭm′ə-lā′tĭd): killed by burning.
2. **longevity** (lŏn-jĕv′ĭ-tē): length of life.

Mini-Lesson Literary Concepts

REVIEWING FORM Remind students that the form of a poem is the physical arrangement of its words and lines on the page. Poets make choices about the form of their poems. Some poems follow a predictable pattern, such as having the same number of syllables in each line and the same number of lines in each stanza. Other poems have an irregular form.

Application Have students describe the form of "Mother to Son" and "the lesson of the moth." Encourage them to notice the irregular forms of these two poems, including the use of short lines, irregular stanzas, and (in Marquis's work) a lack of punctuation. Have them compare the poems in a chart like the one shown.

Mother/Son	Moth
mixes short and long lines	short lines
one long stanza	irregular stanzas
punctuation	lack of punctuation

RESPONDING OPTIONS

FROM PERSONAL RESPONSE TO CRITICAL ANALYSIS

REFLECT 1. Jot down several words that describe your reaction to "the lesson of the moth."

RETHINK 2. Do you think most people share the moth's attitude toward life? Why or why not?
Consider
Close Textual Reading
- the opinions the moth expresses in lines 25–29 and 40–42
- archy's reaction in lines 51–53

3. Look again at the attitude scales you made for the Personal Connection on page 313. Are you more like archy or the moth? Explain your answer.

RELATE 4. In your opinion, would the moth have helpful advice about life to offer the mother in "Mother to Son"? Why or why not? Imagine the mother's encounter with the moth and illustrate it.

Thematic Link
5. How does each of these poems relate to the theme of this part of Unit Three, "Struggling for Survival"? Are the speakers' struggles similar or different? Explain your answer.

Multimodal Learning
ANOTHER PATHWAY
Cooperative Learning

With a small group of classmates, discuss which of these poems you consider to be more optimistic about life. Think about both the positive and the negative images in each poem, and draw pictures of them on poster board or the chalkboard. Also consider the speakers' attitudes.

QUICKWRITES

1. Using an extended metaphor, compose a **poem** titled "Father to Daughter"—or one that deals with some other relationship you would enjoy writing about. In the poem, one person should share his or her attitude toward life with another.

2. Select an organism—plant or animal—other than a cockroach, and write a poetic or prose **monologue** in which the organism teaches a lesson or expresses an attitude toward life.

📁 **PORTFOLIO** Save your writing. You may want to use it later as a springboard to a piece for your portfolio.

LITERARY CONCEPTS

As you have learned, a metaphor involves a comparison between two different things. When a metaphor is continued for several lines or throughout a poem, it is called an **extended metaphor**. In "Mother to Son," what is the extended metaphor for the mother's life? What images are used to develop the metaphor? How well do you think the metaphor works?

MOTHER TO SON / THE LESSON OF THE MOTH 317

From Personal Response to Critical Analysis

1. Responses will vary.
2. Possible response: Although the majority of people probably share archy's point of view, some people might believe that a short life filled with beauty is preferable to a long, boring one.
3. Encourage students to review the poem for specific ideas that correspond to their own thoughts and feelings.
4. Possible response: The moth's advice probably would not help the mother, because the mother believes in endurance and perseverance.
5. Possible response: The mother struggles to survive both literally and spiritually, and the moth is struggling to live intensely—even if it means dying in the process. The speakers' struggles are different—the mother is struggling to provide for a family, whereas the moth's struggle to live brilliantly doesn't seem to be hindered by any family responsibilities.

Another Pathway

Cooperative Learning Before beginning their work, students should plan their group duties. A recorder can keep a list of "positive" and "negative" images in each of the two poems, while two other students illustrate these images. All group members should explain and support their opinions about the optimism of each poem before the group comes to some consensus on the question.

Rubric
3 Full Accomplishment Students list, illustrate, and thoroughly discuss the poems' images and messages to decide which is more optimistic.
2 Substantial Accomplishment Students list, illustrate, and discuss most of the poems' images and messages to decide which is more optimistic.
1 Little or Partial Accomplishment Students list, illustrate, and discuss a few of the poems' images and cannot decide which is more optimistic.

Literary Concepts

Encourage the whole class to discuss the poem, with one student recording suggestions on the chalkboard. Another student may also wish to act as a moderator, by calling on students and keeping order. Have students review the poem for details that support the extended metaphor. Invite students to debate the effectiveness of the poem's extended metaphor comparing life's struggles to a staircase.

QuickWrites

1. Encourage students to convey the personality of their subject, as well as his or her opinions about life. The person does not necessarily have to have strong or unusual attitudes.
2. Have students brainstorm a list of organisms and a list of personal qualities various organisms might possess. Then students can choose one that appeals to them most.

The Writer's Craft
Poetry, pp. 76–80
Scriptwriting, pp. 86–88

Across the Curriculum

Science *Cooperative Learning*
Encourage students to learn about the great variety (approximately 100,000 species) of moths. Divide the class into small groups of three or four. Each group can select a specific moth species to research. Groups should report on moths' benefits for humanity (silk production, weed control, and scientific research), as well as their drawbacks (destruction of plants and fabrics).

ADDITIONAL SUGGESTION

Geography *Harlem* Have students do research to make a map of the United States that shows the wide array of places from which African-American writers, visual artists, and performing artists came to Harlem during the Harlem Renaissance. Students can use colored string or yarn to mark each person's journey. Remind students to include a map key that indicates who is represented by a specific color.

LANGSTON HUGHES

Hughes once said that his poetry was about people such as "workers, roustabouts, and singers, and job hunters on Lenox Avenue in New York, or Seventh Street in Washington or South State in Chicago—people up today and down tomorrow, working this week and fired the next, beaten and baffled, but determined not to be wholly beaten, buying furniture on the installment plan, filling the house with roomers to help pay the rent, hoping to get a new suit for Easter—and pawning that suit before the Fourth of July." During his life Hughes was awarded a Guggenheim fellowship (1935), an American Academy of Arts and Letters grant (1947), and the NAACP's Spingarn Medal (1960).

DON MARQUIS

Early in his career, Don Marquis worked as an assistant to Joel Chandler Harris, the writer who adapted African-American legends to create the Uncle Remus stories. These stories feature talking animal characters, such as Br'er Rabbit and Br'er Fox, and could be the inspiration for Marquis's own use of animals as commentators on life.

Multimodal Learning

ALTERNATIVE ACTIVITIES

With a partner, rewrite one of these poems as a **rap song.** You may wish to find or compose appropriate music to accompany your lyrics. Perform the song for the class, having your performance recorded on videotape if possible.

ACROSS THE CURRICULUM

Science Did you know that the emperor moth has the most powerful sense of smell in nature? See what other surprising moth facts you can find. How many different kinds are there? How are they of benefit to human beings? Why are they drawn to light (often at their own peril)?

LANGSTON HUGHES

1902–1967

Langston Hughes was one of the first African Americans to earn his living solely from writing. Although he wrote novels, short stories, plays, song lyrics, newspaper columns, and radio scripts, he is best known for his poetry. Many of his poems reflect the speech patterns and jazz rhythms he heard on the streets of Harlem in New York City, where he lived as an adult.

Hughes had a lonely childhood, never receiving much support from his separated parents. For much of his youth, he lived like a nomad, moving from place to place. For a time, he lived with his grandmother, who introduced him to books.

After graduating from high school in Cleveland, Hughes spent a short and unhappy time in Mexico before enrolling at Columbia University in New York. He later dropped out and worked odd jobs. In Europe, he was robbed of everything he owned. When he returned to the United States, he began writing and eventually graduated from Lincoln University in Pennsylvania.

Hughes was "discovered" while working as a busboy. He left three of his poems at a table where the poet Vachel Lindsay was dining. Lindsay was impressed with the young poet's works and presented them at one of his own readings. Soon afterward, Hughes's writing career took off.

OTHER WORKS *Not Without Laughter, The Dream Keeper* Extended Reading

DON MARQUIS

1878–1937

One day "the biggest cockroach you ever saw" scampered across Don Marquis's desk at the offices of the *New York Sun,* giving Marquis the idea for a comic character—archy, the philosophical cockroach poet. Later, Marquis created mehitabel, a joyful, adventurous alley cat. Through such characters, Marquis expressed his views on life from 1912 to 1925 in his newspaper column, "Sun Dial." Of this column a well-known writer said, "Most of us didn't consult the leading editorials to know what to think. The almost universal reflex, in New York at any rate, was 'Let's see what Don says about it.'"

Before becoming a prosperous writer, Marquis held a variety of jobs, including drugstore clerk, truck driver, poultry plucker, short-order cook, and teacher. Considered one of America's finest humorists, Marquis wrote novels, plays, short stories, poems, and essays.

318 UNIT THREE PART 1: STRUGGLING FOR SURVIVAL

Alternative Activities

For a rap song based on "Mother to Son," students might decide that the son should be the "speaker" who reports the words of his mother. Some students might wish to add lines in which the son responds to certain ideas of his mother. If students decide to adapt "the lesson of the moth" into a rap song, they might wish to change certain phrases to create rhymes and particular rhythms. This rap could also feature two separate voices (and points of view) in conversation.

PREVIEWING

NONFICTION

Von

"Von," a Vietnamese youth interviewed by Janet Bode

Activating Prior Knowledge
PERSONAL CONNECTION

Imagine that, like the boy in this story, you must flee your country because of political unrest and the dangers of war. Not only are you faced with the uncertainty of what lies ahead, but you can take only one person with you. What will you do? Share your thoughts with the class.

Building Background
HISTORICAL CONNECTION

From 1954 to 1975, Vietnam, a small country in Southeast Asia, was divided into Communist-ruled North Vietnam and non-Communist South Vietnam. The Communists, however, began to wage a war to establish communism in the South. During the 1960s and 1970s, the United States and the South Vietnamese army tried to stop them, but by 1975 the Communists had taken control of the whole of Vietnam.

Like many Vietnamese, Von and his father fled the brutality of the Communists in a crowded, unsafe boat. Such "boat people" risked illness, drowning, and pirate attacks on the South China Sea. Many died. Those who survived went to refugee camps in other Southeast Asian countries until they could be relocated.

Active Reading/Setting a Purpose
READING CONNECTION

Predicting Good readers are active readers, gathering information as they read to predict the events in stories. In addition to predicting during reading, it is useful to begin making predictions before you read. Predict what problems emigrants like Von and his father might face as they leave their homeland, go on their journey, and try to adjust to a new country. Organize your ideas in a word web like the one shown here. Then, in your notebook, jot down predictions you make while you are reading the selection. After your reading, check to see whether your predictions were correct.

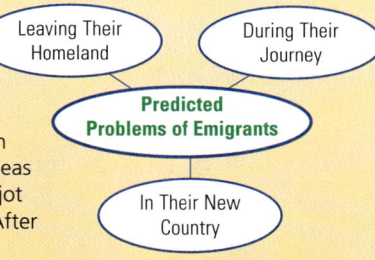

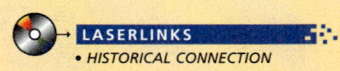
• HISTORICAL CONNECTION
319

OVERVIEW

Objectives
- To understand and appreciate an oral history about a South Vietnamese boy's escape to America
- To enrich reading by predicting outcomes
- To identify and understand an oral history
- To express understanding of the selection through a choice of writing forms, including a journal entry and a letter
- To extend understanding of oral history through a variety of multimodal and cross-curricular activities

Skills

READING SKILLS/STRATEGIES
- Predict

LITERARY CONCEPTS
- Oral history
- Motivation

SPEAKING, LISTENING, AND VIEWING
- Critical viewing
- Group discussion
- Oral presentation

THE WRITER'S STYLE
- Point of view

GRAMMAR
- Using quotation marks

SPELLING
- Final y words with suffixes

STUDY SKILLS
- Reference books

Cross-Curricular Connections

SOCIAL STUDIES
- Vietnamese culture

HISTORY
- Vietnam
- Protecting the rights of refugees

GEOGRAPHY
- Tropical heat

SCIENCE
- Grenades

MATHEMATICS
- Halfway across the globe

 HISTORICAL CONNECTION
Vietnamese Refugees These haunting photographs of Vietnamese adults and children will show students the plight of people forced to flee their homeland.

Side A, Frame 52686

PRINT AND MEDIA RESOURCES

UNIT THREE RESOURCE BOOK
Strategic Reading: Literature, p. 21
Reading SkillBuilder, p. 22
Spelling SkillBuilder, p. 23

GRAMMAR MINI-LESSONS
Transparencies, p. 33
Copymasters, p. 43

WRITING MINI-LESSONS
Transparencies, p. 47

ACCESS FOR STUDENTS ACQUIRING ENGLISH
Selection Summaries
Reading and Writing Support

FORMAL ASSESSMENT
Selection Test, pp. 61–62
 Test Generator

 **AUDIO LIBRARY**
See Reference Card

LASERLINKS
Historical Connection

THE LANGUAGE OF LITERATURE TEACHER'S EDITION **319**

VON

"Von," a Vietnamese youth as interviewed by Janet Bode

SUMMARY

South Vietnamese teenager Von was seven years old when Saigon fell to the Communists in 1975. Because his father feared for his life, he and Von fled the country, leaving the rest of his family behind. They escaped in a small boat, which was robbed by pirates. At last, a Red Cross ship saved them. After months in a refugee camp, Von and his father came to the United States, where they were sponsored and helped to adjust by members of a Detroit synagogue. Eventually Von became a U.S. citizen and prepared to enter a university. He hopes to bring the rest of his family to America someday.

Thematic Link: *Struggle for Survival* A South Vietnamese boy and his father struggle against natural, political, and social forces in their quest for freedom.

CUSTOMIZING FOR
Students Acquiring English

- Use **ACCESS FOR STUDENTS ACQUIRING ENGLISH,** *Reading and Writing Support.*

- Explain that American troops became involved in the war in Vietnam in the 1960s and early 1970s in support of the South Vietnamese. Von's father worked for the United States government during the fighting. This is why Von and his father were later given permission to come to the United States.

- Some students may have left a country that is in upheaval, or they may have left close family members behind in their native country. Ask students to compare and contrast their own experiences with Von's as they read, and invite volunteers to share their thoughts with a group or with the class after they have finished the selection.

① Make sure that students understand that in this context *fell* means "surrendered," not "fell down."

---

① On April 30, 1975, Saigon, the capital of South Vietnam, fell, ending this stage of the tragedy that by then had cost 1.3 million Vietnamese and 56,000 American lives. Von is a survivor of that war and the devastating years that followed. Today when you see him—slim, handsome, with an optimistic and ready grin—it's hard to imagine what his eyes have seen. Over a series of days, we met in hours sandwiched between his busy schedule of school and work. He begins at his beginning.

320 UNIT THREE PART 1: STRUGGLING FOR SURVIVAL

WORDS TO KNOW

ambassador (ăm-băs′ə-dər) *n.* a country's chief diplomatic official in a foreign land (p. 329)

visa (vē′zə) *n.* an official permission to leave or enter a country (p. 329)

Copyright © David Hartung/Gamma Liaison.

VON **321**

STRATEGIC READING FOR
Less-Proficient Readers

Set a Purpose Encourage students to become involved in the story by imagining that they are a newcomer in a foreign country. Ask them what problems they would expect to face. Then have them read to find out how Von's father gets into trouble and what convinces him that he cannot stay in Vietnam.

Use **UNIT THREE RESOURCE BOOK**, p. 21, for guidance in reading the selection.

CUSTOMIZING FOR
Gifted and Talented Students

Have students think about how they could transform Von's story into a dramatic monologue. Encourage them to think, as they read, about the particular scenes that would be especially entertaining or emotionally moving in a performance. Ask them how Von's unique speech patterns would affect the monologue. Ask them how Von's story could be made consistently interesting without elaborate sets or props.

Linking to History

The nation of Vietnam became officially divided by treaty into two separate countries in 1954. Thereafter, Communist North Vietnam and Communists in South Vietnam (known as the Viet Cong) fought to overthrow a series of non-Communist governments in South Vietnam that were supported by the United States, France, and others. President Richard Nixon withdrew most U.S. troops from Vietnam in 1973 and 1974. A year later, South Vietnam fell to the Communists.

Mini-Lesson Reading Skills/Strategies

PREDICTING Explain to students that noting the sequence of events can help them organize information more clearly so that they can make more precise predictions about events that will occur or be revealed later in a story.

Point out to students that it is important to pay attention to the sequence of events in biographies and autobiographies because events often are not revealed in the order in which they occur, or the chronological order. For example, this selection begins with Von in the United States. Then it goes back in time and outlines the events that led to Von's move to Detroit.

Application Encourage students to note the sequence of events as described by both Janet Bode and Von. Have them record the events on a time line or in a chart like the one shown.

Now have students add to or refine the predictions they made in their reading logs.

Reteaching/Reinforcement
• *Unit Three Resource Book*, p. 22

Event	When Occurred
Saigon falls	April 30, 1975
Bode and Von meet	not stated
move to Da Nang	1972

THE LANGUAGE OF LITERATURE TEACHER'S EDITION **321**

Literary Concept:
ORAL HISTORY

A Point out to students that oral histories include personal reactions and factual recollections. Ask students how the information contained in Janet Bode's italicized passage differs from that in Von's sections. *(Possible responses: The italicized sections provide background material and transitions from one part of Von's story to another. These sections summarize parts of Von's story.)*

CUSTOMIZING FOR
Students Acquiring English

2 Point out to students that the Communists were the North Vietnamese.

Active Reading: CONNECT

B Ask students what images, words, or phrases come into their mind when they hear the term *concentration camp*.

Linking to Science

C Grenades are small bombs—usually thrown by hand or shot from a gun—that detonate on impact or are controlled with a timing device. Usually a grenade is filled with pieces of metal or some gas or chemical.

STRATEGIC READING FOR
Less-Proficient Readers

D Check to see that students are clear about the basic events leading to the departure of Von and his father.

- Why is Von's father in trouble? *(He worked for the United States against the Communists; the Communists won the war and now can get revenge on those who fought against them.)* **Drawing Conclusions**

- What convinces Von's father that he cannot stay in Vietnam? *(He is told to "clean out the grenades" under the trees.)* **Relating Cause and Effect**

Set a Purpose Have students read to find out what leads to Von and his father meeting the German sailors and how Von and his father are treated by them.

I was born in Saigon. My father was a navy officer for South Vietnam. He worked for the United States government. I have three brothers and three sisters. I am number four. I'm the only one who came to America with my father. My mother and the rest of them are still in Vietnam. Sometimes on Sundays after church, my father and I talk about our past memories, what brought us here and of the future. I decided that someday I would like to write of my family, and of him and me together. You are the first person I ever told my family's story. . . .

A *In 1972, when Von was four years old, the family moved to Da Nang in the central part of the country. Von's earliest memories of the war were of hiding and eating in bomb shelters while waiting for the daily bombing raids to end.*

2 *When Saigon fell to the Communists in 1975, Von's father could have escaped to the United States, but he made his way back at great peril to rejoin his family. However, the Communists soon put Von's father in a "re-education center." At this center, actually a concentration camp, Von's father worked at hard labor from six in the morning until nine in the evening every day for three years, without breaks or vacations.*

In the meantime, Von's family had to sell everything they owned in order to get enough money to buy food. For several years, Von could no longer go to school, but he continued to try to read on his own. When Von's **B** *father was finally released from the concentration camp in 1978, the government told him he must take only one child and work in the countryside. Von and his father were sent to a place near the border, where fierce battles raged between Cambodia and Vietnam. "We were caught," Von says, "in the middle again."*

One day they told my father, "You, tomorrow, because you were an officer, you must go and clean out the grenades." The Cambodians put **C** grenades under the trees. They put boobytraps everywhere. In the morning when we went to the farms and started working, sometimes people blew up. They blew off their legs and their arms and often they get killed.

Of course my father didn't say "no" to them. He said, "When?" To me he said, "Oh, my God. I have to risk my life for this? NO! I can't take any more." My father, he could not sleep. He thought, it's my life. All this time I work to become a good man. I come back and for this? I will die for nothing? Should I leave or should I stay? If I stay, I will get killed. He kept what he planned a secret. He just said to me, "You and me, we're leaving. We must go back to your mother." **D**

At six o'clock in the morning, we were supposed to be in the mission at work. But at two o'clock at night, we left the house. They weren't strict with him anymore. They let him be free, because they knew him. They knew he'd been in a concentration camp. And they knew he was very good. They didn't think he would leave. It was dark out and I was afraid. Even in the countryside, they have security guards. We did not go on the road. We sneaked through the trees. Finally we got to a place where we could take a bus. We had little money left for the month, but I was so young, my father didn't have to pay for my bus ticket.

> *Should I leave or should I stay? If I stay, I will get killed.*

322 UNIT THREE PART 1: STRUGGLING FOR SURVIVAL

Mini-Lesson — Literary Concepts

REVIEWING MOTIVATION Remind students that a motivation is a reason that explains why a character in a narrative acts, feels, or thinks a certain way. Tell students that a character's motivation can be stated directly in a narrative or inferred by the reader based on the thoughts, dialogue and actions of the character.

Application Have students discuss the motivations for actions by Von and his father. Have them note especially important actions (such as leaving Vietnam) and the reasons that motivated them (the fear of Von's father for his life).

We got back to Saigon, but we could just see my mother for a few hours. It was too dangerous for everybody if we stayed. Too soon, he had to say to my mother, "I must leave you." To me he said, "I must take a younger son with me, you. I take you because you suffer so much. You have a feeling."

I always cared for my mother. I always helped her. My mother said to my father, "Von will be good." She was crying so much. She said, "This is right. This is the way we have to do it. You must leave me."

She said to me, "You take care of your father." And she told my father, "Take care of Von. Get him schooling." My brothers and sisters just looked at me. They were so sad. They knew we were leaving, even though my father didn't tell them. If he told them, they would say, "Why do you take Von? You don't love me?"

My mother said, "I love you." And we left.

At that time, many South Vietnamese people were trying to sneak out of the country. They were looking for navy men who knew how to row the boat, who knew how to get to Thailand. Do you know anything about the boat people? They make a boat and they sail and they try to get to freedom. My father was on the sea for almost twenty-five years. Some people learned this and they said to him, "We offer you a job. We make a fake ID for you and your son. We take care of a boat. We get food and you two can go with us."

My father said, "Okay." But somehow the Communists found out and took the boat and the money, too. He was afraid the government might be looking for him. "I must leave you," he told the people.

My father found another connection. This time poor, poor people came to him. They could pay him no money, but they had a boat. For three months, my father prepared. He mended the motor. He bought a map, a compass. Then with the boat, my father and I sneaked out to the river. We were picking up people as we were going along. People here, people there, all poor, country people who wanted to escape to a better life.

There were fifty-two people in a twelve-foot-long boat. We could not move. I sat with my knees in my face. I could not lie down. There were a lot of men, and a few women. There were some kids, but most of the people were in their early twenties. I was maybe eleven or twelve.

We left on a rainy night. There were military police boats out in the sea looking for the escape boats, looking for the boat people. But with the rain, they went inside. We go and go and go. One night and the next day in the evening, we went all the way down the river to the sea because my father rowed so fast. We go and go and go. We were going to Indonesia. My father knew we shouldn't go to Thailand, because there were a lot of pirates. Most of the people who went to Thailand got killed. After four days we saw a blinking light! Oh, we thought, that's an American ship! We first saw the light around two in the morning, and by six we could see the boat.

The boat was all black. It was so big and it said "Thailand" on it. My father told me, "They are dangerous people." We were afraid they would attack us. They know the boat people often have money and gold. . . . We only had one gun, a shotgun. The people were saying, "What should we do? Shoot them?"

My father said, "No, we cannot. There are

VON **323**

Mini-Lesson Grammar

USING QUOTATION MARKS Point out to students that quotation marks are used at the beginning and end of direct quotations. When writers use another person's exact written or spoken words, they are giving a direct quotation. In written interviews, rules involving capitalization and the use of quotation marks with other punctuation marks apply as usual.

Application Have students add, remove, or change the punctuation to make the following sentences correct.
1. I asked him "if he wanted to return to Vietnam."
2. I love soda Von said and I also love hamburgers.
3. The English teacher said what do you know about verbs?
4. Von said, I came home because you said, "that I should be home at 7:30."

- *Grammar Handbook*, pp. 898–899
- *Grammar Mini-Lessons* copymasters, p. 43, transparencies, p. 33

Quotation Marks, pp. 663–666

Active Reading: CLARIFY

E Have students think about Von's father's words in this passage. Then have them paraphrase his remarks to Von so that they clarify the possible meanings of the sentence, "You have a feeling." (*Von's father seems to imply that Von has suffered more than his siblings. The "feeling" could be some special sadness, fright, or sensitivity in Von that his father has noticed.*)

Literary Concept: ORAL HISTORY

F Point out that scenes of this type must have occurred often in the aftermath of the Vietnam War. Use the scene to help students focus on the special characteristics of an individual account of history as opposed to a conventional textbook history. (*Possible responses: It can give a more personal understanding of a historical event. It can show how an event felt to actual people.*)

Literary Concept: MOTIVATION

G Ask students to explain why Von's father takes so much time to prepare for the trip. (*Possible response: Because he was caught during his first attempt to flee, Von's father is determined to take more care this time. He patiently does the things necessary—improving or obtaining equipment and materials—to increase his chances of success.*)

CUSTOMIZING FOR Multiple Learning Styles

H **Bodily-Kinesthetic Learners** Have volunteers use masking tape to mark off an area in the classroom that is 12 feet long and 5 feet wide, shaped like the bottom of a boat. Then invite the entire class to try to stand in it. Have students describe how crowded conditions such as this might affect an individual both physically and emotionally.

THE LANGUAGE OF LITERATURE TEACHER'S EDITION **323**

Critical Thinking: MAKING JUDGMENTS

I Invite students to evaluate the decision Von's father makes. Ask them if they would have reached the same conclusion if faced with the same dilemma. Why or why not? *(Possible responses: I would have made the same decision because it's no use risking your life just to save some possessions. I would not have made that decision; why not attack at once by surprise rather than meekly let the pirates board the boat and perhaps kill you anyway?)*

Literary Concept: MOTIVATION

J Ask students to comment on why the pirates might have decided to give food to the refugees. *(Possible responses: I think Von is right in saying that they felt sorry for the people in the boat. Even though they felt no qualms about robbing them, apparently the pirates felt like they could not just let them die from starvation.)*

Critical Thinking: ANALYZING

K Ask students to explain why they think the captains of the Dutch and Italian ships did not stop for the refugees. *(Possible responses: They might have felt like they didn't want to get involved in a situation that had nothing to do with them. They might have had a deadline that made them decide they couldn't stop. They might have felt there was nothing they could do for the refugees. They might have been prejudiced against Asian people.)*

I so many of them. If we shoot at them, they will definitely kill us. It is better to let them rob us."

They came on board our little boat. They had knives and hammers. My father said, "Try to act cool." I was so scared I was shaking. Even

Copyright © Patrick Bar/Gamma Liaison.

my feet were shaking. They ordered all the men to go onto their big ship. I was so small that one man took my hand, picked me up, and threw me to another man on their ship. It looked so far and the ship was rocking that I was afraid they would miss me and I would fall into the sea. They would not bother to save me.

The pirates went around our boat checking for gold. They asked for watches and rings and money and said, "If you lie, we'll throw you into the sea." Everybody gave them everything they had, all their savings for their new lives. But after that the pirates gave us food. We were all very hungry people. They took us back to our boat. We were lucky. They didn't kill us. I guess they felt sorry for us. **J**

We were back alone on the sea, and then we saw some more big, big ships. One was from Holland, another from Italy. They saw us and didn't stop! We lay there. We were so hot. Every time we saw a big ship we got so happy. They came so close that then we got afraid that we could get caught in their waves. My father always put a white flash, a message, and it said, "If you want to pick us up, we come close. If no, we stay away." **K**

324 UNIT THREE PART 1: STRUGGLING FOR SURVIVAL

Mini-Lesson The Writer's Style

First-Person Point of View
personal pronouns   I, me, we

POINT OF VIEW Explain to students that in narrative writing (whether it is fiction or nonfiction) point of view refers to who is telling the story. There are three basic points of view: first person, third-person omniscient, and third-person limited. A narrative told by someone who takes part in the action is written from the first-person point of view. In "Von," although Janet Bode conducted the interview, Von is telling his own story.

Application Have students copy the chart of pronouns to the left and write a paragraph in which they use the first-person point of view. Remind them that the first-person point of view does not have to be autobiographical. Students can create a character and then tell the story from that character's point of view.

Reteaching/Reinforcement
• Writing Handbook, anthology p. 836–837
• *Writing Mini-Lessons* transparencies, p. 47

 The Writer's Craft

Point of View, pp. 322–323

324 THE LANGUAGE OF LITERATURE TEACHER'S EDITION

Some of the ships said, "Yes, we take you," and then when we came close, they tried to hit us to make us drown and die in the sea. My father knew they used that trick a lot. They didn't want us there, and if we died, nobody knew. So many people were coming out of Vietnam. Other countries didn't want to take any more. It's even worse today.

We go and go and go. In two weeks we saw a ship from Germany with a red cross on it. My father rowed, rowed, rowed, and he came very nicely right next to the ship. The Germans took us on board their ship. They gave us food, a shower, blankets. They told us to sleep. And they asked to speak to the captain of the boat. My father, he doesn't know German but he knows French, he went and spoke French to them. They said, "Tomorrow we will take you and your people to an island, to a refugee camp."

My father said, "Oh, thank you very much."

The first island they brought us to was one where nobody had lived. It was called Coocoo. The food was poison, the water polluted. And the mosquitoes! People had come there, cut down the trees, and built some houses. But it was dangerous for the people, and a lot of us were sick. Some of us died. They took us to the hospital at the refugee camp. They gave us injections.

After a month we had an interview from the United Nations. They called our names. My father said, "I worked for the United States government in South Vietnam." They took all the information down and then said, "Okay, we will call Washington, D.C. You must wait while we do that."

While we waited, my father worked for the chief commander in the refugee camp in Indonesia. I worked, too. The United Nations had donated some money to build some more houses to make the camp bigger. I sought them out for a job. They said, "If you want to help the people, gather the wood so they can build the barracks."

I said, "Fine, fine, I volunteer."

Most of the people at the refugee camp were Vietnamese. Some of them had so sad stories, oh my. "In Thailand they stole my sister," one said. "My brother and my mother got killed because the boat sink," another said. But on the island, we all lived together in barracks, and life at that time was beautiful. Each day the United Nations gave every person a half cup of rice and a half cup of another food. The American Peace Corps[1] came there, too. We people built a school, and they tried to teach a little English. We stayed there for eight months, until one afternoon we heard our name called again. They told us, "You have a sponsor from the United States."

I thought, Oh wow! A new land! A new life!

I thought, Oh wow! A new land! A new life! The United Nations had a special boat to Singapore. They take the refugees that are leaving to that city, we stay a week, and from there we take an airplane to Hong Kong and on to Alaska.

I looked out the window of the airplane in Alaska and I was so surprised. I tell my father, "Rice! Rice! Rice is falling from the sky!" He explained to me what is snow. From there we went to California, where we stayed in a shelter for a week. The people said, "Enjoy this; soon you will be in your new home, Detroit, and there the weather is very cold."

---

1. **Peace Corps:** a volunteer organization set up by the U.S. government to help people in developing countries.

Critical Thinking: SPECULATING

P Encourage students to speculate about why the woman never came back. *(Possible responses: There may have been too many refugees for her to deal with. She may work for a big bureaucracy that does not care about individuals.)*

Critical Thinking: MAKING JUDGMENTS

Q Ask students who is right in this case—Von or his father? *(Possible responses: Von's father is right, because there is plenty of crime in the United States, and Von is naive to think that all Americans are nice. Von is right—the Americans' unfamiliar ways worry Von's father, and he is overreacting.)*

CUSTOMIZING FOR
Students Acquiring English

4 Some students may not know what a rabbi is. Explain that a rabbi is a Jewish religious leader. In this context, a congregation is a group of people who belong to a particular synagogue.

Active Reading: CLARIFY

R Ask students how Von decides which foods to take home from the supermarket. *(Possible responses: He chooses only foods that he has seen or heard of before. He is in a strange place and chooses what is familiar to him.)*

It was January when we came to Detroit. I said, "What a dirty city." There were a lot of newspapers flying in the air, and it was so cold. A lady met us at the airport and took us in a really strange and crazy hotel filled with new immigrants and mental people.² She said, "Here is fifty dollars. I'll see you in fifteen days." We never saw her again.

At night at the hotel, the people screamed loud. They banged on the walls. We had nothing to cook. We didn't know what to eat. We didn't know what is American food. My father went out to the corner store, and he got some coffee and a sandwich. Then he bought some soup and some rice to cook. He told me, "Stay inside." I said, "Why? American people very nice. They wouldn't hurt anybody." He told me, "Stay inside."

I think of South Vietnam. It is a beautiful country. I think of my mother and brothers and sisters and grandmother. I think new people to America are hungry for their countries. Governments can be so cruel.

After two, three weeks, we had a phone call, a Vietnamese voice. We were excited. There were no other Vietnamese in the hotel. He said, "You will meet your sponsor. It is a rabbi and his congregation. They have found a home for you. One of the ladies speaks French, so you can talk to them."

When we meet them, the lady asks me, "Von, do you drink milk?" I'm too big to drink milk. With Vietnamese, milk is only for a baby. It is too expensive to buy.

I think, this is strange. Why does she ask me this? "How about soda?" she says.

"Oh, yes, I love soda."

"What kind of food do you eat? Hamburger?"

I tell her, "Oh, I love hamburger." I never eat hamburger, but I'd heard of it a lot.

So they took us to our home. It was in the basement, one bedroom and one living room. The Jewish people from the temple, everybody gave a little bit. We got a TV, two beds, some furniture, a table, cups and plates and cooking things. After that the lady and the rabbi took us to a supermarket. They said, "Von, take all the food you want."

I had never seen anything like this supermarket. The lady showed me the shopping cart and what to do. The first thing I grabbed was Coca-Cola. I knew that. And bread. Then I looked around and I didn't see anything to eat. It was all frozen. I'd never seen that in Vietnam. There we had all fresh fruit and vegetables. I got some cans of food. At the refugee camp, I saw those for the first time.

The lady said, "Do you like potato chips?"

I said, "What are potato chips?"

She bought some chicken for us. My father said, "I feel so bad. They brought us here and they had to take us shopping."

That afternoon, three more Jewish ladies came to the house. They showed us how to cook, how to make chicken, how to use the stove, where to put the milk and soda. They were so nice. I didn't understand a word they said, but I always smiled.

The next day they took me and my father shopping for clothes. I was so skinny and the pants were so big. They told my father and me, "You have to come to temple to meet the people." I got shoes, too. They said to my father, "Tomorrow, we will take Von to get a shot so you can put him in school."

---

2. **mental people:** people suffering from mental illness.

326 UNIT THREE PART 1: STRUGGLING FOR SURVIVAL

Multicultural Perspectives

THE MEANINGS OF FOOD Point out to students that the woman who offers milk does not intend to offend Von. She simply doesn't realize that in Vietnam only babies drink milk. The different meanings people attach to food as well as other things may be the causes of cross-cultural misunderstandings. In this example, the difference may be more than just cultural. Lactose intolerance is a condition in which a person cannot digest milk and many dairy products. People with lactose intolerance often think of themselves as being allergic to milk. This condition is common among Asian adults, which may be another reason (in addition to cost) why the adults Von knew did not drink milk. People of European ancestry have a lower incidence of lactose intolerance and make greater use of milk and milk products in cooking.

They got my father a job as a typewriter repairman. He didn't know anything about that. He wanted to work on the ships, but they said to do that you must be a United States citizen. He said, "Okay."

I was very scared to start school after six years. I had to skip a lot of grades. Most of the students looked at me because the way I was dressing was strange. It was so cold, I wore everything I'd bought. I didn't know where anything was. I came late to every class. I was confused and I could not ask people. They told me in sign language, "Go to eat." I went into the cafeteria. There were hundreds of people.

A supervisor knew I was a new student. He took me to the head of the line to get a hamburger, and the other students got angry. "Why does that boy get to go first?" I told the supervisor, "I want to wait in the line. Please." He said, "Don't worry about it. Take the food."

On that day and on other days, when I had a hard problem to solve, or when I felt sad or confused, I always look back on my past. I say, "Wow, what happened in the past is even harder. This is nothing." Let's face it, this is easy here.

There were no Vietnamese kids at the school, and only one Chinese boy, but he became my best friend. After a while I got along with the other students. I met a very nice black boy. He thought I was Chinese and all Chinese know karate and kung fu. He said, "I like your country's movies." I told him, "I'm Vietnamese." But he didn't know what was Vietnamese. He took me home to meet his mother, and, wow, did they have a big TV. He said, "What do you want? Food?" "Yeah." He made food for me and we ate and drank soda. I didn't understand what I was seeing. I couldn't answer his questions, but we understood each other.

Later I invited him to my house. I was doing the laundry, but I didn't know how to do laundry here. In Vietnam we use a brush to scrub it, then take it outside and hang it in the wind. I washed it by hand in the bathtub and left it to dry. Two, three days, and it was not dry! The boy went, "Von, what is this? Why don't you bring it to a laundromat?" He didn't know my family never had even seen a washing machine.

Other kids did bring some trouble to me. They talked about the way my hair looked, my clothes. When they called me "Chinese," they did it to make fun of me. They didn't call me by name. They laughed because I could not speak well. I was really upset about it, but then again I thought, so what?

I took an art class and the teacher said, "You draw whatever you like." I drew a map of Vietnam, the boat I escaped in, my family, and all the blood. One of my drawings I put in my father's bedroom, and on it I wrote, "NO MORE WAR!!!"

I got along well with my teachers. The English teacher gave me vocabulary to learn, like *breakfast, dinner, orange juice*. I'd take it home and translate and study it. The pronunciation was hard for me, words like *brother*. I'd practice my English by recording my voice on a tape recorder. I'd read from a book, then play it back. I watched TV news a lot, CNN.[3]

Even though my father was working, the rabbi paid the rent, the telephone bill, the food, everything for six months! They took us to the temple and made a party to introduce us. They gave us a hat to wear, a yarmulke.[4]

---

3. **CNN:** the Cable News Network.
4. **yarmulke** (yär′məl-kə): a small brimless cap worn by some Jewish men and boys.

Literary Concept: MOTIVATION

W Ask students to explain why Von has such a strong desire to get a job. *(Possible response: He has extremely powerful feelings of pride. Although he greatly appreciates the way that he and his father are being helped by the rabbi and others in the synagogue, Von feels compelled to provide for himself.)*

Active Reading: EVALUATE

X Ask students to evaluate the supermarket manager's actions. Do they think it is fair of him to turn away Von because of his deficient English skills? Why or why not?

Active Reading: CONNECT

Y Ask students to comment on Von's dilemma. If they were in his position, would they concentrate on their schoolwork, or would they try to split their focus between school and a job?

CUSTOMIZING FOR
Gifted and Talented Students

Have students discuss the personal characteristics that Von and his father needed to possess to adapt successfully to American culture. Ask students to explain why they think adapting to a new culture is or is not an entirely positive thing.

We still have it today. They knew it was my birthday. I had never had a birthday party in my life. They made a big cake, and they told me to hold it and blow out the candles. They told me to give a speech. I was only here two, three months. I didn't know anything. My father said, "Whatever people give you, you have to say 'Thank you.'" I said, "Thank you, thank you."

It was wonderful. They gave me the whole cake to take home. I ate it for one month! Every day after school, I cut one piece and ate it. The rabbi always called to see how we were. He said, "If you have any problem, we are here to help."

After six months, I said to my father and the rabbi, "Let me go look for a job." We don't want the temple to pay for us anymore.

The rabbi said, "We wouldn't recommend that you work. You better concentrate on school."

Without telling them, I looked. I saw a lot of students go to work, so I copied them. I started walking from my house. I went into a supermarket. I was interviewed by the manager, and he told me, "Sorry, you have an English problem. Study more and come back in six months." I went into many supermarkets that day, many small stores.

They didn't understand what I was talking about. I didn't understand what I was talking about. But I already knew the words for juice, milk, fruit, so that's why I was interested in those stores. I went home. I was so sad. I didn't want to bother my father. He was very busy, too, learning a new job and studying English in night school.

The next day after school, I went to look again. My school had a work-study program, and a teacher told me about a job at Burger King. I was interviewed and the boss knew that I had an English problem. I begged him, "I can do anything! I can take the cooking test, but I can't take the writing test. I don't know English." So he went check, check, check, like that, on the test and I passed. So my first job in America was to cook hamburgers. I took the frozen hamburger and put it inside the fire. That's all he wanted me to do.

But then I saw customers who didn't throw their food in the trash. I came out and I cleaned the tables. I saw someone had thrown sodas on the floor. I took a mop and cleaned it up. I wanted to show him that I could work. He gave me a uniform and said, "You start today."

I ran home and said to my father, "I must write a letter to the rabbi. I must say, 'Thank you for everything you've done for us. Someday when I have a good job, I will donate money to this temple to keep it forever. Now my father and I both work and won't need any more help.'"

My father said, "Oh, that is great."

The rabbi called my house. He said, "Von,

Copyright © Mark Lewis/Tony Stone Images.

328   UNIT THREE   PART 1: STRUGGLING FOR SURVIVAL

Mini-Lesson Study Skills

REFERENCE BOOKS Point out to students that libraries contain a wide range of useful reference books. Among these are atlases, which contain maps, charts, tables, and other geographical information about the world.

Application Have students use an atlas to locate as many of the places mentioned in the text as possible. Using a good atlas, students should be able to locate countries such as Vietnam, Cambodia, Thailand, and Hong Kong; cities such as Singapore, Ho Chi Minh City (formerly Saigon), Da Nang, and Detroit; and states such as Alaska, California, and Michigan. Unfortunately, most atlases don't show the uninhabited island of Coocoo.

we want to help you. We don't want anything from you. You've only been here a few months. Remember your schoolwork, but you do what you want." I sent my money to my mother.

My father and I have been here for a long time now, eight, nine years. For five years we have had all the papers in order to have my mother and my brothers and my sisters come here. We have sent a letter to the United States <u>ambassador</u> to Thailand. We have written to the United States representative at the United Nations. We contacted our congressman, and he wrote a letter. The congressman said, "Your family is qualified to come to the United States. They are at the top of the list." Still we wait and we wait and we wait. The Communist government doesn't want to give them <u>visas</u>.

This year on July 4th, my father and I became citizens of the United States. I'm a free man! I read the Constitution. We the people are all equal. Now no one can say, if the United States someday has a problem, "You have to go back to Vietnam." I love this country. This country is my country now. I never go back.

My brothers and sisters don't have the opportunities that I do. Today it is September, and I am starting university. I am a very lucky person. And when my family gets here and we are together again, we will make such a celebration! ❖

LITERARY INSIGHT

Foreign Student
BY BARBARA B. ROBINSON

In September she appeared
   row three, seat seven,
   heavy pleated skirt,
   plastic purse,
5   tidy note pad,
there she sat,
silent,
straight from Taipei,
and she bowed
10 when I entered the room.
A model student
I noticed,
every assignment complete,
on time, neat,
15 and she listened
when I talked.

But now it's May,
and Si Lan
is called Lani.
20 She strides in
with Lynne and Susan.
Her gear is crammed
into a macramé
shoulder sack.
25 And she chatters with Pete
during class
and
I'm glad.

WORDS TO KNOW	**ambassador** (ăm-băs′ə-dər) *n.* a country's chief diplomatic official in a foreign land
	visa (vē′zə) *n.* an official permission to leave or enter a country

329

Mini-Lesson Spelling

Y WORDS WITH SUFFIXES Remind students that sometimes suffixes are added to words that end in the letter *y.* If the letter before the final *y* is a vowel, the *y* is not changed before the suffix is added. However, if the letter before the final *y* is a consonant, students must change the *y* to an *i* before adding any suffix except *-ing.* Explain that the letter *y* never changes before *-ing.*

Application Have students add suffixes to the following words, as indicated.

1. apply (-es)
2. convey (-ing)
3. agency (-es)
4. century (-es)
5. attorney (-s)
6. employ (-er)
7. penalty (-es)
8. modify (-ing)

Ask students to look for more words that fit this pattern, in their own writing and in things that they read, and add these words to their personal word lists.

Reteaching/Reinforcement
• *Unit Three Resource Book,* p. 23

STRATEGIC READING FOR
Less-Proficient Readers

Have students explain why Von considers himself lucky. *(Von compares his situation in the United States with that of his family in Vietnam. He considers himself lucky because of all the opportunities, such as attending university, that he has.)* **Summarizing/Making Inferences**

COMPREHENSION CHECK
1. Who put Von's father in a concentration camp? *(the Communist government of Vietnam)*
2. Who sponsors Von and his father in the United States? *(a rabbi and his synagogue in Detroit, Michigan)*
3. Where does Von get his first job in America? *(at a Burger King)*
4. Why is July 4 an important day for Von and his father? *(It is the day they became American citizens.)*

INSIGHT
1. How would you describe the change Si Lan undergoes? *(Possible response: She changes from a girl who dresses and behaves formally to one who looks and acts more "American.")*
2. Why do you think the narrator in the poem ends with the line "I'm glad"? Do you feel the same? Why or why not? *(Possible response: The narrator is glad Si Lan is making friends and interacting with other students in class. This is a good thing, but she might be adapting too much, and this could mean that other students aren't learning about her culture and language.)*

BARBARA B. ROBINSON

In her long career as a writer, Barbara Robinson (born in 1921) has published short stories in magazines such as *Redbook* and the *Toronto Star Weekly.* Her books include *Across from Indian Shore* and *The Best Christmas Pageant Ever.*

country + es = countries
spray + ing = spraying

THE LANGUAGE OF LITERATURE TEACHER'S EDITION 329

From Personal Response to Critical Analysis

1. Responses will vary.
2. Possible responses: Leaving his family was probably Von's most difficult experience. Being on the sea in a crowded boat was Von's most difficult experience because of the fear that the group would not survive.
3. Possible response: Although Von has some tough moments along the way, he basically adjusts well to living in America. His early confusion and unhappiness become a determination to make his own way.
4. Responses will vary. It might be difficult to predict the experience of emigrants unless one has lived through a similar situation.
5. Possible response: The reader learns more about Von's experiences than Lani's. Her adjustment may seem easier, but it probably was a bumpy road, just like Von's. If they met, they might talk about the times they felt awkward and confused in their early days in America.
6. Possible responses: Yes, the United States should accept refugees, because this nation can help refugees live better lives. No, too many refugees will make it difficult for the United States to deal with its own problems.

Another Pathway

Cooperative Learning As students take turns summarizing the successive scenes in "Von," one student can serve as a monitor to ensure that summaries do not get bogged down with unnecessary details.

Rubric

3 Full Accomplishment Students thoroughly and concisely summarize the narrative.

2 Substantial Accomplishment Students devise a good summary of the narrative.

1 Little or Partial Accomplishment Students have difficulty summarizing the narrative.

RESPONDING OPTIONS

FROM PERSONAL RESPONSE TO CRITICAL ANALYSIS

REFLECT
1. What were your thoughts about Von as you read this selection? Jot down your thoughts in your notebook, and then share them with a partner.

RETHINK
Thematic Link

2. Which of Von's experiences do you think were the most difficult for him? Why?

Close Textual Reading

3. Evaluate how well Von adjusts to life in the United States.
   Consider
   - his experience in the hotel during the first weeks
   - his school experiences
   - why he wants to work
   - his attitude toward the United States

4. Review the predictions you made for the Reading Connection on page 319. What problem or problems faced by the emigrants in the selection were you unable to predict? Why do you think you were unable to do so?

RELATE
Literary Link

5. Compare Von's adjustment to a new country with that of Lani in "Foreign Student" (page 329). If Von and Lani were to meet, what might they say to each other about their experiences?

6. In 1993, more than 1 million people immigrated to the United States. Like Von and his father, some of these immigrants were refugees. Should the United States accept all refugees? Explain your answer.

ANOTHER PATHWAY

Cooperative Learning
With a group of classmates, summarize Von's story orally and record the summary on audiotape. One person should recount the beginning, with the next student summarizing the next scene, and so on.

QUICKWRITES

1. What exactly does Von experience during one day and night on a refugee boat? Write a **journal entry** in which Von describes his feelings and experiences in more detail than the selection provides.

2. Write a **letter** Von might have written to the South Vietnamese government to persuade them to let the rest of his family emigrate from Vietnam to the United States.

📁 **PORTFOLIO** Save your writing. You may want to use it later as a springboard to a piece for your portfolio.

LITERARY CONCEPTS

One way to preserve people's stories—their history—is to let them "talk it." This is called **oral history**. Oral history includes personal reactions and factual recollections. In her introduction to the volume in which Von's story appears, Janet Bode wrote, "At times the sentence construction might seem a little awkward. The grammar might not always be perfect." Why do you think she chose not to correct Von's grammatical errors?

330 UNIT THREE PART 1: STRUGGLING FOR SURVIVAL

Literary Concepts

Help students see that Bode wanted to present Von as he really is. If she had corrected his grammatical errors, she might have ended up with a less vivid and less accurate portrayal of him.

QuickWrites

1. Have students take time to imagine what the experience on the boat was like and to jot down ideas. Remind them to think about descriptive details involving each of the senses.
2. Urge students to think about the letter's audience—a government representative. Invite them to consider how this audience will affect the way they communicate the issues.

 **The Writer's Craft**

Sensory Details, p. 256
Audience, pp. 234–235

Multimodal Learning

ALTERNATIVE ACTIVITIES

1. Create a **storyboard**—a series of sketches arranged in sequence—that depicts key events in the selection. Include a caption with each sketch, and share your work with the class.
2. Make a **collage** that portrays Von's experiences in Vietnam, on the boat, and in the United States.

CRITIC'S CORNER

Stephen Tremayne Johnson, a student reader, said about this selection, "I liked how much optimism Von had for his family, his future, and himself." Do you agree? If so, do you think Von is unusual in the optimism he feels? Explain your answer.

WORDS TO KNOW

Define **ambassador** and **visa**, then research the words' origins. Find out what an ambassador does, how a person becomes an ambassador, who needs visas, and how visas are obtained.

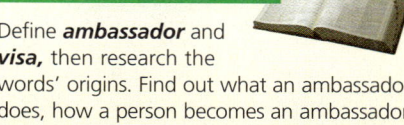

Words to Know

One definition of *ambassador* is "the highest-ranking diplomatic representative appointed by one country or government to represent it in another." The word comes from Middle English and Middle French and is related to the Old High German word *ambaht*, meaning "service." In America, ambassadors are usually chosen by the President. An ambassador acts primarily as a spokesperson—and occasionally as a negotiator—for his or her government.

The word *visa* (which comes from the Latin word *visus*, "seen") can be defined as "an endorsement on a passport, showing that it has been examined by the proper officials of a country and granting entry into or passage through that country." Visas are sometimes necessary to enter certain countries or to stay in them for a certain length of time. Usually visas can be obtained by contacting the embassy of the country to which one wishes to travel. Visas do not take the place of passports but instead work in combination with them.

"VON"

"Von," (1968–) whose name was changed to protect his privacy and the safety of his family, was born in Saigon, South Vietnam, in 1968. His father, an officer in the South Vietnamese army, studied in the United States before Von was born. When Von looked at his father's pictures of California, he secretly hoped, "Maybe someday I be there." As the selection explains, Von and his father eventually came to the United States and became citizens. Many years later, the rest of Von's family finally got permission to emigrate from Vietnam.

JANET BODE

1943–

Janet Bode has written a number of award-winning nonfiction books. Her experiences living in New York City inspired her with the idea for *New Kids on the Block: Oral Histories of Immigrant Teens,* from which "Von" was taken. According to her, "Walking by the diner, the stationery store, the market, the restaurant, and the deli, I pass a United Nations of recent immigrants to this country."

Many of Bode's books and articles explore problems facing today's teenagers, such as sibling rivalry, interracial and cross-cultural dating, and teenage pregnancy.

Bode says, "Women's issues are my primary concern, but I have a strong undercurrent of interest in all people regardless of gender."

OTHER WORKS *Different Worlds: Interracial and Cross-Cultural Dating, Truce: Ending the Sibling War, Beating the Odds: Stories of Unexpected Achievers*

Extended Reading

VON

Von's first memories are of the summer of 1972, known in southern Vietnam as the Hot Summer "because of all the bombing and the many deaths." His mother came from a wealthy Vietnamese family, and his father held a high government position.

JANET BODE

Bode has done extensive research and written several books dealing with people—especially young people—in crisis. Her written works for young adults include *Kids Having Kids: The Unwed Teenage Parent; Rape: Preventing It;* and *Coping with the Legal, Medical and Emotional Aftermath.* In 1975 she used her expertise to coauthor a documentary film for television, *Women Against Rape.*

VON **331**

Alternative Activities

1. Have students reread the text in order to identify what they consider to be its key scenes. Then have them decide which details would best convey the essence of the scene in an illustration.
2. Encourage students to think about ways to express Von's experiences both realistically and abstractly. A less representational image of a person being oppressed by outside forces would also be effective in a collage dealing with the feelings of physical discomfort and fear that Von experienced.

Across the Curriculum

Social Studies *The Culture of Vietnam* Have students do research for a report on the cultural and religious background of the South Vietnamese. Encourage students to present material on Vietnamese cuisine; literature, music, and performing arts; language; and the practice of both Buddhism and Christianity in the country.

Math *Halfway Across the Globe* Have students use an atlas to try to calculate the number of miles that Von and his father traveled between Da Nang and Detroit.

EDITOR'S NOTE *With the permission of the copyright holder, this selection was excerpted from a longer work. The material on page 320 is an introduction by Janet Bode to Von's story. The italicized passage on page 322 summarizes the family's struggles in Vietnam during the years 1972–1978. The rest of the selection is in Von's voice.*

THE LANGUAGE OF LITERATURE TEACHER'S EDITION **331**

OVERVIEW

Objectives

- To understand and appreciate a radio drama about a man's fateful encounter with a spectral hitchhiker
- To identify and understand the concept of foreshadowing
- To express understanding of a radio drama through a choice of writing forms, including a scene and an introduction
- To extend understanding of the drama through a variety of multimodal and cross-curricular activities

Skills

READING SKILLS/ STRATEGIES
- Making inferences

LITERARY CONCEPTS
- Foreshadowing
- Suspense

THE WRITER'S STYLE
- Sensory details

GENRE STUDY
- Drama

GRAMMAR
- Interjections

SPELLING
- Final silent e with suffixes

SPEAKING, LISTENING, AND VIEWING
- Drama Performance
- Drama
- Group discussion
- Oral presentation

Cross-Curricular Connections

MATHEMATICS
- Coast to coast

HISTORY
- Orson Welles's *Mercury Theater on the Air*

SOCIAL STUDIES
- Destination Gallup
- Calling long distance

HISTORICAL CONNECTION

Radio Shows What was radio like in its golden age, before the advent of television? Introduce students to radio shows by playing these excerpts from actual radio broadcasts, complete with photographs of the people who made them happen.

Side A, Frame 22964

PREVIEWING

DRAMA

The Hitchhiker
Lucille Fletcher

Activating Prior Knowledge

PERSONAL CONNECTION

What do you think makes a good horror story? With your class, discuss the criteria for high-quality horror—kinds of settings, types of characters, plot elements, and other characteristics, such as sound effects. Make a diagram like the one shown here to record your ideas.

Building Background

HISTORICAL CONNECTION

In the 1930s and 1940s, before television was a part of daily life, families gathered around the radio to listen to their favorite shows, such as *Fibber McGee and Molly, The Green Hornet,* and *Suspense.* The vivid sounds of radio—voices, laughs, screams, trains, creaking doors—helped create pictures in listeners' imaginations.

The sound effects in *The Hitchhiker,* which was written for radio, helped the audience follow Ronald Adams on his eerie coast-to-coast car trip on Route 66. *The Hitchhiker* was originally produced and narrated by 23-year-old Orson Welles, who later became a well-known actor and movie director.

A radio performer shows off items used to create sound effects for a radio play in 1938.

Setting a Purpose

WRITING CONNECTION

What role do you think a hitchhiker might play in a horror story? Write your prediction in your notebook. After you have read the drama, decide whether your prediction was accurate. If not, how did the hitchhiker's role differ from the role you predicted?

• HISTORICAL CONNECTION

332 UNIT THREE PART 1: STRUGGLING FOR SURVIVAL

PRINT AND MEDIA RESOURCES

UNIT THREE RESOURCE BOOK
Strategic Reading: Literature, p. 27
Vocabulary SkillBuilder, p. 30
Reading SkillBuilder, p. 28
Spelling SkillBuilder, p. 29

WRITING MINI-LESSONS
Transparencies, p. 38

ACCESS FOR STUDENTS ACQUIRING ENGLISH
Selection Summaries
Reading and Writing Support

FORMAL ASSESSMENT
Selection Test, pp. 63–64
 Test Generator

 **AUDIO LIBRARY**
See Reference Card

 **LASERLINKS**
Historical Connection

THE HITCHHIKER

by Lucille Fletcher

A Play for Radio

Cast of Characters:
Orson Welles
Ronald Adams
Adams's Mother
Voice of hitchhiker
Mechanic
Henry, a sleepy man
Woman's Voice (Henry's wife)
Girl
Operator
Long-distance Operator
Albuquerque Operator
New York Operator
Mrs. Whitney

SUMMARY

As he sets out on a cross-country trip, Ronald Adams's mother warns him to be careful driving. As Adams crosses the Brooklyn Bridge in the rain, he barely avoids a hitchhiker in the roadway. As the trip progresses, he repeatedly sees the hitchhiker and grows increasingly anxious that the man is trying to kill him. Eventually, Adams wonders if he is going crazy and phones his mother from New Mexico. A neighbor tells him that Mrs. Adams is in the hospital, recovering from her shock at her son's death in a car crash on the Brooklyn Bridge.

Thematic Link: *Struggling for Survival* A man struggles for survival as he is pursued by a ghostly hitchhiker.

STRATEGIC READING FOR
Less-Proficient Readers

Set a Purpose Encourage students to become involved in the story by asking them to share their feelings about ghost stories and other scary stories. Then have students read to learn where Ronald Adams is going and what promise he makes to his mother.

Use **UNIT THREE RESOURCE BOOK**, p. 27, for guidance in reading the selection.

CUSTOMIZING FOR
Students Acquiring English

- Use **ACCESS FOR STUDENTS ACQUIRING ENGLISH**, *Reading and Writing Support.*
- Explain that this is a story of suspense. Ask students to be aware of how the story makes them feel as they read.
- In addition to these boxes, you may want to use the suggestions under Strategic Reading for Less-Proficient Readers.

WORDS TO KNOW

assurance (ə-shoor′əns) *n.* a guarantee or pledge (p. 334)
lark (lärk) *n.* a carefree adventure (p. 336)
menacing (měn′ĭ-sĭng) *adj.* threatening **menace** *v.* (p. 337)
nondescript (nŏn′dĭ-skrĭpt′) *adj.* lacking in distinctive qualities; drab (p. 336)
sinister (sĭn′ĭ-stər) *adj.* suggestive of evil or misfortune (p. 337)

CUSTOMIZING FOR
Gifted and Talented Students

Have students track the changes in Adams's attitude toward the hitchhiker as the story progresses. Ask them how his changing explanation for the man's presence affects his behavior.

(Possible responses:

Page 336—"I thought probably one of those fast trucks had picked him up...." Adams thinks it's odd to see the man again.

Pages 337–338—"Yet the thought of picking him up, of having him sit beside me, was somehow unbearable." Adams becomes increasingly upset.)

Linking to History

Radio plays flourished in the 1930s and 1940s, before the popularity of television. Among the most popular examples of the genre was Orson Welles's weekly series, *Mercury Theater on the Air*. This series produced *The Hitchhiker* as well as the famous radio adaptation of *The War of the Worlds*.

CUSTOMIZING FOR
Multiple Learning Styles

Ⓐ Musical Learners Encourage students to create music and sound effects for a production of *The Hitchhiker*. Invite students to research sound-effects records and to experiment with ways to create sound effects.

Critical Thinking: CLASSIFYING

Ⓑ Have students describe the difference between a story that appeals to the heart and one that appeals to the spine. *(Possible response: A story that appeals to the heart will leave a reader or listener feeling emotions such as sadness, melancholy, or joy, whereas one that appeals to the spine will leave a reader or listener feeling frightened.)*

Ⓐ **Welles.** Good evening, this is Orson Welles. (*Music in*)

Personally I've never met anybody who didn't like a good ghost story, but I know a lot of people who think there are a lot of people who don't like a good ghost story. For the benefit of these, at least, I go on record at the outset of this evening's entertainment with the sober <u>assurance</u> that although blood may be curdled on this program, none will be spilt. There's no shooting, knifing, throttling, axing, or poisoning here. No clanking chains, no cobwebs, no bony and/or hairy hands appearing from secret panels or, better yet, bedroom curtains. If it's any part of that dear old *phosphorescent*[1] foolishness that people who don't like ghost stories don't like, then again I promise you we haven't got it. What we do have is a thriller. If it's half as good as we think it is, you can call it a shocker; and we present it proudly and without apologies. After all, a story doesn't have to appeal to the heart—it can also appeal to the spine. Sometimes you want your heart to be warmed—sometimes you want your spine to tingle. The tingling, it's to be hoped, will be quite audible as you listen tonight to *The Hitchhiker*—that's the name of our story, *The Hitchhiker*— **Ⓑ**

(*Sound: automobile wheels humming over concrete road*)

(*Music: something weird and shuddery*)

---

1. *phosphorescent* (fŏs´fə-rĕs´ənt): glowing with a cold light.

> **WORDS TO KNOW**
> **assurance** (ə-shoor´əns) *n.* a guarantee or pledge

334

Mini-Lesson — Reading Skills/Strategies

MAKING INFERENCES Remind students that an inference is a logical guess or conclusion based on information not directly stated in a story. By using information in selections and from their own experience, readers can figure out more than the words say. For instance, in this radio drama, one can infer from the title alone that the story will have something to do with automobiles, roads, and a journey.

Application As students read the selection, they will encounter information—sometimes in the form of a single detail—that allows them to make an inference. Encourage them to jot down in their notebooks what they can conclude from details such as the raindrops on the hitchhiker's clothing, the fact that the hitchhiker repeatedly appears *in front of* Adams's car, or the fact that the young female hitchhiker doesn't see the phantom hitchhiker.

Reteaching/Reinforcement
• *Unit Three Resource Book*, p. 28

334 THE LANGUAGE OF LITERATURE **TEACHER'S EDITION**

Drive-In (1974), Howard Kanovitz. Photo courtesy of the artist.

Adams. I am in an auto camp on Route Sixty-six just west of Gallup, New Mexico. If I tell it, perhaps it will help me. It will keep me from going mad. But I must tell this quickly. I am not mad now. I feel perfectly well, except that I am running a slight temperature. My name is Ronald Adams. I am thirty-six years of age, unmarried, tall, dark, with a black mustache. I drive a 1940 Ford V-8, license number 6V-7989. I was born in Brooklyn. All this I know. I know that I am at this moment perfectly sane. That it is not I who have gone mad—but something else—something utterly beyond my control. But I must speak quickly. At any moment the link with life may break. This may be the last thing I ever tell on earth . . . the last night I ever see the stars. . . .

(Music in)

Adams. Six days ago I left Brooklyn to drive to California. . . .

Mother. Goodbye, Son. Good luck to you, my boy. . . .

Adams. Goodbye, Mother. Here—give me a kiss, and then I'll go. . . .

Mother. I'll come out with you to the car.

Adams. No. It's raining. Stay here at the door. Hey—what is this? Tears? I thought you promised me you wouldn't cry.

Mother. I know, dear. I'm sorry. But I—do hate to see you go.

Adams. I'll be back. I'll be on the coast only three months.

Mother. Oh—it isn't that. It's just—the trip. Ronald—I wish you weren't driving.

Adams. Oh—Mother. There you go again. People do it every day.

Mother. I know. But you'll be careful, won't you? Promise me you'll be extra careful.

THE HITCHHIKER   335

STRATEGIC READING FOR
Less-Proficient Readers

E Check to see that students are clear about details in the story's exposition.

- What is Ronald Adams's destination? *(California)* **Noting Relevant Details**
- What does Adams promise his mother? *(He will drive carefully; not fall asleep, drive too fast, or pick up strangers on the road; and contact her when he reaches Hollywood.)* **Summarizing/Noting Relevant Details**

Set a Purpose Have students read to find out what Adams sees beside a roadside stand.

CUSTOMIZING FOR
Students Acquiring English

I Point out that *reckoned* in this context means "calculated or planned." Ask a more fluent student to paraphrase, "But I reckoned without him." *(I planned the trip ahead without considering the man.)*

Active Reading: CLARIFY

F Have students explain exactly why Adams gets "the willies." *(Possible response: He gets spooked because he has seen the same hitchhiker on the Brooklyn Bridge in New York, on the Pulaski Skyway in New Jersey, and on the Pennsylvania Turnpike.)*

Don't fall asleep—or drive fast—or pick up any strangers on the road. . . .

Adams. Lord, no. You'd think I was still seventeen to hear you talk—

Mother. And wire me as soon as you get to Hollywood, won't you, Son?

Adams. Of course I will. Now don't you worry. There isn't anything going to happen. It's just eight days of perfectly simple driving on smooth, decent, civilized roads, with a hotdog or a hamburger stand every ten miles . . . . *(fade)*

(Sound: auto hum)
(Music in)

Adams. I was in excellent spirits. The drive ahead of me, even the loneliness, seemed like a <u>lark</u>. But I reckoned without him.

(Music changes to something weird and empty.)

Adams. Crossing Brooklyn Bridge that morning in the rain, I saw a man leaning against the cables. He seemed to be waiting for a lift. There were spots of fresh rain on his shoulders. He was carrying a cheap overnight bag in one hand. He was thin, <u>nondescript</u>, with a cap pulled down over his eyes. He stepped off the walk, and if I hadn't swerved, I'd have hit him.

(Sound: terrific skidding)
(Music in)

Adams. I would have forgotten him completely, except that just an hour later, while crossing the Pulaski Skyway over the Jersey flats, I saw him again. At least, he looked like the same person. He was standing now, with one thumb pointing west. I couldn't figure out how he'd got there, but I thought probably one of those fast trucks had picked him up, beaten me to the Skyway, and let him off. I didn't stop for him. Then—late that night, I saw him again.

(Music changing)

Adams. It was on the new Pennsylvania Turnpike between Harrisburg and Pittsburgh. It's 265 miles long, with a very high speed limit. I was just slowing down for one of the tunnels—when I saw him—standing under an arc light by the side of the road. I could see him quite distinctly. The bag, the cap, even the spots of fresh rain spattered over his shoulders. He hailed me this time. . . .

Voice *(very spooky and faint).* Hall-ooo. . . . *(echo as through tunnel)* Hall-ooo . . . !

Adams. I stepped on the gas like a shot. That's lonely country through the Alleghenies,[2] and I had no intention of stopping. Besides, the coincidence, or whatever it was, gave me the willies.[3] I stopped at the next gas station.

(Sound: auto tires screeching to stop . . . horn honk)

Mechanic. Yes, sir.

Adams. Fill her up.

Mechanic. Certainly, sir. Check your oil, sir?

Adams. No, thanks.

(Sound: gas being put into car . . . bell tinkle, et cetera)

Mechanic. Nice night, isn't it?

Adams. Yes. It—hasn't been raining here recently, has it?

Mechanic. Not a drop of rain all week.

Adams. I suppose that hasn't done your business any harm.

Mechanic. Oh—people drive through here all kinds of weather. Mostly business, you know.

---

2. **Alleghenies** (ăl′ĭ-gā′nēz): the Allegheny Mountains, a range extending from northern Pennsylvania to western Virginia.
3. **gave me the willies:** made me nervous.

| WORDS TO KNOW | **lark** (lärk) *n.* a carefree adventure
nondescript (nŏn′dĭ-skrĭpt′) *adj.* lacking in distinctive qualities; drab |

336

Mini-Lesson  Genre Study

Drama
performed by actors before an audience

tells the story through dialogue and the actions of the characters

contains stage directions that suggest details about scenery, costumes, lighting, music, sound effects, and how actors should move and speak

Radio Drama
performed by actors for an audience of radio listeners

tells the story through dialogue, narration, and sounds that suggest the actions of the characters

contains no visual elements, but relies on music, sound effects, and how actors speak to communicate the story

DRAMA Draw the chart shown on the left and explain to students that a **radio drama** uses many of the conventions of drama. However, tell students the crucial difference is that a radio drama is written specifically to be heard and not seen.

Application Have students copy the chart in their notebooks. Encourage them to consult it as they look for the characteristics of a radio play in *The Hitchhiker.*

There aren't many pleasure cars out on the turnpike this season of the year.

Adams. I suppose not. *(casually)* What about hitchhikers?

Mechanic *(half laughing).* Hitchhikers *here?*

Adams. What's the matter? Don't you ever see any?

② **Mechanic.** Not much. If we did, it'd be a sight for sore eyes.

Adams. Why?

Mechanic. A guy'd be a fool who started out to hitch rides on this road. Look at it. It's 265 miles long, there's practically no speed limit, and it's a straightaway. Now what car is going to stop to pick up a guy under these conditions? Would you stop?

Adams. No. *(slowly, with puzzled emphasis)* Then you've never seen anybody?

Mechanic. Nope. Mebbe they get the lift before the turnpike starts—I mean, you know, just before the toll house—but then it'd be a mighty long ride. Most cars wouldn't want to pick up a guy for that long a ride. And you know—this is pretty lonesome country here—mountains, and woods. . . . You ain't seen anybody like that, have you?

Ⓖ **Adams.** No. *(quickly)* Oh no, not at all. It was—just a—technical question.

Mechanic. I see. Well—that'll be just a dollar forty-nine—with the tax. . . . *(fade)*

(Sound: auto hum up)

(Music changing)

Adams. The thing gradually passed from my mind, as sheer coincidence. I had a good night's sleep in Pittsburgh. I did not think about the man all next day—until just outside of Zanesville, Ohio, I saw him again.

(Music: dark, ominous note)

Adams. It was a bright, sunshiny afternoon. The peaceful Ohio fields, brown with the autumn stubble, lay dreaming in the golden light. I was driving slowly, drinking it in, when the road suddenly ended in a detour. In front of the barrier, he was standing.

Ⓗ

(Music in)

Adams. Let me explain about his appearance before I go on. I repeat. There was nothing <u>sinister</u> about him. He was as drab as a mud fence. Nor was his attitude <u>menacing</u>. He merely stood there, waiting, almost drooping a little, the cheap overnight bag in his hand. He looked as though he had been waiting there for hours. Then he looked up. He hailed me. He started to walk forward.

Ⓘ

Voice *(far off).* Hall-ooo. . . . Hall-ooo. . . .

Adams. I had stopped the car, of course, for the detour. And for a few moments, I couldn't seem to find the new road. I knew he must be thinking that I had stopped for him.

Voice *(closer).* Hall-ooo. . . . Hallll . . . ooo. . . .

(Sound: gears jamming . . . sound of motor turning over hard . . . nervous accelerator)

Voice *(closer).* Halll . . . oooo. . . .

Adams *(panicky).* No. Not just now. Sorry. . . .

Voice *(closer).* Going to California?

(Sound: starter starting . . . gears jamming)

Adams *(as though <u>sweating blood</u>).* No. Not today. The other way. Going to New York. Sorry . . . sorry. . . . ③

(Sound: Car starts with squeal of wheels on dirt . . . into auto hum.)

(Music in)

Adams. After I got the car back onto the road again, I felt like a fool. Yet the thought of picking him up, of having him sit beside me,

WORDS TO KNOW
sinister (sĭn′ĭ-stər) *adj.* suggestive of evil or misfortune
menacing (mĕn′ĭ-sĭng) *adj.* threatening **menace** *v.*

337

CUSTOMIZING FOR
Students Acquiring English

② The expression "a sight for sore eyes" means something or someone you are glad to see.

③ The expression "sweating blood" indicates that someone is very worried or upset.

Critical Thinking: ANALYZING

Ⓖ Ask students why Ronald Adams answers the mechanic's question with a "no." *(Possible response: Adams has a sense that something is extremely odd about the appearance of this hitchhiker, and he may feel that if the mechanic heard all the details he would not believe him.)*

Literary Concept: FORESHADOWING

Ⓗ Encourage students to identify any hints of Adams's fate that the author provides in this passage. *(Possible response: The fact that the hitchhiker is standing exactly where the road ends in a detour seems more than just coincidence, and it may indicate that this figure has something to do with some sudden change in Adams.)*

Critical Thinking: SPECULATING

Ⓘ Ask students to speculate on the identity of the hitchhiker. *(Nearly every answer is acceptable. Encourage students to furnish reasons for their ideas.)*

Mini-Lesson The Writer's Style

SENSORY DETAILS Remind students that in radio drama, the audience receives all of the information about characters and events through what they hear. The writer of a radio drama can help readers fully experience the drama in two ways: first, through descriptions and second, by using sound effects and music to convey how something looks, smells, tastes, feels, or sounds.

Application Have students identify at least three examples of descriptive details and sound details from the highlighted paragraphs on page 337 that give the audience information. *(descriptions such as* "the peaceful Ohio fields" *and* "drab as a mud fence"; *sounds such as gears jamming, car's motor)* Then have students write a page of a dramatic scene of their own in which they use descriptive details, sound effects, and music.

Reteaching/Reinforcement
- *Writing Handbook,* anthology, p. 831
- *Writing Mini-Lessons* transparencies, p. 38

Sensory details, p. 256

CUSTOMIZING FOR
Students Acquiring English

4 Explain to students that words such as *yep* and *mebbe* indicate that the speaker is speaking in dialect. Have a volunteer tell what these words are in standard English. *(yes; maybe)*

5 Students might not be familiar with the use of the phrase *taking a nip* to mean "drinking alcohol."

STRATEGIC READING FOR
Less-Proficient Readers

J Check that students are clear about Adams's encounters with the hitchhiker.

- What does Adams see beside the roadside stand? *(a suspicious-looking man)* **Noting Relevant Details**
- Who was the man? *(possibly the same hitchhiker he saw several times before)* **Making Inferences**

Set a Purpose Have students read to find out when Adams knows that he is "utterly alone."

---

was somehow unbearable. Yet, at the same time, I felt, more than ever, unspeakably alone.

(*Sound: auto hum up*)

Adams. Hour after hour went by. The fields, the towns ticked off, one by one. The lights changed. I knew now that I was going to see him again. And though I dreaded the sight, I caught myself searching the side of the road, waiting for him to appear.

(*Sound: auto hum up . . . car screeches to a halt . . . impatient honk two or three times . . . door being unbolted*)

Sleepy man's voice. Yep? What is it? What do you want?

Adams (*breathless*). You sell sandwiches and pop here, don't you?

Voice (*cranky*). Yep. We do. In the daytime. But we're closed up now for the night.

Adams. I know. But—I was wondering if you could possibly let me have a cup of coffee—black coffee.

Voice. Not at this time of night, mister. My wife's the cook, and she's in bed. Mebbe farther down the road—at the Honeysuckle Rest. . . .

(*Sound: door squeaking on hinges as though being closed*)

Adams. No—no. Don't shut the door. (*shakily*) Listen—just a minute ago, there was a man standing here—right beside this stand—a suspicious looking man. . . .

Woman's voice (*from distance*). Hen-ry? Who is it, Henry?

Henry. It's nobuddy, Mother. Just a feller thinks he wants a cup of coffee. Go back into bed.

Adams. I don't mean to disturb you. But you see, I was driving along—when I just happened to look—and there he was. . . .

Henry. What was he doing?

Adams. Nothing. He ran off—when I stopped the car.

Henry. Then what of it? That's nothing to wake a man in the middle of his sleep about. (*sternly*) Young man, I've got a good mind to turn you over to the sheriff.

Adams. But—I—

Henry. You've been taking a nip; that's what you've been doing. And you haven't got anything better to do than to wake decent folk out of their hard-earned sleep. Get going. Go on.

Adams. But—he looked as though he were going to rob you.

Henry. I ain't got nothin' in this stand to lose. Now—on your way before I call out Sheriff Oakes. (*fade*)

(*Sound: auto hum up*)

Adams. I got into the car again and drove on slowly. I was beginning to hate the car. If I could have found a place to stop . . . to rest a little. But I was in the Ozark Mountains of Missouri now. The few resort places there were closed. Only an occasional log cabin, seemingly deserted, broke the monotony of the wild, wooded landscape. I had seen him at that roadside stand; I knew I would see him again—perhaps at the next turn of the road. I knew that when I saw him next, I would run him down. . . .

(*Sound: auto hum up*)

Adams. But I did not see him again until late next afternoon. . . .

(*Sound of railroad warning signal at crossroads*)

Adams. I had stopped the car at a sleepy little junction just across the border into Oklahoma—to let a train pass by—when he appeared, across the tracks, leaning against a telephone pole.

338 UNIT THREE PART 1: STRUGGLING FOR SURVIVAL

Mini-Lesson Study Skills

GRAPHIC ORGANIZERS Like most plays and short stories, this radio drama has an identifiable plot structure. Remind students that a typical plot (the sequence of related events that make up a story) contains an exposition, a central conflict, complications, a climax, and a resolution.

Application Have students illustrate the dramatic structure of *The Hitchhiker* by using a diagram, chart, or graph. Urge them to study the script first and identify the exact locations of plot elements before they begin their visual aids.

(*Sound: distant sound of train chugging . . . bell ringing steadily*)

Adams (*very tense*). It was a perfectly airless, dry day. The red clay of Oklahoma was baking under the southwestern sun. Yet there were spots of fresh rain on his shoulders. I couldn't stand that. Without thinking, blindly, I started the car across the tracks.

(*Sound: train chugging closer*)

Adams. He didn't even look up at me. He was staring at the ground. I stepped on the gas hard, veering the wheel sharply toward him. I could hear the train in the distance now, but I didn't care. Then something went wrong with the car. It stalled right on the tracks.

(*Sound: train chugging closer; above this, sound of car stalling*)

Adams. The train was coming closer. I could hear its bell ringing and the cry of its whistle. Still he stood there. And now—I knew that he was beckoning—beckoning me to my death.

(*Sound: Train chugging close. Whistle blows wildly. Then train rushes up and by with pistons going, et cetera.*)

Adams. Well—I frustrated him that time. The starter had worked at last. I managed to back up. But when the train passed, he was gone. I was all alone in the hot, dry afternoon.

(*Sound: Train retreating. Crickets begin to sing.*)
(*Music in*)

Adams. After that, I knew I had to do something. I didn't know who this man was or what he wanted of me. I only knew that from now on, I must not let myself be alone on the road for one moment.

(*Sound: auto hum up; slow down; stop; door opening*)

Adams. Hello, there. Like a ride?

Girl. What do you think? How far you going?

Adams. Amarillo . . . I'll take you to Amarillo.

Girl. Amarillo, Texas?

Adams. I'll drive you there.

Girl. Gee!

(*Sound: Door closes. Car starts.*)
(*Music in*)

Girl. Mind if I take off my shoes? My dogs[4] are killing me.

Adams. Go right ahead.

Girl. Gee, what a break this is. A swell car, a decent guy, and driving all the way to Amarillo. All I been getting so far is trucks.

Adams. Hitchhike much?

Girl. Sure. Only it's tough sometimes, in these great open spaces, to get the breaks.

Adams. I should think it would be. Though I'll bet if you get a good pickup in a fast car, you can get to places faster than—say, another person, in another car?

Girl. I don't get you.

Adams. Well, take me, for instance. Suppose I'm driving across the country, say, at a nice steady clip of about forty-five miles an hour. Couldn't a girl like you, just standing beside the road, waiting for lifts, beat me to town after town—provided she got picked up every time in a car doing from sixty-five to seventy miles an hour?

Girl. I dunno. Maybe she could and maybe she couldn't. What difference does it make?

Adams. Oh—no difference. It's just a—crazy idea I had sitting here in the car.

Girl (*laughing*). Imagine spending your time in a swell car thinking of things like that!

Adams. What would you do instead?

---

4. **dogs:** a slang term for feet.

THE HITCHHIKER **339**

Mini-Lesson Grammar

INTERJECTIONS Point out to students that an interjection is a word or group of words used to express a strong feeling or emotion. Interjections express feelings such as surprise, relief, joy, or pain.

Application Invite students to identify several interjections that Fletcher uses on page 339. Have students name the emotion that the interjection expresses. (*Interjections include "Well—"[relief], "Gee!" [surprise], and "Gee," [relief].*) Have students brainstorm a list of emotions and the interjections that express those emotions; list these on the board. Next, ask two volunteers at a time to role-play a dialogue by using the interjections listed. Have the class determine the situation—who and where they are and what they are doing.

Reteaching/Reinforcement

Interjections, p. 544

CUSTOMIZING FOR
Students Acquiring English

6 Ask students to provide synonyms for *phantom*. (Possible responses: *ghost, apparition*)

7 Explain that the expression "keep your eyes peeled" means "to look closely at or examine."

Literary Concept: SUSPENSE

M Ask students to comment on how the sounds contribute to the feeling of suspense. (Possible response: *The sounds of the crash are frightening because the listener does not know if there has been a collision or what the result of the crash might be. Also, the sound of a car skidding is eerily reminiscent of Adams's skidding on the Brooklyn Bridge, so it adds to the feeling of suspense in this scene.*)

Literary Concept: FORESHADOWING

N Point out to students that the radio drama contains several references to sleep. Invite students to comment on how the girl's recommendation of "a good dose of sleep" might foreshadow some later event in the plot. (Possible response: *The girl implies that Adams needs to stop moving. He has been constantly on the go, and her simple recommendation hints that at some later point he may finally be required to stop or something bad might happen to him.*)

STRATEGIC READING FOR
Less-Proficient Readers

O Ask students to explain what Adams means when he states that he is "utterly alone." (*The girl fails to see the hitchhiker, questions Adams's sanity, and then runs away from him and is picked up by a passing truck. At this point Adams realizes that he is both mentally and physically alone.*) **Relating Cause and Effect/Drawing Conclusions**

Set a Purpose Have students read to find out what news Adams gets from Brooklyn.

Girl (*admiringly*). What would I do? If I was a good-looking fellow like yourself? Why—I'd just enjoy myself—every minute of the time. I'd sit back and relax, and if I saw a good-looking girl along the side of the road. . . . (*sharply*) Hey! Look out!

Adams (*breathlessly*). Did you see him too?

Girl. See who?

Adams. That man. Standing beside the barbed wire fence.

Girl. I didn't see—anybody. There wasn't nothing but a bunch of steers—and the barbed wire fence. What did you think you was doing? Trying to run into the barbed wire fence?

Adams. There was a man there, I tell you . . . a thin, gray man with an overnight bag in his hand. And I was trying to—run him down.

Girl. Run him down? You mean—kill him?

Adams. He's a sort of—phantom. I'm trying to get rid of him—or else prove that he's real. But (*desperately*) you say you didn't see him back there? You're sure?

Girl (*queerly*). I didn't see a soul. And as far as that's concerned, mister . . .

Adams. Watch for him the next time, then. Keep watching. Keep your eyes peeled on the road. He'll turn up again—maybe any minute now. (*excitedly*) There. Look there—

(*Sound: Auto sharply veering and skidding. Girl screams.*)

(*Sound: crash of car going into barbed wire fence; frightened lowing[5] of steer*)

Girl. How does this door work? I—I'm gettin' outta here.

Adams. Did you see him that time?

Girl (*sharply*). No. I didn't see him that time. And personally, mister, I don't expect never to see him. All I want to do is to go on living—and I don't see how I will very long, driving with you—

Adams. I'm sorry. I—I don't know what came over me. (*frightened*) Please—don't go. . . .

Girl. So if you'll excuse me, mister—

Adams. You can't go. Listen, how would you like to go to California? I'll drive you to California.

Girl. Seeing pink elephants all the way? No thanks.

Adams (*desperately*). I could get you a job there. You wouldn't have to be a waitress. I have friends there—my name is Ronald Adams—you can check up.

(*Sound: Door opens.*)

Girl. Uhn-huuh. Thanks just the same.

Adams. Listen. Please. For just one minute. Maybe you think I am half-cracked. But this man. You see, I've been seeing this man all the way across the country. He's been following me. And if you could only help me—stay with me—until I reach the coast—

Girl. You know what I think you need, big boy? Not a girl friend. Just a good dose of sleep. . . . There, I got it now.

(*Sound: Door opens . . . slams.*)

Adams. No. You can't go.

Girl (*screams*). Leave your hands offa me, do you hear! Leave your—

Adams. Come back here, please, come back.

(*Sound: struggle . . . slap . . . footsteps running away on gravel . . . lowing of steer*)

Adams. She ran from me as though I were a monster. A few minutes later, I saw a passing truck pick her up. I knew then that I was utterly alone.

(*Sound: lowing of steer up*)

Adams. I was in the heart of the great Texas

---
5. **lowing:** mooing.

340 UNIT THREE PART 1: STRUGGLING FOR SURVIVAL

Mini-Lesson: Speaking,  Listening, and Viewing

DRAMA PERFORMANCE In all drama, actors say lines in certain ways to communicate specific feelings and ideas. Often stage directions give the actor and director suggestions on how certain sentences might be spoken. In many cases, there is more than one way to achieve a vocal effect or a tone of voice, and actors and directors commonly explore a variety of different ways to read or interpret single lines or entire scenes.

Application Have two student actors and a student director study a scene (such as the one between Adams and the female hitchhiker) and rehearse parts of it in several different ways. For instance, the actor playing the girl might start the scene by using a high-pitched voice. Then she might use frequent laughs and giggles. The actor playing Adams might play the scene once trying to hide his nervousness, another time as if he has just seen a ghost. Encourage the director to come up with other acting ideas for both actors. When their scene is fully rehearsed, have them present it to the class.

Hilco (1989), Kit Boyce. Courtesy of the artist.

prairies. There wasn't a car on the road after the truck went by. I tried to figure out what to do, how to get hold of myself. If I could find a place to rest. Or even if I could sleep right here in the car for a few hours, along the side of the road.... I was getting my winter overcoat out of the back seat to use as a blanket (*hall-ooo*) when I saw him coming toward me (*hall-ooo*), emerging from the herd of moving steer....

Voice. Hall-ooo.... Hall-oooo....

(*Sound: auto starting violently ... up to steady hum*)

(*Music in*)

Adams. I didn't wait for him to come any closer. Perhaps I should have spoken to him then, fought it out then and there. For now he began to be everywhere. Whenever I stopped, even for a moment—for gas, for oil, for a drink of pop, a cup of coffee, a sandwich—he was there.

(*Music faster*)

Adams. I saw him standing outside the auto camp in Amarillo that night when I dared to slow down. He was sitting near the drinking fountain in a little camping spot just inside the border of New Mexico.

(*Music faster*)

Adams. He was waiting for me outside the Navajo Reservation, where I stopped to check my tires. I saw him in Albuquerque,[6] where I bought twelve gallons of gas.... I was afraid now, afraid to stop. I began to drive faster and faster. I was in lunar landscape now—the great arid mesa country of

---

6. **Albuquerque** (ăl′bə-kûr′kē): a city in central New Mexico.

THE HITCHHIKER **341**

Mini-Lesson: Speaking, Listening, and Viewing

DRAMA Actors who perform in radio plays can't use all of their usual expressive tools. Techniques ranging from facial expressions to gestures to posture and gait are useless on radio. Consequently, actors need to be even more inventive about the ways in which they use their voices to communicate their characters' personalities and behavior.

Application Have students write several additional lines that might be spoken by various characters in *The Hitchhiker*. Then encourage them to perform them as spoken by the characters. Record the performances on audiotape and have classmates guess the identities of the characters based on students' vocal intonation, accents, and other verbal details.

Active Reading: CLARIFY

R Have students review the warnings Adams was given by his mother before he left New York to drive across country. Has he followed her advice? You may wish to use the following model to give students ideas of what they might be thinking about.

Think-Aloud Model *Adams's mother told him to be careful, to avoid falling asleep while driving, not to pick up strangers, and to wire from Hollywood. He has followed some of her advice but not all of it. It's too soon to tell if he will wire her from Hollywood.*

Linking to Social Studies

S During the time of this story, local telephone operators connected local calls or transferred a caller to a regional long-distance operator. In *The Hitchhiker*, Adams first speaks with an operator in Gallup, New Mexico; then he is transferred to a long-distance operator in Albuquerque; this operator contacts an operator in New York, and the call is connected. The use of a word (such as *Beechwood*) before a number was common until the 1960s; the first two letters of the word corresponded to the first two numerals of the telephone number. Telephone area codes did not come into existence until the mid-1960s.

Literary Concept: SUSPENSE

T Have students explain how this long scene involving various telephone operators helps create suspense. *(Possible response: The scene interrupts the rapidly unfolding events of the plot. Suddenly the reader is delayed by a succession of details that prolong the mystery of what will happen to Adams.)*

R New Mexico. I drove through it with the indifference of a fly crawling over the face of the moon.

(*Music faster*)

Adams. But now he didn't even wait for me to stop. Unless I drove at eighty-five miles an hour over those endless roads—he waited for me at every other mile. I would see his figure, shadowless, flitting before me, still in its same attitude, over the cold and lifeless ground; flitting over dried-up rivers, over broken stones cast up by old glacial upheavals, flitting in the pure and cloudless air. . . .

(*Music strikes sinister note of finality.*)

Adams. I was beside myself when I finally reached Gallup, New Mexico, this morning. There is an auto camp here—cold, almost deserted at this time of year. I went inside and asked if there was a telephone. I had the feeling that if only I could speak to someone familiar, someone that I loved, I could pull myself together.

(*Sound: nickel put in slot*)

Operator. Number, please?

Adams. Long distance.

(*Sound: return of nickel; buzz.*)

Long-distance opr. This is long distance.

Adams. I'd like to put in a call to my home in Brooklyn, New York. I'm Ronald Adams. The number is Beechwood 2-0828.

Long-distance opr. Thank you. What is your number?

Adams. 312

Albuquerque opr. Albuquerque.

Long-distance opr. New York for Gallup. (*pause*)

New York opr. New York.

S **Long-distance opr.** Gallup, New Mexico, calling Beechwood 2-0828. (*fade*)

Adams. I had read somewhere that love could banish demons. It was the middle of the morning. I knew Mother would be home. I pictured her, tall, white-haired, in her crisp house dress, going about her tasks. It would be enough, I thought, merely to hear the even calmness of her voice. . . .

Long-distance opr. Will you please deposit three dollars and eighty-five cents for the first three minutes? When you have deposited a dollar and a half, will you wait until I have collected the money?

(*Sound: clunk of six coins*)

Long-distance opr. All right, deposit another dollar and a half.

(*Sound: clunk of six coins*)

Long-distance opr. Will you please deposit the remaining eighty-five cents?

(*Sound: clunk of four coins*)

Long-distance opr. Ready with Brooklyn—go ahead, please. **T**

Adams. Hello.

Mrs. Whitney. Mrs. Adams's residence.

Adams. Hello. Hello—Mother?

Mrs. Whitney (*very flat and rather proper . . . dumb, too, in a frizzy sort of way*). This is Mrs. Adams's residence. Who is it you wished to speak to, please?

Adams. Why—who's this?

Mrs. Whitney. This is Mrs. Whitney.

Adams. Mrs. Whitney? I don't know any Mrs. Whitney. Is this Beechwood 2-0828?

Mrs. Whitney. Yes.

Adams. Where's my mother? Where's Mrs. Adams?

Mrs. Whitney. Mrs. Adams is not at home. She is still in the hospital.

Adams. The hospital!

342   UNIT THREE   PART 1: STRUGGLING FOR SURVIVAL

Mrs. Whitney. Yes. Who is this calling, please? Is it a member of the family?

Adams. What's she in the hospital for?

Mrs. Whitney. She's been prostrated⁷ for five days. Nervous breakdown. But who is this calling?

Adams. Nervous breakdown? But—my mother was never nervous. . . .

Mrs. Whitney. It's all taken place since the death of her oldest son, Ronald.

Adams. Death of her oldest son, Ronald . . .? Hey—what is this? What number is this?

Mrs. Whitney. This is Beechwood 2-0828. It's all been very sudden. He was killed just six days ago in an automobile accident on the Brooklyn Bridge.

Operator (*breaking in*). Your three minutes are up, sir. (*silence*) Your three minutes are up, sir. (*pause*) Your three minutes are up, sir. (*fade*) Sir, your three minutes are up. Your three minutes are up, sir.

Adams (*in a strange voice*). And so, I am sitting here in this deserted auto camp in Gallup, New Mexico. I am trying to think. I am trying to get hold of myself. Otherwise, I shall go mad. . . . Outside it is night—the vast, soulless night of New Mexico. A million stars are in the sky. Ahead of me stretch a thousand miles of empty mesa, mountains, prairies—desert. Somewhere among them, he is waiting for me. Somewhere I shall know who he is, and who . . . I . . . am. . . .

(*Music up*) ❖

---

7. **prostrated:** in a state of mental collapse.

THE HITCHHIKER **343**

Literary Concept: CLIMAX

U Ask students to identify the climax of *The Hitchhiker*. (*Possible response: The climax is the moment when Adams hears that he was killed in an automobile accident six days earlier.*)

Literary Concept: FLASHBACK

V Point out to students that this is the end of the long flashback that began near the start of the radio play. The reader has now been brought up-to-date on events that occurred since Adams left Brooklyn.

STRATEGIC READING FOR
Less-Proficient Readers

W Have students explain what Adams learns when he calls Brooklyn. (*He learns that he has been dead for the last six days.*) **Drawing Conclusions**

CUSTOMIZING FOR
Gifted and Talented Students

Have students analyze and discuss the story's extensive imagery involving ideas such as travel and a journey. In what way does this imagery work on a metaphorical or symbolic level?

COMPREHENSION CHECK

1. Who doesn't want Ronald Adams to drive across country? (*his mother*)
2. What greeting does the hitchhiker repeatedly call out to Adams? (*"Hall-ooo"*)
3. Why does Adams drive his car into a barbed-wire fence and a herd of steer? (*He is trying to run down the hitchhiker.*)
4. Why is Adams's mother in the hospital? (*She had a nervous collapse after he was killed on the Brooklyn Bridge.*)

Mini-Lesson Spelling

FINAL SILENT e WITH SUFFIXES
Review with students that a suffix is a word ending that changes the meaning or part of speech of a word. When adding a suffix that begins with a vowel to a word that ends with a silent e, you must drop the final e.

    assure + -ance = **assurance**

    menace + -ing = **menacing**

Application Have students copy the spelling rule into their notebooks and then add suffixes to the following words, as indicated.

1. finance + -ial
2. resemble + -ance
3. picture + -ing
4. commerce + -ial
5. drive + -er
6. take + -ing
7. give + -er
8. adhere + -ing
9. emerge + -ence
10. move + -ing

Ask students to look for more words that fit this pattern, in their own writing and in things they read, and to add these words to their personal word lists.

Reteaching/Reinforcement
• *Unit Three Resource Book*, p. 29

Words ending with silent e + suffix beginning with a vowel drop the final e

HISTORICAL INSIGHT

Route 66

Like Ronald Adams in *The Hitchhiker,* hundreds of thousands of travelers chose Route 66 to go west during the mid-twentieth century. Now part of history, Route 66 was one of America's most famous highways. Starting at Grant Park in Chicago, Illinois, it stretched 2,448 miles across two-thirds of the country and eight states to Los Angeles, California. Unlike today's interstate highways which bypass towns, Route 66 passed through the center of towns and became known as "The Main Street of America."

The idea for Route 66 grew out of a decision by the federal government in 1921 to develop a system of interconnected interstate routes. The resulting system included Route 66 as the main artery linking the East and the West. In the years that followed, this famous two-lane road was highly traveled by people moving west and tourists visiting spectacular sites, like the Grand Canyon. Lyrics from Bobby Troup's hit song of 1946 captured the excitement of the road:

> If you ever plan to motor west
> Travel my way, take the highway that's the best.
> Get your kicks on Route Sixty-six! . . .

By the mid-1950s, despite the fact that the old highway was maintained and was divided into four lanes for long sections, it could not handle the growing traffic. Stretches of Route 66 were being replaced here and there to make way for new interstate highways. Even the popular television series of the early 1960s, *Route 66*, was not able to stop the road's death, and the last stretch of U.S. Highway 66 was bypassed by Interstate 40 in 1984 near Williams, Arizona.

RESPONDING OPTIONS

FROM PERSONAL RESPONSE TO CRITICAL ANALYSIS

REFLECT
1. If you were all alone, listening to this drama on the radio, how do you think you would feel? Explain your answer.

RETHINK
Thematic Link

2. What do you think has happened to Adams? Give reasons for your answer.
   Consider
   - how he thinks the hitchhiker is a threat to his survival
   - whether he is dead
   - whether he is mad or insane
   - other possible explanations for his experiences

3. Who do you think the mysterious hitchhiker is? Use details from the play to support your answer.

Close Textual Reading

4. Do you think *The Hitchhiker* is a good horror story? Why or why not?
   Consider
   - the criteria your class discussed for the Personal Connection on page 332
   - the statements and promises in Orson Welles's introduction
   - how it compares with more modern horror stories

RELATE
5. Horror stories have always fascinated readers and audiences of all ages. Why do you think these stories are so popular?

LITERARY CONCEPTS

Foreshadowing is a writer's hinting at a future event in a story. As this play progresses, Lucille Fletcher drops stronger and stronger hints that the innocent-looking fellow on the road will bring an end to Ronald Adams's story. Find some of these clues and connect them with what happens later.

Multimodal Learning
ANOTHER PATHWAY

Use tracing paper to copy the outline of the United States, then draw Adams's route on the map. At appropriate places along the route, write short sentences to describe the incidents that took place on his trip.

QUICKWRITES

1. The ending of this play leaves the audience hanging. Write an additional **scene** that will leave no questions in readers' minds.

2. How could Ronald Adams's drive to California have been different? Rewrite Welles's **introduction**, putting a different spin on the story or setting up the audience for an entirely different kind of horror story.

📁 **PORTFOLIO** Save your writing. You may want to use it later as a springboard to a piece for your portfolio.

THE HITCHHIKER **345**

From Personal Response to Critical Analysis

1. Responses will vary.
2. Possible responses: Adams was killed on the Brooklyn Bridge, but his spirit or mind is still on some kind of journey. Adams has been driven mad by seeing the image of the hitchhiker, and so he thinks he hears Mrs. Whitney say that he is dead.
3. Possible responses: The hitchhiker is someone Adams once knew. The hitchhiker is some image or memory of Adams himself.
4. Remind students to draw on specific examples from the text when explaining their answers.
5. Possible response: People are fascinated with things that are unknown or mysterious. People like being scared by a story and then feeling comfortable again in real life.

Literary Link

Ask students how Adams is similar to the lawyer in "The Bet." *(Possible response: Both men experience a death of sorts. Adams is dead without realizing it, whereas the lawyer, although living, lives as though he were dead.)*

Another Pathway

Have students review the story, paying special attention to all the locations mentioned. Encourage them to note the events that occur in each place. Remind students that their summaries of events should be concise but should include detailed explanations of what happened.

Rubric
3 Full Accomplishment Students make an accurate map and write concise descriptions of central plot points.
2 Substantial Accomplishment Students map out Adams's journey and write descriptions of several plot points.
1 Little or Partial Accomplishment Students map out parts of Adams's journey and have difficulty writing descriptions of plot points.

Literary Concepts

Have students work in small groups to look for and discuss hints about the hitchhiker. Help students find clues such as the hitchhiker's unchanging appearance, the unlikely places he appears, and the fact that Adams's companion in the car sees nothing except steers along the side of the road.

QuickWrites

1. Have students decide what information or message the scene will convey. Encourage them to write this information in one or two sentences. Then have them think about the best way to dramatize this information.

2. Ask students to sketch out their plans for the alternate version. Then they can go back to Welles's introduction and see what needs to be revised to match their own plan.

The Writer's Craft
Script Writing, pp. 86–88

THE LANGUAGE OF LITERATURE Teacher's Edition **345**

Words to Know

Possible synonyms and antonyms for the words follow:

assurance—*promise, guarantee; doubt, question*

lark—*escapade, adventure; stagnation, inertia*

menacing—*threatening, ominous; peaceful, friendly*

nondescript—*drab, unchanging; dynamic, colorful*

sinister—*evil, wicked; good, wholesome*

Reteaching/Reinforcement
• *Unit Three Resource Book*, p. 30

Across the Curriculum

Mathematics *Coast to Coast* The most direct route would probably be as follows: Interstate 95 to Interstate 70 (Washington, D.C.) to Interstate 44 (St. Louis) to Interstate 40 (Oklahoma City) through Gallup to Interstate 15 (Barstow) to Los Angeles. This route is approximately 3,000 miles. At 55 miles an hour for 8 hours a day, this trip would take almost 7 days.

ADDITIONAL SUGGESTION

 **Social Studies** *Destination Gallup* Have students do research on this city in northwestern New Mexico. Encourage them to seek out information on the community's importance as a transportation center (a shipping hub for cattle, wool, animal hides, and forest products) and as a gathering place for various Native American tribes.

LUCILLE FLETCHER

Other works by Lucille Fletcher include *Night Man, The Daughters of Jasper Clay, Blindfold, The Strange Blue Yawl,* and *The Girl in Cabin B54.*

Multimodal Learning

ALTERNATIVE ACTIVITIES

Cooperative Learning With your classmates, produce *The Hitchhiker* as a radio play. Some students can play roles, while others can provide the necessary music and sound effects. Audiotape the performance for other classes to hear.

ACROSS THE CURRICULUM

Mathematics Use a current road map of the United States to calculate the mileage from Brooklyn, New York, to Los Angeles, California, using the most direct route that will take you through Gallup, New Mexico, and on to Los Angeles. Driving at 55 miles per hour, for 8 hours a day, how long would it take to reach Los Angeles?

WORDS TO KNOW

Review the Words to Know at the bottom of the selection pages. On your paper, create a word web like the one below for each vocabulary word.

Eerie
- Synonym: weird
- Antonym: comforting
- Synonym: frightening
- Antonym: familiar

LUCILLE FLETCHER

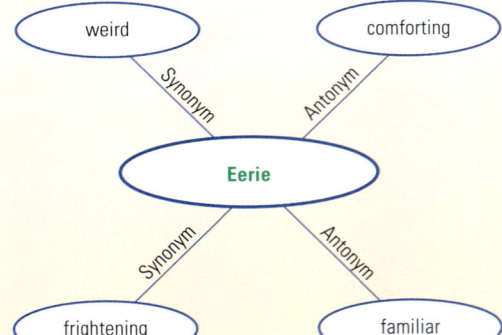

1912–

Lucille Fletcher was born in Brooklyn, New York, where Ronald Adams's frightening trip begins. A graduate of Vassar College, she married another writer, the novelist Douglass Wallop III. They lived on the eastern shore of Maryland's Chesapeake Bay until Wallop's death in 1985.

During the 1930s and 1940s, Fletcher kept radio audiences on the edge of their seats with her chilling mystery dramas. She is best known for her radio play *Sorry, Wrong Number,* a suspense classic. She wrote 20 plays for the radio series *Suspense* and scripts for the television series *Chrysler Theater* and *Lights Out.* Fletcher has also written several mystery novels—including *And Presumed Dead* and *Blindfold,* which were made into movies. Her first Broadway play, *Night Watch,* was produced in 1972 and later made into a movie starring Elizabeth Taylor.

OTHER WORKS *Mirror Image, Eighty Dollars to Stamford* Extended Reading

346 UNIT THREE PART 1: STRUGGLING FOR SURVIVAL

Alternative Activities

Cooperative Learning Thirteen students can play the 13 roles in the radio play, or some students can play more than one small role. Encourage nontraditional casting choices, such as having a boy play one of the telephone operators and a girl play the mechanic. A small group of students can be responsible for collecting previously recorded sounds, as well as coming up with ideas for live sound effects. Remind students to refer to some of their exercises from the speaking, listening, and viewing mini-lessons. Although you may wish to direct the performance yourself, you might also choose one or two capable students to oversee all of the production's artistic considerations.

ON YOUR OWN

 REFLECT & ASSESS

THE FLOOD

by Ralph Helfer

It was
raining that morning,
as usual. For weeks it had
been coming down—sometimes
heavily, with thunder and
lightning, and sometimes with
just a mist of light rain.
But it was always there,
and by now the blankets,
the beds, and the whole
house were constantly damp.

OBJECTIVES

- To promote independent active reading
- To apply and practice skills learned in previous selections
- To provide an opportunity to assess students' performance through an alternative assessment instrument

Reading Pathways

- Encourage students to read independently for enjoyment.
- Have students take notes on questions that occur to them as they read.
- Invite students to choose passages from the nonfiction account to read aloud.
- Evaluate how well students can read, interpret, discuss, and write about the selection on their own by using the Integrated Assessment booklet. Administer the assessment at the end of the unit after students have read all the selections and completed all the writing that was assigned. Set aside two class periods, or about two hours, for the assessment.

PRINT AND MEDIA RESOURCES

UNIT THREE RESOURCE BOOK
Strategic Reading: Literature, p. 33

FORMAL ASSESSMENT
Selection Test, p. 65
Part Test, pp. 67–68
Test Generator

ALTERNATIVE ASSESSMENT
Unit Three Integrated Assessment, pp. 13–18

ACCESS FOR STUDENTS ACQUIRING ENGLISH
Selection Summaries

AUDIO LIBRARY
See Reference Card

THE LANGUAGE OF LITERATURE TEACHER'S EDITION **347**

SUMMARY

Ralph Helfer recalls a flood that devastated his ranch north of Los Angeles, California. The ranch served as a home for a host of exotic animals—including bears, lions, tigers, elephants, and wolves—that Helfer trained to perform in movies and television. As he, his wife Toni, and their assistants work to save the animals from the floodwaters, they find that the animals cooperate with them and also help one another. After three days, the rain lets up and the waters subside, but many animals are injured or missing. Community members offer help. Gradually, almost all of the missing animals turn up and are reunited with the Helfers.

Thematic Link: *Struggling for Survival*
Both human beings and captive wild animals struggle and help one another to survive against deadly floodwaters.

My career was at a peak. I'd spent twelve years struggling to get to the top, and I had finally made it. My life was pretty good. I had just completed the back-to-back shooting of *Daktari* and *Gentle Ben*, and I was living at our new ranch, Africa U.S.A., with 1500 wild animals and a crew of dedicated keepers and trainers.

The ranch was beautiful. Nestled at the bottom of Soledad Canyon, about thirty miles north of Los Angeles, the property snaked for a mile down the canyon beside the banks of the Santa Clarita stream. The highway wound above it on one side, the railroad track on the other.

> **As I left the rhinos, I noticed that I could no longer jump over the stream that ran beside their barn. I was starting to get a little concerned.**

We'd had heavy rains before, and even a few floods, but nothing we couldn't handle. There was a flood-control dam above us, fifteen miles up the canyon, and we weren't too worried about the stream's overflowing. But just to make sure, we had asked the city's flood-control office to advise us. They checked their records for the biggest flood in the office's hundred-year history, and calculated that to handle one that size we would need a channel 100 feet wide, 12 feet deep, and 1 mile long. It cost us $100,000 and three months of hard work, but we built it. It was worth it to feel safe.

Toni and I had grabbed a few hours' sleep before leaving the house, which was located off the ranch up on a hill, and heading out into the rain again early this morning to make sure our animals were dry and safe.

On arriving at the compound, Toni went over to check on the "wild string," a group of lions, tigers, bears, and leopards that had been donated to us by people who never should have had them in the first place. Hopeless animal lovers that we were, we had taken them in, even though we knew that very few spoiled mature animals could ever be indoctrinated with affection training.

I checked at the office for messages, then headed for "Beverly Hills," our nickname for the area where our movie-star animals lived—Gentle Ben, Clarence the cross-eyed lion, Judy the chimp, Bullfrog the "talking" buffalo, Modoc the elephant, and many others. The rain had become a steady downpour by the time I arrived there. Everything seemed to be in order, so I went on to the rhinos. No problems there, either.

As I left the rhinos, I noticed that I could no longer jump over the stream that ran beside their barn. I was starting to get a little concerned. The sky was now opening up with a vengeance. I wrapped my poncho around me and continued my tour of inspection.

I was wondering how Toni was making out with the wild string, when Miguel, a Mexican keeper who had been with us for six years, arrived to care for the animals in the Beverly Hills section. He smiled his broad, gold-capped grin, then disappeared around a bend of the stream.

Then my head trainer, Frank Lamping, arrived. He told me that the earthen dam above us was about to go. To prevent the dam from bursting, the flood-control people were opening the floodgates to release the pressure. We were to watch out for some heavy water coming downstream.

The crew had all been working continuously from morning until night since the rains had

Copyright © Richard R. Hewett/Shooting Star.

Linking to History

The floods that crashed through southern California in the first two months of 1969 left more than 100 people dead and caused extensive property damage. Other notable floods in U.S. history include the following:

- 1889, Johnstown, Pennsylvania—A defective dam burst and caused the Johnstown flood, which killed more than 2,200 people.
- 1972, Man, West Virginia—Torrential rainstorms caused a dam to break; 118 people died when a 17-mile valley was flooded.
- 1972, East Coast—Tropical storm Agnes caused flash floods that killed 129 people along the eastern seaboard.
- 1993, states along the Mississippi River from Minnesota to Missouri—Ten states were affected by two months of heavy rain. The region suffered at least $12 billion in property damage; 70,000 people lost their homes; and nearly 50 people died.

---

begun, to make sure that the ranch was safe. Now we had to redouble our efforts.

I told Frank to check the stock area. A trainer yelled from the roadway above that he had the nursery section under control.

I found some pretty badly undermined cages in my area and set to work with a shovel to fill the erosion. I was looking down at my shovel, working hard, when I heard a noise. It was a low roar, and it was quickly becoming louder and closer. I remember just looking over my shoulder, and suddenly there it was—a wall of water carrying with it full-sized oak trees, sheds, branches. Down it came, crashing and exploding against the compound, uprooting cages, overturning buildings, trucks—anything in its way.

Instantly, everything was in chaos. Sheer panic broke out among the animals in the Beverly Hills section. Lions were roaring and hitting against the sides of their cages; bears were lunging against the bars; chimps were screaming. The water was starting to rock the cages. Some were already floating and were about to be swept downstream.

I didn't know what to do first! I raced for the cages but was thrown down by the weight of the water. Miguel came running over, yelling half in English and half in Spanish. I told him to grab a large coil of rope that was hanging in a tree nearby. I fastened it around me and, with Miguel holding the other end, I started out into the water. If I could just get to the cages, I could unlock them and set the animals free. At least then they could fend for themselves. It was their only chance. Otherwise, they would all drown in their cages.

The water was rushing past me furiously. I struggled through it to Gentle Ben's cage, fumbling for the key. "Don't *drop* it!" I mumbled to myself. The key turned, I threw open the door, and the great old bear landed right on top of me in his panic for freedom.

I grabbed Ben's heavy coat and hung on as his massive body carried me to a group of cages holding more than twenty animals. The water was now five or six feet deep. Cages were starting to come loose from their foundations; the animals were swimming inside them, fighting for breath. I let go of Ben and grabbed onto the steel bars of one of the cages. My heart sank as I saw Ben dog-paddling, trying to reach the embankment. He never did. I could just barely make out his form as he was carried through some rough white water and around a bend before he was lost from view.

One by one I released the animals—leopards, tigers, bears—talking as calmly as I could, even managing an occasional pat or kiss of farewell. I watched as they were carried away, swept along with the torrent of water. Some would come together for a moment and would then be whisked away, as though a giant hand had come up and shoved them. Some went under. I strained to see whether any of these came up again, but I couldn't tell.

My wonderful, beloved animals were all fighting for their lives. I felt sick and helpless.

To my right, about thirty feet out in the water and half submerged, was a large, heavy steel cage on wheels with a row of four compartments in it. I managed to get to it just as the force of the current started to move it. I began to open the compartments, one by one, but now the cage was moving faster downstream, carrying me with it. I looked back to the shore, at Miguel. He saw the problem, and with his end of the rope he threw a dally[1] around a large tree branch. We were running out of time. If the rope came to the end of its slack before I could get it off me and onto the cage, we would lose the cage. It was picking up

---

1. **threw a dally:** looped the rope around an immovable object to keep it from slipping.

350   UNIT THREE   PART 1: STRUGGLING FOR SURVIVAL

speed, and the animals inside were roaring and barking in terror.

I decided to hold the cage myself, with the rope tied around my waist. There were two beautiful wolves in the last cage, Sheba and Rona. Toni and I had raised them since they were pups. I was at their door, fumbling with the lock, when the rope went taut. I thought it would cut me in half. I grabbed the steel bars with both hands, leaving the key in the lock, praying it wouldn't drop out. When I reached down once more to open the lock, the key fell into the water! I was stunned, frozen. I knew I had just signed those animals' death warrants. The water behind the cage was building up a wall of force. I held on as tightly as I could, but finally the cage was ripped out of my hands.

I fell backward into the churning water; when I surfaced, I could see the cage out in the mainstream, racing with the trees, bushes, and sides of buildings, heading on down the raging river. I looked for the last time at Sheba and Rona. They were looking at us quietly as if they knew, but their eyes begged for help. My tears joined the flood as my beloved friends were washed away.

By this time it had become clear to me what had happened. The floodgates on the dam had been opened, all right, but because the ground was already saturated with the thirty inches of rain that had fallen in the last few weeks, it wouldn't absorb any more. At the same time, the new storm had hit, pouring down another fourteen inches in just twenty-four hours. Together, these conditions had caused the flood.

It was a larger flood than any that had been recorded in the area in the last hundred years, and it was made worse because the water had been held up occasionally on its fifteen-mile journey down the canyon by debris in its path. When suddenly released, the water that had built up behind the naturally formed logjams doubled in force. By the time it reached us, huge waves had been built up: the water and debris came crashing down on us like a wall, then subsided, only to come crashing down again. We were to struggle through two days and nights of unbelievable havoc and terror, trying desperately to salvage what we could of the ranch.

> At the same time, the new storm had hit, pouring down another fourteen inches in just twenty-four hours.

The storm grew worse. Heavy sheets of rain filled and overflowed our flood channel, undermining its sides until they caved in. By mid-morning the Santa Clarita had become a raging, murderous torrent, 150 feet wide and 15 feet deep, moving through Africa U.S.A. with the speed and force of an express train. In its fury it wiped out a two-lane highway, full-grown oak trees, generator buildings—everything. Our soundstage was in a full-sized building, 100 feet long by 50 feet wide, but the water just picked it up like a matchbox and carried it away downstream, end over end, rolling it like a toy and depositing it on a sand embankment a mile away. Electric wires flared brightly as the water hit them. We rushed for the main switch to the soundstage, shutting everything down for fear of someone being electrocuted. Everywhere, animals and people were in the water, swimming for safety.

We'd be half drowned, and then we'd make our way to the shore, cough and sputter, and go back into the water. You don't think at a time like that—you *do*.

My people risked their lives over and over again for the animals.

The waves next hit the elephant pens, hard. We moved the elephants out as the building collapsed and was carried downstream. Then the waves caught the camels' cage, pulling it into the water. One huge camel was turning over and over as he was swept along. (I thought at the time that somewhere, someday, if that animal drowned, some archeologist would dig up its bones and say, "My God, there must have been camels in Los Angeles!")

We worked frenziedly. Bears, lions, and tigers were jumping out of their cages and immediately being swept downstream. Others were hanging onto our legs and pulling us under, or we were hanging onto them and swimming for shore. I unlocked the cheetah's cage, and he sprang out over my head, right into the water, and was gone. Animals were everywhere.

I remember grabbing hold of a mature tiger as

 Multicultural Perspectives

AFRICAN ANIMALS Helfer named his ranch "Africa U.S.A." because of the many animals from Africa that he kept and trained there. Africa's animals, such as the lion, giraffe, and elephant, are well-known throughout the world. One reason Africa is the home of such animals is because of its geographic history. Earth can be divided into several distinct geographical regions based on the distribution of mammals. Land masses that have been isolated for a great period of time, such as Africa and Australia, have developed organisms unique to the continent (such as the giraffe in Africa and the kangaroo in Australia).

Unfortunately, changes in the climate, as well as the expansion of the human population, have caused a great reduction in the African animal population. However, through international efforts to save and preserve endangered wildlife, African countries have outlawed the killing of certain animals and established protected game reserves and national parks to provide these animals with a safe place to live. As a result, the exporting of African animals is now more carefully monitored.

he came out of his cage. He carried me on his back to temporary security on the opposite bank as smoothly as if we'd rehearsed it.

Another time I found myself being carried downstream with Zamba, Jr., who was caught in the same whirlpool that I was. I grabbed his mane, and together we swam for the safety of the shore. After resting a bit, I managed to get back to the main area, leaving the lion in as good a spot as any. At least for the moment he was safe.

As the storm rode on, the river was full of animals and people swimming together; there was no "kill" instinct in operation, only that of survival. Men were grabbing fistfuls of fur, clinging for life. A monkey grabbed a lion's tail, which allowed him to make it to safety.

Clarence the cross-eyed lion was in a state of panic. The river had surrounded him and was now flooding his cage. His trainer, Bob, waded across the water, put a chain on Clarence, took him out of his cage, and attempted to jump across the raging stream with him. But the lion wouldn't jump. The water was rising rapidly. Bob threw part of the chain to me. To gain some leverage, I grabbed a pipe that was running alongside a building. As we both pulled, Clarence finally jumped, and just then the pipe I was holding onto came loose. It turned out to be a "hot" electric conduit, for when Clarence leaped and the pipe came loose, we all got a tremendous electric shock! Fortunately, the pipe also pulled the wires loose, so the shock only lasted for an instant. Had it continued, it would certainly have killed us, as we were standing knee-deep in water.

We noticed a group of monkeys trapped in a small outcropping of dirt and debris in the middle of the river. Frank almost died trying to save them: he tied a rope around his waist and started across, but about halfway over he slipped and went under. We didn't know whether to pull on the rope or not. We finally saw him in midstream, trying to stay afloat. Whenever we pulled on the rope, he would go under. (We found out later that the rope had become tangled around his foot, and every time we yanked it we were pulling him under!) But he made it, thank God, and he was able to swim the animals to safety.

We were racing against time. The river was still rising, piling up roots and buildings and pushing them along in front, forming a wall of destruction. The shouts of half-drowned men and the screams of drowning animals filled the air, along with thunder and lightning and the ever-increasing downpour of rain.

Throughout the turmoil and strife one thing was crystal clear to me, and that is that without affection training, all would have been lost. It was extraordinary. As dangerous and frightening as the emergency was, these animals remained calm enough to let themselves be led to safety when it was possible for us to do so.

Imagine yourself in a raging storm, with buildings crashing alongside of you. You make your way to a cage that houses a lion or a tiger, and the animal immediately understands why you're there and is happy to see you. You open the door, put a leash on the animal, and you both jump out into the freezing, swirling water. Together, you're swept down the stream, hitting logs, rolling over and over, as you try to keep your arms around the animal. Together, you get up onto the safety of dry land. You dry off, give your animal a big hug, and then go back in for another one.

There was one big cage left in the back section containing a lion. This lion was a killer who had been fear trained rather than affection trained. We went out to him. The other lions were being saved because we could swim with them, but this fellow was too rough. I got to the cage and opened the door. A couple of my men threw ropes on the lion and pulled, trying to get him out of his potential grave—but he

Linking to Science

Although lions used to roam throughout Europe, Asia, and Africa, now they live mainly in Africa south of the Sahara. Popularly referred to as "the king of beasts," the lion is one of the largest cats: a male lion can stand three feet high and ten feet long from nose to tip of tail and can weigh about 500 pounds. Male lions have impressive manes, which surround their faces with shaggy fur. Females are smaller and do not have manes. The female lion hunts (sometimes in a pack with other females) gazelles, antelopes, giraffes, zebras, and other smaller animals. Lions are part of the genus *(Leo)* that includes the other large, roaring cats: leopards, tigers, jaguars, snow leopards, and clouded leopards.

Linking to Science

An Indian buffalo is the same as a water buffalo. Herds of these huge animals—which are similar to oxen—live wild in swampy areas through much of Southeast Asia. They can be extremely aggressive toward other animals and human beings. Indian buffaloes are also raised in captivity, primarily for milk and butter, as well as for their thick, black hides.

---

wouldn't come out. He was petrified! We pulled and struggled and fought to get him out of the cage, but we couldn't do it, and we finally had to let him go.

Then the "wild string" panicked, and in their hysteria they attacked their rescuers as if they were enemies. In the end, we had to resort to tranquilizer guns. We fired darts into each fear-trained animal, and as they succumbed to the medication, we held their bodies up above the water and carried them to safety. Tragically, there was not enough time to drag all of them to safety; several drowned in their drugged sleep before we could reach them.

> We eventually became stranded with some of the animals on an island—this was all that was left of Africa U.S.A.

The storm continued on into the night, and with the darkness came a nightmare of confusion. We worked on without sleep, sustained by coffee and desperation.

During that first night, it became clear that ancient Modoc, the elephant, the one-eyed wonder of the big top,[2] had by no means outlived her capacity for calmness and courage in the face of disaster. Modoc took over, understanding fully what was at stake and what was required of her. Animal after animal was saved as she labored at the water's edge, hauling their cages to safety on higher ground. When the current tore a cage free and washed it downstream, Modoc got a firmer grip on the rope with her trunk and, with the power of several bulldozers, steadily dragged the cage back to safety. Then a trainer would attach the rope to another endangered pen, and Modoc would resume her labors.

We eventually became stranded with some of the animals on an island—this was all that was left of Africa U.S.A., plus the area alongside the railroad track. When the dam had burst upstream, the wall of water that hit the ranch divided into two fast-moving rivers. As time passed, the rivers widened and deepened until they were impossible to cross. As dusk fell on the second day, we realized that we were cut off from the mainland. Since it was the highest ground on the ranch, the island in the center had become the haven for all the survivors. The office building, the vehicles, and about twenty cages were all well above the flooded zone and so were safe for the time being. The giraffes, some monkeys, and one lion were all housed in makeshift cages on the island. We all hoped the water would not rise any further.

Behind the office building ran a railroad track. By following the tracks for three miles, it would be possible to reach the highway. The problem would then be in crossing the torrent of water to get to the road.

I noticed that Bullfrog, our thousand-pound Indian buffalo, was gone. Buffalos are known to be excellent swimmers. Surely he could survive! I asked around to see whether anyone had seen him. No one had. Bullfrog's cage had been at the entrance to the ranch, because he always greeted visitors with a most unusual bellow that sounded exactly like the word "Hi." Now he was gone, too. Would it ever end? I felt weak. The temperature had dropped, and the wind had come up. The wind-chill factor was now thirty degrees below zero.

There's something horrible about tragedy that occurs in the dark. I could hear the water

---

2. **big top:** the main tent of a traveling circus.

354   UNIT THREE   PART 1: STRUGGLING FOR SURVIVAL

running behind me, and every once in a while I'd hear a big timber go, or an animal cry, or a person shouting. It all seemed very unreal.

Throughout the night and all the next day the rain continued, and we worked on. Luckily, help came from everywhere. The highway, which we could no longer get to but which we could see, was lined with cars. Some people had successfully rigged up a bos'n chair[3] 50 feet in the air and were sending hot food and drink over to us, a distance of some 200 yards. Other people were walking three miles over the hills to bring supplies. Radio communication was set up by a citizens-band club. Gardner McKay, the actor and a true friend, put his Mercedes on the track, deflated the tires, and slowly drove down to help us. One elderly woman prepared ham and coffee and brought it in at two o'clock in the morning, only to find on her return that her car had been broken into and robbed!

Then a train engine came down the track to help (just an engine—no cars). Three girls from the affection-training school volunteered to rescue the snakes. The girls climbed onto the cowcatcher on the front of the engine. We then wrapped about thirty feet of pythons and boa constrictors around their shoulders and told them where to take the snakes once they were on the other side. (There was, of course, no more electricity in the reptile and nursery area, and unless we could get the reptiles to some heat, they would surely die.) Goats, aoudads, and llamas all rode in the coal bin behind the engine. I'll never forget the look on one girl's face as the engine pulled out and a python crawled through her hair.

By four the next morning, some twenty people had, by some method or another, made it over to our island to help. Some chose a dangerous way, tying ropes around their middles and entering the water slowly, with those on the island holding the other ends of the ropes. Then, with the current carrying them quickly downstream, they would look for a logjam or boulder to stop them so they could make their way to where we were.

I was having some coffee in the watchmen's trailer when the scream of an animal shattered the night. I dashed out to find a small group of people huddled together, trying to shine their flashlights on the animal who was out there in the dark, desperately struggling in the raging water. It had succeeded in swimming out of the turbulence in the middle of the stream, but the sides of the river were too slippery for it to get a foothold and climb to safety. In the dark, I couldn't make out which animal it was. Then I heard it: "Hi! Hi!" It was a call of desperation from Bullfrog, the buffalo, as he fought for his life. There was nothing we could do to help him, and his "Hi's" trailed down the dark, black abyss, fading as he was carried away around the bend.

Then Toni screamed at me in the dark, "Ralph, over here!" I fought my way through a maze of debris and water and burst into a clearing. There was Toni, holding a flashlight on—lo and behold—a big steel cage from Beverly Hills! It had been washed downstream and was lodged in the trunk of a toppled tree. It was still upright, but its back was facing us, and we couldn't see inside. We waded out to the cage. Toni kept calling, "Sheba, Rona, are you there? Please answer!" Our hearts were beating fast, and Toni was crying.

Hoping against hope that the wolves were still alive, we rounded the corner, half swimming, half falling. Then we eased up to the front of the cage and looked straight into two sets of the most beautiful eyes I'd ever seen. Rona and

---

3. **bos'n** (bō′sən) **chair:** a sling moved by an arrangement of ropes and pulleys, usually used to transfer people or materials from one ship to another or from a ship to shore.

Copyright © Richard R. Hewett/Shooting Star.

Sheba had survived! They practically jumped out of their skins when they saw us, as though to say, "Is it really *you?*" Toni had her key, and we unlocked the door. Both wolves fell all over us, knocking us into the water. They couldn't seem to stop licking our faces and whimpering. Thank God, at least *they* were safe!

The rain finally let up on the morning of the third day. The sun came out, and at last we had time to stop, look around, and assess the damage. It was devastating, and heartrending.

Most of the animals had been let out of their cages and had totally disappeared, including Judy, Clarence, Pajama Tops the zebra, and Raunchy, our star jaguar. We knew a few others had definitely drowned. Both rhinos were missing, and so were the hippos. Our beloved

Gentle Ben had been washed away, along with hundreds of other animals.

I was sitting there looking at the wreckage when somebody put a cup of hot chocolate in my hand. It was Toni. She stood before me, as exhausted as I was, clothes torn and wet, hair astray, cold and shivering. What a woman! Earlier, she had managed to make her way to the Africa U.S.A. nursery, where all of the baby animals were quartered. Without exception, the babies had all followed her to safety. Not one baby animal had been lost.

The hot liquid felt good going down. I stood up and hugged and kissed Toni, and arm in arm we walked. The sun was just topping the cottonwoods. The river had subsided. All was quiet, except for an occasional animal noise: a yelp, a growl, a snort. All of the animals were happy to see the sun, to feel its warmth.

Toni and I felt only the heavy, leaden feeling of loss. Ten years were, literally, down the drain. We had just signed a contract with Universal Studios to open our beautiful ranch to their tours; this would now be impossible. A million dollars was gone, maybe more. But what was far worse was the loss of some of our beloved animals.

We hiked to a ridge above the railroad track. Something caught my eye, and as we came near an outcrop of trees where we could have a better view, we looked over. There, on top of a nearby hill, we saw an incredible sight. Lying under the tree was Zamba, and at his feet, resting, were a multitude of animals. Deer, bears, tigers, llamas, all lying together peacefully. The animals must have fought their way clear of the treacherous waters and, together, climbed the hill, slept, and then dried off in the morning sun. They hadn't run away. In fact, they seemed to be waiting for our next move. It was as though God had caused the flood to make me realize how powerful affection training is, how deep it had gone. The lamb could truly lie down with the lion, without fear, and could do it by choice!

We called Zam over to us and smothered him with hugs and kisses. As we climbed down to the ranch, the other animals joined us. Camels, giraffes, eland—all came along as we wound our way down.

So many people were there at the ranch! We were once again connected with the rest of the world. Exhausted, wet, wonderful people—true animal lovers. They had come from everywhere. Some were employees, some friends, some strangers. All greeted us as we came down the hill. Their faces expressed hope and love. They cared . . . and it showed.

> The rain finally let up on the morning of the third day. The sun came out, and at last we had time to stop, look around, and assess the damage.

We took the animals one by one and fed, cleaned, and housed them as best we could.

"Ralph, come quickly!" screamed a voice. "He made it, he made it! *He's alive!*"

"Who, who?" I screamed, and was met by a resounding "Hi, Hi!" From around the corner came Bullfrog—disheveled and muddy, but alive!

"Hi, hi!"

Yes, *hi*, you big lovable . . . hi! hi!

We began searching for the animals that were still lost. The ranch was a network of people and animals working together on the massive cleanup effort. Animals were straining to pull big trucks out of the water and muck.

THE FLOOD 357

OPTION 1

Cooperative Learning

CREATING A NARRATIVE MURAL

Have groups of students review "The Flood" to select a scene that they would like to paint in a mural detailing several key moments from Helfer's nonfiction account. Encourage them to think about the differences between a portrait of an animal and a narrative painting that shows an animal in the midst of a scene or story. Point out that the goal of a portrait painter is to convey an animal's physical appearance or essential nature, whereas a narrative painter attempts to convey an animal's behavior as some event unfolds. Of course, often the narrative artist is also able to capture an animal's physical appearance and something of its essential nature.

Teacher's Role You may wish to remind students that they can examine photographs or paintings of animals to help them make decisions about how to create their own work. You might help them work effectively together by having some group members serve as illustrators, some as recorders of details from the text, and at least one group member as a liaison with other groups.

Rubric

3 Full Accomplishment Students create a painting that vividly and accurately conveys a scene from the narrative and that fits into the overall framework of a mural.

2 Substantial Accomplishment Students create a painting that conveys a scene from the narrative and that fits into the overall framework of a mural.

1 Little or Partial Accomplishment Students have difficulty creating a painting that conveys a scene from the narrative or that fits into the overall framework of a mural.

THE LANGUAGE OF LITERATURE TEACHER'S EDITION 357

OPTION 2

Individual Activity

LISTING ANIMALS, EVENTS, AND OUTCOMES

Have students make a list of animals that Ralph Helfer mentions in his account of the flood. Then have them give a brief description of the flood's immediate effect on the animal ("got pulled under the water," "disappeared down the river") and finally the fate of the animal.

Teacher's Role Help students find concise ways to identify each type of animal and to describe the moment when the author loses contact with or saves it.

Rubric

3 Full Accomplishment Students produce a thorough list that notes all animals, as well as the flood's immediate and ultimate effects on them.

2 Substantial Accomplishment Students produce a list that notes most animals, as well as the flood's immediate and ultimate effects on them.

1 Little or Partial Accomplishment Students have difficulty producing a list that notes animals and the flood's immediate and ultimate effects on them.

Bakery trucks were coming by with stale bread for the elephants. Farmers loaned us their skip loaders to round up the hippos and rhinos. (One hippo fell in love with the skip-loader bucket and coyly followed it home!) Charley and Madeline Franks, two loyal helpers, kept hot chili coming and must have dished out hundreds of meals. People from the Humane Society, Fish and Game, Animal Regulation, and the SPCA[4] all helped to comfort and tend the animals.

Everyone was busy constructing makeshift cages. The medical-lab trailer was pulled out of the mud. The nursery building and all of its kitchen storage area had been completely submerged, and some of it had been washed away. However, what could be salvaged was taken up to the island for immediate use.

> **Of 1500 other animals, only 9 had drowned. Five of these were animals that had not been affection trained.**

Outside the ranch, the animals began turning up everywhere. Elephants showed up in people's backyards. Eagles sat in the limbs of trees. Llamas and guanacos cruised the local restaurants and were seen in parking lots. There was no difficulty between animals and people.

We had had dozens of alligators, some weighing two hundred to three hundred pounds. The whole pen had been hit by the water; we lost most of them because the water was ice-cold, and it battered and beat them. For seven months afterward we'd read in the paper that the bodies of alligators were being found everywhere, up to forty-five miles away. There were helicopter and airplane photos of alligators that had been killed, their bodies lying in the sand as the water subsided.

Of 1500 other animals, only 9 had drowned. Five of these were animals that had not been affection trained.

Only one animal remained lost and unaccounted for, and that was old Gentle Ben. I had last seen him being swept sideways down the river. We didn't have much hope for him.

I was starting to feel the full shock of everything that had happened. True, by some miracle most of the animals were safe, but other losses had been enormous. As the emergency lessened and mopping-up operations took over, I felt worse and worse. The shakes set in, and then I developed a high fever. The doctors said it was a walking pneumonia, and that rest, good food, and warmth were in order. But there were still too many things to do—now was not the time to stop. I did, however, need to find a place to sit down and relax for a while.

As I sat on a log, my body trembled with shock as well as illness. In looking over the debris, it seemed to me that everything I had worked for was gone. The emotional pain, the sheer physical exhaustion, and the pneumonia had overloaded me. I just couldn't handle any more. I had no more tears, no pain of any kind. I was numb. I sat in the middle of the chaos with an old blanket wrapped around me, unmoving, unable to give any more orders.

I had closed my eyes and was drifting off to sleep when something warm and wet on my face woke me up. I opened my eyes and saw Ben. *Gentle Ben had come home!!* I hugged him and cried like a big kid. I turned to get up to tell everyone, but I didn't have to. They

---

4. **SPCA:** Society for the Prevention of Cruelty to Animals.

were all there. Toni, joined by the rest, had brought him to me. He'd been found two miles down the canyon, mud-covered and a few pounds lighter, but safe! Tears were in everybody's eyes—and if you looked closely, it seemed that even old Ben had a few.

A beautiful rainbow arched its brilliant colors across the ravaged countryside, then was gone.

There was a time in my life when I felt I had reached the end of the rainbow. I had touched it, had dug my hand deep into its treasures of happiness and prosperity.

Suddenly, everything had changed. All that I had created was gone. I hadn't realized how vulnerable the world is, how delicate the balance of forces that sustain our existence.

I stood up and dusted off my jeans. In the distance I could see the sky clearing, and I knew that some day there would be another rainbow, its treasure awaiting. Until then, we had a job to do. We would need to start all over again. ❖

RALPH HELFER

Ralph Helfer (1931–) says that "blood, sweat, and tears" rebuilt his animal-rental business, the world's largest, after the devastating flood described in this selection from his book *The Beauty of the Beasts*. Whether it is a huge lion charging terrified campers, a python coiling around a screaming woman, or a half-ton grizzly frolicking with a woodsman, Helfer's animals have astounded film audiences around the world.

Many years ago, when Helfer was a Hollywood stuntman, he was attacked by an angry lion. As a result, he vowed to change the way that humans interacted with wild animals. During the three decades of Helfer's animal-training career, his animals collected 26 Patsy awards (the animal equivalent of the Oscar), and many of them became well-known personalities, including Clarence the cross-eyed lion, the bear Gentle Ben, Judy the Daktari chimpanzee, and the Mercury cougar.

No longer running the rental business, Helfer today spends most of his time in Africa, producing animal documentaries, writing books and magazine articles about wild animals, conducting safaris, lecturing, and working with conservation, ecology, and humane organizations to protect wild animals. He believes that his success in quieting the killer instinct in predators may help in the study of ways to control aggressiveness in humans and that his affection-training methods could be applied to the rearing of children. On an experimental basis, Helfer has taught delinquent teenagers to care for and train animals.

RALPH HELFER

Animals trained by Ralph Helfer have appeared in films such as *Zebra in the Kitchen*, *King Dinosaur*, and *Savage Harvest*, and television series such as *Daktari*, *Gentle Ben*, and *Cowboy in Africa*. Helfer belongs to the Wilderness Federation and is president of Eden International, a production company based in Kenya.

OVERVIEW

In the Guided Assignment for this section, students will write an essay evaluating the believability of a story. By evaluating stories, students will better understand how using details to elaborate an idea can make their writing more vivid and convincing. As preparation for this assignment, the Writer's Style will help students recognize three ways that they can use elaboration in their own writing. In Reading the World, students will evaluate the criteria for believability in the visual arts.

Objectives

- To recognize how writers use details to make their work vivid
- To create effective paragraphs
- To make a word or idea more specific through the use of appositives
- To write a critical essay about the believability of a piece of literature
- To evaluate the use of details to create a setting in a picture

Skills

LITERATURE
- Identifying and analyzing methods of elaboration

GRAMMAR AND USAGE
- Using appositives
- Using commas with subordinate clauses

MEDIA LITERACY
- Evaluating the believability of details

ORAL COMMUNICATION
- Giving peer feedback
- Group conferencing

CRITICAL THINKING
- Establishing criteria for evaluation
- Making judgments
- Analyzing

Teaching Strategy: MODELING
In the following models, methods of elaboration—strong sensory details, facts and statistics, and examples—are used to make the readings more clear and persuasive. These techniques are useful for all genres of writing.

A Abel Possible responses: The sight of the bear's "long snout, thick as my thigh" and the smell, "like the forest floor, like crushed moss and damp leaves," help to make the presence of this bear very immediate.

B Helfer Possible response: Facts like "150 feet wide and 15 feet deep" and the statistics about the flood's force and the items it wipes out in its path emphasize the flood's power.

WRITING ABOUT LITERATURE

ASKING QUESTIONS

Every story you read creates its own unique world. Sometimes it's fun to go along with the story, enjoying the elaborate details and interesting scenes, but sometimes it's necessary to take a step back and ask some questions about the writing. Are the characters true to life? Are the details realistic? In these pages you will

- study methods authors use to elaborate on ideas
- write a critical response that questions a story
- question the effectiveness of a real-world setting

The Writer's Style: Elaboration Good writers make their work vivid by including details such as facts, incidents, examples, sensory details, and quotations.

Read the Literature

Notice the kinds of details these writers use to elaborate on their ideas.

Literature Models

A Elaboration with Sensory Details
Sensory details help a reader "take part" in an experience. What details of smell, sight, and touch help you to "experience" the bear?

> With a bear at your side, it is not the simplest thing to play a fish properly, but the presence of this huge animal, and especially her long snout, thick as my thigh, wonderfully concentrates the mind. She smells like the forest floor, like crushed moss and damp leaves.
>
> Robert H. Abel, from "Appetizer"

B Elaboration with Facts and Statistics
How does Helfer use facts and statistics to emphasize the power of the flood?

> The storm grew worse. Heavy sheets of rain filled and overflowed our flood channel, undermining its sides until they caved in. By mid-morning the Santa Clarita had become a raging, murderous torrent, 150 feet wide and 15 feet deep, moving through Africa U.S.A. with the speed and force of an express train. In its fury it wiped out a two-lane highway, full-grown oak trees, generator buildings—everything.
>
> Ralph Helfer, from "The Flood"

360 UNIT THREE: BATTLE FOR CONTROL

PRINT AND MEDIA RESOURCES

UNIT THREE RESOURCE BOOK
Writer's Style, p. 37
Prewriting Guide, p. 38
Elaboration, p. 39
Peer Response Guide, pp. 40–41
Revision and Editing, p. 42
Student Model, p. 43
Rubric, p. 44

GRAMMAR MINI-LESSONS
Transparencies, pp. 30, 47
Copymasters, p. 39

WRITING MINI-LESSONS
Transparencies, p. 29

ACCESS FOR STUDENTS ACQUIRING ENGLISH
Reading and Writing Support

FORMAL ASSESSMENT
Guidelines for Writing Assessment

 WRITING COACH

360 THE LANGUAGE OF LITERATURE TEACHER'S EDITION

Connect to Science

Good newspaper and magazine writers often use examples, as in the paragraph below, to clarify their ideas and to add information. Examples bring specific meaning to a general statement.

Magazine Article

What's so bad about UV? Those rays that fry your skin can also "sunburn" your eyes, causing temporary blindness. This condition is called "snow blindness" because it sometimes strikes skiers when strong rays bounce off the slopes into their eyes, "burning" the corneas (the outside layer of the eye). Fortunately, snow-blind eyes can usually repair themselves in a day or two.

from "Sunglasses"
Zillions, June/July 1995

Elaboration with Examples
What example is given in this article? What is the main idea that is explained?

Try Your Hand: Using Elaboration

1. **Find Examples of Elaboration** With a group, look through a science or history book to find examples of elaboration with examples, facts, and sensory details.

2. **Elaborate on a Main Idea** Choose one of the following ideas and write a paragraph elaborating on it:
   - When I arrived at home, I knew something was up.
   - I think it's best to walk away from an angry friend.

3. **Revise in Portfolio** Take a sentence from one of your finished papers and elaborate on it in three different ways, showing how elaboration can support ideas.

SkillBuilder

GRAMMAR FROM WRITING

Using Appositives
Elaboration can make a word or an idea more specific and easier to understand. One way to elaborate is to use an appositive noun or phrase.

 An appositive noun or phrase explains one or more words in a sentence. Notice how the author Janet Bode uses an appositive in "Von" to add a detail about Saigon:

On April 30, 1975, Saigon, the capital of South Vietnam, fell.

APPLYING WHAT YOU'VE LEARNED
Rewrite the following sentences by elaborating with appositive nouns or phrases.

1. Von had never seen frozen vegetables before.
2. Ralph Helfer was living at Africa U.S.A.

Now try combining these pairs of sentences, using appositives.

1. The bear sat beside him as he fished. The bear was a huge animal.
2. The bear was friendly. This was a surprising trait.

GRAMMAR HANDBOOK

For more information on appositives, see the Grammar Handbook, pages 892–894.

WRITING ABOUT LITERATURE **361**

Teaching Strategy: MODELING

 Possible response: Snow blindness is the example given of the dangers of UV rays. The main idea is that UV rays that damage the skin can also damage the eyes.

Try Your Hand

1. Responses will vary. Most science and history books will provide a lot of support for students' main ideas with facts and statistics and detailed examples. Also, history books may use sensory details to elaborate on a specific experience or situation.

2. Responses will vary. Suggest that students use vivid and concrete details to make their paragraphs lively and convincing. Note the following example:
   - When I arrived home, I knew something was up. The house was in a state of disarray: furniture overturned, bed unmade, dishes broken. Then I discovered the source. Sitting in the kitchen, amid all the clutter, was my cat. She looked at me with pride and satisfaction, for sitting at her feet was the mouse she had waged war with and conquered.

3. Elaborations can use strong sensory details, facts, statistics, and examples to support the ideas in the sentence.

SkillBuilder — GRAMMAR FROM WRITING

USING APPOSITIVES Tell students that using appositives is one way to vary their writing. Remind them that variation makes their writing more interesting and alive for their readers. However, warn students that using too many appositives all together in a piece of writing can seem awkward and monotonous.

Applying What You've Learned Possible responses:
1. Von, new to the United States, had never seen frozen vegetables, hard as rocks, before.
2. Ralph Helfer, the author, was living at Africa U.S.A.

Answers:
1. The bear, a huge animal, sat beside him as he fished.
2. The bear was friendly, a surprising trait.

Additional Suggestions Have students review the selections in this unit to find appositives.

Reteaching/Reinforcement
Grammar Mini-Lessons copymasters, p. 39, transparencies, p. 30

Writer's Craft
Appositives, pp. 311–312

THE LANGUAGE OF LITERATURE TEACHER'S EDITION **361**

Critical Thinking:
MAKING JUDGMENTS

D Ask students whether there are any types or genres of writing that seem more believable than others. For instance, students may argue that science fiction and perhaps fiction in general are less truthful than newspaper reporting or historical writing. However, point out to them that it is often difficult to evaluate a piece of writing that seems factual but is completely made up. Also, tell students that a fictional story can be as believable as a factual one if the ideas are consistent.

Speaking and Listening:
COLLABORATIVE OPPORTUNITY

E Have students work in groups of three or four. Students can read from their chosen selections to the group, emphasizing the details and elaboration. Have the group members evaluate whether they find the details believable. Group members can use the questions from Exploring the Story Elements to assist in evaluating the selection.

CUSTOMIZING FOR
Less-Proficient Writers

F Students may need help in creating a chart, especially if their story element has both believable and unbelievable details. Tell students to keep in mind whether they basically find the element believable or unbelievable but not to omit any relevant details in their charts.

WRITING ABOUT LITERATURE

Criticism

D A good story is hard to put down. Writers who elaborate with well-chosen details can make you believe in people and places that never existed. Sometimes, however, a story isn't so believable. Something about the characters, plot, or setting makes you stop and question what you're reading. Critics, whether they are book reviewers or readers like you, often judge a story by how believable it is.

GUIDED ASSIGNMENT
Write a Critical Essay Evaluate the believability of a story you choose. Judge how well the author has crafted a believable character, setting, or plot, and elaborate on your opinions.

1 Prewrite and Explore

E Choose a story from this unit or one you have read outside of class. You can pick a story you liked or one you didn't believe. Remember that even fantastic creatures and settings can be believable if they make sense in the story's fictional world.

EXPLORING THE STORY ELEMENTS

Read the story a second time, writing down your reactions.

- Which story element do you believe or disbelieve the most?
- What details about the story element seem real? Which seem false?
- Why do you find these details easy or difficult to believe?

ORGANIZING YOUR IDEAS

F Now that you've thought the story over, state your opinion about the believability of one story element. To convince readers that your criticism is fair, you will need to support your opinion with examples from the story. A chart like the one at the right can help organize your examples and ideas.

Student's Idea and Details Chart

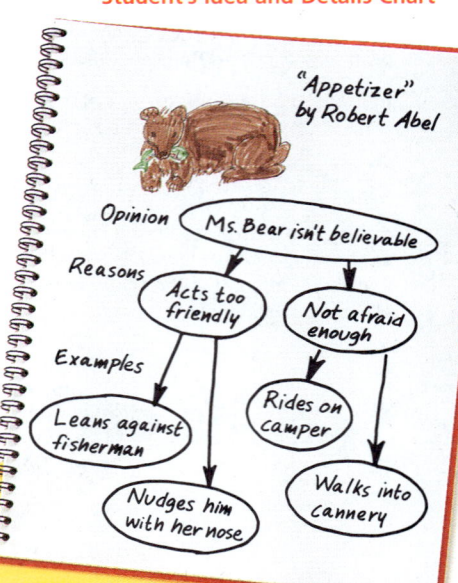

362

Assessment Option

SELF-ASSESSMENT When students have finished the Organizing Your Ideas activity, they can check that their ideas are organized or charted correctly. Students should ask themselves the following questions:
- *Are there any other examples from the selection that I might have used?*
- *Are the examples I chose relevant?*
- *Are my examples grouped together with their respective reasons?*

Tell them that if any ideas or examples are missing or out of place, to revise the organization or chart to make it complete.

2 Write and Analyze a Discovery Draft

Freewriting can help you discover the reasons for your opinion. As you write, ask yourself these questions:

- What experiences have I had that cause me to believe or disbelieve the story element?
- How do my experiences or knowledge support or contradict details in the story?

Student's Discovery Draft

This is one way the bear is sort of believable.

The author thinks he's communicating with the bear. I believe that because I can tell when my cats want to be fed or want attention.

There's still something about the bear I don't believe. Would a big wild Alaskan bear be friendly to a human? Would it stand next to a man, waiting for him to catch a fish, and not attack him? It seems like the bear reasons all this out. Maybe that's what bothers me: the bear seems almost human.

I think I have my main point here: the bear acts too human to be believable.

3 Draft and Share

Use your discovery draft to write a more organized critical essay. Begin with an introduction that describes the story and states your main point. In the body of your essay, support your opinion with reasons and examples from the story. Finish with a conclusion summarizing your ideas. Have a classmate read your draft.

PEER RESPONSE

- What reasons and examples do I give to support my opinion?
- Do you agree or disagree with my criticism? Why or why not?

SkillBuilder

WRITER'S CRAFT

Creating Effective Paragraphs

Organizing your essay into paragraphs helps your readers focus on one main idea at a time. To create clear and interesting paragraphs, follow these guidelines:

- Begin a new paragraph each time you introduce a new idea.
- Try stating your new idea in a topic sentence.
- Elaborate on your idea with reasons or examples.
- Put ideas and examples in a logical order.
- Remove ideas or examples that do not support the main idea.

APPLYING WHAT YOU'VE LEARNED

Look at each paragraph in your essay to see if you have followed the guidelines above. If you need to revise a paragraph, you may want to focus on one guideline at a time.

 WRITING HANDBOOK

For more information on writing paragraphs, see the Writing Handbook, pages 827–829.

WRITING ABOUT LITERATURE **363**

Writing Skill: ELABORATION

 The Discovery Draft provides an opportunity for students to think through and analyze the ideas they have gathered. Encourage students to think of experiences they have had that may be similar to the ones in their chosen selection. Suggest that these examples can be compared to the details in their readings to evaluate whether they believe or disbelieve the story element.

Teaching Strategy: USING THE SKILLBUILDER

 You can help students organize their drafts by teaching the SkillBuilder on Creating Effective Paragraphs at this time. It will help students to write well-ordered and concise paragraphs.

SkillBuilder WRITER'S CRAFT

CREATING EFFECTIVE PARAGRAPHS
Remind students that the basic structure of an essay is an introduction, a body, and a conclusion. The introduction and conclusion should be in separate paragraphs of their own. The main body of the essay can contain several paragraphs. Tell students that the number of paragraphs is determined by the number of new ideas and topic sentences they have. There is no correct number of paragraphs in an essay.

Applying What You've Learned Paragraphs should begin with topic sentences and include only relevant supporting details.

Additional Suggestions If students are having trouble revising the paragraphs in their essay, they can try writing a new paragraph—for example, a new introductory paragraph.

Reteaching/Reinforcement
Writing Mini-Lessons transparencies, p. 29

Paragraphs, pp. 244–254

THE LANGUAGE OF LITERATURE **TEACHER'S EDITION 363**

Critical Thinking: ANALYZING

I To help students evaluate the clarity of their responses, have them answer the following questions:
- *Does each paragraph have a topic sentence?*
- *Is each topic sentence supported with examples?*

Teaching Strategy: MODELING

J Discuss with students how this sample meets the Standards for Evaluation on this page. Point out to them that the second sentence is the main point of the essay. The second paragraph contains two details from the story that show that the bear character is not believable: the bear stands next to the narrator and nudges him, and the bear licks the window of the camper instead of smashing it. Both of these details have supporting argumentation in logical order. In the first example, the writer explains that the bear is behaving like a domestic pet rather than a wild animal. In the second example, the student shows that Abel is attributing human emotions to the bear.

Standards for Evaluation

Ideas and Content
- gives title, author, and a brief summary of the literature
- gives supported evaluation of an element of the selection
- includes examples, quotations, and details that support the evaluation
- has a conclusion that clearly summarizes the evaluation

Structure and Form
- uses well-organized paragraphs and a clear organization
- includes transitional words and phrases to show relationships among ideas

Grammar, Usage, and Mechanics
- contains no more than two or three minor errors in grammar and usage
- correctly integrates quotations into the text
- contains no more than two or three minor errors in spelling, capitalization, and punctuation

---

WRITING ABOUT LITERATURE

4 Revise and Edit

I Now that you're ready to revise your draft, ask yourself if you have presented your response clearly. Read the story again. Do you still have the same opinion? After you finish your draft, read it over and reflect on how well you supported your ideas.

Student's Final Draft

In the story "Appetizer" Robert Abel describes an encounter between a bear and a fisherman. I think that the character of this bear is too human to be believable in the story. When the narrator talks with the bear, he seems to be communicating on a higher level than animals and humans can communicate. The bear is also much more friendly to humans than you would expect from a wild bear in Alaska.

Which sentence explains the main point of the essay?

J *How does the student use details from the story to show that the bear character is not believable?*

When the bear stands right next to the narrator and nudges him with her nose, she communicates like my cat might when he wants attention. However, this is a wild bear! It's not believable that the bear would behave like a household pet. The narrator is convinced that the bear is expressing feelings of affection for him; later, as if to prove her love, she licks the window of his camper instead of smashing it and then won't leave. Unbelievable!

Standards for Evaluation

A critical essay
- has an introduction with a clearly stated criticism
- supports the criticism with appropriate examples
- has a logical organization that is easy to follow
- contains standard grammar and usage
- has a conclusion that clearly summarizes the evaluation

364 UNIT THREE: BATTLE FOR CONTROL

Assessment Option

SELF-ASSESSMENT Students can assess their own writing by asking themselves the following questions:
- *Does my introduction contain a brief description of the story?*
- *Have I used enough details for readers who are not familiar with the story?*
- *Is my opinion clearly stated?*
- *Have I supported my opinion with appropriate examples?*
- *Does my writing have a logical structure?*
- *Could I express myself more clearly?*
- *Is my grammar, spelling, and punctuation correct?*

Grammar in Context

Complex Sentences When revising a critical essay, you can show the relationship between your ideas with complex sentences. A **complex sentence** contains an independent clause, which can stand alone as a sentence, and one or more subordinate clauses, which cannot stand alone.

A complex sentence can effectively show time or cause-and-effect relationships between your ideas. Use conjunctions such as *because, when, after, before, until, unless,* and *if* to connect your ideas.

> The bear was trying to communicate with the fisherman.
> *When*
> ^The bear nudged him with her nose. ^She was trying to tell him
> *If*
> something. ^My dog does the same thing. ^He wants to be fed.
> *After*
> ^The bear told the narrator to fish behind a big boulder. ^He landed a granddaddy fish.

In the example above, the short simple sentences are combined into complex sentences that clarify the relationships between the ideas.

Try Your Hand: Using Complex Sentences

Revise the following paragraph by making some of the simple sentences into complex sentences, using such conjunctions as *because, when, after, before, until, unless,* and *if.*

> Last Wednesday we had an exciting time at the cannery. A big bear came right through the truck ramp for a feast. We don't know how she got there. Most of us saw her coming and ran out. We knew we didn't stand a chance against her. We had a meeting out in front to decide what to do. Frank wanted to use his gun. We agreed that was not the answer. Marty suggested we all go home. The boss said no. Holly thought we should blow the lunch whistle. That finally drove the bear away. We spent the rest of the week cleaning up the mess and making repairs.

SkillBuilder

GRAMMAR FROM WRITING

Using Commas with Subordinate Clauses

One way to add variety to your sentences is to vary the order of the clauses in your complex sentences. If the independent clause comes first, usually no comma is needed.

The bear takes matters into her own hands when the salmon flips into a little side pool.

However, if the subordinate clause comes first, a comma is used before the independent clause.

When the salmon flips into a little side pool, the bear takes matters into her own hands.

APPLYING WHAT YOU'VE LEARNED

Move the subordinate clause to the beginning of each complex sentence below, and punctuate the revised sentence correctly.

1. Ms. Bear seemed distracted after Mr. Bear stopped by.
2. Ms. Bear took a nap on the camper hood although I beeped the horn long and loud.
3. I stayed at the Buckville Tavern because I was still supposed to be on vacation.

 GRAMMAR HANDBOOK

For more help with commas, see pages 892–894 of the Grammar Handbook.

WRITING ABOUT LITERATURE   **365**

Teaching Strategy: STUMBLING BLOCK

K Students are often confused about what is a dependent and what is an independent clause, especially if they have heard of the other common terminology: main and subordinate clauses. Explain that a subordinate clause is a dependent clause. Neither can stand alone, so both are dependent on another clause to make a complete sentence. A main clause is an independent clause and can stand alone. The subordinate or dependent clause modifies the main or independent clause.

Teaching Strategy: USING THE SKILLBUILDER

L You can help students understand and correctly punctuate complex sentences and coordinating conjunctions by teaching the SkillBuilder on Using Commas with Subordinate Clauses at this time.

Try Your Hand

Make sure students choose logical conjunctions and punctuate sentences correctly. The following is a sample:

Last Wednesday we had an exciting time at the cannery because a big bear came right through the truck ramp for a feast. We don't know how she got there. Most of us saw her coming and ran out because we knew we didn't stand a chance against her. We had a meeting out in front to decide what to do. Frank wanted to use his gun, but we agreed that was not the answer. Marty suggested we all go home. Because the boss said no, Holly thought we should blow the lunch whistle. That finally drove the bear away. We spent the rest of the week cleaning up the mess and making repairs.

SkillBuilder GRAMMAR FROM WRITING

USING COMMAS WITH SUBORDINATE CLAUSES Remind students that knowing the common coordinating conjunctions will help them understand how to use commas correctly with subordinating clauses. Tell them that sentences beginning with conjunctions must have an independent clause to complete the sentence.

Common Conjunctions:
because, after, while, when, if, before, since, although

Applying What You've Learned Answers:
1. After Mr. Bear stopped by, Ms. Bear seemed distracted.
2. Although I beeped the horn long and loud, Ms. Bear took a nap on the camper hood.
3. Because I was still supposed to be on vacation, I stayed at the Buckville Tavern.

Additional Suggestions Have students work in pairs to practice writing sentences that contain coordinating conjunctions.

Reteaching/Reinforcement
Grammar Mini-Lessons transparencies, p. 47

 The Writer's Craft

Complex Sentences, pp. 560–568

READING THE WORLD

On pages 360–365, students evaluated the believability of elements of a story. They should be aware that aspects of the real world also can be evaluated in a similar fashion. In this lesson, students apply what they have learned in evaluating writing to evaluating the believability of a setting. Encourage them to imagine they are in the audience, viewing the scene.

Critical Thinking: EVALUATING

M You may need to help students answer the questions by explaining that the setting is a festival or performance set in the past. Point out the age of the building and the style of clothing. Students may notice details in the performers' clothing, shoes, or hairstyles that seem unbelievable because they are from different time periods or seem to come from a variety of countries.

366 THE LANGUAGE OF LITERATURE TEACHER'S EDITION

READING THE WORLD

ELABORATE DETAILS

You've seen how writers use sensory details to make a story more believable to readers. Details can be used for a similar purpose in real life. This picture shows an imaginary setting that has been made to look real with elaborate details. How real does it seem to you?

View What imaginary setting is being created here? What details help to create the scene? What details do not fit? Is there anything that makes this place unbelievable?

Interpret Decide how effective you think this setting is. Write a critical paragraph, supporting your criticism with details from the photograph.

Discuss With a group, discuss what details you would add to or remove from the setting to make it more believable or interesting. What could affect your judgment here? Refer to the SkillBuilder at the right for help with establishing criteria for evaluation.

SkillBuilder

CRITICAL THINKING

Establishing Criteria for Evaluation

As you evaluated the setting in this photograph, you used your own **criteria**, or standards, to make a judgment. Your standards probably depended on what you thought the setting should accomplish. Do you think it should inform visitors—or just entertain them?

Besides thinking about the purpose of the setting, you may also have thought about your own likes and dislikes. Do you enjoy places like this? Would your personal feelings make you judge the setting too easily or harshly?

You may have been unaware of what criteria you were using to evaluate the setting. Think about your criteria now.

APPLYING WHAT YOU'VE LEARNED
With a small group, write criteria for judging the effectiveness of each imaginary setting listed below. Afterwards, discuss reasons for similarities and differences between the criteria.

- a fantasy theme park
- a working colonial farm
- a haunted house
- the set of a realistic play

READING THE WORLD   367

Media Literacy:
INTERPRETING A SETTING

N Students' paragraphs may suggest that the details support the believability of the photograph. Details that make the picture seem believable may include the banners and crests on the building, the people's clothes, and the nature of the dance or performance. Try to ensure that student paragraphs contain topic sentences and support in the form of appropriate examples.

Speaking and Listening:
GROUP DISCUSSION

O Have each group appoint a note taker to record a list of details the group would add or remove to make the scene more believable or interesting. Also encourage groups to examine how they decided what should and should not go into the setting. Encourage them to think of criteria like consistency: the details in the setting all should be from the same time period.

SkillBuilder CRITICAL THINKING

ESTABLISHING CRITERIA FOR EVALUATION Encourage students to imagine the reasons why people may want to visit such a place and performance. They may answer that the reasons for such a setting depend on whether people want to be informed or simply entertained by something that seems historically accurate. If students answer that they do not enjoy places like this, have them imagine other settings they would like to visit. Help them to come up with the details that could be included in such a place. Ask them what criteria they would use to choose the details. Criteria for choosing and evaluating each setting may include accuracy of details or consistency in terms of time and place among the various aspects of the setting.

Applying What You've Learned Reasons for the effectiveness of each setting will vary widely. Students should recognize that the criteria for the effectiveness of each setting are different.

THE LANGUAGE OF LITERATURE TEACHER'S EDITION   367

UNIT THREE
Part 2 Lesson Planner

TIME ALLOTMENTS SHOWN ARE APPROXIMATE. DEPENDING ON YOUR GOALS AND THE NEEDS OF YOUR STUDENTS, YOU MAY WISH TO ALLOW MORE OR LESS TIME FOR CERTAIN PORTIONS OF THE LESSON.

Table of Contents	Discussion	Previewing the Selection	Reading the Selection
PART OPENER **GOING TO EXTREMES** What Do You Think? page 368	**20 MINUTES** • Reflect on the part theme		
SELECTION **The Banana Tree** page 370 CHALLENGING		**20 MINUTES** • PERSONAL CONNECTION • SCIENCE CONNECTION • READING CONNECTION: Understanding dialect	**35 MINUTES** • Introduce vocabulary • Read pp. 370–77 (8 pp.)
SELECTION **The Tell-Tale Heart** page 381 AVERAGE		**20 MINUTES** • PERSONAL CONNECTION • LITERARY CONNECTION • READING CONNECTION: Evaluating	**25 MINUTES** • Introduce vocabulary • Read pp. 381–86 (6 pp.)
SELECTION **Tsali of the Cherokees** page 391 CHALLENGING		**20 MINUTES** • PERSONAL CONNECTION • HISTORICAL CONNECTION • READING CONNECTION: Contrasting	**35 MINUTES** • Introduce vocabulary • Read pp. 391–97 (7 pp.)
SELECTION **Painful Memories of Dating** page 401 AVERAGE		**20 MINUTES** • PERSONAL CONNECTION • MEDIA CONNECTION • READING CONNECTION: Hyperbole	**10 MINUTES** • Introduce vocabulary • Read pp. 401–03 (3 pp.)
SELECTIONS **The Runaway** page 407 AVERAGE **Macavity: The Mystery Cat** page 408 AVERAGE		**20 MINUTES** • PERSONAL CONNECTION • LITERARY CONNECTION • WRITING CONNECTION	**10 MINUTES** • Introduce vocabulary • Read pp. 407–09 (3 pp.)
Writing	Exploring Topics	Prewriting	Drafting and Revising
WRITING FROM EXPERIENCE **Informative Exposition**	**20 MINUTES**	**25 MINUTES**	**75 MINUTES**

Time estimates assume in-class work. You may wish to assign some of these stages as homework.

Responding to the Selection

FROM PERSONAL RESPONSE TO CRITICAL ANALYSIS	OR	ANOTHER PATHWAY	LITERARY CONCEPTS	QUICKWRITES
45 MINUTES				
• Discussion questions	OR	• Television interview	• Protagonist/antagonist	• Dialogue • Personal narrative
50 MINUTES				
• Discussion questions	OR	• Mock trial	• Mood	• Alternative ending • Lead paragraph
40 MINUTES				
• Discussion questions	OR	• Illustrations	• Author's purpose • Oral history	• Paragraph • Epitaph
50 MINUTES				
• Discussion questions	OR	• Comedy episode		• Diary entry • Advice column
45 MINUTES				
• Discussion questions	OR	• Read-aloud	• Rhyme scheme	• Poem • Prose or poem

Extension Activities

	ALTERNATIVE ACTIVITIES	LITERARY LINKS	CRITIC'S CORNER	THE WRITER'S STYLE	ACROSS THE CURRICULUM	ART CONNECTION	WORDS TO KNOW	BIOGRAPHY
40 MINUTES	✓				GEOGRAPHY		✓	✓
45 MINUTES	✓	✓			SCIENCE	✓	✓	✓
45 MINUTES	✓				SOCIAL STUDIES		✓	✓
25 MINUTES	✓						✓	✓
30 MINUTES	✓	✓						✓

Publishing and Reflecting

35 MINUTES

UNIT THREE

Part 2 Cooperative Project

Historical Crimes

Overview

Students will research some of the worst crimes in history, as well as experts' opinions of the causes of those crimes. They will then hold a panel discussion about what might be done to prevent future crimes of a similar nature.

PROJECT AT A GLANCE
The selections in Unit Three, Part 2 are about people who go to extremes for one reason or another, until they are out of control. Things go seriously wrong, usually with tragic consequences. For this project, students will research some of the worst crimes in history and will find out what the experts say about the causes. Students will also investigate some of the programs that have been put into effect as deterrents. They will then hold a panel discussion of the relative success rates of these programs and will come up with their own ideas for how violent crimes can be prevented.

OBJECTIVES
- To research extreme examples of crimes and criminals
- To research some of the possible causes of such behavior
- To form opinions about the success or failure of the programs and support those opinions in a class discussion
- To formulate possible alternative plans for deterring criminal behavior

SUGGESTED GROUP SIZE
3–6 students

MATERIALS
- Various accounts of historical criminal cases (from magazines, newspapers, encyclopedia, and so on)
- Newspapers, magazines, and so on, that analyze current or recent criminal cases

 Getting Started

Arranging the Project
Before students begin, do a little research yourself to see if your school library has sufficient information on famous historical crimes and their analyses by experts in the field of criminal behavior. If not, arrange with a local library for these materials to be available to students, either at the library itself or at your school library by way of a loan. These materials might be temporarily designated as "Research Only" and unavailable for borrowing. This will ensure access for all students, not just for the first ones who get there.

Arranging the Panel Discussion
Arranging the discussion should require only rearranging a bit of furniture in your classroom on the appropriate day. Depending on the number of groups and their topics, you might consider having a four- or five-way discussion, with groups sitting in a circle. You might also pair off groups who chose a similar person or crime for a debate in front of the rest of the class.

The project is basically a student-driven activity. Your job will be to act as discussion moderator, project facilitator, and general adviser.

2 Creating the Debate

Introducing the Project
Explain that students will be working cooperatively to identify some of what society deems the "worst" crimes in history, and to research some of their possible causes. Students also will look into various deterrent programs that have been tried through the ages and will evaluate the apparent success of each. Groups will then brainstorm to develop a program of their own and will present the plan and supporting arguments to the class.

At most times, unfortunately, there seems to be one "big" criminal case in the news that everybody hears about. Discuss such a case with students. You may want to bring in newspaper or magazine articles about this crime and allow students to familiarize themselves with the case. Open a class discussion by asking for opinions about why this person or persons (allegedly) committed the crime. Continue by asking for suggestions about how this might have been prevented. Try to steer the conversation away from gory details and concentrate on causes and effects.

Group Investigations
Divide students into groups of three to six. The groups will research past criminals and select one on which to concentrate their efforts. Although murder is probably the "celebrity" of crimes, point out that other crimes (treason, embezzlement, terrorism, kidnapping) have had very lasting and widespread effects and are worthy of study. After selecting a subject, groups should investigate the background of the person involved and the opinions formed by psychologists and law enforcement officers. Groups should also make an informal study of the success or failure of deterrent programs and form their own ideas of how to possibly prevent such behavior from recurring.

Creating a Project Description
If you find that the same subject has been chosen too often, you can suggest alternative subjects.

Before the discussion, ask groups to write a brief description of their ideas for preventive measures and to outline a few supporting facts. This will help you keep abreast of groups' progress and maintain the focus of the project. Try to meet with each group a few times during the project to help keep them on the correct path and to monitor their work.

OPTION 1: WHAT HAPPENED? Groups can research several crimes and determine the fate of the person or persons involved. Debate might focus on the question, "Does crime really pay?"

OPTION 2: DEATH PENALTY Students can stage a debate on the pros and cons of the death penalty. They should research statistics, interview other students and adults, and read the opinions of experts before they begin.

OPTION 3: TALK TO AN EXPERT Invite, or have students invite, an expert in criminal behavior to speak to the class. Large cities probably have such a person on the police force. If you live in a small town, you might contact a nearby college or university. Students should prepare specific questions to ask the visitor.

OPTION 4: THE "JESSE JAMES" SYNDROME Groups can research famous criminals who became celebrities or were made out to be heroes by the public or the media. Students should form opinions as to the cause of this inappropriate adulation and present an oral argument supporting their opinions.

It may take some supervision on your part to keep students from becoming bogged down by the physical details of the actual crime. Encourage them to think about the causes and effects rather than the blood and gore.

3 Sharing the Deterrent Plans

Groups can be asked to write a one- or two-page paper describing their deterrent plan in some detail. These plans can then be collected and bound together as a class project. Students can spend a few days examining the plans and then can discuss them as a class.

Students in coming years might be interested in looking over these plans for inspiration for their own projects, so keep a copy of them on file in your classroom or in the school library.

Assessing the Project

The following rubric can be used for group or individual assessment.

3 Full Accomplishment Students follow directions and produce a plan for deterring criminal behavior based on solid research and investigation.

2 Substantial Accomplishment Students produce a plan for deterring criminal behavior, but the plan is unrealistic or is not based on solid research.

1 Little or Partial Accomplishment Students' plan is incomplete or does not fulfill the requirements of the assignment.

For the Portfolio
You will want to include a copy of your written assessment in each student's portfolio, as well as a copy of the group's final plan for deterring criminal behavior.

Note: For other assessment options, see the *Teacher's Guide to Assessment and Portfolio Use.*

Cross-Curricular Options

SOCIAL STUDIES

Students can research crimes and crime rates in other societies, eras, or countries to find how the kinds and frequencies differ from those of the modern-day United States. They should also express a fact-based opinion as to why there is a difference, if one exists.

HEALTH AND SAFETY
Students can interview law enforcement officers and solicit from them a list of suggestions on how not to become a victim of crime.

SCIENCE

At one time, scientists proposed that criminals' brains were abnormal or that their heads did not conform to the same measurement ratios as those of "normal" people. Students can research this and other theories, as well as the evidence that supports or disproves each theory.

Resources

Police Lab by Melvin Berger discusses criminal investigations.

Exploring the Mind and Brain by Melvin Berger discusses normal and abnormal functions of the brain.

PART 2

WHAT DO YOU THINK?
Objectives

The activities on this page can be used to
- introduce the Part 2 theme, "Going to Extremes," since each activity is connected to one or more of the selections in Part 2
- create materials for students' personal portfolios that they can later reconsider or revise
- build an understanding of theme that can be reviewed and revised as students progress through the unit

What is worth dying for?
After students have created a list of historical figures, they can jot down important details about these figures and the sacrifices they made. Students can refer to this information during their debate. (See "Tsali of the Cherokees," p. 390.)

To what extremes would you go?
Remind students that the desired things need not be material possessions. When students have finished the activity, you may wish to discuss with them the extremes to which they would go to get something. (See "The Tell-Tale Heart," p. 380, and "The Banana Tree," p. 369.)

How would you visualize a rock video?
Encourage students to brainstorm a list of visuals or images that would capture the idea of going to extremes. Remind students that the images can be based on a particular aspect of the theme of the song or can capture a wide range of possible interpretations of the song title. (All selections are connected to this activity.)

UNIT THREE **PART 2**

GOING TO EXTREMES

WHAT DO Y?u THINK?

REFLECTING ON THEME

Have you ever battled for something you strongly believed in? If so, you know that emotions can become extreme. Use the activities on this page to explore some ways in which people go to extremes. Keep a record of your impressions. Compare them with the thoughts of the characters in Part 2.

What is worth dying for?
Sometimes people may be willing to put even their lives on the line. With your classmates, brainstorm names of people in history who were willing to sacrifice their lives to stand up for what they believed in. Pick several of these, and stage a debate about whether their actions were heroic or foolish.

How would you visualize a rock video?
Imagine that you are producing a music video for a rock group's new song, entitled "Going to Extremes." In your notebook, create a storyboard showing some of the images you might use to convey the theme of the song.

To what extremes would you go?
Have you ever found yourself saying "I'd give anything to have that"? Design a questionnaire on which your classmates can identify three things they have wanted to have for a long time. Provide space for the student to record the extremes to which he or she would be willing to go to get each thing.

Thing Desired
1 _____
2 _____
3 _____

Would you
- use all your free time?
- spend all your savings?
- do something you didn't believe in?

Looking Back
At the beginning of this unit, you thought about some different forms the struggle for survival can take. Did your ideas change as you read the selections in Part 1? What kinds of struggles for survival occur in the selections? What measures do the characters take in their battles for control? How successful are they? Discuss your answers to these questions with a partner.

368

Looking Back
Have students make a chart in which they summarize, for each selection, the struggle for survival that the main character faces. Make sure students also include the measures each character takes and the degree of success he or she has in winning the struggle. Students may refer to this information in their discussions with partners.

PARENTAL INVOLVEMENT
Have students interview a parent or another family member about a situation or an experience in which that relative went to extremes in order to achieve something or to survive a struggle. Suggest that students present the interview in a form that can be shared with the class (essay, oral report, or video or audio presentation). Encourage students to ask questions that will prompt the interviewee to analyze his or her actions and to give reasons why he or she went to extremes.

368 THE LANGUAGE OF LITERATURE **TEACHER'S EDITION**

PREVIEWING

FICTION

The Banana Tree
James Berry

Activating Prior Knowledge
PERSONAL CONNECTION
Each year powerful storms called hurricanes cause death and destruction in many parts of the world. What do you know about hurricanes? Have you ever been caught in one yourself? With a small group of classmates, use a word web like the one shown here to organize your knowledge of hurricanes.

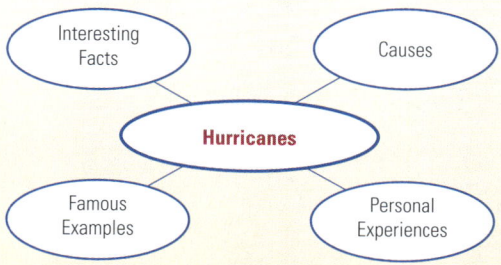

Building Background
SCIENCE CONNECTION
If you lived in Jamaica, the setting of "The Banana Tree," you would probably know a lot about hurricanes. Jamaica is an island nation in the Caribbean Sea. It is located in one of the three regions where most of the world's hurricanes occur.

Hurricanes develop from areas of low atmospheric pressure over warm ocean water. A hurricane produces torrents of rain and winds that swirl at up to 150 miles per hour around a calm spot in the center, called the eye. The eye is about 20 miles in diameter and travels 10 to 15 miles per hour. Picking up strength and speed as it moves, the hurricane may generate large waves that flood nearby coasts. As the hurricane moves over land, it brings heavy rain and strong winds, which cease as the eye passes.

Copyright © World Perspectives/Tony Stone Images.

Active Reading/Setting a Purpose
READING CONNECTION

Understanding Dialect In describing the hurricane in this story, Mr. Bass says, "The storm's bad, chil'run. Really bad. But it'll blow off. It'll spen' itself out." Like most Jamaicans, Mr. Bass speaks in a dialect of English that incorporates words, pronunciations, and expressions from various African languages, Spanish, and French.

In the Jamaican dialect, the last letter of a word may be missing, as in *spen'* for *spend,* or a vowel sound may be changed, as in *chil'run* for *children.* Reading the dialogue in this story aloud may help you figure out the meanings of unfamiliar words.

 LASERLINKS
- SCIENCE CONNECTION
- CULTURAL CONNECTION

369

OVERVIEW

Objectives
- To understand and appreciate a short story about a boy's response to a hurricane
- To enrich reading through an understanding of dialect
- To identify and analyze protagonists and antagonists
- To express understanding of the story through a choice of writing forms, including a personal narrative and a dialogue
- To extend understanding of the story through a variety of multimodal and cross-curricular activities

Skills

READING SKILLS/STRATEGIES
- Using context clues

THE WRITER'S STYLE
- Sentence variety

GRAMMAR
- Verb tenses

SPEAKING, LISTENING, AND VIEWING
- Directing a videotape
- Group discussion
- Oral presentation

LITERARY CONCEPTS
- Allusion
- Dialect
- Protagonist and antagonist

SPELLING
- Words from the French language

Cross-Curricular Connections

HISTORY
- Hurricane Andrew
- Jamaica then and now

GEOGRAPHY
- Bananas

 **SCIENCE CONNECTION**
Hurricanes Satellite photos of hurricanes, news photos showing the devastation they cause, and a map of a region where they are frequent will help activate students' prior knowledge.

Side A, Frame 52692

 **CULTURAL CONNECTION**
People and Places in Jamaica Before students read "The Banana Tree," show them these photographs of the land and people of Jamaica to help them visualize the story's setting.

Side A, Frame 52701

PRINT AND MEDIA RESOURCES

UNIT THREE RESOURCE BOOK
Strategic Reading: Literature, p. 47
Vocabulary SkillBuilder, p. 50
Reading SkillBuilder, p. 48
Spelling SkillBuilder, p. 49

GRAMMAR MINI–LESSONS
Transparencies, p.16
Copymasters, p. 24

WRITING MINI–LESSONS
Transparencies, pp. 40–43

ACCESS FOR STUDENTS ACQUIRING ENGLISH
Selection Summaries
Reading and Writing Support

FORMAL ASSESSMENT
Selection Test, pp. 69–70
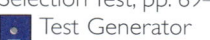 Test Generator

 AUDIO LIBRARY
See Reference Card

 LASERLINKS
Science Connection
Cultural Connection

 INTERNET RESOURCES
McDougal Littell Literature Center at http://www.hmco.com/mcdougal/lit

THE LANGUAGE OF LITERATURE TEACHER'S EDITION **369**

THE BANANA TREE

by James Berry

SUMMARY

Young Gustus Bass, his family, and the rest of the community take shelter in the local school during a hurricane. Neither of his parents notices when Gustus slips out into the storm and heads home to save his banana tree. The tree was planted when he was born, and he hopes to sell the fruit to buy a pair of shoes. Gustus wants the shoes so he can go on outings with his cricket team, competing in a sport that his father thinks is a waste of time. Trying to save the tree, Gustus is knocked unconscious. Mr. Bass and a search party arrive in time to save Gustus, and Mr. Bass tries to give his own boots to Gustus.

Thematic Link: *Going to Extremes*
Gustus is willing to battle the extreme conditions of a hurricane in order to save his banana tree.

CUSTOMIZING FOR
Students Acquiring English

- Use **ACCESS FOR STUDENTS ACQUIRING ENGLISH,** *Reading and Writing Support.*
- Less-fluent students may have difficulty deciphering the Jamaican dialect. Help them to understand what is said by asking a more fluent student to translate into Standard English or to paraphrase statements when necessary.

STRATEGIC READING FOR
Less-Proficient Readers

Set a Purpose To engage students with the selection, ask them to draw a hurricane hitting a small town. Then have them read to see how members of the Bass family interact with one another.

Use **UNIT THREE RESOURCE BOOK,** p. 47, for guidance in reading the selection.

WORDS TO KNOW

debris (də-brē′) *n.* the scattered remains of something broken or destroyed (p. 375)
grimace (grĭm′ĭs) *v.* to make a facial expression that reflects pain (p. 375)
refuse (rĕf′yōos) *n.* trash; garbage (p. 374)
torso (tôr′sō) *n.* the human body excluding the head and limbs; trunk (p. 375)
turbulent (tûr′byə-lənt) *adj.* violently agitated or disturbed; disorderly (p. 375)

In the hours the hurricane stayed, its presence made everybody older. It made Mr. Bass see that not only people and animals and certain valuables were of most importance to be saved.

From its very buildup the hurricane meant to show it was merciless, unstoppable, and, with its might, changed landscapes.

All day the Jamaican sun didn't come out. Then, ten minutes before, there was a swift shower of rain that raced by and was gone like some urgent messenger-rush of wind. And again everything went back to that quiet, that unnatural quiet. It was as if trees crouched quietly in fear. As if, too, birds knew they should shut up. A thick and low black cloud had covered the sky and shadowed everywhere, and made it seem like night was coming on. And the cloud deepened. Its deepening spread more and more over the full stretch of the sea.

The doom-laden afternoon had the atmosphere of Judgment Day[1] for everybody in all the districts about. Everybody knew the hour of disaster was near. Warnings printed in bold lettering had been put up at post offices, police stations, and schoolyard entrances and in clear view on shop walls in village squares.

Carrying children and belongings, people hurried in files and in scattered groups, headed for the big, strong, and safe community buildings. In Canerise Village, we headed for the schoolroom. Loaded with bags and cases, with bundles and lidded baskets, individuals carrying or leading an animal, parents shrieking for children to stay at their heels, we arrived there. And, looking around, anyone would think the whole of Canerise was here in this vast superbarn of a noisy chattering schoolroom.

With violent gusts and squalls the storm broke. Great rushes, huge bulky rushes, of wind struck the building in heavy, repeated thuds, shaking it over and over, and carrying on.

Families were huddled together on the floor. People sang, sitting on benches, desks, anywhere there was room. Some people knelt in loud prayer. Among the refugees' noises a goat bleated, a hen fluttered or cackled, a dog whined.

Mr. Jetro Bass was sitting on a soap box. His broad back leaned on the blackboard against the wall. Mrs. Imogene Bass, largely pregnant, looked a midget beside him. Their children were sitting on the floor. The eldest boy, Gustus, sat farthest from his father. Altogether, the children's heads made seven different levels of height around the parents. Mr. Bass forced a reassuring smile. His toothbrush mustache moved about a little as he said, "The storm's bad, chil'run. Really bad. But it'll blow off. It'll spen' itself out. It'll kill itself."

Except for Gustus's, all the faces of the children turned up with subdued fear and looked at their father as he spoke.

"Das true wha' Pappy say," Mrs. Bass said. "The good Lord won' gi' we more than we can bear."

Mr. Bass looked at Gustus. He stretched fully through the sitting children and put a lumpy, blistery hand—though a huge hand—on the boy's head, almost covering it. The boy's clear brown eyes looked straight and unblinkingly into his father's face. "Wha's the matter, bwoy?" his dad asked.

He shook his head. "Nothin', Pappy."

"Wha' mek you say nothin'? I sure somet'ing bodder you, Gustus. You not a bwoy who frighten easy. Is not the hurricane wha' bodder you? Tell Pappy."

"Is nothin'."

"You're a big bwoy now. Gustus—you nearly thirteen. You strong. You very useful fo' you

---

1. **Judgment Day:** in traditional Christian belief, the day on which the world will end.

THE BANANA TREE   **371**

CUSTOMIZING FOR
Students Acquiring English

2 Be sure all students understand what Mr. Bass has said. What is a synonym for *harborin'*? (keeping; hiding)

Literary Concept: DIALECT

C Ask a volunteer to read aloud what Gustus is thinking (beginning with "What's the good of tellin'") and another student to translate the dialect into Standard English. (*Possible response:* "What is the good of telling, when Pappy doesn't like cricket. He will only get vexed and say it is an evil game for idle hands!")

Critical Thinking: ANALYZE

D Ask students to explain why the community would choose to sing religious songs. (*Possible responses:* They are frightened, and the religious songs are comforting; they are looking for a way to pass the time together.)

STRATEGIC READING FOR
Less-Proficient Readers

E Have students summarize how members of the Bass family interact with one another. (*Mr. Bass is very strict, and his children are afraid of him. Mrs. Bass is pious and appears to be connected to her younger children. Gustus is isolated from the rest of the family, feeling misunderstood and neglected.*)
Summarizing/Classifying

Set a Purpose Ask students to continue reading, paying attention to why Gustus leaves the safety of the school and heads home.

---

age. You good as mi right han'. I depen' on you. But this afternoon—earlier—in the rush, when we so well push to move befo' storm broke, you couldn' rememba a t'ing! Not one t'ing! Why so? Wha' on you mind? You harborin' t'ings from me, Gustus?"

Gustus opened his mouth to speak but closed it again. He knew his father was proud of how well he had grown. To strengthen him, he had always given him "last milk"[2] straight from the cow in the mornings. He was thankful. But to him his strength was only proven in the number of innings he could pitch for his cricket[3] team. The boy's lips trembled. What's the good of tellin', when Pappy don' like cricket. He only get vex an' say it's an evil game for idle hands! He twisted his head and looked away. "I'm harborin' nothin', Pappy."

"Gustus . . ."

> He knew his father was proud of how well he had grown.

At that moment a man called, "Mr. Bass!" He came up quickly. "Got a hymnbook, Mr. Bass? We want you to lead us singing."

The people were sitting with bowed heads, humming a song. As the repressed singing grew louder and louder, it sounded mournful in the room. Mr. Bass shuffled, looking around as if he wished to back out of the suggestion. But his rich voice and singing leadership were too famous. Mrs. Bass already had the hymnbook in her hand, and she pushed it at her husband. He took it and began turning the leaves as he moved toward the center of the room.

Immediately Mr. Bass was surrounded. He started with a resounding chant over the heads of everybody. "Abide wid me; fast fall the eventide. . . ." He joined the singing but broke off to recite the next line. "The darkness deepen; Lord, wid me, abide. . . ." Again, before the last long-drawn note faded from the deeply stirred voices, Mr. Bass intoned musically, "When odder helpers fail, and comfo'ts flee . . ."

In this manner he fired inspiration into the singing of hymn after hymn. The congregation swelled their throats, and their mixed voices filled the room, pleading to heaven from the depths of their hearts. But the wind outside mocked viciously. It screamed. It whistled. It smashed everywhere up.

Mrs. Bass had tightly closed her eyes, singing and swaying in the center of the children who nestled around her. But Gustus was by himself. He had his elbows on his knees and his hands blocking his ears. He had his own worries.

What's the good of Pappy asking all those questions when he treat him so bad? He's the only one in the family without a pair of shoes! Because he's a big boy, he don't need anyt'ing an' must do all the work. He can't stay at school in the evenings an' play cricket because there's work to do at home. He can't have no outings with the other children because he has no shoes. An' now when he was to sell his bunch of bananas an' buy shoes so he can go out with his cricket team, the hurricane is going to blow it down.

It was true: the root of the banana was his "navel string."[4] After his birth the umbilical cord[5] was dressed with castor oil and sprinkled with nutmeg and buried, with the banana tree

---

2. **last milk:** the last milk drawn from a cow; it has a greater fat content than first milk.
3. **cricket:** an English game somewhat akin to baseball.
4. **navel string:** the umbilical cord.
5. **umbilical** (ŭm-bĭl'ĭ-kəl) **cord:** the cord through which a fetus receives nourishment; a person's navel marks the place where it was attached.

372   UNIT THREE PART 2: GOING TO EXTREMES

Mini-Lesson  Literary Concepts

THE EFFECTS OF ALLUSION

Literary allusion enriches the resonance of the character's emotions or feelings: "Paula began her journey like the heroic Odysseus."

Biblical allusion creates a sense of morality through lessons or examples: "To make that decision would require the wisdom of Solomon."

Historical allusion draws parallels between recent events and the past: "The Iran-Contra affair could have developed into Reagan's Watergate."

REVIEWING ALLUSION Remind students that an allusion is a reference to a famous person, place, event, or work of literature. For an allusion to be effective, however, readers must know the reference. See the chart for the effects of allusion.

Application Have students write a series of sentences describing aspects of their daily lives. Each sentence should contain an allusion. For example, "Although I wanted to succeed in math, geometry was my Waterloo."

Hurricane, Bahamas (1898), Winslow Homer. Watercolor and graphite on off-white woven paper, 14½" × 21½", The Metropolitan Museum of Art, Amelia B. Lazarus Fund, 1910 (10.228.7). Copyright © 1989 The Metropolitan Museum of Art.

##

Hurricane, Bahamas by Winslow Homer Although Winslow Homer (1836–1910) is most famous for his depictions of life in coastal New England, his frequent vacations in the Caribbean inspired many of his watercolors. Homer typically used vibrant colors to depict the sun-drenched islands; however, the darkness of the impending hurricane here subdues his palette.

Reading the Art *How does the painting illustrate the contradictory responses of houses and nature to the violent storm?*

Linking to History

 Most hurricanes occur in the late summer and early fall, when the sea is at its warmest. Hurricane Andrew devastated southern Florida in August of 1992, destroying or damaging 85,000 homes, taking 30 lives, and leaving more than 250,000 people homeless. The center of the storm struck 12 miles south of Miami with winds as high as 165 miles per hour.

Multicultural Perspectives

JAMAICA TODAY To help students understand the events of "The Banana Tree," provide them with the following information about life in present-day Jamaica. Most of the island is an elevated plateau with a long spine of mountains that rise to nearly 7,500 feet, although there are low-lying plains along the north and south coasts. The Jamaican economy is based on sugar (mainly in the form of molasses and rum), bauxite (the ore from which aluminum is derived), and tourism. Also, about one-quarter of Jamaicans farm cacao, coconuts, coffee, and yams. Nearly half of all Jamaicans live in rural areas, and over 80 percent of the total population is Christian.

THE LANGUAGE OF LITERATURE **TEACHER'S EDITION** 373

Literary Concept: DIALECT

F Point out to students that dialects make use of unique expressions or word combinations. Have students find dialect words or phrases in this passage and throughout the selection. (*Possible responses: "nana midwife"—a woman who helps deliver and care for children; "nable string"—umbilical cord; "mudder"—mother*)

STRATEGIC READING FOR
Less-Proficient Readers

G Ask students why Gustus leaves the schoolhouse. (*He is determined to save the tree he has carefully nurtured.*)
Summarizing/Noting Relevant Details

Set a Purpose Have students make a note, as they finish reading, of how successful Gustus is in saving his banana tree.

Literary Concept:
PROTAGONIST

H Ask students to pause in their reading and name some of the characters in the story. Then ask who the main character, or protagonist, is. (*Gustus*)

planted over it for him. When he was nine days old, the nana midwife[6] had taken him out into the open for the first time. She had held the infant proudly, and walked the twenty-five yards that separated the house from the kitchen, and at the back showed him his tree. "'Memba when you grow up," her toothless mouth had said, "it's you nable strings feedin' you tree, the same way it feed you from you mudder."

> **His shirt was fluttering from his back like a boat sail.**

Refuse from the kitchen made the plant flourish out of all proportion. But the rich soil around it was loose. Each time the tree gave a shoot, the bunch would be too heavy for the soil to support; so it crashed to the ground, crushing the tender fruit. This time, determined that his banana must reach the market, Gustus had supported his tree with eight props. And as he watched it night and morning, it had become very close to him. Often he had seriously thought of moving his bed to its root.

Muffled cries, and the sound of blowing noses, now mixed with the singing. Delayed impact of the disaster was happening. Sobbing was everywhere. Quickly the atmosphere became sodden[7] with the wave of weeping outbursts. Mrs. Bass's pregnant belly heaved. Her younger children were upset and cried, "Mammy, Mammy, Mammy. . . ."

Realizing that his family, too, was overwhelmed by the surrounding calamity, Mr. Bass bustled over to them. Because their respect for him bordered on fear, his presence quietened all immediately. He looked around. "Where's Gustus! Imogene . . . where's Gustus!"

"He was 'ere, Pappy," she replied, drying her eyes. "I dohn know when he get up."

Briskly Mr. Bass began combing the schoolroom to find his boy. He asked; no one had seen Gustus. He called. There was no answer. He tottered, lifting his heavy boots over heads, fighting his way to the jalousie.[8] He opened it and his eyes gleamed up and down the road but saw nothing of the boy. In despair Mr. Bass gave one last thunderous shout: "Gustus!" Only the wind sneered.

By this time Gustus was halfway on the mile journey to their house. The lone figure in the raging wind and shin-deep road flood was tugging, snapping, and pitching branches out of his path. His shirt was fluttering from his back like a boat sail. And a leaf was fastened to his cheek. But the belligerent wind was

---

6. **nana midwife:** a woman who helps other women give birth and care for their newborn children.
7. **sodden:** soaked.
8. **jalousie** (jăl′ə-sē): a window covering having adjustable slats to let in light and air.

WORDS TO KNOW
refuse (rĕf′yōōs) *n.* trash; garbage

374

Mini-Lesson  The Writer's Style

SENTENCE VARIETY Point out to students that varying sentence structure is one of the most important devices an author can use to make his or her writing interesting. There are three main kinds of sentences.
- Simple sentence: "The Jamaican sun didn't come out."
- Compound sentence: "Mrs. Bass already had the hymnbook in her hand, and she pushed it at her husband."
- Complex sentence: "In the hours the hurricane stayed, its presence made everybody older."

Application Have students write a paragraph that describes the effects of a violent tornado, thunderstorm, or blizzard. The paragraph should contain all three kinds of sentences.

Reteaching/Reinforcement
- *Writing Mini-Lessons* transparency pack, pp. 40–43

The Writer's Craft
Sentence Variety, pp. 302–303

374 THE LANGUAGE OF LITERATURE **TEACHER'S EDITION**

merciless. It bellowed into his ears and drummed a deafening commotion. As he grimaced and covered his ears, he was forcefully slapped against a coconut tree trunk that lay across the road.

When his eyes opened, his round face was turned up to a festered sky. Above the tormented trees a zinc sheet writhed, twisted, and somersaulted in the tempestuous flurry. Leaves of all shapes and sizes were whirling and diving like attackers around the zinc sheet. As Gustus turned to get up, a bullet drop of rain struck his temple. He shook his head, held grimly to the tree trunk, and struggled to his feet.

Where the road was clear, he edged along the bank. Once, when the wind staggered him, he recovered with his legs wide apart. Angrily he stretched out his hands with clenched fists and shouted, "I almos' hol' you that time . . . come solid like that again, an' we fight like man an' man!"

When Gustus approached the river he had to cross, it was flooded and blocked beyond recognition. Pressing his chest against the gritty road bank, the boy closed his weary eyes on the brink of the spating river. The wrecked footbridge had become the harboring fort for all the debris, branches, and monstrous tree trunks which the river swept along its course. The river was still swelling. More accumulation arrived each moment, ramming and pressing the bridge. Under pressure it was cracking and shifting minutely toward a turbulent forty-foot fall.

Gustus had seen it! A feeling of dismay paralyzed him, reminding him of his foolish venture. He scraped his cheek on the bank looking back. But how can he go back? He has no strength to go back. His house is nearer than the school. An' Pappy will only strap him for nothin' . . . for nothin' . . . no shoes, nothin', when the hurricane is gone.

With trembling fingers he tied up the remnants of his shirt. He made a bold step and the wind half lifted him, ducking him in the muddy flood. He sank to his neck. Floating leaves, sticks, coconut husks, dead rat-bats, and all manner of feathered creatures and refuse surrounded him. Forest vines under the water entangled him. But he struggled desperately until he clung to the laden bridge and climbed up among leafless branches.

His legs were bruised and bore deep scratches, but steadily he moved up on the slimy pile. He felt like a man at sea, in the heart of a storm, going up the mast of a ship. He rested his feet on a smooth log that stuck to the water-splashed heap like a black torso. As he strained up for another grip, the torso came to life and leaped from under his feet. Swiftly sliding down, he grimly clutched some brambles.

WORDS TO KNOW
grimace (grĭm′ĭs) *v.* to make a facial expression that reflects pain
debris (də-brē′) *n.* the scattered remains of something broken or destroyed
turbulent (tûr′byə-lənt) *adj.* violently agitated or disturbed; disorderly
torso (tôr′sō) *n.* the human body excluding the head and limbs; trunk

375

Mini-Lesson Grammar

VERB TENSES Different forms of a verb are used to show the time of an action or a state of being. The forms of the verb that indicate time are called tenses. The three simple verb tenses are past, present, and future. They are formed by:
- changing the spelling of the verb, such as search/search**ed** or run/**ran**
- using a helping verb, such as **has** tried/**had** tried/**will** try

Application Point out to students that the account of Gustus's journey home is told in the past tense. Have students refer to the highlighted paragraph on page 375. Ask them to rewrite the paragraph in the present tense. Then ask students to describe how the change in the verb tense affects the action of the story.

Reteaching/Reinforcement
- *Grammar Handbook*, anthology pp. 883–884
- *Grammar Mini-Lessons* copymasters p. 24, transparencies p. 16

 **The Writer's Craft**

Verb Tenses, pp. 483–484

Critical Thinking: HYPOTHESIZE

I Ask students to consider Gustus's return home. Ask students how likely it is that Gustus will make it back safely based on what they have read thus far. *(Possible response: It seems unlikely that Gustus will make it back alive; the wind is too powerful.)*

CUSTOMIZING FOR
Multiple Learning Styles

J Bodily-Kinesthetic Learners
As Gustus fights his way home against the force of the storm, he challenges the hurricane to fight him. Encourage students to pick up details of the physical challenge the journey home presents to Gustus and of how he attempts to use his body to combat the storm.

CUSTOMIZING FOR
Students Acquiring English

3 Call students' attention to the phrase "the brink of the spating river." Ask a student to paraphrase or describe the boy's location. *(Possible response: on the edge of the rushing or flooding river)*

4 Point out the words "like a black torso" and explain that this phrase is a simile—the boy stood on a log that looked like a human body but wasn't really a body.

Active Reading: EVALUATE

K Have students discuss Gustus's decision to keep going. Ask students if he would have been better off returning to the shelter. If students are having problems evaluating the situation, provide them with the following model.

Think-Aloud Model *Even though the school was farther away, I think it would have been better for Gustus to return rather than try to cross the raging river. While I can understand his fear of his father, it is foolish for him to avoid punishment if that means he will be killed.*

THE LANGUAGE OF LITERATURE TEACHER'S EDITION **375**

Active Reading: CONNECT

L Ask students whether they have ever been as determined as Gustus to accomplish a seemingly impossible task. Ask them if they were more successful than Gustus appears to be at this point. If so, ask students how they managed to keep going.

Critical Thinking: MAKING JUDGMENTS

M Have students discuss if Gustus's return home increases the chances of the tree's surviving the hurricane. *(Possible response: Considering that the house has already blown down, there is little Gustus can do to keep the tree from harm. Gustus himself is injured by the storm, so it seems unlikely he can be effective.)*

Literary Concept: ALLUSION

N Have students discuss why Gustus is described as crucified against the banana tree. How does this allusion correspond to other details of the story? *(Possible response: The wind has pushed Gustus against the tree, probably with his arms outstretched. This suggests that Gustus is willing to sacrifice himself for his tree just as Christians believe that Jesus sacrificed himself for humankind.)*

The urgency of getting across became more frightening, and he gritted his teeth and dug his toes into the debris, climbing with maddened determination. But a hard gust of wind slammed the wreck, pinning him like a motionless lizard. For a minute the boy was stuck there, panting, swelling his naked ribs.

He stirred again and reached the top. He was sliding over a breadfruit limb when a flutter startled him. As he looked and saw the clean-head crow and glassy-eyed owl close together, there was a powerful jolt. Gustus flung himself into the air and fell in the expanding water on the other side. When he surfaced, the river had dumped the entire wreckage into the gurgling gully. For once the wind helped. It blew him to land.

Gustus was in a daze when he reached his house. Mud and rotten leaves covered his head and face, and blood caked around a gash on his chin. He bent down, shielding himself behind a tree stump whose white heart was a needly splinter, murdered by the wind.

He could hardly recognize his yard. The terrorized trees that stood were writhing in turmoil. Their thatched house had collapsed like an open umbrella that was given a heavy blow. He looked the other way and whispered, "Is still there! That's a miracle. . . . That's a miracle."

Dodging the wind, he staggered from tree to tree until he got to his own tormented banana tree. Gustus hugged the tree. "My nable string!" he cried. "My nable string! I know you would stan' up to it, I know you would."

The bones of the tree's stalky leaves were broken, and the wind lifted them and harassed them. And over Gustus's head the heavy fruit swayed and swayed. The props held the tree, but they were squeaking and slipping. And around the plant the roots stretched and trembled, gradually surfacing under loose earth.

With the rags of his wet shirt flying off his back, Gustus was down busily on his knees, bracing, pushing, tightening the props. One by one he was adjusting them until a heavy rush of wind knocked him to the ground. A prop fell on him, but he scrambled to his feet and looked up at the thirteen-hand bunch of bananas. "My good tree," he bawled, "hol' you fruit. . . . Keep it to you heart like a mudder savin' her baby! Don't let the wicked wind t'row you to the groun' . . . even if it t'row me to the groun'. I will not leave you."

> **The terrorized trees that stood were writhing in turmoil.**

But several attempts to replace the prop were futile. The force of the wind against his weight was too much for him. He thought of a rope to lash the tree to anything, but it was difficult to make his way into the kitchen, which, separate from the house, was still standing. The invisible hand of the wind tugged, pushed, and forcefully restrained him. He got down and crawled on his belly into the earth-floor kitchen. As he showed himself with the rope, the wind tossed him, like washing on the line, against his tree.

The boy was hurt! He looked crucified against the tree. The spike of the wind was slightly withdrawn. He fell, folded on the ground. He lay there unconscious. And the wind had no mercy for him. It shoved him, poked him, and molested his clothes like muddy newspaper against the tree.

As darkness began to move in rapidly, the wind grew more vicious and surged a mighty gust that struck the resisting kitchen. It was heaved to the ground in a rubbled pile. The brave wooden hut had been shielding the

376 UNIT THREE PART 2: GOING TO EXTREMES

Mini-Lesson: Speaking, Listening, and Viewing

DIRECTING A VIDEOTAPE Explain to students that making a videotape is a creative process that must be carefully planned. Suggest that directing a video encourages the exploration of different elements in the story, rather than an exact transcription of the story's main events.

Application Have students work alone or in small groups to plan how they would film Gustus's struggle to return home. Remind them they would be adapting the story for an American audience, and ask students whom they would choose to play the role of Gustus. Ask students what music or sound effects they would choose to accompany the journey home. If time allows, you might wish to invite interested students to draw storyboards outlining some or all of their proposals.

banana tree but in its death fall missed it by inches. The wind charged again and the soft tree gurgled—the fruit was torn from it and plunged to the ground.

The wind was less fierce when Mr. Bass and a searching party arrived with lanterns. Because the bridge was washed away, the hazardous roundabout journey had badly impeded them.

Talks about safety were mockery to the anxious father. Relentlessly he searched. In the darkness his great voice echoed everywhere, calling for his boy. He was wrenching and ripping through the house wreckage when suddenly he vaguely remembered how the boy had been fussing with the banana tree. Desperate, the man struggled from the ruins, flagging the lantern he carried.

The flickering light above his head showed Mr. Bass the forlorn and pitiful banana tree. There it stood, shivering and twitching like a propped-up man with lacerated throat and dismembered head. Half of the damaged fruit rested on Gustus. The father hesitated. But when he saw a feeble wink of the boy's eyelids, he flung himself to the ground. His bristly chin rubbed the child's face while his unsteady hand ran all over his body. "Mi bwoy!" he murmured. "Mi hurricane bwoy! The Good Lord save you. . . . Why you do this? Why you do this?"

"I did want buy mi shoes, Pappy. I . . . I can't go anywhere 'cause I have no shoes. . . . I didn' go to school outing at the factory. I didn' go to Government House. I didn' go to Ol' Fort in town."

Mr. Bass sank into the dirt and stripped himself of his heavy boots. He was about to lace them to the boy's feet when the onlooking men prevented him. He tied the boots together and threw them over his shoulder.

Gustus's broken arm was strapped to his side as they carried him away. Mr. Bass stroked his head and asked how he felt. Only then grief swelled inside him and he wept. ❖

LITERARY INSIGHT

The Hurricane
BY LUIS PALÉS MATOS

When the hurricane unfolds
Its fierce accordion of winds,
On the tip of its toes,
Agile dancer, it sweeps whirling
Over the carpeted surface of the sea
With the scattered branches of the palm.

THE HURRICANE **377**

STRATEGIC READING FOR
Less-Proficient Readers

Have students discuss whether Gustus was successful in his attempt to save the tree. *(Possible responses: He failed, because the tree fell anyway; he succeeded, because he made his father realize how important playing cricket is to him.)* **Drawing Conclusions**

CUSTOMIZING FOR
Gifted and Talented Students

Invite students to discuss the role poverty plays in the events of the story. Have students discuss how the story might differ if the characters were of another socioeconomic level.

COMPREHENSION CHECK

1. What disaster strikes the village where Gustus lives? *(a hurricane)*
2. Why does Gustus want shoes so badly? *(so he can go on outings with his cricket team)*
3. How does Gustus plan to get money to buy shoes? *(by selling the bananas from his tree)*
4. How does Mr. Bass respond when Gustus tells him of his plans to buy new shoes? *(He tries to give Gustus his own boots.)*

INSIGHT

1. Ask students to think of the hurricane as a character in both the story and the poem. Ask them in which piece they think the hurricane is more vicious. Make sure students cite details that support their responses. *(Possible response: The hurricane in the story is more vicious, because it destroys bridges and trees and almost destroys Gustus.)*
2. What traits does the hurricane have in the poem? in the story? *(Possible responses: The hurricane in the poem is fierce but graceful like a dancer. The hurricane in the story is violent and destructive.)*

PALÉS MATOS

The Puerto Rican poet Palés Matos (1898–1959) grew up in a literary family. He was famous for poetry that celebrated the rhythms of Puerto Ricans of African ancestry. Although not of that ancestry himself, he felt that the African spirit would be lost if its oral and musical traditions were not captured in literature.

Mini-Lesson Spelling

WORDS FROM THE FRENCH LANGUAGE
Many words that are borrowed from the French language use vowel and letter combinations in ways uncommon to English words. Examples from the selection include:

debris (from *débriser*, "to break apart")

grimace (from *grimache*, "mask")

Spelling words borrowed from French is easier if students learn these vowel patterns:

r**ou**te	dun**geon**
sold**ier**	r**es**ta**ur**ant

Application Read the following words aloud. Ask students to write them in their notebooks.
1. coupon
2. carousel
3. sauté
4. silhouette
5. lieutenant
6. surgeon
7. chandelier
8. chauvinist
9. gourmet
10. boulevard

Ask students to look for more words that fit this pattern and to add these words to their personal word lists.

Reteaching/Reinforcement
• *Unit Three Resource Book*, p. 49

THE LANGUAGE OF LITERATURE TEACHER'S EDITION **377**

From Personal Response to Critical Analysis

1. Responses will vary.
2. Possible responses: He wishes he were more sensitive to his son's needs; he feels he has failed Gustus.
3. Possible responses: He is foolish because there is nothing he can do to protect the tree and he might be killed trying to save it; he is courageous to venture out into the storm and risk his life to save the young tree.
4. Possible responses: Putting one's life in jeopardy for the sake of a tree is foolish; risking one's life to protect something or someone else is admirable if you feel strongly about the situation.
5. Possible response: Their relationship is strained; they do not communicate well.
6. Possible response: The poem does not address the violence and destruction of the hurricane; the story does not take into account the hurricane's beauty.
7. Responses will vary.

Another Pathway

Cooperative Learning Have students work in groups of three. Ask each group to brainstorm the questions they would like to ask Mr. Bass and Gustus. Have students decide who will play the roles of the television reporter, Mr. Bass, and Gustus. Invite group members to review the characters' responses before presenting to the class.

Rubric

3 Full Accomplishment Students accurately present details of the characters and the story events.

2 Substantial Accomplishment Students cover some of the actions of the story but fail to present Gustus's and Mr. Bass's feelings accurately.

1 Little or Partial Accomplishment Students conduct the interview with little regard for the details of the characters or story events.

RESPONDING OPTIONS

FROM PERSONAL RESPONSE TO CRITICAL ANALYSIS

REFLECT
1. Do you have stronger feelings about Gustus or about Mr. Bass? Why? Jot down your thoughts in your notebook.

RETHINK
2. Reread the last two paragraphs of the story. What do you think Mr. Bass is thinking and feeling after hearing Gustus's reasons for making the trip to the banana tree?

3. Do you think Gustus is courageous or foolish in trying to protect his tree? Explain your answer.
   Consider
   • what the tree means to him
   • what dangers he faces
   • how his decision might affect his relationship with his father

Thematic Link
4. If you were in Gustus's situation, do you think you would go to the extremes he did to save the tree? Why or why not?

5. How would you describe the relationship between Gustus and his father? Give evidence to support your answer.

RELATE
Literary Link
6. Compare and contrast the image of a hurricane created by Palés Matos in "The Hurricane" (page 377) with the image created by Berry. Are the tones of the works the same, or are they different? Explain your answer.

7. Do you think the ways in which Gustus and his father interact are typical of most father-son relationships? Why or why not?

LITERARY CONCEPTS

The **protagonist** of a work of fiction is the story's main character—the one that arouses the most interest and sympathy in the reader. The protagonist usually struggles or competes against an **antagonist,** who might be another character, a force of nature or society, or a force within the protagonist. Identify the protagonist and the antagonist in "The Banana Tree." Does the personality of the protagonist change? If so, how?

Multimodal Learning
ANOTHER PATHWAY
Cooperative Learning
Imagine that you are a television reporter who has been assigned the task of interviewing Gustus and Mr. Bass after the hurricane. Prepare questions and answers for the interview. Then, with two classmates playing the roles of Gustus and Mr. Bass, present the interview to the class.

QUICKWRITES

1. Write a **dialogue** that might take place between Gustus and his father after Gustus's broken arm is treated.

2. Have you ever, like Gustus, wanted something badly but been unable or unwilling to ask for it? Write a **personal narrative** in which you describe the situation and what happened.

📁 PORTFOLIO *Save your writing. You may want to use it later as a springboard to a piece for your portfolio.*

378 UNIT THREE PART 2: GOING TO EXTREMES

Literary Concepts

In discussing the difference between the protagonist and the antagonist, point out that although there is usually only one protagonist, there may be several antagonists. Students should understand that Gustus is the protagonist. Most students will say that the hurricane is the antagonist, and some will say that, in addition, Mr. Bass is an antagonist. Although the brave and tenacious personality of Gustus is revealed in this story, it is hard to say if it changes.

QuickWrites

1. Students may want to set up their dialogue in a play format, with only minimal stage directions to indicate action.
2. Invite students to share events from their personal experience but allow them to alter names, events, and places if they wish.

 The Writer's Craft

Guidelines for Writing Dialogue, p. 327
Autobiographical Incident, pp. 27–39

ALTERNATIVE ACTIVITIES

Review the ways in which Berry personifies, or gives human qualities to, the hurricane. Then create a **drawing** or **painting** that shows the battle for control between the hurricane and Gustus. If you have a graphics program on your computer, here's a chance to use it.

ACROSS THE CURRICULUM

Geographical Connection The banana is an important food crop in many parts of the world. Find out which countries are the chief producers of bananas. What climate do they have?

WORDS TO KNOW

Review the Words to Know at the bottom of the selection pages. On your paper, draw the answer blanks that follow each clue below, then write the vocabulary word that fits the clue. Unscramble the letters in the boxes to make a word that relates to this story.

1. a trunk that is not used for storage __ __ __ __ ▢
2. a word that describes a raging river ▢ __ __ __ __ __ __ __ __
3. to show pain __ __ __ ▢ __ __ __
4. wreckage from an airplane crash __ __ __ ▢ __ __
5. the contents of a rubbish bin __ __ __ __ ▢ __

JAMES BERRY

1925–

"The Banana Tree" is from *A Thief in the Village and Other Stories,* a collection of stories that are "straight out of my own childhood and later observations," according to James Berry, who was born in Jamaica and emigrated to England in 1948. While working in the British school system, he noticed that there were few books about the experiences of children with African or Caribbean backgrounds. "No one has reported our stories, or the way we saw things," Berry has said. "It's the function of writers and poets to bring in the left-out side of the human family."

Berry's *A Thief in the Village and Other Stories* won the Grand Prix Smarties Prize in 1987 and was named a Coretta Scott King Award honor book in 1988. In these stories, Berry describes the harsh reality of Caribbean life and uses the Jamaican dialect to convey the authentic spirit and voice of the Caribbean culture.

Berry's Jamaican heritage has provided him with material for several of his other books. *Anancy-Spiderman* is a collection of retold West Indian folk tales, based on West African traditions, about a crafty man-spider. *When I Dance* contains poems that focus on the humor, struggles, injustice, and goodness of Jamaican teenage life.

OTHER WORKS *The Girls and Yanga Marshall, The Future-Telling Lady and Other Stories, Celebration Song* Extended Reading

THE BANANA TREE **379**

Words to Know

1. **t**orso
2. **t**urbulent
3. g**r**imace
4. debri**s**
5. refu**s**e

Unscrambled letters: **storm**

Reteaching/Reinforcement
- *Unit Three Resource Book,* p. 50

Across the Curriculum

Geographical Connection
Cooperative Learning Have students consult an encyclopedia or an on-line computer service for information about bananas and where this crop grows. Encourage them to assess how important the banana crop is in the overall economy of each region. You might divide students into groups of four or five and have each group choose a different region or country to research. Then have each group give a class presentation that summarizes its findings. Assign one member of each group to locate or draw maps of the group's chosen region.

ADDITIONAL SUGGESTION
History *Jamaica Then and Now* Encourage students to work in pairs or small groups to research the settlement and colonization of Jamaica. Point out to students that although Jamaica was encountered by Columbus in 1494 and settled by the Spanish in 1509, the British controlled the island, and its precious sugar crop, by 1655. Throughout its history Jamaica has experienced poverty and high rates of unemployment. For this reason, struggles for equal rights and fair economic treatment have characterized much of Jamaica's history.

JAMES BERRY

In addition to locating stories in a Caribbean setting, Berry has written about the contemporary experiences of minorities in England. For instance, in *The Girls and Yanga Marshall,* Berry focuses on the conflicting education the title character receives in school and on the London streets.

Alternative Activities

Before students begin their drawing, painting, or computer graphic, be sure that they isolate one particular event from Gustus's battle with the hurricane. Suggest that they work in a group to select sequential events in the story to illustrate its chronology.

OVERVIEW

Objectives

- To understand and appreciate a classic horror story that depicts extremes in human behavior
- To enrich reading by using active reading strategies
- To identify and analyze mood
- To express understanding of the story through a choice of writing forms, including an alternative ending and lead paragraphs
- To extend understanding of the story through a variety of multimodal and cross-curricular activities

Skills

READING SKILLS/STRATEGIES
- Evaluating

THE WRITER'S STYLE
- Denotation and connotation

SPEAKING, LISTENING, AND VIEWING
- Group presentation
- Oral presentation

GRAMMAR
- Adverbs

LITERARY CONCEPTS
- Tone
- Mood

GENRE STUDY
- Horror fiction

Cross-Curricular Connections

SCIENCE
- Fear and shock

SOCIAL STUDIES
- The evil eye
- 19th-century America

PREVIEWING

FICTION

The Tell-Tale Heart
Edgar Allan Poe

Activating Prior Knowledge
PERSONAL CONNECTION

Some of the most frightening characters in movies originated in literature. Perhaps the most famous of these are Frankenstein's monster and Count Dracula. Though they may not have originated in literature, other movie creatures that draw on the traditions of literary horror include werewolves, King Kong, Godzilla, Freddy Krueger, and the Terminator. What kinds of horror characters scare you the most? What do they have in common? Lower the shades and turn down the lights as you discuss these questions with your classmates!

Building Background
LITERARY CONNECTION

The best horror story writers are experts at scaring the wits out of us. Edgar Allan Poe was one of the first American authors to do this. Oddly enough, his work owes much to his own feverish dreams, to which he applied a rare talent for shaping believable tales. Poe's characters face mysterious forces both within and outside themselves. Underneath the bizarre and frightening details of his stories, Poe explored the conflict in the human soul.

Like Poe, today's master of horror, Stephen King, fully comprehends the frightening power of the unknown and the supernatural. Why do so many people love the horror stories of writers like Poe and King? As one critic put it, "There is no delight the equal of dread."

Active Reading/Setting a Purpose
READING CONNECTION

Evaluating To enjoy "The Tell-Tale Heart" fully, keep your reading log handy as you read, and jot down answers to the questions inserted in the text. When you finish reading, evaluate the story's effectiveness as a horror story. Make judgments about the characters, the setting and mood, and the plot. How believable is the story? How horrifying is it?

Illustration of "The Raven"
The Bettman Archive

380 UNIT THREE PART 2: GOING TO EXTREMES

PRINT AND MEDIA RESOURCES

UNIT THREE RESOURCE BOOK
Strategic Reading: Literature, p. 53
Vocabulary SkillBuilder, p. 55
Reading SkillBuilder, p. 54

GRAMMAR MINI-LESSONS
Transparencies, p. 40
Copymasters, p. 19

WRITING MINI-LESSONS
Transparencies, p. 37

ACCESS FOR STUDENTS ACQUIRING ENGLISH
Selection Summaries
Reading and Writing Support

FORMAL ASSESSMENT
Selection Test, pp. 71–72
 Test Generator

AUDIO LIBRARY
See Reference Card

LASERLINKS
Author Background

INTERNET RESOURCES
McDougal Littell Literature Center at http://www.hmco.com/mcdougal/lit

380 THE LANGUAGE OF LITERATURE TEACHER'S EDITION

The Tell-Tale Heart

by Edgar Allan Poe

True!—nervous—very, very dreadfully nervous I had been and am! but why *will* you say that I am mad? The disease had sharpened my senses—not destroyed—not dulled them. Above all was the sense of hearing acute. I heard all things in the heaven and in the earth. I heard many things in hell. How, then, am I mad? Hearken! and observe how healthily—how calmly I can tell you the whole story.

It is impossible to say how first the idea entered my brain; but once conceived, it haunted me day and night. Object there was none. Passion there was none. I loved the old man. He had never wronged me. He had never given me insult. For his gold I had no desire. I think it was his eye! yes, it was this! He had the eye of a vulture—a pale blue eye, with a film over it. Whenever it

WORDS TO KNOW
acute (ə-kyōōt′) *adj.* sharp; keen
conceived (kən-sēvd′) *adj.* thought of **conceive** *v.*

SUMMARY

While insisting he is not mad, the narrator is upset by an old man's vulturelike eye that is covered with a blue haze. The narrator visits the old man's room for seven nights, and on the eighth, he kills him while the sound of the old man's heart throbs in his ears. He then hides the body under the floor. When the police investigate, the narrator is confident they will find nothing. Later he begins to hear a muffled sound, which grows louder and louder. Convinced that the noise is the old man's heart, the narrator confesses his crime.

Thematic Link: *Going to Extremes*
One man's obsession with another person leads him to the extreme act of murder.

CUSTOMIZING FOR
Students Acquiring English

- Use **ACCESS FOR STUDENTS ACQUIRING ENGLISH,** *Reading and Writing Support.*
- Less-fluent students may become frustrated by difficult grammar and sentence structures. Review the action periodically with the class and ask students to describe the narrator and his behavior at various points in the story.

① Remind students that *mad* here means "crazy," not "angry."

② Ask a more fluent student to change these sentences to a more common construction. *(There was no object. There was no passion.)*

STRATEGIC READING FOR
Less-Proficient Readers

Set a Purpose To engage students, ask them to think of other horror stories they have read or heard or horror films they have seen. Ask them what they expect to find in reading a horror short story. Have students look for how the narrator carries out his plan as they read.

Use **UNIT THREE RESOURCE BOOK,** p. 53, for guidance in reading the selection.

WORDS TO KNOW

acute (ə-kyōōt′) *adj.* sharp; keen (p. 381)
audacity (ô-dăs′ĭ-tē) *n.* shameless daring or boldness (p. 386)
conceived (kən-sēvd′) *adj.* thought of **conceive** *v.* (p. 381)
crevice (krĕv′ĭs) *n.* a crack (p. 383)
derision (dĭ-rĭzh′ən) *n.* ridicule (p. 386)
hypocritical (hĭp′ə-krĭt′ĭ-kəl) *adj.* false or deceptive, like a person who is pretending to be what he or she is not (p. 386)
stealthily (stĕl′thĭ-lē) *adv.* cautiously; secretly (p. 383)
stifled (stī′fəld) *adj.* smothered **stifle** *v.* (p. 382)
vehemently (vē′ə-mənt-lē) *adv.* with intense emotion (p. 386)
vex (vĕks) *v.* to disturb; annoy (p. 382)

CUSTOMIZING FOR
Gifted and Talented Students

Have students discuss the narrator's reliability as they read. Ask students whether it is possible to believe the narrator's version of events if the narrator's sanity is in question. Encourage students to consider the reliability of any narrator, whether insane or not.

Active Reading: QUESTION

 Ask students to concentrate on how the narrator presents himself at the opening of the story. *(Possible responses: He tries to say he is not mad, but he sure sounds like he is insane. He sounds as though he fully believes that his actions were justified.)*

Linking to Social Studies

B The belief in the evil eye is ancient and crosses many cultures. Typically, old women are said to be able to cast misfortune with a glance of their eye toward anyone who offends them. To avoid the evil eye, some people wear blue beads or other charms as protection.

CUSTOMIZING FOR
Students Acquiring English

3 Explain that the minute hand of a clock moves too slowly to be easily seen. Here the narrator uses exaggeration to emphasize how slowly he moved.

Active Reading: CLARIFY

C Draw attention to the fact that the old man knows only that someone is at the threshold of his room; at this point he does not know who stands in his doorway or what that person's intention is.

---

fell upon me, my blood ran cold; and so by degrees—very gradually—I made up my mind to take the life of the old man, and thus rid myself of the eye forever.

Now this is the point. You fancy me mad. Madmen know nothing. But you should have seen *me*. You should have seen how wisely I proceeded—with what caution—with what foresight—with what dissimulation[1] I went to work!

I was never kinder to the old man than during the whole week before I killed him. And every night, about midnight, I turned the latch of his door and opened it—oh, so gently! And then, when I had made an opening sufficient for my head, I put in a dark lantern, all closed, closed, so that no light shone out, and then I thrust in my head. Oh, you would have laughed to see how cunningly I thrust it in! I moved it slowly—very, very slowly, so that I might not disturb the old man's sleep. It took me an hour to place my whole head within the opening so far that I could see him as he lay upon his bed. Ha!—would a madman have been so wise as this? And then, when my head was well in the room, I undid the lantern cautiously—oh, so cautiously—cautiously (for the hinges creaked)—I undid it just so much that a single thin ray fell upon the vulture eye. And this I did for seven long nights—every night just at midnight—but I found the eye always closed; and so it was impossible to do the work; for it was not the old man who <u>vexed</u> me, but his Evil Eye. And every morning, when the day broke, I went boldly into the chamber, and spoke courageously to him, calling him by name in a hearty tone, and inquiring how he had passed the night. So you see he would have been a very profound old man, indeed, to suspect that every night, just at twelve, I looked in upon him while he slept.

QUESTION
What is your first impression of the narrator?
Using a Reading Log

Upon the eighth night I was more than usually cautious in opening the door. A watch's minute hand moves more quickly than did mine. Never before that night had I *felt* the extent of my own powers—of my sagacity.[2] I could scarcely contain my feelings of triumph. To think that there I was, opening the door, little by little, and he not even to dream of my secret deeds or thoughts. I fairly chuckled at the idea; and perhaps he heard me; for he moved on the bed suddenly, as if startled. Now you may think that I drew back—but no. His room was as black as pitch with the thick darkness (for the shutters were close fastened, through fear of robbers), and so I knew that he could not see the opening of the door, and I kept pushing it on steadily, steadily.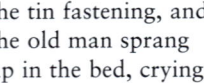

I had my head in, and was about to open the lantern, when my thumb slipped upon the tin fastening, and the old man sprang up in the bed, crying out—"Who's there?"

CLARIFY
Does the old man suspect anything?
Using a Reading Log

I kept quite still and said nothing. For a whole hour I did not move a muscle, and in the meantime I did not hear him lie down. He was still sitting up in the bed listening—just as I have done, night after night, hearkening to the death watches[3] in the wall.

Presently I heard a slight groan, and I knew it was the groan of mortal terror. It was not a groan of pain or grief—oh, no!—it was the low, <u>stifled</u> sound that arises from the bottom of the soul when overcharged with awe. I

---

1. **dissimulation:** a hiding of one's true feelings.
2. **sagacity:** sound judgment; intelligence.
3. **death watches:** deathwatch beetles—wood-burrowing insects that make a tapping sound with their head.

> **WORDS TO KNOW**
> **vex** (vĕks) *v.* to disturb; annoy
> **stifled** (stī'fəld) *adj.* smothered **stifle** *v.*

382

Mini-Lesson — Reading Skills/Strategies

ACTIVE READING: EVALUATING Point out to students that evaluating is a process of judging the worth of something or someone. In evaluating a work of literature, readers form opinions about what they read, including characters and events.

Application Encourage students to create their own lists of criteria for evaluating a work of literature. Ask students the following questions to assist them in developing their evaluative criteria. Then have students apply their criteria to this story.
- How important is it that the piece entertain or amuse me?
- Is it necessary for the characters, events, and dialogue to be believable?
- Do I care if the story moves me emotionally?
- Should I feel enough for the characters to be concerned with the outcome of the story?
- Did the story keep me guessing, or could I predict the outcome?

Have students review the entries they wrote based on the Reading Connection on page 380.

Reteaching/Reinforcement
- *Unit Three Resource Book,* p. 54

knew the sound well. Many a night, just at midnight, when all the world slept, it has welled up from my own bosom, deepening, with its dreadful echo, the terrors that distracted me. I say I knew it well. I knew what the old man felt, and pitied him, although I chuckled at heart. I knew that he had been lying awake ever since the first slight noise, when he had turned in the bed. His fears had been ever since growing upon him. He had been trying to fancy them causeless, but could not. He had been saying to himself—"It is nothing but the wind in the chimney—it is only a mouse crossing the floor," or "it is merely a cricket which has made a single chirp." Yes, he has been trying to comfort himself with these suppositions; but he had found all in vain. *All in vain*; because Death, in approaching him, had stalked with his black shadow before him, and enveloped the victim. And it was the mournful influence of the unperceived shadow that caused him to feel—although he neither saw nor heard—to *feel* the presence of my head within the room.

When I had waited a long time, very patiently, without hearing him lie down, I resolved to open a little—a very, very little crevice in the lantern. So I opened it—you cannot imagine how stealthily, stealthily—until, at length, a single dim ray, like the thread of the spider, shot from out the crevice and fell full upon the vulture eye.

It was open—wide, wide open—and I grew furious as I gazed upon it. I saw it with perfect distinctness—all a dull blue, with a hideous veil over it that chilled the very marrow in my bones; but I could see nothing else of the old man's face or person: for I had directed the ray as if by instinct, precisely upon the damned spot.

And now have I not told you that what you mistake for madness is but over-acuteness of

> Presently I heard a slight groan, and I knew **it was the groan of mortal terror.**

WORDS TO KNOW
crevice (krĕv′ĭs) *n.* a crack
stealthily (stĕl′thĭ-lē) *adv.* cautiously; secretly

383

Literary Concept: MOOD

D Ask students to identify details that increase the atmosphere of horror. *(Possible response: The straining of the old man and the account of his desperate attempt to pretend no one is in the room increase the reader's anticipation and interest.)*

Active Reading: CLARIFY

E Have students explain why it is appropriate for the light to shine on the old man's evil eye. You may wish to provide students with the following model to help in their discussion.

Think-Aloud Model *I think it's appropriate for the light to shine in the old man's vulturelike eye because it was the eye that made the narrator wish to kill him. This was the eighth night in a row that the narrator had approached the room, and until this night, he hadn't seen the eye. This obsession was what sent him away and also what made him come back to commit the crime.*

CUSTOMIZING FOR
Multiple Learning Styles

F **Spatial or Graphic Learners** Have students draw the scene where the lantern falls on the old man's eye. Point out that the figure of the narrator should be barely discernible in the dark, while the old man's eye should be illuminated by the thin ray of light from the lantern.

Mini-Lesson Literary Concepts

REVIEWING TONE Remind students that tone is an author's attitude toward his or her subject. The tone of a story often coincides with its subject matter, such as a serious or sad tone when the story focuses on tragic events. However, sometimes the tone of the story differs from its subject: A humorous or upbeat tone may be used to describe painful or disturbing events.

Application Have students discuss how the tone of "The Tell-Tale Heart" creates a sense of the macabre. Encourage them to answer the questions below to help prompt discussion:

- How does the narrator's belief that he is not mad affect the tone of the story?
- How do the sentence length and word choice of the narrator influence the reader's experience of the story?
- How would students characterize the narrator's attitude toward the old man based on his account? How does this shape how believable the events of the story are to the reader?

Critical Thinking: SPECULATE

G Ask students to speculate why the narrator hears the beating of the old man's heart even when he is some distance away. *(Possible responses: The narrator is insane and he imagines he can hear the beating. He actually hears the beating of a heart, but he mistakes his own heart in his excited state for that of the old man.)*

Literary Concept: TONE

H Ask students what the tone of this passage reveals about the author's attitude toward the narrator. *(Possible response: Through the way the author presents the narrator's frantic thoughts and through the author's use of exclamatory sentences, he seems to be stressing the fact that the narrator is becoming more unbalanced.)*

CUSTOMIZING FOR
Students Acquiring English

4 Have a student paraphrase "do you mark me well?" *(Do you understand me?)* Ask them whom the narrator is addressing. *(Possible responses: the readers; the police as he retells the story)*

5 Explain that "The old man's hour had come!" means that it was time for him to die, according to the narrator.

STRATEGIC READING FOR
Less-Proficient Readers

I Have students explain how the narrator completes his plan to murder the old man. *(He throws the old man on the floor and pulls the heavy bed over him; the old man dies either of fear or by suffocation.)* Noting Relevant Details/Noting Sequence of Events

Set a Purpose Have students read on to see what happens to the old man and the narrator.

Copyright © John Thompson.

the senses?—now, I say, there came to my ears a low, dull, quick sound, such as a watch makes when enveloped in cotton. I knew *that* sound well too. It was the beating of the old man's heart. It increased my fury, as the beating of a drum stimulates the soldier into courage.

But even yet I refrained and kept still. I scarcely breathed. I held the lantern motionless. I tried how steadily I could maintain the ray upon the eye. Meantime the hellish tattoo[4] of the heart increased. It grew quicker and quicker, and louder and louder every instant. The old man's terror *must* have been extreme! It grew louder, I say, louder every moment!—do you mark me well? I have told you that I am nervous: so I am. And now at the dead hour of the night, amid the dreadful silence of that old house, so strange a noise as this excited me to uncontrollable terror. Yet, for some minutes longer I refrained and stood still. But the beating grew louder, louder! I thought the heart must burst. And now a new anxiety seized me—the sound would be heard by a neighbor! The old man's hour had come! With a loud yell, I threw open the lantern and leaped into the room. He shrieked once—once only. In an instant I dragged him to the floor, and pulled the heavy bed over him. I then smiled gaily, to find the deed so far done. But, for many minutes, the heart beat on with a muffled sound. This, however, did not vex me; it would not be heard through the wall. At length it ceased. The old man was dead. I removed the bed and examined the corpse. Yes, he was stone, stone dead. I placed my

---
4. **hellish tattoo:** awful drumming.

384 UNIT THREE PART 2: GOING TO EXTREMES

Mini-Lesson   Genre Study

FICTION Edgar Allan Poe was a master of **horror fiction,** sometimes known as Gothic fiction or Gothic romance in his time. As the genre became popular, Gothic or horror writers established uniform conventions:

- an emphasis on the supernatural, the fantastic, and the grotesque
- a setting among savage landscapes, graveyards, ruins, or haunted castles
- an unsuspecting, innocent victim (typically a young female heroine) who falls prey to a powerful evil character

Application Have students copy the web shown and use it to evaluate how Poe's story conforms to the conventions of Gothic fiction. Ask in what ways Poe departs from the conventions of Gothic writing in "The Tell-Tale Heart."

384 THE LANGUAGE OF LITERATURE TEACHER'S EDITION

hand upon the heart and held it there many minutes. There was no pulsation. He was stone dead. His eye would trouble me no more.

If still you think me mad, you will think so no longer when I describe the wise precautions I took for the concealment of the body. The night waned,[5] and I worked hastily, but in silence. First of all I dismembered the corpse. I cut off the head and the arms and the legs.

I then took up three planks from the flooring of the chamber, and deposited all between the scantlings.[6] I then replaced the boards so cleverly, so cunningly, that no human eye—not even *his*—could have detected anything wrong. There was nothing to wash out—no stain of any kind—no blood-spot whatever. I had been too wary for that. A tub had caught all—ha! ha!

When I made an end of these labors, it was four o'clock—still dark as midnight. As the bell sounded the hour, there came a knocking at the street door. I went down to open it with a light heart,—for what had I *now* to fear? There entered three men, who introduced themselves, with perfect suavity,[7] as officers of the police. A shriek had been heard by a neighbor during the night: suspicion of foul play had been aroused; information had been lodged at the police office, and they (the officers) had been deputed to search the premises.

I smiled,—for *what* had I to fear? I bade the gentlemen welcome. The shriek, I said, was my own in a dream. The old man, I mentioned, was absent in the country. I took my visitors all over the house. I bade them search—search *well*. I led them, at length, to *his* chamber. I showed them his treasures, secure, undisturbed.

PREDICT
Do you think he will be caught?
Using a Reading Log

---

5. **waned:** approached its end.
6. **scantlings:** small wooden beams supporting the floor.
7. **suavity** (swäv′ĭ-tē): smooth courteousness.

He was stone dead. His eye would trouble me no more.

THE TELL-TALE HEART **385**

Active Reading: PREDICT
J Students should predict how the narrator plans to cover up the old man's murder.

Literary Concept: MOOD
K Ask students how the author creates a manic mood in this passage. *(Possible responses: He uses dashes to show the excitement. He repeats words and even has his narrator laugh as he relates the dismemberment.)*

Critical Thinking: HYPOTHESIZE
L Have students hypothesize whether the narrator will manage to fool the police. *(Possible responses: He is too insane not to give himself away sooner or later; sometimes he seems sane in the way he presents himself, so he might not get caught.)*

Mini-Lesson The Writer's Style

DENOTATION AND CONNOTATION
Denotation is the dictionary definition of a word. **Connotation** means the feelings or thoughts that a word suggests other than its strict, literal meanings.

Application Refer students to the highlighted paragraph. Ask them to write both the denotative and connotative meanings of the underlined words in the following phrases:

dark as <u>midnight</u>

light <u>heart</u>

You may wish to extend the activity by having students review other descriptive passages from the selection and note any words whose connotative meanings differ from their denotative, or more literal, meanings.

Reteaching/Reinforcement
• *Writing Mini-Lessons* transparencies, p. 37

The Writer's Craft
Denotation and Connotation, pp. 314, 696

CUSTOMIZING FOR
Students Acquiring English

6 Point out that *ere long* is an old-fashioned way of saying "before long."

7 Explain that trifles are small, unimportant things.

STRATEGIC READING FOR
Less-Proficient Readers

M Have students discuss the return of the old man's heartbeat in the ears of the narrator and explain why it can't be heard by others in the room. *(The beating may be the sound of the narrator's own excited heart, a hallucination, or a signal that the old man seeks revenge from beyond the grave.)* **Making Inferences**

Active Reading: CLARIFY

N Ask students to consider the narrator's sanity in developing their responses. Invite them to contemplate possible feelings of guilt in the narrator.

CUSTOMIZING FOR
Gifted and Talented Students

Have students debate the nature of guilt and revenge in the story. Ask them to consider whether the return of the tell-tale heart is symbolic of the dead man's desire to avenge his horrific murder or if it is a symbol of the narrator's guilt.

COMPREHENSION CHECK

1. Why does the narrator want to kill the old man? *(He hates the old man's pale blue eye.)*
2. What does the narrator do for several nights before committing the murder? *(He watches as the old man sleeps.)*
3. What suddenly makes the narrator decide to kill the old man? *(The old man's heartbeat is so loud he is afraid the neighbors will hear.)*
4. How do the police find out about the murder? *(The narrator blurts out a confession.)*

In the enthusiasm of my confidence, I brought chairs into the room, and desired them *here* to rest from their fatigues, while I myself, in the wild audacity of my perfect triumph, placed my own seat upon the very spot beneath which reposed[8] the corpse of the victim.

The officers were satisfied. My *manner* had convinced them. I was singularly at ease. They sat, and while I answered cheerily, they chatted of familiar things. But, ere long, I felt myself getting pale and wished them gone. My head ached, and I fancied a ringing in my ears: but still they sat and still chatted. The ringing became more distinct:—it continued and became more distinct; I talked more freely to get rid of the feeling: but it continued and gained definitiveness—until, at length, I found that the noise was *not* within my ears.

No doubt I now grew *very* pale;—but I talked more fluently, and with a heightened voice. Yet the sound increased—and what could I do? It was *a low, dull, quick sound—much such a sound as a watch makes when enveloped in cotton.* I gasped for breath—and yet the officers heard it not. I talked more quickly—more vehemently; but the noise steadily increased. I arose and argued about trifles, in a high key and with violent gesticulations,[9] but the noise steadily increased. Why *would* they not be gone? I paced the floor to and fro with heavy strides, as if excited to fury by the observations of the men—but the noise steadily increased. Oh God! what *could* I do? I foamed—I raved—I swore. I swung the chair upon which I had been sitting, and grated it upon the boards, but the noise arose over all and continually increased. It grew louder—louder—*louder!* And still the men chatted pleasantly, and smiled. Was it possible they heard not? Almighty God!—no, no! They heard!—they suspected!—they *knew!*—they were making a *mockery* of my horror!—this I thought, and this I think. But any thing was better than this agony! Any thing was more tolerable than this derision! I could bear those hypocritical smiles no longer! I felt that I must scream or die—and now—again!—hark! louder! louder!! *louder!*—

"Villains!" I shrieked, "dissemble[10] no more! I admit the deed!—tear up the planks—here, here!—it is the beating of his hideous heart!" ❖

CLARIFY
Why didn't the murderer keep quiet?

Using a Reading Log

---

8. **reposed:** rested.
9. **gesticulations** (jĕ-stĭk′yə-lā′shənz): energetic gestures of the hands or arms.
10. **dissemble:** pretend.

WORDS TO KNOW

audacity (ô-dăs′ĭ-tē) *n.* shameless daring or boldness
vehemently (vē′ə-mənt-lē) *adv.* with intense emotion
derision (dĭ-rĭzh′ən) *n.* ridicule
hypocritical (hĭp′ə-krĭt′ĭ-kəl) *adj.* false or deceptive, like a person who is pretending to be what he or she is not

386

Mini-Lesson  Grammar

ADVERBS Remind students that an adverb modifies a verb, an adjective, or another adverb. Most adverbs are formed simply by adding *-ly* to an adjective:

slow   slow**ly**

quick   quick**ly**

When adding *-ly*, it is sometimes necessary to alter the spelling of the original word:

happy   happ**ily**

Application Have students pick out the adverbs in the highlighted passage and answer the questions:

- What adverbs does Poe use repeatedly?
- What is the effect of repeating particular adverbs in the passage?
- How does Poe's selection of adverbs affect the tone and mood of the story?

Reteaching/Reinforcement
- *Grammar Handbook*, anthology p. 878
- *Grammar Mini-Lessons* copymasters p. 19, transparencies p. 40

 The Writer's Craft

Adverbs, pp. 511–512, 696

RESPONDING OPTIONS

FROM PERSONAL RESPONSE TO CRITICAL ANALYSIS

REFLECT
1. In your notebook, describe the part of this story that you found most memorable.

RETHINK
2. What are your impressions of the narrator?
   Consider
   - his insistence that he is sane
   - his obsession with the old man's eye
   - his care in planning the murder
3. Evaluate the narrator's behavior when he is with the police.
4. What do you think might have happened if the police had not come to the old man's house on the night of the murder?

Thematic Link
5. How does this story relate to the theme "Going to Extremes"?
6. Consider your prereading discussion of horror characters and your evaluation of "The Tell-Tale Heart" as a horror story. How does Poe's tale measure up to your favorite horror stories?

RELATE
7. Under most systems of criminal law, an insane person cannot be found guilty of a crime. Defendants declared not guilty by reason of insanity are usually hospitalized until they are no longer considered mentally ill and dangerous. Do you think murderers should be able to use an insanity defense to avoid punishment? Explain your answer.

Multimodal Learning
ANOTHER PATHWAY
Cooperative Learning
With a group of classmates, stage the narrator's trial for murder. Select a jury, a defense attorney, a prosecuting attorney, a judge, witnesses, and a defendant. All participants should use story details in presenting and judging the case.

QUICKWRITES
1. What if the police hadn't come? Write an alternative **ending** for the story, presenting what might have happened.
2. Consider how two different kinds of newspapers might report the murder in "The Tell-Tale Heart"—one a reputable daily newspaper that presents factual, objective reporting; the other a tabloid known for sensational stories. Write the **lead paragraph** of a murder report for each newspaper.

📁 **PORTFOLIO** Save your writing. You may want to use it later as a springboard to a piece for your portfolio.

LITERARY CONCEPTS
The **mood** of a literary work is the feeling or atmosphere that the writer creates for the reader. A story's events and setting and the way these are described all contribute to the mood of the story. One element of "The Tell-Tale Heart" that creates a mood of horror is the description of sounds, such as the victim's groan and the heartbeat. What other details in the story help produce its mood of horror?

THE TELL-TALE HEART 387

From Personal Response to Critical Analysis
1. Responses will vary.
2. Possible response: The narrator is extremely intelligent, but he is obsessively mad, emotionally unstable, and dangerous.
3. Possible responses: He thinks that he is calm, but the police can tell he is agitated; he's actually too calm for someone who supposedly has been awakened by the police.
4. Responses will vary. Some students may say the narrator's guilt would have compelled him to confess sooner or later. Others may say that the narrator would never have confessed without police pressure.
5. Possible responses: The narrator not only dislikes the old man's eye, he kills him because of it; the narrator not only kills the man, he dismembers the body and hides it under the floorboards.
6. Responses will vary.
7. Encourage students to use details from the story in their responses.

Another Pathway
Cooperative Learning Have students form large groups. Students may wish to use small juries or a select number of witnesses to make the groups manageable. Before starting, have the group decide which students will defend the murderer and which will prosecute him. Students who do not have strong opinions should sit on the jury to decide which side of the case was better presented.

Rubric
3 Full Accomplishment Students present a well-rehearsed performance that does justice to the complexity of the story.
2 Substantial Accomplishment Students draw on parts of the story but have not adequately rehearsed their arguments and responses.
1 Little or Partial Accomplishment Students do not relate their staging of the trial to specific events of the story.

Literary Concepts
Ask students to brainstorm a list of adjectives to describe the mood of the story. Explain to students that the mood may shift over the course of the selection but that one mood generally prevails. Thus, although some sections of "The Tell-Tale Heart" may sound more sane than others, the depravity of the narrator gives the story a mood of gloom, anxiety, desperation, and horror throughout. Other details that contribute to this mood include the narrator's eccentric voice, the obsessive quality of the narrator's observations, the night-time setting, and the excited language.

QuickWrites
1. Point out to students that the character of the narrator should not change. Whether they decide he is mad or sane, this judgment should be reflected in their rewriting of the ending.
2. Point out that reputable newspapers try to be less emotional than tabloids, while tabloids take a more "no-holds-barred" approach to the sensational topic.

📁 **The Writer's Craft**
Analyzing a Story, pp. 163–177
Effective Paragraphs, pp. 244–246

Literary Links

Each man must deal with something that upsets him. For the narrator of "The Tell-Tale Heart," it is something real, the old man's eye. For the narrator of "The Hitchhiker," it is a phantom. Each man may start out sane but ends up obsessed with the man whose existence torments him.

Across the Curriculum

Science *Cooperative Learning* Point out that extreme fright can send the body into shock. Encourage students to consult medical reference materials in on-line encyclopedias or similar services to learn the relationship between acute fear and shock. Have students form two groups: one group can describe the symptoms of shock, and the other can describe suggested treatment. Each group can elect a recorder and a presenter to share their findings with the other groups or with another class.

ADDITIONAL SUGGESTION

Social Studies *19th-Century America* Have students research the living conditions of Americans in the early 1800s. Ask students to consider how knowing the way people lived during that time might influence their understanding of the story. Ask students if they think a 19th-century reader would have found the story more or less scary than a modern reader.

LITERARY LINKS

Compare and contrast the narrators of "The Tell-Tale Heart" and "The Hitchhiker" (page 332). Consider their sanity and their personalities.

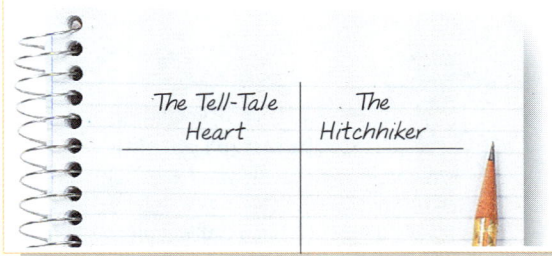

Multimodal Learning

ALTERNATIVE ACTIVITIES

1. With a partner, make an **audiotape** of sound effects for several scenes in the story.
2. Imagine that you have been commissioned by a publisher to illustrate "The Tell-Tale Heart." Choose any memorable scene or image from the story (except one already illustrated in this book), and interpret it in a **painting** or **drawing**.
3. Draw **plans** for an amusement-park house of horrors called House of the Tell-Tale Heart. Include a description of the setting and the scares, thrills, and shocks visitors will experience as they make their way through the house.

ACROSS THE CURRICULUM

Science Find out about the physical effects of sudden fright. What happens to the heart and other parts of the body? Is it possible to become so agitated as to hear blood pounding loudly in one's ears?

ART CONNECTION

Refer to the illustration on page 384. Describe what you see. What aspects of the image do you think make it appropriate for this story? Now notice the artist's use of light and shadow. What does this element lend to the mood of the piece? Share your reaction with a partner.

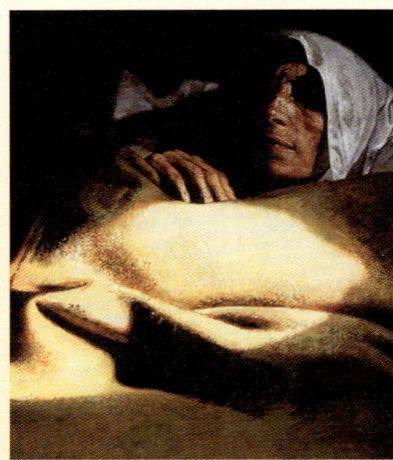

Alternative Activities

1. Encourage students to use many vivid sound effects for their audiotape, including bloodcurdling shrieks and the amplified beating of a heart. The partners should take turns reading sections of the story aloud, while the other person plays the accompanying sound effects.
2. Have students use whatever technique appeals to them in painting or drawing their scenes or images. Once the illustrations are complete, display them on a wall in the classroom.
3. Have students work in small groups. Before drawing their plan, each member of the group should make a list of the elements of the story he or she found most compelling. Then have the group brainstorm how these elements could be incorporated into an amusement park haunted house. Have part of the group draw the plans for the house, while the other students provide a description of the house. Spatial or graphic learners may enjoy sketching their group's plans or creating a poster advertisement for the house.

WORDS TO KNOW

EXERCISE A On your paper, write the letter of the word whose meaning is unrelated to the meanings of the other words in each set.

1. (a) destroyed, (b) wrecked, (c) conceived, (d) ruined
2. (a) insincere, (b) hypocritical, (c) truthful, (d) phony
3. (a) craving, (b) crevice, (c) crack, (d) cranny
4. (a) please, (b) vex, (c) gratify, (d) delight
5. (a) stifled, (b) muffled, (c) smothered, (d) heightened

EXERCISE B Review the Words to Know at the bottom of the selection pages. Then fill in each set of blanks below with the vocabulary word that relates to the sentence. Arrange the circled letters to name a character who sucks his victims' blood.

1. Many years ago the old man's eyesight was very sharp. ☐ _ ☐ _ _
2. The murderer treated his victim with cruel mockery. _ _ ☐ _ _ _ _ _
3. To commit an extreme act of violence requires great boldness. _ _ ☐ _ ☐ _ _ _
4. The thief entered the house as quietly and secretly as possible. _ _ _ ☐ _ _ _ _ _
5. The outraged witness strongly denounced the defendant. _ _ _ _ _ _ _ _ ☐ _

- AUTHOR BACKGROUND

EDGAR ALLAN POE

1809–1849

More than a century after his death, Edgar Allan Poe remains one of the most popular of American writers. Poe was born in Boston, the son of traveling actors. The beginnings of his unhappy life were marked by his father's desertion of the family, followed by the death of his mother when he was two years old. The orphaned Poe was taken in by Mr. and Mrs. John Allan of Virginia, who gave him his middle name but never officially adopted him.

After being expelled from West Point, Poe sought work as a journalist. Although he received recognition for his biting literary reviews, money was scarce. Poverty intensified his despair over the lingering illness and eventual death of his beloved wife, Virginia, whom he had married 14 years earlier. During one of her bouts of illness, Poe wrote, "I became insane, with long intervals of horrible sanity." Deeply depressed, Poe often sought escape in alcohol. He died four days after being found on the streets of Baltimore, sick, delirious, and, in his doctor's words, "haggard, not to say bloated, and unwashed."

Poe was an innovator in the composition of the modern short story, and many critics also credit him with the invention of the detective story. His classic horror tales established his reputation as a master of the macabre. Poe also wrote haunting poetry, such as "The Raven" and "Annabel Lee."

OTHER WORKS "The Black Cat," *The Masque of the Red Death and Other Tales, The Pit and the Pendulum and Five Other Tales* Extended Reading

THE TELL-TALE HEART **389**

Words to Know

Exercise A
1. c
2. c
3. a
4. b
5. d

Exercise B
1. **a**cute
2. **d**erision
3. au**d**acity
4. ste**a**lthily
5. vehementl**y**

Unscrambled letters: **Dracula**

Reteaching/Reinforcement
- *Unit Three Resource Book*, p. 55

EDGAR ALLAN POE

The end of Poe's life was as melodramatic and mysterious as his fiction. In 1849, two years after his wife's death, he became engaged to Elmira Royster Shelton, who had been his childhood sweetheart. On his way to fetch his mother-in-law to the wedding, Poe stopped in Baltimore. What happened over the next three days is unknown. On October 3, Poe was found semiconscious and delirious on a Baltimore street. He died four days later without fully regaining consciousness. His last words were "Lord, help my poor soul."

 **AUTHOR BACKGROUND**

Edgar Allan Poe Images of the author and illustrations for his short stories highlight this informative video presentation. Students will learn more about Poe's life and works.

Side A, Frame 25350

WHAT DO YOU THINK?

Reflecting on Theme

Have students refer back to the questionnaire they designed before they began reading the selections in Part 2. How do they think the narrator of "The Tell-Tale Heart" would answer the questionnaire? Invite them to imagine that they are the narrator and to fill in the questionnaire with his responses. These responses should be consistent with the character and obsessions he reveals as he tells his story.

OVERVIEW

Objectives

- To understand and appreciate an oral history of the Cherokee
- To enrich reading by looking for contrasts
- To identify and analyze the author's purpose in writing
- To express understanding of the story through a choice of writing forms, including a paragraph and an epitaph
- To extend understanding of the story through a variety of multimodal and cross-curricular activities

Skills

READING SKILLS/ STRATEGIES
- Comparing and contrasting

SPEAKING, LISTENING, AND VIEWING
- Group discussion
- Oral presentation

LITERARY CONCEPTS
- Conflict
- Author's purpose
- Oral history

GRAMMAR
- Possessive and plural nouns

Cross-Curricular Connections

SOCIAL STUDIES
- Native American government

HISTORY
- Escaping the Trail of Tears
- The Cherokee alphabet

HISTORICAL CONNECTION

Cherokee History Students will see paintings depicting the Trail of Tears by Robert Lindneux and the Cherokee artist Dorothy Sullivan, as well as images of Sequoyah, the inventor of the Cherokee written language; Chief John Ross, the leader of the Cherokee at the time of the Trail of Tears; and President Andrew Jackson, who signed the act that ordered the forced removal of the Cherokee.

Side A, Frame 52707

PREVIEWING

NONFICTION

Tsali of the Cherokees
Norah Roper
As told to Alice Marriott

Activating Prior Knowledge
PERSONAL CONNECTION

After the United States gained independence from England, and throughout the 1800s, the U.S. government repeatedly pushed Native Americans off their lands. What do you know about the government's treatment of Native Americans? Why might the government have wanted control of their lands? Why do you suppose it acted so forcefully? Discuss these questions with your classmates.

Building Background
HISTORICAL CONNECTION

The Cherokee are a Native American people whose original home was the southeastern United States. In 1838, the Georgia militia forced the Cherokee to leave their homes, because settlers wanted their land. Some Cherokee resisted and were killed. The rest were forced to march to what is now Oklahoma on a route that became known as the Trail of Tears.

Active Reading/Setting a Purpose
READING CONNECTION

Contrast When you contrast groups of people, you look for differences. In this selection, the writer describes sharp cultural differences between the white settlers and a group of Cherokee. These differences in values help explain the conflict between the two groups. As you read, use a chart like the one shown here to note the groups' differences in attitude toward home and family, land, and gold.

	Cherokee	White Settlers
Home and Family		
Land		
Gold		

- HISTORICAL CONNECTION

390 UNIT THREE PART 2: GOING TO EXTREMES

PRINT AND MEDIA RESOURCES

UNIT THREE RESOURCE BOOK
Strategic Reading: Literature, p. 59
Vocabulary SkillBuilder, p. 61
Reading SkillBuilder, p. 60

GRAMMAR MINI-LESSONS
Transparencies, p. 8, 9
Copymasters, p. 10, 11

ACCESS FOR STUDENTS ACQUIRING ENGLISH
Selection Summaries
Reading and Writing Support

FORMAL ASSESSMENT
Selection Test, pp. 73–74
Test Generator

AUDIO LIBRARY
See Reference Card

LASERLINKS
Historical Connection

INTERNET RESOURCES
McDougal Littell Literature Center at http://www.hmco.com/mcdougal/lit

390 THE LANGUAGE OF LITERATURE TEACHER'S EDITION

Tsali of the Cherokees

by Norah Roper, as told to Alice Marriott

In the time when their troubles began, the ordinary Cherokees did not at first understand that anything was really wrong.

They knew that their tribal chiefs traveled back and forth to the white man's place called Washington more often than they used to do. They knew that when the chiefs came back from that place, there were quarrels in the tribal council.

Up in the hills and the back country, where the *Ani Keetoowah*—the true Cherokees—lived, word of the changes came more slowly than the changes themselves came to the valley Cherokees. Many of the hill people never left their farm lands, and those who did went only to the nearest trading post and back. Few travelers ever came into the uplands, where the mists of the Smokies[1] shut out the encroaching world.

So, when the news came that some of the chiefs of the Cherokees had touched the pen, and put their names or their marks on a paper, and agreed by doing so that this was no longer Cherokee country, the *Ani Keetoowah* could not believe what they heard. Surely, they said to each other, this news must be false. No Cherokee—not even a mixed-blood—would sign away his own and his people's lands. But that was what the chiefs had done.

Then the word came that the chiefs were even more divided among themselves and that not all of them had touched the pen. Some were not willing to move away to the new lands across the Mississippi and settle in the hills around Fort Gibson, Oklahoma.

---

1. **Smokies**: the Great Smoky Mountains (part of the Appalachian Mountain system) in North Carolina and Tennessee.

WORDS TO KNOW
encroaching (ĕn-krō'chĭng) *adj.* advancing gradually or sneakily encroach *v.*

WORDS TO KNOW

askew (ə-skyōō') *adv.* crookedly (p. 396)
encroaching (ĕn-krō'chĭng) *adj.* advancing gradually or sneakily **encroach** *v.* (p. 391)
plunder (plŭn'dər) *v.* to take property by force (p. 396)
smolder (smōl'dər) *v.* to burn with smoke but no flame (p. 395)
sulkily (sŭl'kĭ-lē) *adv.* in a resentful or glum manner (p. 393)

CUSTOMIZING FOR
Gifted and Talented Students

Have students discuss the conflict between the U.S. government and Native Americans as they read. Ask them if there were alternatives to relocating Native Americans. If so, ask them what these alternatives might have meant to the development of the United States.

Active Reading: CLARIFY

A Ask students to explain why the author says that "hope is the cruelest curse on mankind." If students have difficulty, provide them with the following model.

Think-Aloud Model *This remark really surprised me because I always thought hope was one of the most important things humans could have. However, I understand that "getting my hopes up too high" sometimes makes it impossible for me to be satisfied. Perhaps the author is only getting us ready for the likely outcome of the story: the Cherokees' loss of their land.*

CUSTOMIZING FOR
Students Acquiring English

3 Explain that missionaries were Christians who tried to convert Native Americans to their religious beliefs.

Literary Concept: CONFLICT

B Have students explain how the differing views of Tsali and the missionary on the land's value leads to conflict between them. *(Possible response: Tsali lives off the land and believes that others would not be able to farm it, while the missionary believes the gold on the land makes it very valuable. The conflict leads the missionary to insult and belittle Tsali.)*

A "Perhaps we should hang on," the *Ani Keetoowah* said to one another. "Perhaps we will not have to go away after all." They waited and hoped, although they knew in their hearts that hope is the cruelest curse on mankind.

One of the leaders of the *Ani Keetoowah* was Tsali. The white men had trouble pronouncing his name, so they called him "Charley" or "Dutch." Tsali was a full blood, and so were his wife and their family. They were of the oldest *Keetoowah* Cherokee blood and would never have let themselves be shamed by having half-breed relatives.

Tsali and his four sons worked two hillsides and the valley between them, in the southern part of the hill country. Tsali and his wife and their youngest son lived in a log house at the head of the hollow. The others had their own homes, spread out along the hillsides. They grew corn and beans, a few English peas, squashes and pumpkins, tobacco and cotton, and even a little sugar cane and indigo.[2] Tsali's wife kept chickens in a fenced run[3] away from the house.

The women gathered wild hemp[4] and spun it; they spun the cotton, and the wool from their sheep. Then they wove the thread into cloth, and sometimes in winter when their few cattle and the sheep had been cared for and the chickens fed and there was not much else to do, the men helped at the looms[5] which they had built themselves. The women did all the cutting and the making of garments for the whole family.

Tsali and his family were not worldly rich, in the way that the chiefs and some of the Cherokees of the valley towns were rich. They had hardly seen white man's metal money in their lives. But Tsali's people never lacked for food, or good clothing, or safe shelter.

3 The missionaries seldom came into the uplands then. Tsali took his sons and their wives, and his own wife, to the great dance ground where the seven *Keetoowah* villages gathered each month at the time of the full moon. There they danced their prayers in time to the beating of the women's terrapin-shell[6] leg rattles, around and around the mound of packed white ashes on top of which bloomed the eternal fire that was the life of all the Cherokees.

The occasional missionaries fussed over the children. They gave them white men's names, so that by Tsali's time everyone had an Indian name and an English one. The Cherokees listened to the missionaries politely, for the missionaries were great gossips, and the Cherokees heard their news and ignored the rest of their words.

"You will have to go soon," said one white preacher to Tsali. "There's no hope this time. The lands have all been sold, and the Georgia troopers are moving in. You'll have to go west."

"We'll never leave," Tsali answered. "This is our land and we belong to it. Who could take it from us—who would want it? It's hard even for us to farm here, and we're used to hill farming. The white men wouldn't want to come here— they'll want the rich lands in the valleys, if the lowland people will give them up." **B**

"They want these hills more than any other land," the missionary said. He sounded almost threatening. "Don't you see, you poor ignorant Indian? They are finding gold—gold, man, gold—downstream in the lower *Keetoowah* country. That means that the source of the gold is in the headwaters of the rivers that flow from here down into the valleys. I've seen gold dust in those streams myself."

---

2. **indigo:** a plant used to make blue dye.
3. **run:** an outdoor enclosed area for domestic animals.
4. **hemp:** a plant from which rope and coarse cloth are made.
5. **looms:** devices on which thread is woven into cloth.
6. **terrapin-shell:** turtle-shell.

392 UNIT THREE PART 2: GOING TO EXTREMES

Mini-Lesson — Reading Skills/Strategies

Topic	Comparison	Contrast
gold	missionary and trader want to get rich from the gold mine	Tsali wants to farm, not mine for gold

COMPARING AND CONTRASTING
Explain to students that when they compare two things, they are looking for ways in which the things are alike. Explain that when they contrast two things, they are looking for ways in which the things differ. For example, if students read the two highlighted passages on page 393, they can compare the reactions of the missionary and the trader to Tsali's gold. These attitudes can be contrasted with Tsali's attitude about gold. See the accompanying chart for an elaboration of this comparison and contrast.

Application Have students reread the story and look for topics where people's opinions and attitudes can be compared and contrasted. For example, students can contrast the trader's opinion of what it means to be rich with Tsali's idea of being rich. Encourage students to record their comparisons and contrasts in a chart like the one shown.

Reteaching/Reinforcement
• *Unit Three Resource Book,* p. 60

392 THE LANGUAGE OF LITERATURE TEACHER'S EDITION

"Gold?" asked Tsali. "You mean this yellow stuff?" And he took a buckskin pouch out of the pouch that hung from his sash, and opened it. At the sight of the yellow dust the pouch contained, the missionary seemed to go a little crazy.

"That's it!" he cried. "Where did you get it? How did you find it? You'll be rich if you can get more."

C "We find it in the rivers, as you said," Tsali replied. "We gather what we need to take to the trader. I have this now because I am going down to the valley in a few days, to get my wife some ribbons to trim her new dress."

D "Show me where you got it," the missionary begged. "We can all be rich. I'll protect you from the other white men, if you make me your partner."

"No, I think I'd better not," said Tsali thoughtfully. "My sons are my partners, as I was my father's. We do not need another partner, and, as long as we have our old squirrel guns, we do not need to be protected. Thank you, but you can go on. We are better off as we are."

The missionary coaxed and threatened, but Tsali stood firm. In the end, the white man went away, without any gold except a pinch that Tsali gave him, because the missionary seemed to value the yellow dust even more than the trader did.

Then it was time to go to the trading post. When Tsali came in the store, the trader said to him, "Well, Chief, glad to see you. I hear you're a rich man these days."

"I have always been a rich man," Tsali answered. "I have my family and we all have our good health. We have land to farm, houses to live in, food on our tables, and enough clothes. Most of all, we have the love in our hearts for each other and our friends. Indeed, you are right. We are very rich."

"That's one way of looking at it," said the trader, "but it isn't what I was thinking about. From what I hear, there's gold on your land. You've got a gold mine."

"A gold man?" repeated Tsali. "I never heard of a gold man."

"No!" shouted the trader. "A gold mine, I said. A place where you can go and pick up gold."

"Oh, that!" Tsali exclaimed. "Yes, we have some places like that on our land. Here's some of the yellow dust we find there."

And he opened the pouch to show the trader. The trader had seen pinches of Tsali's gold dust before, and taken it in trade, without saying much about it. Now he went as crazy as the missionary. "Don't tell anybody else about this, Charley," he whispered, leaning over the counter. "We'll just keep it to ourselves. I'll help you work it out, and I'll keep the other white men away. We'll all be rich." **E**

"Thank you," said Tsali, "but I don't believe I want to be rich that way. I just want enough of this stuff to trade you for ribbons and sugar."

"Oh, all right," answered the trader <u>sulkily</u>, "have it your own way. But don't blame me if you're sorry afterwards."

"I won't blame anybody," said Tsali, and bought his ribbon.

A month later, when the Georgia militia[7] came riding up the valley to Tsali's house, the missionary and the trader were with them. The men all stopped in front of the house, and Tsali's wife came out into the dogtrot, the open-ended passage that divided the two halves of the house and made a cool breezeway where the family sat in warm weather. She spoke to the men.

---

7. **militia** (mə-lĭsh′ə): an army made up of ordinary citizens instead of professional soldiers.

WORDS TO KNOW
sulkily (sŭl′kĭ-lē) *adv.* in a resentful or glum manner

393

Mini-Lesson — Literary Concepts

REVIEWING CONFLICT This selection is an example of narrative nonfiction. As such, it employs many techniques of fiction writing in order to tell a true story. Establishing conflict, for example, is such a technique. Remind students that conflict is the result of a struggle between two opposing forces. It may occur internally, when a character is trying to make a difficult decision, or externally, when the character comes up against another character or is subject to a hostile environment.

Application Point out to students that the conflict of "Tsali of the Cherokees" is entirely external: Tsali and his family come into conflict with the missionary, the trader, and the militia, but the reader is not privy to any internal conflict that the characters may feel. Have students select a moment of conflict in the story, such as when Amanda decides to join her husband and face death rather than leave the land. Have students rewrite this external conflict to show the character's internal conflict. After their rewriting is finished, students can discuss how the inclusion of internal conflict changes their understanding of the story's events.

STRATEGIC READING FOR
Less-Proficient Readers

C Ask students to explain why the missionary desires Tsali's land. *(The gold dust found in the rivers on Tsali's land makes it valuable. The missionary wants the land so he can get rich.)* Noting Relevant Details/Making Judgments

Set a Purpose Have students read to see how Tsali and his family plan to continue living on the land after they are ordered to leave.

Active Reading: QUESTION

D Have students discuss any questions or comments they have at this point regarding Tsali's interaction with the missionary. For instance, ask students if they believe that the missionary's desire to protect Tsali is sincere.

Literary Concept:
AUTHOR'S PURPOSE

E Ask students what the author's purpose may be in having the trader and the missionary both promise to protect Tsali. *(Possible responses: Because her purpose seems to be to inform the reader what the settlers were like, she shows how the white men in the story are all driven by gold. She is trying to persuade her readers that neither character is really acting in Tsali's best interest.)*

Active Reading: CLARIFY

F Ask students why they think Amanda is so polite to the militia and why the captain refuses her hospitality. Provide students with the following model to promote discussion.

Think-Aloud Model It seems strange that Amanda is so cordial to someone who has come to do her harm, but she may be trying to buy herself a little more time or avoid inciting the captain's anger. She also appears to be a strong woman, and she may be trying to cover up her own anxiety. The captain refuses her hospitality because he wants to make it clear that he is there strictly for the business of removing Tsali from his ancestral lands.

Linking to Social Studies

G Whereas settlers believed that all Native American groups were led by a single powerful chief or binding council of chiefs, Native American leadership was actually very different. Often the chief was little more than a spokesperson: he expressed the opinions of the tribe, but his decisions were not binding without the people's support. Most Native American groups were governed by unanimous decision making. After a long series of discussions, the tribe formed a consensus that equally bound all of its members to a particular course of action.

Literary Concept: CONFLICT

H Have students explain the conflict between the militia captain and Amanda. *(The captain has been sent to remove all of Tsali's family from the land, but Amanda counters that the chiefs had no right to sign over the land to the government.)*

Copyright © Smithsonian Institution, Washington, D.C. National Anthropological Archives, Negative # 1000-B.

"Won't you come in and sit down?"

"Where's the old man?" the militia captain asked.

"Why, he's working out in the fields," said Amanda. "Sit down and have a cool drink of water while I send the boy for him."

"Send the boy quickly," the captain ordered. "We'll wait in our saddles and not trouble to get down."

"All right, if you'd rather not," Amanda said. "Do you mind telling me why you're here?"

"We're here to put you off this place," said the captain. "Haven't you heard? This isn't Cherokee land any more; the chiefs signed it over to the government, and now it's open for settlement. One or the other of these two gentlemen will probably claim it."

"They can't do that!" Amanda protested. "It's our land—nobody else's. The chiefs had no right to sign it away. My husband's father worked this place, and his father before him. This is our home. This is where we belong."

"No more," said the captain. "You belong in the removal camps down by the river, with the rest of the Indians. They're going to start shipping the Cherokees west tomorrow morning."

Amanda sat down on the bench in the dogtrot, with her legs trembling under her. "All of us?" she asked.

"Every one of you."

394 UNIT THREE PART 2: GOING TO EXTREMES

Mini-Lesson Study Skills

Taking Essay Tests

1. Be sure you know what you're being tested on beforehand.
2. Read the entire examination and budget your time carefully.
3. Read carefully and underline such key words as *define, explain, effects, compare, distinguish, three examples*.
4. Brainstorm thoughts on the topic and jot down words for key ideas or points.
5. Turn the question around and try to use it as a start for your essay.
6. Decide what you want to say about the question.
7. Make an outline.
8. Write, review, and revise your essay.

TAKING ESSAY TESTS: PLANNING YOUR ANSWERS Many students find essay exams difficult and stressful. However, students' fears may be reduced if they follow the simple guidelines outlined at left.

Application Have students work in small groups to develop essay questions based on "Tsali of the Cherokees." Have groups exchange questions. Then have each student choose a question and independently work through all stages of planning and developing an outline for the essay without actually writing it.

"Let me call my son and send him for his daddy," Amanda said.

"Hurry up!"

Amanda went into the house, calling to the boy, who was just fourteen and had been standing, listening, behind the door. She gave him his father's old squirrel gun, and he sneaked his own blowgun and darts and slid out the back of the house. Amanda went back to the dogtrot and sat and waited. She sat there and waited, while the missionary, the trader, and the captain quarreled about which of their wives should cook in her kitchen. She let them quarrel and hoped her men were all right.

Tsali and his older sons were working the overhill corn field, when the boy came panting up and told them what had happened.

"Is your mother all right?" Tsali asked.

"She was when I left," the boy answered.

"We'll hide in the woods till they're gone," Tsali told his older sons. "If they find us, they'll have to kill us to put us off this land."

"What about the women?" the oldest son asked.

"They'll be all right," Tsali answered. "Your mother's a quick-thinking woman; she'll take care of them. If we can hide in the caves by the river till dark, we'll go back then and get them."

They slipped away into the woods, downhill to the river, taking the boy with them, although he offered to go back and tell the white men he couldn't find his father.

All afternoon Amanda waited. Her daughters-in-law saw the strange men and horses in front of the big house and came to join her. At dusk, the captain gave up and ordered his men to make camp in the front yard. "We'll wait here until the men come back," he said.

With the white men camped all around the house, the women went into the kitchen and barred all the doors. It was a long time before the campfires made from the fence pickets ceased to blaze and began to smolder. It was a longer time until the women heard it—a scratch on the back door, so soft and so light that it would have embarrassed a mouse. Amanda slid back the bar, and Tsali and his sons slipped into the darkened room. There was just enough moonlight for them to make out each other's shapes.

"We came to get you," Tsali said. "Come quickly. Leave everything except your knives. Don't wait a minute."

Amanda and her daughters-in-laws always wore their knives at their belts, so they were ready. One at a time, Tsali last, the whole family crept out of their home and escaped into the woods.

In the morning, when the white men stretched and scratched and woke, the *Ani Keetoowah* were gone.

It was spring, and the weather was warm, but the rain fell and soaked the Cherokees. They had brought no food, and they dared not fire a gun. One of the daughters-in-law was pregnant, and her time was close. Amanda was stiff and crippled with rheumatism.[8] They gathered wild greens, for it was too early for berries or plums, and the men and boy trapped small animals and birds in string snares the women made by pulling out their hair and twisting it.

Day by day, for four weeks, the starving family listened to white men beating through the woods. The Cherokees were tired and cold and hungry, but they were silent. They even began to hope that in time the white men would go away and the Indians would be safe.

---

8. **rheumatism** (rōō′mə-tĭz′əm): an inflammation and stiffness of the joints and muscles.

WORDS TO KNOW

smolder (smōl′dər) *v.* to burn with smoke but no flame

Multicultural Perspectives

THE CHEROKEE NATION At one time, the Cherokee dominated what is now the southeastern United States. However, contact with early colonists in the 1750s led to a smallpox epidemic that destroyed nearly half the population. In 1827, the Cherokee drew up a constitution and established themselves as an independent nation with an elected, republican form of government. Their status as an independent nation was acknowledged by Chief Justice John Marshall in the Supreme Court decision *Worchester v. Georgia* (1832), which prohibited Georgia from expelling the Cherokee.

As Roper's oral history suggests, a fraudulent treaty resulted in the forced relocation known as The Trail of Tears. The forced march on the trail was led by Chief John Ross (Kooweskoowe), who, like Tsali, initially tried to resist. Today, 45,000 Cherokee live in Oklahoma.

STRATEGIC READING FOR
Less-Proficient Readers

L Have students explain what happens to Tsali and his family when they are taken from the woods. *(They are given the choice to either leave the land or be shot. Tsali, Amanda, and his oldest sons decide to remain.)* **Summarizing**

Active Reading: CLARIFY

M Ask students why the daughters-in-law and the youngest son are sent away. *(Possible responses: The daughters-in-law did not grow up on the land, so they do not have the same connection to it. The youngest son is sent away because he has not had a chance to mature, and he will take care of his sisters-in-law on the arduous journey awaiting them.)*

CUSTOMIZING FOR
Gifted and Talented Students

Point out that this selection is an oral history edited by the author. Have students discuss how the events of Tsali's life as described by Norah Roper might have been changed in Alice Marriott's written version. Encourage students to think about how different points of view can change a story and to use details from the selection to support their position.

COMPREHENSION CHECK

1. What does Tsali have that the settlers desperately want? *(gold)*
2. Where do Tsali and his family hide? *(in a cave near the river)*
3. What does the militia plan to do with Tsali and his family? *(send them to the West)*
4. What do Tsali, Amanda, and his eldest sons decide to do? *(They choose to die rather than leave their land.)*

It was not to be. One trooper brought his dog, and the dog caught the human scent. So the dog, with his man behind him, came sniffing into the cave, and Tsali and his family were caught before the men could pick up their loaded guns.

The militiamen shouted, and other white men came thudding through the woods. They tied the Cherokee men's hands behind them and bound them all together along a rope. The militiamen pushed Tsali and his sons through the woods. The women followed, weeping.

At last they were back at their own house, but they would not have recognized it. The troopers had <u>plundered</u> the garden and trampled the plants they didn't eat. The door from the kitchen into the dogtrot hung <u>askew</u>, and the door to the main room had been wrenched off its hinges. Clothes and bedding lay in filthy piles around the yard. What the militiamen could not use, they ruined.

"Oh, my garden!" cried Amanda, and, when she saw the scattered feathers, "Oh, my little hens!"

"What are you going to do with us?" Tsali demanded.

"Take you down to the river. The last boat is loading today. There's still time to get you on it and out of here."

"I—will—not—go," Tsali said quietly. "You—nor you—nor you—nobody can make me go."

"Our orders are to take all the Cherokees. If any resist, shoot them."

"Shoot me, then!" cried Tsali. The captain raised his rifle.

"Stop!" Amanda screamed. She stepped over beside her husband. "If you shoot, shoot us both," she ordered. "Our lives have been one life since we were no older than our boy here. I don't want to go on living without my husband. And I cannot leave our home any more than he can. Shoot us both."

The four sons stepped forward. "We will die with our parents," the oldest one said. "Take our wives to the boat, if that is the only place where they can be safe, but we stay here." He turned to his wife and the other young women.

"That is my order as your husband," Tsali's son said. "You must go away to the west and make new lives for yourselves while you are still young enough to do so." The wives sobbed and held out their arms, but the husbands turned their backs on the women. "We will stay with our parents," all the young men said.

The young boy, too, stood with his brothers, beside his father. "Let this boy go," Tsali said to the white men. "He is so young. A man grows, and plants his seed, and his seed goes on. This is my seed. I planted it. My older sons and I have had our chances. They will leave children, and their names will never be forgotten. But this boy is too young. His seed has not ripened for planting yet. Let him go, to care for his sisters, on the way to the west."

"Very well," said the captain. "He can't do much harm if he does live." He turned to two militiamen. "Take the boy and the young women away," he ordered. "Keep them going till they come to the boats, and load them on board."

The young women and the boy, stunned and silenced, were driven down the road before they could say goodbye, nor would the troopers let them look back. Behind them, as they started on the long main road, they heard the sound of the shots. ❖

L

M

WORDS TO KNOW
plunder (plŭn′dər) *v.* to take property by force
askew (ə-skyōō′) *adv.* crookedly

396

Mini-Lesson Grammar

POSSESSIVE AND PLURAL NOUNS

Remind students that to make a noun plural, they usually add *s*. To make it possessive, they add *'s*. To make the plural possessive form, they add *s'*.

Singular	Plural	Possessive	Plural Possessive
boy	boys	boy's	boys'

Application Write the following sentences on the chalkboard, omitting the apostrophes. Have students come to the board and insert apostrophes where necessary.

1. Tsali's family believed the land was theirs.
2. The militia's disregard for the Native Americans' lives was immoral.
3. Members of the Cherokee lived in the Southeast.
4. We will remember Amanda's courage.

Reteaching/Reinforcement

- *Grammar Handbook*, anthology pp. 870–871
- *Grammar Mini-Lessons* copymasters, pp. 10, 11; transparencies, pp. 8, 9

📁 The Writer's Craft

Plural nouns, pp. 422–423
Possessive nouns, 425

HISTORICAL INSIGHT

The Trail of Tears

Although Tsali's family refused to leave the beautiful, fertile land that had been home to the Cherokee for over 1,000 years, most of the Cherokee did leave. In 1838, about 15,000 of them were forced to make a terrible 800-mile march westward to the so-called Indian Territory in what is now Oklahoma. One out of every four died along what came to be known as the Trail of Tears.

Back in the mid-1700s, the Cherokee had fought the colonists who were moving into their territory. By 1800, however, some Cherokee had begun to live among the colonists, and their economic and political structures began to mirror those of the white settlers. Some Cherokee owned large plantations and kept slaves. The tribe even established a republican form of government called the Cherokee Nation. But before long, white settlers demanded more Native American lands in Tennessee, Georgia, and Alabama for their own farms and plantations. The invention of the cotton gin (which made cotton farming more profitable) and the discovery of gold in Georgia made Cherokee land all the more desirable.

In 1830, a momentous event heralded the eventual doom of the Cherokee and other tribes. President Andrew Jackson signed the Indian Removal Act, requiring tribes east of the Mississippi to move west.

Trail of Tears, Jerome Tiger. Watercolor on paper. The Phillips Petroleum Collection, The Philbrook Museum of Art, Tulsa, Oklahoma.

The Cherokee resisted. Most stood their ground even when, in 1835, a small group of chiefs signed a new treaty with the government. They agreed to give up all remaining Cherokee lands, and many Cherokee left for the west. For those who would not give in, what followed was a tragic forced relocation.

Commanded to abandon homes, livestock, and ancestral burial grounds, the Cherokee were marched 800 miles through mud and manure. Many died during the 189-day journey.

Art Note

Trail of Tears by Jerome Tiger
Contemporary artist Jerome Tiger (1941–1967) was a descendant of Creeks and Seminoles who were resettled in Oklahoma. Tiger depicts the struggle of the Cherokee to survive sickness, bitter cold, and starvation as they trudged across frozen, desolate land.

Reading the Art What kind of relationship between humans and nature is suggested by the painting? What mood is suggested by the painting? What details add to this atmosphere?

INSIGHT

1. *Why did so many Cherokee resist resettlement in Oklahoma?* (Possible responses: They were forced to leave fertile land, livestock, and ancestral homes for the harsh environment of Indian Territory; they were forced to leave prosperous farms and land for an uncertain fate.)

2. *How does the Cherokee recollection given here differ from Marriott's account?* (Possible response: The account given here suggests that Native Americans sadly accepted their fates, whereas Marriott's account illustrates that many were willing to die defending their homes and land.)

From Personal Response to Critical Analysis

1. Encourage students to use sensory details.
2. Possible response: Tsali, Amanda, and their sons refuse to leave the land on which they have always lived. They feel it is better to die than have to live in another place.
3. Charts will vary but should include references to land, monetary wealth, and family. Encourage students to use examples from the selection in their responses.
4. Possible response: Just at the moment the family begins to hope the settlers will go away, they are caught by the militia.
5. Responses will vary.

Literary Link

Have students compare and contrast how the characters of "Tsali of the Cherokees" and those of "The Bet" stand up for the positions they believe in. Ask students how the sense of hope in humanity is similar in the two selections. Ask them how Tsali's actions differ from those of the lawyer and the banker. *(Possible responses: Both Tsali and his family and the lawyer in "The Bet" are willing to go to extremes for their positions. However, whereas the lawyer has lost hope in humanity, Tsali has not. Also, the lawyer begins his self-imposed exile because of the promise of money. Tsali, on the other hand, does not crave monetary gain; he simply wants to retain what's his.)*

Another Pathway

Remind students that illustrations should be from the perspective of the surviving boy.

Rubric

3 Full Accomplishment Drawings clearly illustrate important events from the perspective of the surviving son.

2 Substantial Accomplishment Drawings illustrate some major events partially from the perspective of the surviving son.

1 Little or Partial Accomplishment Drawings indicate little understanding of major events or perspective of the surviving son.

RESPONDING OPTIONS

FROM PERSONAL RESPONSE TO CRITICAL ANALYSIS

REFLECT 1. What is your reaction to Tsali's fatal decision? Jot down your thoughts in your notebook, and share them with a partner.

RETHINK 2. Why do you think Tsali, his wife, and their four sons make the decision they do? Explain your answer.
   Consider
   - Tsali's and his family's feelings about the land
   - the surviving son
   - what happened to those who marched to Oklahoma

3. Review the chart you made for the Reading Connection on page 390. How do the cultural differences between the Cherokee and the white settlers explain the conflict between them?

4. The writer says that "hope is the cruelest curse on mankind." How does the selection support this view?

RELATE 5. In your opinion, should the Cherokee be compensated for the government's actions during the time of the Trail of Tears? If so, how? If not, why not?

Multimodal Learning
ANOTHER PATHWAY

Imagine that you are Tsali's surviving son. Tell the story of your family's tragedy in a series of drawings. Share your illustrations with the class.

LITERARY CONCEPTS

An **author's purpose** is a writer's specific reason for writing. Authors write for four basic purposes: to entertain, to explain or inform, to express opinions, and to persuade readers to do or believe things. What purposes do you think Alice Marriott had in mind when she wrote this account? Which one seems most important to her? Explain your answer.

CONCEPT REVIEW: Oral History Recall that oral histories are stories passed by word of mouth from one generation to the next. How might the account of Tsali have been different if it had been researched and written up rather than told to a writer?

QUICKWRITES

1. In this selection, Tsali explains his conception of a rich man. Make two columns on a sheet of paper. List words and phrases describing Tsali's idea of wealth in one column and your own in the other. Then write a **paragraph** comparing Tsali's ideas with yours.

2. Write an **epitaph** for Tsali and his family. It can be a short prose inscription or a poem.

   📁 **PORTFOLIO** Save your writing. You may want to use it later as a springboard to a piece for your portfolio.

398 UNIT THREE PART 2: GOING TO EXTREMES

Literary Concepts

In order for students to better understand the importance of the author's purpose, have them discuss how the story affected them. For instance, ask students if they felt angry or sad as they read. Students will probably say that the author wanted to inform readers and persuade them that the Cherokee were treated unfairly.

Concept Review Point out to students that this oral history, although based on an interpretation of real events, still reads as if it were a work of fiction. A research-based account would be less like fiction.

QuickWrites

1. Stress that riches are not measured only in material wealth. Encourage students to include intangible as well as material riches as they develop their lists.
2. Remind students that Tsali and his family's way of life was very simple. As students plan their epitaphs, encourage them to create inscriptions or short poems consistent with the family's lifestyle.

 **The Writer's Craft**

Paragraphs at work, p. 123

Multimodal Learning

ALTERNATIVE ACTIVITIES

1. **Cooperative Learning** With five classmates, **role-play** a discussion among the following characters: the captain of the militia, a Cherokee chief who signed the government treaty, Tsali's youngest son, a Cherokee woman who survived the Trail of Tears, the missionary, and the trader. Have each character express his or her opinion about the statement "Tsali and his people should have obeyed the militia's orders."

2. Retell Tsali's story, including important details and some of the dialogue from the selection. If possible, tape-record your **oral version** and share it with younger students.

ACROSS THE CURRICULUM

Social Studies How many Cherokee escaped the Trail of Tears and remained in the Great Smoky Mountains of western North Carolina? What kind of lives did these people lead? Present your findings to the class in the form of a labeled visual display, using copies of old pictures.

WORDS TO KNOW

EXERCISE A Review the Words to Know at the bottom of the selection pages. Then, for each of the five words, create a word map like the one below.

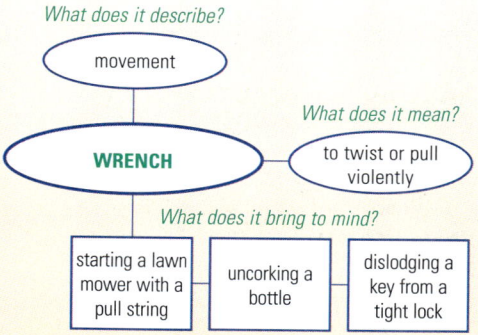

EXERCISE B Sketch or paint a series of five pictures that illustrate the meanings of the vocabulary words. Display them in your classroom.

ALICE MARRIOTT

While her grandfather was visiting the curator of Egyptology at Chicago's Field Museum, five-year-old Alice Marriott (1910–1992) wandered off by herself. To her delight, she found the museum's totem poles. This early interest in ancient cultures blossomed at the University of Oklahoma, where she became the first woman to receive a degree in anthropology. From Oklahoma she traveled to Oregon to study Native Americans: "We lived in tents, interviewed elderly Modoc Indians, and I fell completely and permanently in love with the desert country in general and Oregon in particular."

Marriott later returned to Oklahoma and became "one of the lucky few who worked with Plains Indians while the last of the buffalo hunters were still around." She wrote many books and articles on Native Americans, including "Tsali of the Cherokees," which was told to her by Norah Roper, Tsali's granddaughter. "I am not interesting," claimed Marriott. "It is what I have done with where I have been that is."

OTHER WORKS *Maria, the Potter of San Ildefonso; The Ten Grandmothers; Hell on Horses and Women*

Extended Reading

TSALI OF THE CHEROKEES **399**

Words to Know

Exercise A
Possible responses:

encroaching: movement/advancing gradually/a cat hunting a mouse

sulkily: behavior/resentful or glum/a child who has been denied a treat

smolder: action/smoke but no flame/ashes in a fireplace

plunder: action/take by force/pirates taking gold from a ship

askew: position/crooked/a hat on a head

Exercise B
Be sure that students' illustrations are based on the meanings given.

Reteaching/Reinforcement
- *Unit Three Resource Book*, p. 61

Across the Curriculum

Social Studies Approximately 1,000 Cherokees escaped the forced march by hiding in the remote mountains of western North Carolina, much as Tsali tried to do. These people came to be known as the Eastern Band of Cherokees. Students can find out more about these people in an encyclopedia, reference book, or on-line computer service.

ADDITIONAL SUGGESTION

History *Cherokee Alphabet* Ask students to locate a copy of the Cherokee alphabet that was created by Sequoyah, the great Cherokee leader (1766–1843). Ask students to find out how the alphabet works. Challenge students to practice writing short messages and have other students decode the words.

Alice Marriott

Alice Marriott lived and worked for ten years with various Native American tribes living in Oklahoma, including the Cherokee and the Kiowa. An adopted member of three Native American families, Marriott is remembered for her skilled interpretations of Native American folklore and oral history.

Alternative Activities

1. Before beginning the discussion, have the group plan which student will take on which character. Encourage each group to work together to develop responses for each of the characters. Each student should act as a recorder for the group discussion of his or her own character before expanding these ideas into a more developed statement of the character's opinions.

2. Suggest that students make a rough outline of the events of the story before they begin to record their history. If exact quotes are taken from the selection, they should be short and kept to a minimum. If students tape-record their oral history, have them play it back.

THE LANGUAGE OF LITERATURE TEACHER'S EDITION **399**

OVERVIEW

Objectives
- To understand and appreciate a humorous essay about dating
- To enrich reading by understanding hyperbole
- To express understanding of the story through a choice of writing forms, including a diary entry and an advice column
- To extend understanding of the story through a variety of multimodal and cross-curricular activities

Skills

LITERARY CONCEPTS
- Humor
- Hyperbole

SPEAKING, LISTENING, AND VIEWING
- Group discussion
- Oral presentation

Cross-Curricular Connections

SOCIAL STUDIES
- Dating practices

MEDIA
- Comparing advice columns and editorials

PREVIEWING

NONFICTION

Painful Memories of Dating
Dave Barry

Activating Prior Knowledge
PERSONAL CONNECTION

Think about the title of this selection. How could memories of dating be painful? If you knew that the selection was a humorous newspaper article and that the word *painful* referred to emotions, what might the title suggest to you? Discuss your ideas with your classmates. Use a word web like the one shown to record the class's ideas.

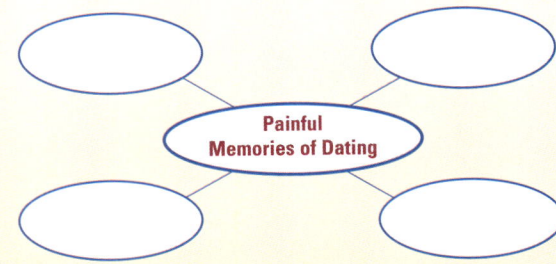

Building Background
MEDIA CONNECTION

Dave Barry writes a weekly humor column for the *Miami Herald*. Through syndication—sale for use by other newspapers—his articles appear in more than 150 papers, including some in foreign countries. Barry's humor depends on several ingredients: humorous references to current events, wild exaggerations of the truth, and irony (saying the opposite of what he means). In the article you are about to read, Barry combines all of these elements as he gives a boy named Eric some advice on dating.

Dave Barry at work

Active Reading/Setting a Purpose
READING CONNECTION

Hyperbole In this article, Barry claims that if a girl had refused his invitation for a date, he would have had to leave junior high school forever and "become a bark-eating hermit." Such extreme exaggeration, called hyperbole, helps make Barry's writing humorous. As you read, look for and jot down other examples of hyperbole.

400 UNIT THREE PART 2: GOING TO EXTREMES

PRINT AND MEDIA RESOURCES

UNIT THREE RESOURCE BOOK
Strategic Reading: Literature, p. 65
Reading SkillBuilder, p. 66

ACCESS FOR STUDENTS ACQUIRING ENGLISH
Selection Summaries
Reading and Writing Support

FORMAL ASSESSMENT
Selection Test, p. 75
 Test Generator

AUDIO LIBRARY
See Reference Card

Painful MEMORIES OF DATING

BY DAVE BARRY

As a mature adult, I feel an obligation to help the younger generation, just as the mother fish guards her unhatched eggs, keeping her lonely vigil day after day, never leaving her post, not even to go to the bathroom, until her tiny babies emerge and she is able, at last, to eat them. "She may be your mom, but she's still a fish" is a wisdom nugget that I would pass along to any fish eggs reading this column.

But today I want to talk about dating. This subject was raised in a letter to me from a young person named Eric Knott, who writes:

"I have got a big problem. There's this girl in my English class who is really good-looking. However, I don't think she knows I exist. I want to ask her out, but I'm afraid she will say no, and I will be the freak of the week. What should I do?"

Eric, you have sent your question to the right mature adult, because as a young person, I spent a lot of time thinking about this very problem. Starting in about 8th grade, my time was divided as follows:

Academic Pursuits: 2 percent
Zits: 16 percent
Trying to Figure Out How to Ask Girls Out: 82 percent

The most sensible way to ask a girl out is to walk directly up to her on foot and say, "So you want to go out or what?" I never did this. I knew, as Eric Knott knows, that there was always the possibility that the girl would say no, thereby leaving me with no viable option but to leave Harold C. Crittenden Junior High School forever and go into the

---

WORDS TO KNOW

spontaneity (spŏn′tə-nē′ĭ-tē) *n.* effortless and unplanned behavior (p. 403)

CUSTOMIZING FOR
Gifted and Talented Students

Remind students that this story is told from a male point of view to a boy. Encourage students to debate whether it is harder for a girl or a boy to arrange for a date. Ask them to discuss the different issues boys and girls face when they date.

CUSTOMIZING FOR
Students Acquiring English

2 Explain that Chip 'n' Dale are chipmunk cartoon characters with very high voices.

Literary Concept: HUMOR

B Have students explain why Barry's description of the woodland creatures is humorous. *(Possible responses: The difference between the animals' appearance and their behavior makes it humorous; the reference to mean cartoon characters adds to the surprise and humor.)*

STRATEGIC READING FOR
Less-Proficient Readers

C Ask students how the comparison of getting a date to maneuvering a nuclear submarine suggests that Barry's advice is not to be taken seriously. *(Possible response: Getting a date is not a search-and-destroy mission.)* **Drawing Conclusions**

Set a Purpose Have students assess, as they finish the selection, how successful the author's date was.

Literary Concept: HYPERBOLE

D Have students discuss the effects of Barry's use of hyperbole to describe his anxiety. *(Possible response: It entertains the reader by making Barry's fears seem even more severe than they probably were.)*

---

woods and become a bark-eating hermit whose only companions would be the gentle and understanding woodland creatures.

"Hey, Zitface!" the woodland creatures would shriek in their cute little Chip 'n' Dale voices while raining acorns down up on my head. "You wanna *date?* Hahahahahaha."

So the first rule of dating is, Never risk direct contact with the girl in question. Your role model should be the nuclear submarine, gliding silently beneath the ocean surface, tracking an enemy target that does not even begin to suspect that the submarine would like to date it. I spent the vast majority of 1960 keeping a girl named Judy under surveillance, maintaining a minimum distance of 50 lockers to avoid the danger that I might somehow get into a conversation with her, which could have led to disaster.

Judy: Hi.
Me: Hi.
Judy: Just in case you have ever thought

Copyright © David Shannon.

402 UNIT THREE PART 2: GOING TO EXTREMES

Assessment Option

Discussion Questions
1. Would you follow Barry's advice for arranging a date? Why or why not?
2. If you don't want to accept a date, is it better to lie and say you're busy or tell the truth?

INFORMAL ASSESSMENT You can informally assess students' understanding of the essay by having the class share how their views on dating compare to Barry's ideas. Organize discussion groups of eight to ten students, with a mixture of male and female students, if possible. Ask a group leader to present the open-ended questions at left to the group, allowing time for each member to express his or her opinion. Stress that students should respect one another's opinions.

Rubric
3 Full Accomplishment Students use specific details from the story and relate their opinions to the essay.
2 Substantial Accomplishment Students remember some details from Barry's story but cannot link their own opinions to the essay.
1 Little or Partial Accomplishment Students are unable to recall the relevant details of Barry's story.

402 THE LANGUAGE OF LITERATURE TEACHER'S EDITION

about having a date with me, the answer is no.

Woodland Creatures: Hahahahahaha.

The only problem with the nuclear-submarine technique is that it's difficult to get a date with a girl who has never, technically, been asked. This is why you need Phil Grant. Phil was a friend of mine who had the ability to talk to girls. It was a mysterious superhuman power he had, comparable to X-ray vision. So, after several thousand hours of intense discussion and planning with me, Phil approached a girl he knew named Nancy, who approached a girl named Sandy, who was a direct personal friend of Judy's and who passed the word back to Phil via Nancy that Judy would be willing to go on a date with me. This procedure protected me from direct humiliation, similar to the way President Reagan was protected from direct involvement in the Iran-Contra scandal[1] by a complex White House chain of command that at one point, investigators now believe, included his horse.

Thus it was that, finally, Judy and I went on an actual date, to see a movie in White Plains, N.Y. If I were to sum up the romantic ambience[2] of this date in four words, those words would be, "My mother was driving." This made for an extremely quiet drive, because my mother, realizing that her presence was hideously embarrassing, had to pretend she wasn't there. If it had been legal, I think she would have got out and sprinted alongside the car, steering through the window. Judy and I, sitting in the back seat about 75 feet apart, were also silent, unable to communicate without the assistance of Phil, Nancy and Sandy.

After what seemed like several years, we got to the movie theater, where my mother went off to sit in the Parents and Lepers Section. The movie was called *North to Alaska*, but I can tell you nothing else about it because I spent the whole time wondering whether it would be necessary to amputate my right arm, which was not getting any blood flow as a result of being perched for two hours like a petrified snake on the back of Judy's seat exactly one molecule away from physical contact.

So it was definitely a fun first date, featuring all the relaxed <u>spontaneity</u> of a real-estate closing,[3] and in later years I did regain some feeling in my arm. My point, Eric Knott, is that the key to successful dating is self-confidence. I bet that good-looking girl in your English class would *love* to go out with you. But *you* have to make the first move. So just do it! Pick up that phone! Call Phil Grant. ❖

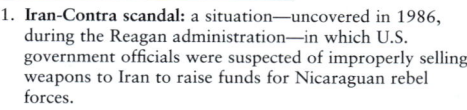

Judy: Just in case you have ever thought about having a date with me, the answer is no.

---

1. **Iran-Contra scandal:** a situation—uncovered in 1986, during the Reagan administration—in which U.S. government officials were suspected of improperly selling weapons to Iran to raise funds for Nicaraguan rebel forces.
2. **ambience** (ăm′bē-əns): the special atmosphere or mood created by an environment.
3. **real-estate closing:** a meeting at which the rights to land or a building are officially transferred from seller to buyer.

WORDS TO KNOW

spontaneity (spŏn′tə-nē′ĭ-tē) *n.* effortless and unplanned behavior

403

From Personal Response to Critical Analysis

1. Responses will vary.
2. Encourage students to use specific details from the selection and to explain why they think something is realistic or exaggerated.
3. Possible responses: Barry goes to extremes both to avoid Judy and to get a date with her. The advice he gives is extreme.
4. The description of a mother fish who eats her young shows that Barry is not giving serious advice.
5. Suggest that students review the events of the date before planning their pantomime.
6. Responses will vary. Note that some students may come from cultural or religious backgrounds whose courtship traditions differ.

Literary Links

Responses will vary. Some students will find McManus's description of the incident in Miss Bindle's math class more humorous because of its greater reliance on broad humor and slapstick. Others may find Barry's description more humorous because of its reliance on the comedy of an awkward situation.

Another Pathway

Cooperative Learning Each group must have at least four students to play the roles of Dave, Phil Grant, Judy, and Mrs. Barry. Have groups review the events leading up to the date as well as the date itself in planning their comedy. Be sure that each group includes the thoughts and feelings of Judy as well as Dave. Point out that since situation comedies usually end on a positive note, Judy and Dave must come to a type of agreement or happy ending.

Rubric

3 Full Accomplishment The group uses details from the story and presents them in a creative and interesting way.

2 Substantial Accomplishment The group picks up some details but misses important elements of the story.

1 Little or Partial Accomplishment The group's comedy does not correspond to the events or character traits in the story.

RESPONDING OPTIONS

FROM PERSONAL RESPONSE TO CRITICAL ANALYSIS

REFLECT 1. What was your reaction to Barry's experiences? Jot down your thoughts in your notebook.

RETHINK 2. Which parts of Barry's article seem realistic? Which parts seem exaggerated? Look back at the examples of hyperbole you jotted down for the Reading Connection on page 400.

Close Textual Reading

3. How does this article relate to the theme "Going to Extremes"?

Thematic Link

4. Reread the first paragraph of Barry's article. What does it reveal about what you can expect from the rest of the article?

5. With a partner, present a humorous pantomime of Dave Barry's date.

RELATE 6. Some dating behaviors have changed since the 1960s, when Barry was a teenager. Judging from Barry's account and your own observations and experiences, what has changed and what has stayed the same?

Multimodal Learning
ANOTHER PATHWAY

Cooperative Learning

With a small group of classmates, create a television situation-comedy episode entitled "Dave's First Date." Plan how you will portray the initial communication and the date itself. Also provide a satisfying conclusion to the episode. Act out the episode for the class.

LITERARY LINKS

Compare Dave Barry's description of his first date with Patrick McManus's description of the incident in Miss Bindle's math class (page 57). Which of the two descriptions do you think is more humorous? Why?

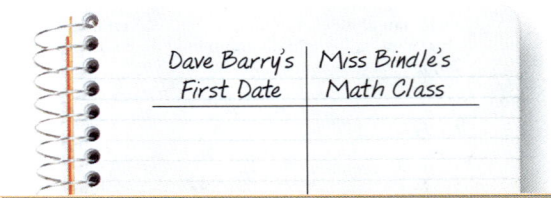

QUICKWRITES

1. Imagine that you are Judy, the girl Barry writes about in this column. Write a **diary entry** describing your first date with Dave.

2. Write a quick draft of an **advice column**, responding as Dave Barry might to a request for advice about a problem that students your age face. Try to capture Dave Barry's humorous tone.

📁 **PORTFOLIO** Save your writing. You may want to use it later as a springboard to a piece for your portfolio.

404   UNIT THREE PART 2: GOING TO EXTREMES

QuickWrites

1. Have students consider how the date was arranged, Judy's thoughts in the car, her awareness of Dave's arm in the movie theater, and whether Judy would be interested in going on another date with Dave.

2. Suggest that students start with a question from a fictitious reader, the way Dave Barry introduces the character of Eric Knott at the opening of his story.

 **The Writer's Craft**

Autobiographical Incidents, pp. 27–39
Developing a Personal Voice, pp. 316–317

Multimodal Learning

ALTERNATIVE ACTIVITIES

Cooperative Learning Produce a **how to video** about dating. First, decide whether you want to approach the subject seriously or humorously. Then start your video with tips on how to ask for a date. Afterwards, give pointers on how to have a successful date. Involve other students in your production by having them role-play various dating situations for your viewers.

WORDS TO KNOW

Review the meaning of **spontaneity** at the bottom of page 403. With a partner or small group, act out a situation that demonstrates the meaning of the word.

Words to Know

Encourage students to use an example of spontaneity from the story in their presentations.

Across the Curriculum

Social Studies *The Dating Game* Point out to students that the anxiety most American teenagers feel about dating is often alleviated in other cultures through special holidays and ceremonies designed to bring young men and women together. For example, the Kikuyu of West Africa have celebrations where young men and women pair off to dance and socialize. Have students research other cultural practices that may ease the pressures of dating.

Media *Dear Abby* Have students photocopy or cut out a variety of advice columns and editorials from different newspapers and magazines. Divide students into small groups and have them read and compare each writer's tone. Ask each group to write a summary describing how different journalists treated their subject matter. Ask them to consider how a reader would know whether or not the advice was sincere.

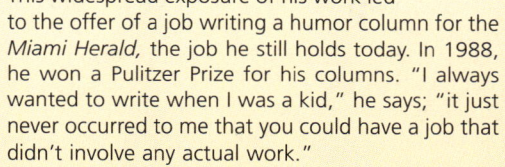

1947–

Born in Armonk, New York, Dave Barry was elected class clown by the Pleasantville High School class of 1965. Despite this honor, he did not immediately consider humor as a career. It was about 15 years later that he started writing freelance humor articles for a small newspaper—articles that soon were picked up by a few other papers, then by more. This widespread exposure of his work led to the offer of a job writing a humor column for the *Miami Herald*, the job he still holds today. In 1988, he won a Pulitzer Prize for his columns. "I always wanted to write when I was a kid," he says; "it just never occurred to me that you could have a job that didn't involve any actual work."

Barry has published 16 books, 2 of which became the basis of the CBS television series *Dave's World*. Often, while thinking about what he is going to write next, he plays a guitar that was once owned by Bruce Springsteen. Occasionally he plays in a "not very good" rock band at charitable functions.

Barry urges young people to write humor "even if it has no redeeming value." He says that thinking of jokes is easy; the hard part is saying it right: "I revise and revise and revise so my readers will feel and experience what is funny to me."

OTHER WORKS *Dave Barry Is Not Making This Up, Dave Barry Talks Back, Dave Barry's Greatest Hits, Bad Habits* Extended Reading

DAVE BARRY

Despite having a successful writing career, Dave Barry once told an interviewer that "writing has always been hard for me." He said of the process of writing his column, "I very rarely have any idea where a column is going when it starts. It's a matter of piling a little piece here and a little piece there, fitting them together, going on to the next part, then going back and gradually shaping the whole piece into something. That's what writing is. That's why it's so painful and slow."

EDITOR'S NOTE *With the permission of the copyright holder, the title has been shortened.*

Alternative Activities

Tell students that how-to videos usually give simple, direct steps on how to achieve a particular goal. Students should collectively brainstorm what they think are the best strategies for getting a date. One should record these suggestions. Suggest that the group divide up into those who will perform the how-to video, those who will make the script, and those who will make and supply props such as top-ten lists of things to avoid when making a date.

OVERVIEW

Objectives

- To understand and appreciate two poems about animals
- To identify and analyze the rhyme scheme of a poem
- To express understanding of the story through a choice of writing forms, including poems and prose
- To extend understanding of the story through a variety of multimodal and cross-curricular activities

Skills

LITERARY CONCEPTS
- Rhythm
- Rhyme scheme

THE WRITER'S STYLE
- Personification

SPEAKING, LISTENING, AND VIEWING
- Poetry reading
- Group discussion
- Oral presentation

Cross-Curricular Connections

HISTORY
- Artistic allies

ALTERNATIVE
Previewing

Instead of writing a narrative describing the human qualities of an animal, students can choose partners and discuss their ideas.

Writing Connection

Discussion Prompts Think about animals you have known whose behavior sometimes seemed human and describe at least one to your partner. Then listen as your partner describes his or her thoughts. The following questions might help you get started:

- What animal are you thinking about?
- Using descriptive details, explain the traits that make it seem human.

As you read the poems, notice the details that the authors use to make the colt and the cat seem human.

STRATEGIC READING FOR
Less-Proficient Readers

Set a Purpose To engage students in the poem, ask them to draw the scene describing the colt. Then have students read Eliot's poem and watch for how visible the cat is to the speaker.

Use **UNIT THREE RESOURCE BOOK**, p. 71, for guidance in reading the selection.

PREVIEWING

POETRY

The Runaway
Robert Frost

Macavity: The Mystery Cat
T. S. Eliot

Activating Prior Knowledge
PERSONAL CONNECTION

Think about all of the animals you have observed—at home, in your neighborhood, on farms, at the zoo, and in the wild. Have you ever seen or heard about any animals that were out of control? How did they behave? Share your observations with the class.

CATS photo courtesy of The CATS Company. Copyright 1991 Martha Swope.

Building Background
LITERARY CONNECTION

You are about to read poems by two of the most famous 20th-century American poets, Robert Frost and T. S. Eliot. In these works, the poets write about unusual animal behavior: Frost focuses on a colt; Eliot, on a cat.

Robert Frost spent much of his life on a farm. He knew and loved the land and the farm animals. One critic has noted that Frost had no peer in his "ability to portray the local truth in nature." He could bring the actions of a colt so fully to life because he had not only observed horses but had handled them.

Similarly, Eliot was no mere observer of cats. He was a great fancier of felines, and was often photographed with his animals. Eliot was so captivated by these independent creatures that, in the 1930s, he was moved to compose for his godchildren and friends the poems that became *Old Possum's Book of Practical Cats*. In 1981, Andrew Lloyd Webber made Eliot's delightful and outrageous cats famous around the world when he adapted the poems for his stage musical *Cats*.

Active Reading/Setting a Purpose
WRITING CONNECTION

As you read these poems, you may find that the colt and the cat seem to have personalities almost like those of people you know. Think about other animals whose behavior sometimes seems human—for example, you might know an angry dog or nervous parakeet. Write a short narrative illustrating the human-like personality traits of one or more of these animals.

406 UNIT THREE PART 2: GOING TO EXTREMES

PRINT AND MEDIA RESOURCES

UNIT THREE RESOURCE BOOK
Strategic Reading: Literature, p. 69

WRITING MINI–LESSONS
Transparencies, p. 39

ACCESS FOR STUDENTS ACQUIRING ENGLISH
Reading and Writing Support

FORMAL ASSESSMENT
Selection Test, p. 77
Part Test, pp. 79–80
 Test Generator

 **AUDIO LIBRARY**
See Reference Card

LASERLINKS
Art Gallery
Author Background

The Runaway
by Robert Frost

Thematic Link: *Going to Extremes*
In the two poems, animals in extreme situations attempt to adapt to their surroundings.

A
Once when the snow of the year was beginning to fall,
We stopped by a mountain pasture to say, "Whose colt?"
A little Morgan¹ had one forefoot on the wall,
The other curled at his breast. He dipped his head
5 And snorted at us. And then he had to bolt.
We heard the miniature thunder where he fled,
And we saw him, or thought we saw him, dim and gray,
Like a shadow against the curtain of falling flakes.
"I think the little fellow's afraid of the snow.
10 He isn't winter-broken. It isn't play
With the little fellow at all. He's running away.
I doubt if even his mother could tell him, 'Sakes,
It's only weather.' He'd think she didn't know!
Where is his mother? He can't be out alone."
15 And now he comes again with clatter of stone,
And mounts the wall again with whited eyes
And all his tail that isn't hair up straight.
He shudders his coat as if to throw off flies.
"Whoever it is that leaves him out so late,
B 20 When other creatures have gone to stall and bin,
Ought to be told to come and take him in."

---

1. **Morgan:** a horse of a breed noted for strength, speed, and endurance.

FROM PERSONAL RESPONSE TO CRITICAL ANALYSIS

REFLECT 1. What are your feelings about the colt in this poem? Jot down your thoughts in your notebook.

RETHINK 2. Think about the human characteristics of the colt's behavior. How do its actions relate to the theme "Going to Extremes"?
Thematic Link

3. Do you think Frost wants readers to learn a lesson about life from the colt's experience? Explain your answer.

THE RUNAWAY **407**

CUSTOMIZING FOR
Students Acquiring English

- Use **ACCESS FOR STUDENTS ACQUIRING ENGLISH,** Reading and Writing Support.
- Read each poem aloud to the class before students begin to read. The setting in "The Runaway" is important to the poem. Ask students to imagine the scene by finding the details in the poem and to draw a picture of the scene described.

Literary Concept:
RHYME SCHEME

A Point out to students the rhyme scheme for the first six lines of "The Runaway." *(ABACBC)* Mention that several lines may pass before an end rhyme occurs. Then complete with students the rhyme scheme for the rest of the poem, lines 7–21. *(DEFDDEFGGHI-HIJJ)*

Active Reading: EVALUATE

B Ask students to evaluate whether the colt is in danger. *(Possible responses: The colt is in danger, because it is panicked and out in the cold; it is not in danger, because the speaker does not sound too worried and the snowfall is not that great.)*

From Personal Response to Critical Analysis

1. Responses will vary.
2. Possible response: Fear is an emotion that is experienced by animals as well as humans, but the speaker at points describes the colt and his mother in terms of a human mother and child.
3. Possible response: Frost is possibly suggesting that young people often have to learn on their own rather than be told by adults.

Mini-Lesson   The Writer's Style

PERSONIFICATION Help students understand that personification is the giving of human qualities to an animal, object, or idea. For instance, in "The Runaway," the young colt is given human qualities. Personification often allows a poet to explore dimensions of the human condition indirectly, through analogy.

Application Have students compile a "character sketch" of the horse, listing its characteristics. Then have them answer the following questions that address Frost's use of personification:

- What kind of person would the horse be?
- How would a human with the same characteristics respond to being caught out in the snow?
- How would the responses differ?

Reteaching/Reinforcement
- Writing Handbook, anthology p. 834
- *Writing Mini-Lessons* transparencies, p. 39

Personification, pp. 319–320

THE LANGUAGE OF LITERATURE TEACHER'S EDITION **407**

CUSTOMIZING FOR
Gifted and Talented Students

Ask students to discuss the relationship of rhythm and rhyme to the subject matter of the poems. Ask them to discuss how rhythm and rhyme work to produce a serious effect in Frost's poem. Then ask them how Eliot, in contrast to Frost, uses rhythm and rhyme for a comic effect.

Literary Concept: RHYTHM

C Tell students that two successive lines that rhyme and have the same rhythm are known as couplets. Have students identify other couplets in the poem. *(The entire poem is a series of couplets.)*

Critical Thinking: SPECULATE

D Before students read further, have them speculate about the crimes a cat might commit. *(Possible responses: stealing food, sleeping where it's not allowed)*

CUSTOMIZING FOR
Students Acquiring English

I Hindu students may be able to describe a fakir. *(a wonder-worker; a person who performs magic feats)* Also explain that *levitate* means "to rise in the air against the laws of gravity."

Literary Concept: RHYME SCHEME

E Point out to students that the end rhyme of lines 3 and 4 repeats in lines 7–10. Encourage students to find other couplets that repeat an earlier end rhyme.

MACAVITY: THE MYSTERY CAT

BY T.S. ELIOT

C Macavity's a Mystery Cat: he's called the Hidden Paw—
For he's the master criminal who can defy the Law.
He's the bafflement of Scotland Yard,[1] the Flying Squad's despair:[2]
D For when they reach the scene of crime—*Macavity's not there!*

5 Macavity, Macavity, there's no one like Macavity,
He's broken every human law, he breaks the law of gravity.
I His powers of levitation would make a fakir stare,
And when you reach the scene of crime—*Macavity's not there!*
E You may seek him in the basement, you may look up in the air—
10 But I tell you once and once again, *Macavity's not there!*

---

1. **Scotland Yard:** the London police department, especially the detective bureau.
2. **the Flying Squad's despair:** a hopeless problem even for the special motorized emergency police unit in London.

408 UNIT THREE PART 2: GOING TO EXTREMES

Mini-Lesson  Literary Concepts

REVIEWING RHYTHM Remind students that the pattern of stressed and unstressed syllables in poetry is called rhythm. When syllables are stressed, or emphasized, in a consistent pattern, the poem has a regular beat. Each unit of stressed (marked ´) and unstressed (marked ˘) syllables is called a foot.

Application Make photocopies of the highlighted passage on page 408, or have students write it. Ask students to mark the pattern of stressed and unstressed syllables. You may wish to invite students to complete a similar exercise for an excerpt from Frost's "The Runaway."

Macavity's a ginger cat, he's very tall and thin;
You would know him if you saw him, for his eyes are sunken in.
His brow is deeply lined with thought, his head is highly domed;
His coat is dusty from neglect, his whiskers are uncombed.
15 He sways his head from side to side, with movements like a snake;
And when you think he's half asleep, he's always wide awake.

Macavity, Macavity, there's no one like Macavity,
For he's a fiend in feline shape, a monster of depravity.
You may meet him in a by-street, you may see him in the square—
20 But when a crime's discovered, then *Macavity's not there!*

He's outwardly respectable. (They say he cheats at cards.)
And his footprints are not found in any file of Scotland Yard's.
And when the larder's looted, or the jewel-case is rifled,
Or when the milk is missing, or another Peke's³ been stifled,
25 Or the greenhouse glass is broken, and the trellis past repair—
Ay, there's the wonder of the thing! *Macavity's not there!*

And when the Foreign Office find a Treaty's gone astray,
Or the Admiralty lose some plans and drawings by the way,
There may be a scrap of paper in the hall or on the stair—
30 But it's useless to investigate—*Macavity's not there!*
And when the loss has been disclosed, the Secret Service say:
"It *must* have been Macavity!"—but he's a mile away.
You'll be sure to find him resting, or a-licking of his thumbs,
Or engaged in doing complicated long division sums.

35 Macavity, Macavity, there's no one like Macavity,
There never was a Cat of such deceitfulness and suavity.
He always has an alibi, and one or two to spare:
At whatever time the deed took place—MACAVITY WASN'T THERE!
And they say that all the Cats whose wicked deeds are widely
   known
40 (I might mention Mungojerrie, I might mention Griddlebone)
Are nothing more than agents for the Cat who all the time
Just controls their operations: the Napoleon⁴ of Crime!

---

3. **Peke:** a Pekingese, a small dog with long hair.
4. **Napoleon** (nə-pōʹlē-ən): emperor of the French, 1804–1814. As a military leader, Napoleon was powerful, clever, and seemingly unconquerable.

MACAVITY: THE MYSTERY CAT **409**

Literary Concept: RHYTHM

F Point out to students that the rhythm of a poem sometimes changes during its course. Invite students to check lines as they read to see if Eliot alters the rhythm of this poem. *(Possible response: The poem's rhythm remains regular.)*

Active Reading: CONNECT

G Have students think about the extraordinary antics of Macavity and other pets and animals they have known. Ask them to describe the unusual characteristics these animals have.

CUSTOMIZING FOR
Students Acquiring English

2 Point out that an alibi is an explanation of why a person could not have committed a crime.

COMPREHENSION CHECK

1. What did the speaker of "The Runaway" encounter in the pasture? *(a colt)*
2. What was the colt trying to do? *(escape from the snow)*
3. Who is the criminal described in Eliot's poem? *(Macavity the cat)*
4. What does Macavity always have that keeps him out of trouble? *(an alibi)*

Mini-Lesson: Speaking, Listening, and Viewing

POETRY READING Explain to students that poetry is intended to be read aloud. Robert Frost and T. S. Eliot were famous not only as writers of poetry but also as interpretive readers of their poems. There is no better way for students to understand the crucial role and relationship of rhythm and rhyme than to listen to a poetry reading.

Application Have students work in groups of three or four. Students should find in their library or bookstore a tape recording of Eliot or Frost reading from his works. When students first listen to the tape, encourage them simply to listen to the reading without following the text and to pause after each poem to write their impressions in their notebooks. On a second reading, have students follow along in the text. Can they hear the effect of the rhyme and rhythm? On a third hearing, encourage the group to read aloud with the poet. Have the group discuss what it is like to read when paying attention to the rhythm and rhyme of the poem.

THE LANGUAGE OF LITERATURE TEACHER'S EDITION **409**

From Personal Response to Critical Analysis

1. Invite students to cite examples from the text in their discussions.
2. Possible response: Macavity steals milk and terrorizes dogs; he also commits human crimes like stealing jewels, breaking glass, and cheating at cards.
3. Responses should include some discussion of the poet's use of personification to describe the cat.
4. Be sure students use specific details to support their comparisons.
5. Possible responses: The mood of "The Runaway" is serious, while that of "Macavity" is humorous. Both poems have a sense of wonder about two very unusual animals.

Another Pathway

Tell students that their performance should reflect the poet's use of rhythm and rhyme. Students who find this difficult may want to tap or beat the rhythm as they practice.

Rubric

3 Full Accomplishment Student reads the poem with attention and care to its rhythm and rhyme.

2 Substantial Accomplishment Student does not fully express the rhythm or the rhyme of the poem.

1 Little or Partial Accomplishment Student has difficulty identifying the poem's rhythm and rhyme.

RESPONDING OPTIONS

FROM PERSONAL RESPONSE TO CRITICAL ANALYSIS

REFLECT
1. Are your feelings about Macavity in "Macavity: The Mystery Cat" different from your feelings about the runaway colt? Explain.

RETHINK
2. What kinds of crimes does Macavity commit? How does he resemble a human criminal?
3. From what you know about cats, can you imagine a cat's behaving like Macavity? Give reasons for your answer.

RELATE
4. Compare and contrast the attitudes of these poems' speakers toward the animals they describe. Use details from the poems to support your conclusions.
5. Compare and contrast the moods of the two poems.

Multimodal Learning
ANOTHER PATHWAY

Plan a read-aloud of either "The Runaway" or "Macavity: The Mystery Cat" for your class. Study the punctuation in the poems and the techniques the poets use to convey particular sounds. You might want to tape practice readings to prepare for your performance.

LITERARY CONCEPTS

The pattern of rhymes in a poem is called the poem's **rhyme scheme.** A rhyme scheme can be described by assigning a different letter to each rhyming sound. Notice, for example, the rhyming words in these lines from "The Runaway":

Once when the snow of the year was beginning to fall,	A
We stopped by a mountain pasture to say, "Whose colt?"	B
A little Morgan had one forefoot on the wall,	A
The other curled at his breast. He dipped his head	C
And snorted at us. And then he had to bolt.	B

On a sheet of paper, write letters indicating the rhyme scheme of the first two stanzas of "Macavity: The Mystery Cat."

QUICKWRITES

1. Follow the example of Frost and Eliot by writing a **poem** about an animal that has human qualities. Use repetition and alliteration to create the sounds you want readers to hear.

2. If the colt and Macavity could talk, what would each say in response to the poem that has been written about him? Write either animal's reaction as a piece of **prose** or a **poem.**

📁 **PORTFOLIO** Save your writing. You may want to use it later as a springboard to a piece for your portfolio.

410 UNIT THREE PART 2: GOING TO EXTREMES

Literary Concepts

Point out to students that rhyming is a key way poets provide a sense of coherence, structure, and musicality to a poem. The rhyme scheme is a charting of this important technique. Students should understand that the rhyme schemes for the first two stanzas of "Macavity: The Mystery Cat" are AABBCCBBBB and DDEEFF. So that students better understand the importance of rhyme scheme—and the difficulty of finding rhymes to fit a pattern—have them write a short poem of six to eight lines on a favorite pet or animal. Have them identify their poem's rhyme scheme.

QuickWrites

1. Remind students that repetition also applies to phrases, lines, and/or grammatical structures. Also remind students that alliteration is the repetition of consonant sounds at the beginning of words.
2. Students should decide how the animal's characteristics relate to human traits before beginning. For example, Macavity may sound sly or aloof and the young colt frightened or wild.

The Writer's Craft

Writing a Poem, pp. 71–83
Effective Paragraphs, pp. 244–254

410 THE LANGUAGE OF LITERATURE TEACHER'S EDITION

Literary Links

Responses will vary. Students might mention "Moco Limping" and "the lesson of the moth," since these poems also describe animals.

Across the Curriculum

History Cooperative Learning
Artistic Allies Robert Frost and T. S. Eliot were born in the United States but moved to Great Britain to focus on writing poetry, Frost for a brief period and Eliot for so long that he became a British citizen. Have groups of three or four students research the cultural and intellectual exchange between the two countries during the period between the world wars. Students' research can focus on the history and development of poetry during the time period, the well-known poets writing during this time, or anthologies or volumes of poetry published. Students may divide research tasks according to sources being searched: reference books, biographies, histories.

ART GALLERY
Farmlands Artworks by Edward Kellogg, Konstantin Rodko, Henry Pember Smith, and Currier and Ives show farms and farm life.

Side A, Frame 52716

Multimodal Learning

ALTERNATIVE ACTIVITIES

In a medium of your choice, create a **portrait** of either the colt or Macavity. Use descriptive details from the poem to guide you in developing your portrait. If you have a graphics program on your computer, here's a chance to use it. Display it in the classroom.

LITERARY LINKS

Think about the poetry you have read in the book so far. Are there any poems that are similar to the two you have just read? Consider the themes or the literary devices the poems might have in common. Discuss specific examples with classmates.

ROBERT FROST

1874–1963

Robert Frost, the most popular American poet of his time, nearly missed his calling. As a young adult, Frost married and worked at many odd jobs—mill hand, shoe salesman, farmer—to support his family. By the time he was 38, he was a discouraged man. His farm had failed, and he had suffered numerous rejections of his poetry. He decided to move his family to England and concentrate on writing.

Frost's work soon began to receive acclaim on both sides of the Atlantic, and he later returned to the United States. He is the only American poet to have won four Pulitzer Prizes, and in 1962 he was awarded a gold medal by Congress. Despite these honors, Frost endured much hardship. By 1940, three of his six children and his beloved wife were dead. Two infant daughters died from illness, and another daughter was committed to a psychiatric hospital, as was Frost's younger sister. His son committed suicide soon after the death of Frost's wife.

Most of Frost's poetry is inspired by rural life and emphasizes the individual's fight to retain an identity and the human struggle against natural forces.
OTHER WORKS *The Road Not Taken: A Selection of Robert Frost's Poems, Poems by Robert Frost: A Boy's Will and North of Boston*

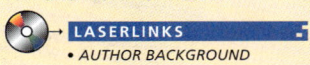
- AUTHOR BACKGROUND
- ART GALLERY

T. S. ELIOT

1888–1965

Thomas Stearns Eliot ranks among the most important poets of the 20th century. Unlike "Macavity: The Mystery Cat," most of Eliot's poetry is written in a serious vein. His famous poem *The Waste Land*, considered by many critics to be the most influential poem of modern times, uses nontraditional techniques to portray a lack of faith and values in a world devastated by World War I.

Eliot was born in St. Louis, Missouri, and educated at Harvard University. Eliot studied at the graduate level in England, becoming a British subject in 1927. He began writing poetry during college and published his first major poem, "The Love Song of J. Alfred Prufrock," in 1915.

Eliot is also known for his plays, including *Murder in the Cathedral* and *The Cocktail Party*, and for his literary criticism. He worked as a literary editor and lectured at many colleges and universities in the United States and England. Eliot received numerous honors, including the 1948 Nobel Prize in literature.
OTHER WORKS *Selected Poems, The Waste Land and Other Poems*

Extended Reading

THE RUNAWAY / MACAVITY: THE MYSTERY CAT **411**

ROBERT FROST

Although Frost was one of America's most popular and respected poets, his use of traditional poetic techniques has made him difficult to place in the development of modern poetry. A number of critics have commented that Frost's poetry is not experimental and makes use of many of the techniques of 19th-century poetry. He is a traditionalist in his use of rhyme and rhythm.

T. S. ELIOT

Eliot received the Nobel Prize for literature in 1948. He was ambivalent about the award, thinking that it had too often signaled that a writer had reached the end of his or her productive career. However, he continued to write, turning out a number of successful plays, including *The Confidential Clerk* (1953) and *The Elder Statesman* (1958). His *Collected Poems* and *Collected Plays* both appeared in 1962.

Alternative Activities

Before students begin, they should list the qualities and characteristics of the animal they have chosen to capture in their portraits. Encourage students who find drawing difficult to create and label a collage of pictures that illustrate certain aspects of either Macavity or the colt.

AUTHOR BACKGROUND
Robert Frost In this interview footage, Frost discusses the cruelty of nature and the impact of his many jobs on his writing.

Side A, Frame 29183

THE LANGUAGE OF LITERATURE TEACHER'S EDITION **411**

OVERVIEW

To gain a deeper appreciation of the nonfiction selections they have read in this unit, students will explore the characteristics of a problem-solution essay and then create their own well-developed example in this lesson.

Objectives

- To plan a problem-solution essay by considering elements such as ideas, research, and organization
- To draft a problem-solution essay and solicit a response
- To revise, edit, and publish a problem-solution essay
- To reflect on the process of writing a problem-solution essay

Skills

LITERATURE
- Examining issues
- Identifying problems and solutions

WRITING AND LANGUAGE
- Evaluating ideas
- Elaborating on ideas
- Creating introductions
- Developing conclusions

GRAMMAR AND USAGE
- Using direct objects

MEDIA LITERACY
- Interpreting statistics
- Studying charts
- Reading a newspaper article
- Researching in newspapers and electronic bulletin boards

SPEAKING, LISTENING, AND VIEWING
- Conducting group discussions
- Debating
- Brainstorming
- Peer evaluations
- Reading aloud

Teaching Strategy: MODELING

A To show students how to generate writing ideas from a springboard, have them look at the models on pages 412 and 413. Ask students to brainstorm a list of possible solutions to each of these problems. You may wish to use these discussion prompts:
- How can the number of bicycle-related deaths be reduced?
- What are some solutions to the low morale at Palmer Middle School?
- How might a community balance the needs of all its members?

WRITING FROM EXPERIENCE

Writing to Explain

If someone asked you to name the problems facing people you know, what would you say? As you have learned in Unit Three, "Battle for Control," problems come in all shapes and sizes. Some are easily solved, but others require the efforts of many people. How effective will you be at solving the problems you face?

GUIDED ASSIGNMENT
Write a Problem-Solution Essay In this lesson, you will have an opportunity to tackle a problem that is important to you. A problem-solution essay can help you evaluate a problem and find a positive solution.

1 Look Around You

A As you read the excerpts and examine the chart on these pages, ask yourself questions about the problem described in each piece. Who is affected by the problem? Do you think there might be more than one point of view? Why should anyone care about the problem?

Reading the News Have you noticed in recent newspaper reports or news broadcasts problems such as those described on these pages? What were the problems? Why do you think they were in the news?

Taking a Poll Think about your own experiences. What would you say is the number one problem in your community? Why? You might take a poll of your classmates to see what they think the biggest problem is. Make a list of your findings.

Student's Journal

Monday June 5
Today Sandra showed me this article from her school paper. She seemed really upset about what's going on at her school.

I think I'll write about the problem in the article Sandra gave me. This is a problem at my school too.

Chart

wheel danger!

Each year there are approximately 1,000 bicycle-related deaths.

62% of those deaths involve head injuries.

38% other

412 UNIT THREE: BATTLE FOR CONTROL

PRINT AND MEDIA RESOURCES

UNIT THREE RESOURCE BOOK
Prewriting Activity, p. 73
Elaboration, p. 74
Peer Response Guide, pp. 75–76
Revising and Proofreading, p. 77
Student Model, p. 78
Rubric, p. 79

FORMAL ASSESSMENT
Guidelines for Writing Assessment

GRAMMAR MINI-LESSONS
Transparencies, pp. 10, 38
Copymasters, p. 13

WRITING MINI-LESSONS
Transparencies, p. 34

 WRITING COACH

ACCESS FOR STUDENTS ACQUIRING ENGLISH
Reading and Writing Support

 LASERLINKS
Writing Springboard

412 THE LANGUAGE OF LITERATURE TEACHER'S EDITION

1

Poll Shows Student Morale at a Record Low
by Lakisha Adams

The results are in on a poll conducted by the Blue and Gold newspaper. Seventy-five percent of the students at Palmer Middle School feel that morale is low. Students listed the new dress code, the football team's string of losses, and the decrease in school clubs as some of the issues bothering them.

"The students have been complaining more than usual these days," Principal Skinner remarked. "However, no one has offered any solutions."

Newspaper Article

Teenagers sing the blues: There's nothing legal to do

When the late singer Eddie Cochran wrote the 1950s song about teenagers of his day, he forever captured the frustrations youths face in dealing with parental authority.

The song's most memorable line: "There ain't no cure for the summertime blues," remains a rallying cry for today's highly mobile teens—struggling against boredom in the 1990s.

But recently, teenagers have begun clashing with another level of authority: suburban municipal officials armed with new laws.

And from Des Plaines to Palos Heights, these officials are taking aim at popular teen pastimes, everything from cruising in cars to gathering for teen dances.

"It's about time we got serious about certain kinds of activity that are a threat to the community," said Des Plaines Ald. Jean Higgason, outraged by large numbers of teens cruising the streets of her community.

"Gang members are infiltrating," Higgason added.

Ironically, some child behavior experts and teens say, wiping out these accessible and popular forms of activities leaves teens with fewer options for filling a critical need: healthy interaction with their peers.

Ray Quintanilla
from *Chicago Tribune*

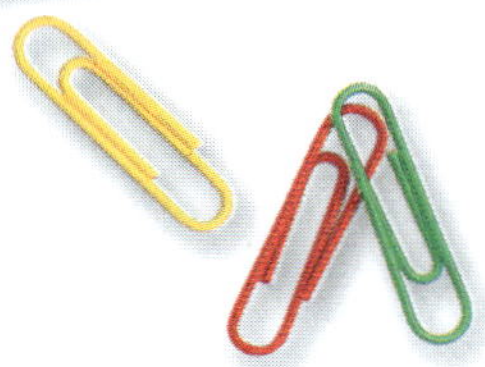

2 Write in Your Journal

Pick two or three of the problems you discovered. If you or a friend were involved in one of the situations, what would you do about it? Write your reactions.

Decision Point Choose a problem you want to write about. It can be one of the problems on these pages or one from your own life, but it should be something that's important to you.

> LASERLINKS
> • WRITING SPRINGBOARD
> WRITING COACH

WRITING FROM EXPERIENCE 413

WRITING SPRINGBOARD
Urban Cowboys in Los Angeles
These cowboys are teaching young people in South Central Los Angeles about riding and roping—and helping them stay away from gangs and drugs.

Side B, Frame 9493

Writing Prompt Think of a problem you have seen or heard about in your community. Write a problem-solution essay that describes the problem and suggests a way of solving it.

CUSTOMIZING FOR
Less-Proficient Writers

D Inexperienced writers often find it difficult to generate solutions. Suggest that they start by identifying the problem. Explain that it is almost impossible to find solutions to problems you don't understand. Guide them to state the problem clearly. Then have students analyze the problem. Arrange them in small groups to describe the problem and ask questions about it. Have groups consider causes and effects in their analysis.

Critical Thinking: ANALYZING

E At this stage of the writing process, have students develop specific goals for their paper. For example, suggest that students decide if it would be sufficient to include a thorough explanation of the problems and possible solutions in their essay, or if they would rather try to persuade their readers that their solutions are best. Direct students to look at the guided assignment on page 412 as they solidify their writing goals.

Writing Skill:
USING THE COMPUTER

F Suggest that students jot down notes and proposed solutions on a computer. Explain that the computer not only allows students to express their ideas quickly but also provides a base for later drafting. Tell students that by working on a computer, they can later easily rearrange text to shape a draft.

PREWRITING

Exploring Solutions

Solutions That Work By now you've identified a problem that's important to you, one that you want to write about. The steps on these pages can help you explore possible solutions.

① Think About Possible Solutions

D Think about the resources you would use to develop a solution to the problem. Two good resources are your own common sense and your friends' opinions. Another source is your school or neighborhood library. Try using the following strategies to explore solutions.

Research Sources

STUDY THE PROBLEM

Restate the situation in your own words. Make sure you understand all the issues involved.

BRAINSTORM IDEAS WITH FRIENDS

You might consider talking over the problem with some of your friends. Think about a time when you or someone you know experienced a similar problem. How did he or she solve that problem? Try brainstorming some additional solutions. The tips in the SkillBuilder on page 415 will help you and your friends work together to build a list of ideas.

E

RESEARCH POSSIBLE SOLUTIONS

Do you need to know more details about the problem? Sources such as your school newspaper, electronic bulletin boards, or daily newspapers can reveal ways people have solved problems similar to yours. You may even want to consult an expert. Use the advice in the Multimedia Handbook for additional research ideas. You might make a web like the one on the next page to keep track of your proposed solutions.

 SkillBuilder   **RESEARCH SKILLS**

COMPUTERIZED REFERENCE SOURCES
Explain that the easiest way to find a book in a library is to use a card catalog. Tell students that more and more card catalogs are on computer. Be sure that students understand they can search for materials by typing in key words, such as the author's name, the book's title, or the paper's subject. The computer matches the entry to items in the library's collection. Also, describe how many computer catalogs allow users to narrow their search by using key words that combine an author's name and the subject. For example, students could look for all the books by an author named Juarez on the subject of bicycle safety. Explain that, in addition to book and other print resources, many on-line card catalogs index video, cassette, and CD materials.

Application Encourage students to use an on-line card catalog to find books and other sources that offer possible solutions to the issues they have raised in their prewriting.

414 THE LANGUAGE OF LITERATURE TEACHER'S EDITION

❷ Evaluate Your Ideas

Before you start your essay, you'll need to evaluate your ideas. How would you carry out each solution? What kinds of support would each require? Would any of your solutions create new problems?

Student's Solution Web

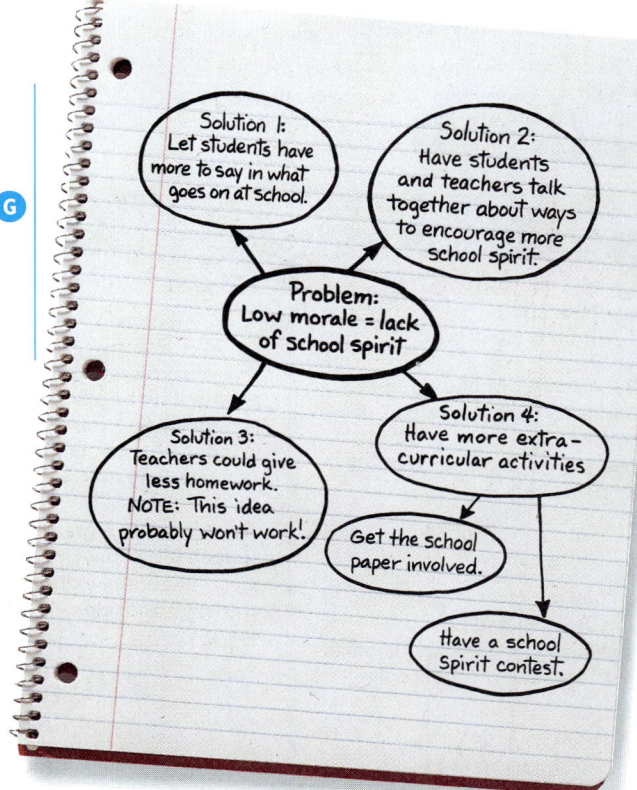

❸ Pick Your Solution

Which solution seems most workable? Can you combine any of your solutions? Look at the web above that one student made for his report. After making this web, he combined some of the ideas to make one solution, which he wrote in his essay. What solution will you write about in your essay?

SkillBuilder

 SPEAKING & LISTENING

Conducting Group Discussions

When it comes to solving problems, you may find that two or three heads are better than one. Why not get your friends together and share some ideas? To keep things orderly, you might need to set some rules.

- Ask "What if?" questions to get at possible solutions. For example, "What if there were more activities at school? How would that solve the problem?"
- If you disagree with someone else's idea, wait until he or she finishes speaking. Then give an alternative solution.

Role-playing can help you develop solutions. One person can pretend to be the person with the problem. Others can take the roles of other people affected by the problem.

APPLYING WHAT YOU'VE LEARNED
Choose a time when you can brainstorm ideas. Make a list of the ideas your group proposes.

THINK & PLAN

Reflecting on Your Ideas

1. What makes this problem really important to you?
2. How will your audience and purpose affect your format?
3. How might you organize your ideas?

CUSTOMIZING FOR
Less-Proficient Writers

G In addition to creating a web, you may wish to help students create a problem-solution chart. Explain that a problem-solution chart can help students find the best solution and develop effective responses to possible objections. The chart can take many forms. Share with the class the two possibilities shown below.

Problem	Results	Solutions

Problem	Solutions	Pros	Cons

Encourage students to refer to their charts as they draft their papers.

Writing Skill:
IDENTIFYING AUDIENCE

H When students are ready to draft, they should ask themselves the following questions:
- *Who is my audience?*
- *Why is my audience interested in this problem?*
- *What does the audience already know about the problem?*
- *Is my solution new to the audience?*
- *How will my solution affect this audience?*

Teaching Strategy: MANAGING THE PAPER LOAD

To enable students to get individual, immediate feedback, confer briefly with them as they gather and organize information. Discuss the student's organizational methods, suggesting alternative ideas as needed.

Mini-Lesson — Speaking and Listening

CONDUCTING GROUP DISCUSSIONS
Suggest that students brainstorm possible solutions by using the "5W and H" questions: *Who? What? When? Where? Why?* and *How?* Have each group member state his or her problem and briefly explain the solution. Suggest that the rest of the group listen and then ask the 5W and H questions. Allow students a few minutes after each interview to jot down notes.

Applying What You've Learned An effective way for students to keep their group on task and to accurately record information is to record their group discussions. Suggest that they play the tape and take notes after the discussion.

Additional Suggestions In addition to role-playing, students can debate the solutions. Divide each group in half and have one side take the *pro* side while the other side takes the *con* side.

Writing Skill: USING THE COMPUTER

I Remind students that a draft can be written in any order and organized later. For example, some writers may find it easier to state the problem first and then tell how it affects people. Other students may want to begin by writing about the solution and return to the problem.

Point out that, since they make reorganizing text easy, computers offer flexibility for those with different writing styles.

Encourage students to draft their papers on the computer and use The Writing Coach, which provides targeted drafting guidelines.

Teaching Strategy: MODELING

J Tell students organizing their writing on a computer that they can create headings in their document such as Introduction, Problem, Solution, and Conclusion. Point out the headings Problem and Solution in the student's rough draft shown here. Describe how writers can move their computer's cursor back and forth to the section they wish to work on.

DRAFTING

Writing Your Ideas

At the Starting Gate Now you're ready to put your ideas into draft form. As you write, you may find that your solution isn't working or that your problem isn't really a problem after all. Don't be afraid to go off in another direction, or even to start over.

❶ Write Your Rough Draft

As you draft your problem-solution essay, ask other people who are interested in the problem to help you develop your solution in more detail. Notice the peer comments in the student model below.

Student's Rough Draft with Peer Comments

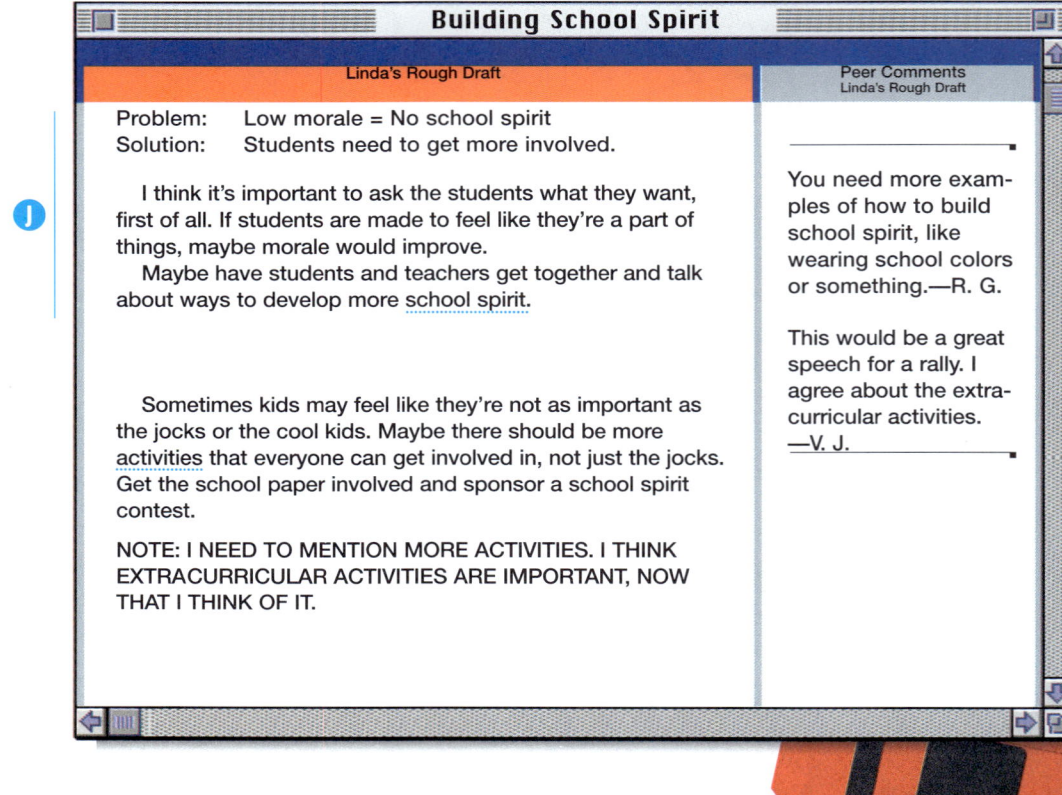

416 UNIT THREE: BATTLE FOR CONTROL

WRITING SPRINGBOARD
Problems to Solve Two students and a teacher at a California high school discuss problems they consider serious, such as prejudice and poverty.

Side B, Frame 12229

Writing Prompt Choose a problem that you consider serious. Write an essay telling how the problem affects you and society as a whole. In your essay, suggest some actions you might take to combat the problem and explain why others should also take action.

❷ Shape Your Writing

As you rework your rough draft, consider the suggestions below to help you present your ideas clearly.

Writing Your Introduction Define or describe the problem, telling why it is a problem and who is affected. Look once more at the student model on the preceding page. How well does it describe the problem?

Making Your Draft Clear and Complete Include details to explain the problem and to support your proposed solution. The first student reviewer's note shows how important it is to use specific examples. Look back at your prewriting notes. Did you include everything you wanted to mention? The SkillBuilder at the right can help you elaborate on your ideas. For tips on organizing your problem-solution essay, see page 841 of the Writing Handbook.

Ending Your Essay Restate the problem and your proposed solution. Then look back at the notes you made during prewriting. What final thoughts can you give your readers?

❸ Evaluate Your Draft

Step back from your draft and look at it as if someone else had written it. Did you clearly state the problem? Do the solutions you proposed make sense? To evaluate the draft you wrote, ask yourself the following questions:

- How can I help the reader better understand the cause of the problem?
- Have I shown why the solution I proposed is a good one?
- Have I thought about the pros and cons of this solution?

 **PEER RESPONSE**

At this point, you may find it helpful to get comments from your peers, particularly the ones who gave you ideas for solutions. Peers can help you see points that you might have missed. Ask them questions like the following:

- How would you summarize the problem and the solution?
- What other solutions might I have overlooked?

SkillBuilder

 WRITER'S CRAFT

Elaborating on Ideas

To help readers understand your recommended solution, add specific details to what you have written. Use these suggestions:

- Add some statistics or other facts to back up your solution.
- Use incidents and examples. In the comments on the student model, the writer was reminded of how to build school spirit. The writer could mention these examples in her final draft.
- Use quotations from people who support the conclusions you have reached.

APPLYING WHAT YOU'VE LEARNED
Now go back and review the ideas you have written. Which ideas need more elaboration? For example, if you are writing about school spirit, what facts or statistics could you include to demonstrate the importance of your solutions?

RETHINK & EVALUATE

Preparing to Revise

1. What do you like best about the way you've stated the problem and its solution?
2. How will you use your peers' feedback to revise your essay?
3. How can you make the solution to your problem more convincing?

WRITING FROM EXPERIENCE **417**

Writing Skill: INTRODUCTION

K Remind students to begin their essays in an interesting way. Direct them to look to the model on page 413 for ideas. Share some possibilities with students, such as using an anecdote, a statistic, a description, a quotation, or a dialogue. Invite volunteers to work in small groups to evaluate each essay's introduction.

CUSTOMIZING FOR
Less-Proficient Writers

L As writers shape their essays, they should make sure that each paragraph contains a separate and distinct idea. Encourage students to check their organization by creating an outline. Students can create their own outlines or use the following model:
 I. Introduction
 II. The problem
 III. Suggested solution
 IV. Objection 1
 V. Objection 2
 VI. Conclusion

Critical Thinking: ANALYZING

M Guide students to critically review their essay's solutions and possible objections one more time. Help students ask themselves whether they have supported their solutions with facts—information that can be verified—rather than with opinions—personal beliefs. If they have used facts, have them examine the facts to make sure they are relevant, timely, and powerful enough to support their conclusions.

SkillBuilder  WRITER'S CRAFT

ELABORATING ON IDEAS To encourage students to use quotations and dialogue, review the rules for punctuating a speaker's exact words. Remind students that dialogue is set off by quotation marks. Any end punctuation that is part of the quote goes inside the punctuation marks. Share the following model with students:

"The solution is not as simple as it sounds," Officer Brown said. "It will take much effort," he continued, "but we can succeed."

Applying What You've Learned Arrange students in pairs. Have partners read each other's papers and underline all elaboration.

Additional Suggestions Have students draw a flowchart to show their problem-solution concepts. Guide students to add details as branches from the main diagram.

Reteaching/Reinforcement
Writing Mini-Lessons transparencies, p. 34

 **The Writer's Craft**
Elaboration, pp. 255–61

Writing Skill: REVISING

N Explain that the strengths and weaknesses of a piece of writing are often easier to recognize if the writer lets some time elapse before revising. Describe how this lets writers look at their work with a fresh eye. If possible, have students set aside their essays for a few hours or a day before revising. Be sure that students use the Standards for Evaluation on page 419 as they revise their papers.

Teaching Strategy: USING THE SKILLBUILDER

O Walk around the room as students revise and edit to see that writers are actually making changes, not just copying the same text to make it appear neater. Also make sure that students are using direct objects correctly. If students need help with direct objects, teach the SkillBuilder on page 419 at this time.

Teaching Strategy: MODELING

P Have a volunteer read the student speech cards to the class. Then discuss with students how the student writer incorporated the peer comments. Students should notice that many more examples of school spirit have been added to the essay.

REVISING AND PUBLISHING

Finishing Your Essay

The Final Steps Now you're ready to take the next step: finalizing your essay. The next two pages will help you through the revision and publishing process. What type of format will you choose to show your readers how strongly you feel about the problem you're presenting?

1 Revise and Edit Your Essay

Here are some suggestions to help you revise and improve your draft:

- Refer to the comments made by your peers to help you make sure your essay gives a clear explanation of the problem and the solution you're proposing.
- Use the Standards for Evaluation and the Editing Checklist to see whether your essay is complete. Is there anything you need to add to your essay?
- Check your conclusion to make sure you have summarized the problem and your solution.
- Look at how one student used examples to complete her draft.

Student's Speech Cards

The problem of low student morale in our school seems to point to a lack of school spirit. In fact, a number of students don't even feel part of the school at all. According to my poll, some kids who aren't involved in sports feel they're not as important as the jocks or the top-of-the-class kids. One solution could be to have more extracurricular activities that everyone can get involved in. That way, all of us will feel like the school is really ours.

Perhaps the paper could sponsor a school spirit contest. Concerned students could form a committee and hand out questionnaires. We could then suggest school clubs that a wider variety of people could get involved in, and we could propose more school-related activities to promote unity. For example, one day we could all wear the school colors or dress like the school mascot. Maybe some students could make a banner for the school's lobby. If students get more involved, maybe more kids would start showing up for games too. The problem of low morale won't be solved until we all feel we have a say in what's going on at school.

How did the student use examples to explain her solution to the problem?

How did the student incorporate the peer comments she received during the drafting stage?

418 UNIT THREE: BATTLE FOR CONTROL

One student used her draft ideas in a speech illustrated by the poster above.

2 Present Your Work

Think about a format that you think will fit your essay. If you want others to feel as strongly as you do about the problem you're discussing, you may choose a public format, such as a speech or a newspaper article.

PUBLISHING IDEAS

- Present your essay as a speech for a rally.
- Create an ad campaign that includes posters like the one above.
- Write an article for the school paper or a letter to your principal.

Standards for Evaluation

An effective problem-solution essay
- gives a clear and concise explanation of the problem and its significance
- presents a workable solution and includes details that explain and support it
- concludes by restating the problem and the solution

SkillBuilder

GRAMMAR FROM WRITING

Using Direct Objects

One way to achieve clarity in an essay is to use direct objects properly. A direct object is a noun or pronoun that follows an action verb. It answers the question *whom* or *what*.

The students formed a committee.

Action Verb	Direct Object
formed	committee

GRAMMAR HANDBOOK

For more information on direct objects in sentences, see pages 876–877 of the Grammar Handbook.

Editing Checklist Ask yourself the following questions:

- Did I include examples to back up my solutions?
- Did I use direct objects correctly?
- Did I proofread my essay?

REFLECT & ASSESS

Evaluating Your Experience

1. How did you come up with the solution to the problem?
2. How could you use your problem-solving skills in other areas of your life?

 PORTFOLIO Add your essay to your portfolio, along with a list of problem-solving tips you found helpful.

WRITING FROM EXPERIENCE 419

Writing Skill: PUBLISHING

 Encourage students to try to publish their essays in the school or community newspaper. If students select this method of publication, they might consider changing the form of their writing from an essay to an editorial or a letter to the editor.

Portfolio

Have students review their portfolios to see which papers they would like to include. If they choose their problem-solution essay, have them include all drafts and any charts or other graphic devices they used.

Standards for Evaluation

Ideas and Content
- Explains problem clearly, and tells why a solution is neccessary
- Presents a workable solution that is explained well
- Supports discussion with quotes, facts, examples, details
- Concludes by restating the problem and the proposed solution, and by providing information necessary for people to take action

Structure and Form
- Uses well-organized paragraphs and a clear organization
- Includes transitional words and phrases to show relationships among ideas
- Uses a variety of sentence structures

Grammar, Usage, and Mechanics
- Contains no more than two or three minor errors in grammar and usage
- Contains no more than two or three minor errors in spelling, capitalization, and punctuation

---

 **GRAMMAR FROM WRITING**

USING DIRECT OBJECTS Tell students that to find the direct object in a sentence, they should ask *what* or *whom* after the verb. The word that answers *what* or *whom* is the direct object. If the sentence does not answer one of these two questions, there is no direct object. Caution students not to confuse direct objects with adverbs that tell *how, where, when,* or *how much*.

Applying What You've Learned Ask students to underline the direct objects (if any) in the following sentences:
1. I set the <u>alarm</u> <u>clock</u> for 7:30.
2. I fed <u>cornflakes</u> to the dog and put <u>dog</u> <u>food</u> in my own bowl!

Reteaching/Reinforcement

Grammar Mini-Lessons copymasters p. 13, transparencies, pp. 10, 38.

The Writer's Craft
Direct Objects, pp. 396–97

UNIT REVIEW

This feature allows students to reflect on what they have learned in Unit Three and to assess how well they understand what they have learned. This feature provides students with multiple opportunities for self-assessment, although you may wish to use some of the activities to informally assess specific skills, such as speaking and listening or cooperative work.

Objectives

- To allow students to reflect on and assess their understanding of theme
- To allow students to reflect on and assess their understanding of literary concepts such as protagonists, antagonists, and mood
- To provide students with the opportunity to assess and build their portfolios

Reflecting on Theme

OPTION 1

Students should skim each selection, paying attention to what each character struggles to achieve. You may wish to have students record their responses in a chart that lists each character in one column and the goals for which he or she is fighting in the other column. Encourage students to organize their thoughts and ideas in a brief outline before they begin to write their journal entries.

OPTION 2

Remind students also to consider in their responses the ways in which characters react to their conflicts. Suggest that they organize their thoughts in charts that detail the similarities and differences between each character's conflict and their own experiences. They can then refer to this information when writing their paragraphs.

OPTION 3

Suggest that students in each group first work alone to generate a list of selections, in order of importance, to include in the book. Then students should share their lists with the rest of their group and work together to come up with a group list. Make sure groups support their choices with detailed explanations.

REFLECT & ASSESS

UNIT THREE: BATTLE FOR CONTROL

The characters in this unit battle for control in a variety of situations. Has reading about their struggles influenced your own thoughts about what is worth fighting for? Have you changed your mind about the extremes to which you would go in a conflict? To explore these questions, complete one or more of the options in each of the following sections.

REFLECTING ON THEME

OPTION 1 **Reading from Within** The characters in this unit would give very different answers to the question "What do you think is worth fighting for?" Jot down how you think the main character of each selection that you have read would respond to the question. Circle the response that most clearly reflects your own opinion, and write a journal entry explaining how you would answer the question.

OPTION 2 **Connecting** In which of this unit's selections do the characters face conflicts that remind you of experiences in your own life? For each case, write a few paragraphs explaining the similarities and differences between the two situations.

OPTION 3 **Making Choices** Get together with a few classmates and imagine that you are putting together a book called *Battle for Control*, intended to teach people how to deal with conflicts. Which of the selections in this unit would you choose to include in the book? Try to agree on a group list of four or five suitable selections, explaining the reasons for your choices.

Self Assessment: Which selections in this unit have had the greatest impact on your own thoughts about dealing with conflict? Which might have the greatest influence on your behavior in the future? List the selection titles in order of the impact the selections have had on you. Next to each, jot down the lesson you have learned from the selection.

REVIEWING LITERARY CONCEPTS

OPTION 1 **Examining Protagonists and Antagonists** After looking through the short stories in this unit, make a chart like the one shown, identifying the protagonist and the antagonist(s) in each story. Assign each protagonist a score, from 1 to 10, to indicate how successfully he or she battles for control, and note the reason for your score.

Story	Protagonist	Antagonist(s)	My Score	Reason
"The Banana Tree"	Gustus	the hurricane Gustus's father	5	Gustus does not stop the hurricane from destroying his tree, but he comes to understand his father better.

420 UNIT THREE: BATTLE FOR CONTROL

Self-Assessment In order to help students answer these questions, encourage them to review the selections in this unit as well as the notes they took while reading them. Have students think about situations in the past that they would handle differently now on the basis of what they have learned from the selections. Suggest that students also consider some of the concrete ways in which the selections will affect their lives in the future.

OPTION 2 Identifying Mood Remember that mood is a feeling or atmosphere that a writer creates for readers. Choose some selections (or parts of selections) that you think have clearly identifiable moods. For each one, jot down the word that best describes the mood. Compare your list of words with a classmate's.

Self-Assessment: Look over the following list of literary terms introduced in this unit. Write a one-sentence definition of each term, then use the Handbook of Reading Terms and Literary Concepts on page 812 to check your definitions.

realistic fiction *oral history*
point of view *foreshadowing*
tone *author's purpose*
extended metaphor *rhyme scheme*

PORTFOLIO BUILDING

- **QuickWrites** The QuickWrites in this unit asked you to write in a variety of forms, including poems, dialogues, diary entries, newspaper articles, and narratives. In which form was your writing most effective? Choose one or two good examples, and write a cover note for each piece, explaining what you like best about it. Then add the pieces and the notes to your portfolio.
- **Writing About Literature** Earlier in this unit, you evaluated the believability of one of the selections. Reread your critical essay, then evaluate it in a sentence or two. Did writing the essay teach you anything that you might bring to future reading?
- **Writing from Experience** Now that you've written a problem-solution essay, do you still feel strongly about the problem? Do you still think that your solution would work? Draft a letter to someone familiar with the problem. Discuss your proposed solution and your thoughts on the matter now. Decide whether to include your letter with your essay.
- **Personal Choice** Look back through your records and evaluations of all the activities you completed in this unit. Also look at activities and writing you have done on your own. In which activity or writing assignment did you resolve a conflict in a way that you were especially pleased about? Write a paragraph explaining what went well, attach it to the work or evaluation, and include both in your portfolio.

Self-Assessment: Organize the work in your portfolio in a way that is not chronological. You could organize your work according to themes, types of activities, or successfulness. Consider the benefits of all of these options, and choose the one that suits you best.

SETTING GOALS

As you completed the reading and writing activities in this unit, you probably discovered topics that interest you—perhaps the history of the Cherokee people or the plight of immigrants to the United States. What kinds of further reading and what kinds of writing tasks might help you find out more about those topics? Record your thoughts in your notebook.

REFLECT & ASSESS **421**

Reviewing Literary Concepts

OPTION 1

Encourage students to skim the stories in order to complete their charts. Make sure students support their scores for each character with details from the selections. You may also wish to have students compare and discuss their charts with other students when they have completed the activity.

OPTION 2

Remind students to pay attention to the writer's descriptions of characters and events to help them determine the mood of each selection. Make sure students are able to adequately support their decisions about the mood of each selection with details from the story.

Self-Assessment For terms that students have difficulty defining, have them apply each term to a selection they have read after checking the definition in the Handbook.

Portfolio Building

You may wish to help students choose options or modify options for them that best suit the needs you have established for the class. Encourage students to incorporate in their portfolios drafts, in addition to final products, so that they can reflect on and assess their development and progress.

Self-Assessment Have students make a list of possible ways to organize their portfolios. Then ask them to choose from their lists and organize their portfolios accordingly. Make sure students consider the strengths and weaknesses of the different ways of organizing their work.

Setting Goals

In order to help students answer these questions and set future goals, have students consider which selections had the greatest impact on them and the ways in which they were affected by them. In addition, have students review their written work to determine the kinds of writing that would best suit their areas of interest. Encourage students to set reasonable goals for the future.

UNIT FOUR

Facing the ENEMY

Kites rise highest against the wind, not with it.

Sir Winston Churchill
Prime minister of Great Britain during World War II

UNIT THEMES

Unit Four
Facing the Enemy In this unit, students will read selections about people who must confront an enemy in one form or another—whether in the guise of another person or a nonhuman force. The unit contains two parts: Part 1, "So Much at Stake," and Part 2, "Unlikely Heroes." Selections in both parts contribute to the unit theme by exploring the great risks some people take when facing an enemy and the ways in which some people unexpectedly rise to face the enemy's challenge.

Part 1
So Much at Stake Selections in Part 1 focus on the dangers that individuals encounter as they face up to their enemies. For example, in the excerpt from *Gifted Hands*, a doctor struggles against death itself as he fights to save the lives of children who are very ill.

Part 2
Unlikely Heroes Selections in Part 2 tell the stories of individuals who meet their enemies head-on with unexpected heroism, such as the little boy who, with his prized marble, staves off an alien invasion of the Earth in "Playing for Keeps."

Links to Unit Six
The Oral Tradition Unit Six contains literature from the oral tradition that connects with the themes in Unit Four. You may wish to begin or end Unit Four by using the following selections from Unit Six that relate to the theme "Facing the Enemy":
- "Racing the Great Bear," p. 762
- "Otoonah," p. 769
- "The Woman in the Snow," p. 775

Greed (1982), Carlos Almaraz. Oil on canvas, 34" × 44". Copyright © 1982 Carlos Almaraz. Courtesy of the Almaraz Estate.

Exploring Theme

To help students explore the connections between the art, the quotation, and the unit theme, have them consider the following questions:

1. What kinds of enemies do you think people face in their lives? *(Possible response: People sometimes face other people who are trying to hurt or harm them, but an enemy doesn't have to be human. A natural event, such as a drought, also can be an enemy.)*

2. According to the remark by Sir Winston Churchill, what is a positive effect of confronting an enemy? *(Possible response: A kite fighting against the wind is like someone struggling against an enemy. Only by fighting the wind can the kite rise higher and higher. Similarly, by confronting our enemies and our problems, we can become stronger, more determined people.)*

3. How well do you think the painting captures the theme of facing the enemy? *(Possible response: The painting is a good example of the theme because the central image is two dogs that are prepared to fight a ferocious battle over a bone. The way the dogs are drawn, with their teeth bared and their hair raised, shows that they consider each other to be a dangerous enemy.)*

4. What kinds of stories do you think you will read in this unit? *(Possible response: The stories will be about the different kinds of enemies that people face in their lives. The stories also may show how different people choose to deal with their enemies and may describe the outcomes of the struggles.)*

5. Discuss a personal experience in which you had to face someone or something you considered an enemy. What did you learn about yourself and about your enemy from the experience? *(Responses will vary.)*

Art Note

Greed by Carlos Almaraz The Mexican-American artist Carlos Almaraz, who was born in 1941, began his formal art training as a high school student in the East Los Angeles barrio. Later in life, Almaraz returned to Los Angeles, where he immersed himself in the Chicano movement as a painter who cared deeply about color and figure drawing.

Reading the Art *How do you think Almaraz's use of color and line relate to the subject matter of the painting?*

THE LANGUAGE OF LITERATURE TEACHER'S EDITION

UNIT FOUR
Part 1 Skills Trace

 DENOTES MINI-LESSON IN TEACHER'S EDITION

Selections	Reading Skills and Strategies	Literary Concepts	Writing Opportunities	Speaking, Listening, and Viewing
FICTION **The Gift of the Magi** O. Henry	In-depth reading, PE p. 425 Clarifying, ML TE p. 428	Classics, PE p. 432 Allusion, ML TE p. 430	Interior monologue, PE p. 432 Paragraph, PE p. 432 List, PE p. 432	Love song, PE p. 433
POETRY **Speech to the Young/Speech to the Progress-Toward** Gwendolyn Brooks **A Man** Nina Cassian		Alliteration, PE p. 437 Repetition, ML TE p. 435	Brief account of an experience, PE p. 434 Speech, PE p. 437 Quotation, PE p. 437	Choreograph a dance, PE p. 438 Poetry reading on audiotape, PE p. 438 Choral reading, ML TE p. 436
NONFICTION **from Lincoln: A Photobiography** Russell Freedman	Using context clues, ML TE p. 441	Biography, PE p. 448 Extended metaphor, ML TE p. 446	Poem with metaphors, PE p. 448 Letter, PE p. 448 Character sketch, PE p. 448 Poem, PE p. 448 Proposal, PE p. 449	Group discussion, TE p. 442 Scoring a poem with music, ML TE p. 447
NONFICTION **from Gifted Hands** Ben Carson, M.D., with Cecil Murphey	Specialized vocabulary, PE p. 450 Evaluating, ML TE p. 454	Autobiography, PE p. 457 Author's purpose, PE p. 457 Description, ML TE p. 453	List of contributions, PE p. 457 Letter to the editor, PE p. 457 Diary entry, PE p. 457	Sneak preview, PE p. 458
DRAMA **Survival** Alfred Brenner	Reading a teleplay, PE p. 459 Visualizing, ML TE p. 471 Distinguishing fact from opinion, ML TE p. 475	Minor characters, PE p. 481 Plot, ML TE p. 466	Newspaper review, PE p. 480 Comparison and contrast essay, PE p. 480 Alternative ending, PE p. 480 Paragraph, PE p. 480	Dramatic performance, PE p. 481 Paired discussion, PE p. 481 Oral summary, ML TE p. 472 Delivering a summation, ML TE p. 479
NONFICTION ON YOUR OWN **Battle by the Breadfruit Tree** Theodore Waldeck				Paired and public reading, TE p. 483

Writing	Reading Skills and Strategies	Literary Concepts	Writing Opportunities	Speaking, Listening, and Viewing
WRITING ABOUT LITERATURE **Direct Response**	Analyzing descriptive language, PE pp. 490–91 Responding to literature, PE pp. 492–95	Analyzing descriptive language, PE pp. 490–91	Use descriptive language, PE p. 491 Write stage directions, PE p. 491 Write a self-description, PE p. 491 Personal response essay, PE pp. 492–95	Viewing a photograph, PE p. 496 Interpreting a photograph, PE p. 496 Discussion, PE p. 496 Observing people, PE p. 497

Grammar, Usage, Mechanics, and Spelling	Multimodal Learning	Research and Study Skills	Vocabulary
Hard and soft c and g, ML TE p. 427 Show, don't tell, ML TE p. 429 Commas with interrupters, ML TE p. 431	Collage, PE p. 432 Love song, PE p. 433 Drawing, painting, or sculpture, PE p. 433		agile inconsequential assertion instigate cascade predominating chronicle prudence coveted subside
	Illustration, PE p. 437 Choreograph a dance, PE p. 438 Poetry reading on audiotape, PE p. 438 Choral reading, ML TE p. 436		
Chronological order, ML TE p. 443 Irregular verbs, ML TE p. 444 Prefixes and roots, ML TE p. 445	Group discussion, ML TE p. 442 Scoring a poem with music, ML TE p. 447	Research the presidential chain of command, PE p. 449	abduction assailant conspiracy revoke vindictiveness
Complex sentences, ML TE p. 452 Suffixes following c and g, ML TE p. 455 Elaboration using examples, ML TE p. 456	Sneak preview, PE p. 458	Research current brain research, PE p. 458	autopsy inevitable dilated malignant dismal radical distraught skepticism galvanize vivacious
The assimilated prefix ad-, ML TE p. 463 Stage directions, ML TE p. 465 Compound subjects, ML TE p. 477	Dramatic performance, PE p. 481 Paired discussion, PE p. 481 Painting, PE p. 481 Diorama, PE p. 481 Oral summary, ML TE p. 472 Delivering a summation, ML TE p. 479	Research 19th-century life on the sea, PE p. 481	apprehend dingy bristle maritime concede morality conjecture ply corroborate testimony
	Creating a group dance, TE p. 486 Creating a landscape painting, TE p. 488		

Grammar, Usage, Mechanics, and Spelling	Multimodal Learning	Research and Study Skills	Media Literacy
Using descriptive language, PE p. 491 Achieving sentence variety, PE p. 493 Using indefinite pronouns, PE p. 495 Pronoun-antecedent agreement, PE p. 495	Viewing a photograph, PE p. 496 Interpreting a photograph, PE p. 496 Discussion, PE p. 496 Observing people, PE p. 497	Charting ideas, PE p. 492	Interpreting a photograph, PE pp. 496–97

UNIT FOUR
Part 2 Skills Trace

 DENOTES MINI-LESSON IN TEACHER'S EDITION

Selections	Reading Skills and Strategies	Literary Concepts	Writing Opportunities	Speaking, Listening, and Viewing
FICTION **Playing for Keeps** Jack C. Haldeman II	Comparing and contrasting, ML TE p. 502	Science fiction, PE p. 505 Humor, PE p. 505 Idioms, ML TE p. 501 Science fiction, ML TE p. 504	Brief account of space invasion, PE p. 499 E-mail note, PE p. 505 Epilogue, PE p. 505 Alternative ending, PE p. 505 Dramatic script, PE p. 506	Group discussion, PE p. 505 Readers theater production, PE p. 506 Viewing westerns, ML TE p. 503
FICTION **The Dinner Party** Mona Gardner	Stereotypes, PE p. 507 Visualizing, ML TE p. 509	Suspense, PE p. 510	Chart, PE p. 510 Interior monologue, PE p. 510 Dialogue, PE p. 510	Group discussion, PE p. 510
FICTION **Flowers for Algernon** Daniel Keyes	Inferences, PE p. 513 Clarifying, ML TE p. 514	Character changes, PE p. 540 Characterization, ML TE p. 517	Progress report, PE p. 539 Letter of recommendation, PE p. 539 Rewrite progress report, PE p. 539 Research paper, PE p. 540 Medical abstract, PE p. 540 Paragraph, ML TE p. 529	Debate, PE p. 539 Group discussion, PE p. 540 Oral report, PE p. 540 Group discussions, ML TE p. 521 Viewing *Bill*, ML TE p. 527 Speeches, ML TE p. 531 Role-play, ML TE p. 538
POETRY **Paul Revere's Ride** Henry Wadsworth Longfellow	Summarizing, PE p. 542 Summarizing, ML TE p. 544	Narrative poem, PE p. 548 Second-person point of view, ML TE p. 546 Imagery, ML TE p. 545	Narrative poem, PE p. 548 News article, PE p. 548 Ballad, PE p. 549	Dramatic reading, PE p. 549 Ballad performance, PE p. 549 Group discussions, ML TE p. 547
NONFICTION **from Harriet Tubman: Conductor on the Underground Railroad** Ann Petry	Motivation, PE p. 550 Relating cause and effect, ML TE p. 552	Biography, PE p. 560 Minor characters, ML TE p. 553	Diary entry, PE p. 560 Description, PE p. 560 Letter, PE p. 560 Storymap, ML TE p. 559	

Writing	Reading Skills and Strategies	Literary Concepts	Writing Opportunities	Speaking, Listening, and Viewing
WRITING FROM EXPERIENCE **Informative Exposition**		Details, PE p. 567 Dialogue, PE p. 567	Writing an eyewitness report, PE pp. 562–69 Drafting, PE pp. 566–67 Revising and publishing, PE pp. 568–69	Taking notes on a conversation, PE p. 565 Group discussion, ML TE p. 564

Grammar, Usage, Mechanics, and Spelling	Multimodal Learning	Research and Study Skills	Vocabulary	
	Group discussion, PE p. 505 Readers theater production, PE p. 506 Solar system model, PE p. 506 Viewing westerns, ML TE p. 503	Research the solar system, PE p. 506	congenial flourish gloat immerse oblivious	
	Group discussion, PE p. 510	Research cobras, PE p. 511	naturalist	
Final e words and suffixes, ML TE p. 523 Sentence variety, ML TE p. 524 Formal English, ML TE p. 532 Run-on sentences, ML TE p. 534	Debate, PE p. 539 Group discussion, PE p. 540 Oral report, PE p. 540 Drawing of the brain, PE p. 540 Group discussions, ML TE p. 521 Viewing *Bill,* ML TE p. 527 Speeches, ML TE p. 531 Role-play, ML TE p. 538	Research functions of the brain, PE p. 540 Research medical abstracts, PE p. 540 Researching information outside of libraries, ML TE p. 537	absurd hypothesis impair introspective naïveté opportunist proportional regression	sensation shrew specialization statistically syndrome tangible vacuous
	Cartoons, PE p. 548 Dramatic reading, PE p. 549 Ballad performance, PE p. 549 Group discussions, ML TE p. 547	Research Revere's ride, PE p. 549		
Gerunds and participles, ML TE p. 554 Words ending in *-able* and *-ible,* ML TE p. 555 Parallelism, ML TE p. 556	Sketch, PE p. 560 Calculation of distance traveled, PE p. 561	Research slave memoirs, PE p. 561 Research routes between Maryland and Ontario, PE p. 561 Graphic organizers, ML TE p. 558	borne cajoling disheveled dispel eloquence	fastidious indomitable instill mutinous sullen

Grammar, Usage, Mechanics, and Spelling	Multimodal Learning	Research and Study Skills	Media Literacy
Sentence combining, PE p. 569		Taking notes on a conversation, PE p. 565 Using an observation chart, PE p. 565	

UNIT FOUR
Recommended Resources

ENRICHMENT RESEARCH

Recommended Novels and Nonfiction

LITERATURE CONNECTIONS WITH SOURCEBOOK FOR TEACHERS

Across Five Aprils
by Irene Hunt

Thematic Links During the Civil War, a young farm boy must step forward and take responsibility when the rest of his family members are split over the war and choose to face varying enemies.
About the Author Irene Hunt (born 1907) grew up in southern Illinois and listened to her grandfather's stories of the Civil War, which she turned into award-winning historical novels for young people.
Other Works by Irene Hunt *The Lottery Rose, No Promises in the Wind, Up a Road Slowly*

LITERATURE CONNECTIONS WITH SOURCEBOOK FOR TEACHERS

Johnny Tremain
by Esther Forbes

Thematic Links In the days before the Revolutionary War, Johnny Tremain has to make a critical adjustment when an injury prevents him from working in his chosen profession.
About the Author Esther Forbes (1891–1967) was a biographer and novelist whose work reflected her fascination with American history and specifically the Revolutionary era.
Other Works by Esther Forbes *A Mirror for Witches, Miss Marrel, Paradise, Paul Revere and the World He Lived In*

Phoenix Rising
by Karen Hesse

Thematic Links A nuclear accident drastically changes the lives of the hero and heroine.
About the Author Karen Hesse (born 1952) was an avid reader as a child and aims her stories at the kind of child she once was. She says she wants to show her readers characters that grow as a result of their problems.
Other Works by Karen Hesse *Wish on a Unicorn, Letters from Rifka*

The Bellmaker
by Brian Jacques

Thematic Links In this fantasy tale, characters face unexpected mishaps and adventures.
About the Author Brian Jacques (born 1939) wrote his first novel as a story for children at a school for the blind. He likes to set stories in the past because it offers better opportunities for romance and adventure.
Other Works by Brian Jacques *Mariel of Redwall, Mossflower, Mattimeo*

Indian Chiefs
by Russell Freedman

Thematic Links Freedman's book portrays six Native American chiefs—Red Cloud, Santana, Quanoh Parker, Washakie, Joseph, and Sitting Bull—and details their encounters with pioneers. Illustrated with historical photographs.
About the Author Newbery Award winning author Russell Freedman (born 1929) writes nonfiction books for young people.
Other Works by Russell Freedman *Teenagers Who Made History, The Wright Brothers: How They Invented the Airplane, Eleanor Roosevelt: A Life of Discovery*

The Young Unicorns
by Madeleine L'Engle

Thematic Links An ex-gang member and a blind musician must face a young gang threatening to kill them. Set in New York City.
About the Author Madeleine L'Engle (born 1918) is best known for her books about young people. She writes about characters who must face serious conflicts and learn to find viable solutions.
Other Works by Madeleine L'Engle *A Wrinkle in Time, A Wind in the Door, A Swiftly Tilting Planet, Many Waters, The Arm of the Starfish, A Ring of Endless Night*

For Teacher **TEACHING LITERATURE**

Farmer, Lesley S.J. *Creative Partnerships: Librarians and Teachers Working Together.* Worthington: Linworth, 1993.

Hook, Peggy. "Pick Your Own Paperbacks." *School Library Journal* (November 1995).

Smith, J. Lea. "Drama in the Middle Level Classroom: Bringing Content to Life." *Middle School Journal* (May 1995).

White, Brian. "Preparing Middle School Students to Respond to Literature (Using Autobiographical Writing Before Reading)." *Middle School Journal* 24 (September 1992) 21–23.

423e UNIT FOUR FACING THE ENEMY

CROSS-CURRICULAR TEACHING   PROFESSIONAL DEVELOPMENT

Recommended Readings in Cross-Curricular Areas

HISTORY/SOCIAL STUDIES

Lincoln
by Peter Hunhardt (1992)
This recent biography combines both lively text and mesmerizing photographs. Links to Russell Freedman's *Lincoln: A Photobiography*.

The American Revolutionaries: A History in Their Own Words, 1750–1800
edited by Milton Meltzer (1987)
Excerpts from letters, diaries, and other autobiographical accounts recount the Revolutionary War. Links to "Paul Revere's Ride."

All Times, All Peoples: A World History of Slavery
by Milton Meltzer (1980)
This book chronicles the history of slavery. Links to *Lincoln: A Photobiography* and Anne Petry's *Harriet Tubman: Conductor on the Underground Railroad*.

SCIENCE

Medical Dilemmas
by Margaret O. Hyde and Elizabeth H. Forsyth (1990)
Explores ethical issues, such as experimentation on humans and a patient's right to privacy. Links to *Gifted Hands* and "Flowers for Algernon."

For Teacher — CROSS-CURRICULAR INSTRUCTION

Burnford, Gail. "Teacher-Action Research Inside an Integrated Curriculum." *Middle School Journal* (November 1994).

Hough, David L. "Achieving Independent Student Responses Through Integrated Instruction (Strategies for Middle School Students)." *Middle School Journal* 25 (May 1994): 35–42.

Meltzer, Milton. *Nonfiction for the Classroom*. Newark, DE: International Reading Association, 1994.

Recommended Media Resources

THE LANGUAGE OF LITERATURE

LASERLINKS
Videodisc, Gr. 8
See *LaserLinks Teacher's Source Book*, pages 36–37, for an overview of Unit Four.

AUDIO LIBRARY
Tapes
Unit Four: Facing the Enemy
Gr. 8, Tape 11: Sides A & B
Gr. 8, Tape 12: Sides A & B

WRITING COACH
Writing Coach Software: Writing About Literature: Direct Response; Interpretive Response

OUTSIDE RESOURCES

Films/Videos/Film Strips/Audiocassettes
Filmstrips About Great Novels: Flowers for Algernon. filmstrip. Listening Library.
Race to Freedom: The Story of the Underground Railroad. videocassette. Xenon Home Video, 1993.
The Civil War. 9 videocassettes. Produced by Ken and Ric Burns in association with WETA-TV, PBS Video, 1989. (70 min. each)

Internet Resources
World Wide Web at
http://www.hmco.com/mcdougal

For Teacher — TEACHING WITH TECHNOLOGY

Dyrli, Odvard Egil. "Integrating Technology into Your Classroom Curriculum." *Technology and Learning* 14 (February 1994): 38–44.

John, Nancy. *The Internet Troubleshooter: Help for the Logged on and Lost.* Chicago, IL: The American Library Association, 1994.

Means, Barbara, et al. *Using Technology to Support Education Reform.* Newton, MA: Education Development Center, Inc., Menlo Park, CA: SRI International, 1993.

Media and Methods. 1429 Walnut St., Philadelphia, PA 19102.

Messages and Meaning: A Media Curriculum Guide. Newark, DE: International Reading Association, 1995.

Wresch, William, ed. *Computer in Composition Instruction.* Urbana, IL: National Council Teachers of English, 1984.

UNIT FOUR
Professional Enrichment

Teleport into Teleplays!

Reading and writing a teleplay allows students to tap different strengths and intelligences—spatial, logical-mathematical, musical, bodily-kinesthetic, interpersonal, and intrapersonal, as well as linguistic.

Besides, teleplays are a lot of fun! Try the following guidelines to help students discover more about literature and themselves through teleplays.

LEARNING THE LINGO!
Teleplay writers consider visual images their principal means of communication. Words function to complement and clarify the images on the screen, not the other way around. You can help your students get the most from creating teleplays by first explaining how a teleplay is constructed. Share the following terms and explanations:
- **Shot list** A *shot list* is a roster of the major scenes that are going to be "shot," or photographed. Quick and simple to prepare, a shot list records all the scenes the director wants to include in the teleplay.
- **Storyboards** A *storyboard* is a visual way of planning the scene. Compare it to the graphic organizers that students use to brainstorm writing ideas. Explore with the class how storyboards enable teleplay writers to think in more detail about what they will include in each scene. Students may be interested in learning that Walt Disney (1901–1966) was the first illustrator to use storyboards to plan cartoons.
- **Scripts** A *script* is a written plan for a teleplay. Scripts can be written in many different ways. For example, some scripts are arranged in columns, with the directions for the crew on the left and the dialogue and stage directions on the right. Scripts for commercials often include storyboards.

WRITING A TELEPLAY
- Encourage students to use realistic dialogue and stage directions to help the performers interpret the characters and actions.
- Have students prepare careful scripts, marking key points with easy-to-understand words and phrases.

EXPRESSING CHARACTERIZATION
Explain that teleplay performers need to combine voice and action to bring the roles they are portraying to life. One of the basic ways they do this is through *characterization*—the process whereby the performer internalizes the character's personality and communicates it to the audience. Characterization is at the heart of performing a teleplay. Discuss these methods of characterization with the performers in your classroom:
- Explain the importance of studying the teleplay in depth so performers understand the plot as well as the emotional and intellectual messages.
- Allow students time to research the teleplay's setting, the time and place of the action.
- Be sure that students remember that characterization is most successful when the performer is able to communicate the character's essence through voice, mannerisms, and physical movement.
- Help students consciously select the mannerisms and physical movements that best reveal the character.
- Remind students to stay in character once a rehearsal or performance has begun. Students must project the character's actions and feelings and not their own.

MEMORIZING THE LINES
"There's no way I can remember all those lines!" your students complain. Reassure them with these helpful hints for memorization:
- Tell students to focus on the material. Have them turn off the TV, radio, and stereo as they memorize.
- Be sure that students understand what they are memorizing. Explain that recalling something you know is easier than recalling something confusing.
- Memorize the entire sequence of thought, not individual words. Learn groups of closely related thoughts.
- Let students know that they will need the most time in the beginning, when the material is unfamiliar. The memorization process gets easier as time goes on. Remind students to review the material often to keep it fresh in their minds.

Related Reading

 Blacker, Irwin R. *The Elements of Screenwriting: A Guide for Film and Television Writers.* New York: Macmillan, 1987.

 Hamlett, Christina. *Humorous Plays for Teen-Agers.* Boston, MA: Plays, 1987.

 Seto, Judith Roberts. *The Young Actor's Workbook.* New York: Grove/Weidenfeld, 1988.

Family and Community Involvement

Family

From the story of a young, poor couple who make personal sacrifices for each other to an account of Harriet Tubman's central role in the Underground Railroad, all of the selections in Unit Four connect to the theme of facing the enemy.

The following Copymasters for Unit Four provide activities related to this theme that students can take home and complete with a parent or other family member.

OPTION 1: DISCUSS THE KINDS OF ENEMIES PEOPLE FACE

- **Connection** All of the selections in Unit Four connect to facing the enemy.
- **Activity** *Copymaster, p. 1* Students and family members discuss some of the kinds of enemies that people face in their lives as well as some of the ways in which people confront these enemies. A chart is provided to help organize their responses.

OPTION 2: DRAW A PICTURE OF YOUR HERO

- **Connection** Many of the selections in Unit Four deal with characters who act heroically.
- **Activity** *Copymaster, p. 2* Students work with family members to select a personal hero and draw a picture that captures the heroic qualities of this person. A word web is provided to organize their thoughts and ideas.

OPTION 3: WRITE A POEM ABOUT AN ENEMY YOU FACED

- **Connection** All of the selections in Unit Four connect to the theme of facing the enemy.
- **Activity** *Copymaster, p. 3* Students work with family members to write a poem that explores their feelings about facing an enemy. A word web is provided to help organize their thoughts and ideas.

 Community

OPTION 1

- **Connection** In "The Dinner Party" a group of dinner guests is threatened by a deadly cobra.
- **Activity** Have students visit a zoo to observe and learn more about cobras and other snakes.

OPTION 2

- **Connection** The excerpt from *Gifted Hands* details the difficulties faced by a heroic surgeon as he struggles to save the lives of terminally ill children.
- **Activity** Invite a pediatric surgeon to the class to discuss his or her work.

OPTION 3

- **Connection** In *Flowers for Algernon* the main character is a 37-year-old mentally handicapped man who undergoes a surgical procedure to increase his intelligence.
- **Activity** Invite a doctor to class to speak to students about intelligence research.

OPTION 4

- **Connection** The excerpt from *Harriet Tubman: Conductor on the Underground Railroad* details one young woman's courage and determination.
- **Activity** Invite a historian to the class to speak to students about the Underground Railroad.
- **Alternative Activity** Encourage students to visit their local public library to find books about the Underground Railroad.

UNIT FOUR
Part 1 Cooperative Project

A High-Stakes Game

Overview

Students will design and implement a competitive game where the losers will be penalized in some form.

PROJECT AT A GLANCE

The selections in Unit Four, Part 1 concern people who are facing an enemy of some sort in a situation where the stakes are high. The stakes vary from personal pride to possible death, but all are of utmost importance to those involved. For this project, students will design and implement a game along the lines of the television game show *Jeopardy*. They will research and make up questions, design a point system, and decide a penalty for the losing team. The culmination of the project will be an actual game played among the student groups.

OBJECTIVES

- To recognize situations where the stakes are high
- To design a game that includes a high-stakes penalty for the losing team
- To play the game with other groups of students

SUGGESTED GROUP SIZE

4–5 students

MATERIALS

- Various reference books (dictionaries, almanacs, atlases, encyclopedias, and so on)
- Several textbooks for eighth grade or lower
- A tape and/or board-game of the television game show *Jeopardy* (optional)
- Index cards for questions
- Medium-size box

Getting Started

Arranging the Project
Gather several reference books for the project. Of special use will be textbooks other than those students are currently using that are at the same grade level or lower. Students can also use dictionaries, encyclopedias, and other reference books in the school library.

Videotape—or ask a student to tape—an episode of the television game show *Jeopardy*. You can use this later to give students an idea for a game format.

Arranging for Game Playing
Look over the options for this project. Two of them require you to make arrangements with your school administration and, possibly, with that of another school. You also may need to schedule a time and place for the game to be held, depending on the option you choose. If you choose an interschool game, you will have to deal with the transportation needs of the students. Consider who would be a good judge for the game and sign him or her up now, even if you plan to have this project culminate in a classroom game.

Creating the Games

Introducing the Project
Explain that students will be working in small groups to create a new game. The game should be played by two teams of students at a time. Groups will design a point system that is fair. Not only should the game offer some reward for the members of the winning team, it should also offer a penalty for the members of the losing team. Students will research and make up questions for the game. All questions will be put into a box and will be drawn randomly during play. You will be the moderator, and another adult will serve as judge to settle any disputes that arise.

Show students the tape of the *Jeopardy* program. Ask that they notice the scoring system and how it provides rewards (adding to the score) and penalties (subtracting from the score). You may certainly fast-forward through the commercials, chitchat, and much of the play to review only pertinent portions.

Group Investigations
Divide students into groups of four or five. Group members will brainstorm to invent a game that can be played by two teams. They will create a scoring system for the game that is fair to all. The game must offer a reward for winning and a penalty for losing. This may be an integral part of play (as on *Jeopardy*) or bestowed after the final winners and losers are determined. Then students may research and write questions. Questions and their answers should be written on index cards and placed in the box. Meet with each group to monitor progress.

Creating a Project Description
When students have formulated their game and scoring system, they should write a complete description of the game. These descriptions can be reviewed by the entire class, who will vote on which game gets to be played. Students may also choose to take portions of several games and make one new class game. Remind them that the questions should be based on academic subjects.

OPTION 1: INTERSCHOOL GAME Students may challenge another eighth-grade class from a different school to a game. If the reward and penalty are not built in to the game, be sure they are something that could be tolerated by both schools. Perhaps the losers can go to a winners' football game and have to cheer for that team.

OPTION 2: INTRASCHOOL GAME Students can challenge another eighth-grade class in your school. You can coordinate the project with the other teacher and allow both classes to contribute to the final game design and pool of questions.

OPTION 3: QUESTION OF THE DAY At the end of every class period, student groups select one question from the box and write an answer before leaving the room. You can collect the cards and check the answers, keeping the groups' scores all the while. At the end of a designated time (two to three weeks), you can announce the winners. (Be sure you ask students *not* to write the answers on the cards if you intend to use this option.)

Depending on how you shape the project, you should specify the number of questions groups are expected to make up. Too many will be better than too few. You might also want to read all the questions to weed out duplications and to make sure they are all legitimate academic questions.

3 Sharing the Game

You might put a little spark in a classroom game by inviting the principal or other teachers to attend. If you have opted for an interschool game, consider holding it at a time when families as well as other teachers can come and cheer on their teams.

As a culminating activity, ask the entire class to reflect on the project and tell what they might do differently next time.

Assessing the Project

The following rubric can be used for group or individual assessment.

3 Full Accomplishment Students follow directions and produce a game that gives winners a reward and penalizes losers.

2 Substantial Accomplishment Students' game is complete but not well-thought-out, or the rewards and penalties are unclear.

1 Little or Partial Accomplishment Students' game is incomplete or does not fulfill the requirements of the assignment.

For the Portfolio
Include a copy of the group's game description in each student's portfolio, as well as a copy of your written assessment of their project. You should keep a copy of the final class game plan for future reference.

Note: For other assessment options, see the *Teacher's Guide to Assessment and Portfolio Use.*

Cross-Curricular Options

MATH

Students can devise a scoring system that will allow anyone to win up until the last moment. You can refer them again to the *Jeopardy* scoring system, where no contestant is really "out of the running" until the last question.

PHYSICAL EDUCATION
Students can design a general athletic contest that involves simple physical contests (running, jumping, throwing a ball) and a scoring system that involves ranking each contestant.

Resources

General reference books such as the latest edition of *The World Almanac* or *Information Please Almanac* provide brief facts that can be used to write questions or check answers.

Puzzle Pursuit by Vera F. Leider provides a collection of challenging word and number puzzles.

Puzzles from Other Worlds by Martin Gardner provides mathematical puzzles from around the world.

COOPERATIVE PROJECT TEACHER'S EDITION **423j**

UNIT FOUR
Part 1 Lesson Planner

TIME ALLOTMENTS SHOWN ARE APPROXIMATE. DEPENDING ON YOUR GOALS AND THE NEEDS OF YOUR STUDENTS, YOU MAY WISH TO ALLOW MORE OR LESS TIME FOR CERTAIN PORTIONS OF THE LESSON.

Table of Contents	Discussion	Previewing the Selection	Reading the Selection
PART OPENER SO MUCH AT STAKE What Do You Think? page 424	**20 MINUTES** • Reflect on the part theme		
SELECTION The Gift of the Magi page 426 CHALLENGING		**20 MINUTES** • PERSONAL CONNECTION • HISTORICAL CONNECTION • READING CONNECTION: In-depth reading	**30 MINUTES** • Introduce vocabulary • Read pp. 426–431 (6 pp.)
SELECTION Speech to the Young/ Speech to the Progress Toward A Man page 435 AVERAGE		**20 MINUTES** • PERSONAL CONNECTION • LITERARY CONNECTION • WRITING CONNECTION	**15 MINUTES** • Read pp. 435–436 (2 pp.)
SELECTION from Lincoln: A Photobiography page 440 AVERAGE		**20 MINUTES** • PERSONAL CONNECTION • HISTORICAL CONNECTION • WRITING CONNECTION	**30 MINUTES** • Introduce vocabulary • Read pp. 440–447 (8 pp.)
SELECTION from Gifted Hands page 451 AVERAGE		**20 MINUTES** • PERSONAL CONNECTION • SCIENCE CONNECTION • READING CONNECTION: Specialized vocabulary	**30 MINUTES** • Introduce vocabulary • Read pp. 451–456 (6 pp.)
SELECTION Survival page 460 AVERAGE		**20 MINUTES** • PERSONAL CONNECTION • SOCIAL STUDIES CONNECTION • READING CONNECTION: Reading a teleplay	**45 MINUTES** • Introduce vocabulary • Read pp. 460–479 (20 pp.)
NONFICTION ON YOUR OWN Battle by the Breadfruit Tree page 483 AVERAGE			**25 MINUTES** • Read pp. 483–489 (7 pp.)
Writing WRITING ABOUT LITERATURE Direct Response	**Writer's Style** **20 MINUTES**	**Prewriting** **20 MINUTES**	**Drafting and Revising** **80 MINUTES**

* Time estimates assume in-class work. You may wish to assign some of these stages as homework.

Responding to the Selection

FROM PERSONAL RESPONSE TO CRITICAL ANALYSIS	OR	ANOTHER PATHWAY	LITERARY CONCEPTS	QUICKWRITES
50 MINUTES				
• Discussion questions	OR	• Collage	• Classics	• Interior monologue • Paragraph • List
35 MINUTES				
• Discussion questions	OR	• Illustration & slogan	• Alliteration	• Speech • Quotation
45 MINUTES				
• Discussion questions	OR	• Poem with metaphors	• Biography	• Letter • Character sketch • Poem
40 MINUTES				
• Discussion questions	OR	• List	• Autobiography • Author's purpose	• Letter to the editor • Diary entry
45 MINUTES				
• Discussion questions	OR	• Review	• Minor characters	• Essay • Alternative ending • Paragraph

Extension Activities

	ALTERNATIVE ACTIVITIES	LITERARY LINKS	CRITIC'S CORNER	THE WRITER'S STYLE	ACROSS THE CURRICULUM	ART CONNECTION	WORDS TO KNOW	BIOGRAPHY
40 MINUTES	✓		✓				✓	✓
45 MINUTES	✓				✓			✓
40 MINUTES	✓				SOCIAL STUDIES		✓	✓
40 MINUTES	✓				SCIENCE		✓	✓
60 MINUTES	✓	✓			SCIENCE / HISTORY		✓	✓
								✓

Publishing and Reflecting
30 MINUTES

Grammar in Context
10 MINUTES

Reading the World
35 MINUTES

PART 1

WHAT DO YOU THINK?
Objectives

The activities on this page can be used to
- introduce the Part 1 theme of "So Much at Stake" since each activity is connected to one or more selections
- create materials for students' personal portfolios that they can return to later for reconsideration or revision
- build an understanding of theme that can be returned to and revised as students progress through the unit

How can you help?
Encourage students to list the day-to-day hardships facing people in poverty in order to make practical suggestions. You may wish to have them briefly read recent newspapers to get a sense of their local government's policies and plans to combat poverty. (See "The Gift of the Magi," p. 425.)

Whom would you choose?
Tell students that they can base their tributes on someone they know, a historical figure, or a fictional character. Encourage students to read their tributes to the class when they have completed the activity. (See the excerpt from *Lincoln: A Photobiography*, p. 439.)

What is at stake?
Have students list aspects which demonstrate the high stakes involved in their chosen professions. Students can then refer to this information when creating their illustrations. (See the excerpt from *Gifted Hands*, p. 450.)

What is most important?
After students have surveyed classmates, they can think about the best way to display the results. You may also wish to have the class work together to generate more qualities to add to the list. (See *Survival*, p. 459, and "Speech to the Young" and "A Man," p. 434.)

UNIT FOUR PART 1

So Much At Stake

WHAT DO YOU THINK?

REFLECTING ON THEME

Have you ever faced up to an enemy? Maybe it wasn't a person, but some impersonal force, such as poverty or disease. In such a conflict, anything can be at stake—from your pride to your very survival. Use the activities on this page to explore what is at stake when people face different kinds of enemies.

How can you help?
Many people must confront poverty in their lives. How should we tackle this "enemy" in society? Working with two other students, create a list of practical suggestions for helping people in the community who do not have adequate food or shelter. Present your ideas in a booklet.

Whom would you choose?
Write a tribute praising someone who bravely faced an enemy such as illness, poverty, or injustice. Describe how the person's attitude or actions were an inspiration to others. What was at stake for him or her?

What is most important?
A person needs certain qualities to be able to face up to his or her enemies. Using the list provided, survey your classmates to find out the qualities they feel are most important. Have them grade the qualities on a scale of 1 to 10, with 10 being the most important. Report your findings in the form of a chart or a graph.

Important Qualities	
caution	generosity
strength	helpfulness
honesty	reliability
intelligence	determination

What is at stake?

In some jobs people must make vital decisions—decisions that sometimes are a matter of life or death. Pick a profession that you admire, in which the stakes are high. Draw a picture illustrating the profession. Show why the stakes are so high, and why you admire the profession.

424

COMMUNITY OUTREACH
As an extension to the "How can you help?" activity on this page, you may wish to have local advocates for the poor and homeless come to speak in your class. Students can work in small groups to generate a list of questions regarding the adequacy of their local government's plans in dealing with this issue as well as alternative ways of helping these communities. Afterward encourage students to find more information about volunteering at local organizations that assist the poor and homeless.

PARENTAL INVOLVEMENT
Invite students to work with a parent or relative to write a newspaper article about an experience facing some sort of conflict. Students can first interview the parent or relative about their experiences facing up to an "enemy" and then write a short article with a catchy headline that one might find in a newspaper. Students may wish to read some newspaper articles to get a sense of form and style. Encourage volunteers to read aloud or display their articles.

PREVIEWING

FICTION

The Gift of the Magi
O. Henry

Activating Prior Knowledge
PERSONAL CONNECTION

Suppose you want to give a special gift to a person you love, but the gift is much more expensive than you can afford. How might you handle the situation? Record your thoughts in an idea map like the one shown here. Then share your ideas with the class.

Special Gift Ideas

Building Background
HISTORICAL CONNECTION

In this story, O. Henry makes an allusion, or reference, to the Magi. According to Christian tradition, the Magi were three wise men or kings named Balthasar, Melchior, and Gaspar. They traveled from the east to Bethlehem, guided by a miraculous star, to present gifts of gold, frankincense, and myrrh to the infant Jesus.

Some scholars suggest that these gifts had both symbolic meanings and practical value. Gold symbolized love; frankincense, worship; and myrrh, sacrifice. Gold obviously had monetary value; frankincense and myrrh, both sweet-smelling tree resins, were burned as incense and used in medicines. Myrrh was also used in ancient times for embalming, or preserving, the bodies of the dead.

READING CONNECTION — Setting a Purpose

In-Depth Reading How you read depends on what you are reading and why. Sometimes you can use skimming and scanning, or quick surface reading, to get information quickly. At other times you need to engage in in-depth reading, in which you slow down and really examine what is in front of you.

Some of O. Henry's vocabulary and references can be difficult to understand. Occasionally, you will need to reread a sentence to comprehend its full meaning. To help you keep track of the events in the selection, use your reading log to jot down answers to the questions inserted in the text. As you read, notice what the characters do to show their love through gifts.

The Three Magi (about A.D. 600–650), unknown artist. Sant' Apollinare Nuovo, Ravenna, Italy, Scala/Art Resource, New York.

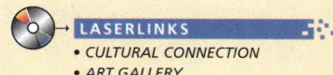
LASERLINKS
- CULTURAL CONNECTION
- ART GALLERY

425

OVERVIEW
Objectives

- To understand and appreciate a classic short story about a young married couple's sacrifices for each other
- To enrich reading by using active reading strategies
- To understand in-depth reading
- To identify and understand the concept of classics
- To appreciate the use of surprise endings
- To express understanding of the short story through a choice of writing forms, including an interior monologue, a paragraph, and a list
- To extend understanding of the autobiographical essay through a variety of multimodal and cross-curricular activities

Skills

READING SKILLS/STRATEGIES
- Clarifying
- In-depth reading

THE WRITER'S STYLE
- Show, don't tell

GRAMMAR
- Commas with interrupters

LITERARY CONCEPTS
- Classics
- Allusions

SPELLING
- Hard and soft *c* and *g*

SPEAKING, LISTENING, AND VIEWING
- Group discussion
- Oral presentation

Cross-Curricular Connections

HISTORY
- Wigs

MATHEMATICS
- Budgetary priorities

CULTURAL CONNECTION
New York in the Early 1900s Help students visualize the setting of the selection by displaying these photographs of people and places of the era.

Side A, Frame 52729

ART GALLERY
The Magi These paintings by renowned artists, including Albrecht Dürer and Sandro Botticelli, show the different ways in which the artists envisioned the Magi.

Side A, Frame 52737

PRINT AND MEDIA RESOURCES

UNIT FOUR RESOURCE BOOK
Strategic Reading: Literature, p. 4
Vocabulary SkillBuilder, p. 7
Reading SkillBuilder, p. 5
Spelling SkillBuilder, p. 6

GRAMMAR MINI–LESSONS
Transparencies, pp. 29–30
Copymasters, pp. 38–39

WRITING MINI–LESSONS
Transparencies, p. 46

ACCESS FOR STUDENTS ACQUIRING ENGLISH
Selection Summaries
Reading and Writing Support

TEACHER'S GUIDE TO ASSESSMENT AND PORTFOLIO USE

FORMAL ASSESSMENT
Selection Test, pp. 81–82
 Test Generator

 **AUDIO LIBRARY**
See Reference Card

 **LASERLINKS**
Cultural Connection
Art Gallery

THE LANGUAGE OF LITERATURE TEACHER'S EDITION **425**

SUMMARY

Della and Jim, young and recently married, love each other deeply and have very little money. Della cuts off her beautiful, long hair and sells it to a wig maker so that she can buy Jim a Christmas gift—an elegant platinum chain for his gold pocket watch. Then she discovers that Jim has sold his watch, his prized possession, to buy a gift for her—a set of elegant combs. The narrator points out that Della and Jim may seem foolish, but they have true wisdom, the wisdom of the Magi (the wise men who brought gifts to the baby Jesus).

Thematic Link: *So Much at Stake*
Despite numbing poverty, two young people sacrifice prized possessions to show their love for each other.

CUSTOMIZING FOR
Students Acquiring English

- Use ACCESS FOR STUDENTS ACQUIRING ENGLISH, *Reading and Writing Support.*
- Some students may not be familiar with the beliefs and traditions surrounding Christmas. Refer students to the Historical Connection on page 425 and, if necessary, explain the gift-giving customs. Invite students to discuss special days or events from their cultures, during which the exchange of gifts is practiced.

STRATEGIC READING FOR
Less-Proficient Readers

Set a Purpose Encourage students to become involved in the story by thinking about some important gift that they saved their money to buy. Have them draw or paint a picture of this prized purchase. Then have students read to find out what Jim's and Della's prized possessions are and how Della gets the money to buy a gift for Jim.

Use UNIT FOUR RESOURCE BOOK, p. 4, for guidance in reading the selection.

The GIFT of the MAGI

by O. Henry

WORDS TO KNOW

agile (ăj'əl) *adj.* able to move quickly and easily (p. 427)
assertion (ə-sûr'shən) *n.* a statement (p. 430)
cascade (kă-skād') *n.* a waterfall (p. 428)
chronicle (krŏn'ĭ-kəl) *n.* a record of events (p. 431)
coveted (kŭv'ĭt-ĭd) *adj.* greedily wish for **covet** *v.* (p. 431)

inconsequential (ĭn-kŏn'sĭ-kwĕn'shəl) *adj.* of no importance (p. 430)
instigate (ĭn'stĭ-gāt') *v.* to stir up; provoke (p. 427)
predominating (prĭ-dŏm'ə-nā'tĭng) *adj.* most important or frequent **predominate** *v.* (p. 427)
prudence (prōōd'ns) *n.* the use of good judgment and common sense (p. 428)
subside (səb-sīd') *v.* to sink down; settle (p. 427)

426 THE LANGUAGE OF LITERATURE TEACHER'S EDITION

One dollar and eighty-seven cents. That was all. And 60 cents of it was in pennies. Pennies saved one and two at a time by bulldozing the grocer and the vegetable man and the butcher until one's cheeks burned with the silent imputation of parsimony[1] that such close dealing implied. Three times Della counted it. One dollar and eighty-seven cents. And the next day would be Christmas.

There was clearly nothing to do but flop down on the shabby little couch and howl. So Della did it. Which <u>instigates</u> the moral reflection that life is made up of sobs, sniffles, and smiles, with sniffles <u>predominating</u>.

While the mistress of the home is gradually <u>subsiding</u> from the first stage to the second, take a look at the home. A furnished flat at $8 per week. It did not exactly beggar description, but it certainly had that word on the lookout for the mendicancy squad.[2]

In the vestibule below belonged to this flat a letterbox into which no letter would go and an electric button from which no mortal finger could coax a ring. Also appertaining[3] thereunto was a card bearing the name "Mr. James Dillingham Young."

CLARIFY
Why is Della crying?
A Using a Reading Log

The "Dillingham" had been flung to the breeze during a former period of prosperity when its possessor was being paid $30 per week. Now, when the income was shrunk to $20, the letters of "Dillingham" looked blurred, as though they were thinking seriously of contracting to a modest and unassuming D. But whenever Mr. James Dillingham Young came home and reached his flat above, he was called "Jim" and greatly hugged by Mrs. James Dillingham Young, already introduced to you as Della. Which is all very good.

Della finished her cry and attended to her cheeks with the powder rag. She stood by the window and looked out dully at a gray cat walking a gray fence in a gray backyard. Tomorrow would be Christmas Day, and she had only $1.87 with which to buy Jim a present. She had been saving every penny she could for months, with this result. Twenty dollars a week doesn't go far. Expenses had been greater than she had calculated. They always are. Only $1.87 to buy a present for Jim. Her Jim. Many a happy hour she had spent planning for something nice for him. Something fine and rare and sterling—something just a little bit near to being worthy of the honor of being owned by Jim.

There was a pier glass[4] between the windows of the room. Perhaps you have seen a pier glass in an $8 flat. A very thin and very <u>agile</u> person may, by observing his reflection in a rapid sequence of longitudinal strips, obtain a fairly accurate conception of his looks. Della, being slender, had mastered the art.

Suddenly she whirled from the window and stood before the glass. Her eyes were shining brilliantly, but her face had lost its color within twenty seconds. Rapidly she pulled down her hair and let it fall to its full length.

Now, there were two possessions of the James Dillingham Youngs in which they both

---

1. **imputation** (ĭm'pyōō-tā'shən) **of parsimony** (pär'sə-mō'nē): suggestion of stinginess.
2. **mendicancy** (mĕn'dĭ-kən-sē) **squad:** a police unit assigned to arrest beggars. The author here is making a play on the word *beggar*, used earlier in the sentence to mean "make inadequate."
3. **appertaining** (ăp'ər-tā'nĭng): belonging as a part; attached.
4. **pier glass:** a narrow mirror set in a wall section between windows.

WORDS TO KNOW
instigate (ĭn'stĭ-gāt') *v.* to stir up; provoke
predominating (prĭ-dŏm'ə-nā'tĭng) *adj.* most important or frequent **predominate** *v.*
subside (səb-sīd') *v.* to sink down; settle
agile (ăj'əl) *adj.* able to move quickly and easily

427

CUSTOMIZING FOR
Gifted and Talented Students

Have students choose a paragraph on this page and rewrite it in simple, vivid language. Encourage students to use these two versions as a springboard for an analysis and evaluation of O. Henry's prose style. Ask students to write a brief critical review arguing whether or not they feel the author's use of language is effective.

CUSTOMIZING FOR
Students Acquiring English

① Explain that a furnished flat is an apartment that has furniture already in it.

② Point out that the husband's full name makes him sound wealthy and important. Because the family is having money problems, the author suggests that a shorter version would better describe the man and his circumstances.

Active Reading: **CLARIFY**

A Help students understand that Della is crying because she and Jim are extremely poor, their home is depressing, and she fears she will not be able to buy a nice Christmas gift for her beloved husband.

Mini-Lesson Spelling

HARD AND SOFT c and g Review for students the basic rules that govern spelling of the hard and soft c and g sounds:

- When the letters *c* and *g* have a hard sound, they are usually followed by the vowels *a, o,* or *u,* or by any consonant except *y.*
- When the letters *c* and *g* have a soft sound, they are usually followed by an *e,* an *i,* or a *y.*
- Many words end with the letters *cle* (*bicycle, spectacle*) or *gle* (*tangle, bungle*). Remind students that these endings cannot be spelled *cel* and *gel* without changing the sound of the *c* and *g.*

instigate   cascade
agile   coveted
prudence   chronicle

Application Have students refer to the chart and spell the following words as you read them aloud.
1. coffee   4. nice
2. could   5. conception
3. regard   6. longitudinal

Reteaching/Reinforcement
- *Unit Four Resource Book,* p. 6

If the *c* or *g* is followed by the letter...	then the *c* or *g* sound is...
e, i, or *y*	soft
a, o, or *u*	hard
any consonant except *y*	hard

Literary Concept: ALLUSIONS

B Point out to students the narrator's allusion to two biblical figures. Ask students why O. Henry might have chosen these allusions. *(Possible responses: The narrator emphasizes the value and beauty of Della's hair and Jim's watch by comparing the couple to wealthy royalty. By alluding to biblical figures, the author prepares the reader for the concluding allusion to the Magi.)*

Cultural Note

C Explain that at the time of the story, wigmakers bought human hair to make hairpieces and wigs. At that time, women grew their hair long and were reluctant to cut it, so Madame Sofronie was willing to pay Della a good amount of money for her hair.

CUSTOMIZING FOR
Students Acquiring English

3 Tell students that the author is addressing the readers when he says, "Forget the hashed metaphor." Ask students why it was "hashed." *(Possible response: "wings that trip" is a mixed metaphor.)*

4 Be sure students know that Jim owns a pocket watch, not a wristwatch.

STRATEGIC READING FOR
Less-Proficient Readers

D Check to see that students understand details of the story's exposition and Della's response to the story's central conflict.

- What are Jim's and Della's prized possessions? *(his gold watch and her long, gorgeous hair)* Summarizing
- How does Della get the money to buy a nice gift for Jim? *(She sells her hair.)* Noting Relevant Details

Set a Purpose Have students read to learn what Christmas gifts Jim and Della buy for each other and how Jim gets the money to buy Della's gift.

---

took a mighty pride. One was Jim's gold watch that had been his father's and his grandfather's. The other was Della's hair. Had the Queen of Sheba[5] lived in the flat across the air shaft, Della would have let her hair hang out the window some day to dry and mocked at Her Majesty's jewels and gifts. Had King Solomon[6] been the janitor, with all his treasures piled up in the basement, Jim would have pulled out his watch every time he passed, just to see him pluck at his beard from envy.

So now Della's beautiful hair fell about her, rippling and shining like a cascade of brown waters. It reached below her knee and made itself almost a garment for her. And then she did it up again nervously and quickly. Once she faltered for a minute and stood still while a tear or two splashed on the worn red carpet.

On went her old brown jacket; on went her old brown hat. With a whirl of skirts and with the brilliant sparkle still in her eyes, she fluttered out the door and down the stairs to the street.

Where she stopped, the sign read "Mme. Sofronie. Hair Goods of All Kinds." One flight up Della ran and collected herself, panting, before Madame, large, too white, chilly, and hardly looking the "Sofronie."

"Will you buy my hair?" asked Della.

"I buy hair," said Madame. "Take yer hat off and let's have a sight at the looks of it."

Down rippled the brown cascade.

"Twenty dollars," said Madame, lifting the mass with a practiced hand.

"Give it to me quick," said Della.

Oh, and the next two hours tripped by on rosy wings. Forget the hashed metaphor. She was ransacking the stores for Jim's present.

She found it at last. It surely had been made for Jim and no one else. There was none other like it in any of the stores, and she had turned all of them inside out. It was a platinum fob chain[7] simple and chaste in design, properly proclaiming its value by substance alone and not by meretricious ornamentation[8]—as all good things should do. It was even worthy of The Watch. As soon as she saw it, she knew that it must be Jim's. It was like him. Quietness and value—the description applied to both. Twenty-one dollars they took from her for it, and she hurried home with the 87 cents. With that chain on his watch Jim might be properly anxious about the time in any company. Grand as the watch was, he sometimes looked at it on the sly on account of the old leather strap that he used in place of a chain.

When Della reached home, her intoxication gave way a little to prudence and reason. She got out her curling irons and lighted the gas and went to work repairing the ravages made by generosity added to love. Which is always a tremendous task, dear friends—a mammoth task.

Within forty minutes her head was covered with tiny, close-lying curls that made her look wonderfully like a truant schoolboy. She looked at her reflection in the mirror long, carefully, and critically.

---

5. **Queen of Sheba:** in the Bible, a rich Arabian queen.
6. **King Solomon:** a biblical king of Israel, known for his wisdom and wealth.
7. **fob chain:** a short chain for a pocket watch.
8. **meretricious** (mĕr′ĭ-trĭsh′əs) **ornamentation:** cheap, gaudy decoration.

WORDS TO KNOW
cascade (kă-skād′) *n.* a waterfall
prudence (prōōd′ns) *n.* the use of good judgment and common sense

428

Mini-Lesson — **Reading Skills/Strategies**

ACTIVE READING: CLARIFY Tell students that clarifying is a reading strategy in which a reader pauses occasionally, as he or she reads, to reflect on what has been read. These breaks in reading are good places for students to clarify events and ideas in a story. One useful technique for clarifying is paraphrasing. By restating and summarizing the events or ideas of a story in their own words, students can clarify their understanding of a selection. For example, a paraphrase of the second highlighted passage above might be as follows: "If Jim wore his watch on that handsome chain, he'd be tempted to check the time in order to show the watch and chain off."

Application Divide the class into pairs. Challenge each pair to write a brief story, using complicated or elaborate language. Then have each pair trade its story with another pair. Ask pairs to clarify their understanding of the stories by paraphrasing main events and ideas.

Reteaching/Reinforcement
- *Unit Four Resource Book,* p. 5

Golden Fall (1940), Joseph Stella. Oil on canvas, 26" × 20", courtesy of Spanierman Gallery, New York.

THE GIFT OF THE MAGI **429**

Art Note

Golden Fall by Joseph Stella

In this painting, the choices of Joseph Stella (1877–1946) to obscure the subject's face, to place her long hair in the foreground, and to bathe the entire canvas in golden tones contribute to an overall effect of radiance and mystery. The hair is beautiful but also carries a subtle note of wildness in its ropelike shapes. Similarly, the design on the woman's garment invites the viewer to associate her with nature, but the floral design also conveys a hint of violence in the sharp, jagged edges of the leaves.

Reading the Art *Why do you think the artist chose the title* Golden Fall *for this image? How would the effect of the painting be different if the figure's face were visible? What words would you choose to describe the mood of this painting?*

Mini-Lesson The Writer's Style

SHOW, DON'T TELL Explain that good writers strengthen their writing by showing instead of telling information. For instance, instead of simply stating that the Youngs were poor, the author shows their poverty by detailing Della's obsession with her $1.87 savings. Similarly, rather than just telling the reader that Della was anxious, O. Henry portrays this through her actions: "Della wriggled off the table and went for him."

Application Have students examine the first highlighted passage on page 428 and identify a sentence in which O. Henry shows, rather than tells, that Della is both sad and excited by what she is about to do. Then have students write three other sentences that O. Henry might have used to convey the same idea.

Reteaching/Reinforcement
- *Writer's Handbook,* anthology pp. 832–833
- *Writing Mini-Lessons* transparencies, p. 46

 **The Writer's Craft**

Show, Don't Tell, pp. 262–266

THE LANGUAGE OF LITERATURE **TEACHER'S EDITION** **429**

Literary Concept: SIMILE

E Ask students to locate the simile used in this paragraph. *("as immovable as a setter at the scent of a quail")* Ask students if they think this simile is effective in conveying Jim's action. *(Possible response: Yes, this phrase conveys Jim's abrupt halt and the fixed intensity of his stare. It's an appropriate description of Jim's shock at the sight of Della's cut hair.)*

Active Reading: CLARIFY

F Help students understand that O. Henry means for the reader to feel slightly confused—along with Della—about Jim's reaction. Ask students what they think Jim's reaction might be. If they need help, share the following model with them:

Think-Aloud Model *I suppose that because his face is registering neither approval nor disapproval, it's best to describe it as blank. I guess his initial reaction could be described as shock.*

Literary Concept: SUSPENSE

G Encourage students to describe the effect of this long passage in which Jim barely speaks and Della is a blur of movement and words. *(Possible response: O. Henry creates suspense by drawing out the scene without making clear Jim's reaction. As Della's anxiety mounts and Jim continues to make ambiguous responses, the reader's own sense of anxiety grows.)*

CUSTOMIZING FOR Students Acquiring English

5 Point out that the author jokingly suggests that readers look away from the couple as they embrace, to protect their privacy.

6 Paraphrase *had me going* as "you had me fooled for a while."

"If Jim doesn't kill me," she said to herself, "before he takes a second look at me, he'll say I look like a Coney Island chorus girl. But what could I do—oh, what could I do with a dollar and eighty-seven cents!"

At 7 o'clock the coffee was made, and the frying pan was on the back of the stove hot and ready to cook the chops.

Jim was never late. Della doubled the fob chain in her hand and sat on the corner of the table near the door that he always entered. Then she heard his step on the stair away down on the first flight, and she turned white for just a moment. She had a habit of saying little silent prayers about the simplest everyday things, and now she whispered: "Please, God, make him think I am still pretty."

The door opened, and Jim stepped in and closed it. He looked thin and very serious. Poor fellow, he was only twenty-two—and to be burdened with a family! He needed a new overcoat, and he was without gloves.

Jim stopped inside the door, as immovable as a setter at the scent of a quail. His eyes were fixed upon Della, and there was an expression in them that she could not read, and it terrified her. It was not anger, nor surprise, nor disapproval, nor horror, nor any of the sentiments that she had been prepared for. He simply stared at her fixedly with that peculiar expression on his face.

CLARIFY
What is Jim's reaction to Della's hair?
Using a Reading Log

Della wriggled off the table and went for him.

"Jim, darling," she cried, "don't look at me that way. I had my hair cut off and sold it because I couldn't have lived through Christmas without giving you a present. It'll grow again—you won't mind, will you? I just had to do it. My hair grows awfully fast. Say 'Merry Christmas!' Jim, and let's be happy. You don't know what a nice—what a beautiful, nice gift I've got for you."

"You've cut off your hair?" asked Jim, laboriously, as if he had not arrived at that patent fact yet even after the hardest mental labor.

"Cut it off and sold it," said Della. "Don't you like me just as well, anyhow? I'm me without my hair, ain't I?"

Jim looked about the room curiously.

"You say your hair is gone?" he said, with an air almost of idiocy.

"You needn't look for it," said Della. "It's sold, I tell you—sold and gone too. It's Christmas Eve, boy. Be good to me, for it went for you. Maybe the hairs of my head were numbered," she went on with a sudden serious sweetness, "but nobody could ever count my love for you. Shall I put the chops on, Jim?"

Out of his trance Jim seemed to quickly wake. He enfolded his Della. For ten seconds let us regard with discreet scrutiny[9] some inconsequential object in the other direction. Eight dollars a week or a million a year—what is the difference? A mathematician or a wit would give you the wrong answer. The magi brought valuable gifts, but that was not among them. This dark assertion will be illuminated later on.

Jim drew a package from his overcoat pocket and threw it upon the table.

"Don't make any mistake, Dell," he said, "about me. I don't think there's anything in the way of a haircut or a shave or a shampoo that could make me like my girl any less. But if you'll unwrap that package, you may see why you had me going awhile at first."

White fingers and nimble tore at the string

---

9. **scrutiny** (skrōōt′n-ē): careful observation.

WORDS TO KNOW
inconsequential (ĭn′kŏn-sĭ-kwĕn′shəl) *adj.* of no importance
assertion (ə-sûr′shən) *n.* a statement

430

Mini-Lesson  Literary Concepts

REVIEWING ALLUSION Remind students that an allusion is a reference to a famous person, place, event, or other work of literature. In the title "The Gift of the Magi," O. Henry makes a biblical allusion to the wise men—in later tradition, the three kings Balthasar, Melchior, and Gaspar—who brought gold, frankincense, and myrrh to the infant Jesus.

Application Have students identify the allusion in the highlighted passage on page 430. *(Coney Island chorus girl)* Encourage them to discuss the meaning and effect of this allusion. Ask them if this allusion is still effective for contemporary readers. You may wish to have students suggest other allusions that would communicate a similar meaning.

430 THE LANGUAGE OF LITERATURE **TEACHER'S EDITION**

and paper. And then an ecstatic scream of joy, and then, alas! a quick feminine change to hysterical tears and wails, necessitating the immediate employment of all the comforting powers of the lord of the flat.

For there lay The Combs—the set of combs, side and back, that Della had worshiped for long in a Broadway window. Beautiful combs, pure tortoise shell, with jeweled rims—just the shade to wear in the beautiful vanished hair. They were expensive combs, she knew, and her heart had simply craved and yearned over them without the least hope of possession. And now, they were hers, but the tresses[10] that should have adorned the coveted adornments[11] were gone.

But she hugged them to her bosom, and at length she was able to look up with dim eyes and a smile and say, "My hair grows so fast, Jim!"

And then Della leaped up like a little singed cat and cried, "Oh, oh!"

Jim had not yet seen his beautiful present. She held it out to him eagerly upon her open palm. The dull, precious metal seemed to flash with a reflection of her bright and ardent spirit.

"Isn't it a dandy, Jim? I hunted all over town to find it. You'll have to look at the time a hundred times a day now. Give me your watch. I want to see how it looks on it."

Instead of obeying, Jim tumbled down on the couch and put his hands under the back of his head and smiled.

"Dell," said he, "let's put our Christmas presents away and keep 'em a while. They're too nice to use just at present. I sold the watch to get the money to buy your combs. And now suppose you put the chops on."

The magi, as you know, were wise men—wonderfully wise men—who brought gifts to the Babe in the manger. They invented the art of giving Christmas gifts. Being wise, their gifts were no doubt wise ones, possibly bearing the privilege of exchange in case of duplication. And here I have lamely related to you the uneventful chronicle of two foolish children in a flat who most unwisely sacrificed for each other the greatest treasures of their house. But in a last word to the wise of these days let it be said that of all who give gifts these two were of the wisest. Of all who give and receive gifts, such as they are the wisest. Everywhere they are the wisest. They are the magi. ❖

"MY HAIR GROWS SO FAST, JIM!"

10. **tresses:** a woman's long, unbound hair.
11. **adornments:** things intended to beautify; ornaments.

WORDS TO KNOW
coveted (kŭv′ĭ-tĭd) *adj.* greedily wished for **covet** *v.*
chronicle (krŏn′ĭ-kəl) *n.* a record of events

Literary Concept: SIMILE

H Ask students to identify the simile in this passage. *(Della jumps up "like a little singed cat.")* Remind students that on page 430 the author compares Jim's stillness to that of "a setter at the scent of a quail." Ask students to explain what effect the author achieves by using these comparisons to animals. *(Animals react instinctively, without thinking.)*

CUSTOMIZING FOR
Students Acquiring English

7 Ask a volunteer to briefly describe the three wise men for students who may be unfamiliar with this religious story.

STRATEGIC READING FOR
Less-Proficient Readers

I Check to see that students are clear about the details of the double surprise at the end of the story.
- What gifts do Della and Jim buy for each other? *(She buys him a platinum watch chain, and he buys her a set of hair combs.)* Summarizing
- How did Jim get the money to buy Della's gift? *(He sold his watch.)* Noting Relevant Details

CUSTOMIZING FOR
Gifted and Talented Students

Have students imagine themselves trying to convince Hollywood studio executives to finance a film adaptation of "The Gift of the Magi." Have them prepare a synopsis of the film as part of their proposal. Ask students to think about which aspects of the story they would play up and which aspects they would downplay to make the film an attractive investment to the studio executives.

Mini-Lesson Grammar

COMMAS WITH INTERRUPTERS Point out to students that commas are used to set off most interrupters in sentences. Remind students that an interrupter is a word or words that interrupt the flow of thought in a sentence. The commas around an interrupter indicate a pause before and after the interruption. Tell students that the highlighted sentence above actually contains two such interrupters. The first ("as you know") is separated from the sentence by commas. O. Henry chose to separate the second interrupter by using dashes, which are slightly stronger than commas.

Application Have students use commas to punctuate the following sentences.
1. The Youngs' rent however was due.
2. The couple I suppose were not foolish after all.
3. Della's beautiful hair of course had disappeared.

Reteaching/Reinforcement
- *Grammar Handbook,* anthology pp. 892–894
- *Grammar Mini-Lessons* copymasters, pp. 38–39, transparencies, pp. 29–30

The Writer's Craft
Commas with Interrupters, p. 646

COMPREHENSION CHECK

1. What are the Youngs' two prized possessions? *(Della's hair and Jim's watch)*
2. What two gifts do they buy each other? *(He buys her hair combs, and she buys him a watch chain.)*
3. How does each get the money to buy the other a gift? *(She sells her hair, and he sells his watch.)*

From Personal Response to Critical Analysis

1. Responses will vary.
2. Possible responses: Della and Jim are foolish because they sell the possessions that are most valuable to them. The selflessness of Della and Jim shows their wisdom—they put their love above everything else, no matter what the cost.
3. Possible responses include *devoted, immature, adoring, reckless, sacrificing, romantic, innocent, ambitious.*
4. Possible response: The enemy in the story is the poverty that threatens Jim and Della's lives.
5. Possible responses: Nothing has changed since the time of the story—there are still people who are willing to sacrifice important things to make other people happy. Today this is rare, because more people look out only for themselves.
6. Responses will vary.

Another Pathway

Cooperative Learning As other students identify key events in the text, one student can record the group's ideas. Encourage all students to participate in gathering images to represent these key events. One student can work to ensure that the group's updating of any events seems accurate.

Rubric

3 Full Accomplishment Students assemble a collage that accurately illustrates all key events in the story.

2 Substantial Accomplishment Students assemble a collage that illustrates most key events in the story.

1 Little or Partial Accomplishment Students have difficulty identifying the story's key events and assembling a collage that accurately illustrates them.

RESPONDING OPTIONS

FROM PERSONAL RESPONSE TO CRITICAL ANALYSIS

REFLECT
1. What were your thoughts about Della and Jim? Write them down in your notebook, then share them with a partner.

RETHINK
2. O. Henry sees Della and Jim as being both foolish and wise. How would you evaluate them?

3. What three words would you use to describe Della and Jim's relationship?

Thematic Link
4. How does this story relate to the unit theme, "Facing the Enemy"? Who or what do you think is the enemy in the story? Explain your answer.

5. Do you think that people today would be willing to make such sacrifices to give gifts to those they love? Give reasons for your answer.

RELATE
6. For most people, exchanging gifts is an experience very different from Della and Jim's. Work with a small group of classmates to examine people's attitudes toward giving and receiving gifts. In the discussion, recount some of your own experiences with gift giving.

LITERARY CONCEPTS

Some works of literature burst on the scene, winning high praise and great popularity, only to be forgotten after a short time. Other works, like the stories of O. Henry, are read year after year by people around the world. Such enduring works are considered **classics.** Classics like "The Gift of the Magi" deal with emotions, behaviors, or truths that human beings of every age, race, and culture share. What aspects of this story do you think make it a classic?

Multimodal Learning
ANOTHER PATHWAY

Cooperative Learning
With a small group of classmates, review the main events of the story. Then work together to create a collage that represents the key events. Your collage might modernize the story by showing how the events could happen in today's world.

QUICKWRITES

1. What might Jim be thinking when he notices Della's short hair? Write an **interior monologue** that expresses his thoughts.

2. Who do you think makes the greater sacrifice—Della or Jim? Write your opinion, and the reasons for it, in the form of a brief **paragraph.**

3. A gift that costs nothing can be the most valuable gift of all. Make a **list** of gifts that cost nothing. Share your list with the class.

📁 **PORTFOLIO** Save your writing. You may want to use it later as a springboard to a piece for your portfolio.

432 UNIT FOUR PART 1: SO MUCH AT STAKE

Literary Concepts

Draw students' attention to "timeless" themes (poverty, sacrifice, and romantic love), as well as to the Christmas setting, as ways of explaining the story's unusual and enduring popularity. Invite students to name more contemporary stories, novels, or films that deal with these themes.

QuickWrites

1. Partners can role-play the scene to help the student playing Jim generate ideas about Jim's frame of mind.
2. Encourage students to make an outline of their argument before they begin writing. Remind them to use supporting details from the story or their own experience.
3. Encourage students to think about activities and experiences that do not cost money.

 **The Writer's Craft**

Writing Dialogue, p. 326
Writing Paragraphs, pp. 244-251

432 THE LANGUAGE OF LITERATURE TEACHER'S EDITION

THE WRITER'S STYLE

O. Henry is a master of the surprise ending. Were you surprised by Jim's sacrifice? Why or why not? Find clues in the story that foreshadow the surprise ending.

Multimodal Learning

ALTERNATIVE ACTIVITIES

1. An example of a gift that costs nothing is a love song. As a gift to Della and Jim, compose a **love song** that captures the essence of their relationship.

2. "The Gift of the Magi" is a story of romantic love and mutual sacrifice. Create a **drawing, painting,** or **sculpture** that serves as a symbol of these romantic concepts and that could be used to illustrate the story.

WORDS TO KNOW

On your paper, write the letter of the word that is most *different* in meaning from the other words in the set. Use a dictionary if you need help.

1. (a) stop, (b) stir, (c) urge, (d) instigate
2. (a) predominating, (b) dominating, (c) ruling, (d) missing
3. (a) increase, (b) subside, (c) lessen, (d) decline
4. (a) history, (b) record, (c) chronicle, (d) prediction
5. (a) stream, (b) river, (c) brook, (d) cascade
6. (a) assertion, (b) declaration, (c) denial, (d) statement
7. (a) desired, (b) coveted, (c) craved, (d) unwanted
8. (a) carelessness, (b) caution, (c) prudence, (d) wisdom
9. (a) limber, (b) agile, (c) clumsy, (d) flexible
10. (a) important, (b) unnecessary, (c) inconsequential, (d) insignificant

O. HENRY

1862–1910

Using the pen name O. Henry, William Sydney Porter wrote nearly 300 short stories that brought him worldwide fame. During the two decades following his death, his short stories were more popular than those of any other American writer. Like his stories, his life was marked by surprises.

Born in Greensboro, North Carolina, Porter was raised by his grandmother and aunt after his mother's death. He left school at 16 to work in his uncle's drugstore. Later he moved to Texas and worked on a ranch there. At the age of 25, he married Athol Estes. After the birth of their child, they moved to Austin, Texas, where Porter became a bank clerk. Several years after leaving this position, he was suspected of having embezzled bank funds. Porter fled to Central America to avoid trial. When he returned to visit his dying wife, he was arrested, convicted, and jailed for three years. Throughout, he maintained his innocence.

It was in jail that Porter refined his short story style, writing stories based on his Western, Central American, and prison experiences.

OTHER WORKS *The Four Million, Heart of the West, The Gentle Grafter, Strictly Business, Whirligigs, Sixes and Sevens, Waifs and Strays,* "The Ransom of Red Chief," "A Retrieved Reformation," "Hearts and Hands" *Extended Reading*

THE GIFT OF THE MAGI **433**

Words to Know

1. a	6. c
2. d	7. d
3. a	8. a
4. d	9. c
5. d	10. a

Reteaching/Reinforcement
- *Unit Four Resource Book,* p. 7

Across the Curriculum

History *Wigs* Have students research and report on the history of wigs and hairpieces. Encourage them to include information on the use of both natural and synthetic hair in wigs, as well as their uses in theatrical productions and daily life.

Mathematics *Budgetary Priorities* Have students calculate what percentage of a month's rent Della spent on her present for her husband. *(The rent was $8 per week; if we assume $32 per month for rent, and we know that Della spent $21 for the watch chain, then she spent approximately 66% of a month's rent on the gift.)* Then have them find out the monthly rent or mortgage for a typical local apartment today. Students can figure out how much they could spend on a gift if they spent the same percentage that Della did.

O. HENRY (WILLIAM SYDNEY PORTER)

After he was released from prison, Porter moved to New York City, where he worked as a newspaper columnist and a fiction writer. One day in a restaurant, he was asked where he found his plots. "Oh, everywhere," he replied. "There are stories in everything." He then picked up the bill for the meal and said, "There's a story in this." He promptly outlined an entire plot for a story that was later published as "Springtime à la Carte."

The Writer's Style

Although most readers are surprised by Jim's sacrifice, O. Henry subtly foreshadows the end of the story in details such as Jim's expression when he enters the apartment, his having bought a gift for Della, and the implied comparison between the Youngs and the Magi (who brought "valuable gifts"). Explain to students that the ending is an example of irony, in which an event occurs that is very different from what might normally be expected.

Writing Conclusions, pp. 281–283

Alternative Activities

1. Students might model their compositions on contemporary love songs. Encourage students to list briefly the important aspects of Della and Jim's relationship that they think should be reflected in the song.
2. Some students might wish to search the text for such an image, whereas others may prefer to develop their own ideas.

OVERVIEW

Objectives
- To understand and appreciate two poems about triumphing over life's adversities
- To identify and understand alliteration
- To express understanding of the poems through a choice of writing forms, including a speech and a quotation
- To extend understanding of the poems through a variety of multimodal and cross-curricular activities

Skills

LITERARY CONCEPTS
- Repetition
- Alliteration

SPEAKING, LISTENING, AND VIEWING
- Choral reading
- Group discussion
- Oral presentation

Cross-Curricular Connections

SOCIAL STUDIES
- The Great Migration

SCIENCE
- Prosthetic devices

ALTERNATIVE
Previewing

Instead of writing about an obstacle they have faced, students can choose partners and discuss their experiences.

Writing Connection

Discussion Prompts: *When has a major obstacle stood in the way of something you wanted to do in your life? How did you respond to it? After considering these questions, describe your experience to your partner. Then listen as your partner describes his or her experience. The following questions might help you get started:*

- *Have you ever been kept from doing something because of some rule?*
- *Have you ever been kept from doing something because of your age or some physical limitation?*
- *How did you deal with this challenge? What did you learn about yourself from the experience?*

As you read the two poems, try to identify the major obstacles that are Gwendolyn Brooks's and Nina Cassian's subjects.

PREVIEWING

POETRY

Speech to the Young
Speech to the Progress-Toward
Gwendolyn Brooks

A Man
Nina Cassian

Activating Prior Knowledge
PERSONAL CONNECTION

The poems you are about to read deal with the challenge of facing life's obstacles. What kinds of obstacles do people commonly encounter in their lives? What kinds of obstacles are extraordinarily difficult to overcome? To help you organize your thoughts, use a concept map like the one shown. Then share your ideas with the class. In your discussion, consider what gives people the courage to overcome obstacles.

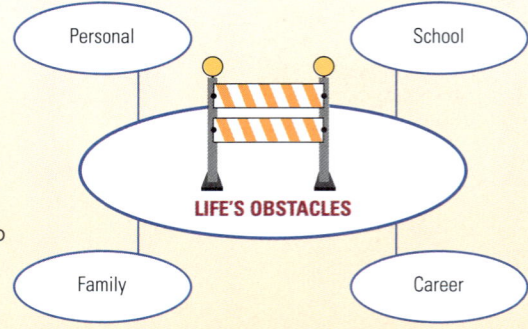

Building Background
LITERARY CONNECTION

Gwendolyn Brooks and Nina Cassian have both overcome obstacles in their lives. Much of Brooks's poetry draws on the painful experience of growing up African American in the early part of this century. She shows a keen awareness of the problems of color and justice in the United States. Though she examines despair and grief in her work, ultimately her attitude is positive.

While Brooks has struggled with the obstacle of racial discrimination, Nina Cassian, a Romanian, has faced political obstacles. Denounced by the Romanian government for failing to uphold Communist ideals in her work, she was forced to seek a new home in the United States in the 1980s.

Setting a Purpose
WRITING CONNECTION

Think of a time in your life when a major obstacle stood in the way of something you wanted to do. How did you deal with it? Write a brief account of your experience. Then, as you read these poems, take note of the speakers' attitudes toward obstacles.

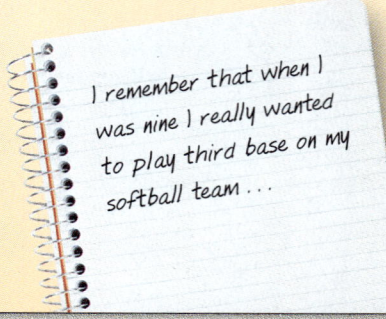

434 UNIT FOUR PART 1: SO MUCH AT STAKE

PRINT AND MEDIA RESOURCES

UNIT FOUR RESOURCE BOOK
Strategic Reading: Literature, p. 11

ACCESS FOR STUDENTS ACQUIRING ENGLISH
Reading and Writing Support

FORMAL ASSESSMENT
Selection Test, p. 83
 Test Generator

AUDIO LIBRARY
See Reference Card

Speech to the Young
Speech to the Progress-Toward
(Among them Nora and Henry III)

by Gwendolyn Brooks

Say to them,
say to the down-keepers,
the sun-slappers,
the self-soilers,
5 the harmony-hushers,
"Even if you are not ready for day
it cannot always be night."
You will be right.
For that is the hard home-run.

10 Live not for battles won.
Live not for the-end-of-the-song.
Live in the along.

Copyright © Nicholas Wilton.

FROM PERSONAL RESPONSE TO CRITICAL ANALYSIS

REFLECT
1. What is your impression of the speaker's advice? Jot down your thoughts in your notebook.

RETHINK
2. What do you think is the meaning of the last stanza of the poem?
3. What does the speaker think is at stake, or in danger of being lost, if young people do not follow the advice given in the poem?
4. What obstacles might make the speaker's advice difficult to follow?
5. What character trait is shared by the people mentioned in lines 2–5? Do you know people like these? Explain your answer.

SPEECH TO THE YOUNG / SPEECH TO THE PROGRESS-TOWARD **435**

Mini-Lesson  Literary Concepts

REVIEWING REPETITION Remind students that repetition is the repeated use of any element of language—a sound, a word, a phrase, a line, or a grammatical structure. Point out that writers—especially poets—use repetition to stress important ideas and to create memorable sound effects. For instance, alliteration is a type of repetition that repeats consonant sounds.

Application Have students identify each instance of repetition in one of the poems. Then have them rewrite those words or phrases to remove all repetition from the poem. After having them perform oral readings of their two versions, encourage students to discuss the importance of repetition to the overall effect of the poem.

Thematic Link: *So Much at Stake*
In each of these two poems, the speaker celebrates a triumph over a challenging life obstacle.

CUSTOMIZING FOR
Students Acquiring English

- Use **ACCESS FOR STUDENTS ACQUIRING ENGLISH**, *Reading and Writing Support*.
- Before reading these poems, you may want to define or act out the terms *optimistic* and *pessimistic* so less fluent students can use these words to talk about the poems later.

① Explain that these descriptive words refer to negative or pessimistic people.

② Ask what the speaker means by "Live in the along." (*Possible response: live in the present*)

STRATEGIC READING FOR
Less-Proficient Readers

Set a Purpose Encourage students to become involved in the poems by asking them how an attitude about life could become an obstacle. Then have them read to find out how the poets address two obstacles—one mental and one physical.

Use **UNIT FOUR RESOURCE BOOK**, p. 11, for guidance in reading the selection.

From Personal Response to Critical Analysis

1. Responses will vary.
2. Possible response: It is more valuable to live in the present than to put too much stock in past or future victories or results.
3. Possible response: If young people are unable to resist the naysayers, or negative people, they could lose hope of ever being fulfilled in life.
4. Possible response: A failure of nerve, a lack of confidence, or a lack of family or peer support would make the speaker's advice hard to follow.
5. Possible response: Those people share the traits of pessimism and hopelessness.

A MAN
by Nina Cassian

Das Buch [The book] (1985), Anselm Kiefer. Lead, steel and tin, 114" × 213½" × 34", Los Angeles County Museum of Art, Modern and Contemporary Art Council Fund and Louise and Harold Held.

While fighting for his country, he lost an arm
and was suddenly afraid:
"From now on, I shall only be able to do things by halves.
I shall reap half a harvest.
5 I shall be able to play either the tune
or the accompaniment on the piano,
but never both parts together.
I shall be able to bang with only one fist
on doors, and worst of all
10 I shall only be able to half hold
my love close to me.
There will be things I cannot do at all,
applaud for example,
at shows where everyone applauds."

15 From that moment on, he set himself to do
    everything with twice as much enthusiasm.
And where the arm had been torn away
a wing grew.

Mini-Lesson: Speaking, Listening, and Viewing

CHORAL READING Remind students that although most writers take great care choosing words, poets are more likely than others to choose words for their sound as well as their meaning.

In "Speech to the Young/Speech to the Progress-Toward," for instance, Gwendolyn Brooks uses simple, direct words to create alliteration, rhythm, and rhyme. In "A Man," Nina Cassian employs repetition of certain words and phrases to create a powerful rhythm that underscores the war veteran's list of fears.

Application Have students study the meanings and sound devices of either poem. Then invite them to rehearse and perform a choral reading of the poem. Invite them to use their voices to underscore gently the poem's particular sounds.

RESPONDING OPTIONS

FROM PERSONAL RESPONSE TO CRITICAL ANALYSIS

REFLECT
1. What is your impression of the man described in "A Man"?

RETHINK
2. Do you think that the man's reaction to his disability is common?
   Consider
   Close Textual Reading
   - his initial reaction in the first stanza
   - how his attitude seems to have changed in the second stanza
   - how you might react if the same thing happened to you

3. What do you think the poet means by "a wing grew"?

Thematic Link
4. What does the man's decision reveal about the way in which he copes with obstacles?

RELATE
5. Which poem—"Speech to the Young . . ." or "A Man"—has a more powerful message for you? Which seems more useful? Explain your choice.

6. Which poem do you consider more hopeful? Why?

Multimodal Learning
ANOTHER PATHWAY
Think of a single image that conveys the messages of both poems. Then make an illustration of that image and think of an inspirational slogan to accompany your illustration. Write the slogan below the illustration.

QUICKWRITES

1. Using either prose or poetry, write your own **speech** to the young, based on your own experiences. Offer advice about how to handle some obstacle they are likely to encounter.

2. Reread the words set in quotation marks in the first stanza of "A Man." Then write a similar **quotation** that reflects the man's new attitude in the second stanza.

📁 **PORTFOLIO** Save your writing. You may want to use it later as a springboard to a piece for your portfolio.

LITERARY CONCEPTS

Alliteration is a repetition of consonant sounds at the beginnings of two or more words, as in "Peter Piper picked a peck of pickled peppers." Poets often use alliteration to emphasize words, to tie lines together, and to give their writing a musical quality. Find examples of alliteration in Brooks's poem. What words and ideas are emphasized by means of the alliteration?

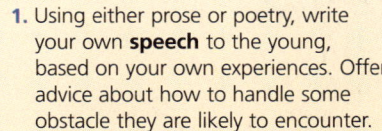

She sells sea shells by the sea shore.

SPEECH TO THE YOUNG/SPEECH TO THE PROGRESS-TOWARD/A MAN **437**

From Personal Response to Critical Analysis

1. Responses will vary.
2. Possible responses: The man's positive response is common because one can see his kind of optimism in such things as the Special Olympics. The man's negative response is common because it is natural for people to have feelings of defeat and depression when they are hurt; however, his ability to overcome these feelings is not something everyone is able to do.
3. Possible response: The poet means that the man discovered some source of hope and confidence in himself and was able to transcend his disability.
4. Possible response: His decision shows that he does not let obstacles—or his own imagination—defeat him, but rather he faces his troubles and overcomes them.
5. Encourage students to support their responses with references to both texts.
6. Possible response: The image of the man growing a wing makes "A Man" more hopeful. There is evidence in the poem itself that a change for the better has taken place.

Another Pathway
Urge students to begin by rereading each poem and expressing its message in a single sentence. Then have them compare the messages and think of an image and slogan that would link them.

Rubric
3 Full Accomplishment Students conceive and present an image and slogan that vividly convey the messages of the poems.
2 Substantial Accomplishment Students conceive and present an image and slogan that convey the message of at least one of the poems.
1 Little or Partial Accomplishment Students have trouble conceiving an image or a slogan that conveys the message of either poem.

Literary Links
Compare the attitudes of the speaker in "A Man" with the mother's attitude in "Mother to Son" (p. 314). *(Possible response: Both the man and the mother have similar attitudes: Although life has been hard, they have not lost their sense of hope or reason for living.)*

Literary Concepts
You might have a volunteer read the poem aloud in order to draw students' attention to the alliteration of the letters *s*, *h*, *l*, and *n*.

QuickWrites
1. Urge students to focus on the specific audience for their speech and consider how it should affect the content and style of their writing. Have them brainstorm anecdotes or details to help communicate their message.
2. Remind students that the poet's use of repetition in the first stanza helped make those lines effective. Encourage them to use repetition in their own quotations.

 The Writer's Craft
Audience, pp. 234–235
Poetry, pp. 76–83

THE LANGUAGE OF LITERATURE TEACHER'S EDITION **437**

GWENDOLYN BROOKS

Brooks has been widely praised for work that embodies large political and social issues, such as race and gender, by shedding light on the small moments of individuals' lives. In a 1967 biography, Brooks described her poetry as "related to life in the broad sense of the word, even though the subject matter relates closest to the Negro. Although I called my first book *A Street in Bronzeville*, I hoped that people would recognize instantly that Negroes are just like other people; they have the same hates and loves and fears, the same tragedies and triumphs and deaths, as people of any race or religion or nationality."

Across the Curriculum

Social Studies *The Great Migration* Like more than five million other African Americans, Gwendolyn Brooks moved from the rural South to a northern city in the years between 1940 and the late 1960s. This extraordinary movement of citizens came to be known as the Great Migration. Have students research and report on the causes and effects of the Great Migration in an oral presentation.

Science Cooperative Learning *Prosthetic Devices* Have students find out information on prostheses—artificial parts that replace missing organs and limbs. Encourage them to explain how these devices help people in their daily lives. Have students work in groups of four. Each group can focus on particular limbs, technological developments of prosthetics, or human-interest accounts of people functioning with artificial limbs.

Art Connection

You might have volunteers present their ideas for illustrating "A Man" to the whole class.

Multimodal Learning

ALTERNATIVE ACTIVITIES

1. Note the words and phrases that appeal to your senses of sight, sound, and touch in these two poems. Then work with a partner to choreograph a **dance** that is a visual interpretation of one of the poems. Perform your dance for the class.
2. Investigate poems having similar themes to the two you have just read. Select several to read on **audiotape,** and play your tape for the class.

ART CONNECTION

Look back to the photograph of the sculpture on page 436. First, think about what the artwork means to you simply as a piece of sculpture. Then, analyze the artwork as it relates to the poem "A Man."

If it were your job to illustrate the poem, describe what you might draw or paint. Discuss your ideas with a partner.

GWENDOLYN BROOKS

1917–

When Gwendolyn Brooks was young, both her parents encouraged her writing. Her father presented her with a writing desk, and her mother excused her from most household chores for the sake of her writing.

In her early poetry, Brooks wrote about the lives of ordinary African Americans, drawing on the experiences of her family and of the poor who lived around her in Chicago. In 1950, Brooks became the first African-American author to receive a Pulitzer Prize (for her collection of poetry *Annie Allen*). Later, she was the first black woman to serve as poetry consultant to the Library of Congress (1985–1936).

Brooks donates money to be given as prizes to winners of poetry contests. She has been Illinois's poet laureate since 1968.

OTHER WORKS *A Street in Bronzeville; Bronzeville Boys and Girls; The Bean Eaters; The Tiger Who Wore White Gloves, or What You Are You Are*

Extended Reading

NINA CASSIAN

1924–

Born in Galati, Romania, Nina Cassian is one of Romania's notable poets of the 20th century. Her life, marked by poverty, political struggles, and exile, has not been easy.

At the age of 15, Cassian became a Communist, and her early volumes of poetry reflect her Communist beliefs. Many years later, however, she came to reject these political views.

In 1985, Cassian sought political asylum in the United States, and she has been teaching poetry at New York University ever since. In recent years, she has written five new volumes of poetry. In 1994, she was named a Literary Lion by the New York Public Library for her writing and literary activities.

OTHER WORKS *Call Yourself Alive?, Cheerleader for a Funeral, Life Sentences: Selected Poems*

Extended Reading

UNIT FOUR PART 1: SO MUCH AT STAKE

Alternative Activities

1. Have students take turns recording the sensory images that the partner identifies in the poems. Then have students discuss and plan how to express these details through dance.
2. Help students focus on lyric poems—perhaps others written by Gwendolyn Brooks. Encourage students to analyze a poem's meaning, imagery, and sound devices before they begin rehearsing a reading.

PREVIEWING

NONFICTION and POETRY

from Lincoln: A Photobiography
Russell Freedman

O Captain! My Captain!
Walt Whitman

Activating Prior Knowledge
PERSONAL CONNECTION

Abraham Lincoln is one of the most famous of U.S. leaders and most respected of men. How much do you know about Abraham Lincoln the president and Abraham Lincoln the man? With a small group of classmates, discuss all that you know. Then share your knowledge with the entire class.

Building Background
HISTORICAL CONNECTION

In 1863, as the Civil War raged, Walt Whitman wrote, "I have finally made up my mind that Mr. Lincoln has done as good as a human being could do—I still think him a pretty big President." Lincoln held the United States together, preserving the Union when powerful proslavery and antislavery forces risked tearing it apart. Little known when he first sought the presidency in 1860, Lincoln was elected with less than 40 percent of the popular vote. By the time of his inauguration, a number of Southern states had seceded and formed their own government. Six weeks later the Civil War began.

In 1864, after several important Union successes in the war, Lincoln was elected to a second term. A few weeks after his inauguration, the Confederacy surrendered, and Lincoln's focus became bringing the Southern states back into the nation through Reconstruction.

After Lincoln's death, Walt Whitman composed "O Captain! My Captain!" in memory of the president. Whitman had never been formally introduced to Lincoln, but during the war he had written, "I see the President almost every day, as I happen to live where he passes to or from his lodging out of town. . . . We have got so that we exchange bows, and very cordial ones."

Setting a Purpose
WRITING CONNECTION

In your notebook, list questions you have about Abraham Lincoln as a man and as a president, and about his assassination. After you read these two selections, look back at your questions to see which have been answered and which you may want to answer by researching them on your own.

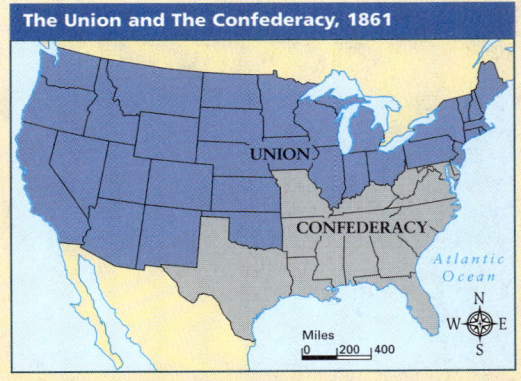
The Union and The Confederacy, 1861

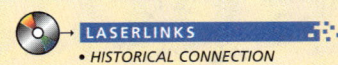
LASERLINKS
• HISTORICAL CONNECTION

OVERVIEW

Objectives
- To understand and appreciate a biography and a poem about Abraham Lincoln
- To identify and understand biography
- To express understanding of the selections through a choice of writing forms, including a letter, a character sketch, and a poem
- To extend understanding of the selection through a variety of multimodal and cross-curricular activities

Skills

READING SKILLS/STRATEGIES
- Using context clues

THE WRITER'S STYLE
- Chronological order

GRAMMAR
- Irregular verbs

LITERARY CONCEPTS
- Biography
- Extended metaphor

SPELLING
- Prefixes and roots

SPEAKING, LISTENING, AND VIEWING
- Scoring a poem with music
- Group discussion
- Oral presentation

Cross-Curricular Connections

SOCIAL STUDIES
- Death and the presidency

HISTORY
- Radical Republicans
- The Lincoln family

GEOGRAPHY
- The route of Lincoln's funeral procession

HISTORICAL CONNECTION
President Lincoln Broaden students' knowledge of Lincoln by showing these illustrations and photographs. Included are scenes of Lincoln with his family, as well as a Mathew Brady photograph of Lincoln reviewing Union troops during the Civil War.

Side A, Frames 52748

PRINT AND MEDIA RESOURCES

UNIT FOUR RESOURCE BOOK
Strategic Reading: Literature, p. 15
Vocabulary SkillBuilder, p. 18
Reading SkillBuilder, p. 16
Spelling SkillBuilder, p. 17

GRAMMAR MINI–LESSONS
Transparencies, p. 20
Copymasters, pp. 27–28

WRITING MINI–LESSONS
Transparencies, p. 33

ACCESS FOR STUDENTS ACQUIRING ENGLISH
Selection Summaries
Reading and Writing Support

FORMAL ASSESSMENT
Selection Test, pp. 85–86
 Test Generator

AUDIO LIBRARY
See Reference Card

LASERLINKS
Historical Connection

INTERNET RESOURCES
McDougal Littell Literature Center at http://www.hmco.com/mcdougal/lit

SUMMARY

Disagreements during the Civil War caused assassination threats against President Lincoln from the time he was elected. Heavily guarded, he did not worry about the threats, but he did once dream that he discovered people in mourning at the White House. He asked, "Who is dead in the White House?" and was told, "The President." Shortly after Lincoln's dream, General Lee surrendered, ending the war. Five days later, Lincoln was killed by John Wilkes Booth, who supported the Confederacy. By describing Lincoln's activities on the day before he died, and by showing how his family, his colleagues, and the public reacted to his death, Freedman reveals the human dimensions as well as the greatness of Abraham Lincoln.

Thematic Link: *So Much at Stake*
Abraham Lincoln's integrity, courage, and intelligence helped him lead the nation through its most critical challenge.

CUSTOMIZING FOR
Students Acquiring English

- Use **ACCESS FOR STUDENTS ACQUIRING ENGLISH,** *Reading and Writing Support.*
- Students may have trouble keeping track of people's names and their political affiliations in this selection. When Lee or Grant, the Confederacy, the rebels, or the Union are mentioned, check for understanding with basic questions, such as: Who were called the rebels? Who supported President Lincoln? Who was threatening the president?

STRATEGIC READING FOR
Less-Proficient Readers

Set a Purpose Encourage students to become involved in the biographical excerpt by having them discuss what it would feel like to have their lives threatened nearly every day. Then have students read to find out why people were concerned for Lincoln's safety and why his bodyguard left his post at Ford's Theater.

Use **UNIT FOUR RESOURCE BOOK,** p. 15, for guidance in reading the selection.

FROM

LINCOLN
A PHOTOBIOGRAPHY

by Russell Freedman

WORDS TO KNOW

abduction (ăb-dŭk′shən) *n.* kidnapping (p. 441)
assailant (ə-sā′lənt) *n.* a person who attacks another (p. 443)
conspiracy (kən-spîr′ə-sē) *n.* an agreement by two or more people to perform an illegal or wrong act (p. 443)
revoke (rĭ-vōk′) *v.* to withdraw or repeal (p. 441)
vindictiveness (vĭn-dĭk′tĭv-nĭs) *n.* a desire for revenge (p. 441)

The president's friends were worried about his safety. They feared that rebel sympathizers would try to kidnap or kill him in a desperate attempt to save the Confederacy.

Lincoln had been living with rumors of abduction and assassination ever since he was first elected. Threatening letters arrived in the mail almost every day. He filed them away in a bulging envelope marked ASSASSINATION.

"I long ago made up my mind that if anyone wants to kill me, he will do it," he told a newspaper reporter. "If I wore a shirt of mail,[1] and kept myself surrounded by a bodyguard, it would be all the same. There are a thousand ways of getting at a man if it is desired that he should be killed."

Even so, his advisors insisted on taking precautions. Soldiers camped on the White House lawn, cavalry troops escorted Lincoln on his afternoon carriage rides, and plainclothes detectives served as his personal bodyguards. He complained about the protection, but he accepted it. Thoughts of death were certainly on his mind. More than once, he had been troubled by haunting dreams.

He told some friends about a dream he had early in April, just before the fall of Richmond.[2] In the dream, he was wandering through the halls of the White House. He could hear people sobbing, but as he went from room to room, he saw no one.

He kept on until he reached the East Room of the White House: "There I met with a sickening surprise. Before me was a . . . corpse wrapped in funeral vestments. Around it were stationed soldiers who were acting as guards; and there was a throng of people, some gazing mournfully upon the corpse, whose face was covered, others weeping pitifully. 'Who is dead in the White House?' I demanded of one of the soldiers. 'The President,' was his answer; 'he was killed by an assassin.' Then came a loud burst of grief from the crowd, which awoke me from my dream. I slept no more that night."

April 14, 1865, was Good Friday. Lee had surrendered just five days earlier, and Washington was in a festive mood. Lincoln arose early as usual, so he could work at his desk before breakfast. He was looking forward to the day's schedule. That afternoon he would tell his wife, "I never felt so happy in my life."

At eleven, he met with his cabinet. He had invited General Grant to attend the meeting as guest of honor. Most of the talk centered on the difficult problems of reconstruction in the conquered South. Lincoln emphasized again that he wanted no persecutions, "no bloody work." Enough blood had been shed. "There are men in Congress," he said, "who possess feelings of hate and vindictiveness in which I do not sympathize and cannot participate."

After lunch he returned to his office to review court-martial sentences.[3] He revoked the death sentence of a Confederate spy. And he pardoned a deserter, signing his name with the comment, "Well, I think this boy can do us more good above ground than under ground."

Late in the afternoon he went for a carriage ride with Mary. That evening they would attend the theater with another couple, but for the moment, they wanted some time to themselves.

---

1. **shirt of mail:** protective armor for the upper part of the body, made of small interlocking metal rings.
2. **the fall of Richmond:** the Union capture of Richmond, Virginia—the Confederate capital—in April 1865. This event assured the victory of the North in the Civil War.
3. **court-martial sentences:** punishments decided by military courts.

WORDS TO KNOW
abduction (ăb-dŭk′shən) *n.* kidnapping
vindictiveness (vĭn-dĭk′tĭv-nĭs) *n.* a desire for revenge
revoke (rĭ-vōk′) *v.* to withdraw or repeal

441

Critical Thinking: SPECULATING

 Ask students to use context clues to speculate on the identity of Willie. *(Possible response: Willie was one of the Lincolns' sons.)*

CUSTOMIZING FOR
Multiple Learning Styles

D **Linguistic Learners** Have students write several diary entries that Mary Todd Lincoln might have written after Willie's death.

Linking to History

E Abraham and Mary Todd Lincoln had four children—Robert Todd, Edward Baker, William Wallace ("Willie"), and Thomas ("Tad," who was reputed to be his father's favorite). Willie Lincoln died in the White House at age 11. In fact, of the four children, only Robert (1843–1926) survived into adulthood. Robert was a lawyer, and he held the posts of secretary of war from 1881 to 1885 and U.S. minister to England from 1889 to 1893.

Literary Concept: BIOGRAPHY

F Encourage students to note the details Russell Freedman uses to portray Lincoln. By providing information about Lincoln's late arrival, eyeglasses, and the rocking chair provided by the theater, Freedman helps the reader to recognize the individual as well as the national hero.

Courtesy of the Illinois State Historical Library.

The war had been hard on both of them. Since **C** Willie's death, Mary had been plagued by depression and imaginary fears, and at times, **D** Lincoln had feared for his wife's sanity. As their carriage rolled through the countryside, they talked hopefully of the years ahead. "We must both be more cheerful in the future," Lincoln said. "Between the war and the loss of our **E** darling Willie, we have been very miserable."

After dinner, Lincoln and Mary left for Ford's Theater in the company of a young army major, Henry R. Rathbone, and his fiancee, Clara Harris. Arriving late, they were escorted up a winding stairway to the flag-draped presidential box overlooking the stage. The play had already started, but as Lincoln's party appeared in the box, the orchestra struck up "Hail to the Chief"[4] and the audience rose for a standing ovation. Lincoln smiled and bowed. He took his place in a rocking chair provided for him by the management and put on a pair of gold-rimmed eyeglasses he had mended with a string. Mary sat beside him, with Major

---

4. **"Hail to the Chief":** a patriotic song played at public appearances of the president of the United States since about 1828. The words, seldom heard, are from Sir Walter Scott's "The Boat Song"; James Sanderson wrote the music.

442 UNIT FOUR PART 1: SO MUCH AT STAKE

Assessment  **Option**

INFORMAL ASSESSMENT You can informally assess students' understanding of the excerpt from *Lincoln: A Photobiography* by dividing students into small discussion groups of four or five. Invite groups to consider the issues that informed Lincoln's political life (and ultimately his death). Encourage them to discuss how slavery, the secession of Southern states from the Union, and the Civil War might have provided reasons for some people to feel hostility toward the president.

Rubric

3 Full Accomplishment Students intelligently and thoroughly discuss the issues that led to the Civil War and to the death of Lincoln.

2 Substantial Accomplishment Students discuss many of the issues that led to the Civil War and to the death of Lincoln.

1 Little or Partial Accomplishment Students have difficulty discussing the issues that led to the Civil War and to the death of Lincoln.

Rathbone and Miss Harris to their right.

The play was *Our American Cousin*, a popular comedy starring Laura Keene, who had already given a thousand performances in the leading role. Lincoln settled back and relaxed. He laughed heartily, turning now and then to whisper to his wife. Halfway through the play, he felt a chill and got up to drape his black overcoat across his shoulders.

During the third act, Mary reached over to take Lincoln's hand. She pressed closer to him. Behind them, the door to the presidential box was closed but not locked. Lincoln's bodyguard that evening, John Parker, had slipped away from his post outside the door to go downstairs and watch the play.

The audience had just burst into laughter when the door swung open. A shadowy figure stepped into the box, stretched out his arm, aimed a small derringer pistol at the back of Lincoln's head, and pulled the trigger. Lincoln's arm jerked up. He slumped forward in his chair as Mary reached out to catch him. Then she screamed.

Major Rathbone looked up to see a man standing with a smoking pistol in one hand and a hunting knife in the other. Rathbone lunged at the gunman, who yelled something and slashed Rathbone's arm to the bone. Then the assailant leaped from the box to the stage, twelve feet below. One of his boot spurs caught on the regimental flag draped over the box. As he crashed onto the stage, he broke the shinbone of his left leg.

The assailant struggled to his feet, faced the audience, and shouted the motto of the commonwealth of Virginia: *"Sic semper tyrannis"*—(Thus always to tyrants). The stunned and disbelieving audience recognized him as John Wilkes Booth, the well-known actor. What was going on? Was this part of the play?

Booth hobbled offstage and out the stage door, where a horse was saddled and waiting. Twelve days later he would be cornered by federal troops and shot in a Virginia barn.

The theater was in an uproar. People were shouting, standing on chairs, shoving for the exits, as Laura Keene cried out from the stage, "The president is shot! The president is shot!"

Two doctors rushed to the president's box. Lincoln had lost consciousness instantly. The bullet had entered his skull above his left ear, cut through his brain, and lodged behind his right eye. The doctors worked over him as Mary hovered beside them, sobbing hysterically. Finally, six soldiers carried the president out of the theater and across the fog-shrouded street to a boardinghouse, where a man with a lighted candle stood beckoning. He was placed on a four-poster bed in a narrow room off the hallway. The bed wasn't long enough for Lincoln. He had to be laid diagonally across its cornhusk mattress.

Five doctors worked over the president that night. Now and then he groaned, but it was obvious that he would not regain consciousness. The room filled with members of the cabinet, with congressmen and high government officials. Mary waited in the front parlor. "Bring Tad—he will speak to Tad—he loves him so," she cried. Tad had been attending another play that evening. Sobbing, "They killed my pa, they killed my pa," he was taken back to the White House to wait.

Robert Lincoln was summoned to join the hushed crowd around his father's bedside. Outside, cavalry patrols clattered down the street. Another assassin had just tried to murder Secretary of State William Seward. Everyone suspected that the attacks were part of a rebel conspiracy to murder several

WORDS TO KNOW
assailant (ə-sā′lənt) *n.* a person who attacks another
conspiracy (kən-spĭr′ə-sē) *n.* an agreement by two or more people to perform an illegal or wrong act

443

Active Reading: CLARIFY

I Have students paraphrase this famous quotation in order to be sure that they understand its meaning. (Possible responses: Now he is dead, but his reputation and name will live on. He is part of history. Now his soul lives in eternity. From now on he will live in the memories and imaginations of people.)

Critical Thinking: SYNTHESIZING

J Encourage students to explain how this scene echoes a previous scene in the excerpt. (Possible response: The last time the East Room of the White House was mentioned, it was in President Lincoln's haunting dream. In that dream and in actuality in this scene, a funeral is held for the president.)

Active Reading: EVALUATE

K Have students offer their opinions about the tradition of viewing the body or coffin of a dead person.

Literary Concept: BIOGRAPHY

L Encourage students to note the way that Freedman suddenly interrupts his chronological narrative. Ask them to comment on the author's decision to jump ahead more than a century to tell about opening the box that held the contents of President Lincoln's pockets. (Possible response: The author's decision to jump ahead to 1976 helps the reader feel connected to Lincoln by providing details about what he had in his pockets when he died.)

Active Reading: CONNECT

M Encourage students to share their thoughts and feelings about what it would be like to be in the public eye, vulnerable to hostility and scorn from all directions.

---

government officials and capture the city.

By dawn, a heavy rain was falling. Lincoln was still breathing faintly. Robert Lincoln surrendered to tears, then others in the room began to cry. At 7:22 A.M. on April 15, Lincoln died at the age of fifty-six. A doctor folded the president's hands across his chest. Gently he smoothed Lincoln's contracted face muscles, closed his eyelids, and drew a white sheet over his head. It was then that Secretary of War Edwin M. Stanton murmured, "Now he belongs to the ages."

The funeral was held in the East Room of the White House four days later, on April 19. Afterwards, the long funeral procession, led by a detachment of black troops, moved slowly up Pennsylvania Avenue to the muffled beat of drums and the tolling of church bells. When the procession reached the Capitol, Lincoln was carried inside to lie in state under the huge Capitol dome. The next day, thousands of people, black and white, soldiers and civilians, stood patiently in the rain, waiting to file past the open coffin.

On April 21, a funeral train set out on a sixteen-hundred-mile journey to Illinois, carrying Abraham Lincoln home to his final resting place in Springfield. The train followed the same route Lincoln had taken when he came to Washington as president-elect. It stopped at major cities along the way, so mourners could again file past the coffin. Where it did not stop, men and women with their children stood silently along the route to watch the train pass.

On the night of May 2, the train left Chicago and puffed its way southward through the rain across the Illinois prairie. People had built bonfires along the railroad tracks, and they stood outlined against the glowing red flames at every prairie village and country crossroads as the funeral train passed through.

At 9 A.M. it approached Springfield with its bell tolling. It steamed slowly through the business center and pulled up at the station, where regiments of soldiers and delegations of officials were waiting to meet it. Tens of thousands of people jammed the streets around the station and stood on nearby rooftops. A military band began to play a funeral dirge. All the bells of Springfield tolled. Guns fired a salute. And the crowd fell silent as the train came to a stop.

On the morning that Lincoln died, someone emptied the contents of his pockets and placed them in a box, which was wrapped in brown paper and tied with a string. Robert Lincoln passed the box on to his daughter, who presented it to the Library of Congress in 1937. Labeled "Do Not Open," it remained locked in a vault until 1976, when the string was untied and the paper unwrapped as the library staff looked on.

The morning he died, Lincoln had in his pockets a pair of small spectacles folded into a silver case; a small velvet eyeglass cleaner; a large linen handkerchief with *A. Lincoln* stitched in red; an ivory pocketknife trimmed with silver; and a brown leather wallet lined with purple silk. The wallet contained a Confederate five-dollar bill bearing the likeness of Jefferson Davis and eight newspaper clippings that Lincoln had cut out and saved. All the clippings praised him. As president, he had been denounced, ridiculed, and damned by a legion of critics. When he saw an article that complimented him, he often kept it.

One clipping found in Lincoln's wallet quotes the British reformer John Bright. Shortly before the presidential election of 1864, Bright wrote to the American newspaper publisher Horace Greeley and said:

"All those who believe that Slavery weakens America's power and tarnishes your good

444 UNIT FOUR PART 1: SO MUCH AT STAKE

Mini-Lesson Grammar

IRREGULAR VERBS Point out to students that certain pairs of irregular verbs are often confused. Several of these verbs and their definitions are listed below:

sit "to be in a seated position"
set "to put or place"
lie "to rest in a flat position"
lay "to put or place"

Application Invite students to choose the correct verb to complete the following sentences.

1. Lincoln asked his wife to (sit/set) down on the chair beside him. *(sit)*
2. Tad Lincoln asked his mother to (lay/lie) down to rest. *(lie)*
3. The doctor asked an assistant to (sit/set) the sponge on the table. *(set)*

Reteaching/Reinforcement
- *Grammar Handbook*, anthology pp. 885–886
- *Grammar Mini-Lessons* copymaster, pp. 27, 28, transparencies p. 20

The Writer's Craft
Irregular Verbs, p. 480

444 THE LANGUAGE OF LITERATURE TEACHER'S EDITION

name throughout the world, and who regard the restoration of your Union as a thing to be desired . . . are heartily longing for the reelection of Mr. Lincoln. . . . they think they have observed in his career a grand simplicity of purpose and a patriotism which knows no change and does not falter." ❖

Abraham Lincoln lying in state.
Courtesy of the Illinois State Historical Library.

FROM PERSONAL RESPONSE TO CRITICAL ANALYSIS

REFLECT 1. Were you surprised by any aspect of this account of Lincoln's death? Write your thoughts in your notebook.

RETHINK 2. Lincoln had always believed that if anyone wanted to kill him, there was nothing he could do to prevent it. Do you think there is anything he could have done? Explain your answer.

3. From this account, what have you learned about the character of Lincoln, the man?

RELATE 4. Today, U.S. presidents are heavily protected when they appear in public. Consider what is good and what is bad about tight security for public figures. Should presidents be so heavily protected? Explain your opinion.

LINCOLN: A PHOTOBIOGRAHY   445

Mini-Lesson Spelling

PREFIXES AND ROOTS Remind students that a root is a word part that cannot stand alone. It must be joined to other parts—a prefix and/or a suffix—to form a word. A root can be joined with many different prefixes to form many different words with different meanings. For instance, the word *abduction* (meaning "kidnapping") is made from the root *duct* (which means "to lead"), the prefix *ab-*, and the suffix *-ion*. By replacing this prefix with the prefix *pro-* (which means "forward"), one creates the word *production*, meaning "the process of bringing forth."

Application Have students study these words in order to create new words by replacing the prefixes.
1. denounced—replace with *pro-* (pronounced)
2. observed—replace with *pre-* (preserved)
3. propose—replace with *ex-* (expose)

Reteaching/Reinforcement
• *Unit Four Resource Book*, p. 17

STRATEGIC READING FOR
Less-Proficient Readers

N Ask students to summarize the contents of Lincoln's pockets and the circumstances leading up to discovery of the contents. *(Possible response: When the President died, the contents of his pockets were collected and stored in a box, which Lincoln's granddaughter gave to the Library of Congress in 1937. The contents included a pair of glasses, an eyeglass cleaner, a handkerchief, a pocketknife, and a wallet.)* **Noting Sequence of Events/Summarizing**

From Personal Response to Critical Analysis

1. Responses will vary.
2. Possible responses: The president could have stayed alive by restricting his activities; it might have been hard to limit himself this way, but it would have been safer than going to a public theater. Lincoln was absolutely right to think that he was ultimately powerless at the hands of a determined assassin.
3. Possible responses: Lincoln was a complex man. For example, he could be charitable about forgiving rebel behavior but fatalistic about the need for bodyguards. Lincoln's humanity is striking—his decency and thoughtfulness as well as his knowledge of his own shortcomings.
4. Possible responses: The good of heavily protecting presidents outweighs the bad because there are many people with weapons and a desire to kill important leaders. It's bad for presidents to be heavily protected, because they can never have normal contact with people, yet they must have this contact to govern fairly.

THE LANGUAGE OF LITERATURE TEACHER'S EDITION   445

O Captain! My Captain!

by Walt Whitman

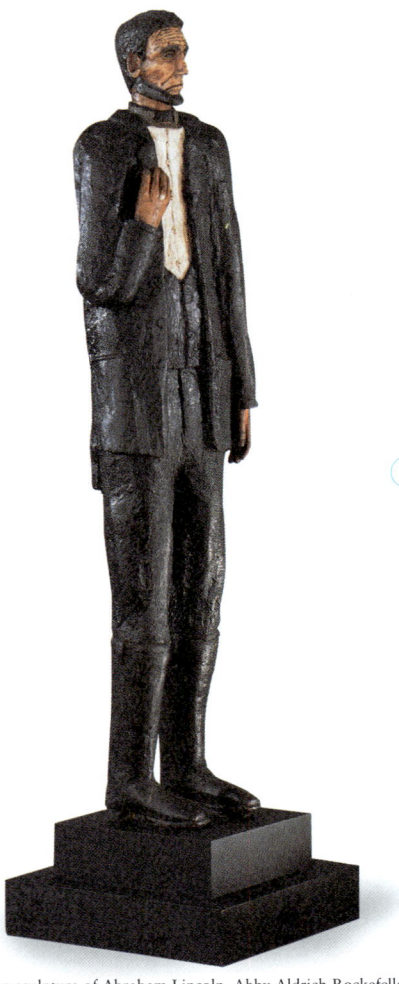

Decorative sculpture of Abraham Lincoln. Abby Aldrich Rockefeller Folk Art Center, Williamsburg, Virginia.

O Captain! my Captain! our fearful trip is done,
The ship has weather'd every rack,[1] the prize we sought is won,
The port is near, the bells I hear, the people all exulting,[2]
While follow eyes the steady keel, the vessel grim and daring;
    But O heart! heart! heart!
      O the bleeding drops of red,
        Where on the deck my Captain lies,
        Fallen cold and dead.

O Captain! my Captain! rise up and hear the bells;
Rise up—for you the flag is flung—for you the bugle trills,
For you bouquets and ribbon'd wreaths—for you the shores a-crowding,
For you they call, the swaying mass, their eager faces turning;
    Here Captain! dear father!
      This arm beneath your head!
        It is some dream that on the deck,
        You've fallen cold and dead.

My Captain does not answer, his lips are pale and still,
My father does not feel my arm, he has no pulse nor will,
The ship is anchor'd safe and sound, its voyage closed and done,
From fearful trip the victor ship comes in with object won:
    Exult O shores, and ring O bells!
      But I with mournful tread,
        Walk the deck my Captain lies,
        Fallen cold and dead.

1. **rack:** a battering, as by a storm.
2. **exulting:** rejoicing.

HISTORICAL INSIGHT

PRESIDENTIAL ASSASSINATIONS

Abraham Lincoln's assassination, the first murder of a president in the young history of the United States, shook the nation to its core, as can be seen in the excerpt from *Lincoln: A Photobiography* and in Whitman's grand poetic tribute. Over the next 36 years, the country was rocked by two more presidential assassinations—those of James A. Garfield and William McKinley. President Garfield was shot in the back by the evangelist Charles J. Guiteau as he walked through a train station in 1881. In 1901, at a public event in New York State, Leon Czolgosz gunned down William McKinley. The assassin seemed to be waiting to shake the president's hand but was hiding a pistol under what looked like an arm bandage.

It would be 62 years before another president—John F. Kennedy—would lose his life to an assassin. After a government investigation, it was determined that the alleged assassin, Lee Harvey Oswald, had acted alone. Some critics, however, believed that he had been part of a group that planned to murder Kennedy.

These tragedies are only part of the historical picture. There have also been numerous unsuccessful attempts on the lives of presidents. The first occurred in 1835, when Richard Lawrence shot two loaded pistols at Andrew Jackson from six feet away; miraculously, neither pistol released a bullet. Botched attempts were also made on the lives of Theodore Roosevelt, President-Elect Franklin D. Roosevelt, Harry S. Truman, Gerald R. Ford, and Ronald Reagan.

Who were these assassins? With the exception of Lincoln's assassin, the actor John Wilkes Booth, they were shy, ordinary people. Most had traumatic childhoods and a history of mental illness. They tended to be loners who nevertheless longed for fame. Most had an irrational dislike of the American way of life and of their victims' political views. Nearly all acted alone.

No one knows exactly how an assassination affects the country, but many historians insist that each killing of a significant U.S. political leader influences the course of U.S. history in a major way. For example, Reconstruction—the reorganization of the governments of the Southern states—might have been very different if Lincoln had lived.

Abraham Lincoln
1809–1865

James A. Garfield
1831–1881

William McKinley
1843–1901

John F. Kennedy
1917–1963

PRESIDENTIAL ASSASSINATIONS **447**

CUSTOMIZING FOR
Gifted and Talented Students

Have students write an appreciation of Abraham Lincoln's characteristics in a poem or song. Remind them to use details from the text, as well as their own intuitions about Lincoln's ethics and personality.

COMPREHENSION CHECK

1. What did President Lincoln receive in the mail nearly every day? *(death threats)*
2. Where was President Lincoln shot? *(at Ford's Theater in Washington, D.C.)*
3. Where was the president buried? *(in Springfield, Illinois)*
4. What does the speaker of "O Captain! My Captain!" see on the deck of the ship? *(The captain lies dead.)*
5. In Whitman's poem, who does the captain represent? *(Lincoln)*

INSIGHT

1. Only one of the four assassinated American presidents was killed since 1901. Why do you think there was only one assassination after 1901 although there were other attempts? *(Possible response: In recent years protection of public figures such as presidents has been increased.)*
2. Why do you think the person who is the President of the United States is a frequent target for assassination attempts? *(Possible response: The President is the highest representative of the United States government and is a symbol of the U.S. government and way of life.)*

Mini-Lesson: Speaking, Listening, and Viewing

SCORING A POEM WITH MUSIC Remind students that poems—especially those with notable sound devices such as rhyme, repetition, and alliteration—often contain strong elements of musicality. Usually a poet attempts to link the effects of particular sounds to the theme and mood of the work. For instance, the writer of a joyful poem about spring might choose words that sound light and buoyant.

Application Have students analyze Whitman's poem in order to determine its mood and central thematic concerns. Then invite students to find a piece of music that would complement an oral reading of the poem. Have students play the music (with or without a reading of the text) for the class.

THE LANGUAGE OF LITERATURE TEACHER'S EDITION **447**

From Personal Response to Critical Analysis

1. Possible response: It conveys the speaker's sense of deep grief.
2. Possible response: The comparison is valid. A ship's captain holds some of the same responsibilities as a president—while the ship is at sea, the captain leads the ship's society, just as Lincoln led the country during the Civil War. People feel respect for both a ship's captain and a president.
3. Possible response: To heighten the tragedy and irony of the captain's death, Whitman contrasts it with the successful completion of a task or journey ("our fearful trip is done"), the people's exultation at the triumph, pealing bells, and beautiful wreaths and flowers.
4. Possible responses: The biographical excerpt conveys a greater sense of loss because the author includes details that bring Abraham Lincoln to life. The poem conveys more loss because its speaker is full of grief and energy, whereas the speaker of the biography is unemotional.
5. Possible response: The country lost a great leader at a time when it was trying to put itself back together, and Lincoln's vision and intelligence and leadership were sorely missed.

Another Pathway

Cooperative Learning As others brainstorm metaphors, one student (a prober) could help the group come up with the best possible choices by asking the group to explain why their ideas are effective. Group members can discuss and decide which set of metaphors would work best in a poem. While some members contribute to the writing of the poem, one member could check for understanding by reviewing the finished draft and offering comments and suggestions.

Rubric

3 Full Accomplishment Students generate several intriguing metaphors, from which they write a vivid poem on the same subject as "O Captain! My Captain!"

2 Substantial Accomplishment Students generate a few metaphors, from which they write a poem on the same subject as "O Captain! My Captain!"

1 Little or Partial Accomplishment Students generate only one or two metaphors and have trouble writing a poem on the same subject as "O Captain! My Captain!"

RESPONDING OPTIONS

FROM PERSONAL RESPONSE TO CRITICAL ANALYSIS

REFLECT
1. What feeling does "O Captain! My Captain!" convey to you?

RETHINK
2. In your opinion, how effective is Whitman's comparison of Lincoln's death to that of a ship's captain?
   Consider
   - what the ship represents
   - the "fearful trip" the ship has completed
   - how the crowd is reacting
   - what is happening on deck

   Close Textual Analysis

3. How does Whitman use contrasts to heighten the tragedy and irony of the captain's death?

RELATE
4. Does the excerpt from *Lincoln: A Photobiography* or "O Captain! My Captain!" convey a greater sense of loss to you? Explain your answer.

   Literary Link

5. Besides the loss of Lincoln himself, what were other consequences of his assassination? What do you think was the worst consequence of this tragedy?

   Thematic Link

Multimodal Learning
ANOTHER PATHWAY
Cooperative Learning
Whitman chose to compare Lincoln to a ship's captain. With other students, think of two or three other metaphors for our country, its leader, the Civil War, and the leader's death. Together, try to write a poem that makes use of your metaphors.

LITERARY CONCEPTS

A **biography** is the true story of a person's life, told by someone else. If possible, a biographer usually tries to interview his or her subject. When the subject is no longer living, a biographer relies on letters, diaries, and any other available information. A biographer cannot help presenting his or her subject from a personal point of view—admiring, critical, or somewhere in between—but skilled biographers try to give as balanced an interpretation as they can.

Review the way in which Russell Freedman presents facts in his account of Lincoln. What is his point of view? Do you think he provides a balanced interpretation? Why or why not?

QUICKWRITES

1. Write a **letter** to President Lincoln in which you try to persuade him not to attend the play on April 14, 1865.
2. Write a **character sketch** of President Lincoln based only on what you can infer from the contents of his pockets at the time of his death.
3. Using "O Captain! My Captain!" as a model, write a **poem** about another loss.

📁 **PORTFOLIO** Save your writing. You may want to use it later as a springboard to a piece for your portfolio.

448 UNIT FOUR PART 1: SO MUCH AT STAKE

Literary Concepts

Encourage students to go back to the text to examine Freedman's tone as well as his choice of words and of details and facts. Students may think that Freedman is basically sympathetic to Lincoln, although he takes care to include information that helps to give the human side of Lincoln. You may wish to have students work in small groups of three or four to design and complete a chart that lists the biographer's inclusion of both Lincoln's strengths and weaknesses as a president.

QuickWrites

1. Have students begin by deciding on the letter writer's identity and relationship to the President.
2. Encourage students to begin by studying the list of the contents of the pocket and jotting down associations that come into their minds.
3. Remind students that their poem need not deal with a loss of life. Assure them that no loss is "too small" to be an appropriate subject for a poem.

Multimodal Learning

ALTERNATIVE ACTIVITIES

Locate a copy of Ford's Theater's seating plan, and find out where President Lincoln sat the night of April 14, 1865. Using the plan as a graphic aid, draft a **proposal** explaining how you would use a team of Secret Service agents to protect Lincoln.

ACROSS THE CURRICULUM

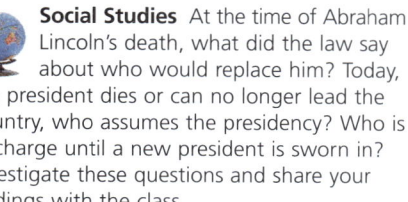

Social Studies At the time of Abraham Lincoln's death, what did the law say about who would replace him? Today, if a president dies or can no longer lead the country, who assumes the presidency? Who is in charge until a new president is sworn in? Investigate these questions and share your findings with the class.

WORDS TO KNOW

Review the Words to Know at the bottom of the selection pages, and list them on your paper. Then match each word with the situation that best fits its meaning.

1. As the mob's hatred grew, so did its thirst for revenge.
2. The boy's millionaire father anxiously awaited the kidnapper's ransom note.
3. The assassin's death sentence was overturned, but he would never be free.
4. Though the three of them plotted for months, their scheme failed.
5. The woman aimed her pistol at the President but shot a bystander.

Words to Know

1. vindictiveness
2. abduction
3. revoke
4. conspiracy
5. assailant

Reteaching/Reinforcement
- *Unit Four Resource Book,* p. 18

Across The Curriculum

Social Studies *Death and the Presidency* Students' research should show that both in Lincoln's time and at the present, the death of a president results in the vice-president becoming president. Today, unlike in Lincoln's time, a detailed line of succession to the presidency is specified. The first part of this line is as follows:
1. vice-president
2. speaker of the House of Representatives
3. president pro tempore of the Senate
4. secretary of state
5. secretary of the treasury

ADDITIONAL SUGGESTION
Geography *Going Home* Have students draw a detailed map that shows the approximate route by which President Lincoln's remains were returned to Springfield, Illinois.

RUSSELL FREEDMAN

1929–

A story about Louis Braille, a blind boy who invented the Braille alphabet at the age of 16, inspired Russell Freedman to write his first book, *Teenagers Who Made History.* Since then he has written almost 40 nonfiction books for young people.

In his later books, Freedman has included photographs because of their ability to "reveal something that words alone can't express" and has returned to writing about people. "When I finish a book, like the one about Lincoln, I feel I know Lincoln better than my friends," he has said. Freedman is a three-time winner of the prestigious Newbery Medal.
OTHER WORKS *The Wright Brothers: How They Invented the Airplane, Eleanor Roosevelt: A Life of Discovery* Extended Reading

WALT WHITMAN

1819–1892

The poetry of Walt Whitman was praised by a few critics during his lifetime but denounced by many others. Abraham Lincoln reportedly read aloud from Whitman's *Leaves of Grass,* even though few bookstores carried it. Today Whitman is considered one of the greatest of American poets.

Born on Long Island, New York, Whitman quit school at the age of 11, working at various times as a printer, a teacher, a newspaper reporter, an editor, and a publisher.

Whitman's concern for others has recently been proved. In 1995, four volumes of Whitman's notes, which had been presumed stolen since the 1940s, resurfaced. The notebooks contain notes Whitman took while working as a nurse in a Union army hospital in Washington during the Civil War.
OTHER WORKS *Drum-Taps, Poems of Walt Whitman*

Extended Reading

LASERLINKS
• AUTHOR BACKGROUND

449

RUSSELL FREEDMAN

In his Newbery Medal acceptance speech in 1988, Freedman noted that "one of the great joys of writing nonfiction for youngsters is the opportunity to explore almost any subject that excites your interest. I picked Lincoln as a subject because I felt I could offer a fresh perspective for today's generation of young readers, but mostly I picked him because I wanted to satisfy my own itch to know."

AUTHOR BACKGROUND

Walt Whitman These images show the poet as a young man and as an old man. Included is the frontispiece engraving of Whitman from the 1855 edition of *Leaves of Grass.*

Side A, Frames 52755

Alternative Activities

Remind students to think in terms of restricting access to the President. They should consider the locations of all doors and passageways leading in and out of the theater, as well as the proximity of the stage to the presidential box. Ask students to decide where Secret Service agents would best be positioned to shield the President from an assailant's bullet.

WALT WHITMAN

Whitman's metaphor of Lincoln as a ship's captain may be a reflection of the poet's fascination with the ocean. He remarked, "Even as a boy, I had the fancy, the wish, to write a piece, perhaps a poem, about the sea-shore.... Hours, days, in my Long Island youth and early manhood, I haunted the shores of Rockaway or Coney Island, or away east to the Hamptons or Montauk."

THE LANGUAGE OF LITERATURE Teacher's Edition **449**

OVERVIEW

Objectives

- To understand and appreciate an autobiography about a surgeon's efforts to help children recover from brain injuries
- To understand specialized medical vocabulary
- To identify and understand an autobiography
- To express understanding of autobiography through a choice of writing forms, including a letter to the editor and a diary entry
- To extend understanding of autobiography through a variety of multimodal and cross-curricular activities

Skills

READING SKILLS/STRATEGIES
- Evaluating
- Using specialized vocabulary

THE WRITER'S STYLE
- Elaboration using examples

GRAMMAR
- Complex sentences

LITERARY CONCEPTS
- Autobiography
- Author's purpose
- Description

SPELLING
- Suffixes following c and g

SPEAKING, LISTENING, AND VIEWING
- Group discussion
- Oral presentation

Cross-Curricular Connections

SCIENCE
- The Hippocratic oath
- Brain research

HISTORY
- The history of surgery

SCIENCE CONNECTION
The Brain Help students understand this complex selection by showing them these photographs of the human brain, brain surgery, and computerized brain scans.

Side A, Frame 52760

PREVIEWING

NONFICTION

from Gifted Hands
Ben Carson, M.D., with Cecil Murphey

Activating Prior Knowledge
PERSONAL CONNECTION

Think about the responsibilities, the problems, the work schedule, the training, and the income of a doctor. What do you think would be satisfying about being a doctor? What would be difficult about it? Record your views in a chart like the one shown, then discuss them with the class.

Being a Doctor	
Satisfactions	Difficulties

Building Background
SCIENCE CONNECTION

This selection describes the specialized work of Ben Carson, a leading pediatric neurosurgeon (pē´dē-ăt´rĭk noor´ō-sûr´jən)— a doctor who operates on the nervous system of children. Most of Dr. Carson's surgery involves the brain, the center of the nervous system.

Dr. Carson is the director of pediatric neurosurgery at Johns Hopkins Hospital in Baltimore, Maryland. Children requiring difficult brain surgery, like the removal of a tumor, are referred to Dr. Carson and other pediatric neurosurgeons by doctors who do not have specialized training in this type of surgery. Patients come to Johns Hopkins from all over the country and around the world.

Performing operations considered unthinkable a short time ago, Dr. Carson and his colleagues develop their own techniques for solving difficult medical problems. Sometimes these procedures work, and patients are cured; at other times the procedures fail. From these failures, the doctors often gain new knowledge that will benefit others.

Setting A Purpose
READING CONNECTION

Specialized Vocabulary Medicine, like other specialized fields, has its own vocabulary. Some medical terms in this selection are defined in the Words to Know boxes and in footnotes. The meanings of others can be inferred from the context. The meaning of *metastasized* on page 456, for example, is suggested by the sentence clue "all over." Still others can be figured out from their word parts. For example in *chemotherapy* (page 455), *chemo-* refers to chemicals or drugs, and *therapy* means "treatment." As you read this account of a doctor's professional experiences, look for definitions and clues that will help you with the meanings of unfamiliar medical terms.

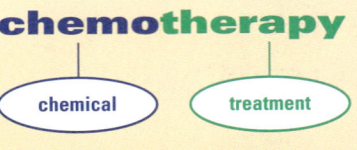

LASERLINKS
• SCIENCE CONNECTION

450 UNIT FOUR PART 1: SO MUCH AT STAKE

PRINT AND MEDIA RESOURCES

UNIT FOUR RESOURCE BOOK
Strategic Reading: Literature, p. 21
Vocabulary SkillBuilder, p. 24
Reading SkillBuilder, p. 22
Spelling SkillBuilder, p. 23

GRAMMAR MINI-LESSONS
Transparencies, pp. 44 and 47

WRITING MINI-LESSONS
Transparencies, p. 34

ACCESS FOR STUDENTS ACQUIRING ENGLISH
Selection Summaries
Reading and Writing Support

FORMAL ASSESSMENT
Selection Test, pp. 87–88
Test Generator

AUDIO LIBRARY
See Reference Card

LASERLINKS
Science Connection
Author Background

INTERNET RESOURCES
McDougal Littell Literature Center at http://www.hmco.com/mcdougal/lit

from
Gifted Hands
by Ben Carson, M.D., with Cecil Murphey

Courtesy of Johns Hopkins Children's Center.

WORDS TO KNOW

autopsy (ô'tŏp'sē) *n.* an examination of a dead body to determine the cause of death (p. 456)
dilated (dī-lā'tĭd) *adj.* enlarged (p. 452)
dismal (dĭz'məl) *adj.* causing gloom or depression (p. 455)
distraught (dĭ-strôt') *adj.* extremely agitated (p. 453)
galvanize (găl'və-nīz) *v.* to arouse; electrify (p. 452)

inevitable (ĭn-ĕv'ĭ-tə-bəl) *adj.* impossible to avoid or prevent; certain (p. 453)
malignant (mə-lĭg'nənt) *adj.* cancerous (p. 455)
radical (răd'ĭ-kəl) *adj.* extreme (p. 453)
skepticism (skĕp'tĭ-sĭz'əm) *n.* a doubting or questioning attitude (p. 455)
vivacious (vĭ-vā'shəs) *adj.* full of life and spirit (p. 453)

SUMMARY

Pediatric neurosurgeon Ben Carson recalls three patients who strengthened his desire to ignore critics and continue treating seemingly hopeless cases. One patient was Bo-Bo, a four-year-old dying of a brain injury. Though other doctors said Carson was wasting his time, he tried radical surgery. Six weeks later, Bo-Bo was completely well. The second patient was Charles, age ten, with brain injuries even worse than Bo-Bo's. Carson tried the same surgery, but Charles responded slowly. Again, other doctors criticized Carson. Yet Charles, too, recovered. The third patient was Danielle, who was five months old and had been born with a cancerous brain tumor. No other doctor would operate. Carson and a partner removed the tumor, but cancer had spread through the baby's body, and she died. Carson felt that if he had operated a month earlier, she might have lived.

Thematic Link: *So Much at Stake* A neurosurgeon works to help children battle life-threatening illnesses and injuries.

CUSTOMIZING FOR
Students Acquiring English

- Use **ACCESS FOR STUDENTS ACQUIRING ENGLISH**, *Reading and Writing Support.*
- As you discuss this selection with students, be sure to define unfamiliar medical terms and personnel.

STRATEGIC READING FOR
Less-Proficient Readers

Set a Purpose Encourage students to become involved in the story by describing their impressions of a hospital operating room. Then have students read to find out about Dr. Carson's handling of Bo-Bo's case and whether she recovers from surgery.

Use **UNIT FOUR RESOURCE BOOK**, p. 21, for guidance in reading the selection.

CUSTOMIZING FOR
Gifted and Talented Students

Have students debate the right of patients to decide the course of their medical treatment. Point out that the issues become especially complicated when a child is involved. Ask students who they think can best speak for the welfare of the ill child—a physician with technical expertise or the parent or guardian. Ask if there are any circumstances in which students think children should have a voice in these decisions.

CUSTOMIZING FOR
Students Acquiring English

1. Explain that doctors visit their hospital patients each day. This is called making rounds.
2. Tell students that the ICU is the intensive care unit. A comatose person is someone who is unconscious.
3. Make sure students understand that the expression "ran into" is not meant literally, but means "to meet accidentally."

Active Reading: EVALUATE

A Have students discuss whether a pediatric neurosurgeon should operate on a patient with a supposedly hopeless illness. *(Possible responses: Yes, surgery should be performed if the doctor thinks there is any chance at all of saving a patient's life; no, neurosurgery is extremely expensive and should only be performed if there is more than a tiny hope that it will be successful.)*

Dr. Ben Carson is an outstanding neurosurgeon. He is famous for successfully performing many operations that others feared to try—such as, in 1987, when he and his team separated twin babies who were joined at the head. Time after time, people have credited him with performing miracles in the operating room on young patients who seemed to be facing certain death.

Three Special Children

The resident[1] flicked off his penlight and straightened up from the bedside of Bo-Bo Valentine. "Don't you think it's time to give up on this little girl?" he asked, nodding toward the 4-year-old child.

It was early Monday morning, and I was making rounds. When I came to Bo-Bo, the house officer explained her situation. "Just about the only thing she has left is pupilary response," he said. (That meant that her pupils still responded to light.) The light he shone in her eyes told him that pressure had built inside her head. The doctors had put Bo-Bo in a barbiturate coma[2] and given her hyperventilation[3] but still couldn't keep the pressures down.

Little Bo-Bo was another of the far-too-many children who run out into a street and are hit by a car. A Good Humor truck struck Bo-Bo. She'd lain in the ICU all weekend, comatose and with an intracranial pressure monitor in her skull. Her blood pressure gradually worsened, and she was losing what little function, purposeful movement, and response to stimuli she had.

Before answering the resident, I bent over Bo-Bo and lifted her eyelids. Her pupils were fixed and <u>dilated</u>. "I thought you told me the pupils were still working?" I said in astonishment.

"I did," he protested. "They were working just before you came in."

"You're telling me this just happened? That her eyes just now dilated?"

"They must have!"

"Four plus emergency," I called loudly but calmly. "We've got to do something right away!" I turned to the nurse standing behind me. "Call the operating room. We're on our way."

"Four plus emergency!" she called even louder and hurried down the corridor.

Although rare, a plus four—for dire emergency—<u>galvanizes</u> everyone into action. The OR[4] staff clears out a room and starts getting the instruments ready. They work with quiet efficiency, and they're quick. No one argues and no one has time to explain.

Two residents grabbed Bo-Bo's bed and half-ran down the hallway. Fortunately surgery hadn't started on the scheduled patient, so we bumped the case.

On my way to the operating room I ran into another neurosurgeon—senior to me and a man I highly respect because of his work with trauma accidents. While the staff was setting up, I explained to him what had happened and what I was going to do.

"Don't do it," he said, as he walked away from me. "You're wasting your time."

His attitude amazed me, but I didn't dwell on it. Bo-Bo Valentine was still alive. We had a chance—extremely small—but still a chance to save her life. I decided I would go ahead and do surgery anyway.

---

1. **resident:** a physician working at a hospital to receive specialized training in the care of patients.
2. **barbiturate coma** (bär-bĭch′ər-ĭt kō′mə): a deep unconsciousness produced by a drug that depresses the nervous system.
3. **hyperventilation** (hī′pər-vĕn′tl-ā′shən): a procedure that increases the rate of breathing, causing a loss of carbon dioxide in the blood and reducing blood pressure.
4. **OR:** an abbreviation of *operating room*.

WORDS TO KNOW
dilated (dī-lā′tĭd) *adj.* enlarged
galvanize (găl′və-nīz) *v.* to arouse; electrify

452

Mini-Lesson Grammar

COMPLEX SENTENCES Point out to students that a complex sentence contains one main clause and one or more subordinate clauses. Remind them that a clause is a group of words that contains a verb and its subject. A main clause is one that can stand on its own; a subordinate clause cannot stand by itself because it does not express a complete thought.

Application Invite students to distinguish the main and subordinate clauses in these sentences:
1. When I came to Bo-Bo *(subordinate)*, the house officer explained her situation *(main)*.
2. Before answering the resident *(subordinate)*, I bent over Bo-Bo and lifted her eyelids *(main)*.
3. While the staff was setting up *(subordinate)*, I explained to him what had happened and what I was going to do *(main)*.

Then have students write a complex sentence about Dr. Carson's decision to operate on Bo-Bo.

Reteaching/Reinforcement
- *Grammar Mini-Lessons* transparencies, pp. 44, 48

Complex Sentences, pp. 560-568

452 THE LANGUAGE OF LITERATURE TEACHER'S EDITION

Bo-Bo was gently positioned on an "egg crate," a soft, flexible pad covering the operating table, and was covered with a pale green sheet. Within minutes the nurses and anesthesiologist had her ready for me to begin.

I did a craniectomy. First I opened her head and took off the front portion of her skull. The skull bone was put in a sterile solution. Then I opened up the covering of her brain—the dura.[5] Between the two halves of the brain is an area called the falx. By splitting the falx, the two halves could communicate together and equalize the pressure between her hemispheres. Using cadaveric dura (dura from a dead person), I sewed it over her brain. This gave her brain room to swell, then heal, and still held everything inside her skull in place. Once I covered the area, I closed the scalp. The surgery took about two hours.

Bo-Bo remained comatose for the next few days. It is heartbreaking to watch parents sit by the bedside of a comatose child, and I felt for them. I could only give them hope; I couldn't promise Bo-Bo's recovery. One morning I stopped by her bed and noted that her pupils were starting to work a little bit. I recall thinking, "Maybe something positive is starting to happen."

After two more days Bo-Bo started moving a little. Sometimes she stretched her legs or shifted her body as if trying to get more comfortable. Over the course of a week she grew alert and responsive. When it became apparent that she was going to recover, we took her back to surgery, and I replaced the portion of her skull that had been removed. Within six weeks Bo-Bo was once again, a normal 4-year-old girl—vivacious, bouncy, and cute.

This is another instance when I'm glad I didn't listen to a critic.

I've actually done one craniectomy since then. Again I encountered opposition.

In the summer of 1988, we had a similar situation except that Charles,* age 10, was in worse shape. He had been hit by a car.

When the head nurse told me that Charles's pupils had become fixed and dilated, that meant we had to take action. The clinic was especially busy that day, so I sent the senior resident to explain to the mother that, in my judgment, we ought to take Charles to the operating room immediately. We would remove a portion of his brain as a last-ditch effort to save his life. "It may not work," the resident told her, "but Dr. Carson thinks it's worth a try."

The poor mother was distraught and shocked. "Absolutely not," she cried. "I can't let you do it. You will not do that to my boy! Just let him die in peace. You're not going to be playing around with my kid."

"But this way we have a chance—"

"A chance? I want more than a chance." She kept shaking her head. "Let him go." Her response was reasonable. By then Charles wasn't responding to anything.

Only three days earlier we had regretfully told her that Charles's condition was so serious that he would probably not recover, and she should come to grips with the inevitable end. Then suddenly a man stood before her, urging her to give her consent to a radical procedure. The resident could give her no assurance that Charles would recover or even be better.

After the resident returned and repeated the

*For the sake of privacy, I have changed his name.

---

5. **dura** (do͝or′ə): the outermost and toughest of the three membranes covering the brain and spinal cord.

WORDS TO KNOW
vivacious (vĭ-vā′shəs) *adj.* full of life and spirit
distraught (dĭ-strôt′) *adj.* extremely agitated
inevitable (ĭn-ĕv′ĭ-tə-bəl) *adj.* impossible to avoid or prevent; certain
radical (răd′ĭ-kəl) *adj.* extreme

453

Mini-Lesson Literary Concepts

REVIEWING DESCRIPTION Remind students that a description is a picture, in words, of a scene, a character, or an object. See the web to the right. In a work of fiction, a description is apt to appeal to the reader's senses. In a nonfiction account, such as an autobiography, descriptions often provide detailed information about people or events.

Application Have students read closely the second paragraph on page 453. Then have them analyze this example of description. Ask students to determine whether the author is describing a person, describing an event, or appealing to the reader's senses. (*He is describing an event—an operation performed on Bo-Bo's brain.*) Then ask students how the author describes the event. (*He describes each step of the operation in considerable detail—for example, "opened up the covering of her brain" and "using cadaveric dura."*) Have students discuss the effect of this descriptive passage. (*It gives the reader a vivid sense of the severity of Bo-Bo's injury and the efforts necessary to bring her back to health.*)

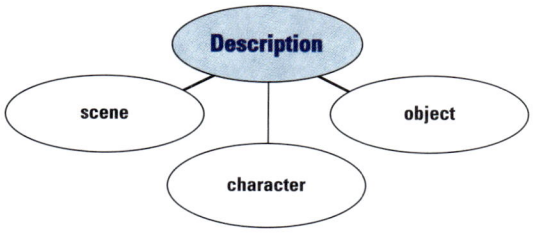

Active Reading: EVALUATE

 Ask students to explain their reaction to this paragraph. Ask them if they agree with the surgeon's philosophy and to explain why or why not. If they need help, you might wish to share the following thought processes with them:

Think-Aloud Model *Charles's mother seems sure about her feelings. But Dr. Carson is making a really important point—if there is a tiny bit of hope, then it just might be worth operating. When he says that "the worst thing that could happen is that Charles dies anyway," his reason makes sense. But maybe the mother thinks that the worst thing might be that Charles will suffer even more and then die. Since it's such an important decision, I think the doctor is probably right in discussing surgery one more time with Charles's mother.*

Linking to Science

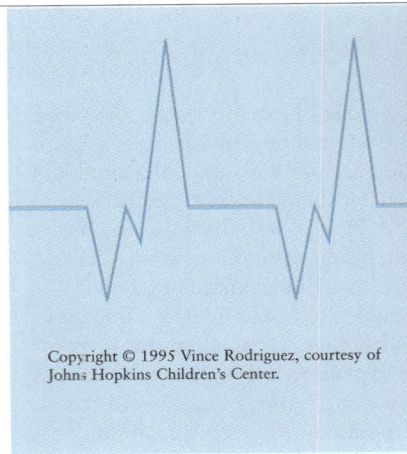 The Hippocratic Oath is a creed of ethical conduct that graduates of many medical schools for centuries have pledged to uphold. Based on the practice and theories of the Greek physician Hippocrates (460?–370? B.C.), the oath states, in part, "The regimen I adopt shall be for the benefit of my patients according to my ability and judgment, and not for their hurt or for any wrong."

Literary Concept: AUTHOR'S PURPOSE

 Have students consider how the information in these several short paragraphs helps the author achieve his purpose. (*Possible response: Carson's purpose is to inform the reader about various situations in which his willingness to perform surgery saved the lives of "hopeless" patients. These short paragraphs show the pressures he faced within the medical establishment.*)

Individual	Specific Event/Behavior	My Evaluation
Charles' mother	refuses surgery	She was justified because she felt as though Charles had already suffered too much.

Copyright © 1995 Vince Rodriguez, courtesy of Johns Hopkins Children's Center.

conversation, I went to see Charles's mother. I spent a long time explaining in detail that we weren't going to cut the boy in pieces. She still hesitated.

"Let me tell you about a similar situation we had here," I said. "She was a sweet little girl named Bo-Bo." When I finished I added, "Look, I don't know about this surgery. It may not work, but I don't see that we can give up in a situation where we still have even a glimmer of hope. Maybe it's the smallest chance of hope, but we can't just throw it away, can we? The worst thing that could happen is that Charles dies anyway."

Once she understood exactly what I would do, she said, "You mean there really is a chance? A possibility that Charles might live?"

"A chance, yes, if we do surgery. Without it, no chance whatsoever."

"In that case," she said, "of course I want you to try. I just didn't want you cutting him up when it didn't make any difference—"

Not defending ourselves that we don't do such things, I again emphasized that this was the only chance we could offer her. She signed the consent form immediately. We rushed the boy off to the operating room.

As with Bo-Bo, it involved removing a portion of the skull, cutting between the two halves of the brain, covering the swollen brain with cadaveric dura, and sewing the scalp back up.

As expected, Charles remained comatose afterward, and for a week nothing changed. More than one staff member said something to me like, "The ball game's over. We're wasting our time."

Someone presented Charles's case in our neurosurgical grand rounds. Neurosurgery grand rounds is a weekly conference attended by all neurosurgeons and residents to discuss interesting cases. Previously scheduled for an important surgery, I couldn't be present, but I was told what was said by several who had been in on the conference.

"What do you think?" the attending doctor asked one intern.

"Isn't this going a little bit beyond the call of duty?"

Another one said quite firmly. "I think it was a foolish thing to do."

Others agreed.

One of the attending neurosurgeons, familiar with the boy's condition, stated, "These types of situations never result in anything good."

Another said, "This patient has not yet recovered, and he's not going to recover. In my opinion, it's inappropriate to attempt a craniectomy."

Would they have been so vocal if I had been present? I'm not sure, yet they were speaking

---

Mini-Lesson — Reading Skills/Strategies

ACTIVE READING: EVALUATE Remind students that evaluating is the process of judging the worth of something or someone. A work of literature or its elements—such as characters, events, specific instances of behavior—may be evaluated by the reader. The works of literature themselves are usually evaluated on standards such as entertainment, believability, originality, or emotional power.

Application Encourage students to make their own evaluations of the behavior of individuals involved in the cases of Bo-Bo, Charles, and Danielle. Ask them what their opinions are about the actions and words of certain physicians and family members. Tell students to place their evaluations in a chart like the one shown.

Reteaching/Reinforcement
• *Unit Four Resource Book*, p. 22

from their own conviction. And since seven days had passed with no change, their <u>skepticism</u> was understandable.

Maybe I'm just stubborn, or maybe I inwardly knew the boy still had a fighting chance. At any rate, I wasn't ready to give up.

On the eighth day a nurse noticed that Charles's eyelids were fluttering. It was the story of Bo-Bo all over again. Soon Charles started to talk, and before a month ended, we sent him to rehab.[6] He has made great strides ever since. In the long run, we believe he's going to be fine.

Bo-Bo won't have any seizures, but Charles may. His condition was more severe, he was older, and he didn't recover as quickly as Bo-Bo. Six months after the event (when I last had contact with the family), Charles had still not fully recovered, although he is active, walking and talking, and is developing a dynamic personality. Most of all, Charles's mother clearly is thankful to have her son alive.

Another case I don't think I'll ever forget involved Detroit-born Danielle. Five months old when I first saw her, she had been born with a tumor on her head that continued growing. By the time I saw Danielle, the tumor bulged out through the skull and was the same size as her head. The tumor had actually eroded the skin, and pus drained out of it.

Friends advised her mother, "Put your baby in an institution and let her die."

"No!" she said. "This is my child. My own flesh and blood."

Danielle's mother was doing the herculean task of taking care of her. Two or three times each day she changed Danielle's dressings, trying to keep the wounds clean.

Danielle's mother called my office because she had read an article about me in the *Ladies Home Journal* in which it stated that I frequently did surgeries that nobody else would touch. She talked to my physician's assistant, Carol James.

"Ben," Carol reported later that day, "I think this one is worth looking into."

After hearing the details, I agreed. "Have the mother send me the medical records and pictures."

> "This patient has not yet recovered, and he's not going to recover. In my opinion, it's inappropriate to attempt a craniectomy."

Less than a week later, I examined everything. I realized immediately that it was a <u>dismal</u> situation. The brain was abnormal, the tumor had spread all over the place, and we didn't know how the skin could be closed.

I called my friend Craig Dufresne, a superb plastic surgeon, and together we tried to figure out a way that we could remove the tumor and close the skull again. We also consulted Dr. Peter Phillips, one of our pediatric neuro-oncologists who specializes in treating kids with brain tumors.

Together we finally devised a way that we would actually get the tumor out. Then Dr. Dufresne would swing up muscle/skin flaps from the back and try to cover the head with them. Once that had healed, Doctors Peter Phillips and Lewis Strauss would come up with a chemotherapy program to kill any remaining <u>malignant</u> cells.

---

6. **rehab:** the hospital department where patients are sent for rehabilitation—therapy intended to restore full health.

WORDS TO KNOW
skepticism (skĕp′tĭ-sĭz′əm) *n.* a doubting or questioning attitude
dismal (dĭz′məl) *adj.* gloomy; depressing
malignant (mə-lĭg′nənt) *adj.* cancerous

455

STRATEGIC READING FOR
Less-Proficient Readers

H Ask students to compare Charles's case to Bo-Bo's. (*Both Charles and Bo-Bo had similar brain damage after being struck by moving vehicles. However, the damage to Charles's head was much more serious. Dr. Carson performed an operation on Charles that was similar to Bo-Bo's. Since Charles's injuries were more extensive and he was older, his recovery was slower than Bo-Bo's.*)
Comparing and Contrasting/Summarizing

Set a Purpose Have students read to find out how Danielle fares before and after surgery.

Literary Concept: DESCRIPTION

I Draw students' attention to this description of Danielle's condition. Ask them to comment on how a poet's or fiction writer's description of Danielle's health might differ from a neurosurgeon's. (*Possible response: Carson is describing the exact physical condition of Danielle when he first observed her, whereas a poet or fiction writer would be more likely to use vivid descriptive or figurative language.*)

CUSTOMIZING FOR
Students Acquiring English

5 Explain that Hercules was a Greek mythical hero with super-human powers. Ask students what the adjective *herculean* might mean in the phrase "herculean task." (*a task of unusual difficulty*)

CUSTOMIZING FOR
Multiple Learning Styles

J Spatial or Graphic Learners Invite students to make a drawing or a model of a normal human brain. Encourage them to include as many details as possible and to label the various parts of the brain.

Mini-Lesson Spelling

SUFFIXES FOLLOWING c AND g Remind students that it is sometimes difficult to choose between the following endings when one is spelling a word: *-ant/-ent, -able/-ible, -uous/-ious, -ance/-ence, -asm/-ism.* Review with students the basic rules governing the use of suffixes after the letters *c* and *g*.

- When the letters *c* and *g* have a hard sound, they are followed by the vowels *a* or *u*. Use the endings *-ance, -ant, -able, -uous, -asm.*

- When the letters *c* and *g* have a soft sound, they are followed by the vowels *e* or *i*. Use the endings *-ence, -ent, -ible, -ious, -ism.*

Examples from the selection: **vivacious, skepticism**

Application Have students spell the following words after you read them aloud.
1. elegant
2. magnificent
3. intelligent
4. significance
5. ambiguous
6. innocence

Reteaching/Reinforcement
- *Unit Four Resource Book,* p. 23

CUSTOMIZING FOR
Students Acquiring English

6 *Metastasized* means that the cancer had spread throughout the body.

STRATEGIC READING FOR
Less-Proficient Readers

K Ask students to explain how Danielle fares before and after surgery. *(Before surgery Danielle's growth and quality of life were impeded by a brain tumor. After surgery she showed signs of recovery but then died.)* **Noting Sequences of Events**

Active Reading: EVALUATE

L Ask students if the effect of the excerpt would be different if all three patients had recovered. *(Possible response: If Carson included only patients who recovered fully, the excerpt might sound self-promoting and egotistical.)*

CUSTOMIZING FOR
Gifted and Talented Students

Have students rewrite this autobiographical excerpt as a one-act play. Students might weave the three narratives together or present them one at a time, as Carson does.

COMPREHENSION CHECK
1. How was Bo-Bo injured? (She was struck by a truck.)
2. What is Bo-Bo's condition six weeks after her surgery? (She is back to normal.)
3. Why do other physicians think operating on Charles was foolish? (They think the boy's chances of surviving are nonexistent.)
4. Why does surgery fail to save Danielle? (Cancer had spread throughout her body.)

We assumed it was going to be a tough case and would require a tremendous amount of time. We were right. The operation to remove the tumor and to sew in the muscle flaps took 19 hours. We had no concern about the time, only the results.

Dr. Dufresne and I tag-teamed the surgery. I needed almost half of the surgery hours to remove the tumor. Then Dufresne spent the next nine hours covering her skull with the muscular cutaneous skin flaps. He was able to get the skin closed over.

> "We know that you're a man of God, and that the Lord has all these things in His hands."

About halfway through the surgery, I said to Dufresne, "I think we're going to come out of this with our socks on."

He nodded, and I could tell he felt as confident as I did.

The surgery was successful. As we had anticipated, in the weeks following the removal of the tumor, Danielle had to go back to the operating room and have the flaps moved to take tension off certain areas and to improve blood circulation to the surgical site.

Initially, Danielle started to do well and responded like a normal infant. I could see the pleasure her parents took in the everyday motions of babyhood most parents can take for granted. Her tiny hand grasping one of their fingers. A little smile. Then Danielle turned the corner and started going in the wrong direction. First, she had a small respiratory problem, followed by gastrointestinal[7] problems. After we cleared them up, her kidneys reacted. We didn't know if these other problems were related to the tumor.

Doctors and nurses in the pediatric ICU worked around the clock trying to keep Danielle's lungs and kidneys going. They were just as involved as we were.

Finally all that could be done had been done, and she died. We did an autopsy, and we found that the tumor had metastasized all over her lungs, kidneys, and gastrointestinal tract. Our surgery for the tumor in her head was a little too late. Had we gotten to her a month earlier, before things had metastasized, we might have been able to save her.

Danielle's parents and grandparents had come from Michigan and stayed in Baltimore to be near her. During the weeks of waiting and hoping for her recovery they had been extremely dedicated, understanding, and encouraging to us in everything we tried. When she died, I marveled at their maturity.

"We want it to be clear that we don't harbor any grudges over anything you folks did here at Hopkins," Danielle's parents said.

"We've just been incredibly thankful," said the grandmother, "that you were willing to undertake a case that everyone else considered impossible anyway."

Especially I remember the words of Danielle's mother. In a voice that was barely audible, she choked back her own grief and said, "We know that you're a man of God, and that the Lord has all these things in His hands. We also believe we've done everything humanly possible to save our daughter. Despite this outcome, we'll always be grateful for everything that was done here."

I share Danielle's story because not all our cases are successful. I can count on my fingers the number of bad outcomes.

---

7. **gastrointestinal** (găs′trō-ĭn-tĕs′tə-nəl): involving the stomach and intestines.

WORDS TO KNOW
autopsy (ô′tŏp′sē) *n.* an examination of a dead person's body to determine the cause of death

456

Mini-Lesson — The Writer's Style

ELABORATION USING EXAMPLES

Explain that there are several methods of using details to elaborate on an idea, all of which are shown on the chalkboard. These include facts, statistics, sensory details, incidents, quotations, graphic aids, and examples.

A well-chosen example can often be more effective than a whole page of explanation of an idea. For example, in this excerpt from *Gifted Hands*, Dr. Carson uses three examples—Bo-Bo, Charles, and Danielle—to elaborate on his ideas about the benefits of radical surgery.

Application Have students write a paragraph that begins with an idea or opinion about some aspect of illness and health. (For example, "I think that health care should be free in this country.") Have them elaborate on this idea by using one or more examples from their own experience.

Reteaching/Reinforcement
- *Writing Handbook*, anthology p. 831
- *Writing Mini-Lessons transparencies*, p. 34

The Writer's Craft
Examples, p. 257

Methods of Elaboration
- facts
- statistics
- sensory details
- incidents
- quotations
- graphic aids
- examples

RESPONDING OPTIONS

FROM PERSONAL RESPONSE TO CRITICAL ANALYSIS

REFLECT 1. What is your impression of Dr. Carson and his work? Record your thoughts in your notebook.

RETHINK 2. Why do you think Dr. Carson accepts cases in which there seems to be little hope?
Consider
- his reasons for wanting to operate on Bo-Bo and Charles
- the satisfaction and other personal benefits he gets from his work

Thematic Link 3. Recall that the theme of this part of Unit Four is "So Much at Stake." Who or what is at stake in decisions of whether to operate on patients with little chance of survival?

RELATE 4. Examine Dr. Carson's presentation of other doctors' attitudes about the operations he describes. Do you feel the attitudes are presented fairly? Explain your opinion.

5. Difficult cases can force doctors to face heart-wrenching questions. What is your opinion about performing radical medical procedures in cases that seem hopeless?

Multimodal Learning
ANOTHER PATHWAY

Imagine that you are part of a committee that will be nominating candidates for an Outstanding Physician of the Year Award. List the contributions to the medical profession that make Dr. Carson worthy of the award. Include examples from the selection.

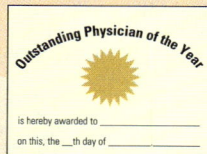

QUICKWRITES

1. Write a **letter to the editor** of your local newspaper, in which you either defend or oppose doctors who perform surgery in cases that appear to be hopeless.

2. Write a **diary entry** that one of the parents in this selection might have written after Dr. Carson performed surgery on his or her child.

📁 **PORTFOLIO** Save your writing. You may want to use it later as a springboard to a piece for your portfolio.

LITERARY CONCEPTS

An **autobiography**, like other kinds of nonfiction, usually contains both facts, or statements that can be proved, and opinions, or statements that express the writer's beliefs and cannot be proved. Because an autobiographer is writing about his or her own beliefs, he or she might state as a fact something that a reader might view as an opinion, such as "We had a chance to save her life." Look for apparent statements of fact in this selection. Which may really be opinions? How might someone else state a conflicting opinion?

CONCEPT REVIEW: Author's Purpose Authors write with specific purposes. What do you think was Ben Carson's purpose for writing about these three patients?

FROM GIFTED HANDS

From Personal Response to Critical Analysis

1. Responses will vary.
2. Possible responses: Carson believes in fighting the odds. His optimism combined with his skills gives him the confidence to save many seemingly hopeless patients.
3. Possible response: Most directly, the patients' lives are at stake. Families often feel torn among various ways of protecting their relatives—either from disease or from unnecessary surgery. Doctors may feel that their reputations are at stake.
4. Possible response: Dr. Carson describes other doctors' opinions as different from his, but he doesn't criticize or judge them.
5. Responses will vary.

Literary Links

Ask students to compare and contrast the enemy in *Gifted Hands* with the one in "The Gift of the Magi" (p. 426). *(Possible responses: Dr. Carson's three patients are fighting against the most fearsome enemy of all—death. Compared to this enemy, there is less at stake in the Youngs' fight against their enemy, poverty.)*

Another Pathway

Encourage students to think not only about Dr. Carson's surgical procedures but also about the personal qualities that he brings to caring for patients and their families before and after surgery.

Rubric
3 Full Accomplishment Students create a thorough and carefully worded list of Dr. Carson's contributions.
2 Substantial Accomplishment Students create a substantial list of descriptions of Dr. Carson's contributions.
1 Little or Partial Accomplishment Students have difficulty listing and describing Dr. Carson's contributions.

Literary Concepts

Have students read aloud certain sentences from the text (such as "the worst thing that could happen is that Charles dies anyway") using the tone and bearing of a surgeon. Encourage them to note how the authority and experience of the speaker may make an opinion sound like a fact.

Concept Review Help students focus on Carson's belief in doing whatever is humanly possible to save even those patients deemed hopeless.

QuickWrites

1. Remind students to present their ideas clearly and logically.
2. Encourage students to write about their fears, hopes, and impressions in any manner that seems natural.

📁 **The Writer's Craft**
Writing Letters, p. 684

Words to Know

Exercise A
1. galvanized
2. dilated
3. dismal
4. skepticism
5. malignant
6. radical
7. distraught
8. inevitable
9. autopsy
10. vivacious

Reteaching/Reinforcement
- *Unit Four Resource Book*, p. 24

Across the Curriculum

Science *Cooperative Learning Brain Research* Students' research might concern recent operating procedures, discoveries about the way the brain processes information, or some psychological aspect of the organ. Divide students into small groups of three or four. Each group can choose a different part of the brain or area of brain research to study. Each member of the group should be responsible for locating one source of information.

ADDITIONAL SUGGESTION

History *The History of Surgery* Have students research the long history of surgical operations. Encourage them to include information on various methods and traditions—including surgery performed by priests and barbers. Modern surgery is usually dated from the introduction of ether anesthesia in 1846, and much of students' information will be about the period following this important development.

AUTHOR BACKGROUND

Ben Carson To augment the author biography, show students this footage of Carson discussing his surgical and writing careers.

Side A, Frame 32178

Multimodal Learning

ALTERNATIVE ACTIVITIES

Cooperative Learning Imagine that a television series is being produced about the life of Dr. Ben Carson. With a small group of classmates, create a **sneak preview** of the first episode of the series by acting out a few events related to one of the three cases discussed in this selection. You may wish to videotape your sneak preview. Share your production with the class.

ACROSS THE CURRICULUM

Science Much brain research is being done currently, and the results of this research are reported in newspapers, magazines, and television programs. Use electronic resources or library resources to investigate one recent discovery about the brain, and then share your findings with the class.

WORDS TO KNOW

Review the Words to Know at the bottom of the selection pages, and list them on your paper. Then choose the best word to fill each blank in the following paragraph. Use each word only once.

The seriously ill boy __(1)__ the OR staff into action. One sign of his condition was his __(2)__ pupils. The patient's physicians had given a discouraging, __(3)__ medical report. Even the chief of surgery was showing great __(4)__. The boy had a __(5)__ tumor growing in his brain, and unless a __(6)__ operation was performed immediately, he would probably not survive.

As the staff prepared the boy for surgery, his __(7)__ parents stayed beside him. The surgeon thought that death was probably __(8)__. If the boy died, he thought, an __(9)__ would reveal the exact cause of death.

Miraculously, the operation was a success. In a few months, the little boy was his __(10)__ self once again.

BEN CARSON, M.D.

Ben Carson grew up poor in inner-city Detroit. When he began failing subjects in school as a young boy, his mother, Sonya Carson, gave him the inspiration and direction to make something of himself. She repeated to him over and over, "Bennie, you can do it. Don't stop believing that for one second." She turned off the television set and made her boys read two books a week. Not only did Ben's grades quickly improve; he began a path of increasing success. He graduated third in his high school class and won a scholarship to Yale University.

About the time he entered medical school, Carson realized he had "an unusual ability—a divine gift of extraordinary eye and hand coordination."

1951–

One of his most difficult cases required him to use his hands for 22 hours in order to separate conjoined twins who were attached at the back of the head. "I've adopted the philosophy that if somebody is going to die if we don't do something, we have nothing to lose by trying," he has said.

Carson, who has been profiled on ABC's *20/20,* struggles to balance his demanding career with the many other aspects of his full life. He devotes time to his wife Candy and their three sons as well as his church. He also enjoys giving inspirational talks to young African-American students all over the country.

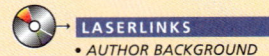
- AUTHOR BACKGROUND

458 UNIT FOUR PART 1: SO MUCH AT STAKE

Alternative Activities

Cooperative Learning Encourage students to reflect on various films and television programs involving medical personnel, themes, and settings that they have seen. Ask students to describe some of the characteristics of these productions. Ask if they are more likely to be dramas or comedies and if they focus more on the medical staff or on the patients. Discuss with students the purpose and style of television promotional spots. Tell students that a sneak preview should leave the audience wanting to see more. To help them get started, ask students the following questions:

- Who are the principal characters?
- What are the main conflicts and complications?
- What is the climax of the story?
- What opportunities for dialogue are there?

Encourage students to be imaginative about new and interesting ways to present a story with a medical theme.

PREVIEWING

DRAMA

Survival
Alfred Brenner

Activating Prior Knowledge
PERSONAL CONNECTION
Television courtroom dramas are often popular. In the same way, major real-life trials are highly newsworthy and can keep Americans glued to their television sets for months at a time. Why do you suppose people are so fascinated with both real-life and fictitious legal battles? Do they fascinate you? Why or why not? As you read this drama, decide how much like a real court case you think it is.

Building Background
SOCIAL STUDIES CONNECTION
Survival is based on a real court case tried 150 years ago. The legal terms used in it are the same as those used today. The **prosecution,** representing the United States, brings the criminal charge of **manslaughter**—murder without the intent of injury—against Holmes. It is the job of the prosecution to convince the jury that Holmes is guilty. Holmes—the **defendant** or **accused**—has an attorney who attempts to establish his innocence.

In a criminal trial, the attorneys on both sides make **opening statements.** Next, each side presents witnesses. The opposing attorney is allowed to **cross-examine** each witness in an attempt to find mistakes in the witness's testimony. Each side is also permitted to **object** to what the other side presents. The judge responds to an objection either by **overruling** it, allowing what has been presented to remain as part of the record, or by **sustaining** it, disallowing what has been said or shown.

The prosecution and the defense **rest** their cases when they have presented all of their evidence. Each may then choose to review the issues in a **summation** before the members of the jury make their decision.

Setting a Purpose
READING CONNECTION
Reading a Teleplay Because *Survival* was written as a television play, the script includes a number of camera and film-editing directions. The chart below explains some key camera and film-editing terms used in the play.

Camera and Film-Editing Terminology	
Fade in/ fade out	A picture, with accompanying sounds, comes in slowly from black or goes out slowly to black.
Over	A picture or sound fades in over another picture or sound continuing in the background.
Pans away	The camera turns to show other characters or another part of the scene.
Cut to	A picture is abruptly replaced by another picture.
Dissolve to	A picture fades out at the same time that the next picture fades in.
Super (superimpose)	One picture is briefly shown on top of another one.
Hit film	One filmed sequence instantly replaces another.

LASERLINKS
- READING CONNECTION
- VISUAL VOCABULARY

SURVIVAL **459**

OVERVIEW

Objectives
- To understand and appreciate a teleplay about the court trial of a man who sacrificed the lives of several men in order to save the lives of others
- To enrich reading by understanding the conventions of a teleplay
- To identify and understand the role of minor characters
- To express understanding of the drama through a choice of writing forms, including an essay, an alternative ending, and a paragraph
- To extend understanding of the teleplay through a variety of multimodal and cross-disciplinary activities

Skills

READING SKILLS/STRATEGIES
- Visualizing
- Distinguishing fact from opinion
- Reading a teleplay

THE WRITER'S STYLE
- Stage directions

GRAMMAR
- Compound subjects

LITERARY CONCEPTS
- Minor characters
- Plot

SPELLING
- The assimilated prefix *ad-*

SPEAKING, LISTENING, AND VIEWING
- Delivering a summation
- Group discussions
- Oral presentations

Cross-Curricular Connections

HISTORY
- Male juries
- The great famine
- Life on the sea

SCIENCE
- Icebergs

READING CONNECTION
All the Angles In this video, a narrator explains many of the film terms used in "Survival."

Side A, Frame 36478

VISUAL VOCABULARY
- crow's nest (krōz nĕst)
- jollyboat (jŏl'ē-bōt)
- longboat (lông'bōt')

Side A, Frame 52767

PRINT AND MEDIA RESOURCES

UNIT FOUR RESOURCE BOOK
Strategic Reading: Literature, p. 27
Vocabulary SkillBuilder, p. 30
Reading SkillBuilder, p. 28
Spelling SkillBuilder, p. 29

GRAMMAR MINI–LESSONS
Transparencies, p. 5
Copymasters, p. 5

ACCESS FOR STUDENTS ACQUIRING ENGLISH
Selection Summaries
Reading and Writing Support

FORMAL ASSESSMENT
Selection Test, pp. 88–89
 Test Generator

 **AUDIO LIBRARY**
See Reference Card

 **LASERLINKS**
Reading Connection
Visual Vocabulary

THE LANGUAGE OF LITERATURE TEACHER'S EDITION **459**

SUMMARY

It is 1842, and the sailor David Holmes is on trial for murdering passenger Frank Askin. Askin's sister bitterly tells of seeing Holmes force her brother out of a lifeboat. But Holmes's lawyer, Armstrong, shows that the lifeboat was too full, and Holmes had to force out the male passengers to prevent the boat from sinking. Armstrong reveals that Holmes sacrificed his own dreams to do what he thought was right. The court finds Holmes guilty, but sentences him to only six months in prison.

Thematic Link: *So Much at Stake* After a shipwreck at sea, a man risks his own life and sacrifices those of several others to save the lives of many passengers.

CUSTOMIZING FOR
Students Acquiring English

- Use **ACCESS FOR STUDENTS ACQUIRING ENGLISH**, *Reading and Writing Support*.

- Because this is a very long selection, recap the action with the class every few pages. You may also wish to have groups of nearly fluent students pre-read, prepare, and act out the scenes on the boat for the rest of the class to make this story come alive.

STRATEGIC READING FOR
Less-Proficient Readers

Set a Purpose Encourage students to become involved in the story by acting out the stereotypical behavior of a courtroom judge, prosecution and defense lawyers, defendants, witnesses, and jury. Then have students read to find out the exact charge against David Holmes and why Holmes's lawyer is angry with him.

Use **UNIT FOUR RESOURCE BOOK**, p. 27, for guidance in reading the selection.

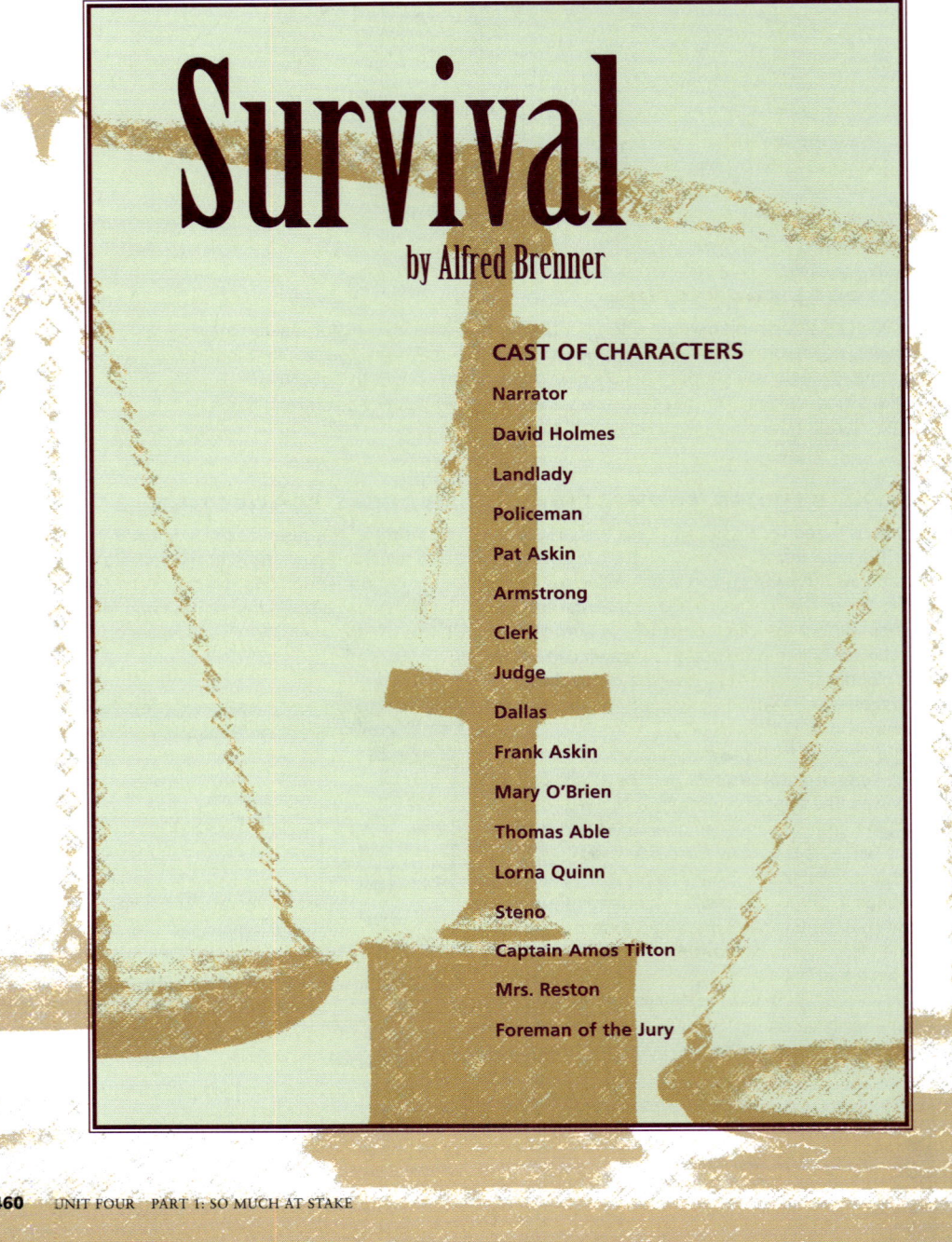

Survival
by Alfred Brenner

CAST OF CHARACTERS

Narrator
David Holmes
Landlady
Policeman
Pat Askin
Armstrong
Clerk
Judge
Dallas
Frank Askin
Mary O'Brien
Thomas Able
Lorna Quinn
Steno
Captain Amos Tilton
Mrs. Reston
Foreman of the Jury

460 UNIT FOUR PART 1: SO MUCH AT STAKE

WORDS TO KNOW

apprehend (ăp'rĭ-hĕnd') *v.* to take into custody; arrest (p. 463)
bristling (brĭs'lĭng) *adj.* to act in an angry and offended way **bristle** *v.* (p. 462)
concede (kən-sēd') *v.* to yield or grant something (p. 468)
conjecture (kən-jĕk'chər) *n.* a conclusion based on guesswork (p. 471)
corroborate (kə-rŏb'ə-rāt') *v.* to support with additional evidence; make more certain (p. 468)

dingy (dĭn'jē) *adj.* shabby; drab (p. 461)
maritime (măr'ĭ-tīm') *adj.* having to do with sailing or shipping on the sea (p. 468)
morality (mə-răl'ĭ-tē) *n.* a set of ideas about right and wrong behavior (p. 478)
ply (plī) *v.* to continue supplying or offering something to (p. 475)
testimony (tĕs'tə-mō'nē) *n.* information given by a witness under oath before a court (p. 468)

ACT ONE

Fade In:

A street in Philadelphia near the waterfront, 1842. A single street lamp drops a vague puddle of light on the cobbles. All we can see are the fronts of several buildings, some barrels, a coil of rope. David Holmes, a thick heavy-set seaman with hard obsessed eyes, about 30, carrying a seabag over his shoulder, is walking slowly along buildings.

Narrator. This story is based upon a real case. It was tried in the U.S. Circuit Court in the City of Philadelphia, on the 13th of April, 1842. It bears the title U.S. versus Holmes.

(*Holmes halts abruptly at the door of a house over which hangs a sign:*

The Jolly Rest
Rooms for Seamen
and Their Guests

He knocks on door. We hear footsteps within, a rusty lock turn; then door opens a crack and we see a landlady in nightdress, holding a candle, peering out suspiciously.)

Landlady (*looking him up and down*). Rent's two dollars a week . . . in advance. . . . (*Holmes reaches for his money bag, takes out several coins, drops them into her hand. She counts them quickly, glances up at him again.*) This way . . . (*He enters a vestibule, follows her a few steps to a door. She opens it, goes into a small* dingy *room containing a bolster bed, small table and chair. He steps in after her.*) You just come off ship? (*He nods.*) What's yer name?

Holmes (*throwing bag down, feeling bed*). Holmes . . .

Landlady (*scrutinizing him carefully*). Say, you ain't the one who brought in that longboat, saved all them women? (*Holmes glances at her swiftly, rigid, tense.*) Wait'll I tell Mrs. Brannigan I got a *hero* boardin' with me. . . .

Holmes (*leaping toward her, grabbing her throat, hissing*). You don't tell nobody who you got! Nobody! (*He slowly drops his hands. They stare at each other. An awkward silence. Suddenly she turns on her heel, leaves. He stands there, staring after her, exhausted. Abruptly he shakes it off, bends down beside his seabag, opens it, takes out several sheets of paper, pen, ink, goes to chest, sits down and begins to write. He writes slowly, painfully. There is no sound except the scratching of the pen. Camera pans away from him, moves slowly around the room.*)

Dissolve to: Holmes slumped across desk, asleep. A partially addressed envelope is lying beside him. A shaft of sunlight lights up his face. It is morning. There is a knock on the door. His eyes open. He jerks up, suddenly awake, springs to his feet.

Holmes. Who is it? (*Door opens. Two policemen, followed by landlady, enter.*)

First Policeman. David Holmes, we have a warrant for your arrest. . . . (*grabs Holmes' arm*)

Holmes (*jerks away rigidly*). Take your hands off me!

(*He walks toward door erectly, almost proudly, exits. Policemen follow him out quickly. Landlady glances around room, notices something on the table. The letter Holmes wrote is still there. She picks up the envelope, looks at it.*)

Cut to: Closeup of envelope. We read the name "Pat Askin" on it.

Dissolve to: Pat Askin, an attractive girl in her

WORDS TO KNOW

dingy (dĭn′jē) *adj.* shabby; drab

461

20's *standing somewhat nervously among a small knot of men and women outside a pair of paneled doors on which is printed:*

U.S. Circuit Court for the
Third Eastern District
of Pennsylvania

A buzz of excited conversation rises from the men and women. Suddenly, Pat *sees someone. Her whole body stiffens. The others, following her eyes, turn, stare at* Holmes, *who had just arrived. Beside him is his attorney,* Armstrong, *a well-dressed man in his 40's holding a briefcase under his arm.* Holmes *catches sight of* Pat, *halts, tenses. But* Armstrong *quickly grabs his arm, pulls him through paneled doors, into courtroom.*

Cut to: Holmes *and* Armstrong *inside courtroom coming down the aisle. Suddenly* Holmes *stops, his eyes fixed rigidly on something just ahead. We are able to distinguish the name, "William Brown," printed on the side of the craft near the bow.*

Armstrong (*glancing at* Holmes). Exhibit A for the prosecution. (*He leads* Holmes *to defense table. They sit down.*) I tried to get a postponement. . . .

Holmes (*bristling*). Who said I wanted a postponement?

Armstrong. If I did everything you wanted, Holmes, there'd be a noose around your neck right now.

Holmes. I'm gonna plead guilty.

Armstrong. No!

Holmes (*defiantly*). I did everything they said I did! I'm not gonna deny it. Armstrong, you didn't have to come all the way down here from Boston to defend me. . . . Why did you?

Armstrong. I'm not sure. Maybe it's because I've never seen Philadelphia before. (Pat Askin *is coming down the aisle.*) Holmes, why don't you stop fighting me?

Holmes (*snapping*). I told you the facts—

Armstrong. I understand the facts! What I need to understand is you! (*But* Holmes *is not listening. He is staring out toward spectators.* Armstrong, *following his eyes, sees* Pat. *She takes a seat among six or seven girls in first row.*) What about Pat Askin?

Holmes (*turning on him angrily*). Listen, Armstrong! Why don't you let them sentence me and be done with it? (*The rapping of a gavel interrupts him.*)

Clerk (*calling out*). Oyez! Oyez![1] The United States Circuit Court, for the Third Eastern

---

1. **Oyez! Oyez!** (ō′yĕs′ ō′yĕs′): "Hear ye, hear ye"; a call for silence and attention to open a court of law.

WORDS TO KNOW

bristling (brĭs′lĭng) *adj.* acting in an angry and offended way **bristle** *v.*

District of Pennsylvania is now in session. The United States versus Holmes. Will everyone rise. (*Everyone rises.* Judge *enters, sits at bench. All are seated.*)

Judge. Is the accused ready for trial? (Armstrong *motions for* Holmes *to rise.*)

Holmes (*on his feet*). Yes, sir . . .

Clerk (*reading aloud from paper in his hands*). "In that David Holmes, ordinary seaman, on or about April 20, 1841, did commit manslaughter by unlawfully and feloniously[2] making an assault upon and casting Frank Askin, a passenger, from a longboat belonging to the merchant ship, the *William Brown,* into the Atlantic Ocean, by means of which Askin was suffocated and drowned. . . ." David Holmes, you have heard the charge against you: how say you, guilty or not guilty . . . ?

Holmes. (*A pause. He looks around hesitantly.*) I . . . Not guilty . . .

Pat (*crying out*). He's lying! I saw him! He . . . (Pat *leaps to her feet. She breaks,[3] sobbing. Several other girls move to her side quickly, hold and comfort her. Sounds of excited conversation . . . confusion in the courtroom.*)

Judge (*pounding the gavel*). Order! Order in the Court! (*Noise gradually ceases. He turns to prosecutor.*) Mr. Dallas, the United States District Attorney, will present the case for the people. . . .

Dallas (*rises, steps toward jury*). Gentlemen of the Jury, four months ago an American merchant ship, the *William Brown,* set sail from Liverpool, England. . . . (*His voice fades.*)

Dissolve to: Dallas *from a different angle, still addressing jury. His jacket is open now, and he is loosening his collar and mopping his brow. He has been talking for a while and is beginning to wind up his address . . .*

. . . Although the members of the crew and the mate have all disappeared and have still not been <u>apprehended</u>, fortunately there are a number of witnesses present who were on that longboat, who saw these horrible deeds with their own eyes . . . (*He turns toward women sitting in first row, who are watching, listening intently.*) . . . Why did Holmes do such a thing? I suggest, gentlemen, you will find the reason . . . the motive, if you will—in the character of the man himself. . . . (*We see* Holmes *sitting in his chair, his right hand clenched on the table. He is motionless, expressionless.* Armstrong *keeps glancing at him.*) A man who in a moment of panic exploded, and sent not only Frank Askin, but eleven of his fellow passengers to their death! (*Dallas turns, walks slowly back to his seat.* Judge *looks questioningly at* Armstrong. Armstrong *says something to* Holmes *who does not react. Finally he rises.*)

Armstrong. Your Honor, the defense will not address the jury at this time. (*He is seated.*)

Judge (*looks at him quizzically, then to* Dallas). Prosecution will proceed . . .

Clerk. Miss Pat Askin will take the stand . . . (Pat *crosses up aisle to stand.* Holmes *watches her intently.*) Raise your right hand—Do you solemnly swear that the testimony you are about to give will be the truth . . . the whole truth and nothing but the truth, so help you God?

Pat. I do. . . .

Clerk. State your name. . . .

---

2. **feloniously** (fə-lō′nē-əs-lē): in a manner that constitutes a felony—a serious crime that merits significant punishment, usually no less than one year in prison.
3. **breaks:** is overcome with emotion and unable to continue.

WORDS TO KNOW

apprehend (ăp′rĭ-hĕnd′) *v.* to take into custody; arrest

463

Critical Thinking:
HYPOTHESIZING

I Ask students why they think the judge asks Armstrong this question. Ask students why they think Armstrong doesn't object. *(Possible response: The judge expects Armstrong to object because Dallas has asked a leading question that could harm Holmes.)*

Linking to History

J In the 19th century, the staple food of Ireland was the potato. When a blight caused all the nation's potatoes to rot in the ground for five successive years (1845–1850), more than a million Irish people died of starvation. Another 2 million people emigrated from the island, and most of these people sailed to the United States. The widespread poverty that devastated Ireland during the famine was intensified by British landowners who evicted peasants unable to pay their rent.

Linking to Science

K An iceberg is a floating chunk of ice that has separated from a glacier. Much of the mass of ice lies below the surface of the water. Even so, some icebergs rise above the water as high as a ten-story building. Such an iceberg caused the Irish monk St. Brendan to use the phrase "floating crystal castle" to describe icebergs.

Critical Thinking:
SPECULATING

L Encourage students to comment on how this demonstration might help the prosecution. *(Possible response: It would help the prosecution if it shows that Pat Askin could have seen from her position in the boat what she claims to have seen.)*

Pat. Patricia Askin. . . .

Dallas (*approaches*). You are the sister of Frank Askin who was thrown off a longboat and drowned in the Atlantic Ocean on April 20th of this year?

Pat. Yes. . . .

Dallas. Were you on the same longboat at that time?

Pat. I was. . . .

Dallas (*points to boat*). Is that the longboat?

Pat. Yes. . . .

Dallas. Miss Askin, did you see the defendant, David Holmes, forcibly throw your brother, Frank, out of *this* longboat and thus cause him to drown?

Pat. Yes . . . I did. . . . (*Murmuring, voices from courtroom. Judge bangs gavel.*)

I Judge. Did I hear an objection, Mr. Armstrong?

Armstrong (*from far away*). What . . . ? No . . . Your Honor . . .

Judge (*to Dallas*). Proceed . . .

Dallas (*to Pat*). You and Frank were not the only passengers aboard the ship, the *William Brown*, were you, Miss Askin?

Pat. No . . . there were about thirty others emigrating with us. . . .

Dallas. Where were you coming from?

Pat. Ireland.

Dallas. Why did you decide to come to America?

J Pat. Well . . . it was the famine . . . my father died. . . . Frank and I decided to sell our little plot and seek a better life in this country.

Dallas. Miss Askin, please tell the court what happened on the night of April 19th.

K Pat. An iceberg hit the ship. . . .

Dallas. Would you describe the circumstances. . . .

Pat. Well, I was asleep when it happened. When I opened my eyes, everyone was in their nightclothes screaming . . . someone was yelling: "On deck! Into the boats!" We piled up the hatchway with the seas crashing down. Some climbed into the little jollyboat.[4] But most of us got into the longboat. . . . Soon after the two boats were lowered into the sea, the ship went down. . . .

Dallas. Miss Askin, I am now going to ask you to step down from the stand and get into the longboat, taking the exact position you were in that night. . . . (*Dallas begins to help her out of stand.*)

Judge. One moment—would the prosecutor please explain the purpose of his procedure?

Dallas. If it please the Court. It is necessary to indicate Miss Askin's position in the boat in order to show that she could see what was going on. . . .

Judge. You may proceed. . . . (*Dallas leads Pat to longboat, helps her inside.*)

Dallas. Is this where you were sitting?

Pat. Yes.

Dallas. What were you doing?

Pat. Bailing[5] . . .

Dallas (*over*). Bailing? There was water in the boat?

Pat. Oh, a great deal.

(*Super: Film, sound of sea, winds up.*)

Pat (*continued*). Besides, we had sprung a leak. . . . My clothes were soaked and I was exhausted. My brother was sitting in front of me. Then I saw Holmes. Beside him were two seamen. He had a terrible look as he faced my brother. (*We are in close, can almost see what Pat is describing.*) Frank asked him what was happening. For a moment there was no reply—

---

4. **jollyboat:** a ship's small boat, used for minor tasks.
5. **bailing:** removing water from a boat by repeatedly filling a container and emptying it over the side.

then Holmes took my brother by the shoulders and said, "It's your turn, Frank. You've got to go." (*There is a look of horror on* Frank's *face.*) Then they threw my brother over the side. (*She screams.*) Leave him be! Leave him be! (*We are in for a closeup of her face.*)

(*Sound of storm down and out. We hear nothing but* Pat's *sobbing. Lights come up on* Dallas *in courtroom.*)

Dallas. On that night, your brother as well as other male passengers were thrown over— Miss Askin, were any of the *crew* thrown overboard?

Pat. No.

Dallas. No further questions. (*begins to help her down*)

Armstrong (*rising*). You may remain where you are, Miss Askin. You just stated that none of the crew members were thrown overboard. Could you tell me why?

Pat. Well . . . they . . . Holmes said they were needed to row.

Armstrong. No more questions. (*He turns away. Court attendant helps* Pat *down.*)

Judge. Is that the extent of your cross-examination of this important witness, Mr. Armstrong?

Armstrong. Miss Askin will be called as a witness for the defense, Your Honor.

Judge. For the *defense?*

Armstrong. Yes, Your Honor. . . .

(Judge *stares at him, shrugs, turns toward clerk.*)

Clerk. Miss Mary O'Brien . . . (Mary *comes forward, glances angrily at* Holmes.)

(*He is gazing across at* Pat. Armstrong *notices the look on his face.*)

Dissolve to: Dallas *at stand.*

Dallas. Miss O'Brien, was Holmes in command of the longboat immediately after the ship went down?

Mary (*in stand*). No sir, John Widdows was— the first mate.

Dallas. Oh?

Mary. Holmes took over later. . . .

Dallas. Took over? Forcibly? Did he fight with the mate?

Mary. Not right away. But he started to argue with him. . . .

Dallas. What about, Miss O'Brien?

Mary. The direction we was to take. . . . The mate told Holmes to head west for land. . . . Holmes refused. He said our only chance was to head south where we might pick up a ship. . . . Well, sir, that's what we did—we went south. . . .

Dallas. Then Holmes actually took command.

Mary. All night long I heard this voice shoutin', cursin', threatenin'. . . . I tell you, I'm not a shrinkin' violet of a woman, but I was scared of him. . . . He's crazy!

Dallas. Crazy?

Mary. Yes, sir . . .

Dallas. Thank you, Miss O'Brien. . . . Your witness . . .

Armstrong (*rising*). How would you describe a man who was crazy, Miss O'Brien?

Mary. Well . . . out of his mind. . . . You know . . .

Armstrong. Would you say that a man who is crazy doesn't know what he's doing?

Mary. Yes, sir! That's it!

Armstrong. You mean Holmes didn't know what he was doing on that longboat?

Mary. I didn't say that. . . .

Armstrong. Well . . . You said he was crazy.

Mary. Well . . . He wasn't exactly crazy. . . . He . . .

Armstrong. No more questions. . . . (*He goes back to table. Camera stays on him and* Holmes.)

Clerk (*over, calling*). Thomas Able.

SURVIVAL 465

Mini-Lesson   The Writer's Style

STAGE DIRECTIONS Explain that stage directions are the instructions to the actors, the director, and (in a teleplay) the film crew in a dramatic script. These instructions may suggest lighting, music, sound effects, camera effects, costumes, and how actors should move and speak. Usually stage directions appear in italic type within parentheses or brackets.

For example, stage directions in the highlighted passage on page 465 indicate that the flashback scene in the longboat fades "down and out" and is replaced by "Dallas in courtroom" once again.

Application Invite students to write a short dramatic scene between Holmes and Armstrong that involves both dialogue and action. Have them include stage directions that give information about the characters' appearance and movements, as well as about lighting, music, and sound or camera effects they think would make the scene effective.

Reteaching/Reinforcement

The Writer's Craft
Plays and Skits, p. 326

Literary Concept:
MINOR CHARACTERS

P Though Thomas Able is a minor character in the drama, his words in the witness stand help the audience (and the jury) better understand David Holmes. Ask students what they learn about Holmes from Able's description of the seaman's actions. *(Possible response: David Holmes is a man of remarkable bravery and physical ability, as well as modesty, but he was also viewed as crazy.)*

Active Reading: EVALUATE

Q Invite students to offer their opinions on whether this exchange between District Attorney Dallas and Thomas Able will be more helpful to the case of the prosecution or that of the defense. *(Possible responses: This testimony will help Holmes's case more because it shows him to be a sober, serious person surrounded by less trustworthy sailors. The prosecution's case will benefit more because Able's testimony shows that Holmes was somewhat eccentric and not really popular—so he might have held a grudge against other sailors.)*

Critical Thinking: ANALYZING

R Urge students to discuss why the author might have included this brief exchange between Armstrong and Holmes. Ask students if they think the exchange could be important in any way. *(Possible response: The exchange shows that Armstrong is familiar with ships, and it gives some indication of how Holmes feels about life at sea.)*

Dissolve to: Witness stand. Thomas Able, *a little wizened seaman, sitting there looking at* Dallas *who has just begun to question him.*

Dallas. Mr. Able, how long were you and Holmes members of the crew of the *William Brown*?

Able. Five years . . .

Dallas. At the time of the sinking, where did you go?

Able. In the jollyboat . . .

Dallas. When you heard what had happened aboard the longboat, were you surprised?

Able. No, sir . . . I wouldn't be surprised at anything Holmes did. . . . He's capable of anything. . . . He's like gunpowder, ready to explode at any time. . . .

Dallas. Had he ever done anything like that before?

Able. No, not exactly . . . but, well, he was proud. . . .

Dallas. Proud?

Able. Well, he always had to be the first one up on the crow's nest[6] . . . even during the worst weather. . . . I seen him hanging on to the top of the mizzenmast[7] once with the ship practically layin' over horizontal with the sea . . . and the mast all icy. . . . An' when he came down later, his hands all bloody, he didn't say one word . . . even when some of the men slapped his shoulder and told him he did a nice job. . . . He was crazy!

Dallas (*smiles*). Did you like him as a shipmate?

Able. Nobody likes him.

Dallas. Why not?

Able. Well, he was different. . . . Kept apart. . . . Never swapped a yarn. . . . On shore leave, he never joined us. . . . Never took a drink. . . . I don't trust a man who don't take a drink. . . . Not a seafarin' man . . .

Dallas. Thank you, Mr. Able . . . (*He returns to table.* Armstrong *approaches stand.*)

Armstrong. Tell me, Mr. Able, is Holmes a good seaman? In your opinion?

Able. Aye . . .

Armstrong. A brave man?

Able. Aye, I guess he's got courage, but it's stupid . . .

Armstrong (*sharply*). Would you just answer my questions, please! Now Mr. Able, in all the years that you knew the defendant, did he ever willfully harm anyone?

Able. Well . . . no. . . .

Armstrong. No further questions . . . (*He turns away.*)

Dallas. That's all, Mr. Able . . . (Able *steps down.*)

Clerk (*calling*). Miss Lorna Quinn . . . (Lorna *rises from among row of women. As she does, we see* Armstrong *at defense table making a few notes.* Holmes *glances at him.*)

Armstrong. That Tom Able reminds me of a man I once shipped with . . .

Holmes. What did *you* ever wanna go to sea for? It was a stupid thing to do.

Dissolve to: Lorna Quinn *on stand being questioned by* Dallas. *She is nervous.*

Dallas. . . . Do you actually mean, Miss Quinn, that on the night of April 20th, the night following the sinking of the *William Brown*, you heard the defendant order the crew to throw the male passengers overboard?

Lorna. I even saw it happen. . . . I saw Holmes and two of the crew go up to Riley and they

---

6. **crow's nest:** a small lookout platform near the top of a ship's mast (a tall pole rising from the deck and supporting the ship's sails).
7. **mizzenmast** (mĭz′ən-məst): the mast third from the front of a ship with three or more masts.

466 UNIT FOUR PART 1: SO MUCH AT STAKE

Mini-Lesson  Literary Concepts

REVIEWING PLOT Remind students that plot is the sequence of related events that make up a story. In other words, it is the action—or what happens—in a story. Most plots follow a regular pattern. The exposition introduces the characters and the conflicts they face. Complications occur as the characters try to resolve the conflict. Eventually, the plot reaches its highest point of interest or suspense; this is called the climax. The final stage of a plot is the resolution, in which the author ties up loose ends and brings the story to a close.

Application Have students track the progress of *Survival*'s plot. Encourage them to note the events that make up the plot and to organize this information in a chart that identifies the exposition, conflict, complications, climax, and resolution.

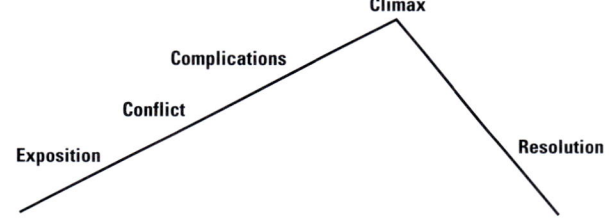

All Hands to the Pump (1888-1889), Henry Scott Tuke. Tate Gallery, London/Art Resource, New York.

Art Note

***All Hands to the Pumps* by Henry Scott Tuke** In this dramatic painting, Tuke (1858–1929) shows a group of sailors in great peril at sea. The danger is evident in the torn sails, the flooded deck, and the churning pumps, as well as in the faces and gestures of the seven men.

Reading the Art What details in the image indicate that the wind is blowing? What words would you use to describe the mood aboard the ship? Are any of the men panicking, in your opinion? Does any one of the figures appear to be in charge?

CUSTOMIZING FOR
Multiple Learning Styles

Spatial or Graphic Learners Invite students to use wood, clay, or some other material to build a model of the courtroom or of the longboat. Encourage students to look at photographs and illustrations of courtrooms or longboats before they design their own.

Active Reading: CLARIFY

S Invite students to offer explanations that clarify Holmes's decision to spare the men whose wives were present. *(Possible responses: Holmes may have felt that it was too cruel to force the wives to watch their husbands being sacrificed for them. Holmes may have feared that the wives' responses to their husbands' deaths would have further endangered the longboat and its passengers.)*

Active Reading: CONNECT

T Invite students to describe the thoughts and feelings they might experience if they were in the judge's position at this point in the story.

Critical Thinking: HYPOTHESIZING

U Ask students to infer why Armstrong might feel comfortable in conceding his right to cross-examine these ten witnesses. *(Possible response: Armstrong may sense that each of these witnesses will say almost exactly the same things that Lorna Quinn did. If this were so—according to what is apparently Armstrong's strategy—he would have no more to say to each of them than he did to Lorna. Since he did get Lorna to answer ambiguously when he asked if she felt safer after Holmes helped her and the others, the defense lawyer may have felt that one seed of doubt is as good as eleven.)*

---

told him to stand up . . . and when Riley stood up, they gave him a shove and he went right overboard. . . .

Dallas. How close were you to Riley when this happened?

Lorna. Well, no further than you are from me right now . . .

Dallas. Then what happened?

Lorna. Well, they threw over Duffy next, then Charlie Conlin. . . . Charlie offered Holmes five sovereigns[8] if he'd spare his life, but Holmes wouldn't even listen to him . . . and, well, this went on until every one of the men passengers except Ed McKenzie and Patrick Whelan, were thrown over. Holmes spared those two because their wives were aboard. . . .

Dallas. Are you able to tell the court—from your own observation—how many men were thrown overboard during that terrible night?

Lorna. Well, there was Riley, Duffy, Charlie Conlin, Frank Askin. . . . There were twelve. . . .

Dallas (*turning away swiftly*). Your witness . . .

Armstrong (*rises, approaches* Lorna). Miss Quinn, did you personally feel safer—when you saw that the boat had been lightened by those men?

Dallas. Objection!

Judge. You are placing the witness in an extremely delicate moral dilemma, Mr. Armstrong. . . .

Armstrong. If it please the Court, the defendant was faced with exactly the same moral dilemma.

Judge (*after a pause*). Objection overruled.

Armstrong. Miss Quinn, I asked you if you felt safer—more secure—when you saw that the boat had been lightened by those. Remember, you're under oath.

Lorna (*almost in tears*). I . . . I . . . don't know. . . .

Armstrong. That's all, Miss Quinn. (*He returns to defense table. She steps down.* Dallas *comes forward.*)

Clerk. Miss Ann Flaherty . . .

Armstrong (*rising*). If the Court please, I understand the U.S. Prosecutor intends to call at least ten survivors as witnesses. . . .

Dallas. That's correct.

Armstrong. The defense concedes that the testimony of these witnesses will corroborate the testimony already heard. . . .

Judge. Mr. Armstrong, you're making a rather crucial concession. . . .

Armstrong. Your honor, the defense does not deny that Holmes was responsible for casting Frank Askin and other male passengers overboard. . . .

Judge (*taken aback*). Oh! (*He studies* Armstrong. *A silence.*) Mr. Armstrong, the Court understands you came all the way down from Boston to conduct this defense. . . .

Armstrong. That's correct, Your Honor. . . .

Judge. You attended college in Boston?

Armstrong. Harvard College, Your Honor.

Judge. Do you have any personal interest in this case, Mr. Armstrong?

Armstrong. Your Honor, the effect of maritime law is felt in Boston as well as in Philadelphia; on land as well as on sea. I believe

---

[8] **sovereigns** (sŏv′ər-ĭnz): gold coins formerly used in Britain.

WORDS TO KNOW
concede (kən-sēd′) *v.* to yield or grant something
testimony (tĕs′tə-mō′nē) *n.* information given by a witness under oath before a court
corroborate (kə-rŏb′ə-rāt′) *v.* to support with additional evidence; make more certain
maritime (măr′ĭ-tīm′) *adj.* having to do with sailing or shipping on the sea

468

Multicultural Perspectives

CHANGING ETHNIC SURNAMES

Historically, the spelling of some immigrants' surnames has changed during the immigration process. Sometimes, it has been common for immigrants to change the spelling of surnames that might mark them as foreign or as members of a particular ethnic group in the United States. Other times, names have been changed by immigration officials as a result of confusion in translating foreign names.

Anglicizing surnames was much less common among the Irish than among many other immigrant groups. With the exception of dropping the *O'* from such names as *O'Sullivan, O'Callaghan, O'Farrell, O'Flaherty, O'Kelly, O'Riley,* and *O'Kennedy,* most Irish immigrants did not voluntarily change their names. For instance, the names of the longboat passengers in *Survival*— including Conlin, Whelan, Duffy, Quinn, O'Brien—have been common in the United States for generations.

that this trial has meaning for all who travel on the sea—seamen and passengers. That is my personal interest.

Judge. The prosecution will proceed. . . . (Armstrong *is seated*.)

Clerk. Captain Amos Tilton . . . (*Captain Tilton lean, hard, tanned, in sea uniform, approaches.*)

Cut to: Armstrong *and* Holmes. Holmes *is tensely watching* Pat. *Then to* Pat.

Dissolve to: Witness stand. Dallas *is questioning the captain.*

Dallas. Captain Tilton, how long were you in command of the *William Brown*?

Captain. Eight years. . . .

Dallas. During her last voyage, how many had she on board?

Captain. A crew of 13 and 39 passengers. Scotch and Irish immigrants, as well as a heavy cargo. . . .

Dallas. What happened when she was hit by the iceberg?

Captain. Well, there was panic among the passengers, sir, but the crew with one exception handled themselves well. . . . The second mate, seven of the crew, two passengers and myself got into the small jollyboat, while the first mate, four seamen and thirty-seven passengers got into the longboat. We in the jollyboat were picked up six days later.

Dallas. How many male passengers were in the longboat?

Captain. Sixteen, sir . . .

Dallas. Captain, you just stated that you in the jollyboat were picked up six days later . . .

Captain. Yes, sir . . .

Dallas. During those six days conditions were extremely difficult. There was the same storm, the same unruly sea as that which the longboat encountered . . . and yet you brought your boat into safety with all aboard?

Captain. Yes, sir . . .

Dallas. Now Captain—had *you* instead of Holmes been in command of the longboat—would you have given the same order—in other words, would you have sacrificed the lives of any of the passengers, just to save your own life?

Armstrong. Objection!

Judge (*quickly*). Overruled! The court considers the captain an expert witness.

Dallas. Well, Captain? Would you have committed manslaughter?

Captain. I . . . no, sir. (*Uproar in court*)

Cut to: Holmes *and* Armstrong *for reaction. Both are deeply shaken. Uproar swells—Quick fade out.*

ACT TWO

Fade In:

The courtroom. No time lapse. Captain Tilton *is in the witness stand. Uproar continues.* Judge *is rapping for order.*

Dallas. Your witness.

Armstrong (*approaches stand*). Captain, in your testimony you stated that the crew with one exception handled themselves well. Please explain the exception.

Captain. John Widdows, first mate . . .

Armstrong (*surprised*). The first mate?

Captain. I would have taken him out of the longboat, but it was impossible due to the storm—the panic and all.

Armstrong. Why?

SURVIVAL 469

Art Note

Shipwreck Off Nantucket by William Bradford In this large oil painting, William Bradford (1823–1892) conveys the awesome force of the Atlantic Ocean during a storm. Bradford creates a kind of hollow in the center of the canvas between representations of two enormous waves. Barely afloat in a small boat in the center of this hollow are several tiny human figures, who are dwarfed by their stricken ship, by the waves, and by the stormy sky.

Reading the Art *How does the effect of this painting compare and contrast with those on pages 467 and 476? Which is the most frightening to you? Why?*

CUSTOMIZING FOR
Students Acquiring English

6 Mention to students that, traditionally, ships have been named after women and referred to as *she* rather than *it*, even if the ship is named after a man.

Critical Thinking:
SYNTHESIZING

Y Encourage students to bear in mind this testimony by Captain Tilton as they review what they know about Holmes's actions in the longboat. Then ask them for a possible explanation for Holmes's behavior. *(Possible response: Holmes may have been aware of the longboat's limited capacity. If he knew this—or if he surmised it from the way the boat felt when it was overloaded—he could have decided to take action to save as many passengers as possible.)*

Literary Concept:
CHARACTERIZATION

Z Ask students what Holmes's volunteering to go on the longboat tells them about his character. *(Possible response: That he probably knew he was in "grave jeopardy" shows his courage and heroism.)*

Shipwreck off Nantucket (1859–1860), William Bradford. Oil on canvas, 40" × 64", The Metropolitan Museum of Art, Purchase, John Osgood and Elizabeth Amis Cameron Blanchard Memorial Fund, Fosburgh Fund, Inc., Gift, and Maria DeWitt Jesup Fund, 1971 (1971.192). Copyright © 1995 The Metropolitan Museum of Art.

Captain. He was a coward.

Armstrong. And so Holmes took over. (Captain *looks down at his hands.*) Captain Tilton, how many people could the longboat normally hold?

Captain. She was built to hold twenty, sir. . . .

Armstrong. And how many were aboard?

Captain. Forty-two.

Armstrong. Captain Tilton, what was the condition of the longboat?

Captain. I felt she was in grave jeopardy, sir. . . .

Armstrong. Captain, based upon your experience, how did you estimate your chances of survival?

Captain. At the time? Not one chance in a hundred.

Armstrong. Were your estimates shared by your crew?

Captain. Yes, sir . . .

Armstrong. When the jollyboat and the longboat were lowered into the water, where did you assign Holmes?

Captain. To the jollyboat.

Armstrong (*surprised*). The jollyboat? How did he get into the longboat? Did you order him to go?

Captain. No, sir. . . . He volunteered. . . .

Armstrong. Do you mean he volunteered to go into the longboat, knowing that he was possibly going to his death?

Captain. Yes.

Armstrong. Do you know why Holmes volunteered?

Captain. No, sir. . . .

470   UNIT FOUR   PART 1: SO MUCH AT STAKE

Armstrong. Did you have an opportunity to observe the defendant at the time the *William Brown* was hit by the iceberg?

Captain. Yes, sir. . . .

Armstrong. How did he act?

Captain. . . . His efforts to save the passengers were conspicuous, sir. Without him I'm sure more lives would have been lost. . . .

Armstrong. Captain, is it possible that Holmes volunteered to go into the longboat because he thought he could save the boat?

Dallas (*jumping up*). Objection! This is conjecture, suggestion. . . . It is not evidence. . . .

Judge. Sustained . . .

Armstrong. All right. . . . Captain, the longboat did survive . . . despite all the odds against her, and she was picked up eventually. . . . How do you account for this? Would you say it was due to Holmes' seamanship?

AA Captain. Well, Holmes is a fine seaman. It was very likely due to—

Armstrong (*quickly*). Due to the fact that the boat was lightened?

Dallas (*shouting*). Objection!

Armstrong. I am merely asking for the captain's expert opinion, Your Honor. It is crucial to this case to establish why this longboat stayed afloat.

Judge. It is a reasonable question. Objection overruled.

Armstrong. Captain, in your opinion, was the lightening of the longboat by approximately a ton important to its survival?

Captain. I cannot answer a question . . .

Judge. This is a court of law, not the deck of a ship. Answer the question!

Captain (*grudgingly*). Yes, it was possible. . . .

Armstrong. Thank you, Captain . . . (*He turns away.* Captain *starts to leave stand.*)

Dallas (*rising*). One moment, Captain . . . (Captain *remains in stand.*) Could the longboat have survived *without* Holmes? If he had *not* lightened the boat by throwing twelve human beings to their doom? Was there any chance at all, Captain?

Captain. There are always miracles, sir. . . .

Dallas (*vehement*). Would you answer my question, please! Yes, or no?

Captain. It was possible, sir. . . .

Dallas (*turning away*). No further questions! (Captain *rises, steps out of stand.*)

Judge (*with sarcasm*). Captain Tilton, you may leave the stand. . . . (Captain *hurries away.*) **BB**

Dallas. Prosecution rests. . . .

Judge. Is defense ready to present its case? **CC**

Armstrong (*rising*). Yes, Your Honor . . .

Judge. Proceed.

(Armstrong *nods to clerk.*)

Clerk (*calling out*). Mrs. Margaret Reston. . . . Please take the stand. . . .

(Mrs. Reston *rises, comes forward.*)

Cut to: Holmes *watching her tensely.*

Dissolve to: Witness stand.

Armstrong. You have a daughter, Mrs. Reston?

Mrs. Reston. Aye . . . Isabel. . . . She's 9 years old.

Armstrong. Mrs. Reston, would you please tell the Court what happened to your daughter on the night the *William Brown* was struck by the iceberg. . . .

Mrs. Reston. Well, she was left behind on the sinking ship. . . .

Armstrong. What did you do when you discovered this?

WORDS TO KNOW
conjecture (kən-jĕk´chər) *n.* a conclusion based on guesswork

471

Literary Concept: PLOT

AA Ask students to explain what effect Captain Tilton's testimony has on the conflict between the defense and the prosecution. *(Possible response: Captain Tilton's testimony complicates the conflict by supplying evidence that may help Holmes. His testimony also helps move the plot toward a climax.)*

Critical Thinking: ANALYZING

BB Ask students to comment on why the stage directions indicate these lines should be spoken sarcastically. *(Possible response: The judge seems to be annoyed with the captain's attitude.)*

Active Reading: EVALUATE

CC Ask students for their opinions on whether Captain Tilton's testimony will help or hurt David Holmes's chances for acquittal. If they need help, share the following model with them:

Think-Aloud Model *Although Captain Tilton is a prosecution witness, he says several important complimentary things about Holmes. I think that his comments about the defendant's bravery and fine seamanship seem likely to help Holmes more than hurt him.*

Mini-Lesson — Reading Skills/Strategies

VISUALIZING Remind students that visualizing is the process of forming a mental picture from a written description. Good readers use details supplied by the writer to picture characters, settings, and events in their mind. Visualizing is especially important when reading the script of a play, film, or television drama.

Application Encourage students to visualize the characters' physical appearances and movements in the courtroom, as well as the action in the longboat. Also, remind students to use their own experiences viewing movies and television programs as a basis for visualizing the script's descriptions of visual effects. You may wish to give students the opportunity to sketch particular scenes from the selection. Allow students who are uncomfortable with drawing to write short paragraphs describing how they visualize characters or events.

Reteaching/Reinforcement
- *Unit Four Resource Book,* p. 28

Active Reading: PREDICT

DD Encourage students to predict what they will learn from Patricia Askin's testimony for the defense.

Critical Thinking: SPECULATING

EE Ask students if they think Armstrong knows the answers to the questions he's asking Patricia Askin. Help them understand that seasoned courtroom lawyers know it is risky to ask a witness a question to which the lawyer doesn't know the answer. Encourage students to point out other examples of this courtroom technique in the text of *Survival*.

STRATEGIC READING FOR
Less-Proficient Readers

FF Check that students understand details contained in the testimony of Pat Askin.

- What interest did Holmes and Frank Askin share, according to Pat Askin? *(They both loved farming.)* **Comparing and Contrasting**

- Who seems to be the only person who knew David Holmes's first love was not the sea? *(Pat Askin)* **Noting Relevant Details**

Set a Purpose Have students read to find out why Holmes worked on ships for so many years and why he volunteered to go on the longboat.

Active Reading: EVALUATE

GG Invite students to offer their opinions of the judge's rulings in this case. Do they feel that he is being fair to both sides? How would they rate his performance in this trial? If they need assistance, you may want to share the following thought processes with them:

Think-Aloud Model *In my opinion, the judge is keeping an orderly courtroom and being perfectly fair—his rulings on the lawyers' objections don't indicate that he favors either side. However, I can see how someone could believe that the judge favors the prosecution because of his repeated questioning of Armstrong's decisions.)*

Mrs. Reston. Well, I was like out of my mind. . . . I cried out for help. . . . And, praise God, one of the seamen, he climbed back on to the ship just as she was keeling over and rescued my daughter. Oh, I'll never forget it. That seaman didn't even know me, yet he risked his life.

Armstrong. Who was that seaman, Mrs. Reston?

Mrs. Reston. David Holmes . . .

Armstrong. Thank you, Mrs. Reston. Your witness.

Dallas. Mrs. Reston, I'm sure there was a great deal of bravery displayed. . . . The question is: Did he voluntarily and feloniously deprive a fellow creature of his life? . . . I therefore ask you: While you were on the longboat, did you see him cause any of the passengers to be thrown into the sea?

Mrs. Reston. I . . . I . . .

Dallas (*glowering*⁹). Well, Mrs. Reston . . . ?

Mrs. Reston. I . . . I . . . Please . . . Please don't ask me. . . . (*She sobs. Armstrong is on his feet.*)

Armstrong. Objection. Is it necessary to browbeat the witness, Your Honor?

Dallas. Your Honor, I would like to reserve the right to re-examine this witness later when she is more capable of answering questions.

Judge. Permission granted.

Dallas. No further questions. (*He turns away. Mrs. Reston comes down from stand.*)

Clerk (*calling out*). Miss Patricia Askin . . .

(*Pat rises nervously, comes forward, takes stand.*)

Armstrong. Miss Askin, when did you first meet the defendant?

Pat. On the *William Brown*. During the first week of the voyage.

Armstrong. Could you describe the circumstances?

Pat. My brother introduced us. . . .

Armstrong. Oh, he knew Holmes then?

Pat. Well, he met him aboard ship, too. . . .

Armstrong. Did he and Holmes see a lot of each other during the voyage?

Pat. Well, yes . . .

Armstrong. Your brother tilled the soil in Ireland, didn't he?

Pat. Yes. Farming was his whole life. His dream was to get to some land in America.

Armstrong. Looking back on it now, doesn't it seem unusual to you that your brother and Holmes should have struck up such a speedy acquaintanceship . . . considering the fact that Holmes is supposed to be such a difficult man to know, that he doesn't mix easily . . . and that *his* first love is the sea?

Pat. David Holmes' first love is *not* the sea. . . .

Armstrong. Oh, no, what is it then?

Pat. Farming. . . .

Armstrong. He told you that?

Pat. Yes. . . . All he wanted was to own a farm. . . .

Armstrong. No one else on board ship was aware of Holmes' attitude toward farming. You must have been quite intimate for him to confide in you like that. . . .

Dallas. Objection! I can see no purpose in this line of questioning, Your Honor. . . .

Armstrong. If it please the Court, I am attempting to show why Holmes volunteered to go into the longboat at the risk of his life. . . . I believe he had a good reason. . . . To understand it, however, it is necessary to understand his relationship with Pat and Frank Askin. . . .

Judge. Objection overruled.

---

9. **glowering** (glou′ər-ĭng): staring angrily.

472 UNIT FOUR PART 1: SO MUCH AT STAKE

Assessment Option

INFORMAL ASSESSMENT You can informally assess students' understanding of *Survival* by having them give an oral summary of plot events from the point of view of David Holmes. Have students begin with the death of Holmes's father in New York and trace the series of events that led eventually to the trial in Philadelphia.

Urge students to begin by jotting down notes about the sequence of events. Then have them review their notes and deliver their summaries orally.

Rubric

3 Full Accomplishment Speaking as David Holmes, students accurately and thoroughly summarize plot events from the time Holmes left New York until the trial.

2 Substantial Accomplishment Speaking as David Holmes, students present a mostly organized summary of many plot events from the time Holmes left New York until the trial.

1 Little or Partial Accomplishment Students have difficulty summarizing plot events and assuming the point of view of David Holmes.

Armstrong. How intimate with the defendant were you, Miss Askin?

Pat. Well, we used to talk a lot . . . that's all. . . .

Armstrong (*quickly*). You liked Holmes, didn't you?

Pat. I was blind. . . .

Armstrong (*sharply*). Were you in love with him?

Pat (*bursting out*). I didn't say that!

Armstrong. Were you?

Pat. Well . . . I . . . don't know. . . .

Armstrong. Was he in love with you?

Pat. I don't know! Ask him!

Armstrong. He thought a great deal of your brother, didn't he?

Pat. I . . . don't know. . . .

Armstrong. Didn't his actions indicate as much?

Pat. I don't know!

Armstrong. Miss Askin, during the ocean crossing, did you or your brother make any plans for the future in which the defendant was included?

Pat (*her voice low, broken*). I made plans, hundreds of them. . . . What good are they now?

Armstrong. Miss Askin, on the morning of April 21st, the morning after that terrible night in which your brother and the others were thrown overboard. . . . Did you think there was any chance of rescue?

Pat. No, I didn't care. . . .

Armstrong. Would you say that David Holmes—by his own exertions and at the risk of his own life—was responsible for saving that longboat?

Dallas (*jumping up*). Objection!

Judge. Sustained!

Armstrong (*turns away*). No further questions . . . (Judge *looks at* Dallas. Dallas *shakes his head*.)

Judge. You may step down, Miss Askin. . . . (*She does*.)

Armstrong (*rises*). I call the accused. . . . (Holmes *stands*.)

Judge. Does the accused request that he be permitted to testify?

Holmes (*after a pause*). I do. . . .

Judge. You have the right to do so. . . . You also have the right not to take the stand. If you don't testify, that fact won't be held against you. If you do, you may be subjected to a rigorous cross-examination.

Holmes. I understand, Your Honor. . . . (Holmes *goes to stand*.)

Clerk. Raise your right hand. (*He does*.) Do you solemnly swear that the evidence you are about to give shall be the truth, the whole truth, and nothing but the truth, so help you God?

Holmes. I do. . . . (*He is seated*.)

Armstrong. David Holmes, how long have you been a seaman?

Holmes. Since I was fourteen . . .

Armstrong. Do you like the sea?

Holmes. I hate it!

Armstrong. Yet you have been a seaman all your life. Why?

Holmes. I had no other occupation . . . no money to buy a farm. . . .

SURVIVAL **473**

Critical Thinking: CLASSIFYING

JJ Point out that both Pat Askin and David Holmes have referred to a similar dedication to a life of farming. Invite students to comment on how life on the sea and on a farm might be different yet also similar. *(Possible response: The most obvious difference is that a life on the sea involves constant movement. Many seafarers desire the rootlessness and the experiences of a sea-going life. In contrast, a life of farming is rooted to one spot. There is little opportunity for change or movement. Farmers and people who work on the sea share an involvement with nature, and may have independent and self-sufficient personalities.)*

Active Reading: EVALUATE

KK Ask students to evaluate Holmes's behavior in this scene and why Armstrong implies that Holmes threw Frank Askin overboard because he was frightened. If they need help, you might wish to share the following thought processes with them:

Think-Aloud Model *Holmes's temper tantrum seems familiar. It's like his irrational behavior at the start of the play, when he threatened Armstrong that he was going to plead guilty. Here his outburst comes after his lawyer asks about his leaving his father's farm. Something about that experience is deeply disturbing to him. But Armstrong knows how to handle Holmes. By saying that Holmes might have been frightened, he may get him to testify to prove Armstrong wrong.)*

Active Reading: CLARIFY

LL Ask students to explain what happened to Holmes's father. *(Possible response: After killing the man who came to take away his farm, he was hanged by a mob.)*

Armstrong. Is that your ambition in life? To own a farm?

Holmes. Yes.

Armstrong. Have you ever worked on a farm?

Holmes. My father's farm . . .

Armstrong. Where was this?

Holmes. New York State. Near Albany.

Armstrong. Did you like the life, the work?

JJ **Holmes.** For me it's the only life. . . .

Armstrong. Why did you leave? (*A long silence.* Holmes *doesn't answer.*) Did you hear my question?

Holmes (*to* Judge). Can I leave the stand?

Judge. Why?

KK **Holmes.** I'm not gonna answer these questions! (*Reaction from jury*)

Armstrong. May it please the Court, I beg for an opportunity to speak to my client. A brief delay. Two minutes.

Judge (*raps gavel*). There will be a two-minute pause in the proceedings.

Armstrong. (*To* Holmes. *Sotto voce.*[10] *Angry.*) If you leave the stand now, I walk out.

Holmes. Go ahead!

Armstrong. Holmes, what are you afraid of? A little rough questioning? Or maybe you threw Frank Askin overboard because you were frightened!

Holmes. No!

Armstrong. Well, prove it then! If not to me, to Pat. Answer the questions I ask you before the whole world. (*He walks away from stand.*)

Judge (*raps gavel*). Mr. Holmes, do you intend to submit to questioning, or do you wish to step down? (*There is a pause.* Holmes *looks across at* Armstrong.) You will not have another opportunity to change your mind. . . .

Holmes. I'll answer.

Armstrong. Your father had a farm. Why did you leave it?

Holmes. They took it away from my father.

Armstrong. Why did they take it away?

Holmes (*resisting*). I dunno! (*Then, after a silence, as* Armstrong *watches him, with great effort*) He owed money on it. . . . He never told anybody. . . . He was too proud. . . . When a man came to take it away, my father shot him dead. I saw it. . . . Then more men came and took my father, and they got a rope. . . . (*His voice chokes, remembering.*) I couldn't stand it . . . I **LL** ran away. . . .

Armstrong. Where did you go?

Holmes. New York City. . . .

Armstrong. What did you do there?

Holmes. I hung around the waterfront, slept in doorways. . . . One night some men came. They beat me unconscious. When I came to I was in the hold of a ship.

Armstrong. How old were you?

Holmes. Fourteen.

Armstrong. What happened on the ship? Did you become part of the crew?

Holmes. The mate sent me up on the mast the first day out. I couldn't stay there. I got dizzy . . . I fell. Musta been laying on the deck for hours. But them seamen—they just laughed. We were at sea eighteen months and they kept laughing at me. I couldn't do anything right. I hated them. (Holmes *is wound up, talking with difficulty, but getting it out of his system.* Armstrong *steps back, listens politely.*) I made up my mind then I'd show them. . . . It took me a year, two, three . . . I don't know how

---

10. **sotto voce** (sŏt′ō vō′chē): in soft tones, so as not to be overheard.

474 UNIT FOUR PART 1: SO MUCH AT STAKE

long. . . . I hated the sea, but I fought it. . . . I fought *them*. . . . I swore an oath to myself that I'd get my father's farm back. . . . Someday I'd return. . . . That's all I lived for. . . . I saved my money. . . .

Armstrong. What money?

Holmes. My pay . . .

Armstrong. What is your pay?

Holmes. Eleven dollars a month.

Armstrong. You mean you thought you could save enough out of that to buy back your father's farm?

Holmes (*triumphantly*). I did! The money is in a bank in New York City right now. . . .

Armstrong. How long did it take you to save that much money?

Holmes. Thirteen years.

Armstrong. Thirteen years? Is that why you never went ashore with your shipmates?

Holmes. I couldn't afford to.

Armstrong. Well, if you had all this money, why didn't you leave the sea?

Holmes. After this trip I was gonna quit.

Armstrong. David Holmes, during the last voyage of the *William Brown,* you became acquainted with Frank Askin. Explain the circumstances.

Holmes. Well . . . I heard some of the passengers one night. . . . I was on the lee'ard[11] watch. . . . Frank Askin was talking about farming. . . . He seemed to know what he was talking about, and he spoke like it really meant something to him. So I sought him out and plied him with questions.

Armstrong. You became friends?

Holmes. Yes. . . .

Armstrong. In the course of your friendship with him, did you often speak with his sister, Pat?

Holmes. Yes. . . .

Armstrong. What was your relationship with her?

Holmes. We got along. . . .

Armstrong. Is that all?

Holmes. We got along!

Armstrong. Did you ask her to marry you?

Holmes. No!

Armstrong. Did you *consider* asking her? (*As Holmes hesitates*) Did you?

Holmes. I considered a lot of things!

Armstrong (*reaches inside his jacket, takes out a letter, shows it to* Judge). Your honor, this has been recorded as Exhibit B for the defense. (*Turns to* Holmes) Have you ever seen this letter before? David Holmes, did you write this letter? Is this your signature? (*shows it to him*) It was given to me by Mrs. Althea Temple, landlady of the boarding house you stayed in on your first night ashore. It is addressed to Miss Pat Askin. Did you write this letter? (Holmes *nods—unable to speak.*) Please read it to the court. (*He hands it to him.*)

Holmes (*choked*). I didn't know what I was doing when I wrote it. . . . I . . .

Armstrong. I appreciate that. Please read it.

Holmes. (*Mumbling, hunched over. After a long pause, reading.*) "Dear Pat. I am going to ship out on the first vessel. I have some money. I want you to have it. Don't think of it as mine. Think of it as Frank's, that he left it for you. . . . Pat I want you to know that I

---

11. **lee'ard** (lōō'ərd): a contraction of *leeward,* referring to the side of the ship opposite to the direction from which the wind is blowing.

WORDS TO KNOW

ply (plī) *v.* to continue supplying or offering something to

475

Art Note

Shipwreck by Robert Loftin Newman
Robert Loftin Newman (1827–1912) depicts the chilling effects of a shipwreck by showing passengers trying to survive in a small craft. The central image of the boat and people is surrounded—in fact, nearly swallowed up—by the green paint that indicates the seawater and its spray.

Reading the Art How would the effect of this painting be different if the human beings and boat were more clearly defined by the artist?

Literary Concept: PLOT

OO Encourage students to identify what they consider to be the climax of *Survival*. Have them explain their answers. *(Possible responses: The climax comes during this scene with the discovery of the relationship between Holmes and Pat, the revelation of the relationship and pact between Holmes and Frank, and Holmes's "confession" on the witness stand. The climax of the plot will come when the jury brings in its verdict—only then is the conflict truly resolved.)*

STRATEGIC READING FOR
Less-Proficient Readers

PP Check that students understand vital details in David Holmes's testimony.

- Why does Holmes say he worked on ships for so many years? *(to earn money to buy back his father's farm)*
  Relating Cause and Effect

- Why did Holmes volunteer to go on the longboat? *(Frank and Pat Askin—all Holmes had—were on that boat.)*
  Making Inferences

Set a Purpose Have students read to find out the verdict in the case.

Shipwreck, Robert L. Newman (1827–1912). Oil on canvas, 12" × 24½", New Britain Museum of American Art, Connecticut, Harriet Russell Stanley Fund (1949.13). Photo by E. Irving Blomstrann.

loved Frank, too. I know you hate me, but there was nothing else I could have done. . . . I don't know if he told you . . ." (*Holmes breaks.* Armstrong *takes letter, continues reading.*)

Armstrong. "I don't know if he told you, but we planned to farm together, as partners. . . . I had hoped you would be with us. . . . I am going to ship out on the first vessel. David Holmes . . ." (*Silence.* Holmes *is sitting there, his head bowed.* Armstrong *looks at him gently.*) Thank you, David. . . . Now can you tell the court why you volunteered to go into the longboat?

Holmes (*his voice low*). To save it. Everything I had was on that boat. (*Then crying out in anguish*) I *had* to save it! And I did. I did what I could! God, what else could I do? But I had to do it. I *had to.* I loved them.

PP *Fade out.*

ACT THREE

Fade In:

The courtroom. Holmes *still on stand.* Dallas, *having just completed his re-examination, returns to table.* Judge *looks across at* Armstrong *questioningly.*

Dallas. No further questions.

Armstrong. No re-examination. . . . Your Honor . . . the defense rests.

Judge. You may leave the stand, Mr. Holmes. (Holmes *steps down. There is a pause as* Judge *checks his notes, looks up.*) Gentlemen, are you ready for summation?

(*The* Foreman of the Jury *rises.*)

Foreman. Just a minute! Your Honor!

(*Commotion in the courtroom*)

Judge (*pounding gavel*). What is the cause of this outburst?

476   UNIT FOUR   PART 1: SO MUCH AT STAKE

Foreman. There's been a mistake in some of the testimony.

Judge (*stern*). Mistake?

Foreman. Your Honor, maybe if you could have a portion of Captain Tilton's and Lorna Quinn's testimony that tells about the number of men thrown overboard . . .

Judge. (*Staring at foreman narrowly. After a long pause, to steno.*[12]) You may comply with the request. . . .

Steno. (*flipping through notes. Reads.*) "Question by Mr. Dallas to Miss Quinn: From your observation, are you able to tell the Court how many men were thrown overboard during that terrible night? Answer: well . . . there was Riley, Duffy, Charlie Conlin, Frank Askin. There were twelve."

Foreman (*quickly*). Now could you read the part where Captain Tilton tells how many men passengers were on the longboat.

Steno. (*Flipping through notes. Reads.*) "Question by Mr. Dallas: How many male passengers were in the longboat? Answer by Captain Tilton: Sixteen, sir . . ."

Foreman. There you are, sir! Since there were sixteen men passengers originally in the longboat, and twelve were thrown overboard, *four* must have survived. . . . But according to Miss Quinn's testimony, only *two* men passengers survived. She said they were not thrown overboard because their wives were present. Well, Your Honor, that leaves two men not accounted for. I'd like to know what happened to them!

Dallas (*rises*). If the Court please, both the defense and the prosecution are aware that two of the male passengers are not accounted for . . . the fact is, no one seems to know what happened to them . . . and it has no bearing on this case.

Judge. Gentlemen, the question you must decide involves only one point: is the defendant, David Holmes, guilty of the manslaughter of Frank Askin? Only Frank Askin. None other.

Foreman. But Your Honor! How can we come to a decision unless the evidence regarding those two men . . .

Judge. You're out of order, sir.

Voice. Your Honor! Your Honor! (*Everyone turns. We see* Mrs. Reston *extremely agitated, coming forward. Suddenly she halts, frightened at the judge's stern look.*) Excuse me, sir . . . I . . . Perhaps I can explain . . . I mean, about those two men . . .

Judge (*narrowly*). Do you know what happened to them?

Mrs. Reston. Yes . . . Yes . . . (*Reaction from the court*)

Armstrong (*rising*). Please the Court! I request that this witness be allowed to take the stand! I have no idea what she will say, but her evidence might have a bearing on this case. . . .

Judge. Any objection, Mr. Dallas?

Dallas. No objection.

Judge. Mrs. Reston, you may take the stand. . . .

Armstrong (*comes forward*). Now, Mrs. Reston, your testimony will bear directly upon the question which is disturbing the jury. . . . It will include nothing else. . . .

Mrs. Reston. Yes . . . (*glancing across at* Holmes *with difficulty*) I didn't say before; I didn't want to hurt anybody—I—but it is gnawing inside me, and I must get it out or I will never be able to look anyone in the face again. It is something I saw. . . .

Armstrong. What did you see?

Mrs. Reston. It was just before dawn (*hit film*)

---

12. **steno:** stenographer—a person who uses shorthand to record testimony during a trial. Today, court stenographers use a keyboard machine that prints shorthand symbols.

Mini-Lesson Grammar

COMPOUND SUBJECTS Point out to students that compound subjects joined by the word *and* take a plural verb. This is true no matter what the number of each part of the compound.

Example Armstrong and Holmes *enter the courtroom together.*

However, when the parts of a subject are joined by *or* or *nor*, the verb agrees with the part of the subject that is nearer to it.

Example Neither the judge nor the spectators *are* able to tell what the witness is saying.

Application Have students choose the correct verb for each of the sentences below.

1. The land and the sea (is/*are*) attractive to different types of people.
2. Neither icebergs nor fire (*is*/are) able to sink this.

Reteaching/Reinforcement
- *Grammar Handbook*, anthology p. 863
- *Grammar Mini-Lessons* copymasters, p. 5, transparencies, p. 5

 The Writer's Craft

Compound Subjects, pp. 68–69, 580

Critical Thinking: ANALYZING

TT Encourage students to imagine the powerful effect of this filmmaking technique. Point out that the courtroom image is instantly replaced with vivid images of the frightful moments on the longboat. However, the voice of Mrs. Reston continues over the images, creating added tension between past and present. Ask students why they think the author did not use just Mrs. Reston's verbal description. *(Possible response: It is much more frightening and exciting to see the extreme situation the passengers find themselves in. The audience gets a powerful reminder of the results of Holmes's actions.)*

CUSTOMIZING FOR
Gifted and Talented Students

UU Invite students to debate this question: Is there any circumstance in which one person has the right to decide who should die and who should live? Remind them that the question is a moral one—the answer would encompass a variety of possible situations. Encourage students to consider various situations as they arrive at their conclusions.

Active Reading: EVALUATE

VV Invite students to evaluate District Attorney Dallas's address to the jury. Ask them how effectively he communicated his ideas and if they agree with his assessment of the case. *(Encourage students to use information from the text to support their ideas about Dallas's performance and reasoning.)*

CUSTOMIZING FOR
Students Acquiring English

8 Ask students what Armstrong wants people to do when he asks them "to look for one moment into your own hearts." *(to put themselves in Holmes's place)*

---

after that awful night. . . . I mean the night the men were cast over. The storm had quieted at that moment, and we were trying to rest when I noticed a movement beneath the canvas on the bottom of the boat . . . two of the men passengers were hidden. Their feet were sticking out. I realized that they had hidden during the night to escape being thrown over. Just then I saw that two of the seamen had also noticed them. They didn't know that I was watching. They bent down and struck and struck, and then they threw the two unconscious bodies overboard. . . . (*film out*) They didn't have to do it. There was no need for it any more. Yet they threw those men over anyway. . . . I sat there too frightened to say anything. (*She is sobbing.*)

Armstrong. Thank you, Mrs. Reston. (*He crosses to defense table, sits beside* Holmes.)

Holmes (*shocked deeply*). I didn't know. . . . I didn't know. . . .

Judge. Mr. Dallas . . . ?

Dallas (*rises*). No questions, Mrs. Reston. (*She leaves stand.*) Your Honor, I waive my right to final summation and would like to address the jury now.

Judge. Mr. Armstrong?

Armstrong. Agreed.

Dallas. Please the Court, Gentlemen of the Jury. The act just described by Mrs. Reston is murder—vicious, stupid, unreasonable killing for its own sake. Why did those seamen cast two human beings into the sea, when any necessity for such an act was clearly at an end? Because they had been ordered to kill and because once they started to kill, all sense of morality broke down. They couldn't stop. Who was responsible for it? The prisoner, David Holmes, for it was he alone who made the decision to take the lives of his fellow men! Did David Holmes have the right to issue such an order? Did he have the right to place himself above his fellow men and select those who should die and those who should live? Does any man have that right? Gentlemen, this case does not deal merely with the guilt or innocence of one man. In a sense we are all on that longboat, and at stake is a question of the most profound significance, a moral law. This law holds that *all* men's lives are sacred, of equal value . . . that in a crisis where some men have to die in order to save the rest, the decisions as to who will go cannot be left to the discretion of one man but must be decided upon equally by all concerned. . . . Gentlemen, David Holmes not only committed manslaughter but he broke the moral law upon which our democracy rests! Therefore you have no choice . . . but to find the defendant GUILTY! (*Uproar of crowd.* Judge *pounds gavel, courtroom becomes quiet. He looks towards* Armstrong. Armstrong *rises slowly now, approaches judge and jury.*)

Armstrong. Your Honor, Gentlemen of the Jury. As you sit here in this courtroom judging David Holmes . . . I ask you to look for one moment into your own hearts. What would *you* have done on the night of April 20th? A hundred leagues[13] from land . . . a boat filled with water . . . women screaming, knowing that at any moment all may perish. . . . What would you have done? Debated the moral law and the democratic process? Taken a ballot? As an experienced seaman, Holmes knew there was only one way to save the boat . . . a

---

13. **leagues** (lēgz): units of distance, each equal to 3 nautical miles or 4.8 kilometers.

WORDS TO KNOW

morality (mə-răl′ĭ-tē) *n.* a set of ideas about right and wrong behavior

478

terrible way. . . . Lighten it. And that is what he did. Considering the women and children first, he gave the order to cast over the male passengers . . . among them a man he loved and admired . . . a man in whom all his hopes for the future were placed—indeed, the very person he had come to save. Can you imagine the dreams which will torment him for the rest of his life? (*Quietly but with rising intensity*) Holmes acted out of duty, because it was his duty to save the boat, and out of love, because he believed human lives to be sacred. . . . And so he saved the majority of the passengers. (*He turns suddenly to face the witnesses.*) Look at them . . . would they be here today if it were not for Holmes? (*Turns swiftly to jury*) How can you declare him guilty?

WW *Fade out.*

Fade in slowly: Holmes *is standing before judge.*

Clerk. Gentlemen of the Jury, have you agreed upon a verdict?

Foreman. We have. . . .

Clerk. And how do you find, gentlemen?

Foreman. We find the defendant . . . guilty. (*We hear a gasp, a cry from spectators.*) But we recommend mercy. . . . (*We hear murmuring in courtroom.*)

Judge (*pounds gavel*). Order. (*Murmuring dies out.*) David Holmes, you have broken the basic moral law upon which our civilization rests. You have abrogated to your own hands a right which lies only in the people at large and in God himself. Although there are many circumstances of this case which are of a character to commend you to the admiration of this court and indeed to all humanity—the law demands punishment. In accordance with the jury's recommendation of mercy, I hereby sentence you, David Holmes, to six months in prison. Court dismissed! (*Noise in court.* Holmes *stands there swaying.* Armstrong *comes up to him, places his arm around his shoulder, leads him slowly down aisle toward doors in rear. As they reach doors,* Pat *approaches.*)

Pat (*choked, trembling*). David . . . I understand . . . (*They look at each other.*) Don't go back to sea. . . . (*Pause*) Buy the farm. . . .

Holmes (*inarticulate*). Yes . . .

(Armstrong *takes him off.* Pat *continues to watch until the two men have disappeared down the corridor. Her eyes are wet.*)

Slow fade.

SURVIVAL **479**

Active Reading: CONNECT

WW Encourage students to imagine themselves as members of the jury. Would they find Holmes guilty or not guilty of manslaughter in the death of Frank Askin? Have them explain their reasoning.

Active Reading: PREDICT

XX Invite students to make predictions about the jury's verdict.

STRATEGIC READING FOR
Less-Proficient Readers

YY Have students explain the verdict in the case. (*Holmes is found guilty but is given a light sentence—six months. He can then buy the farm and leave the sea.*) Summarizing

---

COMPREHENSION CHECK

1. What is the title of the case, and what is the charge against the defendant? (*U.S. versus* Holmes; *manslaughter*)
2. Why did Pat Askin and her brother leave Ireland to go to the United States? (*They were looking for a better life after suffering from the famine in Ireland.*)
3. What two vessels allowed some people to survive the sinking of the *William Brown*? (*a longboat and a jollyboat*)
4. What were David Holmes and Frank Askin planning to do when they arrived in the United States? (*They were going to farm together.*)
5. What verdict does the jury hand down to David Holmes, and what is his sentence? (*He is found guilty and sentenced to six months in prison.*)

Mini-Lesson: Speaking, Listening, and Viewing

DELIVERING A SUMMATION Explain that both the prosecuting attorney and the defense attorney have an opportunity to give a closing statement at the end of a trial. In this summation, the attorneys address the jury directly and review the most important pieces of evidence that prove their cases. An attorney also attempts to appeal to the logic, the common sense, and the emotions of the members of the jury.

Application Have students study the lengthy closing statements of both Dallas and Armstrong. Then have some students rehearse the prosecutor's speech while others rehearse the defense's speech. Finally, have pairs of students deliver the two lawyers' final statements as if they were in an actual courtroom.

From Personal Response to Critical Analysis

1. Responses will vary.
2. Possible responses: The verdict is fair because, although the other seamen's actions should not be blamed on Holmes, he should be held responsible for Frank Askin's death. The verdict is unfair because there wasn't time to sit down and come to some general agreement about what action to take.
3. Possible responses: The light sentence is appropriate because the sacrifice of lives was unavoidable. The sentence is far too lenient because Holmes caused the death of other human beings—no matter what his reasons for doing so.
4. Possible response: Holmes is a very proud, private, courageous man who is extremely self-disciplined and focused on his goals.
5. Possible responses: They should have physically stopped him from doing it—if given a chance, maybe some passengers would have voluntarily sacrificed their lives for the lives of the others. There wasn't anything they could or should have done—that is, if they wanted to survive.
6. Urge students to support their opinions with references to specific parts of the teleplay.
7. Possible responses: This rule is right because children have their whole lives ahead of them and women are the ones who care for them. Children should be protected but it's sexist to protect women over men—how can a man's life be any less valuable than a woman's?

Another Pathway

Encourage students to decide what kind of newspaper they are writing for and to make sure they use the appropriate tone. Remind students to think about the script and the film terms on page 459 when they are writing.

Rubric
3 Full Accomplishment Students create a well-written, original review that analyzes both the script and the use of film techniques.
2 Substantial Accomplishment Students write an organized review that analyzes the script and some film techniques.
1 Little or Partial Accomplishment Students have difficulty developing and organizing their ideas into a review.

RESPONDING OPTIONS

FROM PERSONAL RESPONSE TO CRITICAL ANALYSIS

REFLECT
1. What is your response to David Holmes? Record your thoughts in your notebook.

RETHINK
2. Do you agree or disagree with the jury's verdict? Explain your answer.
   Consider
   - what was at stake for the people on the longboat
   - the prosecution's argument that one man cannot decide the fate of many
   - whether Holmes's actions influenced the seamen to commit murder
3. What is your opinion of the sentence Holmes received? Explain your answer.
4. How would you characterize Holmes?

Close Textual Reading
   Consider
   - his letter to Pat and his reluctance about the trial
   - how he has lived his life and what his plans for the future are
   - the motives for his actions on the longboat
5. What, if anything, do you think the women, children, and crew members on the longboat should have done when Holmes began throwing men overboard?
6. How realistic did you find this drama to be? Explain your opinion.

RELATE
7. The traditional, unwritten rule of the sea is that women and children should be protected first in times of crisis. What are your feelings about this rule?

Multimodal Learning
ANOTHER PATHWAY

What are the characteristics of a successful courtroom drama? Think about this question and refer to your notes for the Personal Connection on page 459. Then write a review of *Survival* that might appear in a newspaper the day after it is broadcast on TV.

QUICKWRITES

1. Draft a short **essay** comparing and contrasting the trial in this drama with a trial you have heard about or watched recently.
2. Write an **alternative ending** for *Survival*, based on a different verdict.
3. Some real trials are shown on television as they happen. What do you think of this practice? Write a **paragraph** presenting the advantages and disadvantages of live courtroom broadcasts.

📁 **PORTFOLIO** Save your writing. You may want to use it later as a springboard to a piece for your portfolio.

480 UNIT FOUR PART 1: SO MUCH AT STAKE

QuickWrites

1. You might suggest that students use a graphic aid to help them compare and contrast the two trials.
2. Ask students if it would be effective to use any camera effects in the closing moments of this alternate script.
3. Encourage students to consider the issue from various points of view—that of the defendant, the plaintiff, the victim, the jury.

The Writer's Craft

Comparison and Contrast, pp. 120–125
Developing a Script, pp. 86–88

LITERARY CONCEPTS

In addition to main characters, short stories and plays usually have a number of **minor characters** who interact with the main characters and with one another, moving the plot along and providing background for the story. Thomas Able and Captain Amos Tilton are among the minor characters in *Survival*. As witnesses, they provide different views of Holmes's personality. What do you learn about Holmes from Able? from the captain?

Multimodal Learning

ALTERNATIVE ACTIVITIES

1. **Cooperative Learning** Work with a small group of classmates to present a **performance** of one scene from *Survival*. Each student can take on a different task in the production; some can be actors, while others can work as members of the crew. If you can, videotape the performance, following as closely as possible the camera directions given in the script. Present your performance to the class.

2. Create a **painting** that depicts the *William Brown* striking the iceberg. You may want to include the dramatic rescue attempt, showing the survivors in the jollyboat and the longboat.

LITERARY LINKS

Compare and contrast the murderer in "The Tell-Tale Heart" (page 380) with David Holmes. How are their motives and their behavior similar? Use a Venn diagram like the one shown to explore this and other questions: How are they different? Is one any more or less guilty than the other? Explain your answers.

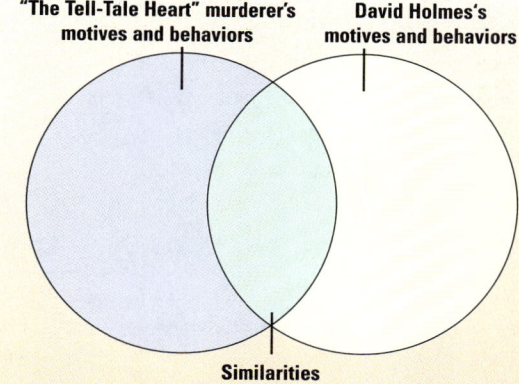

ACROSS THE CURRICULUM

 History *Cooperative Learning* With a small group of classmates, research life on the sea in the 1840s. Each student can investigate a different question: What kinds of ships sailed the Atlantic Ocean? What were the crews' living conditions? What were their jobs? Present a group report to the class.

 Science With a partner, discuss what you know about icebergs. How big do they get? In what seas are they most commonly found? Use references to check your information. Then, if you wish, work together to create an iceberg diorama.

SURVIVAL **481**

Literary Links

Possible responses: *"The Tell-Tale Heart" murderer's motives and behaviors*—hates old man; plans details of the murder; acts paranoid; tries to evade detection

David Holmes's motives and behaviors—wants to be able to live out his dream; wants to save as many lives as possible; courageous; takes control; feels remorse; willing to plead guilty

Similarities—secretive and private men; both driven to their actions by feelings of desperation

Across the Curriculum

History *Cooperative Learning Life on the Sea* You might wish to have one student in each group serve as differentiator by keeping track of each group member's findings. Encourage students to use a variety of sources—books and databases on boat-building and maritime history, encyclopedias, diaries and other eyewitness accounts—to do their research.

Science *Icebergs* Student discussion might include some of the following: icebergs develop in both the Arctic (and float to the North Atlantic Ocean) and Antarctic (where they sometimes float to the Atlantic Ocean and also to the South Pacific Ocean). Antarctic icebergs are often 10 miles long; the largest recorded Arctic iceberg was 4 miles long.

Literary Concepts

If necessary, have students review the testimony of Able (page 466), which informs us that Holmes was a good seaman who performed various daring deeds aboard ship but who did not socialize with other seamen. The testimony of the captain (pages 469–471) provides detailed information about Holmes's behavior in the wake of the iceberg and on the longboat.

Alternative Activities

1. **Cooperative Learning** You might wish to designate a particularly organized or imaginative student as the director of the scene. If necessary, one student could be designated as a researcher or runner and perform many of the tasks of a traditional stage manager.

2. Encourage students to visualize the scene in their own way. They might use oil or acrylic paint, or they may decide to use something lighter such as watercolors.

THE LANGUAGE OF LITERATURE Teacher's Edition **481**

Words to Know

1. apprehend
2. conjecture
3. maritime
4. morality
5. concede
6. dingy
7. testimony
8. ply
9. corroborate
10. bristle

Reteaching/Reinforcement
- *Unit Four Resource Book*, p. 30

WORDS TO KNOW

Review the Words to Know at the bottom of the selection pages, and list them on your paper. Then choose the word most closely related to each of the following situations.

1. a person's being caught picking pockets in the ship's mess
2. a bystander's guessing the time when a crime was committed
3. goods' being imported by ship
4. the sailor's insisting that the mutiny was wrong
5. a defense attorney's admitting defeat
6. a ship cabin's falling into long neglect
7. a witness's describing the details of a murder in court
8. a cook's providing the ship's passengers with dish after dish of food
9. a prosecutor's finding another witness to the crime
10. a red-faced captain's responding to a rude seaman

ALFRED BRENNER

Alfred Brenner (1916–) has said that when he read Eugene O'Neill's seven sea plays as a teenager, they "appealed to his romantic and rebellious nature" and had a significant impact on his life. Deciding to become a playwright, he wasted no time. He wrote during high school and at the University of Wisconsin, and his first play was produced when he was only 21 years old.

Struggling to earn a living as a writer for the theater, Brenner turned in the 1950s to the exciting new medium of television, where he found success as a writer of television dramas. He sold scripts to *The Kraft Playhouse*; *The United States Steel Hour*, on which *Survival* was shown; and other major dramatic programs. When Brenner came across the story he tells in *Survival*, he was intrigued enough to locate the original trial transcript at the New York University Law Library. This drama is frequently produced in high schools and used in college philosophy classes to discuss moral issues.

In 1958, Brenner moved from the East to Hollywood, where there was a greater market for television and film scripts. It was not long before his script *Eddie* won an Emmy Award. Brenner has continued writing television and film scripts and stage plays and has published a handbook for screenwriters. He taught film writing at the University of California, Los Angeles, for almost 25 years. He encourages young people to be writers, saying, "It's a very exciting, very difficult, insecure but wonderful profession."

482 UNIT FOUR PART 1: SO MUCH AT STAKE

WHAT DO YOU THINK?
Reflecting on Theme

Have students think about the tribute they wrote praising someone who bravely faced an enemy. Invite them to write a tribute to David Holmes in which they describe what was at stake for him and how he faced the enemy.

ON YOUR OWN

BATTLE BY THE BREADFRUIT TREE

by Theodore J. Waldeck

Smith and I were anxious to procure motion pictures of a herd of baboons. We had tried and tried, with no success whatever, though we saw many of these creatures.

Our camp was some miles from a little ravine through which a stream ran. Beyond the ravine was a plateau leading back to thick woods. The baboons, scores of them, came out of these woods with their young to play on the plateau, to drink from the stream, and to fight for the favors of the females. Often Smith and I watched them, tried to photograph them, but could never get close enough. The baboons enjoyed what we were doing. They thought it was a game of some sort.

BATTLE BY THE BREADFRUIT TREE   **483**

Objectives
- To promote independent active reading
- To apply and practice skills learned in previous selections
- To provide an opportunity to assess students' performance through an alternative assessment instrument

Reading Pathways
- Encourage students to read this exciting selection independently for enjoyment.
- Invite students to choose partners and do a paired reading.
- Invite students to choose especially vivid passages of the selection to read aloud to their classmates.
- Evaluate how well students can read, interpret, discuss, and write about the selection on their own by using the Integrated Assessment for Unit Four, located in the Alternative Assessment booklet. Administer the assessment at the end of the unit after students have read all the selections and completed all the writing that was assigned. Set aside two class periods, or about two hours, for the assessment.

RESOURCE AND MEDIA ORGANIZER

UNIT FOUR RESOURCE BOOK
Strategic Reading:
Literature, p. 33

FORMAL ASSESSMENT
Selection Test, pp. 91–92
Part Test, pp 93–94
Test Generator

ALTERNATIVE ASSESSMENT
Unit Four Integrated
    Assessment, pp. 19–24

ACCESS FOR STUDENTS ACQUIRING ENGLISH
Selection Summaries

AUDIO LIBRARY
See Reference Card

SUMMARY

Waldeck, a naturalist working in South Africa, witnesses a fight between a mother baboon and a leopard stalking the baboon's infant. The mother baboon is killed during the ferocious fight. Waldeck and his partner Smith are so amazed by the sight that they do not think about helping the baboon. Just before her death, the baboon utters a piercing cry. As the leopard moves to attack the young baboon, Waldeck aims his gun at the leopard. Suddenly a whole herd of baboons appears, summoned by the mother's last cry. They tear the leopard to bits and take the young baboon away with them.

Thematic Link: *So Much at Stake* A mother baboon battles a leopard in order to protect the life of her offspring.

Once we set up the camera at the edge of the plateau in order to take them when they came through the woods at dawn to greet the sun. We didn't even come close, for when the baboons saw us, they charged like a shrieking army of savages. They threw sticks and stones at us, and we fled as though the devil and all his imps were at our heels. A grown bull baboon could have torn either of us to shreds. We didn't even stop to take our camera. We felt sure that our camera would be a wreck when we returned, which could not be until the baboons had retired from the plateau. We went back then, to find it exactly as we had left it. They had not so much as touched it.

"We *must* get those pictures," said Smith, "and I think I know the answer. Those bread-fruit trees[1] this side of the ravine. That big one, with the leafy top . . ."

"Yes?"

"We go there now and build a platform, up among the leaves, set up our camera, take blankets, a Thermos bottle filled with hot tea, and spend the night. Then, when they come out in the morning, we'll be looking right down on them."

I saw that he was right, and we set about it. The trekkers[2] got boards from the camp and carried them to the tree. Big limbs were cut off and lashed high among the leaves at the top of the breadfruit tree. Then the boards were laid across the limbs, the camera set up. We had supper, took our blankets, and went to the tree to spend an uncomfortable night; but however uncomfortable it might be, it would not matter if we got our pictures.

Night. We sat hunched up with our blankets over us listening to the sounds of the night. Now and again we dozed off. I'd have a cigarette; Smith would smoke a pipe. Then we'd waken. The wind blew steadily toward us from the plateau, which we could see dimly in the moonlight. The hours wore on.

Finally, animals began to greet the growing morning, though it would be some time, if they stuck to schedule, before the baboons appeared. I sat back on my blanket now—it was already warm enough to do without it—and watched the day break. I never tired of doing that. The sun comes up in a different way in Africa. First the leaves would be black. Then a grayish haze would outline their shapes. Then the gray would lighten into the green of the leaves. Then the sun itself would strike through, and morning would be with us, covering that part of Africa with a mixture of colors that ran through all the spectrum. Sunlight played upon colors like a mighty organist upon the keys, and the keys were everything the sunlight touched; when the dawn was come, it was music made visible. Not just the music that men played, but the music of Nature herself, with all the sounds that Nature used. A great sword of crimson was like a bloodcurdling scream you could not hear because you came before it sounded or after the sound had passed—and the sword struck deeply into the ravine and raised itself to slash across the plateau on which the baboons usually played. The green of the trees was light and like a touch of agony somehow—not the agony of pain, but the agony of an unexplainable kind of ecstasy. Far away and all around were the mounded hills, with the veldt[3] between them, and some of the hills wore caps of crimson or orange or gold, and some were still touched with the mystery of distance or the night that had not yet left them. Whatever color or combination of colors you cared to

---

1. **breadfruit trees:** tropical trees with seedless round fruit.
2. **trekkers:** people employed to carry equipment on an expedition.
3. **veldt** (vĕlt): an open grassland of southern Africa.

Leopard and Baboon. John Dominis, Life Magazine. Copyright © 1965 Time Inc.

Linking to Science

Baboons are a species of monkey that live in Africa (south of the Sahara) as well as in Asia. They are large, powerful animals that walk on four legs, have large heads with long, doglike muzzles, and powerful jaws containing sharp teeth (almost like tusks on the upper part of the jaw).

Baboons have highly developed social behaviors, and a troop of baboons acts as a tightly knit community. This group is led and protected by a single dominant male. Most troops of baboons contain more adult females than adult males. In most species, grown males leave their mothers and join other groups, while females stay together. Related females are extremely protective of each other.

mention, you could find there. And they came out of the east in a magical rush, like paint of all colors flung across the world by a painter bigger than all the earth itself.

I sighed and drank it in. Smith was looking out through the leaves, watching for the baboons to appear. Then he nudged me, and I made an end, for the moment, of dreaming. I parted the leaves in utter silence, making sure that my lens was uncovered and aimed at the plateau, and looked through. The baboon herd had not come, but a single baboon and her baby. Smith had not actually seen her coming. One moment he had been watching, seeing nothing. Then he had blinked his eyes, and she was there. He signaled me to start the camera. I noted that the wind was toward us. I felt sure that the rest of the baboons would come, following this one. The mother baboon, while her baby played across the plateau behind her, came down to its edge to peer into the ravine, perhaps to dash down for a drink. I started the camera. It was almost silent but not quite. And with the first whirring sound, which we ourselves could scarcely hear, though we were right beside it, the mother jumped up and looked around. Her ears had caught the little sound. She looked in all directions, twisting her head swiftly, and even in this her eyes kept darting to her young one. I stilled the whirring. We did not move or make a sound, even a whisper. She was so close we could see her nose wrinkling as she tried to get our scent. But the wind was toward us, and she got nothing. She even looked several times at the breadfruit tree that hid us.

I was about to start grinding again when a terrific squall came from the baby. It caught at my heart, that sound. I know it caught at the heart of Smith, too, for I could see it in his face. The mother baboon whirled around, so fast one could scarcely see the movement. The baby was jumping swiftly to the top of a rock, which was all too low to be of any use to him, as protection against the creature that was close behind him.

That creature was a hunting leopard, and it, like the baboon, had come so softly and

BATTLE BY THE BREADFRUIT TREE **485**

OPTION 1

Cooperative Learning
CREATING A GROUP DANCE

Have groups of students work on creating dance interpretations of the scene between the baboons and the leopard. Students could work in groups of four—three performers to play the two principal baboons and the leopard, and one student to design and organize the dance's choreography. Remind students that they need not present naturalistic interpretations of the animals (unless they wish to do so). Some students might find it more interesting to portray the behavior and feelings involved in the fight, rather than the animals themselves.

If more than one group works on this activity, encourage students to appreciate how their groups transform the same source material in different ways.

Teacher's Role Encourage students to divide the narrative into scenes. After the arrival of the mother and baby baboon, natural breaks in the narrative occur four times when the two adult animals rest. The fifth scene would include the death of the baboon, the attack of the baboon troop, the death of the leopard, and the rescue of the baby baboon.

Rubric

3 Full Accomplishment Students work well together and succeed in producing a well-thought-out dance and can support their choices with references to the text.

2 Substantial Accomplishment Students work well together, but do not produce a dance interpretation consistent with the narrative and have difficulty supporting their choices with references to the text.

1 Little or Partial Accomplishment Students show little cooperative ability and have difficulty defining dance choices or supporting those choices.

---

silently that we had not seen it. It was simply there, a murderous streak behind the baby baboon. Did the female hesitate for a single moment? Not at all. If the leopard were a streak, so was the mother baboon. She shot toward that leopard and was in the air above him, reaching for his neck, while he was in midleap behind the baby, which now sat upon the rock and uttered doleful screams of terror.

The great cat instantly had his work cut out for him. For the baboon, by gripping his neck from behind, beyond reach of those talons, could break it. And that was what she tried, with hands and feet and killing incisors. But while I knew nothing of this fighting combination, the leopard must have, for he did what any cat would instinctively do in such a case. He spun to his back and reached for the baboon with all four of his brutally armed paws. One stroke across the abdomen of the baboon, and she would be killed outright. But she knew something of leopards.

> **Smith did not make a sound, nor did I. I don't think we even breathed.**

Smith did not make a sound, nor did I. I don't think we even breathed. The great cat recovered himself as the baboon jumped free of the leopard and ran toward her baby. The leopard charged the baboon. The baboon waited until the last minute, shot into the air, allowed the cat to go under her, turned in the air, and dropped back for the killing hold on the back of the neck again.

She got some hair in her mouth, which she spat out disgustedly. The baby kept on squalling. As nearly as I could tell—though I probably would not have heard even the trumpeting of elephants or the roaring of lions—there was no sound other than the screaming of the female baboon, the squalling of her baby, and the spitting and snarling of the leopard.

This time, when the leopard whirled to his back to dislodge the baboon, he managed to sink his claws into the baboon. I saw the blood spurt from the baboon's body, dyeing her fur. I knew that the smell of blood would drive the leopard mad, and it did. He would just as soon eat the meat of a grown baboon if he could not have the baby.

Both stood off for a second, regarding each other, to spit out fur and hair. Then the leopard charged once more. Again the baboon leaped high, started down, reaching for that neck. And this time, when she came down, the leopard had already turned, and she could not entirely avoid landing among those fearful talons. Even a baboon could not jump from a spot in midair. For a brief moment there was a terrific flurry of infighting, from which came the snarling of the leopard, the screaming of the she-baboon. Now we could see the leopard, now the baboon, the latter trying with all her strength and agility to escape a disemboweling stroke from one of the four feet of the killer. Then both were so mixed up, and fighting so much all over the plateau, that we could not distinguish them. We could tell they were together because they formed a ball of fighting fury, and the sounds of the two animals came out of the pinwheel of murderous action.

How long it lasted I do not know. To the she-baboon and her baby it must have seemed ages. It may have been seconds, even a minute. And then they were standing off, catching their breath, spitting out fur, regarding each other again. Both were tired. To my utter amazement the baboon was holding her own with the leopard. At that moment I would not have known which one had the edge, if either. For both were panting, weary, and stained with blood.

Neither gave ground. By common consent they stood for a few seconds, the baboon on her hind legs, the leopard crouching on all fours. Then the leopard charged. Again the baboon went into the air to let the leopard go under her. She knew better, at this stage of the game, than to run away or jump to either side. The leopard could overtake her if she ran, could turn instantly and follow her if she jumped to either side. So up and over was her only chance. Again she came down. But this time she was expecting the cat to whip upon his back and present his talons, and was ready. She twisted aside a little, and to the front, perhaps with some idea of reaching for the neck from the underside, now uppermost. The forepaws of the leopard lashed at her. The sun gleamed on the exposed talons and showed that they were red with baboon blood. I could see long weals[4] across the abdomen of the baboon. She had evaded those slashes at the last moment, each time. Feeling the talons' touch she had got away, just enough to escape disemboweling, not enough to escape deep, parallel gashes that reached inward for her life.

Now I began to see how the fight was going to go, though neither Smith nor I could have done anything about it because we were spellbound, rooted to our place in the breadfruit tree, watching something that few explorers had ever seen: a battle between a leopard and a baboon! And for the best reason in the world—the baboon to protect her baby.

But now the she-baboon was tiring. It was obvious in all her movements, though I knew and the leopard knew that as long as she stood upright and could see him, she was dynamite—fury incarnate,[5] capable of slaying if she got in the blows she wanted. So far she had not made it.

Now she panted more than the leopard did. She did not entirely evade his rushes, though she jumped over him as before. But she did not go as high or twist as quickly in the air. She couldn't. Her body was beginning to weigh too much for her tiring muscles. She was like an arm-weary prizefighter who has almost fought himself out. But her little eyes still glared defiance, her screaming still informed him that she was ready for more. Now there were other slashes upon her face, her head, her chest, and her abdomen—clear down even to her hands and feet. She was a bloody mess. But she never even thought of quitting. They drew apart once more, spitting fur. They glared at each other. Several times I saw the orange eyes of the leopard, and there was hell in them—the hell of hate and fury and thwarted hunger.

Now he charged before the baboon had rested enough. He was getting stronger, the baboon weaker. His second wind[6] came sooner perhaps, and he sorely needed it. Even yet the baboon could break his neck, given the one chance.

Again the baboon went into the air, came down, and was caught in the midst of those four paws. Again the battle raged, the two animals all mixed up together, all over the plateau. The little one squalled from his boulder, and there was despair in his voice. He cried hopeless encouragement to his mother. She heard, I knew she did, and tried to find some reserve with which to meet the attacks of the killer.

That last piece of infighting lasted almost too long. There was no relief from it, and the nerves of the two men who watched were strained to the breaking point, though neither was aware of

---

4. **weals:** ridges on the skin, produced by blows.
5. **incarnate** (ĭn-kär′nĭt): given form; in the flesh.
6. **second wind:** a burst of energy following a period of exhaustion.

Linking to Science

In the wild, some animals live in groups for protection. Baboons, for example, have a system in which dominant males rest or march in the center of the troop and watch the others. If any part of the troop is threatened, the males leave the center to face the danger.

Occasionally, a mother and her infant baboon get separated from the troop. Despite the fact that the average female baboon is less than half the size of a male, she can, if provoked, be a fearsome fighter. Baboon mothers have such powerful protective instincts that they will sacrifice their own lives rather than allow harm to come to their babies.

Individual Activity

CREATING A LANDSCAPE PAINTING

Invite students to paint the scene that Theodore Waldeck describes in the second column of page 484. Encourage students to get ideas for their painting by studying the author's descriptions ("the green of the trees was light" and "some of the hills wore caps of crimson or orange or gold"), as well as passages that suggest some greater magic or mystery about the scene. Remind students that their paintings can range from the representational to the abstract.

Teacher's Role Help students focus on a particular element of the scene or a specific feeling they wish their painting to convey.

Rubric

3 Full Accomplishment Students create a painting that vividly conveys some aspect of the landscape described.

2 Substantial Accomplishment Students create a painting that conveys some aspect of the scene described.

1 Little or Partial Accomplishment Students have difficulty creating a painting related to the scene described.

---

it. How long they had held their breath they did not know.

The two beasts broke apart, and I saw instantly that the leopard had at last succeeded, managing the stroke he had been trying for since the battle began. He had raked deeply into the abdomen of the baboon. The result may be well imagined. The baboon drew off slowly and looked down at herself. What she saw told her the truth—that even if the leopard turned and ran away this minute, she was done.

But did she expect mercy? Death did not grant mercy in Africa—certainly not on this particular morning.

The baboon noted the direction of the leopard's glance. The great cat was crouched well back but facing the rock on which the baby squalled. He licked his chops, looked at the dying she-baboon, and growled, and it was as though he said:

"Not much time now. And when you are gone, nothing will keep me from getting him!"

As if the leopard had actually screamed those words, I got the thought which raced through his evil head. And the baboon got it too. For she turned slowly, like a dead thing walking, and moved to turn her back toward the rock, so that now the baby was almost over her head.

Then she looked at the leopard once more and screamed as though she answered: "Perhaps, but over my dead body!"

The leopard charged again, for the last time. It would be easy now. And as the she-baboon set herself against that last charge, the strangest, most nearly human cry I ever heard went keening[7] out across the veldt. It bounced against the breadfruit trees, dipped into the ravine; it went back through the forest whence the other baboons usually came to play and drink. It went out in all directions, that cry, across the plain. It rolled across the mounded hills. It was a cry that could never be forgotten by those that heard it.

And then, in the midst of the cry—like none she had uttered while the fight had been so fierce—the leopard struck her down. She sprawled, beaten to a pulp, at the base of the boulder, while that last cry of hers still moved across the veldt.

> *It was a cry that could never be forgotten by those that heard it.*

And now, sure that the she-baboon was dead, the leopard backed away, crouched, lifted his eyes to the baby on the rock.

I came to life then, realizing for the first time what I was seeing. I couldn't have moved before. But now, somehow, my rifle was in my hands, at my shoulder, and I was getting the leopard in my sights. Why had I not done it before, saved the life of the mother? I'll never know. Certainly, and sincerely, I had not allowed the fight to continue simply in order to see which would win out. I had simply become a statue, possessing only eyes and ears.

I got the leopard in my sights as he crouched to spring. I had his head for a target. I'd get him before he moved, before he sprang. The baby—looking down, sorrow in his cries, with a knowledge of doom too—had nowhere to go. I tightened the trigger. And then . . .

On the instant, the leopard was blotted out, and for several seconds I could not understand what had happened, what the mother's last cry had meant. But now I did. For living baboons, leaping, screaming, had appeared out of nowhere. They came, the

---

7. **keening:** wailing.

whole herd of them, and the leopard was invisible in their midst. I did not even hear the leopard snarl and spit. I heard nothing save the baboons, saw nothing save the big blur of their bodies, over and around the spot where I had last seen the leopard.

How long that lasted I do not know. But when it was over, another she-baboon jumped to the rock, gathered up the baby, and was gone. After her trailed all the other baboons. Smith and I looked at each other, and if my face was as white and shocked as his, it was white and shocked indeed. Without a word, because we both understood, we slipped down from the tree, crossed the ravine, climbed its far side, crossed the plateau, looked down at the dead she-baboon, then looked away again. One mother had fought to the death for the life of her baby and had saved that life. We looked around for the leopard who had slain her. We couldn't find a piece of it as big as an average man's hand! So the baboons had rallied to the dying cry of the mother baboon.

We went slowly back to the tree, got our camera down, returned with it to our camp. Not until we were back did we realize that neither of us, from the beginning of that fight to its grim and savage end, had thought of the camera, much less touched it.

One of the greatest fights any explorer ever saw was unrecorded. ❖

THEODORE J. WALDECK

Theodore J. Waldeck (1894–) was just a child when both of his parents died. He and his sister were sent from their home in Brooklyn, New York, to live with their grandfather in Vienna, Austria. The grandfather was anxious to have his grandson become a doctor, but Waldeck was more interested in adventure.

When he was 18 years old, Waldeck accompanied a family friend, the Duke of Mecklenburg, on an African expedition. No sooner had they arrived at an African seaport than Waldeck became ill with a tropical fever. The Duke, unable to wait for his ailing friend, continued the expedition and left money for Waldeck to return home when he was fully recovered. However, when Waldeck was well again, he used the money to equip a safari and follow the expedition. "This foolhardy adventure luckily was the turning point in my life," Waldeck once said, "for I became convinced I wanted to be an explorer." Waldeck spent 18 years exploring Africa and leading expeditions. From these adventures came stories, including "Battle by the Breadfruit Tree," part of his book *On Safari*.

With his wife, writer Jo Besse McElveen Waldeck, Waldeck lived for many months among native tribes in the interior of British Guiana, South America (today called Guyana), making friends and learning their languages and customs.

OTHER WORKS *Lions on the Hunt*, *The White Panther*

Class Discussion
SHARING IDEAS

Teacher's Role Engage students in a whole-class discussion using the following questions. Help students see both sides of more difficult questions by acting as a moderator between differing points of view.

1. Did you want the leopard or the baboon to win the fight? Explain your answer. *(Encourage students to give reasons for their choice—or for their refusal to favor one animal over the other.)*

2. At one point the author says he knew what was going through the leopard's "evil head." Do you think the leopard was evil? Why or why not? *(Possible response: The author is just expressing his dismay at the fact that the leopard would gladly kill the baby baboon. Since he's a scientist, he knows that a cat's instinct to kill for food is not evil.)*

3. Do you think Waldeck would have been justified in shooting the leopard? Why or why not? *(Possible responses: Yes, a person can't just sit there and allow a baby baboon to be killed by a fierce predator. No, because the leopard was only doing what was natural. People should not interfere in encounters between wild animals. Leopards are rare, so it would have been irresponsible for Waldeck to kill that animal.)*

4. What effects do you think this experience might have had on Waldeck and Smith? *(Possible response: The men probably gained a new understanding of baboons' fighting abilities, the power of the mother-child relationship, and the sophistication of baboons' communication and group behavior.)*

THEODORE J. WALDECK

The purpose of the expedition on which Waldeck accompanied the Duke of Mecklenburg was to determine the border between what was then British East Africa and German East Africa. Waldeck led other expeditions to Africa that took him to Uganda, Tanganyika, and Abyssinia.

OVERVIEW

In the Guided Assignment for this section, students will write a personal response to a work of literature. By writing a reaction to literature, students learn to use details to support their opinions. As preparation and support for this assignment, The Writer's Style will help students understand the importance of using descriptive language, sentence variety, and indefinite pronouns to create interesting and clear sentences. In Reading the World, students will explore their reactions to nonverbal information such as facial expressions and body language.

Objectives

- To recognize how authors use descriptive language to show action, character, or setting
- To achieve sentence variety and to use descriptive language
- To write effectively by showing and not telling
- To write a personal response to a piece of literature
- To understand reactions to nonverbal information

Skills

LITERATURE
- Recognizing descriptive details that help to show action, character, or setting

GRAMMAR AND USAGE
- Using indefinite pronouns

MEDIA LITERACY
- Reading nonverbal information

ORAL COMMUNICATION
- Peer response
- Group conferencing

CRITICAL THINKING
- Interpreting nonverbal clues
- Synthesizing
- Analyzing

Teaching Strategy: MODELING
In the following models, the authors show their settings and characters rather than telling about them. They use details to create vivid images in the reader's mind.

A Waldeck Possible response: The details make the scene of the sunrise over the open grassland come alive.

B Brenner Possible responses: Readers would not know as much if they were only told about the man on the mast because the description of his actions shows just how crazy or brave he really is.

WRITING ABOUT LITERATURE

SHOW HOW YOU FEEL

As you read the selections in Unit Four, "Facing the Enemy," were you excited? saddened? troubled? all of these? Good writing draws you into the world it depicts. Thoughtful reading allows you to make connections between your reading and your life. In this lesson you will

- see how writers *show* rather than *tell* information
- write a personal response to a piece of literature
- explore ways that people *show* reactions and feelings

Writer's Style: Show, Don't Tell Good writers don't just tell what happens or what something is like. They use details to show action, characters, or setting.

Read the Literature

These writers use details to show a place or character.

Literature Models

A Showing a Place
Why are these details more effective than a simple statement telling you that the sunrise was magnificent?

> Far away and all around were the mounded hills, with the veldt between them, and some of the hills wore caps of crimson or orange or gold, and some were still touched with the mystery of distance or the night that had not yet left them. Whatever color or combination of colors you cared to mention, you could find there. And they came out of the east in a magical rush, like paint of all colors flung across the world.
>
> Theodore Waldeck, from "Battle by the Breadfruit Tree"

B Showing Character
What do Able's examples show about the man on the mast? Why would you see him less clearly if Able said nothing but "He was crazy!"

> **A**ble. Well, he always had to be the first one up on the crow's nest . . . even during the worst weather. . . . I seen him hanging on to the top of the mizzenmast once with the ship practically layin' over horizontal with the sea . . . and the mast all icy. . . . An' when he came down later, his hands all bloody, he didn't say one word . . . even when some of the men slapped his shoulder and told him he did a nice job. . . . He was crazy!
>
> Alfred Brenner, from *Survival*

490 UNIT FOUR: FACING THE ENEMY

PRINT AND MEDIA RESOURCES

UNIT FOUR RESOURCE BOOK
The Writer's Style, p. 37
Prewriting Guide, p. 38
Elaboration, p. 39
Peer Response Guide, pp. 40–41
Revision and Editing, p. 42
Student Model, p. 43–44
Rubric, p. 45

GRAMMAR MINI-LESSONS
Transparencies, pp. 6, 11
Copymasters, p. 6

WRITING MINI-LESSONS
Transparencies, pp. 40–42

ACCESS FOR STUDENTS ACQUIRING ENGLISH
Reading and Writing Support

FORMAL ASSESSMENT
Guidelines for Writing Assessment

Connect to Life

Feature writers use details to show what real people, places, and events are like. Look at the feature article below. Think about how you respond to this description.

Magazine Article

> Now he appears to float the remaining ball across the stage on top of his hands, as if he's nudging a soap bubble. It glides up over his fingertips and into his palm, runs back up one arm, across his chest and down the other arm. He peers at it, and it leaps onto his forehead. He sinks to the floor, puts his hands behind his head and casually crosses his feet, the ball still perched on his forehead. He looks like a man about to daydream beneath his personal moon.
>
> Steve Kemper
> from "The Magical Motion of Michael Moschen"
> *Smithsonian*, August 1995

Showing Action How does the writer help you visualize what the juggler is doing?

Try Your Hand: Showing, Not Telling

1. **Show a Few Things** Rewrite these sentences so that they "show" rather than "tell" about a person, a place, or an event.
   - Herman was annoying.
   - The beach was beautiful.
   - My party was a disaster.

2. **It's Show Time** Write stage directions for the opening moments of a play set on a city sidewalk. The mood of the scene can be tense, lively, or peaceful. Tell how the main character should act as the play begins.

3. **Show Yourself** Complete the statement "I am . . ." with an adjective that describes part of your personality. Then write a paragraph that shows that part of your personality. Share your paragraph with a group of classmates and let them guess what adjective you used to describe yourself.

SkillBuilder

WRITER'S CRAFT

Using Descriptive Language

Good writers use specific nouns, vivid adjectives, and precise verbs to show action, character, and setting in a way that makes readers feel they are there. Look at this example from "Battle by the Breadfruit Tree."

> *We didn't even come close, for when the baboons saw us, they charged like a shrieking army of savages.*

Theodore Waldeck could have written "The baboons were angry," but by using descriptive language to show what happens, he places his readers in the scene.

Try to picture the scene that you are writing about, and pretend you are participating in it yourself. Noticing details and descriptions will help you write.

APPLYING WHAT YOU'VE LEARNED

Rewrite the sentences below, replacing general nouns and verbs with more specific ones and adding adjectives so that the language is descriptive.

1. The animal looked tired.
2. The baboon's eyes were ugly.
3. We went slowly back to the tree.

WRITING HANDBOOK

For more help with descriptive language, see page 832 of the Writing Handbook.

WRITING ABOUT LITERATURE **491**

Teaching Strategy: MODELING

C Kemper Possible response: The details of how the ball moves over the juggler's body, what the juggler does, and how he looks on stage help the reader visualize his actions.

Try Your Hand

1. Responses will vary. Sentences should contain descriptive details about each person and place. Here are some examples:
   - Herman would pull on people's clothing and interrupt their conversations all the time.
   - The beach had white sand and palm trees reaching right down to the water's edge.
   - The music was so boring, the decorations were so sad, and the conversations were so dull that everyone at my party went home early.

2. Help students write purely descriptive stage directions. Here is a sample:
   In the center is an orange front door to an apartment building. Its windows are made of security glass and there is wire over the glass. Graffiti covers the metal gates on both sides of the door. A policeman strolls up to the man leaning against a dirt-stained brick wall.

3. Statements and paragraphs will vary. Here is a sample adjective and paragraph:
   I am cool. I used to hang out with people my age or younger, but now I hang out only with people who are older. I wear the latest fashions. I am learning to write songs, and I go over to my friend's place after school because she's a musician and has her own studio gear.

SkillBuilder WRITER'S CRAFT

USING DESCRIPTIVE LANGUAGE

Encourage students to use a variety of vocabulary words when they write. If they want to use a dictionary, advise them that they should always think about what they want to say rather than just the words they could use to say it. Make sure they always check a word's connotations—the other meanings of a word—before they use that word in their descriptions.

Application Possible responses:
1. The old, mangy leopard looked worn out.
2. The terrified baboon's red eyes were wide open.
3. Carefully and quietly, we crept back to the tall baobab tree.

Additional Suggestions Students can continue adding descriptive details to the following sentences:
1. We hid behind the tree.
2. The campsite was far away.

Reteaching/Reinforcement

 The Writer's Craft

Descriptive Language, pp. 49–61

THE LANGUAGE OF LITERATURE TEACHER'S EDITION **491**

Teaching Strategy:
STUMBLING BLOCK

D Students may be intimidated by the idea of writing a personal response to literature. Assure them that there is no one correct response. Guide students to understand that their emotional reactions to a piece of writing and how they feel about a real event can be the same. A piece of writing may make them feel excited just as the same activity in real life would make them feel excited. Tell them that if they imagine they are actually experiencing the events they read about, they will have more vivid responses.

Critical Thinking: SYNTHESIZING

E Remind students that they will be bringing together their own responses with the events and descriptions in the story. Encourage them to state exactly what it is in the story that provokes the most powerful response. Often, students will have mixed or very complex responses. Advise them that these are excellent reactions and that they should try to convey as many different aspects of their response as possible.

Teaching Strategy: MODELING

F Students may need some time to fill out a Prewriting Chart. Recommend that they keep asking why they feel and think certain things about the story and to write their reactions using the most specific words as possible.

WRITING ABOUT LITERATURE

Personal Response

If a friend told you that a trip she'd taken was "weird," you might not know what she meant until she gave you the details. Describing your response to something you read is much like sharing your reaction to a real event. Details that show your readers why you responded as you did allow them to share your experience. These details could be from the story you read or from your own life.

GUIDED ASSIGNMENT
Write a Personal Response By writing a personal response you make a connection between the literature you read and your life and experiences. You support these thoughts and feelings with details from the selection.

1 Prewrite and Explore

Which piece of literature from Unit Four do you remember best? Which affected you the most when you read it? Choose a selection from this unit or one you have enjoyed on your own and had a strong reaction to.

REVIEWING THE LITERATURE

Look at any notes you took while you were first reading the selection. Read the selection again. Pay attention to what you are thinking or feeling as you read.

- What passages really get your attention? Why?
- What are your feelings about the characters, the events, and the writer's message?
- Is there anything in your own life that helps you to connect to this story in a unique way?

Remember that your reaction can be positive, negative, or anything else you want it to be. There is no wrong way to respond when you are writing about how you really feel.

CHOOSING A TOPIC

Try recording your reactions in a chart like the one at the left. When your chart is complete, decide what interests you the most about the literature and what you want to express to the reader about that topic.

Student's Prewriting Chart

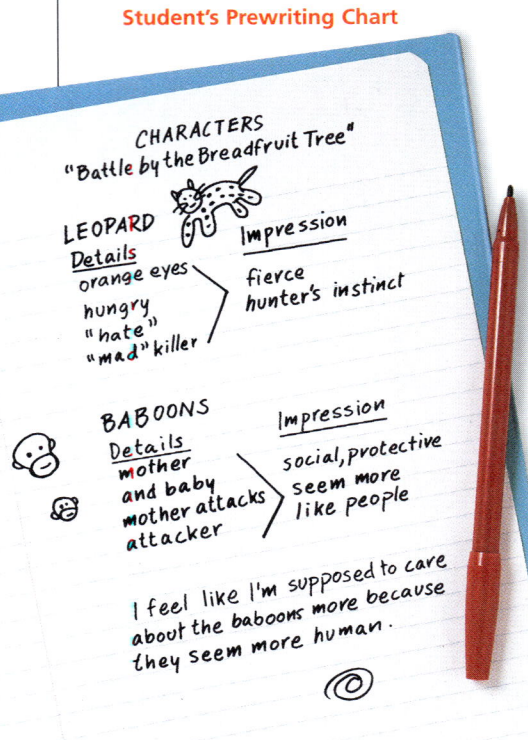

 Assessment Option

SELF-ASSESSMENT After students have completed the Choosing A Topic activity, they can assess their reactions. Students should ask themselves the following questions:
- *Did I record all the details about each passage?*
- *What was my overall reaction to the selection?*
- *What detail or details finally led me to have my main reaction?*
- *Did I record all the emotions and thoughts I had about the selection?*

❷ Write to Understand

Freewriting is one way to think more clearly about your topic before you begin drafting. You may not know where your reactions will take you until you write them down.

- How would you describe your overall reaction to the selection you've chosen? What reasons can you give?
- What life experiences have you had that affected the way you responded to this particular topic?
- What lessons, insights, or goals will you take with you?

Student's Freewriting

This writer makes it sound like the leopard is a horrible creature or something. Horrible creature? It's just an animal. When the leopard sees the baby baboon the writer says, "I got the thought which raced through his evil head." Waldeck, hungry is not the same as evil. It's like when Jimmy and I were fighting and the teacher assumed he was the "victim" just because I'm bigger than he is.

The writer makes the story more exciting by creating a good guy and a bad guy.

The weaker one can be wrong too, but the animal world doesn't have right or wrong.

❸ Draft and Share

As you draft your response, think about how to organize your ideas.

- Begin with an introduction that identifies the work, tells what it's about, and explains the connections you saw.
- In the body, give reasons for your response. Include details that show why you reacted the way you did.
- Finish with a conclusion that summarizes your response.

PEER RESPONSE

- How would you sum up my response?
- Which of the connections I made seem the most logical?

SkillBuilder

WRITER'S CRAFT

Achieving Sentence Variety

Varying the types of sentences you use as well as the way they begin will make your personal response more interesting to read. Try these sentence types.

- Simple sentences have one subject and one predicate.
  The leopard charged.
- Compound sentences consist of two or more simple sentences combined with a conjunction.
  The men ran, and they left the camera.
- Complex sentences contain one main clause and one or more subordinate clauses.
  Even after the baboon got tired, she still had the strength to yell.

Here are some ways to vary the beginning of your sentences.

- Use an adverb.
  Finally, a single baboon and her baby appeared.
- Use an -ing verb form.
  Spinning around, the leopard reached for the baboon.
- Use an adverbial clause.
  As they watched from the tree, the men were spellbound.

APPLYING WHAT YOU'VE LEARNED
Read over your draft and look for opportunities to vary your sentences.

Writing Skill: POINT OF VIEW

G The Write to Understand exercise provides a further opportunity for students to discover how they feel and what they think. Help them to develop their point of view by focusing on what they think about certain events as they reread the selection. Encourage them to imagine themselves as physically present in the scene as an onlooker or as one of the characters. Ask how they would feel in that place while that action is going on.

Teaching Strategy: USING THE SKILLBUILDER

H You can help students add variety to their writing by teaching the SkillBuilder on sentence variety at this time. It reminds students to use simple, compound, and complex sentences to make their writing more interesting.

Teaching Strategy: COLLABORATIVE OPPORTUNITY

I Students can work in pairs to evaluate each other's drafts by checking to make sure they have followed the suggestions on the list in Draft and Share.

SkillBuilder WRITER'S CRAFT

ACHIEVING SENTENCE VARIETY Begin analyzing a selection from this unit to identify the different types of sentences. Then have students continue to identify the sentences in the passage as simple, compound, or complex. Some sentences may be a combination of compound and complex. Encourage students to speculate on the effectiveness of varying long and short sentences.

Application Remind students that varying sentence structure helps make their writing more interesting and clear. You may want to review the use of coordinating and subordinating conjunctions in *The Writer's Craft*, pages 304–305 and 560–561, to help them add sentence variety.

Additional Suggestions Have partners practice revising another piece of their writing. They can work together to identify the sentence types they have used and then change sentences as necessary.

Reteaching/Reinforcement
Writing Mini-Lessons transparencies, pp. 40–42

 The Writer's Craft

Sentence Variety, pp. 302–303

Critical Thinking: ANALYZING

J To evaluate and revise their personal reactions, students should be careful in their choice of specific words to describe their reactions and use many different kinds of sentences to add variety and interest.

Teaching Strategy: MODELING

K Show students how the introduction of the student sample meets the Standards for Evaluation on this page. It identifies and briefly describes the piece of literature being analyzed. The remainder of the sample also follows these guidelines by explaining the reaction in the body of the essay. It then concludes with a summary of the response. Also point out to students where the draft analyzes and reevaluates the first reaction. This occurs in the first paragraph ("When I reread the story, though, I realized . . ."). Help students to see that in the second paragraph, the writer uses the story to reflect on actions in the real world.

Standards for Evaluation

Ideas and Content
- identifies the work by title and author
- gives a brief summary of the work.
- uses details and quotations from the work as well as the writer's personal experience to support the writer's response.
- ends with a summary of the response and a conclusion.

Structure and Form
- demonstrates proper paragraphing.
- includes transitional words and phrases to show relationships among ideas.
- uses variety of sentence structures.

Grammar, Usage, and Mechanics
- contains no more than two or three minor errors in grammar and usage
- contains no more than two or three minor errors in spelling, capitalization, and punctuation

---

WRITING ABOUT LITERATURE

❹ Revise and Edit

J Thoughtful reflection, colorful details, and clear organization make a personal response interesting to read. Consider the connections you have made between your life and this literature. Are they connections you were aware of at first reading? How did your feelings toward the story change as you were writing?

Student's Final Draft

The Big Guy Takes the Rap

"Battle by the Breadfruit Tree" is an exciting true story by Theodore Waldeck about a fight to the death between a leopard and a mother baboon. Waldeck and another wildlife photographer visit the African wilderness and watch the fight from a branch in a breadfruit tree. At first I rooted for the mother baboon to defeat the horrible leopard, just as Waldeck did. When I reread the story, though, I realized that turning the leopard into a villain isn't fair. The leopard is fighting for survival, too, just like the baboon.

K

Waldeck made me feel for the mother baboon and her baby by describing the leopard as a cold-blooded murderer. He describes the leopard as "a murderous streak behind the baby baboon." However, that's just because the leopard is stronger and supposed to be a better hunter. As a kid who always gets blamed for starting fights because I am bigger than the other kids, I understand that it's not wrong to be strong. Also, these animals don't think about right and wrong.

What background information helps the reader understand this response? What sentences describe the student's response?

What details from the story help you understand this student's response?

Standards for Evaluation

A personal response
- has an introduction that gives the title, author, and format of the literary work and introduces the response
- provides enough information about the literary work for the reader to understand the response
- gives reasons for the reaction and supports them with details
- draws an overall conclusion summarizing the response

 Assessment ✓ Option

SELF-ASSESSMENT To help students assess their own personal responses, have them ask themselves the following questions:
- *Have I identified the story for the reader?*
- *Did I include my personal responses in clear and accurate language?*
- *Does my essay use a variety of sentences—simple, complex, and compound?*
- *Have I explained myself fully, even if my reaction was complex or contradictory?*
- *Does my essay supply a conclusion that summarizes my overall response?*

Grammar in Context

Pronoun and Antecedent Agreement When revising your personal response, make sure that the pronouns you use agree with their antecedents. The **antecedent** of a pronoun is the noun (or other pronoun) that the pronoun is replacing.

> The baboons enjoyed what we were doing. They thought it was a game of some sort.

They is the pronoun that replaces *baboons*. *Baboons* is the pronoun's antecedent.

The pronoun must agree with its antecedent in number. If a pronoun's antecedent is singular, the pronoun must be singular. If the antecedent is plural, the pronoun must also be plural.

> Everyone can have ~~their~~ *his or her* own opinion, but when the writer says that the leopard was wrong because it was fierce, ~~they're~~ *he's* not looking at the facts. When the baboons came and attacked ~~them~~ *it*, they were fierce too.

Try Your Hand: Making Pronouns and Antecedents Agree

Fill in the blanks in each sentence with a pronoun that agrees with its antecedent.

1. When a leopard is hungry, ____ doesn't wonder whom to eat or if it is wrong to kill.
2. The men heard the baby baboon cry, and that's when ____ started thinking baboons were weak.
3. Would a hungry Waldeck feel guilty about eating a chicken, knowing ____ was not human?

For more information about pronoun and antecedent agreement, see page 876 of the Grammar Handbook.

SkillBuilder

GRAMMAR FROM WRITING

Using Indefinite Pronouns

Some indefinite pronouns are singular, others are plural, and a few may be either singular or plural. When you are trying to decide what verb form to use, you must first know whether the pronoun is singular or plural.

Singular	Plural
another	both
anybody	few
each	many
neither	several
someone	
Neither wants to give up.	Both are tired and weak.

Some, all, any, none, and *most* take a singular verb when they refer to a singular word.

> All of my film is lost.

When they refer to a plural word or words, they need a plural verb.

> All of the baboons are angry.

APPLYING WHAT YOU'VE LEARNED

Look over your draft to find the indefinite pronouns. Make sure indefinite pronoun subjects and verbs agree.

GRAMMAR HANDBOOK

For more information on subject-verb agreement with indefinite pronouns, see page 867 of the Grammar Handbook.

WRITING ABOUT LITERATURE **495**

CUSTOMIZING FOR
Students Acquiring English

 Some students may have difficulty identifying the antecedent for the pronoun. Advise them that the antecedent can come before or after the pronoun in the sentence. They can check agreement by asking themselves who or what they are discussing at each point in their writing.

Teaching Strategy:
USING THE SKILLBUILDER

 To help students understand the difference between singular and plural pronouns, you may want to teach the SkillBuilder on Using Indefinite Pronouns at this time. It describes the rules for agreement with singular and plural pronouns.

Try Your Hand

1. it (a leopard)
2. they (the men)
3. it (a chicken)

SkillBuilder GRAMMAR FROM WRITING

USING INDEFINITE PRONOUNS Explain to students that a simple way to remember whether an indefinite pronoun is singular or plural is to add the word *one* to the pronoun. If you can put *one* together with the pronoun in the sentence, it is singular—for example, *another one, any one, anybody, each one, neither one,* and *someone.* If you can't add the word *one,* it is a plural indefinite pronoun—"both one," "few one," "many one," and "several one" don't make sense.

Application Help students see that all singular indefinite pronouns need a singular verb and all plural indefinite pronouns need plural verbs.

Additional Suggestions Have students practice with these sentences:
1. All of us (is/<u>are</u>) going behind the tree.
2. Neither of them (<u>is</u>/are) correct.
3. Many of us (was/<u>were</u>) scared.

Reteaching/Reinforcement
Grammar Mini-Lessons, copymaster, p. 6, transparencies, pp. 6, 11

 The Writer's Craft
Pronouns, pp. 435–460

READING THE WORLD

On pages 490–495, students responded to a selection from the unit. The Reading the World on these pages extends this process by asking students to react to facial expressions and body language. This will help them understand the importance of nonverbal communication.

Critical Thinking: ANALYZING

N Encourage students who have never attended or noticed scenes like this to think about where these people might be and what sort of event it is. This may lead students to analyze the dark-haired woman's expression as a sign of satisfaction or pleasure at having won an election. Ask students whether they would think of her expression in the same way if this scene were before an election, not after it.

Media Literacy: INTERPRETING NONVERBAL INFORMATION

O Encourage students to think of how they would feel about the person based only on her facial expressions and gestures. Lead them to compare their reactions to those of the other audience members around the lectern. The woman's gestures may imply that agreeing with her words will make students feel as good as she does.

Speaking and Listening: GROUP DISCUSSION

P Many students will speculate that the politician wants audience members to agree that she is right and to be enthusiastic about her beliefs. Her body language is supposed to show that she is positive and optimistic. Also, some students might say that her body language inspires trust and confidence in her abilities.

READING THE WORLD

SPEAKING WITHOUT WORDS

You know that you respond to what you read in very personal ways. However, do you ever think about how you respond to the people and situations around you? More importantly, do you ever think about exactly what you are responding to? Think about how you would respond if you were part of the event pictured here.

N **View** Look at the scene on these pages. What is each person doing? How would you describe the expression on the dark-haired woman's face? How many other nonverbal signals can you find?

O **Interpret** Decide what each gesture and expression might mean. Be as specific as possible. If you were in the audience, how do you think these signals would make you feel about this politician? How might they affect your reaction to what she said?

P **Discuss** Compare your reactions to those of others in your group. If you were in the audience when this photograph was taken, what might this politician and her supporters want you to believe about her? How might her body language be meant to influence your opinion? Refer to the SkillBuilder at the right for help with understanding nonverbal cues.

SkillBuilder

 CRITICAL THINKING

Interpreting Nonverbal Cues

You may not know it, but you use many forms of nonverbal communication. The expression on your face and the ways you sit, stand, walk, and use your hands can communicate things about you and your message.

Body language sometimes is a truer reflection of someone's thoughts and feelings than words. Body language, however, can often be "read" in more than one way. Can you be sure that your reading is right? You need to be careful of the signals you interpret, as well as of the signals you send.

Some forms of nonverbal communication are standard signals, such as the thumbs-up sign and the V-for-victory sign that are shown here. What about other, less obvious forms of nonverbal communication?

APPLYING WHAT YOU'VE LEARNED
- Observe people in a situation such as a party or a presentation. What examples of nonverbal communication can you find? Are they consistent with each person's verbal communication?
- With a partner, list examples of nonverbal communication. Think of as many likely interpretations as possible. What might influence the ways the signals could be interpreted?

READING THE WORLD 497

SkillBuilder CRITICAL THINKING

INTERPRETING NONVERBAL CLUES

Point out to students that people from a variety of cultural backgrounds use many different nonverbal expressions. Tell them that these differences can be some of the most interesting aspects of a culture. Demonstrate how even the same gesture can mean different things. For instance, hand waving can mean hello or goodbye, but if you are swimming, it can mean you need help. Less-obvious forms of nonverbal communication include a frown, shuffling feet, and, most important, eye movement.

Application

- Students will come up with a variety of examples of nonverbal communication. Encourage them to speculate on what this nonverbal expression means and then compare it to the verbal communication.
- Have one student use an example of a nonverbal communication and "hold" it while the partner analyzes what it could mean. Students may want to use only one example rather than a combination of gesture and facial expression to make the sign less obvious.

UNIT FOUR
Part 2 Lesson Planner

TIME ALLOTMENTS SHOWN ARE APPROXIMATE. DEPENDING ON YOUR GOALS AND THE NEEDS OF YOUR STUDENTS, YOU MAY WISH TO ALLOW MORE OR LESS TIME FOR CERTAIN PORTIONS OF THE LESSON.

Table of Contents	Discussion	Previewing the Selection	Reading the Selection
PART OPENER **UNLIKELY HEROES** **What Do You Think?** page 498	**20 MINUTES** • Reflect on the part theme		
SELECTION **Playing for Keeps** page 500 AVERAGE		**20 MINUTES** • PERSONAL CONNECTION • SCIENCE CONNECTION • WRITING CONNECTION	**20 MINUTES** • Introduce vocabulary • Read pp. 500–504 (5 pp.)
SELECTION **The Dinner Party** page 508 AVERAGE		**20 MINUTES** • PERSONAL CONNECTION • HISTORICAL CONNECTION • READING CONNECTION: Stereotypes	**10 MINUTES** • Introduce vocabulary • Read pp. 508–509 (2 pp.)
SELECTION **Flowers for Algernon** page 514 CHALLENGING		**20 MINUTES** • PERSONAL CONNECTION • SCIENCE CONNECTION • READING CONNECTION: Inferences	**50 MINUTES** • Introduce vocabulary • Read pp. 514–538 (25 pp.)
SELECTION **Paul Revere's Ride** page 543 AVERAGE		**20 MINUTES** • PERSONAL CONNECTION • HISTORICAL CONNECTION • READING CONNECTION: Summarizing	**20 MINUTES** • Read pp. 543–547 (5 pp.)
SELECTION *from* **Harriet Tubman: Conductor on the Underground Railroad** page 551 AVERAGE		**20 MINUTES** • PERSONAL CONNECTION • HISTORICAL CONNECTION • READING CONNECTION: Motivation	**35 MINUTES** • Introduce vocabulary • Read pp. 551–559 (9 pp.)
Writing	Exploring Topics	Prewriting	Drafting and Revising
WRITING FROM EXPERIENCE **Informative Exposition**	**25 MINUTES**	**35 MINUTES**	**90 MINUTES**

Time estimates assume in-class work. You may wish to assign some of these stages as homework.

Responding to the Selection

FROM PERSONAL RESPONSE TO CRITICAL ANALYSIS	OR	ANOTHER PATHWAY	LITERARY CONCEPTS	QUICKWRITES
		45 MINUTES		
• Discussion questions	OR	• Group discussion	• Science fiction • Humor	• E-mail note • Epilogue • Alternative ending
		35 MINUTES		
• Discussion questions	OR	• Discussion/chart	• Suspense	• Interior monologue • Dialogue
		50 MINUTES		
• Discussion questions	OR	• Debate	• Character changes	• Progress report • Letter of recommendation • Rewrite
		40 MINUTES		
• Discussion questions	OR	• Cartoons	• Narrative poem	• Narrative poem • News article
		45 MINUTES		
• Discussion questions	OR	• Sketch	• Biography	• Diary entry • Description • Letter

Extension Activities

• ALTERNATIVE ACTIVITIES • LITERARY LINKS • CRITIC'S CORNER • THE WRITER'S STYLE • ACROSS THE CURRICULUM • ART CONNECTION • WORDS TO KNOW • BIOGRAPHY

Alternative Activities	Literary Links	Critic's Corner	The Writer's Style	Across the Curriculum	Art Connection	Words to Know	Biography
20 MINUTES							
✓	✓			SCIENCE		✓	✓
20 MINUTES							
				SCIENCE		✓	✓
45 MINUTES							
✓			✓	SCIENCE	✓		✓
40 MINUTES							
✓	✓			SOCIAL STUDIES			✓
30 MINUTES							
✓				MATH GEOGRAPHY		✓	✓

Publishing and Reflecting

40 MINUTES

UNIT FOUR
Part 2 Cooperative Project

Historical Dramas

Overview

Students will research an intriguing historical event that involves some level of heroism, and then they will dramatize the event.

PROJECT AT A GLANCE
The selections in Unit Four, Part 2 depict ordinary people who exhibit extraordinary heroism in the face of adversity. For this project, students will work cooperatively to research a historical act of heroism. They will then write a script, assign roles, and act out the drama in front of the rest of the class. The project may culminate in a performance of all the dramatizations for the entire school or for an invited audience.

OBJECTIVES
- To research and choose a historical event that involves an act of heroism by one or more of the participants
- To write a dramatic script describing the event
- To dramatize the event for an audience

SUGGESTED GROUP SIZE
4–5 students

MATERIALS
- Paper and writing utensils
- Props, costumes, and/or scenery (optional)

1 Getting Started

Arranging the Project
Decide what level of performance you expect from the students. The more you expect from them, the more arrangements you will have to make. Do you expect costumes, makeup, line memorization, and props? If so, decide how much responsibility you expect students to take for each of these. This project can be as involved or as simple as you care to make it.

Arranging the Performances
If the performances are to be held in the classroom, you need only rearrange a bit of furniture. Try to allow as much space between the audience and the players as possible.

If the performances are to be held in the auditorium, now is the time to schedule the performances, as well as rehearsal time for each group. Auditorium performances may also require stagehands for opening and closing the curtain and taking care of the lighting. If the school cannot provide you with help, you can ask the Media Club or Drama Club for volunteers to assist you.

2 Creating the Dramas

Introducing the Project
Explain that students will be working together in small groups to select a true historical event of mutual interest. This event should show one or more persons doing something heroic. Students will then dramatize that event by writing a script for a one-act play. Groups will assign roles, hold rehearsals, and give a final performance for an audience.

Open a discussion about heroism with the class. Ask them to remember any recent news that involved ordinary people doing extraordinary things. You might give a generic example of a firefighter rushing in to save a person from a burning building. The firefighter is probably an average person who is "just doing the job," but to the person saved, he or she is a hero(ine).

You might also want to review the form in which scripts are written. Students can look at the dramas in this text to be reminded of the form and to note what is and is not included in the scripts.

Group Investigations
Divide students into groups of four or five. Members should start researching to find examples of true heroism that might be worthy of group consideration. Final selection of a subject and event should be made as a group. Encourage groups to consider recent heroes and events also; *historical* does not necessarily mean "older than dirt." Once a selection has been made, group members can work cooperatively to develop a script that reflects the act of heroism. As students work on their scripts, hold class meetings to keep track of any common problems groups are experiencing.

Creating a Project Description
After groups have selected a subject and event, they should prepare a brief written report naming the person and giving a capsule description of the event. Meet with each group to review progress and discuss their plans and intentions for the script. This meeting will alert you to any problems groups are experiencing and to any special needs their dramatizations will require.

OPTION 1: NARROWING THE TIME PERIOD
You may want to coordinate this project with a history teacher and ask groups to select an event from the specific time period they are currently studying.

OPTION 2: ON CAMERA Students' dramatizations can be videotaped and then played for the class. Videotaping will allow you to review the performances more than once and according to your scheduling needs. You may wish to allow students multiple "takes" to redo scenes if any mistakes are made in the original performance. Groups can then select the best take to represent their performance; or if appropriate equipment is available, they can edit together various takes to create the best overall performance.

OPTION 3: BEFORE AND AFTER Groups can select a person declared a "hero" by the media and research to find out what his or her life was like before and after the event. Students should discuss any significant changes in the person's life.

OPTION 4: A REAL HERO Students can interview local firefighters or police officers and find one who is considered a hero(ine) by co-workers. Groups can then interview the person to find out what it feels like to be a hero(ine) and whether or not life has changed.

Encourage students to be creative in their scripts. Explain that dramatizations are much more than just the bare bones of the events. Groups should expand dialogue beyond the obvious to try to help explain how characters are feeling and what they are thinking.

3 Sharing the Dramas

If possible, allow students to share their dramatizations with other classes or with the entire school. If you are restricted to staging performances in the classroom, you may want to think about videotaping them as they happen (rather than for perfection). These tapes then could be shared with other classes. As always, remind the students in the audience to listen and watch with respect.

Assessing the Project

The following rubric can be used for group or individual assessment.

3 Full Accomplishment Students follow directions and produce a one-act play showing a historical act of heroism.

2 Substantial Accomplishment Students produce a play, but the act of heroism is unclear or poorly depicted.

1 Little or Partial Accomplishment Students' play is incomplete or does not fulfill the requirements of the assignment.

For the Portfolio
You may want to copy the scripts and include them in individual students' portfolios. As always, include a copy of your written assessment of the group's final production.

Note: For other assessment option, see the *Teacher's Guide to Assessment and Portfolio Use.*

Cross-Curricular Options

ART
Have students create a painting, drawing, or collage that could be used to advertise the performances. Encourage them to include an element unique to each performance.

MUSIC
Ask students to research songs that have been written about real-life heroes. Students can perform the songs themselves, or they can audio-tape them and play them for the rest of the class.

SCIENCE

Students can research and dramatize an important scientific discovery or invention.

Resources

Incredible True Adventures and ***More Incredible True Adventures*** by Don L. Wulffson profile men and women who have survived amazing adventures.

Great Lives: Exploration by Milton Lomask describes 25 explorers from ancient Greece to the twentieth century.

PART 2

WHAT DO YOU THINK?
Objectives

The activities on this page can be used to
- introduce the Part 2 theme of "Unlikely Heroes" since each activity is connected to one or more selections
- create materials for students' personal portfolios that they can return to later for reconsideration or revision
- build an understanding of theme that can be returned to and revised as students progress through the unit

What is a hero?
Tell students that their pictures can be based on fictional characters in movies and books, such as a superhero, or even actors associated with heroic roles, such as Arnold Schwarzenegger or Sigourney Weaver. (See "Flowers for Algernon," p. 512, and "Playing for Keeps," p. 499.)

How would a hero handle it?
You may wish to have students work in large groups to complete the activity. Encourage groups to brainstorm first a list of possible situations. Then half of the group can plan a skit in which someone maintains control and the other half can plan a skit about the person who loses control. (See "The Dinner Party," p. 507.)

Whom would you feature?
Students in each group should briefly jot down a list of unlikely heroes on which the entire group can vote. Once 12 heroes have been selected, encourage groups to design and construct calendars with illustrations and photos that can be displayed in the classroom. (See "Harriet Tubman: Conductor on the Underground Railroad," p. 550.)

UNIT FOUR **PART 2**

UNLIKELY HEROES

WHAT DO YOU THINK?

REFLECTING ON THEME

What does it take to act heroically? Sometimes the people who behave most admirably are the people you least expect. Use the activities on this page to consider what it takes to be a hero. Keep a record of your impressions. Later, you can compare them with the experiences of the characters in this part of Unit Four.

What is a hero?
Draw a picture of someone who is "the perfect hero" according to most movies and books. Try to make your drawing humorous, and use labels to point out what is heroic. Then draw the complete opposite—someone whom you would normally *never* expect to be the hero in a movie or book.

How would a hero handle it?
Think of a real-life crisis situation that would require a person to have self-control in order to survive—for example, a situation in which someone witnesses a bank robbery. Work together to create a skit, showing what might happen to someone who loses self-control and to someone who maintains it.

Looking back

At the beginning of this unit, you considered what is at stake when people confront their enemies. Did your ideas change as you read the selections in Part 1? Choose two of the selections and identify the enemies that they feature. What is at stake? How do the characters react? Jot down how you would have reacted under the same circumstances.

Whom would you feature?
History is full of people who rose to the occasion and became heroes. Imagine you are in charge of creating a calendar that features "unlikely heroes from history." Whom would you choose to be pictured each month? Work as a group to create a list of names and vote on your top 12 choices.

Selection
Enemies?
What is at stake?
Reaction
My reaction

498

Cross-Curricular Connections

Science Have students work in small groups to research individuals who have accidentally made important scientific and medical discoveries, such as Alexander Fleming, an English researcher who in 1928 accidentally discovered penicillin. Groups should then write reports on their chosen individuals and present their reports to the class. Encourage groups to use photos, illustrations, and other helpful materials in their presentations.

Looking Back
Have students refer back to the selections in Part 1 and write brief summaries of the two selections they have chosen. They can then refer to this information when completing the activity in their notebooks. Encourage students to be as honest as possible when discussing how they would have reacted in the characters' situations. Students should then share their thoughts with a partner.

PREVIEWING

FICTION

Playing for Keeps
Jack C. Haldeman II

PERSONAL CONNECTION *Activating Prior Knowledge*
What do you know about UFO's—unidentified flying objects? Some people believe that UFO's may be spaceships from distant planets, but others think they have an earthly origin. Discuss with the class your thoughts about UFO's. Before you begin, you may wish to jot down some notes in a diagram like the one shown here.

SCIENCE CONNECTION *Building Background*
If you believe that UFO's come from outer space, you are not alone. According to a recent Gallup poll, almost half of all U.S. citizens are believers. Sightings of UFO's are nothing new, though. As long ago as A.D. 98, ancient Romans reported seeing a round burning shield flashing across the sky. Throughout the Middle Ages people told tales of strange objects and unexplained lights in the sky and on land. Today, UFO's are reported to have frightened animals, caused static on radios, and left marks on the ground when they landed.

In 1947, around the time of a great increase in the number of UFO reports, the U.S. Air Force began an investigation of UFO sightings. When the project ended in 1969, more than 12,000 reports had been studied. It was discovered that in over 90 percent of the cases the observers had actually seen Venus or other planets, bright stars, comets, meteors, strange cloud formations, artificial satellites, balloons, birds, or even insects.

WRITING CONNECTION *Setting A Purpose*
Imagine what might happen if space aliens were to invade and take control of the earth. How would they look? What would human life be like afterward? Let your imagination run wild, and write a brief account of such an invasion.

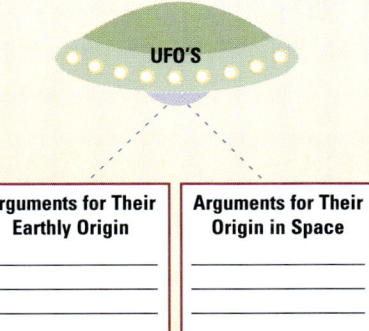

OVERVIEW

Objectives
- To understand a science fiction story about aliens visiting the earth
- To identify and understand science fiction
- To express understanding of the story through a choice of writing forms, including an e-mail note, an epilogue, and an alternative ending
- To extend understanding of the story through a variety of multimodal and cross-curricular activities

Skills

READING SKILLS/ STRATEGIES
- Comparing and contrasting

SPEAKING, LISTENING, AND VIEWING
- Film
- Group discussion
- Oral presentation

LITERARY CONCEPTS
- Science fiction
- Humor
- Idioms

GENRE STUDY
- Science fiction

Cross-Curricular Connections

SCIENCE
- Solar system models

SOCIAL STUDIES
- 1938 War of the Worlds radio broadcast

ALTERNATIVE
Previewing
In lieu of writing their accounts of an alien invasion, students may work in small groups and share their ideas.

Writing Connection
Discussion Prompts: *Think of some of the most vivid examples of aliens you have ever read about or seen in the movies or on television. How are these similar to or different from your own ideas of what an alien might look like or how it might behave? Many stories predict that the world will end after the arrival of aliens. Do you believe this is true, or do you think that there might be the possibility of peaceful coexistence?*

Discuss your ideas with the other members of your group and try to come up with a consensus about the details of an alien invasion. If you wish, present your ideas to other groups.

PRINT AND MEDIA RESOURCES

UNIT FOUR RESOURCE BOOK
Strategic Reading: Literature, p. 49
Vocabulary SkillBuilder, p. 51
Reading SkillBuilder, p. 50

ACCESS FOR STUDENTS ACQUIRING ENGLISH
Selection Summaries
Reading and Writing Support

FORMAL ASSESSMENT
Selection Test, pp. 95–96
 Test Generator

AUDIO LIBRARY
See Reference Card

INTERNET RESOURCES
McDougal Littell Literature Center at http://www.hmco.com/mcdougal/lit

SUMMARY

Evil four-armed, green aliens invade the United States, and Sara and Bill Russell watch the invasion on television. They decide not to tell their eight-year-old son, Johnny, whose wild imagination often causes trouble. The next day, playing alone, Johnny meets an alien. The evil monster draws circles in the dust. He uses small globes to represent the planets and to show that his planet will destroy the earth. Johnny acts quickly. He takes out his prize marble and knocks out of the circles the globe that represents the alien planet. The terrified alien vanishes along with his spaceship, and then all the other aliens and their spaceships disappear.

Thematic Link: *Unlikely Heroes* After the earth has been invaded by aliens, an eight-year-old boy is the unlikely hero who uses his marbles to save the planet.

CUSTOMIZING FOR
Students Acquiring English

- Use **ACCESS FOR STUDENTS ACQUIRING ENGLISH**, *Reading and Writing Support*.
- The author chose to tell this story in a lighthearted manner, even though it could have been written as a horror story. Ask students to be aware, as they read, of the differences between Johnny's fantasy world and the "reality" of the invasion.

I Explain to students that Tarzan and Superman are two heroes represented in comic books, television, and films.

STRATEGIC READING FOR
Less-Proficient Readers

Set a Purpose Ask students to read and take note of what is known about the aliens.

Use **UNIT FOUR RESOURCE BOOK**, p. 49, for guidance in reading the selection.

Literary Concept: IDIOM

A Ask students to explain the difference between the literal meaning of "glued to the tube" and the meaning of the idiom. (*Literally, Sara and Bert would have their faces pasted to the TV picture tube. The idiom suggests that their attention is focused on the television.*)

Playing for Keeps

by Jack C. Haldeman II

Johnny Russell was playing in his backyard when the aliens landed. He was Tarzan in a land of giant ferns while they invaded Philadelphia, but had shifted over to Superman before Baltimore fell. Johnny was eight years old and easily bored. By the time his mother called him in for dinner, the aliens were all over Washington, D.C. Things were a mess. Ugly green monsters were everywhere. Lots of people were real upset, especially Johnny. They were having spinach for dinner.

Johnny hated spinach more than anything else in the world, except maybe brussels sprouts and creamed corn.

He made such a fuss at the table trying to slip the dog his spinach that his parents sent him to bed early. That was too bad, because there was a lot of neat stuff on television that night. Eight years old is just the right age for appreciating a good monster or two. Johnny slept through it all, dreaming that he was flying his tree house over the ocean in search of lost continents.

His parents, on the other hand, were totally immersed in aliens of the real sort. There was no escaping them. Even the 24-hour sports network was full of monsters. Specials followed specials all night long. Bert and Sara stayed glued to the tube,[1] afraid they might miss something. It was an exciting time to watch television, even better than the time the dam burst at Fort Mudge. A good crisis brought out the best in the electronics media, no doubt about that.

They watched the national news for a while and then switched over to the local news. They even tuned in PBS and watched a panel of distinguished professors pointing sticks at an alien's picture. It was exciting. Sara made popcorn and Bert put another six pack of beer in the fridge.

"Don't you think we ought to wake up Johnny?" asked Sara, salting the popcorn.

Bert opened another beer. "No," he said. "We've got to teach him not to play with his food. A parent has certain obligations, you know." Bert had always been the strict one.

"But isn't that a little severe?" asked Sara.

---

1. **glued to the tube:** watching television attentively.

WORDS TO KNOW
immerse (ĭ-mûrs') *v.* to involve completely; absorb the attention of

---

WORDS TO KNOW

congenial (kən-jēn'yəl) *adj.* friendly (p. 502)
flourish (flûr'ĭsh) *n.* a showy or dramatic gesture (p. 504)
gloat (glōt) *v.* to express great pleasure (p. 504)
immerse (ĭ-mûrs') *v.* to involve completely; absorb the attention of (p. 500)
oblivious (ə-blĭv'ē-əs) *adj.* not aware or attentive (p. 504)

Einige Kreise [Several circles] (1926), Wassily Kandinsky. Oil on canvas, 55¼" × 55⅝", Solomon R. Guggenheim Museum, New York, gift of Solomon R. Guggenheim, 1941 (FN 41.283). Copyright © The Solomon R. Guggenheim Foundation, New York. Photo by David Heald.

"After all, he's very fond of hideous beasts."

"No," said Bert. "Remember what he did with the brussels sprouts?"

Sara turned pale. "I thought I'd never get it all out. The air conditioning hasn't worked right since."

"And the creamed corn?"

Sara shuddered at the memory of the bomb squad marching through their living room in knee-deep water. "You're right," she said, passing him the popcorn.

They settled back and watched the early news, the special news, the update news, the fast-break news, the late news, and the late-late news. In between, they watched the news in brief and the news in detail. They were saturated with news and popcorn and all they got out of it was indigestion and no news at all. Nobody knew much of anything about the aliens except they were crawling all over the place and were meaner than junkyard dogs.

Their silver, cigar-shaped spaceships had simply appeared out of nowhere with a shimmering colorful splash of glitter not unlike the special effects of a once-popular TV show still in reruns. It was horrible. People fled in panic, especially when the monsters started coming out of the spaceships.

The aliens stood about eight feet tall with thick, stocky bodies. Their four arms had too many elbows and not enough fingers. Folds of wrinkled green skin covered their neckless teen

PLAYING FOR KEEPS **501**

Art Note

Several Circles by Wassily Kandinsky
Circles played a prominent role in the art of Russian artist Kandinsky (1866–1944). He believed that the circle was a primary form, a shape in balance with both its inside and outside at the same moment.

Reading the Art Why do you think this painting was selected to appear with a science fiction story? What impression do you have of the artist's use of shape and color?

CUSTOMIZING FOR
Gifted and Talented Students

Have students discuss the influence of the imagination on a person's perception of reality. Ask them to consider how people's reading, television viewing, and dreaming affect their understanding of the world.

Active Reading: EVALUATE

B Have students assess the seriousness of the situation. Ask them how people's reliance on television affects their perception of the events. If students are having difficulty, provide them with the following model:

Think-Aloud Model *An alien invasion is a very serious situation, but the author seems to be joking around and making the invasion seem like no big deal. The family watched the news all night and didn't really find out anything about the invasion. The author seems to be making fun of people who count on television to tell them what to do.*

Mini-Lesson Literary Concepts

REVIEWING IDIOMS Remind students that idioms are expressions that have a meaning different from the sum of their individual words. For example, have students look at and discuss the meanings of the following idioms from the selection:
- glued to the tube (p. 500)
- tan his hide (p. 503)
- deadpan (p. 503)

Application Divide the class into groups of three or four. Have each group make a list of idioms, along with their idiomatic meanings. Students may want to refer to special dictionaries that define common American idioms, such as *The New Dictionary of American Slang*, if they are having trouble discerning meanings. Encourage groups to share their lists with the class, noting which phrases are more common and which are less common. Groups can then challenge one another to use a selected idiom in a sentence.

THE LANGUAGE OF LITERATURE **TEACHER'S EDITION** **501**

Literary Concept:
SCIENCE FICTION

C Ask students to identify a common feature of science fiction in this passage. *(Possible response: Many science fiction stories describe people getting killed in some weird way by strange weapons that have advanced technology.)*

STRATEGIC READING FOR
Less-Proficient Readers

D Have students explain what they know about the aliens. *(The aliens stand about eight feet tall, have stocky bodies, four arms, neckless heads with folds of wrinkled green skin, and three unblinking eyes. They travel in silver, cigar-shaped spaceships, are very hostile, and vaporize human beings at will. They appear to be intelligent but do not speak to the humans.)* Summarizing/Noting Relevant Details

Set a Purpose Have students continue reading to learn the outcome of the encounter between the alien and Johnny.

Critical Thinking: SPECULATING

E Have students discuss the likelihood of Johnny having seen the aliens before. Ask what this might suggest about the alien invasion. *(Possible response: Johnny has such an active imagination, it is hard to tell if he actually saw the aliens before. However, if he did, it suggests that the aliens made an earlier trip to the earth to plan their invasion.)*

CUSTOMIZING FOR
Students Acquiring English

 Explain that the idiomatic phrase "messed around" means to play or pass time together in an aimless way.

---

heads, and their three unblinking eyes held what could only be interpreted as malice and contempt for the entire human race.

At first it was hoped that they might be a congenial star-roving race of beings, eager as puppy dogs to give mankind all sorts of marvelous inventions. These hopes were quickly dashed.

C The aliens seemed far more interested in vaporizing[2] people. Helicopters and airplanes that approached the hovering ships vanished in white-hot explosions. People who were foolish enough to make threatening gestures or stray too close went up in smoke. It made for good television footage, but did little to aid any kind of mutual understanding.

Mutual understanding, as a matter of fact, didn't seem to be the aliens' strong suit.[3] They just didn't appear to be interested. Some of the best minds on Earth had attempted to establish communication with the aliens. Some of the best minds on Earth had been vaporized, too. The aliens were obviously intelligent, but they **D** didn't have much to say.

Bert and Sara were about ready to turn in, having watched the instant replay of the destruction of Washington for the fourth or fifth time. It was impressive, but not really all that great. The Japanese had done it better in that movie about the radioactive frog. Sara washed the popcorn bowls.

"I'll bet Johnny will be excited when he wakes up," she said. "Channel Four said they've even seen a couple aliens right here in town. Imagine that."

"I don't think we ought to tell the boy about them," said Bert. "At least not yet."

"For goodness sakes, honey. Why not?"

"The child has an active enough imagination as it is. There's no sense in getting him all riled up. Remember the time he thought he saw that UFO down by the river?"

Sara nearly dropped the bowl she was drying. That had been a near thing. Johnny had pulled every fire alarm in town, and only their friendship with the judge had kept their names out of the paper.

"Besides," said Bert. "What does a kid know about monsters? He's only eight years old."

Sara nodded. He was right, as always.

But Johnny wasn't completely fooled. When little Freddy Nabors didn't show up by twelve o'clock, he knew something was wrong. He and Freddy always messed around together on Saturday afternoon. Sometimes they went on dangerous secret missions, but usually they just played. By twelve-fifteen Johnny had decided a plague must have killed all the kids on Earth but him so he went out into the backyard to play.

He wasn't allowed to go out behind the garage, so naturally it was his favorite place. It was full of old lumber and rusty nails. Lumber was more fun to play with than

---

2. **vaporizing:** turning something solid into a gas; disintegrating.
3. **strong suit:** greatest talent; area of excellence.

WORDS TO KNOW
congenial (kən-jēn′yəl) *adj.* friendly

Mini-Lesson • Reading Skills/Strategies

Comparing
look for similarities

Contrasting
look for differences

COMPARING AND CONTRASTING
Remind students that effective readers use skills such as comparing and contrasting as they read. When readers identify the similarities or differences between two or more things in a selection, they are comparing and contrasting. Tell students they can learn important information about characters and/or events by identifying their similarities and differences. Writers often use comparisons and contrasts as a way of generating meaning in a story.

Application Have students compare and contrast the responses of Bert and Sara, Johnny, and other human beings to the alien invasion. Encourage them to think about what these similarities and differences might tell them about each character and about the characters' relationships with one another.

Reteaching/Reinforcement
• *Unit Four Resource Book,* p. 50

almost anything. Sometimes he built boats out of the scraps, and sometimes spaceships. Today he built a Grand Prix car.[4] It was low and sleek, faster than a bat. He pretended it was orange with black trim. Since he couldn't find any wheels, he used cinder blocks for racing tires.

Diving into the hairpin turn,[5] he had just passed Fangio and was gaining on Andretti[6] when he saw the monster. Johnny was not impressed. He'd seen better ones on television. Sticking his tongue out between his lips and making a rude noise, he downshifted with a raspberry[7] and pulled to the side of the road. After taking off his imaginary helmet and racing gloves, he got out of his fabricated car and stared at the alien. The alien stared back. Three eyes to two, the alien had an edge; but Johnny never flinched. The Lone Ranger[8] wouldn't have backed down, and neither would he.

In the distance Johnny could see one of their spaceships hovering over the river. It looked just like the one he'd seen before. He knew better than to head for the fire alarms this time, though. His father would tan his hide.

The alien grunted and pointed at his ship and then to himself. Johnny stood as firm as Wyatt Earp,[9] his jaw set like Montgomery Clift's, playing for keeps his body held with the stern proudness of John Wayne. He didn't nod, he didn't blink. He stared at the monster with Paul Newman's[10] baby-blue eyes, hard as ice. He wished he'd worn long pants, though. Shorts just didn't cut it when you were staring down a monster.

The alien started waving all its arms in the air, grunting like crazy. Johnny was frightened, but he didn't give an inch. He could have been Gary Cooper standing alone in the middle of a dusty street facing an angry mob with only the badge on his chest and the goodness in his heart to protect him. Johnny could almost hear the people scurrying for cover. The helmet and racing gloves were useless. He should have had his six-shooter.

The alien kicked at the dust, smoothing out an area between them. He bent over and Johnny hunkered down to join him. At least now he knew what to expect. They were about to talk, or *palaver*, as Slim Pickins[11] would say.

The alien picked up a stick and drew a large circle in the dirt. From a fold in his tunic he removed a small golden globe, which he placed precisely in the center. He pointed to the sun and then to the globe. Johnny nodded, his face as deadpan as if he was trying to fill an inside straight.[12]

The monster drew three concentric circles around the golden globe and placed another globe on the third circle. It was smaller than the first and covered with blue and white swirls. He patted the dirt, waved his arms in circles all around them and pointed to the globe. Johnny bit his lip. This was getting complicated.

The alien continued drawing circles in the dust and setting down the small globes. When he had finished, nine of them surrounded the

---

4. **Grand Prix** (grän′ prē′) **car:** a type of racing car used in an international series of road races over difficult courses.
5. **hairpin turn:** a U-shaped curve in a road.
6. **Fangio** (fän′jyō) . . . **Andretti** (ăn-drĕt′ē): Juan Manuel Fangio and Mario Andretti, famous racing-car drivers.
7. **raspberry:** a rude noise made by extending the tongue and exhaling so that the lips vibrate.
8. **Lone Ranger:** a fictional masked crime fighter of the Old West who was one of the great heroes of radio, television, and comics.
9. **Wyatt Earp:** a famous lawman of the American West in the late 19th century.
10. **Montgomery Clift . . . John Wayne . . . Paul Newman:** movie actors who have portrayed Western heroes.
11. **Gary Cooper . . . Slim Pickins:** movie actors who have appeared in Westerns.
12. **as deadpan . . . inside straight:** as without expression as the face of someone trying to bluff poker opponents.

PLAYING FOR KEEPS **503**

Literary Concept: METAPHOR

F In this paragraph and others that follow, the narrator compares Johnny to many famous movie actors and Western heroes. Have students discuss how the metaphors of popular heroes are appropriate to the story. *(Possible response: These heroes are the kind that young boys identify with, so when Johnny must act courageously he probably would use such people as role models for how he behaves.)*

Literary Concept: IDIOM

G Explain to students that the idiom "tan his hide" derives from the process of tanning—making leather from rawhides. Ask students to define the idiom's meaning in the context of Johnny's getting into trouble. *(Possible response: The idiom means to administer a beating or a whipping. Here it refers to the literal or figurative whipping that Johnny will receive from his dad if he pulls the alarm.)*

CUSTOMIZING FOR
Students Acquiring English

3 Tell students that "playing for keeps" means playing a game in which the loser suffers a terrible punishment.

4 Ask a volunteer to explain poker, especially the importance of bluffing an opponent.

CUSTOMIZING FOR
Multiple Learning Styles

H Linguistic and Bodily-Kinesthetic Learners Have students role-play the final shootout scene between Johnny and the alien. Invite linguistic learners to act as translators for Johnny, explaining the meaning of the alien's globe and drawing. Bodily-kinesthetic learners can mime Johnny's actions and words for the alien.

Mini-Lesson: Speaking, Listening, and Viewing

FILM Arrange for students to view clips of Western films such as *Red River* (1948), starring Montgomery Clift and John Wayne, and *Butch Cassidy and the Sundance Kid* (1969), starring Robert Redford and Paul Newman. Have them first review the attributes Johnny admires about each of these actors. *(Clift's set jaw, Wayne's stern pride, Newman's icy blue eyes)* Remind them to look for these attributes as they watch the clips.

Application After students view the film clips, ask them to discuss the following:

- *Do they admire the same qualities in these actors as does Johnny?*
- *Does seeing the actors make it easier to understand what Johnny was thinking as he faced the alien?*
- *Why do they think Johnny admires actors in Westerns?*
- *Does viewing the film clips add to their appreciation of the story?*
- *Can they think of other actors with similar attributes?*

Students can respond to these questions by role-playing professional film reviewers in a discussion.

Active Reading: CLARIFY

I Have students reread the preceding paragraph to help them clarify what the third globe out from the golden globe in the center represents and then have them explain what his actions mean. *(Possible response: The third globe out from the center represents the earth; the alien is communicating he will destroy the earth as he has destroyed the other planets.)*

STRATEGIC READING FOR
Less-Proficient Readers

J Ask students to explain how Johnny defeats the alien. *(Johnny treats the challenge as a game of marbles and, after shooting the alien's marble out of orbit, he keeps the globes.)* Noting Relevant Details/Noting Sequence of Events

Critical Thinking: SPECULATING

K Have students discuss why the alien disappears. *(Possible response: Johnny and the alien were engaged in a symbolic battle over the planet; when Johnny knocked his symbol out, the alien knew he had lost.)*

CUSTOMIZING FOR
Gifted and Talented Students

Remind students that many science fiction stories are set in the future, yet the events of this story seem to have taken place in the past. If necessary, point out the story's dated references to Johnny's media heroes as evidence of this. Have students discuss the role of time in science fiction. Ask if events have to occur in the future, or might they just transcend present human experience.

COMPREHENSION CHECK

1. What has happened to Baltimore, Philadelphia, and Washington, D.C., as the story begins? *(The cities have been taken over by aliens.)*
2. Why won't the Russells wake Johnny so that he can watch the news? *(They are punishing Johnny for playing with his food.)*
3. What happens when Johnny knocks the alien's marble out of the circle? *(The aliens and their spaceship leave.)*

---

larger yellow one. With a <u>flourish</u> he took one more from his tunic. This one was special; it was silver and seemed to glow with a light from within. He set it outside the farthest circle and pointed first to himself, then to the spaceship, and finally to the silver sphere.

Slowly he began rolling the sphere into the ring of circles. As he passed the outermost globe, he snarled and crushed it into the dirt beneath one of his massive thumbs. He continued rolling the silver sphere toward the center, snarling and crushing as he demolished each of the small globes. When he reached the third globe from the center, his lips drew back in a hideous sneer and he rose to his full height, towering over the crouching boy. The alien <u>gloated</u>, roaring with bone-chilling laughter as he crushed the small blue globe under his foot, grinding it into the dirt with a vengeance.[13]

I This, at last, was something Johnny could understand. It was a challenge. Without rising, he reached around to his back pocket. It was still there, as he knew it would be. He'd won it from Freddy Nabors two years ago and he never went anywhere without it. It was his talisman, his good luck piece. It was also his weapon and had never let him down. He gritted his teeth and took it reassuringly in his hand. It was blue with milky white bands, a perfect agate.[14]

He dropped and took quick aim, <u>oblivious</u> to the ranting and raving of the alien. He'd been under pressure before, this was nothing new.

With a flick of his thumb the aggie sailed across the dust, crashing into the silver ball, sending it careening out of orbit into the yellow one. They both flew outside the circle.

He stood—as a man would stand after battle—and retrieved all the marbles. He held them high above his head.

"Keepsies,"[15] he said and slipped them into his pocket.

J

The alien backed away in horror, babbling wildly. With a shimmer and a pop, he disappeared. An instant later the spaceship vanished in a similar fashion, as did all the spaceships and all the aliens all over the world.

K

Johnny climbed back into his Grand Prix car and accelerated through the gears. He was nearly a lap behind by now and would have to do some fancy driving to catch up. Besides, his mother was fixing creamed corn tonight, and the boy who had saved the world had important things on his mind.

As he took the checkered flag he wondered how Conan[16] would have handled creamed corn. ❖

---

13. **with a vengeance:** with a great amount of force.
14. **agate** (ăg′ĭt): a playing marble made of a semiprecious stone.
15. **keepsies:** the marbles won from an opponent in a game of marbles.
16. **Conan:** the hero of a series of stories set in an imaginary prehistoric time; played by Arnold Schwarzenegger in the movie *Conan the Barbarian*.

WORDS TO KNOW	**flourish** (flûr′ĭsh) *n.* a showy or dramatic gesture
	gloat (glōt) *v.* to express great pleasure
	oblivious (ə-blĭv′ē-əs) *adj.* not aware or attentive

504

Mini-Lesson  Genre Study

FICTION Explain to students that **science fiction** is a type of fiction that is based on real or imaginary scientific ideas. Works of science fiction can be divided into two broad categories. First, there are stories such as *E.T.*, in which some aspect of the present world is disrupted by something unusual or alien. The second type includes works set at some other time or in some other place, such as the *Star Wars* and *Star Trek* movies.

Application Have students work in small groups and compile a list of science fiction films and stories, including "Playing for Keeps." Have each group answer the following questions:
- *How would they categorize the different works?*
- *How does this selection compare to other works in the science fiction genre?*
- *Are there any ways each story is unique?*

Then ask the groups to compare their lists to find out if they categorize science fiction works in similar ways. Groups can create a class booklet of capsule reviews of the science fiction analyzed.

RESPONDING OPTIONS

FROM PERSONAL RESPONSE TO CRITICAL ANALYSIS

REFLECT
1. Do you find this story humorous? Why or why not? Write your thoughts in your notebook.

RETHINK
2. Why do you think Johnny is able to save the world when adults cannot?
   Consider
   - what Johnny's parents say about him
   - his interest in television and movie heroes
   - the way he confronts the alien

Close Textual Reading

3. Draw a picture illustrating Johnny's confrontation with the alien. Try to capture the humor of the story.

Thematic Link

4. Do you think Johnny knows he is saving the world? On the basis of your answer, do you consider Johnny to be a hero? Explain your opinion.

RELATE
5. Because of their constant television viewing, the characters in this story can no longer tell the difference between entertainment and a real crisis. Do you think television has this effect in real life? Why or why not?

LITERARY CONCEPTS

Science fiction is fiction that is based on real or possible scientific developments. It frequently presents an imaginary view into the future while still conveying writers' concerns about problems in present-day society. What makes "Playing for Keeps" a science fiction story? How is it similar to and different from other science fiction you've read? Give examples to support your answer.

CONCEPT REVIEW: Humor By treating Johnny's hatred of vegetables as seriously as the alien attack, the author makes light of the crisis and brings humor to "Playing for Keeps." Find another use of humor in the story.

Multimodal Learning
ANOTHER PATHWAY
Cooperative Learning

With a small group of classmates, discuss what aspects (if any) of this story are believable. In your discussion, compare the situations in the selection with the situations you made up for the Writing Connection on page 499.

QUICKWRITES

1. The aliens disappear from the face of the earth at the end of Johnny's "battle" with one of them. Write an **e-mail note** that the defeated alien might transmit to his home planet, telling what has happened.

2. Write one of two possible **epilogues** for this story: either describe what you think happens to the aliens and their spaceships, or predict what happens to Johnny after they leave.

3. What might have happened if Johnny had run away from the alien? Write an **alternative ending** based on this idea.

 **PORTFOLIO** Save your writing. You may want to use it later as a springboard to a piece for your portfolio.

PLAYING FOR KEEPS 505

From Personal Response to Critical Analysis

1. Encourage students to use examples from the selection in their responses.
2. Possible response: Johnny has innocence and imagination that others lack, and he draws on his heroes to defeat the aliens.
3. Encourage students to use their imaginations in creating their humorous pictures of Johnny's confrontation with the alien.
4. Possible responses: Johnny did not know he was saving the world, only that he had to win the game, so he is not a hero. Because Johnny follows the pattern of his personal heroes in his showdown with the alien, he is a hero.
5. Responses will vary.

Another Pathway

Cooperative Learning Before groups begin their discussions, have students review the major events of the story. Ask them to separate these events into a list of believable and unbelievable events. One student can be the discussion leader and another the recorder. Invite students to share the accounts they wrote for the Writing Connection.

Rubric
3 Full Accomplishment Students compose a complete list and link it to their Writing Connection accounts.
2 Substantial Accomplishment Students compose a partial list and relate some of it to their Writing Connection accounts.
1 Little or Partial Accomplishment Students fail to note the main events of the story and cannot link what they know to their Writing Connection accounts.

Literary Concepts

"Playing for Keeps" is science fiction because it is based on possible scientific developments. In this story, the present world is confronted by something alien from outer space. Examples of other science fiction given by students will vary.

Concept Review Responses may include such humorous events as Johnny's Grand Prix fantasy, his parents' discussion of his antics, and his defeat of the alien.

QuickWrites

1. Explain to students that an e-mail note is a short letter transmitted between computers. Encourage students to copy the form of an e-mail file when developing their alien account.
2. Remind students that an epilogue is a brief explanation of what occurred after the main events of the story. Suggest to students that they maintain the story's humorous tone.
3. Encourage students to use specific details from the story to predict what would happen if Johnny had run away from the alien.

The Writer's Craft
Field Notes, pp. 62–65
Writing Conclusions, pp. 281-283

THE LANGUAGE OF LITERATURE TEACHER'S EDITION 505

Words to Know

1. congenial
2. flourish
3. gloat
4. immersed
5. oblivious

Reteaching/Reinforcement
• *Unit Four Resource Book,* p. 51

Literary Links

Ask students to compare the aliens' attempt to destroy the earth in this selection with the human attempt to collect animals from other planets in "The Collecting Team." Ask how the goal of the zoologists compares with the aliens' goal. *(Possible response: The zoologists do not wish to destroy the planet, only to collect specimens for further study.)*

Across the Curriculum

Science Cooperative Learning *Solar System Models* Have students work in small groups. Suggest that the group split up to research not only the order but also the approximate size and color of the planets. Groups may wish to use foam balls, balloons, or clay to construct their models. Challenge students to make their models movable.

ADDITIONAL SUGGESTION

Social Studies *War of the Worlds* Have students find out about the 1938 radio broadcast by Orson Welles of Howard Koch's dramatization of H. G. Wells's science fiction classic *The War of the Worlds.* Many people listening to the broadcast really believed Mars had invaded the earth and they panicked. The broadcast provided one of the first major examples of the electronic media's impact on society. Groups of three or four can research different aspects of this event to find out how the broadcast was performed, why people panicked, and how people reacted after finding out it was just fiction.

ALTERNATIVE ACTIVITIES

With another student, rewrite one of the scenes in this story as a dramatic **script.** Present the scene to your classmates as a Readers Theater production.

ACROSS THE CURRICULUM

Science The alien uses small globes to show Johnny the arrangement of the planets in the solar system. Find out how the planets are arranged around the sun. Make a simple model that shows this arrangement and the relative sizes of the planets. Also, see if you can think of a fun phrase for remembering the order of the planets, like

"Mother Very Easily Makes Jelly Sandwiches Under No Protest."

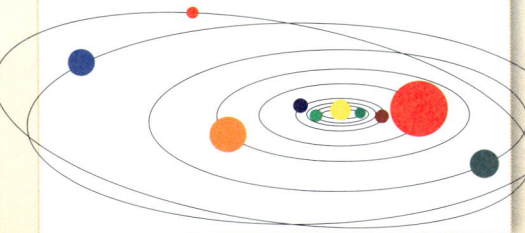

CRITIC'S CORNER

About the end of "Playing for Keeps," Beth Donaldson, a student reader, said, "I loved the way you knew exactly what the alien meant when he was diagramming the solar system, but Johnny didn't." It is often the case that readers of a work of literature know more than the characters in the work. As you read "Playing for Keeps," what else did you know that the characters didn't?

WORDS TO KNOW

Review the Words to Know at the bottom of the selection pages, and list them on your paper. Then choose the word that best fills each numbered blank in the following paragraph.

We were hoping that the aliens would be talkative and __(1)__ so that we could share ideas. Instead, the aliens were hostile. One alien showed his malice toward humans by waving with a __(2)__ the plans to invade our planet. It appeared, from the grin on its face, that the alien was beginning to __(3)__. The media recorded every stage of the crisis, causing the nation to be __(4)__ in the news of the alien attack. The aliens were so confident that they were __(5)__ to our successful efforts to kill their leaders.

JACK C. HALDEMAN II

Jack C. Haldeman II came to science fiction with a scientific background. He had worked as a research assistant and as a medical technician. Haldeman says, "I often draw on my scientific background as well as my sense of humor. Mostly I try to entertain, though I have been known to slip in a message or two.

Haldeman was first known for his stories about futuristic sports events, a rare theme in science fiction. "Louisville Slugger" describes a baseball game that decides the future of humankind. In

1941–

"The Thrill of Victory" and its sequel "The Agony of Defeat" a robotic football team, illegally programmed with the will to win, plays a championship game against genetically altered beings.

Occasionally, Haldeman collaborates with other science fiction writers, including his brother Joe. In addition to writing science fiction, Haldeman works at the University of Florida, doing research in the field of artificial intelligence. He lives in rural Florida.

OTHER WORKS "Thirty Love," *The Fall of Winter*

Extended Reading

Alternative Activities

Have the pair select a particularly active scene, such as when Johnny is sent to his room for playing with his food or when he encounters the alien. Explain to students that in writing their script they have some flexibility in the words and stage directions of the characters, but their scripts should remain faithful to the overall plot of the story.

PREVIEWING

FICTION

The Dinner Party
Mona Gardner

PERSONAL CONNECTION *Activating Prior Knowledge*

Copy the chart shown. Write predictions of what you think most females and most males would do in each situation. Then get together with a small group of classmates and compare predictions. Have female and male students responded differently? Discuss whether people have fixed ideas about male and female behavior.

Situation	Females	Males
1. Seeing a bleeding wound		
2. Getting a flat tire		
3. Seeing a rat or a snake		

Building Background
HISTORICAL CONNECTION

India was under British control for nearly 200 years before gaining its independence in 1947. "The Dinner Party" takes place in British India, the part of the country ruled directly by the British government. Some of the attitudes held by the British people of the time would be considered backward today. Most British officials felt superior to their subjects and rarely socialized with Indians. In addition, most men viewed themselves as superior to women, and that attitude of male superiority becomes an issue in this story.

Active Reading/Setting A Purpose
READING CONNECTION

Stereotypes An oversimplified view of an entire group of people is known as a stereotype. Such sweeping statements as "That's what all police officers are like" and "That's how all rich people act" are based on stereotypes. As you read this story, look for the stereotype expressed by a guest at the dinner party, and see whether it proves to be accurate.

• HISTORICAL CONNECTION

507

OVERVIEW

Objectives

- To understand and appreciate a short story about a cobra at a dinner party
- To identify and understand stereotypes
- To identify and appreciate suspense
- To express understanding of the story through a choice of writing forms, including an interior monologue and a dialogue
- To extend understanding of the story through a variety of multimodal and cross-curricular activities

Skills

READING SKILLS/ STRATEGIES
• Visualizing

LITERARY CONCEPTS
• Stereotypes
• Suspense

SPEAKING, LISTENING, AND VIEWING
• Group discussion
• Oral presentation

Cross-Curricular Connections

SCIENCE
• Cobras

SOCIAL STUDIES
• Sex-role stereotyping

 HISTORICAL CONNECTION
India During British Rule
Introduce your students to the world of colonial India by presenting these photographs of Britons and Indians.

Side A, Frame 226

PRINT AND MEDIA RESOURCES

UNIT FOUR RESOURCE BOOK
Strategic Reading: Literature, p. 55
Reading SkillBuilder, p. 56

ACCESS FOR STUDENTS ACQUIRING ENGLISH
Selection Summaries
Reading and Writing Support

FORMAL ASSESSMENT
Selection Test, p. 97
 Test Generator

 **AUDIO LIBRARY**
See Reference Card

LASERLINKS
Historical Connection

THE LANGUAGE OF LITERATURE TEACHER'S EDITION 507

SUMMARY

At a dinner party in India, guests discuss whether women or men have greater self-control in a crisis. An American scientist sees the hostess become tense and murmur to a servant, who sets a bowl of milk outside the open dining room doors. Knowing that milk is used as bait for snakes, the American realizes there must be a cobra under the table. He calmly takes charge. Without revealing why, he challenges everyone at the table to stay still for five minutes. The cobra slithers out. Once the commotion dies down, the host says the American has proved that men have greater self-control in a crisis. Then the hostess reveals that she had the milk set out after she felt the snake lying across her foot.

Thematic Link: *Unlikely Heroes* A woman surprises her male guests by showing complete self-control in a crisis.

CUSTOMIZING FOR
Students Acquiring English

- Use **ACCESS FOR STUDENTS ACQUIRING ENGLISH,** *Reading and Writing Support.*
- Keep in mind that ideas of gender characteristics vary from country to country. Encourage all students to take part in the previewing discussion. Be sure ideas of gender behavior, characteristics, and equality are included in the discussion.

STRATEGIC READING FOR
Less-Proficient Readers

Set a Purpose To help students become engaged in the selection, point out that the story focuses on how men and women behave under pressure and invite them to discuss how they themselves react in a crisis. Then have them note the different responses of the naturalist, the hostess, and the other guests.

Use **UNIT FOUR RESOURCE BOOK,** p. 55, for guidance in reading the selection.

The Dinner Party

by Mona Gardner

Detail of *Dinner at Haddo House* (1884), Alfred Edward Emslie. National Portrait Gallery, London.

508 UNIT FOUR PART 2: UNLIKELY HEROES

Art Note

***Dinner at Haddo House* by A. E. Emslie (1848–1918)** This painting shows an actual event, the meeting of British Prime Minister William Gladstone with the Earl and Countess of Aberdeen at their home, Haddo House.

Reading the Art *Is the setting of this painting similar to or different from the way you visualize the dining room of "The Dinner Party"? Explain your answer with specific references to the painting and the story.*

WORDS TO KNOW

naturalist (năch′ər-ə-lĭst) *n.* a person who studies living things by observing them directly (p. 509)

The country is India. A large dinner party is being given in an up-country station by a colonial official[1] and his wife. The guests are army officers and government attachés[2] and their wives, and an American naturalist.

At one side of the long table a spirited discussion springs up between a young girl and a colonel. The girl insists women have long outgrown the jumping-on-a-chair-at-sight-of-a-mouse era, that they are not as fluttery as their grandmothers. The colonel says they are, explaining that women haven't the actual nerve control of men. The other men at the table agree with him.

"A woman's unfailing reaction in any crisis," the colonel says, "is to scream. And while a man may feel like it, yet he has that ounce more of control than a woman has. And that last ounce is what counts!"

The American scientist does not join in the argument, but sits watching the faces of the other guests. As he looks, he sees a strange expression come over the face of the hostess. She is staring straight ahead, the muscles of her face contracting slightly. With a small gesture she summons the native boy standing behind her chair. She whispers to him. The boy's eyes widen: he turns quickly and leaves the room. No one else sees this, nor the boy when he puts a bowl of milk on the verandah[3] outside the glass doors.

The American comes to with a start. In India, milk in a bowl means only one thing. It is bait for a snake. He realizes there is a cobra in the room.

He looks up at the rafters—the likeliest place—and sees they are bare. Three corners of the room, which he can see by shifting only slightly, are empty. In the fourth corner a group of servants stand, waiting until the next course can be served. The American realizes there is only one place left—under the table.

His first impulse is to jump back and warn the others. But he knows the commotion will frighten the cobra and it will strike. He speaks quickly, the quality of his voice so arresting that it sobers everyone.

"I want to know just what control everyone at this table has. I will count three hundred—that's five minutes—and not one of you is to move a single muscle. The persons who move will forfeit 50 rupees.[4] Now! Ready!"

The 20 people sit like stone images while he counts. He is saying ". . . two hundred and eighty . . ." when, out of the corner of his eye, he sees the cobra emerge and make for the bowl of milk. Four or five screams ring out as he jumps to slam shut the verandah doors.

"You certainly were right, Colonel!" the host says. "A man has just shown us an example of real control."

"Just a minute," the American says, turning to his hostess, "there's one thing I'd like to know. Mrs. Wynnes, how did you know that cobra was in the room?"

A faint smile lights up the woman's face as she replies. "Because it was lying across my foot." ❖

---

1. **colonial official:** a person holding a position in the British government ruling India.
2. **attachés** (ăt′ə-shāz′): people who assist an ambassador.
3. **verandah:** a long porch, usually roofed, along the side of a building.
4. **rupees** (rōō-pēz′): Indian units of money.

WORDS TO KNOW

naturalist (năch′ər-ə-lĭst) *n.* a person who studies living things by observing them directly

---

Mini-Lesson — Reading Skills/Strategies

VISUALIZING Explain to students that visualizing is the process of forming a mental picture from a written description. This mental picture allows readers to place themselves in the action of the story as firsthand participants, rather than as distanced readers.

Application To assist students in forming a mental picture of the events of "The Dinner Party," ask:
- What does the dining room look like? How are the characters dressed? What food might be served?
- How would you react to the colonel's remarks about women's response to crisis? Would the comments anger you, or would you side with the colonel?
- Pretend you are the American. How does your body respond to the snake in the room?
- If you were a guest, how would you respond when the cobra emerged from under the table?

You may wish to have students form small discussion groups and have each group either respond to all of the questions or address one question only.

Reteaching/Reinforcement
- *Unit Four Resource Book,* p. 56

CUSTOMIZING FOR
Gifted and Talented Students

Have students discuss the Historical Connection on page 507 and the importance of the story's colonial context. Ask how the stereotyping of women by men in this selection parallels the stereotyping by the British of their Indian subjects.

CUSTOMIZING FOR
Students Acquiring English

1 Ask a volunteer to define "springs up." *(comes up quickly)* Then ask for a synonym of this phrase. *(Possible responses: arises; begins)*

2 Explain that the smile on the woman's face lights up her appearance by making her appear happy.

Literary Concept: STEREOTYPE

A Ask students to explain why the colonel's opinion is an example of stereotyping. *(He is saying that all men respond in one way to a crisis and all women respond in another way.)*

Literary Concept: SUSPENSE

B Point out that students must wait to see what will happen to the guests. Ask students what questions come to mind at this moment. *(Possible responses: Will the cobra attack someone? Will men and women respond differently?)*

Active Reading: EVALUATE

C Ask students if the responses of the American and the hostess to the cobra support or contradict the colonel's stereotype. *(Possible response: Although the American calmly distracts the other guests, the hostess shows even more control, since the snake has been on her foot and she hasn't moved or shown any sign of distress.)*

COMPREHENSION CHECK

1. How does the colonel think women respond to a crisis? *(They scream because they have no control.)*
2. How does the American get the guests to sit quietly? *(He makes up a game, with money at stake, to test their control.)*
3. How does the hostess disprove the colonel's theory? *(She stays calm and acts wisely when she feels a cobra lying across her foot.)*

From Personal Response to Critical Analysis

1. Responses will vary.
2. Possible responses: The hostess is an unexpected hero because her behavior contradicts the colonel's stereotype. The American is a hero because he keeps everyone quiet, giving the snake time to leave before anyone panics and gets bitten.
3. Possible responses: I didn't change my ideas because I don't believe that there is one general behavior for men or women. It surprised me because I wouldn't have been so calm in the same situation.
4. Portraits will vary.
5. Possible response: The colonel is insistent in his stereotyping of women, so it is unlikely he'll change. However, the hostess's example so clearly shows that he is wrong, that it will be hard for him to ignore it.

Another Pathway

Cooperative Learning Have each student in the group select a story with a prominent female character. Have one student record the characters and stories. The group should then discuss how each character would react in Mrs. Wynnes's situation. Afterward, have the group fill in a chart with their opinions about the characters. Invite the groups to compare their charts to find out whether each group categorized the female characters in the same way.

Rubric

3 Full Accomplishment Students link Mrs. Wynnes to other female characters and fully complete their chart.

2 Substantial Accomplishment Students partially link Mrs. Wynnes to other female characters and fail to complete their charts.

1 Little or Partial Accomplishment Students fail to link Mrs. Wynnes to other characters.

RESPONDING OPTIONS

FROM PERSONAL RESPONSE TO CRITICAL ANALYSIS

REFLECT
1. What were your reactions to this story? Record them in your notebook.

RETHINK
Thematic Link
2. In your opinion, who behaves heroically in this story? Is the hero an unlikely one in the context of the story's setting? Give reasons for your answers.

3. Review your predictions for the Personal Connection on page 507. How has this story affected your ideas about female and male reactions to tense situations?

4. Draw portraits of the characters in the story. Make sure their faces reflect their feelings and personalities.

RELATE
5. Do you think the incident presented in the story will change the colonel's stereotyped view of women? Explain your answer, using story details and your own experience.

LITERARY CONCEPTS

A writer creates **suspense** by keeping readers guessing about how a story will end. Early in "The Dinner Party," we learn something that most of the characters do not know—that there is a deadly snake loose in the room. We feel suspense as we begin to imagine all the things that could go wrong. How does the naturalist's challenge to the guests add to the suspense?

Multimodal Learning/Literary Link
ANOTHER PATHWAY

Cooperative Learning

With a group of classmates, discuss some of the other female characters you have read about in this book. Which characters, if faced with a crisis, might respond as Mrs. Wynnes does? How would the others respond? Present your ideas to the class in a chart.

QUICKWRITES

1. What do you suppose Mrs. Wynnes is thinking as the cobra lies across her foot? Write Mrs. Wynnes's **interior monologue**—her train of thought—during these tense minutes.

2. Picture the look on the face of the colonel after Mrs. Wynnes tells the group about the cobra. What might the colonel say next? Write a **dialogue** between the colonel and Mrs. Wynnes that could be added to the end of the story.

📁 **PORTFOLIO** Save your writing. You may want to use it later as a springboard to a piece for your portfolio.

510 UNIT FOUR PART 2: UNLIKELY HEROES

Literary Concepts

Point out to students that by counting to 300, the naturalist allows enough time for the cobra to emerge. Notice that the resolution of the suspense comes at nearly the last moment—the naturalist has already counted to 280 when the snake emerges from under the table. Encourage students to point out events that lead up to this climax, such as the naturalist's first awareness of the snake, or his attempt to locate it.

QuickWrites

1. Explain to students that in an interior monologue the reader is aware of nothing other than the character's thoughts. Suggest that students' monologues include whether or not Mrs. Wynnes knows the American is aware of the snake in the room.

2. Students may wish to depart from the prose format of the story and write their dialogue as if part of a play. Suggest that their dialogue relate in some way to the colonel's opening remarks.

Scriptwriting, pp. 86–88
Writing Dialogue, pp. 324–327

ACROSS THE CURRICULUM

Science A common image of the cobra is of the snake's being "charmed" by a man playing music. How is this possible, given that the cobra is one of the world's most dangerous snakes? Find out all you can about the cobra—why it is dangerous, where it lives, how large it grows, what it looks like, what it eats, and whether it can really be "charmed." Report your findings to the class. Include a picture of a cobra or your own drawing of one.

WORDS TO KNOW

Review the word *naturalist.* Then, on your paper, make a word web like the one shown here. Research information about naturalists to complete the web.

- Famous Examples
- Training
- Tools Used
- NATURALIST
- Kinds of Careers
- Nature of the Job

MONA GARDNER

During her childhood in Seattle, Washington, Mona Gardner (1900–1982) frequently visited Japan with her family. There she developed a life-long fascination with the Far East. She graduated from Stanford University in Stanford, California, in 1920. She began a career as a writer, specifically working as a journalist. She moved to Japan, covering the Far East as a correspondent for an American newspaper syndicate. Gardner wrote, "Twelve years of living with the Japanese has filled me with a lifelong interest in these people and in their destiny in the East."

In the 1930s, she spent five months in China, reporting on that country's war with Japan. One of her three books, *The Menacing Sun,* tells of her travels in Indochina, the East Indies, and India. *Extended Reading*

THE DINNER PARTY **511**

Words to Know

Student webs will vary. Be sure that students complete all portions of the word web.

Across the Curriculum

Science Cooperative Learning *Cobras* Students should work in groups of three or four. Encourage them to divide sections of their research among the members of the group. For example, one student may focus on the cobra's habitat, one on snake charmers, another on the cobra's biology, and a fourth on cobra venom. Suggest that part of the group prepare the visual materials and the remainder work on a short summary of the information the group found.

ADDITIONAL SUGGESTION

Social Studies *Sex-role Stereotyping* Explain to students that women are not always thought of as the weaker sex and that women were not always thought of in this way in the past. Anthropologist Margaret Mead found that women in some areas of the South Pacific were trained to be leaders, while men were raised to be passive. Have students look at some of Mead's popular works that deal with the experience of young people, such as *Coming of Age in Samoa* (1928), or *Growing Up in New Guinea* (1930). Set the following purpose for reading: *How does Mead's conclusion that stereotyped behavior based on sex roles comes from cultural learning, not innate differences between the sexes, support the behavior shown in "The Dinner Party"?*

Alternative Activities

1. It can be inferred that Mrs. Wynnes relished making the point that a woman had just as much control as a man in a crisis, because of her smile when she told the American that the snake had been lying across her foot. Ask students what they think she might have said had the cobra incident not occurred. Have students write a response that Mrs. Wynnes might make to the colonel's opinions.

2. Have students draw a sketch of the dinner party setting. Challenge them to show the snake's presence in the room in a way that captures the story's suspense and surprise ending. Ask students to consider how they can provide their audience with a point of view that characters in the story would not have. Students can review the story, reexamine the art on page 508, or do research to make their drawings more detailed.

THE LANGUAGE OF LITERATURE TEACHER'S EDITION **511**

OVERVIEW

Objectives

- To understand and appreciate a short story about the challenges and injustices faced by a mentally challenged man
- To enrich reading by using active reading strategies
- To identify and understand character changes
- To express understanding of the story through a choice of writing forms, including a progress report and a letter of recommendation
- To extend understanding of the story through a variety of multimodal and cross-curricular activities

Skills

READING SKILLS/ STRATEGIES
- Inference
- Clarifying
- Evaluating

LITERARY CONCEPTS
- Characterization
- Allusion
- Character changes

THE WRITER'S STYLE
- Sentence variety
- Formal English

GRAMMAR
- Run-on sentences

SPELLING
- Final e words and suffixes

SPEAKING, LISTENING, AND VIEWING
- Group Discussions
- Film
- Speeches
- Oral presentation

Cross-Curricular Connections

SOCIAL STUDIES
- Subliminal learning
- Judit Polgar
- Laboratory animals

SCIENCE
- Mice and humans
- The human brain
- Medical abstracts

PREVIEWING

FICTION

Flowers for Algernon
Daniel Keyes

Activating Prior Knowledge
PERSONAL CONNECTION

What if you woke up tomorrow and realized you had become a genius overnight? In your notebook or on a sheet of paper, answer the following questions:

- What would your initial reaction be?
- What drawbacks, if any, might there be to being a genius?
- How might your friends and members of your family respond to your intelligence?

Building Background
SCIENCE CONNECTION

Imagine just taking a pill to help you with your math or history homework! What if you could simply swallow a tablet to become smarter? "Smart drugs" include a variety of food supplements and prescription drugs that some people think improve memory and increase concentration and intelligence. Some smart pills are medications that are used for treating mental disorders but which certain individuals have found to sharpen their minds. However, many doctors are skeptical of these effects.

Health-food stores and mail-order companies sell food supplements that they claim will make people feel younger and more energetic. Some health-food bars offer these supplements in "smart drinks" with names like Memory Fuel, Fast Blast, and Mind Mix.

Many scientists say that the only thing smart about these substances is the way they are pushed on the public. There is no scientific evidence—no recognized studies—to support the effectiveness of these drugs and supplements. Moreover, the Food and Drug Administration has not thoroughly tested many smart drugs for safety and effectiveness. Although legitimate drugs to restore lost memory and treat other mental disorders are under development, it will be many years before drugs that improve thinking ability are available to the public.

512 UNIT FOUR PART 2: UNLIKELY HEROES

PRINT AND MEDIA RESOURCES

UNIT FOUR RESOURCE BOOK
Strategic Reading: Literature, p. 59
Vocabulary SkillBuilder, p. 62
Reading SkillBuilder, p. 60
Spelling SkillBuilder, p. 61

GRAMMAR MINI–LESSONS
Transparencies, p. 2
Copymasters, p. 2

WRITING MINI–LESSONS
Transparencies, pp. 36, 40–43

ACCESS FOR STUDENTS ACQUIRING ENGLISH
Selection Summaries
Reading and Writing Support

FORMAL ASSESSMENT
Selection Test, pp. 99–100
Test Generator

INTERNET RESOURCES
McDougal Littell Literature Center at http://www.hmco.com/mcdougal/lit

Active Reading/Setting A Purpose
READING CONNECTION

Inferences

An inference is a logical guess or conclusion based on facts. Making inferences is an important skill in reading nearly all categories of literature, including fiction, poetry, and nonfiction. By paying attention to what you read and applying what you know from your own experience, you can make inferences that go beyond what the words say.

You already know how to do this mental detective work. In the selections you have read thus far, you have picked up clues that helped you understand what was going on. You have made inferences about plots, settings, and characters' feelings and actions. For example, when you read that someone's face turns red, you might infer that the person is embarrassed or ashamed. If further reading does not support the inference, you discard it and make a different inference. You might discover that the red-faced character has, in fact, been mistreated and therefore infer that his or her red face is a sign of anger.

As you read "Flowers for Algernon," you will need to make many inferences. Because the story is presented as a series of progress reports written by the main character, Charlie, you will need to use the evidence in these reports to support your inferences. Look for clues in the spelling, punctuation, and style of Charlie's reports as well as in the events he writes about. Since in the beginning of the story Charlie is less intelligent than you, you will be able to make inferences by simply drawing on your own knowledge and experience. For example, you will know why Charlie's coworkers are laughing before he does.

Let the questions inserted at various points in the selection help you make inferences as you read. In addition, look for clues that can help you make inferences about Charlie's feelings about himself and others, his level of intelligence, and others' reactions to him. The inferences you make should change as the story moves forward. In your notebook, jot down notes to keep track of these changes. Use a chart similar to the one shown here, and you will have your own "progress report" for the story.

READING STRATEGIES

SUMMARY

Charlie Gordon is 37 years old and has low mental ability. As he prepares to undergo a procedure to increase his intelligence, he begins keeping a journal. The changes in his mental ability over the course of months are reflected in his writing. Dr. Nemur and Dr. Strauss perform the same surgery on Charlie that has already tripled the intelligence of a white mouse named Algernon. Charlie's teacher, Miss Kinnian, encourages him but has doubts. He becomes a genius and acquires tremendous academic knowledge, as well as a new and painful awareness of human failings. He begins his own research into techniques for increasing intelligence. Then Algernon, whom Charlie considers his friend, begins to lose his intelligence. Charlie discovers a flaw in his doctors' theories and realizes that he too will begin to lose his intelligence. Ultimately Algernon dies. Charlie returns to his original level of intelligence but is unable to resume his old life. He moves away, asking his friends to put flowers on Algernon's grave as he had always done.

Thematic Link: *Unlikely Heroes* A mentally challenged man undergoes amazing changes during a medical experiment.

I can infer …	On the basis of Progress Reports from…				
	March 5–10	March 15–29	April 3–30	May 15–June 4	June 5–July 28
Charlie's feelings about himself					
Charlie's feelings about others					
Charlie's intelligence level					
Others' reactions to Charlie					

FLOWERS FOR ALGERNON **513**

STRATEGIC READING FOR
Less-Proficient Readers

Set a Purpose Ask students to discuss times they didn't feel smart enough. Then have them read to identify the title character and find out how Algernon competes with Charlie at the lab.

Use **UNIT FOUR RESOURCE BOOK**, p. 59, for guidance in reading the selection.

WORDS TO KNOW

absurd (əb-sûrd′) *adj.* ridiculously unreasonable (p. 529)
hypothesis (hī-pŏth′ĭ-sĭs) *n.* a theory used as a basis for research (p. 533)
impair (ĭm-pâr′) *v.* to weaken; damage (p. 532)
introspective (ĭn′trə-spĕk′tĭv) *adj.* examining one's own thoughts, feelings, and sensations (p. 533)
naïveté (nä′ēv-tā′) *n.* a lack of sophistication; simplicity (p. 531)

opportunist (ŏp′ər-tōō′nĭst) *n.* a person who takes advantage of any opportunity to achieve a goal, with little regard for moral principles (p. 526)
proportional (prə-pôr′shə-nəl) *adj.* having a constant relation in degree or number (p. 533)
regression (rĭ-grĕsh′ən) *n.* a return to a less developed condition (p. 532)
sensation (sĕn-sā′shən) *n.* a state of great interest and excitement (p. 528)
shrew (shrōō) *n.* a mean, nagging woman (p. 526)

specialization (spĕsh′ə-lĭ-zā′shən) *n.* a focus on a particular activity or area of study (p. 529)
statistically (stə-tĭs′tĭ-klē) *adv.* in terms of the principles used to analyze numerical data (p. 533)
syndrome (sĭn′drōm′) *n.* a group of symptoms that characterizes a disease or psychological disorder (p. 533)
tangible (tăn′jə-bəl) *adj.* able to be seen or touched; material (p. 528)
vacuous (văk′yōō-əs) *adj.* showing a lack of intelligence or thought (p. 530)

THE LANGUAGE OF LITERATURE TEACHER'S EDITION **513**

CUSTOMIZING FOR
Students Acquiring English

- Use **ACCESS FOR STUDENTS ACQUIRING ENGLISH,** *Reading and Writing Support.*
- Students may have trouble reading the passages at the beginning of the story because of the misspellings and the ungrammatical structures. Have them read troubling words and phrases aloud, since the misspellings are usually phonetic.

CUSTOMIZING FOR
Gifted and Talented Students

Have students discuss society's attitudes toward the mentally challenged. Ask them in what ways the general public still needs to be educated if it is to treat mentally challenged individuals with the respect they deserve. Have students note the ways different characters treat Charlie before and after his surgery.

CUSTOMIZING FOR
Multiple Learning Styles

A Intrapersonal Learners Point out that the story is told through a series of progress reports written by Charlie, much like journal entries. Have students record in a journal their personal reflections on Charlie's changes. Suggest students consider how their feelings about Charlie are affected by what happens to him.

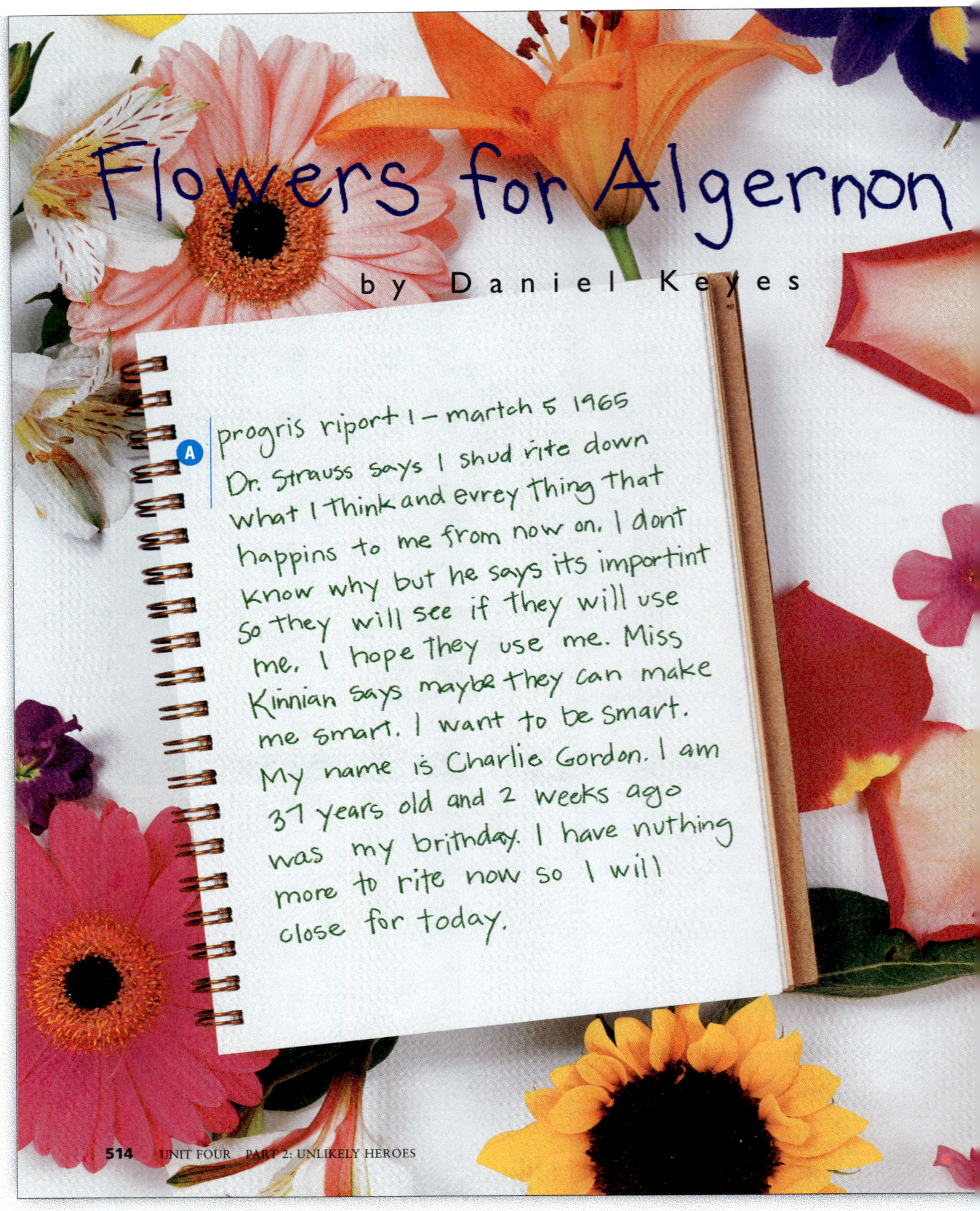

Flowers for Algernon

by Daniel Keyes

A progris riport 1—martch 5 1965
Dr. Strauss says I shud rite down what I think and evrey thing that happins to me from now on. I dont know why but he says its importint so they will see if they will use me. I hope they use me. Miss Kinnian says maybe they can make me smart. I want to be smart. My name is Charlie Gordon. I am 37 years old and 2 weeks ago was my brithday. I have nuthing more to rite now so I will close for today.

Mini-Lesson | **Reading Skills/Strategies**

ACTIVE READING: CLARIFY Explain to students that while stopping to clarify confusing passages may appear to take extra time, in the long run it may actually save time. Point out that unresolved problems only grow and compound each other, forcing students to reread material. Suggest they use their reading logs to keep track of questions and how they resolve them.

Application In the early parts of this story, students may have had difficulty making sense of particular words and expressions Charlie used. This is especially true when Charlie does not understand what is being said, such as when he tries to copy down what his doctors are discussing. For example, refer students to the highlighted passage on page 515. Ask them to clarify the situation by either restating orally or rewriting it in their own words. Then encourage students to discuss any other passages they may have found difficult and how they clarified them.

Reteaching/Reinforcement
- *Unit Four Resource Book,* p. 60

progris riport 2—martch 6

I had a test today. I think I faled it. and I think that maybe now they wont use me. What happind is a nice young man was in the room and he had some white cards with ink spillled all over them. He sed Charlie what do you see on this card. I was very skared even tho I had my rabits foot in my pockit because when I was a kid I always faled tests in school and I spillled ink to.

I told him I saw a inkblot. He said yes and it made me feel good. I thot that was all but when I got up to go he stopped me. He said now sit down Charlie we are not thru yet. Then I dont remember so good but he wantid me to say what was in the ink. I dint see nuthing in the ink but he said there was picturs there other pepul saw some picturs. I coudnt see any picturs. I reely tryed to see. I held the card close up and then far away. Then I said if I had my glases I coud see better I usually only ware my glases in the movies or TV but I said they are in the closit in the hall. I got them. Then I said let me see that card agen I bet Ill find it now.

I tryed hard but I still coudnt find the picturs I only saw the ink. I told him maybe I need new glases. He rote somthing down on a paper and I got skared of faling the test. I told him it was a very nice inkblot with littel points all around the eges. He looked very sad so that wasnt it. I said please let me try agen. Ill get it in a few minits becaus Im not so fast somtimes. Im a slow reeder too in Miss Kinnians class for slow adults but I'm trying very hard.

He gave me a chance with another card that had 2 kinds of ink spillled on it red and blue.

He was very nice and talked slow like Miss Kinnian does and he explaned it to me that it was a *raw shok*.[1] He said pepul see things in the ink. I said show me where. He said think. I told him I think a inkblot but that wasnt rite eather. He said what does it remind you—pretend somthing. I closd my eyes for a long time to pretend. I told him I pretned a fowntan pen with ink leeking all over a table cloth. Then he got up and went out.

I dont think I passd the *raw shok* test.

progris report 3—martch 7

Dr Strauss and Dr Nemur say it dont matter about the inkblots. I told them I dint spill the ink on the cards and I coudnt see anything in the ink. They said that maybe they will still use me. I said Miss Kinnian never gave me tests like that one only spelling and reading. They said Miss Kinnian told that I was her bestist pupil in the adult nite scool becaus I tryed the hardist and I reely wantid to lern. They said how come you went to the adult nite scool all by yourself Charlie. How did you find it. I said I askd pepul and sumbody told me where I shud go to lern to read and spell good. They said why did you want to. I told them becaus all my life I wantid to be smart and not dumb. But its very hard to be smart. They said you know it will probly be tempirery. I said yes. Miss Kinnian told me. I dont care if it herts.

Later I had more crazy tests today. The nice

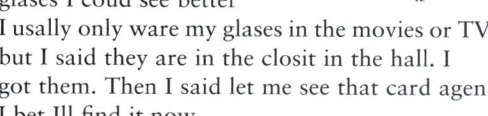

---

1. **raw shok:** Charlie's way of writing *Rorschach* (rôr′shäk′), the name of a test used to analyze people's personalities on the basis of what they see in inkblot designs.

lady who gave it me told me the name and I asked her how do you spellit so I can rite it in my progris riport. THEMATIC APPERCEPTION TEST.² I dont know the frist 2 words but I know what *test* means. You got to pass it or you get bad marks. This test lookd easy becaus I coud see the picturs. Only this time she dint want me to tell her the picturs. That mixd me up. I said the man yesterday said I shoud tell him what I saw in the ink she said that dont make no difrence. She said make up storys about the pepul in the picturs.

I told her how can you tell storys about pepul you never met. I said why shud I make up lies. I never tell lies any more becaus I always get caut.

She told me this test and the other one the raw-shok was for getting personalty. I laffed so hard. I said how can you get that thing from inkblots and fotos. She got sore and put her picturs away. I dont care. It was sily. I gess I faled that test too.

Later some men in white coats took me to a difernt part of the hospitil and gave me a game to play. It was like a race with a white mouse. They called the mouse Algernon. Algernon was in a box with a lot of twists and turns like all kinds of walls and they gave me a pencil and a paper with lines and lots of boxes. On one side it said START and on the other end it said FINISH. They said it was *amazed*³ and that Algernon and me had the same *amazed* to do. I dint see how we coud have the same *amazed* if Algernon had a box and I had a paper but I dint say nothing. Anyway there wasnt time because the race started.

One of the men had a watch he was trying to hide so I woudnt see it so I tryed not to look and that made me nervus.

Anyway that test made me feel worser than all the others because they did it over 10 times with difernt *amazeds* and Algernon won every time. I dint know that mice were so smart.

Maybe thats because Algernon is a white mouse. Maybe white mice are smarter then other mice.

progris riport 4—Mar 8

Their going to use me! Im so exited I can hardly rite. Dr Nemur and Dr Strauss had a argament about it first. Dr Nemur was in the office when Dr Strauss brot me in. Dr Nemur was worryed about using me but Dr Strauss told him Miss Kinnian rekemmended me the best from all the people who she was teaching. I like Miss Kinnian becaus shes a very smart teacher. And she said Charlie your going to have a second chance. If you volunteer for this experament you mite get smart. They dont know if it will be perminint but theirs a chance. Thats why I said ok even when I was scared because she said it was an operashun. She said dont be scared Charlie you done so much with so little I think you deserv it most of all.

So I got scaird when Dr Nemur and Dr Strauss argud about it. Dr Strauss said I had something that was very good. He said I had a good *motor-vation*.⁴ I never even knew I had that. I felt proud when he said that not every body with an eye-q⁵ of 68 had that thing. I dont know what it is or where I got it but he said Algernon had it too.

CLARIFY

Why does Charlie feel so excited?

Using a Reading Log

---

2. **Thematic Apperception** (thĭ-măt′ĭk ăp′ər-sĕp′shən) **Test:** a test for analyzing people's personalities on the basis of the stories they make up about a series of pictures.
3. **amazed:** Charlie's way of writing *a maze*.
4. **motor-vation:** Charlie's way of writing *motivation*, a word referring to the inner drive that makes a person take a particular course of action.
5. **eye-q:** Charlie's way of writing *I.Q.* (an abbreviation of *intelligence quotient*). Based on the results of a standardized test, an I.Q. is a measurement of a person's mental ability relative to a normal level.

Copyright © Guy Billout.

FLOWERS FOR ALGERNON   **517**

Critical Thinking: SPECULATING

G Ask students why Charlie might make this judgment about Algernon. *(Possible response: Charlie bases his judgment on Algernon's color. He may have thought that mice could only be gray or brown in color.)*

Active Reading: CLARIFY

H To help explain Charlie's excitement, draw students' attention to Charlie's belief that he has to pass the tests given to him and also to his growing doubt and tension about having passed them. *(Possible responses: He has been accepted for the experiment that may increase his intelligence. He feels that he has successfully passed the tests he thought he had failed.)*

Mini-Lesson  Literary Concepts

REVIEWING CHARACTERIZATION
Remind students that characterization refers to the techniques a writer uses to create and develop a character. Draw the word web on the chalkboard and point out to students the four basic methods a writer uses to develop a character.

Application Have students review the selection to see how Charlie's character is developed. Ask students to copy the web into their notebooks and add details from the selection that are examples of each method.

- physical description
- character's thoughts, speech, action
- **Characterization**
- thoughts, speech, actions of other characters
- direct comments

THE LANGUAGE OF LITERATURE TEACHER'S EDITION **517**

CUSTOMIZING FOR
Students Acquiring English

2 Explain to students that Charlie uses asterisks to show that he remembers only parts of words. Charlie then summarizes the idea of the conversation in a brief paragraph, "I dint get . . ."

3 Explain that the expression "on my side" means "supports, agrees with." Dr. Strauss supported Charlie and wanted Charlie to participate in the experiment.

4 Explain that fear of black cats and reliance on lucky charms are examples of superstitions. Some people believe that these things affect their luck. Ask students about superstitions in their native countries.

Active Reading: CLARIFY

I Ask volunteers to write a grammatically correct version of these three paragraphs, correctly spelling out the starred words and putting punctuation in correct places. (*Starred words, in order, are: intellectual, mentality, hostile, uncooperative, apathetic, achievement, relativity, comparatively, tremendous, achievement.*)

Critical Thinking: MAKING JUDGMENTS

J Ask students what Dr. Strauss suggests to Charlie about science. (*Possible response: Science is supposedly based on verifiable knowledge, unlike superstition, which is not verifiable and cannot replicate results.*) Ask students if they agree with Dr. Strauss's distinction.

Active Reading: PREDICT

K Ask students to base their predictions on the earlier promises made by the doctors and what Charlie says the operation is for. (*Possible responses: He will become smarter like the mouse. Charlie will remain the same or worse, he will lose intelligence.*)

Algernons *motor-vation* is the cheese they put in his box. But it cant be that because I didnt eat any cheese this week.

Then he told Dr Nemur something I dint understand so while they were talking I wrote down some of the words.

He said Dr Nemur I know Charlie is not what you had in mind as the first of your new brede of intelek** (coudnt get the word) superman. But most people of his low ment** are host** and uncoop** they are usualy dull apath** and hard to reach. He has a good natcher hes intristed and eager to please.

Dr Nemur said remember he will be the first human beeng ever to have his intelijence trippled by surgicle meens.

Dr Strauss said exakly. Look at how well hes lerned to read and write for his low mentel age its as grate an acheve** as you and I lerning einstines therey of **vity[6] without help. That shows the intenss motor-vation. Its comparat** a tremen** achev** I say we use Charlie.

I dint get all the words and they were talking to fast but it sounded like Dr Strauss was on my side and like the other one wasnt.

Then Dr Nemur nodded he said all right maybe your right. We will use Charlie. When he said that I got so exited I jumped up and shook his hand for being so good to me. I told him thank you doc you wont be sorry for giving me a second chance. And I mean it like I told him. After the operashun Im gonna try to be smart. Im gonna try awful hard.

progris ript 5—Mar 10

Im skared. Lots of people who work here and the nurses and the people who gave me the tests came to bring me candy and wish me luck. I hope I have luck. I got my rabits foot and my lucky penny and my horse shoe. Only a black cat crossed me when I was comming to the hospitil. Dr Strauss says dont be superstitis Charlie this is sience. Anyway Im keeping my rabits foot with me.

I asked Dr Strauss if Ill beat Algernon in the race after the operashun and he said maybe. If the operashun works Ill show that mouse I can be as smart as he is. Maybe smarter. Then Ill be abel to read better and spell the words good and know lots of things and be like other people. I want to be smart like other people. If it works perminint they will make everybody smart all over the wurld.

They dint give me anything to eat this morning. I dont know what that eating has to do with getting smart. Im very hungry and Dr Nemur took away my box of candy. That Dr Nemur is a grouch. Dr Strauss says I can have it back after the operashun. You cant eat befor a operashun . . .

Progress Report 6—Mar 15

PREDICT
What's going to happen to Charlie now?
Using a Reading Log

The operashun dint hurt. He did it while I was sleeping. They took off the bandijis from my eyes and my head today so I can make a PROGRESS REPORT. Dr Nemur who looked at some of my other ones says I spell PROGRESS wrong and he told me how to spell it and REPORT too. I got to try and remember that.

I have a very bad memary for spelling. Dr Strauss says its ok to tell about all the things that happin to me but he says I shoud tell more about what I feel and what I think. When I told him I dont know how to think he said try. All the time when the bandijis were on my eyes I tryed to think. Nothing happened. I dont know what to think about. Maybe if I ask him he will tell me how I can think now that Im

---
6. **einstines therey of **vity:** Charlie's way of writing *Einstein's theory of relativity*, a reference to the scientific theory of space and time developed by Albert Einstein.

518 UNIT FOUR PART 2: UNLIKELY HEROES

Copyright © Mark Penberthy.

suppose to get smart. What do smart people think about. Fancy things I suppose. I wish I knew some fancy things alredy.

Progress Report 7—mar 19
Nothing is happening. I had lots of tests and different kinds of races with Algernon. I hate that mouse. He always beats me. Dr Strauss said I got to play those games. And he said some time I got to take those tests over again. Those inkblots are stupid. And those pictures are stupid too. I like to draw a picture of a man and a woman but I wont make up lies about people.

I got a headache from trying to think so much. I thot Dr Strauss was my frend but he dont help me. He dont tell me what to think or when Ill get smart. Miss Kinnian dint come to see me. I think writing these progress reports are stupid too.

FLOWERS FOR ALGERNON 519

Multicultural Perspectives

INTELLIGENCE TESTS Many people believe that intelligence can be gauged by testing a person's memory, problem-solving ability, and learning speed. However, it is difficult to test everyone fairly even in these broad areas.

For example:
- Many people can learn one subject more quickly than another subject.
- People may have difficulty demonstrating their problem-solving capabilities because they do not understand instructions in English.
- Some tests assume that test-takers have a certain cultural knowledge; this puts test-takers from another culture at a disadvantage.
- A person may have talents and skills that are not measured by intelligence tests.

Criticisms like these have caused many people to rethink the use and structure of traditional intelligence tests and to develop alternative assessment methods.

CUSTOMIZING FOR
Multiple Learning Styles

N Mathematical Learners Have students compute what Charlie's IQ will be if it triples. *(Charlie's IQ is 68; 68 × 3 = 204)* Point out that the average score on an IQ test is 100 and that a score above 140 is considered very superior. Have students assess what it means for Charlie to score 204. *(He would be incredibly intelligent, a genius.)*

Linking to Science

O Recently, scientists in the United States have discovered that mice and humans share a gene that assists them in spatial learning, a type of memory that enables a problem solver to return to a certain place by using visible surroundings as clues. Mice that have the gene can return to a specific spot in a maze. This discovery, and others like it, suggests that examining the biology and behavior of mice can be helpful in understanding human behavior and biology.

Active Reading: QUESTION

P Why does the foreman criticize Ernie by saying he's trying to be a Charlie Gordon? *(Possible response: The foreman thinks that because Ernie has lost a package, he has made a stupid mistake; the foreman has little concern for Charlie's feelings and thinks it is funny to use Charlie's deficiencies to criticize an employee.)*

Active Reading: CLARIFY

Q Encourage students to think about Charlie's feelings toward Algernon both before and after the operation to explain why Charlie doesn't want to race with Algernon. *(Possible response: He is frustrated and thinks that he will continue to lose.)*

Progress Report 8—Mar 23

Im going back to work at the factory. They said it was better I shud go back to work but I cant tell anyone what the operashun was for and I have to come to the hospitil for an hour evry night after work. They are gonna pay me mony every month for lerning to be smart.

Im glad Im going back to work because I miss my job and all my frends and all the fun we have there.

N Dr Strauss says I shud keep writing things down but I dont have to do it every day just when I think of something or something speshul happins. He says dont get discoridged because it takes time and it happins slow. He says it took a long time with Algernon before he got 3 times smarter then he was before. Thats why Algernon beats me all the time because he had that operashun too. That makes me feel better. I coud probly do that *amazed* faster than a reglar mouse. Maybe **O** some day Ill beat Algernon. Boy that would be something. So far Algernon looks like he mite be smart perminent.

Mar 25 (I dont have to write PROGRESS REPORT on top any more just when I hand it in once a week for Dr Nemur to read. I just have to put the date on. That saves time)

We had a lot of fun at the factory today. Joe Carp said hey look where Charlie had his operashun what did they do Charlie put some brains in. I was going to tell him but I remembered Dr Strauss said no. Then Frank Reilly said what did you do Charlie forget your key and open your door the hard way. That made me laff. Their really my friends and they like me.

Sometimes somebody will say hey look at Joe or Frank or George he really pulled a Charlie Gordon. I dont know why they say that but they always laff. This morning Amos Borg who is the 4 man at Donnegans used my name when he shouted at Ernie the office boy. Ernie lost a packige. He said Ernie for godsake what are you trying to be a Charlie Gordon. I dont understand why he said that. I never lost any packiges.

Mar 28 Dr Straus came to my room tonight to see why I dint come in like I was suppose to. I told him I dont like to race with Algernon any more. He said I dont have to for a while but I shud come in. He had a present for me only it wasnt a present but just for lend. I thot it was a little television but it wasnt. He said I got to turn it on when I go to sleep. I said your kidding why shud I turn it on when Im going to sleep. Who ever herd of a thing like that. But he said if I want to get smart I got to do what he says. I told him I dint think I was going to get smart and he put his hand on my sholder and said Charlie you dont know it yet but your getting smarter all the time. You wont notice for a while. I think he was just being nice to make me feel good because I dont look any smarter.

Oh yes I almost forgot. I asked him when I can go back to the class at Miss Kinnians school. He said I wont go their. He said that soon Miss Kinnian will come to the hospitil to start and teach me speshul. I was mad at her for not comming to see me when I got the operashun but I like her so maybe we will be frends again.

Mar 29 That crazy TV kept me up all night. How can I sleep with something yelling crazy

> Maybe someday I'll beat Algernon. Boy that would be something.

CLARIFY
Why doesn't Charlie want to race with Algernon anymore?
Using a Reading Log

things all night in my ears. And the nutty pictures. Wow. I dont know what it says when Im up so how am I going to know when Im sleeping.

Dr Strauss says its ok. He says my brains are lerning when I sleep and that will help me when Miss Kinnian starts my lessons in the hospitl (only I found out it isnt a hospitil its a labatory). I think its all crazy. If you can get smart when your sleeping why do people go to school. That thing I dont think will work. I use to watch the late show and the late late show on TV all the time and it never made me smart. Maybe you have to sleep while you watch it.

PROGRESS REPORT 9—April 3
Dr Strauss showed me how to keep the TV turned low so now I can sleep. I don't hear a thing. And I still dont understand what it says. A few times I play it over in the morning to find out what I lerned when I was sleeping and I dont think so. Miss Kinnian says Maybe its another langwidge or something. But most times it sounds american. It talks so fast faster than even Miss Gold who was my teacher in 6 grade and I remember she talked so fast I coudnt understand her.

I told Dr Strauss what good is it to get smart in my sleep. I want to be smart when Im awake. He says its the same thing and I have two minds. Theres the *subconscious* and the *conscious*[7] (thats how you spell it). And one dont tell the other one what its doing. They dont even talk to each other. Thats why I dream. And boy have I been having crazy dreams. Wow. Ever since that night TV. The late late late late late show.

I forgot to ask him if it was only me or if everybody had those two minds.

(I just looked up the word in the dictionary Dr Strauss gave me. The word is *subconscious. adj. Of the nature of mental operations yet not present in consciousness; as, subconscious conflict of desires.*) There's more but I still dont know what it means. This isnt a very good dictionary for dumb people like me.

Anyway the headache is from the party. My frends from the factery Joe Carp and Frank Reilly invited me to go with them to Muggsys Saloon for some drinks. I dont like to drink but they said we will have lots of fun. I had a good time.

Joe Carp said I shoud show the girls how I mop out the toilet in the factory and he got me a mop. I showed them and everyone laffed when I told that Mr Donnegan said I was the best janiter he ever had because I like my job and do it good and never come late or miss a day except for my operashun.

I said Miss Kinnian always said Charlie be proud of your job because you do it good.

Everybody laffed and we had a good time and they gave me lots of drinks and Joe said Charlie is a card when hes potted.[8] I dont know what that means but everybody likes me and we have fun. I cant wait to be smart like my best frends Joe Carp and Frank Reilly.

I dont remember how the party was over but I think I went out to buy a newspaper and coffe for Joe and Frank and when I came back there was no one their. I looked for them all over till late. Then I dont remember so good but I think I got sleepy or sick. A nice cop brot me back home. Thats what my landlady Mrs Flynn says.

But I got a headache and a big lump on my head and black and blue all over. I think maybe I fell but Joe Carp says it was the cop

---

7. **the subconscious** (sŭb-kŏn′shəs) **and the conscious** (kŏn′shəs): psychological terms for two kinds of mental activity. The subconscious consists of all a person's mental activity that he or she is not aware of, and the conscious is the mental activity of which the person is aware.
8. **Charlie is a card when hes potted:** Charlie is funny when he's drunk.

FLOWERS FOR ALGERNON **521**

Mini-Lesson: Speaking, Listening, and Viewing

GROUP DISCUSSIONS Explain that part of the difficulty of reading "Flowers for Algernon" comes from Charlie's nonstandard spelling and punctuation. Charlie writes things in the way he hears them and not according to the rules of proper spelling and grammar.

Application Have students work in small groups. Assign each group a progress report from April 18 to June 5 when Charlie is at the height of his increased intellectual capabilities (pages 523–533).

One student should read the passage (or part of a passage) aloud slowly to the group while students "translate" the words *exactly as they hear them*, disregarding spelling and punctuation rules. Have the group discuss the different versions of the story using the following prompts:

- *Did everyone hear the selection in exactly the same way?*
- *What does this imply about using spelling and grammar errors to make judgments about someone's intelligence?*

STRATEGIC READING FOR
Less-Proficient Readers

(U) Ask students what important event occurs on April 6. *(Charlie beats Algernon at the maze race for the first time.)* **Noting Relevant Details**

- Why is it so important that Charlie is finally able to beat Algernon at the maze? *(It provides concrete evidence that Charlie is getting smarter)* **Making Inferences**

Set a Purpose Have students read to find out why Charlie loses his job at Donnegan's Plastic Box Company.

Linking to Literature

(V) Point out that *The Life and Strange Surprising Adventures of Robinson Crusoe* by Daniel Defoe was published in 1719. Contrary to what Miss Kinnian says, Defoe wrote two more accounts of Robinson Crusoe's adventures.

Ask students why they think Keyes refers to this book. *(Possible response: Crusoe is alone on his island and desperately desires companionship, much as Charlie has a growing awareness of his own isolation from his peers.)*

Active Reading: CLARIFY

(W) Ask students to clarify what is in Miss Kinnian's eye. *(tears)* Then have students discuss the difference between Charlie's perception of why Miss Kinnian is crying and why she is actually crying. *(Possible response: Charlie thinks that she is crying because something got in her eye, but she is really crying because she is upset at the abuse Charlie's co-workers subject him to.)*

---

they beat up drunks some times. I don't think so. Miss Kinnian says cops are to help people. Anyway I got a bad headache and Im sick and hurt all over. I dont think Ill drink anymore.

April 6 I beat Algernon! I dint even know I beat him until Burt the tester told me. Then the second time I lost because I got so exited I fell off the chair before I finished. But after that I beat him 8 more times. I must be getting smart to beat a smart mouse like Algernon. But I dont *feel* smarter.

I wanted to race Algernon some more but Burt said thats enough for one day. They let me hold him for a minit. Hes not so bad. Hes soft like a ball of cotton. He blinks and when he opens his eyes their black and pink on the eges.

I said can I feed him because I felt bad to beat him and I wanted to be nice and make frends. Burt said no Algernon is a very specshul mouse with an operashun like mine, and he was the first of all the animals to stay smart so long. He told me Algernon is so smart that every day he has to solve a test to get his food. Its a thing like a lock on a door that changes every time Algernon goes in to eat so he has to lern something new to get his food. That made me sad because if he coudnt **(U)** lern he woud be hungry.

I dont think its right to make you pass a test to eat. How woud Dr Nemur like it to have to pass a test every time he wants to eat. I think Ill be frends with Algernon.

April 9 Tonight after work Miss Kinnian was at the laboratory. She looked like she was glad to see me but scared. I told her dont worry Miss Kinnian Im not smart yet and she laffed. She said I have confidence in you Charlie the way you struggled so hard to read and right better than all the others. At werst you will have it for a littel wile and your doing somthing for sience.

We are reading a very hard book. I never read such a hard book before. Its called *Robinson Crusoe* about a man who gets merooned on a dessert Iland. Hes smart and figers out all kinds of things so he can have a house and food and hes a good swimmer. Only I feel sorry because hes all alone and has no frends. But I think their must be somebody else on the iland because theres a picture with his funny umbrella looking at footprints. I hope he gets a frend and not be lonly.

April 10 Miss Kinnian teaches me to spell better. She says look at a word and close your eyes and say it over and over until you remember. I have lots of truble with *through* that you say *threw* and *enough* and *tough* that you dont say *enew* and *tew*. You got to say *enuff* and *tuff*. Thats how I use to write it before I started to get smart. Im confused but Miss Kinnian says theres no reason in spelling.

Apr 14 Finished *Robinson Crusoe*. I want to find out more about what happens to him but Miss Kinnian says thats all there is. *Why*

Apr 15 Miss Kinnian says Im lerning fast. She read some of the Progress Reports and she looked at me kind of funny. She says Im a fine person and Ill show them all. I asked her why. She said never mind but I shoudnt feel bad if I find out that everybody isnt nice like I think. She said for a person who god gave so little to you done more then a lot of people with brains they never even used. I said all my frends are smart people but there good. They like me and they never did anything that wasnt nice. Then she got something in her eye and she had to run out to the ladys room.

CLARIFY
What is in Miss Kinnian's eye?
Using a Reading Log

Apr 16 Today, I lerned, the *comma*, this is a comma (,) a period, with a tail, Miss Kinnian, says its important, because, it makes writing, better, she said, somebody, coud lose, a lot of money, if a

522 UNIT FOUR PART 2: UNLIKELY HEROES

comma, isnt, in the, right place, I dont have, any money, and I dont see, how a comma, keeps you, from losing it,

But she says, everybody, uses commas, so Ill use, them too,

Apr 17 I used the comma wrong. Its punctuation. Miss Kinnian told me to look up long words in the dictionary to lern to spell them. I said whats the difference if you can read it anyway. She said its part of your education so now on Ill look up all the words Im not sure how to spell. It takes a long time to write that way but I think Im remembering. I only have to look up once and after that I get it right. Anyway thats how come I got the word *punctuation* right. (Its that way in the dictionary). Miss Kinnian says a period is punctuation too, and there are lots of other marks to lern. I told her I thot all the periods had to have tails but she said no.

You got to mix them up, she showed? me" how. to mix! them(up,. and now; I can! mix up all kinds" of punctuation, in! my writing? There, are lots! of rules? to lern; but Im gettin'g them in my head.

One thing I? like about, Dear Miss Kinnian: (thats the way it goes in a business letter if I ever go into business) is she, always gives me' a reason" when—I ask. She's a gen'ius! I wish! I cou'd be smart" like, her;

(Punctuation, is; fun!)

April 18 What a dope I am! I didn't even understand what she was talking about. I read the grammar book last night and it explanes the whole thing. Then I saw it was the same way as Miss Kinnian was trying to tell me, but I didn't get it. I got up in the middle of the night, and the whole thing straightened out in my mind.

Miss Kinnian said that the TV working in my sleep helped out. She said I reached a plateau. Thats like the flat top of a hill.

After I figgered out how punctuation worked, I read over all my old Progress Reports from the beginning. Boy, did I have crazy spelling and punctuation! I told Miss Kinnian I ought to go over the pages and fix all the mistakes but she said, "No, Charlie, Dr. Nemur wants them just as they are. That's why he let you keep them after they were photostated, to see your own progress. You're coming along fast, Charlie."

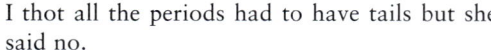

"You're coming along fast, Charlie."

That made me feel good. After the lesson I went down and played with Algernon. We don't race any more.

April 20 I feel sick inside. Not sick like for a doctor, but inside my chest it feels empty like getting punched and a heartburn at the same time.

I wasn't going to write about it, but I guess I got to, because its important. Today was the first time I ever stayed home from work.

Last night Joe Carp and Frank Reilly invited me to a party. There were lots of girls and some men from the factory. I remembered how sick I got last time I drank too much, so I told Joe I didn't want anything to drink. He gave me a plain coke instead. It tasted funny, but I thought it was just a bad taste in my mouth.

We had a lot of fun for a while. Joe said I should dance with Ellen and she would teach me the steps. I fell a few times and I couldn't understand why because no one else was dancing besides Ellen and me. And all the time I was tripping because somebody's foot was always sticking out.

Mini-Lesson Spelling

FINAL e WORDS AND SUFFIXES Tell students that when words ending in a silent e are combined with a suffix starting with a vowel, the silent e is dropped:

specialize + -ation = specialization
amaze + -ing = amazing

However, when words ending in a silent e are combined with a suffix starting with a consonant, the silent e is not dropped:

measure + -ment = measurement
achieve + -ment = achievement

Application Draw the chart on the chalkboard and ask students to complete it by combining the silent e words with the suffixes indicated at left.

Ask students to look for more words that fit this pattern, in their own writing and in things that they read, and to add these words to their personal word lists.

Reteaching/Reinforcement
• *Unit Four Resource Book*, p. 61

Silent *e* word	+ Suffix *-ing*	+ Suffix *-ment*
1. endorse	endorsing	endorsement
2. state	stating	statement
3. amuse	amusing	amusement
4. confine	confining	confinement
5. engage	engaging	engagement

CUSTOMIZING FOR
Students Acquiring English

6 Explain that the idiomatic expression "to ditch" someone, as in "we . . . ditched him," means to leave someone behind without telling him or her.

Literary Concept:
CHARACTERIZATION

AA Invite students to describe how Charlie's increasing intelligence is affecting his reactions to situations. *(Possible responses: As Charlie becomes more intelligent, he also grows more perceptive and self-conscious. He sees flaws and shortcomings in his co-workers.)*

Active Reading: **EVALUATE**

BB Ask students whether they think "Flowers for Algernon" could change readers' attitudes and actions toward people who are mentally challenged. *(Possible responses: Empathizing with Charlie would make people realize that abusing mentally challenged people is wrong.)*

Linking to Social Studies

 CC Some people who are thought to be geniuses are given intensive tutoring in specific subjects. Judit Polgar, who in 1992 at age 16 became the world's top woman chess player, is a good example. She began playing chess with her father when she was four years old; now she goes to school only to take exams so she can concentrate on chess. Judit's father has said, "Genius can be educated into any healthy child."

Then when I got up I saw the look on Joe's face and it gave me a funny feeling in my stomach. "He's a scream," one of the girls said. Everybody was laughing.

Frank said, "I ain't laughed so much since we sent him off for the newspaper that night at Muggsy's and ditched him."

"Look at him. His face is red."

"He's blushing. Charlie is blushing."

"Hey, Ellen, what'd you do to Charlie? I never saw him act like that before."

I didn't know what to do or where to turn. Everyone was looking at me and laughing and I felt naked. I wanted to hide myself. I ran out into the street and I threw up. Then I walked home. It's a funny thing I never knew that Joe and Frank and the others liked to have me around all the time to make fun of me.

Now I know what it means when they say "to pull a Charlie Gordon."

I'm ashamed.

PROGRESS REPORT 11

April 21 Still didn't go into the factory. I told Mrs. Flynn my landlady to call and tell Mr. Donnegan I was sick. Mrs. Flynn looks at me very funny lately like she's scared of me.

I think it's a good thing about finding out how everybody laughs at me. I thought about it a lot. It's because I'm so dumb and I don't even know when I'm doing something dumb. People think it's funny when a dumb person can't do things the same way they can.

Anyway, now I know I'm getting smarter every day. I know punctuation and I can spell good. I like to look up all the hard words in the dictionary and I remember them. I'm reading a lot now, and Miss Kinnian says I read very fast. Sometimes I even understand what I'm reading about, and it stays in my mind. There are times when I can close my eyes and think of a page and it all comes back like a picture.

Besides history, geography, and arithmetic, Miss Kinnian said I should start to learn a few foreign languages. Dr. Strauss gave me some more tapes to play while I sleep. I still don't understand how that conscious and unconscious mind works, but Dr. Strauss says not to worry yet. He asked me to promise that when I start learning college subjects next week I wouldn't read any books on psychology[9]—that is, until he gives me permission.

I feel a lot better today, but I guess I'm still a little angry that all the time people were laughing and making fun of me because I wasn't so smart. When I become intelligent like Dr. Strauss says, with three times my I.Q. of 68, then maybe I'll be like everyone else and people will like me and be friendly.

I'm not sure what an *I.Q.* is. Dr. Nemur said it was something that measured how intelligent you were—like a scale in the drugstore weighs pounds. But Dr. Strauss had a big arguement with him and said an I.Q. didn't weigh intelligence at all. He said an I.Q. showed how much intelligence you could get, like the numbers on the outside of a measuring cup. You still had to fill the cup up with stuff.

Then when I asked Burt, who gives me my intelligence tests and works with Algernon, he said that both of them were wrong (only I had to promise not to tell them he said so). Burt says that the I.Q. measures a lot of different things including some of the things you learned already, and it really isn't any good at all.

So I still don't know what I.Q. is except that mine is going to be over 200 soon. I didn't want to say anything, but I don't see how if they don't know *what* it is, or *where* it is—I don't see how they know *how much* of it you've got.

Dr. Nemur says I have to take a *Rorshach*

---

9. **psychology** (sī-kŏl′ə-jē): the study of mental processes and behavior.

524 UNIT FOUR PART 2: UNLIKELY HEROES

Mini-Lesson The Writer's Style

SENTENCE VARIETY In "Flowers for Algernon," Charlie's progress and deterioration are recorded in his use of language: his spelling and punctuation chart his rise and decline. Keyes also varies sentence length and structure to indicate changes in Charlie's mental processes.

Application Have students compare the highlighted passage on this page with the highlighted passage on page 522 for indications of change in Charlie's mental capacity. Have students note Keyes's use of compound sentences to contrast the difference before and after Charlie learns the punctuation rules.

Reteaching/Reinforcement
- *Writing Handbook*, anthology pp. 836–837
- *Writing Mini-Lessons* transparencies, pp. 40–43

 **The Writer's Craft**

Sentence Variety, pp. 302-303

---

524 THE LANGUAGE OF LITERATURE TEACHER'S EDITION

Test tomorrow. I wonder what *that* is.

April 22 I found out what a *Rorshach* is. It's the test I took before the operation—the one with the inkblots on the pieces of cardboard. The man who gave me the test was the same one.

I was scared to death of those inkblots. I knew he was going to ask me to find the pictures and I knew I wouldn't be able to. I was thinking to myself, if only there was some way of knowing what kind of pictures were hidden there. Maybe there weren't any pictures at all. Maybe it was just a trick to see if I was dumb enough to look for something that wasn't there. Just thinking about that made me sore at him.

"All right, Charlie," he said, "you've seen these cards before, remember?"

"Of course I remember."

The way I said it, he knew I was angry, and he looked surprised. "Yes, of course. Now I want you to look at this one. What might this be? What do you see on this card? People see all sorts of things in these inkblots. Tell me what it might be for you—what it makes you think of."

I was shocked. That wasn't what I had expected him to say at all. "You mean there are no pictures hidden in those inkblots?"

He frowned and took off his glasses. "What?"

"Pictures. Hidden in the inkblots. Last time you told me that everyone could see them and you wanted me to find them too."

He explained to me that the last time he had used almost the exact same words he was using now. I didn't believe it, and I still have the suspicion that he misled me at the time just for the fun of it. Unless—I don't know any more—could I have been *that* feeble-minded?

We went through the cards slowly. One of them looked like a pair of bats tugging at something. Another one looked like two men fencing with swords. I imagined all sorts of things. I guess I got carried away. But I didn't trust him any more, and I kept turning them around and even looking on the back to see if there was anything there I was supposed to catch. While he was making his notes, I peeked out of the corner of my eye to read it. But it was all in code that looked like this:

WF+A DdF-Ad orig. WF–A SF+obj

The test still doesn't make sense to me. It seems to me that anyone could make up lies about things that they didn't really see. How could he know I wasn't making a fool of him by mentioning things that I didn't really imagine? Maybe I'll understand it when Dr. Strauss lets me read up on psychology.

April 25 I figured out a new way to line up the machines in the factory, and Mr. Donnegan says it will save him ten thousand dollars a year in labor and increased production. He gave me a $25 bonus.

I wanted to take Joe Carp and Frank Reilly out to lunch to celebrate, but Joe said he had to buy some things for his wife, and Frank said he was meeting his cousin for lunch. I guess it'll take a little time for them to get used to the changes in me. Everybody seems to be frightened of me. When I went over to Amos Borg and tapped him on the shoulder, he jumped up in the air.

People don't talk to me much any more or kid around the way they used to. It makes the job kind of lonely.

April 27 I got up the nerve today to ask Miss Kinnian to have dinner with me tomorrow night to celebrate my bonus.

So I still don't know what I.Q. is except that mine is going to be over 200 soon.

Literary Concept: IDIOM

GG Have students explain what is meant by the idiom "riding on his coattails." Tell them that the word *opportunist* is an important context clue. (Possible response: to reach a goal or achieve something as a result of one's close association with a more qualified or influential person rather than through one's own efforts)

Active Reading: CLARIFY

HH Remind students that one change in Charlie's behavior is that he analyzes people's actions and motivations more closely. Use the following model to demonstrate a possible thought process:

Think-Aloud Model *It may be that Charlie doesn't understand the figurative idiom "to ride on his coattails" and is trying to understand it literally. Or Charlie might be wondering if Dr. Strauss is really an opportunist who is more concerned with his career than with the experiment that has so radically changed Charlie's life.*

Critical Thinking: ANALYZING

II Ask students to explain why Charlie once thought that Miss Kinnian was "very, very old" even though he actually is older than she is. (Possible response: Before his operation, Charlie was like a child, far behind Miss Kinnian mentally, so she seemed much older. He now is quickly catching up to her, so she no longer seems as old.)

At first she wasn't sure it was right, but I asked Dr. Strauss and he said it was okay. Dr. Strauss and Dr. Nemur don't seem to be getting along so well. They're arguing all the time. This evening when I came in to ask Dr. Strauss about having dinner with Miss Kinnian, I heard them shouting. Dr. Nemur was saying that it was *his* experiment and *his* research, and Dr. Strauss was shouting back that he contributed just as much, because he found me through Miss Kinnian and he performed the operation. Dr. Strauss said that someday thousands of neurosurgeons[10] might be using his technique all over the world.

Dr. Nemur wanted to publish the results of the experiment at the end of this month. Dr. Strauss wanted to wait a while longer to be sure. Dr. Strauss said that Dr. Nemur was more interested in the Chair of Psychology at Princeton[11] than he was in the experiment. Dr. Nemur said that Dr. Strauss was nothing but an <u>opportunist</u> who was trying to ride to glory on *his* coattails.

When I left afterwards, I found myself trembling. I don't know why for sure, but it was as if I'd seen both men clearly for the first time. I remember hearing Burt say that Dr. Nemur had a <u>shrew</u> of a wife who was pushing him all the time to get things published so that he could become famous. Burt said that the dream of her life was to have a big shot husband.

CLARIFY
 What does Charlie mean by this question?
Using a Reading Log

Was Dr. Strauss really trying to ride on his coattails?

April 28 I don't understand why I never noticed how beautiful Miss Kinnian really is. She has brown eyes and feathery brown hair that comes to the top of her neck. She's only thirty-four! I think from the beginning I had the feeling that she was an unreachable genius—and very, very old. Now, every time I see her she grows younger and more lovely.

We had dinner and a long talk. When she said that I was coming along so fast that soon I'd be leaving her behind, I laughed.

"It's true, Charlie. You're already a better reader than I am. You can read a whole page at a glance while I can take in only a few lines at a time. And you remember every single thing you read. I'm lucky if I can recall the main thoughts and the general meaning."

"I don't feel intelligent. There are so many things I don't understand."

She took out a cigarette and I lit it for her. "You've got to be a *little* patient. You're accomplishing in days and weeks what it takes normal people to do in half a lifetime. That's what makes it so amazing. You're like a giant sponge now, soaking things in. Facts, figures, general knowledge. And soon you'll begin to connect them, too. You'll see how the different branches of learning are related. There are many levels, Charlie, like steps on a giant ladder that take you up higher and higher to see more and more of the world around you.

"I can see only a little bit of that, Charlie, and I won't go much higher than I am now, but you'll keep climbing up and up, and see more and more, and each step will open new worlds that you never even knew existed." She frowned. "I hope . . . I just hope to God—"

"What?"

---

10. **neurosurgeons** (nŏŏr´ō-sûr´jənz): doctors who perform operations on the brain and other parts of the nervous system.
11. **Chair of Psychology at Princeton:** the position of head of the Psychology Department at Princeton University.

> WORDS TO KNOW
> **opportunist** (ŏp´ər-tōō´nĭst) *n.* a person who takes advantage of any opportunity to achieve a goal, with little regard for moral principles
> **shrew** (shrōō) *n.* a mean, nagging woman

Max Seabaugh/MAX.

"Never mind, Charles. I just hope I wasn't wrong to advise you to go into this in the first place."

I laughed. "How could that be? It worked, didn't it? Even Algernon is still smart."

We sat there silently for a while, and I knew what she was thinking about as she watched me toying with the chain of my rabbit's foot and my keys. I didn't want to think of that possibility any more than elderly people want to think of death. I *knew* that this was only the beginning. I knew what she meant about levels because I'd seen some of them already. The thought of leaving her behind made me sad.

I'm in love with Miss Kinnian.

PROGRESS REPORT 12

April 30 I've quit my job with Donnegan's Plastic Box Company. Mr. Donnegan insisted that it would be better for all concerned if I left. What did I do to make them hate me so?

The first I knew of it was when Mr. Donnegan showed me the petition. Eight hundred and forty names, everyone connected with the factory, except Fanny Girden. Scanning the list quickly, I saw at once that hers was the only missing name. All the rest demanded that I be fired.

FLOWERS FOR ALGERNON 527

Mini-Lesson: Speaking, Listening, and Viewing

FILM Show students *Bill* (1981), an Emmy-award winning television movie about a mentally challenged man who sets out to live independently after being institutionalized for more than 40 years. Actor Mickey Rooney plays Bill in this movie and its sequel, *Bill: On His Own* (1983). Both films are available from International Video Entertainment.

Application After viewing the film(s), ask students the following questions:

- What are your feelings about the institution? What did it provide and fail to provide for Bill?

- Will Bill face the same problems in the outside world that Charlie does? How will Bill deal with the problems?

- As recently as the early 1970s, mentally challenged individuals were routinely placed in institutions; today, relatively few are. Do the movie and the short story suggest why this policy changed?

Ask students to write a brief film review expressing their reaction to the film and the issues it raises.

Literary Concept: SUSPENSE

JJ Point out that so far the rabbit's foot has brought Charlie good luck. Ask what possible misfortune Charlie now refers to. *(Possible responses: He might leave her intellectually far behind. The operation might reverse itself.)* Ask how this information might add suspense to the story. *(Possible responses: It makes readers wonder what will happen to Charlie, both in terms of his relationship with Miss Kinnian and in regard to the reversal of the effects of the operation.)*

STRATEGIC READING FOR
Less-Proficient Readers

KK Ask students why Charlie loses his job at the plastics company. *(All the workers, except one, petitioned and demanded that he leave, so Charlie was forced to quit or be fired.)* **Noting Relevant Details/Relating Cause and Effect**

- What does his decision to quit reveal about how his co-workers view the effects of the operation? *(They are frightened by the sudden increase in Charlie's intelligence. Once Charlie can no longer be made fun of, his co-workers no longer want him around.)* **Making Judgments**

Set a Purpose Have students read on to discover what Charlie now does with the time he used to spend at the factory.

THE LANGUAGE OF LITERATURE TEACHER'S EDITION 527

Active Reading: CLARIFY

LL Have students clarify why Mr. Donnegan asked Charlie to leave. Encourage them to think about the changes taking place in Charlie's personality and intellectual abilities. *(Possible responses: He wanted to avoid trouble at the factory. The employees put enormous pressure on him to fire Charlie.)*

Literary Concept: ALLUSION

MM Ask students why Charlie's decision to have the operation is compared to Eve's decision to accept the fruit from the tree of knowledge. *(Possible response: Charlie, like Eve, wanted to increase his knowledge; both moved from a state of innocence to one of understanding.)*

Literary Concept: THEME

NN Point out that a major theme of the story is the relationship of intelligence to happiness. Ask students whether they think Charlie has become happier since the operation. *(Possible responses: Charlie is enjoying more of life because his abilities to understand it have increased and he has found a real friend in Miss Kinnian. On the other hand, with this new knowledge he also feels the pain of understanding how others have mistreated him.)*

Joe Carp and Frank Reilly wouldn't talk to me about it. No one else would either, except Fanny. She was one of the few people I'd known who set her mind to something and believed it no matter what the rest of the world proved, said, or did—and Fanny did not believe that I should have been fired. She had been against the petition on principle, and despite the pressure and threats she'd held out.

"Which don't mean to say," she remarked, "that I don't think there's something mighty strange about you, Charlie. Them changes. I don't know. You used to be a good, dependable, ordinary man—not too bright maybe, but honest. Who knows what you done to yourself to get so smart all of a sudden. Like everybody around here's been saying, Charlie, it's not right."

"But how can you say that, Fanny? What's wrong with a man becoming intelligent and wanting to acquire knowledge and understanding of the world around him?"

CLARIFY

Why has Mr. Donnegan asked Charlie to leave his job?
Using a Reading Log

She stared down at her work, and I turned to leave. Without looking at me, she said: "It was evil when Eve listened to the snake and ate from the tree of knowledge. It was evil when she saw that she was naked. If not for that, none of us would ever have to grow old and sick and die.¹²"

Once again now I have the feeling of shame burning inside me. This intelligence has driven a wedge between me and all the people I once knew and loved. Before, they laughed at me and despised me for my ignorance and dullness; now, they hate me for my knowledge and understanding. What in God's name do they want of me?

They've driven me out of the factory. Now I'm more alone than ever before . . .

May 15 Dr. Strauss is very angry at me for not having written any progress reports in two weeks. He's justified because the lab is now paying me a regular salary. I told him I was too busy thinking and reading. When I pointed out that writing was such a slow process that it made me impatient with my poor handwriting, he suggested that I learn to type. It's much easier to write now because I can type nearly seventy-five words a minute. Dr. Strauss continually reminds me of the need to speak and write simply so that people will be able to understand me.

I'll try to review all the things that happened to me during the last two weeks. Algernon and I were presented to the American Psychological Association sitting in convention with the World Psychological Association last Tuesday. We created quite a <u>sensation</u>. Dr. Nemur and Dr. Strauss were proud of us.

I suspect that Dr. Nemur, who is sixty—ten years older than Dr. Strauss—finds it necessary to see <u>tangible</u> results of his work. Undoubtedly the result of pressure by Mrs. Nemur.

Contrary to my earlier impressions of him, I realize that Dr. Nemur is not at all a genius. He has a very good mind, but it struggles under the specter of self-doubt. He wants people to take him for a genius. Therefore, it is important for him to feel that his work is accepted by the world. I believe that Dr. Nemur was afraid of further delay because he worried that someone else might make a discovery along these lines and take the credit from him.

---

12. **It was evil . . . die:** a reference to the biblical story of Adam and Eve (Genesis 2–3). After they ate fruit from the tree of knowledge of good and evil, they were banished from the Garden of Eden, and they and their descendants became subject to illness and death.

WORDS TO KNOW
sensation (sĕn-sā′shən) *n.* a state of great interest and excitement
tangible (tăn′jə-bəl) *adj.* able to be seen or touched; material

Dr. Strauss, on the other hand, might be called a genius, although I feel that his areas of knowledge are too limited. He was educated in the tradition of narrow specialization; the broader aspects of background were neglected far more than necessary—even for a neurosurgeon.

I was shocked to learn that the only ancient languages he could read were Latin, Greek, and Hebrew and that he knows almost nothing of mathematics beyond the elementary levels of the calculus of variations.[13] When he admitted this to me, I found myself almost annoyed. It was as if he'd hidden this part of himself in order to deceive me, pretending—as do many people, I've discovered—to be what he is not. No one I've ever known is what he appears to be on the surface.

Dr. Nemur appears to be uncomfortable around me. Sometimes when I try to talk to him, he just looks at me strangely and turns away. I was angry at first when Dr. Strauss told me I was giving Dr. Nemur an inferiority complex.[14] I thought he was mocking me, and I'm oversensitive at being made fun of.

How was I to know that a highly respected psychoexperimentalist like Nemur was unacquainted with Hindustani[15] and Chinese? It's absurd when you consider the work that is being done in India and China today in the very field of his study.

I asked Dr. Strauss how Nemur could refute Rahajamati's attack on his method and results if Nemur couldn't even read them in the first place. That strange look on Dr. Strauss's face can mean only one of two things. Either he doesn't want to tell Nemur what they're saying in India, or else—and this worries me—Dr. Strauss doesn't know either. I must be careful to speak and write clearly and simply so that people won't laugh.

May 18 I am very disturbed. I saw Miss Kinnian last night for the first time in over a week. I tried to avoid all discussions of intellectual concepts and to keep the conversation on a simple, everyday level, but she just stared at me blankly and asked me what I meant about the mathematical variance equivalent in Dobermann's Fifth Concerto.

Contrary to my earlier impressions of him, I realize that Dr. Nemur is not at all a genius.

When I tried to explain, she stopped me and laughed. I guess I got angry, but I suspect I'm approaching her on the wrong level. No matter what I try to discuss with her, I am unable to communicate. I must review Vrostadt's equations on levels of semantic progression. I find that I don't communicate with people much any more. Thank God for books and music and things I can think about. I am alone in my apartment at Mrs. Flynn's boarding house most of the time and seldom speak to anyone.

---

13. **calculus** (kăl′kyə-ləs) **of variations:** a branch of higher mathematics.
14. **inferiority complex:** a psychological condition involving feelings of personal worthlessness.
15. **Hindustani** (hĭn′dŏŏ-stä′nē): a group of languages used in India.

WORDS TO KNOW
specialization (spĕsh′ə-lĭ-zā′shən) *n.* a focus on a particular activity or area of study
absurd (əb-sûrd′) *adj.* ridiculously unreasonable

529

CUSTOMIZING FOR
Students Acquiring English

8 Mention that *Mazeltov* is a Yiddish word meaning "congratulations" or "good luck." Traditionally it is said at a Jewish wedding after the groom breaks a glass during the ceremony. Ask students to explain why its use here is ironic. *(The glass is broken accidentally by a dishwasher, not deliberately as part of a celebration.)*

Active Reading: CLARIFY

RR Ask students how the responses of the customers to the dishwasher are similar to those of Charlie's co-workers to Charlie. If students are having difficulty, provide them with the following model:

Think-Aloud Model *It is painful for me to read this passage because I can see that the customers are treating the dishwasher the same way that Charlie was once treated. Like Charlie, he responds good-naturedly, unaware that the joke is at his expense. However, the scene is all the more poignant because Charlie can comprehend the injustice of such ill treatment. I don't know if I would have the courage to stand up to a whole roomful of people, but I admire Charlie for doing so.*

Active Reading: CONNECT

SS Ask students to discuss whether they have ever witnessed people making fun of a mentally challenged person. Ask how they responded to the situation. Then ask if reading this story has altered the way they would act in the future.

May 20 I would not have noticed the new dishwasher, a boy of about sixteen, at the corner diner where I take my evening meals if not for the incident of the broken dishes. They crashed to the floor, shattering and sending bits of white china under the tables. The boy stood there, dazed and frightened, holding the empty tray in his hand. The whistles and catcalls from the customers (the cries of "Hey, there go the profits! . . ." "*Mazeltov!* . . ." and "Well, *he* didn't work here very long. . . ." which invariably seem to follow the breaking of glass or dishware in a public restaurant) all seemed to confuse him.

When the owner came to see what the excitement was about, the boy cowered as if he expected to be struck and threw up his arms as if to ward off the blow.

"All right! All right, you dope," shouted the owner, "don't just stand there! Get the broom and sweep that mess up. A broom . . . a broom, you idiot! It's in the kitchen. Sweep up all the pieces."

The boy saw that he was not going to be punished. His frightened expression disappeared, and he smiled and hummed as he came back with the broom to sweep the floor. A few of the rowdier customers kept up the remarks, amusing themselves at his expense.

"Here, sonny, over here there's a nice piece behind you. . . ."

"C'mon, do it again. . . ."

"He's not so dumb. It's easier to break 'em than to wash 'em. . . ."

As his vacant eyes moved across the crowd of amused onlookers, he slowly mirrored their smiles and finally broke into an uncertain grin at the joke which he obviously did not understand.

I felt sick inside as I looked at his dull, <u>vacuous</u> smile, the wide, bright eyes of a child, uncertain but eager to please. They were laughing at him because he was mentally retarded.

And I had been laughing at him too.

Suddenly, I was furious at myself and all those who were smirking at him. I jumped up and shouted, "Shut up! Leave him alone! It's not his fault he can't understand! He can't help what he is! But for God's sake . . . he's still a human being!"

The room grew silent. I cursed myself for losing control and creating a scene. I tried not to look at the boy as I paid my check and walked out without touching my food. I felt ashamed for both of us.

> I cursed myself for losing control and creating a scene.

How strange it is that people of honest feelings and sensibility, who would not take advantage of a man born without arms or legs or eyes—how such people think nothing of abusing a man born with low intelligence. It infuriated me to think that not too long ago, I, like this boy, had foolishly played the clown.

And I had almost forgotten.

I'd hidden the picture of the old Charlie Gordon from myself because now that I was intelligent, it was something that had to be pushed out of my mind. But today in looking at that boy, for the first time I saw what I had been. *I was just like him!*

Only a short time ago, I learned that people laughed at me. Now I can see that unknowingly I joined with them in laughing at myself. That hurts most of all.

I have often reread my progress reports and seen the illiteracy, the childish <u>naïveté</u>, the

---

WORDS TO KNOW
vacuous (văk'yōō-əs) *adj.* showing a lack of intelligence or thought
naïveté (nä'ēv-tā') *n.* a lack of sophistication; simplicity

mind of low intelligence peering from a dark room, through the keyhole, at the dazzling light outside. I see that even in my dullness I knew that I was inferior and that other people had something I lacked—something denied me. In my mental blindness, I thought that it was somehow connected with the ability to read and write, and I was sure that if I could get those skills I would automatically have intelligence too.

Even a feeble-minded man wants to be like other men.

A child may not know how to feed itself, or what to eat, yet it knows of hunger.

This, then, is what I was like. I never knew. Even with my gift of intellectual awareness, I never really knew.

This day was good for me. Seeing the past more clearly, I have decided to use my knowledge and skills to work in the field of increasing human intelligence levels. Who is better equipped for this work? Who else has lived in both worlds? These are my people. Let me use my gift to do something for them.

Tomorrow, I will discuss with Dr. Strauss the manner in which I can work in this area. I may be able to help him work out the problems of widespread use of the technique which was used on me. I have several good ideas of my own.

There is so much that might be done with this technique. If I could be made into a genius, what about thousands of others like myself? What fantastic levels might be achieved by using this technique on normal people? on *geniuses*?

There are so many doors to open. I am impatient to begin.

PROGRESS REPORT 13

May 23 It happened today. Algernon bit me. I visited the lab to see him, as I do occasionally, and when I took him out of his cage, he snapped at my hand. I put him back and watched him for a while. He was unusually disturbed and vicious.

May 24 Burt, who is in charge of the experimental animals, tells me that Algernon is changing. He is less cooperative; he refuses to run the maze any more; general motivation has decreased. And he hasn't been eating. Everyone is upset about what this may mean.

May 25 They've been feeding Algernon, who now refuses to work the shifting-lock problem. Everyone identifies me with Algernon. In a way we're both the first of our kind. They're all pretending that Algernon's behavior is not necessarily significant for me. But it's hard to hide the fact that some of the other animals who were used in this experiment are showing strange behavior.

Dr. Strauss and Dr. Nemur have asked me not to come to the lab any more. I know what they're thinking, but I can't accept it. I am going ahead with my plans to carry their research forward. With all due respect to both of these fine scientists, I am well aware of their limitations. If there is an answer, I'll have to find it out for myself. Suddenly, time has become very important to me.

May 29 I have been given a lab of my own and permission to go ahead with the research. I'm onto something. Working day and night. I've had a cot moved into the lab. Most of my writing time is spent on the notes which I keep in a separate folder, but from time to time I feel it necessary to put down my moods and my thoughts out of sheer habit.

I find the calculus of intelligence to be a fascinating study. Here is the place for the application of all the knowledge I have acquired. In a sense it's the problem I've been concerned with all my life.

May 31 Dr. Strauss thinks I'm working too hard. Dr. Nemur says I'm trying to cram a lifetime of research and thought into a few

---

Mini-Lesson: Speaking, Listening, and Viewing

SPEECHES Explain to students that one purpose of making a speech is to persuade the audience to believe or do something the speaker wishes. Persuasive speakers use their words, voice, and body language to make a strong impression on their audience.

Application Explain that many mentally challenged people lead productive, independent lives. Some people do not believe this, and they resist arguments that are in favor of programs that allow mentally challenged people to live and work in their communities. Divide the class into groups of three or four and ask each group to write a brief speech to persuade doubters to allow a group home for the mentally challenged to be established in their community. Students should use what they have learned from reading the selection and any personal experience they may have with this issue. Each group should elect one person to present their speech to the class. After all the speeches have been given, the class can discuss which arguments were the most persuasive and why.

Active Reading: CLARIFY

Ask students what conclusion Charlie has reached from his research. *(The increase of his intelligence is not permanent.)* Have students identify the parts of the letter that support this conclusion. *(Possible responses: The title of the report links Charlie and Algernon, and readers have just discovered that Algernon has regressed; Charlie's hope of finding an error; his use of the words "failure" and "disproving"; his saying that he is sorry; his mention of "the ashes of the work.")*

Critical Thinking: HYPOTHESIZING

Have students use their own words to form a hypothesis about what will happen to Charlie both physically and mentally. *(Possible responses: Charlie's IQ will start decreasing. He'll become more and more uncoordinated. He'll begin to forget the things he has learned.)*

---

weeks. I know I should rest, but I'm driven on by something inside that won't let me stop. I've got to find the reason for the sharp <u>regression</u> in Algernon. I've got to know *if* and *when* it will happen to me.

June 4
LETTER TO DR. STRAUSS *(copy)*
Dear Dr. Strauss:

Under separate cover I am sending you a copy of my report entitled "The Algernon-Gordon Effect: A Study of Structure and Function of Increased Intelligence," which I would like to have you read and have published.

As you see, my experiments are completed. I have included in my report all of my formulae, as well as mathematical analysis in the appendix. Of course, these should be verified.

Because of its importance to both you and Dr. Nemur (and need I say to myself, too?) I have checked and rechecked my results a dozen times in the hope of finding an error. I am sorry to say the results must stand. Yet for the sake of science, I am grateful for the little bit that I here add to the knowledge of the function of the human mind and of the laws governing the artificial increase of human intelligence.

I recall your once saying to me that an experimental *failure* or the *disproving* of a theory was as important to the advancement of learning as a success would be. I know now that this is true. I am sorry, however, that my own contribution to the field must rest upon the ashes of the work of two men I regard so highly.

Yours truly,
Charles Gordon
encl.: rept.

June 5 I must not become emotional. The facts and the results of my experiments are

Copyright © Vivienne Flesher.

clear, and the more sensational aspects of my own rapid climb cannot obscure the fact that the tripling of intelligence by the surgical technique developed by Drs. Strauss and Nemur must be viewed as having little or no practical applicability (at the present time) to the increase of human intelligence.

As I review the records and data on Algernon, I see that although he is still in his physical infancy, he has regressed mentally. Motor activity[16] is <u>impaired</u>; there is a general reduction of glandular activity; there is an accelerated loss of coordination.

---

16. **motor activity:** movement produced by use of the muscles.

WORDS TO KNOW
regression (rĭ-grĕsh′ən) *n.* a return to a less developed condition
impair (ĭm-pâr′) *v.* to weaken; damage

532

Mini-Lesson ✒ The Writer's Style

FORMAL ENGLISH Explain to students that formal English is marked by a serious tone and by longer and more complex sentences; it often uses specialized vocabulary. Point out to students that in the passages highlighted on pages 532 and 533, Keyes makes almost exclusive use of formal English.

Application To assist students in their understanding of the uses of formal English in this selection, present the following questions for discussion:
- *How do the tone and sentence structure of these passages differ from earlier progress reports?*
- *Does the medical and scientific jargon affect your willingness to believe the unrealistic elements of the story? Why or why not?*

Ask students to describe situations in which the use of formal English is expected and situations in which informal English would be acceptable.

Reteaching/Reinforcement
- *Writing Mini-Lessons* transparencies, p. 36

📁 **The Writer's Craft**
Formal and Informal English, p. 315

---

532 THE LANGUAGE OF LITERATURE TEACHER'S EDITION

There are also strong indications of progressive amnesia.[17]

As will be seen by my report, these and other physical and mental deterioration syndromes can be predicted with statistically significant results by the application of my formula.

The surgical stimulus to which we were both subjected has resulted in an intensification and acceleration of all mental processes. The unforeseen development, which I have taken the liberty of calling the Algernon-Gordon effect, is the logical extension of the entire intelligence speedup. The hypothesis here proven may be described simply in the following terms: Artificially increased intelligence deteriorates at a rate of time directly proportional to the quantity of the increase.

I feel that this, in itself, is an important discovery.

As long as I am able to write, I will continue to record my thoughts in these progress reports. It is one of my few pleasures. However, by all indications, my own mental deterioration will be very rapid.

I have already begun to notice signs of emotional instability and forgetfulness, the first symptoms of the burnout.

June 10 Deterioration progressing. I have become absent-minded. Algernon died two days ago. Dissection shows my predictions were right. His brain had decreased in weight, and there was a general smoothing out of cerebral convolutions as well as a deepening and broadening of brain fissures.[18]

I guess the same thing is or will soon be happening to me. Now that it's definite, I don't want it to happen.

I put Algernon's body in a cheese box and buried him in the back yard. I cried.

June 15 Dr. Strauss came to see me again. I wouldn't open the door, and I told him to go away. I want to be left to myself. I have become touchy and irritable. I feel the darkness closing in. It's hard to throw off thoughts of suicide. I keep telling myself how important this introspective journal will be.

It's a strange sensation to pick up a book that you've read and enjoyed just a few months ago and discover that you don't remember it. I remembered how great I thought John Milton was, but when I picked up *Paradise Lost,* I couldn't understand it at all. I got so angry I threw the book across the room.

I've got to try to hold on to some of it. Some of the things I've learned. Oh, God, please don't take it all away.

June 19 Sometimes, at night, I go out for a walk. Last night I couldn't remember where I lived. A policeman took me home. I have the strange feeling that this has all happened to me before—a long time ago. I keep telling myself I'm the only person in the world who can describe what's happening to me.

June 21 Why can't I remember? I've got to fight. I lie in bed for days, and I don't know

---

17. **progressive amnesia** (ăm-nē′zhə): a steadily worsening loss of memory.
18. **cerebral convolutions** (sĕr′ə-brəl kŏn′və-lōō′shənz) . . . **brain fissures** (fĭsh′ərz): features of the brain. Cerebral convolutions are the ridges or folds on the brain's surface; fissures are grooves that divide the brain into lobes, or sections.

WORDS TO KNOW

syndrome (sĭn′drōm) *n.* a group of symptoms that characterizes a disease or psychological disorder
statistically (stə-tĭs′tĭ-klē) *adv.* in terms of the principles used to analyze numerical data
hypothesis (hī-pŏth′ĭ-sĭs) *n.* a theory used as a basis for research
proportional (prə-pôr′shə-nəl) *adj.* having a constant relation in degree or number
introspective (ĭn′trə-spĕk′tĭv) *adj.* examining one's own thoughts, feelings, and sensations

Critical Thinking:
SYNTHESIZING

C Have students discuss why Charlie's experience of senility, a state of memory loss and lack of coordination that primarily afflicts elderly people, is described as "second childhood." *(Possible responses: He will be dependent on people again just as a child needs special care. He is being "reborn" to his previous mental state, one that is similar to a child's mental development.)*

Copyright © Vivienne Flesher.

C who or where I am. Then it all comes back to me in a flash. Fugues[19] of amnesia. Symptoms of senility—second childhood. I can watch them coming on. It's so cruelly logical. I learned so much and so fast. Now my mind is deteriorating rapidly. I won't let it happen. I'll fight it. I can't help thinking of the boy in the restaurant, the blank expression, the silly smile, the people laughing at him. No—please—not that again . . .

June 22 I'm forgetting things that I learned recently. It seems to be following the classic

---
19. **fugues** (fyo͞ogz): psychological states in which people seem to be acting consciously, although later they have no memory of the activity.

534   UNIT FOUR   PART 2: UNLIKELY HEROES

Mini-Lesson Grammar

RUN-ON SENTENCES   Remind students that a run-on sentence incorrectly combines two or more sentences. Sometimes it is possible to join two complete thoughts with a conjunction, thus avoiding a run-on sentence. Other times, a run-on sentence needs to be broken down into separate sentences.

Application   As Charlie deteriorates, his use of language deteriorates as well. He stops using compound or complex sentences and instead writes run-ons. Have students look at the example highlighted on page 535. Ask students what the sudden appearance of a run-on sentence might suggest about the rate of Charlie's deterioration. Then ask students to rewrite the highlighted sentence on page 536 to practice correcting run-on sentences.

Reteaching/Reinforcement
- Grammar Handbook, anthology pp. 861–862
- *Grammar Mini-Lessons* copymasters p. 2, transparencies p. 2

 **The Writer's Craft**

Run-on Sentences, pp. 406, 557

534   THE LANGUAGE OF LITERATURE   TEACHER'S EDITION

pattern—the last things learned are the first things forgotten. Or is that the pattern? I'd better look it up again . . .

I reread my paper on the Algernon-Gordon effect, and I get the strange feeling that it was written by someone else. There are parts I don't even understand.

Motor activity impaired. I keep tripping over things, and it becomes increasingly difficult to type.

June 23 I've given up using the typewriter completely. My coordination is bad. I feel that I'm moving slower and slower. Had a terrible shock today. I picked up a copy of an article I used in my research, Krueger's "Über psychische Ganzheit," to see if it would help me understand what I had done. First I thought there was something wrong with my eyes. Then I realized I could no longer read German. I tested myself in other languages. All gone.

June 30 A week since I dared to write again. It's slipping away like sand through my fingers. Most of the books I have are too hard for me now. I get angry with them because I know that I read and understood them just a few weeks ago.

I keep telling myself I must keep writing these reports so that somebody will know what is happening to me. But it gets harder to form the words and remember spellings. I have to look up even simple words in the dictionary now, and it makes me impatient with myself.

Dr. Strauss comes around almost every day, but I told him I wouldn't see or speak to anybody. He feels guilty. They all do. But I don't blame anyone. I knew what might happen. But how it hurts.

July 7 I don't know where the week went. Todays Sunday I know because I can see through my window people going to church. I think I stayed in bed all week but I remember Mrs. Flynn bringing food to me a few times. I keep saying over and over Ive got to do something but then I forget or maybe its just easier not to do what I say Im going to do.

I think of my mother and father a lot these days. I found a picture of them with me taken at a beach. My father has a big ball under his arm and my mother is holding me by the hand. I dont remember them the way they are in the picture. All I remember is my father drunk most of the time and arguing with mom about money.

He never shaved much and he used to scratch my face when he hugged me. My mother said he died but Cousin Miltie said he heard his mom and dad say that my father ran away with another woman. When I asked my mother she slapped my face and said my father was dead. I dont think I ever found out which was true but I dont care much. (He said he was going to take me to see cows on a farm once but he never did. He never kept his promises . . .)

July 10 My landlady Mrs. Flynn is very worried about me. She says the way I lay around all day and dont do anything I remind her of her son before she threw him out of the house. She said she doesnt like loafers. If Im sick its one thing, but if Im a loafer thats another thing and she wont have it. I told her I think Im sick.

I try to read a little bit every day, mostly stories, but sometimes I have to read the same thing over and over again because I dont know what it means. And its hard to write. I know I should look up all the words in the dictionary but its so hard and Im so tired all the time.

Then I got the idea that I would only use the easy words instead of the long hard ones. That saves time. I put flowers on Algernons grave about once a week. Mrs Flynn thinks Im crazy to put flowers on a mouses grave but I told her that Algernon was special.

July 14 Its sunday again. I dont have

Literary Concept:
CHARACTERIZATION

H Invite students to describe the impressions they get of Charlie from the details in this entry. *(Possible responses: Charlie is totally isolated and lonely. He is so forgetful and careless he may no longer be capable of caring for himself. Charlie seems worse off now than at the beginning of the story.)*

Critical Thinking:
MAKING JUDGMENTS

I Have students debate the doctor's response to Charlie's condition. Ask what his treatment of Charlie reveals about his knowledge of mentally challenged individuals. *(Possible responses: His treatment of Charlie shows his lack of knowledge about the mentally challenged. He talks down to Charlie as if Charlie were an infant. He reveals the prejudice and lack of respect for mentally challenged people that many people have.)*

CUSTOMIZING FOR
Students Acquiring English

9 Some students may not know that the nonverbal communication of a wink in this case means that the doctor is trying to share a joke with Mrs. Flynn.

Active Reading: EVALUATE

J Ask students why Joe Carp defends Charlie instead of picking on him as he once did. *(Possible responses: Joe may feel guilty for the way he has treated Charlie. He may feel sorry for all that Charlie has had to endure.)* Ask students if they think that Joe's actions really mean that he's Charlie's friend. Supply students with the following model to assist in discussion:

Think-Aloud Model *I'm not sure if Joe's defense of Charlie makes him a friend. Based on the way Joe has treated Charlie in the past, it is surprising that he would stand up for Charlie at all. I also remember that Joe was one of the people who signed the petition for Charlie's dismissal. I am not sure if Joe is motivated by a sense of guilt or by his friendship with Charlie.*

---

anything to do to keep me busy now because my television set is broke and I dont have any money to get it fixed. (I think I lost this months check from the lab. I dont remember)

I get awful headaches and asperin doesnt help me much. Mrs Flynn knows Im really sick and she feels very sorry for me. Shes a wonderful woman whenever someone is sick.

July 22 Mrs Flynn called a strange doctor to see me. She was afraid I was going to die. I told the doctor I wasnt too sick and that I only forget sometimes. He asked me did I have any friends or relatives and I said no I dont have any. I told him I had a friend called Algernon once but he was a mouse and we used to run races together. He looked at me kind of funny like he thought I was crazy.

He smiled when I told him I used to be a genius. He talked to me like I was a baby and he winked at Mrs Flynn. I got mad and chased him out because he was making fun of me the way they all used to.

July 24 I have no more money and Mrs Flynn says I got to go to work somewhere and pay the rent because I havent paid for over two months. I dont know any work but the job I used to have at Donnegans Plastic Box Company. I dont want to go back there because they all knew me when I was smart and maybe they'll laugh at me. But I dont know what else to do to get money.

July 25 I was looking at some of my old progress reports and its very funny but I cant read what I wrote. I can make out some of the words but they dont make sense.

Miss Kinnian came to the door but I said go away I dont want to see you. She cried and I cried too but I wouldnt let her in because I didnt want her to laugh at me. I told her I didn't like her any more. I told her I didnt want to be smart any more. Thats not true. I still love her and I still want to be smart but I had to say that so shed go away. She gave Mrs. Flynn money to pay the rent. I dont want that. I got to get a job.

Please . . . please let me not forget how to read and write . . .

July 27 Mr. Donnegan was very nice when I came back and asked him for my old job of janitor. First he was very suspicious but I told him what happened to me then he looked very sad and put his hand on my shoulder and said Charlie Gordon you got guts.

Everybody looked at me when I came downstairs and started working in the toilet sweeping it out like I used to. I told myself Charlie if they make fun of you dont get sore because you remember their not so smart as you once thot they were. And besides they were once your friends and if they laughed at you that doesnt mean anything because they liked you too.

One of the new men who came to work there after I went away made a nasty crack he said hey Charlie I hear your a very smart fella a real quiz kid. Say something intelligent. I felt bad but Joe Carp came over and grabbed him by the shirt and said leave him alone you lousy cracker or Ill break your neck. I didnt expect Joe to take my part so I guess hes really my friend.

Later Frank Reilly came over and said Charlie if anybody bothers you or trys to take advantage you call me or Joe and we will set em straight. I said thanks Frank and I got choked up so I had to turn around and go into the supply room so he wouldnt see me cry. Its good to have friends.

July 28 I did a dumb thing today I forgot I wasnt in Miss Kinnians class at the adult

Copyright © Alan Cober/Stock Illustration Source.

536   UNIT FOUR   PART 2: UNLIKELY HEROES

Mini-Lesson **Study Skills**

RESEARCHING INFORMATION OUTSIDE OF LIBRARIES Remind students that relying only on libraries for research overlooks many important resources of additional, and perhaps more current, information. Point out to students that they can write to or visit government agencies, public service organizations, and local community centers to obtain up-to-the-minute information.

Application Encourage students to contact a professional, governmental, or local organization that works with mentally challenged people. Students may wish to ask how the organization assists the mentally challenged, or they may want to find out if the organization needs volunteers. Often the names, addresses, and telephone numbers of these organizations are provided in the front part of the telephone book, which lists government agencies. Students may also wish to consult the *Encyclopedia of Associations,* which lists thousands of organizations by subject area.

STRATEGIC READING FOR
Less-Proficient Readers

K Have students explain why Charlie decides to move away. (*Charlie decides to leave New York because he still remembers part of what it was like after his operation. At the same time, he does not want people to feel sorry for him because of his present condition.*)
Summarizing/Making Inferences

CUSTOMIZING FOR
Gifted and Talented Students

Have students debate the use of standardized tests to measure a student's progress in school or acceptance to college. Ask if they feel these tests are a fair measure of a person's capabilities and potential to succeed in life.

Active Reading: CLARIFY

L Remind students of Charlie's changing feelings for the mouse and of Charlie's last request regarding Algernon. (*Possible response: Because both Charlie and Algernon have gone through the same experience, Charlie learns to care for Algernon. He sees the two of them as linked in a special way because of the failed operation.*)

COMPREHENSION CHECK

1. What operation does Charlie undergo? (*brain surgery to increase his IQ*)
2. Who is Algernon? (*a white mouse who had the same operation as Charlie*)
3. What happens to Algernon? (*He gains in intelligence, then regresses mentally, loses his coordination, and eventually dies.*)
4. What happens to Charlie? (*His intelligence grows and then returns to its original level, and he decides to leave New York.*)

---

center any more like I use to be. I went in and sat down in my old seat in the back of the room and she looked at me funny and she said Charles. I dint remember she ever called me that before only Charlie so I said hello Miss Kinnian Im redy for my lesin today only I lost my reader that we was using. She startid to cry and run out of the room and everybody looked at me and I saw they wasnt the same pepul who use to be in my class.

Then all of a suddin I rememberd some things about the operashun and me getting smart and I said holy smoke I reely pulled a Charlie Gordon that time. I went away before she come back to the room.

Thats why Im going away from New York for good. I dont want to do nothing like that agen. I dont want Miss Kinnian to feel sorry for me. Evry body feels sorry at the factery and I dont want that eather so Im going someplace where nobody knows that Charlie Gordon was once a genus and now he cant even reed a book or rite good.

Im taking a cuple of books along and even if I cant reed them Ill practise hard and maybe I wont forget every thing I lerned. If I try reel hard maybe Ill be a littel bit smarter then I was before the operashun. I got my rabits foot and my luky penny and maybe they will help me.

If you ever reed this Miss Kinnian dont be sorry for me Im glad I got a second chanse to be smart becaus I lerned a lot of things that I never even new were in this world and Im grateful that I saw it all for a littel bit. I dont know why Im dumb agen or what I did wrong maybe its becaus I dint try hard enuff. But if I try and practis very hard maybe Ill get a littl smarter and know what all the words are. I remember a littel bit how nice I had a feeling with the blue book that has the torn cover when I red it. Thats why Im gonna keep trying to get smart so I can have that feeling agen. Its a good feeling to know things and be smart. I wish I had it rite now if I did I woud sit down and reed all the time. Anyway I bet Im the first dumb person in the world who ever found out somthing importent for sience. I remember I did somthing but I dont remember what. So I gess its like I did it for all the dumb pepul like me.

Goodbye Miss Kinnian and Dr. Strauss and evreybody. And P.S. please tell Dr Nemur not to be such a grouch when pepul laff at him and he woud have more frends. Its easy to make frends if you let pepul laff at you. Im going to have lots of frends where I go.

P.P.S. Please if you get a chanse put some flowers on Algernons grave in the bak yard. . . . ❖

P.P.S. Please if you get a chanse put some flowers on Algernons grave in the bak yard. . . .

CLARIFY
Why is Algernon special to Charlie?
Using a Reading Log

538 UNIT FOUR PART 2: UNLIKELY HEROES

Assessment ✓ Option

INFORMAL ASSESSMENT Have students work in small groups to role-play characters from the selection. Students should decide how the following characters would respond to reading Charlie's entries:

- Miss Kinnian
- Joe Carp
- Mrs. Flynn
- Dr. Strauss
- Dr. Nemur
- Burt

In their presentations, students should assume the personality of each of the characters and speak only from that character's point of view. Have students review the specific entries that mention their characters before role-playing.

Rubric

3 Full Accomplishment The group captures the personality and perspective of the characters, developing their probable reactions to the entries.

2 Substantial Accomplishment The group speaks from the characters' perspectives, but their interpretations of the characters' reactions are unlikely.

1 Little or Partial Accomplishment Students give their own opinions and do not consider the characters' point of view.

RESPONDING OPTIONS

FROM PERSONAL RESPONSE TO CRITICAL ANALYSIS

REFLECT
1. What is your reaction to Charlie's experiences? Write your thoughts in your notebook.

RETHINK
2. Do you think the doctors should have performed the operation on Charlie? Why or why not?

Thematic Link
3. In your opinion, is Charlie a hero? Give reasons for your answer.

4. Refer to the chart you made for the Reading Connection on page 513, and decide which of the changes that Charlie goes through are most difficult for him. Explain your choices.

5. If Charlie were asked to participate in another experiment to increase his intelligence, do you think he would accept? Give reasons for your opinion.
   Consider
Close Textual Reading
   - how he has felt about becoming intelligent
   - whether he is happier before or after becoming a genius
   - what, if anything, he has gained by the end of the story

6. What do you think might become of Charlie after he leaves New York?

RELATE
7. A patient gives "informed consent" to a medical procedure if his or her agreement is based on a thorough understanding of the risks and benefits involved. Do you think that when a patient cannot completely understand a procedure, doctors should make the decision for the patient? Weigh the possible benefits to the patient or to medical science against the rights of the patient.

Multimodal Learning

ANOTHER PATHWAY

Cooperative Learning

Hold a debate about whether the operation should have been performed on Charlie. To review the events of the story and begin preparing for the debate, you might look over the chart you made for the Reading Connection on page 513.

QUICKWRITES

1. In his progress report of April 28, Charlie writes that he is in love with Miss Kinnian. If Miss Kinnian were also writing progress reports, what might she write about Charlie? Write her **entry** for that day.

2. Charlie says that he is leaving for a place where people won't feel sorry for him. He needs a job. Assume the identity of Mr. Donnegan, Charlie's boss, and write a **letter of recommendation** for Charlie.

3. Rewrite Charlie's **progress report** of "March 6," using correct spelling, punctuation, and grammar. When you have finished, compare your work with that of other students.

📁 **PORTFOLIO** Save your writing. You may want to use it later as a springboard to a piece for your portfolio.

QuickWrites

1. Point out to students that their entries should reflect Miss Kinnian's relationship as a teacher with Charlie.
2. Suggest that students note the way Mr. Donnegan's relationship with Charlie changes when Charlie returns to work.
3. Students' interpretations of the nonstandard language will probably lead to different rewrites.

The Writer's Craft

Paragraphs, pp. 244-251
Letter, p. 684
Correcting Sentence Errors, pp. 296-301

From Personal Response to Critical Analysis

1. Responses will vary.
2. Possible responses: No operation comes with a guarantee, and the doctors believed there was a strong chance of success. The doctors at least should have waited until they saw the results of the experiment with Algernon before involving Charlie in such life-altering research.
3. Possible responses: Charlie is a hero because of his unflagging determination to succeed at what he sets out to do. Charlie shouldn't be considered the hero; the doctors who helped him, even if it was temporary, could qualify as heroes.
4. Most students will identify the period of Charlie's decline as the most difficult stage because of his self-awareness.
5. Possible responses: Yes, because he does not remember much about the previous experiment and still has the desire to learn. No, because he realizes that he was even more isolated from people when his intelligence increased.
6. Possible responses: He will have to find another job and may have to face other people's ridicule again. He will soon die like Algernon.
7. Responses will vary.

Another Pathway

Cooperative Learning In preparation for the debate, poll students as to whether they think the operation should have been performed. If possible, have students work in smaller groups accordingly. When the groups are preparing for the debate, be sure group members not only articulate their own position but also attempt to anticipate the arguments of the opposing group. Instruct both sides to use specific details from the story to support their position.

Rubric

3 Full Accomplishment Student team develops an insightful, well-balanced defense of its position, complete with detailed support.

2 Substantial Accomplishment Student team presents a defense of its position but does not supplement it with relevant details.

1 Little or Partial Accomplishment Student team fails to present a persuasive argument.

Across the Curriculum

Science *The Human Brain* Students' research should reveal that the cerebrum is the part of the brain responsible for thinking processes, memory, and personality. Scientists have "mapped" the cerebrum. If possible, show students such a map.

Science *Medical Abstracts* Students may wish to label each section of their abstract with the headers "description," "hypothesis," "procedure," and "result" to organize the details of the experiment performed on Charlie.

ADDITIONAL SUGGESTION

Social Studies *Cooperative Learning Laboratory Animals* Have students find out more about the use of laboratory animals in scientific research. Divide the class into small groups and have each group find out the different types of animals that are used in scientific research, what sorts of experiments are conducted on them, and the goals of the research. Have students explain the controversy surrounding such research by presenting both sides of the issue. Then have the groups share their results with the class.

Art Connection

Possible response: This image suggests that the brain is a mystery, a puzzle that takes time to understand and put together. As the puzzle is completed, the person becomes whole, and as pieces are taken away, the person becomes incomplete.

LITERARY CONCEPTS

As you filled in the chart for the Reading Connection, you made inferences about dramatic changes in Charlie's personality and intelligence. An author can show **character development** through dialogue, through description, and in other ways. One way in which Daniel Keyes shows change in his main character is through the growth and decline of Charlie's ability to spell correctly. In what other ways does the author show Charlie changing?

Multimodal Learning

ALTERNATIVE ACTIVITIES

1. **Cooperative Learning** With some classmates, watch a videotape of *Charly,* the film based on Keyes's novelization of "Flowers for Algernon." Then get together for a **discussion** in which you compare the film with the short story. Which do you like better? Does the film portray Charlie as you imagine him? What would you do differently if you were filming the story?
2. Research a topic related to this story, such as psychological testing or "smart drugs." Share your findings with the class in an **oral report.**
3. Investigate the controversy surrounding the question of animal experimentation. Find out about the arguments on both sides of the issue, and write a balanced **research paper** on the topic.

540 UNIT FOUR PART 2: UNLIKELY HEROES

ACROSS THE CURRICULUM

Science After the operation, Charlie's ability to reason and solve problems develops dramatically. Find out what part of the brain is responsible for this ability and what other thinking functions it might control. Make a drawing of the brain and label that region.

Science Find an abstract—a summary, usually only one or two paragraphs long, of scientific research—in a scientific journal. Using it as a model, write a medical abstract describing the experiment in which Charlie was involved, including the hypothesis, the procedure, and the results.

ART CONNECTION

Look at the painting reproduced on page 537. What does this image mean to you? Take some time to examine the details of the work. How does it relate to the main character of the story?

Copyright © Alan Cober/Stock Illustration Source.

Literary Concepts

Divide the class into groups of three or four. Encourage them to use both their charts from the Reading Connection and their word webs from the Literary Concepts Mini-Lesson on page 517. Have group members compare their charts and webs and select a way they feel is especially effective in showing character changes, such as Charlie's sudden questioning of the doctor's abilities. Have groups present their choices to the class and explain why they made the choices they did.

Alternative Activities

1. **Cooperative Learning** Have students work in groups of four to six students. Suggest that each group record their discussion.
2. Suggest that students check local social work agencies as a source of information on psychological testing. Health food stores and nutritionists may have current information on "smart drugs" available to consumers.
3. Have students use the *Reader's Guide to Periodical Literature* to research animal experimentation. Give them certain key words to check, such as PETA, laboratory, animals, experimentation, and so forth.

WORDS TO KNOW

On a separate sheet of paper, answer the following questions.

1. If a person calls you **vacuous,** are you being complimented or insulted? Why?
2. Is water **tangible** or not? Explain.
3. Who is probably more **introspective**—a poet or a doctor? Explain.
4. If eyeglasses **impair** your vision, are they good or bad for you?
5. Does an **opportunist** take chances? Why or why not?
6. Besides medicine, what other fields have areas of **specialization?**
7. Is a **hypothesis** true, false, or unproved?
8. Would a **shrew** be popular or unpopular? Why?
9. Who would be more likely to show **naïveté**—a child or an adult?
10. If a person proves an argument **statistically,** what is she using?
11. **Regression** suggests movement in what direction?
12. Which scientific discovery would cause a greater **sensation**—a cure for a foot disease or a cure for AIDS? Explain.
13. If a mouse's growth is directly **proportional** to the amount it eats, how will eating more affect its growth?
14. If someone thought that an idea of yours was **absurd,** would you be happy or sad? Explain.
15. What kind of professional would likely treat a **syndrome?**

DANIEL KEYES

1927–

After Daniel Keyes won a Hugo Award for "Flowers for Algernon" at the World Science Fiction Convention in 1959, he expanded the story into a novel. For the novel, he won a Nebula Award from the Science Fiction Writers of America in 1966. Even *Charly,* the feature film based on the novel, was a winner: Cliff Robertson was presented with an Academy Award in 1968 for his portrayal of Charlie in the movie. "Flowers for Algernon" has also been the basis for TV and stage plays (including a musical) produced in the United States, Canada, Britain, France, Poland, Australia, and Japan.

Given the subject matter of Keyes's famous story, it is not surprising that he majored in psychology at Brooklyn College. He says he is "fascinated by the complexities of the human mind." One of his novels—*The Minds of Billy Milligan,* based on the story of a real person—came about in an unusual way. Billy Milligan, who had 24 personalities, chose Keyes to write the book because several of his "selves" had read "Flowers for Algernon" and agreed that Keyes was the perfect author to tell their tale.

Born in Brooklyn, New York, Keyes joined the U.S. Maritime Service as a teenager, working as a ship's purser on oil tankers. After finishing college, he had jobs in publishing and in fashion photography, then became a teacher at the high school from which he had graduated. Since 1966, he has taught creative writing and American literature at Ohio University. Currently on extended leave in Boca Raton, Florida, he is writing full time.

Words To Know

Responses will vary. The following are possible answers.
1. You are being insulted because you are being called unintelligent.
2. yes, because you can feel water
3. a poet, because he or she deals with thoughts and feelings, while a doctor is concerned with patients
4. bad, because they make your eyesight worse
5. yes, because he or she has to take advantage of a situation
6. Nearly every field of study is specialized, from electronics to history to literature.
7. A hypothesis is only a working idea and remains unproved.
8. unpopular, because the person would be annoying
9. a child, because he or she has not yet acquired sophistication through experience
10. She is using principles to analyze numerical data.
11. a movement backward
12. a cure for AIDS because a foot disease usually is not life-threatening
13. It will grow larger if it eats more.
14. sad, because he or she would think I was ridiculous
15. a medical doctor or psychiatrist, because a syndrome is a physical or mental condition

Reteaching/Reinforcement
- Unit Four Resource Book, p. 62

Literary Links

Have students compare Miss Kinnian's concern for Charlie with Mrs. Teubbes's concern for her class in "White Mice." Ask which teacher is more effective and more supportive of her students. (Mrs. Teubbes is very condescending toward her class in a way that Miss Kinnian is not. For example, it is hard to imagine Mrs. Teubbes paying the rent for one of her student's families.)

WHAT DO YOU THINK?
Reflecting on Theme

Have students think about the drawings they did of a perfect hero before they began reading the selections in Part 2. Ask them to compare their thoughts then and their thoughts now. If their thoughts are different now, invite them to draw a new picture of a perfect hero to reflect those new ideas.

OVERVIEW

Objectives

- To understand and appreciate a narrative poem about Paul Revere
- To enrich reading through summarizing
- To identify and understand the characteristics of a narrative poem
- To express understanding of the poem through a choice of writing forms, including a narrative poem and a newspaper article
- To extend understanding of the poem through a variety of multimodal and cross-curricular activities

Skills

READING SKILLS/ STRATEGIES
- Summarizing

LITERARY CONCEPTS
- Imagery
- Narrative poetry

THE WRITER'S STYLE
- Second-person point of view

SPEAKING, LISTENING, AND VIEWING
- Group discussions
- Oral presentation

Cross-Curricular Connections

HISTORY
- Battle of Concord

SOCIAL STUDIES
- Revere's ride

GEOGRAPHY
- Mapping the area

PREVIEWING

POETRY

Paul Revere's Ride
Henry Wadsworth Longfellow

Activating Prior Knowledge
PERSONAL CONNECTION

In Paul Revere's time, people who showed strong support for, or risked their lives for, American independence were considered patriots. Whom would you consider to be a patriot today? Do you think patriotism is an old-fashioned idea, or is it a timeless concept—one that will never go out of fashion? How is patriotism shown today? Explore these questions, either alone or with a small group of classmates. Jot down your ideas in a chart like the one shown.

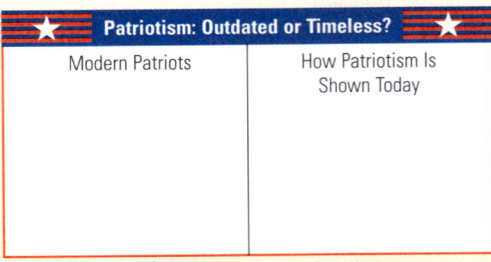

Patriotism: Outdated or Timeless?	
Modern Patriots	How Patriotism Is Shown Today

Building Background
HISTORICAL CONNECTION

On the third Monday of each April, the city of Boston, Massachusetts, celebrates Patriots' Day to commemorate the battles of Lexington and Concord, which marked the beginning of the Revolutionary War. "Paul Revere's Ride" relates the dramatic events that took place on the night before these battles.

By 1775, many American colonists had grown rebellious toward their British rulers. The British decided to arrest the rebel leaders and to march on Concord to seize a stockpile of colonial weapons. The rebels did not know the route the British troops would take. On the night of April 18, Paul Revere nervously awaited the answer from a spy. He had agreed to ride out and warn the colonists of the British advance—and his ride that night would make him famous.

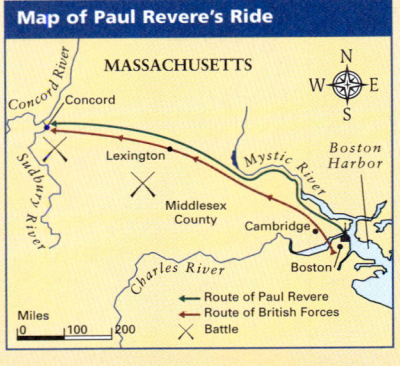

Map of Paul Revere's Ride

Active Reading/Setting A Purpose
READING CONNECTION

Summarizing "Paul Revere's Ride" tells the story of a patriot's daring mission. Summarizing the important ideas in the poem will help you understand and remember what you read. To summarize is to tell briefly in your own words the main ideas of a piece of writing, leaving out unimportant details. First read the poem without taking notes. Then go back and jot down the main ideas and important details in each stanza. Finally, use your notes to write a brief summary of Paul Revere's story.

542 UNIT FOUR PART 2: UNLIKELY HEROES

PRINT AND MEDIA RESOURCES

UNIT FOUR RESOURCE BOOK
Strategic Reading: Literature, p. 65
Reading SkillBuilder, p. 66

WRITING MINI–LESSONS
Transparencies, p. 47

ACCESS FOR STUDENTS ACQUIRING ENGLISH
Reading and Writing Support

FORMAL ASSESSMENT
Selection Test, p. 101
 Test Generator

 **AUDIO LIBRARY**
See Reference Card

 **LASERLINKS**
Historical Connection

Paul Revere's Ride

by Henry Wadsworth Longfellow

Listen, my children, and you shall hear
Of the midnight ride of Paul Revere,
On the eighteenth of April, in Seventy-five;
Hardly a man is now alive
5 Who remembers that famous day and year.

He said to his friend, "If the British march
By land or sea from the town to-night,
Hang a lantern aloft in the belfry arch[1]
Of the North Church tower as a signal light,—
10 One if by land, and two if by sea;
And I on the opposite shore will be,
Ready to ride and spread the alarm
Through every Middlesex[2] village and farm,
For the country folk to be up and to arm."

15 Then he said, "Good-night!" and with muffled oar
Silently rowed to the Charlestown shore,
Just as the moon rose over the bay,
Where swinging wide at her moorings[3] lay
The *Somerset,* British man-of-war;[4]
20 A phantom ship, with each mast and spar[5]
Across the moon like a prison bar,
And a huge black hulk, that was magnified
By its own reflection in the tide.

Meanwhile, his friend, through alley and street
25 Wanders and watches, with eager ears,
Till in the silence around him he hears
The muster of men at the barrack door,
The sound of arms, and the tramp of feet,

Midnight Ride of Paul Revere (1931), Grant Wood. Oil on composition board, 30" × 40", The Metropolitan Museum of Art, Arthur Hoppock Hearn Fund, 1950 (50.117). Copyright © 1996 Estate of Grant Wood/Licensed by VAGA, New York. Photo Copyright © 1988 The Metropolitan Museum of Art.

---

1. **belfry** (bĕl'frē) **arch:** a curved opening in a bell tower.
2. **Middlesex:** a county of eastern Massachusetts, setting for the first battle of the Revolutionary War on April 19, 1775.
3. **moorings:** the place where a ship is docked.
4. **man-of-war:** warship.
5. **spar:** a pole supporting a ship's sail.

Art Note

The Midnight Ride of Paul Revere by Grant Wood
This 1931 painting is an example of Regionalism, a style of painting embraced by some U.S. artists in the 1920s and 1930s. While choosing realistic subject matter, Wood (1892–1942) makes no attempt to be historically accurate—the homes are too well-lit, and the perfect shapes of the buildings and trees heighten reality and give an eerie quality to the painting.

Reading the Art *What does the painting's contrast of the moonlit town with the darkness ahead suggest about Revere's ride?*

Thematic Link: *Unlikely Heroes*
Opposition to British rule inspires a silversmith to heroic actions.

CUSTOMIZING FOR
Students Acquiring English

- Use **ACCESS FOR STUDENTS ACQUIRING ENGLISH,** *Reading and Writing Support.*
- Some students may not be familiar with the historical background of this poem. Briefly explain the status of the thirteen colonies, the Revolutionary War, and the Declaration of Independence (1776).
- ① Make sure students know that the year is 1775.
- ② Have a volunteer define the verb "to arm." *(to take up weapons)*

STRATEGIC READING FOR
Less-Proficient Readers

Set a Purpose Have students volunteer any information they have about the American Revolutionary War. Then have them keep reading to see how many lights are placed in the belfry of the Old North Church and what this signal communicates to the waiting Revere.

- Use **UNIT FOUR RESOURCE BOOK,** p. 65, for guidance in reading the selection.

Active Reading: CLARIFY

Ⓐ Have students explain the plan for announcing the movement of the British troops. *(Possible response: One lantern will be lit from the belfry if the troops move by land, two lanterns if over water; Revere will wait for the signal and ride through the countryside to alert the sleeping colonists.)*

CUSTOMIZING FOR
Gifted and Talented Students

Have students discuss the link between literature and patriotism. Ask if they think songs, novels, and poems today inspire patriotic sentiments similar to those in Longfellow's poems.

Critical Thinking: SPECULATING

B While writing this poem, Longfellow climbed up into the belfry of the Old North Church. Have students speculate how his experience might have influenced the details included in the poem. *(Possible response: He might have witnessed the pigeons, the shadows of the rafters, the trembling ladder, and the view of the water from the church belfry.)*

Literary Concept: IMAGERY

C Have students discuss how the description of the church graveyard and the wind helps to enhance their experience of the poem. *(Possible responses: The silent graveyard with the camp of the dead at night creates a haunting effect. The wind creeping from headstone to headstone like a sentry from tent to tent links the mobilization of the British troops, the impending battle, and the dead who have gone before.)*

Active Reading: CLARIFY

D Ask students to explain the importance of the "line of black ... like a bridge of boats" that Revere's friend spots from atop the bell tower. If students are having difficulty, use the following model:

Think-Aloud Model *I think that these lines continue the sense of danger conveyed by the references to the graveyard and the wind. The lines add to the eerie atmosphere in this part of the poem. However, the line of black also signals to the spy that the British are moving by boat. I expect there will soon be two lights in the church belfry.*

And the measured tread of the grenadiers,[6]
30 Marching down to their boats on the shore.

Then he climbed the tower of the Old North Church,
By the wooden stairs, with stealthy tread,[7]
To the belfry chamber overhead,
And startled the pigeons from their perch
35 On the somber[8] rafters, that round him made
Masses and moving shapes of shade,—
By the trembling ladder, steep and tall,
To the highest window in the wall,
Where he paused to listen and look down
40 A moment on the roofs of the town
And the moonlight flowing over all.

Beneath, in the churchyard, lay the dead,
In their night encampment on the hill,
Wrapped in silence so deep and still
45 That he could hear, like a sentinel's[9] tread,
The watchful night-wind, as it went
Creeping along from tent to tent,
And seeming to whisper, "All is well!"
A moment only he feels the spell
50 Of the place and the hour, and the secret dread
Of the lonely belfry and the dead;
For suddenly all his thoughts are bent
On a shadowy something far away,
Where the river widens to meet the bay,—
55 A line of black that bends and floats
On the rising tide like a bridge of boats.

Meanwhile, impatient to mount and ride,
Booted and spurred, with a heavy stride
On the opposite shore walked Paul Revere.
60 Now he patted his horse's side,
Now he gazed at the landscape far and near,
Then, impetuous,[10] stamped the earth,

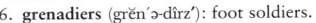

6. **grenadiers** (grĕn′ə-dîrz′): foot soldiers.
7. **stealthy tread:** quiet footsteps.
8. **somber:** gloomy.
9. **sentinel's:** of a guard or sentry.
10. **impetuous** (ĭm-pĕch′o͞o-əs): acting suddenly, on impulse.

544 UNIT FOUR PART 2: UNLIKELY HEROES

Mini-Lesson — Reading Skills/Strategies

SUMMARIZING Remind students that when they summarize, they are putting the main ideas of a piece of writing into their own words. Tell students they should read and, if necessary, reread the material until they fully understand it. Then they can write in their reading logs a one-sentence restatement that captures the main idea. For longer works, students may wish to summarize sections or difficult passages as they read. Explain to students that summarizing makes it easier to remember what they have read.

Application Ask students to reread "Paul Revere's Ride." Then have them write a sentence that captures the main idea of the poem, such as "When the British troops launched their attack, Paul Revere and his friend devised a plan to warn the colonists." Then have students review the major sections of the poem and summarize each event. Invite students to share their summaries for comparison.

Reteaching/Reinforcement
• *Unit Four Resource Book,* p. 66

And turned and tightened his saddle girth;[11]
But mostly he watched with eager search
65 The belfry tower of the Old North Church,
As it rose above the graves on the hill,
Lonely and spectral[12] and somber and still.
And lo! as he looks, on the belfry's height
A glimmer, and then a gleam of light!
70 He springs to the saddle, the bridle he turns,
But lingers and gazes, till full on his sight
A second lamp in the belfry burns.

A hurry of hoofs in a village street,
A shape in the moonlight, a bulk in the dark,
75 And beneath, from the pebbles, in passing, a spark
Struck out by a steed flying fearless and fleet;
That was all! And yet, through the gloom and the light,
The fate of a nation was riding that night;
And the spark struck out by that steed, in his flight,
80 Kindled the land into flame with its heat.
He has left the village and mounted the steep,
And beneath him, tranquil and broad and deep,
Is the Mystic,[13] meeting the ocean tides;
And under the alders[14] that skirt its edge,
85 Now soft on the sand, now loud on the ledge,
Is heard the tramp of his steed as he rides.

It was twelve by the village clock,
When he crossed the bridge into Medford town.
He heard the crowing of the cock,
90 And the barking of the farmer's dog,
And felt the damp of the river fog,
That rises after the sun goes down.

It was one by the village clock,
When he galloped into Lexington.
95 He saw the gilded weathercock
Swim in the moonlight as he passed,
And the meeting-house windows, blank and bare,
Gaze at him with a spectral glare,

---

11. **saddle girth:** the strap attaching a saddle to a horse's body.
12. **spectral:** ghostly.
13. **Mystic:** a short river flowing into Boston Harbor.
14. **alders:** trees of the birch family.

Literary Concept: IMAGERY

H Have students find images in this stanza of a peaceful country village. *(Possible responses: bleating sheep; the twitter of birds; the morning breeze over the meadows; people asleep in bed)* Then ask them to contrast this imagery with the imagery at the end of the stanza. *(Possible response: The peaceful village becomes a battlefield.)*

Linking to History

I At the Battle of Concord (referred to in lines 107–110), three British soldiers and two colonists were killed. The British reached the colonists' main supply depot only after the colonists removed most of the guns and ammunition.

STRATEGIC READING FOR
Less-Proficient Readers

J Ask students to explain what will result from Revere's nighttime ride through the countryside. *(Possible response: The colonists will be better prepared to fight the British, but some of the colonists will still die in the next day's battle.)* **Noting Sequence of Events**

CUSTOMIZING FOR
Students Acquiring English

4 Explain that the British soldiers' uniforms included red coats and therefore were often referred to as "the redcoats."

Critical Thinking:
MAKING JUDGMENTS

K Ask students to discuss how the last lines reveal the poet's purpose in writing the poem. *(Possible response: Longfellow ends the poem by suggesting that he hopes future generations will share Revere's patriotic fervor in times of crisis.)*

As if they already stood aghast[15]
100   At the bloody work they would look upon.

It was two by the village clock,
When he came to the bridge in Concord town.
He heard the bleating[16] of the flock,
And the twitter of birds among the trees,
105   And felt the breath of the morning breeze
Blowing over the meadow brown.
And one was safe and asleep in his bed
Who at the bridge would be first to fall,
Who that day would be lying dead,
110   Pierced by a British musket-ball.

You know the rest. In the books you have read
How the British Regulars[17] fired and fled,—
How the farmers gave them ball for ball,
From behind each fence and farmyard wall,
115   Chasing the redcoats down the lane,
Then crossing the fields to emerge again
Under the trees at the turn of the road,
And only pausing to fire and load.

So through the night rode Paul Revere;
120   And so through the night went his cry of alarm
To every Middlesex village and farm,—
A cry of defiance, and not of fear,
A voice in the darkness, a knock at the door,
And a word that shall echo forevermore!
125   For, borne on the night-wind of the Past,
Through all our history, to the last,
In the hour of darkness and peril[18] and need,
The people will waken and listen to hear
The hurrying hoof-beats of that steed,
130   And the midnight message of Paul Revere.

---

15. **aghast** (ə-găst′): terrified.
16. **bleating:** the crying of sheep.
17. **British Regulars:** members of Great Britain's standing army.
18. **peril:** danger.

546   UNIT FOUR   PART 2: UNLIKELY HEROES

Mini-Lesson The Writer's Style

SECOND-PERSON POINT OF VIEW
Explain to students that by using the pronoun *you* to address his audience, Longfellow is following a long tradition in narrative poetry. It is common in narrative poems for the speaker either to address the source of his or her inspiration or to address the audience directly at the beginning of the poem.

Application Have students discuss their response to the speaker directly addressing them in lines 1–5 and 111–112. Ask them if the use of direct address changes how they relate to the poet and whether it makes them feel more or less involved in the action of the poem. Then have students write a short stanza of rhyming poetry about an exciting event that directly addresses the reader with the pronoun *you*.

Reteaching/Reinforcement
• Writing Mini-Lessons transparencies, p. 47

 **The Writer's Craft**
Point of View, pp. 322–323

HISTORICAL INSIGHT

Paul Revere: The Man

People living in the Boston of 1775 referred to Paul Revere as Bold Revere. His reputation was glowing; his contemporaries knew him to be sensible and even-tempered, living a life in which boldness and good sense were finely balanced. He was the best American silversmith of his time, and the scope of his patriotism extended far beyond his famous "midnight ride."

Born in Boston in 1735, Revere attended school until he was 13, when he began a long apprenticeship with his silversmith father. When Revere was 19, his father died, leaving the teenager in charge of the large family. At the age of 21, although he was against warfare in principle, he served briefly in the French and Indian War at Lake George, New York.

After returning to Boston, he married Sarah Orne and soon became the most accomplished silversmith in the New World, producing a greater variety of works than any other silversmith of his time. It was not long before he joined groups opposed to the British rule of the American colonies. He made frequent trips on horseback to Philadelphia, carrying secret information to revolutionary groups. Although these grueling, dangerous 11-day trips took him away from his work and his growing family, he eventually fathered 16 children—8 with Sarah, who died in 1773, and 8 with his second wife, Rachel, whom he married later that year.

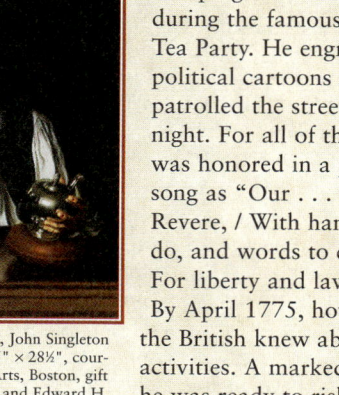

Paul Revere (about 1768), John Singleton Copley. Oil on canvas, 35" × 28½", courtesy of Museum of Fine Arts, Boston, gift of Joseph W., William B., and Edward H. R. Revere (30.781). Copyright © 1995, all rights reserved.

Revere aided in the dumping of British tea during the famous Boston Tea Party. He engraved political cartoons and patrolled the streets at night. For all of this, he was honored in a popular song as "Our . . . bold Revere, / With hands to do, and words to cheer / For liberty and laws . . ." By April 1775, however, the British knew about his activities. A marked man, he was ready to risk his life and all he had on a ride to warn his countrymen of the British advance.

After the Revolutionary War, Revere kept up his feverish pace. Eager to see the U.S. economy become independent of Europe's, he learned how to make hardware, parts for ships, and stoves. He was the first craftsman in the United States to make church bells, producing almost 400 of them. At the age of 65, still far from retirement, Revere opened the first mill for rolling copper sheets in the United States, risking $25,000 of his own money and borrowing another $10,000. Not long before his death in 1818, Revere worked with Robert Fulton, making copper for the boilers of the world's first successful steamboat.

PAUL REVERE: THE MAN **547**

COMPREHENSION CHECK

1. What does the signal of two lanterns tell Paul Revere? *(The British will travel by sea.)*
2. What is the purpose of Paul Revere's ride? *(to alert the colonists that British troops are approaching)*
3. According to the poet, when will Americans hear Paul Revere's message? *(whenever the nation faces peril)*

Art Note

***Portrait of Paul Revere* by John Singleton Copley** Copley (1738–1815) was raised in Boston and today is regarded as the greatest portrait painter of the American colonial era. This portrait shows Revere in his shirtsleeves, holding one of his silver teapots, a casual pose that Copley did not use in any of his other works.

Reading the Art What aspects of Revere's personality does Copley capture in his portrait?

INSIGHT

1. How might Revere's resourcefulness as a silversmith have affected his successful midnight ride? *(Possible response: Revere's success as a silversmith reflects his ambition and ability to overcome difficult circumstances. These attributes may have helped him during his ride.)*
2. In what other ways did Revere show his commitment to the colonies? *(Possible response: Revere served the colonies before the war by carrying messages and taking part in the Boston Tea Party, during the war by engraving political cartoons and patrolling the streets, and after the war by helping with the expansion of the U.S. economy.)*
3. Do you think Revere was successful in balancing his roles as family man, businessman, and patriot? Explain your answer. *(Responses will vary.)*

Mini-Lesson: Speaking, 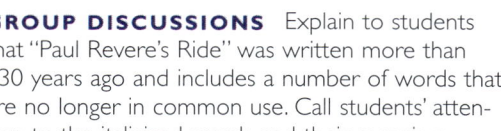 Listening, and Viewing

GROUP DISCUSSIONS Explain to students that "Paul Revere's Ride" was written more than 130 years ago and includes a number of words that are no longer in common use. Call students' attention to the italicized words and their meanings:

line 8: Hang a lantern *aloft* (high)

line 27: The *muster* of men (assembling)

line 76: Struck out by a *steed* (horse)

line 95: the gilded *weathercock* (weathervane)

line 97: the *meeting-house* (church)

Application Have students reread the lines before answering the following questions:
- How do the sounds of the words create a musical quality?
- Would the feeling conveyed by the poem change if the older words were replaced with more modern words?

Have the class select modern-day synonyms to replace the italicized words and write the revised lines on the chalkboard. Then discuss with the whole class how the meaning, mood, rhyme, and rhythm are affected by these changes.

THE LANGUAGE OF LITERATURE **TEACHER'S EDITION** **547**

From Personal Response to Critical Analysis

1. Accept all reasonable responses. Encourage students to include examples from the poem.
2. Possible responses: Yes, because he is an ordinary citizen called upon to do extraordinary duties. No, because he was heroic in all parts of his life.
3. Stanzas and responses will vary.
4. Possible responses: The rhythm of the poem provides a sense of the horse's gallop that would not be possible in prose writing. The prose writing might go into more depth about the background of the ride and the battle.
5. Responses will vary.

Another Pathway

Encourage students to reread and review the events of the poem, their notes, and their summaries to create a list of the major events they will cover in their cartoons. Students can work with partners to provide captions for one another's cartoon series.

Rubric

3 Full Accomplishment Student's cartoon series illustrates all the major events of the poem.

2 Substantial Accomplishment Student illustrates some events from the poem.

1 Little or Partial Accomplishment Student fails to relate his or her series of cartoons to the events of the poem.

RESPONDING OPTIONS

FROM PERSONAL RESPONSE TO CRITICAL ANALYSIS

REFLECT
1. Did anything in this account of Paul Revere's ride surprise you? Jot down your thoughts in your notebook.

RETHINK
Thematic Link

2. Does Paul Revere match your concept of an unlikely hero? Why or why not?

3. Choose a stanza from "Paul Revere's Ride" that you think creates a strong mood. What feeling does the stanza call forth in you? In which lines do poetic devices—such as rhyme, rhythm, and figurative language—help to create the mood?

Close Textual Reading

4. How does the effect of this poem differ from the effect a prose account of Revere's ride would have? Which form do you prefer for the telling of this story? Why?

RELATE
5. Look at the ideas about patriotism you recorded for the Personal Connection on page 542. If you had to name a present-day figure with the patriotic spirit of Paul Revere, whom would you choose? Explain your choice.

Multimodal Learning
ANOTHER PATHWAY

Draw a series of cartoons showing the sequence of events on the night of April 18, 1775. To help you plan your drawings, refer to the notes and summary you made for the Reading Connection on page 542.

LITERARY CONCEPTS

"Paul Revere's Ride" is called a **narrative poem** because it tells a story, or narrative, in poetic form. Like a work of prose fiction, a narrative poem has a setting, a plot, and characters. What is the setting of this poem, and who are its main characters? How might you summarize the poem's plot in a single sentence?

QUICKWRITES

1. With a partner, choose a famous event in U.S. history. Then write a **narrative poem** about the event, imitating the style of "Paul Revere's Ride."

2. Turn the story of Paul Revere's ride into a **news article** that answers the important journalistic questions *who, what, when, where,* and *why.* Include a headline that conveys the drama and importance of the event.

📁 **PORTFOLIO** Save your writing. You may want to use it later as a springboard to a piece for your portfolio.

548 UNIT FOUR PART 2: UNLIKELY HEROES

Literary Concepts

For a description of the setting of this poem, consult the Literary Concept note at the top of page 545. In coming up with a summary sentence, consult the Mini-Lesson on summarizing on page 544.

QuickWrites

1. Students may want to use an irregular pattern of rhythm and rhyme and focus more on capturing the spirit of Longfellow's poem.
2. Remind students to include all the important information, which may be spread out over several stanzas. Also encourage students to use their imagination to develop quotes from the colonists Revere warns.

 **The Writer's Craft**

Poetry, pp. 70–83
Informative Writing, pp. 92–109

Multimodal Learning

ALTERNATIVE ACTIVITIES

1. Plan a **dramatic reading** of "Paul Revere's Ride" or another of Longfellow's narrative poems. You may wish to work with a partner, reading passages alternately to the accompaniment of background music that reflects the mood of the poem. Perform the reading for your classmates.

2. A ballad is a narrative poem that is designed to be sung. Ballads are usually about ordinary people who have unusual adventures; they are often written in four-line stanzas with regular patterns of rhythm and rhyme. With a partner, compose a **ballad** about Paul Revere. Present a live or tape-recorded performance of it to the class.

LITERARY LINKS

Compare and contrast "Paul Revere's Ride" with "O Captain! My Captain!" For what purpose was each poem written? How are the subjects alike, and how are they different? How do the poets' uses of rhythm, rhyme, figures of speech (metaphors, similes, and personification), alliteration, and imagery compare?

ACROSS THE CURRICULUM

 Social Studies Longfellow changed or omitted several key facts about Paul Revere's ride. Research what really happened that night, and report your findings to the class in a talk or a written narrative.

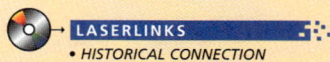
HENRY WADSWORTH LONGFELLOW

1807–1882

When Henry Wadsworth Longfellow was a senior at Bowdoin College, he wrote these words to his father: "I most eagerly aspire after future eminence in literature." Unlike many writers, Longfellow completely achieved his literary aspirations—he was to become the most popular American poet of his time.

Born in Portland, Maine, Longfellow left public school for private school when he was 5 because he was afraid of "rough boys." He was admitted to Bowdoin College at the age of 14 and had published nearly 40 poems by the time he graduated at 18. After his graduation, the skill he had shown in translating a Latin poem led the trustees of Bowdoin to offer him the unprecedented opportunity of becoming the first professor of modern languages there. He created his own texts in this new field and later accepted a professorship at Harvard.

Longfellow's personal life was marked by deep sadness. His first wife died from an illness after four years of marriage. "What a solitary, lonely being I am!" he wrote. Eight years later he married Frances Appleton, with whom he had six children. After 18 happy years, this marriage ended tragically with Frances's death from burns she received when her dress caught fire. Because Longfellow's face and hands had been badly burned while trying to save her, he was unable to attend her funeral, held on the anniversary of their wedding day. His life, Longfellow said, "crumbled away like sand."

OTHER WORKS *The Courtship of Miles Standish, Evangeline: A Tale of Acadia, The Song of Hiawatha,* "The Village Blacksmith," "The Children's Hour"

Extended Reading

LASERLINKS
• HISTORICAL CONNECTION

549

Literary Links

Suggest to students who are having difficulty that they select particular poetic devices in each poem rather than attempting to complete the entire list. In comparing the two poets' purposes, students should find that each poem was written to commemorate an American hero, although Longfellow writes of a figure from the past, and Whitman of a contemporary.

Across The Curriculum

Social Studies *Revere's Ride*
Encourage students to consult a librarian before they begin their research. Point out that they may encounter several versions of the events of April 18, 1775. Have students track the contradictions, and tell which version(s) of the events they find most believable.

HENRY WADSWORTH LONGFELLOW

"Paul Revere's Ride" is part of a larger book of poems, *Tales of a Wayside Inn.* Longfellow patterned this book, in which a group of travelers stops by an inn and passes the night telling stories, after Chaucer's *Canterbury Tales.*

 HISTORICAL CONNECTION
Paul Revere and His Times Paul Revere's famous ride, the Boston Tea Party, and other events of the Revolutionary era are included in these images. Present these paintings and illustrations to increase students' knowledge of Boston's history and geography.

Side A, Frame 232

Alternative Activities

1. Suggest students find recordings of fife and drum music—such as would have been popular in Revere's time—to accompany their dramatic reading. Fife and drum recordings may be found in most libraries under "folk music."

2. Point out to students that most early narrative poems, such as the *Odyssey,* were designed to be sung. Ballads served as an oral history of legendary events. The rhyme and rhythm helped people to remember the events.

THE LANGUAGE OF LITERATURE TEACHER'S EDITION **549**

OVERVIEW

Objectives

- To understand and appreciate a biography about Harriet Tubman
- To enrich reading by identifying motivation
- To identify and understand the elements of a biography
- To express understanding of the selection through a choice of writing forms, including a diary entry, a description, and a letter
- To extend understanding of the selection through a variety of multimodal and cross-curricular activities

Skills

READING SKILLS/STRATEGIES
- Relating cause and effect
- Motivation

LITERARY CONCEPTS
- Minor characters
- Biography

LISTENING, SPEAKING, AND VIEWING
- Group discussion
- Oral presentation

THE WRITER'S STYLE
- Parallelism

GRAMMAR
- Gerunds and participles

SPELLING
- Words ending in -able and -ible

Cross-Curricular Connections

SOCIAL STUDIES
- Quakers

HISTORY
- Fugitive Slave Law
- William Still
- Biographical sketches

GEOGRAPHY/MATH
- The road north

HISTORICAL CONNECTION

Harriet Tubman and the Underground Railroad Posters describing escaped slaves, paintings of travelers on the Underground Railroad, and images of Harriet Tubman will help students understand the importance of Tubman's work.

Side A, Frame 239

PREVIEWING

NONFICTION

from Harriet Tubman: Conductor on the Underground Railroad

Ann Petry

PERSONAL CONNECTION *Activating Prior Knowledge*

In the years immediately preceding the U.S. Civil War, about 4 million African Americans labored as slaves on Southern plantations. Each year, several thousand of these slaves would attempt to escape northward, and many succeeded. Those who were recaptured, however, might be beaten, maimed, or even killed. If you had been a slave at that time, would you have tried to escape? Why or why not? Write down your thoughts for class discussion.

HISTORICAL CONNECTION *Building Background*

The term *Underground Railroad*—referring not to a railroad but to a secret system of individuals who helped slaves escape to the North and to Canada—became popular after a slave named Tice Davids escaped from his Kentucky master in 1831. Davids's bewildered master said that his slave must have "gone off on an underground railroad."

The Underground Railroad had "stations" where fleeing slaves could get food and drink. The "commuter's ticket" was the password "A friend with friends." Most important, the railroad had "conductors" like Harriet Tubman, who helped escort the slaves to freedom. Conducting slaves to freedom became even more risky after the passage of the Fugitive Slave Law of 1850 made it a federal crime to assist a runaway slave.

READING CONNECTION *Active Reading/Setting A Purpose*

Motivation The reasons that move a person to act are his or her motivation. People can be motivated by such things as dedication, love, fear, and guilt. As you read this selection, think about what motivated Harriet Tubman to help so many slaves escape. Take note of her personality, her beliefs, and the circumstances she faced.

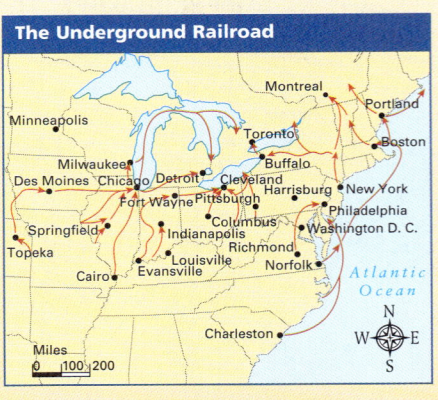

The Underground Railroad

• HISTORICAL CONNECTION

550 UNIT FOUR PART 2: UNLIKELY HEROES

PRINT AND MEDIA RESOURCES

UNIT FOUR RESOURCE BOOK
Strategic Reading: Literature, p. 69
Vocabulary SkillBuilder, p. 72
Reading SkillBuilder, p. 70
Spelling SkillBuilder, p. 71

GRAMMAR MINI-LESSONS
Transparencies, pp. 16, 18
Copymasters, pp. 24–25

ACCESS FOR STUDENTS ACQUIRING ENGLISH
Selection Summaries
Reading and Writing Support

FORMAL ASSESSMENT
Selection Test, pp. 103–104
Part Test, pp. 105–106
 Test Generator

AUDIO LIBRARY
See Reference Card

LASERLINKS
Historical Connection

INTERNET RESOURCES
For a list of Internet sites related to Frederick Douglass, please see the Houghton Mifflin Home Page at http://hmco.com.

550 THE LANGUAGE OF LITERATURE TEACHER'S EDITION

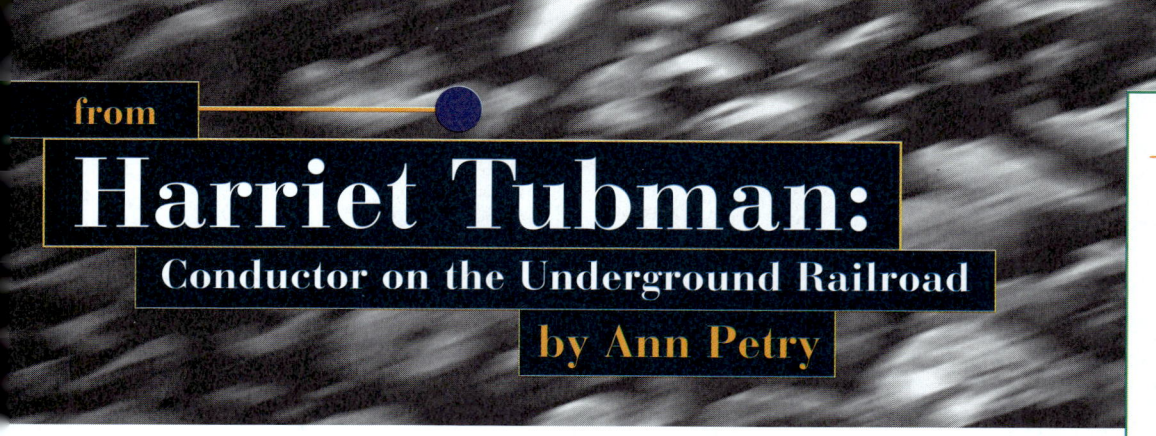

from Harriet Tubman: Conductor on the Underground Railroad
by Ann Petry

The Railroad Runs to Canada

ALONG THE EASTERN SHORE OF MARYLAND, IN DORCHESTER COUNTY, IN CAROLINE COUNTY, THE MASTERS KEPT HEARING WHISPERS ABOUT THE MAN NAMED MOSES, WHO WAS RUNNING OFF SLAVES. AT FIRST THEY DID NOT BELIEVE IN HIS EXISTENCE. THE STORIES ABOUT HIM WERE FANTASTIC, UNBELIEVABLE. YET THEY WATCHED FOR HIM. THEY OFFERED REWARDS FOR HIS CAPTURE.

They never saw him. Now and then they heard whispered rumors to the effect that he was in the neighborhood. The woods were searched. The roads were watched. There was never anything to indicate his whereabouts. But a few days afterward, a goodly number of slaves would be gone from the plantation. Neither the master nor the overseer had heard or seen anything unusual in the quarter.[1] Sometimes one or the other would vaguely remember having heard a whippoorwill call somewhere in the woods, close by, late at night. Though it was the wrong season for whippoorwills.

Sometimes the masters thought they had heard the cry of a hoot owl, repeated, and would remember having thought that the intervals between the low, moaning cry were wrong, that it had been repeated four times in succession instead of three. There was never anything more than that to suggest that all was not well in the quarter. Yet when morning came, they invariably discovered that a group of the finest slaves had taken to their heels.

Unfortunately, the discovery was almost always made on a Sunday. Thus a whole day was lost before the machinery of pursuit could be set in motion. The posters offering rewards for the fugitives could not be printed until Monday. The men who made a living hunting for runaway slaves were out of reach, off in the woods with their dogs and their guns, in pursuit of four-footed game, or they were in camp meetings saying their prayers with their wives and families beside them.

Harriet Tubman could have told them that there was far more involved in this matter of running off slaves than signaling the would-be runaways by imitating the call of a whippoorwill or a hoot owl, far more involved than a

---
1. **quarter:** the area in which slaves lived.

WORDS TO KNOW

borne (bôrn) *adj.* carried **bear** *v.* (p. 552)
cajoling (kə-jō′lĭng) *v.* urging gently; coaxing (p. 556)
disheveled (dĭ-shĕv′əld) *adj.* messy; untidy (p. 553)
dispel (dĭ-spĕl′) *v.* to drive away (p. 553)
eloquence (ĕl′ə-kwəns) *n.* an ability to speak forcefully and persuasively (p. 555)
fastidious (fă-stĭd′ē-əs) *adj.* difficult to please (p. 558)
indomitable (ĭn-dŏm′ĭ-tə-bəl) *adj.* unable to be conquered (p. 556)
instill (ĭn-stĭl′) *v.* to supply gradually (p. 553)
mutinous (myo̅o̅t′n-əs) *adj.* rebelling against a leader (p. 555)
sullen (sŭl′ən) *adj.* showing silent resentment; sulky (p. 555)

CUSTOMIZING FOR
Gifted and Talented Students

Have students discuss the conflict slaves faced between the desire for freedom and the risks of escaping.

Art Note

Forward by Jacob Lawrence Like many African-American artists of the 1920s and 1930s, Lawrence (1917–) used his artistic talents as a way to explore his heritage. He typically did this by painting a series of works on a person or topic specific to the African-American experience, such as Harriet Tubman, Frederick Douglass, and African-American migration.

Reading the Art *What elements of Tubman's character are revealed through this painting? What is the significance of its title?*

Critical Thinking:
HYPOTHESIZING

Ⓐ Explain that ashcake is cornmeal baked in hot ashes; salt herring is dried and salted fish; and a bandanna is a large, colorful handkerchief. Ask students what these details reveal about a slave's life. *(Possible response: They ate simple food, had few possessions, and needed headgear to protect themselves from the sun when working the fields.)*

STRATEGIC READING FOR
Less-Proficient Readers

Ⓑ Ask students to explain who Moses is. *(Harriet Tubman is "the man named Moses." Many plantation owners falsely assumed that the slaves' references to Moses were to a man.)* **Drawing Conclusions**

Set a Purpose Have students find the many hardships the runaways experience on their way.

CAUSE	EFFECT
Tubman's experiences with slavery and desire to prevent more injustices	Tubman helps slaves escape bondage
People's fear of the Fugitive Slave Law	People at the first stop turn away Tubman
Some people's desire to help despite the risk	The German farmer gives them shelter
Abolitionists' experiences and hatred of slavery; their political beliefs	Thomas Garrett and Frederick Douglass help Tubman

Forward (1967), Jacob Lawrence. Tempera on masonite, 23⅞" × 35⅕₆", North Carolina Museum of Art, Raleigh, purchased with funds from the State of North Carolina.

matter of waiting for a clear night when the North Star was visible.

In December 1851, when she started out with the band of fugitives that she planned to take to Canada, she had been in the vicinity of the plantation for days, planning the trip, carefully selecting the slaves that she would take with her.

She had announced her arrival in the quarter by singing the forbidden spiritual—"Go down, Moses, 'way down to Egypt Land"² — singing it softly outside the door of a slave cabin late at night. The husky voice was beautiful even when it was barely more than a murmur <u>borne</u> on the wind.

Once she had made her presence known, word of her coming spread from cabin to cabin. The slaves whispered to each other, ear to mouth, mouth to ear, "Moses is here." "Moses has come." "Get ready. Moses is back again." The ones who had agreed to go north with her put ashcake and salt herring in an old bandanna, hastily tied it into a bundle, and then waited patiently for the signal that meant it was time to start.

There were eleven in this party, including one of her brothers and his wife. It was the largest group that she had ever conducted, but she was determined that more and more slaves should know what freedom was like.

---
2. **"Go down, Moses, 'way down to Egypt Land":** a line from a well-known African-American folk song about Moses leading the enslaved Israelites out of Egypt.

WORDS TO KNOW
borne (bôrn) *adj.* carried **bear** *v.*

552

Mini-Lesson · Reading Skills/Strategies

RELATING CAUSE AND EFFECT
Remind students that events are often connected. One event may cause another event (the effect) to happen. The events in a narrative often reflect this relationship. For example, the passage of the Fugitive Slave Law (cause) led Tubman to guide slaves all the way to Canada (effect).

Application Ask students to explain why understanding a person's or character's motivation (cause) is a key to understanding how he or she will act (effect). Have students complete a chart like the one shown.

Reteaching/Reinforcement
• *Unit Four Resource Book*, p. 70

She had to take them all the way to Canada. The Fugitive Slave Law[3] was no longer a great many incomprehensible words written down on the country's law books. The new law had become a reality. It was Thomas Sims, a boy, picked up on the streets of Boston at night and shipped back to Georgia. It was Jerry and Shadrach, arrested and jailed with no warning.

She had never been in Canada. The route beyond Philadelphia was strange to her. But she could not let the runaways who accompanied her know this. As they walked along, she told them stories of her own first flight; she kept painting vivid word pictures of what it would be like to be free.

But there were so many of them this time. She knew moments of doubt when she was half-afraid and kept looking back over her shoulder, imagining that she heard the sound of pursuit. They would certainly be pursued. Eleven of them. Eleven thousand dollars' worth of flesh and bone and muscle that belonged to Maryland planters. If they were caught, the eleven runaways would be whipped and sold south, but she—she would probably be hanged.

They tried to sleep during the day, but they never could wholly relax into sleep. She could tell by the positions they assumed, by their restless movements. And they walked at night. Their progress was slow. It took them three nights of walking to reach the first stop. She had told them about the place where they would stay, promising warmth and good food, holding these things out to them as an incentive to keep going.

When she knocked on the door of a farmhouse, a place where she and her parties of runaways had always been welcome, always been given shelter and plenty to eat, there was no answer. She knocked again, softly. A voice from within said, "Who is it?" There was fear in the voice.

She knew instantly from the sound of the voice that there was something wrong. She said, "A friend with friends," the password on the Underground Railroad.

The door opened, slowly. The man who stood in the doorway looked at her coldly, looked with unconcealed astonishment and fear at the eleven <u>disheveled</u> runaways who were standing near her. Then he shouted, "Too many, too many. It's not safe. My place was searched last week. It's not safe!" and slammed the door in her face.

She turned away from the house, frowning. She had promised her passengers food and rest and warmth, and instead of that there would be hunger and cold and more walking over the frozen ground. Somehow she would have to <u>instill</u> courage into these eleven people, most of them strangers, would have to feed them on hope and bright dreams of freedom instead of the fried pork and corn bread and milk she had promised them.

They stumbled along behind her, half-dead for sleep, and she urged them on, though she was as tired and as discouraged as they were. She had never been in Canada, but she kept painting wondrous word pictures of what it would be like. She managed to <u>dispel</u> their fear of pursuit so that they would not become hysterical, panic-stricken. Then she had to bring

---

3. **Fugitive Slave Law:** a law passed in 1850, allowing slave owners to recover escaped slaves even if they had reached free states.

> WORDS TO KNOW
> **disheveled** (dĭ-shĕv'əld) *adj.* messy; untidy
> **instill** (ĭn-stĭl') *v.* to supply gradually
> **dispel** (dĭ-spĕl') *v.* to drive away

553

Linking to History

C The Fugitive Slave Law forced the return of escaped slaves throughout the country, causing many of them to settle in Canada. Well-traveled routes ran through Ohio, Indiana, and Pennsylvania, ultimately leading to Canada via Detroit, Niagara Falls, or across Lake Erie.

Active Reading: EVALUATE

D Ask students why Tubman didn't want the runaways to know that she had never been to Canada. If students need help, use the following model to give them ideas of what they might be thinking about:

Think-Aloud Model *I wonder why Tubman didn't want the runaways to know she'd never been to Canada. I know that they were nervous and very aware of the terrible consequences if they were captured. They would need complete confidence in their leader if they were to keep going. If Tubman admitted the route was strange to her, the runaways might be afraid they'd get lost or captured and want to turn back.*

Literary Concept: MINOR CHARACTERS

E Ask students why the farmer reacts this way. *(Possible responses: His house was recently searched. Although the farmer has welcomed Tubman and runaways before, he probably fears the harsher penalties enforced by the new Fugitive Slave Law. His astonishment indicates his surprise that Tubman is still willing to run the risk of helping slaves escape.)*

Mini-Lesson Literary Concepts

REVIEWING MINOR CHARACTERS

Remind students that in addition to main characters, literary works usually have a number of minor characters who interact with the main character and with one another. Minor characters help to move the narrative along, provide background for the selection, and supply information about the main characters. Because this is a biography about Tubman's life, she is the main character and others, such as Frederick Douglass, are minor characters.

Application Have students compile a list of the minor characters mentioned in the biography. Ask them to explain how these characters function in the narrative. *(Possible response: The minor characters help to give information about Tubman and the Underground Railroad.)* Then invite students to select a scene involving a minor character, such as the runaway who wishes to return, or William Still's interviewing of the slaves. Have students rewrite this passage from the point of view of the minor character. Ask them the effect of this change in perspective.

CUSTOMIZING FOR
Students Acquiring English

3 Explain that the expression "afraid of their own shadows" indicates that they were very anxious and nervous about being caught and so were afraid of everything.

STRATEGIC READING FOR
Less-Proficient Readers

F Have students list the difficulties that beset the runaways on their journey. *(They were cold, hungry, without shelter, and without sleep.)* Summarizing

Set a Purpose Have students read to find out how Tubman responds to a slave who finds the hardships too difficult to endure.

Linking to Social Studies

G Quakerism, or The Society of Friends, began in England in the 1600s. It was introduced to the American colonies when William Penn founded Pennsylvania for English Quakers who wished to escape religious persecution. Quakers are known for their commitment to pacifism and justice for all. The Quakers believe that all humans are descended from the same ancestors and therefore should be treated equally. Because of these beliefs, the Quakers were leaders in the movement to abolish slavery.

Literary Concept:
MINOR CHARACTERS

H Point out to students that the German farmer, like the farmer on page 553, is a minor character who has a major effect on the chances of the runaways surviving the trip to Canada. Ask students to compare the German farmer's reaction with that of the previous farmer. *(Possible response: Unlike the other farmer, the German farmer warmly greets Tubman and provides her and the runaways with much needed food and shelter.)*

Identifying Gerunds and Participles

Gerund	Participle
used as a noun	used as a modifier

---

some of the fear back so that they would stay awake and keep walking though they drooped with sleep.

Yet during the day, when they lay down deep in a thicket, they never really slept, because if a twig snapped or the wind sighed in the branches of a pine tree, **they jumped to their feet, afraid of their own shadows, shivering and shaking.** It was very cold, but they dared not make fires because someone would see the smoke and wonder about it.

She kept thinking, Eleven of them. Eleven thousand dollars' worth of slaves. And she had to take them all the way to Canada. Sometimes she told them about Thomas Garrett, in Wilmington. She said he was their friend even though he did not know them. He was the friend of all fugitives. He called them God's poor. He was a Quaker[4] and his speech was a little different from that of other people. His clothing was different, too. He wore the wide-brimmed hat that the Quakers wear.

She said that he had thick white hair, soft, almost like a baby's, and the kindest eyes she had ever seen. He was a big man and strong, but he had never used his strength to harm anyone, always to help people. He would give all of them a new pair of shoes. Everybody. He always did. Once they reached his house in Wilmington, they would be safe. He would see to it that they were.

She described the house where he lived, told them about the store where he sold shoes. She said he kept a pail of milk and a loaf of bread in the drawer of his desk so that he would have food ready at hand for any of God's poor who should suddenly appear before him, fainting with hunger. There was a hidden room in the store. A whole wall swung open, and behind it was a room where he could hide fugitives. On the wall there were shelves filled with small boxes—boxes of shoes—so that you would never guess that the wall actually opened.

While she talked, she kept watching them. They did not believe her. She could tell by their expressions. They were thinking, New shoes, Thomas Garrett, Quaker, Wilmington—what foolishness was this? Who knew if she told the truth? Where was she taking them anyway?

That night they reached the next stop—a farm that belonged to a German. She made the runaways take shelter behind trees at the edge of the fields before she knocked at the door. She hesitated before she approached the door, thinking, Suppose that he, too, should refuse shelter, suppose— Then she thought, Lord, I'm going to hold steady on to You, and You've got to see me through—and knocked softly.

She heard the familiar guttural voice say, "Who's there?"

She answered quickly, "A friend with friends."

He opened the door and greeted her warmly. "How many this time?" he asked.

"Eleven," she said and waited, doubting, wondering.

He said, "Good. Bring them in."

He and his wife fed them in the lamp-lit kitchen, their faces glowing as they offered food and more food, urging them to eat, saying there was plenty for everybody, have more milk, have more bread, have more meat.

They spent the night in the warm kitchen. They really slept, all that night and until dusk the next day. When they left, it was with reluctance. They had all been warm and safe and well-fed. It was hard to exchange the security offered by that clean, warm kitchen for the darkness and the cold of a December night.

---
4. **Quaker:** a member of a religious group known as the Society of Friends.

Mini-Lesson Grammar

GERUNDS AND PARTICIPLES Explain to students that a gerund is a verb form used as a noun. For example, *"Thinking* was difficult when Tubman and the slaves had not slept." However, the present participle of most verbs is also formed by adding *-ing* to the present tense of a verb, such as *shivering* and *shaking* in the highlighted passage on page 554. Tell students that the only way to distinguish a gerund from a participle is to look at how the word is used in a sentence. If it is used as a noun, it is a gerund; if it acts as a modifier, the word is a participle.

Application Read the following sentences aloud. Have students identify whether a gerund or participle is used in the sentence.

1. *Escaping* from slavery meant a chance at freedom. *(gerund)*
2. *Using* whatever they could find, the slaves fought their way north. *(participle)*

Reteaching/Reinforcement
- *Grammar Mini-Lessons* copymasters pp. 24–25, transparencies pp. 16–18

Gerund or Participle? p. 604

"Go On or Die"

Harriet had found it hard to leave the warmth and friendliness, too. But she urged them on. For a while, as they walked, they seemed to carry in them a measure of contentment; some of the serenity and the cleanliness of that big, warm kitchen lingered on inside them. But as they walked farther and farther away from the warmth and the light, the cold and the darkness entered into them. They fell silent, sullen, suspicious. She waited for the moment when some one of them would turn mutinous. It did not happen that night.

Two nights later she was aware that the feet behind her were moving slower and slower. She heard the irritability in their voices, knew that soon someone would refuse to go on.

She started talking about William Still and the Philadelphia Vigilance Committee.[5] No one commented. No one asked any questions. She told them the story of William and Ellen Craft and how they escaped from Georgia. Ellen was so fair that she looked as though she were white, and so she dressed up in a man's clothing, and she looked like a wealthy young planter. Her husband, William, who was dark, played the role of her slave. Thus they traveled from Macon, Georgia, to Philadelphia, riding on the trains, staying at the finest hotels. Ellen pretended to be very ill—her right arm was in a sling, and her right hand was bandaged, because she was supposed to have rheumatism. Thus she avoided having to sign the register at the hotels, for she could not read or write. They finally arrived safely in Philadelphia and then went on to Boston.

No one said anything. Not one of them seemed to have heard her.

She told them about Frederick Douglass,[6] the most famous of the escaped slaves, of his eloquence, of his magnificent appearance. Then she told them of her own first, vain effort at running away, evoking the memory of that miserable life she had led as a child, reliving it for a moment in the telling.

But they had been tired too long, hungry too long, afraid too long, footsore too long. One of them suddenly cried out in despair, "Let me go back. It is better to be a slave than to suffer like this in order to be free."

She carried a gun with her on these trips. She had never used it—except as a threat. Now as she aimed it, she experienced a feeling of guilt, remembering that time, years ago, when she had prayed for the death of Edward Brodas, the Master, and then not too long afterward had heard that great wailing cry that came from the throats of the field hands, and knew from the sound that the Master was dead.

One of the runaways said, again, "Let me go back. Let me go back," and stood still and then turned around and said, over his shoulder, "I am going back."

She lifted the gun, aimed it at the despairing slave. She said, "Go on with us or die." The husky, low-pitched voice was grim.

He hesitated for a moment, and then he joined the others. They started walking again. She tried to explain to them why none of them

---

5. **Philadelphia Vigilance Committee:** a fundraising organization set up before the Civil War to help slaves escaping from the South.
6. **Frederick Douglass:** an African-American leader of the 1800s who worked for the end of slavery in the United States.

WORDS TO KNOW
sullen (sŭl′ən) *adj.* showing silent resentment; sulky
mutinous (myo͞ot′n-əs) *adj.* rebelling against a leader
eloquence (ĕl′ə-kwəns) *n.* an ability to speak forcefully and persuasively

555

Critical Thinking: SPECULATING

I Have students speculate about how Tubman could know a runaway slave would "turn mutinous." *(Possible responses: Tubman knew how hard it was for the runaways to leave the comfort of the warm kitchen. Her previous trips taught her that someone would rebel when forced to continue.)*

Linking to History

J William Still was the son of former slaves; his father had bought his own freedom, while his mother had escaped from slavery. Still was an integral link between the Pennsylvania Society for the Abolition of Slavery and the African-American community. He also tried to end discrimination on Philadelphia railroads.

STRATEGIC READING FOR
Less-Proficient Readers

K Ask students to explain why Tubman threatens to kill the runaway rather than let him return. *(She cannot risk having the group break up. The runaway knows too much about her activities and might betray her, the other slaves, and the people providing them with food, shelter, and help along the way.)* Making Inferences

Set a Purpose Have students read to discover what Tubman does after she reaches Canada.

Mini-Lesson  Spelling

WORDS ENDING IN -able AND -ible Explain to students that the suffix *-able* is usually added to complete words to form adjectives. (However, as the word *indomitable* shows, it is sometimes added to roots rather than to complete words.) The suffix *-ible* is more commonly added to roots than to complete words; it too forms adjectives.

Application Write the following sentences on the chalkboard and ask students to write in their notebooks the correct spelling of the word formed by using the proper suffix, *-able* or *-ible*.

1. Harriet Tubman was courageous and depend(able).
2. Tubman was almost undetect(able) when moving through the woods.
3. The stops on the Underground Railroad were not suscept(ible) to discovery.
4. Frederick Douglass lived a life of incred(ible) adventure and accomplishment.
5. It was not accept(able) for the runaways to question Harriet Tubman's judgment.

Reteaching/Reinforcement
• *Unit Four Resource Book,* p. 71

Active Reading: CONNECT

Ask students if there is any cause for which they would be willing to risk imprisonment, or possibly their lives, as did those who aided the Underground Railroad.

Critical Thinking: ANALYZING

Have students explain what Tubman means by her statement, "freedom's not bought with dust." (*Possible responses: Freedom is not something you gain easily or cheaply. For a runaway to obtain freedom, he or she must be willing to pay the ultimate price—risking one's life for freedom.*)

CUSTOMIZING FOR Multiple Learning Styles

Musical Learners Invite students to discuss how music might have been part of Tubman's strategy to calm the runaways and urge them to continue onward. Encourage students to research spirituals and work songs that would have been popular among slaves in the South during Tubman's day.

Active Reading: CLARIFY

Ask students to explain why Still interviews the runaways. If students have difficulty, provide them with the following model:

Think-Aloud Model *I'm not sure what motivated Still to record the experiences of runaways. Perhaps he thought he might be able to locate other family members if they passed through his store, or maybe he wanted to document the experience of slaves so their lives and suffering would not be forgotten.*

---

could go back to the plantation. If a runaway returned, he would turn traitor; the master and the overseer would force him to turn traitor. The returned slave would disclose the stopping places, the hiding places, the corn stacks they had used with the full knowledge of the owner of the farm, the name of the German farmer who had fed them and sheltered them. These people who had risked their own security to help runaways would be ruined, fined, imprisoned.

She said, "We got to go free or die. And freedom's not bought with dust."

This time she told them about the long agony of the Middle Passage[7] on the old slave ships, about the black horror of the holds, about the chains and the whips. They too knew these stories. But she wanted to remind them of the long, hard way they had come, about the long, hard way they had yet to go. She told them about Thomas Sims, the boy picked up on the streets of Boston and sent back to Georgia. She said when they got him back to Savannah, got him in prison there, they whipped him until a doctor who was standing by watching said, "You will kill him if you strike him again!" His master said, "Let him die!"

Thus she forced them to go on. Sometimes she thought she had become nothing but a voice speaking in the darkness, cajoling, urging, threatening. Sometimes she told them things to make them laugh; sometimes she sang to them and heard the eleven voices behind her blending softly with hers, and then she knew that for the moment all was well with them.

She gave the impression of being a short, muscular, indomitable woman who could never be defeated. Yet at any moment she was liable to be seized by one of those curious fits of sleep,[8] which might last for a few minutes or for hours.

Even on this trip, she suddenly fell asleep in the woods. The runaways, ragged, dirty, hungry, cold, did not steal the gun, as they might have, and set off by themselves or turn back. They sat on the ground near her and waited patiently until she awakened. They had come to trust her implicitly, totally. They, too, had come to believe her repeated statement, "We got to go free or die." She was leading them into freedom, and so they waited until she was ready to go on.

Finally, they reached Thomas Garrett's house in Wilmington, Delaware. Just as Harriet had promised, Garrett gave them all new shoes and provided carriages to take them on to the next stop.

By slow stages they reached Philadelphia, where William Still hastily recorded their names and the plantations whence they had come and something of the life they had led in slavery. Then he carefully hid what he had written, for fear it might be discovered. In 1872 he published this record in book form and called it *The Underground Railroad*. In the foreword to his book he said: "While I knew the danger of keeping strict records, and while I did not then dream that in my day slavery would be blotted out, or that the time would come when I could publish these records, it used to afford me great satisfaction to take them down, fresh from the lips of

---

7. **Middle Passage:** the sea route along which African slaves were transported across the Atlantic Ocean to the Americas.
8. **curious fits of sleep:** mysterious spells of dizziness or unconsciousness experienced by Harriet Tubman.

WORDS TO KNOW
cajoling (kə-jō′lĭng) *adj.* urging gently; coaxing **cajole** *v.*
indomitable (ĭn-dŏm′ĭ-tə-bəl) *adj.* unable to be conquered

556

Mini-Lesson The Writer's Style

PARALLELISM Explain to students that using a similar structure or repeated words in parts of a sentence can add power and detail to a piece of writing. Such parallelism adds both emphasis and rhythm to sentences.

Application Use the following discussion prompts to help students understand parallelism in the highlighted passages on page 556:
- What do these passages have in common?
- What words or phrases are repeated in each passage?
- What is the effect of the repetition?

- If the repetition of similar words or structures was omitted, would the meaning change?
- How does parallelism help carry the reader along? How does it reinforce the author's ideas?

Have students record their responses in their reading logs. Then invite volunteers to share their thoughts with their classmates.

 The Writer's Craft

Parallelism, p. 112

556 THE LANGUAGE OF LITERATURE TEACHER'S EDITION

Daybreak—A Time to Rest (1967), Jacob Lawrence. Tempera on hardboard, 30" × 24", National Gallery of Art, Washington, D.C., anonymous gift. Copyright © Board of Trustees, National Gallery of Art, Washington, D.C.

Art Note

Daybreak—A Time to Rest by Jacob Lawrence Lawrence held his first solo show in 1938 at a YMCA in Harlem. He was hired the same year by the Works Progress Administration (WPA) Federal Art Project. The WPA (1935–1943) was an important New Deal agency that developed building projects to provide jobs for the unemployed. On the place of his work in contemporary art, Lawrence has said that his pictures express his experience (including his national, racial, and class identity) and reflect the American scene.

Reading the Art How does the emphasis placed on feet relate to the theme of rest? Would the meaning change if Lawrence had not included the feet as part of the painting? Why or why not?

Literary Concept: BIOGRAPHY

 Call attention to the author's use of the phrase "almost certainly stayed." Ask students what this reveals about the nature of Petry's biography. *(Possible responses: It indicates that the author is making every effort to present details that are historically accurate. The author is quick to point out where she is making reasonable assumptions based on research.)*

---

fugitives on the way to freedom, and to preserve them as they had given them."

William Still, who was familiar with all the station stops on the Underground Railroad, supplied Harriet with money and sent her and her eleven fugitives on to Burlington, New Jersey.

Harriet felt safer now, though there were danger spots ahead. But the biggest part of her job was over. As they went farther and farther north, it grew colder; she was aware of the wind on the Jersey ferry and aware of the cold damp in New York. From New York they went on to Syracuse, where the temperature was even lower.

In Syracuse she met the Reverend J. W. Loguen, known as "Jarm" Loguen. This was the beginning of a lifelong friendship. Both Harriet and Jarm Loguen were to become friends and supporters of Old John Brown.⁹

From Syracuse they went north again, into a colder, snowier city—Rochester. Here they almost certainly stayed with Frederick Douglass, for he wrote in his autobiography: "On one occasion I had eleven fugitives at

---

9. **Old John Brown:** an antislavery leader executed for leading a raid on the federal arsenal at Harpers Ferry, Virginia, in 1859.

FROM HARRIET TUBMAN: CONDUCTOR ON THE UNDERGROUND RAILROAD **557**

Multicultural Perspectives

THE ABOLITIONIST MOVEMENT (1830–1860)
While their contributions cannot be underestimated, Harriet Tubman, Thomas Garrett, and Frederick Douglass are only a few of the mid-19th-century leaders who sought an end to slavery.

Founded in 1833 by William Lloyd Garrison, the American Anti-Slavery Society distributed literature that documented the horrors of slavery throughout the slave states. The popular poet John Greenleaf Whittier, the novelist Harriet Beecher Stowe, and the orator Wendell Phillips all were outspoken in their call to abolish slavery.

On October 16, 1859, the activist John Brown initiated his plan to lead slaves in an armed rebellion. He and 21 followers stormed the arsenal at Harpers Ferry, Virginia (now in West Virginia). The next morning, Brown was captured by Robert E. Lee and was hanged on December 2, 1859. Brown's sincerity and dignity during his highly publicized trial led many abolitionists to regard him as a martyr.

THE LANGUAGE OF LITERATURE **TEACHER'S EDITION 557**

CUSTOMIZING FOR
Students Acquiring English

4 Explain that "bone-biting cold" is a figurative expression that emphasizes the extreme cold in the Canadian town in the wintertime.

Critical Thinking: ANALYZING

Q Have students explain how life for ex-slaves changed when they settled in Canada. *(There was no slavery. They could vote, run for office, serve on juries, own homes, and in general live like everyone else.)*

Literary Concept: MOTIVATION

R Ask students to discuss what motivated Tubman to make her home in St. Catharines. *(Possible responses: She could help the runaways make it through the harsh winter. It provided her with a place where she could stay in contact with people she cared about. Canada afforded her a safe place of freedom.)*

STRATEGIC READING FOR
Less-Proficient Readers

S Ask students to explain what work Harriet Tubman continued to do after leaving Canada. *(For the next six years, she made two trips a year to rescue slaves.)* **Drawing Conclusions**

CUSTOMIZING FOR
Gifted and Talented Students

Have students research to find other historical times when people were forced to escape enslavement or persecution, such as the ancient Israelites escaping from the Egyptians, Native Americans escaping the reservation system, or Cambodians fleeing the Khmer Rouge. Ask students to write a brief essay comparing these escape efforts to those of slaves in the United States.

---

the same time under my roof, and it was necessary for them to remain with me until I could collect sufficient money to get them to Canada. It was the largest number I ever had at any one time, and I had some difficulty in providing so many with food and shelter, but, as may well be imagined, they were not very fasticious in either direction, and were well content with very plain food, and a strip of carpet on the floor for a bed, or a place on the straw in the barn loft."

Late in December 1851, Harriet arrived in St. Catharines, Canada West (now Ontario), with the eleven fugitives. It had taken almost a month to complete this journey; most of the time had been spent getting out of Maryland.

That first winter in St. Catharines was a terrible one. Canada was a strange, frozen land, snow everywhere, ice everywhere, and a bone-biting cold the like of which none of them had ever experienced before. Harriet rented a small frame house in the town and set to work to make a home. The fugitives boarded with her. They worked in the forests, felling trees, and so did she. Sometimes she took other jobs, cooking or cleaning house for people in the town. She cheered on these newly arrived fugitives, working herself, finding work for them, praying for them, sometimes begging for them.

Often she found herself thinking of the beauty of Maryland, the mellowness of the soil, the richness of the plant life there. The climate itself made for an ease of living that could never be duplicated in this bleak, barren countryside.

In spite of the severe cold, the hard work, she came to love St. Catharines and the other towns and cities in Canada where black men lived. She discovered that freedom meant more than the right to change jobs at will, more than the right to keep the money that one earned. It was the right to vote and to sit on juries. It was the right to be elected to office. In Canada there were black men who were county officials and members of school boards. St. Catharines had a large colony of ex-slaves, and they owned their own homes, kept them neat and clean and in good repair. They lived in whatever part of town they chose and sent their children to the schools.

When spring came, she decided that she would make this small Canadian city her home—as much as any place could be said to be home to a woman who traveled from Canada to the Eastern Shore of Maryland as often as she did.

In the spring of 1852, she went back to Cape May, New Jersey. She spent the summer there, cooking in a hotel. That fall she returned, as usual, to Dorchester County and brought out nine more slaves, conducting them all the way to St. Catharines, in Canada West, to the bone-biting cold, the snow-covered forests—and freedom.

She continued to live in this fashion, spending the winter in Canada and the spring and summer working in Cape May, New Jersey, or in Philadelphia. She made two trips a year into slave territory, one in the fall and another in the spring. She now had a definite, crystallized purpose, and in carrying it out, her life fell into a pattern which remained unchanged for the next six years. ❖

WORDS TO KNOW **fastidious** (fă-stĭd′ē-əs) *adj.* difficult to please

558

Mini-Lesson Study Skills

GRAPHIC ORGANIZERS Tell students that one way to compare and contrast two subjects is to use a Venn diagram. This consists of two overlapping circles. The outside areas contain information unique to each subject. The overlapping area contains information common to both subjects.

Application Suggest that students use Venn diagrams to compare and contrast slave memoirs in the Alternative Activities on page 561. They can use the diagram as the basis for their reports. Students can refer to the sample shown for guidance.

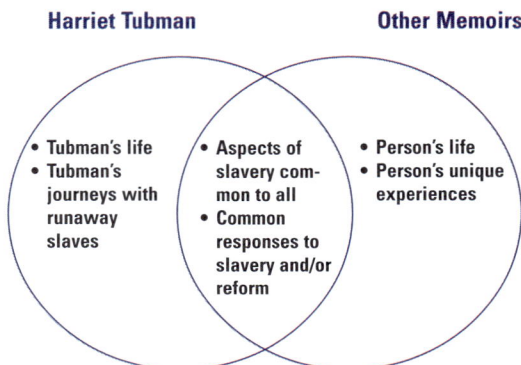

LITERARY INSIGHT

LETTER TO HARRIET TUBMAN
by Frederick Douglass

Rochester, August 29, 1868

Dear Harriet,

I am glad to know that the story of your eventful life has been written by a kindly lady, and that the same is soon to be published. You ask for what you do not need when you call upon me for a word of commendation. I need such words from you far more than you can need them from me, especially where your superior labors and devotion to the cause of the lately enslaved of our land are known as I know them. The difference between us is very marked. Most that I have done and suffered in the service of our cause has been in public, and I have received much encouragement at every step of the way. You, on the other hand, have labored in a private way. I have wrought in the day—you in the night. I have had the applause of the crowd and the satisfaction that comes of being approved by the multitude, while the most that you have done has been witnessed by a few trembling, scarred, and footsore bondmen and women, whom you have led out of the house of bondage, and whose heartfelt "*God Bless you*" has been your only reward. The midnight sky and the silent stars have been the witnesses of your devotion to freedom and of your heroism. Excepting John Brown—of sacred memory—I know of no one who has willingly encountered more perils and hardships to serve our enslaved people than you have. Much that you have done would seem improbable to those who do not know you as I know you. It is to me a great pleasure and a great privilege to bear testimony to your character and your works, and to say to those to whom you may come, that I regard you in every way truthful and trustworthy.

Your friend,
Frederick Douglass

Frederick Douglass (1818–1895, abolitionist, statesman) (1856), unidentified photographer. Ambrotype, 4 3/16" × 3 3/8", gift of an anonymous donor, National Portrait Gallery, Smithsonian Institution/Art Resource, New York.

LETTER TO HARRIET TUBMAN **559**

COMPREHENSION CHECK

1. What was Harriet Tubman's code name? *(Moses)*
2. Where did Tubman lead the runaways to secure their freedom? *(to Canada)*
3. Of what importance was the expression, "A friend with friends?" *(It was the password on the Underground Railroad.)*
4. How did people help the runaways along the way? *(They provided them with food, shelter, clothing, and funds to continue their journey north.)*

INSIGHT

1. How would you characterize the relationship between Douglass and Tubman based on this letter? *(Possible responses: Tubman and Douglass shared a warm and courteous friendship. Each sympathized and supported the other's work and felt respectful toward the other.)*
2. Do Tubman and Douglass appear to have the same relationship in the biography you have read? Explain why or why not. *(Possible response: The relationship between Tubman and Douglass seems less personal in Petry's biography. This could be because Petry was concentrating on the escape of the slaves, not the relationship between the two. If showing this relationship had been Petry's purpose, she would have been more likely to include letters like the one included in the Insight.)*

FREDERICK DOUGLASS (1817–1895)

Douglass, one of the founders of the U.S. civil rights movement, was a slave who escaped to the North as a young man. His famous autobiography, *Narrative of the Life of Frederick Douglass*, helped to convince many people of the injustice of slavery. In his many eloquent speeches and dedicated hard work, Douglass also was instrumental in demanding increased rights for women.

Assessment Option

INFORMAL ASSESSMENT To assess students' understanding of the selection, have them draw a storymap summarizing key events of Tubman's efforts to lead slaves to freedom. To help them organize their ideas, students can use a graphic organizer like a time line or a map marking Tubman's trail north.

Rubric

3 Full Accomplishment Student summarizes all key events, effectively using a graphic organizer to show either the passage of time or stages in Tubman's journey.

2 Substantial Accomplishment Student summarizes most key events and selects appropriate graphic organizer to map them.

1 Little or Partial Accomplishment Student summarizes only a few key events and has difficulty using a graphic organizer to map them.

THE LANGUAGE OF LITERATURE TEACHER'S EDITION **559**

From Personal Response to Critical Analysis

1. Responses will vary.
2. She wanted as many slaves as possible to know freedom.
3. Possible responses: Yes; once I left the plantation, there would be no turning back for me, so I would have to trust her. No; I could trust my life only to someone I had known very well for many years.
4. Possible response: Douglass is very accurate in how he portrays Tubman. However, he is too modest about his own accomplishments.
5. Possible responses: People have a moral obligation to break the law if it is in conflict with their conscience. Even though it was a good thing for people to help the slaves, if citizens broke laws when they didn't like them, there would be no order at all.

Another Pathway

Students' sketches will vary but should include some textual reference to dangers Tubman faced. If necessary, discuss with students the very real possibility of capture and of Tubman's being killed. Explain this was most likely to occur closer to the plantations. Students might consider whether there was more risk at night, when the slaves were moving, or during the daylight, when they rested.

Rubric

3 Full Accomplishment Students identify specific frightening aspects of the escape and fully illustrate them.

2 Substantial Accomplishment Students identify aspects that might have frightened Tubman but fail to sketch them in detail.

1 Little or Partial Accomplishment Students fail to isolate aspects that may have frightened Tubman.

RESPONDING OPTIONS

FROM PERSONAL RESPONSE TO CRITICAL ANALYSIS

REFLECT
1. What impressed you most about Harriet Tubman? Write your thoughts in your notebook, then share them with a partner.

RETHINK
2. What do you think was Tubman's primary motivation for risking her life to help people realize their dream of freedom?

3. Do you think that if you had been a slave who decided to run away, you would have entrusted your life to Harriet Tubman? Explain your answer.
   Consider
   - Tubman's knowledge and experience
   - the risk of getting caught and punished
   - Tubman's threat "Go on with us or die"

Close Textual Reading

RELATE
4. Review the Literary Insight selection on page 559. Do you agree or disagree with Frederick Douglass's evaluation of Harriet Tubman? Explain your opinion.

Literary Link

5. People who opened their homes to escaping slaves broke the Fugitive Slave Law. Do you think that breaking the law is justified in such cases? Why or why not?

Multimodal Learning
ANOTHER PATHWAY

If you had been Harriet Tubman, what aspects of helping slaves to escape would have frightened you most? Why? Draw a sketch, based on details in the selection, to convey your answer. Compare and contrast your response with the responses of other students.

QUICKWRITES

1. Imagine that you are a slave escaping to freedom in Canada. Write a detailed **diary entry** describing one day of your journey.

2. Harriet Tubman helped many people escape from slavery. Think about a person who has helped you through a very difficult situation. Write a **description** of this person.

3. Imagine that you are one of the slaves whom Tubman has led safely to Canada. Write a **letter** to your former master in Maryland, telling him your thoughts now that you are free.

📁 **PORTFOLIO** Save your writing. You may want to use it later as a springboard to a piece for your portfolio.

LITERARY CONCEPTS

A **biography** is a type of nonfiction in which a writer gives an account of someone else's life. Some biographies contain elements of fiction in addition to facts. This excerpt from *Harriet Tubman: Conductor on the Underground Railroad* contains dialogue, for example, as well as descriptions of some of Tubman's thoughts. The author, clearly could not have known what was actually said and thought by Tubman, but she made an educated guess. What do the re-created thoughts and dialogue add to the biography? Support your opinion with examples from the selection.

560 UNIT FOUR PART 2: UNLIKELY HEROES

Literary Concepts

Explain to students that biographers rely on a variety of resources for their reconstruction of a person's life. A writer often may have to make "educated guesses" about what a person said or did, especially if the subject is from the distant past. Point out to students that some of the most effective and dramatic parts of the biography are when Tubman speaks. Her command to "Go on with us or die" would not have the same impact if Petry had written, "Tubman sometimes was forced to threaten people to continue moving."

QuickWrites

1. Point out to students that the major events of the runaway slave's "day" may actually occur while he or she is traveling at night.
2. Students may feel more comfortable if they change names of people or places in their descriptions.
3. Ask students to consider what feelings a former slave would have toward the former master. Their letters should convey these emotions, as well as their thoughts.

 **The Writer's Craft**

Journal Writing, pp. 222–223
Personal Voice, pp. 316–317

560 THE LANGUAGE OF LITERATURE TEACHER'S EDITION

ALTERNATIVE ACTIVITIES

Using a computer database or library resources, research slave memoirs. Then present an oral report, comparing what you have discovered in your research with what you have learned from this selection.

ACROSS THE CURRICULUM

Geography/Mathematics Imagine that you are leading slaves from Dorchester County, Maryland, to freedom in St. Catharines, Ontario, Canada. Do some research to find out what present-day trails and roads would be most suitable for the trip. Select your route and calculate how many miles a day you will have to travel to reach your destination in a month. Also decide on the safest places to stay along the way.

WORDS TO KNOW

EXERCISE A
On your paper, complete each simile (comparison containing *like* or *as*) to illustrate the meaning of the word in dark type.

1. The slave's thin hat was **borne** on the wind like . . .
2. When the master learned of the slaves' escape, he became as **sullen** as . . .
3. After many days on the road, the runaway slave girl looked as **disheveled** as . . .
4. The mistreated slaves became as **mutinous** toward their master as . . .
5. The **fastidious** plantation owner was as difficult to please as . . .

EXERCISE B Use the remaining vocabulary words—*instill, dispel, eloquence, cajole,* and *indomitable*—in a short paragraph that answers the question, How does Harriet Tubman compare with your idea of a hero?

ANN PETRY

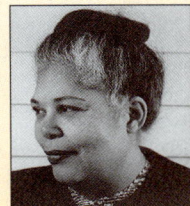
1912–

Ann Petry was born above her father's drugstore in Old Saybrook, Connecticut. As a child in one of only two African-American families in the small town, she heard family tales about her runaway-slave grandfather, and about her father, who had resisted a racial attack when he had opened his own pharmacy.

Despite her interest in writing as a career, Petry graduated from the Connecticut College of Pharmacy and went to work in the family store. There she listened to the stories of townspeople—people who would inspire some of the characters in her writing.

After she married, Petry moved to New York, where she worked as an ad salesperson, a reporter and editor for Harlem newspapers, a recreation specialist at a Harlem elementary school, and an activist for racial justice and women's rights. During this time, a number of her short stories were printed in magazines. One of these attracted the attention of a major publishing company, from which she received a literary fellowship and encouragement to write a novel. The novel she wrote—*The Street*, a story of an African-American woman's struggle to survive in a hostile Harlem neighborhood—made Petry an overnight success. She was the first African-American female to write about problems African-American women face in the slums.

OTHER WORKS *Tituba of Salem Village, Legends of the Saints* Extended Reading

FROM HARRIET TUBMAN: CONDUCTOR ON THE UNDERGROUND RAILROAD

Alternative Activities

Explain to students that slavery was not restricted to the Southern United States but occurred in many regions of the world. Encourage students to research slave memoirs from other areas. For example, the memoir *A History of Mary Prince, A West Indian Slave, Related By Herself* (Ann Arbor: University of Michigan Press, 1993) is an account of slavery in the Caribbean, told by a former slave who escaped to Great Britain.

ANN PETRY

Petry has said that the reason she wrote Tubman's biography was because she felt most textbooks "do not give an adequate or accurate picture of the history of slavery in the United States."

Words To Know

Exercise A
Similes will vary. Accept all reasonable comparisons using *like* or *as*.

Exercise B
Be sure that students use the words correctly in their paragraphs.

Reteaching/Reinforcement
- *Unit Four Resource Book* p. 72

Across the Curriculum

Geography/Mathematics
The Road North Point out to students that they will have to use an atlas-style road map to plan their trip, especially because Tubman could not have taken major highways or roads on her escape. Point out that maps have a scale, and students will have to measure their charted course carefully to compute mileage.

ADDITIONAL SUGGESTION

History Cooperative Learning *Building Biography* Have students work in small groups to compile a short biographical sketch of a civil rights leader using some of the tools biographers use:

- oral histories
- diaries
- newspapers
- interviews
- property records
- memoirs
- other historical accounts

Literary Links

Ask students to compare Harriet Tubman to Mrs. Wynnes in "The Dinner Party." How does the response of the slave owners to Moses mirror the stereotyping Mrs. Wynnes faces from the colonel? How may this stereotyping give Tubman an advantage over her adversaries? *(Possible responses: The colonel expects Mrs. Wynnes to be unable to handle a crisis, and the slave owners assume that only a man could lead slaves to freedom. Tubman may use this stereotype to her advantage, because the slave owners would be looking for a man.)*

OVERVIEW

To gain a deeper appreciation of the nonfiction selections they have read in this unit, students will explore the characteristics of an eyewitness report and then create their own well-developed example in this lesson.

Objectives

- To plan an eyewitness report by considering such elements as topic, focus, and details
- To draft an eyewitness report and solicit a response
- To revise, edit, and publish an eyewitness report
- To reflect on the process of writing an eyewitness report

Skills

LITERATURE
- Using dialogue

WRITING AND LANGUAGE
- Exploring topics
- Adding details
- Using dialogue
- Relating incidents

GRAMMAR AND USAGE
- Sentence combining

MEDIA LITERACY
- Interpreting a program of events
- Studying an article

- Finding the 5 *W*s and an *H* in newspaper articles

SPEAKING, LISTENING, AND VIEWING
- Conferencing
- Holding a television news show
- Reading aloud
- Group discussion

CRITICAL THINKING
- Selecting relevant information

Teaching Strategy:
STUMBLING BLOCK

A Students may be surprised to learn that many writers find a blank sheet of paper (or an empty computer screen) a source of anxiety. Tell students that the most effective way to move past that feeling is to write *something*. Reassure students that once the clean surface has words on it, other ideas will flow more quickly. Tell students that possible jottings might include unrelated ideas, notes, questions, and examples. Guide students to try this technique by jotting down their responses and reactions to this passage in the text.

WRITING FROM EXPERIENCE

WRITING TO EXPLAIN

Think about the selections you've just read in Unit Four, "Facing the Enemy." Could you picture the fight of the mother baboon as you read the story? Could you hear the tolling of the bell on the funeral train as Lincoln was brought to Springfield? The rich details that are included in an eyewitness report can make you feel as if you were there.

GUIDED ASSIGNMENT
Write an Eyewitness Report This lesson will help you write your own eyewitness report of an event that captures the "you-are-there" excitement for readers.

Event Photos

① Look for the Story

Has anyone ever asked you to describe something you've seen? When you describe a scene or situation for a person who wasn't there, you're giving an eyewitness report. The following suggestions can help you explore topics for your own eyewitness report.

Writing About Past Events What events have you seen that you'd like to write about? You might have seen a live performance, such as a concert or a sports event, that grabbed your attention. Make a list of such events, in your journal. Then write a one-paragraph description of an event that you saw.

Hunting for the Story You may not realize it, but exciting events are happening all around you—at school and within your community. Is there an upcoming concert or sports event that you think might be exciting? Think of yourself as a reporter on the hunt for a story. Where can you go?

Program of Events

B What kinds of information does each item give that the other items don't give?

The freestyle event was so exciting! It really ought to be written up

562   UNIT FOUR: FACING THE ENEMY

PRINT AND MEDIA RESOURCES

UNIT FOUR RESOURCE BOOK
Prewriting Activity, p. 75
Elaboration, p. 76
Peer Response Guide, pp. 77–78
Revision and Editing, p. 79
Student Model, p. 80

GRAMMAR MINI-LESSONS
Transparencies, pp. 28, 46, 47

WRITING MINI-LESSONS
Transparencies, pp. 40, 41

ACCESS FOR STUDENTS ACQUIRING ENGLISH
Reading and Writing Support

FORMAL ASSESSMENT
Guidelines for Writing Assessment

 **LASERLINKS**
Writing Springboard

This girl was amazing! I should include her in my report.

This article doesn't sound exciting. I think I'll write my own version of the Special Olympics and send it in.

Special Competition Results in Countless Winners

NEW HAVEN, Conn. The Special Olympics World Games ended Sunday, and almost everyone concerned was happy with the achievements—athletic and otherwise—over the last nine days.

There was almost endless competition for the 7,200 athletes, all mentally retarded and some physically disabled, from 140 nations. They made new friends from far-off nations. And they proved to themselves and to the public that mental retardation is not the end of a productive life, but just one more obstacle to be dealt with.

Frank Litsky
from *Chicago Tribune*

Article

2 Analyze the Information

Take a look at the souvenir items on these pages. How could you use items like these to provide background information for your report?

- **LASERLINKS**
  - WRITING SPRINGBOARD
- **WRITING COACH**

WRITING FROM EXPERIENCE **563**

Teaching Strategy: MODELING

B To show students how to generate writing ideas from a springboard, model how to use the items pictured to spark ideas. Read the article aloud to the class and present the following think-aloud model or one of your own:

Think-Aloud Model: *This Special Olympics article makes me think of the time I helped out in a scouting event for physically challenged kids. That might make a good topic.*

Then invite students to work in small groups to discuss their reactions to these models. Students should note that the program provides a list of events and times. The photograph shows what one athlete looks like. The article tells how many athletes participated.

CUSTOMIZING FOR
Students Acquiring English

C Students may be unfamiliar with the Special Olympics. Explain that it is an international athletic competition for mentally and physically challenged amateur athletes. The winners receive medals. Invite students to share with their classmates any experiences they have had with Special Olympics.

WRITING SPRINGBOARD

Kayaking A group of teenagers kayak down some rapids, and one participant helps another whose kayak has overturned.

Side B, Frame 15307

Writing Prompt Write an eyewitness report about a time you saw people helping one another. For example, you could focus on teammates participating in a sport, or you could write about people's actions during an emergency or a disaster.

THE LANGUAGE OF LITERATURE TEACHER'S EDITION **563**

CUSTOMIZING FOR
Less-Proficient Writers

D Remind these students that freewriting means writing nonstop. Be sure they understand that it means writing whatever comes into their minds without stopping to worry about whether the ideas are good or the spelling is correct. Freewriting is most successful if the writer sets a goal, such as writing for 15 minutes or filling one page. For productive freewriting, remind students not to go back and review, cross anything out, or interrupt flashes of insight.

Writing Skill:
USING A COMPUTER

E Suggest that students who do their freewriting on a computer dim the screen so they cannot see their writing. Reassure them that the computer's memory will still be recording their ideas, but they will not be able to see what they have written until they once again brighten the screen. This will prevent them from stopping and criticizing their writing.

Teaching Strategy:
STUMBLING BLOCK

F Inexperienced writers often have difficulty narrowing a topic. Suggest that students use a triangle, such as the one shown below, to narrow a broad writing topic:

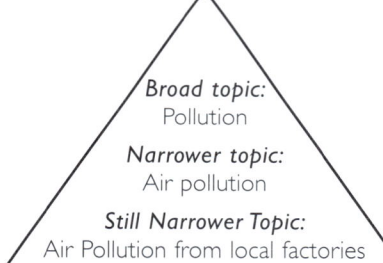

PREWRITING

Uncovering the Story

At-the-Scene Reporting As a reporter, it's your job to find the story. What events can you find that you'd really like to share with others? You can use the suggestions on these two pages to record the details about your event.

❶ Choose Your Topic

Out of all of the events you have witnessed or plan to attend, is there one in particular that really grabs your attention? This might be a humorous event or one that you find powerful, tragic, or inspiring. You might try freewriting **D** **E** about the events you've seen to decide which event interests you the most.

❷ Look for a Focus

If the topic you chose seems broad, you may need to narrow your focus. What part of the event stands out? This could be the focus of **F** your account. For example, one student attended the Special Olympics and wanted to write about what she saw. Since the topic of the Special Olympics is too broad, she decided to write about only one event.

❸ Record the Details

There are different ways to go about recording details about your topic. You might use one or all of the methods described on the next page.

564 UNIT FOUR: FACING THE ENEMY

Mini-Lesson: Speaking Listening and Viewing

GROUP DISCUSSION A very effective way to select and narrow a topic is to discuss it as a group. Explain to students that many professional writers use this technique by conferencing with other writers and editors. A series of questions can be used to focus the discussion. Write these possibilities on the board:
- Why do you find this topic interesting?
- Who are your readers?
- Will they find the topic as interesting as you do? Why or why not?

Application Have students prepare focus questions like those above about their topic. Then arrange students in small groups to talk about their topic choices. Suggest that each group elect a moderator to keep the discussion on track and a recorder to jot down ideas.

Getting the Facts Your main goal is to help your readers watch the event through your eyes. Good reporters take careful notes and ask questions to get the facts for their stories. These questions begin with five w's and an h: *Who, What, When, Where, Why,* and *How.* You can use these kinds of questions to get the facts you need.

- Who participated in the event?
- What happened?
- When did the event take place?
- Where did the event take place?
- Why were these games established?
- How did the event end?

Using an Observation Chart Good reporters also are skilled observers. The SkillBuilder at the right will help you sharpen your observation skills to take in all the details of a scene. As you observe an event, you might make an observation chart similar to the one below, which one student made to record the details she witnessed.

Using Your Camera If you're planning to attend the event you'd like to write about, think about taking a camera or camcorder along. You might use it to help you record some of the excitement and to illustrate your final report.

Observation Chart

SkillBuilder

 CRITICAL THINKING

Selecting Relevant Information

Good reporters take in what they see and hear as they observe an event. A tape recorder is a good tool to help you accurately record what people say. As you play the tape later, choose quotes that will give your readers a clear sense of time, place, and action. Avoid quotes that use vague referents and dull facts. Consider the following quotes that one student overheard at the Special Olympics. Which is clearer?

"She's really doing a good job."

"Today, Alexis can forget about feeling different because she has Down syndrome," her dad said.

APPLYING WHAT YOU'VE LEARNED
Take a few notes on a conversation that occurs in the cafeteria or at the dinner table. How does the dialogue give you a sense of the scene and the action that is taking place?

THINK & PLAN

Reflecting on Your Ideas

1. What details will you include to help your readers "see" the event?
2. How will you use quotes in your draft to help your readers understand the importance of the event?

WRITING FROM EXPERIENCE **565**

Teaching Strategy: MODELING

To demonstrate how reporters use these questions, ask students to bring in some newspaper articles that cover the five w's and an h in the first paragraph or two. Select one article at random and model the process for students. Then distribute the articles and have students work in small groups to isolate the five w's and an h. Have students show their findings in a chart.

Teaching Strategy: STUMBLING BLOCK

Students often believe that observation charts and other graphic organizers must be grammatically correct. Explain that the purpose of an observation chart is to gather and organize details. As a result, grammar, punctuation, and spelling are not critically important at this stage in the writing process. Reassure them that their goal is to group and organize ideas. Also suggest that students organize their chart around a controlling idea, such as the five senses.

SkillBuilder CRITICAL THINKING

SELECTING RELEVANT INFORMATION
Inexperienced writers often have difficulty distinguishing between relevant and irrelevant details. They often include irrelevant details in an essay because these details are true and accurate aspects of the event. Explain to students that their job as writers is to choose their details to fit the picture they are creating. Be sure they understand that just because a detail is true does not necessarily mean that it is relevant.

Application Explain to students that mystery writers often include irrelevant details to throw readers off the track. Have students select a mystery story they have read and isolate the relevant and irrelevant details. Suggest that students show their findings on a chart.

Additional Suggestions Invite students to underline the irrelevant details in the conversation they recorded in the cafeteria.

THE LANGUAGE OF LITERATURE TEACHER'S EDITION **565**

Writing Skill:
USING A COMPUTER

Students may find it easier to write their eyewitness reports on a computer. Students can use The Writing Coach, which provides columns for peer response and revision ideas, as well as preprogrammed tips. If students are using computers, remind them to save all drafts separately on a disk. Before students start writing, show them how to title each draft to make sure that nothing is lost or overwritten in successive drafts.

Teaching Strategy: MANAGING THE PAPER LOAD

Students often desire detailed feedback at this stage of the composing process. Instead, as you read the drafts, concentrate on only the one element that each student finds most troublesome. Students can work out less serious problems in a peer review setting.

DRAFTING

Sharing Your Experience

The Scene in Your Mind Remember how you felt after reading an exciting account of an event? What can you include in your draft to help your readers visualize the scene you witnessed? These pages will help you report on the experience for your readers.

1 Draft and Discover

As you write your draft, try to keep the image of the scene in your mind. The details you use uncover bit by bit the photograph of the event in your mind. You might start by writing everything you remember about the event. Try to use details that will help your readers feel as if they were at the scene with you.

Student's Discovery Draft

> The 100-meter freestyle swimming event at the Special Olympics was very exciting. Lots of people came to the race to support the competitors.
>
> At the start of the race, many of the swimmers didn't look as if they would finish. But their family members and the cheering crowds didn't really seem to care whether anyone won a medal. They just wanted the swimmers to finish the race.
>
> A family nearby was dressed all in blue sweatshirts that had the name "Alexis" stenciled in white lettering. They carried a big sign that read, "Go! Alexis" and cheered for a girl in Lane 1. She looked small and scared next to the others. When the race started, there was so much splashing, Alexis could barely be seen.
>
> Alexis was in last place for a while. Then there were only five people ahead of her. Soon she had caught up with a girl in a red swimming cap. Finally it was over. Alexis came in second place, winning a silver medal.

Maybe I should focus more on Alexis rather than on everyone there.

I can use photos to make a slide presentation.

566

 WRITING SPRINGBOARD
The Chicago Flood This video footage shows how the flooding of underground tunnels created chaos in the city's downtown area—and left fish swimming in the basement of City Hall.

Side B, Frame 17546

Writing Prompt Think of a truly eye-opening event you have seen, and write an eyewitness report about it. The event can be shocking, like a flood or storm, or thrilling, like a concert or other performance.

566 THE LANGUAGE OF LITERATURE TEACHER'S EDITION

2 Check Your Progress

Are there parts of the experience that you are having trouble capturing on paper? You might ask someone else who was there to help you recall some of the details. Snapshots, programs, ticket stubs, or other kinds of memorabilia from the event can also refresh your memory.

3 Sharpen the Focus

Once you have evaluated your writing, you may decide that you need to change a few things as you fine-tune your draft. The following suggestions will help you rework your draft.

Add Colorful Details Good eyewitness reports keep readers' attention by relating facts in interesting ways. Dates, names, and even weather conditions can help make the event clearer for your readers, but by themselves these facts can be boring. The SkillBuilder at the right can help you describe incidents that will enliven your writing.

Show, Don't Tell As you write your draft, try using descriptions that show, rather than tell, what happened. In the student model, the sentence "The 100-meter freestyle swimming event at the Special Olympics was very exciting" is an example of telling. The writer could show the excitement with sentences such as "Alexis's arms moved like windmills. Soon she had passed another swimmer."

Add Some Dialogue Including portions of conversations can be more effective than writing several paragraphs of description. Is there an interesting quote from an official, a participant, or an observer that you can remember?

 PEER RESPONSE

You might ask peer reviewers to read your draft aloud and share their reactions to these questions:

- Which parts of my report did you have trouble "seeing"?
- What images or ideas do you recall most vividly?
- What emotions did you feel as you read my account?

SkillBuilder

 WRITER'S CRAFT

Relating Incidents
Many writers include memorable incidents in their reports to hold readers' interest and to elaborate on the points they wish to make. Make sure the incidents you use relate to an overall theme or an important point that you associate with the event. For example, if a student wanted to point out the camaraderie she saw at the Special Olympics, she would include incidents that show people cheering for competitors or helping in some way.

APPLYING WHAT YOU'VE LEARNED
As you read through each incident of the event, ask yourself, "Does this incident fit in with how I felt about the whole event?" Include incidents that make your point.

 WRITING HANDBOOK

For more information on relating incidents, see page 827 of the Writing Handbook.

RETHINK & EVALUATE

Preparing to Revise

1. What did you discover about the event as you wrote your draft?
2. Has writing your draft changed your view of the experience? Explain how.

WRITING FROM EXPERIENCE 567

Teaching Strategy: MANAGING THE PAPER LOAD

K As you walk around the class, skim the drafts of several students to see how well they are organizing information. Point out any paragraph in which the main idea is unclear, more supporting details and examples are needed, or irrelevant ideas are included. If you see problems, confer with these students.

Writing Skill: DRAFTING

L Explain to students that the reason why some experienced writers prefer to write in longhand is that it gives them more time to think. Some writers find that the slower pace of handwriting, as opposed to inputting at the computer, allows ideas to surface and develop.

CUSTOMIZING FOR
Less-Proficient Writers

M Inexperienced writers often avoid using dialogue because they are unsure of its use. Provide students with these guidelines:

- Use speaker's tags—such as "she said" and "he shouted"—to identify the speaker and tell how things are said.
- Put quotation marks around the speaker's exact words.
- Capitalize the first letter of a quotation. Also, capitalize the first letter of a new sentence within a quotation.
- Place commas and periods inside quotation marks. Place question marks or exclamation points inside quotation marks if they belong to the quotation itself.
- Begin a new paragraph each time the speaker changes.

SkillBuilder WRITER'S CRAFT

RELATING INCIDENTS Remind students to tailor their incidents to match the point they wish to make. Using specific student examples, guide students to cut extraneous details from their incidents and sharpen the points that make their report clear. Help students edit their incidents by providing this checklist:

- What does this incident add to the point I am making?
- Are there any irrelevant details in this incident?
- How would the report change if I cut this incident?
- What sensory details could I add to the incident to hold my reader's interest?

Applications Invite students to work in pairs to read each other's eyewitness reports and discuss the suitability of each incident.

Additional Suggestions Suggest that students reread their previous writings and list examples of incidents they used.

Reteaching/Reinforcement

 The Writer's Craft

Incidents, p. 256

CUSTOMIZING FOR

Students Acquiring English

N These students may find it difficult to proofread their work for spelling errors. You may wish to pair less-proficient students with peers who can help them spot and correct misspelled words. Suggest that students acquiring English begin a personal glossary of words they often misspell. Have students refer to the glossary and add to it when they proofread subsequent assignments.

Teaching Strategy: MODELING

O Invite a volunteer to read the revised student report aloud. List the details, dialogue, and incidents on the board. Point out that the details appeal to the reader's senses and help readers get a more vivid mental picture of the action. The quotations act as description to sharpen the images and make the eyewitness account more specific.

REVISING AND PUBLISHING

Finishing Your Report

An Impression That Lasts Your eyewitness report can make a lasting impression on your readers. As you revise, consider using some or all of the following suggestions to polish your draft.

Student's Final Draft

NewsScope Special Events • August Edition   2

A Race for Silver

by Regina Selkirk

There were plenty of tears and hugs at the 100-meter freestyle swimming event of the Special Olympics.

Many people were there to support the competitors and to pass out hugs. One family all wore blue sweatshirts with the name "Alexis" stenciled in white lettering. They carried a banner with the words, "Go! Alexis" and waved to a girl in Lane 1.

Alexis looked small and scared. When the race started, there was so much splashing that Alexis could barely be seen. Her dad pointed to her yellow cap bobbing above the water.

"Today, Alexis can forget about feeling different because she has Down syndrome," her dad said. "We just want her to have some fun today."

Alexis was in last place for a while, but soon there were only five people ahead of her. "Go, Alex!" her brother yelled. "You can do it!"

Alexis's arms moved like windmills. Soon she had passed another swimmer! Now only a girl in a white cap was ahead of her. Alexis was so close. Could she win a gold medal?

At the finish line, Alexis and the girl in the white cap seemed to reach the wall at the same time. The audience was silent as the judges tried to sort out who had won. The family in blue sweatshirts crossed their fingers. Finally the announcer said that the girl in the white cap had won. Even though Alexis didn't get the gold, her family was thrilled with her silver medal.

568 UNIT FOUR: FACING THE ENEMY

1. Revise and Edit

Use the following tips as you revise your report.

- Add details to show the action rather than tell about it.
- Use the SkillBuilder on the right to help you vary your sentence lengths and create more interest.
- Consult the Standards for Evaluation and the Editing Checklist to be sure you have given readers enough information to understand the event and presented the details in a way that is easy to follow.
- Notice how the student's final draft at the left incorporates interesting details and dialogue.

How do the details this student used help you picture the scene?

What role do the quotations play in the report?

2 Present Your Final Draft

If the topic you wrote about featured dramatic scenes or images, you might consider a more visual format for your final report. This student turned her report into a multimedia presentation describing her experience at the Special Olympics. This presentation included slides and a script. The student presented her report to various organizations. See the Multimedia Handbook for tips on accessing information on-line and for making a multimedia presentation.

PUBLISHING IDEAS

- You might send your report to a special-interest newsletter.
- You might share your report with special-interest groups on the World Wide Web.

Standards for Evaluation

An eyewitness report
- uses sensory details, dialogue, and action verbs to show what was observed, bringing the event to life
- has a clear focus
- provides readers with the information they need to understand the event
- presents details in a sensible order that is easy to follow

---

SkillBuilder

GRAMMAR FROM WRITING

Sentence Combining

One way to vary your sentence lengths and show clearer relationships among ideas is by combining two shorter sentences into one. For example:

Alexis was in last place for a while. Soon there were only five people ahead of her.

Alexis was in last place for a while, but soon there were only five people ahead of her.

GRAMMAR HANDBOOK

For more information on sentence combining, see page 860 in the Grammar Handbook.

Editing Checklist Review the following list as you revise your draft.

- Did you check for misspelled words?
- Did you vary your sentence lengths?
- Did you proofread your draft?

REFLECT & ASSESS

Evaluating the Experience

1. How did you choose the event that you wrote about?
2. How did you help the readers feel as if they were there?

 PORTFOLIO Add your report and any photographs you might have of the event to your portfolio.

WRITING FROM EXPERIENCE 569

Speaking, Listening, and Viewing: TELEVISION NEWS SHOW

P Suggest that students present their eyewitness reports as a live television news show. Arrange students in groups to report on their "late-breaking" news event. To make their newscasts more realistic, have students include props such as microphones, cameras, and signs. If possible, videotape the newscasts so students can watch their performances later.

Teaching Strategy: MANAGING THE PAPER LOAD

Q If students present their eyewitness reports as a TV news show, save time by evaluating only the oral presentations and not their written papers.

PORTFOLIO

Invite students to rank their papers for possible inclusion in their portfolios. Have students devise their own ranking systems to help them sort their work.

Standards for Evaluation

Have students review their eyewitness reports for the following:

Ideas and Content
- has a clear focus
- uses sensory details, dialogue and action verbs to show what was observed, bring the event to life
- provides readers with the information they need to understand the event
- has a strong opening and closing

Structure and Form
- uses well-organized paragraphs and a clear organization
- includes transitional words and phrases to show relationships among ideas
- uses a variety of sentence structures

Grammar, Usage, and Mechanics
- contains no more than two or three minor errors in grammar and usage
- contains no more than two or three minor errors in spelling, capitalization, and punctuation

---

SkillBuilder  GRAMMAR FROM WRITING

SENTENCE COMBINING Show students the following ways to combine sentences:

1. Use conjunctions such as *and, but,* or *or* to join two complete sentences. Place a comma before the conjunction.

2. Drop repeated words and ideas and use *and, but,* or *or* to join the remaining sentence parts. Do not use commas, as in the following example:

   Riding over potholes can damage your bike.

   Riding over bumpy roads can damage your bike.

   Riding over potholes <u>and</u> bumpy roads can damage your bike.

3. Move an important word from one sentence to another, as in this example:

Computers have many uses. The uses are different.
Computers have many different uses.

Application Have students combine the following:
1. I love winter sports. I especially like skiing.
2. I have two cats. I have a parrot.

Reteaching/Reinforcement

Grammar Mini-Lessons transparencies, pp. 28, 46, 47
Writing Mini-Lessons transparencies, pp. 40, 41

The Writer's Craft

Sentence Combining, pp. 304–313

THE LANGUAGE OF LITERATURE TEACHER'S EDITION 569

UNIT REVIEW

This feature allows students to reflect on what they have learned in Unit Four and to assess how well they understand what they have learned. This feature provides students with multiple opportunities for self-assessment, although you may wish to use some of the activities to informally assess specific skills such as speaking and listening or cooperative work.

Objectives

- To allow students to reflect on and assess their understanding of theme
- To allow students to reflect on and assess their understanding of literary concepts such as biography, autobiography, and character changes
- To provide students with the opportunity to assess and build their portfolios

Reflecting on Theme

OPTION 1

Students should skim each selection, taking note of the qualities that make their chosen characters heroic. Suggest that students record this information in charts to which they can refer later when creating their drawings and character sketches.

OPTION 2

Suggest that students organize their thoughts in charts or Venn diagrams that detail the similarities and differences between each character's situation and the ways in which they would handle the same situation. They should then refer to this information when writing their compare-and-contrast paragraphs.

OPTION 3

Remind students that they are preparing an outline which should organize main points and supporting details for their speeches. Suggest that students brainstorm a list of possible enemies and ways to confront these enemies, supporting their choices with details from the selections and their own experience.

REFLECT & ASSESS

UNIT FOUR: FACING THE ENEMY

Whom or what do you consider to be your enemies in life? How do you choose to deal with them? Perhaps the selections in Unit Four have influenced your thoughts on these questions. To explore them further, complete one or more of the options in each of the following sections.

REFLECTING ON THEME

OPTION 1 **Choosing Heroes** Look back through the selections in this unit, picking out two or three characters who you think act the most heroically. Create a "Heroes' Gallery" with drawings and brief character sketches of them.

OPTION 2 **Comparing and Contrasting** From this unit's selections, choose some situations that you found particularly interesting or gripping. How well do the characters handle those situations? How do you think you would react to the situations? Write a few paragraphs, comparing and contrasting the characters' actions with what you think yours would be.

OPTION 3 **Giving Advice** Prepare an outline of a speech entitled "How to Face Up to Your Enemy in Life." First decide who or what might be considered an enemy. Then, in offering your advice, draw on examples from the selections in this unit and from your personal experience.

Self Assessment: Make a list of the most important things that you feel you must personally struggle against in life—perhaps school subjects that you find difficult or attitudes in society that you do not agree with. For each item on your list, make a note of any new ways of tackling them you have learned. Jot down the titles of any selections that have influenced your thinking.

REVIEWING LITERARY CONCEPTS

OPTION 1 **Contrasting Biography and Autobiography** What is the difference between biography and autobiography? What are the strengths and weaknesses of each form? Fill in a chart like the one shown. Then discuss with a partner your ideas about what information can be learned from each form that cannot be learned from the other.

Autobiography		Biography	
Strengths	**Weaknesses**	**Strengths**	**Weaknesses**

Self-Assessment In order to help students answer these questions, encourage them to review the selections in this unit as well as the notes they took while reading them. Have students consider the ways in which the selections influenced their thoughts about personal struggle. Students should then use this information to compile their lists.

OPTION 2 **Examining Character Changes** Many of the characters in Unit Four change in some way. Select three or four characters that you think change in very important ways. Record each change in a chart like the one shown. Then identify the character who you think changes the most. Discuss your choice with a partner. If the two of you don't agree, try to persuade your partner.

Character: _____	
Beginning of the Story	**End of the Story**

PORTFOLIO BUILDING

- **QuickWrites** Look through the QuickWrites assignments that you completed in this unit. Choose one or two pieces that you would like to revise in the light of what you have learned since writing them. For each piece you choose, write a note saying what you would change, attach it to the piece, and add both to your portfolio.
- **Writing About Literature** In this unit, you wrote a personal response to one of the unit's stories or poems. Reread your personal response. How does it sound now? What, if anything, would you add to it or delete from it? Write a sentence or two explaining the subject of your response and the way you responded.
- **Writing from Experience** Earlier in this unit, you wrote an eyewitness report. Reread your report, pretending that you are reading it for the first time. What details stand out? Does the report cover the essential facts? In a note for your portfolio, tell whether you think your report is effective, giving reasons for your opinion.
- **Personal Choice** Look back through your records and evaluations of all the activities you completed in this unit, as well as any activities and writing you have done on your own. In which activity did you best express your own thoughts about facing enemies? Write a paragraph explaining what these thoughts are and how you were able to express them in the activity. Attach the paragraph to your record and add both to your portfolio.

 Self-Assessment: Compare what you have added to your portfolio in Unit Four with the pieces you added in previous units. Can you see any progress in your work? In what areas? Jot down your thoughts in your notebook.

SETTING GOALS

As you completed the reading and writing activities in this unit, you may have identified certain writers whose work you would like to read more of. Write their names in your notebook, noting which of the titles listed in the Other Works section of their biographies sound interesting to you.

 Self-Assessment: With a small group of classmates, discuss how well you feel you understand the following literary terms introduced in this unit. On the basis of your discussion, divide the terms among the members of the group. Briefly explain to the group the meanings of the terms you have been assigned.

classic	science fiction
alliteration	humor
author's purpose	suspense
minor characters	narrative poem

Reviewing Literary Concepts

OPTION 1

Encourage students to skim relevant selections to help them complete their charts. Have students also consider their reactions to and impressions of other biographies and autobiographies they may have read in order to determine the ways in which the form affects the amount and type of information learned.

OPTION 2

Have students skim the selections as they complete their charts and remind them that some characters may undergo change in more than one way. Encourage students to support their opinions with specific details from the selections in order to be as persuasive as possible.

Self-Assessment For terms that students have difficulty explaining to the group, have them write, in their own words, a definition for each term after checking in the Handbook. You may also wish to have them apply each term to a selection they have read.

Portfolio Building

You may wish to help students choose options or modify options for them that best suit the needs you have established for the class. Encourage students to incorporate in their portfolios drafts, in addition to final products, so that they can reflect on and assess their development and progress.

Self-Assessment To help students compare pieces of writing and assess their progress, have them compare how easy or difficult it was to complete more recent writing assignments with earlier ones. Encourage students also to consider how much revision was involved in more recent work in comparison to earlier work.

Setting Goals

In order to help students set future goals, have students consider which writer's work had the greatest impact on them and the ways in which they were affected by the writing. Encourage them to set reasonable goals for outside reading in the future.

UNIT FIVE

UNIT FIVE

Personal Discoveries

How I wish I could pigeon-hole

myself and neatly fix a label on!

But self-knowledge comes too late

and by the time I've known myself

I am no longer what I was.

Mabel Segun
Nigerian Poet

UNIT THEMES

Unit Five

Personal Discoveries In this unit, students will read about people who change and grow by making personal discoveries about themselves and the world they live in. The unit contains two parts: Part 1, "Finding Your Place," and Part 2, "Vital Connections." Selections in both parts contribute to the unit theme by exploring the ways in which characters find their special place in the world and the ways in which important relationships help characters to learn valuable lessons about life.

Part 1

Finding Your Place Selections in Part 1 focus on the role that personal discoveries play in helping characters figure out where they fit into the world. For example, in the story "Dancer," a Native American girl gains self-confidence through a fascination with dance.

Part 2

Vital Connections Selections in Part 2 explore how relationships with other people play an important part in characters' personal discoveries. For example, the young girl in "Raymond's Run" learns the true meaning of achievement from the most important person in her life, her disabled brother.

Links to Unit Six
The Oral Tradition Unit Six contains literature from the oral tradition that connects with the themes in Unit Five. You may wish to begin or end Unit Five by using the following selections from Unit Six that relate to the theme "Personal Discoveries":
- "Strawberries," p. 786
- "No News," p. 789
- "The First Flute," p. 791

Detail of Cross Cultural Dressing (1993), Pacita Abad. Oil, fabric, and plastic buttons on stitched and padded canvas, 100" × 136", courtesy of the artist.

Exploring Theme

To help students explore the connections between the art, the quotation, and the unit theme, have them consider the following questions:

1. Why do you think personal discoveries are important for people? *(Possible responses: Through personal discoveries, people learn about themselves and the world they live in. These discoveries, which can result from both good and bad experiences, allow people to grow.)*

2. What does Mabel Segun's quotation mean to you? *(Possible response: Segun points to a difficulty connected with personal discovery. She says that by the time you've learned something about yourself, you've already developed into someone who is not the same as before. You then must learn about yourself all over again.)*

3. In what ways do you think the art is an example of personal discovery? *(Possible responses: All art can be viewed as a form of personal discovery because artists, through their work, try to express something about themselves. This work, which shows different women from different cultures, might represent what the artist has learned about women. The three women may represent different aspects of the same person, showing that an individual is a complex being.)*

4. What kinds of stories do you think you will read in this unit? *(Possible response: stories about the different kinds of discoveries that people make about themselves as a result of either good or bad situations)*

5. Discuss an important personal discovery that you made recently. What led you to make this discovery? What did you learn? How has this discovery affected your life? *(Responses will vary.)*

Art Note

Detail of *Cross Cultural Dressing* by Pacita Abad Born in the Philippines, Pacita Abad studied painting at art schools in both Washington, D.C., and New York City. She has been awarded numerous grants, including a National Endowment for the Arts Visual Artist Fellowship in 1989, and her work has been exhibited internationally. This particular work incorporates oil paint and fabric.

Reading the Art *How would you describe the overall style of this work? What details about the painter's use of media, color, textures, and line help contribute to this style?*

THE LANGUAGE OF LITERATURE TEACHER'S EDITION

UNIT FIVE
Part 1 Skills Trace

 DENOTES MINI-LESSON IN TEACHER'S EDITION

Selections	Reading Skills and Strategies	Literary Concepts	Writing Opportunities	Speaking, Listening, and Viewing
FICTION **Dancer** Vickie Sears	Voice, PE p. 575 Making judgments, ML TE p. 580	Narrator, PE p. 581 Characterization, ML TE p. 577	Tribal name & explanation, PE p. 581 Paragraph, PE p. 581	Oral report, PE p. 581 Musical accompaniment, PE p. 582
FICTION **The Moustache** Robert Cormier	Clarifying, PE p. 583 Clarifying, ML TE p. 585	Symbol, PE p. 592 Chronological order, ML TE p. 587	Interior monologue, PE p. 592 Character sketch, PE p. 592	Group presentation, PE p. 592 Interviews, PE p. 593
POETRY **The Other Pioneers** Roberto Félix Salazar **Saying Yes** Diana Chang	Contrasting speakers, PE p. 594	Dialogue, PE p. 598 Form, ML TE p. 595	Poem, PE p. 598 Short essay, PE p. 598	Role-playing, PE p. 598 Ethnic music, ML TE p. 597
DRAMA **The Man Without a Country** Edward Everett Hale, dramatized by Walter Hackett	Sequencing, PE p. 601 Questioning, ML TE p. 614	Dynamic/static characters, PE p. 618 Scene, PE p. 618 Theme, ML TE p. 610	Letter, PE p. 617 Diary entry, PE p. 617 Poem or folksong, PE p. 617 Epitaph, PE p. 617 Letters, ML TE p. 613	Mock trial, PE p. 617 Dramatic reading, PE p. 618 Oral interpretation, ML TE p. 611
POETRY ON YOUR OWN **Think As I Think** Stephen Crane **The Choice** Dorothy Parker **I Belong** A. Whiterock **There's This That I Like About Hockey, My Lad** John Kieran **Rice and Rose Bowl Blues** Diane Mei Lin Mark			Journal, TE p. 620 Identity web, TE p. 624	Paired reading, TE p. 620 Class discussion, TE p. 627

Writing	Reading Skills and Strategies	Literary Concepts	Writing Opportunities	Speaking, Listening, and Viewing
WRITING ABOUT LITERATURE **Analysis**	Analyzing poetry, PE pp. 630–33	Sentence variety, PE pp. 628–29 Elements of poetry, PE pp. 630–31	Alternate version of a paragraph, PE p. 629 Paragraph, PE p. 629 Poem, PE p. 629 Analyzing poetry, PE pp. 630–33	Viewing a building, PE p. 635 Interpreting a building, PE p. 635 Discussion, PE p. 635 Brainstorm subjects for analysis, PE p. 635

Grammar, Usage, Mechanics, and Spelling	Multimodal Learning	Research and Study Skills	Vocabulary
Informal English, ML TE p. 579	Oral report, PE p. 581 Musical accompaniment, PE p. 582	Research the Assiniboin, PE p. 582	fixated preening
Capitalization of proper nouns, ML TE p. 586 The prefix com-, ML TE p. 588 Slang, ML TE p. 590	Group presentation, PE p. 592 Interviews, PE p. 593 Elderly-care chart, PE p. 593	Research arteriosclerosis and Alzheimer's disease, PE p. 593 The K-W-L approach, ML TE p. 589	complex lapse lucid pathetic serene
	Role-playing, PE p. 598 Painting, PE p. 599 Posterboard display, PE p. 599 Ethnic music, ML TE p. 597	Research immigration, TE p. 599	
Punctuating items in a series, ML TE p. 603 Dialogue in plays, ML TE p. 604 Words ending with -ous, ML TE p. 608	Mock trial, PE p. 617 Comic book, PE p. 618 Dramatic reading, PE p. 618 Oral interpretation, ML TE p. 611	Research the entry of states into the Union between 1805–1862, PE p. 619 Using graphic organizers, ML TE p. 607	abetting fidelity insignia odious rescind
	Collage, TE p. 626		

Grammar, Usage, Mechanics, and Spelling	Multimodal Learning	Research and Study Skills	Media Literacy
Punctuating poetry, PE p. 631 Verb tense, PE p. 633 Using verb tense in quotations, PE p. 633	Viewing a building, PE p. 635 Interpreting a building, PE p. 635 Discussion, PE p. 635 Brainstorm subjects for analysis, PE p. 635	Analyzing parts of a whole, PE p. 635	Analyzing details of a building, PE pp. 634–35

UNIT FIVE
Part 2 Skills Trace

ML DENOTES MINI-LESSON IN TEACHER'S EDITION

Selections	Reading Skills and Strategies	Literary Concepts	Writing Opportunities	Speaking, Listening, and Viewing
FICTION **Stop the Sun** Gary Paulsen	Connecting, PE p. 637 Connecting, ML TE p. 639	Repetition, PE p. 646 Realistic fiction, PE p. 646 Dialogue, ML TE p. 642	Diary entry, PE p. 645 Advertisement, PE p. 645 Poem, PE p. 645	Musical accompaniment, PE p. 647 Minidrama, PE p. 647 Film viewing, ML TE p. 644
FICTION **Raymond's Run** Toni Cade Bambara	Analyzing, PE p. 648 Summarizing, ML TE p. 653	Slang, PE p. 657 Conflict, ML TE p. 652	Paragraph, PE p. 657 Sports article, PE p. 657	Brainstorming session, PE p. 657 Readers theater, ML TE p. 656
FICTION **Keeping Time** Bill Meissner	Making judgments, ML TE p. 665	Moral, PE p. 666 Similes, ML TE p. 663	Description, PE p. 659 Paragraph, PE p. 666 Pep talk, PE p. 666 Poem, PE p. 666	Role-playing, PE p. 666
NONFICTION **Power of the Powerless: A Brother's Lesson** Christopher de Vinck	Making generalizations, ML TE p. 671	Main idea, ML TE p. 670	Description, PE p. 668 Letter, PE p. 672 Create a diary, PE p. 672 Diary entry, PE p. 672	
POETRY **A Fairy Tale** Leroy V. Quintana **My Mother Really Knew** Wing Tek Lum		Tone, PE p. 677 Free verse, ML TE p. 675	Description, PE p. 674 Paragraph, PE p. 677 Bedtime story, PE p. 677	Storyboard, PE p. 677 Lullaby, PE p. 678 Oral interpretation, ML TE p. 676
POETRY **Sea-Fever** John Masefield **Mi Madre** Pat Mora	Symbol, PE p. 679	Imagery, PE p. 682 Elements of poetry, PE p. 682 Personification, ML TE p. 680	Poem, PE p. 682 Advertisement, PE p. 682	Brainstorming session, PE p. 682 Musical accompaniment, PE p. 683
Writing	**Reading Skills and Strategies**	**Literary Concepts**	**Writing Opportunities**	**Speaking, Listening, and Viewing**
WRITING FROM EXPERIENCE **Persuasion**	Distinguishing fact and opinion, PE pp. 686–87		Writing a persuasive essay, PE pp. 684–91 Paragraph, PE p. 684 Drafting, PE pp. 688–89 Avoiding loaded language, PE p. 689 Revising and publishing, PE pp. 690–91 Newspaper article, PE p. 691	Speech or petition, PE p. 691

Grammar, Usage, Mechanics, and Spelling	Multimodal Learning	Research and Study Skills	Vocabulary
Show, don't tell, ML TE p. 640 Punctuating quotations, ML TE p. 641 Greek prefixes, ML TE p. 643	Father's Day card, PE p. 645 Musical accompaniment, PE p. 647 Minidrama, PE p. 647 Film viewing, ML TE p. 644	Research the Vietnam War, PE p. 646	chant dry founder inert persist
Choosing the right voice, ML TE p. 650 Irregular verbs, ML TE p. 654 The sound f, ML TE p. 655	Brainstorming session, PE p. 657 Newspaper advertisement, PE p. 658 Readers theater ML TE p. 656	Research the Special Olympics, PE p. 658 Calculate distance of race, PE p. 658	prodigy
Chronological order, ML TE p. 661 Silent letters, ML TE p. 662 Adjectives and adverbs, ML TE p. 664	Role-playing, PE p. 666 Abstract art, PE p. 667		benignly chasm diffused spindly subtly
	Illustration or design, PE p. 673		
	Storyboard, PE p. 677 Lullaby, PE p. 678 Artistic representation, PE p. 678 Oral interpretation, ML TE p. 676		
	Brainstorming session, PE p. 682 Musical accompaniment, PE p. 683		

Grammar, Usage, Mechanics, and Spelling	Multimodal Learning	Research and Study Skills	Media Literacy
Avoiding double negatives, PE p. 691	Speech or petition, PE p. 691 Leaflet or brochure, PE p. 691	Gathering evidence, PE pp. 686–87 On-line services, PE p. 687 Evaluating sources, PE p. 687	On-line services, PE p. 687

UNIT FIVE
Recommended Resources

ENRICHMENT   RESEARCH

✓ Recommended Novels and Nonfiction

 LITERATURE CONNECTIONS WITH SOURCEBOOK FOR TEACHERS

The Glory Field
by Walter Dean Myers

Thematic Links In this multi-generational novel, the descendants of a slave discover strength and identity in their vital connection to family and land. Each steps forward in his or her own way.

About the Author Walter Dean Myers (born 1937) has been a prolific writer of both fiction and nonfiction works for young adults. His work has received a number of honors and citations.

Other Works by Walter Dean Myers *Somewhere in the Darkness, Scorpions, Malcolm X: By Any Means Necessary, Fallen Angels, Motown and Didi: A Love Story*

 LITERATURE CONNECTIONS WITH SOURCEBOOK FOR TEACHERS

The Contender
by Robert Lipsyte

Thematic Links Alfred Brooks, a high school dropout, desperately wants to transform his life and prove to himself that he can be somebody. Subjecting himself to the discipline of training to be a boxer, he tries to discover whether he has the heart of a contender. His commitment to boxing leads to new discoveries about himself and his obligations to his friend and his community.

About the Author Robert Lipsyte (born 1938) worked for many years first as a sports reporter and then as a columnist for the *New York Times* and later as a sports correspondent for NBC News. His novels explore issues that confront young people today, such as the possibility of positive change, the need for commitment to one's community, and the real meaning of manhood.

Other Works by Robert Lipsyte *One Fat Summer; The Summerboy; The Brave; Liberty Two; Free to Be Muhammad Ali; Summer Rules; The Chemo Kid*

LITERATURE CONNECTIONS WITH SOURCEBOOK FOR TEACHERS  SPANISH VERSION AVAILABLE

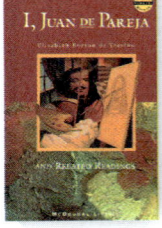

I, Juan De Pareja
by Elizabeth Borton de Treviño

Thematic Links On the threshold of a new life, Juan de Pareja, a Moorish slave in 17th century Spain, reveals his personal discoveries as he tells of his life with his master, the famous Spanish painter Diego Velázquez.

About the Author Elizabeth Borton de Treviño (born 1904) bases her stories on true or historic events that appeal to her imagination. Her stories most often explore the theme of love.

Other Works by Elizabeth Borton de Treviño *Nacar, the White Deer; Casilda of the Rising Moon; Here Is Mexico; Beyond the Gates of Hercules: A Tale of the Lost Atlantis; Juarez: Man of Law; El Güero*

Speaking Out: Teenagers' Take on Race, Sex and Identity
by Susan Kuklin

Thematic Links Students reveal their innermost feelings as they discuss the issues of today's society.

About the Author Susan Kuklin (born 1941) writes books for children and young adults. Many of her books are illustrated with the photographs she takes.

Other Works by Susan Kuklin *Fighting Back: What Some People Are Doing About AIDS*

Memory
by Margaret Mahy

Thematic Links Through his friendship with an elderly woman with Alzheimer's disease, Johnny learns to accept his own past.

About the Author Margaret Mahy (born 1936) writes for readers of many different ages. Her stories for young adults focus on family relationships.

Other Works by Margaret Mahy *The Other Side of Silence, The Tricksters, Aliens in the Family*

For Teacher TEACHING LITERATURE

Burke, Margaret. "Now There's a Novel Idea!: Using Drama in the Secondary English Classroom." *English Quarterly* 25:4 (Summer 1993) 26–28.

Silva, Anita, ed. *Children's Books and Their Creators*. Boston: Houghton Mifflin, 1995.

Stott, Jon C. *Native Americans in Children's Literature*. Phoenix, AZ: Oryx, 1995.

Strickland, Dorothy S. "An Interview with Lois Lowry, 1994 Newbery Medal Winner." *The Reading Teacher* 48:4 (December 1994) 308–09.

Wood, Karen, "Integrating Collaborative Learning Across the Curriculum." *Middle School Journal,* (January 1994).

573e   UNIT FOUR   PERSONAL DISCOVERIES

CROSS-CURRICULAR TEACHING   PROFESSIONAL DEVELOPMENT

Recommended Readings in Cross-Curricular Areas

HISTORY/SOCIAL STUDIES

Asian Americans: An Interpretive History by Sucheng Chan (1990) Contributions made and prejudices faced by Asian Americans. Links to "Saying Yes," "Rice and Rose Bowl Blues," and "My Mother Really Knew."

America After Vietnam: Legacies of a Hated War by Edward F. Dolan, Jr. (1989) Focuses on the effects of the Vietnam War on those returning from combat. Links to Gary Paulsen's "Stop the Sun."

HISTORY

I Am the Fire of Time: The Voices of Native-American Women edited by Jane B. Katz (1977) Anthologizes the writings of Native American women and includes many photographs. Links to Vicki Sears's "Dancer."

PHYSICAL EDUCATION

B-Ball: The Team that Never Lost a Game by Ron Jones (1990) Details the story of the San Francisco Special Olympics basketball team. Links to "Raymond's Run" and *Power of the Powerless: A Brother's Lesson.*

For Teacher — CROSS-CURRICULAR INSTRUCTION

Downs, J. R. "Getting Parents and Students Involved: Using Survey and Interview Techniques." *Social Studies* 84.3 (1993).

Manning, M. L. *Celebrating Diversity: Multi-Cultural Education in Middle-Level Schools.* Columbus, OH: National Middle School Association, 1994.

Orwig, Ann H. "Home/School/Community Connection." *Technology and Learning* (November/December 1994).

Sherman, Paul. "Connecting Kids to Community with Survey Research." *Middle School Journal* (March 1995).

Recommended Media Resources

THE LANGUAGE OF LITERATURE

LASERLINKS
Videodisc, Gr. 8
See *LaserLinks Teacher's Source Book,* pages 48–49, for an overview of Unit Five.

AUDIO LIBRARY
Tapes
Unit Five: Personal Discoveries
Gr. 8, Tape 13: Sides A & B
Gr. 8, Tape 14: Sides A & B

WRITING COACH
Writing Coach Software: Writing About Literature: Interpretive Response; Persuasive Essay

OUTSIDE RESOURCES

Films/Videos/Film Strips/Audiocassettes
Best Boy. videocassette, New York, 1980. (104 min.)
Dancing Feather. videocassette. Beacon Films, 1984. (28 min.)
Dear America: Letters Home from Vietnam. videocassette. New York, 1987. (87 min.)
Dream Big: The Over-the-Rhine Steel Drum Band. videocassette. TV Image, 1994.
Faith Ringgold Paints Crown Heights. videocassette. L&S Video, 1995.

Internet Resources
WorldWide Web at
http://www.hmco.com/mcdougal

For Teacher — TEACHING WITH TECHNOLOGY

Bender, Robert M. "Creating Communities on the Internet: Electronic Discussion Lists in the Classroom." *Computers in Libraries* 15.5 (May 1995), 38–43.

Kinnaman, Daniel E., and Dyrli, Odvard Egil. "Gaining Access to Technology: First Step in Making a Difference for Your Students." *Technology & Learning* 14 (January 1994).

Peterson, Norman K., and Orde, Barbara J. "Implementing Multimedia in the Middle School Curriculum: Pros, Cons, and Lessons Learned." *T.H.E. Journal* 22 (February 1995).

UNIT FIVE
Professional Enrichment

Appreciating Poetry

Do your students groan when they are asked to study poetry? Here's how to help your eighth graders as they read the poems in this unit.

Explain to students that poetry isn't around just to frustrate them! They need to see that poetry can captivate, delight, and dazzle. They also need to understand that poetry can describe, portray, argue, express, explore, prod, and please. Eighth graders must realize that poetry isn't about puzzles; it's about power and pleasure—the power to express oneself and the pleasure of working with language to find fresh ways of doing so. Effective poetry uses imagery, figures of speech, structure, and sound to tell us more about ourselves and how we live.

MAKING POETRY MATTER

How can you make reading and writing poetry matter to your students? Start by making it an important part of your classroom all the time. You can begin by reading poems aloud to your students. Read a poem that appeals to you, for your enthusiasm will be contagious.

In *Side by Side,* Nancie Atwell explains how she helps students learn to interpret a poem. After reading one of her favorite poems aloud, she explains "why I had chosen to read [that] poem—what in the work had spoken to me. I pointed out things I had noticed about the poem on my first and second and third and fourth readings. Most importantly, I asked them what they thought of the poem and why, or what they had learned about how it might be written. I learned to demystify the process of reading a poem so that my students might see how a reader could relish unraveling the difficulties of poetry."

While your students are learning about poetry, give them a chance to write their own. To do that, create a classroom environment that supports experimentation and sharing. The following are some suggestions for helping eighth graders enjoy reading and writing poetry.

- Give students a number of different poems to explore. Allow them to decide which poems to read.
- Introduce poetry by using poems written by writers whose prose works students already know. Bridging prose and poetry this way helps students make connections between the known and unknown.
- Urge students to first enjoy a poem, then analyze it.
- Show students how to ignore the line breaks and look for the punctuation as they read poetry. This will help them find meaning.
- A good way to understand more about a poem is to rewrite it in your own words. Encourage students to use this technique. Have them notice which lines are most difficult to rewrite and how their version differs from the original.
- Students often tend to skip unclear passages rather than question them. Encourage students to work in small groups to clarify confusing lines in a poem.
- To reinforce the concept that personal responses are the building blocks of interpretation, you may wish to have students interpret one of the pieces of fine art in their textbook as a poem. Have students begin by noting how they feel as they look at the artwork. Then lead them in a discussion of the ways in which the artist evokes these feelings, such as color, shape, and form. Finally, have students write their poems about the picture.
- Write your own poetry while students are writing theirs.
- Share your verse with the class. Students will be less likely to be afraid of sharing their efforts if they know that you are not afraid of sharing yours.
- Because interpreting poetry is highly subjective, you may wish to limit your assessment to structural elements.

Related Reading

Doreski, Carol Kiler, and Doreski, William. *How to Read and Interpret Poetry.* New York: Arco, 1988.

Janeczko, Paul. ed. *Preposterous: Poems of Youth.* Danbury, Connecticut: Watts, 1991.

Koch, Kenneth, and Farrell, Kate, eds. *Talking to the Sun: An Illustrated Anthology of Poems for Young People.* New York: Henry Holt, 1985.

Peck, Richard, ed. *Pictures That Storm Inside My Head: Poems for the Inner You.* New York: Avon, 1976.

Sullivan, Charles. ed. *Imaginary Gardens: American Poetry and Art for Young People.* New York: Abrams, 1989.

Family and Community Involvement

Family

All of the selections in Unit Five connect to the theme of personal discoveries.

The following Copymasters provide activities related to that theme that students can take home and complete with a parent or other family member.

OPTION 1: DESIGN AN ALBUM OF YOUR PERSONAL DISCOVERIES
- **Connection** All of the selections in Unit Five connect to personal discoveries.
- **Activity** *Copymaster, p. 1* Students work with family members to design an album that shows the different personal discoveries they have made in life.

OPTION 2: DRAW A MAP OF YOUR CONNECTIONS TO OTHER PEOPLE
- **Connection** Many of the selections in Unit Five deal with the strong bonds that people share with others.
- **Activity** *Copymaster, p. 2* Students work with family members to create a "map" that shows the special bonds they have with other people in their lives. A chart is provided to help organize students' thoughts and ideas.

OPTION 3: READ ABOUT PERSONAL DISCOVERIES
- **Connection** All of the selections in Unit Five connect to the theme of personal discoveries.
- **Activity** *Copymaster, p. 3* Students and family members skim newspapers or magazines for articles about people who have made personal discoveries. After they have taken turns reading the articles aloud, they discuss what they have learned from the articles. A chart is provided for keeping track of the articles.

Community

OPTION 1
- **Connection** The selections in Unit Five all illustrate the theme of personal discoveries.
- **Activity** Invite a guidance counselor from your school to speak with the class about his or her role in helping students to make important discoveries about themselves.

OPTION 2
- **Connection** The main character in "Dancer" is a young Native American girl who becomes part of the Native American community through her fascination with dancing.
- **Activity** Arrange a field trip to see a Native American powwow or visit a museum devoted to Native American history and culture.

OPTION 3
- **Connection** In "Raymond's Run," the narrator learns a vital lesson from her disabled brother.
- **Activity** Invite a doctor to the class to speak with students about people with physical and mental disabilities.

OPTION 4
- **Connection** Many of the selections in Unit Five, such as "Saying Yes" and "Sea-Fever," are poems that deal with personal discoveries.
- **Activity** Have a poet speak to the class about his or her work and the ways in which poetry can uniquely express personal feelings and emotions. You may also wish to have students read their own poetry to the class.

UNIT FIVE
Part 1 Cooperative Project

Time Capsule

Overview

Students will preserve their thoughts about what makes their own generation unique by creating a time capsule.

PROJECT AT A GLANCE

The selections in Unit Five, Part 1 are about making personal discoveries, realizing greater self-knowledge, and discovering how these lead to the development of a personal identity. For this project, students will find or construct a container appropriate for use as a time capsule. They will then research what makes their generation unique and different from those that have gone before. Students will translate these findings into objects to include in the time capsule. Then they will plan and carry out a ceremony during which they either present the capsule to the school administration or bury it in a protected place.

OBJECTIVES

- To define the purpose of a time capsule
- To find or construct a suitable time capsule
- To examine the qualities that make the current generation unique
- To work cooperatively to find appropriate items for inclusion in the capsule
- To plan a ceremony during which to present the time capsule to the school administration or to bury it

SUGGESTED GROUP SIZE
3–4 students

MATERIALS

- Material to construct or adapt a time capsule
- A variety of items as examples

 **Getting Started**

Arranging the Project

If you feel that actually making the time capsule is too involved, you might do some preliminary searching for an available and appropriate container that students can use. This option has the added advantage of letting students see exactly how much space they have to work with from the beginning.

If other teachers are working on the same project, you may want to coordinate the final ceremony with them. Each class could still make their own capsule, but there could be one culminating ceremony.

Arranging for the Ceremony

Contact school administrators as soon as possible to see if they are interested in participating in a ceremony. If they are agreeable, set a date, time, and place now, as well as a list of who will be present. You can still ask students to write formal invitations to the event when the time comes.

Consider asking the administration for permission to bury the capsule on school grounds. Select a spot remote enough that it will not interfere with daily school life, and find a large rock or other item to mark the spot.

If none of these plans is feasible, find a place in the classroom to store the capsule. You may want to save it for a few years and then invite students back to open it and share their thoughts.

 **Creating the Capsules**

Introducing the Project

Explain to students that they will be working in small groups to make a time capsule. They will research a variety of things to include in the capsule that illustrate how their generation is unique from any other. The final decisions about what to include should be made by the entire class. They will then organize and carry out a ceremony during which the capsule will be presented to the school administration or will be buried for safekeeping.

Discuss the purpose of a time capsule with students. You might explain that the original idea came about because so little is known about ancient civilizations. A time capsule preserves for examination in the future documents and items that are exemplary of a particular culture or time period.

Have students look over the items you have brought to class. Some items, such as 8-track audio cassettes, will speak about one specific period of time. Other items might belong to more generalized eras, such as a pair of jeans. Discuss how each item does or does not reflect the generation it belonged to and whether or not students would include it in a time capsule.

Group Investigations

Divide students into groups of three or four. The groups will brainstorm together to come up with about 10 to 15 items that are representative of their generation. Encourage students to get others' opinions about the items they select, especially other members of their generation. Groups should be prepared to explain the reasoning behind their selection of each item in a class meeting.

Each group also should help plan the ceremony for the presentation of the capsule. You might provide students with a list of the administrators to facilitate the planning. Groups should plan any speeches or music that they want to include in the program. Later, they should meet and look over all the plans. They can devise a class plan from the group plans by voting on the best elements and ideas. After the plans are finalized, groups should write formal invitations to the administrators.

Creating a Project Description

After students have gathered a number of items, meet with them and listen to their reasons for including each one. This will help you monitor their progress and will give you a chance to make suggestions about their collection. Meet again when students have a written first draft of their plans for the ceremony. Point out things students might want to consider or specify in the final plans.

OPTION 1: PERSONAL CAPSULE Each group can make a capsule that reflects an interest shared by all its members. For this option, you'll want to assign groups that are as homogeneous as possible. This option also would work well for individual students.

OPTION 2: PAST TIME CAPSULES There are more than 10,000 time capsules currently buried across the United States. Students can research some of the capsules and can learn about the very first one created. They also can discover what items others have deemed important enough to include for posterity.

OPTION 3: FOCUS Ask groups to focus their efforts on one specific aspect of their generation. Possible items for inclusion might reflect the fashions, art, books, movies, sports, or music that this generation prefers.

OPTION 4: KING TUT'S TIME CAPSULE Students can research to discover what was contained in King Tut's unintentional time capsule—his tomb—and what we have learned from the items. You also might assign for study other similar archaeological findings.

The final time capsule should be a manageable size but roomy enough for more than just a few items. If you will be proceeding with the burial of the capsule, you may have to enlist the help of the maintenance staff in digging the hole and covering it up again. Within reason, allow students to include as much as possible in the time capsule.

3 Sharing the Ceremony

If administrators are interested in participating in the ceremony, they should be issued formal invitations to attend and, if appropriate, formal invitations to speak. If your school has a band, it might also be invited to perform. If possible, the entire student body can be asked to participate, or you can hold a more private ceremony.

Hold a class meeting after the ceremony to discuss the outcome of the project.

Assessing the Project

The following rubric can be used for group or individual assessment.

3 Full Accomplishment Students follow directions and select several appropriate items for the time capsule and produce a viable plan for a ceremony.

2 Substantial Accomplishment Students select some appropriate items for the capsule and produce a hasty plan for the ceremony.

1 Little or Partial Accomplishment Students' selection of items is inappropriate or does not fulfill the requirements of the assignment.

For the Portfolio
Include in each student's portfolio a copy of the list of items contributed by his or her group, as well as a copy of the final plan for the ceremony and a copy of your written assessment.

Note: For other assessment options, see the *Teacher's Guide to Assessment and Portfolio Use.*

Cross-Curricular Options

LANGUAGE ARTS
Students can write to the International Time Capsule Society (c/o Oglethorpe University, 4484 Peachtree Road NE, Atlanta, GA 30319) for more information about time capsules. They also might be interested in registering their time capsule with the society.

SOCIAL STUDIES

Have students research Thomwell Jacobs's first time capsule and then write a report explaining how Jacobs's time capsule reflected the times in which he lived.

SCIENCE

At one time, there were plans to send a time capsule into space. Students can contact the Space Arc Program (c/o Rochester Museum and Science Center, 657 East Avenue, Box 1480, Rochester, NY 14603–1480) to learn what happened to the plans, if they were carried out, and what the time capsule contains.

Resources

In Search of Tutankhamun by Piero Ventura and Gian Paolo Ceserani describes the discovery of King Tut's tomb.

Splendors of the Past: Lost Cities of the Ancient World published by National Geographic contains beautiful illustrations of lost cities from seven periods, such as Pompeii and Sumara.

Symbols of America by Hal Morgan provides historical background on well-known American trademarks, such as Aunt Jemima and the "golden arches."

UNIT FIVE
Part 1 Lesson Planner

TIME ALLOTMENTS SHOWN ARE APPROXIMATE. DEPENDING ON YOUR GOALS AND THE NEEDS OF YOUR STUDENTS, YOU MAY WISH TO ALLOW MORE OR LESS TIME FOR CERTAIN PORTIONS OF THE LESSON.

Table of Contents	Discussion	Previewing the Selection	Reading the Selection
PART OPENER **FINDING YOUR PLACE** **What Do You Think?** page 574	**20 MINUTES** • Reflect on the part theme		
SELECTION **Dancer** page 576 AVERAGE		**20 MINUTES** • PERSONAL CONNECTION • CULTURAL CONNECTION • READING CONNECTION: Voice	**20 MINUTES** • Introduce vocabulary • Read pp. 576–80 (5 pp.)
SELECTION **The Moustache** page 584 AVERAGE		**20 MINUTES** • PERSONAL CONNECTION • SOCIAL STUDIES CONNECTION • READING CONNECTION: Clarifying	**30 MINUTES** • Introduce vocabulary • Read pp. 584–91 (8 pp.)
SELECTIONS **The Other Pioneers** page 595 AVERAGE **Saying Yes** page 597 AVERAGE		**20 MINUTES** • PERSONAL CONNECTION • CULTURAL CONNECTION • READING CONNECTION: Contrasting speakers	**15 MINUTES** • Read pp. 595–97 (3 pp.)
SELECTION **The Man Without a Country** page 602 AVERAGE		**25 MINUTES** • PERSONAL CONNECTION • HISTORICAL CONNECTION • READING CONNECTION: Sequencing	**55 MINUTES** • Introduce vocabulary • Read pp. 602–16 (15 pp.)
POETRY ON YOUR OWN **Think As I Think** **The Choice** **I Belong** **There's This That I Like About Hockey, My Lad** **Rice and Rose Bowl Blues** pages 620–627 EASY			**30 MINUTES** • Read pp. 620–27 (8 pp.)
Writing	**Writer's Style**	**Prewriting**	**Drafting and Revising**
WRITING ABOUT LITERATURE **Analysis**	**30 MINUTES**	**20 MINUTES**	**75 MINUTES**

Time estimates assume in-class work. You may wish to assign some of these stages as homework.

Responding to the Selection

FROM PERSONAL RESPONSE TO CRITICAL ANALYSIS	OR	ANOTHER PATHWAY	LITERARY CONCEPTS	QUICKWRITES
		45 MINUTES		
• Discussion questions	OR	• Oral report	• Narrator	• Tribal name • Paragraph
		45 MINUTES		
• Discussion questions	OR	• Group presentation	• Symbol	• Interior monologue • Character sketch
		40 MINUTES		
• Discussion questions	OR	• Role-playing	• Dialogue	• Poem • Short essay
		50 MINUTES		
• Discussion questions	OR	• Mock trial	• Dynamic/static characters • Scene	• Letter • Journal entry • Poem or folk song • Epitaph

Extension Activities

• ALTERNATIVE ACTIVITIES • LITERARY LINKS • CRITIC'S CORNER • THE WRITER'S STYLE • ACROSS THE CURRICULUM • ART CONNECTION • WORDS TO KNOW • BIOGRAPHY

	ALTERNATIVE ACTIVITIES	LITERARY LINKS	CRITIC'S CORNER	THE WRITER'S STYLE	ACROSS THE CURRICULUM	ART CONNECTION	WORDS TO KNOW	BIOGRAPHY
35 MINUTES	✓				SOCIAL STUDIES		✓	✓
40 MINUTES	✓				SCIENCE		✓	✓
25 MINUTES	✓							✓
45 MINUTES	✓	✓			HISTORY	✓	✓	✓

Publishing and Reflecting	Grammar in Context	Reading the World
30 MINUTES	**10 MINUTES**	**25 MINUTES**

PART 1

WHAT DO YOU THINK?
Objectives

The activities on this page can be used to
- introduce the Part 1 theme of "Finding Your Place," since each activity is connected to one or more selections
- create materials for students' personal portfolios that they can return to later for reconsideration or revision
- build an understanding of theme that can be returned to and revised as students progress through the unit

What do you enjoy?
Encourage students to choose an interest or hobby they feel reveals something special about themselves. You may also wish to have students write brief entries in their notebooks discussing what they have learned about their classmates. (See "Dancer," p. 575.)

Do you know them?
Have students create charts in which they detail their impressions of their chosen relatives before and after the interviews. Invite volunteers to read their impressions to the class. (See "The Moustache," p. 583.)

What would you miss?
Have students first write down what they would and would not miss. They can then refer to this information when creating their collages. (See *The Man Without a Country*, p. 600.)

Who are you?
Encourage students to brainstorm first a list of qualities and interests that they can design as puzzle pieces. Have students think of ways in which the puzzle pieces can be designed to represent the specific quality or interest. For instance, students who are musical might shape their puzzles as a musical instrument or note. (This activity is linked to all selections in the unit part.)

UNIT FIVE PART 1

FINDING YOUR PLACE

WHAT DO Y?u THINK?

REFLECTING ON THEME

What kind of person are you? Think about the things that shape who you are—your interests, your ethnicity, your family. Discovering more about yourself can help you find your place in the world. The activities on this page involve the kinds of personal discoveries that help people find their place.

Do you know them?
Our connections with family are often the strongest of all. But how well do you really know your family? Interview an older member of your family about an important event in their life that occurred when they were your age. Afterward, consider whether your impression of your relative has changed.

What would you miss?
Your country can have a great influence on your sense of identity. Imagine you and your family were leaving to live in another country. Create a collage, showing the things you would and would not miss about life in the United States.

What do you enjoy?
Your personal interests and hobbies say a lot about who you are. Pick something you are particularly interested in or enjoy doing. Share an aspect of this activity. If possible, try to show real examples: if you are interested in a certain kind of ethnic cookery, cook something and bring it to class for classmates to try; if you enjoy a particular kind of music, bring in a recording for them to sample.

Who are you?
Think about all the factors that shape who you are. Design a jigsaw puzzle with pieces that express your personality—your qualities, interests, and diversity. Make the shape and design reflect the factors you feel are most important in your life.

Cross-Curricular Connections

 Social Studies Have students work alone to research the way in which a particular community or culture ritually initiates young people into the adult community. Encourage students to consider a diverse range of rituals; these might include religious ceremonies such as confirmations or bar mitzvahs, or individual family customs such as ear piercing or dating. Students should examine how the ritual functions to help young adults find their place within the community. Students can present their findings to the class.

COMMUNITY OUTREACH

Invite students to speak with guidance counselors at your school for more information about organizations that help students with job placement and career goals by evaluating their interests and aptitudes. You may also wish to encourage students to use the reference facilities at your local public library to find more information about job placement services and career counseling for students. Then have students perform preliminary research to find out more about their career interests and goals.

574 THE LANGUAGE OF LITERATURE TEACHER'S EDITION

PREVIEWING

FICTION

Dancer
Vickie Sears

Activating Prior Knowledge
PERSONAL CONNECTION
In "Dancer," a young foster child of Native American descent must adjust to a new household and discover her place in the family. As you try to find your place in the world, how do you define yourself? Jot down what you think makes you the individual that you are. Use a word web, like the one started here, to help you organize your thoughts. Then share your ideas in a small group.

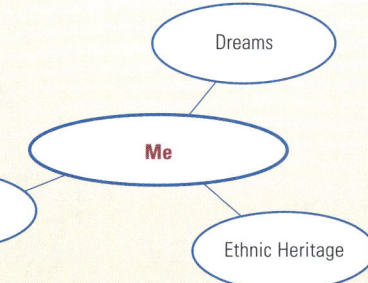

Building Background
CULTURAL CONNECTION
In the Native American culture, ceremonial dances traditionally were performed to bring sun or rain, to ensure good hunting, to prepare for battle, and to get closer to nature. In many Native American communities today, a monthly dance called a powwow is a regular event. The powwow keeps the traditional culture alive. Dances such as the owl dance, the friendship dance, the circle dance, and the hoop dance are performed by Native Americans of all ages. For many of these Native Americans, this reminder of their ethnic heritage helps them to define themselves and often leads to the development of increased self-esteem and self-knowledge.

Native American dancer at an intertribal powwow in New Mexico. Copyright © 1992 Jonathan Meyers/FPG International Corp.

Active Reading/Setting a Purpose
READING CONNECTION
Voice The first thing you may notice as you read this story is the narrator's voice. A Native American woman tells the story in her own distinctive way of speaking. She has an earthy, conversational style. Her language is often non-standard, as when she says, "I don't know nothing from that." Her descriptions are colorful; for example, she describes her foster child's nightmares as "real screamer dreams." As you read, be aware of the narrator's voice and how it makes her come alive on the page.

• CULTURAL CONNECTION   575

OVERVIEW

Objectives
- To understand and appreciate a short story about a Native American girl's discovery of her heritage
- To enrich reading by identifying voice
- To identify and understand the role of the narrator
- To express understanding of the story through a choice of writing forms, including a tribal name and a paragraph
- To extend understanding of the story through a variety of multimodal and cross-disciplinary activities

Skills

READING SKILLS/STRATEGIES
- Making judgments
- Appreciating voice

LITERARY CONCEPTS
- Narrator
- Characterization

THE WRITER'S STYLE
- Informal English

SPEAKING, LISTENING, AND VIEWING
- Group discussion
- Oral presentation

Cross-Curricular Connections

SOCIAL STUDIES
- Traditional Native-American dance
- The Assiniboin
- Powwows

 CULTURAL CONNECTION
Native American Dances Rare footage shows Native American dancers performing the hoop dance, the eagle dance, and other traditional dances. Watching these performances will help students visualize the events in "Dancer."

Side A, Frame 40769

PRINT AND MEDIA RESOURCES

UNIT FIVE RESOURCE BOOK
Strategic Reading: Literature, p. 4
Reading SkillBuilder, p. 5

WRITING MINI–LESSONS
Transparencies, p. 36

ACCESS FOR STUDENTS ACQUIRING ENGLISH
Selection Summaries
Reading and Writing Support

TEACHER'S GUIDE TO ASSESSMENT AND PORTFOLIO USE

FORMAL ASSESSMENT
Selection Test, pp. 107–108
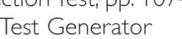 Test Generator

 **AUDIO LIBRARY**
See Reference Card

 LASERLINKS
Cultural Connection
Social Studies Connection

 INTERNET RESOURCES
McDougal Littell Literature Center at http://www.hmco.com/mcdougal/lit

THE LANGUAGE OF LITERATURE TEACHER'S EDITION **575**

SUMMARY

Five-year-old Clarissa, a Native American, is known as a difficult child and is sent to live with a foster mother. Her foster mother is also a Native American, and she ignores Clarissa's reputation. She accepts Clarissa as family and deals matter-of-factly with the child's fear and rage. She also takes Clarissa to monthly gatherings to enjoy dancing, drumming, and singing. The little girl becomes part of the Native American community. Clarissa is fascinated by one dancer, 70-year-old Molly Graybull. Her foster mother and Molly teach Clarissa about dancing and other parts of Native American culture. As the months go by, Clarissa gains confidence and pride. Her broken spirit heals, and she becomes an inspired dancer.

Thematic Link: *Finding Your Place* A troubled girl discovers her Assiniboin heritage through dance.

CUSTOMIZING FOR
Students Acquiring English

- Use **ACCESS FOR STUDENTS ACQUIRING ENGLISH,** *Reading and Writing Support.*
- Less fluent students may have trouble with the nonstandard grammar used by the narrator. Be sure to paraphrase any confusing expressions or passages.

STRATEGIC READING FOR
Less-Proficient Readers

Ask students to volunteer the names of dances that belong to their own cultural heritage. Ask if they know the history of the dance.

Set a Purpose Have students read to find out what Clarissa is drawn to when she attends the powwow.

CUSTOMIZING FOR
Gifted and Talented Students

Have students discuss the importance of knowing one's heritage in developing self-esteem. Ask them to consider, as they read, what Clarissa gains from learning traditional dances and why the dances have this effect on her. *(Possible response: Clarissa hasn't had a home to call her own; she finds her place within the traditions of her people.)*

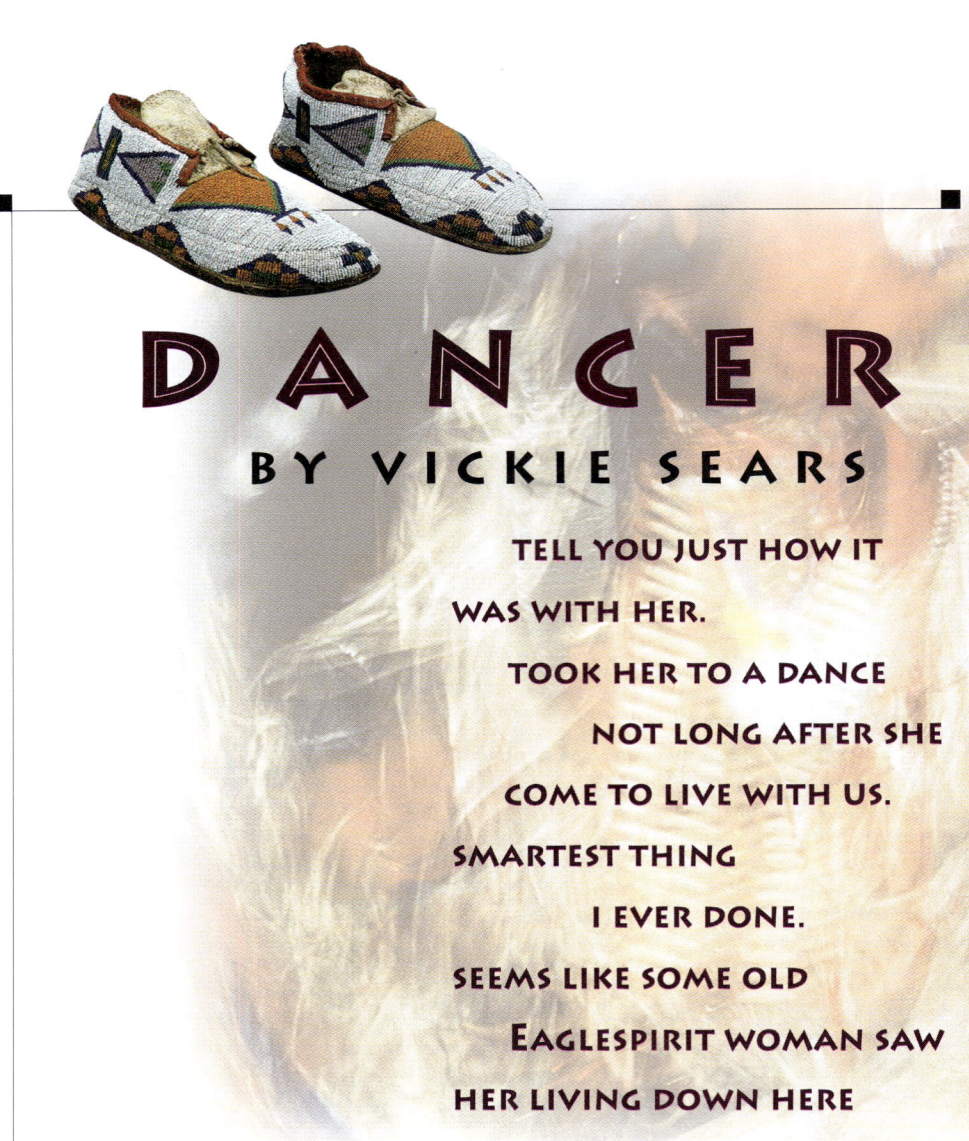

DANCER
BY VICKIE SEARS

TELL YOU JUST HOW IT
WAS WITH HER.
TOOK HER TO A DANCE
NOT LONG AFTER SHE
COME TO LIVE WITH US.
SMARTEST THING
I EVER DONE.
SEEMS LIKE SOME OLD
EAGLESPIRIT WOMAN SAW
HER LIVING DOWN HERE
AND CAME BACK JUST TO
BE WITH CLARISSA.

WORDS TO KNOW

fixated (fĭk′sā-tĭd) *adj.* having one's attention absorbed; engrossed **fixate** *v.* (p. 577)

preening (prē′nĭng) *adj.* showing pride and self-satisfaction **preen** *v.* (p. 577)

A Five years old she was when she come to us. Some foster kids come with lots of stuff, but she came with everything she had in a paper bag. Some dresses that was too short. A pair of pants barely holding a crotch. A pile of ratty underwear and one new nightgown. Mine was her third foster home in as many months. The agency folks said she was *so-cio-path-ic*.[1] I don't know nothing from that. She just seemed like she was all full up with anger and scaredness like lots of the kids who come to me. Only she was a real loner. Not trusting nobody. But she ran just like any other kid, was quiet when needed. Smiled at all the right times. If you could get her to smile, that is. Didn't talk much, though.

B Had these ferocious dreams, too. Real screamer dreams they were. Shake the soul right out of you. She'd be screaming and crying with her little body wriggling on the bed, her hair all matted up on her woody-colored face. One time I got her to tell me what she was seeing, and she told me how she was being chased by a man with a long knife what he was going to kill her with and nobody could hear her calling out for help. She didn't talk too much about them, but they was all bad like that one. Seemed the most fierce dreams I ever remember anybody ever having outside of a vision seek.[2] They said her tribe was Assiniboin,[3] but they weren't for certain. What was for sure was that she was a fine dark-eyed girl just meant for someone to scoop up for loving.

Took her to her first dance in September, like I said, not long after she came. It wasn't like I thought it would be a good thing to do. It was just that we was all going. Me, my own kids, some nieces and nephews and the other children who was living with us. The powwow was just part of what we done all the time. Every month. More often in the summer. But this was the regular first Friday night of the school year. We'd all gather up and go to the school. I was thinking on leaving her home with a sitter 'cause she'd tried to kill one of the cats a couple of days before. We'd had us a big talk and she was grounded, but, well, it seemed like she ought to be with us.

Harold, that's my oldest boy, he and the other kids was mad with her, but he decided to show her around anyhow. At the school he went through the gym telling people, "This here's my sister, Clarissa." Wasn't no fuss or anything. She was just another one of the kids. When they was done meeting folks, he put her on one of the bleachers near the drum and went to join the men. He was in that place where his voice cracks but was real proud to be drumming. Held his hand up to his ear even, some of the time. Anyhow, Clarissa was sitting there, not all that interested in the dance or drum, when Molly Graybull come out in her button dress. Her arms was all stretched out, and she was slipping around, <u>preening</u> on them spindles of legs that get skinnier with every year. She was well into her seventies, and I might as well admit, Molly had won herself a fair share of dance contests. So it wasn't no surprise how a little girl could get so <u>fixated</u> on Molly. Clarissa watched her move around-around-around. Then all the rest of the dancers **C**

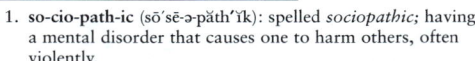

1. **so-cio-path-ic** (sō′sē-ə-păth′ĭk): spelled *sociopathic*; having a mental disorder that causes one to harm others, often violently.
2. **vision seek:** Native American rite in which a person in a dream or trancelike state receives guidance or powers.
3. **Assiniboin** (ə-sĭn′ə-boin′): Native American tribe of northeastern and north central Montana and parts of Canada.

| WORDS TO KNOW | **preening** (prē′nĭng) *adj.* showing pride and self-satisfaction **preen** *v.* |
| | **fixated** (fĭk′sā-tĭd) *adj.* having one's attention absorbed; engrossed **fixate** *v.* |

577

Art Note

***Blackfoot Child* by Charles La Monk**
A traditional painter who used oils and mixed media, Wyoming artist La Monk sought to portray the experiences of Native American peoples. Said La Monk, "I try to capture on canvas the haunting emotion of the Indian people whose every ounce of strength is consumed in daily survival. The somber features and the costumes reveal a determination to live on as they have for generations."

Reading the Art *How would you characterize the girl in this painting? What qualities, such as strength or innocence, might she possess? Is this how you visualize Clarissa? Why or why not?*

Linking to Social Studies

 D Native Americans perform dances for many reasons. The Plains tribes believed that the buffalo dance would bring good hunting. Eastern Woodland tribes celebrated the first summer crops with the green corn dance. The Hopi snake dance was a prayer for rain, and the Plains sun dance fulfilled a vow to a divine spirit.

Blackfoot Child, Charles La Monk. Oil on canvas, 16" × 12". Courtesy of Chuck La Monk, dedicated to Lauren La Monk.

578 UNIT FIVE PART 1: FINDING YOUR PLACE

Multicultural Perspectives

THE ASSINIBOIN The Assiniboin are a Plains tribe that were once part of the Sioux Indians. A nomadic people, the tribe moved throughout parts of Canada and northwestern United States (what is now Ontario, Saskatchewan, Montana, and North Dakota). *Assiniboin* is a name which most likely derives from a Chippewa word meaning "one who cooks by the use of stones." In Canada, the Assiniboin are sometimes referred to as "Stonies" because of their cooking methods, which include dropping hot stones into soup to bring it to a boil. The Assiniboin tribe was devastated by smallpox, which killed almost half the tribe's members around the beginning of the 1800s. Today, many of the Assiniboin live on two reservations in Montana, Fort Belknap and Fort Peck, and on other smaller reservations in Canada. Conditions on the reservations can be harsh and many inhabitants live in poverty. Despite this, many members strive to maintain Assiniboin traditions, and many still speak their native language.

after Molly. She sure took in a good eyeful. Fancy dance. Owl dance. Circle dance. Even a hoop dancer was visiting that night.[4] Everything weaving all slow, then fast. Around-around until that child couldn't see nothing else. Seemed like she was struck silent in the night, too. Never had no dreams at all. Well, not the hollering kind anyways.

Next day she was more quiet than usual, only I could see she was looking at her picture book and tapping the old one-two, one-two. Tapping her toes on the rug with the inside of her head going around and around. As quiet as she could be, she was.

A few days went on before she asks me, "When's there gonna be another dance?"

I tell her in three weeks. She just smiles and goes on outside, waiting on the older kids to come home from school.

The very next day she asks if she can listen to some singing. I give her the tape recorder and some of Joe Washington from up to the Lummi reservation and the Kicking Woman Singers. Clarissa, she takes them tapes and runs out back behind the chicken shed, staying out all afternoon. I wasn't worried none, though, 'cause I could hear the music the whole time. Matter of fact, it like to make me sick of them same songs come the end of three weeks. But that kid, she didn't get into no kind of mischief. Almost abnormal how good she was. Worried me some to see her so caught up but it seemed good too. The angry part of her slowed down so's she wasn't hitting the animals or chopping on herself with sticks like she was doing when she first come. She wasn't laughing much either, but she started playing with the other kids when they come home. Seemed like everybody was working hard to be better with each other.

Come March, Clarissa asks, "Can I dance?"

For sure, the best time for teaching is when a kid wants to listen, so we stood side to side with me doing some steps. She followed along fine. I put on a tape and started moving faster, and Clarissa just kept up all natural. I could tell she'd been practicing lots. She was doing real good.

SHE DIDN'T DANCE AGAIN THAT NIGHT, BUT I COULD SEE THERE WAS DREAMING COMING INTO HER EYES.

Comes the next powwow, which was outside on the track field, I braided Clarissa's hair. Did her up with some ermine and bead ties, then give her a purse to carry. It was all beaded with a rose and leaves. Used to be my aunt's. She held it right next to her side with her chin real high. She joined in a Circle dance. I could see she was watching her feet a little and looking how others do their steps, but mostly she was doing wonderful. When Molly Graybull showed up beside her, Clarissa took to a seat and stared. She didn't dance again that night, but I could see there was dreaming coming into her eyes. I saw that fire

---
4. **Fancy dance. Owl dance. Circle dance. Even a hoop dancer . . . that night:** references to traditional Native American dances—in order, a competitive dance for showing performers' best steps; an expressive dance honoring the sacredness of the owl; a social dance performed in a circle; a dance for a single male performer using hoops.

DANCER **579**

Mini-Lesson The Writer's Style

INFORMAL ENGLISH Help students to understand that informal English is marked by a casual tone. It typically uses sentences that are shorter and vocabulary that is simpler than those of formal English. Readers might expect to find informal English in dialogue, advertisements, diaries, and friendly letters. Sears uses informal English to help give her story a conversational tone.

Application Have students examine the highlighted passage above and then have them change the narrator's informal English to more formal English, adding additional details wherever necessary. Have volunteers read their rewrites aloud. Then reread the original passage to the class. Ask them how their revisions affected the tone of the original passage and their visualization of the narrator. Ask students to record their responses in their reading logs.

Reteaching/Reinforcement
- *Writing Mini-Lessons* transparencies, p. 36

The Writer's Craft
Formal and Informal English, p. 315

CUSTOMIZING FOR
Students Acquiring English

 Have a volunteer paraphrase the idiomatic expression "took in a good eyeful." *(saw many things; looked closely at many different things)*

3 Tell students that *lots* is a slang term meaning "a lot," "often," "very much."

4 Explain that the fire the narrator saw in Clarissa's eyes is not literal fire. Invite volunteers to suggest another way to describe this fire. *(desire, determination)*

Literary Concept: NARRATOR

E Ask students what important information the narrator reveals here about Clarissa. *(Possible responses: Clarissa is interested in listening to the traditional songs. Clarissa's interest in the music is helping her work through some of her emotional problems.)*

Active Reading: CONNECT

F Invite students to tell whether they agree that "the best time for teaching is when a kid wants to listen." To begin discussion, you may wish to provide the following model to the class:

Think-Aloud Model *I think that the only time a person will learn is when he or she really wants to. It is very important to make what is being taught interesting. I know that when I don't find a topic interesting, I may not work as hard to understand it.*

STRATEGIC READING FOR
Less-Proficient Readers

 Ask students to summarize Clarissa's behavior after the powwow. *(Clarissa begins listening to music and asks the narrator to teach her to dance. After she learns, Clarissa spends a lot of time practicing her dancing.)* **Summarizing**

Set a Purpose Have students look for what the traditional dancing means to Clarissa.

THE LANGUAGE OF LITERATURE TEACHER'S EDITION **579**

Literary Concept:
CHARACTERIZATION

H Ask students how Sears uses Clarissa's statement to develop her character. (*Possible response: This is the first time Clarissa has said anything proudly; Sears is showing how her heritage has improved Clarissa's self-image.*)

STRATEGIC READING FOR
Less-Proficient Readers

I Have students explain what Clarissa's new knowledge of Native American dance has given her. (*She has a new sense of her heritage, and a better sense of herself.*) Making Inferences/Drawing Conclusions

CUSTOMIZING FOR
Gifted and Talented Students

Ask students to discuss the role tradition plays in this story. Have students discuss the difficulties of passing on and maintaining traditions.

COMPREHENSION CHECK
1. What problems does Clarissa have when she first arrives? (*She acts violently and has bad dreams.*)
2. What does Clarissa do after the first powwow? (*She listens to music and practices dancing.*)
3. What do Clarissa and Molly do at the end of the story? (*They dance together.*)

INSIGHT

1. Which of the activities mentioned in the poem is the most important to building community? Why? (*Possible responses: dancing, because it supports tradition; talking, because it passes on oral history*)
2. Why do you think the speaker and Clarissa want to participate in the festivities? (*Possible responses: It's enjoyable; it gives them both a sense of belonging.*)

ALONZO LOPEZ

Alonzo Lopez is a member of the Papago Indian tribe of southern Arizona and northwestern Mexico. He wrote "Celebration" when he was a student at the Institute of American Indian Arts in Santa Fe, New Mexico.

---

that said to practice. And she did. I heard her every day in her room. Finally bought her her very own tape recorder so's the rest of us could listen to music too.

Some months passed on. All the kids was getting bigger. Clarissa, she went into the first grade. Harvey went off to community college up in Seattle, and that left me with Ronnie being the oldest at home. Clarissa was keeping herself busy all the time going over to Molly Graybull's. She was coming home with Spider Woman stories and trickster tales.[5] One night she speaks up at supper and says, right clear and loud, "I'm an Assiniboin." Clear as it can be, she says it again. Don't nobody have to say nothing to something that proud said.

Next day I started working on a wing dress for Clarissa. She was going to be needing one for sure real soon.

Comes the first school-year powwow and everyone was putting on their best. I called for Clarissa to come to my room. I told her, "I think it's time you have something special for yourself." Then I held up the green satin and saw her eyes full up with glitter. She didn't say nothing. Only kisses me and runs off to her room.

Just as we're all getting out of the car, Clarissa whispered to me, "I'm gonna dance with Molly Graybull." I put my hand on her shoulder to say, "You just listen to your spirit. That's where your music is."

We all danced an Owl dance, a Friendship dance, and a couple of Circle dances. Things was feeling real warm and good, and then it was time for the women's traditional.[6] Clarissa joined the circle. She opened her arms to something nobody but her seemed to hear.

That's when I saw that old Eagle woman come down and slide right inside of Clarissa, scooping up that child. There Clarissa was, full up with music. All full with that old, old spirit, letting herself dance through Clarissa's feet. Then Molly Graybull come dancing alongside Clarissa, and they was both the same age. ❖

---

5. **Spider Woman stories and trickster tales:** Native American legends about Spider Woman's teachings and gift-giving and about mischievous heroes with magical powers.
6. **women's traditional:** slow Native American dance historically reserved for women.

LITERARY INSIGHT

CELEBRATION
BY ALONZO LOPEZ

I shall dance tonight.
When the dusk comes crawling,
There will be dancing
    and feasting.
5   I shall dance with the others
    in circles,
        in leaps,
            in stomps.
Laughter and talk
10   will weave into the night,
Among the fires
    of my people.
Games will be played
And I shall be
15   a part of it.

Mini-Lesson — **Reading Skills/Strategies**

MAKING JUDGMENTS Explain to students that making judgments means forming opinions about a character and a character's actions or beliefs. These judgments are based on information in the story and on the reader's own beliefs. By examining the narrator's voice (the tone, mood, and opinions the narrator expresses), readers can make their own judgments about the relationship developed in "Dancer." Remind students that this story is presented from the narrator's perspective, with her own judgments expressed in the way she tells the story.

Application Ask students to imagine they are Clarissa as an adult. Tell them to write a letter to the foster mother that expresses Clarissa's views on how she was raised. Tell students that before they begin, they should review the story to infer what the foster mother's opinions on parenting are and decide whether or not they agree with her. Have volunteers share their letters with the class.

Reteaching/Reinforcement
• *Unit Five Resource Book,* p. 5

RESPONDING OPTIONS

FROM PERSONAL RESPONSE TO CRITICAL ANALYSIS

REFLECT
1. What are you left wondering about as the story ends? Jot down your thoughts in your notebook.

RETHINK
2. How would you describe what happens to Clarissa on the dance floor at the end of the story?

3. Explain the influences you think help Clarissa to change and to find her place in the new community.
   Consider
   • her relationship with her foster mother
   • the way the rest of the family treats her
   • her reaction to Molly Graybull's dancing

4. Which character from the story had the greatest effect on you? Give reasons for your answer.

5. Clarissa's love of Native American dance amazes and delights those in her community. What do you predict for Clarissa's future?

RELATE
Thematic Link

6. Clarissa proudly announces, "I'm an Assiniboin." Do you think that learning about your ethnic heritage helps you to define yourself? Why or why not?

7. Compare Clarissa's feelings about dancing at the powwow with the feelings about dancing expressed by the speaker in the Insight poem "Celebration," on page 580.

LITERARY CONCEPTS

In "Dancer," the foster mother, a main character, is the **narrator.** The reader sees the story through her eyes as she shares her thoughts and feelings about Clarissa. Think about how the foster mother's role as narrator affects what you learn about the events and people in the story. Who in "Dancer" do you feel you know best by the end? Why?

Multimodal Learning
ANOTHER PATHWAY

When a child is placed in a foster home, a social worker is assigned to evaluate the care the child receives from the foster family. Imagine that you are Clarissa's social worker and that you are reporting back to your supervisor. Present an oral report to the class concerning Clarissa's progress.

QUICKWRITES

1. Some Native American tribes give each of their members a name that reflects the person's nature. For example, Molly's last name, Graybull, may suggest her importance in the tribe, her wisdom, and her leadership. Think of a tribal name for Clarissa or her foster mother that reflects some important quality or character trait. Write the **tribal name** and a brief **explanation** of why you chose it.

2. Assume the voice of Harold, the narrator's eldest son, and write a **paragraph** giving your impression of Clarissa.

 PORTFOLIO Save your writing. You may want to use it later as a springboard to a piece for your portfolio.

DANCER 581

From Personal Response to Critical Analysis

1. Possible responses: Will Clarissa stay with her foster mother? Did Clarissa feel the Elk Woman spirit inside her as she danced?

2. Possible responses: She is united with the traditions of her people. The special bond between Clarissa and Molly Graybull is represented through the foster mother's vision of an old woman's spirit entering Clarissa's body.

3. Possible responses: She finds love from her foster mother. She is treated like a member of the family by her foster siblings. She is inspired by and identifies with Molly's dancing.

4. Possible response: The narrator had the greatest effect because of her patience with the troubled girl and her seemingly limitless supply of love for all her children.

5. Possible response: No matter what happens in her life, Clarissa will continue to develop her love of Native American dance.

6. Possible response: Yes, because knowing where you come from gives you a sense of who you are. No, because how you define yourself is based on your present situation, not on your past.

7. Possible response: The two are very much alike because both see dancing as a means of acquiring a sense of community and shared traditions.

Another Pathway

Point out to students that a social worker would be likely to use formal English in his or her report about Clarissa. Be sure that the oral reports compare Clarissa's first experiences in her new foster home with her actions after she dances.

Rubric
3 Full Accomplishment Students provide a full account in formal English of Clarissa's experiences.
2 Substantial Accomplishment Students provide a full account of Clarissa's development, but use informal or nonstandard English.
1 Little or Partial Accomplishment Students do not cover the major events of the story and/or cannot determine the difference between formal and informal English.

Literary Concepts

Point out to students that how well they understand the narrator often depends on whether the narrator gives his or her own opinions or is primarily concerned with telling the story of other characters. As students think about which character they know best, suggest they keep in mind that the narrator filters the information readers receive about Clarissa.

QuickWrites

1. Explain to students that many tribal names are composites of two or more characteristics. For example, Sitting Bull was known for his staunch determination, his heroism, and his nobility. Invite students to use imagery from their own experiences in choosing tribal names.

2. Remind students that Harold was quite angry with Clarissa's attempts to injure the family cat; therefore Harold's narration may not be as supportive of Clarissa as his mother's.

The Writer's Craft
Paragraphs, pp. 248–251

Words to Know

Word wheels will vary. Note that students' comparisons, associations, and usage will most likely reflect their understanding of what the words mean to them.

Across the Curriculum

Social Studies *The Assiniboin Tribe* To help students begin their research, you may want to refer them back to the Multicultural Perspective on page 578. About 3,500 Assiniboin now live in Montana and another 3,500 reside in Alberta and Saskatchewan in Canada. Encourage partners to divide the research. For example, one student may focus on the traditional hunting and farming techniques of the Assiniboin, and on the way their families were structured, while the other student examines the contemporary living conditions of the tribe. Partners should integrate their findings before presenting their material to the class.

ADDITIONAL SUGGESTION

Social Studies Cooperative Learning *Powwows* Have students form groups of three or four to research what activities occur at powwows. Each group can focus on a specific aspect, such as food, music, dances, games, or attire. If possible, have students contact a community Native American organization for further information. Students may be able to attend a powwow, many of which are open to the public. Students can present their findings as either written or oral reports. Encourage them to include visuals or audio recordings, if permissible.

Literary Links

Ask students how Clarissa's discovery of her Native American past relates to Tsali and his family's attempt (in Unit Three) to defend their tradition. (Possible response: It is through the efforts of Tsali, his family, and other Native Americans who sacrificed their lives to defend and preserve their traditions that Clarissa now finds inspiration, strength, and a better sense of her self.)

VICKI SEARS

Sears credits many of her ideas for stories to the children she has encountered as a therapist, teacher, and writer. Other collections of stories by Sears include *The Things that Divide Us, Hear the Silence, Gathering Ground,* and *Gathering of Spirit.*

Multimodal Learning

ALTERNATIVE ACTIVITIES

On your own or with a small group, find **music** to accompany a particular type of Native American dance. Bring the music to class and share it with your classmates. You also might tell them about the instruments used and about the history of the dance.

ACROSS THE CURRICULUM

Social Studies *Cooperative Learning*
In a group, research the Assiniboin tribe, using an on-line computer service if possible. Present an exhibit to the class that includes a map showing where the Assiniboin now live; pictures and information about their history, culture, and traditions; and brief statements of what they are most known for and what traditions they still practice. You also may wish to recreate Assiniboin artifacts to include in your display.

WORDS TO KNOW

Make a word wheel, like the one shown for the word *wriggling,* for each of the two Words to Know. Use the following instructions to help you fill in the wheel:

Describe It—Describe what the word means to you.
Compare It—Find similar and different words.
Associate It—What does it make you think of?
Use It—Write a sentence using the word.

Describe It	Compare It
squirming, not violently	moving like a snake, not a bat
Associate It	**Use It**
a person in pain	The boy was wriggling out of her arms.

VICKIE SEARS

1941–

Vickie Sears is part Cherokee, part Spanish, and part English. Like Clarissa, she was a foster child. Always feeling unwanted, she spent her years between 4 and 11 in an orphanage and various foster homes—all "pretty negative" experiences, she says. In her loneliness, she began to write and to dream of having "at least two big houses so I could have all of the children that no one wanted." Sears did not reach that goal, but over the years she did care for 32 Native American foster children. Now adults, all of these young people and their children—Sears's 117 "grandchildren"—gather for a reunion every four years.

After working her way through the University of San Francisco, Sears wrote for an anti–Vietnam War magazine, taught in a ghetto high school, worked on a tree farm, cleaned motels and welfare houses, wrote grants for the War on Poverty, did youth drug and alcohol counseling, and directed a tribal mental health program. Today, she is a therapist and writer in Seattle.

Sears writes short stories, poetry, and professional articles. She views her stories and poems as a "way to heal, as well as a way to create beauty."

OTHER WORKS *Simple Songs: Stories by Vickie Sears*

Extended Reading

582 UNIT FIVE PART 1: FINDING YOUR PLACE

SOCIAL STUDIES CONNECTION
The Assiniboin Present these photographs of traditional Assiniboin dress and lodging to teach students about this Native American culture.

Side A, Frame 52792

Alternative Activities

Suggest that students consult their librarian to locate traditional Native American music. Inform students that in the 1920s and 1930s, anthropologists such as Franz Boas and Ruth Benedict tried to record the customs and stories of Native Americans throughout North America. These early studies still provide some of the best live recordings of Native American music.

PREVIEWING

FICTION

The Moustache
Robert Cormier

Activating Prior Knowledge
PERSONAL CONNECTION

In this story, 17-year-old Mike learns about the plight of the elderly when he visits his grandmother in a nursing home. What do you know about the elderly and the problems they face? If you have ever visited a nursing home, what were your reactions? How do you feel about growing old? On a word web like the one shown here, jot down some of your images of and thoughts about the elderly and growing old.

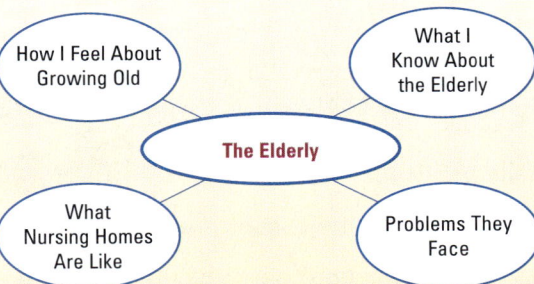

Building Background
SOCIAL STUDIES CONNECTION

Most elderly people in the United States live on their own or with their families. However, about 6 percent of the nation's elderly reside in nursing homes. An older person may decide to live in such a facility if he or she has health problems requiring constant medical attention. Such care is needed for many conditions that afflict the aged, including arteriosclerosis (är-tîr′ē-ō-sklə-rō′sĭs)—commonly known as hardening of the arteries—a disease that affects the grandmother in this story.

Arteriosclerosis narrows the arteries and decreases blood flow to vital organs, such as the brain. It can cause strokes, which may result in dizziness, general weakness, slurred speech, and forgetfulness.

Active Reading/Setting a Purpose
READING CONNECTION

Clarifying As you read "The Moustache," you may need to stop from time to time to clarify what you are reading. Recall that clarifying involves pausing occasionally for a quick review of what you understand so far and drawing conclusions about what is suggested but not stated directly. The questions that appear with this story will help you follow the motives of the characters and understand the theme. Use your reading log to record your responses to the questions inserted throughout the selection.

- *SOCIAL STUDIES CONNECTION*

583

OVERVIEW

Objectives
- To understand and appreciate a short story about a young man's painful discovery of his grandmother's failing mind
- To enrich reading by using active reading strategies
- To identify and understand symbols
- To express understanding of the story through a choice of writing forms, including an interior monologue and a character sketch
- To extend understanding of the story through a variety of multimodal and cross-disciplinary activities

Skills

READING SKILLS/ STRATEGIES
- Clarify
- Connect

LITERARY CONCEPTS
- Chronological order
- Symbols

THE WRITER'S STYLE
- Slang

GRAMMAR
- Capitalization of proper nouns

SPELLING
- The prefix *com-*

SPEAKING, LISTENING, AND VIEWING
- Group discussion
- Oral presentation

Cross-Curricular Connections

HISTORY
- Ethel Barrymore

SCIENCE
- Arteriosclerosis
- Diseases of aging

SOCIAL STUDIES
- Achievements of older people

 SOCIAL STUDIES CONNECTION
Nursing Homes Increase students' knowledge of nursing homes by showing these photographs of residents painting, exercising, and socializing.

Side A, Frame 52796

PRINT AND MEDIA RESOURCES

UNIT FIVE RESOURCE BOOK
Strategic Reading: Literature, p. 9
Vocabulary SkillBuilder, p. 12
Reading SkillBuilder, p. 10
Spelling SkillBuilder, p. 11

GRAMMAR MINI–LESSONS
Transparencies, pp. 25–26
Copymasters, pp. 33–34

WRITING MINI–LESSONS
Transparencies, p. 36

ACCESS FOR STUDENTS ACQUIRING ENGLISH
Selection Summaries
Reading and Writing Support,

FORMAL ASSESSMENT
Selection Test, pp. 109–110
 Test Generator

AUDIO LIBRARY
See Reference Card

 LASERLINKS
Social Studies Connection
Science Connection

THE LANGUAGE OF LITERATURE **TEACHER'S EDITION** 583

The Moustache
by Robert Cormier

At the last minute Annie couldn't go. She was invaded by one of those twenty-four-hour flu bugs that sent her to bed with a fever, moaning about the fact that she'd also have to break her date with Handsome Harry Arnold that night. We call him Handsome Harry because he's actually handsome, but he's also a nice guy, cool, and he doesn't treat me like Annie's kid brother, which I am, but like a regular person. Anyway, I had to go to Lawnrest alone that afternoon. But first of all I had to stand inspection.

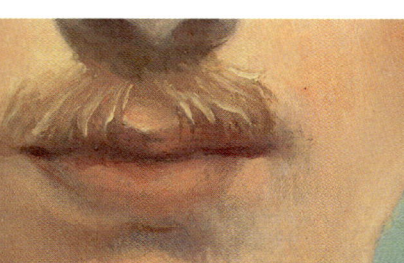

WORDS TO KNOW

complex (kŏm′plĕks′) *n.* an exaggerated concern or preoccupation (p. 586)
lapse (lăps) *v.* to drift or fall (p. 587)
lucid (lōō′sĭd) *adj.* mentally alert; clear-headed (p. 587)
pathetic (pə-thĕt′ĭk) *adj.* pitiful (p. 590)
serene (sə-rēn′) *adj.* calm (p. 591)

My mother lined me up against the wall. She stood there like a one-man firing squad, which is kind of funny because she's not like a man at all, she's very feminine, and we have this great relationship—I mean, I feel as if she really likes me. I realize that sounds strange, but I know guys whose mothers love them and cook special stuff for them and worry about them and all, but there's something missing in their relationship.

Anyway. She frowned and started the routine.

"That hair," she said. Then admitted: "Well, at least you combed it."

I sighed. I have discovered that it's better to sigh than argue.

"And that moustache." She shook her head. "I still say a seventeen-year-old has no business wearing a moustache."

"It's an experiment," I said. "I just wanted to see if I could grow one." To tell the truth, I had proved my point about being able to grow a decent moustache, but I also had learned to like it.

"It's costing you money, Mike," she said.

"I know, I know."

The money was a reference to the movies. The Downtown Cinema has a special Friday night offer—half-price admission for high school couples seventeen or younger. But the woman in the box office took one look at my moustache and charged me full price. Even when I showed her my driver's license. She charged full admission for Cindy's ticket, too, which left me practically broke and unable to take Cindy out for a hamburger with the crowd afterward. That didn't help matters, because Cindy has been getting impatient recently about things like the fact that I don't own my own car and have to concentrate on my studies if I want to win that college scholarship, for instance. Cindy wasn't exactly crazy about the moustache, either.

Now it was my mother's turn to sigh.

"Look," I said, to cheer her up. "I'm thinking about shaving it off." Even though I wasn't. Another discovery: You can build a way of life on postponement.

"Your grandmother probably won't even recognize you," she said. And I saw the shadow fall across her face.

Let me tell you what the visit to Lawnrest was all about. My grandmother is 73 years old. She is a resident—which is supposed to be a better word than *patient*—at the Lawnrest Nursing Home. She used to make the greatest turkey dressing in the world and was a nut about baseball and could even quote batting averages, for crying out loud. She always rooted for the losers. She was in love with the Mets until they started to win. Now she has arteriosclerosis, which the dictionary says is "a chronic disease characterized by abnormal thickening and hardening of the arterial walls." Which really means that she can't live at home anymore or even with us, and her memory has betrayed her as well as her body. She used to wander off and sometimes didn't recognize people. My mother visits her all the time, driving the thirty miles to Lawnrest almost every day. Because Annie was home for a semester break from college, we had decided to make a special Saturday visit. Now Annie was in bed, groaning theatrically—she's a drama major—but I told my mother I'd go, anyway. I hadn't seen my grandmother since she'd been admitted to Lawnrest. Besides, the place is located on the Southwest Turnpike, which meant I could barrel along in my father's new Le Mans. My ambition was to see the speedometer hit 75. Ordinarily, I used the old station wagon, which can barely stagger up to 50.

> **CONNECT**
> Have you ever known an elderly person with health problems similar to those described?

THE MOUSTACHE **585**

Active Reading: CLARIFY

C Have students review the context in which Mike refers to "these figures." *(Possible responses: Mike is making an analogy between the senior residents of Lawnrest and figures in a wax museum. Because many residents are immobile or do not seem to speak, they remind Mike of the statues in wax museums.)*

CUSTOMIZING FOR
Students Acquiring English

5 Explain that the expression "par for the course" refers to the game of golf. When a golfer hits the ball into the hole in the expected or usual number of strokes, the golfer has parred the hole, or made a par. This expression shows that Mike expects to be ignored when he meets girls.

Linking to History

D Ethel Barrymore (1879–1959) was a member of the famous Barrymore family of actors that included her brothers Lionel and John. *None But the Lonely Heart* (1944) was made when Barrymore was in her sixties.

Critical Thinking: HYPOTHESIZING

E Have students hypothesize how Mike's visit with his grandmother will go based on her response when he enters. *(Possible responses: Because she recognizes him immediately, it appears that the visit will be successful. Even though Mike's grandmother seems to know him, there is no guarantee that she will continue to be lucid.)*

Frankly, I wasn't too crazy about visiting a nursing home. They reminded me of hospitals, and hospitals turn me off. I mean, the smell of ether¹ makes me nauseous, and I feel faint at the sight of blood. And as I approached Lawnrest—which is a terrible cemetery kind of name, to begin with—I was sorry I hadn't avoided the trip. Then I felt guilty about it. I'm loaded with guilt <u>complexes</u>. Like driving like a madman after promising my father to be careful. Like sitting in the parking lot, looking at the nursing home with dread and thinking how I'd rather be with Cindy. Then I thought of all the Christmas and birthday gifts my grandmother had given me, and I got out of the car, guilty, as usual.

Inside, I was surprised by the lack of hospital smell, although there was another odor or maybe the absence of an odor. The air was antiseptic, sterile. As if there was no atmosphere at all or I'd caught a cold suddenly and couldn't taste or smell.

A nurse at the reception desk gave me directions—my grandmother was in East Three. I made my way down the tiled corridor and was glad to see that the walls were painted with cheerful colors like yellow and pink. A wheelchair suddenly shot around a corner, self-propelled by an old man, white-haired and toothless, who cackled merrily as he barely missed me. I jumped aside—here I was, almost getting wiped out by a two-mile-an-hour wheelchair after doing seventy-five on the pike. As I walked through the corridors seeking East Three, I couldn't help glancing into the rooms, and it was like some kind of wax museum²—all these figures in various stances and attitudes, sitting in beds or chairs, standing at windows, as if they were frozen forever in these postures. To tell the truth, I began to hurry because I was getting depressed. Finally, I saw a beautiful girl approaching, dressed in white, a nurse or an attendant, and I was so happy to see someone young, someone walking and acting normally, that I gave her a wide smile and a big hello and must have looked like a kind of nut. Anyway, she looked right through me as if I were a window, which is about par for the course whenever I meet beautiful girls.

I finally found the room and saw my grandmother in bed. My grandmother looks like Ethel Barrymore.³ I never knew who Ethel Barrymore was until I saw a terrific movie, *None But the Lonely Heart,* on TV, starring Ethel Barrymore and Cary Grant.⁴ Both my grandmother and Ethel Barrymore have these great craggy faces like the side of a mountain and wonderful voices like syrup being poured. Slowly. She was propped up in bed, pillows puffed behind her. Her hair had been combed out and fell upon her shoulders. For some reason, this flowing hair gave her an almost girlish appearance, despite its whiteness.

She saw me and smiled. Her eyes lit up and her eyebrows arched and she reached out her hands to me in greeting. "Mike, Mike," she said. And I breathed a sigh of relief. This was one of her good days. My mother had warned me that she might not know who I was at first.

CLARIFY
C Who is Mike referring to when he says, "these figures"?

---

1. **ether** (ē′thər): a chemical formerly used by surgeons as an anesthetic.
2. **wax museum:** a museum that displays wax statues of famous people.
3. **Ethel Barrymore** (1879–1959): U.S. stage and screen actress.
4. **Cary Grant** (1904–1986): U.S. movie star.

WORDS TO KNOW — **complex** (kŏm′plĕks′) *n.* an exaggerated concern or preoccupation

586

Mini-Lesson — Grammar

CAPITALIZATION OF PROPER NOUNS
Remind students that common nouns refer to a whole class of persons, places, things, or ideas. Common nouns are not capitalized. A proper noun refers to a specific person, place, thing, or idea and is capitalized to show its importance.

Application In the examples shown on the chart, the words in the left-hand column are taken from the selection. Have students compare the right- and left-hand columns. Then have students correct the capitalization mistakes in the following sentences.

Lawnrest	nursing home
Christmas	holiday
East Three	room
corridor	West Hall
wax museum	Madame Cassant's House of Horror
Ethel Barrymore	movie star
Mike	grandson

1. I think she's going to name her Cat waldo.
2. We drove down main street and parked next to the bank.

Reteaching/Reinforcement
- Grammar Handbook, anthology pp. 887–889
- *Grammar Mini-Lessons* copymasters, pp. 33–34, transparencies, pp. 25–26

The Writer's Craft
Proper Nouns and Proper Adjectives, pp. 616–617

I took her hands in mine. They were fragile. I could actually feel her bones, and it seemed as if they would break if I pressed too hard. Her skin was smooth, almost slippery, as if the years had worn away all the roughness the way the wind wears away the surfaces of stones.

> "Mike, Mike, I didn't think you'd come," she said, so happy, and she was still Ethel Barrymore, that voice like a caress.

"Mike, Mike, I didn't think you'd come," she said, so happy, and she was still Ethel Barrymore, that voice like a caress. "I've been waiting all this time." Before I could reply, she looked away, out the window. "See the birds? I've been watching them at the feeder. I love to see them come. Even the blue jays. The blue jays are like hawks—they take the food that the small birds should have. But the small birds, the chickadees, watch the blue jays and at least learn where the feeder is."

She lapsed into silence, and I looked out the window. There was no feeder. No birds. There was only the parking lot and the sun glinting on car windshields.

She turned to me again, eyes bright. Radiant, really. Or was it a medicine brightness?

CLARIFY
⑥ What do you think is going on with Mike's grandmother?

"Ah, Mike. You look so grand, so grand. Is that a new coat?"

"Not really," I said. I'd been wearing my Uncle Jerry's old army-fatigue jacket for months, practically living in it, my mother said. But she insisted that I wear my raincoat for the visit. It was about a year old but looked new because I didn't wear it much. Nobody was wearing raincoats lately.

"You always loved clothes, didn't you, Mike?" she said.

I was beginning to feel uneasy because she regarded me with such intensity. Those bright eyes. I wondered—are old people in places like this so lonesome, so abandoned that they go wild when someone visits? Or was she so happy because she was suddenly lucid and everything was sharp and clear? My mother had described those moments when my grandmother suddenly emerged from the fog that so often obscured her mind.

I didn't know the answers, but it felt kind of spooky, getting such an emotional welcome from her.

"I remember the time you bought the new coat—the chesterfield,"⁵ she said, looking away again, as if watching the birds that weren't there. "That lovely coat with the velvet collar. Black, it was. Stylish. Remember that, Mike? It was hard times, but you could never resist the glitter."

I was about to protest—I had never heard of a chesterfield, for crying out loud. But I stopped. Be patient with her, my mother had said. Humor her. Be gentle.

We were interrupted by an attendant who pushed a wheeled cart into the room. "Time for juices, dear," the woman said. She was the standard forty- or fifty-year-old woman: glasses, nothing hair, plump cheeks. Her manner was cheerful but a businesslike kind of cheerfulness. I'd hate to be called

---
5. **chesterfield:** an overcoat, usually with concealed buttons and a velvet collar.

WORDS TO KNOW
lapse (lăps) *v.* to drift or fall
lucid (lōō′sĭd) *adj.* mentally alert; clear-headed

CUSTOMIZING FOR
Multiple Learning Styles

Interpersonal Learners Invite students to form groups of three or four and discuss whether they interact differently with friends their own age and with older people. Ask them what are the benefits and drawbacks of each type of relationship. Encourage them to think about what a friendship with an older person can provide that friendship with one's younger friends cannot.

Critical Thinking:
MAKING JUDGMENTS

1 Have students assess how the nurse treats Mike's grandmother. Ask students if they think this is a way that a caregiver should treat patients. *(Possible responses: There is no excuse for the nurse to treat Mike's grandmother like a child. However, juice may be good for her, and it may be difficult for the nurse to get patients like his grandmother to drink juice.)*

Copyright © Susi Kilgore.

588 UNIT FIVE PART 1: FINDING YOUR PLACE

Mini-Lesson  Spelling

Com- +	Form	Examples
m, p, b	com	commend
	compound	
l	col	collapse
	collate	
r	cor	correlation
	correct	
h or vowel	co	coherent
	coalesce	
c, d, f, g, j, n, q, s, t, v	con	concern
	condense	

THE PREFIX Com- Tell students that the prefix *com-* means "with" or "together." When combining *com-* with a root or word beginning with *m*, *p*, or *b*, the prefix does not change.

com-   + plex = **complex**
(together)   (weave) = consisting of two
                        or more parts

When combining *com-* with other roots or words that begin with other letters, frequently the prefix changes to *col-*, *cor-*, *co-*, or *con-* to make the word easier to pronounce.

Application Have students spell the words that are formed when the prefix *com-* is added to the root words listed.

1. respond   4. lection
2. operation 5. pete
3. serve   6. tinue

Ask students to look for more words that fit this pattern, and to add them to their personal word lists.

Reteaching/Reinforcement
• *Unit Five Resource Book*, p. 11

588 THE LANGUAGE OF LITERATURE TEACHER'S EDITION

"dear" by someone getting paid to do it. "Orange or grape or cranberry, dear? Cranberry is good for the bones, you know."

My grandmother ignored the interruption. She didn't even bother to answer, having turned away at the woman's arrival, as if angry about her appearance.

The woman looked at me and winked. A conspiratorial kind of wink. It was kind of horrible. I didn't think people winked like that anymore. In fact, I hadn't seen a wink in years.

"She doesn't care much for juices," the woman said, talking to me as if my grandmother weren't even there. "But she loves her coffee. With lots of cream and two lumps of sugar. But this is juice time, not coffee time." Addressing my grandmother again, she said, "Orange or grape or cranberry, dear?"

"Tell her I want no juices, Mike," my grandmother commanded regally, her eyes still watching invisible birds.

The woman smiled, patience like a label on her face. "That's all right, dear. I'll just leave some cranberry for you. Drink it at your leisure. It's good for the bones."

She wheeled herself out of the room. My grandmother was still absorbed in the view. Somewhere a toilet flushed. A wheelchair passed the doorway—probably that same old driver fleeing a hit-run accident. A television set exploded with sound somewhere, soap-opera voices filling the air. You can always tell soap-opera voices.

I turned back to find my grandmother staring at me. Her hands cupped her face, her index fingers curled around her cheeks like parenthesis marks.

"But you know, Mike, looking back, I think you were right," she said, continuing our conversation as if there had been no interruption. "You always said, 'It's the things of the spirit that count, Meg.' The spirit! And so you

> "You always said, 'It's the things of the spirit that count, Meg.' The spirit!"

bought the baby-grand piano—a baby grand in the middle of the Depression. A knock came on the door and it was the deliveryman. It took five of them to get it into the house." She leaned back, closing her eyes. "How I loved that piano, Mike. I was never that fine a player, but you loved to sit there in the parlor, on Sunday evenings, Ellie on your lap, listening to me play and sing." She hummed a bit, a fragment of melody I didn't recognize. Then she drifted into silence. Maybe she'd fallen asleep. My mother's name is Ellen, but everyone always calls her Ellie. "Take my hand, Mike," my grandmother said suddenly. Then I remembered—my grandfather's name was Michael. I had been named for him.

"Ah, Mike," she said, pressing my hands with all her feeble strength. "I thought I'd lost

CLARIFY
Who does Mike's grandmother think Mike is?

you forever. And here you are, back with me again. . . ."

Her expression scared me. I don't mean scared as if I were in danger but scared because of what could happen to her when she realized the mistake she had made. My mother always said I favored her side of the family. Thinking back to the pictures in the old family albums, I recalled my grandfather as tall and thin. Like me. But the resemblance ended there. He was thirty-five when he died, almost forty years ago. And he wore a moustache. I brought my hand to my face. I also wore a moustache now, of course.

THE MOUSTACHE 589

Mini-Lesson Study Skills

THE KWL APPROACH Explain to students that when they are having difficulty defining their objectives for studying or reading, they can organize their learning with the KWL approach. Students simply ask themselves the three questions shown on the chalkboard. Tell them that by setting clear-cut objectives before, during, and after reading, they can better understand and synthesize information.

Application Have students apply the KWL approach to the materials they will be reading to complete the Across the Curriculum activity on page 593.

> K What do I already **know**?
> W What do I **want** to know?
> L What did I **learn**?

Literary Concept:
CHARACTERIZATION

M Have students explain what new aspects of Mike's character are revealed in this scene. *(Possible responses: He is gentle and tender. His ability to show sympathy here suggests that he is more mature than he may have first appeared.)*

Active Reading: CLARIFY

N Encourage students to clarify what conclusions Mike has reached about his grandmother, and why these realizations scare him. If needed, provide students with the following model:

Think-Aloud Model *Although Mike usually jokes around while telling his story, his tone changes and he becomes serious at this point. From what Mike says, I see that he has viewed his parents and grandmother only in relation to himself—what they provided him. Now he realizes that they all have lives of their own, independent of his needs. I wonder why this scares him. Perhaps he is afraid that he can't have the same comfortable ideas about his parents and grandmother, or maybe he is afraid to find out more about them.*

STRATEGIC READING FOR
Less-Proficient Readers

O Ask students what Mike's grandmother wants forgiveness for after all these years. *(She accused her husband of cheating with another woman, realized she was wrong, but was too proud to apologize before he died.)* Noting Relevant Details/Noting Sequence of Events

Set a Purpose Have students complete the story to discover what Mike decides to tell his mother about his visit.

"I sit here these days, Mike," she said, her voice a lullaby, her hand still holding mine, "and I drift and dream. The days are fuzzy sometimes, merging together. Sometimes it's like I'm not here at all but somewhere else altogether. And I always think of you. Those years we had. Not enough years, Mike, not enough. . . ."

Her voice was so sad, so mournful that I made sounds of sympathy, not words exactly but the kind of soothings that mothers murmur to their children when they awaken from bad dreams.

"And I think of that terrible night, Mike, that terrible night. Have you ever really forgiven me for that night?"

"Listen . . ." I began. I wanted to say: "Nana, this is Mike your grandson, not Mike your husband."

"Sh . . . sh . . ." she whispered, placing a finger as long and cold as a candle against my lips. "Don't say anything. I've waited so long for this moment. To be here. With you. I wondered what I would say if suddenly you walked in that door like other people have done. I've thought and thought about it. And I finally made up my mind—I'd ask you to forgive me. I was too proud to ask before." Her fingers tried to mask her face. "But I'm not proud anymore, Mike." That great voice quivered and then grew strong again. "I hate you to see me this way—you always said I was beautiful. I didn't believe it. The Charity Ball when we led the grand march and you said I was the most beautiful girl there. . . ."

"Nana," I said. I couldn't keep up the pretense any longer, adding one more burden to my load of guilt, leading her on this way, playing a <u>pathetic</u> game of make-believe with an old woman clinging to memories. She didn't seem to hear me.

"But that other night, Mike. The terrible one. The terrible accusations I made. Even Ellie woke up and began to cry. I went to her and rocked her in my arms, and you came into the room and said I was wrong. You were whispering, an awful whisper, not wanting to upset little Ellie but wanting to make me see the truth. And I didn't answer you, Mike. I was too proud. I've even forgotten the name of the girl. I sit here wondering now—was it Laura or Evelyn? I can't remember. Later, I learned that you were telling the truth all the time, Mike. That I'd been wrong. . . ." Her eyes were brighter than ever as she looked at me now, but tear-bright, the tears gathering. "It was never the same after that night, was it, Mike? The glitter was gone. From you. From us. And then the accident . . . and I never had the chance to ask you to forgive me. . . ."

My grandmother. My poor, poor grandmother. Old people aren't supposed to have those kinds of memories. You see their pictures in the family albums, and that's what they are: pictures. They're not supposed to come to life. You drive out in your father's Le Mans doing seventy-five on the pike, and all you're doing is visiting an old lady in a nursing home. A duty call. And then you find out that she's a person. She's *somebody*. She's my grandmother, all right, but she's also herself. Like my own mother and father. They exist outside of their relationship to me. I was scared again. I wanted to get out of there.

"Mike, Mike," my grandmother said. "Say it, Mike."

I felt as if my cheeks would crack if I uttered a word.

"Say you forgive me, Mike. I've waited all these years. . . ."

WORDS TO KNOW
pathetic (pə-thĕt′ĭk) *adj.* pitiful

Mini-Lesson The Writer's Style

SLANG Explain to students that slang expressions are a type of informal English. Cormier uses slang to make Mike's speech sound like that of a teenage boy. Have students look at these phrases:
- "Frankly, I wasn't **too crazy** about visiting a nursing home. They reminded me of hospitals, and hospitals **turn me off**." (p. 586)
- "I . . . must have looked like **a kind of nut**. Anyway, she **looked right through me** as if I were a window, which is about **par for the course** whenever I meet beautiful girls." (p. 586)

Application Have students write a short scene between Mike and one of his friends in which Mike tells about his visit with his grandmother. Instruct students to incorporate slang words and phrases in their scenes to make the conversation realistic.

Reteaching/Reinforcement
- *Writing Mini-Lessons* transparencies, p. 36

 The Writer's Craft
Formal and Informal English, p. 315

I was surprised at how strong her fingers were.

"Say, 'I forgive you, Meg.'"

I said it. My voice sounded funny, as if I were talking in a huge tunnel. "I forgive you, Meg."

Her eyes studied me. Her hands pressed mine. For the first time in my life, I saw love at work. Not movie love. Not Cindy's sparkling eyes when I tell her that we're going to the beach on a Sunday afternoon. But love like something alive and tender, asking nothing in return. She raised her face, and I knew what she wanted me to do. I bent and brushed my lips against her cheek. Her flesh was like a leaf in autumn, crisp and dry.

She closed her eyes and I stood up. The sun wasn't glinting on the cars any longer. Somebody had turned on another television set, and the voices were the show-off voices of the panel shows. At the same time you could still hear the soap-opera dialogue on the other television set.

I waited awhile. She seemed to be sleeping, her breathing <u>serene</u> and regular. I buttoned my raincoat. Suddenly she opened her eyes again and looked at me. Her eyes were still bright, but they merely stared at me. Without recognition or curiosity. Empty eyes. I smiled at her, but she didn't smile back. She made a kind of moaning sound and turned away on the bed, pulling the blankets around her.

I counted to twenty-five and then to fifty and did it all over again. I cleared my throat and coughed tentatively. She didn't move; she didn't respond. I wanted to say, "Nana, it's me." But I didn't. I thought of saying, "Meg, it's me." But I couldn't.

Finally I left. Just like that. I didn't say good-bye or anything. I stalked through the corridors, looking neither to the right nor the left, not caring whether that wild old man with the wheelchair ran me down or not.

> Her eyes studied me. Her hands pressed mine. For the first time in my life, I saw love at work.

On the Southwest Turnpike I did seventy-five—no, eighty—most of the way. I turned the radio up as loud as it could go. Rock music—anything to fill the air. When I got home, my mother was vacuuming the living-room rug. She shut off the cleaner, and the silence was deafening. "Well, how was your grandmother?" she asked.

I told her she was fine. I told her a lot of things. How great Nana looked and how she seemed happy and had called me Mike. I wanted to ask her—hey, Mom, you and Dad really love each other, don't you? I mean—there's nothing to forgive between you, is there? But I didn't.

Instead I went upstairs and took out the electric razor Annie had given me for Christmas and shaved off my moustache. ❖

WORDS TO KNOW
serene (sə-rēn′) *adj.* calm

Multicultural Perspectives

REVERSING STEREOTYPES In our youth-oriented society, many people have stereotyped views of the elderly. Students might be surprised to learn that:
- In 1990, more than 12% of the population in America was over age 65.
- About two-thirds of Americans over 65 describe their health as good to excellent.
- Employees over 65 are absent less often than younger workers and have fewer on-the-job accidents.
- At age 65, people have twice the vocabulary of recent college graduates.

From Personal Response to Critical Analysis

1. Responses will vary.
2. Possible responses: So he will not be confused with his grandfather again. He realizes that it symbolizes a level of maturity and responsibility that he is not quite ready for.
3. Possible responses: Mike feels guilty for not having visited his grandmother sooner. He realizes that she is a person with a complex and difficult past. He returns home with a new perspective on his grandparents and his parents.
4. Possible response: Yes, because it could offer her some peace of mind. No, because it would be deceptive.
5. Possible response: Previously Mike thought of his family as people he could easily understand: a "mother," a "grandmother," a "sister." After the visit he began to see individuals in all their complexity.
6. Responses will vary.

Another Pathway

Cooperative Learning Point out to students that the story has three major sections: before, during, and after Mike visits his grandmother. Have each group use the chronological order of the story to chart Mike's emotions. One student should record the group's list of emotions.

Rubric

3 Full Accomplishment Students identify emotions from each part of the story.

2 Substantial Accomplishment Students act out some emotions but fail to address others.

1 Little or Partial Accomplishment Students act out emotions that do not occur in the story.

RESPONDING OPTIONS

FROM PERSONAL RESPONSE TO CRITICAL ANALYSIS

REFLECT 1. What aspect of the story did you find most moving? Record your thoughts in your notebook.

RETHINK 2. Why do you think Mike shaves off his moustache?

3. How do Mike's feelings about his grandmother change during the course of the story?
   Consider
   - Mike's guilt as he goes to the nursing home
   - his feelings when his grandmother thinks he is her husband
   - his thoughts when he returns home

4. If you were Mike, would you go along with your grandmother's fantasy about her husband? Why or why not?

5. What personal discovery does Mike make? Discuss your ideas with the class.

RELATE 6. When people like Mike's grandmother can no longer take care of themselves, what should they do? Some feel that the elderly should live with their children or grandchildren, whatever the costs. Others believe that the elderly receive better care in nursing homes and that the government should pay for nursing home care for patients who cannot afford it. What do you think?

Multimodal Learning
ANOTHER PATHWAY

Cooperative Learning

Mike reveals different emotions in the story. Working in a group, identify these emotions. Imagine that your group represents all of the feelings that Mike expresses. Each student in the group can choose one emotion to act out. Classmates can try to guess the emotion that is being expressed.

LITERARY CONCEPTS

Sometimes a writer uses a concrete object—a **symbol**—to stand for an idea. For example, in "The Moustache," the piano symbolizes certain things about the grandfather—his generous spirit and his love of life. Similarly, Mike's moustache is a concrete object that symbolizes something about Mike. What do you think Mike's moustache might symbolize?

QUICKWRITES

1. What do you suppose Mike is thinking about as he leaves the nursing home? Write an **interior monologue** expressing his thoughts.

2. Use evidence from the story to make inferences about Mike's grandmother. Then write a **character sketch** that reveals what she was like before and after her husband died. Be sure to include information about her outlook on life.

 **PORTFOLIO** *Save your writing. You may want to use it later as a springboard to a piece for your portfolio.*

592 UNIT FIVE PART 1: FINDING YOUR PLACE

Literary Concepts

Remind students that symbols seldom mean the same thing to all readers. Discuss with students these questions:

- How might Mike's age influence what the moustache symbolizes? *(Like many teenagers, Mike may see it as a sign of coming of age. Mike's growing a mustache and then shaving it off may symbolize his ambivalence about becoming an adult.)*
- Does Mike's moustache symbolize the same thing to Mike and his mother? *(No; to Mike it may be an assertion of his independence; to his mother it may be a symbol of rebellion.)*

QuickWrites

1. Tell students that in an interior monologue readers hear only the voice of Mike. Encourage students to contrast the thrill of speeding in his dad's new car on the way to the nursing home with how he might feel on the way home.

2. Point out to students that most of this character sketch will be inferred from details in the story, although certain details, such as her pride and remorse, may be of use.

The Writer's Craft

Dialogue, pp. 324–327
Analyzing a story, pp. 170–174

Multimodal Learning

ALTERNATIVE ACTIVITIES

1. Create a **biographical sketch** by interviewing one of your older relatives or friends on audiotape or videotape. Request a photograph from his or her youth. Ask the person to tell you some stories about the picture. Play the interview for the class.

2. With a partner, look into the kinds of care provided for the elderly in your community. Then evaluate the availability and quality of care in your community. Present your findings in the form of a **chart**.

ACROSS THE CURRICULUM

Science Two diseases of the elderly are arteriosclerosis and Alzheimer's (älts'hī-mərz) disease. You know from this story some possible effects of arteriosclerosis. Research additional information about this disease as well as the causes and effects of Alzheimer's disease. Compare their causes and effects.

WORDS TO KNOW

EXERCISE A Review the Words to Know at the bottom of the selection pages, and list them on your paper. Write the word that best completes each sentence.

1. Mike thought Lawnrest might be noisy, but it was really ____.
2. It had been a long time since Mike had seen his grandmother, and he had a strong guilt ____.
3. Mike wasn't sure whether his grandmother would be ____ enough to recognize him.
4. He wouldn't know what to do if she were to have a stroke and ____ into a coma.
5. When Mike saw his grandmother, he was struck by how frail and ____ she was.

EXERCISE B Choose the word *lucid, pathetic,* or *serene* and, with another student, create a collage that presents a visual representation of the word.

ROBERT CORMIER

Robert Cormier (1925–), who grew up during the Great Depression, says he was a "skinny kid living in a ghetto type of neighborhood wanting the world to know I existed." His childhood wish came true. Today, he is one of the country's best-known writers of adolescent fiction.

Several of Cormier's books, particularly *The Chocolate War*, have been considered controversial because of their complex themes. The author explains: "We're brought up to expect happy endings. . . . My books go against that: the hero doesn't always win, and sometimes you're not sure who the bad guy is."

Cormier's four children have provided ideas for his stories. "The Moustache" developed when his son, Peter, visited his grandmother in a nursing home. "He returned visibly moved, shaken," the author recalls. Cormier also looks to his ten grandchildren for story ideas.

Cormier's books have won many awards. In 1994, *We All Fall Down* was voted by the American Library Association as one of the best books for young adults written during the last 25 years. It also won a 1993–1994 young adult California Reader Medal, an award voted by teenagers.

OTHER WORKS *In the Middle of the Night, Tunes for Bears to Dance To, Other Bells for Us to Ring, Beyond the Chocolate War*   Extended Reading

LASERLINKS
• SCIENCE CONNECTION

THE MOUSTACHE 593

Words to Know

Exercise A
1. serene
2. complex
3. lucid
4. lapse
5. pathetic

Exercise B
Collages will vary. Suggest that students look at magazines and advertisements as possible resources.

Reteaching/Reinforcement
• *Unit Five Resource Book*, p. 12

Across the Curriculum

Science *Diseases of Aging* Suggest that students do not restrict their research to the library or computer searches. For example, national organizations such as the AARP (American Association of Retired Persons) have current information on all diseases that affect the elderly, including new research and treatment methods.

ADDITIONAL SUGGESTION

Social Studies *Achievements of Older People* Invite students to prepare reports about well-known people who are over 70 and still very active in a particular field. Students may wish to consult an almanac to find the birth dates of famous people to help them begin their research.

SCIENCE CONNECTION

Arteriosclerosis As students view these magnified photos of human arteries, they will see for themselves the difference between a normal artery and one narrowed by arteriosclerosis, the condition that afflicts the narrator's grandmother.

Side A, Frame 52804

ROBERT CORMIER

Before becoming a full-time fiction writer, Robert Cormier worked for more than thirty years as a radio reporter and editor. Although Cormier claims he writes for no specific audience, he notes, "I've aimed for the intelligent reader and have often found that reader is fourteen years old."

Alternative Activities

1. Be sure that students are very clear about the purpose of the interview and respectful of the elderly person's feelings while asking questions. They may wish to organize their questions by asking the person they interview about a specific time mentioned in "The Moustache," such as the Great Depression.

2. Suggest to students that one of the best ways to evaluate the quality of care given to the elderly in their community is to volunteer to work with the elderly. There are many nursing homes and hospitals that welcome readers and companions for their patients.

OVERVIEW

Objectives

- To understand and appreciate two poems about ethnic heritage
- To compare and contrast the speakers of the two poems
- To analyze the use of dialogue in poems
- To express understanding of the poems through a choice of writing forms, including a poem and an essay
- To extend understanding of the story through a variety of multimodal and cross-disciplinary activities

Skills

READING SKILLS/STRATEGIES
- Compare and Contrast

LITERARY CONCEPTS
- Form
- Dialogue

SPEAKING, LISTENING, AND VIEWING
- Ethnic music
- Group discussion
- Oral presentation

Cross-Curricular Connections

SOCIAL STUDIES
- Immigration

ALTERNATIVE Previewing

Students can choose partners and discuss their impressions of each speaker.

Personal Connection

Discussion Prompts *Have students use the following prompts to begin their discussions:*

- *How does each speaker identify with his or her ethnic heritage?*
- *Does that heritage affect how the speaker views the world?*

 CULTURAL CONNECTION
The Spanish Conquistadors This montage will expand students' knowledge of the explorers who sailed from Spain to conquer the Americas.

Side A, Frame 42152

 VISUAL VOCABULARY
- **mesquite** (mĕ-skēt′)
- **nopal** (nō′pəl)

Side A, Frame 52808

594 THE LANGUAGE OF LITERATURE TEACHER'S EDITION

PREVIEWING

POETRY

The Other Pioneers
Roberto Félix Salazar

Saying Yes
Diana Chang

Activating Prior Knowledge
PERSONAL CONNECTION

We often identify one another with one-word labels, such as *jock, Democrat, brain,* and *nerd.* Sometimes people are labeled solely according to their ethnic heritage. Why do you think we label people in this manner rather than describe them in a way that shows their various qualities, interests, and talents? How might one-word labeling keep people from finding their place? Record your thoughts in your notebook, then discuss them with the class.

Building Background
CULTURAL CONNECTION

Who are the people of the United States? Some say that the country's varied racial mix is like a salad bowl overflowing with a rich variety of ingredients that keep their individual flavors. However, many people in this country can claim several cultural backgrounds, or a mix of ethnic identities. It is possible for a single individual to have an ancestry that is Native American, Spanish, African, and Chinese combined.

Fifteen thousand years ago, people now called Native Americans migrated from Asia to North America, and some eventually reached the tip of South America. These pioneers explored the land and discovered valuable resources. When, a little more than 400 years ago, the first white settlers, the Spanish, arrived in the Southwest and in what is now Florida, Native Americans guided them.

Today, immigrants continue to pour into the United States. Almost 1 million arrived in 1992 alone, nearly one-third of them coming from Asia. These immigrants, like those who preceded them, have brought diverse cultural traditions to the United States.

Active Reading/Setting a Purpose
READING CONNECTION

Contrasting Speakers You may recall that the voice that talks to the reader in poetry is called the speaker. As you read, compare and contrast the speakers in "The Other Pioneers" and "Saying Yes." Consider how each speaker identifies with his or her ethnic heritage. Use a chart, similar to the one shown, to record your ideas about each speaker.

Contrasting Speakers	
"The Other Pioneers"	"Saying Yes"

 LASERLINKS
- CULTURAL CONNECTION
- VISUAL VOCABULARY

594   UNIT FIVE   PART 1: FINDING YOUR PLACE

PRINT AND MEDIA RESOURCES

UNIT FIVE RESOURCE BOOK
Strategic Reading: Literature, p. 15

FORMAL ASSESSMENT
Selection Test, p. 111
 Test Generator

ACCESS FOR STUDENTS ACQUIRING ENGLISH
Reading and Writing Support

 **AUDIO LIBRARY**
See Reference Card

LASERLINKS
Cultural Connection
Visual Vocabulary
Contemporary Connection

The Other Pioneers

by Roberto Félix Salazar

California Vaqueros, James Walker. Oil on canvas, 31" × 46". The Anschutz Collection, Denver.

Now I must write
Of those of mine who rode these plains
Long years before the Saxon[1] and the Irish came.
Of those who plowed the land and built the towns
5   And gave the towns soft-woven Spanish names.
Of those who moved across the Rio Grande
Toward the hiss of Texas snake and Indian yell.
Of men who from the earth made thick-walled homes
And from the earth raised churches to their God.
10 And of the wives who bore them sons
And smiled with knowing joy.

---

1. Saxon (săk′sən): English.

CUSTOMIZING FOR
Gifted and Talented Students

Have students discuss how difficult it is to find a "place" to describe one's ethnic identity. Ask students to discuss the different meanings of "place" in each poem. For instance, Salazar's poem suggests a place in history, whereas Chang suggests that there are several places, such as America and China, that shape her identity. Encourage students to use their own or a family member's experience in their discussion.

Active Reading: EVALUATE

C Have students evaluate how the relationship between Native Americans and Spanish settlers is represented in Salazar's poem. Tell them to consider the author's purpose in writing this poem. If students are having difficulty, provide the following model:

Think-Aloud Model *The purpose of the poem is to remember and praise the struggles of early Spanish settlers; however, the speaker's presentation of the Native Americans as cruel warriors does not seem to do justice to the complexity of the situation.*

Literary Concept: REPETITION

D Ask students why the poet repeats the series of Spanish names. (*Possible responses: The repetition emphasizes the poem's theme of pride in one's heritage. It reveals the speaker's view that heritage passes down from fathers to sons.*)

From Personal Response to Critical Analysis

1. Responses will vary.
2. Possible response: The pioneers display courage, hard work, endurance, discipline.
3. Possible response: The poet's purpose was probably to declare his pride in his Spanish heritage and the role his people played in settling Texas.
4. Possible response: By contemporary standards, his views do not seem particularly enlightened, but he is writing from a position of sympathy with the values of the Spanish settlers of the last century.
5. Responses will vary.

They saw the Texas sun rise golden-red with promised wealth
And saw the Texas sun sink golden yet, with wealth unspent.
"Here," they said. "Here to live and here to love."
15 "Here is the land for our sons and the sons of our sons."
And they sang the songs of ancient Spain
And they made new songs to fit new needs.
They cleared the brush and planted the corn
And saw green stalks turn black from lack of rain.
20 They roamed the plains behind the herds
And stood the Indian's cruel attacks.
There was dust and there was sweat.
And there were tears and the women prayed.

And the years moved on.
25 Those who were first placed in graves
Beside the broad mesquite and the tall nopal.²
Gentle mothers left their graces and their arts
And stalwart fathers pride and manly strength.
Salinas, de la Garza, Sánchez, García,
30 Uribe, González, Martínez, de León:
Such were the names of the fathers.
Salinas, de la Garza, Sánchez, García,
Uribe, González, Martínez, de León:
Such are the names of the sons.

---

2. **mesquite** (mĕ-skēt′) . . . **nopal** (nō-päl′): thorny tree or shrub common in the Southwestern United States and in northern Mexico; cactus with reddish flowers, found chiefly in Mexico.

FROM PERSONAL RESPONSE TO CRITICAL ANALYSIS

REFLECT 1. What lines or phrases from this poem linger the longest in your mind? Record your thoughts in your notebook.

RETHINK 2. What qualities do you think these pioneers display?

3. What do you think was the poet's purpose in writing this poem? Explain your answer.

4. What seems to be the speaker's attitude toward Native Americans and toward women? Give reasons for your answer.

RELATE 5. Do you think today's society encourages people to be proud of their ethnic identities? Why or why not? Discuss your thoughts with a partner.

596   UNIT FIVE   PART 1: FINDING YOUR PLACE

Multicultural  Perspectives

SPANISH NAMES Salazar lists several Spanish names at the end of his poem, and describes them as having passed from father to son. However, in Spanish-speaking countries, children often add their mother's maiden name to their father's last name, so that the children's surnames represent both halves of their heritage. Thus, if a Mexican woman's last name is Garza-Ornelas, one can assume that Garza is her father's name and Ornelas was her mother's name before marriage. The Russian tradition is for the children to take a masculine or feminine version of their father's first name; for example, if the father's given name were Alexei, his sons would take the middle name Alexevitch and his daughters that of Alexevna. Last names in Russian also have masculine and feminine endings; hence, in Tolstoy's *War and Peace*, the sister is Natasha Rostova and the brother is called Nikolai Rostov. In Chinese, the family name precedes the given name; the cellist who is known in the West as Yo-Yo Ma is called Ma Yo-Yo in China.

Saying Yes
by Diana Chang

"Are you Chinese?"
"Yes."

"American?"
"Yes."

5 "*Really* Chinese?"
"No . . . not quite."

"*Really* American?"
"Well, actually, you see . . ."

But I would rather say
10 yes

Not neither-nor,
not maybe,
but both, and not only

The homes I've had,
15 the ways I am

I'd rather say it
twice,
yes

Seated Girl With Dog (1944), Milton Avery. Collection of Roy R. Neuberger, New York. Copyright © 1996 Milton Avery Trust/Artists Rights Society (ARS), New York.

SAYING YES **597**

Art Note

Seated Girl with Dog by Milton Avery Avery (1893–1965) tried to find a balance between the abstract and the real in his work. In this painting of a girl and her dog, Avery keeps the forms of the two living things but leaves the details abstract.

Reading the Art *How does this painting reflect issues of identity in the poem?*

Literary Concept: CONFLICT

E Have students discuss the conflict that is revealed in the dialogue between the speaker and the person addressing her. *(Possible response: The person questioning the speaker seems to be trying to pinpoint her ethnic identity: either she is "really" American or she is "really" Chinese, but not both. The speaker's response resists these attempts to label her as one thing or the other.)*

Literary Concept: FORM

F Ask students to compare the first four stanzas of the poem with the last four stanzas. *(Possible response: The first four stanzas each have two lines of dialogue composed of a question and an answer. The form changes in the last four stanzas, becoming less regular. No questions are asked; stanzas 5 and 7 have two lines, and stanzas 6 and 8 have three lines.)*

STRATEGIC READING FOR
Less-Proficient Readers

G Ask students if they think Chang's sense of identification differs from Salazar's. *(Chang seems to be torn between a number of different identifications. Salazar celebrates a generations-old Spanish heritage, while Chang considers the complexity of diverse heritages.)*
Making Inferences/ Drawing Conclusions

Mini-Lesson: Speaking, Listening, and Viewing

ETHNIC MUSIC Discuss with students the poems' theme of ethnic heritage and relate this to the important role music plays in keeping cultural traditions alive. Explain that music, like oral history, can be easily passed from generation to generation. In fact, the lyrics of many folk songs are a form of oral history set to music.

Application Ask students to research and select one or more pieces of music that represent their cultural backgrounds. Have students share this music with their classmates, either by performing it or playing a recording. Ask students to prepare a brief oral presentation that explains something about their choices. Encourage bilingual and multilingual students to translate lyrics for their classmates.

COMPREHENSION CHECK

1. Who are the other pioneers in Salazar's poem? *(early Spanish settlers in the Southwest)*
2. Why is the speaker proud in "The Other Pioneers"? *(because of his ancestors' role in settling Texas)*
3. What is the speaker torn between in "Saying Yes"? *(being labeled as exclusively Chinese or American)*
4. How does the speaker resolve this dilemma? *(by claiming an identification with both)*

From Personal Response to Critical Analysis

1. Responses will vary.
2. Possible response: The speaker is trying to explain that she lives her life in the cultures of both America and China and that she cannot identify her heritage in terms of only one or the other culture.
3. Possible responses: someone who doesn't know the speaker very well; someone who likes things to be in clear categories
4. Possible response: The speaker of "The Other Pioneers" might identify himself with the ethnic label "Spanish-American," "Hispanic," or "Latino." The speaker of "Saying Yes" might refuse to identify herself with any one label, or might refer to herself as Chinese-American.
5. Illustrations will vary. Be sure students clearly demonstrate the connection between theme and illustration.

Another Pathway
Encourage students not to feel restricted by the assumed gender of the speakers in deciding who will take which role. You may wish to direct students to the contrast between the strong ethnic identity of the first speaker and the refusal of the second speaker to limit herself to a single identity.

Rubric
3 Full Accomplishment Both members of the pair participate equally, drawing on specific details from the poem to present both speakers' positions.
2 Substantial Accomplishment Pairs present the position of each speaker, but their dialogue is stilted and has no conversational flow.
1 Little or Partial Accomplishment Students do not present the speakers' concerns.

RESPONDING OPTIONS

FROM PERSONAL RESPONSE TO CRITICAL ANALYSIS

REFLECT 1. What is your impression of the main speaker in "Saying Yes"? Discuss your ideas with a classmate.

RETHINK 2. What idea is the main speaker trying to explain?
Consider
- the questions the speaker is asked
- how the answers change as the questions become more specific
- *Close Textual Reading* • the meaning of lines 9–13
- the main speaker's conclusions

3. Who might be asking the questions in this poem, and why?

RELATE 4. How do the Chinese American and the Hispanics in the two poems identify themselves in relation to their ethnic heritage? Compare how they view themselves culturally. What ethnic label do you think each would choose?

Thematic Link 5. Make an illustration that shows how each poem fits the theme "Finding Your Place."

Multimodal Learning
ANOTHER PATHWAY
Imagine that the speakers in these two poems meet. What might they say to each other? With a partner, write their dialogue. Then act out the conversation for your class.

LITERARY CONCEPTS
Although the use of **dialogue** in poetry is certainly not unheard of, dialogue is used much less frequently in poems than in prose works. You may have noticed that both of the poems you just read contain dialogue. The first half of "Saying Yes" records conversation between the speaker and an unidentified person. In "The Other Pioneers," the pioneers' own words are added to the speaker's description of the pioneers' activities. What do you think the dialogue contributes to the meaning of each poem? Explain your answer.

QUICKWRITES
1. What qualities, interests, and ethnic heritage characterize you? Write a **poem** that conveys your identity.
2. Some people see the United States as a melting pot—a place in which immigrants of various nationalities and races are absorbed into one main culture. Other people see our nation as a salad bowl, with immigrants being part of one nation but retaining strong individual ethnic identities. Which of these concepts do you think the speaker of each poem would support? Why? Write a short **essay** that answers these questions.

📁 **PORTFOLIO** Save your writing. You may want to use it later as a springboard to a piece for your portfolio.

598 UNIT FIVE PART 1: FINDING YOUR PLACE

Literary Concepts
Dialogue enhances the meaning of the poems by representing specific ideas of the speaker, members of his or her ethnic heritage, and also of those trying to understand the speakers' heritage. Point out to students that the dialogue in these two poems is not meant as an actual transcription of a conversation. Dialogue functions to give a representation of what people might have said, not an exact record.

QuickWrites
1. Remind students that assigning specific qualities or interests to ethnic heritage often leads to stereotyping. Be sure that in framing their poems, students avoid such generalizations, focusing instead on their own personal identity.
2. When writing their essays, students should cite specific reasons the speakers would give based on what is said in their poems.

The Writer's Craft
Poetry, pp. 76–80
Evaluating opinion, pp. 364–365

Multimodal Learning

ALTERNATIVE ACTIVITIES

1. Choose a line from "The Other Pioneers" that might inspire a painting. Then create a **painting,** and share your results with the class.
2. Research some aspect of the history of Asian immigration to the United States. Then present your findings to the class in the form of a **posterboard display** containing photographs, drawings, charts, and graphs as well as brief descriptions of these graphics.

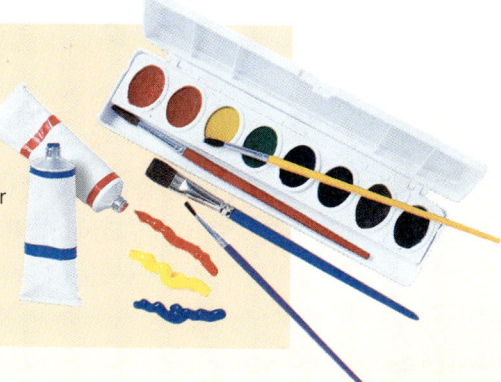

ROBERTO FÉLIX SALAZAR

Roberto Félix Salazar (1921–) is a Mexican-American poet. In "The Other Pioneers," Salazar celebrates his ethnic background and honors the contributions of his Spanish ancestors, who settled the Southwestern United States. Philip Ortego, a professor of Chicano Studies, explains that "The Other Pioneers" was written as a reminder that the early Southwestern pioneers had Spanish names and that many Americans today continue, with great pride, to call themselves by those names.

DIANA CHANG

Diana Chang, a contemporary Chinese-American poet, short story writer, and novelist, often writes about Asian-American identity. Her first novel, *The Frontiers of Love,* published in the 1960s, was criticized by some Asian Americans who said she should write about her own experiences in the United States, not about the experiences of Eurasians (people of mixed European and Asian descent) in China, where the novel is set. The novel has recently been republished and is considered a forerunner of literature about mixed-race people.

The daughter of a Chinese father and a Eurasian mother, Chang was born in the United States and today lives on Long Island, New York. She taught creative writing at Barnard College for ten years. Chang is also a painter, and her acrylics, pastels, and watercolors have been exhibited in both group and solo shows.

She adapted one of her stories, "Falling Free," into a radio play for public radio. About "Saying Yes," Chang remarks, "To my surprise, 'Saying Yes' has been reprinted very often. I can only suppose it's because it is sincere and simple."

LASERLINKS
• CONTEMPORARY CONNECTION

Across the Curriculum

Social Studies *Immigration* Inform students that immigration to the United States has changed dramatically over the course of its history. At one time, the United States practiced an "open door" immigration policy that permitted almost anyone to relocate to the country. However, from the late 19th century on, certain quotas were designed to restrict the number of immigrants allowed in the country from different parts of the world. Have students research during which "wave" of immigration their ancestors were most likely to have settled in the United States and how immigration quotas affect new immigrants that share the same ethnic background.

DIANA CHANG

Although much of her work focuses on her Chinese and American heritage, Diana Chang is often inspired by the landscape where she lives. She uses the rhythms of nature as the starting point for many poems.

Literary Links

Have students compare the way bilingual students in the short story "White Mice" and the speaker of the poem "The Other Pioneers" maintain their ethnic heritage. Ask how their perspectives might differ. *(Possible response: Both the speaker of "The Other Pioneers" and the children in "White Mice" are proud of their Hispanic identity. Salazar's speaker might criticize Mr. and Mrs. Martinez for naming their daughter "America.")*

CONTEMPORARY CONNECTION
Chinese Americans Today As these photographs show, Chinese Americans have become part of the social fabric of the United States but have also maintained links to their Chinese heritage.

Side A, Frame 52811

Alternative Activities

1. Encourage students to select lines with concrete imagery, such as building a house or planting corn, as sources for their painting.
2. **Cooperative Learning** Have the class work in small groups and plan which aspects of the project each student will be responsible for. Some students may be more familiar with doing computer and library research, others may prefer drawing or creating graphs, and others may wish to write the descriptions for the graphics.

OVERVIEW

Objectives

- To understand and appreciate a drama about a man who endures an unusual punishment for treason
- To understand sequencing
- To identify and understand the use of dynamic and static characters, and the function of scene changes
- To express understanding of the story through a choice of writing forms, including a letter, a journal entry, a poem or folk song, and an epitaph
- To extend understanding of the story through a variety of multimodal and cross-disciplinary activities

Skills

READING SKILLS/STRATEGIES
- Sequencing
- Question

THE WRITER'S STYLE
- Dialogue in plays

GRAMMAR
- Punctuating items in a series

LITERARY CONCEPTS
- Dynamic and static characters

- Scene changes
- Theme

SPELLING
- Words ending with *-ous*

SPEAKING, LISTENING, AND VIEWING
- Oral interpretation
- Group discussion
- Oral presentation

Cross-Curricular Connections

HISTORY
- The Federalist Party
- Treason
- The expanding nation

SCIENCE
- Steam power

HISTORICAL CONNECTION
Events During Nolan's Exile, 1805–1862 Seeing these paintings and illustrations will familiarize students with some of the historic events that occurred during the time frame of the play. Among the images are a painting of the Lewis and Clark expedition, an illustration of Nat Turner's rebellion, and an advertisement for *Uncle Tom's Cabin*.

Side A, Frame 52817

PREVIEWING

DRAMA

The Man Without a Country
Edward Everett Hale
Dramatized by Walter Hackett

Activating Prior Knowledge
PERSONAL CONNECTION
The central character in this play becomes separated from his American homeland, an important part of his personal identity. Imagine what it might be like to be forcibly separated from your homeland. How would you react? How might this affect your personal identity? Discuss your ideas with the class.

Building Background
HISTORICAL CONNECTION
"The Man Without a Country" is a dramatized version of a story based on events in American history. The play spans 57 years of American history, beginning in 1805, during the presidency of Thomas Jefferson, and ending in 1862 with the presidency of Abraham Lincoln and the Civil War.

As the play opens, the reader meets real-life figure Aaron Burr, one of U.S. history's most controversial characters. The drama refers to Burr's plot to seize a portion of the United States and start a new country. Burr was in fact involved in such a plot in 1805. He was tried for treason but was later cleared of all charges for lack of evidence. The events of the life of the main character, Philip Nolan, as they are portrayed in the play, are largely fictitious. In reality, Nolan was a well-known horse trader of the American West. It has been written, but not confirmed, that in 1800, near the time of his death, he was preparing a military invasion of the very same land area targeted for seizure by Aaron Burr.

The time line shown here pinpoints other important events that occurred during the course of the play, some of which are referred to in the dialogue.

1800	
1804	Lewis and Clark expedition begins
1812	War with Britain begins
1817	Erie Canal begun
1823	Monroe Doctrine
1825	Steam locomotive invented
1829	Andrew Jackson becomes president
1830	Indian Removal Act
1831	Nat Turner's Rebellion
1835	Seminole War begins
1849	California Gold Rush
1852	*Uncle Tom's Cabin* published
1857	Dred Scott case
1861	Lincoln becomes president/Civil War begins
1865	

PRINT AND MEDIA RESOURCES

UNIT FIVE RESOURCE BOOK
Strategic Reading: Literature, p. 19
Vocabulary SkillBuilder, p. 22
Reading SkillBuilder, p. 20
Spelling SkillBuilder, p. 21

GRAMMAR MINI-LESSONS
Transparencies, p. 31
Copymasters, p. 40

WRITING MINI-LESSONS
Transparencies, p. 48

ACCESS FOR STUDENTS ACQUIRING ENGLISH
Selection Summaries
Reading and Writing Support

FORMAL ASSESSMENT
Selection Test, pp. 113–114
 Test Generator

 AUDIO LIBRARY
See Reference Card

 **LASERLINKS**
Historical Connection
Social Studies Connection

 **INTERNET RESOURCES**
McDougal Littell Literature Center at http://www.hmco.com/mcdougal/lit

Setting a Purpose/Active Reading
READING CONNECTION

Sequencing

When one thing follows another in chronological order, a sequence has been arranged. Events in fiction, nonfiction, and drama occur in a certain order, or sequence. One way to begin to make sense of a story or play is to pay attention to the sequence of events.

Sequencing can be particularly helpful when there is a long chronology of events or changes that the reader must keep track of. In some selections, events are arranged neatly and logically in sequence. In other selections, however, it is up to the reader to organize and make sense of the time order. Writers sometimes use time-order words or phrases to signal a sequence of events. These signal words and phrases include *first, next, then, now, this time,* and *before*.

Being aware of the correct sequence of events in a story or play can help readers explore the impact of events on the characters and determine how characters change. Understanding sequence also allows the reader to predict what might happen next. Refer to the guidelines presented here when you are examining the use of sequencing in a story.

In "The Man Without a Country," events involving Philip Nolan, the main character, occur rapidly, and the setting changes frequently. It will help you to understand what is happening if you keep track of the sequence of events in the plot as they relate to the time frame of the play. What happens first, next, and so on until the play comes to a conclusion? Notice how each event is affected by the event before it.

As you read "The Man Without a Country," make a time line of the play's dramatic events, adding to it the real events from the time line in the Historical Connection. To help you get started, refer to the time line begun for you here.

Strategies for Studying Sequencing

- Ask yourself the questions "What happened first?" and "What happened next?" If you like, keep notes in your notebook.
- Highlight passages in which an event is described.
- Make a list of any time-order words or phrases as they appear in the selection. These signal words help make the sequence clear.
- Use a sequence chart, similar to the one shown, to record information about each event in the selection.

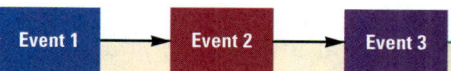

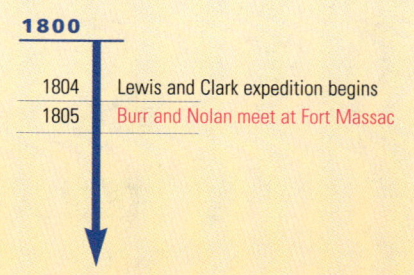

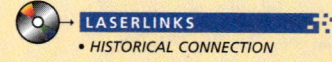
• HISTORICAL CONNECTION

SUMMARY

In 1807, a young army lieutenant named Philip Nolan is convicted of plotting treason with Aaron Burr, a former Vice-President of the United States. Angry at the unjust conviction, Nolan declares that he never wants to hear of the United States again. The court sentences him to spend the rest of his life on various U.S. ships. Nolan is not allowed to return to his country, to hear news about it, or to read about it. In 1862, after a tormented life, Nolan lies dying aboard the ship of Captain Benjamin Rankin. Rankin takes pity on Nolan and tells him of all the major events in the United States during Nolan's 55 years of exile. Nolan's last wish is to be buried at sea but to have a memorial stone in the United States.

Thematic Link: *Finding Your Place* A thoughtless comment made in anger sets into motion a life of exile that dramatizes how important a homeland is to a person's identity.

CUSTOMIZING FOR
Students Acquiring English

- Use **ACCESS FOR STUDENTS ACQUIRING ENGLISH**, *Reading and Writing Support*.
- Be sure that students have a little knowledge of the history of the period. The United States was expanding and gaining more land and new states.
- In addition to these boxes, you may want to use the suggestions under Strategic Reading for Less-Proficient Readers.

WORDS TO KNOW

abetting (ə-bĕt′ĭng) *n.* encouraging or supporting an action or plan, especially one of wrongdoing **abet** *v.* (p. 605)

fidelity (fĭ-dĕl′ĭ-tē) *n.* faithfulness to obligations or duties (p. 605)

insignia (ĭn-sĭg′nē-ə) *n.* a badge of rank or membership (p. 608)

odious (ō′dē-əs) *adj.* deserving hatred; disgusting (p. 605)

rescind (rĭ-sĭnd′) *v.* withdraw, repeal, or cancel (p. 609)

STRATEGIC READING FOR
Less-Proficient Readers

Set a Purpose Encourage students to become involved in the story by thinking about what role nationality plays in identity. Then have students read to find out where there is a place for Philip Nolan, according to Burr.

Use **UNIT FIVE RESOURCE BOOK**, p. 19, for guidance in reading the selection.

CUSTOMIZING FOR
Gifted and Talented Students

Have students discuss the concept of exile. Then have students consider the following questions as they read:

- In what circumstances might exile be an effective means of punishment?
- Would some people be less affected by exile than others?
- Is a country the only thing from which one could be exiled?
- In what specific ways might exile affect a person?

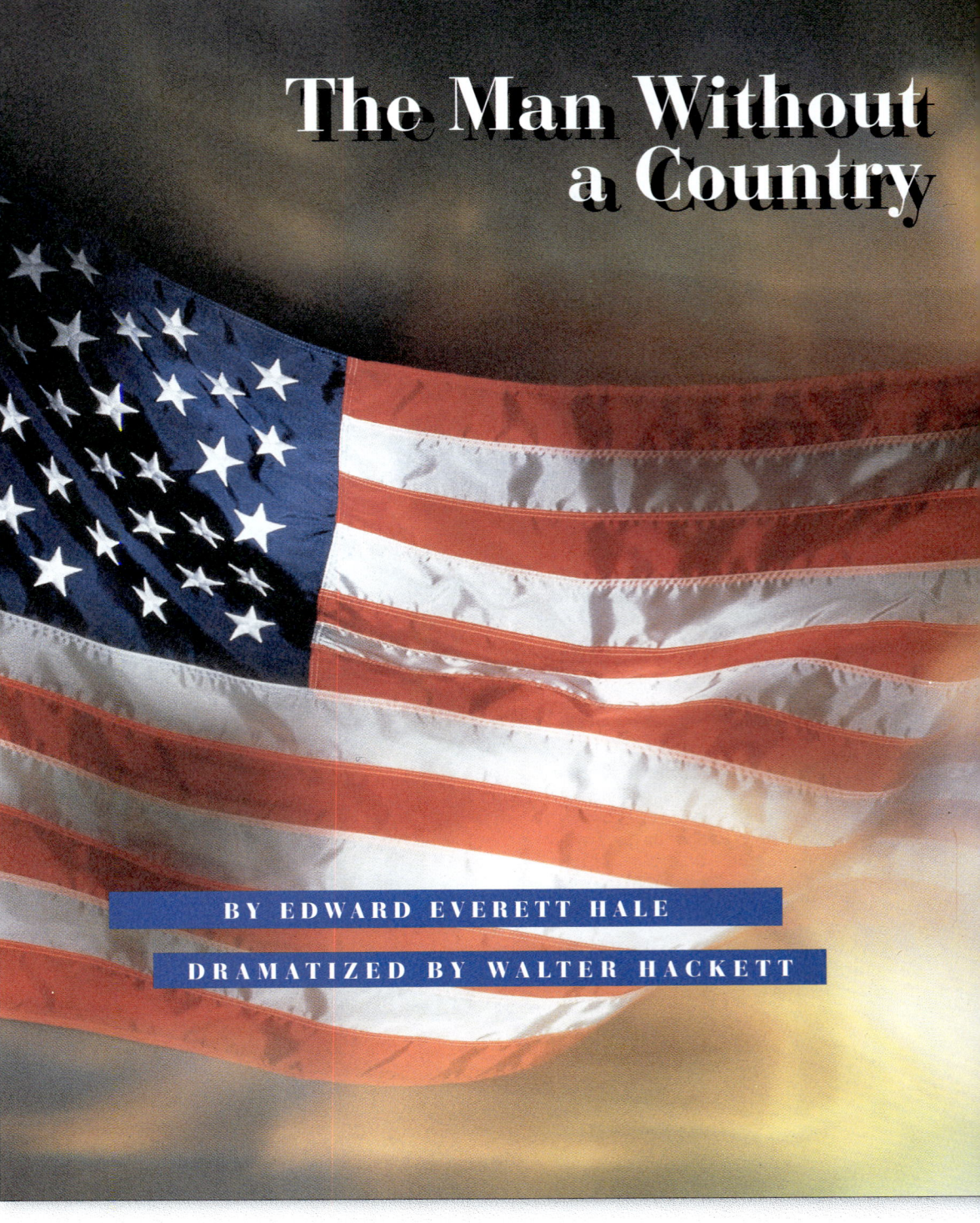

The Man Without a Country

BY EDWARD EVERETT HALE

DRAMATIZED BY WALTER HACKETT

CAST OF CHARACTERS

Voice 1
Voice 2
Narrator
Colonel
Aaron Burr, former Vice-President of the United States
Lieutenant Philip Nolan, junior officer drawn into Burr's plot
Prosecutor
Judge
Counsel
Defense
Thomas Jefferson
Captain Ethan Shaw
Lieutenant Mitchell
Guard
Officer 1
Officer 2
Captain Lane
Sailor
Officer 3
Dr. Bates
Lieutenant Harper
Captain Ben Rankin
Mrs. Anna Rutledge, a friend of Captain Rankin's
Navy Secretary
Doctor

(*Music: a strong Americana theme. Forte[1] and fade under.*)

Voice 1. I understand he's comin' aboard tomorrow. I've never seen him. I wonder what he looks like?

Voice 2. Who you talkin' about?

Voice 1. The Man Without a Country.

(*Music: forte briefly and under again.*)

Narrator. Fort Massac is a small yet strategic United States Army outpost that stands on the muddy banks of the lower Mississippi River. In this year of 1805, its officers and men are none too happy concerning their lonely detail. But on this particular day there is in evidence a more-than-average amount of excitement. A famous guest has come to visit them. At the evening mess[2] he sits in the place of honor, at the commanding officer's right. As the meal progresses the officers stare at the newcomer: Aaron Burr! Aaron Burr, former Vice-President of the United States, rabid Federalist, master politician, smooth-tongued orator; Aaron Burr, the man who had killed Alexander Hamilton[3] in a duel. (*Fading*) The Colonel turns to Burr and says.

(*Music out.*)

Colonel. Are you sure I can't get you to change your mind, Mr. Burr? You're welcome to remain here as long as you wish.

Burr. Thank you, Colonel, but I'm afraid I must be leaving within the next day or so.

Colonel. Pressing business, I imagine.

Burr. Yes, of a sort.

Officer (*away*). Mr. Burr, we had rather imag-

---

1. **Forte** (fôr′tā′): musical direction meaning "loud and forceful."
2. **mess:** meal served to soldiers eating together.
3. **Alexander Hamilton:** (1755?–1804) U.S. secretary of the treasury under President George Washington and long-time political enemy of Aaron Burr.

THE MAN WITHOUT A COUNTRY **603**

Mini-Lesson Grammar

PUNCTUATING ITEMS IN A SERIES
Use the examples shown on the chalkboard to point out to students that they should separate items in a series by placing a comma after every item except the last. A series might consist of three or more nouns, adjectives, verbs, adverbs, phrases, or even clauses.

Application Have students identify the highlighted series in the narrator's passage on page 603. Then have them use commas to correctly punctuate the following sentences.

1. Exile is among the most rare effective and heartless of punishments.
2. Nolan could not get news of America from conversation from books or newspapers or from any contact with the place itself.

Reteaching/Reinforcement
• *Grammar Handbook*, anthology p. 895
• *Grammar Mini-Lessons* copymasters, p. 40, transparencies, p. 31

The Writer's Craft
Commas, pp. 644–653

Literary Concept:
CAST OF CHARACTERS

A Before they begin reading the radio play, students should study its cast of characters. Previewing a drama this way gives the reader an overview of the people (and sometimes the settings) of the play. Ask students what they can tell about this play from its cast of characters. (*Possible responses: There may be scenes set in a courtroom and on a ship. The story concerns military personnel, as well as figures from history, such as Burr and Jefferson.*)

CUSTOMIZING FOR
Students Acquiring English

I Ask a volunteer to simplify the expression "none too happy." (*not too happy, not very happy*)

Linking to History

B The Federalist Party, formed in 1787, was America's first organized political party and held power until 1800, when John Adams's reelection bid failed. In that year, Thomas Jefferson and Aaron Burr tied on election day. As provided by the Constitution, Representatives then voted. Jefferson received the most votes and became president. Aaron Burr came in second and so became vice-president.

The Federalist Party unsuccessfully attempted to regain the presidency until 1816. At that point the party lost nearly all its influence and most of its members joined the Whig Party or the Democratic Party.

Active Reading: CLARIFY

C Ask students to describe what has happened so far in the play. (*Possible response: The script begins with a brief scene between sailors, then shifts to a narrator who fills in the story's basic background, and then follows with a scene involving Aaron Burr.*)

The ship's captain was responsible for the vessel, the cargo, and the sailors.

The judge scowled, blinked, and rubbed his brow.

CUSTOMIZING FOR
Students Acquiring English

2 Ask students where a person would go if he or she were tired. What is a synonym for "quarters"? *(room)*

3 Have students provide a synonym for "going on." *(almost)*

Literary Concept: DYNAMIC AND STATIC CHARACTERS

D Aaron Burr's character undergoes little change in this radio drama, and so he remains a static character. In contrast, Nolan is a dynamic character because he grows and changes.

Critical Thinking: ANALYZING

E Ask students why Nolan is interested in Burr's offer of help. *(Possible response: Nolan is an ambitious young man who wishes to have a more interesting and lucrative position.)*

STRATEGIC READING FOR
Less-Proficient Readers

F Check to see that students understand details of the drama's exposition.

- According to Burr, where is there a place for Nolan? *(in a "new country")*
  Noting Relevant Details

- What is the meaning of Burr's reference to a "new country"? *(He apparently has plans to form a new country.)*
  Making Inferences

Set a Purpose Have students read to find out the details and consequences of Nolan's arrest.

★ ★ ★

ined that this journey of yours was one of pleasure.

Burr. Suppose we call it a journey of observation. You see, gentlemen, my career has never allowed me to relax long enough to seek pleasure. By the way, I hope to talk more with some of you gentlemen before I leave.

Colonel. That is a pleasure all of us will look forward to, sir.

Burr. I hope so. And now if you will excuse me, *(fading)* I'll go to my quarters. I'm rather tired by my journey. *(a pause, then knock on door)*

Burr *(muffled tone).* Yes?

Nolan *(a young voice).* It's Lieutenant Nolan, sir. I have the tobacco you asked for this morning. *(sound of door opening and closing)*

Nolan. Here you are, sir, a pound of fine burley.

Burr. Thank you, er—

Nolan. Lieutenant Nolan.

Burr. First name?

Nolan. Philip, sir.

Burr. Thank you for the tobacco. *(pause)* Sit down.

Nolan. Thank you, Mr. Burr.

Burr. You haven't been in service too long, I take it.

Nolan. No, sir. Going on four years.

Burr. Like the Army?

Nolan *(slowly).* Why, yes, sir.

Burr. The pay of a junior officer isn't very much, eh?

Nolan. No, sir.

Burr. Ever get tired of this duty? *(beat)* Don't be afraid to speak up, Nolan. Remember I once was in the Army, too. I was very young when I enlisted. So I have an idea how you younger officers think.

Nolan *(hesitantly).* Well, Mr. Burr, to be frank . . . *(He shoots it out.)* . . . to be very frank, life on a frontier post like this is just about the most boring existence in the world. *(beat)* Of course I wouldn't want the Colonel to hear me say that.

Burr *(laughs easily).* Of course you wouldn't.

Nolan. Then another thing—*(He hesitates.)*

Burr. Go on.

Nolan. I happen to be in debt. As you just said: an Army lieutenant's pay isn't very much.

Burr *(smoothly).* I'm sorry to hear that.

Nolan. I've been thinking of applying for a transfer.

Burr. Perhaps I could help you on that, Nolan.

Nolan *(eagerly).* Oh, if only you would, Mr. Burr—

Burr. It wouldn't mean you would be transferred to another post.

Nolan *(puzzled).* No?

Burr. No! It would mean a great chance for you. A chance for fame and position and money—a great deal of money.

Nolan. And where is this place, sir?

Burr. In a new country.

Nolan. A new country?

Burr. A new glorious empire. Nolan, there is a place for you in that empire. But before I tell you more, you must swear to say nothing to anyone. Understand—not a word! Will you swear it?

Nolan. Yes . . . I swear it.

(Music: a theme of excitement. Forte and fade under for:)

Voice *(reading rapidly).* "Washington, D.C., July 3, 1807. To all commanding officers of United States Army posts in the Mississippi River sector: You are hereby commanded to apprehend and secure the persons of Aaron

604 UNIT FIVE PART 1: FINDING YOUR PLACE

Mini-Lesson The Writer's Style

DIALOGUE IN PLAYS Remind students that in a literary work a conversation between characters is called dialogue. Plays rely on dialogue more than any other literary form. In dramatic literature, dialogue gives the audience information about characters' thoughts, feelings, and personalities. Dialogue also conveys information about events happening offstage.

Application Encourage students to study the dialogue between Burr and Nolan on page 604. Ask them to explain how the dialogue reflects their different personalities and positions in life. Then invite students to extend the dialogue between Burr and Nolan. Make sure students extend this scene using dialogue that reflects the men's personalities in a consistent manner.

Reteaching/Reinforcement
- *Writing Mini-Lessons* transparencies, p. 48

 **The Writer's Craft**

Writing Dialogue, pp. 326–27

Burr, General James Wilkinson, and any other such conspirators guilty of attempting treason and plotting to seize a portion of these United States, on which to fashion a new country of their own. . . . Signed, John Clarke, Secretary of War."

(*Music up and out.*)

Prosecutor. To sum up my case as prosecution on this board of court-martial: Gentlemen, I accuse the defendant, Lieutenant Philip Nolan, of the crime of treason against the United States of America.

(*A buzz of voices. Sound of gavel on wood.*)

Judge. Silence! The prosecution will proceed.

Prosecutor. This man sitting here is guilty of actively abetting the most odious political plot in the entire history of our beloved country—and I am including the one another gentleman participated in—Mr. Benedict Arnold.[4]

Counsel. Objection.

Judge. Objection overruled.

Counsel. But, sir, I can present conclusive evidence that will prove that Philip Nolan—

(*Gavel rapped.*)

Prosecutor. There is not a bit of doubt that Philip Nolan knowingly entered into a secret and infamous agreement with Aaron Burr; an agreement to undermine the safety of his own native land. You have heard me question him concerning his dealings with Burr. And what has been his reply? That he is under oath to say nothing of what transpired between them.

Counsel. Objection.

Judge. Objection overruled.

Prosecutor. And why did this Judas[5] sell himself? The answer: for the empty promises of an egotistical dreamer, who promised him money and fame. That is why Philip Nolan sold his soul; that is why he broke the solemn oath of fidelity to country that he swore to abide by at the time of his enlistment.

Nolan (*away*). You're a liar.

(*gavel in sharply*)

Judge. I might warn the prisoner that any such further remarks might result in adversely swaying the members of this board of court-martial. The prosecution may proceed.

Prosecutor. I simply repeat what is obvious: Lieutenant Nolan should be adjudged guilty.

Judge. Has the defense anything to say?

Counsel. Sir, Lieutenant Nolan wishes to speak for himself.

Judge. Let *Mr.* Nolan proceed.

Nolan (*quietly*). For two days I have sat here and listened as the charges piled up against me. I have heard the prosecution deliberately distort every statement, every answer I gave.

Prosecutor. I object.

Judge. Sustained.

Nolan. I readily admit that I listened to Burr's offer to join him.

Prosecutor. Then why didn't you come forward and unmask him?

Nolan. Because I was under oath to say nothing.

Defense. I object. Lieutenant Nolan is not now being cross-examined. I request the court that he be allowed to finish uninterrupted.

---

4. **Mr. Benedict Arnold:** (1741–1801) American Revolutionary War general and, later, traitor to the United States. He plotted to surrender West Point to the British in exchange for money, but the plan was foiled.

5. **Judas** (jōō′dəs): person who betrays someone under the pretense of friendship; from *Judas Iscariot*, one of the 12 Apostles and the betrayer of Jesus.

WORDS TO KNOW

abetting (ə-bĕt′ĭng) *n.* encouraging or supporting an action or plan, especially one of wrongdoing **abet** *v.*
odious (ō′dē-əs) *adj.* deserving hatred; disgusting
fidelity (fĭ-dĕl′ĭ-tē) *n.* faithfulness to obligations or duties

---

Linking to History

G The U.S. Constitution defines treason in Article III, Section 3: "Treason against the United States, shall consist only in levying war against them or in adhering to their enemies, giving them aid and comfort. No person shall be convicted of treason unless on the testimony of two witnesses to the same overt act, or on confession in open court."

Active Reading: QUESTION

H Encourage students to share any questions they have as they read this passage. For instance, why does Nolan call the prosecutor a liar? Will such a comment hurt or help Nolan's chances of being found not guilty, or will it not matter?

Critical Thinking: ANALYZING

I Point out that the italic type shows that the judge emphasized "Mr." when he spoke. Ask students why the judge called the defendant "*Mr.* Nolan" rather than "Lieutenant Nolan." (*Possible response: The judge thought Nolan didn't deserve a military title because of his actions.*)

Active Reading: EVALUATE

J Ask students to evaluate the judge's behavior so far. In their opinion, is he behaving in a fair and impartial manner? (*Possible response: No, he's not behaving fairly because his sarcasm toward Nolan, his support of the prosecution's objections, and his denial of the defense's objections show that he wishes Nolan to be found guilty.*)

Art Note

America, Victoria and Albert, and Black Eagle Off the Isle of Wight, 1851 by Tim Thompson This painting, done by a contemporary British artist, captures the great variety of vessels that might be seen in a harbor on a quiet morning in the mid-nineteenth century.

Reading the Art *What is the mood of this piece? Does the overall setting seem hectic or calm? What sorts of sounds and smells might you experience in this scene?*

Active Reading: CLARIFY

K Encourage students to explain why Philip Nolan repeatedly pleads his innocence and why the prosecutor accuses him of treason. *(Possible response: The ambiguous part of the case is how Nolan responded to Burr's invitations. Nolan claims he listened to but did not conspire with Burr, yet could not go back on his pledge to secrecy. The prosecutor argues —and the judge ultimately agrees—that Nolan's failure to report Burr was, in fact, "giving aid and comfort" to him, and that constitutes treason.)*

Critical Thinking: MAKING JUDGMENTS

L Ask students if they believe the court of this radio drama has enough evidence to convict Philip Nolan of treason. *(Possible response: There is not enough evidence to convict Nolan of treason because it is unclear what he agreed to when speaking with Burr.)*

Active Reading: PREDICT

M Invite students to predict the sentence the judge will hand down to Lieutenant Philip Nolan.

Judge. Continue, Mr. Nolan.

Nolan. I swear that I rejected Burr's offer. (*beat*) I realize that military justice is of a necessity swift and sometimes unjust.

Prosecutor. Objection.

Judge. Sustained. The defendant will reword his line of reasoning.

Nolan. I realize that in any court of justice it is possible for an innocent man to be falsely accused of the wrongs done by others. (*His voice rises.*) For the past two weeks I have seen other officers—men actually guilty of the same crime I allegedly committed—go free. Free because this board wished to find them free.

(*Angry ad libs from members. Gavel.*)

Judge. Are you finished, Mr. Nolan?

Nolan. No! I know well what the verdict will be. I know I will be made an example of the fate in store for others.

Judge. Mr. Nolan, I believe it has been easily established that you have been unfaithful to your country, that you have committed against the United States—

Nolan (*angrily*). Damn the United States. I wish I may never hear of the United States again!

(*Music: angry theme up and out into sound of gavel on wood three times.*)

Judge. The prisoner will rise and face the board. (*beat*) Philip Nolan, hear the sentence of this board. The board of court-martial, subject to the approval of the President, decrees that you shall never again hear the name of the United States!

(*Music up and fade under.*)

Judge. Mr. Nolan is to be taken to New Orleans

America, Victoria & Albert, and Black Eagle off the Isle of Wight, 1851, Tim Thompson. Oil on canvas, 20" × 40". Image used under license with T.F.R. Thompson.

and delivered to Lieutenant Mitchell, acting naval commander. You will request that no one will ever mention the United States to the prisoner while he is on board ship. Mr. Nolan is to be confined until further orders.

(*Music up briefly and under.*)

Jefferson. "Washington, D.C., October 28, 1807. To Secretary of Navy Crowninshield. Your deposition⁶ relative to the case of Philip Nolan received and noted. You are hereby empowered to turn the prisoner over to Captain Ethan Shaw, commander of the *Nautilus,* now in New Orleans. Sincerely yours, your obedient servant, Thomas Jefferson, President of the United States."

(*Music up and out into distant sound of ship's bell striking six.*)

Shaw (*on fourth stroke*). Lieutenant Mitchell, I can't say I like this duty.

Mitchell. Sorry, Captain Shaw, but I'm just carrying out my orders.

Shaw. I understand. Go on and read the rest of the order.

Mitchell. "You will provide him with such quarters, rations, and clothing as would be proper for an officer of his late rank. The officers on board your ship will make arrangements agreeable to themselves regarding his society."

Shaw (*gloomily*). That is going to be a pleasant situation. Go on.

Mitchell. "He is to be exposed to no indignity of any kind, nor is he ever unnecessarily to be reminded that he is a prisoner. . . ."

Shaw. And I suppose that is going to be an easy order to obey.

---

6. **deposition** (dĕp′ə-zĭsh′ən): written testimony made by a witness under oath for use in court.

THE MAN WITHOUT A COUNTRY **607**

Active Reading: EVALUATE

Q Ask students to share and back up their opinions about whether the crime of treason warrants a harsh or a mild sentence.

Active Reading: CLARIFY

R Make sure that students are clear about why this particular sentence was given to Philip Nolan. You might ask a student volunteer to state the reason in a single sentence.

CUSTOMIZING FOR
Students Acquiring English

4 Paraphrase for students "How does he take it?" as "How does Nolan feel about his sentence."

Critical Thinking: ANALYZING

S Ask students why orders have been given to remove all insignias from Nolan's uniform. *(Possible responses: He is no longer a representative of the United States. The insignias were a symbol of his relationship with America—now he has no relationship with the nation.)*

Literary Concept: THEME

T Have students discuss how this conversation between two minor characters underscores the play's message about the importance of one's homeland to one's sense of self. *(Possible response: Officer 1 is exhausted and homesick, and he questions whether he will take to the sea again. The conversation draws attention to the freedom these officers have to return to America and claim it as their own. A person might wonder who he or she is if he or she belonged nowhere.)*

★ ★ ★

Q Mitchell. "But under no circumstances is Philip Nolan ever to hear of his country again, nor to see any information regarding it; and you will caution all your officers that these rules are not to be broken. It is the unswerving **R** intention of the government that he shall never again see the country which he has disowned. Before the end of your cruise you will receive orders with regard to transferring the prisoner. Respectfully yours, W. Southard, assistant to the secretary of the Navy."

4 Shaw (*as though shrugging*). Well!—(*beat*) How does he take it?

Mitchell. I don't think he realizes what is going to happen.

Shaw. He'll soon learn. (*abruptly*) Where is he now?

Mitchell. Waiting outside, sir.

Shaw. Bring him in.

(*Chair scraping on floor. Hatch door slid open.*)

Shaw (*calling out*). Guard, bring the prisoner here.

Guard (*off*). Aye, sir. (*as an aside to* Nolan) Step lively, you.

Shaw. You can leave us now, Lieutenant Mitchell.

Mitchell. Thank you, sir.

(*Hatch slid closed.*)

Shaw. Well, Mr. Nolan, I suppose you're wondering quite a few things at the moment.

Nolan. I am.

Shaw. You're to be given quarters. You'll be fairly comfortable. The ship's commissary will supply anything you lack. Your meals will be served to you in your cabin.

Nolan. About my uniforms, the insignia has been removed.

Shaw. You are to be allowed to wear your uniforms minus all insignia.

Nolan. But—

Shaw. Orders.

Nolan. I see. (*pause*) Captain Shaw, exactly what is my position aboard your ship?

Shaw (*fumbling*). Why—why, er—(*quickly recovering himself*) You may consider your position as that of a guest—a slightly underprivileged guest.

Nolan. Am I to sail with you?

Shaw. Naturally.

Nolan. Where?

Shaw. Around the Horn, into the Pacific, and across to Tahiti.

Nolan. Tahiti? That's a long way from the United States.

Shaw. A very long way.

Nolan. How long are we to be gone?

Shaw. Two years!

(*Music: a dramatic theme. Forte and out.*)

Officer 1 (*lazily*). I sometimes wonder why I joined the Navy, rather than the Army. This idea of roaming the seven seas can be tiresome. When we get back to the States, I'm going to put in for shore duty.

Officer 2. I rather like it here in Tahiti. It's warm and peaceful, a nice lazy life.

T Officer 1. It's been almost two years since I last saw my parents. In fact, it's been nine months since we sailed from New Orleans. A couple of nomads, you and I, men without a home.

Officer 2. Much better than being a man without a country.

Officer 1. What's that? Oh, yes. Poor Nolan! At times I feel sorry for him.

WORDS TO KNOW

insignia (ĭn-sĭg'nē-ə) *n.* a badge of rank or membership

608

Mini-Lesson  Spelling

WORDS ENDING WITH -OUS Point out to students that the suffix *-ous* means "full of" or "having certain characteristics." It is added to nouns and verbs to create adjectives.

When the base word ends in silent *e*, the *e* is dropped before adding the suffix—unless the *e* is preceded by a *g*. When this suffix is added to a word that ends in *y*, the *y* is changed to an *i*.

Examples:
odious
outrageous
furious

Application Have students add the suffix *-ous* to the following words.

1. melody
2. courage
3. humor
4. industry
5. marvel
6. moment
7. continue
8. vary
9. injury
10. nerve

Ask students to look for more words that fit this pattern and to add these words to their personal word lists.

Reteaching/Reinforcement
• *Unit Five Resource Book*, p. 21

608 THE LANGUAGE OF LITERATURE TEACHER'S EDITION

Officer 2. Too bad he lost his head. Wonder if the government will ever <u>rescind</u> his sentence?

Officer 1. Hard to say.

Officer 2. It would have been a more merciful thing to have hanged him. Anything in place of being a floating derelict.⁷

Officer 1. (*He lowers his voice.*) Quiet! Here he comes now. Watch what you say.

Nolan. Good afternoon, gentlemen. Grand day, isn't it? (*Officers ad lib greetings.*) Mind if I join you?

Officer 1. Plenty of deck space.

Officer 2. Sit down.

Nolan (*sighs deeply*). Ahh! That sun feels good. Thought I would do a bit of reading. The surgeon passed on this old newspaper to me—an English newspaper.

Officer 2. You're a great reader, Mr. Nolan.

Nolan. Oh, yes. Helps pass away the time, you know. Keeps me in touch with what is taking place. (*pause*) Would you gentlemen tell me something?

Officer 1 (*cautiously*). Why . . . yes.

Nolan. I notice that these newspapers that are passed on to me have certain paragraphs cut out. For example, this one here.

(*Sound of newspaper being unfolded.*)

Nolan. Here! Now here is a story dealing with Napoleon's campaign, and just as it apparently starts to relate the policy of the United States toward The Little Corporal,⁸ I discover that the rest of the account has been sheared out. Peculiar, isn't it? Er, could you tell me why?

Officer 1. No.

Officer 2. Hadn't noticed.

Nolan. Well, I guess it doesn't matter. By the way, what is the latest news from our country?

Officer 2. We have no news.

Nolan. But last night in the wardroom you were talking over the dispatches received from the States. As soon as I came in, you stopped. Why?

Officer 2. I wish you wouldn't ask, Mr. Nolan.

Nolan (*as though shrugging*). Very well. I realize you're not supposed to talk about the United States to me. I thought I could worm some information from you.

Officer 2. We're honor-bound not to discuss the matter with you.

Officer 1. You should understand.

Nolan (*dully*). Yes, I understand.

Officer 1. What about your parents, Mr. Nolan, or your relatives? Couldn't they—?

Nolan. My parents are dead. As for my relatives, they don't know, and I doubt if they'd help. (*a simple dignity*) Now, if you don't mind, I'll go to my quarters.

Officer 1. Nolan.

Nolan. Yes?

Officer 1. If I were in your position, I wouldn't show the courage you're displaying.

(*Music up dramatically and under.*)

Voice. "Belfast, Ireland, June 14, 1810. To Captain James Wyatt, U.S.S. *General Greene*.

---

7. **derelict:** poor, unemployed, friendless person with no home.
8. **Napoleon's campaign . . . The Little Corporal:** Napoleon I—originally Napoleon Bonaparte—emperor of France (1804–1814), was attempting to gain complete control of Europe at the time of the events described. He was called The Little Corporal because of his short stature and because of his courage during a battle in which he himself aimed the cannon, a risky task usually performed by a corporal.

WORDS TO KNOW

rescind (rĭ-sĭnd′) *v.* to withdraw, repeal, or cancel

609

Critical Thinking: MAKING JUDGMENTS

U Have students explain whether they agree or disagree with Officer 2's assessment of Nolan's sentence. *(Possible responses: agree, because as things stand, Nolan is simply being tortured for the rest of his life; disagree, because even a life in exile offers many opportunities to learn things, to know people, and to be happy)*

Critical Thinking: ANALYZING

V Ask students why the stage directions indicate that Officer 1 should speak "cautiously." Ask if they think he is overreacting. *(Possible response: Perhaps Officer 1 senses that Philip Nolan is going to ask him something about the United States. Given that the officer knows that Nolan has just been reading a newspaper and is starved for news of America, such an assumption would be reasonable.)*

CUSTOMIZING FOR Multiple Learning Styles

W **Musical Learners** Sound effects—such as a newspaper being unfolded, a gavel being rapped, a ship's bell striking, doors and hatches opening and closing—and musical selections could make a radio production of *The Man Without a Country* especially effective.

Literary Concept:
RADIO DRAMA

X Remind students that the effectiveness of a radio drama depends in part on the sounds used to tell the story. Ask students to summarize the information conveyed to the listener by this brief scene between the sailor and Captain Lane. *(Possible response: The dialogue conveys the information that Lane is the captain of a ship, that the sailor has a lower rank, and that Nolan wishes to speak to Lane. The sound effects convey the idea that Lane's quarters are private.)*

CUSTOMIZING FOR
Students Acquiring English

5 Paraphrase the idiomatic expression "you don't wink an eye at orders" as "orders must be followed properly and not changed on a whim."

Active Reading: CLARIFY

Y Invite students to explain why Captain Lane instructs Nolan to "go below and remain there" in the event of a battle. *(Possible response: Despite Nolan's interest in helping the captain, the rules of his sentence will not permit it. Nolan cannot be allowed to participate in a military action on behalf of the United States.)*

Critical Thinking: ANALYZING

Z Encourage students to explain what this sound effect might signify to the radio audience. *(Possible response: The audience would be aware of the setting—a gathering involving glasses—from the word* toast. *The audience would infer from the sound of breaking glass that Nolan had dropped his glass in shock, dismay, or anger.)*

You will receive the person of Philip Nolan, who will accompany you on your voyage to the Straits of Gibraltar and through the Mediterranean."

(*Music up briefly and under.*)

Voice 2. "From the log of the U.S.S. *Enterprise.* November 11, 1814. Havana, Cuba. Today we took on fresh supplies for our cruise to the Far East. Also received as passenger Mr. Philip Nolan."

(*Music up and out into knock on door.*)

Lane. Enter.

(*Hatch slid open.*)

Sailor. Mr. Nolan, sir. He would like to speak with you.

Lane. Show him in.

Sailor. Aye, aye, sir. (*slightly away*) The captain will see you.

(*After a beat, hatch slid shut.*)

Lane. Yes, Mr. Nolan?

Nolan. Captain Lane, I have heard scuttlebutt[9] that we may engage the enemy at any moment.

Lane. That's no great secret. What about it?

Nolan. Well, Captain, I have heard you're a bit short-handed. I'm wondering if you can use me.

Lane (*surprised*). Hmmm?

Nolan. I know ship's routine well. Any detail would be welcome, sir, even that of a powder monkey.[10]

Lane. You mean you desire combat duty?

Nolan. Exactly, sir.

Lane (*not unkindly*). That's generous of you, Nolan, but I'm afraid it's impossible. Your position . . . my orders concerning you, they're very strict.

Nolan. Couldn't you forget them, just this once?

Lane. In the Navy you don't wink an eye at orders. In fact, Mr. Nolan, when and if we do engage the enemy, I must ask that you go below and remain there until the action has stopped.

(*Music up briefly and out into voices singing a Christmas carol. They sing one chorus. As they stop:*)

Officer 3. A toast, gentlemen.

Voices. "A toast."

Officer 3. A toast to our ship, the mighty *Constitution.*

Voices. "Hear, hear." "A great fighting ship."

Officer 3. A toast. To this Christmas Day in the year of our Lord, 1821.

Voices. "Merry Christmas." "A great day."

Nolan. Gentlemen, may I propose a toast? (*There is an awkward pause.*)

Officer 3. Go ahead, Mr. Nolan.

Nolan. I propose a toast to the United States. (*another pause*)

Officer 3. Sorry, Mr. Nolan, but that toast will have to be drunk later, when you are not present.

(*Glass broken, as though dropped from Nolan's hand.*)

(*Music up dramatically and out.*)

Captain. Well, gentlemen, who would like to read next? Dr. Bates?

Bates. Thank you, Captain, but I'll remain just a ship's doctor.

Captain. Lieutenant Harper, how about you?

Harper. I'm not much of a hand at reading, but I'll try.

Captain. Try this. It's a new book of poems by

---

9. **scuttlebutt** (skŭt'l-bŭt'): slang for gossip or rumor.
10. **powder monkey:** slang for a person who carries or sets explosives.

610   UNIT FIVE   PART 1: FINDING YOUR PLACE

Mini-Lesson  Literary Concepts

REVIEWING THEME Remind students that the message about life or about human nature that is communicated in a work of literature is its theme. Sometimes an author comes right out and states a theme directly.

In most cases, however, the author states the theme indirectly, and the reader must infer it. One good way of determining a theme is to think about what lessons the main characters have learned and then to apply those lessons to all people.

Application Have students look carefully at the lines from the Scott poem on page 611. Have them think about how the meaning of the poem combines with Nolan's reaction to it. Then have them explain how Edward Everett Hale and Walter Hackett might be using this scene to convey a theme.

that Scotsman, Walter Scott. Let me see. Ah, here's what seems to be a good poem: "The Lay of the Last Minstrel." Right here.

Harper (*He reads poorly.*).
"After due pause, they bade him tell
Why he, who touched the harp so well,
Should thus, with ill-rewarded toil,
Wander a poor and thankless soil,
When the most generous Southern Land
Would well requite his skillful hand . . ."

Nolan (*slightly away*). Stop! Stop!

Captain. What's wrong, Mr. Nolan?

Nolan. With all due respect to Lieutenant Harper, Captain, he's not doing justice to that poem.

(*A few surprised ad libs from others.*)

Harper. At least I thought I was reading intelligently.

Nolan. Perhaps! But with no feeling.

Captain. Are you an expert on Sir Walter Scott's works?

Nolan. As a matter of fact, I've never read this poem, but I do know enough to realize that it isn't being read the way it should.

Harper. Why don't you read it, Mr. Nolan?

Captain. You're at liberty to do so.

Nolan.
"The aged harper, howsoe'er
His friend, his harp, was dear,
Liked not to hear it, ranked so high
Above his flowing poesy:
Less liked he that still that scornful jeer
Misprized the land he loved so dear;
High was the sound as thus again
The bard resumed his minstrel strain.
Breathes there the man, with soul so dead,
(*a bit emotionally*)
Who never to himself hath said—
This is my own, my native land!
Whose heart hath ne'er within him burned
As home (*stumbling a bit*) his footsteps he hath turned
From wandering on a foreign strand?
If such there breathe, go, mark him well.
For him no minstrel raptures swell; (*His voice starts to break.*)
High though his titles, proud his name,
Boundless his wealth as wish can claim,
Despite these titles, power and pelf, (*He shouts.*)
The wretch, concentred all in self . . ."

(*Book dropped to floor.*)

Nolan. (*a beaten voice*). I . . . I guess I'm not such a fine reader, after all.

(*Music: a theme of motion. Forte and under for:*)

Voice 1 (*calling out, as though speaking through a speaking trumpet*). Hooo there, *Constellation.* Stand by to receive our longboat.

Voice 2 (*off in distance*). What have you for us? Any mail?

Voice 1. No mail. We are transferring Philip Nolan.

(*Music up and out.*)

Rankin. It's certainly a pleasure to have you aboard, Anna. Let me see, I haven't seen you in four—no, in five years.

Anna. As soon as I heard word at the Consulate that your ship was coming here, I said to myself: "I'll be the very first American to welcome Ben Rankin."

Rankin. And you kept your word. Your husband sent a message that he'd come aboard late this afternoon. You know, Anna, you don't seem to have aged one bit since I last saw you.

THE MAN WITHOUT A COUNTRY   **611**

Mini-Lesson: Speaking, Listening, and Viewing

ORAL INTERPRETATION Remind students that radio dramas—more than short stories, poetry, and even stage plays and film scripts—rely on sound to communicate their meanings. The way the actors speak the words makes the difference between an interesting story and a boring or confusing one. In order to create an understandable, compelling performance with their voices, actors rely on their understanding of the words, on stage directions in the script, and on instructions given to them by a director.

Application Have students prepare two readings of Sir Walter Scott's "The Lay of the Last Minstrel." In the first reading, have them intentionally read the poem in a flat, unfeeling way, as Harper might have. In the second reading, have them invest the lines with feeling and meaning as in Nolan's reading. Have students discuss how the different readings affect the listener's appreciation of the poem.

Active Reading: QUESTION

DD Invite students to share any questions they have as they read this passage. For instance, students may wonder about the significance of this reference to Naples and why both Anna and Rankin laugh at the line about odors.

CUSTOMIZING FOR
Students Acquiring English

7 Tell students that the dated expression "I'd give a pretty penny" indicates that Anna would really like to see Charleston Harbor.

8 Paraphrase "I'd never as much as laid eyes upon him" as "I had never seen him before."

9 Define "detail" here as "a job or a task."

Active Reading: EVALUATE

EE Invite students to share their opinions of Anna Rutledge's comment about Nolan's suffering. Ask them if their own views are closer to Rankin's or Rutledge's. Make sure students support their opinions.

Literary Concept:
SCENE CHANGES

FF Encourage students to take note of this scene change. Ask them what they might infer about the scene change from the combination of the tragic music and the clock strokes. *(Possible responses: A different kind of music implies a different time, and a clock striking indicates the passage of time.)*

★ ★ ★

Anna. And I can return the compliment. Ben, you look just the same as you did thirty years ago. Yes, that's when we first met, thirty years ago in Charleston. You were just a plain midshipman then. And now look at you—a captain of a man-o-war.

Rankin. And here you are, married.

Anna. I'm a grandmother.

Rankin. How do you like Naples?

Anna. I like everything but the odors. (*Both laugh.*) You know, Ben, I haven't been home in seven years, not since 1840. (*Sighs*) Being wife to an American Consul isn't all sunshine. Right now, I'd give a pretty penny for one good whiff of Charleston Harbor.

Rankin (*suddenly*). Have you ever heard of Philip Nolan?

Anna. Nolan, Nolan!

Rankin. Perhaps you know him better under his other name . . . The Man Without a Country.

Anna. Don't tell me that he's—?

Rankin. Yes, I have him aboard.

Anna. When my husband was stationed at Marseilles[11]—which was six years back—the *Constellation* came in for repairs. Nolan was aboard, but I didn't see him.

(*Off in distance, some of the crew ad libbing.*)

Rankin. I've heard of him ever since I was a midshipman, but until fifteen months ago, I had never as much as laid eyes upon him.

Anna. He's become something of a legend.

Rankin. Practically a Navy tradition. Shifted from one ship to another. Poor man, he's the nearest thing to perpetual motion I have ever encountered.

Anna. Does he give you any trouble?

Rankin. No. I've heard that during the early days, he was quite aggressive, but he's lost all that. Getting fairly old. Must be around, oh, I'd say at least sixty-five. Minds his own business and keeps pretty much to himself. (*He lowers his voice.*) Look! There he is walking toward us. Poor old devil!

Anna. I'm afraid I don't share your sympathy. In my opinion, Nolan deserves to suffer.

Nolan (*fading in*). Captain Rankin, sir.

Rankin. Yes, Mr. Nolan?

Nolan. The second officer wants to know if you have any instructions before the liberty party goes ashore.

Rankin. Anna, will you excuse me for several minutes?

Anna. Certainly.

Rankin. By the way, Anna, this is Mr. Nolan. Mr. Nolan this is Mrs. Rutledge.

Anna. Good afternoon.

Rankin (*fading*). Mr. Jenks, I wish to see you before you go ashore. Have a detail for you. (*Ad lib voices in background gradually die out.*)

Nolan. This is a nice day, don't you think, Mrs. Rutledge?

Anna (*coldly*). Quite comfortable.

Nolan. The last port we touched was Havre. Very interesting place. I wasn't allowed ashore, but I heard the crew talking. These foreign places are fine enough, but not like home. Mrs. Rutledge, what is the news from the United States?

Anna. I thought you were the man who once said he never wanted to hear that name again.

(*Music: a tragic theme up and out into clock striking five strokes.*)

Rankin. (*His voice has grown older. He speaks on the third stroke of the clock.*) Mr.

---

11. **Marseilles** (mär-sā′): France's oldest city, located in the southeast, on the Mediterranean Sea. Dramatic battles took place here in the late 1700s, during the French Revolution.

Old Willie—the Village Worthy (1886), James Guthrie. Oil on canvas, 60.8 cm × 50.8 cm. Glasgow Museums: Art Gallery and Museum, Kelvingrove, Scotland. Photo copyright © Glasgow Museums.

Secretary, it seems to me that you doubt the truth of my story. I assure you, sir, that I am speaking the truth.

Navy Secretary. I—I don't know what to think. I know your word is good, but hang it all, Rankin, the Navy Department's records show absolutely no trace of this man you speak of . . . this Philip Nolan.

Rankin. Naturally not, Mr. Secretary. Those records were destroyed by fire when the British seized Washington during the War of 1812.

Secretary. It all sounds like a fairy tale, like a nightmare.

Rankin. Whether you want to believe it or not, Philip Nolan was sentenced back in 1807, and this is 1859. Mind you, Mr. Secretary, for 52 years Philip Nolan has been shifted from one ship to another. For 52 years he has never set foot on American soil. For 52 years he has not heard the name of the United States even mentioned by anyone. For over a half-century this unfortunate derelict has experienced a living death.

Secretary. Captain Rankin, why do you concern yourself with this matter?

Rankin. Because I like Nolan. He has been com-

Art Note

Old Willie, a Village Worthy by James Guthrie In this portrait, James Guthrie (1859–1930) gives strength and steadiness to his subject by placing him at the center of the canvas, looking straight at the viewer. Other details in the painting reinforce this sense of directness and lack of ornamentation: the man's clothing is formal without being fussy, and his set jaw and sober gaze suggest a man who has common sense and integrity.

Reading the Art *How would the effect of this painting be different if the subject were not looking directly at the viewer? Do you think this painting would be an appropriate illustration for any of the characters in* The Man Without a Country? *If so, which character?*

STRATEGIC READING FOR
Less-Proficient Readers

GG Ask students to explain the length of time Nolan has been in exile at the time of Rankin's conversation with the Navy secretary. *(52 years)* **Noting Relevant Details**

Set a Purpose Have students read to learn what Philip Nolan hopes will happen after his death.

Critical Thinking: ANALYZING

HH Ask students why the phrase "living death" might be an appropriate way to describe Philip Nolan's sentence. *(Possible response: A significant part of Nolan's identity has been taken from him so that he might as well be dead.)*

Assessment Option

INFORMAL ASSESSMENT You can informally assess students' understanding of *The Man Without a Country* by having them write two letters. Tell students to imagine that 52 years have passed since Philip Nolan was convicted.

In the first letter, have them write as Nolan to the judge. The purpose of Nolan's letter is to explain to the judge what he has learned from his long exile. In the second letter, have students write the judge's reply to Nolan. Encourage them to include the judge's reflections on the case, the verdict, and the sentence.

Rubric

3 Full Accomplishment Students use voices appropriate to each character, and their letters detail each man's thoughts.

2 Substantial Accomplishment Students remain partially true to each character's voice and discuss some of each man's thoughts on Nolan's crime and punishment.

1 Little or Partial Accomplishment Students have trouble writing in the voices of the two characters, and their letters mention only a few relevant ideas regarding Nolan's case.

Active Reading: CLARIFY

II Encourage students to explain what Rankin is implying with this comment about the following year's national election. *(Possible response: If the situation were ignored by the secretary and publicized in the newspapers, voters might be inclined not to vote for the current president, under whom the secretary is serving.)*

Literary Concept: DYNAMIC AND STATIC CHARACTERS

JJ Have students comment on how Captain Rankin has changed since his first appearance in this play. *(Possible response: When we first meet Rankin, he treats Nolan respectfully but does not defy the rules of Nolan's sentence. By the end of the play, he risks censure and informs him of the country's recent history.)*

Active Reading: EVALUATE

KK Ask students to comment on Rankin's behavior. Ask them if they think his actions are risky in any way. Ask them if they admire his behavior or if they feel that it is inappropriate. *(Possible responses: He risks being disciplined by his superiors for defying the rules of Nolan's exile. Although his actions break rules, his motives for doing so are humane and are justified in light of Nolan's suffering.)*

---

mitted to my care on two occasions, and each time I found him to be a kind, mild gentleman. *(pleadingly)* Mr. Secretary, won't you investigate his case? The man has only a few years of life ahead of him. Why not let him enjoy them?

Secretary. With the possibility of war with the South growing stronger this department hasn't time for such an investigation.

Rankin. Aren't you trying to tell me that you don't care to unearth any skeletons?

Secretary. An unfortunate choice of words, Captain. *(coldly)* Taking for granted there is such a man as Philip Nolan, he will have to remain an unknown; a legend, if you like.

Rankin *(casually)*. Suppose the newspapers got hold of this story? The national election is only a year off.

Secretary *(significantly)*. It is entirely within my power to depose you from your command. Then there is the Far East. That is a long voyage. *(fading)* You know how many days a voyage to Japan takes, do you not, Captain Rankin? Or don't you?

(A pause, then telegraph buzzer sending message.)

Voice 1. "Washington, D.C., January 12, 1860. To Captain Benjamin Rankin, Newport News, Virginia. . . . Prepare to sail on 27th for extended tour of Far East, including China and Japan. Detailed orders following."

(Buzzer up briefly and under again.)

Voice 2. "Shanghai, China, May 11, 1862. To Captain Benjamin Rankin, aboard U.S.S. *Levant*. . . . Captain Chalmers of the *Ohio* will deliver into your hands the person of Philip Nolan. From past contact with him, you will know how to receive and handle his case."

(Music washes in over sound. Hold briefly and out.)

614 UNIT FIVE PART 1: FINDING YOUR PLACE

Rankin *(low voice)*. You think the end is in sight, doctor?

Doctor. He's liable to go off any minute.

Rankin. Suppose you leave me alone with him?

Doctor. Very well. *(slight fade)* If you need me, I'll be outside.

(Hatch slid open, then closed.)

Rankin. Philip. *(beat)* Philip, it's Rankin.

Nolan. Hello, Captain.

Rankin. Is there anything you wish?

Nolan. Just sit here and talk to me. *(beat)* I know I'm dying. Perhaps now you will tell me what I want to know.

Rankin. Anything you wish.

Nolan *(breathing heavily)*. I want you to know that there is not a man on this ship—that there is not in America, God bless her!—a more loyal man than I. How like a wretched night's dream a boy's idea of personal fame or of separate sovereignty seems, when one looks back on it after such a life as mine.

Rankin *(after pause)*. Now what would you like to hear?

Nolan. Is our country larger?

Rankin. A good many states have been added. Ohio, Kentucky, Michigan, Indiana, and Mississippi; and California and Texas and Oregon.

Nolan. What of America's progress?

Rankin. Our country has made tremendous strides. Her cotton manufacturing is the greatest in the world. We have made great improvements on the steam train.

Nolan. Steam train?

Rankin. Yes. A form of carriage propelled by steam. Then a Naval Academy has been established at Annapolis and a Military Academy at West Point in New York. A great piece of literature has been written by a

---

Mini-Lesson — Reading Skills/Strategies

ACTIVE READING: QUESTION Remind students that good readers ask themselves questions in an effort to understand characters and events. Then they look for the answers as they continue to read. For example, as students read *The Man Without a Country*, they might have asked themselves questions such as the following:
- Why is Burr willing to help a junior officer?
- Is this a trial in a regular American courtroom, or is it a military trial?
- Has it been arranged so that Nolan can't see even the shoreline of America?

Application In the first column of a chart like the one shown, have students jot down the questions they had while reading the selection. Then have students see how many of the answers they have learned by filling in the chart's second column. Students may find it useful to refer to the time lines they created as they read. These time lines will help them locate events that they had questions about or events that they think will help them answer their questions.

Reteaching/Reinforcement
- *Unit Five Resource Book*, p. 20

My Questions	Answers I Find in the Text

woman named Stowe—*Uncle Tom's Cabin.*

Nolan. Are we at peace?

Rankin. There was a war with England.

Nolan. In 1812. I heard rumors of it at the time. I have also heard there is trouble between the North and the South. (*hastily*) No! Don't tell me. I prefer not to know. Who is our President now?

Rankin. A great man named Abraham Lincoln. He's from the state of Illinois, a man who worked his way up from the ranks.

Nolan. Good for him.

Rankin. The United States is fast growing into the greatest democracy in the world.

Nolan (*weakly*). Wonderful . . . wonderful news.

Rankin (*alarmed*). Philip, are you—?

Nolan. Better than I have ever been. You see that old flag against the wall?

Rankin. Yes.

Nolan. I want to be wrapped in it. You'll see to that?

Rankin. I promise.

Nolan. God bless you! (*His voice becomes weaker.*) On the table is a Bible.

Rankin. I have it.

Nolan. Open it. (*pause*) Now read what is written on the flyleaf.

Rankin (*slowly and with simple dignity*). "Bury me in the sea. It has been my home, and I love it. But will not someone set up a stone for my memory somewhere on my native soil, that my disgrace may not be more than I ought to bear? Say on it: 'In memory of Philip Nolan, Lieutenant in the Army of the United States. He loved his country as no other man has loved her; but no man deserved less at her hands.'"

(*Music up to curtain.*)

The End ❖

The Burial at Sea (1896), Sir Frank Brangwyn. Oil on canvas, 154.9 cm × 233.7 cm. Glasgow Museums: Art Gallery and Museum, Kelvingrove, Scotland. Photo copyright © Glasgow Museums.

HISTORICAL INSIGHT

1. Why do you think Aaron Burr might have had a strong desire to start a new country, distinct and separate from the United States? *(Possible responses: Aaron Burr was ambitious for power—after getting to the Senate and the vice-presidency, he wanted to be in control of things himself, and he probably feared that he would never get to be president of the United States. He may have felt that starting a new country was his only chance. It's possible that Aaron Burr was so dissatisfied with the direction that the country was heading in—and with the way the nation's most powerful politicians were governing it—that he felt it was necessary to start something new, something better.)*

2. In what sense did James Wilkinson behave ethically? In what sense did he behave unethically? Do you think he should have been punished by Jefferson? Why or why not? *(Possible response: It could be said that Wilkinson behaved ethically by betraying Aaron Burr and reporting his actions to President Jefferson. However, his conspiring with Burr in the first place was not only illegal but also could be seen as immoral. After all, he was a government employee and thus an ally of Jefferson.)*

HISTORICAL INSIGHT

AARON BURR: PORTRAIT OF A SLY MAN

Esther Burr described her one-year-old son, Aaron, as "a little dirty Noisy Boy . . . Sly and mischievous . . . not so good tempered . . . and requires a good Governor to bring him to terms." Her death six months later prevented her from seeing him grow up, but her words seem to predict the troublesome future of this controversial American.

During the Revolutionary War, Burr was praised for military actions but was never trusted by General George Washington. After the war, he became one of the nation's leading lawyers. He served New York as a state legislator and as its attorney general in 1789. In 1800, Burr ran for the presidency, but he lost to Thomas Jefferson in a run-off election and thereby became vice-president. Burr's longtime political enemy, Alexander Hamilton, used his influence to put Jefferson in office.

Burr's political career was shattered when, four years following his presidential defeat, he challenged Alexander Hamilton to a duel. For years, Burr had endured Hamilton's political opposition and harsh criticism. Burr's outrage peaked when Hamilton helped defeat Burr in the race for the governorship of New York. The duel took place at 7 a.m. on July 11, 1804, in Weehawken, New Jersey. Ten full paces were measured off. Each man fired one shot. Hamilton's bullet snapped a tree limb 12 feet above; Burr's bullet penetrated Hamilton's abdomen. Hamilton died at 2 p.m. the following day. Burr was indicted for murder but never tried.

Burr completed his term as vice-president and then turned to perhaps the strangest chapter in his life. It is alleged that for the next several years, he plotted radical schemes with James Wilkinson, a friend and general-in-chief of the U.S. Army, to rule Louisiana. It is also alleged that he conspired to take Spanish-owned Florida territory, Mexico, and the Southwest to form a new country. Burr was ultimately betrayed by Wilkinson, who arrested him. Burr was turned over to Supreme Court Chief Justice John Marshall and was charged with treason and misdemeanor.

On September 1, 1807, the jury acquitted Burr and his associates for lack of evidence. Certainly Burr was "sly and mischievous," but was he a traitor? You might want to read more about his alleged treason and decide for yourself. Scholars continue to debate the question.

RESPONDING OPTIONS

FROM PERSONAL RESPONSE TO CRITICAL ANALYSIS

REFLECT 1. What is your first reaction to this play? Record your thoughts in your notebook.

RETHINK 2. In your opinion, is Nolan's punishment fair? Why or why not?
   Consider
   - how his outburst about his homeland must have affected the court
   - whether he is guilty of a crime
   - the length of his "sentence"
   - how he was treated by the officers and sailors at sea

   3. List three of Nolan's character traits, and explain the circumstances in which each trait is revealed.

Thematic Link 4. Why do you think Nolan becomes so upset when he reads Sir Walter Scott's poem?

RELATE 5. Does this drama seem real to you? Could something like what happened to Philip Nolan really occur? Explain.

6. Today, heads of state are sometimes banished from their countries when there is a change of government. How do you think these former leaders feel? Compare this kind of banishment with Nolan's punishment.

Ferdinand Marcos, former president of the Philippines, was forced to leave his country in 1986, after widespread protest against him. Reuters/Bettmann.

Multimodal Learning
ANOTHER PATHWAY

Cooperative Learning

Toward the end of the play, Captain Ben Rankin appeals to the Secretary of the Navy to investigate Nolan's case. With a group of students, plan a retrial of Nolan's case at the point in the play at which Rankin makes the appeal. Present the new trial with the rest of the class acting as jury.

QUICKWRITES

1. Imagine that Nolan insists on returning to the United States. Write the **letter** he might send to the President of the United States or the Secretary of the Navy asking to have his sentence revoked.

2. Write a **diary entry** for one of the days in the 55 years Nolan lives aboard ship. Use your imagination and clues from the play.

3. Compose a **poem** or **folksong** about the legend of Philip Nolan.

4. Nolan shows Rankin an epitaph he wants inscribed on a gravestone. Write another **epitaph** for Nolan, either from your point of view or from the point of view of someone who knew him at sea.

 **PORTFOLIO** Save your writing. You may want to use it later as a springboard to a piece for your portfolio.

THE MAN WITHOUT A COUNTRY 617

From Personal Response to Critical Analysis

1. Responses will vary.
2. Possible responses: The punishment is fair because Nolan kept Burr's secret, despite knowing that the plan was treasonous. Nolan was innocent, so the punishment was unfair.
3. Possible responses: Nolan reveals his sense of personal loyalty when he refuses to reveal Burr's plan. He reveals his temper when he has an outburst in court. He reveals his patriotism when he inquires repeatedly about America and tries to find some way to serve America in battle.
4. Possible response: The speaker of the poem, like Nolan, is in exile, and Nolan relates to the speaker's passionate words about his feelings for his home.
5. Encourage students to offer specific reasons for their responses.
6. Possible responses: Probably the feelings of an exiled leader would be similar to those of Nolan. Yet an exiled leader would probably be able to live in luxury and hear news of his or her homeland, making the exile somewhat easier than Nolan's.

Another Pathway

Cooperative Learning Have four students play the roles of Nolan, the judge, a prosecutor, and a defense counsel. You might choose one or more students to direct the performance of the retrial.

Rubric

3 Full Accomplishment The retrial is realistic and imaginative, and performances are entertaining.

2 Substantial Accomplishment The retrial is largely realistic and interesting, and performances are somewhat accurate.

1 Little or Partial Accomplishment Students have difficulty conceiving a realistic retrial, and performances are unfocused.

QuickWrites

1. Have students think about Nolan's character traits—especially near his death—before they draft the letter. Have them consider if Nolan would be apt to present his proposal in a cool, logical way, or emotionally.

2. Encourage students to include small details, as well as others that reveal something of the mental and emotional reality of Nolan's exile. Remind them to refer to their time lines for any events that can be mentioned in their entry.

3. Invite students to think in slightly larger-than-life terms as they compose their poems or songs. Remind them of one or more figures in folklore and popular poetry, such as Casey (at the bat), Dan McGrew, and Barbara Allen.

4. Remind students that epitaphs usually are brief and capture a person in a few words. Encourage them to choose language that fits the message they'd like to convey.

The Writer's Craft

Argument, pp. 142–146
Journal, pp. 222–223
Poetry, pp. 76–80
Point of view, pp. 322–323

Literary Links

Some students may feel that to be incarcerated alone would be worse than being on a ship with other people. Others might feel that constant sea travel would make that imprisonment more difficult to bear.

Across the Curriculum

History *The Expanding Nation*
Students' maps should reflect that the following states existed in 1805: Delaware, Pennsylvania, New Jersey, Georgia, Connecticut, Massachusetts, Maryland, South Carolina, New Hampshire, Virginia, New York, North Carolina, Rhode Island, Vermont, Kentucky, Tennessee, and Ohio. In addition, the country also held the Louisiana Territory, the Indiana Territory, the Mississippi Territory, and the Territory South of the River Ohio.

During the time period of the play, the following states joined the union: Louisiana, Indiana, Mississippi, Illinois, Alabama, Maine, Missouri, Arkansas, Michigan, Florida, Texas, Iowa, Wisconsin, California, Minnesota, Oregon, and Kansas.

ADDITIONAL SUGGESTION

Science *Steam Power*
Have students create a time line that charts important advances in the use of steam in ships, road vehicles, and railroads. Students might include such details as Thomas Savery's 1698 steam engine, Thomas Newcomen's 1705 model, and James Watt's patented 1769 engine. The earliest steam carriages for roads were built in 1769 in France. Steamships were first built in Scotland in 1802. Two years later the Englishman Richard Trevithick introduced a steam locomotive.

Art Connection

Although student responses to the painting may vary somewhat, most students will probably feel that the subject and mood of the painting complement the selection.

LITERARY CONCEPTS

In a short story or play, the main character is usually the one who undergoes the most development and growth. A main character who changes dramatically is said to be a **dynamic character**. The minor characters in a story are often **static characters**, ones who change very little, if at all, as the plot unfolds. Identify the dynamic and static characters in "The Man Without a Country."

In a play, a **scene** is a section presenting events that occur in one place at one time. In a stage play, a curtain is drawn or a set is changed to indicate a change in scene. Such visual cues do not work with a radio play. How are scene changes indicated in "The Man Without a Country"?

Multimodal Learning

ALTERNATIVE ACTIVITIES

1. Present a **dramatic reading** of several scenes in the play. Carefully select appropriate music to fit each scene and include this music in your presentation.
2. Create a **comic book** version of "The Man Without a Country." Follow the sequence of events in the plot. Use dialogue from the play or write your own, and then share your results with the class.

LITERARY LINKS

Philip Nolan was imprisoned on a ship. The lawyer in "The Bet" (page 240) was imprisoned within the room of a house. Which situation do you think would be more difficult to endure, given all of the circumstances of each man's imprisonment? Give reasons for your answer.

ART CONNECTION

Look again at the artwork on pages 606–607. Examine the mood of the piece. What does it convey to you? Notice its content, scale, use of color, and any other elements that communicate the spirit or feeling of the painting. Would you have chosen a similar image to go with this selection? Why or why not?

Literary Concepts

Help students understand that Nolan is a dynamic character because his feelings about America (and himself as an American) change during the play. The only other dynamic character in the play is Rankin, who changes from a rule-abiding officer to one who talks candidly with the dying Nolan.

Concept Review Draw students' attention to passages in the text that show that music and, occasionally, sound effects are used to indicate scene changes. You might also mention to students that the term "scene changes" is typically reserved for plays. The phrase "setting changes" is often used in types of writing other than drama.

Alternative Activities

1. Encourage students to memorize the lines in the scene so they can be free to use their bodies expressively during the reading.
2. Before they begin planning how to illustrate various events in the plot, have students refer to their time lines from page 601 in order to review the sequence of events.

Multimodal Learning
ACROSS THE CURRICULUM

History During the time of Nolan's imprisonment, the number of states in the Union doubled. Find out which states entered the Union during the time frame of the play. Then, make two maps of the United States. The first should show the states and territories that existed before Nolan's imprisonment. The second should present the United States as it appeared at the time of Nolan's death. Indicate on the second map the date of each state's admittance to the Union. Display your results in the classroom.

WORDS TO KNOW

Review the Words to Know at the bottom of the selection pages, and list them on your paper. Identify the word that is most closely related to each description below. Rearrange the boxed letters to form the popular two-word name of the battleship U.S.S. *Constitution*.

1. undying loyalty _ ☐ ☐ _ ☐ _ _ _
2. to do away with ☐ _ ☐ _ _ _ ☐
3. aiding in a criminal action _ _ ☐ _ _ _ _ _
4. extremely detestable ☐ _ _ ☐ _ ☐
5. a sign of a position in the military _ ☐ _ _ _ ☐ _

Words to Know
1. fidelity
2. rescind
3. abetting
4. odious
5. insignia

The battleship is called "Old Ironsides."

Reteaching/Reinforcement
• *Unit Five Resource Book*, p. 22

EDWARD EVERETT HALE

1822–1909

Edward Everett Hale was minister of the South Congregational Church in Boston for 43 years, but he found time to write scores of stories, novels, nonfiction books, poems, songs, and ballads about history and adventure for both children and adults. Hale is known for writing stories about impossible situations that seem starkly real. His most famous story is "The Man Without a Country." First published anonymously during the Civil War, the story was written, Hale said, as a "sentiment of love to the nation."

A grandnephew of the Revolutionary War hero Nathan Hale, the author was born into a large family in Boston. He greatly admired his parents, who "made home the happiest place of all." He asked to go to school at the age of 2. By age 6, he could "rattle off about isosceles triangles"; a few years later, he and his sister "published" a magazine, producing, of course, only one copy per issue. When Hale was 13, he entered Harvard University only to find himself "thoroughly and completely homesick." After college, he taught at the Boston Latin School and studied theology on his own.

A believer in public service, Hale joined the Massachusetts Rifle Corps and the Sanitary Commission during the Civil War. He was a leader in several charitable organizations, including the New England Emigrant Aid Society and the Lend-a-Hand movement. He edited a monthly magazine, *Old and New*, for five years and traveled frequently in the United States and Europe, gathering material for his writing. Hale and his wife had two daughters and six sons. At 81, he was elected chaplain of the U.S. Senate, a post he kept until shortly before his death six years later.

OTHER WORKS *A New England Boyhood*

Extended Reading

EDWARD EVERETT HALE

Edward Everett Hale's *The Man Without a Country* has been adapted for film numerous times—from a silent film in 1917 to a made-for-television version in 1973. The story has also been produced as an opera and has been performed at the Metropolitan Opera in New York City.

SOCIAL STUDIES CONNECTION
The U.S. Navy in the 1800s These images depict typical ships of the early and mid-19th century, as well as some of the naval battles of the War of 1812. Viewing these illustrations and paintings will expand students' knowledge of the U.S. Navy and help them better understand the selection.

Side A, Frame 52827

• SOCIAL STUDIES CONNECTION

WHAT DO YOU THINK?
Reflecting on Theme

Ask students to look again at the collages they made at the beginning of Part One of this unit. Ask them if they listed "news" or "information" about home, or if they assumed that they would be able to hear about events at home. Ask students to now imagine themselves under Nolan's sentence and reevaluate the ideas their collages show. Encourage them to think about how they would change their collages.

Objectives

- To promote independent active reading
- To apply and practice skills learned in previous selections
- To provide an opportunity to assess students' performance through an alternative instrument

Reading Pathways

- Suggest that students read for enjoyment and record their responses to each poem in their journals.
- Invite students to choose partners and do paired readings.
- Encourage groups of students to read the poems together in round-robins.
- Evaluate how well students can read, interpret, discuss, and write about the selection on their own by using the Integrated Assessment for Unit One, located in the Alternative Assessment booklet. Administer the assessment at the end of the unit after students have read all the selections and completed all the writing that was assigned. Set aside two class periods, or about two hours, for the assessment.

Art Note

Frog with Top Hat, Eyeglasses, and Cat-tail, **unknown artist** This work was produced in 1910 by a member of the Society of American Fakirs (SAF), a group of students that existed from 1891 to 1914 at the Art Students' League of New York City. The SAF parodied works by other artists, not simply reproducing them but also transforming them into works filled with a sense of magic and whimsy. In doing so they felt that they could deflate some of the solemnity surrounding the study of great works of art. This portrait is a caricature of Ernest Blumenschein's *Portrait of a Tragedian,* shown at the National Academy of Design in 1910.

Reading the Art *How does the manner and expression of the toad relate to the toad discussed in "Think As I Think"?*

STEPHEN CRANE

The poetry of Stephen Crane was inspired by the work of Emily Dickinson. The son of a Methodist minister, Crane wrote many of his poems on religious themes, as had Dickinson. Unlike Dickinson's poems, however, Crane's anticipate the free-verse movement of the twentieth century.

ON YOUR OWN

Think As I Think

by Stephen Crane

"Think as I think," said a man,
"Or you are abominably wicked;
You are a toad."

And after I had thought of it,
5   I said, "I will, then, be a toad."

Frog with Top Hat, Eyeglasses, and Cat-tail (1910), artist unknown. The Art Students League of New York. Photograph by Ariel Cortes.

STEPHEN CRANE

Although Stephen Crane was dead from tuberculosis by the time he was 28, he is considered one of America's most important writers. He was one of the first American writers to describe in fiction the harsh realities of life. He wrote six novels, more than 100 short stories, and two volumes of poetry.

Born in Newark, New Jersey, the youngest of 14 children, Crane left college to pursue a writing career. Upon reading that artists must experience hardship to be creative, he chose to live in New York City's slums. Out of this experience and his newspaper reporting on slum conditions came his first novel, which was considered so shocking for its time that no publisher would print it. Crane borrowed money to publish it himself. His second novel, *The Red Badge of Courage,* depicts the horrors of the Civil War. A huge success, the book's reputation has continued to the present day.

1871–1900

OTHER WORKS "A Man Said to the Universe," "A Mystery of Heroism"   *Extended Reading*

PRINT AND MEDIA RESOURCES

UNIT FIVE RESOURCE BOOK
Strategic Reading: Literature, p. 25

FORMAL ASSESSMENT
Selection Test, pp. 115–116
Part Test, pp. 117–118
Test Generator

ALTERNATIVE ASSESSMENT
Unit Five Integrated Assessment, pp. 25–30

AUDIO LIBRARY
See Reference Card

The Choice

by Dorothy Parker

He'd have given me rolling lands,
    Houses of marble, and billowing farms,
Pearls, to trickle between my hands,
    Smoldering rubies, to circle my arms.
5 You—you'd only a lilting song,
    Only a melody, happy and high,
You were sudden and swift and strong,—
    Never a thought for another had I.

He'd have given me laces rare,
10   Dresses that glimmered with frosty sheen,
Shining ribbons to wrap my hair,
    Horses to draw me, as fine as a queen.
You—you'd only to whistle low,
    Gaily I followed wherever you led.
15 I took you, and I let him go,—
    Somebody ought to examine my head!

Thematic Link: *Finding Your Place* In the five poems in this selection, the complexities of finding one's place—learning to speak one's mind, choosing someone to love, respecting the environment, playing a sport, balancing family obligations and recreation—are explored.

DOROTHY PARKER

1893–1967

A fiction writer and poet, Dorothy Parker is remembered for her ready wit. Readers have delighted in her ability to find humor even in tragedy—often her own. Her work frequently addresses such themes as lost love, women's issues, and racial oppression. Parker's poetry and fiction appeared in many magazines, including *The New Yorker*, to which she contributed for more than 30 years.

During the 1920s, Parker was known in New York City literary circles as a member of the Algonquin Round Table, a group of writers who met regularly at the Algonquin Hotel and became famous when their conversations were quoted in the press.

Parker's personal life was marked by depression. Her most lasting relationship was with her second husband, actor Alan Campbell. They wrote 16 screenplays together, including *A Star is Born*, which received an Academy Award nomination for best picture.

OTHER WORKS "Penelope," "Prayer for a New Mother"

Extended Reading

DOROTHY PARKER

The above poem is very typical of Dorothy Parker's verse. It sets up a conventional, traditional situation or sentiment and then in the last line punctures the convention with the sharp point of her cynical wit. Much of Parker's work, whether in verse, fiction, or drama, shows this tacking back and forth between sentiment and satire.

Art Note

Mountain Sunset—Southwest Series #181 by Teruko Wilde The artist Teruko Wilde has done a whole series of paintings of southwestern scenes. This canvas is one in a group titled *Southwest Series*.

Reading the Art *What mood does the painter's use of soft, harmonious colors evoke? How do the emotions suggested by the painting relate to the sentiments expressed by the speaker of "I Belong"?*

Mountain Sunset—Southwest Series #181 (1994), Teruko Wilde. Oil on canvas, 44" × 50". Copyright © Teruko Wilde. Courtesy of Third Canyon Gallery, Denver. Photo courtesy of Leapingotis Fine Art Gallery, Vail, Colorado

I Belong
by A. Whiterock

All that I see around me
   I am a part of.

I am the mountain, to stand
   with pride, strength, and faith.
5 I am the tree, to stand tall and straight,
   above all to be honest with myself,
   and to my brothers and my sisters.

I am the grass, to show kindness and love
   to all who surround me and
10 above all
   to love myself as well as others,
   to be more considerate of my
   brothers and my sisters.
To understand more clearly.

15 I am the fire, which is shared among my
   brothers and my sisters
   for survival.
   Sharing also comes from my four-legged
   relations who eat only enough
20 to survive
   and save some for us.

We use the fire to light our Sacred Pipe
   but only to share
   with our Grandfather.
25 No matter how small the flame
   it is still our life
   and we must care for and protect it.

We are the keepers of the fire
   We share this together.

OPTION 1

Individual Activity
CREATING AN IDENTITY WEB

Point out that each poem contains a speaker using a first-person point of view. Invite students to explore how each speaker describes himself or herself in each poem. Then ask students to make a list of possible ways to describe their own identities. Some possibilities are:

- physical appearance
- emotions
- friends and family
- ethnic background
- intellectual interests
- goals and ambitions
- activities

Challenge students to brainstorm for ideas that expand the categories to find a variety of ways to describe themselves. To keep their lists organized, students can vertically fold their paper to make a different column for each of the categories. When they are finished brainstorming, students can convert their lists into "identity webs" similar to the partially completed one shown.

Teacher's Role Encourage students to be open about describing themselves. Some students may need extra attention, particularly if they think there is "nothing special" about themselves.

Rubric
3 Full Accomplishment Student completes all parts of the web, providing detailed descriptions in each category.
2 Substantial Accomplishment Student completes the web, but does not provide detailed descriptions for each category.
1 Little or Partial Accomplishment Student brainstorms ideas, but has difficulty displaying his or her ideas in word web form.

There's This That I Like About Hockey, My Lad

by John Kieran

There's this that I like about hockey, my lad;
   It's a clattering, battering sport.
As a popular pastime it isn't half bad
   For chaps of the sturdier sort.
5 You step on the gas and you let in the clutch;
You start on a skate and come back on a crutch;
Your chance of surviving is really not much;
   It's something like storming a fort.

There's this that I like about hockey, my boy;
10   There's nothing about it that's tame.
The whistle is blown and the players deploy;
   They start in to maul and to maim.
There's a dash at the goal and a crash on the ice;
The left wing goes down when you've swatted him twice;
15 And your teeth by a stick are removed in a trice;
   It's really a rollicking game.

There's this that I like about hockey, old chap;
   I think you'll agree that I'm right;
Although you may get an occasional rap,
20   There's always good fun in the fight.
So toss in the puck, for the players are set;
Sing ho! for the dash on the enemy net;
And ho! for the smash as the challenge is met;
   And hey! for a glorious night!

624   UNIT FIVE   PART 1: FINDING YOUR PLACE

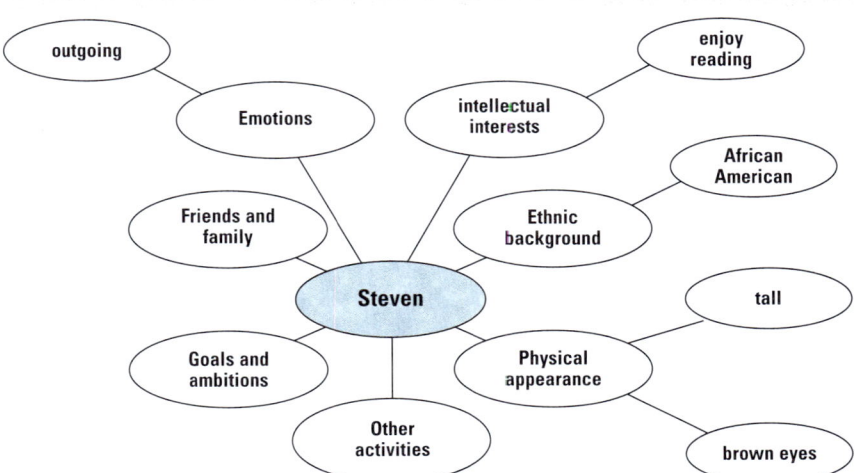

Copyright © Colin Samuels/Photonica.

Linking to Physical Education

Hockey is a team sport developed in Canada. In the 1870s, students at Montreal's McGill University wrote and distributed the first official set of rules for the sport. The International Ice Hockey Federation (IIHF) was established in 1908 as an international amateur association. Its first championship game took place as part of the 1920 Olympic Games. In 1903, the first professional hockey team was organized in Houghton, Michigan. The National Hockey League was formed in 1917 in Montreal.

While hockey is often regarded as one of the most violent of team sports, criticism has resulted in stricter guidelines requiring protective equipment and stronger enforcement of penalty violations. While this once was a sport played only in colder climates, the development of indoor ice rinks since the 1940s has increased hockey's popularity in warmer areas as well.

JOHN KIERAN

1892–1981

By the time John Kieran became, in his 20s, a full-time sportswriter for the *New York Times,* he had graduated from Fordham University, served during World War I, taught in a country school, run a poultry business, and worked as a timekeeper for a sewer construction project.

Kieran covered sports for the *New York Times* from 1915 to 1943. In 1927, he became the first columnist to have a byline in the *Times.* In his long-running column, "Sports of the Times," he was known to use quotations from such ancient writers as Virgil or Plato in discussing the pitching style of a baseball player.

Kieran became known as "a walking encyclopedia" when, from 1938 to 1948, he was a panelist on the radio quiz show *Information, Please!* Kieran turned to ornithology and nature in his later years and wrote books about birds, flowers, and trees.

OTHER WORKS *The Story of the Olympic Games, 776 B.C.–1936 A.D.; A Natural History of New York City*

JOHN KIERAN

Other works written by John Kieran reflect his wide-ranging interests. His works include *The American Sporting Scene, Footnotes on Nature, An Introduction to Birds, A Natural History of New York City, An Introduction to Wild Flowers,* and *Not Under Oath: Recollections and Reflections.*

OPTION 2

Cooperative Learning
COLLAGE

Divide the class into groups of four or five. Each group will construct a collage of images that reflect the personality of one of the five speakers of these poems. Before students begin construction, they should brainstorm a list of qualities they have inferred about the speaker of their choice. One group member can record the group's ideas and another can act as a generator of ideas, suggesting possible images to match the speaker's qualities. Other group members can plan the layout of the collage.

Teacher's Role You may choose to assign poems to individual groups, making sure each group is evenly mixed in terms of gender, or you may wish to allow students to form their own groups according to which speaker's character they would like to explore. Provide students with posterboard and other media such as crayons, markers, paints, and old newspapers and magazines. Challenge students to come up with images other than the specific ones mentioned in the poems. For instance, students might find an image other than the toad to describe the speaker of the first poem.

Rubric
3 **Full Accomplishment** Students work well together and create a collage that demonstrates their ability to make inferences.
2 **Substantial Accomplishment** Students work well together, but their collage indicates that they had some difficulties selecting images to represent the speaker's characteristics.
1 **Little or Partial Accomplishment** Students have difficulties working cooperatively and develop only a few images.

Rice and Rose Bowl Blues

by Diane Mei Lin Mark

I remember the day
Mama called me in from
the football game with brothers
and neighbor boys
5 in our front yard

said it was time
I learned to
wash rice for dinner

glancing out the window
10 I watched a pass interception
setting the other team up
on our 20

*Pour some water
into the pot,*
15 she said pleasantly,
*turning on the tap
Rub the rice
between your hands,
pour out the clouds,*
20 *fill it again*
(I secretly traced
an end run through
the grains in
between pourings)

626 UNIT FIVE PART 1: FINDING YOUR PLACE

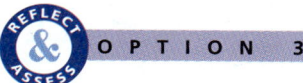

25 with the rice
settled into a simmer
I started out the door
but was called back

the next day
30 Roland from across the street
sneeringly said he heard
I couldn't play football
anymore

I laughed loudly,
35 asking him
where
he'd heard
such a thing

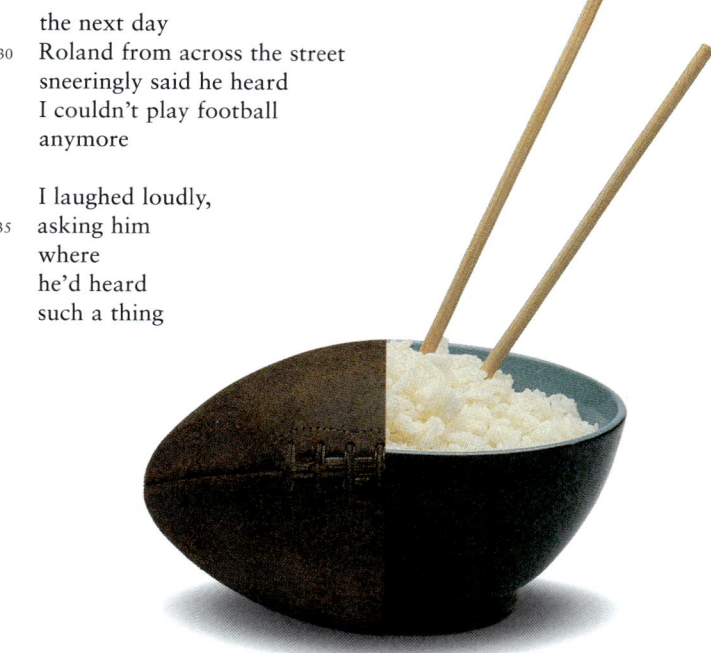

DIANE MEI LIN MARK

Diane Mei Lin Mark's academic pursuits and professional choices reflect her deep interest in Asian Americans. She completed her undergraduate work in English and Asian Studies at Mills College in California and then received a master's degree in American Studies from the University of Hawaii. Later, Mark studied filmmaking at New York University. She traveled and lived in Asia on a scholarship from the East-West Communication Institute.

Mark was a writer and an associate producer of *Pearls,* a documentary film series about Asian Americans that aired on public television. She co-produced the movie *Picture Bride.* Mark also has worked as a newspaper reporter and an oral history researcher.

OTHER WORKS "Suzie Wong Doesn't Live Here," "Liberation," "And The Old Folks Said"

DIANE MEI LIN MARK

Diane Mei Lin Mark has written two books on Chinese-American history and has published poetry in *Asian Women, Third World Women, Asian Americans in Hawaii, Impulse,* and *Breaking Silence: An Anthology of Contemporary Asian American Poets.*

OPTION 3

Class Discussion
SHARING IDEAS

Teacher's Role In developing class discussion, you may wish to discuss each poem separately and then encourage students to develop questions comparing the poems and connecting their themes to students' own lives.

1. Why does the speaker of "Think As I Think" agree to be a toad? *(Possible response: The speaker would rather be a toad than be forced to conform to another person's thinking.)*
2. What choice does the speaker in "The Choice" make? *(Possible response: The speaker chooses between two lovers—one who is obviously wealthy and one who, though lacking wealth, makes her happy.)*
3. Why does the speaker in "The Choice" think she should have her head examined? *(Possible response: She is wondering if she made the right choice, opting for love rather than luxury.)*
4. What attitudes about nature does the speaker of "I Belong" express? *(Possible responses: The speaker feels part of Nature. People must care for and protect the earth.)*
5. What adjectives would the speaker of the fourth poem use to describe hockey? *(Possible responses: exciting, dangerous, thrilling, fast-paced)*
6. Why does the speaker of "Rice and Rose Bowl Blues" laugh at Roland? *(Possible response: She bolsters her courage with a laugh, hoping his belief that she can no longer play football is untrue.)*
7. What are some of the stereotypes about boys and girls that "Rice and Rose Bowl Blues" deals with? *(Possible response: Unfair stereotypes might include that boys should be active and play sports, while girls should stay in the house and help their mothers.)*

WRITING ABOUT LITERATURE

THE SUM OF ITS PARTS

Poets are constantly tinkering with the elements of poetry—images, rhythm, sound, sentences, and meaning. Knowing more about these elements can help you understand the inner workings of a poem, its meaning, and the poet's intentions. In this lesson you will

- see how writers vary sentence structure and length
- identify and analyze the elements of a poem
- analyze the "poetry" of a building's design

Writer's Style: Sentence Variety Writers vary the structure, length, and beginnings of their sentences to add interest and impact to their writing.

Read the Literature

These writers keep the reader's interest by varying sentence structure and length.

Literature Models

A **Varying Structures**
Notice the simple structure of the first sentence. How does the poet depart from that structure in the second sentence?

> I shall dance tonight.
> When the dusk comes crawling,
> There will be dancing
> and feasting.
>
> Alonzo Lopez
> from "Celebration"

B **Varying Length**
How do the short sentence and fragment reflect the character's action and attitude? What effect does the longest sentence have?

> Finally I left. Just like that. I didn't say good-bye or anything. I stalked through the corridors, looking neither to the right nor the left, not caring whether that wild old man with the wheelchair ran me down or not.
>
> Robert Cormier
> from "The Moustache"

628 UNIT FIVE: PERSONAL DISCOVERIES

OVERVIEW

In the Guided Assignment for this section, students will write an analysis of a poem. By examining how a poem works, students will better understand the elements of poetry and how to construct an analysis. As preparation for this assignment, the Writer's Style will help students notice variations in sentence length and understand the effects of this variety on their writing. In Reading the World, students will analyze a building by looking at certain elements and then seeing how these elements are put together to create an effect.

Objectives

- To notice the effects of varying sentence structure and length
- To create sentence variety by using adverb and adjective phrases
- To write an analysis of the elements of a poem
- To analyze the parts and overall effect of a building

Skills

LITERATURE
- Analyzing sentence variety

GRAMMAR AND USAGE
- Using adverb and adjective phrases
- Punctuating poetry
- Using verb tense in quotations

MEDIA LITERACY
- Analyzing a building

ORAL COMMUNICATION
- Peer discussion
- Group discussion
- Group conferencing

CRITICAL THINKING
- Analyzing parts of a whole
- Classifying

Teaching Strategy: MODELING

The following models contain variations in sentence structure and length. These techniques are useful in all genres of writing.

A **Lopez** Possible responses: The poet's second sentence is a longer sentence. Also, it is in two parts, breaking at the end of the second line at the comma.

B **Cormier** Possible response: The short sentence and the fragment reflect the character's impatience and abrupt decision to leave. The longer sentence shows that he continues walking without stopping—just like the sentence.

PRINT AND MEDIA RESOURCES

UNIT FIVE RESOURCE BOOK
Writer's Style, p. 29
Prewriting Guide, p. 30
Elaboration, p. 31
Peer Response Guide, pp. 32–33
Revision and Editing, p. 34
Student Model, pp. 35–36
Rubric, p. 37

GRAMMAR MINI-LESSONS
Transparencies, pp. 16, 44, 46–47
Copymasters, pp. 24, 38, 39

FORMAL ASSESSMENT
Guidelines for Writing Assessment

ACCESS FOR STUDENTS ACQUIRING ENGLISH
Reading and Writing Support

 WRITING COACH

---

628 THE LANGUAGE OF LITERATURE TEACHER'S EDITION

Connect to Life

Sentence variety also adds interest to nonfiction writing. This writer uses different sentence beginnings to spice up her description of a beach house.

Magazine Article

> Home-made chaises fade to gentle turquoise in briny spray and hot sun. Beyond a kitchen-sill display, the sea pervades, as it does on all sides. Swimsuits dry in minutes on the porch rail. In the kitchen, tag-sale chairs and tables display signs of summer, from guests' tote bags to juicy melons.
>
> Carol Prisant
> from "Sun-soaked Beach House"
> *House Beautiful*

Varying Sentence Openers
How does the author vary the way these sentences start?

Try Your Hand: Varying Sentences

1. **Make It Change** Write an alternate version of a paragraph you have read. This time, vary the sentence beginnings. You can change the structure of the sentences completely, but challenge yourself to keep the meaning the same.

2. **Make It Fast** Write a paragraph about one minute in an exciting game, using sentences that get increasingly long. Then write a paragraph in which the sentences get increasingly short. Does the action seem to get faster or slower?

3. **Make It Yours** Write a poem following the form of "Celebration" as closely as possible. For example, you could begin your poem with "I shall study tonight" and write about your evening plans.

SkillBuilder

Using Adverb and Adjective Phrases

You can add details to your sentences by using adjective or adverb prepositional phrases. Beginning with a phrase once in a while can help vary your sentence structure. Look at the magazine article on this page. Two of the sentences begin with adverb phrases.

Beyond a kitchen-sill display, the sea pervades . . .

In the kitchen, tag-sale chairs and tables display . . .

These two phrases modify verbs to tell where the action is taking place. Putting them first gives the reader a nice break from the usual subject-verb construction.

APPLYING WHAT YOU'VE LEARNED

Try to make these sentences more interesting by adding adjective or adverb phrases.

1. I look forward to seeing my friends.
2. It seems as if the day will never end.
3. I'll call my friends and head for town.

 GRAMMAR HANDBOOK

For more about prepositional phrases, see page 902 of the Grammar Handbook.

WRITING ABOUT LITERATURE **629**

Teaching Strategy: USING THE SKILLBUILDER

To help students understand the different types of sentences, you may wish to teach the SkillBuilder on Using Adverb and Adjective Phrases at this time. It explains how placing an adverb or adjective phrase at the beginning of the sentence can add variety to a piece of writing.

Teaching Strategy: MODELING

Prisant If students have read the SkillBuilder on this page, they will probably identify the introductory phrases in the second and fourth sentences. They may also notice that these sentences are longer than any of the other sentences.

Try Your Hand

1. Selections and rewrites will vary. Help students use a variety of sentence openers to retain meaning.
2. Students may find that the action in the paragraph with increasingly long sentences tends to slow down as it progresses. The paragraph with the increasingly short sentences probably builds to a climax in a more effective manner.
3. Poems will vary. Encourage students to follow the sentence structure of the whole poem. This will show students how the form and content of the poem can work together in interesting ways. They may be surprised by how effective their poems are.

SkillBuilder  GRAMMAR FROM WRITING

USING ADVERB AND ADJECTIVE PHRASES Remind students that adverb phrases add more information about the verb, adverb, or adjective in a sentence. These phrases commonly begin with words such as *in, when, after, although,* and *if*. Adjective phrases add more information about the noun in a sentence. They commonly begin with the words *that, which, who, whom,* and *whose*.

Application Possible responses:
1. When school is over, I look forward to seeing my friends.
2. If it is my science class, it seems as if the day will never end.
3. Although I have only a few dollars, I'll call my friends and head for town.

Additional Suggestions You may wish to have students continue with the following sentence.

I'll ask them if they want to get a pizza.

Reteaching/Reinforcement
Grammar Mini-Lessons copymasters pp. 38, 39, transparencies pp. 44, 46, 47

 The Writer's Craft
Adverb Phrases, pp. 540, 564

Critical Thinking: ANALYZING

E Help students understand the purpose of analyzing a poem by previewing the Guided Assignment. Tell them they are analyzing the poem to see how its various elements work to support its main theme.

Critical Thinking: CLASSIFYING

F Guide students to see that they can approach a poem in two ways: they can analyze a poem as a whole or they can analyze the parts of a poem. If they analyze the poem as a whole, they should show how each element of the poem relates to a central idea or central ideas. If they analyze the parts of the poem, they should show how each part stands for or relates to the rest of the poem.

Teaching Strategy: MODELING

G If students are having difficulty understanding what they should look for in a poem, they can look at the student's marked poem to identify certain elements from the list. Students should look in their own poems for recurring elements. For example, this student identified several instances of the future tense in the last few lines.

WRITING ABOUT LITERATURE

Analysis

Poetry can communicate an enormous amount of meaning in very few words. Since every word counts, it is important to study each poetic element carefully to see how it works and what function it serves. Analyzing a poem is like taking apart an engine. It's sometimes easier to understand one piece, or element, at a time.

GUIDED ASSIGNMENT

Analyze a Poem Analyzing poetry means asking questions about how the writing works. It's like opening the poem up to look inside. Write an analysis of a poem, identifying the elements and explaining the use of each one.

1 Prewrite and Explore

Before you can examine the use of different poetic elements, you have to discover which ones are present in the poem you choose.

FINDING A POEM TO ANALYZE

Look back at Unit Five. Which poem touched you? Which had an image or idea you really liked?

When you have decided on a poem, find a few elements or techniques you can analyze closely. Look at the list below to get some ideas. You may want to copy or retype the poem and write your notes directly on your copy, as shown here.

Elements of poetry

Form Analyze the way the poem looks—the lines and stanzas, the arrangement of words.

Sound Rhyme, rhythm, and repetition help the poet create emphasis and patterns in the poem.

Imagery Imagery involves words and phrases that appeal to the five senses. Look for images in the poem.

Figurative Language Identify examples of simile, metaphor, or personification in the poem.

Student's Marked Copy

Celebration
Alonzo Lopez

I shall (dance) tonight. — *this is personification and alliteration*
When the dusk comes crawling,
There will be (dancing)
  and feasting.
I shall (dance) with the others — *this repeats*
  in circles,
    in leaps,
      in stomps. — *this helps me picture it— why did he break it up like this and make it slant?*
Laughter and talk
  will weave into the night,
Among the fires — *alliteration*
  of my people.
Games will be played
And I shall be
  a part of it. — *why is this all in future tense?*

630 UNIT FIVE: PERSONAL DISCOVERIES

Assessment Option

SELF-ASSESSMENT After students have completed Finding a Poem to Analyze, they can assess their analysis of the poem. Students can ask themselves the following questions:
- *Which elements in the poem are repeated?*
- *What do I think is the effect of this repetition?*
- *Is there a tone or central idea to the whole poem?*
- *Are there any other elements that I have overlooked?*

2 Write a Discovery Draft

Try to understand the poem by writing about it. As you write, ask yourself,

- What is the theme or meaning of this poem?
- How does each element contribute to that meaning?
- What was my response to the poem? Which elements affected my response?

Student's Discovery Draft

> I'm pretty sure there's no rhyme in this poem, and there's no simile. There is repetition, though, and personification ("the dusk comes crawling"). There are some images I can talk about also.

Does the feast suggest an image? What are they eating?

Maybe this is supposed to make some kind of dance-like rhythm?

> Forms of the word <u>dance</u> come up in the poem a few times. Why would he repeat it that way? It is probably just for emphasis. What about the repeated rhythm of "in circles, / in leaps, / in stomps"?

3 Draft and Share

Before you draft, consider a few different ways to structure your analysis. You could list the elements one by one, explaining their significance in the poem. Another way would be to discuss the poem one line or idea at a time, dealing with the elements as they come up. Share your draft and use these questions to get feedback.

PEER RESPONSE

- Which elements of the poem did I analyze?
- Did I explain how these elements work together?
- What part of my analysis could I explain more clearly?

SkillBuilder

GRAMMAR FROM WRITING

Punctuating Poetry

Because poetry is a free form of expression, words and ideas often appear in unusual order. Writers try to punctuate their poems in a way that will help the reader understand the meaning. Commas and periods, for example, can help the reader find a change in ideas. If you are confused by a poem, it often helps to figure out where the sentences are.

Look at the poem "Celebration" by Alonzo Lopez. If you read each line by itself, the poem might not make as much sense as when you read the lines as continuous sentences. Line breaks don't always mean the end of an idea. They could signify a pause or a break in the rhythm.

APPLYING WHAT YOU'VE LEARNED

Find all the complete sentences in "Celebration." Write out each sentence in a notebook, and see if this helps you understand the poem.

GRAMMAR HANDBOOK

For more help with punctuation, see page 891 of the Grammar Handbook.

WRITING ABOUT LITERATURE **631**

Writing Skill: POINT OF VIEW

The Discovery Draft provides an opportunity for students to sort through their analysis of the poem and to think about the important elements of the poem. Guide them to think about their initial interest in the poem and what grabbed their attention. Encourage them to focus on the elements that caused this and any other striking effects.

Teaching Strategy: USING THE SKILLBUILDER

You can help students analyze their poems by teaching the SkillBuilder on Punctuating Poetry at this time. It helps students recognize the different ways writers punctuate poems to help readers understand the poem's meaning.

CUSTOMIZING FOR
Less-Proficient Writers

Some writers may have difficulty organizing their information. You may wish to suggest that they try clustering ideas that relate to each other or use a word web to connect analyses to one central element.

SkillBuilder — GRAMMAR FROM WRITING

PUNCTUATING POETRY Remind students that when they read a poem, they should read in complete sentences, pausing at the end of a line only if the writer has supplied a comma, period, or other punctuation mark at that point. Reading in complete sentences and not line by line will make the poet's meaning clearer. Punctuation marks give the reader clues to the meaning the writer intended to communicate.

Application Possible responses:
1. I shall dance tonight.
2. When the dusk comes crawling, there will be dancing and feasting.
3. I shall dance with the others in circles, in leaps, in stomps.
4. Laughter and talk will weave into the night, among the fires of my people.
5. Games will be played and I shall be a part of it.

Additional Suggestions You may wish to have students punctuate the poem with other punctuation marks that still maintain the same pauses. For example, they might replace periods with semicolons or commas with dashes.

Critical Thinking: ANALYZING

K As they revise their writing, students should check that their examples support their opinions, make sure that quotations have been copied accurately, and look for a clear statement of the main idea in the introduction and the conclusion.

Teaching Strategy: MODELING

L Discuss with students how this student draft meets the Standards for Evaluation on this page. It concentrates on particular elements—personification in the first paragraph and imagery in the second paragraph—to make the writing clear. It also shows how these elements are used in the poem and how they affect the reader.

Speaking and Listening: GROUP DISCUSSION

M You may wish to use this opportunity to have students form groups of three to four. Have them discuss the approach to analysis illustrated in the draft as compared to their own. Ask students to discuss whether they concentrated on similar elements. Have them explain their criteria to the group members.

Standards for Evaluation

Ideas and Content
- gives author, title, and brief summary of the literature
- breaks literature down into its elements and identifies each parts job
- analyzes how individual elements work together in the literature
- concludes with a summary of the contribution of each element in the literature

Structure and Form
- uses well-organized paragraphs and a clear organization
- includes transitional words and phrases to show relationships among ideas
- uses a variety of sentences

Grammar, Usage, and Mechanics
- contains no more than two or three minor errors in grammar and usage
- contains no more than two or three minor errors in spelling, capitalization, and punctuation

---

WRITING ABOUT LITERATURE

4 Revise and Edit

K Before you write your final draft, go back and read the entire poem again to be sure you haven't gotten off track. When you are finished, reflect on the first time you read the poem. Now that you have taken apart the poem, reflect on how your analysis helped you understand the writing in new ways.

Student's Final Draft

L Another technique used by Lopez is personification. When the speaker says, "When the dusk comes crawling," he is making the dusk seem human. Crawling is not a very pleasant or normal thing for dusk to do. When the speaker says "crawling," that sounds creepy and makes me think he wants to get away from the dusk. Otherwise why would he have chosen such a scary word? He sees the feast as a way to get away from the crawling dusk, by connecting with people.

The student explains Lopez's purpose by breaking down the poem and looking at one small piece.

M *Notice how the writer has identified the image and explained its purpose.*

Image is an important part of this poem as well. Lopez says, "Laughter and talk / will weave into the night." I can almost see the laughter and talk coming out of the people and weaving themselves into the darkness. This is a very pretty image and it makes the night seem less frightening. I think what Lopez wants to do is weave some sort of protection by laughing and dancing. This will make the night seem good.

Standards for Evaluation

A poetry analysis
- identifies the author and title of the poem
- breaks the poem down into its parts and identifies the job of each part in the poem
- shows how the individual elements work together to create meaning
- includes a conclusion about the poet's choices

Assessment Option

SELF-ASSESSMENT To help students assess their own writing, they can ask themselves the following questions:
- What is the poem about?
- Have I found a reflection of the main idea of the poem in certain elements in the poem?
- Have I used paragraphs to group ideas about one section of the poem or an element?
- Have I used details to support my analysis of each element?

Grammar in Context

Verb Tense When you write your analysis, you will be using examples from the poem to illustrate your points. Sometimes it's difficult to get the verb tense right when you are working with a source. Here are two situations you'll run into. In both situations, it is proper to use present-tense verbs. Use present tense when

- quoting the writer:
  Lopez writes, "Games will be played."
- telling about an action:
  The speaker imagines the celebration.

> The way the speaker ~~repeated~~ *repeats* "I shall dance" must mean that he not only ~~expected~~ *expects* to dance but ~~was~~ *is* looking forward to it. When he ~~said~~ *says*, "in circles, / in leaps, / in stomps," the lines ~~created~~ *create* a rhythm I can follow. The speaker ~~was~~ *is* practically dancing already!

Try Your Hand: Using Verb Tense Correctly

On a separate sheet of paper, revise the paragraph below, using the correct tense.

> The poet wrote, "in circles, / in leaps, / in stomps," putting one phrase on each line. By separating the phrases, he brought out their dancelike rhythm: move pause, move pause, move stop. The look of the lines stepping down the page suggested the motion of the dance the speaker pictured.

SkillBuilder

GRAMMAR FROM WRITING

Using Verb Tense with Quotations

There are two ways to quote a selection in an analysis. One way is to write a direct quotation, in which you repeat the words of a passage exactly:

He says, "I shall dance."

The other way is to write an indirect quotation, in which you put a passage in your own words:

He says that he will dance.

The verb tense you use in explaining a direct or an indirect quote may differ from the tense of the quote itself. The quotes above are in future tense, but the explanatory expression (*He says*) is in present tense.

In the expressions that go with quotes for a selection, use present-tense verbs. That way, even if the tense of the quotes varies, your overall analysis will keep the same tense. Using one tense throughout the analysis will help make it easy to follow.

APPLYING WHAT YOU'VE LEARNED

Change the quotations below from direct to indirect, adjusting verb tense as needed.

1. The speaker says, "There will be dancing."
2. "Laughter and talk," writes Lopez, "will weave into the night."

WRITING ABOUT LITERATURE **633**

Teaching Strategy: STUMBLING BLOCK

Students may be confused about when to use the present tense and when to use the past tense in writing an analysis of a piece of literature. Tell them that the rule is to write in the present tense when analyzing something that occurs or something that a character or narrator says *in* the poem. When discussing what an author does (writes or thinks) or when discussing the poem as an object, use the past tense. So a narrator, speaker, or character *says* something, but a writer *wrote* the poem. Similarly, a part of the poem *is* good, but "I thought the poem *was* good when I first read it."

Try Your Hand

Descriptions of elements in the poem should be in the present tense. Here is a sample:

When the words "in circles, in leaps, in stomps" are written down the page, one line per phrase, it looks like a repeated motion. When the speaker dances in the poem, he is probably repeating his motions as well. This form reflects the content of the poem.

SkillBuilder — GRAMMAR FROM WRITING

USING VERB TENSE IN QUOTATIONS
Remind students that there are two main kinds of quotations: direct and indirect. In either case, the expressions that go with the quotes from a selection should be in the present tense.

Application Possible responses:
1. The speaker says there will be dancing.
2. Lopez writes that laughter and talk will weave into the night.

Additional Suggestions You may wish to add these items to the exercise on quotations.
1. The speaker says, "When the dusk comes crawling."
2. "When the dusk comes crawling," says the speaker, making the dusk seem human.

Reteaching/Reinforcement
Grammar Mini-Lessons copymasters p. 24, transparencies p. 16

The Writer's Craft
Verb Tenses, pp. 483–484

READING THE WORLD

On pages 630–633, students analyzed a poem. They did so by looking at the poem in terms of its various elements, such as form, sound, imagery, or figurative language. In this lesson, they can apply those same skills to analyzing a building. Just as a poem has a structure—a combination of different elements—so too a building has many integrated parts.

Critical Thinking: ANALYZING

O Guide students to notice the vertical rectangle that divides the projecting oblong on the left from the shape on the right. To some students, this shape may look like half an arrow pointing upward. Also draw students' attention to the squares that make up the windows and the large wall. Students can refer to page 630 for some elements of poetry that may apply to the building, such as the form, a repetition of certain elements, and perhaps even a visual rhythm.

Media Literacy: ANALYZING A BUILDING

P Students may interpret the building's design as having some sort of purely functional purpose: something for boats or shipping. Guide them to see that there aren't any cranes or other functional items. The building could be a cultural or civic center. Students may use words like *futuristic*, *weird*, or *modern* to describe the building because of its combination of unusual and even "conflicting" shapes.

Speaking and Listening: GROUP DISCUSSION

Q Group members can note their reactions to each element. Have them appoint a notetaker. The group should guide the notetaker to write a heading that is a certain element of the building. Then the notetaker can list the group's reactions to that part of the building. At the end, the group should have the notetaker make the heading, Overall Reaction, and note the group's response. Encourage groups to respond with opinions that go beyond whether they like or do not like the building. Make sure groups assist the notetaker in making notes, stopping often to review and clarify them.

READING THE WORLD

BREAKING IT DOWN

Often you respond to something without thinking about your reasons. You like or dislike certain sights, people, even buildings—but why? What lies behind your reaction? Just as you analyze a poem by breaking it into pieces, you can analyze an object or a situation.

View How does this building strike you? What do you notice first? Take a closer look. What do you notice as you begin to study it?

Interpret What kind of building might this be? What do you think its purpose is? What words describe the building? dramatic? modern? traditional? What is it about the building that causes you to describe it in this way?

Discuss In a group, discuss your reactions to this building. Try to identify which elements of the building, such as size, shape, and setting, cause you to feel about it the way you do. Refer to the SkillBuilder for more tips on analysis.

SkillBuilder

CRITICAL THINKING

Analyzing Parts of a Whole

Analysis is the process of breaking a subject into its parts in order to understand that subject more easily. For example, what did you do when you were asked to evaluate the building pictured on this page? You probably looked at each element of the building separately: its size, its design, the materials used to build it, and the setting, for example. The purpose can also be important. For instance, how does the fact that this building is the Rock and Roll Hall of Fame affect how you view it?

By breaking a subject into manageable parts and asking thoughtful questions, even a complicated subject can become much easier to understand.

APPLYING WHAT YOU'VE LEARNED
What else besides a poem or a building can you think of that you might analyze? Brainstorm with your group a list of possible subjects.

READING THE WORLD   635

SkillBuilder — CRITICAL THINKING

ANALYZING PARTS OF A WHOLE Advise students that the elements in a poem or building are intentionally chosen by the poet or architect. However, students should be careful in their own writing about guessing a poet's or architect's intentions. Tell students that it is often better to analyze a poem in terms of how it works, how it affects readers, and so on, rather than guessing at an author's intentions.

Application Possible responses:
- Students may think of art objects such as paintings or sculptures or other forms of writing such as stories or speeches. Or they may think of other nonart objects such as clothes, faces, or even nonphysical things such as the aspects of someone's personality.

UNIT FIVE
Part 2 Lesson Planner

TIME ALLOTMENTS SHOWN ARE APPROXIMATE. DEPENDING ON YOUR GOALS AND THE NEEDS OF YOUR STUDENTS, YOU MAY WISH TO ALLOW MORE OR LESS TIME FOR CERTAIN PORTIONS OF THE LESSON.

Table of Contents	Discussion	Previewing the Selection	Reading the Selection
PART OPENER **VITAL CONNECTIONS** What Do You Think page 636	**20 MINUTES** • Reflect on the part theme		
SELECTION **Stop the Sun** page 638 AVERAGE		**20 MINUTES** • PERSONAL CONNECTION • HISTORICAL CONNECTION • READING CONNECTION: Connecting	**25 MINUTES** • Introduce vocabulary • Read pp. 638–44 (7 pp.)
SELECTION **Raymond's Run** page 649 AVERAGE		**20 MINUTES** • PERSONAL CONNECTION • SCIENCE CONNECTION • READING CONNECTION: Analyzing	**30 MINUTES** • Introduce vocabulary • Read pp. 649–56 (8 pp.)
SELECTION **Keeping Time** page 660 AVERAGE		**20 MINUTES** • PERSONAL CONNECTION • PHYSICAL EDUCATION CONNECTION • WRITING CONNECTION	**25 MINUTES** • Introduce vocabulary • Read pp. 660–65 (6 pp.)
SELECTION **Power of the Powerless: A Brother's Lesson** page 669 EASY		**20 MINUTES** • PERSONAL CONNECTION • SCIENCE CONNECTION • WRITING CONNECTION	**10 MINUTES** • Read pp. 669–71 (3 pp.)
SELECTIONS **A Fairy Tale** page 675 AVERAGE **My Mother Really Knew** page 676 AVERAGE		**20 MINUTES** • PERSONAL CONNECTION • CULTURAL CONNECTION • WRITING CONNECTION	**10 MINUTES** • Read pp. 675–76 (2 pp.)
SELECTIONS **Sea-Fever** page 680 CHALLENGING **Mi Madre** page 681 CHALLENGING		**20 MINUTES** • PERSONAL CONNECTION • LITERARY CONNECTION • READING CONNECTION: Symbol	**10 MINUTES** • Read pp. 680–81 (2 pp.)
Writing WRITING FROM EXPERIENCE **Writing to Persuade**	**Exploring Topics** **20 MINUTES**	**Prewriting** **20 MINUTES**	**Drafting and Revising** **75 MINUTES**

Time estimates assume in-class work. You may wish to assign some of these stages as homework.

UNIT FIVE PERSONAL DISCOVERIES

Responding to the Selection

FROM PERSONAL RESPONSE TO CRITICAL ANALYSIS	OR	ANOTHER PATHWAY	LITERARY CONCEPTS	QUICKWRITES
		50 MINUTES		
• Discussion questions	OR	• Father's Day card	• Repetition • Realistic fiction	• Journal entry • Advertisement • Poem
		45 MINUTES		
• Discussion questions	OR	• Brainstorming session	• Slang	• Paragraph • Sports article
		50 MINUTES		
• Discussion questions	OR	• Role-playing	• Moral	• Paragraph • Pep talk • Poem
		35 MINUTES		
• Discussion questions	OR	• Journal		• Letter • Journal entry
		30 MINUTES		
• Discussion questions	OR	• Storyboard	• Tone	• Paragraph • Bedtime story
		35 MINUTES		
• Discussion questions	OR	• Brainstorming session	• Imagery • Elements of poetry	• Poem • Advertisement

Extension Activities

ALTERNATIVE ACTIVITIES	LITERARY LINKS	CRITIC'S CORNER	THE WRITER'S STYLE	ACROSS THE CURRICULUM	ART CONNECTION	WORDS TO KNOW	BIOGRAPHY
55 MINUTES							
✔	✔			HISTORY HEALTH	✔	✔	✔
40 MINUTES							
✔	✔			MATH PHYSICAL EDUCATION		✔	✔
50 MINUTES							
✔		✔				✔	✔
40 MINUTES							
✔	✔	✔				✔	✔
30 MINUTES							
✔							✔
40 MINUTES							
✔	✔						✔

Publishing and Reflecting

30 MINUTES

UNIT FIVE

Part 2 Cooperative Project

Community Awareness Week

Overview

Students will plan a Community Awareness Week, designed to highlight and foster links within the community.

PROJECT AT A GLANCE
The selections in Unit Five, Part 2 deal with how one's environment and other people contribute to the definition and refinement of self-identity. For this project, students will plan a Community Awareness Week whose purpose is to create understanding, respect, and support for the members of the community. The plan may include such things as concerts, speeches, ethnic foods, demonstrations, exhibits, and games. Students will analyze their plans, explaining the purpose of each event and telling how it promotes understanding.

OBJECTIVES
- To understand that people need other people for spiritual, intellectual, and emotional fulfillment
- To understand that relationships are built on understanding and respect
- To plan a Community Awareness Week that will highlight the needs and strengths of the community
- To foster harmony, understanding, and respect through the Community Awareness Week

SUGGESTED GROUP SIZE
4–6 students

MATERIALS
- Paper and writing utensils

1 Getting Started

Arranging the Project
Decide on your level of expectations. This project can go no farther than the classroom, or it can be taken into the streets of the community. The more the community is involved, the more your involvement will be required.

If you choose to keep the project simple and only on paper in the classroom, your job will be to monitor the groups as they proceed. If you choose to actually hold even some of the events students plan, you should coordinate with other teachers and possibly some volunteer adults for extra supervision and support.

Arranging Community Awareness Week
At the most basic level, groups can present their ideas in the classroom and can tell how the ideas would help foster understanding in the community.

For a major project, groups might actually arrange and hold at least a day of activities for the community. If your community already offers a festival or other event, you might look into having a class booth or some other way for the class to participate in the event.

2 Creating the Plan

Introducing the Project
Explain that students will work cooperatively to plan a Community Awareness Week. They will plan a day-by-day calendar of special events, as well as exhibits and booths that will run the entire week. They should plan where and when the festival would be held, as well as any people or groups that would be invited to perform or set up a booth. After the plans and schedule are complete, groups should write a description of each event, exhibit, or booth that also tells why and how it would promote understanding in the community. Groups can be given time to examine and discuss each other's plans. If desired, students can select the best aspects of the plans and make one group plan.

Hold a class discussion about the various nationalities, ethnicities, ages, and religions that make up their community. For heavily urban areas you may want to define the boundaries of what students consider "the community" so everyone is speaking about the same thing. Students who have been to or participated in community festivals might like to share their experiences to help others understand the concept of a community celebration.

Start students off brainstorming the kinds of special exhibits and events they might like to schedule. Encourage them to look around the community to find local bands and artists to schedule. Stress that this is a time when the people of the community can find out what others in the community can do, are doing, and are capable of doing.

Group Investigations
Divide students into groups of four to six. Groups should begin by having each member look around the community for people and things that are special enough to share with others. Students can contact local businesses and other organizations and ask about what they might have to offer. After some serious investigation, groups can meet to begin planning the week in earnest, each member contributing what he or she learned. You might suggest that students make a sketch of the area in which they plan to hold the celebration and mark, for their own reference, where each event will take place. Attend a planning meeting with each group to make sure they maintain the focus of the project.

OPTION 1: NEIGHBORHOOD BLOCK PARTY
Students who live near one another can work together to plan a block party for their immediate neighborhood. The focus of the project would remain the same, but it would be on a much smaller scale. The party need only be held for one day or one evening.

OPTION 2: SCHOOL AWARENESS DAY
Students can plan a day on which the entire school participates in a School Awareness Day. Each class can set up exhibits explaining what they are studying, and students can arrange for tours of the cafeteria kitchen.

OPTION 3: IN-SCHOOL OPEN HOUSE
Students can plan a day when they invite other classes to drop in and see what they are doing in school and out of school. Each student can set up a display of what he or she likes to do outside of school, and all students can be responsible for displays showing class work.

OPTION 4: GETTING TO KNOW YOU
Students can plan a day when they would get to know a segment of the community better. For instance, arrangements might be made for a visit to a senior-citizens center. Students might bring some things that show who they are, and they could get to know some of the senior citizens.

Adapt this project to the needs, resources, and energy level of your students. You might even consider a Getting to Know You day just for the students in your class.

 ## 3 Sharing the Celebration

After groups have made their presentations in class, you might ask them to combine the plans into one comprehensive project. Students could write a cover letter explaining why it would be a good idea to hold an Awareness Week, enclose a copy of the plan, and mail it to the appropriate official.

Be sure to hold a class meeting to discuss the project and its results. Students also should be invited to comment on any difficulties the project presented.

 ## Assessing the Project

The following rubric can be used for group or individual assessment.

3 Full Accomplishment Students follow directions and present a plan for a Community Awareness Week that would foster understanding and harmony in the community.

2 Substantial Accomplishment Students produce a plan, but the aim of fostering understanding in the community is weak or uncertain.

1 Little or Partial Accomplishment Students' plan is incomplete or does not fulfill the requirements of the assignment.

For the Portfolio
If possible, photocopy the groups' explanations for inclusion in each student's portfolio, along with a copy of your written assessment of his or her participation in the project.

Note: For other assessment options, see the *Teacher's Guide to Assessment and Portfolio Use*.

Cross-Curricular Options

MUSIC
Students can find and tape music that would be appropriate for the opening ceremonies of the Community Awareness Week, similar to that presented during the Olympics.

SOCIAL STUDIES
 If your community has a festival or similar event already in place, students can research the impact it has had on the community. They can contact the Chamber of Commerce or other government offices for information.

ART
Students can make a collage of pictures that in some way represent people and events in the community.

FOREIGN LANGUAGE
If your school is in an ethnically mixed area, students can interview several people to find out if they speak another language or know others who do. They can keep a tally of all the languages spoken.

Resources

How to Use Your Community as a Resource by Helen H. Carey and Judith E. Greenburg provides helpful information about ways the community can be used for student projects.

COOPERATIVE PROJECT TEACHER'S EDITION **635d**

PART 2

WHAT DO YOU THINK
Objectives

The activities on this page can be used to
- introduce the Part 2 theme of "Vital Connections," since each activity is connected to one or more selections
- create materials for students' personal portfolios that they can return to later for reconsideration or revision
- build an understanding of theme that can be returned to and revised as students progress through the unit

What are the connections?
Have students first list the important people in their lives. Suggest that students devise symbols to use for showing people's links to them, such as a book for teachers. You may also wish to encourage students to think of alternate ways of designing the diagram, such as a family tree. (This activity provides a general link to all the selections in this unit part.)

How did it affect you?
Remind students that a diary entry need not be written in a formal or highly organized manner. However, students may wish to jot down first some ideas about their conversations with parents or relatives which they then can use in writing their diary entries. (See "Stop the Sun," p. 637, and "Power of the Powerless," p. 668.)

What made you proud?
Have students first draft the postcard to determine what important points they want to make and to help organize their thoughts. You may also wish to encourage students to design an image for the front of the postcard that illustrates their feelings. (See "Raymond's Run," p. 648.)

UNIT FIVE **PART 2**

VITAL CONNECTIONS

WHAT DO Yu THINK?

REFLECTING ON THEME

What have you learned from the key people in your life? Do you feel a strong connection to a particular person? Our links to people are vital to our personal development and happiness. Use the activities on this page to explore the connections that you feel to people around you.

What are the connections?
Who are the important people in your life—family, friends, teachers, acquaintances? Draw a diagram, with you in the middle, that shows all the important people in your life right now. Devise a way of showing what their link is with you and how important you consider it.

How did it affect you?
Have you ever had a discussion with a parent or a close relative about a difficult or serious issue? Did it change your relationship? In your notebook, write a diary entry describing the conversation and your feelings about the experience.

What made you proud?

When were you really proud of a sibling or a friend? Was it because of something the person did, made, or said? Write a postcard to your sibling or friend explaining how you felt and why.

Looking back
At the beginning of this unit, you considered the ways in which people find a sense of identity. Having read the selections in Part 1, do you feel you have a better understanding of the different ways in which people discover what their place is in the world? Make a note of any ways in which the selections remind you of events in your own life or feelings you have experienced.

Looking Back
Have students refer to the selections in the unit as they think about the different ways people discover their place in the world. Encourage students to be as honest as possible when they discuss events in their own life or feelings they have experienced.

PARENTAL INVOLVEMENT
Have students work with their parents or relatives to create a collage that illustrates the importance of "home" to their lives. Students should first jot down their ideas and feelings about home, which they can use to select and design images for their collages. Encourage them to use a wide variety of media in their collages, such as found photos and illustrations from newspapers and magazines as well as their own drawings. Invite students to display their collages in the classroom for everyone to appreciate.

PREVIEWING

FICTION

Stop the Sun
Gary Paulsen

Activating Prior Knowledge

PERSONAL CONNECTION

How much do you know about the Vietnam War and about the problems of Vietnam veterans after the war? With a small group of classmates, or with the whole class, discuss what you already know about the Vietnam War and its veterans. Use a chart like the one started here to organize your ideas.

The Vietnam War	Vietnam Veterans
U.S. troops involved in 1960s and 1970s	no welcome-home parades

Building Background

HISTORICAL CONNECTION

After entering the Vietnam War in 1965, the United States tried unsuccessfully to prevent North Vietnam from invading South Vietnam. Because of the conditions of this particular war, the morale and discipline of the U.S. soldier were worse, some say, than at any other time in U.S. history. By 1970, some military units were approaching collapse. Some men were refusing to engage in combat, and many were addicted to drugs—it was estimated that 10 to 15 percent of American troops were using heroin. In addition, there were reports of barracks thefts, other crimes, and racial strife.

How long does it take a man to get over his war experiences? According to the World War II hero Audie Murphy, one never does. Some Vietnam veterans still suffer from psychological problems stemming from the war. Sometimes referred to as the Vietnam syndrome, the symptoms include nervousness, anger, nightmares, and flashbacks to horrifying encounters on the battlefield.

The Vietnam Veterans Memorial in Washington, D.C. Copyright © Paul Merideth/Tony Stone Images.

Setting a Purpose/Active Reading

READING CONNECTION

Connecting Recall that a reader's process of relating what happens in a story to his or her own experience or knowledge is called connecting. In "Stop the Sun," 13-year-old Terry has trouble communicating with his parents. He finds it particularly difficult to relate to his Vietnam veteran father, by whom he feels greatly embarrassed. As you read, see whether you connect with Terry's experiences. In a class discussion, compare and contrast how Terry relates to his parents with how you relate to yours. Also, to help you understand the story better as you read it, use your reading log to jot down answers to the questions inserted in the text.

 LASERLINKS
• HISTORICAL CONNECTION

OVERVIEW

Objectives

- To understand and appreciate a short story about a son's struggles to communicate with his father about the Vietnam War
- To enrich reading by using active reading strategies
- To identify and understand repetition
- To express understanding of the short story through a choice of writing forms, including a diary entry, an advertisement, and a poem
- To extend understanding of the selection through a variety of multimodal and cross-curricular activities

Skills

READING SKILLS/ STRATEGIES
• Connect

THE WRITER'S STYLE
• Show, don't tell

GRAMMAR
• Punctuating quotations

LITERARY CONCEPTS
• Repetition
• Realistic fiction
• Dialogue

SPELLING
• Greek prefixes

SPEAKING, LISTENING, AND VIEWING
• Vietnam War films
• Group discussion
• Oral presentation

Cross-Curricular Connections

HISTORY
• France and Vietnam
• A day in the Vietnam War

HEALTH
• Vietnam syndrome

 **HISTORICAL CONNECTION**
U.S. Soldiers in Vietnam By watching this combination of photographs and news footage, students will learn more about the causes of the Vietnam War and better understand what it was like to be a soldier there.

Side A, Frame 44743

PRINT AND MEDIA RESOURCES

UNIT FIVE RESOURCE BOOK
Strategic Reading: Literature, p. 41
Vocabulary SkillBuilder, p. 44
Reading SkillBuilder, p. 42
Spelling SkillBuilder, p. 43

GRAMMAR MINI–LESSONS
Transparencies, pp. 33–34
Copymasters, pp. 42–43

WRITING MINI–LESSONS
Transparencies, p. 46

ACCESS FOR STUDENTS ACQUIRING ENGLISH
Selection Summaries
Reading and Writing Support

FORMAL ASSESSMENT
Selection Test, pp. 119–120
 Test Generator

 **AUDIO LIBRARY**
See Reference Card

 **LASERLINKS**
Historical Connection
Author Background

INTERNET RESOURCES
McDougal Littell Literature Center at http://www.hmco.com/mcdougal/lit

THE LANGUAGE OF LITERATURE TEACHER'S EDITION **637**

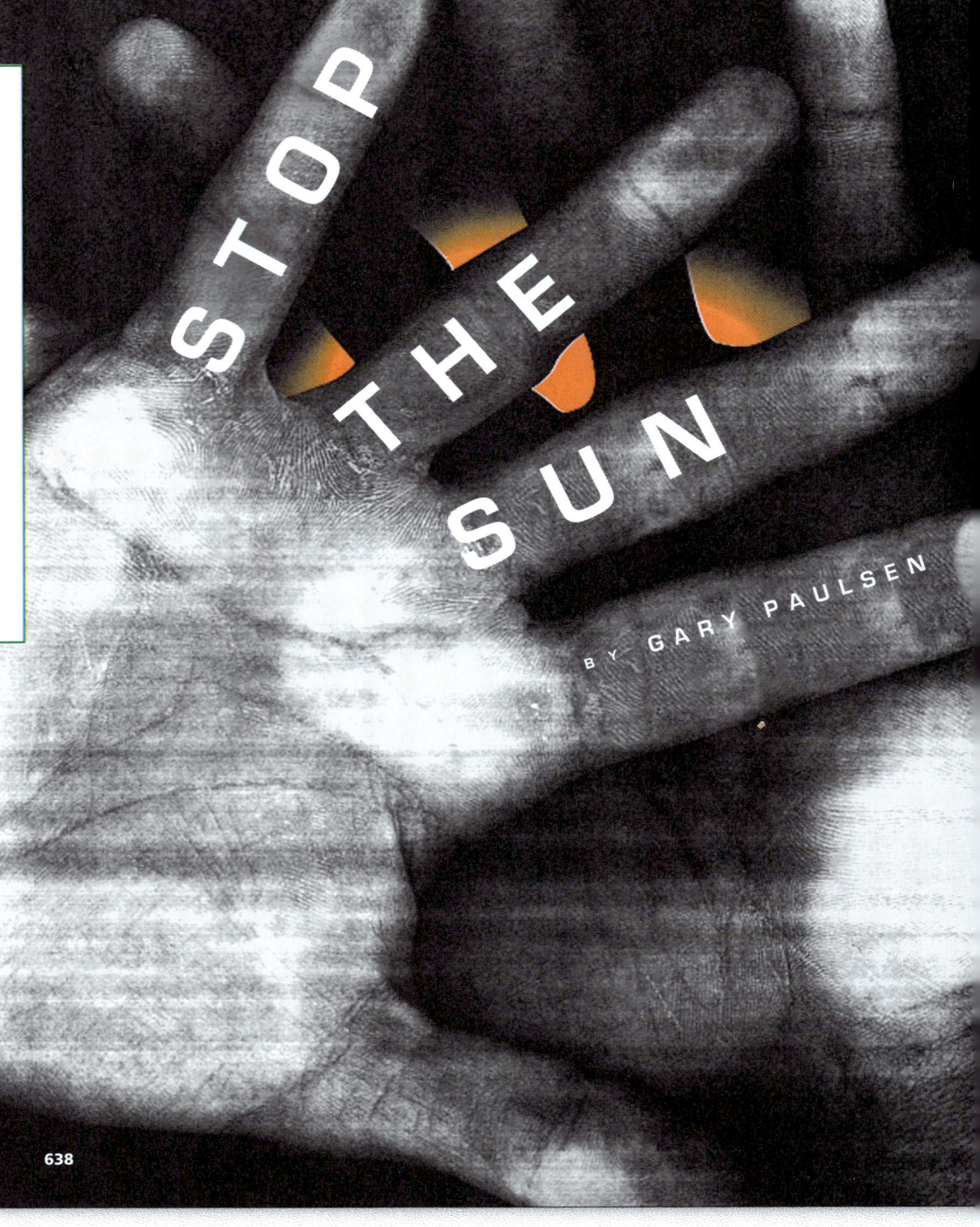

STOP THE SUN
BY GARY PAULSEN

SUMMARY

Terry Erickson, age 13, is embarrassed by his father's strange behavior at a hardware store one day. His father sometimes behaves strangely because of his combat experiences during the Vietnam War. Puzzled, Terry researches the war and finally gets his father to talk. He discovers that his father was the only one of his group who lived through a nighttime raid. The father waited in anguish and terror in the dark, believing that when the sun rose he would be found and killed, and mentally trying to stop the sunrise. He survived only by hiding under the body of a dead friend. Now, years later, he feels dead inside. His strange behavior is linked to his memories and his pain. Terry is filled with new respect and compassion for his father.

Thematic Link: *Vital Connections* A boy forges an intimate connection with his father by asking him to share his wartime memories.

STRATEGIC READING FOR
Less-Proficient Readers

Set a Purpose Encourage students to become involved in the story by asking them if they know anyone who fought in the Vietnam War or any other war. Encourage them to share their impressions of these people and their experiences. Then have students read to find out how his father's behavior affects Terry.

Use **UNIT FIVE RESOURCE BOOK,** p. 41, for guidance in reading the selection.

CUSTOMIZING FOR
Students Acquiring English

- Use **ACCESS FOR STUDENTS ACQUIRING ENGLISH,** *Reading and Writing Support.*
- Some students may not be familiar with the Vietnam War and the controversy it inspired in the United States. They may benefit from reading the Historical Insight on page 644 prior to reading the story.

WORDS TO KNOW

chant (chănt) *n.* something sung or spoken in a rhythmic monotone (p. 642)
dry (drī) *adj.* direct and without emotion; matter-of-fact (p. 639)
founder (foun′dər) *v.* to get stuck; break down (p. 641)
inert (ĭn-ûrt′) *adj.* having no power to move or act; lifeless (p. 642)
persist (pər-sĭst′) *v.* to continue stubbornly (p. 639)

Terry Erickson was a tall boy, 13, starting to fill out with muscle but still a little awkward. He was on the edge of being a good athlete, which meant a lot to him. He felt it coming too slowly, though, and that bothered him.

But what bothered him even more was when his father's eyes went away.

Usually it happened when it didn't cause any particular trouble. Sometimes during a meal his father's fork would stop halfway to his mouth, just stop, and there would be a long pause while the eyes went away, far away.

After several minutes his mother would reach over and take the fork and put it gently down on his plate, and they would go back to eating—or try to go back to eating—normally.

They knew what caused it. When it first started, Terry had asked his mother in private what it was, what was causing the strange behavior.

"It's from the war," his mother had said. "The doctors at the veterans' hospital call it the Vietnam syndrome."

"Will it go away?"

"They don't know. Sometimes it goes away. Sometimes it doesn't. They are trying to help him."

"But what happened? What actually caused it?"

"I told you. Vietnam."

"But there had to be something," Terry persisted. "Something made him like that. Not just Vietnam. Billy's father was there, and he doesn't act that way."

"That's enough questions," his mother said sternly. "He doesn't talk about it, and I don't ask. Neither will you. Do you understand?"

"But, Mom."

"That's enough."

And he stopped pushing it. But it bothered him whenever it happened. When something bothered him, he liked to stay with it until he understood it, and he understood no part of this.

Words. His father had trouble, and they gave him words like Vietnam syndrome. He knew almost nothing of the war, and when he tried to find out about it, he kept hitting walls. Once he went to the school library and asked for anything they might have that could help him understand the war and how it affected his father. They gave him a dry history that described French involvement, Communist involvement, American involvement. But it told him nothing of the war. It was all numbers, cold numbers, and nothing of what had *happened*. There just didn't seem to be anything that could help him.

Another time he stayed after class and tried to talk to Mr. Carlson, who taught history. But some part of Terry was embarrassed. He didn't want to say why he wanted to know about Vietnam, so he couldn't be specific.

"What do you want to know about Vietnam, Terry?" Mr. Carlson had asked. "It was a big war."

Terry had looked at him, and something had started up in his mind, but he didn't let it out. He shrugged. "I just want to know what it was like. I know somebody who was in it."

"A friend?"

"Yessir. A good friend."

Mr. Carlson had studied him, looking into his eyes, but didn't ask any other questions. Instead he mentioned a couple of books Terry had not seen. They turned out to be pretty good. They told about how it felt to be in combat. Still, he couldn't make his father be one of the men he read about.

CONNECT

How do *you* respond when you cannot get answers to questions?
Using Reading Log

WORDS TO KNOW
persist (pər-sĭst′) *v.* to continue stubbornly
dry (drī) *adj.* direct and without emotion; matter-of-fact

639

Literary Concept: REPETITION

C Point out to students that this is the third time that the narrator has used a phrase describing the eyes of Terry's father as "going away." Ask them what this phrase means and what effect its repetition has on the reader. *(Possible response: The phrase suggests that Terry's father is losing connection with his family and perhaps with reality as well. The repetition lodges this important, graphic image in the reader's mind.)*

CUSTOMIZING FOR
Students Acquiring English

3 Explain that the expression "it ate into him" reveals how deeply Terry felt his embarrassment about his father.

4 Point out that "to drop it" is not meant literally. It means giving up on a plan (in this case, asking his father about Vietnam).

STRATEGIC READING FOR
Less-Proficient Readers

D Make sure that students are clear about the ways his father's behavior affects Terry.

- What happens at the hardware store, and how does this incident make Terry feel? *(His father squirms on the floor and cries and pants wildly; Terry feels embarrassed.)* **Making Generalizations**

- Why does Terry cross the street when he sees his father? *(He is embarrassed by his father.)* **Relating Cause and Effect**

Set a Purpose Have students read to learn why Terry's father decides to talk about his war experiences and how Terry feels after hearing his father's story.

Active Reading: PREDICT

E Ask students what they think is wrong with Terry's father. Ask if they think Terry will succeed in getting his father to talk about his problems.

C And it may have gone on and on like that, with Terry never really knowing any more about it except that his father's eyes started going away more and more often. It might have just gone the rest of his life that way except for the shopping mall.

It was easily the most embarrassing thing that ever happened to him.

It started as a normal shopping trip. His father had to go to the hardware store, and he asked Terry to go along.

When they got to the mall they split up. His father went to the hardware store, Terry to a record store to look at albums.

Terry browsed so long that he was late meeting his father at the mall's front door. But his father wasn't there, and Terry looked out to the car to make sure it was still in the parking lot. It was, and he supposed his father had just gotten busy, so he waited.

Still his father didn't come, and he was about to go to the hardware store to find him, when he noticed the commotion. Or not a commotion so much as a sudden movement of people.

Later, he thought of it and couldn't remember when the feeling first came to him that there was something wrong. The people were moving toward the hardware store, and that might have been what made Terry suspicious.

There was a crowd blocking the entry to the store, and he couldn't see what they were looking at. Some of them were laughing small, nervous laughs that made no sense.

Terry squeezed through the crowd until he got near the front. At first he saw nothing unusual. There were still some people in front of him, so he pushed a crack between them. Then he saw it: His father was squirming along the floor on his stomach. He was crying, looking terrified, his breath coming in short, hot pants like some kind of hurt animal.

It burned into Terry's mind, the picture of his father down on the floor. It burned in and in, and he wanted to walk away, but something made his feet move forward. He knelt next to his father and helped the owner of the store get him up on his feet. His father didn't speak at all but continued to make little whimpering sounds, and they led him back into the owner's office and put him in a chair. Then Terry called his mother and she came in a taxi to take them home. Waiting, Terry sat in a chair next to his father, looking at the floor, wanting only for the earth to open and let him drop in a deep hole. He wanted to disappear.

Words. They gave him words like Vietnam syndrome, and his father was crawling through a hardware store on his stomach.

When the embarrassment became so bad that he would cross the street when he saw his father coming, when it ate into him as he went to sleep, Terry realized he had to do something. He had to know this thing, had to understand what was wrong with his father.

When it came, it was simple enough at the start. It had taken some courage, more than Terry thought he could find. His father was sitting in the kitchen at the table and his mother had gone shopping.

PREDICT
What has happened to Terry's father?

Terry wanted it that way; he wanted his father alone. His mother seemed to try to protect him, as if his father could break.

Terry got a soda out of the refrigerator and popped it open. As an afterthought, he handed it to his father and got another for himself. Then he sat at the table.

His father smiled. "You look serious."

"Well . . ."

It went nowhere for a moment, and Terry was just about to drop it altogether. It may be the wrong time, he thought, but there might

3

D

E

4

640   UNIT FIVE   PART 2: VITAL CONNECTIONS

Mini-Lesson   The Writer's Style

SHOW, DON'T TELL Remind students that good writers show rather than tell the reader things as often as possible. Writers use this principle when they are expressing an opinion, making a comparison or contrast, describing an event or a feeling, or explaining an instance of cause and effect. For example, Gary Paulsen shows the father's eccentric behavior in the hardware store rather than simply stating that he acted strangely.

Application Refer students to page 640 and have them list the details that Paulsen uses to show the father's behavior and Terry's embarrassment.

(Possible responses: "squirming along the floor . . . . hurt animal"; "get him on his feet . . . . whimpering sounds.") Have students imagine they have witnessed this account and retell the episode from their perspective, using specific details.

Reteaching/Reinforcement
- *Writing Handbook*, anthology p. 833
- *Writing Mini-Lessons* transparencies, p. 46

Show, Don't Tell, pp. 262–263

640   THE LANGUAGE OF LITERATURE   TEACHER'S EDITION

never be a better one. He tightened his back, took a sip of pop.

"I was wondering if we could talk about something, Dad," Terry said.

His father shrugged. "We already did the bit about girls. Some time ago, as I remember it."

"No. Not that." It was a standing joke between them. When his father finally got around to explaining things to him, they'd already covered it in school. "It's something else."

"Something pretty heavy, judging by your face."

"Yes."

"Well?"

I still can't do it, Terry thought. Things are bad, but maybe not as bad as they could get. I can still drop this thing.

"Vietnam," Terry blurted out. And he thought, there, it's out. It's out and gone.

"No!" his father said sharply. It was as if he had been struck a blow. A body blow.

"But, Dad."

"No. That's another part of my life. A bad part. A rotten part. It was before I met your mother, long before you. It has nothing to do with this family, nothing. No."

So, Terry thought, so I tried. But it wasn't over yet. It wasn't started yet.

"It just seems to bother you so much," Terry said, "and I thought if I could help or maybe understand it better . . ." His words ran until he <u>foundered</u>, until he could say no more. He looked at the table, then out the window. It was all wrong to bring it up, he thought. I blew it. I blew it all up. "I'm sorry."

But now his father didn't hear him. Now his father's eyes were gone again, and a shaft of something horrible went through Terry's heart as he thought he had done this thing to his father, caused his eyes to go away.

"You can't know," his father said after a time. "You can't know this thing."

Terry said nothing. He felt he had said too much.

"This thing that you want to know—there is so much of it that you cannot know it all, and to know only a part is . . . is too awful. I can't tell you. I can't tell anybody what it was really like."

It was more than he'd ever said about Vietnam, and his voice was breaking. Terry hated himself and felt he would hate himself until he was an old man. In one second he had caused such ruin. And all because he had been embarrassed. What difference did it make? Now he had done this, and he wanted to hide, to leave. But he sat, waiting, knowing that it wasn't done.

His father looked to him, through him, somewhere into and out of Terry. He wasn't in the kitchen anymore. He wasn't in the house.

CLARIFY

If Terry's father is not "in the kitchen anymore," where is he?

He was back in the green places, back in the hot places, the wet-hot places.

"You think that because I act strange, that we can talk and it will be all right," his father said. "That we can talk and it will just go away. That's what you think, isn't it?"

Terry started to shake his head, but he knew it wasn't expected.

"That's what the shrinks say," his father continued. "The psychiatrists tell me that if I talk about it, the whole thing will go away. But they don't know. They weren't there. You weren't there. Nobody was there but me and some other dead people, and they can't talk because they couldn't stop the morning."

Terry pushed his soda can back and forth, looking down, frightened at what was happening. *The other dead people,* he'd said, as if he were dead as well. *Couldn't stop the morning.*

WORDS TO KNOW
founder (foun'dər) *v.* to get stuck; break down

Mini-Lesson   Grammar

PUNCTUATING QUOTATIONS Explain that when quoting directly, one usually includes explanatory words, or tags, such as *Terry explained.* If the explanatory words precede the quotation, place a comma after the last explanatory word. If they follow the direct quotation, place a comma after the last quoted word and before the quotation mark.

Sometimes the explanatory words divide a quoted sentence in two. Commas are placed between the last word and the end quotation mark of the first part of the quotation, and after the last word of the explanatory phrase, as in the <u>highlighted</u> example.

Application Write the following sentence on the chalkboard, without punctuation. Have students copy the sentence and add punctuation.

"I was wondering," Terry said, "if we could talk about something, Dad."

Reteaching/Reinforcement
- *Grammar Handbook,* anthology p. 898
- *Grammar Mini-Lessons* copymasters pp. 42–43, transparencies pp. 33–34

📁 **The Writer's Craft**

Quotation Marks, pp. 664–665

Literary Concept:
REALISTIC FICTION

I To help students appreciate "Stop the Sun" as an example of realistic fiction, ask them to identify Paulsen's use of realistic details in this passage. *(Possible response: The untouched can of soda and the jagged, awkward attempts at conversation between father and son help make this scene more realistic.)*

Critical Thinking:
SYNTHESIZING

J Ask students to explain how Terry's experience of his father at this point in the story contrasts with his experience of him in the hardware store. *(Possible response: In the hardware store, Terry could experience only the physical and behavioral effects of what was going on in his father's mind; here he is able to follow his father's thoughts one by one as he describes them in words.)*

CUSTOMIZING FOR
Multiple Learning Styles

K Logical-Mathematical Learners
Have students determine what percentage of the unit was killed by the Vietcong. *(98%)* Then explain to students that 58,000 American soldiers lost their lives during the war.

Literary Concept: DIALOGUE

L Ask students to explain what they learn about the father's character through the dialogue in this scene. *(Possible response: the father's bravery and skill as a soldier, his patience and instinct for survival, as well as his sense of grief and remembered fear)*

"I don't understand, Dad."

"No. You don't." His voice hardened, then softened again, and broke at the edges. "But see, see how it was . . ." He trailed off, and Terry thought he was done. His father looked back down to the table, at the can of soda he hadn't touched, at the tablecloth, at his hands, which were folded, <u>inert</u> on the table.

"We were crossing a rice paddy in the dark," he said, and suddenly his voice flowed like a river breaking loose. "We were crossing the paddy, and it was dark, still dark, so black you couldn't see the end of your nose. There was a light rain, a mist, and I was thinking that during the next break I would whisper and tell Petey Kressler how nice the rain felt, but of course I didn't know there wouldn't be a Petey Kressler."

He took a deep, ragged breath. At that moment Terry felt his brain swirl, a kind of whirlpool pulling, and he felt the darkness and the light rain because it was in his father's eyes, in his voice.

"So we were crossing the paddy, and it was a straight sweep, and then we caught it. We began taking fire from three sides, automatic weapons, and everybody went down and tried to get low, but we couldn't. We couldn't get low enough. We could never get low enough, and you could hear the rounds hitting people. It was just a short time before they brought in the mortars,[1] and we should have moved, should have run, but nobody got up, and after a time nobody *could* get up. The fire just kept coming and coming, and then incoming mortars, and I heard screams as they hit, but there was nothing to do. Nothing to do."

"Dad?" Terry said. He thought, maybe I can stop him. Maybe I can stop him before . . . before it gets to be too much. Before he breaks.

"Mortars," his father went on, "I hated mortars. You just heard them wump as they fired, and you didn't know where they would hit, and you always felt like they would hit your back. They swept back and forth with the mortars, and the automatic weapons kept coming in, and there was no radio, no way to call for artillery. Just the dark to hide in. So I crawled to the side and found Jackson, only he wasn't there, just part of his body, the top part, and I hid under it and waited, and waited, and waited.

"Finally the firing quit. But see, see how it was in the dark with nobody alive but me? I yelled once, but that brought fire again, so I shut up, and there was nothing, not even the screams."

His father cried, and Terry tried to understand, and he thought he could feel part of it. But it was so much, so much and so strange to him.

"You cannot know this," his father repeated. It was almost a <u>chant</u>. "You cannot know the fear. It was dark, and I was the only one left alive out of 54 men, all dead but me, and I knew that the Vietcong[2] were just waiting for light. When the dawn came, 'Charley'[3] would come out and finish everybody off, the way they always did. And I thought if I could stop the dawn, just stop the sun from coming up, I could make it."

Terry felt the fear, and he also felt the tears coming down his cheeks. His hand went out across the table, and he took his father's hand and held it. It was shaking.

---

1. **mortars:** small, portable cannons that fire explosive shells; also, the shells fired by such cannons.
2. **Vietcong:** Communist rebels fighting to overthrow the U.S.-supported South Vietnamese government.
3. **Charley:** a slang term used by U.S. soldiers to refer to the Vietcong.

WORDS TO KNOW
inert (ĭn-ûrt′) *adj.* having no power to move or act; lifeless
chant (chănt) *n.* something sung or spoken in a rhythmic monotone

642

Mini-Lesson • Literary Concepts

Dialogue
• characterization
• furthers plot

REVIEWING DIALOGUE A conversation between two or more characters in a literary work is called a dialogue. Write on the chalkboard the definition of dialogue shown and use it to explain two ways dialogue functions in literature. Dialogue is used for characterization and to further the plot by showing characters responding to each other, making discoveries, or changing in some way. For example, the dialogue between Terry and his mother on page 639 establishes both characters and sets up the conflict and tension regarding the father's behavior.

Application Have students study the dialogue on pages 642 and 643. Then have them explain how the dialogue furthers the plot. *(Possible response: The father's words describe events that have set the whole story in motion. The telling of these events leads Terry to a new understanding of, and empathy for, his father. Their relationship has changed after this dialogue is over.)*

Prometheus Under Fire (1984), Rupert Garcia. Pastel on paper, 29¾" × 84". Courtesy of the artist, Rena Bransten Gallery, San Francisco, and Galerie Claude Samuel, Paris. Copyright © 1995 Rupert Garcia.

"I mean I actually thought that if I could stop the sun from coming up, I could live. I made my brain work on that because it was all I had. Through the rest of the night in the rain in the paddy, I thought I could do it. I could stop the dawn." He took a deep breath. "But you can't, you know. You can't stop it from coming, and when I saw the gray light, I knew I was dead. It would just be minutes, and the light would be full, and I just settled under Jackson's body, and hid."

He stopped, and his face came down into his hands. Terry stood and went around the table to stand in back of him, his hands on his shoulders, rubbing gently.

"They didn't shoot me. They came, one of them poked Jackson's body and went on, and they left me. But I was dead. I'm still dead, don't you see? I died because I couldn't stop the sun. I died. Inside where I am—I died."

Terry was still in back of him, and he nodded, but he didn't see. Not that. He understood only that he didn't understand and that he would probably never know what it was really like, would probably never understand what had truly happened. And maybe his father would never be truly normal.

But Terry also knew that it didn't matter. He would try to understand, and the trying would have to be enough. He would try hard from now on, and he would not be embarrassed when his father's eyes went away. He would not be embarrassed no matter what his father did. Terry had knowledge now. Maybe not enough and maybe not all that he would need.

But it was a start. ❖

Art Note

Prometheus Under Fire by Rupert Garcia Prometheus is a figure in Greek mythology who stole fire from the gods on Mount Olympus and gave it to humankind. For his theft, Prometheus was punished by the gods.

Reading the Art Would the figure of Prometheus be a better symbol for soldiers who fought in Vietnam, Vietnam itself, or the United States?

STRATEGIC READING FOR
Less-Proficient Readers

Ask students why Terry's father begins to share his story. (*He may sense his son's burning desire to know what happened; he may simply need to talk.*) Making Inferences

CUSTOMIZING FOR
Gifted and Talented Students

Have students discuss the idea of survivor's guilt. Explain that this psychological and emotional disturbance can occur in people who survive some terrible event that kills many others.

COMPREHENSION CHECK

1. Why does Terry's father sometimes act strangely? (*He is emotionally scarred by his war experiences.*)
2. What term does Terry's mother say the doctors use to identify what sometimes happens to her husband? (*Vietnam syndrome*)
3. Is the kitchen conversation between Terry and his father important? Explain. (*The conversation is important because it is the first time Terry's father shares memories of the war with his son; the conversation brings them closer together.*)

Mini-Lesson — Spelling

GREEK PREFIXES Tell students that many English words come from the Greek language. Three common prefixes that come from Greek are *syn-*, *psych-*, and *auto-*. Write on the chalkboard the prefixes and their meanings as shown. The selection contains these examples: *syndrome*, *psychiatrists*, and *automatic*.

Application Read aloud the examples above and have students write them in their notebooks. Then write the following sentences on the chalkboard and have students fill in the words that complete the sentences.

1. The _____ urged Terry's father to talk about his war experiences.
2. An _____ weapon can rapidly fire one shot after another.
3. Flashbacks are a symptom of Vietnam _____.

Ask students to look for more words that fit this pattern, and to add these words to their personal word lists.

Reteaching/Reinforcement
• *Unit Five Resource Book*, p. 43

Greek Prefixes
syn- means "with," "together"
psych- means "soul" or "mind"
auto- means "self"

INSIGHT

1. In your opinion, are there any circumstances under which it is right for one nation to support one side or the other in another nation's civil war? *(Possible responses: Such an action might be justified if one of the warring sides were guilty of atrocities. If freedom were at risk, another nation would be right in stepping in. A civil war is no place for soldiers of another country.)*

2. Why do you think that some returning soldiers were able to "ease back into civilian life" but others were not? *(Possible responses: It is understandable that those soldiers who endured horrible events would have a harder time adjusting to civilian life than those soldiers who had the luck to elude such events. Individuals react differently, so it's no surprise that soldiers adapted differently at home.)*

3. What might you say to a returning war veteran suffering from problems like Terry's father? *(Responses will vary.)*

4. Have you learned anything new or different about a soldier's experiences of war? *(Possible response: The effects of war aren't always physical; a person can carry emotional scars for a long time.)*

HISTORICAL INSIGHT

THE VIETNAM WAR

The Vietnam War, lasting from 1957 to 1975, was the longest, most unpopular war the United States ever fought in, and the first in which it did not meet its goals.

In 1954, Vietnam was divided into two nations, South Vietnam and Communist North Vietnam. When the North sought to take over the South, other nations, including the United States, feared Communist expansion and therefore intervened. Although more than 58,000 Americans lost their lives, today a Communist government rules a united Vietnam.

The U.S. role in the war became one of the most debated issues in the nation's history. Some saw it as a necessary battle in the global fight against Communism; others believed it to be morally wrong. Such opponents felt that other nations had no business interfering, much less risking the lives of their citizens, in the civil struggle of the Vietnamese.

Despite protests, the United States entered the war in 1965. While the United States set out to fight a mechanized war, North Vietnam fought a guerrilla war, relying on surprise attacks and hand-laid bombs in a strategy well suited to the jungle landscape. Some have said that the United States was woefully disadvantaged from the start because of the difficult Southeast Asian terrain and the Vietcong's intimate knowledge of it. Describing patrol duty, one soldier asked a friend to imagine walking through thick grass 8 to 15 feet high "while all around you are men possessing the latest automatic weapons who desperately want to kill you." To make matters worse, U.S. troops often could not distinguish between the enemy and the civilians for whom they were fighting: untold numbers of civilians were killed, and many of their villages were burned.

At home, mass antiwar protests hastened the American pullout. The returning soldiers received no ticker-tape parades and little thanks, and there was little national mourning for the dead. Nevertheless, many veterans were able to ease back into civilian life. Others, however—like Terry's father in "Stop the Sun"—were deeply scarred by their experiences and had to live with long-term emotional problems. Many are still wrestling with these problems today.

644 UNIT FIVE PART 2: VITAL CONNECTIONS

Mini-Lesson: Speaking, Listening, and Viewing

FILM Students might enjoy and learn from one of the following films:

Heroes—stars Henry Winkler as a Vietnam veteran suffering from flashbacks.

In Country—stars Emily Lloyd as a young woman coming to terms with the death of her father in Vietnam.

Distant Thunder—stars John Lithgow as a veteran who reunites with his son.

Dear America: Letters Home From Vietnam—uses celebrity voices to dramatize soldiers' personal correspondence to their friends and family.

Application Preview first and then hold a class screening of one of the films mentioned above or another appropriate film. Engage students in a class discussion using these questions:

- What important facts did you learn about the Vietnam War from this film?
- How would you describe the film's point of view? Would you say it was prowar or antiwar?
- Did this film change any attitudes you already had about the Vietnam War, or wars in general? If so, how did your attitudes change?

RESPONDING OPTIONS

FROM PERSONAL RESPONSE TO CRITICAL ANALYSIS

REFLECT
1. Which character do you have the strongest response to—Terry or his father? Jot down your thoughts in your notebook, and share your writing with a partner.

RETHINK
Close Textual Analysis

2. What personal discoveries do you think Terry has made by the end of the story? Explain your ideas.
   Consider
   - Terry's reaction to hearing his father's story
   - the sense of hopelessness felt by his father
   - whether Terry can really understand his father's experiences in Vietnam
   - your own experiences with family discussions of difficult issues

3. For the Reading Connection on page 637, you were asked to connect Terry's experiences with your own. If you were in Terry's place, would you feel as embarrassed by your father as he does? Why or why not?

RELATE
4. Do you agree or disagree with Terry's decision to ask his father about the war? Give reasons for your answer.

5. A number of Vietnam veterans feel that because they fought in an unpopular war, the public and the government have ignored their needs. How do you think the government should respond to these veterans?

A hunger strike held near the White House by Vietnam veterans in 1981. UPI/Bettmann Newsphotos.

Multimodal Learning
ANOTHER PATHWAY
Cooperative Learning
What kind of card might Terry choose to give his father on Father's Day? With a small group of classmates, design and make a card that reflects Terry's new understanding of his father and of himself. Include a meaningful picture or design on the front and a personal message inside.

QUICKWRITES
1. Think back to an embarrassing moment in your life. Write a **diary entry** describing the incident.
2. Imagine you are starting a support group in which Vietnam veterans will gather to talk about their problems. Write an **advertisement** for the support group. Think of statements that might encourage troubled veterans like Terry's father to join the group.
3. Write a Veterans Day **poem** to honor Vietnam veterans. Before you begin, think about what you have learned about the Vietnam War and its veterans from this story. Share the poem with your class.

📁 **PORTFOLIO** Save your writing. You may want to use it later as a springboard to a piece for your portfolio.

STOP THE SUN 645

From Personal Response to Critical Analysis

1. Responses will vary.
2. Possible responses: Terry has discovered a way to connect with his father about Vietnam; he has discovered empathy for his father; he has discovered that his ability to understand things may be more limited.
3. Possible responses: It would be embarrassing because the father's behavior draws the attention of total strangers. It would cause anger at the people who stared rather than embarrassment over the father's behavior.
4. Possible responses: It was necessary for him to ask because—despite what his father says—the experience does have something to do with Terry. Terry's father should be allowed to talk as little as he wishes about those horrific events.
5. Responses will vary.

Another Pathway

Cooperative Learning Encourage students to discuss which emotions or thoughts they want their card to communicate before they begin making it. Assign one student to serve as moderator to help the group come to agreement on the card's message.

Rubric
3 Full Accomplishment Students create a card containing a visually arresting design and a message that clearly reflects Terry's discoveries.
2 Substantial Accomplishment Students create a card containing a pleasant design and a message that suggests Terry's discoveries.
1 Little or Partial Accomplishment Students create a card containing an unclear design and a message that only tangentially reflects Terry's discoveries.

QuickWrites
1. Remind students to include enough background information to provide a context for the incident.
2. Urge students to study a variety of advertisements—including print advertisements, radio advertisements, and promotional brochures—to help them decide which techniques might work best for this ad's audience.
3. Remind students that they are free to write their poems with or without poetic elements such as rhyme, strict meter, and regular stanzas.

The Writer's Craft
Using a Journal, pp. 222–223
Writing a Poem, pp. 76–80

THE LANGUAGE OF LITERATURE TEACHER'S EDITION

Literary Links

In "The Banana Tree," it is the son who is silent, brooding, and troubled and the father who tries to get him to share his thoughts and feelings. Gustus's conflict with his father has to do with his feeling underappreciated and overworked. Gustus handles the conflict by trying to take matters into his own hands. After he has survived the hurricane, his father learns what has been making him unhappy.

It is the opposite situation in "Stop the Sun," which features Terry encouraging his father to talk to him. Terry is embarrassed by his father but finally talks to him about his behavior. When his father shares important memories of the Vietnam War, Terry's feelings of embarrassment are replaced by empathy and patience.

Across the Curriculum

History *A Day in the Vietnam War* Students might enhance their understanding of the newspaper account by consulting a map that shows North Vietnam and South Vietnam as they appeared in the 1960s. If students use a current map, they may encounter some confusing name changes. For instance, the former capital of South Vietnam, Saigon, is now named Ho Chi Minh City.

Science Cooperative Learning *Vietnam syndrome* Vietnam syndrome, or post-Vietnam stress syndrome, can produce dramatic effects, and students might report on symptoms such as depression, flashbacks, feelings of emotional detachment or isolation, alcoholism, drug abuse, and suicide. Have students form small groups of three or four to research further information on this syndrome. Students also may wish to contact local veterans' organizations for information.

Art Connection

Ask students what they think of the colors the artist uses in *Prometheus Under Fire*. How do the reds, yellows, and oranges relate to some of the themes of the story?

LITERARY CONCEPTS

Writers sometimes use **repetition,** a repeated use of certain words or phrases to emphasize important ideas or feelings. Paulsen uses repetition frequently in "Stop the Sun." On page 640, for example, the narrator says, "It burned into Terry's mind, the picture of his father down on the floor. It burned in and in. . . ." Find other examples of repeated words and phrases. What do you think the use of repetition adds to the story?

> That's another part of my life.
> A bad part.
> A rotten part.

CONCEPT REVIEW: Realistic Fiction "Stop the Sun" is realistic fiction, set in the modern, real world. You might recall that the characters in such fiction behave like real people as they deal with typical contemporary problems. Find details in the story that convey this kind of realism.

Multimodal Learning
ART CONNECTION

Refer back to the illustration on page 643. What do you notice about the artist's style? Pay particular attention to the subject matter and use of color. Describe what you see. How might you connect this illustration to the war experiences described in the selection?

Detail of *Prometheus Under Fire* (1984), Rupert Garcia. Pastel on paper, 29¼" × 84". Courtesy of the artist, Rena Bransten Gallery, San Francisco, and Galerie Claude Samuel, Paris. Copyright © 1995 Rupert Garcia.

646 UNIT FIVE PART 2: VITAL CONNECTIONS

LITERARY LINKS

Terry in this story and Gustus in "The Banana Tree" (page 369) struggle in their relationships with their fathers. Compare and contrast the situations that lead to these struggles. Consider how the fathers and sons handle their conflicts and what personal discoveries are made.

ACROSS THE CURRICULUM

 History The peak years of U.S. troop involvement in the Vietnam War were 1965–1969. Choose a particular day in this period, and at your library or via the Internet, locate a newspaper published on that day. Report to the class on what happened in the war on that day. You might try sketching the paper's front page to share with your classmates.

 Science Many Vietnam veterans have, like Terry's father, suffered from "Vietnam syndrome" (also known as post-Vietnam stress syndrome). Research this syndrome—the symptoms that make it up, its effects, and the ways in which it is treated. If possible, interview a physician about the syndrome. Present your findings to the class.

Literary Concepts

You might wish to have students listen to oral readings of certain sections of the story in order to hear repetitions such as "laughing small, nervous laughs"; "burned in and in"; and "a blow. A body blow."

Concept Review Students can work in pairs or small groups to identify details of realistic fiction such as *shopping mall; we already did the bit about girls, shrinks; and got a soda out of the refrigerator and popped it open.*

Multimodal Learning

ALTERNATIVE ACTIVITIES

1. If you were making a movie version of "Stop the Sun," what **music** would you use to convey the emotions of the story? Find or compose a piece of **music** that captures the mood of the father's memory of Vietnam. Play the music for the class.

2. Terry is deeply troubled whenever his father's eyes go "away, far away." Choose a scene in the story when this happens. With a partner, adopt the roles of father and son, study the emotions conveyed in the scene, and perform the scene as a **minidrama** for the class.

WORDS TO KNOW

Review the Words to Know at the bottom of the selection pages. On your paper, write the word or phrase that best answers the question.

1. Is the tone of a **chant** most likely to be flat, lively, or varied?
2. Do people who **persist** when things get rough show cowardice, determination, or laziness?
3. If a company were to **founder**, would it be growing larger, electing a new president, or collapsing?
4. Is a lecture described as **dry** likely to be stirring, intelligent, or uninteresting?
5. Which sight in a city could be accurately described as **inert**—a statue, a subway train, or a flock of pigeons?

Words to Know

1. flat
2. determination
3. collapsing
4. uninteresting
5. statue

Reteaching/Reinforcement
- *Unit Five Resource Book*, p. 44

GARY PAULSEN

Paulsen's passionate opinions about reading may stem from his positive experiences with the friendly librarian who gave him his first library card. "She didn't care if I looked right, wore the right clothes, dated the right girls, was popular at sports—none of those prejudices existed at the public library," he recalls.

In the following years, Paulsen worked as a soldier, a rancher, and an animal trapper. As a trapper for the state of Minnesota, Paulsen was given four sled dogs to help him with his work. However, the time spent with these dogs convinced him that he could no longer kill animals; so he quit trapping and began to write. Paulsen has written often about sled dogs, many of which he now considers part of the family. Some students may have read Paulsen's book *Woodsong*.

AUTHOR BACKGROUND
Gary Paulsen What events caused Gary Paulsen to become a writer? Students may be surprised by the answer he gives in this film. As Paulsen tells it, he became a writer because of a friendly librarian and a very cold night.

Side A, Frame 47017

GARY PAULSEN

1939–

According to the National Council of Teachers of English, Gary Paulsen is one of the most important writers of young adult literature in the world. Paulsen has written 130 fiction and nonfiction books and more than 200 short stories and articles for adults and children. On a bet, he once wrote 11 short stories and articles in four days and sold them all.

Paulsen based his first book, *The Special War*, on interviews with Vietnam veterans. Many of his later works feature teenage characters who find self-awareness through challenging tests of survival in the wilderness. *Dogsong*, for example, is based on his own experience of competing in the Iditarod, a grueling 1,200-mile dogsled race across Alaska. Paulsen has received countless awards, including three prestigious Newbery Medals.

Life has not always been rewarding for the author, however. He spent an unhappy childhood living with alcoholic parents and a series of relatives. According to Paulsen, "I was an 'army brat,' and it was a miserable life." In school, he says, "I was a geek, a nerd, a dweeb. . . . I was the last kid chosen for sports, barely got through high school, didn't have a girlfriend until I was in the army. I would skip school and go fishing or hunting." The one piece of advice he gives young people is to "read like a wolf eats. Read what they tell you not to read and read when they tell you not to. Read all the time."

Paulsen currently spends most of his time on his 44-foot sloop, which he plans to sail across the Pacific Ocean. When he is not on his boat, he lives in northern Minnesota or New Mexico.

OTHER WORKS *Dancing Carl, Hatchet, The Island, The Winter Room, The River,* the Culpepper Adventure Series, the Gary Paulsen World of Adventure Series   Extended Reading

- AUTHOR BACKGROUND

STOP THE SUN   647

Alternative Activities

1. Encourage students to reread the passage in which Terry's father recounts his memories. Have students make a list of words that concisely describe the emotional tone of these recollections. Then have them survey as much music as possible, in order to find or compose a selection that conveys the emotional tone of the words included on the list. You may wish to suggest that students survey both folk music (Joan Baez, Pete Seeger, and Bob Dylan) and rock music (the Rolling Stones, Jefferson Airplane, and the Doors) of the 1960s.

2. The student playing Terry's father should decide exactly what images will pass before his or her eyes during the scene. Encourage this student to perform the scene in a kind of self-made isolation. The student playing Terry, on the other hand, should be sharply attuned to each nuance and change in his father's appearance and behavior.

OVERVIEW

Objectives

- To understand and appreciate a short story about the relationship between a girl and her disabled brother
- To understand the process of analyzing
- To identify and understand slang
- To express understanding of the short story through a choice of writing forms, including a paragraph and an article
- To extend understanding of the story through a variety of multimodal and cross-disciplinary activities

Skills

READING SKILLS/ STRATEGIES
- Summarizing

THE WRITER'S STYLE
- Choosing the right voice

GRAMMAR
- Irregular verbs

LITERARY CONCEPTS
- Slang
- Conflict

SPELLING
- The sound *f*

SPEAKING, LISTENING, AND VIEWING
- Readers theater
- Group discussion
- Oral presentation

Cross-Curricular Connections

PHYSICAL EDUCATION
- The Special Olympics

MATHEMATICS
- The metric system

SCIENCE CONNECTION

Hydrocephalus Diagrams of a normal human brain and a brain with hydrocephalus will help students understand this rare and debilitating disorder, which affects Raymond in "Raymond's Run."

Side A, Frame 52836

PREVIEWING

FICTION

Raymond's Run
Toni Cade Bambara

Activating Prior Knowledge
PERSONAL CONNECTION

This story is about a young girl named Squeaky who has responsibility for her mentally disabled older brother. Imagine yourself in a situation like this. With your classmates, discuss what you think your relationship with your brother might be like and how you would handle the responsibility of caring for him. How would you react if someone made fun of him? If you in fact have a disabled brother or sister, describe your relationship with him or her.

Building Background
SCIENCE CONNECTION

Squeaky's brother Raymond has a medical condition known as *hydrocephalus* (hī'drō-sĕf'ə-ləs), also called "water on the brain." The symptoms of this disorder include a swelling of the head caused by the excessive amount of fluid that collects in the skull. In the disorder's severest form, the excess fluid damages the brain and affects mental processes, as in Raymond's case.

Hydrocephalus may be caused by an infection, a tumor, a major head injury, or a malformation of the brain before birth. Childhood hydrocephalus is fairly rare, occurring in only about 1 of every 1,000 children. If detected early, hydrocephalus can be treated successfully with surgery.

Setting a Purpose/Active Reading
READING CONNECTION

Analyzing The process of breaking something down into its elements and examining each element is called analyzing. Analyzing literature can be a valuable way of enhancing your understanding of it. To analyze the plot of a work of fiction, for example, you might divide the plot into an exposition, a series of complications, a climax, and a resolution.

In this story, you will read about Squeaky's relationships with her brother and the girls in her neighborhood. As you read, analyze the relationships by thinking of words that describe how Squeaky relates to each person. Jot the words down in a chart like the one shown, then discuss with the class how you would characterize Squeaky's relationships.

Analyzing Squeaky's Relationships	
Character	**Descriptive Words**
Raymond	
Gretchen	
Cynthia	
Mary Louise	
Rosie	

• SCIENCE CONNECTION

648 UNIT FIVE PART 2: VITAL CONNECTIONS

PRINT AND MEDIA RESOURCES

UNIT FIVE RESOURCE BOOK
Strategic Reading: Literature, p. 47
Reading SkillBuilder, p. 48
Spelling SkillBuilder, p. 49

GRAMMAR MINI-LESSONS
Transparencies, p. 20
Copymasters, pp. 27–28

ACCESS FOR STUDENTS ACQUIRING ENGLISH
Selection Summaries
Reading and Writing Support

FORMAL ASSESSMENT
Selection Test, pp. 121–122
 Test Generator

 **AUDIO LIBRARY**
See Reference Card

 **LASERLINKS**
Science Connection
Sports Connection

Raymond's Run

by Toni Cade Bambara

I don't have much work to do around the house like some girls. My mother does that. And I don't have to earn my pocket money by hustling; George runs errands for the big boys and sells Christmas cards. And anything else that's got to get done, my father does. All I have to do in life is mind my brother Raymond, which is enough.

SUMMARY

Squeaky lives in a tough, inner-city neighborhood and cares about two things: her disabled brother Raymond and running. Raymond runs with her when she practices, and she defends him—and herself—against ridicule. She plans to win first place, as usual, in the May Day race. Trading insults with her rival Gretchen, Squeaky wonders why few girls she knows have real friendships. The race starts, and Gretchen keeps up with Squeaky. For the first time, Raymond runs his own unofficial race behind a fence on the sidelines. Squeaky realizes that Raymond's achievement means more to her than winning and that she can win at many things other than running. When Squeaky is named winner, she and Gretchen exchange smiles of friendly respect.

Thematic Link: *Vital Connections* A girl's loyalty to, and love for, her brother lead her to make important discoveries about him and about herself.

STRATEGIC READING FOR
Less-Proficient Readers

Set a Purpose Encourage students to become involved in the story by sharing their own experiences with caring for someone or something. Then have students read to find out the sport at which Squeaky excels, as well as who hopes to beat her.

Use **UNIT FIVE RESOURCE BOOK**, p. 47, for guidance in reading the selection.

CUSTOMIZING FOR
Students Acquiring English

- Use **ACCESS FOR STUDENTS ACQUIRING ENGLISH**, *Reading and Writing Support*.
- Students may have trouble with some of the slang words used by the narrator. You may wish to preteach unfamiliar words or phrases found in the story, or pause during reading to define terms.
- ① Define *mind* as "watch and be responsible for; look after."

WORDS TO KNOW

prodigy (prŏd′ə-jē) *n.* a person with an exceptional talent (p. 651)

Art Note

Petite Fille by Loïs Mailou Jones Jones (1905–) was one of the first African-American painters to use African imagery in her work. Since 1960, her work has included Haitian scenes and figures. *Petite fille* is French for "little girl."

Reading the Art *Do you think that the girl in the portrait looks like the picture you have of Squeaky in your mind? If not, how would you describe Squeaky's appearance?*

CUSTOMIZING FOR
Gifted and Talented Students

Have students assess how Squeaky's responsibility for her brother shapes her character. Ask if they think it factors into her success as a runner. *(Possible response: Squeaky's responsibility for Raymond shows that she is a mature and capable person. Her dedication to running is further evidence of her maturity.)*

CUSTOMIZING FOR
Students Acquiring English

② Point out that *'cause* is short for *because*.

③ Paraphrase the expression "in my face" as "right in front of me, face to face."

Literary Concept:
POINT OF VIEW

A Ask students what the point of view is, and how they can tell. *(It is first person, because the narrator tells the story in her own words and uses the pronouns* I, me, *and* my.*)*

Literary Concept: **SETTING**

B Have students identify the clues that suggest the story's setting. *(Possible responses: The fire hydrants suggest a city; Amsterdam Avenue is a street in New York City.)*

Petite Fille [Little girl] (1982), Loïs Mailou Jones. Watercolor, 24″ × 30″. Courtesy of the artist.

② Sometimes I slip and say my little brother Raymond. But as any fool can see he's much bigger and he's older too. But a lot of people call him my little brother 'cause he needs looking after 'cause he's not quite right. And a lot of smart mouths got lots to say about that too, especially when George was minding him. But now, if anybody has anything to say to Raymond, anything to say about his big head,[1] they have to come by me. And I don't play the ③ dozens[2] or believe in standing around with somebody in my face doing a lot of talking. I much rather just knock you down and take my chances even if I am a little girl with skinny arms and a squeaky voice, which is how I got the name Squeaky. And if things get too rough, I run. And as anybody can tell you, I'm the fastest thing on two feet. There is no track meet that I don't win the first place medal. I use to win the twenty-yard dash when I was a little kid in kindergarten. Nowadays, it's the fifty-yard dash. And tomorrow I'm subject to run the quarter-meter relay all by myself and come in first, second, and third. The big kids call me Mercury[3] 'cause I'm the swiftest thing in the neighborhood. Everybody knows that—except two people who know better, my father and me. He can beat me to Amsterdam Avenue with me having a two-fire-hydrant head start and him running with his hands in his pockets

A

B

---

1. **big head:** enlarged skull (a result of Raymond's hydrocephalus).
2. **play the dozens:** exchange rhyming insults.
3. **Mercury:** in Roman mythology, the swift messenger of the gods.

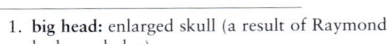

Mini-Lesson — The Writer's Style

CHOOSING THE RIGHT VOICE Remind students that the writing they do in a journal will read very differently from a research report. Nonetheless, if they express their thoughts and feelings in words that come naturally to them, their personal voices will come through in all their writing.

In "Raymond's Run," the author tells the story in the voice of her main character, Squeaky. Rather than altering Squeaky's natural voice to make it sound more proper or impressive, Bambara has Squeaky speak colloquially, so that her personality shines through.

Application Have students write a short narrative about some conflict between them and another person. To help students write in their own natural voices, have them imagine they are describing the conflict to a close friend.

Reteaching/Reinforcement

Developing a Personal Voice, pp. 316–317

and whistling. But that's private information. 'Cause can you imagine some thirty-five-year-old man stuffing himself into PAL shorts to race little kids? So as far as everyone's concerned, I'm the fastest and that goes for Gretchen, too, who has put out the tale that she is going to win the first-place medal this year. Ridiculous. In the second place, she's got short legs. In the third place, she's got freckles. In the first place, no one can beat me and that's all there is to it.

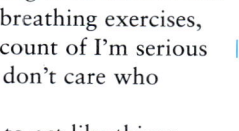

The big kids call me Mercury 'cause I'm the swiftest thing in the neighborhood.

I'm standing on the corner admiring the weather and about to take a stroll down Broadway so I can practice my breathing exercises, and I've got Raymond walking on the inside close to the buildings, 'cause he's subject to fits of fantasy and starts thinking he's a circus performer and that the curb is a tightrope strung high in the air. And sometimes after a rain he likes to step down off his tightrope right into the gutter and slosh around getting his shoes and cuffs wet. Then I get hit when I get home. Or sometimes if you don't watch him he'll dash across traffic to the island in the middle of Broadway and give the pigeons a fit. Then I have to go behind him apologizing to all the old people sitting around trying to get some sun and getting all upset with the pigeons fluttering around them, scattering their newspapers and upsetting the wax-paper lunches in their laps. So I keep Raymond on the inside of me, and he plays like he's driving a stagecoach which is O.K. by me so long as he doesn't run me over or interrupt my breathing exercises, which I have to do on account of I'm serious about my running, and I don't care who knows it.

Now some people like to act like things come easy to them, won't let on that they practice. Not me. I'll high-prance down 34th Street like a rodeo pony to keep my knees strong even if it does get my mother uptight so that she walks ahead like she's not with me, don't know me, is all by herself on a shopping trip, and I am somebody else's crazy child. Now you take Cynthia Procter for instance. She's just the opposite. If there's a test tomorrow, she'll say something like, "Oh, I guess I'll play handball this afternoon and watch television tonight," just to let you know she ain't thinking about the test. Or like last week when she won the spelling bee for the millionth time, "A good thing you got 'receive,' Squeaky, 'cause I would have got it wrong. I completely forgot about the spelling bee." And she'll clutch the lace on her blouse like it was a narrow escape. Oh, brother. But of course when I pass her house on my early morning trots around the block, she is practicing the scales on the piano over and over and over. Then in music class she always lets herself get bumped around so she falls accidentally on purpose onto the piano stool and is so surprised to find herself sitting there that she decides just for fun to try out the ole keys. And what do you know—Chopin's waltzes[4] just spring out of her fingertips and she's the most surprised thing in the world. A regular prodigy. I could kill people like that. I stay up all night studying the words for the spelling

---

4. **Chopin's** (shō-pănz′) **waltzes:** works by the 19th-century pianist and composer Frédéric Chopin.

WORDS TO KNOW
prodigy (prŏd′ə-jē) *n.* a person with an exceptional talent

Active Reading: CONNECT

F Ask students how they would feel about being responsible for Raymond's care.

CUSTOMIZING FOR
Students Acquiring English

7 Students may not recognize the writer's comparison of the confrontation between Squeaky and the other girls to a showdown between gunfighters. Explain that Dodge City, Kansas, became famous for gunfights in its streets and saloons in the 1870s and 1880s. At the time, the frontier town was the commercial center for the huge cattle business in the Southwest.

8 Paraphrase this sentence as "She doesn't want to argue. She'd rather just fight, since arguments turn into physical fights anyway."

Literary Concept: CONFLICT

G Ask students why Squeaky is so ready to fight with these girls. *(Possible response: She dislikes Gretchen because she is her rival in the May Day race, and Mary Louise because she is disloyal, ungrateful, and backbiting. She thinks Rosie is fat, stupid, and insensitive to Raymond.)*

Active Reading: CLARIFY

H Ask students what Squeaky means by saying that Gretchen is "the only one talking in this ventriloquist-dummy routine." If they need help, you might wish to share the following thought processes with them.

Think-Aloud Model *It seems clear from Squeaky's tone that she doesn't think much of the other two girls. As far as she's concerned, she and Gretchen are the only two people there. Perhaps because she views Gretchen as a serious opponent, she sees the other girls as mere puppets or dummies.*

---

bee. And you can see me any time of day practicing running. I never walk if I can trot, and shame on Raymond if he can't keep up. But of course he does, 'cause if he hangs back someone's liable to walk up to him and get smart, or take his allowance from him, or ask him where he got that great big pumpkin head. People are so stupid sometimes.

> **I am not a strawberry.
> I do not dance on my toes.
> I run.**

So I'm strolling down Broadway breathing out and breathing in on counts of seven, which is my lucky number, and here comes Gretchen and her sidekicks: Mary Louise, who used to be a friend of mine when she first moved to Harlem from Baltimore and got beat up by everybody till I took up for her on account of her mother and my mother used to sing in the same choir when they were young girls, but people ain't grateful, so now she hangs out with the new girl Gretchen and talks about me like a dog; and Rosie, who is as fat as I am skinny and has a big mouth where Raymond is concerned and is too stupid to know that there is not a big deal of difference between herself and Raymond and that she can't afford to throw stones. So they are steady coming up Broadway and I see right away that it's going to be one of those Dodge City scenes 'cause the street ain't that big and they're close to the buildings just as we are. First I think I'll step into the candy store and look over the new comics and let them pass. But that's chicken and I've got a reputation to consider. So then I think I'll just walk straight on through them or over them if necessary. But as they get to me, they slow down. I'm ready to fight, 'cause like I said I don't feature a whole lot of chitchat, I much prefer to just knock you down right from the jump and save everybody a lotta precious time.

"You signing up for the May Day races?" smiles Mary Louise, only it's not a smile at all. A dumb question like that doesn't deserve an answer. Besides, there's just me and Gretchen standing there really, so no use wasting my breath talking to shadows.

"I don't think you're going to win this time," says Rosie, trying to signify with her hands on her hips all salty, completely forgetting that I have whupped her behind many times for less salt than that.

"I always win 'cause I'm the best," I say straight at Gretchen who is, as far as I'm concerned, the only one talking in this ventriloquist-dummy routine.[5] Gretchen smiles, but it's not a smile, and I'm thinking that girls never really smile at each other because they don't know how and don't want to know how and there's probably no one to teach us how, 'cause grown-up girls don't know either. Then they all look at Raymond who has just brought his mule team to a standstill. And they're about to see what trouble they can get into through him.

"What grade you in now, Raymond?"

"You got anything to say to my brother, you say it to me, Mary Louise Williams of Raggedy Town, Baltimore."

"What are you, his mother?" sasses Rosie.

"That's right, Fatso. And the next word out of anybody and I'll be their mother too." So they just stand there and Gretchen shifts from one leg to the other and so do they. Then Gretchen puts her hands on her hips and is

---

5. **ventriloquist-dummy routine:** Squeaky thinks that all the girls are speaking Gretchen's thoughts, like dummies being controlled by a ventriloquist.

Mini-Lesson Literary Concepts

REVIEWING CONFLICT Remind students that conflict is a struggle between two opposing forces. In an external conflict, a character struggles against some outside person or force. Internal conflict occurs when the struggle is within the character. Point out, for example, that Squeaky spends much of the story in external conflict with Gretchen, Mary Louise, Rosie, and others. The possibility that Squeaky also feels an internal conflict—which sets her sense of responsibility for Raymond against her own athletic ambitions—surfaces at the end of the story.

Application Have students list the conflicts they see in "Raymond's Run," identifying each as external or internal, and providing details that show the nature of each struggle. Have volunteers share their lists, and then ask students to decide which conflicts are the most important ones in the story.

about to say something with her freckle-face self but doesn't. Then she walks around me looking me up and down but keeps walking up Broadway, and her sidekicks follow her. So me and Raymond smile at each other and he says, "Gidyap," to his team and I continue with my breathing exercises, strolling down Broadway toward the ice man on 145th with not a care in the world 'cause I am Miss Quicksilver[6] herself.

I take my time getting to the park on May Day because the track meet is the last thing on the program. The biggest thing on the program is the May Pole dancing, which I can do without, thank you, even if my mother thinks it's a shame I don't take part and act like a girl for a change. You'd think my mother'd be grateful not to have to make me a white organdy dress with a big satin sash and buy me new white baby-doll shoes that can't be taken out of the box till the big day. You'd think she'd be glad her daughter ain't out there prancing around a May Pole getting the new clothes all dirty and sweaty and trying to act like a fairy or a flower or whatever you're supposed to be when you should be trying to be yourself, whatever that is, which is, as far as I am concerned, a poor Black girl who really can't afford to buy shoes and a new dress you only wear once a lifetime 'cause it won't fit next year.

I was once a strawberry in a Hansel and Gretel pageant when I was in nursery school and didn't have no better sense than to dance on tiptoe with my arms in a circle over my head doing umbrella steps and being a perfect fool just so my mother and father could come dressed up and clap. You'd think they'd know better than to encourage that kind of nonsense. I am not a strawberry. I do not dance on my toes. I run. That is what I am all about. So I always come late to the May Day program, just in time to get my number pinned on and lay in the grass till they announce the fifty-yard dash.

I put Raymond in the little swings, which is a tight squeeze this year and will be impossible next year. Then I look around for Mr. Pearson, who pins the numbers on. I'm really looking for Gretchen, if you want to know the truth, but she's not around. The park is jam-packed. Parents in hats and corsages and breast-pocket handkerchiefs peeking up. Kids in white dresses and light-blue suits. The parkees[7] unfolding chairs and chasing the rowdy kids from Lenox[8] as if they had no right to be there. The big guys with their caps on backwards, leaning against the fence swirling the basketballs on the tips of their fingers, waiting for all these crazy people to clear out the park so they can play. Most of the kids in my class are carrying bass drums and glockenspiels[9] and flutes. You'd think they'd put in a few bongos or something for real like that.

Then here comes Mr. Pearson with his clipboard and his cards and pencils and whistles and safety pins and 50 million other things he's always dropping all over the place with his clumsy self. He sticks out in a crowd because he's on stilts. We used to call him Jack and the Beanstalk to get him mad. But I'm the only one that can outrun him and get away, and I'm too grown for that silliness now.

"Well, Squeaky," he says, checking my name off the list and handing me number seven and two pins. And I'm thinking he's got no right to call me Squeaky if I can't call him Beanstalk.

"Hazel Elizabeth Deborah Parker," I correct him and tell him to write it down on his board.

---

6. **Miss Quicksilver:** a reference to the speed with which quicksilver (the liquid metal mercury) flows.
7. **parkees:** park employees.
8. **Lenox:** a street in the Harlem section of New York City.
9. **glockenspiels** (glŏk′ən-spēlz′): musical instruments having tuned metal bars that are played with light hammers.

RAYMOND'S RUN   653

Mini-Lesson   Reading Skills/Strategies

SUMMARIZING Remind students that a summary retells the main ideas in a piece of writing. Point out that an effective summary includes only the key points, omitting unimportant details.

Application Refer students to the charts they made to analyze Squeaky's relationships (see page 648). Ask them to select one character and to summarize their analyses of Squeaky's relationship with that character. Encourage students to incorporate their descriptive words into their summaries. You may wish to pair students and have them exchange and compare summaries.

Reteaching/Reinforcement
- *Unit Five Resource Book*, p. 48

STRATEGIC READING FOR
Less-Proficient Readers

I Make sure that students are clear about details of Squeaky's relationship with her rivals.

- Do you think Squeaky would like to be friends with the other girls? Why or why not? *(Possible responses: Yes, because she seems to wish that Mary Louise were still her friend, and she may feel jealous of Gretchen. No, because she despises the way they treat Raymond.)* **Drawing Conclusions**

- How does the confrontation between Squeaky and her rivals turn out? *(The girls back off and walk away.)* **Making Generalizations**

Set a Purpose Have students read to learn what Squeaky thinks about right before the start of a race.

Active Reading: CONNECT

J Ask students whether they agree with Squeaky's belief that girls are encouraged to dress up and engage in silly activities. Ask them if they feel that these activities influence the way girls act.

CUSTOMIZING FOR
Multiple Learning Styles

K **Spatial or Graphic Learners** Have students consider Squeaky's defiant declaration, "I am not a strawberry." Encourage them to think of some other non-human entity with which she might be more content to be compared. Invite students to draw or paint a portrait of Squeaky in this other identity.

Critical Thinking: HYPOTHESIZING

L Have students offer their ideas on why Squeaky might be looking for Gretchen. *(Possible response: She may wish to assess whether her rival seems nervous or confident.)*

CUSTOMIZING FOR
Students Acquiring English

9 Mr. Pearson is not really on stilts. Explain that Squeaky describes him this way because of his long legs.

CUSTOMIZING FOR
Students Acquiring English

10 Paraphrase the idiomatic expression that the new girl will give Squeaky "a run for your money" as "the new girl will provide a real challenge."

11 Ask a volunteer to paraphrase "I'm so burnt." (*I'm so angry.*)

Critical Thinking:
MAKING JUDGMENTS

M Ask students to share their opinions of Mr. Pearson's implied suggestion. Ask if they think it would be a good idea for Squeaky to let Gretchen win the race. (*Possible response: It would be a terrible idea, because Gretchen's victory would be worthless if Squeaky were not trying.*)

Literary Concept: SLANG

N Encourage students to find the two examples of slang in this paragraph. (*"psyching"* and *"do my thing"*) Check their understanding of these slang terms by having them reword them in standard English. (*Possible responses: psyching—intimidating someone mentally; do my thing—do my job, do what I do best, do what comes naturally to me, run the race*)

Active Reading: PREDICT

O Invite students to make predictions about the outcome of the race.

"Well, Hazel Elizabeth Deborah Parker, going to give someone else a break this year?" I squint at him real hard to see if he is seriously thinking I should lose the race on purpose just to give someone else a break. "Only six girls running this time," he continues, shaking his head sadly like it's my fault all of New York didn't turn out in sneakers. "That new girl should give you a run for your money." He looks around the park for Gretchen like a periscope in a submarine movie. "Wouldn't it be a nice gesture if you were . . . to ahhh . . ."

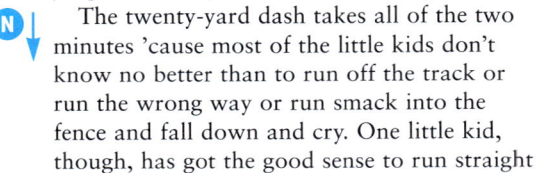

Grownups got a lot of nerve sometimes.

I give him such a look he couldn't finish putting that idea into words. Grownups got a lot of nerve sometimes. I pin number seven to myself and stomp away, I'm so burnt. And I go straight for the track and stretch out on the grass while the band winds up with "Oh, the Monkey Wrapped His Tail Around the Flag Pole," which my teacher calls by some other name. The man on the loudspeaker is calling everyone over to the track and I'm on my back looking at the sky, trying to pretend I'm in the country, but I can't, because even grass in the city feels hard as sidewalk, and there's just no pretending you are anywhere but in a "concrete jungle" as my grandfather says.

The twenty-yard dash takes all of the two minutes 'cause most of the little kids don't know no better than to run off the track or run the wrong way or run smack into the fence and fall down and cry. One little kid, though, has got the good sense to run straight for the white ribbon up ahead so he wins. Then the second-graders line up for the thirty-yard dash and I don't even bother to turn my head to watch 'cause Raphael Perez always wins. He wins before he even begins by psyching the runners, telling them they're going to trip on their shoelaces and fall on their faces or lose their shorts or something, which he doesn't really have to do since he is very fast, almost as fast as I am. After that is the forty-yard dash which I used to run when I was in first grade. Raymond is hollering from the swings 'cause he knows I'm about to do my thing 'cause the man on the loudspeaker has just announced the fifty-yard dash, although he might just as well be giving a recipe for angel food cake 'cause you can hardly make out what he's saying for the static. I get up and slip off my sweatpants and then I see Gretchen standing at the starting line, kicking her legs out like a pro. Then as I get into place I see that ole Raymond is on line on the other side of the fence, bending down with his fingers on the ground just like he knew what he was doing. I was going to yell at him but then I didn't. It burns up your energy to holler.

Every time, just before I take off in a race, I always feel like I'm in a dream, the kind of dream you have when you're sick with fever and feel all hot and weightless. I dream I'm flying over a sandy beach in the early morning sun, kissing the leaves of the trees as I fly by. And there's always the smell of apples, just like in the country when I was little and used to think I was a choo-choo train, running through the fields of corn and chugging up the hill to the orchard. And all the time I'm dreaming this, I get lighter and lighter until I'm flying over the beach again, getting blown through the sky like a feather that weighs nothing at all. But once I spread my fingers in the dirt and crouch over the Get on Your Mark, the dream goes and I am solid again and am telling

654 UNIT FIVE PART 2: VITAL CONNECTIONS

Mini-Lesson  Grammar

Present	Past	Past Participle
begin	began	(have) begun
bring	brought	(have) brought
fall	fell	(have) fallen

IRREGULAR VERBS Remind students that irregular verbs do not follow the regular pattern of adding -d or -ed to form the past and past participle. For many irregular verbs, the past and past participle are spelled the same. Share the examples of irregular verbs on the chalkboard with students.

Application Have students change the verbs to the correct tense in the following sentences.
1. Yesterday I bring Raymond to the park.
2. Squeaky has begin to feel uncomfortable with the way people treat Raymond.
3. Raymond fall into a puddle.

Reteaching/Reinforcement
• *Grammar Mini-Lesson* copymasters pp. 27–28, transparencies p. 20

 **The Writer's Craft**
Irregular Verbs, p. 480

Visa (1951), Stuart Davis. Oil on canvas, 40" × 52". The Museum of Modern Art, New York, gift of Mrs. Gertrud A. Mellon. Copyright ©1996 Estate of Stuart Davis/Licensed by VAGA, New York. Photograph copyright © 1995 The Museum of Modern Art, New York.

myself, Squeaky you must win, you must win, you are the fastest thing in the world, you can even beat your father up Amsterdam if you really try. And then I feel my weight coming back just behind my knees then down to my feet then into the earth and the pistol shot explodes in my blood and I am off and weightless again, flying past the other runners, my arms pumping up and down and the whole world is quiet except for the crunch as I zoom over the gravel in the track. I glance to my left and there is no one. To the right, a blurred Gretchen, who's got her chin jutting out as if it would win the race all by itself. And on the other side of the fence is Raymond with his arms down to his side and the palms tucked up behind him, running in his very own style, and it's the first time I ever saw that and I almost stop to watch my brother Raymond on his first run. But the white ribbon is bouncing toward me and I tear past it, racing into the distance till my feet with a mind of their own start digging up footfuls of dirt and brake me short. Then all the kids standing on the side pile on me, banging me on the back and slapping my head with their May Day programs, for I have won again and everybody on 151st Street can walk tall for another year.

"In first place . . ." the man on the loudspeaker is clear as a bell now. But then he

RAYMOND'S RUN **655**

Art Note

Visa by Stuart Davis Stuart Davis (1894–1964) uses bright colors and short pieces of text to create a work that is suggestive of contemporary urban life. In its use of words, the painting alludes to both advertising and graffiti. In fact, the painting has the overall appearance of a billboard.

Reading the Art Why do you think Davis titled this work *Visa*? What thoughts or feelings does the painting elicit in you? What do you think this painting is about?

Critical Thinking: ANALYZING

P Ask students whether they believe these thoughts and feelings of Squeaky's are intentional or involuntary. Could they be related in any way to her running successes? *(Possible responses: Squeaky doesn't intend to have these thoughts and feelings; they just happen. I think Squeaky consciously prepares for races this way; these fantasies probably help Squeaky loosen her muscles and visualize winning the race.)*

STRATEGIC READING FOR
Less-Proficient Readers

Q Ask students what Squeaky thinks about just before the pistol shot that starts the race. *(She "dreams" that she is flying over a beach, and then she thinks about how fast she is and how she must win the race.)* Summarizing

Set a Purpose Have students read to learn the outcome of the race and about Squeaky's personal discovery.

CUSTOMIZING FOR
Students Acquiring English

12 Explain that the narrator alludes to the pistol shot into the air to begin the race, and that the sound inspired the narrator to run.

Mini-Lesson Spelling

THE SOUND f Use the examples shown on the chalkboard to remind students that the sound *f* can be spelled four ways in English. First, there is the letter *f* itself; then there is the letter doubled as *ff*. However, in some words (all of which have Anglo-Saxon etymologies) the sound of *f* is spelled *gh*. In some other words (all of which have Greek etymologies) the sound of *f* is spelled *ph*.

Application Have students spell the following words as you recite them.
1. footfall
2. tough
3. cuff
4. photograph
5. freckles
6. telephone
7. stuff
8. finish

Ask students to look for more words that fit this pattern, and to add these words to their personal word lists.

Reteaching/Reinforcement
- *Unit Five Resource Book*, p. 49

The Sound f
feather   rough
off   phony

Literary Concept: CONFLICT

R Ask students whether they think Squeaky has felt any internal conflict regarding Raymond. If so, ask how they would define this conflict. *(Possible response: As soon as the idea of Raymond as a runner dawns on her, Squeaky becomes unusually excited. After having been focused on her own running for some time, she proposes a handful of different courses for her own "career." This dramatic change suggests that she feels internal conflict between her fierce desire for athletic excellence and her desire for Raymond to be something more than a tagalong.)*

STRATEGIC READING FOR
Less-Proficient Readers

S Ask students to explain the outcome of the race and what Squeaky discovers about herself. *(After some confusion, it is announced that Squeaky has won the race. More important, Squeaky learns that she cares as much about Raymond's achievements as her own.)* Summarizing/Drawing Conclusions

CUSTOMIZING FOR
Gifted and Talented Students

Have students discuss the ways caring for those who are less able than we are—whether because of age or some physical or mental disability—can be a meaningful learning experience.

COMPREHENSION CHECK

1. Why does Squeaky sometimes call Raymond her "little brother?" *(because he is mentally disabled and needs caretaking)*
2. Who is Squeaky's main rival? *(Gretchen)*
3. Who wins the May Day race? *(Squeaky)*
4. What does Squeaky realize about Raymond after the race? *(He would make a good runner.)*

---

pauses and the loudspeaker starts to whine. Then static. And I lean down to catch my breath and here comes Gretchen walking back, for she's overshot the finish line too, huffing and puffing with her hands on her hips taking it slow, breathing in steady time like a real pro and I sort of like her a little for the first time. "In first place . . ." and then three or four voices get all mixed up on the loudspeaker and I dig my sneaker into the grass and stare at Gretchen who's staring back, we both wondering just who did win. I can hear old Beanstalk arguing with the man on the loudspeaker and then a few others running their mouths about what the stopwatches say. Then I hear Raymond yanking at the fence to call me and I wave to shush him, but he keeps rattling the fence like a gorilla in a cage like in them gorilla movies, but then like a dancer or something he starts climbing up nice and easy but very fast. And it occurs to me, watching how smoothly he climbs hand over hand and remembering how he looked running with his arms down to his side and with the wind pulling his mouth back and his teeth showing and all, it occurred to me that Raymond would make a very fine runner. Doesn't he always keep up with me on my trots? And he surely knows how to breathe in counts of seven 'cause he's always doing it at the dinner table, which drives my brother George up the wall. And I'm smiling to beat the band 'cause if I've lost this race, or if me and Gretchen tied, or even if I've won, I can always retire as a runner and begin a whole new career as a coach with Raymond as my champion. After all, with a little more study I can beat Cynthia and her phony self at the spelling bee. And if I bugged my mother, I could get piano lessons and become a star. And I have a big rep as the baddest thing around. And I've got a roomful of ribbons and medals and awards. But what has Raymond got to call his own?

So I stand there with my new plans, laughing out loud by this time as Raymond jumps down from the fence and runs over with his teeth showing and his arms down to the side, which no one before him has quite mastered as a running style. And by the time he comes over I'm jumping up and down so glad to see him—my brother Raymond, a great runner in the family tradition. But of course everyone thinks I'm jumping up and down because the men on the loudspeaker have finally gotten themselves together and compared notes and are announcing, "In first place—Miss Hazel Elizabeth Deborah Parker." (Dig that.) "In second place—Miss Gretchen P. Lewis." And I look over at Gretchen, wondering what the "P." stands for. And I smile. 'Cause she's good, no doubt about it. Maybe she'd like to help me coach Raymond; she obviously is serious about running, as any fool can see. And she nods to congratulate me and then she smiles. And I smile. We stand there with this big smile of respect between us. It's about as real a smile as girls can do for each other, considering we don't practice real smiling every day, you know, 'cause maybe we too busy being flowers or fairies or strawberries instead of something honest and worthy of respect . . . you know . . . like being people. ❖

Mini-Lesson: Speaking, Listening, and Viewing

READERS THEATER Point out to students that stories written in the first-person point of view—particularly those containing slang or other distinctive linguistic characteristics—are often especially effective when performed aloud.

Application Have students create a Readers Theater production using the text of "Raymond's Run." Students can play the parts of Squeaky, Raymond, Gretchen, Cynthia Proctor, Mary Louise, Rosie, and Mr. Pearson. One or more students can be responsible for providing sound and music effects, and one other student can direct the production. Suggest that students rewrite some of Squeaky's descriptions of encounters with other characters as dialogue.

RESPONDING OPTIONS

FROM PERSONAL RESPONSE TO CRITICAL ANALYSIS

REFLECT
1. What were your strongest impressions of Squeaky? Jot your thoughts in your notebook, or make a drawing of Squeaky as you imagine her to be.

RETHINK
Close Textual Reading

2. In what ways has Squeaky changed by the end of the story?
   Consider
   - her feelings about Raymond
   - her view of her rival
   - her view of herself

Thematic Link

3. Think about Squeaky's vital connection with Raymond. Would Squeaky be a different person if Raymond were not her brother? Explain your answer.

4. Review your analysis of Squeaky's relationships for the Reading Connection on page 648. What does each of her relationships with the other girls reveal about her personality?

RELATE
5. What attitudes toward disabled people are presented in "Raymond's Run"? Do you think these attitudes are typical of the ways in which people respond to disabled individuals?

Multimodal Learning
ANOTHER PATHWAY

Cooperative Learning
Think about the personal discovery with regard to Raymond that Squeaky has made by the end of the story. With a small group of classmates, brainstorm slogans that reflect this discovery. Then create an artistic presentation of each slogan and display the artwork in the classroom.

LITERARY CONCEPTS

Slang is a casual, informal form of language used more often in speaking than in writing. Slang terms may be new words, or they may be established words and phrases that have taken on new meanings. An example of slang in "Raymond's Run" is Squeaky's use of *uptight* to mean "tense" or "nervous."

Look back over the story for particularly colorful examples of slang, and read the examples aloud.

Then choose one passage containing slang and rewrite it in standard, formal English. Is the original better? Why or why not?

QUICKWRITES

1. Squeaky says, "I'm the fastest thing on two feet." What are *you* really good at? Write a **paragraph** that describes a skill that you feel very confident about.

2. Imagine that you are a sportswriter for your local newspaper. Write an **article** about Squeaky's May Day race. Be sure to cover the *who, what, when, where, why,* and *how* of the story. To add an element of human interest, you might mention Raymond's sideline run.

PORTFOLIO Save your writing. You may want to use it later as a springboard to a piece for your portfolio.

RAYMOND'S RUN **657**

From Personal Response to Critical Analysis

1. Responses will vary.
2. Possible responses: Squeaky focuses on Raymond's potential as a runner instead of her own. She comes to respect Gretchen. She realizes her future can contain other successes besides running.
3. Possible responses: No, because she would still have her competitive streak, temper, intelligence, and talent as a runner. Yes, she might be less defensive and ready to fight, or she might be more self-involved.
4. Possible response: Gretchen—reveals Squeaky's competitiveness and respect for others; Cynthia—reveals her genuineness and her contempt for pretense; Mary Louise—reveals her empathy; Rosie—reveals her loyalty to her brother, her intolerance.
5. Possible response: The story indicates that some people make fun of Raymond, reflecting an attitude of ridicule toward people with disabilities.

Another Pathway

Cooperative Learning One student might be designated as a group's integrator, to help students come to agreement on how to turn descriptions of Squeaky's thoughts and feelings into slogans. Each group member can then choose a slogan to illustrate.

Rubric

3 Full Accomplishment Students devise slogans that accurately convey some aspect of Squeaky's discovery, and they create imaginative illustrations of these slogans.

2 Substantial Accomplishment Students generate several slogans, some of which accurately convey some aspect of Squeaky's discovery, and they adequately illustrate these slogans.

1 Little or Partial Accomplishment Students struggle to think of and illustrate slogans relating to Squeaky's discovery.

Literary Concepts

Help students locate examples of slang, such as *smart mouths, play the dozens, in my face, regular, get smart,* and *hangs out.* Help students understand the value of each expression in the context of its use. You may also wish to refer to the support given for Students Acquiring English throughout the selection.

QuickWrites

1. Students might include their own ideas about why they are good at this activity and particular experiences in which they successfully demonstrated their skills.
2. Students' lead paragraph should include the "angle" of the story—its most compelling aspect—as well as the outcome of the race. In subsequent paragraphs they can describe in chronological order how the race developed.

The Writer's Craft

Effective Paragraphs, pp. 244–51
Eyewitness Report, pp. 50–59

Words to Know

Possible responses include: *remarkable, outstanding, driven, intelligent, genius,* and *young.* Encourage students who are having difficulty to consult a thesaurus.

Across the Curriculum

Physical Education *The Special Olympics* Students can do this research in the library with the aid of *Readers' Guide to Periodical Literature* and various indexes to newspapers for recent articles about the Special Olympics.

Mathematics *The Metric System* Students can use an encyclopedia, an almanac, a mathematics textbook, or a dictionary to learn that 50 meters is longer than 50 yards (a yard is 36 inches; a meter is 39.37 inches) and that a marathon is 26 miles and 385 yards (which equals 42.2 kilometers).

Literary Links

Although the protagonist of "A Man" is frightened and depressed at first, he transforms his self-doubting attitude into a confident and life-affirming one. Raymond in "Raymond's Run" seems not to have serious doubts or other emotional limitations. Both figures end up having strong, positive feelings about how they can live happily and productively in the world.

SPORTS CONNECTION
Athletes with Disabilities Many people with disabilities enjoy the competition and fun that sports provide. These photographs from the Special Olympics and the International Games for the Disabled show runners, skiers, and other athletes going for the gold.

Side A, Frame 52838

TONI CADE BAMBARA

"She gave me permission to wonder, to dawdle, to daydream," Bambara remarked about her mother. "My most indelible memory of 1948 is my mother coming upon me in the middle of the kitchen floor with my head in the clouds and my pencil on the paper and her mopping around me. . . . She thought it was wonderful that I could write things that almost made some kind of sense."

Multimodal Activities

ALTERNATIVE ACTIVITIES

With a partner, design a newspaper **advertisement** for a new business—Squeaky and Gretchen's coaching service. Think about what people you want to attract and what statements and images might persuade them to try the service.

ACROSS THE CURRICULUM

Physical Education Use library or Internet resources to research the Special Olympics. Try to find out who sponsors the competitions, where they are held, who competes, and what events are included. Report your findings to the class.

 Mathematics Today, the distances of many running events are measured in meters rather than yards. Which is longer, Squeaky's 50-yard race or a 50-meter race? By how much? What is the length of a marathon in miles and yards? in kilometers?

TONI CADE BAMBARA

Toni Cade Bambara believed that authors "are everyday people who write stories that come out of their neighborhoods." Like the characters in "Raymond's Run" and in many of her other short stories, she grew up in New York City. She wrote about African Americans who show family pride and a strong sense of community. In 1981, she won the American Book Award for her novel *The Salt Eaters*.

Bambara said, "Temperamentally, I move toward the short story because I'm a sprinter rather than a long-distance runner. I cannot sustain characters over a long period of time. Walking around, frying eggs, being a mother, shopping—I cannot have those char-

1939–1995

acters living in my house with me for more than a couple of weeks." Bambara credited her mother with having greatly influenced her work.

After attending college in New York City, Bambara studied theater and mime in Europe and dance and film in the United States. She planned recreational programs for the mentally ill and taught college English and African-American studies. During her later years she lived in Philadelphia, where she taught a writers' workshop, produced documentary videos, and was intensely involved in her community.
OTHER WORKS *Gorilla, My Love; The Seabirds Are Still Alive*

Extended Reading

 **LASERLINKS**
• SPORTS CONNECTION

658 UNIT FIVE PART 2: VITAL CONNECTIONS

Alternative Activities

Encourage students to analyze advertisements in various newspapers, magazines, and directories such as the Yellow Pages. Urge them to ask themselves questions about what services they would offer, what their overall strategy would be, whether the business would compete with any other local businesses, and what particular details or services might attract people's attention to such a business in your area. Suggest that students review one another's advertisements, checking for all the potential information a client might want to know. Then have students revise their work, incorporating one another's changes.

LITERARY LINKS

Look back at the poem "A Man" on page 434. Both Raymond and the man in the poem have disabilities. Compare the feelings or attitudes about living with disabilities that are conveyed by the two works.

WORDS TO KNOW

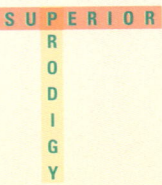

Review the meaning of the word **prodigy** in the selection. Using the model as a guide, write the word vertically on your paper. Use each of the seven letters to form a word that you associate with a prodigy. (One has been done as an example.) Share your results with classmates.

```
        S
      U
P R O D I G Y
      E
      R
      I
      O
      R
```
P
R
O
D
I
G
Y

PREVIEWING

FICTION

Keeping Time
Bill Meissner

Activating Prior Knowledge
PERSONAL CONNECTION

It is the dream of the narrator of this story to play on his high school's baseball team and eventually to become a major-league player. How do you feel about the team-sports program in your school? Consider the ways in which team sports are organized, the ways in which team members are selected, and the pros and cons of athletic competition in general. Record your thoughts in a chart like the one shown, then discuss your ideas with the class.

Team Sports in School	
Arguments For	**Arguments Against**

Building Background
PHYSICAL EDUCATION CONNECTION

For some teenagers, participation in team sports is essential to a fulfilling school career. Many students get involved in sports just for the fun of it; others see organized athletics as a springboard to a career in professional sports. What many young people may not realize is that team sports can be a way to learn important life skills. Accomplished coaches teach discipline, competitiveness, teamwork, and the importance of excellence—qualities that can be applied in almost any field or endeavor.

Too often, however, teenage athletes are encouraged to set their sights on careers in professional sports only to find their dreams dashed. Professional athletics is among the most competitive of careers. Only about 1 out of every 100,000 students who participate in high school athletics goes on to play professionally. Reggie Williams, a former National Football League star, says, "As a society, we have an obsession with sports and put too much emphasis on professional sports and all that big money. That is too dangerous a carrot because the opportunities are too few."

Setting a Purpose
WRITING CONNECTION

Write a description of one of your most important personal goals or dreams. Why is it important to you? How do you plan to attain it? Do you think your dream is likely to be realized?

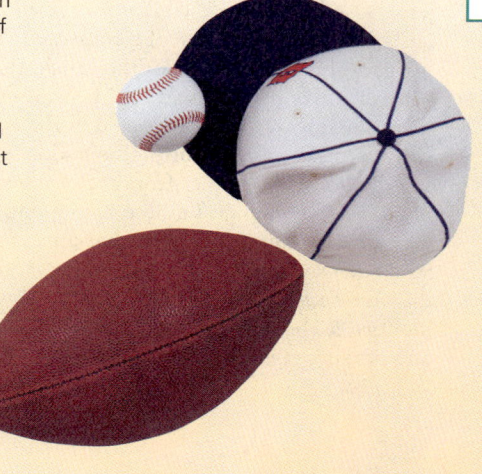

OVERVIEW

Objectives
- To understand and appreciate a short story about the way baseball connects three people across two decades
- To identify and understand the story's moral
- To express understanding of the short story through a choice of writing forms, including a paragraph, a pep talk, and a poem
- To extend understanding of the story through a variety of multimodal and cross-disciplinary activities

Skills

READING SKILLS/ STRATEGIES
- Making judgments

THE WRITER'S STYLE
- Chronological order

GRAMMAR
- Adjectives and adverbs

LITERARY CONCEPTS
- Moral
- Similes

SPELLING
- Silent letters

SPEAKING, LISTENING, AND VIEWING
- Group discussion
- Oral presentation

Cross-Curricular Connections

HISTORY
- Baseball's origins

SCIENCE
- Dissecting a baseball

PRINT AND MEDIA RESOURCES

UNIT FIVE RESOURCE BOOK
Strategic Reading: Literature, p. 53
Vocabulary SkillBuilder, p. 56
Reading SkillBuilder, p. 54
Spelling SkillBuilder, p. 55

GRAMMAR MINI–LESSONS
Transparencies, pp. 12, 13, 39, 40
Copymasters, pp. 19, 20

ACCESS FOR STUDENTS ACQUIRING ENGLISH
Selection Summaries
Reading and Writing Support

FORMAL ASSESSMENT
Selection Test, pp. 123–124
 Test Generator

 **AUDIO LIBRARY**
See Reference Card

LASERLINKS
Contemporary Connection

Keeping

by Bill Meissner

SUMMARY

Coach Brace chooses the narrator's best friend, Steve Lyon, to play on the freshman baseball team, but he does not choose the narrator. Angry and crushed, the narrator gives up his dream of becoming a professional baseball player and does not try out for the team again. He is left with the feeling that the coach is a mean man. Twenty years later, at a high-school reunion, the narrator talks with Coach Brace, who is very ill with cancer. The coach greets the narrator warmly and begins reminiscing about the narrator's days on the team, forgetting that the narrator was not on the team. They talk about baseball and about life. The narrator realizes that his own bitterness has blinded him to the coach's kindness and to the fun and character-building that are baseball's most meaningful rewards.

Thematic Link: Vital Connections A man's conversation with an old baseball coach helps him make an important discovery about enduring human values.

STRATEGIC READING FOR
Less-Proficient Readers

Set a Purpose Encourage students to become involved in the story by asking them to name activities for which they must try out or audition. Call on volunteers to tell how it feels to wait for the results. Then have students read to find out whether the narrator and his best friend make the team.

Use **UNIT FIVE RESOURCE BOOK**, p. 53, for guidance in reading the selection.

CUSTOMIZING FOR
Students Acquiring English

- Use **ACCESS FOR STUDENTS ACQUIRING ENGLISH**, Reading and Writing Support.
- Ask volunteers to explain the sport of baseball, including the meaning of terms such as "fielding grounders," "batting cages," "liner over third base," and so on.
- ① "Sheese" is an exclamation that is used for emphasis.

Sometimes the human heart is the only clock in the world that keeps true time.

Coach John Brace, a pile of team jerseys on his arm, leaned rhythmically left, then right, like a pendulum between the two rows of wooden benches. As he walked down the aisle of that high school locker room, Coach tossed jerseys to the boys he'd chosen for the freshman baseball team after a day of tryouts. I sat in my gym shorts at the end of the bench, the varnished wood sticky and cool beneath my thighs, and though it wasn't cold in the room, shivers rushed outward from the middle of my <u>spindly</u> body like ripples from the center of a pond. I felt as though I'd been sitting on that bench all my life, waiting for that one moment. As Coach rocked closer, I remember watching the blue-and-gold jerseys fluttering, in slow motion, to the outstretched hands of each boy, and praying my hands would be next.

I had practiced tirelessly for that one day of tryouts—I knew it would be my first chance to make a real baseball team. Sometimes, alone in a field behind a warehouse, I bounced a ball off the brick wall and fielded grounders. Sometimes, dropping quarters into the slot, I'd swing and swing in a batting cage until my shoulder muscles ached. But more often than not, during the summer days of seventh and eighth grades, I practiced with my best friend, Steve Lyon, at the old West School field until our crew cuts[1] glistened with sweat. "Sheese, we're improving," Steve often mused afterward as we sat beneath the shade of a billowing elm. "There's no way we won't make the team, man." ①

One day, after our usual routine of batting practice, I was goofing around in the outfield with my ball cap on sideways; I jumped and shook my arms in the air and howled at the

---

1. **crew cuts:** hairstyles in which the hair is cut very close to the head (so called because rowers wore such a style).

WORDS TO KNOW
spindly (spĭnd′lē) *adj.* slender and long in a way that suggests weakness

---

WORDS TO KNOW

benignly (bĭ-nīn′lē) *adv.* in a kind and gentle way (p. 664)
chasm (kăz′əm) *n.* a great difference in feelings or interests (p. 663)
diffused (dĭ-fyōōzd′) *adj.* spread-out; softened **diffuse** *v.* (p. 665)
spindly (spĭnd′lē) *adj.* slender and long in a way that suggests weakness (p. 660)
subtly (sŭt′lē) *adv.* in a way difficult to detect and not immediately obvious (p. 661)

Time

sky as Steve watched, laughing. In the middle of my act, Steve cut the laughter, then pointed subtly with his thumb and I looked behind me. My whole body went numb when I saw Coach Brace in his powder-blue car, watching me from the stoplight. Coach lifted one hand politely to wave to us as he drove off. Upset for the rest of that afternoon, I kept repeating to Steve how ridiculous I must have looked to the man who'd be our baseball coach next year. I knew Coach Brace was serious about baseball, and I cursed my luck that he'd driven by when I was acting stupid instead of when I was hitting a liner over third base or making one of my patented diving catches. I told Steve how I didn't look like a ballplayer but like some clowning kid who didn't care. "Don't worry," Steve assured me, "he'll never remember."

For Career Day in civics class that fall, leaning over my narrow-ruled paper, I scrawled an essay about how I planned to be a major league baseball player. Beneath the bright spotlight of my cone-shaped desk lamp, I wrote that I'd sign a pro baseball contract after high school, play a while in the minor leagues—maybe in nearby Madison or Wausau—then be called up to the majors. As I described each step of my career, the words flowed as easily as players running onto the field at the start of a game. To me, the logic and the progression of the essay seemed so simple, so undeniably true. When I was finished, I printed the title in tall, bold letters at the top: TOMORROW. At school the next morning, the civics teacher, Mrs. Griswald, handed the essay back to me, saying I had written it in pencil and I was supposed to write it in pen. Mrs. Griswald also jotted at the bottom of the essay, in red marker: *What if you don't make it???* As I recopied the essay that night with a black pen, I remember thinking to myself, *I'll make it. I will make it.*

In the locker room after freshman tryouts, we waited on the benches while Coach Brace unlocked the supply room. Somehow, nervous as I felt, I was still aware of the scents in the room: the smell of must[2] and the dank cement floor of the shower, the smell of leather where boys' palms had sweated into their gloves, the

---

2. **must:** staleness; mustiness.

WORDS TO KNOW   **subtly** (sŭt'lē) *adv.* in a way difficult to detect and not immediately obvious

661

Mini-Lesson — The Writer's Style

CHRONOLOGICAL ORDER Remind students that biographies, histories, and stories are usually told in chronological order—the order in which the events occurred. Point out that chronological order is also useful when explaining a process or giving directions.

Transitional words and phrases that express time can help make the order of events clear. For example, in the highlighted passage above, phrases such as "the next morning" and "that night" make it easy for the reader to keep track of the order of events. List on the chalkboard the transitional words and phrases shown here.

Application Have students write an essay describing an experience in which they were disappointed. Have them tell the story in chronological order, using transitional words and time references to keep the order of events clear.

Reteaching/Reinforcement
• Writing Handbook, anthology p. 829

The Writer's Craft
Chronological Order, p. 240

CUSTOMIZING FOR
Gifted and Talented Students

Have students discuss the issues of resentment and forgiveness. Ask if there are situations in which it is acceptable to express one's resentment toward another person, or if it is better to keep these feelings to oneself. Ask students to consider, as they read, how the narrator's resentment has affected his life.

CUSTOMIZING FOR
Students Acquiring English

2 The word *patented* is not used literally here to mean "something unique protected by law." Explain that the narrator felt he had invented a catching style that no one else could duplicate.

Active Reading: EVALUATE

A Invite students to offer their opinions about the narrator's reaction to the coach's witnessing his antics in the outfield. Ask if it is appropriate for him to assume that he looked ridiculous. (*Possible response: He's overreacting—it's natural to clown around and have fun playing baseball informally.*)

Literary Concept: SIMILE

B Have students identify the simile in this passage. Then ask them to explain why they think the author chose this simile to describe the way his words flowed onto the page. (*Possible response: The words flow onto the page like players onto a field. The narrator loves baseball and so the simile comparing words to players comes naturally to him.*)

Critical Thinking: ANALYZING

C Ask students to comment on why Mrs. Griswald asks this question. (*Possible response: She knows how hard it is to become a professional athlete, and she fears that the narrator's goal may be unrealistic.*)

Transitional Words and Phrases

after	then
earlier	the next day
last week	this morning
later	tonight
soon	yesterday

THE LANGUAGE OF LITERATURE TEACHER'S EDITION **661**

Literary Concept: FLASHBACK

D Ask students to describe how the author uses a flashback to open the story. *(Possible response: After starting at a critical moment, he flashes back to explain events. Then he lets events unfold until he returns here to the moment at which the story began—the coach crossing the locker room with an armful of jerseys.)*

CUSTOMIZING FOR
Students Acquiring English

3 Mention that the idiomatic phrase "out a ... window" indicates something that is gone or has disappeared quickly.

STRATEGIC READING FOR
Less-Proficient Readers

E Check that students are clear about the importance of team tryouts to the narrator.

- What is the narrator's life dream? *(He wants only to be a professional baseball player.)* **Making Generalizations**
- Do the narrator and Steve make the team? *(Steve does, but the narrator doesn't.)* **Comparing and Contrasting**

Set a Purpose Have students read to find out what Brace says to the narrator at the reunion and what Steve and the narrator do in the parking lot afterwards.

Literary Concept: SIMILE

F Ask students what the author compares his disappointment to. *(The narrator's disappointment is compared to a crushing weight.)*

faint odor of the damp, loamy April earth tracked in by our cleated shoes.

Coach reappeared with the jerseys and gave a brief speech. He was known throughout the high school and our town as a gentle man, and a great teacher, and he had a reputation for these inspirational speeches, but I was feeling too much anxiety to listen: All I could hear was the soft slapping of water dripping from the showerheads, a sound that seemed to grow louder until it nearly exploded in my ears. Then Coach stepped down the aisle, handing out the jerseys. He leaned left, then right, as if he were dancing a slow waltz.

By the time Coach reached the end of the bench where Steve and I and a couple of other guys waited, only two jerseys were draped over his wrist. Coach hesitated a moment, tossed one jersey to Steve. Then he turned and tossed the second one to a boy who sat across from me.

With that tossed jersey, which I can still see now, a blue-and-gold blur floating softly in the air, the coach threw a young boy's dreams out a locker-room window, and they spiraled miles and miles to the hard ground.

I don't remember what Coach said after that. He might have been saying, "Boys, I'm really sorry," but the loud pain filling my skull blocked out his words.

Walking home with Steve, I couldn't help feeling an anger for Coach Brace, a kind of hatred growing steadily inside me, spreading to every artery and muscle and nerve. I'd never hated anyone before, but in my mind, Coach Brace became meaner and more vindictive by the second. I swore at him, I called him names, I did cruel imitations of his locker-room speeches.

"You got ripped off, man," Steve said, trying to make me feel better. "Plain and simple. You *deserve* to be on that team. You're better than *all* those guys who got jerseys."

I stopped in the middle of the sidewalk and glared at Steve. "Including you, I suppose."

Steve glanced down at the jersey folded on his duffel bag, then back at me. "Yeah," he said. "Including me."

His words didn't help. My world was changing at that moment; nothing could stop it from pivoting away from my future as a baseball player. Nothing could lighten the enormous disappointment that crushed me like a weight. I swore I'd never speak to Coach Brace again.

When we reached my front door, Steve uttered our usual farewell. "Tomorrow," he said.

"Yeah," I said feebly, unable to lift my gaze from the concrete. "Tomorrow."

After supper I pulled my civics class essay from my desk drawer, walked to the corner of the backyard, lit a match, and burned those pages one by one. I watched my looping words darken as the paper curled in on itself like a

662 UNIT FIVE PART 2: VITAL CONNECTIONS

Mini-Lesson Spelling

benign   ghetto
subtle   column
psychic   numb
palm   rhythm

SILENT LETTERS Point out to students that a few consonants are silent when they appear in certain combinations. In the list of words shown on the chalkboard, the underlined letter is silent. Explain that there are no regular rules for spelling words like these. Tell students that they can keep a list of tricky spelling words, and that they also can help themselves remember their spelling by creating interesting memory aids. For example: The *b* in *subtle* is as silent as a submarine gliding undersea.

Application Have students spell these words as you recite them. Then they can use a dictionary to check their spelling.

1. spaghetti   5. align
2. doubt   6. psychology
3. rhyme   7. wrath
4. autumn   8. plumber

Ask students to look for more words that fit this pattern, in their writing and in the things that they read, and have them add these words to their personal word lists.

Reteaching/Reinforcement
- *Unit Five Resource Book*, p. 55

662 THE LANGUAGE OF LITERATURE TEACHER'S EDITION

fist. The ashes fell onto the worn spot in the dirt where home plate used to be.

I never tried out for the baseball team the next three years of high school, even though Steve said I should. I was too hurt, and just couldn't face Coach Brace for another tryout. Steve played well, a star third baseman during our four years of high school, and the team won the conference championship one year. After school on spring days, Steve stopped at his locker next to mine; he pulled his books out quickly, and I knew, as usual, he was headed to baseball practice.

"What's up tonight, buddy?" he asked me once after seventh period.

"Nothing," I shrugged, clicking my locker door shut, then opening it, then clicking it shut again.

"Man, I wish I had your free time," he said.

"I wish I had your practice," I replied.

Suddenly awkward in his untucked madras³ shirt and white jeans, Steve pretended to adjust the cover on his science book. We both knew my being cut from the team created a kind of <u>chasm</u> between us, and neither of us was too comfortable talking about it. Then, before he turned, he gave me a quick grin, nodded, and said, "Tomorrow."

I nodded back as he hurried down the hall toward the locker room. Some afternoons I loitered in the empty hallway until the team took the field and began their warm-up exercises. Through the high, distorted glass of the second-story window, I watched the players wavering in the distance. As those four years passed, I decided it was a stupid, small idea of mine, anyway, to want to be a major leaguer. After all—what were my chances?

Twenty years later, when I returned to town for a high school reunion, someone said that Coach Brace had become seriously ill with cancer. The rumors circulated among my classmates that Coach, who had been our senior class advisor, would try to make it to the gathering that night, but everyone said he looked very bad, the illness eating away at him. Some of my classmates shook their heads and said his chances weren't good.

When Coach Brace walked into the reunion amid a flurry of handshakes and friendly calls from former students, his face looked as though the skin had collapsed inward onto the bone, and shadows, like dark gray bunting,⁴

---

3. **madras** (măd′rəs): a cotton cloth usually printed in a plaid or striped pattern (named for a city in India).
4. **bunting:** strips of cloth used as decorative drapery on festive occasions.

WORDS TO KNOW
chasm (kăz′əm) *n.* a great difference in feelings or interests

---

Active Reading: EVALUATE

G Have students evaluate the narrator's reaction to being cut from the team—burning his essay and not trying out for the team again. Model the following thought process for students:

Think-Aloud Model *The narrator had a very strong reaction—maybe too strong. Burning his essay is a symbolic act that represents his abandonment of his dream. It seems a shame that the narrator didn't try again to make the team. Giving up so easily proves that he wasn't cut out to be a professional athlete.*

CUSTOMIZING FOR Students Acquiring English

4 Point out that Steve and the narrator use slang in their greetings, for example "man," "buddy," and "What's up."

Active Reading: CONNECT

H Encourage students to connect with the narrator at this point in the story. Ask volunteers what advice or feedback they would give him about the decisions he is making.

Literary Concept: CHRONOLOGICAL ORDER

I Point out to students that since the end of the flashback, the author has presented events in chronological order. Then ask what change the author makes at this point in the narrative. *(The author leaps ahead 20 years.)*

Mini-Lesson Literary Concepts

REVIEWING SIMILES Remind students that similes—along with metaphors and personification—are a type of figurative language. A simile compares two unlike things that have some quality in common. Similes make a direct comparison, using the words *like* or *as*. For example, in the highlighted passage on pages 662–63, Bill Meissner uses a simile to compare a burning sheet of paper with a fist.

Application Have students identify two additional similes on pages 663–664 *("shadows, like dark gray bunting"* and *"moment . . . like a huge, undissolved stone").* Then have them create other similes to describe a sheet of burning paper.

Critical Thinking:
SYNTHESIZING

J Have students review the earlier scene in which the narrator feels upset because Coach Brace has seen him clowning around. Invite them to compare and contrast the narrator's assumptions about Brace's reactions with the coach's actual thoughts. *(Possible response: The narrator assumes that Brace thought his behavior stupid and ridiculous. In fact, Brace may have been thinking about how the narrator and Steve were still playing after practice was officially over. He seems to have been impressed with the ability and attitude of the boys.)*

Literary Concept: MORAL

K Explain to students that a moral is a lesson about life. Ask them whether the coach's words convey a moral. *(Possible response: Yes, because he is talking about being a winner in life, not just in baseball.)*

Active Reading: EVALUATE

L Encourage students to discuss whether the narrator was right to not share his feelings with Coach Brace. *(Possible responses: It would have been appropriate for the narrator to express himself honestly—gently and respectfully, but truthfully—to the coach. It wouldn't have been right, given the trouble in the coach's life at this point.)*

---

clung to the skin beneath his eyes. I turned toward him as he made his way through the crowd, and then, when the old hurt rose inside me, I turned away.

After the reunion dinner, Coach stepped to the microphone in the high school gym, his navy blue suit jacket seeming too large for him. During a short speech, he bowed his head slightly, lowered his voice, and told us the illness had been tough on him. "But I'm going to beat this thing," he said, raising his head. "I'm going to beat it. If baseball taught me one thing, it taught me not to give up."

After the speeches, Coach spotted me standing by the makeshift bar in the corner of the gym; he walked over and greeted me. We exchanged small talk for a few minutes, and while we talked, I couldn't stop that locker-room scene from replaying in my mind.

Then, out of nowhere, Coach said, "You always were a good ballplayer. I remember that. I remember seeing you and Steve Lyon practicing by the old West School." He toasted me with his plastic cup of punch. "You guys were always a great addition to my team," he said proudly.

To my team. I was stunned by those last words, and a sudden realization hit me: Coach Brace *never even remembered* cutting me from the team. That moment, which had meant so much to me, that moment I'd carried around for years inside my stomach like a huge, undissolved stone had simply disappeared from his mind. To him, I was just one of his former players who contributed to those conference championship teams. I thought about correcting him, telling him *No, I never played on your team. You cut me, remember?* Thought about telling how because of him, I went home that night and lay for hours in my unlit room, my future abruptly turned to ashes. Instead, I looked into Coach's eyes and what I saw there was the kindness I'd refused to acknowledge all those years. Then I began to visualize his illness—the cancer spreading its gray, deadly branches just beneath his skin.

"So," he said, erasing my vision, "do you still play ball?"

"Yeah," I replied. "Sometimes. With a few older guys, I mean."

He chuckled, grinned <u>benignly</u>. "That's the wonderful thing about baseball. You're never too old." He paused, then added solemnly, "When you've got baseball in your life, you're always a winner. Don't forget that."

His words reverberated in my head and I closed my eyes. I realized that these were the same words he'd spoken to us after the freshman tryouts in the locker room. I had the dizzying sensation that, without realizing it, I was walking on some wide, cyclical path, and I'd just passed a starting point again. I opened my eyes, and, for the first time, I understood those words. "I won't forget," I said.

Coach and I shook hands. Before he turned to leave, he caught me off guard by sliding his arm around me and giving me a hug. His frail hand clapped the back of my shoulder, and in those few seconds all the hurt feelings seemed to slide out of my body, rise through the blue and gold crepe paper wafting over our heads, drift through the ceiling of the high school gym, and evaporate into the endless night sky. My pain, which I'd always considered so enormous, suddenly seemed very small to me; I wondered how I could possibly have carried it for so long.

Later, as Coach walked toward the exit, I knew it might be the last time I'd ever see him. But then, I thought, maybe not. Maybe he'd be there, standing at the podium the next time we got together.

WORDS TO KNOW

benignly (bĭ-nīn′lē) *adv.* in a kind and gentle way

664

Mini-Lesson Grammar

ADJECTIVES AND ADVERBS Remind students that an adjective modifies a noun or a pronoun, whereas an adverb modifies a verb, an adjective, or another adverb. Knowing the difference between these two parts of speech can help a writer decide which word is correct in a sentence. For example, *quick* is an adjective, and *quickly* is an adverb. The author of "Keeping Time" used the adverb form in the clause, "the evening passed too quickly," because the word in question (an adverb) must modify the verb *passed.*

Application Have students choose the correct word from each pair below.
1. The coach walked over and greeted me (warm/<u>warmly</u>).
2. That moment was like a (<u>huge</u>/hugely) stone sitting in my stomach.

Reteaching/Reinforcement
- *Grammar Handbook,* anthology p. 878
- *Grammar Mini-Lesson* copymasters pp. 19, 20, transparencies pp. 12, 13, 39, 40

Adjective or Adverb, p. 514

Adjective modifies
- noun
- pronoun

Adverb modifies
- verb
- adjective
- adverb

664 THE LANGUAGE OF LITERATURE TEACHER'S EDITION

Tomorrow.

During the reunion, Steve and I talked for a while, but the evening passed too quickly, and we never got around to mentioning our ball-playing days. At one A.M. I said farewell to my classmates as we shuffled into the entryway of the gym. I glanced around to find Steve, but I couldn't spot him in the crowd.

Standing by the car with my wife, I heard a voice call to me from behind. "Hey, man," the voice said. "Wanna play some baseball?"

I turned to see Steve leaning against his car, mitt in one hand, beer in the other.

"You mean here?" I gasped. "Now?"

"Why not?"

I glanced at my wife, who smiled and nodded at me. Opening the car trunk, I pulled out my old glove.

Steve and I set down our cans of beer, slipped off our suit jackets, and draped them on posts at the edge of the parking lot. We stood beneath the glow of the full moon, awkward in our white shirts and ties, our waists a little thicker, our hair thinner and grayer, the cells inside our bodies subtly changing second by second. We tossed the ball across the open stretch of black asphalt. It wasn't the best playing surface, we agreed with a laugh as the soles of our shined shoes scuffed across it, but it would do for now. Though neither of us said it, Steve and I knew what each of us was thinking: Tomorrow we'd go to the old West School field, where we used to practice, and we'd play baseball. We'd slip into our worn spikes, torn T-shirts, and faded caps and play baseball. And if the field was gone, then we'd play in the place where it *used* to be. Tomorrow.

That night, in the <u>diffused</u> light, the ball seemed to flutter toward our outstretched gloves. I listened to the rhythmic beat of the ball in the leather pockets. The thought crossed my mind that you could keep time by a game of catch, this heartbeat, this throwing back and forth, back and forth, each swing of the arm like the sweep of a pendulum, each throw another year. It was then that I heard the honk of a horn, and in that instant, time stopped.

We turned to see Coach Brace, idling in his old powder-blue car, watching us from the far end of the lot, lifting his hand in a wave.

WORDS TO KNOW
diffused (dĭ-fyo͞ozd′) *adj.* spread-out; softened **diffuse** *v.*

From Personal Response to Critical Analysis

1. Responses will vary.
2. Possible response: As a teenager, the narrator isn't very realistic or pragmatic about preparing for a career. He's pretty self-absorbed, and he gives up easily when he doesn't immediately succeed. As an adult he is still self-absorbed but his behavior with Brace and Lyon shows that he is actually more flexible and mature than he once was.
3. Possible responses: The blame rests with the narrator because he didn't have enough perseverance to try out again. The coach deserves some blame because of the insensitive way he informed boys that they had failed to make the team.
4. Possible response: The author seems to be saying that time passes whether we want it to or not, and life doesn't always turn out the way we want it to.
5. Possible responses: Hand-picking team members and cutting some people is the best method—it's realistic, and it prepares young people for similar situations later in life. There must be a better way to choose school sports teams, because schools are supposed to be about teaching students and encouraging them to participate, not telling them they can't participate.

Another Pathway

Cooperative Learning Have students review the actual scenes in the text. Invite students to improvise dialogue from starting points found in the story. They might choose to write just what the narrator says, first as a teenager and, second, as an adult, or they might choose to write a dialogue between the narrator and the coach. Students might audiotape these improvisations and use them as the foundation for their two written scenes.

Rubric

3 Full Accomplishment Students write imaginative, believable scripts, and their performances vividly capture the characters' personalities.

2 Substantial Accomplishment Students write realistic dialogue, and their performances generally reflect the characters' personalities.

1 Little or Partial Accomplishment Students have difficulty writing scripts containing believable dialogue and performing the two scenes for the class.

RESPONDING OPTIONS

FROM PERSONAL RESPONSE TO CRITICAL ANALYSIS

REFLECT
1. What was your first impression of the narrator of this story? Jot down your thoughts in your notebook.

RETHINK
Close Textual Analysis

2. Compare the qualities of the narrator as an adult with his qualities as a teenager. In what ways does he remain the same? How does he change? Explain your answers.

Consider
- how he reacts when he does not make the baseball team
- what happens to his dream of playing professional baseball
- the personal discoveries he makes

3. Who do you think is to blame for the fact that the narrator's dream of playing professional baseball is not realized? Explain your opinion.

RELATE
Thematic Link

4. What do you think the title of this story and the statement regarding the human heart at the beginning suggest about time, the nature of dreams, and the narrator's experience?

5. Consider the system in which coaches select members of school sports teams by trying out and handpicking athletes. Do you think the practice of cutting people from teams is fair? Do you think there might be a better selection method? As you discuss these questions with your classmates, give reasons for your answers.

LITERARY CONCEPTS

Some stories convey a **moral**—a lesson about human nature. For example, the well-known children's story "The Tortoise and the Hare" has as its moral "Slow and steady wins the race." In some stories, the moral is directly stated; in others, the reader must infer the moral from the words and actions. In your opinion, what is the moral of "Keeping Time"? Is it stated directly or indirectly?

Multimodal Learning
ANOTHER PATHWAY
Cooperative Learning

In a small group, brainstorm what the narrator, both as a teenager and as an adult, might say directly to the coach. Write two scenes, and role-play them for the class. If possible, you may wish to record your performances on videotape.

QUICKWRITES

1. At the reunion, the coach says to the narrator, "When you've got baseball in your life, you're always a winner." Write a brief **paragraph** explaining what you think he means.

2. While speaking with the coach at the reunion, the narrator makes a personal discovery. Write a **pep talk** he might give to students about this discovery.

3. Write a **poem** about either the locker-room scene or the game of catch after the reunion. Try to capture the emotion of the scene in your poem.

📁 **PORTFOLIO** Save your writing. You may want to use it later as a springboard to a piece for your portfolio.

666 UNIT FIVE PART 2: VITAL CONNECTIONS

Literary Concepts

Encourage students to state in their own words the moral or lesson Meissner wanted to get across. You might wish to draw their attention to the two scenes involving Coach Brace to help them discover the unstated moral of the story. A possible moral of the story is that success has to do with what's inside a person.

QuickWrites

1. As they think about the sentence, students might substitute other activities for baseball to help them infer the author's meaning.
2. Remind students that a pep talk tries to motivate listeners by focusing their attention on positive aspects of a subject.
3. Encourage students to prewrite by jotting down words, phrases, or ideas such a poem might use.

Writing a Poem, pp. 76–80
Developing a Personal Voice, pp. 316–317

Multimodal Learning

ALTERNATIVE ACTIVITIES

On page 662, the narrator describes his anger at not being chosen for the team. Using information from the story and your imagination, create a piece of realistic or abstract **art**—a painting, montage, or collage—that represents his anger.

CRITIC'S CORNER

About "Keeping Time," our student-board reviewer Aaron Fitzstephens said, "It shows you that dreams don't always happen." In your opinion, does this statement express the moral of "Keeping Time"? Why or why not? How would you express the moral of the story?

WORDS TO KNOW

Review the Words to Know at the bottom of the selection pages. Then write the word that is most clearly related to each situation described below.

1. As the sun set behind the pitcher's mound, a soft glow replaced the harsh light of the blindingly sunny day.
2. Finding themselves on two different, brutally competitive teams, the two boys experienced a break in their long-time friendship.
3. Dumbfounded, the ballplayers watched the young deer wobble and collapse onto the field, steady itself on sticklike legs, fall, and right itself once again.
4. The players were happy that the mean-spirited coach was retiring and that his replacement treated them in a more pleasant way.
5. When he spied his girlfriend in the bleachers, the player tipped his cap to her so slightly that she did not notice.

BILL MEISSNER

"Keeping Time" is about the clash between dreams and reality and about forgiveness, says Bill Meissner (1948–). Like the narrator of the story, Meissner failed to make his freshman baseball team and held a grudge against his coach until they both met decades later at a reunion. Explains Meissner, "I had to switch gears quickly because my career goal was to be a major-league player." Unlike the narrator of the story, however, Meissner got back on his feet and forged ahead. He played American Legion baseball during high school. Today, he plays baseball informally with friends.

After graduating from the University of Wisconsin, Meissner received a master's degree in creative writing at the University of Massachusetts. For the last 20 years, he has taught at St. Cloud State University in Minnesota, where he is director of creative writing.

Meissner has published three volumes of poetry that draw on his childhood and adolescent experiences. "Keeping Time" is one of 30 short stories in his 1994 collection *Hitting into the Wind*. These stories use baseball themes to explore growing up and father-son relationships.

According to Meissner, "A story is like a pebble tossed into a still pond. The ripples hopefully reach out to touch the shoreline, the audience." He says he wants his writing "to touch the reader's personal experience."

- CONTEMPORARY CONNECTION

Words to Know

1. diffused
2. chasm
3. spindly
4. benignly
5. subtly

Reteaching/Reinforcement
• *Unit Five Resource Book*, p. 56

Across the Curriculum

 **History** Cooperative Learning *Baseball's Origins* Have students use library or on-line resources to prepare a report on the origins and history of professional baseball. Students might find it useful and interesting to view Ken Burns's video series *Baseball*, which was broadcast on PBS and also is available on video. You may wish to divide students into small groups and have each group research the history of a specific professional team. Have students display their findings by creating baseball history cards similar to baseball trading cards.

 **Science** *Dissecting a Baseball* Obtain an old, discarded baseball (perhaps from the Physical Education department) and have students take it apart to discover its contents. A regulation baseball is made of a center of cork, two layers of rubber, tightly wrapped wool and cotton yarn, a coating of rubber cement, and a cowhide casing stitched with red string.

Literary Links

Compare the narrator's response to rejection with that of Eli in "The Lie." (*Possible response: Whereas the narrator of "Keeping Time" is devastated when he isn't chosen for the baseball team, Eli seems less emotionally responsive to his rejection from Whitehall. This could be because Eli's father is more concerned with Eli's acceptance than Eli is. In fact, there are more similarities between Eli's father and the narrator of "Keeping Time" than between Eli and the narrator.*)

CONTEMPORARY CONNECTION
Nobody Gets Cut The students in these interviews attend a school that allows all students to participate in extracurricular activities, regardless of ability. Hearing other students talk about their love of sports and their fear of not making the team may spark a discussion among your students.

Side A, Frame 49180

Alternative Activities

You might encourage students to experiment with different media to learn how well each can be adapted to an expression of strong emotion. Remind students to think in terms of color, or of lines and shapes, as they compose their image. Encourage students to review the text to refresh their memories of the narrator's feelings. As a preparation for this activity, some students might find it useful to remember a time that they were very angry or to fantasize themselves in the narrator's shoes.

PREVIEWING

OVERVIEW

Objectives
- To understand and appreciate a memoir that shows the power of a brother's love
- To express understanding of the memoir through a choice of writing forms, including a letter and a diary entry
- To extend understanding of the memoir through a variety of multimodal and cross-disciplinary activities

Skills

READING SKILLS/ STRATEGIES
- Making generalizations

LITERARY CONCEPTS
- Main idea

SPEAKING, LISTENING, AND VIEWING
- Group discussion
- Oral presentation

Cross-Curricular Connections

SOCIAL STUDIES
- Legislation for the disabled

SCIENCE
- Birth defects

ALTERNATIVE

Previewing

Students can choose partners and use the following prompts to preview "Power of the Powerless: A Brother's Lesson" verbally.

Writing Connection

Discussion Prompts *Think of a disabled person from whom you or someone you know has learned. Briefly describe this person or what you imagine this person to be like. Perhaps you are yourself disabled. If so, have you learned how to cope with your disability from someone who is also disabled? Listen carefully as your partner describes his or her experiences. If you need help, consider these questions:*

- *How was this person disabled?*
- *Did his or her disabilities prevent him or her from doing various activities?*
- *How did he or she feel about being disabled?*
- *What have you learned from your experiences?*
- *Did your thoughts about disabled people change from this experience?*

As you read, notice how the author describes his brother and what this reveals about his feelings for him.

NONFICTION

Power of the Powerless: A Brother's Lesson
Christopher de Vinck

Activating Prior Knowledge
PERSONAL CONNECTION

In this true story, Christopher de Vinck describes the valuable life lessons he learned from his severely disabled brother Oliver. His relationship with Oliver was a vital connection that deeply affected his life. Have you or anyone you know learned an important lesson from a physically or mentally disabled person? Write your thoughts in a diagram like the one shown. Then share your ideas with a small group of classmates.

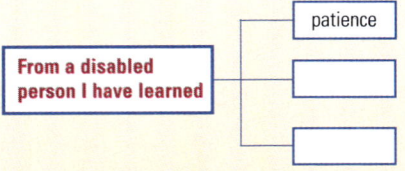

Building Background
SCIENCE CONNECTION

Oliver was born with multiple birth defects. A birth defect can be a visible abnormality in the body's structure, such as a clubfoot (a twisted or curled foot), or an internal defect, such as a hole in the heart. Although there are thousands of types of birth defects, they occur relatively infrequently. Only about two percent of newborn babies in the United States have a recognizable birth defect, and only half of them require treatment.

It has been established that some birth defects are inherited and others have environmental causes. Infants may inherit conditions resulting in defects, such as Down syndrome, from one or both parents.

A pregnant woman's exposure to tobacco smoke or to alcohol or poisonous substances, such as mercury in contaminated food, can also affect the development of a fetus. Such environmental causes have their greatest impact during the first three months of pregnancy. Early in her pregnancy, Oliver's mother was overcome by fumes that had a toxic effect on the child she was carrying.

Setting a Purpose
WRITING CONNECTION

For the Personal Connection, you were asked to consider a disabled person from whom you or someone you know has learned valuable life lessons. Write a brief paragraph describing this person. If you do not know enough about the person to describe him or her, write what you imagine the person to be like.

668 UNIT FIVE PART 2: VITAL CONNECTIONS

PRINT AND MEDIA RESOURCES

UNIT FIVE RESOURCE BOOK
Strategic Reading: Literature, p. 59
Reading SkillBuilder, p. 60

ACCESS FOR STUDENTS ACQUIRING ENGLISH
Selection Summaries
Reading and Writing Support

FORMAL ASSESSMENT
Selection Test, p. 125
Test Generator

AUDIO LIBRARY
See Reference Card

Power of the Powerless:
A Brother's Lesson
by Christopher de Vinck

I grew up in the house where my brother was on his back in his bed for almost 33 years, in the same corner of his room, under the same window, beside the same yellow walls. Oliver was blind, mute. His legs were twisted. He didn't have the strength to lift his head nor the intelligence to learn anything.

Today I am an English teacher, and each time I introduce my class to the play about Helen Keller, "The Miracle Worker," I tell my students about Oliver. One day, during my first year teaching, a boy in the last row raised his hand and said, "Oh, Mr. de Vinck. You mean he was a vegetable."

I stammered for a few seconds. My family and I fed Oliver. We changed his diapers, hung his clothes and bed linen on the basement line in winter, and spread them out white and clean on the lawn in the summer. I always liked to watch the grasshoppers jump on the pillowcases.

We bathed Oliver. Tickled his chest to make him laugh. Sometimes we left the radio on in his room. We pulled the shade down over his bed in the morning to keep the sun from burning his tender skin. We listened to him laugh as we watched television downstairs. We listened to him rock his arms up and down to make the bed squeak. We listened to him cough in the middle of the night.

"Well, I guess you could call him a

Art Note

Sunroom by Winifred Nicholson In this painting, Winifred Nicholson (1893–1981) finds great suggestive power in subtle shadings of color and faintly rendered lines and shapes. The outline of a door (and perhaps a window) is recognizable, but the viewer is stirred primarily by the light and color on the canvas. The open, delicate quality of the image is due as much to what Nicholson chose to omit as to what she actually painted.

Reading the Art Do you think this image is an effective illustration for "Power of the Powerless: A Brother's Lesson"? Why or why not? What role does the sun play in this painting and in the story?

CUSTOMIZING FOR
Gifted and Talented Students

Have students write a composition in which they explain how the brothers' lives might have been different if the family had chosen to place Oliver in an institution rather than to "take him home and love him."

STRATEGIC READING FOR
Less-Proficient Readers

A Make sure that students are clear about the extent of Oliver's physical disabilities.

- What is Oliver's physical condition? *(He is blind and mute, with deformed limbs, useless muscles, and little intelligence.)* **Summarizing**
- How do Oliver's parents realize that he is blind? *(As a baby, he looks directly at the sun.)* **Relating Cause and Effect**

Set a Purpose Have students read to find out why it is so important to the author that a woman named Roe feeds Oliver.

Sunroom (1980), Winifred Nicholson. Copyright © the artist's family.

vegetable. I called him Oliver, my brother. You would have liked him."

One October day in 1946, when my mother was pregnant with Oliver, her second son, she was overcome by fumes from a leaking coal-burning stove. My oldest brother was sleeping in his crib, which was quite high off the ground, so the gas didn't affect him. My father pulled them outside, where my mother revived quickly.

On April 20, 1947, Oliver was born. A healthy looking, plump, beautiful boy.

One afternoon, a few months later, my mother brought Oliver to a window. She held him there in the sun, the bright good sun, and there Oliver looked and looked directly into the sunlight, which was the first moment my mother realized that Oliver was blind. My parents, the true heroes of this story, learned, with the passing months, that blindness was only part of the problem. So they brought Oliver to Mt. Sinai Hospital in New York for tests to determine the extent of his condition.

A

The doctor said that he wanted to make it very clear to both my mother and father that there was absolutely nothing that could be done for Oliver. He didn't want my parents to grasp at false hope. "You could place him in an institution," he said. "But," my parents

670   UNIT FIVE   PART 2: VITAL CONNECTIONS

Mini-Lesson  Literary Concepts

REVIEWING MAIN IDEA Remind students that the main idea is the central idea that a writer expresses in his or her work. Usually the term is used in discussions of nonfiction writing, whereas the term *theme* is applied to fiction, dramatic writing, and poetry.

Explain that the main idea may refer to the central message of the entire work or of just one paragraph within that work. Sometimes the main idea is stated in the topic sentence of a paragraph. Other times the main idea is not directly stated and must be inferred by the reader.

Application Encourage students to draft sentences that they think express the main idea of "Power of the Powerless: A Brother's Lesson." Have them refer to specific passages in the text that inform their responses. *(Possible response: Christopher de Vinck makes an important comment about his family being blessed with "a true presence of peace." This shows the author's main idea—that people who help and love those with disabilities often learn priceless lessons about the importance and meaning of human life.)*

replied, "he is our son. We will take Oliver home of course." The good doctor answered, "Then take him home and love him."

Oliver grew to the size of a 10-year-old. He had a big chest, a large head. His hands and feet were those of a five-year-old, small and soft. We'd wrap a box of baby cereal for him at Christmas and place it under the tree; pat his head with a damp cloth in the middle of a July heat wave. His baptismal certificate hung on the wall above his head. A bishop came to the house and confirmed him.¹

Even now, five years after his death from pneumonia on March 12, 1980, Oliver still remains the weakest, most helpless human being I ever met, and yet he was one of the most powerful human beings I ever met. He could do absolutely nothing except breathe, sleep, eat, and yet he was responsible for action, love, courage, insight. When I was small my mother would say, "Isn't it wonderful that you can see?" And once she said, "When you go to heaven, Oliver will run to you, embrace you, and the first thing he will say is 'Thank you.'" I remember, too, my mother explaining to me that we were blessed with Oliver in ways that were not clear to her at first.

So often parents are faced with a child who is severely retarded, but who is also hyperactive,² demanding or wild, who needs constant care. So many people have little choice but to place their child in an institution. We were fortunate that Oliver didn't need us to be in his room all day. He never knew what his condition was. We were blessed with his presence, a true presence of peace.

When I was in my early 20s I met a girl and fell in love. After a few months I brought her home to meet my family. When my mother went to the kitchen to prepare dinner, I asked the girl, "Would you like to see Oliver?" for I had told her about my brother. "No," she answered.

Soon after, I met Roe, a lovely girl. She asked me the names of my brothers and sisters. She loved children. I thought she was wonderful. I brought her home after a few months to meet my family. Soon it was time for me to feed Oliver. I remember sheepishly asking Roe if she'd like to see him. "Sure," she said.

I sat at Oliver's bedside as Roe watched over my shoulder. I gave him his first spoonful, his second. "Can I do that?" Roe asked with ease, with freedom, with compassion, so I gave her the bowl and she fed Oliver one spoonful at a time.

The power of the powerless. Which girl would you marry? Today Roe and I have three children. ❖

---

1. **confirmed him:** performed the Christian ceremony admitting him into full membership in the church.
2. **hyperactive:** excessively active.

POWER OF THE POWERLESS: A BROTHER'S LESSON 671

From Personal Response to Critical Analysis

1. Responses will vary.
2. Possible responses: Even a person who cannot speak or see can be powerful because of the behavior he or she elicits in other people. People's love for Oliver encourages them to say, feel, and do things in certain ways.
3. Possible response: Oliver's family behaved admirably because they faced his disabilities yet did not blanket him or themselves with pity.
4. Possible response: The author's brother taught him that caring for other people is the most important thing a person can do in the world. The author shows that there are blessings to be found even in tragic circumstances.
5. Possible response: to explain to readers what he had learned about life from an unexpected teacher—his disabled brother
6. Encourage students to consider such factors as the costs of institutional health care, the benefits of expert medical attention versus those of family attention, and the large time commitment home care requires.

Another Pathway

Cooperative Learning Have students begin by brainstorming feelings and thoughts they might have as Oliver's brother—starting with his birth. You might assign one student to serve as a turn-taking monitor during the brainstorming process. Encourage students to write honestly and remind them not to worry about seeming to contradict themselves if conflicting feelings and thoughts arise.

Rubric

3 Full Accomplishment Students create a diary full of rich, imaginative, and interesting entries relating to key events in the lives of Oliver and Christopher.

2 Substantial Accomplishment Students create a diary containing several interesting entries relating to events in the lives of Oliver and Christopher.

1 Little or Partial Accomplishment Students create a diary with few imaginative entries, and they have difficulty generating responses to key events in the lives of Oliver and Christopher.

RESPONDING OPTIONS

FROM PERSONAL RESPONSE TO CRITICAL ANALYSIS

REFLECT 1. What is your reaction to the author of this selection? Record your thoughts in your notebook.

RETHINK 2. De Vinck describes his brother Oliver as being "one of the most powerful human beings I ever met." How could such a helpless person be so powerful?

3. What is your opinion of the family's handling of Oliver's disability? Give reasons for your answer.

Thematic Link 4. How would you express the lesson de Vinck learned from Oliver—and the lesson you have learned from de Vinck?

5. What do you think was the author's purpose in writing this account? Explain your answer.

RELATE 6. Oliver's parents felt strongly about caring for Oliver at home. Many families, however, feel unable to care for disabled children properly at home and choose to put them in institutions. Which choice do you think is appropriate? What factors might affect a family's decision? Why? Discuss your ideas with a partner.

Thematic Link

LITERARY LINKS

How does de Vinck's relationship with Oliver compare with Squeaky's relationship with Raymond in "Raymond's Run" (page 648). In what ways are the relationships alike? In what ways are they different? Compare the attitudes and the lessons conveyed in the two selections.

Multimodal Learning
ANOTHER PATHWAY

Cooperative Learning

Imagine that you are Oliver's brother and you want to keep a diary of key events, reactions, and feelings associated with Oliver's life. Work with a small group of classmates to create such a diary. Use details from the selection, but also use your imagination to fill in important events—for example, Oliver's first birthday.

QUICKWRITES

1. Suppose that Oliver had been able to communicate in writing. What might he have said to his brother? Write a **letter** he might have composed.

2. Imagine how Oliver's mother might have felt when she learned the extent of her baby's disabilities. Keeping in mind what you have learned about her character, record her feelings in the form of a **diary entry**.

📁 **PORTFOLIO** Save your writing. You may want to use it later as a springboard to a piece for your portfolio.

Literary Links

Possible response: The relationships are similar in the sense that both narrators deeply love their siblings and take very good care of them. The two relationships are different because Raymond is much freer to express his own love to his sister than Oliver is to his brother. Both relationships celebrate an attitude of selflessness and caring about the welfare of loved ones around us.

QuickWrites

1. Encourage students to think about what Oliver's writing style might be like. Have them imagine all the things that Oliver would have to say to his brother after years of silence.
2. Remind students that diary entries are generally not intended for others to read. Ask students to consider what feelings Oliver's mother may wish to express in this private format.

 **The Writer's Craft**

Developing a Personal Voice, pp. 316–17
Using a Journal, pp. 222–23

Multimodal Learning

ALTERNATIVE ACTIVITIES

Cooperative Learning On page 671, de Vinck says that his brother was responsible for "action, love, courage, insight." Get together with three of your classmates, each choosing one of the words *action, love, courage,* and *insight*. Make an **illustration** or **design** to convey how your word applies to Oliver. Combine the group's work into one display, and share it with the class.

WORDS TO KNOW

WORDPLAY The word *sheepishly* in this selection (page 671) means "in an embarrassed or bashful way" and contains a reference to the behavior of sheep. With the class divided into two groups, brainstorm some other words that refer to animal-like characteristics, such as *mousy*. Then play a game of vocabulary charades, using the words you listed.

CRITIC'S CORNER

The student-board reviewer Theresa Ernst made the following comment about this selection: "I don't think many kids like to read about people who are disabled, but I think adults find it interesting because they understand disabilities better." Do you agree or disagree with this statement? Explain your opinion.

CHRISTOPHER DE VINCK

Christopher de Vinck (1951–) says that he began writing out of loneliness after a failed romantic relationship. He wrote poetry for ten years before the *Wall Street Journal* published his first essay in 1985. His second article, "Power of the Powerless: A Brother's Lesson," was also published that year by the *Journal*. Hundreds of readers, many with "Olivers" in their lives, responded strongly to de Vinck's work, phoning or writing letters to him. He eventually interviewed many of them for his book *The Power of the Powerless: A Brother's Legacy of Love*.

De Vinck has also published two collections of autobiographical essays and a novel for young people. He says that his prose style comes out of what he learned from writing poetry, which he continues to do. His essays are published in newspapers and magazines, including the *Reader's Digest*.

Since receiving degrees from Ramapo State College and Columbia University, de Vinck has juggled two careers—writing and teaching. He taught English for 16 years and is currently language arts supervisor for kindergarten through 12th grade in Wayne, New Jersey. He and his wife have three children.

After Oliver died, de Vinck's mother gave him Oliver's red dinner bowl. De Vinck keeps it in the room where he writes. He says, "If Oliver could make a contribution with such limited ability, we all can." To young people with disabled brothers or sisters, he offers this advice: "Just love them."

OTHER WORKS *Augusta and Trab*   Extended Reading

POWER OF THE POWERLESS **673**

Alternative Activities

Cooperative Learning Invite students to brainstorm about their chosen word before they start to illustrate it. Students could use a word web or could take turns brainstorming aloud as another student serves as recorder. Encourage students to return to the text of the story to link the concept to some specific passage of text. Then have them begin to experiment with graphic designs and illustrations.

Words to Know

Other words that refer to animals or their characteristics include *catty, bearish, piggish, feline,* and *fishy*.

Across the Curriculum

Social Studies *Legislation for the Disabled* Have students research and gather information on any United States legislation protecting the rights of disabled persons. To guide their research, students should consider the following questions:

- What protections does the legislation offer?
- Who were the main supporters and opponents of the legislation?
- Are there major organizations that represent disabled individuals?

If possible, have students contact local agencies supporting the rights of the disabled and interview their spokespersons. Students can present their findings in an oral or written report.

Science *Cooperative Learning Birth Defects* Have students use library or computer resources to learn more about birth defects. They might focus their research on those disabilities caused by environmental factors (such as happened to Christopher de Vinck's brother, Oliver) or those caused by chromosomal abnormalities. Divide students into groups of three. Each group can focus on a specific type of defect. Members can divide responsibility according to resource—one using the computer, another consulting library references, and a third contacting local health organizations such as a chapter of the March of Dimes.

CHRISTOPHER DE VINCK

Although de Vinck's essay touched the hearts of many, it was initially rejected by the *Reader's Digest*. When it was published on the editorial page of the *Wall Street Journal*, it caught the attention of President Ronald Reagan, and the *New York Post* requested permission to reprint it the following day. *Reader's Digest*, regretting its original rejection, also reprinted the essay.

THE LANGUAGE OF LITERATURE **TEACHER'S EDITION** **673**

OVERVIEW

Objectives
- To understand and appreciate two poems about parent-child relationships
- To identify and understand the concept of tone
- To express understanding of the poems through a choice of writing forms, including a paragraph and a bedtime story
- To extend understanding of the poems through a variety of multimodal and cross-disciplinary activities

Skills

LITERARY CONCEPTS
- Tone
- Free verse

SPEAKING, LISTENING, AND VIEWING
- Oral interpretation
- Group discussion

Cross-Curricular Connections

SOCIAL STUDIES
- Fairy tales around the world

SCIENCE
- Hawaiian Islands

ALTERNATIVE

Previewing

Instead of writing their descriptions of a good father, students can choose partners and discuss their ideas.

Writing Connection

Discussion Prompts *Share your ideas about what characterizes a "good father" with your partner, and then listen carefully to your partner's ideas. Discuss the similarities and differences between your ideas and those of your partner. These questions can help you get started:*

- In your opinion, what would the personality of a "good father" be like?
- What responsibilities should a father fulfill?
- What kind of experiences might a good father share with his family?
- How might a good father respond to his own (or his children's) mistakes and failures?

Read the two poems closely to identify the characteristics that Leroy V. Quintana and Wing Tek Lum consider important in a father.

PREVIEWING

POETRY

A Fairy Tale
Leroy V. Quintana

My Mother Really Knew
Wing Tek Lum

Activating Prior Knowledge
PERSONAL CONNECTION

Each of the two poems you are about to read focuses on the connection between a father and a child. Take a few minutes to think about father-child relationships. What words do you associate with a father's love? Use a diagram like the one started here to help organize your thoughts. Then share your ideas with a small group of classmates.

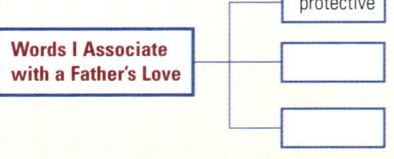

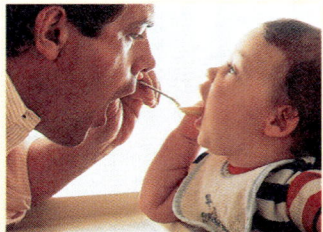

Building Background
CULTURAL CONNECTION

Children depend on their parents for love and the basic necessities of life. In traditional families, the mother runs the home and cares for the children, while the father makes the major family decisions. For many families in the United States and elsewhere, however, the traditional roles are changing.

More and more, parents are making decisions about their children together. Some fathers have even adopted the role of househusband, staying home with the children while their wives work. Today, the ways fathers love and care for their children are, in many cases, vastly different from what they were a century ago. Many fathers feel more comfortable about performing the more intimate tasks of parenting, such as diaper changing and toilet training.

Setting a Purpose
WRITING CONNECTION

What is your idea of a good father? Use the words you listed for the Personal Connection to help you write a description of the qualities of a good father. Share your description with classmates.

674 UNIT FIVE PART 2: VITAL CONNECTIONS

PRINT AND MEDIA RESOURCES

UNIT FIVE RESOURCE BOOK
Strategic Reading: Literature, p. 63

ACCESS FOR STUDENTS ACQUIRING ENGLISH
Reading and Writing Support

FORMAL ASSESSMENT
Selection Test, p. 127
 Test Generator

AUDIO LIBRARY
See Reference Card

---

674 THE LANGUAGE OF LITERATURE TEACHER'S EDITION

A FAIRY TALE

BY LEROY V. QUINTANA

Bedtime. I tell stories, tales
of Robert Rattlesnake, Bennie Beaver,
Yolanda Panda Bear, Jerry Giraffe
and Danny the Dog.
5 And then it's Elisa's turn. She begins
"Once upanza time. . ."
"¡Panza!"[1] I say. "It's not upanza,
it's *once upon* a time. This is a panza,"
and grab her stomach, tickle her
10 until she can laugh no more.
"Once upanza time. . . ."
"No No No No No!" I scream,
"It's *once upon* a time, not *upanza* time.
This is a panza," and I grab her stomach,
15 tickle her again until she's weak from laughter.
"Please tell me a real story," I plead,
"and please don't say panza."
"Once upanza time. . ." she begins.
"O.K.," I say, resigned. "You can say panza."
20 "Once upanza time. . .
there lived a panza
and it lived happily ever after.
Good night, Daddy."

---
1. panza: *Spanish*: belly.

FROM PERSONAL RESPONSE TO CRITICAL ANALYSIS

REFLECT 1. Think of a word or phrase that summarizes your reaction to this poem. Share it with your classmates.

2. How would you evaluate the parenting style of this father?

RETHINK 3. How would you characterize the relationship between the father and his daughter?
Consider
• the father's parenting style
• the activity they are engaged in
• how they interact with each other

RELATE 4. Review the description of a good father you wrote for the Writing Connection on page 674. In your opinion, is the father in this poem a good father? Why or why not?

A FAIRY TALE   675

Mini-Lesson   Literary Concepts

REVIEWING FREE VERSE Remind students that poetry with no regular patterns of rhyme, rhythm, or line length is called free verse. Often poets write in free verse to capture the sounds and rhythms of everyday speech. For example, in "A Fairy Tale," the poet lists characters in bedtime stories ("Robert Rattlesnake, Bennie Beaver,/Yolanda Panda Bear, Jerry Giraffe/and Danny the Dog") in a conversational manner. If the poet had used rhyme or a regular rhythm in these lines, the reader might have had a less distinct sense of everyday language.

Application Have students rewrite four or six lines of either poem using rhyme and the same number of syllables in each line in their rewrites. Then have them discuss the different effects of the original lines and the lines they have written.

CUSTOMIZING FOR

Students Acquiring English

2 Explain that "a tough cookie" is an idiomatic phrase that describes a strong-willed person.

3 The expression "a chip off the old block" means the child behaves as the parent does.

Literary Concept: TONE

B Help students understand that the poet's series of simple declarative statements conveys an earnest tone. Ask them to cite other parts of the text that show that Wing Tek Lum's tone is not lighthearted. *(Possible responses: The poem's final lines convey the seriousness—and the note of melancholy—with which the poet views the love he feels for his parents.)*

CUSTOMIZING FOR

Multiple Learning Styles

C **Bodily-Kinesthetic Learners** Ask students why the mother and brothers coax the speaker to kiss the father. Ask them if it's more important to demonstrate one's love physically or verbally.

Cultural Note

D The islands referred to in this simile are the Hawaiian Islands.

CUSTOMIZING FOR

Gifted and Talented Students

Have students make critical evaluations of these two poems. Encourage them to make judgments about each work, using standards such as originality, emotional power, and the use of poetic devices.

COMPREHENSION CHECK

1. What words does the child in "A Fairy Tale" confuse with *upanza?* *("upon a")*
2. What act is the narrator of "My Mother Really Knew" coaxed into performing? *(kissing his father good night)*

My Mother Really Knew

by Wing Tek Lum

2 My father was a tough cookie,
his friends still tell me with a smile.
He was hot-tempered
and had to have his own way,
but they loved him nonetheless,
and so did I.

I remember that
for maybe the first decade of my life
I had to kiss him every night
B before I went to bed.

There was one time
he got into a big argument
with the rest of us at dinnertime,
and afterwards when he was in his study
I had to go to sleep
and refused to see him,
3 a chip off the old block.

But my mother and elder brothers
coaxed me to his door,
and I ran in
C and pecked his cheek
without saying a word,
and went to bed
thinking of how unfair life was.

Love, my mother really knew,
was like these islands[1]
formed in part
D by tidal waves and hurricanes
and the eruptions of volcanoes,
which suddenly appear
and just as suddenly go away.

1. **these islands:** the Hawaiian Islands.

Mini-Lesson: Speaking, Listening, and Viewing

ORAL INTERPRETATION Remind students that poets choose words not only for their meaning but also for their sounds. Explain that poets often create meaning by arranging words in lines in certain ways, so that the verse conveys various rhythms. An oral interpretation of a poem can convey these sound devices as well as the emotional tone of the work.

Application Have students present a variety of oral interpretations of either poem. Encourage them to experiment with different strategies for delivering each work. Have them rehearse with a tape recorder, if possible.

RESPONDING OPTIONS

FROM PERSONAL RESPONSE TO CRITICAL ANALYSIS

REFLECT 1. What is your response to "My Mother Really Knew"? Record your reactions in your notebook.

RETHINK
Thematic Link

2. What does the last stanza of the poem suggest about parent-child relationships?

3. The speaker of the poem is said to be "a chip off the old block." In what ways might the speaker be like the father? Explain your opinion.

4. What do you think the speaker's mother really knew?

RELATE 5. Recall that the mood of a work of literature is the emotional effect it has on the reader. Compare and contrast the moods of these two poems. What do the moods of the poems reveal about the children's feelings for their fathers?

6. How are the father-child relationships presented in the two poems alike, and how are they different? Use information from the poems to support your conclusions.

Multimodal Learning
ANOTHER PATHWAY

A storyboard is a series of sketches arranged in sequence. Create a storyboard for one of the two poems, showing visually the sequence of events it presents. Label each sketch in the storyboard, then display it in the classroom.

QUICKWRITES

1. The mother in the poem "My Mother Really Knew" shows that she has wisdom about the love between parents and children, and it seems that the speaker benefits from her wisdom. Think of a time when someone showed wisdom that improved your understanding of a person or thing. Write a **paragraph** describing the situation, the nature of the wisdom, and the way it helped you.

2. Create a short **bedtime story** that expands on the story the little girl tells at the end of "A Fairy Tale."

📁 **PORTFOLIO** *Save your writing. You may want to use it later as a springboard to a piece for your portfolio.*

LITERARY CONCEPTS

A writer's expression of his or her attitude toward a subject is called the writer's **tone**. A writer's tone might be described, for example, as angry, sad, humorous, or admiring. Think about the tones of the two poems and then compare them. Do you prefer one poem's tone to the other's? Explain your answer.

A FAIRY TALE/MY MOTHER REALLY KNEW

From Personal Response to Critical Analysis

1. Responses will vary.
2. Possible response: The last stanza suggests that parents and children are bound to experience many arguments and conflicts and hurt feelings, but these are a natural part of love.
3. Possible response: The father is characterized as a stubborn hothead and the narrator demonstrates these same qualities by refusing to kiss the father good night.
4. Possible response: The speaker's mother really knew how much love her husband and the speaker felt for each other, as well as how important it was to demonstrate that love can survive conflict.
5. Possible responses: The first poem's mood is playful—it shows an easy informality that the child and parent have with each other. The serious, reflective mood of the second poem shows a stormier relationship between parent and child.
6. Possible response: In both cases, the parent and the child love each other deeply; the first relationship is more relaxed and playful than the second.

Another Pathway
Urge students to begin by analyzing the poem in order to divide it into sections. Then have them make decisions about how best to illustrate each section. Remind them to use the same artistic style in each successive storyboard.

Rubric
3 Full Accomplishment Students identify all major events and effectively illustrate them in order.
2 Substantial Accomplishment Students identify most major events and illustrate them adequately and in order.
1 Little or Partial Accomplishment Students have trouble identifying major events and illustrate them out of order.

Literary Concepts
You (or student volunteers) might wish to give oral readings of the two poems, in order to help students hear the playful tone of "A Fairy Tale" and contrast it with the earnest tone of "My Mother Really Knew." If students have difficulty identifying tone, ask them to consider the emotions the characters express in each poem—pleasure and anger.

QuickWrites
1. Invite students to brainstorm ideas for their paragraphs. Ask them to think about various people who have taught them things, both important and less important.
2. Encourage students to consider their audiences as they create their bedtime stories. If possible, have them think of a particular child they know, in order to make decisions about what would be most interesting and entertaining to a young child.

The Writer's Craft
Audience, pp. 234–35
Effective Paragraphs, pp. 244–51

Across the Curriculum

Social Studies *Fairy Tales Around the World* Have students investigate fairy tales from various cultures. For instance, they might look into tales from the British Isles and Ireland, Germany (such as those collected by the Brothers Grimm), Scandinavia, Africa, or Mexico. Students can also research the various retellings of particular fairy tales from culture to culture. Ask them to find similarities and differences among versions from different cultures.

Science *Cooperative Learning* *Hawaiian Islands* Have students research the geological history of the Hawaiian Islands. Encourage them to collect information on the volcanoes that formed each of the eight major islands. Divide the class into eight groups and assign each group a specific island. Students can put together a bulletin board to display their findings.

LEROY V. QUINTANA

Quintana is a Vietnam veteran whose two major interests are Vietnam and New Mexico. "In many ways, I'm still basically a small-town New Mexico boy carrying on the oral tradition," he says. "I seem to be tied to a sense of the past; my work reflects the 'sense of place' evoked by New Mexico. I hope I am worthy of portraying the land and its people well."

WING TEK LUM

Lum has published one volume of poetry, *Expounding the Doubtful Points*. This first volume focuses on his family and Chinese-American issues. He is working on a second volume that explores what it was like to live in Honolulu's Chinatown a hundred years ago. He lives on the island of Oahu with his wife and daughter.

Multimodal Activities

ALTERNATIVE ACTIVITIES

1. **Cooperative Learning** With a small group, compose a **lullaby** that the father in "A Fairy Tale" might sing to his daughter at bedtime. Keep in mind the kind of father that he appears to be. Then perform your lullaby for the class.
2. Create an **artistic representation** of the concept of love presented in the last stanza of "My Mother Really Knew." Use any medium or form you want—paint, pencil, collage, or clay, for example.

LEROY V. QUINTANA

1944–

Leroy Quintana is a descendant of the early Spanish settlers in what is now New Mexico. He grew up listening to traditional Mexican folk tales and stories of the Old West told by his grandparents, who raised him. "I have always," he has said, "enjoyed stories—I read comic books by the hundreds, went to the movies, and recited the stanzas in the back of the catechism [a book of religious instruction] religiously."

Drawing on folklore and his childhood experiences, Quintana's first volumes of poetry, *Hijo del Pueblo* and *Sangre*, describe village life in New Mexico. He has twice received the American Book Award for poetry from the Before Columbus Foundation.

Quintana began writing when he was a student at the University of New Mexico. He received graduate degrees in English from New Mexico State University and in counseling from Western New Mexico University. He currently teaches at San Diego Mesa College. His daughter Elisa, now an engineering student, is the girl featured in "A Fairy Tale."
OTHER WORKS *Interrogations, A History of Home*

Extended Readings

WING TEK LUM

According to Wing Tek Lum (1946–), "My Mother Really Knew" is autobiographical. "My mother was a very good person," he says. "My father was more authoritarian—I respected him." Lum's mother died when he was 16 years old; his father, when the poet was 29. "The only way I can hold on to my relationship with them," he states, "is by thinking about them through my poetry."

"I slid into poetry as a hobby," explains Lum. "I am a slow reader and writer. Perhaps that stirred me into writing poetry, not prose. Poetry is like a snapshot, a slice of time. A prose writer sees many slices." Lum's Chinese-born mother and Hawaiian-born father made him aware, he says, of his Chinese roots while encouraging a strong identification with American culture.

An excellent mathematics and science student, Lum left his native Hawaii to study engineering at Brown University in Providence, Rhode Island. He then attended Union Theological Seminary in New York City and did social work in New York and Hong Kong before returning to Hawaii.
OTHER WORKS *Expounding the Doubtful Points*

Extended Readings

Alternative Activities

1. **Cooperative Learning** Suggest groups first discuss any lullabies they already know. They may wish to write new lyrics to a familiar tune. Encourage students to incorporate the father's humor and the poet's free verse style into their compositions.
2. Help students focus on the lines' simile, which compares love with islands. Make sure they understand that, as tidal waves and hurricanes and volcanic eruptions were part of what formed the islands, so emotional storms contribute to the growth of love. Remind students that their representation does not have to be literal; it could, for instance, convey the emotional impact of the lines.

PREVIEWING

POETRY

Sea-Fever
John Masefield

Mi Madre
Pat Mora

Activating Prior Knowledge
PERSONAL CONNECTION

The speakers of the poems you are about to read express their strong feelings for the natural world—specifically, the sea and the desert. To which of the two are you most drawn? What aspects of the desert and the sea appeal to you most? Jot down your thoughts in a word web like the one shown. Compare your ideas with those of your classmates.

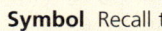

Building Background
LITERARY CONNECTION

Elements of nature move some people to great emotion, compel the truly dedicated to live in the wilderness, and inspire creative expression. Nature has stirred some of our greatest writers. Henry David Thoreau, who in 1844 rejected creature comforts for a cabin in the woods, is among the most famous of America's poetic nature writers. Thoreau wrote, "I seek acquaintance with Nature—to know her moods and manners." His classic work *Walden* is a record of his experiment in living with nature.

In the early 20th century, several desert writers became popular. One of these was Mary Austin, who wrote lyrical sketches of the dry lands of the Southwest. Later, Joseph Wood Krutch, a resident of Arizona, wrote *The Desert Year* (1952) and *The Voice of the Desert* (1955). Also around that time, Anne Morrow Lindbergh described, in *Gift from the Sea,* her search of sea and sand to find "a new pattern of living."

In recent years, because of a heightened public concern with the environment, nature writing has become more popular. Thoreau's sentiment—"Give me the ocean, the desert, or the wilderness!"—probably means more to Americans today than it did 150 years ago.

Setting A Purpose
READING CONNECTION

Symbol Recall that writers sometimes use concrete objects—people, places, or things—as symbols that stand for ideas or qualities. An eagle may be used to symbolize strength, for example, or a rose to stand for love. As you read these poems, think about how the poets make use of symbols.

Walden Pond in Massachusetts, site of Thoreau's cabin. Copyright © Doris De Witt/Tony Stone Images.

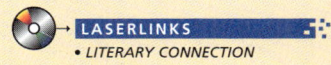
• LITERARY CONNECTION

OVERVIEW

Objectives

- To understand and appreciate two lyric poems about a special connection to nature
- To identify and understand the concept of imagery
- To understand the elements of poetry
- To express understanding of the poems through a choice of writing forms, including a poem and an advertisement
- To extend understanding of the poems through a variety of multimodal and cross-disciplinary activities

Skills

LITERARY CONCEPTS
- Imagery
- Personification

SPEAKING, LISTENING, AND VIEWING
- Group discussion
- Oral presentation

Cross-Curricular Connections

SCIENCE
- Desert blooms

GEOGRAPHY
- Earth's oceans and seas

LITERARY CONNECTION
Desert Scenes Viewing these photographs of the desert will help students envision the images Pat Mora conjures up in "Mi Madre."

Side A, Frame 52848

PRINT AND MEDIA RESOURCES

UNIT FIVE RESOURCE BOOK
Strategic Reading: Literature, p. 67

FORMAL ASSESSMENT
Selection Test, pp. 129–130
Part Test, pp. 131–132
 Test Generator

ALTERNATIVE ASSESSMENT
End-of-Year Integrated Assessment: Reader, pp. 31–42; Student Response Booklet, pp. 43–56

ACCESS FOR STUDENTS ACQUIRING ENGLISH
Selection Summaries

 **AUDIO LIBRARY**
See Reference Card

 **LASERLINKS**
Literary Connection

Sea-Fever

Sea-Fever
by John Masefield

I must go down to the seas again, to the lonely sea and the sky,
And all I ask is a tall ship and a star to steer her by,
And the wheel's kick and the wind's song and the white sail's
    shaking,
And a grey mist on the sea's face and a grey dawn breaking.

5 I must go down to the seas again, for the call of the running tide
Is a wild call and a clear call that may not be denied;
And all I ask is a windy day with the white clouds flying,
And the flung spray and the blown spume[1] and the sea gulls crying.

I must go down to the seas again to the vagrant gypsy life,[2]
10 To the gull's way and the whale's way where the wind's like
    a whetted[3] knife;
And all I ask is a merry yarn from a laughing fellow-rover,
And quiet sleep and a sweet dream when the long trick's over.

---

1. **spume:** foam.
2. **vagrant gypsy life:** a carefree life of wandering from place to place.
3. **whetted:** sharpened.

FROM PERSONAL RESPONSE TO CRITICAL ANALYSIS

REFLECT 1. What is your impression of the speaker of this poem? Discuss your thoughts with the class.

RETHINK 2. Does the speaker ask for simple things or extravagant things? Explain your answer.

3. In the Reading Connection on page 679, you were asked to think about symbols. What do you think the sea symbolizes for the speaker? Give reasons for your answer.
   Consider
   • what the speaker asks of the sea
   • the description of the call of the tide
   • the kind of life the speaker yearns for

4. Explain what the title of the poem means to you.

680 UNIT FIVE PART 2: VITAL CONNECTIONS

Mini-Lesson Literary Concepts

REVIEWING PERSONIFICATION Use the word web shown to remind students that personification is the technique of giving human qualities to an animal, an object, or an idea. For example, in "Sea Fever," John Masefield personifies the sea when he describes it as "lonely" in the first line.

Application Have students identify another example of personification in the poem. (*Possible response: "the sea's face"*) Then have them identify two other things—one animate and one inanimate—that the poet personifies. (*the tide, the sea gulls*) Remind them to note the sensory details Masefield uses to give human qualities to animals, things, and ideas.

Thematic Link: *Vital Connections* In both of these poems, the speaker celebrates a passionate connection to an element of the natural world.

CUSTOMIZING FOR
Students Acquiring English

• Use **ACCESS FOR STUDENTS ACQUIRING ENGLISH,** *Reading and Writing Support.*

1. Remind students that sailors typically refer to their ships as if they were female, in this case as "her."

2. Paraphrase "a merry yarn from a laughing fellow-rover" as "a funny story told by another traveler."

STRATEGIC READING FOR
Less-Proficient Readers

Set a Purpose Have students read to find out how each poet describes a natural landscape.

Use **UNIT FIVE RESOURCE BOOK,** p. 69, for guidance in reading the selection.

Literary Concept: IMAGERY

A Ask students how Masefield uses imagery to convey the idea that the sea is an exciting place to be. (*Possible responses: "wheel's kick," "white sail's shaking," "wild call," "flung spray," "blown spume," "wind's like a whetted knife"*)

From Personal Response to Critical Analysis

1. Responses will vary.
2. Possible response: The speaker asks for simple things—a ship, wind, spray, sea gulls, a merry yarn, sleep and dreams.
3. Possible responses: The sea may symbolize the simple life, freedom, independence, adventure, self-reliance, and so forth.
4. Responses will vary.

680 THE LANGUAGE OF LITERATURE TEACHER'S EDITION

Mi Madre[1] B

BY PAT MORA

I say feed me.
She serves red prickly pear[2] on a spiked cactus. 3

I say tease me.
She sprinkles raindrops in my face on a sunny day.

I say frighten me.
She shouts thunder, flashes lightning.

I say comfort me.
She invites me to lay on her firm body.

I say heal me.
She gives me *manzanilla, orégano, dormilón.*[3]

I say caress me.
She strokes my skin with her warm breath.

I say make me beautiful.
She offers turquoise for my fingers, a pink blossom for my hair.

I say sing to me.
She chants lonely women's songs of femaleness.

I say teach me.
She endures: glaring heat
numbing cold
frightening dryness.

She: the desert
She: strong mother. C

---

1. **mi madre** (mē mä′drĕ) *Spanish:* my mother.
2. **prickly pear:** the pear-shaped edible fruit of a kind of cactus.
3. ***manzanilla*** (män-sä-nē′yä), ***orégano*** (ô-rĕ′gä-nô), ***dormilón*** (dôr-mē-lôn′) *Spanish:* sweet-smelling herbs that can be used to make home medicines.

681

Literary Concept:
PERSONIFICATION

B Point out to students that Pat Mora's personification of the desert begins in the title. Figuratively, she views the desert as her mother. Invite students to search the poem for all the verbs that reinforce the idea of the desert as a human being. *(serves, sprinkles, shouts, invites, gives, strokes, offers, chants, endures)*

CUSTOMIZING FOR
Students Acquiring English

3 Be sure all students understand that "she" here refers to the desert.

CUSTOMIZING FOR
Multiple Learning Styles

C **Linguistic Learners** Using the word *desert* or *sea* as a starting point, students can brainstorm and create a word web of associated imagery.

CUSTOMIZING FOR
Gifted and Talented Students

Have students decide which poem is more dependent on personification for its effects. *("Mi Madre")* Then have them rewrite the poem in such a way that it communicates the same basic ideas but does not use personification. Invite them to discuss the differences between Mora's poem and their rewrites.

COMPREHENSION CHECK

1. What is the speaker of "Sea- Fever" determined to do? *(to sail on the sea)*
2. How many "characters" are there in the poem "Mi Madre"? *(The speaker is the only human being, but the desert—the speaker's "mother"—could be considered a second character.)*

Multicultural Perspectives

EARLY DESERT DWELLERS Among those who have made a life in the deserts of North America, one of the earliest and most important groups are the Cochise. This Native American culture flourished between 8000 and 2000 B.C. in parts of the Great Basin—an area comprising parts of present-day Nevada, Utah, Arizona, and New Mexico.

The Cochise people were a desert culture (as opposed to a hunting culture), and they turned to the desert itself to gather wild plants and seeds. Later some Cochise grew maize, while others made arrows and began hunting small game.

From Personal Response to Critical Analysis

1. Responses will vary.
2. Possible responses: She calls the desert a mother because it provides her with sustenance. Perhaps the speaker is from the desert and thinks of herself as a child of the desert.
3. Possible responses: provides a home for various animals and insects; gives people a sense of simplicity and purity
4. Possible response: The speaker of "Sea-Fever" needs to experience the adventure, movement, and solitude of sailing. The speaker of "Mi Madre" also needs solitude, but she wishes to be tended to in various ways—fed, caressed, healed, comforted, taught, and groomed.
5. Encourage students to supply samples from the texts.

Another Pathway

Cooperative Learning Students might choose individual stanzas to work on, or the whole group could make its way through the poem stanza by stanza. You might wish to assign one student to record ideas and another to explain procedures the group will follow.

Rubric

3 Full Accomplishment Students rewrite the poem, substituting vivid, imaginative descriptions of an ocean landscape for the original's descriptions of the desert.

2 Substantial Accomplishment Students rewrite nearly all of the poem, substituting some imaginative descriptions of an ocean landscape for the original's descriptions of the desert.

1 Little or Partial Accomplishment Students find it difficult to adhere to the structure of "Mi Madre" as they substitute a few descriptions of the ocean for the original's desert descriptions.

RESPONDING OPTIONS

FROM PERSONAL RESPONSE TO CRITICAL ANALYSIS

REFLECT
1. What feeling does "Mi Madre" leave you with? Write your thoughts in your notebook.

RETHINK
Thematic Link
2. Why do you think the speaker calls the desert a mother?
3. Note the ways in which the maternal desert gives of herself. Describe some other ways—ones that the speaker does not mention.

RELATE
4. Compare and contrast the needs of the speakers of these two poems.
5. In your opinion, which speaker paints the most appealing or convincing picture of nature? Explain your choice.

Multimodal Learning
ANOTHER PATHWAY

Cooperative Learning
What if "Mi Madre" were a poem about the sea? With a small group of classmates, reread the poem and brainstorm ways to turn the sentences beginning "She . . ." into statements about the sea. For example, your first stanza might read: "I say feed me. / She releases a scurrying crab on the shore."

LITERARY CONCEPTS

Words and phrases that appeal to readers' five senses are examples of **imagery**. Writers use imagery to convey how things look, feel, smell, sound, and taste. Note how the phrases "the lonely sea" and "red prickly pear on a spiked cactus" help you visualize the objects in these poems. Find other examples of imagery.

CONCEPT REVIEW: Elements of Poetry Make a chart, like the one shown, to analyze the elements of poetry in the poems. Record examples of each element and explain why you think the poet uses it.

Elements of Poetry		
Element	**Example**	**Why It Is Used**
Rhyme and rhythm		
Simile		
Repetition		
Alliteration		
Personification		

QUICKWRITES

1. The speaker of one of these poems has "sea fever." What in nature do you get feverish about? Perhaps you have Arctic fever or mountain fever! Write a **poem** about one of your favorite aspects of nature.

2. Create an **advertisement** for a seaside or desert vacation spot, using words, phrases, and lines from the appropriate poem.

📁 **PORTFOLIO** Save your writing. You may want to use it later as a springboard to a piece for your portfolio.

682 UNIT FIVE PART 2: VITAL CONNECTIONS

Literary Concepts

You might have students use a word web for each of the five senses. On the web they might list such images as *tall ship, wind's song, sail's shaking, red prickly pear, oregano*.

Concept Review Have students list examples first and then reflect on the poet's purpose in using these elements. If necessary, remind students that rhyme, rhythm, alliteration, and repetition all make a poem more musical. Similes help to create vivid descriptions.

QuickWrites

1. You might have students begin by listing descriptive details that relate to each of the five senses. Encourage them to think about how they would like their poem to sound.

2. Invite students to survey any available advertisements—especially for resorts or vacation spots—to familiarize themselves with the particular way that language is used in them.

Writing a Poem, pp. 76–80

LITERARY LINKS

Like Masefield, Elinor Wylie wrote a poem about the sea—"Sea Lullaby" (page 131). Compare and contrast "Sea-Fever" with Wylie's poem. How are the poets' imagery and characterizations of the sea alike, and how are they different? What does the sea symbolize in each poem?

Multimodal Learning

ALTERNATIVE ACTIVITIES

With a partner, choose appropriate **music** to accompany a reading of each poem. After each of you reads one of the poems with musical accompaniment, discuss which poem sounds best when set to music and why that poem sounds best.

JOHN MASEFIELD

1878–1967

As a teenager, John Masefield dreamed of becoming a writer. The adults who knew him had other ideas: "Put this writing-rubbish right out of your head," they would say, or, "Only clever people can be writers." They were undoubtedly surprised when Masefield was named poet laureate of England in 1930. Masefield published more than 30 volumes of poetry, 8 novels, 13 plays, and a number of short stories, biographies, and essays.

After the death of his parents, Masefield was raised in Ledbury, England, by his uncle. When he was 13, he ended his formal education by running away to the sea. For four years he traveled the world, working on ships. He eventually settled in New York City. There, he spent two years working on the waterfront and in a bakery, a stable, a saloon, and a rug mill. He also began to write.

Very unhappy and homesick, Masefield burned most of what he had written and returned to England, where he experimented with different writing styles and forms. "In verse, men must try for something of music and of painting; in prose, for something of drama and of portrait," Masefield once wrote. In 1902, he published his first collection of poems, *Salt-Water Poems and Ballads,* from which "Sea-Fever" is taken.

OTHER WORKS *Jim Davis* Extended Reading

PAT MORA

1942–

"I write," Pat Mora says, "in part, because Hispanic perspectives need to be part of our literary heritage.... I also write because I am fascinated by the pleasure and power of words." Mora's poetry, nonfiction, and short stories prove that she remains true to her words. In her work, she portrays the cultural diversity and visual beauty of the Southwest and the harmony that can exist between nature and human beings.

Mora has spent most of her life in El Paso, Texas, where she was born. (Her four grandparents had migrated from Mexico to El Paso to escape a revolution early in this century.) After receiving a master's degree from the University of Texas at El Paso, she pursued a career in teaching. She also for a time hosted a public-radio show called *Voices: The Mexican-American in Perspective.*

In 1986, Mora received a Kellogg National Fellowship to study ways of preserving cultures. She explains, "I am interested in how we save languages and traditions. What we have inside of our homes and our families is a treasure chest that we don't pay attention to." She urges young people to preserve their heritage by tape-recording their family's stories and finding out about the cultural treasures in their homes.

OTHER WORKS *Chants* Extended Reading

SEA-FEVER/MI MADRE **683**

Literary Links

Wylie characterizes the sea as a violent force—a killer. She uses imagery such as "treacherous smiler" and "savage beguiler" to depict the ocean's capacity for destruction. In contrast, Masefield uses imagery such as "the call of the running tide" and "lonely sea" to characterize the ocean as a welcoming, if moody being. In the former poem the sea symbolizes death, whereas in the latter it symbolizes life and adventure.

Across the Curriculum

Science Cooperative Learning *Desert Blooms* Invite groups to select one of the following types of cacti: ball cactus, barrel cactus, bishop's cap, chin, fishhook, hedgehog, leaf, moon, old man, organ pipe, peyote, pincushion, torch, and prickly pear cactus. One member can look for scientific information about its characteristics and another for illustrations. A third can synthesize and record these findings, and a fourth can present an oral report to the class.

Geography *Earth's Oceans and Seas* Have students use an atlas, almanac, or other reference book to learn more about the world's oceans and seas. They might choose to focus on one ocean, such as the Arctic or Indian.

JOHN MASEFIELD

In an account of his early years, John Masefield wrote, "I was in the garden one day, standing near a clump of honeysuckle and looking north. As I looked, I became aware, for the first time, that I had an imagination, and that I could tell this faculty to imagine all manner of strange things, and at once the strange things, especially fantastic things, would be there in multitude to do my bidding."

PAT MORA

Pat Mora's work includes a volume of poetry, *Agua Santa: Holy Water;* a collection of family stories, *Voices from the Interior;* and two picture books, *Pablo's Tree* and *The Desert Is My Mother: El desierto es mi madre.*

Alternative Activities

Have students sample as wide a variety of musical selections as possible. For instance, have them consider selections in different genres, such as classical, folk (especially songs from Mexico), and ambient music. If possible, have students listen to sea chanteys, as well. Encourage students to experiment by doing readings with music that is more or less rhythmic.

THE LANGUAGE OF LITERATURE TEACHER'S EDITION **683**

OVERVIEW

To gain a deeper appreciation of the nonfiction selections they have read in this unit, students will explore the characteristics of a persuasive essay and then create their own well-developed example in this lesson.

Objectives

- To plan a persuasive essay by considering such elements as support, audience, language, and organization
- To draft a persuasive essay and solicit a response
- To revise, edit, and publish a persuasive essay
- To reflect on the process of writing a persuasive essay

Skills

LITERATURE
- Identifying audience

WRITING AND LANGUAGE
- Evaluating facts
- Crafting an introduction
- Organizing information
- Drafting a conclusion
- Avoiding loaded language

GRAMMAR AND USAGE
- Avoiding double negatives

MEDIA LITERACY
- Interpreting a nutrition chart
- Analyzing news broadcasts
- Studying personal correspondence

SPEAKING, LISTENING, AND VIEWING
- Conferencing
- Campaigning
- Reading aloud

CRITICAL THINKING
- Evaluating sources

Critical Thinking: ANALYZING

A Be sure that students understand that persuasive writing tries to convince readers to accept the writer's opinion on an issue or to take a course of action. Explain that persuasion builds on many of the skills students have already learned, including defining, stating problems and solutions, and comparing and contrasting.

Teaching Strategy: STUMBLING BLOCK

B To make sure that students understand this introduction to persuasion, invite them to list the characteristics of persuasive writing. Possible responses may include:
- a message about a controversial issue
- facts and examples to support that position
- consideration of both sides of the issue

Correct any misconceptions that student responses reflect.

WRITING FROM EXPERIENCE

Writing to Persuade

In Unit Five, "Personal Discoveries," you read about individuals who faced opposition as they struggled to change people's minds. How often have you been in a similar situation? Were you as successful as you had hoped to be? In this lesson, you will learn how to persuade others, as well as to recognize when someone is trying to persuade you!

GUIDED ASSIGNMENT

A **Write a Persuasive Essay** Write an essay persuading others to agree with you about an issue that you feel is important.

1 Discuss the Issues

What situations are reflected in the items on these two pages? Have you heard any of these topics discussed on television or on the radio? Have you thought about any of these issues yourself?

Find the Message Write a summary of each of the topics presented here. Can you identify more than one side of each issue? How does the information each source presents help you understand the issues? What more would you want to know about each topic before forming an opinion?

B **Share the Message** Compare your summaries with those of some of your classmates. In what ways are your summaries alike? How are they different?

2 Choose an Issue

C Make a list of other situations about which people disagree. Choose the issue you feel most strongly about. Write a paragraph briefly telling what the two sides of the issue are. What is your position?

684 UNIT FIVE: PERSONAL DISCOVERIES

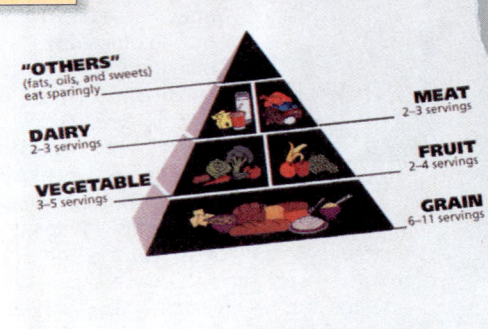

Nutrition Chart
Leading doctors and scientists want the U.S. Department of Agriculture and the Department of Health and Human Services to revise the requirements for a balanced diet. They feel that people should eat more vegetables and less meat.

PRINT AND MEDIA RESOURCES

UNIT FIVE RESOURCE BOOK
Prewriting Activity, p. 71
Elaboration, p. 72
Peer Response Guide, pp. 73–74
Revising and Proofreading, p. 75
Student Model, pp. 76–77
Rubric, p. 78

GRAMMAR MINI-LESSONS
Transparencies, pp. 13–15
Copymasters, p. 21

WRITING MINI-LESSONS
Transparencies, p. 37

ACCESS FOR STUDENTS ACQUIRING ENGLISH
Reading and Writing Support

FORMAL ASSESSMENT
Guidelines for Writing Assessment

 **LASERLINKS**
Writing Springboard

News Broadcast
News Anchor: "Crowds gathered outside a stadium in Minneapolis today to protest sports teams' use of Native American names."

Personal Correspondence

Coach Bradley,
I'd like to try out for the football team this year. I love the game! I play football with my brothers and other kids in my neighborhood all the time.

Sincerely,
Carla Babrick

This is so wrong! I think I'll write about this.

Why shouldn't girls be allowed to try out for football?

LINCOLN MIDDLE SCHOOL

Carla, thanks for your note. I'm sorry, but I think football is too dangerous for girls. Have you thought about trying out for the cheerleading squad?

—Coach Bradley

LASERLINKS
• WRITING SPRINGBOARD

WRITING COACH

WRITING FROM EXPERIENCE   685

Teaching Strategy: USING WRITING SPRINGBOARDS

C Encourage students to respond freely to the writing prompts on pages 684 and 685. Have students begin by discussing their responses in small groups.

Teaching Strategy: MODELING

D Discuss with students the news broadcast and personal correspondence shown on this page. Encourage students to freewrite about one or more of these items in their journals. Remind students that their responses will not be graded and may provide them with useful material for other persuasive writing assignments.

WRITING SPRINGBOARD
Boys Town Changes Kids' Lives
How can going on an old-fashioned cattle drive change your life forever? Two troubled boys who took part in this Boys Town program explain.

Side B, Frame 20022

Writing Prompt Some people say that programs like the ones Boys Town runs are the only way to reach some children. Others contend that these programs are expensive, wasteful, and a reward for bad behavior. What do you think? Write a persuasive essay in favor of or against these programs.

THE LANGUAGE OF LITERATURE Teacher's Edition **685**

CUSTOMIZING FOR
Less-Proficient Writers

E Inexperienced writers often produce inadequate support for their views because they do not know how to use the library to gather facts, details, or other evidence. Review research methods with students, using the mini-lesson on the bottom of this page. In addition, explain some of the latest on-line resources that can present special problems. You may also want to plan individual conferences with students to determine which sources they should use to begin their research.

Media Literacy:
GATHERING FACTS

F Suggest that as students look for facts in various sources, they see themselves as helping to solve some of the problems and issues they discover. Explain that the issues that engage them most fully will probably be the ones they can research most thoroughly and thus write about most convincingly.

Teaching Strategy: MODELING

G Explain that an idea tree works the same way as a cluster diagram to help writers generate ideas. Using the idea tree on this page as a model, describe how students write the general topic at the bottom or top of a sheet of paper. Then they think of ideas that are related to the topic and write them as branches connected to the main topic.

PREWRITING

Building Your Case

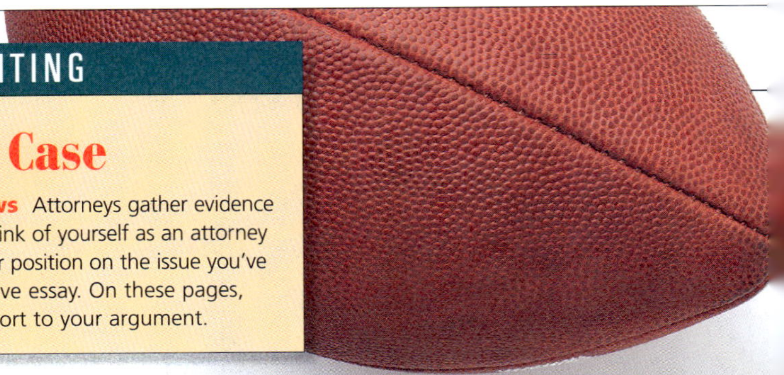

Ways to Support Your Views Attorneys gather evidence to use in their clients' defense. Think of yourself as an attorney out to gather facts to defend your position on the issue you've chosen to argue in your persuasive essay. On these pages, you'll discover ways to add support to your argument.

❶ List Your Views

Make a list of everything you know about the issue. Include any questions you might have. You can make an idea tree like the one below to list what you know and what you need to find out.

❷ Look for Support

As you research your topic, consider including the following types of support.

Facts A fact is a statement that can be proved. Facts are important sources of support because they make your argument more persuasive.

Student's Idea Tree

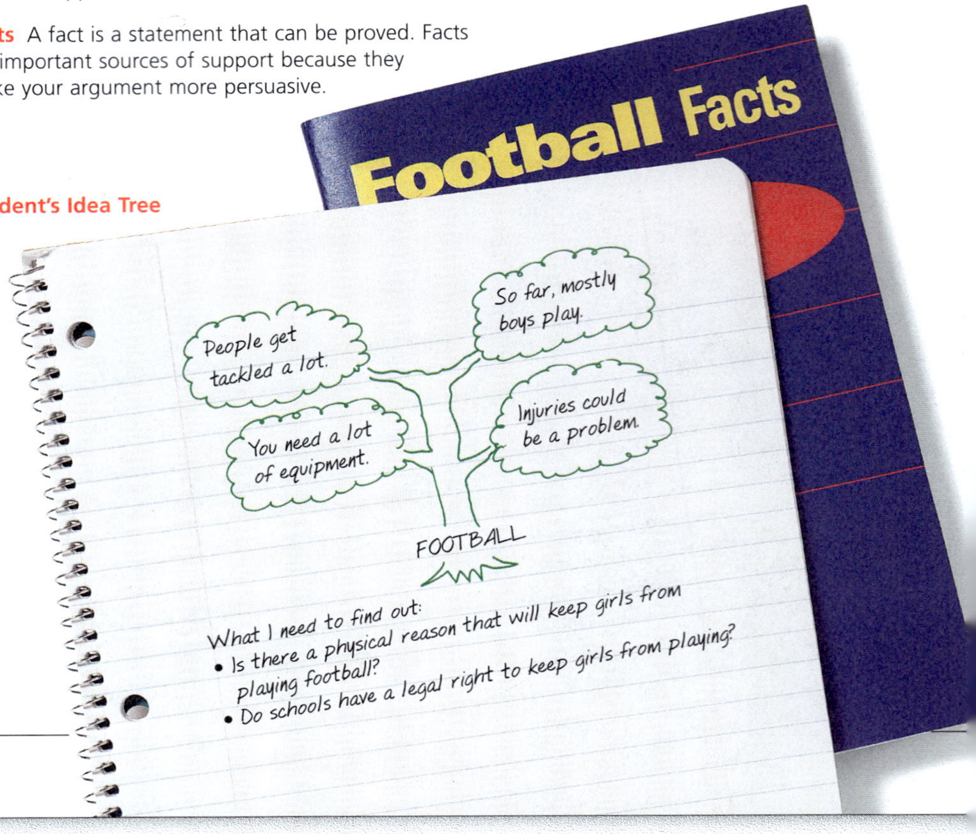

SkillBuilder **RESEARCH SKILLS**

GENERAL REFERENCE SOURCES Provide students with the following overview of reference sources to use as they build their persuasive case:
- Encyclopedias are collections of informational articles written by experts. There are general encyclopedias such as *World Book* and specialized volumes such as *The Encyclopedia of Sports*.
- Almanacs and yearbooks contain current facts and statistics on topics such as government and sports.
- Atlases are books of maps. They provide information about highways, population, government, climates, landforms, and so on.
- Periodicals are newspapers, magazines, and journals. Recent periodicals are kept on open shelves; older ones are stored in back rooms or on a film called microforms.

Application Encourage students to use a wide variety of reference sources to get the most accurate, authoritative, and unbiased information on their topics. As students research a topic, they should keep a list of all sources they investigated.

Opinions Opinions are personal feelings or beliefs. Therefore, they cannot be proved. However, opinions are important sources of support because they may summarize people's points of view. Opinions are also sometimes given by authorities in specific fields, such as doctors and professors.

Page 850 of the Multimedia Handbook offers tips on using on-line services to research facts, opinions, and opposing points of view. You can also do a computer search at your local library or use the card catalog to find books and articles on your subject. The SkillBuilder at the right will help you evaluate the sources you find.

❸ Identify Your Audience

Who is your audience? Decide how much they know about the issue. As you draft, and when you revise, make sure you've given your readers all the information they need to judge your argument.

❹ Explore Both Sides of the Issue

As you plan your essay, you'll need to consider both sides of the issue. You want to address opposing points of view effectively, as well as test your own reasons and support. A pro/con chart, such as the one below, can help you consider opposing viewpoints.

Student's Pro/Con Chart

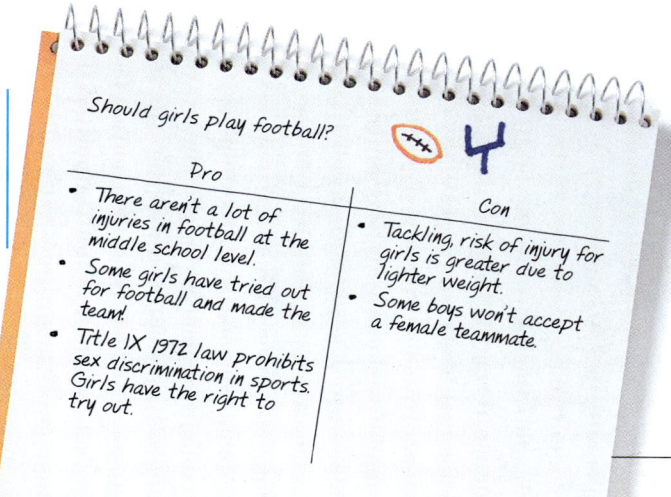

SkillBuilder

 CRITICAL THINKING

Evaluating Sources

The following suggestions can help you evaluate sources to support your arguments.

- Look for material written by authors who are authorities on a particular subject. Check a library catalog to see if an author has written more than one book on the subject.
- Check for biased viewpoints.
- Read a variety of sources to cross-check for accuracy.
- To be sure you're using current material, check the copyright date. Depending on your topic, the information may be outdated if the book is more than two years old.
- Consider where the source was published. An article found in a tabloid newspaper is not a valid source.

APPLYING WHAT YOU'VE LEARNED
List the strengths and weaknesses of your sources. Which sources will you use?

THINK & PLAN

Reflecting on Your Ideas

1. How has your research affected the way you view the issues?
2. How will you use the information you gathered to write your essay?
3. How will your audience affect the way you write your essay?

WRITING FROM EXPERIENCE **687**

Teaching Strategy: STUMBLING BLOCK

H Many students find it difficult to identify and support their own opinions. Students may feel they lack the experience to adequately buttress their beliefs. Reassure students that at this stage in the writing process their opinions can still be tentative. Later, if they still hold the same opinions, they can support their beliefs with information from their research.

Writing Skill: IDENTIFYING AUDIENCE

I Students may need help identifying and writing for their audience. Suggest that they interview some of the people who will eventually read their paper to discover what they know about the topic and their opinions on the issue.

Critical Thinking: ANALYZING

J If students are having a difficult time distinguishing facts from opinions, they can set aside their drafts and study the student's pro-and-con chart at the bottom of this page. Students can work in pairs to isolate facts and opinions, highlighting facts in one color and opinions in another. Extend the activity by having students add at least two more facts and two more opinions to this chart.

SkillBuilder CRITICAL THINKING

EVALUATING SOURCES Suggest that students add these criteria for evaluating sources. The sources should be:
1. Well known: Check several different sources. If the same information appears in all of them, the material is probably reliable.
2. Well supported: Check that each source supports its beliefs with sufficient detail. If the material expresses the author's point of view but offers little to back it up, turn to another source.
3. Balanced: Read the sources to make sure that the tone is balanced and the reasoning is logical.

Application Suggest that students develop a search strategy, a personal and systematic procedure that leads from general to specific sources.

THE LANGUAGE OF LITERATURE TEACHER'S EDITION **687**

Writing Skill: PURPOSE

K Guide students to focus on the purpose of their writing as they draft. *(to persuade)* Suggest that students ask themselves the following questions to focus on their purpose:

- *What effect do I want my writing to have on my readers?*
- *What facts, opinions, examples, and details will convince readers to accept my point of view?*
- *What aspects of this essay will best appeal to my readers?*

Writing Skill: USING THE COMPUTER

L Suggest that students do their drafting on a computer. Explain that the computer allows them to express their ideas quickly and provides a base for revision. Encourage students to use the Writing Coach, which provides detailed, specific guidelines for the drafting stage. You may also want to suggest that students copy their work into several documents. Explain that this allows them to experiment with different ways to organize their material.

DRAFTING

Making Your Point

Your Views, Your Way Now that you've explored the issue, it's time to get your thoughts down on paper. State your case clearly and use strong support for your argument. Here are some suggestions to follow as you write.

1 Draft and Discover

As you write your draft, use facts and statistics, examples and incidents, or graphic aids to elaborate on your ideas and support your position. For example, a student writing in favor of girls playing on the football team chose to use facts from sports doctors and other sports authorities to support her argument. K

Student's Rough Draft

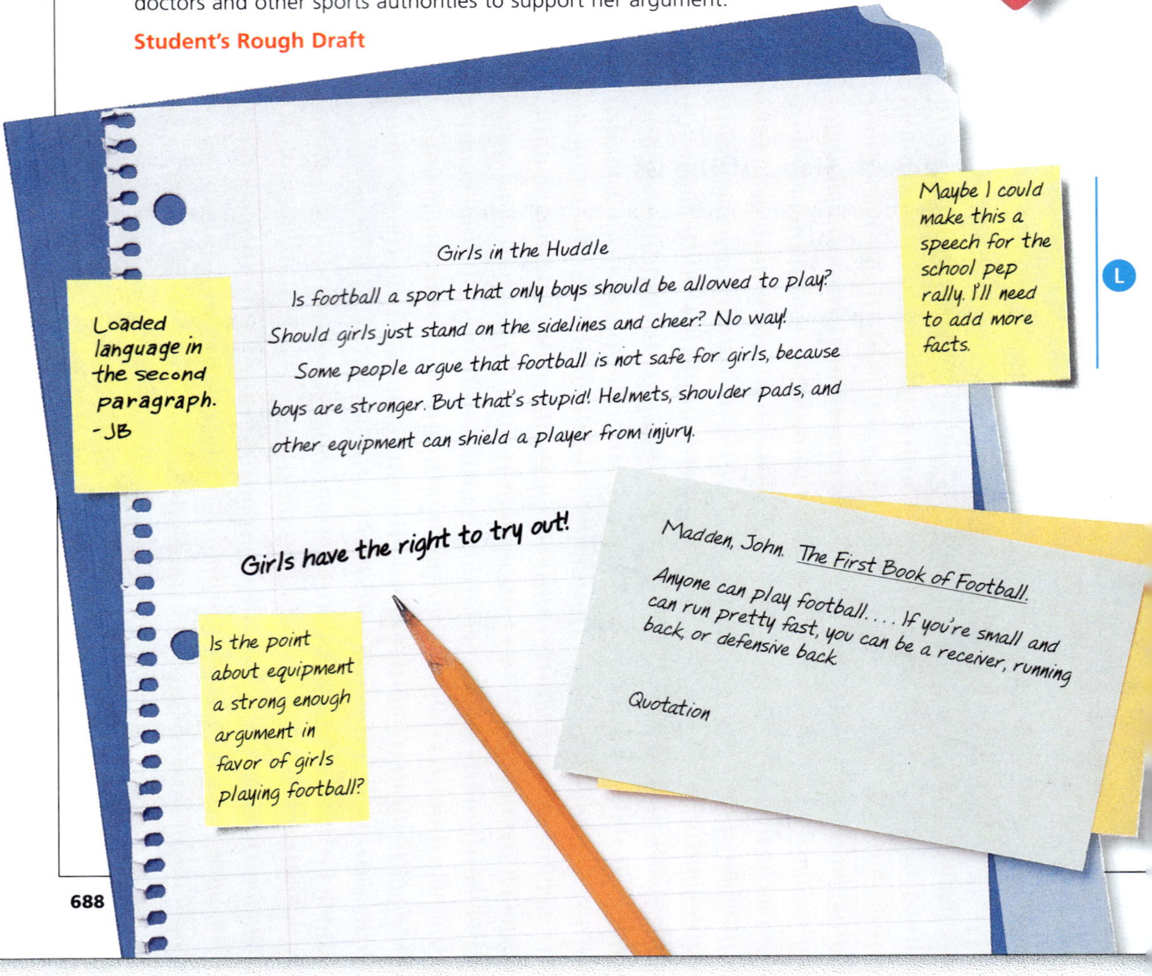

Girls in the Huddle
Is football a sport that only boys should be allowed to play? Should girls just stand on the sidelines and cheer? No way!
Some people argue that football is not safe for girls, because boys are stronger. But that's stupid! Helmets, shoulder pads, and other equipment can shield a player from injury.
Girls have the right to try out!
Loaded language in the second paragraph. -JB
Maybe I could make this a speech for the school pep rally. I'll need to add more facts.
Is the point about equipment a strong enough argument in favor of girls playing football?
Madden, John. The First Book of Football.
Anyone can play football. . . . If you're small and can run pretty fast, you can be a receiver, running back, or defensive back.
Quotation

L

688

WRITING SPRINGBOARD
How Karl Malone Goes Above and Beyond A teenager talks about what it's like to attend Karl Malone's basketball camp and reveals how the star athlete has encouraged and inspired him

Side B, Frame 21603

Writing Prompt Should professional athletes be role models for young people? Should they be held to a higher standard of behavior because of all the attention they receive? Write a persuasive essay that defends your answers.

② Analyze Your Draft

After letting your draft sit for a while, review it again. Have you addressed opposing views? Have any of your views changed? Decide whether the arguments in your rough draft are based mostly on fact or on emotional appeals.

③ Rework Your Draft

The following suggestions can help you present your views in a powerful way.

Writing Your Introduction You'll want to catch your readers' interest at the beginning, as you state your position on the issue. You could use a dramatic incident or a statistic to add interest to your introduction. The sentences that follow should support your position.

Organizing Your Ideas One way to organize your essay is to order the points you want to make from weakest to strongest. Mention your strongest point last, because that is the point that will stick with your reader. See the Writing Handbook, page 844, for more suggestions to help you organize your essay.

Drafting Your Conclusion In your conclusion, be sure to restate your position in some way. You might also consider leaving your readers with a challenging question. See the Writing Handbook for tips on writing conclusions.

PEER RESPONSE

Peer reviewers can help you revise your draft. While you don't want to get into a debate over the issue, you do want to get their feedback on how well you present the issue. Ask a peer reviewer questions like these:

- How would you restate my position?
- Which ideas are strongest? weakest?
- Have I effectively addressed opposing arguments?
- Do you think my audience will be persuaded by my arguments? If not, how can I make my position stronger?

SkillBuilder

 WRITER'S CRAFT

Avoiding Loaded Language

The words you use can appeal to readers' emotions and can sway them to your point of view. **Connotation** is the feeling or thought that a particular word or phrase suggests. Which sentence below has a positive connotation? Which gives you a negative feeling?

The argument that girls can't play football is stupid.

The argument that girls can't play football isn't based on fact.

Emotional appeals usually contain very little information. Be sure to have good, solid support for your argument, rather than relying on loaded language.

APPLYING WHAT YOU'VE LEARNED
Change the adjective in the following sentence to make the connotation positive.

The coach's rash decision kept girls off the team.

RETHINK & EVALUATE

Preparing to Revise

1. What facts do you need to add to strengthen your argument?
2. How well did you present opposing viewpoints?

WRITING FROM EXPERIENCE 689

CUSTOMIZING FOR
Less-Proficient Writers

M Suggest that students work in pairs to analyze their drafts. As one student reads aloud his or her draft, encourage the partner to ask "Who says?" after every fact or opinion. The writer should make sure he or she can respond with an appropriate source, such as "a noted scientist," "a famous musician," or "a well-known government researcher."

Writing Skill: INTRODUCTION

N Remind students that they can use a personal anecdote, statistic, description, quotation, dialogue, or example to open their essay in an exciting way. Invite volunteers to share the openings they used. Have the rest of the class critique each opening and offer praise as well as suggestions for revision.

Teaching Strategy: MANAGING THE PAPER LOAD

Save time checking students' revisions by asking writers to attach to their drafts a note that asks the most important question they want answered about their writing. Examples might include: How can I improve my introduction? How can I organize my ideas? Is my conclusion persuasive enough? As you read the drafts, concentrate on that question, noting other problems only when they are very serious.

SkillBuilder WRITER'S CRAFT

AVOIDING LOADED LANGUAGE Explore with students how loaded language can be dishonest when it is used to cover up the issues. However, when it underscores a well-supported point, it can add emotional appeal to an essay. Invite students to analyze their drafts to see if important words could be replaced by synonyms whose connotations are more effective.

Application Possible responses include *quick, rapid, swift,* and *timely.*

Additional Suggestions Have students explore other uses of language that appeal to emotion, such as glittering generalities, testimonials, and stereotyping.

Reteaching/Reinforcement
Writing Mini-Lessons transparencies, p. 37

 **The Writer's Craft**
Connotation and Denotation, pp. 314, 696

Writing Skill: REVISING

O Remind students that the pro and con points of a persuasive essay are often easier to recognize if the writer puts aside the writing for a time before revising. Doing so lets students look at their work as readers rather than as writers. Tell students they will find it much easier to spot loaded language and inadequate support if they set aside their papers for a few hours or a day before revising. Be sure that students use the Standards for Evaluation as they revise their papers.

Teaching Strategy: MODELING

P Have students compare the final draft on this page to the initial draft on page 688. Ask students how they can tell the writer valued the peer comments. Discuss with the class how the writer added facts, cut the loaded language in the second paragraph, and adjusted the point about equipment. Point out the writer's technique of presenting coaches' ideas about injuries before addressing this item. Discuss the references to sources of facts—several books, a magazine article, and a law.

REVISING AND PUBLISHING

Finishing Your Essay

A Polished Draft Take time to consider your own suggestions and others' responses to your draft. The steps on these pages can help you clarify and strengthen your position.

Student's Final Draft

Girls in the Huddle

Is football a sport for boys only? Should girls just stand on the sidelines and cheer? The answer is no. Here's why.

First of all, there is no physical reason why a girl should not play. According to John Madden in <u>The First Book of Football</u>, "Anyone can play football. . . . If you're small and can run pretty fast, you can be a receiver, running back, or defensive back." An article in the May 1995 <u>Sports Illustrated for Kids</u> proved Madden's point in an interview with a girl who became a starting quarterback on her school's football team. If girls love the game, why should they just be spectators?

Some football coaches have talked about an increased risk of injury for girls. This risk is not great, especially at the middle school level. In two books on sports injuries, doctors mentioned that most injuries don't occur until a player plays football in high school. Players may have to suffer sprains, bumps, or bruises, but nothing more serious.

Another reason that girls should be able to play is that they have a legal right to try out. Under Title IX, a 1972 law, schools getting federal aid cannot discriminate in sports on the basis of sex. That means girls can try out for football.

690 UNIT FIVE: PERSONAL DISCOVERIES

1 Revise and Edit

Review the Standards for Evaluation, the Editing Checklist, and the following steps as you edit your draft.

- Review your position on the issue. Are there any points that need to be explained more clearly?
- Have you effectively used words with connotations?
- Have you ordered your points in a logical manner?
- Does your conclusion restate your position?

How did the student address opposing points of view?

How did the student use facts and opinions to support her argument?

You can turn your essay into a visual display.

2 Show Your Work

The format you choose for your final essay can help you to make a strong impact on your readers. This student chose to create a visual display. You might also choose one of the publishing options below.

PUBLISHING IDEAS

- You might turn your essay into an article for your school newspaper or a letter to the editor of your community newspaper.
- A speech or petition might be a good format for persuading others about the issue.
- You might make a leaflet or brochure and use it as a teaching tool.

Standards for Evaluation

A persuasive essay
- has a strong introduction
- clearly states the issue and the writer's position
- presents ideas logically and effectively
- addresses opposing viewpoints
- ends with a strong argument or summary or a call for action

SkillBuilder

GRAMMAR FROM WRITING

Avoiding Double Negatives

Avoid using two negative words in one clause. Instead, use one negative word to express a negative idea.

Incorrect *Girls didn't have no chance to play football.*

Correct *Girls didn't have a chance to play football.*

GRAMMAR HANDBOOK

For more information on using negatives correctly, see page 880 of the Grammar Handbook.

Editing Checklist Check the following points as you finalize your draft.

- Did you effectively use words with connotations?
- Did you avoid using double negatives?
- Did you proofread for errors in verb agreement?

REFLECT & ASSESS

Evaluating Your Experience

1. What did you learn about yourself or your beliefs?
2. How did people react to the way you presented your views? What does that tell you about your writing?

 PORTFOLIO Include your essay and your research notes in your portfolio.

WRITING FROM EXPERIENCE 691

Speaking, Listening, and Viewing:
CAMPAIGNING

 Suggest that students present their writing as part of a campaign to effect social change. Have students work in small groups to plan their campaign. Encourage them to start by recasting their essay as a brochure or handout. Suggest that they use their plans and handout as the basis for a series of panel discussions, presentations, and multimedia shows.

PORTFOLIO

Guide students to establish a portfolio of their best work. Have students work with partners to evaluate their writing for possible inclusion in their portfolios.

Standards for Evaluation

Ideas and Content
- clearly states the issue and writer's opinion in the introduction
- supports opinions and ideas with observations, facts, and expert opinions
- takes into account and answers opposing views
- uses sound logic and effective language
- concludes with a strong argument, summary, or call to action

Structure and Form
- uses well-organized paragraphs and a clear organization
- includes transitional words and phrases to show relationships among ideas

Grammar, Usage, and Mechanics
- contains no more than two or three minor errors in grammar and usage
- contains no more than two or three minor errors in spelling, capitalization, and punctuation

---

SkillBuilder GRAMMAR FROM WRITING

AVOIDING DOUBLE NEGATIVES Share with students the following list of negatives:

no	not	barely
hardly	scarcely	only
but	verb + n't	nobody
no one	nothing	nowhere
never	neither	

Application Have students correct the double negatives in these examples:
1. He hasn't hardly a friend.
2. You haven't no one to blame but yourself.
3. He couldn't find none.
4. The child isn't barely able to reach the shelf.

Reteaching/Reinforcement
Grammar Mini-Lessons copymasters p. 21, transparencies pp. 13–15

Double Negatives, p. 526

THE LANGUAGE OF LITERATURE TEACHER'S EDITION 691

UNIT REVIEW

This feature allows students to reflect on what they have learned in Unit Five and to assess how well they understand what they have learned. This feature provides students with multiple opportunities for self-assessment, although you may wish to use some of the activities to informally assess specific skills, such as speaking and listening or cooperative work.

Objectives

- To allow students to reflect on and assess their understanding of theme
- To allow students to reflect on and assess their understanding of literary concepts such as symbols and morals
- To provide students with the opportunity to assess and build their portfolios

Reflecting on Theme

OPTION 1

Students should skim each selection and pay attention to the actions of the character whom they feel is the most successful in making discoveries about himself or herself. Students should use this information to compose their letters of advice. Encourage students first to draft their letters in order to organize their thoughts and ideas. You may wish to have students share their drafts with a partner and incorporate their partner's responses in their revised letters.

OPTION 2

Encourage students to reread the poems in this unit in order to determine which ones they will illustrate. As students review the poems, they can list the imagery used and refer to this list when illustrating.

OPTION 3

Encourage students to skim the selections in this unit as well as the notes they took while reading them in order to determine which selections had the greatest impact on them. Make sure students are able to support their choices with details from the selections and their own experiences.

REFLECT & ASSESS

UNIT FIVE: PERSONAL DISCOVERIES

How do you view yourself in relation to others? Have you found your place in the world? These are the kinds of questions that arise for the characters in Unit Five. After reading the selections, are you better able to understand the search for personal identity? Choose one or more of the options in each section below to help you reflect on what you have learned.

REFLECTING ON THEME

OPTION 1 Reading from Within The characters in this unit are forced to examine who they are and how they fit in. Choose two characters—the one you think is the most successful in making discoveries about himself or herself, and the one you think is the least successful in making such discoveries. Then pretend that you are the most successful character and write a letter of advice to the least successful character, telling how he or she can achieve greater self-understanding.

OPTION 2 Focusing on Poetry Review the poetry that you read in this unit. Think about which poems best reflect for you the unit theme, "Personal Discoveries." Then make illustrations for the poems you have selected. Try to convey both the poems' subject matter and the theme of the unit.

OPTION 3 Learning a Lesson Which selections in this unit have had the greatest impact on the way you view yourself, both as an individual and in relation to others? Rate each selection on a scale of 1–10, according to the effect it has had on you. Discuss your ratings with a partner, explaining the reasoning behind them.

Self-Assessment: What is the best way to find your place in the world? What makes you who you are? What have you discovered about yourself? Write a few short paragraphs describing how you would answer these questions now. Then, using a different-colored pen, make notes in the margins, telling which selections have influenced your thoughts.

REVIEWING LITERARY CONCEPTS

OPTION 1 Thinking About Symbols Recall that a symbol is a person, a place, or an object that stands for something beyond itself—as a flag symbolizes a country, for example. Working with a small group of classmates, look back at the fiction, nonfiction, and poetry in this unit. After brainstorming a number of possibilities, select one symbol that stands for a major aspect of each selection. Make a chart like the one shown, drawing pictures of the symbols and explaining their meanings.

Selection	Symbol	Symbolic Meaning
"The Moustache"		stands for Mike's maturity, which increases with experience; stands for his grandfather

692   UNIT FIVE: PERSONAL DISCOVERIES

Self-Assessment In order to help students answer these questions, have them think about situations in the past that they would handle differently now on the basis of what they have learned from the selections. In addition, encourage them to consider attitudes they have held in the past and how they will adjust or change these attitudes in the future.

OPTION 2 **Stating Morals** Identify the selections in this unit from which you can infer a moral, or lesson. Write down each moral in a single sentence, then see if a partner can identify the selections that match the morals.

Self-Assessment: Make a chart like the one shown. Then, after looking at the following list of poetry terms discussed in this unit, write each term in one of the columns to show how well you think you understand it. Once you have targeted the terms you do not understand, find a partner who understands them well. Go back over the poetry in the unit together, reviewing the terms. Also try to help a student understand the terms of which you have a firm grasp.

dialogue in poetry   simile
imagery   repetition
rhyme   alliteration
rhythm   personification

My Knowledge of Poetry Concepts		
Understand Completely	Understand Partially	Do Not Understand

PORTFOLIO BUILDING

- **QuickWrites** Several of this unit's QuickWrites assignments asked you to construct paragraphs, make diary entries, and write poems. From your responses to each kind of assignment, choose one in which you notice an especially strong link to the unit theme, particularly with regard to relationships among loved ones. Write a cover note explaining why you feel good about your responses, then add them, along with the note, to your portfolio.

- **Writing About Literature** Earlier in this unit, you analyzed a poem. Reread the poem and your analysis now. Decide whether you still think your analysis is on target, and jot down a sentence explaining your opinion. Note how your analysis might help you read poetry in the future. You may wish to include your note in your portfolio.

- **Writing from Experience** As you think back on the persuasive essay you wrote in this unit, what part of the research and writing seems to have been the most challenging? What part was the most interesting? Why? What did you learn about understanding both sides of an issue before forming an opinion?

- **Personal Choice** Look back through the records and evaluations of all the activities you completed in this unit. In which activities or responses do you feel you offered a truly creative product or a clever solution to a problem? Write a paragraph giving a favorable critique of your work.

 *Self-Assessment: Compare the poems you have added to your portfolio for Unit Five with those that were already in your portfolio. Do you think you are becoming a better poet? If so, how? Write a note explaining how you feel you have developed as a poet. Attach it to the poetry in your portfolio.*

SETTING GOALS

As you completed the reading and writing activities that focused on the poetry in this unit, you probably identified certain poems you liked. Which poets' works, or which kinds of poetry, would you like to read more of? What kinds of poems would you like to write yourself?

Reviewing Literary Concepts

OPTION 1

Remind students that not all objects or images in a selection are symbols. Have groups consider how the particular symbol functions in the selection and what it means to the characters in order to help them complete their charts.

OPTION 2

Students may want to skim the selections in this unit in order to determine the morals or lessons taught. If partners have difficulty matching selections and morals, encourage students to discuss their impressions of the morals of the selections.

 **Self-Assessment** For terms that students have difficulty understanding, have them write, in their own words, a definition for each term after checking in the Handbook. You may wish to have them apply each term to a poem in the unit. Partners who understand the terms can check to make sure the terms are being used properly.

Portfolio Building

You may wish to help students choose options or modify options for them that best suit the needs you have established for the class. Encourage students to incorporate in their portfolios drafts, in addition to final products, so that they can reflect on and assess their development and progress.

Self-Assessment As students assess their progress, have them consider how easy or difficult it was to write more recent poems compared with earlier poems. Encourage students also to determine how much revision was involved in more recent poems in comparison with earlier ones. Students can use this information when writing their notes.

Setting Goals

In order to help students answer these questions and set future goals, have them consider which poet's work had the greatest impact on them and the ways in which they were affected by the poems. Ask them if they prefer a particular type of poetry—free verse, lyrical, narrative, or haiku. Encourage them to set practical goals for outside reading in the future.

UNIT SIX

UNIT OVERVIEW

In Unit Six, "Across Time and Place: The Oral Tradition," students will read a variety of myths, fables, folk tales, and legends from the oral tradition of many cultures in the Americas. This unit contains five sections, each linked to a previous unit in this book:

Links to Unit One: Changing Perceptions
- Paul Bunyan and the Winter of the Blue Snow
- The Souls in Purgatory
- The Girl in the Lavender Dress

Links to Unit Two: Critical Adjustments
- John Henry
- Brer Possum's Dilemma
- Aunty Misery
- M'su Carencro and Mangeur de Poulet

Links to Unit Three: Battle for Control
- Pecos Bill
- The Five Eggs
- Raven and the Coming of Daylight
- Spotted Eagle and Black Crow

Links to Unit Four: Facing the Enemy
- Racing the Great Bear
- Otoonah
- The Woman in the Snow

Links to Unit Five: Personal Discoveries
- Strawberries
- No News
- The First Flute

You may wish to begin or end Units One through Five with theme-related selections from Unit Six, or you may choose to present the selections from Unit Six as a separate unit.

Discovering the Oral Tradition

Use the following discussion prompts to help students appreciate the oral tradition.
- Olga Loya, the storyteller pictured on page 695, claims that "stories can heal people." What do you think she means by this? Are stories a kind of medicine? What kinds of ailments do you think can be healed by stories? *(Possible response: She's referring to the way most people like to have stories told or read to them. Stories can be very comforting and calming, and they help heal a person's worries or anxieties.)*
- What do you think Loya means by saying that "storytelling is a way for people to find their power"? Do you agree or disagree? *(Possible responses: Loya may be referring to the way that people identify with the characters and events that appear in stories. When people hear stories that have to do with places, people, or issues that they recognize from their own lives, they feel a stronger sense of identity. In this way, stories can help people develop a sense of community—their ethnic or racial or geographical background, for example.)*

UNIT SIX

Across Time and Place

The Oral TRADITION

People can hear a story and relate it to their own lives.

Stories can heal people.

Storytelling is a way for people to find their power.

Olga Loya

Olga Loya is a Mexican American who grew up in East Los Angeles. She strives to keep the oral tradition alive through her storytelling.

Introducing Storytelling

Explain to students that stories that are communicated orally are alive in a way that written stories are not. When a story is committed to paper, it becomes fixed—it is set in print. A person can go back to that story again and again, and it will always be the same.

On the other hand, oral stories are always changing because they are often retold in slightly different ways. Stories change depending on who is speaking, what words that person chooses, and the effect that person wants to achieve by telling the story.

Encourage students to play a simple game to demonstrate how a narrative can change or be embellished when recited orally. Start by reciting a sentence to the class, such as "The two dogs did a little dance on the grass and then rolled on their backs and howled." Then have a student add to your sentence with one of his or her own. Have students successively build the story with their own sentences until each student has contributed to the story. Invite students to discuss any changes they noticed in the story as it was being created.

Mini-Lesson: Speaking, Listening, and Viewing

STORYTELLING IN THE CLASSROOM You might wish to make certain adjustments in your classroom to make the environment more conducive to storytelling. You might include students in this process. Encourage them to share their ideas of ways to change the room so that the atmosphere will be more appropriate for telling and hearing stories.

Possible ideas include: creating a large open space in which students can sit on the floor in a circle; darkening the room (or softening the light in some way); allowing students to sit or lie where they like; having student volunteers suggest some types of music or sound effects that could accompany the stories while they are being told.

THE LANGUAGE OF LITERATURE TEACHER'S EDITION

UNIT SIX
Skills Trace: Links to Units 1–3

 DENOTES MINI-LESSON IN TEACHER'S EDITION

Selections	Reading Skills and Strategies	Literary Concepts	Writing Opportunities	Speaking, Listening, and Viewing
LINKS TO UNIT ONE Paul Bunyan and the Winter of the Blue Snow The Souls in Purgatory The Girl in the Lavender Dress	Recognizing similar stories in the same or other cultures, PE p. 701 Relating to unit theme, PE p. 701 Recognizing cultural features, PE p. 701 Connecting, ML TE p. 708	Exaggeration, ML TE p. 702	Venn diagram, PE p. 715	Storytelling contest, PE p. 714 Television news program, PE p. 715 Readers theater, ML TE p. 707 Ghost stories, ML TE p. 710 Retell story, ML TE p. 712
LINKS TO UNIT TWO John Henry Brer Possum's Dilemma Aunty Misery M'su Carencro and Mangeur de Poulet	Classifying, PE p. 717 Evaluating, PE p. 717 Recognizing morals, PE p. 717 Relating cause and effect, ML TE p. 728	Irony, ML TE p. 724 Personification, ML TE p. 725	Script, PE p. 730 Morals, PE p. 731	Dramatize a tale, PE p. 730 Dramatic reading, ML TE p. 718 Spoken literature, ML TE p. 721
LINKS TO UNIT THREE Pecos Bill The Five Eggs Raven and the Coming of Daylight Spotted Eagle and Black Crow	Evaluating, PE p. 733 Noting relevant details, PE p. 733 Comparing cultures, PE p. 733 Questioning, ML TE p. 740	Myth, ML TE p. 743	Write court arguments, PE p. 750 Introduction, ML TE p. 734 Eulogy, ML TE p. 746	Mock trial, PE p. 750 Dramatic reading, ML TE p. 737 Monologue, ML TE p. 738 Film, ML TE p. 748
Writing	**Reading Skills and Strategies**	**Literary Concepts**	**Writing Opportunities**	**Speaking, Listening, and Viewing**
WRITING ABOUT LITERATURE Creative Response	Responding to a tale or legend, PE pp. 754–757	Using dialogue, PE p. 752–753 Story elements, PE pp. 754–755	Dialogue, PE p. 753 Memorable lines, PE p. 753 Comparable dialogues, PE p. 753 Scene from a dramatic adaptation, PE pp. 754–757 Showing direct address, PE p. 757	Giving a performance, PE p. 755 Viewing different images, PE p. 759 Interpreting changes over time, PE p. 759 Discussion, PE p. 759 Discussing romanticized images, PE p. 759

Grammar, Usage, Mechanics, and Spelling	Multimodal Learning	Research and Study Skills	Vocabulary
Adjectives in comparisons, ML TE p. 703 Words ending with -ous/-us, ML TE p. 704 Using figurative language, ML TE p. 706	Storytelling contest, PE p. 714 Painting, drawing, or sculpture, PE p. 714 Television news program, PE p. 715 *Retablo exvoto,* PE p. 715 Readers theater, ML TE p. 707 Ghost stories, ML TE p. 710 Retell story, ML TE p. 712	Research stories, PE p. 714 Research *El Día de los Muertos,* PE p. 714 Research Mexican history, PE p. 715 Research forest conservation, PE p. 715 Research *retablos,* PE p. 715 Research versions of story, PE p. 715	dumbfounded intercession pungent reproach
Subject-verb agreement in standard English, ML TE p. 722 Double consonants with a suffix, ML TE p. 727	Dramatize a tale, PE p. 730 Classroom display, PE p. 730 Map the railroads, PE p. 731 Time line, PE p. 731 Word web, PE p. 731 Chart, PE p. 731 Dramatic reading, ML TE p. 718 Spoken literature, ML TE p. 721	Research Cajun culture, PE p. 730 Research the history of the railroads, PE p. 731 Research buzzards, PE p. 731	
Words with silent letters, ML TE p. 736 Plural and possessive nouns, ML TE p. 742	Mock trial, PE p. 750 Time line, PE p. 750 Model eagle's nest, PE p. 751 Collage or mobile, PE p. 751 Images of Paul Bunyan and Pecos Bill, PE p. 751 Dramatic reading, ML TE p. 737 Monologue, ML TE p. 738 Film, ML TE p. 748	Research the Native Americans of the Great Plains, PE p. 750 Research eagles, PE p. 751 Research cedar items used by the Haida, PE p. 751 Research the people of Ecuador, PE p. 751	abyss enmity sheer

Grammar, Usage, Mechanics, and Spelling	Multimodal Learning	Research and Study Skills	Media Literacy
Using commas in quotations, PE p. 753 Formatting a script, PE p. 757	Giving a performance, PE p. 755 Viewing different images, PE p. 759 Interpreting changes over time, PE p. 759 Discussion, PE p. 759 Discussing romanticized images, PE p. 759	Analyzing characters, plot, and setting, PE p. 754	Interpreting and evaluating images, PE pp. 758–759

UNIT SIX
Skills Trace: Links to Units 4–5

 DENOTES MINI-LESSON IN TEACHER'S EDITION

Selections	Reading Skills and Strategies	Literary Concepts	Writing Opportunities	Speaking, Listening, and Viewing
LINKS TO UNIT FOUR **Racing the Great Bear** **Otoonah** **The Woman in the Snow**	Noting relevant details, PE p. 761 Making judgments, PE p. 761 Classifying traits, PE p. 761 Comparing and contrasting cultures, PE p. 761 Noting relevant details, ML TE p. 763	Folklore, ML TE p. 769 Foreshadowing, ML TE p. 775	Dust jacket paragraphs, PE p. 782 Newspaper articles, PE p. 782 Paragraphs describing an experience, ML TE p. 765	Compose a song, PE p. 783 Folk tale, ML TE p. 777 Active listening, ML TE p. 778
LINKS TO UNIT FIVE **Strawberries** **No News** **The First Flute**	Identifying fun, PE p. 785 Visualizing, PE p. 785 Evaluating character actions, PE p. 785 Comparing cultures, PE p. 785 Distinguishing fact and opinion, ML TE p. 791	Conflict, ML TE p. 792	Script, PE p. 797 Advice letter, PE p. 797 Origin myth, PE p. 797	Debate, PE p. 796 Television program, PE p. 797 Group discussion, PE p. 797 Indigenous music, ML TE p. 794

Writing	Reading Skills and Strategies	Literary Concepts	Writing Opportunities	Speaking, Listening, and Viewing
WRITING FROM EXPERIENCE **Writing a Report**			Writing a research report, PE pp. 798–805 Statement of controlling purpose, PE p. 800 Drafting, PE pp. 802–803 Crediting sources, PE p. 803 Revising and publishing, PE pp. 804–805	

Grammar, Usage, Mechanics, and Spelling	Multimodal Learning	Research and Study Skills	Vocabulary
Compound words, ML TE p. 764 Troublesome modifiers, ML TE p. 771	Dust jacket, PE p. 782 Newspaper front page, PE p. 782 Diorama, PE p. 783 Illustration, PE p. 783 Time line, PE p. 783 Compose a song, PE p. 783 Complete a chart, PE p. 783 Folk tale, ML TE p. 777 Active listening, ML TE p. 778	Research the Montgomery bus boycott, PE p. 782 Research Kodiak Island, PE p. 783 Research the Iroquois, PE p. 783	brandishing console forlorn petite pivotal plummet recoil savor
The letters *qu*, ML TE p. 786 Sentence fragments, ML TE p. 789	Calculations with Mayan number system, PE p. 796 Report card, PE p. 796 Debate, PE p. 796 Television program, PE p. 797 Illustrations, PE p. 797 Group discussion, PE p. 797 Indigenous music, ML TE p. 794	Research Mayan accomplishments, PE p. 797 Research Cherokee customs, PE p. 797	agitated evading melancholy

Grammar, Usage, Mechanics, and Spelling	Multimodal Learning	Research and Study Skills	Media Literacy
Crediting sources, PE p. 803 Capitalizing titles of created works, PE p. 805		Using a library database, PE p. 800 Using expert advice, PE p. 800 Previewing sources, PE p. 801 Creating source cards, PE p. 801 Taking notes, PE p. 801	Using a library database, PE p. 800

UNIT SIX
Recommended Resources

ENRICHMENT   RESEARCH

Recommended Novels and Collections

Creation Stories from Around the World
by Virginia Hamilton

Thematic Links Includes 25 creation myths from almost every continent.

About the Author Virginia Hamilton (born 1936) often writes about herself, her community, and her family. Her books are award-winners and favorites of her ever-increasing fans.

Other Works by Virginia Hamilton *M.C. Higgins the Great, Zeely, The House of Dies Drear, The Planet of Junior Brown, Her Stories*

The Rain People
by Laurence Yep

Thematic Links Retells 20 traditional Chinese tales.

About the Author Newbery-Award winning Yep (born 1948) has written many books for young adults that combine his experiences as a Chinese American and his love of science fiction. In many of his works, he explores the theme of being an outsider.

Other Works by Laurence Yep *Sweetwater, Dragonwings, Child of the Owl, Sea Glass, Dragon of the Lost Sea, The Serpent's Children, Dragon Steel, The Star Fisher*

The Mermaid's Twin Sister: More Stories from Trinidad
by Lynn Joseph

Thematic Links Realistic, down-to-earth characters combine with the magic and legends of Trinidad.

About the Author Lynn Joseph was born and raised on the island of Trinidad. She credits her mother for her love of books.

Other Works by Lynn Joseph *Coconut Kind of Day, An Island Christmas, Jasmine's Parlour Day, A Wave in her Pocket*

The Golem
by Isaac Bashevis Singer

Thematic Links Retells a 16th-century Jewish tale about a rabbi in old Prague.

About the Author Singer (1904–1991) wrote stories and novels for children and adults based on the culture and traditions of Jewish life in Poland. In 1978 Singer was awarded the Nobel Prize in literature.

Other Works by Isaac Bashevis Singer *Zlateh the Goat and Other Stories, The Fearsome Inn, When Shlemiel Went to Warsaw and Other Stories, A Day of Pleasure: Stories of a Boy Growing Up in Warsaw, Why Noah Chose the Dove*

The Pig's Ploughman
by Bernard Evslin

Thematic Links Pig's Ploughman is an enormous hog in Celtic mythology.

About the Author Bernard Evslin (born 1922) has written numerous books that retell myths and legends. His book *The Green Hero* was nominated for a National Book Award.

Other Works by Bernard Evslin *The Trojan War, Adventures of Ulysses, The Greek Gods and Heroes*

The Magic Orange Tree and Other Haitian Folktales
by Diane Wolkstein

Thematic Links Diane Wolkstein has compiled folktales told primarily by Haitian storytellers.

About the Author She writes about tales from around the world and has worked as a professional storyteller for the New York City Parks Department.

Other Works by Diane Wolkstein *The Banza, The Magic Wings: A Tale from China, Oom Razoom or Go I Know Not Where, Bring Back I Know Not What, The Red Lion: a Persian Story*

For Teacher — TEACHING LITERATURE

Day, Frances Ann. *Multicultural Voices in Contemporary Literature: A Resource for Teachers.* Portsmouth, NH: Heinemann, 1994.

Helbig, Alethea K. *This Land Is Our Land: A Guide to Multicultural Literature for Children and Young Adults.* Westport, CT: Greenwood, 1992.

Miller-Lachmann, Lyn. *Our Family, Our Friends, Our World: An Annotated Guide to Significant Multicultural Books for Children and Teenagers.* New Providence, NJ: R. R. Bowker, 1992.

Templeton, S. *Teaching the Integrated Language Arts.* Boston, MA: Houghton Mifflin, 1991.

Wood, Karen D. *Guiding Readers Through Text.* Newark, DE: International Reading Association, 1992.

CROSS-CURRICULAR TEACHING   PROFESSIONAL DEVELOPMENT

Recommended Readings in Cross-Curricular Areas

SOCIAL STUDIES

Day of the Dead: A Mexican-American Celebration by D. Hoyt-Goldsmith (1994) Two ten-year-old California sisters explain the holiday's history and festivities in a Mexican-American community. Links to "The Souls in Purgatory."

HISTORY

The Iroquois by Barbara Graymont (1988) Provides a historical overview from the tribal union of 1450 to present day. Links to "Racing the Great Bear."

HISTORY/GEOGRAPHY

Cowboys of the Wild by Russell Freedman (1985) Portrays real-life cowboys who worked while cattle roamed the open range. Links to "Pecos Bill."

SCIENCE

Shadows on the Tundra: Alaskan Tales of Predators, Prey and Man by Tom Walker (1989) Tundra inhabitants such as grizzlies and wolves are introduced in a series of illustrated narrative pieces. Links to "Otoonah."

For Teacher — CROSS-CURRICULAR INSTRUCTION

Hough, David L. "Achieving Independent Student Responses Through Integrated Instruction (Strategies for Middle School Students)." *Middle School Journal.* 25 (May 1994) 35–42.

Musser, Louise S. and Evelyn B. Freeman. "Teach Young Students About Native Americans: Use Myths, Legends, and Folktales." *The Social Studies* 80 (January/February 1989) 5–9.

Nelli, Elizabeth. "Mirror of a People: Folktales and Social Studies." *Social Education* 49 (February 1985) 155–58.

Norton, Donna. "Circa 1492 and the Integration of Literature, Reading, and Geography (Engaging Children in Literature)." *Reading Teacher* 46:7 (April 1993) 610–14.

Recommended Media Resources

THE LANGUAGE OF LITERATURE

LASERLINKS
Videodisc, Gr. 8
See *LaserLinks Teacher's Source Book*, page 59.

AUDIO LIBRARY
Unit Six: The Oral Tradition
Gr. 8, Tape 15:
  Sides A & B
Gr. 8, Tape 16:
  Sides A & B

WRITING COACH
Writing Coach Software: Writing About Literature: Direct Response; Explanation of an Idea

OUTSIDE RESOURCES

Films/Videos/Film Strips/Audiocassettes
The American Tall Tales Audio. 4 audiocassettes. Caedmon/Harper Audio, 1992. (60 min.)
Story-telling: Tales and Techniques. videocassette. Folktellers & WSJK TV, 1994.
Stories of American Indian Culture. 3 videos. Best Film and Video, 1990. (20 min. each)
Keepers of the Animals: Native American Animal Stories. 2 audiocassettes. Fulcrum Publishing, 1992.

Internet Resources
World Wide Web at
http://www.hmco.com/mcdougal

For Teacher — TEACHING WITH TECHNOLOGY

Gillespie, Joan. "Cumulative Tales: A Collaborative Computer Activity," *National Middle School Journal* (January 1995).

Hill, Brian. *Making the Most of Video: Technology in Language Learning.* London: Centre for Information on Language Teaching and Research, 1989.

Technology Connection. Linworth Publishing, Inc. 480 E. Wilson Bridge Rd. Worthington, OH 43085–2372

UNIT SIX
Professional Enrichment

The Vanishing Hitchhiker and the Choking Doberman

> Grandma receives a microwave oven for a birthday gift. She is delighted with her children's thoughtfulness and generosity. After they leave, she bathes her adorable poodle. Holding the soaking animal, she gets a great idea: Why not dry him off in the new microwave oven?

The results are not pretty. Another urban legend strikes—the Legend of the Microwaved Pet!

URBAN FOLKLORE

Urban legends are "true" stories that are too good to be true, almost always attributed to a "friend of a friend." They are stories that never happened but that are told as truth. As with other types of folklore, urban legends develop from the oral tradition. Since they are passed down from person to person, the stories change as a result of the telling. Take the "Death Car," for example. The earliest documented telling concerns a $50 Buick cursed with the stench of a corpse. In subsequent retellings, the $50 Buick became a $500 Corvette—although it still has the stench of the corpse! As you can see, there are many slight variations of each work, and the original writers and tellers are no longer known.

Students might be interested to know that increasingly, computers have replaced storytellers as a means of transmitting urban legends. Scores of these stories now appear on the World Wide Web, ripe for the retelling. Students skilled at tapping technology might want to see how many urban legends they can pluck from the Net and share with the class.

Like traditional American tall tales, today's urban legends describe ridiculous events in a serious way. They present simple plots with clear moral lessons. As a result, when these stories are transmitted from person to person, they convey the values and wisdom of modern culture as well as entertain us. To reinforce this with your class, invite students to brainstorm a list of contemporary values, those guideposts students feel are rewarded in society. Here are some possibilities: materialism, appearance, respect, individual rights, athletic ability, enterprise, honesty, and charity. As students read "The Girl in the Lavender Dress," invite them to see how their list compares to the values they find in the story.

ALL-TIME FAVORITE URBAN LEGENDS

Urban legends are tremendously popular. Share these examples with your students. See which ones they have heard—and passed on!

- **"The Severed Fingers"** After a fight with some hoodlums in a drive-in movie, a teenager finds three severed fingers jammed behind his rear bumper.
- **"The Baby on the Roof"** At a rest stop, parents place their baby, buckled in his car seat, on top of the car. They drive off, the baby still on the roof.
- **"The Hare Dryer"** A family assumes their dog killed the neighbor's pet bunny. The family washes the dead bunny, blows its fur dry, and places it back in its hutch. Later, we discover that the dog dug up the already-dead bunny.
- **"The Tummy Ache"** A boy on a hike fills his canteen at a stream. A year later, doctors discover a snake living in his stomach.
- **"The Batter-Fried Rat"** A family stops at a fast-food stand and discovers that more than chicken has been fried.

BRINGING URBAN LEGENDS TO YOUR CLASSROOM

Try these ideas for bringing more urban legends into your classroom:

- Invite your students to create their own urban legends or add twists to existing ones. In keeping with the genre, students should read their legends to the class and invite other students to suggest changes in wording.
- Play a game of "telephone" to create a class urban legend. Arrange students in small groups to tell and retell their legends, incorporating or rejecting misunderstandings.
- Explain to students that urban legends give us a repository of strong images that become part of our imagination and even our daily speech. Invite students to look through books of urban legends to find expressions that have become commonplace.
- Invite students to select an urban legend and recast it as a comic book or comic strip.

Related Reading

 Brunvald, Jan Harold. *The Baby Train.* New York: W.W. Norton, 1993.

 Brunvald, Jan Harold. *The Big Book of Urban Legends.* New York: Paradox Press, 1994.

 Brunvald, Jan Harold. *The Vanishing Hitchhiker.* New York: W.W. Norton, 1982.

Family and Community Involvement

Family

From a Puerto Rican tale about an old woman who attempts to prevent a visit from Death to a Cherokee legend about the first man and woman in the world, all of the selections in Unit Six are part of the oral tradition. By completing some of the following activities, your students, their families, and other community members can make important connections outside the classroom as they explore other examples of the oral tradition.

The following Copymasters for Unit Six provide activities that students can take home and complete with a parent or other family member.

OPTION 1: READ A STORY ALOUD
- **Connection** All of the selections in Unit Six are part of the oral tradition.
- **Activity** *Copymaster, p. 1* Students work with family members to read aloud and appreciate a piece of literature of their own choosing.

OPTION 2: RECORD A FAMILY STORY
- **Connection** All of the selections in Unit Six are part of the oral tradition.
- **Activity** *Copymaster, p. 2* Students work with a family member to tape-record or videotape a family member telling a personal story from their family's personal history.

OPTION 3: WRITING YOUR OWN FOLK TALE
- **Connection** Many of the selections in Unit Six, such as "The Five Eggs" and "The First Flute," are entertaining folk tales.
- **Activity** *Copymaster, p. 3* Students work with a family member to write a short folk tale. A word web is provided to help organize students' ideas and thoughts.

Community

OPTION 1
- **Connection** A few of the selections in Unit Six are examples of African-American oral literature.
- **Activity** Visit a museum devoted to African-American culture.
- **Alternative Activity** Have students visit their local public library to research the importance of the oral tradition in African-American culture.

OPTION 2
- **Connection** Some of the selections in Unit Six, such as "Pecos Bill," are folk tales and legends about the American Wild West.
- **Activity** Arrange to have an expert on Western lore speak to the class about the Wild West.

OPTION 3
- **Connection** All of the selections in Unit Six are part of the oral tradition.
- **Activity** Invite a storyteller, possibly from your local library, to speak to the class about the importance of storytelling and to give them instruction in telling or reading stories aloud.
- **Alternative Activity** Encourage students to attend a story-telling festival.

UNIT SIX
Cooperative Project

Tales From New Lands

Overview

Students will create a background and a collection of folk tales for a fictional culture.

PROJECT AT A GLANCE

The selections in Unit Six help define storytelling as the passing on of oral histories as a means of preserving cultural heritage. For this project, students will work cooperatively to develop a new culture and to create folklore that reflects that culture. Students will decide on some of the characteristics of the new culture's members, as well as their fears and hopes, their likes and dislikes, and their environment. Then students will brainstorm several plot outlines that members will develop into folk tales that reflect the new culture. Groups should also invent a flag, a mode of dress, and food for the culture. Cultures and stories will be presented to the class.

OBJECTIVES

- To identify the characteristics of a culture
- To create a new culture and some of its identifying characteristics
- To write folk tales that reflect the characteristics of the culture
- To create a flag, costumes, food, and other objects that represent and help define the culture
- To present the culture and its tales to classmates in an entertaining way

SUGGESTED GROUP SIZE
3–4 students

MATERIALS
- Art supplies
- A cassette player and an audiotape of a folk tale (optional)

1 Getting Started

Arranging the Project
Decide how you would like to shape this project. One way to approach it is to have each group present a synopsis of its culture and then present the stories. The class can then discuss ways in which the stories reflect the culture.

Another way to approach the project is to ask groups to keep their cultures a secret. The class can take notes during the presentation of the stories and draw their own conclusions about the culture. These conclusions can then be compared to the groups' original descriptions to see how well their messages and ideas came across. Be sure to tell students well ahead of time, so no one gives away any information about their culture.

Arrange art materials, as well as a place to use them. This is also the time to find an audiotape of a folk story that you can play as an example of the art of storytelling.

Arranging for the Storytelling
Move seats into a semi-circle on the day of the event. Tell students in advance if you expect them to read the stories, memorize and recite them, or tell them extemporaneously so they can plan their time appropriately.

2 Creating the Cultures

Introducing the Project
Explain that each group will work together to create a culture on which to base several folk tales. The group should specify where the culture's people or creatures live, what they look like, what they eat, how they dress, what they worship and fear, what personal traits they value, if they have any heroes and why, their forms of recreation, and any other facts that the group deems pertinent. The group also should design a flag, clothing, and other items that would belong to the culture. When each group has established its culture, it should create several plot outlines that reveal the characteristics of that culture. Individual members can flesh out the tales into ones worthy of telling as folklore. Each member of the group should be prepared to tell one of the stories to the class.

If possible, play the audiotape of a storyteller at this point in the project. Have students note some of the things the storyteller does to hold the audience's interest.

You might hold a class discussion about how clues to a culture are found within every folk tale. Point out or have students point out examples from some of the selections in this unit.

Group Investigations
Divide students into groups of three or four. Groups should set off immediately to create a description of their culture. Encourage groups to be imaginative, as this project has no reality requirement. Remind them that folk tales have a point—they either teach lessons or explain phenomena. As groups develop their plot outlines, be sure they describe the function of the narrator, where appropriate.

Creating a Project Description
Meet with groups early in the project to review their lists of cultural characteristics. You can point out missing or conflicting information, as well as offer encouragement. Schedule subsequent meetings when groups have complete written plot outlines for their stories. Allow them to tell you what cultural characteristics each story will reveal and how they will be revealed. You also might use a few minutes of class time to keep track of any obstacles groups are commonly encountering while working on the project.

OPTION 1: ONE ELEMENT OF FOLKLORE
Students can choose one element common to all folk tales and research it across several different cultures. The discoveries can be compared and contrasted and presented orally.

OPTION 2: FOLKLORE FESTIVAL Time and space permitting, students can plan and produce a folklore festival. Groups should select a specific culture and several tales from that culture to tell before an audience. Encourage storytellers to dress in appropriate costumes and decorate their surrounding area to reflect the environment of the culture.

OPTION 3: FOLKLORE AS DRAMA Students can select a folk tale, write a script, and act it out before an audience. Remind groups to include a narrator in their play, if the plot calls for one.

OPTION 4: START A TRADITION Students can write an original folk tale set in today's world. They should write a tale that they could tell to their grandchildren as a means of teaching them a lesson in behavior or explaining a phenomenon to them.

This project is designed to be instructive and fun. Encourage students to write about cultures where pigs dance, cars fly, monkeys are in charge of grocery stores, or any other nonsense occurs—as long as students remain faithful to the purpose of the assignment.

3 Sharing the Cultures

Now your preliminary decision about revealing or not revealing the characteristics of the culture comes into play. If you chose to have the characteristics revealed, groups can make a general presentation before launching into storytelling. If you chose to keep the characteristics secret, be sure to have the audience note the clues that they hear in the stories. The audience can pool their clues and come to conclusions about each culture, then they can compare their conclusions to the group's original description.

Assessing the Project

The following rubric can be used for group or individual assessment.

3 Full Accomplishment Students follow directions and create specific characteristics for a fictional culture and several folk tales that reveal that culture.

2 Substantial Accomplishment Students create specific characteristics for a fictional culture, but the accompanying folk tales are not representative of the culture or fail to reveal its structure.

1 Little or Partial Accomplishment Students do not complete the project to the point of performing, or the performance does not fulfill the requirements of the assignment.

For the Portfolio
You may select groups' original designs for their culture and/or their original plot outlines for inclusion in students' portfolios. As always, keep a copy of your written assessment in the portfolios.

Note: For other assessment options, see the *Teacher's Guide to Assessment and Portfolio Use.*

Cross-Curricular Options

FOREIGN LANGUAGE
Students who speak or are studying a foreign language can research folk tales from a country where that language is spoken. The tales can be compared and contrasted to those of other countries. You may want to solicit assistance from a language teacher for this project.

ART
Students can design and draw or paint a book cover for one folk tale or a collection of folk tales.

LANGUAGE ARTS
Have students research Aesop's fables. They can write an essay telling how the fables are alike and different from the tales in this unit.

PHYSICAL EDUCATION
Students can research a present or past sports figure who has become legendary. They can write a tall tale about this person, exaggerating his or her accomplishments.

Resources

Aesop's Fables by Aesop have been collected in many editions, all containing Aesop's short moral tales from ancient Greece.

Mythical and Fabulous Creatures: A Sourcebook and Research Guide by Malcolm South features 20 essays on how these beasts have been depicted in ancient and modern literature.

Best-Loved Folktales of the World edited by Joanna Cole retells 200 tales, arranged geographically.

UNIT SIX
Lesson Planner: Links to Units 1–3

TIME ALLOTMENTS SHOWN ARE APPROXIMATE. DEPENDING ON YOUR GOALS AND THE NEEDS OF YOUR STUDENTS, YOU MAY WISH TO ALLOW MORE OR LESS TIME FOR CERTAIN PORTIONS OF THE LESSON.

Table of Contents	Discussion	Previewing the Selections	Reading the Selections
PART OPENER **The Oral Tradition** page 694	**30 MINUTES** • Discuss storytellers past and present • Review the history of storytelling		
LINKS TO UNIT ONE **Paul Bunyan and the Winter of the Blue Snow** page 702 AVERAGE **Souls in Purgatory** page 706 AVERAGE **The Girl in the Lavender Dress** page 710 AVERAGE		**10 MINUTES** • NORTHEASTERN UNITED STATES • MEXICO • NORTHEASTERN UNITED STATES	**40 MINUTES** • Introduce vocabulary • Read pp. 702–05 (4 pp.) • Read pp. 706–09 (4 pp.) • Read pp. 710–13 (4 pp.)
LINKS TO UNIT TWO **John Henry** page 718 AVERAGE **Brer Possum's Dilemma** page 721 AVERAGE **Aunty Misery** page 724 AVERAGE **M'su Carencro and Mangeur de Poulet** page 727 EASY		**10 MINUTES** • NORTHEASTERN UNITED STATES • SOUTHEASTERN UNITED STATES • PUERTO RICO • SOUTHEASTERN UNITED STATES	**40 MINUTES** • Read pp. 718–20 (3 pp.) • Read pp. 721–23 (3 pp.) • Read pp. 724–26 (3 pp.) • Read pp. 727–29 (3 pp.)
LINKS TO UNIT THREE **Pecos Bill** page 734 AVERAGE **The Five Eggs** page 740 AVERAGE **Raven and the Coming of Daylight** page 742 AVERAGE **Spotted Eagle and Black Crow** page 745 AVERAGE		**15 MINUTES** • SOUTHWESTERN UNITED STATES • ECUADOR • PACIFIC COAST • GREAT PLAINS	**45 MINUTES** • Read pp. 734–39 (6 pp.) • Read pp. 740–41 (2 pp.) • Read pp. 742–44 (3 pp.) • Read pp. 745–49 (5 pp.)
Writing	**Writer's Style**	**Prewriting**	**Drafting and Revising**
WRITING ABOUT LITERATURE **Creative Response**	**30 MINUTES**	**20 MINUTES**	**90 MINUTES**

Time estimates assume in-class work. You may wish to assign some of these stages as homework.

Responding Options

LITERATURE CONNECTION	CROSS-CURRICULAR CONNECTIONS	CULTURAL CONNECTIONS
	90 MINUTES	
• Plan a storytelling contest	**SOCIAL STUDIES** • Learn about the "Day of the Dead" **HISTORY** • Discover 16th-century Mexico	• Investigate forest conservation • Construct a *retablo* • Compare/contrast tales
	90 MINUTES	
• Adapt a tale into a one-act play	**SOCIAL STUDIES** • Create a Cajun display **HISTORY** • Explore the history of the railroads	• Imagine living forever • Compare animal tales • Research the buzzard • write morals
	90 MINUTES	
• Prepare a civil trial	**SOCIAL STUDIES** • Create a Native American time line **SCIENCE** • Construct an eagle's nest	• Create a collage or mobile • Research creation myths • Investigate the people of Ecuador • Create images of Paul Bunyan and Pecos Bill

Publishing and Reflecting	Grammar in Context	Reading the World
30 MINUTES	5 MINUTES	40 MINUTES

UNIT SIX

OVERVIEW

These pages are designed to introduce students to the tradition of storytelling. Students read a transcript of an interview with Olga Loya, a modern storyteller. Her words give students an opportunity to experience what it is like to feel connected to an ancient tradition and to share stories with a modern audience.

Objectives

- To understand and appreciate the richness of oral storytelling
- To apply and practice skills learned in previous selections

STORYTELLER
Olga Loya Tells "La Cucarachita"

"La Cucarachita" is an original story in the form of a folk tale. "The beginning and the end of the story are my own creation," storyteller Olga Loya says, "but the center part, with the repetition, is similar to stories found in many cultures."

"I chose to tell a story about a cockroach because I like the sound of the words *la cucarachita*," Loya explains. "Also, a cockroach is not something you often think of in a positive way. In Latin American cultures, the cockroach is perceived as very important, and there are stories and songs about *la cucaracha*. But often when I talk about her in front of an Anglo audience, their initial reaction is 'Yuck!'"

"If there's one thing I'd like people to take away from this story, it's that we need to see more of our own beauty—inside and out," Loya adds. "At times, we see everything negatively. We need to look at ourselves with an eye of kindness instead."

Side B, Frames 27905

STORYTELLERS PAST AND PRESENT

OLGA LOYA

A Present Day Storyteller Speaks

Many of Olga Loya's stories come out of her Mexican heritage as well as her own family history. She also shares tales from all over Latin America and from a variety of oral traditions around the world.

I've always told stories. My grandmother was a *curandera* (koo-rän-dĕ′rä), a healer. When she died, her house was filled with flowers from all the people that came to say goodbye to her. She always told stories to get her point across to people and to help them. My father was also a storyteller. He was one of those people who would tell a story that lasted five minutes at first. Then the next time he told it, it would last ten minutes, then fifteen minutes, then twenty.

In 1980 I went to a storytelling conference. It was like a thunderbolt to my heart. I came home and said to my family, "I'm going to be a storyteller." At first I started telling stories from books. Within a year, I realized I had many stories within myself and within my own culture. Some of the first stories I told were from Mexico, because that is my heritage. As time passed, I began to realize that there were many stories within my own family. So now I tell a number of family stories as well as stories from Latin America and all over the world. Once I was invited by some Native Americans to come and tell stories to the elders of the tribe. They honored me by giving me permission to tell some of their stories, too.

There are many types of Latino stories. *Mitos* (mē′tôs), or myths, explain how things came to be. Myths are very powerful because they represent the heart of the culture. The *leyendas* (lĕ-yĕn′däs), or legends, tell of people from times before. Legends are a way of connecting past and present. At one time in the past, the characters were believed to be real, but even now we

696 UNIT SIX: THE ORAL TRADITION

can relate their lives to our own. There are also folk tales, *cuentos* (kwĕn'tôs). Many of these have animal characters. Sometimes these teach a lesson, sometimes they entertain, and often they do both. And there are *fábulas* (fä'bōō-läs), or fables, which always have a moral.

The themes of Latino stories are really universal ones such as honoring your parents, paying attention to how you deal with the land, and not going to extremes in behavior—keeping a balance is important. Another theme that often appears is that of death, but it is often treated in a playful way, which reflects the attitudes of the culture.

I'm always looking for stories that touch my heart. Those are the stories I want to tell, because those are the stories that people will want to listen to. Stories can help people communicate with each other. People can hear a story and relate it to their own lives. Stories can heal people. Storytelling is a way for people to find their power.

We are all storytellers. We all have stories that we carry with us, but some of us don't know we have them. We should be story detectives—find the stories that move us and tell them. Go to your parents and to other members of your family and ask them to tell stories. Take the time to find out your family's stories or they will not be passed on. If you don't have the stories to pass on to your children, the stories will die. They will not stay alive unless someone tells them.

Latin American folklore is a rich blend of Native American traditions and Spanish customs and values. This unique folklore continues to thrive in Hispanic communities throughout the United States.

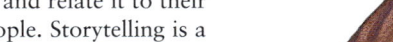
- STORYTELLER: *La Cucarachita*

An Ancient Storyteller
The Mexican-American grandmother of the turn of the century, highly respected in her close-knit extended family, often took responsibility for passing along family tales to her grandchildren.

This Mexican-American woman grew up in Texas. During her childhood, Texas was still a part of Mexico but fought for and won its independence in 1836.

Body language, including hand gestures, is effective in bringing a tale to life.

STORYTELLERS PAST AND PRESENT **697**

Critical Thinking: HYPOTHESIZING

A Ask students to share their ideas about why Olga Loya's father needed more time to tell the same story. *(Possible response: Each time he told the story, he could see which parts especially interested or entertained his listeners. Then he could use this information to add more details to these parts of the story.)*

Critical Thinking: ANALYZING

B Ask students why family stories die if no one tells them. *(Possible response: Since the stories are not written down, they are completely dependent on the oral tradition for their existence. If the stories are not told, they will not be passed on to future generations.)*

Linking to Social Studies

Mexico boasts a rich array of Native American peoples. Approximately seventy distinct languages are spoken in Mexico today. The most common of these languages are Aztec, Yucatec, Quiché-Tzutujil-Cakchiquel, Mam, Kekchí, Mixtec, Zapotec, and Otomí. The tradition of oral storytelling is vital to the continuing existence of languages such as these.

Mini-Lesson: Speaking, Listening, and Viewing

SHARING STORIES Point out to students that they already know certain stories from their families, as well as from the regions or cultures that make up their heritage. Remind students that a story can be extremely short and simple or it can be lengthy and involve subtle details and descriptions.

Application Have students work in pairs or small groups. Invite each student to share one story that he or she identifies with his or her own family or background. You might wish to encourage students to tell the story more than once to a variety of listeners, so that they learn how slight variations in the story can change its effect. Encourage students to record their stories.

THE LANGUAGE OF LITERATURE **TEACHER'S EDITION** **697**

UNIT SIX

TIME LINE
Objectives

- To understand the history and development of oral traditions in the Americas
- To understand and appreciate types of literature in the oral tradition

---

STRATEGIC READING FOR
Less-Proficient Readers

Make sure that students understand the ideas and details included in the time line by asking the following questions.

- What geographical regions relate to the items on the time line before 1570? *(Siberia and North America, the Yucatán Peninsula, the Northwest Coast, Puerto Rico, and Mexico)*
- Which items on the time line include details about conflicts between various cultures, peoples, or nations? *(Cortés ending the Aztec empire, British expelling the Acadians, Ecuador gains independence from Spain, Sioux warriors battle the U.S. Army)*

Critical Thinking:
SPECULATING

A Have students explain why so many items involving conflict or struggle are included on this time line. *(Possible responses: History includes many examples of struggle, and these conflicts are often the basis of historical narrative and the interpretation of history.)*

Literary Concept: **FOLKLORE**

B Help students understand that the four main kinds of folklore—myths, folk tales, fables, and legends—are not always clear-cut. Tales often contain elements of more than one kind of folklore. Also, the status of a story may change within a culture; for example, a myth or legend may be considered to be factually true at one time, while at another time it may be seen as true only in a symbolic way.

KEEPING THE PAST ALIVE

By giving voice to their cultural heritage, storytellers like Olga Loya keep the past alive. Even cultures that vanished centuries ago can be considered to live on as long as their tales are passed on to new listeners. These tales from cultures around the world make up what is called the oral tradition.

The stories in this unit are drawn from a wide range of regions, countries, and cultures in the Americas. The time line at the right illustrates this rich variety in the oral tradition. It shows what cultures the stories are associated with, along with a key event in each culture's history.

A

Besides being a celebration of varied cultures, the stories in this unit show the common elements that run through different types of folklore. These shared elements form a bridge linking tales from ancient civilizations with stories in the modern oral tradition. The chart below shows some of the common elements of folklore.

B

MYTHS	FOLK TALES
• answer basic questions about the world	• are told primarily for entertainment
• are often considered truthful by their originators	• often feature human beings or humanlike animals

COMMON ELEMENTS
- keep the past alive
- teach lessons about human behavior
- reveal the values of the society

FABLES	LEGENDS
• are short tales that illustrate morals	• are often considered factual by those who tell them
• frequently have characters that are animals	• may have some basis in fact
	• are usually set in the past

698 UNIT SIX: THE ORAL TRADITION

ESKIMO

Otoonah 769

. . .

3000–1000 B.C. *Eskimos cross the Bering Sea from Siberia to North America.*

GUATEMALAN

The First Flute 791

. . .

A.D. 300–900 *The Mayan civilization flourishes in the Yucatán Peninsula.*

HAIDA

Raven and the Coming of Daylight 742

. . .

1000–1300 *The Northwest Coast is one of the most heavily populated areas in North America, with an estimated 129,000 inhabitants.*

Mini-Lesson Study Skills

INTERPRETING GRAPHICS Point out to students that graphic organizers help people organize, understand, and retain information by conveying it visually.

A time line is a graphic device that arranges events in chronological order. Time lines can help students see how a certain topic (such as "the oral tradition") relates to different eras. For instance, the time line on pages 698–99 gives information on several eras in the Western Hemisphere, including the prehistoric age, the ancient world, pre-Colonial America, the nineteenth century, and the twentieth century.

Make sure that students understand that, in this time line, each event is represented by a date, an illustration, and a brief description.

Application Have students identify the items on the time line that took place before 1500. Ask them to name the three events that took place between 1500 and 1800; the five events that took place during the 19th century; and the two events that took place in the 20th century.

698 THE LANGUAGE OF LITERATURE TEACHER'S EDITION

PUERTO RICAN
Aunty Misery 724
. . .
1493 Columbus arrives at the island of Puerto Rico.

MEXICAN
The Souls in Purgatory 706
. . .
1521 Cortés conquers Mexico, putting an end to the Aztec empire.

IROQUOIS
Racing the Great Bear 762
. . .
1570 Five tribes of Native Americans form the Iroquois League.

CAJUN
M'su Carencro and Mangeur de Poulet 727
. . .
1754–1763 Settlers are forced to leave the French colony of Acadia, in what is now Canada, during the French and Indian War. Many of them migrate to Louisiana.

CHEROKEE
Strawberries 786
. . .
about **1820** The Cherokee scholar Sequoyah creates a written alphabet for his people.

ECUADORIAN
The Five Eggs 740
. . .
1830 Ecuador declares independence from Spanish rule.

AFRICAN AMERICAN
Brer Possum's Dilemma 721
. . .
about **1850** The prosperity of cotton growers in the South is built upon slave labor.

OGLALA
Spotted Eagle and Black Crow 745
. . .
1860s Chief Red Cloud of the Oglala Teton people leads Sioux warriors in battles against the U.S. Army.

NORTH AMERICAN
John Henry 718
Paul Bunyan and the Winter of the Blue Snow 702
Pecos Bill 734
. . .
1869 The first transcontinental railroad is completed.

MODERN ORAL TRADITION
The Girl in the Lavender Dress 710
No News 789
. . .
1945 World War II ends.

AFRICAN AMERICAN
The Woman in the Snow 775
. . .
1956 The Supreme Court orders integrated seating on public buses in Montgomery, Alabama.

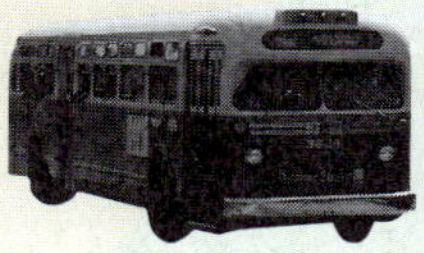

KEEPING THE PAST ALIVE **699**

Linking to History

C In 1824, Sequoyah received a medal from the eastern council of Native American leaders. The message that accompanied the medal said: "In receiving this small tribute from the representative of the people of your native land, in honor of your transcendent invention, you will, I trust, place a proper estimate on the grateful feelings of your fellow countrymen. . . . The present generation have already experienced the great benefits of your incomparable system. The old and the young find no difficulty in learning to read and write in their native language and to correspond with their distant friends with the same facility as the whites do. . . ."

**Critical Thinking:
HYPOTHESIZING**

D Ask students to explain what kinds of stories they think might have grown out of the construction of America's first transcontinental railroad. *(Possible responses: Stories involving difficult physical labor, as well as homesickness; stories about different types of people coming into contact with one another; stories about bravery or grand accomplishments; stories about people moving from one place to another)*

Mini-Lesson   Genre Study

LITERATURE IN THE ORAL TRADITION
Remind students that the four types of literature in the oral tradition are myths, folk tales, fables, and legends.

Application As students proceed through this unit, have them choose two or three selections and create charts that list as many details from the selection as possible that demonstrate the particular qualities of the type of folklore that the selection represents. Remind students that some selections may contain elements from more than one type of folklore.

THE LANGUAGE OF LITERATURE **TEACHER'S EDITION** **699**

OVERVIEW
Objectives
- To understand and appreciate a tall tale, a folk tale, and a legend about mystical or fantastical figures who come into contact with ordinary human beings
- To appreciate the culture of the regions and countries represented
- To extend understanding of the selections through a variety of multimodal and cross-curricular activities

Reading Pathways
- Encourage groups of students to do choral readings of each of the three selections. Assign the readings in advance, so that students can plan and rehearse their oral presentations before sharing them with classmates.
- Invite students to read the tall tale, the folk tale, and the legend aloud to classmates. Encourage listeners to note any confusing passages. Have students form their own questions about these passages and discuss their responses with their classmates.
- After students have read these tales, have them reread them to identify structural elements such as conflict. Encourage them to note whether the selections contain examples of internal conflict, external conflict, or both. Then ask students to identify any similarities and differences among these tales and the selections in the related unit. For example, have students consider how the conflicts in "The Souls in Purgatory" are similar to or different from those in "The Inn of Lost Time."

PREVIEWING

LINKS TO UNIT ONE

Changing Perceptions

Activating Prior Knowledge
In the selections in Unit One, people and events are not always what they seem at first glance. With the benefit of experience, characters go beyond their initial perceptions and gain new insight and understanding. In the stories you are about to read, the characters' perceptions also change in the light of experience.

MEXICO
The Souls in Purgatory
retold by Guadalupe Baca-Vaughn

The first people to bring the Roman Catholic religion to Mexico were missionaries and priests from Spain who arrived in the 16th century. They converted millions of Native Americans to Catholicism, and the great majority of Mexicans now belong to the Roman Catholic Church. However, the ancient beliefs and traditions of the region did not disappear—many of them have been combined with Catholic beliefs. This blend of traditions is reflected in many Mexican customs and folk tales, including this tale of faith.

Building Background

700 UNIT SIX: THE ORAL TRADITION

PRINT AND MEDIA RESOURCES

UNIT SIX RESOURCE BOOK
Strategic Reading: Literature, p. 4
Vocabulary SkillBuilder, p. 7
Reading SkillBuilder, p. 5
Spelling SkillBuilder, p. 6

GRAMMAR MINI-LESSONS
Transparencies, p. 13
Copymasters, p. 20

WRITING MINI-LESSONS
Transparencies, p. 39

ACCESS FOR STUDENTS ACQUIRING ENGLISH
Selection Summaries
Reading and Writing Support

TEACHER'S GUIDE TO ASSESSMENT AND PORTFOLIO USE

FORMAL ASSESSMENT
Selection Test, pp. 133–134
 Test Generator

 **AUDIO LIBRARY**
See Reference Card

INTERNET RESOURCES
McDougal Littell Literature Center at http://www.hmco.com/mcdougal/lit

700 THE LANGUAGE OF LITERATURE TEACHER'S EDITION

NORTHEASTERN U.S.

Paul Bunyan and the Winter of the Blue Snow

retold by Paul Robert Walker

Building Background

In the 19th century, forests covered a much larger area of the United States than they do today. Chopping them down to clear farmland and to provide lumber was an immense task. It was almost certainly the lumberjacks of the northern woods who told the first tall tales about the greatest lumberjack of them all—Paul Bunyan. Tall tales are stories in which exaggerated characters perform incredible feats. This selection is based on several Bunyan tales, including ones told in the logging camps of Michigan.

Building Background

NORTHEASTERN U.S.

The Girl in the Lavender Dress

retold by Maureen Scott

Urban legends are contemporary stories that are told repeatedly in many versions around the world. The people telling them usually claim the stories are true and that they actually happened to a relative or friend of a friend. In fact, urban legends simply represent modern-day folklore. Part of their appeal may be that they combine traditional fears—for example, the fear of ghosts—with more modern fears, such as the fear of random violence or of being stalked.

Setting A Purpose

AS YOU READ . . .

See whether the stories remind you of any other tales from the same culture or other cultures.

Consider how the characters' thoughts and actions fit the theme "Changing Perceptions."

Notice how each story reflects various features of its culture.

LINKS TO UNIT ONE **701**

SUMMARY

Paul Bunyan and the Winter of the Blue Snow Bunyan, a huge lumberjack, and Babe, his giant ox, join a logging camp in the North Woods. Bunyan and Babe go to work: soon 100 million trees have been cut and piled on the frozen river, ready for transport when the ice thaws. The owner of a sawmill along the Mississippi River receives the logs but refuses to pay for them. Paul gets Babe to drink the river, sucking the logs upstream. The owner pays, and the logs flow back down the Mississippi.

The Souls in Purgatory A shy woman, who has few domestic skills, prays regularly to the Souls in Purgatory. Her aunt makes false boasts about her to a merchant in the hope that he will marry her. He tests the woman by asking her to spin three bundles of linen, to sew three shirts, and to embroider a vest. Three lovely ghosts appear and help her because of her devotion to the Poor Souls. They ask to be invited to her wedding. At the wedding, three hags appear and tell the groom that their bent bodies were caused by too much spinning, sewing, and embroidering. He vows never to ask his new wife to perform these tasks again.

The Girl in the Lavender Dress A husband and wife offer a ride to a young woman and the wife lends her a sweater. When they arrive at the house of the young woman's parents, she has vanished from the car. The parents inform the couple that their daughter died four months ago. The next day, the couple finds the girl's gravestone—next to which is the woman's sweater.

CUSTOMIZING FOR
Students Acquiring English

- Use **ACCESS FOR STUDENTS ACQUIRING ENGLISH,** *Reading and Writing Support.*

- Ask students familiar with "The Souls in Purgatory" or those who speak Spanish to read and explain the Spanish words and phrases in this tale to the class.

WORDS TO KNOW

dumbfounded (dŭm'foun'dĭd) *adj.* speechless with shock or amazement (p. 706)

intercession (ĭn'tər-sĕsh'ən) *n.* the asking for something that will benefit someone else (p. 706)

pungent (pŭn'jənt) *adj.* sharp and intense, as an odor (p. 711)

reproach (rĭ-prōch') *v.* to accuse or blame (p. 708)

STRATEGIC READING FOR
Less-Proficient Readers

Set a Purpose Encourage students to become involved in the selections by asking them to share some of their thoughts about ghost stories and other tales that involve supernatural or exaggerated characters. Then have students read to find out what Paul Bunyan and Babe must do to the trees in order to make room to lie down to sleep.

Use **UNIT SIX RESOURCE BOOK**, p. 4, for guidance in reading the selection.

CUSTOMIZING FOR
Gifted and Talented Students

Have students write a story similar to "Paul Bunyan and the Winter of the Blue Snow," using another setting with slightly different characters. Their task is to write a narrative that concerns a larger-than-life figure who helps ordinary humans do difficult work. Rather than set their tales in the North Woods, students could use a desert, ocean, Arctic, jungle, or urban setting. They should feel free to give their hero a different name and a sidekick as entertaining and useful as Babe.

Art Note

Drawing by Rockwell Kent Rockwell Kent (1882–1971) portrays Paul Bunyan as a figure of gigantic stature. In Bunyan's muscular physique and rough-hewn features, Kent creates the impression of an oversized man, as opposed to simply a cartoon or caricature.

Reading the Art What descriptive words would you apply to the figure in this drawing? What details in the drawing indicate that the subject matter is legendary rather than realistic?

Paul Bunyan and the Winter of the Blue Snow

retold by Paul Robert Walker

Illustration by Rockwell Kent. Courtesy of the Rockwell Kent Legacies.

702 UNIT SIX: THE ORAL TRADITION

Mini-Lesson • Literary Concepts

Realistic Description
a big, big man with a bushy black beard, a red woolen cap, a plaid woolen shirt, and leather boots

Exaggeration/Hyperbole
leather boots that were just about as tall as Joe

REVIEWING EXAGGERATION Remind students that an exaggeration is a statement that something is much more than it actually is. An extreme exaggeration made for emphasis or humor is called *hyperbole*. Many folk tales (such as "Paul Bunyan and the Winter of the Blue Snow") use exaggeration and hyperbole for comic effect.

Application Have students make a chart with two columns, similar to the one shown. Then ask them to analyze a few paragraphs of "Paul Bunyan and the Winter of the Blue Snow" and fill in the chart with examples from the text.

Back in the Winter of the Blue Snow, the boys were logging the giant pines of the North Woods. It was a pretty big camp in those days, with a crew of 180 men. And every man was at least seven feet tall and weighed at least 350 pounds.

Joe Muffreau was too small to be a logger, being only six feet fourteen inches tall and weighing only 349 pounds and 53 ounces. But he was the fastest flapjack flipper in the North Woods, so they made him the camp cook.

One night, Joe looked out the window of the cook shack and saw something moving in the darkness. At first he thought it was a couple of pine trees coming in for dinner. But when it got closer, he realized it was a man—a big, big man with a bushy black beard, a red woolen cap, a plaid woolen shirt, and leather boots that were just about as tall as Joe Muffreau. Joe opened the door of the cook shack and smiled up at the stranger.

"You look mighty hungry," said Joe.

"I am," said the stranger. "My name's Paul Bunyan."

"Well, come on in and grab some grub."

Joe had a crew of twenty-two cookeys, and he put them all to work preparing dinner for the big lumberjack. After about three hours, it was all ready, and Paul sat down to have himself a little meal. He ate thirty-three pounds of beef, one whole venison, six hams, two bushels of fried potatoes, twelve four-pound loaves of bread, twelve dozen eggs, and 678 flapjacks topped off with six gallons of maple syrup, and he washed it all down with twenty-two gallons of coffee.

Illustration by Rockwell Kent. Courtesy of the Rockwell Kent Legacies.

When he was finished Paul said, "That'll tide me over. Now what about my ox?"

Joe looked out the window of the cook shack and squinted into the darkness. "What ox?" he asked. "All I see is a mountain covered with blue snow."

"That's no mountain—that's my ox," said Paul. "I call him Babe."

Joe looked out the window again. Sure enough, the mountain was really Babe, the Big Blue Ox. It was a reasonable mistake, because Babe was pretty big. Some folks say he measured fourteen ax handles between the eyes. Others say he measured forty-two and a half ax handles and a can of chewing tobacco. That just shows how people exaggerate. The truth is, Babe measured exactly seven ax handles between the eyes. . . . Of course, ax handles were a lot bigger in those days.

Joe had one of his boys show Paul and Babe to the stables. The stable boss let Babe eat as much as he wanted—which was a year's supply of hay for the entire camp. Then Paul and Babe kicked over a few hundred trees so they could lie down, and they went to sleep in the blue snow.

The next morning was crisp and clear and so cold that the thermometer outside Joe's cook shack froze at sixty below—it was perfect logging weather. After breakfast Paul and Babe went out with the lumberjacks to a section of tall pines. A section is a pretty big piece of land—640 acres—and the boys had been logging it all winter. It was slow, tedious work.

Mini-Lesson Grammar

ADJECTIVES IN COMPARISONS The *comparative* form of an adjective is used to compare two things. The comparative is formed by adding *-er* to the ends of one- or two-syllable adjectives. For longer adjectives, use the word *more*.

The *superlative* form of an adjective is used to compare more than two things. The superlative is formed by adding the ending *-est* for short adjectives or the word *most* for long adjectives.

Application Have students identify one example of the comparative and one example of the superlative in the two highlighted passages (*fastest, bigger*).

Have them write the comparative and superlative forms for each of the following adjectives.
1. small (*smaller, smallest*)
2. tedious (*more tedious, most tedious*)
3. dark (*darker, darkest*)

Reteaching/Reinforcement
- Grammar Handbook, anthology p. 879
- Grammar Mini-Lessons copymasters p. 20, transparencies p. 13

 **The Writer's Craft**

Adjectives in Comparisons, pp. 518–519

Art Note

Babe'd Walk Right Off with It by **Rockwell Kent** To convince the viewer of Babe's enormity, Kent includes two human figures that are a fraction of the ox's size.

Reading the Art What details in the illustration help you understand the action being portrayed? How would the effect of this image be different if the two human figures had been left out?

Literary Concept: EXAGGERATION

A Ask students to identify an example of exaggeration in the first paragraph. (*The men are all at least 7 feet tall and weigh 350 pounds.*) Then ask how exaggeration works in the first sentence of the second paragraph. (*Possible response: There are 12 inches in a foot, so that Joe is actually 7 feet, 2 inches tall; likewise, because there are 16 ounces in a pound, he actually weighs more than 350 pounds.*)

CUSTOMIZING FOR
Students Acquiring English

I Explain to students that *grub* is slang for "food," especially food prepared at a work camp. *Cookeys* is slang for "cooks," the people who prepare the meals.

STRATEGIC READING FOR
Less-Proficient Readers

B Make sure that students are clear about details that establish the exaggerated world of the folk tale by asking the following questions.

- How many men work on the logging crew? (*180*) Noting Relevant Details
- What size are all of these men? (*at least 7 feet tall and 350 pounds*) Summarizing/ Noting Relevant Details
- What do Paul and Babe have to do before they can lie down to sleep? (*They kick over a few hundred trees.*) Relating Cause and Effect

Set a Purpose Have students read to learn what happens when Babe stops drinking river water.

Art Note

Paul . . . Plowed Out an Outlet for It by Rockwell Kent Before studying painting, Kent studied architecture at Columbia University. His affinity for drafting and design is apparent in his use of lines and scale to illustrate the river and mountains, and in the relationship of Bunyan and Babe to the surrounding landscape.

Reaching the Art *Do you think that this drawing effectively illustrates the author's descriptions of the log jam? Why or why not?*

Active Reading: QUESTION

 Encourage students to share any questions they have as they read this passage. For instance, some students may be puzzled about the term *cleverality*. Help them understand that the storyteller may have used this made-up word (the actual noun is *cleverness*) to contribute to the tale's backwoods, homespun tone.

Linking to Math

D Point out to students that 640 acres is exactly one square mile. An acre equals 4,840 square yards or 43,560 square feet. Thus 640 acres is equivalent to 27,878,400 square feet or 3,097,600 square yards.

CUSTOMIZING FOR
Students Acquiring English

(2) Tell students that *dang* is a mild expletive, used for emphasis.

Why, some of those North Woods pines were so big that a two-man team could saw at one side of the trunk for three days before they'd run into another team sawing from the other side.

Of course, Paul didn't work with a partner, and he didn't work with a saw. He stepped right up to the biggest tree he could find, lifted his giant ax, and chopped that North Woods pine down with a single stroke—*Boom!* The sound exploded like thunder in the cold air. Then he stepped over to another tree and did it again—*Boom!* The other loggers stared in wide-eyed wonder. The way Paul was going, they'd be done with the whole section by lunchtime.

Then Paul did something that really surprised them. He set his giant ax on the ground, scratched his bushy black beard, and said, "Boys, I don't mind working hard, but there's gotta be a better method of logging. This is just too slow. First we chop down the trees; then we pull them over the skid roads to the river. It seems like double work." Paul scratched his beard some more, and all the boys could see his cleverality working away in his big brain.

After a few minutes Paul got a light in his eyes. He picked up Babe's leather harness and wrapped it around the whole section—all 640 acres. Then the Big Blue Ox dragged the land, pine trees and all, down to the river. Paul and the boys cut the timber just like they were shearing a sheep, and the logs fell right into the river. Of course, the river was frozen at the time, but this way they were all set for the spring thaw. After the logs were cut, Babe hauled the section back where it belonged, and Paul hitched him up to another one.

With Paul and Babe, the Winter of the Blue Snow turned out to be the biggest logging season in the history of the world. When the spring thaw came, there were one hundred million logs in the river. Paul and the boys floated them down nice and easy at first, but the snow kept melting, the river kept getting higher, the logs kept moving faster, and pretty soon it was out of control. Those hundred million logs started bumping and stopping and sliding and piling, and all of a sudden Paul and the boys had a logjam to beat all jams. The logs were piled two hundred feet high and backed up a mile upriver. Paul stood on the bank, scratching his bushy black beard. The boys could see his cleverality working pretty good. Finally Paul put Babe in the river and grabbed a shotgun. Then he peppered the Big Blue Ox with moose shot. Now, moose shot is good-sized ammunition, but Babe thought it was just a swarm of flies. He started swishing his tail around, stirring that river and stirring it some more, until pretty soon the whole dang river flowed backward and the logs came loose. Then Paul lifted Babe out of the water, and the logs floated downstream again.

Everything went pretty smoothly after that—until they got the logs to the sawmill. You see, Paul and the boys had so many logs, there weren't enough sawmills in the North Woods to buy them. Paul did a little checkin'

Illustration by Rockwell Kent. Courtesy of the Rockwell Kent Legacies.

704 UNIT SIX: THE ORAL TRADITION

Mini-Lesson  Spelling

WORDS ENDING WITH -OUS/-US Remind students of the rules that govern the spelling of words ending with *-ous* and *-us*. The letters *-ous* make up a suffix that is often added to nouns to form adjectives meaning "full of" or "having certain characteristics." For example, the noun *advantage* can be turned into the adjective *advantageous* by adding this suffix. However, *-us* is a noun ending, not a suffix. For example, the nouns *virus* and *surplus* end with these letters.

Example from the selection: *tedious*

Application Have students spell the following words as you recite them aloud.
1. marvelous
2. census
3. outrageous
4. adventurous
5. radius
6. circus

Reteaching/Reinforcement
- *Unit Six Resource Book*, p. 6

---

704 THE LANGUAGE OF LITERATURE TEACHER'S EDITION

around and discovered there was a big sawmill operator down near the Gulf of Mexico who was willing to buy all the logs they had. So the lumberjacks floated fifty million logs down the Mississippi River.

When the logs reached the Gulf of Mexico, the big sawmill operator refused to pay for them. Maybe he figured he was so far from the North Woods that he didn't have to worry about Paul Bunyan and the boys. But that's not the way Paul saw it. Paul never cared much about money—just logging—but a deal is a deal, and that fellow down on the Gulf of Mexico was cheating all the boys—and Babe, too. So Paul started scratching his beard and working his cleverality again. Then he got that light in his eyes, and the boys knew he had a plan.

Paul turned to Joe Muffreau and said, "Joe, I want you to bring me the biggest block of salt you can find."

"What about pepper?" asked Joe.

"No pepper," said Paul. "Just salt."

Joe sent his twenty-two cookeys back to the camp in an eight-horse flapjack wagon. When they came back, they were carrying a block of salt that was almost as big as Joe's cook shack. Paul picked it up in one hand and set it down in front of Babe, the Big Blue Ox. Well, Babe was always partial to salt, so he licked it and licked it until there was nothing left.

Of course, then Babe was pretty thirsty, so Paul led him over to the Mississippi River. Babe started drinking, and it must have tasted mighty good after that salt, because he just kept drinking and drinking until the water came all the way up from the Gulf of Mexico, with the fifty-million logs floating on the top.

Well, the sawmill operator paid right up after that. So Paul told Babe to stop drinking, and the Mississippi River flowed back down to the Gulf of Mexico, carrying the logs right with it. Paul split the profits with all the boys, including Babe. And that's what happened during the Winter of the Blue Snow. ❖

PAUL ROBERT WALKER

Paul Robert Walker (1953–) says he became a writer because "I was born this way. I delight in words, ideas, characters, and the stories they create. I'm fascinated with facts and the blurry line that separates them from—or turns them into—fiction." He admits he really became a writer because of his grandfather, a book called *The Swamp Fox*, and the Los Angeles Times.

Named after his Danish grandfather, who edited a Danish newspaper in the United States and was knighted by the King of Denmark for his writing, Walker thinks he inherited his grandfather's "writing genes." When, at the age of seven, Walker read *The Swamp Fox*, about Revolutionary War General Francis Marion, he discovered "the power of a good book." In 1986, he was hired to write articles for reference books. Although most of what he wrote was never published, Walker turned one of the articles into a full-length book about a baseball player. The book, *Pride of Puerto Rico: The Life of Roberto Clemente*, launched Walker's writing career.

Walker says it is a "totalaciously splendiferous" experience to read his stories to young people because it allows him not only to write but to teach and act.

OTHER WORKS *Big Men, Big Country; Bigfoot and Other Legendary Creatures*

CUSTOMIZING FOR
Students Acquiring English

3 Invite volunteers to provide a more commonly used synonym for *mighty* as it appears here. *(Possible responses: very, really)*

STRATEGIC READING FOR
Less-Proficient Readers

E Ask students to explain what happens when Babe stops drinking from the river. *(The Mississippi begins to flow again into the Gulf of Mexico and the logs are carried back to the sawmill.)*
Relating Cause and Effect

From Personal Response to Critical Analysis

1. What are your impressions of Paul Bunyan? Jot down your thoughts in your notebook. *(Responses will vary.)*
2. Why do you think Paul Bunyan is so warmly received at the logging camp? *(Possible responses: The loggers are isolated but friendly and enjoy meeting new people; Joe and the other loggers see that Paul can be of enormous help to them.)*
3. What personal characteristics does this folk tale celebrate? *(Possible responses: honesty, hard work, ingenuity, physical fitness, generosity)*

COMPREHENSION CHECK
1. Which of Paul Bunyan's facial features is mentioned several times in the narrative? *(his bushy black beard)*
2. What is mistaken for "a mountain covered with blue snow"? *(Babe, the blue ox)*
3. What faster method of logging does Paul Bunyan discover? *(He ties Babe's harness around a whole section of trees and lets Babe tug the whole section to the frozen river.)*
4. How does Bunyan force the sawmill owner to pay his debt? *(He has Babe drink the Mississippi River. This draws the logs back upriver away from the sawmill.)*

THE SOULS

retold by Guadalupe Baca-Vaughn

Si es verdad, allá va, Si es mentira, queda urdida.[1]
(*If it be true, so it is. If it be false, so be it.*)

There was once an old lady who had raised a niece since she was a tiny baby. She had taught the girl to be good, obedient, and industrious, but the girl was very shy and timid and spent much time praying, especially to the Souls in Purgatory.[2]

As the girl grew older and very beautiful, the old woman began to worry that when she died her niece would be left all alone in the world, a world which her niece saw only through innocent eyes. The old lady prayed daily to all the saints in heaven for their intercession to Our Lord that he might send some good man who would fall in love with her niece and marry her; then she could die in peace.

As it happens, the old woman did chores for a *comadre*[3] who had a rooming house. Among her tenants there was a seemingly rich merchant who one day said that he would like to get married if he could find a nice, quiet girl who knew how to keep house and be a good wife and mother to his children when they came.

The old lady opened her ears and began to smile and scheme in her mind, for she could imagine her niece married to the nice gentleman. She told the merchant that he could find all that he was looking for in her niece, who was a jewel, a piece of gold, and so gifted that she could even catch birds while they were flying!

The gentleman became interested and said that he would like to meet the girl and would go to her house the next day.

The old woman ran home as fast as she could; she appeared to be flying. When she got home all out of breath, she called her niece and told her to straighten up the house and get herself ready for the next day, as there was a gentleman who would be calling. She told her to be sure to wash her hair and brush it until it shone like the sun and to put on her best dress, for in this meeting her future was at stake.

The poor timid girl was dumbfounded. She went to her room and knelt before her favorite *retablo*[4] of the Souls in Purgatory. "Please," she prayed, "don't let my aunt do something rash to embarrass us both."

The next day she obediently prepared herself for the meeting. When the merchant arrived, he asked her if she could spin. "Spin?" answered

---

1. *Si es verdad, allá va, / Si es mentira, queda urdida* (sē ĕs vĕr-däd′ ä-yä′ vä sē ĕs mĕn-tē′rä kĕ′dä ōōr-dē′dä) *Spanish*.
2. **Souls in Purgatory:** spirits of dead people in a place where they undergo temporary suffering to make up for their sins on Earth.
3. *comadre* (kô-mä′drĕ) *Spanish*: a female friend.
4. *retablo* (rĕ-tä′blô) *Spanish*: a wooden panel on which a religious picture is painted or carved.

WORDS TO KNOW
intercession (ĭn′tər-sĕsh′ən) *n.* the act of asking for something that will benefit someone else
dumbfounded (dŭm′foun′dĭd) *adj.* speechless with shock or amazement

706

Mini-Lesson | The Writer's Style

USING FIGURATIVE LANGUAGE Good writers use figurative language to compare one thing to something else. Often the things being compared are not considered similar.

The two most common types of figurative language are similes and metaphors. A **simile** uses the words *like* or *as* to compare two things. For instance, *that boy's eyes are like saucers* is a simile that compares human eyes with a type of china. A **metaphor** makes a comparison without using *like* or *as*. The metaphor *our friendship became a prison* compares a relationship with a physical location.

Application Encourage students to identify the metaphor and simile in the highlighted passages on page 706. ("*her niece, who was a jewel, a piece of gold*"; "*her hair . . . shone like the sun*") Then have them write another metaphor that describes the girl and a simile that describes her hair.

Reteaching/Reinforcement
• *Writing Mini-Lessons* transparencies p. 39

Types of Figurative Language, pp. 318–319

In Purgatory

En busqueda de la paz [In search of peace], Alfredo Linares.

the old woman, while the poor embarrassed girl stood by with bowed head. "Spin! The hanks[5] disappear so fast you would think she was drinking them like water."

The merchant left three hanks of linen to be spun by the following day. "What have you done, *Tía?*"[6] the poor girl asked. "You know I can't spin!" "Don't sell yourself short," the old lady replied with twinkling eyes. "Where is your faith in God, the Souls in Purgatory? You pray to them every day. They will help you. Just wait and see!" Sobbing, the girl ran to her room and knelt down beside her bed and began to pray, often raising her head to the *retablo* of the Souls in Purgatory which hung on the wall beside her bed. After she quieted down, she thought she heard a soft sound behind her. She

---

5. **hanks:** bundles of fibers that are spun into thread or yarn.
6. **tía** (tē′ä) *Spanish:* aunt.

Critical Thinking: ANALYZING

D Have students explain the identity of the three ghosts. (Possible response: The juxtaposition of the girl's prayer and the ghosts' appearance is not accidental: they come in response to her prayers. Their words about helping the girl "in gratitude for all the good you have done for us" show that the ghosts are three souls from purgatory.)

Literary Concept: SIMILE

E Have students identify the strange simile in this passage. ("Her sewing is like ripe cherries in the mouth of a dragon.") Encourage students to restate this idea in nonfigurative terms to explore its possible meanings. (Possible responses: The things that she sews are surprising and delectable; her ability is a rare gift that can only be obtained by exercising care and discretion in the face of risk.)

CUSTOMIZING FOR
Multiple Learning Styles

F **Spatial or Graphic Learners** Have students draw or paint an image illustrating the scene in which the ghosts sew the shirts. Alternatively, students might choose to draw a shirt or make a tiny one out of fabric or other materials.

CUSTOMIZING FOR
Students Acquiring English

2 Point out that the expression "he asked the old lady for her niece's hand in marriage" means that he asked the old lady if she would permit her niece to marry him.

Active Reading: CONNECT

G Invite students to connect their lives with that of the young heroine in this tale. Encourage them to share their thoughts and feelings about how they would feel about the aunt's behavior and about the imminent wedding. You may wish to use the following model to give them ideas about what they might be thinking about.

Think-Aloud Model *I'm not so sure if I agree with what the aunt is doing. If I were her niece, I would be unhappy with her for forcing this stranger on me. Also, the aunt seems so sure of herself, but I'm worried about what the merchant will say when he finds out that the aunt and niece have been tricking him.*

D turned and saw three beautiful ghosts dressed in white, smiling at her. "Do not be concerned," they said. "We will help you in gratitude for all the good you have done for us." Saying this, each one took a hank of linen and in a wink spun the linen into thread as fine as hair.

The following day when the merchant came, he was astonished to see the beautiful linen and was very pleased. "Didn't I tell you, sir?" said the old lady with pride and joy. The gentleman asked the girl if she could sew. Before the surprised girl could answer, the old aunt cried, "Sew? Of course she can sew. Her sewing is like ripe cherries in the mouth of a dragon." The merchant then left a piece of the finest linen to be made into three shirts. The poor girl cried bitterly, but her aunt told her not to worry, that her devotion to the Poor Souls would get her out of this one too, as they had shown how much they loved her on the previous day.

E

The three ghosts were waiting for the girl beside her bed when she went into her room, crying miserably. "Don't cry, little girl," they said. "We will help you again, for we know your aunt, and she knows what she is doing and why."

The ghosts went to work cutting and snipping and sewing. In a flash they had three beautiful shirts finished with the finest stitches and the tiniest seams.

F

The next morning when the gentleman came to see if the girl had finished the shirts, he could not believe his eyes. "They are lovely; they seem to have been made in heaven," he said.

This time the merchant left a vest of rare satin to be embroidered. He thought he would try this girl for the third and last time. The girl cried desperately and could not even **reproach** her aunt. She had decided that she would not ask any more favors of the Souls. She went to her room and lay across the bed and cried and cried. When she finally sat up and dried her tears, she saw the three ghosts smiling at her. "We will help you again, but this time we have a condition, and that is that you will invite us to your wedding." "Wedding? Am I going to get married?" she asked in surprise. "Yes," they said, "and very soon."

The next day a very happy gentleman came for his vest, for he was sure that the lovely girl would have it ready for him. But he was not prepared for the beauty of the vest. The colors were vibrant and beautifully matched. The embroidery looked like a painting. It took his breath away. Without hesitation, he asked the old lady for her niece's hand in marriage. "For," he said, "this vest looks as if it was not touched by human hands but by angels!"

The old woman danced with joy and could hardly contain her happiness. She gave her consent at once. The merchant left to arrange for the wedding. Wringing her hands, the poor girl cried, "But *Tía*, what am I going to do when he finds out that I can't do any of those things?" "Don't worry, my *palomita*,[7] the Blessed Souls[8] will get you out of this trouble too. You wait and see!"

G

Almost at once the old woman went to her *comadre* to tell her the good news and to ask her to help get ready for the wedding. Soon everything was ready.

The poor girl did not know how to invite the Souls to her wedding. She timidly went and

> "Wedding? Am I going to get married?"

---
7. *palomita* (pä-lô-mē′tä) *Spanish:* little dove.
8. **Blessed Souls:** the holy spirits of the dead.

WORDS TO KNOW **reproach** (rĭ-prōch′) *v.* to criticize; blame

---

Mini-Lesson | Reading Skills/Strategies

ACTIVE READING: CONNECT Remind students that the process of relating the content of a literary work to their own knowledge or experience is called connecting. Active readers find ways to connect their own experience with the thoughts and feelings of the characters they read about.

Application Have students write a brief essay discussing the ways they connect with the girl at various points in the story. For example, the task of spinning three bundles of linen is impossible for the girl. Students might write a paragraph about a personal experience involving a seemingly impossible task.

Reteaching/Reinforcement
• *Unit Six Resource Book,* p. 5

stood beside her bed and asked the *retablo* to come to her wedding.

The great day finally arrived. The girl looked beautiful in the gown which the merchant had brought as part of her *donas*.[9] Everyone in the village had been invited to the wedding.

During the fiesta when everyone was drinking *brindes*[10] to the bride and groom and the music was playing, three ugly hags came to the *sala*[11] and stood waiting for the groom to come and welcome them in. One of the hags had an arm that reached to the floor and dragged; the other arm was short. The second hag was bent almost double and had to turn her head sideways to look up. The third hag had bulging, bloodshot eyes like a lobster. "Jesús María," cried the groom. "Who are those ugly creatures?" "They are aunts of my father, whom I invited to my wedding," answered the bride, knowing quite well who they might be. The groom, being well-bred, went at once to greet the ugly hags. He took them to their seats and brought them refreshments. Very casually, he asked the first hag, "Tell me, señora, why is one of your arms so long and the other one short?" "My son," she answered, "my arms are like that because I spin so much."

The groom went to his wife and said, "Go at once and tell the servants to burn your spinning wheel, and never let me see a spinning wheel in my house; never let me see you spinning, ever!"

The groom went to the second hag and asked her why she was so humped over. "My son," she replied, "I am that way from embroidering on a frame so much." The groom went to his wife and whispered, "Burn your embroidery frame at once, and never let me see you embroider another thing."

Next, the groom went to the third hag and asked, "Why are your eyes so bloodshot and bulging?" "My son, it is because I sew so much and bend over while sewing." She had hardly finished speaking when the groom went to his wife and said, "Take your needles and thread and bury them. I never want to see you sewing, never! If I see you sewing, I will divorce you and send you far away, for the wise man learns from others' painful experiences."

Well—so the Souls, in spite of being holy, can also be rascals.

Colorín, colorado, ya mi cuento se ha acabado.[12]
(Scarlet or ruby red, my story has been said.) ❖

---

9. *donas* (dô'näs) *Spanish:* wedding presents a man gives to his bride.
10. *brindes* (brēn'dĕs) *Spanish:* drinks to someone's health or happiness; toasts.
11. *sala* (sä'lä) *Spanish:* a large room for entertaining.
12. *Colorín, colorado, ya mi cuento se ha acabado* (cô-lôr-ēn' cô-lô-rä'dô yä mē kwĕn'tô sĕ ä ä-kä-bä'dô) *Spanish.*

GUADALUPE BACA-VAUGHN

As a little girl, Guadalupe Baca-Vaughn (1905–) first heard "The Souls in Purgatory" from her aunt, "who told me the stories she heard as a child in Mexico." Baca-Vaughn was born in New Mexico, the birthplace of her father's family. Her mother's family was from California when it was still part of Mexico.

Baca-Vaughn was an interpreter and censor for the U.S. Government in El Paso, Texas, during World War II. She eventually returned to New Mexico. Over the next 35 years, she taught elementary and junior high school students.

After retiring, she received a grant to teach the history, culture, and stories of Northern New Mexico to children in local schools. Worried about people losing their cultural heritage, she says, "We should know what went before us."

CUSTOMIZING FOR
Multiple Learning Styles

Musical Learners Have students create a music score that might accompany a film version of "The Girl in the Lavender Dress." Encourage them to analyze the story closely in order to identify where scenes begin and end and to decide what the dominant mood of each scene should be. Then have them compose original music or gather pieces of existing music to create a fitting background.

STRATEGIC READING FOR
Less-Proficient Readers

Set a Purpose Have students read to learn who Herbert and his wife see in the headlights of their car and how the young woman responds to Herbert's offer to deliver her to her destination.

The Girl in the Lavender Dress

retold by Maureen Scott

Copyright © Andrea Brooks

UNIT SIX: THE ORAL TRADITION

Mini-Lesson: Speaking, Listening, and Viewing

HEARING GHOST STORIES Explain to students that "The Girl in the Lavender Dress" is a good example of a story that has been passed along orally in many versions around the world. Ghost stories, of course, are prime candidates for this kind of oral retelling.

Point out to students that many effective ghost stories contain descriptive details of both everyday events and events that are out of the ordinary.

Application Encourage students to listen to the way the story sounds as you (or a volunteer) read it aloud. Have them experiment with reading the ghostly passages with different tones and styles. Then ask students to discuss how these differences affect their appreciation of the ghost story.

710 THE LANGUAGE OF LITERATURE TEACHER'S EDITION

My grandmother was, I always believed, a truthful woman. She paid her taxes. She went to church. She considered the Lord's business as her own. When her children told lies, they soon saw the light of truth. They went to bed without any supper, the taste of soap still **pungent** on their tongues.

That's why the story that follows bothers me so much. It just *can't* be true. Of course, Grandma was 92 when she told it to me and her mind had started to fail. She might have really believed it. Who knows? Maybe you will, too.

I'll try to tell the story just the way she told it to me. She was in a nursing home then. It was late at night and the two of us were alone in the TV room. Grandma's eyelids hung low over her eyes. She worked her wrinkled jaw a few times and began:

It all happened about '42 or '43 [Grandma said]. It was during World War II. We didn't have much gas in those days. No one did. So whenever Herbert took the car somewhere, I tried to go along for the ride.

We lived in Vermont in those days. This time I'm thinking of, Herbert had some business in Claremont. That's in New Hampshire, just across the river. Well, seems Herbert had saved up the gas to go by car. About 25 miles. He said we could leave after work Friday. That night we'd have us a good restaurant meal. Maybe see a movie, too. Then we'd stay in a hotel and drive back the next day.

I don't remember the month, exactly. Sometime in the fall, 'cause it was cool. It was a misty night. I remember Herbert had to keep the wipers going. And it was after dusk when we first saw her. I know it was dark, 'cause I remember first seeing her in the lights ahead.

Neither Herbert nor I spoke. He slowed down, and the girl stopped walking. She just stood there on our side of the road. Not hitching, exactly, but she sure looked like she wanted a ride. It was a lonely road, and there weren't many cars.

First Herbert passed her, going real slow. Then he backed up to where she was. I rolled down my window. She was a pretty little thing, about eighteen or twenty. A round face and big round eyes. Brown hair, cut straight. The mist kind of made her face shine. But the funny thing was what she was wearing: only a thin lavender party dress. In that weather!

Well, I don't remember that anybody did any asking. I just opened the door and leaned forward. She climbed into the back seat, and Herbert started up again. Finally I asked her where she was going.

"Claremont." That was all she said at first. She had a light, breathless voice, like it took a whole lungful of air to say that one word.

"You're lucky," Herbert said. "We're going all the way."

The girl didn't reply. We rode on a little ways. I turned around once or twice, but the girl just smiled, sort of sadly. Anyhow, I didn't want to stare at her. But who was she, and why was she walking on a lonely road at night? I've never been the kind to pry into other people's business. So what I did then was, well, I'd taken off my sweater when the car got warm. I offered it to her, and she put it on.

The mist turned to light rain. Just before we got to the river, Herbert broke the silence. "Where are you going in Claremont, Miss?"

There was no reply.

WORDS TO KNOW

pungent (pŭn′jənt) *adj.* sharp and intense, as an odor

STRATEGIC READING FOR
Less-Proficient Readers

D Make sure that students understand the early plot developments of the tale by asking the following questions.

- What do Herbert and his wife see in the headlights? *(a girl standing by the side of the road)* **Noting Relevant Details**
- How does the girl respond to Herbert's offer to deliver her to her destination in Claremont? *(She says that it would be nice.)* **Summarizing**

Set a Purpose Have students read to learn what is lying next to Carol Bullard's gravestone.

Critical Thinking: SPECULATING

E Invite students to offer their own explanations for the empty back seat of the automobile.

Critical Thinking: SYNTHESIZING

F Have students assess whether the passenger that Herbert and his wife picked up was Carol Bullard. *(Possible response: The description that Carol's mother gives fits exactly the description of the hitchhiker on page 711, so it is possible that the hitchhiker was either Carol Bullard or her ghost.)*

CUSTOMIZING FOR
Students Acquiring English

3 Point out the metaphorical language to students and ask a volunteer to describe what a lobster claw on an elbow would feel like. *(a strong, hard pinch)*

"It's coming on to rain," Herbert said. "And we got time to deliver you."

"Oh," the girl breathed. "Could you *really*? That would be—that would be *nice*. To my parents' house. Corner of Bond and Mason."

"Claremont must be a nice place to grow up," I said, but again, there was no sound from the back of the car. You couldn't even hear her breathing. I just settled back into my seat and enjoyed the trip. We crossed the bridge, headed into town, and Herbert turned right onto Bond Street.

Back in the car, we sped away through the night.

We rode along, looking at the street signs. Mason was way out. There was only one house on the corner, on the opposite side. Herbert made a U-turn and stopped the car.

There was no one in the rear seat!

I looked at Herbert. He looked at me, his eyes popping. I pulled myself up so I could see the back floor. Nothing. Just a little wetness where her feet had been.

"Where'd she get out?" Herbert asked.

"At a stoplight?" I wondered. But we both knew it couldn't be. It was a two-door car, so we'd know it if a door opened. Both of us looked at the rear windows. They were closed, as they had been. Neither of us had felt a draft.

Yet there had to be some explanation. "Come," Herbert said. We hurried toward the house. It was a big square boxlike building. Lights were on in nearly every room. Splotches of brightness covered the wet lawn.

The door had a name on it: J. R. Bullard. It was opened by a long-faced man about fifty.

"Excuse me," Herbert said, "but there seems to be some mystery. You see, your daughter—"

"Daughter?" said the man. "Why, we don't have any daughter." A small woman, some years younger, now stood at his side.

"Well—" Herbert began.

"We *did* have a daughter," the woman said. "But Carol is deceased, you see. She was buried in Calhoun Cemetery four months ago."

Herbert gripped my arm. We both knew Calhoun Cemetery: it was on the Vermont side of the river. "Then who—?" Herbert wondered aloud. Suddenly he looked embarrassed. "Excuse us," he muttered. "It's all a—a mistake."

"Just a minute," I said. "Would you mind telling us what Carol looked like?"

The couple exchanged glances. If they were worried, it wasn't about Carol. It was about us. "A little on the short side," the woman said almost to herself. "A round face. Big round eyes. Dark, straight hair, cut in bangs."

Herbert's hand was a lobster claw on my elbow. We excused ourselves in a hurry. Back in the car, we sped away through the night. Then we drove around for a long time, looking. Across the bridge. Down every little road. Back into Claremont. Near every stoplight. Along Bond Street.

But we both knew the search was futile. There was only one answer. What we'd had in our car, sitting on the back seat and even talking, was the ghost of Carol Bullard. And the amazing thing was that we had proof. A ghost, you see, cannot cross water. That was why, when we came to the river, the ghost had only one choice: to disappear!

712 UNIT SIX: THE ORAL TRADITION

Assessment Option

INFORMAL ASSESSMENT You can informally assess students' understanding of "The Girl with the Lavender Dress" by having students tell the story from a different point of view. The most useful exercise might be to tell the story from the point of view of Carol Bullard. Have students begin the story the moment before Carol sees the headlights of the approaching car.

Rubric

3 Full Accomplishment Students vividly retell the story using details that clearly reflect the point of view of Carol Bullard.

2 Substantial Accomplishment Students retell the story mostly from Carol Bullard's point of view, but one or two parts of the story are confusing or out of focus.

1 Little or Partial Accomplishment Students have difficulty retelling the events of the story from Carol Bullard's point of view.

Grandma stopped talking, and I thought that was the end of her incredible story. But no—there was more:

And that isn't all [Grandma went on]. That night—the night that it happened—we were both pretty edgy. Didn't get much sleep, either. Not till the next morning did we think of my sweater. It had disappeared with the ghost.

That was a really good sweater, almost new. You see, we didn't have much money, and it was wartime. Clothes were hard to come by. But once in a while I'd blow a week's pay on something really nice, something that would last for years—like that sweater.

Now listen: it's like this. On the way home, we thought we'd swing around by Calhoun Cemetery. We wanted to find a certain gravestone, the one that would say "Carol Bullard" on it. So we did just that. It took a long time, but finally we found the new graves. And there, at last, was the stone. A small flat stone. Just "Carol Bullard" on it. No dates; nothing more. But next to the stone, neatly folded up, *was my sweater!*

True—or not? You decide. ❖

STRATEGIC READING FOR
Less-Proficient Readers

G Ask students to describe what is lying beside Carol Bullard's gravestone on the Vermont side of the river. *(the grandmother's sweater)* Noting Relevant Details

CUSTOMIZING FOR
Gifted and Talented Students

Have students discuss their ideas about why a "legend" like this one might get passed around. Ask them to consider the themes or aspects of the story that make it a good candidate for oral storytelling.

Literary Links

Ask students to compare the travelers in "The Girl in the Lavender Dress" with the scientists in "Collecting Team." *(Possible response: In both cases, there are errors of perception. The couple believe an apparition to be a living person but find out the truth when they talk to her parents. The scientists believe they are freely pursuing their work but learn they are imprisoned when they cannot leave the planet.)*

From Personal Response to Critical Analysis

1. What is your reaction to the end of this story? Write some of your ideas in your notebook. *(Responses will vary.)*
2. What details in the text hint that there is something unusual about the girl in the lavender dress? *(Possible responses: The girl is wearing a thin party dress on a fall night; her strange voice and sad smile, her silence in the back seat, and her disappearance from the car all seem odd.)*
3. Why do you think Carol Bullard responds to Herbert's offer to deliver her with the question, "Could you really?" *(Possible response: Perhaps she has attempted to get back across the river before and senses that it is impossible.)*

COMPREHENSION CHECK
1. Who narrates the story about the girl in the lavender dress? *(the grandmother of the speaker)*
2. Where does the story take place? *(in Vermont and New Hampshire)*
3. Where does the girl ask the couple to take her? *(to her parents' home in Claremont)*
4. What is in the car's back seat when they reach the house? *(nothing)*
5. What do the parents say about their daughter to the couple? *(She died four months earlier.)*

Literature Connection

Project 1 The team of judges and organizers should create guidelines that establish clear, attainable criteria for judging the stories. Make sure that these guidelines state that existing stories and original stories will be judged equally. The guidelines should also determine how to create the best atmosphere for storytelling in the classroom or other location.

Remind researchers and story writers that the stories will be judged on the way they are conveyed orally.

Encourage storytellers to get feedback from peers and others during rehearsal. Have them work with a tape recorder, if possible.

Rubric

3 Full Accomplishment Students thoroughly plan and smoothly execute a storytelling contest in which two or more imaginative, interesting stories are presented and judged according to fair, clear rules.

2 Substantial Accomplishment Students' planning of the contest is satisfactory, but not all students participate; their performance of at least two stories is spirited and fairly judged.

1 Little or Partial Accomplishment Students have difficulty organizing the contest; the presentation of the stories is lackluster or confusing; and judgments are made without clear, established rules.

RESPONDING OPTIONS

Multimodal Activity

LITERATURE CONNECTION PROJECT 1

Plan a Storytelling Contest Organize a contest that involves the telling of tall tales and stories. Decide who will be organizers and judges, researchers, story writers, storytellers, and designers. Work in teams, and refer to the suggestions presented as you play your part in this project.

Organizers and Judges Decide on the rules of the contest. Include guidelines for judging the storytelling and any other elements that are significant to your contest planning. Assign a team of designers to create the awards that will be given to winners of the contest.

Researchers and Story Writers You can either find existing stories to retell or create your own stories. Keep in mind that tall tales include exaggeration, humor, and incredible feats. Your stories can be funny, strange, or both. Work from an outline or storyboards to create your story.

Storytellers Concentrate on telling the story effectively. Rehearse it several times. If you are using visual aids, practice handling them. Speak at a comfortable pitch, placing extra stress on important words. Let your enthusiasm show, and look people in the eye as if you were having a one-on-one conversation.

Multimodal Activity

SOCIAL STUDIES CONNECTION PROJECT 2

Learn About the "Day of the Dead" Both the native peoples of Mexico and the conquering Roman Catholic Spaniards believed that the spirits of the dead return to Earth to visit the living. An important festival in Mexico today is El Día de los Muertos (ĕl dē′ä dĕ lôs mwĕr′tôs), which means "the Day of the Dead."

Find out about El Día de los Muertos. Research when the festival occurs, and why and how it is celebrated. Your research could include a visit to a museum that features Day of the Dead *ofrendas* (ô-frĕn′däs), or offerings to the dead.

Many Mexican and Mexican-American families celebrate the festival in their homes. Re-create some aspect of the festival in the form of paintings, drawings, or clay sculpture. You could even construct an *ofrenda*. Share your results with the class.

Day of the Dead Festival		
When	Why	How

714 UNIT SIX: THE ORAL TRADITION

Social Studies Connection

Project 2 Students' research might include information on various foods and flowers associated with the three-day festival that celebrates the spirits of the dead. For example, *pan de muertos* (the bread of the dead) and marigolds (the flowers of the dead) are common sights during the festival. Students might also explain customs such as visiting relatives, ringing bells, and lighting fireworks.

An *ofrenda* is an offering placed on a "children's altar" to invite *angelitos*, the spirits of dead children, for a one-night visit. It consists of a small basket of nuts, sugar skulls decorated with one's own name, hot cocoa in cups, flowers, fruits, and toys.

Rubric

3 Full Accomplishment Students' presentation is interesting and thorough.

2 Substantial Accomplishment Students' presentation contains several facts.

1 Little or Partial Accomplishment Students have difficulty researching and presenting information.

Multimodal Activity

HISTORY CONNECTION PROJECT 3

Discover 16th-Century Mexico Find out about how the Spaniards conquered the Aztecs in the early 1500s in what is now south-central Mexico. Present your findings in the form of a television news broadcast with visual aids, perhaps including a historical map and time line. You could use an actual television news program as a model. If possible, a partner could videotape your report.

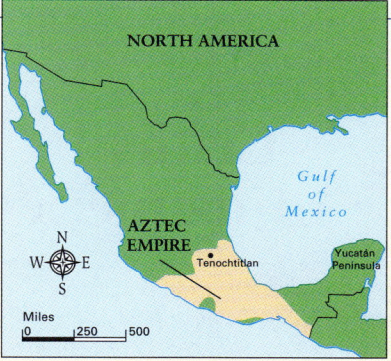

Multimodal Activities

ACROSS CULTURES MINI-PROJECTS

Investigate Forest Conservation In the United States, the early settlers approached the nation's expansive forest land as though it would last forever, clearing land and felling more trees than they really needed. By 1891, a movement to save and manage the forests was underway. Find out about forest conservation from the 1890s to the present, and report your findings to the class. Present your statistics in the form of a graph.

Construct a *Retablo* The girl in "The Souls in Purgatory" prayed before a *retablo*. This painting of religious figures, often on wood, is one kind of *retablo*—a *retablo santo* (sän′tô). Today, another kind of *retablo*—a *retablo exvoto* (ĕs-vô′tô)—is far more common.

Use the library or Internet, or talk with a person of Mexican descent, to learn what is on a *retablo exvoto* and what it is used for. Then create one the girl might have made, or make one for yourself.

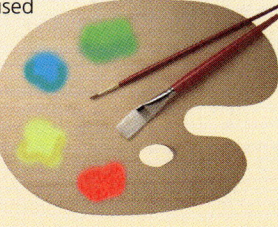

Compare and Contrast Tales There are more than 75 versions of the story "The Girl in the Lavender Dress." In the library, locate a version that is set in a different time or place. Use a Venn diagram, like the one shown, to compare and contrast the version you find in the library with the one in the book.

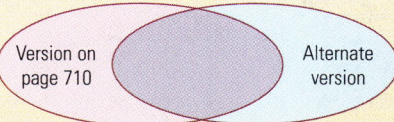

Extended Reading

MORE ABOUT THE CULTURES

- *Bold Journey: West with Lewis and Clark* by Charles Bohner
- *In This Proud Land: The Story of a Mexican-American Family* by Bernard Wolf
- *The United States in the Mexican War* by Don Lawson
- *Windmills, Bridges and Old Machines: Discovering Our Industrial Past* by David Weitzman

LINKS TO UNIT ONE **715**

History Connection

Project 3 Students' presentations might include information on the main Aztec city of Tenochtitlán (founded c. 1325), the surrounding area of central and southern Mexico (gained by the Aztecs between the 12th and 16th centuries through alliance and military victories), and the Aztec god of war, Quetzalcoatl. Students should make clear that the Spanish victory occurred in part because the Spanish forces—unlike the Aztecs—had access to both horses and firearms.

Rubric

3 Full Accomplishment Students accurately research and present a news broadcast that vividly and thoroughly conveys information about the Spanish conquest of the Aztecs.

2 Substantial Accomplishment Students partially research and organize a news broadcast that presents some interesting pieces of information about the Spanish conquest of the Aztecs.

1 Little or Partial Accomplishment Students do little research and have difficulty presenting a news broadcast that coherently explores the topic of the Spanish conquest of the Aztecs.

Across Cultures

Investigate Forest Conservation Students' research might include the following information: 1891—U.S. government sets aside forested areas called *wooded reserves*; 1905—U.S. Forest Service established; 1911 and 1924—passage and expansion of Weeks Law; 1947—Forest Pest Control Act; 1960—Multiple Use-Sustained Yield Act; 1964—Wilderness Act; 1974—Forest and Rangeland Renewable Resources Planning Act.

Construct a Retablo Students' research should show that a *retablo exvoto* is a painting made on a small piece of tin. The painting depicts a miracle and is hung on a wall to show thanks to Christ or the Virgin Mary.

Compare and Contrast Tales Contrasts might include the setting of the story and the age or gender of the hitchhiker. Comparisons might include the untimely death of the hitchhiker and certain details of the behavior of ghosts and apparitions.

OVERVIEW

Objectives

- To understand and appreciate four stories about animals and people who must make adjustments to succeed or survive
- To appreciate the cultures of the regions represented
- To extend understanding of the selections through a variety of multimodal and cross-curricular activities

Reading Pathways

- Encourage volunteers to read the tales aloud to classmates. Have students work by themselves or with partners to plan and rehearse their reading. Encourage the students who are not reading to listen carefully to the readings in order to ask questions about any details or passages they don't understand.

- Have students choose partners and read together the tales. Ask them to consider how the selections are affected by the geography or culture of the tradition that produced them.

- Invite students to compare the tales with the selections they read in Unit Two. For example, encourage students to think about the endings of "Brer Possum's Dilemma" and "White Mice." Challenge them to discuss the ways that both selections have surprise endings.

PREVIEWING

LINKS TO UNIT TWO

Critical Adjustments

Activating Prior Knowledge

In Unit Two, the selections explore decisive actions that the characters must take at critical moments—actions that may change the course of their lives forever. Similarly, in the tales you will read next, the characters find themselves in situations in which they must make crucial decisions and adjustments.

Building Background

SOUTHEASTERN U.S.

Brer Possum's Dilemma
retold by Jackie Torrence

By the middle of the 19th century, slaves made up nearly one-third of the population of the Southern United States. Slavery flourished in the South, which was heavily dependent on cotton and tobacco plantations that required large numbers of workers. Slaves on these plantations came from a variety of African cultures. As they mingled traditions and swapped stories, they produced new kinds of folk tales and fables. Some of these African-American fables featured the "Brer" animals.

M'su Carencro and Mangeur de Poulet
retold by J. J. Reneaux

During the 1750s, the British and French were fighting for control of eastern North America in the French and Indian War. As part of the struggle, the British drove French settlers out of the colony of Acadia in eastern Canada. Many migrated to Louisiana. They brought with them their heritage of Acadian French culture and folk tales such as this one, which they gradually adapted to fit their new land. The Acadians eventually came to be known as Cajuns.

716 UNIT SIX: THE ORAL TRADITION

PRINT AND MEDIA RESOURCES

UNIT SIX RESOURCE BOOK
Strategic Reading: Literature, p. 11
Reading SkillBuilder, p. 12
Spelling SkillBuilder, p. 13

GRAMMAR MINI–LESSONS
Transparencies, p. 3
Copymasters, p. 3

WRITING MINI–LESSONS
Transparencies, p. 39

ACCESS FOR STUDENTS ACQUIRING ENGLISH
Selection Summaries
Reading and Writing Support

FORMAL ASSESSMENT
Selection Test, pp. 135–136
 Test Generator

AUDIO LIBRARY
See Reference Card

INTERNET RESOURCES
McDougal Littell Literature Center at http://www.hmco.com/mcdougal/lit

716 THE LANGUAGE OF LITERATURE TEACHER'S EDITION

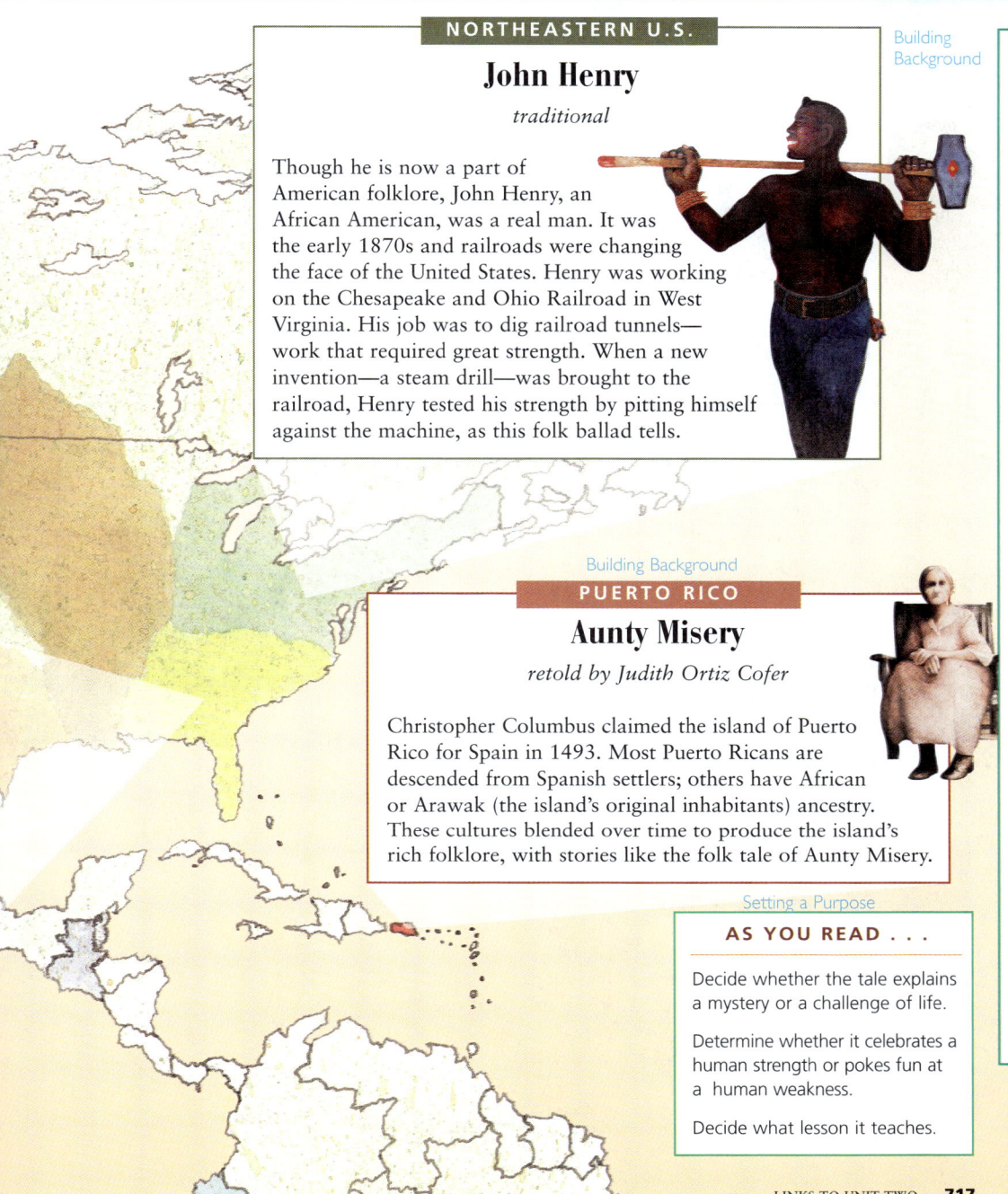

NORTHEASTERN U.S.
John Henry
traditional

Building Background

Though he is now a part of American folklore, John Henry, an African American, was a real man. It was the early 1870s and railroads were changing the face of the United States. Henry was working on the Chesapeake and Ohio Railroad in West Virginia. His job was to dig railroad tunnels—work that required great strength. When a new invention—a steam drill—was brought to the railroad, Henry tested his strength by pitting himself against the machine, as this folk ballad tells.

Building Background

PUERTO RICO
Aunty Misery
retold by Judith Ortiz Cofer

Christopher Columbus claimed the island of Puerto Rico for Spain in 1493. Most Puerto Ricans are descended from Spanish settlers; others have African or Arawak (the island's original inhabitants) ancestry. These cultures blended over time to produce the island's rich folklore, with stories like the folk tale of Aunty Misery.

Setting a Purpose

AS YOU READ . . .

Decide whether the tale explains a mystery or a challenge of life.

Determine whether it celebrates a human strength or pokes fun at a human weakness.

Decide what lesson it teaches.

LINKS TO UNIT TWO   **717**

SUMMARY

John Henry John Henry competes against a steam drill in driving steel. He proudly claims that he would sooner die than let a steam drill beat him. Henry beats the steam drill but ultimately dies. However, before he dies, he tells his baby son that he, too, must be a steel-driving man. Henry's wife goes to the place where her husband died.

Brer Possum's Dilemma Brer Possum finds Brer Snake lying in a hole in the road with a brick on his back. The snake convinces the reluctant possum (who fears a snake bite) to remove the brick, lift him from the hole, and put him in his pocket. Then the now-warm snake announces he will bite the possum. Brer Possum protests, but Brer Snake reminds him that he knew he was a snake.

Aunty Misery Aunty Misery is angry with the children who taunt her and steal pears from her tree. After she shelters a disguised sorcerer, he grants her wish that anyone climbing the tree will be unable to come down without her permission. The children learn to stay away. After Death knocks at Aunty Misery's door, she tricks him into climbing the pear tree. A few years with no death in the world upsets many people. Aunty Misery releases Death on the condition that he spare her.

M'su Carencro and Mangeur de Poulet Mangeur de Poulet, a chicken hawk, teases M'su Carencro, because the hungry buzzard refuses to kill for food. Showing off, the chicken hawk flies high, dives at a rabbit, crashes, and dies. The buzzard then prepares to eat Mangeur de Poulet.

CUSTOMIZING FOR
Students Acquiring English

- Use **ACCESS FOR STUDENTS ACQUIRING ENGLISH,** *Reading and Writing Support.*

- Students may need some assistance with the nonstandard language in "John Henry," "Brer Possum's Dilemma," and "M'su Carencro and Mangeur de Poulet."

STRATEGIC READING FOR
Less-Proficient Readers

Set a Purpose Encourage students to become involved in the selections by having them share their associations with the word ballad. Then have students read to find out what John Henry plans to do before the sun sets.

Use **UNIT SIX RESOURCE BOOK**, p. 11, for guidance in reading the selection.

CUSTOMIZING FOR
Gifted and Talented Students

Have students choose one of the three selections following "John Henry" and rewrite it in the form of a traditional ballad.

Literary Concept: BALLAD

A Explain to students that the ballad—a kind of narrative song—has been a popular form of oral storytelling for centuries. Ballads are characterized by regular stanzas, refrains and other repetitions, and strong story lines involving romance, tragedy, historical events, and the exploits of rebels, outlaws, or underdogs.

CUSTOMIZING FOR
Students Acquiring English

I Ask a volunteer to simplify "he didn't have but a dime." *(He had only a dime.)*

Literary Concept: THEME

B Ask students how John Henry's lack of money is relevant to the values this song celebrates. *(Possible response: "John Henry" celebrates the working class. John Henry is born into poverty and into a life of hard physical labor. His battle against the steam drill represents the struggle of man against the machines that are replacing him.)*

A JOHN HENRY

TRADITIONAL

When John Henry was a little boy,
Sitting upon his father's knee,
His father said, "Look here, my boy,
You must be a steel driving man[1] like me,
5 You must be a steel driving man like me."

John Henry went up on the mountain,
Just to drive himself some steel.
The rocks was so tall and John Henry so small,
He said lay down hammer and squeal,
10 He said lay down hammer and squeal.

John Henry had a little wife,
And the dress she wore was red;
The last thing before he died,
He said, "Be true to me when I'm dead,
15 Oh, be true to me when I'm dead."

I John Henry's wife ask him for fifteen cents,
And he said he didn't have but a dime,
Said, "If you wait till the rising sun goes down,
I'll borrow it from the man in the mine,
20 I'll borrow it from the man in the mine."

John Henry started on the right-hand side,
And the steam drill started on the left.
He said, "Before I'd let that steam drill beat me down,
I'd hammer my fool self to death,
B 25 Oh, I'd hammer my fool self to death."

---
1. **steel driving man:** a person who used a ten-pound hammer to drive a steel drill into rock in order to make holes for explosives.

718   UNIT SIX: THE ORAL TRADITION

Mini-Lesson: Speaking,  Listening, and Viewing

DRAMATIC READING Explain to students that dramatic readings of tales such as "John Henry" can help them more fully appreciate the use of language in the story. For instance, "John Henry" uses repetition to create a strong steady rhythm that, when combined with rhyme, vividly conveys the ballad's subject of hammering and drilling.

Application Divide the class into groups of ten. Have members of each group select speaking roles to perform: narrator, John Henry, his father, his wife, as well as the Captain and the Shaker—both non-speaking parts. The narrator can read the expository sections and those with individual speaking parts can interject. You may wish to suggest that members without specific roles represent a chorus that speaks the repeated last line of each stanza. Groups can perform their reading for each other or, if possible, for other classes.

His Hammer in His Hand, Palmer C. Hayden (1890–1973). From the John Henry Series, Museum of African American Art, Los Angeles, Palmer C. Hayden Collection, gift of Miriam A. Hayden. Photo by Armando Solis.

The steam drill started at half-past six,
John Henry started the same time.
John Henry struck bottom at half-past eight,
And the steam drill didn't bottom till nine,
30   And the steam drill didn't bottom till nine.

John Henry said to his captain,
"A man, he ain't nothing but a man,
Before I'd let that steam drill beat me down,
I'd die with the hammer in my hand,
35   Oh, I'd die with the hammer in my hand."

John Henry said to his shaker,[2]
"Shaker, why don't you sing just a few more rounds?
And before the setting sun goes down,
You're gonna hear this hammer of mine sound,
40   You're gonna hear this hammer of mine sound."

---

2. **shaker:** the person who holds the steel drill for the steel driving man and shakes the drill to remove it from the rock.

Multicultural Perspectives

THE LEGEND OF JOHN HENRY John Henry is considered to be the subject of the most famous American folk ballad. In the folk ballad, John Henry wins the race but dies. The real John Henry is said to have been crushed by rock that fell from the mine tunnel ceiling after winning the race. Various tales and work songs involving John Henry have flourished in America since the mid-nineteenth century. Many of these narratives have made their way into print. In 1931, a collection of ballads was published under the title *John Henry: Tracking Down a Negro Legend.* Also, Langston Hughes and Arna Bontemps included John Henry in their important work, *The Book of Negro Folklore* (published in 1958).

CUSTOMIZING FOR
Students Acquiring English

2 Point out to students that *road* is short for "railroad" here.

Critical Thinking:
SYNTHESIZING

F Have students explain how stanzas 9, 10, and 11 refer to the beginning of the ballad. *(Possible response: Stanza 9 follows up on Henry's earlier comments about preferring death to defeat by the steam drill. Stanza 10 contains echoes of the first stanza, in which John Henry himself was a baby. In stanza 11, his wife's "going where John Henry fell dead" seems to show her following his wish to be true to him after his death, which he requested in stanza 3.)*

STRATEGIC READING FOR
Less-Proficient Readers

G Ask students to describe John Henry's fate. *(John Henry died from out-hammering the steam drill.)*
Summarizing/Making Inferences

From Personal Response to Critical Analysis

1. Was John Henry heroic or foolhardy to battle the steam drill? What other words do you think might be appropriate to describe him? *(Possible responses: He was heroic because he believed in his own ability to win against the machine. He was foolhardy because his pride caused him to lose his life. Other words to describe him might include* tough, stubborn, superhuman, *and* naive.*)*
2. John Henry and his son are born into a particular line of work. Do you think that some people have a destiny to do one particular thing? Why or why not? *(Possible responses: Yes, everyone has some talent that he or she is meant to use, but discovering it is sometimes difficult. No, people can do many different things for many different reasons.)*
3. Like the steam drill in John Henry's day, modern machines often take jobs away from people. Machines, however, can also make people's lives easier. Are there any labor-saving machines today that you think do more harm than good? Explain your answer. *(Answers will vary.)*

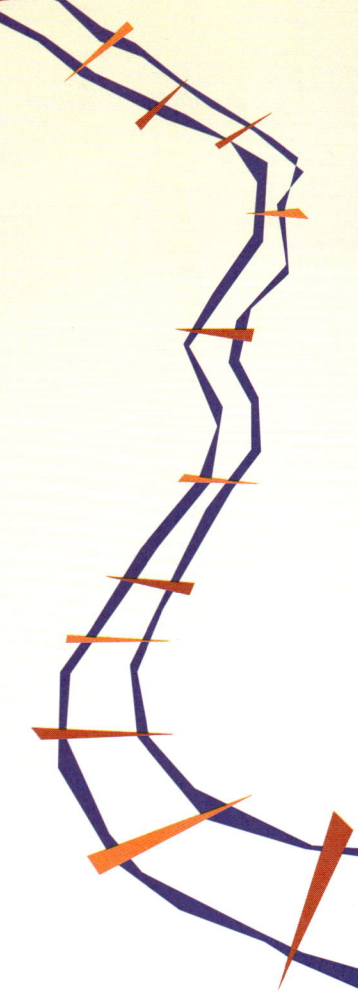

John Henry hammered on the mountain,
He hammered till half-past three,
He said, "This big Bend Tunnel on the C. & O. road[3]
Is going to be the death of me,
45   Lord! is going to be the death of me."

John Henry had a little baby boy,
You could hold him in the palm of your hand.
The last words before he died,
"Son, you must be a steel driving man,
50   Son, you must be a steel driving man."

John Henry had a little woman,
And the dress she wore was red,
She went down the railroad track and never come back,
Said she was going where John Henry fell dead,
55   Said she was going where John Henry fell dead.

John Henry hammering on the mountain,
As the whistle blew for half-past two,
The last word I heard him say,
"Captain, I've hammered my insides in two,
60   Lord, I've hammered my insides in two."

---
3. **big Bend . . . road:** Construction work on the Big Bend Tunnel on the Chesapeake & Ohio Railroad in West Virginia took place from 1870 to 1873.

COMPREHENSION CHECK
1. What was the occupation of John Henry's father? *(steel driving)*
2. After his wife asks him for money, where does John Henry say that he will get it? *(He will borrow it from the man in the mine.)*
3. Does John Henry or the steam drill get to the bottom of the mine first? *(John Henry)*
4. What causes John Henry's death? *(exhaustion, overexertion)*
5. Where does John Henry's wife go? *(down the railroad track to where Henry died)*

Brer Possum's Dilemma

retold by Jackie Torrence

Brer Possum, Barry Moser. From *Jump, Again!* by Van Dyke Parks, published by Harcourt Brace Jovanovich in 1987. Illustration Copyright © Barry Moser. Reprinted with permission from the artist.

STRATEGIC READING FOR
Less-Proficient Readers

Set a Purpose Have students discuss other folk tales, fables, and myths that chronicle the experiences of animals, for example, the fable of the tortoise and the hare. Then have them read to find out how Brer Possum gets outwitted by Brer Snake.

CUSTOMIZING FOR
Multiple Learning Styles

Intrapersonal Learners Have individual students do research to find out about the behavioral traits of opossums and snakes. Encourage them to analyze how well the actions of the animals in "Brer Possum's Dilemma" fit the behavior of the actual animals. Invite students to write a paragraph or two about their observations.

Literary Note
The most popular "Brer" character was Brer Rabbit, a trickster. In all of the stories Brer Rabbit was a winner who outwitted bigger animals. In contrast, Brer Possum is a hapless, good-hearted fool.

You may wish to encourage students to think about what values a character like Brer Possum may have represented to the slaves of the American South.

Mini-Lesson: Speaking, Listening, and Viewing

SPOKEN LITERATURE Have students sample Jackie Torrence's recorded works, such as the stories on *Tales for Scary Times, Country Characters,* or *Mountain Magic: The Jack Tales,* all available on audiocassette from the Earwig Music Co.

Application Have students listen to these tapes and note Torrence's use of intonation and pauses to heighten the effect of her stories. Ask students to explain what qualities she added that are not apparent in written versions of the stories.

You might also wish to have students record their own oral versions of the tale about Brer Possum or another tale in this book. Encourage students to weave music and sound effects into their stories and to make use of the vocal techniques that they noticed in Torrence's performances.

CUSTOMIZING FOR
Students Acquiring English

1 Familiarize students with the dialect of this tale. Define *feller* as "fellow" or "person." Point out the use of a double negative in "he never liked to see no critters in trouble." Also, note that often the first or the last sound of a word is dropped, as in *'imself* and *helpin'*.

2 Define *reckon* as "suppose."

Active Reading: PREDICT

A Encourage students to think about what they know so far about the characters of Brer Possum and Brer Snake. Invite students to make predictions about what Brer Possum will decide to do.

Literary Concept: CHARACTERIZATION

B Ask students to explain how the dialogue gives the reader a better understanding of each character. *(Possible response: Dialogue such as "You're a-goin' to have to give me time to think about this" shows Brer Possum's earnest and somewhat foolish personality because he won't just say "no" to Brer Snake. A line such as "Maybe not. Maybe not. Maaaaaaaybe not" shows Brer Snake's craftiness because he won't give a definite answer.)*

Back in the days when the animals could talk, there lived ol' Brer[1] Possum. He was a fine feller. Why, he never liked to see no critters in trouble. He was always helpin' out, a-doin' somethin' for others.

Ever' night, ol' Brer Possum climbed into a persimmon tree, hung by his tail, and slept all night long. And each mornin', he climbed outa the tree and walked down the road to sun 'imself.

One mornin' as he walked, he come to a big hole in the middle of the road. Now, ol' Brer Possum was kind and gentle, but he was also nosey, so he went over to the hole and looked in. All at once, he stepped back, 'cause layin' in the bottom of that hole was ol' Brer Snake with a brick on his back.

Brer Possum said to 'imself, "I best git on outa here, 'cause ol' Brer Snake is mean and evil and low-down, and if I git to stayin' around 'im, he jist might git to bitin' me."

So Brer Possum went on down the road.

But Brer Snake had seen Brer Possum, and he commenced to callin' for 'im.

"Help me, Brer Possum."

Brer Possum stopped and turned around. He said to 'imself, "That's ol' Brer Snake a-callin' me. What do you reckon he wants?"

Well, ol' Brer Possum was kindhearted, so he went back down the road to the hole, stood at the edge, and looked down at Brer Snake.

"Was that you a-callin' me? What do you want?"

Brer Snake looked up and said, "I've been down here in this hole for a mighty long time with this brick on my back. Won't you help git it offa me?"

Brer Possum thought.

"Now listen here, Brer Snake. I knows you. You's mean and evil and low-down, and if'n I was to git down in that hole and git to liftin' that brick offa your back, you wouldn't do nothin' but bite me."

Ol' Brer Snake just hissed.

"Maybe not. Maybe not. Maaaaaaaybe not."

Brer Possum said, "I ain't sure 'bout you at all. I jist don't know. You're a-goin' to have to let me think about it."

So ol' Brer Possum thought—he thought high, and he thought low—and jist as he was thinkin', he looked up into a tree and saw a dead limb a-hangin' down. He climbed into the tree, broke off the limb, and with that ol' stick, pushed that brick offa Brer Snake's back. Then he took off down the road.

Brer Possum thought he was away from ol' Brer Snake, when all at once he heard somethin'.

"Help me, Brer Possum."

Brer Possum said, "Oh, no, that's him agin."

But bein' so kindhearted, Brer Possum turned around, went back to the hole, and stood at the edge.

"Brer Snake, was that you a-callin' me? What do you want now?"

Ol' Brer Snake looked up outa the hole and hissed.

"I've been down here for a mighty long time, and I've gotten a little weak, and the sides of this ol' hole are too slick for me to climb. Do you think you can lift me outa here?"

Brer Possum thought.

"Now, you jist wait a minute. If'n I was to git down into that hole and lift you outa there, you wouldn't do nothin' but bite me."

Brer Snake hissed.

"Maybe not. Maybe not. Maaaaaaaybe not."

Brer Possum said, "I jist don't know. You're a-goin' to have to give me time to think about this."

So ol' Brer Possum thought.

And as he thought, he jist happened to look down there in that hole and see that ol' dead limb. So he pushed the limb underneath ol' Brer Snake, and he lifted 'im outa the hole,

---

1. **Brer** *Southern dialect:* Brother.

722 UNIT SIX: THE ORAL TRADITION

Mini-Lesson Grammar

SUBJECT-VERB AGREEMENT IN STANDARD ENGLISH Point out to students that subjects and verbs in a sentence must always agree in number: Singular subjects must be used with singular verbs, and plural subjects must be used with plural verbs.

In the present tense, plural verbs do not end in the letter *s*. Moreover, only verbs in the third person singular show any change—they end in *s*.

Application Have students choose the correct verb form in each of the following sentences.

1. Each morning Brer Possum (<u>strolls</u>/stroll) down the road to warm himself in the sun.
2. The first words of Brer Snake in the tale (is/<u>are</u>) "Help me, Brer Possum."

Reteaching/Reinforcement
- *Grammar Handbook,* anthology, p. 863
- *Grammar Mini-Lessons* copymasters p. 3, transparencies p. 3

The Writer's Craft
Making Subjects and Verbs Agree in Number, p. 578

way up into the air, and throwed 'im into the high grass.

Brer Possum took off a-runnin' down the road.

Well, he thought he was away from ol' Brer Snake when all at once he heard somethin'.

"Help me, Brer Possum."

Brer Possum thought, "That's him agin."

But bein' so kindhearted, he turned around, went back to the hole, and stood there a-lookin' for Brer Snake. Brer Snake crawled outa the high grass just as slow as he could, stretched 'imself out across the road, rared up, and looked at ol' Brer Possum.

Then he hissed. "I've been down there in that ol' hole for a mighty long time, and I've gotten a little cold 'cause the sun didn't shine. Do you think you could put me in your pocket and git me warm?"

Brer Possum said, "Now you listen here, Brer Snake. I knows you. You's mean and evil and low-down, and if'n I put you in my pocket, you wouldn't do nothin' but bite me."

Brer Snake hissed.

"Maybe not. Maybe not. Maaaaaaaybe not."

"No, sireee, Brer Snake. I knows you. I jist ain't a-goin' to do it."

But jist as Brer Possum was talkin' to Brer Snake, he happened to git a real good look at 'im. He was a-layin' there lookin' so pitiful, and Brer Possum's great big heart began to feel sorry for ol' Brer Snake.

"All right," said Brer Possum. "You must be cold. So jist this once I'm a-goin' to put you in my pocket."

So ol' Brer Snake coiled up jist as little as he could, and Brer Possum picked 'im up and put 'im in his pocket.

Brer Snake laid quiet and still—so quiet and still that Brer Possum even forgot that he was a-carryin' 'im around. But all of a sudden, Brer Snake commenced to crawlin' out, and he turned and faced Brer Possum and hissed.

"I'm a-goin' to bite you."

But Brer Possum said, "Now wait a minute. Why are you a-goin' to bite me? I done took that brick offa your back, I got you outa that hole, and I put you in my pocket to git you warm. Why are you a-goin' to bite me?"

Brer Snake hissed.

"You knowed I was a snake before you put me in your pocket."

And when you're mindin' your own business and you spot trouble, don't never trouble trouble 'til trouble troubles you. ❖

JACKIE TORRENCE

1944–

Growing up in North Carolina, Jackie Torrence loved hearing the stories told by her family, including her grandfather, who was the son of a slave. She first heard "Brer Possum's Dilemma" from her Aunt Mildred.

But it was not until a chance incident in 1972 that Torrence began her storytelling career at the library where she worked. She was asked to substitute for a storyteller. Soon she was captivating children and adults across the country, and she became known as The Story Lady. Now Torrence spends most of the year away from her North Carolina home, telling folk tales and ghost stories and conducting workshops.

Torrence says, "I decided that I had a dream and I was either going to let it take me down or I was going to ride it and see where it goes. I'm still riding."

OTHER WORKS available on audiocassette: *Brer Rabbit Stories, Tales for Scary Times, Country Characters*

STRATEGIC READING FOR
Less-Proficient Readers

Set a Purpose Have students read to learn why Aunty Misery will never die.

Critical Thinking: ANALYZING

A Encourage students to comment on the reasons that most folk tales—including this one—contain few details about the setting of the story. *(Possible responses: Oral tales are essentially about the plot of a story and not about the details of setting. The lack of a specific setting helps readers feel that the tale happened in a time and place of enchantment; the fact that there are few details of setting gives the tale a universal appeal that can last from generation to generation.)*

CUSTOMIZING FOR
Students Acquiring English

I Explain that *crazy* in this sentence is not meant literally. The children annoyed the old woman very much.

Literary Concept: FOLKLORE

B Have students point out features of this passage that are common to many tales. *(Possible responses: the presence of a stranger who may possess supernatural or magical powers; the granting of a wish)*

Literary Links

Invite students to compare and contrast the attitude of the children toward Aunty Misery to that of the speaker in "In a Neighborhood in Los Angeles" (p. 158) toward his grandmother. *(Possible response: The children showed their disrespect for Aunty Misery by taunting her and stealing her fruit. The speaker in Alarcón's poem remembers his grandmother with fondness and respect for all that she taught him.)*

Aunty Misery

retold by Judith Ortiz Cofer

This is a story about an old, very old woman who lived alone in her little hut with no other company than a beautiful pear tree that grew at her door. She spent all her time taking care of her pear tree. But the neighborhood children drove the old woman crazy by stealing her fruit. They would climb her tree, shake its delicate limbs, and run away with armloads of golden pears, yelling insults at "Aunty Misery," as they called her.

One day, a pilgrim[1] stopped at the old woman's hut and asked her permission to spend the night under her roof. Aunty Misery saw that he had an honest face and bade the traveler come in. She fed him and made a bed for him in front of her hearth. In the morning while he was getting ready to leave, the stranger told her that he would show his gratitude for her hospitality by granting her one wish.

"There is only one thing that I desire," said Aunty Misery.

"Ask, and it shall be yours," replied the stranger, who was a sorcerer[2] in disguise.

"I wish that anyone who climbs up my pear tree should not be able to come back down until I permit it."

"Your wish is granted," said the stranger, touching the pear tree as he left Aunty Misery's house.

And so it happened that when the children came back to taunt[3] the old woman and to steal her fruit, she stood at her window watching them. Several of them shimmied up the trunk of the pear tree and immediately got stuck to it as

---

1. **pilgrim:** a wanderer; traveler.
2. **sorcerer:** a person who practices witchcraft or magic.
3. **taunt** (tônt): to make fun of in a mean way.

724 UNIT SIX: THE ORAL TRADITION

Mini-Lesson  Literary Concepts

REVIEWING IRONY Remind students that irony is a contrast between what is expected and what actually exists or happens. Authors and storytellers use irony to create effects ranging from humor to strong emotion.

For example, in "M'su Carencro and Mangeur de Poulet," it is ironic that the buzzard's next meal turns out to be the dead chicken hawk—the character who was so intent on getting the buzzard to hunt live prey.

Application Have students identify passages in "Aunty Misery" that show the presence of irony. Then have students explain why the passage is ironic. *(Students might focus on Death's fallibility or the reactions of human beings to the absence of Death in the world.)*

Twilight (1971), Hubert Shuptrine. Copyright © 1971, 1994 Hubert Shuptrine, all rights reserved.

Art Note

Twilight by Hubert Shuptrine Hubert Shuptrine (1936–) exploits an unusual perspective to force the viewer to confront the subject straight on. The artist has positioned the old woman in such a way that her knees and hands are in the center of the canvas. Because of the artist's low vantage point, the woman (as well as the chair in which she sits) seems oversized. This distortion combines with the dark shadowy representation of the woman's eyes to give an atmosphere of mystery to the image.

Reading the Art *How would you describe the subject of the painting? What two meanings could the title of this painting have? What details in the image support either interpretation? Do you think this is an appropriate illustration for "Aunty Misery"? Why or why not?*

Mini-Lesson The Writer's Style

PERSONIFICATION Point out to students that authors or storytellers use personification by giving human qualities to an animal, an object, a plant, a place, or an idea. Personification (like simile and metaphor) is a type of figurative language. Storytellers use figurative language to create vivid pictures and sensations for the reader.

In "Brer Possum's Dilemma," the possum and the snake are personified, and in "M'su Carencro and Mangeur de Poulet," the birds are personified. This use of figurative language creates lively characters and comic effects.

Application Have students refer to the chart and identify the personification in "Aunty Misery." Have them explain what effects this use of personification has on the reader. *(Possible response: The storyteller personifies death and misery. The personification makes these two ideas vivid and entertaining.)*

Reteaching/Reinforcement
- *Writing Mini-Lessons* transparencies p. 39

The Writer's Craft

Personification, pp. 319–320

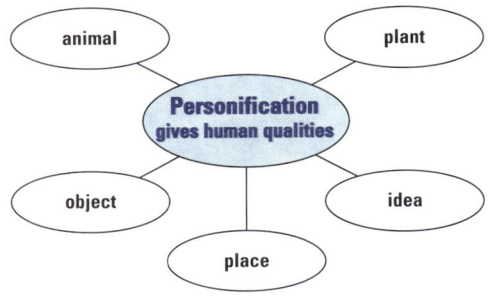

Literary Concept: PERSONIFICATION

C Tell students that folklore often features personifications of natural forces or of big concepts such as life and death. Encourage students to discuss the ways death is sometimes portrayed or pictured in popular culture and folk literature. *(Possible response: as the "grim reaper," a skeleton dressed in black and carrying a scythe; as the Angel of Death)* Then ask students how they would describe what Aunty Misery personifies. *(Possible responses: misery, pain, suffering)*

Literary Concept: IRONY

D Invite students to explain the irony of people's reactions to the absence of death. *(Possible responses: You expect that people would be thrilled to live forever, but instead they protest the lack of death; you would expect eternal life to bring happiness, but instead it can also bring misery.)*

STRATEGIC READING FOR
Less-Proficient Readers

E Ask students why Aunty Misery will never die. *(She has released Death from the pear tree in return for his promise not to come back for her.)*
Summarizing

From Personal Response to Critical Analysis

1. What do you think of the bargain Aunty Misery makes with Death? Write your thoughts in your notebook. *(Responses will vary.)*
2. Why do you think Misery is portrayed as a woman and Death as a man? *(Responses will vary.)*
3. How would you explain why misery exists in the world? *(Responses will vary.)*

---

if with glue. She let them cry and beg her for a long time before she gave the tree permission to let them go, on the condition that they never again steal her fruit or bother her.

Time passed, and both Aunty Misery and her tree grew bent and gnarled with age. One day another traveler stopped at her door. This one looked suffocated and exhausted, so the old woman asked him what he wanted in her village. He answered her in a voice that was dry and hoarse, as if he had swallowed a desert: "I am Death, and I have come to take you with me."

Thinking fast, Aunty Misery said, "All right, but before I go I would like to pluck some pears from my beloved pear tree to remember how much pleasure it brought me in this life. But I am a very old woman and cannot climb to the tallest branches where the best fruit is; will you be so kind as to do it for me?"

With a heavy sigh like wind through a catacomb,[4] Death climbed the pear tree. Immediately he became stuck to it as if with glue. And no matter how much he cursed and threatened, Aunty Misery would not give the tree permission to release Death.

Many years passed, and there were no deaths in the world. The people who make their living from death began to protest loudly. The doctors claimed no one bothered to come in for examinations or treatments anymore, because they did not fear dying; the pharmacists' business suffered too, because medicines are, like magic potions, bought to prevent or postpone the inevitable; the priests and undertakers were unhappy with the situation also, for obvious reasons. There were also many old folks tired of life who wanted to pass on to the next world to rest from the miseries of this one.

Aunty Misery realized all this, and not wishing to be unfair, she made a deal with her prisoner, Death: if he promised not ever to come for her again, she would give him his freedom. He agreed. And that is why so long as the world is the world, Aunty Misery will always live. ❖

---

4. **catacomb** (kăt′ə-kōm′): an underground arrangement of tunnels or chambers, used as a burial place.

JUDITH ORTIZ COFER

1952–

As a child, Judith Ortiz Cofer grew up in two different worlds—she was born in Puerto Rico but moved to Paterson, New Jersey, as a young child. Where she lived depended on her father's U.S. Navy assignments—whenever he was at sea, she returned to Puerto Rico. Both worlds influenced her writing.

In Puerto Rico, she listened to her grandmother's stories in Spanish under a giant mango tree, surrounded by her extended family. It was there, Ortiz Cofer says, "that I first began to feel the power of words."

In New Jersey, she spent much time by herself, building up "an arsenal of [English] words by becoming an insatiable reader of books." She also served as her mother's interpreter.

Ortiz Cofer left her two worlds to attend college in Georgia and then to teach. She has won such honors as the 1990 Pushcart Prize for Nonfiction and the 1994 O. Henry Award for outstanding American short stories.

In a 1992 article in *Glamour* magazine, Ortiz Cofer wrote, "With the stories I tell . . . I try to get my audience past the particulars of my skin color, my accent or my clothes."

OTHER WORKS *Silent Dancing: A Partial Remembrance of a Puerto Rican Childhood*

COMPREHENSION CHECK

1. At the beginning of the story, how does the old woman spend all her time? *(taking care of her beloved pear tree)*
2. What powers does the old woman's overnight visitor possess? *(As sorcerer, he has the power to grant one wish.)*
3. Who is Aunty Misery's next visitor? *(Death)*
4. What does she make her visitor promise before she releases him? *(She makes Death promise not to come for her again.)*

M'su Carencro and Mangeur de Poulet

retold by J. J. Reneaux

Detail of *Buzzards' Roost* (1985), Hubert Shuptrine. Copyright © 1985 S. Hill Corporation, all rights reserved, used with permission.

STRATEGIC READING FOR
Less-Proficient Readers

Set a Purpose Have students read to learn what M'su Carencro eats for supper.

Linking to Science

The buzzard is actually a type of large hawk. As a rule, buzzards are birds of prey that feed on insects and small mammals. The term *buzzard* is often misapplied to the turkey vulture and the black vulture. These vultures are the true models for the character M'su Carencro. Vultures rarely attack living creatures; rather, they feed (often in groups) on dead animals.

The chicken hawk is a slightly smaller type of hawk that is notable for its aggressiveness.

Mini-Lesson Spelling

DOUBLE CONSONANTS WITH A SUFFIX
Explain to students that before a suffix that begins with a vowel the final consonant of a word is doubled. For example, when the suffix -*est* is added to *sad*, the word changes to *saddest*. However, when the suffix begins with a consonant, the final consonant of the word is not doubled—for instance, the word *sadly*.

Application Have students spell words by adding endings to the base words.
1. rebel + ious *(rebellious)*
2. dip + ed *(dipped)*
3. concur + ent *(concurrent)*
4. omit + ed *(omitted)*
5. fat + ness *(fatness)*
6. glad + ly *(gladly)*
7. equip + ing *(equipping)*
8. drop + ed *(dropped)*

Ask students to look for more words that fit this pattern, and to add these words to their personal word lists.

Reteaching/ Reinforcement
• *Unit Six Resource Book,* p. 13

THE LANGUAGE OF LITERATURE TEACHER'S EDITION **727**

Art Note

Buzzards' Roost by Hubert Shuptrine
In this painting, Shuptrine uses contrast to create a vivid image that suggests the harsh side of nature. The three birds seem plump and substantial next to the veinlike branches on which they are perching. The stark branches and muted hues indicate that winter has set in.

Reading the Art What do you think the artist is trying to convey in this picture? What details make you think so?

CUSTOMIZING FOR
Students Acquiring English

(1) Describe a *know-it-all* as someone who is conceited and acts superior to others.

(2) Ask a student to pronounce and spell *don'tcha* in standard English. *(don't you)*

(3) Point out to students that in this context *Number One* means "yourself." Chicken Hawk thinks that everyone has to think of himself or herself first.

Active Reading: CONNECT

 Invite students to comment on which character they more deeply identify with and why.

Literary Links

 Ask students to compare M'su Carencro with the speaker of "my enemy was dreaming." *(Possible responses: Carencro is a patient, humble character who feels a responsibility to behave according to Nature's plan; the speaker of the poem is a warrior who has a compassionate side to his character. Both characters seem to share an essential humility about their places in the universe; both choose not to take the life of a rival.)*

One day M'su Carencro,¹ the buzzard, was sitting on a fence post real patient-like, just waiting for something to drop dead so he could have his supper, when who should come flapping up but ol' Mangeur de Poulet,² the chicken hawk. Mangeur de Poulet calls out, "Hey, *ça va, mon padnat?*"³

M'su Carencro shook his head and sighed, "*Ça va mal!*⁴ Not good at all! I am so hungry. I been waitin' for days for somethin' to drop dead so I can have my supper."

(1) "What you talkin' 'bout?" says know-it-all Chicken Hawk. "If you're so hungry, why (2) don'tcha get out there and hunt you some good fresh meat? You got eyes, you got wings, you got a beak. Go for it! You got to look out for Number One in this world, *mon ami.*"⁵

"*Non, non, non,*" says Buzzard, "you don't understand. I'm s'posed to wait for somethin' to drop dead before I eat it. It's my job. That's

---

1. **M'su Carencro** (mə-sōō′ kä-răn-krô′) *Cajun dialect:* Mr. Buzzard. *M'su* is a short form of *Monsieur* (mə-syœ′), the French word for "Mister."
2. **Mangeur de Poulet** (män-zhür′ də pōō-lā′) *French:* The literal translation of this name is "Chicken Eater."
3. **ça va, mon padnat?** (sä vä′ môn päd-nä′) *French and Cajun dialect:* how's it going, partner?
4. **Ça va mal!** (sä-vä-mäl′) *French:* It's going badly!
5. **mon ami** (mô′ nä-mē′) *French:* my friend.

Mini-Lesson — Reading Skills/Strategies

RELATING CAUSE AND EFFECT Help students understand that cause and effect describes a relationship between events in stories or other narrative accounts. One event brings about, or causes, a second event. The first event in time is the cause; the second event is the effect.

Application Encourage students to trace cause and effect in the events in "M'su Carencro and Mangeur de Poulet." You might wish to have them use a two-column chart like the one shown. Remind students that each effect becomes a cause for another effect.

Reteaching/Reinforcement
• *Unit Six Resource Book*, p. 12

Cause	Effect

just the way *le Bon Dieu*⁶ made me."

"*Le Bon Dieu?* Aw, *non!* Don't waste your breath talkin' 'bout the Good God," says Chicken Hawk. "Besides, *mon ami*, even if there is a God, what makes you think he cares whether you get your supper? You gotta do like me, look out fo' yourself. Here, let ol' Chicken Hawk show you how to do that thang."

With that, Mangeur de Poulet leaped into the air and started wildly flapping about in daring loop-the-loops and crazy figure eights, showing off like you've never seen. All of a sudden, he spied a juicy little rabbit right down there next to Buzzard's fence post.

"Aw, this'll show Buzzard," he thought. Chicken Hawk took dead aim, and down he zoomed after that rabbit, faster and faster. But Rabbit was smart-smart. She saw Chicken Hawk's shadow closing in on her, and she jumped down her hole just as the big showoff came zooming in. By this time, Chicken Hawk was speeding so fast that his brakes couldn't save him, and he slammed smack dab into that fence post! And down he dropped—thunk!—deader than the post itself, right at Buzzard's feet.

Buzzard looked down at that dead chicken hawk. Then he looked up to heaven. He grins real big and says, "*Merci beaucoup,*⁷ *mon Grand Bon Dieu!* Good God Almighty, thank you!" Then he jumps down off the fence post, smacks his lips, and says, "Suppertime!" ❖

---
6. **le Bon Dieu** (lə bôn dyœ′) *French:* the Good Lord.
7. **merci beaucoup** (mĕr-sē′ bō-kōō′) *French:* thank you very much.

J. J. RENEAUX

J. J. Reneaux (1955–) is "mostly Cajun," with a little Choctaw Indian and Irish mixed in. She grew up in southern Louisiana in a storytelling family. Reneaux carefully researches her culture and draws on her own experiences to tell traditional and contemporary Cajun stories and other "down-home" Southern tales. She likes stories that bring people together. "As my Daddy says, 'We're all fishing out of the same bass boat.'"

About the traditional tales she tells, Reneaux says, "We are lost in a forest. Our ancestors' stories are the bread crumbs. They give us answers. They tell us who we are." She thinks that the tales also reflect the zest for life so central to Cajun culture. A talented guitar player, Reneaux combines music and stories in her performances. "For me, telling stories without music is like eating gumbo without hot sauce."

In addition to performing at schools, festivals, and clubs across the United States and Canada, Reneaux has told her award-winning Cajun stories on national television and radio. Before becoming a storyteller, she was a tree planter, a fry cook, a nurse's aide, a session singer and musician, and an oil-rig worker. Not surprisingly, she describes herself as "a graduate of the school of life."

OTHER WORKS *Haunted Bayou and other Cajun Ghost Stories;* available on audiocassette: *Cajun Folktales, Cajun Ghost Stories*

Active Reading: EVALUATE

C Have students evaluate the two characters in this fable. Ask them what words they would choose to explain how each character approaches life. If they need help, you may wish to use the following model.

Think-Aloud Model *I think that the buzzard is patient and humble. It seems as though he approaches life in an easy-going manner. On the other hand, the chicken hawk is arrogant, reckless, and pushy.*

STRATEGIC READING FOR Less Proficient Readers

D Ask students what M'su Carancro eats for dinner. *(Mangeur de Poulet)* Noting Relevant Details/Summarizing

CUSTOMIZING FOR Gifted and Talented Students

Several characters in these four selections say that their personalities or life's work were determined for them at birth. Have students discuss whether or not they believe human beings are born with behavioral characteristics that can never be changed.

From Personal Response to Critical Analysis

1. What is your reaction to the end of this tale? Write your thoughts in your notebook. *(Responses will vary.)*
2. What message do you think this story is intended to convey? *(Possible responses: Behave in a natural way. Life will be good if you are calm and humble and reasonable—but if you show off or act recklessly, you'll pay for it.)*

COMPREHENSION CHECK
1. What is M'su Carancro, the buzzard, doing at the beginning of the story? *(waiting for something to drop dead so he can have his supper)*
2. What does Mangeur de Poulet, the chicken hawk, advise M'su Carancro, the buzzard, to do? *(kill something for supper)*
3. According to M'su Carancro, why can't he kill something for supper? *(He believes that God made him not to kill but to eat things that are already dead.)*
4. What does M'su Carancro eat for supper? *(Mangeur de Poulet, the chicken hawk)*

Literature Connection

Project 1 Students' first task is to choose a tale. One student might ensure that every group member's opinion is considered. After a tale has been chosen, students should determine how many people will be needed to perform each task. Encourage students to make sure that people are evenly distributed.

Remind writers that breaking down a story into a series of causes and effects can help them understand the story's structure. Encourage them to answer questions about the story's plot, such as "What is the conflict in the story?" "What complications arise?" and "What is the climax?"

Encourage the stage crew to consult with the writers about what props are needed. You might wish to participate in these discussions, to make sure that students' plans for costumes, props, makeup, and sound are practical.

Remind actors to practice "getting into character." Have them spend time thinking about their motivations for each specific line or action they will perform in the play.

Rubric
3 Full Accomplishment Students work together productively to plan, develop, and perform an imaginative and entertaining stage adaptation.
2 Substantial Accomplishment Students work together well as they plan, develop, and perform a competent stage adaptation.
1 Little or Partial Accomplishment Students have difficulty working together and struggle to plan, develop, and perform their adaptation.

RESPONDING OPTIONS

LITERATURE CONNECTION PROJECT 1 — Multimodal Activity

Adapt a Tale into a One-Act Play Working in groups, choose one of the tales you have just read, or pick another tale from one of the same cultures. For example, you could find and adapt another Brer story.

Assign tasks within your group—writers, actors, costumers, stage builders, and so on. Refer to these suggestions as you produce your play.

Writers Map out the plot in outline form or on storyboards. Use plays in this book as models for formatting the script.

Actors After learning your lines, work on expressing your character's personal qualities.

Stage Crew List the costumes and props you will need. If you are adapting an animal story, consider how to design costumes or make-up that represents the animals. If possible, find appropriate music from the story's culture to accompany the performance.

Stage all of the plays in a drama festival. If possible, you could videotape the festival for other students in your school.

SOCIAL STUDIES CONNECTION PROJECT 2 — Multimodal Activity

Create a Cajun Display "M'su Carencro and Mangeur de Poulet" is a folk tale from Louisiana's Cajun people. Research Cajun culture. Then create a display for your classroom showing your findings.

- Make a map with captions showing the native country of the Cajuns and how their ancestors came to settle in Louisiana. Include pictures of the Louisiana bayou.
- Explore other Cajun folk tales and music of the culture.
- You could select and include a passage from Henry Wadsworth Longfellow's poem "Evangeline," which is about the Cajuns' Louisiana migration.
- Investigate Cajun food and include some recipes in your display.

730 UNIT SIX: THE ORAL TRADITION

Social Studies Connection

Project 2 Students' maps should clearly show that the native land of the Cajuns is present-day Nova Scotia and Prince Edward Island in eastern Canada. Students might include the name *Acadia* on their maps, this term being the origin of the name *Cajun*. In Louisiana, the Acadians settled mainly along the Teche, Lafourche, and Vermilion bayous in the south-central part of the state.

Students' research might include information on such folk tales as "Why Alligator Hates Dog" and a number of traditional ghost stories. Cajun music is notable for its use of folk instruments such as fiddles, as well as drums and accordions. Students may include information on Cajun food such as gumbo (a fish soup) and shrimp and crawfish, usually prepared with spicy sauces.

Rubric
3 Full Accomplishment Students' research is thorough and accurate, and their presentation of information is clear and vivid.
2 Substantial Accomplishment Students research one of the topics and present their findings in a well-organized, careful manner.
1 Little or Partial Accomplishment Students' research is insubstantial, and their presentation of information is vague and incomplete.

HISTORY CONNECTION PROJECT 3 Multimodal Activity

Explore the History of the Railroads The building of the railroads played a major role in the development of the United States in the 19th century. Research the history of the railroads. Use encyclopedias and computer databases to find out details.

- Create a map of the United States. Use one color to show railroads that existed in 1835, a few years after the first tracks were laid. Use another color to show railroads existing in 1875. With a third color, show the railroads that existed by the end of the century.

- Then record your key findings on a time line. Add drawings or pictures of the locomotives and of the machines used to build the railroads.

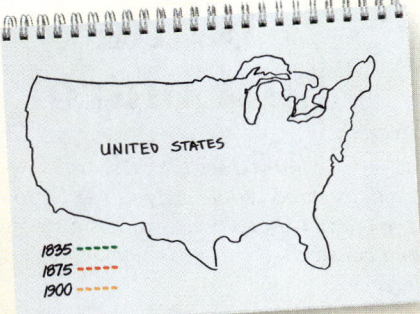

History Connection

Project 3 After students have completed their research, encourage them to organize their findings in ways that will make referring to the information easier when creating their maps and time lines.

Rubric

3 Full Accomplishment Students complete thorough and accurate research on several aspects of American railroads and display their findings clearly.

2 Substantial Accomplishment Students complete satisfactory research on some aspects of American railroads and display their findings clearly.

1 Little or Partial Accomplishment Students do inadequate research and display their few findings in a map and three time lines that are incomplete.

ACROSS CULTURES MINI-PROJECTS Multimodal Activities

Living Forever Imagine that you could live forever, like Aunty Misery. Make a word web showing your thoughts about the joys and sorrows of never dying.

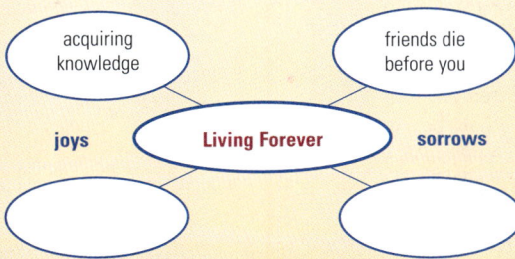

Ask an adult you know to do the same activity. Compare the similarities and differences between his or her word web and your own.

Compare Animal Tales Design a chart that indicates the similarities and differences between the two animal tales you have just read. Consider the purpose of each story, the animals' behavior, and how each story reflects its culture.

Research the Buzzard In the Cajun tale, M'su Carencro is referred to as the buzzard. In fact, the term "buzzard" is given to many species of birds around the world. Go to a library or use a computer database to find out about buzzards and their behavior. Which kind of bird do you think is featured in the story?

Write Morals The tale of Brer Possum ends with a moral—a lesson to be learned from the story. What lessons can be learned from the other stories? Write suitable morals for them.

> *Extended Social Studies Reading*
>
> **MORE ABOUT THE CULTURES**
>
> - *America's Immigrants: Adventure in Eyewitness History* by Rhoda Hoff
> - *The French and Indian Wars* by American Heritage
> - *Railroads in the Days of Steam* by American Heritage
> - *Slavery in America* by Robert Liston

LINKS TO UNIT TWO 731

Across Cultures

Living Forever Students might give the adult an empty word web with the words Living Forever in the center and have the adult complete the web. Or, students could tape-record the adult's responses to the phrase.

Compare Animal Tales Students' charts might show that both stories are intended to teach a lesson as well as to entertain. They might note that each character's behavior seems appropriate to the animal it represents.

Research the Buzzard Students' research should indicate that the buzzard is a type of hawk. This term is often erroneously used to indicate a bird rightly known as a turkey vulture or a black vulture. The buzzard in the story is based on one of these vultures.

Write Morals Students' morals should be concise, and their messages should be unambiguous. Encourage students to use simple language to express the stories' ideas.

OVERVIEW
Objectives
- To understand and appreciate four stories about people and animals who come into conflict with one another
- To appreciate the cultures of the regions represented
- To extend understanding of the selections through a variety of multimodal and cross-curricular activities.

Reading Pathways
- Invite volunteers to read the folk tales, myth, and legend aloud to classmates. Have students work in pairs to plan and practice this reading. Urge the rest of the class to listen for passages in which readers convey a character or attitude vividly.

- After students have finished reading "The Five Eggs," they can read it again to trace the cause-and-effect chain of events that leads the couple through the story. Then have students identify similarities and differences between this selection and the selections in Unit Three. For example, students might consider how the couple's battle in "The Five Eggs" is similar to or different from the struggle faced by the characters in "Getting the Facts of Life."

- Read "Spotted Eagle and Black Crow" aloud to the class. You might wish to pause at certain points in the narrative, to allow students to compare and contrast customs, traditions, and beliefs of Oglala culture with those of the students' cultures.

PREVIEWING

LINKS TO UNIT THREE

Battle for Control

Activating Prior Knowledge
What battles for control does life present? To what lengths should someone go in order to win? Each of the tales in Unit Three explores a struggle for control and considers the ways in which it affects the characters' lives.

Building Background

PACIFIC COAST

Raven and the Coming of Daylight
retold by Gail Robinson and Douglas Hill

The Haida (hī′də) were one of the Native American peoples who lived along the Pacific Northwest Coast. Resources in the area were plentiful, and the Haida developed an advanced society. This Haida myth is a trickster tale. Tricksters in folk tales are characters, often animals, who use cleverness to get what they want.

ECUADOR

Building Background

The Five Eggs
retold by Frank Henius

Ecuador is a small South American country of great geographical variety. The mighty Andes mountains stand in stark contrast to the coastal lowlands in the west and the rain forests in the east. This geographical diversity and the mix of different traditions in Ecuador's history have contributed to its rich culture. The folk tale of "The Five Eggs" probably originated with the native mountain people, who had no written language.

732   UNIT SIX: THE ORAL TRADITION

PRINT AND MEDIA RESOURCES

UNIT SIX RESOURCE BOOK
Strategic Reading: Literature, p. 17
Reading SkillBuilder, p. 18
Spelling SkillBuilder, p. 19

GRAMMAR MINI-LESSONS
Transparencies, pp. 8, 9
Copymasters, pp. 10, 11

ACCESS FOR STUDENTS ACQUIRING ENGLISH
Selection Summaries
Reading and Writing Support

FORMAL ASSESSMENT
Selection Test, pp. 137–138
 Test Generator

 **AUDIO LIBRARY**
See Reference Card

 **INTERNET RESOURCES**
McDougal Littell Literature Center at http://www.hmco.com/mcdougal/lit

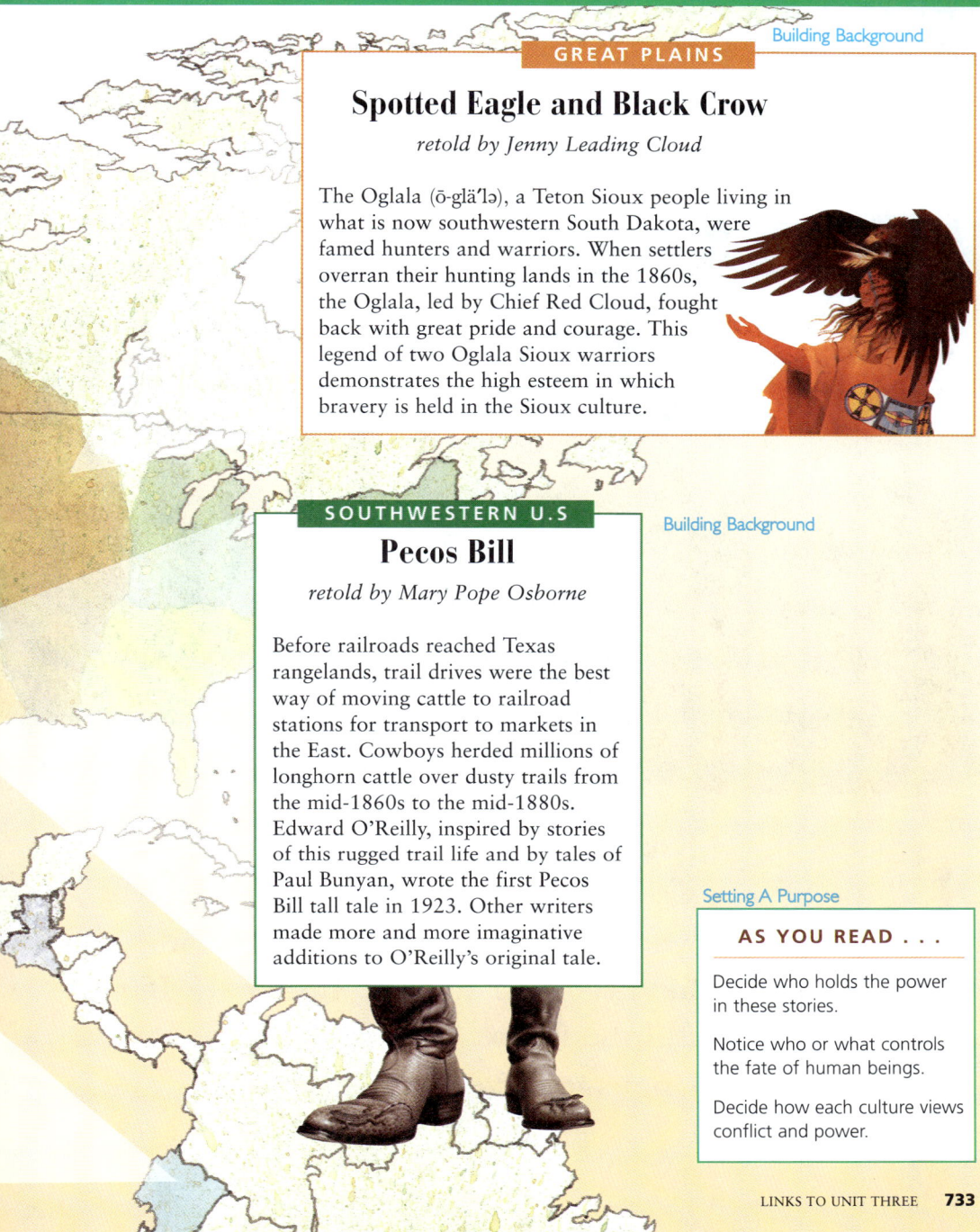

Building Background

GREAT PLAINS
Spotted Eagle and Black Crow
retold by Jenny Leading Cloud

The Oglala (ō-glä′lə), a Teton Sioux people living in what is now southwestern South Dakota, were famed hunters and warriors. When settlers overran their hunting lands in the 1860s, the Oglala, led by Chief Red Cloud, fought back with great pride and courage. This legend of two Oglala Sioux warriors demonstrates the high esteem in which bravery is held in the Sioux culture.

SOUTHWESTERN U.S

Building Background

Pecos Bill
retold by Mary Pope Osborne

Before railroads reached Texas rangelands, trail drives were the best way of moving cattle to railroad stations for transport to markets in the East. Cowboys herded millions of longhorn cattle over dusty trails from the mid-1860s to the mid-1880s. Edward O'Reilly, inspired by stories of this rugged trail life and by tales of Paul Bunyan, wrote the first Pecos Bill tall tale in 1923. Other writers made more and more imaginative additions to O'Reilly's original tale.

Setting A Purpose

AS YOU READ . . .

Decide who holds the power in these stories.

Notice who or what controls the fate of human beings.

Decide how each culture views conflict and power.

LINKS TO UNIT THREE **733**

SUMMARY

Pecos Bill Bill is reared by Texas coyotes, but at 17 he learns that he's human and decides to be the greatest cowboy of all. Bill becomes the leader of the Hell's Gate Gang and controls the entire Southwest. During a drought he ropes a cyclone and wrings water from it. Later he falls in love with Slue-foot Sue, and on their wedding day Bill's horse bucks her into the sky. Bill ropes her and is pulled skyward too, and the two now live with their children on the moon.

The Five Eggs Juan and Juanica are very poor and are starving. Juan begs for money on the street and is able to buy five eggs. He and his wife argue about who should get to eat three of the eggs. Juanica pretends to die of grief, but Juan outsmarts her by nearly having her buried alive. At the edge of the grave, Juanica says that Juan can eat all five eggs. At home, however, Juanica sets five eggs on the table and eats three.

Raven and the Coming of Daylight Gull, the keeper of daylight, will not let the sun out of its box. Other creatures ask Raven to reason with his cousin. When Gull continues to refuse, Raven magically puts a thorn in Gull's foot and insists that he needs some daylight to pull it out. Gull flings open the box and lets the sun out.

Spotted Eagle and Black Crow Two Oglala warriors love Red Bird. Black Crow is jealous because Red Bird prefers Spotted Eagle. One day, Black Crow leaves his friend to die stranded on a cliff; he tells Red Bird that Spotted Eagle is dead, and he marries her. Spotted Eagle befriends eagles on the cliff, and they fly him to safety. In the village he says nothing of Black Crow's act. During a battle, Black Crow asks Spotted Eagle to forgive him and rescue him. Spotted Eagle forgives him but says that he must fight alone. Black Crow dies, and Spotted Eagle marries Red Bird. Later he takes gifts to the eagles who helped him and pledges friendship with the Eagle Nation.

WORDS TO KNOW

abyss (ə-bĭs′) *n.* a seemingly bottomless hole (p. 746)

enmity (ĕn′mĭ-tē) *n.* a bitter hatred (p. 748)

sheer (shîr) *adj.* very steep; vertical (p. 746)

CUSTOMIZING FOR
Gifted and Talented Students

Have students rewrite one of the selections by setting it in a contemporary scene. For instance, students might set the events of "Pecos Bill" in a small American city in the 1990s. Encourage them to rethink descriptions that link the story to Texas. Ask students to consider how they might convey Pecos Bill's exploits and character traits in a context other than that of cowboys in the American Southwest.

STRATEGIC READING FOR
Less-Proficient Readers

Set a Purpose Encourage students to become involved in the selections by asking them to identify some mythical or legendary figures with whom they are familiar. Then have students read to find out how Pecos Bill spent his childhood and why he sets out with the cowpoke for the nearest ranch.

Use **UNIT SIX RESOURCE BOOK,** p. 17, for guidance in reading the selection.

CUSTOMIZING FOR
Students Acquiring English

- Use **ACCESS FOR STUDENTS ACQUIRING ENGLISH,** *Reading and Writing Support.*
- Some students may have difficulty with the nonstandard pronunciations and words contained in the selection.
- In addition to these boxes, you may want to use the suggestions under Strategic Reading for Less-Proficient Readers.

Pecos Bill

retold by Mary Pope Osborne

Copyright © Colin Poole.

Ask any coyote near the Pecos River in western Texas who was the best cowboy who ever lived, and he'll throw back his head and howl, "Ah-hooo!" If you didn't know already, that's coyote language for *Pecos Bill.*

734 UNIT SIX: THE ORAL TRADITION

| Mini-Lesson The Writer's Style |

INTRODUCTIONS Point out to students the importance of writing interesting and snappy introductions. Remind them that an introduction is intended to capture the audience's attention and to present the main idea of the writing.

One of the best ways that writers use to capture an audience's imagination and lead it into the world of the story is to begin with a vivid description. Storytellers, like prose writers, rely on vivid descriptions to grab their listeners' attention.

Application Have students list words and phrases that contribute to the vivid description in the first two paragraphs of "Pecos Bill." Then have them write a vivid description that introduces a family story that they know.

Reteaching/Reinforcement
- Writing Handbook, anthology p. 826

 **The Writer's Craft**

Introductions, p. 278

When Pecos Bill was a little baby, he was as tough as a pine knot. He teethed on horseshoes instead of teething rings and played with grizzly bears instead of teddy bears. He could have grown up just fine in the untamed land of eastern Texas. But one day his pappy ran in from the fields, hollering, "Pack up, Ma! Neighbors movin' in fifty miles away! It's gettin' too crowded!"

Before sundown Bill's folks loaded their fifteen kids and all their belongings into their covered wagon and started west.

As they clattered across the desolate land of western Texas, the crushing heat nearly drove them all crazy. Baby Bill got so hot and cross that he began to wallop his big brothers. Pretty soon all fifteen kids were going at one another tooth and nail. Before they turned each other into catfish bait, Bill fell out of the wagon and landed *kerplop* on the sun-scorched desert.

The others were so busy fighting that they didn't even notice the baby was missing until it was too late to do anything about it.

Well, tough little Bill just sat there in the dirt, watching his family rattle off in a cloud of dust, until an old coyote walked over and sniffed him.

"Goo-goo!" Bill said.

Now it's an amazing coincidence, but "Goo-goo" happens to mean something similar to "Glad to meet you" in coyote language. Naturally the old coyote figured he'd come across one of his own kind. He gave Bill a big lick and picked him up by the scruff of the neck and carried him home to his den.

Bill soon discovered the coyote's kinfolk were about the wildest, roughest bunch you could imagine. Before he knew it, he was roaming the prairies with the pack. He howled at the moon, sniffed the brush, and chased lizards across the sand. He was having such a good time, scuttling about naked and dirty on all fours, that he completely forgot what it was like to be a human.

Pecos Bill's coyote days came to an end about seventeen years later. One evening as he was sniffing the sagebrush, a cowpoke came loping by on a big horse. "Hey, you!" he shouted. "What in the world are you?"

Bill sat on his haunches and stared at the feller.

"What *are* you?" asked the cowpoke again.

"Varmint," said Bill hoarsely, for he hadn't used his human voice in seventeen years.

"No, you ain't!"

"Yeah, I am. I got fleas, don't I?"

"Well, that don't mean nothing. A lot of Texans got fleas. The thing varmints got that you ain't got is a tail."

"Oh, yes. I do have a tail," said Pecos Bill.

"Lemme see it then," said the cowpoke.

Bill turned around to look at his rear end, and for the first time in his life he realized he didn't have a tail.

"Dang," he said. "But if I'm not a varmint, what am I?"

"You're a cowboy! So start acting like one!"

Bill just growled at the feller like any coyote worth his salt would. But deep down in his heart of hearts he knew the cowpoke was right. For the last seventeen years he'd had a sneaking suspicion that he was different from that pack of coyotes. For one thing, none of them seemed to smell quite as bad as he did.

So with a heavy heart he said good-bye to his four-legged friends and took off with the cowpoke for the nearest ranch.

Acting like a human wasn't all that easy for Pecos Bill. Even though he soon started dressing right, he never bothered to shave or comb his hair. He'd just throw some water on his face in the morning and go around the rest of the day looking like a wet dog. Ignorant cowpokes claimed Bill wasn't too smart. Some of the meaner ones liked to joke that he wore a ten-dollar hat on a five-cent head.

Linking to Social Studies

D The first cowboys were employed by Spanish ranchers in Mexico during the 16th century. Since their ranches covered vast areas of land, the ranchers could let their cattle roam. They trained local Native American peoples to herd the cattle on the open range. These early cowboys were called *vaqueros*, after *vaca*, Spanish for "cow."

Critical Thinking: ANALYZING

E Ask students why the storyteller uses the descriptive details "licking his dinner plate" and "his ears perked up" in this passage. *(Possible response: The storyteller describes Pecos Bill this way to remind the reader of his upbringing with coyotes. Despite his awareness of being human, Bill still has some of the traits he learned from them.)*

CUSTOMIZING FOR
Students Acquiring English

3 Explain that a cowboy would "holler whoa" to stop a horse from running. This expression indicates that Pecos Bill left before anyone had a chance to stop him.

4 Paraphrase "didn't give a spit for" as "didn't care at all about."

5 Point out that someone would "cry uncle" to surrender in a fight.

Literary Concept: TALL TALE

F Point out to students that tellers of tall tales rely on exaggeration to achieve a humorous, entertaining effect. Have students explain what makes this a classic scene from a tall tale. *(Possible response: Bill's action—wrestling with, saddling, and riding a mountain lion—and his casual approach to doing it are exaggerated descriptive details that are typical of tall tales.)*

D The truth was, Pecos Bill would soon prove to be one of the greatest cowboys who ever lived. He just needed to find the kind of folks who'd appreciate him. One night when he was licking his dinner plate, his ears **E** perked up. A couple of ranch hands were going on about a gang of wild cowboys.

"Yep. Those fellas are more animal than human," one ranch hand was saying.

"Yep. Them's the toughest bunch I ever come across. Heck, they're so tough they can kick fire out of flint rock with their bare toes!"

"Yep. 'N' they like to bite nails in half for fun!"

"Who are these fellers?" asked Bill.

"The Hell's Gate Gang," said the ranch hand. "The mangiest, meanest, most low-down bunch of lowlife varmints that ever grew hair."

"Sounds like my kind of folks," said Bill, and before anyone could holler whoa, he **3** jumped on his horse and took off for Hell's Gate Canyon.

Bill hadn't gone far when disaster struck. His horse stepped in a hole and broke its ankle.

"Dang!" said Bill as he stumbled up from the spill. He draped the lame critter around his neck and hurried on.

After he'd walked about a hundred more miles, Bill heard some mean rattling. Then a fifty-foot rattlesnake reared up its ugly head and stuck out its long, forked tongue, ready to fight.

"Knock it off, you scaly-hided fool. I'm in a hurry," Bill said.

4 The snake didn't give a spit for Bill's plans. He just rattled on.

Before the cussed varmint could strike, Bill had no choice but to knock him cross-eyed. "Hey, feller," he said, holding up the dazed snake. "I like your spunk. Come go with us." Then he wrapped the rattler around his arm and continued on his way.

After Bill had hiked another hundred miles with his horse around his neck and his snake around his arm, he heard a terrible growl. A huge mountain lion was crouching on a cliff, getting ready to leap on top of him.

"Don't jump, you mangy bobtailed fleabag!" Bill said.

Well, call any mountain lion a mangy bobtailed fleabag, and he'll jump on your back for sure. After this one leaped onto Bill, so much fur began to fly that it darkened the sky. Bill wrestled that mountain lion into a headlock, then squeezed him so tight that the big cat had **5** to cry uncle.

When the embarrassed old critter started to slink off, Bill felt sorry for him. "Aw, c'mon, you big silly," he said. "You're more like me than most humans I meet."

He saddled up the cat, jumped on his back, and the four of them headed for the canyon, with the mountain lion screeching, the horse neighing, the rattler rattling, and Pecos Bill hollering a wild war whoop.

When the Hell's Gate Gang heard those noises coming from the prairie, they nearly fainted. They dropped their dinner plates, and their faces turned as white as bleached desert bones. Their knees knocked and their six-guns shook.

"Hey, there!" Bill said as he sidled up to their campfire, grinning. "Who's the boss around here?"

A nine-foot feller with ten pistols at his sides stepped forward and in a shaky voice said, "Stranger, I was. But from now on, it'll be you."

"Well, thanky, pardner," said Bill. "Get on with your dinner, boys. Don't let me interrupt."

Once Bill settled down with the Hell's Gate Gang, his true genius revealed itself. With his gang's help, he put together the biggest ranch in the Southwest. He used New Mexico as a corral and Arizona as a pasture. He invented tarantulas and scorpions as practical jokes. He also invented roping. Some say his rope was exactly as long as the equator; others argue it was two feet shorter.

F

736   UNIT SIX: THE ORAL TRADITION

Mini-Lesson Spelling

WORDS WITH SILENT LETTERS

Explain to students that many words contain silent letters. A few consonants are silent in certain combinations. You might wish to write some consonant combinations on the board, pointing out that the underlined letter is silent. Examples:

folk (fōk)
knock (näk)
wring (ring)

Application Have students spell the following words as you recite them aloud.

Silent Consonants

| lk | kn | wr |
| st | wh | mb |

1. thumb
2. talk
3. knuckle
4. knave
5. wrestle
6. whirled
7. bustle
8. stalk
9. whistle
10. climber

Ask students to look for more words that fit this pattern, in their own writing and in things that they read, and to add these words to their personal word lists.

Reteaching/Reinforcement
• *Unit Six Resource Book*, p. 19

---

736   THE LANGUAGE OF LITERATURE   TEACHER'S EDITION

The truth was, Pecos Bill would soon prove to be one of the greatest cowboys who ever lived.

Illustration by J. W. Stewart.

PECOS BILL 737

Literary Note

Tall tales are almost an exclusively American subgenre of folklore. The most famous figures from tall tales are Paul Bunyan, the huge lumberjack from the Pacific Northwest; Davy Crockett, the expert rifleman from Tennessee; John Henry, the strong African-American railroad builder; Daniel Boone, the Kentucky frontiersman; and Johnny Appleseed, the planter of orchards from coast to coast.

Two important 19th century American writers—Washington Irving and Mark Twain—made liberal use of tall tales in their works.

Linking to Geography

 The Pecos is a branch of the Rio Grande. The source of the Pecos River lies near Baldy Peak in the vicinity of Santa Fe, New Mexico. The Pecos flows southeast some 800 miles—finally feeding into the Rio Grande in Texas.

Mini-Lesson: Speaking, Listening, and Viewing

DRAMATIC READING Tell students that in a dramatic reading the different speakers read aloud the words of characters with a narrator reading the remaining text. Remind students that effective speakers use dialect, intonation, and pacing to convey the personality and mood of their characters.

Application Have students organize and perform a dramatic reading of "Pecos Bill." Have students determine who will read aloud the parts of speaking characters and which students will be narrators. Encourage students to work in pairs or small groups to practice the dialect found in the tale.

THE LANGUAGE OF LITERATURE TEACHER'S EDITION 737

Active Reading: PREDICT

G Invite students to make predictions about what events will occur next in the tale. Encourage students to support their ideas with information in the text.

Literary Concept: PERSONIFICATION

H Encourage students to note the way the storyteller uses personification to describe the cyclone as a wild animal. Ask students to identify descriptive details that convey this idea. (*Possible responses: around its neck; by the ears; onto her back; bucked, arched, and screamed like a wild bronco*) Help students understand that the storyteller uses personification to convey the impression of the storm as a living beast. This creates drama and humor in the passage.

Critical Thinking: SPECULATING

I Ask students why Pecos Bill named the colt Widow Maker. (*Possible response: The name Widow Maker suggests that the colt is wild and fierce. The widows he will make are going to be the wives of the men who try to ride him. The name implies that no one can ride him and survive.*)

CUSTOMIZING FOR
Students Acquiring English

6 Paraphrase the expression *having a ball* as "having a good time."

Things were going fine for Bill until Texas began to suffer the worst drought in its history. It was so dry that all the rivers turned as powdery as biscuit flour. The parched grass was catching fire everywhere. For a while Bill and his gang managed to lasso water from the Rio Grande. When that river dried up, they lassoed water from the Gulf of Mexico.

No matter what he did, though, Bill couldn't get enough water to stay ahead of the drought. All his horses and cows were starting to dry up and blow away like balls of tumbleweed. It was horrible.

Just when the end seemed near, the sky turned a deep shade of purple. From the distant mountains came a terrible roar. The cattle began to stampede, and a huge black funnel of a cyclone appeared, heading straight for Bill's ranch.

The rest of the Hell's Gate Gang shouted, "Help!" and ran.

But Pecos Bill wasn't scared in the least. "Yahoo!" he hollered, and he swung his lariat and lassoed that cyclone around its neck.

Bill held on tight as he got sucked up into the middle of the swirling cloud. He grabbed the cyclone by the ears and pulled himself onto her back. Then he let out a whoop and headed that twister across Texas.

The mighty cyclone bucked, arched, and screamed like a wild bronco. But Pecos Bill just held on with his legs and used his strong hands to wring the rain out of her wind. He wrung out rain that flooded Texas, New Mexico, and Arizona, until finally he slid off the shriveled-up funnel and fell into California. The earth sank about two hundred feet below sea level in the spot where Bill landed, creating the area known today as Death Valley.[1]

"There. That little waterin' should hold things for a while," he said, brushing himself off.

After his cyclone ride, no horse was too wild for Pecos Bill. He soon found a young colt that was as tough as a tiger and as crazy as a streak of lightning. He named the colt Widow Maker and raised him on barbed wire and dynamite. Whenever the two rode together, they back flipped and somersaulted all over Texas, loving every minute of it.

One day when Bill and Widow Maker were bouncing around the Pecos River, they came across an awesome sight: a wild-looking, red-haired woman riding on the back of the biggest catfish Bill had ever seen. The woman looked like she was having a ball, screeching, "Ride 'em, cowgirl!" as the catfish whipped her around in the air.

"What's your name?" Bill shouted.

"Slue-foot Sue! What's it to you?" she said. Then she war-whooped away over the windy water.

Thereafter all Pecos Bill could think of was Slue-foot Sue. He spent more and more time away from the Hell's Gate Gang as he wandered the barren cattle lands, looking for her. When he finally found her lonely little cabin, he was so love-struck he reverted to some of his old coyote ways. He sat on his haunches in the moonlight and began a-howling and ah-hooing.

Well, the good news was that Sue had a bit of coyote in her too, so she completely understood Bill's language. She stuck her head out her window and ah-hooed back to him that she loved him, too. Consequently Bill and Sue decided to get married.

On the day of the wedding Sue wore a beautiful white dress with a steel-spring bustle,

---

1. **Death Valley:** a desert area of California and Nevada, site of the Western Hemisphere's lowest point.

738 UNIT SIX: THE ORAL TRADITION

Mini-Lesson: Speaking, Listening, and Viewing

MONOLOGUE Tell students that in the oral tradition, stories are told from the third-person point of view, with the storyteller as the narrator. In contrast, a monologue is told using a first-person point of view. Monologues can be addressed to other characters, to the audience, or may be a character talking to him- or herself.

Application Invite students to select an episode in the story and tell it from the first-person point of view of either Pecos Bill or Slue-foot Sue. Students can perform their monologues for the class.

and Bill appeared in an elegant buckskin suit.

But after a lovely ceremony, a terrible catastrophe occurred. Slue-foot Sue got it into her head that she just had to have a ride on Bill's wild bronco, Widow Maker.

"You can't do that, honey," Bill said. "He won't let any human toss a leg over him but me."

"Don't worry," said Sue. "You know I can ride anything on four legs, not to mention what flies or swims."

Bill tried his best to talk Sue out of it, but she wouldn't listen. She was dying to buck on the back of that bronco. Wearing her white wedding dress with the bustle, she jumped on Widow Maker and kicked him with her spurs.

Well, that bronco didn't need any thorns in his side to start bucking to beat the band. He bounded up in the air with such amazing force that suddenly Sue was flying high into the Texas sky. She flew over plains and mesas, over canyons, deserts, and prairies. She flew so high that she looped over the new moon and fell back to earth.

But when Sue landed on her steel-spring bustle, she rebounded right back into the heavens! As she bounced back and forth between heaven and earth, Bill whirled his lariat above his head, then lassoed her. But instead of bringing Sue back down to earth, he got yanked into the night sky alongside her!

Together Pecos Bill and Slue-foot Sue bounced off the earth and went flying to the moon. And at that point Bill must have gotten some sort of foothold in a moon crater— because neither he nor Sue returned to earth. Not ever.

Folks figure those two must have dug their boot heels into some moon cheese and raised a pack of wild coyotes just like themselves. Texans'll tell you that every time you hear thunder rolling over the desolate land near the Pecos River, it's just Bill's family having a good laugh upstairs. When you hear a strange ah-hooing in the dark night, don't be fooled— that's the sound of Bill howling *on* the moon instead of *at* it. And when lights flash across the midnight sky, you can bet it's Bill and Sue riding the backs of some white-hot shooting stars. ❖

MARY POPE OSBORNE

When Mary Pope Osborne (1949–) was four, her father was in the army and was stationed in Austria along with his family. In her imagination, a nearby castle on a cliff became the home of Cinderella or Sleeping Beauty. She dreamed of worlds that she would later write about.

She studied drama, mythology, and religion at the University of North Carolina at Chapel Hill. After college, she traveled to faraway Eastern European and Asian countries, camping in a cave and riding in a rickety van.

One night, while attending the opening of a musical in Washington, D.C., she fell in love with Will Osborne, who was playing the role of Jesse James. Three years after their marriage, she wrote her first book, *Run, Run as Fast as You Can.* "Finally," Osborne says, "I knew exactly what I wanted to be when I grew up."

Since then, she has won many awards for her more than 25 books for children and young adults. "For years, I've been afraid of getting caught," says Osborne, "afraid that some day an authority figure will knock on my door and say, 'I think you're having too much fun here. Time to get serious and get a real job.'"

OTHER WORKS *Favorite Greek Myths; Haunted Waters; Best Wishes, Joe Brady; Mermaid Tales from Around the World*

STRATEGIC READING FOR
Less-Proficient Readers

Set a Purpose Have students read to find out why Juan and Juanica are fighting and how the five eggs are finally divided between them.

Cultural Note
A More than 10 million people were estimated to live in Ecuador at the beginning of the 1990s. Approximately 4 million Ecuadorians are Indians, and another 4 million are *mestizos,* or people of mixed Indian and Spanish heritage.

The majority of the nation's Indians are descendants of the ancient Incas; they speak various dialects of the Quechua language and live in the Ecuadorian highlands. Today some Indians live in towns and cities.

Active Reading: PREDICT
B Encourage students to note the unusual detail in the plan that Juan describes. Ask them whether they are surprised that Juan mentions getting *five* eggs. Invite students to make predictions about how this number of eggs might figure in the plot.

Active Reading: EVALUATE
C Invite students to share their opinions about the behavior of both Juan and Juanica. Ask them how they would evaluate their marriage and if they think that one or the other has more of a right to the "extra" egg. You may wish to use the following model to give students ideas of what they might be thinking about.

Think-Aloud Model *Judging from what I have read so far, it seems as though Juan and Juanica do not cooperate very well. Rather than trying to get more food for themselves, they should be working together to find a way to share what they have equally.*

The Five

retold by Frank Henius

A In the fields near the city there lived two poor peasants named Juan and Juanica. They loved each other devotedly, but since they were very poor, they would sometimes go two or even three days without eating.

Once, after they had had nothing to eat for three days, Juanica asked her husband, "How long are we going to keep on living if we don't eat?"

"Don't worry," he said, "I will go **B** to town today to see if I can manage to find money to buy five eggs for us to boil and eat."

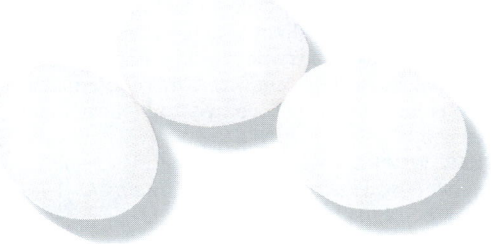

Immediately he set out for town. On arrival, he stood on a corner to wait for a passerby from whom he could ask alms.[1] When he saw a man coming, he said to him, "Listen, my friend! Would you be good enough to give me four cents to buy an egg?" And the man, who was very charitable, gave him the four cents. That happened five times, and the peasant was fortunate enough not to have one of the five refuse him. When he had enough to buy the five eggs, he went on and bought them. And when he had bought them he returned home to tell his wife the good news.

When he reached home, he told his wife to boil the eggs at once, for he was so hungry he could eat a burro. When the eggs were all boiled, his wife said to him, "Juan, come eat your two eggs; I shall eat three because I cooked them."

But he immediately said no, that he was the one to have the three eggs and she should have only two. And he kept on by saying, "Three for me and two for you." But his wife was stubborn, maintaining that she was to have three and he two. And that went on and on.

After they had wasted a good deal of time talking, Juanica decided to tell Juan that if he did not give her the three eggs to eat, she would die. But he said to her, very indifferently, "All right, that makes no difference to me. Go ahead and die!"

So she fell to the ground as though dead. Then he began to weep, "Oh, my poor wife, I

---
1. **alms** (ämz): money given to the needy.

740 UNIT SIX: THE ORAL TRADITION

Mini-Lesson  Reading Skills/Strategies

ACTIVE READING: QUESTIONING Point out to students that the process of raising questions while reading is called questioning. Active readers ask themselves questions in an effort to understand characters and events better. Then they look for the answers to their questions as they continue reading.

Application Have students construct a chart like the one shown that identifies the questions they had while reading the selection. For instance, most students will wonder how Juan and Juanica will resolve their dispute over the fifth egg. Students should also identify answers they found to their questions while reading. If students have questions left unanswered in their charts, you may wish to have the class discuss and answer these questions.

Reteaching/Reinforcement
- *Unit Six Resource Book,* p. 18

My Questions	Answers in the Text

Eggs

loved her so. Oh, my poor wife!" And after he had wept until he was tired, he whispered in her ear, "Juanica, don't be so silly. I'll eat three and you two." But she answered, "No, I am going to eat three and you two, or else you can bury me." But he kept on weeping.

After he saw that his wife refused to come to life again, he decided to go and look for his best friend. But he had five friends, and when he reached their homes, he told them that he had come to ask them please to bury his wife, who had just died, and that he was counting on them, for he did not have a single cent to buy a casket. But his friends said not to worry, that they would see to that.

On his return home, he found her still playing dead. Then Juan burst into tears again, "Oh, Juanica, do not leave me alone, please!" And so that no one would see him, he slipped near where she lay to whisper in her ear, "I am going to eat three and you two." But she said no, that she was to eat the three and he the two. Then he said to her, "Take care, for we are going to bury you." And she replied, "That's nothing; bury me whenever you like."

After waiting a good while, they put her in the casket to carry her to the cemetery. And on the way, Juan kept on crying, "Oh, my poor wife, don't leave me!" And he made them stop the funeral procession, supposedly to kiss her, but really to tell her that he was going to eat three and she two. But her reply was always the same. When they reached the cemetery, they bore her to the edge of the grave dug to receive her. Then he went up to her and whispered in her ear, "Look, you are on the edge of the grave, and we are about to put you in it." Then, when she realized he was telling the truth, she sat up in the casket and said, "All right, then; you can eat all five of them."

So she got up out of the casket, and they both went home. But once they arrived there, Juanica set the five eggs on the table—and ate *three!* ❖

FRANK HENIUS

Not one to stay put, Frank Henius (1882–1955), born in Denmark, went to school in Germany, trained on a sailing ship, and immigrated to the United States.

Becoming a foreign trader and a trade counselor suited his adventurous spirit and frequently took him to South America during his 40-year career. He worked hard to open up United States trade relations with South America. Henius wrote three books on foreign trade, including *The ABC of Foreign Trade* in 1920. He also collected and published *Songs and Games of the Americas* and *Stories from the Americas* from which "The Five Eggs" is taken. These stories from twenty Central and South American countries were selected by Latin Americans as favorites of their children.

His wife, Gertruda, comments that "whenever there was a dispute, my husband was always for the underdog."

COMPREHENSION CHECK
1. In what region do Juan and Juanica live? *(in the fields near the city)*
2. How does Juan get the money to buy the five eggs? *(He goes to the city and asks for donations from five different people.)*
3. Why does Juanica feel she should get three of the five eggs? *(because she cooked them)*
4. Why does Juan feel he should get three of the five eggs? *(because he got the money and bought the eggs)*
5. What is the final solution to the problem? *(Juanica tells Juan he can eat all of the eggs, but she then eats three eggs herself.)*

Literary Links

D Ask students to discuss the differences between how Juan and Juanica approach their problems and how Von's parents deal with their struggles in "Von." *(Possible response: Juan and Juanica disagree about who should receive more to eat and forget that they should cooperate. Von's parents face their situation together and make difficult decisions for the benefit of all.)*

Critical Thinking: HYPOTHESIZING

E Encourage students to discuss why native Ecuadorians might have developed and passed along this oral folk tale. *(Possible responses: They might have devised a story that addressed issues that affected them, such as poverty. They might have wished to teach a lesson about the importance of generosity, empathy, and love.)*

STRATEGIC READING FOR Less-Proficient Readers

F Make sure that students are clear about the sequence of events in the folk tale by asking the following questions.

- Why do Juan and Juanica argue? *(They argue about how they should divide five eggs between them.)* **Noting Relevant Details**
- Who gets the extra egg? *(Juanica)* **Noting Relevant Details**

From Personal Response to Critical Analysis

1. What are your thoughts about Juan and Juanica and their behavior? Write your ideas in your notebook. *(Responses will vary.)*
2. In your opinion, what might have been a better solution to the couple's dilemma? *(Possible responses: They could have drawn lots for the extra egg. They could have scrambled all five eggs; they could have given away one egg.)*

Art Note

Raven Opened the Box of Daylight by Dale DeArmond Dale DeArmond is an Alaskan artist who specializes in woodcuts. In 1975, she published a book of woodcuts illustrating folk tales from the Tlingit (a Northwest Coast Indian tribe) culture. *Raven Opened the Box of Daylight* derives its style from Tlingit art. The face of the sun is very much like that in the art of these people who live along the western coast of Canada and Alaska.

Reading the Art *In what sense is the artist's use of color surprising? What words would you use to describe the figure of the sun? Why do you think woodcuts are a popular art form for illustrating folk tales and myths?*

STRATEGIC READING FOR
Less-Proficient Readers

Set a Purpose Have students read to find out what Raven does to try to get the sun released.

Cultural Note
There remain a few hundred Native Americans who speak the Haida language today. At one time, the Haida were a dominant tribe on the Queen Charlotte Islands (off British Columbia) and Prince of Wales Island (off Alaska). The Haida were notable for a highly stratified social system that included wealthy slave-owning upper classes, as well as a hereditary nobility. They were highly skilled in fishing, hunting, wood carving, and canoe- and house-building.

RAVEN and the

Raven Opened the Box of Daylight (1970), Dale DeArmond. Woodblock. Courtesy of the Anchorage (Alaska) Museum of History and Art.

742 UNIT SIX: THE ORAL TRADITION

Mini-Lesson Grammar

PLURAL AND POSSESSIVE NOUNS
Explain to students that the plural of most nouns is formed by adding -s. However, when a singular noun ends in the letters *s, sh, ch, x,* or *z,* the ending -es is added.

Point out to students the importance of distinguishing between plural nouns and possessive nouns. A singular possessive noun ends in 's, and a plural possessive noun ends in s'.

Application Have students correct the errors involving singular and plural nouns and possessive nouns in the following sentences.

1. Even the dark moss's (mosses) wither, and food is scarce.
2. So all the People complained of Gulls' (Gull's) arrogance and thoughtless self-importance.

Reteaching/Reinforcement
- *Grammar Handbook,* anthology p. 870
- *Grammar Mini-Lessons* copymasters pp. 10, 11, transparencies pp. 8, 9

 **The Writer's Craft**

Singular and Plural Nouns, pp. 422–423
Forming Possessives and Plurals, pp. 660–661

742 THE LANGUAGE OF LITERATURE TEACHER'S EDITION

COMING OF DAYLIGHT
retold by Gail Robinson and Douglas Hill

When the earth was very young, it was dark and cold like a winter's night through all the year's seasons. Gull was the Custodian of Daylight, and he kept it locked tight in a cedar box beneath his wing. Being Custodian made Gull feel very important, and he was not going to lose his position by letting Daylight out of the box.

"He is too vain!" screeched Owl, at a meeting of the People upon Meeting Hill.

"We can never travel, in this darkness, to our half-homes in the south," cried Robin. Her breast was bleached of color for the lack of light.

"Even the dark mosses wither, and food is scarce," whimpered Rabbit.

"One person is like another because I cannot map his face," shouted Bear. "Enemies pretend to be friends to share my blanket and bowl."

"I cannot see my tail, to clean it of burrs," whined Fox.

So all the People complained of Gull's arrogance and thoughtless self-importance.

Then Squirrel turned to Raven and said, "Gull is your cousin. Perhaps he will listen to you. Perhaps you can tell him of your cold blood and your blunderings in the darkness and make him change his mind."

So it was settled that Raven should meet Gull on Meeting Hill the next day—or the next night, since without Daylight there was no difference between day and night.

Gull agreed to come to the meeting. But it was clear, when he came, that he was not going to change his mind or listen to what Raven said. He had come only because it made him feel even more important to have Raven pleading with him.

"I was made Custodian of Daylight in the beginning of things," said Gull. "I am to keep Daylight safe. And I *will* keep it safe." And he curved his wing tighter round the cedar box.

Raven had run out of words to make Gull see the People's need for light. He thought angrily to himself, "I wish this Gull would step on a large thorn."

No sooner had he shaped this thought than Gull cried out, "Squee! My foot!"

"A thorn, Cousin?" asked Raven innocently. "Let me see—I will take it out for you."

But of course it was so dark that he could not see the thorn to remove it.

"I must have light to take out the thorn," said Raven.

"Light? Never!" said Gull.

"Then the thorn will remain."

Gull complained and hopped on one foot and wept, and he finally opened his cedar box a crack, so narrow that out glanced a shaft of light no brighter than a single star.

Raven put his hand to Gull's foot, then pretended not to see the thorn. Instead, he pushed it in deeper.

"Squee!" cried Gull. "My foot!"

"More light, more light!" shouted Raven.

RAVEN AND THE COMING OF DAYLIGHT 743

Mini-Lesson — Literary Concepts

REVIEWING MYTH Remind students that a myth is a traditional story that explains how something came to be or describes the actions of gods and heroes. The authorship of most myths is unknown. Often myths explain such things as human nature, the world's origin, nature's mysteries, or social customs. Most myths were once believed to be literally true and were tied to a particular society's religious beliefs.

Application Have students review the narrative in order to write a single sentence that conveys the myth's central conflict. *(Possible response: the efforts of animals and people to convince or force Gull to bring sunlight to the world).*

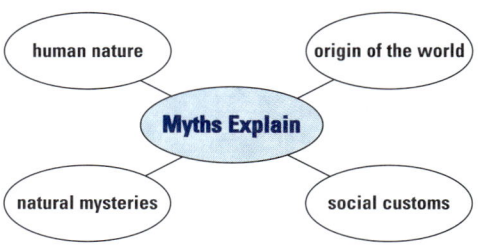

Literary Concept: MYTH

A Ask students to point out the common nouns that are repeatedly capitalized in this selection. *(Gull, Daylight, Custodian, Owl, Raven, People)* Help students understand that this is common in myths, which feature symbolic characters and events.

Cultural Note

B Some students might be confused by the term *People*. Help students understand that the term is used here to describe Owl, Robin, Rabbit, Bear, Fox, Squirrel, and other animals. Remind students that in many Native American cultures, there is a much closer identification of people with animals and other aspects of nature.

Active Reading: CONNECT

C Encourage students to reflect on how the world—and human life—would be different without daylight. Ask them to think about the effect it would have on people's emotions. Invite students to share their thoughts about a world where there is no day.

CUSTOMIZING FOR
Students Acquiring English

I Ask a volunteer to paraphrase the expression "had run out of words." *(didn't have anything more to say)*

Literary Links

D Both "Raven and the Coming of Daylight" and "The Flood" are concerned with the relationship between animals and natural phenomena. Ask students to explain the differences between the two relationships. *(Possible response: In "Raven and the Coming of Daylight," the animals are in control of the elements of nature. In "The Flood," natural forces are larger and more powerful than the animals. This difference could be based, in part, on the fact that "Raven and the Coming of Daylight" is a myth told from the point of view of the animals while "The Flood" is nonfiction told from the point of view of the human who saves the animals.)*

STRATEGIC READING FOR
Less-Proficient Readers

Ask students how Raven gets Gull to open the box and let the sun out. *(He keeps pushing the thorn farther into Gull's foot, saying he needs more light to remove the thorn.)* **Summarizing**

From Personal Response to Critical Analysis

1. What were your impressions of Gull and Raven? Write your ideas in your notebook. *(Responses will vary.)*
2. Was Gull right to keep daylight from the world? Was Raven right to act as he did? Explain your answers. *(Possible responses: Raven was right, since everyone needed daylight. Gull was right, since he was trying to protect his job. Neither was right—Gull was selfish and Raven was cruel.)*
3. In animal tales, animals often behave like human beings. Which human characteristics do Gull and Raven exhibit? *(Possible responses: They are able to speak; Raven can plan an elaborate trick; Gull is vain and selfish; Raven is clever and mean.)*

Nootka raven spirit mask, northwest coast. The Philbrook Museum of Art, Tulsa, Oklahoma, Ellis Soper Collection.

And the lid of the box rose a further crack, so that light gleamed forth like a winter moon. Then Raven reached again for the thorn and pushed it even further into the soft flesh of Gull's foot.

"More light!" roared Raven.

"Squee, squee, squee!" screamed Gull, and in his pain he flung off the lid of the cedar box.

Like a molten fish the sun slithered from the box, and light and warmth blazed out over the world.

Nor was it ever to be recaptured, no matter how loudly or how sadly Gull called to it to return to its safe hiding place beneath his wing. ❖

GAIL ROBINSON

Gail Robinson (1935–) is a well-known Canadian poet and folklorist who heard firsthand many of the Native American tales she has recorded. Together with Douglas Hill, she published *Coyote the Trickster: Legends of the North American Indians,* which includes "Raven and the Coming of Daylight."

The publication of *Coyote the Trickster* coincided with the first appearance of Robinson's poems in book form. After a ten-year break from writing, she has put together a collection of short stories set in western Canada.

OTHER WORKS *Raven the Trickster*

DOUGLAS HILL

Douglas Hill (1935–) has published many books, including the first comprehensive history of western Canada. Influenced by his childhood heroes, Buck Rogers and Flash Gordon, he has written science fiction for young adults. "I was encouraged by the fact that television and films were creating a huge audience for space adventure, even in 1977 B.S.W. [Before *Star Wars*]."

OTHER WORKS *Master of Fiends; Blade of the Poisoner*

744 UNIT SIX: THE ORAL TRADITION

COMPREHENSION CHECK

1. What did Gull control? *(daylight)*
2. Why is the earth dark? *(Gull is Custodian of Daylight, and he keeps it locked up so he can feel important.)*
3. Why is Raven chosen to negotiate with Gull? *(They are cousins, so perhaps Gull will listen to Raven.)*
4. Why does Gull open the cedar box a crack? *(to enable Raven to remove the thorn from Gull's foot)*
5. What allows daylight to come into the world? *(Gull opens the box after Raven has pushed the thorn deeper into Gull's foot.)*

Spotted Eagle and Black Crow

retold by Jenny Leading Cloud

When the Eagle Spoke to Me (1979), Jerry Ingram (Choctaw). Watercolor on paper, 18"× 24", by permission of the artist.

Art Note

When the Eagle Spoke to Me by Jerry Ingram In this watercolor painting, Jerry Ingram (1941–) captures an experience of critical significance in the culture of various Native Americans of the Great Plains. Ingram has focused on the moment when a warrior is visited by a vision and thus finds spiritual power. During the vision depicted, the eagle instructs the warrior in a sacred power song, tells him how to make a medicine bundle, and gives him his sacred symbol design. From this moment on, the eagle is the warrior's guardian.

Reading the Art Why do you think the artist decided to paint the warrior with his arm and hand extended in this way? Do you see any similarities between the eagle and the warrior? Do you think the artist intended there to be a similarity? Why or why not?

STRATEGIC READING FOR
Less-Proficient Readers

Set a Purpose Have students read to find out what happens between Black Crow and Spotted Eagle and whether Spotted Eagle and Red Bird are able to be happy together.

Linking to History

 A Chief Red Cloud (1822–1909), an important figure in Sioux history, dominated the northern plains in the last half of the nineteenth century. Born with the Sioux name Mahpiya Luta, he rose to the position of chief not through heredity but through force of character and repeated triumphs on the battlefield.

When the U.S. government threatened to build a road through Sioux hunting grounds in 1865, Red Cloud and his warriors resisted federal troops. For two years, in what has been called "Red Cloud's War," the Sioux successfully stopped the development of the road.

Officials of the federal government then invited Red Cloud to Washington, D.C., where his forceful speeches built support for his cause. The American public pressured the government into signing the Second Treaty of Fort Laramie in 1868. The treaty stated that the U.S. government would abandon army forts and stop building roads in Sioux territory in Montana, South Dakota, and Wyoming.

Cultural Note

B A Sioux sweat bath was essentially a ritual steam bath. It was conducted in a sweat lodge—a frame of willow sticks covered with buffalo skins. Cold water poured over hot rocks provided the purifying steam. Sioux boys took a sweat bath before going on their most important initiation rite, the vision quest.

Active Reading: EVALUATE

C Encourage students to share their opinions about whether Black Crow had planned this action previously, or whether the idea occurred to him only at this moment.

A This is a story of two warriors, of jealousy, and of eagles. This legend is supposed to have been a favorite of the great *Mahpiya Luta*—Chief Red Cloud of the Oglalas.

Many lifetimes ago, there lived two brave warriors. One was named *Wanblee Gleska*—Spotted Eagle. The other's name was *Kangi Sapa*—Black Crow. They were friends but, as it happened, they both loved the same girl, *Zintkala Luta Win*—Red Bird. She was beautiful, a fine tanner and quillworker,[1] and she liked Spotted Eagle best, which made Black Crow very jealous.

Black Crow went to his friend and said, "Let us, you and I, go on a war party against the Pahani. Let us get ourselves some fine horses and earn eagle feathers."[2] Spotted Eagle thought this a good idea. The two young men **B** purified themselves in a sweat bath. They got out their war medicine[3] and their war shields. They painted their faces. They did all that warriors should do before a raid. Then they went against the Pahani.

Their raid was not a success. The Pahani were watchful. The young warriors got nowhere near the Pahani horse herd. Not only did they capture no ponies, but they even lost their own mounts, because while they were trying to creep up to their enemies' herd, the Pahani found their horses. The two young men had a hard time getting away on foot because the enemy were searching for them everywhere. At one time they had to hide themselves in a lake, under the water, breathing through long, hollow reeds which were sticking up above the surface. They were so clever at hiding themselves that the Pahani finally gave up searching for them.

The young men had to travel home on foot. It was a long way. Their moccasins were tattered, their feet bleeding. At last they came to a high cliff. "Let us go up there," said Black Crow, "and see whether the enemy is following us." They climbed up. They could see no one following them; but on a ledge far below them, halfway up the cliff, they spied a nest with two young eagles in it. "Let us at least get those eagles," Black Crow proposed. There was no way one could climb down the sheer rock wall, but Black Crow took his rawhide lariat, made a loop in it, put the rope around Spotted Eagle's chest under his armpits, and lowered him down. When his friend was on the ledge with the nest, Black Crow said to himself, "I will leave him there to die. I will come home alone, and then Red Bird will marry me." And he threw his end of the rawhide thong down and left without looking back and without listening to Spotted Eagle's cries of what had happened to the lariat and to Black Crow. **C**

Spotted Eagle cried in vain. He got no answer, only silence. At last it dawned on him that his companion had betrayed him, that he had been left to die. The lariat was much too short for him to lower himself to the ground; there was an abyss of two hundred feet yawning beneath him. He was left with the two young eagles screeching at him, angered that this strange, two-legged creature had invaded their home.

Black Crow came back to his village. "Spotted Eagle died a warrior's death," he told

---

1. **tanner and quillworker:** a person who turns animal skins into leather and who weaves porcupine quills into decorations.
2. **earn eagle feathers:** to perform acts of bravery, for which a warrior was given eagle feathers to wear in his headdress.
3. **war medicine:** herbs, roots, and magical objects believed to provide protection during battle.

> **WORDS TO KNOW**
> **sheer** (shîr) *adj.* very steep; vertical
> **abyss** (ə-bĭs′) *n.* a seemingly bottomless hole

Assessment Option

SELF-ASSESSMENT Students can assess their understanding of this story by writing a eulogy that the leader of the tribe would give for Spotted Eagle, when he was believed dead, or for Black Crow, after he was killed. Then have students answer the following questions:

- Why did I choose the character I eulogized?
- What part of the story was most helpful to me as I wrote the eulogy?
- Would the eulogy have been different if it had been given by the surviving friend instead of the tribe's leader? Why or why not?

Up 'N' Down (1994), Howard Carr. Oil on canvas, 30" × 24", by permission of the artist. Photo by Bill McLemore Photography.

the people. "The Pahani killed him." There was loud wailing throughout the village because everybody had liked Spotted Eagle. Red Bird grieved more than the others. She slashed her arms with a sharp knife and cut her hair to make plain her sorrow to all. But in the end she became Black Crow's wife, because life must go on.

But Spotted Eagle did not die on his lonely ledge. The eagles got used to him. The old eagles brought plenty of food—rabbits, prairie dogs, or sage hens—and Spotted Eagle shared this raw meat with the two chicks. Maybe it was the eagle medicine in his bundle which he carried on his chest that made the eagles accept him. Still, he had a very hard time on that ledge. It was so narrow that when he wanted to rest, he had to tie himself with the rawhide thong to a little rock sticking out of the cliff, for fear of falling off the ledge in his sleep. In this way he spent a few very uncomfortable weeks; after all, he was a human being and not a bird to whom such a crack in the rock face is home.

At last the young eagles were big enough to practice flying. "What will become of me

Literary Links

F Encourage students to analyze the way human beings interact with animals in "Appetizer" and in "Spotted Eagle and Black Crow." Ask them how the fisherman views the fish and the bears and how Spotted Eagle views the eagles. *(Possible response: Both human beings interact with animals directly, but Spotted Eagle seems to have a deep bond with animals, whereas the fisherman feels no such connection. Certainly he seems comfortable fishing in the river until the bear appears, but there doesn't seem to be any sense of a spiritual connection or understanding between him and the bear.)*

CUSTOMIZING FOR
Students Acquiring English

2 Ask students to provide a synonym for "the Ones Above." *(Possible response: the gods)*

Critical Thinking: MAKING JUDGMENTS

G Encourage students to share their opinions of Spotted Eagle's behavior. Ask if they think his refusal to tell the whole story is dishonest, foolhardy, noble, or wise. Have students consider the pros and cons of his actions. *(Possible responses: It is wise for him to say little, because this is the way of his people. His instincts about what to do are the most important thing. Spotted Eagle could get what he wants more easily if he would simply tell what happened. What Black Crow did was terrible, so Spotted Eagle shouldn't worry about telling other tribe members about it.)*

Active Reading: CONNECT

H Invite students to imagine themselves in Spotted Eagle's position. Ask them how they would respond to Black Crow's request and what thoughts or feelings would cause them to react in this way.

---

now?" thought the young warrior. "Once these fledglings have flown the nest for good, the old birds won't be bringing any more food up here." Then he had an inspiration. "Perhaps I will die. Very likely I will die. But I will try it. I will not just sit here and give up." He took his little pipe out of the medicine bundle and lifted it to the sky and prayed, "*Wakan Tanka, onshimala ye*. Great Spirit, pity me. You have created man and his cousin, the eagle. You have given me the eagle's name. I have decided to try to let the eagles carry me to the ground. Let the eagles help me, let me succeed."

He smoked and felt a surge of confidence. He grabbed hold of the legs of the two young eagles. "Brothers," he told them, "you have accepted me as one of your own. Now we will live together, or die together. *Hokahay*." And he jumped off the ledge. He expected to be shattered on the ground below, but with a mighty flapping of wings the two young eagles broke his fall and all landed safely. Spotted Eagle said a prayer of thanks to the Ones Above. He thanked the eagles, telling them that one day he would be back with gifts and have a giveaway in their honor.

Spotted Eagle returned to his village. The excitement was great. He had been dead and had come back to life. Everybody asked him how it happened that he was not dead, but he would not tell them. "I escaped," he said, "and that is all." He saw his love married to his treacherous friend, but he bore it in silence. He was not one to bring enmity to his people, to set one family against the other. Besides, what happened could not be changed. Thus he accepted his fate.

A year or so later, a great war party of Pahani attacked his village. The enemy outnumbered them tenfold, and there was no chance of victory for Spotted Eagle's band. All the warriors could do was to fight a slow rear-guard action, which would give the helpless ones—the women, children, and old folks—a chance to escape across the river. Guarding their people this way, the few warriors at hand fought bravely, charging the enemy again and again, making them halt and regroup. Each time, the warriors retreated a little, taking up a new position on a hill or across a gully. In this way they could save their families.

Showing the greatest courage, exposing their bodies freely, were Spotted Eagle and Black Crow. In the end they alone faced the enemy. Then, suddenly, Black Crow's horse was hit by several arrows in succession and collapsed under him. "Brother, forgive me for what I have done," he cried to Spotted Eagle. "Let me jump up on your horse behind you."

Spotted Eagle answered, "You are a Fox. Pin yourself and fight. Then, if you survive, I will forgive you; and if you die, I will forgive you also."

What Spotted Eagle meant was this: Black Crow was a member of the Fox Warrior Society. The braves who belong to it sing this song:

I am a Fox.
If there is anything daring,
If there is anything dangerous to do,
That is a task for me to perform.
Let it be done by me.

Foxes wear a long, trailing sash, decorated with quillwork, which reaches all the way to the ground even when the warrior is on horseback. In the midst of battle, a Fox will sometimes defy death by pinning his sash to the earth with a special wooden pin or with a

WORDS TO KNOW
enmity (ĕn′mĭ-tē) *n.* a bitter hatred

748

Mini-Lesson: Speaking, Listening, and Viewing

IN LEGEND AND ON FILM *Dances with Wolves* (1990), is an award-winning film about a United States Army soldier who eventually becomes a member of a Sioux tribe in the Dakotas. While a class screening of the film may not be possible because of the film's length, you may wish to preview the film and select scenes that relate to this selection. For example, there is a realistic portrayal of a battle with another tribe. Afterward, invite students to have a class discussion that centers around the following questions:

- In your opinion, do the actions and attitudes of the Sioux in the film reflect some of the same values as those held by Spotted Eagle and Black Crow?
- Think about the setting of "Spotted Eagle and Black Crow." What do you see in the setting of this film that reminds you of the legend? Do the Sioux in the movie seem to give special importance to their relationships with animals?
- Were the Sioux in this film similar to or different from Native Americans you have seen in other films? How and why?

knife or arrow. This means: I will stay here, rooted to this spot, facing my foes, until someone comes to release the pin, or until the enemies flee, or until I die.

Black Crow pinned his sash to the ground. There was no one to release him, and the enemy did not flee. Black Crow sang his death song. He was hit by lances and arrows and died a warrior's death. Many Pahani died with him.

Spotted Eagle had been the only one to see this. He finally joined his people, safe across the river. The Pahani had lost all taste to follow them there. "Your husband died well," Spotted Eagle told Red Bird. After some time had passed, Spotted Eagle married Red Bird. And much, much later he told his parents, and no one else, how Black Crow had betrayed him. "I forgive him now," he said, "because once he was my friend, and because he died like a warrior should, fighting for his people, and also because Red Bird and I are happy now."

After a long winter, when spring came again, Spotted Eagle told his wife, "I must go away for a few days to fulfill a promise. I must go alone." He rode off by himself to that cliff. Again he stood at its foot, below the ledge where the eagles' nest had been. He pointed his sacred pipe to the four directions, down to Grandmother Earth and up to the Grandfather, letting the smoke ascend to the sky, calling out: "*Wanblee, misunkala.* Little eagle brothers, hear me."

High above him in the clouds appeared two black dots, circling. These were the eagles who had saved his life. They came at his call, their huge wings spread majestically, uttering a shrill cry of joy and recognition. Swooping down, they alighted at his feet. He stroked them with a feather fan, and thanked them many times, and fed them choice morsels of buffalo meat, and fastened small medicine bundles around their legs as a sign of friendship, and spread sacred tobacco offerings around the foot of the cliff. Thus he made a pact of friendship and brotherhood between *Wanblee Oyate*—the Eagle Nation—and his own people. After he had done all this, the stately birds soared up again into the sky, circling motionless, carried by the wind, disappearing into the clouds. Spotted Eagle turned his horse's head homeward, going happily back to Red Bird. ❖

JENNY LEADING CLOUD

1890?–1980?

Jenny Leading Cloud lived in White River, a little town on the Rosebud Sioux Reservation in South Dakota. There she was an outspoken advocate for the rights of Native Americans. As a result of an investigation by Jenny Leading Cloud, a wealthy white rancher was brought to trial, though not convicted, for the murder of her grandson.

She never wrote down the stories she heard but told them to her children and her grandchildren. "Spotted Eagle and Black Crow," one of her favorites, was first told by Chief Red Cloud of the Oglala Sioux.

SPOTTED EAGLE AND BLACK CROW **749**

COMPREHENSION CHECK

1. In what sense are Black Crow and Spotted Eagle rivals? *(They both love Red Bird.)*
2. Why does Black Crow leave Spotted Eagle on the ledge with the eagles' nest? *(Black Crow leaves him there to die so that he can marry Red Bird himself.)*
3. How does Spotted Eagle safely reach the ground below? *(He hangs onto the legs of two eagles as they fly to the ground.)*
4. What happens when Black Crow requests Spotted Eagle's help in battle? *(Spotted Eagle refuses, and Black Crow must die fighting the enemy.)*
5. Does Spotted Eagle ever tell about Black Crow's betrayal? *(Yes, he tells his own parents years later.)*

STRATEGIC READING FOR
Less-Proficient Readers

Make sure that students understand the sequence of events in this Oglala legend.

- How does Black Crow try to kill his friend? *(He leaves him stranded on the side of a cliff.)* **Noting Relevant Details**
- How does Spotted Eagle survive? *(He shares the eagles' nest and food and finally flies to the ground with them.)* **Summarizing**
- Are Spotted Eagle and Red Bird able to be happy together? *(yes, after Black Crow's death, their marriage, and Spotted Eagle's pact with the two eagles)* **Making Generalizations**

CUSTOMIZING FOR
Gifted and Talented Students

Have students discuss the concept of betrayal. Ask students how people sometimes betray one another and how different people respond to betrayal. Have them consider how to react when one has been betrayed.

From Personal Response to Critical Analysis

1. What were your thoughts as you finished reading this legend? Write them in your notebook. *(Responses will vary.)*
2. Do you think Spotted Eagle should have saved Black Crow's life? Why or why not? *(Possible responses: It would have been nobler to save his friend's life; by letting Black Crow die, Spotted Eagle lowered himself to Black Crow's level. No, he owed nothing to Black Crow. No—by putting Black Crow in a position to fight to the death to save his tribe, he gave Black Crow a chance to redeem his honor.)*
3. Using this legend as a guide, what character traits would you say the Oglalas believe are most important? *(Possible responses: loyalty; courage; fighting skill; endurance; acceptance of fate; living in harmony with each other and with animals)*

THE LANGUAGE OF LITERATURE **TEACHER'S EDITION** **749**

Literature Connection

Project 1 Encourage students to study the text of their chosen story carefully in order to choose and define a complaint that seems appropriate—that is, fair, reasonable, and potentially winnable. You might suggest that students brainstorm ideas about how to support a suit based on a complaint in order to test how it might play out in a trial.

Encourage students on either side of the case to make adequate preparations for the trial. Students presenting the plaintiff's case should make exhaustive lists of examples, details, and reasons why their complaint is legitimate. In preparation they should also try to anticipate the defendant's case by brainstorming ideas that the other side might use against the plaintiff. Students who present the defendant's case should prepare exactly the same way.

You might wish to review certain rules, roles, and behavioral expectations in a typical courtroom by asking volunteers to research courtroom manners and traditions and present them to the class.

Rubric

3 Full Accomplishment Students prepare their cases with thoroughness and intelligence, and they present their arguments with eloquence and persuasiveness.

2 Substantial Accomplishment Students do significant research and planning for their cases, and they present their arguments in an organized and clear way.

1 Little or Partial Accomplishment Students make incomplete preparations for the trial, and they present their arguments with little regard for logic or fairness.

RESPONDING OPTIONS

LITERATURE CONNECTION PROJECT 1 — Multimodal Activity

Prepare a Civil Trial Civil trials are designed to settle conflicts between individuals. Following official court procedure as much as possible, organize a civil trial that settles a dispute presented in one of the four stories. Conduct some research if necessary. Refer to the suggestions provided as you prepare for the trial.

Describe the Dispute and Assign Roles Working in a small group, read through the story and consider the dispute that you want to bring to trial. In a civil lawsuit, the plaintiff files a complaint, or suit, against another person or organization, called the defendant. Decide who will be the plaintiff and defendant.

Write Arguments
- Half of your group can brainstorm ideas to present the plaintiff's side of the argument in a statement of complaint. In this document, injuries or losses are declared.
- The other half of the group can brainstorm ideas to present the defendant's case. In response to the plaintiff's complaint, the defendant files a document called an answer, which gives the defendant's version of the facts of the case. Anticipate the other side's arguments and prepare counter-arguments.

Act Out Court Procedure Small groups can present their arguments to the class as a whole. Taking on the role of judge and jury, the class decides the outcome of each case.

SOCIAL STUDIES CONNECTION PROJECT 2 — Multimodal Activity

 Create a Native American Time Line By the mid-1860s in the United States, white settlers were forcing their way onto Native American lands in great numbers. Once the transcontinental railroad was completed in 1869, the rush of settlers became a stampede. Like many of the Native Americans during this period, the Sioux suffered at the hands of the U.S. government. Create a sequencing time line like the one started to show the conflict between the Native Americans of the Great Plains and the federal government from 1851 to 1890. Begin your research at the library or use a computer database.

Native Americans of the Great Plains 1851–1890

750   UNIT SIX: THE ORAL TRADITION

Social Studies Connection

Project 2 Students' time lines might include the following information: 1866–68: U.S. Army builds forts in Montana and Wyoming, and Red Cloud leads successful raids against forts; 1868: Tetons agree to live on federal reservations; 1875: Crazy Horse and other Oglalas refuse to enter reservations; 1876: U.S. Cavalry tries to defeat Crazy Horse, mistakenly attacks Cheyenne village; 1876: Crazy Horse defeats General George Crook in the Battle of the Rosebud; defeats General Custer in the Battle of the Little Bighorn; 1877: Crazy Horse voluntarily surrenders to U.S. troops; later dies; 1881: Sitting Bull surrenders to U.S. Army.

Rubric

3 Full Accomplishment Time lines contain detailed, accurate information that clearly illustrates the chronology of conflicts.

2 Substantial Accomplishment Time lines contain accurate, mostly well-organized information that illustrates the chronology of the conflicts.

1 Little or Partial Accomplishment Students do little research and have difficulty creating useful time lines.

Science Connection

Project 3 The eagles in this Oglala legend may have been golden eagles (*Aquila chrisaetos*). This eagle is common in Mexico, on the Pacific coast, and through the area of the Rocky Mountains.

Students' research should show that eagles—like most birds—build nests to house their eggs, their young, and themselves. They build their nests in inaccessible places such as cliff caves or lone trees. Eagles' nests are among the largest of all birds' nests—the largest reaching as much as 6 feet in diameter. Mostly, they are built with twigs, leaves, mud, and feathers.

Eagles (birds that are believed to mate for life) usually lay two to four eggs that incubate for 40–45 days. Usually only one of these eggs produces a bird that survives to adulthood three to four years later. Eagles begin to fly about three months after being hatched.

Golden eagles catch live prey by hunting for rabbits and other small mammals. They also eat small game birds, such as grouse, as well as snakes. Contrary to the Oglala legend, golden eagles cannot lift or carry much more than their own weight.

For centuries eagles have symbolized power and war.

Rubric
3 Full Accomplishment Students' thorough and well-organized research helps them construct an accurate model of an eagle's nest.

2 Substantial Accomplishment Students find some facts about eagles and their nests, and they construct an approximate model of an eagle's nest.

1 Little or Partial Accomplishment Students do little research and construct a model of an eagle's nest that is not especially accurate.

Multimodal Activity

SCIENCE CONNECTION PROJECT 3

Construct an Eagle's Nest What is an eagle's nest really like? Find out what species of eagles inhabit the western plains where the Oglala Sioux lived. Then create a scientifically accurate, but much smaller, example of a typical eagle's nest. Use classroom materials to approximate the general look and feel of a real nest. Make a display that allows you to include information about the eagle's life cycle, what it eats, and the symbolism of this great bird.

ACROSS CULTURES MINI-PROJECTS

Create a Collage or Mobile From the cedar tree, which was central to the lives of the Haida people, houses, canoes, and other products were made. Find out what other items the Haida made from cedar. For what purposes is cedar most commonly used today? Create a collage or mobile that depicts cedar items from the early Haida and products used in the United States today.

Research Creation Myths Many cultures have myths describing the creation of some natural element or animal in nature, such as daylight or the butterfly. In a group, identify examples of these myths, share them with one another, and then compare them. What do these myths tell you about the values and beliefs of the societies that created them?

Investigate the People of Ecuador Use the library or the Internet to investigate the daily lives of Ecuador's rural people and its urban population. How do their lives differ? Which group makes up the largest percentage of the population? Present your findings in a classroom display.

Multimodal Activity

Create Images of Paul Bunyan and Pecos Bill As a class, brainstorm similarities and differences between the legendary heroes Paul Bunyan and Pecos Bill. Then, use an art software program, if possible, or traditional art materials to create side-by-side images of these heroes. Label the images to highlight the similarities and differences between the two.

Extended Social Studies Reading

MORE ABOUT THE CULTURES

- *Buffalo Hunt* by Russell Freedman
- *Cowboys of the Wild West* by Russell Freedman
- *Men of the Wild Frontier* by Bennet Wayne
- *The Way It Was—1876* by Suzanne Hilton

LINKS TO UNIT THREE **751**

Across Cultures

Create a Collage or Mobile Students' research should show that the Haida used cedar also to build elaborate boxes, masks, grave markers, and utensils. Today cedar is most often used to make furniture, pencils, and fence posts.

Research Creation Myths Students might report on creation myths from such cultures as the Aztecs, various African or Native American tribes, as well as from places such as China, Egypt, Greece, Iran, Korea, and Japan.

Investigate the People of Ecuador Students' research should show that approximately 55 percent of Ecuador's population of 10 million lives in urban areas. City-dwellers work at manufacturing jobs—especially those involving oil, food, and textiles. Rural Ecuadorians are primarily farmers.

Create Images of Paul Bunyan and Pecos Bill Students' images might highlight distinctive details such as Bunyan's lumberjack attire and axe. Students also might wish to show Bunyan's extraordinary size. Pecos Bill's cowboy attire and lariat should figure in students' images, as well as his coarse features and sloppy grooming.

OVERVIEW

In the Guided Assignment for this section, students will write a scene for a play based on a fable or legend. By writing a play, students learn more about the ways folk tales change and get continually updated. The Writer's Style will help students understand what an audience needs in order to follow the characters and dialogue in stories. In Reading the World, students will analyze the changing image of Pocahontas. By doing so, they can come to understand why and how images of a person or a historical event change.

Objectives

- To understand how authors use dialogue to provide essential information in their writing
- To show direct address
- To present information through writing dialogue
- To respond to a folk tale by writing a scene for a play
- To analyze the way real-world images change over time

Skills

LITERATURE
- Analyzing dialogue for information

GRAMMAR AND USAGE
- Using commas in quotations

MEDIA LITERACY
- Analyzing images from history and today

ORAL COMMUNICATION
- Reading aloud with peers
- Discussion with friends
- Peer conferencing

CRITICAL THINKING
- Separating fiction from reality
- Classifying
- Analyzing

Teaching Strategy: MODELING

In the following models, important information is revealed through dialogue. Students will use these techniques to create their own scenes in a play.

A **Osborne** Possible response: The important information is that Bill is now the boss, whereas the "nine-foot feller" used to be. It is important to the plot because it leads to Bill's next actions.

B **Reneaux** Possible response: Chicken Hawk is confident in giving advice. Buzzard is more patient and accepting than Chicken Hawk. Students may infer that Buzzard is the "good guy."

WRITING ABOUT LITERATURE

STORIES ON STAGE

When you read a story, do you imagine that you can hear the characters speaking? Do you picture each event as it occurs? When you see a play, the characters really do speak, and you actually see what they are doing. The characters tell the story through their actions and words. In this lesson you will

- learn how writers use dialogue
- write a scene based on a legend you have read
- respond to and interpret a modern legend

Writer's Style: Using Dialogue Writers use dialogue to provide important information. In stories, dialogue often reveals character and advances the plot.

Read the Literature

How would you read these excerpts if you were speaking aloud?

Literature Models

A **Dialogue Advances the Plot**
What important event is shown through this dialogue? Why is it important to the plot?

"Hey, there!" Bill said as he sidled up to their campfire, grinning. "Who's the boss around here?"

A nine-foot feller with ten pistols at his sides stepped forward and in a shaky voice said, "Stranger, I was. But from now on, it'll be you."

"Well, thanky, pardner," said Bill.

from "Pecos Bill," retold by Mary Pope Osborne

B **Dialogue Reveals Character**
What type of a character is the chicken hawk? What type is the buzzard? Which one is the "good guy"?

"What you talkin' 'bout?" says know-it-all Chicken Hawk. "If you're so hungry, why don'tcha get out there and hunt you some good fresh meat? You got eyes, you got wings, you got a beak. Go for it! You got to look out for Number One in this world, *mon ami*."

"*Non, non, non*," says Buzzard, "you don't understand. I'm s'posed to wait for somethin' to drop dead before I eat it. It's my job. That's just the way *le Bon Dieu* made me."

from "M'su Carencro and Mangeur de Poulet," retold by J. J. Reneaux

752 UNIT SIX: THE ORAL TRADITION

PRINT AND MEDIA RESOURCES

UNIT SIX RESOURCE BOOK
Writer's Style, p. 23
Prewriting Guide, p. 24
Elaboration, p. 25
Peer Response Guide, pp. 26–27
Revision and Editing, p. 28
Student Model, pp. 29-30
Rubric, p. 31

WRITING MINI-LESSONS
Transparencies, p. 48

GRAMMAR MINI-LESSONS
Transparencies, pp. 32–34
Copymasters, pp. 41–43

ACCESS FOR STUDENTS ACQUIRING ENGLISH
Reading and Writing Support

FORMAL ASSESSMENT
Guidelines for Writing Assessment

 WRITING COACH

Connect to Life

Interviews give celebrities a chance to tell their own stories. In this segment Martina Navratilova and Steffi Graf interview each other about careers they would pick if they couldn't play tennis.

Interview

Navratilova. I think all tennis players want to be rock stars, personally. I could handle that. *[both laugh]* But for me, it would have been an athlete of some kind, because I like to move; I like to see the limits of my body while it's still capable of pushing the limits. I'll explore the limits of my mind later, when the body's not willing anymore. What about you, Steffi?

Graf. The thing is, I got into tennis so early, I didn't give much thought about what else I would have wanted to be. As a kid, I loved animals. I always wanted to be an animal doctor, like any kid. But I was kind of led into tennis. There was no other choice.

from "The Martina and Steffi Dream Team"
Interview magazine

Dialogue Presents Information

What information do you learn from this excerpt? What facts can you gather?

Try Your Hand: Writing Dialogue

1. **Where Are You?** Write a dialogue between two characters. Have them react to a setting without saying where they are. Can you describe the scene through dialogue only?

2. **One-liners** When you think about movies, you often remember certain lines that were especially funny, scary, or dramatic. Write down a couple of lines you remember, and ask yourself what those lines told you about the speaker.

3. **Spectator Sport** Write a few lines of dialogue in which two characters describe an action that they are witnessing. Then write a few lines of dialogue between the characters that are involved in the action directly. Which method is clearer?

SkillBuilder

GRAMMAR FROM WRITING

Using Commas in Quotations

When you are quoting a word, phrase, or clause from a story, use quotation marks to show that it is a quotation. If a comma directly follows a quotation, it is placed inside the quotation marks. In each sentence below, the two clauses are separated by a comma.

When Pecos Bill invented the word "Yahoo," he probably didn't know about Gulliver's Travels.

Osborne writes, "He teethed on horseshoes," but that is an exaggeration to make Bill seem tougher.

Never follow quotation marks with a comma.

APPLYING WHAT YOU'VE LEARNED

Put the quotation marks and commas into these sentences.

1. Bill says You can't do that but Slue-foot Sue wants to ride Widow Maker anyway.
2. Sue should have said I told you so but she was busy riding that horse to the moon.

GRAMMAR HANDBOOK

For more help with using commas in quotations, see page 898 of the Grammar Handbook.

WRITING ABOUT LITERATURE **753**

CUSTOMIZING FOR
Students Acquiring English

C Students may be surprised by the format of this interview, as it does not have the usual interviewer (short question)—interviewee (long answer) structure. Explain to students that this interview is more like a conversation. The two tennis players are discussing what they wanted to be when they were young.

Teaching Strategy: MODELING

D Possible responses: Readers learn about each player's childhood desires. They also get an idea of each player's upbringing and their motivations and values. Navratilova might have wanted to be a rock star, but she looked up to athletes because of her interest in fitness. Graf began earlier so, despite her interest in animals, she became a tennis player when she was very young.

Try Your Hand

1. Dialogues will vary. Students can indicate setting by naming a place or by discussing an activity that is specific to one place.

2. Responses will vary. Encourage students to think about what situation their characters were in and what they may have been thinking as they said these lines.

3. Responses will vary. Here is a sample:
   Paula. Ooh, I don't like that.
   Tim. Well, they seem to. They're eating it all.
   Paula. But it's full of cream and sugar.
   Tim. You don't have to order dessert.
   or
   Paula. Ooh, I don't like this.
   Tim. I do. I've eaten all of mine.
   Paula. How could you? It's full of cream and sugar.
   Tim. I'll eat your dessert if you don't want it.

SkillBuilder — GRAMMAR FROM WRITING

USING COMMAS IN QUOTATIONS

Remind students that only the word or words from the story go inside quotation marks. Students' own writing does not appear inside quotation marks. Have students review the selections in this unit to look for examples of dialogue and quotations. Encourage them to notice commas and other punctuation marks and their position in these passages. Point out that the phrase introducing the quotation often is followed by a comma.

Applying What You've Learned Answers:
1. Bill says, "You can't do that," but Slue-foot Sue wants to ride Widow Maker anyway.
2. Sue should have said "I told you so," but she was busy riding that horse to the moon.

Reteaching/Reinforcement

Grammar Mini-Lessons copymasters pp. 42–43, transparencies pp. 33–34

The Writer's Craft

Commas in Quotations, pp. 651, 664

THE LANGUAGE OF LITERATURE TEACHER'S EDITION **753**

Critical Thinking: CLASSIFYING

E Students can learn more about folk tales by reviewing the selections in this unit. Guide them to find good examples of folk tales, and encourage them to identify which elements are common to folk tales.

Critical Thinking: ANALYZING

F Encourage students to choose one idea or a part of a story on which to base their scene. Then have them imagine ways they can build on that idea or story. Start students off by having them think about numbers of characters, the story they want to use, and where their story will take place.

Writing Skill: DEVELOPING PLOT

G The Plan Your Scene section provides an opportunity for students to think through their ideas and analyze the information they have gathered. Often students have difficulty coming up with plots. Help them to develop their stories by first imagining how many (and which) characters they want and the setting of their scene. Then encourage them to create a situation or situations that will show their story. Ask if there will be a central conflict and how they will develop it in this story.

WRITING ABOUT LITERATURE

Creative Response

E Folk tales present heroic figures, explain natural phenomena, or give moral lessons. Folk tales are also entertaining, but a folk tale survives when it explains or identifies an important belief or element of a community's culture. As the culture changes, the folk tales change or new ones are created that reflect new ideas. Modern writers sometimes bring folk tales to a new audience by turning them into plays.

GUIDED ASSIGNMENT
Write a Play Respond to a tale or legend by writing a scene for a play version of the story.

❶ Prewrite and Explore

F You could respond to a folk tale by updating it for modern times, or you could simply change certain elements. You could even make up a story on your own that is specific to your community. Use questions such as these to brainstorm ideas:

- How could I update the story of Paul Bunyan and his amazing feats?
- If Nima-Cux were a politician's daughter today, what lesson might she be learning?
- Is there something in the natural world that I could explain by writing a legend?

❷ Plan Your Scene

Here are a few ideas to help you get started.

Characters Which characters will you use? Make a list of characters and describe them.

G **Plot** What will happen in your scene? Decide on the events that will take place.

Setting At the beginning of your scene, you'll want to describe the setting in detail. Make a sketch of your stage set to help organize your thoughts.

Write a rough draft of your play that includes your main ideas.

Student's Sketch

754 UNIT SIX: THE ORAL TRADITION

Assessment  Option

SELF-ASSESSMENT After students have completed the Plan Your Scene draft, they can assess their understanding of writing a scene. Students can ask themselves the following questions:
- *Is my scene about one main idea?*
- *How many characters do I have?*
- *Does my plot follow a logical order?*
- *Do I have enough details to make my plot realistic?*
- *Does my stage set have enough details to make it realistic?*

Student's Plan

OLD CHARACTERS	NEW CHARACTERS
Pecos Bill	Bronco Betty
Slue-foot Sue	Buckskin Bob
Hell's Gate Gang	Texas Roping Team

Setting: *a pickup truck center stage, a fence against the back wall, two cow heads leaning over the fence.*

Plot: *Bronco Betty meets up with the Texas Roping Team and plans to lasso a factory and remove it from the desert.*

If I made this a rodeo, there would be different problems to tackle.

3. Draft and Share

When you sit down to write your actual draft, think about everything that you need to express to your audience. Your dialogue and the characters' actions will get the story across. You'll have to think carefully about making every word and movement count.

- Write dialogue to advance the plot, develop characters, or provide information. Don't write dialogue just to fill in time. Think about every line you write.
- Use stage directions that show what the actors are doing. When you write a story, you might say "Bill punched the wall" to show that Bill is angry. In a play, you can't tell the audience that Bill is angry. His words and actions must show it.

Check the Grammar in Context on page 757 to help you format your scene. Try reading your play aloud with a couple of friends, and then ask them these questions.

 **PEER RESPONSE**

- Where did the action and dialogue sound the best?
- What do you think of my set?
- Which character did you like best? Why?

SkillBuilder

 SPEAKING & LISTENING

Giving a Performance

You may have a chance to produce your scene and act in it yourself. If so, you'll want to develop good performance skills such as those below so you can share your scene with friends.

- Speak loudly and clearly and project your voice. Looking at the floor or ceiling directs your voice away from your audience.
- Use gestures to emphasize your lines. Think about the character and what gestures he or she would use. Try to make physical motions as well as words describe the character.
- Exaggerate slightly when you are on stage. Remember that the audience is far away and won't necessarily catch every facial expression or line if you're too subtle.

APPLYING WHAT YOU'VE LEARNED

Get together with some friends and read one another's plays aloud. Critique yourself and your fellow actors, using the suggestions above as criteria.

WRITING ABOUT LITERATURE **755**

Mini-Lesson: Speaking, Listening, and Viewing

GIVING A PERFORMANCE Some students may be hesitant about acting. Help them to get over their reluctance by positioning all actors on stage for maximum effect. If students are reading from scripts, guide them to hold the pages in one hand and direct their voices at the audience and not at the floor.

Applying What You've Learned Remind students to critique each other constructively. If they feel improvements can be made, students should suggest examples to show how. Remind students that performance styles will differ from actor to actor. Point out that the most effective way to play a role is to imagine you are that character.

Additional Suggestions While students are trying out their plays, the audience should take notes and make comments. Often someone not involved in putting on the play can have very useful suggestions.

Teaching Strategy: MODELING

Point out to students that this student's plan is rewriting and updating Mary Pope Osborne's "Pecos Bill." Draw their attention to the lists of characters, the number of details in the setting, and the amount of plot description. Ask how this student has revised the original story. Encourage students to follow this model if they are basing their tales on older stories. Students who are making up new tales or who are revising old stories can also follow this model for extra help.

Writing Skill: DIALOGUE

Remind students that dialogue should sound conversational and show something about a character. Encourage them to imagine actors speaking their words out loud. Students can develop this by imagining how they would respond to other characters, to the scene, and to the events taking place. Help them to develop their plots by making sure their dialogue reveals enough information for their audience.

Speaking and Listening: ROLE-PLAY

Students can work in small groups to try out their scenes. They may need to make copies of their drafts so each character has one. The writer can watch classmates act out the scene, or he or she can act in the scene. For the most effective self-assessment and peer response, writers should try to do both: act and watch.

Critical Thinking: ANALYZING

K To evaluate and analyze their scene, students should use dialogue to give details and to provide information; they should also examine the setting and the characters and think about ways to make the plot more realistic and entertaining

Teaching Strategy: USING THE SKILLBUILDER

L You can help students write their scenes clearly by teaching the SkillBuilder on Direct Address before they begin revising their scenes. It explains how dialogue is presented in a play.

Teaching Strategy: MODELING

M Discuss with students how this sample meets the Standards for Evaluation on this page. Explain that the writer uses dialogue to develop character and plot and to provide information. Betty appears to be a strong and practical character. Bob's words reveal information about the factory. The fact that it is polluting the valley is the central problem. The setting and the whole scene are clearly laid out.

Standards for Evaluation

Ideas and Content
- uses dialogue that enhances and advances the plot
- presents central problem or conflict through plot
- includes stage directions that establish setting, describe action, and give clues to character
- reveals mood and character through dialogue and action

Structure and Form
- is formatted clearly and accurately according to guidelines
- organizes scene effectively so audience can follow story line

Grammar, Usage, and Mechanics
- contains no more than two or three minor errors in grammar and usage
- contains no more than two or three minor errors in spelling, capitalization, and punctuation

---

WRITING ABOUT LITERATURE

4 Revise and Edit

As you continue to work on your scene, you'll probably notice a few things that you want to fix. The most important thing to work on is making sure your audience will be able to follow your story line. Consider producing your scene in class or with some friends, or recording it on video. How would you direct your scene?

Student's Script

Notice that the character descriptions are short.

> **Bronco Betty**
> A Scene for Six Players
>
> Cast of Characters
>
> **Bronco Betty,** who'd rope a comet if it were a challenge
> **Buckskin Bob,** who owns a large ranch and a million cattle
> **Texas Roping Team,** Betty's gang of wild rodeo girls
>
> Scene 1
>
> (*pickup truck in the middle of the stage, cacti on floor, a fence at the back of the stage with two cow heads peering over*)

Betty (*entering stage left*). What seems to be the trouble, rancher? You look perplexed, and I don't think it's just your cowlicks.

Bob. You know what the trouble is.

Betty. Do not. I just rode into town.

Bob. It's that factory. It spits out foul and smelly filth all over the valley and into my horses' and cows' food. I've never seen such trash. It would shame a rat!

Betty. What do they make at that factory? Besides filth?

What information is communicated through this dialogue?

Standards for Evaluation

An effective scene
- uses dialogue that enhances character and advances the plot
- includes stage directions that establish the setting, describe the action, and give clues to character
- presents a central problem or conflict
- is formatted clearly and accurately according to guidelines

756 UNIT SIX: THE ORAL TRADITION

Assessment Option

SELF-ASSESSMENT To help students assess their own writing, they can ask themselves the following questions:
- Have I followed the conventions for showing direct address?
- Did I give short character descriptions?
- Are my characters clearly defined through the use of dialogue?
- Have I provided enough information for my plot to be understood easily?
- Did I describe the setting?

Grammar in Context

Formatting a Script Writing a script is very different from writing a story. Here are a few key points to remember:

- Single-space character and setting descriptions. Double-space speakers' dialogue.
- Center the title of the scene on the page.
- Indent every line of the characters' speeches except the first line.
- Capitalize names of characters in setting descriptions and in dialogue tags.
- Use parentheses to set off your description of the setting at the beginning of the scene or to set off sections of action on stage without dialogue. Use parentheses to set off stage directions within the dialogue.
- Use a period after the character's name at the beginning of a line to show who is speaking. It is not necessary to use quotation marks in a play.

Here's an example of a line of dialogue that shows the correct capitalization, parentheses, and punctuation:

Betty (*motions wildly to the ropers*). Why, you folks are just the kind of maniacs I'm looking for!

The best way to figure out the correct format for a script is to look at a play that has been written correctly. Keep it handy so you can refer to it as you work.

Try Your Hand: Formatting a Script

Rework the draft of your play. Be sure that you have included enough stage direction so that the actors will know exactly what to do and how to say their lines. Use proper formatting to make sure that all of your directions are clear.

SkillBuilder
WRITER'S CRAFT

Showing Direct Address

When you read a play, it's important to know whom the characters are talking to. If someone screams "NO!" how is the reader or actor to know who is talking to whom? There are three ways to show direct address in scripts.

1. Make it obvious through content. Because of the words that are said, the reader can figure out who is hearing them.
   Bob. You're just a woman!
2. Have the character who is speaking say the other character's name in the dialogue, set off by commas.
   Betty. That's right, Bob.
3. Point out in the stage directions whom the actor should be looking at or talking to.
   Bob (*shakes finger at Betty*). You should know better!

APPLYING WHAT YOU'VE LEARNED

Write a few lines for a play in which Slue-foot Sue tells Pecos Bill to go bring in the horses and then tells her maid to cook dinner. Use all three ways of showing direct address.

Writing Skill: FORMATTING A SCRIPT

Guide students to examine their own writing by checking the formatting of their scene. They may need to copy their scenes over to reformat them correctly. Explain that double-spacing means skipping a line before beginning the next character's speech. Advise them that it may take time to format their scenes correctly.

Try Your Hand

Scripts will vary, but all should follow the correct format. Here is a sample:

"Lost in Space"
Cast of Characters
Viv, the captain
Patra, the copilot

(*The planet Atam. Piles of books and papers on the ground. Many desks and chairs form a small hill in the background. Patra is sitting in the middle of the books and papers, looking through them very slowly.*)

Viv (*entering from right*). You've been here all evening. You found the rocket plans yet?

Patra (*looking through books and papers much faster*). I'm sure they were right here. (*panicking*) How're we going to get home? We'll be stuck here all night!

Viv (*firmly*). Rubbish! We'll call home and get the master plans.

Patra (*nervously*). Er . . . 'bout that radio. Seems like we lost that too.

SkillBuilder — WRITER'S CRAFT

SHOWING DIRECT ADDRESS Remind students that these guidelines apply when there are more than two characters on stage. However, writers can use these techniques for any number of players. Show students how these techniques can be combined with revealing details in dialogue and in the characters' actions to show more about the characters.

Applying What You've Learned Responses will vary. Here is a sample:

Sue. (*turning to Bill*). Fetch'em horses when I tell ya.

Bill. You always tellin' me to run for you. Get the maid here to do it for you.

Sue. No way. While you's gettin' them, Bill, she's fixin' me some beans. (*to maid*) Go on, girl. Get to work.

Reteaching/Reinforcement
Writing Mini-Lessons transparencies, p. 48

The Writer's Craft
Dialogue, pp. 324–327

READING THE WORLD

On pages 754–757, students wrote a scene from a play based on a folk tale or fable. Some will have updated the old story. In this lesson, students will examine how a story changes over time. Students will examine the ways that images of Pocahontas, the legendary Powhatan princess, are different depending on the time they were created.

Critical Thinking: ANALYZING

O Students may have difficulty recognizing that these are images of the same person. Explain that this is another example of how the representation of a legendary figure can change. Draw their attention to the clothing and setting of the images. Ask students how much Pocahontas looks like a Native American.

Media Literacy: INTERPRETING AN IMAGE

P Students' suggestions for stories will vary. They may suggest that the image at bottom left suggests a slightly different interpretation from the other two, one that may occur in a more urban setting. The princess at top left seems to be a happy, present-day princess. The one at lower left appears to be intelligent and wealthy. The one at lower right seems thoughtful and content in a natural setting.

Speaking and Listening: GROUP DISCUSSION

Q Students may want to change their perceptions of these images after they have read the SkillBuilder. Students may choose any image as the most real one. Have students speculate why they find a certain image of her most appealing. They may think she has inspired so many interpretations because she seems to have been important and young in a time long ago.

Copyright © The Walt Disney Company, photo courtesy of Photofest.

Painting by an English artist (about 1616)

Still photo from an animated film (1995)

758 UNIT SIX: THE ORAL TRADITION

758 THE LANGUAGE OF LITERATURE TEACHER'S EDITION

READING THE WORLD

REAL OR IDEAL?

In this unit, you've seen how folklore and legends survive and change as a culture changes. Perhaps you responded creatively to one of these tales by updating it as a play. The adaptation of legends over time can take many forms, as the legend of Pocahontas illustrates.

View The images on these pages are all of the Native American princess Pocahontas. Jot down your initial reactions. Note how the images are like and unlike one another.

Interpret These different images came from different time periods. Why do you think these artists portrayed Pocahontas as they did? What kind of princess does each image show?

Discuss Share your reactions. Which image seems most real to you? most appealing? Why do you think Pocahontas inspired so many interpretations? Refer to the SkillBuilder at the right for help in evaluating these images.

SkillBuilder

CRITICAL THINKING

Separating Fiction from Reality

When people tell "true" stories, they often tend to romanticize people and events. Romanticizing means making something seem much more interesting, more dramatic, or more beautiful than it actually is. Romanticizing can also be done to better reflect the values or culture of the times at which a story is told.

For example, some historians believe that Pocahontas was about 12 years old at the time she played the part of the sponsor in a ritual of adoption that was arranged by her father for political reasons. How does the romanticized version of the Pocahontas tale make her story seem more dramatic?

When you hear a story or look at an image, it is important to think about whether what you are seeing or hearing is real or an idealized version of the truth.

APPLYING WHAT YOU'VE LEARNED
Make a list of other stories or people that may have been romanticized. John Henry, Betsy Ross, and the cowhands of the Old West are some examples. Discuss how these stories were romanticized and why you think people tell these stories as they do. What are they trying to accomplish?

Engraving by an American artist (1800s)

SkillBuilder — CRITICAL THINKING

SEPARATING FICTION FROM REALITY
Guide students to understand that they can evaluate stories or images by comparing the image or legend of a person or object to the known facts. In this way, they can see what has been done to that person or thing over time. Encourage students to think of other people or things that are romanticized in the world around them, such as the novelty of a new video game or the bravery or cleverness of someone they admire greatly.

Applying What You've Learned Students' responses will vary but should all consider possible reasons for someone or something being romanticized. For example, students might discuss Paul Revere. They may suggest that Revere's famous ride may not have been exactly as it has been related in fiction. They may further suggest that this romanticizing results from Revere being viewed as a Revolutionary War hero.

UNIT SIX
Lesson Planner: Links to Units 4–5

TIME ALLOTMENTS SHOWN ARE APPROXIMATE. DEPENDING ON YOUR GOALS AND THE NEEDS OF YOUR STUDENTS, YOU MAY WISH TO ALLOW MORE OR LESS TIME FOR CERTAIN PORTIONS OF THE LESSON.

Table of Contents	Discussion	Previewing the Selections	Reading the Selections
LINKS TO UNIT FOUR **Racing the Great Bear** page 762 AVERAGE **Otoonah** page 769 CHALLENGING **The Woman in the Snow** page 775 AVERAGE		**10 MINUTES** • NORTHEASTERN UNITED STATES • PACIFIC COAST • SOUTHEASTERN UNITED STATES	**60 MINUTES** • Introduce vocabulary • Read pp. 762–68 (7 pp.) • Read pp. 769–74 (6 pp.) • Read pp. 775–81 (7 pp.)
LINKS TO UNIT FIVE **Strawberries** page 786 AVERAGE **No News** page 789 EASY **The First Flute** page 791 AVERAGE		**10 MINUTES** • SOUTHEASTERN UNITED STATES • NORTHEASTERN UNITED STATES • GUATEMALA	**30 MINUTES** • Introduce vocabulary • Read pp. 786–88 (3 pp.) • Read pp. 789–90 (2 pp.) • Read pp. 791–95 (5 pp.)

Writing	Exploring Topics	Prewriting	Drafting and Revising
WRITING FROM EXPERIENCE **Writing a Report**	**15 MINUTES**	**30 MINUTES**	**75 MINUTES**

Time estimates assume in-class work. You may wish to assign some of these stages as homework.

Responding Options

- **LITERATURE CONNECTION**
- **CROSS-CURRICULAR CONNECTIONS**
- **CULTURAL CONNECTIONS**

90 MINUTES

LITERATURE CONNECTION	CROSS-CURRICULAR CONNECTIONS	CULTURAL CONNECTIONS
• Create a dust jacket for a book	**SOCIAL STUDIES** • Design a newspaper's front page **SCIENCE** • Construct a diorama of an ecosystem	• Find the enemy in stories • Create an Iroquois time line • Compose a song • Compare/contrast characters

90 MINUTES

• Make a character "report card"	**MATH** • Use the Mayan number system **SOCIAL STUDIES** • Produce a television program	• Tell a story through drawings • Write a letter of advice • Tell an origin myth • Investigate Cherokee beliefs and customs

Publishing and Reflecting

15 MINUTES

LESSON PLANNER TEACHER'S EDITION **759b**

OVERVIEW

Objectives

- To understand and appreciate three tales about how different people have faced their enemies
- To appreciate the distinctive cultures and histories of Iroquois, Eskimo, and African Americans as they are represented in three stories
- To extend understanding of the selection through a variety of multimodal and cross-curricular activities

Reading Pathways

- After students have read these tales once, they can reread them to identify literary techniques such as foreshadowing, exaggeration, onomatopoeia, informal language, and suspense.
- Read the stories aloud to the class, pausing to discuss the cultural and historical background of each. Have students record how this additional information increases their understanding of the story and how it relates to their own cultures.
- Invite volunteers to present each tale to the class. Give students enough time to prepare their oral presentations. Encourage students to practice reading aloud in order to familiarize themselves with the story.

PREVIEWING

LINKS TO UNIT FOUR

Facing the Enemy

Activating Prior Knowledge

Who or what is an enemy? A soldier with a rifle, an impersonal force such as poverty, or an attitude within our own hearts? The selections in Unit Four examine the ways in which people meet a wide range of enemies. Confronting an enemy is an important theme in folklore. The three tales you are about to read feature characters who must stand up to their own enemies.

Building Background

PACIFIC COAST

Otoonah

retold by Robert D. San Souci (săn soo-sē′)

The native peoples of Alaska arrived in North America between 3000 and 1000 B.C. Their way of life changed little until the arrival of European fur traders and whalers in the 1800s. In their bitter-cold world, they have lived by an unwritten rule: help one another to survive and find food. This legend tells how this rule was broken by one family of the Sugpiaq—the people who first settled Kodiak Island, off the coast of Alaska.

760 UNIT SIX: THE ORAL TRADITION

PRINT AND MEDIA RESOURCES

UNIT SIX RESOURCE BOOK
Strategic Reading: Literature, p. 32
Vocabulary SkillBuilder, p. 35
Reading SkillBuilder, p. 33
Spelling SkillBuilder, p. 34

GRAMMAR MINI-LESSONS
Transparencies, p. 15
Copymasters, p. 23

WRITING MINI-LESSONS
Transparencies, p. 46

ACCESS FOR STUDENTS ACQUIRING ENGLISH
Selection Summaries
Reading and Writing Support

FORMAL ASSESSMENT
Selection Test, pp. 139–140
Test Generator

AUDIO LIBRARY
See Reference Card

INTERNET RESOURCES
McDougal Littell Literature Center at http://www.hmco.com/mcdougal/lit

NORTHEASTERN U.S.

Building Background

Racing the Great Bear
retold by Joseph Bruchac (brook´chäk´)

Centered in northern New York State, the Iroquois are not one Native American people but several. In 1570, tribes formed a confederacy known as the League of the Iroquois or the League of Five Nations. Later, the Iroquois became involved in four wars that took place between 1689 and 1763, in which the British and French battled for control of North America. The Iroquois sided with the British. The tribes excelled at warfare. As this legend shows, the Iroquois placed great importance on fighting skills.

Building Background

SOUTHEASTERN U.S.

The Woman in the Snow
retold by Patricia C. McKissack

Unlike legends from the distant past, this one comes out of a modern event—African Americans' struggle for civil rights. By the mid-1950s, several rulings by the U.S. Supreme Court had already brought gains to the fight for equality. The events upon which this tale is based—the bus boycott in Montgomery, Alabama—focused the nation's attention on the boycott's leader, Martin Luther King, Jr. This legend reflects the struggle of King, and of all African Americans, for equal treatment.

Setting a Purpose

AS YOU READ...

Notice the customs of each culture.

Decide what is considered to be good behavior and how it is rewarded.

Decide what traits are seen as negative.

Consider how other cultures value these positive and negative traits.

LINKS TO UNIT FOUR

SUMMARY

Racing the Great Bear When the young men of a Seneca village mysteriously disappear, Swift Runner accepts the chief's challenge to find them. He encounters Nyagwahe, the monster bear who has killed the men. A great chase begins, and Swift Runner eventually catches Nyagwahe. He spares the bear's life after removing his large teeth. Swift Runner brings the dead warriors back to life and returns home as a hero.

Otoonah Faced with starvation, the family of Otoonah decide to send her away to a deserted island. Otoonah is aided by an old man who appears to her in a dream, telling her where to find water and a knife that help her survive. In the spring, she meets her brothers when she is out fishing. They do not believe that she has survived without the help of a man, and they challenge her to a hunt. Otoonah wins, and her brothers try to steal her knife. Otoonah catches the brothers and makes it safely to land during a violent storm that kills them. She returns to her parents' island and later saves the life of the man she marries.

The Woman in the Snow While completing his bus route in a terrible snowstorm, a racist driver refuses to take a young African-American woman and her sick child to the hospital because she does not have the fare. A year later during another snowstorm, the ghost of the woman appears. The frightened driver accidentally hits the gas pedal and is killed after crashing. Twenty-five years later, an African American driver is assigned to the same route. When the ghost appears to him, he allows her to board the bus. He takes her to the hospital, explaining the changes in civil rights that have occurred. The ghost is never seen again.

WORDS TO KNOW

brandishing (brăn´dĭsh-ĭng) *adj.* waving something (such as a weapon) in a threatening manner
brandish *v* (p.774)
console (kən-sōl´) *v.* to comfort (p. 780)
forlorn (fər-lôrn´) *adj.* sad and desperate because of being abandoned (p. 773)
petite (pə-tēt´) *adj.* small and slender (p. 778)
pivotal (pĭv´ə-tl) *adj.* being of central importance (p. 775)
plummet (plŭm´ĭt) *v.* to fall suddenly and steeply (p. 777)
recoil (rĭ-koil´) *v.* to shrink back, as in fear or disgust (p. 778)
savor (sā´vər) *v.* to take great pleasure in (p. 772)

Art Note

Sauk and Fox Bear Claw Necklace (1880) Most Native American tribes considered the claws of bears and the feathers of eagles to possess medicinal powers. Bear claws often were made into decorative necklaces. Besides having medicinal purposes, these objects symbolized social rank.

Reading the Art What does this necklace tell you about the Seneca people's relationship to bears? What social position do you think the wearer would occupy? Explain.

STRATEGIC READING FOR
Less-Proficient Readers

Set a Purpose Before students begin to read, point out that the People of the Longhouse have just made peace after a long period of war. Then have them read to discover why the disappearance of Seneca men on their way to visit the Onondaga threatens this peace.

CUSTOMIZING FOR
Gifted and Talented Students

Challenge students to make a distinction between ordinary time and mythic time as it occurs in the story. Ask how the storyteller's use of time affects their understanding of the story's events.

Linking to Social Studies

A Longhouses were typically 18 to 25 feet wide and 50 to 150 feet long. The roof was formed by arched wooden poles and had holes for smoke to escape from the cooking fires inside. The walls were covered with bark. Many families lived in one longhouse. Each family had a small section that was split into two levels: a top platform where the family could store its possessions, and a lower level where the family slept.

RACING THE GREAT BEAR

RETOLD BY JOSEPH BRUCHAC

NE ONENDJI. HEAR MY STORY, WHICH HAPPENED LONG AGO. FOR MANY GENERATIONS, THE FIVE NATIONS OF THE HAUDENOSAUNEE, THE PEOPLE OF THE LONGHOUSE,[1] HAD BEEN AT WAR WITH ONE ANOTHER.

No one could say how the wars began, but each time a man of one nation was killed, his relatives sought revenge in the blood feud, and so the fighting continued. Then the Creator took pity on his people and sent a messenger of peace. The Peacemaker traveled from nation to nation, convincing the people of the Five Nations—the Mohawk, the Oneida, the Onondaga, the Cayuga, and the Seneca—that it was wrong for brothers to kill one another. It

---

1. **the Longhouse:** a large group dwelling used by some Native American groups, particularly the five tribes of the Iroquois Nation.

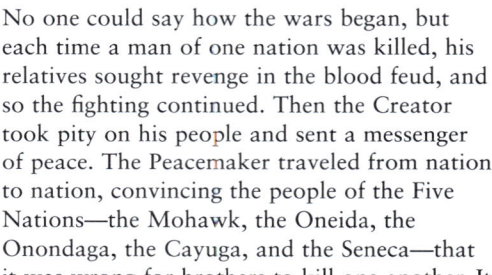

Multicultural Perspectives

IROQUOIS WOMEN The old chief's consultation of the clan mothers shows that women had a great deal of power in Iroquois society. The Iroquois were matrilocal—young married couples went to live in the house of the woman's mother. They were also matrilineal, meaning that a person's descent was traced through the mother's family rather than the father's. All of the family's possessions belonged to the women. Additionally, although the council that governed each tribe of the Iroquois nation was composed exclusively of men, the women elected each member and could remove any member with whom they were dissatisfied.

was not easy, but finally the nations agreed, and the Great Peace began. Most welcomed that peace, though there were some beings with bad hearts who wished to see the return of war.

One day, not long after the Great Peace had been established, some young men in a Seneca village decided they would pay a visit to the Onondaga people.

"It is safe now to walk the trail between our nations," the young men said. "We will return after the sun has risen and set seven times."

Then they set out. They walked toward the east until they were lost from sight in the hills. But many more than seven days passed, and those young men never returned. Now another group of young men left, wanting to find out where their friends had gone. They, too, did not return.

The people grew worried. Parties were sent out to look for the vanished young men, but no sign was found. And the searchers who went too far into the hills did not return, either.

The old chief of the village thought long and hard. He asked the clan mothers, those wise women whose job it was to choose the chiefs and give them good advice, what should be done.

"We must find someone brave enough to face whatever danger is out there," the clan mothers said.

So the old chief called the whole village to a council meeting. He held up a white strand of wampum beads[2] made from quahog[3] clamshells as he spoke.

"Hear me," he said. "I am of two minds about what has happened to our people. It may be that the Onondaga have broken the peace and captured them. It may be there is something with an evil mind that wishes to destroy this new peace and so has killed our people. Now someone must go and find out. Who is brave enough? Who will come and take this wampum from my hand?"

Many men were gathered in that council. Some were known to speak of themselves as brave warriors. Still, though they muttered to one another, no man stepped forward to take the strand of wampum. The old chief began to walk about the circle, holding the wampum in front of each man in turn. But each man only lowered his eyes to the ground. No man lifted his hand to take the wampum.

Just outside the circle stood a boy who had not yet become a man. His parents were dead, and he lived with his grandmother in her old lodge at the edge of the village. His clothing was always torn and his face dirty because his grandmother was too old to care for him as a mother would. The other young men made fun of him, and as a joke they called him Swift Runner—even though no one had ever seen him run and it was thought that he was weak and lazy. All he ever seemed to do was play with his little dog or sit by the fire and listen when the old people were talking.

"Our chief has forgotten our greatest warrior," one of the young men said to another, tilting his head toward Swift Runner.

"*Nyoh,*" the other young man said, laughing. "Yes. Why does he not offer the wampum to Swift Runner?"

The chief looked around the circle of men, and the laughing stopped. He walked out of the circle to the place where the small boy in torn clothes stood. He held out the wampum, and Swift Runner took it without hesitating.

"I accept this," Swift Runner said. "It is right that I be the one to face the danger. In the eyes of the people I am worthless, so if I do not return, it will not matter. I will leave when the sun rises tomorrow."

---

2. **wampum beads:** beads that are made from seashells and that were first used for ceremonial and historical purposes, and then also used as money.
3. **quahog** (kwô′hôg′): a type of clam with a hard, rounded shell.

RACING THE GREAT BEAR   763

CUSTOMIZING FOR
Multiple Learning Styles

Bodily-Kinesthetic Learners Have students chart the physical challenges that Swift Runner faces in his race to catch up with the Great Bear. Encourage students to compare what these challenges would correspond to in modern terms; for example, wearing through a pair of moccasins might be similar to wearing out a pair of sneakers.

Art Note

***Orion in December* by Charles Burchfield** In Greek mythology, the mortal hunter Orion was accidentally killed by Artemis, the goddess of the hunt. After his death, Orion's body was lifted into the sky and can still be seen in the constellation that bears his name. In *Orion in December*, Burchfield (1893–1967) draws attention to the earthly origins of the constellation—the stars seem to reach down through the steely white of the winter landscape.

Reading the Art *Does this night sky look threatening or inviting? Explain. How would you describe the painting's depiction of the trees and stars?*

Orion in December (1959), Charles E. Burchfield. Watercolor and pencil on paper, 39⅞" × 32⅞", National Museum of American Art, gift of S. C. Johnson & Son, Inc., Smithsonian Institution, Washington, D.C./Art Resource, New York.

764 UNIT SIX: THE ORAL TRADITION

Mini-Lesson Spelling

COMPOUND WORDS Tell students that a compound word is made up of two smaller words, for example, *grandmother* and *afternoon*.

Application Have students spell the following compound words as you dictate them.

1. longhouse
2. peacemaker
3. daylight
4. Thanksgiving
5. nightmare
6. wonderland
7. headlights
8. cornmeal
9. hummingbird
10. whirlwind
11. driftwood
12. themselves
13. everywhere
14. something

Ask students to look for more words that fit this pattern, in their own writing and in things that they read, and to add these words to their personal words lists.

Reteaching/ Reinforcement
- *Unit Six Resource Book*, p 34

764 THE LANGUAGE OF LITERATURE   TEACHER'S EDITION

When Swift Runner arrived home at his grandmother's lodge, the old woman was waiting for him.

"Grandson," she said, "I know what you have done. The people of this village no longer remember, but your father was a great warrior. Our family is a family that has power."

Then she reached up into the rafters and took down a heavy bow. It was blackened with smoke and seemed so thick that no man could bend it.

"If you can string this bow, Grandson," the old woman said, "you are ready to face whatever waits for you on the trail."

Swift Runner took the bow. It was as thick as a man's wrist, but he bent it with ease and strung it.

"Wah-hah!" said his grandmother. "You are the one I knew you would grow up to be. Now you must sleep. At dawn we will make you ready for your journey."

It was not easy for Swift Runner to sleep, but when he woke the next morning, he felt strong and clear-headed. His grandmother was sitting by the fire with a cap in her hand.

"This was your grandfather's cap," she said. "I have sewed four hummingbird feathers on it. It will make your feet more swift."

Swift Runner took the cap and placed it on his head.

His grandmother held up four pairs of moccasins. "Carry these tied to your waist. When one pair wears out, throw them aside and put on the next pair."

Swift Runner took the moccasins and tied them to his belt.

Next his grandmother picked up a small pouch. "In this pouch is cornmeal mixed with maple sugar," she said. "It is the only food you will need as you travel. It will give you strength when you eat it each evening."

Swift Runner took the pouch and hung it from his belt by the moccasins.

"The last thing I must give you," said the old woman, "is this advice. Pay close attention to your little dog. You have treated him well, and so he is your great friend. He is small, but his eyes and nose are keen. Keep him always in front of you. He will warn you of danger before it can strike you."

Then Swift Runner set out on his journey. His little dog stayed ahead of him, sniffing the air and sniffing the ground. By the time the sun was in the middle of the sky, they were far from the village. The trail passed through deep woods, and it seemed to the boy as if something was following them among the trees. But he could see nothing in the thick brush.

The trail curved toward the left, and the boy felt even more the presence of something watching. Suddenly his little dog ran into the brush at the side of the trail, barking loudly. There were the sounds of tree limbs breaking and heavy feet running. Then out of the forest came a Nyagwahe, a monster bear. Its great teeth were as long as a man's arm. It was twice as tall as a moose. Close at its heels was Swift Runner's little dog.

"I see you," Swift Runner shouted. "I am after you. You cannot escape me."

Swift Runner had learned those words by listening to the stories the old people told. They were the very words a monster bear speaks when it attacks, words that terrify anyone who hears them. On hearing those words, the great bear turned and fled from the boy.

"You cannot escape me," Swift Runner shouted again. Then he ran after the bear.

The Nyagwahe turned toward the east, with Swift Runner and his dog close behind. It left the trail and plowed through the thick forest, breaking down great trees and leaving a path of destruction like that of a whirlwind. It ran up the tallest hills and down through the swamps, but the boy and the dog stayed at its heels. They ran past a great cave in the rocks.

RACING THE GREAT BEAR **765**

Active Reading: CLARIFY

D Ask students to explain how the account by Swift Runner's grandmother of their family's past enriches readers' understanding of the story. To promote discussion, you may wish to provide students with the following model:

Think-Aloud Model *I think that the grandmother's discussion about Swift Runner's family is very important because no one in the whole tribe thinks he is capable of the challenge before him. Since he comes from a family known for its warriors, it does not appear strange that Swift Runner would try to discover what happened to the lost men. By showing that he is capable of stringing the bow, Swift Runner demonstrates he can match the power and courage of his father.*

Critical Thinking: SPECULATING

E Have students review the items and advice that his grandmother gives to Swift Runner. *(She gives him four pairs of moccasins and a pouch of food, and warns him to stay close to his dog.)* Ask students what these items and advice might suggest about Swift Runner's journey. *(Possible responses: The moccasins suggest that he will travel a great distance; the food pouch suggests that he will have little time to find food; and the advice to stay close to his dog suggests that he may be attacked before the story is over.)*

Literary Concept: CONFLICT

F Ask students to explain what conflicts Swift Runner has faced so far in the story. *(Possible response: Swift Runner has had to face the entire tribe, his own doubts about his abilities, and Nyagwahe.)*

CUSTOMIZING FOR
Students Acquiring English

4 Explain that *at its heels* means "close behind him."

Mini-Lesson The Writer's Style

SHOW, DON'T TELL Help students understand that the oral nature of storytelling makes it important that the storyteller show his or her listening audience the events of the story. Explain that richness of detail is necessary to keep listeners' attention, especially if the plot is complex or if the story is long.

Application In the passage highlighted above, Joseph Bruchac not only tells his listeners that Swift Runner comes from a line of warriors but also shows the boy performing the daunting task of stringing an enormous bow. Have students write two or three paragraphs about an experience where they demonstrated a talent or an ability to someone else. Pair students and have them exchange their work. Each partner should review and comment on how well the writer has shown readers the event.

Reteaching/Reinforcement
- *Writing Handbook*, anthology p. 833
- *Writing Mini-Lessons* transparencies p. 46

 Show, Don't Tell, pp. 262–66

STRATEGIC READING FOR
Less-Proficient Readers

G Ask students to review the two explanations the chief had for why the men disappeared. Ask them which of the two proved to be correct. *(The chief's idea that an unknown evil was threatening to undermine the new peace was right. It was not the Onondaga that were responsible for the men's death, even though many blamed them.)*
Summarizing/Noting Relevant Details

Set a Purpose Have students read to see what Swift Runner does with the bones of the young men.

Active Reading: CONNECT

H Ask students to put themselves in the place of Swift Runner. Ask them if they think they would be able to sleep after meeting Nyagwahe. *(Possible responses: I would be so terrified if visited by a creature like Nyagwahe, even in his human form, that I probably would not sleep for days. If I had the knowledge and the confidence in my abilities that Swift Runner seems to have, I also would be able to sleep easily.)*

Literary Concept: HYPERBOLE

I Have students discuss whether the storyteller is exaggerating elements of the story to increase listeners' interest, or if the story is meant to be taken literally. *(Possible responses: It is doubtful that anyone could run as long as Swift Runner, and creatures like Nyagwahe do not really exist, so the storyteller is exaggerating to increase listeners' interest.)*

HE TOOK OFF HIS FIRST PAIR OF MOCCASINS, WHOSE SOLES WERE WORN AWAY TO NOTHING. HE THREW THEM ASIDE AND PUT ON A NEW PAIR.

All around the cave were the bones of people the bear had caught and eaten.

"My relatives," Swift Runner called as he passed the cave, "I will not forget you. I am after the one who killed you. He will not escape me."

Throughout the day, the boy and his dog chased the great bear, growing closer bit by bit. At last, as the sun began to set, Swift Runner stopped at the head of a small valley and called his small dog to him.

"We will rest here for the night," the boy said. He took off his first pair of moccasins, whose soles were worn away to nothing. He threw them aside and put on a new pair. Swift Runner made a fire and sat beside it with his dog. Then he took out the pouch of cornmeal and maple sugar, sharing his food with his dog.

"Nothing will harm us," Swift Runner said. "Nothing can come close to our fire." He lay down and slept.

In the middle of the night, he was awakened by the growling of his dog. He sat up with his back to the fire and looked into the darkness. There, just outside the circle of light made by the flames, stood a dark figure that looked like a tall man. Its eyes glowed green.

"I am Nyagwahe," said the figure. "This is my human shape. Why do you pursue me?"

"You cannot escape me," Swift Runner said. "I chase you because you killed my people. I will not stop until I catch you and kill you."

The figure faded back into the darkness.

"You cannot escape me," Swift Runner said again. Then he patted his small dog and went to sleep.

As soon as the first light of the new day appeared, Swift Runner rose. He and his small dog took the trail. It was easy to follow the monster's path, for trees were uprooted and the earth torn by its great paws. They ran all through the morning. When the sun was in the middle of the sky, they reached the head of another valley. At the other end they saw the great bear running toward the east. Swift Runner pulled off his second pair of moccasins, whose soles were worn away to nothing. He put on his third pair and began to run again.

All through that day, they kept the Nyagwahe in sight, drawing closer bit by bit. When the

Kit Fox Society bow-lance, No Two Horns (Hunkpapa). State Historical Society of North Dakota (SHSND 10491).

766 UNIT SIX: THE ORAL TRADITION

Art Note

Kit Fox Society bow-lance by No Two Horns No Two Horns (1852–1942) was a member of the Kit Fox Society of the Hunkpapa. The Kit Fox Society earned its name because of the "active and wily" character of society members during battle. This decorated bow with a spear at one end was used as a weapon, as a social banner, and as a stick. In battle, the bow would be stuck into the ground and fighting would occur near it; it was thought to provide protection.

Reading the Art Is this how you pictured Swift Runner's bow? If not, explain your thoughts.

sun began to set, Swift Runner stopped to make camp. He took off the third pair of moccasins, whose soles were worn away to nothing, and put on the last pair.

"Tomorrow," he said to his small dog, "we will catch the monster and kill it." He reached for his pouch of cornmeal and maple sugar, but when he opened it, he found it filled with worms. The magic of the Nyagwahe had done this. Swift Runner poured out the pouch and said in a loud voice, "You have spoiled our food, but it will not stop me. I am on your trail. You cannot escape me."

That night, once again, he was awakened by the growling of his dog. A dark figure stood just outside the circle of light. It looked smaller than the night before, and the glow of its eyes was weak.

"I am Nyagwahe," the dark figure said. "Why do you pursue me?"

"You cannot escape me," Swift Runner said. "I am on your trail. You killed my people. You threatened the Great Peace. I will not rest until I catch you."

"Hear me," said the Nyagwahe. "I see your power is greater than mine. Do not kill me. When you catch me, take my great teeth. They are my power, and you can use them for healing. Spare my life, and I will go far to the north and never again bother the People of the Longhouse."

"You cannot escape me," Swift Runner said. "I am on your trail."

The dark figure faded back into the darkness, and Swift Runner sat for a long time, looking into the night.

At the first light of day, the boy and his dog took the trail. They had not gone far when they saw the Nyagwahe ahead of them. Its sides puffed in and out as it ran. The trail was beside a big lake with many alder trees close to the water. As the great bear ran past, the leaves were torn from the trees. Fast as the bear went, the boy and his dog came closer, bit by bit. At last, when the sun was in the middle of the sky, the giant bear could run no longer. It fell heavily to the earth, panting so hard that it stirred up clouds of dust.

Swift Runner unslung his grandfather's bow and notched an arrow to the sinewy string.

"Shoot for my heart," said the Nyagwahe. "Aim well. If you cannot kill me with one arrow, I will take your life."

"No," Swift Runner said. "I have listened to the stories of my elders. Your only weak spot is the sole of your foot. Hold up your foot and I will kill you."

The great bear shook with fear. "You have defeated me," it pleaded. "Spare my life and I will leave forever."

"You must give me your great teeth," Swift Runner said. "Then you must leave and never bother the People of the Longhouse again."

"I shall do as you say," said the Nyagwahe. "Take my great teeth."

Swift Runner lowered his bow. He stepped forward and pulled out the great bear's teeth. It rose to its feet and walked to the north, growing smaller as it went. It went over the hill and was gone.

RACING THE GREAT BEAR **767**

Active Reading: PREDICT

J Ask students what the changed appearance of the Nyagwahe suggests about the ending of the chase. *(Possible responses: Although Swift Runner's strength may be diminished because of his lack of food, Nyagwahe's physical appearance has visibly changed. This suggests that Swift Runner will soon be able to overtake and defeat the monster.)*

Critical Thinking: SYNTHESIZING

K Have students compare the two visits of the Nyagwahe. Ask them how the response of Swift Runner changed the second night. *(Possible response: Although he still says that he will not stop until he catches the Great Bear, Swift Runner does not immediately fall back to sleep. He considers whether he should kill the monster or spare his life to gain his power.)*

Literary Links

L Have students examine the experiences of Swift Runner and Paul Revere as Henry Wadsworth Longfellow portrayed him in "Paul Revere's Ride." Ask how their missions are alike and different. *(Possible response: Both Swift Runner and Revere must accomplish their dangerous tasks alone, and both are racing either to catch up to or outrun their enemy for the good of their entire community. However, Revere is already an accomplished silversmith at the time of his ride, while Swift Runner is still an unproven youth.)*

Multicultural Perspectives

THE IROQUOIS LEAGUE OF NATIONS

According to legend, the idea for peace between warring tribes appeared to a holy man named Deganawidah in a vision. He pictured the tribes gathered under a great tree, with a giant eagle perched in its top branches to warn of approaching enemies. Hiawatha, a Mohawk, heard of Deganawidah's dream, and went from tribe to tribe in an effort to secure peace. By 1570, he managed to unite the Mohawk, Seneca, Onondaga, Cayuga, and Oneida tribes into the League of Five Nations.

The Great Council of the League of Five Nations was a democratic body composed of 50 members. It met each year in Onondaga territory, near what is now Syracuse, New York. Each member of the Great Council was known as a sachem, and he was expected to stand before the council and give advice on problems facing the Five Nations. It was only after all members had come to a unanimous decision that action could be taken on an issue before the council. In 1715, the Tuscarora Indians joined with the other tribes to create the League of Six Nations.

Carrying the teeth of the Nyagwahe over his shoulder, Swift Runner turned back to the west, his dog at his side. He walked for three moons before he reached the place where the bones of his people were piled in front of the monster's empty cave. He collected those bones and walked around them four times. "Now," he said. "I must do something to make my people wake up." He went to a big hickory tree and began to push it over so that it would fall on the pile of bones.

"My people," he shouted, "get up quickly or this tree will land on you."

The bones of the people who had been killed all came together and jumped up, alive again and covered with flesh. They were filled with joy and gathered around Swift Runner.

"Great one," they said, "who are you?"

"I am Swift Runner," he said.

"How can that be?" one of the men said. "Swift Runner is a skinny little boy. You are a tall, strong man."

Swift Runner looked at himself and saw that it was so. He was taller than the tallest man, and his little dog was bigger than a wolf.

"I am Swift Runner," he said. "I was that boy, and I am the man you see before you."

Then Swift Runner led his people back to the village. He carried with him the teeth of the Nyagwahe, and those who saw what he carried rejoiced. The trails were safe again, and the Great Peace would not be broken. Swift Runner went to his grandmother's lodge and embraced her.

"Grandson," she said, "you are now the man I knew you would grow up to be. Remember to use your power to help the people."

So it was that Swift Runner ran with the great bear and won the race. Throughout his long life, he used the teeth of the Nyagwahe to heal the sick, and he worked always to keep the Great Peace.

Da neho. I am finished. ❖

JOSEPH BRUCHAC

Joseph Bruchac (1942–), whose ancestors include members of the Abenaki tribe, shares his extensive knowledge of Native American culture through his books, poetry, storytelling, and music.

Bruchac was raised by his grandparents in the foothills of the Adirondack Mountains. For years his grandfather denied that Bruchac had any Native American heritage because he did not want him to encounter prejudice. It was not until Bruchac was an adult that he uncovered the truth and began to appreciate the rich folklore of his Native American ancestors.

Bruchac has authored or co-authored more than 50 books. He states that one of the reasons he writes is "to share my insights into the beautiful and all too fragile world of human life and living things." In 1970, he and his wife founded the Greenfield Review Press, which publishes multicultural literature.

Bruchac has won many awards, including a Cherokee Nation Prose Award, and several National Endowment for the Arts grants. He writes "not to be a man apart, but to share."

OTHER WORKS *Dawn Land; Flying with the Eagle, Racing the Great Bear; The Girl Who Married the Moon* (with Gayle Ross); *Native American Stories*

768   UNIT SIX: THE ORAL TRADITION

OTOONAH

RETOLD BY ROBERT D. SAN SOUCI

A Man Cooking Fish as His Wife Softens Kamiks, unknown Inuit artist. Stonecut, 25″ × 39¼″, by permission of the Amway Environmental Foundation.

In those days of the past, there was an Eskimo family—the parents, two brothers, and a sister—who lived in a village near the ocean. Summer was nearly at an end, and bitter winter was coming soon. For one family, the hunting had been especially bad: they had found few edible plants and berries to store, and they had fewer fish and eggs to bury in the ground, where they wouldn't spoil.

One day, the brothers sent their younger sister to gather driftwood from the beach near the family's sod house. When she was gone, the older brother, Nanoona, said to his parents, "There is not enough food for five people. We must send our sister away. She is weak and does not hunt, yet she eats our food. Soon my brother and I will grow too weak to hunt. Then we will all starve."

Next the younger brother, Avraluk, said, "Four can live when five cannot. We will row our sister across the sea to one of the islands and leave her there."

Sadly, the parents agreed to this.

When the girl, Otoonah, returned with an armful of wood, her brothers told her what they had decided. "*Ahpah!* Father! *Ahkah!* Mother!" the wretched girl cried. But her parents turned away and would not look at her. Then her brothers put her in the family's large sealskin boat and rowed her to an island

---

Mini-Lesson Genre Study

FOLKLORE One of the most common folklore stories is the hero-myth. The three parts common to every hero-myth are outlined on the chart.

Application Have students choose one of the selections and review it, looking for the elements of the hero-myth. Have students create a story map of the selection's plot and compare it to the three elements. Group students according to their selection choices and have them discuss their comparisons. Encourage them to consider how the idea of a hero is similar in the different stories they have read in this unit.

> 1. The separation of the hero from his or her home, either willingly or unwillingly, on a journey or quest.
> 2. The hero is isolated and faces difficult or impossible tasks.
> 3. The successful hero returns to his or her society and is presented with some form of reward.

Art Note

A Man Cooking Fish as His Wife Softens Kamiks by Unknown Artist

This Inuit stonecut details a man and woman performing everyday tasks. The stonecut indicates how much of the couple's life is dependent on nature—their clothes, their food, even their art works.

Reading the Art *What does this stonecut suggest about the lives of the couple depicted?*

STRATEGIC READING FOR
Less-Proficient Readers

Set a Purpose Have students read to find out what skills Otoonah develops to survive on her own.

Linking to Social Studies

A *Eskimo* is a Native American word that means "eaters of raw meat." The Eskimo live throughout the Arctic Circle, from the northeastern tip of Russia, across Alaska, northern Canada, and Greenland. The Eskimo refer to themselves as "the people." They are *Inupiat* and *Yupik* in Alaska, *Inuit* in Canada, and *Yuit* in Siberia.

Literary Links

B In both "Otoonah" and "Battle by the Breadfruit Tree," families are put in difficult situations. Have students compare the responses of Otoonah's family to that of the baboons. (*Possible response: When faced with possible starvation, Otoonah's family decides to preserve itself by sacrificing her. When facing a situation that threatens the lives of herself and her offspring, the baboon mother sacrifices her own life in order to protect her baby.*)

Cultural Note

C The abandonment of a member of a family was never an acceptable practice for the Eskimo. In fact, most family relationships, particularly between parents and children, were very loving and permissive.

Cultural Note

D The Eskimo believed in many types of spirits, which corresponded to different aspects of nature. One of the most important of these was a sea goddess named Sedna who lived at the bottom of the ocean. It was important to please her because she controlled the whales, seals, and sea animals the Eskimo depended on for survival. In order to appease her, the Eskimo in Alaska saved parts of the seals they killed to use as offerings in a special yearly ceremony.

STRATEGIC READING FOR
Less-Proficient Readers

E Ask students to review the skills Otoonah develops that help her survive alone. *(She makes weapons to hunt with, becomes a skilled hunter, makes her own clothing and kayak, and lines her hut with furs for warmth.)* **Noting Relevant Details**

Set a Purpose Have students read to discover how Otoonah's hunting skills compare to those of her brothers.

Active Reading: CONNECT

F Invite students to imagine that they are Otoonah. Ask them how they might feel if they were in her place. Provide students with the following model to assist in discussion:

Think-Aloud Model *I don't know if I would be able to live like Otoonah. She has many practical skills that enable her to survive, and on top of that she seems especially resourceful for someone young and on her own. It would be particularly hard for me to live with the isolation, especially after having been abandoned by my family.*

---

below the horizon. There they left her with only the poorest caribou hide that the family owned and flints to start a fire.

For a long time, she did nothing but sob. All the time she stared in the direction where the sun rises and imagined she could see traces of the mainland. Over and over she sang,

> Oh poor me!
> Oh unhappy daughter!
> So sad am I, so sad
> And so lonely!

Finally, when her hunger grew too much to bear, she gathered seaweed from the shore to eat. Then, piling up stones, she made herself a tiny hut. She wrapped herself in the skin at night. When she awoke, she ate more seaweed. But she grew weaker and weaker.

Then, one night, in her makeshift shelter of stones, an old man came to her in a dream. "Walk to the west until you find a broad, swift-flowing stream beside sweet berry bushes. Drink two times from the water, but do not drink again. And do not eat even one berry. But you will find there one other thing that you may take with you."

She awoke soon after this and walked for a long time over the stony ground until she found the broad, swift-flowing stream bordered with berry bushes.

Kneeling, she cupped her hands and drank. The first time she sipped the water, she felt her strength returning. The second time, she felt herself growing stronger still. Although she was still thirsty and hungry, she did as the old man in the dream had told her. She did not take a single drop more or taste a single ripe berry.

Looking across the current, she saw an *ulu*, a knife, with a carved ivory handle lying on a flat rock. With her newfound strength, she lifted a tree trunk and set it over the stream. Then she claimed the knife.

In the days that followed, she used the knife to make a bird spear, harpoon, and a bow and arrows for herself. She practiced throwing the spear and harpoon and shooting arrows until she became skilled at using these weapons.

At the same time, she explored the island and discovered that it was a plentiful hunting ground, with ptarmigans[1] and hares and seals that would sun themselves on the rocks. So she was able to provide plenty of food for herself. Then she made herself clothing, boots, and a cape of sealskin that she had scraped and stretched on the ground to dry. As the days grew cold, she even built a kayak.[2]

Sitting by herself in the warmth of her hut, over which she had packed dirt and which was filled with furs, she often dreamed of sailing home across the sea. She vowed to punish her brothers and her parents who had abandoned her so heartlessly.

Ice began to form on ponds and on the sea. Otoonah could no longer take her kayak out because the ice would pierce its skin cover. Snow fell and piled up against the hut; winds began to howl across the island. But she had plenty of dried seal meat and fish. Inside the shelter it was warm, lit by the yellow flame of a lamp that she had carved from soapstone. The wick was made of moss, and the basin was filled with oil from blubber that she had chewed to release the fuel. Several dried seal stomachs hung on the wall, holding more oil.

When the storms were at their worst and she was weathered in, the young woman sat on her bed platform covered with shrubs and skins and sang songs. Some she remembered her mother singing to her; some she made up:

---

1. **ptarmigans** (tär′mĭ-gənz): birds that are a basic part of the traditional Eskimo diet.
2. **kayak** (kī′ăk′): a watertight canoe completely covered with skins except for a small opening in the center.

770 UNIT SIX: THE ORAL TRADITION

Multicultural Perspectives

THE ARCTIC CLIMATE Students may be interested to learn that most of the Arctic is composed of huge, frozen plains known as tundra. Contrary to popular belief, there is a low level of snowfall in the Arctic, only about 6 to 10 inches of precipitation a year. However, this snow has little chance of melting and can build up for many months. Thick sheets of ice also cover most of the northern Arctic Circle, and the lakes and rivers are frozen for most of the year.

Because the ground is frozen for much of the year, only a few shrubs and bushes can grow, and there are no trees or forests. However, in the summer, lichens, mosses, and even wildflowers grow.

Besides the fishing, there are a number of animals the Eskimo hunt for food. There are Arctic hares and foxes, musk oxen, and polar bears. For several months a year, caribou migrate north, as do ducks, geese, and other birds.

Art Note

Proud Hunter by Pudlo Pudlat In this stonecut by Pudlo Pudlat, a hunter proudly displays his catch. The similarities between the animal and the hunter's coat suggest that successful hunting is not only a source of pride for the hunter but also a source of survival.

Reading the Art How does this stonecut suggest or resemble Otoonah's situation? Explain your answer.

Linking to Geography

G Throughout the Arctic Circle, the winters are long and severe. Temperatures during the winter months average from −20°F to −30°F (−29°C to −34°C). Strong winds make these bitter temperatures seem colder.

Critical Thinking: MAKING JUDGMENTS

H Have students discuss the brothers' response to seeing their sister alive and well after the winter. *(Possible responses: The brothers are shocked that Otoonah is still alive and do not know what to say to her. The brothers may be envious of her good health and prosperity.)*

---

happy songs about summer warmth, bitter songs about loneliness, or boastful songs that she would someday sing when she returned well-fed to mock her starving family.

G The long Arctic night arrived. At noon, the sun—too weary to climb above the horizon—spread the thin light of false dawn over a world blanketed with snow and ice.

Now the young woman hunted seals by finding one of their breathing holes in the icebound sea. She would pile up blocks of snow and sit motionlessly. When she heard a seal snort, she would instantly plunge her harpoon straight down, haul the unhappy creature onto the ice, and finish it off.

In time, she recognized the promise of spring as the first rays of sunlight touched the highest peaks far inland. Although terrible cold still gripped the island, the coming of daylight made hunting easier. Soon the ice mass covering the sea began to break apart into smaller floes.[3]

One day, approaching her favorite hunting area, the young woman heard human voices. At first the sound alone startled her. She was even more astounded to discover that she knew those voices. Running forward, she met her brothers, who were just beaching their kayaks on the shore. At the sight of them, the young woman forgot all her thoughts of revenge.

The two men raised their harpoons at the sight of this strange person running toward them. But they lowered them when they heard her call out, "Nanoona! Avraluk! I am your sister. I am Otoonah!"

Hungry for the sound of human voices, she asked them many questions about her old home and her parents. But they merely shrugged and spoke a few words. They could only stare at the fine furs she wore and the **glow of well-fed, good health in her face.** **H**

Proud Hunter (1987), Pudlo Pudlat. Stonecut, 21½" × 24", by permission of the Amway Environmental Foundation.

3. **floes** (flōz): sheets of floating ice.

OTOONAH **771**

Mini-Lesson Grammar

TROUBLESOME MODIFIERS Remind students that *good* is always an adjective and modifies nouns or pronouns. *Well* is often used as an adverb and so modifies a verb. *Well* also can be used as an adjective, usually to describe someone's health, as in "I feel well." Refer students to the highlighted passage to demonstrate the correct usage of the modifiers:

well-fed: *well* is an adverb modifying the verb *fed*;

good health: *good* is an adjective modifying the noun *health*.

Application Have students choose the word that correctly completes each sentence.

1. The brothers did not behave very (good, <u>well</u>) when they sent Otoonah away. They were far from being (well, <u>good</u>) men.
2. Although the food Otoonah gave her brothers was (<u>good</u>, well), they did not thank her for it.

Reteaching/Reinforcement
- *Grammar Handbook*, anthology p. 881
- *Grammar Mini-Lessons* copymasters p. 23, transparencies p. 15

 The Writer's Craft

Good and *Well*, pp. 516, 689

THE LANGUAGE OF LITERATURE **TEACHER'S EDITION** **771**

Art Note

***Walrus Hunt* by Lucassie Tukaluk** In this stonecut, an Inuit hunter is poised to kill his prey. The simply rendered scene communicates the drama of the situation by suggesting the physical abilities needed to successfully complete a hunt.

Reading the Art *Is it easy to imagine Otoonah killing a walrus in this manner? Why or why not?*

Linking to Social Studies

 Most Eskimo practice bilateral kinship—they trace their descent from both their mother and their father. As a result, there is a high degree of equality between the sexes in daily Eskimo life. However, as this passage suggests, certain jobs such as hunting were done primarily by men, leading the brothers to misunderstand Otoonah's abilities.

STRATEGIC READING FOR
Less-Proficient Readers

Have students discuss how Otoonah's hunting skills compare to her brothers' skills. *(The brothers think that because Otoonah is a woman, she cannot possibly compete with them. They are sure that she will lose if they go out hunting. Although she is angered by her brothers' attitude, Otoonah accepts their challenge. When she wins the hunt, her brothers are furious.)* **Summarizing**

Set a Purpose Ask students to finish reading and notice how Otoonah's hunting abilities help save the man she wants to marry.

Walrus Hunt (1986), Lucassie Tukaluk. Stonecut, 14½″ × 18″, by permission of the Amway Environmental Foundation.

"What man has given you so much food and such fine furs?" her older brother demanded.

"Your husband must give us a portion of what he has," said her younger brother, "since he has married our sister."

Angrily, she said, "No man has given me anything. What I have I have been given by the Old Woman of the Sea who let me take some of the seals and fish in her keeping."

"No woman is such a good hunter," said her older brother. Then they both laughed at her.

"If you are such a hunter," Nanoona continued, "I would challenge you to a hunt."

"And I," Avraluk added.

Angered by their laughter, the young woman said, "I accept your challenge."

They waited until she had launched her own kayak. Then they zigzagged swiftly amid the ice floes. Soon each was lost to the sight of the other.

For the young woman, the hunting was good. By the time she returned, she had two seals lashed to the narrow deck of her kayak. As she rowed with her single paddle which she held in the middle, dipping first right and then left, she sang a little song of thanksgiving to the Old Woman of the Sea.

Both her brothers returned much later, angry and empty-handed. She was already roasting some meat when they came to her hut. She invited them to share her food and spend the night. She did not mock them because she knew they were chewing on bitter defeat with every mouthful of meat—even as she was savoring her victory. When they had finished eating, they did not thank her. They sat apart and whispered together.

In the morning, she awoke and discovered that her brothers were gone. They had also stolen her ivory-handled *ulu* in the fish-skin pouch she had made for it, and most of her

WORDS TO KNOW

savor (sā'vər) *v.* to take great pleasure in

furs and meat. Running to the shore, she saw the two of them far out to sea.

Angry at this second betrayal, she pursued them. She was stronger than either of them; and her boat was sturdier and swifter. Soon she overtook them. She shook her harpoon and cried, "Return what you have stolen, or I will gut your kayaks as I would a fish."

The two were cowards and quickly surrendered the stolen goods. Then the young woman laughed at *them*. To the shamefaced men, it sounded as though her laughter had been picked up by the roaring wind. Soon the sky itself was roaring with dark laughter, as a terrible storm arose.

The young woman, her goods safely tied down, paddled quickly back toward the island through a heavy sea. She called to her brothers to come back with her, but they ignored her. Stubbornly, they paddled on into the heart of the storm. Soon, she heard their calls for help as loud and <u>forlorn</u> as petrels'[4] cries. But although she turned around and tried to find them, they had vanished beneath the waves.

Barely escaping with her own life, she reached safe harbor. For a day and a night she huddled in her shelter, until the wind blew itself out.

When the storm subsided, the young woman took as much meat as she could carry. Then she rowed across to her old village. There she found her parents grieving for their lost sons and fearful that they would soon starve with no one to provide for them. Their grief turned to amazement when they saw Otoonah, her arms laden with food, coming up the beach toward them.

"*Punnick!* Daughter! Have you come home?" her father asked.

"I have come back because it is time for me to return," Otoonah said. "I will give you food from now on." So happy was she to be home that when she searched her heart, she found there no wish to hurt her parents any longer.

After this, she brought all her goods from the island and built herself a new hut, very close to the one in which her parents lived. She soon proved herself the best hunter in the village. Then she was sought by many men, each of whom wanted her to become his wife.

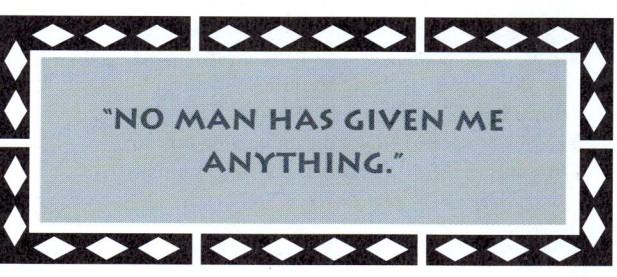

"NO MAN HAS GIVEN ME ANYTHING."

But she set her heart on one man, Apatasok. However, he alone would have no part of her because she insisted on taking a man's role in the hunt. "A woman is supposed to take care of the hunter," he said, "and watch out for his clothes. No more."

"Still, I am determined to have you for my husband," Otoonah said stubbornly.

"A girl does not take a husband of her own choosing. Her parents should seek a husband for her."

Then he walked away before she could argue any more.

---

4. **petrels'**: belonging to a group of sea birds.

WORDS TO KNOW
forlorn (fər-lôrn′) *adj.* sad and desperate because of being abandoned

773

Literary Concept: ONOMATOPOEIA

K Point out to students that the wind does not actually "roar," but that the word describes the sound the wind makes. Challenge students to come up with other words that evoke the sound the wind makes. (*Possible responses: howl, screech, whisper, moan*)

Active Reading: EVALUATE

L Ask students to discuss why, when Otoonah returns home, she not only forgives her parents, but also offers to get food for them. Supply students who are having difficulty with the following model:

Think-Aloud Model *After being alone in a fierce winter, Otoonah may have been so happy to see her parents that her love outweighed her anger. This is the only community she knows, and she must try to live in it the best she can. Besides, the brothers who tried to hurt her are now dead, and her parents are facing starvation.*

CUSTOMIZING FOR
Students Acquiring English

I Paraphrase the expression *would have no part of her* as "he was not interested in being with her at all."

Literary Links

M Have students compare Otoonah and the hostess of "The Dinner Party." Ask them whether the women show similar strength in life-and-death situations. (*Possible response: Both women show self-control and resourcefulness in responding to danger. However, Otoonah must survive on her own while the hostess of the dinner party has the assistance of an intelligent young man to keep the room quiet until the cobra leaves.*)

Multicultural Perspectives

MARRIAGE CUSTOMS It may be difficult for some students to understand why Otoonah cannot choose her own husband. Arranged marriages were part of Eskimo culture. In most cases, the man and woman knew little, if anything, about the person they were to marry. Often, marriages were arranged between families even before a child was born. For example, a contract may have been sealed between two men with the promise that the firstborn daughter would marry the firstborn son. In the United States and Europe, arranged marriages were still common through the late 19th century. Although children had more control over whom they married, they were often dependent on their families to arrange introductions and approve of the marriage. Even today, it is not unheard of for a man to ask the bride's father for her "hand," and in many wedding ceremonies, the father customarily "gives away" the bride.

STRATEGIC READING FOR

Less-Proficient Readers

N Ask students how Otoonah's skill at hunting helps save the man she wants to marry. *(At the last moment, she kills a polar bear that is attacking the man she has chosen to marry.)* Making Inferences

From Personal Response To Critical Analysis

1. In your notebook, describe your thoughts on Otoonah and her family. *(Responses will vary.)*

2. What qualities or emotions allowed Otoonah to face her enemies and win? *(Possible responses: Otoonah's bravery and skill in hunting helped her survive the brutal Arctic conditions; her pride and sense of achievement allowed her to face and overcome her brothers' and others' doubts about her abilities.)*

3. Myths and folk tales often are meant to convey a moral or social truth to their listeners. What moral(s) may this story be communicating? *(Possible responses: The moral of the story is that although some people think men are better able to do certain jobs, women and men must work together if a community is to survive. The story has a special message for women—that even though the odds may not be in their favor, they can overcome adversity and eventually succeed.)*

4. How does the story of Otoonah connect to the current debate over what jobs women and men are capable of performing successfully? *(Possible response: The story suggests that not only can women do the same tasks as men but that they may be able to do many of them better.)*

However, the following winter, when they were hunting near each other on the edge of the frozen sea, Apatasok killed a seal. But while he was loading it on his sled, he discovered to his dismay that the scent of the kill had drawn a polar bear.

Quick-thinking Otoonah cut the traces[5] on her own sled dogs and sent them to harass the bear. Then, with a cry of encouragement to her fellow hunter, she charged behind them, brandishing her harpoon.

The bear fought the dogs with its paws and teeth. Two dogs were felled by crushing blows. But the beast could not move because the circling huskies would attack at every opening. The young man rushed forward, trying to spear the bear in its heart. But the bear turned sharply, its paw shattering the hunter's spear and tumbling the man into the snow. The angered bear turned toward the man to finish him off. But, at that instant, the young woman charged forward, putting all of her weight behind her harpoon. The weapon pierced the bear's heart, and it dropped on the spot.

When the young man got to his feet and stared at the young woman standing beside the slain creature, he began to laugh. But the woman recognized that he was laughing because he was still alive, and because here was an unlooked-for supply of meat, and because he saw the foolishness of his refusal to marry a woman who hunted as well as any man.

Soon she was laughing, too.

When they returned to the village, they were wed. And the polar bear meat provided a marriage feast for their families and neighbors. Afterwards, they became a familiar sight as they hunted together, paddling their kayaks side by side. ❖

---

5. **traces:** straps or chains connecting a harnessed animal to a vehicle.

ROBERT D. SAN SOUCI

"As far back as I can remember," says Robert San Souci (1946–), "I loved stories." He wrote his first "book," illustrated by his brother Daniel, when he was in second grade. Since then, he has written more than 50 books, several of which were illustrated by his brother.

San Souci's stories are set in such varied places as medieval Japan, Native American homelands, the Philippines, and the Bahamas. "I have always had a fascination with traveling to magical places. . . . I guess I'm the ultimate escapist."

He has won many awards, including ones from Parents' Choice, the American Library Association, and the Children's Book Council. *Cut From the Same Cloth: American Women in Myth, Legend, and Tall Tale,* from which "Otoonah" is taken, won a 1993 Aesop Prize from the American Folklore Society.

San Souci finds ideas in many places—from odd articles in newspapers, which he clips and saves in his "Weird File," and from just observing people in general. He has always had a love of folklore. In addition to writing books for young people, San Souci writes thrillers for adults.

A lifelong resident of the San Francisco area, San Souci worked at various jobs—teacher, book buyer, bookstore manager, copywriter, editor—before he was able to support himself through writing.

OTHER WORKS *Song of Sedna: An Eskimo (Inuit) Legend; Short and Shivery; More Short and Shivery: 30 More Terrifying Tales*

WORDS TO KNOW

brandishing (brăn′dĭsh-ĭng) *adj.* waving something (such as a weapon) in a threatening manner **brandish** *v.*

COMPREHENSION CHECK

1. Why do Otoonah's brothers send her to a deserted island? *(The family is in danger of starving and they decide Otoonah should go rather than everyone starve.)*

2. How does Otoonah manage to survive alone? *(A man comes to her in a dream and tells her how to find a magic knife. Otoonah uses the knife to make what she needs.)*

3. What happens when the brothers return to the island? *(They are amazed that Otoonah is still alive and think a man has helped her.)*

4. Why do the brothers steal Otoonah's knife? *(They are jealous that she is a better hunter than they are.)*

5. Why does Apatasok agree to marry Otoonah? *(She kills a polar bear that attacked him on a hunt.)*

The Woman in the Snow

retold by Patricia C. McKissack

The year-long Montgomery, Alabama, bus boycott in 1955–56 was a pivotal event in the American civil rights movement. Blacks refused to ride the buses until their demand of fair and equal treatment for all fare-paying passengers was met. Today the right to sit anywhere on a public bus may seem a small victory over racism and discrimination. But that single issue changed the lives of African Americans everywhere. After the successful boycott in Montgomery, blacks in other cities challenged bus companies, demanding not only the right to sit wherever they chose but also employment opportunities for black bus drivers. Many cities had their own "bus" stories. Some are in history books, but this story is best enjoyed by the fireplace on the night of the first snowfall.

Grady Bishop had just been hired as a driver for Metro Bus Service. When he put on the gray uniform and boarded his bus, nothing mattered, not his obesity,[1] not his poor education, not growing up the eleventh child of the town drunk. Driving gave him power. And power mattered.

One cold November afternoon Grady clocked in for the three-to-eleven shift. "You've got Hall tonight," Billy, the route manager, said matter-of-factly.

"The Blackbird Express." Grady didn't care who knew about his nickname for the route. "Not again." He turned around, slapping his hat against his leg.

"Try the *Hall Street Express*," Billy corrected Grady, then hurried on, cutting their conversation short. "Snow's predicted. Try to keep on schedule, but if it gets too bad out there, forget it. Come on in."

Grady popped a fresh stick of gum into his mouth. "You're the boss. But tell me. How am I s'posed to stay on schedule? What do those people care about time?"

Most Metro drivers didn't like the Hall Street assignment in the best weather, because the road twisted and turned back on itself like

---

1. **obesity** (ō-bē′sĭ-tē): extreme fatness.

WORDS TO KNOW
pivotal (pĭv′ə-tl) *adj.* being of central importance

775

Mini-Lesson Literary Concepts

REVIEWING FORESHADOWING Remind students that foreshadowing refers to a writer's use of hints to suggest events that will occur later in a story. Foreshadowing alerts listeners to upcoming events in the story before they happen.

Refer students to the highlighted passage above (and continuing on to page 777) and point out that its discussion of the bad weather and difficulty driving the Hall Street route foreshadows the trouble that occurs later on Grady's shift.

Application Have students write a paragraph that foreshadows a later event in the story. Have them identify where in the story they would place their paragraph to be most effective. Remind the students that foreshadowing hints at possible later events but does not reveal exactly what will happen. Invite students to read aloud their paragraphs to the class.

CUSTOMIZING FOR
Multiple Learning Styles

Interpersonal Learners Encourage students to examine how characters relate to one another. Invite them to examine the following set of parallel relationships:

- Grady and his co-workers
- Grady and Eula Mae
- Ray and his co-workers
- Ray and Eula Mae

Illustration Copyright © 1992 Brian Pinkney. From *The Dark-Thirty* by Patricia McKissack, reprinted by permission of Alfred A. Knopf, Inc.

776 UNIT SIX: THE ORAL TRADITION

a retreating snake. When slick with ice and snow, it was even more hazardous. But Grady had his own reason for hating the route. The Hall Street Express serviced black domestics[2] who rode out to the fashionable west end in the mornings and back down to the lower east side in the evenings.

"You know I can't stand being a chauffeur for a bunch of colored maids and cooks," he groused.[3]

"Take it or leave it," Billy said, walking away in disgust.

Grady started to say something but thought better of it. He was still on probation,[4] lucky even to have a job, especially during such hard times.

Snow had already begun to fall when Grady pulled out of the garage at 3:01. It fell steadily all afternoon, creating a frosted wonderland on the manicured lawns that lined West Hall. But by nightfall the winding, twisting, and bending street was a driver's nightmare.

The temperature plummeted, too, adding a new challenge to the mounting snow. "Hurry up! Hurry up! I can't wait all day," Grady snapped at the boarding passengers. "Get to the back of the bus," he hustled them on impatiently. "You people know the rules."

The regulars recognized Grady, but except for a few muffled groans they paid their fares and rode in sullen silence out to the east side loop.

"Auntie! Now, just why are you taking your own good time getting off this bus?" Grady grumbled at the last passenger.

The woman struggled down the wet, slippery steps. At the bottom she looked over her shoulder. Her dark face held no clue of any emotion. "Auntie? Did you really call me *Auntie?*" she said, laughing sarcastically. "Well, well, well! I never knew my brother had a white son." And she hurried away, chuckling.

Grady's face flushed with surprise and anger. He shouted out the door, "Don't get uppity with me! Y'all know *Auntie* is what we call all you old colored women." Furious, he slammed the door against the bitter cold. He shook his head in disgust. "It's a waste of time trying to be nice," he told himself.

But one look out the window made Grady refocus his attention to a more immediate problem. The weather had worsened. He checked his watch. It was a little past nine. Remarkably, he was still on schedule, but that didn't matter. He had decided to close down the route and take the bus in.

That's when his headlights picked up the figure of a woman running in the snow, without a hat, gloves, or boots. Although she'd pulled a shawl over the lightweight jacket and flimsy dress she was wearing, her clothing offered very little protection against the elements. As she pressed forward against the driving snow and wind, Grady saw that the woman was very young, no more than twenty. And she was clutching something close to her body. What was it? Then Grady saw the baby, a small

---

2. **domestics:** household servants.
3. **groused:** complained.
4. **on probation:** working for a trial period before being permanently employed.

WORDS TO KNOW
plummet (plŭm′ĭt) *v.* to fall suddenly and steeply

Active Reading: CONNECT

E Ask students if they have ever been in a position where they were expected to enforce a rule but felt they should bend it. Ask what they would do in Grady's situation based on their previous experience. If necessary, provide students with the following model:

Think-Aloud Model *I believe that upholding rules is very important. If they are broken too easily, rules or laws can quickly become meaningless. However, I do believe there are certain situations when rules should be bent. It is inhumane of Grady not to bend the rules for a woman so desperate she would give her wedding ring as fare to save her baby.*

STRATEGIC READING FOR
Less-Proficient Readers

F Ask students how Grady treats African-American passengers. *(He is rude to them and makes racist remarks. He refuses to take the desperate young woman with a baby to the hospital.)* Summarizing

- What do these actions reveal about Grady? *(He is a racist; he is cold-hearted and insensitive to the death he is responsible for.)* Making Inferences/ Drawing Conclusions

Set a Purpose Have students read to find out how Ray Hammond treats the woman's ghost when she appears on his route.

Literary Concept:
FORESHADOWING

G Point out to students that the same conditions that occurred a year ago are recurring. Ask them what this repetition might foreshadow. *(Possible responses: The recurrence of the weather conditions suggests that Grady will meet another person in need; the similarity in conditions may suggest that the storm will bring back the ghost of the woman.)*

---

bundle wrapped in a faded pink blanket.

"These people," Grady sighed, opening the door. The woman stumbled up the steps, escaping the wind that mercilessly ripped at her petite frame.

"Look here. I've closed down the route. I'm taking the bus in."

In big gulping sobs the woman laid her story before him. "I need help, please. My husband's gone to Memphis looking for work. Our baby's sick, real sick. She needs to get to the hospital. I know she'll die if I don't get help."

"Well, I got to go by the hospital on the way back to the garage. You can ride that far." Grady nodded for her to pay. The woman looked at the floor. "Well? Pay up and get on to the back of the bus so I can get out of here."

"I—I don't have the fare," she said, quickly adding, "but if you let me ride, I promise to bring it to you in the morning."

"Give an inch, y'all want a mile. You know the rules. No money, no ride!"

"Oh, please!" the young woman cried. "Feel her little head. It's so hot." She held out the baby to him. Grady recoiled.

Desperately the woman looked for something to bargain with. "Here," she said, taking off her wedding ring. "Take this. It's gold. But please don't make me get off this bus."

He opened the door. The winds howled savagely. "Please," the woman begged.

"Go on home, now. You young gals get hysterical over a little fever. Nothing. It'll be fine in the morning." As he shut the door the last sounds he heard were the mother's sobs, the baby's wail, and the moaning wind.

Grady dismissed the incident until the next morning, when he read that it had been a record snowfall. His eyes were drawn to a small article about a colored woman and child found frozen to death on Hall Street. No one seemed to know where the woman was going or why. No one but Grady.

"That gal should have done like I told her and gone on home," he said, turning to the comics.

It was exactly one year later, on the anniversary of the record snowstorm, that Grady was assigned the Hall Street Express again. Just as before, a storm heaped several inches of snow onto the city in a matter of hours, making driving extremely hazardous.

By nightfall Grady decided to close the route. But just as he was making the turn-around at the east side loop, his headlight picked up a woman running in the snow—the same woman he'd seen the previous year. Death hadn't altered her desperation. Still holding on to the blanketed baby, the small-framed woman pathetically struggled to reach the bus.

Grady closed his eyes but couldn't keep them shut. She was still coming, but from where? The answer was too horrible to consider, so he chose to let his mind find a more reasonable explanation. From some dark corner of his childhood he heard his father's voice, slurred by alcohol, mocking him. *It ain't the same woman, dummy. You know how they all look alike!*

Grady remembered his father with bitterness and swore at the thought of him. This *was* the same woman, Grady argued with his father's memory, taking no comfort in being right. Grady watched the woman's movements breathlessly as she stepped out of the headlight beam and approached the door. She stood outside the door waiting . . . waiting.

The gray coldness of Fear slipped into the driver's seat. Grady sucked air into his lungs in big gulps, feeling out of control. Fear moved

| WORDS TO KNOW | **petite** (pə-tēt′) *adj.* small and slender |
| | **recoil** (rĭ-koil′) *v.* to shrink back, as in fear or disgust |

Mini-Lesson: Speaking, Listening, and Viewing

ACTIVE LISTENING Explain to students that becoming an active listener can be as difficult a task as becoming an active reader. Students who find it difficult to concentrate on what a person is saying may have a particularly hard time following the plot of a folk tale because they fail to note relevant details. Explain that active listeners, like active readers, can better understand a story if they evaluate which details are likely to be important to the story.

Application Divide students into small groups. Each group should work with the same folk tale. Have the group take turns reading passages from the selection. Students should concentrate on the events they feel are most important. Encourage students to make "mental notes" of these events. When the group has finished reading the folk tale, each member can write the five details he or she thought were the most relevant, then compare their list with other members in the group. Have one person act as a reporter to compile the most frequent events on students' lists.

his foot to the gas pedal, careening[5] the bus out into oncoming traffic. Headlights. A truck. Fear made Grady hit the brakes. The back of the bus went into a sliding spin, slamming into a tree. Grady's stomach crushed against the steering wheel, rupturing his liver and spleen. *You've really done it now, lunkhead.* As he drifted into the final darkness, he heard a woman's sobs, a baby wailing—or was it just the wind?

Twenty-five years later, Ray Hammond, a war hero with two years of college, became the first black driver Metro hired. A lot of things had happened during those two and a half decades to pave the way for Ray's new job. The military had integrated its forces during the Korean War. In 1954 the Supreme Court had ruled that segregated schools were unequal. And one by one, unfair laws were being challenged by civil rights groups all over the South. Ray had watched the Montgomery bus boycott with interest, especially the boycott's leader, Dr. Martin Luther King, Jr.

Ray soon found out that progress on the day-to-day level can be painfully slow. Ray was given the Hall Street Express.

"The white drivers call my route the Blackbird Express," Ray told his wife. "I'm the first driver to be given that route as a permanent assignment. The others wouldn't take it."

"What more did you expect?" his wife answered, tying his bow tie. "Just do your best so it'll be easier for the ones who come behind you."

In November, Ray worked the three-to-eleven shift. "Snow's predicted," the route manager barked one afternoon. "Close it down if it gets bad out there, Ray."

The last shift on the Hall Street Express.

Since he was a boy, Ray had heard the story of the haunting of that bus route. Every first snowfall, passengers and drivers testified that they'd seen the ghost of Eula Mae Daniels clutching her baby as she ran through the snow.

"Good luck with Eula Mae tonight," one of the drivers said, snickering.

"I didn't know white folk believed in haints,"[6] Ray shot back.

But parked at the east side loop, staring into the swirling snow mixed with ice, Ray felt tingly, as if he were dangerously close to an electrical charge. He'd just made up his mind to close down the route and head back to the garage when he saw her. Every hair on his head stood on end.

He wished her away, but she kept coming. He tried to think, but his thoughts were jumbled and confused. He wanted to look away, but curiosity fixed his gaze on the advancing horror.

Just as the old porch stories had described her, Eula Mae Daniels was a small-framed woman frozen forever in youth. "So young," Ray whispered. "Could be my Carolyn in a few more years." He watched as the ghost came around to the doors. She was out there, waiting in the cold. Ray heard the baby crying. "There but for the grace of God goes one of mine," he said, compassion overruling his fear. "Nobody deserves to be left out in this weather.

> No one seemed to know where the woman was going or why. No one but Grady.

---

5. **careening:** causing to swerve or lean to one side while in motion.
6. **haints** *Southern dialect:* ghosts.

THE WOMAN IN THE SNOW 779

STRATEGIC READING FOR
Less-Proficient Readers

K Ask students to describe how Ray treats the woman's ghost when she appears on his route. *(Ray, seeing in Eula Mae a troubled spirit in need of help, overcomes his fear and lets her on the bus.)* **Making Inferences/Summarizing**

Active Reading: EVALUATE

L Have students evaluate Ray's "loan" to Eula Mae. Ask them to compare Ray's response to Grady's. *(Possible response: Ray is not only willing to bend the rules, he is willing to pay out of his own pocket to get around them. Grady is not only unwilling to break the rules, he turned Eula Mae away rather than use his own money.)*

Literary Links

Ask students to compare the bus driver Ray Hammond to the title character of Ann Petry's "Harriet Tubman: Conductor on the Underground Railroad." Ask how their experiences and responses to racial oppression are similar and how they differ. *(Possible response: Both Ray and Tubman have had to live with racial oppression—Ray in a period of segregation and Tubman during slavery. Both respond with compassion and assistance to other people in need. However, Ray's payment of the fare was small in comparison to Tubman's sacrifice; unlike Tubman, he did not risk his life in helping Eula Mae.)*

Ghost or not, she deserves better." And he swung open the doors.

The woman had form but no substance. Ray could see the snow falling *through* her. He pushed fear aside. "Come on, honey, get out of the cold," Ray said, waving her on board.

Eula Mae stood stony still, looking up at Ray with dark, questioning eyes. The driver understood. He'd seen that look before, not from a dead woman but from plenty of his passengers. "It's okay. I'm for real. Ray Hammond, the first Negro to drive for Metro. Come on, now, get on," he coaxed her gently.

Eula Mae moved soundlessly up the steps. She held the infant to her body. Ray couldn't remember ever feeling so cold, not even the Christmas he'd spent in a Korean foxhole. He'd seen so much death, but never anything like this.

The ghost mother <u>consoled</u> her crying baby. Then with her head bowed she told her story in quick bursts of sorrow, just as she had twenty-five years earlier. "My husband is in Memphis looking for work. Our baby is sick. She'll die if I don't get help."

"First off," said Ray. "Hold your head up. You got no cause for shame."

"I don't have any money," she said. "But if you let me ride, I promise to bring it to you tomorrow. I promise."

Ray sighed deeply. "The rule book says no money, no ride. But the book doesn't say a word about a personal loan." He took a handful of change out of his pocket, fished around for a dime, and dropped it into the pay box. "You're all paid up. Now, go sit yourself down while I try to get this bus back to town."

Eula Mae started to the back of the bus.

"No you don't," Ray stopped her. "You don't have to sit in the back anymore. You can sit right up front."

The ghost woman moved to a seat closer, but still not too close up front. The baby fretted. The young mother comforted her as best she could.

They rode in silence for a while. Ray checked in the rearview mirror every now and then. She gave no reflection, but when he looked over his shoulder, she was there, all right. "Nobody will ever believe this," he mumbled. "*I* don't believe it.

"Things have gotten much better since you've been . . . away," he said, wishing immediately that he hadn't opened his mouth. Still he couldn't—or wouldn't—stop talking.

"I owe this job to a little woman just about your size named Mrs. Rosa Parks. Down in Montgomery, Alabama, one day, Mrs. Parks refused to give up a seat she'd paid for just because she was a colored woman."

Eula Mae sat motionless. There was no way of telling if she had heard or not. Ray kept talking. "Well, they arrested her. So the colored people decided to boycott the buses. Nobody rode for over a year. Walked everywhere, formed car pools, or just didn't go, rather than ride a bus. The man who led the boycott was named Reverend King. Smart man. We're

> "It's okay. I'm for real. Ray Hammond, the first Negro to drive for Metro. Come on, now, get on."

WORDS TO KNOW **console** (kən-sōl′) *v.* to comfort

780

Multicultural Perspectives

DR. MARTIN LUTHER KING, JR. The boycott to end segregation on the Montgomery bus lines was only the first of a long series of nonviolent protests King organized. He founded the Southern Christian Leadership Conference to end racial oppression.

In 1963, riots broke out in Birmingham, Alabama, over police brutality and maltreatment. King was arrested, and while in prison wrote "Letter from Birmingham Jail" explaining his use of nonviolent protest. In the same year, King led more than 200,000 "Freedom Fighters" in a March on Washington where he delivered his famous "I Have a Dream" speech. In 1964, King was awarded the Nobel Peace Prize.

During the 1965 voter registration drive in Selma, Alabama, violence broke out. King lead a protest march of more than 4,000 people from Selma to Montgomery, the state capital. In 1968, while organizing a multiracial Poor People's March, King was shot and killed in Memphis, Tennessee, by James Earl Ray.

sure to hear more about him in the future. . . . You still with me?" Ray looked around. Yes, she was there. The baby had quieted. It was much warmer on the bus now.

Slowly Ray inched along on the icy road, holding the bus steady, trying to keep the back wheels from racing out of control. "Where was I?" he continued. "Oh yeah, things changed after that Montgomery bus boycott. This job opened up. More changes are on the way. Get this: they got an Irish Catholic running for President. Now, what do you think of that?

About that time Ray pulled the bus over at Seventeenth Street. The lights at Gale Hospital sent a welcome message to those in need on such a frosty night. "This is it."

Eula Mae raised her head. "You're a kind man," she said. "Thank you."

Ray opened the door. The night air gusted up the steps and nipped at his ankles. Soundlessly, Eula Mae stepped off the bus with her baby.

"Excuse me," Ray called politely. "About the bus fare. No need for you to make a special trip . . . back. Consider it a gift."

He thought he saw Eula Mae Daniels smile as she vanished into the swirling snow, never to be seen again. ❖

Patricia C. McKissack

Patricia C. McKissack (1944–) has written one award-winning book after another. Writing separately and together, she and her husband, Fredrick, have written more than 100 books for children and teenagers. Most are about the lives of African Americans and Native Americans—some famous, and others who are "left out of history books."

Their lives, McKissack says, were influenced by the civil rights movement of the 1960s, when "African Americans were really looking up, coming out of darkness, segregation, and discrimination, and doors were beginning to open—ever so slightly, but still opening."

Before becoming a full-time writer, McKissack taught eighth graders and college students, and edited children's books. When she found no biography of Paul Laurence Dunbar for her eighth graders, she wrote one herself. Among the many awards her books have won are three Coretta Scott King Awards and a Newbery Honor Award. She has also written radio and television scripts and an award-winning movie script.

McKissack was born in Smyrna, Tennessee. "We did not have television and I grew up sitting on the front porch listening to family and community stories," she says. She and her husband graduated from Tennessee State University. The McKissacks have three grown sons and live in St. Louis, Missouri.

OTHER WORKS *Christmas in the Big House—Christmas in the Quarters, Sojourner Truth: Ain't I a Woman?*

CUSTOMIZING FOR
Gifted and Talented Students

Have students compare the internal and external conflicts the characters in these three stories must overcome in facing their enemies. In their discussion, students may wish to consider

- whether characters act alone or in a group;
- social pressures or norms they are struggling against;
- reasons why the characters are successful in their struggles.

From Personal Response To Critical Analysis

1. How do you feel about Grady enforcing the rules of his job and refusing to take Eula Mae to the hospital? Write your ideas in your notebook. *(Responses will vary.)*
2. What are the possible implications of Eula Mae finally resting in peace? *(Possible responses: Even though racism wasn't eliminated, Eula Mae was comforted enough by the changes she saw happening to rest in peace finally. Eula Mae was searching for a person who would treat her decently and with human kindness, and she found driver Ray Hammond to be that person.)*
3. Why do you think people like Grady continue to try to oppress people of other races? *(Possible response: People are not born racist; rather, racism is something they learn. Grady was not alone in the segregated South in his attempt to dominate people of color. However, his own feelings of inferiority from his past may have made his racism even more vicious.)*

COMPREHENSION CHECK
1. What is Grady's nickname for the Hall Street Express? *(Blackbird Express)*
2. Why does Grady refuse to take Eula Mae to the hospital? *(because she does not have the fare)*
3. What happens to Eula Mae when she is turned away by Grady? *(She and her baby freeze to death.)*
4. How often does the ghost of Eula Mae return? *(every year during the first snowfall)*
5. What does Ray Hammond do when he encounters Eula May? *(Ray not only lets Eula Mae on the bus, he also pays her fare.)*
6. What happens to Eula Mae after Ray takes her to the hospital? *(She is never seen again.)*

Literature Connection

Project 1 Suggest that students review some of their favorite books to get ideas for their book jackets. Students may wish to research computer databases or conduct library research to find photographs or illustrations for the cultures they are representing on their book jackets.

Rubric
3 **Full Accomplishment** Students complete a dust jacket that is relevant to the story's culture and has fully developed copy and creative illustrations.
2 **Substantial Accomplishment** Students provide copy and illustrations for the dust jacket but do not fully understand the story or the story's culture.
1 **Little or Partial Accomplishment** Students fail to provide copy or illustrations that are relevant to the story.

RESPONDING OPTIONS

Multimodal Activity
LITERATURE CONNECTION PROJECT 1

Create a Dust Jacket for a Book A dust jacket is a paper cover that protects a book and promotes the story to readers. Working in small groups, choose one of the stories you have just read. Imagine that the story is a book, and create a dust jacket for it. Decide who will create each component of the jacket. Refer to these suggestions as you carry out the project.

Cover Design and illustrate the front of the jacket. You could research the artwork of the story's culture and use elements of it in your design.

Back Select a short excerpt from the story that can go on the back of the jacket. Choose an excerpt that makes the reader want to find out more about the story.

Back Inside Flap Interview some classmates and write down their critical reactions to the story. Select three or four favorable quotations from these student reactions to put on the back inside flap.

Front Inside Flap Write a few paragraphs to go on the inside flap of the dust jacket. These should give an idea of what the story is about but not give the whole story away. The purpose of this text is to generate reader interest, so make it as engaging and exciting as possible.

Multimodal Activity
SOCIAL STUDIES CONNECTION PROJECT 2

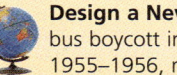

Design a Newspaper's Front Page The bus boycott in Montgomery, Alabama, in 1955–1956, marked a turning point in the civil rights movement in the United States.
   Imagine you are a journalist. Working with a group of classmates, create the front page of a newspaper for the day the boycott ended. Use books or computer databases, if possible, to carry out your research. As you plan your articles for the page, investigate the parts played by Rosa Parks and Dr. Martin Luther King, Jr. Lay out your spread on a computer if possible.

782 UNIT SIX: THE ORAL TRADITION

Social Studies Connection

Project 2 Some students may not have access to a computer or to programs capable of re-creating a newspaper layout. Suggest they use poster board and paste or tape to create a page layout. Remind students to sketch the layout of their front page before cutting and pasting the stories in place. Encourage students to research newspapers and magazines from the period in order to see how those news stories were first portrayed.

Rubric
3 **Full Accomplishment** The group creates a front page that accurately and effectively uses historical information and illustrations.
2 **Substantial Accomplishment** The group creates a well-designed front page, but it is missing valuable aspects of the boycott.
1 **Little or Partial Accomplishment** The group either fails to complete the page or has not done enough research to communicate vital information about the boycott.

Multimodal Activity

SCIENCE CONNECTION PROJECT 3

Construct a Diorama of an Ecosystem
The story "Otoonah" comes from Kodiak Island, off the Alaskan coast. Find out more about this island's natural environment. Investigate the climate. What is the name of this kind of environment? Make a list of the animals and plants that live in it. Are they all mentioned in the story? How does this environment change from season to season? Create a diorama of this natural environment. Write a key that explains the different parts of the diorama and that gives extra information.

Multimodal Activities

ACROSS CULTURES MINI-PROJECTS

Find the Enemy The enemy in these stories may be a real person or an animal, or it may be something less concrete, such as an attitude or situation. Who or what is the enemy in each story? Select a story from Unit Four that features an enemy similar to one you have just read about. Draw a picture that illustrates the similarities between the two.

Create an Iroquois Time Line Make a time line, like the one started here, showing the main events in the history of the Iroquois. Work with another student to select the dates you wish to feature.

The five tribes unite to form the League of the Iroquois.

1570

Compose a Song Discover who the Peacemaker referred to on the first page of "Racing the Great Bear" was. Then find out all you can about this person. Choose a style of music that you think is appropriate—pop, blues, ballad—and write a modern song about the Peacemaker. Share it with your class.

Compare Characters Compare and contrast Carol Bullard—the ghost in "The Girl in the Lavender Dress" (page 710)—and Eula Mae Daniels of "The Woman in the Snow." Begin by listing the qualities of each character. Then record their similarities and differences in a chart like the one shown.

Carol Bullard and Eula Mae Daniels	
Similarities	Differences

Extended Social Studies Reading

MORE ABOUT THE CULTURES

- *American Indians Today* by Judith Harlan
- *The Iroquois* by Barbara A. McCall
- *The Life and Words of Martin Luther King, Jr.* by Ira Peck
- *The Montgomery Bus Boycott, December, 1955* by Janet Stevenson

LINKS TO UNIT FOUR **783**

Science Connection

Project 3 Remind students that the ocean is a major part of the environment for the Eskimo of Kodiak Island and should be represented in their diorama. Also, students may wish to focus more on aspects of the winter seasons because they are much longer.

Rubric

3 Full Accomplishment Students create a diorama that accurately details the environment, climate, plant and animal life, and seasonal variation of Kodiak Island.

2 Substantial Accomplishment Students fail to account for the full range of environmental, seasonal, and subsistence factors that affect Kodiak Island.

1 Little or Partial Accomplishment The diorama does not correspond to the ecology of Kodiak Island.

Across Cultures

Find the Enemy Encourage students to pick a selection from Unit Four that they found particularly moving or inspiring. Remind students to explain why they have made their particular choice and invite them to supply specific examples from both stories in their explanation.

Create an Iroquois Time Line Suggest that students set the limits of the time frame before they begin to make the project more manageable, for example, from 1570 to 1770.

Compose a Song Invite students to use rhythm, rhyme, and repetition as a way to organize their song. Remind students that these devices will make it easier for listeners to follow the song.

Compare Characters Suggest that students examine the historical period, ethnic background, and issues facing each character as a way of focusing their comparison.

OVERVIEW
Objectives

- To understand and appreciate three tales that describe people who learn about their relationships, about events at home, and about what they want in life
- To appreciate the distinctive cultures and histories of Cherokee and Mayan cultures as they are represented in the stories
- To extend understanding of the stories through a variety of multimodal and cross-curricular activities

Reading Pathways

- Assign one or several students to read the tales aloud to the class. On a second reading, challenge the rest of the class to keep a chronology of events that take place in each story. Have students compare these chronologies with those in the selections from Unit 5.

- Read the tales aloud to the class, pausing to discuss the cultural and historical background to the story. Have students record how this additional information increases their understanding of the story and how it relates to their own cultures.

- After students have read "No News" once, they can read it again to identify the similarities and differences between it and "Raymond's Run" from Unit 5. Ask students to describe how information is presented to readers in each of the two stories.

PREVIEWING

LINKS TO UNIT FIVE

Personal Discoveries

Activating Prior Knowledge

In Unit Five, painful as well as joyous experiences lead individuals to make discoveries about themselves. They gain a deeper insight into who they are and what they believe in. The characters in the tales you are about to read also follow their own paths to greater self-knowledge.

Building Background

SOUTHEASTERN U.S.

Strawberries

retold by Gayle Ross

Up until the early 1800s, the Cherokee people lived and hunted in the southern Appalachian region, an area that included what is now part of North Carolina. These early Cherokee people believed their homeland was the center of the world. They pictured the earth as a floating island attached to the sky by four cords. In their mythology, the first man and the first woman were Kana'ti and Selu, who are featured in this myth.

784 UNIT SIX: THE ORAL TRADITION

PRINT AND MEDIA RESOURCES

UNIT SIX RESOURCE BOOK
Strategic Reading: Literature, p. 39
Vocabulary SkillBuilder, p. 42
Reading SkillBuilder, p. 40
Spelling SkillBuilder, p. 41

GRAMMAR MINI-LESSONS
Transparencies, p. 1
Copymasters, p. 1

ACCESS FOR STUDENTS ACQUIRING ENGLISH
Selection Summaries
Reading and Writing Support

FORMAL ASSESSMENT
Selection Test, pp. 141–142
Unit Test, pp. 143–144
Test Generator

ALTERNATIVE ASSESSMENT
End-of-Year Integrated Assessment
  Reader, pp. 31–42; Student Response Booklet, pp. 43–56

AUDIO LIBRARY
See Reference Card

INTERNET RESOURCES
McDougal Littell Literature Center at http://www.hmco.com/mcdougal/lit

---

784 THE LANGUAGE OF LITERATURE TEACHER'S EDITION

NORTHEASTERN U.S.

No News

retold by Connie Regan-Blake and Barbara Freeman

Building Background

"No News" is the kind of folk tale one hears, with subtle variations, across many cultures. Regan-Blake and Freeman first heard this story told about Down Easters, a term New Englanders sometimes use for people from Maine who are east of or downwind from Boston. These storytellers adapted the tale to their Southern culture.

GUATEMALA

Building Background

The First Flute

retold by Dorothy Sharp Carter

The Maya thrived in Guatemala—as well as in parts of what is now Mexico, Belize, El Salvador, and Honduras—between A.D. 250 and 900. Prospering in a difficult tropical forest ecosystem, the Maya built one of the most remarkable civilizations. "The First Flute" takes place during this period, long before the Spanish conquered the Maya in the 1500s.

Setting a Purpose

AS YOU READ...

Think about what is fun about these tales.

Imagine their being repeated from generation to generation.

Consider the ways in which the characters have the ability to laugh at themselves.

Note how the cultures differ from each other and from your own.

LINKS TO UNIT FIVE **785**

SUMMARY

Strawberries The first man and the first woman have a terrible quarrel, and eventually the woman leaves and heads to the east. The man is so miserable and lonely that a spirit takes pity on him. The spirit tries to slow down the woman by making berries and fruit ripen before her eyes. The woman ignores all of the fruit until the spirit places strawberries in her path. When the woman tramples the berries underfoot, the smell is so appetizing that she cannot help but bend her head and eat them. The man catches up with her, and the two renew their relationship. They spend the rest of their lives in happiness together.

No News A woman recovering from an illness meets a friend at a railroad station on her return. Although the friend initially tells her that there is no news to report, the woman quickly learns that her dog has died, her horse has died in a barn fire after her house has burned down, her mother-in-law has died, and her husband has run off.

The First Flute The young princess Nima-Cux has a beautiful voice and is loved by her father, but on her sixteenth birthday she becomes very depressed. After consulting a sorcerer, the chief learns it is because she has not married. Contests are held, but the princess is bored by every competitor except the last, a minstrel who sings her love songs. The princess agrees to marry him, but only if he learns the songs of all the birds of the forest. However, there are so many birds that it is impossible for the man to learn them all. A god takes pity on the man and makes a chirimia or flute for the minstrel. Nima-Cux and the minstrel are married and live in happiness in the chief's palace.

CUSTOMIZING FOR
Students Acquiring English

- Use **ACCESS FOR STUDENTS ACQUIRING ENGLISH**, Reading and Writing Support.

WORDS TO KNOW

agitated (ăj′ĭ-tāt′əd) *adj.* emotionally excited or disturbed (p. 792)

evading (ĭ-vā′dĭng) *adj.* escaping or avoiding

evade *v.* (p. 794)

melancholy (mĕl′ən-kŏl′ē) *adj.* sad and gloomy (p. 792)

THE LANGUAGE OF LITERATURE **TEACHER'S EDITION** **785**

STRATEGIC READING FOR
Less-Proficient Readers

Set a Purpose Ask students what people do when they quarrel. Then have students read and focus on the relationship of the man and the woman. Have students read to find out how their conflict gets resolved.

CUSTOMIZING FOR
Gifted and Talented Students

Invite students to retell "Strawberries" from a first-person point of view as the man, the woman, or the spirit. After students finish their retellings, they can discuss how this shift in point of view affected how they told the story.

CUSTOMIZING FOR
Students Acquiring English

I Ask students to provide a synonym for *quarreled*. (argued; fought)

Critical Thinking: CLASSIFYING

A Have students compare the reactions of the man and the woman. Based on the opening events of the story, ask them what speculations they can make about the status of a Cherokee woman in her society. *(Possible response: When the man and woman quarrel, the woman leaves and the man chases after her. This suggests that women were capable of acting independently.)*

STRAWBERRIES

RETOLD BY GAYLE ROSS

Long ago, in the very first days of the world, there lived the first man and the first woman. They lived together as husband and wife, and they loved one another dearly.

But one day, they quarreled. Although neither later could remember what the quarrel was about, the pain grew stronger with every word that was spoken, until finally, in anger and in grief, the woman left their home and began walking away—to the east, toward the rising sun.

The man sat alone in his house. But as time went by, he grew lonelier and lonelier. The anger left him, and all that remained was a terrible grief and despair, and he began to cry.

A spirit heard the man crying and took pity on him. The spirit said, "Man, why do you cry?"

The man said, "My wife has left me."

The spirit said, "Why did your woman leave?"

The man just hung his head and said nothing.

The spirit asked, "You quarreled with her?"

And the man nodded.

Mini-Lesson Spelling

THE LETTERS QU The letters *qu* can be pronounced two ways. When a word ends *que*, the letters are pronounced *k* (as in *clique*). When *qu* appears in the middle of some words, it is pronounced *k* (as in *lacquer*) or *kw* (as in *acquaint*). When *qu* appears at the beginning of words, it is pronounced *kw* (as in *quick*).

Application Ask students to spell these words as you dictate them.

clique	pronounced k
lacquer	pronounced k
acquaint	pronounced kw
quick	pronounced kw

1. unique
2. quarrel
3. acquire
4. questionnaire
5. plaque
6. banquet
7. adequate
8. quench
9. conquer
10. quotation

Ask students to look for more words that fit this pattern, in their own writing and in things that they read, and to add these words to their personal word lists.

Reteaching/Reinforcement
• *Unit Six Resource Book*, p. 41

Strawberry Dance (1983), G. Peter Jemison (Seneca Nation, Heron Clan). Mixed media on handmade paper, 22″ × 30″, private collection, by permission of the artist.

B "Would you quarrel with her again?" asked the spirit.

The man said, "No." He wanted only to live with his wife as they had lived before—in peace, in happiness, and in love.

C "I have seen your woman," the spirit said. "She is walking to the east toward the rising sun."

The man followed his wife, but he could not overtake her. Everyone knows an angry woman walks fast.

Finally, the spirit said, "I'll go ahead and see if I can make her slow her steps." So the spirit found the woman walking, her footsteps fast and angry and her gaze fixed straight ahead. There was pain in her heart.

The spirit saw some huckleberry bushes growing along the trail, so with a wave of his hand, he made the bushes burst into bloom and ripen into fruit. But the woman's gaze remained fixed. She looked neither to the right nor to the left, and she didn't see the berries. Her footsteps didn't slow.

Again, the spirit waved his hand, and one

STRAWBERRIES   **787**

Art Note

Strawberry Dance (Paper Bag Series) by G. Peter Jemison A Seneca Indian, Jemison (1945–) has been active both politically and artistically in promoting the contemporary work of Native American artists. He asserts the right and need for Native American artists to break with traditional imagery and materials in their art. In the Paper Bag series, Jemison made a number of paper containers covered with complex, colorful designs. Each container illustrates one moment in an ongoing event or story. The Strawberry Dance is a traditional dance of the Iroquois.

Reading the Art *Do you think that this painting is well suited to its title? Why or why not? If not, what would you name the painting?*

Active Reading: EVALUATE

B Ask students why the spirit decides to help the man find the fleeing woman. *(Possible response: The spirit asks why the man desires to have the woman back. Seeing that his answer is sincere and not selfish, the spirit decides to help him.)*

Literary Note

C Direction often has carried significant meanings in folk tales. For instance, *north* and *east* were commonly understood as positive directions; *north* was associated with spiritual purity or mysticism, and east with renewal and adventure. On the other hand, *south* and *west* tended to have more negative associations: *south* was often a place of evil and dangerous, if not impossible, tasks, and *west* was connected with a return from adventure or death.

Multicultural Perspectives

EARLY MIGRATION Even though European colonizers referred to North and South America as the "New World," Native American civilizations in the Western Hemisphere were some of the oldest and the most developed in the world.

While there is some disagreement over when humans first migrated across the Bering Strait from northeast Asia, the earliest migrations are thought to have begun before 30,000 B.C. There were large bands of seminomadic hunters in the Great Plains by 20,000 B.C., and by 8000 B.C., Indians had settled throughout North and South America.

From 5000 B.C. to 1000 B.C., Native American groups developed unique forms of pottery, agriculture, and complex social systems that marked the end of the Stone Age. These early cultures were the forerunners of great civilizations such as the Mound Builders, Aztec, Pueblo, and Inca.

Literary Links

D Have students compare Salazar's "Other Pioneers" to "Strawberries." Ask students to consider how the speaker's pride in his ancestors relates to this origin myth. *(Possible response: Both the poem and this tale address the idea of a new start and a new beginning. Salazar's poem speaks of the settling of Southwestern territories and "Strawberries" tells of the first man and woman.)*

STRATEGIC READING FOR
Less-Proficient Readers

E Ask students how the conflict between the first man and the first woman is resolved. *(A spirit helps the man to catch up to the woman by placing strawberries in her path. The woman finds their aroma irresistible and stops. When the man catches up to her, the woman's anger leaves her, and the two reunite happily.)* Summarizing/Noting Relevant Details

From Personal Response to Critical Analysis

1. What is it like to argue with someone you care about? How might those feelings relate to the feelings of the woman and the man? *(Possible responses: It is very difficult to argue with a person you care about. I can understand the woman's desire to get away; sometimes cooling off is the best thing one can do.)*
2. What may be the purpose of the storyteller recounting the tale? *(Possible responses: Part of the purpose is to entertain listeners with a story about two people in love, as well as to explain where strawberries come from. It shows how women and men should relate together.)*
3. What other stories can you think of that are set at the beginning of creation? *(Responses will vary.)*

---

by one, all of the berries growing along the trail burst into bloom and ripened into fruit. But still, the woman's gaze remained fixed. She saw nothing but her anger and pain, and her footsteps didn't slow.

And again, the spirit waved his hand, and, one by one, the trees of the forest—the peach, the pear, the apple, the wild cherry—burst into bloom and ripened into fruit. But still, the woman's eyes remained fixed, and even still, she saw nothing but her anger and pain. And her footsteps didn't slow.

Then finally, the spirit thought, "I will create an entirely new fruit—one that grows very, very close to the ground so the woman must forget her anger and bend her head for a moment." So the spirit waved his hand, and a thick green carpet began to grow along the trail. Then the carpet became starred with tiny white flowers, and each flower gradually ripened into a berry that was the color and shape of the human heart.

As the woman walked, she crushed the tiny berries, and the delicious aroma came up through her nose. She stopped and looked down, and she saw the berries. She picked one and ate it, and she discovered its taste was as sweet as love itself. So she began walking slowly, picking berries as she went, and as she leaned down to pick a berry, she saw her husband coming behind her.

The anger had gone from her heart, and all that remained was the love she had always known. So she stopped for him, and together, they picked and ate the berries. Finally, they returned to their home, where they lived out their days in peace, happiness, and love.

And that's how the world's very first strawberries brought peace between men and women in the world and why to this day they are called the berries of love. ❖

GAYLE ROSS

Gayle Ross says, "For me, being Cherokee is a true identification—a very real part of who I am." Ross is the great-great-great-granddaughter of John Ross, principal chief of the Cherokees before and during the Trail of Tears.

From her grandmother, Ross first heard the Cherokee stories she retells in books and to audiences across the country. "I don't want anyone to feel guilty about the Trail of Tears," she says. "Instead, I want us to learn from this tragic experience."

Ross left her studies in radio and television at the University of Texas to work in broadcasting, but

1951–

soon became dissatisfied. A trip to a storytelling festival changed her life. Ross quit her job and, with a partner, began performing as The Twelve Moons Storytellers throughout the United States.

Always looking for stories to tell, Ross may find "a piece of a story or a skeletal version" that she "fleshes out with accurate cultural context" and her imagination.

OTHER WORKS *How Rabbit Tricked Otter and Other Cherokee Trickster Stories, Second Best Stories at the National Storytelling Festival, The Girl Who Married the Moon* (with Joseph Bruchac)

788 UNIT SIX: THE ORAL TRADITION

COMPREHENSION CHECK

1. Why does the woman leave the man? *(because they have had a serious quarrel)*
2. In what direction does the woman travel? *(She heads toward the east.)*
3. Who helps the man find his wife? *(a spirit)*
4. What does the spirit try initially to stop the woman from walking? *(The spirit makes all the fruits and berries in the woman's path blossom.)*
5. What finally makes the woman stop walking? *(The spirit creates strawberries, which the woman bends down to eat.)*
6. What happens when the man catches up with the woman? *(Her anger fades, and they are reunited.)*

No News

retold by Connie Regan-Blake and Barbara Freeman

Dorothy and Netti (1974), Alex Katz. Oil on canvas, 72 × 96″, collection of the artist, courtesy of Marlborough Gallery, New York. Copyright © Alex Katz.

A certain Southern lady was returning home after recuperating in the mountains for three months. Her friend Georgeanne met her at the railway station.

"Georgeanne, has there been any news while I've been away?"

"Oh, no, there's no news."

"No news? Surely something has occurred in my absence. Why, I've been gone for nearly three months, and I'm anxious for any little bit of news you may have."

Art Note

***Dorothy and Netti* by Alex Katz**
Katz (1927–) is an American figurative painter. During the 1950s, his large, billboard-like paintings with flat, smooth compositions anticipated the Pop Art movement.

Reading the Art *How would you describe the setting of this painting? What relationship do you think the two women may have? Use details from the painting to explain your response.*

STRATEGIC READING FOR
Less-Proficient Readers

Set a Purpose Ask students to read to find out what happens to the woman's mother-in-law.

Literary Concept: MOOD

Ⓐ Remind students that the mood of a story is the feeling created in the reader. What mood does the opening of the story convey to readers? *(Possible responses: The opening of the story suggests that Georgeanne might be hiding something from her friend. This creates a mood of suspense.)*

CUSTOMIZING FOR
Students Acquiring English

Ⓘ Ask students what is meant by "news." *(Possible response: information about the woman's family or about the town)*

NO NEWS 789

Mini-Lesson Grammar

SENTENCE FRAGMENTS Remind students that in most cases, they should avoid using sentence fragments in their writing. Explain, however, that writers sometimes use sentence fragments for a reason. For example, in "No News," the authors use fragments to capture the sound of how real people talk.

Application Have students examine page 790 for examples of sentence fragments. If necessary, point out the  fragments. Invite students to place the fragments in a chart like the one shown and rewrite them as complete sentences. Then have them read the complete sentences aloud.

Reteaching/Reinforcement
- *Grammar Handbook*, anthology p. 860
- *Grammar Mini-Lessons* copymasters p. 1, transparencies p. 1

📁 The Writer's Craft
Guidelines for Writing Dialogue, p. 327
Sentences and Sentence Fragments, p. 382
Avoiding Sentence Fragments, p. 561

Sentence Fragment	Complete Sentence
"Burnt horseflesh?"	"Did my dog die from eating burnt horseflesh?"

THE LANGUAGE OF LITERATURE TEACHER'S EDITION **789**

Literary Links

B Point out to students that the woman's dog serves as a vital connection to all the events that have happened while she has been away. Ask them to explain if Mike's moustache serves a similar function in Robert Cormier's "The Moustache." *(Possible response: Yes, just as the dog's death serves as a trigger to all the other events recited by Georgeanne, Mike's moustache triggers a string of memories in his grandmother.)*

STRATEGIC READING FOR
Less-Proficient Readers

C Ask students to explain what happened to the woman's mother-in-law. *(Her mother-in-law died of shock after hearing that the woman's husband had run away with another woman.)* Relating Cause and Effect

Literary Concept: HUMOR

D Explain to students that while exaggeration is a common method in humorous writing, understatement can be equally funny. Ask students to discuss why this folk tale about terrible events is funny. *(Possible response: Although the events are horrible, the writers' method of presenting them little by little as if they were "no news" is funny.)*

From Personal Response to Critical Thinking

1. What would it be like to return home and be met by such a list of bad news? *(Responses will vary.)*
2. Is Georgeanne really the woman's friend? *(Possible responses: If Georgeanne really cared about the woman, she would tell her all the news straight off. Perhaps Georgeanne is trying to minimize the dreadful things that have happened to lessen the shock.)*
3. How would you tell another person bad news if faced with a similar situation? *(Responses will vary.)*

"Oh, now, since you mentioned it—'course it don't amount to much—but since you've been away, your dog died."

"My dog died? How did my dog die?"

"He ate some of the burnt horseflesh, and that's what killed the dog."

"Burnt horseflesh?"

"Well, after the fire cooled off, the dog ate some of the burnt horseflesh, and that's what killed the dog."

"Fire cooled off?"

"Well, the barn burned down, burned up all of the cows and horses, and when the fire cooled down, the dog ate some of the burnt horseflesh, and that's what killed the dog."

"My barn burned down? How did my barn burn down?"

"Oh, it was a spark from the house. Blew over, lit the roof of the barn, burned down the barn, burned up all the cows and horses, and when the fire cooled off, the dog ate some of the burnt horseflesh, and that's what killed the dog."

"A spark from the house?"

"Oh, yes, now that's completely burned down."

"But how did my house burn down?"

"It was the candle flame that lit the curtains, shot up the side of the wall, and burned down the house; a spark flew over on the roof of the barn, burned down the barn, burned up all of the cows and horses, and when the fire cooled off, the dog ate some of the burnt horseflesh, and that's what killed the dog."

"Candles? I don't even allow candles in my house. How did the candles get into my house?"

"Oh, they were around the coffin."

"Coffin? Who died?"

"Oh, now you needn't worry about that. Since you've been away, your mother-in-law died."

"Oh, my mother-in-law. What a pity. How did she die?"

"Well, some folks say that it was the shock of hearing that your husband had run away with the choir leader. But other than that, there ain't been no news." ❖

CONNIE REGAN-BLAKE AND BARBARA FREEMAN

Connie Regan-Blake (1947–) and Barbara Freeman (1944–) are Southern cousins. As children, they spent summers at an uncle's farm where they made up stories to tell. Little did they know at the time that they would travel together as adults telling stories for a living.

In 1971, they left their secure library jobs in Chattanooga, Tennessee, and began touring the country collecting and telling stories. Calling themselves The Folktellers, they developed a unique style of tandem storytelling in which they take turns delivering a line, but also pronounce lines in unison.

Regan-Blake and Freeman have been telling stories, many from Appalachia, for 20 years now. They have recorded audiotapes that have won awards from the American Library Association and *Parents' Choice* magazine. They have also produced videos.

The two women also perform solo. Regan-Blake tells tales accompanied by a chamber music trio; Freeman tells humorous mountain tales and true stories of Christian saints and martyrs.

COMPREHENSION CHECK

1. Why has the woman been away? *(She was recuperating in the mountains for three months.)*
2. What is the first thing that Georgeanne tells the woman? *(Her dog has died.)*
3. What has happened to the woman's house and barn? *(They have burned down.)*
4. What has happened to the woman's mother-in-law? *(She has died of shock.)*
5. Where is the woman's husband? *(He has gone off with the leader of the choir.)*

THE FIRST FLUTE

retold by Dorothy Sharp Carter

During the glory of the Mayan[1] civilization, years before the coming of the Spanish, there lived a *cacique*[2] who had a beautiful daughter, the Princess Nima-Cux, whom he loved dearly.

Not only was Nima-Cux beautiful, she was possessed of talents. She could plait grass into fine baskets.

---

1. **Mayan** (mä′yən): belonging to the Maya, a Native American people of southern Mexico and northern Central America.
2. *cacique* (kə-sēk′): a Native American chief.

THE FIRST FLUTE   791

STRATEGIC READING FOR
Less-Proficient Readers

Set a Purpose Have students read to see how Princess Nima-Cux changes after her 16th birthday.

Linking to History

A The history of the Maya is divided into three periods:

Preclassic (1500 B.C.–A.D. 300)—Maize was first cultivated and a sophisticated calendar, chronology, and system of hieroglyphic writing were developed.

Classic (300–900 A.D.)—Mayan culture spread throughout the Yucatan and Chiapas in Mexico, most of Guatemala, and western Honduras. Chichén Itzá, a large government complex, was founded in 900 and occupied until 1200.

Postclassic (900–1700 A.D.)—Marked by a series of civil wars and strife, culminating in the Spanish conquest beginning in 1546.

CUSTOMIZING FOR
Multiple Learning Styles

B **Linguistic Learners** Point out to students that this selection makes use of many Spanish words. Challenge students to find out which words are still commonly used and which are not.

Mini-Lesson   Reading Skills/Strategies

DISTINGUISHING FACT AND OPINION
Point out to students that facts are verifiable events, such as the amount of rain that fell one day or the number of people who voted in the last presidential election. Opinion, on the other hand, expresses the sentiments or ideas of a person or group but cannot be proven.

Application Read the following sentences to the class and invite them to decide whether they describe a fact or an opinion:
1. A Mayan chief was called a *cacique*. *(fact)*
2. The coati has a long, ringed tail. *(fact)*
3. The puma is the most beautiful of the big cats. *(opinion)*
4. The Maya lived in southern Mexico and northern Central America, including Guatemala. *(fact)*

If students disagree, encourage them to support their responses by addressing whether each statement can be proven true.

Reteaching/Reinforcement
- *Unit Six Resource Book*, p. 40

THE LANGUAGE OF LITERATURE TEACHER'S EDITION   791

CUSTOMIZING FOR
Students Acquiring English

I Paraphrase *counted his blessings* as "thought about all the good things in his life."

Critical Thinking: ANALYZING

C Ask students what they think the princess means when she says she "just *was*." (Possible responses: She didn't feel much of anything at all; her sadness appears to have no cause, but simply possesses her.)

STRATEGIC READING FOR
Less-Proficient Readers

D Have students characterize Princess Nima-Cux before and after her 16th birthday. (*Before turning 16, Nima-Cux had everything she wanted, and in addition to her many skills, she could sing like a bird. After her birthday, Nima-Cux suddenly became sad and melancholy; nothing made her happy, even though nothing was terribly wrong.*)

Noting Sequence of Events/ Summarizing

Set a Purpose Invite students to read to find out why the minstrel is able to make Nima-Cux smile once again.

Literary Concept: SETTING

E Have students explain how the author keeps the listener aware of the setting of the story. (Possible response: The author mentions native foods, animals, and plants of Guatemala, such as hearts of palm, monkeys, and orchids.)

She could mold little animals out of clay—and you even knew exactly which animals they were supposed to be. The coati[3] had a long, ringed tail. The puma[4] had an open mouth showing sharp teeth. The tapir's[5] snout was definitely snoutish. The snake wound round and round and round—and if you unwound him, he reached from Nima-Cux's toes to her earlobes.

Above all, Nima-Cux could sing like a bird. Her voice tripped up and down the scale as easily as her feet tripped up and down the steps. The *cacique* sat back and counted his blessings. They all had to do with Nima-Cux, her beauty, her baskets, her clay work, and, especially, her voice.

As princesses should, Nima-Cux had everything she asked for—besides some things she hadn't thought of requesting. There were finely carved dolls, necklaces of rare shells, a cape of bright parrot feathers, an enormous garden filled with flowers and blossoming trees and singing birds and pet animals. No wonder Nima-Cux was happy.

Thus life flowed along contentedly for everyone in the household until Nima-Cux neared her sixteenth birthday. Suddenly she became sad and melancholy. Nothing made her happy. Then again, nothing made her unhappy. She just *was*, for no reason at all, she said.

Detail from *Aviary Triptych* (1992), Carol Cottone-Kolthoff. By permission of the artist. Copyright © 1992 Carol Cottone-Kolthoff.

The *cacique* was greatly agitated. He strode up and down the garden, wondering, wondering what would please Nima-Cux. Another doll? A bright fish? A golden plate for her breast-of-pheasant? But to whatever he proposed, Nima-Cux would only murmur politely, "No. But thank you, Papa."

The cook sent boys scampering up the tallest palm trees to bring back heart of palm for Nima-Cux's dinner.

Hunters were ordered into the jungle to capture monkeys. "Mind you, *funny* monkeys to entertain the princess. Not a sad one in the crowd—or off comes your head."

Maidens roamed the royal gardens gathering orchids to ornament the princess' bedchamber.

What happened? Nima-Cux would peer at the rare *palmito*[6] and moan softly, "I am not hungry."

She would stare at the monkeys cavorting[7] on the branches, while the royal household

---

3. **coati** (kō-ä′tē): a raccoonlike animal of the tropical Americas and the southwestern United States.
4. **puma** (pyōō′mə): a mountain lion.
5. **tapir's** (tā′pərz): belonging to a large, hoglike animal.
6. **palmito** (päl-mē′tô) *Spanish*: a bud of a palm tree, used as a food.
7. **cavorting** (kə-vôrt′ĭng): leaping about.

WORDS TO KNOW
melancholy (mĕl′ən-kŏl′ē) *adj.* depressed and gloomy
agitated (ăj′ĭ-tāt′əd) *adj.* emotionally excited or disturbed

792

Mini-Lesson ⟡ Literary Concepts

CONFLICT Use the word web shown to remind students that conflict may occur within a person's mind (internal conflict) or it may occur when a character struggles against an outside person or force (external conflict). In some cases the author explains the cause of a conflict; in others, the reader must use details from the story to infer why the character is experiencing conflict.

Application Have students place *I* in the blank for internal conflict and *E* for external conflict.

1. __I__ In deciding whether she would tell the woman about the death of her dog, Georgeanne tried to think of what she would want her friend to do in the same situation.
2. __E__ As the woman ran toward the east, the spirit continually placed fruit trees in her path in an attempt to slow her down.
3. __I__ Nima-Cux is unsure why she is unhappy. She wonders if her unhappiness is justified or if she is being selfish.

792 THE LANGUAGE OF LITERATURE TEACHER'S EDITION

screamed in amusement, and would whisper, "Yes, yes, very comical," and sigh deeply. The household would hush its laughter and echo her sighs.

The orchids went unnoticed until they dropped to the floor with a dry rustle.

Herb doctors came. Witch doctors came. Old hunched crones said to know the secrets of life came. They all said, "But she seems quite well and normal. A bit pale. A trifle listless. Perhaps a good tonic . . ."

Nima-Cux was annoyed enough to argue about the tonic. "That smelly stuff? I won't even taste it."

Finally a sorcerer somewhat wiser than the others spoke to the *cacique*. "After all, the princess is practically sixteen. Other girls her age are married. Find a good husband for the Princess Nima-Cux—and she will again shine radiant as a star."

The *cacique* shook his head. A *husband*? How could a mere husband bring her happiness if her own father could not? A poor suggestion. What were sorcerers coming to?

He peeked once more at Nima-Cux's dismal face—and in desperation sent messengers throughout his kingdom. The young man skillful enough to impress the princess and coax a smile to her lips would become her husband. In a week the first tournament would be held.

During the next week the roads were worn into holes by the thousands of footsteps.

Detail from *Aviary Triptych* (1992), Carol Cottone-Kolthoff. By permission of the artist. Copyright © 1992 Carol Cottone-Kolthoff.

Everyone in the kingdom hurried to the palace either to take part or to watch the take-parters (or is it takers-part?). Seats were constructed for the nobility. Those not so noble found a patch of thick grass, a loop of vine, or a high branch. The *cacique* and Nima-Cux sat on a canopied stand. The tournaments began.

The first contestant marched out, proud and arrogant in his gold tunic, attended by a troop of warriors. A handsome youth he was. Maidens fainted with joy at the sight of him. The rest of the contestants growled and trembled.

But Nima-Cux frowned and asked, "What can he *do*? Besides prance and preen, worse than any *quetzal*?"[8]

The *cacique* sighed and made a sign for the warrior to display his talents—if any. The soldiers stood before the young man and threw ears of corn into the air. With his bow and arrows the warrior shot kernels from the ears in regimental procession. One row, then the next and next until all the kernels were gone.

The spectators cheered and shouted with admiration. Such skill—and such elegance! Ayyyyyy! The other contestants ground their teeth and sobbed.

---

8. *quetzal* (kĕt-säl′): a Central American bird with brilliant green and red feathers.

THE FIRST FLUTE **793**

Literary Concept: INTERNAL CONFLICT

F Have students discuss whether the sorcerer is correct in his explanation of the princess's internal conflict. *(Possible responses: He is right, because the sadness comes on suddenly about the time most girls in her culture are married. He is wrong, because real happiness depends on an individual's inner self, not on his or her relationship with another.)*

Active Reading: EVALUATE

G Ask students why the *cacique* suggests that the sorcerers were not very good. *(Possible response: The cacique may not be ready for his daughter to marry; he may be jealous of another man becoming more important to her than he is.)*

Active Reading: CLARIFY

H Ask students why the author of the story would decide to ask readers if it is more correct to say "take-parters" or "takers-part." If necessary, provide the following model:

Think-Aloud Model *It first struck me as very odd to read this question thrown into the story. Usually, authors decide what ways words should be written and put them into place. Perhaps, because this story is meant to be spoken, the writer wants to capture some of the same feeling of interaction between the storyteller and audience. This kind of question keeps me interested in reading more.*

Literary Links

I Encourage students to discuss Nima-Cux's attitude toward the eligible suitors and the speaker's attitude in Dorothy Parker's "The Choice." *(Possible response: Both characters have similar attitudes towards the suitors who are deemed most eligible—they are not interested in these men. Instead, they are looking for someone who can make them happy.)*

Multicultural Perspectives

MAYAN KNOWLEDGE Besides developing a uniquely complex pictorial language, the Maya were proficient in astronomy and mathematics. They used two calendars simultaneously, one for sacred rituals and the other based on the sun's orbit.

The sacred calendar was 260 days long. Each day was called by one of 20 names and assigned a number from 1 to 13 (20 × 13 = 260 days). Each day also had a god or goddess connected to it. By studying the combination of gods, goddesses, and numbers, the priests made predictions about how lucky or unlucky a particular day might be.

The calendar that was based on the sun's orbit was more accurate than the Gregorian calendar used today. It had 18 months of 20 days each, with 5 days at the end of the year. These 5 days were considered extremely unlucky, and all unnecessary work was strictly prohibited throughout Mayan territory.

Linking to Social Studies

J Mayan society was rigidly stratified. The cacique was a member of the ruling class that controlled an agriculturally based peasantry from large cities. This elite group also controlled the government, warfare, religion, and trade. Architects were especially valued, as the Maya constructed large public-works projects that rivaled the size of the Great Pyramids of Egypt—and without the benefit of the wheel or beasts of burden.

CUSTOMIZING FOR
Students Acquiring English

2 Explain that "the Mayan youth competed with each other for the favor of Nima-Cux" means that each young man was trying to impress Nima-Cux and convince her to marry him.

Critical Thinking: ANALYZING

K Have students explain the difference between the minstrel and other competitors. Ask if they are surprised by the princess's response to this competitor. *(Possible responses: The minstrel is the least vain or boastful of all the competitors. It seems unlikely he could win the attention of the princess after so many others have failed. On the other hand, the princess was turned off by the other competitor's arrogance, so it is not altogether surprising that she likes the more humble minstrel.)*

Literary Links

L Ask students to compare the importance of music for Nima-Cux and Clarissa in Vickie Sears's "The Dancer." *(Possible response: Both Nima-Cux and Clarissa find pleasure in music. Music and singing are the center of Nima-Cux's relationship to Mayan culture. Clarissa, on the other hand, develops a relationship with her culture through dance.)*

Nima-Cux yawned and asked politely, "May we see the second match, Papa? The first has taken up *so* much time."

The *cacique* sighed again and motioned for the tournament to continue.

The second competitor strode out as confident and proud as the first. He walked alone, bearing a large basket. When he set it down, out slithered a tremendous snake of a poisonous variety, its eyes glaring with malevolence.

The spectators gasped with horror. Maidens fainted with fear. The remaining rivals watched with relish.

The youth engaged the angry snake in combat, artfully evading its deadly fangs. The spectators held their breaths.

"How boring!" muttered Nima-Cux, staring into the distance.

"Really? Really, daughter? You don't like it?" asked the *cacique* with regret. (He was enjoying the contests immensely.)

He motioned for more action. The youth complied by squeezing the life from the snake. Then he bowed to the applause of the crowd. Or most of the crowd. Nima-Cux was already on her way to the palace and her couch with a headache.

For days the tournaments continued. The most handsome and courageous of the Mayan youth competed with each other for the favor of Nima-Cux— favor that was nowhere to be seen. Certainly not on her lips, which remained clamped in a sulky line. Nor in her eyes, which gazed sadly at the competition without seeing it.

Finally the last contestant appeared, a merry boy wearing the tattered dress of a minstrel.[9] The spectators smiled. The other contestants laughed scornfully. With a quick bow to the princess, the boy began to sing. He sang of the lakes, the forests, the hills of the highlands. He sang of the crystal stars flashing from the dark river of night. He sang of love.

Not bad, not bad, nodded the *cacique*. Not, of course, to compare with Nima-Cux's singing. He glanced at his daughter. What astonishment! Her eyes resembled the crystal of the song. Her lips were open and curving—upward. She was smiling! The *cacique* sat back and pondered the puzzle of life and love.

"I like him, Papa. We can sing together. I will marry him. Only first, he must learn the song of each bird of the forest. Then he can teach me."

---
9. **minstrel** (mĭn′strəl): a singer or musician.

Detail from *Aviary Triptych* (1992), Carol Cottone-Kolthoff. By permission of the artist. Copyright © 1992 Carol Cottone-Kolthoff.

WORDS TO KNOW
evading (ĭ-vā′ dĭng) *adj.* escaping or avoiding **evade** *v.*

794

Mini-Lesson: Speaking, Listening, and Viewing

INDIGENOUS MUSIC Explain to students that—like social customs, foods, clothing, and traditions—music varies from culture to culture. Sometimes these differences may seem minimal or even nonexistent. Other times, the patterns, harmonies, and instruments differ greatly and may sound strange to an unaccustomed listener.

Application Encourage students to research the indigenous music of areas that were once part of Mayan territory: Guatemala, Mexico, Belize, El Salvador, and Honduras. Students should be able to find such music at a public library or a local music store. Have students attempt to identify the following components:
- the instruments used in the performance
- the language in which the music is performed
- elements that rhyme or repeat, such as a chorus or melody
- the purpose for which it may have originally been intended, such as music for a celebration or a festival

The minstrel was happy to oblige. He had *meant* it when he sang of love. At once he disappeared into the jungle.

Day after day he practiced, imitating this bird, then that one. But Guatemala is home to hundreds, thousands of birds. Some whistle a complicated tune. The minstrel began to despair of his task.

The god of the forest, after listening for days to the young minstrel's efforts, took pity on him. Also on the birds and other wild inhabitants of the woods—not to mention himself. He appeared before the minstrel, wearing a kindly smile.

"Perhaps I can help you," he offered. "It is a difficult exercise you are engaged in."

Severing a small limb from a tree, the god removed the pith and cut a series of holes in the tube. "Now attend carefully," he said. And he instructed the young man exactly how to blow into one end while moving his fingers over the holes. The notes of the birds tumbled out, clear and sweet.

With a torrent of thanks, the minstrel flew on his way, carrying the *chirimia,* or flute. Just in time. Nima-Cux, anxious that the chore she had assigned her lover had been impossible, was on the point of another decline. She received the youth with joy. Enchanted she was with the flute and its airs[10] . . . with the minstrel and his airs.

The two were married and lived long and happily in the palace of the *cacique.* And today the Indians of Guatemala will point to the *chirimia,* the most typical of native instruments, and tell you this is the way it came about. ❖

---

10. **airs:** melodies.

Dorothy Sharp Carter

Dorothy Sharp Carter (1921–) developed a strong affinity for Latin American folklore during her 11 years in South and Central America, where her husband worked as a United States foreign service officer.

When she returned to the United States, she entered a graduate program in library science at the University of Texas. One of her projects was collecting and translating Latin American folk tales. Impressed with her work, her professor sent the manuscript to a publisher. It was accepted, and *The Enchanted Orchard and Other Folktales of Central America,* from which "The First Flute" is taken, was published in 1973. Her stories have been published in the magazines *Travel, Nature, Highlights for Children,* and *Humpty Dumpty.*

She was born in Chicago and grew up in Galveston, Texas. Later, Carter went to Mills College in California and taught high school in California and Costa Rica, where she met her husband. They currently live in Texas, spending part of their time on a ranch on the Pedernales River, where they enjoy Texas wildlife.

OTHER WORKS *Greedy Mariani and Other Folktales of the Antilles; His Majesty, Queen Hatshepsut*

Literature Connection

Project 1 Suggest that students focus on major characters, as there will be more evidence on which to base an evaluation for these characters. Students should select five or six qualities to evaluate. As students debate each quality, they should cite evidence in the story to support the grade.

Rubric

3 Full Accomplishment Students produce a report card that accurately represents many qualities of the character they selected.

2 Substantial Accomplishment Students produce a report card that accurately reflects several qualities of the character they selected.

1 Little or Partial Accomplishment Students produce a report card that lists few qualities and does not reflect the character they selected.

RESPONDING OPTIONS

Multimodal Activity

LITERATURE CONNECTION PROJECT 1

Make a Character "Report Card" Working in small groups, select a character from one of the selections you have just read. Prepare a "report card" to evaluate the character's personality, using the following guidelines.

The Character's Qualities Begin by deciding on the qualities you wish to evaluate—courage, kindness, greed, ingenuity, and so on.

The Grading Scale Then decide on the grades you will use to assess the character. You could use letters, numbers, or even symbols.

Group Debate and Class Report Within your group, discuss and debate each quality of the character. Assign a grade when your entire group is in agreement. Report your decision back to the class.

Report Card			
Character	courage	kindness	ingenuity
Nima-Cux			

Multimodal Activity

MATHEMATICS CONNECTION PROJECT 2

Use the Mayan Number System The Maya developed a mathematical system based on the number 20, instead of 10 as in the decimal system we use. They used a dot to represent 1, a line for 5, and a shell or egg-shaped symbol for zero.

Given what you now know about the Mayan numerical system, identify the other Mayan numbers shown.

From the information provided thus far, figure out and write the Mayan numbers for 8, 16, and 80. Then working with a partner, see if you can figure out the Mayan number for 100.

796 UNIT SIX: THE ORAL TRADITION

Mathematics Connection

Project 2 The other Mayan numbers shown are 9, 15, and 60. 8 is written as 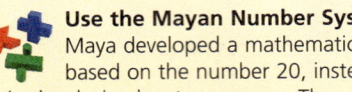. 16 is written as ⬚. 80 is written as ⬚. 100 is written as ⬚. To help students find the first two answers, remind them to substitute a ⬚ for each grouping of five. To find the last two answers, remind students that 20 is a special number in the Mayan number system. Ask students how they could rewrite 80 and 100 in groups of 20. ($20 \times 4 = 80$; $20 \times 5 = 100$) Point out the relationship between the number of dots over the egg-shaped symbol for 20 and 40 and the number of groupings of 20 for that number ($1 \times 20 = 20$; $2 \times 20 = 40$). Some students may suggest putting five dots over the egg-shaped symbol for 100. Remind them that five is represented by a line. Encourage students to write other Mayan numerals on one side of flash cards and work in pairs to identify them.

Multimodal Activity

SOCIAL STUDIES CONNECTION PROJECT 3

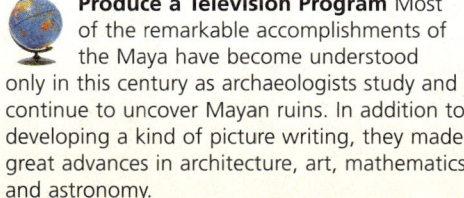

Produce a Television Program Most of the remarkable accomplishments of the Maya have become understood only in this century as archaeologists study and continue to uncover Mayan ruins. In addition to developing a kind of picture writing, they made great advances in architecture, art, mathematics, and astronomy.

Use your school library to research Mayan accomplishments. If you have access to a computer, you could use an encyclopedia program or an on-line service to start your research. Visit a museum with Mayan artifacts if one is nearby. Then produce an educational television program using the following suggestions as a guide:

- Decide on the program's length.
- Write a script from your research, including a brief introduction that explains who the Maya were. You might also include information about their descendants today.
- Gather visual material, and rehearse the show to fit the time slot.
- Make a videotape of the program and show it to your class and other classes.

Multimodal Activities

ACROSS CULTURES MINI-PROJECTS

Tell a Story Through Drawings Adapt one of the three stories to a present-day setting, and tell it through a series of drawings. Keep explanatory text to a minimum. You might want to create a comic strip, picture book, flipbook, or a series of illustrations on wall-sized posterboard. Share your results with classmates.

Write a Letter of Advice Imagine you are training to be a counselor. Your assignment is to analyze the relationship of the couple in "Strawberries" or the couple in "No News." On the basis of your analysis of their behavior, write a letter of advice to the newly married couple in "The First Flute," suggesting how they might build a strong relationship.

Tell an Origin Myth Many cultures have origin myths similar to "Strawberries" and "The First Flute." Choose a nonliving thing in nature, an object such as a musical instrument, or a fruit or vegetable, and write an origin myth about it. Present your tale to the class.

Investigate Cherokee Beliefs and Customs All cultures have distinct beliefs and customs about marriage and family life. Cherokee women held great power, and families were matrilineal, tracing their descent through women instead of men. Find out more about Cherokee customs. Then form small discussion groups and compare and contrast traditional Cherokee beliefs to your own cultural standards.

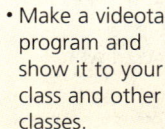

Extended Social Studies Reading

MORE ABOUT THE CULTURES

- *The Cherokees* by Elaine Landau
- *Indians of the Southeast: Then and Now* By Jesse Burt and Robert B. Ferguson
- *Lost Kingdoms of the Maya* by Gene S. Stuart and George E. Stuart
- *The Mysteries of the Ancient Maya* by Carolyn Meyer and C. Gallenkamp

LINKS TO UNIT FIVE

Social Studies Connection

Project 3 A full-length television program is a lot of work. Suggest that students try to complete a five- to seven-minute feature about the Maya. If students do not have access to videotape, invite them to stage the television program as it might be shot in a studio. Students may wish to create large pictures of Mayan temples or architecture to serve as backdrops for the program. Be sure students have a developed and rehearsed script before they begin videotaping.

Rubric

3 Full Accomplishment Students make or stage a television feature that highlights major contributions of the Mayan culture.

2 Substantial Accomplishment Students finish the project, but their information is not detailed.

1 Little or Partial Accomplishment Students fail to complete the project or present data that are factually incorrect.

Across Cultures

Tell a Story Through Drawings Before they begin to draw, students should outline the most important events of the story.

Write a Letter of Advice Suggest to students the difference between the successful couple in "Strawberries" and the failed couple in "No News" may be the degree of involvement each partner has in the other's life. The degree of involvement Nima-Cux has in the minstrel's life and vice versa may be a key determinant of the success or failure of the relationship.

Tell an Origin Myth Challenge students to develop tales about how things began that involve modern technology, such as the development of a cellular telephone or the computer.

Investigate Cherokee Beliefs and Customs If possible, each discussion group should contain students of several cultures. Each student could concentrate on one aspect of Cherokee culture and compare it to his or her own culture. For example, extended families in Cherokee and Asian cultures; harvest festivals in Native American and Jewish cultures.

OVERVIEW

To gain a deeper appreciation of the nonfiction selections they have read in this unit, students will explore the characteristics of a research report and then create their own well-developed example in this lesson.

Objectives

- To plan a research report by considering such elements as topic, thesis statement, examples, and organization
- To draft a research report and solicit a response
- To revise, edit, and publish a research report
- To reflect on the process of writing a research report

Skills

LITERATURE
- Ordering details

WRITING AND LANGUAGE
- Writing a thesis statement
- Making an outline
- Crediting sources

GRAMMAR AND USAGE
- Capitalizing titles

MEDIA LITERACY
- Interpreting a comic strip

- Analyzing a company disclaimer
- Studying a letter
- Using on-line research sources

SPEAKING, LISTENING, AND VIEWING
- Interviewing
- Storytelling
- Reading aloud

RESEARCH SKILLS
- Taking notes
- Using KWL charts

Teaching Strategy: STUMBLING BLOCK

A Writing something original based on several sources is a challenge. As a result, many students treat the report as an exercise in restating what they have read. The paper becomes a string of quotations, paraphrases, and summaries that lack purpose and focus—and often contain plagiarism. Urge students to regard the paper as a chance to answer a question for a particular audience.

Teaching Strategy: MODELING

B Ask students if they have heard similar stories and discuss the popularity of such stories. Students may suggest that these stories are so popular because they are shocking or bizarre and people like to discuss the unbelievable.

WRITING FROM EXPERIENCE

Writing a Report

In Unit Six, "Across Time and Place: The Oral Tradition," you read several stories from different cultures. New folklore continues to develop as stories, tales, and urban legends. Investigating and researching these stories can be fascinating.

GUIDED ASSIGNMENT

A **Write a Research Report** In this lesson you will get a chance to research the culture of a story, folk tale, myth, fable, or urban legend. Then you'll write a report about your findings.

1 Look for a New Angle

What new and interesting facts can you discover about folklore?

Stories You've Read Which of the selections in the unit did you enjoy the most? Would you like to find out more about this type of story or the country it came from?

Cultural Connection Are there stories you've heard from your own culture or from that of a friend that you'd like to learn more about? Have you ever wondered about the stories represented in folk art, song, or dance?

Stories in the News The items on these pages represent some well-known urban legends. These stories describe scary or humorous experiences in urban settings. Usually they happened to "a friend of a friend." Have you heard similar stories? Make a list of such stories and any questions you might have about them.

Company Disclaimer

To Our Customers
The widespread rumor that a customer discovered a rat in her bucket of Krispy Krunchy Chicken is false. Our standards for sanitation and proper food preparation procedures are among the highest in the industry. We regret the confusion this rumor has caused.

I've heard something similar to this. I thought the story was true when I heard it.

B These incidents are variations of stories told throughout the United States and Canada. The stories are usually reported as fact. Why do you think these stories are so popular?

798 UNIT SIX: THE ORAL TRADITION

PRINT AND MEDIA RESOURCES

UNIT SIX RESOURCE BOOK
Prewriting Activity, p. 45
Elaboration, p. 46
Peer Response Guide, pp. 47–48
Revising and Proofreading, p. 49
Student Model, pp. 50–52
Rubric, p. 53

GRAMMAR MINI-LESSONS
Transparencies, p. 27
Copymasters, p. 36

WRITING MINI-LESSONS
Transparencies, pp. 60–61

ACCESS FOR STUDENTS ACQUIRING ENGLISH
Reading and Writing Support

FORMAL ASSESSMENT
Guidelines for Writing Assessment

 LASERLINKS
Writing Springboard

 WRITING COACH

---

798 THE LANGUAGE OF LITERATURE TEACHER'S EDITION

Letter

March 1

Dear Debbie,

Hey, girl, how are you?

I went camping last week, and my cousin told me a story that I keep thinking about. We were talking about bears, and she told me about a man and a woman who went camping with their baby and saw a bear. They wanted a picture of their kid with the bear, so they spread honey all over the kid's face and hands. The bear started to attack the kid, and the people barely escaped with their lives. Can you believe someone would actually do that? It made me nervous the rest of the trip. Do you think it's true?

Write me soon, or else!

Love,
Melvonne

Hey! Someone else told me this story too!

Comic Strip

Mother Goose and Grimm

I've heard this one before. Could it possibly be true?

❷ Choose and Explore

Of all the kinds of folk tales you've read about or heard, which kind interests you most? Choose one type of folk tale and write a paragraph explaining what you already know about this kind of story. What more do you want to find out? What angle would you like to explore further?

LASERLINKS
- WRITING SPRINGBOARD

WRITING COACH

WRITING FROM EXPERIENCE 799

Teaching Strategy: MODELING

C To show students how to generate writing ideas from springboards such as letters, cartoons, and company disclaimers, invite volunteers to read aloud the models on pages 798 and 799. Point out the handwritten comments in the margins and have students work in pairs to generate their own questions. Possibilities include:
- What makes this an urban legend? How could I find out sources for these stories?
- How did these stories get started? Why do people find these folk tales so interesting?

Writing Skill: FINDING WRITING IDEAS

D Be sure students understand that a report is based on material from outside sources rather than on personal knowledge. Explain that the folk tale chosen as the report's subject should be interesting to the writer and the audience. Remind students to choose a topic narrow enough for a short report and for which there is enough background information available.

CUSTOMIZING FOR Less-Proficient Writers

E Beginning writers may have a hard time figuring out how much research a topic will need and how to locate the information. Evaluate the folk tales and the new angles students have chosen and help them judge the availability of information. If necessary, guide students toward topics for which information is easily accessible.

WRITING SPRINGBOARD

Modern Legends Legends aren't just from the distant past. New ones are cropping up every day. You may have heard of some of the modern legends discussed in this lighthearted video presentation.

Side B, Frame 25362

Writing Prompt Write a research report about modern legends. Discuss how they begin, how they grow, and themes that appear many times.

THE LANGUAGE OF LITERATURE TEACHER'S EDITION 799

Teaching Strategy:
STUMBLING BLOCK

F Students often write more effective reports if they find a focus *after* they have read some research material and taken some notes. Finding a focus may well depend on how much information is gathered during the initial search process and how students evaluate and categorize that information. Suggest that students having difficulty finding a focus begin their preliminary research and note taking, and develop a focus as they proceed.

Media Literacy:
GATHERING FACTS

G Students who are having difficulty getting information about a topic may benefit from working with partners. Together they can use the library database and other on-line sources.

Critical Thinking: ANALYZING

H Students are apt to consider any published sources as reliable, pertinent, and equally valid. Remind students to approach all sources critically. Guide students to understand what the author of a source is trying to accomplish and what audience is being addressed. Remind students to treat facts as claims that can be challenged or interpreted differently.

PREWRITING

Researching Folklore

The Search for Answers The questions you have about your topic may be the starting point for your research. The kinds of information you want will point you toward the kinds of research sources you need. These pages will help you plan your research.

❶ Find a Focus

F Try to find the most interesting aspect of your topic. If your topic is too broad, you won't be able to cover everything about it in one report. If your topic is too narrow, you won't have enough information. Try writing a statement of controlling purpose, a one- or two-sentence description of what your report will be about.

❷ Plan Your Research

After selecting a focus, you need a plan for finding information. The following tips can help you decide where to go to find sources.

Library Hunt You can complete a resource search quickly by using a library database. List all the possible sources you find and group them by call numbers or location. Back copies of articles are kept on microfilm or microfiche. See the Multimedia Handbook, page 850, for information about on-line sources.

G

Expert Advice If you're looking for information on a culture or on another topic, you can look for newsletters or brochures written by groups or organizations associated with the culture or topic. You might also ask a librarian to help you find reference books, pamphlets, or other literature.

H

INFOTRAC

Infotrac   *Magazine Index Plus
(Backfile)
Heading   URBAN FOLKLORE

1.   Heard the one about the man-eating squirrel? (coping with urban legends) by Andre Henderson il v7 Governing July '94 p25 (1)

ABSTRACT / HEADINGS

Source Cards

Encyclopedia

Dundes, Alan. "Folklore." The World Book Encyclopedia. 1995 ed.

School Library   031
                    WOR
                    V.4

Brunvand, Jan Harold. The Vanishing Hitchhiker: American Urban Legends and Their Meanings. New York: Norton, 1981.

Public Library   398.2
                    BRU

Book

Morris, Scot. "Paper Chase: Searching for modern folklore on the office bulletin board." OMNI. Apr. 1991: Vol. 13, No. 7.

Public Library

Magazine

800   UNIT SIX: THE ORAL TRADITION

SkillBuilder RESEARCH SKILLS

USING KWL CHARTS Tell students that using a KWL chart can help them plan their research for their report. Describe how a KWL chart uses questions to tap prior knowledge and arrange facts, details, statistics, and examples. Write the model shown on the board. Explain what KWL stands for:
K: What do I already *know* about the topic?
W: What do I *want* to learn?
L: What did I *learn*?

Application Have students work in small groups to fill in a KWL chart for their topic and use it as they research and write.

Topic: The Truth of Urban Legends		
K	**W**	**L**
Urban legends tell fantastic stories.	Are these stories true? How did they start? How can I prove them?	

800 THE LANGUAGE OF LITERATURE TEACHER'S EDITION

3. Gather Information

Once you've found your sources, take some time to plan your fact-gathering process. Take the following steps to be as prepared as possible for writing your report.

Preview Sources Scan the tables of contents and indexes in the books and periodicals you've chosen. Do their contents seem to offer information that will help you? If not, you may need to choose another source.

Create Source Cards As you gather facts, you'll need to keep track of the sources you find. List the author's name and the publication information of each source on a separate index card. Be sure to number each card. This will help you stay organized when you take notes.

Take Notes The SkillBuilder on this page can help you take notes. Write information that you want to use on a note card. Paraphrase, or write in your own words, the main ideas and supporting details from the passage. This will help you avoid plagiarism, or using a person's words without giving him or her credit. Include the source number and indicate whether the information is a quote, a paraphrase, or general knowledge—a widely known fact that can be found in many sources.

Note Cards

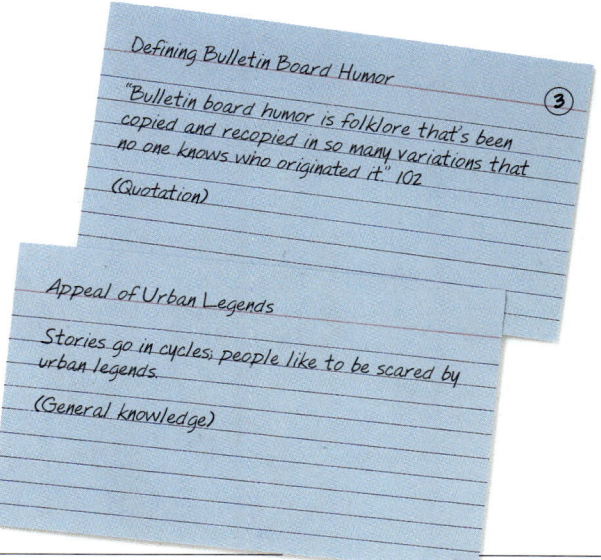

SkillBuilder

RESEARCH SKILLS

Taking Notes

Note taking is a helpful way to collect the information you find in sources. Here are some strategies for taking notes:

Paraphrase the main ideas of the material. Paraphrasing means using your own words to restate someone else's ideas. You still must credit the sources, however.

Quote a source directly if it states the idea in a particularly interesting way. Be sure to use quotation marks and to note that the information is a quote.

APPLYING WHAT YOU'VE LEARNED

Use your own words as you take notes, unless you plan to quote something exactly. In either case, credit your sources.

WRITING HANDBOOK

For more information on note taking and research report writing, see page 846 of the Writing Handbook.

THINK & PLAN

Reflecting on Your Ideas

1. How has the research material you found helped you better understand your topic?
2. What aspect of your topic do you find the most interesting? Why?

Teaching Strategy: MODELING

I Point out the sample source cards shown on page 800. Although students don't have to worry about grammar and punctuation in their notes, they must take care to spell the names of people and places correctly. Remind students that it is very difficult to go back and double-check source information, so it's important to make sure the notes are accurate from the very beginning.

Research Skill: TAKING NOTES

J Suggest that students save time and space by using abbreviations as they take notes. Share these common abbreviations with students:

&	and	=	equals
w/	with	w/o	without
Eng	English	def	definition
y	why	re	regarding

SkillBuilder RESEARCH SKILLS

TAKING NOTES Paraphrasing can be a difficult skill. Many students incorrectly believe that changing one or two words is sufficient. They also do not understand that adapting another writer's entire report structure—even if the words are changed—is still considered plagiarism. Review the note cards on this page, pointing out that the writer put the main idea in his or her own words. Provide additional examples by having students work independently or in teams to paraphrase the letter and company disclaimer on pages 798 and 799.

Applying What You've Learned Remind students that they still have to provide credit for paraphrased material if it is not common knowledge. Model this process with students.

Additional Suggestions Have students review the correct punctuation for quotations. Be sure they surround an author's exact words with quotation marks.

Teaching Strategy:
STUMBLING BLOCK

K Suggest that students who are having difficulty writing their thesis statement go back to the questions that guided their research. Share with students this method of narrowing a topic to a thesis statement by writing the following model on the board:
- Topic: Urban legends
- Research focus: What are the sources for urban legends?
- Thesis statement: Urban legends come from oral stories, such as traditional folk tales.

Writing Skill: OUTLINING

L Remind students to indent each subdivision of the outline, capitalize the first word in each line, and avoid single subheadings. Help students create an outline by sharing the following model outline with them:
I. Introduction
II. First main point
  A. First subpoint
    1. Details for A
    2. Details for A
  B. Second subpoint
    1. Details for B
    2. Details for B
III. Second main point
  [same format as II]
IV. Third main point
  [same format as II]
V. Conclusion

Writing Skill: USING THE COMPUTER

M Encourage students to draft their reports on a computer for ease in recording and revising ideas as they come up. Suggest that students apply the preprogrammed tips of the Writing Coach as they draft on the computer.

DRAFTING

Reporting the Facts

A Way with Words With organized notes and a clear idea of what your report is all about, you're already at the halfway point. Now you're ready to take the next step—writing your report.

Student's Outline and Draft

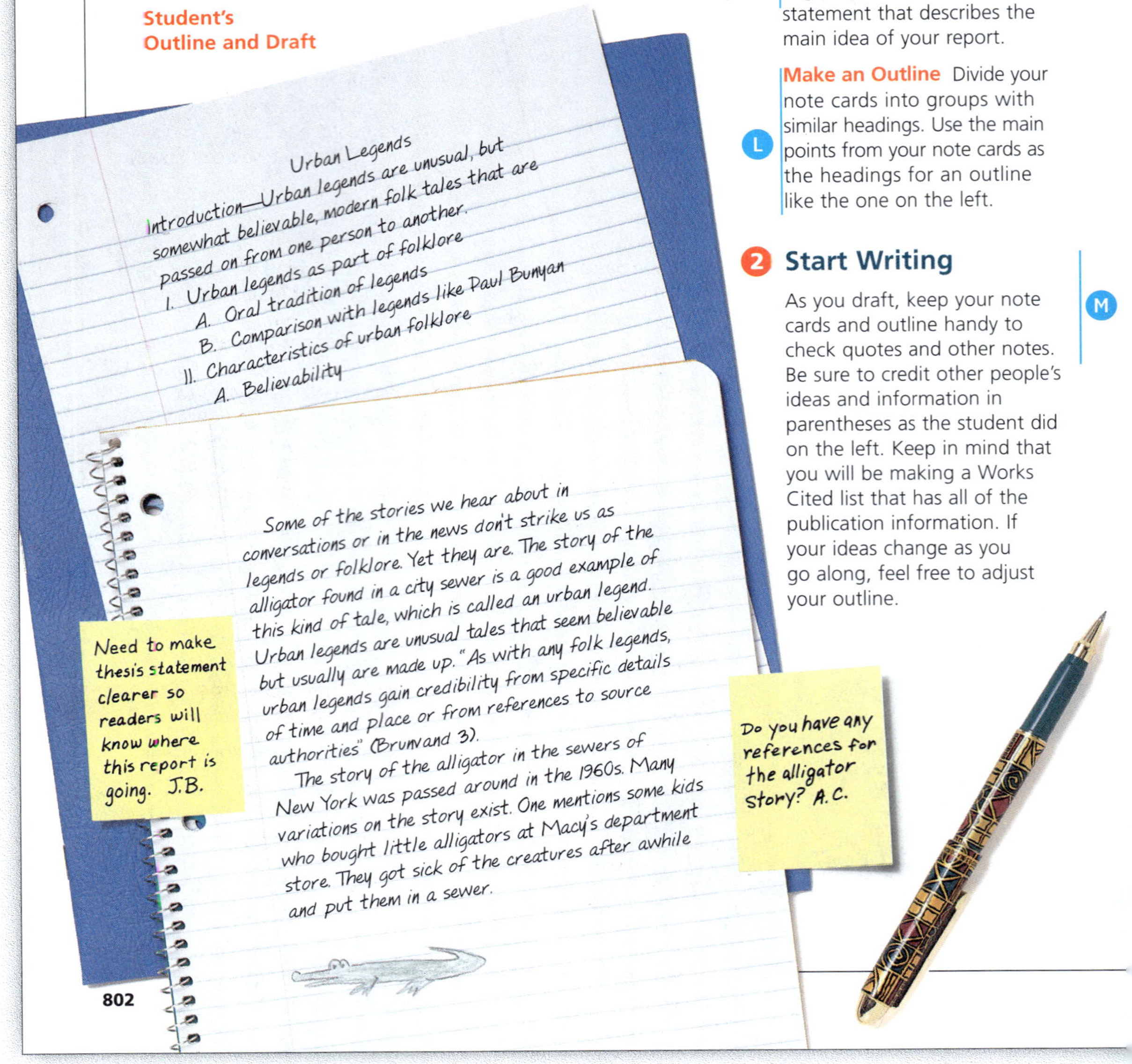

> Urban Legends
> Introduction—Urban legends are unusual, but somewhat believable, modern folk tales that are passed on from one person to another.
> I. Urban legends as part of folklore
>   A. Oral tradition of legends
>   B. Comparison with legends like Paul Bunyan
> II. Characteristics of urban folklore
>   A. Believability

> Some of the stories we hear about in conversations or in the news don't strike us as legends or folklore. Yet they are. The story of the alligator found in a city sewer is a good example of this kind of tale, which is called an urban legend. Urban legends are unusual tales that seem believable but usually are made up. "As with any folk legends, urban legends gain credibility from specific details of time and place or from references to source authorities" (Brunvand 3).
> The story of the alligator in the sewers of New York was passed around in the 1960s. Many variations on the story exist. One mentions some kids who bought little alligators at Macy's department store. They got sick of the creatures after awhile and put them in a sewer.

Need to make thesis statement clearer so readers will know where this report is going. J.B.

Do you have any references for the alligator story? A.C.

802

① Organize Your Ideas

The suggestions below will help you organize your ideas before you begin drafting.

Write a Thesis Statement
K Use your statement of controlling purpose to write a thesis statement that describes the main idea of your report.

Make an Outline Divide your note cards into groups with similar headings. Use the main points from your note cards as the headings for an outline like the one on the left.

② Start Writing

As you draft, keep your note cards and outline handy to check quotes and other notes. Be sure to credit other people's ideas and information in parentheses as the student did on the left. Keep in mind that you will be making a Works Cited list that has all of the publication information. If your ideas change as you go along, feel free to adjust your outline.

M

WRITING SPRINGBOARD
Olga Loya The Mexican American storyteller performs "La Cucarachita," a tale about discovering and learning to like the real you.

Side B, Frame 27905

Writing Prompt Different groups in the Americas have created many types of stories and folklore. Choose one ethnic group in the Americas and research its oral tradition. Then write a research paper that shares your findings.

802 THE LANGUAGE OF LITERATURE **TEACHER'S EDITION**

③ Analyze Your Draft

What new questions about your topic came to mind as you were writing? You might want to do some additional research to answer them. Make a list of your questions. Where will you go to find answers?

④ Rework and Share

Try these suggestions for organizing and polishing your draft.

Write Your Introduction Try to write an opening paragraph that will draw your readers in. Remember, your first or second paragraph will probably develop around your thesis statement. You might open with an interesting anecdote or a hypothetical question. For more on writing introductions, see page 826 of the Writing Handbook.

Order Your Details Make sure that the ideas and details in your report flow logically. If you're researching the origin of a myth or a culture, for example, you might organize your details chronologically. If you're tracing the variations of a myth, you might compare and contrast the details of each variation.

Write a Conclusion End your report by summarizing your main points in the conclusion.

Credit Your Sources Double-check that you have credited any experts or authors you quote. The SkillBuilder on this page will help you credit sources properly.

PEER RESPONSE

Peer feedback will help you know if your ideas are interesting and coherent. Ask a peer reviewer questions like these:

- What would you say is the main point of my report?
- Are there instances where you aren't sure that I used my own words? Explain.
- Have I organized my report in a way that is easy to follow?
- Is there a better word I can use to describe a particular idea?

SkillBuilder

WRITER'S CRAFT

Crediting Sources
If you quote or paraphrase, the author's last name and the page number of the source should appear in parentheses after the reference.

Work by	Example
one author	(Silverberg 3)
two or three authors	(Erdoes and Ortiz 87)
three or more authors	(Milner et al. 21)
One of two or more works by the same author	(Silverberg, The Old Ones 145)

APPLYING WHAT YOU'VE LEARNED
As you make a Works Cited list, check your source cards for the proper spelling of authors' names and source titles.

WRITING HANDBOOK

For more information on crediting sources, see page 849 of the Writing Handbook.

RETHINK & EVALUATE

Preparing to Revise

1. How have you used quotes from sources to elaborate on your ideas?
2. If you created an outline, how easy was it to write your report based on the outline?

Speaking, Listening, and Viewing: INTERVIEWING

N Since the process of drafting and revising varies from writer to writer, suggest that students gain insight into their own strengths and weaknesses by interviewing each other about how they approach these stages when writing a report. Have pairs of students interview each other, using these questions:

- Do you organize your cards in piles? Why or why not?
- Did you write your draft with your notes in front of you?
- Is your first draft complete? Explain.
- When do you insert documentation of sources cited?

Writing Skill: INTRODUCTION

O Give students examples of ways the different types of introductions they have learned about can be adapted to reports. Focus on these four types of introductions: startling fact, question, quotation, and anecdote. Encourage students to try writing one of these types of interesting openings for their report.

CUSTOMIZING FOR
Less-Proficient Writers

P Inexperienced writers may have a difficult time ordering the details in their report. Suggest that students check for a clear topic sentence in each paragraph. If the topic sentence is missing, have students add one. Then arrange students in pairs. Have partners exchange reports and use the topic sentences to check the relevance and order of the details in their partner's paragraphs.

SkillBuilder WRITER'S CRAFT

CREDITING SOURCES Explain that a credited source signals a place in a report where material from another source is paraphrased or quoted. It shows exactly where the material is located in the source and enables the reader to find the source on the Works Cited page. Have students work in small groups to prepare and check each other's documentation.

Applying What You've Learned Remind students to double-check any unusual spellings or dates. Urge students to take the time to prepare a valid list of sources.

Additional Suggestions Tell students that documentation often uses Latin abbreviations. Have students research *ibid.* and *et al.*

Reteaching/Reinforcement
Writing Mini-Lessons transparencies, pp. 60–61

Research Reports, pp. 187–205

Teaching Strategy: MODELING

Q Invite volunteers to read the final report aloud. Explore how the writer has improved the introduction by sharpening the thesis statement and using a question to draw the reader's attention. You might also want to point out the arresting punctuation in the introduction—the dashes—and the effective sentence variation. Also draw students' attention to the thesis statement and how it is supported in the report.

REVISING AND PUBLISHING

Finishing Your Report

A Final Look When you revise your draft, keep your analysis and the peer comments in mind. The suggestions on these pages also can help you get your report into its final form.

Student's Final Report

Myth-Information

Chan 1

Debbie Chan
Mr. Samuelson
5th Period English
11 March 1997

The Truth About Urban Legends

Do you believe that alligators roam the sewers of New York City? You've probably heard this story—or a version of it—and wondered whether it was true. Actually, it's an urban legend, an unusual tale that seems believable but usually is made up. Urban legends pop up in conversations on TV and in newspapers. People often hear these tales, wonder about them, and then pass them on to someone else as if they were true. Urban legends may not seem as literary as the folk tales and myths we've heard all our lives, but they are actually very similar. They have also become an accepted part of modern folklore.

One characteristic of urban legends is their believability. Jan Harold Brunvand, who teaches at the University of Utah, has studied many urban myths over the years. Brunvand writes, "As with any folk legends, urban legends gain credibility from specific details of time and place or from references to source authorities" (Brunvand 3). In other words, urban legends are believable because they contain so many realistic details.

804 UNIT SIX: THE ORAL TRADITION

---

① Revise and Edit

The Standards for Evaluation and the Editing Checklist will help you revise your research report. Here are other points to keep in mind.

- Use facts and statistics to elaborate on your points.
- Make sure you credited sources correctly.

② Prepare Your Final Copy

As you prepare your final copy, remember that your last step is to create a Works Cited list. The student model on the opposite page, as well as page 849 of the Writing Handbook, will help you.

Notice how the thesis statement sets up the main idea of the report.

How has the introduction changed since the rough draft?

Look at how one student incorporated quotes and examples in his research report.

Chan 5

Works Cited

Brunvand, Jan Harold. <u>The Vanishing Hitchhiker: American Urban Legends and Their Meanings</u>. New York: Norton, 1981.

Dundes, Alan. "Folklore." <u>The World Book Encyclopedia</u>. 1995 ed.

Morris, Scot. "Paper Chase: Searching for modern folklore on the office bulletin board." <u>OMNI</u> Apr. 1991: Vol. 13, No. 7.

Nicolini, Mary B. "Is There a FOAF in Your Future? Urban Folk Legends in Room 112." <u>English Journal</u> Dec. 1989: Vol. 78, No. 8.

" 'So there's this guy, see . . .'." <u>Maclean's</u> 2 Dec. 1991: Vol. 104, No. 48.

SkillBuilder

GRAMMAR FROM WRITING

Capitalizing Titles of Created Works

As you list sources, be sure to capitalize all proper nouns. For titles of works, capitalize the first word, the last word, and all other important words. Prepositions of fewer than five letters, articles, and conjunctions are not capitalized. Use italics or underlining to set off the title.

GRAMMAR HANDBOOK

For more information on capitalizing titles of created works, see page 890 of the Grammar Handbook.

Editing Checklist

- Did you check the spellings of authors' names for accuracy?
- Did you proofread all quotes to make sure no words were left out?

REFLECT & ASSESS

Evaluating the Experience

1. Compare writing a research paper with writing an eyewitness report. How are they similar? different?
2. Were you surprised by what you learned during the research phase? Explain.

 PORTFOLIO As you add your report to your portfolio, include a paragraph listing the research skills you gained.

WRITING FROM EXPERIENCE **805**

Standards for Evaluation

A research report
- has an interesting introduction that clearly states the topic and the purpose
- contains facts and details to support main ideas
- presents information in a logical order
- uses information from multiple sources
- gives credit for the ideas and facts of others
- ends with a strong conclusion
- includes a Works Cited list

Teaching Strategy: MODELING

R Using this sample Works Cited page as a model, point out that the sources are arranged in alphabetical order by the author's last name. Show students that the title is used for alphabetizing when there is no author. Remind students that the entries are not numbered and that the second and all subsequent lines of each entry are indented.

Speaking, Listening, and Viewing: STORYTELLING

Suggest that students publish their reports as booklets and read them to their classmates. Or have students read both the original story, folk tale, or urban legend and their report to their classmates or younger students. Remind readers to vary their pitch, volume, and pacing as they read aloud.

PORTFOLIO

Encourage students to add to their portfolio any writing they feel reflects their best efforts.

Standards for Evaluation

Have students review their reports for the following:

Ideas and Content
- includes an introduction that hooks the reader and clearly states the topic and purpose
- presents information from several sources
- contains facts and details to support the main ideas
- concludes with a summary of main points

Structure and Form
- presents information in a logical order
- gives credit for ideas and statements of others
- includes a Work Cited list and credits sources correctly

Grammar, Usage, and Mechanics
- contains no more than two or three minor errors in grammar and usage
- contains no more than two or three minor errors in spelling, capitalization, and punctuation

---

SkillBuilder — GRAMMAR FROM WRITING

CAPITALIZING TITLES OF CREATED WORKS If students are handwriting their papers, remind them to make sure their handwriting distinguishes between capital and lowercase letters. Also remind students to underline or italicize the titles of longer works such as books, movies, magazines, and newspapers. Tell them that they should use quotation marks with titles of shorter works such as legends, folk tales, articles, short stories, and poems.

Applying What You've Learned Have students work in pairs to review their papers for errors in capitalization. Caution students to pay close attention to typographical errors.

Reteaching/Reinforcement
Grammar Mini-Lessons copymasters p. 36, transparencies p. 27

Titles, p. 628

UNIT REVIEW

This feature allows students to reflect on what they have learned in Unit Six and to assess how well they understand what they have learned. This feature provides students with multiple opportunities for self-assessment, although you may wish to use some of the activities to informally assess specific skills, such as speaking and listening or cooperative work.

Objectives

- To allow students to reflect on and assess their understanding of theme
- To allow students to reflect on and assess their understanding of literary concepts such as values and characterization
- To provide students with the opportunity to assess and build their portfolios

Reflecting on Theme

OPTION 1

For each picture, have students brainstorm a list of words they would use to describe each unit theme. Students should then skim the selections in Unit Six in order to identify scenes that illustrate the words on their lists. They can then refer to this information when designing pictures for each unit.

OPTION 2

Before groups design their theme webs, have them create charts that list the five unit themes in the book and record the titles of the selections in Unit Six under any appropriate themes. Groups should then use this information to construct their theme webs. Make sure groups can support their choices for the strongest thematic connection with details from the selections.

OPTION 3

Encourage students to skim the selections in this unit as well as the notes they took while reading them in order to determine which culture's folklore had the greatest impact on them. Make sure students are able to support their choices with details from the selections and their own experiences in their oral reports.

REFLECT & ASSESS

UNIT SIX: THE ORAL TRADITION

The folklore in this unit is linked to the themes of the previous five units. Consider how you have analyzed those themes in Units One through Five. Has reading folklore in the oral tradition changed how you view the five themes? How? To explore these questions further, complete one or more of the options in each of the following sections.

REFLECTING ON THEME

OPTION 1 Writing from Within Look back at the works of art chosen to introduce each unit in this book. If you had to replace these works of art with pictures of scenes from Unit Six—scenes that reflect the unit themes—what scenes would you choose? Draw a picture or write a description of a scene for each unit.

OPTION 2 Discussion With a small group of classmates, consider how specific folklore selections might link to various unit themes. For example, "The Souls in Purgatory," which is here linked to the theme "Changing Perceptions," could also be connected to "Personal Discoveries" and "Critical Adjustments." Design a theme web to illustrate any connections your group sees. Do any of your new links seem stronger than the ones suggested in this unit? Present an oral report to the class, explaining how certain stories link to various themes.

OPTION 3 Looking at Cultures Get together with a group of classmates and discuss the cultures whose folklore you found especially interesting. Select two or three of the cultures and, for each one, jot down what you learned about it in this unit. Share your thoughts with the class in an oral report.

Self-Assessment: To what extent have this unit's selections changed how you understand the previous units' themes? For each theme, write a short paragraph explaining how your views of it have changed as a result of reading the folklore.

REVIEWING LITERARY CONCEPTS

OPTION 1 Looking at Values Much folklore reveals the values of the society from which it comes. Choose three or four selections in which you think you can pinpoint certain values of a society most clearly. Then fill in a chart like the one shown. Review your chart with a classmate, discussing whether the values revealed are relevant to our own society.

Story	Values of Society Revealed
"Otoonah"	The need for people to cooperate

Self-Assessment In order to help students answer these questions, have them look back at the notes they took while reading the selections in each unit. Make sure they pay attention to their thoughts and ideas regarding the unit themes in each case. Having read Unit Six, students should then consider their impressions of the other unit themes and assess any changes in their understanding of these themes.

OPTION 2 **Examining Characterization** Many stories in the oral tradition feature animals. With a group of classmates, discuss the ways in which animals are portrayed in the stories in this unit. Consider the following questions:
- What personal qualities are the animals shown to have?
- How are the portrayals similar to and different from the portrayals of these animals in your own culture?
- Can you see any links with portrayals of animals in other folklore that you know?

PORTFOLIO BUILDING

- **Mini-Project Writing** Look back at the writing you did for the mini-projects in this unit. Choose the piece that you think represents your best treatment of an element of folklore. (For example, you might be pleased with the morals you wrote for the Links to Unit Two.) Write a cover note explaining why you like that piece, then add the note and the piece to your portfolio.
- **Writing About Literature** By now you've responded to one of the unit's selections by writing a scene from a play. Write a review of your scene. Tell what the experience of writing it was like for you—what did you find challenging or enjoyable? Include your review in your portfolio.
- **Writing from Experience** Now that you've written a research report, explore your memory of the experience. Is the topic of folk tales easier or harder to research than other topics? In what ways? What methods did you use that you might employ in other research?
- **Personal Choice** Look back through the records and evaluations of all the activities you completed in this unit. In which of the major projects did you find your exploration of a culture or subject most

 Self-Assessment: Look at the following list of literary terms that relate to fiction. If you are uncertain about the meanings of any, look them up in the Handbook of Reading Terms and Literary Concepts on page 812. Then choose a tale from Unit Six that you particularly like, and write a few paragraphs in which you use the terms to analyze it.

characterization	dialogue
climax	mood
conflict	plot
description	theme

interesting? Make a brief note that explains your reaction, then add the note and the project evaluation to your portfolio.

 Self-Assessment: Now is your chance to review all of the work in your portfolio. Decide on a final organization of what you have included, and write a brief table of contents to show where everything is and why you have included each piece of work.

SETTING GOALS

As you completed the reading and writing activities in this unit, you probably discovered folklore that especially interested you. What kinds of folklore—myths, folk tales, fables, and legends—would you like to read more of? Are there any cultures whose folklore you would like to explore further?

Reviewing Literary Concepts

OPTION 1

Suggest that students skim the selections in this unit in order to help them complete their charts. Encourage students to consider concrete examples of society's values today to compare with those they have read about from other cultures.

OPTION 2

Students may want to skim the selections in this unit in order to determine the ways in which animals are represented. You may wish to have students record their responses in a chart that lists each animal in one column and the ways in which the animal is portrayed in different cultures in separate columns. Students should refer to this information when discussing their thoughts with their classmates.

Self-Assessment For terms that students have difficulty understanding, have them write, in their own words, a definition for each term after checking in the Handbook. You may wish to have students share their paragraphs with a partner who understands the terms.

Portfolio Building

You may wish to help students choose options or modify options for them that best suit the needs you have established for the class. Encourage students to incorporate in their portfolios drafts, in addition to final products, so that they can reflect on and assess their development and progress.

 Self-Assessment Suggest that students skim the work in their portfolio and compile a list of possible ways to organize their work. Have students consider the strengths and weaknesses of each way of organizing their work in order to determine the best way to arrange their portfolios.

Setting Goals

In order to help students answer these questions and set future goals, have them consider which kinds of folklore had the greatest impact on them and the ways in which they were affected by the folklore. Encourage them to set practical goals for outside reading in the future.

Student Resource Bank

Words to Know Access Guide 810

Handbook of Reading Terms and Literary Concepts 812

Writing Handbook
1 The Writing Process 820
2 Building Blocks of Good Writing 826
3 Narrative Writing 836
4 Explanatory Writing 838
5 Persuasive Writing 844
6 Research Report Writing 846

Multimedia Handbook
1 Getting Information Electronically 850
2 Word Processing 852
3 Using Visuals 855
4 Creating a Multimedia Presentation 857

Grammar Handbook
1 Writing Complete Sentences 860
2 Making Subjects and Verbs Agree 863
3 Using Nouns and Pronouns 870
4 Using Modifiers Effectively 878
5 Using Verbs Correctly 883
6 Correcting Capitalization 887
7 Correcting Punctuation 891
8 Grammar Glossary 900

Index of Fine Art 904

Index of Skills 906

Index of Titles and Authors 915

Words to Know: Access Guide

A
abduction, 441
abetting, 605
abominably, 49
absurd, 529
abyss, 746
accommodation, 189
acute, 381
ad-libbing, 191
adulterate, 49
adversary, 168
agile, 427
agitated, 792
ajar, 19
ambassador, 329
appalling, 50
apprehend, 463
apt, 51
ardent, 48
ardor, 230
askew, 396
assailant, 443
assertion, 430
assess, 300
assurance 334
audacity, 386
autopsy, 456

B-C
benignly, 664
blithe, 111
blunt, 221
bonanza, 110
borne, 552
brandishing, 774
bristling, 462
bureaucrat, 35
burly, 305
cajoling, 556
capricious, 243
cascade, 428
catastrophic, 85
chant, 642
chasm, 663
chronicle, 431
clarity, 221
commence, 21
communion, 222
compensate, 95
competent, 188
complex, 586
comply, 290
component, 230
concede, 468
conceived, 381
congenial, 502
conjecture, 471
consequence, 187
conservative, 254
console, 780
conspiracy, 443
copious, 60
corroborate, 468
coveted, 431
cow, 168
crevice, 383

D
debris, 375
decrepit, 92
delusion, 98
derision, 386
desolate, 92
deter, 34
devastating, 50
diffused, 665
dilated, 452
dingy, 461
discreet, 196
disdainfully, 165
disheveled, 553
dismal, 455
dispel, 553
distraught, 453
diversion, 186
docile, 84
dry, 639
dubious, 309
dumbfounded, 706

E-F
eccentric, 190
ecologically, 111
ecstasy, 225
eloquence, 555
encroaching, 391
enmity, 748
evading, 794
excess, 32
fastidious, 558
fidelity, 605
fixated, 577
flourish, 504
forlorn, 773
founder, 641
furtively, 302
futile, 109

G-H
galvanize, 452
gilded, 95
gloat, 504
gnarled, 22
grimace, 375
gusto, 233
haphazardly, 245
hodgepodge, 113
homage, 163
humane, 243
hypocritical, 386
hypothesis, 533

I
immerse, 500
immoral, 243
impact, 254
impair, 532
impeccable, 164
impel, 223
implication, 100
imposing, 166
impromptu, 19
inadequate, 221
incessantly, 243
inconceivable, 34
incongruously, 151
inconsequential, 430
inconsistency, 102
incredulity, 38
indomitable, 556
inducing, 59
inert, 642
inevitable, 453
infested, 49
insignia, 608
insolence, 170
instigate, 427
instill, 553
instinctive, 222
inter, 157
intercession, 706
intimidate, 231
introspective, 533

J-M
judicious, 198
kindling, 221
lapse, 587
lark, 336
laudable, 50
lucid, 587
malevolent, 60
malice, 84
malignant, 455
maritime, 468
median, 292
melancholy, 792
menacing, 337
meticulously, 256
millennium, 151
mirth, 61
morality, 478
motivator, 59
mutinous, 555

N-O
naïveté, 530
naturalist, 509
nebulous, 113
nondescript, 336
nostalgia, 302
novice, 168
nuance, 60
oblivious, 504
obsolete, 243
odious, 605
ominous, 23
opportunist, 526

P
palate, 236
partitioned, 289
pathetic, 590
periphery, 151
persevering, 234
persist, 639
petite, 778
pivotal, 775
placid, 86
plummet, 777
plunder, 396
ply, 475
poignant, 92
posterity, 247
precarious, 194
predominating, 427
preening, 577
preliminaries, 114
preposterous, 110
prodigy, 651
profound, 306
prone, 230
proportional, 533
prudence, 428
psyche, 59
pungent, 711

Q-R
qualm, 103
radical, 453
rapt, 92
rapture, 243
rebuke, 190
recoil, 778
refuse, 374
regression, 532
reluctant, 100
remit, 101
renunciation, 248
repertoire, 53
repress, 109
reproach, 708
rescind, 609
reserve, 32
reside, 290
resignation, 38
resort, 308
responsive, 254
retribution, 169
revoke, 441
ricochet, 58

S
sabotaged, 113
sarcasm, 58
savor, 772
scrutinize, 231
sensation, 528
serene, 591
sheer, 746
shrew, 526
sinister, 337
skepticism, 455
smolder, 395
smug, 305
soberly, 50
specialization, 529
speculation, 306
spindly, 660
spontaneity, 403
statistically, 533
stealthily, 383
stifled, 382
stipulated, 248
subdued, 40
subside, 427
subtly, 661
sulkily, 393
sullen, 555
superfluous, 308
syndrome, 533

T
tangible, 528
tantalizing, 94
tentatively, 19
testimony, 468
torso, 375
transitional, 230
traumatic, 100
tuition, 34
turbulent, 375

U-Z
unrepentant, 33
unwary, 100
vacuous, 530
vain, 86
vault, 19
vehemently, 386
verdancy, 151
verify, 291
vex, 382
vigilant, 232
vindictiveness, 441
visa, 329
vivacious, 453
vogue, 254
writhe, 61
zealot, 164

Pronunciation Key

Symbol	Examples	Symbol	Examples	Symbol	Examples
ă	at, gas	m	man, seem	v	van, save
ā	ape, day	n	night, mitten	w	web, twice
ä	father, barn	ng	sing, anger	y	yard, lawyer
âr	fair, dare	ŏ	odd, not	z	zoo, reason
b	bell, table	ō	open, road, grow	zh	treasure, garage
ch	chin, lunch	ô	awful, bought, horse	ə	awake, even, pencil, pilot, focus
d	dig, bored	oi	coin, boy		
ĕ	egg, ten	ŏŏ	look, full	ər	perform, letter
ē	evil, see, meal	ōō	root, glue, through		
f	fall, laugh, phrase	ou	out, cow		**Sounds in Foreign Words**
g	gold, big	p	pig, cap	KH	German *ich*, *auch*; Scottish *loch*
h	hit, inhale	r	rose, star		
hw	white, everywhere	s	sit, face	N	French *entre*, *bon*, *fin*
ĭ	inch, fit	sh	she, mash	œ	French *feu*, *cœur*; German *schön*
ī	idle, my, tried	t	tap, hopped		
îr	dear, here	th	thing, with	ü	French *utile*, *rue*; German *grün*
j	jar, gem, badge	*th*	then, other		
k	keep, cat, luck	ŭ	up, nut		
l	load, rattle	ûr	fur, earn, bird, worm		

Stress Marks

′ This mark indicates that the preceding syllable receives the primary stress. For example, in the word *language*, the first syllable is stressed: lăng′gwĭj.

′ This mark is used only in words in which more than one syllable is stressed. It indicates that the preceding syllable is stressed, but somewhat more weakly than the syllable receiving the primary stress. In the word *literature*, for example, the first syllable receives the primary stress, and the last syllable receives a weaker stress: lĭt′ər-ə-chŏŏr′.

Adapted from *The American Heritage Dictionary of the English Language*, Third Edition; Copyright © 1992 by Houghton Mifflin Company. Used with the permission of Houghton Mifflin Company.

Reading Terms and Literary Concepts

Act An act is a major section of a play. Each act may be further divided into **scenes.** *Survival* has three acts.

Alliteration Alliteration is a repetition of consonant sounds at the beginning of words. Writers use alliteration for emphasis and to give their writing a musical quality. Note the repetition of the *s* sound in this line from "Macavity: The Mystery Cat":

> He s̲ways his head from s̲ide to s̲ide, with movements like a s̲nake

Allusion An allusion is a reference to a famous person, place, event, or work of literature. In "Playing for Keeps," the narrator makes an allusion to Wyatt Earp, a famous lawman of the American West, when he describes how Johnny stood up to the alien.

Analysis Analysis is a process of breaking something down into its elements so that they can be examined individually. In analyzing a poem, for example, one might consider such elements as form, rhyme, rhythm, figurative language, imagery, mood, and theme.

Anecdote An anecdote is a brief account of an interesting incident or event, usually intended to entertain or make a point. Dave Barry's humorous account of an early experience in "Painful Memories of Dating" can be considered an anecdote.

Antagonist In a story, an antagonist is a force working against the protagonist, or main character; it may be another character, society, a force of nature, or even a force within the main character. In "Getting the Facts of Life," poverty is an antagonist.

Aphorism An aphorism is a short statement that expresses a general observation about life in a clever or pointed way. The sentence at the beginning of "Keeping Time"—"Sometimes the human heart is the only clock in the world that keeps true time"—is an example of an aphorism.

Author's Purpose An author's purpose is his or her reason for creating a particular work. The purpose may be to entertain, to explain or inform, to express an opinion, or to persuade readers to do or believe something. An author may have more than one purpose for writing, but usually one is most important.

Autobiography An autobiography is a form of nonfiction in which a person tells the story of his or her own life. The excerpts from *Once Upon a Time When We Were Colored* and *Gifted Hands* are examples of autobiography.
See also **Memoir** *and* **Oral History.**

Biography A biography is the story of a person's life, written by someone else. The subjects of biographies are often famous people, as in the excerpts from *Lincoln: A Photobiography* and *Harriet Tubman: Conductor on the Underground Railroad.*

Cast of Characters In the script of a play, a cast of characters is a list of all the characters in the play, often in order of appearance. The list is usually found at the beginning of the script.

Cause and Effect Two events are related as cause and effect when one event brings about the other. The event that happens first is the cause; the one that follows is the effect. In "The Dinner Party," the placing of a bowl of milk on the verandah is the cause that produces a desired effect—the removal of the snake from the dining room.

Character A character is a person, an animal, or an imaginary creature that takes part in the action of a literary work. Generally, a work focuses on one or more **main characters. Minor characters** are less important characters who interact with the main characters and with one another, moving the plot along and providing background for the story.

Character Development Characters that grow or change during a story are said to undergo character development. A character that changes significantly is called a **dynamic character;** one that changes only a little or not at all is said to be a **static character.** Main characters often develop the most. In "Otoonah," for example, the title character is a dynamic character who changes dramatically during the course of the story.

Characterization Characterization consists of all the techniques writers use to create and develop characters. There are four basic methods of developing a character: (1) physical description of the character, (2) presentation of the character's thoughts, speech, and actions, (3) presentation of other characters' thoughts about, speech to, and actions toward the character, and (4) direct comments about the character's nature.

Clarifying The process of pausing occasionally while reading, to quickly review what one understands, is called clarifying. By clarifying as they read, good readers are able to draw conclusions about what is suggested but not stated directly.

Classic Classics are enduring works of literature that are read year after year by people around the world. They deal with emotions, behaviors, and truths that human beings of every age, race, and culture share. "The Gift of the Magi" is an example of a classic work of literature.

Climax In the plot of a story or play, the climax (or turning point) is the point of maximum interest. At the climax, the conflict is resolved and the outcome of the plot becomes clear. The climax of "Raymond's Run," for example, occurs when Squeaky wins the race.
See also **Conflict** and **Plot.**

Comparison The process of identifying similarities is called comparison. In "Stop the Sun," for example, the father's terrified breathing is compared to the panting of "some kind of hurt animal."

Conflict Conflict is a struggle between opposing forces. In an **external conflict,** such as the battle between Gustus and the hurricane in "The Banana Tree," a character struggles against another person or some outside force. **Internal conflict,** on the other hand, is a struggle within a character. In "The Splendid Outcast," the narrator experiences inner conflict about what to do at the auction.

Connecting A reader's process of relating the content of a literary work to his or her own knowledge and experience is called connecting. In "The Moustache," for example, readers may connect with Mike's feelings as he interacts with his grandmother.

Context Clues Unfamiliar words are often surrounded by words or phrases—called context clues—that help readers understand their meaning. A context clue may be a definition, a synonym, an example, a comparison or contrast, or any other expression that enables readers to infer the word's meaning.

Contrast The process of pointing out differences between things is called contrast. In "Dancer," for example, the narrator contrasts Clarissa with other children when she says, "Some foster kids come with lots of stuff, but she came with everything she had in a paper bag."

Description A description is a picture, in words, of a scene, a character, or an object. Descriptions can be used to appeal to readers' senses or to provide detailed information about characters or events.

Dialect A dialect is a form of language that is spoken in a particular place or by a particular group of people. Dialects of a language may differ from one another in pronunciation, vocabulary, and grammar.

Some of the dialogue in *All Things Bright and Beautiful* features the dialect of Yorkshire, in the north of England.

Dialogue The words that characters speak aloud are called dialogue. In most literary works, dialogue is set off with quotation marks. In play scripts, however, each character's dialogue simply follows his or her name, without being indicated by quotation marks.

Drama A drama, or play, is a form of literature meant to be performed by actors before an audience. In drama, the characters' dialogue and actions tell the story.

Dynamic Character
See **Character Development**.

Essay An essay is a short work of nonfiction that deals with a single subject. A **formal essay** is highly organized, thoroughly researched, and serious in tone. **Informal essays** are lighter in tone and usually reflect their writers' feelings and personalities.

Evaluating Evaluating is the process of judging the worth of something or someone. A work of literature, or any of its elements, may be evaluated in terms of such criteria as entertainment, believability, originality, and emotional power.

Exaggeration An overstating of an idea is called exaggeration. For example, in "White Mice," one student exaggerates the consistency of the food in a pot by asking, "Is this porridge or cement?" Extreme exaggeration for the purpose of emphasis or humor is called **hyperbole**.

Exposition Exposition, which is usually found at the beginning of a story or play, serves to introduce the main characters, to describe the setting, and sometimes to establish the conflict. In "Spotted Eagle and Black Crow," for example, the first two paragraphs provide most of the exposition.
See also **Plot**.

Extended Metaphor
See **Metaphor**.

External Conflict
See **Conflict**.

Fable A fable is a brief tale that teaches a lesson about human nature. Many fables feature animals that act and speak like human beings, and many end with statements of their moral, or lesson. "Brer Possum's Dilemma" is an African-American fable.

Fact and Opinion A fact is a statement that can be proved. An opinion, in contrast, is a statement that reflects a writer's belief and cannot be proved. Much nonfiction contains both facts and opinions, and it is important for readers to distinguish between the two.

Fiction Fiction is prose writing that tells an imaginary story. The writer of a fictional work may invent all the events and characters in it or may base parts of the story on real people or events.
See also **Novel** and **Short Story**.

Figurative Language Writers use figurative language—expressions that are not literally true—to create fresh and original descriptions. For example, "The Banana Tree" contains a figurative description of Gustus's shirt "fluttering from his back like a boat sail."
See also **Metaphor, Personification,** and **Simile**.

First-Person Point of View
See **Point of View**.

Flashback In a literary work, a flashback is an interruption of the action to present events that took place at an earlier time. A flashback may provide information that helps readers understand a character's current situation. In "The Bet," for example, a flashback is used to present the banker's recollection of a party he gave 15 years earlier.

Folk Tale A folk tale is a simple story that has been passed from generation to generation by word of mouth. The characters in folk tales may be animals, people, or superhuman beings. Folk tales are told primarily to entertain rather than to explain something or teach a lesson. "The Five Eggs" is a folk tale from Ecuador.

Foreshadowing Foreshadowing occurs when a writer provides hints that suggest future events in a story. For example, in "The Inn of Lost Time" the folk tale about Urashima Taro anticipates elements in, and gives readers hints about, Zenta's story.

Form A literary work's form is its structure or organization. The form of a poem includes the arrangement of words and lines on the page. Some poems follow predictable patterns, with the same number of syllables in each line and the same number of lines in each stanza. Others, like "Foreign Student," have irregular forms. In some cases, a poem is given a form that reflects its content—as in "Mixed Singles," where the arrangement of words and lines suggests the movement of a tennis ball.

Frame Story Frame stories are stories that contain or connect other stories. For example, "The Inn of Lost Time" consists of a frame story containing two other stories.

Free Verse Poetry without regular patterns of rhyme and rhythm is called free verse. Some poets use free verse to capture the sounds and rhythms of ordinary speech. "Rice and Rose Bowl Blues" is an example of a poem written in free verse.

Generalization A generalization is a broad statement about an entire group, such as "Whales are larger than salmon." Not all generalizations are true. Some are too broad or not supported by sufficient evidence, like the statement "All eighth graders like yogurt."

Genre A type or category of literature is called a genre. There are four main literary genres: fiction, nonfiction, poetry, and drama.

Humor Humor is a quality that provokes laughter or amusement. Writers create humor through exaggeration, sarcasm, amusing descriptions, irony, and witty and insightful dialogue. "The Clown" is an example of a humorous work.

Hyperbole
See **Exaggeration**.

Idiom An idiom is an expression whose meaning is different from the sum of the meanings of its individual words. The expression "break her date" in "The Moustache" is an example of an idiom.

Imagery Imagery consists of words and phrases that appeal to readers' five senses. Writers use sensory details to help readers imagine how things look, feel, smell, sound, and taste. Note the imagery in this description of the bear in "Appetizer":

> She smells like the forest floor, like crushed moss and damp leaves, and she is as warm as a radiator back in my Massachusetts home, the thought of which floods me with a terrible nostalgia.

In-Depth Reading A reader who reads slowly and deliberately, carefully examining what he or she is reading, is engaging in in-depth reading. Works that contain specialized or challenging vocabulary—like "The Splendid Outcast"—usually require in-depth reading.

Inference An inference is a logical guess or conclusion based on evidence. By combining the information a writer provides with what they know from their own experience, readers can figure out more than the words say. For example, from James Herriot's handling of the bird's death in *All Things Bright and Beautiful,* readers can infer that he is willing to deceive the bird's owner in order to protect her feelings.

Informative Nonfiction
See **Nonfiction**.

Internal Conflict
See **Conflict**.

Irony Irony is a contrast between what is expected and what actually exists or happens. In "The Lie," for example, it is ironic that Dr. Remenzel, after lecturing Eli about not expecting special treatment, himself asks for Eli to be treated specially.

Legend A legend is a story handed down from the past about a specific person—usually someone of heroic accomplishments. Legends often have some basis in historical fact. "Spotted Eagle and Black Crow" is an Oglala legend.

Literary Nonfiction
See **Nonfiction**.

Lyric Poetry Lyric poetry is poetry that presents

the thoughts and feelings of a single speaker. "I Belong" is an example of a lyric poem.

Main Character
See **Character**.

Main Idea A main idea is a writer's principal message. It may be the central idea of an entire work or of a single paragraph. (The main idea of a paragraph is often stated in a **topic sentence.**) Usually, the term *main idea* is used in discussions of nonfiction.

Memoir A memoir is a first-person recollection of an experience or event. "The Home Front: 1941–1945" is an example of a memoir.

Metaphor A metaphor is a comparison of two things that have something in common. Unlike a simile, a metaphor does not contain an explicit word of comparison, such as *like, as,* or *resembles*. In "Moco Limping," for example, the reference to the dog's "stick of a leg" is a metaphor.

In an **extended metaphor,** two things are compared at some length and in several ways. The poem "Mother to Son" is based on an extended metaphor in which the course of the speaker's life is compared to a dark staircase.

Minor Character
See **Character**.

Mood A mood, or atmosphere, is a feeling that a literary work conveys to readers. In "The Woman in the Snow," for example, the description of the ghostly figure and her baby in the snow creates an ominous and heart-wrenching mood.

Moral A moral is a lesson that a story teaches. Morals are often stated directly at the end of fables—like the warning, in "Brer Possum's Dilemma," that one should not go looking for trouble.

Motivation A character's motivation is the reason why he or she acts, feels, or thinks a certain way. For example, Tsali in "Tsali of the Cherokees" is motivated by his Cherokee heritage and love of family.

Myth A myth is a traditional story, usually of unknown authorship, that answers basic questions about the world. Myths attempt to explain such things as human nature, the origin of the world, mysteries of nature, and social customs. "Raven and the Coming of Daylight" is a Haida myth that explains how daylight came into the world.

Narrative Any writing that tells a story is a narrative. The events in a narrative may be real or imagined. Narratives dealing with real events include biographies and autobiographies. Fictional narratives include myths, short stories, novels, and narrative poems.

Narrative Poetry Poetry that tells a story is called narrative poetry. Like fiction, narrative poetry contains characters, settings, and plots. It may also contain such elements of poetry as rhyme, rhythm, imagery, and figurative language. "Paul Revere's Ride" is an example of a narrative poem.

Narrator A narrator is the teller of a story.
See also **Point of View**.

Nonfiction Writing that tells about real people, places, and events is called nonfiction. **Literary nonfiction** is written to be read in much the same way as fiction. **Informative nonfiction** is written mainly to provide factual information.
See also **Autobiography, Biography,** *and* **Essay**.

Nonstandard English Nonstandard English is English that does not follow some of the accepted standards of grammar and usage. It can be used to convey the way some people naturally talk, thus lending an authentic, conversational style to writing. For example, the story "Dancer" is narrated in nonstandard English:

> One night she speaks up at supper and says, right clear and loud, "I'm an Assiniboin." . . . Don't nobody have to say nothing to something that proud said.

Novel A novel is a work of fiction that is longer and more complex than a short story. In a novel, setting, plot, and characters are usually developed in great detail.

Oral History When people relate the stories of their lives by word of mouth, they are creating oral histories. These histories usually include both factual recollections and personal reactions. An oral history may be preserved in writing, like Janet Bode's account of the Vietnamese youth known as Von.

Personification The giving of human qualities to an animal, object, or idea is known as personification. In "The Hurricane," for example, the storm is personified as an "agile dancer" that whirls "on the tip of its toes."

Perspective
See **Point of View**.

Persuasion Persuasion is a type of writing that is meant to sway readers' feelings, beliefs, or actions. Persuasion normally appeals to both the mind and the emotions of readers.

Play
See **Drama**.

Plot A story's plot is the sequence of related events that make up the story; it includes all the action, everything that happens. Typically, a plot begins with **exposition** that introduces the characters and the conflict they face. **Complications** arise as the characters try to resolve the conflict. Eventually, the plot reaches a **climax,** the point of greatest interest or suspense. In the **resolution** that follows, loose ends are tied up and the story is brought to a close.

Poetry Poetry is a type of literature in which ideas and feelings are expressed in compact, imaginative, and musical language. Poets arrange words in ways designed to touch readers' senses, emotions, and minds. Most poems are written in lines, which may contain regular patterns of rhyme and rhythm. These lines may, in turn, be grouped in stanzas.

Point of View The perspective from which a story is told is called its point of view. When a story is told from the **first-person** point of view, the narrator is a character in the story and uses first-person pronouns, such as *I, me,* and *we.* This is the point of view used in "The Splendid Outcast," for example. In a story told from the **third-person** point of view, on the other hand, the narrator is not a character; he or she uses third-person pronouns, such as *he, she,* and *it.* "The Banana Tree" is an example of a story told from the third-person point of view.

Predicting Using what you know to guess what may happen is called predicting. While reading stories, good readers gather information and combine it with prior knowledge to predict upcoming events. This process of predicting keeps the readers involved in what they are reading.

Prose Prose is the ordinary form of spoken and written language—that is, it is language that lacks the special features of poetry.

Protagonist In a story, a protagonist is a main character who is involved in the story's conflict. A story may have more than one protagonist—for example, Della and Jim are the protagonists of "The Gift of the Magi."

Questioning The process of raising questions while reading is called questioning. Good readers ask themselves questions in an effort to understand characters and events, looking for the answers as they continue to read.

Radio Play A drama written specifically to be heard and not seen is called a radio play. *The Hitchhiker* is an example of a radio play.

Realistic Fiction Realistic fiction is imaginative writing set in the real, modern world. The characters act like real people, using ordinary human abilities to cope with problems and conflicts typical of modern life. "The Treasure of Lemon Brown" is an example of realistic fiction.

Repetition Repetition is the use of any element of language—a sound, a word, a phrase, or a grammatical structure—more than once. Writers use repetition to stress important ideas and feelings and to create memorable sound effects, as in "Mi Madre," with its repetition of the words "I say."
See also **Alliteration** and **Rhyme**.

Resolution
See **Plot**.

Rhyme Rhyme is a repetition of sounds at the end

of words. Words rhyme when their accented vowels and all letters that follow have identical sounds. *Cat* and *bat* rhyme, as do *whether* and *feather.*

The most common form of rhyme in poetry is **end rhyme,** in which the rhyming words are at the end of lines. Rhyme that occurs within a line is called **internal rhyme.** These lines from "O Captain! My Captain!" show both end and internal rhyme:

> The ship is anchor'd safe and sound, its voyage closed and done,
> From fearful trip the victor ship comes in with object won

Rhyme Scheme The pattern of rhymes in a poem is the poem's rhyme scheme. A rhyme scheme can be described by using a different letter to represent each rhyming sound. In these lines from Dorothy Parker's "The Choice," words at the end of alternate lines rhyme:

> He'd have given me rolling lands,   a
> Houses of marble, and billowing farms,   b
> Pearls, to trickle between my hands,   a
> Smoldering rubies, to circle my arms.   b

Rhythm Rhythm is a pattern of stressed and unstressed syllables in poetry. When the stressed syllables—the syllables that are emphasized—are arranged in a consistent pattern in a poem, the poem is said to have a regular beat. Note the rhythm in this line from "O Captain! My Captain!" (the mark ´ indicates a stressed syllable; the mark ˘, an unstressed syllable):

> The port is near, the bells I hear, the people all exulting,

Scanning Scanning is the process of searching through writing for a particular fact or piece of information. When you scan, your eyes sweep across a page, looking for key words that may lead you to the information you want.

Scene In a play, a scene is a section presenting events that occur in one place at one time.

Science Fiction Science fiction is fiction based on real or imaginary scientific developments. It frequently presents an imaginative view into the future, as in "Collecting Team."

Sequencing Sequencing is a way of beginning to make sense of a story by paying attention to how the events are ordered chronologically. Understanding the sequence of events in a story allows readers to explore the impact of events on the characters and to predict what might happen next. A writer may use signal words—such as *first, next, then, now, this time,* and *before*—to indicate the sequence of events.

Setting The setting of a story, poem, or play is the time and place of the action. Sometimes the setting is clear and well-defined; at other times, it is left to readers' imagination. Elements of setting may include geographic location, historical period (past, present, or future), season, time of day, and the customs and manners of a society.

Short Story A short story is a brief work of fiction that can generally be read in one sitting. A short story usually focuses on one or two main characters who face a single problem or conflict.

Simile A simile is a comparison of two things that have some quality in common. In a simile, the comparison is expressed by means of a word such as *like, as,* or *resembles.* One of the similes in "Simile: Willow and Ginkgo" is "The ginkgo is leathery as an old bull."

Skimming Skimming is the process of reading quickly to find a main idea or to get an overview of a work or passage. It involves reading the title, the headings, the words in special type, and the first sentence of each paragraph, along with any charts, graphs, and time lines that accompany the writing.

Slang Slang is a casual, informal form of language used more often in speaking than in writing. Slang terms may be new words, or they may be established words and phrases that have taken on new meanings. In "The Treasure of Lemon Brown," for example, the slang term *bigheaded* is used to mean "smart."

Speaker In a poem, the speaker is the voice that

talks to the reader—like the narrator in a work of fiction. In some poems, such as "Saying Yes," the speaker expresses the feelings of the poet. In others, the speaker's attitude may not be the same as the poet's.

Specialized Vocabulary The words unique to a specific subject or profession make up a specialized vocabulary. The excerpt from *Gifted Hands,* for example, contains a number of terms drawn from the specialized vocabulary of the medical profession.

Stage Directions In the script of a play, the instructions to the actors, director, and stage crew are called stage directions. They may suggest scenery, lighting, music, sound effects, and ways for actors to move and speak. In this book, stage directions appear within parentheses and in italic type.

Stanza A group of lines within a poem is called a stanza. A stanza is like a paragraph in prose writing. "Sea Lullaby," for example, contains six stanzas.

Static Character
See **Character Development.**

Stereotype A stereotype is a broad generalization or oversimplified view that disregards individual differences. Stereotypes can lead to unfair judgments of people on the basis of race, ethnic background, or physical appearance.

Style A style is a manner of writing; it involves *how* something is said rather than *what* is said. The style of the poem "Mother to Son," for example, might be described as conversational—it reflects the speaker's usual, informal way of talking. Many elements contribute to style, including word choice, sentence length, tone, and figurative language.

Summarizing Summarizing is telling the main ideas of a piece of writing briefly in one's own words, omitting unimportant details.

Surprise Ending An unexpected twist in the plot at the end of a story is called a surprise ending. "White Mice" is an example of a story with a surprise ending.

Suspense Suspense is a feeling of growing tension and excitement felt by a reader. Writers create suspense by raising questions in readers' minds about what might happen. For example, in "Battle by the Breadfruit Tree" a suspenseful moment occurs when the baboon fights to protect her baby from the leopard.

Symbol A symbol is a person, a place, an object, or an action that stands for something beyond itself. A flag, for example, may symbolize a state or country. The toad in "The Horned Toad" may be said to symbolize the need for personal freedom.

Teleplay A teleplay is a drama written specifically for television. In a teleplay, the stage directions usually include instructions for camera movements and editing. *Survival* is an example of a teleplay.

Theme A theme is a message about life or human nature that is communicated by a literary work. In many cases, readers must infer what the writer's message is. One way of figuring out a theme is to apply the lessons learned by the main characters to all people. For example, a theme of "The Lie" is that parents should avoid putting undue pressure on their children.

Third-Person Point of View
See **Point of View.**

Tone The tone of a work expresses the writer's attitude toward his or her subject. Words such as *angry, sad,* and *humorous* can be used to describe different tones. "Appetizer," for example, can be said to have a humorous tone.

Topic Sentence
See **Main Idea.**

Visualizing The process of forming a mental picture based on a written description is called visualizing. Good readers use the details supplied by writers to picture characters, settings, and events in their minds.

Voice An author's or narrator's voice is his or her distinctive style or manner of expression. It may reveal much about the author's or narrator's personality—as does the voice of Squeaky, the narrator of "Raymond's Run," for example.

1 The Writing Process

The writing process consists of four stages: prewriting, drafting, revising and editing, and publishing and reflecting. As the graphic to the right shows, these stages are not steps that you must complete in a set order. Rather, you may return to any one at any time in your writing process, using feedback from your readers along the way.

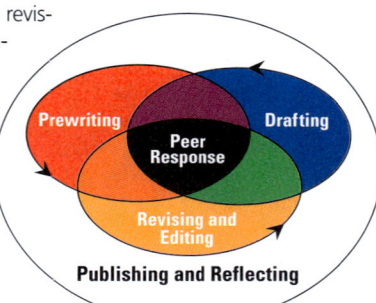

1.1 Prewriting

In the prewriting stage, you explore your ideas and discover what you want to write about.

Choosing a Topic

Ideas for writing can come from just about anywhere: experiences, memories, conversations, dreams, or imaginings. The following techniques can help you to generate ideas for writing and to choose a topic you care about.

Personal Techniques
Make a list of people, places, and activities that have had an effect on you.
Ask who, what, when, where, and why about an important event.
Ask what-if questions about everyday life.
Browse through magazines, newspapers, and on-line bulletin boards for ideas.

Sharing Techniques
With a group, brainstorm a topic by trying to come up with as many ideas as you can. Do not stop to evaluate your ideas for at least five minutes.
With a group, discuss a topic in depth, sharing your questions and ideas.

Writing Techniques
Use a word or picture as a starting point for freewriting.
Freewrite for a short time and then circle the ideas you would like to explore.
Pick a topic and list all the related ideas that occur to you.

Graphic Techniques
Create a time line of memorable events in your life.
Make a cluster diagram of subtopics related to a general topic.

Determining Your Purpose

At some time during your writing process, you need to consider your purpose, or general reason, for writing. Your purpose may be one of the following: to express yourself, to entertain, to inform, to explain, to describe, to analyze, or to persuade. To clarify your purpose, ask yourself questions like these:

- Why did I choose to write about my topic?
- What aspects of the topic mean the most to me?
- What do I want others to think or feel after they read my writing?

Identifying Your Audience

Knowing who will read your writing can help you clarify your purpose, focus your topic, and choose the details and tone that will best communicate your ideas. As you think about your readers, ask yourself questions like these:

- What does my audience already know about my topic?
- What will they be most interested in?
- What language is most appropriate for this audience?

1.2 Drafting

In the drafting stage, you put your ideas on paper and allow them to develop and change as you write.

There's no right or wrong way to draft. Sometimes you might be adventuresome and just dive right into your writing. At other times, you might draft slowly, planning carefully beforehand. You can combine aspects of these approaches to suit yourself and your writing projects.

LINK TO LITERATURE

Inspiration for your writing can come from everyday events. Robert Cormier got the idea for the short story "The Moustache," on page 583, from an actual experience his teenage son had while visiting his grandmother in a nursing home.

LINK TO LITERATURE

Describing the approach she uses to draft stories like "Raymond's Run" on page 648, Toni Cade Bambara says, "I babble along, heading I think in one direction, only to discover myself tugged in another, or sometimes I'm absolutely snatched into an alley."

Discovery drafting is a good approach when you've gathered some information on your topic or have a rough idea for writing but are not quite sure how you feel about your subject or what exactly you want to say. You just plunge into your draft and let your ideas lead you where they will. After finishing a discovery draft, you may decide to start another draft, do more prewriting, or revise your first draft.

Planned drafting may work better for reports and other kinds of formal writing. Try thinking through a writing plan or making an outline before you begin drafting. Then, as you write, you can develop your ideas and fill in the details.

1.3 Using Peer Response

The suggestions and comments your peers or classmates make about your writing are called peer response.

Talking with peers about your writing can help you discover what you want to say or how well you have communicated your ideas. You can ask a peer reader for help at any point in the writing process. For example, your peers can help you develop a topic, narrow your focus, discover confusing passages, or organize your writing.

Questions for Your Peer Readers

You can help your peer readers provide you with the most useful kinds of feedback by following these guidelines:

- Tell readers where you are in the writing process. Are you still trying out ideas, or have you completed a draft?
- Ask questions that will help you get specific information about your writing. Open-ended questions that require more than yes-or-no answers are more likely to give you information you can use as you revise.
- Give your readers plenty of time to respond thoughtfully to your writing.
- Encourage your readers to be honest when they respond to your work. It's OK if you don't agree with them—you always get to decide which changes to make.

The chart on the following page explains different peer-response techniques you might use when you're ready to share your work with others.

Technique	When to Use It	Questions to Ask
Sharing	Use this when you are just exploring ideas or when you want to celebrate the completion of a piece of writing by sharing it with another person.	Will you please read or listen to my writing without criticizing it or making suggestions afterward?
Summarizing	Use this when you want to know if your main idea or goals are clear to readers.	What do you think I'm trying to say? What's my main idea?
Telling	Use this to find out which parts of your writing are affecting readers the way you want and which parts are confusing.	What did you think or feel as you read my words? Which passage were you reading when you had that response?
Replying	Use this when you want to get some new ideas to use in your writing.	What are your ideas about my topic? What do you think about what I have said in my piece?
Identifying	Use this when you want to identify the strengths and weaknesses of your writing.	Where do you like the wording, and where can it be improved? Does the organization make sense? What parts were confusing?

Tips for Being a Peer Reader

Remember these guidelines when you act as a peer reader:

- Respect the writer's feelings.
- Make sure you understand what kind of feedback the writer is looking for before you respond, and then limit your comments accordingly.
- Use "I" statements, such as "I like . . . ," "I think . . . ," or "It would help me if. . . ." Remember that your impressions and opinions may not be the same as someone else's.

1.4 Revising and Editing

In the revising and editing stage, you improve your draft, choose the words that best express your ideas, and proofread for mistakes in spelling, grammar, usage, and punctuation.

WRITING TIP

You may want to ask peer readers questions if their comments are not clear or helpful to you. For example, if a reader says, "This part is confusing," you can probe to find out why. Ask, "What are you confused about? What do you think might make this clearer?"

> **WRITING TIP**
>
> When you finish a draft, take a break before rereading it. The break will help you distance yourself from your writing and allow you to evaluate it more objectively. You may decide to make several drafts—in which you change direction or even start over—before you're ready to revise and polish a piece of writing.

> **WRITING TIP**
>
> For help identifying and correcting problems that are listed in the Proofreading Checklist, see the Grammar Handbook, pages 860–899.

The changes you make in your writing during this stage usually fall into three categories: revising for ideas, revising for form, and editing to correct mistakes. Use the questions and suggestions that follow to help you assess problems in your draft and determine what kinds of changes would improve it.

Revising for Ideas

- Have I discovered the main idea or focus of my writing? Have I expressed it clearly in my draft?
- Have I accomplished my purpose?
- Do my readers have all the information they need, or would adding more details help?
- Are any of my ideas unnecessary?

Revising for Form and Language

- Is my writing unified? Are all the ideas directly related to my main idea or focus?
- Is my writing organized well? Are the relationships among ideas clear?
- Is my writing coherent? Is the flow of sentences and paragraphs smooth and logical?

Editing to Improve Your Writing

When you are satisfied with your draft, proofread and edit it, correcting any mistakes you might have made in spelling, grammar, usage, and punctuation. You may want to proofread your writing several times, looking for different types of mistakes each time. The following checklist may help you proofread your work.

\	Proofreading Checklist
Sentence Structure and Agreement	Are there any run-on sentences or sentence fragments? Do all verbs agree with their subjects? Do all pronouns agree with their antecedents? Are verb tenses correct and consistent?
Forms of Words	Do adverbs and adjectives modify the appropriate words? Are all forms of *be* and other irregular verbs used correctly? Are pronouns used correctly? Are comparative and superlative forms of adjectives correct?
Capitalization, Punctuation, and Spelling	Is any punctuation mark missing or not needed? Are all words spelled correctly? Are all proper nouns, all proper adjectives, and the first words of all sentences capitalized?

Use the proofreading symbols shown below to mark your draft with the changes that you need to make. See the Grammar Handbook for models that use these symbols.

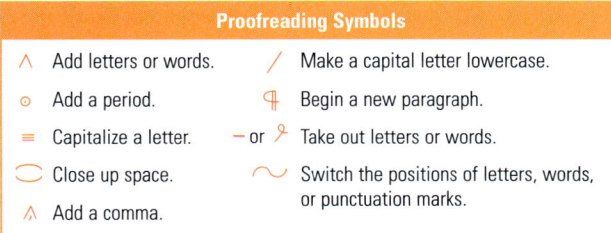

Proofreading Symbols	
∧ Add letters or words.	/ Make a capital letter lowercase.
⊙ Add a period.	¶ Begin a new paragraph.
= Capitalize a letter.	— or ⌒ Take out letters or words.
⌒ Close up space.	∼ Switch the positions of letters, words, or punctuation marks.
∧ Add a comma.	

1.5 Publishing and Reflecting

After you've completed a writing project, consider sharing it with a wider audience—even when you've produced it for a class assignment. Reflecting on your writing process is another good way to bring closure to a writing project.

Creative Publishing Ideas

Following are some ideas for publishing and sharing your writing:

- Display your writing on a school bulletin board.
- Working with other students in your class, create an anthology, or a collection of stories, poems, plays, and other writing.
- Give a dramatic reading of your work for another class or group.
- Submit your writing to a local newspaper or a magazine that publishes student writing.
- Enter your piece in a writing contest.
- Go on-line with your writing by posting it on an electronic bulletin board or sending it to others via e-mail.
- Create a multimedia presentation and share it with classmates.

Reflecting on Your Writing

Think about your writing process and consider whether you'd like to add your writing to your portfolio. You might write yourself a note answering questions like these and attach it to your work:

- What did I learn about myself and my subject?
- Which parts of the writing process did I most and least enjoy?
- As I wrote, what was my biggest problem? How did I solve it?
- What did I learn that I can use the next time I write?

WRITING TIP

If you write a narrative for younger children, ask a grade school teacher if you may read it to his or her students. Afterward, you might ask the students to draw pictures of memorable scenes in your story.

 Building Blocks of Good Writing

2.1 Introductions

A good introduction catches your reader's interest and often presents the main idea of your writing. To introduce your writing effectively, try one of these methods.

Share a Fact

Beginning with an interesting fact can make your reader think, I'd like to learn more about that. In the example below, the surprising size of the items captures the reader's interest.

> A 45-foot-tall clothespin stands in front of Philadelphia's City Hall; a 74,000-pound flashlight stands beam-end down on the University of Nevada campus. These giant items are the work of artists Claes Oldenburg and Coosje van Bruggen, who prove that fine art can be fun.

Present a Description

A vivid description sets a mood and brings a scene to life for your reader. The contrasting details below paint a dramatic picture.

> On a July afternoon, fingers of cool water refreshed and pressed smooth the sizzling, footprinted sand of a beach dotted with rainbow-colored umbrellas. A week later, black, oily water stained the white sand and deposited dead fish and birds on the otherwise deserted shore.

Ask a Question

Beginning with a question can make your reader want to read on to find out the answer. Note how the introduction that follows invites the reader to learn more about a great sports achievement.

WRITING TIP

Writing an introduction does not need to be your first task when you begin a writing project. Instead, begin with any part of your piece that you feel ready to write. Once your ideas come into better focus, you'll probably get a good idea about how to introduce your piece.

826 WRITING HANDBOOK

What did Baltimore Oriole Cal Ripken, Jr., do in 1995 that no other baseball player had ever done? He set a record for the most consecutive games played, breaking Lou Gehrig's record of 2,130 games. For more than 13 years, Ripken was motivated by his love of baseball and his desire to compete at the highest level.

Relate an Incident

An engaging story that includes sensory details or dialogue can help catch your reader's attention. After reading the anecdote below, your reader will want to find out more.

Just when I think I know my mother, she proves me wrong. "I was engaged to another man when I met your father," she mentioned casually one day.

Use Dialogue

As you can see from the example above, quoting a person's words can be an effective beginning to a piece of writing. You can also write fictional dialogue to draw readers into your piece, as shown in the introduction below.

"A little change?" asked a man bundled in old sweaters.
"Sure," I responded, reaching inside my pockets.
"You're a good kid," he said, as I walked away. "I hope you win the lottery someday."
Unfortunately, a person stands a far greater chance of becoming homeless than of winning the lottery.

WRITING TIP

When writing dialogue, be sure to start a new paragraph every time the speaker changes, as in the example at the left. For help with punctuation and capitalization in quotations, see page 898 of the Grammar Handbook.

2.2 Paragraphs

A paragraph is made up of sentences that work together to develop an idea or accomplish a purpose. Whether or not a paragraph contains a topic sentence stating the main idea, it must have both unity and coherence.

WRITING HANDBOOK 827

Topic Sentences

A topic sentence makes the main idea or purpose of a paragraph clear to your reader. A topic sentence can appear anywhere in a paragraph, but when it is the first sentence, it can capture the reader's attention and clearly suggest what will follow.

> *The peregrine falcon, which was nearly extinct in the early 1970s, may soon be taken off the endangered-species list.* After World War II, ornithologists began noticing that falcon populations were declining. Finally, in the 1960s they learned that the pesticide DDT was poisoning the birds, causing them to lay thin-shelled eggs that broke in the nest or otherwise failed to hatch. Ever since DDT was banned in 1972, the falcons have been making a comeback. In the United States alone, there are now more than 1,200 pairs of peregrine falcons.

LINK TO LITERATURE

Notice the strong topic sentence that begins the paragraph about the blue-star banners on page 262 of Hazel Shelton Abernethy's "The Home Front: 1941–1945."

Unity

A paragraph has unity if every sentence in it supports the same main idea or purpose. One way to achieve unity in a paragraph is to state the main idea in a topic sentence and be sure that all the other sentences support that idea, as in the example above. You can create unity in a paragraph without using a topic sentence, however. Decide on a goal for your paragraph and make sure that each sentence supports that goal. Sentences should logically flow from one to the next, as shown in the narrative paragraph below.

> Maria approached her teacher shyly. "I didn't turn in the paper," she whispered. Ms. Williams, unaware of Maria's quiet presence, continued making red marks in her grade book. I'll say it just once more, Maria thought. At that moment, Ms. Williams glanced up to see her most bashful student wringing her hands and gazing at the floor.

WRITING TIP

When you revise your writing, be sure to delete any details that do not relate to the main idea of each paragraph. If a paragraph contains two main ideas, you may break it into two separate paragraphs.

Coherence

In a coherent paragraph, details are presented in a clear, sensible order. Notice that the following paragraph is coherent because the events of Pocahontas's life are related in chronological order.

According to the English colonist John Smith, Pocahontas saved his life. A few years later, she was kidnapped by other colonists. While living with them, she fell in love with John Rolfe, and they were married. Later, Pocahontas, her husband, and their infant son traveled to England, where Pocahontas was introduced to the king.

2.3 Transitions

Transitions are words that show the connections between details, such as relationships in time and space, order of importance, causes and effects, and similarities or differences.

Chronological Order

Some transitions help to clarify the order in which events take place. To arrange details chronologically, as in the example below, use transitional words such as *first, second, always, then, next, later, soon, before, finally, after, earlier, afterward,* and *tomorrow.*

It's easy to make a hummus sandwich. *First,* chop some tomatoes, onions, and lettuce. *Next,* heat the pita bread. *After* spreading hummus on the pita, add the vegetables and it's ready to eat.

Spatial Order

Transitional words and phrases such as *in front, behind, next to, nearest, lowest, above, below, underneath, on the left,* and *in the middle* can help show where items are located. The following example describes the arrangement of photos on a dresser.

On my mother's dresser you can read the history of our family. *On the left,* a picture shows my parents' wedding. The picture *in the middle* is of my older brother as a baby, still toothless. The picture *on the right* shows all of us children in our fanciest clothes.

LINK TO LITERATURE

Look at the anecdote about loading the ice truck on page 255 of the excerpt from *Once Upon a Time When We Were Colored.* Notice how Clifton Taulbert uses transitions to show the chronological order of events.

WRITING HANDBOOK **829**

> **WRITING TIP**
>
> When you begin a sentence with a transition such as *most important, therefore, nevertheless, still,* or *instead,* set the transition off with a comma.

Degree

Transitions such as *mainly, strongest, weakest, first, second, most important, least important, worst,* and *best* show degree of importance or rank order of details, as in the model below.

> I look for several qualities in a friend. *Most important*, I like someone who shares my interests. *Second*, I want someone who can keep a secret. *Least important*, my new friend should get along with all my other friends.

Compare and Contrast

Words and phrases such as *similarly, likewise, also, like, as, neither . . . nor,* and *either . . . or* show similarity or likeness between details. *However, by contrast, yet, but, unlike, instead, whereas,* and *while* show contrast or difference. Note the use of both types of transitions in the model below.

> *Like* the lawyer in "The Bet," Jerry in "A Mother in Mannville" spent much of his time alone. *Both* characters experienced loneliness. *However*, as an orphan, Jerry never willingly chose to be alone, *whereas* the lawyer had agreed to his solitary confinement.

Cause and Effect

To show that details are linked in a cause-and-effect relationship, use transition words and phrases such as *since, because, thus, therefore, so, due to, for this reason,* and *as a result.* Transitions in the following example help readers understand the causes of the writer's attachment to an old notebook.

> My notebook might look tattered and worn, but I treasure it *because* Silvio gave it to me. He was my best friend, but he moved to New Jersey. *Since* the notebook is all I have to remember him by, I will never throw it away.

2.4 Elaboration

To develop the main idea of a paragraph or a longer piece, you need to provide elaboration, or details, so that your readers aren't left with unanswered questions.

Facts and Statistics

A fact is a statement that can be proved, while a statistic is a fact stated in numbers. As in the model below, the facts and statistics you use should strongly support the statements you make.

> The population is booming in cities in the Sunbelt. Between 1980 and 1990, 19 of the 20 fastest-growing U.S. cities were located in California, Arizona, Texas, Florida, and Nevada.

WRITING TIP

Facts and statistics are especially useful in supporting opinions. Be sure that you double-check in your original sources the accuracy of all facts and statistics you cite.

Sensory Details

By showing how something looks, sounds, smells, tastes, and feels, sensory details like the ones in the model below can help your readers more fully experience your subject.

> On the second day of the heat wave, the temperature hit a sweltering 106 degrees. Outside, the sun melted the soft tar of newly paved streets. Inside, people sipped sweet, cool lemonade and hovered around whirring old fans.

Incidents

Describing a brief incident can help to explain or develop an idea. The writer of the model below includes an incident to help make a point about safety.

> Pedestrians, like drivers, should follow certain rules of the road, such as looking both ways before crossing the street. I learned how dangerous it can be to break that rule when I was nearly hit by a driver who was traveling the wrong direction down a one-way street.

LINK TO LITERATURE

Look at the entry for April 20 in "Flowers for Algernon" on page 523. Notice how Daniel Keyes uses an example to develop his point that Charlie's new intelligence has driven a wedge between Charlie and all the people he once knew and loved.

Examples

The model below shows how using an example can help support or clarify an idea. A well-chosen example often can be more effective than a lengthy explanation.

> Fables frequently teach practical lessons. For example, in "Brer Possum's Dilemma," Brer Snake teaches Brer Possum to distrust a companion with an evil nature, despite the companion's reassurances that he's changed.

Quotations

Choose quotations that clearly support your points and be sure that you copy each quotation word for word. Remember to always credit the source.

> In his autobiography, *Once Upon a Time When We Were Colored*, Clifton Taulbert makes his readers feel the chill of the ice in his uncle's icehouse: "As we walked into the icehouse, all I could see was a cold vapor rising from hundreds of blocks of ice."

2.5 Description

Descriptive writing conveys images and impressions of a person, a place, an event, or a thing.

Descriptive writing appears almost everywhere, from reference books to poems. You might use a description to introduce a character in a narrative or to create a strong closing to a persuasive essay. Whatever your purpose and wherever you use description, the following guidelines for good descriptive writing will help you.

Include Plenty of Details

Vivid sensory details help the reader feel like an on-the-scene observer of the subject. The sensory details of the following scene appeal to the senses of sight, sound, smell, touch, and even taste.

832 WRITING HANDBOOK

> Davis slouched at the table and gazed out the coffee shop window, his worn shirt soaked with perspiration. A fly began buzzing furiously against the torn window screen, so Davis took aim with a rolled-up newspaper. When an order of fried eggs and grits was served at the next table, his mouth watered and his stomach growled.

Organize Your Details

Details that are presented in a logical order help the reader form a mental picture of the subject. Descriptive details may be organized chronologically, spatially, by order of importance, or by order of impression, as in the model below.

> The new teacher's towering height and her icy, blue eyes drew our attention immediately. As she strode firmly to the board, our gaze followed her nervously. Only when she finally spoke, in a tone that was warm and friendly, did we begin to relax.

Show, Don't Tell

Instead of just telling about a subject in a general way, provide details and quotations that expand and support what you want to say and that enable your readers to share your experience. The following example just tells and doesn't show.

> It was a terrible day because I ruined my hair.

The paragraph below uses descriptive details to show what the writer experienced on this terrible day.

> I began the day feeling daring and adventuresome, but by the time I went to sleep that night, I felt like crawling in a hole. It all started when, against my mother's better judgment, I tried to dye my hair blond. I wanted to look like the ravishing beauty on the front of the box. By the time I was through, my hair was the color of strained peas.

LINK TO LITERATURE

Try to use vivid, descriptive details to help your reader visualize the subject of your writing. Gary Soto's "Mother and Daughter," on page 203, uses a variety of descriptive details, each presented in order of impression.

WRITING HANDBOOK **833**

WRITING TIP

Metaphors and similes can help you create more vivid, memorable descriptions. Remember that a metaphor compares things directly (*The sun in its chariot streaked across the sky*), while a simile is a comparison using *like* or *as* (*He was caught like a fly in a spider's web*).

Use Precise Language

To create a clear image in your reader's mind, use vivid and precise words. Instead of using general nouns, verbs, and adjectives (*boat, throw, sad*), use specific ones (*canoe, hurl, gloomy*). Notice what happens when vague, general words are replaced with precise words, as in the examples below.

> Joe was smiling.
> Joe was grinning from ear to ear.
>
> The tree fell to the ground.
> The old pine crashed to the forest floor.

2.6 Conclusions

A conclusion should leave readers with a strong final impression. Try any of these approaches for concluding a piece of writing.

Restate the Main Idea

Close by returning to your central idea and stating it in a new way. Link the beginning of your conclusion with the information you have presented, as the model below shows.

> It is therefore essential that environmental activists from countries around the world begin working together if our goal is to be achieved. Without international communication and cooperation, our individual efforts to improve the planet may not make a measurable difference.

Ask a Question

Try asking a question that sums up what you have said and gives readers something to think about. The following example from a piece of persuasive writing ends with a question that suggests a course of action.

Therefore, since it takes many times more grain to feed animals than it takes to feed people, doesn't it make sense to reduce meat consumption?

Make a Recommendation

When you are writing to persuade, you can use your conclusion to tell readers what you want them to do. The conclusion below is from an essay on homelessness.

Shawn, Maria, and José are all real children. The next time you see a homeless person, remember these children and what you can do to help.

End with the Last Event

If you're telling a story, you may end with the last thing that happens. Here, a story ends with an important moment of understanding.

The room was mine—something I had wished for every time my sister and I had had a fight. But the prize I had dreamed about so long seemed completely hollow now.

Generalize About Your Information

The model below concludes by making a specific statement about the importance of the subject.

The anecdotes in *Reflections on the Civil War* show the young volunteers' eagerness to fight as well as the painful consequences of battle. These stories communicate the senselessness of war in general—a powerful message for any age or time.

 LINK TO LITERATURE

"The Gift of the Magi," on page 425, contains one of the most famous surprise endings in American literature. Notice how aptly this conclusion fits the story.

WRITING HANDBOOK **835**

3 Narrative Writing

Narrative writing tells a story. If you write a story from your imagination, it is called a fictional narrative. A true story about actual events is called a nonfictional narrative.

Key Techniques of Narrative Writing

Writing Standards

Good narrative writing

- includes descriptive details and dialogue to develop the characters, setting, and plot
- has a clear beginning, middle, and end
- maintains a consistent tone and point of view
- uses language that is appropriate for the audience
- demonstrates the significance of the events or ideas

Define the Conflict
The conflict of a narrative is the problem that the main character faces. In the example below, the conflict is between the character and the Alaskan wilderness.

Example
When the temperature dropped and our tent wasn't enough to keep us warm, we weren't sure whether we should search for better shelter or go home.

Clearly Organize the Events
Choose the important events and explain them in an order that is easy to understand. In a fictional narrative, this series of events is the story's plot.

Example
- Jeff and I go winter camping to take photos.
- The temperature falls dangerously low.
- We decide not to leave but to look for better shelter.
- We find abandoned igloo and take shelter.
- We get photos the next day.

Depict Characters Vividly
Use vivid details to show your readers what your characters look like, what they say, and what they think.

Example
"I don't give up easily," I told Jeff. "If we quit now, I'll wonder later if we could have made it."

Organizing Narrative Writing

One way to organize a piece of narrative writing is to arrange the events in chronological order, as shown in Option 1 below.

Option 1

Focus on Events
- Introduce characters and setting
- Show event 1
- Show event 2
- End, perhaps showing the significance of the events

Example
- Jeff and I went winter camping to take nature photos.
- The temperature dropped and it was too cold to stay in our tent. We had to decide whether to go home or stay and seek better shelter.
- We decided to stay and began seeking an abandoned igloo Jeff had heard about.
- We found the igloo, took shelter from the cold, and were able to stay and get the photos the next day.

You may prefer to focus on characters, especially if a change in character—the way someone thinks, feels, or behaves—is important to the outcome of the story. In that case, try organizing your story according to Option 2. Try Option 3 if you plan to focus on a conflict that a character experiences within himself or herself or with society, nature, or another character.

Option 2

Focus on Character
- Introduce the main character
- Describe the conflict the character faces
- Relate the events and the changes the character goes through as a result of the conflict
- Present the final change or new understanding

Option 3

Focus on Conflict
- Present the characters and setting
- Introduce the conflict
- Describe the events that develop from the initial conflict
- Show the struggle of the main character with the conflict
- Resolve the conflict

Remember: Good narrative writing is organized logically, with clues to help the reader understand the order of events.

WRITING TIP

Introductions Try hooking your reader's interest by opening a story with an exciting event or some attention-grabbing dialogue. After your introduction, you may need to go back in time and relate the incidents that led up to the opening event.

LINK TO LITERATURE

Realistic dialogue is important for creating believable characters. What characters say in a story should sound like natural speech. Notice how Paulette Childress White uses contractions, slang expressions, and dialect in the conversation on page 294 of "Getting the Facts of Life."

Explanatory Writing

▶ **LINK TO LITERATURE**

Explanatory writing techniques provide tools for exploring the issues presented by or in literature. The examples on the following pages examine Ralph Helfer's nonfiction narrative "The Flood," on page 347, and James Berry's fictional story about a hurricane, "The Banana Tree," on page 370.

Explanatory writing is writing that informs and explains. You can use it to explain how to cook spaghetti, to explore the origins of the universe, or even to compare pieces of literature.

Types of Explanatory Writing

Problem-Solution
Problem-solution writing examines a problem and proposes a solution to it.

Example
Ralph Helfer faces the ongoing problem of flooding on his wild-animal ranch.

Analysis
Analysis explains how something works, how it is defined, or what its parts are.

Example
Ralph Helfer faces physical, emotional, and intellectual challenges in the narrative "The Flood."

Compare and Contrast
Compare-and-contrast writing explores the similarities and differences between two or more subjects.

Example
Both Ralph Helfer and Gustus, a character from "The Banana Tree," face the challenges of natural disasters to save something they value.

Cause-and-Effect
Cause-and-effect writing explains why something happened, why certain conditions exist, or what resulted from an action or a condition.

Example
The flood's destruction leads Ralph Helfer to think and feel differently about his life.

838 WRITING HANDBOOK

4.1 Compare and Contrast

Compare-and-contrast writing explores the similarities and differences between two or more subjects.

Organizing Compare-and-Contrast Writing

When you compare and contrast subjects, you can organize your information in different ways. Two of your options are shown below.

Option 1

Feature by Feature
- Feature 1
  - Subject A
  - Subject B
- Feature 2
  - Subject A
  - Subject B

Example
- Ralph Helfer and Gustus both face natural disasters to save something they value.
- Ralph Helfer risks his life to save his trained animals from the flood waters.
- Gustus risks his life to protect his banana tree from the hurricane.
- Helfer values his animals for different reasons than Gustus does his banana tree.

Option 2

Subject by Subject
- Subject A
  - Feature 1
  - Feature 2
  - Feature 3
- Subject B
  - Feature 1
  - Feature 2
  - Feature 3

Example
- Ralph Helfer risks his life to save his trained animals from the flood waters.
- He acts bravely, crossing dangerous waters.
- His motivation is love for his animals.
- His solution is not completely effective.
- Gustus risks his life to protect his banana tree.
- He acts fearlessly, facing dangerous winds to prop up his tree.
- His motivation is a desire to buy shoes.
- His solution proves to be dangerous.

Writing Standards

Good compare-and-contrast writing
- clearly states the subjects being compared and shows how they are alike and different
- introduces the subjects in an interesting way and gives a reason for the comparison
- uses transitions to signal similarities and differences
- ends with a conclusion that explains the decision made or that provides a new understanding of the subjects compared

 WRITING TIP

The goal of compare-and-contrast writing is to reveal something about the subjects that you wouldn't normally see. The example at left compares the challenges faced in a fictional account of a hurricane and a nonfiction narrative about a flood.

WRITING TIP

See page 829 of the Writing Handbook for information on using transitions in your compare-and-contrast writing.

Writing Standards
Good cause-and-effect writing
▸ clearly states the cause-and-effect relationship being examined
▸ shows clear connections between causes and effects
▸ presents causes and effects in a logical order and uses transition words to indicate order
▸ uses facts, examples, and other details to illustrate each cause and effect

WRITING TIP

You may want to include in your essay a diagram or chart that visually portrays the cause-and-effect relationship explained in your writing.

4.2 Cause and Effect

Cause-and-effect writing explains why something happened, why certain conditions exist, or what resulted from an action or a condition.

Organizing Cause-and-Effect Writing

Your organization will depend on your topic and purpose for writing. If your focus is on explaining the effects of an event such as the passage of a law, you might first state the cause and then explain the effects (Option 1). If you want to explain the causes of an event like the closing of a factory, you might first state the effect and then examine its causes (Option 2). Sometimes you'll want to describe a chain of cause-and-effect relationships (Option 3) to explore a topic such as the disappearance of tropical rain forests or the development of home computers.

Option 1 — **Example**

Cause to Effect	
Cause	The dam opened and the water crashed down the canyon toward Helfer's ranch.
• Effect 1	Trees and boulders were torn from the ground.
• Effect 2	The force of the water pulled sheds apart and overturned trucks.
• Effect 3	Animal cages were swept downstream into the swirling water.

Option 2

Effect to Cause
Effect
• Cause 1
• Cause 2
• Cause 3

Option 3

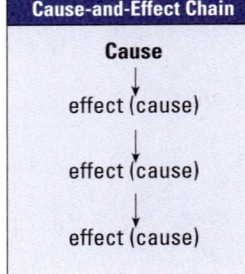

Cause-and-Effect Chain

Remember: Don't assume that a cause-and-effect relationship exists simply because one event follows another. Be sure facts show that the effect couldn't have happened without the cause.

4.3 Problem-Solution

Problem-solution writing clearly states a problem, analyzes the problem, and proposes a solution to the problem.

Writing Standards

Good problem-solution writing
- gives a clear and concise explanation of the problem and its significance
- presents a workable solution and includes details that explain and support it
- concludes by restating the problem

Organizing Problem-Solution Writing

Your organization will depend on the goal of your problem-solution piece, your intended audience, and the specific problem you choose to address. The organizational methods outlined below are effective for different kinds of problem-solution writing.

Option 1

Simple Problem-Solution
- Description of problem
- Why it needs to be solved
- Recommended solution
- Explanation of solution
- Conclusion

Example
- Even with a drainage channel in place, Helfer's property is still vulnerable to flooding.
- He knows the ranch will flood again sometime.
- Helfer should develop a good evacuation plan to move the animals at the first sign of a flood.
- He won't have to rely on uncertain safety measures, like the drainage channel, and he will have a routine in place to keep the animals safe.
- Helfer should keep the safety measures but not rely on them, because nature is unpredictable.

Option 2

Deciding Between Solutions
- Description of Problem
- Solution A
  - Pros
  - Cons
- Solution B
  - Pros
  - Cons
- Recommendation

Example
- Even with a drainage channel in place, Helfer's property is still vulnerable to flooding.
- He can develop a plan to move the animals to safety at the first sign of a flood.
- This way, Helfer can stay at his ranch.
- However, Helfer will have to treat every potential flood as an emergency and evacuate the animals before the flooding is serious.
- Helfer can move his ranch to a new location.

WRITING TIP

Anticipate possible objections to your solution. You can strengthen your arguments by responding to the objections in a clear, reasonable way.

Writing Standards
A good analysis
▸ has a strong introduction and conclusion
▸ clearly explains the subject and its parts
▸ uses a specific organizing structure
▸ uses transitions to connect thoughts
▸ uses language and details appropriate for the audience

4.4 Analysis

In an analysis you try to help your readers understand a subject by explaining how it works, how it is defined, or what its parts are.

The details you include will depend upon the kind of analysis you're writing.

- A **process analysis** should provide background information—such as definitions of terms and a list of needed equipment—and then explain each important step or stage in the process. For example, you might explain the steps to program a VCR or the stages in a plant's growth cycle.
- A **definition** should include the most important characteristics of the subject. To define a quality, such as honesty, you might include the characteristic of truthfulness.
- A **parts analysis** should describe each of the parts, groups, or types that make up the subject. For example, you might analyze the parts of the human brain, the groups affected by a new law, or the types of jazz music.

Organizing Your Analysis

Organize your details in a logical order appropriate for the kind of analysis you're writing. A process analysis is usually organized chronologically, with steps or stages in the order they occur.

Option 1 — **Process Analysis**

Process Analysis	Example
Introduce topic	Carefully following flood evacuation procedures can save your life.
Background information	You need a battery-operated radio tuned to the radio station that provides emergency information.
Explain steps	
• Step 1	As soon as you sense danger, turn on the radio for evacuation instructions.
• Step 2	Once the flood begins, leave before the water gets too deep to drive through.
• Step 3	Finally, be sure to follow recommended escape routes.

WRITING HANDBOOK

You can organize the details in a definition or parts analysis in order of importance or impression. Characteristics in the following definition are organized from most to least obvious.

Option 2

Definition	Example
Introduce term	Ralph Helfer is a hero in the narrative "The Flood."
General definition	Heroes are usually described as being strong and brave and having a noble purpose.
Explain qualities	Helfer shows heroic characteristics while battling a flood on his ranch.
• Quality 1	His strength of action and character is shown as he drags the caged animals from the flooded water.
• Quality 2	His bravery is shown as he faces the danger of the flood to save his animals.
• Quality 3	His noble purpose is shown by his goal of saving his animals from the flood.

In the following parts analysis, the challenge of battling a flood is broken down into three parts.

Option 3

Parts Analysis	Example
Introduce subject	Ralph Helfer faces many demands in the narrative "The Flood."
Explain how subject can be broken into parts	His challenges are intellectual, physical, and emotional.
• Part 1	He faces the intellectual challenge of figuring out how to rescue the animals.
• Part 2	Helfer faces the physical challenges of the flood water, dragging animals to shore, and working for three days and nights.
• Part 3	He faces the emotional challenge of watching as some of his beloved animals are swept away.

> **WRITING TIP**
>
> **Introductions** You may want to begin with a vivid description of the subject to capture the reader's attention. For example, a description of people caught in a flood could introduce the analysis of flood evacuation procedures.

> **WRITING TIP**
>
> **Conclusions** Try ending an analysis by stating the importance of the subject to the reader. An analysis of Ralph Helfer's heroic qualities could end with a statement about his successful rescue effort.

5 Persuasive Writing

Persuasive writing allows you to use the power of language to inform and influence others.

Key Techniques of Persuasive Writing

Writing Standards

Good persuasive writing
- has a strong introduction
- clearly states the issue and the writer's position
- presents ideas logically
- answers opposing viewpoints
- ends with a strong argument or summary or a call for action

State Your Opinion
Taking a stand on an issue and clearly stating your opinion are essential to every piece of persuasive writing you do.

Example
Public tax dollars should continue to fund Green Park Zoo.

Know Your Audience
Knowing who will read your writing will help you decide what information you need to share and what tone you should use to communicate your message. In the example below, the writer has chosen a formal tone that is appropriate for a letter to a politician or for a newspaper editorial.

Example
In fact, an increase in funding will enable Green Park Zoo to expand its highly successful breeding program.

Support Your Opinion
Using reasons, examples, facts, statistics, and anecdotes to support your opinion will show your audience why you feel the way you do. Below, the writer uses an example to support her opinion.

Example
The zoo's breeding program concentrates on the conservation of endangered species such as orangutans.

Organizing Persuasive Writing

In persuasive writing, you need to gather information to support your opinions. Here are some ways you can organize that material to convince your audience.

Option 1

Reasons for Your Opinion	Example
Your opinion	Public tax dollars should continue to fund Green Park Zoo.
• Reason 1	This zoo enables scientists to learn more about the habits and diseases of animals.
• Reason 2	The zoo educates city dwellers about nature.
• Reason 3	Most important, the zoo breeds endangered species to protect them from extinction.

Depending on the purpose and form of your writing, you may want to show the weaknesses of other opinions as you explain the strength of your own. Two options for organizing writing that includes more than just your side of the issue are shown below.

Option 2

Why Your Opinion Is Stronger

Your opinion
• your reasons

Other opinion
• evidence refuting reasons for other opinion and showing strengths of your opinion

Option 3

Why Another Opinion Is Weaker

Other opinion
• reasons

Your opinion
• reasons supporting your opinion and pointing out the weaknesses of the other side

Remember: Effective persuasion often builds from the weakest argument to the strongest. Keep this in mind when you organize the reasons that support your opinion.

WRITING TIP

Introductions Start a persuasive piece with a question, a surprising fact, or an anecdote to capture your readers' interest and make them want to keep reading.

WRITING TIP

Conclusions The ending of a persuasive piece is often the part that sticks in a reader's mind. Your conclusion might summarize the two sides of an issue, restate your position, invite readers to make up their own minds, or call for some action.

6 Research Report Writing

In research report writing, you can find answers to questions about a topic you're interested in. Your writing organizes information from various sources and presents it to your readers as a unified and coherent whole.

Writing Standards

Good research report writing
- clearly states the purpose of the report in a thesis statement
- contains only accurate and relevant information
- documents sources correctly
- develops the topic logically
- reflects careful research on the topic

Key Techniques of Research Report Writing

Clarify Your Thesis
Your thesis statement explains to your readers the question your report will answer. In the example below, the thesis statement answers the question "How did Frederick Douglass draw support for the antislavery movement in a way that others could not?"

Example
Speaking and writing as a former slave, Frederick Douglass openly criticized racism in the United States and drew support for the antislavery movement.

Support Your Ideas
You need to support your ideas with details and facts from reliable sources. In the example below, the writer supports the claim that Douglass risked his freedom.

Example
Douglass wrote his autobiography at the risk of being arrested as a runaway slave. According to writer Richard Conniff, Douglass revealed his true identity because people doubted his stories about slavery.

Document Your Sources
You need to document, or credit, the sources where you found your information. In the example below, the writer quotes Douglass and documents the source.

Example
Douglass stated that the slaveholders tried to "disgust their slaves with freedom" so that the slaves would think they were better off in captivity (Douglass 85).

846 WRITING HANDBOOK

Finding and Evaluating Sources

Begin your research by looking for information on your topic in books, magazines, newspapers, and computer databases. In addition to using your library's card or computer catalog, look up your subject in indexes, such as the *Readers' Guide to Periodical Literature* or the *New York Times Index*. The bibliographies in books that you find during your research may also lead to additional sources. The following checklist will help you evaluate the reliability of the sources you find.

Checklist for Evaluating Your Sources	
Authoritative	Someone who has written several books or articles on your subject or whose work has been published in a well-respected newspaper or journal may be considered an authority.
Up-to-date	Check the publication dates to see if the source reflects the most current research on your subject.
Respected	In general, tabloid newspapers and popular-interest magazines are not reliable sources. If you have questions about whether you are using a respected source, ask your librarian.

LINK TO LITERATURE

Your reading can inspire ideas for research topics. For example, after reading Frederick Douglass's letter to Harriet Tubman, on page 559, you may be interested in learning more about him. The research demonstrated in this part of the Writing Handbook was inspired by Douglass's statement "Most that I have done and suffered in the service of our cause has been in public."

Making Source Cards

For each source you find, record the bibliographic information on a separate index card. You will need this information to give credit to the sources you use in your paper. The samples at the right show how to make source cards for encyclopedia entries, magazine articles, and books. You will use the source number on each card to identify the notes you take during your research.

Taking Notes

As you find material that suits the purpose of your report, record each piece of information on a separate note card. You will probably use all three of the note-taking methods listed on the following page.

> Douglass's lectures Main idea   Source number (2)
> "What, to the American slave, is
> your Fourth of July? ... To him your
> celebration is a sham." 115
>   Page number
>
> Type of note
> (Quotation)

- Paraphrase, or restate in your own words, the main ideas and supporting details from a passage.
- Summarize, or rephrase the original material in fewer words, trying to capture the key ideas.
- Quote, or copy the original text word for word, if you think the author's own words best clarify a particular point. Use quotation marks to signal the beginning and the end of the quotation.

Writing a Thesis Statement

A thesis statement in a research report defines the main idea, or overall purpose, of your report. A clear one-sentence answer to your main question will result in a good thesis statement.

Question: How did Frederick Douglass draw support for the antislavery movement in a way that others could not?

Thesis Statement: Speaking and writing as a former slave, Frederick Douglass openly criticized racism in the United States and drew support for the antislavery movement.

Making an Outline

To organize your report, group your note cards into main ideas and arrange them in a logical order. With your notes, make a topic outline, beginning with a shortened version of your thesis statement. Key ideas are listed after Roman numerals and subpoints are listed after uppercase letters and Arabic numerals, as in the following example.

> **WRITING TIP**
>
> Use the same form for items of the same rank in your outline. For example, if A is a noun, then B and C should be nouns.

> Frederick Douglass: A Voice for Freedom
> Introduction—Douglass's influence as a lecturer and writer
> I. Douglass's early life and background
>   A. Enslavement
>   B. Education
> II. Douglass's campaign against slavery
>   A. Involvement with Massachusetts Anti-Slavery Society
>   1. Treatment of slaves
>   2. Criticism of Northern racism
>   B. Publication of his autobiography
>   C. Publication of the North Star, Douglass's newspaper
> III. Douglass's achievements in the antislavery movement

Documenting Your Sources

When you quote one of your sources or write in your own words information you have found in a source, you need to credit that source, using parenthetical documentation.

Guidelines for Parenthetical Documentation	
Work by One Author	Put the author's last name and the page reference in parentheses: (Douglass 12). If you mention the author's name in the sentence, put only the page reference in parentheses: (12).
Work by Two or Three Authors	Put the authors' last names and the page reference in parentheses: (Meier and Rudwick 146).
Work by More Than Three Authors	Give the first author's last name followed by *et al.*, and the page reference: (Ripley et al. 14).
Work with No Author Given	Give the title or a shortened version and the page reference: ("Abolitionism" 35).
One of Two or More Works by Same Author	Give the author's last name, the title or a shortened version, and the page reference: (Conniff, "Frederick Douglass" 117).

 WRITING TIP

Plagiarism Presenting someone else's writing or ideas as your own is plagiarism. To avoid plagiarism, you need to credit sources as noted at the left. However, if a piece of information is common knowledge—available in several sources—you do not need to credit the source. For an example of parenthetical documentation, see the report on page 804.

Creating a Works Cited Page

At the end of your research report, you need to include a Works Cited page. Any source that you have documented needs to be listed alphabetically by the author's last name. If there is no author, use the editor's last name or the title of the work. Note the guidelines for spacing and punctuation on the model page.

Indent additional lines ½"
Double-space between all lines

Center heading — 1" — *Student's last name Page number*
½"
Chan 14

Works Cited

"Abolitionism." <u>Encyclopaedia Britannica: Micropaedia</u>. 15th ed. 1992.

Conniff, Richard. "Frederick Douglass Always Knew He Was Meant to Be Free." <u>Smithsonian</u> Feb. 1995: 114–27.

Douglass, Frederick. <u>Narrative of the Life of Frederick Douglass, an American Slave</u>. New York: Signet, 1968.

Meier, August, and Elliott Rudwick. <u>From Plantation to Ghetto</u>. 3rd ed. American Century Series. New York: Hill and Wang, 1976.

2 spaces after periods

1 Getting Information Electronically

Electronic resources provide you with a convenient and efficient way to gather information.

1.1 On-line Resources

When you use your computer to communicate with another computer or with another person using a computer, you are working "on-line." On-line resources include commercial information services and information available on the Internet.

Commercial Information Services

You can subscribe to various services that offer information such as the following:

- up-to-date news, weather, and sports reports
- access to encyclopedias, magazines, newspapers, dictionaries, almanacs, and databases (collections of information)
- electronic mail (e-mail) to and from other users
- forums, or ongoing electronic conversations among users interested in a particular topic

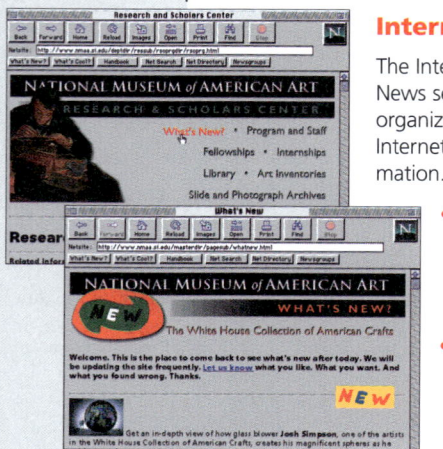

Internet

The Internet is a vast network of computers. News services, libraries, universities, researchers, organizations, and government agencies use the Internet to communicate and to distribute information. The Internet includes two key features:

- **World Wide Web,** which provides you with information on particular subjects and links you to related topics and resources (such as the linked Web pages shown at the left)
- **Electronic mail** (e-mail), which allows you to communicate with other e-mail users worldwide

MULTIMEDIA HANDBOOK

1.2 CD-ROM

A CD-ROM (compact disc–read-only memory) stores data that may include text, sound, photographs, and video.

Almost any kind of information can be found on CD-ROMs, which you can purchase or you can use at the library, including

- encyclopedias, almanacs, and indexes
- other reference books on a variety of subjects
- news reports from newspapers, magazines, television, or radio
- museum art collections
- back issues of magazines
- literature collections

1.3 Library Computer Services

Many libraries offer computerized catalogs and a variety of other electronic resources.

Computerized Catalogs

You may search for a book in a library by typing the title, author, subject, or key words into a computer terminal. When you find the book you're looking for, the screen will display the kind of information shown at right, including the book's call number and whether it is on the shelf or checked out of the library. When a particular work is not available, you may be able to search the catalogs of other libraries.

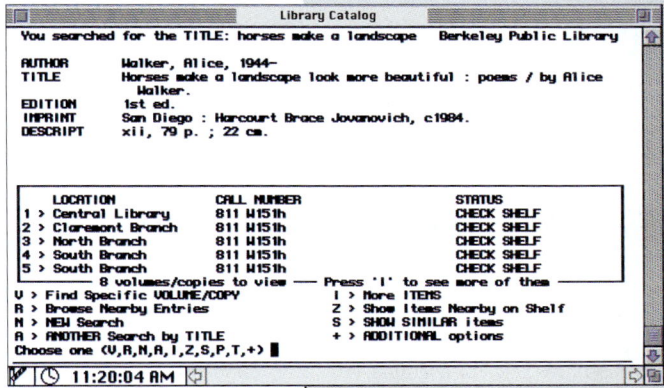

Other Electronic Resources

In addition to computerized catalogs, many libraries offer electronic versions of books or other reference materials. They may also have a variety of indexes on CD-ROM, which allow you to search for magazine or newspaper articles on any topic you choose. Ask your librarian for assistance in using these resources.

WHAT YOU'LL NEED

- To access on-line resources, you need a computer with a modem linked to a telephone line. Your school computer lab or resource center may be linked to the Internet or to a commercial information service.
- To use CD-ROMs, you need a computer system with a CD-ROM player.

2 Word Processing

WHAT YOU'LL NEED

- Computer
- Word-processing program
- Printer

Many word-processing programs allow you to draft, revise, edit, and format your writing and to produce neat, professional-looking papers. They also allow you to share your writing with others.

2.1 Revising and Editing

Improving the quality of your writing becomes easier when you use a word-processing program to revise and edit.

Revising a Document

Most word-processing programs allow you to make the following kinds of changes:

- add or delete words
- move text from one location in your document to another
- undo a change you have made in the text
- save a document with a new name, allowing you to keep old drafts for reference
- view more than one document at a time, so you can copy text from one document and add it to another

Editing a Document

Many word-processing programs have the following features to help you catch errors and polish your writing:

- The **spell checker** automatically finds misspelled words and suggests possible corrections.
- The **grammar checker** spots possible grammatical errors and suggests ways you might correct them.
- The **thesaurus** suggests synonyms for a word you want to replace.
- The **dictionary** will give you the definitions of words so you can be sure you have used words correctly.
- The **search and replace** feature searches your whole document and corrects every occurrence of something you want to change, such as a misspelled name.

WRITING TIP

Even if you use a spell checker, you should still proofread your draft carefully to make sure you've used the right words. For example, you may have used *there* or *they're* when you meant to use *their*.

852 MULTIMEDIA HANDBOOK

2.2 Formatting Your Work

Format is the layout and appearance of your writing on the page. You may choose your formatting options before or after you write.

Formatting Type

You may want to make changes in the typeface, type size, and type style of the words in your document. For each of these, your word-processing program will most likely have several options to choose from. These options allow you to

- change the typeface to create a different look for the words in your document
- change the type size of the entire document or of just the headings of sections in the paper
- change the type style when necessary; for example, use italics or underline for the titles of books and magazines

Typeface	Size	Style
Geneva	7-point Times	*Italic*
Times	10-point Times	**Bold**
Chicago	12-point Times	Underline
Courier	14-point Times	

Formatting Pages

Not only can you change the way individual words look; you can also change the way they are arranged on the page. Some of the formatting decisions you make will depend on how you plan to use a printout of a draft or on the guidelines of an assignment.

- Set the line spacing, or the amount of space you need between lines of text. Double spacing is commonly used for final drafts.
- Set the margins, or the amount of white space around the edges of your text. A one-inch margin on all sides is commonly used for final drafts.
- Create a header for the top of the page or a footer for the bottom if you want to include such information as your name, the date, or the page number on every page.
- Determine the alignment of your text. The screen at the left shows your options.

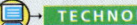

WRITING TIP

Keep your format simple. Your goal is to create not only an attractive document but also one that is easy to read. Your readers will have difficulty if you change the type formatting frequently.

TECHNOLOGY TIP

Some word-processing programs or other software packages provide preset templates, or patterns, for writing outlines, memos, letters, newsletters, or invitations. If you use one of these templates, you will not need to adjust the formatting.

MULTIMEDIA HANDBOOK 853

2.3 Working Collaboratively

Computers allow you to share your writing electronically. Send a copy of your work to someone via e-mail or put it in someone's drop box if your computer is linked to other computers on a network. Then use the feedback of your peers to help you improve the quality of your writing.

Peer Editing on a Computer

The writer and the reader can both benefit from the convenience of peer editing "on screen," or at the computer.

- Be sure to save your current draft and then make a copy of it for each of your peer readers.
- You might have your peer readers enter their comments in a different typeface or type style from the one you used for your text.
- Ask each of your readers to include his or her initials in the file name.
- If your computer allows you to open more than one file at a time, open each reviewer's file and refer to the files as you revise your draft.

TECHNOLOGY TIP

Some word-processing programs, such as the Writing Coach software referred to in this book, allow you to leave notes for your peer readers in the side column or in a separate text box. If you wish, leave those areas blank so your readers can write comments or questions.

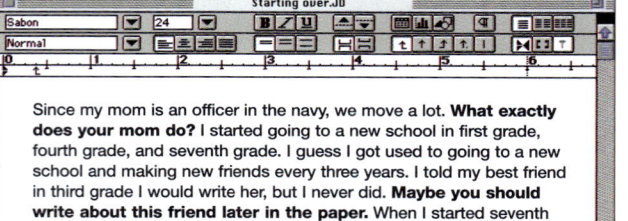

Since my mom is an officer in the navy, we move a lot. **What exactly does your mom do?** I started going to a new school in first grade, fourth grade, and seventh grade. I guess I got used to going to a new school and making new friends every three years. I told my best friend in third grade I would write her, but I never did. **Maybe you should write about this friend later in the paper.** When I started seventh grade, I figured I would be in the same school for three years again, but for some reason, my mom was transferred again this year. This time it wasn't so easy. I hardly got to know people last year. **Didn't you make any friends?** I think that you need two or three years to get settled in a place.

Peer Editing on a Printout

Some peer readers prefer to respond to a draft on paper rather than on the computer.

- Double- or triple-space your document so that your peer editor can make suggestions and changes between the lines.
- Leave extra-wide margins to give your readers room to note their reactions and questions as they read.
- Print out your draft and photocopy it if you want to share it with more than one reader.

Using Visuals

Tables, graphs, diagrams, and pictures often communicate information more effectively than words alone do. Many computer programs allow you to create visuals to use with written text.

3.1 When to Use Visuals

Use visuals in your work to illustrate complex concepts and processes or to make a page look more interesting.

Although you should not expect a visual to do all the work of written text, combining words and pictures or graphics can increase the understanding and enjoyment of your writing. Many computer programs allow you to create and insert graphs, tables, time lines, diagrams, and flow charts into your document. An art program allows you to create border designs for a title page or to draw an unusual character or setting for narrative or descriptive writing. You may also be able to add clip art, or premade pictures, to your document. Clip art can be used to illustrate an idea or concept in your writing or to make your writing more appealing for young readers.

WHAT YOU'LL NEED

- A graphics program to create visuals
- Access to clip-art files from a CD-ROM, a computer disk, or an on-line service

3.2 Kinds of Visuals

The visuals you choose will depend on the type of information you want to present to your readers.

TECHNOLOGY TIP

A spreadsheet program provides you with a preset table for your statistics and performs any necessary calculations.

Tables

Tables allow you to arrange facts or numbers into rows and columns so that your reader can compare information more easily. In many word-processing programs, you can create a table by choosing the number of vertical columns and horizontal rows you need and then entering information in each box, as the illustration shows.

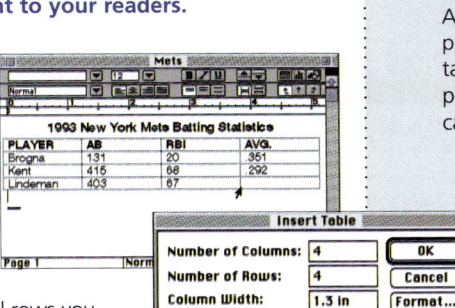

MULTIMEDIA HANDBOOK 855

TECHNOLOGY TIP

To help your readers easily understand the different parts of a pie chart or bar graph, use a different color or shade of gray for each section.

Graphs and Charts

You can sometimes use a graph or chart to help communicate complex information in a clear visual image. For example, you could use a line graph to show how a trend changes over time, a bar graph like the one at the right to compare statistics from different years, or a pie chart to compare percentages. You might want to explore displaying data in more than one visual format before deciding which will work best for you.

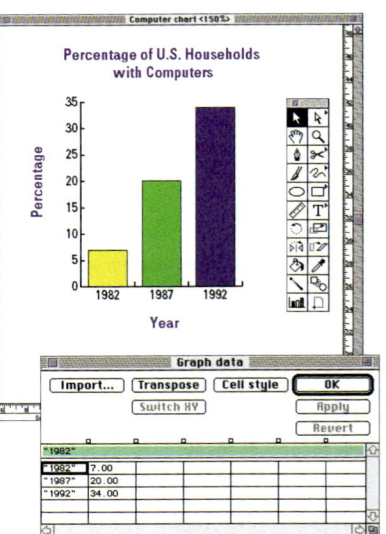

Other Visuals

Art and design programs allow you to create visuals for your writing. Many programs include the following features:

- drawing tools that allow you to draw, color, and shade pictures
- clip art that you can copy or change with drawing tools
- page borders that you can use to decorate title pages, invitations, or brochures
- text options that allow you to combine words with your illustrations
- tools for making geometric shapes in flow charts, time lines, and diagrams that show a process or sequence of events

Creating a Multimedia Presentation

A multimedia presentation is a combination of text, sound, and visuals such as photographs, videos, and animation. Your audience reads, hears, and sees your presentation at a computer, following different "paths" you create to lead the user through the information you have gathered.

4.1 Features of Multimedia Programs

To start planning your multimedia presentation, you need to know what options are available to you. You can combine sound, photos, videos, and animation to enhance any text you write about your topic.

Sound

Including sound in your presentation can help your audience understand information in your written text. For example, the user may be able to listen and learn from

- the pronunciation of an unfamiliar or foreign word
- a speech
- a recorded news interview
- a music selection
- a dramatic reading of a work of literature

Photos and Videos

Photographs and live-action videos can make your subject come alive for the user. Here are some examples:

- videotaped news coverage of a historical event
- videos of music, dance, or theater performances
- charts and diagrams
- photos of an artist's work
- photos or video of a geographical setting that is important to the written text

WHAT YOU'LL NEED

- Individual programs to create and edit the text, graphics, sound, and videos you will use
- A multimedia authoring program that allows you to combine these elements and create links between the screens

MULTIMEDIA HANDBOOK **857**

TECHNOLOGY TIP

You can download photos, sound, and video from Internet sources onto your computer. This process allows you to add elements to your multimedia presentation that would usually require complex editing equipment.

TECHNOLOGY TIP

You can now find CD-ROMs with videos of things like wildlife, weather, street scenes, and events, and other CD-ROMs with recordings of famous speeches, musical selections, and dramatic readings.

Animation

Many graphics programs allow you to add animation, or movement, to the visuals in your presentation. Animated figures add to the user's enjoyment and understanding of what you present. You can use animation to illustrate

- what happens in a story
- the steps in a process
- changes in a chart, graph, or diagram
- how your user can explore information in your presentation

4.2 Planning Your Presentation

To create a multimedia presentation, first choose your topic and decide what you want to include. Then plan how you want your user to move through your presentation.

Imagine that you are creating a multimedia presentation about the great jazz musician "Duke" Ellington. You know you want to include the following items:

- text about his influence on jazz
- a portrait of him
- a recording of him playing a song
- a photograph of him leading his band
- a videotape of his band in concert, audio included
- a recording of a radio interview with him
- text of interesting anecdotes from his concert tours

You can choose one of the following ways to organize your presentation:

- step by step with only one path, or order, in which the user can see and hear the information
- a branching path that allows users to make some choices about what they will see and hear, and in what order

A flow chart can help you figure out the path a user can take through your presentation. Each box in the flow chart on the following page represents something about Ellington for the user to read, see, or hear. The arrows on the flow chart show a branching path the user can follow.

858 MULTIMEDIA HANDBOOK

Whenever boxes branch in more than one direction, it means that the user can choose which item to see or hear first.

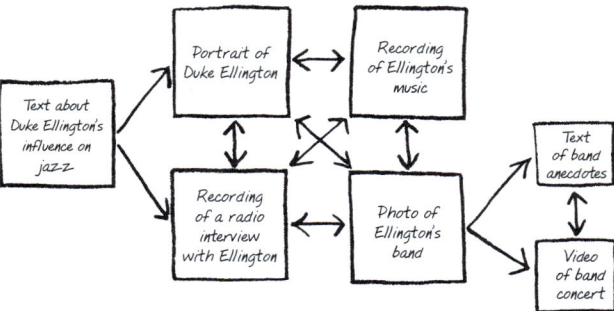

4.3 Guiding Your User

Your user will need directions to follow the path you have planned for your multimedia presentation.

Most multimedia authoring programs allow you to create screens that include text or audio directions that guide the user from one part of your presentation to the next. In the example below, the user can choose between several paths, and directions on the screen explain how to make the choice.

If you need help creating your multimedia presentation, ask your school's technology adviser. You may also be able to get help from your classmates or your software manual.

> **WRITING TIP**
>
> You usually need permission from the person or organization that owns the copyright on materials if you want to copy them. You do not need permission, however, if you are not making money from your presentation, if you use it only for educational purposes, and if you use only a small percentage of the original material.

The user clicks on a button to select any of these options.

Navigational buttons can take the user back and forth, one screen at a time.

This screen shows the portrait of Ellington.

MULTIMEDIA HANDBOOK **859**

GRAMMAR HANDBOOK

1 Writing Complete Sentences

1.1 Sentence Fragments

A sentence fragment is a group of words that does not express a complete thought. It may be missing a subject, a predicate, or both. A sentence fragment makes you wonder *What is this about?* or *What happened?*

Missing Subject or Predicate

You can correct a sentence fragment by adding the missing subject or predicate to complete the thought.

> ∧ Sound effects
> Play an important part in a radio drama. The chug of
> an oncoming train. A car engine stalls. Blows frantically.
> ∧ signals danger   ∧ The train whistle

Phrase and Subordinate-Clause Fragments

When the fragment is a phrase or subordinate clause, you may join the fragment to an existing sentence.

> In a radio drama, The music also stirs the listener's emotions. As the music speeds up, The tension builds. Suddenly, terror grips the listener, Because the music has ended abruptly.

APPLY WHAT YOU'VE LEARNED

Rewrite this paragraph, correcting the sentence fragments.

¹Like *The Hitchhiker*, the dramatization of *The War of the Worlds* was produced for radio by Orson Welles. ²Reporting a Martian invasion of the United States. ³Broadcast October 30, 1938. ⁴An announcer interrupted the broadcast several times. ⁵Said that it was just a play. ⁶However, the story and the acting were so convincing that millions of Americans thought it was a real news report. ⁷Terror struck. ⁸Spreading quickly across the country. ⁹Reports of panic-stricken people in the streets. ¹⁰Welles later apologized to the nation. ¹¹The radio station also. ¹²The Federal Communications Commission made new regulations after the broadcast. ¹³To make sure a radio drama would never cause such panic again.

1.2 Run-On Sentences

A run-on sentence consists of two or more sentences written incorrectly as one. A run-on sentence occurs because the writer either used no end mark or used a comma instead of a period to end the first complete thought. A run-on sentence may confuse readers because it does not show where one thought ends and the next begins.

Forming Separate Sentences

One way to correct a run-on sentence is to form two separate sentences. Use a period or other end punctuation after the first sentence, and capitalize the first letter of the next sentence.

> In "The Treasure of Lemon Brown" Lemon Brown lived in an abandoned building he slept on a pile of rags. Homeless people have to live by their wits they don't have many other defenses against robbery and other dangers.

 REVISING TIP

To correct run-on sentences, read them to yourself, noticing where you naturally pause between ideas. The pause usually indicates where you should place end punctuation.

1.1 Sentence Fragments

Answers will vary. See typical answers below.

Like *The Hitchhiker*, *The War of the Worlds* was a radio drama produced by Orson Welles. Reporting a Martian invasion of the United States, it was broadcast October 30, 1938. An announcer interrupted the broadcast several times and said that it was just a play. However, the story and the acting were so convincing that millions of Americans thought it was a real news report. Terror struck, spreading quickly across the country. There were reports of panic-stricken people in the streets. Welles later apologized to the nation and the radio station. The Federal Communications Commission made new regulations after the broadcast to make sure a radio drama would never cause such panic again.

GRAMMAR HANDBOOK **861**

Forming Compound Sentences

You can also correct a run-on sentence by rewriting it to form a compound sentence. One way to do this is by using a comma and a coordinating conjunction.

Never join simple sentences with a comma alone, or a run-on sentence will result. You need a comma followed by the conjunction *and, but,* or *or* to hold the sentences together.

> Lemon Brown was homeless, **but** he still had his treasure and his memories to comfort him.

You may use a semicolon to join two ideas that are closely related.

In addition, you can correct a run-on sentence by using a semicolon and a conjunctive adverb. Commonly used conjunctive adverbs are *however, therefore, nevertheless,* and *besides.*

> Lemon Brown had an interesting past**;** he had once been a famous blues singer. Homeless people are often ignored**; however,** Greg learned an important lesson by taking time to get to know Lemon Brown.

APPLY WHAT YOU'VE LEARNED

Rewrite this paragraph, correcting the run-on sentences.

¹In "The Treasure of Lemon Brown" we learn a little about what it's like to be homeless, it's not the whole picture. ²It has been estimated that 250,000 to 3 million homeless people are living in the United States today two-thirds of these people are children. ³In fact, children are the fastest-growing segment of the homeless population their average age is three years old. ⁴Many of these kids face other problems health is a particularly big concern. ⁵In 1993 nearly half of the children in New York City's homeless shelters did not have up-to-date immunizations. ⁶Education is another problem, homeless children are more likely to repeat a grade, and they are more likely to drop out or be placed in a special education program.

862 GRAMMAR HANDBOOK

1.2 Run-On Sentences

Answers will vary. See typical answers below.

1 In "The Treasure of Lemon Brown" we learn a little about what it's like to be homeless, but it's not the whole picture. **2** It has been estimated that 250,000 to 3 million homeless people are living in the United States today. Two-thirds of these people are children. **3** In fact, children are the fastest-growing segment of the homeless population; their average age is three years old. **4** Many of these kids face other problems. Health is a particularly big concern. **5** In 1993 nearly half of the children in New York City's homeless shelters did not have up-to-date immunizations. **6** Education is another problem; homeless children are more likely to repeat a grade, and they are more likely to drop out or be placed in a special education program.

Making Subjects and Verbs Agree

2.1 Simple and Compound Subjects

A verb must agree in number with its subject. *Number* refers to whether a word is singular or plural. When a word refers to one thing, it is singular. When it refers to more than one thing, it is plural.

Agreement with Simple Subjects

Use a singular verb with a singular subject.

When the subject is a singular noun, you use the singular form of the verb. The present-tense singular form of a regular verb usually ends in *s* or *es*.

> In "Appetizer" a bear touch[-es] the narrator to show her affection.

Use a plural verb with a plural subject.

> These stories prove[s] what I have always believed. Wild animals communicate[s] with human beings.

Agreement with Compound Subjects

Use a plural verb with a compound subject whose parts are joined by *and*, regardless of the number of each part.

> The man and the bear develop[s] a cautious friendship.

LINK TO LITERATURE

Notice the agreement of subjects with present-tense verbs on page 301 of "Appetizer" by Robert Abel. The present-tense verbs used by the narrator give the reader a sense of observing the action as it unfolds.

REVISING TIP

To find the subject of a sentence, first find the verb. Then ask *who* or *what* performs the action of the verb. Say the subject and the verb together to see if they agree.

GRAMMAR HANDBOOK **863**

When the parts of a compound subject are joined by *or* or *nor*, make the verb agree in number with the part that is closer to it.

> Neither the man nor the bear want to hurt the other. [wants]
> However, the bear's appetite or her "gentle" nudges is likely to endanger the man. [are]

APPLY WHAT YOU'VE LEARNED

Write the correct form of the verb given in parentheses.

1. In "Appetizer" the narrator (encounter, encounters) some kind of Alaskan brown bear.
2. The Kodiak bear and the peninsula brown bear (live, lives) in Alaska.
3. Both bears (grow, grows) up to 9 feet long and 1,500 pounds in weight.
4. These bears (varies, vary) in color from yellowish to almost black.
5. Of the two kinds of brown bears, the grizzly (tends, tend) to be more dangerous.
6. In general, neither a mother bear nor her cubs willingly (approaches, approach) people.
7. However, if you're in the woods, either a grizzly or an Alaskan brown bear (represent, represents) danger.

2.2 Pronoun Subjects

When a pronoun is used as a subject, the verb must agree with it in number.

Agreement with Personal Pronouns

When the subject is a singular personal pronoun, use a singular verb. When the subject is a plural personal pronoun, use a plural verb.

Singular pronouns are *I, you, he, she,* and *it.* Plural pronouns are *we, you,* and *they.* With *I* and *you,* use the plural verb form.

> We disagrees about Philip Nolan in "The Man Without a Country." He claim to be innocent, and he try [tries] to prove it. You believes the charges against him. I thinks Philip Nolan got an unfair trial.

2.1 Simple and Compound Subjects

1. encounters
2. live
3. grow
4. vary
5. tends
6. approach
7. represents

When *he*, *she*, or *it* is the part of the subject closer to the verb in a compound subject containing *or* or *nor*, use a singular verb. When a pronoun is part of a compound subject containing *and*, use a plural verb.

> The judge appears to be prejudiced. Neither the prosecutor nor he seem[s] to have any doubt that Nolan is guilty of treason. The prosecutor and he wants Nolan to be convicted.

Agreement with Indefinite Pronouns

When the subject is a singular indefinite pronoun, use the singular form of the verb.

The following are singular indefinite pronouns: *another, either, nobody, nothing, anybody, everybody, somebody, no one, anyone, everyone, someone, one, anything, everything, something, each,* and *neither*.

> My friends sympathize with Nolan. Nobody believe[s] his crime justifies his punishment. Someone know[s] a story of a similar trial that had a happier ending than Nolan's trial had.

When the subject is a plural indefinite pronoun (*both, few, many,* or *several*), use the plural form of the verb.

> Few imagines being happy in Nolan's place, cut off from all news of his homeland. However, several hopes to live in another country someday.

GRAMMAR HANDBOOK **865**

The indefinite pronouns *some, all, any, none,* and *most* can be either singular or plural. When the pronoun refers to one thing, use a singular verb. When the pronoun refers to several things, use a plural verb.

> In class we took a vote to see how many students agree with Nolan's punishment. Most thinks he was treated unfairly. Of all the evidence against Nolan, none seem to prove his guilt.

2.2 Pronoun Subjects

1. know
2. wonders
3. believe
4. talk
5. asks
6. talk; gets
7. know; depart
8. passes
9. believe; returns; claims
10. explain

APPLY WHAT YOU'VE LEARNED

Choose the correct verb form from each pair.

¹Among students of history, some (know, knows) of Aaron Burr. ²Everybody (wonder, wonders) whether Burr really could have carried out his plot. ³Many (believe, believes) that Burr even raised his own private army. ⁴In the play Nolan and he (talk, talks) about starting a new country. ⁵He (ask, asks) Nolan to help him. ⁶They only (talk, talks) about Burr's plan; neither Nolan nor he (get, gets) the chance to take action because of their arrest. ⁷We (know, knows) that after Burr is found guilty of treason, he and his grand plan (depart, departs) for Europe. ⁸He spends much time in Europe. Most (pass, passes) in a search for foreign support for his plan. ⁹Few (believe, believes) him when he (return, returns) five years later and (claim, claims) innocence of any wrongdoing. ¹⁰I have read several stories about Aaron Burr. None (explain, explains) the reasons behind his foolish plans.

2.3 Common Agreement Problems

Several other situations can cause problems in subject-verb agreement.

Interrupting Words and Phrases

Be sure the verb agrees with its subject when words or phrases come between them.

Sometimes one or more words come between the subject and the verb. These interrupting words do not affect the number of the subject. The subject of a verb is never found in a prepositional phrase or an appositive, which may follow the subject and come before the verb.

> The images in the poem describes hockey as a "battering sport." The poet, a masterful crafter of words, put you in the middle of the action.

REVISING TIP

Look carefully at words that come before the verb to find the subject. Remember that the subject may not be the noun or pronoun closest to the verb.

Phrases beginning with *including, as well as, along with, such as,* and *in addition to* are not part of the subject.

> A hockey game, as well as other contact sports, often result in physical harm to the players. Even noncontact sports, such as baseball or basketball, causes injuries to players.

Inverted Sentences

When the subject comes after the verb, be sure the verb agrees with the subject in number.

A sentence in which the subject follows the verb is called an inverted sentence. Questions are usually in inverted form, as are sentences beginning with *here, there,* and *where.* (For example, Where are the players? There is a game today.)

> There is many references to fighting in the poem. Across the ice rushes the players to maul the enemy. Down go the left wing. Where in all this confusion is the referees?

REVISING TIP

To check subject-verb agreement in inverted sentences, place the subject before the verb. For example, change *there are many references* to *many references are there.*

LINK TO LITERATURE

In "There's This That I Like About Hockey, My Lad" on page 624, notice how the poet repeats the use of inverted sentences starting with *There's* to add emphasis to his images and give the poem structure.

Singular Nouns with Plural Forms

Be sure to use a singular verb when the subject is a noun that is singular in meaning but appears to be plural.

Words like *mumps, news,* and *molasses* appear to be plural because they end in *-s*. However, these words are singular in meaning. Words ending in *ics* that refer to sciences or branches of study (*physics, mathematics, genetics, politics*) are also singular.

> The news about hockey games often sound[s] like the poem, with players bashing each other. Physics teach[es] that for every action, there is a reaction. Athletics often follow[s] this law.

Collective Nouns

Use a singular verb when the subject is a collective noun—such as *class, team, crowd,* or *flock*—that refers to a group acting as a unit. Use a plural verb when the collective noun refers to members of the group acting individually.

> Our hockey team play[s] hard. The majority of players agree[s] with the poet's view.

Nouns of Time, Weight, or Measure

Use a singular verb with a subject that identifies a period of time, a weight, a measure, or a number.

> On average, nine-tenths of a game are [is] spent playing. By my calculations three to four hours were [was] the total penalty time that our team lost last season.

868 GRAMMAR HANDBOOK

Titles

Use a singular verb when the subject is the title of a work of art, literature, or music, even though the title may contain plural words.

> Kiernan's poem could be describing our team, the Rams. "Battering Rams" sound_̂s_ like a better title than the one that the poet picked.

 REVISING TIP

The fact that a title is set off by quotation marks, italics, or underscoring helps to remind you that it is singular and takes a singular verb.

APPLY WHAT YOU'VE LEARNED

Write the correct form of each verb given in parentheses.

1. "There's This That I Like About Hockey, My Lad" (take, takes) a humorous look at the very serious subject of sports injuries.
2. The injuries of a hockey player often (come, comes) from fighting, but there (are, is) many sports injuries from too much exercise.
3. Among the most common sports injuries (are, is) soreness of the leg and back muscles.
4. My track team often (get, gets) cases of sore muscles.
5. Two to 24 hours (pass, passes) after your workout, and then the pain in your legs (start, starts).
6. The best treatment for sore muscles (are, is) rest and an ice pack.
7. Aerobics often (cause, causes) a muscle pull if the person doing the exercises (don't, doesn't) warm up first.
8. Our gym class always (do, does) stretching exercises before an aerobic workout to prevent muscle pulls.
9. Several injuries, including stiff neck and tennis elbow, often (have, has) plagued tennis players.
10. For your neck and elbow, there (are, is) an ice pack to bring relief.
11. *Women's Sports & Fitness* (have, has) many tips on sports injuries, and TV news also (give, gives) some information.
12. Among the best ways to prevent injuries (are, is) a slow start and a gradual cool-down.

2.3 Common Agreement Problems

1. takes
2. come; are
3. is
4. get
5. passes; starts
6. is
7. causes; doesn't
8. does
9. have
10. is
11. has; gives
12. are

GRAMMAR HANDBOOK **869**

3 Using Nouns and Pronouns

3.1 Plural and Possessive Nouns

Nouns refer to people, places, things, and ideas. A noun is plural when it refers to more than one person, place, thing, or idea. Possessive nouns show who or what owns something.

Plural Nouns

Follow these guidelines to form noun plurals.

Nouns	To Form Plural	Examples
Most nouns	add -s	tree—trees
Most nouns that end in *s*, *sh*, *ch*, *x*, or *z*	add -es	dress—dresses brush—brushes
Most nouns that end in *ay*, *ey*, *oy*, or *uy*	add -s	essay—essays monkey—monkeys
Most nouns that end in a consonant and *y*	change *y* to *i* and add -es	story—stories duty—duties
Most nouns that end in *o*	add -s	photo—photos patio—patios cameo—cameos
Some nouns that end in a consonant and *o*	add -es	echo—echoes hero—heroes veto—vetoes
Most nouns that end in *f* or *fe*	change *f* to *v* and add -es or -s	leaf—leaves wife—wives *but* belief—beliefs

Some nouns have the same spelling in both singular and plural: *series, trout, sheep*. Some nouns have irregular plurals that don't follow any rule: *children, teeth*.

> **REVISING TIP**
>
> The plurals of many musical terms that end in *o* preceded by a consonant are formed by adding -s. These nouns include *pianos, solos,* and *sopranos*.

> **REVISING TIP**
>
> The dictionary usually lists the plural form of a noun if the plural is formed irregularly or if it might be formed in more than one way. Dictionary listings are especially helpful for nouns that end in *o, f,* and *fe*.

870 GRAMMAR HANDBOOK

"Getting the Facts of Life" looks at different varietys [ies] of power: the poweres [powers] of money, of work, and of rules. In this story Minerva sees how heros [heroes]—her mother, in particular—can be forged in the struggle for survival, how lifes [lives] can be changed by its outcome.

Possessive Nouns

Follow these guidelines to form possessive nouns.

Nouns	To Form Possessive	Examples
Singular nouns	add apostrophe and -s	girl—girl's
Plural nouns ending in s	add apostrophe	fields—fields' plays—plays'
Plural nouns not ending in s	add apostrophe and -s	men—men's oxen—oxen's

Minerva could easily have quieted the childrens [children's] ruckus. Her sister Stellas [Stella's] approach was to turn up the radio and drown out the noise.

 **REVISING TIP**

Be careful when placing apostrophes in possessive plural nouns. A misplaced apostrophe sometimes changes the word's meaning. For example, *girl's* refers to possession by one girl, but *girls'* refers to possession by more than one girl.

APPLY WHAT YOU'VE LEARNED

Write the correct noun given in parentheses.

¹"Getting the Facts of Life" explores change in a (families, family's) life. ²Growing up is a change (childs, children) can't avoid. ³In the Blue family, the (parent's, parents') (lives, lifes) change when they move from the rural South to Detroit. ⁴(Changes', Changes) are not good for them. ⁵The (fathers, father's) job is gone. ⁶The (mothers, mother's) battles with the welfare system are endless. ⁷Yet (citys, cities) have many attractions. ⁸Shopping for (radios, radioes) and TV sets at stores whose (shelfs, shelves) are packed can be a child's dream. ⁹Instead of working hard to grow (corn, corns), the family can go to the store and buy some.

GRAMMAR HANDBOOK

3.1 Plural and Possessive Nouns

1. family's
2. children
3. parents'; lives
4. Changes
5. father's
6. mother's
7. cities
8. radios; shelves
9. corn

3.2 Pronoun Forms

A personal pronoun is a pronoun that can be used in the first, second, or third person. A personal pronoun has three forms: the subject form, the object form, and the possessive form.

Subject Pronouns

Use the subject form of a pronoun when it is the subject of a sentence or the subject of a clause. *I, you, he, she, it, we,* **and** *they* **are subject pronouns.**

Using the correct pronoun form is seldom a problem when there is just one pronoun in a sentence. Problems can arise, however, when a noun and a pronoun, or two pronouns, are used in a compound subject or compound object. To see if you are using the correct pronoun form, read the sentence with only one pronoun.

> "The Flood" describes a disaster at Toni and Ralph Helfer's wild-animal ranch. Toni and him [he] had to think fast to save the animals.

> **LINK TO LITERATURE**
>
> Notice how Ralph Helfer uses pronouns to avoid repetition of the same nouns and to link ideas in different sentences on page 348 of "The Flood."

Use the subject form of a pronoun when it is a predicate pronoun following a linking verb.

You often hear the object form used as a predicate pronoun in casual conversation (*It is her*). For this reason, the subject form may sound awkward to you, though it is preferred for more formal writing.

> As the waters rose, an elephant dragged the animals in cages to safety. There is no doubt about who was a hero. It was her [she].

> **REVISING TIP**
>
> To check the form of a predicate pronoun, see if the sentence still makes sense when the subject and the predicate pronoun are reversed. (*It was she. She was it.*)

Object Pronouns

Use the object form of a pronoun when it is the object of a sentence, the object of a clause, or the object of a preposition. *Me, you, him, her, it, us,* and *them* are object pronouns.

> Ralph grabbed a lion's mane. The flood water carried the lion and he ⁀*him* to safety.

Possessive Pronouns

Never use an apostrophe in the possessive form of a pronoun. *My, mine, your, yours, his, her, hers, its, our, ours, their,* and *theirs* are possessive pronouns.

Writers often confuse the possessive pronouns *its, your,* and *their* with the contractions *it's, you're,* and *they're*. Remember that the pairs are spelled differently and have different meanings.

> By the time the flood had run it's course, nine animals had lost they're *their* lives.

APPLY WHAT YOU'VE LEARNED

Write the correct pronoun form given in parentheses.

¹After I read "The Flood" by Ralph Helfer, my family and (I, me) saw a museum display about the Johnstown flood of 1829. ²The one most impressed by the display was (I, me). ³The flood at the Helfers' ranch hit Ralph's wife, Toni, and (he, him) hard and killed nine animals of (their's, theirs). ⁴However, between (they, them) and the people of Johnstown, I think the people of Johnstown suffered more. ⁵Imagine many of the people in (you're, your) community losing (they're, their) homes. ⁶In the Johnstown flood, an entire town and (it's, its) buildings were washed away. ⁷More than 2,000 people from the town lost (its, their) lives. ⁸Then a fire broke out and killed many of (they, them) who had survived the flood. ⁹My dad promised to take my mother and (I, me) to see the site of the flood. ¹⁰(He, Him) and (I, me) agree that Ralph and Toni Helfer were lucky. ¹¹The flood left (they, them) and most of (they're, their) animals alive.

GRAMMAR HANDBOOK **873**

3.2 Pronoun Forms

1. I
2. I
3. him; theirs
4. them
5. your; their
6. its
7. their
8. them
9. me
10. He; I
11. them; their

3.3 Pronoun Antecedents

An antecedent is the noun or pronoun to which a personal pronoun refers. The antecedent usually precedes the pronoun.

Pronoun and Antecedent Agreement

A pronoun must agree with its antecedent in
- number—singular or plural
- person—first, second, or third
- gender—masculine, feminine, or neuter

Use a singular pronoun to refer to a singular antecedent; use a plural pronoun to refer to a plural antecedent.

Do not allow interrupting words to determine the number of the personal pronoun.

> If Nima-Cux in "The First Flute" had explored one of her talents, she might have found that they could have made her happy.

If the antecedent is a noun that could be either male or female, use *he or she* (*him or her*, *his or her*), or reword the sentence to avoid the need for a singular pronoun.

> Every other member of the household seemed to be content as they worked for the cacique.
>
> Or
>
> Every other member of the household seemed to be content as they worked for the cacique.

Be sure that the antecedent of a pronoun is clear.

In most cases, do not use a pronoun to refer to an entire idea or clause. Writing is much clearer if the exact reference is repeated.

Herb doctors, witch doctors, and old hunched crones came with different cures, but ~~they~~ *these people* did not help Nima-Cux at all. ~~This~~ *All this failed effort* shows that she should not have waited for someone else to make her happy. But then her father found a young man to become Nima-Cux's husband; ~~he~~ *her father* finally made her happy.

Indefinite Pronouns as Antecedents

When a singular indefinite pronoun is the antecedent, use *he or she* (*him or her*, *his or her*), or rewrite the sentence to avoid the need for a singular pronoun.

Anybody can appreciate the beautiful music of the flute, which brings ~~them~~ *him or her* so much pleasure.

Or

~~Anybody~~ *All* can appreciate the beautiful music of the flute, which brings them so much pleasure.

Indefinite Pronouns					
Singular Indefinite Pronouns	another anybody anyone anything	each either	everybody everyone everything	neither nobody no one nothing one	somebody someone something
Plural Indefinite Pronouns	both	few	many	several	
Singular or Plural Indefinite Pronouns	all	any	most	none	some

REVISING TIP

To avoid vague pronoun reference, do not use *this* or *that* alone to start a clause. Instead, include a word that clarifies what *this* or *that* refers to—*this method, this grouping, that idea.*

REVISING TIP

Avoid the indefinite use of *you* and *they*.

People could always tell what animal Nima-Cux molded. ~~In her tribe they~~ *The tribe members* all knew she had talent.

GRAMMAR HANDBOOK **875**

3.3 Pronoun Antecedents

1 "The First Flute" is a Mayan legend about a competition. One Mayan sport was a game called *pok-a-tok*; every Mayan city had a ball court where the people played it. **2** Two teams of players knocked a small rubber ball through a stone ring on the court's wall just above their heads. **3** No one on either team was allowed to use his or her hands or feet to knock the ball. **4** Instead, players moved the ball by bouncing it off their padded hips, shoulders, or forearms. **5** Men and women bet their entire fortunes on the outcome of games. **6** The winning team could take the spectators' jewelry and clothing, while the losing team might have their heads cut off. **7** Given such high stakes, spectators often fled at the end of a match, hoping to retain their possessions.

APPLY WHAT YOU'VE LEARNED

Rewrite this paragraph, correcting the pronouns.

¹"The First Flute" is a Mayan legend about a competition. One Mayan sport was a game called *pok-a-tok*; every Mayan city had a ball court where they played it. **²**Two teams of players knocked a small rubber ball through a stone ring on the court's wall just above its heads. **³**No one on either team was allowed to use their hands or feet to knock the ball. **⁴**Instead, players moved the ball by bouncing them off his padded hips, shoulders, or forearms. **⁵**Men and women bet its entire fortunes on the outcome of games. **⁶**The winning team could take the spectators' jewelry and clothing, while the losing team might have its heads cut off. **⁷**Given such high stakes, spectators often fled at the end of a match, hoping to retain his or her possessions.

REVISING TIP

In the first sentence of the example, *who* is the subject of the clause *who would be affected most*. In the second sentence, *whoever* is the subject of the sentence.

REVISING TIP

Whom should replace *who* in each sentence in the example:
To whom—object of the preposition
Whom do—direct object of the verb *do want*
Give whom—indirect object of *will give*

3.4 Pronoun Usage

The form that a pronoun takes is always determined by its function within its own clause or sentence.

Who and Whom

Use *who* or *whoever* as the subject of a clause or sentence.

If things were rationed, as in "The Home Front: 1941–1945," whom would be affected most? Whomever needs the rationed items most should receive them first.

Use *whom* as the direct or indirect object of a verb or verbal and as the object of a preposition.

People often use *who* for *whom* when speaking informally. However, in written English the pronouns should be used correctly.

The Rationing Boss might say, "To who should I issue these sports car stamps?" or "Who do I want behind the wheel of a dump truck?" or "I will give who the bicycle?"

In determining the correct pronoun form, ignore interrupters that come between the subject and the verb.

In the example that follows, *who* should replace *whom* because the pronoun is the subject of the clause "Who . . . deserves the 'hot' cars?"

> Whom̷ do you think deserves the "hot" cars?
>   ^who

Pronouns in Contractions

Do not confuse the contractions *it's, they're, who's,* and *you're* with possessive pronouns that sound the same—*its, their, whose,* and *your*.

> When ~~your~~ talking about a big issue like rationing, you
>   ^you're
> must consider ~~whose~~ affected.
>   ^who's

Pronouns with Nouns

Determine the correct form of the pronoun in phrases such as *we girls* and *us boys* by saying the sentence without the noun.

> I repeat, ~~us~~ girls need some of those vehicles!
>   ^we

APPLY WHAT YOU'VE LEARNED

Write the correct pronoun given in parentheses.

1. (Who, Whom), of all the people during World War II, would want to relive the times described in "The Home Front"?
2. (Who, Whom) remembers Hollywood's role on the home front?
3. No doubt the memory remains in those for (who, whom) movies like *Why We Fight* were the inspiration to enlist.
4. Consider all the people (whose, who's) lives changed after seeing such movies.
5. Hollywood produced movies for the U.S. government, praising (its, it's) allies.
6. Ask (whoever, whomever) you know has seen *Casablanca* whether he or she knows that this movie was meant to unite U.S. and French citizens.
7. When Hollywood went to war, (we, us) citizens went too.

3.4 Pronoun Usage

1. Who
2. Who
3. whom
4. whose
5. its
6. whoever
7. we

GRAMMAR HANDBOOK

Using Modifiers Effectively

4.1 Adjective or Adverb?

Use an adjective to modify a noun or a pronoun. Use an adverb to modify a verb, an adjective, or another adverb.

> In "The Lie" Eli's father slow ^ly^ came to understand what was bothering Eli. He had been absolute ^ly^ sure Eli was accepted at Whitehall, a privately ^∘^ school for boys.

Use an adjective after a linking verb to describe the subject.

Remember that in addition to forms of the verb *be,* the following are linking verbs: *become, seem, appear, look, sound, feel, taste, grow,* and *smell.*

> Eli seemed sickly ^∘^ when he knew his actions were about to be discovered. He felt sadly ^∘^ that his parents might think different ^ly^ about him after hearing the truth.

 REVISING TIP

Always determine first which word is being modified. For example, in the second sentence of the example, *sure* is the word being modified; since *sure* is an adjective, the modifier must be an adverb.

APPLY WHAT YOU'VE LEARNED

Write the correct modifier given in parentheses.

1. "The Lie" is a story by the (popular, popularly) author, Kurt Vonnegut, Jr.
2. Even though his stories are often (humorous, humorously), they have (serious, seriously) important messages.
3. The messages in many of his stories are (simple, simply), like treat one another (kind, kindly).
4. Vonnegut's (sad, sadly) experiences as a soldier during World War II (particular, particularly) affected his outlook.
5. He was captured by the Germans and (prompt, promptly) imprisoned in Dresden.
6. Later, he saw the (beautiful, beautifully) city (complete, completely) destroyed by British and American bombs in 1945.
7. His stories show how people's (foolish, foolishly) actions can affect the world.

878 GRAMMAR HANDBOOK

4.1 Adjective or Adverb?

1. popular
2. humorous; seriously
3. simple; kindly
4. sad; particularly
5. promptly
6. beautiful; completely
7. foolish

4.2 Comparisons and Negatives

Comparative and Superlative Adjectives

Use the comparative form of an adjective when comparing two things.

Comparative adjectives are formed by adding *-er* to short adjectives (*fierce—fiercer*) or by using the word *more* with longer adjectives (*unusual—more unusual*).

> In the story "Otoonah," Otoonah's main challenges were finding food and shelter; she dealt with the easiest one first. Shelter was difficulter to find.
>
> (editing marks: easiest → easier; difficulter → more difficult)

Use the superlative form when comparing three or more things.

Superlatives are formed by adding *-est* to short adjectives (*great—greatest*) or by using the word *most* with longer adjectives (*remarkable—most remarkable*).

> Otoonah proved she was the successfulest hunter in her family. She found the larger number of animals.
>
> (editing marks: successfulest → most successful; larger → largest)

 REVISING TIP

When comparing something with everything else of its kind, do not leave out the word *other*. (*Ilga is taller than any **other** girl in the class.*)

The comparative and superlative forms of some adjectives are irregular.

Adjective	Comparative	Superlative
good	better	best
bad	worse	worst
ill	worse	worst
little	less *or* lesser	least
much	more	most
many	more	most

GRAMMAR HANDBOOK 879

Comparative and Superlative Adverbs

When comparing two actions, use a comparative adverb, formed by adding -er or the word more.

When attacking the young hunter, the polar bear moved quickest and skillfuler than the man.
[corrections: quickest → quicker; skillfuler → more skillfully]

When comparing more than two actions, use a superlative adverb, formed by adding -est or the word most.

The songs Otoonah sang more enthusiastically were the boastful ones.
[correction: more → most]

Double Negatives

To avoid double negatives, use only one negative word in a clause. *Not*, *no*, *never*, *none*, and *nobody* are negatives.

Besides the compounds formed with *no*, the words *barely*, *hardly*, and *scarcely* also function as negative words.

Returning home, Otoonah didn't have no hard feelings toward her parents. They couldn't hardly believe Otoonah was alive.
[corrections: no → any; couldn't → could]

> **REVISING TIP**
>
> Do not use both *-er* and *more* or *-est* and *most*.
>
> His car is ~~more~~ faster than hers. It has the ~~most~~ biggest tires I've ever seen.

APPLY WHAT YOU'VE LEARNED

Rewrite this paragraph, correcting mistakes in modifiers.

¹One hundred years ago, the greater challenge facing Eskimos like those in the story "Otoonah" was finding enough food to feed a family during the harsh winters. ²Compared to Eskimos today, a family like Otoonah's was worst off. ³Hunting was more hard than it is today. ⁴A handmade harpoon couldn't never match the rifle for ease of use and accuracy. ⁵An Eskimo using a rifle hunted efficiently, while the Eskimo using a harpoon worked hardest. ⁶Also, of the two methods of hunting, using a harpoon is most dangerous. ⁷Of the two types of hunters, the one throwing the harpoon is likely to lose his balance and fall into the freezing waters.

4.2 Comparisons and Negatives

1 One hundred years ago, the greatest challenge facing Eskimos like those in the story "Otoonah" was finding enough food to feed a family during the harsh winters. **2** Compared to Eskimos today, a family like Otoonah's was worse off. **3** Hunting was harder than it is today. **4** A handmade harpoon could never match the rifle for ease of use and accuracy. **5** An Eskimo using a rifle hunted efficiently, while the Eskimo using a harpoon worked harder. **6** Also, of the two methods of hunting, using a harpoon is more dangerous. **7** Of the two types of hunters, the one throwing the harpoon is more likely to lose his balance and fall into the freezing waters.

4.3 Special Problems with Modifiers

Although the following terms are frequently misused in spoken English, they should be used correctly in written English.

Them and Those

Them is always a pronoun and never a modifier of a noun. **Those** is a pronoun when it stands alone. It is an adjective when followed by a noun.

> In "The Other Pioneers" the poet honors ~~them~~ *those* settlers who plowed the land. He admires them for their strength and courage.

Bad and Badly

Always use *bad* as an adjective, whether before a noun or after a linking verb. *Badly* should generally be used to modify an action verb.

> The settlers wanted so bad*ly* to be part of this country, but many times they felt ~~badly~~ *bad* about leaving their homeland.

This, That, These, and Those

Whether used as adjectives or pronouns, *this* and *these* refer to people and things that are nearby, and *that* and *those* refer to people and things that are farther away.

> Reading about "stalwart fathers" and "gentle mothers," I could tell the poet admires th~~o~~*e*se hardworking people more than th~~e~~*o*se wealthy enough to have a life of ease. More people plowed the land at ~~this~~ *that* long-ago time than do in ~~that~~ *this* day.

LINK TO LITERATURE

Notice how the writer of "The Other Pioneers," Roberto Félix Salazar, has used *those* throughout the first stanza to replace *ancestors*. Not only does *those* enhance the rhythm of the poem, but it also imparts a feeling of mystery and a sense of wider connection to the past.

REVISING TIP

Avoid the use of *here* with *this* and *these*; also, do not use *there* with *that* and *those*.

> This ~~here~~ was a good movie. We hardly breathed as that ~~there~~ image appeared onscreen.

GRAMMAR HANDBOOK **881**

Good and Well

Good is always an adjective, never an adverb. Use *well* as either an adjective or an adverb, depending on the sentence.

When used as an adjective, *well* usually refers to a person's health. As an adverb, *well* modifies an action verb. In the expression "feeling good," *good* refers to being happy, comfortable, or pleased.

> When the weather was ~~well~~ *good*, the crops grew ~~good~~ *well*. The immigrants felt ~~well~~ *good* about settling in a land that held so much promise for their children.

Few and Little, Fewer and Less

Few refers to numbers of things that can be counted; *little* refers to amounts or quantities. **Fewer** is used when comparing numbers of things; *less* is used when comparing amounts or quantities.

> Early settlers got ~~few~~ *little* help from the government and ~~little~~ *few* opportunities to rest. Who knows whether immigrants then had ~~less~~ *fewer* problems than immigrants now?

APPLY WHAT YOU'VE LEARNED

Write the modifier from each pair that fits the meaning of the sentence.

1"The Other Pioneers" is written in English, but (those, this) poem actually honors early Spanish-speaking settlers of the southwestern United States. **2**At (that, this) time there were far (less, fewer) Spanish-speaking Americans than there are at (that, this) time. **3**(Less, Few) early immigrants could speak English (good, well). **4**(Few, Little) languages have escaped the influence of English words, and Spanish is no exception. **5**Whether you think this influence is (well, good) or (bad, badly), the Spanish language had (fewer, less) words when Spaniards first came to the Americas. **6**(Them, Those) explorers brought the speech of Castilla, a province in Spain, with them; however, (this, that) dialect had words added to it by the Spaniards who settled in America. **7**Spanish is a rich language: it adapts (good, well) to song lyrics.

882 GRAMMAR HANDBOOK

4.3 Special Problems with Modifiers

1. this
2. that; fewer; this
3. Few; well
4. Few
5. good; bad; fewer
6. Those; that
7. well

Using Verbs Correctly

5

5.1 Verb Tenses and Forms

Verb tense shows the time of an action or condition. Writers sometimes cause confusion when they use different verb tenses in describing actions that occur at the same time.

Consistent Use of Tenses

When two or more actions occur at the same time or in a sequence, use the same verb tense to describe the actions.

> The narrator of "The Splendid Outcast" goes^(went) to England, attended a horse auction, and finds^(found) that the horse she wanted is^(was) not the only outcast at the auction.

A shift in tense is necessary when two events occur at different times or out of sequence. The tenses of the verbs should clearly indicate that one action precedes the other.

> Each outcast was punished for things he did^(had done) at some time in the past. Although the horse ^(had)killed a man and ^(had)injured others, the author still wanted him.

Tense	Verb Form
Present	walk/walks
Past	walked
Future	will walk
Present perfect	have/has walked
Past perfect	had walked
Future perfect	will/shall have walked

> **REVISING TIP**
>
> In telling a story, be careful not to shift tenses so often that the reader has difficulty keeping the sequence of events straight.

> **LINK TO LITERATURE**
>
> In "The Splendid Outcast" Beryl Markham uses the past tense to tell her story. However, notice on page 165 how she switches to the present tense for the flashback scene at the auction. Thus, she creates a sense of immediacy, a "you are there" feeling.

GRAMMAR HANDBOOK 883

Past Tense and the Past Participle

The simple past form of a verb can always stand alone. Always use the past participles of the following irregular verbs when the verbs follow helping verbs.

Present	Past	Past Participle
be	was/were	(have, had) been
begin	began	(have, had) begun
break	broke	(have, had) broken
bring	brought	(have, had) brought
choose	chose	(have, had) chosen
come	came	(have, had) come
do	did	(have, had) done
drink	drank	(have, had) drunk
eat	ate	(have, had) eaten
fall	fell	(have, had) fallen
freeze	froze	(have, had) frozen
give	gave	(have, had) given
go	went	(have, had) gone
grow	grew	(have, had) grown
lose	lost	(have, had) lost

> Although held firmly by two attendants, the horse ~~begun~~ *began* to act up. He would have broke^ away if the man had not ~~brung~~ *brought* him under control.

APPLY WHAT YOU'VE LEARNED

Write the correct verb for each sentence.

1. The setting of Beryl Markham's story "The Splendid Outcast" (was, is, will be) Newmarket, England.
2. Since the early 1600s, when James I (began, is beginning, begun) the racing tradition there, Newmarket (become, has became, has become) a center of horse racing.
3. In 1634—before he (losed, lost, will lose) his kingdom and his head in a civil war—Charles I offered a gold cup as the prize in a Newmarket race.
4. People (come, have came, have come) to the race every year since it (is starting, started, will have started).
5. Today, people (called, had called, call) horse racing the sport of kings.
6. Racing is now and probably (remained, remains, will remain) popular.

884 GRAMMAR HANDBOOK

5.1 Verb Tenses and Forms

1. is
2. began; has become
3. lost
4. have come; started
5. call
6. will remain

5.2 Commonly Confused Verbs

The following verb pairs are often confused.

Let and Leave

Let means "to allow or permit." **Leave** means "to depart" or "to allow something to remain where it is."

> ~~Leave~~ **Let** me tell you the tale of Pecos Bill. First, though, you must ~~let~~ **leave** behind your ideas of what is real.

Lie and Lay

Lie means "to rest in a flat position" or "to be in a certain place." **Lay** means "to put or place."

> When baby Bill fell off the family wagon, he didn't just ~~lay~~ **lie** there and scream. He met a coyote who carried him off and ~~lay~~ **laid** him down in its den.

REVISING TIP

If you're uncertain about which verb to use, check to see if the verb has an object. The verbs *lie*, *sit*, and *rise* never have objects.

Sit and Set

Sit means "to be in a seated position." **Set** means "to put or place."

> Bill just ~~set~~ **sat** in the dirt, not worrying. Bill always seemed to ~~sit~~ **set** his problems on a stump so they'd blow away.

Rise and Raise

Rise means "to move upward." **Raise** means "to move something upward."

> When Bill's horse couldn't ~~raise~~ **rise** after breaking his ankle, Bill just ~~rose~~ **raised** the horse in his arms and carried him.

GRAMMAR HANDBOOK **885**

Learn and Teach

Learn means "to gain knowledge or skill." **Teach** means "to help someone learn."

> It was strange how quickly the coyotes could ~~learn~~ *teach* Bill all their ways.

Here are the principal parts of these troublesome verb pairs.

Present	Past	Past Participle
let	let	(have, had) let
leave	left	(have, had) left
lie	lay	(have, had) lain
lay	laid	(have, had) laid
sit	sat	(have, had) sat
set	set	(have, had) set
rise	rose	(have, had) risen
raise	raised	(have, had) raised
learn	learned	(have, had) learned
teach	taught	(have, had) taught

APPLY WHAT YOU'VE LEARNED

Choose the correct verb from each pair of words.

1. Tall tales like "Pecos Bill" (rise, raise) many questions about the real life of cowboys.
2. The true life of cowboys (lies, lays) hidden from most Americans.
3. However, it's important to (set, sit) people straight and to (learn, teach) them the truth.
4. For example, if you (let, leave) people to their storybook understanding of the Old West, they'll never know that almost one-fourth of all cowboys were African American.
5. People should be (learned, taught) that almost another fourth of all cowboys were Mexican.
6. Today, more than ever, we must (rise, raise) people's awareness about who helped settle the West.

886 GRAMMAR HANDBOOK

5.2 Commonly Confused Verbs

1. raise
2. lies
3. set; teach
4. leave
5. taught
6. raise

Correcting Capitalization

6

6.1 Proper Nouns and Adjectives

A common noun names a whole class of persons, places, things, or ideas. A proper noun names a particular person, place, thing, or idea. A proper adjective is an adjective formed from a proper noun. All proper nouns and proper adjectives are capitalized.

Names and Personal Titles

Capitalize the name and title of a person.

Also capitalize initials and abbreviations of titles. *Clarissa Harlowe Barton, C. H. Barton, Senator Charles Sumner,* and *Mr. Dred Scott* are capitalized correctly.

> Some of the young men whose Civil War experiences are described in *Reflections on the Civil War* idolized general robert e. lee.

Capitalize a word referring to a family relationship when it is used as someone's name (*Uncle Al*) but not when it is used to identify a person (*Jill's uncle*).

> Some soldiers called Lee uncle bobby, even though he wasn't their Uncle.

REVISING TIP

Do not capitalize personal titles used as common nouns. (*The **senator** spoke to us.*)

GRAMMAR HANDBOOK 887

Languages, Nationalities, Religious Terms

Capitalize the names of languages and nationalities as well as religious names and terms.

Capitalize words referring to languages and nationalities, such as *Hindi, Sanskrit, Afrikaans, Korean, German,* and *Nigerian.* Capitalize religious names and terms, such as *God, Buddha, Bible,* and *Koran.*

> While young soldiers prayed for god's help in battle, Confederate diplomats sought french and british loans.

School Subjects

Capitalize the name of a specific school course (*Biology I, World History*). Do not capitalize a general reference to a school subject (*mathematics, history, music*).

> Most of the young soldiers had little knowledge of History. We studied the Civil War in u.s. history.

Organizations, Institutions

Capitalize the important words in the official names of organizations and institutions (*Congress, Duke University*).

Do not capitalize words that refer to kinds of organizations or institutions (*school, church, university*) or words that refer to specific organizations but are not their official names (*at the university*).

> Decisions made in the house of representatives cost many young soldiers their lives. The Government ran the war, but soldiers had to fight it.

REVISING TIP

Do not capitalize minor words in a proper noun that is made up of several words. (*University of Illinois*)

Geographical Names, Events, Time Periods

Capitalize geographical names, as well as the names of events, historical periods and documents, holidays, and months and days, but not the names of seasons or directions.

Names	Examples
Continents	North America, Asia
Bodies of water	Atlantic Ocean, Ohio River, Lake Louise
Political units	China, Kentucky, Moscow
Sections of a country	New England, the Midwest
Public areas	Central Park, Civic Plaza
Roads and structures	Main Street, Aswan Dam, Acme Building
Historical events	Battle of Shiloh, Gettysburg Address
Documents	the Constitution, the Treaty of Ghent
Periods of history	Reconstruction, the Renaissance
Holidays	Christmas, Presidents' Day, Fourth of July
Months and days	June, Tuesday
Seasons	winter, spring
Directions	east, west

The civil war began at ft. sumter in the south on april 12, 1861. By the time the War ended in the Spring of 1865, it had raged across the united states from pennsylvania South to the gulf of mexico.

REVISING TIP

Don't capitalize a reference that does not use the full name of a place, event, or period. (*We went to Fort McHenry, but the **fort** was closed.*)

APPLY WHAT YOU'VE LEARNED

Write the correct forms of the words given in parentheses.

1. *Reflections on the Civil War* tells about the (Men, men) who fought in the Civil (War, war).
2. Both sides in the (War, war) lost twice as many men to disease as on the (Battlefield, battlefield).
3. Women served as nurses, set up hospitals, and organized relief for both (Union, union) and (Confederate, confederate) armies.
4. One such woman, (Clara, clara) Barton, went on to found the (American Red Cross, american red cross).
5. Barton also formed a (Bureau, bureau) that marked soldiers' graves at Andersonville (Cemetery, cemetery) in (Georgia, georgia).
6. Mary Rice Livermore formed the (United States Sanitary Commission, united states sanitary commission).
7. Union soldiers were aided by this (Commission, commission), whose members insisted on fresh food and (Sanitary, sanitary) hospitals.

6.1 Proper Nouns and Adjectives

1. men; War
2. war; battlefield
3. Union; Confederate
4. Clara; American Red Cross
5. bureau; Cemetery; Georgia
6. United States Sanitary Commission
7. commission; sanitary

6.2 Titles of Created Works

Titles follow certain capitalization rules.

Books, Plays, Magazines, Newspapers, Films

Capitalize the first word, the last word, and all other important words in the title of a book, play or musical, magazine, newspaper, or film. Underline or italicize the title to set it off.

Within a title, don't capitalize articles, conjunctions, and prepositions of fewer than five letters.

> Perhaps Yollie in Gary Soto's "Mother and Daughter" might have thought reading the play <u>the merchant of Venice</u> would help her to prepare for college.

Poems, Stories, Articles

Capitalize the first word, the last word, and all other important words in the title of a poem, a story, or an article. Enclose the title in quotation marks.

> She might have enjoyed the poem "Dover beach." Writing a report about it, she might have come across the article "Matthew Arnold—poet and critic."

APPLY WHAT YOU'VE LEARNED

Rewrite this paragraph, correcting the punctuation and capitalization of titles.

¹Like Yollie's mother in Gary Soto's story mother and daughter, I enjoy monster movies. ²For me, a movie like the monster from the ocean floor is a true classic. ³I used to learn about such movies in magazines like famous monsters of filmland. ⁴Stephen King, author of the horror novels it, pet sematary, and the stand, supposedly read the magazine when he was growing up. ⁵However, I find it hard to believe that someone who wrote a story as scary as the langoliers was inspired by the movie i was a teenage werewolf. ⁶For me, Edgar Allan Poe's poem the raven is much scarier than the movie destroy all monsters, but the movie is more fun.

890 GRAMMAR HANDBOOK

6.2 Titles of Created Works

1 Like Yollie's mother in Gary Soto's story "Mother and Daughter," I enjoy monster movies. **2** For me, a movie like *The Monster from the Ocean Floor* is a true classic. **3** I used to learn about such movies in magazines like *Famous Monsters of Filmland*. **4** Stephen King, author of the horror novels *It*, *Pet Sematary*, and *The Stand*, supposedly read the magazine when he was growing up. **5** However, I find it hard to believe that someone who wrote a story as scary as "The Langoliers" was inspired by the movie *I Was a Teenage Werewolf*. **6** For me, Edgar Allan Poe's poem "The Raven" is much scarier than the movie *Destroy All Monsters*, but the movie is more fun.

Correcting Punctuation

7.1 Compound Sentences

Punctuation helps organize longer sentences that have several clauses.

Commas in Compound Sentences

Use a comma before the conjunction that joins the clauses of a compound sentence.

> In *Gifted Hands* Ben Carson describes his work as a neurosurgeon and he retells his experiences with three young patients.

Semicolons in Compound Sentences

Use a semicolon between the clauses of a compound sentence when no conjunction is used. Use a semicolon before, and a comma after, a conjunctive adverb that joins the clauses of a compound sentence.

Conjunctive adverbs include *therefore, however, so, then, nevertheless, consequently,* and *besides.*

> Two of his patients, Bo-Bo and Charles, live however, one patient, Danielle, dies. Charles's condition left him very little chance at life his doctors were at their wits' end.

LINK TO LITERATURE

Notice on pages 452–455 of *Gifted Hands* how Ben Carson uses compound and complex sentences to combine ideas and merge pieces of information in a way that shows their relation to one another.

REVISING TIP

Even when clauses are connected by a coordinating conjunction, you may use a semicolon between them if one or both clauses contain a comma. (*Two students, Joe and Jill, got perfect test scores;* **but** *Jill had a better overall average.*)

7.1 Compound Sentences

1. Ben Carson wrote *Gifted Hands* as a factual record, and he wanted to give hope to future patients.
2. Carson, a pediatric neurosurgeon, observed subtle changes in his patients; his sharp eye often saved their lives.
3. Signs and symptoms of brain tumors include seizures and trouble speaking; however, these symptoms are sometimes absent.
4. Brain surgery is always major, and the outcome cannot be guaranteed.
5. The bones of the human skull are fused in the adult, but they are free to slide and overlap in babies during the birth process.
6. The adult skull is a solid case; it began development as some 30 separate pieces of membrane and cartilage.

APPLY WHAT YOU'VE LEARNED

Rewrite these sentences, adding commas and semicolons where necessary.

1. Ben Carson wrote *Gifted Hands* as a factual record and he wanted to give hope to future patients.
2. Carson, a pediatric neurosurgeon, observed subtle changes in his patients his sharp eye often saved their lives.
3. Signs and symptoms of brain tumors include seizures and trouble speaking however these symptoms are sometimes absent.
4. Brain surgery is always major and the outcome cannot be guaranteed.
5. The bones of the human skull are fused in the adult but they are free to slide and overlap in babies during the birth process.
6. The adult skull is a solid case it began development as some 30 separate pieces of membrane and cartilage.

7.2 Elements Set Off in a Sentence

Most elements that are not essential to a sentence are set off by commas to highlight the main idea of the sentence.

Introductory Words

Use a comma to separate an introductory word or phrase from the rest of the sentence.

A single introductory prepositional phrase need not be set off with a comma. However, you should use a comma to set off more than one prepositional phrase.

> In class, we read *Harriet Tubman: Conductor on the Underground Railroad.* For several chapters of the book, the author tells about how Harriet Tubman brought people out of slavery to safety in Canada. Clearly, she was an extraordinary woman.

In a complex sentence, set off an introductory subordinate clause with a comma.

Although they were cold and afraid, Harriet and the fugitives struggled toward freedom in the North. Whenever they felt discouraged, Harriet kept them going.

Nouns of Address
Use commas to set off a name or noun in direct address.

Perhaps Harriet said goodbye to their host in Wilmington with the words "Believe me, Thomas, we all thank you for the food and lodging."

Appositives
Use commas to set off some appositives.

When an appositive is necessary for the meaning of a sentence, it is not set off with commas.

That famous conductor, Harriet, told her exhausted travelers that Frederick Douglass, a famous escaped slave, had achieved great things once he gained freedom.

Unclear Elements
Use a comma to prevent misreading or misunderstanding.

Despite all their trying, to cross the Canadian border seemed to be an impossible dream for most runaways.

REVISING TIP

Sometimes when a comma is missing, parts of a sentence can be grouped in more than one way by a reader. A comma separates the parts so they can be read in only one way.

Interrupters

Use commas to set off a word or a group of words that interrupts the flow of a sentence.

> Harriet tired as could be walked bravely forward and urged the fugitives to follow.

When a subordinate clause interrupts the main clause in a sentence, set it off with commas.

> Harriet though she was risking her own freedom, helped escaped slaves time and again. Thomas Garrett because he wanted to help gave shelter and new shoes to the fugitives.

The words shown here are commonly used to begin subordinate clauses. When such words appear in introductory or interrupting clauses, the clauses need to be set off with one or more commas.

Words Often Used to Introduce Subordinate Clauses				
Subordinating Conjunctions	after although as as if as long as as though	because before if in order that provided since	so that than though till unless until	whatever when whenever where wherever while
Relative Pronouns	that	which	who whom	whose

894 GRAMMAR HANDBOOK

APPLY WHAT YOU'VE LEARNED

Rewrite these sentences. Add commas where necessary.

1. Tell me Susan who was nicknamed Moses in *Harriet Tubman: Conductor on the Underground Railroad?*
2. Jim it was Harriet Tubman the one who led a group of escaping slaves.
3. Born a slave on a plantation in Maryland Tubman became very strong from her hard work.
4. In 1849 she escaped walking at night through strange territory.
5. She avoided capture and finally reached Pennsylvania a free state.
6. When she found work in Philadelphia William Still a leader in the Underground Railroad made her one of its conductors.
7. Tubman who was soon famous as an Underground Railroad conductor may have helped as many as 300 slaves escape.
8. After the Civil War ended she worked tirelessly to help African Americans now free from slavery to get an education and voting rights.

7.3 Elements in a Series

Commas should be used to separate three or more elements in a series and to separate adjectives preceding a noun.

Subjects, Verbs, Objects, and Other Elements

Use a comma after every item except the last in a series of three or more items.

The three or more items can be nouns, verbs, adjectives, adverbs, phrases, independent clauses, or other parts of a sentence.

> Theodore Waldeck's "Battle by the Breadfruit Tree" shows conflict involving a tribe of baboons⌃ a leopard⌃ and a baby baboon.

REVISING TIP

Note in the example that a comma followed by a conjunction precedes the last element in the series. That comma is always used.

Two or More Adjectives

In most sentences, use a comma after each, except the last, of two or more adjectives that precede a noun.

7.2 Elements Set Off in a Sentence

1. Tell me, Susan, who was nicknamed Moses in *Harriet Tubman: Conductor on the Underground Railroad?*
2. Jim, it was Harriet Tubman, the one who led a group of escaping slaves.
3. Born a slave on a plantation in Maryland, Tubman became very strong from her hard work.
4. In 1849 she escaped, walking at night through strange territory.
5. She avoided capture and finally reached Pennsylvania, a free state.
6. When she found work in Philadelphia, William Still, a leader in the Underground Railroad, made her one of its conductors.
7. Tubman, who was soon famous as an Underground Railroad conductor, may have helped as many as 300 slaves escape.
8. After the Civil War ended, she worked tirelessly to help African Americans, now free from slavery, to get an education and voting rights.

GRAMMAR HANDBOOK 895

If you can reverse the order of adjectives without changing the meaning or if you can use *and* between them, separate them with commas.

> The slashing͜ snarling͜ screaming baboon and leopard were locked in a fierce͟, death struggle.

7.3 Elements in a Series

1. A baboon is a large, powerful, intelligent monkey.
2. It has a large head, sharp teeth, and a doglike muzzle.
3. There are five species of baboon; some have short, stumpy tails, but others have long tails.
4. They all tend to eat eggs, fruits, grass, insects, leaves, and roots.
5. Many farmers in Africa consider them pests because they destroy crops, make lots of noise, and are quite bold.
6. Their enormous teeth, powerful limbs, and habit of traveling in groups make them the kind of animal it is best not to cross.
7. When a member gives a doglike bark of alarm, the group responds by racing to the scene, making lots of noise, and attacking the predator.

APPLY WHAT YOU'VE LEARNED

Rewrite each sentence, inserting commas where they are needed.

1. A baboon is a large powerful intelligent monkey.
2. It has a large head sharp teeth and a doglike muzzle.
3. There are five species of baboon; some have short stumpy tails, but others have long tails.
4. They all tend to eat eggs fruits grass insects leaves and roots.
5. Many farmers in Africa consider them pests because they destroy crops make lots of noise and are quite bold.
6. Their enormous teeth powerful limbs and habit of traveling in groups make them the kind of animal it is best not to cross.
7. When a member gives a doglike bark of alarm, the group responds by racing to the scene making lots of noise and attacking the predator.

7.4 Dates, Addresses, and Letters

Punctuation in dates, addresses, and letters makes information easy to understand.

Dates

Use a comma between the day of the month and the year. If the date falls in the middle of a sentence, use another comma after the year.

> Marjorie Kinnan Rawlings, who was born on August 8͜, 1896͜ wrote "A Mother in Mannville." In this story she created the character of Jerry.

896 GRAMMAR HANDBOOK

Addresses

Use a comma to separate the city and the state in an address. If the address falls in the middle of a sentence, use a comma after the state too.

> If the narrator had written to Jerry, the return address on her letters might have been Anchorage, Alaska, or Miami, Florida.

Parts of a Letter

Use a comma after the greeting and after the closing in a letter.

> Dear Jerry,
> I hope you like the roller skates in this package.
>   Sincerely,
>   The lady at the cabin

APPLY WHAT YOU'VE LEARNED

Rewrite the following sentences, correcting the comma errors.

1. The author Marjorie Kinnan Rawlings died on December 14 1953 after having lived in Florida for 25 years.
2. Previously, she had worked for the *Courier-Journal* in Louisville Kentucky.
3. Her first Florida residence was in Cross Creek Florida.
4. She moved to Hawthorn Florida when she decided to become a full-time novelist.
5. My grandmother wrote the following to the author after reading *The Yearling:*
   Dear Marjorie
   I think *The Yearling* should be a movie because it is a wonderful book.
        Sincerely
        Myrtle C. Beech
6. On September 14 1943 Grandma purchased Rawlings's cookbook *Cross Creek Cookery*.
7. Here is Grandma's next fan letter to Rawlings:
   Dear Marjorie
   My family loves your cookbook. Keep writing!
        Best wishes
        Myrtle
8. Grandma moved to Orlando Florida on June 14 1948 and always hoped to meet Rawlings somewhere.

7.4 Dates, Addresses, and Letters

1. The author M. K. Rawlings died on December 14, 1953, after having lived in Florida for 25 years.
2. Previously, she had worked for the *Courier-Journal* in Louisville, Kentucky.
3. Her first Florida residence was in Cross Creek, Florida.
4. She moved to Hawthorn, Florida, when she decided to become a full-time novelist.
5. My grandmother wrote the following to the author after reading *The Yearling:*

   Dear Marjorie,
   I think *The Yearling* should be a movie because it is a wonderful book.
        Sincerely,
        Myrtle C. Beech
6. On September 14, 1943, Grandma purchased Rawlings's cookbook *Cross Creek Cookery.*
7. Here is Grandma's next fan letter to Rawlings:

   Dear Marjorie,
   My family loves your cookbook. Keep writing!
        Best wishes,
        Myrtle
8. Grandma moved to Orlando, Florida, on June 14, 1948, and always hoped to meet Rawlings somewhere.

7.5 Quotations

Quotation marks let readers know exactly who said what. Incorrectly placed or missing quotation marks lead to misunderstanding.

Quotation Marks

Use quotation marks at the beginning and the end of direct quotations and to set off titles of short works.

> In class our group chose to analyze Robert Silverberg's "Collecting Team." Diego said,⌄Let's check out the author's use of dialogue.⌄

Capitalize the first word of a direct quotation, especially of a piece of dialogue.

> Monica disagreed with the group, saying, "that's going to be too easy."

End Punctuation

Place periods inside quotation marks. Place question marks and exclamation points inside quotation marks if they belong to the quotation; place them outside if they do not belong to the quotation. Place semicolons outside quotation marks.

> Ira asked, "What do you suggest, Mieko"?
> Mieko said, "Let's discuss Silverberg's use of irony".
> Ira said, "I agree;" then he smiled.

REVISING TIP

If quoted words are from a written source and are not complete sentences, they can begin with a lowercase letter. (*Jefferson said that all people have a right to "life, liberty, and the pursuit of happiness."*)

898 GRAMMAR HANDBOOK

Use a comma to end a quotation that is a complete sentence but is followed by explanatory words.

"I'm in favor of Diego's idea" said Frank.

Divided Quotations

Capitalize the first word of the second part of a direct quotation if it begins a new sentence.

"Let's vote on it," said Diego. "there are five of us, so majority rules."

REVISING TIP

Should the first word of the second part of a divided quotation be capitalized? Imagine the quotation without the explanatory words. If a capital letter would not be used, then do not use one in the divided quotation.

Do not capitalize the first word of the second part of a divided quotation if it does not begin a new sentence.

"I'll record the points of our discussion on the board," said Ira, "If we agree that's a good idea."

APPLY WHAT YOU'VE LEARNED

Rewrite this paragraph, inserting quotation marks and other appropriate punctuation and correcting capitalization.

¹How can you go there. my sister said. zoos are just wrong. ²What are you talking about? I replied. Do you think that animals live in harmony out in the wild? No way. It's eat or be eaten! ³Why, if I were a gazelle, I concluded, I'd much rather be in a lion-free pen than out on the plains running for my life. ⁴Well, she replied, let's say I lock you in your room for the next 50 years so that you won't get hit by a car. ⁵That's ridiculous, I scoffed. ⁶Oh, is it? she said. It's the same exact logic you used in your argument. We take risks every time we step outside, she continued, but that doesn't mean we're better off locked up. ⁷She obviously had me there, but I refused to give in. ⁸Oh, yeah? I said, just as our father called, Dinner's ready! interrupting my brilliant response.

7.5 Quotations

1 "How can you go there?" my sister said. "Zoos are just wrong." 2 "What are you talking about?" I replied. "Do you think that animals live in harmony out in the wild? No way. It's eat or be eaten!" 3 "Why, if I were a gazelle," I concluded, "I'd much rather be in a lion-free pen than out on the plains running for my life." 4 "Well," she replied, "let's say I lock you in your room for the next 50 years so that you won't get hit by a car." 5 "That's ridiculous," I scoffed. 6 "Oh, is it?" she said. "It's the same exact logic you used in your argument. We take risks every time we step outside," she continued, "but that doesn't mean we're better off locked up." 7 She obviously had me there, but I refused to give in. 8 "Oh, yeah?" I said, just as our father called, "Dinner's ready!" interrupting my brilliant response.

Grammar Glossary

This glossary contains various terms you need to understand when you use the Grammar Handbook. Used as a reference source, this glossary will help you explore grammar concepts and how they relate to one another.

Adjective An adjective modifies, or describes, a noun or pronoun. (*fine* day, *poor* me)

A **predicate adjective** follows a linking verb and describes the subject. (I am *happy*.)

A **proper adjective** is formed from a proper noun. (*Spanish* rice)

The **comparative** form of an adjective compares two items. (*more elegant*, *stronger*)

The **superlative** form of an adjective compares three or more items. (*most alert*, *strongest*)

What Adjectives Tell	Examples
How many	*few* friends *many* painters
What kind	*new* techniques *older* buildings
Which one(s)	*this* painting *those* children

Adverb An adverb modifies a verb, an adjective, or another adverb. (Mieko jumped *quickly*.)

The **comparative** form of an adverb compares two actions. (*more slowly*, *sooner*)

The **superlative** form of an adverb compares three or more actions. (*most slowly*, *soonest*)

What Adverbs Tell	Examples
How	walk *carefully* skate *smoothly*
When	*Now* I see. *once* upon a time
Where	She went *out*. *here* in the forest
To what extent	I am *very* pleased. This is *quite* fine.

Agreement Sentence parts that correspond with one another are said to be in agreement.

In **pronoun-antecedent agreement**, a pronoun and the word it refers to are the same in number, gender, and person. (The *girl* lost *her* key. The *girls* lost *their* key.)

In **subject-verb agreement**, the subject and verb in a sentence are the same in number. (*I fly* home. H*e flies* to Rio.)

Antecedent An antecedent is a noun or a pronoun to which a pronoun refers. (Because *Dan* practiced *his* backstroke, *he* improved.)

Appositive An appositive is a noun or phrase that explains one or more words in a sentence. (Julie, *a good student*, found algebra simple.)

Article Articles are the special adjectives *a*, *an*, and *the*. (*the* car, *a* bug, *an* apple)

A **definite article** (the word *the*) is used when a noun refers to a specific thing. (*the* boat)

An **indefinite article** indicates that a noun is not unique but is one of many of its kind. (*a* plate, *an* apple)

Clause A clause is a group of words that contains a verb and its subject. (*I wondered*.)

A **main (independent) clause** can stand by itself as a sentence.

A **subordinate (dependent) clause** does not express a complete thought and cannot stand by itself as a sentence.

Clause	Example
Main (independent)	The robot began operating
Subordinate (dependent)	before we were out of bed.

Collective noun. *See* **Noun.**

Common noun. *See* **Noun.**

Complete predicate The complete predicate of a sentence consists of the main verb plus any words that modify or complete the verb's meaning. (The sun *shimmered in the heat*.)

900 GRAMMAR HANDBOOK

Complete subject The complete subject of a sentence consists of the simple subject plus any words that modify or describe the simple subject. (*The vast canyon* lay before us.)

Complex sentence A complex sentence contains one main clause and one or more subordinate clauses. (*When I get home, I will call you.*)

Compound sentence A compound sentence consists of two or more independent clauses. (*Sue will play, and the rest of us will cheer.*)

Compound sentence part A sentence element that consists of two or more subjects, verbs, or objects is compound. (*Jim* and *Jo* moved. Di *buys* and *sells* rings. Jan plays *soccer* and *tennis*.)

Conjunction A conjunction is a word that links other words or groups of words.

   A ***coordinating conjunction*** connects related words, groups of words, or sentences. (*and, but, or*)

   A ***correlative conjunction*** is one of a pair of conjunctions that work together to connect sentence parts. (*either . . . or, neither . . . nor*)

   A ***subordinating conjunction*** introduces a subordinate clause. (*unless, while, if*)

Conjunctive adverb A conjunctive adverb joins the clauses of a compound sentence. (*however, therefore, besides*)

Contraction A contraction is formed by joining two words and substituting an apostrophe for letters left out of one of the words. (*hasn't*)

Coordinating conjunction. *See* **Conjunction.**

Correlative conjunction. *See* **Conjunction.**

Demonstrative pronoun. *See* **Pronoun.**

Dependent clause. *See* **Clause.**

Direct object A direct object receives the action of a verb. (Stanley hit the *ball*.)

Double negative A double negative is an incorrect use of two negative words when only one is needed. (It's so dark I *can't hardly* see.)

End mark An end mark is any of the several punctuation marks that can end a sentence. See punctuation chart on page 903.

Fragment. *See* **Sentence fragment.**

Future tense. *See* **Verb tense.**

Gerund A gerund is a verbal that ends in *-ing* and functions as a noun. (*Hitting* a home run is easy.)

Helping verb. *See* **Verb.**

Indefinite pronoun. *See* **Pronoun.**

Independent clause. *See* **Clause.**

Indirect object An indirect object tells to or for whom (sometimes to or for what) something is done. (She told *Beth* a joke.)

Infinitive An infinitive is a verbal that begins with the word *to;* the two words create a phrase. (*to see*)

Intensive pronoun. *See* **Pronoun.**

Interjection An interjection is a word or phrase used to express strong feeling. (*Oh!*)

Interrogative pronoun. *See* **Pronoun.**

Inverted sentence An inverted sentence is one in which the subject comes after the verb. (*Where are my shoes? Here is the prize.*)

Irregular verb. *See* **Verb.**

Linking verb. *See* **Verb.**

Main clause. *See* **Clause.**

Modifier A modifier makes another word more precise; modifiers most often are adjectives or adverbs. (*sunny* day, scowled *grimly*)

Noun A noun names a person, a place, a thing, or an idea. (*Don, home, plant, honor*)

   An ***abstract noun*** names an idea, a quality, or a feeling. (*truth*)

   A ***collective noun*** names a group of things. (*herd*)

   A ***common noun*** is the general name of a person, a place, a thing, or an idea. (*girl, mountain, snow, logic*)

   A ***compound noun*** contains two or more words. (*folklore, sidewalk, son-in-law*)

   A ***noun of direct address*** is the name of a person being directly spoken to. (*Sam,* will you do the dishes?)

   A ***possessive noun*** shows who or what owns something. (*Carl's* jacket, the *sun's* light)

GRAMMAR HANDBOOK

A **predicate noun** follows a linking verb and renames the subject. (She is a good *friend*.)

A **proper noun** names a particular person, place, or thing. (*Drew Smith, Maine, Eiffel Tower*)

Number A word is **singular** in number if it refers to just one person, place, thing, idea, or action, and **plural** in number if it refers to more than one person, place, thing, idea, or action. (The words *she, hat,* and *eats* are singular. The words *they, hats,* and *eat* are plural.)

Object of a preposition The object of a preposition is the noun or pronoun after the preposition. (We climbed over the *fence*.)

Object of a verb The object of a verb receives the action of a verb. (They moved *mountains*.)

Participle A participle is often used as part of a verb phrase. (had *danced*) It can also be used as a verbal that functions as an adjective. (the *shining* star)

The **present participle** is formed by adding *-ing* to the present tense of a verb. (*Skating* rapidly, we circled the rink.)

The **past participle** of a regular verb is formed by adding *-d* or *-ed* to the present tense. (*Astonished*, they opened the gift.) The past participle of irregular verbs does not follow this pattern.

Past tense. *See* **Verb tense.**

Perfect tenses. *See* **Verb tense.**

Person The person of a pronoun depends on the noun to which it refers.

A **first-person** pronoun refers to the person speaking. (*I* jumped.)

A **second-person** pronoun refers to the person spoken to. (*You* sat.)

A **third-person** pronoun refers to some other person(s) or thing(s) being spoken of. (*They* sang.)

Personal pronoun. *See* **Pronoun.**

Phrase A phrase is a group of related words that lacks both a subject and a verb. (*gracefully leaping*)

Possessive A noun or pronoun that is possessive shows ownership. (*Dean's* job, *her* sister)

Possessive noun. *See* **Noun.**

Possessive pronoun. *See* **Pronoun.**

Predicate The predicate of a sentence tells what the subject is or does. (The deer *ran away quickly*.)

Predicate adjective. *See* **Adjective.**

Predicate noun. *See* **Noun.**

Predicate pronoun. *See* **Pronoun.**

Preposition A preposition relates a word to another part of the sentence or to the sentence as a whole. (Carlos read *about* the book.)

Prepositional phrase A prepositional phrase consists of a preposition, its object, and the object's modifiers. (king *of the dark forest*)

Present tense. *See* **Verb tense.**

Pronoun A pronoun replaces a noun or another pronoun. Some pronouns allow a writer or speaker to avoid repeating a particular noun. Other pronouns let a writer show a situation in which some information is not known.

A **demonstrative pronoun** singles out one or more persons or things. (*this* boat)

An **indefinite pronoun** refers to an unknown or unidentified person or thing. (*Someone* called.)

An **intensive pronoun** emphasizes a noun or pronoun. (She *herself* performed the surgery.)

An **interrogative pronoun** asks a question. (*Who* took my wrench?)

A **personal pronoun** refers to the first, second, or third person. (*I* spoke. *You* heard. *He* won.)

A **possessive pronoun** shows ownership. (*Your* story is in the folder. Are these notes *his*?)

A **predicate pronoun** follows a linking verb and renames the subject. (The caller was *he*.)

A **reflexive pronoun** reflects an action back on the subject of the sentence. (Ed treated *himself* to a soda.)

A **relative pronoun** relates a subordinate clause to the word it modifies in the main clause. (We gave our reasons, *which* were very strong.)

Pronoun-antecedent agreement. *See* **Agreement.**

Pronoun forms

The **subject form of a pronoun** is used when the pronoun is the subject of a sentence or follows a linking verb as a predicate pronoun. (*He* subtracted. It is *she*.)

The **object form of a pronoun** is used when a personal pronoun is the direct or indirect object of a verb or the object of a preposition or verbal. (I gave *her* a clue. with *them*)

Proper adjective. *See* **Adjective.**

Proper noun. *See* **Noun.**

Punctuation Punctuation clarifies the structure of sentences. See punctuation chart on facing page.

Reflexive pronoun. *See* **Pronoun.**

Regular verb. *See* **Verb.**

Relative pronoun. *See* **Pronoun.**

Run-on sentence A run-on sentence consists of two or more sentences written incorrectly as one. (*I said OK Jim said no.*)

Sentence A sentence expresses a complete thought. The chart below shows the four kinds of sentences.

Kind of Sentence	Example
Declarative (statement)	They went home.
Exclamatory (strong feeling)	We won!
Imperative (request, command)	Let the dog out.
Interrogative (question)	Where is Ronnie?

Sentence fragment A sentence fragment is a group of words that is only part of a sentence. (*As I walked; Was coming to the door*)

Subject The subject is the part of a sentence that tells whom or what the sentence is about. (*Gene* drove.)

Subject-verb agreement. *See* **Agreement.**

Subordinate clause. *See* **Clause.**

Verb A verb expresses an action, a condition, or a state of being. (*swim, is, seems*)

The subject of an **active verb** performs the action of a sentence. (Danielle *soared*.)

The subject of a **passive verb** receives the verb's action or expresses the result of action. (The story *was told*.)

A **helping verb** is used with the main verb; together they make up a verb phrase. (*has* gone)

A **linking verb** expresses a state of being or connects the subject with a word or words that describe the subject. (The ice *feels* cold.)

The past tense and past participle of a **regular verb** are formed by adding -*d* or -*ed*. (*sail, sailed*) An **irregular verb** does not follow this pattern. (*grow, grew, grown*)

Verb phrase A verb phrase consists of a main verb and one or more helping verbs. (*should have been working*)

Verb tense Verb tense shows the time of an action or a state of being. (*go, went, am, seemed*)

The **present tense** places an action or condition in the present. (We *walk* down the street.)

The **past tense** places an action or condition in the past. (They *left*.)

The **future tense** places an action or condition in the future. (They *will go*.)

The **present perfect tense** describes an action that was completed in an indefinite past time or that began in the past and continues in the present. (*has observed, have danced*)

The **past perfect tense** describes one action that happened before another action in the past. (*had wondered, had analyzed*)

The **future perfect tense** describes a future event that will be finished before another future action begins. (*will have fallen*)

Verbal A verbal is formed from a verb and acts as a noun, an adjective, or an adverb. *See* **Gerund; Infinitive; Participle.**

Punctuation	Uses	Examples
Apostrophe (')	Shows possession Forms contractions	John's bike Sara's car We'll go. The train's here.
Colon (:)	Introduces a list or long quotation	these games: tennis, golf, and soccer
Comma (,)	Separates ideas Separates modifiers Separates items in series	I went home, and I fed my iguana. The bored, restless children. She brought apples, pears, and grapes.
Exclamation point (!)	Ends an exclamatory sentence	Let's win this tournament!
Hyphen (-)	Joins words in some compound nouns	sister-in-law, great-grandfather
Period (.)	Ends a declarative sentence Indicates most abbreviations	We saw white-tailed deer and crows. lb. oz. St. Mr. Sept.
Question mark (?)	Ends an interrogative sentence	How are you?
Semicolon (;)	Joins some compound sentences Separates items in series that contain commas	I'm fine; my brother broke his leg. Edwina found a tiny, flat stone; a dark, fragile fossil; and a shiny, spiky seashell.

GRAMMAR HANDBOOK **903**

Index of Fine Art

xi, 98–99	Detail of mountain landscape, Sesshu Tōyō (1420–1506).
xiii, 248	*Gauguin's Armchair* (1888), Vincent van Gogh.
xvii, 552	*Forward* (1967), Jacob Lawrence.
xix, 670	*Sunroom* (1980), Winifred Nicholson.
xxi, 784 *bottom*, 792–794	Detail from *Aviary Triptych* (1992), Carol Cottone-Kolthoff.
xxiv–1	*Moebius Strip II*, M. C. Escher
6	*Three Kings* (about 1950), unknown Puerto Rican artist.
18	*Study of Williams* (1976), Hubert Shuptrine.
23	*Sitting In at Baron's* (1980), Romare Bearden.
24–25	*Midtown Sunset* (1981), Romare Bearden.
33	*Jerry* (1955, repainted 1975), Fairfield Porter.
36	*Amherst Campus No. 1* (1969), Fairfield Porter.
64	*The Garden Road* (1962), Fairfield Porter.
69	*Lizzie and Bruno* (1970), Fairfield Porter.
72	*Hilltop—Farmhouse* (1929), Marie Atkinson Hull.
91	Detail of *Portrait of Sato Issai* (1824), Watanabe Kazan.
94	*The Actor Onoe Baiko VII as Mokuzume in* Tamamo no Mae Kumoi no Hareginu (1984), Tsuruya Kokei.
146–147	*Zwei Köpfe* [Two heads] (1932), Paul Klee.
153	*Nito Herrera in Springtime* (1960), Peter Hurd.
156	*A medio día/Pedacito de mi corazón* [At high noon/A little piece of my heart] (1986), Carmen Lomas Garza.
162	*Whistlejacket* (1762), George Stubbs.
166	Detail of *Portrait of Mrs. Whelan* (about 1911), Harold Gilman.
170–171	*Showing at Tattersall's*, Robert Bevan.
184	*Going to the City, Hansom Cab*, (1879), James J. Tissot.
189	*Liverpool Quay by Moonlight* (1887), John Atkinson Grimshaw.
192	*Lord Ribblesdale* (1902), John Singer Sargent.
197	*Les adieux* [The goodbye] (1871), James J. Tissot.
205	*Colombiane* (1978), Fernando Botero.
206	*Yucateca Sentada* (1979), Alfredo Zalce.
222	*Autumn Leaves* (1873), Winslow Homer.
224	*After the Chase* (1965), Andrew Wyeth.
230	*Pleased With Herself* (1989), Marjorie McDonald.
235	*Empanadas* [Turnovers] (1991), Carmen Lomas Garza.
242	*Portrait of Henri Matisse* (1905), André Derain.
268	*The Branch* (1993), Lee Teter.
269	*Cheyenne in New Mexico* (1993), Malcolm Furlow.
282–283	*Prairie Fire* (about 1953), Blackbear Bosin.
286–287	*Main Street* (1968), Billy Morrow Jackson.
291	*Pink Lace* (1993), Stephen Scott Young.
314	*Stairs, Provincetown* (1920), Charles Demuth.
316	*Candle, Eigg* (1980), Winifred Nicholson.

334–335	*Hamptons Drive-In* (1974), Howard Kanovitz.
341	*Hilco* (1989), Kit Boyce.
373	*Hurricane, Bahamas* (1898), Winslow Homer.
397	*Trail of Tears,* Jerome Tiger.
422–423	*Greed* (1982), Carlos Almaraz.
425	*The Three Magi* (about a.d. 600–650), unknown artist.
429	*Golden Fall* (1940), Joseph Stella.
436	*Das Buch* [The book] (1985), Anselm Kiefer.
467	*All Hands to the Pump* (1888–1889), Henry Scott Tuke.
470	*Shipwreck off Nantucket* (1859–1860), William Bradford.
476	*Shipwreck,* Robert L. Newman (1827–1912).
501	*Einige Kreise* [Several circles] (1926), Wassily Kandinsky.
508	Detail of *Dinner at Haddo House* (1884), Alfred Edward Emslie.
543	*Midnight Ride of Paul Revere* (1931), Grant Wood.
557	*Daybreak—A Time to Rest* (1967), Jacob Lawrence.
572–573	Detail of *Cross Cultural Dressing* (1993), Pacita Abad.
578	Blackfoot Child, Charles La Monk.
595	California Vaqueros, James Walker.
597	Seated Girl with Dog (1944), Milton Avery.
606–607, 618 *bottom*	*America, Victoria & Albert and Black Eagle off the Isle of Wight,* 1851, Tim Thompson.
613	*Old Willie—the Village Worthy* (1886), James Guthrie.
615	*The Burial at Sea* (1896), Sir Frank Brangwyn.
620	*Frog with Top Hat, Eyeglasses, and Cattail* (1910), unknown artist.
622	*Mountain Sunset—South West Series #181* (1994), Teruko Wilde.
643	*Prometheus Under Fire* (1984), Rupert Garcia.
650	*Petite fille* [Little girl] (1982), Loïs Mailou Jones.
655	*Visa* (1951), Stuart Davis.
698 *middle*	*Ballplayer* (about a.d. 600–900), Mayan.
699 *left, second from top*	Detail from Codex Borbonicus, Aztec.
700	Detail of *En busqueda de la paz* [In search of peace], Alfredo Linares.
719	*His Hammer in His Hand,* Palmer C. Hayden.
725	*Twilight* (1971), Hubert Shuptrine.
728	*Buzzards' Roost* (1985), Hubert Shuptrine.
732 left, 744	Nootka raven spirit mask, Northwest Coast.
742	*Raven Opened the Box of Daylight* (1970), Dale DeArmond.
745	*When the Eagle Spoke to Me* (1979), Jerry Ingram.
747	*Up 'N' Down* (1994), Howard Carr.
760, 771	*Proud Hunter* (1987), Pudlo Pudlat.
764	*Orion in December* (1959), Charles E. Burchfield.
766, 767	*Kit Fox Society Bow-lance,* No Two Horns.
769	*A Man Cooking Fish as His Wife Softens Kamiks,* unknown artist.
772	*Walrus Hunt* (1986), Lucassie Tukaluk.
785 *bottom,* 786	*Strawberry Dance* (1983), G. Peter Jemison.
785 *top,* 789	*Dorothy and Netti* (1974), Alex Katz

Index of Skills

Literary Concepts

Alliteration, 437, 812
Allusion, 173, 812
Anecdote, 54, 812
Antagonist, 378, 812
Aphorism, 313, 812
Author's purpose, 299, 398, 457, 812
Autobiography, 43, 257, 812
Ballad, 549
Beat. *See* Rhythm.
Biography, 43–44, 448, 560, 812
Cast of characters, 181, 812
Character, 15, 813
    antagonist, 378, 812
    development of, 285, 540, 570, 618, 813
    dynamic, 618, 813
    main, 15, 618, 813
    minor, 15, 481, 618, 813
    protagonist, 378, 817
    static, 618, 813
Characterization, 27, 813
Classic, 432, 813
Climax, 16, 121, 249, 813, 817
Complications, 16, 817
Conflict, 15, 813
    external and internal, 226, 813
Description, 813
Dialogue, 17, 181, 598, 814
Drama, 181–82, 814
    acts in, 182, 812
    cast of characters in, 181, 812
    dialogue in, 181, 814
    radio play, 817
    resolution in, 817
    scenes in, 182, 618, 818
    script of, 181–82
    sound effects in, 181–82
    stage directions in, 181–82, 819
    teleplay, 459, 819
End rhyme, 134, 818
Epitaph, 159
Essay, 44, 814
Exaggeration, 57, 814
Exposition, 15, 814
Fable, 699, 814
Fact, 44, 457, 814
Fiction, 15–16, 814
    characters in, 15
    novel, 15
    plot in, 15–16
    realistic, 296, 646, 817
    science, 107, 505, 818
    setting in, 15, 104, 173, 226, 818
    short story, 15, 818
    theme in, 16, 238, 819
Figurative language, 124, 131, 814. *See also* Metaphor; Personification; Simile.
Flashback, 249, 814
Folk tale, 699, 814
Foreshadowing, 345, 814
Form, 123, 129, 815
Frame story, 90, 815
Free verse, 123, 267, 815
Generalization, 815
Genre, 815
Humor, 62, 505, 815
Hyperbole, 400, 815
Idiom, 121, 815
Imagery, 124, 682, 815
Internal rhyme, 818
Irony, 41, 62, 815
Legend, 698, 815
Lyric poetry, 815
Main idea, 45, 816
Memoir, 43, 265, 816
Metaphor, 124, 816
    extended, 317, 816
Mood, 270, 387, 816
Moral, 666, 816
Motivation, 550, 816
Myth, 699, 816
Narrative, 816
Narrative poetry, 548, 816
Narrator, 581, 816. *See also* Point of view.
Nonfiction, 43–44, 816
    autobiography, 43, 257, 812
    biography, 43–44, 448, 560, 812
    essay, 44, 814
    informative, 43, 815
    literary, 43, 815
    memoir, 43, 265, 816
    topic sentences in, 45
Novel, 15, 816
Opinion, 44, 457
Oral history, 330, 398, 816
Oral tradition, 696–97, 699
Personification, 124, 131, 817
Perspective. *See* Point of view.
Persuasion, 817
Play. *See* Drama.
Plot, 15–16, 182, 817
    climax, 16, 121, 249, 813, 817
    complications, 16, 817

exposition, 15, 814, 817
resolution, 16, 200, 817
surprise ending, 238, 819
Poetry, 123–24, 817
    ballad, 549
    dialogue in, 598
    figurative language in, 124, 131
    form of, 123, 129, 815
    free verse, 123, 267, 815
    imagery in, 124
    lyric, 815
    narrative, 548, 816
    repetition in, 123–24
    rhyme in, 123, 134, 817
    rhyme scheme of, 410, 818
    rhythm in, 123, 134, 818
    sound devices in, 123–24
    speaker in, 125, 594, 818
    stanzas in, 123, 819
    theme in, 124, 179
Point of view, 817
    first-person, 159, 296, 817
    third-person, 41, 817
Prose, 817
Protagonist, 378, 817
Purpose. *See* Author's purpose.
Radio play, 817
Realistic fiction, 296, 646, 817
Repetition, 123–24, 646, 817
Resolution, 16, 200, 817
Rhyme, 123, 134, 817
Rhyme scheme, 410, 818
Rhythm, 123, 134, 818
Science fiction, 107, 505, 818
Script, 181–82
Setting, 15, 104, 173, 183, 226, 818
Short story, 15, 818
Simile, 124, 131, 818
Slang, 657, 818
Sound devices, 123–24. *See also* Alliteration; Repetition; Rhyme; Rhythm.
Speaker, 125, 594, 818
Stage directions, 181–82, 819
Stanza, 123, 819
Stereotype, 238, 507, 819
Style, 88, 819
Surprise ending, 238, 819
Suspense, 16, 510, 819
Symbol, 592, 679, 819
Teleplay, 459, 819
Theme, 16, 124, 179, 238, 819. *See also* Moral.
Tone, 311, 677, 819
Topic sentence, 45, 819
Turning point. *See* Climax.
Voice, 575, 819

Reading and Critical Thinking Skills

Activating prior knowledge, 16, 45, 83, 90, 137–43, 228, 257, 369, 390, 410, 424, 434, 439, 499, 583, 637, 674, 798
Analyzing, 27, 41, 54, 80–81, 107, 120, 129, 159, 173, 179, 182, 216–17, 226, 227, 238, 257, 265, 268, 270, 378, 581, 598, 617, 635, 648, 657, 812
Applying
    ideas to literature, 16, 29, 41, 44, 45, 54, 74–75, 76–79, 132, 148, 175, 200, 267, 284, 332, 398, 400
    literature to life, 16, 45, 136, 149, 159, 406, 424, 448, 457, 499, 548, 575, 581, 657, 659, 668
Brainstorming, 179, 368, 414
Categorizing, 17, 45, 64, 65, 76, 125, 136, 137, 219, 240, 252, 285, 390, 425, 434, 450, 480, 499, 507, 513, 582, 648, 659
Cause and effect, 159, 238, 241, 581, 592, 645, 812
Clarifying, 5, 10, 11, 16, 38, 44, 93, 164, 166, 168, 170, 176, 243, 245, 268, 293, 382, 386, 427, 430, 516, 520, 522, 526, 528, 538, 583, 586, 587, 589, 641, 813
Classifying and diagramming, 17, 27, 29, 45, 55, 64, 65, 76, 83, 89, 90, 125, 129, 131, 136, 161, 173, 175, 183, 201, 219, 228, 240, 241, 249, 252, 257, 259, 265, 267, 284, 285, 296, 319, 332, 346, 362, 368, 369, 390, 400, 412, 424, 425, 434, 449, 450, 459, 499, 507, 513, 542, 575, 583, 594, 600, 648, 658, 668, 687, 714, 750, 783, 855–56, 859, 870, 871, 875, 879, 883, 884, 886, 889, 894, 900, 903. *See also* Classifying and diagramming *under* Writing Skills, Modes, and Formats.
Compare and contrast, 41, 54, 55, 104, 105, 129, 134, 159, 173, 183, 202, 226, 238, 239, 250, 265, 271, 295, 296, 311, 314, 330, 388, 390, 398, 404, 410, 424, 437, 448, 480, 498, 510, 548, 549, 581, 594, 598, 617, 658, 666, 672, 677, 684, 687, 715, 731, 751, 783, 797, 805, 813
Connecting, 5, 7, 9, 14, 16, 27, 29, 41, 45, 54, 57, 62, 75, 83, 88, 90, 104, 107, 120, 124, 125, 131, 134, 136, 137, 148, 149, 161, 173, 175, 183, 200, 218, 219, 228, 240, 248, 252, 257, 259, 265, 267, 270, 284, 285, 289, 295, 298, 311, 314, 317, 319, 330, 345, 368, 369, 378, 380, 382, 387, 390, 398, 404, 407, 412, 424, 425, 432, 434, 437, 439, 448, 457, 459, 480, 491, 498, 505, 507, 510, 539, 560, 574, 581, 585, 592, 594, 598, 600, 617, 636, 637, 645, 646, 648, 657, 659, 666, 668, 674, 677, 679, 714–15, 730, 750, 782, 796, 813
Contrasting, 390, 813. *See also* Comparison/contrast.
Cooperative learning. *See* Working in groups in the Speaking, Listening, and Viewing index.
Drawing conclusions, 27, 41, 80–81, 88, 120, 148, 159, 238, 265, 295, 311, 330, 345, 378, 398, 410, 432, 437, 457, 480, 510, 592, 617, 645, 666, 677
Evaluating, 5, 7, 8, 10, 11, 16, 27, 32, 41, 44, 62, 64, 80–81, 88, 104, 120, 127, 132, 134, 136, 139, 159, 173, 176, 177, 200, 201, 226, 238, 248, 257, 265, 268, 270, 277, 279, 295, 296, 299, 311, 317, 330, 345, 378, 380, 387, 398, 404, 407, 432, 437, 480, 496–97, 539, 548, 560, 569, 581, 583, 637, 656, 657, 666, 668, 677, 687, 691, 814

Fact and opinion, distinguishing, 44, 814
Fiction and reality, distinguishing, 759
Generalizations, recognizing, 815
Generalizing, 74–75, 80–81, 120, 317, 378, 437, 480, 505
In-depth reading, 425, 815
Inferences, making, 513, 815
Judgment, 54, 62, 88, 104, 120, 129, 134, 159, 173, 177, 179, 200, 238, 270, 311, 330, 378, 387, 398, 404, 437, 480, 539, 560, 581, 583, 598, 668, 677
Nonverbal communication, 496–97
Opinion, 14, 44, 62, 88, 104, 120, 129, 134, 159, 173, 176, 179, 200, 226, 238, 249, 257, 270, 295, 314, 317, 345, 362, 387, 398, 412, 413, 432, 448, 457, 480, 505, 510, 539, 548, 560, 583, 617, 667, 668, 673, 677, 687
Peer interaction, 27, 28, 29, 41, 42, 55, 104, 159, 173, 179, 200, 201, 238, 249. *See also* Working in groups *under* Speaking, Listening, and Viewing.
Peer response, 77, 213, 226, 278, 363, 416, 417, 493, 567, 631, 684, 689, 691, 822–23, 854
Personal response, 14, 16, 27, 44, 75, 121, 125, 127, 131, 132, 134, 136, 139, 148, 149, 159, 173, 176, 177, 200, 218, 228, 238, 240, 248, 249, 250, 257, 264, 295, 317, 368, 378, 407, 412, 424, 434, 439, 457, 480, 490–95, 496–97, 498, 505, 507, 548, 574, 575, 583, 600, 635, 636, 637, 648, 659, 668, 674, 677, 679, 714, 715, 805
Perspectives and perceptions
    discussing, 80–81, 136, 216–17, 367, 496–97
    exploring, 74–75, 80–81, 136–37, 136, 216–17, 700
    interpreting, 80–81, 216–17, 367, 496–97
    viewing, 80–81, 216–27, 367, 496–97
Predicting, 5, 7, 8, 11, 16, 34, 44, 95, 148, 159, 228, 238, 244, 295, 319, 330, 332, 345, 384, 507, 518, 581, 640, 817
Previewing, 16, 44, 124
Questioning, 5, 7, 8, 9, 14, 16, 27, 29, 32, 41, 44, 45, 54, 57, 62, 76, 83, 88, 90, 96, 100, 105, 107, 120, 121, 125, 129, 131, 134, 136, 148, 149, 160, 173, 200, 201, 216–17, 218, 219, 226, 227, 238, 248, 257, 259, 265, 267, 285, 296, 298, 311, 313, 317, 319, 330, 331, 332, 345, 368, 369, 378, 379, 380, 382, 387, 390, 398, 399, 400, 404, 406, 410, 412, 415, 432, 434, 437, 439, 480, 499, 510, 511, 512, 539, 540, 541, 542, 548, 549, 550, 560, 561, 575, 635, 656, 659, 674, 684, 805, 817
Recalling prior experience, 14, 16, 82, 125, 131, 136, 137–43, 148, 161, 219, 252, 259, 284, 285, 404, 406, 432, 434, 583, 636
Reflecting on theme, 2, 136, 148, 218, 284, 368, 424, 498, 574, 636
Scanning, 425, 818
Sequencing, 601, 818
Similarities and differences. *See* Comparison/contrast.
Skimming, 452, 818
Strategies for reading, 5. *See also* Clarifying; Connecting; Evaluating; Predicting; Questioning.
    drama, 182
    fiction, 16
    nonfiction, 44
    poetry, 124

Summarizing, 542, 819
Synthesizing, 129, 159, 257, 378
Theme, reflecting on. *See* Reflecting on theme.
Visualizing, 16, 75, 77, 120, 124, 127, 132, 179, 219, 249, 257, 265, 268, 295, 311, 330, 345, 378, 387, 404, 407, 410, 432, 437, 457, 505, 510, 539, 560, 583, 668, 819

Grammar, Usage, and Mechanics

Abbreviations, 903
Adjective, 900
    comparative form of, 879, 900
    modified by adverb, 878
    as modifier, 878
    phrase, 629
    predicate, 900
    proper, 887, 900
    superlative form of, 879, 900
Adverb, 900
    comparative form of, 880, 900
    conjunctive, 891, 901
    introductory, 892
    as modifier, 878
    phrase, 629
    superlative form of, 880, 900
Agreement
    pronoun-antecedent, 495, 874–76, 900
    subject-verb, 215, 863–69, 900
Antecedent, 495, 874–76, 900
Apostrophe, 871, 901, 903
Appositive, 361, 893, 900
Article, 900
Bad and *badly*, 881
Capitalization, 887–91
    of geographical names, events, time periods, 889
    of languages, nationalities, religious terms, 888
    of names, personal titles, 887
    of organizations, institutions, 888
    of proper nouns, proper adjectives, 887–89
    of school courses, class names, 888
    of titles of created works, 805, 890
Clause
    main (independent), 894, 900
    as sentence fragment, 79, 860
    subordinate (dependent), 365, 860, 894, 900
Collective noun, 868, 901
Colon, 903
Commas, 79, 891–97, 903
    in addresses, 897
    between adjectives of equal rank, 895–96
    in dates, 896, 897
    in complex sentences, 365
    in compound sentences, 891, 892
    with coordinating conjunctions, 862
    in greetings and closings in a letter, 897
    to prevent misreading, 893

with quotation marks, 753, 899
    in series, 895
    with subordinate clauses, 365
Common noun, 901
Comparative, 879, 880, 900
Complex sentence, 365, 901
Compound parts of sentences, 901
Compound sentence, 891, 892, 901
Conjunction
    coordinating, 862, 901
    correlative, 901
    subordinating, 894, 901
Conjunctive adverb, 891, 901
Contraction, 901
    pronoun in, 873, 877
Demonstrative pronoun, 902
Dependent (subordinate) clause, 365, 860, 894, 900
Direct object, 902
Double negative, 691, 880, 901
End mark, 901
Exclamation point, 898, 903
Few and *little*, 882
Fewer and *less*, 882
First-person pronoun, 75, 902
Fragment, sentence, 79, 860–61, 901, 903
Future tense, 903
Gerund, 901
Good and *well*, 882
Grammar, analyzing, in literature, 863, 868, 872, 881, 883, 891
Helping verb, 901
He or *she*, 874, 875
Hyphen, 903
Independent (main) clause, 894, 900
Indirect object, 901
Infinitive, 901
Interjection, 211, 901
Interrupting words and phrases, 866–67
Inverted sentence, 215, 867, 901
It's and *its*, 877
Italics, 805, 868, 890
Learn and *teach*, 886
Let and *leave*, 885
Lie and *lay*, 885
Modifier, 878–82, 901. *See also* Adjective; Adverb.
Names, capitalization of, 887–89. *See also* Titles.
Negatives, 880, 901
Noun, 901
    abstract, 901
    collective, 868, 901
    common, 901
    compound, 901
    of direct address, 893, 901
    modified by adjective, 878
    plural, 870–71
    possessive, 871, 901
    predicate, 902
    with pronoun, 877
    proper, 887–89, 902
    singular, 868
    of time, weight, or measure, 868
    verbal, 903
Number, 902. *See also* Plural; Singular.
Object
    direct, 902
    form of pronoun, 872, 873, 902
    indirect, 901
    of preposition, 902
    of verb, 902
    whom as, 876–77
Participle
    past, 884, 902
    present, 902
Past tense, 903
Perfect tenses, 903
Period, 898, 903
Person of pronoun, 902
Phrase, 902
    adjective/adverb, 629
    comma after, 892–93
    interrupting, 866–67, 894
    introductory, 892–93
    prepositional, 902
    as sentence fragment, 860–61
    verb, 903
Plural
    noun, 870–71
    possessive, 871
    pronoun, 864–65, 874, 875
    verb, 863–69
Possessive nouns and pronouns, 871, 902
Predicate, 902
    complete, 901
    missing, 861
Predicate adjective, 900
Preposition, 902
Prepositional phrase, 902
Pronoun, 902
    agreement with antecedent, 495, 874–76, 900
    in contraction, 873, 877
    demonstrative, 902
    first-person, 75, 159
    he or *she*, 874, 875
    indefinite, 495, 865–66, 875, 901, 902
    intensive, 902
    interrogative, 902
    misused, 881
    with noun, 877
    object form of, 872, 873, 902
    personal, 865, 872, 902
    plural, 864–65, 874, 875
    point of view and, 75
    possessive, 871, 873, 902
    predicate, 872, 902
    reflexive, 902
    relative, 894, 902

second-person, 902
singular, 864–65, 874, 875
subject form of, 864–66, 872, 902
third-person, 41, 75, 874, 875, 902
who and *whom*, 876–77
Proper adjective, 887, 900
Punctuation, 903
apostrophe, 871, 901, 903
colon, 903
comma, 79, 365, 753, 891–97, 899, 903
end, 898–99, 901
exclamation point, 898, 903
hyphen, 903
period, 898, 903
in poetry, 631
question mark, 898, 903
quotation marks, 868, 890, 898–99
semicolon, 862, 891–92, 898, 903
Question mark, 898, 903
Quotation, divided, 899
Quotation marks, 868, 890, 898–99
commas with, 753, 899
with titles of created works, 868, 890, 898
Revising tips, grammatical, 862, 863, 867, 871, 872, 875, 878, 879, 880, 881, 883, 885, 888, 889, 891, 895, 898, 899
Rise and *raise*, 885
Run-on sentence, 79, 861–62, 902
Script, formatting, 757
Second-person pronoun, 902
Semicolon, 862, 891–92, 898, 903
Sentence, 903
combining, 569
complete, 631, 860–62
complex, 365, 901
compound, 861–62, 891–92
compound parts of, 901
declarative, 903
exclamatory, 903
fragment, 79, 860–61, 901, 903
imperative, 903
interrogative, 903
inverted, 215, 867, 901
run-on, 79, 861–62, 902
variety, 493
Singular
noun, 868
possessive, 871
pronoun, 864–65, 874, 875
verb, 863–69
Sit and *set*, 885
Subject, 903
agreement with verb, 215, 863–69, 900
collective noun as, 868
complete, 901
compound, 863–865
in inverted sentence, 215, 867, 901
missing, 861

noun of time, weight, or measure as, 868
phrase between verb and, 866–67
plural, 863–69
pronoun as, 864, 872
simple, 863
who as, 876
Subordinate (dependent) clause, 365, 860, 894, 900
Superlative 879, 880, 900
Tenses of verbs, 903
consistent use of, 883
future, 903
future perfect, 903
past, 884, 903
past perfect, 903
present, 884, 903
present perfect, 903
with quotations, 633
shift in, 883
Them and *those*, 881
These and *those*, 881
They, indefinite, 875
They're and *their*, 877
Third-person pronoun, 41, 75, 874, 875, 902
This and *that*, 881
Titles
of created works, 805, 868, 890, 898
lowercase words in, 888
of persons, 887
shortened or unofficial forms of, 888, 889
Verbal, 903
Verb phrase, 903
Verb, 883–86, 903
active, 903
agreement with subject, 215, 863–69, 900
confusing pairs, 885–86
future tense, 903
gerund, 901
helping, 901, 903
infinitive, 901
in inverted sentence, 215, 867, 901
irregular, 903
linking, 872, 903
modified by adverb, 878
participle, 884, 902
passive, 903
phrase between subject and, 866–67
plural, 863–69
precise, 279
predicates, 902
regular, 903
singular, 863–69
tenses of, 633, 883–84, 903
Who and *what* questions, 863
Who and *whom*, 876–77
You, indefinite, 875

Writing Skills, Modes, and Formats

Analysis, 838, 842–43
Audience, identifying, 821, 844
Cause-and-effect writing, 838, 840
Classifying and diagramming
    chart, 27, 183, 201, 855, 856
    diagram, 668, 674
    flow chart, 858–59
    graph, 856
    time line, 275, 601, 783
    Venn diagram, 202, 481, 715
    word map, 258, 297, 399
    word web, 175, 346, 415, 511, 679, 731
    word wheel, 582
Compare-and-contrast writing, 838–39
Conclusions, 213, 834–35, 843, 845
Descriptive writing, 832–34
    character sketch, 27, 200, 295, 448, 592
    explanation, 257
    eyewitness report, 562–69
    interview, 574
Drafting, 821–22
    discovery, 77, 213, 276, 363, 416–17, 492, 566, 631, 688, 754–55, 802–3, 822
    final, 78, 138–43, 214, 278–79, 364, 418, 494, 568, 569, 632, 689, 690–91, 804–5
Editing. *See* Revising and editing.
Elaborating, 831–32
    with examples, 360, 417, 832
    with facts and statistics, 360, 417
    with quotations, 417, 832
    with sensory details, 360, 490, 567
Emphasis, creating, 210–11
Explanatory writing, 838–43
    encyclopedia entry, 265
    informative paragraph, 265
    problem-solution essay, 412–19, 838, 841
    public service announcement, 265
Facts, 686
Firsthand and expressive writing
    advice, 179, 404
    editorial, 218
    E-mail note, 505
    epitaph, 159, 398, 617
    family history, 136–43
    fictional narrative, 272–79
    graffiti, 249
    humorous memoir, 57
    interior monologue, 104, 432, 510, 592
    journal, 80–81, 159, 177, 249, 330, 332, 387, 404, 412, 413, 424, 457, 539, 560, 617, 645, 672
    letter, 159, 330, 448, 560, 617, 672
    letter to the editor, 457
    memoir, 266
    monologue, 317
    personal ad, 226
    personal essay, 88
    personal narrative, 41, 173, 179, 238, 378
    poem, 129, 173, 179, 226, 295, 317, 598
    postcard, 636
    tribute, 424
Freewriting, 492
Gathering information, 76, 136, 212, 272, 360–61, 362, 412, 490–92, 562–63, 628–30, 798–99, 801, 847. *See also* On-line resources *under* Research and Study Skills.
Informative writing
    biography, 593
    character analysis, 270
    lead paragraph, 387
    medical abstract, 540
    newspaper article, 54, 129, 311, 548, 657
    newspaper front page, 782
    newspaper headlines, 173
    print ad, 265
    progress reports, 539
    research report, 798–805
    society-page report, 200
    survey/poll, 201
    TV program, 200, 797
Introductions, 77, 213, 826–27, 837, 843, 845
Journal. *See* Firsthand and expressive writing.
Narrative and literary writing, 836–37
    anecdote, 54
    bedtime story, 677
    dialogue, 27, 257, 295, 311, 378, 506, 510, 752–53, 757, 827, 837
    dramatic scene, 754–57
    epilogue, 226, 505
    essay, 598
    folksong, 617
    letter, 41, 54
    narrative, 62
    novel, 15
    origin myth, 797
    poem, 62, 125, 129, 134, 173, 226, 410, 448, 548, 617, 645, 666
    quatrain, 41
    radio play, 28
    realistic fiction, 296
    report, 55
    script, 200
    short story, 15, 272–79
    teleplay, 459
Opinion, 687, 844–45
Organizing
    analysis, 842–43
    body of essay, 213
    cause-and-effect writing, 840
    climax, 277
    compare-and-contrast writing, 839
    conclusion, 213, 834–35, 843, 845
    details, 362, 832–33
    form, 123
    introduction, 77, 213, 826–27, 837, 843, 845

order of events, 44, 275, 829
  narrative, 837
  paragraphs, 827–29
  persuasive writing, 845
  problem-solution writing, 841
  statement of purpose, 800
  theme, 124, 179
  thesis statement, 847
  topics, 799–800, 858–59
  topic sentence, 45, 828
  transitions for, 829–30
Paragraphs, 827–29
Paraphrasing, 801
Peer response, 77, 213, 226, 278, 363, 416, 417, 493, 567, 631, 684, 689, 691, 755, 822–23, 854
Persuasive writing, 844–45
  advertisement, 65, 105, 645, 658
  fund-raising letter, 201
  letter of recommendation, 539
  pep talk, 666
  persuasive essay, 684–91
Prewriting, 76–77, 212, 272–75, 362, 414–15, 492, 564–65, 628–30, 686–87, 754, 800–1, 820–21
Problem-solution writing, 838, 841
Purpose, setting, 74, 76–77, 129, 136, 212, 272–74, 362, 414–15, 492, 562–64, 630, 684–87, 798–800, 821
Reflecting on writing, 139, 279, 419, 567, 569, 687, 805, 825
Research report writing, 846–49
Revising and editing, 54, 75, 76, 78, 88, 104, 136, 214, 238, 270, 277–78, 345, 364, 417–18, 480, 505, 567, 568, 690, 731, 756, 804–5, 823–25, 875. *See also* Word processing.
Standards for evaluation
  analysis, 842
  cause-and-effect writing, 840
  compare-and-contrast writing, 839
  creative response, 78
  critical essay, 364
  eyewitness report, 569
  firsthand narrative, 139
  interpretive essay, 214
  narrative writing, 836
  personal response, 494
  persuasive writing, 691, 844
  poetry analysis, 632
  problem-solution writing, 419, 841
  research report, 805, 846
  scene, 756
  short story, 279
Transitions, 829–30
Word processing, 852–56
Writing about literature
  analyzing point of view, 74–75
  asking questions about a story, 360–61
  changing a story element, 76–79
  character analysis, 270
  character "report card," 796
  character sketch, 27
  comparing and contrasting characters, 64, 296, 388, 481, 645
  comparing and contrasting poems, 125, 129, 134, 437
  comparing and contrasting points of view, 74–75
  comparing and contrasting selections, 159, 202, 239, 250, 311, 330, 448
  critical essay, 360–65
  finding a message, 210–11
  interpreting the meaning, 212–15
  literary analysis, 210–15
  overview, 137
  personal response, 27, 28, 41, 42, 54, 62, 104, 257, 266, 317, 318, 330, 490–95, 510
  play, 752–57
  poetry analysis, 127, 132, 176, 177, 268, 410, 598, 628–35
  responding as character, 27, 28, 42, 62, 104, 249, 250, 257, 399, 404, 410, 432, 539, 560, 645
  responding to characters, 27, 29, 41, 62, 63, 64, 88, 104–5, 120, 159, 200, 216, 270, 285, 295, 378, 387, 398, 407, 432, 457, 480, 539, 560, 666
  responding to plot, 120, 173, 238, 345, 387, 548, 581, 592, 617
  responding to speaker of poem, 125, 127, 132, 176, 268, 410, 598
  responding to theme, 505
  rewriting, 54, 76–79, 88, 104, 120, 137, 238, 506
Writing from experience
  eyewitness report, 562–69
  family history, 136–43
  persuasive essay, 684–91
  problem-solution essay, 412–19
  research report, 798–805
  short story, 272–79

Vocabulary Skills

Antonyms, 42, 89, 202, 313, 346
Colloquialisms, 55
Connotation, 28, 689
Context clues, 83, 106, 251, 297, 379, 388, 449, 458, 506, 593, 813
Definitions, 42, 56, 122, 160, 161, 331, 405, 433, 482, 541, 619, 647, 658, 669
Descriptive language, 491, 834
Dialect, 369, 813
Difficult words, 161
Figurative language, 124, 131, 317, 630. *See also* Similes.
Film terminology, 459
Idioms, 121
Legal terminology, 459
Loaded language, 689
Metaphors, 124, 317
Nonstandard English, 258, 816
Root words, 266
Similes, 124, 131, 134, 174, 561

Slang, 657, 819
Specialized vocabulary, 450, 819
Synonyms, 161, 202, 227, 239, 312, 346, 388
Vocabulary charades, 673
Word choice, 210

Research and Study Skills

Bibliography. *See* Works Cited list.
Dictionaries, 852, 870
Commercial information services, 850.
Copyrighted material, 859
Electronic mail, 850
Electronic resources
    CD-ROMs, 851
    library, 800, 851
    on-line, 850
Indexes, 801, 847
Internet, 850
Library research, 800, 847, 851
Note taking, 801, 847
On-line resources, *See* Electronic resources.
Outlining, 848
Plagiarism, avoiding, 801, 849
Research activities
    Alaskan brown bear, 312
    Asian immigration to United States, 599
    Assiniboin tribe, 582
    brain, 458, 540
    buzzards, 731
    Cajun culture, 731
    cobras, 511
    creation myths, 751
    Day of the Dead, 714
    eagle's nest, 751
    echoes, 65
    ecosystems, 121
    Ecuador, 751
    elderly, 593
    environmental problems, 175
    exchange rates, 201
    folklore, 798–805
    forest conservation, 715
    Great Britain in 19th century, 200, 201
    guided research assignment, 798–805
    horned toads, 160
    icebergs, 481
    islands, 64
    Japanese screen painting, 105
    Mayas, 797
    Mexican history, 714, 715
    Native Americans, 271, 797
    Paul Revere's ride, 549
    physiology of sudden fright, 388
    railroads, history of, 730
    scientific abstracts, 540
    solar system, 506
    Spanish words, 160
    Special Olympics, 658
    storytelling contest, 714
    survey/poll, 201
    unusual poems, 130
    U.S. roads, 561
    Vietnam syndrome, 646
    welfare system, 296
    World War II, 266
Source cards, 801–2, 847
Sources of information, 798–801, 847–48. *See also* Gathering information *under* Writing Skills, Modes, and Formats.
    documenting, 846, 849
    electronic, 850–51
    expert advice, 800
    library, 800, 847, 851
    news reports, 798, 850
    personal background, 798
    previewing, 801
    prior knowledge, 798–99
World Wide Web, 850
Works Cited list, 804–5, 849

Speaking, Listening, and Viewing

Cooperative learning. See Working in groups.
Creative response
    art, 106, 174, 250, 296, 331, 379, 399, 411, 424, 433, 481, 510, 599, 667, 673, 678, 715, 758–59, 797
    booklet, 130
    collage, 14, 574, 751
    comic book, 618
    dance, 438
    diorama, 121, 783
    drama. *See* Dramatic reading/presentation.
    dust jacket, 782
    graph/time line, 173
    guided written assignment, 74–79
    illustrations, 105, 130, 271
    map, 345
    mobile, 751
    montage, 227
    multimedia presentation, 857–59
    music/song, 27, 121, 296, 318, 433, 549, 647, 678, 783
    photographs, 857
    poster, 160
    posterboard display, 599
    Spanish match game, 160
    standards for evaluating, 78
    storyboard, 331, 368
Dramatic reading/presentation
    audiotape, 330, 399
    group reading, 271
    how-to videotape, 405
    The Man Without a Country, 618

"The Million-Pound Bank Note," 200
minidrama, 647
music video, 368
one-act play, 730
"Paul Revere's Ride," 549
radio play, 181, 346
Readers Theater, 295
scene/passage, 174, 250, 270, 498, 755
telephone conversation, 296
TV show, 284, 404, 797
videotape, 139, 200, 227, 266, 368, 405, 481, 857

Multimedia presentation, 857–59

Public speaking
civil trial, 750
debate, 296, 539
oral reading, 121, 124, 182, 410
oral report, 201, 266, 561
speech, 437

Reading aloud, 124, 182. *See also* Dramatic reading/presentation; Public speaking.

Technology. *See also* Word processing *under* Writing Skills, Modes, and Formats.
animation, 858
art and design programs, 856
CD-ROMs, 855, 858
clip-art files, 855, 856
databases, 850
E-mail, 850
LaserLinks, 17, 28, 29, 42, 83, 107, 149, 160, 174, 175, 183, 219, 252, 259, 273, 413, 425, 438, 439, 449, 450, 459, 499, 507, 512, 542, 550, 561, 697, 799
spreadsheet, 855
visuals and graphics, 855–56

Working in groups, 216, 251, 266, 361, 498, 673
brainstorming, 179, 368, 414
group discussion, 415, 496–97
poster designing, 265
role-playing, 399, 405
small-group activities, 80–81, 136, 317, 432, 458, 582, 592, 637, 750, 796, 797

Index of Titles and Authors

A
Abel, Robert H., 298, *312*
Abernethy, Hazel Shelton, 259, *266*
Adoff, Arnold, 125, *130*
Alarcón, Francisco X., 158
All Things Bright and Beautiful, from, 83
Appetizer, 298
Apprentice, The, 64
Aunty Misery, 724

B
Baca-Vaughn, Guadalupe, 700, *709*
Bambara, Toni Cade, 648, *658*
Banana Tree, The, 369
Barry, Dave, 400, *405*
Battle by the Breadfruit Tree, 483
Berry, James, 369, *379*
Bet, The, 240
Bode, Janet, 319, *331*
Brenner, Alfred, 459, *482*
Brer Possum's Dilemma, 721
Brooks, Gwendolyn, 434, *438*
Bruchac, Joseph, 760, *768*

C
Carson, Ben, M.D., 450, *458*
Carter, Dorothy Sharp, 784, *795*
Cassian, Nina, 434, *438*
Catton, Bruce, 45, *56*
Celebration, 580
Chang, Diana, 594, *599*
Chekhov, Anton, 240, *251*
Choice, The, 621
Cisneros, Sandra, 6
Clown, The, 57
Cofer, Judith Ortiz, 716, *726*
Collecting Team, 107
Cormier, Robert, 583, *593*
Crane, Stephen, 620

D
Dancer, 575
de Vinck, Christopher, 668, *673*
Dinner Party, The, 507
Dirge Without Music, 53
Douglass, Frederick, 559

E
Eliot, T. S., 406, *411*

F
Fairy Tale, A, 674
First Flute, The, 791
Fisher, Dorothy Canfield, 64, *73*
Five Eggs, The, 740
Fletcher, Lucille, 332, *346*
Flood, The, 347
Flowers for Algernon, 512
Foreign Student, 329
Freedman, Russell, 439, *449*
Freeman, Barbara, 784, *790*
Frost, Robert, 406, *411*

G
Gardner, Mona, 507, *511*
Getting the Facts of Life, 285
Gifted Hands, from, 450
Gift of the Magi, The, 425
Girl in the Lavender Dress, The, 710

H
Hackett, Walter, 183, 600
Haldeman, Jack C., II, 499, *506*
Hale, Edward Everett, 600, *619*
Hard Questions, 175
Harriet Tubman: Conductor on the Underground Railroad, from, 550
Haslam, Gerald, 149, *160*
Helfer, Ralph, 347, *359*
Henius, Frank, 732, *741*

Henry, O., 425, *433*
Herriot, James, 83, *89*
Hill, Douglas, 732, *744*
Hitchhiker, The, 332
Home Front: 1941-1945, The, 259
Horned Toad, The, 149
Hughes, Langston, 313, *318*
Hurricane, The, 377

I
I Belong, 622
Ignacio, Bruce, 267, *271*
In a Neighborhood in Los Angeles, 158
Inn of Lost Time, The, 90

J
John Henry, 718

K
Keeping Time, 659
Keyes, Daniel, 512, *541*
Kieran, John, 624, *625*
Koriyama, Naoshi, 175, *180*

L
Leading Cloud, Jenny, 732, *749*
lesson of the moth, the, 313
Letter to Harriet Tubman, 559
Lie, The, 29
Lincoln: A Photobiography, from, 439
Longfellow, Henry Wadsworth, 542, *549*
Lopez, Alonzo, 580
Lost, 267
Lum, Wing Tek, 674, *677*

M
Macavity: The Mystery Cat, 406
Man, A, 434
Man Without a Country, The, 600
Mark, Diane Mei Lin, 626, *627*
Markham, Beryl, 161, *174*
Marquis, Don, 313, *318*
Marriott, Alice, 390, *399*
Masefield, John, 679, *683*
Matos, Luis Palés, 377
McKissack, Patricia C., 760, *781*
McManus, Patrick F., 57, *63*

Meissner, Bill, 659, *667*
Merriam, Eve, 131, *135*
Millay, Edna St. Vincent, 53
Million-Pound Bank Note, The, 183
Mi Madre, 679
Mixed Singles, 125
Moco Limping, 125
Monreal, David Nava, 125, *130*
Mora, Pat, 679, *683*
Mother and Daughter, 203
Mother in Mannville, A, 219
Mother to Son, 313
Moustache, The, 583
M'su Carencro and Mangeur de Poulet, 716
Murphey, Cecil, 450
my enemy was dreaming, 267
Myers, Walter Dean, 17, *28*
My Mother Really Knew, 674

N
Namioka, Lensey, 90, 106
No News, 789

O
O Captain! My Captain!, 446
oil crisis, 178
Once Upon a Time When We Were Colored, from, 252
Ortiz Cofer, Judith, 716, *726*
Osborne, Mary Pope, 732, *739*
Other Pioneers, The, 594
Otoonah, 769

P
Painful Memories of Dating, 400
Palés Matos, Luis, 377
Parker, Dorothy, *621*
Paul Bunyan and the Winter of the Blue Snow, 700
Paul Revere's Ride, 542
Paulsen, Gary, 637, *647*
Pecos Bill, 734
Petry, Ann, 550, *561*
Playing for Keeps, 499
Poe, Edgar Allan, 380, *389*
Power of the Powerless: A Brother's Lesson, 668

Q
Quintana, Leroy V., 674, *677*

R
Racing the Great Bear, 762
Raven and the Coming of Daylight, 742
Rawlings, Marjorie Kinnan, 219, *227*
Raymond's Run, 648
Reflections on the Civil War, from, 45
Regan-Blake, Connie, 784, *790*
Reneaux, J. J., 716, *729*
Rice and Rose Bowl Blues, 626
Robinson, Barbara B., *329*
Robinson, Gail, 732, *744*
Roper, Norah, 390, *399*
Ross, Gayle, 784, *788*
Runaway, The, 406
Russell, Norman, 267, *271*

S
Sálaz-Márquez, Rubén, 228, *239*
Salazar, Roberto Félix, 594, *599*
San Souci, Robert D., 760, *774*
Saying Yes, 594
Scott, Maureen, 700
Sea-Fever, 679
Sea Lullaby, 131
Sears, Vickie, 575, *582*
Silverberg, Robert, 107, *122*
Simile: Willow and Ginkgo, 131
Soto, Gary, 203, *209*
Souls in Purgatory, The, 700
Speech to the Young / Speech to the Progress-Toward, 434
Splendid Outcast, The, 161
Spotted Eagle and Black Crow, 745
Stop the Sun, 637
Strawberries, 786
Survival, 459

T
Taulbert, Clifton L., 252, *258*
Tell-Tale Heart, The, 380
There's This That I Like About Hockey, My Lad, 624
Think As I Think, 620
Three Wise Guys: Un Cuento de Navidad/A Christmas Tale, 6
Torrence, Jackie, 716, *723*
Treasure of Lemon Brown, The, 17
Tsali of the Cherokees, 390
Tsuda, Margaret, 175, *180*
Twain, Mark, 183, *202*

V
Von, 319
"Von," 319, *331*
Vonnegut, Kurt, Jr., 29, *42*

W
Waldeck, Theodore J., 483, *489*
Walker, Alice, 175, *180*
Walker, Paul Robert, 700, *705*
We Alone, 175
White Mice, 228
White, Paulette Childress, 285, *297*
Whiterock, A., 622
Whitman, Walt, 439, *449*
Woman in the Snow, The, 775
World Is Not a Pleasant Place to Be, The, 225
Wylie, Elinor, 131, *135*

Acknowledgments *(continued)*

Henry Holt and Company, Inc.: "The Clown," from *Real Ponies Don't Go Oink!* by Patrick F. McManus; Copyright © 1974, 1981, 1985, 1989, 1990, 1991 by Patrick F. McManus. By permission of Henry Holt and Company, Inc.

Vivian Hixson: "The Apprentice," by Dorothy Canfield Fisher. By permission of Vivian Hixson, executor.

St. Martin's Press, Inc., and Harold Ober Associates, Inc.: Excerpt from *All Things Bright and Beautiful* by James Herriot; Copyright © 1973 and 1974 by James Herriot. By permission of St. Martin's Press, Inc., and Harold Ober Associates, Inc.

Ruth Cohen, Inc.: "The Inn of Lost Time" by Lensey Namioka, from *Short Stories by Outstanding Writers for Young Adults*, edited by Donald R. Gallo. By permission of Ruth Cohen, Inc. All rights reserved by the author.

Ralph M. Vicinanza, Ltd.: "Collecting Team," from *Explorers of Space: Eight Stories of Science Fiction* by Robert Silverberg; Copyright © 1975 by Headline Publications, Inc. By permission of Robert Silverberg, c/o Ralph M. Vicinanza, Ltd.

F. E. Albi: "Moco Limping" by David Nava Monreal, from *Sighs and Songs of Aztlan;* Copyright © 1975 by F. E. Albi and J. G. Nieto. Reprinted by permission of F. E. Albi, editor.

HarperCollins Publishers, Inc.: "Mixed Singles," from *Sports Pages* by Arnold Adoff; Copyright © 1986 by Arnold Adoff. By permission of HarperCollins Publishers, Inc.

Marian Reiner: "Simile: Willow and Ginkgo" from *A Sky Full of Poems* by Eve Merriam; Copyright © 1964, 1970, 1973 by Eve Merriam. By permission of Marian Reiner.

Alfred A. Knopf, Inc.: "Sea Lullaby," from *Collected Poems of Elinor Wylie* by Elinor Wylie; Copyright 1921 by Alfred A. Knopf, Inc., renewed by William Rose Benet 1949. Reprinted by permission of Alfred A. Knopf, Inc.

Unit Two

University of Nevada Press: "The Horned Toad" from *That Constant Coyote* by Gerald W. Haslam; Copyright © 1990 by the University of Nevada Press. By permission of the University of Nevada Press.

Chronicle Books: "In a Neighborhood in Los Angeles" from *Body in Flames* by Francisco X. Alarcón; Copyright © 1990. By permission of Chronicle Books.

Estate of Beryl Markham: "The Splendid Outcast" from *The Splendid Outcast: Beryl Markham's African Stories* by Beryl Markham. By permission of the Estate of Beryl Markham and Laurence Pollinger Ltd., London.

Harcourt Brace & Company: "We Alone" from *Horses Make a Landscape Look More Beautiful* by Alice Walker; Copyright © 1984 by Alice Walker. "Mother and Daughter," from *Baseball and Other Stories* by Gary Soto; Copyright © 1990 by Gary Soto.
By permission of Harcourt Brace & Company.

The Wilderness Society: "Hard Questions" by Margaret Tsuda, from *The Living Wilderness*, Autumn, 1970; Copyright © 1970 by The Wilderness Society. By permission of the the Wilderness Society.

Naoshi Koriyama: "oil crisis," from *Selected Poems, 1954–1985* by Naoshi Koriyama; Copyright © 1989 by Naoshi Koriyama. By permission of the author.

Plays, Inc.: *The Million-Pound Bank Note* by Walter Hackett, adapted from a story by Mark Twain, from *Radio Plays for Young People,* edited by Walter Hackett; Copyright © 1950 by Plays, Inc. By permission of Plays, Inc., Publishers, 120 Boylston St., Boston, MA 02116 USA.

Atheneum Books for Young Readers: "A Mother in Mannville," from *When the Whippoorwill* by Marjorie Kinnan Rawlings; Copyright 1936, 1940 Marjorie Kinnan Rawlings; copyright renewed © 1964, 1968 by Norton Baskin. Reprinted with the permission of Atheneum Books for Young Readers, an imprint of Simon & Schuster Children's Publishing Division.

William Morrow & Company, Inc.: "The World Is Not a Pleasant Place to Be," from *My House* by Nikki Giovanni; Copyright © 1972 by Nikki Giovanni. By permission of William Morrow & Company, Inc.

Cosmic House, Inc.: "White Mice" by Rubén Sálaz-Márquez, from *Voces: An Anthology of Nuevo Mexicano Writers,* edited by Rudolfo A. Anaya. By permission of Mr. Sal Justin of Cosmic House, Inc., Alameda, N.M., on behalf of Mr. Sálaz-Márquez.

Council Oak Publishing, Inc.: Excerpt from *Once upon a Time When We Were Colored* by Clifton L. Taulbert; Copyright © 1989 by Clifton L. Taulbert. By permission of Council Oak Publishing, Tulsa, Oklahoma.

Hazel Shelton Abernethy: "Home Front," from *Nacogdoches Sampler* by Hazel Shelton Abernethy. By permission of the author.

Norman Russell: "my enemy was dreaming" by Normal Russell, from *The Dekalb Literary Arts Review,* Fall/Winter 1969; Copyright © 1969 by Norman Russell. By permission of Norman Russell.

South Dakota Review: "Lost" by Bruce Ignacio, from *South Dakota Review,* Summer 1969; Copyright © 1969 by the South Dakota Review. By permission of South Dakota Review, Vermillion, SD.

Range Road Music Inc., Quartet Music Inc., and Abilene Music Inc.: "What a Wonderful World" by Bob Thiele and George David Weiss; Copyright © 1967 by Range Road Music Inc. and Quartet Music Inc. Copyright renewed and assigned to Range Road Music Inc., Quartet Music Inc., and Abilene Music. Used by permission. All rights reserved.

Unit Three

Paulette Childress White: "Getting the Facts of Life" by Paulette Childress White, from *Memory of Kin, Stories About Family by Black Writers,* edited by Mary Ellen Washington. Reprinted by permission of the author.

University of Georgia Press: "Appetizer," from *Ghost Traps* by Robert H. Abel; Copyright © 1991 by Robert H. Abel. By permission of University of Georgia Press, Athens, GA.

Harold Ober Associates: "Mother to Son" from *Selected Poems of Langston Hughes* by Langston Hughes; Copyright © 1959 by Langston Hughes, renewed 1990 by George Houston Bass. Reprinted by permission of Harold Ober Associates, Inc.

Doubleday Books: "the lesson of the moth," from *archy and mehitabel* by Don Marquis; Copyright 1927, renewed 1933. By permission of Doubleday Books, a division of Bantam Doubleday Dell Publishing Group, Inc.

Franklin Watts, Inc.: "Von," from *New Kids on the Block: Oral Histories of Immigrant Teens* by Janet Bode; Copyright © 1989 by Janet Bode. By permission of Franklin Watts, Inc., New York.

National Council of Teachers of English: "Foreign Student," from *English Journal,* May 1976, by Barbara Robinson; Copyright © 1976 by the National

Council of Teachers of English. By permission of National Council of Teachers of English.

William Morris Agency, Inc.: "The Hitchhiker" by Lucille Fletcher, from *Radio's Best Plays*; Copyright 1947 by Lucille Fletcher. By permission of the William Morris Agency, Inc., on behalf of the author.

Putnam Publishing Group and Jeremy P. Tarcher, Inc.: Excerpt from *The Beauty of the Beasts* by Ralph Helfer; Copyright © 1990. By permission of Putnam Publishing Group, Inc., and Jeremy P. Tarcher, Inc.

Orchard Books: "The Banana Tree," from *A Thief in the Village and Other Stories* by James Berry; Copyright © 1988 by James Berry. By permission of Orchard Books, New York.

Anna Palés Matos: "The Hurricane" by Luis Palés Matos, translated by Alida Wright Malkus. By permission of Anna Palés Matos.

HarperCollins Publishers, Inc.: "Tsali of the Cherokees," from *American Indian Mythology* by Alice Marriot and Carol K. Rachlin; Copyright © 1968 by Alice Marriot and Carol K. Rachlin. By permission of HarperCollins Publishers, Inc.

Crown Publishers, Inc.: "Oh, he's a crude oper-a-tor," from *Dave Barry Is Not Making This Up* by Dave Barry; Copyright © 1992, renewed 1994 by Dave Barry. By permission of Crown Publishers, Inc., a division of Random House, Inc.

Henry Holt and Company, Inc.: "The Runaway," from *The Poetry of Robert Frost* by Robert Frost, edited by Edward Connery Lathem; Copyright 1951 by Robert Frost. Copyright 1923, renewed © 1969 by Henry Holt and Co., Inc. By permission of Henry Holt and Co., Inc. Reprinted by permission of Henry Holt and Company, Inc.

Harcourt Brace & Company and Faber and Faber Ltd.: "Macavity the Mystery Cat," from *Old Possum's Book of Practical Cats* by T. S. Eliot; Copyright 1939 by T. S. Eliot and renewed © 1967 by Esme Valerie Eliot, reprinted by permission of Harcourt Brace & Company and Faber and Faber Ltd.

Unit Four

Gwendolyn Brooks: "Speech to the Young / Speech to the Progress-Toward," by Gwendolyn Brooks; Copyright © 1991 by Third World Press, Chicago. By permission of the author.

Peter Owen Ltd., Publishers: "A Man" by Nina Cassian, from *The Other Voice: Twentieth-Century Women's Poetry in Translation*. By permission of Peter Owen Ltd., Publishers, London.

Houghton Mifflin Company: "Who Is Dead in the White House?" from *Lincoln: A Photobiography* by Russell Freedman; Copyright © 1987 by Russell Freedman. By permission of Clarion Books/Houghton Mifflin Company. All rights reserved.

Zondervan Publishing House: *Gifted Hands* by Ben Carson, M.D.; Copyright © 1990 by Riview & Harold® Publishing Association. By permission of Zondervan Publishing House.

Alfred Brenner: *Survival* by Alfred Brenner; Copyright © 1957 by Alfred Brenner. By permission of Alfred Brenner.

Viking Penguin: "Battle by the Breadfruit Tree," from *On Safari* by Theodore J. Waldeck; Copyright 1940 by Theodore J. Waldeck, renewed © 1968 by Jo Besse McElveen Waldeck. Reprinted by permission of Viking Penguin, a division of Penguin Books USA, Inc.

Jack C. Haldeman II: "Playing for Keeps" by Jack. C. Haldeman II, from *Isaac Asimov's Science Fiction Magazine,* Copyright © 1982 by Davis Publications. Reprinted by permission of the author.

Bill Berger Associates, Inc.: "The Dinner Party" by Mona Gardner, from *The Saturday Review;* Copyright 1942, renewed © 1970 by *The Saturday Review*. By permission of Bill Berger Associates, Inc.

Daniel Keyes: "Flowers for Algernon" by Daniel Keyes, from *Magazine of Fantasy and Science Fiction*, April 1959, Vol. 16 #4. By permission of the author.

Russell and Volkening, Inc.: Excerpt from *Harriet Tubman: Conductor on the Underground Railroad* by Ann Petry; Copyright 1955, renewed © 1983. By permission of Russell and Volkening, Inc.

Unit Five

Firebrand Books: "Dancer," from *Simple Songs* by Vickie Sears; Copyright © 1990 by Vickie Sears. By permission of Firebrand Books, Ithaca, New York.

T. D. Allen: "Celebration" by Alonzo Lopez, from *The Whispering Wind: Poetry by Young American Indians,* compiled by Terry D. Allen. Used by permission of T. D. Allen and the author.

Pantheon Books: "The Moustache," from *Eight Plus One* by Robert Cormier; Copyright © 1975 by Robert Cormier. By permission of Pantheon Books, a division of Random House, Inc.

Larry Trejo & Associates: "The Other Pioneers" by Roberto Félix Salazar, from *The LULAC National*, July 1939; Copyright 1939 by The LULAC National. By permission of Larry Trejo & Associates.

Diana Chang: "Saying Yes" by Diana Chang, from *Asian American Heritage: An Anthology of Prose and Poetry,* edited by David Hsin-fu Wand. By permission of the author.

Plays, Inc.: *The Man Without a Country* by Walter Hackett, based on a story by Edward Everett Hale, from *Radio Plays for Young People,* edited by Walter Hackett; Copyright © 1950 by Plays, Inc. By permission of Walter Hackett and Plays, Inc., Publishers, 120 Boylston St., Boston, MA 02116 U.S.A.

Viking Penguin: "The Choice," from *The Portable Dorothy Parker* by Dorothy Parker; Copyright 1926, copyright renewed 1954 by Dorothy Parker. By permission of Viking Penguin, a division of Penguin Books USA, Inc.

Indian Historian Press: "I Belong" by A. Whiterock, from *The Weewish Tree,* February 1978. Reprinted by permission of Indian Historian Press.

Scribner: "There's This That I Like About Hockey, My Lad," from *The American Sporting Scene* by John Kieran; Copyright 1941 by John Kieran and Joseph Golinkin, renewed © 1988 by John Kieran. By permission of Scribner, a division of Simon & Schuster, Inc.

Diane Mei Lin Mark: "Rice and Rose Bowl Blues," by Diane Mei Lin Mark from *Breaking Silence, An Anthology of Contemporary Asian American Poets,* edited by Joseph Bruchac. Reprinted by permission of Diane Mei Lin Mark.

Jennifer Flannery, Literary Representative: "Stop the Sun" by Gary Paulsen, from *Boy's Life,* January 1986; Copyright © 1986 by Gary Paulsen. By permission of Jennifer Flannery as literary representative of Gary Paulsen.

Random House, Inc.: "Raymond's Run," from *Gorilla, My Love* by Toni Cade Bambara; Copyright © 1971 by Toni Cade Bambara.
"Keeping Time," from *Hitting Into the Wind* by Bill Meissner; Copyright © 1994 by Bill Meissner.

Used by permission of Random House, Inc.

Wall Street Journal: "Power of the Powerless," by Christopher de Vinck from the *Wall Street Journal,* April 10, 1985; Copyright © 1985 by Dow Jones & Company, Inc. By permission of the Wall Street Journal. All rights reserved.

Leroy V. Quintana: "A Fairy Tale" by Leroy V. Quintana, from *Hispanics in the United States: An Anthology of Creative Literature,* edited by Gary D. Keller and Francisco Jiménez. By permission of Leroy V. Quintana.

Wing Tek Lum: "My Mother Really Knew," from *Expanding the Doubtful Points* by Wing Tek Lum. By permission of the author.

The Society of Authors: "Sea Fever," from *Poems* by John Masefield. By the permission of The Society of Authors as the literary representative of the Estate of John Masefield.

Arte Publico Press: "Mi Madre," from *Chants* by Pat Mora; Copyright © 1984 by Arte Publico Press—University of Houston. By permission of Arte Publico Press.

Unit Six

Harcourt Brace & Company: "Paul Bunyan and the Winter of the Blue Snow," from *Big Men, Big Country: A Collection of American Tall Tales* by Paul Robert Walker; Copyright © 1992 by Paul Robert Walker.
"The First Flute," from *The Enchanted Orchard and Other Folktales of Central America* by Dorothy Sharp Carter; Copyright © 1973 by Dorothy Sharp Carter. By permission of Harcourt Brace & Company.

Guadalupe Baca-Vaughn: "The Souls in Purgatory," by Guadalupe Baca-Vaughn, from *Voces: An Anthology of Nuevo Mexicano Writers,* edited by Rudolfo A. Anaya. By permission of Guadalupe Baca-Vaughn.

The Globe Book Company: "The Girl in the Lavender Dress," retold by Maureen Scott, from *The American Anthology;* Copyright © 1987. By permission of the Globe Book Company.

Jackie Torrence: "Brer Possum's Dilemma" as told by Jackie Torrence, from *Homespun-Tales from America's Favorite Storytellers* . Reprinted by permission of Jackie Torrence, The Story Lady.

Judith Ortiz Cofer: "Aunty Misery," by Judith Ortiz Cofer. By permission of the author.

August House Publishers, Inc.: "M'su Carenco and Mangeur de Poulet," from *Cajun Folktales* by J. J. Reneaux. By permission of August House Publishers, Inc.

Alfred A. Knopf, Inc.: "Pecos Bill," from *American Tall Tales* by Mary Pope Osborne. Text copyright © 1991 by Mary Pope Osborne. Reprinted by permission of Alfred A. Knopf, Inc.

Scribner: "The Five Eggs," from *Stories from the Americas* by Frank Henius; Copyright 1944 Charles Scribner's Sons; copyright renewed © 1972 Gertrude Henius. By the permission of Scribner, an imprint of Simon & Schuster, Inc.

Watson Little, Ltd.: "Raven and the Coming of Daylight," from *Coyote the Trickster: Legends of the North American Indians* by Gail Robinson and Douglas Hill, originally published by Chatto and Windus, Ltd. By permission of Watson Little, Ltd.

Random House, Inc.: "Spotted Eagle and Black Crow" by Jenny Leading Cloud, from *The Sound of Flutes and Other Indian Legends;* Text copyright © 1976 by Richard Erdoes and Alfonso Ortiz. By permission of Pantheon Books, a division of Random House, Inc.

Staniels Associates: "Racing the Great Bear," from *Flying with the Eagle,*

Racing the Great Bear: Stories from Native North America by Joseph Bruchac; Copyright © 1993 by Joseph Bruchac. By permission of Staniels Associates as agent for BridgeWater Books, an imprint of Troll Associates, Inc.

Philomel Books: "Otoonah," from *Cut from the Same Cloth: American Women of Myth, Legend, and Tall Tale* by Robert D. San Souci; Copyright © 1993 by Robert D. San Souci. Reprinted by permission of Philomel Books, an imprint of the Putnam Publishing Group.

Alfred A. Knopf, Inc.: "The Woman in the Snow," from *The Dark Thirty: Southern Tales of the Supernatural* by Patricia McKissack; Copyright © 1992 by Patricia McKissack. Reprinted by permission of Alfred A. Knopf, Inc.

Gayle Ross: "Strawberries," a traditional Cherokee story retold by Gayle Ross. By permission of the author.

The Folktellers: "No News," retold by Connie Regan-Blake and Barbara Freeman. By permission of the Folktellers.

The following sections were prepared by **Ligature, Inc., of Chicago, Illinois:** Learning the Language of Literature, Writing about Literature, Writing from Experience, Writing Handbook, Multimedia Handbook, and Grammar Handbook.

Art Credits

The editors have made every effort to trace the ownership of all copyrighted art and photography found in this book and to make full acknowledgment for their use.

Author Photographs and Portraits
42, 56, 73, 89, 174, 227, 318 *bottom*, 625 AP/Wide World Photos, Inc. 63 George Desaintrat. 106 Richard McNamee. 122, 506, 541 Jay Kay Klein. 135 *top*, 438 *left* Copyright © Layle Silbert. 135 *bottom*, 620–621, 683 *left* The Granger Collection, New York. 180 Jean Weisinger. 251 Itar Tass/Sovfoto. 312 University of Georgia Press. 318 *top*, 411 *right* National Portrait Gallery, Smithsonian Institution, Washington, D.C./Art Resource, New York. 346 By permission of the Vassar College Library. 389 The Edgar Allan Poe Museum of the Poe Foundation, Richmond, Virginia. 411 *left* National Archives. 433, 549 Stock Montage. 438 *left* Howard Simmons. 449 *left* Copyrighted © Chicago Tribune Company. All rights reserved, used with permission. 449 *right* Museum of the City of New York. 458 Johns Hopkins Children's Center, Office of Public Affairs. 582 Courtesy of Firebird Books. 599 Gordon Robotham. 619 Culver Pictures. 658 The Schomburg Center for Research in Black Culture, The New York Public Library, Astor, Lenox and Tilden Foundations. 683 *right*, 726 Courtesy of Arte Publico Press. 749 Courtesy of Richard Erdoes.

Commissioned Art and Photography
2 *top*, 212 *bottom*, 279, 416–418, 569, 684, 685 *bottom*, 686 *top*, 687, 690, 754 *bottom*, 804 Allan Landau.
4, 5, 74, 76, 78, 88, 91 *background*, 126, 132, 136–144, 210–214, 229, 231–232, 237, 272–275, 278, 284, 300, 303, 305, 308, 310, 312, 320–323, 324

Maps: **694–695, 698–701, 716–717, 732–733, 760–761, 784–785** John Sandford. **695–696** Gordon Lewis. **697** Richard Waldrep. Maps on all other Previewing pages and on all Responding pages: Robert Voights.

Miscellaneous Art Credits

xi Detail of mountain landscape, Sesshu Toyo (1420–1506). Six-fold screen, ink and color on paper, 161.0 cm × 351.2 cm, Japan, Muromachi Period, courtesy of the Freer Gallery of Art, Smithsonian Institution, Washington, D.C. (58.5). **xiii** *Gauguin's Armchair* (1888), Vincent van Gogh. Van Gogh Museum, Amsterdam, the Netherlands, Art Resource/New York. **xv** Copyright © David Shannon. **xvii** *Forward* (1967), Jacob Lawrence. Tempera on masonite, 23 7/8″ × 35 15/16″, North Carolina Museum of Art, Raleigh, purchased with funds from the State of North Carolina. **xix** *Sunroom* (1980), Winifred Nicholson. Copyright © the artist's family. **xxi, 784** *bottom* Detail of *Aviary Triptych* (1992), Carol Cottone-Kolthoff. By permission of the artist. Copyright © 1992 Carol Cottone-Kolthoff. **xxiv–1** *Moebius II*, M. C. Escher. Copyright © 1995 M. C. Escher/Cordon Art, Baarn, Holland, all rights reserved. **2** *center* Copyright © Peter Dean/Tony Stone Images; *bottom* Tass/Sovfoto. **3** *top* Copyright © Jim Ballard/Tony Stone Images; *top insets* Courtesy of Jim Ochsenreiter; *bottom* Copyright © Mark E. Gibson. **14** Copyright © 1990 Paul Barton/The Stock Market. **17** Copyright © David Young Wolff/Tony Stone Images. **18** Detail of *Midtown Sunset* (1981), Romare Bearden. Courtesy of the Estate of Romare Bearden. **31** *detail* Copyright © Fred Lynch. **45** Confederate cap worn during the Battle of Gettysburg. Private collection. From *Echoes of Glory: Arms & Equipment of the Confederacy*. Copyright © 1991 Time-Life Books Inc. Photo by Larry Sherer. **46, 550** Reproduced from the collections of the Library of Congress. **47** *top* Courtesy of the Bureau of State Office Buildings, Commonwealth of Massachusetts. Photo by Douglas Christian; *bottom* The Bettmann Archive. **49** Private Edwin Jennison. Reproduced from the collections of the Library of Congress. **50** Walter Miles Parker. Reproduced from the collections of the Library of Congress. **65, 67, 70, 73** Copyright © Renee Lynn/Tony Stone Images. **80–81** Copyright © 1996 Joseph Gillette/Swanstock. **82** P. Degginer/H. Armstrong Roberts. **83** Copyright © Andy Sacks/Tony Stone Images. **84** ZEFA-U.K./H. Armstrong Roberts. **88** From *All Creatures Great and Small* by James Herriot. Copyright © 1972 James Herriot. Used by permission of Bantam Books, a division of Bantam Doubleday Dell Publishing Group, Inc. **90** Copyright © Dana Levy/Photo Researchers, Inc. **119** UPI/Bettmann. **126** *Fido*, Laura McDougall. Copyright © Laura McDougall. **128** Brent Bear/H. Armstrong Roberts. **131** *top* Copyright © Lefever/Grushow from Grant Heilman Photography, Inc.; *bottom* Copyright © S. W. Carter/Photo Researchers, Inc. **138** *top insets* Courtesy of Linda Washington. **146–147** *background*, **422–423** *background*, **595** *background*, **596, 627** *top*, **665, 681, 724** Copyright © 1995 PhotoDisc, Inc. **148** Photo Library International Ltd./Leo de Wys Inc. **150, 155** Detail of *A medio día/Pedacito de mi corazón* [At high noon/A little piece of my heart] (1986), Carmen Lomas Garza. Gouache on cotton rag paper, 28″ × 20″. Copyright © 1986 Carmen Lomas Garza. Photo by Wolfgang Dietze. **160** Copyright © Steven C. Wilson/Entheos. **161** Paramount Film Library. **175** Copyright © David Hiser/Tony Stone Images. **176–178** *detail* Copyright © Roxana Villa/SIS. **183** Christie's Images. **203** *top* Detail of *Colombiane* (1978), Fernando Botero. ©

1995 Fernando Botero/Licensed by VAGA, New York, courtesy of Marlborough Gallery, New York; *bottom* Detail of *Yucateca Sentada* [Seated Yucatecan woman](1979), Alfredo Zalce. Acrylic on wood, 60 cm × 80 cm, courtesy of the Mexican Fine Arts Center Museum, Chicago. **216–217** Copyright © Bernie Boston. **218** Copyright © Kevin Schafer/Tony Stone Images. **220** Detail of Autumn leaf (1991), Hilary Page. Watercolor, courtesy of the artist. From page 28 of *Watercolor Right from the Start*, Watson-Guptill 1992. **224** *background* Detail of Autumn leaves (1991), Hilary Page. Watercolor, courtesy of the artist. From p. 28 of *Watercolor Right from the Start*, Watson-Guptill 1992. **245, 247** Detail of *Portrait of Henri Matisse* (1905), André Derain. Tate Gallery, London/Art Resource, New York. Copyright © 1996 Artists Rights Society (ARS), New York/ADAGP, Paris. **259** The Granger Collection, New York. **260** Photo by Douglas K. Meyer. **264** The Bettmann Archive. **266** D-day assault by U.S. troops, Normandy, France. UPI/Bettmann. **273** *top left* Bourseiller/Durieux/HOA–QUI, Paris. **298** Copyright © Ron Sanford/Tony Stone Images. **313** Copyright © Deborah Davis/Photonica. **315** Detail of *Candle, Eigg* (1980), Winifred Nicholson. 58 cm × 43 cm, private collection. Copyright © The artist's family. Photo by John Webb. **331** Photos by Nicole Nelson. **332** Copyright © FPG International Corp. **347, 351, 354, 357–358** Copyright © Michael Orton/Tony Stone Images. **366–367** Copyright © Craig Aurness/Westlight. **370** Phototone. **379** Copyright © 1989 Bildarchiv Okapia/Photo Researchers, Inc. **380** *top left* Archive Photos; *top right* The Bettmann Archive. **381** *detail* Copyright © John Thompson. **405** *top*, **574** Copyright © Don Smetzer/Tony Stone Images. **426** *comb* Copyright © Kei Muto/Photonica; *watch* Copyright © Susumu Yasui/Photonica. **428** Copyright © Susumu Yasui/Photonica. **431** Copyright © Kei Muto/Photonica. **447** *left*, *near left* The Bettmann Archive; *right*, *near right* UPI/Bettmann. **451** Courtesy of Johns Hopkins Children's Center. **483** Copyright © James P. Rowan/Tony Stone Images. **490–494** Breadfruit leaves courtesy of The National Tropical Botanical Garden, Lawai, Kauai, Hawaii, and the Missouri Botanical Garden, St. Louis. **496–497** Reuters/Bettmann. **511** Copyright © Alan Smith/Tony Stone Images. **550** Reproduced from the collections of the Library of Congress. **562** *photos* Copyright © Rick Stewart/Allsport USA. **564** *bottom* Copyright © Bob Thomas/Tony Stone Images. **566** *top* Copyright © Al Bello/Allsport. **576** *background* Copyright © Gary Holscher/Tony Stone Images; *top* Assiniboine, or Gros Ventre, moccasins (about 1890), unknown Native American craftworker from Fort Belknap Reservation, Montana. Buckskin, rawhide, glass, 26 cm wide, Detroit Institute of Arts, Richard and Marion Pohrt Collection (cp-141). Photo Copyright © Dirk Bakker/Detroit Institute of Arts. **579** Copyright © Gary Holscher/Tony Stone Images. **602–603, 606–607** *background* Copyright © J. A. Nemeth/Picturesque Inc. **616** Copyright © The Bettmann Archive. **618** *top* Copyright © 1995 Classic PIO Partners; *bottom America, Victoria & Albert and Black Eagle off the Isle of Wight, 1851,* Tim Thompson. Oil on canvas, 20″ × 40″. Image used under license with T. F. R. Thompson. **634–635** Copyright © Timothy Hursley. **648** Copyright © Cathlyn Melloan/Tony Stone Images. **649, 651–652, 654** Copyright © M. Yamazaki/Photonica. **662** Copyright © Takahisa Ide/Photonica. **663** Copyright © Steven Edson/Photonica. **674** Copyright © 1991 Arthur Tilley/FPG International Corp. **685** *top* Courtesy Image Club Graphics, Inc. For a free catalog call: 1-800-661-9410; *top inset* Copyright © Eric Haase/Contact Press Images. **691** *left inset* Wyatt McSpadden; *right inset* Courtesy Elizabeth Buggy. **698** *top* Kayak with a sealskin vest, Greenland. The Greenland Museum, Werner Forman/Art Resource, New York; *middle* Ballplayer (about A.D. 600–900), unknown Mayan artist. Copyright © Lee Boltin; *bottom* Shaman rattle in the form of a crane with a figure representing a shaman on its back, Native American artist from Northwest Coast. Field Museum of Natural History, Chicago, Werner Forman/Art Resource, New York. **699** *top left* The Granger Collection, New York; *top right* The Bettmann Archive; *left, second from top* Detail from Codex Borbonicus (about A.D. 1200–1500), unknown Aztec artist. Bibliothèque du Palais Bourbon, Paris, Giraudon/Art Resource, New York; *left, second from bottom* Moccasins (1830), unknown Iroquois craftworker. Buckskin, wool, cotton, glass beads. The Detroit Institute of Arts, Founders Society Purchase with funds from Flint Ink Corporation (1988.32). Photo by Dirk Bakker. Photo Copyright © 1995 The Detroit Institute of Arts; *lower left* The Granger Collection, New York; *center, second from bottom* Copyright © L. Nelson/H. Armstrong Roberts; *center bottom* Red Cloud. The Bettmann Archive; *bottom right* H. Armstrong Roberts. **700** Detail of *En busqueda de la paz* [In search of peace], Alfredo Linares. **701** *top* Detail of Illustration by Rockwell Kent. Courtesy of the Rockwell Kent Legacies; *bottom* Detail Copyright © Andrea Brooks. **716** Detail of *Brer Possum*, Barry Moser. From *Jump, Again!* by Van Dyke Parks, published by Harcourt Brace Jovanovich in 1987. Illustration Copyright © Barry Moser. Reprinted with permission from the artist. **717** *top* Detail from *His Hammer in His Hand*, Palmer C. Hayden (1890–1973). From the John Henry Series, Museum of African American Art, Los Angeles, Palmer C. Hayden Collection, gift of Miriam A. Hayden. Photo by Armando Solis; *center* Detail of *Twilight* (1971), Hubert Shuptrine. Copyright © 1971, 1994 Hubert Shuptrine, all rights reserved. **728** *Buzzards' Roost* (1985), Hubert Shuptrine. Copyright © by S. Hill Corporation. All rights reserved. Used with permission. **732** *left* Nootka raven spirit mask, northwest coast. The Philbrook Museum of Art, Tulsa, Oklahoma, Ellis Soper Collection. **733** *top* Detail of *When the Eagle Spoke to Me* (1979), Jerry Ingram (Choctaw). Watercolor on paper, 18″ × 24″, by permission of the artist; *bottom* Detail Copyright © Colin Poole. **758** *top* Copyright © The Walt Disney Company, photo courtesy of Photofest; *bottom* Portrait of Pocahontas (after 1616), unknown artist, English School, after an engraving by Simon de Passe. National Portrait Gallery, Smithsonian Institution, Washington, D.C./Art Resource, New York. **759** *bottom* The Bettmann Archive. **760** *Proud Hunter* (1987), Pudlo Pudlat. Stonecut, 21 1/2″ × 24″, by permission of the Amway Environmental Foundation. **761** *bottom* Illustration Copyright © 1992 Brian Pinkney. From *The Dark-Thirty* by Patricia McKissack, reprinted by permission of Alfred A. Knopf, Inc.; **761** *top*, **762** From *The Spirit of Native America* by Anna Lee Walters. Copyright © 1989, published by Chronicle Books. **785** *top, Dorothy and Netti* (1974), Alex Katz. Oil on canvas, 72″ × 96″, collection of the artist, courtesy of Marlborough Gallery, New York. Copyright © Alex Katz; *bottom, Strawberry Dance* (1983), G. Peter Jemison (Seneca Nation, Heron Clan). Mixed media on handmade paper, 22″ × 30″, private collection, by permission of the artist. **791** Illustration from *La Ruta Maya: Yucatan, Guatemala and Belize—a travel survival kit* (first edition) by Tom Brosnahan. By permission of Lonely Planet Publications. **799** Reprinted by permission of Tribune Media Services. **836** Copyright © Jeff Schultz/Alaska Stock Images. **838** Copyright © Terry

Farmer/Tony Stone Images. **844** Copyright © James P. Rowan/Tony Stone Images. **846** UPI/Bettmann. **850** *Vaquero* [Cowboy] (1980), Luis Jimenez. Copyright © Luis Jimenez. Homepage (http://www.nmaa.si.edu) Copyright © National Museum of American Art, Smithsonian Institution. Netscape, Netscape Navigator, and the Netscape Communications Corporation Logo are trademarks of Netscape Communications Corporation. **853–855** Screen shots reprinted with permission from Microsoft Corporation. **856** Used with express permission. Adobe and Adobe Illustrator are trademarks of Adobe Systems Incorporated. **857, 859** Photofest.

Teacher Review Panels *(continued)*

Bonnie Garrett, Davis Middle School, Compton School District

Sally Jackson, Madrona Middle School, Torrance Unified School District

Sharon Kerson, Los Angeles Center for Enriched Studies, Los Angeles Unified School District

Gail Kidd, Center Middle School, Azusa School District

Corey Lay, ESL Department Chairperson, Chester Nimitz Middle School, Los Angeles Unified School District

Myra LeBendig, Forshay Learning Center, Los Angeles Unified School District

Dan Manske, Elmhurst Middle School, Oakland Unified School District

Joe Olague, Language Arts Department Chairperson, Alder Middle School, Fontana School District

Pat Salo, 6th Grade Village Leader, Hidden Valley Middle School, Escondido Elementary School District

FLORIDA

Judi Briant, English Department Chairperson, Armwood High School, Hillsborough County School District

Beth Johnson, Polk County English Supervisor, Polk County School District

Sharon Johnston, Learning Resource Specialist, Evans High School, Orange County School District

Eileen Jones, English Department Chairperson, Spanish River High School, Palm Beach County School District

Jan McClure, Winter Park High School Orange County School District

Wanza Murray, English Department Chairperson (retired), Vero Beach Senior High School, Indian River City School District

Shirley Nichols, Language Arts Curriculum Specialist Supervisor, Marion County School District

Debbie Nostro, Ocoee Middle School, Orange County School District

Barbara Quinaz, Assistant Principal, Horace Mann Middle School, Dade County School District

OHIO

Joseph Bako, English Department Chairperson, Carl Shuler Middle School, Cleveland City School District

Deb Delisle, Language Arts Department Chairperson, Ballard Brady Middle School, Orange School District

Ellen Geisler, English/Language Arts Department Chairperson, Mentor Senior High School, Mentor School District

Dr. Mary Gove, English Department Chairperson, Shaw High School, East Cleveland School District

Loraine Hammack, Executive Teacher of the English Department, Beachwood High School, Beachwood City School District

Sue Nelson, Shaw High School, East Cleveland School District

Mary Jane Reed, English Department Chairperson, Solon High School, Solon City School District

Nancy Strauch, English Department Chairperson, Nordonia High School, Nordonia Hills City School District

Ruth Vukovich, Hubbard High School, Hubbard Exempted Village School District

TEXAS

Anita Arnold, English Department Chairperson, Thomas Jefferson High School, San Antonio Independent School District

Gilbert Barraza, J.M. Hanks High School, Ysleta School District

Sandi Capps, Dwight D. Eisenhower High School, Alding Independent School District

Judy Chapman, English Department Chairperson, Lawrence D. Bell High School, Hurst-Euless-Bedford School District

Pat Fox, Grapevine High School, Grapevine-Colley School District

LaVerne Johnson, McAllen Memorial High School, McAllen Independent School District

Donna Matsumura, W.H. Adamson High School, Dallas Independent School District

Ruby Mayes, Waltrip High School, Houston Independent School District

Mary McFarland, Amarillo High School, Amarillo Independent School District

Adrienne Thrasher, A.N. McCallum High School, Austin Independent School Distric

Manuscript Reviewers *(continued)*

Maryann Lyons, Literacy Specialist, Mentor teacher, San Francisco Unified School District, San Francisco, California

Karis MacDonnell, Ed.D., Dario Middle School, Miami, Florida

Bonnie J. Mansell, Downey Adult School, Downey, California

Martha Mitchell, Memorial Middle School, Orlando, Florida

Nancy Nachman, Landmark High School, Jacksonville, Florida

Karen Williams Perry, English Department Chairperson, Kennedy Jr. High School, Lisle, Illinois

Julia Pferdehirt, free-lance writer, former Special Education teacher, Middleton, Wisconsin

Phyllis Stewart Rude, English Department Head, Mears Jr./Sr. High School, Anchorage, Alaska

Leo Schubert, Bettendorf Middle School, Bettendorf, Iowa

Gertrude H. Vannoy, Curriculum Liaison Specialist, Gifted and Horizon teacher, Meany Middle School, Seattle, Washington

Richard Wagner, Language Arts Curriculum Coordinator, Paradise Valley School District, Phoenix, Arizona

Stephen J. Zadravec, Newmarket Jr./Sr. High School, Newmarket, New Hampshire